The Complete Weird-Fiction Works of

H.P. LOVECRAFT:

In One Volume.

THE COMPLETE WEIRD-FICTION WORKS OF

H.P. LOVECRAFT

In One Volume

Includes
Collaborations &
Ghostwritings

By H.P. LOVECRAFT

Edited and annotated by FINN J.D. JOHN

Hardcover Compact Edition
Build 2021.01
http://pulp-lit.com/360

ISBNs:

Hardcover Compact Edition:	978-1-63591-361-3
E-book:	978-1-63591-364-4
Audiobook, retail:	978-1-63591-365-1
Audiobook, library edition:	978-1-63591-366-8
PDF:	978-1-63591-368-2

Dustjacket art:

Cover art adopted from Margaret Brundage's cover illustration for the May 1935 issue of *Weird Tales* magazine.

Pulp-Lit Productions
Corvallis, Oregon

http://pulp-lit.com

Table of Contents.

Foreword.

Howard Phillips Lovecraft was born on August 10, 1890 — a product of the late Victorian era. In many ways, he remained a late-Victorian man (although he himself would likely not agree) until his death in 1937. Along the way, he produced a body of weird-fiction work that, sparse though it is, has had a tremendous influence on 20th- and 21st-century literature.

That body of work is contained in this omnibus edition, now collected for the first time into a single volume: all of Lovecraft's prose-fiction output published between 1917, when he first turned from the witty-but-opaque nonfiction and turgid Georgian poetry that he then favored, until his death from cancer in 1937. Unlike most other collections, it includes all his known ghostwritten works, along with a few key pieces of poetry, as well as the full text of his seminal and transformative "master's thesis," *Supernatural Horror in Literature.*

It's important to note that, with one or two exceptions, this collection includes only Lovecraft's prose fiction. It is not everything Lovecraft wrote — not even close. It excludes most of his juvenilia (most of which he destroyed); his philosophical ruminations and scientific observations; his travelogues and other nonfiction writings; most of his poetry; and, of course, his letters.

Taken together, these other works dwarf the weird-fiction writings contained in this volume. His letters alone total many times more than everything else he wrote put together; estimates of his total production range from 30,000 to 100,000 letters sent to family members, friends, and fellow writers. Nor were these letters light reading; when courting his wife, Sonia Greene, he regularly sent her letters in the 40-to-50-page range. Late in his life, when his circumstances were really straitened, he actually skipped meals to finance the postage on these colossal missives.

ABOUT PRONUNCIATIONS.

When Lovecraft was writing these stories, there was no expectation that the names and incantations he created would ever have to be voiced. Moreover, some of them — including the names "Cthulhu" and "R'lyeh" — were intended to be sounds that the human vocal apparatus was not equipped to produce. One can find plenty of debate among hardcore Lovecraft aficionados over how one should pronounce all these "Cthuvian" words, and the ancient spells in *The Case of Charles Dexter Ward*, and so forth; but in the audio edition of this collection, we have opted to use the pronunciations most commonly used for them. They may not be correct, but then, by definition, no human can really get them right anyway; so we have opted to prioritize clarity over accuracy.

ABOUT THE COLLABORATIONS.

This volume is unusual among H.P. Lovecraft collections in that it aspires to absolute completeness — including those works of weird fiction that H.P. Lovecraft ghostwrote or collaborated with other writers upon.

Although only one or two of these rises to the level of quality of the best of Lovecraft's own by-lined work, all of the collaborations and ghostwritings are nonetheless wonderful stories. They have a real contribution to make to the meta-story of Lovecraft's creative life; and they reveal aspects to Lovecraft's personality (especially his sense of humor) that his more serious works seldom allow us to glimpse.

The reason for this is easily understood. When writing or revising a story for another writer, Lovecraft was able to fully relax. He knew (or thought he knew) that these stories would not affect his reputation as a literary figure; his name was not on them; someone else's was. So the terrible pressure of self-doubt that grew and strengthened throughout his career, the pressure that kept him in a state of virtual creative paralysis for the last several years of his life, fell away like an old cloak, and his real style — his relaxed, erudite, chatting-with-friends style — was able to shine through.

In the collaborative stories we get to see glimpses of Lovecraft's wry humor, kindly and benevolent but with a sort of gently sardonic edge to it. We also get to roll in the kind of over-the-top campiness that you just don't see in most of his by-lined stuff after the *Herbert West, Reanimator* era. Especially in the Hazel Heald stories, the campiness often reaches the point where one wonders if he's secretly engaging in a little self-parody.

We also get to see some halfhearted copy, especially in stories done or revised for people who didn't pay him well. But this is not uniformally a bad thing. One of the reasons Lovecraft's output was so scant was that his almost obsessive perfectionism and severe self-criticism kept him diligently polishing and revising many of his stories long past the point at which it made sense to continue doing so. This he could certainly not afford to do in a work-for-hire job that would pay him only $15 or $20. So in these anonymized stories we get to see Lovecraft's work as it might have appeared in his second drafts, or maybe third — rough, sometimes unsubtle, often crammed with all-too-familiar buzzwords like "eldritch" and "Cyclopean," yet eminently, fundamentally, and wonderfully Lovecraftian.

Lovecraft provided consultation, revision, and ghostwriting services to dozens of clients during his lifetime. However, the majority of such work was for nonfiction writers such as David Van Bush (known for self-help titles such as *Fear, Man's Worst Enemy*; *Smile, Smile, Smile*; and *Applied Psychology and Scientific Living*) and Anne Tillery Renshaw (proprietress of the Renshaw School of Speech in Washington, D.C.). These nonfiction undertakings are, of course, not included here.

Throughout his writing life, H.P. Lovecraft persistently followed British standard spelling, disdaining the American "reformed" spelling introduced by Noah Webster a century before. Lovecraft went so far in defense (or should we say defence?) of the British standard as to stipulate to *Weird Tales* and other publishers that his work not be copy-edited to fit the style of the other stories in the magazine.

Pulp-Lit Productions is, of course, an American company, and its house style follows all of Mr. Webster's decrees with appropriate faithfulness; but we have honored (honoured) Mr. Lovecraft's wishes with respect to his stories themselves, and they retain their British styling.

ABOUT 1920s RACISM.

There is another issue that must be addressed in any serious collection of the work of H.P. Lovecraft, and that is the question of racism. Recently it has become somewhat fashionable to claim that Lovecraft was an unusually toxic racist even by the standards of his own age. Whole books have been published by credentialed academic writers in which his stories and letters are cherry-picked to support the assertion that, far from being a mere "product of his time," Lovecraft was a hateful racist of reptilian proportions, an outlier even in an age of Jim Crow laws, poll taxes, eugenic sterilization laws, the widespread lynching of African-American combat veterans, and a popular American president who praised the Ku Klux Klan in the opening credits of the most popular movie in the land.

This position is, obviously, misguided to the point of silliness. But it's important not to react to its strident excessiveness by allowing ourselves to minimize the degree to which endemic racism really did influence H.P. Lovecraft and his work, and the degree to which Lovecraft — especially early in his career as a writer — contributed to it. Put simply, nearly every white person in the 1920s was a white supremacist. The concept of "race," and the assumption that some "races" were more intelligent or advanced or virtuous than others, and that one's own was the very best one, simply wasn't in debate in mainstream white society, especially among writers and readers of the mainstream commercial fiction that filled the old pulp magazines. Racism was in the water Lovecraft drank and the air Lovecraft breathed. And especially after the 1919 Red Scare crystallized white America's war-spawned existential fears around an ethnically defined "other," many white Americans — Lovecraft included — said and wrote some things of which they ought to have been deeply ashamed.

But to single Lovecraft out of this vast cohort of benighted Americans for special censure because he failed to rise above their level — as, to their everlasting credit, many did, including Lovecraft's almost-girlfriend Winifred Virginia Jackson — is to wield history as a rhetorical weapon rather than as a tool for better understanding.

Lovecraft made it very clear in his letters that he shared the ethnic chauvinism of his age. This makes some of his writings very awkward for modern readers. It is well to keep this in mind while reading his stories — and also to remember that they are cultural artifacts of a very different society from our own.

In the end, the question of Lovecraft and racism boils down to two words: "It's complicated." Reading his work, especially early work, occasionally requires that one hold one's nose. But the alternative is, in the words of the old cliché, to throw the baby out with the bathwater, and that, above all, is what we must not do.

GETTING TO KNOW H.P.L.

In the next section, you will find a brief biography of our author. It is by no means intended to replace a real, detailed biography, but rather to help fit his stories together into a coherent canon, to aid the reader in getting familiar with the sequence, circumstances, and context of each of Lovecraft's works as they are presented herein. (You will also find a detailed timeline of Lovecraft's life in the Appendix, at the very end of this volume.)

Biographical information is helpful in reading any author's work; but it's especially important with Lovecraft. This is for two reasons: First, because Lovecraft was a true autodidact who never stopped learning and reading and traveling in search of new ideas and better stories. His early work is noticeably different from — and, most scholars agree, technically inferior to — his later work. In 1919, Lovecraft was almost a recluse, and his work from that period reflects that lack of socialization; fifteen years later, he was possibly the most well-traveled man in Rhode Island, with a nationwide network of friends and a growing reputation for his keen wit and generosity of spirit. In other words, "The Street" and "The Colour out of Space" were written by very different men, and it is well to know this before tucking into reading Lovecraft for the first time.

The second reason a biographical background is useful is that throughout his career, each of the stories Lovecraft wrote built on his previous work, and frequently picked up threads from other writers' works as well.

Lovecraft's writings were created in the context both of his life, and of a growing fictional universe to which his works make contributions, additions and references; being familiar with that context, and with it that fictional universe, adds a whole new dimension to the enjoyment of his work. And it's that familiarity that this collection seeks to make available to the casual reader and the experienced, hardcore Lovecraft fan alike.

Readers who are interested in a more in-depth treatment of the life and times of this fascinating man have a wide selection of options to choose from. And it pays to be picky: a number of avid Lovecraft fans have taken advantage of the new self-publishing tools to put out fan biographies of him. Some of these are great, but don't make a very good entry point for those new to the subject. Of the more professional attempts, all are noticeably different one from another, and each has its own set of flaws and idiosyncrasies. In several cases these flaws are egregious enough to nearly ruin the work.

The scholarly works of S.T. Joshi are, most agree, by far the best and most complete — especially *I Am Providence: The Life and Times of H.P. Lovecraft* (two-volume set, Hippocampus Press, 2010; 564 and 598 pages, respectively).

Also worthy of note is the first real biography of Lovecraft, L. Sprague de Camp's *H.P. Lovecraft: A Biography* (Ballantine Books, 1976; 480 pages).

De Camp's work, although controversial, does have something to contribute to Lovecraft scholarship, if for no other reason than that it was the first. But de Camp makes many assumptions based on his own relatively mainstream sensibilities, and trades on some pseudo-Freudian theories of his own, which have to be dismissed out of hand.

Also, it must also be noted that there is a real sense, in reading de Camp, that he considers all pulp writers, Lovecraft included, to be somewhat beneath his own literary level. There is a subtle sense of condescension throughout de Camp's treatment, as if he is pandering to the unsophisticated — a Cordon Bleu chef preparing lunch for a crew of hard-hats. Like some of the others who have over the years had a go at interpreting and expanding Lovecraft's work in the world, he appears not to actually understand it — but believes and assumes that he does, and that it's just a bunch of jump scares and black magic that for some reason amuses the marginally literate. This attitude can be very irritating for readers, who may develop a sense that they are being secretly sneered at.

BIOGRAPHICAL NOTES.

The youthful H.P. Lovecraft was a bright, precocious little tyke, who took to reciting poetry when he was three and writing it when he was six. When he was three, his father developed some kind of psychosis and was committed to an insane asylum, where he died five years later. (Speculation continues to this day as to whether the cause of this psychosis might have been tertiary-stage syphilis; most scholars believe it was, although there is no solid proof. If so, he was at least able to avoid transmitting it to his wife.) Left in the family were his mother, an aunt, and his grandfather, Whipple van Buren Phillips.

Whipple took a particular interest in young Howard, particularly as the boy showed great interest in literary topics. The old man provided him with exciting books and told him wild Gothic terror-tales, stirring the youngster's interest in horror stories. Despite the loss of his father, these were wonderful times for little Howard, full of people who loved him and completely free of any concern about money. Whipple Phillips had been a successful businessman, and the family lived a comfortable upper-class life.

But just after 1900, Whipple started suffering business reversals. Before they could be straightened out, Whipple died, in 1904. The loss hit young Howard hard, and the finances of his family were hit harder. They had to move out of the mansion in which they'd lived, the first in a series of economizing moves made necessary by ever-dwindling resources.

As a youth, Lovecraft showed great intelligence and promise. He seemed destined for an academic life, perhaps as an astronomy professor. He read voraciously and conducted scientific experiments in a basement chemical laboratory. He was 13 when he got his first telescope, and used it to relentlessly observe the heavens. He even began publishing two amateur scientific journals, the *Scientific Gazette* (first issue: 1899) and

Rhode Island Journal of Astronomy (first issue: 1903), both of which he printed himself using a hectograph apparatus.

By 1906, at the age of 16, Lovecraft was writing a monthly column on astronomy in the daily *Providence Evening Tribune*. He also was still producing the *Rhode Island Journal of Astronomy*, and he also had a small printing press, with which he produced notecards.

But after 1908 or so, he abruptly ended this phenomenal run of intellectual productivity, and plunged into a eight-year season of lethargy. This was just about the time he should have been graduating from high school; however, instead of doing that, he suffered a nervous breakdown and dropped out of sight. Biographer S.T. Joshi makes a fairly convincing case that this breakdown may have been precipitated by Lovecraft's realization that his lack of aptitude for mathematics would make his lifelong goal of becoming a scientist impossible. It also seems likely that it had to do with a realization that his family wouldn't be able to afford to send him to university, regardless of his math scores. Perhaps it was a little of both.

Whatever the cause, Lovecraft, at age 18, went into a half-decade-long retreat from the world. During this time, he continued reading voraciously and omnivorously, of both high-culture classics and low-brow dime novels; and he pounded out thousands of lines of poetry, most of it stilted, formal stuff in iambic pentameter, in the style of the 1700s. It wasn't bad poetry; in fact, as time went on, practice made it remarkably good, although never (by most accounts) truly great. (The best poems Lovecraft wrote during this period, or at least the most appealing ones, were arguably the ones he didn't take too seriously, such as "Unda; or, The Bride of the Sea" and the Georgian drinking song reproduced in "The Tomb.")

But, be it good or bad, Lovecraft's poetry of this period wasn't taking him anywhere; after all, it was two centuries out of fashion.

Thus, Lovecraft lumbered along in near-total obscurity for a good five years, reading and producing reams of writings that, although very good and steadily improving, weren't marketable — a set of circumstances that will sound very familiar to anyone who's pursued a bachelor's degree in college. Lovecraft, a lifelong autodidact, was giving himself his own particular undergraduate education, although he surely wasn't self-aware enough to think of it in that way.

Then, in 1913, he found himself moved to complain in a letter to the editor of the classic pulp magazine *The Argosy* about the quality of stories it had published by inspirational-romance author Fred Jackson.

The letter sparked a flurry of responses from Jackson's fans, who rose to his defense. In the letters section of *The Argosy*, Lovecraft gave as good as he got, but did so with an erudite good humor that prevented things from getting truly nasty; soon he found himself with several new friends among those arguing against him. This led to his introduction to the hobby that would change him profoundly and shape the course of the rest of his life: Amateur journalism.

Here it is vital to understand that for a Regency or early-Victorian-age gentleman (as H.P. Lovecraft always styled himself to be), the word "amateur" meant something quite different from what it conjures today. To Lovecraft, "amateur" meant not a mediocre bodger or tyro, but rather a gentleman of leisure engaging in an activity for love of knowledge rather than for hope of gain. Charles Darwin was an amateur naturalist. James Clerk Maxwell (Lord Kelvin) was (or, at least, later became) an amateur physicist. Lord Edward Bullwer-Lytton was an amateur novelist. And H.P. Lovecraft was now going to be an amateur publisher.

By 1915, Lovecraft was publishing his own amateur magazine: *The Conservative*. It was, naturally, a great place to look for Georgian poetry, if one were interested in that sort of thing, along with whatever else Lovecraft's friends might have had to contribute to the title.

Amateur journalism was to the early 20th century what blogging and podcasting are to the early 21st. Indeed, the parallels are striking. Amateur journalists purchased small and inexpensive hand-operated printing presses and produced regular small-run periodicals circulated among friends, just as modern bloggers purchase inexpensive shared-host Internet accounts, install Wordpress on them, and produce regular columns. The quality of amateur-press work varied just as widely as does the quality of blogs today. And as with blogs today, circles of friends among amateur-press enthusiasts contributed content for each other's periodicals, met up for social events, collaborated on big storytelling projects, fell in love with one another, squabbled and fought with one another, formed and re-formed cliques, and generally behaved like what they were: a community. More specifically, they were a community of like-minded souls who appreciated Lovecraft, Georgian poetry and all, and made him feel welcome and at home.

It is to this community that we owe the greatest thanks for Lovecraft having been pushed out of his stodgy pre-Revolutionary literary rut and into the vanguard of a brand-new twist on the old 19th-century Gothic horror story: Weird fiction. We especially owe that word of thanks to one particular highly respected member of the amateur-press community, W. Paul Cook. Cook persuaded Lovecraft to publish his best piece of juvenilia, a very promising short story written when Lovecraft was still in high school titled "The Alchemist," in *United Amateur* in late 1916.

Response to "The Alchemist" was enthusiastic enough to persuade Lovecraft to set aside his poetry and try his hand at the writing of weird fiction. He took his first steps toward doing this at the age of 27, in 1917.

This biography will be continued year by year in the brief introductory articles that introduce each year of Lovecraft's creative life — starting with 1908, on the next page.

1908.

Refuge in Poetry.

H.P. Lovecraft was, by most accounts, a child prodigy. He mastered the alphabet while still a toddler; wrote his first poem at age 7; and launched his first publishing enterprise, the *Scientific Gazette*, when he was 9.

Regrettably, Lovecraft destroyed most of his juvenilia in 1908 when he experienced the nervous breakdown that took him out of high school. But he did not destroy all of it. One particular piece that he wrote before his 18th birthday would later play an unexpectedly big role in his career — "The Alchemist," the best story of all his juvenilia, which he wrote shortly before his 18th birthday, just before his nervous collapse.

In addition, we are including one other example of Lovecraft's juvenilia, because, like "The Alchemist," it was published in an amateur journal more than a decade after it was written: "The Beast in the Cave," drafted in 1904 and finished in 1905.

The Beast in the Cave.

2,500-WORD SHORT STORY; 1905.

This short story is possibly the most impressive piece of Lovecraft's juvenilia still existing today; he wrote the first draft when he was 14 years old. It is a surprisingly competent piece of work for a high-school freshman. It is included here because it is the first piece of publishable weird fiction Lovecraft ever wrote.

And indeed it was published, many years later, in the June 1918 issue of W. Paul Cook's amateur journal, The Vagrant.

The horrible conclusion which had been gradually obtruding itself upon my confused and reluctant mind was now an awful certainty. I was lost, completely, hopelessly lost in the vast and labyrinthine recesses of the Mammoth Cave. Turn as I might, in no direction could my straining vision seize on any object capable of serving as a guidepost to set me on the outward path. That nevermore should I behold the blessed light of day, or scan the pleasant hills and dales of the beautiful world outside, my reason could no longer entertain the slightest unbelief. Hope had departed. Yet, indoctrinated as I was by a life of philosophical study, I derived no small measure of satisfaction from my unimpassioned demeanour; for although I had frequently read of the wild frenzies into which were thrown the victims of similar situations, I experienced none of these, but stood quiet as soon as I clearly realised the loss of my bearings.

Nor did the thought that I had probably wandered beyond the utmost limits of an ordinary search cause me to abandon my composure even for a moment. If I must die, I reflected, then was this terrible yet majestic cavern as welcome a sepulchre as that which any churchyard might afford; a conception which carried with it more of tranquility than of despair.

Starving would prove my ultimate fate; of this I was certain. Some, I knew, had gone mad under circumstances such as these, but I felt that this end would not be mine. My disaster was the result of no fault save my own, since unbeknown to the guide I had separated myself from the regular party of sightseers; and, wandering for over an hour in forbidden avenues of the cave, had found myself unable to retrace the devious windings which I had pursued since forsaking my companions.

Already my torch had begun to expire; soon I would be enveloped by the total and almost palpable blackness of the bowels of the earth. As I stood in the waning, unsteady light, I idly wondered over the exact circumstances of my coming end. I remembered the accounts which I had heard of the colony of consumptives, who, taking their residence in this gigantic grotto to find health from the apparently salubrious air of the underground world, with its steady, uniform temperature, pure air, and peaceful quiet, had found, instead, death in strange and ghastly form. I had seen the sad remains of their ill-made cottages as I passed them by with the party, and had wondered what unnatural influence a long sojourn in this immense and silent cavern would exert upon one as healthy and as vigorous as I. Now, I grimly told myself, my opportunity for settling this point had arrived, provided that want of food should not bring me too speedy a departure from this life.

As the last fitful rays of my torch faded into obscurity, I resolved to leave no stone unturned, no possible means of escape neglected; so summoning all the powers possessed by my lungs, I set up a series of loud shoutings, in the vain hope of attracting the attention of the guide by my clamour. Yet, as I called, I believed in my heart that my cries were to no purpose, and that my voice, magnified and reflected by the numberless ramparts of the black maze about me, fell upon no ears save my own. All at once, however, my attention was fixed with a start as I fancied that I heard the sound of soft approaching steps on the rocky floor of the cavern. Was my deliverance about to be accomplished so soon? Had, then, all my horrible apprehensions been for naught, and was the guide, having marked my unwarranted absence from the party, following my course and seeking me out in this limestone labyrinth? Whilst these joyful queries arose in my brain, I was on the point of renewing my cries, in order that my discovery might come the sooner, when in an instant my delight was turned to horror as I listened; for my ever acute ear, now sharpened in even greater degree by the complete silence of the cave, bore to my benumbed understanding the unexpected and dreadful knowledge that these footfalls were not like those of any mortal man. In the unearthly stillness of this subterranean region, the tread of the booted guide would have sounded like a series of sharp and incisive blows. These impacts were soft, and stealthy, as of the padded paws of some feline. Besides, at times, when I listened carefully, I seemed to trace the falls of four instead of two feet.

I was now convinced that I had by my cries aroused and attracted some wild beast, perhaps a mountain lion which had accidentally strayed within the cave. Perhaps, I considered, the Almighty had chosen for me a swifter and more merciful death than that of hunger. Yet the instinct of self-preservation, never wholly dormant, was stirred in my breast, and though escape from the oncoming peril might but spare me for a sterner and more lingering end, I determined nevertheless to part with my life at as high a price as I could command. Strange as it may seem, my mind conceived of no intent on the part of the visitor save that of hostility. Accordingly, I became very quiet, in the hope that the unknown beast would, in the absence of a guiding sound, lose its direction as had I, and thus pass me by. But this hope was not destined for realisation, for the strange footfalls steadily advanced, the animal evidently having obtained my scent, which in an atmosphere so absolutely free from all distracting influences as is that of the cave, could doubtless be followed at great distance.

Seeing therefore that I must be armed for defence against an uncanny and unseen attack in the dark, I grouped about me the largest of the fragments of rock which were strown upon all parts of the floor of the cavern in the vicinity, and, grasping one in each hand for immediate use, awaited with resignation the inevitable result. Meanwhile the hideous pattering of the paws drew near. Certainly, the conduct of the creature was exceedingly strange. Most of the time, the tread seemed to be that of a quadruped, walking with a singular lack of unison betwixt hind and fore feet, yet at brief and infrequent intervals I fancied that but two feet were engaged in the process of locomotion. I wondered what species of animal was to confront me; it must, I thought, be some unfortunate beast who had paid for its curiosity to investigate one of the entrances of the fearful grotto with a lifelong confinement in its interminable recesses. It doubtless obtained as food the eyeless fish, bats, and rats of the cave, as well as some of the ordinary fish that are wafted in at every freshet of Green River, which communicates in some occult manner with the waters of the cave. I occupied my terrible vigil with grotesque conjectures of what alterations cave life might have wrought in the physical structure of the beast, remembering the awful appearances ascribed by local tradition to the consumptives who had died after long residence in the cavern. Then I remembered with a start that, even should I succeed in killing my antagonist, I should never behold its form, as my torch had long since been extinct, and I was entirely unprovided with matches. The tension on my brain now became frightful. My disordered fancy conjured up hideous and fearsome shapes from the sinister darkness that surrounded me, and that actually seemed to press upon my body. Nearer, nearer, the dreadful footfalls approached. It seemed that I must give vent to a piercing scream, yet had I been sufficiently irresolute to attempt such a thing, my voice could scarce have responded. I was petrified, rooted to the spot. I doubted if my right arm would allow me to hurl its missile at the oncoming thing when the crucial moment should arrive. Now the steady pat, pat, of the steps was close at hand; now, very close. I could hear the laboured breathing of the animal, and terror-struck as I was, I realised that it must have come from a considerable distance, and was correspondingly fatigued. Suddenly the spell broke. My right hand, guided by my ever trustworthy sense of hearing, threw with full force the sharp-angled bit of limestone which it contained, toward that point in the darkness from which emanated the breathing and pattering, and, wonderful to relate, it nearly reached its goal, for I heard the thing jump, landing at a distance away, where it seemed to pause.

Having readjusted my aim, I discharged my second missile, this time most effectively, for with a flood of joy I listened as the creature fell in what sounded like a complete collapse, and evidently remained prone and unmoving. Almost overpowered by the great relief which rushed over me, I reeled back against the wall. The breathing continued, in heavy, gasping inhalations and expirations, whence I realised that I had no more than wounded the creature. And now all desire to examine the thing ceased. At last something allied to groundless, superstitious, fear had entered my brain, and I did not approach the body, nor did I continue to cast stones at it in order to complete the extinction of its life. Instead, I ran at full speed in what was, as nearly as I could estimate in my frenzied condition, the direction from which I had come. Suddenly I heard a sound, or rather, a regular succession of sounds. In another instant they had resolved themselves into a series of sharp, metallic clicks. This time there was no doubt. It was the guide. And then I shouted, yelled, screamed, even shrieked with joy as I beheld in the vaulted arches above the faint and glimmering effulgence which I knew to be the reflected light of an approaching torch. I ran to meet the flare, and before I could completely understand what had occurred, was lying upon the ground at the feet of the guide, embracing his boots, and gibbering, despite my boasted reserve, in a most meaningless and idiotic manner, pouring out my terrible story, and at the same time overwhelming my auditor with protestations of gratitude. At length I awoke to something like my normal consciousness. The guide had noted my absence upon the arrival of the party at the entrance of the cave, and had, from his own intuitive sense of direction, proceeded to make a thorough canvass of the by-passages just ahead of where he had last spoken to me, locating my whereabouts after a quest of about four hours.

By the time he had related this to me, I, emboldened by his torch and his company, began to reflect upon the strange beast which I had wounded but a short distance back in the darkness, and suggested that we ascertain, by the rushlight's aid, what manner of creature was my victim. Accordingly I retraced my steps, this time with a courage born of companionship, to the scene of my terrible experience. Soon we descried a white object upon the floor, an object whiter even than the gleaming limestone itself. Cautiously advancing, we gave vent to a simultaneous ejaculation of wonderment, for of all the unnatural monsters either of us had in our lifetimes beheld, this was in surpassing degree the strangest. It appeared to be an anthropoid ape of large proportions, escaped, perhaps, from some itinerant menagerie. Its hair was snow-white, a thing due no doubt to the bleaching action of a long existence within the inky confines of the cave, but it was also surprisingly thin, being indeed largely absent save on the head, where it was of such length and abundance that it fell over the shoulders in considerable profusion. The face was turned away from us, as the creature lay almost directly upon it. The inclination of the limbs was very singular, explaining, however, the alternation in their use which I had before noted, whereby the beast used sometimes all four, and on other occasions but two for its progress. From the tips of the fingers or toes long nail-like claws extended. The hands or feet were not prehensile, a fact that I ascribed to that long residence in the cave which, as I before mentioned, seemed evident from the all-pervading and almost unearthly whiteness so characteristic of the whole anatomy. No tail seemed to be present.

The respiration had now grown very feeble, and the guide had drawn his pistol with the evident intent of despatching the creature, when a sudden sound emitted by the latter caused the weapon to fall unused. The sound was of a nature difficult to describe. It was not like the normal note of any known species of simian, and I wondered if this unnatural quality were not the result of a long-continued and complete silence, broken by the sensations produced by the advent of the light, a thing which the beast could not have seen since its first entrance into the cave. The sound, which I might feebly attempt to classify as a kind of deep-toned chattering, was faintly continued. All at once a fleeting spasm of energy seemed to pass through the frame of the beast. The paws went through a convulsive motion, and the limbs contracted. With a jerk, the white body rolled over so that its face was turned in our direction. For a moment I was so struck with horror at the eyes thus revealed that I noted nothing else. They were black, those eyes, deep, jetty black, in hideous contrast to the snow-white hair and flesh. Like those of other cave denizens, they were deeply sunken in their orbits, and were entirely destitute of iris. As I looked more closely, I saw that they were set in a face less prognathous than that of the average ape, and infinitely more hairy. The nose was quite distinct.

As we gazed upon the uncanny sight presented to our vision, the thick lips opened, and several sounds issued from them, after which the thing relaxed in death.

The guide clutched my coat-sleeve and trembled so violently that the light shook fitfully, casting weird, moving shadows on the walls about us.

I made no motion, but stood rigidly still, my horrified eyes fixed upon the floor ahead.

Then fear left, and wonder, awe, compassion, and reverence succeeded in its place, for the sounds uttered by the stricken figure that lay stretched out on the limestone had told us the awesome truth. The creature I had killed, the strange beast of the unfathomed cave was, or had at one time been, a MAN!!!

The Alchemist.

3,700-WORD SHORT STORY; 1908.

This story pushes the limits of the term "juvenilia" a bit, as it was written just before Lovecraft turned 18. It was the last serious piece of weird fiction Lovecraft wrote before he fell into the nervous breakdown that ended his high-school career.

This is the story that, reprinted nearly a decade after it was written in the November 1916 issue of The United Amateur, *brought Lovecraft's weird-fiction talents to the attention of the amateur-press community and convinced him to turn away from scholarly treatises and turgid Georgian poetry and embark on a career as a fiction writer.*

High up, crowning the grassy summit of a swelling mound whose sides are wooded near the base with the gnarled trees of the primeval forest, stands the old chateau of my ancestors. For centuries its lofty battlements have frowned down upon the wild and rugged countryside about, serving as a home and stronghold for the proud house whose honoured line is older even than the moss-grown castle walls. These ancient turrets, stained by the storms of generations and crumbling under the slow yet mighty pressure of time, formed in the ages of feudalism one of the most dreaded and formidable fortresses in all France. From its machicolated parapets and mounted battlements barons, counts, and even kings had been defied, yet never had its spacious halls resounded to the footsteps of the invader.

But since those glorious years all is changed. A poverty but little above the level of dire want, together with a pride of name that forbids its alleviation by the pursuits of commercial life, have prevented the scions of our line from maintaining their estates in pristine splendour; and the falling stones of the walls, the overgrown vegetation in the parks, the dry and dusty moat, the ill-paved courtyards, and toppling towers without, as well as the sagging floors, the worm-eaten wainscots, and the faded tapestries within, all tell a gloomy tale of fallen grandeur. As the ages passed, first one, then another of the four great turrets were left to ruin, until at last but a single tower housed the sadly reduced descendants of the once mighty lords of the estate.

It was in one of the vast and gloomy chambers of this remaining tower that I, Antoine, last of the unhappy and accursed Comtes de C——, first saw the light of day, ninety long years ago. Within these walls, and amongst the dark and shadowy forests, the wild ravines and grottoes of the hillside below, were spent the first years of my troubled life. My parents I never knew. My father had been killed at the age of thirty-two, a month before I was born, by the fall of a stone somehow dislodged from one of the deserted parapets of the castle; and my mother having died at my birth, my care and education devolved solely upon one remaining servitor, an old and trusted man of considerable intelligence, whose name I remember as Pierre. I was an only child, and the lack of companionship which this fact entailed upon me was augmented by the strange care exercised by my aged guardian in excluding me from the society of the peasant children whose abodes were scattered here and there upon the plains that surround the base of the hill. At the time, Pierre said that this restriction was imposed upon me because my noble birth placed me above association with such plebeian company. Now I know that its real object was to keep from my ears the idle tales of the dread curse upon our line, that were nightly told and magnified by the simple tenantry as they conversed in hushed accents in the glow of their cottage hearths.

Thus isolated, and thrown upon my own resources, I spent the hours of my childhood in poring over the ancient tomes that filled the shadow-haunted library of the chateau, and in roaming without aim or purpose through the perpetual dusk of the spectral wood that clothes the side of the hill near its foot. It was perhaps an effect of such surroundings that my mind early acquired a shade of melancholy. Those studies and pursuits which partake of the dark and occult in Nature most strongly claimed my attention.

Of my own race I was permitted to learn singularly little, yet what small knowledge of it I was able to gain, seemed to depress me much. Perhaps it was at first only the manifest reluctance of my old preceptor to discuss with me my paternal ancestry that gave rise to the terror which I ever felt at the mention of my great house; yet as I grew out of childhood, I was able to piece together disconnected fragments of discourse, let slip from the unwilling tongue which had begun to falter in approaching senility, that had a sort of relation to a certain circumstance which I had always deemed strange, but which now became dimly terrible. The circumstance to which I allude is the early age at which all the Comtes of my line had met their end. Whilst I had hitherto considered this but a natural attribute of a family of short-lived men, I afterward pondered long upon these premature deaths, and began to connect them with the wanderings of the old man, who often spoke of a curse which for centuries had prevented the lives of the holders of my title from much exceeding the span of thirty-two years. Upon my twenty-first birthday, the aged Pierre gave to me a family document which he said had for many generations been handed down from father to son, and continued by each possessor. Its contents were of the most startling nature, and its perusal confirmed the gravest of my apprehensions. At this time, my belief in the supernatural was firm and deep-seated, else I should have dismissed with scorn the incredible narrative unfolded before my eyes.

The paper carried me back to the days of the thirteenth century, when the old castle in which I sat had been a feared and impregnable fortress. It told of a certain ancient man who had once dwelt on our estates, a person of no small accomplishments, though little above the rank of peasant; by name, Michel, usually designated by the surname of Mauvais, the Evil, on account of his sinister reputation. He had studied beyond the custom of his kind, seeking such things as the Philosopher's Stone, or the Elixir of Eternal Life, and was reputed wise in the terrible secrets of Black Magic and Alchemy. Michel Mauvais had one son, named Charles, a youth as proficient as himself in the hidden arts, and who had therefore been called Le Sorcier, or the Wizard. This pair, shunned by all honest folk, were suspected of the most hideous practices. Old Michel was said to have burnt his wife alive as a sacrifice to the Devil, and the unaccountable disappearances of many small peasant children were laid at the dreaded door of these two. Yet through the dark natures of the father and the son ran one redeeming ray of humanity; the evil old man loved his offspring with fierce intensity, whilst the youth had for his parent a more than filial affection.

One night the castle on the hill was thrown into the wildest confusion by the vanishment of young Godfrey, son to Henri the Comte. A searching party, headed by the frantic father, invaded the cottage of the sorcerers and there came upon old Michel Mauvais, busy over a huge and violently boiling cauldron. Without certain cause, in the ungoverned madness of fury and despair, the Comte laid hands on the aged wizard, and ere he released his murderous hold his victim was no more. Meanwhile joyful servants were proclaiming the finding of young Godfrey in a distant and unused chamber of the great edifice, telling too late that poor Michel had been killed in vain. As the Comte and his associates turned away from the lowly abode of the alchemists, the form of Charles Le Sorcier appeared through the trees. The excited chatter of the menials standing about told him what had occurred, yet he seemed at first unmoved at his father's fate. Then, slowly advancing to meet the Comte, he pronounced in dull yet terrible accents the curse that ever afterward haunted the house of C——.

"May ne'er a noble of thy murd'rous line — Survive to reach a greater age than thine!" spake he, when, suddenly leaping backwards into the black wood, he drew from his tunic a phial of colourless liquid which he threw into the face of his father's slayer as he disappeared behind the inky curtain of the night. The Comte died without utterance, and was buried the next day, but little more than two and thirty years from the hour of his birth. No trace of the assassin could be found, though relentless bands of peasants scoured the neighbouring woods and the meadow-land around the hill.

Thus time and the want of a reminder dulled the memory of the curse in the minds of the late Comte's family, so that when Godfrey, innocent cause of the whole tragedy and now bearing the title, was killed by an arrow whilst hunting, at the age of thirty-two, there were no thoughts save those of grief at his demise. But when, years afterward, the next young Comte, Robert by name, was found dead in a nearby field from no apparent cause, the peasants told in whispers that their seigneur had but lately passed his thirty-second birthday when surprised by early death. Louis, son to Robert, was found drowned in the moat at the same fateful age, and thus down through the centuries ran the ominous chronicle; Henris, Roberts, Antoines, and Armands snatched from happy and virtuous lives when little below the age of their unfortunate ancestor at his murder.

That I had left at most but eleven years of further existence was made certain to me by the words which I read. My life, previously held at small value, now became dearer to me each day, as I delved deeper and deeper into the mysteries of the hidden world of black magic. Isolated as I was, modern science had produced no impression upon me, and I laboured as in the Middle Ages, as rapt as had been old Michel and young Charles themselves in the acquisition of daemonological and alchemical learning. Yet read as I might, in no manner could I account for the strange curse upon my line. In unusually rational moments, I would even go so far as to seek a natural explanation, attributing the early deaths of my ancestors to the sinister Charles Le Sorcier and his heirs; yet having found upon careful inquiry that there were no known descendants of the alchemist, I would fall back to occult studies, and once more endeavour to find a spell that would release my house from its terrible burden. Upon one thing I was absolutely resolved. I should never wed, for since no other branches of my family were in existence, I might thus end the curse with myself.

As I drew near the age of thirty, old Pierre was called to the land beyond. Alone I buried him beneath the stones of the courtyard about which he had loved to wander in life. Thus was I left to ponder on myself as the only human creature within the great fortress, and in my utter solitude my mind began to cease its vain protest against the impending doom, to become almost reconciled to the fate which so many of my ancestors had met. Much of my time was now occupied in the exploration of the ruined and abandoned halls and towers of the old chateau, which in youth fear had caused me to shun, and some of which, old Pierre had once told me, had not been trodden by human foot for over four centuries. Strange and awesome were many of the objects I encountered. Furniture, covered by the dust of ages and crumbling with the rot of long dampness, met my eyes. Cobwebs in a profusion never before seen by me were spun everywhere, and huge bats flapped their bony and uncanny wings on all sides of the otherwise untenanted gloom.

Of my exact age, even down to days and hours, I kept a most careful record, for each movement of the pendulum of the massive clock in the library told off so much more of my doomed existence. At length I approached that time which I had so long viewed with apprehension. Since most of my ancestors had been seized some little while before they reached the exact age of Comte Henri at his end, I was every moment on the watch for the coming of the unknown death. In what strange form the curse should overtake me, I knew not; but I was resolved, at least, that it should not find me a cowardly or a passive victim. With new vigour I applied myself to my examination of the old chateau and its contents.

It was upon one of the longest of all my excursions of discovery in the deserted portion of the castle, less than a week before that fatal hour which I felt must mark the utmost limit of my stay on earth, beyond which I could have not even the slightest hope of continuing to draw breath, that I came upon the culminating event of my whole life. I had spent the better part of the morning in climbing up and down half-ruined staircases in one of the most dilapidated of the ancient turrets. As the afternoon progressed, I sought the lower levels, descending into what appeared to be either a mediaeval place of confinement, or a more recently excavated storehouse for gunpowder. As I slowly traversed the nitre-encrusted passageway at the foot of the last staircase, the paving became very damp, and soon I saw by the light of my flickering torch that a blank, water-stained wall impeded my journey. Turning to retrace my steps, my eye fell upon a small trap-door with a ring, which lay directly beneath my feet. Pausing, I succeeded with difficulty in raising it, whereupon there was revealed a black aperture, exhaling noxious fumes which caused my torch to sputter, and disclosing in the unsteady glare the top of a flight of stone steps. As soon as the torch, which I lowered into the repellent depths, burned freely and steadily, I commenced my descent. The steps were many, and led to a narrow stone-flagged passage which I knew must be far underground. The passage proved of great length, and terminated in a massive oaken door, dripping with the moisture of the place, and stoutly resisting all my attempts to open it. Ceasing after a time my efforts in this direction, I had proceeded back some distance toward the steps, when there suddenly fell to my experience one of the most profound and maddening shocks capable of reception by the human mind. Without warning, I heard the heavy door behind me creak slowly open upon its rusted hinges. My immediate sensations are incapable of analysis. To be confronted in a place as thoroughly deserted as I had deemed the old castle with evidence of the presence of man or spirit, produced in my brain a horror of the most acute description. When at last I turned and faced the seat of the sound, my eyes must have started from their orbits at the sight that they beheld. There in the ancient Gothic doorway stood a human figure. It was that of a man clad in a skull-cap and long mediaeval tunic of dark colour. His long hair and flowing beard were of a terrible and intense black hue, and of incredible profusion. His forehead, high beyond the usual dimensions; his cheeks, deep-sunken and heavily lined with wrinkles; and his hands, long, claw-like, and gnarled, were of such a deathly, marble-like whiteness as I have never elsewhere seen in man. His figure, lean to the proportions of a skeleton, was strangely bent and almost lost within the voluminous folds of his peculiar garment. But strangest of all were his eyes; twin caves of abysmal blackness, profound in expression of understanding, yet inhuman in degree of wickedness. These were now fixed upon me, piercing my soul with their hatred, and rooting me to the spot whereon I stood. At last the figure spoke in a rumbling voice that chilled me through with its dull hollowness and latent malevolence. The language in which the discourse was clothed was that debased form of Latin in use amongst the more learned men of the Middle Ages, and made familiar to me by my prolonged researches into the works of the old alchemists and daemonologists. The apparition spoke of the curse which had hovered over my house, told me of my coming end, dwelt on the wrong perpetrated by my ancestor against old Michel Mauvais, and gloated over the revenge of Charles Le Sorcier. He told how the young Charles had escaped into the night, returning in after years to kill Godfrey the heir with an arrow just as he approached the age which had been his father's at his assassination; how he had secretly returned to the estate and established himself, unknown, in the even then deserted subterranean chamber whose doorway now framed the hideous narrator; how he had seized Robert, son of Godfrey, in a field, forced poison down his throat, and left him to die at the age of thirty-two, thus maintaining the foul provisions of his vengeful curse. At this point I was left to imagine the solution of the greatest mystery of all, how the curse had been fulfilled since that time when Charles Le Sorcier must in the course of Nature have died, for the man digressed into an account of the deep alchemical studies of the two wizards, father and son, speaking most particularly of the researches of Charles Le Sorcier concerning the elixir which should grant to him who partook of it eternal life and youth.

His enthusiasm had seemed for the moment to remove from his terrible eyes the hatred that had at first so haunted them, but suddenly the fiendish glare returned, and with a shocking sound like the hissing of a serpent, the stranger raised a glass phial with the evident intent of ending my life as had Charles Le Sorcier, six hundred years before, ended that of my ancestor. Prompted by some preserving instinct of self-defence, I broke through the spell that had hitherto held me immovable, and flung my now dying torch at the creature who menaced my existence. I heard the phial break harmlessly against the stones of the passage as the tunic of the strange man caught fire and lit the horrid scene with a ghastly radiance. The shriek of fright and impotent malice emitted by the would-be assassin proved too much for my already shaken nerves, and I fell prone upon the slimy floor in a total faint.

When at last my senses returned, all was frightfully dark, and my mind remembering what had occurred, shrank from the idea of beholding more; yet curiosity overmastered all. Who, I asked myself, was this man of evil, and how came he within the castle walls? Why should he seek to avenge the death of poor Michel Mauvais, and how had the curse been carried on through all the long centuries since the time of Charles Le Sorcier? The dread of years was lifted from my shoulders, for I knew that he whom I had felled was the source of all my danger from the curse; and now that I was free, I burned with the desire to learn more of the sinister thing which had haunted my line for centuries, and made of my own youth one long-continued nightmare. Determined upon further exploration, I felt in my pockets for flint and steel, and lit the unused torch which I had with me. First of all, the new light revealed the distorted and blackened form of the mysterious stranger. The hideous eyes were now closed. Disliking the sight, I turned away and entered the chamber beyond the Gothic door. Here I found what seemed much like an alchemist's laboratory. In one corner was an immense pile of a shining yellow metal that sparkled gorgeously in the light of the torch. It may have been gold, but I did not pause to examine it, for I was strangely affected by that which I had undergone. At the farther end of the apartment was an opening leading out into one of the many wild ravines of the dark hillside forest. Filled with wonder, yet now realising how the man had obtained access to the chateau, I proceeded to return. I had intended to pass by the remains of the stranger with averted face, but as I approached the body, I seemed to hear emanating from it a faint sound, as though life were not yet wholly extinct. Aghast, I turned to examine the charred and shrivelled figure on the floor. Then all at once the horrible eyes, blacker even than the seared face in which they were set, opened wide with an expression which I was unable to interpret. The cracked lips tried to frame words which I could not well understand. Once I caught the name of Charles Le Sorcier, and again I fancied that the words "years" and "curse" issued from the twisted mouth. Still I was at a loss to gather the purport of his disconnected speech. At my evident ignorance of his meaning, the pitchy eyes once more flashed malevolently at me, until, helpless as I saw my opponent to be, I trembled as I watched him.

Suddenly the wretch, animated with his last burst of strength, raised his hideous head from the damp and sunken pavement. Then, as I remained, paralysed with fear, he found his voice and in his dying breath screamed forth those words which have ever afterward haunted my days and my nights. "Fool," he shrieked, "can you not guess my secret? Have you no brain whereby you may recognise the will which has through six long centuries fulfilled the dreadful curse upon your house? Have I not told you of the great elixir of eternal life? Know you not how the secret of Alchemy was solved? I tell you, it is I! I! I! that have lived for six hundred years to maintain my revenge, FOR I AM CHARLES LE SORCIER!"

1917.

A Return to the Field.

H.P. Lovecraft was 27 years old in 1917, when he turned his literary talents once again to the writing of weird fiction after nine years of writing almost nothing but nonfiction and obsolescent poetry.

"I wish I had not dropped [fiction] writing in the nine years between 1908 and 1917," he wrote in a letter that year.

But if a decade of immersion in the style and conventions of the late 1700s hadn't left Lovecraft with much marketable poetry, it turned out to have been a fantastic training regimen for the kind of fiction writing that would shortly make him famous — although, alas, never rich. And Lovecraft clearly saw immediately that he had found a new literary passion.

These short works — "The Tomb" and "Dagon" especially — were very well received among Lovecraft's amateur-press colleagues. However, it's important to remember that at this time, weird fiction was strictly a hobby for Lovecraft — or, more accurately, a minor part of a hobby. During 1917, Lovecraft's primary preoccupation was with his amateur-press activities — publishing, writing nonfiction and hammering out poetry in the style of the 1700s. He may have suspected he was onto something good, but he had yet to figure out how important fiction writing would be in his life, and in the lives of generations of like-minded souls in years to come.

The Tomb.

4,100-WORD SHORT STORY; 1917.

This 4,000-word short story was H.P. Lovecraft's first professional-grade contribution to the field of weird fiction. Although its plot was not up to the standards of Lovecraft's later work, it's still a whacking great story, already drenched with the layered ambiance of sublime, cryptic dread that would soon make its author famous. Possibly the best thing about "The Tomb" is the Georgian poetry which Lovecraft deftly mixes into it, making it a nice transition between his old writing practice and the new one on which he was just embarking.

"The Tomb" was written in June of 1917, at around the same time Lovecraft was starting into writing patriotic poems and exhortations in support of the Allied war effort in the First World War. It was published for the first time considerably later, in the March 1922 issue of W. Paul Cook's amateur journal, The Vagrant.

Sedibus ut saltem placidis in morte quiescam.

— VIRGIL.

In relating the circumstances which have led to my confinement within this refuge for the demented, I am aware that my present position will create a natural doubt of the authenticity of my narrative. It is an unfortunate fact that the bulk of humanity is too limited in its mental vision to weigh with patience and intelligence those isolated

The Tomb

by H. P. Lovecraft

Weird Tales, January 1926

phenomena, seen and felt only by a psychologically sensitive few, which lie outside its common experience. Men of broader intellect know that there is no sharp distinction betwixt the real and the unreal; that all things appear as they do only by virtue of the delicate individual physical and mental media through which we are made conscious of them; but the prosaic materialism of the majority condemns as madness the flashes of super-sight which penetrate the common veil of obvious empiricism.

My name is Jervas Dudley, and from earliest childhood I have been a dreamer and a visionary. Wealthy beyond the necessity of a commercial life, and temperamentally unfitted for the formal studies and social recreations of my acquaintances, I have dwelt ever in realms apart from the visible world; spending my youth and adolescence in ancient and little-known books, and in roaming the fields and groves of the region near my ancestral home. I do not think that what I read in these books or saw in these fields and groves was exactly what other boys read and saw there; but of this I must say little, since detailed speech would but confirm those cruel slanders upon my intellect which I sometimes overhear from the whispers of the stealthy attendants around me. It is sufficient for me to relate events without analysing causes.

I have said that I dwelt apart from the visible world, but I have not said that I dwelt alone. This no human creature may do; for lacking the fellowship of the living, he inevitably draws upon the companionship of things that are not, or are no longer, living. Close by my home there lies a singular wooded hollow, in whose twilight deeps I spent most of my time; reading, thinking and dreaming. Down its moss-covered slopes my first steps of infancy were taken, and around its grotesquely gnarled oak trees my first fancies of boyhood were woven. Well did I come to know the presiding dryads of those trees, and often have I watched their wild dances in the struggling beams of waning moon — but of these things I must not now speak. I will tell only of the lone tomb in the darkest of the hillside thickets; the deserted tomb of the Hydes, an old and exalted family whose last direct descendant had been laid within its black recesses many decades before my birth.

The vault to which I refer is an ancient granite, weathered and discoloured by the mists and dampness of generations. Excavated back into the hillside, the structure is visible only at the entrance. The door, a ponderous and forbidding slab of stone, hangs upon rusted iron hinges, and is fastened ajar in a queerly sinister way by means of heavy iron chains and padlocks, according to a gruesome fashion of half a century ago. The abode of the race whose scions are inurned had once crowned the declivity which holds the tomb, but had long since fallen victim to the flames which sprang up from a disastrous stroke of lightning. Of the midnight storm which destroyed this gloomy mansion, the older inhabitants of the region sometimes speak in hushed and uneasy voices; alluding to what they call "divine wrath" in a manner that in later years vaguely increased the always strong fascination which I felt for the forest-darkened sepulchre. One man only had perished in the fire. When the last of the Hydes was buried in this place of shade and stillness, the sad urnful of ashes had come from a distant land; to which the family had repaired when the mansion burned down. No one remains to lay flowers before the granite portal, and few care to brave the depressing shadows which seem to linger strangely about the water-worn stones.

I shall never forget the afternoon when first I stumbled upon the half-hidden house of the dead. It was in mid-summer, when the alchemy of Nature transmutes the sylvan landscape to one vivid and almost homogeneous mass of green; when the senses are well-nigh intoxicated with the surging seas of moist verdure and the subtly indefinable odours of the soil and the vegetation. In such surroundings the mind loses its perspective; time and space become trivial and unreal, and echoes of a forgotten prehistoric past beat insistently upon the enthralled consciousness. All day I had been wandering through the mystic groves of the hollow; thinking thoughts I need not discuss, and conversing with things I need not name. In years a child of ten, I had seen and heard many wonders unknown to the throng; and was oddly aged in certain respects. When, upon forcing my way between two savage clumps of briers, I suddenly encountered the entrance of the vault, I had no knowledge of what I had discovered. The dark blocks of granite, the door so curiously ajar, and the funereal carvings above the arch, arounsed in me no associations of mournful or terrible character. Of graves and tombs I knew and imagined much, but had on account of my peculiar temperament been kept from all personal contact with churchyards and cemeteries. The strange stone house on the woodland slope was to me only a source of interest and speculation; and its cold, damp interior, into which I vainly peered through the aperture so tantalisingly left, contained for me no hint of death or decay. But in that instant of curiosity was born the madly unreasoning desire which has brought me to this hell of confinement. Spurred on by a voice which must have come from the hideous soul of the forest, I resolved to enter the beckoning gloom in spite of the ponderous chains which barred my passage. In the waning light of day I alternately rattled the rusty impediments with a view to throwing wide the stone door, and essayed to squeeze my slight form through the space already provided; but neither plan met with success. At first curious, I was now frantic; and when in the thickening twilight I returned to my home, I had sworn to the hundred gods of the grove that at any cost I would some day force an entrance to the black chilly depths that seemed calling out to me. The physician with the iron-grey beard who comes each day to my room once told a visitor that this decision marked the beginnings of a pitiful monomania; but I will leave final judgement to my readers when they shall have learnt all.

The months following my discovery were spent in futile attempts to force the complicated padlock of the slightly open vault, and in carefully guarded inquiries regarding the nature and history of the structure. With the traditionally receptive ears of the small boy, I learned much; though an habitual secretiveness caused me to tell no one of my information or my resolve. It is perhaps worth mentioning that I was not at all surprised or terrified on learning of the nature of the vault. My rather original ideas regarding life and death had caused me to associate the cold clay with the breathing body in a vague fashion; and I felt that the great sinister family of the burned-down mansion was in some way represented within the stone space I sought to explore. Mumbled tales of the weird rites and godless revels of bygone years in the ancient hall gave to me a new and potent interest in the tomb, before whose door I would sit for hours at a time each day. Once I thrust a candle within the nearly closed entrance, but could see nothing save a flight of damp stone steps leading downward. The odour of the place repelled yet bewitched me. I felt I had known it before, in a past remote beyond all recollection; beyond even my tenancy of the body I now possess.

The year after I first beheld the tomb, I stumbled upon a worm-eaten translation of Plutarch's Lives in the book-filled attic of my home. Reading the life of Theseus, I was much impressed by that passage telling of the great stone beneath which the boyish hero was to find his tokens of destiny whenever he should become old enough to lift its enourmous weight. This legend had the effect of dispelling my keenest impatience to enter the vault, for it made me feel that the time was not yet ripe. Later, I told myself, I should grow to a strength and ingenuity which might enable me to unfasten the heavily chained door with ease; but until then I would do better by conforming to what seemed the will of Fate.

Accordingly my watches by the dank portal became less persistent, and much of my time was spent in other though equally strange pursuits. I would sometimes rise very quietly in the night, stealing out to walk in those churchyards and places of burial from which I had been kept by my parents. What I did there I may not say, for I am not now sure of the reality of certain things; but I know that on the day after such a nocturnal ramble I would often astonish those about me with my knowledge of topics almost forgotten for many generations. It was after a night like this that I shocked the community with a queer conceit about the burial of the rich and celebrated Squire Brewster, a maker of local history who was interred in 1711, and whose slate headstone, bearing a graven skull and crossbones, was slowly crumbling to power. In a moment of childish imagination I vowed not only that the undertaker, Goodman Simpson, had stolen the silver-buckled shoes, silken hose, and satin small-clothes of the deceased before burial; but that the Squire himself, not fully inanimate, had turned twice in his mound-covered coffin on the day of interment.

But the idea of entering the tomb never left my thoughts; being indeed stimulated by the unexpected genealogical discover that my own maternal ancestry possessed at least a slight link with the supposedly extinct family of the Hydes. Last of my paternal race, I was likewise the last of this older and more mysterious line. I began to feel that the tomb was mine, and to look forward with hot eagerness to the time when I might pass within that stone door and down those slimy stone steps in the dark. I now formed the habit of listening very intently at the slightly open portal, choosing my favourite hours of midnight stillness for the odd vigil. By the time I came of age, I had made a small clearing in the thicket before the mould-stained facade of the hillside, allowing the surrounding vegetation to encircle and overhang the space like the walls and rzoof of sylvan bower. This bower was my temple, the fastened door my shrine, and here I would lie outstretched on the mossy ground, thinking strange thoughts and dreaming of strange dreams.

The night of the first revelation was a sultry one. I must have fallen asleep from fatigue, for it was with a distinct sense of awakening that I heard the voices. Of those tones and accents I hesitate to speak; of their quality I will not speak; but I may say that they presented certain uncanny differences in vocabulary, pronunciation, and mode of utterance. Every shade of New England dialect, from the uncouth syllables of the Puritan colonists to the precise rhetoric of fifty years ago, seemed represented in that shadowy colloquy, though it was only later that I noticed the fact. At the time, indeed, my attention was distracted from this matter by another phenomenon; a phenomenon so fleeting that I could not take oath upon its reality. I barely fancied that as I awoke, a light had been hurriedly extinguished within the sunken sepulchre. I do not think I was either astounded or panic-stricken, but I know that I was greatly and permanently changed that night. Upon returning home I went with much directness to a rotting chest in the attic, wherein I found the key which next day unlocked with ease the barrier I had so long stormed in vain.

It was in the soft glow of late afternoon that I first entered the vault on the abandoned slope. A spell was upon me, and my heart leaped with an exultation I can but ill describe. As I closed the door behind me and descended the dripping steps by the light of my lone candle, I seemed to know the way; and though the candle sputtered with the stifling reek of the place, I felt singularly at home in the musty, charnel-house air. Looking about me, I beheld many marble slabs bearing coffins, or the remains of coffins. Some of these were sealed and intact, but others had nearly vanished, leaving the silver handles and plates isolated amidst certain curious heaps of whitish dust. Upon one plate I read the name of Sir Geoffrey Hyde, who had come from Sussex in 1640 and died here a few years later. In a conspicuous alcove was one fairly well-preserved and untenanted casket, adorned with a single name which brought to me both a smile and a shudder. An odd impulse caused me to climb upon the broad slab, extinguish my candle, and lie down within the vacant box.

In the grey light of dawn I staggered from the vault and locked the chain of the door behind me. I was no longer a young man, though but twenty-one winters had chilled my bodily frame. Early-rising villagers who observed my homeward progress looked at me strangely, and marvelled at the signs of ribald revelry which they saw in one whose life was known to be sober and solitary. I did not appear before my parents till after a long and refreshing sleep.

Henceforward I haunted the tomb each night; seeing, hearing, and doing things I must never reveal. My speech, always susceptible to environmental influences, was the first thing to succumb to the change; and my suddenly acquired archaism of diction was soon remarked upon. Later a queer boldness and recklessness came into my demeanour, till I unconsciously grew to possess the bearing of a man of the world despite my lifelong seclusion. My formerly silent tongue waxed voluble with the easy grace of a Chesterfield or the godless cynicism of a Rochester. I displayed a peculiar erudition utterly unlike the fantastic, monkish lore over which I had pored in youth; and covered the flyleaves of my books with facile impromptu epigrams which brought up suggestions of Gay, Prior, and the sprightliest of Augustan wits and rimesters. One morning at breakfast I came close to disaster by declaiming in palpably liquourish accents an effusion of eighteenth-century Bacchanalian mirth; a bit of Georgian playfulness never recorded in a book, which ran something like this:

Come hither, my lads, with your tankards of ale,
And drink to the present before it shall fail;
Pile each on your platter a mountain of beef,
For 'tis eating and drinking that bring us relief:
So fill up your glass,
So life will soon pass;
When you're dead ye'll ne'er drink to your king or your lass!

Anacreon had a red nose, so they say;
But what's a red nose if ye're happy and gay?
Gad split me! I'd rather be red whilst I'm here,
Than white as a lily — and dead half a year!
So Betty, my miss,
Come give me kiss;
In hell there's no innkeeper's daughter like this!

Young Harry, propp'd up just as straight as he's able,
Will soon lose his wig and slip under the table;
But fill up your goblets and pass 'em around —
Better under the table than under the ground!
So revel and chaff
As ye thirstily quaff:
Under six feet of dirt 'tis less easy to laugh!

The fiend strike me blue! I'm scarce able to walk,
And damn me if I can stand upright or talk!
Here, landlord, bid Betty to summon a chair;
I'll try home for a while, for my wife is not there!
So lend me a hand;
I'm not able to stand,
But I'm gay whilst I linger on top of the land!

About this time I conceived my present fear of fire and thunderstorms. Previously indifferent to such things, I had now an unspeakable horror of them; and would retire to the innermost recesses of the house whenever the heavens threatened an electrical display. A favourite haunt of mine during the day was the ruined cellar of the mansion that had burned down, and in fancy I would picture the structure as it had been in its prime. On one occasion I startled a villager by leading him confidently to a shallow sub-cellar, of whose existence I seemed to know in spite of the fact that it had been unseen and forgotten for many generations.

At last came that which I had long feared. My parents, alarmed at the altered manner and appearance of their only son, commenced to exert over my movements a kindly espionage which threatened to result in disaster. I had told no one of my visits to the tomb, having guarded my secret purpose with religious zeal since childhood; but now I was forced to exercise care in threading the mazes of the wooded hollow, that I might throw off a possible pursuer. My key to the vault I kept suspended from a cord about my neck, its presence known only to me. I never carried out of the sepulchre any of the things I came upon whilst within its walls.

One morning as I emerged from the damp tomb and fastened the chain of the portal with none too steady hand, I beheld in an adjacent thicket the dreaded face of a watcher. Surely the end was near; for my bower was discovered, and the objective of my nocturnal journeys revealed. The man did not accost me, so I hastened home in an effort to overhear what he might report to my careworn father. Were my sojourns beyond the chained door about to be proclaimed to the world? Imagine my delighted astonishment on hearing the spy inform my parent in cautious whisper that I had spent the night in the bower outside the tomb; my sleep-filmed eyes fixed upon the crevice where the padlocked portal stood ajar! By what miracle had the watcher been thus deluded? I was now convinced that a supernatural agency protected me. Made bold by this heaven-sent circumstance, I began to resume perfect openness in going to the vault; confident that no one could witness my entrance. For a week I tasted to the full the joys of that charnel conviviality which I must not describe, when the thing happened, and I was borne away to this accursed abode of sorrow and monotony.

I should not have ventured out that night; for the taint of thunder was in the clouds, and hellish phosphorescence rose from the rank swamp at the bottom of the hollow. The call of the dead, too, was different. Instead of the hillside tomb, it was the charred cellar on the crest of the slope whose presiding daemon beckoned to me with unseen fingers. As I emerged from an intervening grove upon the plain before the ruin, I beheld in the misty moonlight a thing I had always vaguely expected. The mansion, gone for a century, once more reared its stately height to the raptured vision; every window ablaze with the splendour of many candles. Up the long drive rolled the coaches of the Boston gentry, whilst on foot came a numerous assemblage of powdered exquisites from the neighbouring mansions. With this throng I mingled, though I knew I belonged with the hosts rather than the guests. Inside the hall were music, laughter, and wine on every hand. Several faces I recognised; though I should have known them better had they been shrivelled or eaten away by death and decomposition. Amidst a wild and reckless throng I was the wildest and most abandoned. Gay blasphemy poured in torrents from my lips, and in my shocking sallies I heeded no law of God, Man, or Nature. Suddenly a peal of thunder, resonant even above the din of the swinish revelry, clave the very roof and laid a hush of fear upon the boisterous company. Red tongues of flame and searing gusts of heat engulfed the house; and the roysterers, struck with terror at the descent of a calamity which seemed to transcend the bounds of unguided Nature, fled shrieking into the night. I alone remained, riveted to my seat by a grovelling fear which I had never felt before. And then a second horror took possession of my soul. Burnt alive to ashes, my body dispersed by the four winds, I might never lie in the tomb of Hydes! Was not my coffin prepared for me? Had I not a right to rest till eternity amongst the descendants of Sir Geoffrey Hyde? Aye! I would claim my heritage of death, even though my soul go seeking through the ages for another corporeal tenement to represent it on that vacant slab in the alcove of the vault. Jervas Hyde should never share the sad fate of Palinurus!

As the phantom of the burning house faded, I found myself screaming and struggling madly in the arms of two men, one of whom was the spy who had followed me to the tomb. Rain was pouring down in torrents, and upon the southern horizon were flashes of the lightning that had so lately passed over our heads. My father, his face lined with sorrow, stood by as I shouted my demands to be laid within the tomb; frequently admonishing my captors to treat me as gently as they could. A blackened circle on the floor of the ruined cellar told of a violent stroke from the heavens; and from this spot a group of curious villagers with lanterns were prying a small box of antique workmanship which the thunderbolt had brought to light. Ceasing my futile and now objectless writhing, I watched the spectators as they viewed the treasure-trove, and was permitted to share in their discoveries. The box, whose fastenings were broken by the stroke which had unearthed it, contained many papers and objects of value; but I had eyes for one thing alone. It was the porcelain miniature of a young man in a smartly curled bag-wig, and bore the initials "J.H." The face was such that as I gazed, I might well have been studying my mirror.

On the following day I was brought to this room with the barred windows, but I have been kept informed of certain things through an aged and simple-minded servitor, for whom I bore a fondness in infancy, and who like me loves the churchyard. What I have dared relate of my experiences within the vault has brought me only pitying smiles. My father, who visits me frequently, declares that at no time did I pass the chained portal, and swears that the rusted padlock had not been touched for fifty years when he examined it. He even says that all the village knew of my journeys to the tomb, and that I was often watched as I slept in the bower outside the grim facade, my half-open eyes fixed on the crevice that leads to the interior. Against these assertions I have no tangible proof to offer, since my key to the padlock was lost in the struggle on that night of horrors. The strange things of the past which I learnt during those nocturnal meetings with the dead he dismisses as the fruits of my lifelong and omnivorous browsing amongst the ancient volumes of the family library. Had it not been for my old servant Hiram, I should have by this time become quite convinced of my madness.

But Hiram, loyal to the last, has held faith in me, and has done that which impels me to make public at least a part of my story. A week ago he burst open the lock which chains the door of the tomb perpetually ajar, and descended with a lantern into the murky depths. On a slab in an alcove he found an old but empty coffin whose tarnished plate bears the single word "Jervas." In that coffin and in that vault they have promised me I shall be buried.

Dagon.

2,200-WORD SHORT STORY; 1917.

This short story became one of H.P. Lovecraft's most influential tales, if not a particularly famous one. It is in "Dagon" that we first see the "cyclopean ruins rising from the depths of the sea" motif, which has become almost a cliché, along with the borrowing of made-up "half-forgotten myths" of gods of ancient civilizations. It also clearly stakes out Lovecraft's intended focus, in his weird fiction, of maintaining plausibility; nothing that happens in "Dagon" is physically impossible, and nothing in the story depends on supernatural or magical forces to work.

"Dagon" may have been inspired by a short story Lovecraft had read in a pulp magazine four years earlier: "Fishhead," by Irwin S. Cobb. But it's completely different from Cobb's story, and in no sense derivative.

It was written in July of 1917, a month or so after "The Tomb," and was published, to considerable acclaim, in the November 1919 issue of W. Paul Cook's amateur journal, The Vagrant.

I am writing this under an appreciable mental strain, since by tonight I shall be no more. Penniless, and at the end of my supply of the drug which alone makes life endurable, I can bear the torture no longer; and shall cast myself from this garret window into the squalid street below. Do not think from my slavery to morphine that I am a weakling or a degenerate. When you have read these hastily scrawled pages you may guess, though never fully realise, why it is that I must have forgetfulness or death.

It was in one of the most open and least frequented parts of the broad Pacific that the packet of which I was supercargo fell a victim to the German sea-raider. The great war was then at its very beginning, and the ocean forces of the Hun had not completely sunk to their later degradation; so that our vessel was made legitimate prize, whilst we of her crew were treated with all the fairness and consideration due us as naval prisoners. So liberal, indeed, was the discipline of our captors, that five days after we were taken I managed to escape alone in a small boat with water and provisions for a good length of time.

When I finally found myself adrift and free, I had but little idea of my surroundings. Never a competent navigator, I could only guess vaguely by the sun and stars that I was somewhat south of the equator. Of the longitude I knew nothing, and no island or coast-line was in sight. The weather kept fair, and for uncounted days I drifted aimlessly beneath the scorching sun; waiting either for some passing ship, or to be cast on the shores of some habitable land. But neither ship nor land appeared, and I began to despair in my solitude upon the heaving vastnesses of unbroken blue.

The change happened whilst I slept. Its details I shall never know; for my slumber, though troubled and dream-infested, was continuous. When at last I awaked, it was to discover myself half sucked into a slimy expanse of hellish black mire which extended about me in monotonous undulations as far as I could see, and in which my boat lay grounded some distance away.

Though one might well imagine that my first sensation would be of wonder at so prodigious and unexpected a transformation of scenery, I was in reality more horrified than astonished; for there was in the air and in the rotting soil a sinister quality which chilled me to the very core. The region was putrid with the carcasses of decaying fish, and of other less describable things which I saw protruding from the nasty mud of the unending plain. Perhaps I should not hope to convey in mere words the unutterable hideousness that can dwell in absolute silence and barren immensity. There was nothing within hearing, and nothing in sight save a vast reach of black slime; yet the very completeness of the stillness and homogeneity of the landscape oppressed me with a nauseating fear.

Weird Tales, October 1923

The sun was blazing down from a sky which seemed to me almost black in its cloudless cruelty; as though reflecting the inky marsh beneath my feet. As I crawled into the stranded boat I realised that only one theory could explain my position. Through some unprecedented volcanic upheaval, a portion of the ocean floor must have been thrown to the surface, exposing regions which for innumerable millions of years had lain hidden under unfathomable watery depths. So great was the extent of the new land which had risen beneath me, that I could not detect the faintest noise of the surging ocean, strain my ears as I might. Nor were there any sea-fowl to prey upon the dead things.

For several hours I sat thinking or brooding in the boat, which lay upon its side and afforded a slight shade as the sun moved across the heavens. As the day progressed, the ground lost some of its stickiness, and seemed likely to dry sufficiently for travelling purposes in a short time. That night I slept but little, and the next day I made for myself a pack containing food and water, preparatory to an overland journey in search of the vanished sea and possible rescue.

On the third morning I found the soil dry enough to walk upon with ease. The odour of the fish was maddening; but I was too much concerned with graver things to mind so slight an evil, and set out boldly for an unknown goal. All day I forged steadily westward, guided by a far-away hummock which rose higher than any other elevation on the rolling desert. That night I encamped, and on the following day still travelled toward the hummock, though that object seemed scarcely nearer than when I had first espied it. By the fourth evening I attained the base of the mound which turned out to be much higher than it had appeared from a distance, an intervening valley setting it out in sharper relief from the general surface. Too weary to ascend, I slept in the shadow of the hill.

I know not why my dreams were so wild that night; but ere the waning and fantastically gibbous moon had risen far above the eastern plain, I was awake in a cold perspiration, determined to sleep no more. Such visions as I had experienced were too much for me to endure again. And in the glow of the moon I saw how unwise I had been to travel by day. Without the glare of the parching sun, my journey would have cost me less energy; indeed, I now felt quite able to perform the ascent which had deterred me at sunset. Picking up my pack, I started for the crest of the eminence.

I have said that the unbroken monotony of the rolling plain was a source of vague horror to me; but I think my horror was greater when I gained the summit of the mound and looked down the other side into an immeasurable pit or canyon, whose black recesses the moon had not yet soared high enough to illuminate. I felt myself on the edge of the world; peering over the rim into a fathomless chaos of eternal night. Through my terror ran curious reminiscences of Paradise Lost, and of Satan's hideous climb through the unfashioned realms of darkness.

As the moon climbed higher in the sky, I began to see that the slopes of the valley were not quite so perpendicular as I had imagined. Ledges and outcroppings of rock afforded fairly easy foot-holds for a descent, whilst after a drop of a few hundred feet, the declivity became very gradual. Urged on by an impulse which I cannot definitely analyse, I scrambled with difficulty down the rocks and stood on the gentler slope beneath, gazing into the Stygian deeps where no light had yet penetrated.

All at once my attention was captured by a vast and singular object on the opposite slope, which rose steeply about an hundred yards ahead of me; an object that gleamed whitely in the newly bestowed rays of the ascending moon. That it was merely a gigantic piece of stone, I soon assured myself; but I was conscious of a distinct impression that its contour and position were not altogether the work of Nature. A closer scrutiny filled me with sensations I cannot express; for despite its enormous magnitude, and its position in an abyss which had yawned at the bottom of the sea since the world was young, I perceived beyond a doubt that the strange object was a well-shaped monolith whose massive bulk had known the workmanship and perhaps the worship of living and thinking creatures.

Dazed and frightened, yet not without a certain thrill of the scientist's or archaeologist's delight, I examined my surroundings more closely. The moon, now near the zenith, shone weirdly and vividly above the towering steeps that hemmed in the chasm, and revealed the fact that a far-flung body of water flowed at the bottom, winding out of sight in both directions, and almost lapping my feet as I stood on the slope. Across the chasm, the wavelets washed the base of the Cyclopean monolith; on whose surface I could now trace both inscriptions and crude sculptures. The writing was in a system of hieroglyphics unknown to me, and unlike anything I had ever seen in books; consisting for the most part of conventionalised aquatic symbols such as fishes, eels, octopi, crustaceans, molluscs, whales, and the like. Several characters obviously represented marine things which are unknown to the modern world, but whose decomposing forms I had observed on the ocean-risen plain.

It was the pictorial carving, however, that did most to hold me spellbound. Plainly visible across the intervening water on account of their enormous size, were an array of bas-reliefs whose subjects would have excited the envy of Doré. I think that these things were supposed to depict men — at least, a certain sort of men; though the creatures were shewn disporting like fishes in waters of some marine grotto, or paying homage at some monolithic shrine which appeared to be under the waves as well. Of their faces and forms I dare not speak in detail; for the mere remembrance makes me grow faint. Grotesque beyond the imagination of a Poe or a Bulwer, they were damnably human in general outline despite webbed hands and feet, shockingly wide and flabby lips, glassy, bulging eyes, and other features less pleasant to recall. Curiously enough, they seemed to have been chiselled badly out of proportion with their scenic background; for one of the creatures was shewn in the act of killing a whale represented as but little larger than himself. I remarked, as I say, their grotesqueness and strange size, but in a moment decided that they were merely the imaginary gods of some primitive fishing or seafaring tribe; some tribe whose last descendant had perished eras before the first ancestor of the Piltdown or Neanderthal Man was born. Awestruck at this unexpected glimpse into a past beyond the conception of the most daring anthropologist, I stood musing whilst the moon cast queer reflections on the silent channel before me.

Then suddenly I saw it. With only a slight churning to mark its rise to the surface, the thing slid into view above the dark waters. Vast, Polyphemus-like, and loathsome, it darted like a stupendous monster of nightmares to the monolith, about which it flung its gigantic scaly arms, the while it bowed its hideous head and gave vent to certain measured sounds. I think I went mad then.

Of my frantic ascent of the slope and cliff, and of my delirious journey back to the stranded boat, I remember little. I believe I sang a great deal, and laughed oddly when I was unable to sing. I have indistinct recollections of a great storm some time after I reached the boat; at any rate, I know that I heard peals of thunder and other tones which Nature utters only in her wildest moods.

When I came out of the shadows I was in a San Francisco hospital; brought thither by the captain of the American ship which had picked up my boat in mid-ocean. In my delirium I had said much, but found that my words had been given scant attention. Of any land upheaval in the Pacific, my rescuers knew nothing; nor did I deem it necessary to insist upon a thing which I knew they could not believe. Once I sought out a celebrated ethnologist, and amused him with peculiar questions regarding the ancient Philistine legend of Dagon, the Fish-God; but soon perceiving that he was hopelessly conventional, I did not press my inquiries.

It is at night, especially when the moon is gibbous and waning, that I see the thing. I tried morphine; but the drug has given only transient surcease, and has drawn me into its clutches as a hopeless slave. So now I am to end it all, having written a full account for the information or the contemptuous amusement of my fellow-men. Often I ask myself if it could not all have been a pure phantasm — a mere freak of fever as I lay sun-stricken and raving in the open boat after my escape from the German man-of-war. This I ask myself, but ever does there come before me a hideously vivid vision in reply. I cannot think of the deep sea without shuddering at the nameless things that may at this very moment be crawling and floundering on its slimy bed, worshipping their ancient stone idols and carving their own detestable likenesses on submarine obelisks of water-soaked granite. I dream of a day when they may rise above the billows to drag down in their reeking talons the remnants of puny, war-exhausted mankind — of a day when the land shall sink, and the dark ocean floor shall ascend amidst universal pandemonium.

The end is near. I hear a noise at the door, as of some immense slippery body lumbering against it. It shall not find me. God, that hand! The window! The window!

A Reminiscence of Dr. Samuel Johnson.

BY HUMPHREY LITTLEWIT, ESQ.

2,000-WORD SHORT STORY; 1917.

This witty little pseudo-memoir was a sort of wry tip of the hat to the Georgian-era phase of earlier times, and Lovecraft used the pseudonym "Humphrey Littlewit, Esq." when publishing it. It was apparently a playfully self-inflicted parody of Lovecraft's own affectations, as he was well known for styling himself as a Georgian gentleman.

He wrote it in August of 1917, and it first saw publication the following month, in the September 1917 issue of United Amateur.

The Privilege of Reminiscence, however rambling or tiresome, is one generally allow'd to the very aged; indeed, 'tis frequently by means of such Recollections that the obscure occurrences of History, and the lesser Anecdotes of the Great, are transmitted to Posterity.

Tho' many of my readers have at times observ'd and remark'd a Sort of antique Flow in my Stile of Writing, it hath pleased me to pass amongst the Members of this Generation as a young Man, giving out the Fiction that I was born in 1890, in America. I am now, however, resolv'd to unburthen myself of a Secret which I have hitherto kept thro' Dread of Incredulity; and to impart to the Publick a true knowledge of my long years, in order to gratifie their taste for authentick Information of an Age with whose famous Personages I was on familiar Terms. Be it then known that I was born on the family Estate in Devonshire, of the 10th day of August, 1690 (or in the new Gregorian Stile of Reckoning, the 20th of August), being therefore now in my 228th year. Coming early to London, I saw as a Child many of the celebrated Men of King William's Reign, including the lamented Mr. Dryden, who sat much at the Tables of Will's Coffee-House. With Mr. Addison and Dr. Swift I later became very well acquainted, and was an even more familiar Friend to Mr. Pope, whom I knew and respected till the Day of his Death. But since it is of my more recent Associate, the late Dr. Johnson, that I am at this time desir'd to write; I will pass over my Youth for the present.

I had first Knowledge of the Doctor in May of the year 1738, tho' I did not at that Time meet him. Mr. Pope had just compleated his Epilogue to his Satires (the Piece beginning: "Not twice a Twelvemonth you appear in Print."), and had arrang'd for its Publication. On the very Day it appear'd, there was also publish'd a Satire in Imitation of Juvenal, intitul'd "London," by the then unknown Johnson; and this so struck the Town, that many Gentlemen of Taste declared, it was the Work of a greater Poet than Mr. Pope. Notwithstanding what some Detractors have said of Mr. Pope's petty jealousy, he gave the Verses of his new Rival no small Praise; and having learnt thro' Mr. Richardson who the Poet was, told me, 'that Mr. Johnson wou'd soon be deterré'.

I had no personal Acquaintance with the Doctor till 1763, when I was presented to him at the Mitre Tavern by Mr. James Boswell, a young Scotchman of excellent Family and great Learning, but small Wit, whose metrical Effusions I had sometimes revis'd.

Dr. Johnson, as I beheld him, was a full, pursy Man, very ill drest, and of slovenly Aspect. I recall him to have worn a bushy Bob-Wig, untyed and without Powder, and much too small for his Head. His cloaths were of rusty brown, much wrinkled, and with more than one Button missing. His Face, too full to be handsom, was likewise marred by the Effects of some scrofulous Disorder; and his Head was continually rolling about in a sort of convulsive way. Of this Infirmity, indeed, I had known before; having heard of it from Mr. Pope, who took the Trouble to make particular Inquiries.

Being nearly seventy-three, full nineteen Years older than Dr. Johnson (I say Doctor, tho' his Degree came not till two Years afterward), I naturally expected him to have some Regard for my Age; and was therefore not in that Fear of him, which others confess'd. On my asking him what he thought of my favourable Notice of his Dictionary in The Londoner, my periodical Paper, he said: Sir, I possess no Recollection of having perus'd your Paper, and have not a great Interest in the Opinions of the less thoughtful Part of Mankind." Being more than a little piqued at the Incivility of one whose Celebrity made me solicitous of his Approbation, I ventur'd to retaliate in kind, and told him, I was surpris'd that a Man of Sense shou'd judge the Thoughtfulness of one whose Productions he admitted never having read. "Why, Sir," reply'd Johnson, "I do not require to become familiar with a Man's Writings in order to estimate the Superficiality of his Attainments, when he plainly shews it by his Eagerness to mention his own Productions in the first Question he puts to me." Having thus become Friends, we convers'd on many Matters. When, to agree with him, I said I was distrustful of the Authenticity of Ossian's Poems, Mr. Johnson said: "That, Sir, does not do your Understanding particular Credit; for what all the Town is sensible of, is no great Discovery for a Grub-Street Critick to make. You might as well say, you have a strong Suspicion that Milton wrote Paradise Lost!"

I thereafter saw Johnson very frequently, most often at Meetings of *THE LITERARY CLUB,* which was founded the next Year by the Doctor, together with Mr. Burke, the parliamentary Orator, Mr. Beauclerk, a Gentleman of Fashion, Mr. Langton, a pious Man and Captain of Militia, Sir J. Reynolds, the widely known Painter, Dr. Goldsmith, the prose and poetick Writer, Dr. Nugent, father-in-law to Mr. Burke, Sir John Hawkins, Mr. Anthony Charmier, and my self. We assembled generally at seven o'clock of an Evening, once a Week, at the Turk's-Head, in Gerrard-Street, Soho, till that Tavern was sold and made into a private Dwelling; after which Event we mov'd our Gatherings successively to Prince's in Sackville-Street, Le Tellier's in Dover-Street, and Parsloe's and The Thatched House in St. James's-Street. In these Meetings we preserv'd a remarkable Degree of Amity and Tranquillity, which contrasts very favourably with some of the Dissensions and Disruptions I observe in the literary and amateur Press Associations of today. This Tranquillity was the more remarkable, because we had amongst us Gentlemen of very opposed Opinions. Dr. Johnson and I, as well as many others, were high Tories; whilst Mr. Burke was a Whig, and against the American War, many of his Speeches on that Subject having been widely publish'd. The least congenial Member was one of the Founders, Sir John Hawkins, who hath since written many misrepresentations of our Society. Sir John, an eccentrick Fellow, once declin'd to pay his part of the Reckoning for Supper, because 'twas his Custom at Home to eat no Supper. Later he insulted Mr. Burke in so intolerable a Manner, that we all took Pains to shew our Disapproval; after which Incident he came no more to our Meetings. However, he never openly fell out with the Doctor, and was the Executor of his Will; tho' Mr. Boswell and others have Reason to question the genuineness of his Attachment. Other and later Members of the *CLUB* were Mr. David Garrick, the Actor and early Friend of Dr. Johnson, Messieurs Tho. and Jos. Warton, Dr. Adam Smith, Dr. Percy, Author of the Reliques, Mr. Edw. Gibbon, the Historian, Dr. Burney, the Musician, Mr. Malone, the Critick, and Mr. Boswell. Mr. Garrick obtain'd Admittance only with Difficulty; for the Doctor, notwithstanding his great Friendship, was for ever affecting to decry the Stage and all Things connected with it. Johnson, indeed, had a most singular Habit of speaking for Davy when others were against him, and of arguing against him, when others were for him. I have no Doubt that he sincerely lov'd Mr. Garrick, for he never alluded to him as he did to Foote, who was a very coarse Fellow despite his comick Genius. Mr. Gibbon was none too well lik'd, for he had an odious sneering Way which offended even those of us who most admir'd his historical Productions. Mr. Goldsmith, a little Man very vain of his Dress and very deficient in Brilliancy of Conversation, was my particular Favourite; since I was equally unable to shine in the Discourse. He was vastly jealous of Dr. Johnson, tho' none the less liking and respecting him. I remember that once a Foreigner, a German, I think, was in our Company; and that whilst Goldsmith was speaking, he observ'd the Doctor preparing to utter something. Unconsciously looking upon Goldsmith as a meer Encumbrance when compar'd to the greater Man, the Foreigner bluntly interrupted him and incurr'd his lasting Hostility by crying, "Hush, Toctor Shonson iss going to speak!"

In this luminous Company I was tolerated more because of my Years than for my Wit or Learning; being no Match at all for the rest. My Friendship for the celebrated Monsieur Voltaire was ever a Cause of Annoyance to the Doctor; who was deeply orthodox, and who us'd to say of the French Philosopher: "Vir est acerrimi Ingenii et paucarum Literarum."

Mr. Boswell, a little teazing Fellow whom I had known for some Time previously, us'd to make Sport of my aukward Manners and old-fashion'd Wig and Cloaths. Once coming in a little the worse for Wine (to which he was addicted) he endeavour'd to lampoon me by means of an Impromptu in verse, writ on the Surface of the Table; but lacking the Aid he usually had in his Composition, he made a bad grammatical Blunder. I told him, he shou'd not try to pasquinade the Source of his Poesy. At another Time Bozzy (as we us'd to call him) complain'd of my Harshness toward new Writers in the Articles I prepar'd for The Monthly Review. He said, I push'd every Aspirant off the Slopes of Parnassus. "Sir," I reply'd, "you are mistaken. They who lose their Hold do so from their own Want of Strength; but desiring to conceal their Weakness, they attribute the Absence of Success to the first Critick that mentions them." I am glad to recall that Dr. Johnson upheld me in this Matter.

Dr. Johnson was second to no Man in the Pains he took to revise the bad Verses of others; indeed, 'tis said that in the book of poor blind old Mrs. Williams, there are scarce two lines which are not the Doctor's. At one Time Johnson recited to me some lines by a Servant to the Duke of Leeds, which had so amus'd him, that he had got them by Heart. They are on the Duke's Wedding, and so much resemble in Quality the Work of other and more recent poetick Dunces, that I cannot forbear copying them:

When the Duke of Leeds shall marry'd be
To a fine young Lady of high Quality
How happy will that Gentlewoman be
In his Grace of Leeds' good Company.

I ask'd the Doctor, if he had ever try'd making Sense of this Piece; and upon his saying he had not, I amus'd myself with the following Amendment of it:

When Gallant LEEDS auspiciously shall wed
The virtuous Fair, of antient Lineage bred,
How must the Maid rejoice with conscious Pride
To win so great an Husband to her Side!

On shewing this to Dr. Johnson, he said, "Sir, you have

straightened out the Feet, but you have put neither Wit nor Poetry into the Lines."

It wou'd afford me Gratification to tell more of my Experiences with Dr. Johnson and his circle of Wits; but I am an old Man, and easily fatigued. I seem to ramble along without much Logick or Continuity when I endeavour to recall the Past; and fear I light upon but few Incidents which others have not before discuss'd. Shou'd my present Recollections meet with Favour, I might later set down some further Anecdotes of old Times of which I am the only Survivor. I recall many things of Sam Johnson and his Club, having kept up my Membership in the Latter long after the Doctor's Death, at which I sincerely mourn'd. I remember how John Burgoyne, Esq., the General, whose Dramatick and Poetical Works were printed after his Death, was blackballed by three Votes; probably because of his unfortunate Defeat in the American War, at Saratoga. Poor John! His Son fared better, I think, and was made a Baronet. But I am very tired. I am old, very old, and it is Time for my Afternoon Nap.

Nemesis.

Poetry; 1917.

"Nemesis" is H.P. Lovecraft's most well-known poem, and stands close behind Edgar Allan Poe's "The Raven" in any ranking of the most appealing pieces of weird poetry of all time. It is one of several particularly relevant Lovecraft poems that we have included in this collection because of the outsize contribution they make to their author's literary legacy.

Lovecraft claimed, in a letter to Rheinhart Kleiner, that he dashed off "Nemesis" "in the sinister small hours of the black morning after Hallowe'en 1917." The first of its dozens of publishings happened a few months later, in the June 1918 issue of W. Paul Cook's amateur journal, The Vagrant.

Thro' the ghoul-guarded gateways of slumber,
Past the wan-moon'd abysses of night,
I have liv'd o'er my lives without number,
I have sounded all things with my sight;
And I struggle and shriek ere the daybreak,
    being driven to madness with fright.

I have whirl'd with the earth at the dawning,
When the sky was a vaporous flame;
I have seen the dark universe yawning,
Where the black planets roll without aim;
Where they roll in their horror unheeded,
    without knowledge or lustre or name.

I had drifted o'er seas without ending,
Under sinister grey-clouded skies
That the many-fork'd lightning is rending,
That resound with hysterical cries;
With the moans of invisible daemons
    that out of the green waters rise.

I have plung'd like a deer thro' the arches
Of the hoary primoridal grove,
Where the oaks feel the presence that marches
And stalks on where no spirit dares rove;
And I flee from a thing that surrounds me,
    and leers thro' dead branches above.

I have stumbled by cave-ridden mountains
That rise barren and bleak from the plain,
I have drunk of the fog-foetid fountains
That ooze down to the marsh and the main;
And in hot cursed tarns I have seen things
    I care not to gaze on again.

I have scann'd the vast ivy-clad palace,
I have trod its untenanted hall,
Where the moon writhing up from the valleys
Shews the tapestried things on the wall;
Strange figures discordantly woven,
    which I cannot endure to recall.

I have peer'd from the casement in wonder
At the mouldering meadows around,
At the many-roof'd village laid under
The curse of a grave girdled ground;
And from rows of white urn-carven marble
    I listen intently for sound.

I have haunted the tombs of the ages,
I have flown on the pinions of fear
Where the smoke-belching Erebus rages,
Where the jokulls loom snow-clad and drear:
And in realms where the sun of the desert
    consumes what it never can cheer.

I was old when the Pharaohs first mounted
The jewel-deck'd throne by the Nile;
I was old in those epochs uncounted
When I, and I only, was vile;
And Man, yet untainted and happy,
    dwelt in bliss on the far Arctic isle.

Oh, great was the sin of my spirit,
And great is the reach of its doom;
Not the pity of Heaven can cheer it,
Nor can respite be found in the tomb:
Down the infinite aeons come beating
    the wings of unmerciful gloom.

Thro' the ghoul-guarded gateways of slumber,
Past the wan-moon'd abysses of night,
I have liv'd o'er my lives without number,
I have sounded all things with my sight;
And I struggle and shriek ere the daybreak,
    being driven to madness with fright.

1918.

Starry Darkness.

Although H.P. Lovecraft did not contribute much to his weird-fiction canon during 1918, it was a pivotal year for him. This is the year in which he first received payment for his literary output (other than a prize won in his youth). His poem "On Receiving a Picture of the Marshes of Ipswitch," written the year before, was published in *The National Magazine* that year.

This was also the year in which Lovecraft really rose to prominence in the small but cultish world of amateur press, serving as the 1917-1918 president of the United Amateur Press Association.

Also in 1918, Lovecraft discovered that the friends and colleagues he had met through his hobby of amateur journalism would actually pay him for editorial services — from proofreading manuscripts up to and including ghost-writing full manuscripts, a service for which he charged $2.25 per manuscript page.

Within a year or so, ghostwriting, collaboration and editorial services would become Lovecraft's primary line of work. For the rest of his life, helping others with their manuscripts would be his main occupation, with his own work thrown in as a sort of a side hustle.

Psychopompos: A Tale in Rhyme.

BROADSIDE BALLAD;
1918.

At nearly 2,500 words, this poem is longer than many of Lovecraft's short stories; but, of course, that's exactly what it is — a short story set in iambic pentameter, with a two-stanza mood-setting introduction.

The story itself is the kind of old-fashioned, traditional werewolf tale that Lovecraft generally eschewed. But the combination of stilted, formal poetic form and wryly ironic narrative style yield an unusual literary experience for most modern readers — partly **because** *of the hackneyed plot concept.*

The real reason Lovecraft wrote it, however, may have been that he was making a study of the chapbooks and broadside ballads of the 16th and 17th centuries. These were cheap, poorly printed stories sold by itinerant author-vendors among the few English commoners who could read. Many of these were great big doggerelly poems (ballads) which told a complete story . . . in other words, something very similar to "Psychopompos." If you think about it, the format makes good sense for its time and place: since so few people could read, and all printed material was valuable, there was a demand for long-form stories phrased in such a way that they could be fairly easily memorized and even added to or "riffed on."

Perhaps Lovecraft wanted to see if that which was old could be made new again, and tried his hand at an imitation broadside ballad with a few tongue-in-cheek witticisms tucked into its text for the entertainment of his more modern readers. Or maybe he was simply indulging his antiquarianism. Either way, it's not an experiment that he ever repeated, so far as we know.

Lovecraft wrote it toward the end of the First World War, in June of 1918, shortly after writing a patriotic poem titled "The Volunteer," which was widely reprinted in regional and national newspapers.

As for "Psychopompos," it was first published in the October 1919 issue of W. Paul Cook's amateur journal, The Vagrant.

I am He who howls in the night;
I am He who moans in the snow;
I am He who hath never seen light;
I am He who mounts from below.

My car is the car of Death;
My wings are the wings of dread;
My breath is the north wind's breath;
My prey are the cold and the dead.

In old Auvergne, when schools were poor and few,
And peasants fancy'd what they scarcely knew,
When lords and gentry shunn'd their Monarch's throne
For solitary castles of their own,
There dwelt a man of rank, whose fortress stood
In the hush'd twilight of a hoary wood.
De Blois his name; his lineage high and vast,
A proud memorial of an honour'd past;
But curious swains would whisper now and then
That Sieur De Blois was not as other men.
In person dark and lean, with glossy hair,
And gleaming teeth that he would often bare,
With piercing eye, and stealthy roving glance,
And tongue that clipt the soft, sweet speech of France;
The Sieur was little lov'd and seldom seen,
So close he kept within his own demesne.

The castle servants, few, discreet, and old,
Full many a tale of strangeness might have told;
But bow'd with years, they rarely left the door
Wherein their sires and grandsires serv'd before.
Thus gossip rose, as gossip rises best,
When mystery imparts a keener zest;
Seclusion oft the poison tongue attracts,
And scandal prospers on a dearth of facts.
'Twas said, the Sieur had more than once been spy'd
Alone at midnight by the river's side,
With aspect so uncouth, and gaze so strange,
That rustics cross'd themselves to see the change;
Yet none, when press'd, could clearly say or know
Just what it was, or why they trembled so.
De Blois, as rumour whisper'd, fear'd to pray,
Nor us'd his chapel on the Sabbath day;
Howe'er this may have been, 'twas known at least
His household had no chaplain, monk, or priest.
But if the Master liv'd in dubious fame,
Twice fear'd and hated was his noble Dame;
As dark as he, in features wild and proud,
And with a weird supernal grace endow'd,
The haughty mistress scorn'd the rural train
Who sought to learn her source, but sought in vain.
Old women call'd her eyes too bright by half,
And nervous children shiver'd at her laugh;
Richard, the dwarf (whose word had little weight),
Vow'd she was like a serpent in her gait,
Whilst ancient Pierre (the aged often err)
Laid all her husband's mystery to her.
Still more absurd were those odd mutter'd things
That calumny to curious list'ners brings;
Those subtle slanders, told with downcast face,
And muffled voice — those tales no man may trace;
Tales that the faith of old wives can command,
Tho' always heard at sixth or seventh hand.
Thus village legend darkly would imply
That Dame De Blois possess'd an evil eye;
Or going further, furtively suggest
A lurking spark of sorcery in her breast;
Old Mère Allard (herself half witch) once said
The lady's glance work'd strangely on the dead.
So liv'd the pair, like many another two
That shun the crowd, and shrink from public view.
They scorn'd the doubts by ev'ry peasant shewn,
And ask'd but one thing — to be let alone!

'Twas Candlemas, the dreariest time of year,
With fall long gone, and spring too far to cheer,
When little Jean, the bailiff's son and heir,
Fell sick and threw the doctors in despair.
A child so stout and strong that few would think
An hour might carry him to death's dark brink,
Yet pale he lay, tho' hidden was the cause,
And Galens search'd in vain thro' Nature's laws.
But stricken sadness could not quite suppress
The roving thought, or wrinkled grandam's guess:
Tho' spoke by stealth, 'twas known to half a score
That Dame De Blois rode by the day before;
She had (they said) with glances weird and wild
Paus'd by the gate to view the prattling child,
Nor did they like the smile which seem'd to trace
New lines of evil on her proud, dark face.
These things they whisper'd, when the mother's cry
Told of the end — the gentle soul gone by;
In genuine grief the kindly watcher wept,
Whilst the lov'd babe with saints and angels slept.
The village priest his simple rites went thro',
And good Michel nail'd up the box of yew;

Around the corpse the holy candles burn'd,
The mourners sighed, the parents dumbly yearn'd.
Then one by one each sought his humble bed,
And left the lonely mother with her dead.

Late in the night it was, when o'er the vale
The storm-king swept with pandemoniac gale;
Deep pil'd the cruel snow, yet strange to tell,
The lightning sputter'd while the white flakes fell;
A hideous presence seem'd abroad to steal,
And terror sounded in the thunder's peal.
Within the house of grief the tapers glow'd
Whilst the poor mother bow'd beneath her load;
Her salty eyes too tired now to weep,
Too pain'd to see, too sad to close in sleep.
The clock struck three, above the tempest heard,
When something near the lifeless infant stirr'd;
Some slipp'ry thing, that flopp'd in awkward way,
And climb'd the table where the coffin lay;
With scaly convolutions strove to find
The cold, still clay that death had left behind.
The nodding mother hears — starts broad awake —
Empower'd to reason, yet too stunn'd to shake;
The pois'nous thing she sees, and nimbly foils
The ghoulish purpose of the quiv'ring coils:
With ready axe the serpent's head she cleaves,
And thrills with savage triumph whilst she grieves.
The injur'd reptile hissing glides from sight,
And hides its cloven carcass in the night.

The weeks slipp'd by, and gossip's tongue began
To call the Sieur De Blois an alter'd man;
With curious mien he oft would pace along
The village street, and eye the gaping throng.
Yet whilst he shew'd himself as ne'er before,
His wild-eyed lady was observ'd no more.
In course of time, 'twas scarce thought odd or ill
That he his ears with village lore should fill;
Nor was the town with special rumour rife
When he sought out the bailiff and his wife:
Their tale of sorrow, with its ghastly end,
Was told, indeed, by ev'ry wond'ring friend.
The Sieur heard all, and low'ring rode away,
Nor was he seen again for many a day.

When vernal sunshine shed its cheering glow,
And genial zephyrs blew away the snow,
To frighten'd swains a horror was reveal'd
In the damp herbage of a melting field.
There (half preserv'd by winter's frigid bed)
Lay the dark Dame De Blois, untimely dead;
By some assassin's stroke most foully slain,
Her shapely brow and temples cleft in twain.
Reluctant hands the dismal burden bore
To the stone arches of the husband's door,
Where silent serfs the ghastly thing receiv'd,
Trembling with fright, but less amaz'd than griev'd;
The Sieur his dame beheld with blazing eyes,
And shook with anger, more than with surprise.
(At least 'tis thus the stupid peasants told
Their wide-mouth'd wives when they the tale unroll'd.)
The village wonder'd why De Blois had kept
His spouse's loss unmention'd and unwept,
Nor were there lacking sland'rous tongues to claim
That the dark master was himself to blame.
But village talk could scarcely hope to solve
A crime so deep, and thus the months revolve:
The rural train repeat the gruesome tale,
And gape and marvel more than they bewail.

Swift flew the sun, and winter once again
With icy talons gripp'd the frigid plain.
December brought its store of Christmas cheer,
And grateful peasants hail'd the op'ning year;
But by the hearth as Candlemas drew nigh,
The whisp'ring ancients spoke of things gone by.
Few had forgot the dark demoniac lore
Of things that came the Candlemas before,
And many a crone intently eyed the house
Where dwelt the sadden'd bailiff and his spouse.
At last the day arriv'd, the sky o'erspread
With dark'ning messengers and clouds of lead;
Each neighb'ring grove Aeolian warnings sigh'd,
And thick'ning terrors broadcast seem'd to bide.
The good folk, tho' they knew not why, would run
Swift past the bailiff's door, the scene to shun;
Within the house the grieving couple wept,
And mourn'd the child who now forever slept.
On rush'd the dusk in doubly hideous form,
Borne on the pinions of the gath'ring storm;
Unusual murmurs fill'd the rainless wind,
The rising river lash'd the troubled shore;
Black thro' the night the awful storm-god prowl'd,
And froze the list'ners' life-blood as he howl'd;
Gigantic trees like supple rushes sway'd,
Whilst for his home the trembling cotter pray'd.

Now falls a sudden lull amidst the gale;
With less'ning force the circling currents wail;
Far down the stream that laves the neighb'ring mead
Burst a new ululation, wildly key'd;
The peasant train a frantic mien assume,
And huddle closer in the spectral gloom:
To each strain'd ear the truth too well is known,
For that dread sound can come from wolves alone!
The rustics close attend, when ere they think,
A lupine army swarms the river's brink;
From out the waters leap a howling train

That rend the air, and scatter o'er the plain:
With flaming orbs the frothing creatures fly,
And chant with hellish voice their hungry cry.
First of the pack a mighty monster leaps
With fearless tread, and martial order keeps;
Th' attendant wolves his yelping tones obey,
And form in columns for the coming fray:
No frighten'd swain they harm, but silent bound
With a fix'd purpose o'er the frozen ground.
Straight course the monsters thro' the village street,
Unholy vigour in their flying feet;
Thro' half-shut blinds the shelter'd peasants peer,
And wax in wonder as they lose in fear.
Th' excited pack at last their goal perceive,
And the vex'd air with deaf'ning clamour cleave;
The churls, astonish'd, watch th' unnatural herd
Flock round a cottage at the leader's word:
Quick spreads the fearsome fact, by rumour blown,
That the doom'd cottage is the bailiff's own!

Round and around the howling daemons glide,
Whilst the fierce leader scales the vine-clad side;
The frantic wind its horrid wail renews,
And mutters madly thro' the lifeless yews.
In the frail house the bailiff calmly waits
The rav'ning horde, and trusts th' impartial Fates,
But the wan wife revives with curious mien
Another monster and an older scene;
Amidst th' increasing wind that rocks the walls,
The dame to him the serpent's deed recalls:
Then as a nameless thought fills both their minds,
The bare-fang'd leader crashes thro' the blinds.
Across the room, with murd'rous fury rife,
Leaps the mad wolf, and seizes on the wife;
With strange intent he drags his shrieking prey
Close to the spot where once the coffin lay.
Wilder and wilder roars the mounting gale
That sweeps the hills and hurtles thro' the vale;
The ill-made cottage shakes, the pack without
Dance with new fury in demoniac rout.
Quick as his thought, the valiant bailiff stands
Above the wolf, a weapon in his hands;
The ready axe that serv'd a year before,
Now serves as well to slay one monster more.
The creature drops inert, with shatter'd head,
Full on the floor, and silent as the dead;
The rescu'd wife recalls the dire alarms,
And faints from terror in her husband's arms.
But as he holds her, all the cottage quakes,
And with full force the titan tempest breaks:
Down crash the walls, and o'er their shrinking forms
Burst the mad revels of the storm of storms.
Th' encircling wolves advance with ghastly pace,
Hunger and murder in each gleaming face,
But as they close, from out the hideous night
Flashes a bolt of unexpected light:
The vivid scene to ev'ry eye appears,
And peasants shiver with returning fears.
Above the wreck the scatheless chimney stays,
Its outline glimm'ring in the fitful rays,
Whilst o'er the hearth still hangs the household shrine,
The Saviour's image and the Cross divine!
Round the blest spot a lambent radiance glows,
And shields the cotters from their stealthy foes:
Each monstrous creature marks the wondrous glare,
Drops, fades, and vanishes in empty air!
The village train with startled eyes adore,
And count their beads in rev'rence o'er and o'er.
Now fades the light, and dies the raging blast,
The hour of dread and reign of horror past.
Pallid and bruis'd, from out his toppled walls
The panting bailiff with his good wife crawls:
Kind hands attend them, whilst o'er all the town
A strange sweet peace of spirit settles down.
Wonder and fear are still'd in soothing sleep,
As thro' the breaking clouds the moon rays peep.

Here paus'd the prattling grandam in her speech,
Confus'd with age, the tale half out of reach;
The list'ning guest, impatient for a clue,
Fears 'tis not one tale, but a blend of two;
He fain would know how far'd the widow'd lord
Whose eerie ways th' initial theme afford,
And marvels that the crone so quick should slight
His fate, to babble of the wolf-wrack'd night.
The old wife, press'd, for greater clearness strives,
Nods wisely, and her scatter'd wits revives;
Yet strangely lingers on her latter tale
Of wolf and bailiff, miracle and gale.
When (quoth the crone) the dawn's bright radiance bath'd
Th' eventful scene, so late in terror swath'd,
The chatt'ring churls that sought the ruin'd cot
Found a new marvel in the gruesome spot.
From fallen walls a trail of gory red,
As of the stricken wolf, erratic led;
O'er road and mead the new-dript crimson wound,
Till lost amidst the neighb'ring swampy ground:
With wonder unappeas'd the peasants burn'd,
For what the quicksand takes is ne'er return'd.

Once more the grandam, with a knowing eye,
Stops in her tale, to watch a hawk soar by;
The weary list'ner, baffled, seeks anew
For some plain statement, or enlight'ning clue.
Th' indulgent crone attends the puzzled plea,
Yet strangely mutters o'er the mystery.
The Sieur? Ah, yes — that morning all in vain
His shaking servants scour'd the frozen plain;

No man had seen him since he rode away
In silence on the dark preceding day.
His horse, wild-eyed with some unusual fright,
Came wand'ring from the river-bank that night.
His hunting-hound, that mourn'd with piteous woe,
Howl'd by the quicksand swamp, his grief to shew.
The village folk thought much, but utter'd less;
The servants' search wore out in emptiness:
For Sieur De Blois (the old wife's tale is o'er)
Was lost to mortal sight for evermore.

Polaris.

1,500-WORD SHORT STORY;
1918.

This short story marks the first appearance of the Land of Lomar, located near the North Pole before the onset of the Ice Age, in Lovecraft's work. It appears to have been inspired by a dream, which he described in a letter to Maurice Moe in May of 1918; sometime over the following month or two, he spun the dream into "Polaris."

"Polaris" is also the first appearance in Lovecraft's fiction of the technique of blending elements from the real world into his story-world, to create an enhanced sense of plausibility — most notably, the regrettably-offensively-described "Esquimaux" people. This blending would become one of the signal characteristics of his most famous stories in years to come.

It was first published in December 1920, in the inaugural issue of Alfred Galpin's amateur journal, The Philosopher.

Into the north window of my chamber glows the Pole Star with uncanny light. All through the long hellish hours of blackness it shines there. And in the autumn of the year, when the winds from the north curse and whine, and the red-leaved trees of the swamp mutter things to one another in the small hours of the morning under the horned waning moon, I sit by the easement and watch that star. Down from the heights reels the glittering Cassiopeia as the hours wear on, while Charles' Wain lumbers up from behind the vapour-soaked swamp trees that sway in the night-wind. Just before dawn Arcturus winks ruddily from above the cemetery on the low hillock, and Coma Berenices shimmers weirdly afar off in the mysterious east; but still the Pole Star leers down from the same place in the black vault, winking hideously like an insane watching eye which strives to convey some strange message, yet recalls nothing save that it once had a message to convey. Sometimes, when it is cloudy, I can sleep.

Well do I remember the night of the great Aurora, when over the swamp played the shocking coruscations of the daemon-light. After the beams came clouds, and then I slept.

And it was under a horned waning moon that I saw the

city for the first time. Still and somnolent did it lie, on a strange plateau in a hollow betwixt strange peaks. Of ghastly marble were its walls and its towers, its columns, domes, and pavements. In the marble streets were marble pillars, the upper parts of which were carven into the images of grave bearded men. The air was warm and stirred not. And overhead, scarce ten degrees from the zenith, glowed that watching Pole Star. Long did I gaze on the city, but the day came not. When the red Aldebaran, which blinked low in the sky but never set, had crawled a quarter of the way around the horizon, I saw light and motion in the houses and the streets. Forms strangely robed, but at once noble and familiar, walked abroad, and under the horned waning moon men talked wisdom in a tongue which I understood, though it was unlike any language I had ever known. And when the red Aldebaran had crawled more than half way around the horizon, there were again darkness and silence.

When I awaked, I was not as I had been. Upon my memory was graven the vision of the city, and within my soul had arisen another and vaguer recollection, of whose nature I was not then certain. Thereafter, on the cloudy nights when I could sleep, I saw the city often; sometimes under that horned waning moon, and sometimes under the hot yellow rays of a sun which did not set, but which wheeled low around the horizon. And on the clear nights the Pole Star leered as never before.

Gradually I came to wonder what might be my place in that city on the strange plateau betwixt strange peaks. At first content to view the scene as an all-observant uncorporeal presence, I now desired to define my relation to it, and to speak my mind amongst the grave men who conversed each day in the public squares. I said to myself, "This is no dream, for by what means can I prove the greater reality of that other life in the house of stone and brick south of the sinister swamp and the cemetery on the low hillock, where the Pole Star peers into my north window each night?"

One night as I listened to the discourse in the large square containing many statues, I felt a change; and perceived that I had at last a bodily form. Nor was I a stranger in the streets of Olathoë, which lies on the plateau of Sarkis, betwixt the peaks Noton and Kadiphonek. It was my friend Alos who spoke, and his speech was one that pleased my soul, for it was the speech of a true man and patriot. That night had the news come of Daikos' fall, and of the advance of the Inutos; squat, hellish, yellow fiends who five years ago appeared out of the unknown west to ravage the confines of our kingdom, and finally to besiege our towns. Having taken the fortified places at the foot of the mountains, their way now lay open to the plateau, unless every citizen could resist with the strength of ten men. For the squat creatures were mighty in the arts of war, and knew not the scruples of honour which held back our tall, grey-eyed men of Lomar from ruthless conquest.

Alos, my friend, was commander of all the forces of the plateau, and in him lay the last hope of our country. On this occasion he spoke of the perils to be faced, and exhorted the men of Olathoë, bravest of the Lomarians, to sustain the traditions of their ancestors, who when forced to move southward from Zobna before the advance of the great ice-sheet (even as our descendants must some day flee from the land of Lomar), valiantly and victoriously swept aside the hairy, long-armed, cannibal Gnophkehs that stood in their way. To me Alos denied a warrior's part, for I was feeble and given to strange faintings when subjected to stress and hardships. But my eyes were the keenest in the city, despite the long hours I gave each day to the study of the Pnakotic manuscripts and the wisdom of the Zobnarian Fathers; so my friend, desiring not to doom me to inaction, rewarded me with that duty which was second nothing in importance. To the watch-tower of Thapnen he sent me, there to serve as the eyes of our army. Should the Inutos attempt to gain the citadel by the narrow pass behind the peak Noton, and thereby surprise the garrison, I was to give the signal of fire which would warn the waiting soldiers and save the town from immediate disaster.

Alone I mounted the tower, for every man of stout body was needed in the passes below. My brain was sore dazed with excitement and fatigue, for I had not slept in many days; yet was my purpose firm, for I loved my native land of Lomar, and the marble city of Olathoë that lies betwixt the peaks of Noton and Kadiphonek.

But as I stood in the tower's topmost chamber, I beheld the horned waning moon, red and sinister, quivering through the vapours that hovered over the distant valley of Banof. And through an opening in the roof glittered the pale Pole Star, fluttering as if alive, and leering like a fiend and tempter. Methought its spirit whispered evil counsel, soothing me to traitorous somnolence with a damnable rhythmical promise which it repeated over and over:

Slumber, watcher, till the spheres
Six and twenty thousand years
Have revolv'd, and I return
To the spot where now I burn.
Other stars anon shall rise
To the axis of the skies;
Stars that soothe and stars that bless
With a sweet forgetfulness:
Only when my round is o'er
Shall the past disturb thy door.

Vainly did I struggle with my drowsiness, seeking to connect these strange words with some lore of the skies which I had learnt from the Pnakotic manuscripts. My head, heavy and reeling, drooped to my breast, and when next I looked up it was in a dream; with the Pole Star grinning at me through a window from over the horrible swaying trees of a dream-swamp. And I am still dreaming.

In my shame and despair I sometimes scream frantically, begging the dream-creatures around me to waken me ere the Inutos steal up the pass behind the peak Noton and take the citadel by surprise; but these creatures are daemons, for they laugh at me and tell me I am not dreaming. They mock me whilst I sleep, and whilst the squat yellow foe may be creeping silently upon us. I have failed in my duty and betrayed the marble city of Olathoë; I have proven false to Alos, my friend and commander. But still these shadows of my dream deride me. They say there is no land of Lomar, save in my nocturnal imaginings; that in those realms where the Pole Star shines high and red Aldebaran crawls low around the horizon, there has been naught save ice and snow for thousands of years, and never a man save squat yellow creatures, blighted by the cold, whom they call "Esquimaux."

And as I writhe in my guilty agony, frantic to save the city whose peril every moment grows, and vainly striving to shake off this unnatural dream of a house of stone and brick south of a sinister swamp and a cemetery on a low hillock; the Pole Star, even and monstrous, leers down from the black vault, winking hideously like an insane watching eye which strives to convey some strange message, yet recalls nothing save that it once had a message to convey.

1919.

The Gentleman Fictioneer.

For Howard Phillips Lovecraft, 1919 was a remarkably productive year. His budding ghost-writing trade was bearing fruit, although his best client was a dreadfully tendentious and hucksterish pop-psychology writer named David Van Bush, author of such titles as *Will Power and Success*; *Psychology of Sex: How to Make Love and Marry*; and *Grit and Gumption*. Still, business was business, and Bush, unlike most of Lovecraft's clients, paid well and promptly.

Lovecraft also started collaborating with a poet named Winifred Virginia Jackson, a particularly attractive divorcée 14 years his senior. He worked with Jackson on "The Green Meadow" and, in 1920, "The Crawling Chaos"—both of which later ran under her by-line. There were, and still are, rumors of a love affair, although no one really knows; if there was an affair, it was almost certainly a Platonic one.

Lovecraft's high level of output during 1919 is all the more surprising because that's the year in which a rather traumatic event took place: His mother, Sarah Susan Phillips Lovecraft, entered the Butler Hospital for the Insane, the same mental hospital in which his father had died when Howard was a small boy. The anxiety with which Sarah Susan had struggled all her life had reached debilitating proportions, and she needed help. She first went to her older sister's house, where she struggled for a couple months with alternating bouts of hysteria and depression, then checked into the hospital.

Lovecraft, although he wrote constantly and visited frequently, never actually entered the hospital itself, meeting his mother in spaces outside when he came. This apparently stemmed from some sort of fear or dread of such places, possibly a leftover from visits to his father in the 1890s.

The other key event that happened for Lovecraft in 1919 was his discovery, in August of that year, of the works of Lord Dunsany (Edward J.M.D. Plunkett, 18th Baron Dunsany). Lord Dunsany's work had a colossal impact on Lovecraft, second only to that of Edgar Allan Poe, and he was therewith launched into what is sometimes referred to as his Dunsany period—starting with "The White Ship," written a few weeks later, in which Dunsany's influence is unmistakable.

In addition to "The White Ship," Lovecraft put up some of the best work of his early career in 1919—reflecting the fact that he was still experimenting with approaches, stretching his storytelling muscles, and finding his style. He also produced some of his worst work, after getting caught up in the hysterical popular response to the first "Red Scare."

"Beyond the Wall of Sleep," "Memory," "Old Bugs," "The Transition of Juan Romero," "The Doom that Came to Sarnath," "The Street" and "The Statement of Randolph Carter" all flew off his pen in 1919. All were published in his friends' amateur-press journals; it would be another three years before Lovecraft started publishing his work in professional venues.

Beyond the Wall of Sleep.

4,300-WORD SHORT STORY;
1919.

This mid-sized short story was written sometime in the spring of 1919, shortly after Sarah Susan Lovecraft had been admitted to Butler Hospital. It is likely that Lovecraft drew some inspiration for it from some of the scenes he saw at the Butler Hospital.

It was first published in the October 1919 issue of John Clinton Pryor's amateur journal, Pine Cones.

What strange, splendid yet terrible experiences came to the poor mountaineer in the hours of sleep?

— A STORY OF A SUPERNAL BEING FROM ALGOL, THE DEMON-STAR.

I have often wondered if the majority of mankind ever pause to reflect upon the occasionally titanic significance of dreams, and of the obscure world to which they belong. Whilst the greater number of our nocturnal visions are perhaps no more than faint and fantastic reflections of our waking experiences — Freud to the contrary with his puerile symbolism — there are still a certain remainder whose immundane and ethereal character permits of no ordinary interpretation, and whose vaguely exciting and disquieting effect suggests possible minute glimpses into a sphere of mental existence no less important than physical life, yet separated from that life by an all but impassable barrier. From my experience I cannot doubt but that man, when lost to terrestrial consciousness, is indeed sojourning in another and uncorporeal life of far different nature from the life we know, and of which only the slightest and most indistinct memories linger after waking. From those blurred and fragmentary memories we may infer much, yet prove little. We may guess that in dreams life, matter, and vitality, as the earth knows such things, are not necessarily constant; and that time and space do not exist as our waking selves comprehend them. Sometimes I believe that this less material life is our truer life, and that our vain presence on the terraqueous globe is itself the secondary or merely virtual phenomenon.

It was from a youthful revery filled with speculations of this sort that I arose one afternoon in the winter of 1900-01, when to the state psychopathic institution in which I served as an intern was brought the man whose case has ever since haunted me so unceasingly. His name, as given on the records, was Joe Slater, or Slaader, and his appearance was that of the typical denizen of the Catskill Mountain region; one of those strange, repellent scions of a primitive Colonial peasant stock whose isolation for nearly three centuries in the hilly fastnesses of a little-traveled countryside has caused them to sink to a kind of barbaric degeneracy, rather than advance with their more fortunately placed brethren of the thickly settled districts. Among these odd folk, who correspond exactly to the decadent element of "white trash" in the South, law and morals are non-existent; and their general mental status is probably below that of any other section of the native American people.

Joe Slater, who came to the institution in the vigilant custody of four state policemen, and who was described as a highly dangerous character, certainly presented no evidence of his perilous disposition when I first beheld him. Though well above the middle stature, and of somewhat brawny frame, he was given an absurd appearance of harmless stupidity by the pale, sleepy blueness of his small watery eyes, the scantiness of his neglected and never-shaven growth of yellow beard, and the listless drooping of his heavy nether lip. His age was unknown, since among his kind neither family records nor permanent family ties exist; but from the baldness of his head in front, and from the decayed condition of his teeth, the head surgeon wrote him down as a man of about forty.

From the medical and court documents we learned all that could be gathered of his case: This man, a vagabond, hunter and trapper, had always been strange in the eyes of his primitive associates. He had habitually slept at night beyond the ordinary time, and upon waking would often talk of unknown things in a manner so bizarre as to inspire fear even in the hearts of an unimaginative populace. Not that his form of language was at all unusual, for he never spoke save in the debased patois of his environment; but the tone and tenor of his utterances were of such mysterious wildness, that none might listen without apprehension. He himself was generally as terrified and baffled as his auditors, and within an hour after awakening would forget all that he had said, or at least all that had caused him to say what he did; relapsing into a bovine, half-amiable normality like that of the other hill-dwellers.

As Slater grew older, it appeared, his matutinal aberrations had gradually increased in frequency and violence; till about a month before his arrival at the institution had occurred the shocking tragedy which caused his arrest by the authorities. One day near noon, after a profound sleep begun in a whisky debauch at about five of the previous afternoon, the man had roused himself most suddenly, with ululations so horrible and

Weird Tales, March 1938

"We shall meet again, perhaps in the shining mists of Orion's sword."

unearthly that they brought several neighbors to his cabin — a filthy sty where he dwelt with a family as indescribable as himself. Rushing out into the snow, he had flung his arms aloft and commenced a series of leaps directly upward in the air; the while shouting his determination to reach some "big, big cabin with brightness in the roof and walls and floor and the loud queer music far away." As two men of moderate size sought to restrain him, he had struggled with maniacal force and fury, screaming of his desire and need to find and kill a certain "thing that shines and shakes and laughs." At length, after temporarily felling one of his detainers with a sudden blow, he had flung himself upon the other in a demoniac ecstasy of blood-thirstiness, shrieking fiendishly that he would "jump high in the air and burn his way through anything that stopped him."

Family and neighbors had now fled in a panic, and when the more courageous of them returned, Slater was gone, leaving behind an unrecognizable pulp-like thing that had been a living man but an hour before. None of the mountaineers had dared to pursue him, and it is likely that they would have welcomed his death from the cold; but when several mornings later they heard his screams from a distant ravine they realized that he had somehow managed to survive, and that his removal in one way or another would be necessary. Then had followed an armed searching-party, whose purpose (whatever it may have been originally) became that of a sheriff's posse after one of the seldom popular state troopers had by accident observed, then questioned, and finally joined the seekers.

On the third day Slater was found unconscious in the hollow of a tree, and taken to the nearest jail, where alienists from Albany examined him as soon as his senses returned. To them he told a simple story. He had, he said, gone to sleep one afternoon about sundown after drinking much liquor. He had awaked to find himself standing bloody-handed in the snow before his cabin, the mangled corpse of his neighbor Peter Slader at his feet. Horrified, he had taken to the woods in a vague effort to escape from the scene of what must have been his crime. Beyond these tidings he seemed to know nothing, nor could the expert questioning of his interrogators bring out a single additional fact.

That night Slater slept quietly, and the next morning he wakened with no singular feature save a certain alteration of expression. Doctor Barnard, who had been watching the patient, thought he noticed in the pale blue eyes a certain gleam of peculiar quality, and in the flaccid lips an all but imperceptible tightening, as if of intelligent determination. But when questioned, Slater relapsed into the habitual vacancy of the mountaineer, and only reiterated what he had said on the preceding day.

On the third morning occurred the first of the man's mental attacks. After some show of uneasiness in sleep, he burst forth into a frenzy so powerful that the combined efforts of four men were needed to bind him in a straitjacket. The alienists listened with keen attention to his words, since their curiosity had been aroused to a high pitch by the suggestive yet mostly conflicting and incoherent stories of his family and neighbors. Slater raved for upward of fifteen minutes, babbling in his backwoods dialect of green edifices of light, oceans of space, strange music, and shadowy mountains and valleys. But most of all did he dwell upon some mysterious blazing entity that shook and laughed and mocked at him. This vast, vague personality seemed to have done him a terrible wrong, and to kill it in triumphant revenge was his paramount desire. In order to reach it, he said, he would soar through abysses of emptiness, burning every obstacle that stood in his way. Thus ran his discourse, until with the greatest suddenness he ceased. The fire of madness died from his eyes, and in dull wonder he looked at his questioners and asked why he was bound. Dr. Barnard unbuckled the leather harness and did not restore it till night, when he succeeded in persuading Slater to don it of his own volition, for his own good. The man had now admitted that he sometimes talked queerly, though he knew not why.

Within a week two more attacks appeared, but from them the doctors learned little. On the source of Slater's visions they speculated at length, for since he could neither read nor write, and had apparently never heard a legend or fairy-tale, his gorgeous imagery was quite inexplicable. That it could not come from any known myth or romance was made especially clear by the fact that the unfortunate lunatic expressed himself only in his own simple manner. He raved of things he did not understand and could not interpret; things which he claimed to have experienced, but which he could not have learned through any normal or connected narration. The alienists soon agreed that abnormal dreams were the foundation of the trouble; dreams whose vividness could for a time completely dominate the waking mind of this basically inferior man. With due formality Slater was tried for murder, acquitted on the ground of insanity, and committed to the institution wherein I held so humble a post.

I have said that I am a constant speculator concerning dream-life, and from this you may judge of the eagerness with which I applied myself to the study of the new patient as soon as I had fully ascertained the facts of his case. He seemed to sense a certain friendliness in me, born no doubt of the interest I could not conceal, and the gentle manner in which I questioned him. Not that he ever recognized me during his attacks, when I hung breathlessly upon his chaotic but cosmic word-pictures; but he knew me in his quiet hours, when he would sit by his barred window—weaving baskets of straw and willow, and perhaps pining for the mountain freedom he could never again enjoy. His family never called to see him; probably it had found another temporary head, after the manner of decadent mountain folk.

By degrees I commenced to feel an overwhelming wonder at the mad and fantastic conceptions of Joe Slater. The man himself was pitiably inferior in mentality and language alike; but his glowing, titanic visions, though described in a barbarous disjointed jargon, were assuredly things which only a superior or even exceptional brain could conceive. How, I often asked myself, could the stolid imagination of a Catskill degenerate conjure up sights whose very possession argued a lurking spark of genius? How could any backwoods dullard have gained so much as an idea of those glittering realms of supernal radiance and space about which Slater ranted in his furious delirium? More and more I inclined to the belief that in the pitiful personality who cringed before me lay the disordered nucleus of something beyond my comprehension; something infinitely beyond the comprehension of my more experienced but less imaginative medical and scientific colleagues.

And yet I could extract nothing definite from the man. The sum of all my investigation was, that in a kind of semi-corporeal dream-life Slater wandered or floated through resplendent and prodigious valleys, meadows, gardens, cities, and palaces of light, in a region unbounded and unknown to man; that there he was no peasant or degenerate, but a creature of importance and vivid life, moving proudly and dominantly, and checked only by a certain deadly enemy, who seemed to be a being of visible yet ethereal structure, and who did not appear to be of human shape, since Slater never referred to it as a man, or as aught save a thing. This thing had done Slater some hideous but unnamed wrong, which the maniac (if maniac he were) yearned to avenge.

From the manner in which Slater alluded to their dealings, I judged that he and the luminous thing had met on equal terms; that in his dream existence the man was himself a luminous thing of the same race as his enemy. This impression was sustained by his frequent references to flying through space and burning all that impeded his progress. Yet these conceptions were formulated in rustic words wholly inadequate to convey them, a circumstance which drove me to the conclusion that if a true dream world indeed existed, oral language was not its medium for the transmission of thought. Could it be that the dream soul inhabiting this inferior body was desperately struggling to speak things which the simple and halting tongue of dullness could not utter? Could it be that I was face to face with intellectual emanations which would explain the mystery if I could but learn to discover and read them? I did not tell the older physicians of these things, for middle age is skeptical, cynical, and disinclined to accept new ideas. Besides, the head of the institution had but lately warned me in his paternal way that I was overworking; that my mind needed a rest.

It had long been my belief that human thought consists basically of atomic or molecular motion, convertible into ether waves of radiant energy like heat, light and electricity. This belief had early led me to contemplate the possibility of telepathy or mental communication by means of suitable apparatus, and I had in my college days prepared a set of transmitting and receiving instruments somewhat similar to the cumbrous devices employed in wireless telegraphy at that crude, pre-radio period. These I had tested with a fellow-student, but achieving no result, had soon packed them away with other scientific odds and ends for possible future use.

Now, in my intense desire to probe into the dream-life of Joe Slater, I sought these instruments again, and spent several days in repairing them for action. When they were complete once more I missed no opportunity for their trial. At each outburst of Slater's violence, I would fit the transmitter to his forehead and the receiver to my own, constantly making delicate adjustments for various hypothetical wave-lengths of intellectual energy. I had but little notion of how the thought-impressions would, if successfully conveyed, arouse an intelligent response in my brain, but I felt certain that I could detect and interpret them. Accordingly I continued my experiments, though informing no one of their nature.

It was on the twenty-first of February, 1901, that the thing occurred. As I look back across the years I realize how unreal it seems, and sometimes half wonder if old Doctor Fenton was not right when he charged it all to my excited imagination. I recall that he listened with great kindness and patience when I told him, but afterward gave me a nerve-powder and arranged for the half-year's vacation on which I departed the next week.

That fateful night I was wildly agitated and perturbed, for despite the excellent care he had received, Joe Slater was unmistakably dying. Perhaps it was his mountain freedom that he missed, or perhaps the turmoil in his brain had grown too acute for his rather sluggish physique; but at all events the flame of vitality flickered low in the decadent body. He was drowsy near the end, and as darkness fell he dropped off into a troubled sleep.

I did not strap on the strait jacket as was customary when he slept, since I saw that he was too feeble to be dangerous, even if he woke in mental disorder once more before passing away. But I did place upon his head and mine the two ends of my cosmic "radio," hoping against hope for a first and last message from the dream world in the brief time remaining. In the cell with us was one nurse, a mediocre fellow who did not understand the purpose of the apparatus, or think to inquire into my course. As the hours wore on I saw his head droop awkwardly in sleep, but I did not disturb him. I myself, lulled by the rhythmical breathing of the healthy and the dying man, must have nodded a little later.

The sound of weird lyric melody was what aroused me. Chords, vibrations, and harmonic ecstasies echoed passionately on every hand, while on my ravished sight burst the stupendous spectacle of ultimate beauty. Walls, columns, and architraves of living fire blazed effulgently around the spot where I seemed to float in air, extending upward to an infinitely high vaulted dome of indescribable splendor. Blending with this display of palatial magnificence, or rather, supplanting it at times in kaleidoscopic rotation, were glimpses of wide plains and graceful valleys, high mountains and inviting grottoes, covered with every lovely attribute of scenery which my delighted eyes could conceive of, yet formed wholly of some glowing, ethereal plastic entity, which in consistency partook as much of spirit as of matter. As I gazed, I perceived that my own brain held the key to these enchanting metamorphoses; for each vista which appeared to me was the one my changing mind most wished to behold. Amidst this elysian realm I dwelt not as a stranger, for each sight and sound was familiar to me; just as it had been for uncounted eons of eternity before, and would be for like eternities to come.

Then the resplendent aura of my brother of light drew near and held colloquy with me, soul to soul, with silent and perfect interchange of thought. The hour was one of approaching triumph, for was not my fellow-being escaping at last from a degrading periodic bondage; escaping for ever, and preparing to follow the accursed oppressor even unto the uttermost fields of ether, that upon it might be wrought a flaming cosmic vengeance which would shake the spheres? We floated thus for a little time, when I perceived a slight blurring and fading of the objects around us, as though some force were recalling me to earth — where I least wished to go. The form near me seemed to feel a change also, for it gradually brought its discourse toward a conclusion, and itself prepared to quit the scene, fading from my sight at a rate somewhat less rapid than that of the other objects. A few more thoughts were exchanged, and I knew that the luminous one and I were being recalled to bondage, though for my brother of light it would be the last time. The sorry planet shell being well-nigh spent, in less than an hour my fellow would be free to pursue the oppressor along the Milky Way and past the hither stars to the very confines of infinity.

A well-defined shock separates my final impression of the fading scene of light from my sudden and somewhat shamefaced awakening and straightening up in my chair as I saw the dying figure on the couch move hesitantly. Joe Slater was indeed awaking, though probably for the last time. As I looked more closely, I saw that in the sallow cheeks shone spots of color which had never before been present. The lips, too, seemed unusual, being tightly compressed, as if by the force of a stronger character than had been Slater's. The whole face finally began to grow tense, and the head turned restlessly with closed eyes.

I did not rouse the sleeping nurse, but readjusted the slightly disarranged headbands of my telepathic "radio," intent to catch any parting message the dreamer might have to deliver. All at once the head turned sharply in my direction and the eyes fell open, causing me to stare in blank amazement at what I beheld. The man who had been Joe Slater, the Catskill decadent, was now gazing at me with a pair of luminous, expanding eyes whose blue seemed subtly to have deepened. Neither mania nor degeneracy was visible in that gaze, and I felt beyond a doubt that I was viewing a face behind which lay an active mind of high order.

At this juncture my brain became aware of a steady external influence operating upon it. I closed my eyes to concentrate my thoughts more profoundly, and was rewarded by the positive knowledge that my long-sought mental message had come at last. Each transmitted idea formed rapidly in my mind, and though no actual language was employed, my habitual association of conception and expression was so great that I seemed to be receiving the message in ordinary English.

"Joe Slater is dead," came the soul-petrifying voice of an agency from beyond the wall of sleep. My opened eyes sought the couch of pain in curious horror, but the blue eyes were still calmly gazing, and the countenance was still intelligently animated. "He is better dead, for he was unfit to bear the active intellect of cosmic entity. His gross body could not undergo the needed adjustments between ethereal life and planet life. He was too much an animal, too little a man; yet it is through his deficiency that you have come to discover me, for the cosmic and planet souls rightly should never meet. He has been my torment and diurnal prison for forty-two of your terrestrial years.

"I am an entity like that which you yourself become in the freedom of dreamless sleep. I am your brother of light, and have floated with you in the effulgent valleys. It is not permitted me to tell your waking earth-self of your real self, but we are all roamers of vast spaces and travelers in many ages. Next year I may be dwelling in the Egypt which you call ancient, or in the cruel empire of Tsan Chan which is to come three thousand years hence. You and I have drifted to the worlds that reel about the red Arcturus, and dwelt in the bodies of the insect-philosophers that crawl proudly over the fourth moon of Jupiter. How little does the earth self know life and its extent! How little, indeed, ought it to know for its own tranquillity!

"Of the oppressor I cannot speak. You on earth have unwittingly felt its distant presence—you who without knowing idly gave the blinking beacon the name of the Algol, the Demon-Star. It is to meet and conquer the oppressor that I have vainly striven for eons, held back by bodily encumbrances. Tonight I go as a Nemesis bearing just and blazingly cataclysmic vengeance. Watch me in the sky close by the Demon-Star.

"I cannot speak longer, for the body of Joe Slater grows cold and rigid, and the coarse brains are ceasing to vibrate as I wish. You have been my only friend on this planet—the only soul to sense and seek for me within the repellent form which lies on this couch. We shall meet again—perhaps in the shining mists of Orion's Sword, perhaps on a bleak plateau in prehistoric Asia, perhaps in unremembered dreams tonight, perhaps in some other form an eon hence, when the solar system shall have been swept away."

At this point the thought-waves abruptly ceased, and the pale eyes of the dreamer—or can I say dead man?—commenced to glaze fishily. In a half-stupor I crossed over to the couch and felt of his wrist, but found it cold, stiff, and pulseless. The sallow cheeks paled again, and the thick lips fell open, disclosing the repulsively rotten fangs of the degenerate Joe Slater. I shivered, pulled a blanket over the hideous face, and awakened the nurse. Then I left the cell and went silently to my room. I had an instant and unaccountable craving for a sleep whose dreams I should not remember.

The climax? What plain tale of science can boast of such a rhetorical effect? I have merely set down certain things appealing to me as facts, allowing you to construe them as you will. As I have already admitted, my superior, old Doctor Fenton, denies the reality of everything I have related. He vows that I was broken down with nervous strain, and badly in need of the long vacation on full pay which he so generously gave me. He assures me on his professional honor that Joe Slater was but a low-grade paranoiac, whose fantastic notions must have come from the crude hereditary folk-tales which circulate in even the most decadent of communities. All this he tells me—yet I cannot forget what I saw in the sky on the night after Slater died. Lest you think me a biased witness, another pen must add this final testimony, which may perhaps supply the climax you expect. I will quote the following account of the star Nova

Persei verbatim from the pages of that eminent astronomical authority, Professor Garrett P. Serviss:

> *On February 22, 1901, a marvelous new star was discovered by Doctor Anderson of Edinburgh, not very far from Algol. No star had been visible at that point before. Within twenty-four hours the stranger had become so bright that it outshone Capella. In a week or two it had visibly faded, and in the course of a few months it was hardly discernible with the naked eye.*

Memory.

400-WORD PROSE-POEM; 1919.

This dark, diminuitive prose-poem was written around the same time as "Beyond the Wall of Sleep," just after H.P. Lovecraft's mother was admitted to the psychiatric hospital.

It was first published in the June 1919 issue of the United Amateur Press Association's United Cooperative.

In the valley of Nis the accursed waning moon shines thinly, tearing a path for its light with feeble horns through the lethal foliage of a great upas-tree. And within the depths of the valley, where the light reaches not, move forms not meet to be beheld. Rank is the herbage on each slope, where evil vines and creeping plants crawl amidst the stones of ruined palaces, twining tightly about broken columns and strange monoliths, and heaving up marble pavements laid by forgotten hands. And in trees that grow gigantic in crumbling courtyards leap little apes, while in and out of deep treasure-vaults writhe poison serpents and scaly things without a name.

Vast are the stones which sleep beneath coverlets of dank moss, and mighty were the walls from which they fell. For all time did their builders erect them, and in sooth they yet serve nobly, for beneath them the grey toad makes his habitation.

At the very bottom of the valley lies the river Than, whose waters are slimy and filled with weeds. From hidden springs it rises, and to subterranean grottoes it flows, so that the Daemon of the Valley knows not why its waters are red, nor whither they are bound.

The Genie that haunts the moonbeams spake to the Daemon of the Valley, saying, "I am old, and forget much. Tell me the deeds and aspect and name of them who built these things of stone." And the Daemon replied, "I am Memory, and am wise in lore of the past, but I too am old. These beings were like the waters of the river Than, not to be understood. Their deeds I recall not, for they were but of the moment. Their aspect I recall dimly, for it was like to that of the little apes in the trees.

Their name I recall clearly, for it rhymed with that of the river. These beings of yesterday were called Man."

So the Genie flew back to the thin horned moon, and the Daemon looked intently at a little ape in a tree that grew in a crumbling courtyard.

The Green Meadow.

BY WINIFRED V. JACKSON AND H.P. LOVECRAFT

2,300-WORD SHORT STORY; 1919.

"The Green Meadow" was written in early 1919 — after Lovecraft's own "Polaris," and most likely just before "Beyond the Wall of Sleep" — but it wasn't actually published until the Spring 1927 issue of W. Paul Cook's amateur-press magazine, The Vagrant. *It was H.P. Lovecraft's first collaborative weird-fiction story, and was written soon after he returned to the craft following a decade or so as a nonfiction writer and poet.*

The story itself is based on a dream which Jackson had in late 1918; and with its reminiscent and contemplative tone, its style is true to its origin. Jackson's contributions to the actual writing of the story were probably very scant; the prose style is recognizably Lovecraft's.

It's likely that "The Green Meadow" represents an exploration of a storytelling style rather than an attempt to craft a cohesive tale. In terms of plot, the story goes absolutely nowhere; and the frame story, involving a strange book found embedded in a meteorite and apparently written by a Greek-speaking philosopher two millennia before, is extremely difficult to suspend disbelief and "play along" with. It's the tone and style that make this story special.

It's worth noting that this story was written just a few months before Lovecraft discovered the early writings of Lord Dunsany in August 1919. So "The Green Meadow" may be the best example of Lovecraft's pre-Dunsany dreamy-writing style. A comparison of its tone and approach with the other Jackson story — "The Crawling Chaos" — clearly showcases the difference.

ABOUT WINIFRED V. JACKSON (1876-1959).

Winifred Virginia Jackson was a very attractive 43-year-old Boston woman, freshly divorced from her first husband, Horace Jordan. Primarily a poet, she had gotten involved in the Boston amateur-press community shortly after marrying Jordan in 1915, and she and Lovecraft were soon working closely together. Lovecraft published a number of her poems in his amateur journal, The Conservative, *starting in early 1916; and, when she published an amateur journal of her own, he returned the favor. She also served as second vice-president under him when he was president of the United Amateur Press Association (UAPA) in 1917 and 1918.*

There were persistent rumors of a romance between the two of them; and there may very well have been something of that sort. Lovecraft's wife, Sonia Haft Greene, later recalled that she had "stole[n] HPL away from Winifred Jackson."

If there was a romance, it was either a wholly Platonic affair, or very nearly so. But there's a good bit of circumstantial evidence that some kind of special connection existed. Furthermore, after Lovecraft and Greene started seeing each other seriously, Jackson — formerly one of the most active members of UAPA — seems to have retired from the scene almost entirely.

Not much is known about Winifred Jackson today, beyond the usual sort of information one finds in obituaries and between the lines in letters to friends. And this is particularly unfortunate, because what we know hints at a very interesting person. In 1915, at close to the high-water mark of institutionalized racism in the post-Civil-War United States, she married Horace Jordan — a Black man. And just after her presumed romance with Lovecraft, she started a long-term affair with William Stanley Braithwaite, literary editor of the Boston Transcript, *the most prominent Black literary critic in the country. Also, she was a gifted poet, particularly in the arena of the weird.*

INTRODUCTORY NOTE.

The following very singular narrative, or record of impressions, was discovered under circumstances so extraordinary that they deserve careful description. On the evening of Wednesday, August 27, 1913, at about eight-thirty o'clock, the population of the small seaside village of Potowonket, Maine, U.S.A., was aroused by a thunderous report accompanied by a blinding flash; and persons near the shore beheld a mammoth ball of fire dart from the heavens into the sea but a short distance out, sending up a prodigious column of water. The following Sunday a fishing party composed of John Richmond, Peter B. Carr, and Simon Canfield, caught in their trawl and dragged ashore a mass of metallic rock, weighing 360 pounds, and looking (as Mr. Canfield said) like a piece of slag. Most of the inhabitants agreed that this heavy body was none other than the fireball which had fallen from the sky four days before; and Dr. Richard M. Jones, the local scientific authority, allowed that it must be an aerolite or meteoric stone. In chipping off specimens to send to an expert Boston analyst, Dr. Jones discovered imbedded in the semi-metallic mass the strange book containing the ensuing tale, which is still in his possession.

In form the discovery resembles an ordinary notebook, about five by three inches in size, and containing thirty leaves. In material, however, it presents marked peculiarities. The covers are apparently of some dark stony substance unknown to geologists, and unbreakable by any mechanical means. No chemical reagent seems to act upon them. The leaves are much the same, save that they are lighter in colour, and so infinitely thin as to be quite flexible. The whole is bound by some process not very clear to those who have observed it; a process involving the adhesion of the leaf substance to the cover substance. These substances cannot now be separated, nor can the leaves be torn by any amount of force. The writing is Greek of the purest classical quality, and several students of palaeography declare that the characters are in a cursive hand used about the second century B.C. There is little in the text to determine the date. The mechanical mode of writing cannot be deduced beyond the fact that it must have resembled that of the modern slate and slate-pencil. During the course of analytical efforts made by the late Professor Chambers of Harvard, several pages, mostly at the conclusion of the narrative, were blurred to the point of utter effacement before being read; a circumstance forming a well-nigh irreparable loss. What remains of the contents was done into modern Greek letters by the palaeographer, Rutherford, and in this form submitted to the translators.

Professor Mayfield of the Massachusetts Institute of Technology, who examined samples of the strange stone, declares it a true meteorite; an opinion in which Dr. von Winterfeldt of Heidelberg (interned in 1918 as a dangerous enemy alien) does not concur. Professor Bradley of Columbia College adopts a less dogmatic ground; pointing out that certain utterly unknown ingredients are present in large quantities, and warning that no classification is as yet possible.

The presence, nature, and message of the strange book form so momentous a problem, that no explanation can even be attempted. The text, as far as preserved, is here rendered as literally as our language permits, in the hope that some reader may eventually hit upon an interpretation and solve one of the greatest scientific mysteries of recent years.

THE BOOK.

It was a narrow place, and I was alone. On one side, beyond a margin of vivid waving green, was the sea; blue, bright, and billowy, and sending up vapourous exhalations which intoxicated me. So profuse, indeed, were these exhalations, that they gave me an odd impression of a coalescence of sea and sky; for the heavens were likewise bright and blue. On the other side was the forest, ancient almost as the sea itself, and stretching infinitely inland. It was very dark, for the trees were grotesquely huge and luxuriant, and incredibly numerous. Their giant trunks were of a horrible green which blended weirdly with the narrow green tract whereon I stood. At some distance away, on either side of me, the strange forest extended down to the water's edge, obliterating the shoreline and completely hemming in the narrow tract. Some of the trees, I observed, stood in the water itself, as though impatient of any barrier to their progress.

I saw no living thing, nor sign that any living thing save myself had ever existed. The sea and the sky and the wood encircled me, and reached off into regions beyond my imagination. Nor was there any sound save of the wind-tossed wood and of the sea.

As I stood in this silent place, I suddenly commenced to tremble; for though I knew not how I came there, and could scarce remember what my name and rank had been, I felt that I should go mad if I could understand what lurked about me. I recalled things I had learned, things I had dreamed, things I had imagined and yearned for in some other distant life. I thought of long nights when I had gazed up at the stars of heaven and cursed the gods that my free soul could not traverse the vast abysses which were inaccessible to my body. I conjured up ancient blasphemies, and terrible delvings into the papri of Democritus; but as memories appeared, I shuddered in deeper fear, for I knew that I was alone — horribly alone. Alone, yet close to sentient impulses of vast, vague kind, which I prayed never to comprehend nor encounter. In the voice of the swaying green branches I fancied I could detect a kind of malignant hatred and demoniac triumph. Sometimes they struck me as being in horrible colloquy with ghastly and unthinkable things which the scaly green bodies of the trees half-hid; hid from sight, but not from consciousness.

The most oppressive of my sensations was a sinister feeling of alienage. Though I saw about me objects which I could name; trees, grass, sea, and sky; I felt that their relation to me was not the same as that of the trees, grass, sea, and sky I knew in another and dimly remembered life. The nature of the difference I could not tell, yet I shook in stark fright as it impressed itself upon me.

And then, in a spot where I had before discerned nothing but the misty sea, I beheld the Green Meadow, separated from me by a vast expanse of blue rippling water with sun-tipped wavelets, yet strangely near. Often I would peep fearfully over my right shoulder at the trees, but I preferred to look at the Green Meadow, which affected me oddly.

It was while my eyes were fixed upon this singular tract, that I first felt the ground in motion beneath me. Beginning with a kind of throbbing agitation which held a fiendish suggestion of conscious action, the bit of bank on which I stood detached itself from the grassy shore and commenced to float away; borne slowly onward as if by some current of resistless force. I did not move, astonished and startled as I was by the unprecedented phenomenon, but stood rigidly still until a wide lane of water yawned betwixt me and the land of trees. Then I sat down in a sort of daze, and again looked at the sun-tipped water and the Green Meadow.

Behind me the trees and the things they may have been hiding seemed to radiate infinite menace. This I knew without turning to view them, for as I grew more used to the scene I became less and less dependent upon the five senses that once had been my sole reliance. I knew the green scaly forest hated me, yet now I was safe from it, for my bit of bank had drifted far from the shore.

But though one peril was past, another loomed up before me. Pieces of earth were constantly crumbling from the floating isle which held me, so that death could not be far distant in any event. Yet even then I seemed to sense that death would be death to me no more, for I turned again to watch the Green Meadow, imbued with a curious feeling of security in strange contrast to my general horror.

Then it was that I heard, at a distance immeasurable, the sound of falling water. Not that of any trival cascade such as I had known, but that which might be heard in the far Scythian lands if all the Mediterranean were poured down an unfathomable abyss. It was toward this sound that my shrinking island was drifting, yet I was content.

Far in the rear were happening weird and terrible things; things which I turned to view, yet shivered to behold. For in the sky dark vapourous forms hovered fantastically, brooding over trees and seeming to answer the challenge of the waving green branches. Then a thick mist arose from the sea to join the sky-forms, and the shore was erased from my sight. Though the sun — what sun I knew not — shone brightly on the water around me, the land I had left seemed involved in a demoniac tempest where dashed the will of the hellish trees and what they hid, with that of the sky and the sea. And when the mist vanished, I saw only the blue sky and the blue sea, for the land and the trees were no more.

It was at this point that my attention was arrested by the singing in the Green Meadow. Hitherto, as I have said, I had encountered no sign of human life; but now there arose to my ears a dull chant whose origin and nature were apparently unmistakable. While the words were utterly undistinguishable, the chant awaked in me a peculiar train of associations; and I was reminded of some vaguely disquieting lines I had once translated out of an Egyptian book, which in turn were taken from a papyrus of ancient Meroë. Through my brain ran lines that I fear to repeat; lines telling of very antique things and forms of life in the days when our earth was exceeding young. Of things which thought and moved and were alive, yet which gods and men would not consider alive. It was a strange book.

As I listened, I became gradually conscious of a circumstance which had before puzzled me only subconsciously. At no time had my sight distinguished any definite objects in the Green Meadow, an impression of vivid homogeneous verdure being the sum total of my perception. Now, however, I saw that the current would cause my island to pass the shore at but a little distance; so that I might learn more of the land and of the singing thereon. My curiosity to behold the singers had mounted high, though it was mingled with apprehension.

Bits of sod continued to break away from the tiny tract which carried me, but I heeded not their loss; for I felt that I was not to die with the body (or appearance of a body) which I seemed to possess. That everything about me, even life and death, was illusory; that I had overleaped the bounds of mortality and corporeal entity, becoming a free, detached thing; impressed me as almost certain. Of my location I knew nothing, save that I felt I could not be on the earth-planet once so familiar to me. My sensations, apart from a kind of haunting terror, were those of a traveller just embarked upon an unending voyage of discovery. For a moment I thought of the lands and persons I had left behind, and of strange ways whereby I might some day tell them of my adventurings, even though I might never return.

I had now floated very near the Green Meadow, so that the voices were clear and distinct; but though I knew many languages I could not quite interpret the words of the chanting. Familiar they indeed were, as I had subtly felt when at a greater distance, but beyond a sensation of vague and awesome remembrance I could make nothing of them. A most extraordinary quality in the voices — a quality which I cannot describe — at once frightened and fascinated me.

My eyes could now discern several things amidst the omnipresent verdure-rocks, covered with bright green moss, shrubs of considerable height, and less definable shapes of great magnitude which seemed to move or vibrate amidst the shrubbery in a peculiar way. The chanting, whose authors I was so anxious to glimpse, seemed loudest at points where these shapes were most numerous and most vigorously in motion.

And then, as my island drifted closer and the sound of the distant waterfall grew louder, I saw clearly the source of the chanting, and in one horrible instant remembered everything. Of such things I cannot, dare not tell, for therein was revealed the hideous solution of all which had puzzled me; and that solution would drive you mad, even as it almost drove me . . . I knew now the change through which I had passed, and through which certain others who once were men had passed! and I knew the endless cycle of the future which none like me may escape . . . I shall live forever, be conscious forever, though my soul cries out to the gods for the boon of death and oblivion . . . All is before me: beyond the deafening torrent lies the land of Stethelos, where young men are infinitely old . . . The Green Meadow . . . I will send a message across the horrible immeasurable abyss . . . .

(At this point the text becomes illegible.)

Old Bugs.

AN EXTEMPORANEOUS SOB STORY
BY MARCUS LOLLIUS, PROCONSUL OF GAUL.

3,000-WORD SHORT STORY;
1919.

As its tongue-in-cheek subtitle suggests, "Old Bugs" was written in a playful spirit. In July of 1919, just before Prohibition took effect, Lovecraft's young amateur-journalism protegé, Alfred Galpin, decided to give liquor a try while the law still allowed him to do so. Accordingly, he bought a bottle each of rye whiskey and port wine, slipped out into the woods behind the golf course in his home town of Appleton, Wisconsin, and had a little solitary pastoral spree

When he mentioned this to Lovecraft in a letter, Lovecraft — whose attitude toward alcohol was that of a strict teetotaler — replied with the manuscript of "Old Bugs," followed by a one-line message: "NOW will you be good?!"

Although it seems strange that such a fun little tidbit should have remained unpublished in one amateur journal or another, it wasn't until 1959 that "Old Bugs" saw print, in The Shuttered Room and Other Pieces, *one of the collections published by August Derleth's Arkham House.*

Sheehan's Pool Room, which adorns one of the lesser alleys in the heart of Chicago's stockyard district, is not a nice place. Its air, freighted with a thousand odours such as Coleridge may have found at Cologne, too seldom knows the purifying rays of the sun; but fights for space with the acrid fumes of unnumbered cheap cigars and cigarettes which dangle from the coarse lips of unnumbered human animals that haunt the place day and night. But the popularity of Sheehan's remains unimpaired; and for this there is a reason — a reason obvious to anyone who will take the trouble to analyse the mixed stenches prevailing there. Over and above the fumes and sickening closeness rises an aroma once familiar throughout the land, but now happily banished to the back streets of life by the edict of a benevolent government — the aroma of strong, wicked whiskey — a precious kind of forbidden fruit indeed in this year of grace 1950.

Sheehan's is the acknowledged centre to Chicago's subterranean traffic in liquor and narcotics, and as such has a certain dignity which extends even to the unkempt attachés of the place; but there was until lately one who lay outside the pale of that dignity — one who shared the squalor and filth, but not the importance, of Sheehan's. He was called "Old Bugs," and was the most disreputable object in a disreputable environment. What he had once been, many tried to guess; for his language and mode of utterance when intoxicated to a certain degree were such as to excite wonderment; but what he was, presented less difficulty — for "Old Bugs," in superlative degree, epitomised the pathetic species known as the "bum" or the "down-and-outer." Whence he had come, no one could tell. One night he had burst wildly into Sheehan's, foaming at the mouth and screaming for whiskey and hasheesh; and having been supplied in exchange for a promise to perform odd jobs, had hung about ever since, mopping floors, cleaning cuspidors and glasses, and attending to an hundred similar menial duties in exchange for the drink and drugs which were necessary to keep him alive and sane.

He talked but little, and usually in the common jargon of the underworld; but occasionally, when inflamed by an unusually generous dose of crude whiskey, would burst forth into strings of incomprehensible polysyllables and snatches of sonorous prose and verse which led certain habitués to conjecture that he had seen better days. One steady patron — a bank defaulter under cover — came to converse with him quite regularly, and from the tone of his discourse ventured the opinion that he had been a writer or professor in his day. But the only tangible clue to Old Bugs' past was a faded photograph which he constantly carried about with him — the photograph of a young woman of noble and beautiful features. This he would sometimes draw from his tattered pocket, carefully unwrap from its covering of tissue paper, and gaze upon for hours with an expression of ineffable sadness and tenderness. It was not the portrait of one whom an underworld denizen would be likely to know, but of a lady of breeding and quality, garbed in the quaint attire of thirty years before. Old Bugs himself seemed also to belong to the past, for his nondescript clothing bore every hallmark of antiquity. He was a man of immense height, probably more than six feet, though his stooping shoulders sometimes belied this fact. His hair, a dirty white and falling out in patches, was never combed; and over his lean face grew a mangy stubble of coarse beard which seemed always to remain at the bristling stage — never shaven — yet never long enough to form a respectable set of whiskers. His features had perhaps been noble once, but were now seamed with the ghastly effects of terrible dissipation. At one time — probably in middle life — he had evidently been grossly fat; but now he was horribly lean, the purple flesh hanging in loose pouches under his bleary eyes and upon his cheeks. Altogether, Old Bugs was not pleasing to look upon.

The disposition of Old Bugs was as odd as his aspect. Ordinarily he was true to the derelict type — ready to do anything for a nickel or a dose of whiskey or hasheesh — but at rare intervals he shewed the traits which earned him his name. Then he would try to straighten up, and a certain fire would creep into the sunken eyes. His demeanour would assume an unwonted grace and even dignity; and the sodden creatures around him would sense something of superiority — something which made them less ready to give the usual kicks and cuffs to the poor butt and drudge. At these times he would shew a sardonic humour and make remarks which the folk of Sheehan's deemed foolish and irrational. But the spells would soon pass, and once more Old Bugs would resume his eternal floor-scrubbing and cuspidor-cleaning.

But for one thing Old Bugs would have been an ideal slave to the establishment — and that one thing was his conduct when young men were introduced for their first drink. The old man would then rise from the floor in anger and excitement, muttering threats and warnings, and seeking to dissuade the novices from embarking upon their course of "seeing life as it is." He would sputter and fume, exploding into sesquipedalian admonitions and strange oaths, and animated by a frightful earnestness which brought a shudder to more than one drug-racked mind in the crowded room. But after a time his alcohol-enfeebled brain would wander from the subject, and with a foolish grin he would turn once more to his mop or cleaning-rag.

I do not think that many of Sheehan's regular patrons will ever forget the day that young Alfred Trever came. He was rather a "find" — a rich and high-spirited youth who would "go the limit" in anything he undertook — at least, that was the verdict of Pete Schultz, Sheehan's "runner," who had come across the boy at Lawrence College, in the small town of Appleton, Wisconsin. Trever was the son of prominent parents in Appleton. His father, Karl Trever, was an attorney and citizen of distinction, whilst his mother had made an enviable reputation as a poetess under her maiden name of Eleanor Wing. Alfred was himself a scholar and poet of distinction, though cursed with a certain childish irresponsibility which made him an ideal prey for Sheehan's runner. He was blond, handsome, and spoiled; vivacious and eager to taste the several forms of dissipation about which he had read and heard. At Lawrence he had been prominent in the mock-fraternity of "Tappa Tappa Keg," where he was the wildest and merriest of the wild and merry young roysterers; but this immature, collegiate frivolity did not satisfy him. He knew deeper vices through books, and he now longed to know them at first hand. Perhaps this tendency toward wildness had been stimulated somewhat by the repression to which he had been subjected at home; for Mrs. Trever had particular reason for training her only child with rigid severity. She had, in her own youth, been deeply and permanently impressed with the horror of dissipation by the case of one to whom she had for a time been engaged.

Young Galpin, the fiancé in question, had been one of

Appleton's most remarkable sons. Attaining distinction as a boy through his wonderful mentality, he won vast fame at the University of Wisconsin, and at the age of twenty-three returned to Appleton to take up a professorship at Lawrence and to slip a diamond upon the finger of Appleton's fairest and most brilliant daughter. For a season all went happily, till without warning the storm burst. Evil habits, dating from a first drink taken years before in woodland seclusion, made themselves manifest in the young professor; and only by a hurried resignation did he escape a nasty prosecution for injury to the habits and morals of the pupils under his charge. His engagement broken, Galpin moved east to begin life anew; but before long, Appletonians heard of his dismissal in disgrace from New York University, where he had obtained an instructorship in English. Galpin now devoted his time to the library and lecture platform, preparing volumes and speeches on various subjects connected with belles lettres, and always shewing a genius so remarkable that it seemed as if the public must sometime pardon him for his past mistakes. His impassioned lectures in defence of Villon, Poe, Verlaine, and Oscar Wilde were applied to himself as well, and in the short Indian summer of his glory there was talk of a renewed engagement at a certain cultured home on Park Avenue. But then the blow fell. A final disgrace, compared to which the others had been as nothing, shattered the illusions of those who had come to believe in Galpin's reform; and the young man abandoned his name and disappeared from public view. Rumour now and then associated him with a certain "Consul Hasting" whose work for the stage and for motion-picture companies attracted a certain degree of attention because of its scholarly breadth and depth; but Hasting soon disappeared from the public eye, and Galpin became only a name for parents to quote in warning accents. Eleanor Wing soon celebrated her marriage to Karl Trever, a rising young lawyer, and of her former admirer retained only enough memory to dictate the naming of her only son, and the moral guidance of that handsome and headstrong youth. Now, in spite of all that guidance, Alfred Trever was at Sheehan's and about to take his first drink.

"Boss," cried Schultz, as he entered the vile-smelling room with his young victim, "meet my friend Al Trever, bes' li'l' sport up at Lawrence — tha's 'n Appleton, Wisconsin, y' know. Some swell guy, too — 's father's a big corp'ration lawyer up in his burg, 'n 's mother's some fiery genius. He wants to see life as she is — wants to know what the real lightnin' juice tastes like — so jus' remember he's me friend an' treat 'im right."

As the names Trever, Lawrence, and Appleton fell on the air, the loafers seemed to sense something unusual. Perhaps it was only some sound connected with the clicking balls of the pool tables or the rattling glasses that were brought from the cryptic regions in the rear — perhaps only that, plus some strange rustling of the dirty draperies at the one dingy window — but many thought that someone in the room had gritted his teeth and drawn a very sharp breath.

"Glad to know you, Sheehan," said Trever in a quiet, well-bred tone. "This is my first experience in a place like this, but I am a student of life, and don't want to miss any experience. There's poetry in this sort of thing, you know — or perhaps you don't know, but it's all the same."

"Young feller," responded the proprietor, "ya come tuh th' right place tuh see life. We got all kinds here — reel life an' a good time. The damn' government can try tuh make folks good if it wants tuh, but it can't stop a feller from hittin' 'er up when he feels like it. Whaddya want, feller — booze, coke, or some other sorta dope? Yuh can't ask for nothin' we ain't got."

Habitués say that it was at this point they noticed a cessation in the regular, monotonous strokes of the mop.

"I want whiskey — good old-fashioned rye!" exclaimed Trever enthusiastically. "I'll tell you, I'm good and tired of water after reading of the merry bouts fellows used to have in the old days. I can't read an Anacreontic without watering at the mouth — and it's something a lot stronger than water that my mouth waters for!"

"Anacreontic — what'n hell's that?" Several hangers-on looked up as the young man went slightly beyond their depth. But the bank defaulter under cover explained to them that Anacreon was a gay old dog who lived many years ago and wrote about the fun he had when all the world was just like Sheehan's.

"Let me see, Trever," continued the defaulter, "didn't Schultz say your mother is a literary person, too?"

"Yes, damn it," replied Trever, "but nothing like the old Teian! She's one of those dull, eternal moralisers that try to take all the joy out of life. Namby-pamby sort — ever heard of her? She writes under her maiden name of Eleanor Wing."

Here it was that Old Bugs dropped his mop.

"Well, here's yer stuff," announced Sheehan jovially as a tray of bottles and glasses was wheeled into the room. "Good old rye, an' as fiery as ya kin find anyw'eres in Chi."

The youth's eyes glistened and his nostrils curled at the fumes of the brownish fluid which an attendant was pouring out for him. It repelled him horribly, and revolted all his inherited delicacy; but his determination to taste life to the full remained with him, and he maintained a bold front. But before his resolution was put to the test, the unexpected intervened. Old Bugs, springing up from the crouching position in which he had hitherto been, leaped at the youth and dashed from his hands the uplifted glass, almost simultaneously attacking the tray of bottles and glasses with his mop, and scattering the contents upon the floor in a confusion of odoriferous fluid and broken bottles and tumblers. Numbers of men, or things which had been men, dropped to the floor and began lapping at the puddles of spilled liquor, but most remained immovable, watching the unprecedented actions of the barroom drudge and derelict. Old Bugs straightened up before the astonished Trever, and in a mild and cultivated voice said, "Do not do this thing. I was like you once, and I did it. Now I am like — this."

"What do you mean, you damned old fool?" shouted Trever. "What do you mean by interfering with a gentleman in his pleasures?" Sheehan, now recovering from his astonishment, advanced and laid a heavy hand on the old waif's shoulder.

"This is the last time far you, old bird!" he exclaimed furiously. "When a gen'l'man wants tuh take a drink here, by God, he shall, without you interferin'. Now get th' hell outa here afore I kick hell outa ya."

But Sheehan had reckoned without scientific knowledge of abnormal psychology and the effects of nervous stimulus. Old Bugs, obtaining a firmer hold on his mop, began to wield it like the javelin of a Macedonian hoplite, and soon cleared a considerable space around himself, meanwhile shouting various disconnected bits of quotation, among which was prominently repeated, " . . . the sons of Belial, blown with insolence and wine."

The room became pandemonium, and men screamed and howled in fright at the sinister being they had aroused. Trever seemed dazed in the confusion, and shrank to the wall as the strife thickened. "He shall not drink! He shall not drink!" Thus roared Old Bugs as he seemed to run out of — or rise above — quotations. Policemen appeared at the door, attracted by the noise, but for a time they made no move to intervene. Trever, now thoroughly terrified and cured forever of his desire to see life via the vice route, edged closer to the blue-coated newcomers. Could he but escape and catch a train for Appleton, he reflected, he would consider his education in dissipation quite complete.

Then suddenly Old Bugs ceased to wield his javelin and stopped still — drawing himself up more erectly than any denizen of the place had ever seen him before. "Ave, Caesar, moriturus te saluto!" he shouted, and dropped to the whiskey-reeking floor, never to rise again.

Subsequent impressions will never leave the mind of young Trever. The picture is blurred, but ineradicable. Policemen ploughed a way through the crowd, questioning everyone closely both about the incident and about the dead figure on the floor. Sheehan especially did they ply with inquiries, yet without eliciting any information of value concerning Old Bugs. Then the bank defaulter remembered the picture, and suggested that it be viewed and filed for identification at police headquarters. An officer bent reluctantly over the loathsome glassyeyed form and found the tissue-wrapped cardboard, which he passed around among the others.

"Some chicken!" leered a drunken man as he viewed the beautiful face, but those who were sober did not leer, looking with respect and abashment at the delicate and spiritual features. No one seemed able to place the subject, and all wondered that the drug-degraded derelict should have such a portrait in his possession — that is, all but the bank defaulter, who was meanwhile eyeing the intruding bluecoats rather uneasily. He had seen a little deeper beneath Old Bugs' mask of utter degradation.

Then the picture was passed to Trever, and a change came over the youth. After the first start, he replaced the tissue wrapping around the portrait, as if to shield it from the sordidness of the place. Then he gazed long and searchingly at the figure on the floor, noting its great height, and the aristocratic cast of features which seemed to appear now that the wretched flame of life had flickered out. No, he said hastily, as the question was put to him, he did not know the subject of the picture. It was so old, he added, that no one now could be expected to recognise it.

But Alfred Trever did not speak the truth, as many guessed when he offered to take charge of the body and secure its interment in Appleton. Over the library mantel in his home hung the exact replica of that picture, and all his life he had known and loved its original.

For the gentle and noble features were those of his own mother.

The Transition of Juan Romero.

2,700-WORD SHORT STORY; 1919.

No one will ever mistake "The Transition of Juan Romero" for H.P. Lovecraft's best work, but it's not as awful as he seems to have thought it was after he had written it. Shortly after he finished it, on Sept. 16, 1919, Lovecraft put it away, and would not allow it to be published, even in the most obscure of his friends' amateur journals. It did not see print until 1944, well after Lovecraft's death, when it appeared in Marginalia, *one of the Arkham House collections.*

There certainly are some flaws that can be, and have been, pointed to; and this is one of the Lovecraft stories in which his early casual racism mars his work. However, one can also see the early stirrings of Lovecraft's style taking shape.

Of the events which took place at the Norton Mine on October 18th and 19th, 1894, I have no desire to speak. A sense of duty to science is all that impels me to recall, in the last years of my life, scenes and happenings fraught with a terror doubly acute because I cannot wholly define it. But I believe that before I die I should tell what I know of the — shall I say transition — of Juan Romero.

My name and origin need not be related to posterity; in fact, I fancy it is better that they should not be, for when a man suddenly migrates to the States or the Colonies, he leaves his past behind him. Besides, what I once was is not in the least relevant to my narrative; save perhaps the fact that during my service in India I was more at home amongst white-bearded native teachers than amongst my brother-officers. I had delved not a little into odd Eastern lore when overtaken by the calamities which brought about my new life in America's vast West — a life wherein I found it well to accept a name — my present one — which is very common and carries no meaning.

In the summer and autumn of 1894 I dwelt in the drear expanses of the Cactus Mountains, employed as a common labourer at the celebrated Norton Mine, whose discovery by an aged prospector some years before had turned the surrounding region from a nearly unpeopled waste to a seething cauldron of sordid life. A cavern of gold, lying deep beneath a mountain lake, had enriched its venerable finder beyond his wildest dreams, and now formed the seat of extensive tunneling operations on the part of the corporation to which it had finally been sold. Additional grottoes had been found, and the yield of yellow metal was exceedingly great; so that a mighty and heterogeneous army of miners toiled day and night in the numerous passages and rock hollows. The Superintendent, a Mr. Arthur, often discussed the singularity of the local geological formations; speculating on the probable extent of the chain of caves, and estimating the future of the titanic mining enterprises. He considered the auriferous cavities the result of the action of water, and believed the last of them would soon be opened.

It was not long after my arrival and employment that Juan Romero came to the Norton Mine. One of the large herd of unkempt Mexicans attracted thither from the neighbouring country, he at first attracted attention only because of his features; which though plainly of the Red Indian type, were yet remarkable for their light colour and refined conformation, being vastly unlike those of the average "greaser" or Piute of the locality. It is curious that although he differed so widely from the mass of Hispanicised and tribal Indians, Romero gave not the least impression of Caucasian blood. It was not the Castilian conquistador or the American pioneer, but the ancient and noble Aztec, whom imagination called to view when the silent peon would rise in the early morning and gaze in fascination at the sun as it crept above the eastern hills, meanwhile stretching out his arms to the orb as if in the performance of some rite whose nature he did not himself comprehend. But save for his face, Romero was not in any way suggestive of nobility. Ignorant and dirty, he was at home amongst the other brown-skinned Mexicans; having come (so I was afterward told) from the very lowest sort of surroundings. He had been found as a child in a crude mountain hut, the only survivor of an epidemic which had stalked lethally by. Near the hut, close to a rather unusual rock fissure, had lain two skeletons, newly picked by vultures, and presumably forming the sole remains of his parents. No one recalled their identity, and they were soon forgotten by the many. Indeed, the crumbling of the adobe hut and the closing of the rock-fissure by a subsequent avalanche had helped to efface even the scene from recollection. Reared by a Mexican cattle-thief who had given him his name, Juan differed little from his fellows.

The attachment which Romero manifested toward me was undoubtedly commenced through the quaint and ancient Hindoo ring which I wore when not engaged in active labour. Of its nature, and manner of coming into my possession, I cannot speak. It was my last link with a chapter of my life forever closed, and I valued it highly. Soon I observed that the odd-looking Mexican was likewise interested; eyeing it with an expression that banished all suspicion of mere covetousness.

Its hoary hieroglyphs seemed to stir some faint recollection in his untutored but active mind, though he could not possibly have beheld their like before. Within a few weeks after his advent, Romero was like a faithful servant to me; this notwithstanding the fact that I was myself but an ordinary miner. Our conversation was necessarily limited. He knew but a few words of English, while I found my Oxonian Spanish was something quite different from the patois of the peon of New Spain.

The event which I am about to relate was unheralded by long premonitions. Though the man Romero had interested me, and though my ring had affected him peculiarly, I think that neither of us had any expectation of what was to follow when the great blast was set off. Geological considerations had dictated an extension of the mine directly downward from the deepest part of the subterranean area; and the belief of the Superintendent that only solid rock would be encountered, had led to the placing of a prodigious charge of dynamite. With this work Romero and I were not connected, wherefore our first knowledge of extraordinary conditions came from others. The charge, heavier perhaps than had been estimated, had seemed to shake the entire mountain. Windows in shanties on the slope outside were shattered by the shock, whilst miners throughout the nearer passages were knocked from their feet. Jewel Lake, which lay above the scene of action, heaved as in a tempest. Upon investigation it was seen that a new abyss yawned indefinitely below the seat of the blast; an abyss so monstrous that no handy line might fathom it, nor any lamp illuminate it. Baffled, the excavators sought a conference with the Superintendent, who ordered great lengths of rope to be taken to the pit, and spliced and lowered without cessation till a bottom might be discovered.

Shortly afterward the pale-faced workmen apprised the Superintendent of their failure. Firmly though respectfully, they signified their refusal to revisit the chasm or indeed to work further in the mine until it might be sealed. Something beyond their experience was evidently confronting them, for so far as they could ascertain, the void below was infinite. The Superintendent did not reproach them. Instead, he pondered deeply, and made plans for the following day. The night shift did not go on that evening.

At two in the morning a lone coyote on the mountain began to howl dismally. From somewhere within the works a dog barked an answer; either to the coyote — or to something else. A storm was gathering around the peaks of the range, and weirdly shaped clouds scudded horribly across the blurred patch of celestial light which marked a gibbous moon's attempts to shine through many layers of cirro-stratus vapours. It was Romero's voice, coming from the bunk above, that awakened me, a voice excited and tense with some vague expectation I could not understand:

"*Madre de Dios! — el sonido — ese sonido — oiga Vd! — lo oye Vd? — señor,* THAT SOUND!"

I listened, wondering what sound he meant. The coyote, the dog, the storm, all were audible; the last named now gaining ascendancy as the wind shrieked more and more frantically. Flashes of lightning were visible through the bunk-house window. I questioned the nervous Mexican, repeating the sounds I had heard:

"El coyote — el perro — el viento?"

But Romero did not reply. Then he commenced whispering as in awe:

"El ritmo, señor — el ritmo de la tierra — THAT THROB DOWN IN THE GROUND!"

And now I also heard; heard and shivered and without knowing why. Deep, deep, below me was a sound — a rhythm, just as the peon had said — which, though exceedingly faint, yet dominated even the dog, the coyote, and the increasing tempest. To seek to describe it was useless — for it was such that no description is possible. Perhaps it was like the pulsing of the engines far down in a great liner, as sensed from the deck, yet it was not so mechanical; not so devoid of the element of the life and consciousness. Of all its qualities, remoteness in the earth most impressed me. To my mind rushed fragments of a passage in Joseph Glanvil which Poe has quoted with tremendous effect: " . . . the vastness, profundity, and unsearchableness of His works, which have a depth in them greater than the well of Democritus."[1]

Suddenly Romero leaped from his bunk, pausing before me to gaze at the strange ring on my hand, which glistened queerly in every flash of lightning, and then staring intently in the direction of the mine shaft. I also rose, and both of us stood motionless for a time, straining our ears as the uncanny rhythm seemed more and more to take on a vital quality. Then without apparent volition we began to move toward the door, whose rattling in the gale held a comforting suggestion of earthly reality. The chanting in the depths — for such the sound now seemed to be — grew in volume and distinctness; and we felt irresistibly urged out into the storm and thence to the gaping blackness of the shaft.

We encountered no living creature, for the men of the night shift had been released from duty, and were doubtless at the Dry Gulch settlement pouring sinister rumours into the ear of some drowsy bartender. From the watchman's cabin, however, gleamed a small square of yellow light like a guardian eye. I dimly wondered how the rhythmic sound had affected the watchman; but Romero was moving more swiftly now, and I followed without pausing.

As we descended the shaft, the sound beneath grew definitely composite. It struck me as horribly like a sort of Oriental ceremony, with beating of drums and chanting of many voices. I have, as you are aware, been much in India. Romero and I moved without material hesitancy through drifts and down ladders; ever toward the thing that allured us, yet ever with a pitifully helpless fear and reluctance. At one time I fancied I

1. *Motto of* A Descent Into the Maelstrom.

had gone mad — this was when, on wondering how our way was lighted in the absence of lamp or candle, I realized that the ancient ring on my finger was glowing with eerie radiance, diffusing a pallid lustre through the damp, heavy air around.

It was without warning that Romero, after clambering down one of the many wide ladders, broke into a run and left me alone. Some new and wild note in the drumming and chanting, perceptible but slightly to me, had acted on him in a startling fashion; and with a wild outcry he forged ahead unguided in the cavern's gloom. I heard his repeated shrieks before me, as he stumbled awkwardly along the level places and scrambled madly down the rickety ladders. And frightened as I was, I yet retained enough of my perception to note that his speech, when articulate, was not of any sort known to me. Harsh but impressive polysyllables had replaced the customary mixture of bad Spanish and worse English, and of these, only the oft repeated cry "Huitzilopotchli" seemed in the least familiar. Later I definitely placed that word in the works of a great historian[1] — and shuddered when the association came to me.

The climax of that awful night was composite but fairly brief, beginning just as I reached the final cavern of the journey. Out of the darkness immediately ahead burst a final shriek from the Mexican, which was joined by such a chorus of uncouth sound as I could never hear again and survive. In that moment it seemed as if all the hidden terrors and monstrosities of earth had become articulate in an effort to overwhelm the human race. Simultaneously the light from my ring was extinguished, and I saw a new light glimmering from lower space but a few yards ahead of me. I had arrived at the abyss, which was now redly aglow, and which had evidently swallowed up the unfortunate Romero. Advancing, I peered over the edge of that chasm which no line could fathom, and which was now a pandemonium of flickering flame and hideous uproar. At first I beheld nothing but a seething blur of luminosity; but then shapes, all infinitely distant, began to detach themselves from the confusion, and I saw — was it Juan Romero? — but God! I dare not tell you what I saw! . . . Some power from heaven, coming to my aid, obliterated both sights and sounds in such a crash as may be heard when two universes collide in space. Chaos supervened, and I knew the peace of oblivion.

I hardly know how to continue, since conditions so singular are involved; but I will do my best, not even trying to differentiate betwixt the real and the apparent. When I awakened, I was safe in my bunk and the red glow of dawn was visible at the window. Some distance away the lifeless body of Juan Romero lay upon a table, surrounded by a group of men, including the camp doctor. The men were discussing the strange death of the Mexican as he lay asleep; a death seemingly connected in some way with the terrible bolt of lightning which had struck and shaken the mountain. No direct cause was evident, and an autopsy failed to show any reason why Romero should not be living. Snatches of conversation indicated beyond a doubt that neither Romero nor I had left the bunk-house during the night; that neither of us had been awake during the frightful storm which had passed over the Cactus range. That storm, said men who had ventured down the mine shaft, had caused extensive caving-in, and had completely closed the deep abyss which had created so much apprehension the day before. When I asked the watchman what sounds he had heard prior to the mighty thunder-bolt; he mentioned a coyote, a dog, and the snarling mountain wind — nothing more. Nor do I doubt his word.

Upon the resumption of work, Superintendent Arthur called upon some especially dependable men to make a few investigations around the spot where the gulf had appeared. Though hardly eager, they obeyed, and a deep boring was made. Results were very curious. The roof of the void, as seen when it was open, was not by any means thick; yet now the drills of the investigators met what appeared to be a limitless extent of solid rock. Finding nothing else, not even gold, the Superintendent abandoned his attempts; but a perplexed look occasionally steals over his countenance as he sits thinking at his desk.

One other thing is curious. Shortly after waking on that morning after the storm, I noticed the unaccountable absence of my Hindoo ring from my finger. I had prized it greatly, yet nevertheless felt a sensation of relief at its disappearance. If one of my fellow-miners appropriated it, he must have been quite clever in disposing of his booty, for despite advertisements and a police search, the ring was never seen again. Somehow I doubt if it was stolen by mortal hands, for many strange things were taught me in India.

My opinion of my whole experience varies from time to time. In broad daylight, and at most seasons I am apt to think the greater part of it a mere dream; but sometimes in the autumn, about two in the morning when the winds and animals howl dismally, there comes from inconceivable depths below a damnable suggestion of rhythmical throbbing . . . and I feel that the transition of Juan Romero was a terrible one indeed.

1 *Prescott,* Conquest of Mexico.

The White Ship.

2,500-WORD SHORT STORY; 1919.

This short story is the first of a series of H.P. Lovecraft's stories written in conscious imitation of the style of Lord Dunsany, whose work he had just discovered when he wrote it in October 1919.

Lord Dunsany, the Anglo-Irish fantaisiste, *had a substantial effect on Lovecraft's writing style from the moment Lovecraft discovered him, shortly after penning "The Transition of Juan Romero." Biographers have lamented the influence from time to time, since for a year or two after this much of Lovecraft's work acquired the characteristic dreamy, poetic style of a Dunsany pastiche.*

"The White Ship" was first published in the November 1919 issue of United Amateur.

I am Basil Elton, Keeper of the North Point Light that my father and grandfather kept before me. Far from the shore stands the gray lighthouse, above sunken slimy rocks that are seen when the tide is low, but unseen when the tide is high. Past that beacon for a century have swept the majestic barques of the seven seas. In the days of my grandfather there were many; in the days of my father not so many; and now there are so few that I sometimes feel strangely alone, as though I were the last man on our planet.

From far shores came those white-sailed argosies of old; from far Eastern shores where warm suns shine and sweet odors linger about strange gardens and gay temples. The old captains of the sea came often to my grandfather and told him of these things which in turn he told to my father, and my father told to me in the long autumn evenings when the wind howled eerily from the East. And I have read more of these things, and of many things besides, in the books men gave me when I was young and filled with wonder.

But more wonderful than the lore of old men and the lore of books is the secret lore of ocean. Blue, green, gray, white or black; smooth, ruffled, or mountainous; that ocean is not silent. All my days have I watched it and listened to it, and I know it well. At first it told to me only the plain little tales of calm beaches and near ports, but with the years it grew more friendly and spoke of other things; of things more strange and more distant in space and time. Sometimes at twilight the gray vapors of the horizon have parted to grant me glimpses of the ways beyond; and sometimes at night the deep waters of the sea have grown clear and phosphorescent, to grant me glimpses of the ways beneath. And these glimpses have been as often of the ways that were and the ways that might be, as of the ways that are; for ocean is more ancient than the mountains, and freighted with the memories and the dreams of Time.

Out of the South it was that the White Ship used to come when the moon was full and high in the heavens. Out of the South it would glide very smoothly and silently over the sea. And whether the sea was rough or calm, and whether the wind was friendly or adverse, it would always glide smoothly and silently, its sails distant and its long strange tiers of oars moving rhythmically. One night I espied upon the deck a man, bearded and robed, and he seemed to beckon me to embark for far unknown shores. Many times afterward I saw him under the full moon, and ever did he beckon me.

Very brightly did the moon shine on the night I answered the call, and I walked out over the waters to the White Ship on a bridge of moonbeams. The man who had beckoned now spoke a welcome to me in a soft language I seemed to know well, and the hours were filled with soft songs of the oarsmen as we glided away into a mysterious South, golden with the glow of that full, mellow moon.

And when the day dawned, rosy and effulgent, I beheld the green shore of far lands, bright and beautiful, and to me unknown. Up from the sea rose lordly terraces of verdure, tree-studded, and shewing here and there the gleaming white roofs and colonnades of strange temples. As we drew nearer the green shore the bearded man told me of that land, the land of Zar, where dwell all the dreams and thoughts of beauty that come to men once and then are forgotten. And when I looked upon the terraces again I saw that what he said was true, for among the sights before me were many things I had once seen through the mists beyond the horizon and in the phosphorescent depths of ocean. There too were forms and fantasies more splendid than any I had ever known; the visions of young poets who died in want before the world could learn of what they had seen and dreamed. But we did not set foot upon the sloping meadows of Zar, for it is told that he who treads them may nevermore return to his native shore.

As the White Ship sailed silently away from the templed terraces of Zar, we beheld on the distant horizon ahead the spires of a mighty city; and the bearded man said to me, "This is Thalarion, the City of a Thousand Wonders, wherein reside all those mysteries that man has striven in vain to fathom." And I looked again, at closer range, and saw that the city was greater than any city I had known or dreamed of before. Into the sky the spires of its temples reached, so that no man might behold their peaks; and far back beyond the horizon stretched the grim, gray walls, over which one might spy only a few roofs, weird and ominous, yet adorned with rich friezes and alluring sculptures. I yearned mightily to enter this fascinating yet repellent city, and besought the bearded man to land me at the stone pier by the huge carven gate Akariel; but he gently denied my wish, saying, "Into Thalarion, the City of a Thousand Wonders, many have passed but none returned. Therein walk only daemons and mad things that are no longer men, and the streets are white with the unburied bones of those who have looked upon the eidolon Lathi, that reigns over the city." So the White Ship sailed on past the walls of Thalarion, and followed for many days a southward-flying bird, whose glossy plumage matched the sky out of which it had appeared.

Then came we to a pleasant coast gay with blossoms of every hue, where as far inland as we could see basked lovely groves and radiant arbors beneath a meridian sun. From bowers beyond our view came bursts of song and snatches of lyric harmony, interspersed with faint laughter so delicious that I urged the rowers onward in my eagerness to reach the scene. And the bearded man spoke no word, but watched me as we approached the lily-lined shore. Suddenly a wind blowing from over the flowery meadows and leafy woods brought a scent at which I trembled. The wind grew stronger, and the air was filled with the lethal, charnel odor of plague-stricken towns and uncovered cemeteries. And as we sailed madly away from that damnable coast the bearded man spoke at last, saying, "This is Xura, the Land of Pleasures Unattained."

So once more the White Ship followed the bird of heaven, over warm blessed seas fanned by caressing, aromatic breezes. Day after day and night after night did we sail, and when the moon was full we would listen to soft songs of the oarsmen, sweet as on that distant night when we sailed away from my far native land. And it was by moonlight that we anchored at last in the harbor of Sona-Nyl, which is guarded by twin headlands of crystal that rise from the sea and meet in a resplendent arch. This is the Land of Fancy, and we walked to the verdant shore upon a golden bridge of moonbeams.

In the Land of Sona-Nyl there is neither time nor space, neither suffering nor death; and there I dwelt for many aeons. Green are the groves and pastures, bright and fragrant the flowers, blue and musical the streams, clear and cool the fountains, and stately and gorgeous the temples, castles, and cities of Sona-Nyl. Of that land there is no bound, for beyond each vista of beauty rises another more beautiful. Over the countryside and amidst the splendor of cities can move at will the happy folk, of whom all are gifted with unmarred grace and unalloyed happiness. For the aeons that I dwelt there I wandered blissfully through gardens where quaint pagodas peep from pleasing clumps of bushes, and where the white walks are bordered with delicate blossoms. I climbed gentle hills from whose summits I could see entrancing panoramas of loveliness, with steepled towns nestling in verdant valleys, and with the golden domes of gigantic cities glittering on the infinitely distant horizon. And I viewed by moonlight the sparkling sea, the crystal headlands, and the placid harbor wherein lay anchored the White Ship.

It was against the full moon one night in the immemorial year of Tharp that I saw outlined the beckoning form of the celestial bird, and felt the first stirrings of unrest. Then I spoke with the bearded man, and told him of my new yearnings to depart for remote Cathuria, which no man hath seen, but which all believe to lie beyond the basalt pillars of the West. It is the Land of Hope, and in it shine the perfect ideals of all that we know elsewhere; or at least so men relate. But the bearded man said to me, "Beware of those perilous seas wherein men say Cathuria lies. In Sona-Nyl there is no pain or death, but who can tell what lies beyond the basalt pillars of the West?" Natheless at the next full moon I boarded the White Ship, and with the reluctant bearded man left the happy harbor for untraveled seas.

And the bird of heaven flew before, and led us toward the basalt pillars of the West, but this time the oarsmen sang no soft songs under the full moon. In my mind I would often picture the unknown Land of Cathuria with its splendid groves and palaces, and would wonder what new delights there awaited me. "Cathuria," I would say to myself, "is the abode of gods and the land of unnumbered cities of gold. Its forests are of aloe and sandalwood, even as the fragrant groves of Camorin, and among the trees flutter gay birds sweet with song. On the green and flowery mountains of Cathuria stand temples of pink marble, rich with carven and painted glories, and having in their courtyards cool fountains of silver, where purr with ravishing music the scented waters that come from the grotto-born river Narg. And the cities of Cathuria are cinctured with golden walls, and their pavements also are of gold. In the gardens of these cities are strange orchids, and perfumed lakes whose beds are of coral and amber. At night the streets and the gardens are lit with gay lanthorns fashioned from the three-colored shell of the tortoise, and here resound the soft notes of the singer and the lutanist. And the houses of the cities of Cathuria are all palaces, each built over a fragrant canal bearing the waters of the sacred Narg. Of marble and porphyry are the houses, and roofed with glittering gold that reflects the rays of the sun and enhances the splendor of the cities as blissful gods view them from the distant peaks. Fairest of all is the palace of the great monarch Dorieb, whom some say to be a demi-god and others a god. High is the palace of Dorieb, and many are the turrets of marble upon its walls. In its wide halls many multitudes assemble, and here hang the trophies of the ages. And the roof is of pure gold, set upon tall pillars of ruby and azure, and having such carven figures of gods and heroes that he who looks up to those heights seems to gaze upon the living Olympus. And the floor of the palace is of glass, under which flow the cunningly lighted waters of the Narg, gay with gaudy fish not known beyond the bounds of lovely Cathuria."

Thus would I speak to myself of Cathuria, but ever would

the bearded man warn me to turn back to the happy shore of Sona-Nyl; for Sona-Nyl is known of men, while none hath ever beheld Cathuria.

And on the thirty-first day that we followed the bird, we beheld the basalt pillars of the West. Shrouded in mist they were, so that no man might peer beyond them or see their summits — which indeed some say reach even to the heavens. And the bearded man again implored me to turn back, but I heeded him not; for from the mists beyond the basalt pillars I fancied there came the notes of singers and lutanists; sweeter than the sweetest songs of Sona-Nyl, and sounding mine own praises; the praises of me, who had voyaged far from the full moon and dwelt in the Land of Fancy. So to the sound of melody the White Ship sailed into the mist betwixt the basalt pillars of the West. And when the music ceased and the mist lifted, we beheld not the Land of Cathuria, but a swift-rushing resistless sea, over which our helpless barque was borne toward some unknown goal. Soon to our ears came the distant thunder of falling waters, and to our eyes appeared on the far horizon ahead the titanic spray of a monstrous cataract, wherein the oceans of the world drop down to abysmal nothingness. Then did the bearded man say to me, with tears on his cheek, "We have rejected the beautiful Land of Sona-Nyl, which we may never behold again. The gods are greater than men, and they have conquered." And I closed my eyes before the crash that I knew would come, shutting out the sight of the celestial bird which flapped its mocking blue wings over the brink of the torrent.

Out of that crash came darkness, and I heard the shrieking of men and of things which were not men. From the East tempestuous winds arose, and chilled me as I crouched on the slab of damp stone which had risen beneath my feet. Then as I heard another crash I opened my eyes and beheld myself upon the platform of that lighthouse whence I had sailed so many aeons ago. In the darkness below there loomed the vast blurred outlines of a vessel breaking up on the cruel rocks, and as I glanced out over the waste I saw that the light had failed for the first time since my grandfather had assumed its care.

And in the later watches of the night, when I went within the tower, I saw on the wall a calendar which still remained as when I had left it at the hour I sailed away. With the dawn I descended the tower and looked for wreckage upon the rocks, but what I found was only this: a strange dead bird whose hue was as of the azure sky, and a single shattered spar, of a whiteness greater than that of the wave-tips or of the mountain snow.

And thereafter the ocean told me its secrets no more; and though many times since has the moon shone full and high in the heavens, the White Ship from the South came never again.

The Street.

2,200-WORD SHORT STORY; 1919.

S. T. Joshi calls "The Street" "probably the single worst tale Lovecraft ever wrote." For most modern readers, it is hard to disagree. Later in his life, Lovecraft himself came to believe the story was terrible.

But this is a story that cannot be understood outside its historical context. It was written late in the year 1919, which was a year in which a plot by terrorists to send mail bombs to J. P. Morgan, Oliver Wendell Holmes, and 34 other prominent Americans was exposed, in April; two months later, an Italian-born radical accidentally blew himself up trying to kill Attorney General Alexander Palmer. Palmer responded by launching, with the help of J. Edgar Hoover and under cover of a concerted propaganda effort, the notorious "Palmer Raids," and one of the most dramatic of these was a day of violent raids against offices of the Union of Russian Workers, on Nov. 7, 1919.

It is a near-certainty that these raids, staged just a few days before Lovecraft set pen to paper to write this story, had a lot to do with his writing it. Thanks in part to the success of Palmer's propaganda campaign, Americans were very much afraid of something just like the conspiracy depicted in "The Street"; there is ample reason to believe Lovecraft was no exception. To attribute the fears articulated in this story to simple racism, as so many critics have done, is to, at the very least, oversimplify its context.

"The Street" was first published in the December 1920 issue of Horace L. Lawson's amateur journal, The Wolverine.

There be those who say that things and places have souls, and there be those who say they have not; I dare not say, myself, but I will tell of The Street.

Men of strength and honour fashioned that Street: good valiant men of our blood who had come from the Blessed Isles across the sea. At first it was but a path trodden by bearers of water from the woodland spring to the cluster of houses by the beach. Then, as more men came to the growing cluster of houses and looked about for places to dwell, they built cabins along the north side, cabins of stout oaken logs with masonry on the side toward the forest, for many Indians lurked there with fire-arrows. And in a few years more, men built cabins on the south side of The Street.

Up and down The Street walked grave men in conical hats, who most of the time carried muskets or fowling pieces. And there were also their bonneted wives and sober children. In the evening these men with their wives and children would sit about gigantic hearths and read and speak. Very simple were the things of which they read and spoke, yet things which gave them courage and goodness and helped them by day to subdue the forest and till the fields. And the children would listen and learn of the laws and deeds of old, and of that dear England which they had never seen or could not remember.

There was war, and thereafter no more Indians troubled The Street. The men, busy with labour, waxed prosperous and as happy as they knew how to be. And the children grew up comfortable, and more families came from the Mother Land to dwell on The Street. And the children's children, and the newcomers' children, grew up. The town was now a city, and one by one the cabins gave place to houses — simple, beautiful houses of brick and wood, with stone steps and iron railings and fanlights over the doors. No flimsy creations were these houses, for they were made to serve many a generation. Within there were carven mantels and graceful stairs, and sensible, pleasing furniture, china, and silver, brought from the Mother Land.

So The Street drank in the dreams of a young people and rejoiced as its dwellers became more graceful and happy. Where once had been only strength and honour, taste and learning now abode as well. Books and paintings and music came to the houses, and the young men went to the university which rose above the plain to the north. In the place of conical hats and small-swords, of lace and snowy periwigs, there were cobblestones over which clattered many a blooded horse and rumbled many a gilded coach; and brick sidewalks with horse blocks and hitching-posts.

There were in that Street many trees: elms and oaks and maples of dignity; so that in the summer, the scene was all soft verdure and twittering bird-song. And behind the houses were walled rose-gardens with hedged paths and sundials, where at evening the moon and stars would shine bewitchingly while fragrant blossoms glistened with dew.

So The Street dreamed on, past wars, calamities, and change. Once, most of the young men went away, and some never came back. That was when they furled the old flag and put up a new banner of stripes and stars. But though men talked of great changes, The Street felt them not, for its folk were still the same, speaking of the old familiar things in the old familiar accounts. And the trees still sheltered singing birds, and at evening the moon and stars looked down upon dewy blossoms in the walled rose-gardens.

In time there were no more swords, three-cornered hats, or periwigs in The Street. How strange seemed the inhabitants with their walking-sticks, tall beavers, and cropped heads! New sounds came from the distance — first strange puffings and shrieks from the river a mile away, and then, many years later, strange puffings and shrieks and rumblings from other directions. The air was not quite so pure as before, but the spirit of the place had not changed. The blood and soul of their ancestors had fashioned The Street. Nor did the spirit change when they tore open the earth to lay down strange pipes, or when they set up tall posts bearing weird wires. There was so much ancient lore in that Street, that the past could not easily be forgotten.

Then came days of evil, when many who had known The Street of old knew it no more, and many knew it who had not known it before, and went away, for their accents were coarse and strident, and their mien and faces unpleasing. Their thoughts, too, fought with the wise, just spirit of The Street, so that The Street pined silently as its houses fell into decay, and its trees died one by one, and its rose-gardens grew rank with weeds and waste. But it felt a stir of pride one day when again marched forth young men, some of whom never came back. These young men were clad in blue.

With the years, worse fortune came to The Street. Its trees were all gone now, and its rose-gardens were displaced by the backs of cheap, ugly new buildings on parallel streets. Yet the houses remained, despite the ravages of the years and the storms and worms, for they had been made to serve many a generation. New kinds of faces appeared in The Street, swarthy, sinister faces with furtive eyes and odd features, whose owners spoke unfamiliar words and placed signs in known and unknown characters upon most of the musty houses. Push-carts crowded the gutters. A sordid, undefinable stench settled over the place, and the ancient spirit slept.

Great excitement once came to The Street. War and revolution were raging across the seas; a dynasty had collapsed, and its degenerate subjects were flocking with dubious intent to the Western Land. Many of these took lodgings in the battered houses that had once known the songs of birds and the scent of roses. Then the Western Land itself awoke and joined the Mother Land in her titanic struggle for civilization. Over the cities once more floated the old flag, companioned by the new flag, and by a plainer, yet glorious tricolour. But not many flags floated over The Street, for therein brooded only fear and hatred and ignorance. Again young men went forth, but not quite as did the young men of those other days. Something was lacking. And the sons of those young men of other days, who did indeed go forth in olive-drab with the true spirit of their ancestors, went from distant places and knew not The Street and its ancient spirit.

Over the seas there was a great victory, and in triumph most of the young men returned. Those who had lacked something lacked it no longer, yet did fear and hatred and ignorance still brood over The Street; for many had stayed behind, and many strangers had come from distance places to the ancient houses. And the young men who had returned dwelt there no longer. Swarthy and sinister were most of the strangers, yet among them one might find a few faces like those who fashioned The Street and moulded its spirit. Like and yet unlike, for there was in the eyes of all a weird, unhealthy glitter as of greed, ambition, vindictiveness, or misguided zeal. Unrest and treason were abroad amongst an evil few who plotted to strike the Western Land its death blow, that they might mount to power over its ruins, even as assassins had mounted in that unhappy, frozen land from whence most of them had come. And the heart of that plotting was in The Street, whose crumbling houses teemed with alien makers of discord and echoed with the plans and speeches of those who yearned for the appointed day of blood, flame and crime.

Of the various odd assemblages in The Street, the Law said much but could prove little. With great diligence did men of hidden badges linger and listen about such places as Petrovitch's Bakery, the squalid Rifkin School of Modern Economics, the Circle Social Club, and the Liberty Cafe. There congregated sinister men in great numbers, yet always was their speech guarded or in a foreign tongue. And still the old houses stood, with their forgotten lore of nobler, departed centuries; of sturdy Colonial tenants and dewy rose-gardens in the moonlight. Sometimes a lone poet or traveler would come to view them, and would try to picture them in their vanished glory; yet of such travelers and poets there were not many.

The rumour now spread widely that these houses contained the leaders of a vast band of terrorists, who on a designated day were to launch an orgy of slaughter for the extermination of America and of all the fine old traditions which The Street had loved. Handbills and papers fluttered about filthy gutters; handbills and papers printed in many tongues and in many characters, yet all bearing messages of crime and rebellion. In these writings the people were urged to tear down the laws and virtues that our fathers had exalted, to stamp out the soul of the old America — the soul that was bequeathed through a thousand and a half years of Anglo-Saxon freedom, justice, and moderation. It was said that the swart men who dwelt in The Street and congregated in its rotting edifices were the brains of a hideous revolution, that at their word of command many millions of brainless, besotted beasts would stretch forth their noisome talons from the slums of a thousand cities, burning, slaying, and destroying till the land of our fathers should be no more. All this was said and repeated, and many looked forward in dread to the fourth day of July, about which the strange writings hinted much; yet could nothing be found to place the guilt. None could tell just whose arrest might cut off the damnable plotting at its source. Many times came bands of blue-coated police to search the shaky houses, though at last they ceased to come; for they too had grown tired of law and order, and had abandoned all the city to its fate. Then men in olive-drab came, bearing muskets, till it seemed as if in its sad sleep The Street must have some haunting dreams of those other days, when musketbearing men in conical hats walked along it from the woodland spring to the cluster of houses by the beach. Yet could no act be performed to check the impending cataclysm, for the swart, sinister men were old in cunning.

So The Street slept uneasily on, till one night there gathered in Petrovitch's Bakery, and the Rifkin School of Modern Economics, and the Circle Social Club, and Liberty Cafe, and in other places as well, vast hordes of men whose eyes were big with horrible triumph and expectation. Over hidden wires strange messages traveled, and much was said of still stranger messages yet to travel; but most of this was not guessed till afterward, when the Western Land was safe from the peril. The men in olive-drab could not tell what was happening, or what they ought to do; for the swart, sinister men were skilled in subtlety and concealment.

And yet the men in olive-drab will always remember that night, and will speak of The Street as they tell of it to their grandchildren; for many of them were sent there toward morning on a mission unlike that which they had expected. It was known that this nest of anarchy was old, and that the houses were tottering from the ravages of the years and the storms and worms; yet was the happening of that summer night a surprise because of its very queer uniformity. It was, indeed, an exceedingly singular happening, though after all, a simple one. For without warning, in one of the small hours beyond midnight, all the ravages of the years and the storms and the worms came to a tremendous climax; and after the crash there was nothing left standing in The Street save two ancient chimneys and part of a stout brick wall. Nor did anything that had been alive come alive from the ruins. A poet and a traveler, who came with the mighty crowd that sought the scene, tell odd stories. The poet says that all through the hours before dawn he beheld sordid ruins indistinctly in the glare of the arc-lights; that there loomed above the wreckage another picture wherein he could describe moonlight and fair houses and elms and oaks and maples of dignity. And the traveler declares that instead of the place's wonted stench there lingered a delicate fragrance as of roses in full bloom. But are not the dreams of poets and the tales of travelers notoriously false?

There be those who say that things and places have souls, and there be those who say they have not; I dare not say, myself, but I have told you of The Street.

The Doom that Came to Sarnath.

2,600-WORD SHORT STORY; 1919.

This short story is one of Lovecraft's strongly Lord Dunsany-inspired tales. It differs from Dunsany's work, however, in that it is presented not as a story set in a dream-world or realm of fantasy, but as a prehistorical event from the dawn of time on our own Earth. This, of course, transformed the tale from a melancholy but insignificant morsel of daydreaming into an unsettling meditation on what might have been and what might one day again be.

"The Doom that Came to Sarnath" was written on Dec. 3, 1919, and first published in the June 1920 issue of Gavin T. McColl's amateur journal, The Scot.

There is in the land of Mnar a vast still lake that is fed by no stream, and out of which no stream flows. Ten thousand years ago there stood by its shore the mighty city of Sarnath, but Sarnath stands there no more.

It is told that in the immemorial years when the world was young, before ever the men of Sarnath came to the land of Mnar, another city stood beside the lake; the gray stone city of Ib, which was old as the lake itself, and peopled with beings not pleasing to behold. Very odd and ugly were these beings, as indeed are most beings of a world yet inchoate and rudely fashioned. It is written on the brick cylinders of Kadatheron that the beings of Ib were in hue as green as the lake and the mists that rise above it; that they had bulging eyes, pouting, flabby lips, and curious ears, and were without voice. It is also written that they descended one night from the moon in a mist; they and the vast still lake and gray stone city Ib. However this may be, it is certain that they worshipped a sea-green stone idol chiseled in the likeness of Bokrug, the great water-lizard; before which they danced horribly when the moon was gibbous. And it is written in the papyrus of Ilarnek, that they one day discovered fire, and thereafter kindled flames on many ceremonial occasions. But not much is written of these beings, because they lived in very ancient times, and man is young, and knows but little of the very ancient living things.

After many eons men came to the land of Mnar, dark shepherd folk with their fleecy flocks, who built Thraa, Ilarnek, and Kadatheron on the winding river Ai. And certain tribes, more hardy than the rest, pushed on to the border of the lake and built Sarnath at a spot where precious metals were found in the earth.

Not far from the gray city of Ib did the wandering tribes lay the first stones of Sarnath, and at the beings of Ib they marveled greatly. But with their marveling was mixed hate, for they thought it not meet that beings of such aspect should walk about the world of men at dusk. Nor did they like the strange sculptures upon the gray monoliths of Ib, for why those sculptures lingered so late in the world, even until the coming of men, none can tell; unless it was because the land of Mnar is very still, and remote from most other lands, both of waking and of dream.

As the men of Sarnath beheld more of the beings of Ib their hate grew, and it was not less because they found the beings weak, and soft as jelly to the touch of stones and arrows. So one day the young warriors, the slingers and the spearmen and the bowmen, marched against Ib and slew all the inhabitants thereof, pushing the queer bodies into the lake with long spears, because they did not wish to touch them. And because they did not like the gray sculptured monoliths of Ib they cast these also into the lake; wondering from the greatness of the labor how ever the stones were brought from afar, as they must have been, since there is naught like them in the land of Mnar or in the lands adjacent.

Thus of the very ancient city of Ib was nothing spared, save the sea-green stone idol chiseled in the likeness of Bokrug, the water-lizard. This the young warriors took back with them as a symbol of conquest over the old gods and beings of Ib, and as a sign of leadership in Mnar. But on the night after it was set up in the temple, a terrible thing must have happened, for weird lights were seen over the lake, and in the morning the people found the idol gone and the high-priest Taran-Ish lying dead, as from some fear unspeakable. And before he died, Taran-Ish had scrawled upon the altar of chrysolite with coarse shaky strokes the sign of DOOM.

After Taran-Ish there were many high-priests in Sarnath but never was the sea-green stone idol found. And many centuries came and went, wherein Sarnath prospered exceedingly, so that only priests and old women remembered what Taran-Ish had scrawled upon the altar of chrysolite. Betwixt Sarnath and the city of Ilarnek arose a caravan route, and the precious metals from the earth were exchanged for other metals and rare cloths and jewels and books and tools for artificers and all things of luxury that are known to the people who dwell along the winding river Ai and beyond. So Sarnath waxed mighty and learned and beautiful, and sent forth conquering armies to subdue the neighboring cities; and in time there sat upon a throne in Sarnath the kings of all the land of Mnar and of many lands adjacent.

The wonder of the world and the pride of all mankind was Sarnath the magnificent. Of polished desert-quarried marble were its walls, in height three hundred cubits and in breadth seventy-five, so that chariots might pass each other as men drove them along the top. For full five hundred stadia did they run, being open only on the side toward the lake where a green stone sea-wall kept back the waves that rose oddly once a year at the festival of the destroying of Ib. In Sarnath were fifty streets from the lake to the gates of the caravans, and fifty more intersecting them. With onyx were they paved, save those whereon the horses and camels and elephants trod, which were paved with granite. And the gates of Sarnath were as many as the landward ends of the streets, each of bronze, and flanked by the figures of lions and elephants carven from some stone no longer known among men. The houses of Sarnath were of glazed brick and chalcedony, each having its walled garden and crystal lakelet. With strange art were they builded, for no other city had houses like them; and travelers from Thraa and Ilarnek and Kadatheron marveled at the shining domes wherewith they were surmounted.

But more marvelous still were the palaces and the temples, and the gardens made by Zokkar the olden king. There were many palaces, the last of which were mightier than any in Thraa or Ilarnek or Kadatheron. So high were they that one within might sometimes fancy himself beneath only the sky; yet when lighted with torches dipt in the oil of Dother their walls showed vast paintings of kings and armies, of a splendor at once inspiring and stupefying to the beholder. Many were the pillars of the palaces, all of tinted marble, and carven into designs of surpassing beauty. And in most of the palaces the floors were mosaics of beryl and lapis lazuli and sardonyx and carbuncle and other choice materials, so disposed that the beholder might fancy himself walking over beds of the rarest flowers. And there were likewise fountains, which cast scented waters about in pleasing jets arranged with cunning art. Outshining all others was the palace of the kings of Mnar and of the lands adjacent. On a pair of golden crouching lions rested the throne, many steps above the gleaming floor. And it was wrought of one piece of ivory, though no man lives who knows whence so vast a piece could have come. In that palace there were also many galleries, and many amphitheaters where lions and men and elephants battled at the pleasure of the kings. Sometimes the amphitheaters were flooded with water conveyed from the lake in mighty aqueducts, and then were enacted stirring sea-fights, or combats betwixt swimmers and deadly marine things.

Lofty and amazing were the seventeen tower-like temples of Sarnath, fashioned of a bright multi-colored stone not known elsewhere. A full thousand cubits high stood the greatest among them, wherein the high-priests dwelt with a magnificence scarce less than that of the kings. On the ground were halls as vast and splendid as those of the palaces; where gathered throngs in worship of Zo-Kalar and Tamash and Lobon, the chief gods of Sarnath, whose incense-enveloped shrines were as the thrones of monarchs. Not like the eikons of other gods were those of Zo-Kalar and Tamash and Lobon. For so close to life were they that one might swear the graceful bearded gods themselves sat on the ivory thrones. And up unending steps of zircon was the tower-chamber, wherefrom the high-priests looked out over the city and the plains and the lake by day; and at the cryptic moon and significant stars and planets, and their reflections in the lake, at night. Here was done the very secret and ancient rite in detestation of Bokrug, the water-lizard, and here rested the altar of chrysolite which bore the Doom-scrawl of Taran-Ish.

Wonderful likewise were the gardens made by Zokkar the olden king. In the center of Sarnath they lay, covering a great space and encircled by a high wall. And they were surmounted by a mighty dome of glass, through which shone the sun and moon and planets when it was clear, and from which were hung fulgent images of the sun and moon and stars and planets when it was not clear. In summer the gardens were cooled with fresh odorous breezes skilfully wafted by fans, and in winter they were heated with concealed fires, so that in those gardens it was always spring. There ran little streams over bright pebbles, dividing meads of green and gardens of many hues, and spanned by a multitude of bridges. Many were the waterfalls in their courses, and many were the hued lakelets into which they expanded. Over the streams and lakelets rode white swans, whilst the music of rare birds chimed in with the melody of the waters. In ordered terraces rose the green banks, adorned here and there with bowers of vines and sweet blossoms, and seats and benches of marble and porphyry. And there were many small shrines and temples where one might rest or pray to small gods.

Each year there was celebrated in Sarnath the feast of the destroying of Ib, at which time wine, song, dancing, and merriment of every kind abounded. Great honors were then paid to the shades of those who had annihilated the odd ancient beings, and the memory of those beings and of their elder gods was derided by dancers and lutanists crowned with roses from the gardens of Zokkar. And the kings would look out over the lake and curse the bones of the dead that lay beneath it.

At first the high-priests liked not these festivals, for there had descended amongst them queer tales of how the sea-green eikon had vanished, and how Taran-Ish had died from fear and left a warning. And they said that from their high tower they sometimes saw lights beneath the waters of the lake. But as many years passed without calamity even the priests laughed and cursed and joined in the orgies of the feasters. Indeed, had they not themselves, in their high tower, often performed the very ancient and secret rite in detestation of Bokrug, the water-lizard? And a thousand years of riches and delight passed over Sarnath, wonder of the world.

Gorgeous beyond thought was the feast of the thousandth year of the destroying of Ib. For a decade had it been talked of in the land of Mnar, and as it drew nigh there came to Sarnath on horses and camels and elephants men from Thraa, Ilarnek, and Kadetheron, and all the cities of Mnar and the lands beyond. Before the marble walls on the appointed night were pitched the pavilions of princes and the tents of travelers. Within his banquet-hall reclined Nargis-Hei, the king, drunken with ancient wine from the vaults of conquered Pnoth, and surrounded by feasting nobles and hurrying slaves. There were eaten many strange delicacies at that feast; peacocks from the distant hills of Linplan, heels of camels from the Bnazic desert, nuts and spices from Sydathrian groves, and pearls from wave-washed Mtal dissolved in the vinegar of Thraa. Of sauces there were an untold number, prepared by the subtlest cooks in all Mnar, and suited to the palate of every feaster. But most prized of all the viands were the great fishes from the lake, each of vast size, and served upon golden platters set with rubies and diamonds.

Whilst the king and his nobles feasted within the palace, and viewed the crowning dish as it awaited them on golden platters, others feasted elsewhere. In the tower of the great temple the priests held revels, and in pavilions without the walls the princes of neighboring lands made merry. And it was the high-priest Gnai-Kah who first saw the shadows that descended from the gibbous moon into the lake, and the damnable green mists that arose from the lake to meet the moon and to shroud in a sinister haze the towers and the domes of fated Sarnath. Thereafter those in the towers and without the walls beheld strange lights on the water, and saw that the gray rock Akurion, which was wont to rear high above it near the shore, was almost submerged. And fear grew vaguely yet swiftly, so that the princes of Ilarnek and of far Rokol took down and folded their tents and pavilions and departed, though they scarce knew the reason for their departing.

Then, close to the hour of midnight, all the bronze gates of Sarnath burst open and emptied forth a frenzied throng that blackened the plain, so that all the visiting princes and travelers fled away in fright. For on the faces of this throng was writ a madness born of horror unendurable, and on their tongues were words so terrible that no hearer paused for proof. Men whose eyes were wild with fear shrieked aloud of the sight within the king's banquet-hall, where through the windows were seen no longer the forms of Nargis-Hei and his nobles and slaves, but a horde of indescribable green voiceless things with bulging eyes, pouting, flabby lips, and curious ears; things which danced horribly, bearing in their paws golden platters set with rubies and diamonds and containing uncouth flames. And the princes and travelers, as they fled from the doomed city of Sarnath on horses and camels and elephants, looked again upon the mist-begetting lake and saw the gray rock Akurion was quite submerged. Through all the land of Mnar and the land adjacent spread the tales of those who had fled from Sarnath, and caravans sought that accursed city and its precious metals no more. It was long ere any travelers went thither, and even then only the brave and adventurous young men of yellow hair and blue eyes, who are no kin to the men of Mnar. These men indeed went to the lake to view Sarnath; but though they found the vast still lake itself, and the gray rock Akurion which rears high above it near the shore, they beheld not the wonder of the world and pride of all mankind. Where once had risen walls of three hundred cubits and towers yet higher, now stretched only the marshy shore, and where once had dwelt fifty million of men now crawled the detestable water-lizard. Not even the mines of precious metal remained. DOOM had come to Sarnath.

But half buried in the rushes was spied a curious green idol; an exceedingly ancient idol chiseled in the likeness of Bokrug, the great water-lizard. That idol, enshrined in the high temple at Ilarnek, was subsequently worshipped beneath the gibbous moon throughout the land of Mnar.

The Statement of Randolph Carter.

2,500-WORD SHORT STORY; 1919.

This short story was written in late December 1919, and Lovecraft wrote that it was a near-transcription of a dream he had had earlier that month. In the dream, the part of "Harley Warren" was played by Samuel Loveman; and the part of "Randolph Carter," of course, was played by Lovecraft himself.

It was first published in W. Paul Cook's amateur journal, The Vagrant, *in the May 1920 issue.*

I repeat to you, gentlemen, that your inquisition is fruitless. Detain me here for ever if you will; confine or execute me if you must have a victim to propitiate the illusion you call justice; but I can say no more than I have said already. Everything that I can remember, I have told with perfect candor. Nothing has been distorted or concealed, and if anything remains vague, it is only because of the dark cloud which has come over my mind—that cloud and the nebulous nature of the horrors which brought it upon me.

Again I say, I do not know what has become of Harley Warren, though I think—almost hope that he is in peaceful oblivion, if there be anywhere so blessed a thing. It is true that I have for five years been his closest friend, and a partial sharer of his terrible researches into the unknown. I will not deny, though my memory is uncertain and indistinct, that this witness of yours may have seen us together as he says, on the Gainsville pike, walking toward Big Cypress Swamp, at half past eleven on that awful night. That we bore electric lanterns, spades, and a curious coil of wire with attached instruments, I will even affirm; for these things all played a part in the single hideous scene which remains burned into my shaken recollection. But of what followed, and of the reason I was found alone and dazed on the edge of the swamp next morning, I must insist that I know nothing save what I have told you over and over again. You say to me that there is nothing in the swamp or near it which could form the setting of that frightful episode. I reply that I knew nothing beyond what I saw. Vision or nightmare it may have been—vision or nightmare I fervently hope it was—yet it is all that my mind retains of what took place in those shocking hours after we left the sight of men. And why Harley Warren did not return, he or his shade—or some nameless thing I cannot describe—alone can tell.

As I have said before, the weird studies of Harley Warren were well known to me, and to some extent shared by me. Of his vast collection of strange, rare books on forbidden subjects I have read all that are written in the languages of which I am master; but these are few as compared with those in languages I cannot understand. Most, I believe, are in Arabic; and the fiend-inspired book which brought on the end—the book which he carried in his pocket out of the world—was written in characters whose like I never saw elsewhere. Warren would never tell me just what was in that book. As to the nature of our studies—must I say again that I no longer retain full comprehension? It seems to me rather merciful that I do not, for they were terrible studies, which I pursued more through reluctant fascination than through actual inclination. Warren always dominated me, and sometimes I feared him. I remember how I shuddered at his facial expression on the night before the awful happening, when he talked so incessantly of his theory, why certain corpses never decay, but rest firm and fat in their tombs for a thousand years. But I do not fear him now, for I suspect that he has known horrors beyond my ken. Now I fear for him.

Once more I say that I have no clear idea of our object on that night. Certainly, it had much to do with something in the book which Warren carried with him—that ancient book in undecipherable characters which had come to him from India a month before—but I swear I do not know what it was that we expected to find. Your witness says he saw us at half past eleven on the Gainsville pike, headed for Big Cypress Swamp. This is probably true, but I have no distinct memory of it. The picture seared into my soul is of one scene only, and the hour must have been long after midnight; for a waning crescent moon was high in the vaporous heavens.

The place was an ancient cemetery; so ancient that I trembled at the manifold signs of immemorial years. It was in a deep, damp hollow, overgrown with rank grass, moss, and curious creeping weeds, and filled with a vague stench which my idle fancy associated absurdly with rotting stone. On every hand were the signs of neglect and decrepitude, and I seemed haunted by the notion that Warren and I were the first living creatures to invade a lethal silence of centuries. Over the valley's rim a wan, waning crescent moon peered through the noisome vapors that seemed to emanate from unheard-of catacombs, and by its feeble, wavering beams I could distinguish a repellent array of antique slabs, urns, cenotaphs, and mausoleum facades; all crumbling, moss-grown, and moisture-stained, and partly concealed by the gross luxuriance of the unhealthy vegetation.

Weird Tales, February 1925

My first vivid impression of my own presence in this terrible necropolis concerns the act of pausing with Warren before a certain half-obliterated sepulcher and of throwing down some burdens which we seemed to have been carrying. I now observed that I had with me an electric lantern and two spades, whilst my companion was supplied with a similar lantern and a portable telephone outfit. No word was uttered, for the spot and the task seemed known to us; and without delay we seized our spades and commenced to clear away the grass, weeds, and drifted earth from the flat, archaic mortuary. After uncovering the entire surface, which consisted of three immense granite slabs, we stepped back some distance to survey the charnel scene; and Warren appeared to make some mental calculations. Then he returned to the sepulcher, and using his spade as a lever, sought to pry up the slab lying nearest to a stony ruin which may have been a monument in its day. He did not succeed, and motioned to me to come to his assistance. Finally our combined strength loosened the stone, which we raised and tipped to one side.

The removal of the slab revealed a black aperture, from which rushed an effluence of miasmal gases so nauseous that we started back in horror. After an interval, however, we approached the pit again, and found the exhalations less unbearable. Our lanterns disclosed the top of a flight of stone steps, dripping with some detestable ichor of the inner earth, and bordered by moist walls encrusted with niter. And now for the first time my memory records verbal discourse, Warren addressing me at length in his mellow tenor voice; a voice singularly unperturbed by our awesome surroundings.

"I'm sorry to have to ask you to stay on the surface," he said, "but it would be a crime to let anyone with your frail nerves go down there. You can't imagine, even from what you have read and from what I've told you, the things I shall have to see and do. It's fiendish work, Carter, and I doubt if any man without ironclad sensibilities could ever see it through and come up alive and sane. I don't wish to offend you, and Heaven knows I'd be glad enough to have you with me; but the responsibility is in a certain sense mine, and I couldn't drag a bundle of nerves like you down to probable death or madness. I tell you, you can't imagine what the thing is really like! But I promise to keep you informed over the telephone of every move—you see I've enough wire here to reach to the center of the earth and back!"

I can still hear, in memory, those coolly spoken words; and I can still remember my remonstrances. I seemed desperately anxious to accompany my friend into those sepulchral depths, yet he proved inflexibly obdurate. At one time he threatened to abandon the expedition if I remained insistent; a threat which proved effective, since he alone held the key to the thing. All this I can still remember, though I no longer know what manner of thing we sought. After he had obtained my reluctant acquiescence in his design, Warren picked up the reel of wire and adjusted the instruments. At his nod I took one of the latter and seated myself upon an aged, discolored gravestone close by the newly uncovered aperture. Then he shook my hand, shouldered the coil of wire, and disappeared within that indescribable ossuary.

For a minute I kept sight of the glow of his lantern, and heard the rustle of the wire as he laid it down after him; but the glow soon disappeared abruptly, as if a turn in the stone staircase had been encountered, and the sound died away almost as quickly. I was alone, yet bound to the unknown depths by those magic strands whose insulated surface lay green beneath the struggling beams of that waning crescent moon.

In the lone silence of that hoary and deserted city of the dead, my mind conceived the most ghastly fantasies and illusions; and the grotesque shrines and monoliths seemed to assume a hideous personality—a half-sentience. Amorphous shadows seemed to lurk in the darker recesses of the weed-choked hollow and to flit as in some blasphemous ceremonial procession past the portals of the mouldering tombs in the hillside; shadows which could not have been cast by that pallid, peering crescent moon.

I constantly consulted my watch by the light of my electric lantern, and listened with feverish anxiety at the receiver of the telephone; but for more than a quarter of an hour heard nothing. Then a faint clicking came from the instrument, and I called down to my friend in a tense voice. Apprehensive as I was, I was nevertheless unprepared for the words which came up from that uncanny vault in accents more alarmed and quivering than any I had heard before from Harley Warren. He who had so calmly left me a little while previously, now called from below in a shaky whisper more portentous than the loudest shriek:

"God! If you could see what I am seeing!"

I could not answer. Speechless, I could only wait. Then came the frenzied tones again:

"Carter, it's terrible—monstrous—unbelievable!"

This time my voice did not fail me, and I poured into the transmitter a flood of excited questions. Terrified, I continued to repeat, "Warren, what is it? What is it?"

Once more came the voice of my friend, still hoarse with fear, and now apparently tinged with despair:

"I can't tell you, Carter! It's too utterly beyond thought—I dare not tell you—no man could know it and live—Great God! I never dreamed of this!"

Stillness again, save for my now incoherent torrent of shuddering inquiry. Then the voice of Warren in a pitch of wilder consternation:

"Carter! for the love of God, put back the slab and get out of this if you can! Quick!—leave everything else and make for the outside—it's your only chance! Do as I say, and don't ask me to explain!"

I heard, yet was able only to repeat my frantic questions. Around me were the tombs and the darkness and the shadows; below me, some peril beyond the radius of the human imagination. But my friend was in greater danger than I, and through my fear I felt a vague resentment that he should deem me capable of deserting him under such circumstances. More clicking, and after a pause a piteous cry from Warren:

"Beat it! For God's sake, put back the slab and beat it, Carter!"

Something in the boyish slang of my evidently stricken companion unleashed my faculties. I formed and shouted a resolution, "Warren, brace up! I'm coming down!" But at this offer the tone of my auditor changed to a scream of utter despair:

"Don't! You can't understand! It's too late—and my own fault. Put back the slab and run—there's nothing else you or anyone can do now!"

The tone changed again, this time acquiring a softer quality, as of hopeless resignation. Yet it remained tense through anxiety for me.

"Quick—before it's too late!"

I tried not to heed him; tried to break through the paralysis which held me, and to fulfil my vow to rush down to his aid. But his next whisper found me still held inert in the chains of stark horror.

"Carter—hurry! It's no use—you must go—better one than two—the slab—"

A pause, more clicking, then the faint voice of Warren:

"Nearly over now—don't make it harder—cover up those damned steps and run for your life—you're losing time—so long, Carter—won't see you again."

Here Warren's whisper swelled into a cry; a cry that gradually rose to a shriek fraught with all the horror of the ages:

"Curse these hellish things—legions—My God! Beat it! Beat it! BEAT IT!"

After that was silence. I know not how many interminable eons I sat stupefied; whispering, muttering, calling, screaming into that telephone. Over and over again through those eons I whispered and muttered, called, shouted, and screamed, "Warren! Warren! Answer me—are you there?"

And then there came to me the crowning horror of all—the unbelievable, unthinkable, almost unmentionable thing. I have said that eons seemed to elapse after Warren shrieked forth his last despairing warning, and that only my own cries now broke the hideous silence. But after a while there was a further clicking in the receiver, and I strained my ears to listen. Again I called down, "Warren, are you there?" and in answer heard the thing which has brought this cloud over my mind. I do not try, gentlemen, to account for that thing—that voice—nor can I venture to describe it in detail, since the first words took away my consciousness and created a mental blank which reaches to the time of my awakening in the hospital. Shall I say that the voice was deep; hollow; gelatinous; remote; unearthly; inhuman; disembodied? What shall I say? It was the end of my experience, and is the end of my story. I heard it, and knew no more—heard it as I sat petrified in that unknown cemetery in the hollow, amidst the crumbling stones and the falling tombs, the rank vegetation and the miasmal vapors—heard it well up from the innermost depths of that damnable open sepulcher as I watched amorphous, necrophagous shadows dance beneath an accursed waning moon.

And this is what it said:

"You fool, Warren is DEAD!"

1920.

Out of the Chrysalis.

H.P. Lovecraft's Lord Dunsany-inspired burst of literary energy carried him into 1920 with some of his most excellent early stories. It was quite clear that, although his early inspiration from the likes of Edgar Allan Poe and Ambrose Bierce had not been replaced, it had certainly been augmented. There was a new god in Lovecraft's literary pantheon.

Although Lovecraft wrote a number of stories in 1920, those among them that were published that year went out in amateur-press magazines such as *The United Amateur*, *Tryout*, and *Wolverine*. Some of them would, of course, be published later on in magazines that paid — for instance, "The Temple" would later grace the September 1925 issue of *Weird Tales* — but that sort of success was still in the future for Lovecraft.

In addition to "The Temple," 1920 saw "The Terrible Old Man," "The Tree," "The Cats of Ulthar," "Facts Concerning the Late Arthur Jermyn and his Family," "From Beyond," "Celephaïs," "Nyarlarthotep," and "The Picture in the House" roll off Lovecraft's pen.

Something else happened in 1920 as well. The Hub Club, a Boston amateur-press organization, held its convention in July, and several of its members visited Lovecraft in Providence and talked him into going.

Upon his arrival in Boston for the meeting, Lovecraft found himself not just corresponding with kindred spirits, but kibitzing with them in real life as well — and the feeling of being a welcome and somewhat celebrated part of a community of like-minded souls was intoxicating for the reclusive and introverted writer. His deadpan humor and spot-on imitation of an 18th-century English gentleman was a big hit with this geeky crowd. Lovecraft had found a circle of accepting friends who admired and respected his wit and talents, as he admired and respected theirs. From then on, he was a regular at Hub Club events in Boston.

Ex Oblivione.

BY WARD PHILLIPS

700-WORD PROSE-POEM; 1920.

We don't know exactly when this short, bleak prose-poem was written, beyond the fact that it was sometime in 1920.

It was published in the March 1921 issue of United Amateur *under the pseudonym "Ward Phillips."*

When the last days were upon me, and the ugly trifles of existence began to drive me to madness like the small drops of water that torturers let fall ceaselessly upon one spot of their victim's body, I loved the irradiate refuge of sleep. In my dreams I found a little of the beauty I had vainly sought in life, and wandered through old gardens and enchanted woods.

Once when the wind was soft and scented I heard the south calling, and sailed endlessly and languorously under strange stars.

Once when the gentle rain fell I glided in a barge down a sunless stream under the earth till I reached another world of purple twilight, iridescent arbours, and undying roses.

And once I walked through a golden valley that led to shadowy groves and ruins, and ended in a mighty wall green with antique vines, and pierced by a little gate of bronze.

Many times I walked through that valley, and longer and longer would I pause in the spectral half-light where the giant trees squirmed and twisted grotesquely, and the grey ground stretched damply from trunk to trunk, sometimes disclosing the mould-stained stones of buried temples. And always the goal of my fancies was the mighty vine-grown wall with the little gate of bronze therein.

After a while, as the days of waking became less and less bearable from their greyness and sameness, I would often drift in opiate peace through the valley and the shadowy groves, and wonder how I might seize them for my eternal dwelling-place, so that I need no more crawl back to a dull world stript of interest and new colours. And as I looked upon the little gate in the mighty wall, I felt that beyond it lay a dream-country from which, once it was entered, there would be no return.

So each night in sleep I strove to find the hidden latch of the gate in the ivied antique wall, though it was exceedingly well hidden. And I would tell myself that the realm beyond the wall was not more lasting merely, but more lovely and radiant as well.

Then one night in the dream-city of Zakarion I found a yellowed papyrus filled with the thoughts of dream-sages who dwelt of old in that city, and who were too wise ever to be born in the waking world. Therein were written many things concerning the world of dream, and among them was lore of a golden valley and a sacred grove with temples, and a high wall pierced by a little bronze gate. When I saw this lore, I knew that it touched on the scenes I had haunted, and I therefore read long in the yellowed papyrus.

Some of the dream-sages wrote gorgeously of the wonders beyond the irrepassable gate, but others told of horror and disappointment. I knew not which to believe, yet longed more and more to cross forever into the unknown land; for doubt and secrecy are the lure of lures, and no new horror can be more terrible than the daily torture of the commonplace. So when I learned of the drug which would unlock the gate and drive me through, I resolved to take it when next I awaked.

Last night I swallowed the drug and floated dreamily into the golden valley and the shadowy groves; and when I came this time to the antique wall, I saw that the small gate of bronze was ajar. From beyond came a glow that weirdly lit the giant twisted trees and the tops of the buried temples, and I drifted on songfully, expectant of the glories of the land from whence I should never return.

But as the gate swung wider and the sorcery of the drug and the dream pushed me through, I knew that all sights and glories were at an end; for in that new realm was neither land nor sea, but only the white void of unpeopled and illimitable space. So, happier than I had ever dared hope to be, I dissolved again into that native infinity of crystal oblivion from which the daemon Life had called me for one brief and desolate hour.

The Terrible Old Man.

1,100-WORD SHORT STORY; 1920.

This diminutive short story introduces us for the first time to the fictional town of Kingsport. The story is somewhat reminiscent of "The Street," in that it involves a horrible doom falling upon a group of suspicious and up-to-no-good foreigners, and although this time the foreigners are not Russian, it remains very much in the spirit of the post-war "Red Scare."

It was first published in the May 1920 issue of W. Paul Cook's amateur journal, The Vagrant.

It was the design of Angelo Ricci and Joe Czanek and Manuel Silva to call on the Terrible Old Man. This old man dwells all alone in a very ancient house on Water Street near the sea, and is reputed to be both exceedingly rich and exceedingly feeble; which forms a situation very attractive to men of the profession of Messrs. Ricci, Czanek, and Silva, for that profession was nothing less dignified than robbery.

The inhabitants of Kingsport say and think many things about the Terrible Old Man which generally keep him safe from the attention of gentlemen like Mr. Ricci and his colleagues, despite the almost certain fact that he hides a fortune of indefinite magnitude somewhere about his musty and venerable abode. He is, in truth, a very strange person, believed to have been a captain of East India clipper ships in his day; so old that no one can remember when he was young, and so taciturn that few know his real name. Among the gnarled trees in the front yard of his aged and neglected place he maintains a strange collection of large stones, oddly grouped and painted so that they resemble the idols in some obscure Eastern temple. This collection frightens away most of the small boys who love to taunt the Terrible Old Man about his long white hair and beard, or to break the small-paned windows of his dwelling with wicked missiles; but there are other things which frighten the older and more curious folk who sometimes steal up to the house to peer in through the dusty panes. These folk say that on a table in a bare room on the ground floor are many peculiar bottles, in each a small piece of lead suspended pendulum-wise from a string. And they say that the Terrible Old Man talks to these bottles, addressing them by such names as Jack, Scar-Face, Long Tom, Spanish Joe, Peters, and Mate Ellis, and that whenever he speaks to a bottle the little lead pendulum within makes certain definite vibrations as if in answer.

Those who have watched the tall, lean, Terrible Old Man in these peculiar conversations, do not watch him again. But Angelo Ricci and Joe Czanek and Manuel Silva were not of Kingsport blood; they were of that new and heterogeneous alien stock which lies outside the charmed circle of New England life and traditions, and they saw in the Terrible Old Man merely a tottering, almost helpless grey-beard, who could not walk without the aid of his knotted cane, and whose thin, weak hands shook pitifully. They were really quite sorry in their way for the lonely, unpopular old fellow, whom everybody shunned, and at whom all the dogs barked singularly. But business is business, and to a robber whose soul is in his profession, there is a lure and a challenge about a very old and very feeble man who has no account at the bank, and who pays for his few necessities at the village store with Spanish gold and silver minted two centuries ago.

Messrs. Ricci, Czanek, and Silva selected the night of April 11th for their call. Mr. Ricci and Mr. Silva were to interview the poor old gentleman, whilst Mr. Czanek waited for them and their presumable metallic burden with a covered motor-car in Ship Street, by the gate in the tall rear wall of their host's grounds. Desire to avoid needless explanations in case of unexpected police intrusions prompted these plans for a quiet and unostentatious departure.

As prearranged, the three adventurers started out separately in order to prevent any evil-minded suspicions afterward. Messrs. Ricci and Silva met in Water Street by the old man's front gate, and although they did not like the way the moon shone down upon the painted stones through the budding branches of the gnarled trees, they had more important things to think about than mere idle superstition. They feared it might be unpleasant work making the Terrible Old Man loquacious concerning his hoarded gold and silver, for aged sea-captains are notably stubborn and perverse. Still, he was very old and very feeble, and there were two visitors. Messrs. Ricci and Silva were experienced in the art of making unwilling persons voluble, and the screams of a weak and exceptionally venerable man can be easily muffled. So they moved up to the one lighted window and heard the Terrible Old Man talking childishly to his bottles with pendulums. Then they donned masks and knocked politely at the weather-stained oaken door.

Waiting seemed very long to Mr. Czanek as he fidgeted restlessly in the covered motor-car by the Terrible Old Man's back gate in Ship Street. He was more than ordinarily tender-hearted, and he did not like the hideous screams he had heard in the ancient house just after the hour appointed for the deed. Had he not told his colleagues to be as gentle as possible with the pathetic old sea-captain? Very nervously he watched that narrow oaken gate in the high and ivy-clad stone wall. Frequently he consulted his watch, and wondered at the delay. Had the old man died before revealing where his treasure was hidden, and had a thorough search become necessary? Mr. Czanek did not like to wait so long in the dark in such a place. Then he sensed a soft tread or tapping on the walk inside the gate, heard a gentle fumbling at the rusty latch, and saw the narrow, heavy door swing inward. And in the pallid glow of the single dim street-lamp he strained his eyes to see what his colleagues had brought out of that sinister house which loomed so close behind. But when he looked, he did not see what he had expected; for his colleagues were not there at all, but only the Terrible Old Man leaning quietly on his knotted cane and smiling hideously. Mr. Czanek had never before noticed the colour of that man's eyes; now he saw that they were yellow.

Little things make considerable excitement in little towns, which is the reason that Kingsport people talked all that spring and summer about the three unidentifiable bodies, horribly slashed as with many cutlasses, and horribly mangled as by the tread of many cruel boot-heels, which the tide washed in. And some people even spoke of things as trivial as the deserted motor-car found in Ship Street, or certain especially inhuman cries, probably of a stray animal or migratory bird, heard in the night by wakeful citizens. But in this idle village gossip the Terrible Old Man took no interest at all. He was by nature reserved, and when one is aged and feeble, one's reserve is doubly strong. Besides, so ancient a sea-captain must have witnessed scores of things much more stirring in the far-off days of his unremembered youth.

The Tree.

1,600-WORD SHORT STORY; 1920.

This short story was finished in early- to mid-1920, but Lovecraft had been pondering the concept for over a year. It is sometimes listed among his Dunsany-influenced stories, and its prose style likely borrowed some of its cadence from the Irishman's work; but the plot predates Lovecraft's discovery of Dunsany.

In later years Lovecraft repudiated "The Tree," and listed it among his least favorite backlist titles; but it isn't clear why that is. Although short, it's a fine story, and it isn't just anyone who could make a story set in the ancient Greco-Roman world ring true, as this one unquestionably does.

It was first published in the October 1921 issue of Charles W. "Tryout" Smith's famously poorly copy-edited amateur journal, Tryout.

On a verdant slope of Mount Maenalus, in Arcadia, there stands an olive grove about the ruins of a villa. Close by is a tomb, once beautiful with the sublimest sculptures, but now fallen into as great decay as the house. At one end of that tomb, its curious roots displacing the time-stained blocks of Pentelic marble, grows an unnaturally large olive tree of oddly repellent shape; so like to some grotesque man, or death-distorted body of a man, that the country folk fear to pass it at night when the moon shines faintly through the crooked boughs. Mount Maenalus is a chosen haunt of dreaded Pan, whose queer companions are many, and simple swains believe that the tree must have some hideous kinship to these weird Panisci; but an old bee-keeper who lives in the neighboring cottage told me a different story.

Many years ago, when the hillside villa was new and resplendent, there dwelt within it the two sculptors Kalos and Musides. From Lydia to Neapolis the beauty of their work was praised, and none dared say that the one excelled the other in skill. The Hermes of Kalos stood in a marble shrine in Corinth, and the Pallas of Musides surmounted a pillar in Athens near the

Parthenon. All men paid homage to Kalos and Musides, and marvelled that no shadow of artistic jealousy cooled the warmth of their brotherly friendship.

But though Kalos and Musides dwelt in unbroken harmony, their natures were not alike. Whilst Musides revelled by night amidst the urban gaieties of Tegea, Kalos would remain at home; stealing away from the sight of his slaves into the cool recesses of the olive grove. There he would meditate upon the visions that filled his mind, and there devise the forms of beauty which later became immortal in breathing marble. Idle folk, indeed, said that Kalos conversed with the spirits of the grove, and that his statues were but images of the fauns and dryads he met there for he patterned his work after no living model.

So famous were Kalos and Musides, that none wondered when the Tyrant of Syracuse sent to them deputies to speak of the costly statue of Tyche which he had planned for his city. Of great size and cunning workmanship must the statue be, for it was to form a wonder of nations and a goal of travellers. Exalted beyond thought would be he whose work should gain acceptance, and for this honor Kalos and Musides were invited to compete. Their brotherly love was well known, and the crafty Tyrant surmised that each, instead of concealing his work from the other, would offer aid and advice; this charity producing two images of unheard of beauty, the lovelier of which would eclipse even the dreams of poets.

With joy the sculptors hailed the Tyrant's offer, so that in the days that followed their slaves heard the ceaseless blows of chisels. Not from each other did Kalos and Musides conceal their work, but the sight was for them alone. Saving theirs, no eyes beheld the two divine figures released by skillful blows from the rough blocks that had imprisoned them since the world began.

At night, as of yore, Musides sought the banquet halls of Tegea whilst Kalos wandered alone in the olive Grove. But as time passed, men observed a want of gaiety in the once sparkling Musides. It was strange, they said amongst themselves that depression should thus seize one with so great a chance to win art's loftiest reward. Many months passed yet in the sour face of Musides came nothing of the sharp expectancy which the situation should arouse.

Then one day Musides spoke of the illness of Kalos, after which none marvelled again at his sadness, since the sculptors' attachment was known to be deep and sacred. Subsequently many went to visit Kalos, and indeed noticed the pallor of his face; but there was about him a happy serenity which made his glance more magical than the glance of Musides who was clearly distracted with anxiety and who pushed aside all the slaves in his eagerness to feed and wait upon his friend with his own hands. Hidden behind heavy curtains stood the two unfinished figures of Tyche, little touched of late by the sick man and his faithful attendant.

As Kalos grew inexplicably weaker and weaker despite the ministrations of puzzled physicians and of his assiduous friend, he desired to be carried often to the grove which he so loved. There he would ask to be left alone, as if wishing to speak with unseen things. Musides ever granted his requests, though his eyes filled with visible tears at the thought that Kalos should care more for the fauns and the dryads than for him. At last the end drew near, and Kalos discoursed of things beyond this life. Musides, weeping, promised him a sepulchre more lovely than the tomb of Mausolus; but Kalos bade him speak no more of marble glories. Only one wish now haunted the mind of the dying man; that twigs from certain olive trees in the grove be buried by his resting place — close to his head. And one night, sitting alone in the darkness of the olive grove, Kalos died. Beautiful beyond words was the marble sepulchre which stricken Musides carved for his beloved friend. None but Kalos himself could have fashioned such bas-reliefs, wherein were displayed all the splendours of Elysium. Nor did Musides fail to bury close to Kalos' head the olive twigs from the grove.

As the first violence of Musides' grief gave place to resignation, he labored with diligence upon his figure of Tyche. All honour was now his, since the Tyrant of Syracuse would have the work of none save him or Kalos. His task proved a vent for his emotion and he toiled more steadily each day, shunning the gaieties he once had relished. Meanwhile his evenings were spent beside the tomb of his friend, where a young olive tree had sprung up near the sleeper's head. So swift was the growth of this tree, and so strange was its form, that all who beheld it exclaimed in surprise; and Musides seemed at once fascinated and repelled.

Three years after the death of Kalos, Musides despatched a messenger to the Tyrant, and it was whispered in the agora at Tegea that the mighty statue was finished. By this time the tree by the tomb had attained amazing proportions, exceeding all other trees of its kind, and sending out a singularly heavy branch above the apartment in which Musides labored. As many visitors came to view the prodigious tree, as to admire the art of the sculptor, so that Musides was seldom alone. But he did not mind his multitude of guests; indeed, he seemed to dread being alone now that his absorbing work was done. The bleak mountain wind, sighing through the olive grove and the tomb-tree, had an uncanny way of forming vaguely articulate sounds.

The sky was dark on the evening that the Tyrant's emissaries came to Tegea. It was definitely known that they had come to bear away the great image of Tyche and bring eternal honour to Musides, so their reception by the proxenoi was of great warmth. As the night wore on a violent storm of wind broke over the crest of Maenalus, and the men from far Syracuse were glad that they rested snugly in the town. They talked of their illustrious Tyrant, and of the splendour of his capital and exulted in the glory of the statue which Musides had wrought for him. And then the men of Tegea spoke of the goodness of Musides, and of his heavy grief for his friend and how not even the coming laurels of art could console him in the absence of Kalos, who might have worn those laurels instead. Of the tree which grew by the tomb, near the head of Kalos, they also spoke. The wind shrieked more horribly, and both the Syracusans and the Arcadians prayed to Aiolos.

In the sunshine of the morning the proxenoi led the Tyrant's messengers up the slope to the abode of the sculptor, but the night wind had done strange things. Slaves' cries ascended from a scene of desolation, and no more amidst the olive grove rose the gleaming colonnades of that vast hall wherein Musides had dreamed and toiled. Lone and shaken mourned the humble courts and the lower walls, for upon the sumptuous greater peristyle had fallen squarely the heavy overhanging bough of the strange new tree, reducing the stately poem in marble with odd completeness to a mound of unsightly ruins. Strangers and Tegeans stood aghast, looking from the wreckage to the great, sinister tree whose aspect was so weirdly human and whose roots reached so queerly into the sculptured sepulchre of Kalos. And their fear and dismay increased when they searched the fallen apartment, for of the gentle Musides, and of the marvellously fashioned image of Tyche, no trace could be discovered. Amidst such stupendous ruin only chaos dwelt, and the representatives of two cities left disappointed; Syracusans that they had no statue to bear home, Tegeans that they had no artist to crown. However, the Syracusans obtained after a while a very splendid statue in Athens, and the Tegeans consoled themselves by erecting in the agora a marble temple commemorating the gifts, virtues, and brotherly piety of Musides.

But the olive grove still stands, as does the tree growing out of the tomb of Kalos, and the old bee-keeper told me that sometimes the boughs whisper to one another in the night wind, saying over and over again. "*Oida! Oida!*—I know! I know!"

The Cats of Ulthar

1,300-WORD SHORT STORY; 1920.

It should come as no surprise that H.P. Lovecraft continued to cherish this story all his life, considering its subject matter. Lovecraft, although he never kept one of his own after childhood, loved cats.

This snack-size short story was written on June 14, 1920, and the influence of Lord Dunsany can be easily detected in it. It first saw print in Charles W. "Tryout" Smith's amateur journal, Tryout, *in the November 1920 issue.*

It is said that in Ulthar, which lies beyond the river Skai, no man may kill a cat; and this I can verily believe as I gaze upon him who sitteth purring before the fire. For the cat is cryptic, and close to strange things which men cannot see. He is the soul of antique Aegyptus, and bearer of tales from forgotten cities in Meroe and Ophir. He is the kin of the jungle's lords, and heir to the secrets of hoary and sinister Africa. The Sphinx is his cousin, and he speaks her language; but he is more ancient than the Sphinx, and remembers that which she hath forgotten.

In Ulthar, before ever the burgesses forbade the killing of cats, there dwelt an old cotter and his wife who delighted to trap and slay the cats of their neighbors. Why they did this I know not; save that many hate the voice of the cat in the night, and take it ill that cats should run stealthily about yards and gardens at twilight. But whatever the reason, this old man and woman took pleasure in trapping and slaying every cat which came near to their hovel; and from some of the sounds heard after dark, many villagers fancied that the manner of slaying was exceedingly peculiar. But the villagers did not discuss such things with the old man and his wife; because of the habitual expression on the withered faces of the two, and because their cottage was so small and so darkly hidden under spreading oaks at the back of a neglected yard. In truth, much as the owners of cats hated these odd folk, they feared them more; and instead of berating them as brutal assassins, merely took care that no cherished pet or mouser should stray toward the remote hovel under the dark trees. When through some unavoidable oversight a cat was missed, and sounds heard after dark, the loser would lament impotently; or console himself by thanking Fate that it was not one of his children who had thus vanished. For the people of Ulthar were simple, and knew not whence it is all cats first came.

One day a caravan of strange wanderers from the South entered the narrow cobbled streets of Ulthar. Dark wanderers they were, and unlike the other roving folk who passed through the village twice every year. In the market-place they told fortunes for silver, and bought gay beads from the merchants. What was the land of these wanderers none could tell; but it was seen that they were given to strange prayers, and that they had painted on the sides of their wagons strange figures with human bodies and the heads of cats, hawks, rams and lions. And the leader of the caravan wore a headdress with two horns and a curious disk betwixt the horns.

There was in this singular caravan a little boy with no father or mother, but only a tiny black kitten to cherish. The plague had not been kind to him, yet had left him this small furry thing to mitigate his sorrow; and when one is very young, one can find great relief in the lively antics of a black kitten. So the boy whom the dark people called Menes smiled more often than he wept as he sat playing with his graceful kitten on the steps of an oddly painted wagon.

On the third morning of the wanderers' stay in Ulthar, Menes could not find his kitten; and as he sobbed aloud in the market-place certain villagers told him of the old man and his wife, and of sounds heard in the night. And when he heard these things his sobbing gave place to meditation, and finally to prayer. He stretched out his arms toward the sun and prayed in a tongue no villager could understand; though indeed the villagers did not try very hard to understand, since their attention was mostly taken up by the sky and the odd shapes the clouds were assuming. It was very peculiar, but as the little boy uttered his petition there seemed to form overhead the shadowy, nebulous figures of exotic things; of hybrid creatures crowned with horn-flanked disks. Nature is full of such illusions to impress the imaginative.

That night the wanderers left Ulthar, and were never seen again. And the householders were troubled when they noticed that in all the village there was not a cat to be found. From each hearth the familiar cat had vanished; cats large and small, black, grey, striped, yellow and white. Old Kranon, the burgomaster, swore that the dark folk had taken the cats away in revenge for the killing of Menes' kitten; and cursed the caravan and the little boy. But Nith, the lean notary, declared that the old cotter and his wife were more likely persons to suspect; for their hatred of cats was notorious and increasingly bold. Still, no one durst complain to the sinister couple; even when little Atal, the innkeeper's son, vowed that he had at twilight seen all the cats of Ulthar in that accursed yard under the trees, pacing very slowly and solemnly in a circle around the cottage, two abreast, as if in performance of some unheard-of rite of beasts. The villagers did not know how much to believe from so small a boy; and though they feared that the evil pair had charmed the cats to their death, they preferred not to chide the old cotter till they met him outside his dark and repellent yard.

So Ulthar went to sleep in vain anger; and when the people awakened at dawn — behold! every cat was back at his accustomed hearth! Large and small, black, grey, striped, yellow and white, none was missing. Very sleek and fat did the cats appear, and sonorous with purring content. The citizens talked with one another of the affair, and marveled not a little. Old Kranon again insisted that it was the dark folk who had taken them, since cats did not return alive from the cottage of the ancient man and his wife. But all agreed on one thing: that the refusal of all the cats to eat their portions of meat or drink their saucers of milk was exceedingly curious. And for two whole days the sleek, lazy cats of Ulthar would touch no food, but only doze by the fire or in the sun.

It was fully a week before the villagers noticed that no lights were appearing at dusk in the windows of the cottage under the trees. Then the lean Nith remarked that no one had seen the old man or his wife since the night the cats were away. In another week the burgomaster decided to overcome his fears and call at the strangely silent dwelling as a matter of duty, though in so doing he was careful to take with him Shang the blacksmith and Thul the cutter of stone as witnesses. And when they had broken down the frail door they found only this: two cleanly picked human skeletons on the earthen floor, and a number of singular beetles crawling in the shadowy corners.

There was subsequently much talk among the burgesses of Ulthar. Zath, the coroner, disputed at length with Nith, the lean notary; and Kranon and Shang and Thul were overwhelmed with questions. Even little Atal, the innkeeper's son, was closely questioned and given a sweetmeat as reward. They talked of the old cotter and his wife, of the caravan of dark wanderers, of small Menes and his black kitten, of the prayer of Menes and of the sky during that prayer, of the doings of the cats on the night the caravan left, and of what was later found in the cottage under the dark trees in the repellent yard.

And in the end the burgesses passed that remarkable law which is told of by traders in Hatheg and discussed by travelers in Nir; namely, that in Ulthar no man may kill a cat.

The Temple.

5,400-WORD SHORT STORY;
1920.

Quite why H.P. Lovecraft decided to circle back around to the topic of the First World War in the summer of 1920 is not clear. Perhaps "The Temple" was a concept he developed during the war, two years earlier, and he simply never had the inclination or inspiration to develop it until now.

Regardless of the motivation, the result was a story that has been generally panned by critics and Lovecraft scholars, but actually has a lot to recommend it.

For one thing, it is written from a point of view hostile to the assumed sympathies of the readers: a cold-blooded sea-wolf of a German U-boat commander. The commander is presented very unsympathetically; yet Lovecraft almost forces us to admire him as he marches bravely to his certain doom.

Furthermore, in the final few paragraphs, Lovecraft shows one of the signal characteristics of his work: a finely tuned instinct for just how much to tell, and how much to leave tantalizingly unrevealed, in the dénouement *of a story.*

Owing no doubt to its length, "The Temple" did not find a home in the amateur journals that were, in the early 1920s, Lovecraft's only outlet. It was, however, picked up later by editor Edwin Baird of Weird Tales *magazine, and published in the September 1925 issue.*

(Manuscript found on the coast of Yucutan)

On August 20, 1917, I, Karl Heinrich, Graf von Altberg-Ehrenstein, Lieutenant-Commander in the Imperial German Navy and in charge of the submarine *U-29*, deposit this bottle and record in the Atlantic Ocean at a point to me unknown but probably about N. Latitude 20 degrees, W. Longitude 35 degrees, where my ship lies disabled on the ocean floor. I do so because of my desire to set certain unusual facts before the public; a thing I shall not in all probability survive to accomplish in person, since the circumstances surrounding me are as menacing as they are extraordinary, and involve not only the hopeless crippling of the *U-29*, but the impairment of my iron German will in a manner most disastrous.

On the afternoon of June 18, as reported by wireless to the *U-61*, bound for Kiel, we torpedoed the British freighter *Victory*, New York to Liverpool, in N. Latitude 45 degrees 16 minutes, W. Longitude 28 degrees 34 minutes; permitting the crew to leave in boats in order to obtain a good cinema view for the admiralty records. The ship sank quite picturesquely, bow first, the stem rising high out of the water whilst the hull shot down perpendicularly to the bottom of the sea. Our camera missed nothing, and I regret that so fine a reel of film should never reach Berlin. After that we sank the lifeboats with our guns and submerged.

When we rose to the surface about sunset, a seaman's body was found on the deck, hands gripping the railing in curious fashion. The poor fellow was young, rather dark, and very handsome; probably an Italian or Greek, and undoubtedly of the *Victory's* crew. He had evidently sought refuge on the very ship which had been forced to destroy his own — one more victim of the unjust war of aggression which the English pig-dogs are waging upon the Fatherland. Our men searched him for souvenirs, and found in his coat pocket a very odd bit of ivory carved to represent a youth's head crowned with laurel. My fellow-officer, Lieutenant Kienze, believed that the thing was of great age and artistic value, so took it from the men for himself. How it had ever come into the possession of a common sailor neither he nor I could imagine.

As the dead man was thrown overboard there occurred two incidents which created much disturbance amongst the crew. The fellow's eyes had been closed; but in the dragging of his body to the rail they were jarred open, and many seemed to entertain a queer delusion that they gazed steadily and mockingly at Schmidt and Zimmer, who were bent over the corpse. Boatswain Muller, an elderly man who would have known better had he not been a superstitious Alsatian swine, became so excited by this impression that he watched the body in the water; and swore that after it sank a little it drew its limbs into a swimming position and sped away to the south under the waves. Kienze and I did not like these displays of peasant ignorance, and severely reprimanded the men, particularly Muller.

The next day a very troublesome situation was created by the indisposition of some of the crew. They were evidently suffering from the nervous strain of our long voyage, and had had bad dreams. Several seemed quite dazed and stupid; and after satisfying myself that they were not feigning their weakness, I excused them from their duties. The sea was rather rough, so we descended to a depth where the waves were less troublesome. Here we were comparatively calm, despite a somewhat puzzling southward current which we could not identify from our oceanographic charts. The moans of the sick

Weird Tales, September 1925

men were decidedly annoying; but since they did not appear to demoralize the rest of the crew, we did not resort to extreme measures. It was our plan to remain where we were and intercept the liner *Dacia*, mentioned in information from agents in New York.

In the early evening we rose to the surface, and found the sea less heavy. The smoke of a battleship was on the northern horizon, but our distance and ability to submerge made us safe. What worried us more was the talk of Boatswain Muller, which grew wilder as night came on. He was in a detestably childish state, and babbled of some illusion of dead bodies drifting past the undersea portholes; bodies which looked at him intensely, and which he recognized in spite of bloating as having seen dying during some of our victorious German exploits. And he said that the young man we had found and tossed overboard was their leader. This was very gruesome and abnormal, so we confined Muller in irons and had him soundly whipped. The men were not pleased at his punishment, but discipline was necessary. We also denied the request of a delegation headed by Seaman Zimmer, that the curious carved ivory head be cast into the sea.

On June 20, Seaman Bohin and Schmidt, who had been ill the day before, became violently insane. I regretted that no physician was included in our complement of officers, since German lives are precious; but the constant ravings of the two concerning a terrible curse were most subversive of discipline, so drastic steps were taken. The crew accepted the event in a sullen fashion, but it seemed to quiet Muller; who thereafter gave us no trouble. In the evening we released him, and he went about his duties silently.

In the week that followed we were all very nervous, watching for the *Dacia*. The tension was aggravated by the disappearance of Muller and Zimmer, who undoubtedly committed suicide as a result of the fears which had seemed to harass them, though they were not observed in the act of jumping overboard. I was rather glad to be rid of Muller, for even his silence had unfavorably affected the crew. Everyone seemed inclined to be silent now, as though holding a secret fear. Many were ill, but none made a disturbance. Lieutenant Kienze chafed under the strain, and was annoyed by the merest trifle — such as the school of dolphins which gathered about the *U-29* in increasing numbers, and the growing intensity of that southward current which was not on our chart.

It at length became apparent that we had missed the *Dacia* altogether. Such failures are not uncommon, and we were more pleased than disappointed, since our return to Wilhelmshaven was now in order. At noon June 28 we turned northeastward, and despite some rather comical entanglements with the unusual masses of dolphins, were soon under way.

The explosion in the engine room at 2 a.m. was wholly a surprise. No defect in the machinery or carelessness in the men had been noticed, yet without warning the ship was racked from end to end with a colossal shock. Lieutenant Kienze hurried to the engine room, finding the fuel-tank and most of the mechanism shattered, and Engineers Raabe and Schneider instantly killed. Our situation had suddenly become grave indeed; for though the chemical air regenerators were intact, and though we could use the devices for raising and submerging the ship and opening the hatches as long as compressed air and storage batteries might hold out, we were powerless to propel or guide the submarine. To seek rescue in the life-boats would be to deliver ourselves into the hands of enemies unreasonably embittered against our great German nation, and our wireless had failed ever since the Victory affair to put us in touch with a fellow U-boat of the Imperial Navy.

From the hour of the accident till July 2 we drifted

constantly to the south, almost without plans and encountering no vessel. Dolphins still encircled the *U-29*, a somewhat remarkable circumstance considering the distance we had covered. On the morning of July 2 we sighted a warship flying American colors, and the men became very restless in their desire to surrender. Finally Lieutenant Menze had to shoot a seaman named Traube, who urged this un-German act with especial violence. This quieted the crew for the time, and we submerged unseen.

The next afternoon a dense flock of sea-birds appeared from the south, and the ocean began to heave ominously. Closing our hatches, we awaited developments until we realized that we must either submerge or be swamped in the mounting waves. Our air pressure and electricity were diminishing, and we wished to avoid all unnecessary use of our slender mechanical resources; but in this case there was no choice. We did not descend far, and when after several hours the sea was calmer, we decided to return to the surface. Here, however, a new trouble developed; for the ship failed to respond to our direction in spite of all that the mechanics could do. As the men grew more frightened at this undersea imprisonment, some of them began to mutter again about Lieutenant Kienze's ivory image, but the sight of an automatic pistol calmed them. We kept the poor devils as busy as we could, tinkering at the machinery even when we knew it was useless.

Kienze and I usually slept at different times; and it was during my sleep, about 5 a.m., July 4, that the general mutiny broke loose. The six remaining pigs of seamen, suspecting that we were lost, had suddenly burst into a mad fury at our refusal to surrender to the Yankee battleship two days before, and were in a delirium of cursing and destruction. They roared like the animals they were, and broke instruments and furniture indiscriminately; screaming about such nonsense as the curse of the ivory image and the dark dead youth who looked at them and swam away. Lieutenant Kienze seemed paralyzed and inefficient, as one might expect of a soft, womanish Rhinelander. I shot all six men, for it was necessary, and made sure that none remained alive.

We expelled the bodies through the double hatches and were alone in the *U-29*. Kienze seemed very nervous, and drank heavily. It was decided that we remain alive as long as possible, using the large stock of provisions and chemical supply of oxygen, none of which had suffered from the crazy antics of those swine-hound seamen. Our compasses, depth gauges, and other delicate instruments were ruined; so that henceforth our only reckoning would be guess work, based on our watches, the calendar, and our apparent drift as judged by any objects we might spy through the portholes or from the conning tower. Fortunately we had storage batteries still capable of long use, both for interior lighting and for the searchlight. We often cast a beam around the ship, but saw only dolphins, swimming parallel to our own drifting course. I was scientifically interested in those dolphins; for though the ordinary *Delphinus Delphis* is a cetacean mammal, unable to subsist without air, I watched one of the swimmers closely for two hours, and did not see him alter his submerged condition.

With the passage of time Kienze and I decided that we were still drifting south, meanwhile sinking deeper and deeper. We noted the marine fauna and flora, and read much on the subject in the books I had carried with me for spare moments. I could not help observing, however, the inferior scientific knowledge of my companion. His mind was not Prussian, but given to imaginings and speculations which have no value. The fact of our coming death affected him curiously, and he would frequently pray in remorse over the men, women, and children we had sent to the bottom; forgetting that all things are noble which serve the German state. After a time he became noticeably unbalanced, gazing for hours at his ivory image and weaving fanciful stories of the lost and forgotten things under the sea. Sometimes, as a psychological experiment, I would lead him on in the wanderings, and listen to his endless poetical quotations and tales of sunken ships. I was very sorry for him, for I dislike to see a German suffer; but he was not a good man to die with. For myself I was proud, knowing how the Fatherland would revere my memory and how my sons would be taught to be men like me.

On August 9, we espied the ocean floor, and sent a powerful beam from the searchlight over it. It was a vast undulating plain, mostly covered with seaweed, and strewn with the shells of small mollusks. Here and there were slimy objects of puzzling contour, draped with weeds and encrusted with barnacles, which Kienze declared must be ancient ships lying in their graves. He was puzzled by one thing, a peak of solid matter, protruding above the oceanbed nearly four feet at its apex; about two feet thick, with flat sides and smooth upper surfaces which met at a very obtuse angle. I called the peak a bit of outcropping rock, but Kienze thought he saw carvings on it. After a while he began to shudder, and turned away from the scene, as if frightened; yet could give no explanation save that he was overcome with the vastness, darkness, remoteness, antiquity, and mystery of the oceanic abysses. His mind was tired, but I am always a German, and was quick to notice two things: that the *U-29* was standing the deep-sea pressure splendidly, and that the peculiar dolphins were still about us, even at a depth where the existence of high organisms is considered impossible by most naturalists. That I had previously overestimated our depth, I was sure; but none the less we must still have been deep enough to make these phenomena remarkable. Our southward speed, as gauged by the ocean floor, was about as I had estimated from the organisms passed at higher levels.

It was at 3:15 PM., August 12, that poor Kienze went wholly mad. He had been in the conning tower using the searchlight when I saw him bound into the library compartment where I sat reading, and his face at once betrayed him. I will repeat here what he said, underlining the words he emphasized: "He is calling! He is calling! I hear him! We must go!" As he spoke he took his ivory image from the table, pocketed it, and seized my arm in an effort to drag me up the companionway to the deck. In a moment I understood that he meant to open the hatch and plunge with me into the water outside, a vagary of suicidal and homicidal mania for which I was scarcely prepared. As I hung back and attempted to soothe him he grew more violent, saying: "Come now — do not wait until later; it is better to repent and be forgiven than to defy and be condemned." Then I tried the opposite of the soothing plan, and told him he was mad — pitifully demented. But he was unmoved, and cried: "If I am mad, it is mercy. May the gods pity the man who in his callousness can remain sane to the hideous end! Come and be mad whilst he still calls with mercy!"

This outburst seemed to relieve a pressure in his brain; for as he finished he grew much milder, asking me to let him depart alone if I would not accompany him. My course at once became clear. He was a German, but only a Rhinelander and a commoner; and he was now a potentially dangerous madman. By complying with his suicidal request I could immediately free myself from one who was no longer a companion but a menace. I asked him to give me the ivory image before he went, but this request brought from him such uncanny laughter that I did not repeat it. Then I asked him if he wished to leave any keepsake or lock of hair for his family in Germany in case I should be rescued, but again he gave me that strange laugh. So as he climbed the ladder I went to the levers and, allowing proper time-intervals, operated the machinery which sent him to his death. After I saw that he was no longer in the boat I threw the searchlight around the water in an effort to obtain a last glimpse of him since I wished to ascertain whether the water pressure would flatten him as it theoretically should, or whether the body would be unaffected, like those extraordinary dolphins. I did not, however, succeed in finding my late companion, for the dolphins were massed thickly and obscuringly about the conning tower.

That evening I regretted that I had not taken the ivory image surreptitiously from poor Kienze's pocket as he left, for the memory of it fascinated me. I could not forget the youthful, beautiful head with its leafy crown, though I am not by nature an artist. I was also sorry that I had no one with whom to converse. Kienze, though not my mental equal, was much better than no one. I did not sleep well that night, and wondered exactly when the end would come. Surely, I had little enough chance of rescue.

The next day I ascended to the conning tower and commenced the customary searchlight explorations. Northward the view was much the same as it had been all the four days since we had sighted the bottom, but I perceived that the drifting of the *U-29* was less rapid. As I swung the beam around to the south, I noticed that the ocean floor ahead fell away in a marked declivity, and bore curiously regular blocks of stone in certain places, disposed as if in accordance with definite patterns. The boat did not at once descend to match the greater ocean depth, so I was soon forced to adjust the searchlight to cast a sharply downward beam. Owing to the abruptness of the change a wire was disconnected, which necessitated a delay of many minutes for repairs; but at length the light streamed on again, flooding the marine valley below me.

I am not given to emotion of any kind, but my amazement was very great when I saw what lay revealed in that electrical glow. And yet as one reared in the best Kultur of Prussia, I should not have been amazed, for geology and tradition alike tell us of great transpositions in oceanic and continental areas. What I saw was an extended and elaborate array of ruined edifices; all of magnificent though unclassified architecture, and in various stages of preservation. Most appeared to be of marble, gleaming whitely in the rays of the searchlight, and the general plan was of a large city at the bottom of a narrow valley, with numerous isolated temples and villas on the steep slopes above. Roofs were fallen and columns were broken, but there still remained an air of immemorially ancient splendor which nothing could efface.

Confronted at last with the Atlantis I had formerly deemed largely a myth, I was the most eager of explorers. At the bottom of that valley a river once had flowed; for as I examined the scene more closely I beheld the remains of stone and marble bridges and sea-walls, and terraces and embankments once verdant and beautiful. In my enthusiasm I became nearly as idiotic and sentimental as poor Kienze, and was very tardy in noticing that the southward current had ceased at last, allowing the *U-29* to settle slowly down upon the sunken city as an airplane settles upon a town of the upper earth. I was slow, too, in realizing that the school of unusual dolphins had vanished.

In about two hours the boat rested in a paved plaza close to the rocky wall of the valley. On one side I could view the entire city as it sloped from the plaza down to the old river-bank; on the other side, in startling proximity, I was confronted by the richly ornate and perfectly preserved facade of a great building, evidently a temple, hollowed from the solid rock. Of the original workmanship of this titanic thing I can only make conjectures. The facade, of immense magnitude, apparently covers a continuous hollow recess; for its windows are many and widely distributed. In the center yawns a great open door, reached by an impressive flight of steps, and surrounded by exquisite carvings like the figures of Bacchanals in relief. Foremost of all are the great columns and friezes, both decorated with sculptures of inexpressible beauty; obviously portraying idealized pastoral scenes and processions of priests and priestesses bearing strange ceremonial devices in adoration of a radiant god. The art is of the most phenomenal perfection, largely Hellenic in idea, yet strangely individual. It imparts an impression of terrible antiquity, as though it were the remotest rather than the immediate ancestor of Greek art. Nor can I doubt that every detail of this massive product was fashioned from the virgin hillside rock of our planet. It is palpably a part of the valley wall, though how the vast interior was ever excavated I cannot imagine. Perhaps a cavern or series of caverns furnished the nucleus. Neither age nor submersion has corroded the pristine grandeur of this awful fane — for fane indeed it must be — and today after thousands of years it rests untarnished and inviolate in the endless night and silence of an ocean-chasm.

I cannot reckon the number of hours I spent in gazing at the sunken city with its buildings, arches, statues, and bridges, and the colossal temple with its beauty and mystery. Though I knew that death was near, my curiosity was consuming; and I threw the searchlight beam about in eager quest. The shaft of light permitted me to learn many details, but refused to show anything within the gaping door of the rock-hewn temple; and after a time I turned off the current, conscious of the need of conserving power. The rays were now perceptibly dimmer than they had been during the weeks of drifting. And as if sharpened by the coming deprivation of light, my desire to explore the watery secrets grew. I, a German, should be the first to tread those eon-forgotten ways!

I produced and examined a deep-sea diving suit of jointed metal, and experimented with the portable light and air regenerator. Though I should have trouble in managing the double hatches alone, I believed I could overcome all obstacles with my scientific skill and actually walk about the dead city in person.

On August 16 I effected an exit from the *U-29*, and laboriously made my way through the ruined and mud-choked streets to the ancient river. I found no skeletons or other human remains, but gleaned a wealth of archeological lore from sculptures and coins. Of this I cannot now speak save to utter my awe at a culture in the full noon of glory when cave dwellers roamed Europe and the Nile flowed unwatched to the sea. Others, guided by this manuscript if it shall ever be found, must unfold the mysteries at which I can only hint. I returned to the boat as my electric batteries grew feeble, resolved to explore the rock temple on the following day.

On the 17th, as my impulse to search out the mystery of the temple waxed still more insistent, a great disappointment befell me; for I found that the materials needed to replenish the portable light had perished in the mutiny of those pigs in July. My rage was unbounded, yet my German sense forbade me to venture unprepared into an utterly black interior which might prove the lair of some indescribable marine monster or a labyrinth of passages from whose windings I could never extricate myself. All I could do was to turn on the waning searchlight of the *U-29*, and with its aid walk up the temple steps and study the exterior carvings. The shaft of light entered the door at an upward angle, and I peered in to see if I could glimpse anything, but all in vain. Not even the roof was visible; and though I took a step or two inside after testing the floor with a staff, I dared not go farther. Moreover, for the first time in my life I experienced the emotion of dread. I began to realize how some of poor Kienze's moods had arisen, for as the temple drew me more and more, I feared its aqueous abysses with a blind and mounting terror. Returning to the submarine, I turned off the lights and sat thinking in the dark. Electricity must now be saved for emergencies.

Saturday the 18th I spent in total darkness, tormented by thoughts and memories that threatened to overcome my German will. Kienze had gone mad and perished before reaching this sinster remnant of a past unwholesomely remote, and had advised me to go with him. Was, indeed, Fate preserving my reason only to draw me irresistibly to an end more horrible and unthinkable than any man has dreamed of? Clearly, my nerves were sorely taxed, and I must cast off these impressions of weaker men.

I could not sleep Saturday night, and turned on the lights regardless of the future. It was annoying that the electricity should not last out the air and provisions. I revived my thoughts of euthanasia, and examined my automatic pistol. Toward morning I must have dropped asleep with the lights on, for I awoke in darkness yesterday afternoon to find the batteries dead. I struck several matches in succession, and desperately regretted the improvidence which had caused us long ago to use up the few candles we carried.

After the fading of the last match I dared to waste, I sat very quietly without a light. As I considered the inevitable end my mind ran over preceding events, and developed a hitherto dormant impression which would have caused a weaker and more superstitious man to shudder. The head of the radiant god in the sculptures on the rock temple is the same as that carven bit of ivory which the dead sailor brought from the sea and which poor Kienze carried back into the sea.

I was a little dazed by this coincidence, but did not become terrified. It is only the inferior thinker who hastens to explain the singular and the complex by the primitive shortcut of supernaturalism. The coincidence was strange, but I was too sound a reasoner to connect circumstances which admit of no logical connection, or to associate in any uncanny fashion the disastrous events which had led from the Victory affair to my present plight. Feeling the need of more rest, I took a sedative and secured some more sleep. My nervous condition was reflected in my dreams, for I seemed to hear the cries of drowning persons, and to see dead faces pressing against the portholes of the boat. And among the dead faces was the living, mocking face of the youth with the ivory image.

I must be careful how I record my awakening today, for I am unstrung, and much hallucination is necessarily mixed with fact. Psychologically my case is most interesting, and I regret that it cannot be observed scientifically by a competent German authority. Upon opening my eyes my first sensation was an overmastering desire to visit the rock temple; a desire which grew every instant, yet which I automatically sought to resist through some emotion of fear which operated in the reverse direction. Next there came to me the impression of light amidst the darkness of dead batteries, and I seemed to see a sort of phosphorescent glow in the water through the porthole which opened toward the temple. This aroused my curiosity, for I knew of no deep-sea organism capable of emitting such luminosity.

But before I could investigate there came a third impression which because of its irrationality caused me to doubt the objectivity of anything my senses might record. It was an aural delusion; a sensation of rhythmic, melodic sound as of some wild yet beautiful chant or choral hymn, coming from the outside through the absolutely sound-proof hull of the U-29. Convinced of my psychological and nervous abnormality, I lighted some matches and poured a stiff dose of sodium bromide solution, which seemed to calm me to the extent of dispelling the illusion of sound. But the phosphorescence remained, and I had difficulty in repressing a childish impulse to go to the porthole and seek its source. It was horribly realistic, and I could soon distinguish by its aid the familiar objects around me, as well as the empty sodium bromide glass of which I had had no former visual impression in its present location. This last circumstance made me ponder, and I crossed the room and touched the glass. It was indeed in the place where I had seemed to see it. Now I knew that the light was either real or part of an hallucination so fixed and consistent that I could not hope to dispel it, so abandoning all resistance I ascended to the conning tower to look for the luminous agency. Might it not actually be another U-boat, offering possibilities of rescue?

It is well that the reader accept nothing which follows as objective truth, for since the events transcend natural law, they are necessarily the subjective and unreal creations of my overtaxed mind. When I attained the conning tower I found the sea in general far less luminous than I had expected. There was no animal or vegetable phosphorescence about, and the city that sloped down to the river was invisible in blackness. What I did see was not spectacular, not grotesque or terrifying, yet it removed my last vestige of trust in my consciousness. For the door and windows of the undersea temple hewn from the rocky hill were vividly aglow with a flickering radiance, as from a mighty altar-flame far within.

Later incidents are chaotic. As I stared at the uncannily lighted door and windows, I became subject to the most extravagant visions — visions so extravagant that I cannot even relate them. I fancied that I discerned objects in the temple; objects both stationary and moving; and seemed to hear again the unreal chant that had floated to me when first I awaked. And over all rose thoughts and fears which centered in the youth from the sea and the ivory image whose carving was duplicated on the frieze and columns of the temple before me. I thought of poor Kienze, and wondered where his body rested with the image he had carried back into the sea. He had warned me of something, and I had not heeded — but he was a soft-headed Rhinelander who went mad at troubles a Prussian could bear with ease.

The rest is very simple. My impulse to visit and enter the temple has now become an inexplicable and imperious command which ultimately cannot be denied. My own German will no longer controls my acts, and volition is henceforward possible only in minor matters. Such madness it was which drove Kienze to his death, bare-headed and unprotected in the ocean; but I am a Prussian and a man of sense, and will use to the last what little will I have. When first I saw that I must go, I prepared my diving suit, helmet, and air regenerator for instant donning, and immediately commenced to write this hurried chronicle in the hope that it may some day reach the world. I shall seal the manuscript in a bottle and entrust it to the sea as I leave the *U-29* for ever.

I have no fear, not even from the prophecies of the madman Kienze. What I have seen cannot be true, and I know that this madness of my own will at most lead only to suffocation when my air is gone. The light in the temple is a sheer delusion, and I shall die calmly like a German, in the black and forgotten depths. This demoniac laughter which I hear as I write comes only from my own weakening brain. So I will carefully don my suit and walk boldly up the steps into the primal shrine, that silent secret of unfathomed waters and uncounted years.

Poetry and the Gods.

BY ANNA HELEN CROFTS AND H.P. LOVECRAFT

2,500-WORD SHORT STORY; 1920.

Unlike the Winifred Jackson collaborations, "Poetry and the Gods" appears to have been largely written by the collaborator rather than Lovecraft; some passages have the distinctive style and writing voice of post-Lord Dunsany Lovecraft, but others do not. It also, unusually for Lovecraft, features a female protagonist, a modern young woman named Marcia; and it even goes so far as to describe her attire ("a low cut black evening dress"), which is something Lovecraft would never do.

It is worth noting, also, that the story as a whole has the feel of a Paradise Lost-style religious allegory, only directed at the canon of Western literature rather than at God. It is weird fiction only in the widest and most inclusive sense. This, and the lack of information about Crofts, make this story a real outlier in Lovecraft's oeuvre.

"On the whole, 'Poetry and the Gods' is simply a curiosity," biographer S.T. Joshi writes, in I Am Providence; *"and will become of interest only if more information on its writing and its collaborator emerges."*

He is, of course, absolutely correct.

"Poetry and the Gods" was written in mid-1920, around the time Lovecraft was writing "The Tree," "The Cats of Ulthar," and "The Temple." It was first published in the September 1920 issue of United Amateur.

ABOUT ANNA HELEN CROFTS (1888-1975).

Very little is known about Anna Helen Crofts of North Adams, Massachusetts, with whom Lovecraft collaborated on only this one story. Even biographer S.T. Joshi, who has probably spent more time going through Lovecraft's correspondence and the surviving records of amateur-press publications than anyone alive today, confesses himself largely baffled. He was able to find only one other example of her by-line, a one-page story in the March 1921 issue of United Amateur; and he found no references of any kind to her in Lovecraft's correspondence.

There is a theory that Anna Helen Crofts is a pseudonym used by Winifred Jackson; but a close reading of "Poetry and the Gods" seems to all but rule that possibility out. The story as a whole is very different from "The Green Meadow" and "The Crawling Chaos," and when the story lapses into poetry the work sounds completely unlike the usual styles of either Jackson or Lovecraft.

A damp gloomy evening in April it was, just after the close of the Great War, when Marcia found herself alone with strange thoughts and wishes, unheard-of yearnings which floated out of the spacious twentieth-century drawing room, up the deeps of the air, and eastward to olive groves in distant Arcady which she had seen only in her dreams. She had entered the room in abstraction, turned off the glaring chandeliers, and now reclined on a soft divan by a solitary lamp which shed over the reading table a green glow as soothing as moonlight when it issued through the foliage about an antique shrine.

Attired simply, in a low-cut black evening dress, she appeared outwardly a typical product of modern civilization; but tonight she felt the immeasurable gulf that separated her soul from all her prosaic surroundings. Was it because of the strange home in which she lived, that abode of coldness where relations were always strained and the inmates scarcely more than strangers? Was it that, or was it some greater and less explicable misplacement in time and space, whereby she had been born too late, too early, or too far away from the haunts of her spirit ever to harmonize with the unbeautiful things of contemporary reality?

To dispel the mood which was engulfing her more and more deeply each moment, she took a magazine from the table and searched for some healing bit of poetry. Poetry had always relieved her troubled mind better than anything else, though many things in the poetry she had seen detracted from the influence. Over parts of even the sublimest verses hung a chill vapour of sterile ugliness and restraint, like dust on a window-pane through which one views a magnificent sunset.

Listlessly turning the magazine's pages, as if searching for an elusive treasure, she suddenly came upon something which dispelled her languor. An observer could have read her thoughts and told that she had discovered some image or dream which brought her nearer to her unattained goal than any image or dream she had seen before. It was only a bit of vers libre, that pitiful compromise of the poet who overleaps prose yet falls short of the divine melody of numbers; but it had in it all the unstudied music of a bard who lives and feels, who gropes ecstatically for unveiled beauty. Devoid of regularity, it yet had the harmony of winged, spontaneous words, a harmony missing from the formal, convention-bound verse she had known. As she read on, her surroundings gradually faded, and soon there lay about her only the mists of dream, the purple, star-strewn mists beyond time, where only Gods and dreamers walk.

Moon over Japan,
White butterfly moon!
Where the heavy-lidded Buddhas dream
To the sound of the cuckoo's call . . .
The white wings of moon butterflies
Flicker down the streets of the city,
Blushing into silence the useless wicks of sound-lanterns in the hands of girls

Moon over the tropics,
A white-curved bud
Opening its petals slowly in the warmth of heaven . . .
The air is full of odours
And languorous warm sounds . . .
A flute drones its insect music to the night
Below the curving moon-petal of the heavens.

Moon over China,
Weary moon on the river of the sky,
The stir of light in the willows is like the flashing of a thousand silver minnows
Through dark shoals;
The tiles on graves and rotting temples flash like ripples,
The sky is flecked with clouds like the scales of a dragon.

Amid the mists of dream the reader cried to the rhythmical stars, of her delight at the coming of a new age of song, a rebirth of Pan. Half closing her eyes, she repeated words whose melody lay hidden like crystals at the bottom of a stream before dawn, hidden but to gleam effulgently at the birth of day.

Moon over Japan,
White butterfly moon!

Moon over the tropics,
A white curved bud
Opening its petals slowly in the warmth of heaven.
The air is full of odours
And languorous warm sounds . . .

Moon over China,
Weary moon on the river of the sky . . .

Out of the mists gleamed godlike the form of a youth, in winged helmet and sandals, caduceus-bearing, and of a beauty like to nothing on earth. Before the face of the sleeper he thrice waved the rod which Apollo had given him in trade for the nine-corded shell of melody, and upon her brow he placed a wreath of myrtle and roses. Then, adoring, Hermes spoke:

"O Nymph more fair than the golden-haired sisters of Cyene or the sky-inhabiting Atlantides, beloved of Aphrodite and blessed of Pallas, thou hast indeed discovered the secret of the Gods, which lieth in beauty and song. O Prophetess more lovely than the Sybil of Cumae when Apollo first knew her, thou has truly spoken of the new age, for even now on Maenalus, Pan sighs and stretches in his sleep, wishful to wake and behold about him the little rose-crowned fauns and the antique Satyrs. In thy yearning hast thou divined what no mortal, saving only a few whom the world rejects, remembereth: that the Gods were never dead, but only sleeping the sleep and dreaming the dreams of Gods in lotos-filled Hesperian gardens beyond the golden sunset. And now draweth nigh the time of their awakening, when coldness and ugliness shall perish, and Zeus sit once more on Olympus. Already the sea about Paphos trembleth into a foam which only ancient skies have looked on before, and at night on Helicon the shepherds hear strange murmurings and half-remembered notes. Woods and fields are tremulous at twilight with the shimmering of white saltant forms, and immemorial Ocean yields up curious sights beneath thin moons. The Gods are patient, and have slept long, but neither man nor giant shall defy the Gods forever. In Tartarus the Titans writhe and beneath the fiery Aetna groan the children of Uranus and Gaea. The day now dawns when man must answer for centuries of denial, but in sleeping the Gods have grown kind and will not hurl him to the gulf made for deniers of Gods. Instead will their vengeance smite the darkness, fallacy and ugliness which have turned the mind of man; and under the sway of bearded Saturnus shall mortals, once more sacrificing unto him, dwell in beauty and delight. This night shalt thou know the favour of the Gods, and behold on Parnassus those dreams which the Gods have through ages sent to earth to show that they are not dead. For poets are the dreams of Gods, and in each and every age someone hath sung unknowingly the message and the promise from the lotos-gardens beyond the sunset."

Then in his arms Hermes bore the dreaming maiden through the skies. Gentle breezes from the tower of Aiolas wafted them high above warm, scented seas, till suddenly they came upon Zeus, holding court upon double-headed Parnassus, his golden throne flanked by Apollo and the Muses on the right hand, and by ivy-wreathed Dionysus and pleasure-flushed Bacchae on the left hand. So much of splendour Marcia had never seen before, either awake or in dreams, but its radiance did her no injury, as would have the radiance of lofty Olympus; for in this lesser court the Father of Gods had tempered his glories for the sight of mortals.

Before the laurel-draped mouth of the Corycian cave sat in a row six noble forms with the aspect of mortals, but the countenances of Gods. These the dreamer recognized from images of them which she had beheld, and she knew that they were none else than the divine Maeonides, the avernian Dante, the more than mortal Shakespeare, the chaos-exploring Milton, the cosmic Goethe and the musalan Keats. These were those messengers whom the Gods had sent to tell men that Pan had passed not away, but only slept; for it is in poetry that Gods speak to men. Then spake the Thunderer:

"O Daughter — for, being one of my endless line, thou art indeed my daughter — behold upon ivory thrones of honour the august messengers Gods have sent down that in the words and writing of men there may be still some traces of divine beauty. Other bards have men justly crowned with enduring laurels, but these hath Apollo crowned, and these have I set in places apart, as mortals who have spoken the language of the Gods. Long have we dreamed in lotos-gardens beyond the West, and spoken only through our dreams; but the time approaches when our voices shall not be silent. It is a time of awakening and change. Once more hath Phaeton ridden low, searing the fields and drying the streams. In Gaul lone nymphs with disordered hair weep beside fountains that are no more, and pine over rivers turned red with the blood of mortals. Ares and his train have gone forth with the madness of Gods and have returned Deimos and Phobos glutted with unnatural delight. Tellus moons with grief, and the faces of men are as the faces of Erinyes, even as when Astraea fled to the skies, and the waves of our bidding encompassed all the land saving this high peak alone. Amidst this chaos, prepared to herald his coming yet to conceal his arrival, even now toileth our latest born messenger, in whose dreams are all the images which other messengers have dreamed before him. He it is that we have chosen to blend into one glorious whole all the beauty that the world hath known before, and to write words wherein shall echo all the wisdom and the loveliness of the past. He it is who shall proclaim our return and sing of the days to come when Fauns and Dryads shall haunt their accustomed groves in beauty. Guided was our choice by those who now sit before the Corycian grotto on thrones of ivory, and in whose songs thou shalt hear notes of sublimity by which years hence thou shalt know the greater messenger when he cometh. Attend their voices as one by one they sing to thee here. Each note shalt thou hear again in the poetry which is to come, the poetry which shall bring peace and pleasure to thy soul, though search for it through bleak years thou must. Attend with diligence, for each chord that vibrates away into hiding shall appear again to thee after thou hast returned to earth, as Alpheus, sinking his waters into the soul of Hellas, appears as the crystal arethusa in remote Sicilia."

Then arose Homeros, the ancient among bards, who took his lyre and chanted his hymn to Aphrodite. No word of Greek did Marcia know, yet did the message not fall vainly upon her ears, for in the cryptic rhythm was that which spake to all mortals and Gods, and needed no interpreter.

So too the songs of Dante and Goethe, whose unknown words clave the ether with melodies easy to ready and adore. But at last remembered accents resounded before the listener. It was the Swan of Avon, once a God among men, and still a God among Gods:

Write, write, that from the bloody course of war,
My dearest master, your dear son, may hie;
Bless him at home in peace, whilst I from far,
His name with zealous fervour sanctify.

Accents still more familiar arose as Milton, blind no more, declaimed immortal harmony:

Or let thy lamp at midnight hour
Be seen in some high lonely tower,
Where I might oft outwatch the Bear
With thrice-great Hermes, or unsphere
The spirit of Plato, to unfold
What worlds or what vast regions hold
The immortal mind, that hath forsook
Her mansion in this fleshy nook.
Sometime let gorgeous tragedy
In sceptered pall come sweeping by,
Presenting Thebes, or Pelop's line,
Or the tale of Troy divine.

Last of all came the young voice of Keats, closest of all the messengers to the beauteous faun-folk:

Heard melodies are sweet, but those unheard
Are sweeter, therefore, yet sweet pipes, play on . . .
When old age shall this generation waste,
Thou shalt remain, in midst of other woe
Than ours, a friend to man, to whom thou say'st
"Beauty is truth — truth beauty" — that is all
Ye know on earth, and all ye need to know.

As the singer ceased, there came a sound in the wind blowing from far Egypt, where at night Aurora mourns by the Nile for her slain Memnon. To the feet of the Thunderer flew the rosy-fingered Goddess and, kneeling, cried, "Master, it is time I unlocked the Gates of the East." And Phoebus, handing his lyre to Calliope, his bride among the Muses, prepared to depart for the jewelled and column-raised Palace of the Sun, where fretted the steeds already harnessed to the golden car of Day. So Zeus descended from his carven throne and placed his hand upon the head of Marcia, saying:

"Daughter, the dawn is nigh, and it is well that thou shouldst return before the awakening of mortals to thy home. Weep not at the bleakness of thy life, for the shadow of false faiths will soon be gone and the Gods shall once more walk among men. Search thou unceasingly for our messenger, for in him wilt thou find peace and comfort. By his word shall thy steps be guided to happiness, and in his dreams of beauty shall thy spirit find that which it craveth." As Zeus ceased, the young Hermes gently seized the maiden and bore her up toward the fading stars, up and westward over unseen seas.

Many years have passed since Marcia dreamt of the Gods and of their Parnassus conclave. Tonight she sits in the same spacious drawing-room, but she is not alone. Gone is the old spirit of unrest, for beside her is one whose name is luminous with celebrity: the young poet of poets at whose feet sits all the world. He is reading from a manuscript words which none has ever heard before, but which when heard will bring to men the dreams and the fancies they lost so many centuries ago, when Pan lay down to doze in Arcady, and the great Gods withdrew to sleep in lotos-gardens beyond the lands of the Hesperides. In the subtle cadences and hidden melodies of the bard the spirit of the maiden had found rest at last, for there echo the divinest notes of Thracian Orpheus, notes that moved the very rocks and trees by Hebrus' banks.

The singer ceases, and with eagerness asks a verdict, yet what can Marcia say but that the strain is "fit for the Gods"?

And as she speaks there comes again a vision of Parnassus and the far-off sound of a mighty voice saying, "By his word shall thy steps be guided to happiness, and in his dreams of beauty shall thy spirit find all that it craveth."

Facts Concerning the Late Arthur Jermyn and His Family.

3,700-WORD SHORT STORY; 1920.

This mid-size short story is one of the most polarizing titles in Lovecraft's canon. But those who detest it and those who admire it generally agree that it is a competent and chilling tale — the more so because it never spells out its culminating horror in words.

Modern readers tend to find the basic concept of "Arthur Jermyn" awkward, because it is, at its basis, grounded in fears of miscegenation. In this case, though, the miscegenation is not what used to be called "race-mixing" in the benighted Jim Crow days of the post-Civil-War South — but, rather, a more primal sort of miscegenation, what one might call "species-mixing." Lovecraft would later expand on this theme, far more effectively, in The Shadow over Innsmouth.

"Facts Concerning the Late Arthur Jermyn and his Family" was written late in the summer of 1920, shortly after Lovecraft helped Anna Helen Crofts with "Poetry and the Gods." It was first published as a two-part serial in Horace L. Lawson's amateur journal, Wolverine.

I.

Life is a hideous thing, and from the background behind what we know of it peer daemoniacal hints of truth which make it sometimes a thousandfold more hideous. Science, already oppressive with its shocking revelations, will perhaps be the ultimate exterminator of our human species — if separate species we be — for its reserve of unguessed horrors could never be borne by mortal brains if loosed upon the world. If we knew what we are, we should do as Sir Arthur Jermyn did; and Arthur Jermyn soaked himself in oil and set fire to his clothing one night. No one placed the charred fragments in an urn or set a memorial to him who had been; for certain papers and a certain boxed object were found which made men wish to forget. Some who knew him do not admit that he ever existed.

Arthur Jermyn went out on the moor and burned himself after seeing the boxed object which had come from Africa. It was this object, and not his peculiar personal appearance, which made him end his life. Many would have disliked to live if possessed of the peculiar features of Arthur Jermyn, but he had been a poet and scholar and had not minded. Learning was in his blood, for his great-grandfather, Sir Robert Jermyn, Bt., had been an anthropologist of note, whilst his great-great-great-grandfather, Sir Wade Jermyn, was one of the earliest explorers of the Congo region, and had written eruditely of its tribes, animals, and supposed antiquities. Indeed, old Sir Wade had possessed an intellectual zeal amounting almost to a mania; his bizarre conjectures on a prehistoric white Congolese civilisation earning him much ridicule when his book, *Observation on the Several Parts of Africa*, was published. In 1765 this fearless explorer had been placed in a madhouse at Huntingdon.

Madness was in all the Jermyns, and people were glad there were not many of them. The line put forth no branches, and Arthur was the last of it. If he had not been, one can not say what he would have done when the object came. The Jermyns never seemed to look quite right — something was amiss, though Arthur was the worst, and the old family portraits in Jermyn House showed fine faces enough before Sir Wade's time. Certainly, the madness began with Sir Wade, whose wild stories of Africa were at once the delight and terror of his few friends. It showed in his collection of trophies and specimens, which were not such as a normal man would accumulate and preserve, and appeared strikingly in the Oriental seclusion in which he kept his wife. The latter, he had said, was the daughter of a Portuguese trader whom he had met in Africa; and did not like English ways. She, with an infant son born in Africa, had accompanied him back from the second and longest of his trips, and had gone with him on the third and last, never returning. No one had ever seen her closely, not even the servants; for her disposition had been violent and singular. During her brief stay at Jermyn House she occupied a remote wing, and was waited on by her husband alone. Sir Wade was, indeed, most peculiar in his solicitude for his family; for when he returned to Africa he would permit no one to care for his young son save a loathsome black woman from Guinea. Upon coming back, after the death of Lady Jermyn, he himself assumed complete care of the boy.

But it was the talk of Sir Wade, especially when

Weird Tales, April 1924

in his cups, which chiefly led his friends to deem him mad. In a rational age like the eighteenth century it was unwise for a man of learning to talk about wild sights and strange scenes under a Congo moon; of the gigantic walls and pillars of a forgotten city, crumbling and vine-grown, and of damp, silent, stone steps leading interminably down into the darkness of abysmal treasure-vaults and inconceivable catacombs. Especially was it unwise to rave of the living things that might haunt such a place; of creatures half of the jungle and half of the impiously aged city — fabulous creatures which even a Pliny might describe with scepticism; things that might have sprung up after the great apes had overrun the dying city with the walls and the pillars, the vaults and the weird carvings. Yet after he came home for the last time Sir Wade would speak of such matters with a shudderingly uncanny zest, mostly after his third glass at the Knight's Head; boasting of what he had found in the jungle and of how he had dwelt among terrible ruins known only to him. And finally he had spoken of the living things in such a manner that he was taken to the madhouse. He had shown little regret when shut into the barred room at Huntingdon, for his mind moved curiously. Ever since his son had commenced to grow out of infancy, he had liked his home less and less, till at last he had seemed to dread it. The Knight's Head had been his headquarters, and when he was confined he expressed some vague gratitude as if for protection. Three years later he died.

Wade Jermyn's son Philip was a highly peculiar person. Despite a strong physical resemblance to his father, his appearance and conduct were in many particulars so coarse that he was universally shunned. Though he did not inherit the madness which was feared by some, he was densely stupid and given to brief periods of uncontrollable violence. In frame he was small, but intensely powerful, and was of incredible agility. Twelve years after succeeding to his title he married the daughter of his gamekeeper, a person said to be of gypsy extraction, but before his son was born joined the navy as a common sailor, completing the general disgust which his habits and misalliance had begun. After the close of the American war he was heard of as sailor on a merchantman in the African trade, having a kind of reputation for feats of strength and climbing, but finally disappearing one night as his ship lay off the Congo coast.

In the son of Sir Philip Jermyn the now accepted family peculiarity took a strange and fatal turn. Tall and fairly handsome, with a sort of weird Eastern grace despite certain slight oddities of proportion, Robert Jermyn began life as a scholar and investigator. It was he who first studied scientifically the vast collection of relics which his mad grandfather had brought from Africa, and who made the family name as celebrated in ethnology as in exploration. In 1815 Sir Robert married a daughter of the seventh Viscount Brightholme and was subsequently blessed with three children, the eldest and youngest of whom were never publicly seen on account of deformities in mind and body. Saddened by these family misfortunes, the scientist sought relief in work, and made two long expeditions in the interior of Africa. In 1849 his second son, Nevil, a singularly repellent person who seemed to combine the surliness of Philip Jermyn with the hauteur of the Brightholmes, ran away with a vulgar dancer, but was pardoned upon his return in the following year. He came back to Jermyn House a widower with an infant son, Alfred, who was one day to be the father of Arthur Jermyn.

Friends said that it was this series of griefs which unhinged the mind of Sir Robert Jermyn, yet it was probably merely a bit of African folklore which caused the disaster. The elderly scholar had been collecting legends of the Onga tribes near the field of his grandfather's and his own explorations, hoping in some way to account for Sir Wade's wild tales of a lost city peopled by strange hybrid creatures. A certain consistency in the strange papers of his ancestor suggested that the madman's imagination might have been stimulated by native myths. On October 19, 1852, the explorer Samuel Seaton called at Jermyn House with a manuscript of notes collected among the Ongas, believing that certain legends of a gray city of white apes ruled by a white god might prove valuable to the ethnologist. In his conversation he probably supplied many additional details; the nature of which will never be known, since a hideous series of tragedies suddenly burst into being. When Sir Robert Jermyn emerged from his library he left behind the strangled corpse of the explorer, and before he could be restrained, had put an end to all three of his children; the two who were never seen, and the son who had run away. Nevil Jermyn died in the successful defence of his own two-year-old son, who had apparently been included in the old man's madly murderous scheme. Sir Robert himself, after repeated attempts at suicide and a stubborn refusal to utter an articulate sound, died of apoplexy in the second year of his confinement.

Sir Alfred Jermyn was a baronet before his fourth birthday, but his tastes never matched his title. At twenty he had joined a band of music-hall performers, and at thirty-six had deserted his wife and child to travel with an itinerant American circus. His end was very revolting. Among the animals in the exhibition with which he travelled was a huge bull gorilla of lighter colour than the average; a surprisingly tractable beast of much popularity with the performers. With this gorilla Alfred Jermyn was singularly fascinated, and on many occasions the two would eye each other for long periods through the intervening bars. Eventually Jermyn asked and obtained permission to train the animal, astonishing audiences and fellow performers alike with his success. One morning in Chicago, as the gorilla and Alfred Jermyn were rehearsing an exceedingly clever boxing match, the former delivered a blow of more than the usual force, hurting both the body and the dignity of the amateur trainer. Of what followed, members of "The Greatest Show On Earth" do not like to speak. They did not expect to hear Sir Alfred Jermyn emit a shrill, inhuman scream, or to see him seize his clumsy antagonist with both hands, dash it to the floor of the cage, and bite fiendishly at its hairy throat. The gorilla was off its guard, but not for long, and before anything could be done by the regular trainer, the body which had belonged to a baronet was past recognition.

II.

Arthur Jermyn was the son of Sir Alfred Jermyn and a music-hall singer of unknown origin. When the husband and father deserted his family, the mother took the child to Jermyn House, where there was none left to object to her presence. She was not without notions of what a nobleman's dignity should be, and saw to it that her son received the best education which limited money could provide. The family resources were now sadly slender, and Jermyn House had fallen into woeful disrepair, but young Arthur loved the old edifice and all its contents. He was not like any other Jermyn who had ever lived, for he was a poet and a dreamer. Some of the neighbouring families who had heard tales of old Sir Wade Jermyn's unseen Portuguese wife declared that her Latin blood must be showing itself; but most persons merely sneered at his sensitiveness to beauty, attributing it to his music-hall mother, who was socially unrecognised. The poetic delicacy of Arthur Jermyn was the more remarkable because of his uncouth personal appearance. Most of the Jermyns had possessed a subtly odd and repellent cast, but Arthur's case was very striking. It is hard to say just what he resembled, but his expression, his facial angle, and the length of his arms gave a thrill of repulsion to those who met him for the first time.

It was the mind and character of Arthur Jermyn which atoned for his aspect. Gifted and learned, he took highest honours at Oxford and seemed likely to redeem the intellectual fame of his family. Though of poetic rather than scientific temperament, he planned to continue the work of his forefathers in African ethnology and antiquities, utilising the truly wonderful though strange collection of Sir Wade. With his fanciful mind he thought often of the prehistoric civilisation in which the mad explorer had so implicitly believed, and would weave tale after tale about the silent jungle city mentioned in the latter's wilder notes and paragraphs. For the nebulous utterances concerning a nameless, unsuspected race of jungle hybrids he had a peculiar feeling of mingled terror and attraction, speculating on the possible basis of such a fancy, and seeking to obtain light among the more recent data gleaned by his great-grandfather and Samuel Seaton amongst the Ongas.

In 1911, after the death of his mother, Sir Arthur Jermyn determined to pursue his investigations to the utmost extent. Selling a portion of his estate to obtain the requisite money, he outfitted an expedition and sailed for the Congo. Arranging with the Belgian authorities for a party of guides, he spent a year in the Onga and Kahn country, finding data beyond the highest of his expectations. Among the Kaliris was an aged chief called Mwanu, who possessed not only a highly retentive memory, but a singular degree of intelligence and interest in old legends. This ancient confirmed every tale which Jermyn had heard, adding his own account of the stone city and the white apes as it had been told to him.

According to Mwanu, the gray city and the hybrid creatures were no more, having been annihilated by the warlike N'bangus many years ago. This tribe, after destroying most of the edifices and killing the live beings, had carried off the stuffed goddess which had been the object of their quest; the white ape-goddess which the strange beings worshipped, and which was held by Congo tradition to be the form of one who had reigned as a princess among these beings. Just what the white apelike creatures could have been, Mwanu had no idea, but he thought they were the builders of the ruined city. Jermyn could form no conjecture, but by close questioning obtained a very picturesque legend of the stuffed goddess.

The ape-princess, it was said, became the consort of a great white god who had come out of the West. For a long time they had reigned over the city together, but when they had a son, all three went away. Later the god and princess had returned, and upon the death of the princess her divine husband had mummified the body and enshrined it in a vast house of stone, where it was worshipped. Then he departed alone. The legend here seemed to present three variants. According to one story, nothing further happened save that the stuffed goddess became a symbol of supremacy for whatever tribe might possess it. It was for this reason that the N'bangus carried it off. A second story told of a god's return and death at the feet of his enshrined wife. A third told of the return of the son, grown to manhood—or apehood or godhood, as the case might be—yet unconscious of his identity. Surely the imaginative blacks had made the most of whatever events might lie behind the extravagant legendry.

Of the reality of the jungle city described by old Sir Wade, Arthur Jermyn had no further doubt; and was hardly astonished when early in 1912 he came upon what was left of it. Its size must have been exaggerated, yet the stones lying about proved that it was no mere Negro village. Unfortunately no carvings could be found, and the small size of the expedition prevented operations toward clearing the one visible passageway that seemed to lead down into the system of vaults which Sir Wade had mentioned. The white apes and the stuffed goddess were discussed with all the native chiefs of the region, but it remained for a European to improve on the data offered by old Mwanu. M. Verhaeren, Belgian agent at a trading-post on the Congo, believed that he could not only locate but obtain the stuffed goddess, of which he had vaguely heard; since the once mighty N'bangus were now the submissive servants of King Albert's government, and with but little persuasion could be induced to part with the gruesome deity they had carried off. When Jermyn sailed for England, therefore, it was with the exultant probability that he would within a few months receive a priceless ethnological relic confirming the wildest of his great-great-great-grandfather's narratives—that is, the wildest which he had ever heard. Countrymen near Jermyn House had perhaps heard wilder tales handed down from ancestors who had listened to Sir Wade around the tables of the Knight's Head.

Arthur Jermyn waited very patiently for the expected box from M. Verhaeren, meanwhile studying with increased diligence the manuscripts left by his mad ancestor. He began to feel closely akin to Sir Wade, and to seek relics of the latter's personal life in England as well as of his African exploits. Oral accounts of the mysterious and secluded wife had been numerous, but no tangible relic of her stay at Jermyn House remained. Jermyn wondered what circumstance had prompted or permitted such an effacement, and decided that the husband's insanity was the prime cause. His great-great-great-grandmother, he recalled, was said to have been the daughter of a Portuguese trader in Africa. No doubt her practical heritage and superficial knowledge of the Dark Continent had caused her to flout Sir Wade's tales of the interior, a thing which such a man would not be likely to forgive. She had died in Africa, perhaps dragged thither by a husband determined to prove what he had told. But as Jermyn indulged in these reflections he could not but smile at their futility, a century and a half after the death of both his strange progenitors.

In June, 1913, a letter arrived from M. Verhaeren, telling of the finding of the stuffed goddess. It was, the Belgian averred, a most extraordinary object; an object quite beyond the power of a layman to classify. Whether it was human or simian only a scientist could determine, and the process of determination would be greatly hampered by its imperfect condition. Time and the Congo climate are not kind to mummies; especially when their preparation is as amateurish as seemed to be the case here. Around the creature's neck had been found a golden chain bearing an empty locket on which were armorial designs; no doubt some hapless traveller's keepsake, taken by the N'bangus and hung upon the goddess as a charm. In commenting on the contour of the mummy's face, M. Verhaeren suggested a whimsical comparison; or rather, expressed a humorous wonder just how it would strike his corespondent, but was too much interested scientifically to waste many words in levity. The stuffed goddess, he wrote, would arrive duly packed about a month after receipt of the letter.

The boxed object was delivered at Jermyn House on the afternoon of August 3, 1913, being conveyed immediately to the large chamber which housed the collection of African specimens as arranged by Sir Robert and Arthur. What ensued can best be gathered from the tales of servants and from things and papers later examined. Of the various tales, that of aged Soames, the family butler, is most ample and coherent. According to this trustworthy man, Sir Arthur Jermyn dismissed everyone from the room before opening the box, though the instant sound of hammer and chisel showed that he did not delay the operation. Nothing was heard for some time; just how long Soames cannot exactly estimate, but it was certainly less than a quarter of an hour later that the horrible scream, undoubtedly in Jermyn's voice, was heard. Immediately afterward Jermyn emerged from the room, rushing frantically toward the front of the house as if pursued by some hideous enemy. The expression on his face, a face ghastly enough in repose, was beyond description. When near the front door he seemed to think of something, and turned back in his flight, finally disappearing down the stairs to the cellar. The servants were utterly dumbfounded, and watched at the head of the stairs, but their master did not return. A smell of oil was all that came up from the regions below. After dark a rattling was heard at the door leading from the cellar into the courtyard; and a stable-boy saw Arthur Jermyn, glistening from head to foot with oil and redolent of that fluid, steal furtively out and vanish on the black moor surrounding the house. Then, in an exaltation of supreme horror, everyone saw the end. A spark appeared on the moor, a flame arose, and a pillar of human fire reached to the heavens. The house of Jermyn no longer existed.

The reason why Arthur Jermyn's charred fragments were not collected and buried lies in what was found afterward, principally the thing in the box. The stuffed goddess was a nauseous sight, withered and eaten away, but it was clearly a mummified white ape of some unknown species, less hairy than any recorded variety, and infinitely nearer mankind—quite shockingly so. Detailed description would be rather unpleasant, but two salient particulars must be told, for they fit in revoltingly with certain notes of Sir Wade Jermyn's African expeditions and with the Congolese legends of the white god and the ape-princess. The two particulars in question are these: the arms on the golden locket about the creature's neck were the Jermyn arms, and the jocose suggestion of M. Verhaeren about certain resemblance as connected with the shrivelled face applied with vivid, ghastly, and unnatural horror to none other than the sensitive Arthur Jermyn, great-great-great-grandson of Sir Wade Jermyn and an unknown wife. Members of the Royal Anthropological Institute burned the thing and threw the locket into a well, and some of them do not admit that Arthur Jermyn ever existed.

Celephaïs.

2,500-WORD SHORT STORY; 1920.

This dreamy, bittersweet short story (or, perhaps, long prose poem) is one of the most admired of Lovecraft's Lord Dunsany-inspired stories. It is hard not to contemplate the parallels between Kuranes and his author, and to wonder how much autobiographical influence there is in this story.

"Celephaïs" was written in early November 1920, and published in the May 1922 issue of Sonia Haft Greene's amateur journal, The Rainbow.

In a dream Kuranes saw the city in the valley, and the seacoast beyond, and the snowy peak overlooking the sea, and the gaily painted galleys that sail out of the harbour toward distant regions where the sea meets the sky. In a dream it was also that he came by his name of Kuranes, for when awake he was called by another name.

Perhaps it was natural for him to dream a new name; for he was the last of his family, and alone among the indifferent millions of London, so there were not many to speak to him and to remind him who he had been. His money and lands were gone, and he did not care for the ways of the people about him, but preferred to dream and write of his dreams. What he wrote was laughed at by those to whom he showed it, so that after a time he kept his writings to himself, and finally ceased to write.

The more he withdrew from the world about him, the more wonderful became his dreams; and it would have been quite futile to try to describe them on paper. Kuranes was not modern, and did not think like others who wrote. Whilst they strove to strip from life its embroidered robes of myth and to show in naked ugliness the foul thing that is reality, Kuranes sought for beauty alone. When truth and experience failed to reveal it, he sought it in fancy and illusion, and found it on his very doorstep, amid the nebulous memories of childhood tales and dreams.

There are not many persons who know what wonders are opened to them in the stories and visions of their youth; for when as children we listen and dream, we think but half-formed thoughts, and when as men we try to remember, we are dulled and prosaic with the poison of life. But some of us awake in the night with strange phantasms of enchanted hills and gardens, of fountains that sing in the sun, of golden cliffs overhanging murmuring seas, of plains that stretch down to sleeping cities of bronze and stone, and of shadowy companies of heroes that ride caparisoned white horses along the edges of thick forests; and then we know that we have looked back through the ivory gates into that world of wonder which was ours before we were wise and unhappy.

Kuranes came very suddenly upon his old world of childhood. He had been dreaming of the house where he had been born; the great stone house covered with ivy, where thirteen generations of his ancestors had lived, and where he had hoped to die. It was moonlight, and he had stolen out into the fragrant summer night, through the gardens, down the terraces, past the great oaks of the park, and along the long white road to the village. The village seemed very old, eaten away at the edge like the moon which had commenced to wane, and Kuranes wondered whether the peaked roofs of the small houses hid sleep or death. In the streets were spears of long grass, and the window-panes on either side broken or filmily staring. Kuranes had not lingered, but had plodded on as though summoned toward some goal. He dared not disobey the summons for fear it might prove an illusion like the urges and aspirations of waking life, which do not lead to any goal. Then he had been drawn down a lane that led off from the village street toward the channel cliffs, and had come to the end of things, to the precipice and the abyss where all the village and all the world fell abruptly into the unechoing emptiness of infinity, and where even the sky ahead was empty and unlit by the crumbling moon and the peering stars. Faith had urged him on, over the precipice and into the gulf, where he had floated down, down, down; past dark, shapeless, undreamed dreams, faintly glowing spheres that may have been partly dreamed dreams, and laughing winged things that seemed to mock the dreamers of all the worlds. Then a rift seemed to open in the darkness before him, and he saw the city of the valley, glistening radiantly far, far below, with a background of sea and sky, and a snowcapped mountain near the shore.

Kuranes had awakened the very moment he beheld the city, yet he knew from his brief glance that it was none other than Celephaïs, in the Valley of Ooth-Nargai beyond the Tanarian Hills where his spirit had dwelt all the eternity of an hour one summer afternoon very long ago, when he had slipt away from his nurse and let the warm sea-breeze lull him to sleep as he watched the clouds from the cliff near the village. He had protested then, when they had found him, waked him, and carried him home, for just as he was aroused he had been about to sail in a golden galley for those alluring regions where the sea meets the sky. And now he was equally resentful of awaking, for he had found his fabulous city after forty weary years.

But three nights afterward Kuranes came again to Celephaïs. As before, he dreamed first of the village that was asleep or dead, and of the abyss down which one must float silently; then the rift appeared again, and he beheld the glittering minarets of the city, and saw the graceful galleys riding at anchor in the blue harbour, and watched the gingko trees of Mount Aran swaying in the sea-breeze. But this time he was not snatched away, and like a winged being settled gradually over a grassy hillside 'til finally his feet rested gently on the turf. He had indeed come back to the Valley of Ooth-Nargai and the splendid city of Celephaïs.

Marvel Tales, May 1934

"And then the luminous vapours spread apart to reveal a greater brightness, the brightness of the city Celephaïs."

Down the hill amid scented grasses and brilliant flowers walked Kuranes, over the bubbling Naraxa on the small wooden bridge where he had carved his name so many years ago, and through the whispering grove to the great stone bridge by the city gate. All was as of old, nor were the marble walls discoloured, nor the polished bronze statues upon them tarnished. And Kuranes saw that he need not tremble lest the things he knew be vanished; for even the sentries on the ramparts were the same, and still as young as he remembered them. When he entered the city, past the bronze gates and over the onyx pavements, the merchants and camel-drivers greeted him as if he had never been away; and it was the same at the turquoise temple of Nath-Horthath, where the orchid-wreathed priests told him that there is no time in Ooth-Nargai, but only perpetual youth. Then Kuranes walked through the Street of Pillars to the seaward wall, where gathered the traders and sailors, and strange men from the regions where the sea meets the sky. There he stayed long, gazing out over the bright harbour where the ripples sparkled beneath an unknown sun, and where rode lightly the galleys from far places over the water. And he gazed also upon Mount Aran rising regally from the shore, its lower slopes green with swaying trees and its white summit touching the sky.

More than ever Kuranes wished to sail in a galley to the far places of which he had heard so many strange tales, and he sought again the captain who had agreed to carry him so long ago. He found the man, Athib, sitting on the same chest of spice he had sat upon before, and Athib seemed not to realize that any time had passed. Then the two rowed to a galley in the harbour, and giving orders to the oarmen, commenced to sail out into the billowy Cerenarian Sea that leads to the sky. For several days they glided undulatingly over the water, till finally they came to the horizon, where the sea meets the sky.

Here the galley paused not at all, but floated easily in the blue of the sky among fleecy clouds tinted with rose. And far beneath the keel Kuranes could see strange lands and rivers and cities of surpassing beauty, spread indolently in the sunshine which seemed never to lessen or disappear. At length Athib told him that their journey was near its end, and that they would soon enter the harbour of Serannian, the pink marble city of the clouds, which is built on that ethereal coast where the west wind flows into the sky; but as the highest of the city's carven towers came into sight there was a sound somewhere in space, and Kuranes awaked in his London garret.

For many months after that Kuranes sought the marvellous city of Celephaïs and its sky-bound galleys in vain; and though his dreams carried him to many gorgeous and unheard-of places, no one whom he met could tell him how to find Ooth-Nargai beyond the Tanarian Hills. One night he went flying over dark mountains where there were faint, lone campfires at great distances apart, and strange, shaggy herds with tinkling bells on the leaders, and in the wildest part of this hilly country, so remote that few men could ever have seen it, he found a hideously ancient wall or causeway of stone zigzagging along the ridges and valleys; too gigantic ever to have risen by human hands, and of such a length that neither end of it could be seen. Beyond that wall in the grey dawn he came to a land of quaint gardens and cherry trees, and when the sun rose he beheld such beauty of red and white flowers, green foliage and lawns, white paths, diamond brooks, blue lakelets, carven bridges, and red-roofed pagodas, that he for a moment forgot Celephaïs in sheer delight. But he remembered it again when he walked down a white path toward a red-roofed pagoda, and would have questioned the people of this land about it, had he not found that there were no people there, but only birds and bees and butterflies. On another night Kuranes walked up a damp stone spiral stairway endlessly, and came to a tower window overlooking a mighty plain and river lit by the full moon; and in the silent city that spread away from the river bank he thought he beheld some feature or arrangement which he had known before. He would have descended and asked the way to Ooth-Nargai had not a fearsome aurora sputtered up from some remote place beyond the horizon, showing the ruin and antiquity of the city, and the stagnation of the reedy river, and the death lying upon that land, as it had lain since King Kynaratholis came home from his conquests to find the vengeance of the gods.

So Kuranes sought fruitlessly for the marvellous city of Celephaïs and its galleys that sail to Serannian in the sky, meanwhile seeing many wonders and once barely escaping from the high-priest not to be described, which wears a yellow silken mask over its face and dwells all alone in a prehistoric stone monastery in the cold desert plateau of Leng. In time he grew so impatient of the bleak intervals of day that he began buying drugs in order to increase his periods of sleep. Hasheesh helped a great deal, and once sent him to a part of space where form does not exist, but where glowing gases study the secrets of existence. And a violet-coloured gas told him that this part of space was outside what he had called infinity. The gas had not heard of planets and organisms before, but identified Kuranes merely as one from the infinity where matter, energy, and gravitation exist. Kuranes was now very anxious to return to minaret-studded Celephaïs, and increased his doses of drugs; but eventually he had no more money left, and could buy no drugs. Then one summer day he was turned out of his garret, and wandered aimlessly through the streets, drifting over a bridge to a place where the houses grew thinner and thinner. And it was there that fulfillment came, and he met the cortege of knights come from Celephaïs to bear him thither forever.

Handsome knights they were, astride roan horses and clad in shining armour with tabards of cloth-of-gold curiously emblazoned. So numerous were they, that Kuranes almost mistook them for an army, but they were sent in his honour; since it was he who had created Ooth-Nargai in his dreams, on which account he was now to be appointed its chief god for evermore. Then they gave Kuranes a horse and placed him at the head of the cavalcade, and all rode majestically through the downs of Surrey and onward toward the region where Kuranes and his ancestors were born. It was very strange, but as the riders went on they seemed to gallop back through time; for whenever they passed through a village in the twilight they saw only such houses and villagers as Chaucer or men before him might have seen, and sometimes they saw knights on horseback with small companies of retainers. When it grew dark they travelled more swiftly, till soon they were flying uncannily as if in the air. In the dim dawn they came upon the village which Kuranes had seen alive in his childhood, and asleep or dead in his dreams. It was alive now, and early villagers curtsied as the horsemen clattered down the street and turned off into the lane that ends in the abyss of dreams. Kuranes had previously entered that abyss only at night, and wondered what it would look like by day; so he watched anxiously as the column approached its brink. Just as they galloped up the rising ground to the precipice a golden glare came somewhere out of the west and hid all the landscape in effulgent draperies. The abyss was a seething chaos of roseate and cerulean splendour, and invisible voices sang exultantly as the knightly entourage plunged over the edge and floated gracefully down past glittering clouds and silvery coruscations. Endlessly down the horsemen floated, their chargers pawing the aether as if galloping over golden sands; and then the luminous vapours spread apart to reveal a greater brightness, the brightness of the city Celephaïs, and the sea coast beyond, and the snowy peak overlooking the sea, and the gaily painted galleys that sail out of the harbour toward distant regions where the sea meets the sky.

And Kuranes reigned thereafter over Ooth-Nargai and all the neighboring regions of dream, and held his court alternately in Celephaïs and in the cloud-fashioned Serannian. He reigns there still, and will reign happily for ever, though below the cliffs at Innsmouth the channel tides played mockingly with the body of a tramp who had stumbled through the half-deserted village at dawn; played mockingly, and cast it upon the rocks by ivy-covered Trevor Towers, where a notably fat and especially offensive millionaire brewer enjoys the purchased atmosphere of extinct nobility.

From Beyond.

3,000-WORD SHORT STORY; 1920.

This is another of Lovecraft's early works that, although generally panned by Lovecraft's most erudite scholarly admirers, is remarkably effective as a story and is well worth reading. It explores the idea of technology being used to bridge two different dimensions or planes of existence — our material plane, and some unknown other; and it explores the full implications of what it might mean to be in direct physical contact with extradimensional beings.

"From Beyond" was not published until 14 years after it was written, when it appeared in the June 1934 issue of Fantasy Fan.

Horrible beyond conception was the change which had taken place in my best friend, Crawford Tillinghast. I had not seen him since that day, two months and a half before, when he told me toward what goal his physical and metaphysical researches were leading; when he had answered my awed and almost frightened remonstrances by driving me from his laboratory and his house in a burst of fanatical rage. I had known that he now remained mostly shut in the attic laboratory with that accursed electrical machine, eating little and excluding even the servants, but I had not thought that a brief period of ten weeks could so alter and disfigure any human creature. It is not pleasant to see a stout man suddenly grown thin, and it is even worse when the baggy skin becomes yellowed or grayed, the eyes sunken, circled, and uncannily glowing, the forehead veined and corrugated, and the hands tremulous and twitching. And if added to this there be a repellent unkemptness, a wild disorder of dress, a bushiness of dark hair white at the roots, and an unchecked growth of white beard on a face once clean-shaven, the cumulative effect is quite shocking. But such was the aspect of Crawford Tilllinghast on the night his half coherent message brought me to his door after my weeks of exile; such was the specter that trembled as it admitted me, candle in hand, and glanced furtively over its shoulder as if fearful of unseen things in the ancient, lonely house set back from Benevolent Street.

That Crawford Tillinghast should ever have studied science and philosophy was a mistake. These things should be left to the frigid and impersonal investigator, for they offer two equally tragic alternatives to the man of feeling and action; despair, if he fail in his quest, and terrors unutterable and unimaginable if he succeed. Tillinghast had once been the prey of failure, solitary and melancholy; but now I knew, with nauseating fears of my own, that he was the prey of success. I had indeed warned him ten weeks before, when he burst forth with his tale of what he felt himself about to discover. He had been flushed and excited then, talking in a high and unnatural, though always pedantic, voice.

"What do we know," he had said, "of the world and the universe about us? Our means of receiving impressions are absurdly few, and our notions of surrounding objects infinitely narrow. We see things only as we are constructed to see them, and can gain no idea of their absolute nature. With five feeble senses we pretend to comprehend the boundlessly complex cosmos, yet other beings with wider, stronger, or different range of senses might not only see very differently the things we see, but might see and study whole worlds of matter, energy, and life which lie close at hand yet can never be detected with the senses we have. I have always believed that such strange, inaccessible worlds exist at our very elbows, and now I believe I have found a way to break down the barriers. I am not joking. Within twenty-four hours that machine near the table will generate waves acting on unrecognized sense organs that exist in us as atrophied or rudimentary vestiges. Those waves will open up to us many vistas unknown to man and several unknown to anything we consider organic life. We shall see that at which dogs howl in the dark, and that at which cats prick up their ears after midnight. We shall see these things, and other things which no breathing creature has yet seen. We shall overleap time, space, and dimensions, and without bodily motion peer to the bottom of creation."

When Tillinghast said these things I remonstrated, for I knew him well enough to be frightened rather than amused; but he was a fanatic, and drove me from the house. Now he was no less a fanatic, but his desire to speak had conquered his resentment, and he had written me imperatively in a hand I could scarcely recognize. As I entered the abode of the friend so suddenly metamorphosed to a shivering gargoyle, I became infected with the terror which seemed stalking in all the shadows. The words and beliefs expressed ten weeks before seemed bodied forth in the darkness beyond the small circle of candle light, and I sickened at the hollow, altered voice of my host. I wished the servants were about, and did not like it when he said they had all left three days previously. It seemed strange that old Gregory, at least, should desert his master without telling as tried a friend as I. It was he who had given me all the information I had of Tillinghast after I was repulsed in rage.

Yet I soon subordinated all my fears to my growing curiosity and fascination. Just what Crawford Tillinghast now wished of me I could only guess, but that he had some stupendous secret or discovery to impart, I could not doubt. Before I had protested at his unnatural pryings into the unthinkable; now that he had evidently succeeded to some degree I almost shared his spirit, terrible though the cost of victory appeared. Up through the dark emptiness of the house I followed the bobbing candle in the hand of this shaking parody of man. The electricity seemed to be turned off, and when I asked my guide he said it was for a definite reason.

"It would be too much . . . I would not dare," he continued to mutter. I especially noted his new habit of muttering, for it was not like him to talk to himself. We entered the laboratory in the attic, and I observed that detestable electrical machine, glowing with a sickly, sinister violet luminosity. It was connected with a powerful chemical battery, but seemed to be receiving no current; for I recalled that in its experimental stage it had sputtered and purred when in action. In reply to my question Tillinghast mumbled that this permanent glow was not electrical in any sense that I could understand.

He now seated me near the machine, so that it was on my right, and turned a switch somewhere below the crowning cluster of glass bulbs. The usual sputtering began, turned to a whine, and terminated in a drone so soft as to suggest a return to silence. Meanwhile the luminosity increased, waned again, then assumed a pale, outrè colour or blend of colours which I could neither place nor describe. Tillinghast had been watching me, and noted my puzzled expression.

"Do you know what that is?" he whispered, "That is ultra-violet." He chuckled oddly at my surprise. "You thought ultra-violet was invisible, and so it is — but you can see that and many other invisible things now.

"Listen to me! The waves from that thing are waking a thousand sleeping senses in us; senses which we inherit from aeons of evolution from the state of detached electrons to the state of organic humanity. I have seen the truth, and I intend to show it to you. Do you wonder how it will seem? I will tell you." Here Tillinghast seated himself directly opposite me, blowing out his candle and staring hideously into my eyes. "Your existing sense-organs — ears first, I think — will pick up many of the impressions, for they are closely connected with the dormant organs. Then there will be others. You have heard of the pineal gland? I laugh at the shallow endocrinologist, fellow-dupe and fellow-parvenu of the Freudian. That gland is the great sense organ of organs — I have found out. It is like sight in the end, and transmits visual pictures to the brain. If you are normal, that is the way you ought to get most of it . . . I mean get most of the evidence from beyond."

I looked about the immense attic room with the sloping south wall, dimly lit by rays which the everyday eye cannot see. The far corners were all shadows and the whole place took on a hazy unreality which obscured its nature and invited the imagination to symbolism and phantasm. During the interval that Tillinghast was long silent I fancied myself in some vast incredible temple of long-dead gods; some vague edifice of innumerable black stone columns reaching up from a floor of damp slabs to a cloudy height beyond the range of my vision. The picture was very vivid for a while, but gradually gave way to a more horrible conception; that of utter, absolute solitude in infinite, sightless, soundless space. There seemed to be a void, and nothing more, and I felt a childish fear which prompted me to draw from my hip pocket the revolver I carried after dark since the night I was held up in East Providence. Then from the farthermost regions of remoteness, the sound softly glided into existence. It was infinitely faint, subtly vibrant, and unmistakably musical, but held a quality of surpassing wildness which made its impact feel like a delicate torture of my whole body. I felt sensations like those one feels when accidentally scratching ground glass. Simultaneously there developed something like a cold draught, which apparently swept past me from the direction of the distant sound. As I waited breathlessly I perceived that both sound and wind were increasing; the effect being to give me an odd notion of myself as tied to a pair of rails in the path of a gigantic approaching locomotive. I began to speak to Tillinghast, and as I did so all the unusual impressions abruptly vanished. I saw only the man, the glowing machines, and the dim apartment. Tillinghast was grinning repulsively at the revolver which I had almost unconsciously drawn, but from his expression I was sure he had seen and heard as much as I, if not a great deal more. I whispered what I had experienced and he bade me to remain as quiet and receptive as possible.

"Don't move," he cautioned, "for in these rays we are able to be seen as well as to see. I told you the servants left, but I didn't tell you how. It was that thick-witted house-keeper — she turned on the lights downstairs after I had warned her not to, and the wires picked up sympathetic vibrations. It must have been frightful — I could hear the screams up here in spite of all I was seeing and hearing from another direction, and later it was rather awful to find those empty heaps of clothes around the house. Mrs. Updike's clothes were close to the front hall switch — that's how I know she did it. It got them all. But so long as we don't move we're fairly safe. Remember we're dealing with a hideous world in which we are practically helpless . . . Keep still!"

The combined shock of the revelation and of the abrupt command gave me a kind of paralysis, and in my terror my mind again opened to the impressions coming from what Tillinghast called "beyond." I was now in a vortex of sound and motion, with confused pictures before my eyes. I saw the blurred outlines of the room, but from some point in space there seemed to be pouring a seething column of unrecognizable shapes or clouds, penetrating the solid roof at a point ahead and to the right of me. Then I glimpsed the temple-like effect again, but this time the pillars reached up into an aerial ocean of light, which sent down one blinding beam along the path of the cloudy column I had seen before. After that the scene was almost wholly kaleidoscopic, and in the jumble of sights, sounds, and unidentified sense-impressions I felt that I was about to dissolve or in some way lose the solid form. One definite flash I shall always remember. I seemed for an instant to behold a patch of strange night sky filled with shining, revolving spheres, and as it receded I saw that the glowing suns formed a constellation or galaxy of settled shape; this shape being the distorted face of Crawford Tillinghast. At another time I felt the huge animate things brushing past me and occasionally walking or drifting through my supposedly solid body, and thought I saw Tillinghast look at them as though his better trained senses could catch them visually. I recalled what he had said of the pineal gland, and wondered what he saw with this preternatural eye.

Suddenly I myself became possessed of a kind of augmented sight. Over and above the luminous and shadowy chaos arose a picture which, though vague, held the elements of consistency and permanence. It was indeed somewhat familiar, for the unusual part was superimposed upon the usual terrestrial scene much as a cinema view may be thrown upon the painted curtain of a theater. I saw the attic laboratory, the electrical machine, and the unsightly form of Tillinghast opposite me; but of all the space unoccupied by familiar objects not one particle was vacant. Indescribable shapes both alive and otherwise were mixed in disgusting disarray, and close to every known thing were whole worlds of alien, unknown entities. It likewise seemed that all the known things entered into the composition of other unknown things and vice versa. Foremost among the living objects were inky, jellyfish monstrosities which flabbily quivered in harmony with the vibrations from the machine. They were present in loathsome profusion, and I saw to my horror that they overlapped; that they were semi-fluid and capable of passing through one another and through what we know as solids. These things were never still, but seemed ever floating about with some malignant purpose. Sometimes they appeared to devour one another, the attacker launching itself at its victim and instantaneously obliterating the latter from sight. Shudderingly I felt that I knew what had obliterated the unfortunate servants, and could not exclude the thing from my mind as I strove to observe other properties of the newly visible world that lies unseen around us. But Tillinghast had been watching me and was speaking.

"You see them? You see them? You see the things that float and flop about you and through you every moment of your life? You see the creatures that form what men call the pure air and the blue sky? Have I not succeeded in breaking down the barrier; have I not shown you worlds that no other living men have seen?" I heard his scream through the horrible chaos, and looked at the wild face thrust so offensively close to mine. His eyes were pits of flame, and they glared at me with what I now saw was overwhelming hatred. The machine droned detestably.

"You think those floundering things wiped out the servants? Fool, they are harmless! But the servants are gone, aren't they? You tried to stop me; you discouraged me when I needed every drop of encouragement I could get; you were afraid of the cosmic truth, you damned coward, but now I've got you! What swept up the servants? What made them scream so loud? . . . Don't know, eh! You'll know soon enough. Look at me — listen to what I say — do you suppose there are really any such things as time and magnitude? Do you fancy there are such things as form or matter? I tell you, I have struck depths that your little brain can't picture. I have seen beyond the bounds of infinity and drawn down demons from the stars . . . I have harnessed the shadows that stride from world to world to sow death and madness . . . Space belongs to me, do you hear? Things are hunting me now — the things that devour and dissolve — but I know how to elude them. It is you they will get, as they got the servants . . . Stirring, dear sir? I told you it was dangerous to move, I have saved you so far by telling you to keep still — saved you to see more sights and to listen to me. If you had moved, they would have been at you long ago. Don't worry, they won't hurt you. They didn't hurt the servants — it was the seeing that made the poor devils scream so. My pets are not pretty, for they come out of places where aesthetic standards are — very different. Disintegration is quite painless, I assure you — but I want you to see them. I almost saw them, but I knew how to stop. You are curious? I always knew you were no scientist. Trembling, eh. Trembling with anxiety to see the ultimate things I have discovered. Why don't you move, then? Tired? Well, don't worry, my friend, for they are coming . . . Look, look, curse you, look . . . it's just over your left shoulder . . ."

What remains to be told is very brief, and may be familiar to you from the newspaper accounts. The police heard a shot in the old Tillinghast house and found us there — Tillinghast dead and me unconscious. They arrested me because the revolver was in my hand, but released me in three hours, after they found it was apoplexy which had finished Tillinghast and saw that my shot had been directed at the noxious machine which now lay hopelessly shattered on the laboratory floor. I did not tell very much of what I had seen, for I feared the coroner would be skeptical; but from the evasive outline I did give, the doctor told me that I had undoubtedly been hypnotized by the vindictive and homicidal madman.

I wish I could believe that doctor. It would help my shaky nerves if I could dismiss what I now have to think of the air and the sky about and above me. I never feel alone or comfortable, and a hideous sense of pursuit sometimes comes chillingly on me when I am weary. What prevents me from believing the doctor is one simple fact — that the police never found the bodies of those servants whom they say Crawford Tillinghast murdered.

Nyarlarthotep.

1,100-WORD PROSE-POEM; 1920.

Sleepwalking is, of course, a serious medical issue. But, if we are to believe Lovecraft's account in a letter he sent to Rheinhart Kleiner, the first paragraph of this story is the product of an episode of "sleepwriting."

"Nyarlarthotep" is a prose-poem based closely on a dream from which Lovecraft apparently awoke with pen in hand and words already written on the page.

The picture this prose-poem conjures is a remarkable one — remarkable, and bleak. It's the decline and destruction of civilization in just over 1,000 words.

"Nyarlarthotep" was written in late 1920, around the same time as "The Crawling Chaos," the dream-story on which Lovecraft collaborated with Winifred Jackson, the title of which was taken from "Nyarlarthotep's" first line. It was first published in the November 1920 issue of United Amateur, *which got out late and most likely was not mailed until several months into 1921.*

Nyarlathotep . . . the Crawling Chaos . . . I am the last . . . I will tell the audient void . . . .

I do not recall distinctly when it began, but it was months ago. The general tension was horrible. To a season of political and social upheaval was added a strange and brooding apprehension of hideous physical danger; a danger widespread and all-embracing, such a danger as may be imagined only in the most terrible phantasms of the night. I recall that the people went about with pale and worried faces, and whispered warnings and prophecies which no one dared consciously repeat or acknowledge to himself that he had heard. A sense of monstrous guilt was upon the land, and out of the abysses between the stars swept chill currents that made men shiver in dark and lonely places. There was a daemoniac alteration in the sequence of the seasons — the autumn heat lingered fearsomely, and everyone felt that the world and perhaps the universe had passed from the control of known gods or forces to that of gods or forces which were unknown.

And it was then that Nyarlathotep came out of Egypt. Who he was, none could tell, but he was of the old native blood and looked like a Pharaoh. The fellahin knelt when they saw him, yet could not say why. He said he had risen up out of the blackness of twenty-seven centuries, and that he had heard messages from places not on this planet. Into the lands of civilisation came Nyarlathotep, swarthy, slender, and sinister, always buying strange instruments of glass and metal and combining them into instruments yet stranger. He spoke much of the sciences — of electricity and psychology — and gave exhibitions of power which sent his spectators away speechless, yet which swelled his fame to exceeding magnitude. Men advised one another to see Nyarlathotep, and shuddered. And where Nyarlathotep went, rest vanished; for the small hours were rent with the screams of nightmare. Never before had the screams of nightmare been such a public problem; now the wise men almost wished they could forbid sleep in the small hours, that the shrieks of cities might less horribly disturb the pale, pitying moon as it glimmered on green waters gliding under bridges, and old steeples crumbling against a sickly sky.

I remember when Nyarlathotep came to my city — the great, the old, the terrible city of unnumbered crimes. My friend had told me of him, and of the impelling fascination and allurement of his revelations, and I burned with eagerness to explore his uttermost mysteries. My friend said they were horrible and impressive beyond my most fevered imaginings; and what was thrown on a screen in the darkened room prophesied things none but Nyarlathotep dared prophesy, and in the sputter of his sparks there was taken from men that which had never been taken before yet which shewed only in the eyes. And I heard it hinted abroad that those who knew Nyarlathotep looked on sights which others saw not.

It was in the hot autumn that I went through the night with the restless crowds to see Nyarlathotep; through the stifling night and up the endless stairs into the choking room. And shadowed on a screen, I saw hooded forms amidst ruins, and yellow evil faces peering from behind fallen monuments. And I saw the world battling against blackness; against the waves of destruction from ultimate space; whirling, churning, struggling around the dimming, cooling sun. Then the sparks played amazingly around the heads of the spectators, and hair stood up on end whilst shadows more grotesque than I can tell came out and squatted on the heads. And when I, who was colder and more scientific than the rest, mumbled a trembling protest about "imposture" and "static electricity," Nyarlathotep drove us all out, down the dizzy stairs into the damp, hot, deserted midnight streets. I screamed aloud that I was not afraid; that I never could be afraid; and others screamed with me for solace. We swore to one another that the city was exactly the same, and still alive; and when the electric lights began to fade we cursed the company over and over again, and laughed at the queer faces we made.

I believe we felt something coming down from the greenish moon, for when we began to depend on its light we drifted into curious involuntary marching formations and seemed to know our destinations though we dared not think of them. Once we looked at the pavement and found the blocks loose and displaced by grass, with scarce a line of rusted metal to shew where the tramways had run. And again we saw a tram-car, lone, windowless, dilapidated, and almost on its side. When we gazed around the horizon, we could not find the third tower by the river, and noticed that the silhouette of the second tower was ragged at the top. Then we split up into narrow columns, each of which seemed drawn in a different direction. One disappeared in a narrow alley to the left, leaving only the echo of a shocking moan. Another filed down a weed-choked subway entrance, howling with a laughter that was mad. My own column was sucked toward the open country, and presently I felt a chill which was not of the hot autumn; for as we stalked out on the dark moor, we beheld around us the hellish moon-glitter of evil snows. Trackless, inexplicable snows, swept asunder in one direction only, where lay a gulf all the blacker for its glittering walls. The column seemed very thin indeed as it plodded dreamily into the gulf. I lingered behind, for the black rift in the green-litten snow was frightful, and I thought I had heard the reverberations of a disquieting wail as my companions vanished; but my power to linger was slight. As if beckoned by those who had gone before, I half-floated between the titanic snowdrifts, quivering and afraid, into the sightless vortex of the unimaginable.

Screamingly sentient, dumbly delirious, only the gods that were can tell. A sickened, sensitive shadow writhing in hands that are not hands, and whirled blindly past ghastly midnights of rotting creation, corpses of dead worlds with sores that were cities, charnel winds that brush the pallid stars and make them flicker low. Beyond the worlds vague ghosts of monstrous things; half-seen columns of unsanctified temples that rest on nameless rocks beneath space and reach up to dizzy vacua above the spheres of light and darkness. And through this revolting graveyard of the universe the muffled, maddening beating of drums, and thin, monotonous whine of blasphemous flutes from inconceivable, unlighted chambers beyond Time; the detestable pounding and piping whereunto dance slowly, awkwardly, and absurdly the gigantic, tenebrous ultimate gods — the blind, voiceless, mindless gargoyles whose soul is Nyarlathotep.

The Crawling Chaos.

BY WINIFRED V. JACKSON
AND H.P. LOVECRAFT

**3,000-WORD SHORT STORY;
1920.**

"The Crawling Chaos," the second of Lovecraft's collaborations with Winifred Virginia Jackson, is very similar to "The Green Meadow." It is another dream-story, but this time the dream is induced by opium administered during a medical procedure. Like "The Green Meadow," it's probably entirely Lovecraft's work, building from a story idea supplied by Jackson.

Once again the prose is trance-like and drifting, although one can now definitely detect the influence of Lord Dunsany in it; and Lovecraft plays with ambiguity and subtext much more, leaving riddles behind for the reader to puzzle over. Furthermore, the frame story, if one can call it that — the taking of the opium dose — is much more believable.

"The Crawling Chaos" was written in late 1920, shortly after Lovecraft wrote his own prose-poem "Nyarlarthotep," from the first line of which he sourced the title of the story. It was first published in the April 1921 issue of the United Co-Operative.

Of the pleasures and pains of opium much has been written. The ecstasies and horrors of De Quincey and the *artificiels* of Baudelaire are preserved and interpreted with an art which makes them immortal, and the world knows well the beauty, the terror and the mystery of those obscure realms into which the inspired dreamer is transported. But much as has been told, no man has yet dared intimate the nature of the phantasms thus unfolded to the mind, or hint at the direction of the unheard-of roads along whose ornate and exotic course the partaker of the drug is so irresistibly borne. De Quincey was drawn back into Asia, that teeming land of nebulous shadows whose hideous antiquity is so impressive that "the vast age of the race and name overpowers the sense of youth in the individual," but farther than that he dared not go. Those who have gone farther seldom returned, and even when they have, they have been either silent or quite mad.

I took opium but once — in the year of the plague, when doctors sought to deaden the agonies they could not cure. There was an overdose — my physician was worn out with horror and exertion — and I travelled very far indeed. In the end I returned and lived, but my nights are filled with strange memories, nor have I ever permitted a doctor to give me opium again.

The pain and pounding in my head had been quite unendurable when the drug was administered. Of the future I had no heed; to escape, whether by cure, unconsciousness, or death, was all that concerned me. I was partly delirious, so that it is hard to place the exact moment of transition, but I think the effect must have begun shortly before the pounding ceased to be painful. As I have said, there was an overdose; so my reactions were probably far from normal. The sensation of falling, curiously dissociated from the idea of gravity or direction, was paramount; though there was subsidiary impression of unseen throngs in incalculable profusion, throngs of infinitely diverse nature, but all more or less related to me. Sometimes it seemed less as though I were falling, than as though the universe or the ages were falling past me.

Suddenly my pain ceased, and I began to associate the pounding with an external rather than internal force. The falling had ceased also, giving place to a sensation of uneasy, temporary rest; and when I listened closely, I fancied the pounding was that of the vast, inscrutable sea as its sinister, colossal breakers lacerated some desolate shore after a storm of titanic magnitude. Then I opened my eyes.

For a moment my surroundings seemed confused, like a projected image hopelessly out of focus, but gradually I realised my solitary presence in a strange and beautiful room lighted by many windows. Of the exact nature of the apartment I could form no idea, for my thoughts were still far from settled, but I noticed van-coloured rugs and draperies, elaborately fashioned tables, chairs, ottomans, and divans, and delicate vases and ornaments which conveyed a suggestion of the exotic without being actually alien. These things I noticed, yet they were not long uppermost in my mind. Slowly but inexorably crawling upon my consciousness and rising above every other impression, came a dizzying fear of the unknown; a fear all the greater because I could not analyse it, and seeming to concern a stealthily approaching menace; not death, but some nameless, unheard-of thing inexpressibly more ghastly and abhorrent.

Presently I realised that the direct symbol and excitant of my fear was the hideous pounding whose incessant reverberations throbbed maddeningly against my exhausted brain. It seemed to come from a point outside and below the edifice in which I stood, and to associate itself with the most terrifying mental images. I felt that some horrible scene or object lurked beyond the silk-hung walls, and shrank from glancing through the arched, latticed windows that opened so bewilderingly on every hand.

Perceiving shutters attached to these windows, I closed

them all, averting my eyes from the exterior as I did so. Then, employing a flint and steel which I found on one of the small tables, I lit the many candles reposing about the walls in arabesque sconces. The added sense of security brought by closed shutters and artificial light calmed my nerves to some degree, but I could not shut out the monotonous pounding.

Now that I was calmer, the sound became as fascinating as it was fearful, and I felt a contradictory desire to seek out its source despite my still powerful shrinking. Opening a portière at the side of the room nearest the pounding, I beheld a small and richly draped corridor ending in a carven door and large oriel window.

To this window I was irresistibly drawn, though my ill-defined apprehensions seemed almost equally bent on holding me back. As I approached it I could see a chaotic whirl of waters in the distance. Then, as I attained it and glanced out on all sides, the stupendous picture of my surroundings burst upon me with full and devastating force.

I beheld such a sight as I had never beheld before, and which no living person can have seen save in the delirium of fever or the inferno of opium. The building stood on a narrow point of land — or what was now a narrow point of land — fully three hundred feet above what must lately have been a seething vortex of mad waters. On either side of the house there fell a newly washed-out precipice of red earth, whilst ahead of me the hideous waves were still rolling in frightfully, eating away the land with ghastly monotony and deliberation. Out a mile or more there rose and fell menacing breakers at least fifty feet in height, and on the far horizon ghoulish black clouds of grotesque contour were resting and brooding like unwholesome vultures. The waves were dark and purplish, almost black, and clutched at the yielding red mud of the bank as if with uncouth, greedy hands. I could not but feel that some noxious marine mind had declared a war of extermination upon all the solid ground, perhaps abetted by the angry sky.

Recovering at length from the stupor into which this unnatural spectacle had thrown me, I realized that my actual physical danger was acute. Even whilst I gazed, the bank had lost many feet, and it could not be long before the house would fall undermined into the awful pit of lashing waves. Accordingly I hastened to the opposite side of the edifice, and finding a door, emerged at once, locking it after me with a curious key which had hung inside.

I now beheld more of the strange region about me, and marked a singular division which seemed to exist in the hostile ocean and firmament. On each side of the jutting promontory different conditions held sway. At my left as I faced inland was a gently heaving sea with great green waves rolling peacefully in under a brightly shining sun. Something about that sun's nature and position made me shudder, but I could not then tell, and cannot tell now, what it was. At my right also was the sea, but it was blue, calm, and only gently undulating, while the sky above it was darker and the washed-out bank more nearly white than reddish.

I now turned my attention to the land, and found occasion for fresh surprise; for the vegetation resembled nothing I had ever seen or read about. It was apparently tropical or at least sub-tropical — a conclusion borne out by the intense heat of the air. Sometimes I thought I could trace strange analogies with the flora of my native land, fancying that the well-known plants and shrubs might assume such forms under a radical change of climate; but the gigantic and omnipresent palm trees were plainly foreign. The house I had just left was very small — hardly more than a cottage — but its material was evidently marble, and its architecture was weird and composite, involving a quaint fusion of Western and Eastern forms. At the corners were Corinthian columns, but the red tile roof was like that of a Chinese pagoda. From the door inland there stretched a path of singularly white sand, about four feet wide, and lined on either side with stately palms and unidentifiable flowering shrubs and plants. It lay toward the side of the promontory where the sea was blue and the bank rather whitish. Down this path I felt impelled to flee, as if pursued by some malignant spirit from the pounding ocean. At first it was slightly uphill, then I reached a gentle crest. Behind me I saw the scene I had left; the entire point with the cottage and the black water, with the green sea on one side and the blue sea on the other, and a curse unnamed and unnamable lowering over all. I never saw it again, and often wonder . . . After this last look I strode ahead and surveyed the inland panorama before me.

The path, as I have intimated, ran along the right-hand shore as one went inland. Ahead and to the left I now viewed a magnificent valley comprising thousands of acres, and covered with a swaying growth of tropical grass higher than my head. Almost at the limit of vision was a colossal palm tree which seemed to fascinate and beckon me. By this time wonder and escape from the imperilled peninsula had largely dissipated my fear, but as I paused and sank fatigued to the path, idly digging with my hands into the warm, whitish-golden sand, a new and acute sense of danger seized me. Some terror in the swishing tall grass seemed added to that of the diabolically pounding sea, and I started up crying aloud and disjointedly, "Tiger? Tiger? Is it Tiger? Beast? Beast? Is it a Beast that I am afraid of?"

My mind wandered back to an ancient and classical story of tigers which I had read; I strove to recall the author, but had difficulty. Then in the midst of my fear I remembered that the tale was by Rudyard Kipling; nor did the grotesqueness of deeming him an ancient author occur to me; I wished for the volume containing this story, and had almost started back toward the doomed cottage to procure it when my better sense and the lure of the palm prevented me.

Whether or not I could have resisted the backward beckoning without the counter-fascination of the vast palm tree, I do not know. This attraction was now dominant, and I left the path and crawled on hands and knees down the valley's slope despite my fear of the grass and of the serpents it might contain. I resolved to fight for life and reason as long as possible against all menaces of sea or land, though I sometimes feared defeat as the maddening swish of the uncanny grasses joined the still audible and irritating pounding of the distant breakers. I would frequently pause and put my hands to my ears for relief, but could never quite shut out the detestable sound. It was, as it seemed to me, only after ages that I finally dragged myself to the beckoning palm tree and lay quiet beneath its protecting shade.

There now ensued a series of incidents which transported me to the opposite extremes of ecstasy and horror; incidents which I tremble to recall and dare not seek to interpret. No sooner had I crawled beneath the overhanging foliage of the palm, than there dropped from its branches a young child of such beauty as I never beheld before. Though ragged and dusty, this being bore the features of a faun or demigod, and seemed almost to diffuse a radiance in the dense shadow of the tree. It smiled and extended its hand, but before I could arise and speak I heard in the upper air the exquisite melody of singing; notes high and low blent with a sublime and ethereal harmoniousness. The sun had by this time sunk below the horizon, and in the twilight I saw that an aureole of lambent light encircled the child's head.

Then in a tone of silver it addressed me:

"It is the end. They have come down through the gloaming from the stars. Now all is over, and beyond the Arinurian streams we shall dwell blissfully in Teloë."

As the child spoke, I beheld a soft radiance through the leaves of the palm tree, and rising, greeted a pair whom I knew to be the chief singers among those I had heard. A god and goddess they must have been, for such beauty is not mortal; and they took my hands, saying, "Come, child, you have heard the voices, and all is well. In Teloë beyond the Milky Way and the Arinurian streams are cities all of amber and chalcedony. And upon their domes of many facets glisten the images of strange and beautiful stars. Under the ivory bridges of Teloë flow rivers of liquid gold bearing pleasure-barges bound for blossomy Cytharion of the Seven Suns. And in Teloë and Cytharion abide only youth, beauty, and pleasure, nor are any sounds heard, save of laughter, song, and the lute. Only the gods dwell in Teloë of the golden rivers, but among them shalt thou dwell."

As I listened, enchanted, I suddenly became aware of a change in my surroundings. The palm tree, so lately overshadowing my exhausted form, was now some distance to my left and considerably below me. I was obviously floating in the atmosphere; companioned not only by the strange child and the radiant pair, but by a constantly increasing throng of half-luminous, vine-crowned youths and maidens with wind-blown hair and joyful countenance. We slowly ascended together, as if borne on a fragrant breeze which blew not from the earth but from the golden nebulae, and the child whispered in my ear that I must look always upward to the pathways of light, and never backward to the sphere I had just left. The youths and maidens now chanted mellifluous choriambics to the accompaniment of lutes, and I felt enveloped in a peace and happiness more profound than any I had in life imagined, when the intrusion of a single sound altered my destiny and shattered my soul. Through the ravishing strains of the singers and the lutanists, as if in mocking, daemoniac concord, throbbed from gulfs below the damnable, the detestable pounding of that hideous ocean. As those black breakers beat their message into my ears I forgot the words of the child and looked back, down upon the doomed scene from which I thought I had escaped.

Down through the aether I saw the accursed earth slowly turning, ever turning, with angry and tempestuous seas gnawing at wild desolate shores and dashing foam against the tottering towers of deserted cities. And under a ghastly moon there gleamed sights I can never describe, sights I can never forget; deserts of corpselike clay and jungles of ruin and decadence where once stretched the populous plains and villages of my native land, and maelstroms of frothing ocean where once rose the mighty temples of my forefathers. Round the northern pole steamed a morass of noisome growths and miasmal vapours, hissing before the onslaught of the ever-mounting waves that curled and fretted from the shuddering deep.

Then a rending report clave the night, and athwart the desert of deserts appeared a smoking rift. Still the black ocean foamed and gnawed, eating away the desert on either side as the rift in the centre widened and widened. There was now no land left but the desert, and still the fuming ocean ate and ate. All at once I thought even the pounding sea seemed afraid of something, afraid of dark gods of the inner earth that are greater than the evil god of waters, but even if it was it could not turn back; and the desert had suffered too much from those nightmare waves to help them now.

So the ocean ate the last of the land and poured into the smoking gulf, thereby giving up all it had ever conquered. From the new-flooded lands it flowed again, uncovering death and decay; and from its ancient and immemorial bed it trickled loathsomely, uncovering nighted secrets of the years when Time was young and the gods unborn.

Above the waves rose weedy remembered spires. The moon laid pale lilies of light on dead London, and Paris stood up from its damp grave to be sanctified with star-dust. Then rose spires and monoliths that were weedy but not remembered; terrible spires and monoliths of lands that men never knew were lands. There was not any pounding now, but only the unearthly roaring and hissing of waters tumbling into the rift. The smoke of that rift had changed to steam, and almost hid the world as it grew denser and denser. It seared my face and hands, and when I looked to see how it affected my companions I found they had all disappeared.

Then very suddenly it ended, and I knew no more till I awaked upon a bed of convalescence. As the cloud of steam from the Plutonic gulf finally concealed the entire surface from my sight, all the firmament shrieked at a sudden agony of mad reverberations which shook the trembling aether. In one delirious flash and burst it happened; one blinding, deafening holocaust of fire, smoke, and thunder that dissolved the wan moon as it sped outward to the void.

And when the smoke cleared away, and I sought to look upon the earth, I beheld against the background of cold, humorous stars only the dying sun and the pale mournful planets searching for their sister.

The Picture in the House.

3,300-WORD SHORT STORY; 1920.

This compact tale is widely regarded as the first really great Lovecraft story. It is the first of his stories to truly exploit the weird potential of New England, and the first to include the fictional city of Arkham and the fictional Miskatonic Valley.

It was written on Dec. 12, 1920, and published in the "July 1919" issue of National Amateur *— which for various reasons did not come out until the summer of 1921.*

Searchers after horror haunt strange, far places. For them are the catacombs of Ptolemais, and the carven mausolea of the nightmare countries. They climb to the moonlit towers of ruined Rhine castles, and falter down black cobwebbed steps beneath the scattered stones of forgotten cities in Asia. The haunted wood and the desolate mountain are their shrines, and they linger around the sinister monoliths on uninhabited islands.

But the true epicure in the terrible, to whom a new thrill of unutterable ghastliness is the chief end and justification of existence, esteems most of all the ancient, lonely farmhouses of backwoods New England; for there the dark elements of strength, solitude, grotesqueness and ignorance combine to form the perfection of the hideous.

Most horrible of all sights are the little unpainted wooden houses remote from travelled ways, usually squatted upon some damp grassy slope or leaning against some gigantic outcropping of rock. Two hundred years and more they have leaned or squatted there, while the vines have crawled and the trees have swelled and spread. They are almost hidden now in lawless luxuriances of green and guardian shrouds of shadow; but the small-paned windows still stare shockingly, as if blinking through a lethal stupor which wards off madness by dulling the memory of unutterable things.

In such houses have dwelt generations of strange people, whose like the world has never seen. Seized with a gloomy and fanatical belief which exiled them from their kind, their ancestors sought the wilderness for freedom. There the scions of a conquering race indeed flourished free from the restrictions of their fellows, but cowered in an appalling slavery to the dismal phantasms of their own minds. Divorced from the enlightenment of civilization, the strength of these Puritans turned into singular channels; and in their isolation, morbid self-repression, and struggle for life with relentless Nature, there came to them dark furtive traits from the prehistoric depths of their cold Northern heritage. By necessity practical and by philosophy stern, these folks were not beautiful in their sins. Erring as all mortals must, they were forced by their rigid code to seek concealment above all else; so that they came to use less and less taste in what they concealed. Only the silent, sleepy, staring houses in the backwoods can tell all that has lain hidden since the early days, and they are not communicative, being loath to shake off the drowsiness which helps them forget. Sometimes one feels that it would be merciful to tear down these houses, for they must often dream.

It was to a time-battered edifice of this description that I was driven one afternoon in November, 1896, by a rain of such chilling copiousness that any shelter was preferable to exposure. I had been travelling for some time amongst the people of the Miskatonic Valley in quest of certain genealogical data; and from the remote, devious, and problematical nature of my course, had deemed it convenient to employ a bicycle despite the lateness of the season. Now I found myself upon an apparently abandoned road which I had chosen as the shortest cut to Arkham, overtaken by the storm at a point far from any town, and confronted with no refuge save the antique and repellent wooden building which blinked with bleared windows from between two huge leafless elms near the foot of a rocky hill. Distant though it is from the remnant of a road, this house none the less impressed me unfavorably the very moment I espied it. Honest, wholesome structures do not stare at travellers so slyly and hauntingly, and in my genealogical researches I had encountered legends of a century before which biased me against places of this kind. Yet the force of the elements was such as to overcome my scruples, and I did not hesitate to wheel my machine up the weedy rise to the closed door which seemed at once so suggestive and secretive.

I had somehow taken it for granted that the house was abandoned, yet as I approached it I was not so sure, for though the walks were indeed overgrown with weeds, they seemed to retain their nature a little too well to argue complete desertion. Therefore instead of trying the door I knocked, feeling as I did so a trepidation I could scarcely explain. As I waited on the rough, mossy rock which served as a door-step, I glanced at the neighboring windows and the panes of the transom above me, and noticed that although old, rattling, and almost opaque with dirt, they were not broken. The building, then, must still be inhabited, despite its isolation and general neglect. However, my rapping evoked no response, so after repeating the summons I tried the rusty latch and found the door unfastened. Inside was a little vestibule with walls from which the plaster was falling, and through the doorway came a faint but peculiarly hateful odour. I entered, carrying my bicycle, and closed the door behind me. Ahead rose a narrow staircase, flanked by a small door probably leading to the cellar, while to the left and right were closed doors leading to rooms on the ground floor.

Leaning my cycle against the wall I opened the door at the left, and crossed into a small low-ceiled chamber but dimly lighted by its two dusty windows and furnished in the barest and most primitive possible way. It appeared to be a kind of sitting-room, for it had a table and several chairs, and an immense fireplace above which ticked an antique clock on a mantel. Books and papers were very few, and in the prevailing gloom I could not readily discern the titles. What interested me was the uniform air of archaism as displayed in every visible detail. Most of the houses in this region I had found rich in relics of the past, but here the antiquity was curiously complete; for in all the room I could not discover a single article of definitely post-revolutionary date. Had the furnishings been less humble, the place would have been a collector's paradise.

As I surveyed this quaint apartment, I felt an increase in that aversion first excited by the bleak exterior of the house. Just what it was that I feared or loathed, I could by no means define; but something in the whole atmosphere seemed redolent of unhallowed age, of unpleasant crudeness, and of secrets which should be forgotten. I felt disinclined to sit down, and wandered about examining the various articles which I had noticed. The first object of my curiosity was a book of medium size lying upon the table and presenting such an antediluvian aspect that I marvelled at beholding it outside a museum or library. It was bound in leather with metal fittings, and was in an excellent state of preservation; being altogether an unusual sort of volume to encounter in an abode so lowly. When I opened it to the title page my wonder grew even greater, for it proved to be nothing less rare than Pigafetta's account of the Congo region, written in Latin from the notes of the sailor Lopex and printed at Frankfurt in 1598. I had often heard of this work, with its curious illustrations by the brothers De Bry, hence for a moment forgot my uneasiness in my desire to turn the pages before me. The engravings were indeed interesting, drawn wholly from imagination and careless descriptions, and represented negroes with white skins and Caucasian features; nor would I soon have closed the book had not an exceedingly trivial circumstance upset my tired nerves and revived my sensation of disquiet. What annoyed me was merely the persistent way in which the volume tended to fall open of itself at Plate XII, which represented in gruesome detail a butcher's shop of the cannibal Anziques. I experienced some shame at my susceptibility to so slight a thing, but the drawing nevertheless disturbed me, especially in connection with some adjacent passages descriptive of Anzique gastronomy.

I had turned to a neighboring shelf and was examining its meagre literary contents — an eighteenth century Bible, a *Pilgrim's Progress* of like period, illustrated with grotesque woodcuts and printed by the almanack-maker Isaiah Thomas, the rotting bulk of Cotton Mather's *Magnalia Christi Americana*, and a few other books of evidently equal age — when my attention was aroused by the unmistakable sound of walking in the room overhead. At first astonished and startled, considering the lack of response to my recent knocking at the door, I immediately afterward concluded that the walker had just awakened from a sound sleep, and listened with less surprise as the footsteps sounded on the creaking stairs. The tread was heavy, yet seemed to contain a curious quality of cautiousness; a quality which I disliked the more because the tread was heavy. When I had entered the room I had shut the door behind me. Now, after a moment of silence during which the walker may have been inspecting my bicycle in the hall, I heard a fumbling at the latch and saw the paneled portal swing open again.

In the doorway stood a person of such singular appearance that I should have exclaimed aloud but for the restraints of good breeding. Old, white-bearded, and ragged, my host possessed a countenance and physique which inspired equal wonder and respect. His height could not have been less than six feet, and despite a general air of age and poverty he was stout and powerful in proportion. His face, almost hidden by a long beard which grew high on the cheeks, seemed abnormally ruddy and less wrinkled than one might expect; while over a high forehead fell a shock of white hair little thinned by the years. His blue eyes, though a trifle bloodshot, seemed inexplicably keen and burning. But for his horrible unkemptness the man would have been as distinguished-looking as he was impressive. This unkemptness, however, made him offensive despite his face and figure. Of what his clothing consisted I could hardly tell, for it seemed to me no more than a mass of tatters surmounting a pair of high, heavy boots; and his lack of cleanliness surpassed description.

The appearance of this man, and the instinctive fear he inspired, prepared me for something like enmity; so that I almost shuddered through surprise and a sense of uncanny incongruity when he motioned me to a chair and addressed me in a thin, weak voice full of fawning respect and ingratiating hospitality. His speech was very curious, an extreme form of Yankee dialect I had thought long extinct; and I studied it closely as he sat down opposite me for conversation.

"Ketched in the rain, be ye?" he greeted. "Glad ye was nigh the haouse en' hed the sense ta come right in. I calc'late I was alseep, else I'd a heerd ye — I ain't as young as I uster be, an' I need a paowerful sight o' naps naowadays. Trav'lin fur? I hain't seed many folks 'long this rud sence they tuk off the Arkham stage."

I replied that I was going to Arkham, and apologized for my rude entry into his domicile, whereupon he continued.

"Glad ta see ye, young Sir — new faces is scurce arount here, an' I hain't got much ta cheer me up these days. Guess yew hail from Bosting, don't ye? I never ben thar, but I kin tell a taown man when I see 'im — we hed one fer deestrick schoolmaster in 'eighty-four, but he quit suddent an' no one never heerd on 'im sence —" here the old man lapsed into a kind of chuckle, and made no explanation when I questioned him. He seemed to be in an aboundingly good humor, yet to possess those eccentricities which one might guess from his grooming. For some time he rambled on with an almost feverish geniality, when it struck me to ask him how he came by so rare a book as Pigafetta's "Regnum Congo." The effect of this volume had not left me, and I felt a certain hesitancy in speaking of it, but curiosity overmastered all the vague fears which had steadily accumulated since my first glimpse of the house. To my relief, the question did not seem an awkward one, for the old man answered freely and volubly.

"Oh, that Afriky book? Cap'n Ebenezer Holt traded me thet in 'sixty-eight — him as was kilt in the war." Something about the name of Ebenezer Holt caused me to look up sharply. I had encountered it in my genealogical work, but not in any record since the Revolution. I wondered if my host could help me in the task at which I was laboring, and resolved to ask him about it later on. He continued.

"Ebenezer was on a Salem merchantman for years, an' picked up a sight o' queer stuff in every port. He got this in London, I guess — he uster like ter buy things at the shops. I was up ta his haouse onct, on the hill, tradin' hosses, when I see this book. I relished the picters, so he give it in on a swap. 'Tis a queer book — here, leave me git on my spectacles —" The old man fumbled among his rags, producing a pair of dirty and amazingly antique glasses with small octagonal lenses and steel bows. Donning these, he reached for the volume on the table and turned the pages lovingly.

"Ebenezer cud read a leetle o' this — 'tis Latin — but I can't. I had two er three schoolmasters read me a bit, and Passon Clark, him they say got draownded in the pond — kin yew make anything outen it?" I told him that I could, and translated for his benefit a paragraph near the beginning. If I erred, he was not scholar enough to correct me; for he seemed childishly pleased at my English version. His proximity was becoming rather obnoxious, yet I saw no way to escape without offending him. I was amused at the childish fondness of this ignorant old man for the pictures in a book he could not read, and wondered how much better he could read the few books in English which adorned the room. This revelation of simplicity removed much of the ill-defined apprehension I had felt, and I smiled as my host rambled on:

"Queer haow picters kin set a body thinkin'. Take this un here near the front. Hey yew ever seed trees like thet, with big leaves a floppin' over an' daown? And them men — them can't be niggers — they dew beat all. Kinder like Injuns, I guess, even ef they be in Afriky. Some o' these here critters looks like monkeys, or half monkeys an' half men, but I never heerd o' nothin' like this un." Here he pointed to a fabulous creature of the artist, which one might describe as a sort of dragon with the head of an alligator.

"But naow I'll show ye the best un — over here nigh the middle —" The old man's speech grew a trifle thicker and his eyes assumed a brighter glow; but his fumbling hands, though seemingly clumsier than before, were entirely adequate to their mission. The book fell open, almost of its own accord and as if from frequent consultation at this place, to the repellent twelfth plate showing a butcher's shop amongst the Anzique cannibals. My sense of restlessness returned, though I did not exhibit it. The especially bizarre thing was that the artist had made his Africans look like white men — the limbs and quarters hanging about the walls of the shop were ghastly, while the butcher with his axe was hideously incongruous. But my host seemed to relish the view as much as I disliked it.

"What d'ye think o' this — ain't never see the like hereabouts, eh? When I see this I telled Eb Holt, 'That's suthin' ta stir ye up an' make yer blood tickle.' When I read in Scripter about slayin' — like them Midianites was slew — I kinder think things, but I ain't got no picter of it. Here a body kin see all they is to it — I s'pose 'tis sinful, but ain't we all born an' livin' in sin? — Thet feller bein' chopped up gives me a tickle every time I look at 'im — I hev ta keep lookin' at 'im — see whar the butcher cut off his feet? Thar's his head on thet bench, with one arm side of it, an' t'other arm's on the other side o' the meat block."

As the man mumbled on in his shocking ecstasy the expression on his hairy, spectacled face became indescribable, but his voice sank rather than mounted. My own sensations can scarcely be recorded. All the terror I had dimly felt before rushed upon me actively and vividly, and I knew that I loathed the ancient and abhorrent creature so near me with an infinite intensity. His madness, or at least his partial perversion, seemed beyond dispute. He was almost whispering now, with a huskiness more terrible than a scream, and I trembled as I listened.

"As I says, 'tis queer haow picters sets ye thinkin'. D'ye know, young Sir, I'm right sot on this un here. Arter I got the book off Eb I uster look at it a lot, especial when I'd heerd Passon Clark rant o' Sundays in his big wig. Onct I tried suthin' funny — here, young Sir, don't git skeert — all I done was ter look at the picter afore I kilt the sheep for market — killin' sheep was kinder more fun arter lookin' at it — " The tone of the old man now sank very low, sometimes becoming so faint that his words were hardly audible. I listened to the rain, and to the rattling of the bleared, small-paned windows, and marked a rumbling of approaching thunder quite unusual for the season. Once a terrific flash and peal shook the frail house to its foundations, but the whisperer seemed not to notice it.

"Killin' sheep was kinder more fun — but d'ye know, 'twan't quite satisfyin'. Queer haow a cravin' gits a holt on ye — As ye love the Almighty, young man, don't tell nobody, but I swar ter Gawd thet picter begun to make me hungry fer victuals I couldn't raise nor buy — here, set still, what's ailin' ye? — I didn't do nothin', only I wondered haow 'twud be ef I did — They say meat makes blood an' flesh, an' gives ye new life, so I wondered ef 'twudn't make a man live longer an' longer ef 'twas more the same — " But the whisperer never continued. The interruption was not produced by my fright, nor by the rapidly increasing storm amidst whose fury I was presently to open my eyes on a smoky solitude of blackened ruins. It was produced by a very simple though somewhat unusual happening.

The open book lay flat between us, with the picture staring repulsively upward. As the old man whispered the words "more the same" a tiny splattering impact was heard, and something showed on the yellowed paper of the upturned volume. I thought of the rain and of a leaky roof, but rain is not red. On the butcher's shop of the Anzique cannibals a small red spattering glistened picturesquely, lending vividness to the horror of the engraving. The old man saw it, and stopped whispering even before my expression of horror made it necessary; saw it and glanced quickly toward the floor of the room he had left an hour before. I followed his glance, and beheld just above us on the loose plaster of the ancient ceiling a large irregular spot of wet crimson which seemed to spread even as I viewed it. I did not shriek or move, but merely shut my eyes. A moment later came the titanic thunderbolt of thunderbolts; blasting that accursed house of unutterable secrets and bringing the oblivion which alone saved my mind.

1921.

A Style of Literary High Camp.

The year of 1921 brought much of the wonderful and the awful to young H.P. Lovecraft. On the one hand, his new Boston friends were the best thing that could have happened to the shy, secluded H.P. This was also the year in which Lovecraft first met, at a Hub Club event, the tall, striking woman who would later become his wife: fellow amateur journalist Sonia Haft Greene.

In February he gave a speech at the Hub Club, in which he told his colleagues, to great applause, of the joy that amateur journalism had brought into his life; and he was able to proudly report this enthusiastic reception back to his still-hospitalized mother.

But he would not long have the chance to share such triumphs with Sarah Susan. In May of that year, she went under the surgeon's knife for a gall-bladder operation. All seemed to go well — but within just a few days she was in terrible and growing pain.

Finally, on May 24, Sarah Susan Phillips Lovecraft succumbed to a growing infection in her gall bladder — a common enough occurrence in those dark pre-antibiotic days.

Howard was devastated. He retreated to his room and for several months did little other than write letters and pen maudlin ruminations about the futility of life.

Eventually, though, his friends and aunts brought him around. On June 9, he called on a new member of his amateur-press association, a retired college professor named Miss M.A. Little, and the next month he emerged from his shell a little more with another trip to the Hub Club in Boston.

Finally, late in the year, a fellow amateur-press publisher, George J. Houtain, contracted with him for a series of weird tales at $5 each. Houtain was going to make the jump to professional magazine publishing, and wanted some good stuff to go with his new spicy humor magazine, called (rather racily, as this was in the early days of Prohibition) *Home Brew*.

The result was *Herbert West, Reanimator*.

Another thing happened to Lovecraft in 1921 as well . . . or, perhaps, started to happen. His correspondence with Sonia Greene continued to blossom, and late that year she came to Providence to see him. Their acquaintance slowly started to become more serious, and by the end of 1921 one might almost say that the two were dating, albeit in a non-romantic way.

In addition to *Herbert West, Reanimator*, Lovecraft's 1921 weird-fiction output under his own name included "The Nameless City," "The Quest of Iranon," "Ex Oblivione," "The Moon Bog," "The Outsider," "The Other Gods," and "The Music of Erich Zann."

The Nameless City.

5,000-WORD SHORT STORY; 1921.

This substantial short story features the first mention of the mad Arab Abdul Alhazred, and although the Necronomicon *is not mentioned, it is quoted from. Although "The Nameless City" is not usually counted among Lovecraft's greatest tales, biographer W. Scott Poole makes a compelling case for it as an underappreciated masterpiece. Perhaps its reputation suffers because, for reasons that will be obvious to readers who have read both stories, it is often compared with* At the Mountains of Madness, *which nearly everyone agrees is one of the best works of weird fiction ever written.*

"The Nameless City" was written a few days before Jan. 26, 1921, and was first published in the November 1921 issue of Horace Lawson's amateur journal, Wolverine.

When I drew nigh the nameless city I knew it was accursed. I was traveling in a parched and terrible valley under the moon, and afar I saw it protruding uncannily above the sands as parts of a corpse may protrude from an ill-made grave. Fear spoke from the age-worn stones of this hoary survivor of the deluge, this great-grandfather of the eldest pyramid; and a viewless aura repelled me and bade me retreat from antique and sinister secrets that no man should see, and no man else had dared to see.

Remote in the desert of Araby lies the nameless city, crumbling and inarticulate, its low walls nearly hidden by the sands of uncounted ages. It must have been thus before the first stones of Memphis were laid, and while the bricks of Babylon were yet unbaked. There is no legend so old as to give it a name, or to recall that it was ever alive; but it is told of in whispers around campfires and muttered about by grandams in the tents of sheiks so that all the tribes shun it without wholly knowing why. It was of this place that Abdul Alhazred the mad poet dreamed the night before he sang his unexplained couplet:

That is not dead which can eternal lie,
And with strange aeons even death may die.

I should have known that the Arabs had good reason for shunning the nameless city, the city told of in strange tales but seen by no living man, yet I defied them and went into the untrodden waste with my camel. I alone have seen it, and that is why no other face bears such hideous lines of fear as mine; why no other man shivers so horribly when the night wind rattles the windows. When I came upon it in the ghastly stillness of unending sleep it looked at me, chilly from the rays of a cold moon amidst the desert's heat. And as I returned its look I forgot my triumph at finding it, and stopped still with my camel to wait for the dawn.

For hours I waited, till the east grew grey and the stars faded, and the grey turned to roseate light edged with gold. I heard a moaning and saw a storm of sand stirring among the antique stones though the sky was clear and the vast reaches of desert still. Then suddenly above the desert's far rim came the blazing edge of the sun, seen through the tiny sandstorm which was passing away, and in my fevered state I fancied that from some remote depth there came a crash of musical metal to hail the fiery disc as Memnon hails it from the banks of the Nile. My ears rang and my imagination seethed as I led my camel slowly across the sand to that unvocal place; that place which I alone of living men had seen.

In and out amongst the shapeless foundations of houses and places I wandered, finding never a carving or inscription to tell of these men, if men they were, who built this city and dwelt therein so long ago. The antiquity of the spot was unwholesome, and I longed to encounter some sign or device to prove that the city was indeed fashioned by mankind. There were certain proportions and dimensions in the ruins which I did not like. I had with me many tools, and dug much within the walls of the obliterated edifices; but progress was slow, and nothing significant was revealed. When night and the moon returned I felt a chill wind which brought new fear, so that I did not dare to remain in the city. And as I went outside the antique walls to sleep, a small sighing sandstorm gathered behind me, blowing over the grey stones though the moon was bright and most of the desert still.

I awakened just at dawn from a pageant of horrible dreams, my ears ringing as from some metallic peal. I saw the sun peering redly through the last gusts of a little sandstorm that hovered over the nameless city, and marked the quietness of the rest of the landscape. Once more I ventured within those brooding ruins that swelled beneath the sand like an ogre under a coverlet, and again dug vainly for relics of the forgotten race. At noon I rested, and in the afternoon I spent much time tracing the walls and bygone streets, and the outlines of the nearly vanished buildings. I saw that the city had been mighty indeed, and wondered at the sources of its greatness. To myself I pictured all the spendours of an age so distant that Chaldaea could not recall it, and thought of Sarnath the Doomed, that

Weird Tales, November 1938

"When I drew nigh the nameless city I knew it was accursed."

stood in the land of Mnar when mankind was young, and of Ib, that was carven of grey stone before mankind existed.

All at once I came upon a place where the bedrock rose stark through the sand and formed a low cliff; and here I saw with joy what seemed to promise further traces of the antediluvian people. Hewn rudely on the face of the cliff were the unmistakable facades of several small, squat rock houses or temples; whose interiors might preserve many secrets of ages too remote for calculation, though sandstorms had long effaced any carvings which may have been outside.

Very low and sand-choked were all the dark apertures near me, but I cleared on with my spade and crawled through it, carrying a torch to reveal whatever mysteries it might hold. When I was inside I saw that the cavern was indeed a temple, and beheld plain signs of the race that had lived and worshiped before the desert was a desert. Primitive altars, pillars, and niches, all curiously low, were not absent; and though I saw no sculptures or frescoes, there were many singular stones clearly shaped into symbols by artificial means. The lowness of the chiseled chamber was very strange, for I could hardly kneel upright; but the area was so great that my torch showed only part of it at a time. I shuddered oddly in some of the far corners; for certain altars and stones suggested forgotten rites of terrible, revolting and inexplicable nature and made me wonder what manner of men could have made and frequented such a temple. When I had seen all that the place contained,

I crawled out again, avid to find what the temples might yield.

Night had now approached, yet the tangible things I had seen made curiosity stronger than fear, so that I did not flee from the long mooncast shadows that had daunted me when first I saw the nameless city. In the twilight I cleared another aperture and with a new torch crawled into it, finding more vague stones and symbols, though nothing more definite than the other temple had contained. The room was just as low, but much less broad, ending in a very narrow passage crowded with obscure and cryptical shrines. About these shrines I was prying when the noise of a wind and my camel outside broke through the stillness and drew me forth to see what could have frightened the beast.

The moon was gleaming vividly over the primitive ruins, lighting a dense cloud of sand that seemed blown by a strong but decreasing wind from some point along the cliff ahead of me. I knew it was this chilly, sandy wind which had disturbed the camel and was about to lead him to a place of better shelter when I chanced to glance up and saw that there was no wind atop the cliff. This astonished me and made me fearful again, but I immediately recalled the sudden local winds that I had seen and heard before at sunrise and sunset, and judged it was a normal thing. I decided it came from some rock fissure leading to a cave, and watched the troubled sand to trace it to its source; soon perceiving that it came from the black orifice of a temple a long distance south of me, almost out of sight. Against the choking sand-cloud I plodded toward this temple, which as I neared it loomed larger than the rest, and shewed a doorway far less clogged with caked sand. I would have entered had not the terrific force of the icy wind almost quenched my torch. It poured madly out of the dark door, sighing uncannily as it ruffled the sand and spread among the weird ruins. Soon it grew fainter and the sand grew more and more still, till finally all was at rest again; but a presence seemed stalking among the spectral stones of the city, and when I glanced at the moon it seemed to quiver as though mirrored in unquiet waters. I was more afraid than I could explain, but not enough to dull my thirst for wonder; so as soon as the wind was quite gone I crossed into the dark chamber from which it had come.

This temple, as I had fancied from the outside, was larger than either of those I had visited before; and was presumably a natural cavern since it bore winds from some region beyond. Here I could stand quite upright, but saw that the stones and altars were as low as those in the other temples. On the walls and roof I beheld for the first time some traces of the pictorial art of the ancient race, curious curling streaks of paint that had almost faded or crumbled away; and on two of the altars I saw with rising excitement a maze of well-fashioned curvilinear carvings. As I held my torch aloft it seemed to me that the shape of the roof was too regular to be natural, and I wondered what the prehistoric cutters of stone had first worked upon. Their engineering skill must have been vast.

Then a brighter flare of the fantastic flame showed that form which I had been seeking, the opening to those remoter abysses whence the sudden wind had blown; and I grew faint when I saw that it was a small and plainly artificial door chiseled in the solid rock. I thrust my torch within, beholding a black tunnel with the roof arching low over a rough flight of very small, numerous and steeply descending steps. I shall always see those steps in my dreams, for I came to learn what they meant. At the time I hardly knew whether to call them steps or mere footholds in a precipitous descent. My mind was whirling with mad thoughts, and the words and warning of Arab prophets seemed to float across the desert from the land that men know to the nameless city that men dare not know. Yet I hesitated only for a moment before advancing through the portal and commencing to climb cautiously down the steep passage, feet first, as though on a ladder.

It is only in the terrible phantasms of drugs or delirium that any other man can have such a descent as mine. The narrow passage led infinitely down like some hideous haunted well, and the torch I held above my head could not light the unknown depths toward which I was crawling. I lost track of the hours and forgot to consult my watch, though I was frightened when I thought of the distance I must have been traversing. There were changes of direction and of steepness; and once I came to a long, low, level passage where I had to wriggle my feet first along the rocky floor, holding torch at arm's length beyond my head. The place was not high enough for kneeling. After that were more of the steep steps, and I was still scrambling down interminably when my failing torch died out. I do not think I noticed it at the time, for when I did notice it I was still holding it above me as if it were ablaze. I was quite unbalanced with that instinct for the strange and the unknown which had made me a wanderer upon earth and a haunter of far, ancient, and forbidden places.

In the darkness there flashed before my mind fragments of my cherished treasury of daemonic lore; sentences from Alhazred the mad Arab, paragraphs from the apocryphal nightmares of Damascus, and infamous lines from the delirious *Image du Monde* of Gauthier de Metz. I repeated queer extracts, and muttered of Afrasiab and the daemons that floated with him down the Oxus; later chanting over and over again a phrase from one of Lord Dunsany's tales — "The unreveberate blackness of the abyss." Once when the descent grew amazingly steep I recited something in sing-song from Thomas Moore until I feared to recite more:

A reservoir of darkness, black
As witches' cauldrons are, when fill'd
With moon-drugs in th' eclipse distill'd
Leaning to look if foot might pass
Down thro' that chasm, I saw, beneath,
As far as vision could explore,
The jetty sides as smooth as glass,

Looking as if just varnish'd o'er
With that dark pitch the Seat of Death
Throws out upon its slimy shore.

Time had quite ceased to exist when my feet again felt a level floor, and I found myself in a place slightly higher than the rooms in the two smaller temples now so incalculably far above my head. I could not quite stand, but could kneel upright, and in the dark I shuffled and crept hither and thither at random. I soon knew that I was in a narrow passage whose walls were lined with cases of wood having glass fronts. As in that Palaeozoic and abysmal place I felt of such things as polished wood and glass I shuddered at the possible implications. The cases were apparently ranged along each side of the passage at regular intervals, and were oblong and horizontal, hideously like coffins in shape and size. When I tried to move two or three for further examination, I found that they were firmly fastened.

I saw that the passage was a long one, so floundered ahead rapidly in a creeping run that would have seemed horrible had any eye watched me in the blackness; crossing from side to side occasionally to feel of my surroundings and be sure the walls and rows of cases still stretched on. Man is so used to thinking visually that I almost forgot the darkness and pictured the endless corridor of wood and glass in its low-studded monotony as though I saw it. And then in a moment of indescribable emotion I did see it.

Just when my fancy merged into real sight I cannot tell; but there came a gradual glow ahead, and all at once I knew that I saw the dim outlines of a corridor and the cases, revealed by some unknown subterranean phosphorescence. For a little while all was exactly as I had imagined it, since the glow was very faint; but as I mechanically kept stumbling ahead into the stronger light I realized that my fancy had been but feeble. This hall was no relic of crudity like the temples in the city above, but a monument of the most magnificent and exotic art. Rich, vivid, and daringly fantastic designs and pictures formed a continuous scheme of mural paintings whose lines and colours were beyond description. The cases were of a strange golden wood, with fronts of exquisite glass, and containing the mummified forms of creatures outreaching in grotesqueness the most chaotic dreams of man.

To convey any idea of these monstrosities is impossible. They were of the reptile kind, with body lines suggesting sometimes the crocodile, sometimes the seal, but more often nothing of which either the naturalist or the palaeontologist ever heard. In size they approximated a small man, and their fore-legs bore delicate and evident feet curiously like human hands and fingers. But strangest of all were their heads, which presented a contour violating all known biological principles. To nothing can such things be well compared — in one flash I thought of comparisons as varied as the cat, the bullfrog, the mythic Satyr, and the human being. Not Jove himself had had so colossal and protuberant a forehead, yet the horns and the noselessness and the alligator-like jaw placed the things outside all established categories. I debated for a time on the reality of the mummies, half suspecting they were artificial idols; but soon decided they were indeed some palaeogean species which had lived when the nameless city was alive. To crown their grotesqueness, most of them were gorgeously enrobed in the costliest of fabrics, and lavishly laden with ornaments of gold, jewels, and unknown shining metals.

The importance of these crawling creatures must have been vast, for they held first place among the wild designs on the frescoed walls and ceiling. With matchless skill had the artist drawn them in a world of their own, wherein they had cities and gardens fashioned to suit their dimensions; and I could not help but think that their pictured history was allegorical, perhaps shewing the progress of the race that worshiped them. These creatures, I said to myself, were to men of the nameless city what the she-wolf was to Rome, or some totem-beast is to a tribe of Indians.

Holding this view, I could trace roughly a wonderful epic of the nameless city; the tale of a mighty seacoast metropolis that ruled the world before Africa rose out of the waves, and of its struggles as the sea shrank away, and the desert crept into the fertile valley that held it. I saw its wars and triumphs, its troubles and defeats, and afterwards its terrible fight against the desert when thousands of its people — here represented in allegory by the grotesque reptiles — were driven to chisel their way down though the rocks in some marvelous manner to another world whereof their prophets had told them. It was all vividly weird and realistic, and its connection with the awesome descent I had made was unmistakable. I even recognized the passages.

As I crept along the corridor toward the brighter light I saw later stages of the painted epic — the leave-taking of the race that had dwelt in the nameless city and the valley around for ten million years; the race whose souls shrank from quitting scenes their bodies had known so long where they had settled as nomads in the earth's youth, hewing in the virgin rock those primal shrines at which they had never ceased to worship. Now that the light was better I studied the pictures more closely and, remembering that the strange reptiles must represent the unknown men, pondered upon the customs of the nameless city. Many things were peculiar and inexplicable. The civilization, which included a written alphabet, had seemingly risen to a higher order than those immeasurably later civilizations of Egypt and Chaldaea, yet there were curious omissions. I could, for example, find no pictures to represent deaths or funeral customs, save such as were related to wars, violence, and plagues; and I wondered at the reticence shown concerning natural death. It was as though an ideal of immortality had been fostered as a cheering illusion.

Still nearer the end of the passage was painted scenes of the utmost picturesqueness and extravagance: contrasted views of the nameless city in its desertion and growing ruin, and of the strange new realm of paradise to which the race had hewed its way through the stone. In these views the city and the desert valley were shewn always by moonlight, golden nimbus hovering over the fallen walls, and half-revealing the splendid perfection of former times, shown spectrally and elusively by the artist. The paradisal scenes were almost too extravagant to be believed, portraying a hidden world of eternal day filled with glorious cities and ethereal hills and valleys. At the very last I thought I saw signs of an artistic anticlimax. The paintings were less skillful, and much more bizarre than even the wildest of the earlier scenes. They seemed to record a slow decadence of the ancient stock, coupled with a growing ferocity toward the outside world from which it was driven by the desert. The forms of the people — always represented by the sacred reptiles — appeared to be gradually wasting away, though their spirit as shewn hovering above the ruins by moonlight gained in proportion. Emaciated priests, displayed as reptiles in ornate robes, cursed the upper air and all who breathed it; and one terrible final scene shewed a primitive-looking man, perhaps a pioneer of ancient Irem, the City of Pillars, torn to pieces by members of the elder race. I remember how the Arabs fear the nameless city, and was glad that beyond this place the grey walls and ceiling were bare.

As I viewed the pageant of mural history I had approached very closely to the end of the low-ceiled hall, and was aware of a gate through which came all of the illuminating phosphorescence. Creeping up to it, I cried aloud in transcendent amazement at what lay beyond; for instead of other and brighter chambers there was only an illimitable void of uniform radiance, such one might fancy when gazing down from the peak of Mount Everest upon a sea of sunlit mist. Behind me was a passage so cramped that I could not stand upright in it; before me was an infinity of subterranean effulgence.

Reaching down from the passage into the abyss was the head of a steep flight of steps — small numerous steps like those of black passages I had traversed — but after a few feet the glowing vapours concealed everything. Swung back open against the left-hand wall of the passage was a massive door of brass, incredibly thick and decorated with fantastic bas-reliefs, which could if closed shut the whole inner world of light away from the vaults and passages of rock. I looked at the step, and for the nonce dared not try them. I touched the open brass door, and could not move it. Then I sank prone to the stone floor, my mind aflame with prodigious reflections which not even a death-like exhaustion could banish.

As I lay still with closed eyes, free to ponder, many things I had lightly noted in the frescoes came back to me with new and terrible significance — scenes representing the nameless city in its heyday — the vegetations of the valley around it, and the distant lands with which its merchants traded. The allegory of the crawling creatures puzzled me by its universal prominence, and I wondered that it would be so closely followed in a pictured history of such importance. In the frescoes the nameless city had been shewn in proportions fitted to the reptiles. I wondered what its real proportions and magnificence had been, and reflected a moment on certain oddities I had noticed in the ruins. I thought curiously of the lowness of the primal temples and of the underground corridor, which were doubtless hewn thus out of deference to the reptile deities there honoured; though it perforce reduced the worshipers to crawling. Perhaps the very rites here involved crawling in imitation of the creatures. No religious theory, however, could easily explain why the level passages in that awesome descent should be as low as the temples — or lower, since one cold not even kneel in it. As I thought of the crawling creatures, whose hideous mummified forms were so close to me, I felt a new throb of fear. Mental associations are curious, and I shrank from the idea that except for the poor primitive man torn to pieces in the last painting, mine was the only human form amidst the many relics and symbols of the primordial life.

But as always in my strange and roving existence, wonder soon drove out fear; for the luminous abyss and what it might contain presented a problem worthy of the greatest explorer. That a weird world of mystery lay far down that flight of peculiarly small steps I could not doubt, and I hoped to find there those human memorials which the painted corridor had failed to give. The frescoes had pictured unbelievable cities, and valleys in this lower realm, and my fancy dwelt on the rich and colossal ruins that awaited me.

My fears, indeed, concerned the past rather than the future. Not even the physical horror of my position in that cramped corridor of dead reptiles and antediluvian frescoes, miles below the world I knew and faced by another world of eerie light and mist, could match the lethal dread I felt at the abysmal antiquity of the scene and its soul. An ancientness so vast that measurement is feeble seemed to leer down from the primal stones and rock-hewn temples of the nameless city, while the very latest of the astounding maps in the frescoes shewed oceans and continents that man has forgotten, with only here and there some vaguely familiar outlines. Of what could have happened in the geological ages since the paintings ceased and the death-hating race resentfully succumbed to decay, no man might say. Life had once teemed in these caverns and in the luminous realm beyond; now I was alone with vivid relics, and I trembled to think of the countless ages through which these relics had kept a silent deserted vigil.

Suddenly there came another burst of that acute fear which had intermittently seized me ever since I first saw the terrible valley and the nameless city under a cold moon, and despite my exhaustion I found myself starting frantically to a sitting posture and gazing back along the black corridor toward the tunnels that rose to the outer world. My sensations were like those which had made me shun the nameless city at night, and were as inexplicable as they were poignant. In another moment, however, I received a still greater shock in the form of a definite sound — the first which had broken the utter silence of these tomb-like depths. It was a deep, low moaning, as of a distant throng of condemned spirits, and came from the direction in which I was staring. Its volume rapidly grew, till it soon reverberated frightfully through the low passage, and at the same time I became conscious of an increasing draught of cold air, likewise flowing from the tunnels and the city above. The touch of this air seemed to restore my balance, for I instantly recalled the sudden gusts which had risen around the mouth of the abyss each sunset and sunrise, one of which had indeed revealed the hidden tunnels to me. I looked at my watch and saw that sunrise was near, so I braced myself to resist the gale that was sweeping down to its cavern home as it had swept forth at evening. My fear again waned low, since a natural phenomenon tends to dispel broodings over the unknown.

More and more madly poured the shrieking, moaning night wind into the gulf of the inner earth. I dropped prone again and clutched vainly at the floor for fear of being swept bodily through the open gate into the phosphorescent abyss. Such fury I had not expected, and as I grew aware of an actual slipping of my form toward the abyss I was beset by a thousand new terrors of apprehension and imagination. The malignancy of the blast awakened incredible fancies; once more I compared myself shudderingly to the only human image in that frightful corridor, the man who was torn to pieces by the nameless race, for in the fiendish clawing of the swirling currents there seemed to abide a vindictive rage all the stronger because it was largely impotent. I think I screamed frantically near the last — I was almost mad — of the howling wind-wraiths. I tried to crawl against the murderous invisible torrent, but I could not even hold my own as I was pushed slowly and inexorably toward the unknown world. Finally reason must have wholly snapped; for I fell babbling over and over that unexplainable couplet of the mad Arab Alhazred, who dreamed of the nameless city:

That is not dead which can eternal lie,
And with strange aeons even death may die.

Only the grim brooding desert gods know what really took place — what indescribable struggles and scrambles in the dark I endured or what Abaddon guided me back to life, where I must always remember and shiver in the night wind till oblivion — or worse — claims me. Monstrous, unnatural, colossal, was the thing — too far beyond all the ideas of man to be believed except in the silent damnable small hours of the morning when one cannot sleep.

I have said that the fury of the rushing blast was infernal — cacodaemoniacal — and that its voices were hideous with the pent-up viciousness of desolate eternities. Presently these voices, while still chaotic before me, seemed to my beating brain to take articulate form behind me; and down there in the grave of unnumbered aeon-dead antiquities, leagues below the dawn-lit world of men, I heard the ghastly cursing and snarling of strange-tongued fiends. Turning, I saw outlined against the luminous aether of the abyss what could not be seen against the dusk of the corridor — a nightmare horde of rushing devils; hate distorted, grotesquely panoplied, half transparent devils of a race no man might mistake — the crawling reptiles of the nameless city.

And as the wind died away I was plunged into the ghoul-pooled darkness of earth's bowels; for behind the last of the creatures the great brazen door clanged shut with a deafening peal of metallic music whose reverberations swelled out to the distant world to hail the rising sun as Memnon hails it from the banks of the Nile.

The Quest of Iranon.

2,800-WORD SHORT STORY; 1921.

This short story is arguably the most Dunsanian of Lovecraft's Lord Dunsany-inspired stories. At first glance, it looks a bit like a long prose-poem, self-consciously seeking after lyric beauty, and therefore vulnerable to charges of mawkishness — in later years Lovecraft himself came to see it that way. But the story has a philosophical depth and complexity to it that is often overlooked by those who mistake it for a mere bit of melancholic mood-mongering in slavish imitation of Lord Dunsany.

"The Quest of Iranon" was written on Feb. 28, 1921. Lovecraft was initially very proud of it, and wanted to save it for his own amateur journal, The Conservative*; but by the time he had an issue ready for release, in early 1923, he apparently had started to sour on the story. It remained in his file of unpublished manuscripts until finally it was published in the July-August 1935 issue of Lloyd Arthur Eshbach's amateur magazine,* The Galleon.

Into the granite city of Teloth wandered the youth, vine-crowned, his yellow hair glistening with myrrh and his purple robe torn with briers of the mountain Sidrak that lies across the antique bridge of stone. The men of Teloth are dark and stern, and dwell in square houses, and with frowns they asked the stranger whence he had come and what were his name and fortune. So the youth answered:

"I am Iranon, and come from Aira, a far city that I recall only dimly but seek to find again. I am a singer of songs that I learned in the far city, and my calling is to make beauty with the things remembered of childhood. My wealth is in little memories and dreams, and in hopes that I sing in gardens when the moon is tender and the west wind stirs the lotus-buds."

When the men of Teloth heard these things they whispered to one another; for though in the granite city there is no laughter or song, the stern men sometimes look to the Karthian hills in the spring and think of the lutes of distant Oonai whereof travellers have told. And thinking thus, they bade the stranger stay and sing in the square before the Tower of Mlin, though they liked not the colour of his tattered robe, nor the myrrh in his hair, nor his chaplet of vine-leaves, nor the youth in his golden voice. At evening Iranon sang, and while he sang an old man prayed and a blind man said he saw a nimbus over the singer's head. But most of the men of Teloth yawned, and some laughed and some went to sleep; for Iranon told nothing useful, singing only his memories, his dreams, and his hopes.

"I remember the twilight, the moon, and soft songs, and the window where I was rocked to sleep. And through the window was the street where the golden lights came, and where the shadows danced on houses of marble. I remember the square of moonlight on the floor, that was not like any other light, and the visions that danced on the moonbeams when my mother sang to me. And too, I remember the sun of morning bright above the many-coloured hills in summer, and the sweetness of flowers borne on the south wind that made the trees sing.

"Oh Aira, city of marble and beryl, how many are thy beauties! How I loved the warm and fragrant groves across the hyaline Nithra, and the falls of the tiny Kra that flowed though the verdant valley! In those groves and in the vale the children wove wreaths for one another, and at dusk I dreamed strange dreams under the yath-trees on the mountain as I saw below me the lights of the city, and the curving Nithra reflecting a ribbon of stars.

"And in the city were the palaces of veined and tinted marble, with golden domes and painted walls, and green gardens with cerulean pools and crystal fountains. Often I played in the gardens and waded in the pools, and lay and dreamed among the pale flowers under the trees. And sometimes at sunset I would climb the long hilly street to the citadel and the open place, and look down upon Aira, the magic city of marble and beryl, splendid in a robe of golden flame.

"Long have I missed thee, Aira, for I was but young when we went into exile; but my father was thy King and I shall come again to thee, for it is so decreed of Fate. All through seven lands have I sought thee, and some day shall I reign over thy groves and gardens, thy streets and palaces, and sing to men who shall know whereof I sing, and laugh not nor turn away. For I am Iranon, who was a Prince in Aira."

That night the men of Teloth lodged the stranger in a stable, and in the morning an archon came to him and told him to go to the shop of Athok the cobbler, and be apprenticed to him.

"But I am Iranon, a singer of songs, " he said, "and have no heart for the cobbler's trade."

"All in Teloth must toil," replied the archon, "for that is the law." Then said Iranon:

"Wherefore do ye toil; is it not that ye may live and be happy? And if ye toil only that ye may toil more, when shall happiness find you? Ye toil to live, but is not life made of beauty and song? And if ye suffer no singers among you, where shall be the fruits of your toil? Toil without song is like a weary journey without an end. Were not death more pleasing?" But

Weird Tales, March 1939

"Beyond the Karthian Hills lieth Oonai, the city of lutes and dancing."

the archon was sullen and did not understand, and rebuked the stranger.

"Thou art a strange youth, and I like not thy face nor thy voice. The words thou speakest are blasphemy, for the gods of Teloth have said that toil is good. Our gods have promised us a haven of light beyond death, where shall be rest without end, and crystal coldness amidst which none shall vex his mind with thought or his eyes with beauty. Go thou then to Athok the cobbler or be gone out of the city by sunset. All here must serve, and song is folly."

So Iranon went out of the stable and walked over the narrow stone streets between the gloomy square house of granite, seeking something green, for all was of stone. On the faces of men were frowns, but by the stone embankment along the sluggish river Zuro sat a young boy with sad eyes gazing into the waters to spy green budding branches washed down from the hills by the freshets. And the boy said to him:

"Art thou not indeed he of whom the archons tell, who seekest a far city in a fair land? I am Romnod, and born of the blood of Teloth, but am not old in the ways of the granite city, and yearn daily for the warm groves and the distant lands of beauty and song. Beyond the Karthian hills lieth Oonai, the city of lutes and dancing, which men whisper of and say is both lovely and terrible. Thither would I go were I old enough to find the way, and thither shouldst thou go and thou wouldst sing and have men listen to thee. Let us leave the city of Teloth and fare together among the hills of spring. Thou shalt shew me the ways of travel and I will attend thy songs at evening when the stars one by one bring dreams to the minds of dreamers. And peradventure it may be that Oonai the city of lutes and dancing is even the fair Aira thou seekest, for it is told that thou hast not known Aira since the old days, and a name often changeth. Let us go to Oonai, O Iranon of the golden head, where men shall know our longings and welcome us as brothers, nor even laugh or frown at what we say." And Iranon answered:

"Be it so, small one; if any in this stone place yearn for beauty he must seek the mountains and beyond, and I would not leave thee to pine by the sluggish Zuro. But think not that delight and understanding dwell just across the Karthian hills, or in any spot thou canst find in a day's, or a year's, or a lustrum's journey. Behold, when I was small like thee I dwelt in the valley of Narthos by the frigid Xari, where none would listen to my dreams; and I told myself that when older I would go to Sinara on the southern slope, and sing to smiling dromedary-men in the marketplace. But when I went to Sinara I found the dromedary men all drunken and ribald, and saw that their songs were not as mine, so I travelled in a barge down the Xari to onyx-walled Jaren. And the soldiers at Jaren laughed at me and drove me out, so that I wandered to many cities. I have seen Stethelos that is below the great cataract, and have gazed on the marsh where Sarnath once stood. I have been to Thraa, Ilarnek, and Kadatheron on the winding river Ai, and have dwelt long in Olathoe in the land of Lomar. But though I have had listeners sometimes, they have ever been few. and I know that welcome shall wait me only in Aira, the city of marble and beryl where my father once ruled as King. So for Aira shall we seek, though it were well to visit distant and lute-blessed Oonai across the Karthian hills, which may indeed be Aira, though I think not. Aira's beauty is past imagining, and none can tell of it without rapture, whilst of Oonai the camel-drivers whisper leeringly."

At the sunset Iranon and small Romnod went forth from Teloth, and for long wandered amidst the green hills and cool forests. The way was rough and obscure, and never did they seem nearer to Oonai the city of lutes and dancing; but in the dusk as the stars came out Iranon would sing of Aira and its beauties and Romnod would listen, so that they were both happy after a fashion. They ate plentifully of fruit and red berries, and marked not the passing of time, but many years must have slipped away. Small Romnod was now not so small, and spoke deeply instead of shrilly, though Iranon was always the same, and decked his golden hair with vines and fragrant resins found in the woods. So it came to pass that Romnod seemed older than Iranon, though he had been very small when Iranon had found him watching for green budding branches in Teloth beside the sluggish stone-banked Zuro.

Then one night when the moon was full the travellers came to a mountain crest and looked down upon the myriad lights of Oonai. Peasants had told them they were near, and Iranon knew that this was not his native city of Aira. The lights of Oonai were not like those of Aira; for they were harsh and glaring, while the lights of Aira shine as softly and magically as shone the moonlight on the floor by the window where Iranon's mother once rocked him to sleep with song. But Oonai was a city of lutes and dancing, so Iranon and Romnod went down the steep slope that they might find men to whom songs and dreams would bring pleasure. And when they were come into the town they found rose-wreathed revellers bound from house to house and leaning from windows and balconies, who listened to the songs of Iranon and tossed him flowers and applauded when he was done. Then for a moment did Iranon believe he had found those who thought and felt even as he, though the town was not a hundredth as fair as Aira.

When dawn came Iranon looked about with dismay, for the domes of Oonai were not golden in the sun, but grey and dismal. And the men of Oonai were pale with revelling, and dull with wine, and unlike the radient men of Aira. But because the people had thrown him blossoms and acclaimed his sings Iranon stayed on, and with him Romnod, who liked the revelry of the town and wore in his dark hair roses and myrtle. Often at night Iranon sang to the revellers, but he was always as before, crowned only in the vine of the mountains and remembering the marble streets of Aira and the hyaline Nithra. In the frescoed halls of the Monarch did he sing, upon a crystal dais raised over a floor that was a mirror, and as he sang, he brought pictures to his hearers till the floor seemed to reflect old, beautiful, and half-remembered things instead of the wine-reddened feasters who pelted him with roses. And the King bade him put away his tattered purple, and clothed him in satin and cloth-of-gold, with rings of green jade and bracelets of tinted ivory, and lodged him in a gilded and tapestried chamber on a bed of sweet carven wood with canopies and coverlets of flower-embroidered silk. Thus dwelt Iranon in Oonai, the city of lutes and dancing.

It is not known how long Iranon tarried in Oonai, but one day the King brought to the palace some wild whirling dancers from the Liranian desert, and dusky flute-players from Drinen in the East, and after that the revellers threw their roses not so much at Iranon as at the dancers and flute-players. And day by day that Romnod who had been a small boy in granite Teloth grew coarser and redder with wine, till he dreamed less and less, and listened with less delight to the songs of Iranon. But though Iranon was sad, he ceased not to sing, and at evening told again of his dreams of Aira, the city of marble and beryl. Then one night the reddened and fattened Romnod snorted heavily amidst the poppied silks of his banquet-couch and died writhing, whilst Iranon, pale and slender, sang to himself in a far corner. And when Iranon had wept over the grave of Romnod and strewn it with green branches, such as Romnod used to love, he put aside his silks and gauds and went forgotten out of Oonai the city of lutes and dancing clad only in the ragged purple in which he had come, and garlanded with fresh vines from the mountains.

Into the sunset wandered Iranon, seeking still for his native land and for men who would understand his songs and dreams. In all the cities of Cydathria and in the lands beyond the Bnazie desert gay-faced children laughed at his olden songs and tattered robe of purple; but Iranon stayed ever young, and wore wreaths upon his golden head whilst he sang of Aira, delight of the past and hope of the future.

So came he one night to the squalid cot of an antique shepherd, bent and dirty, who kept flocks on a stony slope above a quicksand marsh. To this man Iranon spoke, as to so many others:

"Canst thou tell me where I may find Aira, the city of marble and beryl, where flows the hyaline Nithra and where the falls of the tiny Kra sing to the verdant valleys and hills forested with yath trees?" and the shepherd, hearing, looked long and strangely at Iranon, as if recalling something very far away in time, and noted each line of the stranger's face, and his golden hair, and his crown of vine-leaves. But he was old, and shook his head as he replied:

"O stranger, I have indeed heard the name of Aira, and the other names thou hast spoken, but they come to me from afar down the waste of long years. I heard them in my youth from the lips of a playmate, a beggar's boy given to strange dreams, who would weave long tales about the moon and the flowers and the west wind. We used to laugh at him, for we knew him from his birth though he thought himself a King's son. He was comely, even as thou, but full of folly and strangeness; and he ran away when small to find those who would listen gladly to his songs and dreams. How often hath he sung to me of lands that never were, and things that never can be! Of Aira did he speak much; of Aira and the river Nithra, and the falls of the tiny Kra. There would he ever say he once dwelt as a Prince, though here we knew him from his birth. Nor was there ever a marble city of Aira, or those who could delight in strange songs, save in the dreams of mine old playmate Iranon who is gone."

And in the twilight, as the stars came out one by one and the moon cast on the marsh a radiance like that which a child sees quivering on the floor as he is rocked to sleep at evening, there walked into the lethal quicksands a very old man in tattered purple, crowned with withered vine-leaves and gazing ahead as if upon the golden domes of a fair city where dreams are understood. That night something of youth and beauty died in the elder world.

The Moon Bog.

3,400-WORD SHORT STORY; 1921.

This mid-size short story was written for a gathering of amateur journalists who met in a member's home in Boston on March 10, 1921. The purpose of the evening was for each member to share what he or she had written for the occasion from a shared writing prompt, and the work judged best would receive a prize. The evening had a St. Patrick's Day theme. And although it did not win the prize, "The Moon Bog" was well received and roundly praised.

The story remained unpublished at the time, but was later picked up for the June 1926 issue of Weird Tales.

Somewhere, to what remote and fearsome region I know not, Denys Barry has gone. I was with him the last night he lived among men, and heard his screams when the thing came to him; but all the peasants and police in County Meath could never find him, or the others, though they searched long and far. And now I shudder when I hear the frogs piping in swamps, or see the moon in lonely places.

I had known Denys Barry well in America, where he had grown rich, and had congratulated him when he bought back the old castle by the bog at sleepy Kilderry. It was from Kilderry that his father had come, and it was there that he wished to enjoy his wealth among ancestral scenes. Men of his blood had once ruled over Kilderry and built and dwelt in the castle, but those days were very remote, so that for generations the castle had been empty and decaying. After he went to Ireland, Barry wrote me often, and told me how under his care the gray castle was rising tower by tower to its ancient splendor, how the ivy was climbing slowly over the restored walls as it had climbed so many centuries ago, and how the peasants blessed him for bringing back the old days with his gold from over the sea. But in time there came troubles, and the peasants ceased to bless him, and fled away instead as from a doom. And then he sent a letter and asked me to visit him, for he

Weird Tales, June 1927

was lonely in the castle with no one to speak to save the new servants and laborers he had brought from the North.

The bog was the cause of all these troubles, as Barry told me the night I came to the castle. I had reached Kilderry in the summer sunset, as the gold of the sky lighted the green of the hills and groves and the blue of the bog, where on a far islet a strange olden ruin glistened spectrally. That sunset was very beautiful, but the peasants at Ballylough had warned me against it and said that Kilderry had become accursed, so that I almost shuddered to see the high turrets of the castle gilded with fire. Barry's motor had met me at the Ballylough station, for Kilderry is off the railway. The villagers had shunned the car and the driver from the North, but had whispered to me with pale faces when they saw I was going to Kilderry. And that night, after our reunion, Barry told me why.

The peasants had gone from Kilderry because Denys Barry was to drain the great bog. For all his love of Ireland, America had not left him untouched, and he hated the beautiful wasted space where peat might be cut and land opened up. The legends and superstitions of Kilderry did not move him, and he laughed when the peasants first refused to help, and then cursed him and went away to Ballylough with their few belongings as they saw his determination. In their place he sent for laborers from the North, and when the servants left he replaced them likewise. But it was lonely among strangers, so Barry had asked me to come.

When I heard the fears which had driven the people from Kilderry, I laughed as loudly as my friend had laughed, for these fears were of the vaguest, wildest, and most absurd character. They had to do with some preposterous legend of the bog, and a grim guardian spirit that dwelt in the strange olden ruin on the far islet I had seen in the sunset. There were tales of dancing lights in the dark of the moon, and of chill winds when the night was warm; of wraiths in white hovering over the waters, and of an imagined city of stone deep down below the swampy surface. But foremost among the weird fancies, and alone in its absolute unanimity, was that of the curse awaiting him who should dare to touch or drain the vast reddish morass. There were secrets, said the peasants, which must not be uncovered; secrets that had lain hidden since the plague came to the children of Partholan in the fabulous years beyond history. In the Book of Invaders it is told that these sons of the Greeks were all buried at Tallaght, but old men in Kilderry said that one city was overlooked save by its patron moon-goddess; so that only the wooded hills buried it when the men of Nemed swept down from Scythia in their thirty ships.

Such were the idle tales which had made the villagers leave Kilderry, and when I heard them I did not wonder that Denys Barry had refused to listen. He had, however, a great interest in antiquities, and proposed to explore the bog thoroughly when it was drained. The white ruins on the islet he had often visited, but though their age was plainly great, and their contour very little like that of most ruins in Ireland, they were too dilapidated to tell the days of their glory. Now the work of drainage was ready to begin, and the laborers from the North were soon to strip the forbidden bog of its green moss and red heather, and kill the tiny shell-paved streamlets and quiet blue pools fringed with rushes.

After Barry had told me these things I was very drowsy, for the travels of the day had been wearying and my host had talked late into the night. A man-servant showed me to my room, which was in a remote tower overlooking the village and the plain at the edge of the bog, and the bog itself; so that I could see from my windows in the moonlight the silent roofs from which the peasants had fled and which now sheltered the laborers from the North, and too, the parish church with its antique spire, and far out across the brooding bog the remote olden ruin on the islet gleaming white and spectral. Just as I dropped to sleep I fancied I heard faint sounds from the distance; sounds that were wild and half musical, and stirred me with a weird excitement which colored my dreams. But when I awaked next morning I felt it had all been a dream, for the visions I had seen were more wonderful than any sound of wild pipes in the night. Influenced by the legends that Barry had related, my mind had in slumber hovered around a stately city in a green valley, where marble streets and statues, villas and temples, carvings and inscriptions, all spoke in certain tones the glory that was Greece. When I told this dream to Barry we had both laughed; but I laughed the louder, because he was perplexed about his laborers from the North. For the sixth time they had all overslept, waking very slowly and dazedly, and acting as if they had not rested, although they were known to have gone early to bed the night before.

That morning and afternoon I wandered alone through the sun-gilded village and talked now and then with idle laborers, for Barry was busy with the final plans for beginning his work of drainage. The laborers were not as happy as they might have been, for most of them seemed uneasy over some dream which they had had, yet which they tried in vain to remember. I told them of my dream, but they were not interested till I spoke of the weird sounds I thought I had heard. Then they looked oddly at me, and said that they seemed to remember weird sounds, too.

In the evening Barry dined with me and announced that he would begin the drainage in two days. I was glad, for although I disliked to see the moss and the heather and the little streams and lakes depart, I had a growing wish to discern the ancient secrets the deep-matted peat might hide. And that night my dreams of piping flutes and marble peristyles came to a sudden and disquieting end; for upon the city in the valley I saw a pestilence descend, and then a frightful avalanche of wooded slopes that covered the dead bodies in the streets and left unburied only the temple of Artemis on the high peak, where the aged moon-priestess Cleis lay cold and silent with a crown of ivory on her silver head.

I have said that I awaked suddenly and in alarm. For some time I could not tell whether I was waking or sleeping, for the sound of flutes still rang shrilly in my ears; but when I saw on the floor the icy moonbeams and the outlines of a latticed gothic window, I decided I must be awake and in the castle of Kilderry. Then I heard a clock from some remote landing below strike the hour of two, and knew I was awake. Yet still there came that monstrous piping from afar; wild, weird airs that made me think of some dance of fauns on distant Maenalus. It would not let me sleep, and in impatience I sprang up and paced the floor. Only by chance did I go to the north window and look out upon the silent village and the plain at the edge of the bog. I had no wish to gaze abroad, for I wanted to sleep; but the flutes tormented me, and I had to do or see something. How could I have suspected the thing I was to behold?

There in the moonlight that flooded the spacious plain was a spectacle which no mortal, having seen it, could ever forget. To the sound of reedy pipes that echoed over the bog there glided silently and eerily a mixed throng of swaying figures, reeling through such a revel as the Sicilians may have danced to Demeter in the old days under the harvest moon beside the Cyane. The wide plain, the golden moonlight, the shadowy moving forms, and above all the shrill monotonous piping, produced an effect which almost paralyzed me; yet I noted amidst my fear that half of these tireless mechanical dancers were the laborers whom I had thought asleep, whilst the other half were strange airy beings in white, half-indeterminate in nature, but suggesting pale wistful naiads from the haunted fountains of the bog. I do not know how long I gazed at this sight from the lonely turret window before I dropped suddenly in a dreamless swoon, out of which the high sun of morning aroused me.

My first impulse on awaking was to communicate all my fears and observations to Denys Barry, but as I saw the sunlight glowing through the latticed east window I became sure that there was no reality in what I thought I had seen. I am given to strange fantasms, yet am never weak enough to believe in them; so on this occasion contented myself with questioning the laborers, who slept very late and recalled nothing of the previous night save misty dreams of shrill sounds. This matter of the spectral piping harassed me greatly, and I wondered if the crickets of autumn had come before their time to vex the night and haunt the visions of men. Later in the day I watched Barry in the library poring over his plans for the great work which was to begin on the morrow, and for the first time felt a touch of the same kind of fear that had driven the peasants away. For some unknown reason I dreaded the thought of disturbing the ancient bog and its sunless secrets, and pictured terrible sights lying black under the unmeasured depth of age-old peat. That these secrets should be brought to light seemed injudicious, and I began to wish for an excuse to leave the castle and the village. I went so far as to talk casually to Barry on the subject, but did not dare continue after he gave his resounding laugh. So I was silent when the sun set fulgently over the far hills, and Kilderry blazed all red and gold in a flame that seemed a portent.

Whether the events of that night were of reality or illusion I shall never ascertain. Certainly they transcend anything we dream of in nature and the universe; yet in no normal fashion can I explain those disappearances which were known to all men after it was over. I retired early and full of dread, and for a long time could not sleep in the uncanny silence of the tower. It was very dark, for although the sky was clear the moon was now well in the wane, and would not rise till the small hours. I thought as I lay there of Denys Barry, and of what would befall that bog when the day came, and found myself almost frantic with an impulse to rush out into the night, take Barry's car, and drive madly to Ballylough out of the menaced lands. But before my fears could crystallize into action I had fallen asleep, and gazed in dreams upon the city in the valley, cold and dead under a shroud of hideous shadow.

Probably it was the shrill piping that awaked me, yet that piping was not what I noticed first when I opened my eyes. I was lying with my back to the east window overlooking the bog, where the waning moon would rise, and therefore expected to see light cast on the opposite wall before me; but I had not looked for such a sight as now appeared. Light indeed glowed on the panels ahead, but it was not any light that the moon gives. Terrible and piercing was the shaft of ruddy refulgence that streamed through the gothic window, and the whole chamber was brilliant with a splendor intense and unearthly. My immediate actions were peculiar for such a situation, but it is only in tales that a man does the dramatic and foreseen thing. Instead of looking out across the bog toward the source of the new light, I kept my eyes from the window in panic fear, and clumsily drew on my clothing with some dazed idea of escape. I remember seizing my revolver and hat, but before it was over I had lost them both without firing the one or donning the other. After a time the fascination of the red radiance overcame my fright, and I crept to the east window and looked out whilst the maddening, incessant piping whined and reverberated through the castle and over all the village.

Over the bog was a deluge of flaring light, scarlet and sinister, and pouring from the strange olden ruin on the far islet. The aspect of that ruin I can not describe — I must have been mad, for it seemed to rise majestic and undecayed, splendid and column-cinctured, the flame-reflecting marble of its entablature piercing the sky like the apex of a temple on a mountain-top. Flutes shrieked and drums began to beat, and as I watched in awe and terror I thought I saw dark saltant forms silhouetted grotesquely against the vision of marble and effulgence. The effect was titanic — altogether unthinkable — and I might have stared indefinitely had not the sound of the piping seemed to grow stronger at my left. Trembling with a terror oddly mixed with ecstasy, I crossed the circular room to the north window from which I could see the village and the plain at the edge of the bog. There my eyes dilated again with a wild wonder as great as if I had not just turned from a scene beyond the pale of nature, for on the ghastly red-litten plain was moving a procession of beings in such a manner as none ever saw before save in nightmares.

Half gliding, half floating in the air, the white-clad bog-wraiths were slowly retreating toward the still waters and the island ruin in fantastic formations suggesting some ancient and solemn ceremonial dance. Their waving translucent arms, guided by the detestable piping of those unseen flutes, beckoned in uncanny rhythm to a throng of lurching laborers who followed doglike with blind, brainless, floundering steps as if dragged by a clumsy but resistless demon-will. As the naiads neared the bog, without altering their course, a new line of stumbling stragglers zigzagged drunkenly out of the castle from some door far below my window, groped sightiessly across the courtyard and through the intervening bit of village, and joined the floundering column of laborers on the plain. Despite their distance below me I at once knew they were the servants brought from the North, for I recognized the ugly and unwieldy form of the cook, whose very absurdness had now become unutterably tragic. The flutes piped horribly, and again I heard the beating of the drums from the direction of the island ruin. Then silently and gracefully the naiads reached the water and melted one by one into the ancient bog; while the line of followers, never checking their speed, splashed awkwardly after them and vanished amidst a tiny vortex of unwholesome bubbles which I could barely see in the scarlet light. And as the last pathetic straggler, the fat cook, sank heavily out of sight in that sullen pool, the flutes and the drums grew silent, and the blinding red rays from the ruins snapped instantaneously out, leaving the village of doom lone and desolate in the wan beams of a new-risen moon.

My condition was now one of indescribable chaos. Not knowing whether I was mad or sane, sleeping or waking, I was saved only by a merciful numbness. I believe I did ridiculous things such as offering prayers to Artemis, Latona, Demeter, Persephone, and Plouton. All that I recalled of a classic youth came to my lips as the horrors of the situation roused my deepest superstitions. I felt that I had witnessed the death of a whole village, and knew I was alone in the castle with Denys Barry, whose boldness had brought down a doom. As I thought of him, new terrors convulsed me, and I fell to the floor; not fainting, but physically helpless. Then I felt the icy blast from the east window where the moon had risen, and began to hear the shrieks in the castle far below me. Soon those shrieks had attained a magnitude and quality which can not be written of, and which makes me faint as I think of them. All I can say is that they came from something I had known as a friend.

At some time during this shocking period the cold wind and the screaming must have roused me, for my next impression is of racing madly through inky rooms and corridors and out across the courtyard into the hideous night. They found me at dawn wandering mindless near Ballylough, but what unhinged me utterly was not any of the horrors I had seen or heard before. What I muttered about as I came slowly out of the shadows was a pair of fantastic incidents which occurred in my flight: incidents of no significance, yet which haunt me unceasingly when I am alone in certain marshy places or in the moonlight.

As I fled from that accursed castle along the bog's edge I heard a new sound: common, yet unlike any I had heard before at Kilderry. The stagnant waters, lately quite devoid of animal life, now teemed with a horde of slimy enormous frogs which piped shrilly and incessantly in tones strangely out of keeping with their size. They glistened bloated and green in the moonbeams, and seemed to gaze up at the fount of light. I followed the gaze of one very fat and ugly frog, and saw the second of the things which drove my senses away.

Stretching directly from the strange olden ruin on the far islet to the waning moon, my eyes seemed to trace a beam of faint quivering radiance having no reflection in the waters of the bog. And upward along that pallid path my fevered fancy pictured a thin shadow slowly writhing; a vague contorted shadow struggling as if drawn by unseen demons. Crazed as I was, I saw in that awful shadow a monstrous resemblance — a nauseous, unbelievable caricature — a blasphemous effigy of him who had been Denys Barry.

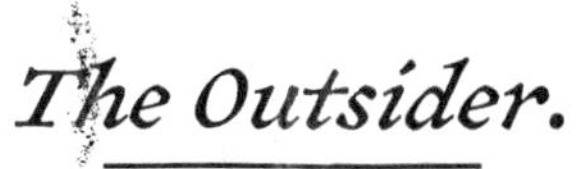

The Outsider.

2,600-WORD SHORT STORY; 1921.

Most readers and critics have agreed, over the years, that "The Outsider" is a fabulous story, one of the very best of Lovecraft's early efforts. In later years the author himself came to disdain it, calling its plotting overly mechanical and its language excessively florid; nearly everyone who has ever read the tale disagrees.

"The Outsider" was written sometime in mid-1921, probably the spring or early summer. It most likely was the first thing Lovecraft wrote after recovering from the death of his mother, and as such has come in for its share of quasi-biographical interpretations by readers and critics over the years. It was not published for several years after Lovecraft wrote it, finally seeing print in the April 1926 issue of Weird Tales.

Unhappy is he to whom the memories of childhood bring only fear and sadness. Wretched is he who looks back upon lone hours in vast and dismal chambers with brown hangings and maddening rows of antique books, or upon awed watches in twilight groves of grotesque, gigantic, and vine-encumbered trees that silently wave twisted branches far aloft. Such a lot the gods gave to me — to me, the dazed, the disappointed; the barren, the broken. And yet I am strangely content and cling desperately to those sere memories, when my mind momentarily threatens to reach beyond to the other.

I know not where I was born, save that the castle was infinitely old and infinitely horrible, full of dark passages and having high ceilings where the eye could find only cobwebs and shadows. The stones in the crumbling corridors seemed always hideously damp, and there was an accursed smell everywhere, as of the piled-up corpses of dead generations. It was never light, so that I used sometimes to light candles and gaze steadily at them for relief, nor was there any sun outdoors, since the terrible trees grew high above the topmost accessible tower. There was one black tower which reached above the trees into the unknown outer sky, but that was partly ruined and could

"To my horror I saw in its eaten-away and bone-revealing outlines a leering, abhorrent travesty on the human shape; and in its mouldy, disintegrating apparel an unspeakable quality that chilled me even more."

Weird Tales, April 1926

not be ascended save by a well-nigh impossible climb up the sheer wall, stone by stone.

I must have lived years in this place, but I cannot measure the time. Beings must have cared for my needs, yet I cannot recall any person except myself, or anything alive but the noiseless rats and bats and spiders. I think that whoever nursed me must have been shockingly aged, since my first conception of a living person was that of somebody mockingly like myself, yet distorted, shrivelled, and decaying like the castle. To me there was nothing grotesque in the bones and skeletons that strewed some of the stone crypts deep down among the foundations. I fantastically associated these things with everyday events, and thought them more natural than the coloured pictures of living beings which I found in many of the mouldy books. From such books I learned all that I know. No teacher urged or guided me, and I do not recall hearing any human voice in all those years — not even my own; for although I had read of speech, I had never thought to try to speak aloud. My aspect was a matter equally unthought of, for there were no mirrors in the castle, and I merely regarded myself by instinct as akin to the youthful figures I saw drawn and painted in the books. I felt conscious of youth because I remembered so little.

Outside, across the putrid moat and under the dark mute trees, I would often lie and dream for hours about what I read in the books; and would longingly picture myself amidst gay crowds in the sunny world beyond the endless forests. Once I tried to escape from the forest, but as I went farther from the castle the shade grew denser and the air more filled with brooding fear; so that I ran frantically back lest I lose my way in a labyrinth of nighted silence.

So through endless twilights I dreamed and waited, though I knew not what I waited for. Then in the shadowy solitude my longing for light grew so frantic that I could rest no more, and I lifted entreating hands to the single black ruined tower that reached above the forest into the unknown outer sky. And at last I resolved to scale that tower, fall though I might; since it were better to glimpse the sky and perish, than to live without ever beholding day.

In the dank twilight I climbed the worn and aged stone stairs till I reached the level where they ceased, and thereafter clung perilously to small footholds leading upward. Ghastly and terrible was that dead, stairless cylinder of rock; black, ruined, and deserted, and sinister with startled bats whose wings made no noise. But more ghastly and terrible still was the slowness of my progress; for climb as I might, the darkness overhead grew no thinner, and a new chill as of haunted and venerable mould assailed me. I shivered as I wondered why I did not reach the light, and would have looked down had I dared. I fancied that night had come suddenly upon me, and vainly groped with one free hand for a window embrasure, that I might peer out and above, and try to judge the height I had once attained.

All at once, after an infinity of awesome, sightless, crawling up that concave and desperate precipice, I felt my head touch a solid thing, and I knew I must have gained the roof, or at least some kind of floor. In the darkness I raised my free hand and tested the barrier, finding it stone and immovable. Then came a deadly circuit of the tower, clinging to whatever holds the slimy wall could give; till finally my testing hand found the barrier yielding, and I turned upward again, pushing the slab or door with my head as I used both hands in my fearful ascent. There was no light revealed above, and as my hands went higher I knew that my climb was for the nonce ended; since the slab was the trapdoor of an aperture leading to a level stone surface of greater circumference than the lower tower, no doubt the floor of some lofty and capacious observation chamber. I crawled through carefully, and tried to prevent the heavy slab from falling back into place, but failed in the latter attempt. As I lay exhausted on the stone floor I heard the eerie echoes of its fall, hoped when necessary to pry it up again.

Believing I was now at prodigious height, far above the accursed branches of the wood, I dragged myself up from the floor and fumbled about for windows, that I might look for the first time upon the sky, and the moon and stars of which I had read. But on every hand I was disappointed; since all that I found were vast shelves of marble, bearing odious oblong boxes of disturbing size. More and more I reflected, and wondered what hoary secrets might abide in this high apartment so many aeons cut off from the castle below. Then unexpectedly my hands came upon a doorway, where hung a portal of stone, rough with strange chiselling. Trying it, I found it locked; but with a supreme burst of strength I overcame all obstacles and dragged it open inward. As I did so there came to me the purest ecstasy I have ever known; for shining tranquilly through an ornate grating of iron, and down a short stone passageway of steps that ascended from the newly found doorway, was the radiant full moon, which I had never before seen save in dreams and in vague visions I dared not call memories.

Fancying now that I had attained the very pinnacle of the castle, I commenced to rush up the few steps beyond the door; but the sudden veiling of the moon by a cloud caused me to stumble, and I felt my way more slowly in the dark. It was still very dark when I reached the grating — which I tried carefully and found unlocked, but which I did not open for fear of falling from the amazing height to which I had climbed. Then the moon came out.

Most demoniacal of all shocks is that of the abysmally unexpected and grotesquely unbelievable. Nothing I had before undergone could compare in terror with what I now saw; with the bizarre marvels that sight implied. The sight itself was as simple as it was stupefying, for it was merely this: instead of a dizzying prospect of treetops seen from a lofty eminence, there stretched around me on the level through the grating nothing less than the solid ground, decked and diversified by marble slabs and columns, and overshadowed by an ancient stone church, whose ruined spire gleamed spectrally in the moonlight.

Half unconscious, I opened the grating and staggered out upon the white gravel path that stretched away in two directions. My mind, stunned and chaotic as it was, still held the frantic craving for light; and not even the fantastic wonder which had happened could stay my course. I neither knew nor cared whether my experience was insanity, dreaming, or magic; but was determined to gaze on brilliance and gaiety at any cost. I knew not who I was or what I was, or what my surroundings might be; though as I continued to stumble along I became conscious of a kind of fearsome latent memory that made my progress not wholly fortuitous. I passed under an arch out of that region of slabs and columns, and wandered through the open country; sometimes following the visible road, but sometimes leaving it curiously to tread across meadows where only occasional ruins bespoke the ancient presence of a forgotten road. Once I swam across a swift river where crumbling, mossy masonry told of a bridge long vanished.

Over two hours must have passed before I reached what seemed to be my goal, a venerable ivied castle in a thickly wooded park, maddeningly familiar, yet full of perplexing strangeness to me. I saw that the moat was filled in, and that some of the well-known towers were demolished, whilst new wings existed to confuse the beholder. But what I observed with chief interest and delight were the open windows — gorgeously ablaze with light and sending forth sound of the gayest revelry. Advancing to one of these I looked in and saw an oddly dressed company indeed; making merry, and speaking brightly to one another. I had never, seemingly, heard human speech before and could guess only vaguely what was said. Some of the faces seemed to hold expressions that brought up incredibly remote recollections, others were utterly alien.

I now stepped through the low window into the brilliantly lighted room, stepping as I did so from my single bright moment of hope to my blackest convulsion of despair and realization. The nightmare was quick to come, for as I entered, there occurred immediately one of the most terrifying demonstrations I had ever conceived. Scarcely had I crossed the sill when there descended upon the whole company a sudden and unheralded fear of hideous intensity, distorting every face and evoking the most horrible screams from nearly every throat. Flight was universal, and in the clamour and panic several fell in a swoon and were dragged away by their madly fleeing companions. Many covered their eyes with their hands, and plunged blindly and awkwardly in their race to escape, overturning furniture and stumbling against the walls before they managed to reach one of the many doors.

The cries were shocking; and as I stood in the brilliant apartment alone and dazed, listening to their vanishing echoes, I trembled at the thought of what might be lurking near me unseen. At a casual inspection the room seemed deserted, but when I moved towards one of the alcoves I thought I detected a presence there — a hint of motion beyond the golden-arched doorway leading to another and somewhat similar room. As I approached the arch I began to perceive the presence more clearly; and then, with the first and last sound I ever uttered — a ghastly ululation that revolted me almost as poignantly as its noxious cause — I beheld in full, frightful vividness the inconceivable, indescribable, and unmentionable monstrosity which had by its simple appearance changed a merry company to a herd of delirious fugitives.

I cannot even hint what it was like, for it was a compound of all that is unclean, uncanny, unwelcome, abnormal, and detestable. It was the ghoulish shade of decay, antiquity, and dissolution; the putrid, dripping eidolon of unwholesome revelation, the awful baring of that which the merciful earth should always hide. God knows it was not of this world — or no longer of this world — yet to my horror I saw in its eaten-away and bone-revealing outlines a leering, abhorrent travesty on the human shape; and in its mouldy, disintegrating apparel an unspeakable quality that chilled me even more.

I was almost paralysed, but not too much so to make a feeble effort towards flight; a backward stumble which failed to break the spell in which the nameless, voiceless monster held me. My eyes bewitched by the glassy orbs which stared loathsomely into them, refused to close; though they were mercifully blurred, and showed the terrible object but indistinctly after the first shock. I tried to raise my hand to shut out the sight, yet so stunned were my nerves that my arm could not fully obey my will. The attempt, however, was enough to disturb my balance; so that I had to stagger forward several steps to avoid falling. As I did so I became suddenly and agonizingly aware of the nearness of the carrion thing, whose hideous hollow breathing I half fancied I could hear. Nearly mad, I found myself yet able to throw out a hand to ward off the foetid apparition which pressed so close; when in one cataclysmic second of cosmic nightmarishness and hellish accident my fingers touched the rotting outstretched paw of the monster beneath the golden arch.

I did not shriek, but all the fiendish ghouls that ride the nightwind shrieked for me as in that same second there crashed down upon my mind a single fleeting avalanche of soul-annihilating memory. I knew in that second all that had been; I remembered beyond the frightful castle and the trees, and recognized the altered edifice in which I now stood; I recognized, most terrible of all, the unholy abomination that stood leering before me as I withdrew my sullied fingers from its own.

But in the cosmos there is balm as well as bitterness, and that balm is nepenthe. In the supreme horror of that second I forgot what had horrified me, and the burst of black memory vanished in a chaos of echoing images. In a dream I fled from that haunted and accursed pile, and ran swiftly and silently in the moonlight. When I returned to the churchyard place of marble and went down the steps I found the stone trap-door immovable; but I was not sorry, for I had hated the antique castle and the trees. Now I ride with the mocking and friendly ghouls on the night-wind, and play by day amongst the catacombs of Nephren-Ka in the sealed and unknown valley of Hadoth by the Nile. I know that light is not for me, save that of the moon over the rock tombs of Neb, nor any gaiety save the unnamed feasts of Nitokris beneath the Great Pyramid; yet in my new wildness and freedom I almost welcome the bitterness of alienage.

For although nepenthe has calmed me, I know always that I am an outsider; a stranger in this century and among those who are still men. This I have known ever since I stretched out my fingers to the abomination within that great gilded frame; stretched out my fingers and touched a cold and unyielding surface of polished glass.

The Other Gods.

2,000-WORD SHORT STORY; 1921.

This short story runs neck-and-neck with "The Quest of Iranon" as the most Dunsanian of H.P. Lovecraft's Lord Dunsany-inspired stories. Indeed, it may have an edge, because it's more than just a story — it's a piece of foundational mythology for a new storyworld, like The Gods of Pegaña *was.*

This parallel may have caused some trouble for Lovecraft's legacy, as the mythology hinted at here invited certain readers — August Derleth chief among them — to assume that Lovecraft was undertaking the creation of a narratively complete, Bullfinch-style pseudomythology of his own, and to hunt through his work cherry-picking references that appeared to support such an interpretation.

It is undeniable that characters and features first introduced in "The Other Gods" are featured and referenced in many other later Lovecraft stories, just as they would have been had Lovecraft intended to create such a mythology. But it seems clear that although Lovecraft did intend to conjure a cycle of mythology connected with forgotten entities from the dawn of time, he intended that it remain nebulous, vague, sinister, and above all plausible — which all but demanded that it be always fearfully hinted at, and never be spelled out in full prosaic detail. That, of course, is not how Derleth interpreted it.

"The Other Gods" was written on Aug. 14, 1921, and it's the last story Lovecraft wrote in the full Old-Testament-inspired style of Lord Dunsany's work. It remained unpublished for a decade after Lovecraft wrote it, finally seeing print in the November 1933 issue of Fantasy Fan.

Atop the tallest of Earth's peaks dwell the gods of earth, and suffer not man to tell that he hath looked upon them. Lesser peaks they once inhabited; but ever the men from the plains would scale the slopes of rock and snow, driving the gods to higher and higher mountains till now only the last remains. When they left their old peaks they took with them all signs of themselves, save once, it is said, when they left a carven image on the face of the mountain which they called Ngranek.

But now they have betaken themselves to unknown Kadath in the cold waste where no man treads, and are grown stern, having no higher peak whereto to flee at the coming of men. They are grown stern, and where once they suffered men to displace them, they now forbid men to come; or coming, to depart. It is well for men that they know not of Kadath in the cold waste; else they would seek injudiciously to scale it.

Sometimes when earth's gods are homesick they visit in the still of the night the peaks where once they dwelt, and weep softly as they try to play in the olden way on remembered slopes. Men have felt the tears of the gods on white-capped Thurai, though they have thought it rain; and have heard the sighs of the gods in the plaintive dawn-winds of Lerion. In cloud-ships the gods are wont to travel, and wise cotters have legends that keep them from certain high peaks at night when it is cloudy, for the gods are not lenient as of old.

In Ulthar, which lies beyond the river Skai, once dwelt an old man avid to behold the gods of earth; a man deeply learned in the seven cryptical books of Hsan, and familiar with the Pnakotic Manuscripts of distant and frozen Lomar. His name was Barzai the Wise, and the villagers tell of how he went up a mountain on the night of the strange eclipse.

Barzai knew so much of the gods that he could tell of their comings and goings, and guessed so many of their secrets that he was deemed half a god himself. It was he who wisely advised the burgesses of Ulthar when they passed their remarkable law against the slaying of cats, and who first told the young priest Atal where it is that black cats go at midnight on St. John's Eve. Barzai was learned in the lore of the earth's gods, and had gained a desire to look upon their faces. He believed that his great secret knowledge of gods could shield him from their wrath, so resolved to go up to the summit of high and rocky Hatheg-Kla on a night when he knew the gods would be there.

Hatheg-Kla is far in the stony desert beyond Hatheg, for which it is named, and rises like a rock statue in a silent temple. Around its peak the mists play always mournfully, for mists are the memories of the gods, and the gods loved Hatheg-Kla when they dwelt upon it in the old days. Often the gods of earth visit Hatheg-Kla in their ships of clouds, casting pale vapors over the slopes as they dance reminiscently on the summit under a clear moon. The villagers of Hatheg say it is ill to climb the Hatheg-Kla at any time, and deadly to climb it by night when pale vapors hide the summit and the moon; but Barzai heeded them not when he came from neighboring Ulthar with the young priest Atal, who was his disciple. Atal was only the son of an innkeeper, and was sometimes afraid; but Barzai's father had been a landgrave who dwelt in an ancient castle, so he had no common superstition in his blood, and only laughed at the fearful cotters.

Barzai and Atal went out of Hatheg into the stony desert despite the prayers of peasants, and talked of earth's gods by their campfires at night. Many days they traveled, and from afar saw lofty Hatheg-Kla with his aureole of mournful mist. On the thirteenth day they reached the mountain's lonely base, and Atal spoke of his fears. But Barzai was old and learned and had no fears, so led the way up the slope that no man had scaled since the time of Sansu, who is written of with fright in the moldy Pnakotic Manuscripts.

The way was rocky, and made perilous by chasms, cliffs, and falling stones. Later it grew cold and snowy; and Barzai and Atal often slipped and fell as they hewed and plodded upward with staves and axes. Finally the air grew thin, and the sky changed color, and the climbers found it hard to breathe; but still they toiled up and up, marveling at the strangeness of the scene and thrilling at the thought of what would happen on the summit when the moon was out and the pale vapours spread around. For three days they climbed higher and higher toward the roof of the world; then they camped to wait for the clouding of the moon.

For four nights no clouds came, and the moon shone down cold through the thin mournful mist around the silent pinnacle. Then on the fifth night, which was the night of the full moon, Barzai saw some dense clouds far to the north, and stayed up with Atal to watch them draw near. Thick and majestic they sailed, slowly and deliberately onward; ranging themselves round the peak high above the watchers, and hiding the moon and the summit from view. For a long hour the watchers gazed, whilst the vapours swirled and the screen of clouds grew thicker and more restless. Barzai was wise in the lore of earth's gods, and listened hard for certain sounds, but Atal felt the chill of the vapours and the awe of the night, and feared much. And when Barzai began to climb higher and beckon eagerly, it was long before Atal would follow.

So thick were the vapours that the way was hard, and though Atal followed at last, he could scarce see the gray shape of Barzai on the dim slope above in the clouded moonlight. Barzai forged very far ahead, and seemed despite his age to climb more easily than Atal; fearing not the steepness that began to grow too great for any save a strong and dauntless man, nor pausing at wide black chasms that Atal could scarce leap. And so they went up wildly over rocks and gulfs, slipping and stumbling, and sometimes awed at the vastness and horrible silence of bleak ice pinnacles and mute granite steeps.

Very suddenly Barzai went out of Atal's sight, scaling a hideous cliff that seemed to bulge outward and block the path for any climber not inspired of earth's gods. Atal was far below, and planning what he should do when he reached the place, when curiously he noticed that the light had grown strong, as if the cloudless peak and moonlit meetingplace of the gods were very near. And as he scrambled on toward the bulging cliff and litten sky he felt fears more shocking than any he had known before. Then through the high mists he heard the voice of Barzai shouting wildly in delight:

"I have heard the gods. I have heard earth's gods singing in revelry on Hatheg-Kla! The voices of earth's gods are known to Barzai the Prophet! The mists are thin and the moon is bright, and I shall see the gods dancing wildly on Hatheg-Kla that they loved in youth. The wisdom of Barzai hath made him greater than earth's gods, and against his will their spells and barriers are as naught; Barzai will behold the gods, the proud gods, the secret gods, the gods of earth who spurn the sight of man!"

Atal could not hear the voices Barzai heard, but he was now close to the bulging cliff and scanning it for footholds. Then he heard Barzai's voice grow shriller and louder:

"The mist is very thin, and the moon casts shadows on the slope; the voices of earth's gods are high and wild, and they fear the coming of Barzai the Wise, who is greater than they . . . The moon's light flickers, as earth's gods dance against it; I shall see the dancing forms of the gods that leap and howl in the moonlight . . . The light is dimmer and the gods are afraid . . ."

Whilst Barzai was shouting these things Atal felt a spectral change in all the air, as if the laws of earth were bowing to greater laws; for though the way was steeper than ever, the upward path was now grown fearsomely easy, and the bulging cliff proved scarce an obstacle when he reached it and slid perilously up its convex face. The light of the moon had strangely failed, and as Atal plunged upward through the mists he heard Barzai the Wise shrieking in the shadows:

"The moon is dark, and the gods dance in the night; there is terror in the sky, for upon the moon hath sunk an eclipse foretold in no books of men or of earth's gods . . . There is unknown magic on Hatheg-Kla, for the screams of the frightened gods have turned to laughter, and the slopes of ice shoot up endlessly into the black heavens whither I am plunging . . . Hei! Hei! At last! In the dim light I behold the gods of earth!"

And now Atal, slipping dizzily up over inconceivable steeps, heard in the dark a loathsome laughing, mixed with such a cry as no man else ever heard save in the Phlegethon of unrelatable nightmares; a cry wherein reverberated the horror and anguish of a haunted lifetime packed into one atrocious moment:

"The other gods! The other gods! The gods of the outer hells that guard the feeble gods of earth! . . . Look away . . . Go back . . . Do not see! Do not see! The vengeance of the infinite abysses . . . That cursed, that damnable pit . . . Merciful gods of earth, I am falling into the sky!"

And as Atal shut his eyes and stopped his ears and tried to hump downward against the frightful pull from unknown heights, there resounded on Hatheg-Kla that terrible peal of thunder which awaked the good cotters of the plains and the honest burgesses of Hatheg, Nir and Ulthar, and caused them to behold through the clouds that strange eclipse of the moon that no book ever predicted. And when the moon came out at last Atal was safe on the lower snows of the mountain without sight of earth's gods, or of the other gods.

Now it is told in the moldy Pnakotic Manuscripts that Sansu found naught but wordless ice and rock when he did climb Hatheg-Kla in the youth of the world. Yet when the men of Ulthar and Nir and Hatheg crushed their fears and scaled that haunted steep by day in search of Barzai the Wise, they found graven in the naked stone of the summit a curious and cyclopean symbol fifty cubits wide, as if the rock had been riven by some titanic chisel. And the symbol was like to one that learned men have discerned in those frightful parts of the Pnakotic Manuscripts which were too ancient to be read. This they found.

Barzai the Wise they never found, nor could the holy priest Atal ever be persuaded to pray for his soul's repose. Moreover, to this day the people of Ulthar and Nir and Hatheg fear eclipses, and pray by night when pale vapors hide the mountain-top and the moon. And above the mists on Hatheg-Kla, earth's gods sometimes dance reminiscently; for they know they are safe, and love to come from unknown Kadath in ships of clouds and play in the olden way, as they did when earth was new and men not given to the climbing of inaccessible places.

The Music of Erich Zann.

3,500-WORD SHORT STORY; 1921.

This short story is widely acknowledged as one of Lovecraft's best works, and it was one of his own personal favorites. It is, without a doubt, his most opaque piece of storytelling. So much is left in subtext in the telling of this story that it almost feels as if one is being deliberately teased by the withholding of vital information.

There may have been a reason for this; the story was written in December 1921, just after Lovecraft finished the first two parts of Herbert West, Reanimator, *a story which revels humorously in over-the-top pop horror. Lovecraft may have needed to write something obscure and subtle as a sort of palate cleanser.*

It was published, for the first of many times, in the March 1922 issue of National Amateur.

I have examined maps of the city with the greatest care, yet have never again found the Rue d'Auseil. These maps have not been modern maps alone, for I know that names change. I have, on the contrary, delved deeply into all the antiquities of the place, and have personally explored every region, of whatever name, which could possibly answer to the street I knew as the Rue d'Auseil. But despite all I have done, it remains an humiliating fact that I cannot find the house, the street, or even the locality, where, during the last months of my impoverished life as a student of metaphysics at the university, I heard the music of Erich Zann.

That my memory is broken, I do not wonder; for my health, physical and mental, was gravely disturbed throughout the period of my residence in the Rue d'Auseil, and I recall that I took none of my few acquaintances there. But that I cannot find the place again is both singular and perplexing; for it was within a half-hour's walk of the university and was distinguished by peculiarities which could hardly be forgotten by any one who had been there. I have never met a person who has seen the Rue d'Auseil.

Weird Tales, May 1925

The Rue d'Auseil lay across a dark river bordered by precipitous brick blear-windowed warehouses and spanned by a ponderous bridge of dark stone. It was always shadowy along that river, as if the smoke of neighboring factories shut out the sun perpetually. The river was also odorous with evil stenches which I have never smelled elsewhere, and which may some day help me to find it, since I should recognize them at once. Beyond the bridge were narrow cobbled streets with rails; and then came the ascent, at first gradual, but incredibly steep as the Rue d'Auseil was reached.

I have never seen another street as narrow and steep as the Rue d'Auseil. It was almost a cliff, closed to all vehicles, consisting in several places of flights of steps, and ending at the top in a lofty ivied wall. Its paving was irregular, sometimes stone slabs, sometimes cobblestones, and sometimes bare earth with struggling greenish-grey vegetation. The houses were tall, peaked-roofed, incredibly old, and crazily leaning backward, forward, and sidewise. Occasionally an opposite pair, both leaning forward, almost met across the street like an arch; and certainly they kept most of the light from the ground below. There were a few overhead bridges from house to house across the street.

The inhabitants of that street impressed me peculiarly. At first I thought it was because they were all silent and reticent; but later decided it was because they were all very old. I do not know how I came to live on such a street, but I was not myself when I moved there. I had been living in many poor places, always evicted for want of money; until at last I came upon that tottering house in the Rue d'Auseil kept by the paralytic Blandot. It was the third house from the top of the street, and by far the tallest of them all.

My room was on the fifth story; the only inhabited room there, since the house was almost empty. On the night I arrived I heard strange music from the peaked garret overhead, and the next day asked old Blandot about it. He told me it was an old German viol-player, a strange dumb man who signed his name as Erich Zann, and who played evenings in a cheap theater orchestra; adding that Zann's desire to play in the night after his return from the theater was the reason he had chosen this lofty and isolated garret room, whose single gable window was the only point on the street from which one could look over the terminating wall at the declivity and panorama beyond.

Thereafter I heard Zann every night, and although he kept me awake, I was haunted by the weirdness of his music. Knowing little of the art myself, I was yet certain that none of his harmonies had any relation to music I had heard before; and concluded that he was a composer of highly original genius. The longer I listened, the more I was fascinated, until after a week I resolved to make the old man's acquaintance.

One night as he was returning from his work, I intercepted Zann in the hallway and told him that I would like to know him and be with him when he played. He was a small, lean, bent person, with shabby clothes, blue eyes, grotesque, satyrlike face, and nearly bald head; and at my first words seemed both angered and frightened. My obvious friendliness, however, finally melted him; and he grudgingly motioned to me to follow him up the dark, creaking and rickety attic stairs. His room, one of only two in the steeply pitched garret, was on the west side, toward the high wall that formed the upper end of the street. Its size was very great, and seemed the greater because of its extraordinary barrenness and neglect. Of furniture there was only a narrow iron bedstead, a dingy wash-stand, a small table, a large bookcase, an iron music-rack, and three old-fashioned chairs. Sheets of music were piled in disorder about the floor. The walls were of bare boards, and had probably never known plaster; whilst the abundance of dust and cobwebs made the place seem more deserted than inhabited. Evidently Erich Zann's world of beauty lay in some far cosmos of the imagination.

Motioning me to sit down, the dumb man closed the door, turned the large wooden bolt, and lighted a candle to augment the one he had brought with him. He now removed his viol from its motheaten covering, and taking it, seated himself in the least uncomfortable of the chairs. He did not employ the music-rack, but, offering no choice and playing from memory, enchanted me for over an hour with strains I had never heard before; strains which must have been of his own devising. To describe their exact nature is impossible for one unversed in music. They were a kind of fugue, with recurrent passages of the most captivating quality, but to me were notable for the absence of any of the weird notes I had overheard from my room below on other occasions.

Those haunting notes I had remembered, and had often hummed and whistled inaccurately to myself, so when the player at length laid down his bow I asked him if he would render some of them. As I began my request the wrinkled satyrlike face lost the bored placidity it had possessed during the playing, and seemed to show the same curious mixture of anger and fright which I had noticed when first I accosted the old man. For a moment I was inclined to use persuasion, regarding rather lightly the whims of senility; and even tried to awaken my host's weirder mood by whistling a few of the strains to which I had listened the night before. But I did not pursue this course for more than a moment; for when the dumb musician recognized the whistled air his face grew suddenly distorted with an expression wholly beyond analysis, and his long, cold, bony right hand reached out to stop my mouth and silence the crude imitation. As he did this he further demonstrated his eccentricity by casting a startled glance toward the lone curtained window, as if fearful of some intruder — a glance doubly absurd, since the garret stood high and inaccessible above all the adjacent roofs, this window being the only point on the steep street, as the concierge had told me, from which one could see over the wall at the summit.

The old man's glance brought Blandot's remark to my mind, and with a certain capriciousness I felt a wish to look out over the wide and dizzying panorama of moonlit roofs and city lights beyond the hilltop, which of all the dwellers in the Rue d'Auseil only this crabbed musician could see. I moved toward the window and would have drawn aside the nondescript curtains, when with a frightened rage even greater than before, the dumb lodger was upon me again; this time motioning with his head toward the door as he nervously strove to drag me thither with both hands. Now thoroughly disgusted with my host, I ordered him to release me, and told him I would go at once. His clutch relaxed, and as he saw my disgust and offense, his own anger seemed to subside. He tightened his relaxing grip, but this time in a friendly manner, forcing me into a chair; then with an appearance of wistfulness crossing to the littered table, where he wrote many words with a pencil, in the labored French of a foreigner.

The note which he finally handed me was an appeal for tolerance and forgiveness. Zann said that he was old, lonely, and afflicted with strange fears and nervous disorders connected with his music and with other things. He had enjoyed my listening to his music, and wished I would come again and not mind his eccentricities. But he could not play to another his weird harmonies, and could not bear hearing them from another; nor could he bear having anything in his room touched by another. He had not known until our hallway conversation that I could overhear his playing in my room, and now asked me if I would arrange with Blandot to take a lower room where I could not hear him in the night. He would, he wrote, defray the difference in rent.

As I sat deciphering the execrable French, I felt more lenient toward the old man. He was a victim of physical and nervous suffering, as was I; and my metaphysical studies had taught me kindness. In the silence there came a slight sound from the window — the shutter must have rattled in the night wind, and for some reason I started almost as violently as did Erich Zann. So when I had finished reading, I shook my host by the hand, and departed as a friend.

The next day Blandot gave me a more expensive room on the third floor, between the apartments of an aged money-lender and the room of a respectable upholsterer. There was no one on the fourth floor.

It was not long before I found that Zann's eagerness for my company was not as great as it had seemed while he was persuading me to move down from the fifth story. He did not ask me to call on him, and when I did call he appeared uneasy and played listlessly. This was always at night — in the day he slept and would admit no one. My liking for him did not grow, though the attic room and the weird music seemed to hold an odd fascination for me. I had a curious desire to look out of that window, over the wall and down the unseen slope at the glittering roofs and spires which must lie outspread there. Once I went up to the garret during theater hours, when Zann was away, but the door was locked.

What I did succeed in doing was to overhear the nocturnal playing of the dumb old man. At first I would tip-toe up to my old fifth floor, then I grew bold enough to climb the last creaking staircase to the peaked garret. There in the narrow hall, outside the bolted door with the covered keyhole, I often heard sounds which filled me with an indefinable dread — the dread of vague wonder and brooding mystery. It was not that the sounds were hideous, for they were not; but that they held vibrations suggesting nothing on this globe of earth, and that at certain intervals they assumed a symphonic quality which I could hardly conceive as produced by one player. Certainly, Erich Zann was a genius of wild power. As the weeks passed, the playing grew wilder, whilst the old musician acquired an increasing haggardness and furtiveness pitiful to behold. He now refused to admit me at any time, and shunned me whenever we met on the stairs.

Then one night as I listened at the door, I heard the shrieking viol swell into a chaotic babel of sound; a pandemonium which would have led me to doubt my own shaking sanity had there not come from behind that barred portal a piteous proof that the horror was real — the awful, inarticulate cry which only a mute can utter, and which rises only in moments of the most terrible fear or anguish. I knocked repeatedly at the door, but received no response. Afterward I waited in the black hallway, shivering with cold and fear, till I heard the poor musician's feeble effort to rise from the floor by the aid of a chair. Believing him just conscious after a fainting fit, I renewed my rapping, at the same time calling out my name reassuringly. I heard Zann stumble to the window and close both shutter and sash, then stumble to the door, which he falteringly unfastened to admit me. This time his delight at having me present was real; for his distorted face gleamed with relief while he clutched at my coat as a child clutches at its mother's skirts.

Shaking pathetically, the old man forced me into a chair whilst he sank into another, beside which his viol and bow lay carelessly on the floor. He sat for some time inactive, nodding oddly, but having a paradoxical suggestion of intense and frightened listening. Subsequently he seemed to be satisfied, and crossing to a chair by the table wrote a brief note, handed it to me, and returned to the table, where he began to write rapidly and incessantly. The note implored me in the name of mercy, and for the sake of my own curiosity, to wait where I was while he prepared a full account in German of all the marvels and terrors which beset him. I waited, and the dumb man's pencil flew.

It was perhaps an hour later, while I still waited and while the old musician's feverishly written sheets still continued to pile up, that I saw Zann start as from the hint of a horrible shock. Unmistakably he was looking at the curtained window and listening shudderingly. Then I half fancied I heard a sound myself; though it was not a horrible sound, but rather an exquisitely low and infinitely distant musical note, suggesting a player in one of the neighboring houses, or in some abode beyond the lofty wall over which I had never been able to look. Upon Zann the effect was terrible, for, dropping his pencil, suddenly he rose, seized his viol, and commenced to rend the night with the wildest playing I had ever heard from his bow save when listening at the barred door.

It would be useless to describe the playing of Erich Zann on that dreadful night. It was more horrible than anything I had ever overheard, because I could now see the expression of his face, and could realize that this time the motive was stark fear. He was trying to make a noise; to ward something off or drown something out — what, I could not imagine, awesome though I felt it must be. The playing grew fantastic, delirious, and hysterical, yet kept to the last the qualities of supreme genius which I knew this strange old man possessed. I recognized the air — it was a wild Hungarian dance popular in the theaters, and I reflected for a moment that this was the first time I had ever heard Zann play the work of another composer.

Louder and louder, wilder and wilder, mounted the shrieking and whining of that desperate viol. The player was dripping with an uncanny perspiration and twisted like a monkey, always looking frantically at the curtained window. In his frenzied strains I could almost see shadowy satyrs and bacchanals dancing and whirling insanely through seething abysses of clouds and smoke and lightning. And then I thought I heard a shriller, steadier note that was not from the viol; a calm, deliberate, purposeful, mocking note from far away in the West.

At this juncture the shutter began to rattle in a howling night wind which had sprung up outside as if in answer to the mad playing within. Zann's screaming viol now outdid itself emitting sounds I had never thought a viol could emit. The shutter rattled more loudly, unfastened, and commenced slamming against the window. Then the glass broke shiveringly under the persistent impacts, and the chill wind rushed in, making the candles sputter and rustling the sheets of paper on the table where Zann had begun to write out his horrible secret. I looked at Zann, and saw that he was past conscious observation. His blue eyes were bulging, glassy and sightless, and the frantic playing had become a blind, mechanical, unrecognizable orgy that no pen could even suggest.

A sudden gust, stronger than the others, caught up the manuscript and bore it toward the window. I followed the flying sheets in desperation, but they were gone before I reached the demolished panes. Then I remembered my old wish to gaze from this window, the only window in the Rue d'Auseil from which one might see the slope beyond the wall, and the city outspread beneath. It was very dark, but the city's lights always burned, and I expected to see them there amidst the rain and wind. Yet when I looked from that highest of all gable windows, looked while the candles sputtered and the insane viol howled with the night-wind, I saw no city spread below, and no friendly lights gleamed from remembered streets, but only the blackness of space illimitable; unimagined space alive with motion and music, and having no semblance of anything on earth. And as I stood there looking in terror, the wind blew out both the candles in that ancient peaked garret, leaving me in savage and impenetrable darkness with chaos and pandemonium before me, and the demon madness of that night-baying viol behind me.

I staggered back in the dark, without the means of striking a light, crashing against the table, overturning a chair, and finally groping my way to the place where the blackness screamed with shocking music. To save myself and Erich Zann I could at least try, whatever the powers opposed to me. Once I thought some chill thing brushed me, and I screamed, but my scream could not be heard above that hideous viol. Suddenly out of the blackness the madly sawing bow struck me, and I knew I was close to the player. I felt ahead, touched the back of Zann's chair, and then found and shook his shoulder in an effort to bring him to his senses.

He did not respond, and still the viol shrieked on without slackening. I moved my hand to his head, whose mechanical nodding I was able to stop, and shouted in his ear that we must both flee from the unknown things of the night. But he neither answered me nor abated the frenzy of his unutterable music, while all through the garret strange currents of wind seemed to dance in the darkness and babel. When my hand touched his ear I shuddered, though I knew not why — knew not why till I felt the still face; the ice-cold, stiffened, unbreathing face whose glassy eyes bulged uselessly into the void. And then, by some miracle, finding the door and the large wooden bolt, I plunged wildly away from that glassy-eyed thing in the dark, and from the ghoulish howling of that accursed viol whose fury increased even as I plunged.

Leaping, floating, flying down those endless stairs through the dark house; racing mindlessly out into the narrow, steep, and ancient street of steps and tottering houses; clattering down steps and over cobbles to the lower streets and the putrid canyon-walled river; panting across the great dark bridge to the broader, healthier streets and boulevards we know; all these are terrible impressions that linger with me. And I recall that there was no wind, and that the moon was out, and that all the lights of the city twinkled.

Despite my most careful searches and investigations, I have never since been able to find the Rue d'Auseil. But I am not wholly sorry; either for this or for the loss in undreamable abysses of the closely-written sheets which alone could have explained the music of Erich Zann.

Herbert West, Reanimator.

12,000-WORD SERIAL NOVELETTE; 1921.

H.P. Lovecraft did not often indulge in humourous writing, although there is ample reason to believe that if he had, he would have been very good at it. But it is most likely that if he had, Herbert West, Reanimator *would be categorized as comedy.*

Herbert West, Reanimator *was written to order as a six-part serial in a startup magazine provocatively titled* Home Brew, *and subtitled — for anyone too thick to get the Prohibition reference — "A Thirst Quencher for Lovers of Personal Liberty."*

Home Brew *was not an amateur journal, although careless scholars still sometimes categorize it as one. It was, rather, an amateur journalist's first foray into professional magazine publishing. As such, it paid for its stories, and Lovecraft received $5 for each of them — the first writing pay cheque he ever earned.*

Herbert West, Reanimator *has a campy quality to it that grows stronger as the story goes on, which leads biographer S.T. Joshi to suggest that, although it may not have started out as a self-parody, it had become one by the time Lovecraft wrote the last installment. It was, after all, appearing in a humour magazine. When in Rome, right?*

But it is also possible, and in fact rather likely, that Lovecraft had his tongue planted firmly in his cheek from the very start of this project, and that the increasingly delicious campiness of parts 5 and 6 (the latter subtitled, with rich and ironic melodrama, "The Tomb-Legions") was the result of Lovecraft warming to the task and hitting his full stride.

Lovecraft started writing Herbert West, Reanimator *in October 1921, and finished the last episode in June 1922; it was published under the title of "Grewsome Tales" in the February through July issues of* Home Brew. *For more details of the writing and publication schedule, see the timeline of Lovecraft's life and work, in the Appendix.*

To be dead, to be truly dead, must be glorious. There are far worse things awaiting man than death.

— COUNT DRACULA.

I.
FROM THE DARK.

Of Herbert West, who was my friend in college and in after life, I can speak only with extreme terror. This terror is not due altogether to the sinister manner of his recent disappearance, but was engendered by the whole nature of his life-work, and first gained its acute form more than seventeen years ago, when we were in the third year of our course at the Miskatonic University Medical School in Arkham. While he was with me, the wonder and diabolism of his experiments fascinated me utterly, and I was his closest companion. Now that he is gone and the spell is broken, the actual fear is greater. Memories and possibilities are ever more hideous than realities.

The first horrible incident of our acquaintance was the greatest shock I ever experienced, and it is only with reluctance that I repeat it. As I have said, it happened when we were in the medical school where West had already made himself notorious through his wild theories on the nature of death and the possibility of overcoming it artificially. His views, which were widely ridiculed by the faculty and by his fellow-students, hinged on the essentially mechanistic nature of life; and concerned means for operating the organic machinery of mankind by calculated chemical action after the failure of natural processes. In his experiments with various animating solutions, he had killed and treated immense numbers of rabbits, guinea-pigs, cats, dogs, and monkeys, till he had become the prime nuisance of the college. Several times he had actually obtained signs of life in animals supposedly dead; in many cases violent signs. But he soon saw that the perfection of his process, if indeed possible, would necessarily involve a lifetime of research. It likewise became clear that, since the same solution never worked alike on different organic species, he would require human subjects for further and more specialised progress. It was here that he first came into conflict with the college authorities, and was debarred from future experiments by no less a dignitary than the dean of the medical school himself — the learned and benevolent Dr. Allan Halsey, whose work in behalf of the stricken is recalled by every old resident of Arkham.

I had always been exceptionally tolerant of West's pursuits, and we frequently discussed his theories, whose ramifications and corollaries were almost infinite. Holding with Haeckel that all life is a chemical and physical process, and that the so-called "soul" is a myth, my friend believed that artificial reanimation of the dead can depend only on the condition of the tissues; and that unless actual decomposition has set in, a corpse fully equipped with organs may with suitable measures be set going again in the peculiar fashion known as life. That the psychic or intellectual life might be impaired by the slight deterioration of sensitive brain-cells which even a short period of death would be apt to cause, West fully realised. It had at first been his hope to find a reagent which would restore vitality before the actual advent of death, and only repeated failures on animals had shewn him that the natural and artificial life-motions were incompatible. He then sought extreme freshness in his specimens, injecting his solutions into the blood immediately after the extinction of life. It was this circumstance which made the professors so carelessly sceptical, for they felt that true death had not occurred in any case. They did not stop to view the matter closely and reasoningly.

It was not long after the faculty had interdicted his work that West confided to me his resolution to get fresh human bodies in some manner, and continue in secret the experiments he could no longer perform openly. To hear him discussing ways and means was rather ghastly, for at the college we had never procured anatomical specimens ourselves. Whenever the morgue proved inadequate, two local negroes attended to this matter, and they were seldom questioned. West was then a small, slender, spectacled youth with delicate features, yellow hair, pale blue eyes, and a soft voice, and it was uncanny to hear him dwelling on the relative merits of Christchurch Cemetery and the potter's field. We finally decided on the potter's field, because practically every body in Christchurch was embalmed, a thing of course ruinous to West's researches.

I was by this time his active and enthralled assistant, and helped him make all his decisions, not only concerning the source of bodies but concerning a suitable place for our loathsome work. It was I who thought of the deserted Chapman farmhouse beyond Meadow Hill, where we fitted up on the ground floor an operating room and a laboratory, each with dark curtains to conceal our midnight doings. The place was far from any road, and in sight of no other house, yet precautions were none the less necessary, since rumours of strange lights, started by chance nocturnal roamers, would soon bring disaster on our enterprise. It was agreed to call the whole thing a chemical laboratory if discovery should occur. Gradually we equipped our sinister haunt of science with materials either purchased in Boston or quietly borrowed from the college — materials carefully made unrecognisable save to expert eyes — and provided spades and picks for the many burials we should have to make in the cellar. At the college we used an incinerator, but the apparatus was too costly for our unauthorised laboratory. Bodies were always a nuisance — even the small guinea-pig bodies from the slight clandestine experiments in West's room at the boardinghouse.

We followed the local death-notices like ghouls, for our specimens demanded particular qualities. What we wanted were corpses interred soon after death and without artificial preservation; preferably free from malforming disease, and certainly with all organs present. Accident victims were our best hope. Not for many weeks did we hear of anything suitable;

Weird Tales, November 1943

though we talked with morgue and hospital authorities, ostensibly in the college's interest, as often as we could without exciting suspicion. We found that the college had first choice in every case, so that it might be necessary to remain in Arkham during the summer, when only the limited summer-school classes were held. In the end, though, luck favoured us; for one day we heard of an almost ideal case in the potter's field; a brawny young workman drowned only the morning before in Summer's Pond, and buried at the town's expense without delay or embalming. That afternoon we found the new grave, and determined to begin work soon after midnight.

It was a repulsive task that we undertook in the black small hours, even though we lacked at that time the special horror of graveyards which later experiences brought to us. We carried spades and oil dark lanterns, for although electric torches were then manufactured, they were not as satisfactory as the tungsten contrivances of today. The process of unearthing was slow and sordid — it might have been gruesomely poetical if we had been artists instead of scientists — and we were glad when our spades struck wood. When the pine box was fully uncovered, West scrambled down and removed the lid, dragging out and propping up the contents. I reached down and hauled the contents out of the grave, and then both toiled hard to restore the spot to its former appearance. The affair made us rather nervous, especially the stiff form and vacant face of our first trophy, but we managed to remove all traces of our visit. When we had patted down the last shovelful of earth, we put the specimen in a canvas sack and set out for the old Chapman place beyond Meadow Hill.

On an improvised dissecting-table in the old farmhouse, by the light of a powerful acetylene lamp, the specimen was not very spectral looking. It had been a sturdy and apparently unimaginative youth of wholesome plebeian type — large-framed, grey-eyed, and brown-haired — a sound animal without psychological subtleties, and probably having vital processes of the simplest and healthiest sort. Now, with the eyes closed, it looked more asleep than dead; though the expert test of my friend soon left no doubt on that score. We had at last what West had always longed for — a real dead man of the ideal kind, ready for the solution as prepared according to the most careful calculations and theories for human use. The tension on our part became very great. We knew that there was scarcely a chance for anything like complete success, and could not avoid hideous fears at possible grotesque results of partial animation. Especially were we apprehensive concerning the mind and impulses of the creature, since in the space following death some of the more delicate cerebral cells might well have suffered deterioration. I, myself, still held some curious notions about the traditional "soul" of man, and felt an awe at the secrets that might be told by one returning from the dead. I wondered what sights this placid youth might have seen in inaccessible spheres, and what he could relate if fully restored to life. But my wonder was not overwhelming, since for the most part I shared the materialism of my friend. He was calmer than I as he forced a large quantity of his fluid into a vein of the body's arm, immediately binding the incision securely.

The waiting was gruesome, but West never faltered. Every now and then he applied his stethoscope to the specimen, and bore the negative results philosophically. After about three-quarters of an hour without the least sign of life he disappointedly pronounced the solution inadequate, but determined to make the most of his opportunity and try one change in the formula before disposing of his ghastly prize. We had that afternoon dug a grave in the cellar, and would have to fill it by dawn — for although we had fixed a lock on the house, we wished to shun even the remotest risk of a ghoulish discovery. Besides, the body would not be even approximately fresh the next night. So taking the solitary acetylene lamp into the adjacent laboratory, we left our silent guest on the slab in the dark, and bent every energy to the mixing of a new solution; the weighing and measuring supervised by West with an almost fanatical care.

The awful event was very sudden, and wholly unexpected. I was pouring something from one test-tube to another, and West was busy over the alcohol blast-lamp which had to answer for a Bunsen burner in this gasless edifice, when from the pitch-black room we had left there burst the most appalling and daemoniac succession of cries that either of us had ever heard. Not more unutterable could have been the chaos of hellish sound if the pit itself had opened to release the agony of the damned, for in one inconceivable cacophony was centered all the supernal terror and unnatural despair of animate nature. Human it could not have been — it is not in man to make such sounds — and without a thought of our late employment or its possible discovery, both West and I leaped to the nearest window like stricken animals; overturning tubes, lamp, and retorts, and vaulting madly into the starred abyss of the rural night. I think we screamed ourselves as we stumbled frantically toward the town, though as we reached the outskirts we put on a semblance of restraint — just enough to seem like belated revellers staggering home from a debauch.

We did not separate, but managed to get to West's room, where we whispered with the gas up until dawn. By then we had calmed ourselves a little with rational theories and plans for investigation, so that we could sleep through the day — classes being disregarded. But that evening two items in the paper, wholly unrelated, made it again impossible for us to sleep. The old deserted Chapman house had inexplicably burned to an amorphous heap of ashes; that we could understand because of the upset lamp. Also, an attempt had been made to disturb a new grave in the potter's field, as if by futile and spadeless clawing at the earth. That we could not understand, for we had patted down the mould very carefully.

And for seventeen years after that West would look frequently over his shoulder, and complain of fancied footsteps behind him. Now he has disappeared.

II.

THE PLAGUE-DAEMON.

I shall never forget that hideous summer sixteen years ago, when like a noxious afrite from the halls of Eblis typhoid stalked leeringly through Arkham. It is by that satanic scourge that most recall the year, for truly terror brooded with bat-wings over the piles of coffins in the tombs of Christchurch Cemetery; yet for me there is a greater horror in that time — a horror known to me alone now that Herbert West has disappeared.

West and I were doing post-graduate work in summer classes at the medical school of Miskatonic University, and my friend had attained a wide notoriety because of his experiments leading toward the revivification of the dead. After the scientific slaughter of uncounted small animals the freakish work had ostensibly stopped by order of our sceptical dean, Dr. Allan Halsey; though West had continued to perform certain secret tests in his dingy boarding house room, and had on one terrible and unforgettable occasion taken a human body from its grave in the potter's field to a deserted farmhouse beyond Meadow Hill.

I was with him on that odious occasion, and saw him inject into the still veins the elixir which he thought would to some extent restore life's chemical and physical processes. It had ended horribly — in a delirium of fear which we gradually came to attribute to our own overwrought nerves — and West had never afterward been able to shake off a maddening sensation of being haunted and hunted. The body had not been quite fresh enough; it is obvious that to restore normal mental attributes a body must be very fresh indeed; and the burning of the old house had prevented us from burying the thing. It would have been better if we could have known it was underground.

After that experience West had dropped his researches for some time; but as the zeal of the born scientist slowly returned, he again became importunate with the college faculty, pleading for the use of the dissecting-room and of fresh human specimens for the work he regarded as so overwhelmingly important. His pleas, however, were wholly in vain; for the decision of Dr. Halsey was inflexible, and the other professors all endorsed the verdict of their leader. In the radical theory of reanimation they saw nothing but the immature vagaries of a youthful enthusiast whose slight form, yellow hair, spectacled blue eyes, and soft voice gave no hint of the supernormal — almost

"We laid the specimen on an improvised dissecting table in the old farmhouse. Then we set to work . . . ."

Weird Tales, March 1942

diabolical — power of the cold brain within. I can see him now as he was then — and I shiver. He grew sterner of face, but never elderly. And now Sefton Asylum has had the mishap and West has vanished.

West clashed disagreeably with Dr. Halsey near the end of our last undergraduate term in a wordy dispute that did less credit to him than to the kindly dean in point of courtesy. He felt that he was needlessly and irrationally retarded in a supremely great work; a work which he could of course conduct to suit himself in later years, but which he wished to begin while still possessed of the exceptional facilities of the university. That the tradition-bound elders should ignore his singular results on animals, and persist in their denial of the possibility of reanimation, was inexpressibly disgusting and almost incomprehensible to a youth of West's logical temperament. Only greater maturity could help him understand the chronic mental limitations of the "professor-doctor" type — the product of generations of pathetic Puritanism; kindly, conscientious, and sometimes gentle and amiable, yet always narrow, intolerant, custom-ridden, and lacking in perspective. Age has more charity for these incomplete yet high-souled characters, whose worst real vice is timidity, and who are ultimately punished by general ridicule for their intellectual sins — sins like Ptolemaism, Calvinism, anti-Darwinism, anti-Nietzscheism, and every sort of Sabbatarianism and sumptuary legislation. West, young despite his marvellous scientific acquirements, had scant patience with good Dr. Halsey and his erudite colleagues; and nursed an increasing resentment, coupled with a desire to prove his theories to these obtuse worthies in some striking and dramatic fashion. Like most youths, he indulged in elaborate daydreams of revenge, triumph, and final magnanimous forgiveness.

And then had come the scourge, grinning and lethal, from the nightmare caverns of Tartarus. West and I had graduated about the time of its beginning, but had remained for additional work at the summer school, so that we were in Arkham when it broke with full daemoniac fury upon the town. Though not as yet licenced physicians, we now had our degrees, and were pressed frantically into public service as the numbers of the stricken grew. The situation was almost past management, and deaths ensued too frequently for the local undertakers fully to handle. Burials without embalming were made in rapid succession, and even the Christchurch Cemetery receiving tomb was crammed with coffins of the unembalmed dead. This circumstance was not without effect on West, who thought often of the irony of the situation — so many fresh specimens, yet none for his persecuted researches! We were frightfully overworked, and the terrific mental and nervous strain made my friend brood morbidly.

But West's gentle enemies were no less harassed with prostrating duties. College had all but closed, and every doctor of the medical faculty was helping to fight the typhoid plague. Dr. Halsey in particular had distinguished himself in sacrificing service, applying his extreme skill with whole-hearted energy to cases which many others shunned because of danger or apparent hopelessness. Before a month was over the fearless dean had become a popular hero, though he seemed unconscious of his fame as he struggled to keep from collapsing with physical fatigue and nervous exhaustion. West could not withhold admiration for the fortitude of his foe, but because of this was even more determined to prove to him the truth of his amazing doctrines. Taking advantage of the disorganisation of both college work and municipal health regulations, he managed to get a recently deceased body smuggled into the university dissecting-room one night, and in my presence injected a new modification of his solution. The thing actually opened its eyes, but only stared at the ceiling with a look of soul-petrifying horror before collapsing into an inertness from which nothing could rouse it. West said it was not fresh enough — the hot summer air does not favour corpses. That time we were almost caught before we incinerated the thing, and West doubted the advisability of repeating his daring misuse of the college laboratory.

The peak of the epidemic was reached in August. West and I were almost dead, and Dr. Halsey did die on the 14th. The students all attended the hasty funeral on the 15th, and bought an impressive wreath, though the latter was quite overshadowed by the tributes sent by wealthy Arkham citizens and by the municipality itself. It was almost a public affair, for the dean had surely been a public benefactor. After the entombment we were all somewhat depressed, and spent the afternoon at the bar of the Commercial House; where West, though shaken by the death of his chief opponent, chilled the rest of us with references to his notorious theories. Most of the students went home, or to various duties, as the evening advanced; but West persuaded me to aid him in "making a night of it." West's landlady saw us arrive at his room about two in the morning, with a third man between us; and told her husband that we had all evidently dined and wined rather well.

Apparently this acidulous matron was right; for about 3 a.m. the whole house was aroused by cries coming from West's room, where when they broke down the door, they found the two of us unconscious on the blood-stained carpet, beaten, scratched, and mauled, and with the broken remnants of West's bottles and instruments around us. Only an open window told what had become of our assailant, and many wondered how he himself had fared after the terrific leap from the second story to the lawn which he must have made. There were some strange garments in the room, but West upon regaining consciousness said they did not belong to the stranger, but were specimens collected for bacteriological analysis in the course of investigations on the transmission of germ diseases. He ordered them burnt as soon as possible in the capacious fireplace. To the police we both declared ignorance of our late companion's identity. He was, West nervously said, a congenial stranger whom we had met at some downtown bar of uncertain location. We had all been rather jovial, and West and I did not wish to have our pugnacious companion hunted down.

That same night saw the beginning of the second Arkham horror — the horror that to me eclipsed the plague itself. Christchurch Cemetery was the scene of a terrible killing; a watchman having been clawed to death in a manner not only too hideous for description, but raising a doubt as to the human agency of the deed. The victim had been seen alive considerably after midnight — the dawn revealed the unutterable thing. The manager of a circus at the neighbouring town of Bolton was questioned, but he swore that no beast had at any time escaped from its cage. Those who found the body noted a trail of blood leading to the receiving tomb, where a small pool of red lay on the concrete just outside the gate. A fainter trail led away toward the woods, but it soon gave out.

The next night devils danced on the roofs of Arkham, and unnatural madness howled in the wind. Through the fevered town had crept a curse which some said was greater than the plague, and which some whispered was the embodied daemon-soul of the plague itself. Eight houses were entered by a nameless thing which strewed red death in its wake — in all, seventeen maimed and shapeless remnants of bodies were left behind by the voiceless, sadistic monster that crept abroad. A few persons

Weird Tales, July 1942

had half seen it in the dark, and said it was white and like a malformed ape or anthropomorphic fiend. It had not left behind quite all that it had attacked, for sometimes it had been hungry. The number it had killed was fourteen; three of the bodies had been in stricken homes and had not been alive.

On the third night frantic bands of searchers, led by the police, captured it in a house on Crane Street near the Miskatonic campus. They had organised the quest with care, keeping in touch by means of volunteer telephone stations, and when someone in the college district had reported hearing a scratching at a shuttered window, the net was quickly spread. On account of the general alarm and precautions, there were only two more victims, and the capture was effected without major casualties. The thing was finally stopped by a bullet, though not a fatal one, and was rushed to the local hospital amidst universal excitement and loathing.

For it had been a man. This much was clear despite the nauseous eyes, the voiceless simianism, and the daemoniac savagery. They dressed its wound and carted it to the asylum at Sefton, where it beat its head against the walls of a padded cell for sixteen years—until the recent mishap, when it escaped under circumstances that few like to mention. What had most disgusted the searchers of Arkham was the thing they noticed when the monster's face was cleaned—the mocking, unbelievable resemblance to a learned and self-sacrificing martyr who had been entombed but three days before—the late Dr. Allan

Halsey, public benefactor and dean of the medical school of Miskatonic University.

To the vanished Herbert West and to me the disgust and horror were supreme. I shudder tonight as I think of it; shudder even more than I did that morning when West muttered through his bandages, "Damn it, it wasn't quite fresh enough!"

III.

SIX SHOTS BY MIDNIGHT.

It is uncommon to fire all six shots of a revolver with great suddenness when one would probably be sufficient, but many things in the life of Herbert West were uncommon. It is, for instance, not often that a young physician leaving college is obliged to conceal the principles which guide his selection of a home and office, yet that was the case with Herbert West. When he and I obtained our degrees at the medical school of Miskatonic University, and sought to relieve our poverty by setting up as general practitioners, we took great care not to say that we chose our house because it was fairly well isolated, and as near as possible to the potter's field.

Reticence such as this is seldom without a cause, nor indeed was ours; for our requirements were those resulting from a life-work distinctly unpopular. Outwardly we were doctors only, but beneath the surface were aims of far greater and more terrible moment — for the essence of Herbert West's existence was a quest amid black and forbidden realms of the unknown, in which he hoped to uncover the secret of life and restore to perpetual animation the graveyard's cold clay. Such a quest demands strange materials, among them fresh human bodies; and in order to keep supplied with these indispensable things one must live quietly and not far from a place of informal interment.

West and I had met in college, and I had been the only one to sympathise with his hideous experiments. Gradually I had come to be his inseparable assistant, and now that we were out of college we had to keep together. It was not easy to find a good opening for two doctors in company, but finally the influence of the university secured us a practice in Bolton — a factory town near Arkham, the seat of the college. The Bolton Worsted Mills are the largest in the Miskatonic Valley, and their polyglot employees are never popular as patients with the local physicians. We chose our house with the greatest care, seizing at last on a rather run-down cottage near the end of Pond Street; five numbers from the closest neighbour, and separated from the local potter's field by only a stretch of meadow land, bisected by a narrow neck of the rather dense forest which lies to the north. The distance was greater than we wished, but we could get no nearer house without going on the other side of the field, wholly out of the factory district. We were not much displeased, however, since there were no people between us and our sinister source of supplies. The walk was a trifle long, but we could haul our silent specimens undisturbed.

Our practice was surprisingly large from the very first — large enough to please most young doctors, and large enough to prove a bore and a burden to students whose real interest lay elsewhere. The mill-hands were of somewhat turbulent inclinations; and besides their many natural needs, their frequent clashes and stabbing affrays gave us plenty to do. But what actually absorbed our minds was the secret laboratory we had fitted up in the cellar — the laboratory with the long table under the electric lights, where in the small hours of the morning we often injected West's various solutions into the veins of the things we dragged from the potter's field. West was experimenting madly to find something which would start man's vital motions anew after they had been stopped by the thing we call death, but had encountered the most ghastly obstacles. The solution had to be differently compounded for different types — what would serve for guinea-pigs would not serve for human beings, and different human specimens required large modifications.

The bodies had to be exceedingly fresh, or the slight decomposition of brain tissue would render perfect reanimation impossible. Indeed, the greatest problem was to get them fresh enough — West had had horrible experiences during his secret college researches with corpses of doubtful vintage. The results of partial or imperfect animation were much more hideous than were the total failures, and we both held fearsome recollections of such things. Ever since our first daemoniac session in the deserted farmhouse on Meadow Hill in Arkham, we had felt a brooding menace; and West, though a calm, blond, blue-eyed scientific automaton in most respects, often confessed to a shuddering sensation of stealthy pursuit. He half felt that he was followed — a psychological delusion of shaken nerves, enhanced by the undeniably disturbing fact that at least one of our reanimated specimens was still alive — a frightful carnivorous thing in a padded cell at Sefton. Then there was another — our first — whose exact fate we had never learned.

We had fair luck with specimens in Bolton — much better than in Arkham. We had not been settled a week before we got an accident victim on the very night of burial, and made it open its eyes with an amazingly rational expression before the solution failed. It had lost an arm — if it had been a perfect body we might have succeeded better. Between then and the next January we secured three more; one total failure, one case of marked muscular motion, and one rather shivery thing — it rose of itself and uttered a sound. Then came a period when luck was poor; interments fell off, and those that did occur were of specimens either too diseased or too maimed for use. We kept track of all the deaths and their circumstances with systematic care.

One March night, however, we unexpectedly obtained a specimen which did not come from the potter's field. In Bolton the prevailing spirit of Puritanism had outlawed the sport of boxing — with the usual result. Surreptitious and ill-conducted bouts among the mill-workers were common, and occasionally professional talent of low grade was imported. This late winter night there had been such a match; evidently with disastrous results, since two timorous Poles had come to us with incoherently whispered entreaties to attend to a very secret and desperate case. We followed them to an abandoned barn, where the remnants of a crowd of frightened foreigners were watching a silent black form on the floor.

The match had been between Kid O'Brien — a lubberly and now quaking youth with a most un-Hibernian hooked nose — and Buck Robinson, "The Harlem Smoke." The negro had been knocked out, and a moment's examination shewed us that he would permanently remain so. He was a loathsome, gorilla-like thing, with abnormally long arms which I could not help calling fore legs, and a face that conjured up thoughts of unspeakable Congo secrets and tom-tom poundings under an eerie moon. The body must have looked even worse in life — but the world holds many ugly things. Fear was upon the whole pitiful crowd, for they did not know what the law would exact of them if the affair were not hushed up; and they were grateful when West, in spite of my involuntary shudders, offered to get rid of the thing quietly — for a purpose I knew too well.

There was bright moonlight over the snowless landscape, but we dressed the thing and carried it home between us through the deserted streets and meadows, as we had carried a similar thing one horrible night in Arkham. We approached the house from the field in the rear, took the specimen in the back door and down the cellar stairs, and prepared it for the usual experiment. Our fear of the police was absurdly great, though we had timed our trip to avoid the solitary patrolman of that section.

The result was wearily anticlimactic. Ghastly as our prize appeared, it was wholly unresponsive to every solution we injected in its black arm; solutions prepared from experience with white specimens only. So as the hour grew dangerously near to dawn, we did as we had done with the others — dragged the thing across the meadows to the neck of the woods near the potter's field, and buried it there in the best sort of grave the frozen ground would furnish. The grave was not very deep, but fully as good as that of the previous specimen — the thing which had risen of itself and uttered a sound. In the light of our dark lanterns we carefully covered it with leaves and dead vines, fairly certain that the police would never find it in a forest so dim and dense.

The next day I was increasingly apprehensive about the police, for a patient brought rumours of a suspected fight and death. West had still another source of worry, for he had been called in the afternoon to a case which ended very threateningly. An Italian woman had become hysterical over her missing child — a lad of five who had strayed off early in the morning and failed to appear for dinner — and had developed symptoms highly alarming in view of an always weak heart. It was a very foolish hysteria, for the boy had often run away before; but Italian peasants are exceedingly superstitious, and this woman seemed as much harassed by omens as by facts. About seven o'clock in the evening she had died, and her frantic husband had made a frightful scene in his efforts to kill West, whom he wildly blamed for not saving her life. Friends had held him when he drew a stiletto, but West departed amidst his inhuman shrieks, curses and oaths of vengeance. In his latest affliction the fellow seemed to have forgotten his child, who was still missing as the night advanced. There was some talk of searching the woods, but most of the family's friends were busy with the dead woman and the screaming man. Altogether, the nervous strain upon West must have been tremendous. Thoughts of the police and of the mad Italian both weighed heavily.

We retired about eleven, but I did not sleep well. Bolton had a surprisingly good police force for so small a town, and I could not help fearing the mess which would ensue if the affair of the night before were ever tracked down. It might mean the end of all our local work — and perhaps prison for both West and me. I did not like those rumours of a fight which were floating about. After the clock had struck three the moon shone in my eyes, but I turned over without rising to pull down the shade. Then came the steady rattling at the back door.

I lay still and somewhat dazed, but before long heard West's rap on my door. He was clad in dressing-gown and slippers, and had in his hands a revolver and an electric flashlight. From the revolver I knew that he was thinking more of the crazed Italian than of the police.

"We'd better both go," he whispered. "It wouldn't do not to answer it anyway, and it may be a patient — it would be like one of those fools to try the back door."

So we both went down the stairs on tiptoe, with a fear partly justified and partly that which comes only from the soul of the weird small hours. The rattling continued, growing somewhat louder. When we reached the door I cautiously unbolted it and threw it open, and as the moon streamed revealingly down on the form silhouetted there, West did a peculiar thing. Despite the obvious danger of attracting notice and bringing down on our heads the dreaded police investigation — a thing which after all was mercifully averted by the relative isolation of our cottage — my friend suddenly, excitedly, and unnecessarily emptied all six chambers of his revolver into the nocturnal visitor.

For that visitor was neither Italian nor policeman. Looming hideously against the spectral moon was a gigantic misshapen thing not to be imagined save in nightmares — a glassy-eyed, ink-black apparition nearly on all fours, covered with bits of mould, leaves, and vines, foul with caked blood, and having between its glistening teeth a snow-white, terrible, cylindrical object terminating in a tiny hand.

IV.

THE SCREAM OF THE DEAD.

The scream of a dead man gave to me that acute and added horror of Dr. Herbert West which harassed the latter years of our companionship. It is natural that such a thing as a dead man's scream should give horror, for it is obviously, not a pleasing or ordinary occurrence; but I was used to similar experiences, hence suffered on this occasion only because of a particular circumstance. And, as I have implied, it was not of the dead man himself that I became afraid.

Herbert West, whose associate and assistant I was, possessed scientific interests far beyond the usual routine of a village physician. That was why, when establishing his practice in Bolton, he had chosen an isolated house near the potter's field. Briefly and brutally stated, West's sole absorbing interest was a secret study of the phenomena of life and its cessation, leading toward the reanimation of the dead through injections of an excitant solution. For this ghastly experimenting it was necessary to have a constant supply of very fresh human bodies; very fresh because even the least decay hopelessly damaged the brain structure, and human because we found that the solution had to be compounded differently for different types of organisms. Scores of rabbits and guinea-pigs had been killed and treated, but their trail was a blind one. West had never fully succeeded because he had never been able to secure a corpse sufficiently fresh. What he wanted were bodies from which vitality had only just departed; bodies with every cell intact and capable of receiving again the impulse toward that mode of motion called life. There was hope that this second and artificial life might be made perpetual by repetitions of the injection, but we had learned that an ordinary natural life would not respond to the action. To establish the artificial motion, natural life must be extinct — the specimens must be very fresh, but genuinely dead.

The awesome quest had begun when West and I were students at the Miskatonic University Medical School in Arkham, vividly conscious for the first time of the thoroughly mechanical nature of life. That was seven years before, but West looked scarcely a day older now — he was small, blond, clean-shaven, soft-voiced, and spectacled, with only an occasional flash of a cold blue eye to tell of the hardening and growing fanaticism of his character under the pressure of his terrible investigations. Our experiences had often been hideous in the extreme; the results of defective reanimation, when lumps of graveyard clay had been galvanised into morbid, unnatural, and brainless motion by various modifications of the vital solution.

One thing had uttered a nerve-shattering scream; another had risen violently, beaten us both to unconsciousness, and run amuck in a shocking way before it could be placed behind asylum bars; still another, a loathsome African monstrosity, had clawed out of its shallow grave and done a deed — West had had to shoot that object. We could not get bodies fresh enough to shew any trace of reason when reanimated, so had perforce created nameless horrors. It was disturbing to think that one, perhaps two, of our monsters still lived — that thought haunted us shadowingly, till finally West disappeared under frightful circumstances. But at the time of the scream in the cellar laboratory of the isolated Bolton cottage, our fears were subordinate to our anxiety for extremely fresh specimens. West was more avid than I, so that it almost seemed to me that he looked half-covetously at any very healthy living physique.

It was in July, 1910, that the bad luck regarding specimens began to turn. I had been on a long visit to my parents in Illinois, and upon my return found West in a state of singular elation. He had, he told me excitedly, in all likelihood solved the problem of freshness through an approach from an entirely new angle — that of artificial preservation. I had known that he was working on a new and highly unusual embalming compound, and was not surprised that it had turned out well; but until he explained the details I was rather puzzled as to how such a compound could help in our work, since the objectionable staleness of the specimens was largely due to delay occurring before we secured them. This, I now saw, West had clearly recognised; creating his embalming compound for future rather than immediate use, and trusting to fate to supply again some very recent and unburied corpse, as it had years before when we obtained the negro killed in the Bolton prize-fight. At last fate had been kind, so that on this occasion there lay in the secret cellar laboratory a corpse whose decay could not by any possibility have begun. What would happen on reanimation, and whether we could hope for a revival of mind and reason, West did not venture to predict. The experiment would be a landmark in our studies, and he had saved the new body for my return, so that both might share the spectacle in accustomed fashion.

West told me how he had obtained the specimen. It had been a vigorous man; a well-dressed stranger just off the train on his way to transact some business with the Bolton Worsted Mills. The walk through the town had been long, and by the time the traveller paused at our cottage to ask the way to the factories, his heart had become greatly overtaxed. He had refused a stimulant, and had suddenly dropped dead only a moment later. The body, as might be expected, seemed to West a heaven-sent gift. In his brief conversation the stranger had made it clear that he was unknown in Bolton, and a search of his pockets subsequently revealed him to be one Robert Leavitt of St. Louis, apparently without a family to make instant inquiries about his disappearance. If this man could not be restored to life, no one would know of our experiment. We buried our materials in a dense strip of woods between the house and the potter's field. If, on the other hand, he could be restored, our fame would be brilliantly and perpetually established. So without delay West had injected into the body's wrist the compound which would hold it fresh for use after my arrival. The matter of the presumably weak heart, which to my mind imperilled the success of our experiment, did not appear to trouble West extensively. He hoped at last to obtain what he had never obtained before — a rekindled spark of reason and perhaps a normal, living creature.

So on the night of July 18, 1910, Herbert West and I stood in the cellar laboratory and gazed at a white, silent figure beneath the dazzling arc-light. The embalming compound had worked

Weird Tales, November 1942

uncannily well, for as I stared fascinatedly at the sturdy frame which had lain two weeks without stiffening, I was moved to seek West's assurance that the thing was really dead. This assurance he gave readily enough; reminding me that the reanimating solution was never used without careful tests as to life, since it could have no effect if any of the original vitality were present. As West proceeded to take preliminary steps, I was impressed by the vast intricacy of the new experiment; an intricacy so vast that he could trust no hand less delicate than his own. Forbidding me to touch the body, he first injected a drug in the wrist just beside the place his needle had punctured when injecting the embalming compound. This, he said, was to neutralise the compound and release the system to a normal relaxation so that the reanimating solution might freely work when injected. Slightly later, when a change and a gentle tremor seemed to affect the dead limbs, West stuffed a pillow-like object violently over the twitching face, not withdrawing it until the corpse appeared quiet and ready for our attempt at reanimation. The pale enthusiast now applied some last perfunctory tests for absolute lifelessness, withdrew satisfied, and finally injected into the left arm an accurately measured amount of the vital elixir, prepared during the afternoon with a greater care than we had used since college days, when our feats were new and groping. I cannot express the wild, breathless suspense with which we waited for results on this first really fresh specimen — the first we could reasonably expect to open its lips in rational speech, perhaps to tell of what it had seen beyond the unfathomable abyss.

West was a materialist, believing in no soul and attributing all the working of consciousness to bodily phenomena; consequently he looked for no revelation of hideous secrets from gulfs and caverns beyond death's barrier. I did not wholly disagree with him theoretically, yet held vague instinctive remnants of the primitive faith of my forefathers; so that I could not help eyeing the corpse with a certain amount of awe and terrible expectation. Besides — I could not extract from my memory that hideous, inhuman shriek we heard on the night we tried our first experiment in the deserted farmhouse at Arkham.

Very little time had elapsed before I saw the attempt was not to be a total failure. A touch of colour came to cheeks hitherto chalk-white, and spread out under the curiously ample stubble of sandy beard. West, who had his hand on the pulse of the left wrist, suddenly nodded significantly; and almost simultaneously a mist appeared on the mirror inclined above the body's mouth. There followed a few spasmodic muscular motions, and then an audible breathing and visible motion of the chest. I looked at the closed eyelids, and thought I detected a quivering. Then the lids opened, shewing eyes which were grey, calm, and alive, but still unintelligent and not even curious.

In a moment of fantastic whim I whispered questions to the reddening ears; questions of other worlds of which the memory might still be present. Subsequent terror drove them from my mind, but I think the last one, which I repeated, was: "Where have you been?" I do not yet know whether I was answered or not, for no sound came from the well-shaped mouth; but I do know that at that moment I firmly thought the thin lips moved silently, forming syllables which I would have vocalised as "only now" if that phrase had possessed any sense or relevancy. At that moment, as I say, I was elated with the conviction that the one great goal had been attained; and that for the first time a reanimated corpse had uttered distinct words impelled by actual reason. In the next moment there was no doubt about the triumph; no doubt that the solution had truly accomplished, at least temporarily, its full mission of restoring rational and articulate life to the dead. But in that triumph there came to me the greatest of all horrors — not horror of the thing that spoke, but of the deed that I had witnessed and of the man with whom my professional fortunes were joined.

For that very fresh body, at last writhing into full and terrifying consciousness with eyes dilated at the memory of its last scene on earth, threw out its frantic hands in a life and death struggle with the air, and suddenly collapsing into a second and final dissolution from which there could be no return, screamed out the cry that will ring eternally in my aching brain:

"Help! Keep off, you cursed little tow-head fiend — keep that damned needle away from me!"

V.

THE HORROR FROM THE SHADOWS.

Many men have related hideous things, not mentioned in print, which happened on the battlefields of the Great War. Some of these things have made me faint, others have convulsed me with devastating nausea, while still others have made me tremble and look behind me in the dark; yet despite the worst of them I believe I can myself relate the most hideous thing of all — the shocking, the unnatural, the unbelievable horror from the shadows.

In 1915 I was a physician with the rank of First Lieutenant in a Canadian regiment in Flanders, one of many Americans to precede the government itself into the gigantic struggle. I had not entered the army on my own initiative, but rather as a natural result of the enlistment of the man whose indispensable assistant I was — the celebrated Boston surgical specialist, Dr. Herbert West. Dr. West had been avid for a chance to serve as surgeon in a great war, and when the chance had come, he carried me with him almost against my will. There were reasons why I could have been glad to let the war separate us; reasons why I found the practice of medicine and the companionship of West more and more irritating; but when he had gone to Ottawa and through a colleague's influence secured a medical commission as Major, I could not resist the imperious persuasion of one determined that I should accompany him in my usual capacity.

When I say that Dr. West was avid to serve in battle, I do not mean to imply that he was either naturally warlike or anxious for the safety of civilisation. Always an ice-cold intellectual machine; slight, blond, blue-eyed, and spectacled; I think he secretly sneered at my occasional martial enthusiasms and censures of supine neutrality. There was, however, something he wanted in embattled Flanders; and in order to secure it had had to assume a military exterior. What he wanted was not a thing which many persons want, but something connected with the peculiar branch of medical science which he had chosen quite clandestinely to follow, and in which he had achieved amazing and occasionally hideous results. It was, in fact, nothing more or less than an abundant supply of freshly killed men in every stage of dismemberment.

Herbert West needed fresh bodies because his life-work was the reanimation of the dead. This work was not known to the fashionable clientele who had so swiftly built up his fame after his arrival in Boston; but was only too well known to me, who had been his closest friend and sole assistant since the old days in Miskatonic University Medical School at Arkham. It was in those college days that he had begun his terrible experiments, first on small animals and then on human bodies shockingly obtained. There was a solution which he injected into the veins of dead things, and if they were fresh enough they responded in strange ways. He had had much trouble in discovering the proper formula, for each type of

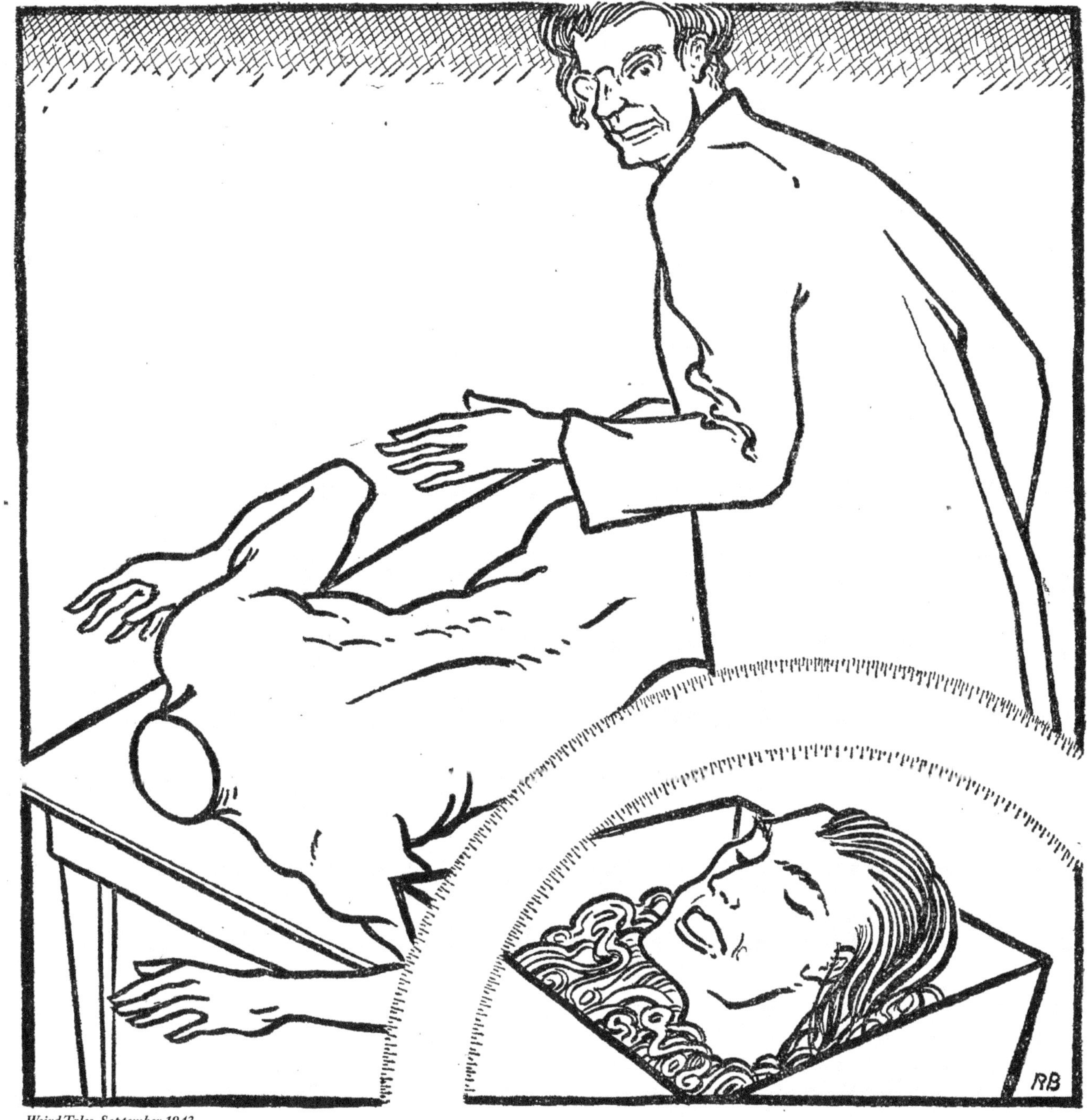

Weird Tales, September 1943

organism was found to need a stimulus especially adapted to it. Terror stalked him when he reflected on his partial failures; nameless things resulting from imperfect solutions or from bodies insufficiently fresh. A certain number of these failures had remained alive — one was in an asylum while others had vanished — and as he thought of conceivable yet virtually impossible eventualities he often shivered beneath his usual stolidity.

West had soon learned that absolute freshness was the prime requisite for useful specimens, and had accordingly resorted to frightful and unnatural expedients in body-snatching. In college, and during our early practice together in the factory town of Bolton, my attitude toward him had been largely one of fascinated admiration; but as his boldness in methods grew, I began to develop a gnawing fear. I did not like the way he looked at healthy living bodies; and then there came a nightmarish session in the cellar laboratory when I learned that a certain specimen had been a living body when he secured it. That was the first time he had ever been able to revive the quality of rational thought in a corpse; and his success, obtained at such a loathsome cost, had completely hardened him.

Of his methods in the intervening five years I dare not speak. I was held to him by sheer force of fear, and witnessed sights that no human tongue could repeat. Gradually I came to find Herbert West himself more horrible than anything he did — that was when it dawned on me that his once normal scientific zeal for prolonging life had subtly degenerated into a mere morbid and ghoulish curiosity and secret sense of charnel picturesqueness. His interest became a hellish and perverse addiction to the repellently and fiendishly abnormal; he gloated calmly over artificial monstrosities which would make most healthy men drop dead from fright and disgust; he became, behind his pallid intellectuality, a fastidious Baudelaire of physical experiment — a languid Elagabalus of the tombs.

Dangers he met unflinchingly; crimes he committed unmoved. I think the climax came when he had proved his point that rational life can be restored, and had sought new worlds to conquer by experimenting on the reanimation of detached parts of bodies. He had wild and original ideas on the independent vital properties of organic cells and nerve-tissue separated from natural physiological systems; and achieved some hideous preliminary results in the form of never-dying, artificially nourished tissue obtained from the nearly hatched eggs of an indescribable tropical reptile. Two biological points he was exceedingly anxious to settle — first, whether any amount of consciousness and rational action be possible without the brain, proceeding from the spinal cord and various nerve-centres; and second, whether any kind of ethereal, intangible relation distinct from the material cells may exist to link the surgically separated parts of what has previously been a single living organism. All this research work required a prodigious supply of freshly slaughtered human flesh — and that was why Herbert West had entered the Great War.

The phantasmal, unmentionable thing occurred one midnight late in March, 1915, in a field hospital behind the lines of St. Eloi. I wonder even now if it could have been other than a daemoniac dream of delirium. West had a private laboratory in an east room of the barn-like temporary edifice, assigned him on his plea that he was devising new and radical methods for the treatment of hitherto hopeless cases of maiming. There he worked like a butcher in the midst of his gory wares — I could never get used to the levity with which he handled and classified certain things. At times he actually did perform marvels of surgery for the soldiers; but his chief delights were of a less public and philanthropic kind, requiring many explanations of sounds which seemed peculiar even amidst that babel of the damned. Among these sounds were frequent revolver-shots — surely not uncommon on a battle-field, but distinctly uncommon in an hospital. Dr. West's reanimated specimens were not meant for long existence or a large audience. Besides human tissue, West employed much of the reptile embryo tissue which he had cultivated with such singular results. It was better than human material for maintaining life in organless fragments, and that was now my friend's chief activity. In a dark corner of the laboratory, over a queer incubating burner, he kept a large covered vat full of this reptilian cell-matter, which multiplied and grew puffily and hideously.

On the night of which I speak we had a splendid new specimen — a man at once physically powerful and of such high mentality that a sensitive nervous system was assured. It was rather ironic, for he was the officer who had helped West to his commission, and who was now to have been our associate. Moreover, he had in the past secretly studied the theory of reanimation to some extent under West. Major Sir Eric Moreland Clapham-Lee, D.S.O., was the greatest surgeon in our division, and had been hastily assigned to the St. Eloi sector when news of the heavy fighting reached headquarters. He had come in an aeroplane piloted by the intrepid Lieut. Ronald Hill, only to be shot down when directly over his destination. The fall had been spectacular and awful; Hill was unrecognisable afterward, but the wreck yielded up the great surgeon in a nearly decapitated but otherwise intact condition. West had greedily seized the lifeless thing which had once been his friend and fellow-scholar; and I shuddered when he finished severing the head, placed it in his hellish vat of pulpy reptile-tissue to preserve it for future experiments, and proceeded to treat the decapitated body on the operating table. He injected new blood, joined certain veins, arteries, and nerves at the headless neck, and closed the ghastly aperture with engrafted skin from an unidentified specimen which had borne an officer's uniform. I knew what he wanted — to see if this highly organised body could exhibit, without its head, any of the signs of mental life which had distinguished Sir Eric Moreland Clapham-Lee. Once a student of reanimation, this silent trunk was now gruesomely called upon to exemplify it.

I can still see Herbert West under the sinister electric light as he injected his reanimating solution into the arm of the headless body. The scene I cannot describe — I should faint if I tried it, for there is madness in a room full of classified charnel things, with blood and lesser human debris almost ankle-deep on the slimy floor, and with hideous reptilian abnormalities sprouting, bubbling, and baking over a winking bluish-green spectre of dim flame in a far corner of black shadows.

The specimen, as West repeatedly observed, had a splendid nervous system. Much was expected of it; and as a few twitching motions began to appear, I could see the feverish interest on West's face. He was ready, I think, to see proof of his increasingly strong opinion that consciousness, reason, and personality can exist independently of the brain — that man has no central connective spirit, but is merely a machine of nervous matter, each section more or less complete in itself. In one triumphant demonstration West was about to relegate the mystery of life to the category of myth. The body now twitched more vigorously, and beneath our avid eyes commenced to heave in a frightful way. The arms stirred disquietingly, the legs drew up, and various muscles contracted in a repulsive kind of writhing.

Then the headless thing threw out its arms in a gesture which was unmistakably one of desperation — an intelligent desperation apparently sufficient to prove every theory of Herbert West. Certainly, the nerves were recalling the man's last act in life; the struggle to get free of the falling aeroplane.

What followed, I shall never positively know. It may have been wholly an hallucination from the shock caused at that instant by the sudden and complete destruction of the building in a cataclysm of German shell-fire — who can gainsay it, since West and I were the only proved survivors? West liked to think that before his recent disappearance, but there were times when he could not; for it was queer that we both had the same hallucination. The hideous occurrence itself was very simple, notable only for what it implied.

The body on the table had risen with a blind and terrible groping, and we had heard a sound. I should not call that sound a voice, for it was too awful. And yet its timbre was not the most awful thing about it. Neither was its message — it had merely screamed, "Jump, Ronald, for God's sake, jump!" The awful thing was its source.

For it had come from the large covered vat in that ghoulish corner of crawling black shadows.

VI.

THE TOMB-LEGIONS.

When Dr. Herbert West disappeared a year ago, the Boston police questioned me closely. They suspected that I was holding something back, and perhaps suspected graver things; but I could not tell them the truth because they would not have believed it. They knew, indeed, that West had been connected with activities beyond the credence of ordinary men; for his hideous experiments in the reanimation of dead bodies had long been too extensive to admit of perfect secrecy; but the final soul-shattering catastrophe held elements of daemoniac phantasy which make even me doubt the reality of what I saw.

I was West's closest friend and only confidential assistant. We had met years before, in medical school, and from the first I had shared his terrible researches. He had slowly tried to perfect a solution which, injected into the veins of the newly deceased, would restore life; a labour demanding an abundance of fresh corpses and therefore involving the most unnatural actions. Still more shocking were the products of some of the experiments — grisly masses of flesh that had been dead, but that West waked to a blind, brainless, nauseous animation. These were the usual results, for in order to reawaken the mind it was necessary to have specimens so absolutely fresh that no decay could possibly affect the delicate brain-cells.

This need for very fresh corpses had been West's moral undoing. They were hard to get, and one awful day he had secured his specimen while it was still alive and vigorous. A struggle, a needle, and a powerful alkaloid had transformed it to a very fresh corpse, and the experiment had succeeded for a brief and memorable moment; but West had emerged with a soul calloused and seared, and a hardened eye which sometimes glanced with a kind of hideous and calculating appraisal at men of especially sensitive brain and especially vigorous physique. Toward the last I became acutely afraid of West, for he began to look at me that way. People did not seem to notice his glances, but they noticed my fear; and after his disappearance used that as a basis for some absurd suspicions.

West, in reality, was more afraid than I; for his abominable pursuits entailed a life of furtiveness and dread of every shadow. Partly it was the police he feared; but sometimes his nervousness was deeper and more nebulous, touching on certain indescribable things into which he had injected a morbid life, and from which he had not seen that life depart. He usually finished his experiments with a revolver, but a few times he had not been quick enough. There was that first specimen on whose rifled grave marks of clawing were later seen. There was also that Arkham professor's body which had done cannibal things before it had been captured and thrust unidentified into a madhouse cell at Sefton, where it beat the walls for sixteen years. Most of the other possibly surviving results were things less easy to speak of — for in later years West's scientific zeal had degenerated to an unhealthy and fantastic mania, and he had spent his chief skill in vitalising not entire human bodies but isolated parts of bodies, or parts joined to organic matter other than human. It had become fiendishly disgusting by the time he disappeared; many of the experiments could not even be hinted at in print. The Great War, through which both of us served as surgeons, had intensified this side of West.

In saying that West's fear of his specimens was nebulous, I have in mind particularly its complex nature. Part of it came merely from knowing of the existence of such nameless monsters, while another part arose from apprehension of the bodily harm they might under certain circumstances do him. Their disappearance added horror to the situation — of them all, West knew the whereabouts of only one, the pitiful asylum thing. Then there was a more subtle fear — a very fantastic sensation resulting from a curious experiment in the Canadian army in 1915. West, in the midst of a severe battle, had reanimated Major Sir Eric Moreland Clapham-Lee, D.S.O., a fellow-physician who knew about his experiments and could have duplicated them. The head had been removed, so that the possibilities of quasi-intelligent life in the trunk might be investigated. Just as the building was wiped out by a German shell, there had been a success. The trunk had moved intelligently; and, unbelievable to relate, we were both sickeningly sure that articulate sounds had come from the detached head as it lay in a shadowy corner of the laboratory. The shell had been merciful, in a way — but West could never feel as certain as he wished, that we two were the only survivors. He used to make shuddering conjectures about the possible actions of a headless physician with the power of reanimating the dead.

West's last quarters were in a venerable house of much elegance, overlooking one of the oldest burying-grounds in

Boston. He had chosen the place for purely symbolic and fantastically aesthetic reasons, since most of the interments were of the colonial period and therefore of little use to a scientist seeking very fresh bodies. The laboratory was in a sub-cellar secretly constructed by imported workmen, and contained a huge incinerator for the quiet and complete disposal of such bodies, or fragments and synthetic mockeries of bodies, as might remain from the morbid experiments and unhallowed amusements of the owner. During the excavation of this cellar the workmen had struck some exceedingly ancient masonry; undoubtedly connected with the old burying ground, yet far too deep to correspond with any known sepulchre therein. After a number of calculations West decided that it represented some secret chamber beneath the tomb of the Averills, where the last interment had been made in 1768. I was with him when he studied the nitrous, dripping walls laid bare by the spades and mattocks of the men, and was prepared for the gruesome thrill which would attend the uncovering of centuried grave-secrets; but for the first time West's new timidity conquered his natural curiosity, and he betrayed his degenerating fibre by ordering the masonry left intact and plastered over. Thus it remained till that final hellish night; part of the walls of the secret laboratory. I speak of West's decadence, but must add that it was a purely mental and intangible thing. Outwardly he was the same to the last — calm, cold, slight, and yellow-haired, with spectacled blue eyes and a general aspect of youth which years and fears seemed never to change. He seemed calm even when he thought of that clawed grave and looked over his shoulder; even when he thought of the carnivorous thing that gnawed and pawed at Sefton bars.

The end of Herbert West began one evening in our joint study when he was dividing his curious glance between the newspaper and me. A strange headline item had struck at him from the crumpled pages, and a nameless titan claw had seemed to reach down through sixteen years. Something fearsome and incredible had happened at Sefton Asylum fifty miles away, stunning the neighbourhood and baffling the police. In the small hours of the morning a body of silent men had entered the grounds, and their leader had aroused the attendants. He was a menacing military figure who talked without moving his lips and whose voice seemed almost ventriloquially connected with an immense black case he carried. His expressionless face was handsome to the point of radiant beauty, but had shocked the superintendent when the hall light fell on it — for it was a wax face with eyes of painted glass. Some nameless accident had befallen this man. A larger man guided his steps; a repellent hulk whose bluish face seemed half eaten away by some unknown malady. The speaker had asked for the custody of the cannibal monster committed from Arkham sixteen years before; and upon being refused, gave a signal which precipitated a shocking riot. The fiends had beaten, trampled, and bitten every attendant who did not flee; killing four and finally succeeding in the liberation of the monster. Those victims who could recall the event without hysteria swore that the creatures had acted less like men than like unthinkable automata guided by the wax-faced leader. By the time help could be summoned, every trace of the men and of their mad charge had vanished.

From the hour of reading this item until midnight, West sat almost paralysed. At midnight the doorbell rang, startling him fearfully. All the servants were asleep in the attic, so I answered the bell. As I have told the police, there was no wagon in the street, but only a group of strange-looking figures bearing a large square box which they deposited in the hallway after one of them had grunted in a highly unnatural voice, "Express — prepaid." They filed out of the house with a jerky tread, and as I watched them go I had an odd idea that they were turning toward the ancient cemetery on which the back of the house abutted. When I slammed the door after them West came downstairs and looked at the box. It was about two feet square, and bore West's correct name and present address. It also bore the inscription, "From Eric Moreland Clapham-Lee, St. Eloi, Flanders." Six years before, in Flanders, a shelled hospital had fallen upon the headless reanimated trunk of Dr. Clapham-Lee, and upon the detached head which — perhaps — had uttered articulate sounds.

West was not even excited now. His condition was more ghastly. Quickly he said, "It's the finish — but let's incinerate — this." We carried the thing down to the laboratory — listening. I do not remember many particulars — you can imagine my state of mind — but it is a vicious lie to say it was Herbert West's body which I put into the incinerator. We both inserted the whole unopened wooden box, closed the door, and started the electricity. Nor did any sound come from the box, after all.

It was West who first noticed the falling plaster on that part of the wall where the ancient tomb masonry had been covered up. I was going to run, but he stopped me. Then I saw a small black aperture, felt a ghoulish wind of ice, and smelled the charnel bowels of a putrescent earth. There was no sound, but just then the electric lights went out and I saw outlined against some phosphorescence of the nether world a horde of silent toiling things which only insanity — or worse — could create. Their outlines were human, semi-human, fractionally human, and not human at all — the horde was grotesquely heterogeneous. They were removing the stones quietly, one by one, from the centuried wall. And then, as the breach became large enough, they came out into the laboratory in single file; led by a talking thing with a beautiful head made of wax. A sort of mad-eyed monstrosity behind the leader seized on Herbert West. West did not resist or utter a sound. Then they all sprang at him and tore him to pieces before my eyes, bearing the fragments away into that subterranean vault of fabulous abominations. West's head was carried off by the wax-headed leader, who wore a Canadian officer's uniform. As it disappeared I saw that the blue eyes behind the spectacles were hideously blazing with their first touch of frantic, visible emotion.

Servants found me unconscious in the morning. West was gone. The incinerator contained only unidentifiable ashes.

Detectives have questioned me, but what can I say? The Sefton tragedy they will not connect with West; not that, nor the men with the box, whose existence they deny. I told them of the vault, and they pointed to the unbroken plaster wall and laughed. So I told them no more. They imply that I am either a madman or a murderer — probably I am mad. But I might not be mad if those accursed tomb-legions had not been so silent.

1922.

A Year of Grewsome Tales.

The start of 1922 saw young H.P. Lovecraft in the middle of one of the most productive phases of his life. He was in the middle of the series of commissioned stories later titled *Herbert West, Reanimator*, in *Home Brew* magazine. Although publisher George Houtain had become tardy with his payments for each episode, payment did eventually come, and when the assignment ended, he was commissioned to start another serial in *Home Brew*—which became *The Lurking Fear*. He contributed copiously to the journals and publications of his amateur-press friends. Perhaps inspired by the increasingly melodramatic excess of "Herbert West," Lovecraft seems at this time to have been seriously exploring the possibilities of building his literary *oeuvre* on a foundation of "grewsome" work, with campy horror overcooked to the point of self-parody.

Also, 1922 was the year in which the *Necronomicon* — the fictional book of black magic penned by the fictional mad Arab Abdul Alhazred, which may actually have better name recognition than Lovecraft himself— made its literary debut, in "The Hound."

In April of 1922, at the invitation of his not-quite-yet-girlfriend, Sonia Greene, Lovecraft came to New York City for the first time; Sonia and various other amateur-press cronies had assured him it was the place to come to level up his professional writing career.

He didn't come to stay, not at first; it was more of a scouting trip. He joined several other amateur-press writers there, along with a young weird-fiction newbie named Frank Belknap Long. Lovecraft and Hub Club colleague Samuel Loveman stayed in Greene's apartment while she demurely stayed in a neighbor's guest room, and they explored the big city for days.

In 1922, Lovecraft also discovered Clark Ashton Smith, the fellow weird-fictioneer and gifted poet from northern California, whose artwork would feature in later stories and who would later become, with Lovecraft and Robert E. Howard, one of the "Three Musketeers of *Weird Tales*."

Something else happened to Lovecraft in 1922, too. He had bestowed upon him what he claimed was his first kiss, from Sonia Greene, under rather astonishing (not to mention goofily romantic) circumstances. He had helped her with a story plot (for the story that would become "The Horror at Martin's Beach," published under Sonia's by-line in the November 1923 issue of *Weird Tales*). She stayed up all night hashing it out, and the next morning, upon reading her synopsis, Lovecraft was so enthusiastic about it that the exhausted, punchy Sonia forgot herself so much as to throw her arms around him and kiss him. Lovecraft, of course, turned red with fright and embarrassment and disconcertedness, but it was pretty clear that he liked it.

For her part, Sonia was thoroughly charmed. After Lovecraft returned to Providence, she confided in several close friends that she missed him greatly, and hinted of a hoped-for marriage proposal down the line.

Sweet Ermengarde; or, The Heart of a Country Girl.

BY PERCY SIMPLE

2,700-WORD SHORT STORY; DATE UNKNOWN.

This witty and delightful work of satire, titled with a semicolon in the grand old style of the 1800s dime novel, is unique in that no one seems to know just when it was actually written. Most scholars theorize it's from the 1919-1921 era; yet it reads a bit like it could be a spoof of one of the lightweight yarns of Fred Jackson, the author whose syrupy romance tales in The Argosy *had first brought Lovecraft out of his shell and into the world of amateur journalism when he launched into that spirited and poetic exchange of denunciations in the letters-to-the-editor section.*

But the "Jackson War," as biographer De Camp jocosely calls it, broke out in 1913 and raged on in the pages of The Argosy *for a year, or at most two; it seems unlikely that Lovecraft would have carried the torch of this lighthearted poetic feud for seven years before suddenly developing an urge, seemingly out of nowhere, to write a satire of Jackson's style.*

The references to bootlegging and the 18th Amendment in the story suggest it was written sometime after the Volstead Act passed in 1919; but bootlegging in Vermont was going on long before the Volstead Act in the state's several dry counties. In 1906 a Franklin County shopkeeper's son was jailed for three years for selling bootleg liquor laced with wood alcohol, killing three customers. This suggests another possibility — that it was written in 1913 or 1914 and then pulled out and hastily freshened up for publication in a friend's amateur-press journal in the early 1920s (although if it was published in one, we don't know the details; its first known appearance in print was in Beyond the Wall of Sleep, *an Arkham House collection published in 1943).*

It is, of course, equally likely that the target of Lovecraft's satire wasn't Jackson at all, but rather the whole genre of "plucky young lad makes good" stories popularized around the turn of the century by writers like Horatio Alger; in which case he could have written it at any time.

I.

A SIMPLE RUSTIC MAID.

Ermengarde Stubbs was the beauteous blonde daughter of Hiram Stubbs, a poor but honest farmer-bootlegger of Hogton, Vt. Her name was originally Ethyl Ermengarde, but her father persuaded her to drop the praenomen after the passage of the 18th Amendment, averring that it made him thirsty by reminding him of ethyl alcohol, C^2H^5OH. His own products contained mostly methyl or wood alcohol, CH^3OH. Ermengarde confessed to sixteen summers, and branded as mendacious all reports to the effect that she was thirty. She had large black eyes, a prominent Roman nose, light hair which was never dark at the roots except when the local drugstore was short on supplies, and a beautiful but inexpensive complexion. She was about five feet, 5.33 inches tall, weighed 115.47 pounds on her father's copy scales — also off them — and was adjudged most lovely by all the village swains who admired her father's farm and liked his liquid crops.

Ermengarde's hand was sought in matrimony by two ardent lovers. 'Squire Hardman, who had a mortgage on the old home, was very rich and elderly. He was dark and cruelly handsome, and always rode horseback and carried a riding-crop. Long had he sought the radiant Ermengarde, and now his ardour was fanned to fever heat by a secret known to him alone — for upon the humble acres of Farmer Stubbs he had discovered a vein of rich GOLD!!

"Aha!" said he, "I will win the maiden ere her parent knows of his unsuspected wealth, and join to my fortune a greater fortune still!" And so he began to call twice a week instead of once as before.

But alas for the sinister designs of a villain — 'Squire Hardman was not the only suitor for the fair one. Close by the village dwelt another, the handsome Jack Manly, whose curly yellow hair had won the sweet Ermengarde's affection when both were toddling youngsters at the village school. Jack had long been too bashful to declare his passion, but one day while strolling along a shady lane by the old mill with Ermengarde, he had found courage to utter that which was within his heart.

"O light of my life," said he, "my soul is so overburdened that I must speak! Ermengarde, my ideal *[he pronounced it i-deel!]*, life has become an empty thing without you. Beloved of my spirit, behold a suppliant kneeling in the dust before thee. Ermengarde — oh, Ermengarde, raise me to an heaven of joy and say that you will some day be mine! It is true that I am poor, but have I not youth and strength to fight my way to fame? This I can do only for you, dear Ethyl — pardon me, Ermengarde — my only, my most precious —"

But here he paused to wipe his eyes and mop his brow, and the fair one responded: "Jack — my angel — at last — I mean, this is so unexpected and quite unprecedented! I had never dreamed that you entertained sentiments of affection in connexion with one so lowly as Farmer Stubbs' child — for I am still but a child! Such is your natural nobility that I had feared—I mean thought—you would be blind to such slight charms as I possess, and that you would seek your fortune in the great city; there meeting and wedding one of those more comely damsels whose splendour we observe in fashion books.

"But, Jack, since it is really I whom you adore, let us waive all needless circumlocution. Jack—my darling—my heart has long been susceptible to your manly graces. I cherish an affection for thee—consider me thine own and be sure to buy the ring at Perkins' hardware store where they have such nice imitation diamonds in the window."

"Ermengarde, me love!"

"Jack—my precious!"

"My darling!"

"My own!"

"My Gawd!"

[Curtain]

II.

AND THE VILLAIN STILL PURSUED HER.

But these tender passages, sacred though was their fervour, did not pass unobserved by profane eyes; for crouched in the bushes and gritting his teeth was the dastardly 'Squire Hardman! When the lovers had finally strolled away he leapt out into the lane, viciously twirling his moustache and riding-crop, and kicking an unquestionably innocent cat who was also out strolling.

"Curses!" he cried—Hardman, not the cat—"I am foiled in my plot to get the farm and the girl! But Jack Manly shall never succeed! I am a man of power—and we shall see!"

Thereupon he repaired to the humble Stubbs' cottage, where he found the fond father in the still-cellar washing bottles under the supervision of the gentle wife and mother, Hannah Stubbs. Coming directly to the point, the villain spoke:

"Farmer Stubbs, I cherish a tender affection of long standing for your lovely offspring, Ethyl Ermengarde. I am consumed with love, and wish her hand in matrimony. Always a man of few words, I will not descend to euphemism: Give me the girl or I will foreclose the mortgage and take the old home!"

"But, Sir," pleaded the distracted Stubbs while his stricken spouse merely glowered, "I am sure the child's affections are elsewhere placed."

"She must be mine!" sternly snapped the sinister 'Squire. "I will make her love me—none shall resist my will! Either she becomes muh wife or the old homestead goes!"

And with a sneer and flick of his riding-crop 'Squire Hardman strode out into the night.

Scarce had he departed, when there entered by the back door the radiant lovers, eager to tell the senior Stubbses of their new-found happiness. Imagine the universal consternation which reigned when all was known! Tears flowed like white ale, till suddenly Jack remembered he was the hero and raised his head, declaiming in appropriately virile accents:

"Never shall the fair Ermengarde be offered up to this beast as a sacrifice while I live! I shall protect her—she is mine, mine, mine—and then some! Fear not, dear father- and mother-to-be—I will defend you all! You shall have the old home still—" adverb, not noun, although Jack was by no means out of sympathy with Stubbs' kind of farm produce—"and I shall lead to the altar the beauteous Ermengarde, loveliest of her sex! To perdition with the cruel 'Squire and his ill-gotten gold—the right shall always win, and a hero is always in the right! I will go to the great city and there make a fortune to save you all ere the mortgage fall due! Farewell, my love—I leave you now in tears, but I shall return to pay off the mortgage and claim you as my bride!"

"Jack, my protector!"

"Ermie, my sweet roll! Dearest!"

"Darling!—and don't forget that ring at Perkins'."

"Oh!"

"Ah!"

[Curtain]

III.

A DASTARDLY ACT.

But the resourceful 'Squire Hardman was not so easily to be foiled. Close by the village lay a disreputable settlement of unkempt shacks, populated by a shiftless scum who lived by thieving and other odd jobs. Here the devilish villain secured two accomplices—ill-favoured fellows who were very clearly no gentlemen. And in the night the evil three broke into the Stubbs cottage and abducted the fair Ermengarde, taking her to a wretched hovel in the settlement and placing her under the charge of Mother Maria, a hideous old hag. Farmer Stubbs was quite distracted, and would have advertised in the papers if the cost had been less than a cent a word for each insertion. Ermengarde was firm, and never wavered in her refusal to wed the villain.

"Aha, my proud beauty," quoth he, "I have ye in me power, and sooner or later I will break that will of thine! Meanwhile think of your poor old father and mother as turned out of hearth and home and wandering helpless through the meadows!"

"Oh, spare them, spare them!" said the maiden.

"Never . . . ha ha ha ha!" leered the brute.

And so the cruel days sped on, while all in ignorance young Jack Manly was seeking fame and fortune in the great city.

IV.

SUBTLE VILLAINY.

One day as 'Squire Hardman sat in the front parlour of his expensive and palatial home, indulging in his favourite pastime of gnashing his teeth and swishing his riding-crop, a great thought came to him; and he cursed aloud at the statue of Satan on the onyx mantelpiece.

"Fool that I am!" he cried. "Why did I ever waste all this trouble on the girl when I can get the farm by simply foreclosing? I never thought of that! I will let the girl go, take the farm, and be free to wed some fair city maid like the leading lady of that burlesque troupe which played last week at the Town Hall!"

And so he went down to the settlement, apologised to Ermengarde, let her go home, and went home himself to plot new crimes and invent new modes of villainy.

The days wore on, and the Stubbses grew very sad over the coming loss of their home, and still nobody seemed able to do anything about it. One day a party of hunters from the city chanced to stray over the old farm, and one of them found the gold!! Hiding his discovery from his companions, he feigned rattlesnake-bite and went to the Stubbs' cottage for aid of the usual kind. Ermengarde opened the door and saw him. He also saw her, and in that moment resolved to win her and the gold. "For my old mother's sake I must"— he cried loudly to himself. "No sacrifice is too great!"

V.

THE CITY CHAP.

Algernon Reginald Jones was a polished man of the world from the great city, and in his sophisticated hands our poor little Ermengarde was as a mere child. One could almost believe that sixteen-year-old stuff. Algy was a fast worker, but never crude. He could have taught Hardman a thing or two about finesse in sheiking. Thus only a week after his advent to the Stubbs family circle, where he lurked like the vile serpent that he was, he had persuaded the heroine to elope! It was in the night that she went, leaving a note for her parents, sniffing the familiar mash for the last time, and kissing the cat goodbye — touching stuff! On the train Algernon became sleepy and slumped down in his seat, allowing a paper to fall out of his pocket by accident. Ermengarde, taking advantage of her supposed position as a bride-elect, picked up the folded sheet and read its perfumed expanse — when lo! she almost fainted! It was a love letter from another woman!!

"Perfidious deceiver!" she whispered at the sleeping Algernon, "so this is all that your boasted fidelity amounts to! I am done with you for all eternity!"

So saying, she pushed him out the window and settled down for a much needed rest.

VI.

ALONE IN THE GREAT CITY.

When the noisy train pulled into the dark station at the city, poor helpless Ermengarde was all alone without the money to get back to Hogton. "Oh why," she sighed in innocent regret, "didn't I take his pocketbook before I pushed him out? Oh well, I should worry! He told me all about the city so I can easily earn enough to get home if not to pay off the mortgage!"

But alas for our little heroine — work is not easy for a greenhorn to secure, so for a week she was forced to sleep on park benches and obtain food from the bread-line. Once a wily and wicked person, perceiving her helplessness, offered her a position as dish-washer in a fashionable and depraved cabaret; but our heroine was true to her rustic ideals and refused to work in such a gilded and glittering palace of frivolity — especially since she was offered only $3.00 per week with meals but no board. She tried to look up Jack Manly, her one-time lover, but he was nowhere to be found. Perchance, too, he would not have known her; for in her poverty she had perforce become a brunette again, and Jack had not beheld her in that state since school days.

One day she found a neat but costly purse in the park; and after seeing that there was not much in it, took it to the rich lady whose card proclaimed her ownership. Delighted beyond words at the honesty of this forlorn waif, the aristocratic Mrs. Van Itty adopted Ermengarde to replace the little one who had been stolen from her so many years ago. "How like my precious Maude," she sighed, as she watched the fair brunette return to blondeness. And so several weeks passed, with the old folks at home tearing their hair and the wicked 'Squire Hardman chuckling devilishly.

VII.

HAPPY EVER AFTERWARD.

One day the wealthy heiress Ermengarde S. Van Itty hired a new second assistant chauffeur. Struck by something familiar in his face, she looked again and gasped. Lo! it was none other than the perfidious Algernon Reginald Jones, whom she had pushed from a car window on that fateful day! He had survived — this much was almost immediately evident. Also, he had wed the other woman, who had run away with the milkman and all the money in the house. Now wholly humbled, he asked forgiveness of our heroine, and confided to her the whole tale of the gold on her father's farm. Moved beyond words, she raised his salary a dollar a month and resolved to gratify at last that always unquenchable anxiety to relieve the worry of the old folks. So one bright day Ermengarde motored back to Hogton and arrived at the farm just as 'Squire Hardman was foreclosing the mortgage and ordering the old folks out.

"Stay, villain!" she cried, flashing a colossal roll of bills. "You are foiled at last! Here is your money — now go, and never darken our humble door again!"

Then followed a joyous reunion, whilst the 'Squire twisted his moustache and riding-crop in bafflement and dismay. But hark! What is this? Footsteps sound on the old gravel walk, and who should appear but our hero, Jack Manly — worn and seedy, but radiant of face. Seeking at once the downcast villain, he said:

"'Squire — lend me a ten-spot, will you? I have just come back from the city with my beauteous bride, the fair Bridget Goldstein, and need something to start things on the old farm." Then turning to the Stubbses, he apologised for his inability to pay off the mortgage as agreed.

"Don't mention it," said Ermengarde, "prosperity has come to us, and I will consider it sufficient payment if you will forget forever the foolish fancies of our childhood."

All this time Mrs. Van Itty had been sitting in the motor waiting for Ermengarde; but as she lazily eyed the sharp-faced Hannah Stubbs a vague memory started from the back of her brain. Then it all came to her, and she shrieked accusingly at the agrestic matron.

"You — you — Hannah Smith — I know you now! Twenty-eight years ago you were my baby Maude's nurse and stole her from the cradle!! Where, oh, where is my child?" Then a thought came as the lightning in a murky sky. "Ermengarde — you say she is your daughter . . . . She is mine! Fate has restored to me my old chee-ild — my tiny Maudie! Ermengarde — Maude — come to your mother's loving arms!!!"

But Ermengarde was doing some tall thinking. How could she get away with the sixteen-year-old stuff if she had been stolen twenty-eight years ago? And if she was not Stubbs' daughter the gold would never be hers. Mrs. Van Itty was rich, but 'Squire Hardman was richer. So, approaching the dejected villain, she inflicted upon him the last terrible punishment.

"'Squire, dear," she murmured, "I have reconsidered all. I love you and your naïve strength. Marry me at once or I will have you prosecuted for that kidnapping last year. Foreclose your mortgage and enjoy with me the gold your cleverness discovered. Come, dear!"

And the poor dub did.

[The End]

Hypnos.

2,800-WORD SHORT STORY; 1922.

This short story, which Lovecraft came to dislike in later years, is a very interesting piece of storytelling. It is told from the point of view of an unreliable narrator, and speculations about the narrator's mental condition form a significant part of the subtext: Is this a dream? Reality? A drug-induced madness?

"Hypnos" was written in March 1922. It was first published in the May 1923 issue of National Amateur.

> *Apropos of sleep, that sinister adventure of all our nights, we may say that men go to bed daily with an audacity that would be incomprehensible if we did not know that it is the result of ignorance of the danger.*
>
> — Baudelaire

May the merciful gods, if indeed there be such, guard those hours when no power of the will, or drug that the cunning of man devises, can keep me from the chasm of sleep. Death is merciful, for there is no return therefrom, but with him who has come back out of the nethermost chambers of night, haggard and knowing, peace rests nevermore. Fool that I was to plunge with such unsanctioned frensy into mysteries no man was meant to penetrate; fool or god that he was — my only friend, who led me and went before me, and who in the end passed into terrors which may yet be mine!

We met, I recall, in a railway station, where he was the center of a crowd of the vulgarly curious. He was unconscious, having fallen in a kind of convulsion which imparted to his slight black-clad body a strange rigidity. I think he was then approaching forty years of age, for there were deep lines in the face, wan and hollow-cheeked, but oval and actually beautiful; and touches of gray in the thick, waving hair and small full beard which had once been of the deepest raven black. His brow was white as the marble of Pentelicus, and of a height and breadth almost god-like.

I said to myself, with all the ardor of a sculptor, that this man was a faun's statue out of antique Hellas, dug from a temple's ruins and brought somehow to life in our stifling age only to feel the chill and pressure of devastating years. And when he opened his immense, sunken, and wildly luminous black eyes I knew he would be thenceforth my only friend — the only friend of one who had never possessed a friend before — for I saw that such eyes must have looked fully upon the grandeur and the terror of realms beyond normal consciousness and reality; realms which I had cherished in fancy, but vainly sought. So as I drove the crowd away I told him he must come home with me and be my teacher and leader in unfathomed mysteries, and he assented without speaking a word. Afterward I found that his voice was music — the music of deep viols and of crystalline spheres. We talked often in the night, and in the day, when I chiseled busts of him and carved miniature heads in ivory to immortalize his different expressions.

Weird Tales, May 1924

Of our studies it is impossible to speak, since they held so slight a connection with anything of the world as living men conceive it. They were of that vaster and more appalling universe of dim entity and consciousness which lies deeper than matter, time, and space, and whose existence we suspect only in certain forms of sleep — those rare dreams beyond dreams which come never to common men, and but once or twice in the lifetime of imaginative men. The cosmos of our waking knowledge, born from such an universe as a bubble is born from the pipe of a jester, touches it only as such a bubble may touch its sardonic source when sucked back by the jester's whim. Men of learning suspect it little and ignore it mostly. Wise men have interpreted dreams, and the gods have laughed. One man with Oriental eyes has said that all time and space are relative, and men have laughed. But even that man with Oriental eyes has done no more than suspect. I had wished and tried to do more than suspect, and my friend had tried and partly succeeded. Then we both tried together, and with exotic drugs courted terrible and forbidden dreams in the tower studio chamber of the old manor-house in hoary Kent.

Among the agonies of these after days is that chief of torments — inarticulateness. What I learned and saw in those hours of impious exploration can never be told — for want of symbols or suggestions in any language. I say this because from first to last our discoveries partook only of the nature of sensations; sensations correlated with no impression which the nervous system of normal humanity is capable of receiving. They were sensations, yet within them lay unbelievable elements of time and space — things which at bottom possess no distinct and definite existence. Human utterance can best convey the general character of our experiences by calling them plungings or soarings; for in every period of revelation some part of our minds broke boldly away from all that is real and present, rushing aerially along shocking, unlighted, and fear-haunted abysses, and occasionally tearing through certain well-marked and typical obstacles describable only as viscous, uncouth clouds of vapors.

In these black and bodiless flights we were sometimes alone and sometimes together. When we were together, my friend was always far ahead; I could comprehend his presence despite the absence of form by a species of pictorial memory whereby his face appeared to me, golden from a strange light and frightful with its weird beauty, its anomalously youthful cheeks, its burning eyes, its Olympian brow, and its shadowing hair and growth of beard.

Of the progress of time we kept no record, for time had become to us the merest illusion. I know only that there must have been something very singular involved, since we came at length to marvel why we did not grow old. Our discourse was unholy, and always hideously ambitious — no god or demon could have aspired to discoveries and conquest like those which we planned in whispers. I shiver as I speak of them, and dare not be explicit; though I will say that my friend once wrote on paper a wish which he dared not utter with his tongue, and which made me burn the paper and look affrightedly out of the window at the spangled night sky. I will hint — only hint — that he had designs which involved the rulership of the visible universe and more; designs whereby the earth and the stars would move at his command, and the destinies of all living things be his. I affirm — I swear — that I had no share in these extreme aspirations. Anything my friend may have said or written to the contrary must be erroneous, for I am no man of strength to risk the unmentionable spheres by which alone one might achieve success.

There was a night when winds from unknown spaces whirled us irresistibly into limitless vacum beyond all thought and entity. Perceptions of the most maddeningly untransmissible sort thronged upon us; perceptions of infinity which at the time convulsed us with joy, yet which are now partly lost to my memory and partly incapable of presentation to others. Viscous obstacles were clawed through in rapid succession, and at length I felt that we had been borne to realms of greater remoteness than any we had previously known.

My friend was vastly in advance as we plunged into this awesome ocean of virgin aether, and I could see the sinister exultation on his floating, luminous, too-youthful memory-face. Suddenly that face became dim and quickly disappeared, and in a brief space I found myself projected against an obstacle which I could not penetrate. It was like the others, yet incalculably denser; a sticky clammy mass, if such terms can be applied to analogous qualities in a non-material sphere.

I had, I felt, been halted by a barrier which my friend and leader had successfully passed. Struggling anew, I came to the end of the drug-dream and opened my physical eyes to the tower studio in whose opposite corner reclined the pallid and still unconscious form of my fellow dreamer, weirdly haggard and wildly beautiful as the moon shed gold-green light on his marble features.

Then, after a short interval, the form in the corner stirred; and may pitying heaven keep from my sight and sound another thing like that which took place before me. I cannot tell you how he shrieked, or what vistas of unvisitable hells gleamed for a second in black eyes crazed with fright. I can only say that I fainted, and did not stir till he himself recovered and shook me in his frensy for someone to keep away the horror and desolation.

That was the end of our voluntary searchings in the caverns of dream. Awed, shaken, and portentous, my friend who had been beyond the barrier warned me that we must never venture within those realms again. What he had seen, he dared not tell me; but he said from his wisdom that we must sleep as little as possible, even if drugs were necessary to keep us awake. That he was right, I soon learned from the unutterable fear which engulfed me whenever consciousness lapsed.

After each short and inevitable sleep I seemed older, whilst my friend aged with a rapidity almost shocking. It is hideous to see wrinkles form and hair whiten almost before one's eyes. Our mode of life was now totally altered. Heretofore a recluse so far as I know — his true name and origin never having passed his lips — my friend now became frantic in his fear of solitude. At night he would not be alone, nor would the company of a few persons calm him. His sole relief was obtained in revelry of the most general and boisterous sort; so that few assemblies of the young and gay were unknown to us.

Our appearance and age seemed to excite in most cases a ridicule which I keenly resented, but which my friend considered a lesser evil than solitude. Especially was he afraid to be out of doors alone when the stars were shining, and if forced to this condition he would often glance furtively at the sky as if hunted by some monstrous thing therein. He did not always glance at the same place in the sky — it seemed to be a different place at different times. On spring evenings it would be low in the northeast. In the summer it would be nearly overhead. In the autumn it would be in the northwest. In winter it would be in the east, but mostly if in the small hours of morning.

Midwinter evenings seemed least dreadful to him. Only after two years did I connect this fear with anything in particular; but then I began to see that he must be looking at a special spot on the celestial vault whose position at different times corresponded to the direction of his glance — a spot roughly marked by the constellation Corona Borealis.

We now had a studio in London, never separating, but never discussing the days when we had sought to plumb the mysteries of the unreal world. We were aged and weak from our drugs, dissipations, and nervous overstrain, and the thinning hair and beard of my friend had become snow-white. Our freedom from long sleep was surprising, for seldom did we succumb more than an hour or two at a time to the shadow which had now grown so frightful a menace.

Then came one January of fog and rain, when money ran

low and drugs were hard to buy. My statues and ivory heads were all sold, and I had no means to purchase new materials, or energy to fashion them even had I possessed them. We suffered terribly, and on a certain night my friend sank into a deep-breathing sleep from which I could not awaken him. I can recall the scene now — the desolate, pitch-black garret studio under the eaves with the rain beating down; the ticking of our lone clock; the fancied ticking of our watches as they rested on the dressing-table; the creaking of some swaying shutter in a remote part of the house; certain distant city noises muffled by fog and space; and, worst of all, the deep, steady, sinister breathing of my friend on the couch — a rhythmical breathing which seemed to measure moments of supernal fear and agony for his spirit as it wandered in spheres forbidden, unimagined, and hideously remote.

The tension of my vigil became oppressive, and a wild train of trivial impressions and associations thronged through my almost unhinged mind. I heard a clock strike somewhere — not ours, for that was not a striking clock — and my morbid fancy found in this a new starting-point for idle wanderings. Clock s — time — space — infinity — and then my fancy reverted to the locale as I reflected that even now, beyond the roof and the fog and the rain and the atmosphere, Corona Borealis was rising in the northeast. Corona Borealis, which my friend had appeared to dread, and whose scintillant semicircle of stars must even now be glowing unseen through the measureless abysses of aether. All at once my feverishly sensitive ears seemed to detect a new and wholly distinct component in the soft medley of drug-magnified sounds — a low and damnably insistent whine from very far away; droning, clamoring, mocking, calling, from the northeast.

But it was not that distant whine which robbed me of my faculties and set upon my soul such a seal of fright as may never in life be removed; not that which drew the shrieks and excited the convulsions which caused lodgers and police to break down the door. It was not what I heard, but what I saw; for in that dark, locked, shuttered, and curtained room there appeared from the black northeast corner a shaft of horrible red-gold light — a shaft which bore with it no glow to disperse the darkness, but which streamed only upon the recumbent head of the troubled sleeper, bringing out in hideous duplication the luminous and strangely youthful memory-face as I had known it in dreams of abysmal space and unshackled time, when my friend had pushed behind the barrier to those secret, innermost and forbidden caverns of nightmare.

And as I looked, I beheld the head rise, the black, liquid, and deep-sunken eyes open in terror, and the thin, shadowed lips part as if for a scream too frightful to be uttered. There dwelt in that ghastly and flexible face, as it shone bodiless, luminous, and rejuvenated in the blackness, more of stark, teeming, brain-shattering fear than all the rest of heaven and earth has ever revealed to me.

No word was spoken amidst the distant sound that grew nearer and nearer, but as I followed the memory-face's mad stare along that cursed shaft of light to its source, the source whence also the whining came, I, too, saw for an instant what it saw, and fell with ringing ears in that fit of shrieking epilepsy which brought the lodgers and the police. Never could I tell, try as I might, what it actually was that I saw; nor could the still face tell, for although it must have seen more than I did, it will never speak again. But always I shall guard against the mocking and insatiate Hypnos, lord of sleep, against the night sky, and against the mad ambitions of knowledge and philosophy.

Just what happened is unknown, for not only was my own mind unseated by the strange and hideous thing, but others were tainted with a forgetfulness which can mean nothing if not madness. They have said, I know not for what reason, that I never had a friend; but that art, philosophy, and insanity had filled all my tragic life. The lodgers and police on that night soothed me, and the doctor administered something to quiet me, nor did anyone see what a nightmare event had taken place. My stricken friend moved them to no pity, but what they found on the couch in the studio made them give me a praise which sickened me, and now a fame which I spurn in despair as I sit for hours, bald, gray-bearded, shriveled, palsied, drug-crazed, and broken, adoring and praying to the object they found.

For they deny that I sold the last of my statuary, and point with ecstasy at the thing which the shining shaft of light left cold, petrified, and unvocal. It is all that remains of my friend; the friend who led me on to madness and wreckage; a godlike head of such marble as only old Hellas could yield, young with the youth that is outside time, and with beauteous bearded face, curved, smiling lips, Olympian brow, and dense locks waving and poppy-crowned. They say that that haunting memory-face is modeled from my own, as it was at twenty-five; but upon the marble base is carven a single name in the letters of Attica — HYPNOS.

Azathoth.

500-WORD FRAGMENT;
1922.

"Azathoth" was originally intended to be a novel, a novel in the dreamy spirit of William Beckford's Vathek, *which Lovecraft had read and been deeply impressed by in 1921.*

Lovecraft's description of his intentions with this novel presage The Dream-Quest of Unknown Kadath — *he planned to write it as a continuous narrative, without chapter divisions; to create (or explore) in it a whole mythology, a la Lord Dunsany's Pegaña; and to try to recapture in its creation the creative spirit of his young childhood when, under the tutelage of Grandfather Whipple, he had stormed the ramparts of imagination and conquered narrative realms with the innocent forthrightness of youth.*

It must not have worked the way he'd hoped it would, for only 500 words or so of "Azathoth" were penned before Lovecraft turned his attention to other things.

Lovecraft wrote this fragment in June of 1922. It was published just after Lovecraft's death, in the 1938 issue of Robert H. Barlow's amateur journal, Leaves.

When age fell upon the world, and wonder went out of the minds of men; when grey cities reared to smoky skies tall towers grim and ugly, in whose shadow none might dream of the sun or of spring's flowering meads; when learning stripped earth of her mantle of beauty, and poets sang no more save of twisted phantoms seen with bleared and inward-looking eyes; when these things had come to pass, and childish hopes had gone away forever, there was a man who travelled out of life on a quest into the spaces whither the world's dreams had fled.

Of the name and abode of this man but little is written, for they were of the waking world only; yet it is said that both were obscure. It is enough to know that he dwelt in a city of high walls where sterile twilight reigned, and that he toiled all day among shadow and turmoil, coming home at evening to a room whose one window opened not on the fields and groves but on a dim court where other windows stared in dull despair. From that casement one might see only walls and windows, except sometimes when one leaned far out and peered aloft at the small stars that passed. And because mere walls and windows must soon drive to madness a man who dreams and reads much, the dweller in that room used night after night to lean out and peer aloft to glimpse some fragment of things beyond the waking world and the greyness of tall cities. After years he began to call the slow-sailing stars by name, and to follow them in fancy when they glided regretfully out of sight; till at length his vision opened to many secret vistas whose existence no common eye suspects. And one night a mighty gulf was bridged, and the dream-haunted skies swelled down to the lonely watcher's window to merge with the close air of his room and make him a part of their fabulous wonder.

There came to that room wild streams of violet midnight glittering with dust of gold; vortices of dust and fire, swirling out of the ultimate spaces and heavy with perfumes from beyond the worlds. Opiate oceans poured there, litten by suns that the eye may never behold and having in their whirlpools strange dolphins and sea-nymphs of unrememberable deeps. Noiseless infinity eddied around the dreamer and wafted him away without even touching the body that leaned stiffly from the lonely window; and for days not counted in men's calendars the tides of far spheres bare him gently to join the dreams for which he longed; the dreams that men have lost. And in the course of many cycles they tenderly left him sleeping on a green sunrise shore, a green shore fragrant with lotos-blossoms and starred by red camalotes.

What the Moon Brings.

700-WORD PROSE-POEM; 1922.

Prose-poetry seems unusually well suited to transcribing and communicating dreams, and it is that purpose to which Lovecraft puts the form in this brief and rather chilling piece. Of particular note is the way in which, toward the end, he makes corpse-worms feel like a salutary and wholesome alternative to another thing—which, of course, goes unnamed.

"What the Moon Brings" was written on June 5, 1922, and published for the first time in the May 1923 issue of The National Amateur.

I hate the moon—I am afraid of it—for when it shines on certain scenes familiar and loved it sometimes makes them unfamiliar and hideous.

It was in the spectral summer when the moon shone down on the old garden where I wandered; the spectral summer of narcotic flowers and humid seas of foliage that bring wild and many-coloured dreams. And as I walked by the shallow crystal stream I saw unwonted ripples tipped with yellow light, as if those placid waters were drawn on in resistless currents to strange oceans that are not in the world. Silent and sparkling, bright and baleful, those moon-cursed waters hurried I knew not whither; whilst from the embowered banks white lotos-blossoms fluttered one by one in the opiate night-wind and dropped despairingly into the stream, swirling away horribly under the arched, carven bridge, and staring back with the sinister resignation of calm, dead faces.

And as I ran along the shore, crushing sleeping flowers with heedless feet and maddened ever by the fear of unknown things and the lure of the dead faces, I saw that the garden had no end under that moon; for where by day the walls were, there stretched now only new vistas of trees and paths, flowers and shrubs, stone idols and pagodas, and bendings of the yellow-litten stream past grassy banks and under grotesque bridges of marble. And the lips of the dead lotos-faces whispered sadly, and bade me follow, nor did I cease my steps till the stream became a river, and joined amidst marshes of swaying reeds and beaches of gleaming sand the shore of a vast and nameless sea.

Upon that sea the hateful moon shone, and over its unvocal waves weird perfumes breeded. And as I saw therein the lotos-faces vanish, I longed for nets that I might capture them and learn from them the secrets which the moon had brought upon the night. But when that moon went over to the west and the still tide ebbed from the sullen shore, I saw in that light old spires that the waves almost uncovered, and white columns gay with festoons of green seaweed. And knowing that to this sunken place all the dead had come, I trembled and did not wish again to speak with the lotos-faces.

Yet when I saw afar out in the sea a black condor descend from the sky to seek rest on a vast reef, I would fain have questioned him, and asked him of those whom I had known when they were alive. This I would have asked him had he not been so far away, but he was very far, and could not be seen at all when he drew nigh that gigantic reef.

So I watched the tide go out under that sinking moon, and saw gleaming the spires, the towers, and the roofs of that dead, dripping city. And as I watched, my nostrils tried to close against the perfume-conquering stench of the world's dead; for truly, in this unplaced and forgotten spot had all the flesh of the churchyards gathered for puffy sea-worms to gnaw and glut upon.

Over these horrors the evil moon now hung very low, but the puffy worms of the sea need no moon to feed by. And as I watched the ripples that told of the writhing of worms beneath, I felt a new chill from afar out whither the condor had flown, as if my flesh had caught a horror before my eyes had seen it.

Nor had my flesh trembled without cause, for when I raised my eyes I saw that the waters had ebbed very low, shewing much of the vast reef whose rim I had seen before. And when I saw that the reef was but the black basalt crown of a shocking eikon whose monstrous forehead now shone in the dim moonlight and whose vile hooves must paw the hellish ooze miles below, I shrieked and shrieked lest the hidden face rise above the waters, and lest the hidden eyes look at me after the slinking away of that leering and treacherous yellow moon.

And to escape this relentless thing I plunged gladly and unhesitantly into the stinking shallows where amidst weedy walls and sunken streets fat sea-worms feast upon the world's dead.

Four O'Clock.

BY SONIA HAFT GREENE AND H.P. LOVECRAFT

1,800-WORD SHORT STORY; 1922.

It is hard to know what to make of "Four O'Clock," the first weird-fiction story written by Sonia Greene and (allegedly) revised by H.P. Lovecraft. Actually, "revised" might be too strong a word; Greene later wrote that he only suggested a few minor wording changes to it, essentially providing a copy-edit.

Most critics, approaching it, seem to have sort of assumed that she wrote it in an attempt to ape the weird fiction writing for which Lovecraft was becoming so well known, and they point to its many ostensible flaws as evidence of her lack of talent. The implication is that, seeking to connect with Lovecraft, she crafted an overcooked, ponderous ghost-story narrative and showed it to him, and he gave her a little feedback as a less awkward alternative to coming right out and telling her how bad it was.

It's an explanation. It fits the available data. And it fits in with certain assumptions that are sometimes made about Greene's talents and abilities. But on closer scrutiny, it's so very hard to read "Four O'Clock" without bursting out laughing at certain phrases and word-pictures — starting right in the first paragraph — that one has to at least consider the possibility that it was written as a light-hearted spoof. Moreover, it was written in late June or early July, shortly after the deliciously overcooked and campy Herbert West, Reanimator *started to appear, serialized, in the humor magazine* Home Brew, *and less than a month after Lovecraft wrote the sixth and final episode, "The Tomb-Legion."*

We don't really know, of course. But it's at least a strong possibility that "Four O'Clock" was written with the goal of producing laughs rather than shudders.

It remained unpublished until 1949, when it appeared in Something About Cats and Other Pieces, *the collection published by August Derleth's Arkham House.*

ABOUT SONIA HAFT GREENE (1883-1972).

Sonia Haft Greene was a tall, charismatic woman with striking dark eyes, possessed of considerable executive ability and referred to by more than one Lovecraft associate as "Junoesque." A native of Ukraine, she came to America when she was nine years old. An early marriage, contracted when she was 15, was apparently an unhappy one; but in 1916 her husband died, leaving her a widow.

Greene took some courses at Columbia University to enhance her employment prospects, and parlayed them into a position as a millinery specialist for a chic New York retailer, pulling down $10,000 a year — the equivalent of about $125,000 a year in modern currency. (Hats, in the 1920s, were a very important part of every American's everyday wardrobe.)

Then, in the early 1920s, she got involved in the amateur press community, and through it, in July 1921, she met H.P. Lovecraft.

Greene was taken with Lovecraft from the start — she recalled having not been much impressed with his physical appearance, but she was very attracted by his wit and intellect, right from the start.

Sonia Haft Greene would go on to marry H.P. Lovecraft three years after they first met. During this courtship, Lovecraft was largely a cordial but passive participant, and Greene had to take the initiative — which, after a suitable interval of waiting for him to make a move, she did, coming to Providence to visit him for a weekend. She also spent a great deal of time and money in the amateur-press community, contributing $50 (equivalent to $600 today) to the United Amateur Press Association organ fund and publishing a remarkably professional-looking journal titled The Rainbow.

It was during those years of courtship that Greene wrote the two weird-fiction stories on which she collaborated with her future husband. And if the quality of these stories is seen to be below Lovecraft's usual level, even for collaborations, it must be remembered that for Greene, they were probably at least partly intended as a pretext for spending time with Lovecraft, and flirting with him. In other words, her mind wasn't on the job — and, if she was doing it right, neither was his.

About two in the morning I knew it was coming. The great black silences of night's depth told me, and a monstrous cricket, chirping with a persistence too hideous to be unmeaning, made it certain. It is to be at four o'clock — at four in the dusk before dawn, just as he said it would be. I had not fully believed it previously, because the prophecies of vindictive madmen are seldom to be taken with seriousness. Besides, I was not justly to be blamed for what had befallen him at four o'clock on that other morning; that terrible morning whose memory will never leave me. And when, at length, he had died and was buried in the ancient cemetery just across the road from my east windows, I was certain that his curse could not harm me. Had I not seen his lifeless clay securely pinned down by huge shovelfuls of mould? Might I not feel assured that his crumbling bones would be powerless to bring me the doom at a day and an hour so precisely stated? Such, indeed, had been my thoughts until this shocking night itself; this night of incredible chaos, of shattered certainties, and of nameless portents.

I had retired early, hoping fatuously to snatch a few hours of sleep despite the prophecy which haunted me. Now that the time was so close at hand, I found it harder and harder to dismiss the vague fears which had always lain beneath my conscious thoughts. As the cooling sheets soothed my fevered body, I could find nothing to soothe my still more fevered mind; but lay tossing and uneasily awake, trying first one position and then another in a desperate effort to banish with slumber that one damnably insistent notion — *that it is to occur at four o'clock.*

Was this frightful unrest due to my surroundings; to the fateful locality in which I was sojourning after so many years? Why, I now asked myself bitterly, had I permitted circumstance to place me on this night of all nights, in that well-remembered house and that well-remembered room whose east windows overlook the lonely road and the ancient country cemetery beyond? In my mind's eye every detail of that unpretentious necropolis rose before me — its white fence, its ghost-like granite shafts, and the hovering auras of those on whom the worms fed. Finally the force of the conception led my vision to depths more remote and more forbidden, and I saw under the neglected grass the silent shapes of the things from which the auras came — the calm sleepers, the rotting things, the things which had twisted frantically in their coffins before sleep came, and the peaceful bones in every stage of disintegration from the complete and coherent skeleton to the huddled handful of dust. Most of all I envied the dust.

Then new terror came as my fancy encountered his grave. Into that sepulchre I dared not let my thought stray, and I should have screamed had not something forestalled the malign power that pulled my mental sight. That something was a sudden gust of wind, sprung from nowhere amidst the calm night, which unfastened the shutter of the nearest window, throwing it back with a shivery slam and uncovering to my actual waking glance the antique cemetery itself, brooding spectrally beneath an early morning moon.

I speak of this gust as something merciful, yet know now that it was only transiently and mockingly so. For no sooner had my eyes compassed the moonlight scene than I became aware of a fresh omen, this time too unmistakable to be classed as an empty phantasm, which arose from among the gleaming tombs across the road. Having glanced with instinctive apprehension toward the spot where *he* lay mouldering — a spot cut off from my gaze by the window-frame — I perceived with trepidation the approach of an indescribable something which flowed menacingly from that very direction; a vague, vapourous, formless mass of greyish-white substance or spirit, dull and tenuous as yet, but every moment increasing in awesome and cataclysmic potentiality. Try as I might to dismiss it as a natural meteorological phenomenon, its fearsomely portentous and *deliberate* character grew upon me amidst new thrills of horror and apprehension; so that I was scarcely unprepared for the definitely purposeful and malevolent culmination which soon occurred.

That culmination, bringing with it a hideous symbolic foreshadowing of the end, was equally simple and threatening. The vapour each moment thickened and piled up, assuming at last a half tangible aspect; while the surface toward me gradually became circular in outline, and markedly concave; as it slowly ceased its advance and stood spectrally at the end of the road. And as it stood there, faintly quivering in the damp night air under that unwholesome moon, I saw that its aspect was that of the pallid and gigantic dial of a distorted clock.

Hideous events now followed in demoniac succession. There took shape in the lower right-hand part of the vapourous dial a black and formidable creature, shapeless and only half seen, yet having four prominent claws which reached out greedily at me — claws redolent of noxious fatality in their very contour and location; since they formed too plainly the dreaded outlines, and filled too unmistakably the exact position, of the numeral IV on the quivering dial of doom.

Presently the monstrosity stepped or wriggled out of the concave surface of the dial, and began to approach me by some unexplained kind of locomotion. The four talons, long, thin, and straight, were now seen to be tipped by disgusting, thread-like tentacles, each with a vile intelligence of its own, which groped about incessantly, slowly at first, but gradually increasing in velocity until I was nearly driven mad by the sheer dizziness of their motion. And as a crowning horror I began to hear all the subtle and cryptical noises that pierced the intensified night silence; a thousand-fold magnified, and in one voice reminding me of the abhorred hour of four. In vain I tried to pull up the coverlet to shut them out; in vain I tried to drown them with my screams. I was mute and paralyzed, yet agonizingly aware of every unnatural sight and sound in that devastating, moon-cursed stillness. Once I managed to get my head beneath the covers — once when the cricket's shrieking of that hideous phrase, *four-o'clock*, seemed about to shatter my brain — but that only aggravated the terror, making the roars of that detestable creature strike me like the blows of a titanic sledgehammer.

And now, as I withdrew my tortured head from its fruitless protection, I found augmented diabolism to harass my eyes. Upon the newly painted wall of my apartment, as if called forth by the tentacled monster from the tomb, there danced mockingly before me a myriad company of beings, black, grey, and white, such as only the fancy of the god-stricken might visualize. Some were of infinitesimal smallness; others covered vast areas. In minor details each had a grotesque and horrible individuality, in general outlines they all conformed to the same nightmare pattern despite their vastly varied size. Again I tried to shut out the abnormalities of the night, but vainly as before. The dancing things on the wall waxed and waned in magnitude, approaching and receding as they trod their morbid and menacing measure. And the aspect of each was that of some demon clock-face with one sinister hour always figured thereon — the dreaded, the doom-delivering hour of *four*.

Baffled in every attempt to shake off the circling and relentless delirium, I glanced once more toward the unshuttered window and beheld again the monster which had come from the grave. Horrible it had been before; indescribable it had now become. The creature, formerly of indeterminate substance, was now formed of red and malignant fire; and waved repulsively its four tentacled claws — unspeakable tongues of living flame. It stared and stared at me out of the blackness; sneeringly, mockingly; now advancing, now retiring. Then, in the tenebrous silence, those four writhing talons of fire beckoned invitingly to their demoniacally dancing counterparts on the walls, and seemed to beat time rhythmically to the shocking saraband till the world was one ghoulishly gyrating vortex of leaping, prancing, gliding, leering, taunting, threatening four o'clocks.

Somewhere, beginning afar off and advancing slowly over the sphinx-like sea and the febrile marshes, I heard the early morning wind come soughing; faintly at first, then louder and louder until its unceasing burden flowed as a deluge of whirring, buzzing cacophony bringing always the hideous threat, "four o'clock, *four o'clock*, FOUR O'CLOCK." Monotonously it grew from a whimper to a deafening roar, as of a giant cataract, but finally reached a climax and began to subside. As it receded into the distance it left upon my sensitive ears such a vibration as is left by the passing of a swift and ponderous railway train; this, and a stark dread whose intensity gave it something of the tranquillity of resignation.

The end is near. All sound and vision have become one vast chaotic maelstrom of lethal, clamorous menace, wherein are fused all the ghastly and unhallowed four o'clocks which have existed since immemorial time began, and all which will exist in eternities to come. The flaming monster is advancing closely now, its charnel tentacles brushing my face and its talons curving hungrily as they grope toward my throat. At last I can see its face through the churning and phosphorescent vapours of the graveyard air, and with devastating pangs I realize that it is in essence an awful, colossal, gargoyle-like caricature of his face — the face of him from whose uneasy grave it has issued. Now I know that my doom is indeed sealed; that the wild threats of the madman were in truth the demon maledictions of a potent fiend, and that my innocence will prove no protection against the malign volition which craves a causeless vengeance. He is determined to pay me with interest for what he suffered at that spectral hour; determined to drag me out of the world into realms which only the mad and the devil-ridden know.

And as amidst the seething of hell's flames and the tumult of the damned those fiery claws point murderously at my throat, I hear upon the mantel the faint whirring sound of a timepiece; the whirring which tells me that it is about to strike the hour whose name now flows incessantly from the death-like and cavernous throat of the rattling, jeering, croaking grave-monster before me — the accursed, the infernal hour of *four o'clock*.

The Horror at Martin's Beach.

BY SONIA HAFT GREENE AND H.P. LOVECRAFT

2,400-WORD SHORT STORY; 1922.

This is the story Sonia Haft Greene is most known for, on which she collaborated considerably with H.P. Lovecraft.

"The Horror at Martin's Beach" includes some fine writing, although it suffers from a significant plot flaw that makes it difficult for a reader to fully suspend disbelief.

The story is most interesting for its role in the courtship of Lovecraft and the woman who was soon to marry him. The story, as Green tells it, is that she and Lovecraft had been up all night brainstorming the story, and when he came up with a perfect phrase for it she was so excited that she threw her arms around him and kissed him for the first time.

Like "Four O'Clock," "The Horror at Martin's Beach" was written in mid-1922 shortly after Lovecraft completed the sixth and final installment of Herbert West, Reanimator. *It was first published in the November 1923 issue of* Weird Tales.

I have never heard an even approximately adequate explanation of the horror at Martin's Beach. Despite the large number of witnesses, no two accounts agree; and the testimony taken by local authorities contains the most amazing discrepancies.

Perhaps this haziness is natural in view of the unheard-of character of the horror itself, the almost paralytic terror of all who saw it, and the efforts made by the fashionable Wavecrest Inn to hush it up after the publicity created by Prof. Ahon's article, "Are Hypnotic Powers Confined to Recognized Humanity?"

Against all these obstacles I am striving to present a coherent version; for I beheld the hideous occurrence, and believe it should be known in view of the appalling possibilities it suggests. Martin's Beach is once more popular as a watering-place, but I shudder when I think of it. Indeed, I cannot look at the ocean at all now without shuddering.

Fate is not always without a sense of drama and climax, hence the terrible happening of August 8, 1922, swiftly followed a period of minor and agreeably wonder-fraught excitement at Martin's Beach. On May 17 the crew of the fishing smack *Alma* of Gloucester, under Capt. James P. Orne, killed, after a battle of nearly forty hours, a marine monster whose size and aspect produced the greatest possible stir in scientific circles and caused certain Boston naturalists to take every precaution for its taxidermic preservation.

The object was some fifty feet in length, of roughly cylindrical shape, and about ten feet in diameter. It was unmistakably a gilled fish in its major affiliations; but with certain curious modifications such as rudimentary forelegs and six-toed feet in place of pectoral fins, which prompted the widest speculation. Its extraordinary mouth, its thick and scaly hide, and its single, deep-set eye were wonders scarcely less remarkable than its colossal dimensions; and when the naturalists pronounced it an infant organism, which could not have been hatched more than a few days, public interest mounted to extraordinary heights.

Capt. Orne, with typical Yankee shrewdness, obtained a vessel large enough to hold the object in its hull, and arranged for the exhibition of his prize. With judicious carpentry he prepared what amounted to an excellent marine museum, and, sailing south to the wealthy resort district of Martin's Beach, anchored at the hotel wharf and reaped a harvest of admission fees.

The intrinsic marvelousness of the object, and the importance which it clearly bore in the minds of many scientific visitors from near and far, combined to make it the season's sensation. That it was absolutely unique — unique to a scientifically revolutionary degree — was well understood. The naturalists had shown plainly that it radically differed from the similarly immense fish caught off the Florida coast; that, while it was obviously an inhabitant of almost incredible depths, perhaps thousands of feet, its brain and principal organs indicated a development startlingly vast, and out of all proportion to anything hitherto associated with the fish tribe.

On the morning of July 20 the sensation was increased by the loss of the vessel and its strange treasure. In the storm of the preceding night it had broken from its moorings and vanished forever from the sight of man, carrying with it the guard who had slept aboard despite the threatening weather. Capt. Orne, backed by extensive scientific interests and aided by large numbers of fishing boats from Gloucester, made a thorough and exhaustive searching cruise, but with no result other than the prompting of interest and conversation. By August 7 hope was abandoned, and Capt. Orne had returned to the Wavecrest Inn to wind up his business affairs at Martin's Beach and confer with certain of the scientific men who remained there.

The horror came on August 8.

It was in the twilight, when grey sea-birds hovered low near the shore and a rising moon began to make a glittering path across the waters. The scene is important to remember, for every impression counts. On the beach were several strollers and a few late bathers; stragglers from the distant cottage colony that rose modestly on a green hill to the north, or from the adjacent cliff-perched Inn whose imposing towers proclaimed its allegiance to wealth and grandeur.

Well within viewing distance was another set of spectators, the loungers on the Inn's high-ceiled and lantern-lighted veranda, who appeared to be enjoying the dance music from the sumptuous ballroom inside. These spectators, who included Capt. Orne and his group of scientific confrères, joined the beach group before the horror progressed far; as did many more from the Inn. Certainly there was no lack of witnesses, confused though their stories be with fear and doubt of what they saw.

There is no exact record of the time the thing began, although a majority say that the fairly round moon was "about a foot" above the low-lying vapours of the horizon. They mention the moon because what they saw seemed subtly connected with it — a sort of stealthy, deliberate, menacing ripple which rolled in from the far skyline along the shimmering lane of reflected moonbeams, yet which seemed to subside before it reached the shore.

Many did not notice this ripple until reminded by later events, but it seems to have been very marked, differing in height and motion from the normal waves around it. Some called it cunning and calculating. And as it died away craftily by the black reefs afar out, there suddenly came belching up out of the glitter-streaked brine a cry of death; a scream of anguish and despair that moved pity even while it mocked it.

First to respond to the cry were the two life guards then on duty; sturdy fellows in white bathing attire, with their calling proclaimed in large red letters across their chests. Accustomed as they were to rescue work, and to the screams of the drowning, they could find nothing familiar in the unearthly ululation; yet with a trained sense of duty they ignored the strangeness and proceeded to follow their usual course.

Hastily seizing an air-cushion, which with its attached coil of rope lay always at hand, one of them ran swiftly along the shore to the scene of the gathering crowd; whence, after whirling it about to gain momentum, he flung the hollow disc far out in the direction from which the sound had come. As the cushion disappeared in the waves, the crowd curiously awaited a sight of the hapless being whose distress had been so great; eager to see the rescue made by the massive rope.

But that rescue was soon acknowledged to be no swift and easy matter; for, pull as they might on the rope, the two muscular guards could not move the object at the other end. Instead, they found that object pulling with equal or even greater force in the very opposite direction, till in a few seconds they were dragged off their feet and into the water by the strange power which had seized on the proffered life-preserver.

One of them, recovering himself, called immediately for help from the crowd on the shore, to whom he flung the remaining coil of rope; and in a moment the guards were seconded by all the hardier men, among whom Capt. Orne was foremost. More than a dozen strong hands were now tugging desperately at the stout line, yet wholly without avail.

Hard as they tugged, the strange force at the other end tugged harder; and since neither side relaxed for an instant, the rope became rigid as steel with the enormous strain. The struggling participants, as well as the spectators, were by this time consumed with curiosity as to the nature of the force in the sea. The idea of a drowning man had long been dismissed; and hints of whales, submarines, monsters, and demons now passed freely around. Where humanity had first led the rescuers, wonder kept them at their task; and they hauled with a grim determination to uncover the mystery.

It being decided at last that a whale must have swallowed the air-cushion, Capt. Orne, as a natural leader, shouted to those on shore that a boat must be obtained in order to approach, harpoon, and land the unseen leviathan. Several men at once prepared to scatter in quest of a suitable craft, while others came to supplant the captain at the straining rope, since his place was logically with whatever boat party might be formed. His own idea of the situation was very broad, and by no means limited to whales, since he had to do with a monster so much stranger. He wondered what might be the acts and manifestations of an adult of the species of which the fifty-foot creature had been the merest infant.

And now there developed with appalling suddenness the crucial fact which changed the entire scene from one of wonder to one of horror, and dazed with fright the assembled band of toilers and onlookers. Capt. Orne, turning to leave his post at the rope, found his hands held in their place with unaccountable strength; and in a moment he realized that he was unable to let go of the rope. His plight was instantly divined, and as each companion tested his own situation the same condition was encountered. The fact could not be denied — every struggler was irresistibly held in some mysterious bondage to the hempen line which was slowly, hideously, and relentlessly pulling them out to sea.

Speechless horror ensued; a horror in which the spectators were petrified to utter inaction and mental chaos. Their complete demoralization is reflected in the conflicting accounts they give, and the sheepish excuses they offer for their seemingly callous inertia. I was one of them, and know.

Even the strugglers, after a few frantic screams and futile groans, succumbed to the paralyzing influence and kept silent and fatalistic in the face of unknown powers. There they stood in the pallid moonlight, blindly pulling against a spectral doom and swaying monotonously backward and forward as the water rose first to their knees, then to their hips. The moon went partly under a cloud, and in the half-light the line of swaying men resembled some sinister and gigantic centipede, writhing in the clutch of a terrible creeping death.

Harder and harder grew the rope, as the tug in both directions increased, and the strands swelled with the undisturbed soaking of the rising waves. Slowly the tide advanced, till the sands so lately peopled by laughing children and whispering lovers were now swallowed by the inexorable flow. The herd of panic-stricken watchers surged blindly backward as the water crept above their feet, while the frightful line of strugglers swayed hideously on, half submerged, and now at a substantial distance from their audience. Silence was complete.

The crowd, having gained a huddling-place beyond reach of the tide, stared in mute fascination; without offering a word of advice or encouragement, or attempting any kind of assistance. There was in the air a nightmare fear of impending evils such as the world had never before known.

Minutes seemed lengthened into hours, and still that human snake of swaying torsos was seen above the fast rising tide. Rhythmically it undulated; slowly, horribly, with the seal of doom upon it. Thicker clouds now passed over the ascending moon, and the glittering path on the waters faded nearly out.

Very dimly writhed the serpentine line of nodding heads, with now and then the livid face of a backward-glancing victim gleaming pale in the darkness. Faster and faster gathered the clouds, till at length their angry rifts shot down sharp tongues of febrile flame. Thunders rolled, softly at first, yet soon increasing to a deafening, maddening intensity. Then came a culminating crash — a shock whose reverberations seemed to shake land and sea alike — and on its heels a cloudburst whose drenching violence overpowered the darkened world as if the heavens themselves had opened to pour forth a vindictive torrent.

The spectators, instinctively acting despite the absence of conscious and coherent thought, now retreated up the cliff steps to the hotel veranda. Rumours had reached the guests inside, so that the refugees found a state of terror nearly equal to their own. I think a few frightened words were uttered, but cannot be sure.

Some, who were staying at the Inn, retired in terror to their rooms; while others remained to watch the fast sinking victims as the line of bobbing heads showed above the mounting waves in the fitful lightning flashes. I recall thinking of those heads, and the bulging eyes they must contain; eyes that might well reflect all the fright, panic, and delirium of a malignant universe — all the sorrow, sin, and misery, blasted hopes and unfulfilled desires, fear, loathing and anguish of the ages since time's beginning; eyes alight with all the soul-racking pain of eternally blazing infernos.

And as I gazed out beyond the heads, my fancy conjured up still another eye; a single eye, equally alight, yet with a purpose so revolting to my brain that the vision soon passed. Held in the clutches of an unknown vice, the line of the damned dragged on; their silent screams and unuttered prayers known only to the demons of the black waves and the night-wind.

There now burst from the infuriate sky such a mad cataclysm of satanic sound that even the former crash seemed dwarfed. Amidst a blinding glare of descending fire the voice of heaven resounded with the blasphemies of hell, and the mingled agony of all the lost reverberated in one apocalyptic, planet-rending peal of Cyclopean din. It was the end of the storm, for with uncanny suddenness the rain ceased and the moon once more cast her pallid beams on a strangely quieted sea.

There was no line of bobbing heads now. The waters were calm and deserted, and broken only by the fading ripples of what seemed to be a whirlpool far out in the path of the moonlight whence the strange cry had first come. But as I looked along that treacherous lane of silvery sheen, with fancy fevered and senses overwrought, there trickled upon my ears from some abysmal sunken waste the faint and sinister echoes of a laugh.

The Hound.

3,000-WORD SHORT STORY; 1922.

This particularly chilling short story was inspired by a trip that Lovecraft made with Rheinhart Kleiner to the 18th-century Dutch Reformed Church on Flatbush Avenue in Brooklyn — and to its adjacent graveyard, full of grave markers dating from the mid-1700s. While there, Lovecraft pocketed a piece of one of the grave markers; and it set him to thinking about the possibilities of a story plot in which a vengeful tomb-denizen, resenting a similar act of souvenir-taking, claws its way out of the grave to track down the desecrator.

That story idea led him directly to "The Hound."

Lovecraft's execution of "The Hound" is rich with melodramatic excess, and this was clearly a stylistic decision on his part. S. T. Joshi, in "I Am Providence," calls the story "an obvious self-parody," and he may be right; but the story Lovecraft worked on just before this one was "The Horror at Martin's Beach," and he was, at the time, freshly finished with Herbert West, Reanimator. *Perhaps he was just going through a phase of his writing life in which he was exploring the limits of campy melodrama as a delivery vehicle for real literary art. If so, the experiment can safely be classified as a failure, or at most a very mixed success.*

It's also a distinct possibility that he was just having fun.

Lovecraft, in later years, came to despise this story, calling it "a dead dog"; this tends to suggest that it was not intended as self-parody.

Penned in October 1922, "The Hound" was one of the five tales Lovecraft submitted to Weird Tales *when he first made contact with editor Edwin Baird in 1923. It was, of course, accepted, and published in the February 1924 issue.*

In my tortured ears there sounds unceasingly a nightmare whirring and flapping, and a faint distant baying as of some gigantic hound. It is not dream — it is not, I fear, even madness — for too much has already happened to give me these merciful doubts.

Weird Tales, February 1924

St. John is a mangled corpse; I alone know why, and such is my knowledge that I am about to blow out my brains for fear I shall be mangled in the same way. Down unlit and illimitable corridors of eldritch phantasy sweeps the black, shapeless Nemesis that drives me to self-annihilation.

May heaven forgive the folly and morbidity which led us both to so monstrous a fate! Wearied with the commonplaces of a prosaic world; where even the joys of romance and adventure soon grow stale, St. John and I had followed enthusiastically every aesthetic and intellectual movement which promised respite from our devastating ennui. The enigmas of the symbolists and the ecstasies of the pre-Raphaelites all were ours in their time, but each new mood was drained too soon, of its diverting novelty and appeal.

Only the somber philosophy of the decadents could help us, and this we found potent only by increasing gradually the depth and diabolism of our penetrations. Baudelaire and Huysmans were soon exhausted of thrills, till finally there remained for us only the more direct stimuli of unnatural personal experiences and adventures. It was this frightful emotional need which led us eventually to that detestable course which even in my present fear I mention with shame and timidity—that hideous extremity of human outrage, the abhorred practice of grave-robbing.

I cannot reveal the details of our shocking expedition, or catalogue even partly the worst of the trophies adorning the nameless museum in which we jointly dwelt, alone and servantless. Our museum was a blasphemous, unthinkable place, where with the satanic taste of neurotic virtuosi we had assembled an universe of terror and a secret room, far, far, underground; where huge winged daemons carven of basalt and onyx vomited from wide grinning mouths weird green and orange light, and hidden pneumatic pipes ruffled into kaleidoscopic dances of death the line of red charnel things hand in hand woven in voluminous black hangings. Through these pipes came at will the odors our moods most craved; sometimes the scent of pale funeral lilies; sometimes the narcotic incense of imagined Eastern shrines of the kingly dead, and sometimes — how I shudder to recall it! — the frightful, soul-upheaving stenches of the uncovered grave.

Around the walls of this repellent chamber were cases of antique mummies alternating with comely, lifelike bodies perfectly stuffed and cured by the taxidermist's art, and with headstones snatched from the oldest churchyards of the world. Niches here and there contained skulls of all shapes, and heads preserved in various stages of dissolution. There one might find the rotting, bald pates of famous noblemen, and the flesh and radiantly golden heads of new-buried children.

Statues and painting there were, all of fiendish subjects and some executed by St. John and myself. A locked portfolio, bound in tanned human skin, held certain unknown and unnameable drawings which it was rumored Goya had perpetrated but dared not acknowledge. There were nauseous musical instruments, stringed, brass, wood-wind, on which St. John and I sometimes produced dissonances of exquisite morbidity and cacodaemoniacal ghastliness; whilst in a multitude of inlaid ebony cabinets reposed the most incredible and unimaginable variety of tomb-loot ever assembled by human madness and perversity. It is of this loot in particular that I must not speak. Thank God I had the courage to destroy it long before I thought of destroying myself!

The predatory excursions on which we collected our unmentionable treasures were always artistically memorable events. We were no vulgar ghouls, but worked only under certain conditions of mood, landscape, environment, weather, season, and moonlight. These pastimes were to us the most exquisite form of aesthetic expression, and we gave their details a fastidious technical care. An inappropriate hour, a jarring lighting effect, or a clumsy manipulation of the damp sod, would almost totally destroy for us that ecstatic titillation which followed the exhumation of some ominous, grinning secret of the earth. Our quest for novel scenes and piquant conditions was feverish and insatiate — St John was always the leader, and he it was who led the way at last to that mocking, accursed spot which brought us our hideous and inevitable doom.

By what malign fatality were we lured to that terrible Holland churchyard? I think it was the dark rumor and legendry, the tales of one buried for five centuries, who had himself been a ghoul in his time and had stolen a potent thing from a mighty sepulchre. I can recall the scene in these final moments — the pale autumnal moon over the graves, casting long horrible shadows; the grotesque trees, drooping sullenly to meet the neglected grass and the crumbling slabs; the vast legions of strangely colossal bats that flew against the moon; the antique ivied church pointing a huge spectral finger at the livid sky; the phosphorescent insects that danced like death-fires under the yews in a distant corner; the odors of mould, vegetation, and less explicable things that mingled feebly with the night-wind from over far swamps and seas; and, worst of all, the faint deep-toned baying of some gigantic hound which we could neither see nor definitely place. As we heard this suggestion of baying we shuddered, remembering the tales of the peasantry; for he whom we sought had centuries before been found in this self same spot, torn and mangled by the claws and teeth of some unspeakable beast.

I remember how we delved in the ghoul's grave with our spades, and how we thrilled at the picture of ourselves, the grave, the pale watching moon, the horrible shadows, the grotesque trees, the titanic bats, the antique church, the dancing death-fires, the sickening odors, the gently moaning night-wind, and the strange, half-heard directionless baying of whose objective existence we could scarcely be sure.

Then we struck a substance harder than the damp mould, and beheld a rotting oblong box crusted with mineral deposits from the long undisturbed ground. It was incredibly tough and thick, but so old that we finally pried it open and feasted our eyes on what it held.

Much — amazingly much — was left of the object despite the lapse of five hundred years. The skeleton, though crushed in places by the jaws of the thing that had killed it, held together with surprising firmness, and we gloated over the clean white skull and its long, firm teeth and its eyeless sockets that once had glowed with a charnel fever like our own. In the coffin lay an amulet of curious and exotic design, which had apparently been worn around the sleeper's neck. It was the oddly conventionalised figure of a crouching winged hound, or sphinx with a semi-canine face, and was exquisitely carved in antique Oriental fashion from a small piece of green jade. The expression of its features was repellent in the extreme, savoring at once of death, bestiality and malevolence. Around the base was an inscription in characters which neither St. John nor I could identify; and on the bottom, like a maker's seal, was graven a grotesque and formidable skull.

Immediately upon beholding this amulet we knew that we must possess it; that this treasure alone was our logical pelf from the centuried grave. Even had its outlines been unfamiliar we would have desired it, but as we looked more closely we saw that it was not wholly unfamiliar. Alien it indeed was to all art and literature which sane and balanced readers know, but we recognized it as the thing hinted of in the forbidden *Necronomicon* of the mad Arab Abdul Alhazred; the ghastly soul-symbol of the corpse-eating cult of inaccessible Leng, in Central Asia. All too well did we trace the sinister lineaments described by the old Arab daemonologist; lineaments, he wrote, drawn from some obscure supernatural manifestation of the souls of those who vexed and gnawed at the dead.

Seizing the green jade object, we gave a last glance at the bleached and cavern-eyed face of its owner and closed up the grave as we found it. As we hastened from the abhorrent spot, the stolen amulet in St. John's pocket, we thought we saw the bats descend in a body to the earth we had so lately rifled, as if seeking for some cursed and unholy nourishment. But the autumn moon shone weak and pale, and we could not be sure.

So, too, as we sailed the next day away from Holland to our home, we thought we heard the faint distant baying of some gigantic hound in the background. But the autumn wind moaned sad and wan, and we could not be sure.

Less than a week after our return to England, strange things began to happen. We lived as recluses; devoid of friends, alone, and without servants in a few rooms of an ancient manor-house on a bleak and unfrequented moor; so that our doors were seldom disturbed by the knock of the visitor.

Now, however, we were troubled by what seemed to be a frequent fumbling in the night, not only around the doors but around the windows also, upper as well as lower. Once we fancied that a large, opaque body darkened the library window when the moon was shining against it, and another time we thought we heard a whirring or flapping sound not far off. On each occasion investigation revealed nothing, and we began to ascribe the occurrences to imagination which still prolonged in our ears the faint far baying we thought we had heard in the Holland churchyard. The jade amulet now reposed in a niche in our museum, and sometimes we burned a strangely scented candle before it. We read much in Alhazred's *Necronomicon* about its properties, and about the relation of ghosts' souls to the objects it symbolized; and were disturbed by what we read.

Then terror came.

On the night of September 24, 19—, I heard a knock at my chamber door. Fancying it St. John's, I bade the knocker enter, but was answered only by a shrill laugh. There was no one in the corridor. When I aroused St. John from his sleep, he professed entire ignorance of the event, and became as worried as I. It was the night that the faint, distant baying over the moor became to us a certain and dreaded reality.

Four days later, whilst we were both in the hidden museum, there came a low, cautious scratching at the single door which led to the secret library staircase. Our alarm was now divided, for, besides our fear of the unknown, we had always entertained a dread that our grisly collection might be discovered. Extinguishing all lights, we proceeded to the door and threw it suddenly open; whereupon we felt an unaccountable rush of air, and heard, as if receding far away, a queer combination of rustling, tittering, and articulate chatter. Whether we were mad, dreaming, or in our senses, we did not try to determine. We only realized, with the blackest of apprehensions, that the apparently disembodied chatter was beyond a doubt in the Dutch language.

After that we lived in growing horror and fascination. Mostly we held to the theory that we were jointly going mad from our life of unnatural excitements, but sometimes it pleased us more to dramatize ourselves as the victims of some creeping and appalling doom. Bizarre manifestations were now too frequent to count. Our lonely house was seemingly alive with the presence of some malign being whose nature we could not guess, and every night that daemoniac baying rolled over the wind-swept moor, always louder and louder. On October 29 we found in the soft earth underneath the library window a series of footprints utterly impossible to describe. They were as baffling as the hordes of great bats which haunted the old manor-house in unprecedented and increasing numbers.

The horror reached a culmination on November 18, when St. John, walking home after dark from the dismal railway station, was seized by some frightful carnivorous thing and torn to ribbons. His screams had reached the house, and I had hastened to the terrible scene in time to hear a whir of wings and see a vague black cloudy thing silhouetted against the rising moon.

My friend was dying when I spoke to him, and he could not answer coherently. All he could do was to whisper, "The amulet — that damned thing — "

Then he collapsed, an inert mass of mangled flesh.

I buried him the next midnight in one of our neglected gardens, and mumbled over his body one of the devilish rituals he had loved in life. And as I pronounced the last daemoniac sentence I heard afar on the moor the faint baying of some gigantic hound. The moon was up, but I dared not look at it. And when I saw on the dim-lighted moor a wide, nebulous shadow sweeping from mound to mound, I shut my eyes and threw myself face down upon the ground. When I arose, trembling, I know not how much later, I staggered into the house and made shocking obeisances before the enshrined amulet of green jade.

Being now afraid to live alone in the ancient house on the moor, I departed on the following day for London, taking with me the amulet after destroying by fire and burial the rest of the impious collection in the museum. But after three nights I heard the baying again, and before a week was over felt strange eyes upon me whenever it was dark. One evening as I strolled on Victoria Embankment for some needed air, I saw a black shape obscure one of the reflections of the lamps in the water. A wind, stronger than the night-wind, rushed by, and I knew that what had befallen St. John must soon befall me.

The next day I carefully wrapped the green jade amulet and sailed for Holland. What mercy I might gain by returning the thing to its silent, sleeping owner I knew not; but I felt that I must try any step conceivably logical. What the hound was, and why it had pursued me, were questions still vague; but I had first heard the baying in that ancient churchyard, and every subsequent event including St. John's dying whisper had served to connect the curse with the stealing of the amulet. Accordingly I sank into the nethermost abysses of despair when, at an inn in Rotterdam, I discovered that thieves had despoiled me of this sole means of salvation.

The baying was loud that evening, and in the morning I read of a nameless deed in the vilest quarter of the city. The rabble were in terror, for upon an evil tenement had fallen a red death beyond the foulest previous crime of the neighborhood. In a squalid thieves' den an entire family had been torn to shreds by an unknown thing which left no trace, and those around had heard all night a faint, deep, insistent note as of a gigantic hound.

So at last I stood again in the unwholesome churchyard where a pale winter moon cast hideous shadows and leafless trees drooped sullenly to meet the withered, frosty grass and cracking slabs, and the ivied church pointed a jeering finger at the unfriendly sky, and the night-wind howled maniacally from over frozen swamps and frigid seas. The baying was very faint now, and it ceased altogether as I approached the ancient grave I had once violated, and frightened away an abnormally large horde of bats which had been hovering curiously around it.

I know not why I went thither unless to pray, or gibber out insane pleas and apologies to the calm white thing that lay within; but, whatever my reason, I attacked the half frozen sod with a desperation partly mine and partly that of a dominating will outside myself. Excavation was much easier than I expected, though at one point I encountered a queer interruption; when a lean vulture darted down out of the cold sky and pecked frantically at the grave-earth until I killed him with a blow of my spade. Finally I reached the rotting oblong box and removed the damp nitrous cover. This is the last rational act I ever performed.

For crouched within that centuried coffin, embraced by a closepacked nightmare retinue of huge, sinewy, sleeping bats, was the bony thing my friend and I had robbed; not clean and placid as we had seen it then, but covered with caked blood and shreds of alien flesh and hair, and leering sentiently at me with phosphorescent sockets and sharp ensanguined fangs yawning twistedly in mockery of my inevitable doom. And when it gave from those grinning jaws a deep, sardonic bay as of some gigantic hound, and I saw that it held in its gory filthy claw the lost and fateful amulet of green jade, I merely screamed and ran away idiotically, my screams soon dissolving into peals of hysterical laughter.

Madness rides the star-wind . . . claws and teeth sharpened on centuries of corpses . . . dripping death astride a bacchanale of bats from nigh-black ruins of buried temples of Belial . . . . Now, as the baying of that dead fleshless monstrosity grows louder and louder, and the stealthy whirring and flapping of those accursed web-wings circles closer and closer, I shall seek with my revolver the oblivion which is my only refuge from the unnamed and unnameable.

The Lurking Fear.

7,300-WORD SERIAL NOVELETTE; 1922.

This four-part serial was H.P. Lovecraft's second story written for a pay cheque, and it was a follow-up to the "Grewsome Tales" of Herbert West and his assistant. It continues the melodramatic vein that runs through much of Lovecraft's work in 1921-1922, and carries it off better than his earlier work.

It's also the high-water mark for artistic high camp in Lovecraft's writing. Following the completion of this story, it would be six months before Lovecraft produced another; and upon its release, it would be very clear that the era of experimentation with overheated melodrama was over.

Unlike Herbert West, Reanimator, The Lurking Fear *was written all at once, all four parts, in late November 1922. It was published in the January through April issues of* Home Brew.

I.
THE SHADOW ON THE CHIMNEY.

There was thunder in the air on the night I went to the deserted mansion atop Tempest Mountain to find the lurking fear. I was not alone, for foolhardiness was not then mixed with that love of the grotesque and the terrible which has made my career a series of quests for strange horrors in literature and in life. With me were two faithful and muscular men for whom I had sent when the time came; men long associated with me in my ghastly explorations because of their peculiar fitness.

We had started quietly from the village because of the reporters who still lingered about after the eldritch panic of a month before — the nightmare creeping death. Later, I thought, they might aid me; but I did not want them then. Would to God I had let them share the search, that I might not have had to bear the secret alone so long; to bear it alone for fear the world would call me mad or go mad itself at the demon implications of the thing. Now that I am telling it anyway, lest the brooding make me a maniac, I wish I had never concealed it.

Weird Tales, June 1928

"They were slithering shadows of red madness."

For I, and I only, know what manner of fear lurked on that spectral and desolate mountain.

In a small motor-car we covered the miles of primeval forest and hill until the wooded ascent checked it. The country bore an aspect more than usually sinister as we viewed it by night and without the accustomed crowds of investigators, so that we were often tempted to use the acetylene headlight despite the attention it might attract. It was not a wholesome landscape after dark, and I believe I would have noticed its morbidity even had I been ignorant of the terror that stalked there. Of wild creatures there were none — they are wise when death leers close. The ancient lightning-scarred trees seemed unnaturally large and twisted, and the other vegetation unnaturally thick and feverish, while curious mounds and hummocks in the weedy, fulgurite-pitted earth reminded me of snakes and dead men's skulls swelled to gigantic proportions.

Fear had lurked on Tempest Mountain for more than a century. This I learned at once from newspaper accounts of the catastrophe which first brought the region to the world's notice. The place is a remote, lonely elevation in that part of the Catskills where Dutch civilization once feebly and transiently penetrated, leaving behind as it receded only a few mined mansions and a degenerate squatter population inhabiting pitiful hamlets on isolated slopes. Normal beings seldom visited the locality till the state police were formed, and even now only infrequent troopers patrol it. The fear, however, is an old tradition throughout the neighboring villages; since it is a prime topic in the simple discourse of the poor mongrels who sometimes leave their valleys to trade handwoven baskets for such primitive necessities as they cannot shoot, raise, or make.

The lurking fear dwelt in the shunned and deserted Martense mansion, which crowned the high but gradual eminence whose liability to frequent thunderstorms gave it the name of Tempest Mountain. For over a hundred years the antique, grove-circled stone house had been the subject of stories incredibly wild and monstrously hideous; stories of a silent colossal creeping death which stalked abroad in summer. With whimpering insistence the squatters told tales of a demon which seized lone wayfarers after dark, either carrying them off or leaving them in a frightful state of gnawed dismemberment; while sometimes they whispered of blood trails toward the distant mansion. Some said the thunder called the lurking fear out of its habitation, while others said the thunder was its voice.

No one outside the backwoods had believed these varying and conflicting stories, with their incoherent, extravagant descriptions of the hall-glimpsed fiend; yet not a farmer or villager doubted that the Martense mansion was ghoulishly haunted. Local history forbade such a doubt, although no ghostly evidence was ever found by such investigators as had visited the building after some especially vivid tale of the squatters. Grandmothers told strange myths of the Martense spectre; myths concerning the Martense family itself, its queer hereditary dissimilarity of eyes, its long, unnatural annals, and the murder which had cursed it.

The terror which brought me to the scene was a sudden and portentous confirmation of the mountaineers' wildest legends. One summer night, after a thunderstorm of unprecedented violence, the countryside was aroused by a squatter stampede which no mere delusion could create. The pitiful throngs of natives shrieked and whined of the unnamable horror which had descended upon them, and they were not doubted. They had not seen it, but had heard such cries from one of their hamlets that they knew a creeping death had come.

In the morning citizens and state troopers followed the shuddering mountaineers to the place where they said the death had come. Death was indeed there. The ground under one of the squatter's villages had caved in after a lightning stroke, destroying several of the malodorous shanties; but upon this property damage was superimposed an organic devastation which paled it to insignificance. Of a possible seventy-five natives who had inhabited this spot, not one living specimen was visible. The disordered earth was covered with blood and human debris bespeaking too vividly the ravages of demon teeth and talons; yet no visible trail led away from the carnage. That some hideous animal must be the cause, everyone quickly agreed; nor did any tongue now revive the charge that such cryptic deaths formed merely the sordid murders common in decadent communities. That charge was revived only when about twenty-five of the estimated population were found missing from the dead; and even then it was hard to explain the murder of fifty by half that number. But the fact remained that on a summer night a bolt had come out of the heavens and left a dead village whose corpses were horribly mangled, chewed, and clawed.

The excited countryside immediately connected the horror with the haunted Martense mansion, though the localities were over three miles apart. The troopers were more skeptical, including the mansion only casually in their investigations, and dropping it altogether when they found it thoroughly deserted. Country and village people, however, canvassed the place with infinite care; overturning everything in the house, sounding ponds and brooks, beating down bushes, and ransacking the nearby forests. All was in vain; the death that had come had left no trace save destruction itself.

By the second day of the search the affair was fully treated by the newspapers, whose reporters overran Tempest Mountain. They described it in much detail, and with many interviews to elucidate the horror's history as told by local grandams. I followed the accounts languidly at first, for I am a connoisseur in horrors; but after a week I detected an atmosphere which stirred me oddly, so that on August 5th, 1921, I registered among the reporters who crowded the hotel at Lefferts Corners, nearest village to Tempest Mountain and acknowledged headquarters of the searchers. Three weeks more, and the dispersal of the reporters left me free to begin a terrible exploration based on the minute inquiries and surveying with which I had meanwhile busied myself.

So on this summer night, while distant thunder rumbled, I left a silent motor-car and tramped with two armed companions up the last mound-covered reaches of Tempest Mountain, casting the beams of an electric torch on the spectral grey walls that began to appear through giant oaks ahead. In this morbid night solitude and feeble shifting illumination, the vast boxlike pile displayed obscure hints of terror which day could not uncover; yet I did not hesitate, since I had come with fierce resolution to test an idea. I believed that the thunder called the death-demon out of some fearsome secret place; and be that demon solid entity or vaporous pestilence, I meant to see it.

I had thoroughly searched the ruin before, hence knew my plan well; choosing as the seat of my vigil the old room of Jan Martense, whose murder looms so great in the rural legends. I felt subtly that the apartment of this ancient victim was best for my purposes. The chamber, measuring about twenty feet square, contained like the other rooms some rubbish which had once been furniture. It lay on the second story, on the southeast corner of the house, and had an immense east window and narrow south window, both devoid of panes or shutters. Opposite the large window was an enormous Dutch fireplace with scriptural tiles representing the prodigal son, and opposite the narrow window was a spacious bed built into the wall.

As the tree-muffled thunder grew louder, I arranged my plan's details. First I fastened side by side to the ledge of the large window three rope ladders which I had brought with me. I knew they reached a suitable spot on the grass outside, for I had tested them. Then the three of us dragged from another room a wide four-poster bedstead, crowding it laterally against the window. Having strewn it with fir boughs, all now rested on it with drawn automatics, two relaxing while the third watched. From whatever direction the demon might come, our potential escape was provided. If it came from within the house, we had the window ladders; if from outside the door and the stairs. We did not think, judging from precedent, that it would pursue us far even at worst.

I watched from midnight to one o'clock, when in spite of the sinister house, the unprotected window, and the approaching thunder and lightning, I felt singularly drowsy. I was between my two companions, George Bennett being toward the window and William Tobey toward the fireplace. Bennett was asleep, having apparently felt the same anomalous drowsiness which affected me, so I designated Tobey for the next watch although even he was nodding. It is curious how intently I had been watching the fireplace.

The increasing thunder must have affected my dreams, for in the brief time I slept there came to me apocalyptic visions. Once I partly awaked, probably because the sleeper toward the window had restlessly flung an arm across my chest. I was not sufficiently awake to see whether Tobey was attending to his duties as sentinel, but felt a distinct anxiety on that score. Never before had the presence of evil so poignantly oppressed me. Later I must have dropped asleep again, for it was out of a phantasmal chaos that my mind leaped when the night grew hideous with shrieks beyond anything in my former experience or imagination.

In that shrieking the inmost soul of human fear and agony clawed hopelessly and insanely at the ebony gates of oblivion. I awoke to red madness and the mockery of diabolism, as farther and farther down inconceivable vistas that phobic and crystalline anguish retreated and reverberated. There was no light, but I knew from the empty space at my right that Tobey was gone, God alone knew whither. Across my chest still lay the heavy arm of the sleeper at my left.

Then came the devastating stroke of lightning which shook the whole mountain, lit the darkest crypts of the hoary grove, and splintered the patriarch of the twisted trees. In the demon flash of a monstrous fireball the sleeper started up suddenly while the glare from beyond the window threw his shadow vividly upon the chimney above the fireplace from which my eyes had never strayed. That I am still alive and sane, is a marvel I cannot fathom. I cannot fathom it, for the shadow on that chimney was not that of George Bennett or of any other human creature, but a blasphemous abnormality from hell's nethermost craters; a nameless, shapeless abomination which no mind could fully grasp and no pen even partly describe. In another second I was alone in the accursed mansion, shivering and gibbering. George Bennett and William Tobey had left no trace, not even of a struggle. They were never heard of again.

II.

A PASSER IN THE STORM.

For days after that hideous experience in the forest-swathed mansion I lay nervously exhausted in my hotel room at Lefferts Corners. I do not remember exactly how I managed to reach the motor-car, start it, and slip unobserved back to the village; for I retain no distinct impression save of wild-armed titan trees, demoniac mutterings of thunder, and Charonian shadows athwart the low mounds that dotted and streaked the region.

As I shivered and brooded on the casting of that brain-blasting shadow, I knew that I had at last pried out one of earth's supreme horrors — one of those nameless blights of outer voids whose faint demon scratchings we sometimes hear on the farthest rim of space, yet from which our own finite vision has given us a merciful immunity. The shadow I had seen, I hardly dared to analyse or identify. Something had lain between me and the window that night, but I shuddered whenever I could not cast off the instinct to classify it. If it had only snarled, or bayed, or laughed titteringly — even that would have relieved the abysmal hideousness. But it was so silent. It had rested a heavy arm or foreleg on my chest . . . .

Obviously it was organic, or had once been organic . . . Jan Martense, whose room I had invaded, was buried in the graveyard near the mansion . . . I must find Bennett and Tobey, if they lived . . . why had it picked them, and left me for the last? . . . Drowsiness is so stifling, and dreams are so horrible . . . .

In a short time I realised that I must tell my story to someone or break down completely. I had already decided not to abandon the quest for the lurking fear, for in my rash ignorance it seemed to me that uncertainty was worse than enlightenment, however terrible the latter might prove to be. Accordingly I resolved in my mind the best course to pursue; whom to select for my confidences, and how to track down the thing which had obliterated two men and cast a nightmare shadow.

My chief acquaintances at Lefferts Corners had been the affable reporters, of whom several had still remained to collect final echoes of the tragedy. It was from these that I determined to choose a colleague, and the more I reflected the more my preference inclined toward one Arthur Munroe, a dark, lean man of about thirty-five, whose education, taste, intelligence, and temperament all seemed to mark him as one not bound to conventional ideas and experiences.

On an afternoon in early September, Arthur Munroe listened to my story. I saw from the beginning that he was both interested and sympathetic, and when I had finished he analysed and discussed the thing with the greatest shrewdness and judgement. His advice, moreover, was eminently practical; for he recommended a postponement of operations at the Martense mansion until we might become fortified with more detailed historical and geographical data. On his initiative we combed the countryside for information regarding the terrible Martense family, and discovered a man who possessed a marvelously illuminating ancestral diary. We also talked at length with such of the mountain mongrels as had not fled from the terror and confusion to remoter slopes, and again scanned for dens and caves, but all without result. And yet, as I have said, vague new fears hovered menacingly over us, as if giant bat-winged gryphons looked on transcosmic gulfs.

As the afternoon advanced, it became increasingly difficult

to see; and we heard the rumble of a thunderstorm gathering over Tempest Mountain. This sound in such a locality naturally stirred us, though less than it would have done at night. As it was, we hoped desperately that the storm would last until well after dark; and with that hope turned from our aimless hillside searching toward the nearest inhabited hamlet to gather a body of squatters as helpers in the investigation. Timid as they were, a few of the younger men were sufficiently inspired by our protective leadership to promise such help.

We had hardly more than turned, however, when there descended such a blinding sheet of torrential rain that shelter became imperative. The extreme, almost nocturnal darkness of the sky caused us to stumble badly, but guided by the frequent flashes of lightning and by our minute knowledge of the hamlet we soon reached the least porous cabin of the lot, an heterogeneous combination of logs and boards whose still existing door and single tiny window both faced Maple Hill. Barring the door after us against the fury of the wind and rain, we put in place the crude window shutter which our frequent searches had taught us where to find. It was dismal sitting there on rickety boxes in the pitchy darkness, but we smoked pipes and occasionally flashed our pocket lamps about. Now and then we could see the lightning through cracks in the wall; the afternoon was so incredibly dark that each flash was extremely vivid.

The stormy vigil reminded me shudderingly of my ghastly night on Tempest Mountain. My mind turned to that odd question which had kept recurring ever since the nightmare thing had happened; and again I wondered why the demon, approaching the three watchers either from the window or the interior, had begun with the men on each side and left the middle man till the last, when the titan fireball had scared it away. Why had it not taken its victims in natural order, with myself second, from whichever direction it had approached? With what manner of far-reaching tentacles did it prey? Or did it know that I was the leader, and saved me for a fate worse than that of my companions?

In the midst of these reflections, as if dramatically arranged to intensify them, there fell nearby a terrific bolt of lightning followed by the sound of sliding earth. At the same time the wolfish wind rose to demoniac crescendos of ululation. We were sure that the one tree on Maple Hill had been struck again, and Munroe rose from his box and went to the tiny window to ascertain the damage. When he took down the shutter the wind, and rain howled deafeningly in, so that I could not hear what he said; but I waited while he leaned out and tried to fathom Nature's pandemonium.

Gradually a calming of the wind and dispersal of the unusual darkness told of the storm's passing. I had hoped it would last into the night to help our quest, but a furtive sunbeam from a knothole behind me removed the likelihood of such a thing. Suggesting to Munroe that we had better get some light even if more showers came, I unbarred and opened the crude door. The ground outside was a singular mass of mud and pools, with fresh heaps of earth from the slight landslide; but I saw nothing to justify the interest which kept my companion silently leaning out the window. Crossing to where he leaned, I touched his shoulder; but he did not move. Then, as I playfully shook him and turned him around, I felt the strangling tendrils of a cancerous horror whose roots reached into illimitable pasts and fathomless abysms of the night that broods beyond time.

For Arthur Munroe was dead. And on what remained of his chewed and gouged head there was no longer a face.

III.

WHAT THE RED GLARE MEANT.

On the tempest-racked night of November 8, 1921, with a lantern which cast charnel shadows, I stood digging alone and idiotically in the grave of Jan Martense. I had begun to dig in the afternoon, because a thunderstorm was brewing, and now that it was dark and the storm had burst above the maniacally thick foliage I was glad.

I believe that my mind was partly unhinged by events since August 5th; the demon shadow in the mansion, the general strain and disappointment, and the thing that occurred at the hamlet in an October storm. After that thing I had dug a grave for one whose death I could not understand. I knew that others could not understand either, so let them think Arthur Munroe had wandered away. They searched, but found nothing. The squatters might have understood, but I dared not frighten them more. I myself seemed strangely callous. That shock at the mansion had done something to my brain, and I could think only of the quest for a horror now grown to cataclysmic stature in my imagination; a quest which the fate of Arthur Munroe made me vow to keep silent and solitary.

The scene of my excavations would alone have been enough to unnerve any ordinary man. Baleful primal trees of unholy size, age, and grotesqueness leered above me like the pillars of some hellish Druidic temple, muffling the thunder, hushing the clawing wind, and admitting but little rain. Beyond the scarred trunks in the background, illumined by faint flashes of filtered lightning, rose the damp ivied stones of the deserted mansion, while somewhat nearer was the abandoned Dutch garden whose walks and beds were polluted by a white, fungous, foetid, over-nourished vegetation that never saw full daylight. And nearest of all was the graveyard, where deformed trees tossed insane branches as their roots displaced unhallowed slabs and sucked venom from what lay below. Now and then, beneath the brown pall of leaves that rotted and festered in the antediluvian forest darkness, I could trace the sinister outlines of some of those low mounds which characterized the lightning-pierced region.

History had led me to this archaic grave. History, indeed, was all I had after everything else ended in mocking Satanism. I now believed that the lurking fear was no material being, but a wolf-fanged ghost that rode the midnight lightning. And I believed, because of the masses of local tradition I had unearthed in search with Arthur Munroe, that the ghost was that of Jan

Martense, who died in 1762. This is why I was digging idiotically in his grave.

The Martense mansion was built in 1670 by Gerrit Martense, a wealthy New Amsterdam merchant who disliked the changing order under British rule, and had constructed this magnificent domicile on a remote woodland summit whose untrodden solitude and unusual scenery pleased him. The only substantial disappointment encountered in this site was that which concerned the prevalence of violent thunderstorms in summer. When selecting the hill and building his mansion, Mynheer Martense had laid these frequent natural outbursts to some peculiarity of the year; but in time he perceived that the locality was especially liable to such phenomena. At length, having found these storms injurious to his head, he fitted up a cellar into which he could retreat from their wildest pandemonium.

Of Gerrit Martense's descendants less is known than of himself; since they were all reared in hatred of the English civilisation, and trained to shun such of the colonists as accepted it. Their life was exceedingly secluded, and people declared that their isolation had made them heavy of speech and comprehension. In appearance all were marked by a peculiar inherited dissimilarity of eyes; one generally being blue and the other brown. Their social contacts grew fewer and fewer, till at last they took to intermarrying with the numerous menial class about the estate. Many of the crowded family degenerated, moved across the valley, and merged with the mongrel population which was later to produce the pitiful squatters. The rest had stuck sullenly to their ancestral mansion, becoming more and more clannish and taciturn, yet developing a nervous responsiveness to the frequent thunderstorms.

Most of this information reached the outside world through young Jan Martense, who from some kind of restlessness joined the colonial army when news of the Albany Convention reached Tempest Mountain. He was the first of Gerrit's descendants to see much of the world; and when he returned in 1760 after six years of campaigning, he was hated as an outsider by his father, uncles, and brothers, in spite of his dissimilar Martense eyes. No longer could he share the peculiarities and prejudices of the Martenses, while the very mountain thunderstorms failed to intoxicate him as they had before. Instead, his surroundings depressed him; and he frequently wrote to a friend in Albany of plans to leave the paternal roof.

In the spring of 1763 Jonathan Gifford, the Albany friend of Jan Martense, became worried by his correspondent's silence; especially in view of the conditions and quarrels at the Martense mansion. Determined to visit Jan in person, he went into the mountains on horseback. His diary states that he reached Tempest Mountain on September 20, finding the mansion in great decrepitude. The sullen, odd-eyed Martenses, whose unclean animal aspect shocked him, told him in broken gutterals that Jan was dead. He had, they insisted, been struck by lightning the autumn before; and now lay buried behind the neglected sunken gardens. They showed the visitor the grave, barren and devoid of markers. Something in the Martenses' manner gave Gifford a feeling of repulsion and suspicion, and a week later he returned with spade and mattock to explore the sepulchral spot. He found what he expected — a skull crushed cruelly as if by savage blows — so returning to Albany he openly charged the Martenses with the murder of their kinsman.

Legal evidence was lacking, but the story spread rapidly round the countryside; and from that time the Martenses were ostracised by the world. No one would deal with them, and their distant manor was shunned as an accursed place. Somehow they managed to live on independently by the product of their estate, for occasional lights glimpsed from far-away hills attested their continued presence. These lights were seen as late as 1810, but toward the last they became very infrequent.

Meanwhile there grew up about the mansion and the mountain a body of diabolic legendry. The place was avoided with doubled assiduousness, and invested with every whispered myth tradition could supply. It remained unvisited till 1816, when the continued absence of lights was noticed by the squatters. At that time a party made investigations, finding the house deserted and partly in ruins.

There were no skeletons about, so that departure rather than death was inferred. The clan seemed to have left several years before, and improvised penthouses showed how numerous it had grown prior to its migration. Its cultural level had fallen very low, as proved by decaying furniture and scattered silverware which must have been long abandoned when its owners left. But though the dreaded Martenses were gone, the fear of the haunted house continued; and grew very acute when new and strange stories arose among the mountain decadents. There it stood; deserted, feared, and linked with the vengeful ghost of Jan Martense. There it still stood on the night I dug in Jan Martense's grave.

I have described my protracted digging as idiotic, and such it indeed was in object and method. The coffin of Jan Martense had soon been unearthed — it now held only dust and nitre — but in my fury to exhume his ghost I delved irrationally and clumsily down beneath where he had lain. God knows what I expected to find — I only felt that I was digging in the grave of a man whose ghost stalked by night.

It is impossible to say what monstrous depth I had attained when my spade, and soon my feet, broke through the ground beneath. The event, under the circumstances, was tremendous; for in the existence of a subterranean space here, my mad theories had terrible confirmation. My slight fall had extinguished the lantern, but I produced an electric pocket lamp and viewed the small horizontal tunnel which led away indefinitely in both directions. It was amply large enough for a man to wriggle through; and though no sane person would have tried at that time, I forgot danger, reason, and cleanliness in my single-minded fever to unearth the lurking fear. Choosing the direction toward the house, I scrambled recklessly into the narrow burrow; squirming ahead blindly and rapidly, and flashing but seldom the lamp I kept before me.

What language can describe the spectacle of a man lost in infinitely abysmal earth; pawing, twisting, wheezing; scrambling madly through sunken convolutions of immemorial blackness without an idea of time, safety, direction, or definite object? There is something hideous in it, but that is what I did. I did it for so long that life faded to a far memory, and I became one with the moles and grubs of nighted depths. Indeed, it was only by accident that after interminable writhings I jarred my forgotten electric lamp alight, so that it shone eerily along the burrow of caked loam that stretched and curved ahead.

I had been scrambling in this way for some time, so that my battery had burned very low, when the passage suddenly inclined sharply upward, altering my mode of progress. And as I raised my glance it was without preparation that I saw glistening in the distance two demoniac reflections of my expiring lamp; two reflections glowing with a baneful and unmistakable effulgence, and provoking maddeningly nebulous memories. I stopped automatically, though lacking the brain to retreat. The eyes approached, yet of the thing that bore them I could distinguish only a claw. But what a claw! Then far overhead I heard a faint crashing which I recognized. It was the wild thunder of the mountain, raised to hysteric fury—I must have been crawling upward for some time, so that the surface was now quite near. And as the muffled thunder clattered, those eyes still stared with vacuous viciousness.

Thank God I did not then know what it was, else I should have died. But I was saved by the very thunder that had summoned it, for after a hideous wait there burst from the unseen outside sky one of those frequent mountainward bolts whose aftermath I had noticed here and there as gashes of disturbed earth and fulgurites of various sizes. With Cyclopean rage it tore through the soil above that damnable pit, blinding and deafening me, yet not wholly reducing me to a coma. In the chaos of sliding, shifting earth I clawed and floundered helplessly till the rain on my head steadied me and I saw that I had come to the surface in a familiar spot; a steep unforested place on the southwest slope of the mountain. Recurrent sheet lightnings illumed the tumbled ground and the remains of the curious low hummock which had stretched down from the wooded higher slope, but there was nothing in the chaos to show my place of egress from the lethal catacomb. My brain was as great a chaos as the earth, and as a distant red glare burst on the landscape from the south I hardly realised the horror I had been through.

But when two days later the squatters told me what the red glare meant, I felt more horror than that which the mould-burrow and the claw and eyes had given; more horror because of the overwhelming implications. In a hamlet twenty miles away an orgy of fear had followed the bolt which brought me above ground, and a nameless thing had dropped from an overhanging tree into a weak-roofed cabin. It had done a deed, but the squatters had fired the cabin in frenzy before it could escape. It had been doing that deed at the very moment the earth caved in on the thing with the claw and eyes.

IV.

THE HORROR IN THE EYES.

There can be nothing normal in the mind of one who, knowing what I knew of the horrors of Tempest Mountain, would seek alone for the fear that lurked there. That at least two of the fear's embodiments were destroyed, formed but a slight guarantee of mental and physical safety in this Acheron of multiform diabolism; yet I continued my quest with even greater zeal as events and revelations became more monstrous. When, two days after my frightful crawl through that crypt of the eyes and claw, I learned that a thing had malignly hovered twenty miles away at the same instant the eyes were glaring at me, I experienced virtual convulsions of fright. But that fright was so mixed with wonder and alluring grotesqueness, that it was almost a pleasant sensation. Sometimes, in the throes of a nightmare when unseen powers whirl one over the roofs of strange dead cities toward the grinning chasm of Nis, it is a relief and even a delight to shriek wildly and throw oneself voluntarily along with the hideous vortex of dream-doom into whatever bottomless gulf may yawn. And so it was with the walking nightmare of Tempest Mountain; the discovery that two monsters had haunted the spot gave me ultimately a mad craving to plunge into the very earth of the accursed region, and with bare hands dig out the death that leered from every inch of the poisonous soil.

As soon as possible I visited the grave of Jan Martense and dug vainly where I had dug before. Some extensive cave-in had obliterated all trace of the underground passage, while the rain had washed so much earth back into the excavation that I could not tell how deeply I had dug that other day. I likewise made a difficult trip to the distant hamlet where the death-creature had been burnt, and was little repaid for my trouble. In the ashes of the fateful cabin I found several bones, but apparently none of the monster's. The squatters said the thing had had only one victim; but in this I judged them inaccurate, since besides the complete skull of a human being, there was another bony fragment which seemed certainly to have belonged to a human skull at some time. Though the rapid drop of the monster had been seen, no one could say just what the creature was like; those who had glimpsed it called it simply a devil. Examining the great tree where it had lurked, I could discern no distinctive marks. I tried to find some trail into the black forest, but on this occasion could not stand the sight of those morbidly large boles, or of those vast serpent-like roots that twisted so malevolently before they sank into the earth.

My next step was to reexamine with microscopic care the deserted hamlet where death had come most abundantly, and where Arthur Munroe had seen something he never lived to describe. Though my vain previous searches had been exceedingly minute, I now had new data to test; for my horrible grave-crawl convinced me that at least one of the phases of the monstrosity had been an underground creature. This time, on the 14th of November, my quest concerned itself mostly with the slopes of Cone Mountain and Maple Hill where they overlook the unfortunate hamlet, and I gave particular attention to the loose earth of the landslide region on the latter eminence.

The afternoon of my search brought nothing to light, and dusk came as I stood on Maple Hill looking down at the hamlet and across the valley to Tempest Mountain. There had been a gorgeous sunset, and now the moon came up, nearly full and shedding a silver flood over the plain, the distant mountainside, and the curious low mounds that rose here and there. It was a peaceful Arcadian scene, but knowing what it hid I hated it. I hated the mocking moon, the hypocritical plain, the festering mountain, and those sinister mounds. Everything seemed to me tainted with a loathsome contagion, and inspired by a noxious alliance with distorted hidden powers.

Presently, as I gazed abstractedly at the moonlit panorama, my eye became attracted by something singular in the nature and arrangement of a certain topographical element. Without having any exact knowledge of geology, I had from the first been interested in the odd mounds and hummocks of the region. I had noticed that they were pretty widely distributed around Tempest Mountain, though less numerous on the plain than near the hilltop itself, where prehistoric glaciation had doubtless found feebler opposition to its striking and fantastic caprices. Now, in the light of that low moon which cast long weird shadows, it struck me forcibly that the various points and lines of the mound system had a peculiar relation to the summit of Tempest Mountain. That summit was undeniably a centre from which the lines or rows of points radiated indefinitely and irregularly, as if the unwholesome Martense mansion had thrown visible tentacles of terror. The idea of such tentacles gave me an unexplained thrill, and I stopped to analyse my reason for believing these mounds glacial phenomena.

The more I analysed the less I believed, and against my newly opened mind there began to beat grotesque and horrible analogies based on superficial aspects and upon my experience beneath the earth. Before I knew it I was uttering frenzied and disjointed words to myself: "My God! . . . Molehills . . . the damned place must be honeycombed . . . how many . . . that night at the mansion . . . they took Bennett and Tobey first . . . on each side of us . . ." Then I was digging frantically into the mound which had stretched nearest me; digging desperately, shiveringly, but almost jubilantly; digging and at last shrieking aloud with some unplaced emotion as I came upon a tunnel or burrow just like the one through which I had crawled on the other demoniac night.

After that I recall running, spade in hand; a hideous run across moon-litten, mound-marked meadows and through diseased, precipitous abysses of haunted hillside forest; leaping screaming, panting, bounding toward the terrible Martense mansion. I recall digging unreasonably in all parts of the brier-choked cellar; digging to find the core and centre of that malignant universe of mounds. And then I recall how I laughed when I stumbled on the passageway; the hole at the base of the old chimney, where the thick weeds grew and cast queer shadows in the light of the lone candle I had happened to have with me. What still remained down in that hell-hive, lurking and waiting for the thunder to arouse it, I did not know. Two had been killed; perhaps that had finished it. But still there remained that burning determination to reach the innermost secret of the fear, which I had once more come to deem definite, material, and organic.

My indecisive speculation whether to explore the passage alone and immediately with my pocket-light or to try to assemble a band of squatters for the quest, was interrupted after a time by a sudden rush of wind from the outside which blew out the candle and left me in stark blackness. The moon no longer shone through the chinks and apertures above me, and with a sense of fateful alarm I heard the sinister and significant rumble of approaching thunder. A confusion of associated ideas possessed my brain, leading me to grope back toward the farthest corner of the cellar. My eyes, however, never turned away from the horrible opening at the base of the chimney; and I began to get glimpses of the crumbling bricks and unhealthy weeds as faint glows of lightning penetrated the weeds outside and illumined the chinks in the upper wall. Every second I was consumed with a mixture of fear and curiosity. What would the storm call forth — or was there anything left for it to call? Guided by a lightning flash I settled myself down behind a dense clump of vegetation, through which I could see the opening without being seen.

If heaven is merciful, it will some day efface from my consciousness the sight that I saw, and let me live my last years in peace. I cannot sleep at night now, and have to take opiates when it thunders. The thing came abruptly and unannounced; a demon, ratlike scurrying from pits remote and unimaginable, a hellish panting and stifled grunting, and then from that opening beneath the chimney a burst of multitudinous and leprous life — a loathsome night-spawned flood of organic corruption more devastatingly hideous than the blackest conjurations of mortal madness and morbidity. Seething, stewing, surging, bubbling like serpents' slime it rolled up and out of that yawning hole, spreading like a septic contagion and streaming from the cellar at every point of egress — streaming out to scatter through the accursed midnight forests and strew fear, madness, and death.

God knows how many there were — there must have been thousands. To see the stream of them in that faint intermittent lightning was shocking. When they had thinned out enough to be glimpsed as separate organisms, I saw that they were dwarfed, deformed hairy devils or apes — monstrous and diabolic caricatures of the monkey tribe. They were so hideously silent; there was hardly a squeal when one of the last stragglers turned with the skill of long practice to make a meal in accustomed fashion of a weaker companion. Others snapped up what it left and ate with slavering relish. Then, in spite of my daze of fright and disgust, my morbid curiosity triumphed; and as the last of the monstrosities oozed up alone from that nether world of unknown nightmare, I drew my automatic pistol and shot it under cover of the thunder.

Shrieking, slithering, torrential shadows of red viscous madness chasing one another through endless, ensanguined corridors of purple fulgurous sky . . . formless phantasms and kaleidoscopic mutations of a ghoulish, remembered scene; forests of monstrous over-nourished oaks with serpent roots twisting and sucking unnamable juices from an earth verminous with millions of cannibal devils; mound-like tentacles groping from underground nuclei of polypous perversion . . . insane lightning over malignant ivied walls and demon arcades choked with fungous vegetation . . . Heaven be thanked for the instinct which led me unconscious to places where men dwell; to the peaceful village that slept under the calm stars of clearing skies.

I had recovered enough in a week to send to Albany for a gang of men to blow up the Martense mansion and the entire top of Tempest Mountain with dynamite, stop up all the discoverable mound-burrows, and destroy certain over-nourished trees whose very existence seemed an insult to sanity. I could sleep a little after they had done this, but true rest will never come as long as I remember that nameless secret of the lurking fear. The thing will haunt me, for who can say the extermination is complete, and that analogous phenomena do not exist all over the world? Who can, with my knowledge, think of the earth's unknown caverns without a nightmare dread of future possibilities? I cannot see a well or a subway entrance without shuddering . . . why cannot the doctors give me something to make me sleep, or truly calm my brain when it thunders?

What I saw in the glow of flashlight after I shot the unspeakable straggling object was so simple that almost a minute elapsed before I understood and went delirious. The object was nauseous; a filthy whitish gorilla thing with sharp yellow fangs and matted fur. It was the ultimate product of mammalian degeneration; the frightful outcome of isolated spawning, multiplication, and cannibal nutrition above and below the ground; the embodiment of all the snarling and chaos and grinning fear that lurk behind life. It had looked at me as it died, and its eyes had the same odd quality that marked those other eyes which had stared at me underground and excited cloudy recollections. One eye was blue, the other brown. They were the dissimilar Martense eyes of the old legends, and I knew in one inundating cataclysm of voiceless horror what had become of that vanished family, the terrible and thunder-crazed house of Martense.

1923.

Dawning of the Weird Tales Era.

For H.P. Lovecraft and his fans, 1923 was a real red-letter year. That was the year that saw the launch of *Weird Tales*—the legendary pulp magazine that would become his most important and widely circulated (and best paying) outlet.

It was Lovecraft's amateur-journalism friends who persuaded him to reach out to *Weird Tales*' editor, Edwin F. Baird. Finally he did so—writing Baird a truly awful and self-deprecating cover letter that would have gotten anybody else's resume dumped in the trash. Luckily, Baird was familiar with Lovecraft's work already, and was very pleased to hear from him.

Lovecraft was still publishing his own amateur-press magazine, *The Conservative*, at the start of 1923; but he dropped the project after the July issue that year, and never resumed it. He also claimed he was quitting amateur journalism—not for the first time—but continued attending meetings and contributing to friends' journals. He also, in the middle of the year, agreed to serve as editor of the United Amateur Press Association (of which Sonia had been elected President)—a post he would hold until mid-1925.

Also in 1923, Lovecraft met young Clifford Eddy, a fellow Providence resident and weird-fiction writer. The two of them became good friends, and Lovecraft shared some of his ghost-writing jobs with Eddy; he also worked with the younger writer, providing feedback and beta-readings on some articles for *Weird Tales*, including one (published the following year) that may have saved the magazine from an early business failure (or not). It was titled "The Loved Dead," and told the story of a psychotic serial-killer funeral director obsessed with corpses. It strongly hints at necrophilia, and ends with the funeral director's suicide. This dark story sparked widespread outrage and resulted in sales of the title being temporarily banned in the state of Indiana; it firmly established *Weird Tales* as the Aleister Crowley of pulp magazines, crowning it with a dark aura of repellent fascination that (the theory goes) ensured strong if secretive future sales for the next decade. On the other hand, it left *Weird Tales*' editorial staff nearly petrified with fear of offending state censorship authorities, and for the next decade anything even slightly off-color—including some of Lovecraft's best stories—ended up on the spike.

Lovecraft also did a good deal of traveling in 1923, going back and forth to Boston several times on amateur-press business and making sightseeing excursions to Salem, Marblehead, Pascoag, New York, and rural New Hampshire.

In the summer of 1923, Lovecraft discovered the weird-fiction writings of Arthur Machen, who was to be the third major literary influence on his writing style. Machen's influence came like a splash of cold water on the overheated, campy style that Lovecraft's work was developing through late 1922, and when next he put pen to paper with "The Rats in the Walls," the change would be noticeable—and, most readers and critics would agree, welcome.

Meanwhile, Lovecraft's relationship with Sonia Greene was deepening, and by the end of the year he was openly courting her—although, of course, she had to take more of a leading role in that courtship than is customary, owing to his inexperience and bashfulness. He wrote to her constantly, and the letters he sent sometimes topped 50 pages. By the end of the year, Lovecraft had decided to leave Providence and move to New York permanently, to be near Sonia and to further his writing career.

In addition to "The Rats in the Walls," Lovecraft's weird-fiction writings of 1923 includes"The Unnamable" and "The Festival."

The Rats in the Walls.

7,300-WORD NOVELETTE; 1923.

This short novelette was the first weird tale to roll off H.P. Lovecraft's pen in 1923, and it wasn't written until early September. Lovecraft spent the first nine months of the year on various amateur-press activities, courting Sonia Greene, and reading the work of his new favorite novelist, Arthur Machen.

When Lovecraft did sit down to write "The Rats in the Walls," it was his first story in nearly a full year. Both the influence of Machen and his waning interest in developing an artistic strain of campy melodrama are immediately obvious in it. It was first published in Weird Tales *in the March 1924 issue.*

As a side note, it was this story that, when it was reprinted for a second time in Weird Tales *in the June 1930 issue, prompted a young Texas writer and scholar named Robert E. Howard to write to Lovecraft, initiating one of the most famous epistolatory relationships of either writer's life.*

On 16 July, 1923, I moved into Exham Priory after the last workman had finished his labours. The restoration had been a stupendous task, for little had remained of the deserted pile but a shell-like ruin; yet because it had been the seat of my ancestors, I let no expense deter me. The place had not been inhabited since the reign of James the First, when a tragedy of intensely hideous, though largely unexplained, nature had struck down the master, five of his children, and several servants; and driven forth under a cloud of suspicion and terror the third son, my lineal progenitor and the only survivor of the abhorred line.

With this sole heir denounced as a murderer, the estate had reverted to the crown, nor had the accused man made any attempt to exculpate himself or regain his property. Shaken by some horror greater than that of conscience or the law, and expressing only a frantic wish to exclude the ancient edifice from his sight and memory, Walter de la Poer, eleventh Baron Exham, fled to Virginia and there founded the family which by the next century had become known as Delapore.

Exham Priory had remained untenanted, though later allotted to the estates of the Norrys family and much studied because of its peculiarly composite architecture; an architecture involving Gothic towers resting on a Saxon or Romanesque substructure, whose foundation in turn was of a still earlier order or blend of orders — Roman, and even Druidic or native Cymric, if legends speak truly. This foundation was a very singular thing, being merged on one side with the solid limestone of the precipice from whose brink the priory overlooked a desolate valley three miles west of the village of Anchester.

Architects and antiquarians loved to examine this strange relic of forgotten centuries, but the country folk hated it. They had hated it hundreds of years before, when my ancestors lived there, and they hated it now, with the moss and mould of abandonment on it. I had not been a day in Anchester before I knew I came of an accursed house. And this week workmen have blown up Exham Priory, and are busy obliterating the traces of its foundations.

The bare statistics of my ancestry I had always known, together with the fact that my first American forebear had come to the colonies under a strange cloud. Of details, however, I had been kept wholly ignorant through the policy of reticence always maintained by the Delapores. Unlike our planter neighbours, we seldom boasted of crusading ancestors or other mediaeval and Renaissance heroes; nor was any kind of tradition handed down except what may have been recorded in the sealed envelope left before the Civil War by every squire to his eldest son for posthumous opening. The glories we cherished were those achieved since the migration; the glories of a proud and honourable, if somewhat reserved and unsocial Virginia line.

During the war our fortunes were extinguished and our whole existence changed by the burning of Carfax, our home on the banks of the James. My grandfather, advanced in years, had perished in that incendiary outrage, and with him the envelope that had bound us all to the past. I can recall that fire today as I saw it then at the age of seven, with the federal soldiers shouting, the women screaming, and the negroes howling and praying. My father was in the army, defending Richmond, and after many formalities my mother and I were passed through the lines to join him.

When the war ended we all moved north, whence my mother had come; and I grew to manhood, middle age, and ultimate wealth as a stolid Yankee. Neither my father nor I ever knew what our hereditary envelope had contained, and as I merged into the greyness of Massachusetts business life I lost all interest in the mysteries which evidently lurked far back in my family tree. Had I suspected their nature, how gladly I would have left Exham Priory to its moss, bats and cobwebs!

My father died in 1904, but without any message to leave to me, or to my only child, Alfred, a motherless boy of ten. It was this boy who reversed the order of family information, for although I could give him only jesting conjectures about the past, he wrote me of some very interesting ancestral legends when the late war took him to England in 1917 as an aviation officer. Apparently the Delapores had a colourful and perhaps sinister history, for a friend of my son's, Capt. Edward Norrys of the Royal Flying Corps, dwelt near the family seat at Anchester and related some peasant superstitions which few novelists could equal for wildness and incredibility. Norrys himself, of course, did not take them so seriously; but they amused my son and made good material for his letters to me. It was this legendry which definitely turned my attention to my transatlantic heritage, and made me resolve to purchase and restore the family seat which Norrys showed to Alfred in its picturesque desertion, and offered to get for him at a surprisingly reasonable figure, since his own uncle was the present owner.

I bought Exham Priory in 1918, but was almost immediately distracted from my plans of restoration by the return of my son as a maimed invalid. During the two years that he lived I thought of nothing but his care, having even placed my business under the direction of partners.

In 1921, as I found myself bereaved and aimless, a retired manufacturer no longer young, I resolved to divert my remaining years with my new possession. Visiting Anchester in December, I was entertained by Capt. Norrys, a plump, amiable young man who had thought much of my son, and secured his assistance in gathering plans and anecdotes to guide in the coming restoration. Exham Priory itself I saw without emotion, a jumble of tottering mediaeval ruins covered with lichens and honeycombed with rooks' nests, perched perilously upon a precipice, and denuded of floors or other interior features save the stone walls of the separate towers.

As I gradually recovered the image of the edifice as it had been when my ancestors left it over three centuries before, I began to hire workmen for the reconstruction. In every case I was forced to go outside the immediate locality, for the Anchester villagers had an almost unbelievable fear and hatred of the place. The sentiment was so great that it was sometimes communicated to the outside labourers, causing numerous desertions; whilst its scope appeared to include both the priory and its ancient family.

My son had told me that he was somewhat avoided during his visits because he was a de la Poer, and I now found myself subtly ostracized for a like reason until I convinced the peasants how little I knew of my heritage. Even then they sullenly disliked me, so that I had to collect most of the village traditions through the mediation of Norrys. What the people could not forgive, perhaps, was that I had come to restore a symbol so abhorrent to them; for, rationally or not, they viewed Exham Priory as nothing less than a haunt of fiends and werewolves.

Piecing together the tales which Norrys collected for me, and supplementing them with the accounts of several savants who had studied the ruins, I deduced that Exham Priory stood on the site of a prehistoric temple, a Druidical or ante-Druidical thing which must have been contemporary with Stonehenge. That indescribable rites had been celebrated there, few doubted,

Weird Tales, March 1924

and there were unpleasant tales of the transference of these rites into the Cybele worship which the Romans had introduced.

Inscriptions still visible in the sub-cellar bore such unmistakable letters as "DIV . . . OPS . . . MAGNA MAT . . . ," sign of the Magna Mater whose dark worship was once vainly forbidden to Roman citizens. Anchester had been the camp of the third Augustan legion, as many remains attest, and it was said that the temple of Cybele was splendid and thronged with worshippers who performed nameless ceremonies at the bidding of a Phrygian priest. Tales added that the fall of the old religion did not end the orgies at the temple, but that the priests lived on in the new faith without real change. Likewise was it said that the rites did not vanish with the Roman power, and that certain among the Saxons added to what remained of the temple, and gave it the essential outline it subsequently preserved, making it the centre of a cult feared through half the heptarchy. About 1000 A.D. the place is mentioned in a chronicle as being a substantial stone priory housing a strange and powerful monastic order and surrounded by extensive gardens which needed no walls to exclude a frightened populace. It was never destroyed by the Danes, though after the Norman Conquest it must have declined tremendously, since there was no impediment when Henry the Third granted the site to my ancestor, Gilbert de la Poer, First Baron Exham, in 1261.

Of my family before this date there is no evil report, but something strange must have happened then. In one chronicle there is a reference to a de la Poer as "cursed of God in 1307," whilst village legendry had nothing but evil and frantic fear to tell of the castle that went up on the foundations of the old temple and priory. The fireside tales were of the most grisly description, all the ghastlier because of their frightened reticence and cloudy evasiveness. They represented my ancestors as a race of hereditary daemons beside whom Gilles de Retz and the Marquis de Sade would seem the veriest tyros, and hinted whisperingly at their responsibility for the occasional disappearances of villagers through several generations.

The worst characters, apparently, were the barons and their direct heirs; at least, most was whispered about these. If of healthier inclinations, it was said, an heir would early and mysteriously die to make way for another more typical scion. There seemed to be an inner cult in the family, presided over by the head of the house, and sometimes closed except to a few members. Temperament rather than ancestry was evidently the basis of this cult, for it was entered by several who married into the family. Lady Margaret Trevor from Cornwall, wife of Godfrey, the second son of the fifth baron, became a favourite bane of children all over the countryside, and the daemon heroine of a particularly horrible old ballad not yet extinct near the Welsh border. Preserved in balladry, too, though not illustrating the same point, is the hideous tale of Lady Mary de la Poer, who shortly after her marriage to the Earl of Shrewsfield was killed by him and his mother, both of the slayers being absolved and blessed by the priest to whom they confessed what they dared not repeat to the world.

These myths and ballads, typical as they were of crude superstition, repelled me greatly. Their persistence, and their application to so long a line of my ancestors, were especially annoying; whilst the imputations of monstrous habits proved unpleasantly reminiscent of the one known scandal of my immediate forebears — the case of my cousin, young Randolph Delapore of Carfax who went among the negroes and became a voodoo priest after he returned from the Mexican War.

I was much less disturbed by the vaguer tales of wails and

howlings in the barren, windswept valley beneath the limestone cliff; of the graveyard stenches after the spring rains; of the floundering, squealing white thing on which Sir John Clave's horse had trod one night in a lonely field; and of the servant who had gone mad at what he saw in the priory in the full light of day. These things were hackneyed spectral lore, and I was at that time a pronounced sceptic. The accounts of vanished peasants were less to be dismissed, though not especially significant in view of mediaeval custom. Prying curiosity meant death, and more than one severed head had been publicly shown on the bastions — now effaced — around Exham Priory.

A few of the tales were exceedingly picturesque, and made me wish I had learnt more of the comparative mythology in my youth. There was, for instance, the belief that a legion of bat-winged devils kept witches' sabbath each night at the priory — a legion whose sustenance might explain the disproportionate abundance of coarse vegetables harvested in the vast gardens. And, most vivid of all, there was the dramatic epic of the rats — the scampering army of obscene vermin which had burst forth from the castle three months after the tragedy that doomed it to desertion — the lean, filthy, ravenous army which had swept all before it and devoured fowl, cats, dogs, hogs, sheep, and even two hapless human beings before its fury was spent. Around that unforgettable rodent army a whole separate cycle of myths revolves, for it scattered among the village homes and brought curses and horrors in its train.

Such was the lore that assailed me as I pushed to completion, with an elderly obstinacy, the work of restoring my ancestral home. It must not be imagined for a moment that these tales formed my principal psychological environment. On the other hand, I was constantly praised and encouraged by Capt. Norrys and the antiquarians who surrounded and aided me. When the task was done, over two years after its commencement, I viewed the great rooms, wainscoted walls, vaulted ceilings, mullioned windows, and broad staircases with a pride which fully compensated for the prodigious expense of the restoration.

Every attribute of the Middle Ages was cunningly reproduced and the new parts blended perfectly with the original walls and foundations. The seat of my fathers was complete, and I looked forward to redeeming at last the local fame of the line which ended in me. I could reside here permanently, and prove that a de la Poer (for I had adopted again the original spelling of the name) need not be a fiend. My comfort was perhaps augmented by the fact that, although Exham Priory was mediaevally fitted, its interior was in truth wholly new and free from old vermin and old ghosts alike.

As I have said, I moved in on 16 July 1923. My household consisted of seven servants and nine cats, of which latter species I am particularly fond. My eldest cat, "Nigger-Man," was seven years old and had come with me from my home in Bolton, Massachusetts; the others I had accumulated whilst living with Capt. Norrys' family during the restoration of the priory.

For five days our routine proceeded with the utmost placidity, my time being spent mostly in the codification of old family data. I had now obtained some very circumstantial accounts of the final tragedy and flight of Walter de la Poer, which I conceived to be the probable contents of the hereditary paper lost in the fire at Carfax. It appeared that my ancestor was accused with much reason of having killed all the other members of his household, except four servant confederates, in their sleep, about two weeks after a shocking discovery which changed his whole demeanour, but which, except by implication, he disclosed to no one save perhaps the servants who assisted him and afterwards fled beyond reach.

This deliberate slaughter, which included a father, three brothers, and two sisters, was largely condoned by the villagers, and so slackly treated by the law that its perpetrator escaped honoured, unharmed, and undisguised to Virginia; the general whispered sentiment being that he had purged the land of an immemorial curse. What discovery had prompted an act so terrible, I could scarcely even conjecture. Walter de la Poer must have known for years the sinister tales about his family, so that this material could have given him no fresh impulse. Had he, then, witnessed some appalling ancient rite, or stumbled upon some frightful and revealing symbol in the priory or its vicinity? He was reputed to have been a shy, gentle youth in England. In Virginia he seemed not so much hard or bitter as harassed and apprehensive. He was spoken of in the diary of another gentleman adventurer, Francis Harley of Bellview, as a man of unexampled justice, honour, and delicacy.

On 22 July occurred the first incident which, though lightly dismissed at the time, takes on a preternatural significance in relation to later events. It was so simple as to be almost negligible, and could not possibly have been noticed under the circumstances; for it must be recalled that since I was in a building practically fresh and new except for the walls, and surrounded by a well-balanced staff of servitors, apprehension would have been absurd despite the locality.

What I afterward remembered is merely this — that my old black cat, whose moods I know so well, was undoubtedly alert and anxious to an extent wholly out of keeping with his natural character. He roved from room to room, restless and disturbed, and sniffed constantly about the walls which formed part of the Gothic structure. I realize how trite this sounds — like the inevitable dog in the ghost story, which always growls before his master sees the sheeted figure — yet I cannot consistently suppress it.

The following day a servant complained of restlessness among all the cats in the house. He came to me in my study, a lofty west room on the second storey, with groined arches, black oak panelling, and a triple Gothic window overlooking the limestone cliff and desolate valley; and even as he spoke I saw the jetty form of Nigger-Man creeping along the west wall and scratching at the new panels which overlaid the ancient stone.

I drowsed away the noontime, and in the afternoon called again on Capt. Norrys, who became exceedingly interested in what I told him. The odd incidents — so slight yet so curious — appealed to his sense of the picturesque and elicited from him a number of reminiscenses of local ghostly lore. We were genuinely perplexed at the presence of rats, and Norrys lent me some traps and Paris Green, which I had the servants place in strategic localities when I returned.

I retired early, being very sleepy, but was harassed by dreams of the most horrible sort. I seemed to be looking down from an immense height upon a twilit grotto, knee-deep with filth, where a white-bearded daemon swineherd drove about with his staff a flock of fungous, flabby beasts whose appearance filled me with unutterable loathing. Then, as the swineherd paused and nodded over his task, a mighty swarm of rats rained down on the stinking abyss and fell to devouring beasts and man alike.

From this terrific vision I was abruptly awakened by the motions of Nigger-Man, who had been sleeping as usual across my feet. This time I did not have to question the source of his snarls and hisses, and of the fear which made him sink his claws into my ankle, unconscious of their effect; for on every side of the chamber the walls were alive with nauseous sound — the verminous slithering of ravenous, gigantic rats. There was now no aurora to show the state of the arras — the fallen section of which had been replaced — but I was not too frightened to switch on the light.

As the bulbs leapt into radiance I saw a hideous shaking all over the tapestry, causing the somewhat peculiar designs to execute a singular dance of death. This motion disappeared almost at once, and the sound with it. Springing out of bed, I poked at the arras with the long handle of a warming-pan that rested near, and lifted one section to see what lay beneath. There was nothing but the patched stone wall, and even the cat had lost his tense realization of abnormal presences. When I examined the circular trap that had been placed in the room, I found all of the openings sprung, though no trace remained of what had been caught and had escaped.

Further sleep was out of the question, so lighting a candle, I opened the door and went out in the gallery towards the stairs to my study, Nigger-Man following at my heels. Before we had reached the stone steps, however, the cat darted ahead of me and vanished down the ancient flight. As I descended the stairs myself, I became suddenly aware of sounds in the great room below; sounds of a nature which could not be mistaken.

The oak-panelled walls were alive with rats, scampering and milling whilst Nigger-Man was racing about with the fury of a baffled hunter. Reaching the bottom, I switched on the light, which did not this time cause the noise to subside. The rats continued their riot, stampeding with such force and distinctness that I could finally assign to their motions a definite direction. These creatures, in numbers apparently inexhaustible, were engaged in one stupendous migration from inconceivable heights to some depth conceivably or inconceivably below.

I now heard steps in the corridor, and in another moment two servants pushed open the massive door. They were searching the house for some unknown source of disturbance which had thrown all the cats into a snarling panic and caused them to plunge precipitately down several flights of stairs and squat, yowling, before the closed door to the sub-cellar. I asked them if they had heard the rats, but they replied in the negative. And when I turned to call their attention to the sounds in the panels, I realized that the noise had ceased.

With the two men, I went down to the door of the sub-cellar, but found the cats already dispersed. Later I resolved to explore the crypt below, but for the present I merely made a round of the traps. All were sprung, yet all were tenantless. Satisfying myself that no one had heard the rats save the felines and me, I sat in my study till morning, thinking profoundly and recalling every scrap of legend I had unearthed concerning the building I inhabited. I slept some in the forenoon, leaning back in the one comfortable library chair which my mediaeval plan of furnishing could not banish. Later I telephoned to Capt. Norrys, who came over and helped me explore the sub-cellar.

Absolutely nothing untoward was found, although we could not repress a thrill at the knowledge that this vault was built by Roman hands. Every low arch and massive pillar was Roman — not the debased Romanesque of the bungling Saxons, but the severe and harmonious classicism of the age of the Caesars; indeed, the walls abounded with inscriptions familiar to the antiquarians who had repeatedly explored the place: things like “P. GETAE. PROP . . . TEMP . . . DONA . . .” and “L. PRAEG . . . VS . . . PONTIFI . . . ATYS . . .”

The reference to Atys made me shiver, for I had read Catullus and knew something of the hideous rites of the Eastern god, whose worship was so mixed with that of Cybele. Norrys and I, by the light of lanterns, tried to interpret the odd and nearly effaced designs on certain irregularly rectangular blocks of stone generally held to be altars, but could make nothing of them. We remembered that one pattern, a sort of rayed sun, was held by students to imply a non-Roman origin suggesting that these altars had merely been adopted by the Roman priests from some older and perhaps aboriginal temple on the same site. On one of these blocks were some brown stains which made me wonder. The largest, in the centre of the room, had certain features on the upper surface which indicated its connection with fire — probably burnt offerings.

Such were the sights in that crypt before whose door the cats howled, and where Norrys and I now determined to pass the night. Couches were brought down by the servants, who were told not to mind any nocturnal actions of the cats, and Nigger-Man was admitted as much for help as for companionship. We decided to keep the great oak door — a modern replica with slits for ventilation — tightly closed; and, with this attended to, we retired with lanterns still burning to await whatever might occur.

The vault was very deep in the foundations of the priory, and undoubtedly far down on the face of the beetling limestone cliff overlooking the waste valley. That it had been the goal of the scuffling and unexplainable rats I could not doubt, though why, I could not tell. As we lay there expectantly, I found my vigil occasionally mixed with half-formed dreams from which the uneasy motions of the cat across my feet would rouse me.

These dreams were not wholesome, but horribly like the one I had had the night before. I saw again the twilit grotto, and the swineherd with his unmentionable fungous beasts wallowing in filth, and as I looked at these things they seemed nearer and more distinct — so distinct that I could almost observe their features. Then I did observe the flabby features of one of them — and awakened with such a scream that Nigger-Man started up, whilst Capt. Norrys, who had not slept, laughed considerably. Norrys might have laughed more — or perhaps less — had he known what it was that made me scream. But I did not remember myself till later. Ultimate horror often paralyses memory in a merciful way.

Norrys waked me when the phenomena began. Out of the same frightful dream I was called by his gentle shaking and his urging to listen to the cats. Indeed, there was much to listen to, for beyond the closed door at the head of the stone steps was a veritable nightmare of feline yelling and clawing, whilst Nigger-Man, unmindful of his kindred outside, was running excitedly round the bare stone walls, in which I heard the same babel of scurrying rats that had troubled me the night before.

An acute terror now rose within me, for here were anomalies which nothing normal could well explain. These rats, if not the creatures of a madness which I shared with the cats alone, must be burrowing and sliding in Roman walls I had thought to be solid limestone blocks ... unless perhaps the action of water through more than seventeen centuries had eaten winding tunnels which rodent bodies had worn clear and ample ... But even so, the spectral horror was no less; for if these were living vermin why did not Norrys hear their disgusting commotion? Why did he urge me to watch Nigger-Man and listen to the cats outside, and why did he guess wildly and vaguely at what could have aroused them?

By the time I had managed to tell him, as rationally as I could, what I thought I was hearing, my ears gave me the last fading impression of scurrying; which had retreated still downward, far underneath this deepest of sub-cellars till it seemed as if the whole cliff below were riddled with questing rats. Norrys was not as sceptical as I had anticipated, but instead seemed profoundly moved. He motioned to me to notice that the cats at the door had ceased their clamour, as if giving up the rats for lost; whilst Nigger-Man had a burst of renewed restlessness, and was clawing frantically around the bottom of the large stone altar in the centre of the room, which was nearer Norrys' couch than mine.

My fear of the unknown was at this point very great. Something astounding had occurred, and I saw that Capt. Norrys, a younger, stouter, and presumably more naturally materialistic man, was affected fully as much as myself — perhaps because of his lifelong and intimate familiarity with local legend. We could for the moment do nothing but watch the old black cat as he pawed with decreasing fervour at the base of the altar, occasionally looking up and mewing to me in that persuasive manner which he used when he wished me to perform some favour for him.

Norrys now took a lantern close to the altar and examined the place where Nigger-Man was pawing; silently kneeling and scraping away the lichens of the centuries which joined the massive pre-Roman block to the tessellated floor. He did not find anything, and was about to abandon his efforts when I noticed a trivial circumstance which made me shudder, even though it implied nothing more than I had already imagined.

I told him of it, and we both looked at its almost imperceptible manifestation with the fixedness of fascinated discovery and acknowledgment. It was only this — that the flame of the lantern set down near the altar was slightly but certainly flickering from a draught of air which it had not before received, and which came indubitably from the crevice between floor and altar where Norrys was scraping away the lichens.

We spent the rest of the night in the brilliantly-lighted study, nervously discussing what we should do next. The discovery that some vault deeper than the deepest known masonry of the Romans underlay this accursed pile, some vault unsuspected by the curious antiquarians of three centuries, would have been sufficient to excite us without any background of the sinister. As it was, the fascination became two-fold; and we paused in doubt whether to abandon our search and quit the priory forever in superstitious caution, or to gratify our sense of adventure and brave whatever horrors might await us in the unknown depths.

By morning we had compromised, and decided to go to London to gather a group of archaeologists and scientific men fit to cope with the mystery. It should be mentioned that before leaving the sub-cellar we had vainly tried to move the central altar which we now recognized as the gate to a new pit of nameless fear. What secret would open the gate, wiser men than we would have to find.

During many days in London Capt. Norrys and I presented our facts, conjectures, and legendary anecdotes to five eminent authorities, all men who could be trusted to respect any family disclosures which future explorations might develop. We found most of them little disposed to scoff but, instead, intensely interested and sincerely sympathetic. It is hardly necessary to name them all, but I may say that they included Sir William Brinton, whose excavations in the Troad excited most of the world in their day. As we all took the train for Anchester I felt myself poised on the brink of frightful revelations, a sensation symbolized by the air of mourning among the many Americans at the unexpected death of the President on the other side of the world.

On the evening of 7 August we reached Exham Priory, where the servants assured me that nothing unusual had occurred. The cats, even old Nigger-Man, had been perfectly placid, and not a trap in the house had been sprung. We were to begin exploring on the following day, awaiting which I assigned well-appointed rooms to all my guests.

I myself retired in my own tower chamber, with Nigger-Man across my feet. Sleep came quickly, but hideous dreams assailed me. There was a vision of a Roman feast like that of Trimalchio, with a horror in a covered platter. Then came that damnable, recurrent thing about the swineherd and his filthy drove in the twilit grotto. Yet when I awoke it was full daylight, with normal sounds in the house below. The rats, living or spectral, had not troubled me; and Nigger-Man was still quietly asleep. On going down, I found that the same tranquillity had prevailed elsewhere; a condition which one of the assembled servants — a fellow named Thornton, devoted to the psychic — rather absurdly laid to the fact that I had now been shown the thing which certain forces had wished to show me.

All was now ready, and at 11 a.m. our entire group of seven men, bearing powerful electric searchlights and implements of excavation, went down to the sub-cellar and bolted the door behind us. Nigger-Man was with us, for the investigators found no occasion to depise his excitability, and were indeed anxious that he be present in case of obscure rodent manifestations. We noted the Roman inscriptions and unknown altar designs only briefly, for three of the savants had already seen them, and all knew their characteristics. Prime attention was paid to the momentous central altar, and within an hour Sir William Brinton had caused it to tilt backward, balanced by some unknown species of counterweight.

There now lay revealed such a horror as would have overwhelmed us had we not been prepared. Through a nearly square opening in the tiled floor, sprawling on a flight of stone steps so prodigiously worn that it was little more than an inclined plane at the centre, was a ghastly array of human or semi-human bones. Those which retained their collocation as skeletons showed attitudes of panic fear, and over all were the marks of rodent gnawing. The skulls denoted nothing short of utter idiocy, cretinism, or primitive semi-apedom.

Above the hellishly littered steps arched a descending passage seemingly chiselled from the solid rock, and conducting a current of air. This current was not a sudden and noxious rush as from a closed vault, but a cool breeze with something of freshness in it. We did not pause long, but shiveringly began to clear a passage down the steps. It was then that Sir William, examining the hewn walls, made the odd observation that the passage, according to the direction of the strokes, must have been chiselled from beneath.

I must be very deliberate now, and choose my words. After ploughing down a few steps amidst the gnawed bones we saw that there was light ahead; not any mystic phosphorescence, but a filtered daylight which could not come except from unknown fissures in the cliff that overlooked the waste valley. That such fissures had escaped notice from outside was hardly remarkable, for not only is the valley wholly uninhabited, but the cliff is so high and beetling that only an aeronaut could study its face in detail. A few steps more, and our breaths were literally snatched from us by what we saw; so literally that Thornton, the psychic investigator, actually fainted in the arms of the dazed men who stood behind him. Norrys, his plump face utterly white and flabby, simply cried out inarticulately; whilst I think that what I did was to gasp or hiss, and cover my eyes.

The man behind me — the only one of the party older than I — croaked the hackneyed "My God!" in the most cracked voice I ever heard. Of seven cultivated men, only Sir William Brinton retained his composure, a thing the more to his credit because he led the party and must have seen the sight first.

It was a twilit grotto of enormous height, stretching away farther than any eye could see; a subterraneous world of limitless mystery and horrible suggestion. There were buildings and other architectural remains — in one terrified glance I saw a weird pattern of tumuli, a savage circle of monoliths, a low-domed Roman ruin, a sprawling Saxon pile, and an early English edifice of wood — but all these were dwarfed by the ghoulish spectacle presented by the general surface of the ground. For yards about the steps extended an insane tangle of human bones, or bones at least as human as those on the steps. Like a foamy sea they stretched, some fallen apart, but others wholly or partly articulated as skeletons; these latter invariably in postures of daemoniac frenzy, either fighting off some menace or clutching other forms with cannibal intent.

When Dr. Trask, the anthropologist, stopped to classify the skulls, he found a degraded mixture which utterly baffled him. They were mostly lower than the Piltdown man in the scale of evolution, but in every case definitely human. Many were of higher grade, and a very few were the skulls of supremely and sensitively developed types. All the bones were gnawed, mostly by rats, but somewhat by others of the half-human drove. Mixed with them were many tiny bones of rats — fallen members of the lethal army which closed the ancient epic.

I wonder that any man among us lived and kept his sanity through that hideous day of discovery. Not Hoffman nor Huysmans could conceive a scene more wildly incredible, more frenetically repellent, or more Gothically grotesque than the twilit grotto through which we seven staggered; each stumbling on revelation after revelation, and trying to keep for the nonce from thinking of the events which must have taken place there three hundred, or a thousand, or two thousand or ten thousand years ago. It was the antechamber of hell, and poor Thornton fainted again when Trask told him that some of the skeleton things must have descended as quadrupeds through the last twenty or more generations.

Horror piled on horror as we began to interpret the architectural remains. The quadruped things — with their occasional recruits from the biped class — had been kept in stone pens, out of which they must have broken in their last delirium of hunger or rat-fear. There had been great herds of them, evidently fattened on the coarse vegetables whose remains could be found as a sort of poisonous ensilage at the bottom of the huge stone bins older than Rome. I knew now why my ancestors had had such excessive gardens — would to heaven I could forget! The purpose of the herds I did not have to ask.

Sir William, standing with his searchlight in the Roman ruin, translated aloud the most shocking ritual I have ever known; and told of the diet of the antediluvian cult which the priests of Cybele found and mingled with their own. Norrys, used as he was to the trenches, could not walk straight when he came out of the English building. It was a butcher shop and kitchen — he had expected that — but it was too much to see familiar English implements in such a place, and to read familiar English graffiti there, some as recent as 1610. I could not go in that building — that building whose daemon activities were stopped only by the dagger of my ancestor Walter de la Poer.

What I did venture to enter was the low Saxon building whose oaken door had fallen, and there I found a terrible row of ten stone cells with rusty bars. Three had tenants, all skeletons of high grade, and on the bony forefinger of one I found a seal ring with my own coat-of-arms. Sir William found a vault with far older cells below the Roman chapel, but these cells were empty. Below them was a low crypt with cases of formally arranged bones, some of them bearing terrible parallel inscriptions carved in Latin, Greek, and the tongue of Phyrgia.

Meanwhile, Dr. Trask had opened one of the prehistoric tumuli, and brought to light skulls which were slightly more human than a gorilla's, and which bore indescribably ideographic carvings. Through all this horror my cat stalked unperturbed. Once I saw him monstrously perched atop a mountain of bones, and wondered at the secrets that might lie behind his yellow eyes.

Having grasped to some slight degree the frightful revelations of this twilit area — an area so hideously foreshadowed by my recurrent dream — we turned to that apparently boundless depth of midnight cavern where no ray of light from the cliff could penetrate. We shall never know what sightless Stygian worlds yawn beyond the little distance we went, for it was decided that such secrets are not good for mankind. But there was plenty to engross us close at hand, for we had not gone far before the searchlights showed that accursed infinity of pits in which the rats had feasted, and whose sudden lack of replenishment had driven the ravenous rodent army first to turn on the living herds of starving things, and then to burst forth from the priory in that historic orgy of devastation which the peasants will never forget.

God! those carrion black pits of sawed, picked bones and opened skulls! Those nightmare chasms choked with the pithecanthropoid, Celtic, Roman, and English bones of countless unhallowed centuries! Some of them were full, and none can say how deep they had once been. Others were still bottomless to our searchlights, and peopled by unnamable fancies. What, I thought, of the hapless rats that stumbled into such traps amidst the blackness of their quests in this grisly Tartarus?

Once my foot slipped near a horribly yawning brink, and I had a moment of ecstatic fear. I must have been musing a long time, for I could not see any of the party but plump Capt. Norrys. Then there came a sound from that inky, boundless, farther distance that I thought I knew; and I saw my old black cat dart past me like a winged Egyptian god, straight into the illimitable gulf of the unknown. But I was not far behind, for there was no doubt after another second. It was the eldritch scurrying of those fiend-born rats, always questing for new horrors, and determined to lead me on even unto those grinning caverns of earth's centre where Nyarlathotep, the mad faceless god, howls blindly in the darkness to the piping of two amorphous idiot flute-players.

My searchlight expired, but still I ran. I heard voices, and yowls, and echoes, but above all there gently rose that impious, insidious scurrying; gently rising, rising, as a stiff bloated corpse gently rises above an oily river that flows under the endless onyx bridges to a black, putrid sea.

Something bumped into me — something soft and plump. It must have been the rats; the viscous, gelatinous, ravenous army that feast on the dead and the living .... Why shouldn't rats eat a de la Poer as a de la Poer eats forbidden things? ... The war ate my boy, damn them all ... and the Yanks ate Carfax with flames and burnt Grandsire Delapore and the secret. .. . No, no, I tell you, I am not that daemon swineherd in the twilit grotto! It was not Edward Norrys' fat face on that flabby fungous thing! Who says I am a de la Poer? He lived, but my boy died! ... Shall a Norrys hold the land of a de la Poer? ... It's voodoo, I tell you ... that spotted snake ... Curse you, Thornton, I'll teach you to faint at what my family do! ... 'Sblood, thou stinkard, I'll learn ye how to gust ... wolde ye swynke me thilke wys? ... Magna Mater! Magna Mater! ... Atys ... Dia ad aghaidh's ad aodaun ... agus bas dunarch ort! Dhonas 's dholas ort, agus leat-sa! ... Ungl unl ... rrlh ... chchch ...

This is what they say I said when they found me in the blackness after three hours; found me crouching in the blackness over the plump, half-eaten body of Capt. Norrys, with my own cat leaping and tearing at my throat. Now they have blown up Exham Priory, taken my Nigger-Man away from me, and shut me into this barred room at Hanwell with fearful whispers about my heredity and experience. Thornton is in the next room, but they prevent me from talking to him. They are trying, too, to suppress most of the facts concerning the priory. When I speak of poor Norrys they accuse me of this hideous thing, but they must know that I did not do it. They must know it was the rats; the slithering scurrying rats whose scampering will never let me sleep; the daemon rats that race behind the padding in this room and beckon me down to greater horrors than I have ever known; the rats they can never hear; the rats, the rats in the walls.

Ashes.

BY C.M. EDDY AND H.P. LOVECRAFT

3,200-WORD SHORT STORY; 1923.

"Ashes" was one of four stories by fellow weird-fictioneer Clifford M. Eddy that H.P. Lovecraft helped prepare for submission to Weird Tales. *Eddy had submitted it along with "The Ghost Eater" previously, and both had been rejected; but Lovecraft helped him revise both stories, and they were accepted when Eddy resubmitted them.*

Of the four stories, "Ashes" is the weakest, and shows the smallest degree of influence by Lovecraft. As the two Providence writers worked together over the following year or so, the influence of Lovecraft on Eddy's style would become increasingly visible; this story, of course, was written before the two started working together, and is the sort of dialogue-heavy story (with a romantic subplot, no less) that Lovecraft tended to avoid.

It was first published in the March 1924 issue of Weird Tales *magazine.*

ABOUT C.M. EDDY (1896-1967).

Clifford M. Eddy was a fellow resident of Providence, and he and his wife Muriel socialized with H.P. Lovecraft a good deal after they discovered each other's presence in 1923. Eddy had already launched a career as a professional pulp writer, having placed a story titled "Sign of the Dragon" in the September 1919 issue of Mystery Magazine. *His style was quite different from Lovecraft's, and certainly more conventional; the difference soon shrank after the two began working together, and Lovecraft's influence on Eddy's later writing is noticeable.*

Lovecraft collaborated with Eddy on a total of four stories before he packed up and moved to New York in early 1924. As mentioned earlier, one of these, "The Loved Dead," a short one about a necrophilic funeral director, got Weird Tales *put onto the naughty list by would-be magazine censors across the country in 1924 and went a long way toward earning for the publication its dark, edgy reputation. It also got the magazine banned from newsstands in Illinois, and established an enduring fear of state censorship boards that, over the years, formed a real problem for its writers.*

After Lovecraft's return to Providence in 1926, he and Eddy don't seem to have collaborated on any more works. By then, Clifford Eddy had started working as a theatrical booking agent for Vaudeville acts. However, their friendship endured, and Muriel Eddy later wrote a memoir of their adventures together.

Eddy's style, as a horror writer, was very much in the high-camp style in which Lovecraft was working in 1923 or so — his Herbert West, Reanimator *phase. Even as Lovecraft was clearly influencing Eddy's style, Eddy may have actually been an important influence on Lovecraft during that time as well, moving him more fully into the embrace of "grewsome" melodrama in the months before Lovecraft discovered Arthur Machen's work.*

"Hello, Bruce. Haven't seen you in a dog's age. Come in."

I threw open the door, and he followed me into the room. His gaunt, ungainly figure sprawled awkwardly into the chair I indicated, and he twirled his hat between nervous fingers. His deep-set eyes wore a worried, hunted look, and he glanced furtively around the room as if searching for a hidden something which might unexpectedly pounce upon him. His face was haggard and colourless. The corners of his mouth twitched spasmodically.

"What's the matter, old man? You look as if you'd seen a ghost. Brace up!" I crossed to the buffet, and poured a small glass of wine from the decanter. "Drink this!"

He downed it with a hasty gulp, and took to toying with his hat again.

"Thanks, Prague — I don't feel quite myself tonight."

"You don't look it, either! What's wrong?"

Malcolm Bruce shifted uneasily in his chair.

I eyed him in silence for a moment wondering what could possibly affect the man so strongly. I knew Bruce as a man of steady nerves and iron will. To find him visibly upset was, in itself, unusual. I passed cigars, and he selected one, automatically.

It was not until the second cigar had been lighted that Bruce broke the silence. His nervousness was apparently gone. Once more he was the dominant self-reliant figure I knew of old.

"Prague," he began, "I've just been through the most devilish, gruesome experience that ever befell a man. I don't know whether I dare tell it or not, for fear you will think I've gone crazy — and I wouldn't blame you if you did! But it's true, every word of it!"

He paused, dramatically, and blew a few rings of smoke in the air.

I smiled. Many a weird tale I had listened to over that

self-same table. There must have been some kink in my personality that inspired confidence, for I had been told stories that some men would have given years of their life to have heard. And yet, despite my love of the bizarre and dangerous, and my longing to explore far reaches of little-known lands, I had been doomed to a life of prosaic, flat, uneventful business.

"Do you happen to have heard of Professor Van Allister?" asked Bruce.

"You don't mean Arthur Van Allister?"

"The same! Then you know him?"

"I should say so! Known him for years. Ever since he resigned as Professor of Chemistry at the College so he could have more time for his experiments. Why, I even helped him choose the plans for that sound-proof laboratory of his, on the top floor of his home. Up to a year or so ago, we were pals. Then he got so busy with his confounded experiments he couldn't find time to be chummy!"

"You may recall, Prague, that when we were in college together, I used to dabble quite a bit in chemistry?"

I nodded, and Bruce continued:

"About four months ago I found myself out of a job. Then Allister advertised for an assistant, and I answered. He remembered me from college days, and I managed to convince him I knew enough about chemistry to warrant a trial.

"He had a young lady doing his secretarial work — a Miss Marjorie Purdy. She was one of these strict-attention-to-business types, and as good-looking as she was efficient. She had been helping Van Allister a bit in his laboratory, and I soon discovered she took a genuine interest in puttering around, making experiments of her own. Indeed, she spent nearly all her spare time with us in the laboratory.

"It was only natural that such companionship should result in a close friendship, and it wasn't long before I began to depend on her to help me in difficult experiments when the Professor was busy. I never could seem to stump her. That girl took to chemistry as a duck takes to water!

"About two months ago then Allister had the laboratory partitioned off, and made a separate work room for himself. He told us that he was about to enter upon a series of experiments which, if successful, would bring him everlasting fame. He flatly refused to make us his confidants in any way, shape or manner.

"From that time on, Miss Purdy and I were left alone more and more. For days at a time the Professor would retire to the seclusion of his new workshop, sometimes not even appearing for his meals.

"That meant, too, that we had more spare time on our hands. Our friendship ripened. I felt a growing admiration for the trim young woman who seemed perfectly content to fuss around smelly bottles and sticky messes, gowned in white from head to foot, even to the rubber gloves she wore.

"The day before yesterday, then, Allister invited us into his workshop.

"'At last I have achieved success,' he announced, holding up for our inspection a small bottle containing a colourless liquid. 'I have here what will rank as the greatest chemical discovery ever known. I am going to prove its efficacy right before your eyes. Bruce, will you bring me one of the rabbits, please?'

"I went back into the other room and brought him one of the rabbits we kept, together with guinea pigs, for experimental purposes.

"He put the little animal into a small glass box just large enough to hold it, and closed the cover. Then he set a glass funnel in a hole in the top of the box, and we drew nearer to watch the experiment.

"He uncorked the bottle, and poised it above the rabbit's prison.

"'Now to prove whether my weeks of effort have resulted in success or failure!'

"Slowly, methodically, he emptied the contents of the bottle into the funnel, and we watched it trickle into the compartment with the frightened animal.

"Miss Purdy uttered a suppressed cry, and I rubbed my eyes to be sure they had not deceived me. For, in the case where but a moment before there had been a live, terrified rabbit, there was now nothing but a little pile of soft, white ashes!"

"Professor Van Allister turned to us with an air of supreme satisfaction. His face radiated ghoulish glee and his eyes were alight with a weird, insane gleam. When he spoke, his voice took on a tone of mastery.

"'Bruce — and you, too, Miss Purdy — it has been your privilege to witness the first successful trial of a preparation that will revolutionize the world. It will instantaneously reduce to a fine ash anything which it comes in contact with, except glass! Just think what that means. An army equipped with glass bombs filled with my compound could annihilate the world! Wood, metal, stone, brick — *everything* — swept away before them, leaving no more trace than the rabbit I have just experimented upon — just a pile of soft, white ashes!'

"I glanced at Miss Purdy. Her face had gone as white as the apron she wore.

"We watched Van Allister as he transferred all that was left of the bunny to a small bottle, and neatly labelled it. I'll admit that I was suffering a mental chill myself by the time he dismissed us, and we left him alone behind the tightly closed doors of his workshop.

"Once safely outside, Miss Purdy's nerves gave way completely. She reeled, and would have fallen had I not caught her in my arms.

"The feel of her soft, yielding body held close to my own was the last straw. I cast prudence to the winds and crushed her tightly to my breast. Kiss after kiss I pressed upon her full red lips, until her eyes opened and I saw the lovelight reflected in them.

"After a delicious eternity we came back to earth again

— long enough to realize that the laboratory was no place for such ardent demonstrations. At any moment Van Allister might come out of his retreat, and if he should discover our love-making — in his present state of mind — we dared not think what might happen.

"For the rest of the day I was like a man in a dream. It's a wonder to me that I succeeded in accomplishing anything at all. My body was merely an automaton, a well-trained machine, going about its appointed tasks, while my mind soared into faraway realms of delightful day-dreaming.

"Marjorie kept busy with her secretarial work for the rest of the day, and not once did I lay eyes upon her until my tasks in the laboratory were completed.

"That night we gave over to the joys of our new-found happiness. Prague, I shall remember that night as long as I live! The happiest moment I have ever known was when Marjorie Purdy promised to become my wife.

"Yesterday was another day of unalloyed bliss. All day long my sweetheart and I worked side-by-side. Then followed another night of lovemaking. If you've never been in love with the only girl in the world, Prague, you can't understand the delirious joy that comes from the very thought of her! And Marjorie returned my devotion a hundredfold. She gave herself unreservedly into my keeping.

"Along about noon time, today, I needed something to complete an experiment, and I stepped over to the drugstore for it.

"When I returned I missed Marjorie. I looked for her hat and coat and they were gone. The professor had not shown himself since the experiment upon the rabbit, and was locked in his workshop.

"I asked the servants, but none of them had seen her leave the house nor had she left any message for me.

"As the afternoon wore on I grew frantic. Evening came and still no sight of my dear little girl.

"All thought of work was forgotten. I paced the floor of my room like a caged lion. Every jangle of the phone or ring at the door bolstered my faltering hopes of some word from her, but each time I was doomed to disappointment. Each minute seemed an hour; each hour an eternity!

"Good God, Prague! You can't imagine how I suffered! From the heights of sublime love I mentally plunged to the darkest depths of despair. I conjured visions of all sorts of terrible fates overtaking her. Still, not a word did I hear.

"It seemed to me that I had lived a life-time but my watch told me it was only 7:30 when the butler told me that Van Allister wanted me in the laboratory.

"I was in no mood for experiments, but while I was under his roof he was my master, and it was time for me to obey.

"The Professor was in his workshop, the door slightly ajar. He called to me to close the door of the laboratory and join him in the little room.

"In my state of mind my brain photographed every minute detail of the scene which met my eyes. In the center of the room, on a marble-top table, was a glass case of about the shape and size of a coffin. It was filled almost to the brim with that same colourless liquid which the small bottle had contained, two days before.

"At the left, on a glass-top tabourette, was a newly-labelled glass jar. I could not repress an involuntary shudder as I realized that it was filled with soft white ashes. Then I saw something that almost made my heart stop beating!

"On a chair, in a far corner of the workshop, was the hat and coat of the girl who had pledged her life to mine — the girl whom I had vowed to cherish and protect while life should last!

"My senses were numbed, my soul surcharged with horror, as realization flashed over me. There could be but one explanation. *The ashes in that jar were the ashes of Marjorie Purdy!*

"The world stood still for one long, terrible moment, and then I went mad — start, staring mad!

"The next I can remember, the Professor and I were locked in a desperate struggle. Old as he was, he still possessed a strength nearly equal to mine, and he had the added advantage of calm self-possession.

"Closer and closer he forced me to the glass coffin. A few moments more and my ashes would join those of the girl I had loved. I stumbled against the tabourette, and my fingers closed over the jar of ashes. With one, last, super-human effort, I raised it high above my head, and brought it down with crushing force upon the skull of my antagonist! His arm relaxed, his limp form dropped in a senseless heap on the floor.

"Still acting upon impulse, I raised the silent form of the Professor and carefully, lest I should spill some of it on the floor, lowered the body into the casket of death!

"A moment, and it was over. Professor and liquid, both, were gone, and in their place was a little pile of soft, white ashes!

"As I gazed at my handiwork the brainstorm passed away, and I came face-to-face with the cold, hard truth that I had killed a fellow-being. An unnatural calm possessed me. I knew that there was not one single shred of evidence against me, barring the fact that I was the last one known to be alone with the Professor. Nothing remained but ashes!

"I put on my hat and coat, told the Butler that the Professor had left word he was not to be disturbed, and that I was going out for the evening. Once outside, all my self-possession vanished. My nerves were shot to pieces. I don't know where I went — only that I wandered aimlessly, here and there, until I found myself outside your apartment, just a little while ago.

"Prague, I felt as if I must talk with someone, that I must unburden my tortured mind. I knew that I could trust you, old pal, so I've told you the entire story. Here I am — do with me as you will. Life holds nothing more for me, now that — Marjorie — is — gone!"

Bruce's voice trembled with emotion and broke as he mentioned the name of the girl he loved.

I leaned across the table, and gazed searchingly into the eyes of the abject figure that slouched dejectedly in the big chair. Then I rose, put on my hat and coat, and crossed to Bruce, who had buried his head in his arms and was shaking with silent sobs.

"Bruce!"

Malcolm Bruce raised his eyes.

"Bruce, listen to me. *Are you sure Marjorie Purdy is dead?*"

"Am I sure that —" his eyes widened at the suggestion, and he sat erect with a sudden start.

"Exactly," I went on. "Are you positive that the ashes in that jar were the ashes of Marjorie Purdy?"

"Why — I — see here, Prague! What are you driving at?"

"Then you're *not* sure. You saw the girl's hat and coat in that chair, and in your state of mind you jumped at conclusions. 'The ashes must be those of the missing girl . . . The Professor must have made away with her . . .' and all that. Come now, did Van Allister *tell* you anything —"

"I don't know what he said. I tell you I went *berserk* — mad!"

"Then you come along with me. If she's not dead, she must be somewhere in that house, and if she is there, we're going to find her!"

On the street we hailed a taxi, and in a few moments the butler admitted us to Van Allister's home. Bruce let us into the laboratory with his key. The door of the workshop was still ajar.

My eyes swept the room in a comprehensive survey. At the left, over near the window, was a closed door. I strode across the room and tried the knob, but it refused to yield.

"Where does that lead?"

"Just an anteroom, where the Professor keeps his apparatus."

"All the same, that doors coming open," I returned, grimly. Stepping back a pace or two, I planted a well-directed kick upon the door. Another, and still another, and the frame-work around the lock gave way.

Bruce, with an inarticulate cry, sped across the room to a huge mahogany chest. He selected one of the keys on his ring, inserted it in the lock, and flung back the cover with trembling hands.

"Here she is, Prague — quick! Get her out where there's air!

Together, we bore the limp figure of the girl into the laboratory. Bruce hastily mixed a concoction which he forced between her lips. A second dose, and her eyes slowly opened.

Her bewildered glance traveled around the room, at last resting on Bruce, and her eyes lighted with sudden, happy recognition.

Later, after the first few moments of reunion, the girl told us her story:

"After Malcolm came out, this afternoon, the Professor sent word to me to come into the workshop. As he often summoned me to do one errand or another, I thought nothing of it, and to save time, took my hat and coat along. He closed the door of the little room, and without warning, attacked me from behind. He overpowered me, tied me hand and foot. It was needless to gag me. As you know, the laboratory is absolutely sound-proof.

"Then he produced a huge Newfoundland dog he had secured from somewhere or other, reduced it to ashes before my very eyes, and put the ashes in a glass jar that was on a tabourette in the workshop.

"He went into the anteroom and, from the chest where you found me, took out the glass casket. At least, it seemed a casket to my terror-stricken eyes! He mixed enough of this horrible liquid to fill it almost to the brim.

"Then he told me that but one thing remained. That was — to perform the experiment upon a human being!" She shuddered at the recollection. "He dilated at length upon what a privilege it would be for anyone to sacrifice his life in such a manner, for such a cause. Then he calmly informed me that he had selected you as the subject of his experiment, and that I was to play the role of witness! I fainted.

"The Professor must have feared some sort of intrusion, for the next I remember is waking inside the chest where you discovered me. It was stifling! Every breath I took came harder and harder. I thought of you, Malcolm — thought of the wonderful, happy hours we had spent together the last few days. I wondered what I would do when you were gone! I even prayed that he would kill me, too! My throat grew parched and dry — everything went black before my eyes.

"Next, I opened them to find myself here — with you, Malcolm." Her voice sank to a horse, nervous whisper. "Where — where is the Professor?"

Bruce silently led her into the workshop. She shivered as the coffin of glass came within range of her vision. Still silently, he crossed directly to the casket, and taking up a handful of the soft white ashes, let them sift slowly through his fingers.

The Ghost Eater.

BY C.M. EDDY
AND H.P. LOVECRAFT

3,900-WORD SHORT STORY;
1923.

"The Ghost Eater" was published in the April 1924 issue of Weird Tales, *and it is one of the two stories Clifford Eddy had just received back from* Weird Tales *with a rejection slip when he met Lovecraft. Lovecraft helped him revise it for resubmission; and thereupon editor Edwin Baird accepted it. It's not clear how much Lovecraft did on the actual manuscript; the writing is recognizably Eddy's, but the story does have many Lovecraftian touches. Whether these were put there by Lovecraft himself, or added by Eddy in conscious imitation of Lovecraft's style, isn't known.*

I.

Moon-madness? A touch of fever? I wish I could think so! But when I am alone after dark in the waste places where my wanderings take me, and hear across infinite voids the demon echoes of those screams and snarls, and that detestable crunching of bones, I shudder again the memory of that eldritch night.

I knew less of woodcraft in those days, though the wilderness called just as strongly to me as it does now. Up to that night I had always been careful to employ a guide, but circumstances now suddenly forced me to a trial of my own skill. It was midsummer in Maine, and, despite my great need to get from Mayfair to Glendale by the next noon, I could find no person willing to pilot me. Unless I took the long route through Potowisset, which would not bring me to my goal in time, there would be dense forests to penetrate; yet whenever I asked for a guide I was met with refusal and evasion.

Stranger that I was, it seemed odd that everyone should have such glib excuses. There was too much "important business" on hand for such a sleepy village, and I knew that the natives were lying. But they all had "imperative duties," or said they had; and would do no more than assure me that the trail through the woods was very plain, running due north, and not in the least difficult for a vigorous young fellow. If I started while the morning was still early, they averred, I could get to Glendale by sundown and avoid a night in the open.

Even then I suspected nothing. The prospect seemed good, and I resolved to try it alone, let the lazy villagers hang back as they might. Probably I would have tried it even if I had suspected; for youth is stubborn, and from childhood I had only laughed at superstition and old wives' tales.

So before the sun was high I had started off through the trees at a swinging stride, lunch in my hand, guardian automatic in my pocket, and belt filled with crisp bills of large denominations. From the distances given me and a knowledge of my own speed, I had figured on making Glendale a little after sunset; but I knew that even if detained overnight through some miscalculation, I had plenty of camping experience to fall back on. Besides, my presence at my destination was not really necessary till the following noon.

It was the weather that set my plans awry. As the sun rose higher, it scorched through even the thickets of the foliage, and burned up my energy at every step. By noon my clothes were soaking with perspiration, and I felt myself faltering in spite of all my resolution. As I pushed deeper into the woods I found the trail greatly obstructed with underbrush, and at many points nearly effaced. It must have been weeks — perhaps months — since anyone had broken his way through; and I began to wonder if I could, after all, live up to my schedule.

At length, having grown very hungry, I looked for the deepest patch of shade I could find, and proceeded to eat the lunch which the hotel had prepared for me. There were some indifferent sandwiches, a piece of stale pie, and a bottle of very light wine; by no means sumptuous fare, but welcome enough to one in my state of overheated exhaustion. It was too hot for smoking to be of any solace, so I did not take out my pipe. Instead, I stretched myself at full length under the trees when my meal was done, intent on stealing a few moments' rest before commencing the last lap of my journey. I suppose I was a fool to drink that wine; for, light though it was, it proved just enough to finish the work the sultry, oppressive day had begun. My plan called for the merest momentary relaxation, yet, with scarcely a warning yawn, I dropped off into a sound slumber.

II.

When I opened my eyes twilight was closing in about me. A wind fanned my cheeks, restoring me quickly to full perception; and as I glanced up at the sky I saw with apprehension that black racing clouds were leading on a solid wall of darkness prophetic of a violent thunderstorm. I knew now that I could not reach Glendale before morning, but the prospect of a night in the woods — my first night of lone forest camping — became very repugnant under these trying conditions. In a moment I decided to push along for a while at least, in the hope of finding some shelter before the tempest should break.

Darkness spread over the woods like a heavy blanket. The lowering clouds grew more threatening, and the wind increased to a veritable gale. A flash of distant lightning illuminated the sky, followed by an ominous rumble that seemed to hint of malign pursuit. Then I felt a drop of rain on my outstretched hand; and though still walking on automatically, resigned myself to the inevitable.

Another moment and I had seen the light; the light of the window through the trees and the darkness. Eager only for shelter, I hastened toward it — would to God I had turned and fled!

There was a sort of imperfect clearing on the farther side of which, with its back against the primeval wood, stood a building. I had expected a shanty or log-cabin, but stopped short in surprise when I beheld a neat and tasteful little house of two stories; some seventy years old by its architecture, yet still in a state of repair betokening the closest and most civilized attention. Through the small panes of one of the lower windows a bright light shone, and toward this — spurred by the impact of another raindrop — I presently hurried across the clearing, rapping loudly on the doors as soon as I gained the steps.

With startling promptness my knock was answered by a deep, pleasant voice which uttered the single syllable, "Come!"

Pushing open the unlocked door, I entered a shadowy hall lighted by an open doorway at the right, beyond which was a book-lined room with the gleaming window. As I closed the outer door behind me I could not help noticing a peculiar odour about the house; a faint, elusive, scarcely definable odour which somehow suggested animals. My host, I surmised, must be a hunter or trapper, with his business conducted on the premises.

The man who had spoken sat in a capacious easy-chair before a marble-topped centre table, a long lounging robe of grey swathing his lean form. The light from a powerful argand lamp threw his features into prominence, and as he eyed me curiously I studied him in no less detail. He was strikingly handsome, with thin, clean-shaven face, glossy, flaxen hair neatly brushed, long, regular eyebrows that met in a slanting angle

Weird Tales, April 1924

above his nose, shapely ears set low and well back on the head, and large expressive grey eyes almost luminous in their animation. When he smiled a welcome he showed a magnificently even set of firm white teeth, and as he waved me to a chair I was struck by the fineness of his slender hands, with their long, tapering fingers whose ruddy, almond-shaped nails were slightly curved and exquisitely manicured. I could not help wondering why a man of such an engaging personality should choose the life of a recluse.

"Sorry to intrude," I ventured, "but I've given up the hope of making Glendale before morning, and there's a storm coming on which sent me looking for cover."

As if to corroborate my words, there came at this point a vivid flash, a crashing reverberation, and the first breaking of a torrential downpour that beat maniacally against the windows.

My host seemed oblivious to the elements and flashed me another smile when he answered. His voice was soothing and well modulated, and his eyes held a calmness almost hypnotic.

"You are welcome to whatever hospitality I can offer, but I'm afraid it won't be much. I've a game leg, so you'll have to do most of the waiting on yourself. If you are hungry you'll find plenty in the kitchen — plenty of food, if not of ceremony!"

It seemed to me that I could detect the slightest trace of a foreign accent in his tone, though his language was fluently correct and idiomatic.

Rising to an impressive height, he headed for the door with long, limping steps, and I noticed the huge hairy arms that hung at his side in such curious contrast with his delicate hands.

"Come," he suggested. "Bring the lamp along with you. I might as well sit in the kitchen as here."

I followed him into the hall and the room across it, and at his direction ransacked the woodpile in the corner and the cupboard on the wall. A few moments later, when the fire was going nicely, I asked him if I might not prepare food for both; but he courteously declined.

"It's too hot to eat," he told me. "Besides I had a bite before you came."

After washing the dishes left from my lone meal, I sat down for a while, smoking my pipe contentedly. My host asked a few questions about the neighbouring villages, but lapsed into sullen taciturnity when he learned I was an outsider. As he brooded there silently I could not help feeling a quality of strangeness in him; some subtle alienage that could hardly be analysed. I was quite certain, for one thing, that he was tolerating me because of the storm rather than welcoming me with genuine hospitality.

As for the storm, it seemed almost to have spent itself. Outside, it was already growing lighter — for there was a full moon behind the clouds — and the rain had dwindled to a trivial drizzle. Perhaps, I thought, I could now resume my journey after all; an idea which I suggested to my host.

"Better wait till morning," he remarked. "You say you're afoot, and it's a good three hours to Glendale. I've two bedrooms upstairs, and you're welcome to one of them if you care to stay."

There was a sincerity in his invitation which dispelled any doubts I had held regarding his hospitality, and I now concluded that his silences must be the result of long isolation from his fellows in the wilderness. After sitting without a word through three fillings of my pipe, I finally began to yawn.

"It's been rather a strenuous day for me," I admitted, "and I guess I'd better be making tracks for bed. I want to be up at sunrise, you know, and on my way."

My host waved his arm toward the door, through which I could see the hall and the staircase.

"Take the lamp with you," he instructed. "It's the only one I have, but I don't mind sitting in the dark, really. Half the time I don't light it all when I'm alone. Oil is so hard to get out here, and I go to the village so seldom. Your room is the one on the right, at the head of the stairs."

Taking the lamp and turning in the hall to say good-night, I could see his eyes glowing almost phosphorescently in the darkened room I had left; and I was half reminded for a moment of the jungle, and the circles of eyes that sometimes glowed just beyond the radius of the campfire. Then I started upstairs.

As I reached the second floor I could hear my host limping across the hall to the other room below, and perceived that he moved with owlish sureness despite the darkness. Truly, he had but little need of the lamp.

The storm was over, and as I entered the room assigned me I found it bright with the rays of a full moon that streamed on the bed from an un-curtained south window. Blowing out the lamp and leaving the house in darkness but for moonbeams, I sniffed at the pungent odour that rose above the scent of the kerosene — the quasi-animal odour I had noticed on first entering the place. I crossed to the window and threw it wide, breathing deep of the cool, fresh night air.

When I started to undress I paused almost instantly, recalling my money belt, still in its place about my waist. Possibly, I reflected, it would be well not to be too hasty or unguarded; for I had read of men who seize just such an opportunity to rob and even to murder the stranger within their dwelling. So, arranging the bedclothes to look as if they covered a sleeping figure, I drew the room's only chair into the concealing shadows, filled and lighted my pipe again, and sat down to rest or watch, as the occasion might demand.

III.

I could not have been sitting there long when my sensitive ears caught the sound of footsteps ascending the stairs. All the old lore of robber landlords rushed on me afresh, when another moment revealed that the steps were plain, loud, and careless, with no attempt at concealment; while my host's tread, as I had heard it from the head of the staircase, was a soft limping stride. Shaking the ashes from my pipe, I slipped it in my pocket. Then, seizing and drawing my automatic, I rose from the chair, tiptoed across the room, and crouched tensely in a spot which the opening door would cover.

The door opened, and into the shaft of moonlight stepped a man I had never seen before. Tall, broad-shouldered, and distinguished, his face half hidden by a heavy square-cut beard and his neck buried in a high black stock of a pattern long obsolete in America, he was indubitably a foreigner. How he could have entered the house without my knowledge was quite beyond me, nor could I believe for an instant that he had been concealed in either of the two rooms or the hall below me. As I gazed intently at him in the insidious moonbeams it seemed to me that I could see directly through his sturdy form; but perhaps this was only an illusion that came from my shock of surprise.

Noticing the disarray of the bed, but evidently missing the intended effect of occupancy, the stranger muttered something to himself in a foreign tongue and proceeded to disrobe. Flinging his clothes into the chair I had vacated, he crept into bed, pulled the covers over him, and in a moment or two was breathing with the regular respiration of a sound sleeper.

My first thought was to seek out my host and demand an explanation, but a second later I deemed it better to make sure that the whole incident was not a mere delusive after-effect of my wine-drugged sleep in the woods. I still felt weak and faint, and despite my recent supper was as hungry as if I had not eaten since that noonday lunch.

I crossed to the bed, reached out, and grasped at the shoulder of the sleeping man. Then, barely checking a cry of mad frightened dizzy astonishment, I fell back with pounding pulse and dilated eyes. *For my clutching fingers had passed directly through the sleeping form, and seized only the sheets below!*

A complete analysis of my jarred and jumbled sensations would be futile. The man was intangible, yet I could still see him there, hear his regular breathing, and watch his figure is it half-turned beneath the clothes. And then, as I was quite certain of my own madness or hypnosis, I heard other footsteps on the stairs; soft, padded, doglike, limping footsteps, pattering up, up, up . . . And again that pungent animal smell, this time in redoubled volume. Dazed and dream-drowsed, I crept once more behind the protecting opened door, shaken to the marrow, but now resigned to any fate known or nameless.

Then into that shaft of eerie moonlight stepped the gaunt form of a great grey wolf. Limped, I should have said, for one hind foot was held in the air, as though wounded by some stray shot. The beast turned its head in my direction, and as it did so the pistol dropped from my twitching fingers and clattered unheeded to the floor. The ascending succession of horrors was fast paralysing my will and consciousness, *for the eyes that now glared toward me from that hellish head were the grey phosphorescent eyes of my host as they had peered at me through the darkness of the kitchen.*

I do not yet know whether it saw me. The eyes turned from my direction to the bed, and gazed gluttonously on the spectral sleeping form there. Then the head tilted back, and from that demon throat came the most shocking ululation I have ever heard; a thick, nauseous, lupine howl that made my heart stand still. The form on the bed stirred, opened his eyes, and shrank from what he saw. The animal crouched quiveringly, and then — as the ethereal figure uttered a shriek of mortal human anguish and terror that no ghost of legend could counterfeit — sprang straight for its victim's throat, its white, firm, even teeth flashing in the moonlight as they closed on the jugular vein of the screaming phantasm. The scream ended in a blood-choked gurgle, and the frightened human eyes turned glassy.

That scream had roused me to action, and in a second I had retrieved my automatic and emptied its entire contents into the wolfish monstrosity before me. *But I heard the unhindered thud of each bullet as it embedded itself in the opposite wall.*

My nerves gave way. Blind fear hurled me towards the door, and blind fear prompted the one backward glance in which I saw that the wolf had sunk its teeth into the body of its quarry. Then came the culminating sensory impression and the devastating thought to which it gave birth. This was the same body I had thrust my hand through a few moments before . . . And yet as I plunged down that black nightmare staircase *I could hear the crunching of bones.*

IV.

How I found the trail to Glendale, or how I managed to traverse it, I suppose I shall never know. I only know that sunrise found me on the hill at the edge of the woods, with the steepled village outspread below me, and the blue thread of the Cataqua sparkling in the distance. Hatless, coatless, ashen-faced, and as soaked with perspiration as if I had spent the night abroad in the storm, I hesitated to enter the village till I had recovered at least some outward semblance of composure. At last I picked my way downhill and through the narrow streets with their flagstone sidewalks and Colonial doorways till I reached the Lafayette House, whose proprietor eyed me askance.

"Where from so early, son? And why the wild look?"

"I've just come through the woods from Mayfair."

"You — came — through — the Devil's Woods — *last night* — and *alone?*" The old man stared with a queer look of alternate horror and incredulity.

"Why not?" I countered. "I couldn't have made it in time through Potowisset, and I had to be here not later than this noon."

"And last night was *full moon!* My Gawd!" He eyed me curiously. "See anything of Vasili Oukranikov or the Count?"

"Say, do I look that simple? What are you trying to do — jolly me?"

But his tone was his grave as a priest's as he replied. "You must be new to these parts, sonny. If you weren't you'd know all about Devil's Woods and the full moon and Vasili and the rest." I felt anything but flippant, yet I knew I must not seem serious after my earlier remarks. "Go on — I know you're dying to tell me. I'm like a donkey — all ears."

Then he told the legend in his dry way, stripping it of vitality and convincingness through lack of coloring, detail, and atmosphere. But for me it needed no vitality or convincingness that any poet could have given. Remember what I had witnessed, and remember that I had never heard of the tale until *after* I had had the experience and fled from the terror of those crunched phantom bones.

"There used to be quite a few Russians scattered betwixt here and Mayfair — they came after one of their nihilist troubles back in Russia. Vasili Oukranikov was one of 'em — a tall, thin, handsome chap with shiny yellow hair and a wonderful manner. They said, though, that he was a servant of the devil — a werewolf and eater of men.

"He built him a house in the woods about a third of the way from here to Mayfair and lived all alone. Every once in a while a traveler would come out of the woods with some pretty strange tale about being chased by a big grey wolf with shining human eyes — like Oukranikov's. One night somebody took a potshot at the wolf, and the next time the Russian came into Glendale he walked with a limp. That settled it. There wasn't any mere suspicion now, but hard facts.

"Then he sent to Mayfair for the Count — his name was Feodor Tchemevsky and he had bought the old gambrel-roof Fowler place up State Street — to come out and see him. They all warned the Count, for he was a fine man and a splendid neighbour, but he said he could take care of himself all right. It was the night of the full moon. He was brave as they make 'em, and all he did was to tell some men he had around the place to follow him to Vasili's if he didn't show up in decent time. They did — and you tell me, sonny, that you've been through those woods at night?"

"Sure I tell him you" — I tried to appear nonchalant — "I'm no Count, and here I am to tell the tale! . . . But what did the men find at Oukranikov's house?"

"They found the Count's mangled body, sonny, and a gaunt grey wolf hovering over it with blood-slavering jaws. You can guess who the wolf was. And folks do say that it every full moon — but sonny, didn't you see or hear anything?"

"Not a thing, pop! And say, what became of the wolf — or Vasili Oukranikov?"

"Why, son, they killed it — filled it full of lead and buried it in the house, and then burned the place down — you know all this was sixty years ago when I was a little shaver, but I remember it as if 'twas yesterday."

I turned away with a shrug of my shoulders. It was all so quaint and silly and artificial in the full light of day. But sometimes when I am alone after dark in the waste places, and hear the demon echoes of those screams and snarls, and that detestable crunching of bones, I shudder again at the memory of that eldritch night.

The Unnamable.

2,900-WORD SHORT STORY; 1923.

This short story, the second of Lovecraft's tales to involve the Randolph Carter character, comes off more like a writing exercise involving philosophical exploration than a real, professional story. It's almost as if Lovecraft were firming up his new attitude toward graveyard horrors, and at the same time broadening and deepending his use of New England settings in general, and Arkham in particular, in his horror-story construction.

It was written sometime in September or October of 1923, possibly before "The Rats in the Walls" (it feels somewhat like a warm-up to that story) but more likely after. It was first published in the July 1925 issue of Weird Tales.

We were sitting on a dilapidated seventeenth-century tomb in the late afternoon of an autumn day at the old burying ground in Arkham, and speculating about the unnamable. Looking toward the giant willow in the cemetery, whose trunk had nearly engulfed an ancient, illegible slab, I had made a fantastic remark about the spectral and unmentionable nourishment which the colossal roots must be sucking from that hoary, charnel earth; when my friend chided me for such nonsense and told me that since no interments had occurred there for over a century, nothing could possibly exist to nourish the tree in other than an ordinary manner. Besides, he added, my constant talk about "unnamable" and "unmentionable" things was a very puerile device, quite in keeping with my lowly standing as an author. I was too fond of ending my stories with sights or sounds which paralyzed my heroes' faculties and left them without courage, words, or associations to tell what they had experienced. We know things, he said, only through our five senses or our intuitions; wherefore it is quite impossible to refer to any object or spectacle which cannot be clearly depicted by the solid definitions of fact or the correct doctrines of theology — preferably those of the Congregationalist, with whatever modifications tradition and Sir Arthur Conan Doyle may supply.

With this friend, Joel Manton, I had often languidly disputed. He was principal of the East High School, born and bred in Boston and sharing New England's self-satisfied deafness to the delicate overtones of life. It was his view that only our normal, objective experiences possess any esthetic significance, and that it is the province of the artist not so much to rouse strong emotion by action, ecstasy, and astonishment, as to maintain a placid interest and appreciation by accurate, detailed transcripts of everyday affairs. Especially did he object to my preoccupation with the mystical and the unexplained; for although believing in the supernatural much more fully than I, he would not admit that it is sufficiently commonplace for literary treatment. That a mind can find its greatest pleasure in escapes from the daily treadmill, and in original and dramatic recombinations of images usually thrown by habit and fatigue into the hackneyed patterns of actual existence, was something virtually incredible to his clear, practical, and logical intellect. With him all things and feelings had fixed dimensions, properties, causes, and effects; and although he vaguely knew that the mind sometimes holds visions and sensations of far less geometrical, classifiable, and workable nature, he believed himself justified in drawing an arbitrary line and ruling out of court all that cannot be experienced and understood by the average citizen. Besides, he was almost sure that nothing can be really "unnamable." It didn't sound sensible to him.

Though I well realized the futility of imaginative and metaphysical arguments against the complacency of an orthodox sun-dweller, something in the scene of this afternoon colloquy moved me to more than usual contentiousness. The crumbling slate slabs, the patriarchal trees, and the centuried gambrel roofs of the witch-haunted old town that stretched around, all combined to rouse my spirit in defense of my work; and I was soon carrying my thrusts into the enemy's own country. It was not, indeed, difficult to begin a counter-attack, for I knew that Joel Manton actually half clung to many old-wives' superstitions which sophisticated people had long outgrown; beliefs in the appearance of dying persons at distant places, and in the impressions left by old faces on the windows through which they had gazed all their lives. To credit these whisperings of rural grandmothers, I now insisted, argued a faith in the existence of spectral substances on the earth apart from and subsequent to their material counterparts. It argued a capability of believing in phenomena beyond all normal notions; for if a dead man can transmit his visible or tangible image half across the world, or down the stretch of the centuries, how can it be absurd to suppose that deserted houses are full of queer sentient things, or that old graveyards teem with the terrible, unbodied intelligence of generations? And since spirit, in order to cause all the manifestations attributed to it, cannot be limited by any of the laws of matter, why is it extravagant to imagine psychically living dead things in shapes — or absences of shapes — which must for human spectators be utterly and appallingly "unnamable"? "Common sense" in reflecting on these subjects, I assured my friend with some warmth, is merely a stupid absence of imagination and mental flexibility.

Twilight had now approached, but neither of us felt any wish to cease speaking. Manton seemed unimpressed by my arguments, and eager to refute them, having that confidence in his own opinions which had doubtless caused his success as a teacher; whilst I was too sure of my ground to fear defeat. The dusk fell, and lights faintly gleamed in some of the distant windows, but we did not move. Our seat on the tomb was very comfortable, and I knew that my prosaic friend would not mind the cavernous rift in the ancient, root-disturbed brickwork close behind us, or the utter blackness of the spot brought by the intervention of a tottering, deserted seventeenth-century house between us and the nearest lighted road. There in the dark, upon that riven tomb by the deserted house, we talked on about the "unnamable" and after my friend had finished his scoffing I told him of the awful evidence behind the story at which he had scoffed the most.

My tale had been called The Attic Window, and appeared in the January, 1922, issue of *Whispers*. In a good many places, especially the South and the Pacific coast, they took the magazines off the stands at the complaints of silly milk-sops; but New England didn't get the thrill and merely shrugged its shoulders at my extravagance. The thing, it was averred, was biologically impossible to start with; merely another of those crazy country mutterings which Cotton Mather had been gullible enough to dump into his chaotic *Magnalia Christi Americana*, and so poorly authenticated that even he had not ventured to name the locality where the horror occurred. And as to the way I amplified the bare jotting of the old mystic — that was quite impossible, and characteristic of a flighty and notional scribbler! Mather had indeed told of the thing as being born, but nobody but a cheap sensationalist would think of having it grow up, look into people's windows at night, and be hidden in the attic of a house, in flesh and in spirit, till someone saw it at the window centuries later and couldn't describe what it was that turned his hair gray. All this was flagrant trashiness, and my friend Manton was not slow to insist on that fact.

Then I told him what I had found in an old diary kept between 1706 and 1723, unearthed among family papers not a mile from where we were sitting; that, and the certain reality of the scars on my ancestor's chest and back which the diary described. I told him, too, of the fears of others in that region, and how they were whispered down for generations; and how no mythical madness came to the boy who in 1793 entered an abandoned house to examine certain traces suspected to be there.

It had been an eldritch thing — no wonder sensitive students shudder at the Puritan age in Massachusetts. So little is known of what went on beneath the surface — so little, yet such a ghastly festering as it bubbles up putrescently in occasional ghoulish glimpses. The witchcraft terror is a horrible ray of light on what was stewing in men's crushed brains, but even that is a trifle. There was no beauty, no freedom — we can see that from the architectural and household remains, and the poisonous sermons of the cramped divines. And inside that rusted iron straitjacket lurked gibbering hideousness, perversion, and diabolism. Here, truly, was the apotheosis ofThe Unnamable.

Cotton Mather, in that demoniac sixth book which no one should read after dark, minced no words as he flung forth his anathema. Stern as a Jewish prophet, and laconically un-amazed as none since his day could be, he told of the beast that had brought forth what was more than beast but less than man — the thing with the blemished eye — and of the screaming drunken wretch that hanged for having such an eye. This much he baldly told, yet without a hint of what came after. Perhaps he did not know, or perhaps he knew and did not dare to tell. Others knew, but did not dare to tell — there is no public hint of why they whispered about the lock on the door to the attic stairs in the house of a childless, broken, embittered old man who had put up a blank slate slab by an avoided grave, although one may trace enough evasive legends to curdle the thinnest blood.

It is all in that ancestral diary I found; all the hushed innuendoes and furtive tales of things with a blemished eye seen at windows in the night or in deserted meadows near the woods. Something had caught my ancestor on a dark valley road, leaving him with marks of horns on his chest and of apelike claws on his back; and when they looked for prints in the trampled dust they found the mixed marks of split hooves and vaguely anthropoid paws. Once a post-rider said he saw an old man chasing and calling to a frightful loping, nameless thing on Meadow Hill in the thinly moonlit hours before dawn, and many believed him. Certainly, there was strange talk one night in 1710 when the childless, broken old man was buried in the crypt behind his own house in sight of the blank slate slab. They never unlocked that attic door, but left the whole house as it was, dreaded and deserted. When noises came from it, they whispered and shivered; and hoped that the lock on that attic door was strong. Then they stopped hoping when the horror occurred at the parsonage, leaving not a soul alive or in one piece.

With the years the legends take on a spectral character — I suppose the thing, if it was a living thing, must have died. The memory had lingered hideously — all the more hideous because it was so secret.

During this narration my friend Manton had become very silent, and I saw that my words had impressed him. He did not laugh as I paused, but asked quite seriously about the boy who went mad in 1793, and who had presumably been the hero of my fiction. I told him why the boy had gone to that shunned, deserted house, and remarked that he ought to be interested, since he believed that windows latent images of those who had sat at them. The boy had gone to look at the windows of that horrible attic, because of tales of things seen behind them, and had come back screaming maniacally.

Manton remained thoughtful as I said this, but gradually reverted to his analytical mood. He granted for the sake of argument that some unnatural monster had really existed, but reminded me that even the most morbid perversion of nature need not be unnamable or scientifically indescribable. I admired his clearness and persistence, and added some further revelations I had collected among the old people. Those later spectral legends, I made plain, related to monstrous apparitions more frightful than anything organic could be; apparitions of gigantic bestial forms sometimes visible and sometimes only tangible, which floated about on moonless nights and haunted the old house, the crypt behind it, and the grave where a sapling had sprouted beside an illegible slab. Whether or not such apparitions had ever gored or smothered people to death, as told in uncorroborated traditions, they had produced a strong and consistent impression; and were yet darkly feared by very aged natives, though largely forgotten by the last two generations — perhaps dying for lack of being thought about. Moreover, so far as esthetic theory was involved, if the psychic emanations of human creatures be grotesque distortions, what coherent representation could express or portray so gibbous and infamous a nebulosity as the specter of a malign, chaotic perversion, itself a morbid blasphemy against nature? Molded by the dead brain of a hybrid nightmare, would not such a vaporous terror constitute in all loathsome truth the exquisitely, the shriekingly unnamable?

The hour must now have grown very late. A singularly noiseless bat brushed by me, and I believe it touched Manton also, for although I could not see him I felt him raise his arm. Presently he spoke.

"But is that house with the attic window still standing and deserted?"

"Yes," I answered, "I have seen it."

"And did you find anything there — in the attic or anywhere else?"

"There were some bones up under the eaves. They may have been what that boy saw — if he was sensitive he wouldn't have needed anything in the window-glass to unhinge him. If they all came from the same object it must have been an hysterical, delirious monstrosity. It would have been blasphemous to leave such bones in the world, so I went back with a sack and took them to the tomb behind the house. There was an opening where I could dump them in. Don't think I was a fool — you ought to have seen that skull. It had four-inch horns, but a face and jaw something like yours and mine."

At last I could feel a real shiver run through Manton, who had moved very near. But his curiosity was undeterred.

"And what about the window-panes?"

"They were all gone. One window had lost its entire frame, and in all the others there was not a trace of glass in the little diamond apertures. They were that kind — the old lattice windows that went out of use before 1700. I don't believe they've had any glass for a hundred years or more — maybe the boy broke 'em if he got that far; the legend doesn't say."

Manton was reflecting again.

"I'd like to see that house, Carter. Where is it? Glass or no glass, I must explore it a little. And the tomb where you put those bones, and the other grave without an inscription — the whole thing must be a bit terrible."

"You did see it — until it got dark."

My friend was more wrought upon than I had suspected, for at this touch of harmless theatricalism he started neurotically away from me and actually cried out with a sort of gulping gasp which released a strain of previous repression. It was an odd cry, and all the more terrible because it was answered. For as it was still echoing, I heard a creaking sound through the pitchy blackness, and knew that a lattice window was opening in that accursed old house beside us. And because all the other frames were long since fallen, I knew that it was the grisly glassless frame of that demoniac attic window.

Then came a noxious rush of noisome, frigid air from that same dreaded direction, followed by a piercing shriek just beside me on that shocking rifted tomb of man and monster. In another instant I was knocked from my gruesome bench by the devilish threshing of some unseen entity of titanic size but undetermined nature; knocked sprawling on the root-clutched mold of that abhorrent graveyard, while from the tomb came such a stifled uproar of gasping and whirring that my fancy peopled the rayless gloom with Miltonic legions of the misshapen damned. There was a vortex of withering, ice-cold wind, and then the rattle of loose bricks and plaster; but I had mercifully fainted before I could learn what it meant.

Manton, though smaller than I, is more resilient; for we opened our eyes at almost the same instant, despite his greater injuries. Our couches were side by side, and we knew in a few seconds that we were in St. Mary's Hospital. Attendants were grouped about in tense curiosity, eager to aid our memory by telling us how we came there, and we soon heard of the farmer who had found us at noon in a lonely field beyond Meadow Hill, a mile from the old burying ground, on a spot where an ancient slaughterhouse is reputed to have stood. Manton had two malignant wounds in the chest, and some less severe cuts or gougings in the back. I was not so seriously hurt, but was covered with welts and contusions of the most bewildering character, including the print of a split hoof. It was plain that Manton knew more than I, but he told nothing to the puzzled and interested physicians till he had learned what our injuries were. Then he said we were the victims of a vicious bull — though the animal was a difficult thing to place and account for.

After the doctors and nurses had left, I whispered an awe-struck question:

"Good God, Manton, but what was it? Those scars — was it like that?"

And I was too dazed to exult when he whispered back a thing I had half expected —

"No — it wasn't that way at all. It was everywhere — a gelatin — a slime yet it had shapes, a thousand shapes of horror beyond all memory. There were eyes — and a blemish. It was the pit — the maelstrom — the ultimate abomination. Carter, it was the unnamable!"

The Festival.

3,600-WORD SHORT STORY; 1923.

This is one of the most remarkable stories in Lovecraft's oeuvre, *not for the tale it tells but for the creamy, melancholic style in which it's written. It is, as S. T. Joshi has noted, "a virtual 3,000-word prose poem."*

"The Festival" was written during the same fertile period of September and October 1923, probably but not certainly after "The Rats in the Walls." It was published in the January 1925 issue of Weird Tales.

Efficiunt Daemones, ut quae non sunt, sic tamen quasi sint, conspicienda hominibus exhibeant. (Devils so work that things which are not appear to men as if they were real.)

— LACTANTIUS

I was far from home, and the spell of the eastern sea was upon me. In the twilight I heard it pounding on the rocks, and I knew it lay just over the hill where the twisting willows writhed against the clearing sky and the first stars of evening. And because my fathers had called me to the old town beyond, I pushed on through the shallow, new-fallen snow along the road that soared lonely up to where Aldebaran twinkled among the trees, on toward the very ancient town I had never seen but often dreamed of.

It was the Yuletide, that men call Christmas though they know in their hearts it is older than Bethlehem and Babylon, older than Memphis and mankind. It was the Yuletide, and I had come at last to the ancient sea town where my people had dwelt and kept festival in the elder time when festival was forbidden; where also they had commanded their sons to keep festival once every century, that the memory of primal secrets might not be forgotten. Mine were an old people, and were old even when this land was settled three hundred years before. And they were strange, because they had come as dark furtive folk from opiate southern gardens of orchids, and spoken another tongue before they learnt the tongue of the blue-eyed fishers. And now they were scattered, and shared only the rituals of mysteries that none living could understand. I was the only one who came back that night to the old fishing town as legend bade, for only the poor and the lonely remember.

Then beyond the hill's crest I saw Kingsport outspread frostily in the gloaming; snowy Kingsport with its ancient vanes and steeples, ridgepoles and chimney-pots, wharves and small bridges, willow-trees and graveyards; endless labyrinths of steep, narrow, crooked streets, and dizzy church-crowned central peak that time durst not touch; ceaseless mazes of colonial houses piled and scattered at all angles and levels like a child's disordered blocks; antiquity hovering on grey wings over winter-whitened gables and gambrel roofs; fanlights and small-paned windows one by one gleaming out in the cold dusk to join Orion and the archaic stars. And against the rotting wharves the sea pounded; the secretive, immemorial sea out of which the people had come in the elder time.

Beside the road at its crest a still higher summit rose, bleak and windswept, and I saw that it was a burying-ground where black gravestones stuck ghoulishly through the snow like the decayed fingernails of a gigantic corpse. The printless road was very lonely, and sometimes I thought I heard a distant horrible creaking as of a gibbet in the wind. They had hanged four kinsmen of mine for witchcraft in 1692, but I did not know just where.

As the road wound down the seaward slope I listened for the merry sounds of a village at evening, but did not hear them. Then I thought of the season, and felt that these old Puritan folk might well have Christmas customs strange to me, and full of silent hearthside prayer. So after that I did not listen for merriment or look for wayfarers, but kept on down past the hushed lighted farmhouses and shadowy stone walls to where the signs of ancient shops and sea taverns creaked in the salt breeze, and the grotesque knockers of pillared doorways glistened along deserted unpaved lanes in the light of little, curtained windows.

I had seen maps of the town, and knew where to find the home of my people. It was told that I should be known and welcomed, for village legend lives long; so I hastened through Back Street to Circle Court, and across the fresh snow on the one full flagstone pavement in the town, to where Green Lane leads off behind the Market House. The old maps still held good, and I had no trouble; though at Arkham they must have lied when they said the trolleys ran to this place, since I saw not a wire overhead. Snow would have hid the rails in any case. I was glad I had chosen to walk, for the white village had seemed very beautiful from the hill; and now I was eager to knock at the door of my people, the seventh house on the left in Green Lane, with an ancient peaked roof and jutting second storey, all built before 1650.

There were lights inside the house when I came upon it, and I saw from the diamond window-panes that it must have been kept very close to its antique state. The upper part overhung the narrow grass-grown street and nearly met the overhanging part of the house opposite, so that I was almost in a tunnel, with the low stone doorstep wholly free from snow. There was no sidewalk, but many houses had high doors reached by double flights of steps with iron railings. It was an odd scene, and because I was strange to New England I had never known its like before. Though it pleased me, I would have relished it better if there had been footprints in the snow, and people in the streets, and a few windows without drawn curtains.

When I sounded the archaic iron knocker I was half afraid. Some fear had been gathering in me, perhaps because of the strangeness of my heritage, and the bleakness of the evening, and the queerness of the silence in that aged town of curious customs. And when my knock was answered I was fully afraid, because I had not heard any footsteps before the door creaked open. But I was not afraid long, for the gowned, slippered old man in the doorway had a bland face that reassured me; and though he made signs that he was dumb, he wrote a quaint and ancient welcome with the stylus and wax tablet he carried.

He beckoned me into a low, candle-lit room with massive exposed rafters and dark, stiff, sparse furniture of the seventeenth century. The past was vivid there, for not an attribute was missing. There was a cavernous fireplace and a spinning-wheel at which a bent old woman in loose wrapper and deep poke-bonnet sat back toward me, silently spinning despite the festive season. An indefinite dampness seemed upon the place, and I marvelled that no fire should be blazing. The high-backed settle faced the row of curtained windows at the left, and seemed to be occupied, though I was not sure. I did not like everything about what I saw, and felt again the fear I had had. This fear grew stronger from what had before lessened it, for the more I looked at the old man's bland face the more its very blandness terrified me. The eyes never moved, and the skin was too much like wax. Finally I was sure it was not a face at all, but a fiendishly cunning mask. But the flabby hands, curiously gloved, wrote genially on the tablet and told me I must wait a while before I could be led to the place of the festival.

Pointing to a chair, table, and pile of books, the old man now left the room; and when I sat down to read I saw that the books were hoary and mouldy, and that they included old Morryster's wild *Marvels of Science*, the terrible *Saducismus Triumphatus* of Joseph Glanvil, published in 1681, the shocking *Daemonolatreja* of Remigius, printed in 1595 at Lyons, and worst of all, the unmentionable *Necronomicon* of the mad Arab Abdul Alhazred, in Olaus Wormius' forbidden Latin translation; a book which I had never seen, but of which I had heard monstrous things whispered. No one spoke to me, but I could hear the creaking of signs in the wind outside, and the whir of the wheel as the bonneted old woman continued her silent

Weird Tales, January 1925

spinning, spinning. I thought the room and the books and the people very morbid and disquieting, but because an old tradition of my fathers had summoned me to strange feastings, I resolved to expect queer things. So I tried to read, and soon became tremblingly absorbed by something I found in that accursed *Necronomicon*; a thought and a legend too hideous for sanity or consciousness, but I disliked it when I fancied I heard the closing of one of the windows that the settle faced, as if it had been stealthily opened. It had seemed to follow a whirring that was not of the old woman's spinning-wheel. This was not much, though, for the old woman was spinning very hard, and the aged clock had been striking. After that I lost the feeling that there were persons on the settle, and was reading intently and shudderingly when the old man came back booted and dressed in a loose antique costume, and sat down on that very bench, so that I could not see him. It was certainly nervous waiting, and the blasphemous book in my hands made it doubly so. When eleven struck, however, the old man stood up, glided to a massive carved chest in a corner, and got two hooded cloaks; one of which he donned, and the other of which he draped round the old woman, who was ceasing her monotonous spinning. Then they both started for the outer door; the woman lamely creeping, and the old man, after picking up the very book I had been reading, beckoning me as he drew his hood over that unmoving face or mask.

We went out into the moonless and tortuous network of that incredibly ancient town; went out as the lights in the curtained windows disappeared one by one, and the Dog Star leered at the throng of cowled, cloaked figures that poured silently from every doorway and formed monstrous processions up this street and that, past the creaking signs and antediluvian gables, the thatched roofs and diamond-paned windows; threading precipitous lanes where decaying houses overlapped and crumbled together; gliding across open courts and churchyards where the bobbing lanthorns made eldritch drunken constellations.

Amid these hushed throngs I followed my voiceless guides; jostled by elbows that seemed preternaturally soft, and pressed by chests and stomachs that seemed abnormally pulpy; but seeing never a face and hearing never a word. Up, up, up, the eery columns slithered, and I saw that all the travellers were converging as they flowed near a sort of focus of crazy alleys at the top of a high hill in the centre of the town, where perched a great white church. I had seen it from the road's crest when I looked at Kingsport in the new dusk, and it had made me shiver because Aldebaran had seemed to balance itself a moment on the ghostly spire.

There was an open space around the church; partly a churchyard with spectral shafts, and partly a half-paved square swept nearly bare of snow by the wind, and lined with unwholesomely archaic houses having peaked roofs and overhanging gables. Death-fires danced over the tombs, revealing gruesome vistas, though queerly failing to cast any shadows. Past the churchyard, where there were no houses, I could see over the hill's summit and watch the glimmer of stars on the harbour, though the town was invisible in the dark. Only once in a while a lantern bobbed horribly through serpentine alleys on its way to overtake the throng that was now slipping speechlessly into the church. I waited till the crowd had oozed into the black doorway, and till all the stragglers had followed. The old man was pulling at my sleeve, but I was determined to be the last. Crossing the threshold into the swarming temple of unknown darkness, I turned once to look at the outside world as the churchyard phosphorescence cast a sickly glow on the hilltop pavement. And as I did so I shuddered. For though the wind had not left much snow, a few patches did remain on the path near the door; and in that fleeting backward look it seemed to my troubled eyes that they bore no mark of passing feet, not even mine.

The church was scarce lighted by all the lanthorns that had entered it, for most of the throng had already vanished. They had streamed up the aisle between the high pews to the trap-door of the vaults which yawned loathsomely open just before the pulpit, and were now squirming noiselessly in. I followed dumbly down the foot-worn steps and into the dark, suffocating crypt. The tail of that sinuous line of night-marchers seemed very horrible, and as I saw them wriggling into a venerable tomb they seemed more horrible still. Then I noticed that the tomb's floor had an aperture down which the throng was sliding, and in a moment we were all descending an ominous staircase of rough-hewn stone; a narrow spiral staircase damp and peculiarly odorous, that wound endlessly down into the bowels of the hill past monotonous walls of dripping stone blocks and crumbling mortar. It was a silent, shocking descent, and I observed after a horrible interval that the walls and steps were changing in nature, as if chiseled out of the solid rock. What mainly troubled me was that the myriad footfalls made no sound and set up no echoes.

After more aeons of descent I saw some side passages or burrows leading from unknown recesses of blackness to this shaft of nighted mystery. Soon they became excessively numerous, like impious catacombs of nameless menace; and their pungent odour of decay grew quite unbearable. I knew we must have passed down through the mountain and beneath the earth of Kingsport itself, and I shivered that a town should be so aged and maggoty with subterraneous evil.

Then I saw the lurid shimmering of pale light, and heard the insidious lapping of sunless waters. Again I shivered, for I did not like the things that the night had brought, and wished bitterly that no forefather had summoned me to this primal rite. As the steps and the passage grew broader, I heard another sound, the thin, whining mockery of a feeble flute; and suddenly there spread out before me the boundless vista of an inner world—a vast fungous shore litten by a belching column of sick greenish flame and washed by a wide oily river that flowed from abysses frightful and unsuspected to join the blackest gulfs of immemorial ocean.

Fainting and gasping, I looked at that unhallowed Erebus of titan toadstools, leprous fire and slimy water, and saw the cloaked throngs forming a semicircle around the blazing pillar. It was the Yule-rite, older than man and fated to survive him; the primal rite of the solstice and of spring's promise beyond the snows; the rite of fire and evergreen, light and music.

And in the stygian grotto I saw them do the rite, and adore the sick pillar of flame, and throw into the water handfuls gouged out of the viscous vegetation which glittered green in the chlorotic glare. I saw this, and I saw something amorphously squatted far away from the light, piping noisomely on a flute; and as the thing piped I thought I heard noxious muffled flutterings in the foetid darkness where I could not see. But what frightened me most was that flaming column; spouting volcanically from depths profound and inconceivable, casting no shadows as healthy flame should, and coating the nitrous stone with a nasty, venomous verdigris. For in all that seething combustion no warmth lay, but only the clamminess of death and corruption.

The man who had brought me now squirmed to a point directly beside the hideous flame, and made stiff ceremonial motions to the semi-circle he faced. At certain stages of the ritual they did grovelling obeisance, especially when he held above his head that abhorrent *Necronomicon* he had taken with him; and I shared all the obeisances because I had been summoned to this festival by the writings of my forefathers. Then the old man made a signal to the half-seen flute-player in the darkness, which player thereupon changed its feeble drone to a scarce louder drone in another key; precipitating as it did so a horror unthinkable and unexpected. At this horror I sank nearly to the lichened earth, transfixed with a dread not of this or any world, but only of the mad spaces between the stars.

Out of the unimaginable blackness beyond the gangrenous glare of that cold flame, out of the tartarean leagues through which that oily river rolled uncanny, unheard, and unsuspected, there flopped rhythmically a horde of tame, trained, hybrid winged things that no sound eye could ever wholly grasp, or sound brain ever wholly remember. They were not altogether crows, nor moles, nor buzzards, nor ants, nor vampire bats, nor decomposed human beings; but something I cannot and must not recall. They flopped limply along, half with their webbed feet and half with their membranous wings; and as they reached the throng of celebrants the cowled figures seized and mounted them, and rode off one by one along the reaches of that unlighted river, into pits and galleries of panic where poison springs feed frightful and undiscoverable cataracts.

The old spinning woman had gone with the throng, and the old man remained only because I had refused when he motioned me to seize an animal and ride like the rest. I saw when I staggered to my feet that the amorphous flute-player had rolled out of sight, but that two of the beasts were patiently standing by. As I hung back, the old man produced his stylus and tablet and wrote that he was the true deputy of my fathers who had founded the Yule worship in this ancient place; that it had been decreed I should come back, and that the most secret mysteries were yet to be performed. He wrote this in a very ancient hand, and when I still hesitated he pulled from his loose robe a seal ring and a watch, both with my family arms, to prove that he was what he said. But it was a hideous proof, because I knew from old papers that that watch had been buried with my great-great-great-great-grandfather in 1698.

Presently the old man drew back his hood and pointed to the family resemblance in his face, but I only shuddered, because I was sure that the face was merely a devilish waxen mask. The flopping animals were now scratching restlessly at the lichens, and I saw that the old man was nearly as restless himself. When one of the things began to waddle and edge away, he turned quickly to stop it; so that the suddenness of his motion dislodged the waxen mask from what should have been his head. And then, because that nightmare's position barred me from the stone staircase down which we had come, I flung myself into the oily underground river that bubbled somewhere to the caves of the sea; flung myself into that putrescent juice of earth's inner horrors before the madness of my screams could bring down upon me all the charnel legions these pest-gulfs might conceal.

At the hospital they told me I had been found half-frozen in Kingsport Harbour at dawn, clinging to the drifting spar that accident sent to save me. They told me I had taken the wrong fork of the hill road the night before, and fallen over the cliffs at Orange Point; a thing they deduced from prints found in the snow. There was nothing I could say, because everything was wrong. Everything was wrong, with the broad windows showing a sea of roofs in which only about one in five was ancient, and the sound of trolleys and motors in the streets below. They insisted that this was Kingsport, and I could not deny it. When I went delirious at hearing that the hospital stood near the old churchyard on Central Hill, they sent me to St. Mary's Hospital in Arkham, where I could have better care. I liked it there, for the doctors were broad-minded, and even lent me their influence in obtaining the carefully sheltered copy of Alhazred's objectionable *Necronomicon* from the library of Miskatonic University. They said something about a "psychosis" and agreed I had better get any harassing obsessions off my mind.

So I read that hideous chapter, and shuddered doubly because it was indeed not new to me. I had seen it before, let footprints tell what they might; and where it was I had seen it were best forgotten. There was no one — in waking hours — who could remind me of it; but my dreams are filled with terror, because of phrases I dare not quote. I dare quote only one paragraph, put into such English as I can make from the awkward Low Latin.

"The nethermost caverns," wrote the mad Arab, "are not for the fathoming of eyes that see; for their marvels are strange and terrific. Cursed the ground where dead thoughts live new and oddly bodied, and evil the mind that is held by no head. Wisely did Ibn Schacabao say, that happy is the tomb where no wizard hath lain, and happy the town at night whose wizards are all ashes. For it is of old rumour that the soul of the devil-bought hastes not from his charnel clay, but fats and instructs the very worm that gnaws; till out of corruption horrid life springs, and the dull scavengers of earth wax crafty to vex it and swell monstrous to plague it. Great holes secretly are digged where earth's pores ought to suffice, and things have learnt to walk that ought to crawl."

The Loved Dead.

BY C.M. EDDY
AND H.P. LOVECRAFT

4,000-WORD SHORT STORY;
1923.

"The Loved Dead" shows the influence of Lovecraft in Clifford Eddy's writing very strongly, and based on this many readers have assumed that it was actually ghostwritten by him, or at least is primarily his work. However, a close reading suggests another explanation — that Eddy, who admired Lovecraft very much, was simply adopting his style and working to incorporate it into his own, as Lovecraft himself had done with the writing of Lord Dunsany several years before.

This would explain the presence of several (admittedly half-hearted) protestations of horror and self-disgust by the narrator, which strike a very un-Lovecraftian note in this story.

This story caused a real sensation when it was published. Moreover, the issue of Weird Tales *in which it came out was the May/June/July 1924 issue, so it was on the stands for an unusually long time. This issue was also the last one published under the direction of editor Edwin Baird. It was assembled and released under the direction of new editor Farnsworth Wright — so one of Wright's first experiences as the new editor of the magazine was the firestorm of protest that broke out over this story.* Weird Tales *was removed from newsstands statewide in Indiana, and in several other smaller jurisdictions as well.*

The episode seems to have put the fear of God into Farnsworth Wright, who operated for the remainder of his tenure as editor in fear of state censorship boards. Oddly, it doesn't seem to have occurred to him that those boards might object to Margaret Brundage's famous covers, which frequently involved nude women (with their more intimate parts barely concealed by a curl of smoke or an intervening leaf); so, after this issue, Weird Tales *came to be characterized by extraordinarily racy covers wrapped around fairly cautious and conservative stories.*

It is midnight. Before dawn they will find me and take me to a black cell where I shall languish interminably, while insatiable desires gnaw at my vitals and wither up my heart, till at last I become with the dead that I love.

My seat is the foetid hollow of an aged grave; my desk is the back of a fallen tombstone worn smooth by devastating centuries; my light is that of the stars and a thin-edged moon, yet I can see as clearly as though it were midday. Around me on every side, sepulchral sentinels guarding unkempt graves, the tilting, decrepit headstones lie half-hidden in masses of hideous, rotting vegetation. Above the rest, silhouetted against the livid sky, an august monument lifts its austere, tapering spire like the spectral chieftain of a Lemurian horde. The air is heavy with the noxious odours of fungi and the scent of damp, mouldy earth, but to me it is the aroma of Elysium. It is still — terrifyingly still — with a silence whose very profundity bespeaks the solemn and the hideous. Could I choose my habitation it would be in the heart of some such city of putrefying flesh and crumbling bones; for their nearness sends ecstatic thrills through my soul, causing the stagnant blood to race through my veins and my torpid heart to pound with delirious joy — for the presence of death is life to me!

My early childhood was one long, prosaic and monotonous apathy. Strictly ascetic, wan, pallid, undersized, and subject to protracted spells of morbid moroseness, I was ostracized by the healthy, normal youngsters of my own age. They dubbed me a spoil-sport, and "old woman," because I had no interest in the rough, childish games they played, or any stamina to participate in them, had I so desired.

Like all rural villages, Fenham had its quota of poison-tongued gossips. Their prying imaginations hailed my lethargic temperament as some abhorrent abnormality; they compared me with my parents and shook their heads in ominous doubt at the vast difference. Some of the more superstitious openly pronounced me a changeling, while others who knew something of my ancestry called attention to the vague mysterious rumours concerning a great-great-grand uncle who had been burned at the stake as a necromancer.

Had I lived in some larger town, with greater opportunities for congenial companionship, perhaps I could have overcome this early tendency to be a recluse. As I reached my teens I grew more sullen, morbid, and apathetic. My life lacked motivation. I seemed in the grip of something that dulled my senses, stunted my development, retarded my activities, and left me unaccountably dissatisfied.

I was sixteen when I attended my first funeral. A funeral in Fenham was a pre-eminent social event, for our town was noted for the longevity of its inhabitants. When, moreover, the funeral was that of such a well-known character as my grandfather, it was safe to assume that the townspeople would turn out en masse to pay due homage to his memory. Yet I did not view the approaching ceremony with even latent interest. Anything that tended to lift me out of my habitual inertia held for me only the promise of physical and mental disquietude.

In deference to my parents' importunings, mainly to give myself relief from their caustic condemnations of what they chose to call my un-filial attitude, I agreed to accompany them.

There was nothing out of the ordinary about my grandfather's funeral unless it was the voluminous array of floral tributes; but this, remember, was my first initiation to the solemn rites of such an occasion. Something about the darkened room, the oblong coffin with its sombre drapings, the banked masses of fragrant blooms, the dolorous manifestations of the assembled villagers, stirred me from my normal listlessness and arrested my attention. Roused from my momentary reverie by a nudge from my mother's sharp elbow, I followed her across the room to the casket where the body of my grandparent lay.

For the first time I was face to face with Death. I looked down upon the calm, placid face lined with its multitudinous wrinkles, and saw nothing to cause so much of sorrow. Instead, it seemed to me that grandfather was immeasurably content, blandly satisfied. I felt swayed by some strange discordant sense of elation. So slowly, so steadily had it crept over me, that I could scarcely define its coming. As I mentally review that portentous hour it seems to me that it must have originated with my first glimpse of that funeral scene, silently strengthening its grip with a subtle insidiousness. A baleful malignant influence that seemed to emanate from the corpse itself held me with magnetic fascination. My whole being seemed charged with some ecstatic electrifying force, and I felt my form straighten without conscious volition. My eyes were trying to burn beneath the closed lids of the dead man's and read some secret message they concealed. My heart gave a sudden leap of unholy glee, and pounded against my ribs with demoniacal force as if to free itself from the confining walls of my frail frame. Wild, wanton, soul-satisfying sensuality engulfed me.

Once more the vigorous prod of the maternal elbow jarred me into activity. I had made my way to the sable-shrouded coffin with leaden tread; I walked away with new-found animation.

I accompanied the cortege to the cemetery, my whole physical being permeated with this mystic enlivening experience. It was as if I had quaffed deep draughts of some esoteric elixir — some abominable concoction brewed from blasphemous formulae in the archives of Belial.

The townsfolk were so intent upon the ceremony that the radical change in my demeanour passed unnoticed by all save my father and my mother, but in the fortnight that followed, the village busybodies found fresh material for their vitriolic tongues in my altered bearing. At the end of the fortnight, however, the potency of the stimulus began to lose its effectiveness. Another day or two and I had completely reverted to my old-time languor, though not to the complete and engulfing insipidity of the past. Before, there had been an utter lack of desire to emerge from the enervation; now vague and indefinable unrest disturbed me. Outwardly I had become myself again, and the scandal-mongers turned to some more engrossing subject. Had they even so much as dreamed of the true cause of my exhilaration they would have shunned me as if I were a filthy, leprous thing. Had I visioned the execrable power behind my brief period of elation I would have locked myself forever from the rest of the world and spent my remaining years in penitent solitude.

Tragedy often runs in trilogies; hence despite the proverbial longevity of our townspeople the next five years brought the death of both parents. My mother went first, in an accident of the most unexpected nature; and so genuine was my grief that I was honestly surprised to find its poignancy mocked and contradicted by that almost forgotten feeling of supreme and diabolical ecstasy. Once more my heart leaped wildly within me, once more it pounded at trip-hammer speed and sent the hot blood coursing through my veins with meteoric fervour. I shook from my shoulders the harassing cloak of stagnation only to replace it with the infinitely more horrible burden of loathsome, unhallowed desire. I haunted the death-chamber where the body of my mother lay, my soul athirst for the devilish nectar that seemed to saturate the air of the darkened room. Every breath strengthened me, lifted me to towering heights of seraphic satisfaction. I knew, now, that it was but a sort of drugged delirium which must soon pass and leave me correspondingly weakened by its malign power; yet I could no more control my longing than I could untwist the Gordian knots in the already tangled skein of my destiny.

I knew, too, that through some strange Satanic curse my life depended upon the dead for its motive force; that there was a singularity in my makeup which responded only to the awesome presence of some lifeless clod.

A few days later, frantic for the bestial intoxicant on which the fullness of my existence depended, I interviewed Fenham's sole undertaker and talked him into taking me on as a sort of apprentice.

The shock of my mother's demise had visibly affected my father. I think that if I had broached the idea of such an outré employment at any other time he would have been emphatic in his refusal. As it was he nodded acquiescence after a moment's sober thought. How little did I dream that he would be the object of my first practical lesson!

He, too, died suddenly, developing some hitherto-unsuspected heart affliction. My octogenarian employer tried his best to dissuade me from the unthinkable task of embalming his body, nor did he detect the rapturous glint in my eyes as I finally won him over to my damnable point of view. I cannot hope to express the reprehensible, the unutterable thoughts that swept in tumultuous waves of passion through my racing heart as I laboured over the lifeless clay. Unsurpassed love was the keynote of these concepts, a love greater — far greater — than any I had ever borne him while he was still alive.

My father was not a rich man, but he had possessed enough

of worldly goods to make them comfortably independent. As his sole heir I found myself in rather a paradoxical position. My early youth had totally failed to fit me for contact with the modern world, but yet the primitive life of Fenham, with its attendant isolation, palled upon me. Indeed, the longevity of the inhabitants defeated my sole motive in arranging my indenture.

After settling the estate it proved an easy matter to secure my release, and I headed for Bayboro, a city some 50 miles away.

Here my year of apprenticeship stood me in good stead. I had no trouble in establishing a favourable connection as an assistant with the Gresham Corporation, a concern that maintained the largest funeral parlours in the city. I even prevailed upon them to let me sleep upon the premises — for the already the proximity of the dead was becoming an obsession.

I applied myself to the task with unwonted zeal. No case was too gruesome for my impious sensibilities, and I soon became master at my chosen vocation. Each fresh corpse brought into the establishment meant a fulfilled promise of ungodly gladness, of irreverent gratification, a return to that rapturous tumult of the arteries which transformed my grisly task into one of beloved devotion — yet every carnal satiation exacted its toll. I came to dread the days that brought no dead for me to gloat over, and prayed to all the obscene gods of the nethermost abysses to bring swift, sure death upon the residents of the city.

Then came the nights when a skulking figure stole surreptitiously through the shadowy streets of the suburbs; pitch-dark nights when the midnight moon was obscured by heavy lowering clouds. It was a furtive figure that blended with the trees and cast fugitive glances over its shoulder, a figure bent on some malignant mission. After one of these prowlings the morning papers would scream to their sensation-mad clientele the details of some nightmare crime; column on column of lurid gloating over abominable atrocities; paragraph on paragraph of impossible solutions and extravagant, conflicting suspicions. Through it all I felt the supreme sense of security, for who would for a moment suspect an employee in an undertaking establishment, where Death was supposedly an everyday affair, of seeking surcease from unnameable urgings in the cold-blooded slaughter of his fellow-beings? I planned each crime with maniacal cunning, varying the manner of my murders so that no one would ever even dream that all were the work of one blood-stained pair of hands. The aftermath of each nocturnal venture was an ecstatic hour of pleasure, pernicious and unalloyed; a pleasure always heightened by the chance that its delicious source might later be assigned to my gloating administrations in the course of my regular occupation. Sometimes that double and ultimate pleasure did occur — O rare and delicious memory!

During long nights when I clung close to the shelter of my sanctuary, I was prompted by the mausoleum silence to devise new and unspeakable ways of lavishing my affections upon the dead that I loved — the dead that gave me life!

One morning Mr. Gresham came much earlier than usual — came to find me stretched out upon a cold slab deep in ghoulish slumber, my arms wrapped around the stark, stiff, naked body of a foetid corpse!

He roused me from my salacious dreams, his eyes filled with mingled detestation and pity. Gently but firmly he told me that I must go, that my nerves were unstrung, that I needed a long rest from the repellent tasks my vocation required, that my impressionable youth was too deeply affected by the dismal atmosphere of my environment. How little did he know of the demoniacal desires that spurred me on in my disgusting infirmities! I was wise enough to see that argument would only strengthen his belief in my potential madness — it was far better to leave than to invite discovery of the motive underlying my actions.

After this I dared not stay long in one place for fear some overt act would lay bare my secret to an unsympathetic world. I drifted from city to city, from town to town. I worked in morgues, around cemeteries, once in a crematory — anywhere that afforded me an opportunity to be near the dead that I so craved.

Then came the world war. I was one of the first to go across, one of the last to return. Four years of blood-red charnel hell . . . sickening slime of rain-rotten trenches . . . deafening bursting of hysterical shells . . . monotonous droning of sardonic bullets . . . smoking frenzies of Phlegethon's fountains . . . stifling fumes of murderous gases . . . grotesque remnants of smashed and shredded bodies . . . four years of transcendent satisfaction.

In every wanderer there is a latent urge to return to the scenes of his childhood. A few months later found me making my way through the familiar byways of Fenham. Vacant dilapidated farmhouses lined the adjacent roadsides, while the years had brought equal retrogression to the town itself. A mere handful of the houses were occupied, but among those was the one I had once called home. The tangled, weed-choked driveway, the broken window panes, the uncared-for acres that stretched behind, all bore mute confirmation of the tales that guarded inquiries had elicited — that it now sheltered a dissolute drunkard who eked out a meagre existence from the chores his few neighbours gave him out of sympathy for the mistreated wife and undernourished child who shared his lot. All in all, the glamour surrounding my youthful environment was entirely dispelled; so, prompted by some errant foolhardy thought, I next turned my steps toward Bayboro.

Here, too, the years had brought changes, but in reverse order. The small city I remembered had almost doubled in size despite its wartime depopulation. Instinctively I sought my former place of employment, finding it still there but with an unfamiliar name and "successor to" above the door, for the influenza epidemic had claimed Mr. Gresham, while the boys were overseas. Some faithful mood impelled me to ask for work. I referred to my tutelage under Mr. Gresham with some trepidation, but my fears were groundless — my late employer had carried the secret of my unethical conduct with him to the grave. An opportune vacancy insured my immediate re-installation.

Then came vagrant haunting memories of scarlet nights of impious pilgrimages, and an uncontrollable desire to renew those illicit joys. I cast caution to the winds and launched upon another series of damnable debaucheries. Once more the yellow sheets found welcome material in the devilish detail of my crimes, comparing them to the red weeks of horror that had appalled the city years before. Once more the police sent out their dragnet and drew into its enmeshing folds — nothing!

My thirst for the noxious nectar of the dead grew to a consuming fire, and I began to shorten the periods between my odious exploits. I realized that I was treading on dangerous ground, but demoniac desire gripped me in its torturing tentacles and urged me on.

All this time my mind is becoming more and more benumbed to any influence except the satiation of my insane longings. Little details vitally important to one bent on such evil escapades escaped me. Somehow, somewhere, I left a vague trace, an elusive clue behind — not enough to warrant my arrest, but sufficient to turn the tide of suspicion in my direction. I sensed this espionage, yet was helpless to stem the surging demand for more dead to quicken my enervated soul.

Then came the night when the shrill whistle of the police roused me from my fiendish gloating over the body of my latest victim, a gory razor still clutched tightly in my hand. With one dexterous motion I closed the blade and thrust it into the pocket of the coat I wore. Nightsticks beat a lusty tattoo upon the door. I crashed the window with a chair, thanking fate I had chosen one of the cheaper tenement districts for my locale. I dropped into a dingy alley as blue-coated forms burst through the shattered door. Over shaky fences, through filthy back yards, past squalid ramshackle houses, down dimly-lighted narrow streets I fled. I thought at once of the wooded marshes that lay beyond the city and stretched for half a hundred miles till they touched the outskirts of Fenham. If I could reach this goal I would be temporarily safe.

Before dawn I was plunging headlong through the forebidding wasteland, stumbling over the rotting roots of half-dead trees whose naked branches stretched out like grotesque arms striving to encumber me with mocking embraces.

The imps of the nefarious gods to whom I offered my idolatrous prayers must have guided my footsteps through that menacing morass.

A week later, wan, bedraggled, and emaciated, I lurked in the woods a mile from Fenham. So far I had eluded my pursuers, yet I dared not show myself, for I knew that the alarm must have been sent broadcast. I vaguely hoped I had thrown them off the trail. After that first frenetic night I had heard no sound of alien voices, no crashing of heavy bodies through the underbrush. Perhaps they had concluded that my body lay hidden in some stagnant pool or had vanished forever in the tenacious quagmire.

Hunger gnawed at my vitals with poignant pangs, thirst left my throat parched and dry. Yet far worse was the unbearable hunger of my starving soul for the stimulus I found only in the nearness of the dead. My nostrils quivered in sweet recollection. No longer could I delude myself with the thought that this desire was a mere whim of the heated imagination. I knew now that it was an integral part of life itself; that without it I should burn out like an empty lamp. I summoned all my remaining energy to fit me for the task of satisfying my accursed appetite. Despite the peril attending my move I set out to reconnoiter, skirting the sheltering shadows like an obscene wraith.

Once more I felt that strange sensation of being led by some unseen satellite of Satan. Yet even my sin-steeped soul revolted for a moment when I found myself before my native abode, the scene of my youthful hermitage.

Then these disquieting memories faded. In their place came the overwhelming lustful desire. Behind the rotting walls of this old house lay my prey. A moment later I had raised one of the shattered windows and clambered over the sill. I listened for a moment, every sense alert, every muscle tensed for action. The silence reassured me. With cat-like tread I stole through the familiar rooms until stentorous snores indicated the place where I was to find surcease from my sufferings.

I allowed myself a sigh of anticipated ecstasy as I pushed open the door of the bedchamber. Panther-like I made my way to the supine form stretched out in drunken stupor. The wife and child — where were they? — well, they could wait. My clutching fingers groped for his throat . . . .

Hours later I was again the fugitive, but a newfound stolen strength was mine. Three silent forms slept to wake no more. It was not until the garish light of day penetrated my hiding place that I visualized the certain consequences of my rashly purchased relief. By this time the bodies must have been discovered. Even the most obtuse of the rural police must surely link the tragedy with my flight from the nearby city. Besides, for the first time I had been careless enough to leave some tangible proof of my identity — my fingerprints on the throats of the newly dead.

All day I shivered in nervous apprehension. The mere crackling of the dry twigs beneath my feet conjured mental images that appalled me. That night, under cover of the protecting darkness, I skirted Fenham and made for the woods that lay beyond. Before dawn came the first definite hint of renewed pursuit — the distant baying of hounds.

Through the long night I pressed on, but by morning I could feel my artificial strength ebbing. Noon brought once more the insistent call of the contaminating curse, and I knew I must fall by the way unless I could once more experience that exotic intoxication that came only with the proximity of the loved dead. I had traveled in a wide semicircle. If I pushed steadily ahead, midnight would bring me to the cemetery where I had lain away my parents years before. My only hope, I felt certain, lay in reaching this goal before I was overtaken. With a silent prayer to the devils that dominated my destiny I turned leaden feet in the direction of my last stronghold.

God! Can it be that a scant twelve hours have passed since I started for my ghostly sanctuary? I have lived an eternity in each leaden hour. But I have reached a rich reward. The noxious odours of this neglected spot are frankincense to my suffering soul!

The first streaks of dawn are greying the horizon. They are coming! My sharp ears catch the far-off howling of the dogs! It is but a matter of minutes before they find me, and shut me away forever from the rest of the world, to spend my days in ravaging yearnings till at last I join the dead I love!

They shall not take me! A way of escape is open! A coward's choice, perhaps, but better — far better — than endless months of nameless misery. I will leave this record behind me that some soul may perhaps understand why I make this choice.

The razor! It has nestled forgotten in my pocket since my flight from Bayboro. Its bloodstained blade gleams oddly in the waning light of the thin-edged moon. One slashing stroke across my left wrist and deliverance is assured . . .

Warm, fresh blood spatters grotesque patterns on dingy, decrepit slabs . . . phantasmal hordes swarm over the rotting graves . . . spectral fingers beckon me . . . ethereal fragments of unwritten melodies rise in celestial crescendo . . . distant stars dance drunkenly in demoniac accompaniment . . . a thousand tiny hammers beat hideous dissonances on anvils inside my chaotic brain . . . great ghosts of slaughtered spirits parade in mocking silence before me . . . scorching tongues of invisible flames sear the brand of hell upon my sickened soul . . . .

I can — write — no — more . . . .

1924.

The Family Man.

Nineteen-twenty-four was something of a high point in H.P. Lovecraft's life. But, looking back on the year from its end, the poor fellow may have wondered if all the great things that had filled the first half of the year were some kind of cynical set-up for the bitter disappointments to follow.

Within the first month or two of 1924, Lovecraft and Sonia Greene became engaged to marry. They followed through on their plans almost immediately, tying the knot on March 3; but there wasn't much time for a honeymoon, because the manuscript for a ghostwriting job was due at *Weird Tales*, and Lovecraft was scrambling to get it ready. It was a story titled "Under the Pyramids," by Harry Houdini — whom Lovecraft had met and struck up a friendship with early that year.

Meanwhile, Sonia had taken some of Lovecraft's work samples to the offices of a friend, Gertrude Tucker, who published a general-interest magazine called *The Reading Lamp*, at which he hoped to get a regular job as a reviewer. Tucker was enthusiastic, and proposed also that Lovecraft should write a nonfiction book covering witchcraft and haunted houses in New England, which she would represent to publishers as his agent. Things were looking very positive.

Lovecraft clearly enjoyed married life, at least at first. Sonia, concerned about his gaunt frame, embarked upon a campaign to fatten him up a bit, and by the end of the year had him up from 140 to 190 pounds.

But things were already starting to go wrong. In May, editor Edwin Baird left *Weird Tales*; the publisher, J.C. Henneberger, was left scrambling to keep the magazine going, and looking for a new editor. So he reached out to Lovecraft, suggesting that he might take over as editor of *Weird Tales*. Lovecraft responded with his customary diffidence, perhaps expecting the publisher to press the case a little; but Henneberger wasn't used to dealing with Lovecraft, and apparently assumed the cool response was a hint that the writer was not interested. (On the other hand, it's entirely possible that he really was not interested; *Weird Tales* was known to be in a shaky financial condition, and was based in Chicago, a city for which the inveterate antiquarian certainly felt no great enthusiasm.)

In any case, the magazine's creditors shortly thereafter took over operations and placed Farnsworth Wright in the editorship. Lovecraft would have a less cordial relationship with Wright than he'd had with his predecessor.

Ex-publisher Henneberger then announced plans to launch a new magazine, *Ghost Stories*, and hired Lovecraft at $40 a week as editor. For two months, Lovecraft was left hanging, engaged but unpaid, while the publisher sought financial backing to launch his title. Finally, in November, he admitted defeat. Lovecraft's job — a dream job for a man like him — had been a cruel tease, and he was paid off with a merchandise credit at a bookstore which he tried, unsuccessfully, to redeem for cash.

By this time, Lovecraft's other iron in the fire had long gone cold as well. For reasons unknown, Gertrude Tucker had decided not to hire him as a reviewer for *The Reading Lamp*, and for good measure had left him high and dry on the nonfiction book project, which he'd put considerable time and effort into.

This wouldn't have been a big problem if not for the fact that Sonia, apparently in an effort to find a line of work that required less travel and let her be home with her new husband more, had quit her $10,000-a-year job and opened a hat store. This move turned out to be a disaster. By the end of the year, the new hat store had failed, probably because the capital she'd anticipated using to cover the business's first one or two money-losing years was lost in a bank failure shortly after she opened her shop.

So starting in July, Lovecraft canvassed the city looking for literary work. But his combination of lack of employment experience and diffident, self-deprecating style kept him relentlessly unemployed, fully dependent on the meager earnings from his ghostwriting business and from his wife.

Toward the end of the year, he seemed to have all but given up on the possibility of finding a position, and was spending less and less of his time pursuing work and more and more of his time loafing around in various cafeterias and automats around New York with the fellow writers he knew. They formed a sort of informal literary circle, calling themselves the Kalem Club (because their last names all started with K, L, or M — George Willard Kirk, Rheinhart Kleiner, and Herman Charles Koenig; Arthur Leeds, Frank Belknap Long, H.P. Lovecraft, and Samuel Loveman; and Henry Everett McNeil and James Ferdinand Morton Jr.) Lovecraft took to referring to them as "the gang" and spending most of his waking hours with them. Increasingly, Sonia found herself competing with the Kalem Club for Lovecraft's time and attention, even as she struggled to support him financially.

The pressure on Sonia was tremendous, and in October she checked into a hospital with what turned out to be psychosomatic symptoms of extreme stress — essentially, a panic attack.

After leaving the hospital, with no other prospects at hand, Sonia accepted a job offer at a department store in Cincinnati. On the last day of 1924, she left for her new job in that city, leaving Lovecraft behind in New York to continue his job search.

There was no reason for Lovecraft to think 1925 would be any kinder to him than 1924 had been, but presumably, on that lonely first New Year's Eve of his married life, he hoped it would be.

It wouldn't.

Deaf, Dumb and Blind.

BY C.M. EDDY
AND H.P. LOVECRAFT

**6,500-WORD SHORT STORY;
1924.**

"Deaf, Dumb and Blind" was the last of the four Clifford Eddy stories on which H.P. Lovecraft collaborated; he worked on it with Eddy in early 1924, just before he moved to New York, but it took several months before Farnsworth Wright was ready for another C.M. Eddy story after the "The Loved Dead" fiasco. It was published in the April 1925 issue of Weird Tales.

This story is the longest of the four, and it either benefitted from a great deal of direct intervention by Lovecraft or (as is more likely) from Lovecraft's inspiration and influence on Eddy.

A little after noon on the 28th day of June, 1924, Dr. Morehouse stopped his machine before the Tanner place and four men alighted. The stone building, in perfect repair and freshness, stood near the road, and but for the swamp in the rear it would have possessed no trace of dark suggestion. The spotless white doorway was visible across a trim lawn for some distance down the road; and as the doctor's party approached, it could be seen that the heavy portal yawned wide open. Only the screen door was closed. The close proximity of the house had imposed a kind of nervous silence on the four men, for what lurked therein could only be imagined with vague terror. This terror underwent a marked abatement when the explorers heard distinctly the sound of Richard Blake's typewriter.

Less than an hour before, a grown man had fled from that house, hatless, coatless, and screaming, to fall upon the doorstep of his nearest neighbour, half a mile away, babbling incoherently of "house," "dark," "swamp," and "room." Dr. Morehouse had needed no further spur to excited action when told that a slavering, maddened creature had burst out of the swamp. He had known that something would happen when the two men had taken the accursed stone house — the man who had fled,

Weird Tales, April 1925

and his master, Richard Blake, the author-poet from Boston, the genius who had gone into the war with every nerve and sense alert and had come out as he was now, still debonair though half a paralytic, still walking with song among the sights and sounds of living fantasy though shut forever from the physical world, deaf, dumb, and blind!

Blake had reveled in the weird traditions and shuddering hints about the house and its former tenants. Such eldritch lore was an imaginative asset from whose enjoyment his physical state might not bar him. He had smiled at the prognostications of the superstitious natives. Now, with his sole companion fled in a mad ecstasy of panic fright, and himself left helpless with whatever had caused that fright, Blake might have less occasion to revel and smile! This, at least, was Dr. Morehouse's reflection as he had faced the problem of the fugitive and called on the puzzled cottager to help him track the matter down. The Morehouses were an old Fenham family, and the doctor's grandfather had been one of those who burned the hermit Simeon Tanner's body in 1819. Not even at this distance could the trained physician escape a spinal tingle at what was recorded of that burning — at the naïve inferences drawn by ignorant countrymen from a slight and meaningless conformation of the deceased. That tingle he knew to be foolish, for trifling bony protuberances on the forepart of the skull are of no significance, and often observable in bald-headed men.

Among the four men who ultimately set resolute faces toward that abhorrent house in the doctor's car, there occurred a singularly awed exchange of vague legends and half-furtive scraps of gossip handed down from curious grandmothers — legends and hints seldom repeated and almost never systematically compared. They extended as far back as 1692, when a Tanner had perished on Gallows Hill in Salem after a witchcraft trial, but did not grow intimate till the time the house was built — 1747, though the ell was more recent. Not even then were the tales very numerous, for queer though the Tanners all were, it was only the last of them, old Simeon, whom people desperately feared. He added to what he had inherited — added horribly, everyone whispered — and bricked up the windows of the southeast room, whose east wall gave on the swamp. That was his study and library, and it had a door of double thickness with braces. It had been chopped through with axes that terrible winter night in 1819 when the stinking smoke had poured from the chimney and they found Tanner's body in there — with that *expression* on its face. It was because of that *expression* — not because of the two bony protuberances beneath the bushy white hair — that they had burned the body and the books and manuscripts it had had in that room. However, the short distance to the Tanner place was covered before much important historical matter could be correlated.

As the doctor, at the head of the party, opened the screen door and entered the arched hallway, it was noticed that the sound of typewriting had suddenly ceased. At this point two of the men also thought they noticed a faint effusion of cold air strangely out of keeping with the great heat of the day, though they afterward refused to swear to this. The hall was in perfect order, as were the various rooms entered in quest of the study where Blake was presumably to be found. The author had furnished his home in exquisite Colonial taste; and though having no help but the one manservant, he had succeeded in maintaining it in a state of commendable neatness.

Dr. Morehouse led his men from room to room through the wide-open doors and archways, at last finding the library or study which he sought — a fine southerly room on the ground floor adjoining the once-dreaded study of Simeon Tanner, lined with the books which the servant communicated through an ingenious alphabet of touches, and the bulky Braille volumes which the author himself read with sensitive finger-tips. Richard Blake, of course, was there, seated as usual before his typewriter with the draft-scattered stack of newly written pages on the table and floor, and one sheet still in the machine. He had stopped work, it appeared, with some suddenness; perhaps because of a chill which had caused him to draw together the neck of his dressing-gown; and his head was turned toward the doorway of the sunny adjoining room in a manner quite singular for one whose lack of sight and hearing shuts out all sense of the external world.

On drawing nearer and crossing to where he could see the author's face, Dr. Morehouse turned very pale and motioned the others to stand back. He needed time to steady himself, and to dispel all possibility of hideous illusion. No longer did he need to speculate why they had burned old Simeon Tanner's body on that wintry night because of the *expression* it wore, for here was something only a well-disciplined mind could confront. The late Richard Blake, whose typewriter had ceased its nonchalant clicking only as the men had entered the house, had seen *something* despite his blindness, and had been affected by it. Humanity had nothing to do with the look that was on his face, or with the glassy morbid vision that blazed in great, blue, bloodshot eyes shut to this world's images for six years. Those eyes were fixed with an ecstasy of clear-sighted horror on the doorway leading to Simeon Tanner's old study, where the sun blazed on walls once shrouded in bricked-up blackness. And Dr. Arlo Morehouse reeled dizzily when he saw that for all the dazzling daylight, the inky pupils of those eyes were dilated as cavernously as those of a cat's eyes in the dark.

The doctor closed the staring blind eyes before he let the others view the face of the corpse. Meanwhile he examined the lifeless form with feverish diligence, using scrupulous technical care, despite his throbbing nerves and almost shaking hands. Some of his results he communicated from time to time to the awed and inquisitive trio around him; other results he judiciously withheld, lest they lead to speculations more disquieting than human speculations should be. It was not from any word of his, but from shrewd independent observation, that one of the men muttered about the body's tousled black hair and the way the papers were scattered. This man said it was as if a strong breeze had blown through the open doorway which the dead man faced; whereas, although the once-bricked windows beyond were indeed fully open to the warm June air, there had been scarcely a breath of wind during the entire day.

When one of the men began to gather the sheets of newly written manuscript as they lay on the floor and table, Dr. Morehouse stopped him with an alarmed gesture. He had seen the sheet that remained in the machine, and had hastily removed and pocketed it after a sentence or two blanched his face afresh. This incident prompted him to collect the scattered sheets himself, and stuff them bulkily into an inside pocket without stopping to arrange them. And not even what he had read terrified him half so much as what he now noticed — the subtle difference in touch and heaviness of typing which distinguished the sheets he picked up from the one he had found on the typewriter. This shadowy impression he could not divorce from that other horrible circumstance which he was so zealously concealing from the men who had heard the machine's clicking not ten minutes before — the circumstance he was trying to exclude from even his own mind till he could be alone and resting in the merciful depths of his Morris chair. One may judge of the fear he felt at that circumstance by considering what he braved to keep it suppressed. In more than thirty years of professional practice he had never regarded the medical examiner as one from whom a fact might be withheld; yet through all the formalities which now followed, no man ever knew that when he examined this staring, contorted, blind man's body he had seen at once *that death must have occurred at least half an hour before discovery.*

Dr. Morehouse presently closed the outer door and led the party through every corner of the ancient structure in search of any evidence which might directly illuminate the tragedy. Never was a result more completely negative. He knew that the trap-door of old Simeon Tanner had been removed as soon as that recluse's books and body had been burnt, and that the sub-cellar and the sinuous tunnel under the swamp had been filled up as soon as they were discovered, some thirty-five years later. Now he saw that no fresh abnormalities had come to replace them, and that the whole establishment exhibited only the normal neatness of modern restoration and tasteful care.

Telephoning for the sheriff at Fenham and for the county medical examiner at Bayboro, he awaited the arrival of the former, who, when he came, insisted on swearing in two of the men as deputies until the examiner should arrive. Dr. Morehouse, knowing the mystifications and futility confronting the officials, could not help smiling wryly as he left with the villager whose house still sheltered the man who had fled.

They found the patient exceedingly weak, but conscious and fairly composed. Having promised the sheriff to extract and transmit all possible information from the fugitive, Dr. Morehouse began some calm and tactful questioning, which was received in a rational and compliant spirit and baffled only by effacement of memory. Much of the man's quiet must have come from merciful inability to recollect, for all he could now tell was that he had been in the study with his master and had seemed to see the next room suddenly grow dark — the room where sunshine had for more than 100 years replaced the gloom of bricked-up windows. Even this memory, which indeed he half doubted, greatly disturbed the unstrung nerves of the patient, and it was with the utmost gentleness and circumspection that Dr. Morehouse told him his master was dead — a natural victim of the cardiac weakness which his terrible war-time injuries must have caused. The man was grieved, for he had been devoted to the crippled author; but he promised to show fortitude in taking the body back to the family in Boston after the close of the medical examiner's formal inquiry.

The physician, after satisfying as vaguely as possible the curiosity of the householder and his wife, and urging them to shelter the patient and keep him from the Tanner house until his departure with the body, next drove home in a growing tremble of excitement. At last he was free to read the typed manuscript of the dead man, and to gain at least an inkling of what hellish thing had defied those shattered senses of sight and sound and penetrated so disastrously to the delicate intelligence that brooded in eternal darkness and silence. He knew it would be a grotesque and terrible perusal, and he did not hasten to begin it. Instead, he very deliberately put his car in the garage, made himself comfortable in a dressing gown, and placed a stand of sedative and restorative medicines beside the great chair he was to occupy. Even after that he obviously wasted time as he slowly arranged the numbered sheets, carefully avoiding any comprehensive glance at their text.

What the manuscript did to Dr. Morehouse we all know. It would never have been read by another had his wife not picked it up as he lay inert in his chair an hour later, breathing heavily and unresponsive to a knocking which one would have thought violent enough to arouse a mummified Pharaoh. Terrible as the document is, particularly in the obvious *change of style* near the end, we cannot avoid the belief that to the folklore-wise physician it presented some *added and supreme horror* which no other will ever be so unfortunate as to receive. Certainly, it is the general opinion of Fenham that the doctor's wide familiarity with the mutterings of old people and the tales his grandfather told him in youth furnished him some special information, in the light of which Richard Blake's hideous chronicle acquired a new, clear and devastating significance nearly insupportable to the normal human mind. That would explain the slowness of his recovery on that June evening, the reluctance with which he permitted his wife and son to read the manuscript, the singular ill grace with which he acceded to their determination not to burn a document so darkly remarkable, and, most of all, the peculiar rashness with which he hastened to purchase the old Tanner property, destroy the house with dynamite, and cut down the trees of the swamp for a substantial distance from the road. Concerning the whole subject he now maintains an inflexible reticence, and it is certain that there will die with him a knowledge without which the world is better off.

The manuscript, as here appended, was copied through the courtesy of Floyd Morehouse, Esq., son of the physician. A few omissions, indicated by asterisks, have been made in the interest of the public peace of mind; still others have been occasioned by the indefiniteness of the text, where the stricken author's lightning-like touch-typing seems shaken into incoherence or ambiguity. In three places, where lacunae are fairly well elucidated by the context, the task of recension has been attempted. Of the *change in style* near the end it were best to say nothing. Surely it is plausible enough to attribute the phenomenon, as regards both content and physical aspect of typing, to the racked and tottering mind of a victim whose former handicaps had paled to nothing before that which he now faced. Bolder minds are at liberty to supply their own deductions.

Here, then, is the document, written in an accursed house by a brain closed to the world's sights and sounds — a brain left alone and unwarned to the mercies and mockeries of powers that no seeing, hearing man has ever stayed to face. Contradictory as it is to all that we know of the universe through physics, chemistry, and biology, the logical mind will classify it as a singular product of dementia — a dementia communicated in some sympathetic way to the man who burst out of that house in time. And thus, indeed, may it very well be regarded so long as Dr. Arlo Morehouse maintains his silence.

THE MANUSCRIPT.

Vague misgivings of the last quarter hour are now becoming definite fears. To begin with, I am thoroughly convinced that something must have happened to Dobbs. For the first time since we have been together he has failed to answer my summons. When he did not respond to my repeated ringing I decided that the bell must be out of order, but I have pounded on the table with vigour enough to rouse a charge of Charon. At first I thought he might have slipped out of the house for a breath of fresh air, for it has been hot and sultry all the forenoon, but it is not like Dobbs to stay away so long without first making sure that I would want nothing.

It is, however, the unusual occurrence of the last few minutes which confirms my suspicion that Dobbs' absence is a matter beyond his control. It is this same happening which prompts me to put my impressions and conjectures on paper in the hope that the mere act of recording them may relieve a certain sinister suggestion of impending tragedy. Try as I will, I cannot free my mind from the legends connected with this old house — mere superstitious fol-de-rol for dwarfed brains to revel in, and on which I would not even waste a thought if Dobbs were here.

Through the years that I have been shut away from the world I used to know, Dobbs has been my sixth sense. Now, for the first time since my incapacitation, I realize the full extent of my impotency. It is Dobbs who has compensated for my sightless eyes, my useless ears, my voiceless throat and my crippled legs. There is a glass of water on my typewriter table. Without Dobbs to fill it when it has been emptied, my plight will be like that of Tantalus. Few have come to this house since we have lived here — there is little in common between garrulous country folk and a paralytic who cannot see, hear or speak to them — it may be days before anyone else appears. Alone ... with only my thoughts to keep me company; disquieting thoughts which have been in no wise assuaged by the sensations of the last few minutes. I do not like these sensations, either, for more and more they are converting mere village gossip into a fantastic imagery which affects my emotions in a most peculiar and almost unprecedented manner.

It seems hours since I started to write this, but I know it can be only a few minutes, for I have just inserted this fresh page into the machine. The mechanical action of switching the sheets, brief though it was, has given me a fresh grip on myself. Perhaps I can shake off the sense of approaching danger long enough to recount that which has already happened.

At first it was no more than a mere tremor, something similar to the shivering of a cheap tenement block when a heavy truck rumbles close by the curb — but this is no loosely built frame structure. Perhaps I am super-sensitive to such things, and it may be that I am allowing my imagination to play tricks; but it seemed to me that the disturbance was more pronounced directly in front of me — and my chair faces the southeast wing; away from the road, directly in line with the swamp at the rear of the dwelling! Delusion though this may have been, there is no denying what followed. I was reminded of moments when I have felt the ground tremble beneath my feet at the bursting of giant shells; times when I have seen ships tossed like chaff before the fury of a typhoon. The house shook like a Dweurgarlan cinder in the sieves of Niflheim. Every timber in the floor beneath my feet quivered like a suffering thing. My typewriter trembled till I could imagine that the keys were chattering of their fear.

A brief moment and it was over. Everything is as calm as before. Altogether too calm! It seems impossible that such a thing could happen and yet leave everything exactly as it was before. No, not exactly — I am thoroughly convinced that something has happened to Dobbs! It is this conviction, added to this unnatural calm, which accentuates the premonitory fear that persists in creeping over me. Fear? Yes — though I am trying to reason sanely with myself that there is nothing of which to be afraid. Critics have both praised and condemned my poetry because of what they term a vivid imagination. At such a time as this I can heartily agree with those who cry "too vivid." Nothing can be very much amiss or ...

Smoke! Just a faint sulphurous trace, but one which is unmistakable to my keenly attuned nostrils. So faint, indeed, that it is impossible for me to determine whether it comes from some part of the house or drifts through the window of the adjoining room, which opens on the swamp. The impression is rapidly becoming more clearly defined. I am sure, now, that it does not come from outside. Vagrant visions of the past, sombre scenes of other days, flashed before me in stereoscopic review. A flaming factory ... hysterical screams of terrified women penned in by walls of fire; a blazing schoolhouse ... pitiful cries of helpless children trapped by collapsing stairs; a theatre fire ... frantic babel of panic-stricken people fighting to freedom over blistering floors; and, overall, impenetrable clouds of black, noxious, malicious smoke polluting the peaceful sky. The air of the room is saturated with thick, heavy, stifling waves ... at any moment I expect to feel hot tongues of flame lick eagerly at my useless legs ... my eyes smart ... my ears throb ... I cough and choke to rid my lungs of the Ocypetian fumes ... smoke such as is associated only with appalling catastrophes ... acrid, stinking, mephitic smoke permeated with the revolting odour of burning flesh.

[***]

Once more I am alone with this portentous calm. The welcome breeze that fans my cheeks is fast restoring my vanished courage. Clearly, the house cannot be on fire, for every vestige of the torturous smoke is gone. I cannot detect a single trace of it, though I have been sniffling like a bloodhound. I am beginning to wonder if I am going mad; if the years of solitude have unhinged my mind — but the phenomenon has been too definite to permit me to class it as mere hallucination. Sane or insane, I cannot conceive these things as aught but actualities — and the moment I catalogue them as such I can come to only one logical conclusion. The inference in itself is enough to upset one's mental stability. To concede this is to grant the truth of the superstitious rumours which Dobbs compiled from the villagers and transcribed for my sensitive fingertips to read — unsubstantiated hearsay that my materialistic mind instinctively condemns as asininity!

I wish the throbbing in my ears would stop! It is as if mad spectral players were beating a duet upon the aching drums. I suppose it is merely a reaction to the suffocating sensations I have just experienced. A few more drafts of this refreshing air ....

Something — someone is in this room! I am as sure I am no longer alone as if I could see the presence I sense so infallibly. It is an impression quite similar to one which I have had while elbowing my way through a crowded street — the definite notion that eyes were singling me out from the rest of the throng with a gaze intense enough to arrest my subconscious attention — the same sensation, only magnified a thousandfold. Who — what — can it be? After all, my fears may be groundless, perhaps it means only that Dobbs has returned. No ... it is not Dobbs. As I anticipated, the tattoo upon my ears has ceased and a low whisper has caught my attention ... the overwhelming significance of the thing has just registered itself upon my bewildered brain ... *I can hear!*

It is not a single whispering voice, but many! [***] Lecherous buzzing of bestial blowflies ... Satanic humming of libidinous bees ... sibilant hissing of obscene reptiles ... a whispering chorus no human throat could sing! It is gaining in volume ... the room rings with demoniacal chanting; tuneless, toneless and grotesquely grim ... a diabolical choir rehearsing unholy litanies . . . paeans of Mephistophelian misery set to music of wailing souls . . . a hideous crescendo of pagan pandemonium [***]

The voices that surround me are drawing closer to my chair. The chanting has come to an abrupt end and the whispering has resolved itself into intelligible sounds. I strain my ears to distinguish the words. Closer . . . and still closer. They are clear, now — too clear! Better had my ears been blocked forever than forced to listen to their hellish mouthings [***]

Impious revelations of soul-sickening Saturnalia [***] ghoulish conceptions of devastating debaucheries [***] profane bribes of Cabirian orgies [***] malevolent threats of unimagined punishments [***]

It is cold. Unseasonably cold! As if inspired by the cacodemoniacal presences that harass me, the breeze that was so friendly a few minutes ago growls angrily about my ears — an icy gale that rushes in from the swamp and chills me to the bone.

If Dobbs has deserted me I do not blame him. I hold no brief for cowardice or craven fear, but there are some things [***] I only hope his fate has been nothing worse than to have departed in time!

My last doubt is swept away. I am doubly glad, now, that I have held to my resolve to write down my impressions . . . not that I expect anyone to understand . . . or believe . . . it has been a relief from the maddening strain of idly waiting for each new manifestation of psychic abnormality. As I see it, there are but three courses that may be taken: to flee from this accursed place and spend the torturous years that lie ahead in trying to forget — but flee I cannot; to yield to an abominable alliance with forces so malign that Tartarus to them would seem but an alcove of paradise — but yield I will not; to die — far rather would I have my body torn limb from limb than to contaminate my soul in barbarous barter with such emissaries of Belial [***]

I have had to pause for a moment to blow upon my fingers. The room is cold with the foetid frigor of the tomb . . . a peaceful numbness is creeping over me . . . I must fight off this lassitude; it is undermining my determination to die rather than give in to the insidious importunings . . . I vow, anew, to resist until the end . . . the end that I know cannot be far away [***]

The wind is colder than ever, if such a thing be possible . . . A wind freighted with the stench of dead-alive things [***] O merciful God who took my sight! [***] a wind so cold it burns where it should freeze . . . it has become a blistering sirocco [***]

Unseen fingers grip me . . . ghost fingers that lack the physical strength to force me from my machine . . . icy fingers that force me into a vile vortex of vice . . . devil-fingers that draw me down into a cesspool of eternal iniquity . . . death-fingers that shut off my breath and make my sightless eyes feel they must burst with the pain [***] Frozen points press against my temples [***] Hard, bony knobs, akin to horns [***] boreal breath of some long dead thing kisses my fevered lips and sears my hot throat with frozen flame [***]

It is dark. [***] Not the darkness that is part of years of blindness [***] the impenetrable darkness of sin-steeped night [***] the pitch-black darkness of purgatory [***]

I see [***] *Spes mea Christus!* [***] It is the end [***] [***]

Not for mortal mind is any resisting of force beyond human imagination. Not for immortal spirit is any conquering of that which hath probed the depths and made of immortality a transient moment. The end? Nay! It is but the blissful beginning . . .

Under the Pyramids.

(ALTERNATE TITLE: IMPRISONED WITH THE PHARAOHS)

BY HARRY HOUDINI
AND H.P. LOVECRAFT

11,000-WORD NOVELETTE; 1924.

"Under the Pyramids" is a strong and competently told novelette that's almost like a travelogue with a twist. Lovecraft wrote it just before he and Sonia Haft Greene were married, and the $100 cheque with which he was promptly rewarded for it essentially financed his honeymoon; unfortunately, it seems also to have ruined his wedding night, because he lost the typescript in a railway station the day before the wedding and had to press his new bride into service to help him retype the whole thing.

"When that manuscript was finished, we were too tired and exhausted for honey-mooning or anything else," Sonia later recalled.

This story probably went from manuscript to magazine page faster than anything else Lovecraft ever wrote. He wrote it in March of 1924, and it was published in the May 1924 issue of Weird Tales.

ABOUT HARRY HOUDINI (1874-1926).

Even today, nearly 100 years after his death, Harry Houdini really doesn't need an introduction. "Houdini," of course, was a stage name; his real name was Erik Weisz, and he was born in Budapest in 1874, the son of a rabbi there. He came to the United States three years later with his family.

Houdini made his name in Vaudeville, in which he was for many years the top-paid performer in the country. He started as a magician, but soon found his talents more suited to escape performances.

By early 1924, when Houdini was recruited to lend his name to a series of ghostwritten articles and columns in Weird Tales, *his was a household name of the first water, associated with numerous famous escape stunts: the Chinese Water Torture Cell, the Milk Can Escape, the Overboard Box Escape, and many more. He'd three times clawed his way out of freshly filled graves after being buried alive. And — perhaps as an indirect countermeasure against critics who claimed some of his stunts were faked — he had also made a name for himself as a debunker of mystical mediums and psychics.*

Houdini's short-lived ghostwritten column in Weird Tales, *"Ask Houdini," and his first two ghostwritten stories in the magazine, "The Spirit-Fakirs of Hermannstadt" and "The Hoax of the Spirit-Lover," appeared between March and July of 1924. These first pieces were all ghostwritten by someone else — possibly future* Weird Tales *editor Farnsworth Wright, possibly Walter B. Gibson (creator of The Shadow).*

"The Spirit-Fakirs" and "The Spirit-Lover" had been written but not yet published when, in February 1924, Weird Tales *publisher J.C. Henneberger commissioned Lovecraft to ghostwrite the third and final installment: "Under the Pyramids."*

Houdini and Lovecraft got along very well indeed, and after working with him on the story Houdini actually talked about helping Lovecraft break through as a known literary figure; but, not long after that, Houdini contracted appendicitis, and mistook its symptoms for soreness resultant from having been sucker-punched in the abdomen by a friend a few days before. As a result, he didn't seek help until it was too late, and he died on Halloween Day in 1926.

As a side note, it's interesting that Houdini and Lovecraft each died on such a traditionally sinister day — the one on All Hallows' Eve, the other on the Ides of March.

I.

Mystery attracts mystery. Ever since the wide appearance of my name as a performer of unexplained feats, I have encountered strange narratives and events which my calling has led people to link with my interests and activities. Some of these have been trivial and irrelevant, some deeply dramatic and absorbing, some productive of weird and perilous experiences and some involving me in extensive scientific and historical research. Many of these matters I have told and shall continue to tell very freely; but there is one of which I speak with great reluctance, and which I am now relating only after a session of grilling persuasion from the publishers of this magazine, who had heard vague rumors of it from other members of my family.

The hitherto guarded subject pertains to my non-professional visit to Egypt fourteen years ago, and has been avoided by me for several reasons. For one thing, I am averse to exploiting certain unmistakably actual facts and conditions obviously unknown to the myriad tourists who throng about the pyramids and apparently secreted with much diligence by the authorities at Cairo, who cannot be wholly ignorant of them. For another thing, I dislike to recount an incident in which my own fantastic imagination must have played so great a part. What I saw — or thought I saw — certainly did not take place; but is rather to be viewed as a result of my then recent readings in Egyptology, and of the speculations anent this theme which my environment

Weird Tales

THE UNIQUE MAGAZINE

ANNIVERSARY
NUMBER 50c
FIFTY DISTINCT FEATURE
NOVELS, SHORT STORIES
AND NOVELETTES.
THRILLS! MYSTERY!
ADVENTURE!

Weird Tales, May/June/July 1924

naturally prompted. These imaginative stimuli, magnified by the excitement of an actual event terrible enough in itself, undoubtedly gave rise to the culminating horror of that grotesque night so long past.

In January, 1910, I had finished a professional engagement in England and signed a contract for a tour of Australian theatres. A liberal time being allowed for the trip, I determined to make the most of it in the sort of travel which chiefly interests me; so accompanied by my wife I drifted pleasantly down the Continent and embarked at Marseilles on the P&O steamer *Malwa*, bound for Port Said. From that point I proposed to visit the principal historical localities of lower Egypt before leaving finally for Australia.

The voyage was an agreeable one, and enlivened by many of the amusing incidents which befall a magical performer apart from his work. I had intended, for the sake of quiet travel, to keep my name a secret; but was goaded into betraying myself by a fellow-magician whose anxiety to astound the passengers with ordinary tricks tempted me to duplicate and exceed his feats in a manner quite destructive of my incognito. I mention this because of its ultimate effect — an effect I should have foreseen before unmasking to a shipload of tourists about to scatter throughout the Nile valley. What it did was to herald my identity wherever I subsequently went, and deprive my wife and me of all the placid inconspicuousness we had sought. Traveling to seek curiosities, I was often forced to stand inspection as a sort of curiosity myself!

We had come to Egypt in search of the picturesque and the mystically impressive, but found little enough when the ship edged up to Port Said and discharged its passengers in small boats. Low dunes of sand, bobbing buoys in shallow water, and a drearily European small town with nothing of interest save the great De Lesseps statue, made us anxious to get to something more worth our while. After some discussion we decided to proceed at once to Cairo and the Pyramids, later going to Alexandria for the Australian boat and for whatever Greco-Roman sights that ancient metropolis might present.

The railway journey was tolerable enough, and consumed only four hours and a half. We saw much of the Suez Canal, whose route we followed as far as Ismailiya and later had a taste of Old Egypt in our glimpse of the restored fresh-water canal of the Middle Empire. Then at last we saw Cairo glimmering through the growing dusk; a winkling constellation which became a blaze as we halted at the great Gare Centrale.

But once more disappointment awaited us, for all that we beheld was European save the costumes and the crowds. A prosaic subway led to a square teeming with carriages, taxicabs, and trolley-cars and gorgeous with electric lights shining on tall buildings; whilst the very theatre where I was vainly requested to play and which I later attended as a spectator, had recently been renamed the "American Cosmograph." We stopped at Shepheard's Hotel, reached in a taxi that sped along broad, smartly built-up streets; and amidst the perfect service of its restaurant, elevators and generally Anglo-American luxuries the mysterious East and immemorial past seemed very far away.

The next day, however, precipitated us delightfully into the heart of the Arabian Nights atmosphere; and in the winding ways and exotic skyline of Cairo, the Bagdad of Harun-al-Rashid seemed to live again. Guided by our Baedeker, we had struck east past the Ezbekiyeh Gardens along the Mouski in quest of the native quarter, and were soon in the hands of a clamorous cicerone who — notwithstanding later developments — was assuredly a master at his trade.

Not until afterward did I see that I should have applied at the hotel for a licensed guide. This man, a shaven, peculiarly hollow-voiced and relatively cleanly fellow who looked like a Pharaoh and called himself "Abdul Reis el Drogman," appeared to have much power over others of his kind; though subsequently the police professed not to know him, and to suggest that *reis* is merely a name for any person in authority, whilst "Drogman" is obviously no more than a clumsy modification of the word for a leader of tourist parties — *dragoman*.

Abdul led us among such wonders as we had before only read and dreamed of. Old Cairo is itself a story-book and a dream — labyrinths of narrow alleys redolent of aromatic secrets; Arabesque balconies and oriels nearly meeting above the cobbled streets; maelstroms of Oriental traffic with strange cries, cracking whips, rattling carts, jingling money, and braying donkeys, kaleidoscopes of polychrome robes, veils, turbans, and tarbushes; water-carriers and dervishes, dogs and cats, soothsayers and barbers; and over all the whining of blind beggars crouched in alcoves, and the sonorous chanting of muezzins from minarets limned delicately against a sky of deep, unchanging blue.

The roofed, quieter bazaars were hardly less alluring. Spice, perfume, incense beads, rugs, silks, and brass — old Mahmoud Suleiman squats cross-legged amidst his gummy bottles while chattering youths pulverize mustard in the hollowed-out capital of an ancient classic column — a Roman Corinthian, perhaps from neighboring Heliopolis, where Augustus stationed one of his three Egyptian legions. Antiquity begins to mingle with exoticism. And then the mosques and the museum — we saw them all, and tried not to let our Arabian revel succumb to the darker charm of Pharaonic Egypt which the museum's priceless treasures offered. That was to be our climax, and for the present we concentrated on the mediaeval Saracenic glories of the Caliphs whose magnificent tomb-mosques form a glittering faery necropolis on the edge of the Arabian Desert.

At length Abdul took us along the Sharia Mohammed Ali to the ancient mosque of Sultan Hassan, and the tower-flanked Babel-Azab, beyond which climbs the steep-walled pass to the mighty citadel that Saladin himself built with the stones of forgotten pyramids. It was sunset when we scaled that cliff, circled the modern mosque of Mohammed Ali, and looked down from the dizzy parapet over mystic Cairo — mystic

Cairo all golden with its carven domes, its ethereal minarets and its flaming gardens.

Far over the city towered the great Roman dome of the new museum; and beyond it — across the cryptic yellow Nile that is the mother of eons and dynasties — lurked the menacing sands of the Libyan Desert, undulant and iridescent and evil with older arcana.

The red sun sank low, bringing the relentless chill of Egyptian dusk; and as it stood poised on the world's rim like that ancient god of Heliopolis — Re-Harakhte, the Horizon-Sun — we saw silhouetted against its vermeil holocaust the black outlines of the Pyramids of Gizeh — the palaeogean tombs there were hoary with a thousand years when Tut-Ankh-Amen mounted his golden throne in distant Thebes. Then we knew that we were done with Saracen Cairo, and that we must taste the deeper mysteries of primal Egypt — the black Kem of Re and Amen, Isis and Osiris.

The next morning we visited the Pyramids, riding out in a Victoria across the island of Chizereh with its massive lebbakh trees, and the smaller English bridge to the western shore. Down the shore road we drove, between great rows of lebbakhs and past the vast Zoological Gardens to the suburb of Gizeh, where a new bridge to Cairo proper has since been built. Then, turning inland along the Sharia-el-Haram, we crossed a region of glassy canals and shabby native villages till before us loomed the objects of our quest, cleaving the mists of dawn and forming inverted replicas in the roadside pools. Forty centuries, as Napoleon had told his campaigners there, indeed looked down upon us.

The road now rose abruptly, till we finally reached our place of transfer between the trolley station and the Mena House Hotel. Abdul Reis, who capably purchased our Pyramid tickets, seemed to have an understanding with the crowding, yelling and offensive Bedouins who inhabited a squalid mud village some distance away and pestiferously assailed every traveler; for he kept them very decently at bay and secured an excellent pair of camels for us, himself mounting a donkey and assigning the leadership of our animals to a group of men and boys more expensive than useful. The area to be traversed was so small that camels were hardly needed, but we did not regret adding to our experience this troublesome form of desert navigation.

The pyramids stand on a high rock plateau, this group forming next to the northernmost of the series of regal and aristocratic cemeteries built in the neighborhood of the extinct capital Memphis, which lay on the same side of the Nile, somewhat south of Gizeh, and which flourished between 3400 and 2000 B.C. The greatest pyramid, which lies nearest the modern road, was built by King Cheops or Khufu about 2800 B.C., and stands more than 450 feet in perpendicular height. In a line southwest from this are successively the Second Pyramid, built a generation later by King Khephren, and though slightly smaller, looking even larger because set on higher ground, and the radically smaller Third Pyramid of King Mycerinus, built about 2700 B.C. Near the edge of the plateau and due east of the Second Pyramid, with a face probably altered to form a colossal portrait of Khephren, its royal restorer, stands the monstrous Sphinx — mute, sardonic, and wise beyond mankind and memory.

Minor pyramids and the traces of ruined minor pyramids are found in several places, and the whole plateau is pitted with the tombs of dignitaries of less than royal rank. These latter were originally marked by mastabas, or stone bench-like structures about the deep burial shafts, as found in other Memphian cemeteries and exemplified by Perneb's Tomb in the Metropolitan Museum of New York. At Gizeh, however, all such visible things have been swept away by time and pillage; and only the rock-hewn shafts, either sand-filled or cleared out by archaeologists, remain to attest their former existence. Connected with each tomb was a chapel in which priests and relatives offered food and prayer to the hovering ka or vital principle of the deceased. The small tombs have their chapels contained in their stone mastabas or superstructures, but the mortuary chapels of the pyramids, where regal Pharaohs lay, were separate temples, each to the east of its corresponding pyramid, and connected by a causeway to a massive gate-chapel or propylon at the edge of the rock plateau.

The gate-chapel leading to the Second Pyramid, nearly buried in the drifting sands, yawns subterraneously south-east of the Sphinx. Persistent tradition dubs it the "Temple of the Sphinx"; and it may perhaps be rightly called such if the Sphinx indeed represents the Second Pyramid's builder Khephren. There are unpleasant tales of the Sphinx before Khephren — but whatever its elder features were, the monarch replaced them with his own that men might look at the colossus without fear.

It was in the great gateway-temple that the life-size diorite statue of Khephren now in the Cairo museum was found; a statue before which I stood in awe when I beheld it. Whether the whole edifice is now excavated I am not certain, but in 1910 most of it was below ground, with the entrance heavily barred at night. Germans were in charge of the work, and the war or other things may have stopped them. I would give much, in view of my experience and of certain Bedouin whisperings discredited or unknown in Cairo, to know what has developed in connection with a certain well in a transverse gallery where statues of the Pharaoh were found in curious juxtaposition to the statues of baboons.

The road, as we traversed it on our camels that morning, curved sharply past the wooden police quarters, post office, drug store and shops on the left, and plunged south and east in a complete bend that scaled the rock plateau and brought us face to face with the desert under the lee of the Great Pyramid. Past Cyclopean masonry we rode, rounding the eastern face and looking down ahead into a valley of minor pyramids beyond which the eternal Nile glistened to the east, and the eternal desert shimmered to the west. Very close loomed the three major pyramids, the greatest devoid of outer casing and showing its bulk of great stones, but the others retaining here and there the neatly fitted covering which had made them smooth and finished in their day.

Presently we descended toward the Sphinx, and sat silent beneath the spell of those terrible unseeing eyes. On the vast stone breast we faintly discerned the emblem of Re-Harakhte, for whose image the Sphinx was mistaken in a late dynasty; and though sand covered the tablet between the great paws, we recalled what Thutmosis IV inscribed thereon, and the dream he had when a prince. It was then that the smile of the Sphinx vaguely displeased us, and made us wonder about the legends of subterranean passages beneath the monstrous creature, leading down, down, to depths none might dare hint at — depths connected with mysteries older than the dynastic Egypt we excavate, and having a sinister relation to the persistence of abnormal, animal-headed gods in the ancient Nilotic pantheon. Then, too, it was I asked myself an idle question whose hideous significance was not to appear for many an hour.

Other tourists now began to overtake us, and we moved on to the sand-choked Temple of the Sphinx, fifty yards to the southeast, which I have previously mentioned as the great gate of the causeway to the Second Pyramid's mortuary chapel on the plateau. Most of it was still underground, and although we dismounted and descended through a modern passageway to its alabaster corridor and pillared hall, I felt that Abdul and the local German attendant had not shown us all there was to see.

After this we made the conventional circuit of the pyramid plateau, examining the Second Pyramid and the peculiar ruins of its mortuary chapel to the east, the Third Pyramid and its miniature southern satellites and ruined eastern chapel, the rock tombs and the honeycombings of the Fourth and Fifth dynasties, and the famous Campbell's Tomb whose shadowy shaft sinks precipitously for fifty-three feet to a sinister sarcophagus which one of our camel drivers divested of the cumbering sand after a vertiginous descent by rope.

Cries now assailed us from the Great Pyramid, where Bedouins were besieging a party of tourists with offers of speed in the performance of solitary trips up and down. Seven minutes is said to be the record for such an ascent and descent, but many lusty sheiks and sons of sheiks assured us they could cut it to five if given the requisite impetus of liberal baksheesh. They did not get this impetus, though we did let Abdul take us up, thus obtaining a view of unprecedented magnificence which included not only remote and glittering Cairo with its crowned citadel background of gold-violet hills, but all the pyramids of the Memphian district as well, from Abu Roash on the north to the Dashur on the south. The Sakkara step-pyramid, which marks the evolution of the low mastaba into the true pyramid, showed clearly and alluringly in the sandy distance. It is close to this transition-monument that the famed tomb of Perneb was found — more than four hundred miles north of the Theban rock valley where Tut-Ankh-Amen sleeps. Again I was forced to silence through sheer awe. The prospect of such antiquity, and the secrets each hoary monument seemed to hold and brood over, filled me with a reverence and sense of immensity nothing else ever gave me.

Fatigued by our climb, and disgusted with the importunate Bedouins whose actions seemed to defy every rule of taste, we omitted the arduous detail of entering the cramped interior passages of any of the pyramids, though we saw several of the hardiest tourists preparing for the suffocating crawl through Cheops' mightiest memorial. As we dismissed and overpaid our local bodyguard and drove back to Cairo with Abdul Reis under the afternoon sun, we half regretted the omission we had made. Such fascinating things were whispered about lower pyramid passages not in the guide books; passages whose entrances had been hastily blocked up and concealed by certain uncommunicative archaeologists who had found and begun to explore them.

Of course, this whispering was largely baseless on the face of it; but it was curious to reflect how persistently visitors were forbidden to enter the Pyramids at night, or to visit the lowest burrows and crypt of the Great Pyramid. Perhaps in the latter case it was the psychological effect which was feared — the effect on the visitor of feeling himself huddled down beneath a gigantic world of solid masonry; joined to the life he has known by the merest tube, in which he may only crawl, and which any accident or evil design might block. The whole subject seemed so weird and alluring that we resolved to pay the pyramid plateau another visit at the earliest possible opportunity. For me this opportunity came much earlier than I expected.

That evening, the members of our party feeling somewhat tired after the strenuous program of the day, I went alone with Abdul Reis for a walk through the picturesque Arab quarter. Though I had seen it by day, I wished to study the alleys and bazaars in the dusk, when rich shadows and mellow gleams of light would add to their glamor and fantastic illusion. The native crowds were thinning, but were still very noisy and numerous when we came upon a knot of reveling Bedouins in the Suken-Nahhasin, or bazaar of the coppersmiths. Their apparent leader, an insolent youth with heavy features and saucily cocked tarbush, took some notice of us, and evidently recognized with no great friendliness my competent but admittedly supercilious and sneeringly disposed guide.

Perhaps, I thought, he resented that odd reproduction of the Sphinx's half-smile which I had often remarked with amused irritation; or perhaps he did not like the hollow and sepulchral resonance of Abdul's voice. At any rate, the exchange of ancestrally opprobrious language became very brisk; and before long Ali Ziz, as I heard the stranger called when called by no worse name, began to pull violently at Abdul's robe, an action quickly reciprocated and leading to a spirited scuffle in which both combatants lost their sacredly cherished headgear and would have reached an even direr condition had I not intervened and separated them by main force.

My interference, at first seemingly unwelcome on both sides, succeeded at last in effecting a truce. Sullenly each belligerent composed his wrath and his attire, and with an assumption of dignity as profound as it was sudden, the two formed a curious pact of honor which I soon learned is a custom of great antiquity in Cairo — a pact for the settlement of their difference by means of a nocturnal fist fight atop the Great Pyramid, long after the departure of the last moonlight sightseer. Each duelist was to assemble a party of seconds, and the affair was to begin at midnight, proceeding by rounds in the most civilized possible fashion.

In all this planning there was much which excited my interest. The fight itself promised to be unique and spectacular, while the thought of the scene on that hoary pile overlooking the antediluvian plateau of Gizeh under the wan moon of the pallid small hours appealed to every fiber of imagination in me. A request found Abdul exceedingly willing to admit me to his party of seconds; so that all the rest of the early evening I accompanied him to various dens in the most lawless regions of the town — mostly northeast of the Ezbekiyeh — where he gathered one by one a select and formidable band of congenial cutthroats as his pugilistic background.

Shortly after nine our party, mounted on donkeys bearing such royal or tourist-reminiscent names as "Rameses," "Mark Twain," "J. P. Morgan," and "Minnehaha," edged through street labyrinths both Oriental and Occidental, crossed the muddy and mast-forested Nile by the bridge of the bronze lions, and cantered philosophically between the lebbakhs on the road to Gizeh. Slightly over two hours were consumed by the trip, toward the end of which we passed the last of the returning tourists, saluted the last inbound trolley-car, and were alone with the night and the past and the spectral moon.

Then we saw the vast pyramids at the end of the avenue, ghoulish with a dim atavistical menace which I had not seemed to notice in the daytime. Even the smallest of them held a hint of the ghastly — for was it not in this that they had buried Queen Nitocris alive in the Sixth Dynasty; subtle Queen Nitocris, who once invited all her enemies to a feast in a temple below the Nile, and drowned them by opening the water-gates? I recalled that the Arabs whisper things about Nitocris, and shun the Third Pyramid at certain phases of the moon. It must have been over her that Thomas Moore was brooding when he wrote a thing muttered about by Memphian boatmen:

The subterranean nymph that dwells
'Mid sunless gems and glories hid —
The lady of the Pyramid!"

Early as we were, Ali Ziz and his party were ahead of us; for we saw their donkeys outlined against the desert plateau at Kafrel-Haram; toward which squalid Arab settlement, close to the Sphinx, we had diverged instead of following the regular road to the Mena House, where some of the sleepy, inefficient police might have observed and halted us. Here, where filthy Bedouins stabled camels and donkeys in the rock tombs of Khephren's courtiers, we were led up the rocks and over the sand to the Great Pyramid, up whose time-worn sides the Arabs swarmed eagerly, Abdul Reis offering me the assistance I did not need.

As most travelers know, the actual apex of this structure has long been worn away, leaving a reasonably flat platform twelve yards square. On this eerie pinnacle a squared circle was formed, and in a few moments the sardonic desert moon leered down upon a battle which, but for the quality of the ringside cries, might well have occurred at some minor athletic club in America. As I watched it, I felt that some of our less-desirable institutions were not lacking; for every blow, feint, and defense bespoke "stalling" to my not-inexperienced eye. It was quickly over, and despite my misgivings as to methods I felt a sort of proprietary pride when Abdul Reis was adjudged the winner.

Reconciliation was phenomenally rapid, and amidst the singing, fraternizing and drinking that followed, I found it difficult to realize that a quarrel had ever occurred. Oddly enough, I myself seemed to be more a center of notice than the antagonists; and from my smattering of Arabic I judged that they were discussing my professional performances and escapes from every sort of manacle and confinement, in a manner which indicated not only a surprising knowledge of me, but a distinct hostility and skepticism concerning my feats of escape. It gradually dawned on me that the elder magic of Egypt did not depart without leaving traces, and that fragments of a strange secret lore and priestly cult-practices have survived surreptitiously amongst the fellaheen to such an extent that the prowess of a strange hahwi or magician is resented and disputed. I thought of how much my hollow-voiced guide Abdul Reis looked like an old Egyptian priest or Pharaoh or smiling Sphinx . . . and wondered.

Suddenly something happened which in a flash proved the correctness of my reflections and made me curse the denseness whereby I had accepted this night's events as other than the empty and malicious "frame-up" they now showed themselves to be. Without warning, and doubtless in answer to some subtle sign from Abdul, the entire band of Bedouins precipitated itself upon me; and having produced heavy ropes, soon had me bound as securely as I was ever bound in the course of my life, either on the stage or off.

I struggled at first, but soon saw that one man could make no headway against a band of over twenty sinewy barbarians. My hands were tied behind my back, my knees bent to their fullest extent, and my wrists and ankles stoutly linked together with unyielding cords. A stifling gag was forced into my mouth, and a blindfold fastened tightly over my eyes. Then, as Arabs bore me aloft on their shoulders and began a jouncing descent of the pyramid, I heard the taunts of my late guide Abdul, who mocked and jeered delightedly in his hollow voice, and assured me that I was soon to have my "magic powers" put to a supreme test — which would quickly remove any egotism I might have gained through triumphing over all the tests offered by America and Europe. Egypt, he reminded me, is very old, and full of inner mysteries and antique powers not even conceivable to the experts of today, whose devices had so uniformly failed to entrap me.

How far or in what direction I was carried, I cannot tell; for the circumstances were all against the formation of any accurate judgment. I know, however, that it could not have been a great distance; since my bearers at no point hastened beyond a walk, yet kept me aloft a surprisingly short time. It is this perplexing brevity which makes me feel almost like shuddering whenever I think of Gizeh and its plateau—for one is oppressed by hints of the closeness to everyday tourist routes of what existed then and must exist still.

The evil abnormality I speak of did not become manifest at first. Setting me down on a surface which I recognized as sand rather than rock, my captors passed a rope around my chest and dragged me a few feet to a ragged opening in the ground, into which they presently lowered me with much rough handling. For apparent eons I bumped against the stony irregular sides of a narrow hewn well which I took to be one of the numerous burial-shafts of the plateau until the prodigious, almost incredible depth of it robbed me of all bases of conjecture.

The horror of the experience deepened with every dragging second. That any descent through the sheer solid rock could be so vast without reaching the core of the planet itself, or that any rope made by man could be so long as to dangle me in these unholy and seemingly fathomless profundities of nether earth, were beliefs of such grotesqueness that it was easier to doubt my agitated senses than to accept them. Even now I am uncertain, for I know how deceitful the sense of time becomes when one is removed or distorted. But I am quite sure that I preserved a logical consciousness that far; that at least I did not add any full-grown phantoms of imagination to a picture hideous enough in its reality, and explicable by a type of cerebral illusion vastly short of actual hallucination.

All this was not the cause of my first bit of fainting. The shocking ordeal was cumulative, and the beginning of the later terrors was a very perceptible increase in my rate of descent. They were paying out that infinitely long rope very swiftly now, and I scraped cruelly against the rough and constricted sides of the shaft as I shot madly downward. My clothing was in tatters, and I felt the trickle of blood all over, even above the mounting and excruciating pain. My nostrils, too, were assailed by a scarcely definable menace: a creeping odor of damp and staleness curiously unlike anything I had ever smelled before, and having faint overtones of spice and incense that lent an element of mockery.

Then the mental cataclysm came. It was horrible—hideous beyond all articulate description because it was all of the soul, with nothing of detail to describe. It was the ecstasy of nightmare and the summation of the fiendish. The suddenness of it was apocalyptic and demoniac—one moment I was plunging agonizingly down that narrow well of million-toothed torture, yet the next moment I was soaring on bat-wings in the gulfs of hell; swinging free and swooping through illimitable miles of boundless, musty space; rising dizzily to measureless pinnacles of chilling ether, then diving gaspingly to sucking nadirs of ravenous, nauseous lower vacua . . . Thank God for the mercy that shut out in oblivion those clawing Furies of consciousness which half unhinged my faculties, and tore harpy-like at my spirit! That one respite, short as it was, gave me the strength and sanity to endure those still greater sublimations of cosmic panic that lurked and gibbered on the road ahead.

II.

It was very gradually that I regained my senses after that eldritch flight through stygian space. The process was infinitely painful, and colored by fantastic dreams in which my bound and gagged condition found singular embodiment. The precise nature of these dreams was very clear while I was experiencing them, but became blurred in my recollection almost immediately afterward, and was soon reduced to the merest outline by the terrible events—real or imaginary—which followed. I dreamed that I was in the grasp of a great and horrible paw; a yellow, hairy, five-clawed paw which had reached out of the earth to crush and engulf me. And when I stopped to reflect what the paw was, it seemed to me that it was Egypt. In the dream I looked back at the events of the preceding weeks, and saw myself lured and enmeshed little by little, subtly and insidiously, by some hellish ghoul-spirit of the elder Nile sorcery; some spirit that was in Egypt before ever man was, and that will be when man is no more.

I saw the horror and unwholesome antiquity of Egypt, and the grisly alliance it has always had with the tombs and temples of the dead. I saw phantom processions of priests with the heads of bulls, falcons, cats, and ibises; phantom processions marching interminably through subterraneous labyrinths and avenues of titanic propylaea beside which a man is as a fly, and offering unnamable sacrifice to indescribable gods. Stone colossi marched in endless night and drove herds of grinning androsphinxes down to the shores of illimitable stagnant rivers of pitch. And behind it all I saw the ineffable malignity of primordial necromancy, black and amorphous, and fumbling greedily after me in the darkness to choke out the spirit that had dared to mock it by emulation.

In my sleeping brain there took shape a melodrama of sinister hatred and pursuit, and I saw the black soul of Egypt singling me out and calling me in inaudible whispers; calling and luring me, leading me on with the glitter and glamor of a Saracenic surface, but ever pulling me down to the age-mad catacombs and horrors of its dead and abysmal pharaonic heart.

Then the dream faces took on human resemblances, and I saw my guide Abdul Reis in the robes of a king, with the sneer of the Sphinx on his features. And I knew that those features were the features of Khephren the Great, who raised the Second Pyramid, carved over the Sphinx's face in the likeness of his own and built that titanic gateway temple whose myriad corridors the archaeologists think they have dug out of the cryptical sand and the uninformative rock. And I looked at the long, lean rigid hand of Khephren; the long, lean, rigid hand as I had seen it on the diorite statue in the Cairo Museum — the statue they had found in the terrible gateway temple — and wondered that I had not shrieked when I saw it on Abdul Reis . . . that hand! It was hideously cold, and it was crushing me; it was the cold and cramping of the sarcophagus . . . the chill and constriction of unrememberable Egypt . . . It was nighted, necropolitan Egypt itself . . . that yellow paw . . . and they whisper such things of Khephren . . . .

But at this juncture I began to wake — or at least, to assume a condition less completely that of sleep than the one just preceding. I recalled the fight atop the pyramid, the treacherous Bedouins and their attack, my frightful descent by rope through endless rock depths, and my mad swinging and plunging in a chill void redolent of aromatic putrescence. I perceived that I now lay on a damp rock floor, and that my bonds were still biting into me with unloosened force. It was very cold, and I seemed to detect a faint current of noisome air sweeping across me. The cuts and bruises I had received from the jagged sides of the rock shaft were paining me woefully, their soreness enhanced to a stinging or burning acuteness by some pungent quality in the faint draft, and the mere act of rolling over was enough to set my whole frame throbbing with untold agony.

As I turned I felt a tug from above, and concluded that the rope whereby I was lowered still reached to the surface. Whether or not the Arabs still held it, I had no idea; nor had I any idea how far within the earth I was. I knew that the darkness around me was wholly or nearly total, since no ray of

Weird Tales, May/June/July 1924

moonlight penetrated my blindfold; but I did not trust my senses enough to accept as evidence of extreme depth the sensation of vast duration which had characterized my descent.

Knowing at least that I was in a space of considerable extent reached from the above surface directly by an opening in the rock, I doubtfully conjectured that my prison was perhaps the buried gateway chapel of old Khephren — the Temple of the Sphinx — perhaps some inner corridors which the guides had not shown me during my morning visit, and from which I might easily escape if I could find my way to the barred entrance. It would be a labyrinthine wandering, but no worse than others out of which I had in the past found my way.

The first step was to get free of my bonds, gag, and blindfold; and this I knew would be no great task, since subtler experts than these Arabs had tried every known species of fetter upon me during my long and varied career as an exponent of escape, yet had never succeeded in defeating my methods.

Then it occurred to me that the Arabs might be ready to meet and attack me at the entrance upon any evidence of my probable escape from the binding cords, as would be furnished by any decided agitation of the rope which they probably held. This, of course, was taking for granted that my place of confinement was indeed Khephren's Temple of the Sphinx. The direct opening in the roof, wherever it might lurk, could not be beyond easy reach of the ordinary modern entrance near the Sphinx; if in truth it were any great distance at all on the surface, since the total area known to visitors is not at all enormous. I had not noticed any such opening during my daytime pilgrimage, but knew that these things are easily overlooked amidst the drifting sands.

Thinking these matters over as I lay bent and bound on the rock floor, I nearly forgot the horrors of abysmal descent and cavernous swinging which had so lately reduced me to a coma. My present thought was only to outwit the Arabs, and I accordingly determined to work myself free as quickly as possible, avoiding any tug on the descending line which might betray an effective or even problematical attempt at freedom.

This, however, was more easily determined than effected. A few preliminary trials made it clear that little could be accomplished without considerable motion; and it did not surprise me when, after one especially energetic struggle, I began to feel the coils of falling rope as they piled up about me and upon me. Obviously, I thought, the Bedouins had felt my movements and released their end of the rope; hastening no doubt to the temple's true entrance to lie murderously in wait for me.

The prospect was not pleasing — but I had faced worse in my time without flinching, and would not flinch now. At present I must first of all free myself of bonds, then trust to ingenuity to escape from the temple unharmed. It is curious how implicitly I had come to believe myself in the old temple of Khephren beside the Sphinx, only a short distance below the ground.

That belief was shattered, and every pristine apprehension of preternatural depth and demoniac mystery revived, by a circumstance which grew in horror and significance even as I formulated my philosophical plan. I have said that the falling rope was piling up about and upon me. Now I saw that it was continuing to pile, as no rope of normal length could possibly do. It gained in momentum and became an avalanche of hemp, accumulating mountainously on the floor and half burying me beneath its swiftly multiplying coils. Soon I was completely engulfed and gasping for breath as the increasing convolutions submerged and stifled me.

My senses tottered again, and I vaguely tried to fight off a menace desperate and ineluctable. It was not merely that I was tortured beyond human endurance — not merely that life and breath seemed to be crushed slowly out of me — it was the knowledge of what those unnatural lengths of rope implied, and the consciousness of what unknown and incalculable gulfs of inner earth must at this moment be surrounding me. My endless descent and swinging flight through goblin space, then, must have been real, and even now I must be lying helpless in some nameless cavern world toward the core of the planet. Such a sudden confirmation of ultimate horror was insupportable, and a second time I lapsed into merciful oblivion.

When I say oblivion, I do not imply that I was free from dreams. On the contrary, my absence from the conscious world was marked by visions of the most unutterable hideousness. God! ... If only I had not read so much Egyptology before coming to this land which is the fountain of all darkness and terror! This second spell of fainting filled my sleeping mind anew with shivering realization of the country and its archaic secrets, and through some damnable chance my dreams turned to the ancient notions of the dead and their sojournings in soul and body beyond those mysterious tombs which were more houses than graves. I recalled, in dream-shapes which it is well that I do not remember, the peculiar and elaborate construction of Egyptian sepulchers; and the exceedingly singular and terrific doctrines which determined this construction.

All these people thought of was death and the dead. They conceived of a literal resurrection of the body which made them mummify it with desperate care, and preserve all the vital organs in canopic jars near the corpse; whilst besides the body they believed in two other elements, the soul, which after its weighing and approval by Osiris dwelt in the land of the blest, and the obscure and portentous ka or life-principle which wandered about the upper and lower worlds in a horrible way, demanding occasional access to the preserved body, consuming the food offerings brought by priests and pious relatives to the mortuary chapel, and sometimes — as men whispered — taking its body or the wooden double always buried beside it and stalking noxiously abroad on errands peculiarly repellent.

For thousands of years those bodies rested gorgeously encased and staring glassily upward when not visited by the ka, awaiting the day when Osiris should restore both ka and soul, and lead forth the stiff legions of the dead from the sunken houses of sleep. It was to have been a glorious rebirth — but not all souls were approved, nor were all tombs inviolate, so that certain grotesque mistakes and fiendish abnormalities were to be looked for. Even today the Arabs murmur of unsanctified convocations and unwholesome worship in forgotten nether abysses, which only winged invisible kas and soulless mummies may visit and return unscathed.

Perhaps the most leeringly blood-congealing legends are those which relate to certain perverse products of decadent priestcraft — composite mummies made by the artificial union of human trunks and limbs with the heads of animals in imitation of the elder gods. At all stages of history the sacred animals were mummified, so that consecrated bulls, cats, ibises, crocodiles and the like might return some day to greater glory. But only in the decadence did they mix the human and the animal in the same mummy — only in the decadence, when they did not understand the rights and prerogatives of the *ka* and the soul.

What happened to those composite mummies is not told of — at least publicly — and it is certain that no Egyptologist ever found one. The whispers of Arabs are very wild, and cannot be relied upon. They even hint that old Khephren — he of the Sphinx, the Second Pyramid and the yawning gateway temple — lives far underground wedded to the ghoul-queen Nitocris and ruling over the mummies that are neither of man nor of beast.

It was of these — of Khephren and his consort and his strange armies of the hybrid dead — that I dreamed, and that is why I am glad the exact dream-shapes have faded from my memory. My most horrible vision was connected with an idle question I had asked myself the day before when looking at the great carven riddle of the desert and wondering with what unknown depth the temple close to it might be secretly connected. That question, so innocent and whimsical then, assumed in my dream a meaning of frenetic and hysterical madness . . . what huge and loathsome abnormality was the Sphinx originally carven to represent?

My second awakening — if awakening it was — is a memory of stark hideousness which nothing else in my life — save one thing which came after — can parallel; and that life has been full and adventurous beyond most men's. Remember that I had lost consciousness whilst buried beneath a cascade of falling rope whose immensity revealed the cataclysmic depth of my present position. Now, as perception returned, I felt the entire weight gone; and realized upon rolling over that although I was still tied, gagged and blindfolded, some agency had removed completely the suffocating hempen landslide which had overwhelmed me. The significance of this condition, of course, came to me only gradually; but even so I think it would have brought unconsciousness again had I not by this time reached such a state of emotional exhaustion that no new horror could make much difference. I was alone . . . with what?

Before I could torture myself with any new reflection, or make any fresh effort to escape from my bonds, an additional circumstance became manifest. Pains not formerly felt were racking my arms and legs, and I seemed coated with a profusion of dried blood beyond anything my former cuts and abrasions could furnish. My chest, too, seemed pierced by a hundred wounds, as though some malign, titanic ibis had been pecking at it. Assuredly the agency which had removed the rope was a hostile one, and had begun to wreak terrible injuries upon me when somehow impelled to desist.

Yet at the same time my sensations were distinctly the reverse of what one might expect. Instead of sinking into a bottomless pit of despair, I was stirred to a new courage and action; for now I felt that the evil forces were physical things which a fearless man might encounter on an even basis.

On the strength of this thought I tugged again at my bonds, and used all the art of a lifetime to free myself as I had so often done amidst the glare of lights and the applause of vast crowds. The familiar details of my escaping process commenced to engross me, and now that the long rope was gone I half regained my belief that the supreme horrors were hallucinations after all, and that there had never been any terrible shaft, measureless abyss or interminable rope. Was I after all in the gateway temple of Khephren beside the Sphinx, and had the sneaking Arabs stolen in to torture me as I lay helpless there? At any rate, I must be free. Let me stand up unbound, ungagged, and with eyes open to catch any glimmer of light which might come trickling from any source, and I could actually delight in the combat against evil and treacherous foes!

How long I took in shaking off my encumbrances I cannot tell. It must have been longer than in my exhibition performances, because I was wounded, exhausted, and enervated by the experiences I had passed through. When I was finally free, and taking deep breaths of a chill, damp, evilly spiced air all the more horrible when encountered without the screen of gag and blindfold edges, I found that I was too cramped and fatigued to move at once. There I lay, trying to stretch a frame bent and mangled, for an indefinite period, and straining my eyes to catch a glimpse of some ray of light which would give a hint as to my position.

By degrees my strength and flexibility returned, but my eyes beheld nothing. As I staggered to my feet I peered diligently in every direction, yet met only an ebony blackness as great as that I had known when blindfolded. I tried my legs, blood-encrusted beneath my shredded trousers, and found that I could walk; yet could not decide in what direction to go. Obviously I ought not to walk at random, and perhaps retreat directly from the entrance I sought; so I paused to note the difference of the cold, fetid, natron-scented air-current which I had never ceased to feel. Accepting the point of its source as the possible entrance to the abyss, I strove to keep track of this landmark and to walk consistently toward it.

I had a match-box with me, and even a small electric flashlight; but of course the pockets of my tossed and tattered clothing were long since emptied of all heavy articles. As I walked cautiously in the blackness, the draft grew stronger and more offensive, till at length I could regard it as nothing less than a tangible stream of detestable vapor pouring out of some aperture like the smoke of the genie from the fisherman's jar in the Eastern tale. The East . . . Egypt . . . truly, this dark cradle of civilization was ever the wellspring of horrors and marvels unspeakable!

The more I reflected on the nature of this cavern wind, the greater my sense of disquiet became; for although despite its odor I had sought its source as at least an indirect clue to the outer world, I now saw plainly that this foul emanation could have no admixture or connection whatsoever with the clean air of the Libyan Desert, but must be essentially a thing vomited from sinister gulfs still lower down. I had, then, been walking in the wrong direction!

After a moment's reflection I decided not to retrace my steps. Away from the draft I would have no landmarks, for the roughly level rock floor was devoid of distinctive configurations. If, however, I followed up the strange current, I would undoubtedly arrive at an aperture of some sort, from whose gate I could perhaps work round the walls to the opposite side of this Cyclopean and otherwise unnavigable hall. That I might fail, I well realized. I saw that this was no part of Khephren's gateway temple which tourists know, and it struck me that this particular hall might be unknown even to archaeologists, and merely stumbled upon by the inquisitive and malignant Arabs who had imprisoned me. If so, was there any present gate of escape to the known parts or to the outer air?

What evidence, indeed, did I now possess that this was the gateway temple at all? For a moment all my wildest speculations rushed back upon me, and I thought of that vivid *mélange* of impressions — descent, suspension in space, the rope, my wounds, and the dreams that were frankly dreams. Was this the end of life for me? Or indeed, would it be merciful if this moment were the end? I could answer none of my own questions, but merely kept on, till Fate for a third time reduced me to oblivion.

This time there were no dreams, for the suddenness of the incident shocked me out of all thought either conscious or subconscious. Tripping on an unexpected descending step at a point where the offensive draft became strong enough to offer an actual physical resistance, I was precipitated headlong down a black flight of huge stone stairs into a gulf of hideousness unrelieved.

That I ever breathed again is a tribute to the inherent vitality of the healthy human organism. Often I look back to that night and feel a touch of actual humor in those repeated lapses of consciousness; lapses whose succession reminded me at the time of nothing more than the crude cinema melodramas of that period. Of course, it is possible that the repeated lapses never occurred; and that all the features of that underground nightmare were merely the dreams of one long coma which began with the shock of my descent into that abyss and ended with the healing balm of the outer air and of the rising sun which found me stretched on the sands of Gizeh before the sardonic and dawn-flushed face of the Great Sphinx.

I prefer to believe this latter explanation as much as I can, hence was glad when the police told me that the barrier to Krephren's gateway temple had been found unfastened, and that a sizeable rift to the surface did actually exist in one corner of the still buried part. I was glad, too, when the doctors pronounced my wounds only those to be expected from my seizure, blindfolding, lowering, struggling with bonds, falling some distance — perhaps into a depression in the temple's inner gallery — dragging myself to the outer barrier and escaping from it, and experiences like that . . . a very soothing diagnosis. And yet I know that there must be more than appears on the surface. That extreme descent is too vivid a memory to be dismissed — and it is odd that no one has ever been able to find a man answering the description of my guide, Abdul Reis el Drogman — the tomb-throated guide who looked and smiled like King Khephren.

I have digressed from my connected narrative — perhaps in the vain hope of evading the telling of that final incident; that incident which of all is most certainly an hallucination. But I promised to relate it, and I do not break promises. When I recovered — or seemed to recover — my senses after that fall down the black stone stairs, I was quite as alone and in darkness as before. The windy stench, bad enough before, was now fiendish; yet I had acquired enough familiarity by this time to bear it stoically. Dazedly I began to crawl away from the place whence the putrid wind came, and with my bleeding hands felt the colossal blocks of a mighty pavement. Once my head struck against a hard object, and when I felt of it I learned that it was the base of a column — a column of unbelievable immensity — whose surface was covered with gigantic chiseled hieroglyphics very perceptible to my touch.

Crawling on, I encountered other titan columns at incomprehensible distances apart; when suddenly my attention was captured by the realization of something which must have been impinging on my subconscious hearing long before the conscious sense was aware of it.

From some still lower chasm in earth's bowels were proceeding certain sounds, measured and definite, and like nothing I had ever heard before. That they were very ancient and distinctly ceremonial I felt almost intuitively; and much reading in Egyptology led me to associate them with the flute, the sambuke, the sistrum, and the tympanum. In their rhythmic piping, droning, rattling and beating I felt an element of terror beyond all the known terrors of earth — a terror peculiarly dissociated from personal fear, and taking the form of a sort of objective pity for our planet, that it should hold within its depths such horrors as must lie beyond these aegipanic cacophonies. The sounds increased in volume, and I felt that they were approaching. Then — and may all the gods of all pantheons unite to keep the like from my ears again — I began to hear, faintly and afar off, the morbid and millennial tramping of the marching things.

It was hideous that footfalls so dissimilar should move in such perfect rhythm. The training of unhallowed thousands of years must lie behind that march of earth's inmost monstrosities . . . padding, clicking, walking, stalking, rumbling, lumbering, crawling . . . and all to the abhorrent discords of those mocking instruments. And then — God keep the memory of those Arab legends out of my head! — the mummies without souls . . . the meeting-place of the wandering kas . . . the hordes of the devil-cursed pharaonic dead of forty centuries . . . the composite mummies led through the uttermost onyx voids by King Khephren and his ghoul-queen Nitocris . . . .

The tramping drew nearer — Heaven save me from the sound of those feet and paws and hooves and pads and talons as it commenced to acquire detail! Down limitless reaches of sunless pavement a spark of light flickered in the malodourous wind and I drew behind the enormous circumference of a Cyclopic column that I might escape for a while the horror that was stalking million-footed toward me through gigantic hypostyles of inhuman dread and phobic antiquity. The flickers increased, and the tramping and dissonant rhythm grew sickeningly loud. In the quivering orange light there stood faintly forth a scene of such stony awe that I gasped from sheer wonder that conquered even fear and repulsion. Bases of columns whose middles were higher than human sight . . . mere bases of things that must each dwarf the Eiffel Tower to insignificance . . . hieroglyphics carved by unthinkable hands in caverns where daylight can be only a remote legend . . . .

I would not look at the marching things. That I desperately resolved as I heard their creaking joints and nitrous wheezing above the dead music and the dead tramping. It was merciful that they did not speak . . . but God! their crazy torches began to cast shadows on the surface of those stupendous columns. Hippopotami should not have human hands and carry torches . . . men should not have the heads of crocodiles . . . .

I tried to turn away, but the shadows and the sounds and the stench were everywhere. Then I remembered something I used to do in half-conscious nightmares as a boy, and began to repeat to myself, 'This is a dream! This is a dream!' But it was of no use, and I could only shut my eyes and pray . . . at least, that is what I think I did, for one is never sure in visions — and I know this can have been nothing more. I wondered whether I should ever reach the world again, and at times would furtively open my eyes to see if I could discern any feature of the place other than the wind of spiced putrefaction, the topless columns, and the thaumatropically grotesque shadows of abnormal horror. The sputtering glare of multiplying torches now shone, and unless this hellish place were wholly without walls, I could not fail to see some boundary or fixed landmark soon. But I had to shut my eyes again when I realized how many of the things were assembling — and when I glimpsed a certain object walking solemnly and steadily without any body above the waist.

A fiendish and ululant corpse-gurgle or death-rattle now split the very atmosphere — the charnel atmosphere poisonous with naftha and bitumen blasts — in one concerted chorus from the ghoulish legion of hybrid blasphemies. My eyes, perversely shaken open, gazed for an instant upon a sight which no human creature could even imagine without panic, fear and physical exhaustion. The things had filed ceremonially in one direction, the direction of the noisome wind, where the light of their torches showed their bended heads — or the bended heads of such as had heads. They were worshipping before a great black fetor-belching aperture which reached up almost out of sight, and which I could see was flanked at right angles by two giant staircases whose ends were far away in shadow. One of these was indubitably the staircase I had fallen down.

The dimensions of the hole were fully in proportion with those of the columns — an ordinary house would have been lost in it, and any average public building could easily have been moved in and out. It was so vast a surface that only by moving the eye could one trace its boundaries . . . so vast, so hideously black, and so aromatically stinking . . . Directly in front of this yawning Polyphemus-door the things were throwing objects — evidently sacrifices or religious offerings, to judge by their gestures. Khephren was their leader; sneering King Khephren or the guide Abdul Reis, crowned with a golden pshent and intoning endless formulae with the hollow voice of the dead. By his side knelt beautiful Queen Nitocris, whom I saw in profile for a moment, noting that the right half of her face was eaten away by rats or other ghouls. And I shut my eyes again when I saw what objects were being thrown as offerings to the fetid aperture or its possible local deity.

It occurred to me that, judging from the elaborateness of this worship, the concealed deity must be one of considerable importance. Was it Osiris or Isis, Horus or Anubis, or some vast unknown God of the Dead still more central and supreme? There is a legend that terrible altars and colossi were reared to an Unknown One before ever the known gods were worshipped . . . .

And now, as I steeled myself to watch the rapt and sepulchral adorations of those nameless things, a thought of escape flashed upon me. The hall was dim, and the columns heavy with shadow. With every creature of that nightmare throng absorbed in shocking raptures, it might be barely possible for me to creep past to the far-away end of one of the staircases and ascend unseen; trusting to Fate and skill to deliver me from the upper reaches. Where I was, I neither knew nor seriously reflected upon — and for a moment it struck me as amusing to plan a serious escape from that which I knew to be a dream. Was I in some hidden and unsuspected lower realm of Khephren's gateway temple — that temple which generations have persistently called the Temple of the Sphinx? I could not conjecture, but I resolved to ascend to life and consciousness if wit and muscle could carry me.

Wriggling flat on my stomach, I began the anxious journey toward the foot of the left-hand staircase, which seemed the more accessible of the two. I cannot describe the incidents and sensations of that crawl, but they may be guessed when one reflects on what I had to watch steadily in that malign, wind-blown torchlight in order to avoid detection. The bottom of the staircase was, as I have said, far away in shadow, as it had to be to rise without a bend to the dizzy parapeted landing above the titanic aperture. This placed the last stages of my crawl at some distance from the noisome herd, though the spectacle chilled me even when quite remote at my right.

At length I succeeded in reaching the steps and began to climb; keeping close to the wall, on which I observed decorations of the most hideous sort, and relying for safety on the absorbed, ecstatic interest with which the monstrosities watched the foul-breezed aperture and the impious objects of nourishment they had flung on the pavement before it. Though the staircase was huge and steep, fashioned of vast porphyry blocks as if for the feet of a giant, the ascent seemed virtually interminable. Dread of discovery and the pain which renewed exercise had brought to my wounds combined to make that upward crawl a thing of agonizing memory. I had intended, on reaching the landing, to climb immediately onward along whatever upper staircase might mount from there; stopping for no last look at the carrion abominations that pawed and genuflected some seventy or eighty feet below—yet a sudden repetition of that thunderous corpse-gurgle and death-rattle chorus, coming as I had nearly gained the top of the flight and showing by its ceremonial rhythm that it was not an alarm of my discovery, caused me to pause and peer cautiously over the parapet.

The monstrosities were hailing something which had poked itself out of the nauseous aperture to seize the hellish fare proffered it. It was something quite ponderous, even as seen from my height; something yellowish and hairy, and endowed with a sort of nervous motion. It was as large, perhaps, as a good-sized hippopotamus, but very curiously shaped. It seemed to have no neck, but five separate shaggy heads springing in a row from a roughly cylindrical trunk; the first very small, the second good-sized, the third and fourth equal and largest of all, and the fifth rather small, though not so small as the first.

Out of these heads darted curious rigid tentacles which seized ravenously on the excessively great quantities of unmentionable food placed before the aperture. Once in a while the thing would leap up, and occasionally it would retreat into its den in a very odd manner. Its locomotion was so inexplicable that I stared in fascination, wishing it would emerge farther from the cavernous lair beneath me.

Then it did emerge . . . it did emerge, and at the sight I turned and fled into the darkness up the higher staircase that rose behind me; fled unknowingly up incredible steps and ladders and inclined planes to which no human sight or logic guided me, and which I must ever relegate to the world of dreams for want of any confirmation. It must have been a dream, or the dawn would never have found me breathing on the sands of Gizeh before the sardonic dawn-flushed face of the Great Sphinx.

The Great Sphinx! God!—that idle question I asked myself on that sun-blest morning before . . . what huge and loathsome abnormality was the Sphinx originally carven to represent?

Accursed is the sight, be it in dream or not, that revealed to me the supreme horror—the unknown God of the Dead, which licks its colossal chops in the unsuspected abyss, fed hideous morsels by soulless absurdities that should not exist. The five-headed monster that emerged . . . that five-headed monster as large as a hippopotamus . . . the five headed monster—and that of which it is the merest forepaw . . . .

But I survived, and I know it was only a dream.

The Shunned House.

10,800-WORD NOVELETTE; 1924.

With all the drama and upheaval, it's not surprising that Lovecraft produced only one story for his own by-line in 1924 — one written while Sonia was in the hospital recovering from her nervous breakdown. This was "The Shunned House," a tale pulled from local Providence legend and augmented in strategic and subtle ways to maximize its impact.

The most interesting thing about "The Shunned House" is Lovecraft's dexterous mixing of real history and actual legendry with made-up bits, to generate an unusual horror story — one that feels as if it just might be true. This technique of mixing fact with fiction in artful ways would become a very important tool in Lovecraft's fiction kit for the rest of his life, and would lead to the the literary accomplishment he's perhaps best known for — the creation of the shadowy shared pseudo-mythology that's come to be known as the Cthulhu Mythos, used by several different writers to give all their stories greater verisimilitude.

"The Shunned House" was written on Oct. 19, 1924, the same day Sonia Haft Greene was taken ill and had to be taken to the hospital. Lovecraft showed it to his fellow Kalem Club members, who were gratifyingly enthusiastic about it.

"The Shunned House" was the first Lovecraft title to be published as a book — although its publication would not be complete until after his death. In 1927, W. Paul Cook proposed publishing it as a chapbook. In 1928 a short run was published under his Recluse Press imprint, but Cook was unable to finance having the pages bound. Eventually 150 of them were acquired by Arkham House; of these, 50 were sold unbound, and the remaining 100 were bound and sold as an Arkham House title. Today they are the rarest Arkham House publication; the genuine articles fetch $14,000 or more, and potential buyers have to keep a sharp eye out for counterfeits.

I.

From even the greatest of horrors irony is seldom absent. Sometimes it enters directly into the composition of the events, while sometimes it relates only to their fortuitous position among persons and places. The latter sort is splendidly exemplified by a case in the ancient city of Providence, where in the late forties Edgar Allan Poe used to sojourn often during his unsuccessful wooing of the gifted poetess, Mrs. Whitman. Poe generally stopped at the Mansion House in Benefit Street — the renamed Golden Ball Inn whose roof has sheltered Washington, Jefferson, and Lafayette — and his favorite walk led northward along the same street to Mrs. Whitman's home and the neighboring hillside churchyard of St. John's, whose hidden expanse of Eighteenth Century gravestones had for him a peculiar fascination.

Now the irony is this. In this walk, so many times repeated, the world's greatest master of the terrible and the bizarre was obliged to pass a particular house on the eastern side of the street; a dingy, antiquated structure perched on the abruptly rising side hill, with a great unkempt yard dating from a time when the region was partly open country. It does not appear that he ever wrote or spoke of it, nor is there any evidence that he even noticed it. And yet that house, to the two persons in possession of certain information, equals or outranks in horror the wildest fantasy of the genius who so often passed it unknowingly, and stands starkly leering as a symbol of all that is unutterably hideous.

The house was — and for that matter still is — of a kind to attract the attention of the curious. Originally a farm or semifarm building, it followed the average New England colonial lines of the middle Eighteenth Century — the prosperous peaked-roof sort, with two stories and dormerless attic, and with the Georgian doorway and interior panelling dictated by the progress of taste at that time. It faced south, with one gable end buried to the lower windows in the eastward rising hill, and the other exposed to the foundations toward the street. Its construction, over a century and a half ago, had followed the grading and straightening of the road in that especial vicinity; for Benefit Street — at first called Back Street — was laid out as a lane winding amongst the graveyards of the first settlers, and straightened only when the removal of the bodies to the North Burial Ground made it decently possible to cut through the old family plots.

At the start, the western wall had lain some twenty feet up a precipitous lawn from the roadway; but a widening of the street at about the time of the Revolution sheared off most of the intervening space, exposing the foundations so that a brick basement wall had to be made, giving the deep cellar a street frontage with door and one window above ground, close to the new line of public travel. When the sidewalk was laid out a century ago the last of the intervening space was removed; and Poe in his walks must have seen only a sheer ascent of dull gray

Weird Tales, October 1937

". . . that awful door in Benefit Street which I had left ajar . . ."

brick flush with the sidewalk and surmounted at a height of ten feet by the antique shingled bulk of the house proper.

The farm-like ground extended back very deeply up the hill, almost to Wheaton Street. The space south of the house, abutting on Benefit Street, was of course greatly above the existing sidewalk level, forming a terrace bounded by a high bank wall of damp, mossy stone pierced by a steep flight of narrow steps which led inward between canyon-like surfaces to the upper region of mangy lawn, rheumy brick walks, and neglected gardens whose dismantled cement urns, rusted kettles fallen from tripods of knotty sticks, and similar paraphernalia set off the weather-beaten front door with its broken fanlight, rotting Ionic pilasters, and wormy triangular pediment.

What I heard in my youth about the shunned house was merely that people died there in alarmingly great numbers. That, I was told, was why the original owners had moved out some twenty years after building the place. It was plainly unhealthy, perhaps because of the dampness and fungous growths in the cellar, the general sickish smell, the drafts of the hallways, or the quality of the well and pump water. These things were bad enough, and these were all that gained belief among the persons whom I knew. Only the notebooks of my antiquarian uncle, Doctor Elihu Whipple, revealed to me at length the darker, vaguer surmises which formed an undercurrent of folklore among old-time servants and humble folk; surmises which never travelled far, and which were largely forgotten when Providence grew to be a metropolis with a shifting modern population.

The general fact is, that the house was never regarded by the solid part of the community as in any real sense "haunted." There were no widespread tales of rattling chains, cold currents of air, extinguished lights, or faces at the window. Extremists sometimes said the house was "unlucky," but that is as far as even they went. What was really beyond dispute is that a frightful proportion of persons died there; or more accurately, had died there, since after some peculiar happenings over sixty years ago the building had become deserted through the sheer impossibility of renting it. These persons were not all cut off suddenly by any one cause; rather did it seem that their vitality was insidiously sapped, so that each one died the sooner from whatever tendency to weakness he may have naturally had. And those who did not die displayed in varying degree a type of anemia or consumption, and sometimes a decline of the mental faculties, which spoke ill for the salubriousness of the building. Neighboring houses, it must be added, seemed entirely free from the noxious quality.

This much I knew before my insistent questioning led my uncle to show me the notes which finally embarked us both on our hideous investigation. In my childhood the shunned house was vacant, with barren, gnarled and terrible old trees, long, queerly pale grass and nightmarishly misshapen weeds in the high terraced yard where birds never lingered. We boys used to overrun the place, and I can still recall my youthful terror not only at the morbid strangeness of this sinister vegetation, but at the eldritch atmosphere and odor of the dilapidated house, whose unlocked front door was often entered in quest of shudders. The small-paned windows were largely broken, and a nameless air of desolation hung round the precarious panelling, shaky interior shutters, peeling wall-paper, falling plaster, rickety staircases, and such fragments of battered furniture as still remained. The dust and cobwebs added their touch of the fearful; and brave indeed was the boy who would voluntarily ascend the ladder to the attic, a vast raftered length lighted only by small blinking windows in the gable ends, and filled with a massed wreckage of chests, chairs, and spinning-wheels which infinite years of deposit had shrouded and festooned into monstrous and hellish shapes.

But after all, the attic was not the most terrible part of the house. It was the dank, humid cellar which somehow exerted the strongest repulsion on us, even though it was wholly above ground on the street side, with only a thin door and window-pierced brick wall to separate it from the busy sidewalk. We scarcely knew whether to haunt it in spectral fascination, or to shun it for the sake of our souls and our sanity. For one thing, the bad odor of the house was strongest there; and for another thing, we did not like the white fungous growths which occasionally sprang up in rainy summer weather from the hard earth floor. Those fungi, grotesquely like the vegetation in the yard outside, were truly horrible in their outlines; detestable parodies of toadstools and Indian-pipes, whose like we had never seen in any other situation. They rotted quickly, and at one stage became slightly phosphorescent; so that nocturnal passers-by sometimes spoke of witch-fires glowing behind the broken panes of the foetor-spreading windows.

We never — even in our wildest Halloween moods — visited this cellar by night, but in some of our daytime visits could detect the phosphorescence, especially when the day was dark and wet. There was also a subtler thing we often thought we detected — a very strange thing which was, however, merely suggestive at most. I refer to a sort of cloudy whitish pattern on the dirt floor — a vague, shifting deposit of mold or niter which we sometimes thought we could trace amidst the sparse fungous growths near the huge fireplace of the basement kitchen. Once in a while it struck us that this patch bore an uncanny resemblance to a doubled-up human figure, though generally no such kinship existed, and often there was no whitish deposit whatever.

On a certain rainy afternoon when this illusion seemed phenomenally strong, and when, in addition, I had fancied I glimpsed a kind of thin, yellowish, shimmering exhalation rising from the nitrous pattern toward the yawning fireplace, I spoke to my uncle about the matter. He smiled at this odd conceit, but it seemed that his smile was tinged with reminiscence. Later I heard that a similar notion entered into some of the wild ancient tales of the common folk — a notion likewise alluding to ghoulish, wolfish shapes taken by smoke from the great chimney, and queer contours assumed by certain of the sinuous tree-roots that thrust their way into the cellar through the loose foundation-stones.

II.

Not till my adult years did my uncle set before me the notes and data which he had collected concerning the shunned house. Doctor Whipple was a sane, conservative physician of the old school, and for all his interest in the place was not eager to encourage young thoughts toward the abnormal. His own view, postulating simply a building and location of markedly unsanitary qualities, had nothing to do with abnormality; but he realized that the very picturesqueness which aroused his own interest would in a boy's fanciful mind take on all manner of gruesome imaginative associations.

The doctor was a bachelor; a white-haired, clean-shaven, old-fashioned gentleman, and a local historian of note, who had often broken a lance with such controversial guardians of tradition as Sidney S. Rider and Thomas W. Bicknell. He lived with one man-servant in a Georgian homestead with knocker and iron-railed steps, balanced eerily on the steep ascent of North Court Street beside the ancient brick court and colony house where his grandfather — a cousin of that celebrated privateersman, Captain Whipple, who burnt His Majesty's armed schooner Gaspee in 1772 — had voted in the legislature on May 4, 1776, for the independence of the Rhode Island Colony. Around him in the damp, low-ceiled library with the musty white panelling, heavy carved overmantel and small-paned, vine-shaded windows, were the relics and records of his ancient family, among which were many dubious allusions to the shunned house in Benefit Street. That pest spot lies not far distant — for Benefit runs edgewise just above the court house along the precipitous hill up which the first settlement climbed.

When, in the end, my insistent pestering and maturing years evoked from my uncle the hoarded lore I sought, there lay before me a strange enough chronicle. Long-winded, statistical, and drearily genealogical as some of the matter was, there ran through it a continuous thread of brooding, tenacious horror and preternatural malevolence which impressed me even more than it had impressed the good doctor. Separate events fitted together uncannily, and seemingly irrelevant details held mines of hideous possibilities. A new and burning curiosity grew in me, compared to which my boyish curiosity was feeble and inchoate.

The first revelation led to an exhaustive research, and finally to that shuddering quest which proved so disastrous to myself and mine. For at the last my uncle insisted on joining the search I had commenced, and after a certain night in that house he did not come away with me. I am lonely without that gentle soul whose long years were filled only with honor, virtue, good taste, benevolence, and learning. I have reared a marble urn to his memory in St. John's churchyard — the place that Poe loved — the hidden grove of giant willows on the hill, where tombs and headstones huddle quietly between the hoary bulk of the church and the houses and bank walls of Benefit Street.

The history of the house, opening amidst a maze of dates, revealed no trace of the sinister either about its construction or about the prosperous and honorable family who built it. Yet from the first a taint of calamity, soon increased to boding significance, was apparent. My uncle's carefully compiled record began with the building of the structure in 1763, and followed the theme with an unusual amount of detail. The shunned house, it seems, was first inhabited by William Harris and his wife Rhoby Dexter, with their children, Elkanah, born in 1755; Abigail, born in 1757; William, Jr., born in 1759; and Ruth, born in 1761. Harris was a substantial merchant and seaman in the West India trade, connected with the firm of Obadiah Brown and his nephews. After Brown's death in 1761, the new firm of Nicholas Brown & Company made him master of the brig Prudence, Providence-built, of 120 tons, thus enabling him to erect the new homestead he had desired ever since his marriage.

The site he had chosen — a recently straightened part of the new and fashionable Back Street, which ran along the side of the hill above crowded Cheapside — was all that could be wished, and the building did justice to the location. It was the best that moderate means could afford, and Harris hastened to move in before the birth of a fifth child which the family expected. That child, a boy, came in December; but was stillborn. Nor was any child to be born alive in that house for a century and a half.

The next April, sickness occurred among the children, and Abigail and Ruth died before the month was over. Doctor Job Ives diagnosed the trouble as some infantile fever, though others declared it was more of a mere wasting-away or decline. It seemed, in any event, to be contagious; for Hannah Bowen, one of the two servants, died of it in the following June. Eli Lideason, the other servant, constantly complained of weakness; and would have returned to his father's farm in Rehoboth but for a sudden attachment for Mehitabel Pierce, who was hired to succeed Hannah. He died the next year — a sad year indeed, since it marked the death of William Harris himself, enfeebled as he was by the climate of Martinique, where his occupation had kept him for considerable periods during the preceding decade.

The widowed Rhoby Harris never recovered from the shock of her husband's death, and the passing of her first-born Elkanah two years later was the final blow to her reason. In 1768 she fell victim to a mild form of insanity, and was thereafter confined to the upper part of the house; her elder maiden sister, Mercy Dexter, having moved in to take charge of the family. Mercy was a plain, raw-boned woman of great strength; but her health visibly declined from the time of her advent. She was greatly devoted to her unfortunate sister, and had an especial affection for her only surviving nephew, William, who from a sturdy infant had become a sickly, spindling lad. In this year the servant Mehitabel died, and the other servant, Preserved Smith, left without coherent explanation — or at least, with only some wild tales and a complaint that he disliked the smell of the place. For a time Mercy could secure no more help, since the seven deaths and case of madness, all occurring within five years' space, had begun to set in motion the body of fireside rumor which later became so bizarre. Ultimately, however, she obtained new servants from out of town; Ann White, a morose woman from that part of North Kingstown now set off as the township of Exeter, and a capable Boston man named Zenas Low.

It was Ann White who first gave definite shape to the sinister idle talk. Mercy should have known better than to hire anyone from the Nooseneck Hill country, for that remote bit of backwoods was then, as now, a seat of the most uncomfortable superstitions. As lately as 1892 an Exeter community exhumed a dead body and ceremoniously burnt its heart in order to prevent certain alleged visitations injurious to the public health and peace, and one may imagine the point of view of the same section in 1768. Ann's tongue was perniciously active, and within a few months Mercy discharged her, filling her place with a faithful and amiable Amazon from Newport, Maria Robbins.

Meanwhile poor Rhoby Harris, in her madness, gave voice to dreams and imaginings of the most hideous sort. At times her screams became insupportable, and for long periods she would utter shrieking horrors which necessitated her son's temporary residence with his cousin, Peleg Harris, in Presbyterian Lane near the new college building. The boy would seem to improve after these visits, and had Mercy been as wise as she was well-meaning, she would have let him live permanently with Peleg. Just what Mrs. Harris cried out in her fits of violence, tradition hesitates to say; or rather, presents such extravagant accounts that they nullify themselves through sheer absurdity. Certainly it sounds absurd to hear that a woman educated only in the rudiments of French often shouted for hours in a coarse and idiomatic form of that language, or that the same person, alone and guarded, complained wildly of a staring thing which bit and chewed at her. In 1772 the servant Zenas died, and when Mrs. Harris heard of it she laughed with a shocking delight utterly foreign to her. The next year she herself died, and was laid to rest in the North Burial Ground beside her husband.

Upon the outbreak of trouble with Great Britain in 1775, William Harris, despite his scant sixteen years and feeble constitution, managed to enlist in the Army of Observation under General Greene; and from that time on enjoyed a steady rise in health and prestige. In 1780, as a captain in the Rhode Island forces in New Jersey under Colonel Angell, he met and married Phebe Hetfield of Elizabethtown, whom he brought to Providence upon his honorable discharge in the following year.

The young soldier's return was not a thing of unmitigated happiness. The house, it is true, was still in good condition; and the street had been widened and changed in name from Back Street to Benefit Street. But Mercy Dexter's once robust frame had undergone a sad and curious decay, so that she was now a stooped and pathetic figure with hollow voice and disconcerting pallor — qualities shared to a singular degree by the one remaining servant Maria. In the autumn of 1782 Phebe Harris gave birth to a still-born daughter, and on the fifteenth of the next May Mercy Dexter took leave of a useful, austere, and virtuous life.

William Harris, at last thoroughly convinced of the radically unhealthful nature of his abode, now took steps toward quitting it and closing it for ever. Securing temporary quarters for himself and his wife at the newly opened Golden Ball Inn, he arranged for the building of a new and finer house in Westminster Street, in the growing part of the town across the Great Bridge. There, in 1785, his son Dutee was born; and there the family dwelt till the encroachments of commerce drove them back across the river and over the hill to Angell Street, in the newer East Side residence district, where the late Archer Harris built his sumptuous but hideous French-roofed mansion in 1876. William and Phebe both succumbed to the yellow fever epidemic of 1797, but Dutee was brought up by his cousin Rathbone Harris, Peleg's son.

Rathbone was a practical man, and rented the Benefit Street house despite William's wish to keep it vacant. He considered it an obligation to his ward to make the most of all the boy's property, nor did he concern himself with the deaths and illnesses which caused so many changes of tenants, or the steadily growing aversion with which the house was generally regarded. It is likely that he felt only vexation when, in 1804, the town council ordered him to fumigate the place with sulfur, tar, and gum camphor on account of the much-discussed deaths of four persons, presumably caused by the then diminishing fever epidemic. They said the place had a febrile smell.

Dutee himself thought little of the house, for he grew up to be a privateersman, and served with distinction on the *Vigilant* under Captain Cahoone in the War of 1812. He returned unharmed, married in 1814, and became a father on that memorable night of September 23, 1815, when a great gale drove the waters of the bay over half the town, and floated a tall sloop well up Westminster Street so that its masts almost tapped the Harris windows in symbolic affirmation that the new boy, Welcome, was a seaman's son.

Welcome did not survive his father, but lived to perish gloriously at Fredericksburg in 1862. Neither he nor his son Archer knew of the shunned house as other than a nuisance almost impossible to rent — perhaps on account of the mustiness and sickly odor of unkempt old age. Indeed, it never was rented after a series of deaths culminating in 1861, which the excitement of the war tended to throw into obscurity. Carrington Harris, last of the male line, knew it only as a deserted and somewhat picturesque center of legend until I told him my experience. He had meant to tear it down and build an apartment house on the site, but after my account decided to let it stand, install plumbing, and rent it. Nor has he yet had any difficulty in obtaining tenants. The horror has gone.

III.

It may well be imagined how powerfully I was affected by the annals of the Harrises. In this continuous record there seemed to me to brood a persistent evil beyond anything in nature as I had known it, an evil clearly connected with the house and not with the family. This impression was confirmed by my uncle's less systematic array of miscellaneous data — legends transcribed from servant gossip, cuttings from the papers, copies of death certificates by fellow-physicians, and the like. All of this material I cannot hope to give, for my uncle was a tireless antiquarian and very deeply interested in the shunned house; but I may refer to several dominant points which earn notice by their recurrence through many reports from diverse sources. For example, the servant gossip was practically unanimous in attributing to the fungous and malodorous cellar of the house a vast supremacy in evil influence. There had been servants — Ann White especially — who would not use the cellar kitchen, and at least three well-defined legends bore upon the queer quasi-human or diabolic outlines assumed by tree-roots and patches of mold in that region. These latter narratives interested me profoundly, on account of what I had seen in my boyhood, but I felt that most of the significance had in each case been largely obscured by additions from the common stock of local ghost lore.

Ann White, with her Exeter superstition, had promulgated the most extravagant and at the same time most consistent tale, alleging that there must lie buried beneath the house one of those vampires — the dead who retain their bodily form and live on the blood or breath of the living — whose hideous legions send their preying shapes or spirits abroad by night. To destroy a vampire one must, the grandmothers say, exhume it and burn its heart, or at least drive a stake through that organ; and Ann's dogged insistence on a search under the cellar had been prominent in bringing about her discharge.

Her tales, however, commanded a wide audience, and were the more readily accepted because the house indeed stood on land once used for burial purposes. To me their interest depended less on this circumstance than on the peculiarly appropriate way in which they dovetailed with certain other things — the complaint of the departing servant Preserved Smith, who had preceded Ann and never heard of her, that something "sucked his breath" at night; the death-certificates of the fever victims of 1804, issued by Doctor Chad Hopkins, and showing the four deceased persons all unaccountably lacking in blood; and the obscure passages of poor Rhoby Harris's ravings, where she complained of the sharp teeth of a glassy-eyed, half-visible presence.

Free from unwarranted superstitition though I am, these things produced in me an odd sensation, which was intensified by a pair of widely separated newspaper cuttings relating to deaths in the shunned house — one from the *Providence Gazette and Country-Journal* of April 12, 1815, and the other from the *Daily Transcript and Chronicle* of October 27, 1845 — each of which detailed an appallingly grisly circumstance whose duplication was remarkable. It seems that in both instances the dying person, in 1815 a gentle old lady named Stafford and in 1845 a schoolteacher of middle age named Eleazar Durfee, became transfigured in a horrible way, glaring glassily and attempting to bite the throat of the attending physician. Even more puzzling, though, was the final case which put an end to the renting of the house — a series of anemia deaths preceded by progressive madnesses wherein the patient would craftily attempt the lives of his relatives by incisions in the neck or wrist.

This was in 1860 and 1861, when my uncle had just begun his medical practise; and before leaving for the front he heard much of it from his elder professional colleagues. The really inexplicable thing was the way in which the victims — ignorant people, for the ill-smelling and widely shunned house could now be rented to no others — would babble maledictions in French, a language they could not possibly have studied to any extent. It made one think of poor Rhoby Harris nearly a century before, and so moved my uncle that he commenced collecting historical data on the house after listening, some time subsequent to his return from the war, to the first-hand account of Doctors Chase and Whitmarsh. Indeed, I could see that my uncle had thought deeply on the subject, and that he was glad of my own interest — an open-minded and sympathetic interest which enabled him to discuss with me matters at which others would merely have laughed. His fancy had not gone so far as mine, but he felt that the place was rare in its imaginative potentialities, and worthy of note as an inspiration in the field of the grotesque and macabre.

For my part, I was disposed to take the whole subject with profound seriousness, and began at once not only to review the evidence, but to accumulate as much more as I could. I talked with the elderly Archer Harris, then owner of the house, many times before his death in 1916; and obtained from him and his still surviving maiden sister Alice an authentic corroboration of all the family data my uncle had collected. When, however, I asked them what connection with France or its language the house could have, they confessed themselves as frankly baffled and ignorant as I. Archer knew nothing, and all that Miss Harris could say was that an old allusion her grandfather, Dutee Harris, had heard of might have shed a little light. The old seaman, who had survived his son Welcome's death in battle by two years, had not himself known the legend, but recalled that his earliest nurse, the ancient Maria Robbins, seemed darkly aware of something that might have lent a weird significance to the French raving of Rhoby Harris, which she had so often heard during the last days of that hapless woman. Maria had been at the shunned house from 1769 till the removal of the family in 1783, and had seen Mercy Dexter die. Once she hinted to the child Dutee of a somewhat peculiar circumstance in Mercy's last moments, but she had soon forgotten all about it save that it was something peculiar. The granddaughter, moreover, recalled even this much with difficulty. She and her brother were not so much interested in the house as was Archer's son Carrington, the present owner, with whom I talked after my experience.

Having exhausted the Harris family of all the information it could furnish, I turned my attention to early town records and deeds with a zeal more penetrating than that which my uncle had occasionally shown in the same work. What I wished was a comprehensive history of the site from its very settlement in 1636 — or even before, if any Narragansett Indian legend could be unearthed to supply the data. I found, at the start, that the land had been part of the long strip of home lot granted originally to John Throckmorton; one of many similar strips beginning at the Town Street beside the river and extending up over the hill to a line roughly corresponding with the modern Hope Street. The Throckmorton lot had later, of course, been much subdivided; and I became very assiduous in tracing that section through which Back or Benefit Street was later run. It had, as rumor indeed said, been the Throckmorton graveyard; but as I examined the records more carefully, I found that the graves had all been transferred at an early date to the North Burial Ground on the Pawtucket West Road.

Then suddenly I came — by a rare piece of chance, since it was not in the main body of records and might easily have been missed — upon something which aroused my keenest eagerness, fitting in as it did with several of the queerest phases of the affair. It was the record of a lease, in 1697, of a small tract of ground to an Étienne Roulet and wife. At last the French element had appeared — that, and another deeper element of horror which the name conjured up from the darkest recesses of my weird and heterogeneous reading — and I feverishly studied the platting of the locality as it had been before the cutting through and partial straightening of Back Street between 1747 and 1758. I found what I had half expected, that where the shunned house now stood the Roulets had laid out their graveyard behind a one-story-and-attic cottage, and that no record of any transfer of graves existed; the document, indeed, ended in much confusion, and I was forced to ransack both the Rhode Island Historical Society and Shepley Library before I could find a local door which the name of Étienne Roulet would unlock. In the end I did find something; something of such vague but monstrous import that I set about at once to examine the cellar of the shunned house itself with a new and excited minuteness.

The Roulets, it seemed, had come in 1696 from East Greenwich, down the west shore of Narragansett Bay. They were Huguenots from Canude, and had encountered much opposition before the Providence selectmen allowed them to settle in the town. Unpopularity had dogged them in East Greenwich, whither they had come in 1686, after the revocation of the Edict of Nantes, and rumor said that the cause of dislike extended beyond mere racial and national prejudice, or the land disputes which involved other French settlers with the English in rivalries which not even Governor Andros could quell. But their ardent Protestantism — too ardent, some whispered — and their evident distress when virtually driven from the village down the bay, had moved the sympathy of the town fathers. Here the strangers had been granted a haven; and the swarthy Étienne Roulet, less apt at agriculture than at reading queer books and drawing queer diagrams, was given a clerical post in the warehouse at Pardon Tillinghast's wharf, far south in Town Street. There had, however, been a riot of some sort later on — perhaps forty years later, after old Roulet's death — and no one seemed to hear of the family after that.

For a century and more, it appeared, the Roulets had been well remembered and frequently discussed as vivid incidents in the quiet life of a New England seaport. Étienne's son Paul, a surly fellow whose erratic conduct had probably provoked the riot which wiped out the family, was particularly a source of speculation; and though Providence never shared the witchcraft panics of her Puritan neighbors, it was freely intimated by old wives that his prayers were neither uttered at the proper time nor directed toward the proper object. All this had undoubtedly formed the basis of the legend known by old Maria Robbins. What relation it had to the French ravings of Rhoby Harris and other inhabitants of the shunned house, imagination or future discovery alone could determine. I wondered how many of those who had known the legends realized that additional link with the terrible which my wider reading had given me; that ominous item in the annals of morbid horror which tells of the creature Jacques Roulet, of Caude, who in 1598 was condemned to death as a demoniac but afterward saved from the stake by the Paris Parliament and shut in a madhouse. He had been found covered with blood and shreds of flesh in a wood, shortly after the killing and rending of a boy by a pair of wolves. One wolf was seen to lope away unhurt. Surely a pretty hearthside tale, with a queer significance as to name and place; but I decided that the Providence gossips could not have generally known of it. Had they known, the coincidence of names would have brought some drastic and frightened action — indeed, might not its limited whispering have precipitated the final riot which erased the Roulets from the town?

I now visited the accursed place with increased frequency; studying the unwholesome vegetation of the garden, examining all the walls of the building, and poring over every inch of the earthen cellar floor. Finally, with Carrington Harris's permission, I fitted a key to the disused door opening from the cellar directly upon Benefit Street, preferring to have a more immediate access to the outside world than the dark stairs, ground-floor hall, and front door could give. There, where morbidity lurked most thickly, I searched and poked during long afternoons when the sunlight filtered in through the cobwebbed above-ground windows, and a sense of security glowed from the unlocked door which placed me only a few feet from the placid sidewalk outside. Nothing new rewarded my efforts — only the same depressing mustiness and faint suggestions of noxious odors and nitrous outlines on the floor — and I fancy that many pedestrians must have watched me curiously through the broken panes.

At length, upon a suggestion of my uncle's, I decided to try the spot nocturnally; and one stormy midnight ran the beams of an electric torch over the moldy floor with its uncanny shapes and distorted, half-phosphorescent fungi. The place had dispirited me curiously that evening, and I was almost prepared when I saw — or thought I saw — amidst the whitish deposits a particularly sharp definition of the "huddled form" I had suspected from boyhood. Its clearness was astonishing and unprecedented — and as I watched I seemed to see again the thin, yellowish, shimmering exhalation which had startled me on that rainy afternoon so many years before.

Above the anthropomorphic patch of mold by the fireplace it rose; a subtle, sickish, almost luminous vapor which as it hung trembling in the dampness seemed to develop vague and shocking suggestions of form, gradually trailing off into nebulous decay and passing up into the blackness of the great chimney with a fetor in its wake. It was truly horrible, and the more so to me because of what I knew of the spot. Refusing to flee, I watched it fade — and as I watched I felt that it was in turn watching me greedily with eyes more imaginable than visible. When I told my uncle about it he was greatly aroused; and after a tense hour of reflection, arrived at a definite and drastic decision. Weighing in his mind the importance of the matter, and the significance of our relation to it, he insisted that we both test—and if possible destroy—the horror of the house by a joint night or nights of aggressive vigil in that musty and fungus-cursed cellar.

IV.

On Wednesday, June 25, 1919, after a proper notification of Carrington Harris which did not include surmises as to what we expected to find, my uncle and I conveyed to the shunned house two camp chairs and a folding camp cot, together with some scientific mechanism of greater weight and intricacy. These we placed in the cellar during the day, screening the windows with paper and planning to return in the evening for our first vigil. We had locked the door from the cellar to the ground floor; and having a key to the outside cellar door, were prepared to leave our expensive and delicate apparatus—which we had obtained secretly and at great cost—as many days as our vigils might be protracted. It was our design to sit up together till very late, and then watch singly till dawn in two-hour stretches, myself first and then my companion; the inactive member resting on the cot.

The natural leadership with which my uncle procured the instruments from the laboratories of Brown University and the Cranston Street Armory, and instinctively assumed direction of our venture, was a marvelous commentary on the potential vitality and resilience of a man of eighty-one. Elihu Whipple had lived according to the hygienic laws he had preached as a physician, and but for what happened later would be here in full vigor today. Only two persons suspected what did happen—Carrington Harris and myself; I had to tell Harris because he owned the house and deserved to know what had gone out of it. Then too, we had spoken to him in advance of our quest; and I felt after my uncle's going that he would understand and assist me in some vitally necessary public explanations. He turned very pale, but agreed to help me, and decided that it would now be safe to rent the house.

To declare that we were not nervous on that rainy night of watching would be an exaggeration both gross and ridiculous. We were not, as I have said, in any sense childishly superstitious, but scientific study and reflection had taught us that the known universe of three dimensions embraces the merest fraction of the whole cosmos of substance and energy. In this case an overwhelming preponderance of evidence from numerous authentic sources pointed to the tenacious existence of certain forces of great power and, so far as the human point of view is concerned, exceptional malignancy. To say that we actually believed in vampires or werewolves would be a carelessly inclusive statement. Rather must it be said that we were not prepared to deny the possibility of certain unfamiliar and unclassified modifications of vital force and attenuated matter; existing very infrequently in three-dimensional space because of its more intimate connection with other spatial units, yet close enough to the boundary of our own to furnish us occasional manifestations which we, for lack of a proper vantage-point, may never hope to understand.

In short, it seemed to my uncle and me that an incontrovertible array of facts pointed to some lingering influence in the shunned house; traceable to one or another of the ill-favored French settlers of two centuries before, and still operative through rare and unknown laws of atomic and electronic motion. That the family of Roulet had possessed an abnormal affinity for outer circles of entity—dark spheres which for normal folk hold only repulsion and terror—their recorded history seemed to prove. Had not, then, the riots of those bygone seventeen-thirties set moving certain kinetic patterns in the morbid brain of one or more of them—notably the sinister Paul Roulet—which obscurely survived the bodies murdered and buried by the mob, and continued to function in some multiple-dimensioned space along the original lines of force determined by a frantic hatred of the encroaching community?

Such a thing was surely not a physical or biochemical impossibility in the light of a newer science which includes the theories of relativity and intra-atomic action. One might easily imagine an alien nucleus of substance or energy, formless or otherwise, kept alive by imperceptible or immaterial subtractions from the life-force or bodily tissue and fluids of other and more palpably living things into which it penetrates and with whose fabric it sometimes completely merges itself. It might be actively hostile, or it might be dictated merely by blind motives of self-preservation. In any case such a monster must of necessity be in our scheme of things an anomaly and an intruder, whose extirpation forms a primary duty with every man not an enemy to the world's life, health, and sanity.

What baffled us was our utter ignorance of the aspect in which we might encounter the thing. No sane person had ever seen it, and few had ever felt it definitely. It might be pure energy—a form ethereal and outside the realm of substance—or it might be partly material; some unknown and equivocal mass of plasticity, capable of changing at will to nebulous approximations of the solid, liquid, gaseous, or tenuously unparticled states. The anthropomorphic patch of mold on the floor, the form of the yellowish vapor, and the curvature of the tree-roots in some of the old tales, all argued at least a remote and reminiscent connection with the human shape; but how representative or permanent that similarity might be, none could say with any kind of certainty.

We had devised two weapons to fight it; a large and specially fitted Crookes tube operated by powerful storage batteries and provided with peculiar screens and reflectors, in case it proved intangible and opposable only by vigorously destructive ether radiations; and a pair of military flame-throwers of the sort used in the World War, in case it proved partly material and susceptible of mechanical destruction — for like the superstitious Exeter rustics, we were prepared to burn the thing's heart out if heart existed to burn. All this aggressive mechanism we set in the cellar in positions carefully arranged with reference to the cot and chairs, and to the spot before the fireplace where the mold had taken strange shapes. That suggestive patch, by the way, was only faintly visible when we placed our furniture and instruments, and when we returned that evening for the actual vigil. For a moment I half doubted that I had ever seen it in the more definitely limned form — but then I thought of the legends.

Our cellar vigil began at ten p.m., daylight saving time, and as it continued we found no promise of pertinent developments. A weak, filtered glow from the rain-harassed street-lamps outside, and a feeble phosphorescence from the detestable fungi within, showed the dripping stone of the walls, from which all traces of whitewash had vanished; the dank, fetid and mildew-tainted hard earth floor with its obscene fungi; the rotting remains of what had been stools, chairs, and tables, and other more shapeless furniture; the heavy planks and massive beams of the ground floor overhead; the decrepit plank door leading to bins and chambers beneath other parts of the house; the crumbling stone staircase with ruined wooden hand-rail; and the crude and cavernous fireplace of blackened brick where rusted iron fragments revealed the past presence of hooks, and irons, spit, crane, and a door to the Dutch oven — these things, and our austere cot and camp chairs, and the heavy and intricate destructive machinery we had brought.

We had, as in my own former explorations, left the door to the street unlocked, so that a direct and practical path of escape might lie open in case of manifestations beyond our power to deal with. It was our idea that our continued nocturnal presence would call forth whatever malign entity lurked there; and that being prepared, we could dispose of the thing with one or the other of our provided means as soon as we had recognized and observed it sufficiently. How long it might require to evoke and extinguish the thing, we had no notion. It occurred to us, too, that our venture was far from safe; for in what strength the thing might appear no one could tell. But we deemed the game worth the hazard, and embarked on it alone and unhesitatingly; conscious that the seeking of outside aid would only expose us to ridicule and perhaps defeat our entire purpose. Such was our frame of mind as we talked — far into the night, till my uncle's growing drowsiness made me remind him to lie down for his two-hour sleep.

Something like fear chilled me as I sat there in the small hours alone — I say alone, for one who sits by a sleeper is indeed alone, perhaps more alone than he can realize. My uncle breathed heavily, his deep inhalations and exhalations accompanied by the rain outside, and punctuated by another nerve-wracking sound of distant dripping water within — for the house was repulsively damp even in dry weather, and in this storm positively swamp-like. I studied the loose, antique masonry of the walls in the fungus-light and the feeble rays which stole in from the street through the screened window; and once, when the noisome atmosphere of the place seemed about to sicken me, I opened the door and looked up and down the street, feasting my eyes on familiar sights and my nostrils on wholesome air. Still nothing occurred to reward my watching; and I yawned repeatedly, fatigue getting the better of apprehension.

Then the stirring of my uncle in his sleep attracted my notice. He had turned restlessly on the cot several times during the latter half of the first hour, but now he was breathing with unusual irregularity, occasionally heaving a sigh which held more than a few of the qualities of a choking moan.

I turned my electric flashlight on him and found his face averted; so rising and crossing to the other side of the cot, I again flashed the light to see if he seemed in any pain. What I saw unnerved me most surprisingly, considering its relative triviality. It must have been merely the association of any odd circumstance with the sinister nature of our location and mission, for surely the circumstance was not in itself frightful or unnatural. It was merely that my uncle's facial expression, disturbed no doubt by the strange dreams which our situation prompted, betrayed considerable agitation, and seemed not at all characteristic of him. His habitual expression was one of kindly and well-bred calm, whereas now a variety of emotions seemed struggling within him. I think, on the whole, that it was this variety which chiefly disturbed me. My uncle, as he gasped and tossed in increasing perturbation and with eyes that had now started open, seemed not one but many men, and suggested a curious quality of alienage from himself.

All at once he commenced to mutter, and I did not like the look of his mouth and teeth as he spoke. The words were at first indistinguishable, and then — with a tremendous start — I recognized something about them which filled me with icy fear till I recalled the breadth of my uncle's education and the interminable translations he had made from anthropological and antiquarian articles in the *Revue des Deux Mondes*. For the venerable Elihu Whipple was muttering in French, and the few phrases I could distinguish seemed connected with the darkest myths he had ever adapted from the famous Paris magazine.

Suddenly a perspiration broke out on the sleeper's forehead, and he leaped abruptly up, half awake. The jumble of French changed to a cry in English, and the hoarse voice shouted excitedly, "My breath, my breath!" Then the awakening became complete, and with a subsidence of facial expression to the normal state my uncle seized my hand and began to relate a dream whose nucleus of significance I could only surmise with a kind of awe.

He had, he said, floated off from a very ordinary series of dream-pictures into a scene whose strangeness was related to nothing he had ever read. It was of this world, and yet not of it — a shadowy geometrical confusion in which could be seen elements of familiar things in most unfamiliar and perturbing combinations. There was a suggestion of queerly disordered pictures superimposed one upon another; an arrangement in which the essentials of time as well as of space seemed dissolved and mixed in the most illogical fashion. In this kaleidoscopic vortex of phantasmal images were occasional snap-shots, if one might use the term, of singular clearness but unaccountable heterogeneity.

Once my uncle thought he lay in a carelessly dug open pit, with a crowd of angry faces framed by straggling locks and three-cornered hats frowning down on him. Again he seemed to be in the interior of a house — an old house, apparently — but the details and inhabitants were constantly changing, and he could never be certain of the faces or the furniture, or even of the room itself, since doors and windows seemed in just as great a state of flux as the presumably more mobile objects. It was queer — damnably queer — and my uncle spoke almost sheepishly, as if half expecting not to be believed, when he declared that of the strange faces many had unmistakably borne the features of the Harris family. And all the while there was a personal sensation of choking, as if some pervasive presence had spread itself through his body and sought to possess itself of his vital processes.

I shuddered at the thought of those vital processes, worn as they were by eighty-one years of continuous functioning, in conflict with unknown forces of which the youngest and strongest system might well be afraid; but in another moment reflected that dreams are only dreams, and that these uncomfortable visions could be, at most, no more than my uncle's reaction to the investigations and expectations which had lately filled our minds to the exclusion of all else.

Conversation, also, soon tended to dispel my sense of strangeness; and in time I yielded to my yawns and took my turn at slumber. My uncle seemed now very wakeful, and welcomed his period of watching even though the nightmare had aroused him far ahead of his alotted two hours.

Sleep seized me quickly, and I was at once haunted with dreams of the most disturbing kind. I felt, in my visions, a cosmic and abysmal loneness; with hostility surging from all sides upon some prison where I lay confined. I seemed bound and gagged, and taunted by the echoing yells of distant multitudes who thirsted for my blood. My uncle's face came to me with less pleasant association than in waking hours, and I recall many futile struggles and attempts to scream. It was not a pleasant sleep, and for a second I was not sorry for the echoing shriek which clove through the barriers of dream and flung me to a sharp and startled awakeness in which every actual object before my eyes stood out with more than natural clearness and reality.

V.

I had been lying with my face away from my uncle's chair, so that in this sudden flash of awakening I saw only the door to the street, the window, and the wall and floor and ceiling toward the north of the room, all photographed with morbid vividness on my brain in a light brighter than the glow of the fungi or the rays from the street outside. It was not a strong or even a fairly strong light; certainly not nearly strong enough to read an average book by. But it cast a shadow of myself and the cot on the floor, and had a yellowish, penetrating force that hinted at things more potent than luminosity. This I perceived with unhealthy sharpness despite the fact that two of my other senses were violently assailed. For on my ears rang the reverberations of that shocking scream, while my nostrils revolted at the stench which filled the place. My mind, as alert as my senses, recognized the gravely unusual; and almost automatically I leaped up and turned about to grasp the destructive instruments which we had left trained on the moldy spot before the fireplace. As I turned, I dreaded what I was to see; for the scream had been in my uncle's voice, and I knew not against what menace I should have to defend him and myself.

Yet after all, the sight was worse than I had dreaded. There are horrors beyond horrors, and this was one of those nuclei of all dreamable hideousness which the cosmos saves to blast an accursed and unhappy few. Out of the fungus-ridden earth steamed up a vaporous corpse-light, yellow and diseased, which bubbled and lapped to a gigantic height in vague outlines half human and half monstrous, through which I could see the chimney and fireplace beyond. It was all eyes — wolfish and mocking — and the rugose insect-like head dissolved at the top to a thin stream of mist which curled putridly about and finally vanished up the chimney. I say that I saw this thing, but it is only in conscious retrospection that I ever definitely traced its damnable approach to form. At the time, it was to me only a seething, dimly phosphorescent cloud of fungous loathsomeness, enveloping and dissolving to an abhorrent plasticity the one object on which all my attention was focussed. That object was my uncle — the venerable Elihu Whipple — who with blackening and decaying features leered and gibbered at me, and reached out dripping claws to rend me in the fury which this horror had brought.

It was a sense of routine which kept me from going mad. I had drilled myself in preparation for the crucial moment, and blind training saved me. Recognizing the bubbling evil as no substance reachable by matter or material chemistry, and therefore ignoring the flame-thrower which loomed on my left, I threw on the current of the Crookes tube apparatus, and focussed toward that scene of immortal blasphemousness the strongest ether radiations which man's art can arouse from the spaces and fluids of nature. There was a bluish haze and a frenzied sputtering, and the yellowish phosphorescence grew dimmer to my eyes. But I saw the dimness was only that of contrast, and that the waves from the machine had no effect whatever.

Then, in the midst of that demoniac spectacle, I saw a fresh horror which brought cries to my lips and sent me fumbling and staggering toward that unlocked door to the quiet street, careless of what abnormal terrors I loosed upon the world, or what thoughts or judgments of men I brought down upon my head. In that dim blend of blue and yellow the form of my uncle had commenced a nauseous liquefaction whose essence eludes all description, and in which there played across his vanishing face such changes of identity as only madness can conceive. He was at once a devil and a multitude, a charnel-house and a pageant. Lit by the mixed and uncertain beams, that gelatinous face assumed a dozen — a score — a hundred — aspects; grinning, as it sank to the ground on a body that melted like tallow, in the caricatured likeness of legions strange and yet not strange.

I saw the features of the Harris line, masculine and feminine, adult and infantile, and other features old and young, coarse and refined, familiar and unfamiliar. For a second there flashed a degraded counterfeit of a miniature of poor mad Rhoby Harris that I had seen in the School of Design museum, and another time I thought I caught the raw-boned image of Mercy Dexter as I recalled her from a painting in Carrington Harris's house. It was frightful beyond conception; toward the last, when a curious blend of servant and baby visages flickered close to the fungous floor where a pool of greenish grease was spreading, it seemed as though the shifting features fought against themselves and strove to form contours like those of my uncle's kindly face. I like to think that he existed at that moment, and that he tried to bid me farewell. It seems to me I hiccupped a farewell from my own parched throat as I lurched out into the street; a thin stream of grease following me through the door to the rain-drenched sidewalk.

The rest is shadowy and monstrous. There was no one in the soaking street, and in all the world there was no one I dared tell. I walked aimlessly south past College Hill and the Athenæum, down Hopkins Street, and over the bridge to the business section where tall buildings seemed to guard me as modern material things guard the world from ancient and unwholesome wonder. Then gray dawn unfolded wetly from the east, silhouetting the archaic hill and its venerable steeples, and beckoning me to the place where my terrible work was still unfinished. And in the end I went, wet, hatless, and dazed in the morning light, and entered that awful door in Benefit Street which I had left ajar, and which still swung cryptically in full sight of the early householders to whom I dared not speak.

The grease was gone, for the moldy floor was porous. And in front of the fireplace was no vestige of the giant doubled-up form traced in niter. I looked at the cot, the chairs, the instruments, my neglected hat, and the yellowed straw hat of my uncle. Dazedness was uppermost, and I could scarcely recall what was dream and what was reality. Then thought trickled back, and I knew that I had witnessed things more horrible than I had dreamed. Sitting down, I tried to conjecture as nearly as sanity would let me just what had happened, and how I might end the horror, if indeed it had been real. Matter it seemed not to be, nor ether, nor anything else conceivable by mortal mind. What, then, but some exotic emanation; some vampirish vapor such as Exeter rustics tell of as lurking over certain churchyards? This I felt was the clue, and again I looked at the floor before the fireplace where the mold and niter had taken strange forms.

In ten minutes my mind was made up, and taking my hat I set out for home, where I bathed, ate, and gave by telephone an order for a pickax, a spade, a military gas-mask, and six carboys of sulfuric acid, all to be delivered the next morning at the cellar door of the shunned house in Benefit Street. After that I tried to sleep; and failing, passed the hours in reading and in the composition of inane verses to counteract my mood.

At eleven a.m. the next day I commenced digging. It was sunny weather, and I was glad of that. I was still alone, for as much as I feared the unknown horror I sought, there was more fear in the thought of telling anybody. Later I told Harris only through sheer necessity, and because he had heard odd tales from old people which disposed him ever so little toward belief. As I turned up the stinking black earth in front of the fireplace, my spade causing a viscous yellow ichor to ooze from the white fungi which it severed, I trembled at the dubious thoughts of what I might uncover. Some secrets of inner earth are not good for mankind, and this seemed to me one of them.

My hand shook perceptibly, but still I delved; after a while standing in the large hole I had made. With the deepening of the hole, which was about six feet square, the evil smell increased; and I lost all doubt of my imminent contact with the hellish thing whose emanations had cursed the house for over a century and a half. I wondered what it would look like — what its form and substance would be, and how big it might have waxed through long ages of life-sucking. At length I climbed out of the hole and dispersed the heaped-up dirt, then arranging the great carboys of acid around and near two sides, so that when necessary I might empty them all down the aperture in quick succession. After that I dumped earth only along the other two sides; working more slowly and donning my gas-mask as the smell grew. I was nearly unnerved at my proximity to a nameless thing at the bottom of a pit.

Suddenly my spade struck something softer than earth. I shuddered, and made a motion as if to climb out of the hole, which was now as deep as my neck. Then courage returned, and I scraped away more dirt in the light of the electric torch I had provided. The surface I uncovered was fishy and glassy — a kind of semi-putrid congealed jelly with suggestions of translucency. I scraped further, and saw that it had form. There was a rift where a part of the substance was folded over. The exposed area was huge and roughly cylindrical; like a mammoth soft blue-white stovepipe doubled in two, its largest part some two feet in diameter. Still more I scraped, and then abruptly I leaped out of the hole and away from the filthy thing; frantically unstopping and tilting the heavy carboys, and precipitating their corrosive contents one after another down that charnel gulf and upon the unthinkable abnormality whose titan elbow I had seen.

The blinding maelstrom of greenish-yellow vapor which surged tempestuously up from that hole as the floods of acid descended, will never leave my memory. All along the hill people tell of the yellow day, when virulent and horrible fumes arose from the factory waste dumped in the Providence River, but I know how mistaken they are as to the source. They tell, too, of the hideous roar which at the same time came from some disordered water-pipe or gas main underground — but again I could correct them if I dared. It was unspeakably shocking, and I do not see how I lived through it. I did faint after emptying the fourth carboy, which I had to handle after the fumes had began to penetrate my mask; but when I recovered I saw that the hole was emitting no fresh vapors.

The two remaining carboys I emptied down without particular result, and after a time I felt it safe to shovel the earth back into the pit. It was twilight before I was done, but fear had gone out of the place. The dampness was less fetid, and all the strange fungi had withered to a kind of harmless grayish powder which blew ash-like along the floor. One of earth's nethermost terrors had perished for ever; and if there be a hell, it had received at last the demon soul of an unhallowed thing. And as I patted down the last spadeful of mold, I shed the first of the many tears with which I have paid unaffected tribute to my beloved uncle's memory.

The next spring no more pale grass and strange weeds came up in the shunned house's terraced garden, and shortly afterward Carrington Harris rented the place. It is still spectral, but its strangeness fascinates me, and I shall find mixed with my relief a queer regret when it is torn down to make way for a tawdry shop or vulgar apartment building. The barren old trees in the yard have begun to bear small, sweet apples, and last year the birds nested in their gnarled boughs.

1925.

In Exile.

For H.P. Lovecraft, 1925 was probably the most miserable year of his life (with the obvious exception of the year of his death). Sonia had left for Cincinnati, and although she returned frequently for visits and attempted to move back, the nuclear Lovecraft family was essentially lost and gone. To make matters worse, on one of her return trips she took him shopping and outfitted him with new suits; within a few weeks thieves had broken into his apartment and stolen nearly everything but the clothes on his back. Ten months later he was still fuming about this, and it seems to have pushed him over into a dark place of rage and hatred for New York—in spite of the fine times he was still having gallivanting around with "the gang."

After about the middle of 1925, Lovecraft's yearning for a return to Providence became almost unbearable, as did the corresponding loathing for New York—and for its incomprehensible ethnic minorities and neighborhoods, which Lovecraft took to referring to as "mongrels" and "bastard races." It was during this time that the depressive, xenophobic side of his personality was at its ickiest, and his ethnic chauvinism reached levels that are painful to modern readers, no matter what their ethnicity might be.

In fairness, it's important to note that Lovecraft's hostility to non-"Nordics," as he called them, seems to have been solely applied rhetorically and in the abstract sense, and not to actual individuals. According to Frank Belknap Long, had he come upon, say, a Chinese man injured in the street, he would have raced to his aid with no less care and solicitude than if the injured party had been a blond Teuton. He was able and frequently willing to rant about "the Jews," even in the presence of his Jewish wife, and he seemed not to understand the paradox that posed.

Nonetheless, 1925 saw Lovecraft's xenophobia and racism at its very worst, and it got bad. He seems to have, at least in part, transferred much of his disappointment and disgust over his entire New York experience onto the ethnic communities he found there.

With Sonia out of town, Lovecraft's job search faded to a desultory shadow of what it had been. Essentially, he had given up. He also lost all the sleekness that Sonia had painstakingly put into him, dropping back to 146 pounds again by June on a diet of bread, baked beans and cheese.

It wasn't all horrible, though. There was always something going on with the other members of the Kalem Club. On the other hand, the Kalem Club sometimes proved as much of a pain as a pleasure, as the other writers would drop by at odd hours when he was trying to work.

Nonetheless, the year was relatively productive. He leveraged his growing loathing of New York to produce "The Horror at Red Hook," "He," and "In the Vault."

It's also worth noting that he sketched out the initial plan for his most famous story, "The Call of Cthulhu," in 1925—although he wouldn't actually write the story until the following year, after his return to Providence.

The Horror at Red Hook.

8,300-WORD NOVELETTE; 1925.

This bombastic novelette is often cited as the worst of Lovecraft's long works. It's also marred by levels of racist hostility comparable to those found in "The Street." Lovecraft, at the time he was writing it, was simply in a foul mood, and was giving free rein to his inner darkness.

"The Horror at Red Hook" was written on Aug. 2, 1925, just after Lovecraft had seen Sonia off on her return to work in Cleveland and well before he got word of his impending return to Providence. It was published in the January 1927 issue of Weird Tales.

> *There are sacraments of evil as well as of good about us, and we live and move to my belief in an unknown world, a place where there are caves and shadows and dwellers in twilight. It is possible that man may sometimes return on the track of evolution, and it is my belief that an awful lore is not yet dead.*
>
> — Arthur Machen

I.

Not many weeks ago, on a street corner in the village of Pascoag, Rhode Island, a tall, heavily built, and wholesome-looking pedestrian furnished much speculation by a singular lapse of behaviour. He had, it appears, been descending the hill by the road from Chepachet; and encountering the compact section, had turned to his left into the main thoroughfare where several modest business blocks convey a touch of the urban. At this point, without visible provocation, he committed his astonishing lapse, staring queerly for a second at the tallest of the buildings before him, and then, with a series of terrified, hysterical shrieks, breaking into a frantic run which ended in a stumble and fall at the next crossing. Picked up and dusted off by ready hands, he was found to be conscious, organically unhurt, and evidently cured of his sudden nervous attack. He muttered some shamefaced explanations involving a strain he had undergone, and with downcast glance turned back up the Chepachet road, trudging out of sight without once looking behind him. It was a strange incident to befall so large, robust, normal-featured, and capable-looking a man, and the strangeness was not lessened by the remarks of a bystander who had recognised him as the boarder of a well-known dairyman on the outskirts of Chepachet.

He was, it developed, a New York police detective named Thomas F. Malone, now on a long leave of absence under medical treatment after some disproportionately arduous work on a gruesome local case which accident had made dramatic. There had been a collapse of several old brick buildings during a raid in which he had shared, and something about the wholesale loss of life, both of prisoners and of his companions, had peculiarly appalled him. As a result, he had acquired an acute and anomalous horror of any buildings even remotely suggesting the ones which had fallen in, so that in the end mental specialists forbade him the sight of such things for an indefinite period. A police surgeon with relatives in Chepachet had put forward that quaint hamlet of wooden colonial houses as an ideal spot for the psychological convalescence; and thither the sufferer had gone, promising never to venture among the brick-lined streets of larger villages till duly advised by the Woonsocket specialist with whom he was put in touch. This walk to Pascoag for magazines had been a mistake, and the patient had paid in fright, bruises, and humiliation for his disobedience.

So much the gossips of Chepachet and Pascoag knew; and so much, also, the most learned specialists believed. But Malone had at first told the specialists much more, ceasing only when he saw that utter incredulity was his portion. Thereafter he held his peace, protesting not at all when it was generally agreed that the collapse of certain squalid brick houses in the Red Hook section of Brooklyn, and the consequent death of many brave officers, had unseated his nervous equilibrium. He had worked too hard, all said, in trying to clean up those nests of disorder and violence; certain features were shocking enough, in all conscience, and the unexpected tragedy was the last straw.

This was a simple explanation which everyone could understand, and because Malone was not a simple person he perceived that he had better let it suffice. To hint to unimaginative people of a horror beyond all human conception — a horror of houses and blocks and cities leprous and cancerous with evil dragged from elder worlds — would be merely to invite a padded cell instead of a restful rustication, and Malone was a man of sense despite his mysticism. He had the Celt's far vision of weird and hidden things, but the logician's quick eye for the outwardly unconvincing; an amalgam which had led him far afield in the forty-two years of his life, and set him in strange places for a Dublin University man born in a Georgian villa near Phoenix Park.

And now, as he reviewed the things he had seen and felt and apprehended, Malone was content to keep unshared the

The HORROR AT RED HOOK

by

H. P. LOVECRAFT

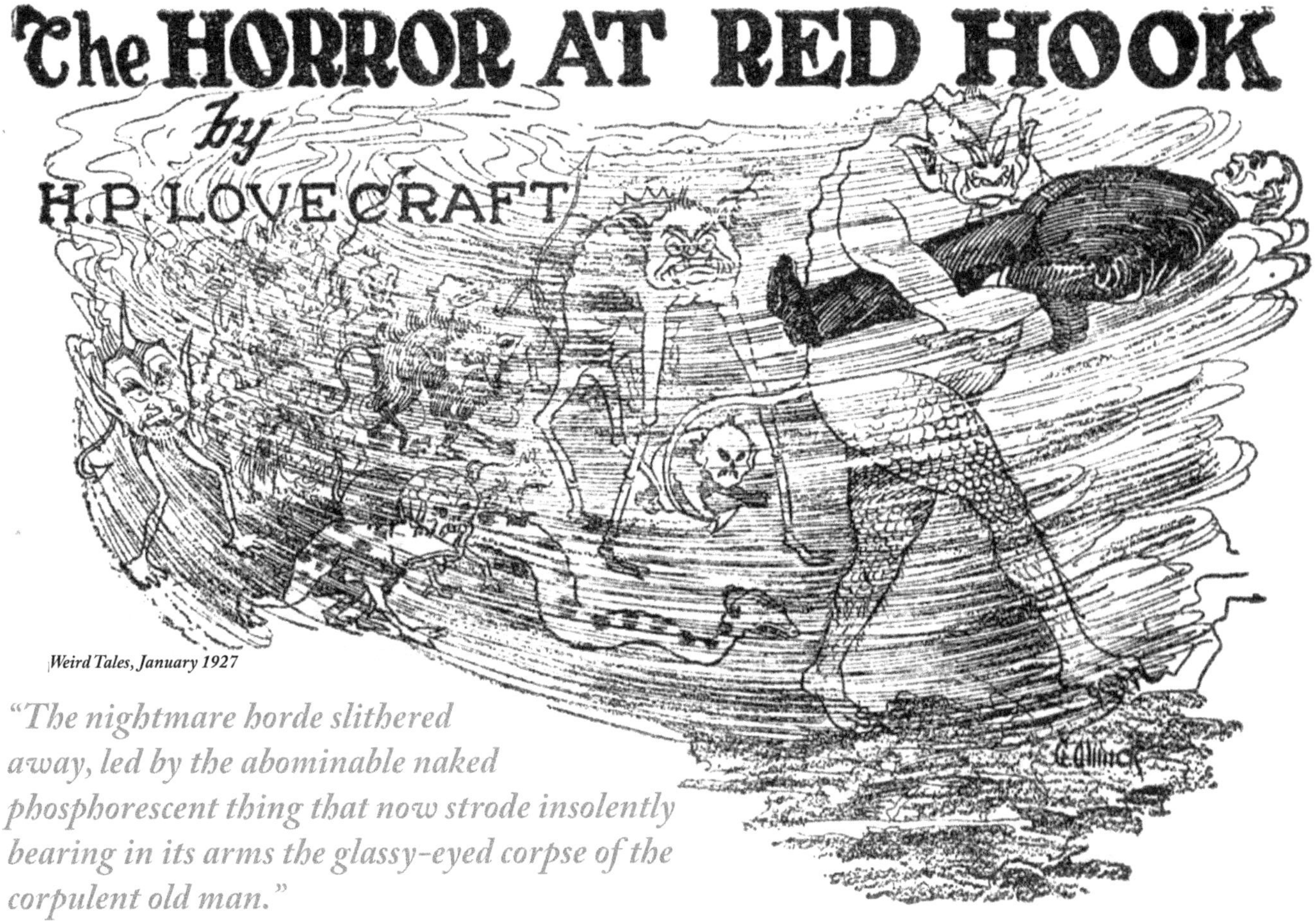

Weird Tales, January 1927

"The nightmare horde slithered away, led by the abominable naked phosphorescent thing that now strode insolently bearing in its arms the glassy-eyed corpse of the corpulent old man."

secret of what could reduce a dauntless fighter to a quivering neurotic; what could make old brick slums and seas of dark, subtle faces a thing of nightmare and eldritch portent. It would not be the first time his sensations had been forced to bide uninterpreted — for was not his very act of plunging into the polyglot abyss of New York's underworld a freak beyond sensible explanation? What could he tell the prosaic of the antique witcheries and grotesque marvels discernible to sensitive eyes amidst the poison cauldron where all the varied dregs of unwholesome ages mix their venom and perpetuate their obscene terrors? He had seen the hellish green flame of secret wonder in this blatant, evasive welter of outward greed and inward blasphemy, and had smiled gently when all the New Yorkers he knew scoffed at his experiment in police work. They had been very witty and cynical, deriding his fantastic pursuit of unknowable mysteries and assuring him that in these days New York held nothing but cheapness and vulgarity. One of them had wagered him a heavy sum that he could not — despite many poignant things to his credit in the Dublin Review — even write a truly interesting story of New York low life; and now, looking back, he perceived that cosmic irony had justified the prophet's words while secretly confuting their flippant meaning. The horror, as glimpsed at last, could not make a story — for like the book cited by Poe's Germany authority, "*es lässt sich nicht lesen* — it does not permit itself to be read."

II.

To Malone the sense of latent mystery in existence was always present. In youth he had felt the hidden beauty and ecstasy of things, and had been a poet; but poverty and sorrow and exile had turned his gaze in darker directions, and he had thrilled at the imputations of evil in the world around. Daily life had for him come to be a phantasmagoria of macabre shadow-studies, now glittering and leering with concealed rottenness as in Beardsley's best manner, now hinting terrors behind the commonest shapes and objects as in the subtler and less obvious work of Gustave Doré. He would often regard it as merciful that most persons of high intelligence jeer at the inmost mysteries; for, he argued, if superior minds were ever placed in fullest contact with the secrets preserved by ancient and lowly cults, the resultant abnormalities would soon not only wreck the world, but threaten the very integrity of the universe. All this reflection was no doubt morbid, but keen logic and a deep sense of humour ably offset it. Malone was satisfied to let his notions remain as half-spied and forbidden visions to be lightly played with; and hysteria came only when duty flung him into a hell of revelation too sudden and insidious to escape.

He had for some time been detailed to the Butler Street

station in Brooklyn when the Red Hook matter came to his notice. Red Hook is a maze of hybrid squalor near the ancient waterfront opposite Governor's Island, with dirty highways climbing the hill from the wharves to that higher ground where the decayed lengths of Clinton and Court streets lead off toward the Borough Hall. Its houses are mostly of brick, dating from the first quarter to the middle of the nineteenth century, and some of the obscurer alleys and byways have that alluring antique flavour which conventional reading leads us to call "Dickensian." The population is a hopeless tangle and enigma; Syrian, Spanish, Italian, and Negro elements impinging upon one another, and fragments of Scandinavian and American belts lying not far distant. It is a babel of sound and filth, and sends out strange cries to answer the lapping of oily waves at its grimy piers and the monstrous organ litanies of the harbour whistles. Here long ago a brighter picture dwelt, with clear-eyed mariners on the lower streets and homes of taste and substance where the larger houses line the hill. One can trace the relics of this former happiness in the trim shapes of the buildings, the occasional graceful churches, and the evidences of original art and background in bits of detail here and there — a worn flight of steps, a battered doorway, a wormy pair of decorative columns or pilasters, or a fragment of once green space with bent and rusted iron railing. The houses are generally in solid blocks, and now and then a many-windowed cupola arises to tell of days when the households of captains and ship-owners watched the sea.

From this tangle of material and spiritual putrescence the blasphemies of an hundred dialects assail the sky. Hordes of prowlers reel shouting and singing along the lanes and thoroughfares, occasional furtive hands suddenly extinguish lights and pull down curtains, and swarthy, sin-pitted faces disappear from windows when visitors pick their way through. Policemen despair of order or reform, and seek rather to erect barriers protecting the outside world from the contagion. The clang of the patrol is answered by a kind of spectral silence, and such prisoners as are taken are never communicative. Visible offences are as varied as the local dialects, and run the gamut from the smuggling of rum and prohibited aliens through diverse stages of lawlessness and obscure vice to murder and mutilation in their most abhorrent guises. That these visible affairs are not more frequent is not to the neighbourhood's credit, unless the power of concealment be an art demanding credit. More people enter Red Hook than leave it — or at least, than leave it by the landward side — and those who are not loquacious are the likeliest to leave.

Malone found in this state of things a faint stench of secrets more terrible than any of the sins denounced by citizens and bemoaned by priests and philanthropists. He was conscious, as one who united imagination with scientific knowledge, that modern people under lawless conditions tend uncannily to repeat the darkest instinctive patterns of primitive half-ape savagery in their daily life and ritual observances; and he had often viewed with an anthropologist's shudder the chanting, cursing processions of blear-eyed and pockmarked young men which wound their way along in the dark small hours of morning. One saw groups of these youths incessantly; sometimes in leering vigils on street corners, sometimes in doorways playing eerily on cheap instruments of music, sometimes in stupefied dozes or indecent dialogues around cafeteria tables near Borough Hall, and sometimes in whispering converse around dingy taxicabs drawn up at the high stoops of crumbling and closely shuttered old houses. They chilled and fascinated him more than he dared confess to his associates on the force, for he seemed to see in them some monstrous thread of secret continuity; some fiendish, cryptical, and ancient pattern utterly beyond and below the sordid mass of facts and habits and haunts listed with such conscientious technical care by the police. They must be, he felt inwardly, the heirs of some shocking and primordial tradition; the sharers of debased and broken scraps from cults and ceremonies older than mankind. Their coherence and definiteness suggested it, and it shewed in the singular suspicion of order which lurked beneath their squalid disorder. He had not read in vain such treatises as Miss Murray's *Witch-Cult in Western Europe*; and knew that up to recent years there had certainly survived among peasants and furtive folk a frightful and clandestine system of assemblies and orgies descended from dark religions antedating the Aryan world, and appearing in popular legends as Black Masses and Witches' Sabbaths. That these hellish vestiges of old Turanian-Asiatic magic and fertility-cults were even now wholly dead he could not for a moment suppose, and he frequently wondered how much older and how much blacker than the very worst of the muttered tales some of them might really be.

III.

It was the case of Robert Suydam which took Malone to the heart of things in Red Hook. Suydam was a lettered recluse of ancient Dutch family, possessed originally of barely independent means, and inhabiting the spacious but ill-preserved mansion which his grandfather had built in Flatbush when that village was little more than a pleasant group of colonial cottages surrounding the steepled and ivy-clad Reformed Church with its iron-railed yard of Netherlandish gravestones. In his lonely house, set back from Martense Street amidst a yard of venerable trees, Suydam had read and brooded for some six decades except for a period a generation before, when he had sailed for the Old World and remained there out of sight for eight years. He could afford no servants, and would admit but few visitors to his absolute solitude, eschewing close friendships and receiving his rare acquaintances in one of the three ground-floor rooms which he kept in order — a vast, high-ceiled library whose walls were solidly packed with tattered books of ponderous, archaic, and vaguely repellent aspect. The growth of the town and its final absorption in the Brooklyn district had meant nothing to Suydam, and he had come to mean less and less to the town. Elderly people still pointed him out on the streets, but to most of the recent population he was merely a queer, corpulent old fellow whose unkempt white hair, stubbly beard, shiny black clothes, and gold-headed cane earned him an amused glance and nothing more. Malone did not know him by sight till duty called him to the case, but had heard of him indirectly as a really profound authority on mediaeval superstition, and had once idly meant to look up an out-of-print pamphlet of his on the Kabbalah and the Faustus legend, which a friend had quoted from memory.

Suydam became a "case" when his distant and only relatives sought court pronouncements on his sanity. Their action seemed sudden to the outside world, but was really undertaken only after prolonged observation and sorrowful debate. It was based on certain odd changes in his speech and habits; wild references to impending wonders, and unaccountable hauntings of disreputable Brooklyn neighbourhoods. He had been growing shabbier and shabbier with the years, and now prowled about like a veritable mendicant; seen occasionally by humiliated friends in subway stations, or loitering on the benches around Borough Hall in conversation with groups of swarthy, evil-looking strangers. When he spoke it was to babble of unlimited powers almost within his grasp, and to repeat with knowing leers such mystical words or names as "Sephiroth," "Ashmodai," and "Samaël." The court action revealed that he was using up his income and wasting his principal in the purchase of curious tomes imported from London and Paris, and in the maintenance of a squalid basement flat in the Red Hook district where he spent nearly every night, receiving odd delegations of mixed rowdies and foreigners, and apparently conducting some kind of ceremonial service behind the green blinds of secretive windows. Detectives assigned to follow him reported strange cries and chants and prancing of feet filtering out from these nocturnal rites, and shuddered at their peculiar ecstasy and abandon despite the commonness of weird orgies in that sodden section. When, however, the matter came to a hearing, Suydam managed to preserve his liberty. Before the judge his manner grew urbane and reasonable, and he freely admitted the queerness of demeanour and extravagant cast of language into which he had fallen through excessive devotion to study and research. He was, he said, engaged in the investigation of certain details of European tradition which required the closest contact with foreign groups and their songs and folk dances. The notion that any low secret society was preying upon him, as hinted by his relatives, was obviously absurd, and shewed how sadly limited was their understanding of him and his work. Triumphing with his calm explanations, he was suffered to depart unhindered; and the paid detectives of the Suydams, Corlears, and Van Brunts were withdrawn in resigned disgust.

It was here that an alliance of Federal inspectors and police, Malone with them, entered the case. The law had watched the Suydam action with interest, and had in many instances been called upon to aid the private detectives. In this work it developed that Suydam's new associates were among the blackest and most vicious criminals of Red Hook's devious lanes, and that at least a third of them were known and repeated offenders in the matter of thievery, disorder, and the importation of illegal immigrants. Indeed, it would not have been too much to say that the old scholar's particular circle coincided almost perfectly with the worst of the organised cliques which smuggled ashore certain nameless and unclassified Asian dregs wisely turned back by Ellis Island. In the teeming rookeries of Parker Place — since renamed — where Suydam had his basement flat, there had grown up a very unusual colony of unclassified slant-eyed folk who used the Arabic alphabet but were eloquently repudiated by the great mass of Syrians in and around Atlantic Avenue. They could all have been deported for lack of credentials, but legalism is slow-moving, and one does not disturb Red Hook unless publicity forces one to.

These creatures attended a tumbledown stone church, used Wednesdays as a dance-hall, which reared its Gothic buttresses near the vilest part of the waterfront. It was nominally Catholic; but priests throughout Brooklyn denied the place all standing and authenticity, and policemen agreed with them when they listened to the noises it emitted at night. Malone used to fancy he heard terrible cracked bass notes from a hidden organ far underground when the church stood empty and unlighted, whilst all observers dreaded the shrieking and drumming which accompanied the visible services. Suydam, when questioned, said he thought the ritual was some remnant of Nestorian Christianity tinctured with the Shamanism of Thibet. Most of the people, he conjectured, were of Mongoloid stock, originating somewhere in or near Kurdistan — and Malone could not help recalling that Kurdistan is the land of the Yezidis, last survivors of the Persian devil-worshippers. However this may have been, the stir of the Suydam investigation made it certain that these unauthorised newcomers were flooding Red Hook in increasing numbers; entering through some marine conspiracy unreached by revenue officers and harbour police, overrunning Parker Place and rapidly spreading up the hill, and welcomed with curious fraternalism by the other assorted denizens of the region. Their squat figures and characteristic squinting physiognomies, grotesquely combined with flashy American clothing, appeared more and more numerously among the loafers and nomad gangsters of the Borough Hall section; till at length it was deemed necessary to compute their numbers, ascertain their sources and occupations, and find if possible a way to round them up and deliver them to the proper immigration authorities. To this task Malone was assigned by agreement of Federal and city forces, and as he commenced his canvass of Red Hook he felt poised upon the brink of nameless terrors, with the shabby, unkempt figure of Robert Suydam as arch-fiend and adversary.

IV.

Police methods are varied and ingenious. Malone, through unostentatious rambles, carefully casual conversations, well-timed offers of hip-pocket liquor, and judicious dialogues with frightened prisoners, learned many isolated facts about the movement whose aspect had become so menacing. The newcomers were indeed Kurds, but of a dialect obscure and puzzling to exact philology. Such of them as worked lived mostly as dock-hands and unlicenced pedlars, though frequently serving in Greek restaurants and tending corner news stands. Most of them, however, had no visible means of support; and were obviously connected with underworld pursuits, of which smuggling and "bootlegging" were the least indescribable. They had come in steamships, apparently tramp freighters, and had been unloaded by stealth on moonless nights in rowboats which stole under a certain wharf and followed a hidden canal to a secret subterranean pool beneath a house. This wharf, canal, and house Malone could not locate, for the memories of his informants were exceedingly confused, while their speech was to a great extent beyond even the ablest interpreters; nor could he gain any real data on the reasons for their systematic importation. They were reticent about the exact spot from which they had come, and were never sufficiently off guard to reveal the agencies which had sought them out and directed their course. Indeed, they developed something like acute fright when asked the reasons for their presence. Gangsters of other breeds were equally taciturn, and the most that could be gathered was that some god or great priesthood had promised them unheard-of powers and supernatural glories and rulerships in a strange land.

The attendance of both newcomers and old gangsters at Suydam's closely guarded nocturnal meetings was very regular, and the police soon learned that the erstwhile recluse had leased additional flats to accommodate such guests as knew his password; at last occupying three entire houses and permanently harbouring many of his queer companions. He spent but little time now at his Flatbush home, apparently going and coming only to obtain and return books; and his face and manner had attained an appalling pitch of wildness. Malone twice interviewed him, but was each time brusquely repulsed. He knew nothing, he said, of any mysterious plots or movements, and had no idea how the Kurds could have entered or what they wanted. His business was to study undisturbed the folklore of all the immigrants of the district; a business with which policemen had no legitimate concern. Malone mentioned his admiration for Suydam's old brochure on the Kabbalah and other myths, but the old man's softening was only momentary. He sensed an intrusion, and rebuffed his visitor in no uncertain way; till Malone withdrew disgusted, and turned to other channels of information.

What Malone would have unearthed could he have worked continuously on the case, we shall never know. As it was, a stupid conflict between city and Federal authority suspended the investigations for several months, during which the detective was busy with other assignments. But at no time did he lose interest, or fail to stand amazed at what began to happen to Robert Suydam. Just at the time when a wave of kidnappings and disappearances spread its excitement over New York, the unkempt scholar embarked upon a metamorphosis as startling as it was absurd. One day he was seen near Borough Hall with clean-shaved face, well-trimmed hair, and tastefully immaculate attire, and on every day thereafter some obscure improvement was noticed in him. He maintained his new fastidiousness without interruption, added to it an unwonted sparkle of eye and crispness of speech, and began little by little to shed the corpulence which had so long deformed him. Now frequently taken for less than his age, he acquired an elasticity of step and buoyancy of demeanour to match the new tradition, and shewed a curious darkening of the hair which somehow did not suggest dye. As the months passed, he commenced to dress less and less conservatively, and finally astonished his new friends by renovating and redecorating his Flatbush mansion, which he threw open in a series of receptions, summoning all the acquaintances he could remember, and extending a special welcome to the fully forgiven relatives who had so lately sought his restraint. Some attended through curiosity, others through duty; but all were suddenly charmed by the dawning grace and urbanity of the former hermit. He had, he asserted, accomplished most of his allotted work; and having just inherited some property from a half-forgotten European friend, was about to spend his remaining years in a brighter second youth which ease, care, and diet had made possible to him. Less and less was he seen at Red Hook, and more and more did he move in the society to which he was born. Policemen noted a tendency of the gangsters to congregate at the old stone church and dance-hall instead of at the basement flat in Parker Place, though the latter and its recent annexes still overflowed with noxious life.

Then two incidents occurred — wide enough apart, but both of intense interest in the case as Malone envisaged it. One was a quiet announcement in the *Eagle* of Robert Suydam's engagement to Miss Cornelia Gerritsen of Bayside, a young woman of excellent position, and distantly related to the elderly bridegroom-elect; whilst the other was a raid on the dance-hall church by city police, after a report that the face of a kidnapped child had been seen for a second at one of the basement windows. Malone had participated in this raid, and studied the place with much care when inside. Nothing was found — in fact, the building was entirely deserted when visited — but the sensitive Celt was vaguely disturbed by many things about the interior. There were crudely painted panels he did not like — panels which depicted sacred faces with peculiarly worldly and sardonic expressions, and which occasionally took liberties that even a layman's sense of decorum could scarcely countenance. Then, too, he did not relish the Greek inscription on the wall above the pulpit; an ancient incantation which he had once stumbled upon in Dublin college days, and which read, literally translated,

> *O friend and companion of night, thou who rejoicest in the baying of dogs and spilt blood, who wanderest in the midst of shades among the tombs, who longest for blood and bringest terror to mortals, Gorgo, Mormo, thousand-faced moon, look favourably on our sacrifices!*

When he read this he shuddered, and thought vaguely of the cracked bass organ notes he fancied he had heard beneath the church on certain nights. He shuddered again at the rust around the rim of a metal basin which stood on the altar, and paused nervously when his nostrils seemed to detect a curious and ghastly stench from somewhere in the neighbourhood. That organ memory haunted him, and he explored the basement with particular assiduity before he left. The place was very hateful to him; yet after all, were the blasphemous panels and inscriptions more than mere crudities perpetrated by the ignorant?

By the time of Suydam's wedding the kidnapping epidemic had become a popular newspaper scandal. Most of the victims were young children of the lowest classes, but the increasing number of disappearances had worked up a sentiment of the strongest fury. Journals clamoured for action from the police, and once more the Butler Street station sent its men over Red Hook for clues, discoveries, and criminals. Malone was glad to be on the trail again, and took pride in a raid on one of Suydam's Parker Place houses. There, indeed, no stolen child was found, despite the tales of screams and the red sash picked up in the areaway; but the paintings and rough inscriptions on the peeling walls of most of the rooms, and the primitive chemical laboratory in the attic, all helped to convince the detective that he was on the track of something tremendous. The paintings were appalling—hideous monsters of every shape and size, and parodies on human outlines which cannot be described. The writing was in red, and varied from Arabic to Greek, Roman, and Hebrew letters. Malone could not read much of it, but what he did decipher was portentous and cabbalistic enough. One frequently repeated motto was in a sort of Hebraised Hellenistic Greek, and suggested the most terrible daemon-evocations of the Alexandrian decadence:

> *HEL · HELOYM · SOTHER · EMMANVEL · SABAOTH · AGLA · TETRAGRAMMATON · AGYROS · OTHEOS · ISCHYROS · ATHANATOS · IEHOVA · VA · ADONAI · SADAY · HOMOVSION · MESSIAS · ESCHEREHEYE.*

Circles and pentagrams loomed on every hand, and told indubitably of the strange beliefs and aspirations of those who dwelt so squalidly here. In the cellar, however, the strangest thing was found—a pile of genuine gold ingots covered carelessly with a piece of burlap, and bearing upon their shining surfaces the same weird hieroglyphics which also adorned the walls. During the raid the police encountered only a passive resistance from the squinting Orientals that swarmed from every door. Finding nothing relevant, they had to leave all as it was; but the precinct captain wrote Suydam a note advising him to look closely to the character of his tenants and protégés in view of the growing public clamour.

V.

Then came the June wedding and the great sensation. Flatbush was gay for the hour about high noon, and pennanted motors thronged the streets near the old Dutch church where an awning stretched from door to highway. No local event ever surpassed the Suydam-Gerritsen nuptials in tone and scale, and the party which escorted bride and groom to the Cunard Pier was, if not exactly the smartest, at least a solid page from the Social Register. At five o'clock adieux were waved, and the ponderous liner edged away from the long pier, slowly turned its nose seaward, discarded its tug, and headed for the widening water spaces that led to old world wonders. By night the outer harbour was cleared, and late passengers watched the stars twinkling above an unpolluted ocean.

Whether the tramp steamer or the scream was first to gain attention, no one can say. Probably they were simultaneous, but it is of no use to calculate. The scream came from the Suydam stateroom, and the sailor who broke down the door could perhaps have told frightful things if he had not forthwith gone completely mad—as it is, he shrieked more loudly than the first victims, and thereafter ran simpering about the vessel till caught and put in irons.

The ship's doctor who entered the stateroom and turned on the lights a moment later did not go mad, but told nobody what he saw till afterward, when he corresponded with Malone in Chepachet. It was murder—strangulation—but one need not say that the claw-mark on Mrs. Suydam's throat could not have come from her husband's or any other human hand, or that upon the white wall there flickered for an instant in hateful red a legend which, later copied from memory, seems to have been nothing less than the fearsome Chaldee letters of the word "LILITH." One need not mention these things because they vanished so quickly—as for Suydam, one could at least bar others from the room until one knew what to think oneself. The doctor has distinctly assured Malone that he did not see IT. The open porthole, just before he turned on the lights, was clouded for a second with a certain phosphorescence, and for a moment there seemed to echo in the night outside the suggestion of a faint and hellish tittering; but no real outline met the eye. As proof, the doctor points to his continued sanity.

Then the tramp steamer claimed all attention. A boat put off, and a horde of swart, insolent ruffians in officers' dress swarmed aboard the temporarily halted Cunarder. They wanted Suydam or his body—they had known of his trip, and for certain reasons were sure he would die. The captain's deck was almost a pandemonium; for at the instant, between the doctor's report from the stateroom and the demands of the men from the tramp, not even the wisest and gravest seaman could think what to do. Suddenly the leader of the visiting mariners, an Arab with a hatefully negroid mouth, pulled forth a dirty, crumpled paper and handed it to the captain. It was signed by Robert Suydam, and bore the following odd message.

> *In case of sudden or unexplained accident or death on my part, please deliver me or my body unquestioningly into the hands of the bearer and his associates. Everything, for me, and perhaps for you, depends on absolute compliance. Explanations can come later — do not fail me now.*
>
> — ROBERT SUYDAM.

Captain and doctor looked at each other, and the latter whispered something to the former. Finally they nodded rather helplessly and led the way to the Suydam stateroom. The doctor directed the captain's glance away as he unlocked the door and admitted the strange seamen, nor did he breathe easily till they filed out with their burden after an unaccountably long period of preparation. It was wrapped in bedding from the berths, and the doctor was glad that the outlines were not very revealing. Somehow the men got the thing over the side and away to their tramp steamer without uncovering it. The Cunarder started again, and the doctor and a ship's undertaker sought out the Suydam stateroom to perform what last services they could. Once more the physician was forced to reticence and even to mendacity, for a hellish thing had happened. When the undertaker asked him why he had drained off all of Mrs. Suydam's blood, he neglected to affirm that he had not done so; nor did he point to the vacant bottle-spaces on the rack, or to the odour in the sink which shewed the hasty disposition of the bottles' original contents. The pockets of those men — if men they were — had bulged damnably when they left the ship. Two hours later, and the world knew by radio all that it ought to know of the horrible affair.

VI.

That same June evening, without having heard a word from the sea, Malone was desperately busy among the alleys of Red Hook. A sudden stir seemed to permeate the place, and as if apprised by "grapevine telegraph" of something singular, the denizens clustered expectantly around the dance-hall church and the houses in Parker Place. Three children had just disappeared — blue-eyed Norwegians from the streets toward Gowanus — and there were rumours of a mob forming among the sturdy Vikings of that section. Malone had for weeks been urging his colleagues to attempt a general cleanup; and at last, moved by conditions more obvious to their common sense than the conjectures of a Dublin dreamer, they had agreed upon a final stroke. The unrest and menace of this evening had been the deciding factor, and just about midnight a raiding party recruited from three stations descended upon Parker Place and its environs. Doors were battered in, stragglers arrested, and candlelighted rooms forced to disgorge unbelievable throngs of mixed foreigners in figured robes, mitres, and other inexplicable devices. Much was lost in the melee, for objects were thrown hastily down unexpected shafts, and betraying odours deadened by the sudden kindling of pungent incense. But spattered blood was everywhere, and Malone shuddered whenever he saw a brazier or altar from which the smoke was still rising.

He wanted to be in several places at once, and decided on Suydam's basement flat only after a messenger had reported the complete emptiness of the dilapidated dance-hall church. The flat, he thought, must hold some clue to a cult of which the occult scholar had so obviously become the centre and leader; and it was with real expectancy that he ransacked the musty rooms, noted their vaguely charnel odour, and examined the curious books, instruments, gold ingots, and glass-stoppered bottles scattered carelessly here and there. Once a lean, black-and-white cat edged between his feet and tripped him, overturning at the same time a beaker half full of a red liquid. The shock was severe, and to this day Malone is not certain of what he saw; but in dreams he still pictures that cat as it scuttled away with certain monstrous alterations and peculiarities. Then came the locked cellar door, and the search for something to break it down. A heavy stool stood near, and its tough seat was more than enough for the antique panels. A crack formed and enlarged, and the whole door gave way — but from the other side; whence poured a howling tumult of ice-cold wind with all the stenches of the bottomless pit, and whence reached a sucking force not of earth or heaven, which, coiling sentiently about the paralysed detective, dragged him through the aperture and down unmeasured spaces filled with whispers and wails, and gusts of mocking laughter.

Of course it was a dream. All the specialists have told him so, and he has nothing to prove the contrary. Indeed, he would rather have it thus; for then the sight of old brick slums and dark foreign faces would not eat so deeply into his soul. But at the time it was all horribly real, and nothing can ever efface the memory of those nighted crypts, those titan arcades, and those half-formed shapes of hell that strode gigantically in silence holding half-eaten things whose still surviving portions screamed for mercy or laughed with madness. Odours of incense and corruption joined in sickening concert, and the black air was alive with the cloudy, semi-visible bulk of shapeless elemental things with eyes. Somewhere dark sticky water was lapping at onyx piers, and once the shivery tinkle of raucous little bells pealed out to greet the insane titter of a naked phosphorescent thing which swam into sight, scrambled ashore, and climbed up to squat leeringly on a carved golden pedestal in the background.

Avenues of limitless night seemed to radiate in every direction, till one might fancy that here lay the root of a contagion destined to sicken and swallow cities, and engulf nations in the foetor of hybrid pestilence. Here cosmic sin had entered, and festered by unhallowed rites had commenced the grinning march of death that was to rot us all to fungous abnormalities too hideous for the grave's holding. Satan here held his Babylonish court, and in the blood of stainless childhood the leprous limbs of phosphorescent Lilith were laved. Incubi and succubae howled praise to Hecate, and headless moon-calves bleated to the Magna Mater. Goats leaped to the sound of thin accursed flutes, and Ægypans chased endlessly after misshapen fauns over rocks twisted like swollen toads. Moloch and Ashtaroth were not absent; for in this quintessence of all damnation the bounds of consciousness were let down, and man's fancy lay open to vistas of every realm of horror and every forbidden dimension that evil had power to mould. The world and Nature were helpless against such assaults from unsealed wells of night, nor could any sign or prayer check the Walpurgis-riot of horror which had come when a sage with the hateful key had stumbled on a horde with the locked and brimming coffer of transmitted daemon-lore.

Suddenly a ray of physical light shot through these phantasms, and Malone heard the sound of oars amidst the blasphemies of things that should be dead. A boat with a lantern in its prow darted into sight, made fast to an iron ring in the slimy stone pier, and vomited forth several dark men bearing a long burden swathed in bedding. They took it to the naked phosphorescent thing on the carved golden pedestal, and the thing tittered and pawed at the bedding. Then they unswathed it, and propped upright before the pedestal the gangrenous corpse of a corpulent old man with stubbly beard and unkempt white hair. The phosphorescent thing tittered again, and the men produced bottles from their pockets and anointed its feet with red, whilst they afterward gave the bottles to the thing to drink from.

All at once, from an arcaded avenue leading endlessly away, there came the daemoniac rattle and wheeze of a blasphemous organ, choking and rumbling out the mockeries of hell in a cracked, sardonic bass. In an instant every moving entity was electrified; and forming at once into a ceremonial procession, the nightmare horde slithered away in quest of the sound — goat, satyr, and Ægypan, incubus, succuba and lemur, twisted toad and shapeless elemental, dog-faced howler and silent strutter in darkness — all led by the abominable naked phosphorescent thing that had squatted on the carved golden throne, and that now strode insolently bearing in its arms the glassy-eyed corpse of the corpulent old man. The strange dark men danced in the rear, and the whole column skipped and leaped with Dionysiac fury. Malone staggered after them a few steps, delirious and hazy, and doubtful of his place in this or in any world. Then he turned, faltered, and sank down on the cold damp stone, gasping and shivering as the daemon organ croaked on, and the howling and drumming and tinkling of the mad procession grew fainter and fainter.

Vaguely he was conscious of chanted horrors and shocking croakings afar off. Now and then a wail or whine of ceremonial devotion would float to him through the black arcade, whilst eventually there rose the dreadful Greek incantation whose text he had read above the pulpit of that dance-hall church.

"O friend and companion of night, thou who rejoicest in the baying of dogs (here a hideous howl burst forth) and spilt blood (here nameless sounds vied with morbid shriekings) who wanderest in the midst of shades among the tombs, (here a whistling sigh occurred) who longest for blood and bringest terror to mortals, (short, sharp cries from myriad throats) Gorgo, (repeated as response) Mormo, (repeated with ecstasy) thousand-faced moon, (sighs and flute notes) look favourably on our sacrifices!"

As the chant closed, a general shout went up, and hissing sounds nearly drowned the croaking of the cracked bass organ. Then a gasp as from many throats, and a babel of barked and bleated words — "Lilith, Great Lilith, behold the Bridegroom!" More cries, a clamour of rioting, and the sharp, clicking footfalls of a running figure. The footfalls approached, and Malone raised himself to his elbow to look.

The luminosity of the crypt, lately diminished, had now slightly increased; and in that devil-light there appeared the fleeing form of that which should not flee or feel or breathe — the glassy-eyed, gangrenous corpse of the corpulent old man, now needing no support, but animated by some infernal sorcery of the rite just closed. After it raced the naked, tittering, phosphorescent thing that belonged on the carven pedestal, and still farther behind panted the dark men, and all the dread crew of sentient loathsomenesses. The corpse was gaining on its pursuers, and seemed bent on a definite object, straining with every rotting muscle toward the carved golden pedestal, whose necromantic importance was evidently so great. Another moment and it had reached its goal, whilst the trailing throng laboured on with more frantic speed. But they were too late, for in one final spurt of strength which ripped tendon from tendon and sent its noisome bulk floundering to the floor in a state of jellyish dissolution, the staring corpse which had been Robert Suydam achieved its object and its triumph. The push had been tremendous, but the force had held out; and as the pusher collapsed to a muddy blotch of corruption the pedestal he had pushed tottered, tipped, and finally careened from its onyx base into the thick waters below, sending up a parting gleam of carven gold as it sank heavily to undreamable gulfs of lower Tartarus. In that instant, too, the whole scene of horror faded to nothingness before Malone's eyes; and he fainted amidst a thunderous crash which seemed to blot out all the evil universe.

VII.

Malone's dream, experienced in full before he knew of Suydam's death and transfer at sea, was curiously supplemented by some odd realities of the case; though that is no reason why anyone should believe it.

The three old houses in Parker Place, doubtless long rotten with decay in its most insidious form, collapsed without visible cause while half the raiders and most of the prisoners were inside; and of both the greater number were instantly killed. Only in the basements and cellars was there much saving of life, and Malone was lucky to have been deep below the house of Robert Suydam. For he really was there, as no one is disposed to deny. They found him unconscious by the edge of a night-black pool, with a grotesquely horrible jumble of decay and bone, identifiable through dental work as the body of Suydam, a few feet away. The case was plain, for it was hither that the smugglers' underground canal led; and the men who took Suydam from the ship had brought him home. They themselves were never found, or at least never identified; and the ship's doctor is not yet satisfied with the simple certitudes of the police.

Suydam was evidently a leader in extensive man-smuggling operations, for the canal to his house was but one of several subterranean channels and tunnels in the neighbourhood. There was a tunnel from this house to a crypt beneath the dance-hall church; a crypt accessible from the church only through a narrow secret passage in the north wall, and in whose chambers some singular and terrible things were discovered. The croaking organ was there, as well as a vast arched chapel with wooden benches and a strangely figured altar. The walls were lined with small cells, in seventeen of which — hideous to relate — solitary prisoners in a state of complete idiocy were found chained, including four mothers with infants of disturbingly strange appearance. These infants died soon after exposure to the light; a circumstance which the doctors thought rather merciful. Nobody but Malone, among those who inspected them, remembered the sombre question of old Delrio: *"An sint unquam daemones incubi et succubae, et an ex tali congressu proles nasci queat?"*

Before the canals were filled up they were thoroughly dredged, and yielded forth a sensational array of sawed and split bones of all sizes. The kidnapping epidemic, very clearly, had been traced home; though only two of the surviving prisoners could by any legal thread be connected with it. These men are now in prison, since they failed of conviction as accessories in the actual murders. The carved golden pedestal or throne so often mentioned by Malone as of primary occult importance was never brought to light, though at one place under the Suydam house the canal was observed to sink into a well too deep for dredging. It was choked up at the mouth and cemented over when the cellars of the new houses were made, but Malone often speculates on what lies beneath. The police, satisfied that they had shattered a dangerous gang of maniacs and man-smugglers, turned over to the Federal authorities the unconvicted Kurds, who before their deportation were conclusively found to belong to the Yezidi clan of devil-worshippers. The tramp ship and its crew remain an elusive mystery, though cynical detectives are once more ready to combat its smuggling and rum-running ventures. Malone thinks these detectives shew a sadly limited perspective in their lack of wonder at the myriad unexplainable details, and the suggestive obscurity of the whole case; though he is just as critical of the newspapers, which saw only a morbid sensation and gloated over a minor sadist cult which they might have proclaimed a horror from the universe's very heart. But he is content to rest silent in Chepachet, calming his nervous system and praying that time may gradually transfer his terrible experience from the realm of present reality to that of picturesque and semi-mythical remoteness.

Robert Suydam sleeps beside his bride in Greenwood Cemetery. No funeral was held over the strangely released bones, and relatives are grateful for the swift oblivion which overtook the case as a whole. The scholar's connexion with the Red Hook horrors, indeed, was never emblazoned by legal proof; since his death forestalled the inquiry he would otherwise have faced. His own end is not much mentioned, and the Suydams hope that posterity may recall him only as a gentle recluse who dabbled in harmless magic and folklore.

As for Red Hook — it is always the same. Suydam came and went; a terror gathered and faded; but the evil spirit of darkness and squalor broods on amongst the mongrels in the old brick houses, and prowling bands still parade on unknown errands past windows where lights and twisted faces unaccountably appear and disappear. Age-old horror is a hydra with a thousand heads, and the cults of darkness are rooted in blasphemies deeper than the well of Democritus. The soul of the beast is omnipresent and triumphant, and Red Hook's legions of blear-eyed, pockmarked youths still chant and curse and howl as they file from abyss to abyss, none knows whence or whither, pushed on by blind laws of biology which they may never understand. As of old, more people enter Red Hook than leave it on the landward side, and there are already rumours of new canals running underground to certain centres of traffic in liquor and less mentionable things.

The dance-hall church is now mostly a dance-hall, and queer faces have appeared at night at the windows. Lately a policeman expressed the belief that the filled-up crypt has been dug out again, and for no simply explainable purpose. Who are we to combat poisons older than history and mankind? Apes danced in Asia to those horrors, and the cancer lurks secure and spreading where furtiveness hides in rows of decaying brick.

Malone does not shudder without cause — for only the other day an officer overheard a swarthy squinting hag teaching a small child some whispered patois in the shadow of an areaway. He listened, and thought it very strange when he heard her repeat over and over again,

"O friend and companion of night, thou who rejoicest in the baying of dogs and spilt blood, who wanderest in the midst of shades among the tombs, who longest for blood and bringest terror to mortals, Gorgo, Mormo, thousand-faced moon, look favourably on our sacrifices!"

He.

4,300-WORD SHORT STORY; 1925.

This short story was dashed off in a cheap notebook that Lovecraft bought while out on a walk through Greenwich Village. It seems highly likely that it was intended as a distillation of Lovecraft's ongoing distress at being stuck in New York; taken in sequence with "The Horror at Red Hook," it is as if the writer is going through the stages of grief, from anger to despair.

The story was written a week after "Red Hook," on Aug. 11, 1925; it was published in the September 1926 issue of Weird Tales.

I saw him on a sleepless night when I was walking desperately to save my soul and my vision. My coming to New York had been a mistake; for whereas I had looked for poignant wonder and inspiration in the teeming labyrinths of ancient streets that twist endlessly from forgotten courts and squares and waterfronts to courts and squares and waterfronts equally forgotten, and in the Cyclopean modern towers and pinnacles that rise blackly Babylonian under waning moons, I had found instead only a sense of horror and oppression which threatened to master, paralyze, and annihilate me.

The disillusion had been gradual. Coming for the first time upon the town, I had seen it in the sunset from a bridge, majestic above its waters, its incredible peaks and pyramids rising flowerlike and delicate from pools of violet mist to play with the flaming clouds and the first stars of evening. Then it had lighted up window by window above the shimmering tides where lanterns nodded and glided and deep horns bayed weird harmonies, and had itself become a starry firmament of dream, redolent of faery music, and one with the marvels of Carcassonne and Samarcand and El Dorado and all glorious and half-fabulous cities. Shortly afterward I was taken through those antique ways so dear to my fancy — narrow, curving alleys and passages where rows of red Georgian brick blinked with small-paned dormers above pillared doorways that had looked on gilded sedans and paneled coaches — and in the first flush of realization of these long-wished things I thought I had indeed achieved such treasures as would make me in time a poet.

But success and happiness were not to be. Garish daylight showed only squalor and alienage and the noxious elephantiasis of climbing, spreading stone where the moon had hinted of loveliness and elder magic; and the throngs of people that seethed through the flume-like streets were squat, swarthy strangers with hardened faces and narrow eyes, shrewd strangers without dreams and without kinship to the scenes about them, who could never mean aught to a blue-eyed man of the old folk, with the love of fair green lanes and white New England village steeples in his heart.

So instead of the poems I had hoped for, there came only a shuddering blackness and ineffable loneliness; and I saw at last a fearful truth which no one had ever dared to breathe before — the unwhisperable secret of secrets — the fact that this city of stone and stridor is not a sentient perpetuation of Old New York as London is of Old London and Paris of Old Paris, but that it is in fact quite dead, its sprawling body imperfectly embalmed and infested with queer animate things which have nothing to do with it as it was in life. Upon making this discovery I ceased to sleep comfortably; though something of resigned tranquillity came back as I gradually formed the habit of keeping off the streets by day and venturing abroad only at night, when darkness calls forth what little of the past still hovers wraith-like about, and old white doorways remember the stalwart forms that once passed through them. With this mode of relief I even wrote a few poems, and still refrained from going home to my people lest I seem to crawl back ignobly in defeat.

Then, on a sleepless night's walk, I met the man. It was in a grotesque hidden courtyard of the Greenwich section, for there in my ignorance I had settled, having heard of the place as the natural home of poets and artists. The archaic lanes and houses and unexpected bits of square and court had indeed delighted me, and when I found the poets and artists to be loud-voiced pretenders whose quaintness is tinsel and whose lives are a denial of all that pure beauty which is poetry and art, I stayed on for love of these venerable things. I fancied them as they were in their prime, when Greenwich was a placid village not yet engulfed by the town; and in the hours before dawn, when all the revellers had slunk away, I used to wander alone among their cryptical windings and brood upon the curious arcana which generations must have deposited there. This kept my soul alive, and gave me a few of those dreams and visions for which the poet far within me cried out.

The man came upon me at about two one cloudy August morning, as I was threading a series of detached courtyards; now accessible only through the unlighted hallways of intervening buildings, but once forming parts of a continuous network of picturesque alleys. I had heard of them by vague rumor, and realized that they could not be upon any map of today; but the fact that they were forgotten only endeared them to me, so that I had sought them with twice my usual eagerness.

Now that I had found them, my eagerness was again redoubled; for something in their arrangement dimly hinted that they might be only a few of many such, with dark, dumb counterparts wedged obscurely betwixt high blank walls and deserted rear tenements, or lurking lamplessly behind archways unbetrayed by hordes of the foreign-speaking or guarded by furtive and uncommunicative artists whose practises do not invite publicity or the light of day.

He spoke to me without invitation, noting my mood and glances as I studied certain knockered doorways above iron-railed steps, the pallid glow of traceried transoms feebly lighting my face. His own face was in shadow, and he wore a wide-brimmed hat which somehow blended perfectly with the out-of-date cloak he affected; but I was subtly disquieted even before he addressed me. His form was very slight; thin almost to cadaverousness; and his voice proved phenomenally soft and hollow, though not particularly deep. He had, he said, noticed me several times at my wanderings; and inferred that I resembled him in loving the vestiges of former years. Would I not like the guidance of one long practiced in these explorations, and possessed of local information profoundly deeper than any which an obvious newcomer could possibly have gained?

As he spoke, I caught a glimpse of his face in the yellow beam from a solitary attic window. It was a noble, even a handsome elderly countenance; and bore the marks of a lineage and refinement unusual for the age and place. Yet some quality about it disturbed me almost as much as its features pleased me perhaps it was too white, or too expressionless, or too much out of keeping with the locality, to make me feel easy or comfortable. Nevertheless I followed him; for in those dreary days my quest for antique beauty and mystery was all that I had to keep my soul alive, and I reckoned it a rare favor of Fate to fall in with one whose kindred seekings seemed to have penetrated so much farther than mine.

Something in the night constrained the cloaked man to silence and for a long hour he led me forward without needless words; making only the briefest of comments concerning ancient names and dates and changes, and directing my progress very largely by gestures as we squeezed through interstices, tiptoed through corridors, clambered over brick walls, and once crawled on hands and knees through a low, arched passage of stone whose immense length and tortuous twistings effaced at last every hint of geographical location I had managed to preserve. The things we saw were very old and marvelous, or at least they seemed so in the few straggling rays of light by which I viewed them, and I shall never forget the tottering Ionic columns and fluted pilasters and urn-headed iron fenceposts and flaring-linteled windows and decorative fanlights that appeared to grow quainter and stranger the deeper we advanced into this inexhaustible maze of unknown antiquity.

We met no person, and as time passed the lighted windows became fewer and fewer. The streetlights we first encountered had been of oil, and of the ancient lozenge pattern. Later I noticed some with candles; and at last, after traversing a horrible unlighted court where my guide had to lead with his gloved hand through total blackness to a narrow wooded gate in a high wall, we came upon a fragment of alley lit only by lanterns in front of every seventh house—unbelievably Colonial tin lanterns with conical tops and holes punched in the sides. This alley led steeply uphill—more steeply than I thought possible in this part of New York—and the upper end was blocked squarely by the ivy-clad wall of a private estate, beyond which I could see a pale cupola, and the tops of trees waving against a vague lightness in the sky. In this wall was a small, low-arched gate of nail-studded black oak, which the man proceeded to unlock with a ponderous key. Leading me within, he steered a course in utter blackness over what seemed to be a gravel path, and finally up a flight of stone steps to the door of the house, which he unlocked and opened for me.

We entered, and as we did so I grew faint from a reek of infinite mustiness which welled out to meet us, and which must have been the fruit of unwholesome centuries of decay. My host appeared not to notice this, and in courtesy I kept silent as he piloted me up a curving stairway, across a hall, and into a room whose door I heard him lock behind us. Then I saw him pull the curtains of the three small-paned windows that barely showed themselves against the lightening sky; after which he crossed to the mantel, struck flint and steel, lighted two candles of a candelabrum of twelve sconces, and made a gesture enjoining soft-toned speech.

In this feeble radiance I saw that we were in a spacious, well-furnished and paneled library dating from the first quarter of the Eighteenth Century, with splendid doorway pediments, a delightful Doric cornice, and a magnificently carved overmantel with scroll-and-urn top. Above the crowded bookshelves at intervals along the walls were well-wrought family portraits; all tarnished to an enigmatical dimness, and bearing an unmistakable likeness to the man who now motioned me to a chair beside the graceful Chippendale table. Before seating himself across the table from me, my host paused for a moment as if in embarrassment; then, tardily removing his gloves, wide-brimmed hat, and cloak, stood theatrically revealed in full mid-Georgian costume from queued hair and neck ruffles to knee-breeches, silk hose, and the buckled shoes I had not previously noticed. Now slowly sinking into a lyre-back chair, he commenced to eye me intently.

Without his hat he took on an aspect of extreme age which was scarcely visible before, and I wondered if this unperceived mark of singular longevity were not one of the sources of my disquiet. When he spoke at length, his soft, hollow, and carefully muffled voice not infrequently quavered; and now and then I had great difficulty in following him as I listened with a thrill of amazement and half-disavowed alarm which grew each instant.

"You behold, Sir," my host began, "a man of very eccentrical habits for whose costume no apology need be offered to one with your wit and inclinations. Reflecting upon better times, I have not scrupled to ascertain their ways, and adopt their dress

Weird Tales, September 1926

"The old man clawed and spat at me through the mouldy air, and barked things in his throat as he swayed with the yellow curtain he clutched."

and manners; an indulgence which offends none if practised without ostentation. It hath been my good fortune to retain the rural seat of my ancestors, swallowed though it was by two towns, first Greenwich, which built up hither after 1800, then New York, which joined on near 1830. There were many reasons for the close keeping of this place in my family, and I have not been remiss in discharging such obligations. The squire who succeeded to it in 1768 studied sartain arts and made sartain discoveries, all connected with influences residing in this particular plot of ground, and eminently desarving of the strongest guarding. Some curious effects of these arts and discoveries I now purpose to show you, under the strictest secrecy; and I believe I may rely on my judgement of men enough to have no distrust of either your interest or your fidelity."

He paused, but I could only nod my head. I have said that I was alarmed, yet to my soul nothing was more deadly than the material daylight world of New York, and whether this man were a harmless eccentric or a wielder of dangerous arts, I had no choice save to follow him and slake my sense of wonder on whatever he might have to offer. So I listened.

"To — my ancestor," he softly continued, "there appeared to reside some very remarkable qualities in the will of mankind; qualities having a little-suspected dominance not only over the acts of one's self and of others, but over every variety of force and substance in Nature, and over many elements and dimensions deemed more universal than Nature herself. May I say that he flouted the sanctity of things as great as space and time and that he put to strange uses the rites of sartain half-breed red Indians once encamped upon this hill? These Indians showed choler when the place was built, and were plaguey pestilent in asking to visit the grounds at the full of the moon. For years they stole over the wall each month when they could, and by stealth performed sartain acts. Then, in '68, the new squire catched them at their doings, and stood still at what he saw. Thereafter he bargained with them and exchanged the free access of his grounds for the exact inwardness of what they did, larning that their grandfathers got part of their custom from red ancestors and part from an old Dutchman in the time of the States-General. And pox on him, I'm afeared the squire must have sarved them monstrous bad rum — whether or not by intent — for a week after he larnt the secret he was the only man living that knew it. You, Sir, are the first outsider to be told there is a secret, and split me if I'd have risked tampering that much with — the powers — had ye not been so hot after bygone things."

I shuddered as the man grew colloquial — and with the familiar speech of another day. He went on.

"But you must know, Sir, that what — the squire — got

from those mongrel savages was but a small part of the larning he came to have. He had not been at Oxford for nothing, nor talked to no account with an ancient chymist and astrologer in Paris. He was, in fine, made sensible that all the world is but the smoke of our intellects; past the bidding of the vulgar, but by the wise to be puffed out and drawn in like any cloud of prime Virginia tobacco. What we want, we may make about us; and what we don't want, we may sweep away. I won't say that all this is wholly true in body, but 'tis sufficient true to furnish a very pretty spectacle now and then. You, I conceive, would be tickled by a better sight of sartain other years than your fancy affords you; so be pleased to hold back any fright at what I design to show. Come to the window and be quiet."

My host now took my hand to draw me to one of the two windows on the long side of the malodorous room, and at the first touch of his ungloved fingers I turned cold. His flesh, though dry and firm, was of the quality of ice; and I almost shrank away from his pulling. But again I thought of the emptiness and horror of reality, and boldly prepared to follow whithersoever I might be led.

Once at the window, the man drew apart the yellow silk curtains and directed my stare into the blackness outside. For a moment I saw nothing save a myriad of tiny dancing lights, far, far before me. Then, as if in response to an insidious motion of my host's hand, a flash of heat-lightning played over the scene, and I looked out upon a sea of luxuriant foliage — foliage unpolluted, and not the sea of roofs to be expected by any normal mind. On my right the Hudson glittered wickedly, and in the distance ahead I saw the unhealthy shimmer of a vast salt marsh constellated with nervous fireflies. The flash died, and an evil smile illumined the waxy face of the aged necromancer.

"That was before my time — before the new squire's time. Pray let us try again."

I was faint, even fainter than the hateful modernity of that accursed city had made me.

"Good God!" I whispered, "can you do that for any time?" And as he nodded, and bared the black stumps of what had once been yellow fangs, I clutched at the curtains to prevent myself from falling. But he steadied me with that terrible, ice-cold claw, and once more made his insidious gesture.

Again the lightning flashed — but this time upon a scene not wholly strange. It was Greenwich, the Greenwich that used to be, with here and there a roof or row of houses as we see it now, yet with lovely green lanes and fields and bits of grassy common. The marsh still glittered beyond, but in the farther distance I saw the steeples of what was then all of New York; Trinity and St. Paul's and the Brick Church dominating their sisters, and a faint haze of wood smoke hovering over the whole. I breathed hard, but not so much from the sight itself as from the possibilities my imagination terrifiedly conjured up.

"Can you — dare you — go far?" I spoke with awe and I think he shared it for a second, but the evil grin returned.

"Far? What I have seen would blast ye to a mad statue of stone! Back, back — forward, forward — look, ye puling lackwit!"

And as he snarled the phrase under his breath he gestured anew bringing to the sky a flash more blinding than either which had come before. For full three seconds I could glimpse that pandemoniac sight, and in those seconds I saw a vista which will ever afterward torment me in dreams. I saw the heavens verminous with strange flying things, and beneath them a hellish black city of giant stone terraces with impious pyramids flung savagely to the moon, and devil-lights burning from unnumbered windows. And swarming loathsomely on aerial galleries I saw the yellow, squint-eyed people of that city, robed horribly in orange and red, and dancing insanely to the pounding of fevered kettle-drums, the clatter of obscene crotala, and the maniacal moaning of muted horns whose ceaseless dirges rose and fell undulantly like the wave of an unhallowed ocean of bitumen.

I saw this vista, I say, and heard as with the mind's ear the blasphemous domdaniel of cacophony which companioned it. It was the shrieking fulfilment of all the horror which that corpse-city had ever stirred in my soul, and forgetting every injunction to silence I screamed and screamed and screamed as my nerves gave way and the walls quivered about me.

Then, as the flash subsided, I saw that my host was trembling too; a look of shocking fear half-blotting from his face the serpent distortion of rage which my screams had excited. He tottered, clutched at the curtains as I had done before, and wriggled his head wildly, like a hunted animal. God knows he had cause, for as the echoes of my screaming died away there came another sound so hellishly suggestive that only numbed emotion kept me sane and conscious. It was the steady, stealthy creaking of the stairs beyond the locked door, as with the ascent of a barefoot or skin-shod horde; and at last the cautious, purposeful rattling of the brass latch that glowed in the feeble candlelight. The old man clawed and spat at me through the moldy air, and barked things in his throat as he swayed with the yellow curtain he clutched.

"The full moon — damn ye — ye . . . ye yelping dog — ye called 'em, and they've come for me! Moccasined feet — dead men — Gad sink ye, ye red devils, but I poisoned no rum o' yours — han't I kept your pox-rotted magic safe — ye swilled yourselves sick, curse ye, and yet must needs blame the squire — let go, you! Unhand that latch — I've naught for ye here — "

At this point three slow and very deliberate raps shook the panels of the door, and a white foam gathered at the mouth of the frantic magician. His fright, turning to steely despair, left room for a resurgence of his rage against me; and he staggered a step toward the table on whose edge I was steadying myself. The curtains, still clutched in his right hand as his left clawed out at me, grew taut and finally crashed down from their lofty fastenings; admitting to the room a flood of that full moonlight which the brightening of the sky had presaged. In those greenish beams the candles paled, and a new semblance of decay spread over the musk-reeking room with its wormy paneling, sagging floor, battered mantel, rickety furniture, and ragged draperies. It spread over the old man, too, whether from the same source or because of his fear and vehemence, and I saw him shrivel and blacken as he lurched near and strove to rend me with vulturine talons. Only his eyes stayed whole, and they glared with a propulsive, dilated incandescence which grew as the face around them charred and dwindled.

The rapping was now repeated with greater insistence, and this time bore a hint of metal. The black thing facing me had become only a head with eyes, impotently trying to wriggle across the sinking floor in my direction, and occasionally emitting feeble little spits of immortal malice. Now swift and splintering blows assailed the sickly panels, and I saw the gleam of a tomahawk as it cleft the rending wood. I did not move, for I could not; but watched dazedly as the door fell in pieces to admit a colossal, shapeless influx of inky substance starred with shining, malevolent eyes. It poured thickly, like a flood of oil bursting a rotten bulkhead, overturned a chair as it spread, and finally flowed under the table and across the room to where the blackened head with the eyes still glared at me. Around that head it closed, totally swallowing it up, and in another moment it had begun to recede; bearing away its invisible burden without touching me, and flowing again out that black doorway and down the unseen stairs, which creaked as before, though in reverse order.

Then the floor gave way at last, and I slid gaspingly down into the nighted chamber below, choking with cobwebs and half-swooning with terror. The green moon, shining through broken windows, showed me the hall door half open; and as I rose from the plaster-strewn floor and twisted myself free from the sagged ceiling, I saw sweep past it an awful torrent of blackness, with scores of baleful eyes glowing in it. It was seeking the door to the cellar, and when it found it, vanished therein. I now felt the floor of this lower room giving as that of the upper chamber had done, and once a crashing above had been followed by the fall past the west window of some thing which must have been the cupola. Now liberated for the instant from the wreckage, I rushed through the hall to the front door and finding myself unable to open it, seized a chair and broke a window, climbing frenziedly out upon the unkempt lawn where moon light danced over yard-high grass and weeds. The wall was high and all the gates were locked but moving a pile of boxes in a corner I managed to gain the top and cling to the great stone urn set there.

About me in my exhaustion I could see only strange walls and windows and old gambrel roofs. The steep street of my approach was nowhere visible, and the little I did see succumbed rapidly to a mist that rolled in from the river despite the glaring moonlight. Suddenly the urn to which I clung began to tremble, as if sharing my own lethal dizziness; and in another instant my body was plunging downward to I knew not what fate.

The man who found me said that I must have crawled a long way despite my broken bones, for a trail of blood stretched off as far as he dared look. The gathering rain soon effaced this link with the scene of my ordeal, and reports could state no more than that I had appeared from a place unknown, at the entrance to a little black court off Perry Street.

I never sought to return to those tenebrous labyrinths, nor would I direct any sane man thither if I could. Of who or what that ancient creature was, I have no idea; but I repeat that the city is dead and full of unsuspected horrors. Whither he has gone, I do not know; but I have gone home to the pure New England lanes up which fragrant sea-winds sweep at evening.

In the Vault.

3,400-WORD SHORT STORY; 1925.

This third and final short story to roll off Lovecraft's pen in 1925 is very different from the other two. It is far from Lovecraft's best work; but it lacks the poison air of depression and hostility that taints "He" and all but ruins "The Horror at Red Hook."

Perhaps that's because Lovecraft was feeling a little bit hopeful once again. He had developed an idea the previous month, which he was mapping out and hoping to develop into a short novel; he was already calling it "The Call of Cthulhu." But before he started into that project in earnest, he dashed off "In the Vault."

"In the Vault" was first published in Charles W. "Tryout" Smith's amateur journal, Tryout, *in the November 1925 issue. This would be the last article Lovecraft would send directly to an amateur journal after writing it; starting in 1926, he was thinking exclusively in terms of professional publication, usually in* Weird Tales.

There is nothing more absurd, as I view it, than that conventional association of the homely and the wholesome which seems to pervade the psychology of the multitude. Mention a bucolic Yankee setting, a bungling and thick-fibred village undertaker, and a careless mishap in a tomb, and no average reader can be brought to expect more than a hearty albeit grotesque phase of comedy. God knows, though, that the prosy tale which George Birch's death permits me to tell has in it aspects beside which some of our darkest tragedies are light.

Birch acquired a limitation and changed his business in 1881, yet never discussed the case when he could avoid it. Neither did his old physician Dr. Davis, who died years ago. It was generally stated that the affliction and shock were results of an unlucky slip whereby Birch had locked himself for nine hours in the receiving tomb of Peck Valley Cemetery, escaping only by crude and disastrous mechanical means; but while this much was undoubtedly true, there were other and blacker things which the man used to whisper to me in his drunken delirium toward the last. He confided in me because I was his doctor, and because he probably felt the need of confiding in someone else after Davis died. He was a bachelor, wholly without relatives.

Birch, before 1881, had been the village undertaker of Peck Valley; and was a very calloused and primitive specimen even as such specimens go. The practices I heard attributed to him would be unbelievable today, at least in a city; and even Peck Valley would have shuddered a bit had it known the easy ethics of its mortuary artist in such debatable matters as the ownership of costly "laying-out" apparel invisible beneath the casket's lid, and the degree of dignity to be maintained in posing and adapting the unseen members of lifeless tenants to containers not always calculated with sublimest accuracy. Most distinctly Birch was lax, insensitive, and professionally undesirable; yet I still think he was not an evil man. He was merely crass of fibre and function — thoughtless, careless, and liquorish, as his easily avoidable accident proves, and without that modicum of imagination which holds the average citizen within certain limits fixed by taste.

Just where to begin Birch's story I can hardly decide, since I am no practiced teller of tales. I suppose one should start in the cold December of 1880, when the ground froze and the cemetery delvers found they could dig no more graves till spring. Fortunately the village was small and the death rate low, so that it was possible to give all of Birch's inanimate charges a temporary haven in the single antiquated receiving tomb. The undertaker grew doubly lethargic in the bitter weather, and seemed to outdo even himself in carelessness. Never did he knock together flimsier and ungainlier caskets, or disregard more flagrantly the needs of the rusty lock on the tomb door which he slammed open and shut with such nonchalant abandon.

At last the spring thaw came, and graves were laboriously prepared for the nine silent harvests of the grim reaper which waited in the tomb. Birch, though dreading the bother of removal and interment, began his task of transference one disagreeable April morning, but ceased before noon because of a heavy rain that seemed to irritate his horse, after having laid but one mortal tenement to its permanent rest. That was Darius Peck, the nonagenarian, whose grave was not far from the tomb. Birch decided that he would begin the next day with little old Matthew Fenner, whose grave was also near by; but actually postponed the matter for three days, not getting to work till Good Friday, the 15th. Being without superstition, he did not heed the day at all; though ever afterward he refused to do anything of importance on that fateful sixth day of the week. Certainly, the events of that evening greatly changed George Birch.

On the afternoon of Friday, April 15th, then, Birch set out for the tomb with horse and wagon to transfer the body of Matthew Fenner. That he was not perfectly sober, he subsequently admitted; though he had not then taken to the wholesale drinking by which he later tried to forget certain things.

Weird Tales, April 1932

"Instinct guided him in his wriggle through the transom."

He was just dizzy and careless enough to annoy his sensitive horse, which as he drew it viciously up at the tomb neighed and pawed and tossed its head, much as on that former occasion when the rain had vexed it. The day was clear, but a high wind had sprung up; and Birch was glad to get to shelter as he unlocked the iron door and entered the side-hill vault. Another might not have relished the damp, odorous chamber with the eight carelessly placed coffins; but Birch in those days was insensitive, and was concerned only in getting the right coffin for the right grave. He had not forgotten the criticism aroused when Hannah Bixby's relatives, wishing to transport her body to the cemetery in the city whither they had moved, found the casket of Judge Capwell beneath her headstone.

The light was dim, but Birch's sight was good, and he did not get Asaph Sawyer's coffin by mistake, although it was very similar. He had, indeed, made that coffin for Matthew Fenner; but had cast it aside at last as too awkward and flimsy, in a fit of curious sentimentality aroused by recalling how kindly and generous the little old man had been to him during his bankruptcy five years before. He gave old Matt the very best his skill could produce, but was thrifty enough to save the rejected specimen, and to use it when Asaph Sawyer died of a malignant fever. Sawyer was not a lovable man, and many stories were told of his almost inhuman vindictiveness and tenacious memory for wrongs real or fancied. To him Birch had felt no compunction in assigning the carelessly made coffin which he now pushed out of the way in his quest for the Fenner casket.

It was just as he had recognised old Matt's coffin that the door slammed to in the wind, leaving him in a dusk even deeper than before. The narrow transom admitted only the feeblest of rays, and the overhead ventilation funnel virtually none at all; so that he was reduced to a profane fumbling as he made his halting way among the long boxes toward the latch. In this funereal twilight he rattled the rusty handles, pushed at the iron panels, and wondered why the massive portal had grown so suddenly recalcitrant. In this twilight too, he began to realise the truth and to shout loudly as if his horse outside could do more than neigh an unsympathetic reply. For the long-neglected latch was obviously broken, leaving the careless undertaker trapped in the vault, a victim of his own oversight.

The thing must have happened at about three-thirty in the afternoon. Birch, being by temperament phlegmatic and practical, did not shout long; but proceeded to grope about for some tools which he recalled seeing in a corner of the tomb. It is doubtful whether he was touched at all by the horror and exquisite weirdness of his position, but the bald fact of imprisonment so far from the daily paths of men was enough to exasperate him thoroughly. His day's work was sadly interrupted, and unless chance presently brought some rambler hither, he might have to remain all night or longer. The pile of tools soon reached, and a hammer and chisel selected, Birch returned over the coffins to the door. The air had begun to be exceedingly unwholesome; but to this detail he paid no attention as he toiled, half by feeling, at the heavy and corroded metal of the latch. He would have given much for a lantern or bit of candle; but lacking these, bungled semi-sightlessly as best he might.

When he perceived that the latch was hopelessly unyielding, at least to such meagre tools and under such tenebrous conditions as these, Birch glanced about for other possible points of escape. The vault had been dug from a hillside, so that the narrow ventilation funnel in the top ran through several feet of earth, making this direction utterly useless to consider. Over the door, however, the high, slit-like transom in the brick facade gave promise of possible enlargement to a diligent worker; hence upon this his eyes long rested as he racked his brains for means to reach it. There was nothing like a ladder in the tomb, and the coffin niches on the sides and rear — which Birch seldom took the trouble to use — afforded no ascent to the space above the door. Only the coffins themselves remained as potential stepping-stones, and as he considered these he speculated on the best mode of transporting them. Three coffin-heights, he reckoned, would permit him to reach the transom; but he could do better with four. The boxes were fairly even, and could be piled up like blocks; so he began to compute how he might most stably use the eight to rear a scalable platform four deep. As he planned, he could not but wish that the units of his contemplated staircase had been more securely made. Whether he had imagination enough to wish they were empty, is strongly to be doubted.

Finally he decided to lay a base of three parallel with the wall, to place upon this two layers of two each, and upon these a single box to serve as the platform. This arrangement could be ascended with a minimum of awkwardness, and would furnish the desired height. Better still, though, he would utilise only two boxes of the base to support the superstructure, leaving one free to be piled on top in case the actual feat of escape required an even greater altitude. And so the prisoner toiled in the twilight, heaving the unresponsive remnants of mortality with little ceremony as his miniature Tower of Babel rose course by course. Several of the coffins began to split under the stress of handling, and he planned to save the stoutly built casket of little Matthew Fenner for the top, in order that his feet might have as certain a surface as possible. In the semi-gloom he trusted mostly to touch to select the right one, and indeed came upon it almost by accident, since it tumbled into his hands as if through some odd volition after he had unwittingly placed it beside another on the third layer.

The tower at length finished, and his aching arms rested by a pause during which he sat on the bottom step of his grim device, Birch cautiously ascended with his tools and stood abreast of the narrow transom. The borders of the space were entirely of brick, and there seemed little doubt but that he could shortly chisel away enough to allow his body to pass. As his hammer blows began to fall, the horse outside whinnied in a tone which may have been encouraging and to others may have been mocking. In either case it would have been appropriate; for the unexpected tenacity of the easy-looking brickwork was surely a sardonic commentary on the vanity of mortal hopes, and the source of a task whose performance deserved every possible stimulus.

Dusk fell and found Birch still toiling. He worked largely by feeling now, since newly gathered clouds hid the moon; and though progress was still slow, he felt heartened at the extent of his encroachments on the top and bottom of the aperture. He could, he was sure, get out by midnight — though it is characteristic of him that this thought was untinged with eerie implications. Undisturbed by oppressive reflections on the time, the place, and the company beneath his feet, he philosophically chipped away the stony brickwork; cursing when a fragment hit him in the face, and laughing when one struck the increasingly excited horse that pawed near the cypress tree. In time the hole grew so large that he ventured to try his body in it now and then, shifting about so that the coffins beneath him rocked and creaked. He would not, he found, have to pile another on his platform to make the proper height; for the hole was on exactly the right level to use as soon as its size might permit.

It must have been midnight at least when Birch decided he could get through the transom. Tired and perspiring despite many rests, he descended to the floor and sat a while on the bottom box to gather strength for the final wriggle and leap to the ground outside. The hungry horse was neighing repeatedly and almost uncannily, and he vaguely wished it would stop. He was curiously unelated over his impending escape, and almost dreaded the exertion, for his form had the indolent stoutness of early middle age. As he remounted the splitting coffins he felt his weight very poignantly; especially when, upon reaching the topmost one, he heard that aggravated crackle which bespeaks the wholesale rending of wood. He had, it seems, planned in vain when choosing the stoutest coffin for the platform; for no sooner was his full bulk again upon it than the rotting lid gave way, jouncing him two feet down on a surface which even he did not care to imagine. Maddened by the sound, or by the stench which billowed forth even to the open air, the waiting horse gave a scream that was too frantic for a neigh, and plunged madly off through the night, the wagon rattling crazily behind it.

Birch, in his ghastly situation, was now too low for an easy scramble out of the enlarged transom; but gathered his energies for a determined try. Clutching the edges of the aperture, he sought to pull himself up, when he noticed a queer retardation in the form of an apparent drag on both his ankles. In another moment he knew fear for the first time that night; for struggle as he would, he could not shake clear of the unknown grasp which held his feet in relentless captivity. Horrible pains, as of savage wounds, shot through his calves; and in his mind was a vortex of fright mixed with an unquenchable materialism that suggested splinters, loose nails, or some other attribute of a breaking wooden box. Perhaps he screamed. At any rate he kicked and squirmed frantically and automatically whilst his consciousness was almost eclipsed in a half-swoon.

Instinct guided him in his wriggle through the transom, and in the crawl which followed his jarring thud on the damp ground. He could not walk, it appeared, and the emerging moon must have witnessed a horrible sight as he dragged his bleeding ankles toward the cemetery lodge; his fingers clawing the black mould in brainless haste, and his body responding with that maddening slowness from which one suffers when chased by the phantoms of nightmare. There was evidently, however, no pursuer; for he was alone and alive when Armington, the lodge-keeper, answered his feeble clawing at the door.

Armington helped Birch to the outside of a spare bed and sent his little son Edwin for Dr. Davis. The afflicted man was fully conscious, but would say nothing of any consequence; merely muttering such things as "Oh, my ankles!," "Let go!," or "Shut in the tomb." Then the doctor came with his medicine-case and asked crisp questions, and removed the patient's outer clothing, shoes, and socks. The wounds — for both ankles were frightfully lacerated about the Achilles' tendons — seemed to puzzle the old physician greatly, and finally almost to frighten him. His questioning grew more than medically tense, and his hands shook as he dressed the mangled members; binding them as if he wished to get the wounds out of sight as quickly as possible.

For an impersonal doctor, Davis' ominous and awestruck cross-examination became very strange indeed as he sought to drain from the weakened undertaker every least detail of his horrible experience. He was oddly anxious to know if Birch were sure — absolutely sure — of the identity of that top coffin of the pile; how he had chosen it, how he had been certain of it as the Fenner coffin in the dusk, and how he had distinguished it from the inferior duplicate coffin of vicious Asaph Sawyer. Would the firm Fenner casket have caved in so readily? Davis, an old-time village practitioner, had of course seen both at the respective funerals, as indeed he had attended both Fenner and Sawyer in their last illnesses. He had even wondered, at Sawyer's funeral, how the vindictive farmer had managed to lie straight in a box so closely akin to that of the diminutive Fenner.

After a full two hours Dr. Davis left, urging Birch to insist at all times that his wounds were caused entirely by loose nails and splintering wood. What else, he added, could ever in any case be proved or believed? But it would be well to say as little as could be said, and to let no other doctor treat the wounds. Birch heeded this advice all the rest of his life till he told me his story; and when I saw the scars — ancient and whitened as they then were — I agreed that he was wise in so doing. He always remained lame, for the great tendons had been severed; but I think the greatest lameness was in his soul. His thinking processes, once so phlegmatic and logical, had become ineffaceably scarred; and it was pitiful to note his response to certain chance allusions such as "Friday," "Tomb," "Coffin," and words of less obvious concatenation. His frightened horse had gone home, but his frightened wits never quite did that. He changed his business, but something always preyed upon him. It may have been just fear, and it may have been fear mixed with a queer belated sort of remorse for bygone crudities. His drinking, of course, only aggravated what it was meant to alleviate.

When Dr. Davis left Birch that night he had taken a lantern and gone to the old receiving tomb. The moon was shining on the scattered brick fragments and marred facade, and the latch of the great door yielded readily to a touch from the outside. Steeled by old ordeals in dissecting rooms, the doctor entered and looked about, stifling the nausea of mind and body that everything in sight and smell induced. He cried aloud once, and a little later gave a gasp that was more terrible than a cry. Then he fled back to the lodge and broke all the rules of his calling by rousing and shaking his patient, and hurling at him a succession of shuddering whispers that seared into the bewildered ears like the hissing of vitriol.

"It was Asaph's coffin, Birch, just as I thought! I knew his teeth, with the front ones missing on the upper jaw — never, for God's sake, show those wounds! The body was pretty badly gone, but if ever I saw vindictiveness on any face — or former face . . . . You know what a fiend he was for revenge — how he ruined old Raymond thirty years after their boundary suit, and how he stepped on the puppy that snapped at him a year ago last August . . . . He was the devil incarnate, Birch, and I believe his eye-for-an-eye fury could beat old Father Death himself. God, what a rage! I'd hate to have it aimed at me!

"Why did you do it, Birch? He was a scoundrel, and I don't blame you for giving him a cast-aside coffin, but you always did go too damned far! Well enough to skimp on the thing some way, but you knew what a little man old Fenner was.

"I'll never get the picture out of my head as long as I live. You kicked hard, for Asaph's coffin was on the floor. His head was broken in, and everything was tumbled about. I've seen sights before, but there was one thing too much here. An eye for an eye! Great heavens, Birch, but you got what you deserved. The skull turned my stomach, but the other was worse — those ankles cut neatly off to fit Matt Fenner's cast-aside coffin!"

1926.

The Supernatural Horror in Literature Era.

H.P. Lovecraft's exile in New York City ended, it seems, just in time; fellow Kalem Club member Samuel Loveman reports that he had taken to carrying a small bottle of poison with him at all times (although biographer S.T. Joshi is very skeptical of this claim). But at the end of March, his aunt Lillian wrote him that a small duplex in Providence was available for rent, and would he like for her to secure it for them — with her in one side, and him in the other?

He would indeed.

So on April 17, Lovecraft was on his way home. Sonia had been planning on accompanying him, but stayed behind for a job interview; she rejoined him a little later. Unfortunately, upon her arrival, Lovecraft's two aunts firmly informed her that neither they nor H.P. would tolerate the scandal of her, as his wife, working outside the home. That sort of modern flapper lifestyle was fine in New York, they told her, but in Providence it was not — especially when it involved a scion of the Phillips family.

(Biographer W. Scott Poole posits that this refusal was motivated by anti-Semitism on Lovecraft's aunts' part. He doesn't cite any evidence for this claim, though, so it is possible, and perhaps likely, that it is pure speculation.)

Whatever the motivation, the result was that Lovecraft was forced to choose between offending his aunts and driving away his wife. He remained silent, letting the power struggle play out as it would, and in the end the aunts won. His marriage, already in rough shape, was now unquestionably over, and he seems to have accepted that — although it would be a while before Sonia would.

During the move from New York, Lovecraft was still toiling away on his "master's thesis" — *Supernatural Horror in Literature*, the first few chapters of which he had by now already completed. This, along with the various processes of settling in, kept him very busy for the first half of 1926, although he did find time in February of that year to dash off "Cool Air," a tale very similar to earlier Poe-inspired short stories but noticeably smoother, tighter and better controlled than his previous work. "Cool Air" is the first post-*Supernatural Horror in Literature* story. It marks the start of the golden age of Lovecraft's work.

The second half of 1926, after *Supernatural Horror* was more or less complete, saw a relative explosion of literary output. First, Lovecraft completed his most famous story, the legendary 12,000-word novelette "The Call of Cthulhu," which he'd outlined just before leaving New York. He finished the year off with "Pickman's Model," "The Strange High House in the Mist," and "The Silver Key." All of them show a marked increase in craftsmanship over Lovecraft's work of the year before.

It was shortly after Lovecraft's return to Providence that he first struck up his correspondence with the young August Derleth, a prolific and precocious writer of commercial fiction and historical nonfiction, whose influence over Lovecraft's literary legacy after his death would be extensive and controversial.

Toward the end of the year, Lovecraft started on a dream-fantasy story, in the style of "The Silver Key" and showing once again some influence of Lord Dunsany, which took flight beneath his pen. By the time he brought it to a close early the following year, he found it had grown into a 43,000-word novel — the longest thing he had yet written. This was *The*

Dream-Quest of Unknown Kadath — probably Lovecraft's most polarizing work; his fans tend to either feel it's his best work, or one of his worst.

THE TRIUMPH OF ENTROPY.

Lovecraft's departure from New York, coincident with his undertaking of *Supernatural Horror in Literature*, forms one of the most important inflection points in his life. I've compared his New York time with that of a caterpillar in its chrysalis. But it can also be compared with a consumptive patient leaving the hospital for the last time, going home to die.

As we've discussed, Lovecraft was born into an old-line family with aristocratic aspirations. His childhood was as idyllic as can be imagined, or at least it started out that way. But starting around the age of three, Lovecraft would watch his lifestyle follow a steady arc downward from that lofty height, like an Achaean galley circling the maw of Charybdis.

First, at age 3, he lost his father to insanity. Then his family's fortune dwindled away, and with it all the doors that would have been open to a youth of Lovecraft's talent and promise, as his beloved grandfather, Whipple Phillips, suffered business reversals. Then, at age 14, Lovecraft lost grandfather Whipple himself, when the older man had a stroke and died.

At age 18, Lovecraft lost his dream of becoming a professional astronomer.

He lost his mother twice — once to anxiety-related mental illness, and two years later to death.

And 1925 was the year in which, having dared to dream that he could interrupt this pattern, he lost his dream of making it as a writer in New York City, and with it the barely-tasted domestic happiness of married life with Sonia Greene.

It is this background of ruthless personal entropy that hung behind Lovecraft, like a once-opulent tapestry now worn and threadbare, as he faced 1926.

All of this is not, of course, to claim that Lovecraft knew no successes and joys during the first 35 years of his life. But it's important to notice that they appeared against a backdrop of steady decline, a fading-away from a barely remembered golden time when everything had been perfect and lovely. And you can feel the wistful quality of hearkening back toward a lost golden age in Lovecraft's work, throughout his life — the loving wistfulness of a man looking to the past to try to recapture something he knows he will never have again.

Lovecraft's return to Providence had a certain quality of exquisite melancholy. He could not go back in time, of course, to retreat to his remembered and cherished childhood home, as Randolph Carter would do in "The Silver Key." So he was settling for going back in space, and surrounding himself with the old furnishings of the 1890s, and dressing himself in his father's Edwardian-age garments, and styling himself as a late-Victorian gentleman — getting as close to that golden past as he could. And the delight he expressed when the opportunity to do so presented itself has a real poignancy to it. One is happy for him, of course; but one also senses that this is it. He has given up.

At the same time, without his sojourn in New York, there is a good chance Lovecraft would never have developed the deep, rich appreciation for his native New England that enabled him to create his classic stories around Arkham, the Miskatonic Valley, Innsmouth, and Kingsport, which really got started at this time. A fish swimming in the ocean does not consider the wetness of the water until it is caught in a net and left on the deck of a fishing boat for a few minutes to gasp in the thin, dry air. When that fish wriggles over the rail and back into the sea, only then does it know what it means to be "wet," and — just to strain our analogy to the breaking point — only then is the fish able to write fully and appreciatively of the experience of the "wet places" of the world.

Likewise, Lovecraft, pining for home from his place in exile, learned to appreciate its true potential as a setting for the kinds of stories he was writing. A year before he left, he was already mapping out some New England-based stories. And upon his reappearance on the scene in Providence, he was ready to get right to work.

ABOUT COSMICISM.

At the same time Lovecraft was undergoing this profound transition, his stories were undergoing a subtle but powerful shift as well — the shift that would transform Lovecraft from a gifted teller of tales of supernatural terror into the founder of a new sub-genre of horror, one springing from a literary philosophy that's come to be known as "cosmicism."

Cosmicism posits that nothing supernatural exists — no god or gods, no universal morality, nothing but cold matter and bleak space — and in that space, humans are as insignificant, unimportant and ignorant as ants on a sidewalk. Moreover, just as that ant on the sidewalk is barely able to perceive a tiny part of its world and can never possibly know more, so it is with humans, who can only see what's slightly larger than themselves. And just as that ant may one day, when it least expects it, be annihilated by the stray footstep of a passing child, humanity may one day be similarly obliterated by something that neither notices its presence nor cares.

That inability to see more than just a horrifying hint of the cosmic enormities from beyond is, for Lovecraft, the heart of true horror, evocative of far more existential dread than an entire menagerie of night-gaunts, ghasts, gugs and ghouls. It is this cosmic horror for which Lovecraft traded the campy, dread-dripping melodrama he was toying with in 1922 and 1923 — before his move to his chrysalis in New York.

Thus, at the same time Lovecraft was emerging from that chrysalis and moving back to Providence, his fiction writing was undergoing a profound but subtle change — from the old Poe-inspired spooky supernatural stories into a new kind of dark, opaque, sinister science fiction. Where once his writing was full of pseudo-mythic supernatural fantasy, he was now finding ways to ground those pseudo-myths in an objective and material (and therefore believable) reality — witches who function by manipulating the fourth dimension, races of creatures with access to sense organs we know nothing about, the genetic-engineering experiments of ancient aliens still running amok beneath the polar icecaps. It would be this approach, more than anything else, that would infuse his later stories with horror and plausibility simultaneously, creating the cocktail of thrilling, lingering dread that would remain a Lovecraft hallmark even in his weakest prose.

Supernatural Horror in Literature.

28,000-WORD DISSERTATION; 1926.

This novella-length essay was a project H.P. Lovecraft launched in 1925, while he was still stuck in New York, for fellow amateur journalist W. Paul Cook. Cook wanted to serialize it in a new magazine he was launching, The Recluse.

Lovecraft started on it in December, and blasted through the first four chapters in a month or so. After that, his progress slowed, as things started to happen in his life that distracted him from his writing — in particular, the opportunity to return to Providence. The last chapter wasn't fully drafted until April, and Lovecraft would still be putting the finishing touches on the work a year after that. In the end, it came in at just under 30,000 words — somewhat longer than the average master's thesis.

The comparison to a thesis covers more than just word count. The publication of this essay, and the extensive research and analysis which Lovecraft put into it, appear to have made an immediate impact on Lovecraft's writing, starting with the very first thing he wrote after undertaking the project — "Cool Air," in February 1926. Lovecraft's undertaking of Supernatural Horror in Literature *stands like a great signpost on the border between early pieces like "The Outsider," "The Shunned House," and "In the Vault" — works sometimes touched with greatness, but checkered in their execution and not always worthy of his muse — and the real masterpieces that would pour from his pen just afterward, the ones nearly everyone agrees are his best: "The Call of Cthulhu," "The Colour out of Space,"* At the Mountains of Madness, *and others.*

Lovecraft's early tales were solid, competent stories, to be sure. But going from "The Horror at Red Hook" to "Pickman's Model" is like going from hamburgers to rib-eye steaks. Something happened to Lovecraft's overall level of mastery and competence at the very end of 1925. That something was almost certainly the process of researching and writing the "master's thesis" that you are about to read. (Or, skip over, depending on what kind of reading you're in the mood to do right now.)

Like any good master's thesis, Supernatural Horror in Literature *is a bit dry and academic, more focused on sharing knowledge with readers than entertaining them. It is, however, packed with useful and interesting insights for the scholastically inclined aficionado of weird fiction.*

I.
INTRODUCTION.

The oldest and strongest emotion of mankind is fear, and the oldest and strongest kind of fear is fear of the unknown. These facts few psychologists will dispute, and their admitted truth must establish for all time the genuineness and dignity of the weirdly horrible tale as a literary form. Against it are discharged all the shafts of materialistic sophistication which clings to frequently felt emotions and external events, and of a naïvely insipid idealism which deprecates the aesthetic motive and calls for a didactic literature to "uplift" the reader toward a suitable degree of smirking optimism. But in spite of all this opposition the weird tale has survived, developed, and attained remarkable heights of perfection; founded as it is on a profound and elementary principle whose appeal, if not always universal, must necessarily be poignant and permanent to minds of the requisite sensitiveness.

The appeal of the spectrally macabre is generally narrow because it demands from the reader a certain degree of imagination and a capacity for detachment from every-day life. Relatively few are free enough from the spell of the daily routine to respond to rappings from outside, and tales of ordinary feelings and events, or of common sentimental distortions of such feelings and events, will always take first place in the taste of the majority; rightly, perhaps, since of course these ordinary matters make up the greater part of human experience. But the sensitive are always with us, and sometimes a curious streak of fancy invades an obscure corner of the very hardest head; so that no amount of rationalisation, reform, or Freudian analysis can quite annul the thrill of the chimney-corner whisper or the lonely wood. There is here involved a psychological pattern or tradition as real and as deeply grounded in mental experience as any other pattern or tradition of mankind; coeval with the religious feeling and closely related to many aspects of it, and too much a part of our inmost biological heritage to lose keen potency over a very important, though not numerically great, minority of our species.

Man's first instincts and emotions formed his response to the environment in which he found himself. Definite feelings based on pleasure and pain grew up around the phenomena whose causes and effects he understood, whilst around those which he did not understand—and the universe teemed with them in the early days—were naturally woven such personifications, marvellous interpretations, and sensations of awe and fear as would be hit upon by a race having few and simple ideas and limited experience. The unknown, being likewise the unpredictable, became for our primitive forefathers a terrible and omnipotent source of boons and calamities visited upon mankind for cryptic and wholly extra-terrestrial reasons, and thus clearly belonging to spheres of existence whereof we know nothing and wherein we have no part. The phenomenon of dreaming likewise helped to build up the notion of an unreal or spiritual world; and in general, all the conditions of savage dawn-life so strongly conduced toward a feeling of the supernatural, that we need not wonder at the thoroughness with which man's very hereditary essence has become saturated with religion and superstition. That saturation must, as matter of plain scientific fact, be regarded as virtually permanent so far as the subconscious mind and inner instincts are concerned; for though the area of the unknown has been steadily contracting for thousands of years, an infinite reservoir of mystery still engulfs most of the outer cosmos, whilst a vast residuum of powerful inherited associations clings round all the objects and processes that were once mysterious, however well they may now be explained. And more than this, there is an actual physiological fixation of the old instincts in our nervous tissue, which would make them obscurely operative even were the conscious mind to be purged of all sources of wonder.

Because we remember pain and the menace of death more vividly than pleasure, and because our feelings toward the beneficent aspects of the unknown have from the first been captured and formalised by conventional religious rituals, it has fallen to the lot of the darker and more maleficent side of cosmic mystery to figure chiefly in our popular supernatural folklore. This tendency, too, is naturally enhanced by the fact that uncertainty and danger are always closely allied; thus making any kind of an unknown world a world of peril and evil possibilities. When to this sense of fear and evil the inevitable fascination of wonder and curiosity is super-added, there is born a composite body of keen emotion and imaginative provocation whose vitality must of necessity endure as long as the human race itself. Children will always be afraid of the dark, and men with minds sensitive to hereditary impulse will always tremble at the thought of the hidden and fathomless worlds of strange life which may pulsate in the gulfs beyond the stars, or press hideously upon our own globe in unholy dimensions which only the dead and the moonstruck can glimpse.

With this foundation, no one need wonder at the existence of a literature of cosmic fear. It has always existed, and always will exist; and no better evidence of its tenacious vigour can be cited than the impulse which now and then drives writers of totally opposite leanings to try their hands at it in isolated tales, as if to discharge from their minds certain phantasmal shapes which would otherwise haunt them. Thus Dickens wrote several eerie narratives; Browning, the hideous poem *Childe Roland*; Henry James, *The Turn of the Screw*; Dr. Holmes, the subtle novel *Elsie Venner*; F. Marion Crawford, *The Upper Berth* and a number of other examples; Mrs. Charlotte Perkins Gilman, social worker, *The Yellow Wall Paper*; whilst the humourist W. W. Jacobs produced that able melodramatic bit called *The Monkey's Paw*.

This type of fear-literature must not be confounded with a type externally similar but psychologically widely different; the literature of mere physical fear and the mundanely gruesome. Such writing, to be sure, has its place, as has the conventional or even whimsical or humorous ghost story where formalism or the author's knowing wink removes the true sense of cosmic fear in its purest sense. The true weird tale has something more than secret murder, bloody bones, or a sheeted form clanking chains according to rule. A certain atmosphere of breathless and unexplainable dread of outer, unknown forces must be present; and there must be a hint, expressed with a seriousness and portentousness becoming its subject, of that most terrible conception of the human brain — a malign and particular suspension or defeat of those fixed laws of Nature which are our only safeguard against the assaults of chaos and the daemons of unplumbed space.

Naturally we cannot expect all weird tales to conform absolutely to any theoretical model. Creative minds are uneven, and the best of fabrics have their dull spots. Moreover, much of the choicest weird work is unconscious; appearing in memorable fragments scattered through material whose massed effect may be of a very different cast. Atmosphere is the all-important thing, for the final criterion of authenticity is not the dovetailing of a plot but the creation of a given sensation. We may say, as a general thing, that a weird story whose intent is to teach or produce a social effect, or one in which the horrors are finally explained away by natural means, is not a genuine tale of cosmic fear; but it remains a fact that such narratives possess, in isolated sections, atmospheric touches which fulfill every condition of true supernatural horror-literature. Therefore we must judge a weird tale not by the author's intent, or by the mere mechanics of the plot; but by the emotional level which it attains at its least mundane point. If the proper sensations are excited, such a "high spot" must be admitted on its own merits as weird literature, no matter how prosaically it is later dragged down. The one test of the really weird is simply this — whether or not there be excited in the reader a profound sense of dread, and of contact with unknown spheres and powers; a subtle attitude of awed listening, as if for the beating of black wings or the scratching of outside shapes and entities on the known universe's utmost rim. And of course, the more completely and unifiedly a story conveys this atmosphere, the better it is as a work of art in the given medium.

II.

THE DAWN OF THE HORROR-TALE.

As may naturally be expected of a form so closely connected with primal emotion, the horror-tale is as old as human thought and speech themselves.

Cosmic terror appears as an ingredient of the earliest folklore of all races, and is crystalised in the most archaic ballads, chronicles, and sacred writings. It was, indeed, a prominent feature of the elaborate ceremonial magic, with its rituals for the evocation of daemons and spectres, which flourished from prehistoric times, and which reached its highest development in Egypt and the Semitic nations. Fragments like the *Book of Enoch* and the *Claviculae of Solomon* well illustrate the power of the weird over the ancient Eastern mind, and upon such things were based enduring systems and traditions whose echoes extend obscurely even to the present time. Touches of this transcendental fear are seen in classic literature, and there is evidence of its still greater emphasis in a ballad literature which paralleled the classic stream but vanished for lack of a written medium. The Middle Ages, steeped in fanciful darkness, gave it an enormous impulse toward expression; and East and West alike were busy preserving and amplifying the dark heritage, both of random folklore and of academically formulated magic and cabbalism, which had descended to them. Witch, werewolf, vampire, and ghoul brooded ominously on the lips of bard and grandam, and needed but little encouragement to take the final step across the boundary that divides the chanted tale or song from the formal literary composition. In the Orient, the weird tale tended to assume a gorgeous colouring and sprightliness which almost transmuted it into sheer phantasy. In the West, where the mystical Teuton had come down from his black Boreal forests and the Celt remembered strange sacrifices in Druidic groves, it assumed a terrible intensity and convincing seriousness of atmosphere which doubled the force of its half-told, half-hinted horrors.

Much of the power of Western horror-lore was undoubtedly due to the hidden but often suspected presence of a hideous cult of nocturnal worshippers whose strange customs — descended from pre-Aryan and pre-agricultural times when a squat race of Mongoloids roved over Europe with their flocks and herds — were rooted in the most revolting fertility-rites of immemorial antiquity. This secret religion, stealthily handed down amongst peasants for thousands of years despite the outward reign of the Druidic, Graeco-Roman, and Christian faiths in the regions involved, was marked by wild "Witches' Sabbaths" in lonely woods and atop distant hills on Walpurgis-Night and Hallowe'en, the traditional breeding-seasons of the goats and sheep and cattle; and became the source of vast riches of sorcery-legend, besides provoking extensive witchcraft-prosecutions of which the Salem affair forms the chief American example. Akin to it in essence, and perhaps connected with it in fact, was the frightful secret system of inverted theology or Satan-worship which produced such horrors as the famous "Black Mass"; whilst operating toward the same end we may note the activities of those whose aims were somewhat more scientific or philosophical — the astrologers, cabbalists, and alchemists of the Albertus Magnus or Raymond Lully type, with whom such rude ages invariably abound. The prevalence and depth of the mediaeval horror-spirit in Europe, intensified by the dark despair which waves of pestilence brought, may be fairly gauged by the grotesque carvings slyly introduced into much of the finest later Gothic ecclesiastical work of the time; the daemonic gargoyles of Notre Dame and Mont St. Michel being among the most famous specimens. And throughout the period, it must be remembered, there existed amongst educated and uneducated alike a most unquestioning faith in every form of the supernatural; from the gentlest of Christian doctrines to the most monstrous morbidities of witchcraft and black magic. It was from no empty background that the Renaissance magicians and alchemists — Nostradamus, Trithemius, Dr. John Dee, Robert Fludd, and the like — were born.

In this fertile soil were nourished types and characters of sombre myth and legend which persist in weird literature to this day, more or less disguised or altered by modern technique. Many of them were taken from the earliest oral sources, and form part of mankind's permanent heritage. The shade which appears and demands the burial of its bones, the daemon lover who comes to bear away his still living bride, the death-fiend or psychopomp riding the night-wind, the man-wolf, the sealed chamber, the deathless sorcerer — all these may be found in that curious body of mediaeval lore which the late Mr. Baring-Gould so effectively assembled in book form. Wherever the mystic Northern blood was strongest, the atmosphere of the popular tales became most intense; for in the Latin races there is a touch of basic rationality which denies to even their strangest superstitions many of the overtones of glamour so characteristic of our own forest-born and ice-fostered whisperings.

Just as all fiction first found extensive embodiment in poetry, so is it in poetry that we first encounter the permanent entry of the weird into standard literature. Most of the ancient instances, curiously enough, are in prose; as the werewolf incident in Petronius, the gruesome passage in Apuleius, the brief but celebrated letter of Pliny the Younger to Sura, and the odd compilation *On Wonderful Events* by the Emperor Hadrian's Greek freedman, Phlegon. It is in Phlegon that we first find that hideous tale of the corpse-bride, *Philinnion and Machates*, later related by Proclus and in modern forming the inspiration of Goethe's *Bride of Corinth* and Washington Irving's *German Student*. But by the time the old Northern myths take literary form, and in that later time when the weird appears as a steady element in the literature of the day, we find it mostly in metrical dress; as indeed we find the greater part of the strictly imaginative writing of the Middle Ages and Renaissance. The Scandinavian Eddas and Sagas thunder with cosmic horror, and shake with the stark fear of Ymir and his shapeless spawn; whilst our own Anglo-Saxon *Beowulf* and the later Continental Nibelung tales are full of eldritch weirdness. Dante is a pioneer in the classic capture of macabre atmosphere, and in Spenser's stately stanzas will be seen more than a few touches of fantastic terror in landscape, incident, and character. Prose literature gives us Mallory's *Morte d'Arthur*, in which are presented many ghastly situations taken from early ballad sources — the theft of the sword and silk from the corpse in Chapel Perilous by Sir Launcelot, the ghost of Sir Gawaine, and the tomb-fiend seen by Sir Galahad — whilst other and cruder specimens were doubtless set forth in cheap and sensational "chapbooks" vulgarly hawked about and devoured by the ignorant. In Elizabethan drama, with its *Dr. Faustus*, the witches in *Macbeth*, the ghost in *Hamlet*, and the horrible gruesomeness of Webster, we may easily discern the strong hold of the daemoniac on the public mind; a hold intensified by the very real fear of living witchcraft, whose terrors, first wildest on the Continent, begin to echo loudly in English ears as the witch-hunting crusades of James the First gain headway. To the lurking mystical prose of the ages is added a long line of treatises on witchcraft and daemonology which aid in exciting the imagination of the reading world.

Through the seventeenth and into the eighteenth century we behold a growing mass of fugitive legendry and balladry of darksome cast; still, however, held down beneath the surface of polite and accepted literature. Chapbooks of horror and weirdness multiply, and we glimpse the eager interest of the people through fragments like Defoe's *Apparition of Mrs. Veal*, a homely tale of a dead woman's spectral visit to a distant friend, written to advertise covertly a badly selling theological disquisition on death. The upper orders of society were now losing faith in the supernatural, and indulging in a period of classic rationalism. Then, beginning with the translations of Eastern tales in Queen Anne's reign and taking definite form toward the middle of the century, comes the revival of romantic feeling — the era of new joy in Nature, and in the radiance of past times, strange scenes, bold deeds, and incredible marvels. We felt it first in the poets, whose utterances take on new qualities of wonder, strangeness, and shuddering. And finally, after the timid appearance of a few weird scenes in the novels of the day — such as Smollett's *Adventures of Ferdinand, Count Fathom* — the released instinct precipitates itself in the birth of a new school of writing; the "Gothic" school of horrible and fantastic prose fiction, long and short, whose literary posterity is destined to become so numerous, and in many cases so resplendent in artistic merit. It is, when one reflects upon it, genuinely remarkable that weird narration as a fixed and academically recognised literary form should have been so late of final birth. The impulse and atmosphere are as old as man, but the typical weird tale of standard literature is a child of the eighteenth century.

III.
THE EARLY GOTHIC NOVEL.

The shadow-haunted landscapes of Ossian, the chaotic visions of William Blake, the grotesque witch-dances in Burns's *Tam O'Shanter*, the sinister daemonism of Coleridge's *Christabel* and *Ancient Mariner*, the ghostly charm of James Hogg's *Kilmeny*, and the more restrained approaches to cosmic horror in *Lamia* and many of Keats's other poems, are typical British illustrations of the advent of the weird to formal literature. Our Teutonic cousins of the Continent were equally receptive to the rising flood, and Brüger's *Wild Huntsman* and the even more famous daemon-bridegroom ballad of *Lenore*—both imitated in English by Scott, whose respect for the supernatural was always great—are only a taste of the eerie wealth which German song had commenced to provide. Thomas Moore adapted from such sources the legend of the ghoulish statue-bride (later used by Prosper Mérimée in *The Venus of Ille*, and traceable back to great antiquity) which echoes so shiveringly in his ballad of *The Ring*; whilst Goethe's deathless masterpiece *Faust*, crossing from mere balladry into the classic, cosmic tragedy of the ages, may be held as the ultimate height to which this German poetic impulse arose.

But it remained for a very sprightly and worldly Englishman—none other than Horace Walpole himself—to give the growing impulse definite shape and become the actual founder of the literary horror-story as a permanent form. Fond of mediaeval romances and mystery as a dilettante's diversion, and with a quaintly imitated Gothic castle as his abode at Strawberry Hill, Walpole in 1764 published *The Castle of Otranto*; a tale of the supernatural which, though thoroughly unconvincing and mediocre in itself, was destined to exert an almost unparalleled influence on the literature of the weird. First venturing it only as a "translation" by one "William Marshal, Gent." from the Italian of a mythical "Onuphrio Muralt," the author later acknowledged his connexion with the book and took pleasure in its wide and instantaneous popularity—a popularity which extended to many editions, early dramatisation, and wholesale imitation both in England and in Germany.

The story—tedious, artificial, and melodramatic—is further impaired by a brisk and prosaic style whose urbane sprightliness nowhere permits the creation of a truly weird atmosphere. It tells of Manfred, an unscrupulous and usurping prince determined to found a line, who after the mysterious sudden death of his only son Conrad on the latter's bridal morn, attempts to put away his wife Hippolita and wed the lady destined for the unfortunate youth—the lad, by the way, having been crushed by the preternatural fall of a gigantic helmet in the castle courtyard. Isabella, the widowed bride, flees from this design; and encounters in subterranean crypts beneath the castle a noble young preserver, Theodore, who seems to be a peasant yet strangely resembles the old lord Alfonso who ruled the domain before Manfred's time. Shortly thereafter supernatural phenomena assail the castle in divers ways; fragments of gigantic armour being discovered here and there, a portrait walking out of its frame, a thunderclap destroying the edifice, and a colossal armoured spectre of Alfonso rising out of the ruins to ascend through parting clouds to the bosom of St. Nicholas. Theodore, having wooed Manfred's daughter Matilda and lost her through death—for she is slain by her father by mistake—is discovered to be the son of Alfonso and rightful heir to the estate. He concludes the tale by wedding Isabella and preparing to live happily ever after, whilst Manfred—whose usurpation was the cause of his son's supernatural death and his own supernatural harassing—retires to a monastery for penitence; his saddened wife seeking asylum in a neighbouring convent.

Such is the tale; flat, stilted, and altogether devoid of the true cosmic horror which makes weird literature. Yet such was the thirst of the age for those touches of strangeness and spectral antiquity which it reflects, that it was seriously received by the soundest readers and raised in spirit of its intrinsic ineptness to a pedestal of lofty importance in literary history. What it did above all else was to create a novel type of scene, puppet-characters, and incidents; which, handled to better advantage by writers more naturally adapted to weird creation, stimulated growth of an imitative Gothic school which in turn inspired the real weavers of cosmic terror—the line of actual artists beginning with Poe. This novel dramatic paraphernalia consisted first of all of the Gothic castle, with its awesome antiquity, vast distances and rambling, deserted, or ruined wings, damp corridors, unwholesome hidden catacombs, and galaxy of ghosts and appalling legends, as a nucleus of suspense and daemoniac fright. In addition, it included the tyrannical and malevolent nobleman as villain; the saintly, long-persecuted, and generally insipid heroine who undergoes the major terrors and serves as a point of view and focus for the reader's sympathies; the valorous and immaculate hero, always of high birth but often in humble disguise; the convention of high-sounding foreign names, mostly Italian, for the characters; and the infinite array of stage properties which includes strange lights, damp trap-doors, extinguished lamps, mouldy hidden manuscripts, creaking hinges, shaking arras, and the like. All this paraphernalia reappears with amusing sameness, yet sometimes with tremendous effect, throughout the history of the Gothic novel; and is by no means extinct even today, though subtler technique now forces it to assume a less naïve and obvious form. An harmonious milieu for a new school had been found, and the writing world was not slow to grasp the opportunity.

German romance at once responded to the Walpole influence, and soon became a byword for the weird and ghastly. In England one of the first imitators was the celebrated Mrs. Barbauld, then Miss Aikin, who in 1773 published an unfinished fragment called *Sir Bertrand*, in which the strings of genuine terror were truly touched with no clumsy hand. A nobleman on a dark and lonely moor, attracted by a tolling bell and distant light, enters a strange and ancient turreted castle whose doors open and close and whose bluish will-o'-the-wisps lead up mysterious staircases toward dead hands and animated black statues. A coffin with a dead lady, whom Sir Bertrand kisses, is finally reached; and upon the kiss the scene dissolves to give place to a splendid apartment where the lady, restored to life, holds a banquet in honour of her rescuer. Walpole admired this tale, though he accorded less respect to an even more prominent offspring of his *Otranto*—*The Old English Baron*, by Clara Reeve, published in 1777. Truly enough, this tale lacks the real vibration to the note of outer darkness and mystery which distinguishes Mrs. Barbauld's fragment; and though less crude than Walpole's novel, and more artistically economical of horror in its possession of only one spectral figure, it is nevertheless too definitely insipid for greatness. Here again we have the virtuous heir to the castle disguised as a peasant and restored to his heritage through the ghost of his father; and here again we have a case of wide popularity leading to many editions, dramatisation, and ultimate translation into French. Miss Reeve wrote another weird novel, unfortunately unpublished and lost.

The Gothic novel was now settled as a literary form, and instances multiply bewilderingly as the eighteenth century draws toward its close. *The Recess*, written in 1758 by Mrs. Sophia Lee, has the historic element, revolving round the twin daughters of Mary, Queen of Scots; and though devoid of the supernatural, employs the Walpole scenery and mechanism with great dexterity. Five years later, and all existing lamps are paled by the rising of a fresh luminary of wholly superior order — Mrs. Ann Radcliffe (1764-1823), whose famous novels made terror and suspense a fashion, and who set new and higher standards in the domain of macabre and fear-inspiring atmosphere despite a provoking custom of destroying her own phantoms at the last through laboured mechanical explanations. To the familiar Gothic trappings of her predecessors Mrs. Radcliffe added a genuine sense of the unearthly in scene and incident which closely approached genius; every touch of setting and action contributing artistically to the impression of illimitable frightfulness which she wished to convey. A few sinister details like a track of blood on castle stairs, a groan from a distant vault, or a weird song in a nocturnal forest can with her conjure up the most powerful images of imminent horror; surpassing by far the extravagant and toilsome elaboration of others. Nor are these images in themselves any the less potent because they are explained away before the end of the novel. Mrs. Radcliffe's visual imagination was very strong, and appears as much in her delightful landscape touches — always in broad, glamorously pictorial outline, and never in close detail — as in her weird phantasies. Her prime weaknesses, aside from the habit of prosaic disillusionment, are a tendency toward erroneous geography and history and a fatal predilection for bestrewing her novels with insipid little poems, attributed to one or another of her characters.

Mrs. Radcliffe wrote six novels, *The Castles of Athlin and Dunbayne* (1789), *A Sicilian Romance* (1794), *The Romance of the Forest* (1791), *The Mysteries of Udolpho* (1794), *The Italian* (1797), and *Gaston de Blondeville*, composed in 1802 but first published posthumously in 1826. Of these *Udolpho* is by far the most famous, and may be taken as a type of early Gothic tale at its best. It is the chronicle of Emily, a young Frenchwoman transplanted to an ancient and portentous castle in the Appennines through the death of her parents and the marriage of her aunt to the lord of the castle — the scheming nobleman Montoni. Mysterious sounds, opened doors, frightful legends, and a nameless horror in a niche behind a black veil all operate in quick succession to unnerve the heroine and her faithful attendant Annette; but finally, after the death of her aunt, she escapes with the aid of a fellow-prisoner whom she has discovered. On the way home she stops at a chateau filled with fresh horrors — the abandoned wing where the departed chatelaine dwelt, and the bed of death with the black pall — but is finally restored to security and happiness with her lover Valacourt, after the clearing-up of a secret which seemed for a time to involve her birth in mystery. Clearly, this is only the familiar material re-worked; but it is so well re-worked that *Udolpho* will always be a classic. Mrs. Radcliffe's characters are puppets, but they are less markedly so than those of her forerunners. And in atmospheric creation she stands preëminent among those of her time.

Of Mrs. Radcliffe's countless imitators, the American novelist Charles Brockden Brown stands the closest in spirit and method. Like her, he injured his creations by natural explanations; but also like her, he had an uncanny atmospheric power which gives his horrors a frightful vitality as long as they remain unexplained. He differed from her in contemptuously discarding the external Gothic paraphernalia and properties and choosing modern American scenes for his mysteries; but his repudiation did not extend to the Gothic spirit and type of incident. Brown's novels involve some memorably frightful scenes, and excel even Mrs. Radcliffe's in describing the operations of the perturbed mind. *Edgar Huntly* starts with a sleep-walker digging a grave, but is later impaired by touches of Godwinian didacticism. *Ormond* involves a member of a sinister secret brotherhood. That and *Arthur Mervyn* both describe the plague of yellow fever, which the author had witnessed in Philadelphia and New York. But Brown's most famous book is *Wieland; or, The Transformation* (1798), in which a Pennsylvania German, engulfed by a wave of religious fanaticism, hears "voices" and slays his wife and children as a sacrifice. His sister Clara, who tells the story, narrowly escapes. The scene, laid at the woodland estate of Mittingen on the Schuylkill's remote reaches, is drawn with extreme vividness; and the terrors of Clara, beset by spectral tones, gathering fears, and the sound of strange footsteps in the lonely house, are all shaped with truly artistic force. In the end a lame ventriloquial explanation is offered, but the atmosphere is genuine while it lasts. Carwin, the malign ventriloquist, is a typical villain of the Manfred or Montoni type.

IV.

THE APEX OF GOTHIC ROMANCE.

Horror in literature attains a new malignity in the work of Matthew Gregory Lewis (1775-1818), whose novel *The Monk* (1796) achieved marvellous popularity and earned him the nickname of "Monk" Lewis. This young author, educated in Germany and saturated with a body of wild Teuton lore unknown to Mrs. Radcliffe, turned to terror in forms more violent than his gentle predecessor had ever dared to think of; and produced as a result a masterpiece of active nightmare whose general Gothic cast is spiced with added stores of ghoulishness. The story is one of a

Spanish monk, Ambrosio, who from a state of over-proud virtue is tempted to the very nadir of evil by a fiend in the guise of the maiden Matilda; and who is finally, when awaiting death at the Inquisition's hands, induced to purchase escape at the price of his soul from the Devil, because he deems both body and soul already lost. Forthwith the mocking Fiend snatches him to a lonely place, tells him he has sold his soul in vain since both pardon and a chance for salvation were approaching at the moment of his hideous bargain, and completes the sardonic betray by rebuking him for his unnatural crimes, and casting his body down a precipice whilst his soul is borne off forever to perdition. The novel contains appalling descriptions such as the incantation in the vaults beneath the convent cemetery, the burning of the convent, and the final end of the wretched abbot. In the sub-plot where the Marquis de las Cisternas meets the spectre of his erring ancestress, The Bleeding Nun, there are many enormously potent strokes; notably the visit of the animated corpse to the Marquis's bedside, and the cabbalistic ritual whereby the Wandering Jew helps him to fathom and banish his dead tormentor. Nevertheless *The Monk* drags sadly when read as a whole. It is too long and too diffuse, and much of its potency is marred by flippancy and by an awkwardly excessive reaction against those canons of decorum which Lewis at first despised as prudish. One great thing may be said of the author; that he never ruined his ghostly visions with a natural explanation. He succeeded in breaking up the Radcliffian tradition and expanding the field of the Gothic novel.

Lewis wrote much more than *The Monk*. His drama, *The Castle Spectre*, was produced in 1798, and he later found time to pen other fictions in ballad form — *Tales of Terror* (1799), *Tales of Wonder* (1801), and a succession of translations from the German.

Gothic romances, both English and German, now appeared in multitudinous and mediocre profusion. Most of them were merely ridiculous in the light of mature taste, and Miss Austen's famous satire *Northanger Abbey* was by no means an unmerited rebuke to a school which had sunk far toward absurdity. This particular school was petering out, but before its final subordination there arose its last and greatest figure in the person of Charles Robert Maturin (1782-1824), an obscure and eccentric Irish clergyman. Out of an ample body of miscellaneous writing which includes one confused Radcliffian imitation called *The Fatal Revenge; or, The Family of Montorio* (1807), Maturin at length evolved the vivid horror-masterpiece of *Melmoth the Wanderer* (1820), in which the Gothic tale climbed to altitudes of sheer spiritual fright which it had never known before.

Melmoth is the tale of an Irish gentleman who, in the seventeenth century, obtained a preternaturally extended life from the Devil at the price of his soul. If he can persuade another to take the bargain off his hands, and assume his existing state, he can be saved; but this he can never manage to effect, no matter how assiduously he haunts those whom despair has made reckless and frantic. The framework of the story is very clumsy; involving tedious length, digressive episodes, narratives within narratives, and laboured dovetailing and coincidences; but at various points in the endless rambling there is felt a pulse of power undiscoverable in any previous work of this kind — a kinship to the essential truth of human nature, an understanding of the profoundest sources of actual cosmic fear, and a white heat of sympathetic passion on the writer's part which makes the book a true document of aesthetic self-expression rather than a mere clever compound of artifice. No unbiased reader can doubt that with *Melmoth* an enormous stride in evolution of the horror-tale is represented. Fear is taken out of the realm of the conventional and exalted into a hideous cloud over mankind's very destiny. Maturin's shudders, the work of one capable of shuddering himself, are of the sort that convince. Mrs. Radcliffe and Lewis are fair game for the parodist, but it would be difficult to find a false note in the feverishly intensified action and high atmospheric tension of the Irishman whose less sophisticated emotions and strain of Celtic mysticism gave him the finest possible natural equipment for his task. Without a doubt Maturin is a man of authentic genius, and he was so recognised by Balzac, who grouped *Melmoth* with Molière's *Don Juan*, Goethe's *Faust*, and Byron's *Manfred* as the supreme allegorical figures of modern European literature, and wrote a whimsical piece called *Melmoth Reconciled*, in which the Wanderer succeeds in passing his infernal bargain to a Parisian bank defaulter, who in turn hands it along a chain of victims until a reveling gambler dies with it in his possession, and by his damnation ends the curse. Scott, Rossetti, Thackeray, and Baudelaire are the other titans who gave Maturin their unqualified admiration, and there is much significance in the fact that Oscar Wilde, after his disgrace and exile, chose for his last days in Paris the assumed name of "Sebastian Melmoth."

Melmoth contains scenes which even now have not lost their power to evoke dread. It begins with a deathbed — an old miser is dying of sheer fright because of something he has seen, coupled with a manuscript he has read and a family portrait which hangs in an obscure closet of his centuried home in County Wicklow. He sends to Trinity College, Dublin, for his nephew John; and the latter upon arriving notes many uncanny things. The eyes of the portrait in the closet glow horribly, and twice a figure strangely resembling the portrait appears momentarily at the door. Dread hangs over the house of the Melmoths, one of whose ancestors, "J. Melmoth, 1646," the portrait represents. The dying miser declares that this man — at a date slightly before 1800 — is alive. Finally the miser dies, and the nephew is told in the will to destroy both the portrait and the manuscript to be found in a certain drawer. Reading the manuscript, which was written late in the seventeenth century by an Englishman named Stanton, young John learns of a terrible incident in Spain in 1677, when the writer met a horrible fellow-countryman and was told of how he had stared to death a priest who tried to denounce him as one filled with fearsome evil. Later, after meeting the man again in London, Stanton is cast into a madhouse and visited by the stranger, whose approach is heralded by spectral music and whose eyes have a more than mortal glare. Melmoth the Wanderer — for such is the malign visitor — offers the captive freedom if he will take over his bargain with the Devil; but like all others whom Melmoth has approached, Stanton is proof against temptation. Melmoth's description of the horrors of a life in a madhouse, used to tempt Stanton, is one of the most potent passages of the book. Stanton is at length liberated, and spends the rest of his life tracking down Melmoth, whose family and ancestral abode he discovers. With the family he leaves the manuscript, which by young John's time is sadly ruinous and fragmentary. John destroys both portrait and manuscript, but in sleep is visited by his horrible ancestor, who leaves a black and blue mark on his wrist.

Young John soon afterward receives as a visitor a shipwrecked Spaniard, Alonzo de Monçada, who has escaped from compulsory monasticism and from the perils of the Inquisition. He has suffered horribly — and the descriptions of his experiences under torment and in the vaults through which he once essays escape are classic — but had the strength to resist Melmoth the Wanderer when approached at his darkest hour in prison. At the house of a Jew who sheltered him after his escape he discovers a wealth of manuscript relating other exploits of Melmoth, including his wooing of an Indian island maiden, Immalee, who later comes to her birthright in Spain and is known as Donna Isidora; and of his horrible marriage to her by the corpse of a dead anchorite at midnight in the ruined chapel of a shunned and abhorred monastery. Monçada's narrative to young John takes up the bulk of Maturin's four-volume book; this disproportion being considered one of the chief technical faults of the composition.

At last the colloquies of John and Monçada are interrupted by the entrance of Melmoth the Wanderer himself, his piercing eyes now fading, and decrepitude swiftly overtaking him. The term of his bargain has approached its end, and he has come home after a century and a half to meet his fate. Warning all others from the room, no matter what sounds they may hear in the night, he awaits the end alone. Young John and Monçada hear frightful ululations, but do not intrude till silence comes toward morning. They then find the room empty. Clayey footprints lead out a rear door to a cliff overlooking the sea, and near the edge of the precipice is a track indicating the forcible dragging of some heavy body. The Wanderer's scarf is found on a crag some distance below the brink, but nothing further is ever seen or heard of him.

Such is the story, and none can fail to notice the difference between this modulated, suggestive, and artistically moulded horror and — to use the words of Professor George Saintsbury — "the artful but rather *jejune* rationalism of Mrs. Radcliffe, and the too often puerile extravagance, the bad taste, and the sometimes slipshod style of Lewis." Maturin's style in itself deserves particular praise, for its forcible directness and vitality lift it altogether above the pompous artificialities of which his predecessors are guilty. Professor Edith Birkhead, in her history of the Gothic novel, justly observes that "with all his faults Maturin was the greatest as well as the last of the Goths." *Melmoth* was widely read and eventually dramatised, but its late date in the evolution of the Gothic tale deprived it of the tumultuous popularity of *Udolpho* and *The Monk.*

V.
THE AFTERMATH OF GOTHIC FICTION.

Meanwhile other hands had not been idle, so that above the dreary plethora of trash like Marquis von Grosse's *Horrid Mysteries* (1796), Mrs. Roche's *Children of the Abbey* (1796), Miss Dacre's *Zofloya; or, The Moor* (1806), and the poet Shelley's schoolboy effusions *Zastrozzi* (1810) and *St. Irvyne* (1811) (both imitations of Zofloya), there arose many memorable weird works both in English and German. Classic in merit, and markedly different from its fellows because of its foundation in the Oriental tale rather than the Walpolesque Gothic Novel, is the celebrated *History of the Caliph Vathek* by the wealthy dilettante William Beckford, first written in the French language but published in an English translation before the appearance of the original. Eastern tales, introduced to European literature early in the eighteenth century through Galland's French translation of the inexhaustibly opulent *Arabian Nights*, had become a reigning fashion; being used both for allegory and for amusement. The sly humour which only the Eastern mind knows how to mix with weirdness had captivated a sophisticated generation, till Bagdad and Damascus names became as freely strewn through popular literature as dashing Italian and Spanish ones were soon to be. Beckford, well read in Eastern romance, caught the atmosphere with unusual receptivity; and in his fantastic volume reflected very potently the haughty luxury, sly diffusion, bland cruelty, urbane treachery, and shadowy spectral horror of the Saracen spirit. His seasoning of the ridiculous seldom mars the force of his sinister theme, and the tale marches onward with a phantasmagoric pomp in which the laughter is that of skeletons feasting under Arabesque domes. *Vathek* is a tale of the grandson of the Caliph Haroun, who, tormented by that ambition for super-terrestrial power, pleasure, and learning which animates the average Gothic villain or Byronic hero (essentially cognate types), is lured by an evil genius to seek the subterranean throne of the mighty and fabulous pre-Adamite sultans in the fiery halls of Eblis, the Mahometan Devil. The descriptions of Vathek's palaces and diversions, of his scheming sorceress-mother Carathis and her witch-tower with the fifty one-eyed negresses, of his pilgrimage to the haunted ruins of Istakhar (Persepolis) and of the impish bride Nouronihar whom he treacherously acquired on the way, of Istakhar's primordial towers and terraces in the burning moonlight of the waste, and of the terrible Cyclopean halls of Eblis, where, lured by glittering promises, each victim is compelled to wander in anguish forever, his right hand upon his blazingly ignited and eternally burning heart, are triumphs of weird colouring which raise the book to a permanent place in English letters. No less notable are the three *Episodes of Vathek*, intended for insertion in the tale as narratives of Vathek's fellow-victims in Eblis' infernal halls, which remained unpublished throughout the author's lifetime and were discovered as recently as 1909 by the scholar Lewis Melville whilst collecting material for his *Life and Letters of William Beckford.* Beckford, however, lacks the essential mysticism which marks the acutest form of the weird; so that his tales have a certain knowing Latin hardness and clearness preclusive of sheer panic fright.

But Beckford remained alone in his devotion to the Orient. Other writers, closer to the Gothic tradition and to European life in general, were content to follow more faithfully in the lead of Walpole. Among the countless producers of terror-literature in these times may be mentioned the Utopian economic theorist William Godwin, who followed his famous non-supernatural *Caleb Williams* (1794) with the intendedly weird *St. Leon* (1799), in which the theme of the elixir of life, as developed by the imaginary secret order of "Rosicrucians," is handled with ingeniousness if not with atmospheric convincingness. This element of Rosicrucianism, fostered by a wave of popular magical interest exemplified in the vogue of the charlatan Cagliostro and the publication of Francis Barrett's *The Magus* (1801), a curious and compendious treatise on occult principles and ceremonies, of which a reprint was made as lately as 1896, figures in Bulwer-Lytton and many late Gothic novels, especially that remote and enfeebled posterity which strangled far down into the nineteenth century and was represented by George W. M. Reynold's *Faust and the Demon* and *Wagner, the Wehr-Wolf.* Caleb Williams, though non-supernatural, has many authentic touches of terror. It is the tale of a servant persecuted by a master whom he has found guilty of murder, and displays an invention and skill which have kept it alive in a fashion to this day. It was dramatised as *The Iron Chest*, and in that form was almost equally celebrated. Godwin, however, was too much the conscious teacher and prosaic man of thought to create a genuine weird masterpiece.

His daughter, the wife of Shelley, was much more successful; and her inimitable *Frankenstein; or, The Modern Prometheus* (1818) is one of the horror-classics of all time. Composed in competition with Lord Byron, Dr. John William Polidori, and her husband in an effort to prove supremacy in horror-making, Mrs. Shelley's *Frankenstein* was the only one of the rival narratives to be brought to an elaborate completion; and criticism has failed to prove that the best parts are due to Shelley rather than to her. The novel, somewhat tinged but scarcely marred by moral didacticism, tells of the artificial human being moulded from charnel fragments by Victor Frankenstein, a young Swiss medical student. Created by its designer "in the mad pride of intellectuality," the monster possesses full intelligence but owns a hideously loathsome form. It is rejected by mankind, becomes embittered, and at length begins the successive murder of all whom young Frankenstein loves best, friends and family. It demands that Frankenstein create a wife for it; and when the student finally refuses in horror lest the world be populated with such monsters, it departs with a hideous threat "to be with him on his wedding night." Upon that night the bride is strangled, and from that time on Frankenstein hunts down the monster, even into the wastes of the Arctic. In the end, whilst seeking shelter on the ship of the man who tells the story, Frankenstein himself is killed by the shocking object of his search and creation of his presumptuous pride. Some of the scenes in *Frankenstein* are unforgettable, as when the newly animated monster enters its creator's room, parts the curtains of his bed, and gazes at him in the yellow moonlight with watery eyes — "if eyes they may be called." Mrs. Shelley wrote other novels, including the fairly notable *Last Man*, but never duplicated the success of her first effort. It has the true touch of cosmic fear, no matter how much the movement may lag in places. Dr. Polidori developed his competing idea as a long short story, *The Vampyre*; in which we behold a suave villain of the true Gothic or Byronic type, and encounter some excellent passages of stark fright, including a terrible nocturnal experience in a shunned Grecian wood.

In this same period Sir Walter Scott frequently concerned himself with the weird, weaving it into many of his novels and poems, and sometimes producing such independent bits of narration as "The Tapestried Chamber" or "Wandering Willie's tale" in *Redguantlet*, in the latter of which the force of the spectral and the diabolic is enhanced by a grotesque homeliness of speech and atmosphere. In 1830 Scott published his *Letters of Demonology and Witchcraft*, which still forms one of our best compendia of European witch-lore. Washington Irving is another famous figure not unconnected with the weird; for though most of his ghosts are too whimsical and humorous to form genuinely spectral literature, a distinct inclination in this direction is to be noted in many of his productions. "The German Student" in *Tales of the Traveler* (1824) is a slyly concise and effective presentation of the old legend of the dead bride, whilst woven into the comic tissue of "The Money-Diggers" in the same volume is more than one hint of piratical apparitions in the realms which Captain Kidd once roamed. Thomas Moore also joined the ranks of the macabre artists in *Alciphron, A Poem*, which he later elaborated in the prose novel of *The Epicurean* (1827). Though merely relating the adventures of a young Athenian duped by the artifice of cunning Egyptian priests, Moore manages to infuse much genuine horror into his account of subterranean frights and wonders beneath the primordial temples of Memphis. De Quincey more than once revels in grotesque and arabesque terrors, though with a desultoriness and learned pomp which deny him the rank of specialist.

This era likewise saw the rise of William Harrison Ainsworth, whose romantic novels teem with the eerie and the gruesome. Capt. Marryat, beside writing such short tales as *The Werewolf*, made a memorable contribution in *The Phantom Ship* (1839), founded on the legend of the Flying Dutchman, whose spectral and accursed vessel sails forever near the Cape of Good Hope. Dickens now rises with the occasional weird bits like *The Signalman*, a tale of ghostly warning conforming to a very common pattern and touched with a verisimilitude which allies it as much with the coming psychological school as with the dying Gothic school. At this time a wave of interest in spiritualist charlatanry, mediumism, Hindoo theosophy, and such matters, much like that of the present day, was flourishing; so that the number of weird tales with a "psychic" or pseudo-scientific basis became considerable. For a number of these the prolific and popular Lord Edward Bulwer-Lytton was responsible; and despite the large doses of turgid rhetoric and empty romanticism in his products, his success in the weaving of a certain kind of bizarre charm cannot be denied.

The House and the Brain, which hints of Rosicrucianism and at a malign and deathless figure perhaps suggested by Louis XV's mysterious courtier St. Germain, yet survives as one of the best short haunted-house tales ever written. The novel *Zanoni* (1842) contains similar elements more elaborately handled, and introduces a vast unknown sphere of being pressing on our own world and guarded by a horrible "Dweller of the Threshold" who haunts those who try to enter and fail. Here we have a benign brotherhood kept alive from age to age till finally reduced to a single member, and as a hero an ancient Chaldaean sorcerer surviving in the pristine bloom of youth to perish on the guillotine of the French Revolution. Though full of the conventional spirit of romance, marred by a ponderous network of symbolic and didactic meanings, and left unconvincing through lack of perfect atmospheric realisation of the situations hinging on the spectral world, *Zanoni* is really an excellent performance as a romantic novel; and can be read with genuine interest today by the not-too-sophisticated reader. It is amusing to note that in describing an attempted initiation into the ancient brotherhood the author cannot escape using the stock Gothic castle of Walpolian lineage.

In *A Strange Story* (1862) Bulwer-Lytton shews a marked improvement in the creation of weird images and moods. The novel, despite enormous length, a highly artificial plot bolstered up by opportune coincidences, and an atmosphere of homiletic pseudo-science designed to please the matter-of-fact and purposeful Victorian reader, is exceedingly effective as a narrative; evoking instantaneous and unflagging interest, and furnishing many potent — if somewhat melodramatic — tableaux and climaxes. Again we have the mysterious user of life's elixir in the person of the soulless magician Margrave, whose dark exploits stand out with dramatic vividness against the modern background of a quiet English town and of the Australian bush; and again we have shadowy intimations of a vast spectral world of the unknown in the very air about us — this time handled with much greater power and vitality than in *Zanoni*. One of the two great incantation passages, where the hero is driven by a luminous evil spirit to rise at night in his sleep, take a strange Egyptian wand, and evoke nameless presences in the haunted and mausoleum-facing pavilion of a famous Renaissance alchemist, truly stands among the major terror scenes of literature. Just enough is suggested, and just little enough is told. Unknown words are twice dictated to the sleep-walker, and as he repeats them the ground trembles, and all the dogs of the countryside begin to bay at half-seen amorphous shadows that stalk athwart the moonlight. When a third set of unknown words is prompted, the sleep-walker's spirit suddenly rebels at uttering them, as if the soul could recognise ultimate abysmal horrors concealed from the mind; and at last an apparition of an absent sweetheart and good angel breaks the malign spell. This fragment well illustrates how far Lord Lytton was capable of progressing beyond his usual pomp and stock romance toward that crystalline essence of artistic fear which belongs to the domain of poetry. In describing certain details of incantations, Lytton was greatly indebted to his amusingly serious occult studies, in the course of which he came in touch with that odd French scholar and cabbalist Alphonse-Louis Constant ("Eliphas Lévi"), who claimed to possess the secrets of ancient magic, and to have evoked the spectre of the Old Grecian wizard Apollonius of Tyana, who lived in Nero's time.

The romantic, semi-Gothic, quasi-moral tradition here represented was carried far down the nineteenth century by such authors as Joseph Sheridan Lefanu, Thomas Preskett Prest with his famous *Varney, the Vampyre* (1847), Wilkie Collins, the late Sir H. Rider Haggard (whose *She* is really remarkably good), Sir A. Conan Doyle, H. G. Wells, and Robert Louis Stevenson — the latter of whom, despite an atrocious tendency toward jaunty mannerisms, created permanent classics in *Markheim*, *The Body-Snatcher*, and *Dr. Jekyll and Mr. Hyde*. Indeed, we may say that this school still survives; for to it clearly belong such of our contemporary horror-tales as specialise in events rather than atmospheric details, address the intellect rather than the impressionistic imagination, cultivate a luminous glamour rather than a malign tensity or psychological verisimilitude, and take a definite stand in sympathy with mankind and its welfare. It has its undeniable strength, and because of its "human element" commands a wider audience than does the sheer artistic nightmare. If not quite so potent as the latter, it is because a diluted product can never achieve the intensity of a concentrated essence.

Quite alone both as a novel and as a piece of terror-literature stands the famous *Wuthering Heights* (1847) by Emily Brontë, with its mad vista of bleak, windswept Yorkshire moors and the violent, distorted lives they foster. Though primarily a tale of life, and of human passions in agony and conflict, its epically cosmic setting affords room for horror of the most spiritual sort. Heathcliff, the modified Byronic villain-hero, is a strange dark waif found in the streets as a small child and speaking only a strange gibberish till adopted by the family he ultimately ruins. That he is in truth a diabolic spirit rather than a human being is more than once suggested, and the unreal is further approached in the experience of the visitor who encounters a plaintive child-ghost at a bough-brushed upper window. Between Heathcliff and Catherine Earnshaw is a tie deeper and more terrible than human love. After her death he twice disturbs her grave, and is haunted by an impalpable presence which can be nothing less than her spirit. The spirit enters his life more and more, and at last he becomes confident of some imminent mystical reunion. He says he feels a strange change approaching, and ceases to take nourishment. At night he either walks abroad or opens the casement by his bed. When he dies the casement is still swinging open to the pouring rain, and a queer smile pervades the stiffened face. They bury him in a grave beside the mound he has haunted for eighteen years, and small shepherd boys say that he yet walks with his Catherine in the churchyard and on the moor when it rains. Their faces, too, are sometimes seen on rainy nights behind the upper casement at Wuthering Heights.

Miss Brontë's eerie terror is no mere Gothic echo, but a tense expression of man's shuddering reaction to the unknown. In this respect, *Wuthering Heights* becomes the symbol of a literary transition, and marks the growth of a new and sounder school.

VI.

SPECTRAL LITERATURE ON THE CONTINENT.

On the Continent literary horror fared well. The celebrated short tales and novels of Ernst Theodor Wilhelm Hoffmann (1776-1822) are a byword for mellowness of background and maturity of form, though they incline to levity and extravagance, and lack the exalted moments of stark, breathless terror which a less sophisticated writer might have achieved. Generally they convey the grotesque rather than the terrible. Most artistic of all the Continental weird tales is the German classic *Undine* (1811), by Friedrich Heinrich Karl, Baron de la Motte Fouqué. In this story of a water-spirit who married a mortal and gained a human soul there is a delicate fineness of craftsmanship which makes it notable in any department of literature, and an easy naturalness which places it close to the genuine folk-myth. It is, in fact, derived from a tale told by the Renaissance physician and alchemist Paracelsus in his Treatise on Elemental Sprites.

Undine, daughter of a powerful water-prince, was exchanged by her father as a small child for a fisherman's daughter, in order that she might acquire a soul by wedding a human being. Meeting the noble youth Huldbrand at the cottage of her foster-father by the sea at the edge of a haunted wood, she soon marries him, and accompanies him to his ancestral castle of Ringstetten. Huldbrand, however, eventually wearies of his wife's supernatural affiliations, and especially of the appearances of her uncle, the malicious woodland waterfall-spirit Kühleborn; a weariness increased by his growing affection for Bertalda, who turns out to be the fisherman's child for whom Undine was exchanged. At length, on a voyage down the Danube, he is provoked by some innocent act of his devoted wife to utter the angry words which consign her back to her supernatural element; from which she can, by the laws of her species, return only once — to kill him, whether she will or no, if ever he prove unfaithful to her memory. Later, when Huldbrand is about to be married to Bertalda, Undine returns for her sad duty, and bears his life away in tears. When he is buried among his fathers in the village churchyard a veiled, snow-white female figure appears among the mourners, but after the prayer is seen no more. In her place is seen a little silver spring, which murmurs its way almost completely around the new grave, and empties into a neighbouring lake. The villagers shew it to this day, and say that Undine, and her Huldbrand are thus united in death. Many passages and atmospheric touches in this tale reveal Fouqué as an accomplished artist in the field of the macabre; especially the descriptions of the haunted wood with its gigantic snow-white man and various unnamed terrors, which occur early in the narrative.

Not so well-known as *Undine*, but remarkable for its convincing realism and freedom from Gothic stock devices, is *The Amber Witch* of Wilhelm Meinhold, another product of the German fantastic genius of the earlier nineteenth century. This tale, which is laid in the time of the Thirty Years' War, purports to be a clergyman's manuscript found in an old church at Coserow, and centres round the writer's daughter, Maria Schweidler, who is wrongly accused of witchcraft. She has found a deposit of amber which she keeps secret for various reasons, and the unexplained wealth obtained from this lends colour to the accusation; an accusation instigated by the malice of the wolf-hunting nobleman Wittich Appelmann, who has vainly pursued her with ignoble designs. The deeds of a real witch, who afterwards comes to a horrible supernatural end in prison, are glibly imputed to the hapless Maria; and after a typical witchcraft trial with forced confessions under torture she is about to be burned at the stake when saved just in time by her lover, a noble youth from a neighbouring district. Meinhold's great strength is in his air of casual and realistic verisimilitude, which intensifies our suspense and sense of the unseen by half persuading us that the menacing events must somehow be either the truth or very close to the truth. Indeed, so thorough is this realism that a popular magazine once published the main points of *The Amber Witch* as an actual occurrence of the seventeenth century!

In the present generation German horror-fiction is most notably represented by Hannis Heinz Ewers, who brings to bear on his dark conceptions an effective knowledge of modern psychology. Novels like *The Sorcerer's Apprentice* and *Alraune*, and short stories like "The Spider," contain distinctive qualities which raise them to a classic level.

But France as well as Germany has been active in the realm of weirdness. Victor Hugo, in such tales as *Hans of Iceland*, and Balzac, in *The Wild Ass's Skin, Séraphîta*, and *Louis Lambert*, both employ supernaturalism to a greater or less extent; though generally only as a means to some more human end, and without the sincere and daemonic intensity which characterises the born artist in shadows. It is in Théophile Gautier that we first seem to find an authentic French sense of the unreal world, and here there appears a spectral mastery which though not continuously used, is recognizable at once as something alike genuine and profound. Short tales like "Avatar," "The Foot of the Mummy," and "Clarimonde" display glimpses of forbidden visits that allure, tantalize, and sometimes horrify; whilst the Egyptian visions evoked in *One of Cleopatra's Nights* are of the keenest and most expressive potency. Gautier captured the inmost soul of aeon-weighted Egypt, with its cryptic life and Cyclopean architecture, and uttered once and for all the eternal horror of its nether world of catacombs, where to the end of time millions of stiff, spiced corpses will stare up in blackness with glassy eyes, awaiting some awesome and unrelatable summons. Gustave Flaubert ably continued the tradition of Gautier in orgies of poetic phantasy like *The Temptation of St. Anthony*, and but for a strong realistic bias might have been an arch-weaver of tapestried terrors. Later on we see the stream divide, producing strange poets and *fantaisistes* of the Symbolist and Decadent schools whose dark interests really centre more in abnormalities of human though and instinct than in the actual supernatural, and subtle story-tellers whose thrills are quite directly derived from the night-black wells of cosmic unreality. Of the former class of "artists in sin" the illustrious poet Baudelaire, influenced vastly by Poe, is the supreme type; whilst the psychological novelist Joris-Karl Huysmans, a true child of the eighteen-nineties, is at once the summation and finale. The latter and purely narrative class is continued by Prosper Mérimée, whose *Venus of Ille* presents in terse and convincing prose the same ancient statue-bride theme which Thomas Moore cast in ballad form in *The Ring*.

The horror-tales of the powerful and cynical Guy de Maupassant, written as his final madness gradually overtook him, present individualities of their own; being rather the morbid outpourings of a realistic mind in a pathological state than the healthy imaginative products of a vision naturally disposed toward phantasy and sensitive to the normal illusions of the unseen. Nevertheless they are of the keenest interest and poignancy; suggesting with marvelous force the imminence of nameless terrors, and the relentless dogging of all ill-starred individual by hideous and menacing representatives of the outer blackness. Of these stories *The Horla* is generally regarded as the masterpiece. Relating the advent to France of an invisible being who lives on water and milk, sways the minds of others, and seems to be the vanguard of a horde of extra-terrestrial organisms arrived on earth to subjugate and overwhelm mankind, this tense narrative is perhaps without a peer in its particular department; notwithstanding its indebtedness to a tale by American Fitz-James O'Brien for details in describing the actual presence of the unseen monster. Other potently dark creations of de Maupassant are *Who Knows?, The Spectre, He, The Diary of a Madman, The White Wolf, On the River*, and the grisly verses entitled *Horror*.

The collaborators Erckmann-Chatrian enriched French literature with many spectral fancies like *The Man-Wolf*, in which a transmitted curse works toward its end in a traditional Gothic-castle setting. Their power of creating a shuddering midnight atmosphere was tremendous despite a tendency toward natural explanations and scientific wonders; and few short tales contain greater horror than *The Invisible Eye*, where a malignant old hag weaves nocturnal hypnotic spells which induce the successive occupants of a certain inn chamber to hang themselves on a cross-beam. *The Owl's Ear* and *The Waters of Death* are full of engulfing darkness and mystery, the latter embodying the familiar overgrown-spider theme so frequently employed by weird fictionists. Villiers de l'Isle-Adam likewise followed the macabre school; his *Torture by Hope*, the tale of a stake-condemned prisoner permitted to escape in order to feel the pangs of recapture, being held by some to constitute the most harrowing short story in literature. This type, however, is less a part of the weird tradition than a class peculiar to itself — the so-called *conte cruel*, in which the wrenching of the emotions is accomplished through dramatic tantalisations, frustrations, and gruesome physical horrors. Almost wholly devoted to this form is the living writer Maurice Level, whose very brief episodes have lent themselves so readily to theatrical adaptation in "thrillers" of the Grand Guignol. As a matter of fact, the French genius is more naturally suited to this dark realism than to the suggestion of the unseen; since the latter process requires, for its best and most sympathetic development on a large scale, the inherent mysticism of the Northern mind.

A very flourishing, though till recently quite hidden, branch of weird literature is that of the Jews, kept alive and nourished in obscurity by the sombre heritage of early Eastern magic, apocalyptic literature, and cabbalism. The Semitic mind, like the Celtic and Teutonic, seems to possess marked mystical inclinations; and the wealth of underground horror-lore surviving in ghettoes and synagogues must be much more considerable than is generally imagined. Cabbalism itself, so prominent during the Middle Ages, is a system of philosophy explaining the universe as emanations of the Deity, and involving the existence of strange spiritual realms and beings apart from the visible world, of which dark glimpses may be obtained through certain secret incantations. Its ritual is bound up with mystical interpretations of the Old Testament, and attributes an esoteric significance to each letter of the Hebrew alphabet — a circumstance which has imparted to Hebrew letters a sort of spectral glamour and potency in the popular literature of magic. Jewish folklore has preserved much of the terror and mystery of the past, and when more thoroughly studied is likely to exert considerable influence on weird fiction. The best example of its literary use so far are the German novel *The Golem*, by Gustav Meyrink, and the drama *The Dybbuk*, by the Jewish writer using the pseudonym "Ansky." The former, with its haunting shadowy suggestions of marvels and horrors just beyond reach, is laid in Prague, and describes with singular mastery that city's ancient ghetto with its spectral, peaked gables. The name is derived from a fabulous artificial giant supposed to be made and animated by mediaeval rabbis according to a certain cryptic formula. *The Dybbuk*, translated and produced in America in 1925, and more recently produced as an opera, describes with singular power the possession of a living body by the evil soul of a dead man. Both golems and dybbuks are fixed types, and serve as frequent ingredients of later Jewish tradition.

VII.

EDGAR ALLAN POE.

In the 1830s occurred a literary dawn directly affecting not only the history of the weird tale, but that of short fiction as a whole; and indirectly moulding the trends and fortunes of a great European æsthetic school. It is our good fortune as Americans to be able to claim that dawn as our own, for it came in the person of our most illustrious and unfortunate fellow-countryman Edgar Allan Poe. Poe's fame has been subject to curious undulations, and it is now a fashion amongst the "advanced intelligentsia" to minimize his importance both as an artist and as an influence; but it would be hard for any mature and reflective critic to deny the tremendous value of his work and the persuasive potency of his mind as an opener of artistic vistas. True, his type of outlook may have been anticipated; but it was he who first realized its possibilities and gave it supreme form and systematic expression. True also, that subsequent writers may have produced greater single tales than his; but again we must comprehend that it was only he who taught them by example and precept the art which they, having the way cleared for them and given an explicit guide, were perhaps able to carry to greater lengths. Whatever his limitations, Poe did that which no one else ever did or could have done; and to him we owe the modern horror-story in its final and perfected state.

Before Poe the bulk of weird writers had worked largely in the dark; without an understanding of the psychological basis of the horror appeal, and hampered by more or less of conformity to certain empty literary conventions such as the happy ending, virtue rewarded, and in general a hollow moral didacticism, acceptance of popular standards and values, and striving of the author to obtrude his own emotions into the story and take sides with the partisans of the majority's artificial ideas. Poe, on the other hand, perceived the essential impersonality of the real artist; and knew that the function of creative fiction is merely to express and interpret events and sensations as they are, regardless of how they tend or what they prove — good or evil, attractive or repulsive, stimulating or depressing, with the author always acting as a vivid and detached chronicler rather than as a teacher, sympathizer, or vendor of opinion. He saw clearly that all phases of life and thought are equally eligible as a subject matter for the artist, and being inclined by temperament to strangeness and gloom, decided to be the interpreter of those powerful feelings and frequent happenings which attend pain rather than pleasure, decay rather than growth, terror rather than tranquility, and which are fundamentally either adverse or indifferent to the tastes and traditional outward sentiments of mankind, and to the health, sanity, and normal expansive welfare of the species.

Poe's spectres thus acquired a convincing malignity possessed by none of their predecessors, and established a new standard of realism in the annals of literary horror. The impersonal and artistic intent, moreover, was aided by a scientific attitude not often found before; whereby Poe studied the human mind rather than the usages of Gothic fiction, and worked with an analytical knowledge of terror's true sources which doubled the force of his narratives and emancipated him from all the absurdities inherent in merely conventional shudder-coining. This example having been set, later authors were naturally forced to conform to it in order to compete at all; so that in this way a definite change begin to affect the main stream of macabre writing. Poe, too, set a fashion in consummate craftsmanship; and although today some of his own work seems slightly melodramatic and unsophisticated, we can constantly trace his influence in such things as the maintenance of a single mood and achievement of a single impression in a tale, and the rigorous paring down of incidents to such as have a direct bearing on the plot and will figure prominently in the climax. Truly may it be said that Poe invented the short story in its present form. His elevation of disease, perversity, and decay to the level of artistically expressible themes was likewise infinitely far-reaching in effect; for avidly seized, sponsored, and intensified by his eminent French admirer Charles Pierre Baudelaire, it became the nucleus of the principal æsthetic movements in France, thus making Poe in a sense the father of the Decadents and the Symbolists.

Poet and critic by nature and supreme attainment, logician and philosopher by taste and mannerism, Poe was by no means immune from defects and affectations. His pretence to profound and obscure scholarship, his blundering ventures in stilted and laboured pseudo-humor, and his often vitriolic outbursts of critical prejudice must all be recognized and forgiven. Beyond and above them, and dwarfing them to insignificance, was a master's vision of the terror that stalks about and within us, and the worm that writhes and slavers in the hideously close abyss. Penetrating to every festering horror in the gaily painted mockery called existence, and in the solemn masquerade called human thought and feeling, that vision had power to project itself in blackly magical crystalisations and transmutations; till there bloomed in the sterile America of the thirties and forties such a moon-nourished garden of gorgeous poison fungi as not even the nether slopes of Saturn might boast. Verses and tales alike sustain the burthen of cosmic panic. The raven whose noisome beak pierces the heart, the ghouls that toll iron bells in pestilential steeples, the vault of Ulalume in the black October night, the shocking spires and domes under the sea, the "wild, weird clime that lieth, sublime, out of Space — out of Time" — all these things and more leer at us amidst maniacal rattlings in the seething nightmare of the poetry. And in the prose there yawn open for us the very jaws of the pit — inconceivable abnormalities slyly hinted into a horrible half-knowledge by words whose innocence we scarcely doubt till the cracked tension of the speaker's hollow voice bids us fear their nameless implications; dæmoniac patterns and presences slumbering noxiously till waked for one phobic instant into a shrieking revelation that cackles itself to sudden madness or explodes in memorable and cataclysmic echoes. A Witches' Sabbath of horror flinging off decorous robes is flashed before us — a sight the more monstrous because of the scientific skill with which every particular is marshaled and brought into an easy apparent relation to the known gruesomeness of material life.

Poe's tales, of course, fall into several classes; some of which contain a purer essence of spiritual horror than others. The tales of logic and ratiocination, forerunners of the modern detective story, are not to be included at all in weird literature; whilst certain others, probably influenced considerably by Hoffmann, possess an extravagance which relegates them to the borderline of the grotesque. Still a third group deal with abnormal psychology and monomania in such a way as to express terror but not weirdness. A substantial residuum, however, represent the literature of supernatural horror in its acutest form; and give their author a permanent and unassailable place as deity and fountainhead of all modern diabolic fiction. Who can forget the terrible swollen ship poised on the billow-chasm's edge in *MS. Found in a Bottle* — the dark intimations of her unhallowed age and monstrous growth, her sinister crew of unseeing greybeards, and her frightful southward rush under full sail through the ice of the Antarctic night, sucked onward by some resistless devil-current toward a vortex of eldritch enlightenment which must end in destruction?

Then there is the unutterable M. Valdemar, kept together by hypnotism for seven months after his death, and uttering frantic sounds but a moment before the breaking of the spell leaves him "a nearly liquid mass of loathsome, of detestable putrescence." In the *Narrative of Arthur Gordon Pym of Nantucket* the voyagers reach first a strange south polar land of murderous savages where nothing is white and where vast rocky ravines have the form of titanic Egyptian letters spelling terrible primal arcana of earth; and thereafter a still more mysterious realm where everything is white, and where shrouded giants and snowy-plumed birds guard a cryptic cataract of mist which empties from immeasurable celestial heights into a torrid milky sea. *Metzengerstein* horrifies with its malign hints of a monstrous metempsychosis — the mad nobleman who burns the stable of his hereditary foe; the colossal unknown horse that issues from the blazing building after the owner has perished therein; the vanishing bit of ancient tapestry where was shown the giant horse of the victim's ancestor in the Crusades; the madman's wild and constant riding on the great horse, and his fear and hatred of the steed; the meaningless prophecies that brood obscurely over the warring houses; and finally, the burning of the madman's palace and the death therein of the owner, borne helpless into the flames and up the vast staircase astride the beast he had ridden so strangely. Afterward the rising smoke of the ruins take the form of a gigantic horse. *The Man of the Crowd*, telling of one who roams day and night to mingle with streams of people as if afraid to be alone, has quieter effects, but implies nothing less of cosmic fear. Poe's mind was never far from terror and decay, and we see in every tale, poem, and philosophical dialogue a tense eagerness to fathom unplumbed wells of night, to pierce the veil of death, and to reign in fancy as lord of the frightful mysteries of time and space.

Certain of Poe's tales possess an almost absolute perfection of artistic form which makes them veritable beacon-lights in the province of the short story. Poe could, when he wished, give to his prose a richly poetic cast; employing that archaic and Orientalised style with jeweled phrase, quasi-Biblical repetition, and recurrent burthen so successfully used by later writers like Oscar Wilde and Lord Dunsany; and in the cases where he has done this we have an effect of lyrical phantasy almost narcotic in essence — an opium pageant of dream in the language of dream, with every unnatural colour and grotesque image bodied forth in a symphony of corresponding sound. *The Masque of the Red Death, Silence, A Fable*, and *Shadow, a Parable*, are assuredly poems in every sense of the word save the metrical one, and owe as much of their power to aural cadence as to visual imagery. But it is in two of the less openly poetic tales, *Ligeia* and *The Fall of the House of Usher* — especially the latter — that one finds those very summits of artistry whereby Poe takes his place at the head of fictional miniaturists. Simple and straightforward in plot, both of these tales owe their supreme magic to the cunning development which appears in the selection and collocation of every least incident. *Ligeia* tells of a first wife of lofty and mysterious origin, who after death returns through a preternatural force of will to take possession of the body of a second wife; imposing even her physical appearance on the temporary reanimated corpse of her victim at the last moment. Despite a suspicion of prolixity and topheaviness, the narrative reaches its terrific climax with relentless power. *Usher*, whose superiority in detail and proportion is very marked, hints shudderingly of obscure life in inorganic things, and displays an abnormally linked trinity of entities at the end of a long and isolated family history — a brother, his twin sister, and their incredibly ancient house all sharing a single soul and meeting one common dissolution at the same moment.

These bizarre conceptions, so awkward in unskillful hands, become under Poe's spell living and convincing terrors to haunt our nights; and all because the author understood so perfectly the very mechanics and physiology of fear and strangeness — the essential details to emphasise, the precise incongruities and conceits to select as preliminaries or concomitants to horror, the exact incidents and allusions to throw out innocently in advance as symbols or prefigurings of each major step toward the hideous dénouement to come, the nice adjustments of cumulative force and the unerring accuracy in linkage of parts which make for faultless unity throughout and thunderous effectiveness at the climactic moment, the delicate nuances of scenic and landscape value to select in establishing and sustaining the desired mood and vitalising the desired illusion — principles of this kind, and dozens of obscurer ones too elusive to be described or even fully comprehended by any ordinary commentator. Melodrama and unsophistication there may be — we are told of one fastidious Frenchman who could not bear to read Poe except in Baudelaire's urbane and Gallically modulated translation — but all traces of such things are wholly overshadowed by a potent and inborn sense of the spectral, the morbid, and the horrible which gushed forth from every cell of the artist's creative mentality and stamped his macabre work with the ineffaceable mark of supreme genius. Poe's weird tales are alive in a manner that few others can ever hope to be.

Like most *fantaisistes*, Poe excels in incidents and broad narrative effects rather than in character drawing. His typical protagonist is generally a dark, handsome, proud, melancholy, intellectual, highly sensitive, capricious, introspective, isolated, and sometimes slightly mad gentleman of ancient family and opulent circumstances; usually deeply learned in strange lore, and darkly ambitious of penetrating to forbidden secrets of the universe. Aside from a high-sounding name, this character obviously derives little from the early Gothic novel; for he is clearly neither the wooden hero nor the diabolical villain of Radcliffian or Ludovician romance. Indirectly, however, he does possess a sort of genealogical connection; since his gloomy, ambitious and anti-social qualities savour strongly of the typical Byronic hero, who in turn is definitely an offspring, of the Gothic Manfreds, Montonis, and Ambrosios. More particular qualities appear to be derived from the psychology of Poe himself, who certainly possessed much of the depression, sensitiveness, mad aspiration, loneliness, and extravagant freakishness which he attributes to his haughty and solitary victims of Fate.

VIII.

THE WEIRD TRADITION IN AMERICA.

The public for whom Poe wrote, though grossly unappreciative of his art, was by no means unaccustomed to the horrors with which he dealt. America, besides inheriting the usual dark folk-lore of Europe, had an additional fund of weird associations to draw upon; so that spectral legends had already been recognised as fruitful subject-matter for literature. Charles Brockden Brown had achieved phenomenal fame with his Radcliffian romances, and Washington Irving's lighter treatment of eerie themes had quickly become classic. This additional fund proceeded, as Paul Elmer More has pointed out, from the keen spiritual and theological interests of the first colonists, plus the strange and forbidding nature of the scene into which they were plunged. The vast and gloomy virgin forests in whose perpetual twilight all terrors might well lurk; the hordes of coppery Indians whose strange, saturnine visages and violent customs hinted strongly at traces of infernal origin; the free rein given under the influence of Puritan theocracy to all manner of notions respecting man's relation to the stern and vengeful God of the Calvinists, and to the sulphurous Adversary of that God, about whom so much was thundered in the pulpits each Sunday; and the morbid introspection developed by an isolated backwoods life devoid of normal amusements and of the recreational mood, harassed by commands for theological self-examination, keyed to unnatural emotional repression, and forming above all a mere grim struggle for survival — all these things conspired to produce an environment in which the black whisperings of sinister grandams were heard far beyond the chimney corner, and in which tales of witchcraft and unbelievable secret monstrosities lingered long after the dread days of the Salem nightmare.

Poe represents the newer, more disillusioned, and more technically finished of the weird schools that rose out of this propitious milieu. Another school — the tradition of moral values, gentle restraint, and mild, leisurely phantasy tinged more or less with the whimsical — was represented by another famous, misunderstood, and lonely figure in American letters — the shy and sensitive Nathaniel Hawthorne, scion of antique Salem and great-grandson of one of the bloodiest of the old witchcraft judges. In Hawthorne we have none of the violence, the daring, the high colouring, the intense dramatic sense, the cosmic malignity, and the undivided and impersonal artistry of Poe. Here, instead, is a gentle soul cramped by the Puritanism of early New England; shadowed and wistful, and grieved at an unmoral universe which everywhere transcends the conventional patterns thought by our forefathers to represent divine and immutable law. Evil, a very real force to Hawthorne, appears on every hand as a lurking and conquering adversary; and the visible world becomes in his fancy a theatre of infinite tragedy and woe, with unseen half-existent influences hovering over it and through it, battling for supremacy and moulding the destinies of the hapless mortals who form its vain and self-deluded population. The heritage of American weirdness was his to a most intense degree, and he saw a dismal throng of vague spectres behind the common phenomena of life; but he was not disinterested enough to value impressions, sensations, and beauties of narration for their own sake. He must needs weave his phantasy into some quietly melancholy fabric of didactic or allegorical cast, in which his meekly resigned cynicism may display with naïve moral appraisal the perfidy of a human race which he cannot cease to cherish and mourn despite his insight into its hypocrisy. Supernatural horror, then, is never a primarily object with Hawthorne; though its impulses were so deeply woven into his personality that he cannot help suggesting it with the force of genius when he calls upon the unreal world to illustrate the pensive sermon he wishes to preach.

Hawthorne's intimations of the weird, always gentle, elusive, and restrained, may be traced throughout his work. The mood that produced them found one delightful vent in the Teutonised retelling of classic myths for children contained in *A Wonder Book* and *Tanglewood Tales*, and at other times exercised itself in casting a certain strangeness and intangible witchery or malevolence over events not meant to be actually supernatural; as in the macabre posthumous novel *Dr. Grimshawe's Secret*, which invests with a peculiar sort of repulsion a house existing to this day in Salem, and abutting on the ancient Charter Street Burying Ground. In *The Marble Faun*, whose design was sketched out in an Italian villa reputed to be haunted, a tremendous background of genuine phantasy and mystery palpitates just beyond the common reader's sight; and glimpses of fabulous blood in mortal veins are hinted at during the course of a romance which cannot help being interesting despite the persistent incubus of moral allegory, anti-Popery propaganda, and a Puritan prudery which has caused the modern writer D. H. Lawrence to express a longing to treat the author in a highly undignified manner. *Septimius Felton*, a posthumous novel whose idea was to have been elaborated and incorporated into the unfinished *Dolliver Romance*, touches on the Elixir of Life in a more or less capable fashion whilst the notes for a never-written tale to be called *The Ancestral Footstep* show what Hawthorne would have done with an intensive treatment of an old English superstition — that of an ancient and accursed line whose members left footprints of blood as they walked — which appears incidentally in both *Septimius Felton* and *Dr. Grimshawe's Secret*.

Many of Hawthorne's shorter tales exhibit weirdness, either of atmosphere or of incident, to a remarkable degree. "Edward Randolph's Portrait," in *Legends of the Province House*, has its diabolic moments. "The Minister's Black Veil" (founded on an actual incident) and "The Ambitious Guest" imply much more than they state, whilst "Ethan Grand" — a fragment of a longer work never completed — rises to genuine heights of cosmic fear with its vignette of the wild hill country and the blazing, desolate lime-kilns, and its delineation of the Byronic "unpardonable sinner," whose troubled life ends with a peal of fearful laughter in the night as he seeks rest amidst the flames of the furnace. Some of Hawthorne's notes tell of weird tales he would have written had he lived longer — an especially vivid plot being that concerning a baffling stranger who appeared now and then in public assemblies, and who was at last followed and found to come and go from a very ancient grave.

But foremost as a finished, artistic unit among all our author's weird material is the famous and exquisitely wrought novel, *The House of the Seven Gables*, in which the relentless working-out of an ancestral curse is developed with astonishing power against the sinister background of a very ancient Salem house — one of those peaked Gothic affairs which formed the first regular building-up of our New England coast towns but which gave way after the seventeenth century to the more familiar gambrel-roofed or classic Georgian types now known as "Colonial." Of these old gabled Gothic houses scarcely a dozen are to be seen today in their original condition throughout the United States, but one well known to Hawthorne still stands in Turner Street, Salem, and is pointed out with doubtful authority as the scene and inspiration of the romance. Such an edifice, with its spectral peaks, its clustered chimneys, its overhanging second story, its grotesque corner-brackets, and its diamond-paned lattice windows, is indeed an object well calculated to evoke sombre reflections; typifying as it does the dark Puritan age of concealed horror and witch-whispers which preceded the beauty, rationality, and spaciousness of the eighteenth century. Hawthorne saw many in his youth, and knew the black tales connected with some of them. He heard, too, many rumours of a curse upon his own line as the result of his great-grandfather's severity as a witchcraft judge in 1692.

From this setting came the immortal tale — New England's greatest contribution to weird literature — and we can feel in an instant the authenticity of the atmosphere presented to us. Stealthy horror and disease lurk within the weather-blackened, moss-crusted, and elm-shadowed walls of the archaic dwelling so vividly displayed, and we grasp the brooding malignity of the place when we read that its builder — old Colonel Pyncheon — snatched the land with peculiar ruthlessness from its original settler, Matthew Maule, whom he condemned to the gallows as a wizard in the year of the panic. Maule died cursing old Pyncheon — "God will give him blood to drink" — and the waters of the old well on the seized land turned bitter. Maule's carpenter son consented to build the great gabled house for his father's triumphant enemy, but the old Colonel died strangely on the day of its dedication. Then followed generations of odd vicissitudes, with queer whispers about the dark powers of the Maules, and sometimes terrible ends befalling the Pyncheons.

The overshadowing malevolence of the ancient house — almost as alive as Poe's House of Usher, though in a subtler way — pervades the tale as a recurrent motif pervades in operatic tragedy; and when the main story is reached, we behold the modern Pyncheons in a pitiable state of decay. Poor old Hepzibah, the eccentric reduced gentlewoman; childlike, unfortunate Clifford, just released from undeserved imprisonment; sly and treacherous judge Pyncheon, who is the old Colonel all over again — all these figures are tremendous symbols, and are well matched by the stunted vegetation and anæmic fowls in the garden. It was almost a pity to supply a fairly happy ending, with a union of sprightly Phœbe, cousin and last scion of the Pyncheons, to the prepossessing young man who turns out to be the last of the Maules. This union, presumably, ends the curse. Hawthorne avoids all violence of diction or movement, and keeps his implications of terror well in the background; but occasional glimpses amply serve to sustain the mood and redeem the work from pure allegorical aridity. Incidents like the bewitching of Alice Pyncheon in the early eighteenth century, and the spectral music of her harpsichord which precedes a death in the family — the latter a variant of an immemorial type of Aryan myth—link the action directly with the supernatural; whilst the dead nocturnal vigil of old judge Pyncheon in the ancient parlour, with his frightfully ticking watch, is stark horror of the most poignant and genuine sort. The way in which the judge's death is first adumbrated by the motions and sniffing of a strange cat outside the window, long before the fact is suspected by the reader or by any of the characters, is a stroke of genius which Poe could not have surpassed. Later the strange cat watches intently outside that same window in the night and on the next day, for—something. It is clearly the psychopomp of primeval myth, fitted and adapted with infinite deftness to its latter-day setting.

But Hawthorne left no well-defined literary posterity. His mood and attitude belonged to the age which closed with him, and it is the spirit of Poe—who so clearly and realistically understood the natural basis of the horror-appeal and the correct mechanics of its achievement—which survived and blossomed. Among the earliest of Poe's disciples may be reckoned the brilliant young Irishman Fitz-James O'Brien (1828-1862), who became naturalised as an American and perished honourably in the Civil War. It is he who gave us *What Was It?*, the first well-shaped short story of a tangible but invisible being, and the prototype of de Maupassant's *The Horla*; he also who created the inimitable *The Diamond Lens*, in which a young microscopist falls in love with a maiden of an infinitesimal world which he has discovered in a drop of water. O'Brien's early death undoubtedly deprived us of some masterful tales of strangeness and terror, though his genius was not, properly speaking, of the same titan quality which characterised Poe and Hawthorne.

Closer to real greatness was the eccentric and saturnine journalist Ambrose Bierce, born in 1842; who likewise entered the Civil War, but survived to write some immortal tales and to disappear in 1913 in as great a cloud of mystery as any he ever evoked from his nightmare fancy. Bierce was a satirist and pamphleteer of note, but the bulk of his artistic reputation must rest upon his grim and savage short stories, a large number of which deal with the Civil War and form the most vivid and realistic expression which that conflict has yet received in fiction. Virtually all of Bierce's tales are tales of horror; and whilst many of them treat only of the physical and psychological horrors within Nature, a substantial proportion admit the malignly supernatural and form a leading element in America's fund of weird literature. Mr. Samuel Loveman, a living poet and critic who was personally acquainted with Bierce, thus sums up the genius of the great "shadow-maker" in the preface to some of his letters:

> *In Bierce the evocation of horror becomes for the first time not so much the prescription or perversion of Poe and Maupassant, but an atmosphere definite and uncannily precise. Words, so simple that one would be prone to ascribe them to the limitations of a literary hack, take on an unholy horror, a new and unguessed transformation. In Poe one finds it a tour de force, in Maupassant a nervous engagement of the flagellated climax. To Bierce, simply and sincerely, diabolism held in its tormented death a legitimate and reliant means to the end. Yet a tacit confirmation with Nature is in every instance insisted upon.*
>
> *In* The Death of Halpin Frayser *flowers, verdure, and the boughs and leaves of trees are magnificently placed as an opposing foil to unnatural malignity. Not the accustomed golden world, but a world pervaded with the mystery of blue and the breathless recalcitrance of dreams is Bierce's. Yet, curiously, inhumanity is not altogether absent.*

The "inhumanity" mentioned by Mr. Loveman finds vent in a rare strain of sardonic comedy and graveyard humour, and a kind of delight in images of cruelty and tantalising disappointment. The former quality is well illustrated by some of the subtitles in the darker narratives; such as "One does not always eat what is on the table," describing a body laid out for a coroner's inquest, and "A man though naked may be in rags," referring to a frightfully mangled corpse.

Bierce's work is in general somewhat uneven. Many of the stories are obviously mechanical, and marred by a jaunty and commonplacely artificial style derived from journalistic models; but the grim malevolence stalking through all of them is unmistakable, and several stand out as permanent mountain-peaks of American weird writing. *The Death of Halpin Frayser*, called by Frederic Taber Cooper the most fiendishly ghastly tale in the literature of the Anglo-Saxon race, tells of a body skulking by night without a soul in a weird and horribly ensanguined wood, and of a man beset by ancestral memories who met death at the claws of that which had been his fervently loved mother. *The Damned Thing*, frequently copied in popular anthologies, chronicles the hideous devastations of an invisible entity that waddles and flounders on the hills and in the wheatfields by night and day. *The Suitable Surroundings* evokes with singular subtlety yet apparent simplicity a piercing sense of the terror which may reside in the written word. In the story the weird author Colston says to his friend Marsh, "You are brave enough to read me in a street-car, but—in a deserted house—alone—in the forest—at night! Bah! I have a manuscript in my pocket that would kill you!" Marsh reads the manuscript in "the suitable surroundings" —and it does kill him. *The Middle Toe of the Right Foot* is clumsily developed, but has a powerful climax. A man named Manton has horribly killed his two children and his wife, the latter of whom lacked the middle toe of the right foot. Ten years later he returns much altered to the neighbourhood; and, being secretly recognised, is provoked into a bowie-knife duel in the dark, to be held in the now abandoned house where his crime was committed. When the moment of the duel arrives a trick is played upon him; and he is left without an antagonist, shut in a night-black ground floor room of the reputedly haunted edifice, with the thick dust of a decade on every hand. No knife is drawn against him, for only a thorough scare is intended; but on the next day he is found crouched in a corner with distorted face, dead of sheer fright at something he has seen. The only clue visible to the discoverers is one having terrible implications: "In the dust of years that lay thick upon the floor — leading from the door by which they had entered, straight across the room to within a yard of Manton's crouching corpse — were three parallel lines of footprints — light but definite impressions of bare feet, the outer ones those of small children, the inner a woman's. From the point at which they ended they did not return; they pointed all one way." And, of course, the woman's prints showed a lack of the middle toe of the right foot. *The Spook House*, told with a severely homely air of journalistic verisimilitude, conveys terrible hints of shocking mystery. In 1858 an entire family of seven persons disappears suddenly and unaccountably from a plantation house in eastern Kentucky, leaving all its possessions untouched — furniture, clothing, food supplies, horses, cattle, and slaves. About a year later two men of high standing are forced by a storm to take shelter in the deserted dwelling, and in so doing stumble into a strange subterranean room lit by an unaccountable greenish light and having an iron door which cannot be opened from within. In this room lie the decayed corpses of all the missing family; and as one of the discoverers rushes forward to embrace a body he seems to recognise, the other is so overpowered by a strange foetor that he accidentally shuts his companion in the vault and loses consciousness. Recovering his senses six weeks later, the survivor is unable to find the hidden room; and the house is burned during the Civil War. The imprisoned discoverer is never seen or heard of again.

Bierce seldom realises the atmospheric possibilities of his themes as vividly as Poe; and much of his work contains a certain touch of naïveté, prosaic angularity, or early-American provincialism which contrasts somewhat with the efforts of later horror-masters. Nevertheless the genuineness and artistry of his dark intimations are always unmistakable, so that his greatness is in no danger of eclipse. As arranged in his definitively collected works, Bierce's weird tales occur mainly in two volumes, *Can Such Things Be?* and *In the Midst of Life*. The former, indeed, is almost wholly given over to the supernatural.

Much of the best in American horror-literature has come from pens not mainly devoted to that medium. Oliver Wendell Holmes's historic *Elsie Venner* suggests with admirable restraint an unnatural Ophidian element in a young woman prenatally influenced, and sustains the atmosphere with finely discriminating landscape touches. *In The Turn of the Screw* Henry James triumphs over his inevitable pomposity and prolixity sufficiently well to create a truly potent air of sinister menace; depicting the hideous influence of two dead and evil servants, Peter Quint and the governess, Miss Jessel, over a small boy and girl who had been under their care. James is perhaps too diffuse, too unctuously urbane, and too much addicted to subtleties of speech to realise fully all the wild and devastating horror in his situations; but for all that there is a rare and mounting tide of fright, culminating in the death of the little boy, which gives the novelette a permanent place in its special class.

F. Marion Crawford produced several weird tales of varying quality, now collected in a volume entitled *Wandering Ghosts*. "For the Blood Is the Life" touches powerfully on a case of moon-cursed vampirism near an ancient tower on the rocks of the lonely South Italian seacoast. "The Dead Smile" treats of family horrors in an old house and an ancestral vault in Ireland, and introduces the banshee with considerable force. "The Upper Berth," however, is Crawford's weird masterpiece; and is one of the most tremendous horror-stories in all literature. In this tale of a suicide-haunted stateroom such things as the spectral saltwater dampness, the strangely open porthole, and the nightmare struggle with the nameless object are handled with incomparable dexterity.

Very genuine, though not without the typical mannered extravagance of the eighteen-nineties, is the strain of horror in the early work of Robert W. Chambers, since renowned for products of a very different quality. *The King in Yellow*, a series of vaguely connected short stories having as a background a monstrous and suppressed book whose perusal brings fright, madness, and spectral tragedy, really achieves notable heights of cosmic fear in spite of uneven interest and a somewhat trivial and affected cultivation of the Gallic studio atmosphere made popular by Du Maurier's *Trilby*. The most powerful of its tales, perhaps, is "The Yellow Sign," in which is introduced a silent and terrible churchyard watchman with a face like a puffy graveworm's. A boy, describing a tussle he has had with this creature, shivers and sickens as he relates a certain detail. "Well, it's Gawd's truth that when I 'it 'im 'e grabbed me wrists, Sir, and when I twisted 'is soft, mushy fist one of 'is fingers come off in me 'and." An artist, who after seeing him has shared with another a strange dream of a nocturnal hearse, is shocked by the voice with which the watchman accosts him. The fellow emits a muttering sound that fills the head "like thick oily smoke from a fat-rendering vat or an odour of noisome decay." What he mumbles is merely this: "Have you found the Yellow Sign?"

A weirdly hieroglyphed onyx talisman, picked up on the street by the sharer of his dream, is shortly given the artist; and after stumbling queerly upon the hellish and forbidden book of horrors the two learn, among other hideous things which no sane mortal should know, that this talisman is indeed the nameless Yellow Sign handed down from the accursed cult of Hastur — from primordial Carcosa, whereof the volume treats, and some nightmare memory of which seeks to lurk latent and ominous at the back of all men's minds. Soon they hear the rumbling of the black-plumed hearse driven by the flabby and corpse-faced watchman. He enters the night-shrouded house in quest of the Yellow Sign, all bolts and bars rotting at his touch. And when the people rush in, drawn by a scream that no human throat could utter, they find three forms on the floor — two dead and one dying. One of the dead shapes is far gone in decay. It is the churchyard watchman, and the doctor exclaims, "That man must have been dead for months." It is worth observing that the author derives most of the names and allusions connected with his eldritch land of primal memory from the tales of Ambrose Bierce. Other early works of Mr. Chambers displaying the outré and macabre element are *The Maker of Moons* and *In Search of the Unknown*. One cannot help regretting that he did not further develop a vein in which he could so easily have become a recognised master.

Horror material of authentic force may be found in the work of the New England realist Mary E. Wilkins, whose volume of short tales, *The Wind in the Rosebush*, contains a number of noteworthy achievements. "In The Shadows on the Wall" we are shown with consummate skill the response of a staid New England household to uncanny tragedy; and the sourceless shadow of the poisoned brother well prepares us for the climactic moment when the shadow of the secret murderer, who has killed himself in a neighbouring city, suddenly appears beside it. Charlotte Perkins Gilman, in *The Yellow Wall Paper*, rises to a classic level in subtly delineating the madness which crawls over a woman dwelling in the hideously papered room where a madwoman was once confined.

In *The Dead Valley* the eminent architect and mediævalist Ralph Adams Cram achieves a memorably potent degree of vague regional horror through subtleties of atmosphere and description.

Still further carrying on our spectral tradition is the gifted and versatile humourist Irvin S. Cobb, whose work both early and recent contains some finely weird specimens. "Fishhead," an early achievement, is banefully effective in its portrayal of unnatural affinities between a hybrid idiot and the strange fish of an isolated lake, which at the last avenge their biped kinsman's murder. Later work of Mr. Cobb introduces an element of possible science, as in the tale of hereditary memory where a modern man with a negroid strain utters words in African jungle speech when run down by a train under visual and aural circumstances recalling the maiming of his black ancestor by a rhinoceros a century before.

Extremely high in artistic stature is the novel *The Dark Chamber* (1927) by the late Leonard Cline. This is the tale of a man who — with the characteristic ambition of the Gothic or Byronic hero-villain — seeks to defy nature and recapture every moment of his past life through the abnormal stimulation of memory. To this end he employs endless notes, records, mnemonic objects, and pictures — and finally odours, music, and exotic drugs. At last his ambition goes beyond his personal life and readies toward the black abysses of hereditary memory — even back to pre-human days amidst the steaming swamps of the carboniferous age, and to still more unimaginable deeps of primal time and entity. He calls for madder music and takes stranger drugs, and finally his great dog grows oddly afraid of him. A noxious animal stench encompasses him, and he grows vacant-faced and subhuman. In the end he takes to the woods, howling at night beneath windows. He is finally found in a thicket, mangled to death. Beside him is the mangled corpse of his dog. They have killed each other. The atmosphere of this novel is malevolently potent, much attention being paid to the central figure's sinister home and household.

A less subtle and well-balanced but nevertheless highly effective creation is Herbert S. Gorman's novel, *The Place Called Dagon*, which relates the dark history of a western Massachusetts back-water where the descendants of refugees from the Salem witchcraft still keep alive the morbid and degenerate horrors of the Black Sabbat.

Sinister House, by Leland Hall, has touches of magnificent atmosphere but is marred by a somewhat mediocre romanticism.

Very notable in their way are some of the weird conceptions of the novelist and short-story writer Edward Lucas White, most of whose themes arise from actual dreams. *The Song of The Siren* has a very persuasive strangeness, while such things as *Lukundoo* and *The Snout* arouse darker apprehensions. Mr. White imparts a very peculiar quality to his tales — an oblique sort of glamour which has its own distinctive type of convincingness.

Of younger Americans, none strikes the note of cosmic horror so well as the California poet, artist and fictionist Clark Ashton Smith, whose bizarre writing, drawings, paintings and stories are the delight of a sensitive few. Mr. Smith has for his background a universe of remote and paralysing fright jungles of poisonous and iridescent blossoms on the moons of Saturn, evil and grotesque temples in Atlantis, Lemuria, and forgotten elder worlds, and dank morasses of spotted death-fungi in spectral countries beyond earth's rim. His longest and most ambitious poem, *The Hashish-Eater*, is in pentameter blank verse; and opens up chaotic and incredible vistas of kaleidoscopic nightmare in the spaces between the stars. In sheer dæmonic strangeness and fertility of conception, Mr. Smith is perhaps unexcelled by any other writer dead or living. Who else has seen such gorgeous, luxuriant, and feverishly distorted visions of infinite spheres and multiple dimensions and lived to tell the tale? His short stories deal powerfully with other galaxies, worlds, and dimensions, as well as with strange regions and æons on the earth. He tells of primal Hyperborea and its black amorphous god Tsathoggua; of the lost continent Zothique, and of the fabulous, Vampire-curst land of Averoigne in mediæval France. Some of Mr. Smith's best work can be found in the brochure entitled *The Double Shadow and Other Fantasies*.

IX.

THE WEIRD TRADITION IN THE BRITISH ISLES.

Recent British literature, besides including the three or four greatest *fantaisistes* of the present age, has been gratifyingly fertile in the element of the weird. Rudyard Kipling has often approached it, and has, despite the omnipresent mannerisms, handled it with indubitable mastery in such tales as *The Phantom Rickshaw, The Finest Story in the World, The Recrudescence of Imray*, and *The Mark of the Beast*. This latter is of particular poignancy; the pictures of the naked leper-priest who mewed like an otter, of the spots which appeared on the chest of the man that priest cursed, of the growing carnivorousness of the victim and of the fear which horses began to display toward him, and of the eventually half-accomplished transformation of that victim into a leopard, being things which no reader is ever likely to forget. The final defeat of the malignant sorcery does not impair the force of the tale or the validity of its mystery.

Lafcadio Hearn, strange, wandering, and exotic, departs still farther from the realm of the real; and with the supreme artistry of a sensitive poet weaves phantasies impossible to an author of the solid roast beef type. His *Fantastics*, written in America, contains some of the most impressive ghoulishness in all literature; whilst his *Kwaidan*, written in Japan, crystalises with matchless skill and delicacy the eerie lore and whispered legends of that richly colourful nation. Still more of Helm's wizardry of language is shown in some of his translations from the French, especially from Gautier and Flaubert. His version of the latter's *Temptation of St. Anthony* is a classic of fevered and riotous imagery clad in the magic of singing words.

Oscar Wilde may likewise be given a place amongst weird writers, both for certain of his exquisite fairy tales, and for his vivid *Picture of Dorian Gray*, in which a marvellous portrait for years assumes the duty of aging and coarsening instead of its original, who meanwhile plunges into every excess of vice and crime without the outward loss of youth, beauty, and freshness. There is a sudden and potent climax when Dorian Gray, at last become a murderer, seeks to destroy the painting whose changes testify to his moral degeneracy. He stabs it with a knife, and a hideous cry and crash are heard; but when the servants enter they find it in all its pristine loveliness. "Lying on the floor was a dead man, in evening dress, with a knife in his heart. He was withered, wrinkled, and loathsome of visage. It was not until they had examined the rings that they recognised who he was."

Matthew Phipps Shiel, author of many weird, grotesque, and adventurous novels and tales, occasionally attains a high level of horrific magic. *Xelucha* is a noxiously hideous fragment, but is excelled by Mr. Shiel's undoubted masterpiece, *The House of Sounds*, floridly written in the "yellow nineties," and recast with more artistic restraint in the early twentieth century. This story, in final form, deserves a place among the foremost things of its kind. It tells of a creeping horror and menace trickling down the centuries on a sub-arctic island off the coast of Norway; where, amidst the sweep of daemon winds and the ceaseless din of hellish waves and cataracts, a vengeful dead man built a brazen tower of terror. It is vaguely like, yet infinitely unlike, Poe's *Fall of the House of Usher*. In the novel *The Purple Cloud* Mr. Shiel describes with tremendous power a curse which came out of the arctic to destroy mankind, and which for a time appears to have left but a single inhabitant on our planet. The sensations of this lone survivor as he realises his position, and roams through the corpse-littered and treasure-strewn cities of the world as their absolute master, are delivered with a skill and artistry falling little short of actual majesty. Unfortunately the second half of the book, with its conventionally romantic element, involves a distinct letdown.

Better known than Shiel is the ingenious Bram Stoker, who created many starkly horrific conceptions in a series of novels whose poor technique sadly impairs their net effect. *The Lair of the White Worm*, dealing with a gigantic primitive entity that lurks in a vault beneath an ancient castle, utterly ruins a magnificent idea by a development almost infantile. *The Jewel of Seven Stars*, touching on a strange Egyptian resurrection, is less crudely written. But best of all is the famous *Dracula*, which has become almost the standard modern exploitation of the frightful vampire myth. Count Dracula, a vampire, dwells in a horrible castle in the Carpathians, but finally migrates to England with the design of populating the country with fellow vampires. How an Englishman fares within Dracula's stronghold of terrors, and how the dead fiend's plot for domination is at last defeated, are elements which unite to form a tale now justly assigned a permanent place in English letters. Dracula evoked many similar novels of supernatural horror, among which the best are perhaps *The Beetle*, by Richard Marsh, *Brood of the Witch-Queen*, by "Sax Rohmer" (Arthur Sarsfield Ward), and *The Door of the Unreal*, by Gerald Bliss. The latter handles quite dexterously the standard werewolf superstition. Much subtler and more artistic, and told with singular skill through the juxtaposed narratives of the several characters, is the novel *Cold Harbour*, by Francis Brett Young, in which an ancient house of strange malignancy is powerfully delineated. The mocking and well-nigh omnipotent fiend Humphrey Furnival holds echoes of the Manfred-Montoni type of early Gothic "villain," but is redeemed from triteness by many clever individualities. Only the slight diffuseness of explanation at the close, and the somewhat too free use of divination as a plot factor, keep this tale from approaching absolute perfection.

In the novel *Witch Wood* John Buchan depicts with tremendous force a survival of the evil Sabbat in a lonely district of Scotland. The description of the black forest with the evil stone, and of the terrible cosmic adumbrations when the horror is finally extirpated, will repay one for wading through the very gradual action and plethora of Scottish dialect. Some of Mr. Buchan's short stories are also extremely vivid in their spectral intimations; "The Green Wildebeest," a tale of African witchcraft, "The Wind in the Portico," with its awakening of dead Britanno-Roman horrors, and "Skule Skerry," with its touches of sub-arctic fright, being especially remarkable.

Clemence Housman, in the brief novelette *The Werewolf*, attains a high degree of gruesome tension and achieves to some extent the atmosphere of authentic folklore. In *The Elixir of Life* Arthur Ransome attains some darkly excellent effects despite a general naïveté of plot, while H. B. Drake's *The*

Shadowy Thing summons up strange and terrible vistas. George Macdonald's *Lilith* has a compelling bizarrerie all its own, the first and simpler of the two versions being perhaps the more effective.

Deserving of distinguished notice as a forceful craftsman to whom an unseen mystic world is ever a close and vital reality is the poet Walter de la Mare, whose haunting verse and exquisite prose alike bear consistent traces of a strange vision reaching deeply into veiled spheres of beauty and terrible and forbidden dimensions of being. In the novel *The Return* we see the soul of a dead man reach out of its grave of two centuries and fasten itself upon the flesh of the living, so that even the face of the victim becomes that which had long ago returned to dust. Of the shorter tales, of which several volumes exist, many are unforgettable for their command of fear's and sorcery's darkest ramifications; notably "Seaton's Aunt," in which there lowers a noxious background of malignant vampirism; "The Tree," which tells of a frightful vegetable growth in the yard of a starving artist; "Out of the Deep," wherein we are given leave to imagine what thing answered the summons of a dying wastrel in a dark lonely house when he pulled a long-feared bell-cord in the attic of his dread-haunted boyhood; "A Recluse," which hints at what sent a chance guest flying from a house in the night; "Mr. Kempe," which shows us a mad clerical hermit in quest of the human soul, dwelling in a frightful sea-cliff region beside an archaic abandoned chapel; and "All-Hallows," a glimpse of dæmoniac forces besieging a lonely mediaeval church and miraculously restoring the rotting masonry. De la Mare does not make fear the sole or even the dominant element of most of his tales, being apparently more interested in the subtleties of character involved. Occasionally he sinks to sheer whimsical phantasy of the Barrie order. Still he is among the very few to whom unreality is a vivid, living presence; and as such he is able to put into his occasional fear-studies a keen potency which only a rare master can achieve. His poem *The Listeners* restores the Gothic shudder to modern verse.

The weird short story has fared well of late, an important contributor being the versatile E. F. Benson, whose "The Man Who Went Too Far" breathes whisperingly of a house at the edge of a dark wood, and of Pan's hoof-mark on the breast of a dead man. Mr. Benson's volume, *Visible and Invisible*, contains several stories of singular power; notably "Negotiam Perambulans," whose unfolding reveals an abnormal monster from an ancient ecclesiastical panel which performs an act of miraculous vengeance in a lonely village on the Cornish coast, and "The Horror-Horn," through which lopes a terrible half-human survival dwelling on unvisited Alpine peaks. "The Face," in another collection, is lethally potent, in its relentless aura of doom. H. R. Wakefield, in his collections, *They Return at Evening* and *Others Who Return*, manages now and then to achieve great heights of horror despite a vitiating air of sophistication. The most notable stories are "The Red Lodge" with its slimy aqueous evil, "He Cometh and He Passeth By," "And He Shall Sing," "The Cairn," "Look Up There," "Blind Man's Bluff," and that bit of lurking millennial horror, "The Seventeenth Hole at Duncaster." Mention has been made of the weird work of H.G. Wells and A. Conan Doyle. The former, in "The Ghost of Fear," reaches a very high level while all the items in *Thirty Strange Stories* have strong fantastic implications. Doyle now and then struck a powerfully spectral note, as in "The Captain of the Pole-Star," a tale of arctic ghostliness, and "Lot No. 249," wherein the reanimated mummy theme is used with more than ordinary skill. Hugh Walpole, of the same family as the founder of Gothic fiction, has sometimes approached the bizarre with much success, his short story "Mrs. Lunt" carrying a very poignant shudder. John Metcalfe, in the collection published as *The Smoking Leg*, attains now and then a rare pitch of potency, the tale entitled "The Bad Lands" containing graduations of horror that strongly savour of genius. More whimsical and inclined toward the amiable and innocuous phantasy of Sir J. M. Barrie are the short tales of E.M. Forster, grouped under the title of *The Celestial Omnibus*. Of these only one, dealing with a glimpse of Pan and his aura of fright, may be said to hold the true element of cosmic horror. Mrs. H.D. Everett, though adhering to very old and conventional models, occasionally reaches singular heights of spiritual terror in her collection of short stories, *The Death Mask*. L. P. Hartley is notable for his incisive and extremely ghastly tale, "A Visitor from Down Under," May Sinclair's *Uncanny Stories* contain more of traditional "occultism" than of that creative treatment of fear which marks mastery in this field, and are inclined to lay more stress on human emotions and psychological delving than upon the stark phenomena of a cosmos utterly unreal. It may be well to remark here that occult believers are probably less effective than materialists in delineating the spectral and the fantastic, since to them the phantom world is so commonplace a reality that they tend to refer to it with less awe, remoteness, and impressiveness than do those who see in it an absolute and stupendous violation of the natural order.

Of rather uneven stylistic quality, but vast occasional power in its suggestion of lurking worlds and beings behind the ordinary surface of life, is the work of William Hope Hodgson, known today far less than it deserves to be. Despite a tendency toward conventionally sentimental conceptions of the universe, and of man's relation to it and to his fellows, Mr. Hodgson is perhaps second only to Algernon Blackwood in his serious treatment of unreality. Few can equal him in adumbrating the nearness of nameless forces and monstrous besieging entities through casual hints and insignificant details, or in conveying feelings of the spectral and the abnormal in connection with regions or buildings.

In *The Boats of the Glen Carrig* (1907) we are shown a variety of malign marvels and accursed unknown lands as encountered by the survivors of a sunken ship. The brooding menace in the earlier parts of the book is impossible to surpass, though a letdown in the direction of ordinary romance and adventure occurs toward the end. An inaccurate and pseudo-romantic attempt to reproduce eighteenth-century prose detracts from the general effect, but the really profound nautical erudition everywhere displayed is a compensating factor.

The House on the Borderland (1908) — perhaps the greatest of all Mr. Hodgson's works — tells of a lonely and evilly regarded house in Ireland which forms a focus for hideous otherworld forces and sustains a siege by blasphemous hybrid anomalies from a hidden abyss below. The wanderings of the narrator's spirit through limitless light-years of cosmic space and Kalpas of eternity, and its witnessing of the solar system's final destruction, constitute something almost unique in standard literature. And everywhere there is manifest the author's power to suggest vague, ambushed horrors in natural scenery. But for a few touches of commonplace sentimentality this book would be a classic of the first water.

The Ghost Pirates (1909), regarded by Mr. Hodgson as rounding out a trilogy with the two previously mentioned works, is a powerful account of a doomed and haunted ship on its last voyage, and of the terrible sea-devils (of quasi-human aspect, and perhaps the spirits of bygone buccaneers) that besiege it and finally drag it down to an unknown fate. With its command of maritime knowledge, and its clever selection of hints and incidents suggestive of latent horrors in nature, this book at times reaches enviable peaks of power.

The Night Land (1912) is a long-extended (538 pp.) tale of the earth's infinitely remote future — billions of billions of years ahead, after the death of the sun. It is told in a rather clumsy fashion, as the dreams of a man in the seventeenth century, whose mind merges with its own future incarnation; and is seriously marred by painful verboseness, repetitiousness, artificial and nauseously sticky romantic sentimentality, and an attempt at archaic language even more grotesque and absurd than that in *Glen Carrig*.

Allowing for all its faults, it is yet one of the most potent pieces of macabre imagination ever written. The picture of a night-black, dead planet, with the remains of the human race concentrated in a stupendously vast mental pyramid and besieged by monstrous, hybrid, and altogether unknown forces of the darkness, is something that no reader can ever forget: Shapes and entities of an altogether non-human and inconceivable sort — the prowlers of the black, man-forsaken, and unexplored world outside the pyramid — are suggested and partly described with ineffable potency; while the night-land landscape with its chasms and slopes and dying volcanism takes on an almost sentient terror beneath the author's touch.

Midway in the book the central figure ventures outside the pyramid on a quest through death-haunted realms untrod by man for millions of years — and in his slow, minutely described, day-by-day progress over unthinkable leagues of immemorial blackness there is a sense of cosmic alienage, breathless mystery, and terrified expectancy unrivaled in the whole range of literature. The last quarter of the book drags woefully, but fails to spoil the tremendous power of the whole.

Mr. Hodgson's later volume, *Carnacki, the Ghost-Finder*, consists of several longish short stories published many years before in magazines. In quality it falls conspicuously below the level of the other books. We here find a more or less conventional stock figure of the "infallible detective" type — the progeny of M. Dupin and Sherlock Holmes, and the close kin of Algernon Blackwood's *John Silence* — moving through scenes and events badly marred by an atmosphere of professional "occultism." A few of the episodes, however, are of undeniable power, and afford glimpses of the peculiar genius characteristic of the author.

Naturally it is impossible in brief sketch to trace out all the classic modern uses of the terror element. The ingredient must of necessity enter into all work, both prose and verse, treating broadly of life; and we are therefore not surprised to find a share in such writers as the poet Browning, whose *Childe Roland to the Dark Tower Came* is instinct with hideous menace, or the novelist Joseph Conrad, who often wrote of the dark secrets within the sea, and of the dæmoniac driving power of Fate as influencing the lives of lonely and maniacally resolute men. Its trail is one of infinite ramifications; but we must here confine ourselves to its appearance in a relatively unmixed state, where it determines and dominates the work of art containing it.

Somewhat separate from the main British stream is that current of weirdness in Irish literature which came to the fore in the Celtic Renaissance of the later nineteenth and early twentieth centuries. Ghost and fairy lore have always been of great prominence in Ireland, and for over a hundred years have been recorded by a line of such faithful transcribers and translators as William Carleton, T. Crofton Croker, Lady Wilde — mother of Oscar Wilde — Douglas Hyde, and W.B. Yeats. Brought to notice by the modern movement, this body of myth has been carefully collected and studied; and its salient features reproduced in the work of later figures like Yeats, J. M. Synge, "A. E.," Lady Gregory, Padraic Colum, James Stephens and their colleagues.

Whilst on the whole more whimsically fantastic than terrible, such folklore and its consciously artistic counterparts contain much that falls truly within the domain of cosmic horror. Tales of burials in sunken churches beneath haunted lakes, accounts of death-heralding banshees and sinister changelings, ballads of spectres and "the unholy creatures of the Raths" — all these have their poignant and definite shivers, and mark a strong and distinctive element in weird literature. Despite homely grotesqueness and absolute naïveté, there is genuine nightmare in the class of narrative represented by the yarn of Teig O'Kane, who in punishment for his wild life was ridden all night by a hideous corpse that demanded burial and drove him from churchyard to churchyard as the dead rose up loathsomely in each one and refused to accommodate the newcomer with a berth. Yeats, undoubtedly the greatest figure of the Irish revival if not the greatest of all living poets, has accomplished notable things both in original work and in the codification of old legends.

X.
MODERN MASTERS.

The best horror-tales of today, profiting by the long evolution of the type, possess a naturalness, convincingness, artistic smoothness, and skillful intensity of appeal quite beyond comparison with anything in the Gothic work of a century or more ago. Technique, craftsmanship, experience, and psychological knowledge have advanced tremendously with the passing years, so that much of the older work seems naïve and artificial; redeemed, when redeemed at all, only by a genius which conquers heavy limitations. The tone of jaunty and inflated romance, full of false motivation and investing every conceivable event with a counterfeit significance and carelessly inclusive glamour, is now confined to lighter and more whimsical phases of supernatural writing. Serious weird stories are either made realistically intense by close consistency and perfect fidelity to Nature except in the one supernatural direction which the author allows himself, or else cast altogether in the realm of phantasy, with atmosphere cunningly adapted to the visualisation of a delicately exotic world of unreality beyond space and time, in which almost anything may happen if it but happen in true accord with certain types of imagination and illusion normal to the sensitive human brain. This, at least, is the dominant tendency; though of course many great contemporary writers slip occasionally into some of the flashy postures of immature romanticism or into bits of the equally empty and absurd jargon of pseudo-scientific "occultism," now at one of its periodic high tides.

Of living creators of cosmic fear raised to its most artistic pitch, few if any can hope to equal the versatile Arthur Machen, author of some dozen tales long and short, in which the elements of hidden horror and brooding fright attain an almost incomparable substance and realistic acuteness. Mr. Machen, a general man of letters and master of an exquisitely lyrical and expressive prose style, has perhaps put more conscious effort into his picaresque *Chronicles of Clemendy*, his refreshing essays, his vivid autobiographical volumes, his fresh and spirited translations, and above all his memorable epic of the sensitive æsthetic mind, *The Hill of Dreams*, in which the youthful hero responds to the magic of that ancient Welsh environment which is the author's own, and lives a dream-life in the Roman city of Isca Silurum, now shrunk to the relic-strewn village of Caerleon-on-Usk. But the fact remains that his powerful horror-material of the nineties and earlier nineteen-hundreds stands alone in its class, and marks a distinct epoch in the history of this literary form.

Mr. Machen, with an impressionable Celtic heritage linked to keen youthful memories of the wild domed hills, archaic forests, and cryptical Roman ruins of the Gwent countryside, has developed an imaginative life of rare beauty, intensity, and historic background. He has absorbed the mediaeval mystery of dark woods and ancient customs, and is a champion of the Middle Ages in all things—including the Catholic faith. He has yielded, likewise, to the spell of the Britanno-Roman life which once surged over his native region; and finds strange magic in the fortified camps, tessellated pavements, fragments of statues, and kindred things which tell of the day when classicism reigned and Latin was the language of the country. A young American poet, Frank Belknap Long, has well summarised this dreamer's rich endowments and wizardry of expression in the sonnet *On Reading Arthur Machen*:

There is a glory in the autumn wood,
The ancient lanes of England wind and climb
Past wizard oaks and gorse and tangled thyme
To where a fort of mighty empire stood:

There is a glamour in the autumn sky;
The reddened clouds are writhing in the glow
Of some great fire, and there are glints below
Of tawny yellow where the embers die.

I wait, for he will show me, clear and cold,
High-rais'd in splendour, sharp against the North,
The Roman eagles, and through mists of gold
The marching legions as they issue forth:

I wait, for I would share with him again
The ancient wisdom, and the ancient pain.

Of Mr. Machen's horror-tales the most famous is perhaps *The Great God Pan* (1894) which tells of a singular and terrible experiment and its consequences. A young woman, through surgery of the brain-cells, is made to see the vast and monstrous deity of Nature, and becomes an idiot in consequence, dying less than a year later. Years afterward a strange, ominous, and foreign-looking child named Helen Vaughan is placed to board with a family in rural Wales, and haunts the woods in unaccountable fashion. A little boy is thrown out of his mind at sight of someone or something he spies with her, and a young girl comes to a terrible end in similar fashion. All this mystery is strangely interwoven with the Roman rural deities of the place, as sculptured in antique fragments. After another lapse of years, a woman of strangely exotic beauty appears in society, drives her husband to horror and death, causes an artist to paint unthinkable paintings of Witches' Sabbaths, creates an epidemic of suicide among the men of her acquaintance, and is finally discovered to be a frequenter of the lowest dens of vice in London, where even the most callous degenerates are shocked at her enormities. Through the clever comparing of notes on the part of those who have had word of her at various stages of her career, this woman is discovered to be the girl

Helen Vaughan, who is the child—by no mortal father—of the young woman on whom the brain experiment was made. She is a daughter of hideous Pan himself, and at the last is put to death amidst horrible transmutations of form involving changes of sex and a descent to the most primal manifestations of the life-principle.

But the charm of the tale is in the telling. No one could begin to describe the cumulative suspense and ultimate horror with which every paragraph abounds without following fully the precise order in which Mr. Machen unfolds his gradual hints and revelations. Melodrama is undeniably present, and coincidence is stretched to a length which appears absurd upon analysis; but in the malign witchery of the tale as a whole these trifles are forgotten, and the sensitive reader reaches the end with only an appreciative shudder and a tendency to repeat the words of one of the characters: "It is too incredible, too monstrous; such things can never be in this quiet world .... Why, man, if such a case were possible, our earth would be a nightmare."

Less famous and less complex in plot than *The Great God Pan*, but definitely finer in atmosphere and general artistic value, is the curious and dimly disquieting chronicle called *The White People*, whose central portion purports to be the diary or notes of a little girl whose nurse has introduced her to some of the forbidden magic and soul-blasting traditions of the noxious witch-cult—the cult whose whispered lore was handed down long lines of peasantry throughout Western Europe, and whose members sometimes stole forth at night, one by one, to meet in black woods and lonely places for the revolting orgies of the Witches' Sabbath. Mr. Machen's narrative, a triumph of skillful selectiveness and restraint, accumulates enormous power as it flows on in a stream of innocent childish prattle, introducing allusions to strange "nymphs," "Dols," "voolas," "white, green, and scarlet ceremonies," "Aklo letters," "Chian language," "Mao games," and the like. The rites learned by the nurse from her witch grandmother are taught to the child by the time she is three years old, and her artless accounts of the dangerous secret revelations possess a lurking terror generously mixed with pathos. Evil charms well known to anthropologists are described with juvenile naïveté, and finally there comes a winter afternoon journey into the old Welsh hills, performed under an imaginative spell which lends to the wild scenery an added weirdness, strangeness, and suggestion of grotesque sentience. The details of this journey are given with marvelous vividness, and form to the keen critic a masterpiece of fantastic writing, with almost unlimited power in the intimation of potent hideousness and cosmic aberration. At length the child—whose age is then thirteen—comes upon a cryptic and banefully beautiful thing in the midst of a dark and inaccessible wood. In the end horror overtakes her in a manner deftly prefigured by an anecdote in the prologue, but she poisons herself in time. Like the mother of Helen Vaughan in *The Great God Pan*, she has seen that frightful deity. She is discovered dead in the dark wood beside the cryptic thing she found; and that thing—a whitely luminous statue of Roman workmanship about which dire mediæval rumours had clustered—is affrightedly hammered into dust by the searchers.

In the episodic novel of *The Three Impostors*, a work whose merit as a whole is somewhat marred by an imitation of the jaunty Stevenson manner, occur certain tales which perhaps represent the high-water mark of Machen's skill as a terror-weaver. Here we find in its most artistic form a favourite weird conception of the author's; the notion that beneath the mounds and rocks of the wild Welsh hills dwell subterraneously that squat primitive race whose vestiges gave rise to our common folk legends of fairies, elves, and the "little people," and whose acts are even now responsible for certain unexplained disappearances, and occasional substitutions of strange dark "changelings" for normal infants. This theme receives its finest treatment in the episode entitled *The Novel of the Black Seal*; where a professor, having discovered a singular identity between certain characters scrawled on Welsh limestone rocks and those existing in a prehistoric black seal from Babylon, sets out on a course of discovery which leads him to unknown and terrible things. A queer passage in the ancient geographer Solinus, a series of mysterious disappearances in the lonely reaches of Wales, a strange idiot son born to a rural mother after a fright in which her inmost faculties were shaken; all these things suggest to the professor a hideous connection and a condition revolting to any friend and respecter of the human race. He hires the idiot boy, who jabbers strangely at times in a repulsive hissing voice, and is subject to odd epileptic seizures. Once, after such a seizure in the professor's study by night, disquieting odours and evidences of unnatural presences are found; and soon after that the professor leaves a bulky document and goes into the weird hills with feverish expectancy and strange terror in his heart. He never returns, but beside a fantastic stone in the wild country are found his watch, money, and ring, done up with catgut in a parchment bearing the same terrible characters as those on the black Babylonish seal and the rock in the Welsh mountains.

The bulky document explains enough to bring up the most hideous vistas. Professor Gregg, from the massed evidence presented by the Welsh disappearances, the rock inscription, the accounts of ancient geographers, and the black seal, has decided that a frightful race of dark primal beings of immemorial antiquity and wide former diffusion still dwell beneath the hills of unfrequented Wales. Further research has unriddled the message of the black seal, and proved that the idiot boy, a son of some father more terrible than mankind, is the heir of monstrous memories and possibilities. That strange night in the study the professor invoked "the awful transmutation of the hills" by the aid of the black seal, and aroused in the hybrid idiot the horrors of his shocking paternity. He "saw his body swell and become distended as a bladder, while the face blackened ...." And then the supreme effects of the invocation appeared, and Professor Gregg knew the stark frenzy of cosmic panic in its darkest form. He knew the abysmal gulfs of abnormality that he had opened, and went forth into the wild hills prepared and resigned. He would meet the unthinkable "Little People" — and his document ends with a rational observation: "If unhappily I do not return from my journey, there is no need to conjure up here a picture of the awfulness of my fate."

Also in *The Three Imposters* is the *Novel of the White Powder*, which approaches the absolute culmination of loathsome fright. Francis Leicester, a young law student nervously worn out by seclusion and overwork, has a prescription filled by an old apothecary none too careful about the state of his drugs. The substance, it later turns out, is an unusual salt which time and varying temperature have accidentally changed to something very strange and terrible; nothing less, in short, than the mediæval *vinum sabbati*, whose consumption at the horrible orgies of the Witches' Sabbath gave rise to shocking transformations and — if injudiciously used — to unutterable consequences. Innocently enough, the youth regularly imbibes the powder in a glass of water after meals; and at first seems substantially benefited. Gradually, however, his improved spirits take the form of dissipation; he is absent from home a great deal, and appears to have undergone a repellent psychological change. One day an odd livid spot appears on his right hand, and he afterward returns to his seclusion; finally keeping himself shut within his room and admitting none of the household. The doctor calls for an interview, and departs in a palsy of horror, saying that he can do no more in that house. Two weeks later the patient's sister, walking outside, sees a monstrous thing at the sickroom window; and servants report that food left at the locked door is no longer touched. Summons at the door bring only a sound of shuffling and a demand in a thick gurgling voice to be let alone. At last an awful happening is reported by a shuddering housemaid. The ceiling of the room below Leicester's is stained with a hideous black fluid, and a pool of viscid abomination has dripped to the bed beneath. Dr. Haberden, now persuaded to return to the house, breaks down the young man's door and strikes again and again with an iron bar at the blasphemous semiliving thing he finds there. It is "a dark and putrid mass, seething with corruption and hideous rottenness, neither liquid nor solid, but melting and changing." Burning points like eyes shine out of its midst, and before it is dispatched it tries to lift what might have been an arm. Soon afterward the physician, unable to endure the memory of what he has beheld, dies at sea while bound for a new life in America.

Mr. Machen returns to the dæmoniac "Little People" in *The Red Hand* and *The Shining Pyramid*; and in *The Terror*, a wartime story, he treats with very potent mystery the effect of man's modern repudiation of spirituality on the beasts of the world, which are thus led to question his supremacy and to unite for his extermination. Of utmost delicacy, and passing from mere horror into true mysticism, is *The Great Return, a story of the Graal*, also a product of the war period. Too well known to need description here is the tale of *The Bowmen*; which, taken for authentic narration, gave rise to the widespread legend of the "Angels of Mons" — ghosts of the old English archers of Crecy and Agincourt who fought in 1914 beside the hard-pressed ranks of England's glorious "Old Contemptibles."

Less intense than Mr. Machen in delineating the extremes of stark fear, yet infinitely more closely wedded to the idea of an unreal world constantly pressing upon ours is the inspired and prolific Algernon Blackwood, amidst whose voluminous and uneven work may be found some of the finest spectral literature of this or any age. Of the quality of Mr. Blackwood's genius there can be no dispute; for no one has even approached the skill, seriousness, and minute fidelity with which he records the overtones of strangeness in ordinary things and experiences, or the preternatural insight with which he builds up detail by detail the complete sensations and perceptions leading from reality into supernormal life or vision. Without notable command of the poetic witchery of mere words, he is the one absolute and unquestioned master of weird atmosphere; and can evoke what amounts almost to a story from a simple fragment of humourless psychological description. Above all others he understands how fully some sensitive minds dwell forever on the borderland of dream, and how relatively slight is the distinction betwixt those images formed from actual objects and those excited by the play of the imagination.

Mr. Blackwood's lesser work is marred by several defects such as ethical didacticism, occasional insipid whimsicality, the flatness of benignant supernaturalism, and a too free use of the trade jargon of modern "occultism." A fault of his more serious efforts is that diffuseness and long windedness which results from an excessively elaborate attempt, under the handicap of a somewhat bald and journalistic style devoid of intrinsic magic, colour, and vitality, to visualise precise sensations and nuances of uncanny suggestion. But in spite of all this, the major products of Mr. Blackwood attain a genuinely classic level, and evoke as does nothing else in literature an awed convinced sense of the imminence of strange spiritual spheres of entities.

The well-nigh endless array of Mr. Blackwood's fiction includes both novels and shorter tales, the latter sometimes independent and sometimes arrayed in series. Foremost of all must be reckoned *The Willows*, in which the nameless presences on a desolate Danube island are horribly felt and recognised by a pair of idle voyagers. Here art and restraint in narrative reach their very highest development, and an impression of lasting poignancy is produced without a single strained passage or a single false note. Another amazingly potent though less artistically finished tale is *The Wendigo*, where we are confronted by horrible evidences of a vast forest dæmon about which North Woods lumbermen whisper at evening. The manner in which certain footprints tell certain unbelievable things is really a marked triumph in craftsmanship. In *An Episode in a Lodging House* we behold frightful presences summoned out of black space by a sorcerer, and *The Listener* tells of the awful psychic residuum creeping about an old house where a leper died. In the volume titled *Incredible Adventures* occur some of the finest tales which the author has yet produced, leading the fancy to wild rites on nocturnal hills, to secret and terrible aspects lurking behind stolid scenes, and to unimaginable vaults of mystery below the sands and pyramids of Egypt; all with a serious finesse and delicacy that convince where a cruder or lighter treatment would merely amuse. Some of these accounts are hardly stories at all, but rather studies in elusive impressions and half-remembered snatches of dream. Plot is everywhere negligible, and atmosphere reigns untrammeled.

John Silence—Physician Extraordinary is a book of five related tales, through which a single character runs his triumphant course. Marred only by traces of the popular and conventional detective-story atmosphere—for Dr. Silence is one of those benevolent geniuses who employ their remarkable powers to aid worthy fellow-men in difficulty—these narratives contain some of the author's best work, and produce an illusion at once emphatic and lasting. The opening tale, "A Psychical Invasion," relates what befell a sensitive author in a house once the scene of dark deeds, and how a legion of fiends was exorcised. "Ancient Sorceries," perhaps the finest tale in the book, gives an almost hypnotically vivid account of an old French town where once the unholy Sabbath was kept by all the people in the form of cats. In "The Nemesis of Fire" a hideous elemental is evoked by new-spilt blood, whilst "Secret Worship" tells of a German school where Satanism held sway, and where long afterward an evil aura remained. "The Camp of the Dog" is a werewolf tale, but is weakened by moralisation and professional "occultism."

Too subtle, perhaps, for definite classification as horror-tales, yet possibly more truly artistic in an absolute sense, are such delicate phantasies as *Jimbo or The Centaur*. Mr. Blackwood achieves in these novels a close and palpitant approach to the inmost substance of dream, and works enormous havoc with the conventional barriers between reality and imagination.

Unexcelled in the sorcery of crystalline singing prose, and supreme in the creation of a gorgeous and languorous world of iridescently exotic vision, is Edward John Moreton Drax Plunkett, Eighteenth Baron Dunsany, whose tales and short plays form an almost unique element in our literature. Inventor of a new mythology and weaver of surprising folklore, Lord Dunsany stands dedicated to a strange world of fantastic beauty, and pledged to eternal warfare against the coarseness and ugliness of diurnal reality. His point of view is the most truly cosmic of any held in the literature of any period. As sensitive as Poe to dramatic values and the significance of isolated words and details, and far better equipped rhetorically through a simple lyric style based on the prose of the King James Bible, this author draws with tremendous effectiveness on nearly every body of myth and legend within the circle of European culture; producing a composite or eclectic cycle of phantasy in which Eastern colour, Hellenic form, Teutonic sombreness and Celtic wistfulness are so superbly blended that each sustains and supplements the rest without sacrifice of perfect congruity and homogeneity. In most cases Dunsany's lands are fabulous—"beyond the East," or "at the edge of the world." His system of original personal and place names, with roots drawn from classical, Oriental, and other sources, is a marvel of versatile inventiveness and poetic discrimination; as one may see from such specimens as "Argimenes," "Bethmoora," "Poltarnees," "Camorak," "Iluriel," or "Sardathrion."

Beauty rather than terror is the keynote of Dunsany's work. He loves the vivid green of jade and of copper domes, and the delicate flush of sunset on the ivory minarets of impossible dream-cities. Humour and irony, too, are often present to impart a gentle cynicism and modify what might otherwise possess a naïve intensity. Nevertheless, as is inevitable in a master of triumphant unreality, there are occasional touches of cosmic fright which come well within the authentic tradition. Dunsany loves to hint slyly and adroitly of monstrous things and incredible dooms, as one hints in a fairy tale. In *The Book of Wonder* we read of Hlo-Hlo, the gigantic spider-idol which does not always stay at home; of what the Sphinx feared in the forest; of Slith, the thief who jumps over the edge of the world after seeing a certain light lit and knowing who lit it; of the anthropophagous; Gibbelins, who inhabit an evil tower and guard a treasure; of the Gnoles, who live in the forest and from whom it is not well to steal; of the City of Never, and the eyes that watch in the Under Pits; and of kindred things of darkness. *A Dreamer's Tales* tells of the mystery that sent forth all men from Bethmoora in the desert; of the vast gate of Perdondaris, that was carved from a single piece of ivory; and of the voyage of poor old Bill, whose captain cursed the crew and paid calls on nasty-looking isles new-risen from the sea, with low thatched cottages having evil, obscure windows.

Many of Dunsany's short plays are replete with spectral fear. In *The Gods of the Mountain* seven beggars impersonate the seven green idols on a distant hill, and enjoy ease and honour in a city of worshippers until they hear that the real idols are missing from their wonted seats. A very ungainly sight in the dusk is reported to them— "rock should not walk in the evening"—and at last, as they sit awaiting the arrival of a troop of dancers, they note that the approaching footsteps are heavier than those of good dancers ought to be. Then things ensue, and in the end the presumptuous blasphemers are turned to green jade statues by the very walking statues whose sanctity they outraged. But mere plot is the very least merit of this marvelously effective play. The incidents and developments are those of a supreme master, so that the whole forms one of the most important contributions of the present age not only to drama, but to literature in general. *A Night at an Inn* tells of four thieves who have stolen the emerald eye of Klesh, a monstrous Hindoo god. They lure to their room and succeed in slaying the three priestly avengers who are on their track, but in the night Mesh comes gropingly for his eye; and having gained it and departed, calls each of the despoilers out into the darkness for an unnamed punishment. In *The Laughter of the Gods* there is a doomed city at the jungle's edge, and a ghostly lutanist heard only by those about to die (cf. Alice's spectral harpsichord in Hawthorne's *House of the Seven Gables*); whilst

The Queen's Enemies retells the anecdote of Herodotus in which a vengeful princess invites her foes to a subterranean banquet and lets in the Nile to drown them. But no amount of mere description can convey more than a fraction of Lord Dunsany's pervasive charm. His prismatic cities and unheard of rites are touched with a sureness which only mastery can engender, and we thrill with a sense of actual participation in his secret mysteries. To the truly imaginative he is a talisman and a key unlocking rich storehouses of dream and fragmentary memory; so that we may think of him not only as a poet, but as one who makes each reader a poet as well.

At the opposite pole of genius from Lord Dunsany, and gifted with an almost diabolic power of calling horror by gentle steps from the midst of prosaic daily life, is the scholarly Montague Rhodes James, Provost of Eton College, antiquary of note, and recognized authority on mediæval manuscripts and cathedral history. Dr. James, long fond of telling spectral tales at Christmastide, has become by slow degrees a literary weird fictionist of the very first rank; and has developed a distinctive style and method likely to serve as models for an enduring line of disciples.

The art of Dr. James is by no means haphazard, and in the preface to one of his collections he has formulated three very sound rules for macabre composition. A ghost story, he believes, should have a familiar setting in the modern period, in order to approach closely the reader's sphere of experience. Its spectral phenomena, moreover, should be malevolent rather than beneficent; since fear is the emotion primarily to be excited. And finally, the technical patois of "occultism" or pseudo-science ought carefully to be avoided, lest the charm of casual verisimilitude be smothered in unconvincing pedantry.

Dr. James, practicing what he preaches, approaches his themes in a light and often conversational way. Creating the illusion of every-day events, he introduces his abnormal phenomena cautiously and gradually; relieved at every turn by touches of homely and prosaic detail, and sometimes spiced with a snatch or two of antiquarian scholarship. Conscious of the close relation between present weirdness and accumulated tradition, he generally provides remote historical antecedents for his incidents; thus being able to utilise very aptly his exhaustive knowledge of the past, and his ready and convincing command of archaic diction and colouring. A favourite scene for a James tale is some centuried cathedral, which the author can describe with all the familiar minuteness of a specialist in that field.

Sly humourous vignettes and bits of lifelike genre portraiture and characterisation are often to be found in Dr. James's narratives, and serve in his skilled hands to augment the general effect rather than to spoil it, as the same qualities would tend to do with a lesser craftsman. In inventing a new type of ghost, he has departed considerably from the conventional Gothic tradition; for where the older stock ghosts were pale and stately, and apprehended chiefly through the sense of sight, the average James ghost is lean, dwarfish, and hairy — a sluggish, hellish sight, an abomination midway betwixt beast and man — and usually touched before it is seen. Sometimes the spectre is of still more eccentric composition; a roll of flannel with spidery eyes, or an invisible entity which moulds itself in bedding and shows a face of crumpled linen. Dr. James has, it is clear, an intelligent and scientific knowledge of human nerves and feelings; and knows just how to apportion statement, imagery, and subtle suggestions in order to secure the best results with his readers. He is an artist in incident and arrangement rather than in atmosphere, and reaches the emotions more often through the intellect than directly. This method, of course, with its occasional absences of sharp climax, has its drawbacks as well as its advantages; and many will miss the thorough atmospheric tension which writers like Machen are careful to build up with words and scenes. But only a few of the tales are open to the charge of tameness. Generally the laconic unfolding of abnormal events in adroit order is amply sufficient to produce the desired effect of cumulative horror.

The short stories of Dr. James are contained in four small collections, entitled respectively *Ghost Stories of an Antiquary*, *More Ghost Stories of an Antiquary*, *A Thin Ghost and Others*, and *A Warning to the Curious*. There is also a delightful juvenile phantasy, *The Five Jars*, which has its spectral adumbrations. Amidst this wealth of material it is hard to select a favourite or especially typical tale, though each reader will no doubt have such preferences as his temperament may determine.

Count Magnus is assuredly one of the best, forming as it does a veritable Golconda of suspense and suggestion. Mr. Wraxall is an English traveler of the middle nineteenth century, sojourning in Sweden to secure material for a book. Becoming interested in the ancient family of De La Gardie, near the village of Raback, he studies its records; and finds particular fascination in the builder of the existing Manor-house, one Count Magnus, of whom strange and terrible things are whispered. The Count, who flourished early in the seventeenth century, was a stern landlord, and famous for his severity toward poachers and delinquent tenants. His cruel punishments were bywords, and there were dark rumours of influences which even survived his interment in the great mausoleum he built near the church — as in the case of the two peasants who hunted on his preserves one night a century after his death. There were hideous screams in the woods, and near the tomb of Count Magnus an unnatural laugh and the clang of a great door. Next morning the priest found the two men; one a maniac, and the other dead, with the flesh of his face sucked from the bones.

Mr. Wraxall hears all these tales, and stumbles on more guarded references to a Black Pilgrimage once taken by the Count, a pilgrimage to Chorazin in Palestine, one of the cities denounced by Our Lord in the Scriptures, and in which old priests say that Antichrist is to be born. No one dares to hint just what that Black Pilgrimage was, or what strange being or thing the Count brought back as a companion. Meanwhile Mr. Wraxall is increasingly anxious to explore the mausoleum of Count Magnus, and finally secures permission to do so, in the company of a deacon. He finds several monuments and three copper sarcophagi, one of which is the Count's. Round the edge of this latter are several bands of engraved scenes, including a singular and hideous delineation of a pursuit — the pursuit of a frantic man through a forest by a squat muffled figure with a devil-fish's tentacle, directed by a tall cloaked man on a neighbouring hillock. The sarcophagus has three massive steel padlocks, one of which is lying open on the floor, reminding the traveler of a metallic clash he heard the day before when passing the mausoleum and wishing idly that he might see Count Magnus.

His fascination augmented, and the key being accessible, Mr. Wraxall pays the mausoleum a second and solitary visit and finds another padlock unfastened. The next day, his last in Raback, he again goes alone to bid the long-dead Count farewell. Once more queerly impelled to utter a whimsical wish for a meeting with the buried nobleman, he now sees to his disquiet that only one of the padlocks remains on the great sarcophagus. Even as he looks, that last lock drops noisily to the floor, and there comes a sound as of creaking hinges. Then the monstrous lid appears very slowly to rise, and Mr. Wraxall flees in panic fear without refastening the door of the mausoleum.

During his return to England the traveler feels a curious uneasiness about his fellow-passengers on the canal-boat which he employs for the earlier stages. Cloaked figures make him nervous, and he has a sense of being watched and followed. Of twenty-eight persons whom he counts, only twenty-six appear at meals; and the missing two are always a tall cloaked man and a shorter muffled figure. Completing his water travel at Harwich, Mr. Wraxall takes frankly to flight in a closed carriage, but sees two cloaked figures at a crossroad. Finally he lodges at a small house in a village and spends the time making frantic notes. On the second morning he is found dead, and during the inquest seven jurors faint at sight of the body. The house where he stayed is never again inhabited, and upon its demolition half a century later his manuscript is discovered in a forgotten cupboard.

In *The Treasure of Abbot Thomas* a British antiquary unriddles a cipher on some Renaissance painted windows, and thereby discovers a centuried hoard of gold in a niche halfway down a well in the courtyard of a German abbey. But the crafty depositor had set a guardian over that treasure, and something in the black well twines its arms around the searcher's neck in such a manner that the quest is abandoned, and a clergyman sent for. Each night after that the discoverer feels a stealthy presence and detects a horrible odour of mould outside the door of his hotel room, till finally the clergyman makes a daylight replacement of the stone at the mouth of the treasure-vault in the well — out of which something had come in the dark to avenge the disturbing of old Abbot Thomas's gold. As he completes his work the cleric observes a curious toad-like carving on the ancient well-head, with the Latin motto "*Depositum custodi* — keep that which is committed to thee."

Other notable James tales are "The Stalls of Barchester Cathedral," in which a grotesque carving comes curiously to life to avenge the secret and subtle murder of an old Dean by his ambitious successor; "Oh, Whistle, and I'll Come to You," which tells of the horror summoned by a strange metal whistle found in a mediævel church ruin; and "An Episode of Cathedral History," where the dismantling of a pulpit uncovers an archaic tomb whose lurking daemon spreads panic and pestilence. Dr. James, for all his light touch, evokes fright and hideousness in their most shocking form, and will certainly stand as one of the few really creative masters in his darksome province.

For those who relish speculation regarding the future, the tale of supernatural horror provides an interesting field. Combated by a mounting wave of plodding realism, cynical flippancy, and sophisticated disillusionment, it is yet encouraged by a parallel tide of growing mysticism, as developed both through the fatigued reaction of "occultists" and religious fundamentalists against materialistic discovery and through the stimulation of wonder and fancy by such enlarged vistas and broken barriers as modern science has given us with its intra-atomic chemistry, advancing astrophysics, doctrines of relativity, and probings into biology and human thought. At the present moment the favouring forces would appear to have somewhat of an advantage; since there is unquestionably more cordiality shown toward weird writings than when, thirty years ago, the best of Arthur Machen's work fell on the stony ground of the smart and cocksure 'nineties. Ambrose Bierce, almost unknown in his own time, has now reached something like general recognition.

Startling mutations, however, are not to be looked for in either direction. In any case an approximate balance of tendencies will continue to exist; and while we may justly expect a further subtilisation of technique, we have no reason to think that the general position of the spectral in literature will be altered. It is a narrow though essential branch of human expression, and will chiefly appeal as always to a limited audience with keen special sensibilities. Whatever universal masterpiece of tomorrow may be wrought from phantasm or terror will owe its acceptance rather to a supreme workmanship than to a sympathetic theme. Yet who shall declare the dark theme a positive handicap? Radiant with beauty, the Cup of the Ptolemies was carven of onyx.

Cool Air.

3,400-word short story; 1926.

This compact short story is a pivot point in H.P. Lovecraft's literary canon. It is the last of the stories Lovecraft wrote while living in New York, and, most readers agree, the best of them. It is also the first of the stories Lovecraft wrote after embarking on the course of studying, reading, and writing that would culminate in Supernatural Horror in Literature *the following year.*

S. T. Joshi, in "I am Providence," refers to "Cool Air" as "a compact exposition of pure physical loathsomeness." This sounds right, but it misses the mark by just a bit, because the physical loathsomeness in "Cool Air" is never actually described in expository writing. Lovecraft evokes it through the subtext of his narrator's reaction to it, and in consequence the scene gains vastly in power and horror. A comparison of this tale with "The Outsider" will showcase the difference.

It's a powerful demonstration that, although Lovecraft had only just started his intensive study of the masters of horror fiction, he was already drawing insights from their work that were empowering him to take his rightful place in their first rank.

"Cool Air" was written sometime in February of 1926; it was subsequently published in the March 1928 issue of Tales of Magic and Mystery.

You ask me to explain why I am afraid of a draught of cool air; why I shiver more than others upon entering a cold room, and seem nauseated and repelled when the chill of evening creeps through the heat of a mild autumn day. There are those who say I respond to cold as others do to a bad odour, and I am the last to deny the impression. What I will do is to relate the most horrible circumstance I ever encountered, and leave it to you to judge whether or not this forms a suitable explanation of my peculiarity.

It is a mistake to fancy that horror is associated inextricably with darkness, silence, and solitude. I found it in the glare of mid-afternoon, in the clangour of a metropolis, and in the teeming midst of a shabby and commonplace rooming-house with a prosaic landlady and two stalwart men by my side. In the spring of 1923 I had secured some dreary and unprofitable magazine work in the city of New York; and being unable to pay any substantial rent, began drifting from one cheap boarding establishment to another in search of a room which might combine the qualities of decent cleanliness, endurable furnishings, and very reasonable price. It soon developed that I had only a choice between different evils, but after a time I came upon a house in West Fourteenth Street which disgusted me much less than the others I had sampled.

The place was a four-story mansion of brownstone, dating apparently from the late forties, and fitted with woodwork and marble whose stained and sullied splendour argued a descent from high levels of tasteful opulence. In the rooms, large and lofty, and decorated with impossible paper and ridiculously ornate stucco cornices, there lingered a depressing mustiness and hint of obscure cookery; but the floors were clean, the linen tolerably regular, and the hot water not too often cold or turned off, so that I came to regard it as at least a bearable place to hibernate till one might really live again. The landlady, a slatternly, almost bearded Spanish woman named Herrero, did not annoy me with gossip or with criticisms of the late-burning electric light in my third-floor front hall room; and my fellow-lodgers were as quiet and uncommunicative as one might desire, being mostly Spaniards a little above the coarsest and crudest grade. Only the din of street cars in the thoroughfare below proved a serious annoyance.

I had been there about three weeks when the first odd incident occurred. One evening at about eight I heard a spattering on the floor and became suddenly aware that I had been smelling the pungent odour of ammonia for some time. Looking about, I saw that the ceiling was wet and dripping; the soaking apparently proceeding from a corner on the side toward the street. Anxious to stop the matter at its source, I hastened to the basement to tell the landlady; and was assured by her that the trouble would quickly be set right.

"Doctair Muñoz," she cried as she rushed upstairs ahead of me, "he have speel hees chemicals. He ees too seeck for doctair heemself—seecker and seecker all the time—but he weel not have no othair for help. He ees vairy queer in hees seeckness—all day he take funnee-smelling baths, and he cannot get excite or warm. All hees own housework he do—hees leetle room are full of bottles and machines, and he do not work as doctair. But he was great once—my fathair in Barcelona have hear of heem—and only joost now he feex a arm of the plumber that get hurt of sudden. He nevair go out, only on roof, and my boy Esteban he breeng heem hees food and laundry and mediceens and chemicals. My Gawd, the sal-ammoniac that man use for keep heem cool!"

Mrs. Herrero disappeared up the staircase to the fourth floor, and I returned to my room. The ammonia ceased to drip, and as I cleaned up what had spilled and opened the window for air, I heard the landlady's heavy footsteps above me. Dr. Muñoz I had never heard, save for certain sounds as of some gasoline-driven mechanism; since his step was soft and gentle.

Weird Tales, September 1939

"He groped his way out with face tightly bandaged, and I never saw his eyes again."

I wondered for a moment what the strange affliction of this man might be, and whether his obstinate refusal of outside aid were not the result of a rather baseless eccentricity. There is, I reflected tritely, an infinite deal of pathos in the state of an eminent person who has come down in the world.

I might never have known Dr. Muñoz had it not been for the heart attack that suddenly seized me one forenoon as I sat writing in my room. Physicians had told me of the danger of those spells, and I knew there was no time to be lost; so remembering what the landlady had said about the invalid's help of the injured workman, I dragged myself upstairs and knocked feebly at the door above mine. My knock was answered in good English by a curious voice some distance to the right, asking my name and business; and these things being stated, there came an opening of the door next to the one I had sought.

A rush of cool air greeted me; and though the day was one of the hottest of late June, I shivered as I crossed the threshold into a large apartment whose rich and tasteful decoration surprised me in this nest of squalor and seediness. A folding couch now filled its diurnal role of sofa, and the mahogany furniture, sumptuous hangings, old paintings, and mellow bookshelves all bespoke a gentleman's study rather than a boarding-house bedroom. I now saw that the hall room above mine—the "leetle room" of bottles and machines which Mrs. Herrero had mentioned—was merely the laboratory of the doctor; and that his main living quarters lay in the spacious adjoining room whose convenient alcoves and large contiguous bathroom permitted him to hide all dressers and obtrusive utilitarian devices. Dr. Muñoz, most certainly, was a man of birth, cultivation, and discrimination.

The figure before me was short but exquisitely proportioned, and clad in somewhat formal dress of perfect cut and fit. A high-bred face of masterful though not arrogant expression was adorned by a short iron-grey full beard, and an old-fashioned pince-nez shielded the full, dark eyes and surmounted an aquiline nose which gave a Moorish touch to a physiognomy otherwise dominantly Celtiberian. Thick, well-trimmed hair that argued the punctual calls of a barber was parted gracefully above a high forehead; and the whole picture was one of striking intelligence and superior blood and breeding.

Nevertheless, as I saw Dr. Muñoz in that blast of cool air, I felt a repugnance which nothing in his aspect could justify. Only his lividly inclined complexion and coldness of touch could have afforded a physical basis for this feeling, and even these things should have been excusable considering the man's known invalidism. It might, too, have been the singular cold that alienated me; for such chilliness was abnormal on so hot a day, and the abnormal always excites aversion, distrust, and fear.

But repugnance was soon forgotten in admiration, for the strange physician's extreme skill at once became manifest despite the ice-coldness and shakiness of his bloodless-looking hands. He clearly understood my needs at a glance, and ministered to them with a master's deftness; the while reassuring me in a finely modulated though oddly hollow and timbreless voice that he was the bitterest of sworn enemies to death, and had sunk his fortune and lost all his friends in a lifetime of bizarre experiment devoted to its bafflement and extirpation. Something of the benevolent fanatic seemed to reside in him, and he rambled on almost garrulously as he sounded my chest and mixed a suitable draught of drugs fetched from the smaller laboratory room. Evidently he found the society of a well-born man a rare novelty in this dingy environment, and was moved to unaccustomed speech as memories of better days surged over him.

His voice, if queer, was at least soothing; and I could not even perceive that he breathed as the fluent sentences rolled urbanely out. He sought to distract my mind from my own seizure by speaking of his theories and experiments; and I remember his tactfully consoling me about my weak heart by insisting that will and consciousness are stronger than organic life itself, so that if a bodily frame be but originally healthy and carefully preserved, it may through a scientific enhancement of these qualities retain a kind of nervous animation despite the most serious impairments, defects, or even absences in the battery of specific organs. He might, he half jestingly said, some day teach me to live—or at least to possess some kind of conscious existence—without any heart at all! For his part, he was afflicted with a complication of maladies requiring a very exact regimen which included constant cold. Any marked rise in temperature might, if prolonged, affect him fatally; and the frigidity of his habitation—some 55 or 56 degrees Fahrenheit—was maintained by an absorption system of ammonia cooling, the gasoline engine of whose pumps I had often heard in my own room below.

Relieved of my seizure in a marvellously short while, I left the shivery place a disciple and devotee of the gifted recluse. After that I paid him frequent overcoated calls; listening while he told of secret researches and almost ghastly results, and trembling a bit when I examined the unconventional and astonishingly ancient volumes on his shelves. I was eventually, I may add, almost cured of my disease for all time by his skillful ministrations. It seems that he did not scorn the incantations of the mediaevalists, since he believed these cryptic formulae to contain rare psychological stimuli which might conceivably have singular effects on the substance of a nervous system from which organic pulsations had fled. I was touched by his account of the aged Dr. Torres of Valencia, who had shared his earlier experiments and nursed him through the great illness of eighteen years before, whence his present disorders proceeded. No sooner had the venerable practitioner saved his colleague than he himself succumbed to the grim enemy he had fought. Perhaps the strain had been too great; for Dr. Muñoz made it whisperingly clear—though not in detail—that the methods of healing had been most extraordinary, involving scenes and processes not welcomed by elderly and conservative Galens.

As the weeks passed, I observed with regret that my new friend was indeed slowly but unmistakably losing ground physically, as Mrs. Herrero had suggested. The livid aspect of his countenance was intensified, his voice became more hollow and indistinct, his muscular motions were less perfectly coordinated, and his mind and will displayed less resilience and initiative. Of this sad change he seemed by no means unaware, and little by little his expression and conversation both took on a gruesome irony which restored in me something of the subtle repulsion I had originally felt.

He developed strange caprices, acquiring a fondness for exotic spices and Egyptian incense till his room smelled like the vault of a sepulchred Pharaoh in the Valley of Kings. At the same time his demands for cold air increased, and with my aid he amplified the ammonia piping of his room and modified the pumps and feed of his refrigerating machine till he could keep the temperature as low as 34 degrees or 40 degrees, and finally even 28 degrees; the bathroom and laboratory, of course, being less chilled, in order that water might not freeze, and that chemical processes might not be impeded. The tenant adjoining him complained of the icy air from around the connecting door, so I helped him fit heavy hangings to obviate the difficulty. A kind of growing horror, of outré and morbid cast, seemed to possess him. He talked of death incessantly, but laughed hollowly when such things as burial or funeral arrangements were gently suggested.

All in all, he became a disconcerting and even gruesome companion; yet in my gratitude for his healing I could not well abandon him to the strangers around him, and was careful to dust his room and attend to his needs each day, muffled in a heavy ulster which I bought especially for the purpose. I likewise did much of his shopping, and gasped in bafflement at some of the chemicals he ordered from druggists and laboratory supply houses.

An increasing and unexplained atmosphere of panic seemed to rise around his apartment. The whole house, as I have said, had a musty odour; but the smell in his room was worse — and in spite of all the spices and incense, and the pungent chemicals of the now incessant baths which he insisted on taking unaided. I perceived that it must be connected with his ailment, and shuddered when I reflected on what that ailment might be. Mrs. Herrero crossed herself when she looked at him, and gave him up unreservedly to me; not even letting her son Esteban continue to run errands for him. When I suggested other physicians, the sufferer would fly into as much of a rage as he seemed to dare to entertain. He evidently feared the physical effect of violent emotion, yet his will and driving force waxed rather than waned, and he refused to be confined to his bed. The lassitude of his earlier ill days gave place to a return of his fiery purpose, so that he seemed about to hurl defiance at the death-daemon even as that ancient enemy seized him. The pretence of eating, always curiously like a formality with him, he virtually abandoned; and mental power alone appeared to keep him from total collapse.

He acquired a habit of writing long documents of some sort, which he carefully sealed and filled with injunctions that I transmit them after his death to certain persons whom he named — for the most part lettered East Indians, but including a once celebrated French physician now generally thought dead, and about whom the most inconceivable things had been whispered. As it happened, I burned all these papers undelivered and unopened. His aspect and voice became utterly frightful, and his presence almost unbearable. One September day an unexpected glimpse of him induced an epileptic fit in a man who had come to repair his electric desk lamp; a fit for which he prescribed effectively whilst keeping himself well out of sight. That man, oddly enough, had been through the terrors of the Great War without having incurred any fright so thorough.

Then, in the middle of October, the horror of horrors came with stupefying suddenness. One night about eleven the pump of the refrigerating machine broke down, so that within three hours the process of ammonia cooling became impossible. Dr. Muñoz summoned me by thumping on the floor, and I worked desperately to repair the injury while my host cursed in a tone whose lifeless, rattling hollowness surpassed description. My amateur efforts, however, proved of no use; and when I had brought in a mechanic from a neighbouring all-night garage, we learned that nothing could be done till morning, when a new piston would have to be obtained. The moribund hermit's rage and fear, swelling to grotesque proportions, seemed likely to shatter what remained of his failing physique, and once a spasm caused him to clap his hands to his eyes and rush into the bathroom. He groped his way out with face tightly bandaged, and I never saw his eyes again.

The frigidity of the apartment was now sensibly diminishing, and at about 5 a.m. the doctor retired to the bathroom, commanding me to keep him supplied with all the ice I could obtain at all-night drug stores and cafeterias. As I would return from my sometimes discouraging trips and lay my spoils before the closed bathroom door, I could hear a restless splashing within, and a thick voice croaking out the order for "More — more!" At length a warm day broke, and the shops opened one by one. I asked Esteban either to help with the ice-fetching whilst I obtained the pump piston, or to order the piston while I continued with the ice; but instructed by his mother, he absolutely refused.

Finally I hired a seedy-looking loafer whom I encountered on the corner of Eighth Avenue to keep the patient supplied with ice from a little shop where I introduced him, and applied myself diligently to the task of finding a pump piston and engaging workmen competent to install it. The task seemed interminable, and I raged almost as violently as the hermit when I saw the hours slipping by in a breathless, foodless round of vain telephoning, and a hectic quest from place to place, hither and thither by subway and surface car. About noon I encountered a suitable supply house far downtown, and at approximately 1:30 p.m. arrived at my boarding-place with the necessary paraphernalia and two sturdy and intelligent mechanics. I had done all I could, and hoped I was in time.

Black terror, however, had preceded me. The house was in utter turmoil, and above the chatter of awed voices I heard a man praying in a deep basso. Fiendish things were in the air, and lodgers told over the beads of their rosaries as they caught the odour from beneath the doctor's closed door. The lounger I had hired, it seems, had fled screaming and mad-eyed not long after his second delivery of ice; perhaps as a result of excessive curiosity. He could not, of course, have locked the door behind him; yet it was now fastened, presumably from the inside. There was no sound within save a nameless sort of slow, thick dripping.

Briefly consulting with Mrs. Herrero and the workmen despite a fear that gnawed my inmost soul, I advised the breaking down of the door; but the landlady found a way to turn the key from the outside with some wire device. We had previously opened the doors of all the other rooms on that hall, and flung all the windows to the very top. Now, noses protected by handkerchiefs, we tremblingly invaded the accursed south room which blazed with the warm sun of early afternoon.

A kind of dark, slimy trail led from the open bathroom door to the hall door, and thence to the desk, where a terrible little pool had accumulated. Something was scrawled there in pencil in an awful, blind hand on a piece of paper hideously smeared as though by the very claws that traced the hurried last words. Then the trail led to the couch and ended unutterably.

What was, or had been, on the couch I cannot and dare not say here. But this is what I shiveringly puzzled out on the stickily smeared paper before I drew a match and burned it to a crisp; what I puzzled out in terror as the landlady and two mechanics rushed frantically from that hellish place to babble their incoherent stories at the nearest police station. The nauseous words seemed well-nigh incredible in that yellow sunlight, with the clatter of cars and motor trucks ascending clamorously from crowded Fourteenth Street, yet I confess that I believed them then. Whether I believe them now I honestly do not know. There are things about which it is better not to speculate, and all that I can say is that I hate the smell of ammonia, and grow faint at a draught of unusually cool air.

"The end," ran that noisome scrawl, "is here. No more ice — the man looked and ran away. Warmer every minute, and the tissues can't last. I fancy you know — what I said about the will and the nerves and the preserved body after the organs ceased to work. It was good theory, but couldn't keep up indefinitely. There was a gradual deterioration I had not foreseen. Dr. Torres knew, but the shock killed him. He couldn't stand what he had to do — he had to get me in a strange, dark place when he minded my letter and nursed me back. And the organs never would work again. It had to be done my way — artificial preservation — for you see I died that time eighteen years ago."

The Call of Cthulhu.

11,000-WORD NOVELETTE; 1926.

This legendary novelette was the first piece of writing to come off H.P. Lovecraft's pen after settling into his new home in his old home town of Providence. By the time he finished it, he had fully drafted Supernatural Horror in Literature *and was mostly just fine-tuning it; but the insights he had gleaned in the course of his researches were finding more and more full expression in his fiction. At the same time, his profound sense of relief at being away from New York, of joy at being home again, and of focus at having had his social calendar cleared of all the Kalem Club activities, were combining to set him up for the most productive and satisfying phase of his writing life. In the following 12 months Lovecraft would produce more than 150,000 words, including some of his most iconic works — starting, of course, with this one.*

"The Call of Cthulhu" was conceived and planned out a year earlier, when Lovecraft envisioned making a short novel out of it. He appears to have put it away, saving it for a time when he would have the emotional resources to do it justice; in New York, of course, he did not. Now, happily installed at 10 Barnes Street, "The Call of Cthulhu" was the first order of literary business.

Lovecraft finished the story in August of 1926. Famously and inexplicably, Weird Tales *editor Farnsworth Wright rejected the story when it was first submitted; but later, after one of Lovecraft's friends mentioned to him that Lovecraft was shopping it around at other places, he wrote to ask for it back, and published it in the February 1928 issue.*

> *Of such great powers or beings there may be conceivably a survival . . . a survival of a hugely remote period when . . . consciousness was manifested, perhaps, in shapes and forms long since withdrawn before the tide of advancing humanity . . . forms of which poetry and legend alone have caught a flying memory and called them gods, monsters, mythical beings of all sorts and kinds . . .*
>
> — ALGERNON BLACKWOOD.

(Found Among the Papers of the Late Francis Wayland Thurston, of Boston)

I.

THE HORROR IN CLAY.

The most merciful thing in the world, I think, is the inability of the human mind to correlate all its contents. We live on a placid island of ignorance in the midst of black seas of infinity, and it was not meant that we should voyage far. The sciences, each straining in its own direction, have hitherto harmed us little; but some day the piecing together of dissociated knowledge will open up such terrifying vistas of reality, and of our frightful position therein, that we shall either go mad from the revelation or flee from the deadly light into the peace and safety of a new dark age.

Theosophists have guessed at the awesome grandeur of the cosmic cycle wherein our world and human race form transient incidents. They have hinted at strange survival in terms which would freeze the blood if not masked by a bland optimism. But it is not from them that there came the single glimpse of forbidden aeons which chills me when I think of it and maddens me when I dream of it. That glimpse, like all dread glimpses of truth, flashed out from an accidental piecing together of separated things — in this case an old newspaper item and the notes of a dead professor. I hope that no one else will accomplish this piecing-out; certainly, if I live, I shall never knowingly supply a link in so hideous a chain. I think that the professor, too, intended to keep silent regarding the part he knew, and that he would have destroyed his notes had not sudden death seized him.

My knowledge of the thing began in the winter of 1926-27 with the death of my great-uncle, George Gammell Angell, Professor Emeritus of Semitic Languages in Brown University, Providence, Rhode Island. Professor Angell was widely known as an authority on ancient inscriptions, and had frequently been resorted to by the heads of prominent museums; so that his passing at the age of ninety-two may be recalled by many. Locally, interest was intensified by the obscurity of the cause of death. The professor had been stricken whilst returning from the Newport boat; falling suddenly, as witnesses said, after having been jostled by a nautical-looking negro who had come from one of the queer dark courts on the precipitous hillside which formed a short cut from the waterfront to the deceased's home in Williams Street. Physicians were unable to find any visible disorder, but concluded after perplexed debate that some obscure lesion of the heart, induced by the brisk ascent of so steep a hill by so elderly a man, was responsible for the end. At the time I saw no reason to dissent from this dictum, but latterly I am inclined to wonder — and more than wonder.

As my great-uncle's heir and executor, for he died a childless widower, I was expected to go over his papers with some thoroughness; and for that purpose moved his entire set of files and boxes to my quarters in Boston. Much of the material which I correlated will be later published by the American Archaeological Society, but there was one box which I found exceedingly puzzling, and which I felt much averse from showing to other eyes. It had been locked, and I did not find the key till it occurred to me to examine the personal ring which the professor carried always in his pocket. Then, indeed, I succeeded in opening it, but when I did so seemed only to be confronted by a greater and more closely locked barrier. For what could be the meaning of the queer clay bas-relief and the disjointed jottings, ramblings and cuttings which I found? Had my uncle, in his latter years, become credulous of the most superficial impostures? I resolved to search out the eccentric sculptor responsible for this apparent disturbance of an old man's peace of mind.

The bas-relief was a rough rectangle less than an inch thick and about five by six inches in area, obviously of modern origin. Its designs, however, were far from modern in atmosphere and suggestion; for, although the vagaries of cubism and futurism are many and wild, they do not often reproduce that cryptic regularity which lurks in prehistoric writing. And writing of some kind the bulk of these designs seemed certainly to be; though my memory, despite much familiarity with the papers and collections of my uncle, failed in any way to identify this particular species, or even hint at its remotest affiliations.

Above these apparent hieroglyphics was a figure of evidently pictorial intent, though its impressionistic execution forbade a very clear idea of its nature. It seemed to be a sort of monster, or symbol representing a monster, of a form which only a diseased fancy could conceive. If I say that my somewhat extravagant imagination yielded simultaneous pictures of an octopus, a dragon, and a human caricature, I shall not be unfaithful to the spirit of the thing. A pulpy, tentacled head surmounted a grotesque and scaly body with rudimentary wings; but it was the general outline of the whole which made it most shockingly frightful. Behind the figure was a vague suggestion of a Cyclopean architectural background.

The writing accompanying this oddity was, aside from a stack of press cuttings, in Professor Angell's most recent hand; and made no pretension to literary style. What seemed to be the main document was headed "CTHULHU CULT" in characters painstakingly printed to avoid the erroneous reading of a word so unheard-of. This manuscript was divided into two sections, the first of which was headed "1925 — Dream and Dream Work of H. A. Wilcox, 7 Thomas St., Providence, R. I.," and the second, "Narrative of Inspector John R. Legrasse, 121 Bienville St., New Orleans, La., at 1908 A. A. S. Mtg. — Notes on Same, & Prof. Webb's Acct." The other manuscript papers were all brief notes, some of them accounts of the queer dreams of different persons, some of them citations from theosophical books and magazines (notably W. Scott-Elliot's *Atlantis and the Lost Lemuria*), and the rest comments on long-surviving secret societies and hidden cults, with references to passages in such mythological and anthropological

Weird Tales, February 1928

"The ring of worshippers moved in endless baccanale between the ring of bodies and the ring of fire."

source-books as Frazer's *Golden Bough* and Miss Murray's *Witch-Cult in Western Europe*. The cuttings largely alluded to outré mental illness and outbreaks of group folly or mania in the spring of 1925.

The first half of the principal manuscript told a very peculiar tale. It appears that on 1 March 1925, a thin, dark young man of neurotic and excited aspect had called upon Professor Angell bearing the singular clay bas-relief, which was then exceedingly damp and fresh. His card bore the name of Henry Anthony Wilcox, and my uncle had recognized him as the youngest son of an excellent family slightly known to him, who had latterly been studying sculpture at the Rhode Island School of Design and living alone at the Fleur-de-Lys Building near that institution. Wilcox was a precocious youth of known genius but great eccentricity, and had from childhood excited attention through the strange stories and odd dreams he was in the habit of relating. He called himself "psychically hypersensitive," but the staid folk of the ancient commercial city dismissed him as merely "queer." Never mingling much with his kind, he had dropped gradually from social visibility, and was now known only to a small group of aesthetes from other towns. Even the Providence Art Club, anxious to preserve its conservatism, had found him quite hopeless.

On the occasion of the visit, ran the professor's manuscript, the sculptor abruptly asked for the benefit of his host's archaeological knowledge in identifying the hieroglyphics on the bas-relief. He spoke in a dreamy, stilted manner which suggested pose and alienated sympathy; and my uncle showed some sharpness in replying, for the conspicuous freshness of the tablet implied kinship with anything but archaeology. Young Wilcox's rejoinder, which impressed my uncle enough to make him recall and record it verbatim, was of a fantastically poetic cast which must have typified his whole conversation, and which I have since found highly characteristic of him. He said, "It is new, indeed, for I made it last night in a dream of strange cities; and dreams are older than brooding Tyre, or the contemplative Sphinx, or garden-girdled Babylon."

It was then that he began that rambling tale which suddenly played upon a sleeping memory and won the fevered interest of my uncle. There had been a slight earthquake tremor the night before, the most considerable felt in New England for some years; and Wilcox's imaginations had been keenly affected. Upon retiring, he had had an unprecedented dream of great Cyclopean cities of Titan blocks and sky-flung monoliths, all dripping with green ooze and sinister with latent horror. Hieroglyphics had covered the walls and pillars, and from some undetermined point below had come a voice that was not a voice; a chaotic sensation which only fancy could transmute into sound, but which he attempted to render by the almost unpronounceable jumble of letters, "Cthulhu fhtagn."

This verbal jumble was the key to the recollection which excited and disturbed Professor Angell. He questioned the sculptor with scientific minuteness; and studied with almost frantic intensity the bas-relief on which the youth had found himself working, chilled and clad only in his nightclothes, when waking had stolen bewilderingly over him. My uncle blamed his old age, Wilcox afterward said, for his slowness in recognizing both hieroglyphics and pictorial design. Many of his questions seemed highly out of place to his visitor, especially those which tried to connect the latter with strange cults or societies; and Wilcox could not understand the repeated promises of silence which he was offered in exchange for an admission of membership in some widespread mystical or paganly religious body. When Professor Angell became convinced that the sculptor was indeed ignorant of any cult or system of cryptic lore, he besieged his visitor with demands for future reports of dreams. This bore regular fruit, for after the first interview the manuscript records daily calls of the young man, during which he related startling fragments of nocturnal imagery whose burden was always some terrible Cyclopean vista of dark and dripping stone, with a subterrene voice or intelligence shouting monotonously in enigmatical sense-impacts uninscribable save as gibberish. The two sounds most frequently repeated are those rendered by the letters "Cthulhu" and "R'lyeh."

On 23 March, the manuscript continued, Wilcox failed to appear; and inquiries at his quarters revealed that he had been stricken with an obscure sort of fever and taken to the home of his family in Waterman Street. He had cried out in the night, arousing several other artists in the building, and had manifested since then only alternations of unconsciousness and delirium. My uncle at once telephoned the family, and from that time forward kept close watch of the case; calling often at the Thayer Street office of Dr. Tobey, whom he learned to be in charge. The youth's febrile mind, apparently, was dwelling on strange things; and the doctor shuddered now and then as he spoke of them. They included not only a repetition of what he had formerly dreamed, but touched wildly on a gigantic thing "miles high" which walked or lumbered about. He at no time fully described this object, but occasional frantic words, as repeated by Dr. Tobey, convinced the professor that it must be identical with the nameless monstrosity he had sought to depict in his dream-sculpture. Reference to this object, the doctor added, was invariably a prelude to the young man's subsidence into lethargy. His temperature, oddly enough, was not greatly above normal; but the whole condition was otherwise such as to suggest true fever rather than mental disorder.

On 2 April at about 3 p.m. every trace of Wilcox's malady suddenly ceased. He sat upright in bed, astonished to find himself at home and completely ignorant of what had happened in dream or reality since the night of 22 March. Pronounced well by his physician, he returned to his quarters in three days; but to Professor Angell he was of no further assistance. All traces of strange dreaming had vanished with his recovery, and my uncle kept no record of his night-thoughts after a week of pointless and irrelevant accounts of thoroughly usual visions.

Here the first part of the manuscript ended, but references to certain of the scattered notes gave me much material for thought — so much, in fact, that only the ingrained skepticism then forming my philosophy can account for my continued distrust of the artist. The notes in question were those descriptive of the dreams of various persons covering the same period as that in which young Wilcox had had his strange visitations. My uncle, it seems, had quickly instituted a prodigiously far-flung body of inquiries amongst nearly all the friends whom he could question without impertinence, asking for nightly reports of their dreams, and the dates of any notable visions for some time past. The reception of his request seems to have been varied; but he must, at the very least, have received more responses than any ordinary man could have handled without a secretary. This original correspondence was not preserved, but his notes formed a thorough and really significant digest. Average people in society and business — New England's traditional "salt of the earth" — gave an almost completely negative result, though scattered cases of uneasy but formless nocturnal impressions appear here and there, always between 23 March and 2 April — the period of young Wilcox's delirium. Scientific men were little more affected, though four cases of vague description suggest fugitive glimpses of strange landscapes, and in one case there is mentioned a dread of something abnormal.

It was from the artists and poets that the pertinent answers came, and I know that panic would have broken loose had they been able to compare notes. As it was, lacking their original letters, I half suspected the compiler of having asked leading questions, or of having edited the correspondence in corroboration of what he had latently resolved to see. That is why I continued to feel that Wilcox, somehow cognizant of the old data which my uncle had possessed, had been imposing on the veteran scientist. These responses from aesthetes told a disturbing tale. From 28 February to 2 April a large proportion of them had dreamed very bizarre things, the intensity of the dreams being immeasurably the stronger during the period of the sculptor's delirium. Over a fourth of those who reported anything, reported scenes and half-sounds not unlike those which Wilcox had described; and some of the dreamers confessed acute fear of the gigantic nameless thing visible towards the last. One case, which the note describes with emphasis, was very sad. The subject, a widely known architect with leanings towards theosophy and occultism, went violently insane on the date of young Wilcox's seizure, and expired several months later after incessant screamings to be saved from some escaped denizen of hell. Had my uncle referred to these cases by name instead of merely by number, I should have attempted some corroboration and personal investigation; but as it was, I succeeded in tracing down only a few. All of these, however, bore out the notes in full. I have often wondered if all the objects of the professor's questioning felt as puzzled as did this fraction. It is well that no explanation shall ever reach them.

The press cuttings, as I have intimated, touched on cases of panic, mania, and eccentricity during the given period. Professor Angell must have employed a cutting bureau, for the number of extracts was tremendous, and the sources scattered throughout the globe. Here was a nocturnal suicide in London, where a lone sleeper had leaped from a window after a shocking cry. Here likewise a rambling letter to the editor of a paper in South America, where a fanatic deduces a dire future from visions he has seen. A dispatch from California describes a theosophist colony as donning white robes en masse for some "glorious fulfilment" which never arrives, whilst items from India speak guardedly of serious native unrest towards the end of March. Voodoo orgies multiply in Haiti, and African outposts report ominous mutterings. American officers in the Philippines find certain tribes bothersome about this time, and New York policemen are mobbed by hysterical Levantines on the night of 22-23 March. The west of Ireland, too, is full of wild rumour and legendry, and a fantastic painter named Ardois-Bonnot hangs a blasphemous Dream Landscape in the Paris spring salon of 1926. And so numerous are the recorded troubles in insane asylums that only a miracle can have stopped the medical fraternity from noting strange parallelisms and drawing mystified conclusions. A weird bunch of cuttings, all told; and I can at this date scarcely envisage the callous rationalism with which I set them aside. But I was then convinced that young Wilcox had known of the older matters mentioned by the professor.

II.

THE TALE OF INSPECTOR LEGRASSE.

The older matters which had made the sculptor's dream and bas-relief so significant to my uncle formed the subject of the second half of his long manuscript. Once before, it appears, Professor Angell had seen the hellish outlines of the nameless monstrosity, puzzled over the unknown hieroglyphics, and heard the ominous syllables which can be rendered only as "Cthulhu"; and all this in so stirring and horrible a connection that it is small wonder he pursued young Wilcox with queries and demands for data.

This earlier experience had come in 1908, seventeen years before, when the American Archaeological Society held its annual meeting in St. Louis. Professor Angell, as befitted one of his authority and attainments, had had a prominent part in all the deliberations, and was one of the first to be approached by the several outsiders who took advantage of the convocation to offer questions for correct answering and problems for expert solution.

The chief of these outsiders, and in a short time the focus of interest for the entire meeting, was a commonplace-looking middle-aged man who had travelled all the way from New Orleans for certain special information unobtainable from any local source. His name was John Raymond Legrasse, and he was by profession an inspector of police. With him he bore the subject of his visit, a grotesque, repulsive, and apparently very ancient stone statuette whose origin he was at a loss to determine.

It must not be fancied that Inspector Legrasse had the least interest in archaeology. On the contrary, his wish for enlightenment was prompted by purely professional considerations. The statuette, idol, fetish, or whatever it was, had been captured some months before in the wooden swamps south of New Orleans during a raid on a supposed voodoo meeting; and so singular and hideous were the rites connected with it, that the police could not but realize that they had stumbled on a dark cult totally unknown to them, and infinitely more diabolic than even the blackest of the African voodoo circles. Of its origin, apart from the erratic and unbelievable tales extorted from the captured members, absolutely nothing was to be discovered; hence the anxiety of the police for any antiquarian lore which might help them to place the frightful symbol, and through it track down the cult to its fountain-head.

Inspector Legrasse was scarcely prepared for the sensation which his offering created. One sight of the thing had been enough to throw the assembled men of science into a state of tense excitement, and they lost no time in crowding around him to gaze at the diminutive figure whose utter strangeness and air of genuinely abysmal antiquity hinted so potently at unopened and archaic vistas. No recognized school of sculpture had animated this terrible object, yet centuries and even thousands of years seemed recorded in its dim and greenish surface of unplaceable stone.

The figure, which was finally passed slowly from man to man for close and careful study, was between seven and eight inches in height, and of exquisitely artistic workmanship. It represented a monster of vaguely anthropoid outline, but with an octopus-like head whose face was a mass of feelers, a scaly, rubbery-looking body, prodigious claws on hind and fore feet, and long, narrow wings behind. This thing, which seemed instinct with a fearsome and unnatural malignancy, was of a somewhat bloated corpulence, and squatted evilly on a rectangular block or pedestal covered with undecipherable characters. The tips of the wings touched the back edge of the block, the seat occupied the centre, whilst the long, curved claws of the doubled-up, crouching hind legs gripped the front edge and extended a quarter of the way down towards the bottom of the pedestal. The cephalopod head was bent forward, so that the ends of the facial feelers brushed the backs of huge fore-paws which clasped the croucher's elevated knees. The aspect of the whole was abnormally lifelike, and the more subtly fearful because its source was so totally unknown. Its vast, awesome, and incalculable age was unmistakable; yet not one link did it show with any known type of art belonging to civilization's youth — or indeed to any other time.

Totally separate and apart, its very material was a mystery; for the soapy, greenish-black stone with its golden or iridescent flecks and striations resembled nothing familiar to geology or mineralogy. The characters along the base were equally baffling; and no member present, despite a representation of half the world's expert learning in this field, could form the least notion of even their remotest linguistic kinship. They, like the subject and material, belonged to something horribly remote and distinct from mankind as we know it; something frightfully suggestive of old and unhallowed cycles of life in which our world and our conceptions have no part.

And yet, as the members severally shook their heads and confessed defeat at the inspector's problem, there was one man in that gathering who suspected a touch of bizarre familiarity in the monstrous shape and writing, and who presently told with some diffidence of the odd trifle he knew. This person was the late William Channing Webb, professor of anthropology in Princeton University, and an explorer of no slight note.

Professor Webb had been engaged, forty-eight years before, in a tour of Greenland and Iceland in search of some Runic inscriptions which he failed to unearth; and whilst high up on the West Greenland coast had encountered a singular tribe or cult of degenerate Eskimos whose religion, a curious form of devil-worship, chilled him with its deliberate bloodthirstiness and repulsiveness. It was a faith of which other Eskimos knew little, and which they mentioned only with shudders, saying that it had come down from horribly ancient aeons before ever the world was made. Besides nameless rites and human sacrifices there were certain queer hereditary rituals addressed to a supreme elder devil or tornasuk; and of this Professor Webb had taken a careful phonetic copy from an aged angekok or wizard-priest, expressing the sounds in Roman letters as best he knew how. But just now of prime significance was the fetish which this cult had cherished, and around which they danced when the aurora leaped high over the ice cliffs. It was, the professor stated, a very crude bas-relief of stone, comprising a hideous picture and some cryptic writing. And as far as he could tell, it was a rough parallel in all essential features of the bestial thing now lying before the meeting.

These data, received with suspense and astonishment by the assembled members, proved doubly exciting to Inspector Legrasse; and he began at once to ply his informant with questions. Having noted and copied an oral ritual among the swamp cult-worshippers his men had arrested, he besought the professor to remember as best he might the syllables taken down amongst the diabolist Eskimos. There then followed an exhaustive comparison of details, and a moment of really awed silence when both detective and scientist agreed on the virtual identity of the phrase common to two hellish rituals so many worlds of distance apart. What, in substance, both the Eskimo wizards and the Louisiana swamp-priests had chanted to their kindred idols was something very like this — the word-divisions being guessed at from traditional breaks in the phrase as chanted aloud:

"Ph'nglui mglw'nafh Cthulhu R'lyeh wgah'nagl fhtagn."

Legrasse had one point in advance of Professor Webb, for several among his mongrel prisoners had repeated to him what older celebrants had told them the words meant. This text, as given, ran something like this:

"In his house at R'lyeh dead Cthulhu waits dreaming."

And now, in response to a general and urgent demand, Inspector Legrasse related as fully as possible his experience with the swamp worshippers; telling a story to which I could see my uncle attached profound significance. It savoured of the wildest dreams of myth-maker and theosophist, and disclosed an astonishing degree of cosmic imagination among such half-castes and pariahs as might be least expected to possess it.

On 1 November 1907, there had come to New Orleans police a frantic summons from the swamp and lagoon country to the south. The squatters there, mostly primitive but good-natured descendants of Lafitte's men, were in the grip of stark terror from an unknown thing which had stolen upon them in the night. It was voodoo, apparently, but voodoo of a more terrible sort than they had ever known; and some of their women and children had disappeared since the malevolent tom-tom had begun its incessant beating far within the black haunted woods where no dweller ventured. There were insane shouts and harrowing screams, soul-chilling chants and dancing devil-flames; and, the frightened messenger added, the people could stand it no more.

So a body of twenty police, filling two carriages and an automobile, had set out in the late afternoon with the shivering squatter as a guide. At the end of the passable road they alighted, and for miles splashed on in silence through the terrible cypress woods where day never came. Ugly roots and malignant hanging nooses of Spanish moss beset them, and now and then a pile of dank stones or fragments of a rotting wall intensified by its hint of morbid habitation a depression which every malformed tree and every fungous islet combined to create. At length the squatter settlement, a miserable huddle of huts, hove in sight; and hysterical dwellers ran out to cluster around the group of bobbing lanterns. The muffled beat of tom-toms was now faintly audible far, far ahead; and a curdling shriek came at infrequent intervals when the wind shifted. A reddish glare, too, seemed to filter through the pale undergrowth beyond endless avenues of forest night. Reluctant even to be left alone again, each one of the cowed squatters refused point-blank to advance another inch towards the scene of unholy worship, so Inspector Legrasse and his nineteen colleagues plunged on unguided into black arcades of horror that none of them had ever trod before.

The region now entered by the police was one of traditionally evil repute, substantially unknown and untraversed by white men. There were legends of a hidden lake unglimpsed by mortal sight, in which dwelt a huge, formless white polypus thing with luminous eyes; and squatters whispered that bat-winged devils flew up out of caverns in inner earth to worship it at midnight. They said it had been there before D'Iberville, before La Salle, before the Indians, and before even the wholesome beasts and birds of the woods. It was nightmare itself, and to see it was to die. But it made men dream, and so they knew enough to keep away. The present voodoo orgy was, indeed, on the merest fringe of this abhorred area, but that location was bad enough; hence perhaps the very place of the worship had terrified the squatters more than the shocking sounds and incidents.

Only poetry or madness could do justice to the noises heard by Legrasse's men as they ploughed on through the black morass towards the red glare and the muffled tom-toms. There are vocal qualities peculiar to men, and vocal qualities peculiar to beasts; and it is terrible to hear the one when the source should yield the other. Animal fury and orgiastic licence here whipped themselves to demoniac heights by howls and squawking ecstasies that tore and reverberated through those nighted woods like pestilential tempests from the gulfs of hell. Now and then the less organized ululations would cease, and from what seemed a well-drilled chorus of hoarse voices would rise in singsong chant that hideous phrase or ritual:

"Ph'nglui mglw'nafh Cthulhu R'lyeh wgah'nagl fhtagn."

Then the men, having reached a spot where the trees were thinner, came suddenly in sight of the spectacle itself. Four of them reeled, one fainted, and two were shaken into a frantic cry which the mad cacophony of the orgy fortunately deadened. Legrasse dashed swamp water on the face of the fainting man, and all stood trembling and nearly hypnotized with horror.

In a natural glade of the swamp stood a grassy island of perhaps an acre's extent, clear of trees and tolerably dry. On this now leaped and twisted a more indescribable horde of human abnormality than any but a Sime or an Angarola could paint. Void of clothing, this hybrid spawn were braying, bellowing and writhing about a monstrous ringshaped bonfire; in the centre of which, revealed by occasional rifts in the curtain of flame, stood a great granite monolith some eight feet in height; on top of which, incongruous in its diminutiveness, rested the noxious carven statuette. From a wide circle of ten scaffolds set up at regular intervals with the flame-girt monolith as a centre hung, head downward, the oddly marred bodies of the helpless squatters who had disappeared. It was inside this circle that the ring of worshippers jumped and roared, the general direction of the mass motion being from left to right in endless bacchanale between the ring of bodies and the ring of fire.

It may have been only imagination and it may have been only echoes which induced one of the men, an excitable Spaniard, to fancy he heard antiphonal responses to the ritual from some far and unillumined spot deeper within the wood of ancient legendry and horror. This man, Joseph D. Galvez, I later met and questioned; and he proved distractingly imaginative. He indeed went so far as to hint of the faint beating of great wings, and of a glimpse of shining eyes and a mountainous white bulk beyond the remotest trees — but I suppose he had been hearing too much native superstition.

Actually, the horrified pause of the men was of comparatively brief duration. Duty came first; and although there must have been nearly a hundred mongrel celebrants in the throng, the police relied on their firearms and plunged determinedly into the nauseous rout. For five minutes the resultant din and chaos were beyond description. Wild blows were struck, shots were fired, and escapes were made; but in the end Legrasse was able to count some forty-seven sullen prisoners, whom he forced to dress in haste and fall into line between two rows of policemen. Five of the worshippers lay dead, and two severely wounded ones were carried away on improvised stretchers by their fellow-prisoners. The image on the monolith, of course, was carefully removed and carried back by Legrasse.

Examined at headquarters after a trip of intense strain and weariness, the prisoners all proved to be men of a very low, mixed-blooded, and mentally aberrant type. Most were seamen, and a sprinkling of negroes and mulattos, largely West Indians or Brava Portuguese from the Cape Verde Islands, gave a colouring of voodooism to the heterogeneous cult. But before many questions were asked, it became manifest that something far deeper and older than negro fetishism was involved. Degraded and ignorant as they were, the creatures held with surprising consistency to the central idea of their loathsome faith.

They worshipped, so they said, the Great Old Ones who lived ages before there were any men, and who came to the young world out of the sky. These Old Ones were gone now, inside the earth and under the sea; but their dead bodies had told their secrets in dreams to the first men, who formed a cult which had never died. This was that cult, and the prisoners said it had always existed and always would exist, hidden in distant wastes and dark places all over the world until the time when the great priest Cthulhu, from his dark house in the mighty city of R'lyeh under the waters, should rise and bring the earth again beneath his sway. Some day he would call, when the stars were ready, and the secret cult would always be waiting to liberate him.

Meanwhile no more must be told. There was a secret which even torture could not extract. Mankind was not absolutely alone among the conscious things of earth, for shapes came out of the dark to visit the faithful few. But these were not the Great Old Ones. No man had ever seen the Old Ones. The carven idol was great Cthulhu, but none might say whether or not the others were precisely like him. No one could read the old writing now, but things were told by word of mouth. The chanted ritual was not the secret — that was never spoken aloud, only whispered. The chant meant only this: "In his house at R'lyeh dead Cthulhu waits dreaming."

Only two of the prisoners were found sane enough to be hanged, and the rest were committed to various institutions. All denied a part in the ritual murders, and averred that the killing had been done by Black-Winged Ones which had come to them from their immemorial meeting-place in the haunted wood. But of those mysterious allies no coherent account could ever be gained. What the police did extract came mainly from an immensely aged mestizo named Castro, who claimed to have sailed to strange ports and talked with undying leaders of the cult in the mountains of China.

Old Castro remembered bits of hideous legend that paled the speculations of theosophists and made man and the world seem recent and transient indeed. There had been aeons when other Things ruled on the earth, and They had had great cities. Remains of Them, he said the deathless Chinamen had told him, were still to be found as Cyclopean stones on islands in the Pacific. They all died vast epochs of time before men came, but there were arts which could revive Them when the stars had come round again to the right positions in the cycle of eternity. They had, indeed, come themselves from the stars, and brought Their images with Them.

These Great Old Ones, Castro continued, were not composed altogether of flesh and blood. They had shape — for did not this star-fashioned image prove it? — but that shape was not made of matter. When the stars were right, They could plunge from world to world through the sky; but when the stars were wrong, They could not live. But although They no longer lived, They would never really die. They all lay in stone houses in Their great city of R'lyeh, preserved by the spells of mighty Cthulhu for a glorious resurrection when the stars and the earth might once more be ready for Them. But at that time some force from outside must serve to liberate Their bodies. The spells that preserved them intact likewise prevented Them from making an initial move, and They could only lie awake in the dark and think whilst uncounted millions of years rolled by. They knew all that was occurring in the universe, for Their mode of speech was transmitted thought. Even now They talked in Their tombs. When, after infinities of chaos, the first men came, the Great Old Ones spoke to the sensitive among them by moulding their dreams; for only thus could Their language reach the fleshy minds of mammals.

Then, whispered Castro, those first men formed the cult around small idols which the Great Ones showed them; idols brought in dim eras from dark stars. That cult would never die till the stars came right again, and the secret priests would take great Cthulhu from His tomb to revive His subjects and resume His rule of earth. The time would be easy to know, for then mankind would have become as the Great Old Ones; free and wild and beyond good and evil, with laws and morals thrown aside and all men shouting and killing and revelling in joy. Then the liberated Old Ones would teach them new ways to shout and kill and revel and enjoy themselves, and all the earth would flame with a holocaust of ecstasy and freedom. Meanwhile the cult, by appropriate rites, must keep alive the memory of those ancient ways and shadow forth the prophecy of their return.

In the elder time chosen men had talked with the entombed Old Ones in dreams, but then something had happened. The great stone city R'lyeh, with its monoliths and sepulchres, had sunk beneath the waves; and the deep waters, full of the one primal mystery through which not even thought can pass, had cut off the spectral intercourse. But memory never died, and high priests said that the city would rise again when the stars were right. Then came out of the earth the black spirits of earth, mouldy and shadowy, and full of dim rumours picked up in caverns beneath forgotten sea-bottoms. But of them old Castro dared not speak much. He cut himself off hurriedly, and no amount of persuasion or subtlety could elicit more in this direction. The size of the Old Ones, too, he curiously declined to mention. Of the cult, he said that he thought the centre lay amid the pathless deserts of Arabia, where Irem, the City of Pillars, dreams hidden and untouched. It was not allied to the European witch-cult, and was virtually unknown beyond its members. No book had ever really hinted of it, though the deathless Chinamen said that there were double meanings in the *Necronomicon* of the mad Arab Abdul Alhazred which the initiated might read as they chose, especially the much-discussed couplet:

That is not dead which can eternal lie,
And with strange aeons even death may die.

Legrasse, deeply impressed and not a little bewildered, had inquired in vain concerning the historic affiliations of the cult. Castro, apparently, had told the truth when he said that it was wholly secret. The authorities at Tulane University could shed no light upon either cult or image, and now the detective had come to the highest authorities in the country and met with no more than the Greenland tale of Professor Webb.

The feverish interest aroused at the meeting by Legrasse's tale, corroborated as it was by the statuette, is echoed in the subsequent correspondence of those who attended, although scant mention occurs in the formal publication of the society.

Caution is the first care of those accustomed to face occasional charlatanry and imposture. Legrasse for some time lent the image to Professor Webb, but at the latter's death it was returned to him and remains in his possession, where I viewed it not long ago. It is truly a terrible thing, and unmistakably akin to the dream-sculpture of young Wilcox.

That my uncle was excited by the tale of the sculptor I did not wonder, for what thoughts must arise upon hearing, after a knowledge of what Legrasse had learned of the cult, of a sensitive young man, who had dreamed not only the figure and exact hieroglyphics of the swamp-found image and the Greenland devil tablet, but had come in his dreams upon at least three of the precise words of the formula uttered alike by Eskimo diabolists and mongrel Louisianans? Professor Angell's instant start on an investigation of the utmost thoroughness was eminently natural; though privately I suspected young Wilcox of having heard of the cult in some indirect way, and of having invented a series of dreams to heighten and continue the mystery at my uncle's expense. The dream-narratives and cuttings collected by the professor were, of course, strong corroboration; but the rationalism of my mind and the extravagance of the whole subject led me to adopt what I thought the most sensible conclusions. So, after thoroughly studying the manuscript again and correlating the theosophical and anthropological notes with the cult narrative of Legrasse, I made a trip to Providence to see the sculptor and give him the rebuke I thought proper for so boldly imposing upon a learned and aged man.

Wilcox still lived alone in the Fleur-de-Lys Building in Thomas Street, a hideous Victorian imitation of seventeenth century Breton architecture which flaunts its stuccoed front amidst the lovely Colonial houses on the ancient hill, and under the very shadow of the finest Georgian steeple in America. I found him at work in his rooms, and at once conceded from the specimens scattered about that his genius is indeed profound and authentic. He will, I believe, be heard from some time as one of the great decadents; for he has crystallized in clay and will one day mirror in marble those nightmares and phantasies which Arthur Machen evokes in prose, and Clark Ashton Smith makes visible in verse and in painting.

Dark, frail, and somewhat unkempt in aspect, he turned languidly at my knock and asked me my business without rising. When I told him who I was, he displayed some interest; for my uncle had excited his curiosity in probing his strange dreams, yet had never explained the reason for the study. I did not enlarge his knowledge in this regard, but sought with some subtlety to draw him out.

In a short time I became convinced of his absolute sincerity, for he spoke of the dreams in a manner none could mistake. They and their subconscious residuum had influenced his art profoundly, and he showed me a morbid statue whose contours almost made me shake with the potency of its black suggestion. He could not recall having seen the original of this thing except in his own dream bas-relief, but the outlines had formed themselves insensibly under his hands. It was, no doubt, the giant shape he had raved of in delirium. That he really knew nothing of the hidden cult, save from what my uncle's relentless catechism had let fall, he soon made clear; and again I strove to think of some way in which he could possibly have received the weird impressions.

He talked of his dreams in a strangely poetic fashion, making me see with terrible vividness the damp Cyclopean city of slimy green stone — whose geometry, he oddly said, was all wrong — and hear with frightened expectancy the ceaseless, half-mental calling from underground: "Cthulhu fhtagn, Cthulhu fhtagn."

These words had formed part of that dread ritual which told of dead Cthulhu's dream-vigil in his stone vault at R'lyeh, and I felt deeply moved despite my rational beliefs. Wilcox, I was sure, had heard of the cult in some casual way, and had soon forgotten it amidst the mass of his equally weird reading and imagining. Later, by virtue of its sheer impressiveness, it had found subconscious expression in dreams, in the bas-relief, and in the terrible statue I now beheld; so that his imposture upon my uncle had been a very innocent one. The youth was of a type, at once slightly affected and slightly ill-mannered, which I could never like; but I was willing enough now to admit both his genius and his honesty. I took leave of him amicably, and wish him all the success his talent promises.

The matter of the cult still remained to fascinate me, and at times I had visions of personal fame from researches into its origin and connections. I visited New Orleans, talked with Legrasse and others of that old-time raiding party, saw the frightful image, and even questioned such of the mongrel prisoners as still survived. Old Castro, unfortunately, had been dead for some years. What I now heard so graphically at first hand, though it was really no more than a detailed confirmation of what my uncle had written, excited me afresh; for I felt sure that I was on the track of a very real, very secret, and very ancient religion whose discovery would make me an anthropologist of note. My attitude was still one of absolute materialism, as I wish it still were; and I discounted with a most inexplicable perversity the coincidence of the dream notes and odd cuttings collected by Professor Angell.

One thing which I began to suspect, and which I now fear I know, is that my uncle's death was far from natural. He fell on a narrow hill street leading up from an ancient waterfront swarming with foreign mongrels, after a careless push from a negro sailor. I did not forget the mixed blood and marine pursuits of the cult-members in Louisiana, and would not be surprised to learn of secret methods and poison needles as ruthless and as anciently known as the cryptic rites and beliefs. Legrasse and his men, it is true, have been let alone; but in Norway a certain seaman who saw things is dead. Might not the deeper inquiries of my uncle after encountering the sculptor's data have come to sinister ears? I think Professor Angell died because he knew too much, or because he was likely to learn too much. Whether I shall go as he did remains to be seen, for I have learned much now.

III.

THE MADNESS FROM THE SEA.

If Heaven ever wishes to grant me a boon, it will be a total effacing of the results of a mere chance which fixed my eye on a certain stray piece of shelf-paper. It was nothing on which I would naturally have stumbled in the course of my daily round, for it was an old number of an Australian journal, the Sydney Bulletin for April 18, 1925. It had escaped even the cutting bureau which had at the time of its issuance been avidly collecting material for my uncle's research.

I had largely given over my inquiries into what Professor Angell called the "Cthulhu Cult," and was visiting a learned friend in Paterson, New Jersey, the curator of a local museum and a mineralogist of note. Examining one day the reserve specimens roughly set on the storage shelves in a rear room of the museum, my eye was caught by an odd picture in one of the old papers spread beneath the stones. It was the Sydney Bulletin I have mentioned, for my friend had wide affiliations in all conceivable foreign parts; and the picture was a half-tone cut of a hideous stone image almost identical with that which Legrasse had found in the swamp.

Eagerly clearing the sheet of its precious contents, I scanned the item in detail; and was disappointed to find it of only moderate length. What it suggested, however, was of portentous significance to my flagging quest; and I carefully tore it out for immediate action. It read as follows:

MYSTERY DERELICT FOUND AT SEA.

Vigilant Arrives With Helpless Armed New Zealand Yacht in Tow.

One Survivor and Dead Man Found Aboard.

TALE OF DESPERATE BATTLE AND DEATHS AT SEA

Rescued Seaman Refuses Particulars of Strange Experience.

Odd Idol Found in His Possession.

INQUIRY TO FOLLOW.

The Morrison Co.'s freighter Vigilant, *bound from Valparaiso, arrived this morning at its wharf in Darling Harbour, having in tow the battled and disabled but heavily armed steam yacht* Alert *of Dunedin, N.Z., which was sighted April 12th in S. Latitude 34° 21', W. Longitude 152° 17', with one living and one dead man aboard.*

The Vigilant *left Valparaiso March 25th, and on April 2nd was driven considerably south of her course by exceptionally heavy storms and monster waves. On April 12th the derelict was sighted; and though apparently deserted, was found upon boarding to contain one survivor in a half-delirious condition and one man who had evidently been dead for more than a week.*

The living man was clutching a horrible stone idol of unknown origin, about one foot in height, regarding whose nature authorities at Sydney University, the Royal Society, and the Museum in College Street all profess complete bafflement, and which the survivor says he found in the cabin of the yacht, in a small carved shrine of common pattern.

This man, after recovering his senses, told an exceedingly strange story of piracy and slaughter. He is Gustaf Johansen, a Norwegian of some intelligence, and had been second mate of the two-masted schooner Emma *of Auckland, which sailed for Callao February 20th with a complement of eleven men.*

The Emma, *he says, was delayed and thrown widely south of her course by the great storm of March 1st, and on March 22nd, in S. Latitude 49° 51' W. Longitude 128° 34', encountered the* Alert, *manned by a queer and evil-looking crew of Kanakas and half-castes. Being ordered peremptorily to turn back, Capt. Collins refused; whereupon the strange crew began to fire savagely and without warning upon the schooner with a peculiarly heavy battery of brass cannon forming part of the yacht's equipment.*

The Emma's *men showed fight, says the survivor, and though the schooner began to sink from shots beneath the water-line they managed to heave alongside their enemy and board her, grappling with the savage crew on the yacht's deck, and being forced to kill them all, the number being slightly superior, because of their particularly abhorrent and desperate though rather clumsy mode of fighting.*

Three of the Emma's *men, including Capt. Collins and First Mate Green, were killed; and the remaining eight under Second Mate Johansen proceeded to navigate the captured yacht, going ahead in their original direction to see if any reason for their ordering back had existed.*

The next day, it appears, they raised and landed on a small island, although none is known to exist in that part of the ocean; and six of the men somehow died ashore, though Johansen is queerly reticent about this part of his story, and speaks only of their falling into a rock chasm.

Later, it seems, he and one companion boarded the yacht and tried to manage her, but were beaten about by the storm of April 2nd.

From that time till his rescue on the 12th the man remembers little, and he does not even recall when William Briden, his companion, died. Briden's death reveals no apparent cause, and was probably due to excitement or exposure.

Cable advices from Dunedin report that the Alert *was well known there as an island trader, and bore an evil reputation along the waterfront. It was owned by a curious group of half-castes whose frequent meetings and night trips to the woods attracted no little curiosity; and it had set sail in great haste just after the storm and earth tremors of March 1st.*

Our Auckland correspondent gives the Emma *and her crew an excellent reputation, and Johansen is described as a sober and worthy man.*

The admiralty will institute an inquiry on the whole matter beginning tomorrow, at which every effort will be made to induce Johansen to speak more freely than he has done hitherto.

This was all, together with the picture of the hellish image; but what a train of ideas it started in my mind! Here were new treasuries of data on the Cthulhu Cult, and evidence that it had strange interests at sea as well as on land. What motive prompted the hybrid crew to order back the Emma as they sailed about with their hideous idol? What was the unknown island on which six of the Emma's crew had died, and about which the mate Johansen was so secretive? What had the vice-admiralty's investigation brought out, and what was known of the noxious cult in Dunedin? And most marvelous of all, what deep and more than natural linkage of dates was this which gave a malign and now undeniable significance to the various turns of events so carefully noted by my uncle?

March First — or February 28th according to the International Date Line — the earthquake and storm had come. From Dunedin the *Alert* and her noisome crew had darted eagerly forth as if imperiously summoned, and on the other side of the earth poets and artists had begun to dream of a strange, dank Cyclopean city whilst a young sculptor had moulded in his sleep the form of the dreaded Cthulhu. March 23rd the crew of the Emma landed on an unknown island and left six men dead; and on that date the dreams of sensitive men assumed a heightened vividness and darkened with dread of a giant monster's malign pursuit, whilst an architect had gone mad and a sculptor had lapsed suddenly into delirium! And what of this storm of April 2nd — the date on which all dreams of the dank city ceased, and Wilcox emerged unharmed from the bondage of strange fever? What of all this — and of those hints of old Castro about the sunken, star-born Old Ones and their coming reign; their faithful cult and their mastery of dreams? Was I tottering on the brink of cosmic horrors beyond man's power to bear? If so, they must be horrors of the mind alone, for in some way the second of April had put a stop to whatever monstrous menace had begun its siege of mankind's soul.

That evening, after a day of hurried cabling and arranging, I bade my host *adieu* and took a train for San Francisco. In less than a month I was in Dunedin; where, however, I found that little was known of the strange cult-members who had lingered in the old sea-taverns. Waterfront scum was far too common for special mention; though there was vague talk about one inland trip these mongrels had made, during which faint drumming and red flame were noted on the distant hills. In Auckland I learned that Johansen had returned with yellow hair turned white after a perfunctory and inconclusive questioning at Sydney, and had thereafter sold his cottage in West Street and sailed with his wife to his old home in Oslo. Of his stirring experience he would tell his friends no more than he had told the admiralty officials, and all they could do was to give me his Oslo address.

After that I went to Sydney and talked profitlessly with seamen and members of the vice-admiralty court. I saw the *Alert*, now sold and in commercial use, at Circular Quay in Sydney Cove, but gained nothing from its non-committal bulk. The crouching image with its cuttlefish head, dragon body, scaly wings, and hieroglyphed pedestal, was preserved in the Museum at Hyde Park; and I studied it long and well, finding it a thing of balefully exquisite workmanship, and with the same utter mystery, terrible antiquity, and unearthly strangeness of material which I had noted in Legrasse's smaller specimen. Geologists, the curator told me, had found it a monstrous puzzle; for they vowed that the world held no rock like it. Then I thought with a shudder of what Old Castro had told Legrasse about the Old Ones; "They had come from the stars, and had brought Their images with Them."

Shaken with such a mental resolution as I had never before known, I now resolved to visit Mate Johansen in Oslo. Sailing for London, I reembarked at once for the Norwegian capital; and one autumn day landed at the trim wharves in the shadow of the Egeberg. Johansen's address, I discovered, lay in the Old Town of King Harold Haardrada, which kept alive the name of Oslo during all the centuries that the greater city masqueraded as "Christiana." I made the brief trip by taxicab, and knocked with palpitant heart at the door of a neat and ancient building with plastered front. A sad-faced woman in black answered my summons, and I was stung with disappointment when she told me in halting English that Gustaf Johansen was no more.

He had not long survived his return, said his wife, for the doings at sea in 1925 had broken him. He had told her no more than he told the public, but had left a long manuscript — of "technical matters" as he said — written in English, evidently in order to guard her from the peril of casual perusal. During a walk through a narrow lane near the Gothenburg dock, a bundle of papers falling from an attic window had knocked him down. Two Lascar sailors at once helped him to his feet, but before the ambulance could reach him he was dead. Physicians found no adequate cause in the end, and laid it to heart trouble and a weakened constitution. I now felt gnawing at my vitals that dark terror which will never leave me till I, too, am at rest, "accidentally" or otherwise. Persuading the widow that my connection with her husband's "technical matters" was sufficient to entitle me to his manuscript, I bore the document away and began to read it on the London boat.

It was a simple, rambling thing — a naïve sailor's effort at a post-facto diary — and strove to recall day by day that last awful voyage. I cannot attempt to transcribe it verbatim in all its cloudiness and redundance, but I will tell its gist enough to show why the sound of the water against the vessel's sides became so unendurable to me that I stopped my ears with cotton.

Johansen, thank God, did not know quite all, even though

he saw the city and the Thing, but I shall never sleep calmly again when I think of the horrors that lurk ceaselessly behind life in time and in space, and of those unhallowed blasphemies from elder stars which dream beneath the sea, known and favoured by a nightmare cult ready and eager to loose them upon the world whenever another earthquake shall heave their monstrous stone city again to the sun and air.

Johansen's voyage had begun just as he told it to the vice-admiralty. The Emma, in ballast, had cleared Auckland on February 20th, and had felt the full force of that earthquake-born tempest which must have heaved up from the sea-bottom the horrors that filled men's dreams. Once more under control, the ship was making good progress when held up by the *Alert* on March 22nd, and I could feel the mate's regret as he wrote of her bombardment and sinking. Of the swarthy cult-fiends on the *Alert* he speaks with significant horror. There was some peculiarly abominable quality about them which made their destruction seem almost a duty, and Johansen shows ingenuous wonder at the charge of ruthlessness brought against his party during the proceedings of the court of inquiry. Then, driven ahead by curiosity in their captured yacht under Johansen's command, the men sight a great stone pillar sticking out of the sea, and in S. Latitude 47° 9', W. Longitude 126° 43', come upon a coastline of mingled mud, ooze, and weedy Cyclopean masonry which can be nothing less than the tangible substance of earth's supreme terror — the nightmare corpse-city of R'lyeh, that was built in measureless aeons behind history by the vast, loathsome shapes that seeped down from the dark stars. There lay great Cthulhu and his hordes, hidden in green slimy vaults and sending out at last, after cycles incalculable, the thoughts that spread fear to the dreams of the sensitive and called imperiously to the faithful to come on a pilgrimage of liberation and restoration. All this Johansen did not suspect, but God knows he soon saw enough!

I suppose that only a single mountain-top, the hideous monolith-crowned citadel whereon great Cthulhu was buried, actually emerged from the waters. When I think of the extent of all that may be brooding down there I almost wish to kill myself forthwith. Johansen and his men were awed by the cosmic majesty of this dripping Babylon of elder daemons, and must have guessed without guidance that it was nothing of this or of any sane planet. Awe at the unbelievable size of the greenish stone blocks, at the dizzying height of the great carven monolith, and at the stupefying identity of the colossal statues and bas-reliefs with the queer image found in the shrine on the *Alert*, is poignantly visible in every line of the mate's frightened description.

Without knowing what futurism is like, Johansen achieved something very close to it when he spoke of the city; for instead of describing any definite structure or building, he dwells only on broad impressions of vast angles and stone surfaces — surfaces too great to belong to anything right or proper for this earth, and impious with horrible images and hieroglyphs. I mention his talk about angles because it suggests something Wilcox had told me of his awful dreams. He said that the geometry of the dream-place he saw was abnormal, non-Euclidean, and loathsomely redolent of spheres and dimensions apart from ours. Now an unlettered seaman felt the same thing whilst gazing at the terrible reality.

Johansen and his men landed at a sloping mud-bank on this monstrous Acropolis, and clambered slipperily up over titan oozy blocks which could have been no mortal staircase. The very sun of heaven seemed distorted when viewed through the polarising miasma welling out from this sea-soaked perversion, and twisted menace and suspense lurked leeringly in those crazily elusive angles of carven rock where a second glance showed concavity after the first showed convexity.

Something very like fright had come over all the explorers before anything more definite than rock and ooze and weed was seen. Each would have fled had he not feared the scorn of the others, and it was only half-heartedly that they searched — vainly, as it proved — for some portable souvenir to bear away.

It was Rodriguez the Portuguese who climbed up the foot of the monolith and shouted of what he had found. The rest followed him, and looked curiously at the immense carved door with the now familiar squid-dragon bas-relief. It was, Johansen said, like a great barn-door; and they all felt that it was a door because of the ornate lintel, threshold, and jambs around it, though they could not decide whether it lay flat like a trap-door or slantwise like an outside cellar-door. As Wilcox would have said, the geometry of the place was all wrong. One could not be sure that the sea and the ground were horizontal, hence the relative position of everything else seemed phantasmally variable.

Briden pushed at the stone in several places without result. Then Donovan felt over it delicately around the edge, pressing each point separately as he went. He climbed interminably along the grotesque stone moulding — that is, one would call it climbing if the thing was not after all horizontal — and the men wondered how any door in the universe could be so vast. Then, very softly and slowly, the acre-great lintel began to give inward at the top; and they saw that it was balanced.

Donovan slid or somehow propelled himself down or along the jamb and rejoined his fellows, and everyone watched the queer recession of the monstrously carven portal. In this phantasy of prismatic distortion it moved anomalously in a diagonal way, so that all the rules of matter and perspective seemed upset.

The aperture was black with a darkness almost material. That tenebrousness was indeed a positive quality; for it obscured such parts of the inner walls as ought to have been revealed, and actually burst forth like smoke from its aeon-long imprisonment, visibly darkening the sun as it slunk away into the shrunken and gibbous sky on flapping membraneous wings. The odour rising from the newly opened depths was intolerable, and at length the quick-eared Hawkins thought he heard a nasty, slopping sound down there. Everyone listened, and everyone was listening still when It lumbered slobberingly into sight and gropingly squeezed Its gelatinous green immensity through the black doorway into the tainted outside air of that poison city of madness.

Poor Johansen's handwriting almost gave out when he wrote of this. Of the six men who never reached the ship, he thinks two perished of pure fright in that accursed instant. The Thing cannot be described — there is no language for such abysms of shrieking and immemorial lunacy, such eldritch contradictions of all matter, force, and cosmic order. A mountain walked or stumbled. God! What wonder that across the earth a great architect went mad, and poor Wilcox raved with fever in that telepathic instant? The Thing of the idols, the green, sticky spawn of the stars, had awaked to claim his own. The stars were right again, and what an age-old cult had failed to do by design, a band of innocent sailors had done by accident. After vigintillions of years great Cthulhu was loose again, and ravening for delight.

Three men were swept up by the flabby claws before anybody turned. God rest them, if there be any rest in the universe. They were Donovan, Guerrera, and Angstrom. Parker slipped as the other three were plunging frenziedly over endless vistas of green-crusted rock to the boat, and Johansen swears he was swallowed up by an angle of masonry which shouldn't have been there; an angle which was acute, but behaved as if it were obtuse. So only Briden and Johansen reached the boat, and pulled desperately for the *Alert* as the mountainous monstrosity flopped down the slimy stones and hesitated, floundering at the edge of the water.

Steam had not been suffered to go down entirely, despite the departure of all hands for the shore; and it was the work of only a few moments of feverish rushing up and down between wheel and engines to get the *Alert* under way. Slowly, amidst the distorted horrors of that indescribable scene, she began to churn the lethal waters; whilst on the masonry of that charnel shore that was not of earth the titan Thing from the stars slavered and gibbered like Polypheme cursing the fleeing ship of Odysseus. Then, bolder than the storied Cyclops, great Cthulhu slid greasily into the water and began to pursue with vast wave-raising strokes of cosmic potency. Briden looked back and went mad, laughing shrilly as he kept on laughing at intervals till death found him one night in the cabin whilst Johansen was wandering deliriously.

But Johansen had not given out yet. Knowing that the Thing could surely overtake the *Alert* until steam was fully up, he resolved on a desperate chance; and, setting the engine for full speed, ran lightning-like on deck and reversed the wheel. There was a mighty eddying and foaming in the noisome brine, and as the steam mounted higher and higher the brave Norwegian drove his vessel head on against the pursuing jelly which rose above the unclean froth like the stern of a daemon galleon. The awful squid-head with writhing feelers came nearly up to the bowsprit of the sturdy yacht, but Johansen drove on relentlessly. There was a bursting as of an exploding bladder, a slushy nastiness as of a cloven sunfish, a stench as of a thousand opened graves, and a sound that the chronicler could not put on paper. For an instant the ship was befouled by an acrid and blinding green cloud, and then there was only a venomous seething astern; where — God in heaven! — the scattered plasticity of that nameless sky-spawn was nebulously recombining in its hateful original form, whilst its distance widened every second as the *Alert* gained impetus from its mounting steam.

That was all. After that Johansen only brooded over the idol in the cabin and attended to a few matters of food for himself and the laughing maniac by his side. He did not try to navigate after the first bold flight, for the reaction had taken something out of his soul. Then came the storm of April 2nd, and a gathering of the clouds about his consciousness. There is a sense of spectral whirling through liquid gulfs of infinity, of dizzying rides through reeling universes on a comet's tail, and of hysterical plunges from the pit to the moon and from the moon back again to the pit, all livened by a cachinnating chorus of the distorted, hilarious elder gods and the green, bat-winged mocking imps of Tartarus.

Out of that dream came rescue — the *Vigilant*, the vice-admiralty court, the streets of Dunedin, and the long voyage back home to the old house by the Egeberg. He could not tell — they would think him mad. He would write of what he knew before death came, but his wife must not guess. Death would be a boon if only it could blot out the memories.

That was the document I read, and now I have placed it in the tin box beside the bas-relief and the papers of Professor Angell. With it shall go this record of mine — this test of my own sanity, wherein is pieced together that which I hope may never be pieced together again. I have looked upon all that the universe has to hold of horror, and even the skies of spring and the flowers of summer must ever afterward be poison to me. But I do not think my life will be long. As my uncle went, as poor Johansen went, so I shall go. I know too much, and the cult still lives.

Cthulhu still lives, too, I suppose, again in that chasm of stone which has shielded him since the sun was young. His accursed city is sunken once more, for the *Vigilant* sailed over the spot after the April storm; but his ministers on earth still bellow and prance and slay around idol-capped monoliths in lonely places. He must have been trapped by the sinking whilst within his black abyss, or else the world would by now be screaming with fright and frenzy. Who knows the end? What has risen may sink, and what has sunk may rise. Loathsomeness waits and dreams in the deep, and decay spreads over the tottering cities of men. A time will come — but I must not and cannot think! Let me pray that, if I do not survive this manuscript, my executors may put caution before audacity and see that it meets no other eye.

Pickman's Model.

5,500-WORD SHORT STORY; 1926.

This short story is plainly an experiment, in which Lovecraft is trying a more colloquial narrative style. Whether it suits him well or not is a matter of personal taste. It's not what most readers come to Lovecraft hoping to find; on the other hand, it's quite possibly as close as we can come to the experience of sitting down and talking with Lovecraft in person. In his letters, he did not try to "sound" the same way he spoke in person; in this story, he does exactly that — although in doing so he is playing the role of Thurber.

In any case, he seems to have abandoned the colloquial approach after this story, which is, arguably, unfortunate, because although critics have often been unkind to "Pickman's Model," the conversational wit displayed in this story makes it something really special, and an outlier in Lovecraft's canon.

"Pickman's Model" does suffer from some of the loss of subtlety that was Lovecraft's primary critique of work appearing in Weird Tales *— his own and that of others. It telegraphs its conclusion fairly broadly, and few readers will have failed to figure it out before the last line delivers the "shocking" confirmation.*

Nonetheless, the case can be made that "Pickman's Model" is the perfect pulp story — not too long, not too dense, not too deep, full of interesting and slightly exaggerated characters and situations, and tremendously satisfying and fun to read.

Lovecraft wrote this story in early September 1926, and submitted it to Weird Tales *shortly thereafter. Not surprisingly, editor Farnsworth Wright snapped "Pickman's Model" up immediately upon receiving it, and published it promptly in the October 1927 issue.*

You needn't think I'm crazy, Eliot — plenty of others have queerer prejudices than this. Why don't you laugh at Oliver's grandfather, who won't ride in a motor? If I don't like that damned subway, it's my own business; and we got here more quickly anyhow in the taxi. We'd have had to walk up the hill from Park Street if we'd taken the car.

I know I'm more nervous than I was when you saw me last year, but you don't need to hold a clinic over it. There's plenty of reason, God knows, and I fancy I'm lucky to be sane at all. Why the third degree? You didn't use to be so inquisitive.

Well, if you must hear it, I don't know why you shouldn't. Maybe you ought to, anyhow, for you kept writing me like a grieved parent when you heard I'd begun to cut the Art Club and keep away from Pickman. Now that he's disappeared I go round to the club once in a while, but my nerves aren't what they were.

No, I don't know what's become of Pickman, and I don't like to guess. You might have surmised I had some inside information when I dropped him — and that's why I don't want to think where he's gone. Let the police find what they can — it won't be much, judging from the fact that they don't know yet of the old North End place he hired under the name of Peters. I'm not sure that I could find it again myself — not that I'd ever try, even in broad daylight!

Yes, I do know, or am afraid I know, why he maintained it. I'm coming to that. And I think you'll understand before I'm through why I don't tell the police. They would ask me to guide them, but I couldn't go back there even if I knew the way. There was something there — and now I can't use the subway or (and you may as well have your laugh at this, too) go down into cellars any more.

I should think you'd have known I didn't drop Pickman for the same silly reasons that fussy old women like Dr. Reid or Joe Minot or Rosworth did. Morbid art doesn't shock me, and when a man has the genius Pickman had I feel it an honour to know him, no matter what direction his work takes. Boston never had a greater painter than Richard Upton Pickman. I said it at first and I say it still, and I never swerved an inch, either, when he showed that "Ghoul Feeding." That, you remember, was when Minot cut him.

You know, it takes profound art and profound insight into Nature to turn out stuff like Pickman's. Any magazine-cover hack can splash paint around wildly and call it a nightmare or a Witches' Sabbath or a portrait of the devil, but only a great painter can make such a thing really scare or ring true. That's because only a real artist knows the actual anatomy of the terrible or the physiology of fear — the exact sort of lines and proportions that connect up with latent instincts or hereditary memories of fright, and the proper colour contrasts and lighting effects to stir the dormant sense of strangeness. I don't have to tell you why a Fuseli really brings a shiver while a cheap ghost-story frontispiece merely makes us laugh. There's something those fellows catch — beyond life — that they're able to make us catch for a second. Doré had it. Sime has it. Angarola of Chicago has it. And Pickman had it as no man ever had it before or — I hope to Heaven — ever will again.

Don't ask me what it is they see. You know, in ordinary art, there's all the difference in the world between the vital, breathing things drawn from Nature or models and the artificial truck

"He had painted a monstrous being on that awful canvas."

Weird Tales, October 1927

that commercial small fry reel off in a bare studio by rule. Well, I should say that the really weird artist has a kind of vision which makes models, or summons up what amounts to actual scenes from the spectral world he lives in. Anyhow, he manages to turn out results that differ from the pretender's mince-pie dreams in just about the same way that the life painter's results differ from the concoctions of a correspondence-school cartoonist. If I had ever seen what Pickman saw—but no! Here, let's have a drink before we get any deeper. God, I wouldn't be alive if I'd ever seen what that man—if he was a man—saw!

You recall that Pickman's forte was faces. I don't believe anybody since Goya could put so much of sheer hell into a set of features or a twist of expression. And before Goya you have to go back to the mediaeval chaps who did the gargoyles and chimaeras on Notre Dame and Mont Saint-Michel. They believed all sorts of things—and maybe they saw all sorts of things, too, for the Middle Ages had some curious phases. I remember your asking Pickman yourself once, the year before you went away, wherever in thunder he got such ideas and visions. Wasn't that a nasty laugh he gave you? It was partly because of that laugh that Reid dropped him. Reid, you know, had just taken up comparative pathology, and was full of pompous "inside stuff" about the biological or evolutionary significance of this or that mental or physical symptom. He said Pickman repelled him more and more every day, and almost frightened him towards the last—that the fellow's features and expression were slowly developing in a way he didn't like, in a way that wasn't human. He had a lot of talk about diet, and said Pickman must be abnormal and eccentric to the last degree. I suppose you told Reid, if you and he had any correspondence over it, that he'd let Pickman's paintings get on his nerves or harrow up his imagination. I know I told him that myself—then.

But keep in mind that I didn't drop Pickman for anything like this. On the contrary, my admiration for him kept growing; for that "Ghoul Feeding" was a tremendous achievement. As you know, the club wouldn't exhibit it, and the Museum of Fine Arts wouldn't accept it as a gift; and I can add that nobody would buy it, so Pickman had it right in his house till he went. Now his father has it in Salem—you know Pickman comes of old Salem stock, and had a witch ancestor hanged in 1692.

I got into the habit of calling on Pickman quite often, especially after I began making notes for a monograph on weird art. Probably it was his work which put the idea into my head, and anyhow, I found him a mine of data and suggestions when I came to develop it. He showed me all the paintings and drawings he had about; including some pen-and-ink sketches that would, I verily believe, have got him kicked out of the club if many of the members had seen them. Before long I was pretty nearly a devotee, and would listen for hours like a schoolboy to art theories and philosophic speculations wild enough to qualify him for the Danvers asylum. My hero-worship, coupled with the fact that people generally were commencing to have less and less to do with him, made him get very confidential with me; and one evening he hinted that if I were fairly close-mouthed and none too squeamish, he might show me something rather unusual—something a bit stronger than anything he had in the house.

"You know," he said, "there are things that won't do for Newbury Street—things that are out of place here, and that can't be conceived here, anyhow. It's my business to catch the overtones of the soul, and you won't find those in a parvenu set of artificial streets on made land. Back Bay isn't Boston—it isn't anything yet, because it's had no time to pick up memories and attract local spirits. If there are any ghosts here, they're the tame ghosts of a salt marsh and a shallow cove; and I want human ghosts—the ghosts of beings highly organized enough to have looked on hell and known the meaning of what they saw.

"The place for an artist to live is the North End. If any aesthete were sincere, he'd put up with the slums for the sake of the massed traditions. God, man! Don't you realize that places like that weren't merely made, but actually grew? Generation after generation lived and felt and died there, and in days when people weren't afraid to live and feel and die. Don't you know there was a mill on Copp's Hill in 1632, and that half the present streets were laid out by 1650? I can show you houses that have stood two centuries and a half and more; houses that have witnessed what would make a modern house crumble into powder. What do moderns know of life and the forces behind it? You call the Salem witchcraft a delusion, but I'll wager my four-times-great-grandmother could have told you things. They hanged her on Gallows Hill, with Cotton Mather looking sanctimoniously on. Mather, damn him, was afraid somebody might succeed in kicking free of this accursed cage of monotony—I wish someone had laid a spell on him or sucked his blood in the night!

"I can show you a house he lived in, and I can show you another one he was afraid to enter in spite of all his fine bold talk. He knew things he didn't dare put into that stupid Magnalia or that puerile Wonders of the Invisible World. Look here, do you know the whole North End once had a set of tunnels that kept certain people in touch with each other's houses, and the burying ground, and the sea? Let them prosecute and persecute above ground—things went on every day that they couldn't reach, and voices laughed at night that they couldn't place!

"Why, man, out of ten surviving houses built before 1700 and not moved since I'll wager that in eight I can show you something queer in the cellar. There's hardly a month that you don't read of workmen finding bricked-up arches and wells leading nowhere in this or that old place as it comes down—you could see one near Henchman Street from the elevated last year. There were witches and what their spells summoned; pirates and what they brought in from the sea; smugglers; privateers—and I tell you, people knew how to live, and how to enlarge the bounds of life, in the old time! This wasn't the only world a bold and wise man could know—faugh! And to think of today in contrast, with such pale-pink brains that even a club of supposed artists gets shudders and convulsions if a picture goes beyond the feelings of a Beacon Street tea-table!

"The only saving grace of the present is that it's too damned stupid to question the past very closely. What do maps and records and guide-books really tell of the North End? Bah! At a guess I'll guarantee to lead you to thirty or forty alleys and networks of alleys north of Prince Street that aren't suspected by ten living beings outside of the foreigners that swarm them. And what do those Dagoes know of their meaning? No, Thurber, these ancient places are dreaming gorgeously and over-flowing with wonder and terror and escapes from the commonplace, and yet there's not a living soul to understand or profit by them. Or rather, there's only one living soul—for I haven't been digging around in the past for nothing!

"See here, you're interested in this sort of thing. What if I told you that I've got another studio up there, where I can catch the night-spirit of antique horror and paint things that I couldn't even think of in Newbury Street? Naturally I don't tell those cursed old maids at the club—with Reid, damn him, whispering even as it is that I'm a sort of monster bound down the toboggan of reverse evolution. Yes, Thurber, I decided long ago that one must paint terror as well as beauty from life, so I did some exploring in places where I had reason to know terror lives.

"I've got a place that I don't believe three living Nordic men besides myself have ever seen. It isn't so very far from the elevated as distance goes, but it's centuries away as the soul goes. I took it because of the queer old brick well in the cellar—one of the sort I told you about. The shack's almost tumbling down so that nobody else would live there, and I'd hate to tell you how little I pay for it. The windows are boarded up, but I like that all the better, since I don't want daylight for what I do. I paint in the cellar, where the inspiration is thickest, but I've other rooms furnished on the ground floor. A Sicilian owns it, and I've hired it under the name of Peters.

"Now, if you're game, I'll take you there tonight. I think you'd enjoy the pictures, for, as I said, I've let myself go a bit there. It's no vast tour—I sometimes do it on foot, for I don't want to attract attention with a taxi in such a place. We can take the shuttle at the South Station for Battery Street, and after that the walk isn't much."

Well, Eliot, there wasn't much for me to do after that harangue but to keep myself from running instead of walking for the first vacant cab we could sight. We changed to the elevated at the South Station, and at about twelve o'clock had climbed down the steps at Battery Street and struck along the old waterfront past Constitution Wharf. I didn't keep track of the cross streets, and can't tell you yet which it was we turned up, but I know it wasn't Greenough Lane.

When we did turn, it was to climb through the deserted length of the oldest and dirtiest alley I ever saw in my life, with crumbling-looking gables, broken small-paned windows, and archaic chimneys that stood out half-disintegrated against the moonlit sky. I don't believe there were three houses in sight that hadn't been standing in Cotton Mather's time—certainly I glimpsed at least two with an overhang, and once I thought I saw a peaked roof-line of the almost forgotten pre-gambrel type, though antiquarians tell us there are none left in Boston.

From that alley, which had a dim light, we turned to the left into an equally silent and still narrower alley with no light at all: and in a minute made what I think was an obtuse-angled bend towards the right in the dark. Not long after this Pickman produced a flashlight and revealed an antediluvian ten-panelled door that looked damnably worm-eaten. Unlocking it, he ushered me into a barren hallway with what was once splendid dark-oak panelling—simple, of course, but thrillingly suggestive of the times of Andros and Phipps and the Witchcraft. Then he took me through a door on the left, lighted an oil lamp, and told me to make myself at home.

Now, Eliot, I'm what the man in the street would call fairly "hard-boiled," but I'll confess that what I saw on the walls of that room gave me a bad turn. They were his pictures, you know—the ones he couldn't paint or even show in Newbury Street—and he was right when he said he had "let himself go." Here—have another drink—I need one anyhow!

There's no use in my trying to tell you what they were like, because the awful, the blasphemous horror, and the unbelievable loathsomeness and moral foetor came from simple touches quite beyond the power of words to classify. There was none of the exotic technique you see in Sidney Sime, none of the trans-Saturnian landscapes and lunar fungi that Clark Ashton Smith uses to freeze the blood. The backgrounds were mostly old churchyards, deep woods, cliffs by the sea, brick tunnels, ancient panelled rooms, or simple vaults of masonry. Copp's Hill Burying Ground, which could not be many blocks away from this very house, was a favourite scene.

The madness and monstrosity lay in the figures in the foreground—for Pickman's morbid art was pre-eminently one of demoniac portraiture. These figures were seldom completely human, but often approached humanity in varying degree. Most of the bodies, while roughly bipedal, had a forward slumping, and a vaguely canine cast. The texture of the majority was a kind of unpleasant rubberiness. Ugh! I can see them now! Their occupations—well, don't ask me to be too precise. They were usually feeding—I won't say on what. They were sometimes shown in groups in cemeteries or underground passages, and often appeared to be in battle over their prey—or rather, their treasure-trove. And what damnable expressiveness Pickman sometimes gave the sightless faces of this charnel booty! Occasionally the things were shown leaping through open windows at night, or squatting on the chests of sleepers, worrying at their throats. One canvas showed a ring of them baying about a hanged witch on Gallows Hill, whose dead face held a close kinship to theirs.

But don't get the idea that it was all this hideous business of theme and setting which struck me faint. I'm not a three-year-old kid, and I'd seen much like this before. It was the faces, Eliot, those accursed faces, that leered and slavered out of the canvas with the very breath of life! By God, man, I verily believe they were alive! That nauseous wizard had waked the fires of hell in pigment, and his brush had been a nightmare-spawning wand. Give me that decanter, Eliot!

There was one thing called "The Lesson"—Heaven pity me, that I ever saw it! Listen—can you fancy a squatting circle of nameless dog-like things in a churchyard teaching a small child how to feed like themselves? The price of a changeling, I suppose—you know the old myth about how the weird people leave their spawn in cradles in exchange for the human babes they steal. Pickman was showing what happens to those stolen babes—how they grow up—and then I began to see a hideous relationship in the faces of the human and non-human figures. He was, in all his gradations of morbidity between the frankly non-human and the degradedly human, establishing a sardonic linkage and evolution. The dog-things were developed from mortals!

And no sooner had I wondered what he made of their own young as left with mankind in the form of changelings, than my eye caught a picture embodying that very thought. It was that of an ancient Puritan interior—a heavily beamed room with lattice windows, a settle, and clumsy seventeenth-century furniture, with the family sitting about while the father read from the Scriptures. Every face but one showed nobility and reverence, but that one reflected the mockery of the pit. It was that of a young man in years, and no doubt belonged to a supposed son of that pious father, but in essence it was the kin of the unclean things. It was their changeling—and in a spirit of supreme irony Pickman had given the features a very perceptible resemblance to his own.

By this time Pickman had lighted a lamp in an adjoining room and was politely holding open the door for me; asking me if I would care to see his "modern studies." I hadn't been able to give him much of my opinions—I was too speechless with fright and loathing—but I think he fully understood and felt highly complimented. And now I want to assure you again, Eliot, that I'm no mollycoddle to scream at anything which shows a bit of departure from the usual. I'm middle-aged and decently sophisticated, and I guess you saw enough of me in France to know I'm not easily knocked out. Remember, too, that I'd just about recovered my wind and gotten used to those frightful pictures which turned colonial New England into a kind of annex of hell. Well, in spite of all this, that next room forced a real scream out of me, and I had to clutch at the doorway to keep from keeling over. The other chamber had shown a pack of ghouls and witches over-running the world of our forefathers, but this one brought the horror right into our own daily life!

God, how that man could paint! There was a study called "Subway Accident," in which a flock of the vile things were clambering up from some unknown catacomb through a crack in the floor of the Boston Street subway and attacking a crowd of people on the platform. Another showed a dance on Copp's Hill among the tombs with the background of today. Then there were any number of cellar views, with monsters creeping in through holes and rifts in the masonry and grinning as they squatted behind barrels or furnaces and waited for their first victim to descend the stairs.

One disgusting canvas seemed to depict a vast cross-section of Beacon Hill, with ant-like armies of the mephitic monsters squeezing themselves through burrows that honeycombed the ground. Dances in the modern cemeteries were freely pictured, and another conception somehow shocked me more than all the rest—a scene in an unknown vault, where scores of the beasts crowded about one who had a well-known Boston guidebook and was evidently reading aloud. All were pointing to a certain passage, and every face seemed so distorted with epileptic and reverberant laughter that I almost thought I heard the fiendish echoes. The title of the picture was, "Holmes, Lowell and Longfellow Lie Buried in Mount Auburn."

As I gradually steadied myself and got readjusted to this second room of deviltry and morbidity, I began to analyse some of the points in my sickening loathing. In the first place, I said to myself, these things repelled because of the utter inhumanity and callous crudity they showed in Pickman. The fellow must be a relentless enemy of all mankind to take such glee in the torture of brain and flesh and the degradation of the mortal tenement. In the second place, they terrified because of their very greatness. Their art was the art that convinced—when we saw the pictures we saw the demons themselves and were afraid of them. And the queer part was, that Pickman got none of his power from the use of selectiveness or bizarrerie. Nothing was blurred, distorted, or conventionalized; outlines were sharp and lifelike, and details were almost painfully defined. And the faces!

It was not any mere artist's interpretation that we saw; it was pandemonium itself, crystal clear in stark objectivity. That was it, by Heaven! The man was not a *fantaisiste* or romanticist at all—he did not even try to give us the churning, prismatic ephemera of dreams, but coldly and sardonically reflected some stable, mechanistic, and well-established horror-world which he saw fully, brilliantly, squarely, and unfalteringly. God knows what that world can have been, or where he ever glimpsed the blasphemous shapes that loped and trotted and crawled through it; but whatever the baffling source of his images, one thing was plain. Pickman was in every sense—in conception and in execution—a thorough, painstaking, and almost scientific realist.

My host was now leading the way down the cellar to his actual studio, and I braced myself for some hellish efforts among the unfinished canvases. As we reached the bottom of the damp stairs he turned his flash-light to a corner of the large open space at hand, revealing the circular brick curb of what was evidently a great well in the earthen floor. We walked nearer, and I saw that it must be five feet across, with walls a good foot thick and some six inches above the ground level—solid work of the seventeenth century, or I was much mistaken. That, Pickman said, was the kind of thing he had been talking about—an aperture of the network of tunnels that used to undermine the hill. I noticed idly that it did not seem to be bricked up, and that a heavy disc of wood formed the apparent cover. Thinking of the things this well must have been connected with if Pickman's wild hints had not been mere rhetoric, I shivered slightly; then turned to follow him up a step and through a narrow door into a room of fair size, provided with a wooden floor and furnished as a studio. An acetylene gas outfit gave the light necessary for work.

The unfinished pictures on easels or propped against the walls were as ghastly as the finished ones upstairs, and showed the painstaking methods of the artist. Scenes were blocked out with extreme care, and pencilled guide lines told of the minute exactitude which Pickman used in getting the right perspective and proportions. The man was great—I say it even now, knowing as much as I do. A large camera on a table excited my notice, and Pickman told me that he used it in taking scenes for backgrounds, so that he might paint them from photographs in the studio instead of carting his oufit around the town for this or that view. He thought a photograph quite as good as an actual scene or model for sustained work, and declared he employed them regularly.

There was something very disturbing about the nauseous sketches and half-finished monstrosities that leered round from every side of the room, and when Pickman suddenly unveiled a huge canvas on the side away from the light I could not for my life keep back a loud scream—the second I had emitted that night. It echoed and echoed through the dim vaultings of that ancient and nitrous cellar, and I had to choke back a flood of reaction that threatened to burst out as hysterical laughter. Merciful Creator! Eliot, but I don't know how much was real and how much was feverish fancy. It doesn't seem to me that earth can hold a dream like that!

It was a colossal and nameless blasphemy with glaring red eyes, and it held in bony claws a thing that had been a man, gnawing at the head as a child nibbles at a stick of candy. Its position was a kind of crouch, and as one looked one felt that at any moment it might drop its present prey and seek a juicier morsel. But damn it all, it wasn't even the fiendish subject that made it such an immortal fountain-head of all panic — not that, nor the dog face with its pointed ears, bloodshot eyes, flat nose, and drooling lips. It wasn't the scaly claws nor the mould-caked body nor the half-hooved feet — none of these, though any one of them might well have driven an excitable man to madness.

It was the technique, Eliot — the cursed, the impious, the unnatural technique! As I am a living being, I never elsewhere saw the actual breath of life so fused into a canvas. The monster was there — it glared and gnawed and gnawed and glared — and I knew that only a suspension of Nature's laws could ever let a man paint a thing like that without a model — without some glimpse of the nether world which no mortal unsold to the Fiend has ever had.

Pinned with a thumb-tack to a vacant part of the canvas was a piece of paper now badly curled up — probably, I thought, a photograph from which Pickman meant to paint a background as hideous as the nightmare it was to enhance. I reached out to uncurl and look at it, when suddenly I saw Pickman start as if shot. He had been listening with peculiar intensity ever since my shocked scream had waked unaccustomed echoes in the dark cellar, and now he seemed struck with a fright which, though not comparable to my own, had in it more of the physical than of the spiritual. He drew a revolver and motioned me to silence, then stepped out into the main cellar and closed the door behind him.

I think I was paralysed for an instant. Imitating Pickman's listening, I fancied I heard a faint scurrying sound somewhere, and a series of squeals or beats in a direction I couldn't determine. I thought of huge rats and shuddered. Then there came a subdued sort of clatter which somehow set me all in goose-flesh — a furtive, groping kind of clatter, though I can't attempt to convey what I mean in words. It was like heavy wood falling on stone or brick — wood on brick — what did that make me think of?

It came again, and louder. There was a vibration as if the wood had fallen farther than it had fallen before. After that followed a sharp grating noise, a shouted gibberish from Pickman, and the deafening discharge of all six chambers of a revolver, fired spectacularly as a lion tamer might fire in the air for effect. A muffled squeal or squawk, and a thud. Then more wood and brick grating, a pause, and the opening of the door — at which I'll confess I started violently. Pickman reappeared with his smoking weapon, cursing the bloated rats that infested the ancient well.

"The deuce knows what they eat, Thurber," he grinned, "for those archaic tunnels touched graveyard and witch-den and sea-coast. But whatever it is, they must have run short, for they were devilish anxious to get out. Your yelling stirred them up, I fancy. Better be cautious in these old places — our rodent friends are the one drawback, though I sometimes think they're a positive asset by way of atmosphere and colour."

Well, Eliot, that was the end of the night's adventure. Pickman had promised to show me the place, and Heaven knows he had done it. He led me out of that tangle of alleys in another direction, it seems, for when we sighted a lamp-post we were in a half-familiar street with monotonous rows of mingled tenement blocks and old houses. Charter Street, it turned out to be, but I was too flustered to notice just where we hit it. We were too late for the elevated, and walked back downtown through Hanover Street. I remember that wall. We switched from Tremont up Beacon, and Pickman left me at the corner of Joy, where I turned off. I never spoke to him again.

Why did I drop him? Don't be impatient. Wait till I ring for coffee. We've had enough of the other stuff, but I for one need something. No — it wasn't the paintings I saw in that place; though I'll swear they were enough to get him ostracised in nine-tenths of the homes and clubs of Boston, and I guess you won't wonder now why I have to steer clear of subways and cellars. It was — something I found in my coat the next morning. You know, the curled-up paper tacked to the frightful canvas in the cellar; the thing I thought was a photograph of some scene he meant to use as a background for that monster. That last scare had come while I was reaching to uncurl it, and it seems I had vacantly crumpled it into my pocket. But here's the coffee — take it black, Eliot, if you're wise.

Yes, that paper was the reason I dropped Pickman; Richard Upton Pickman, the greatest artist I have ever known — and the foulest being that ever leaped the bounds of life into the pits of myth and madness. Eliot — old Reid was right. He wasn't strictly human. Either he was born in strange shadow, or he'd found a way to unlock the forbidden gate. It's all the same now, for he's gone — back into the fabulous darkness he loved to haunt. Here, let's have the chandelier going.

Don't ask me to explain or even conjecture about what I burned. Don't ask me, either, what lay behind that mole-like scrambling Pickman was so keen to pass off as rats. There are secrets, you know, which might have come down from old Salem times, and Cotton Mather tells even stranger things. You know how damned lifelike Pickman's paintings were — how we all wondered where he got those faces.

Well — that paper wasn't a photograph of any background, after all. What it showed was simply the monstrous being he was painting on that awful canvas. It was the model he was using — and its background was merely the wall of the cellar studio in minute detail. But by God, Eliot, it was a photograph from life!

Two Black Bottles.

BY WILFRED BLANCH TALMAN AND H.P. LOVECRAFT

5,000-WORD SHORT STORY; 1926.

"Two Black Bottles" is one of the more entertaining of the Lovecraft collaborations. Talman brought it to Lovecraft in the summer of 1926. It may not have been Talman's first weird story, but it was certainly one of his first; the young writer was just 22 years old, and he likely felt a little self-conscious about putting his work out into the world. Lovecraft took the story in hand, made a number of revisions to it, and helped Talman send it off to Weird Tales, *where it was quickly snapped up.*

Talman complained a bit, in later years, about some of the changes Lovecraft made to the story. His additions and subtractions from the plot were apparently solid and welcome, but he also tweaked the dialogue in ways that made it not ring true to its old-Dutch New York roots.

It is, nonetheless, a fantastic spooky story, and the atmosphere — the damp old church across the swampy moor, the semi-twilight that falls when the sun drops behind the steep mountains, the gravestones gathered around the ruined church like worshippers around a shrine — is among the most effective in all Lovecraft's work.

Written in mid-1926 at around the same time as "Pickman's Model," it first saw publication roughly one year later in the August 1927 issue of Weird Tales *magazine.*

ABOUT WILFRED BLANCH TALMAN (1904-1986).

Wilfred Talman met H.P. Lovecraft through the amateur-press movement in 1925, during Lovecraft's time in New York; he soon became a "member" of the Kalem Club, the informal association of writing friends to which Lovecraft belonged. He would go on to be a reporter and editor of some note, working for the New York Times *and later the* Texaco Star.

Talman was also an accomplished draftsman, and it was he who designed H.P. Lovecraft's personal bookplate for him.

A descendant of one of the old Dutch families of New York State, Talman had a rich cultural heritage to milk for spooky stories; but although he did enjoy moderate success in the pulps for a few years, he soon thereafter turned his attention to more lucrative pursuits. This, if "Two Black Bottles" is any indication of his abilities, is unfortunate.

Not all of the few remaining inhabitants of Daalbergen, that dismal little village in the Ramapo Mountains, believe that my uncle, old Dominie Johannes Vanderhoof, is really dead. Some of them believe he is suspended somewhere between heaven and hell because of the old sexton's curse. If it had not been for that old magician, he might still be preaching in the little damp church across the moor.

After what has happened to me in Daalbergen, I can almost share the opinion of the villagers. I am not sure that my uncle is dead, but I am very sure that he is not alive upon this earth. There is no doubt that the old sexton buried him once, but he is not in that grave now. I can almost feel him behind me as I write, impelling me to tell the truth about those strange happenings in Daalbergen so many years ago.

It was the fourth day of October when I arrived at Daalbergen in answer to a summons. The letter was from a former member of my uncle's congregation, who wrote that the old man had passed away and that there should be some small estate which I, as his only living relative, might inherit.

Having reached the secluded little hamlet by a wearying series of changes on branch railways, I found my way to the grocery store of Mark Haines, writer of the letter, and he, leading me into a stuffy back room, told me a peculiar tale concerning Dominie Vanderhoof's death.

"Y' should be careful, Hoffman," Haines told me, "when y' meet that old sexton, Abel Foster. He's in league with the devil, sure's you're alive. 'Twa'n't two weeks ago Sam Pryor, when he passed the old graveyard, heared him mumblin t' the dead there. 'Twa'n't right he should talk that way — an' Sam does vow that there was a voice answered him — a kind o' half-voice, hollow and muffled-like, as though it come out o' th' ground. There's others, too, as could tell y' about seein' him standin' afore old Dominie Slott's grave — that one right agin' the church wall — a-wringin' his hands an' a-talkin' t' th' moss on th' tombstone as though it was the old Dominie himself."

Old Foster, Haines said, had come to Daalbergen about ten years before, and had been immediately engaged by Vanderhoof to take care of the damp stone church at which most of the villagers worshipped. No one but Vanderhoof seemed to like him, for his presence brought a suggestion almost of the uncanny. He would sometimes stand by the door when the people came to church, and the men would coldly return his servile bow while the women brushed past in haste, holding their skirts aside to avoid touching him. He could be seen on

TWO BLACK BOTTLES

by Wilfred Blanch Talman

"A gigantic, loathsome black shadow was climbing from the grave and floundering gruesomely toward the church."

Weird Tales, August 1927

weekdays cutting the grass in the cemetery and tending the flowers around the graves, now and then crooning and muttering to himself. And few failed to notice the particular attention he paid to the grave of the Reverend Guilliam Slott, first pastor of the church in 1701.

It was not long after Foster's establishment as a village fixture that disaster began to lower. First came the failure of the mountain mine where most of the men worked. The vein of iron had given out, and many of the people moved away to better localities, while those who had large holdings of land in the vicinity took to farming and managed to wrest a meagre living from the rocky hillsides.

Then came the disturbances in the church. It was whispered about that the Reverend Johannes Vanderhoof had made a compact with the devil, and was preaching his word in the house of God. His sermons had become weird and grotesque — redolent with sinister things which the ignorant people of Daalbergen did not understand. He transported them back over ages of fear and superstition to regions of hideous, unseen spirits, and peopled their fancy with night-haunting ghouls. One by one the congregation dwindled, while the elders and deacons vainly pleaded with Vanderhoof to change the subject of his sermons. Though the old man continually promised to comply, he seemed to be enthralled by some higher power which forced him to do its will. A giant in stature, Johannes Vanderhoof was known to be weak and timid at heart, yet even when threatened with expulsion he continued his eerie sermons, until scarcely a handful of people remained to listen to him on Sunday morning. Because of weak finances, it was found impossible to call a new pastor, and before long not one of the villagers dared venture near the church or the parsonage which adjoined it. Everywhere there was fear of those spectral wraiths with whom Vanderhoof was apparently in league.

My uncle, Mark Haines told me, had continued to live in the parsonage because there was no one with sufficient courage to tell him to move out of it. No one ever saw him again, but lights were visible in the parsonage at night, and were even glimpsed in the church from time to time. It was whispered about the town that Vanderhoof preached regularly in the church every Sunday morning, unaware that his congregation was no longer there to listen. He had only the old sexton, who lived in the basement of the church, to take care of him, and Foster made a weekly visit to what remained of the business section of the village to buy provisions. He no longer bowed servilely to everyone he met, but instead seemed to harbor a demoniac and ill-concealed hatred. He spoke to no one except as was necessary to make his purchases, and glanced from left to right out of evil-filled eyes as he walked the street with his cane tapping the uneven pavements. Bent and shrivelled with extreme age, his presence could actually be felt by anyone near him, so powerful was that personality which, said the townspeople, had made Vanderhoof accept the devil as his master.

No person in Daalbergen doubted that Abel Foster was at the bottom of all the town's ill luck, but not a one dared lift a finger against him, or could even approach him without a tremor of fear. His name, as well as Vanderhoof's, was never mentioned aloud. Whenever the matter of the church across the moor was discussed, it was in whispers; and if the conversation chanced to be nocturnal, the whisperers would keep glancing over their shoulders to make sure that nothing shapeless or sinister crept out of the darkness to bear witness to their words. The churchyard continued to be kept just as green and beautiful as when the church was in use, and the flowers near the graves in the cemetery were tended just as carefully as in times gone by. The old sexton could occasionally be seen working there, as if still being paid for his services, and those who dared venture near said that he maintained a continual conversation with the devil and with those spirits which lurked within the graveyard walls.

One morning, Haines went on to say, Foster was seen digging a grave where the steeple of the church throws its shadow in the afternoon, before the sun goes down behind the mountain and puts the entire village in semi-twilight. Later, the church bell, silent for months, tolled solemnly for a half-hour. And at sundown those who were watching from a distance saw Foster bring a coffin from the parsonage on a wheelbarrow, dump it into the grave with slender ceremony, and replace the earth in the hole.

The sexton came to the village the next morning, ahead of his usual weekly schedule, and in much better spirits than was customary. He seemed willing to talk, remarking that Vanderhoof had died the day before, and that he had buried his body beside that of Dominie Slott near the church wall. He smiled from time to time, and rubbed his hands in an untimely and unaccountable glee. It was apparent that he took a perverse and diabolic delight in Vanderhoof's death. The villagers were conscious of an added uncanniness in his presence, and avoided him as much as they could. With Vanderhoof gone they felt more insecure than ever, for the old sexton was now free to cast his worst spells over the town from the church across the moor.

Muttering something in a tongue which no one understood, Foster made his way back along the road over the swamp. It was then, it seems, that Mark Haines remembered having heard Dominie Vanderhoof speak of me as his nephew. Haines accordingly sent for me, in the hope that I might know something which would clear up the mystery of my uncle's last years. I assured my summoner, however, that I knew nothing about my uncle or his past, except that my mother had mentioned him as a man of gigantic physique but with little courage or power of will.

Having heard all that Haines had to tell me, I lowered the front legs of my chair to the floor and looked at my watch. It was late afternoon. "How far is it out to the church?" I inquired. "Think I can make it before sunset?"

"Sure, lad, y' ain't goin' out there t'night! Not t' that place!" The old man trembled noticeably in every limb and half rose from his chair, stretching out a lean, detaining hand. "Why, it's plumb foolishness!" he exclaimed.

I laughed aside his fears and informed him that, come what may, I was determined to see the old sexton that evening and get the whole matter over as soon as possible. I did not intend to accept the superstitions of ignorant country folk as truth, for I was convinced that all I had just heard was merely a chain of events which the over-imaginative people of Daalbergen had happened to link with their ill-luck. I felt no sense of fear or horror whatever.

Seeing that I was determined to reach my uncle's house before nightfall, Haines ushered me out of his office and reluctantly gave me the few required directions, pleading from time to time that I change my mind. He shook my hand when I left, as though he never expected to see me again. "Take keer that old devil, Foster, don't git ye!" he warned, again and again. "I wouldn't go near him after dark fer love n'r money. No siree!" He re-entered his store, solemnly shaking his head, while I set out along a road leading to the outskirts of the town.

I had walked barely two minutes before I sighted the moor of which Haines had spoken. The road, flanked by a whitewashed fence, passed over the great swamp, which was overgrown with clumps of underbrush dipping down into the dank, slimy ooze. An odour of deadness and decay filled the air, and even in the sunlit afternoon little wisps of vapour could be seen rising from the unhealthful spot.

On the opposite side of the moor I turned sharply to the left, as I had been directed, branching from the main road. There were several houses in the vicinity, I noticed; houses which were scarcely more than huts, reflecting the extreme poverty of their owners. The road here passed under the drooping branches of enormous willows which almost completely shut out the rays of the sun. The miasmal odour of the swamp was still in my nostrils, and the air was damp and chilly. I hurried my pace to get out of that dismal tunnel as soon as possible.

Presently I found myself in the light again. The sun, now hanging like a red ball upon the crest of the mountain, was beginning to dip low, and there, some distance ahead of me, bathed in its bloody iridescence, stood the lonely church.

I began to sense that uncanniness which Haines had mentioned; that feeling of dread which made all Daalbergen shun the place. The squat, stone hulk of the church itself, with its blunt steeple, seemed like an idol to which the tombstones that surrounded it bowed down and worshipped, each with an arched top like the shoulders of a kneeling person, while over the whole assemblage the dingy, grey parsonage hovered like a wraith.

I had slowed my pace a trifle as I took in the scene. The sun was disappearing behind the mountain very rapidly now, and the damp air chilled me. Turning my coat collar up about my neck, I plodded on. Something caught my eye as I glanced up again. In the shadow of the church wall was something white — a thing which seemed to have no definite shape. Straining my eyes as I came nearer, I saw that it was a cross of new timber, surmounting a mound of freshly turned earth.

The discovery sent a new chill through me. I realized that this must be my uncle's grave, but something told me that it was not like the other graves near it. It did not seem like a dead grave. In some intangible way it appeared to be living, if a grave can be said to live. Very close to it, I saw as I came nearer, was another grave; an old mound with a crumbling stone about it. Dominie Slott's tomb, I thought, remembering Haines's story.

There was no sign of life anywhere about the place. In the semi-twilight I climbed the low knoll upon which the parsonage stood, and hammered upon the door. There was no answer. I skirted the house and peered into the windows. The whole place seemed deserted. The lowering mountains had made night fall with disarming suddenness the minute the sun was fully hidden. I realized that I could see scarcely more than a few feet ahead of me. Feeling my way carefully, I rounded a corner of the house and paused, wondering what to do next. Everything was quiet. There was not a breath of wind, nor were there even the usual noises made by animals in their nocturnal ramblings. All dread had been forgotten for a time, but in the presence of that sepulchral calm my apprehensions returned. I imagined the air peopled with ghastly spirits that pressed around me, making the air almost unbreathable. I wondered, for the hundredth time, where the old sexton might be.

As I stood there, half expecting some sinister demon to creep from the shadows, I noticed two lighted windows glaring from the belfry of the church. I then remembered what Haines had told me about Foster's living in the basement of the building. Advancing cautiously through the blackness, I found a side door of the church ajar. The interior had a musty and mildewed odour. Everything I touched was covered with a cold, clammy moisture. I struck a match and began to explore, to discover, if I could, how to get into the belfry.

Suddenly I stopped in my tracks. A snatch of song, loud and obscene, sung in a voice that was guttural and thick with drink, came from above me. The match burned my fingers, and I dropped it. Two pin-points of light pierced the darkness of the farther wall of the church, and below them, to one side, I could see a door outlined where light filtered through its cracks. The song stopped as abruptly as it had commenced, and there was absolute silence again.

My heart was thumping and blood racing through my temples. Had I not been petrified with fear, I should have fled immediately. Not caring to light another match, I felt my way among the pews until I stood in front of the door. So deep was the feeling of depression which had come over me that I felt as though I were acting in a dream. My actions were almost involuntary. The door was locked, as I found when I turned the knob. I hammered upon it for some time, but there was no answer. The silence was as complete as before.

Feeling around the edge of the door, I found the hinges, removed the pins from them, and allowed the door to fall toward me. Dim light flooded down a steep flight of steps. There was a sickening odour of whisky. I could now hear someone stirring in the belfry room above. Venturing a low halloo, I thought I heard a groan in reply, and cautiously climbed the stairs.

My first glance into that unhallowed place was indeed startling. Strewn about the little room were old and dusty books and manuscripts — strange things that bespoke almost unbelievable age. On rows of shelves which reached to the ceiling were horrible things in glass jars and bottles — snakes and lizards and bats. Dust and mould and cobwebs encrusted everything. In the centre, behind a table upon which was a lighted candle, a nearly empty bottle of whisky, and a glass, was a motionless figure with a thin, scrawny, wrinkled face and wild eyes that stared blankly through me. I recognized Abel Foster, the old sexton, in an instant. He did not move or speak as I came slowly and fearfully toward him.

"Mr. Foster?" I asked, trembling with unaccountable fear when I heard my voice echo within the close confines of the room. There was no reply, and no movement from the figure behind the table. I wondered if he had not drunk himself to insensibility, and went behind the table to shake him. At the mere touch of my arm upon his shoulder, the strange old man started from his chair as though terrified. His eyes, still having in them that same blank stare, were fixed upon me. Swinging his arms like flails, he backed away. "Don't!" he screamed. "Don't touch me! Go back — go back!"

I saw that he was both drunk and struck with some kind of a nameless terror. Using a soothing tone, I told him who I was and why I had come. He seemed to understand vaguely and sank back into his chair, sitting limp and motionless. "I thought ye was him," he mumbled. "I thought ye was him come back fer it. He's been a-tryin' t' get out — a-tryin' t' get out sence I put him in there." His voice again rose to a scream and he clutched his chair. "Maybe he's got out now! Maybe he's out!"

I looked about, half expecting to see some spectral shape coming up the stairs. "Maybe who's out?" I inquired.

"Vanderhoof!" he shrieked. "Th' cross over his grave keeps fallin' down in th' night! Every morning the earth is loose, and gets harder t' pat down. He'll come out an' I won't be able t' do nothin'."

Forcing him back into the chair, I seated myself on a box near him. He was trembling in mortal terror, with the saliva dripping from the corners of his mouth. From time to time I felt that sense of horror which Haines had described when he told me of the old sexton. Truly, there was something uncanny about the man. His head had now sunk forward upon his breast, and he seemed calmer, mumbling to himself.

I quietly arose and opened a window to let out the fumes of whisky and the musty odour of dead things. Light from a dim moon, just risen, made objects below barely visible. I could just see Dominie Vanderhoof's grave from my position in the belfry, and blinked my eyes as I gazed at it. That cross was tilted! I remembered that it had been vertical an hour ago.

Fear took possession of me again. I turned quickly. Foster sat in his chair watching me. His glance was saner than before. "So ye're Vanderhoof's nephew," he mumbled in a nasal tone. "Waal, ye might's well know it all. He'll be back after me afore long, he will — jus' as soon as he can get out o' that there grave. Ye might's well know all about it now."

His terror appeared to have left him. He seemed resigned to some horrible fate which he expected any minute. His head dropped down upon his chest again, and he went on muttering in that nasal monotone. "Ye see all them there books and papers? Waal, they was once Dominie Slott's — Dominie Slott, who was here years ago. All them things is got t' do with magic — black magic that th' old Dominie knew afore he come t' this country. They used t' burn 'em an' boil 'em in oil fer knowin' that over there, they did. But old Slott knew, and he didn't go fer t' tell nobody. No sir, old Slott used to preach here generations ago, an' he used to come up here an' study them books, an' use all them dead things in jars, an' pronounce magic curses an' things, but he didn't let nobody know it. No, nobody knowed it but Dominie Slott an' me."

"You?" I ejaculated, leaning across the table toward him.

"That is, me after I learned it." His face showed lines of trickery as he answered me. "I found all this stuff here when I come t' be church sexton, an' I used t' read it when I wa'n't at work. An' I soon got t' know all about it."

The old man droned on, while I listened, spellbound. He told about learning the difficult formulae of demonology, so that, by means of incantations, he could cast spells over human beings. He had performed horrible occult rites of his hellish creed, calling down anathema upon the town and its inhabitants. Crazed by his desires, he tried to bring the church under his spell, but the power of God was too strong.

Finding Johannes Vanderhoof very weak-willed, he bewitched him so that he preached strange and mystic sermons which struck fear into the simple hearts of the country folk. From his position in the belfry room, he said, behind a painting of the temptation of Christ which adorned the rear wall of the church, he would glare at Vanderhoof while he was preaching, through holes which were the eyes of the Devil in the picture. Terrified by the uncanny things which were happening in their midst, the congregation left one by one, and Foster was able to do what he pleased with the church and with Vanderhoof.

"But what did you do with him?" I asked in a hollow voice as the old sexton paused in his confession.

He burst into a cackle of laughter, throwing back his head in drunken glee. "I took his soul!" he howled in a tone that set me trembling. "I took his soul and put it in a bottle — in a little black bottle! And I buried him! But he ain't got his soul, an' he cain't go neither t' heaven n'r hell! But he's a-comin' back after it. He's a-trying' t' get out o' his grave now. I can hear him pushin' his way up through the ground, he's that strong!"

As the old man had proceeded with his story, I had become more and more convinced that he must be telling me the truth, and not merely gibbering in drunkenness. Every detail fitted what Haines had told me. Fear was growing upon me by degrees. With the old wizard now shouting with demoniac laughter, I was tempted to bolt down the narrow stairway and leave that accursed neighbourhood.

To calm myself, I rose and again looked out of the window. My eyes nearly started from their sockets when I saw that the cross above Vanderhoof's grave had fallen perceptibly since I had last looked at it. It was now tilted to an angle of forty-five degrees!

"Can't we dig up Vanderhoof and restore his soul?" I asked almost breathlessly, feeling that something must be done in a hurry.

The old man rose from his chair in terror. "No, no, no!" he screamed. "He'd kill me! I've fergot th' formula, an' if he gets out he'll be alive, without a soul. He'd kill us both!"

"Where is the bottle that contains his soul?" I asked, advancing threateningly toward him. I felt that some ghastly thing was about to happen, which I must do all in my power to prevent.

"I won't tell ye, ye young whelp!" he snarled. I felt, rather than saw, a queer light in his eyes as he backed into a corner. "An' don't ye touch me, either, or ye'll wish ye hadn't!" I moved a step forward, noticing that on a low stool behind him there were two black bottles.

Foster muttered some peculiar words in a low singsong voice. Everything began to turn grey before my eyes, and something within me seemed to be dragged upward, trying to get out at my throat. I felt my knees become weak. Lurching forward, I caught the old sexton by the throat, and with my free arm reached for the bottles on the stool. But the old man fell backward, striking the stool with his foot, and one bottle fell to the floor as I snatched the other. There was a flash of blue flame, and a sulphurous smell filled the room. From the little heap of broken glass a white vapour rose and followed the draft out the window.

"Curse ye, ye rascal!" sounded a voice that seemed faint and far away. Foster, whom I had released when the bottle broke, was crouching against the wall, looking smaller and more shriveled than before. His face was slowly turning greenish-black. "Curse ye!" said the voice again, hardly sounding as though it came from his lips. "I'm done fer! That one in there was mine! Dominie Slott took it out two hundred years ago!"

He slid slowly toward the floor, gazing at me with hatred in eyes that were rapidly dimming. His flesh changed from white to black, and then to yellow. I saw with horror that his body seemed to be crumbling away and his clothing falling into limp folds.

The bottle in my hand was growing warm. I glanced at it, fearfully. It glowed with a faint phosphorescence. Stiff with fright, I set it upon the table, but could not keep my eyes from it. There was an ominous moment of silence as its glow became brighter, and then there came distinctly to my ears the sound of sliding earth. Gasping for breath, I looked out of the window.

The moon was now well up in the sky, and by its light I could see that the fresh cross above Vanderhoof's grave had completely fallen. Once again there came the sound of trickling gravel, and no longer able to control myself, I stumbled down the stairs and found my way out of doors. Falling now and then as I raced over the uneven ground, I ran on in abject terror.

When I had reached the foot of the knoll, at the entrance to that gloomy tunnel beneath the willows, I heard a horrible roar behind me. Turning, I glanced back toward the church. Its wall reflected the light of the moon, and silhouetted against it was a gigantic, loathsome, black shadow climbing from my uncle's grave and floundering gruesomely toward the church.

I told my story to a group of villagers in Haines's store the next morning. They looked from one to the other with little smiles during my tale, I noticed, but when I suggested that they accompany me to the spot, gave various excuses for not caring to go. Though there seemed to be a limit to their credulity, they cared to run no risks. I informed them that I would go alone, though I must confess that the project did not appeal to me.

As I left the store, one old man with a long, white beard hurried after me and caught my arm. "I'll go wi' ye, lad," he said. "It do seem that I once heared my gran'pap tell o' su'thin' o' the sort concernin' old Dominie Slott. A queer old man I've heared he were, but Vanderhoof's been worse."

Dominie Vanderhoof's grave was open and deserted when we arrived. Of course it could have been grave-robbers, the two of us agreed, and yet . . . .

In the belfry the bottle which I had left upon the table was gone, though the fragments of the broken one were found on the floor. And upon the heap of yellow dust and crumpled clothing that had once been Abel Foster were certain immense footprints. After glancing at some of the books and papers strewn about the belfry room, we carried them down the stairs and burned them, as something unclean and unholy. With a spade which we found in the church basement we filled in the grave of Johannes Vanderhoof, and, as an afterthought, flung the fallen cross upon the flames.

Old wives say that now, when the moon is full, there walks about the churchyard a gigantic and bewildered figure clutching a bottle and seeking some unremembered goal.

The Strange High House in the Mist.

3,800-WORD SHORT STORY; 1926.

We now come to a trio of stories that represent something like the swan song of H.P. Lovecraft's Lord Dunsany period: "The Strange High House in the Mist," "The Silver Key," and The Dream-Quest of Unknown Kadath. *All were written at roughly the same time — Lovecraft started on* Dream-Quest *first, in the late fall of 1926, and worked steadily on it until January of 1927; the other two stories were dashed off while he was doing that, both in November. It isn't clear which of the two was written first.*

"The Strange High House in the Mist" is the most Dunsanian of the three, and the only one for which we know a precise date: Nov. 9. It was first published in the October 1931 issue of Weird Tales.

In the morning, mist comes up from the sea by the cliffs beyond Kingsport. White and feathery it comes from the deep to its brothers the clouds, full of dreams of dank pastures and caves of Leviathan. And later, in still summer rains on the steep roofs of poets, the clouds scatter bits of those dreams, that men shall not live without rumor of old strange secrets, and wonders that planets tell planets alone in the night. When tales fly thick in the grottoes of tritons, and conchs in seaweed cities blow wild tunes learned from the Elder Ones, then great eager mists flock to heaven laden with lore, and oceanward eyes on the rocks see only a mystic whiteness, as if the cliff's rim were the rim of all earth, and the solemn bells of buoys tolled free in the aether of faery.

Now north of archaic Kingsport the crags climb lofty and curious, terrace on terrace, till the northernmost hangs in the sky like a gray frozen wind-cloud. Alone it is, a bleak point jutting in limitless space, for there the coast turns sharp where the great Miskatonic pours out of the plains past Arkham, bringing woodland legends and little quaint memories of New England's hills. The sea-folk of Kingsport look up at that cliff as other sea-folk look up at the pole-star, and time the night's watches by the way it hides or shows the Great Bear, Cassiopeia and the Dragon. Among them it is one with the firmament, and truly, it is hidden from them when the mist hides the stars or the sun.

Some of the cliffs they love, as that whose grotesque profile they call Father Neptune, or that whose pillared steps they term "The Causeway"; but this one they fear because it is so near the sky. The Portuguese sailors coming in from a voyage cross themselves when they first see it, and the old Yankees believe it would be a much graver matter than death to climb it, if indeed that were possible. Nevertheless there is an ancient house on that cliff, and at evening men see lights in the small-paned windows.

The ancient house has always been there, and people say One dwells within who talks with the morning mists that come up from the deep, and perhaps sees singular things oceanward at those times when the cliff's rim becomes the rim of all earth, and solemn buoys toll free in the white aether of faery. This they tell from hearsay, for that forbidding crag is always unvisited, and natives dislike to train telescopes on it. Summer boarders have indeed scanned it with jaunty binoculars, but have never seen more than the gray primeval roof, peaked and shingled, whose eaves come nearly to the gray foundations, and the dim yellow light of the little windows peeping out from under those eaves in the dusk. These summer people do not believe that the same One has lived in the ancient house for hundreds of years, but can not prove their heresy to any real Kingsporter. Even the Terrible Old Man who talks to leaden pendulums in bottles, buys groceries with centuried Spanish gold, and keeps stone idols in the yard of his antediluvian cottage in Water Street can only say these things were the same when his grandfather was a boy, and that must have been inconceivable ages ago, when Belcher or Shirley or Pownall or Bernard was Governor of His Majesty's Province of the Massachusetts-Bay.

Then one summer there came a philosopher into Kingsport. His name was Thomas Olney, and he taught ponderous things in a college by Narragansett Bay. With stout wife and romping children he came, and his eyes were weary with seeing the same things for many years, and thinking the same well-disciplined thoughts. He looked at the mists from the diadem of Father Neptune, and tried to walk into their white world of mystery along the titan steps of The Causeway. Morning after morning he would lie on the cliffs and look over the world's rim at the cryptical aether beyond, listening to spectral bells and the wild cries of what might have been gulls. Then, when the mist would lift and the sea stand out prosy with the smoke of steamers, he would sigh and descend to the town, where he loved to thread the narrow olden lanes up and down hill, and study the crazy tottering gables and odd-pillared doorways which had sheltered so many generations of sturdy sea-folk. And he even talked with the Terrible Old Man, who was not fond of strangers, and was invited into his fearsomely archaic cottage where low ceilings and wormy panelling hear the echoes of disquieting soliloquies in the dark small hours.

Weird Tales, October 1931

"Nevertheless there is an ancient house on that cliff, and at evening men see lights in the small-paned windows."

Of course it was inevitable that Olney should mark the gray unvisited cottage in the sky, on that sinister northward crag which is one with the mists and the firmament. Always over Kingsport it hung, and always its mystery sounded in whispers through Kingsport's crooked alleys. The Terrible Old Man wheezed a tale that his father had told him, of lightning that shot one night up from that peaked cottage to the clouds of higher heaven; and Granny Orne, whose tiny gambrel-roofed abode in Ship Street is all covered with moss and ivy, croaked over something her grandmother had heard at second-hand, about shapes that flapped out of the eastern mists straight into the narrow single door of that unreachable place — for the door is set close to the edge of the crag toward the ocean, and glimpsed only from ships at sea.

At length, being avid for new strange things and held back by neither the Kingsporter's fear nor the summer boarder's usual indolence, Olney made a very terrible resolve. Despite a conservative training — or because of it, for humdrum lives breed wistful longings of the unknown — he swore a great oath to scale that avoided northern cliff and visit the abnormally antique gray cottage in the sky. Very plausibly his saner self argued that the place must be tenanted by people who reached it from inland along the easier ridge beside the Miskatonic's estuary. Probably they traded in Arkham, knowing how little Kingsport liked their habitation or perhaps being unable to climb down the cliff on the Kingsport side. Olney walked out along the lesser cliffs to where the great crag leaped insolently up to consort with celestial things, and became very sure that no human feet could mount it or descend it on that beetling southern slope. East and north it rose thousands of feet perpendicular from the water so only the western side, inland and toward Arkham, remained.

One early morning in August Olney set out to find a path to the inaccessible pinnacle. He worked northwest along pleasant back roads, past Hooper's Pond and the old brick powder-house to where the pastures slope up to the ridge above the Miskatonic and give a lovely vista of Arkham's white Georgian steeples across leagues of river and meadow. Here he found a shady road to Arkham, but no trail at all in the seaward direction he wished. Woods and fields crowded up to the high bank of the river's mouth, and bore not a sign of man's presence; not even a stone wall or a straying cow, but only the tall grass and giant trees and tangles of briars that the first Indian might have seen. As he climbed slowly east, higher and higher above the estuary on his left and nearer and nearer the sea, he found the way growing in difficulty till he wondered how ever the dwellers in that disliked place managed to reach the world outside, and whether they came often to market in Arkham.

Then the trees thinned, and far below him on his right he saw the hills and antique roofs and spires of Kingsport. Even Central Hill was a dwarf from this height, and he could just make out the ancient graveyard by the Congregational Hospital beneath which rumor said some terrible caves or burrows lurked. Ahead lay sparse grass and scrub blueberry bushes, and beyond them the naked rock of the crag and the thin peak of the dreaded gray cottage. Now the ridge narrowed, and Olney grew dizzy at his loneness in the sky, south of him the frightful precipice above Kingsport, north of him the vertical drop of nearly a mile to the river's mouth. Suddenly a great chasm opened before him, ten feet deep, so that he had to let himself down by his hands and drop to a slanting floor, and then crawl perilously up a natural defile in the opposite wall. So this was the way the folk of the uncanny house journeyed betwixt earth and sky!

When he climbed out of the chasm a morning mist was gathering, but he clearly saw the lofty and unhallowed cottage ahead; walls as gray as the rock, and high peak standing bold against the milky white of the seaward vapors. And he perceived that there was no door on this landward end, but only a couple of small lattice windows with dingy bull's-eye panes leaded in seventeenth century fashion. All around him was cloud and chaos, and he could see nothing below the whiteness of illimitable space. He was alone in the sky with this queer and very disturbing house; and when he sidled around to the front and saw that the wall stood flush with the cliff's edge, so that the single narrow door was not to be reached save from the empty aether, he felt a distinct terror that altitude could not wholly explain. And it was very odd that shingles so worm-eaten could survive, or bricks so crumbled still form a standing chimney.

As the mist thickened, Olney crept around to the windows on the north and west and south sides, trying them but finding them all locked. He was vaguely glad they were locked, because the more he saw of that house the less he wished to get in. Then a sound halted him. He heard a lock rattle and a bolt shoot, and a long creaking follow as if a heavy door were slowly and cautiously opened. This was on the oceanward side that he could not see, where the narrow portal opened on blank space thousands of feet in the misty sky above the waves.

Then there was heavy, deliberate tramping in the cottage, and Olney heard the windows opening, first on the north side opposite him, and then on the west just around the corner. Next would come the south windows, under the great low eaves on the side where he stood; and it must be said that he was more than uncomfortable as he thought of the detestable house on one side and the vacancy of upper air on the other. When a fumbling came in the nearer casements he crept around to the west again, flattening himself against the wall beside the now opened windows. It was plain that the owner had come home; but he had not come from the land, nor from any balloon or airship that could be imagined. Steps sounded again, and Olney edged round to the north; but before he could find a haven a voice called softly, and he knew he must confront his host.

Stuck out of the west window was a great black-bearded face whose eyes were phosphorescent with the imprint of unheard-of sights. But the voice was gentle, and of a quaint olden kind, so that Olney did not shudder when a brown hand reached out to help him over the sill and into that low room of black oak wainscots and carved Tudor furnishings. The man was clad in very ancient garments, and had about him an unplaceable nimbus of sea-lore and dreams of tall galleons. Olney does not recall many of the wonders he told, or even who he was; but says that he was strange and kindly, and filled with the magic of unfathomed voids of time and space. The small room seemed green with a dim aqueous light, and Olney saw that the far windows to the east were not open, but shut against the misty aether with dull panes like the bottoms of old bottles.

That bearded host seemed young, yet looked out of eyes steeped in the elder mysteries; and from the tales of marvelous ancient things he related, it must be guessed that the village folk were right in saying he had communed with the mists of the sea and the clouds of the sky ever since there was any village to watch his taciturn dwelling from the plain below. And the day wore on, and still Olney listened to rumors of old times and far places, and heard how the kings of Atlantis fought with the slippery blasphemies that wriggled out of rifts in ocean's floor, and how the pillared and weedy temple of Poseidon is still glimpsed at midnight by lost ships, who knew by its sight that they are lost. Years of the Titans were recalled, but the host grew timid when he spoke of the dim first age of chaos before the gods or even the Elder Ones were born, and when the other gods came to dance on the peak of Hatheg-Kla in the stony desert near Ulthar, beyond the River Skai.

It was at this point that there came a knocking on the door; that ancient door of nail-studded oak beyond which lay only the abyss of white cloud. Olney started in fright, but the bearded man motioned him to be still, and tiptoed to the door to look out through a very small peephole. What he saw he did not like, so pressed his fingers to his lips and tiptoed around to shut and lock all the windows before returning to the ancient settle beside his guest. Then Olney saw lingering against the translucent squares of each of the little dim windows in succession a queer black outline as the caller moved inquisitively about before leaving; and he was glad his host had not answered the knocking. For there are strange objects in the great abyss, and the seeker of dreams must take care not to stir up or meet the wrong ones.

Then the shadows began to gather; first little furtive ones under the table, and then bolder ones in the dark panelled corners. And the bearded man made enigmatical gestures of prayer, and lit tall candles in curiously wrought brass candlesticks. Frequently he would glance at the door as if he expected some one, and at length his glance seemed answered by a singular rapping which must have followed some very ancient and secret code. This time he did not even glance through the peep-hole, but swung the great oak bar and shot the bolt, unlatching the heavy door and flinging it wide to the stars and the mist.

And then to the sound of obscure harmonies there floated into that room from the deep all the dreams and memories of earth's sunken Mighty Ones. And golden flames played about weedy locks, so that Olney was dazzled as he did them homage. Trident-bearing Neptune was there, and sportive tritons and fantastic nereids, and upon dolphins' backs was balanced a vast crenulate shell wherein rode the gay and awful form of primal Nodens, Lord of the Great Abyss. And the conchs of the tritons gave weird blasts, and the nereids made strange sounds by striking on the grotesque resonant shells of unknown lurkers in black seacaves. Then hoary Nodens reached forth a wizened hand and helped Olney and his host into the vast shell, whereat the conchs and the gongs set up a wild and awesome clamor. And out into the limitless aether reeled that fabulous train, the noise of whose shouting was lost in the echoes of thunder.

All night in Kingsport they watched that lofty cliff when the storm and the mists gave them glimpses of it, and when toward the small hours the little dim windows went dark they whispered of dread and disaster. And Olney's children and stout wife prayed to the bland proper god of Baptists, and hoped that the traveller would borrow an umbrella and rubbers unless the rain stopped by morning. Then dawn swam dripping and mist-wreathed out of the sea, and the buoys tolled solemn in vortices of white aether. And at noon elfin horns rang over the ocean as Olney, dry and lightfooted, climbed down from the cliffs to antique Kingsport with the look of far places in his eyes. He could not recall what he had dreamed in the skyperched hut of that still nameless hermit, or say how he had crept down that crag untraversed by other feet. Nor could he talk of these matters at all save with the Terrible Old Man, who afterward mumbled queer things in his long white beard; vowing that the man who came down from that crag was not wholly the man who went up, and that somewhere under that gray peaked roof, or amidst inconceivable reaches of that sinister white mist, there lingered still the lost spirit of him who was Thomas Olney.

And ever since that hour, through dull dragging years of grayness and weariness, the philosopher has labored and eaten and slept and done uncomplaining the suitable deeds of a citizen. Not any more does he long for the magic of farther hills, or sigh for secrets that peer like green reefs from a bottomless sea. The sameness of his days no longer gives him sorrow and well-disciplined thoughts have grown enough for his imagination. His good wife waxes stouter and his children older and prosier and more useful, and he never fails to smile correctly with pride when the occasion calls for it. In his glance there is not any restless light, and if he ever listens for solemn bells or far elfin horns it is only at night when old dreams are wandering. He has never seen Kingsport again, for his family disliked the funny old houses and complained that the drains were impossibly bad. They have a trim bungalow now at Bristol Highlands, where no tall crags tower, and the neighbors are urban and modern.

But in Kingsport strange tales are abroad, and even the Terrible Old Man admits a thing untold by his grandfather. For now, when the wind sweeps boisterous out of the north past the high ancient house that is one with the firmament, there is broken at last that ominous, brooding silence ever before the bane of Kingsport's maritime cotters. And old folk tell of pleasing voices heard singing there, and of laughter that swells with joys beyond earth's joys; and say that at evening the little low windows are brighter than formerly. They say, too, that the fierce aurora comes oftener to that spot, shining blue in the north with visions of frozen worlds while the crag and the cottage hang black and fantastic against wild coruscations. And the mists of the dawn are thicker, and sailors are not quite so sure that all the muffled seaward ringing is that of the solemn buoys.

Worst of all, though, is the shrivelling of old fears in the hearts of Kingsport's young men, who grow prone to listen at night to the north wind's faint distant sounds. They swear no harm or pain can inhabit that high peaked cottage, for in the new voices gladness beats, and with them the tinkle of laughter and music. What tales the sea-mists may bring to that haunted and northernmost pinnacle they do not know, but they long to extract some hint of the wonders that knock at the cliff-yawning door when clouds are thickest. And patriarchs dread lest some day one by one they seek out that inaccessible peak in the sky, and learn what centuried secrets hide beneath the steep shingled roof which is part of the rocks and the stars and the ancient fears of Kingsport. That those venturesome youths will come back they do not doubt, but they think a light may be gone from their eyes, and a will from their hearts. And they do not wish quaint Kingsport with its climbing lanes and archaic gables to drag listless down the years while voice by voice the laughing chorus grows stronger and wilder in that unknown and terrible eyrie where mists and the dreams of mists stop to rest on their way from the sea to the skies.

They do not wish the souls of their young men to leave the pleasant hearths and gambrel-roofed taverns of old Kingsport, nor do they wish the laughter and song in that high rocky place to grow louder. For as the voice which has come has brought fresh mists from the sea and from the north fresh lights, so do they say that still other voices will bring more mists and more lights, till perhaps the olden gods (whose existence they hint only in whispers for fear the Congregational parson shall hear) may come out of the deep and from unknown Kadath in the cold waste and make their dwelling on that evilly appropriate crag so close to the gentle hills and valleys of quiet, simple fisher folk. This they do not wish, for to plain people things not of earth are unwelcome; and besides, the Terrible Old Man often recalls what Olney said about a knock that the lone dweller feared, and a shape seen black and inquisitive against the mist through those queer translucent windows of leaded bull's-eyes.

All these things, however, the Elder Ones only may decide; and meanwhile the morning mist still comes up by that lovely vertiginous peak with the steep ancient house, that gray, low-eaved house where none is seen but where evening brings furtive lights while the north wind tells of strange revels. White and feathery it comes from the deep to its brothers the clouds, full of dreams of dank pastures and caves of Leviathan. And when tales fly thick in the grottoes of tritons, and conchs in seaweed cities blow wild tunes learned from the Elder Ones, then great eager vapors flock to heaven laden with lore; and Kingsport, nestling uneasy in its lesser cliffs below that awesome hanging sentinel of rock, sees oceanward only a mystic whiteness, as if the cliff's rim were the rim of all earth, and the solemn bells of the buoys tolled free in the aether of faery.

The Silver Key.

4,900-WORD SHORT STORY; 1926.

This philosophical disquisition in short-story form is the closest H.P. Lovecraft ever came to an autobiographical account of his growth as an artist over the course of his literary life. For readers who are familiar with Lovecraft's biographical details, the parallels are hard to miss.

Scholar S.T. Joshi, in I Am Providence, *hints that "The Silver Key" might be viewed as an epitaph for Lovecraft's once-worshipful regard of Lord Dunsany and his realms of fantasy. Certainly his description of Randolph Carter's literary life, in this story, parallels Dunsany's far more than it does Lovecraft's. This theory cannot be further elucidated here without spoiling the ending, but the reader might bear it in mind as something to ponder after finishing the story.*

The story was written in November 1926, around the same time as "The Strange High House in the Mist" and during a brief break from working on The Dream-Quest of Unknown Kadath. *Although he appears to have written it primarily for himself, Lovecraft submitted it to* Weird Tales, *where it was promptly rejected; however, Farnsworth Wright reconsidered and asked to see it again. Eventually it was published in the January 1929 issue. It was not very well received by the readers, but it made a great impression on fellow writer E. Hoffman Price. Price later prevailed upon Lovecraft to collaborate with him in the writing of a pulpy, action-packed sequel titled "Through the Gates of the Silver Key," which appears later in this collection.*

When Randolph Carter was thirty he lost the key of the gate of dreams. Prior to that time he had made up for the prosiness of life by nightly excursions to strange and ancient cities beyond space, and lovely, unbelievable garden lands across ethereal seas; but as middle age hardened upon him he felt those liberties slipping away little by little, until at last he was cut off altogether. No more could his galleys sail up the river Oukranos past the

Weird Tales, January 1929

"There the bearded and finny Gnorri build their labyrinths."

gilded spires of Thran, or his elephant caravans tramp through perfumed jungles in Kled, where forgotten palaces with veined ivory columns sleep lovely and unbroken under the moon.

He had read much of things as they are, and talked with too many people. Well-meaning philosophers had taught him to look into the logical relations of things, and analyse the processes which shaped his thoughts and fancies. Wonder had gone away, and he had forgotten that all life is only a set of pictures in the brain, among which there is no difference betwixt those born of real things and those born of inward dreamings, and no cause to value the one above the other. Custom had dinned into his ears a superstitious reverence for that which tangibly and physically exists, and had made him secretly ashamed to dwell in visions. Wise men told him his simple fancies were inane and childish, and even more absurd because their actors persist in fancying them full of meaning and purpose as the blind cosmos grinds aimlessly on from nothing to something and from something back to nothing again, neither heeding nor knowing the wishes or existence of the minds that flicker for a second now and then in the darkness.

They had chained him down to things that are, and had then explained the workings of those things till mystery had gone out of the world. When he complained, and longed to escape into twilight realms where magic moulded all the little vivid fragments and prized associations of his mind into vistas of breathless expectancy and unquenchable delight, they turned him instead toward the new-found prodigies of science, bidding him find wonder in the atom's vortex and mystery in the sky's dimensions. And when he had failed to find these boons in things whose laws are known and measurable, they told him he lacked imagination, and was immature because he preferred dream-illusions to the illusions of our physical creation.

So Carter had tried to do as others did, and pretended that the common events and emotions of earthy minds were more important than the fantasies of rare and delicate souls. He did not dissent when they told him that the animal pain of a stuck pig or dyspeptic ploughman in real life is a greater thing than the peerless beauty of Narath with its hundred carven gates and domes of chalcedony, which he dimly remembered from his dreams; and under their guidance he cultivated a painstaking sense of pity and tragedy.

Once in a while, though, he could not help seeing how shallow, fickle, and meaningless all human aspirations are, and how emptily our real impulses contrast with those pompous ideals we profess to hold. Then he would have recourse to the polite laughter they had taught him to use against the extravagance and artificiality of dreams; for he saw that the daily life of our world is every inch as extravagant and artificial, and far less worthy of respect because of its poverty in beauty and its silly reluctance to admit its own lack of reason and purpose. In this way he became a kind of humorist, for he did not see that even humour is empty in a mindless universe devoid of any true standard of consistency or inconsistency.

In the first days of his bondage he had turned to the gentle churchly faith endeared to him by the naïve trust of his fathers, for thence stretched mystic avenues which seemed to promise escape from life. Only on closer view did he mark the starved fancy and beauty, the stale and prosy triteness, and the owlish gravity and grotesque claims of solid truth which reigned boresomely and overwhelmingly among most of its professors; or feel to the full the awkwardness with which it sought to keep alive as literal fact the outgrown fears and guesses of a primal race confronting the unknown. It wearied Carter to see how solemnly people tried to make earthly reality out of old myths which every step of their boasted science confuted, and this misplaced seriousness killed the attachment he might have kept for the ancient creeds had they been content to offer the sonorous rites and emotional outlets in their true guise of ethereal fantasy.

But when he came to study those who had thrown off the old myths, he found them even more ugly than those who had not. They did not know that beauty lies in harmony, and that loveliness of life has no standard amidst an aimless cosmos save only its harmony with the dreams and the feelings which have gone before and blindly moulded our little spheres out of the rest of chaos. They did not see that good and evil and beauty and ugliness are only ornamental fruits of perspective, whose sole value lies in their linkage to what chance made our fathers think and feel, and whose finer details are different for every race and culture. Instead, they either denied these things altogether or transferred them to the crude, vague instincts which they shared with the beasts and peasants; so that their lives were dragged malodorously out in pain, ugliness, and disproportion, yet filled with a ludicrous pride at having escaped from something no more unsound than that which still held them. They had traded the false gods of fear and blind piety for those of license and anarchy.

Carter did not taste deeply of these modern freedoms; for their cheapness and squalor sickened a spirit loving beauty alone while his reason rebelled at the flimsy logic with which their champions tried to gild brute impulse with a sacredness stripped from the idols they had discarded. He saw that most of them, in common with their cast-off priestcraft, could not escape from the delusion that life has a meaning apart from that which men dream into it; and could not lay aside the crude notion of ethics and obligations beyond those of beauty, even when all Nature shrieked of its unconsciousness and impersonal unmorality in the light of their scientific discoveries. Warped and bigoted with preconceived illusions of justice, freedom, and consistency, they cast off the old lore and the old way with the old beliefs; nor ever stopped to think that that lore and those ways were the sole makers of their present thoughts and judgments, and the sole guides and standards in a meaningless universe without fixed aims or stable points of reference. Having lost these artificial settings, their lives grew void of direction and dramatic interest; till at length they strove to drown their ennui in bustle and pretended usefulness, noise and excitement, barbaric display and animal sensation. When these things palled, disappointed, or grew nauseous through revulsion, they cultivated irony and bitterness, and found fault with the social order. Never could they realize that their brute foundations were as shifting and contradictory as the gods of their elders, and that the satisfaction of one moment is the bane of the next. Calm, lasting beauty comes only in a dream, and this solace the world had thrown away when in its worship of the real it threw away the secrets of childhood and innocence.

Amidst this chaos of hollowness and unrest Carter tried to live as befitted a man of keen thought and good heritage. With his dreams fading under the ridicule of the age he could not believe in anything, but the love of harmony kept him close to the ways of his race and station. He walked impassive through the cities of men, and sighed because no vista seemed fully real; because every flash of yellow sunlight on tall roofs and every glimpse of balustraded plazas in the first lamps of evening served only to remind him of dreams he had once known, and to make him homesick for ethereal lands he no longer knew how to find. Travel was only a mockery; and even the Great War stirred him but little, though he served from the first in the Foreign Legion of France. For a while he sought friends, but soon grew weary of the crudeness of their emotions, and the sameness and earthiness of their visions. He felt vaguely glad that all his relatives were distant and out of touch with him, for they would not have understood his mental life. That is, none but his grandfather and great-uncle Christopher could, and they were long dead.

Then he began once more the writing of books, which he had left off when dreams first failed him. But here, too, was there no satisfaction or fulfillment; for the touch of earth was upon his mind, and he could not think of lovely things as he had done of yore. Ironic humor dragged down all the twilight minarets he reared, and the earthy fear of improbability blasted all the delicate and amazing flowers in his faery gardens. The convention of assumed pity spilt mawkishness on his characters, while the myth of an important reality and significant human events and emotions debased all his high fantasy into thin-veiled allegory and cheap social satire. His new novels were successful as his old ones had never been; and because he knew how empty they must be to please an empty herd, he burned them and ceased his writing. They were very graceful novels, in which he urbanely laughed at the dreams he lightly sketched; but he saw that their sophistication had sapped all their life away.

It was after this that he cultivated deliberate illusion, and dabbled in the notions of the bizarre and the eccentric as an antidote for the commonplace. Most of these, however, soon showed their poverty and barrenness; and he saw that the popular doctrines of occultism are as dry and inflexible as those of science, yet without even the slender palliative of truth to redeem them. Gross stupidity, falsehood, and muddled thinking are not dream; and form no escape from life to a mind trained above their own level. So Carter bought stranger books and sought out deeper and more terrible men of fantastic erudition; delving into arcana of consciousness that few have trod, and learning things about the secret pits of life, legend, and immemorial antiquity which disturbed him ever afterward. He decided to live on a rarer plane, and furnished his Boston home to suit his changing moods; one room for each, hung in appropriate colours, furnished with befitting books and objects, and provided with sources of the proper sensations of light, heat, sound, taste, and odour.

Once he heard of a man in the south, who was shunned and feared for the blasphemous things he read in prehistoric books and clay tablets smuggled from India and Arabia. Him he visited, living with him and sharing his studies for seven years, till horror overtook them one midnight in an unknown and archaic graveyard, and only one emerged where two had entered. Then he went back to Arkham, the terrible witch-haunted old town of his forefathers in New England, and had experiences in the dark, amidst the hoary willows and tottering gambrel roofs, which made him seal forever certain pages in the diary of a wild-minded ancestor. But these horrors took him only to the edge of reality, and were not of the true dream country he had known in youth; so that at fifty he despaired of any rest or contentment in a world grown too busy for beauty and too shrewd for dreams.

Having perceived at last the hollowness and futility of real things, Carter spent his days in retirement, and in wistful disjointed memories of his dream-filled youth. He thought it rather silly that he bothered to keep on living at all, and got from a South American acquaintance a very curious liquid to take him to oblivion without suffering. Inertia and force of habit, however, caused him to defer action; and he lingered indecisively among thoughts of old times, taking down the strange hangings from his walls and refitting the house as it was in his early boyhood — purple panes, Victorian furniture, and all.

With the passage of time he became almost glad he had lingered, for his relics of youth and his cleavage from the world made life and sophistication seem very distant and unreal; so much so that a touch of magic and expectancy stole back into his nightly slumbers. For years those slumbers had known only such twisted reflections of every-day things as the commonest slumbers know, but now there returned a flicker of something stranger and wilder; something of vaguely awesome imminence which took the form of tensely clear pictures from his childhood days, and made him think of little inconsequential things he had long forgotten. He would often awake calling for his mother and grandfather, both in their graves a quarter of a century.

Then one night his grandfather reminded him of the key. The grey old scholar, as vivid as in life, spoke long and earnestly of their ancient line, and of the strange visions of the delicate and sensitive men who composed it. He spoke of the flame-eyed Crusader who learnt wild secrets of the Saracens that held him captive; and of the first Sir Randolph Carter who studied magic when Elizabeth was queen. He spoke, too, of that Edmund Carter who had just escaped hanging in the Salem witchcraft, and who had placed in an antique box a great silver key handed down from his ancestors. Before Carter awaked, the gentle visitant had told him where to find that box; that carved oak box of archaic wonder whose grotesque lid no hand had raised for two centuries.

In the dust and shadows of the great attic he found it, remote and forgotten at the back of a drawer in a tall chest. It was about a foot square, and its Gothic carvings were so fearful that he did not marvel no person since Edmund Carter had dared to open it. It gave forth no noise when shaken, but was mystic with the scent of unremembered spices. That it held a key was indeed only a dim legend, and Randolph Carter's father had never known such a box existed. It was bound in rusty iron, and no means was provided for working the formidable lock. Carter vaguely understood that he would find within it some key to the lost gate of dreams, but of where and how to use it his grandfather had told him nothing.

An old servant forced the carven lid, shaking as he did so at the hideous faces leering from the blackened wood, and at some unplaced familiarity. Inside, wrapped in a discoloured parchment, was a huge key of tarnished silver covered with cryptical arabesques; but of any legible explanation there was none. The parchment was voluminous, and held only the strange hieroglyphs of an unknown tongue written with an antique reed. Carter recognized the characters as those he had seen on a certain papyrus scroll belonging to that terrible scholar of the South who had vanished one midnight in a nameless cemetery. The man had always shivered when he read this scroll, and Carter shivered now.

But he cleaned the key, and kept it by him nightly in its aromatic box of ancient oak. His dreams were meanwhile increasing in vividness, and though showing him none of the strange cities and incredible gardens of the old days, were assuming a definite cast whose purpose could not be mistaken. They were calling him back along the years, and with the mingled wills of all his fathers were pulling him toward some hidden and ancestral source. Then he knew he must go into the past and merge himself with old things, and day after day he thought of the hills to the north where haunted Arkham and the rushing Miskatonic and the lonely rustic homestead of his people lay.

In the brooding fire of autumn Carter took the old remembered way past graceful lines of rolling hill and stone-walled meadow, distant vale and hanging woodland, curving road and nestling farmstead, and the crystal windings of the Miskatonic, crossed here and there by rustic bridges of wood or stone. At one bend he saw the group of giant elms among which an ancestor had oddly vanished a century and a half before, and shuddered as the wind blew meaningly through them. Then there was the crumbling farmhouse of old Goody Fowler the witch, with its little evil windows and great roof sloping nearly to the ground on the north side. He speeded up his car as he passed it, and did not slacken till he had mounted the hill where his mother and her fathers before her were born, and where the old white house still looked proudly across the road at the breathlessly lovely panorama of rocky slope and verdant valley, with the distant spires of Kingsport on the horizon, and hints of the archaic, dream-laden sea in the farthest background.

Then came the steeper slope that held the old Carter place he had not seen in over forty years. Afternoon was far gone when he reached the foot, and at the bend half way up he paused to scan the outspread countryside golden and glorified in the slanting floods of magic poured out by a western sun. All the strangeness and expectancy of his recent dreams seemed present in this hushed and unearthly landscape, and he thought of the unknown solitudes of other planets as his eyes traced out the velvet and deserted lawns shining undulant between their tumbled walls, and clumps of faery forest setting off far lines of purple hills beyond hills, and the spectral wooded valley dipping down in shadow to dank hollows where trickling waters crooned and gurgled among swollen and distorted roots.

Something made him feel that motors did not belong in the realm he was seeking, so he left his car at the edge of the forest, and putting the great key in his coat pocket walked on up the hill. Woods now engulfed him utterly, though he knew the house was on a high knoll that cleared the trees except to the north. He wondered how it would look, for it had been left vacant and untended through his neglect since the death of his strange great-uncle Christopher thirty years before. In his boyhood he had revelled through long visits there, and had found weird marvels in the woods beyond the orchard.

Shadows thickened around him, for the night was near. Once a gap in the trees opened up to the right, so that he saw off across leagues of twilight meadow and spied the old Congregational steeple on Central Hill in Kingsport; pink with the last flush of day, the panes of the little round windows blazing with reflected fire. Then, when he was in deep shadow again, he recalled with a start that the glimpse must have come from childish memory alone, since the old white church had long been torn down to make room for the Congregational Hospital. He had read of it with interest, for the paper had told about some strange burrows or passages found in the rocky hill beneath.

Through his puzzlement a voice piped, and he started again at its familiarity after long years. Old Benijah Corey had been his Uncle Christopher's hired man, and was aged even in those far-off times of his boyhood visits. Now he must be well over a hundred, but that piping voice could come from no one else. He could distinguish no words, yet the tone was haunting and unmistakable. To think that "Old Benijy" should still be alive!

"Mister Randy! Mister Randy! Whar be ye? D'ye want to skeer yer Aunt Marthy plumb to death? Hain't she tuld ye to keep nigh the place in the arternoon an' git back afur dark? Randy! Ran . . . dee! . . . He's the beatin'est boy fer runnin' off in the woods I ever see; haff the time a-settin' moonin' raound that snake-den in the upper timberlot! . . . Hey yew, Ran . . . dee!"

Randolph Carter stopped in the pitch darkness and rubbed his hand across his eyes. Something was queer. He had been somewhere he ought not to be; had strayed very far away to places where he had not belonged, and was now inexcusably late. He had not noticed the time on the Kingsport steeple, though he could easily have made it out with his pocket telescope; but he knew his lateness was something very strange and unprecedented. He was not sure he had his little telescope with him, and put his hand in his blouse pocket to see. No, it was not there, but there was the big silver key he had found in a box somewhere. Uncle Chris had told him something odd once about an old unopened box with a key in it, but Aunt Martha had stopped the story abruptly, saying it was no kind of thing to tell a child whose head was already too full of queer fancies. He tried to recall just where he had found the key, but something seemed very confused. He guessed it was in the attic at home in Boston, and dimly remembered bribing Parks with half his week's allowance to help him open the box and keep quiet about it; but when he remembered this, the face of Parks came up very strangely, as if the wrinkles of long years had fallen upon the brisk little Cockney.

"Ran . . . dee! Ran . . . dee! Hi! Hi! Randy!"

A swaying lantern came around the black bend, and old Benijah pounced on the silent and bewildered form of the pilgrim.

"Durn ye, boy, so thar ye be! Ain't ye got a tongue in yer head, that ye can't answer a body! I ben callin' this haff hour, an' ye must a heerd me long ago! Dun't ye know yer Aunt Marthy's all a-fidget over yer bein' off arter dark? Wait till I tell yer Uncle Chris when he gits hum! Ye'd orta know these here woods ain't no fitten place to be traipsin' this hour! They's things abroad what dun't do nobody no good, as my gran'-sir knowed afur me. Come, Mister Randy, or Hannah wunt keep supper no longer!"

So Randolph Carter was marched up the road where wondering stars glimmered through high autumn boughs. And dogs barked as the yellow light of small-paned windows shone out at the farther turn, and the Pleiades twinkled across the open knoll where a great gambrel roof stood black against the dim west. Aunt Martha was in the doorway, and did not scold too hard when Benijah shoved the truant in. She knew Uncle Chris well enough to expect such things of the Carter blood. Randolph did not show his key, but ate his supper in silence and protested only when bedtime came. He sometimes dreamed better when awake, and he wanted to use that key.

In the morning Randolph was up early, and would have run off to the upper timberlot if Uncle Chris had not caught him and forced him into his chair by the breakfast table. He looked impatiently around the low-pitched room with the rag carpet and exposed beams and corner-posts, and smiled only when the orchard boughs scratched at the leaded panes of the rear window. The trees and the hills were close to him, and formed the gates of that timeless realm which was his true country.

Then, when he was free, he felt in his blouse pocket for the key; and being reassured, skipped off across the orchard to the rise beyond, where the wooded hill climbed again to heights above even the treeless knoll. The floor of the forest was mossy and mysterious, and great lichened rocks rose vaguely here and there in the dim light like Druid monoliths among the swollen and twisted trunks of a sacred grove. Once in his ascent Randolph crossed a rushing stream whose falls a little way off sang runic incantations to the lurking fauns and aegipans and dryads.

Then he came to the strange cave in the forest slope, the dreaded "snake-den" which country folk shunned, and away from which Benijah had warned him again and again. It was deep; far deeper than anyone but Randolph suspected, for the boy had found a fissure in the farthermost black corner that led to a loftier grotto beyond—a haunting sepulchral place whose granite walls held a curious illusion of conscious artifice. On this occasion he crawled in as usual, lighting his way with matches filched from the sitting-room matchsafe, and edging through the final crevice with an eagerness hard to explain even to himself. He could not tell why he approached the farther wall so confidently, or why he instinctively drew forth the great silver key as he did so. But on he went, and when he danced back to the house that night he offered no excuses for his lateness, nor heeded in the least the reproofs he gained for ignoring the noon-tide dinner-horn altogether.

Now it is agreed by all the distant relatives of Randolph Carter that something occurred to heighten his imagination in his tenth year. His cousin, Ernest B. Aspinwall, Esq., of Chicago, is fully ten years his senior; and distinctly recalls a change in the boy after the autumn of 1883. Randolph had looked on scenes of fantasy that few others can ever have beheld, and stranger still were some of the qualities which he showed in relation to very mundane things. He seemed, in fine, to have picked up an odd gift of prophecy; and reacted unusually to things which, though at the time without meaning, were later found to justify the singular impressions. In subsequent decades as new inventions, new names, and new events appeared one by one in the book of history, people would now and then recall wonderingly how Carter had years before let fall some careless word of undoubted connection with what was then far in the future. He did not himself understand these words, or know why certain things made him feel certain emotions; but fancied that some unremembered dream must be responsible. It was as early as 1897 that he turned pale when some traveller mentioned the French town of Belloy-en-Santerre, and friends remembered it when he was almost mortally wounded there in 1916, while serving with the Foreign Legion in the Great War.

Carter's relatives talk much of these things because he has lately disappeared. His little old servant Parks, who for years bore patiently with his vagaries, last saw him on the morning he drove off alone in his car with a key he had recently found. Parks had helped him get the key from the old box containing it, and had felt strangely affected by the grotesque carvings on the box, and by some other odd quality he could not name. When Carter left, he had said he was going to visit his old ancestral country around Arkham.

Half way up Elm Mountain, on the way to the ruins of the old Carter place, they found his motor set carefully by the roadside; and in it was a box of fragrant wood with carvings that frightened the countrymen who stumbled on it. The box held only a queer parchment whose characters no linguist or palaeographer has been able to decipher or identify. Rain had long effaced any possible footprints, though Boston investigators had something to say about evidences of disturbances among the fallen timbers of the Carter place. It was, they averred, as though someone had groped about the ruins at no distant period. A common white handkerchief found among forest rocks on the hillside beyond cannot be identified as belonging to the missing man.

There is talk of apportioning Randolph Carter's estate among his heirs, but I shall stand firmly against this course because I do not believe he is dead. There are twists of time and space, of vision and reality, which only a dreamer can divine; and from what I know of Carter I think he has merely found a way to traverse these mazes. Whether or not he will ever come back, I cannot say. He wanted the lands of dream he had lost, and yearned for the days of his childhood. Then he found a key, and I somehow believe he was able to use it to strange advantage.

I shall ask him when I see him, for I expect to meet him shortly in a certain dream-city we both used to haunt. It is rumoured in Ulthar, beyond the River Skai, that a new king reigns on the opal throne of Ilek-Vad, that fabulous town of turrets atop the hollow cliffs of glass overlooking the twilight sea wherein the bearded and finny Gnorri build their singular labyrinths, and I believe I know how to interpret this rumour. Certainly, I look forward impatiently to the sight of that great silver key, for in its cryptical arabesques there may stand symbolised all the aims and mysteries of a blindly impersonal cosmos.

1927.

Dawn of a Golden Age.

Nineteen-twenty-seven was Lovecraft's first full year back in Providence, living in one side of what amounted to a duplex with his aunt occupying the other side. During the first few months of the year, he was still putting the finishing touches on his longest work to date, *The Dream-Quest of Unknown Kadath*; but before the year ended, he would have created an even longer one: *The Case of Charles Dexter Ward*.

The Case of Charles Dexter Ward is one of Lovecraft's most beloved tales today, but after he had written it, Lovecraft's own judgement of it was quite harsh — a foreshadowing of the crushing hypercriticality that would, in partnership with an increasing sensitivity to rejection, begin to really cripple his output after 1931.

This was also the year in which Lovecraft wrote one of his most iconic stories — one that, like *The Case of Charles Dexter Ward*, was deeply infused with the spirit of the New England countryside which he had now started to explore in earnest: "The Colour out of Space." Like "The Call of Cthulhu," this was actually a science-fiction story — part of Lovecraft's new(-ish) cosmicist approach to his storytelling.

Lovecraft's ghostwriting business prospered in 1927, although, of course, he charged too little for his services and had great difficulty collecting even that. The year brought some non-monetary gratification, though, when "The Horror at Red Hook" was published in a British anthology of horror stories titled *You'll Need a Night Light* — representing the first time Lovecraft's work had appeared in a hardcover book — and when "The Colour out of Space" was picked for Edward J. O'Brien's *Best Short Stories* volume for 1938.

In addition to "The Colour out of Space" and *The Case of Charles Dexter Ward*, Lovecraft also wrote "The Very Old Folk" — actually a transcript of a letter posted off to Donald Wandrei describing a particularly vivid dream.

The Dream-Quest of Unknown Kadath.

42,600-WORD NOVEL; 1926.

"Actually, it isn't much good; but forms useful practice for later and more authentic attempts in the novel form."

With these modest words, H.P. Lovecraft dismissed his then-half-finished short novel, The Dream-Quest of Unknown Kadath. *And ever since, Lovecraft aficionados have vehemently disagreed over whether he was correct in his assessment.*

Dream-Quest *is a unique novel, bereft of chapter breaks even though there are several places where it seems naturally to lend itself to them; it's one long flowing anecdote, almost a stream of consciousness, running for nearly 43,000 words without pausing for breath. Reading it all in one sitting is an experience not unlike that of a pharmaceutical Argonaut who has taken too large a dose of LSD and finds himself stuck in a long, strange "trip" that seems destined to go on forever. Many Lovecraft fans absolutely love it. Many others think it's as close to actual bad writing as H.P. Lovecraft ever got.*

But it's important to remember that he never intended it for publication. After he finished it in January of 1927, Lovecraft refused several offers to help him prepare a typescript, and it's only because Robert Barlow pestered him for weeks that he passed the manuscript along to him.

It was eventually published, but not until August Derleth included it in Beyond the Wall of Sleep, *the Arkham House collection published in 1943.*

Three times Randolph Carter dreamed of the marvelous city, and three times was he snatched away while still he paused on the high terrace above it. All golden and lovely it blazed in the sunset, with walls, temples, colonnades and arched bridges of veined marble, silver-basined fountains of prismatic spray in broad squares and perfumed gardens, and wide streets marching between delicate trees and blossom-laden urns and ivory statues in gleaming rows; while on steep northward slopes climbed tiers of red roofs and old peaked gables harbouring little lanes of grassy cobbles. It was a fever of the gods, a fanfare of supernal trumpets and a clash of immortal cymbals. Mystery hung about it as clouds about a fabulous unvisited mountain; and as Carter stood breathless and expectant on that balustraded parapet there swept up to him the poignancy and suspense of almost-vanished memory, the pain of lost things and the maddening need to place again what once had been an awesome and momentous place.

He knew that for him its meaning must once have been supreme; though in what cycle or incarnation he had known it, or whether in dream or in waking, he could not tell. Vaguely it called up glimpses of a far forgotten first youth, when wonder and pleasure lay in all the mystery of days, and dawn and dusk alike strode forth prophetic to the eager sound of lutes and song, unclosing fiery gates toward further and surprising marvels. But each night as he stood on that high marble terrace with the curious urns and carven rail and looked off over that hushed sunset city of beauty and unearthly immanence he felt the bondage of dream's tyrannous gods; for in no wise could he leave that lofty spot, or descend the wide marmoreal flights flung endlessly down to where those streets of elder witchery lay outspread and beckoning.

When for the third time he awakened with those flights still undescended and those hushed sunset streets still untraversed, he prayed long and earnestly to the hidden gods of dream that brood capricious above the clouds on unknown Kadath, in the cold waste where no man treads. But the gods made no answer and shewed no relenting, nor did they give any favouring sign when he prayed to them in dream, and invoked them sacrificially through the bearded priests of Nasht and Kaman-Thah, whose cavern-temple with its pillar of flame lies not far from the gates of the waking world. It seemed, however, that his prayers must have been adversely heard, for after even the first of them he ceased wholly to behold the marvellous city; as if his three glimpses from afar had been mere accidents or oversights, and against some hidden plan or wish of the gods.

At length, sick with longing for those glittering sunset streets and cryptical hill lanes among ancient tiled roofs, nor able sleeping or waking to drive them from his mind, Carter resolved to go with bold entreaty whither no man had gone before, and dare the icy deserts through the dark to where unknown Kadath, veiled in cloud and crowned with unimagined stars, holds secret and nocturnal the onyx castle of the Great Ones.

In light slumber he descended the seventy steps to the cavern of flame and talked of this design to the bearded priests of Nasht and Kaman-Thah. And the priests shook their pshent-bearing heads and vowed it would be the death of his soul. They pointed out that the Great Ones had shown already their wish, and that it is not agreeable to them to be harassed by insistent pleas. They reminded him, too, that not only had no man ever been to Kadath, but no man had ever suspected in what part of space it may lie; whether it be in the dreamlands around our own world, or in those surrounding some unguessed companion of Fomalhaut or Aldebaran. If in our dreamland, it might conceivably be reached, but only three human souls since time began had ever crossed and recrossed the black impious gulfs to other dreamlands, and of that three, two had come back quite mad. There were, in such voyages, incalculable local dangers; as well as that shocking final peril which gibbers unmentionably outside the ordered universe, where no dreams reach; that last amorphous blight of nethermost confusion which blasphemes and bubbles at the centre of all infinity — the boundless daemon sultan Azathoth, whose name no lips dare speak aloud, and who gnaws hungrily in inconceivable, unlighted chambers beyond time amidst the muffled, maddening beating of vile drums and the thin, monotonous whine of accursed flutes; to which detestable pounding and piping dance slowly, awkwardly, and absurdly the gigantic Ultimate gods, the blind, voiceless, tenebrous, mindless Other gods whose soul and messenger is the crawling chaos Nyarlathotep.

Of these things was Carter warned by the priests Nasht and Kaman-Thah in the cavern of flame, but still he resolved to find the gods on unknown Kadath in the cold waste, wherever that might be, and to win from them the sight and remembrance and shelter of the marvellous sunset city. He knew that his journey would be strange and long, and that the Great Ones would be against it; but being old in the land of dream he counted on many useful memories and devices to aid him. So asking a formal blessing of the priests and thinking shrewdly on his course, he boldly descended the seven hundred steps to the Gate of Deeper Slumber and set out through the Enchanted Wood.

In the tunnels of that twisted wood, whose low prodigious oaks twine groping boughs and shine dim with the phosphorescence of strange fungi, dwell the furtive and secretive Zoogs; who know many obscure secrets of the dream world and a few of the waking world, since the wood at two places touches the lands of men, though it would be disastrous to say where. Certain unexplained rumours, events, and vanishments occur among men where the Zoogs have access, and it is well that they cannot travel far outside the world of dreams. But over the nearer parts of the dream world they pass freely, flitting small and brown and unseen and bearing back piquant tales to beguile the hours around their hearths in the forest they love. Most of them live in burrows, but some inhabit the trunks of the great trees; and although they live mostly on fungi it is muttered that they have also a slight taste for meat, either physical or spiritual, for certainly many dreamers have entered that wood who have not come out. Carter, however, had no fear; for he was an old dreamer and had learnt their fluttering language and made many a treaty with them; having found through their help the splendid city of Celephaïs in Ooth-Nargai beyond the Tanarian Hills, where reigns half the year the great King Kuranes, a man he had known by another name in life. Kuranes was the one soul who had been to the star-gulfs and returned free from madness.

Threading now the low phosphorescent aisles between those gigantic trunks, Carter made fluttering sounds in the manner of the Zoogs, and listened now and then for responses. He remembered one particular village of the creatures was in the centre of the wood, where a circle of great mossy stones in what was once a clearing tells of older and more terrible dwellers long forgotten, and toward this spot he hastened. He traced his way by the grotesque fungi, which always seem better nourished as one approaches the dread circle where elder beings danced and sacrificed. Finally the great light of those thicker fungi revealed a sinister green and grey vastness pushing up through the roof of the forest and out of sight. This was the nearest of the great ring of stones, and Carter knew he was close to the Zoog village. Renewing his fluttering sound, he waited patiently; and was at last rewarded by an impression of many eyes watching him. It was the Zoogs, for one sees their weird eyes long before one can discern their small, slippery brown outlines.

Out they swarmed, from hidden burrow and honeycombed tree, till the whole dim-litten region was alive with them. Some of the wilder ones brushed Carter unpleasantly, and one even nipped loathsomely at his ear; but these lawless spirits were soon restrained by their elders. The Council of Sages, recognizing the visitor, offered a gourd of fermented sap from a haunted tree unlike the others, which had grown from a seed dropt down by someone on the moon; and as Carter drank it ceremoniously a very strange colloquy began. The Zoogs did not, unfortunately, know where the peak of Kadath lies, nor could they even say whether the cold waste is in our dream world or in another. Rumours of the Great Ones came equally from all points; and one might only say that they were likelier to be seen on high mountain peaks than in valleys, since on such peaks they dance reminiscently when the moon is above and the clouds beneath.

Then one very ancient Zoog recalled a thing unheard-of by the others; and said that in Ulthar, beyond the River Skai, there still lingered the last copy of those inconceivably old Pnakotic Manuscripts made by waking men in forgotten boreal kingdoms and borne into the land of dreams when the hairy cannibal Gnophkehs overcame many-templed Olathoe and slew all the heroes of the land of Lomar. Those manuscripts he said, told much of the gods, and besides, in Ulthar there were men who had seen the signs of the gods, and even one old priest who had scaled a great mountain to behold them dancing by moonlight. He had failed, though his companion had succeeded and perished namelessly.

So Randolph Carter thanked the Zoogs, who fluttered amicably and gave him another gourd of moon-tree wine to take with him, and set out through the phosphorescent wood for the other side, where the rushing Skai flows down from the slopes of Lerion, and Hatheg and Nir and Ulthar dot the plain. Behind him, furtive and unseen, crept several of the curious Zoogs; for they wished to learn what might befall him, and bear back the legend to their people. The vast oaks grew thicker as he pushed on beyond the village, and he looked sharply for a certain spot where they would thin somewhat, standing quite dead or dying among the unnaturally dense fungi and the rotting mould and mushy logs of their fallen brothers. There he would turn sharply aside, for at that spot a mighty slab of stone rests on the forest floor; and those who have dared approach it say that it bears an iron ring three feet wide. Remembering the archaic circle of great mossy rocks, and what it was possibly set up for, the Zoogs do not pause near that expansive slab with its huge ring; for they realise that all which is forgotten need not necessarily be dead, and they would not like to see the slab rise slowly and deliberately.

Carter detoured at the proper place, and heard behind him the frightened fluttering of some of the more timid Zoogs. He had known they would follow him, so he was not disturbed; for one grows accustomed to the anomalies of these prying creatures.

It was twilight when he came to the edge of the wood, and the strengthening glow told him it was the twilight of morning. Over fertile plains rolling down to the Skai he saw the smoke of cottage chimneys, and on every hand were the hedges and ploughed fields and thatched roofs of a peaceful land. Once he stopped at a farmhouse well for a cup of water, and all the dogs barked affrightedly at the inconspicuous Zoogs that crept through the grass behind. At another house, where people were stirring, he asked questions about the gods, and whether they danced often upon Lerion; but the farmer and his wife would only make the Elder Sign and tell him the way to Nir and Ulthar.

At noon he walked through the one broad high street of Nir, which he had once visited and which marked his farthest former travels in this direction; and soon afterward he came to the great stone bridge across the Skai, into whose central piece the masons had sealed a living human sacrifice when they built it thirteen-hundred years before. Once on the other side, the frequent presence of cats (who all arched their backs at the trailing Zoogs) revealed the near neighborhood of Ulthar; for in Ulthar, according to an ancient and significant law, no man may kill a cat. Very pleasant were the suburbs of Ulthar, with their little green cottages and neatly fenced farms; and still pleasanter was the quaint town itself, with its old peaked roofs and overhanging upper stories and numberless chimney-pots and narrow hill streets where one can see old cobbles whenever the graceful cats afford space enough. Carter, the cats being somewhat dispersed by the half-seen Zoogs, picked his way directly to the modest Temple of the Elder Ones where the priests and old records were said to be; and once within that venerable circular tower of ivied stone — which crowns Ulthar's highest hill — he sought out the patriarch Atal, who had been up the forbidden peak Hatheg-Kla in the stony desert and had come down again alive.

Atal, seated on an ivory dais in a festooned shrine at the top of the temple, was fully three centuries old; but still very keen of mind and memory. From him Carter learned many things about the gods, but mainly that they are indeed only Earth's gods, ruling feebly our own dreamland and having no power or habitation elsewhere. They might, Atal said, heed a man's prayer if in good humour; but one must not think of climbing to their onyx stronghold atop Kadath in the cold waste. It was lucky that no man knew where Kadath towers, for the fruits of ascending it would be very grave. Atal's companion Barzai the Wise had been drawn screaming into the sky for climbing merely the known peak of Hatheg-Kla. With unknown Kadath, if ever found, matters would be much worse; for although Earth's gods may sometimes be surpassed by a wise mortal, they are protected by the Other Gods from Outside, whom it is better not to discuss. At least twice in the world's history the Other Gods set their seal upon Earth's primal granite; once in antediluvian times, as guessed from a drawing in those parts of the Pnakotic Manuscripts too ancient to be read, and once on Hatheg-Kla when Barzai the Wise tried to see Earth's gods dancing by moonlight. So, Atal said, it would be much better to let all gods alone except in tactful prayers.

Carter, though disappointed by Atal's discouraging advice and by the meagre help to be found in the Pnakotic Manuscripts and the Seven Cryptical Books of Hsan, did not wholly despair. First he questioned the old priest about that marvellous sunset city seen from the railed terrace, thinking that perhaps he might find it without the gods' aid; but Atal could tell him nothing. Probably, Atal said, the place belonged to his especial dream world and not to the general land of vision that many know; and conceivably it might be on another planet. In that case Earth's gods could not guide him if they would. But this was not likely, since the stopping of the dreams shewed pretty clearly that it was something the Great Ones wished to hide from him.

Then Carter did a wicked thing, offering his guileless host so many draughts of the moon-wine which the Zoogs had given him that the old man became irresponsibly talkative. Robbed of his reserve, poor Atal babbled freely of forbidden things; telling of a great image reported by travellers as carved on the solid rock of the mountain Ngranek, on the isle of Oriab in the Southern Sea, and hinting that it may be a likeness which Earth's gods once wrought of their own features in the days when they danced by moonlight on that mountain. And he hiccoughed likewise that the features of that image are very strange, so that one might easily recognize them, and that they are sure signs of the authentic race of the gods.

Now the use of all this in finding the gods became at once apparent to Carter. It is known that in disguise the younger among the Great Ones often espouse the daughters of men, so that around the borders of the cold waste wherein stands Kadath the peasants must all bear their blood. This being so, the way to find that waste must be to see the stone face on Ngranek and mark the features; then, having noted them with care, to search for such features among living men. Where they are plainest and thickest, there must the gods dwell nearest; and whatever stony waste lies back of the villages in that place must be that wherein stands Kadath.

Much of the Great Ones might be learnt in such regions, and those with their blood might inherit little memories very useful to a seeker. They might not know their parentage, for the gods so dislike to be known among men that none can be found who has seen their faces wittingly; a thing which Carter realized even as he sought to scale Kadath. But they would have queer lofty thoughts misunderstood by their fellows, and would sing of far places and gardens so unlike any known even in the dreamland that common folk would call them fools; and from all this one could perhaps learn old secrets of Kadath, or gain hints of the marvellous sunset city which the gods held secret. And more, one might in certain cases seize some well-loved child of a god as hostage; or even capture some young god himself, disguised and dwelling amongst men with a comely peasant maiden as his bride.

Atal, however, did not know how to find Ngranek on its isle of Oriab; and recommended that Carter follow the singing Skai under its bridges down to the Southern Sea; where no burgess of Ulthar has ever been, but whence the merchants come in boats or with long caravans of mules and two-wheeled carts. There is a great city there, Dylath-Leen, but in Ulthar its reputation is bad because of the black three-banked galleys that sail to it with rubies from no clearly named shore. The traders that come from those galleys to deal with the jewellers are human, or nearly so, but the rowers are never beheld; and it is not thought wholesome in Ulthar that merchants should trade with black ships from unknown places whose rowers cannot be exhibited.

By the time he had given this information Atal was very drowsy, and Carter laid him gently on a couch of inlaid ebony and gathered his long beard decorously on his chest. As he turned to go, he observed that no suppressed fluttering followed him, and wondered why the Zoogs had become so lax in their curious pursuit. Then he noticed all the sleek complacent cats of Ulthar licking their chops with unusual gusto, and recalled the spitting and caterwauling he had faintly heard, in lower parts of the temple while absorbed in the old priest's conversation. He recalled, too, the evilly hungry way in which an especially impudent young Zoog had regarded a small black kitten in the cobbled street outside. And because he loved nothing on earth more than small black kittens, he stooped and petted the sleek cats of Ulthar as they licked their chops, and did not mourn because those inquisitive Zoogs would escort him no farther.

It was sunset now, so Carter stopped at an ancient inn on a steep little street overlooking the lower town. And as he went out on the balcony of his room and gazed down at the sea of red tiled roofs and cobbled ways and the pleasant fields beyond, all mellow and magical in the slanted light, he swore that Ulthar would be a very likely place to dwell in always, were not the memory of a greater sunset city ever goading one onward toward unknown perils. Then twilight fell, and the pink walls of the plastered gables turned violet and mystic, and little yellow lights floated up one by one from old lattice windows. And sweet bells pealed in the temple tower above, and the first star winked softly above the meadows across the Skai. With the night came song, and Carter nodded as the lutanists praised ancient days from beyond the filigreed balconies and tesselated courts of simple Ulthar. And there might have been sweetness even in the voices of Ulthar's many cats, but that they were mostly heavy and silent from strange feasting. Some of them stole off to those cryptical realms which are known only to cats and which villagers say are on the moon's dark side, whither the cats leap from tall housetops, but one small black kitten crept upstairs and sprang in Carter's lap to purr and play, and curled up near his feet when he lay down at last on the little couch whose pillows were stuffed with fragrant, drowsy herbs.

In the morning Carter joined a caravan of merchants bound for Dylath-Leen with the spun wool of Ulthar and the cabbages of Ulthar's busy farms. And for six days they rode with tinkling bells on the smooth road beside the Skai; stopping some nights at the inns of little quaint fishing towns, and on other nights camping under the stars while snatches of boatmen's songs came from the placid river. The country was very beautiful, with green hedges and groves and picturesque peaked cottages and octagonal windmills.

On the seventh day a blur of smoke rose on the horizon ahead, and then the tall black towers of Dylath-Leen, which is built mostly of basalt. Dylath-Leen with its thin angular towers looks in the distance like a bit of the Giant's Causeway, and its streets are dark and uninviting. There are many dismal sea-taverns near the myriad wharves, and all the town is thronged with the strange seamen of every land on earth and of a few which are said to be not on earth. Carter questioned the oddly robed men of that city about the peak of Ngranek on the isle of Oriab, and found that they knew of it well.

Ships came from Baharna on that island, one being due to return thither in only a month, and Ngranek is but two days' zebra-ride from that port. But few had seen the stone face of the god, because it is on a very difficult side of Ngranek, which overlooks only sheer crags and a valley of sinister lava. Once the gods were angered with men on that side, and spoke of the matter to the Other Gods.

It was hard to get this information from the traders and sailors in Dylath-Leen's sea taverns, because they mostly preferred to whisper of the black galleys. One of them was due in a week with rubies from its unknown shore, and the townsfolk dreaded to see it dock. The mouths of the men who came from it to trade were too wide, and the way their turbans were humped up in two points above their foreheads was in especially bad taste. And their shoes were the shortest and queerest ever seen in the Six Kingdoms. But worst of all was the matter of the unseen rowers. Those three banks of oars moved too briskly and accurately and vigorously to be comfortable, and it was not right for a ship to stay in port for weeks while the merchants traded, yet to give no glimpse of its crew. It was not fair to the tavern-keepers of Dylath-Leen, or to the grocers and butchers, either; for not a scrap of provisions was ever sent aboard. The merchants took only gold and stout black slaves from Parg across the river. That was all they ever took, those unpleasantly featured merchants and their unseen rowers; never anything from the butchers and grocers, but only gold and the fat black men of Parg whom they bought by the pound. And the odours from those galleys which the south wind blew in from the wharves are not to be described. Only by constantly smoking strong thagweed could even the hardiest denizen of the old sea-taverns bear them. Dylath-Leen would never have tolerated the black galleys had such rubies been obtainable elsewhere, but no mine in all Earth's dreamland was known to produce their like.

Of these things Dylath-Leen's cosmopolitan folk chiefly gossiped whilst Carter waited patiently for the ship from Baharna, which might bear him to the isle whereon carven Ngranek towers lofty and barren. Meanwhile he did not fail to seek through the haunts of far travellers for any tales they might have concerning Kadath in the cold waste or a marvellous city of marble walls and silver fountains seen below terraces in the sunset. Of these things, however, he learned nothing; though he once thought that a certain old slant-eyed merchant looked queerly intelligent when the cold waste was spoken of. This man was reputed to trade with the horrible stone villages on the icy desert plateau of Leng, which no healthy folk visit and whose evil fires are seen at night from afar. He was even rumoured to have dealt with that High-Priest Not To Be Described, which wears a yellow silken mask over its face and dwells all alone in a prehistoric stone monastery. That such a person might well have had nibbling traffick with such beings as may conceivably dwell in the cold waste was not to be doubted, but Carter soon found that it was no use questioning him.

Then the black galley slipped into the harbour past the basalt wale and the tall lighthouse, silent and alien, and with a strange stench that the south wind drove into the town. Uneasiness rustled through the taverns along that waterfront, and after a while the dark wide-mouthed merchants with humped turbans and short feet clumped steathily ashore to seek the bazaars of the jewellers. Carter observed them closely, and disliked them more the longer he looked at them. Then he saw them drive the stout black men of Parg up the gangplank grunting and sweating into that singular galley, and wondered in what lands — or if in any lands at all — those fat pathetic creatures might be destined to serve.

And on the third evening of that galley's stay one of the uncomfortable merchants spoke to him, smirking sinfully and hinting of what he had heard in the taverns of Carter's quest. He appeared to have knowledge too secret for public telling; and although the sound of his voice was unbearably hateful, Carter felt that the lore of so far a traveller must not be overlooked. He bade him therefore be his guest in locked chambers above, and drew out the last of the Zoogs' moon-wine to loosen his tongue. The strange merchant drank heavily, but smirked unchanged by the draught. Then he drew forth a curious bottle with wine of his own, and Carter saw that the bottle was a single hollowed ruby, grotesquely carved in patterns too fabulous to be comprehended. He offered his wine to his host, and though Carter took only the least sip, he felt the dizziness of space and the fever of unimagined jungles. All the while the guest had been smiling more and more broadly, and as Carter slipped into blankness the last thing he saw was that dark odious face convulsed with evil laughter and something quite unspeakable where one of the two frontal puffs of that orange turban had become disarranged with the shakings of that epileptic mirth.

Carter next had consciousness amidst horrible odours beneath a tent-like awning on the deck of a ship, with the marvellous coasts of the Southern Sea flying by in unnatural swiftness. He was not chained, but three of the dark sardonic merchants stood grinning nearby, and the sight of those humps in their turbans made him almost as faint as did the stench that filtered up through the sinister hatches. He saw slip past him the glorious lands and cities of which a fellow-dreamer of earth — a lighthouse-keeper in ancient Kingsport — had often discoursed in the old days, and recognized the templed terraces of Zak, abode of forgotten dreams; the spires of infamous Thalarion, that daemon-city of a thousand wonders where the eidolon Lathi reigns; the charnel gardens of Zura, land of pleasures unattained, and the twin headlands of crystal, meeting above in a resplendent arch, which guard the harbour of Sona-Nyl, blessed land of fancy.

Past all these gorgeous lands the malodourous ship flew unwholesomely, urged by the abnormal strokes of those unseen rowers below. And before the day was done Carter saw that the steersman could have no other goal than the Basalt Pillars of the West, beyond which simple folk say splendid Cathuria lies, but which wise dreamers well know are the gates of a monstrous cataract wherein the oceans of earth's dreamland drop wholly to abysmal nothingness and shoot through the empty spaces toward other worlds and other stars and the awful voids outside the ordered universe where the daemon sultan Azathoth gnaws hungrily in chaos amid pounding and piping and the hellish dancing of the Other Gods, blind, voiceless, tenebrous, and mindless, with their soul and messenger Nyarlathotep.

Meanwhile the three sardonic merchants would give no word of their intent, though Carter well knew that they must be leagued with those who wished to hold him from his quest. It is understood in the land of dream that the Other Gods have many agents moving among men; and all these agents, whether wholly human or slightly less than human, are eager to work the will of those blind and mindless things in return for the favour of their hideous soul and messenger, the crawling chaos Nyarlathotep. So Carter inferred that the merchants of the humped turbans, hearing of his daring search for the Great Ones in their castle of Kadath, had decided to take him away and deliver him to Nyarlathotep for whatever nameless bounty might be offered for such a prize. What might be the land of those merchants in our known universe or in the eldritch spaces outside, Carter could not guess; nor could he imagine at what hellish trysting-place they would meet the crawling chaos to give him up and claim their reward. He knew, however, that no beings as nearly human as these would dare approach the ultimate nighted throne of the daemon Azathoth in the formless central void.

At the set of sun the merchants licked their excessively wide lips and glared hungrily and one of them went below and returned from some hidden and offensive cabin with a pot and basket of plates. Then they squatted close together beneath the awning and ate the smoking meat that was passed around. But when they gave Carter a portion, he found something very terrible in the size and shape of it; so that he turned even paler than before and cast that portion into the sea when no eye was on him. And again he thought of those unseen rowers beneath, and of the suspicious nourishment from which their far too mechanical strength was derived.

It was dark when the galley passed betwixt the Basalt Pillars of the West and the sound of the ultimate cataract swelled portentous from ahead. And the spray of that cataract rose to obscure the stars, and the deck grew damp, and the vessel reeled in the surging current of the brink. Then with a queer whistle and plunge the leap was taken, and Carter felt the terrors of nightmare as earth fell away and the great boat shot silent and comet-like into planetary space. Never before had he known what shapeless black things lurk and caper and flounder all through the aether, leering and grinning at such voyagers as may pass, and sometimes feeling about with slimy paws when some moving object excites their curiosity. These are the nameless larvae of the Other Gods, and like them are blind and without mind, and possessed of singular hungers and thirsts.

But that offensive galley did not aim as far as Carter had feared, for he soon saw that the helmsman was steering a course directly for the moon. The moon was a crescent shining larger and larger as they approached it, and shewing its singular craters and peaks uncomfortably. The ship made for the edge, and it soon became clear that its destination was that secret and mysterious side which is always turned away from earth, and which no fully human person, save perhaps the dreamer Snireth-Ko, has ever beheld. The close aspect of the moon as the galley drew near proved very disturbing to Carter, and he did not like the size and shape of the ruins which crumbled here and there. The dead temples on the mountains were so placed that they could have glorified no suitable or wholesome gods, and in the symmetries of the broken columns there seemed to be some dark and inner meaning which did not invite solution. And what the structure and proportions of the olden worshippers could have been, Carter steadily refused to conjecture.

When the ship rounded the edge, and sailed over those lands unseen by man, there appeared in the queer landscape certain signs of life, and Carter saw many low, broad, round cottages in fields of grotesque whitish fungi. He noticed that these cottages had no windows, and thought that their shape suggested the huts of Esquimaux. Then he glimpsed the oily waves of a sluggish sea, and knew that the voyage was once more to be by water — or at least through some liquid. The galley struck the surface with a peculiar sound, and the odd elastic way the waves received it was very perplexing to Carter.

They now slid along at great speed, once passing and hailing another galley of kindred form, but generally seeing nothing but that curious sea and a sky that was black and star-strewn even though the sun shone scorchingly in it.

There presently rose ahead the jagged hills of a leprous-looking coast, and Carter saw the thick unpleasant grey towers of a city. The way they leaned and bent, the manner in which they were clustered, and the fact that they had no windows at all, was very disturbing to the prisoner; and he bitterly mourned the folly which had made him sip the curious wine of that merchant with the humped turban. As the coast drew nearer, and the hideous stench of that city grew stronger, he saw upon the jagged hills many forests, some of whose trees he recognized as akin to that solitary moon-tree in the enchanted wood of earth, from whose sap the small brown Zoogs ferment their curious wine.

Carter could now distinguish moving figures on the noisome wharves ahead, and the better he saw them the worse he began to fear and detest them. For they were not men at all, or even approximately men, but great greyish white slippery things which could expand and contract at will, and whose principal shape — though it often changed — was that of a sort of toad without any eyes, but with a curious vibrating mass of short pink tentacles on the end of its blunt, vague snout. These objects were waddling busily about the wharves, moving bales and crates and boxes with preternatural strength, and now and then hopping on or off some anchored galley with long oars in their forepaws. And now and then one would appear driving a herd of clumping slaves, which indeed were approximate human beings with wide mouths like those merchants who traded in Dylath-Leen; only these herds, being without turbans or shoes or clothing, did not seem so very human after all. Some of the slaves — the fatter ones, whom a sort of overseer would pinch experimentally — were unloaded from ships and nailed in crates which workers pushed into the low warehouses or loaded on great lumbering vans.

Once a van was hitched and driven off, and the fabulous thing which drew it was such that Carter gasped, even after having seen the other monstrosities of that hateful place. Now and then a small herd of slaves dressed and turbaned like the dark merchants would be driven aboard a galley, followed by a great crew of the slippery toad-things as officers, navigators, and rowers. And Carter saw that the almost-human creatures were reserved for the more ignominious kinds of servitude which required no strength, such as steering and cooking, fetching and carrying, and bargaining with men on the earth or other planets where they traded. These creatures must have been convenient on earth, for they were truly not unlike men when dressed and carefully shod and turbaned, and could haggle in the shops of men without embarrassment or curious explanations. But most of them, unless lean or ill-favoured, were unclothed and packed in crates and drawn off in lumbering lorries by fabulous things. Occasionally other beings were unloaded and crated; some very like these semi-humans, some not so similar, and some not similar at all. And he wondered if any of the poor stout black men of Parg were left to be unloaded and crated and shipped inland in those obnoxious drays.

When the galley landed at a greasy-looking quay of spongy rock a nightmare horde of toad-things wiggled out of the hatches, and two of them seized Carter and dragged him ashore. The smell and aspect of that city are beyond telling, and Carter held only scattered images of the tiled streets and black doorways and endless precipices of grey vertical walls without windows. At length he was dragged within a low doorway and made to climb infinite steps in pitch blackness. It was, apparently, all one to the toad-things whether it were light or dark. The odour of the place was intolerable, and when Carter was locked into a chamber and left alone he scarcely had strength to crawl around and ascertain its form and dimensions. It was circular, and about twenty feet across.

From then on time ceased to exist. At intervals food was pushed in, but Carter would not touch it. What his fate would be, he did not know; but he felt that he was held for the coming of that frightful soul and messenger of infinity's Other Gods, the crawling chaos Nyarlathotep. Finally, after an unguessed span of hours or days, the great stone door swung wide again, and Carter was shoved down the stairs and out into the red-litten streets of that fearsome city. It was night on the moon, and all through the town were stationed slaves bearing torches.

In a detestable square a sort of procession was formed; ten of the toad-things and twenty-four almost human torch-bearers, eleven on either side, and one each before and behind. Carter was placed in the middle of the line; five toad-things ahead and five behind, and one almost-human torch-bearer on either side of him. Certain of the toad-things produced disgustingly carven flutes of ivory and made loathsome sounds. To that hellish piping the column advanced out of the tiled streets and into nighted plains of obscene fungi, soon commencing to climb one of the lower and more gradual hills that lay behind the city. That on some frightful slope or blasphemous plateau the crawling chaos waited, Carter could not doubt; and he wished that the suspense might soon be over. The whining of those impious flutes was shocking, and he would have given worlds for some even half-normal sound; but these toad-things had no voices, and the slaves did not talk.

Then through that star-specked darkness there did come a normal sound. It rolled from the higher hills, and from all the jagged peaks around it was caught up and echoed in a swelling pandaemoniac chorus. It was the midnight yell of the cat, and Carter knew at last that the old village folk were right when they made low guesses about the cryptical realms which are known only to cats, and to which the elders among cats repair by stealth nocturnally, springing from high housetops. Verily, it is to the moon's dark side that they go to leap and gambol on the hills and converse with ancient shadows, and here amidst that column of foetid things Carter heard their homely, friendly cry, and thought of the steep roofs and warm hearths and little lighted windows of home.

Now much of the speech of cats was known to Randolph Carter, and in this far terrible place he uttered the cry that was suitable. But that he need not have done, for even as his lips opened he heard the chorus wax and draw nearer, and saw swift shadows against the stars as small graceful shapes leaped from hill to hill in gathering legions. The call of the clan had been given, and before the foul procession had time even to be frightened a cloud of smothering fur and a phalanx of murderous claws were tidally and tempestuously upon it. The flutes stopped, and there were shrieks in the night. Dying almost-humans screamed, and cats spit and yowled and roared, but the toad-things made never a sound as their stinking green ichor oozed fatally upon that porous earth with the obscene fungi.

It was a stupendous sight while the torches lasted, and Carter had never before seen so many cats. Black, grey, and white; yellow, tiger, and mixed; common, Persian, and Manx; Thibetan, Angora, and Egyptian; all were there in the fury of battle, and there hovered over them some trace of that profound and inviolate sanctity which made their goddess great in the temples of Bubastis. They would leap seven strong at the throat of an almost-human or the pink tentacled snout of a toad-thing and drag it down savagely to the fungous plain, where myriads of their fellows would surge over it and into it with the frenzied claws and teeth of a divine battle-fury. Carter had seized a torch from a stricken slave, but was soon overborne by the surging waves of his loyal defenders. Then he lay in the utter blackness hearing the clangour of war and the shouts of the victors, and feeling the soft paws of his friends as they rushed to and fro over him in the fray.

At last awe and exhaustion closed his eyes, and when he opened them again it was upon a strange scene. The great shining disc of the earth, thirteen times greater than that of the moon as we see it, had risen with floods of weird light over the lunar landscape; and across all those leagues of wild plateau and ragged crest there squatted one endless sea of cats in orderly array. Circle on circle they reached, and two or three leaders out of the ranks were licking his face and purring to him consolingly. Of the dead slaves and toad-things there were not many signs, but Carter thought he saw one bone a little way off in the open space between him and the warriors.

Carter now spoke with the leaders in the soft language of cats, and learned that his ancient friendship with the species was well known and often spoken of in the places where cats congregate. He had not been unmarked in Ulthar when he passed through, and the sleek old cats had remembered how he patted them after they had attended to the hungry Zoogs who looked evilly at a small black kitten. And they recalled, too, how he had welcomed the very little kitten who came to see him at the inn, and how he had given it a saucer of rich cream in the morning before he left. The grandfather of that very little kitten was the leader of the army now assembled, for he had seen the evil procession from a far hill and recognized the prisoner as a sworn friend of his kind on earth and in the land of dream.

A yowl now came from the farther peak, and the old leader paused abruptly in his conversation. It was one of the army's outposts, stationed on the highest of the mountains to watch the one foe which Earth's cats fear; the very large and peculiar cats from Saturn, who for some reason have not been oblivious of the charm of our moon's dark side. They are leagued by treaty with the evil toad-things, and are notoriously hostile to our earthly cats; so that at this juncture a meeting would have been a somewhat grave matter.

After a brief consultation of generals, the cats rose and assumed a closer formation, crowding protectingly around Carter and preparing to take the great leap through space back to the housetops of our earth and its dreamland. The old field-marshal advised Carter to let himself be borne along smoothly and passively in the massed ranks of furry leapers, and told him how to spring when the rest sprang and land gracefully when the rest landed. He also offered to deposit him in any spot he desired, and Carter decided on the city of Dylath-Leen whence the black galley had set out; for he wished to sail thence for Oriab and the carven crest Ngranek, and also to warn the people of the city to have no more traffick with black galleys, if indeed that traffick could be tactfully and judiciously broken off. Then, upon a signal, the cats all leaped gracefully with their friend packed securely in their midst; while in a black cave on an unhallowed summit of the moon-mountains still vainly waited the crawling chaos Nyarlathotep.

The leap of the cats through space was very swift; and being surrounded by his companions Carter did not see this time the great black shapelessnesses that lurk and caper and flounder in the abyss. Before he fully realised what had happened he was back in his familiar room at the inn at Dylath-Leen, and the stealthy, friendly cats were pouring out of the window in streams. The old leader from Ulthar was the last to leave, and as Carter shook his paw he said he would be able to get home by cockcrow. When dawn came, Carter went downstairs and learned that a week had elapsed since his capture and leaving. There was still nearly a fortnight to wait for the ship bound toward Oriab, and during that time he said what he could against the black galleys and their infamous ways. Most of the townsfolk believed him; yet so fond were the jewellers of great rubies that none would wholly promise to cease trafficking with the wide-mouthed merchants. If aught of evil ever befalls Dylath-Leen through such traffick, it will not be his fault.

In about a week the desiderate ship put in by the black wale and tall lighthouse, and Carter was glad to see that she was a barque of wholesome men, with painted sides and yellow lateen sails and a grey captain in silken robes. Her cargo was the fragrant resin of Oriab's inner groves, and the delicate pottery baked by the artists of Baharna, and the strange little figures carved from Ngranek's ancient lava. For this they were paid in the wool of Ulthar and the iridescent textiles of Hatheg and the ivory that the black men carve across the river in Parg. Carter made arrangements with the captain to go to Baharna and was told that the voyage would take ten days. And during his week of waiting he talked much with that captain of Ngranek, and was told that very few had seen the carven face thereon; but that most travellers are content to learn its legends from old people and lava-gatherers and image-makers in Baharna and afterward say in their far homes that they have indeed beheld it. The captain was not even sure that any person now living had beheld that carven face, for the wrong side of Ngranek is very difficult and barren and sinister, and there are rumours of caves near the peak wherein dwell the night-gaunts. But the captain did not wish to say just what a night-gaunt might be like, since such cattle are known to haunt most persistently the dreams of those who think too often of them. Then Carter asked that captain about unknown Kadath in the cold waste, and the marvellous sunset city, but of these the good man could truly tell nothing.

Carter sailed out of Dylath-Leen one early morning when the tide turned, and saw the first rays of sunrise on the thin angular towers of that dismal basalt town. And for two days they sailed eastward in sight of green coasts, and saw often the pleasant fishing towns that climbed up steeply with their red roofs and chimney-pots from old dreaming wharves and beaches where nets lay drying. But on the third day they turned sharply south where the roll of water was stronger, and soon passed from sight of any land. On the fifth day the sailors were nervous, but the captain apologized for their fears, saying that the ship was about to pass over the weedy walls and broken columns of a sunken city too old for memory, and that when the water was clear one could see so many moving shadows in that deep place that simple folk disliked it. He admitted, moreover, that many ships had been lost in that part of the sea; having been hailed when quite close to it, but never seen again.

That night the moon was very bright, and one could see a great way down in the water. There was so little wind that the ship could not move much, and the ocean was very calm. Looking over the rail Carter saw many fathoms deep the dome of the great temple, and in front of it an avenue of unnatural sphinxes leading to what was once a public square. Dolphins sported merrily in and out of the ruins, and porpoises revelled clumsily here and there, sometimes coming to the surface and leaping clear out of the sea. As the ship drifted on a little the floor of the ocean rose in hills, and one could clearly mark the lines of ancient climbing streets and the washed-down walls of myriad little houses.

Then the suburbs appeared, and finally a great lone building on a hill, of simpler architecture than the other structures, and in much better repair. It was dark and low and covered four sides of a square, with a tower at each corner, a paved court in the centre, and small curious round windows all over it. Probably it was of basalt, though weeds draped the greater part; and such was its lonely and impressive place on that far hill that it may have been a temple or a monastery. Some phosphorescent fish inside it gave the small round windows an aspect of shining, and Carter did not blame the sailors much for their fears. Then by the watery moonlight he noticed an odd high monolith in the middle of that central court, and saw that something was tied to it. And when after getting a telescope from the captain's cabin he saw that that bound thing was a sailor in the silk robes of Oriab, head downward and without any eyes, he was glad that a rising breeze soon took the ship ahead to more healthy parts of the sea.

The next day they spoke with a ship with violet sails bound for Zar, in the land of forgotten dreams, with bulbs of strange coloured lilies for cargo. And on the evening of the eleventh day they came in sight of the isle of Oriab with Ngranek rising jagged and snow-crowned in the distance. Oriab is a very great isle, and its port of Baharna a mighty city. The wharves of Baharna are of porphyry, and the city rises in great stone terraces behind them, having streets of steps that are frequently arched over by buildings and the bridges between buildings. There is a great canal which goes under the whole city in a tunnel with granite gates and leads to the inland lake of Yath, on whose farther shore are the vast clay-brick ruins of a primal city whose name is not remembered. As the ship drew into the harbour at evening the twin beacons Thon and Thal gleamed a welcome, and in all the million windows of Baharna's terraces mellow lights peeped out quietly and gradually as the stars peep out overhead in the dusk, till that steep and climbing seaport became a glittering constellation hung between the stars of heaven and the reflections of those stars in the still harbour.

The captain, after landing, made Carter a guest in his own small house on the shores of Yath where the rear of the town slopes down to it; and his wife and servants brought strange toothsome foods for the traveller's delight. And in the days after that Carter asked for rumours and legends of Ngranek in all the taverns and public places where lava-gatherers and image-makers meet, but could find no one who had been up the higher slopes or seen the carven face. Ngranek was a hard mountain with only an accursed valley behind it, and besides, one could never depend on the certainty that night-gaunts are altogether fabulous.

When the captain sailed back to Dylath-Leen Carter took quarters in an ancient tavern opening on an alley of steps in the original part of the town, which is built of brick and resembles the ruins of Yath's farther shore. Here he laid his plans for the ascent of Ngranek, and correlated all that he had learned from the lava-gatherers about the roads thither. The keeper of the tavern was a very old man, and had heard so many legends that he was a great help. He even took Carter to an upper room in that ancient house and shewed him a crude picture which a traveller had scratched on the clay wall in the old days when men were bolder and less reluctant to visit Ngranek's higher slopes. The old tavern-keeper's great-grandfather had heard from his great-grandfather that the traveller who scratched that picture had climbed Ngranek and seen the carven face, here drawing it for others to behold, but Carter had very great doubts, since the large rough features on the wall were hasty and careless, and wholly overshadowed by a crowd of little companion shapes in the worst possible taste, with horns and wings and claws and curling tails.

At last, having gained all the information he was likely to gain in the taverns and public places of Baharna, Carter hired a zebra and set out one morning on the road by Yath's shore for those inland parts wherein towers stony Ngranek. On his right were rolling hills and pleasant orchards and neat little stone farmhouses, and he was much reminded of those fertile fields that flank the Skai. By evening he was near the nameless ancient ruins on Yath's farther shore, and though old lava-gatherers had warned him not to camp there at night, he tethered his zebra to a curious pillar before a crumbling wall and laid his blanket in a sheltered corner beneath some carvings whose meaning none could decipher. Around him he wrapped another blanket, for the nights are cold in Oriab; and when upon awaking once he thought he felt the wings of some insect brushing his face he covered his head altogether and slept in peace till roused by the magah birds in distant resin groves.

The sun had just come up over the great slope whereon leagues of primal brick foundations and worn walls and occasional cracked pillars and pedestals stretched down desolate to the shore of Yath, and Carter looked about for his tethered zebra. Great was his dismay to see that docile beast stretched prostrate beside the curious pillar to which it had been tied, and still greater was he vexed on finding that the steed was quite dead, with its blood all sucked away through a singular wound in its throat. His pack had been disturbed, and several shiny knickknacks taken away, and all round on the dusty soil' were great webbed footprints for which he could not in any way account. The legends and warnings of lava-gatherers occurred to him, and he thought of what had brushed his face in the night. Then he shouldered his pack and strode on toward Ngranek, though not without a shiver when he saw close to him as the highway passed through the ruins a great gaping arch low in the wall of an old temple, with steps leading down into darkness farther than he could peer.

His course now lay uphill through wilder and partly wooded country, and he saw only the huts of charcoal-burners and the camp of those who gathered resin from the groves. The whole air was fragrant with balsam, and all the magah birds sang blithely as they flashed their seven colours in the sun. Near sunset he came on a new camp of lava-gatherers returning with laden sacks from Ngranek's lower slopes; and here he also camped, listening to the songs and tales of the men, and overhearing what they whispered about a companion they had lost. He had climbed high to reach a mass of fine lava above him, and at nightfall did not return to his fellows. When they looked for him the next day they found only his turban, nor was there any sign on the crags below that he had fallen. They did not search any more, because the old man among them said it would be of no use.

No one ever found what the night-gaunts took, though those beasts themselves were so uncertain as to be almost fabulous. Carter asked them if night-gaunts sucked blood and liked shiny things and left webbed footprints, but they all shook their heads negatively and seemed frightened at his making such an inquiry. When he saw how taciturn they had become he asked them no more, but went to sleep in his blanket.

The next day he rose with the lava-gatherers and exchanged farewells as they rode west and he rode east on a zebra he bought of them. Their older men gave him blessings and warnings, and told him he had better not climb too high on Ngranek, but while he thanked them heartily he was in no wise dissuaded. For still did he feel that he must find the gods on unknown Kadath; and win from them a way to that haunting and marvellous city in the sunset. By noon, after a long uphill ride, he came upon some abandoned brick villages of the hill-people who had once dwelt thus close to Ngranek and carved images from its smooth lava. Here they had dwelt till the days of the old tavernkeeper's grandfather, but about that time they felt that their presence was disliked. Their homes had crept even up the mountain's slope, and the higher they built the more people they would miss when the sun rose. At last they decided it would be better to leave altogether, since things were sometimes glimpsed in the darkness which no one could interpret favourably; so in the end all of them went down to the sea and dwelt in Baharna, inhabiting a very old quarter and teaching their sons the old art of image-making which to this day they carry on. It was from these children of the exiled hill-people that Carter had heard the best tales about Ngranek when searching through Baharna's ancient taverns.

All this time the great gaunt side of Ngranek was looming up higher and higher as Carter approached it. There were sparse trees on the lower slopes and feeble shrubs above them, and then the bare hideous rock rose spectral into the sky, to mix with frost and ice and eternal snow. Carter could see the rifts and ruggedness of that sombre stone, and did not welcome the prospect of climbing it. In places there were solid streams of lava, and scoriac heaps that littered slopes and ledges. Ninety aeons ago, before even the gods had danced upon its pointed peak, that mountain had spoken with fire and roared with the voices of the inner thunders. Now it towered all silent and sinister, bearing on the hidden side that secret titan image whereof rumour told. And there were caves in that mountain, which might be empty and alone with elder darkness, or might — if legend spoke truly — hold horrors of a form not to be surmised.

The ground sloped upward to the foot of Ngranek, thinly covered with scrub oaks and ash trees, and strewn with bits of rock, lava, and ancient cinder. There were the charred embers of many camps, where the lava-gatherers were wont to stop, and several rude altars which they had built either to propitiate the Great Ones or to ward off what they dreamed of in Ngranek's high passes and labyrinthine caves. At evening Carter reached the farthermost pile of embers and camped for the night, tethering his zebra to a sapling and wrapping himself well in his blankets before going to sleep. And all through the night a voonith howled distantly from the shore of some hidden pool, but Carter felt no fear of that amphibious terror, since he had been told with certainty that not one of them dares even approach the slope of Ngranek.

In the clear sunshine of morning Carter began the long ascent, taking his zebra as far as that useful beast could go, but tying it to a stunted ash tree when the floor of the thin wood became too steep. Thereafter he scrambled up alone; first through the forest with its ruins of old villages in overgrown clearings, and then over the tough grass where anaemic shrubs grew here and there. He regretted coming clear of the trees, since the slope was very precipitous and the whole thing rather dizzying. At length he began to discern all the countryside spread out beneath him whenever he looked about; the deserted huts of the image-makers, the groves of resin trees and the camps of those who gathered from them, the woods where prismatic magahs nest and sing, and even a hint very far away of the shores of Yath and of those forbidding ancient ruins whose name is forgotten. He found it best not to look around, and kept on climbing and climbing till the shrubs became very sparse and there was often nothing but the tough grass to cling to.

Then the soil became meagre, with great patches of bare rock cropping out, and now and then the nest of a condor in a crevice. Finally there was nothing at all but the bare rock, and had it not been very rough and weathered, he could scarcely have ascended farther. Knobs, ledges, and pinnacles, however, helped greatly; and it was cheering to see occasionally the sign of some lava-gatherer scratched clumsily in the friable stone, and know that wholesome human creatures had been there before him. After a certain height the presence of man was further shewn by handholds and footholds hewn where they were needed, and by little quarries and excavations where some choice vein or stream of lava had been found. In one place a narrow ledge had been chopped artificially to an especially rich deposit far to the right of the main line of ascent. Once or twice Carter dared to look around, and was almost stunned by the spread of landscape below. All the island betwixt him and the coast lay open to his sight, with Baharna's stone terraces and the smoke of its chimneys mystical in the distance. And beyond that the illimitable Southern Sea with all its curious secrets.

Thus far there had been much winding around the mountain, so that the farther and carven side was still hidden. Carter now saw a ledge running upward and to the left which seemed to head the way he wished, and this course he took in the hope that it might prove continuous. After ten minutes he saw it was indeed no cul-de-sac, but that it led steeply on in an arc which would, unless suddenly interrupted or deflected, bring him after a few hours' climbing to that unknown southern slope overlooking the desolate crags and the accursed valley of lava. As new country came into view below him he saw that it was bleaker and wilder than those seaward lands he had traversed. The mountain's side, too, was somewhat different; being here pierced by curious cracks and caves not found on the straighter route he had left. Some of these were above him and some beneath him, all opening on sheerly perpendicular cliffs and wholly unreachable by the feet of man. The air was very cold now, but so hard was the climbing that he did not mind it. Only the increasing rarity bothered him, and he thought that perhaps it was this which had turned the heads of other travellers and excited those absurd tales of night-gaunts whereby they explained the loss of such climbers as fell from these perilous paths. He was not much impressed by travellers' tales, but had a good curved scimitar in case of any trouble. All lesser thoughts were lost in the wish to see that carven face which might set him on the track of the gods atop unknown Kadath.

At last, in the fearsome iciness of upper space, he came round fully to the hidden side of Ngranek and saw in infinite gulfs below him the lesser crags and sterile abysses of lava which marked the olden wrath of the Great Ones. There was unfolded, too, a vast expanse of country to the south; but it was a desert land without fair fields or cottage chimneys, and seemed to have no ending. No trace of the sea was visible on this side, for Oriab is a great island. Black caverns and odd crevices were still numerous on the sheer vertical cliffs, but none of them was accessible to a climber. There now loomed aloft a great beetling mass which hampered the upward view, and Carter was for a moment shaken with doubt lest it prove impassable. Poised in windy insecurity miles above earth, with only space and death on one side and only slippery walls of rock on the other, he knew for a moment the fear that makes men shun Ngranek's hidden side. He could not turn round, yet the sun was already low. If there were no way aloft, the night would find him crouching there still, and the dawn would not find him at all.

But there was a way, and he saw it in due season. Only a very expert dreamer could have used those imperceptible foot-holds, yet to Carter they were sufficient. Surmounting now the outward-hanging rock, he found the slope above much easier than that below, since a great glacier's melting had left a generous space with loam and ledges. To the left a precipice dropped straight from unknown heights to unknown depths, with a cave's dark mouth just out of reach above him. Elsewhere, however, the mountain slanted back strongly, and even gave him space to lean and rest.

He felt from the chill that he must be near the snow line, and looked up to see what glittering pinnacles might be shining in that late ruddy sunlight. Surely enough, there was the snow uncounted thousands of feet above, and below it a great beetling crag like that he had just climbed; hanging there forever in bold outline. And when he saw that crag he gasped and cried out aloud, and clutched at the jagged rock in awe; for the titan bulge had not stayed as earth's dawn had shaped it, but gleamed red and stupendous in the sunset with the carved and polished features of a god.

Stern and terrible shone that face that the sunset lit with fire. How vast it was no mind can ever measure, but Carter knew at once that man could never have fashioned it. It was a god chiselled by the hands of the gods, and it looked down haughty and majestic upon the seeker. Rumour had said it was strange and not to be mistaken, and Carter saw that it was indeed so; for those long narrow eyes and long-lobed ears, and that thin nose and pointed chin, all spoke of a race that is not of men but of gods.

He clung overawed in that lofty and perilous eyrie, even though it was this which he had expected and come to find; for there is in a god's face more of marvel than prediction can tell, and when that face is vaster than a great temple and seen looking downward at sunset in the scyptic silences of that upper world from whose dark lava it was divinely hewn of old, the marvel is so strong that none may escape it.

Here, too, was the added marvel of recognition; for although he had planned to search all dreamland over for those whose likeness to this face might mark them as the god's children, he now knew that he need not do so. Certainly, the great face carven on that mountain was of no strange sort, but the kin of such as he had seen often in the taverns of the seaport Celephaïs which lies in Ooth-Nargai beyond the Tanarian Hills and is ruled over by that King Kuranes whom Carter once knew in waking life. Every year sailors with such a face came in dark ships from the north to trade their onyx for the carved jade and spun gold and little red singing birds of Celephaïs, and it was clear that these could be no others than the half-gods he sought. Where they dwelt, there must the cold waste lie close, and within it unknown Kadath and its onyx castle for the Great Ones. So to Celephaïs he must go, far distant from the isle of Oriab, and in such parts as would take him back to Dylath-Teen and up the Skai to the bridge by Nir, and again into the enchanted wood of the Zoogs, whence the way would bend northward through the garden lands by Oukranos to the gilded spires of Thran, where he might find a galleon bound over the Cerenarian Sea.

But dusk was now thick, and the great carven face looked down even sterner in shadow. Perched on that ledge night found the seeker; and in the blackness he might neither go down nor go up, but only stand and cling and shiver in that narrow place till the day came, praying to keep awake lest sleep loose his hold and send him down the dizzy miles of air to the crags and sharp rocks of the accursed valley. The stars came out, but save for them there was only black nothingness in his eyes; nothingness leagued with death, against whose beckoning he might do no more than cling to the rocks and lean back away from an unseen brink. The last thing of earth that he saw in the gloaming was a condor soaring close to the westward precipice beside him, and darting screaming away when it came near the cave whose mouth yawned just out of reach.

Suddenly, without a warning sound in the dark, Carter felt his curved scimitar drawn stealthily out of his belt by some unseen hand. Then he heard it clatter down over the rocks below. And between him and the Milky Way he thought he saw a very terrible outline of something noxiously thin and horned and tailed and bat-winged. Other things, too, had begun to blot out patches of stars west of him, as if a flock of vague entities were flapping thickly and silently out of that inaccessible cave in the face of the precipice. Then a sort of cold rubbery arm seized his neck and something else seized his feet, and he was lifted inconsiderately up and swung about in space. Another minute and the stars were gone, and Carter knew that the night-gaunts had got him.

They bore him breathless into that cliffside cavern and through monstrous labyrinths beyond. When he struggled, as at first he did by instinct, they tickled him with deliberation. They made no sound at all themselves, and even their membranous wings were silent. They were frightfully cold and damp and slippery, and their paws kneaded one detestably. Soon they were plunging hideously downward through inconceivable abysses in a whirling, giddying, sickening rush of dank, tomb-like air; and Carter felt they were shooting into the ultimate vortex of shrieking and daemonic madness. He screamed again and again, but whenever he did so the black paws tickled him with greater subtlety. Then he saw a sort of grey phosphorescence about, and guessed they were coming even to that inner world of subterrene horror of which dim legends tell, and which is litten only by the pale death-fire wherewith reeks the ghoulish air and the primal mists of the pits at earth's core.

At last far below him he saw faint lines of grey and ominous pinnacles which he knew must be the fabled Peaks of Throk. Awful and sinister they stand in the haunted disc of sunless and eternal depths; higher than man may reckon, and guarding terrible valleys where the Dholes crawl and burrow nastily. But Carter preferred to look at them than at his captors, which were indeed shocking and uncouth black things with smooth, oily, whale-like surfaces, unpleasant horns that curved inward toward each other, bat wings whose beating made no sound, ugly prehensile paws, and barbed tails that lashed needlessly and disquietingly. And worst of all, they never spoke or laughed, and never smiled because they had no faces at all to smile with, but only a suggestive blankness where a face ought to be. All they ever did was clutch and fly and tickle; that was the way of night-gaunts.

As the band flew lower the Peaks of Throk rose grey and towering on all sides, and one saw clearly that nothing lived on that austere and impressive granite of the endless twilight. At still lower levels the death-fires in the air gave out, and one met only the primal blackness of the void save aloft where the thin peaks stood out goblin-like. Soon the peaks were very far away, and nothing about but great rushing winds with the dankness of nethermost grottoes in them. Then in the end the night-gaunts landed on a floor of unseen things which felt like layers of bones, and left Carter all alone in that black valley. To bring him thither was the duty of the night-gaunts that guard Ngranek; and this done, they flapped away silently. When Carter tried to trace their flight he found he could not, since even the Peaks of Throk had faded out of sight. There was nothing anywhere but blackness and horror and silence and bones.

Now Carter knew from a certain source that he was in the vale of Pnoth, where crawl and burrow the enormous Dholes; but he did not know what to expect, because no one has ever seen a Dhole or even guessed what such a thing may be like. Dholes are known only by dim rumour, from the rustling they make amongst mountains of bones and the slimy touch they have when they wriggle past one. They cannot be seen because they creep only in the dark. Carter did not wish to meet a Dhole, so listened intently for any sound in the unknown depths of bones about him. Even in this fearsome place he had a plan and an objective, for whispers of Pnoth were not unknown to one with whom he had talked much in the old days. In brief, it seemed fairly likely that this was the spot into which all the ghouls of the waking world cast the refuse of their feastings; and that if he but had good luck he might stumble upon that mighty crag taller even than Throk's peaks which marks the edge of their domain. Showers of bones would tell him where to look, and once found he could call to a ghoul to let down a ladder; for strange to say, he had a very singular link with these terrible creatures.

A man he had known in Boston — a painter of strange pictures with a secret studio in an ancient and unhallowed alley near a graveyard — had actually made friends with the ghouls and had taught him to understand the simpler part of their disgusting meeping and glibbering. This man had vanished at last, and Carter was not sure but that he might find him now, and use for the first time in dreamland that far-away English of his dim waking life. In any case, he felt he could persuade a ghoul to guide him out of Pnoth; and it would be better to meet a ghoul, which one can see, than a Dhole, which one cannot see.

So Carter walked in the dark, and ran when he thought he heard something among the bones underfoot. Once he bumped into a stony slope, and knew it must be the base of one of Throk's peaks. Then at last he heard a monstrous rattling and clatter which reached far up in the air, and became sure he had come nigh the crag of the ghouls. He was not sure he could be heard from this valley miles below, but realised that the inner world has strange laws. As he pondered he was struck by a flying bone so heavy that it must have been a skull, and therefore realising his nearness to the fateful crag he sent up as best he might that meeping cry which is the call of the ghoul.

Sound travels slowly, so it was some time before he heard an answering glibber. But it came at last, and before long he was told that a rope ladder would be lowered. The wait for this was very tense, since there was no telling what might not have been stirred up among those bones by his shouting. Indeed, it was not long before he actually did hear a vague rustling afar off. As this thoughtfully approached, he became more and more uncomfortable; for he did not wish to move away from the spot where the ladder would come. Finally the tension grew almost unbearable, and he was about to flee in panic when the thud of something on the newly heaped bones nearby drew his notice from the other sound. It was the ladder, and after a minute of groping he had it taut in his hands. But the other sound did not cease, and followed him even as he climbed. He had gone fully five feet from the ground when the rattling beneath waxed emphatic, and was a good ten feet up when something swayed the ladder from below. At a height which must have been fifteen or twenty feet he felt his whole side brushed by a great slippery length which grew alternately convex and concave with wriggling; and hereafter he climbed desperately to escape the unendurable nuzzling of that loathsome and overfed Dhole whose form no man might see.

For hours he climbed with aching and blistered hands, seeing again the grey death-fire and Throk's uncomfortable pinnacles. At last he discerned above him the projecting edge of the great crag of the ghouls, whose vertical side he could not glimpse; and hours later he saw a curious face peering over it as a gargoyle peers over a parapet of Notre Dame. This almost made him lose his hold through faintness, but a moment later he was himself again; for his vanished friend Richard Pickman had once introduced him to a ghoul, and he knew well their canine faces and slumping forms and unmentionable idiosyncrasies. So he had himself well under control when that hideous thing pulled him out of the dizzy emptiness over the edge of the crag, and did not scream at the partly consumed refuse heaped at one side or at the squatting circles of ghouls who gnawed and watched curiously.

He was now on a dim-litten plain whose sole topographical features were great boulders and the entrances of burrows. The ghouls were in general respectful, even if one did attempt to pinch him while several others eyed his leanness speculatively. Through patient glibbering he made inquiries regarding his vanished friend, and found he had become a ghoul of some prominence in abysses nearer the waking world. A greenish elderly ghoul offered to conduct him to Pickman's present habitation, so despite a natural loathing he followed the creature into a capacious burrow and crawled after him for hours in the blackness of rank mould. They emerged on a dim plain strewn with singular relics of earth — old gravestones, broken urns, and grotesque fragments of monuments — and Carter realised with some emotion that he was probably nearer the waking world than at any other time since he had gone down the seven hundred steps from the cavern of flame to the Gate of Deeper Slumber.

There, on a tombstone of 1768 stolen from the Granary Burying Ground in Boston, sat a ghoul which was once the artist Richard Upton Pickman. It was naked and rubbery, and had acquired so much of the ghoulish physiognomy that its human origin was already obscure. But it still remembered a little English, and was able to converse with Carter in grunts and monosyllables, helped out now and then by the glibbering of ghouls. When it learned that Carter wished to get to the enchanted wood and from there to the city Celephaïs in Ooth-Nargai beyond the Tanarian Hills, it seemed rather doubtful; for these ghouls of the waking world do no business in the graveyards of upper dreamland (leaving that to the red-footed wamps that are spawned in dead cities), and many things intervene betwixt their gulf and the enchanted wood, including the terrible kingdom of the Gugs.

The Gugs, hairy and gigantic, once reared stone circles in that wood and made strange sacrifices to the Other Gods and the crawling chaos Nyarlathotep, until one night an abomination of theirs reached the ears of earth's gods and they were banished to caverns below. Only a great trap door of stone with an iron ring connects the abyss of the earth-ghouls with the enchanted wood, and this the Gugs are afraid to open because of a curse. That a mortal dreamer could traverse their cavern realm and leave by that door is inconceivable; for mortal dreamers were their former food, and they have legends of the toothsomeness of such dreamers even though banishment has restricted their diet to the ghasts, those repulsive beings which die in the light, and which live in the vaults of Zin and leap on long hind legs like kangaroos.

So the ghoul that was Pickman advised Carter either to leave the abyss at Sarkomand, that deserted city in the valley below Leng where black nitrous stairways guarded by winged diarote lions lead down from dreamland to the lower gulfs, or to return through a churchyard to the waking world and begin the quest anew down the seventy steps of light slumber to the cavern of flame and the seven hundred steps to the Gate of Deeper Slumber and the enchanted wood. This, however, did not suit the seeker; for he knew nothing of the way from Leng to Ooth-Nargai, and was likewise reluctant to awake lest he forget all he had so far gained in this dream. It was disastrous to his quest to forget the august and celestial faces of those seamen from the north who traded onyx in Celephaïs, and who, being the sons of gods, must point the way to the cold waste and Kadath where the Great Ones dwell.

After much persuasion the ghoul consented to guide his guest inside the great wall of the Gugs' kingdom. There was one chance that Carter might be able to steal through that twilight realm of circular stone towers at an hour when the giants would be all gorged and snoring indoors, and reach the central tower with the sign of Koth upon it, which has the stairs leading up to that stone trap door in the enchanted wood. Pickman even consented to lend three ghouls to help with a tombstone lever in raising the stone door; for of ghouls the Gugs are somewhat afraid, and they often flee from their own colossal graveyards when they see them feasting there.

He also advised Carter to disguise as a ghoul himself; shaving the beard he had allowed to grow (for ghouls have none), wallowing naked in the mould to get the correct surface, and loping in the usual slumping way, with his clothing carried in a bundle as if it were a choice morsel from a tomb. They would reach the city of Gugs — which is coterminous with the whole kingdom — through the proper burrows, emerging in a cemetery not far from the stair-containing Tower of Koth. They must beware, however, of a large cave near the cemetery; for this is the mouth of the vaults of Zin, and the vindictive ghasts are always on watch there murderously for those denizens of the upper abyss who hunt and prey on them. The ghasts try to come out when the Gugs sleep and they attack ghouls as readily as Gugs, for they cannot discriminate. They are very primitive, and eat one another. The Gugs have a sentry at a narrow in the vaults of Zin, but he is often drowsy and is sometimes surprised by a party of ghasts. Though ghasts cannot live in real light, they can endure the grey twilight of the abyss for hours.

So at length Carter crawled through endless burrows with three helpful ghouls bearing the slate gravestone of Col. Nepemiah Derby, obit 1719, from the Charter Street Burying Ground in Salem. When they came again into open twilight they were in a forest of vast lichened monoliths reaching nearly as high as the eye could see and forming the modest gravestones of the Gugs. On the right of the hole out of which they wriggled, and seen through aisles of monoliths, was a stupendous vista of cyclopean round towers mounting up illimitable into the grey air of inner earth. This was the great city of the Gugs, whose doorways are thirty feet high. Ghouls come here often, for a buried Gug will feed a community for almost a year, and even with the added peril it is better to burrow for Gugs than to bother with the graves of men. Carter now understood the occasional titan bones he had felt beneath him in the vale of Pnoth.

Straight ahead, and just outside the cemetery, rose a sheer perpendicular cliff at whose base an immense and forbidding cavern yawned. This the ghouls told Carter to avoid as much as possible, since it was the entrance to the unhallowed vaults of Zin where Gugs hunt ghasts in the darkness. And truly, that warning was soon well justified; for the moment a ghoul began to creep toward the towers to see if the hour of the Gugs' resting had been rightly timed, there glowed in the gloom of that great cavern's mouth first one pair of yellowish-red eyes and then another, implying that the Gugs were one sentry less, and that ghasts have indeed an excellent sharpness of smell. So the ghoul returned to the burrow and motioned his companions to be silent. It was best to leave the ghasts to their own devices, and there was a possibility that they might soon withdraw, since they must naturally be rather tired after coping with a Gug sentry in the black vaults. After a moment something about the size of a small horse hopped out into the grey twilight, and Carter turned sick at the aspect of that scabrous and unwholesome beast, whose face is so curiously human despite the absence of a nose, a forehead, and other important particulars.

Presently three other ghasts hopped out to join their fellow, and a ghoul glibbered softly at Carter that their absence of battle-scars was a bad sign. It proved that they had not fought the Gug sentry at all, but had merely slipped past him as he slept, so that their strength and savagery were still unimpaired and would remain so till they had found and disposed of a victim. It was very unpleasant to see those filthy and disproportioned animals which soon numbered about fifteen, grubbing about and making their kangaroo leaps in the grey twilight where titan towers and monoliths arose, but it was still more unpleasant when they spoke among themselves in the coughing gutturals of ghasts. And yet, horrible as they were, they were not so horrible as what presently came out of the cave after them with disconcerting suddenness.

It was a paw, fully two feet and a half across, and equipped with formidable talons. After it came another paw, and after that a great black-furred arm to which both of the paws were attached by short forearms. Then two pink eyes shone, and the head of the awakened Gug sentry, large as a barrel, wabbled into view. The eyes jutted two inches from each side, shaded by bony protuberances overgrown with coarse hairs. But the head was chiefly terrible because of the mouth. That mouth had great yellow fangs and ran from the top to the bottom of the head, opening vertically instead of horizontally.

But before that unfortunate Gug could emerge from the cave and rise to his full twenty feet, the vindictive ghasts were upon him. Carter feared for a moment that he would give an alarm and arouse all his kin, till a ghoul softly glibbered that Gugs have no voice but talk by means of facial expression. The battle which then ensued was truly a frightful one. From all sides the venomous ghasts rushed feverishly at the creeping Gug, nipping and tearing with their muzzles, and mauling murderously with their hard pointed hooves. All the time they coughed excitedly, screaming when the great vertical mouth of the Gug would occasionally bite into one of their number, so that the noise of the combat would surely have aroused the sleeping city had not the weakening of the sentry begun to transfer the action farther and farther within the cavern. As it was, the tumult soon receded altogether from sight in the blackness, with only occasional evil echoes to mark its continuance.

Then the most alert of the ghouls gave the signal for all to advance, and Carter followed the loping three out of the forest of monoliths and into the dark noisome streets of that awful city whose rounded towers of cyclopean stone soared up beyond the sight. Silently they shambled over that rough rock pavement, hearing with disgust the abominable muffled snortings from great black doorways which marked the slumber of the Gugs. Apprehensive of the ending of the rest hour, the ghouls set a somewhat rapid pace; but even so the journey was no brief one, for distances in that town of giants are on a great scale. At last, however, they came to a somewhat open space before a tower even vaster than the rest; above whose colossal doorway was fixed a monstrous symbol in bas-relief which made one shudder without knowing its meaning. This was the central tower with the sign of Koth, and those huge stone steps just visible through the dusk within were the beginning of the great flight leading to upper dreamland and the enchanted wood.

There now began a climb of interminable length in utter blackness: made almost impossible by the monstrous size of the steps, which were fashioned for Gugs, and were therefore nearly a yard high. Of their number Carter could form no just estimate, for he soon became so worn out that the tireless and elastic ghouls were forced to aid him. All through the endless climb there lurked the peril of detection and pursuit; for though no Gug dares lift the stone door to the forest because of the Great One's curse, there are no such restraints concerning the tower and the steps, and escaped ghasts are often chased, even to the very top. So sharp are the ears of Gugs, that the bare feet and hands of the climbers might readily be heard when the city awoke; and it would of course take but little time for the striding giants, accustomed from their ghast-hunts in the vaults of Zin to seeing without light, to overtake their smaller and slower quarry on those cyclopean steps. It was very depressing to reflect that the silent pursuing Gugs would not be heard at all, but would come very suddenly and shockingly in the dark upon the climbers. Nor could the traditional fear of Gugs for ghouls be depended upon in that peculiar place where the advantages lay so heavily with the Gugs. There was also some peril from the furtive and venomous ghasts, which frequently hopped up onto the tower during the sleep hour of the Gugs. If the Gugs slept long, and the ghasts returned soon from their deed in the cavern, the scent of the climbers might easily be picked up by those loathsome and ill-disposed things; in which case it would almost be better to be eaten by a Gug.

Then, after aeons of climbing, there came a cough from the darkness above; and matters assumed a very grave and unexpected turn.

It was clear that a ghast, or perhaps even more, had strayed into that tower before the coming of Carter and his guides; and it was equally clear that this peril was very close. After a breathless second the leading ghoul pushed Carter to the wall and arranged his kinfolk in the best possible way, with the old slate tombstone raised for a crushing blow whenever the enemy might come in sight. Ghouls can see in the dark, so the party was not as badly off as Carter would have been alone. In another moment the clatter of hooves revealed the downward hopping of at least one beast, and the slab-bearing ghouls poised their weapon for a desperate blow. Presently two yellowish-red eyes flashed into view, and the panting of the ghast became audible above its clattering. As it hopped down to the step above the ghouls, they wielded the ancient gravestone with prodigious force, so that there was only a wheeze and a choking before the victim collapsed in a noxious heap.

There seemed to be only this one animal, and after a moment of listening the ghouls tapped Carter as a signal to proceed again. As before, they were obliged to aid him; and he was glad to leave that place of carnage where the ghast's uncouth remains sprawled invisible in the blackness.

At last the ghouls brought their companion to a halt; and feeling above him, Carter realised that the great stone trap door was reached at last. To open so vast a thing completely was not to be thought of, but the ghouls hoped to get it up just enough to slip the gravestone under as a prop, and permit Carter to escape through the crack. They themselves planned to descend again and return through the city of the Gugs, since their elusiveness was great, and they did not know the way overland to spectral Sarkomand with its lion-guarded gate to the abyss.

Mighty was the straining of those three ghouls at the stone of the door above them, and Carter helped push with as much strength as he had. They judged the edge next the top of the staircase to be the right one, and to this they bent all the force of their disreputably nourished muscles. After a few moments a crack of light appeared; and Carter, to whom that task had been entrusted, slipped the end of the old gravestone in the aperture. There now ensued a mighty heaving; but progress was very slow, and they had of course to return to their first position every time they failed to turn the slab and prop the portal open.

Suddenly their desperation was magnified a thousand fold by a sound on the steps below them. It was only the thumping and rattling of the slain ghast's hooved body as it rolled down to lower levels; but of all the possible causes of that body's dislodgement and rolling, none was in the least reassuring. Therefore, knowing the ways of Gugs, the ghouls set to with something of a frenzy; and in a surprisingly short time had the door so high that they were able to hold it still whilst Carter turned the slab and left a generous opening. They now helped Carter through, letting him climb up to their rubbery shoulders and later guiding his feet as he clutched at the blessed soil of the upper dreamland outside. Another second and they were through themselves, knocking away the gravestone and closing the great trap door while a panting became audible beneath. Because of the Great One's curse no Gug might ever emerge from that portal, so with a deep relief and sense of repose Carter lay quietly on the thick grotesque fungi of the enchanted wood while his guides squatted near in the manner that ghouls rest.

Weird as was that enchanted wood through which he had fared so long ago, it was verily a haven and a delight after those gulfs he had now left behind. There was no living denizen about, for Zoogs shun the mysterious door in fear and Carter at once consulted with his ghouls about their future course. To return through the tower they no longer dared, and the waking world did not appeal to them when they learned that they must pass the priests Nasht and Kaman-Thah in the cavern of flame. So at length they decided to return through Sarkomand and its gate of the abyss, though of how to get there they knew nothing. Carter recalled that it lies in the valley below Leng, and recalled likewise that he had seen in Dylath-Leen a sinister, slant-eyed old merchant reputed to trade on Leng, therefore he advised the ghouls to seek out Dylath-Leen, crossing the fields to Nir and the Skai and following the river to its mouth. This they at once resolved to do, and lost no time in loping off, since the thickening of the dusk promised a full night ahead for travel. And Carter shook the paws of those repulsive beasts, thanking them for their help and sending his gratitude to the beast which once was Pickman; but could not help sighing with pleasure when they left. For a ghoul is a ghoul, and at best an unpleasant companion for man. After that Carter sought a forest pool and cleansed himself of the mud of nether earth, thereupon reassuming the clothes he had so carefully carried.

It was now night in that redoubtable wood of monstrous trees, but because of the phosphorescence one might travel as well as by day; wherefore Carter set out upon the well-known route toward Celephaïs, in Ooth-Nargai beyond the Tanarian Hills. And as he went he thought of the zebra he had left tethered to an ash-tree on Ngranek in far-away Oriab so many aeons ago, and wondered if any lava-gatherers had fed and released it. And he wondered, too, if he would ever return to Baharna and pay for the zebra that was slain by night in those ancient ruins by Yath's shore, and if the old tavernkeeper would remember him. Such were the thoughts that came to him in the air of the regained upper dreamland.

But presently his progress was halted by a sound from a very large hollow tree. He had avoided the great circle of stones, since he did not care to speak with Zoogs just now; but it appeared from the singular fluttering in that huge tree that important councils were in session elsewhere. Upon drawing nearer he made out the accents of a tense and heated discussion; and before long became conscious of matters which he viewed with the greatest concern. For a war on the cats was under debate in that sovereign assembly of Zoogs. It all came from the loss of the party which had sneaked after Carter to Ulthar, and which the cats had justly punished for unsuitable intentions. The matter had long rankled; and now, or at least within a month, the marshalled Zoogs were about to strike the whole feline tribe in a series of surprise attacks, taking individual cats or groups of cats unawares, and giving not even the myriad cats of Ulthar a proper chance to drill and mobilise. This was the plan of the Zoogs, and Carter saw that he must foil it before leaving upon his mighty quest.

Very quietly therefore did Randolph Carter steal to the edge of the wood and send the cry of the cat over the starlit fields. And a great grimalkin in a nearby cottage took up the burden and relayed it across leagues of rolling meadow to warriors large and small, black, grey, tiger, white, yellow, and mixed, and it echoed through Nir and beyond the Skai even into Ulthar, and Ulthar's numerous cats called in chorus and fell into a line of march. It was fortunate that the moon was not up, so that all the cats were on earth. Swiftly and silently leaping, they sprang from every hearth and housetop and poured in a great furry sea across the plains to the edge of the wood. Carter was there to greet them, and the sight of shapely, wholesome cats was indeed good for his eyes after the things he had seen and walked with in the abyss. He was glad to see his venerable friend and one-time rescuer at the head of Ulthar's detachment, a collar of rank around his sleek neck, and whiskers bristling at a martial angle. Better still, as a sub-lieutenant in that army was a brisk young fellow who proved to be none other than the very little kitten at the inn to whom Carter had given a saucer of rich cream on that long-vanished morning in Ulthar. He was a strapping and promising cat now, and purred as he shook hands with his friend. His grandfather said he was doing very well in the army, and that he might well expect a captaincy after one more campaign.

Carter now outlined the peril of the cat tribe, and was rewarded by deep-throated purrs of gratitude from all sides. Consulting with the generals, he prepared a plan of instant action which involved marching at once upon the Zoog council and other known strongholds of Zoogs; forestalling their surprise attacks and forcing them to terms before the mobilization of their army of invasion. Thereupon without a moment's loss that great ocean of cats flooded the enchanted wood and surged around the council tree and the great stone circle. Flutterings rose to panic pitch as the enemy saw the newcomers and there was very little resistance among the furtive and curious brown Zoogs. They saw that they were beaten in advance, and turned from thoughts of vengeance to thoughts of present self-preservation.

Half the cats now seated themselves in a circular formation with the captured Zoogs in the centre, leaving open a lane down which were marched the additional captives rounded up by the other cats in other parts of the wood. Terms were discussed at length, Carter acting as interpreter, and it was decided that the Zoogs might remain a free tribe on condition of rendering to the cats a large tribute of grouse, quail, and pheasants from the less fabulous parts of the forest. Twelve young Zoogs of noble families were taken as hostages to be kept in the Temple of Cats at Ulthar, and the victors made it plain that any disappearances of cats on the borders of the Zoog domain would be followed by consequences highly disastrous to Zoogs. These matters disposed of, the assembled cats broke ranks and permitted the Zoogs to slink off one by one to their respective homes, which they hastened to do with many a sullen backward glance.

The old cat general now offered Carter an escort through the forest to whatever border he wished to reach, deeming it likely that the Zoogs would harbour dire resentment against him for the frustration of their warlike enterprise. This offer he welcomed with gratitude; not only for the safety it afforded, but because he liked the graceful companionship of cats. So in the midst of a pleasant and playful regiment, relaxed after the successful performance of its duty, Randolph Carter walked with dignity through that enchanted and phosphorescent wood of titan trees, talking of his quest with the old general and his grandson whilst others of the band indulged in fantastic gambols or chased fallen leaves that the wind drove among the fungi of that primeval floor. And the old cat said that he had heard much of unknown Kadath in the cold waste, but did not know where it was. As for the marvellous sunset city, he had not even heard of that, but would gladly relay to Carter anything he might later learn.

He gave the seeker some passwords of great value among the cats of dreamland, and commended him especially to the old chief of the cats in Celephaïs, whither he was bound. That old cat, already slightly known to Carter, was a dignified maltese; and would prove highly influential in any transaction.

It was dawn when they came to the proper edge of the wood, and Carter bade his friends a reluctant farewell. The young sub-lieutenant he had met as a small kitten would have followed him had not the old general forbidden it, but that austere patriarch insisted that the path of duty lay with the tribe and the army. So Carter set out alone over the golden fields that stretched mysterious beside a willow-fringed river, and the cats went back into the wood.

Well did the traveller know those garden lands that lie betwixt the wood of the Cerenerian Sea, and blithely did he follow the singing river Oukianos that marked his course. The sun rose higher over gentle slopes of grove and lawn, and heightened the colours of the thousand flowers that starred each knoll and dangle. A blessed haze lies upon all this region, wherein is held a little more of the sunlight than other places hold, and a little more of the summer's humming music of birds and bees; so that men walk through it as through a faery place, and feel greater joy and wonder than they ever afterward remember.

By noon Carter reached the jasper terraces of Kiran which slope down to the river's edge and bear that temple of loveliness wherein the King of Ilek-Vad comes from his far realm on the twilight sea once a year in a golden palanquin to pray to the god of Oukianos, who sang to him in youth when he dwelt in a cottage by its banks. All of jasper is that temple, and covering an acre of ground with its walls and courts, its seven pinnacled towers, and its inner shrine where the river enters through hidden channels and the god sings softly in the night. Many times the moon hears strange music as it shines on those courts and terraces and pinnacles, but whether that music be the song of the god or the chant of the cryptical priests, none but the King of Ilek-Vad may say; for only he had entered the temple or seen the priests. Now, in the drowsiness of day, that carven and delicate fane was silent, and Carter heard only the murmur of the great stream and the hum of the birds and bees as he walked onward under the enchanted sun.

All that afternoon the pilgrim wandered on through perfumed meadows and in the lee of gentle riverward hills bearing peaceful thatched cottages and the shrines of amiable gods carven from jasper or chrysoberyl. Sometimes he walked close to the bank of Oukianos and whistled to the sprightly and iridescent fish of that crystal stream, and at other times he paused amidst the whispering rushes and gazed at the great dark wood on the farther side, whose trees came down clear to the water's edge. In former dreams he had seen quaint lumbering buopoths come shyly out of that wood to drink, but now he could not glimpse any. Once in a while he paused to watch a carnivorous fish catch a fishing bird, which it lured to the water by showing its tempting scales in the sun, and grasped by the beak with its enormous mouth as the winged hunter sought to dart down upon it.

Toward evening he mounted a low grassy rise and saw before him flaming in the sunset the thousand gilded spires of Thran. Lofty beyond belief are the alabaster walls of that incredible city, sloping inward toward the top and wrought in one solid piece by what means no man knows, for they are more ancient than memory. Yet lofty as they are with their hundred gates and two hundred turrets, the clustered towers within, all white beneath their golden spires, are loftier still; so that men on the plain around see them soaring into the sky, sometimes shining clear, sometimes caught at the top in tangles of cloud and mist, and sometimes clouded lower down with their utmost pinnacles blazing free above the vapours. And where Thran's gates open on the river are great wharves of marble, with ornate galleons of fragrant cedar and calamander riding gently at anchor, and strange bearded sailors sitting on casks and bales with the hieroglyphs of far places. Landward beyond the walls lies the farm country, where small white cottages dream between little hills, and narrow roads with many stone bridges wind gracefully among streams and gardens.

Down through this verdant land Carter walked at evening, and saw twilight float up from the river to the marvellous golden spires of Thran. And just at the hour of dusk he came to the southern gate, and was stopped by a red-robed sentry till he had told three dreams beyond belief, and proved himself a dreamer worthy to walk up Thran's steep mysterious streets and linger in the bazaars where the wares of the ornate galleons were sold. Then into that incredible city he walked; through a wall so thick that the gate was a tunnel, and thereafter amidst curved and undulant ways winding deep and narrow between the heavenward towers. Lights shone through grated and balconied windows, and the sound of lutes and pipes stole timid from inner courts where marble fountains bubbled. Carter knew his way, and edged down through darker streets to the river, where at an old sea tavern he found the captains and seamen he had known in myriad other dreams. There he bought his passage to Celephaïs on a great green galleon, and there he stopped for the night after speaking gravely to the venerable cat of that inn, who blinked dozing before an enormous hearth and dreamed of old wars and forgotten gods.

In the morning Carter boarded the galleon bound for Celephaïs, and sat in the prow as the ropes were cast off and the long sail down to the Cerenerian Sea begun. For many leagues the banks were much as they were above Thran, with now and then a curious temple rising on the farther hills toward the right, and a drowsy village on the shore, with steep red roofs and nets spread in the sun. Mindful of his search, Carter questioned all the mariners closely about those whom they had met in the taverns of Celephaïs, asking the names and ways of the strange men with long, narrow eyes, long-lobed ears, thin noses, and pointed chins who came in dark ships from the north and traded onyx for the carved jade and spun gold and little red singing birds of Celephaïs. Of these men the sailors knew not much, save that they talked but seldom and spread a kind of awe about them.

Their land, very far away, was called Inquanok, and not many people cared to go thither because it was a cold twilight land, and said to be close to unpleasant Leng; although high impassable mountains towered on the side where Leng was thought to lie, so that none might say whether this evil plateau with its horrible stone villages and unmentionable monastery were really there, or whether the rumour were only a fear that timid people felt in the night when those formidable barrier peaks loomed black against a rising moon. Certainly, men reached Leng from very different oceans. Of other boundaries of Inquanok those sailors had no notion, nor had they heard of the cold waste and unknown Kadath save from vague unplaced report. And of the marvellous sunset city which Carter sought they knew nothing at all. So the traveller asked no more of far things, but bided his time till he might talk with those strange men from cold and twilight Inquanok who are the seed of such gods as carved their features on Ngranek.

Late in the day the galleon reached those bends of the river which traverse the perfumed jungles of Kied. Here Carter wished he might disembark, for in those tropic tangles sleep wondrous palaces of ivory, lone and unbroken, where once dwelt fabulous monarchs of a land whose name is forgotten. Spells of the Elder Ones keep those places unharmed and undecayed, for it is written that there may one day be need of them again; and elephant caravans have glimpsed them from afar by moonlight, though none dares approach them closely because of the guardians to which their wholeness is due. But the ship swept on, and dusk hushed the hum of the day, and the first stars above blinked answers to the early fireflies on the banks as that jungle fell far behind, leaving only its fragrance as a memory that it had been. And all through the night that galleon floated on past mysteries unseen and unsuspected. Once a lookout reported fires on the hills to the east, but the sleepy captain said they had better not be looked at too much, since it was highly uncertain just who or what had lit them.

In the morning the river had broadened out greatly, and Carter saw by the houses along the banks that they were close to the vast trading city of Hlanith on the Cerenerian Sea. Here the walls are of rugged granite, and the houses peakedly fantastic with beamed and plastered gables. The men of Hlanith are more like those of the waking world than any others in dreamland; so that the city is not sought except for barter, but is prized for the solid work of its artisans. The wharves of Hlanith are of oak, and there the galleon made fast while the captain traded in the taverns. Carter also went ashore, and looked curiously upon the rutted streets where wooden ox carts lumbered and feverish merchants cried their wares vacuously in the bazaars. The sea taverns were all close to the wharves on cobbled lanes salted with the spray of high tides, and seemed exceedingly ancient with their low black-beamed ceilings and casements of greenish bull's-eye panes. Ancient sailors in those taverns talked much of distant ports, and told many stories of the curious men from twilight Inquanok, but had little to add to what the seamen of the galleon had told. Then at last, after much unloading and loading, the ship set sail once more over the sunset sea, and the high walls and gables of Hlanith grew less as the last golden light of day lent them a wonder and beauty beyond any that men had given them.

Two nights and two days the galleon sailed over the Cerenerian Sea, sighting no land and speaking but one other vessel. Then near sunset of the second day there loomed up ahead the snowy peak of Aran with its gingko-trees swaying on the lower slope, and Carter knew that they were come to the land of Ooth-Nargai and the marvellous city of Celephaïs. Swiftly there came into sight the glittering minarets of that fabulous town, and the untarnished marble walls with their bronze statues, and the great stone bridge where Naraxa joins the sea. Then rose the gentle hills behind the town, with their groves and gardens of asphodels and the small shrines and cottages upon them; and far in the background the purple ridge of the Tanarians, potent and mystical, behind which lay forbidden ways into the waking world and toward other regions of dream.

The harbour was full of painted galleys, some of which were from the marble cloud-city of Serannian, that lies in ethereal space beyond where the sea meets the sky, and some of which were from more substantial parts of dreamland. Among these the steersman threaded his way up to the spice-fragrant wharves, where the galleon made fast in the dusk as the city's million lights began to twinkle out over the water. Ever new seemed this deathless city of vision, for here time has no power to tarnish or destroy. As it has always been is still the turquoise of Nath-Horthath, and the eighty orchid-wreathed priests are the same who builded it ten thousand years ago. Shining still is the bronze of the great gates, nor are the onyx pavements ever worn or broken. And the great bronze statues on the walls look down on merchants and camel drivers older than fable, yet without one grey hair in their forked beards.

Carter did not once seek out the temple or the palace or the citadel, but stayed by the seaward wall among traders and sailors. And when it was too late for rumours and legends he sought out an ancient tavern he knew well, and rested with dreams of the gods on unknown Kadath whom he sought.

The next day he searched all along the quays for some of the strange mariners of Inquanok, but was told that none were now in port, their galley not being due from the north for full two weeks. He found, however, one Thorabonian sailor who had been to Inquanok and had worked in the onyx quarries of that twilight place; and this sailor said there was certainly a descent to the north of the peopled region, which everybody seemed to fear and shun. The Thorabonian opined that this desert led around the utmost rim of impassable peaks into Leng's horrible plateau, and that this was why men feared it; though he admitted there were other vague tales of evil presences and nameless sentinels. Whether or not this could be the fabled waste wherein unknown Kadath stands he did not know; but it seemed unlikely that those presences and sentinels, if indeed they existed, were stationed for nought.

On the following day Carter walked up the Street of the Pillars to the turquoise temple and talked with the High-Priest. Though Nath-Horthath is chiefly worshipped in Celephaïs, all the Great Ones are mentioned in diurnal prayers; and the priest was reasonably versed in their moods. Like Atal in distant Ulthar, he strongly advised against any attempts to see them; declaring that they are testy and capricious, and subject to strange protection from the mindless Other Gods from Outside, whose soul and messenger is the crawling chaos Nyarlathotep. Their jealous hiding of the marvellous sunset city shewed clearly that they did not wish Carter to reach it, and it was doubtful how they would regard a guest whose object was to see them and plead before them. No man had ever found Kadath in the past, and it might be just as well if none ever found it in the future. Such rumours as were told about that onyx castle of the Great Ones were not by any means reassuring.

Having thanked the orchid-crowned High-Priest, Carter left the temple and sought out the bazaar of the sheep-butchers, where the old chief of Celephaïs' cats dwelt sleek and contented. That grey and dignified being was sunning himself on the onyx pavement, and extended a languid paw as his caller approached. But when Carter repeated the passwords and introductions furnished him by the old cat general of Ulthar, the furry patriarch became very cordial and communicative; and told much of the secret lore known to cats on the seaward slopes of Ooth-Nargai. Best of all, he repeated several things told him furtively by the timid waterfront cats of Celephaïs about the men of Inquanok, on whose dark ships no cat will go.

It seems that these men have an aura not of earth about them, though that is not the reason why no cat will sail on their ships. The reason for this is that Inquanok holds shadows which no cat can endure, so that in all that cold twilight realm there is never a cheering purr or a homely mew. Whether it be because of things wafted over the impassable peaks from hypothetical Leng, or because of things filtering down from the chilly desert to the north, none may say; but it remains a fact that in that far land there broods a hint of outer space which cats do not like, and to which they are more sensitive than men. Therefore they will not go on the dark ships that seek the basalt quays of Inquanok.

The old chief of the cats also told him where to find his friend King Kuranes, who in Carter's latter dreams had reigned alternately in the rose-crystal Palace of the Seventy Delights at Celephaïs and in the turreted cloud-castle of sky-floating Serannian. It seemed that he could no more find content in those places, but had formed a mighty longing for the English cliffs and downlands of his boyhood; where in little dreaming villages England's old songs hover at evening behind lattice windows, and where grey church towers peep lovely through the verdure of distant valleys. He could not go back to these things in the waking world because his body was dead; but he had done the next best thing and dreamed a small tract of such countryside in the region east of the city where meadows roll gracefully up from the sea-cliffs to the foot of the Tanarian Hills. There he dwelt in a grey Gothic manor-house of stone looking on the sea, and tried to think it was ancient Trevor Towers, where he was born and where thirteen generations of his forefathers had first seen the light. And on the coast nearby he had built a little Cornish fishing village with steep cobbled ways, settling therein such people as had the most English faces, and seeking ever to teach them the dear remembered accents of old Cornwall fishers. And in a valley not far off he had reared a great Norman Abbey whose tower he could see from his window, placing around it in the churchyard grey stones with the names of his ancestors carved thereon, and with a moss somewhat like Old England's moss. For though Kuranes was a monarch in the land of dream, with all imagined pomps and marvels, splendours and beauties, ecstasies and delights, novelties and excitements at his command, he would gladly have resigned forever the whole of his power and luxury and freedom for one blessed day as a simple boy in that pure and quiet England, that ancient, beloved England which had moulded his being and of which he must always be immutably a part.

So when Carter bade that old grey chief of the cats adieu, he did not seek the terraced palace of rose crystal but walked out the eastern gate and across the daisied fields toward a peaked gable which he glimpsed through the oaks of a park sloping up to the sea-cliffs. And in time he came to a great hedge and a gate with a little brick lodge, and when he rang the bell there hobbled to admit him no robed and annointed lackey of the palace, but a small stubby old man in a smock who spoke as best he could in the quaint tones of far Cornwall. And Carter walked up the shady path between trees as near as possible to England's trees, and climbed the terraces among gardens set out as in Queen Anne's time. At the door, flanked by stone cats in the old way, he was met by a whiskered butler in suitable livery; and was presently taken to the library where Kuranes, Lord of Ooth-Nargai and the Sky around Serannian, sat pensive in a chair by the window looking on his little seacoast village and wishing that his old nurse would come in and scold him because he was not ready for that hateful lawn-party at the vicar's, with the carriage waiting and his mother nearly out of patience.

Kuranes, clad in a dressing gown of the sort favoured by London tailors in his youth, rose eagerly to meet his guest; for the sight of an Anglo-Saxon from the waking world was very dear to him, even if it was a Saxon from Boston, Massachusetts, instead of from Cornwall. And for long they talked of old times, having much to say because both were old dreamers and well versed in the wonders of incredible places. Kuranes, indeed, had been out beyond the stars in the ultimate void, and was said to be the only one who had ever returned sane from such a voyage.

At length Carter brought up the subject of his quest, and asked of his host those questions he had asked of so many others. Kuranes did not know where Kadath was, or the marvellous sunset city; but he did know that the Great Ones were very dangerous creatures to seek out, and that the Other Gods had strange ways of protecting them from impertinent curiosity. He had learned much of the Other Gods in distant parts of space, especially in that region where form does not exist, and coloured gases study the innermost secrets. The violet gas S'ngac had told him terrible things of the crawling chaos Nyarlathotep, and had warned him never to approach the central void where the daemon sultan Azathoth gnaws hungrily in the dark.

Altogether, it was not well to meddle with the Elder Ones; and if they persistently denied all access to the marvellous sunset city, it were better not to seek that city.

Kuranes furthermore doubted whether his guest would profit aught by coming to the city even were he to gain it. He himself had dreamed and yearned long years for lovely Celephaïs and the land of Ooth-Nargai, and for the freedom and colour and high experience of life devoid of its chains, and conventions, and stupidities. But now that he was come into that city and that land, and was the king thereof, he found the freedom and the vividness all too soon worn out, and monotonous for want of linkage with anything firm in his feelings and memories. He was a king in Ooth-Nargai, but found no meaning therein, and drooped always for the old familiar things of England that had shaped his youth. All his kingdom would he give for the sound of Cornish church bells over the downs, and all the thousand minarets of Celephais for the steep homely roofs of the village near his home. So he told his guest that the unknown sunset city might not hold quite that content he sought, and that perhaps it had better remain a glorious and half-remembered dream. For he had visited Carter often in the old waking days, and knew well the lovely New England slopes that had given him birth.

At the last, he was very certain, the seeker would long only for the early remembered scenes; the glow of Beacon Hill at evening, the tall steeples and winding hill streets of quaint Kingsport, the hoary gambrel roofs of ancient and witch-haunted Arkham, and the blessed meads and valleys where stone walls rambled and white farmhouse gables peeped out from bowers of verdure. These things he told Randolph Carter, but still the seeker held to his purpose. And in the end they parted each with his own conviction, and Carter went back through the bronze gate into Celephaïs and down the Street of Pillars to the old sea wall, where he talked more with the mariners of far ports and waited for the dark ship from cold and twilight Inquanok, whose strange-faced sailors and onyx-traders had in them the blood of the Great Ones.

One starlit evening when the pharos shone splendid over the harbour the longed-for ship put in, and strange-faced sailors and traders appeared one by one and group by group in the ancient taverns along the sea wall. It was very exciting to see again those living faces so like the godlike features of Ngranek, but Carter did not hasten to speak with the silent seamen. He did not know how much of pride and secrecy and dim supernal memory might fill those children of the Great Ones, and was sure it would not be wise to tell them of his quest or ask too closely of that cold desert stretching north of their twilight land. They talked little with the other folk in those ancient sea taverns; but would gather in groups in remote comers and sing among themselves the haunting airs of unknown places, or chant long tales to one another in accents alien to the rest of dreamland. And so rare and moving were those airs and tales that one might guess their wonders from the faces of those who listened, even though the words came to common ears only as strange cadence and obscure melody.

For a week the strange seamen lingered in the taverns and traded in the bazaars of Celephaïs, and before they sailed Carter had taken passage on their dark ship, telling them that he was an old onyx miner and wishful to work in their quarries. That ship was very lovely and cunningly wrought, being of teakwood with ebony fittings and traceries of gold, and the cabin in which the traveller lodged had hangings of silk and velvet. One morning at the turn of the tide the sails were raised and the anchor lifted, and as Carter stood on the high stern he saw the sunrise-blazing walls and bronze statues and golden minarets of ageless Celephaïs sink into the distance, and the snowy peak of Mount Man grow smaller and smaller. By noon there was nothing in sight save the gentle blue of the Cerenerian Sea, with one painted galley afar off bound for that realm of Serannian where the sea meets the sky.

And the night came with gorgeous stars, and the dark ship steered for Charles' Wain and the Little Bear as they swung slowly round the pole. And the sailors sang strange songs of unknown places, and they stole off one by one to the forecastle while the wistful watchers murmured old chants and leaned over the rail to glimpse the luminous fish playing in bowers beneath the sea. Carter went to sleep at midnight, and rose in the glow of a young morning, marking that the sun seemed farther south than was its wont. And all through that second day he made progress in knowing the men of the ship, getting them little by little to talk of their cold twilight land, of their exquisite onyx city, and of their fear of the high and impassable peaks beyond which Leng was said to be. They told him how sorry they were that no cats would stay in the land of Inquanok, and how they thought the hidden nearness of Leng was to blame for it. Only of the stony desert to the north they would not talk. There was something disquieting about that desert, and it was thought expedient not to admit its existence.

On later days they talked of the quarries in which Carter said he was going to work. There were many of them, for all the city of Inquanok was builded of onyx, whilst great polished blocks of it were traded in Rinar, Ogrothan, and Celephaïs and at home with the merchants of Thraa, Flarnek, and Kadatheron, for the beautiful wares of those fabulous ports. And far to the north, almost in the cold desert whose existence the men of Inquanok did not care to admit, there was an unused quarry greater than all the rest; from which had been hewn in forgotten times such prodigious lumps and blocks that the sight of their chiselled vacancies struck terror to all who beheld. Who had mined those incredible blocks, and whither they had been transported, no man might say; but it was thought best not to trouble that quarry, around which such inhuman memories might conceivably cling. So it was left all alone in the twilight, with only the raven and the rumoured Shantak-bird to brood on its immensities. When Carter heard of this quarry he was moved to deep thought, for he knew from old tales that the Great Ones' castle atop unknown Kadath is of onyx.

Each day the sun wheeled lower and lower in the sky, and the mists overhead grew thicker and thicker. And in two weeks there was not any sunlight at all, but only a weird grey twilight shining through a dome of eternal cloud by day, and a cold starless phosphorescence from the underside of that cloud by night. On the twentieth day a great jagged rock in the sea was sighted from afar, the first land glimpsed since Man's snowy peak had dwindled behind the ship. Carter asked the captain the name of that rock, but was told that it had no name and had never been sought by any vessel because of the sounds that came from it at night. And when, after dark, a dull and ceaseless howling arose from that jagged granite place, the traveller was glad that no stop had been made, and that the rock had no name. The seamen prayed and chanted till the noise was out of earshot, and Carter dreamed terrible dreams within dreams in the small hours.

Two mornings after that there loomed far ahead and to the east a line of great grey peaks whose tops were lost in the changeless clouds of that twilight world. And at the sight of them the sailors sang glad songs, and some knelt down on the deck to pray, so that Carter knew they were come to the land of Inquanok and would soon be moored to the basalt quays of the great town bearing that land's name. Toward noon a dark coastline appeared, and before three o'clock there stood out against the north the bulbous domes and fantastic spires of the onyx city. Rare and curious did that archaic city rise above its walls and quays, all of delicate black with scrolls, flutings, and arabesques of inlaid gold. Tall and many-windowed were the houses, and carved on every side with flowers and patterns whose dark symmetries dazzled the eye with a beauty more poignant than light. Some ended in swelling domes that tapered to a point, others in terraced pyramids whereon rose clustered minarets displaying every phase of strangeness and imagination. The walls were low, and pierced by frequent gates, each under a great arch rising high above the general level and capped by the head of a god chiselled with that same skill displayed in the monstrous face on distant Ngranek. On a hill in the centre rose a sixteen-angled tower greater than all the rest and bearing a high pinnacled belfry resting on a flattened dome. This, the seamen said, was the Temple of the Elder Ones, and was ruled by an old High-Priest sad with inner secrets.

At intervals the clang of a strange bell shivered over the onyx city, answered each time by a peal of mystic music made up of horns, viols, and chanting voices. And from a row of tripods on a galley round the high dome of the temple there burst flares of flame at certain moments; for the priests and people of that city were wise in the primal mysteries, and faithful in keeping the rhythms of the Great Ones as set forth in scrolls older than the Pnakotic Manuscripts.

As the ship rode past the great basalt breakwater into the harbour the lesser noises of the city grew manifest, and Carter saw the slaves, sailors, and merchants on the docks. The sailors and merchants were of the strange-faced race of the gods, but the slaves were squat, slant-eyed folk said by rumour to have drifted somehow across or around the impassable peaks from the valleys beyond Leng. The wharves reached wide outside the city wall and bore upon them all manner of merchandise from the galleys anchored there, while at one end were great piles of onyx both carved and uncarved awaiting shipment to the far markets of Rinar, Ograthan and Celephaïs.

It was not yet evening when the dark ship anchored beside a jutting quay of stone, and all the sailors and traders filed ashore and through the arched gate into the city. The streets of that city were paved with onyx and some of them were wide and straight whilst others were crooked and narrow. The houses near the water were lower than the rest, and bore above their curiously arched doorways certain signs of gold said to be in honour of the respective small gods that favoured each. The captain of the ship took Carter to an old sea tavern where flocked the mariners of quaint countries, and promised that he would next day shew him the wonders of the twilight city, and lead him to the taverns of the onyx-miners by the northern wall. And evening fell, and little bronze lamps were lighted, and the sailors in that tavern sang songs of remote places. But when from its high tower the great bell shivered over the city, and the peal of the horns and viols and voices rose cryptical in answer thereto, all ceased their songs or tales and bowed silent till the last echo died away. For there is a wonder and a strangeness on the twilight city of Inquanok, and men fear to be lax in its rites lest a doom and a vengeance lurk unsuspectedly close.

Far in the shadows of that tavern Carter saw a squat form he did not like, for it was unmistakably that of the old slant-eyed merchant he had seen so long before in the taverns of Dylath-Leen, who was reputed to trade with the horrible stone villages of Leng which no healthy folk visit and whose evil fires are seen at night from afar, and even to have dealt with that High-Priest Not To Be Described, which wears a yellow silken mask over its face and dwells all alone in a prehistoric stone monastery. This man had seemed to shew a queer gleam of knowing when Carter asked the traders of Dylath-Leen about the cold waste and Kadath; and somehow his presence in dark and haunted Inquanok, so close to the wonders of the north, was not a reassuring thing. He slipped wholly out of sight before Carter could speak to him, and sailors later said that he had come with a yak caravan from some point not well determined, bearing the colossal and rich-flavoured eggs of the rumoured Shantak-bird to trade for the dextrous jade goblets that merchants brought from Ilarnek.

On the following morning the ship-captain led Carter through the onyx streets of Inquanok, dark under their twilight sky. The inlaid doors and figured house-fronts, carven balconies and crystal-paned oriels all gleamed with a sombre and polished loveliness; and now and then a plaza would open out with black pillars, colonnades, and the statues of curious beings both human and fabulous. Some of the vistas down long and unbending streets, or through side alleys and over bulbous domes, spires, and arabesqued roofs, were weird and beautiful beyond words; and nothing was more splendid than the massive heights of the great central Temple of the Elder Ones with its sixteen carven sides, its flattened dome, and its lofty pinnacled belfry, overtopping all else, and majestic whatever its foreground. And always to the east, far beyond the city walls and the leagues of pasture land, rose the gaunt grey sides of those topless and impassable peaks across which hideous Leng was said to lie.

The captain took Carter to the mighty temple, which is set with its walled garden in a great round plaza whence the streets go as spokes from a wheel's hub. The seven arched gates of that garden, each having over it a carven face like those on the city's gates, are always open, and the people roam reverently at will down the tiled paths and through the little lanes lined with grotesque termini and the shrines of modest gods. And there are fountains, pools, and basins there to reflect the frequent blaze of the tripods on the high balcony, all of onyx and having in them small luminous fish taken by divers from the lower bowers of ocean. When the deep clang from the temple belfry shivers over the garden and the city, and the answer of the horns and viols and voices peals out from the seven lodges by the garden gates, there issue from the seven doors of the temple long columns of masked and hooded priests in black, bearing at arm's length before them great golden bowls from which a curious steam rises. And all the seven columns strut peculiarly in single file, legs thrown far forward without bending the knees, down the walks that lead to the seven lodges, wherein they disappear and do not appear again. It is said that subterrene paths connect the lodges with the temple, and that the long files of priests return through them; nor is it unwhispered that deep flights of onyx steps go down to mysteries that are never told. But only a few are those who hint that the priests in the masked and hooded columns are not human beings.

Carter did not enter the temple, because none but the Veiled King is permitted to do that. But before he left the garden the hour of the bell came, and he heard the shivering clang deafening above him, and the wailing of the horns and viols and voices loud from the lodges by the gates. And down the seven great walks stalked the long files of bowl-bearing priests in their singular way, giving to the traveller a fear which human priests do not often give. When the last of them had vanished he left that garden, noting as he did so a spot on the pavement over which the bowls had passed. Even the ship-captain did not like that spot, and hurried him on toward the hill whereon the Veiled King's palace rises many-domed and marvellous.

The ways to the onyx palace are steep and narrow, all but the broad curving one where the king and his companions ride on yaks or in yak-drawn chariots. Carter and his guide climbed up an alley that was all steps, between inlaid walls bearing strange signs in gold, and under balconies and oriels whence sometimes floated soft strains of music or breaths of exotic fragrance. Always ahead loomed those titan walls, mighty buttresses, and clustered and bulbous domes for which the Veiled King's palace is famous; and at length they passed under a great black arch and emerged in the gardens of the monarch's pleasure. There Carter paused in faintness at so much beauty, for the onyx terraces and colonnaded walks, the gay porterres and delicate flowering trees espaliered to golden lattices, the brazen urns and tripods with cunning bas-reliefs, the pedestalled and almost breathing statues of veined black marble, the basalt-bottomed lagoon's tiled fountains with luminous fish, the tiny temples of iridescent singing birds atop carven columns, the marvellous scrollwork of the great bronze gates, and the blossoming vines trained along every inch of the polished walls all joined to form a sight whose loveliness was beyond reality, and half-fabulous even in the land of dreams. There it shimmered like a vision under that grey twilight sky, with the domed and fretted magnificence of the palace ahead, and the fantastic silhouette of the distant impassable peaks on the right. And ever the small birds and the fountains sang, while the perfume of rare blossoms spread like a veil over that incredible garden. No other human presence was there, and Carter was glad it was so. Then they turned and descended again the onyx alley of steps, for the palace itself no visitor may enter; and it is not well to look too long and steadily at the great central dome, since it is said to house the archaic father of all the rumoured Shantak-birds, and to send out queer dreams to the curious.

After that the captain took Carter to the north quarter of the town, near the Gate of the Caravans, where are the taverns of the yak-merchants and the onyx-miners. And there, in a low-ceiled inn of quarrymen, they said farewell; for business called the captain whilst Carter was eager to talk with miners about the north. There were many men in that inn, and the traveller was not long in speaking to some of them; saying that he was an old miner of onyx, and anxious to know somewhat of Inquanok's quarries. But all that he learned was not much more than he knew before, for the miners were timid and evasive about the cold desert to the north and the quarry that no man visits. They had fears of fabled emissaries from around the mountains where Leng is said to lie, and of evil presences and nameless sentinels far north among the scattered rocks. And they whispered also that the rumoured Shantak-birds are no wholesome things; it being indeed for the best that no man has ever truly seen one (for that fabled father of Shantaks in the king's dome is fed in the dark).

The next day, saying that he wished to look over all the various mines for himself and to visit the scattered farms and quaint onyx villages of Inquanok, Carter hired a yak and stuffed great leathern saddle-bags for a journey. Beyond the Gate of the Caravans the road lay straight betwixt tilled fields, with many odd farmhouses crowned by low domes. At some of these houses the seeker stopped to ask questions; once finding a host so austere and reticent, and so full of an unplaced majesty like to that in the huge features on Ngranek, that he felt certain he had come at last upon one of the Great Ones themselves, or upon one with full nine-tenths of their blood, dwelling amongst men. And to that austere and reticent cotter he was careful to speak very well of the gods, and to praise all the blessings they had ever accorded him.

That night Carter camped in a roadside meadow beneath a great lygath-tree to which he tied his yak, and in the morning resumed his northward pilgrimage. At about ten o'clock he reached the small-domed village of Urg, where traders rest and miners tell their tales, and paused in its taverns till noon. It is here that the great caravan road turns west toward Selarn, but Carter kept on north by the quarry road. All the afternoon he followed that rising road, which was somewhat narrower than the great highway, and which now led through a region with more rocks than tilled fields. And by evening the low hills on his left had risen into sizable black cliffs, so that he knew he was close to the mining country. All the while the great gaunt sides of the impassable mountains towered afar off at his right, and the farther he went, the worse tales he heard of them from the scattered farmers and traders and drivers of lumbering onyx-carts along the way.

On the second night he camped in the shadow of a large black crag, tethering his yak to a stake driven in the ground. He observed the greater phosphorescence of the clouds at this northerly point, and more than once thought he saw dark shapes outlined against them. And on the third morning he came in sight of the first onyx quarry, and greeted the men who there laboured with picks and chisels. Before evening he had passed eleven quarries; the land being here given over altogether to onyx cliffs and boulders, with no vegetation at all, but only great rocky fragments scattered about a floor of black earth, with the grey impassable peaks always rising gaunt and sinister on his right. The third night he spent in a camp of quarry men whose flickering fires cast weird reflections on the polished cliffs to the west. And they sang many songs and told many tales, shewing such strange knowledge of the olden days and the habits of gods that Carter could see they held many latent memories of their sires the Great Ones. They asked him whither he went, and cautioned him not to go too far to the north; but he replied that he was seeking new cliffs of onyx, and would take no more risks than were common among prospectors. In the morning he bade them adieu and rode on into the darkening north, where they had warned him he would find the feared and unvisited quarry whence hands older than men's hands had wrenched prodigious blocks. But he did not like it when, turning back to wave a last farewell, he thought he saw approaching the camp that squat and evasive old merchant with slanting eyes, whose conjectured traffick with Leng was the gossip of distant Dylath-Leen.

After two more quarries the inhabited part of Inquanok seemed to end, and the road narrowed to a steeply rising yak-path among forbidding black cliffs. Always on the right towered the gaunt and distant peaks, and as Carter climbed farther and farther into this untraversed realm he found it grew darker and colder. Soon he perceived that there were no prints of feet or hooves on the black path beneath, and realised that he was indeed come into strange and deserted ways of elder time. Once in a while a raven would croak far overhead, and now and then a flapping behind some vast rock would make him think uncomfortably of the rumoured Shantak-bird. But in the main he was alone with his shaggy steed, and it troubled him to observe that this excellent yak became more and more reluctant to advance, and more and more disposed to snort affrightedly at any small noise along the route.

The path now contracted between sable and glistening walls, and began to display an even greater steepness than before. It was a bad footing, and the yak often slipped on the stony fragments strewn thickly about. In two hours Carter saw ahead a definite crest, beyond which was nothing but dull grey sky, and blessed the prospect of a level or downward course. To reach this crest, however, was no easy task; for the way had grown nearly perpendicular, and was perilous with loose black gravel and small stones. Eventually Carter dismounted and led his dubious yak; pulling very hard when the animal balked or stumbled, and keeping his own footing as best he might. Then suddenly he came to the top and saw beyond, and gasped at what he saw.

The path indeed led straight ahead and slightly down, with the same lines of high natural walls as before; but on the left hand there opened out a monstrous space, vast acres in extent, where some archaic power had riven and rent the native cliffs of onyx in the form of a giant's quarry. Far back into the solid precipice ran that cyclopean gouge, and deep down within earth's bowels its lower delvings yawned. It was no quarry of man, and the concave sides were scarred with great squares, yards wide, which told of the size of the blocks once hewn by nameless hands and chisels. High over its jagged rim huge ravens flapped and croaked, and vague whirrings in the unseen depths told of bats or urhags or less mentionable presences haunting the endless blackness. There Carter stood in the narrow way amidst the twilight with the rocky path sloping down before him; tall onyx cliffs on his right that led on as far as he could see and tall cliffs on the left chopped off just ahead to make that terrible and unearthly quarry.

All at once the yak uttered a cry and burst from his control, leaping past him and darting on in a panic till it vanished down the narrow slope toward the north. Stones kicked by its flying hooves fell over the brink of the quarry and lost themselves in the dark without any sound of striking bottom; but Carter ignored the perils of that scanty path as he raced breathlessly after the flying steed. Soon the left-behind cliffs resumed their course, making the way once more a narrow lane; and still the traveller leaped on after the yak whose great wide prints told of its desperate flight.

Once he thought he heard the hoofbeats of the frightened beast, and doubled his speed from this encouragement. He was covering miles, and little by little the way was broadening in front till he knew he must soon emerge on the cold and dreaded desert to the north. The gaunt grey flanks of the distant impassable peaks were again visible above the right-hand crags, and ahead were the rocks and boulders of an open space which was clearly a foretaste of the dark arid limitless plain. And once more those hoofbeats sounded in his ears, plainer than before, but this time giving terror instead of encouragement because he realised that they were not the frightened hoofbeats of his fleeing yak. The beats were ruthless and purposeful, and they were behind him.

Carter's pursuit of the yak became now a flight from an unseen thing, for though he dared not glance over his shoulder he felt that the presence behind him could be nothing wholesome or mentionable. His yak must have heard or felt it first, and he did not like to ask himself whether it had followed him from the haunts of men or had floundered up out of that black quarry pit. Meanwhile the cliffs had been left behind, so that the oncoming night fell over a great waste of sand and spectral rocks wherein all paths were lost. He could not see the hoofprints of his yak, but always from behind him there came that detestable clopping; mingled now and then with what he fancied were titanic flappings and whirrings. That he was losing ground seemed unhappily clear to him, and he knew he was hopelessly lost in this broken and blasted desert of meaningless rocks and untravelled sands. Only those remote and impassable peaks on the right gave him any sense of direction, and even they were less clear as the grey twilight waned and the sickly phosphorescence of the clouds took its place.

Then dim and misty in the darkling north before him he glimpsed a terrible thing. He had thought it for some moments a range of black mountains, but now he saw it was something more. The phosphorescence of the brooding clouds shewed it plainly, and even silhouetted parts of it as vapours glowed behind. How distant it was he could not tell, but it must have been very far. It was thousands of feet high, stretching in a great concave arc from the grey impassable peaks to the unimagined westward spaces, and had once indeed been a ridge of mighty onyx hills. But now these hills were hills no more, for some hand greater than man's had touched them. Silent they squatted there atop the world like wolves or ghouls, crowned with clouds and mists and guarding the secrets of the north forever. All in a great half circle they squatted, those dog-like mountains carven into monstrous watching statues, and their right hands were raised in menace against mankind.

It was only the flickering light of the clouds that made their mitred double heads seem to move, but as Carter stumbled on he saw arise from their shadowy caps great forms whose motions were no delusion. Winged and whirring, those forms grew larger each moment, and the traveller knew his stumbling was at an end. They were not any birds or bats known elsewhere on earth or in dreamland, for they were larger than elephants and had heads like a horse's. Carter knew that they must be the Shantak-birds of ill rumour, and wondered no more what evil guardians and nameless sentinels made men avoid the boreal rock desert. And as he stopped in final resignation he dared at last to look behind him, where indeed was trotting the squat slant-eyed trader of evil legend, grinning astride a lean yak and leading on a noxious horde of leering Shantaks to whose wings still clung the rime and nitre of the nether pits.

Trapped though he was by fabulous and hippocephalic winged nightmares that pressed around in great unholy circles, Randolph Carter did not lose consciousness. Lofty and horrible those titan gargoyles towered above him, while the slant-eyed merchant leaped down from his yak and stood grinning before the captive. Then the man motioned Carter to mount one of the repugnant Shantaks, helping him up as his judgement struggled with his loathing. It was hard work ascending, for the Shantak-bird has scales instead of feathers, and those scales are very slippery. Once he was seated, the slant-eyed man hopped up behind him, leaving the lean yak to be led away northward toward the ring of carven mountains by one of the incredible bird colossi.

There now followed a hideous whirl through frigid space, endlessly up and eastward toward the gaunt grey flanks of those impassable mountains beyond which Leng was said to be. Far above the clouds they flew, till at last there lay beneath them those fabled summits which the folk of Inquanok have never seen, and which lie always in high vortices of gleaming mist. Carter beheld them very plainly as they passed below, and saw upon their topmost peaks strange caves which made him think of those on Ngranek; but he did not question his captor about these things when he noticed that both the man and the horse-headed Shantak appeared oddly fearful of them, hurrying past nervously and shewing great tension until they were left far in the rear.

The Shantak now flew lower, revealing beneath the canopy of cloud a grey barren plain whereon at great distances shone little feeble fires. As they descended there appeared at intervals lone huts of granite and bleak stone villages whose tiny windows glowed with pallid light. And there came from those huts and villages a shrill droning of pipes and a nauseous rattle of crotala which proved at once that Inquanok's people are right in their geographic rumours. For travellers have heard such sounds before, and know that they float only from the cold desert plateau which healthy folk never visit; that haunted place of evil and mystery which is Leng.

Around the feeble fires dark forms were dancing, and Carter was curious as to what manner of beings they might be; for no healthy folk have ever been to Leng, and the place is known only by its fires and stone huts as seen from afar. Very slowly and awkwardly did those forms leap, and with an insane twisting and bending not good to behold; so that Carter did not wonder at the monstrous evil imputed to them by vague legend, or the fear in which all dreamland holds their abhorrent frozen plateau. As the Shantak flew lower, the repulsiveness of the dancers became tinged with a certain hellish familiarity; and the prisoner kept straining his eyes and racking his memory for clues to where he had seen such creatures before.

They leaped as though they had hooves instead of feet, and seemed to wear a sort of wig or headpiece with small horns. Of other clothing they had none, but most of them were quite furry. Behind they had dwarfish tails, and when they glanced upward he saw the excessive width of their mouths. Then he knew what they were, and that they did not wear any wigs or headpieces after all. For the cryptic folk of Leng were of one race with the uncomfortable merchants of the black galleys that traded rubies at Dylath-Leen; those not quite human merchants who are the slaves of the monstrous moon-things! They were indeed the same dark folk who had shanghaied Carter on their noisome galley so long ago, and whose kith he had seen driven in herds about the unclean wharves of that accursed lunar city, with the leaner ones toiling and the fatter ones taken away in crates for other needs of their polypous and amorphous masters. Now he saw where such ambiguous creatures came from, and shuddered at the thought that Leng must be known to these formless abominations from the moon.

But the Shantak flew on past the fires and the stone huts and the less than human dancers, and soared over sterile hills of grey granite and dim wastes of rock and ice and snow. Day came, and the phosphorescence of low clouds gave place to the misty twilight of that northern world, and still the vile bird winged meaningly through the cold and silence. At times the slant-eyed man talked with his steed in a hateful and guttural language, and the Shantak would answer with tittering tones that rasped like the scratching of ground glass. All this while the land was getting higher, and finally they came to a wind-swept table-land which seemed the very roof of a blasted and tenantless world. There, all alone in the hush and the dusk and the cold, rose the uncouth stones of a squat windowless building, around which a circle of crude monoliths stood. In all this arrangement there was nothing human, and Carter surmised from old tales that he was indeed come to that most dreadful and legendary of all places, the remote and prehistoric monastery wherein dwells uncompanioned the High-Priest Not To Be Described, which wears a yellow silken mask over its face and prays to the Other Gods and their crawling chaos Nyarlathotep.

The loathsome bird now settled to the ground, and the slant-eyed man hopped down and helped his captive alight. Of the purpose of his seizure Carter now felt very sure; for clearly the slant-eyed merchant was an agent of the darker powers, eager to drag before his masters a mortal whose presumption had aimed at the finding of unknown Kadath and the saying of a prayer before the faces of the Great Ones in their onyx castle. It seemed likely that this merchant had caused his former capture by the slaves of the moon-things in Dylath-Leen, and that he now meant to do what the rescuing cats had baffled; taking the victim to some dread rendezvous with monstrous Nyarlathotep and telling with what boldness the seeking of unknown Kadath had been tried. Leng and the cold waste north of Inquanok must be close to the Other Gods, and there the passes to Kadath are well guarded.

The slant-eyed man was small, but the great hippocephalic bird was there to see he was obeyed; so Carter followed where he led, and passed within the circle of standing rocks and into the low arched doorway of that windowless stone monastery. There were no lights inside, but the evil merchant lit a small clay lamp bearing morbid bas-reliefs and prodded his prisoner on through mazes of narrow winding corridors. On the walls of the corridors were printed frightful scenes older than history, and in a style unknown to the archaeologists of earth. After countless aeons their pigments were brilliant still, for the cold and dryness of hideous Leng keep alive many primal things. Carter saw them fleetingly in the rays of that dim and moving lamp, and shuddered at the tale they told.

Through those archaic frescoes Leng's annals stalked; and the horned, hooved, and wide-mouthed almost-humans danced evilly amidst forgotten cities. There were scenes of old wars, wherein Leng's almost-humans fought with the bloated purple spiders of the neighbouring vales; and there were scenes also of the coming of the black galleys from the moon, and of the submission of Leng's people to the polypous and amorphous blasphemies that hopped and floundered and wriggled out of them. Those slippery greyish-white blasphemies they worshipped as gods, nor ever complained when scores of their best and fatted males were taken away in the black galleys. The monstrous moon-beasts made their camp on a jagged isle in the sea, and Carter could tell from the frescoes that this was none other than the lone nameless rock he had seen when sailing to Inquanok; that grey accursed rock which Inquanok's seamen shun, and from which vile howlings reverberate all through the night.

And in those frescoes was shewn the great seaport and capital of the almost-humans; proud and pillared betwixt the cliffs and the basalt wharves, and wondrous with high fanes and carven places. Great gardens and columned streets led from the cliffs and from each of the six sphinx-crowned gates to a vast central plaza, and in that plaza was a pair of winged colossal lions guarding the top of a subterrene staircase. Again and again were those huge winged lions shewn, their mighty flanks of diarite glistening in the grey twilight of the day and the cloudy phosphorescence of the night. And as Carter stumbled past their frequent and repeated pictures it came to him at last what indeed they were, and what city it was that the almost-humans had ruled so anciently before the coming of the black galleys. There could be no mistake, for the legends of dreamland are generous and profuse. Indubitably that primal city was no less a place than storied Sarkomand, whose ruins had bleached for a million years before the first true human saw the light, and whose twin titan lions guard eternally the steps that lead down from dreamland to the Great Abyss.

Other views shewed the gaunt grey peaks dividing Leng from Inquanok, and the monstrous Shantak-birds that build nests on the ledges half way up. And they shewed likewise the curious caves near the very topmost pinnacles, and how even the boldest of the Shantaks fly screaming away from them. Carter had seen those caves when he passed over them, and had noticed their likeness to the caves on Ngranek. Now he knew that the likeness was more than a chance one, for in these pictures were shewn their fearsome denizens; and those bat-wings, curving horns, barbed tails, prehensile paws and rubbery bodies were not strange to him. He had met those silent, flitting and clutching creatures before; those mindless guardians of the Great Abyss whom even the Great Ones fear, and who own not Nyarlathotep but hoary Nodens as their lord. For they were the dreaded night-gaunts, who never laugh nor smile because they have no faces, and who flop unendingly in the dark betwixt the Vale of Pnath and the passes to the outer world.

The slant-eyed merchant had now prodded Carter into a great domed space whose walls were carved in shocking bas-reliefs, and whose centre held a gaping circular pit surrounded by six malignly stained stone altars in a ring. There was no light in this vast evil-smelling crypt, and the small lamp of the sinister merchant shone so feebly that one could grasp details only little by little. At the farther end was a high stone dais reached by five steps; and there on a golden throne sat a lumpish figure robed in yellow silk figured with red and having a yellow silken mask over its face. To this being the slant-eyed man made certain signs with his hands, and the lurker in the dark replied by raising a disgustingly carven flute of ivory in silk-covered paws and blowing certain loathsome sounds from beneath its flowing yellow mask. This colloquy went on for some time, and to Carter there was something sickeningly familiar in the sound of that flute and the stench of the malodorous place. It made him think of a frightful red-litten city and of the revolting procession that once filed through it; of that, and of an awful climb through lunar countryside beyond, before the rescuing rush of earth's friendly cats. He knew that the creature on the dais was without doubt the High-Priest Not To Be Described, of which legend whispers such fiendish and abnormal possibilities, but he feared to think just what that abhorred High-Priest might be.

Then the figured silk slipped a trifle from one of the greyish-white paws, and Carter knew what the noisome High-Priest was. And in that hideous second, stark fear drove him to something his reason would never have dared to attempt, for in all his shaken consciousness there was room only for one frantic will to escape from what squatted on that golden throne. He knew that hopeless labyrinths of stone lay betwixt him and the cold table-land outside, and that even on that table-land the noxious Shantek still waited; yet in spite of all this there was in his mind only the instant need to get away from that wriggling, silk-robed monstrosity.

The slant-eyed man had set the curious lamp upon one of the high and wickedly stained altar-stones by the pit, and had moved forward somewhat to talk to the High-Priest with his hands. Carter, hitherto wholly passive, now gave that man a terrific push with all the wild strength of fear, so that the victim toppled at once into that gaping well which rumour holds to reach down to the hellish Vaults of Zin where Gugs hunt ghasts in the dark. In almost the same second he seized the lamp from the altar and darted out into the frescoed labyrinths, racing this way and that as chance determined and trying not to think of the stealthy padding of shapeless paws on the stones behind him, or of the silent wrigglings and crawlings which must be going on back there in lightless corridors.

After a few moments he regretted his thoughtless haste, and wished he had tried to follow backward the frescoes he had passed on the way in. True, they were so confused and duplicated that they could not have done him much good, but he wished none the less he had made the attempt. Those he now saw were even more horrible than those he had seen then, and he knew he was not in the corridors leading outside. In time he became quite sure he was not followed, and slackened his pace somewhat; but scarce had he breathed in half relief when a new peril beset him. His lamp was waning, and he would soon be in pitch blackness with no means of sight or guidance.

When the light was all gone he groped slowly in the dark, and prayed to the Great Ones for such help as they might afford. At times he felt the stone floor sloping up or down, and once he stumbled over a step for which no reason seemed to exist. The farther he went the damper it seemed to be, and when he was able to feel a junction or the mouth of a side passage he always chose the way which sloped downward the least. He believed, though, that his general course was down; and the vault-like smell and incrustations on the greasy walls and floor alike warned him he was burrowing deep in Leng's unwholesome table-land.

But there was not any warning of the thing which came at last; only the thing itself with its terror and shock and breath-taking chaos. One moment he was groping slowly over the slippery floor of an almost level place, and the next he was shooting dizzily downward in the dark through a burrow which must have been well-nigh vertical.

Of the length of that hideous sliding he could never be sure, but it seemed to take hours of delirious nausea and ecstatic frenzy. Then he realized he was still, with the phosphorescent clouds of a northern night shining sickly above him. All around were crumbling walls and broken columns, and the pavement on which he lay was pierced by straggling grass and wrenched asunder by frequent shrubs and roots. Behind him a basalt cliff rose topless and perpendicular; its dark side sculptured into repellent scenes, and pierced by an arched and carven entrance to the inner blacknesses out of which he had come. Ahead stretched double rows of pillars, and the fragments and pedestals of pillars, that spoke of a broad and bygone street; and from the urns and basins along the way he knew it had been a great street of gardens. Far off at its end the pillars spread to mark a vast round plaza, and in that open circle there loomed gigantic under the lurid night clouds a pair of monstrous things. Huge winged lions of diarite they were, with blackness and shadow between them. Full twenty feet they reared their grotesque and unbroken heads, and snarled derisive on the ruins around them. And Carter knew right well what they must be, for legend tells of only one such twain. They were the changeless guardians of the Great Abyss, and these dark ruins were in truth primordial Sarkomand.

Carter's first act was to close and barricade the archway in the cliff with fallen blocks and odd debris that lay around. He wished no follower from Leng's hateful monastery, for along the way ahead would lurk enough of other dangers. Of how to get from Sarkomand to the peopled parts of dreamland he knew nothing at all; nor could he gain much by descending to the grottoes of the ghouls, since he knew they were no better informed than he. The three ghouls which had helped him through the city of Gugs to the outer world had not known how to reach Sarkomand in their journey back, but had planned to ask old traders in Dylath-Leen. He did not like to think of going again to the subterrene world of Gugs and risking once more that hellish tower of Koth with its Cyclopean steps leading to the enchanted wood, yet he felt he might have to try this course if all else failed. Over Leng's plateau past the lone monastery he dared not go unaided; for the High-Priest's emissaries must be many, while at the journey's end there would no doubt be the Shantaks and perhaps other things to deal with. If he could get a boat he might sail back to Inquanok past the jagged and hideous rock in the sea, for the primal frescoes in the monastery labyrinth had shewn that this frightful place lies not far from Sarkomand's basalt quays. But to find a boat in this aeon-deserted city was no probable thing, and it did not appear likely that he could ever make one.

Such were the thoughts of Randolph Carter when a new impression began beating upon his mind. All this while there had stretched before him the great corpse-like width of fabled Sarkomand with its black broken pillars and crumbling sphinx-crowned gates and titan stones and monstrous winged lions against the sickly glow of those luminous night clouds. Now he saw far ahead and on the right a glow that no clouds could account for, and knew he was not alone in the silence of that dead city. The glow rose and fell fitfully, flickering with a greenish tinge which did not reassure the watcher. And when he crept closer, down the littered street and through some narrow gaps between tumbled walls, he perceived that it was a campfire near the wharves with many vague forms clustered darkly around it; and a lethal odour hanging heavily over all. Beyond was the oily lapping of the harbour water with a great ship riding at anchor, and Carter paused in stark terror when he saw that the ship was indeed one of the dreaded black galleys from the moon.

Then, just as he was about to creep back from that detestable flame, he saw a stirring among the vague dark forms and heard a peculiar and unmistakable sound. It was the frightened meeping of a ghoul, and in a moment it had swelled to a veritable chorus of anguish.

Secure as he was in the shadow of monstrous ruins, Carter allowed his curiosity to conquer his fear, and crept forward again instead of retreating. Once in crossing an open street he wriggled worm-like on his stomach, and in another place he had to rise to his feet to avoid making a noise among heaps of fallen marble. But always he succeeded in avoiding discovery, so that in a short time he had found a spot behind a titan pillar where he could watch the whole green-litten scene of action. There around a hideous fire fed by the obnoxious stems of lunar fungi, there squatted a stinking circle of the toadlike moonbeasts and their almost-human slaves. Some of these slaves were heating curious iron spears in the leaping flames, and at intervals applying their white-hot points to three tightly trussed prisoners that lay writhing before the leaders of the party. From the motions of their tentacles Carter could see that the blunt-snouted moonbeasts were enjoying the spectacle hugely, and vast was his horror when he suddenly recognised the frantic meeping and knew that the tortured ghouls were none other than the faithful trio which had guided him safely from the abyss, and had thereafter set out from the enchanted wood to find Sarkomand and the gate to their native deeps.

The number of malodorous moonbeasts about that greenish fire was very great, and Carter saw that he could do nothing now to save his former allies. Of how the ghouls had been captured he could not guess; but fancied that the grey toadlike blasphemies had heard them inquire in Dylath-Leen concerning the way to Sarkomand and had not wished them to approach so closely the hateful plateau of Leng and the High-Priest Not To Be Described. For a moment he pondered on what he ought to do, and recalled how near he was to the gate of the ghouls' black kingdom. Clearly it was wisest to creep east to the plaza of twin lions and descend at once to the gulf, where assuredly he would meet no horrors worse than those above, and where he might soon find ghouls eager to rescue their brethren and perhaps to wipe out the moonbeasts from the black galley. It occurred to him that the portal, like other gates to the abyss, might be guarded by flocks of night-gaunts; but he did not fear these faceless creatures now. He had learned that they are bound by solemn treaties with the ghouls, and the ghoul which was Pickman had taught him how to glibber a password they understood.

So Carter began another silent crawl through the ruins, edging slowly toward the great central plaza and the winged lions. It was ticklish work, but the moonbeasts were pleasantly busy and did not hear the slight noises which he twice made by accident among the scattered stones. At last he reached the open space and picked his way among the stunned trees and vines that had grown up therein. The gigantic lions loomed terrible above him in the sickly glow of the phosphorescent night clouds, but he manfully persisted toward them and presently crept round to their faces, knowing it was on that side he would find the mighty darkness which they guard. Ten feet apart crouched the mocking-faced beasts of diarite, brooding on cyclopean pedestals whose sides were chiselled in fearsome bas-reliefs. Betwixt them was a tiled court with a central space which had once been railed with balusters of onyx. Midway in this space a black well opened, and Carter soon saw that he had indeed reached the yawning gulf whose crusted and mouldy stone steps lead down to the crypts of nightmare.

Terrible is the memory of that dark descent in which hours wore themselves away whilst Carter wound sightlessly round and round down a fathomless spiral of steep and slippery stairs. So worn and narrow were the steps, and so greasy with the ooze of inner earth, that the climber never quite knew when to expect a breathless fall and hurtling down to the ultimate pits; and he was likewise uncertain just when or how the guardian night-gaunts would suddenly pounce upon him, if indeed there were any stationed in this primeval passage. All about him was a stifling odour of nether gulfs, and he felt that the air of these choking depths was not made for mankind. In time he became very numb and somnolent, moving more from automatic impulse than from reasoned will; nor did he realize any change when he stopped moving altogether as something quietly seized him from behind. He was flying very rapidly through the air before a malevolent tickling told him that the rubbery night-gaunts had performed their duty.

Awaked to the fact that he was in the cold, damp clutch of the faceless flutterers, Carter remembered the password of the ghouls and glibbered it as loudly as he could amidst the wind and chaos of flight. Mindless though night-gaunts are said to be, the effect was instantaneous; for all tickling stopped at once, and the creatures hastened to shift their captive to a more comfortable position. Thus encouraged Carter ventured some explanations; telling of the seizure and torture of three ghouls by the moonbeasts, and of the need of assembling a party to rescue them. The night-gaunts, though inarticulate, seemed to understand what was said; and shewed greater haste and purpose in their flight.

Suddenly the dense blackness gave place to the grey twilight of inner earth, and there opened up ahead one of those flat sterile plains on which ghouls love to squat and gnaw. Scattered tombstones and osseous fragments told of the denizens of that place; and as Carter gave a loud meep of urgent summons, a score of burrows emptied forth their leathery, dog-like tenants. The night-gaunts now flew low and set their passenger upon his feet, afterward withdrawing a little and forming a hunched semicircle on the ground while the ghouls greeted the newcomer.

Carter glibbered his message rapidly and explicitly to the grotesque company, and four of them at once departed through different burrows to spread the news to others and gather such troops as might be available for a rescue. After a long wait a ghoul of some importance appeared, and made significant signs to the night-gaunts, causing two of the latter to fly off into the dark. Thereafter there were constant accessions to the hunched flock of night-gaunts on the plain, till at length the slimy soil was fairly black with them. Meanwhile fresh ghouls crawled out of the burrows one by one, all glibbering excitedly and forming in crude battle array not far from the huddled night-gaunts. In time there appeared that proud and influential ghoul which was once the artist Richard Pickman of Boston, and to him Carter glibbered a very full account of what had occurred. The erstwhile Pickman, pleased to greet his ancient friend again, seemed very much impressed, and held a conference with other chiefs a little apart from the growing throng.

Finally, after scanning the ranks with care, the assembled chiefs all meeped in unison and began glibbering orders to the crowds of ghouls and night-gaunts. A large detachment of the horned flyers vanished at once, while the rest grouped themselves two by two on their knees with extended forelegs, awaiting the approach of the ghouls one by one. As each ghoul reached the pair of night-gaunts to which he was assigned, he was taken up and borne away into the blackness; till at last the whole throng had vanished save for Carter, Pickman, and the other chiefs, and a few pairs of night-gaunts. Pickman explained that night-gaunts are the advance guard and battle steeds of the ghouls, and that the army was issuing forth to Sarkomand to deal with the moonbeasts. Then Carter and the ghoulish chiefs approached the waiting bearers and were taken up by the damp, slippery paws. Another moment and all were whirling in wind and darkness; endlessly up, up, up to the gate of the winged and the special ruins of primal Sarkomand.

When, after a great interval, Carter saw again the sickly light of Sarkomand's nocturnal sky, it was to behold the great central plaza swarming with militant ghouls and night-gaunts. Day, he felt sure, must be almost due; but so strong was the army that no surprise of the enemy would be needed. The greenish flare near the wharves still glimmered faintly, though the absence of ghoulish meeping shewed that the torture of the prisoners was over for the nonce. Softly glibbering directions to their steeds and to the flock of riderless night-gaunts ahead, the ghouls presently rose in wide whirring columns and swept on over the bleak ruins toward the evil flame. Carter was now beside Pickman in the front rank of ghouls, and saw as they approached the noisome camp that the moonbeasts were totally unprepared. The three prisoners lay bound and inert beside the fire, while their toadlike captors slumped drowsily about in no certain order. The almost-human slaves were asleep, even the sentinels shirking a duty which in this realm must have seemed to them merely perfunctory.

The final swoop of the night-gaunts and mounted ghouls was very sudden, each of the greyish toadlike blasphemies and their almost-human slaves being seized by a group of night-gaunts before a sound was made. The moonbeasts, of course, were voiceless; and even the slaves had little chance to scream before rubbery paws choked them into silence. Horrible were the writhings of those great jellyfish abnormalities as the sardonic night-gaunts clutched them, but nothing availed against the strength of those black prehensile talons. When a moonbeast writhed too violently, a night-gaunt would seize and pull its quivering pink tentacles; which seemed to hurt so much that the victim would cease its struggles. Carter expected to see much slaughter, but found that the ghouls were far subtler in their plans. They glibbered certain simple orders to the night-gaunts which held the captives, trusting the rest to instinct; and soon the hapless creatures were borne silently away into the Great Abyss, to be distributed impartially amongst the Dholes, Gugs, ghasts and other dwellers in darkness whose modes of nourishment are not painless to their chosen victims. Meanwhile the three bound ghouls had been released and consoled by their conquering kinsfolk, whilst various parties searched the neighborhood for possible remaining moonbeasts, and boarded the evil-smelling black galley at the wharf to make sure that nothing had escaped the general defeat. Surely enough, the capture had been thorough, for not a sign of further life could the victors detect. Carter, anxious to preserve a means of access to the rest of dreamland, urged them not to sink the anchored galley; and this request was freely granted out of gratitude for his act in reporting the plight of the captured trio. On the ship were found some very curious objects and decorations, some of which Carter cast at once into the sea.

Ghouls and night-gaunts now formed themselves in separate groups, the former questioning their rescued fellow anent past happenings. It appeared that the three had followed Carter's directions and proceeded from the enchanted wood to Dylath-Leen by way of Nir and the Skai, stealing human clothes at a lonely farmhouse and loping as closely as possible in the fashion of a man's walk. In Dylath-Leen's taverns their grotesque ways and faces had aroused much comment; but they had persisted in asking the way to Sarkomand until at last an old traveller was able to tell them. Then they knew that only a ship for Lelag-Leng would serve their purpose, and prepared to wait patiently for such a vessel.

But evil spies had doubtless reported much; for shortly a black galley put into port, and the wide-mouthed ruby merchants invited the ghouls to drink with them in a tavern. Wine was produced from one of those sinister bottles grotesquely carven from a single ruby, and after that the ghouls found themselves prisoners on the black galley as Carter had found himself. This time, however, the unseen rowers steered not for the moon but for antique Sarkomand; bent evidently on taking their captives before the High-Priest Not To Be Described. They had touched at the jagged rock in the northern sea which Inquanok's mariners shun, and the ghouls had there seen for the first time the red masters of the ship; being sickened despite their own callousness by such extremes of malign shapelessness and fearsome odour. There, too, were witnessed the nameless pastimes of the toadlike resident garrison-such pastimes as give rise to the night-howlings which men fear. After that had come the landing at ruined Sarkomand and the beginning of the tortures, whose continuance the present rescue had prevented.

Future plans were next discussed, the three rescued ghouls suggesting a raid on the jagged rock and the extermination of the toadlike garrison there. To this, however, the night-gaunts objected; since the prospect of flying over water did not please them. Most of the ghouls favoured the design, but were at a loss how to follow it without the help of the winged night-gaunts. Thereupon Carter, seeing that they could not navigate the anchored galley, offered to teach them the use of the great banks of oars; to which proposal they eagerly assented.

Grey day had now come, and under that leaden northern sky a picked detachment of ghouls filed into the noisome ship and took their seats on the rowers' benches. Carter found them fairly apt at learning, and before night had risked several experimental trips around the harbour. Not till three days later, however, did he deem it safe to attempt the voyage of conquest. Then, the rowers trained and the night-gaunts safely stowed in the forecastle, the party set sail at last; Pickman and the other chiefs gathering on deck and discussing models of approach and procedure.

On the very first night the howlings from the rock were heard. Such was their timbre that all the galley's crew shook visibly; but most of all trembled the three rescued ghouls who knew precisely what those howlings meant. It was not thought best to attempt an attack by night, so the ship lay to under the phosphorescent clouds to wait for the dawn of a greyish day. When the light was ample and the howlings still the rowers resumed their strokes, and the galley drew closer and closer to that jagged rock whose granite pinnacles clawed fantastically at the dull sky. The sides of the rock were very steep; but on ledges here and there could be seen the bulging walls of queer windowless dwellings, and the low railings guarding travelled highroads. No ship of men had ever come so near the place, or at least, had never come so near and departed again; but Carter and the ghouls were void of fear and kept inflexibly on, rounding the eastern face of the rock and seeking the wharves which the rescued trio described as being on the southern side within a harbour formed of steep headlands.

The headlands were prolongations of the island proper, and came so closely together that only one ship at a time might pass between them. There seemed to be no watchers on the outside, so the galley was steered boldly through the flume-like strait and into the stagnant putrid harbour beyond. Here, however, all was bustle and activity; with several ships lying at anchor along a forbidding stone quay, and scores of almost-human slaves and moonbeasts by the waterfront handling crates and boxes or driving nameless and fabulous horrors hitched to lumbering lorries. There was a small stone town hewn out of the vertical cliff above the wharves, with the start of a winding road that spiralled out of sight toward higher ledges of the rock. Of what lay inside that prodigious peak of granite none might say, but the things one saw on the outside were far from encouraging.

At sight of the incoming galley the crowds on the wharves displayed much eagerness; those with eyes staring intently, and those without eyes wriggling their pink tentacles expectantly. They did not, of course, realize that the black ship had changed hands; for ghouls look much like the horned and hooved almost-humans, and the night-gaunts were all out of sight below. By this time the leaders had fully formed a plan; which was to loose the night-gaunts as soon as the wharf was touched, and then to sail directly away, leaving matters wholly to the instincts of those almost-mindless creatures. Marooned on the rock, the horned flyers would first of all seize whatever living things they found there, and afterward, quite helpless to think except in terms of the homing instinct, would forget their fears of water and fly swiftly back to the abyss; bearing their noisome prey to appropriate destinations in the dark, from which not much would emerge alive.

The ghoul that was Pickman now went below and gave the night-gaunts their simple instructions, while the ship drew very near to the ominous and malodorous wharves. Presently a fresh stir rose along the waterfront, and Carter saw that the motions of the galley had begun to excite suspicion. Evidently the steersman was not making for the right dock, and probably the watchers had noticed the difference between the hideous ghouls and the almost-human slaves whose places they were taking. Some silent alarm must have been given, for almost at once a horde of the mephitic moonbeasts began to pour from the little black doorways of the windowless houses and down the winding road at the right. A rain of curious javelins struck the galley as the prow hit the wharf felling two ghouls and slightly wounding another; but at this point all the hatches were thrown open to emit a black cloud of whirring night-gaunts which swarmed over the town like a flock of horned and cyclopean bats.

The jellyish moonbeasts had procured a great pole and were trying to push off the invading ship, but when the night-gaunts struck them they thought of such things no more. It was a very terrible spectacle to see those faceless and rubbery ticklers at their pastime, and tremendously impressive to watch the dense cloud of them spreading through the town and up the winding roadway to the reaches above. Sometimes a group of the black flutterers would drop a toadlike prisoner from aloft by mistake, and the manner in which the victim would burst was highly offensive to the sight and smell. When the last of the night-gaunts had left the galley the ghoulish leaders glibbered an order of withdrawal, and the rowers pulled quietly out of the harbour between the grey headlands while still the town was a chaos of battle and conquest.

The Pickman ghoul allowed several hours for the night-gaunts to make up their rudimentary minds and overcome their fear of flying over the sea, and kept the galley standing about a mile off the jagged rock while he waited, and dressed the wounds of the injured men. Night fell, and the grey twilight gave place to the sickly phosphorescence of low clouds, and all the while the leaders watched the high peaks of that accursed rock for signs of the night-gaunts' flight. Toward morning a black speck was seen hovering timidly over the top-most pinnacle, and shortly afterward the speck had become a swarm. Just before daybreak the swarm seemed to scatter, and within a quarter of an hour it had vanished wholly in the distance toward the northeast. Once or twice something seemed to fall from the thick swarm into the sea; but Carter did not worry, since he knew from observation that the toadlike moonbeasts cannot swim.

At length, when the ghouls were satisfied that all the night-gaunts had left for Sarkomand and the Great Abyss with their doomed burdens, the galley put back into the harbour betwixt the grey headlands; and all the hideous company landed and roamed curiously over the denuded rock with its towers and eyries and fortresses chiselled from the solid stone.

Frightful were the secrets uncovered in those evil and windowless crypts; for the remnants of unfinished pastimes were many, and in various stages of departure from their primal state. Carter put out of the way certain things which were after a fashion alive, and fled precipitately from a few other things about which he could not be very positive. The stench-filled houses were furnished mostly with grotesque stools and benches carven from moon-trees, and were painted inside with nameless and frantic designs. Countless weapons, implements, and ornaments lay about, including some large idols of solid ruby depicting singular beings not found on the earth. These latter did not, despite their material, invite either appropriation or long inspection; and Carter took the trouble to hammer five of them into very small pieces. The scattered spears and javelins he collected, and with Pickman's approval distributed among the ghouls. Such devices were new to the doglike lopers, but their relative simplicity made them easy to master after a few concise hints.

The upper parts of the rock held more temples than private homes, and in numerous hewn chambers were found terrible carven altars and doubtfully stained fonts and shrines for the worship of things more monstrous than the wild gods atop Kadath. From the rear of one great temple stretched a low black passage which Carter followed far into the rock with a torch till he came to a lightless domed hall of vast proportions, whose vaultings were covered with demoniac carvings and in whose centre yawned a foul and bottomless well like that in the hideous monastery of Leng where broods alone the High-Priest Not

To Be Described. On the distant shadowy side, beyond the noisome well, he thought he discerned a small door of strangely wrought bronze; but for some reason he felt an unaccountable dread of opening it or even approaching it, and hastened back through the cavern to his unlovely allies as they shambled about with an ease and abandon he could scarcely feel. The ghouls had observed the unfinished pastimes of the moonbeasts, and had profited in their fashion. They had also found a hogshead of potent moon-wine, and were rolling it down to the wharves for removal and later use in diplomatic dealings, though the rescued trio, remembering its effect on them in Dylath-Leen, had warned their company to taste none of it. Of rubies from lunar mines there was a great store, both rough and polished, in one of the vaults near the water; but when the ghouls found they were not good to eat they lost all interest in them. Carter did not try to carry any away, since he knew too much about those which had mined them.

Suddenly there came an excited meeping from the sentries on the wharves, and all the loathsome foragers turned from their tasks to stare seaward and cluster round the waterfront. Betwixt the grey headlands a fresh black galley was rapidly advancing, and it would be but a moment before the almost-humans on deck would perceive the invasion of the town and give the alarm to the monstrous things below. Fortunately the ghouls still bore the spears and javelins which Carter had distributed amongst them; and at his command, sustained by the being that was Pickman, they now formed a line of battle and prepared to prevent the landing of the ship. Presently a burst of excitement on the galley told of the crew's discovery of the changed state of things, and the instant stoppage of the vessel proved that the superior numbers of the ghouls had been noted and taken into account. After a moment of hesitation the new comers silently turned and passed out between the headlands again, but not for an instant did the ghouls imagine that the conflict was averted. Either the dark ship would seek reinforcements or the crew would try to land elsewhere on the island; hence a party of scouts was at once sent up toward the pinnacle to see what the enemy's course would be.

In a very few minutes the ghoul returned breathless to say that the moonbeasts and almost-humans were landing on the outside of the more easterly of the rugged grey headlands, and ascending by hidden paths and ledges which a goat could scarcely tread in safety. Almost immediately afterward the galley was sighted again through the flume-like strait, but only for a second. Then a few moments later, a second messenger panted down from aloft to say that another party was landing on the other headland; both being much more numerous than the size of the galley would seem to allow for. The ship itself, moving slowly with only one sparsely manned tier of oars, soon hove in sight betwixt the cliffs, and lay to in the foetid harbour as if to watch the coming fray and stand by for any possible use.

By this time Carter and Pickman had divided the ghouls into three parties, one to meet each of the two invading columns and one to remain in the town. The first two at once scrambled up the rocks in their respective directions, while the third was subdivided into a land party and a sea party. The sea party, commanded by Carter, boarded the anchored galley and rowed out to meet the under-manned galley of the newcomers; whereat the latter retreated through the strait to the open sea. Carter did not at once pursue it, for he knew he might be needed more acutely near the town.

Meanwhile the frightful detachments of the moonbeasts and almost-humans had lumbered up to the top of the headlands and were shockingly silhouetted on either side against the grey twilight sky. The thin hellish flutes of the invaders had now begun to whine, and the general effect of those hybrid, half-amorphous processions was as nauseating as the actual odour given off by the toadlike lunar blasphemies. Then the two parties of the ghouls swarmed into sight and joined the silhouetted panorama. Javelins began to fly from both sides, and the swelling meeps of the ghouls and the bestial howls of the almost-humans gradually joined the hellish whine of the flutes to form a frantick and indescribable chaos of daemon cacophony. Now and then bodies fell from the narrow ridges of the headlands into the sea outside or the harbour inside, in the latter case being sucked quickly under by certain submarine lurkers whose presence was indicated only by prodigious bubbles.

For half an hour this dual battle raged in the sky, till upon the west cliff the invaders were completely annihilated. On the east cliff, however, where the leader of the moonbeast party appeared to be present, the ghouls had not fared so well; and were slowly retreating to the slopes of the pinnacle proper. Pickman had quickly ordered reinforcements for this front from the party in the town, and these had helped greatly in the earlier stages of the combat. Then, when the western battle was over, the victorious survivors hastened across to the aid of their hard-pressed fellows; turning the tide and forcing the invaders back again along the narrow ridge of the headland. The almost-humans were by this time all slain, but the last of the toadlike horrors fought desperately with the great spears clutched in their powerful and disgusting paws. The time for javelins was now nearly past, and the fight became a hand-to-hand contest of what few spearmen could meet upon that narrow ridge.

As fury and recklessness increased, the number falling into the sea became very great. Those striking the harbour met nameless extinction from the unseen bubblers, but of those striking the open sea some were able to swim to the foot of the cliffs and land on tidal rocks, while the hovering galley of the enemy rescued several moonbeasts. The cliffs were unscalable except where the monsters had debarked, so that none of the ghouls on the rocks could rejoin their battle-line. Some were killed by javelins from the hostile galley or from the moonbeasts above, but a few survived to be rescued.

When the security of the land parties seemed assured, Carter's galley sallied forth between the headlands and drove the hostile ship far out to sea; pausing to rescue such ghouls as were on the rocks or still swimming in the ocean. Several moonbeasts washed on rocks or reefs were speedily put out of the way.

Finally, the moonbeast galley being safely in the distance and the invading land army concentrated in one place, Carter landed a considerable force on the eastern headland in the enemy's rear; after which the fight was short-lived indeed. Attacked from both sides, the noisome flounderers were rapidly cut to pieces or pushed into the sea, till by evening the ghoulish chiefs agreed that the island was again clear of them. The hostile galley, meanwhile, had disappeared; and it was decided that the evil jagged rock had better be evacuated before any overwhelming horde of lunar horrors might be assembled and brought against the victors.

So by night Pickman and Carter assembled all the ghouls and counted them with care, finding that over a fourth had been lost in the day's battles. The wounded were placed on bunks in the galley, for Pickman always discouraged the old ghoulish custom of killing and eating one's own wounded, and the able-bodied troops were assigned to the oars or to such other places as they might most usefully fill. Under the low phosphorescent clouds of night the galley sailed, and Carter was not sorry to be departing from the island of unwholesome secrets, whose lightless domed hall with its bottomless well and repellent bronze door lingered restlessly in his fancy.

Dawn found the ship in sight of Sarkomand's ruined quays of basalt, where a few night-gaunt sentries still waited, squatting like black horned gargoyles on the broken columns and crumbling sphinxes of that fearful city which lived and died before the years of man.

The ghouls made camp amongst the fallen stones of Sarkomand, despatching a messenger for enough night-gaunts to serve them as steeds. Pickman and the other chiefs were effusive in their gratitude for the aid Carter had lent them. Carter now began to feel that his plans were indeed maturing well, and that he would be able to command the help of these fearsome allies not only in quitting this part of dreamland, but in pursuing his ultimate quest for the gods atop unknown Kadath, and the marvellous sunset city they so strangely withheld from his slumbers. Accordingly he spoke of these things to the ghoulish leaders; telling what he knew of the cold waste wherein Kadath stands and of the monstrous Shantaks and the mountains carven into double-headed images which guard it. He spoke of the fear of Shantaks for night-gaunts, and of how the vast hippocephalic birds fly screaming from the black burrows high up on the gaunt grey peaks that divide Inquanok from hateful Leng. He spoke, too, of the things he had learned concerning night-gaunts from the frescoes in the windowless monastery of the High-Priest Not To Be Described; how even the Great Ones fear them, and how their ruler is not the crawling chaos Nyarlathotep at all, but hoary and immemorial Nodens, Lord of the Great Abyss.

All these things Carter glibbered to the assembled ghouls, and presently outlined that request which he had in mind and which he did not think extravagant considering the services he had so lately rendered the rubbery doglike lopers. He wished very much, he said, for the services of enough night-gaunts to bear him safely through the aft past the realm of Shantaks and carven mountains, and up into the cold waste beyond the returning tracks of any other mortal. He desired to fly to the onyx castle atop unknown Kadath in the cold waste to plead with the Great Ones for the sunset city they denied him, and felt sure that the night-gaunts could take him thither without trouble; high above the perils of the plain, and over the hideous double heads of those carven sentinel mountains that squat eternally in the grey dusk. For the horned and faceless creatures there could be no danger from aught of earth since the Great Ones themselves dread them. And even were unexpected things to come from the Other Gods, who are prone to oversee the affairs of earth's milder gods, the night-gaunts need not fear; for the outer hells are indifferent matters to such silent and slippery flyers as own not Nyarlathotep for their master, but bow only to potent and archaic Nodens.

A flock of ten or fifteen night-gaunts, Carter glibbered, would surely be enough to keep any combination of Shantaks at a distance, though perhaps it might be well to have some ghouls in the party to manage the creatures, their ways being better known to their ghoulish allies than to men. The party could land him at some convenient point within whatever walls that fabulous onyx citadel might have, waiting in the shadows for his return or his signal whilst he ventured inside the castle to give prayer to the gods of earth. If any ghouls chose to escort him into the throne-room of the Great Ones, he would be thankful, for their presence would add weight and importance to his plea. He would not, however, insist upon this but merely wished transportation to and from the castle atop unknown Kadath; the final journey being either to the marvellous sunset city itself, in case the gods proved favourable, or back to the earthward Gate of Deeper Slumber in the Enchanted Wood in case his prayers were fruitless.

Whilst Carter was speaking all the ghouls listened with great attention, and as the moments advanced the sky became black with clouds of those night-gaunts for which messengers had been sent. The winged steeds settled in a semicircle around the ghoulish army, waiting respectfully as the doglike chieftains considered the wish of the earthly traveller. The ghoul that was Pickman glibbered gravely with his fellows and in the end Carter was offered far more than he had at most expected. As he had aided the ghouls in their conquest of the moonbeasts, so would they aid him in his daring voyage to realms whence none had ever returned; lending him not merely a few of their allied night-gaunts, but their entire army as then encamped, veteran fighting ghouls and newly assembled night-gaunts alike, save only a small garrison for the captured black galley and such spoils as had come from the jagged rock in the sea. They would set out through the aft whenever he might wish, and once arrived on Kadath a suitable train of ghouls would attend him in state as he placed his petition before earth's gods in their onyx castle.

Moved by a gratitude and satisfaction beyond words, Carter made plans with the ghoulish leaders for his audacious voyage. The army would fly high, they decided, over hideous Leng with its nameless monastery and wicked stone villages; stopping only at the vast grey peaks to confer with the Shantak-frightening night-gaunts whose burrows honeycombed their summits. They would then, according to what advice they might receive from those denizens, choose their final course; approaching unknown Kadath either through the desert of carven mountains north of Inquanok, or through the more northerly reaches of repulsive Leng itself. Doglike and soulless as they are, the ghouls and night-gaunts had no dread of what those untrodden deserts might reveal; nor did they feel any deterring awe at the thought of Kadath towering alone with its onyx castle of mystery.

About midday the ghouls and night-gaunts prepared for flight, each ghoul selecting a suitable pair of horned steeds to bear him. Carter was placed well up toward the head of the column beside Pickman, and in front of the whole a double line of riderless night-gaunts was provided as a vanguard. At a brisk meep from Pickman the whole shocking army rose in a nightmare cloud above the broken columns and crumbling sphinxes of primordial Sarkomand; higher and higher, till even the great basalt cliff behind the town was cleared, and the cold, sterile table-land of Leng's outskirts laid open to sight. Still higher flew the black host, till even this table-land grew small beneath them; and as they worked northward over the wind-swept plateau of horror Carter saw once again with a shudder the circle of crude monoliths and the squat windowless building which he knew held that frightful silken-masked blasphemy from whose clutches he had so narrowly escaped. This time no descent was made as the army swept batlike over the sterile landscape, passing the feeble fires of the unwholesome stone villages at a great altitude, and pausing not at all to mark the morbid twistings of the hooved, horned almost-humans that dance and pipe eternally therein. Once they saw a Shantak-bird flying low over the plain, but when it saw them it screamed noxiously and flapped off to the north in grotesque panic.

At dusk they reached the jagged grey peaks that form the barrier of Inquanok, and hovered about these strange caves near the summits which Carter recalled as so frightful to the Shantaks. At the insistent meeping of the ghoulish leaders there issued forth from each lofty burrow a stream of horned black flyers with which the ghouls and night-gaunts of the party conferred at length by means of ugly gestures. It soon became clear that the best course would be that over the cold waste north of Inquanok, for Leng's northward reaches are full of unseen pitfalls that even the night-gaunts dislike; abysmal influences centering in certain white hemispherical buildings on curious knolls, which common folklore associates unpleasantly with the Other Gods and their crawling chaos Nyarlathotep.

Of Kadath the flutterers of the peaks knew almost nothing, save that there must be some mighty marvel toward the north, over which the Shantaks and the carven mountains stand guard. They hinted at rumoured abnormalities of proportion in those trackless leagues beyond, and recalled vague whispers of a realm where night broods eternally; but of definite data they had nothing to give. So Carter and his party thanked them kindly; and, crossing the topmost granite pinnacles to the skies of Inquanok, dropped below the level of the phosphorescent night clouds and beheld in the distance those terrible squatting gargoyles that were mountains till some titan hand carved fright into their virgin rock.

There they squatted in a hellish half-circle, their legs on the desert sand and their mitres piercing the luminous clouds; sinister, wolflike, and double-headed, with faces of fury and right hands raised, dully and malignly watching the rim of man's world and guarding with horror the reaches of a cold northern world that is not man's. From their hideous laps rose evil Shantaks of elephantine bulk, but these all fled with insane titters as the vanguard of night-gaunts was sighted in the misty sky. Northward above those gargoyle mountains the army flew, and over leagues of dim desert where never a landmark rose. Less and less luminous grew the clouds, till at length Carter could see only blackness around him; but never did the winged steeds falter, bred as they were in earth's blackest crypts, and seeing not with any eyes, but with the whole dank surface of their slippery forms. On and on they flew, past winds of dubious scent and sounds of dubious import; ever in thickest darkness, and covering such prodigious spaces that Carter wondered whether or not they could still be within earth's dreamland.

Then suddenly the clouds thinned and the stars shone spectrally above. All below was still black, but those pallid beacons in the sky seemed alive with a meaning and directiveness they had never possessed elsewhere. It was not that the figures of the constellations were different, but that the same familiar shapes now revealed a significance they had formerly failed to make plain. Everything focussed toward the north; every curve and asterism of the glittering sky became part of a vast design whose function was to hurry first the eye and then the whole observer onward to some secret and terrible goal of convergence beyond the frozen waste that stretched endlessly ahead. Carter looked toward the east where the great ridge of barrier peaks had towered along all the length of Inquanok and saw against the stars a jagged silhouette which told of its continued presence. It was more broken now, with yawning clefts and fantastically erratic pinnacles; and Carter studied closely the suggestive turnings and inclinations of that grotesque outline, which seemed to share with the stars some subtle northward urge.

They were flying past at a tremendous speed, so that the watcher had to strain hard to catch details; when all at once he beheld just above the line of the topmost peaks a dark and moving object against the stars, whose course exactly paralleled that of his own bizarre party. The ghouls had likewise glimpsed it, for he heard their low glibbering all about him, and for a moment he fancied the object was a gigantic Shantak, of a size vastly greater than that of the average specimen. Soon, however, he saw that this theory would not hold; for the shape of the thing above the mountains was not that of any hippocephalic bird. Its outline against the stars, necessarily vague as it was, resembled rather some huge mitred head, or pair of heads infinitely magnified; and its rapid bobbing flight through the sky seemed most peculiarly a wingless one. Carter could not tell which side of the mountains it was on, but soon perceived that it had parts below the parts he had first seen, since it blotted out all the stars in places where the ridge was deeply cleft.

Then came a wide gap in the range, where the hideous reaches of transmontane Leng were joined to the cold waste on this side by a low pass through which the stars shone wanly. Carter watched this gap with intense care, knowing that he might see outlined against the sky beyond it the lower parts of the vast thing that flew undulantly above the pinnacles. The object had now floated ahead a trifle, and every eye of the party was fixed on the rift where it would presently appear in full-length silhouette. Gradually the huge thing above the peaks neared the gap, slightly slackening its speed as if conscious of having outdistanced the ghoulish army. For another minute suspense was keen, and then the brief instant of full silhouette and revelation came; bringing to the lips of the ghouls an awed and half-choked meep of cosmic fear, and to the soul of the traveller a chill that never wholly left it. For the mammoth bobbing shape that overtopped the ridge was only a head — a mitred double head — and below it in terrible vastness loped the frightful swollen body that bore it; the mountain-high monstrosity that walked in stealth and silence; the hyaena-like distortion of a giant anthropoid shape that trotted blackly against the sky, its repulsive pair of cone-capped heads reaching half way to the zenith.

Carter did not lose consciousness or even scream aloud, for he was an old dreamer; but he looked behind him in horror and shuddered when he saw that there were other monstrous heads silhouetted above the level of the peaks, bobbing along stealthily after the first one. And straight in the rear were three of the mighty mountain shapes seen full against the southern stars, tiptoeing wolflike and lumberingly, their tall mitres nodding thousands of feet in the aft. The carven mountains, then, had not stayed squatting in that rigid semicircle north of Inquanok, with right hands uplifted. They had duties to perform, and were not remiss. But it was horrible that they never spoke, and never even made a sound in walking.

Meanwhile the ghoul that was Pickman had glibbered an order to the night-gaunts, and the whole army soared higher into the air. Up toward the stars the grotesque column shot, till nothing stood out any longer against the sky; neither the grey granite ridge that was still nor the carven mitred mountains that walked. All was blackness beneath as the fluttering legion surged northward amidst rushing winds and invisible laughter in the aether, and never a Shantak or less mentionable entity rose from the haunted wastes to pursue them. The farther they went, the faster they flew, till soon their dizzying speed seemed to pass that of a rifle ball and approach that of a planet in its orbit. Carter wondered how with such speed the earth could still stretch beneath them, but knew that in the land of dream dimensions have strange properties. That they were in a realm of eternal night he felt certain, and he fancied that the constellations overhead had subtly emphasized their northward focus; gathering themselves up as it were to cast the flying army into the void of the boreal pole, as the folds of a bag are gathered up to cast out the last bits of substance therein.

Then he noticed with terror that the wings of the night-gaunts were not flapping any more. The horned and faceless steeds had folded their membranous appendages, and were resting quite passive in the chaos of wind that whirled and chuckled as it bore them on. A force not of earth had seized on the army, and ghouls and night-gaunts alike were powerless before a current which pulled madly and relentlessly into the north whence no mortal had ever returned. At length a lone pallid light was seen on the skyline ahead, thereafter rising steadily as they approached, and having beneath it a black mass that blotted out the stars. Carter saw that it must be some beacon on a mountain, for only a mountain could rise so vast as seen from so prodigious a height in the air.

Higher and higher rose the light and the blackness beneath it, till all the northern sky was obscured by the rugged conical mass. Lofty as the army was, that pale and sinister beacon rose above it, towering monstrous over all peaks and concernments of earth, and tasting the atomless aether where the cryptical moon and the mad planets reel. No mountain known of man was that which loomed before them. The high clouds far below were but a fringe for its foothills. The groping dizziness of topmost air was but a girdle for its loins. Scornful and spectral climbed that bridge betwixt earth and heaven, black in eternal night, and crowned with a pshent of unknown stars whose awful and significant outline grew every moment clearer. Ghouls meeped in wonder as they saw it, and Carter shivered in fear lest all the hurtling army be dashed to pieces on the unyielding onyx of that cyclopean cliff.

Higher and higher rose the light, till it mingled with the loftiest orbs of the zenith and winked down at the flyers with lurid mockery. All the north beneath it was blackness now; dread, stony blackness from infinite depths to infinite heights, with only that pale winking beacon perched unreachably at the top of all vision. Carter studied the light more closely, and saw at last what lines its inky background made against the stars. There were towers on that titan mountaintop; horrible domed towers in noxious and incalculable tiers and clusters beyond any dreamable workmanship of man; battlements and terraces of wonder and menace, all limned tiny and black and distant against the starry pshent that glowed malevolently at the uppermost rim of sight. Capping that most measureless of mountains was a castle beyond all mortal thought, and in it glowed the daemon-light. Then Randolph Carter knew that his quest was done, and that he saw above him the goal of all forbidden steps and audacious visions; the fabulous, the incredible home of the Great Ones atop unknown Kadath.

Even as he realised this thing, Carter noticed a change in the course of the helplessly wind-sucked party. They were rising abruptly now, and it was plain that the focus of their flight was the onyx castle where the pale light shone. So close was the great black mountain that its sides sped by them dizzily as they shot upward, and in the darkness they could discern nothing upon it. Vaster and vaster loomed the tenebrous towers of the nighted castle above, and Carter could see that it was well-nigh blasphemous in its immensity. Well might its stones have been quarried by nameless workmen in that horrible gulf rent out of the rock in the hill pass north of Inquanok, for such was its size that a man on its threshold stood even as air out on the steps of earth's loftiest fortress. The pshent of unknown stars above the myriad domed turrets glowed with a sallow, sickly flare, so that a kind of twilight hung about the murky walls of slippery onyx. The pallid beacon was now seen to be a single shining window high up in one of the loftiest towers, and as the helpless army neared the top of the mountain Carter thought he detected unpleasant shadows flitting across the feebly luminous expanse. It was a strangely arched window, of a design wholly alien to earth.

The solid rock now gave place to the giant foundations of the monstrous castle, and it seemed that the speed of the party was somewhat abated. Vast walls shot up, and there was a glimpse of a great gate through which the voyagers were swept. All was night in the titan courtyard, and then came the deeper blackness of inmost things as a huge arched portal engulfed the column. Vortices of cold wind surged dankly through sightless labyrinths of onyx, and Carter could never tell what Cyclopean stairs and corridors lay silent along the route of his endless aerial twisting. Always upward led the terrible plunge in darkness, and never a sound, touch or glimpse broke the dense pall of mystery. Large as the army of ghouls and night-gaunts was, it was lost in the prodigious voids of that more than earthly castle. And when at last there suddenly dawned around him the lurid light of that single tower room whose lofty window had served as a beacon, it took Carter long to discern the far walls and high, distant ceiling, and to realize that he was indeed not again in the boundless air outside.

Randolph Carter had hoped to come into the throne-room of the Great Ones with poise and dignity, flanked and followed by impressive lines of ghouls in ceremonial order, and offering his prayer as a free and potent master among dreamers. He had known that the Great Ones themselves are not beyond a mortal's power to cope with, and had trusted to luck that the Other Gods and their crawling chaos Nyarlathotep would not happen to come to their aid at the crucial moment, as they had so often done before when men sought out earth's gods in their home or on their mountains. And with his hideous escort he had half hoped to defy even the Other Gods if need were, knowing as he did that ghouls have no masters, and that night-gaunts own not Nyarlathotep but only archaic Nodens for their lord. But now he saw that supernal Kadath in its cold waste is indeed girt with dark wonders and nameless sentinels, and that the Other Gods are of a surety vigilant in guarding the mild, feeble gods of earth. Void as they are of lordship over ghouls and night-gaunts, the mindless, shapeless blasphemies of outer space can yet control them when they must; so that it was not in state as a free and potent master of dreamers that Randolph Carter came into the Great Ones' throne-room with his ghouls. Swept and herded by nightmare tempests from the stars, and dogged by unseen horrors of the northern waste, all that army floated captive and helpless in the lurid light, dropping numbly to the onyx floor when by some voiceless order the winds of fright dissolved.

Before no golden dais had Randolph Carter come, nor was there any august circle of crowned and haloed beings with narrow eyes, long-lobed ears, thin nose, and pointed chin whose kinship to the carven face on Ngranek might stamp them as those to whom a dreamer might pray. Save for the one tower room the onyx castle atop Kadath was dark, and the masters were not there. Carter had come to unknown Kadath in the cold waste, but he had not found the gods. Yet still the lurid light glowed in that one tower room whose size was so little less than that of all outdoors, and whose distant walls and roof were so nearly lost to sight in thin, curling mists. Earth's gods were not there, it was true, but of subtler and less visible presences there could be no lack. Where the mild gods are absent, the Other Gods are not unrepresented; and certainly, the onyx castle of castles was far from tenantless. In what outrageous form or forms terror would next reveal itself Carter could by no means imagine. He felt that his visit had been expected, and wondered how close a watch had all along been kept upon him by the crawling chaos Nyarlathotep. It is Nyarlathotep, horror of infinite shapes and dread soul and messenger of the Other Gods, that the fungous moonbeasts serve; and Carter thought of the black galley that had vanished when the tide of battle turned against the toadlike abnormalities on the jagged rock in the sea.

Reflecting upon these things, he was staggering to his feet in the midst of his nightmare company when there rang without warning through that pale-litten and limitless chamber the hideous blast of a daemon trumpet. Three times pealed that frightful brazen scream, and when the echoes of the third blast had died chucklingly away Randolph Carter saw that he was alone. Whither, why and how the ghouls and night-gaunts had been snatched from sight was not for him to divine. He knew only that he was suddenly alone, and that whatever unseen powers lurked mockingly around him were no powers of earth's friendly dreamland. Presently from the chamber's uttermost reaches a new sound came. This, too, was a rhythmic trumpeting; but of a kind far removed from the three raucous blasts which had dissolved his goodly cohorts. In this low fanfare echoed all the wonder and melody of ethereal dream; exotic vistas of unimagined loveliness floating from each strange chord and subtly alien cadence. Odours of incense came to match the golden notes; and overhead a great light dawned, its colours changing in cycles unknown to earth's spectrum, and following the song of the trumpets in weird symphonic harmonies. Torches flared in the distance, and the beat of drums throbbed nearer amidst waves of tense expectancy.

Out of the thinning mists and the cloud of strange incenses filed twin columns of giant black slaves with loin-cloths of iridescent silk. Upon their heads were strapped vast helmet-like torches of glittering metal, from which the fragrance of obscure balsams spread in fumous spirals. In their right hands were crystal wands whose tips were carven into leering chimaeras, while their left hands grasped long thin silver trumpets which they blew in turn. Armlets and anklets of gold they had, and between each pair of anklets stretched a golden chain that held its wearer to a sober gait. That they were true black men of earth's dreamland was at once apparent, but it seemed less likely that their rites and costumes were wholly things of our earth. Ten feet from Carter the columns stopped, and as they did so each trumpet flew abruptly to its bearer's thick lips. Wild and ecstatic was the blast that followed, and wilder still the cry that chorused just after from dark throats somehow made shrill by strange artifice.

Then down the wide lane betwixt the two columns a lone figure strode; a tall, slim figure with the young face of an antique Pharaoh, gay with prismatic robes and crowned with a golden pshent that glowed with inherent light. Close up to Carter strode that regal figure; whose proud carriage and smart features had in them the fascination of a dark god or fallen archangel, and around whose eyes there lurked the languid sparkle of capricious humour. It spoke, and in its mellow tones there rippled the wild music of Lethean streams.

"Randolph Carter," said the voice, "you have come to see the Great Ones whom it is unlawful for men to see. Watchers have spoken of this thing, and the Other Gods have grunted as they rolled and tumbled mindlessly to the sound of thin flutes in the black ultimate void where broods the daemon-sultan whose name no lips dare speak aloud.

"When Barzai the Wise climbed Hatheg-Kla to see the Greater Ones dance and howl above the clouds in the moonlight he never returned. The Other Gods were there, and they did what was expected. Zenig of Aphorat sought to reach unknown Kadath in the cold waste, and his skull is now set in a ring on the little finger of one whom I need not name.

"But you, Randolph Carter, have braved all things of earth's dreamland, and burn still with the flame of quest. You came not as one curious, but as one seeking his due, nor have you failed ever in reverence toward the mild gods of earth. Yet have these gods kept you from the marvellous sunset city of your dreams, and wholly through their own small covetousness; for verily, they craved the weird loveliness of that which your fancy had fashioned, and vowed that henceforward no other spot should be their abode.

"They are gone from their castle on unknown Kadath to dwell in your marvellous city. All through its palaces of veined marble they revel by day, and when the sun sets they go out in the perfumed gardens and watch the golden glory on temples and colonnades, arched bridges and silver-basined fountains, and wide streets with blossom-laden urns and ivory statues in gleaming rows. And when night comes they climb tall terraces in the dew, and sit on carved benches of porphyry scanning the stars, or lean over pale balustrades to gaze at the town's steep northward slopes, where one by one the little windows in old peaked gables shine softly out with the calm yellow light of homely candles.

"The gods love your marvellous city, and walk no more in the ways of the gods. They have forgotten the high places of earth, and the mountains that knew their youth. The earth has no longer any gods that are gods, and only the Other Ones from outer space hold sway on unremembered Kadath. Far away in a valley of your own childhood, Randolph Carter, play the heedless Great Ones. You have dreamed too well, O wise arch-dreamer, for you have drawn dream's gods away from the world of all men's visions to that which is wholly yours; having builded out of your boyhood's small fancies a city more lovely than all the phantoms that have gone before.

"It is not well that earth's gods leave their thrones for the spider to spin on, and their realm for the Others to sway in the dark manner of Others. Fain would the powers from outside bring chaos and horror to you, Randolph Carter, who are the cause of their upsetting, but that they know it is by you alone that the gods may be sent back to their world. In that half-waking dreamland which is yours, no power of uttermost night may pursue; and only you can send the selfish Great Ones gently out of your marvellous sunset city, back through the northern twilight to their wonted place atop unknown Kadath in the cold waste.

"So, Randolph Carter, in the name of the Other Gods I spare you and charge you to seek that sunset city which is yours, and to send thence the drowsy truant gods for whom the dream world waits. Not hard to find is that roseal fever of the gods, that fanfare of supernal trumpets and clash of immortal cymbals, that mystery whose place and meaning have haunted you through the halls of waking and the gulfs of dreaming, and tormented you with hints of vanished memory and the pain of lost things awesome and momentous. Not hard to find is that symbol and relic of your days of wonder, for truly, it is but the stable and eternal gem wherein all that wonder sparkles crystallised to light your evening path. Behold! It is not over unknown seas but back over well-known years that your quest must go; back to the bright strange things of infancy and the quick sun-drenched glimpses of magic that old scenes brought to wide young eyes.

"For know you, that your gold and marble city of wonder

is only the sum of what you have seen and loved in youth. It is the glory of Boston's hillside roofs and western windows aflame with sunset, of the flower-fragrant Common and the great dome on the hill and the tangle of gables and chimneys in the violet valley where the many-bridged Charles flows drowsily. These things you saw, Randolph Carter, when your nurse first wheeled you out in the springtime, and they will be the last things you will ever see with eyes of memory and of love. And there is antique Salem with its brooding years, and spectral Marblehead scaling its rocky precipices into past centuries! And the glory of Salem's towers and spires seen afar from Marblehead's pastures across the harbour against the setting sun.

"There is Providence quaint and lordly on its seven hills over the blue harbour, with terraces of green leading up to steeples and citadels of living antiquity, and Newport climbing wraithlike from its dreaming breakwater. Arkham is there, with its moss-grown gambrel roofs and the rocky rolling meadows behind it; and antediluvian Kingsport hoary with stacked chimneys and deserted quays and overhanging gables, and the marvel of high cliffs and the milky-misted ocean with tolling buoys beyond.

"Cool vales in Concord, cobbled lands in Portsmouth, twilight bends of rustic New Hampshire roads where giant elms half hide white farmhouse walls and creaking well-sweeps. Gloucester's salt wharves and Truro's windy willows. Vistas of distant steepled towns and hills beyond hills along the North Shore, hushed stony slopes and low ivied cottages in the lee of huge boulders in Rhode Island's back country. Scent of the sea and fragrance of the fields; spell of the dark woods and joy of the orchards and gardens at dawn. These, Randolph Carter, are your city; for they are yourself. New England bore you, and into your soul she poured a liquid loveliness which cannot die. This loveliness, moulded, crystallised, and polished by years of memory and dreaming, is your terraced wonder of elusive sunsets; and to find that marble parapet with curious urns and carven rail, and descend at last these endless balustraded steps to the city of broad squares and prismatic fountains, you need only to turn back to the thoughts and visions of your wistful boyhood.

"Look! through that window shine the stars of eternal night. Even now they are shining above the scenes you have known and cherished, drinking of their charm that they may shine more lovely over the gardens of dream. There is Antares — he is winking at this moment over the roofs of Tremont Street, and you could see him from your window on Beacon Hill. Out beyond those stars yawn the gulfs from whence my mindless masters have sent me. Some day you too may traverse them, but if you are wise you will beware such folly; for of those mortals who have been and returned, only one preserves a mind unshattered by the pounding, clawing horrors of the void. Terrors and blasphemies gnaw at one another for space, and there is more evil in the lesser ones than in the greater; even as you know from the deeds of those who sought to deliver you into my hands, whilst I myself harboured no wish to shatter you, and would indeed have helped you hither long ago had I not been elsewhere busy, and certain that you would yourself find the way. Shun then, the outer hells, and stick to the calm, lovely things of your youth. Seek out your marvellous city and drive thence the recreant Great Ones, sending them back gently to those scenes which are of their own youth, and which wait uneasy for their return.

"Easier even then the way of dim memory is the way I will prepare for you. See! There comes hither a monstrous Shantak, led by a slave who for your peace of mind had best keep invisible. Mount and be ready — there! Yogash the Black will help you on the scaly horror. Steer for that brightest star just south of the zenith — it is Vega, and in two hours will be just above the terrace of your sunset city. Steer for it only till you hear a far-off singing in the high aether. Higher than that lurks madness, so rein your Shantak when the first note lures. Look then back to earth, and you will see shining the deathless altar-flame of Ired-Naa from the sacred roof of a temple. That temple is in your desiderate sunset city, so steer for it before you heed the singing and are lost.

"When you draw nigh the city steer for the same high parapet whence of old you scanned the outspread glory, prodding the Shantak till he cry aloud. That cry the Great Ones will hear and know as they sit on their perfumed terraces, and there will come upon them such a homesickness that all of your city's wonders will not console them for the absence of Kadath's grim castle and the pshent of eternal stars that crowns it.

"Then must you land amongst them with the Shantak, and let them see and touch that noisome and hippocephalic bird; meanwhile discoursing to them of unknown Kadath, which you will so lately have left, and telling them how its boundless halls are lovely and unlighted, where of old they used to leap and revel in supernal radiance. And the Shantak will talk to them in the manner of Shantaks, but it will have no powers of persuasion beyond the recalling of elder days.

"Over and over must you speak to the wandering Great Ones of their home and youth, till at last they will weep and ask to be shewn the returning path they have forgotten. Thereat can you loose the waiting Shantak, sending him skyward with the homing cry of his kind; hearing which the Great Ones will prance and jump with antique mirth, and forthwith stride after the loathly bird in the fashion of gods, through the deep gulfs of heaven to Kadath's familiar towers and domes.

"Then will the marvellous sunset city be yours to cherish and inhabit for ever, and once more will earth's gods rule the dreams of men from their accustomed seat. Go now — the casement is open and the stars await outside. Already your Shantak wheezes and titters with impatience. Steer for Vega through the night, but turn when the singing sounds. Forget not this warning, lest horrors unthinkable suck you into the gulf of shrieking and ululant madness. Remember the Other Gods; they are great and mindless and terrible, and lurk in the outer voids. They are good gods to shun.

"Hei! Aa-shanta 'nygh! You are off! Send back earth's gods to their haunts on unknown Kadath, and pray to all space that you may never meet me in my thousand other forms. Farewell, Randolph Carter, and beware; for I am Nyarlathotep, the Crawling Chaos."

And Randolph Carter, gasping and dizzy on his hideous Shantak, shot screamingly into space toward the cold blue glare of boreal Vega; looking but once behind him at the clustered and chaotic turrets of the onyx nightmare wherein still glowed the lone lurid light of that window above the air and the clouds of earth's dreamland. Great polypous horrors slid darkly past, and unseen bat wings beat multitudinous around him, but still he clung to the unwholesome mane of that loathly and hippocephalic scaled bird. The stars danced mockingly, almost shifting now and then to form pale signs of doom that one might wonder one had not seen and feared before; and ever the winds of nether howled of vague blackness and loneliness beyond the cosmos.

Then through the glittering vault ahead there fell a hush of portent, and all the winds and horrors slunk away as night things slink away before the dawn. Trembling in waves that golden wisps of nebula made weirdly visible, there rose a timid hint of far-off melody, droning in faint chords that our own universe of stars knows not. And as that music grew, the Shantak raised its ears and plunged ahead, and Carter likewise bent to catch each lovely strain. It was a song, but not the song of any voice. Night and the spheres sang it, and it was old when space and Nyarlathotep and the Other Gods were born.

Faster flew the Shantak, and lower bent the rider, drunk with the marvel of strange gulfs, and whirling in the crystal coils of outer magic. Then came too late the warning of the evil one, the sardonic caution of the daemon legate who had bidden the seeker beware the madness of that song. Only to taunt had Nyarlathotep marked out the way to safety and the marvellous sunset city; only to mock had that black messenger revealed the secret of these truant gods whose steps he could so easily lead back at will. For madness and the void's wild vengeance are Nyarlathotep's only gifts to the presumptuous; and frantick though the rider strove to turn his disgusting steed, that leering, tittering Shantak coursed on impetuous and relentless, flapping its great slippery wings in malignant joy and headed for those unhallowed pits whither no dreams reach; that last amorphous blight of nether-most confusion where bubbles and blasphemes at infinity's centre the mindless daemon-sultan Azathoth, whose name no lips dare speak aloud.

Unswerving and obedient to the foul legate's orders, that hellish bird plunged onward through shoals of shapeless lurkers and caperers in darkness, and vacuous herds of drifting entities that pawed and groped and groped and pawed; the nameless larvae of the Other Gods, that are like them blind and without mind, and possessed of singular hungers and thirsts.

Onward unswerving and relentless, and tittering hilariously to watch the chuckling and hysterics into which the risen song of night and the spheres had turned, that eldritch scaly monster bore its helpless rider; hurtling and shooting, cleaving the uttermost rim and spanning the outermost abysses; leaving behind the stars and the realms of matter, and darting meteor-like through stark formlessness toward those inconceivable, unlighted chambers beyond time wherein Azathoth gnaws shapeless and ravenous amidst the muffled, maddening beat of vile drums and the thin, monotonous whine of accursed flutes.

Onward — onward — through the screaming, cackling, and blackly populous gulfs — and then from some dim blessed distance there came an image and a thought to Randolph Carter the doomed. Too well had Nyarlathotep planned his mocking and his tantalising, for he had brought up that which no gusts of icy terror could quite efface. Home — New England — Beacon Hill — the waking world.

"For know you, that your gold and marble city of wonder is only the sum of what you have seen and loved in youth ... the glory of Boston's hillside roofs and western windows aflame with sunset; of the flower-fragrant Common and the great dome on the hill and the tangle of gables and chimneys in the violet valley where the many-bridged Charles flows drowsily ... this loveliness, moulded, crystallised, and polished by years of memory and dreaming, is your terraced wonder of elusive sunsets; and to find that marble parapet with curious urns and carven rail, and descend at last those endless balustraded steps to the city of broad squares and prismatic fountains, you need only to turn back to the thoughts and visions of your wistful boyhood."

Onward — onward — dizzily onward to ultimate doom through the blackness where sightless feelers pawed and slimy snouts jostled and nameless things tittered and tittered and tittered. But the image and the thought had come, and Randolph Carter knew clearly that he was dreaming and only dreaming, and that somewhere in the background the world of waking and the city of his infancy still lay. Words came again — "You need only turn back to the thoughts and visions of your wistful boyhood." Turn — turn — blackness on every side, but Randolph Carter could turn.

Thick though the rushing nightmare that clutched his senses, Randolph Carter could turn and move. He could move, and if he chose he could leap off the evil Shantak that bore him hurtlingly doomward at the orders of Nyarlathotep. He could leap off and dare those depths of night that yawned interminably down, those depths of fear whose terrors yet could not exceed the nameless doom that lurked waiting at chaos' core. He could turn and move and leap — he could — he would — he would — he would.

Off that vast hippocephalic abomination leaped the doomed and desperate dreamer, and down through endless voids of sentient blackness he fell. Aeons reeled, universes died and were born again, stars became nebulae and nebulae became stars, and still Randolph Carter fell through those endless voids of sentient blackness.

Then in the slow creeping course of eternity the utmost

cycle of the cosmos churned itself into another futile completion, and all things became again as they were unreckoned kalpas before. Matter and light were born anew as space once had known them; and comets, suns and worlds sprang flaming into life, though nothing survived to tell that they had been and gone, been and gone, always and always, back to no first beginning.

And there was a firmament again, and a wind, and a glare of purple light in the eyes of the falling dreamer. There were gods and presences and wills; beauty and evil, and the shrieking of noxious night robbed of its prey. For through the unknown ultimate cycle had lived a thought and a vision of a dreamer's boyhood, and now there were remade a waking world and an old cherished city to body and to justify these things. Out of the void S'ngac the violet gas had pointed the way, and archaic Nodens was bellowing his guidance from unhinted deeps.

Stars swelled to dawns, and dawns burst into fountains of gold, carmine, and purple, and still the dreamer fell. Cries rent the aether as ribbons of light beat back the fiends from outside. And hoary Nodens raised a howl of triumph when Nyarlathotep, close on his quarry, stopped baffled by a glare that seared his formless hunting-horrors to grey dust. Randolph Carter had indeed descended at last the wide marmoreal flights to his marvellous city, for he was come again to the fair New England world that had wrought him.

So to the organ chords of morning's myriad whistles, and dawn's blaze thrown dazzling through purple panes by the great gold dome of the State House on the hill, Randolph Carter leaped shoutingly awake within his Boston room. Birds sang in hidden gardens and the perfume of trellised vines came wistful from arbours his grandfather had reared. Beauty and light glowed from classic mantel and carven cornice and walls grotesquely figured, while a sleek black cat rose yawning from hearthside sleep that his master's start and shriek had disturbed. And vast infinities away, past the Gate of Deeper Slumber and the enchanted wood and the garden lands and the Cerenarian Sea and the twilight reaches of Inquanok, the crawling chaos Nyarlathotep strode brooding into the onyx castle atop unknown Kadath in the cold waste, and taunted insolently the mild gods of earth whom he had snatched abruptly from their scented revels in the marvellous sunset city.

The Case of Charles Dexter Ward.

51,000-WORD NOVEL; 1926.

H.P. Lovecraft tucked into the writing of this, his longest novel, almost immediately upon finishing up with The Dream-Quest of Unknown Kadath. *Initially he envisioned it as a novelette, but it grew and grew, and by the time it was done, it was three or four times the length he'd expected.*

The oddest thing about this novel is Lovecraft's low opinion of it. Today it is one of his most widely admired and universally loved works; but after publishing it, he was so down on it that he never considered shopping it around, and when a book publisher contacted him to inquire about publishing a novel from him, he didn't even mention its existence, replying instead with a proposal to publish a collection of short stories. This proposal went nowhere, such collections having been out of fashion at the time; but it's hard not to speculate on what might have happened if Lovecraft had sent them The Case of Charles Dexter Ward.

Lovecraft finished writing the story on Jan. 28, 1927; but it was not published until the May 1941 issue of Weird Tales, *when publication started in a two-part serial.*

A note on pronunciations: The historically proper pronunciation of "ye" as it was used in the 1600s, like in Joseph Curwen's letters in this story, is "the"; the "y" character represents a thorn. To retain the archaic feel of the printed version in the audiobook edition, however, we have employed the modern mispronunciation "yuh," as it would probably have been read that way by most 20th-century readers both within the story and among its readers.

The essential Saltes of Animals may be so prepared and preserved, that an ingenious Man may have the whole Ark of Noah in his own Studie, and raise the fine Shape of an Animal out of its Ashes at his Pleasure; and by the lyke Method from the essential Saltes of humane Dust, a

Philosopher may, without any criminal Necromancy, call up the Shape of any dead Ancestour from the Dust whereinto his Bodie has been incinerated.

— BORELLUS.

PART ONE:
A RESULT AND A PROLOGUE.

I.

From a private hospital for the insane near Providence, Rhode Island, there recently disappeared an exceedingly singular person. He bore the name of Charles Dexter Ward, and was placed under restraint most reluctantly by the grieving father who had watched his aberration grow from a mere eccentricity to a dark mania involving both a possibility of murderous tendencies and a profound and peculiar change in the apparent contents of his mind. Doctors confess themselves quite baffled by his case, since it presented oddities of a general physiological as well as psychological character.

In the first place, the patient seemed oddly older than his twenty-six years would warrant. Mental disturbance, it is true, will age one rapidly; but the face of this young man had taken on a subtle cast which only the very aged normally acquire. In the second place, his organic processes shewed a certain queerness of proportion which nothing in medical experience can parallel. Respiration and heart action had a baffling lack of symmetry; the voice was lost, so that no sounds above a whisper were possible; digestion was incredibly prolonged and minimised, and neural reactions to standard stimuli bore no relation at all to anything heretofore recorded, either normal or pathological. The skin had a morbid chill and dryness, and the cellular structure of the tissue seemed exaggeratedly coarse and loosely knit. Even a large olive birthmark on the right hip had disappeared, whilst there had formed on the chest a very peculiar mole or blackish spot of which no trace existed before. In general, all physicians agree that in Ward the processes of metabolism had become retarded to a degree beyond precedent.

Psychologically, too, Charles Ward was unique. His madness held no affinity to any sort recorded in even the latest and most exhaustive of treatises, and was conjoined to a mental force which would have made him a genius or a leader had it not been twisted into strange and grotesque forms. Dr. Willett, who was Ward's family physician, affirms that the patient's gross mental capacity, as gauged by his response to matters outside the sphere of his insanity, had actually increased since the seizure. Ward, it is true, was always a scholar and an antiquarian; but even his most brilliant early work did not shew the prodigious grasp and insight displayed during his last examinations by the alienists. It was, indeed, a difficult matter to obtain a legal commitment to the hospital, so powerful and lucid did the youth's mind seem; and only on the evidence of others, and on the strength of many abnormal gaps in his stock of information as distinguished from his intelligence, was he finally placed in confinement. To the very moment of his vanishment he was an omnivorous reader and as great a conversationalist as his poor voice permitted; and shrewd observers, failing to foresee his escape, freely predicted that he would not be long in gaining his discharge from custody.

Only Dr. Willett, who brought Charles Ward into the world and had watched his growth of body and mind ever since, seemed frightened at the thought of his future freedom. He had had a terrible experience and had made a terrible discovery which he dared not reveal to his sceptical colleagues. Willett, indeed, presents a minor mystery all his own in his connexion with the case. He was the last to see the patient before his flight, and emerged from that final conversation in a state of mixed horror and relief which several recalled when Ward's escape became known three hours later. That escape itself is one of the unsolved wonders of Dr. Waite's hospital. A window open above a sheer drop of sixty feet could hardly explain it, yet after that talk with Willett the youth was undeniably gone. Willett himself has no public explanations to offer, though he seems strangely easier in mind than before the escape. Many, indeed, feel that he would like to say more if he thought any considerable number would believe him. He had found Ward in his room, but shortly after his departure the attendants knocked in vain. When they opened the door the patient was not there, and all they found was the open window with a chill April breeze blowing in a cloud of fine bluish-grey dust that almost choked them. True, the dogs howled some time before; but that was while Willett was still present, and they had caught nothing and shewn no disturbance later on. Ward's father was told at once over the telephone, but he seemed more saddened than surprised. By the time Dr. Waite called in person, Dr. Willett had been talking with him, and both disavowed any knowledge or complicity in the escape. Only from certain closely confidential friends of Willett and the senior Ward have any clues been gained, and even these are too wildly fantastic for general credence. The one fact which remains is that up to the present time no trace of the missing madman has been unearthed.

Charles Ward was an antiquarian from infancy, no doubt gaining his taste from the venerable town around him, and from the relics of the past which filled every corner of his parents' old mansion in Prospect Street on the crest of the hill. With the years his devotion to ancient things increased; so that history, genealogy, and the study of colonial architecture, furniture, and craftsmanship at length crowded everything else from his sphere of interests. These tastes are important to remember in considering his madness; for although they do not form its absolute nucleus, they play a prominent part in its superficial form. The gaps of information which the alienists noticed were all related to modern matters, and were invariably offset by a correspondingly excessive though outwardly concealed knowledge of bygone matters as brought out by adroit questioning; so that one would have fancied the patient literally transferred

THE CASE OF

Charles Dexter Ward

H. P. LOVECRAFT

HARRY FERMAN

Weird Tales, May 1945

to a former age through some obscure sort of auto-hypnosis. The odd thing was that Ward seemed no longer interested in the antiquities he knew so well. He had, it appears, lost his regard for them through sheer familiarity; and all his final efforts were obviously bent toward mastering those common facts of the modern world which had been so totally and unmistakably expunged from his brain. That this wholesale deletion had occurred, he did his best to hide; but it was clear to all who watched him that his whole programme of reading and conversation was determined by a frantic wish to imbibe such knowledge of his own life and of the ordinary practical and cultural background of the twentieth century as ought to have been his by virtue of his birth in 1902 and his education in the schools of our own time. Alienists are now wondering how, in view of his vitally impaired range of data, the escaped patient manages to cope with the complicated world of today; the dominant opinion being that he is "lying low" in some humble and unexacting position till his stock of modern information can be brought up to the normal.

The beginning of Ward's madness is a matter of dispute among alienists. Dr. Lyman, the eminent Boston authority, places it in 1919 or 1920, during the boy's last year at the Moses Brown School, when he suddenly turned from the study of the past to the study of the occult, and refused to qualify for college on the ground that he had individual researches of much greater importance to make. This is certainly borne out by Ward's altered habits at the time, especially by his continual search through town records and among old burying-grounds for a certain grave dug in 1771; the grave of an ancestor named Joseph Curwen, some of whose papers he professed to have found behind the panelling of a very old house in Olney Court, on Stampers' Hill, which Curwen was known to have built and occupied. It is, broadly speaking, undeniable that the winter of 1919-20 saw a great change in Ward; whereby he abruptly stopped his general antiquarian pursuits and embarked on a desperate delving into occult subjects both at home and abroad, varied only by this strangely persistent search for his forefather's grave.

From this opinion, however, Dr. Willett substantially dissents; basing his verdict on his close and continuous knowledge of the patient, and on certain frightful investigations and discoveries which he made toward the last. Those investigations and discoveries have left their mark upon him; so that his voice trembles when he tells them, and his hand trembles when he tries to write of them. Willett admits that the change of 1919-20 would ordinarily appear to mark the beginning of a progressive decadence which culminated in the horrible and uncanny alienation of 1928; but believes from personal observation that a finer distinction must be made. Granting freely that the boy was always ill-balanced temperamentally, and prone to be unduly susceptible and enthusiastic in his responses to phenomena around him, he refuses to concede that the early alteration marked the actual passage from sanity to madness; crediting instead Ward's own statement that he had discovered or rediscovered something whose effect on human thought was likely to be marvellous and profound. The true madness, he is certain, came with a later change; after the Curwen portrait and the ancient papers had been unearthed; after a trip to strange foreign places had been made, and some terrible invocations chanted under strange and secret circumstances; after certain answers to these invocations had been plainly indicated, and a frantic letter penned under agonising and inexplicable conditions; after the wave of vampirism and the ominous Pawtuxet gossip; and after the patient's memory commenced to exclude contemporary images whilst his voice failed and his physical aspect underwent the subtle modification so many subsequently noticed.

It was only about this time, Willett points out with much acuteness, that the nightmare qualities became indubitably linked with Ward; and the doctor feels shudderingly sure that enough solid evidence exists to sustain the youth's claim regarding his crucial discovery. In the first place, two workmen of high intelligence saw Joseph Curwen's ancient papers found. Secondly, the boy once shewed Dr. Willett those papers and a page of the Curwen diary, and each of the documents had every appearance of genuineness. The hole where Ward claimed to have found them was long a visible reality, and Willett had a very convincing final glimpse of them in surroundings which can scarcely be believed and can never perhaps be proved. Then there were the mysteries and coincidences of the Orne and Hutchinson letters, and the problem of the Curwen penmanship and of what the detectives brought to light about Dr. Allen; these things, and the terrible message in mediaeval minuscules found in Willett's pocket when he gained consciousness after his shocking experience.

And most conclusive of all, there are the two hideous results which the doctor obtained from a certain pair of formulae during his final investigations; results which virtually proved the authenticity of the papers and of their monstrous implications at the same time that those papers were borne forever from human knowledge.

II.

One must look back at Charles Ward's earlier life as at something belonging as much to the past as the antiquities he loved so keenly. In the autumn of 1918, and with a considerable show of zest in the military training of the period, he had begun his junior year at the Moses Brown School, which lies very near his home. The old main building, erected in 1819, had always charmed his youthful antiquarian sense; and the spacious park in which the academy is set appealed to his sharp eye for landscape. His social activities were few; and his hours were spent mainly at home, in rambling walks, in his classes and drills, and in pursuit of antiquarian and genealogical data at the City Hall, the State House, the Public Library, the Athenaeum, the Historical Society, the John Carter Brown and John Hay

Libraries of Brown University, and the newly opened Shepley Library in Benefit Street. One may picture him yet as he was in those days; tall, slim, and blond, with studious eyes and a slight stoop, dressed somewhat carelessly, and giving a dominant impression of harmless awkwardness rather than attractiveness.

His walks were always adventures in antiquity, during which he managed to recapture from the myriad relics of a glamorous old city a vivid and connected picture of the centuries before. His home was a great Georgian mansion atop the well-nigh precipitous hill that rises just east of the river; and from the rear windows of its rambling wings he could look dizzily out over all the clustered spires, domes, roofs, and skyscraper summits of the lower town to the purple hills of the countryside beyond. Here he was born, and from the lovely classic porch of the double-bayed brick facade his nurse had first wheeled him in his carriage; past the little white farmhouse of two hundred years before that the town had long ago overtaken, and on toward the stately colleges along the shady, sumptuous street, whose old square brick mansions and smaller wooden houses with narrow, heavy-columned Doric porches dreamed solid and exclusive amidst their generous yards and gardens.

He had been wheeled, too, along sleepy Congdon Street, one tier lower down on the steep hill, and with all its eastern homes on high terraces. The small wooden houses averaged a greater age here, for it was up this hill that the growing town had climbed; and in these rides he had imbibed something of the colour of a quaint colonial village. The nurse used to stop and sit on the benches of Prospect Terrace to chat with policemen; and one of the child's first memories was of the great westward sea of hazy roofs and domes and steeples and far hills which he saw one winter afternoon from that great railed embankment, all violet and mystic against a fevered, apocalyptic sunset of reds and golds and purples and curious greens. The vast marble dome of the State House stood out in massive silhouette, its crowning statue haloed fantastically by a break in one of the tinted stratus clouds that barred the flaming sky.

When he was larger his famous walks began; first with his impatiently dragged nurse, and then alone in dreamy meditation. Farther and farther down that almost perpendicular hill he would venture, each time reaching older and quainter levels of the ancient city. He would hesitate gingerly down vertical Jenckes Street with its bank walls and colonial gables to the shady Benefit Street corner, where before him was a wooden antique with an Ionic-pilastered pair of doorways, and beside him a prehistoric gambrel-roofer with a bit of primal farmyard remaining, and the great Judge Durfee house with its fallen vestiges of Georgian grandeur. It was getting to be a slum here; but the titan elms cast a restoring shadow over the place, and the boy used to stroll south past the long lines of the pre-Revolutionary homes with their great central chimneys and classic portals. On the eastern side they were set high over basements with railed double flights of stone steps, and the young Charles could picture them as they were when the street was new, and red heels and periwigs set off the painted pediments whose signs of wear were now becoming so visible.

Westward the hill dropped almost as steeply as above, down to the old "Town Street" that the founders had laid out at the river's edge in 1636. Here ran innumerable little lanes with leaning, huddled houses of immense antiquity; and fascinated though he was, it was long before he dared to thread their archaic verticality for fear they would turn out a dream or a gateway to unknown terrors. He found it much less formidable to continue along Benefit Street past the iron fence of St. John's hidden churchyard and the rear of the 1761 Colony House and the mouldering bulk of the Golden Ball Inn where Washington stopped. At Meeting Street — the successive Gaol Lane and King Street of other periods — he would look upward to the east and see the arched flight of steps to which the highway had to resort in climbing the slope, and downward to the west, glimpsing the old brick colonial schoolhouse that smiles across the road at the ancient Sign of Head where the *Providence Gazette and Country-Journal* was printed before the Revolution. Then came the exquisite First Baptist Church of 1775, luxurious with its matchless Gibbs steeple, and the Georgian roofs and cupolas hovering by. Here and to the southward the neighbourhood became better, flowering at last into a marvellous group of early mansions; but still the little ancient lanes led off down the precipice to the west, spectral in their many-gabled archaism and dipping to a riot of iridescent decay where the wicked old waterfront recalls its proud East India days amidst polyglot vice and squalor, rotting wharves, and blear-eyed ship-chandleries, with such surviving alley names as Packet, Bullion, Gold, Silver, Coin, Doubloon, Sovereign, Guilder, Dollar, Dime, and Cent.

Sometimes, as he grew taller and more adventurous, young Ward would venture down into this maelstrom of tottering houses, broken transoms, tumbling steps, twisted balustrades, swarthy faces, and nameless odours; winding from South Main to South Water, searching out the docks where the bay and sound steamers still touched, and returning northward at this lower level past the steep-roofed 1816 warehouses and the broad square at the Great Bridge, where the 1773 Market House still stands firm on its ancient arches. In that square he would pause to drink in the bewildering beauty of the old town as it rises on its eastward bluff, decked with its two Georgian spires and crowned by the vast new Christian Science dome as London is crowned by St. Paul's. He liked mostly to reach this point in the late afternoon, when the slanting sunlight touches the Market House and the ancient hill roofs and belfries with gold, and throws magic around the dreaming wharves where Providence Indiamen used to ride at anchor. After a long look he would grow almost dizzy with a poet's love for the sight, and then he would scale the slope homeward in the dusk past the old white church and up the narrow precipitous ways where yellow gleams would begin to peep out in small-paned windows and through fanlights set high over double flights of steps with curious wrought-iron railings.

At other times, and in later years, he would seek for vivid contrasts; spending half a walk in the crumbling colonial regions northwest of his home, where the hill drops to the lower eminence of Stampers' Hill with its ghetto and negro quarter clustering round the place where the Boston stage coach used to start before the Revolution, and the other half in the gracious southerly realm about George, Benevolent, Power, and Williams Streets, where the old slope holds unchanged the fine estates and bits of walled garden and steep green lane in which so many fragrant memories linger. These rambles, together with the diligent studies which accompanied them, certainly account for a large amount of the antiquarian lore which at last crowded the modern world from Charles Ward's mind; and illustrate the mental soil upon which fell, in that fateful winter of 1919-20, the seeds that came to such strange and terrible fruition.

Dr. Willett is certain that, up to this ill-omened winter of first change, Charles Ward's antiquarianism was free from every trace of the morbid. Graveyards held for him no particular attraction beyond their quaintness and historic value, and of anything like violence or savage instinct he was utterly devoid. Then, by insidious degrees, there appeared to develop a curious sequel to one of his genealogical triumphs of the year before; when he had discovered among his maternal ancestors a certain very long-lived man named Joseph Curwen, who had come from Salem in March of 1692, and about whom a whispered series of highly peculiar and disquieting stories clustered.

Ward's great-great-grandfather Welcome Potter had in 1785 married a certain "Ann Tillinghast, daughter of Mrs. Eliza, daughter to Capt. James Tillinghast," of whose paternity the family had preserved no trace. Late in 1918, whilst examining a volume of original town records in manuscript, the young genealogist encountered an entry describing a legal change of name, by which in 1772 a Mrs. Eliza Curwen, widow of Joseph Curwen, resumed, along with her seven-year-old daughter Ann, her maiden name of Tillinghast; on the ground "that her Husband's name was become a public Reproach by Reason of what was knowne after his Decease; the which confirming an antient common Rumour, tho' not to be credited by a loyall Wife till so proven as to be wholely past Doubting." This entry came to light upon the accidental separation of two leaves which had been carefully pasted together and treated as one by a laboured revision of the page numbers.

It was at once clear to Charles Ward that he had indeed discovered a hitherto unknown great-great-great-grandfather. The discovery doubly excited him because he had already heard vague reports and seen scattered allusions relating to this person; about whom there remained so few publicly available records, aside from those becoming public only in modern times, that it almost seemed as if a conspiracy had existed to blot him from memory. What did appear, moreover, was of such a singular and provocative nature that one could not fail to imagine curiously what it was that the colonial recorders were so anxious to conceal and forget; or to suspect that the deletion had reasons all too valid.

Before this, Ward had been content to let his romancing about old Joseph Curwen remain in the idle stage; but having discovered his own relationship to this apparently "hushed-up" character, he proceeded to hunt out as systematically as possible whatever he might find concerning him. In this excited quest he eventually succeeded beyond his highest expectations; for old letters, diaries, and sheaves of unpublished memoirs in cobwebbed Providence garrets and elsewhere yielded many illuminating passages which their writers had not thought it worth their while to destroy. One important sidelight came from a point as remote as New York, where some Rhode Island colonial correspondence was stored in the Museum at Fraunces' Tavern. The really crucial thing, though, and what in Dr, Willett's opinion formed the definite source of Ward's undoing, was the matter found in August 1919 behind the panelling of the crumbling house in Olney Court. It was that, beyond a doubt, which opened up those black vistas whose end was deeper than the pit.

PART TWO:

AN ANTECEDENT AND A HORROR.

I.

Joseph Curwen, as revealed by the rambling legends embodied in what Ward heard and unearthed, was a very astonishing, enigmatic, and obscurely horrible individual. He had fled from Salem to Providence — that universal haven of the odd, the free, and the dissenting — at the beginning of the great witchcraft panic; being in fear of accusation because of his solitary ways and queer chemical or alchemical experiments. He was a colourless-looking man of about thirty, and was soon found qualified to become a freeman of Providence; thereafter buying a home lot just north of Gregory Dexter's at about the foot of Olney Street. His house was built on Stampers' Hill west of the Town Street, in what later became Olney Court; and in 1761 he replaced this with a larger one, on the same site, which is still standing.

Now the first odd thing about Joseph Curwen was that he did not seem to grow much older than he had been on his arrival. He engaged in shipping enterprises, purchased wharfage near Mile-End Cove, helped rebuild the Great Bridge in 1713, and in 1723 was one of the founders of the Congregational Church on the hill; but always did he retain the nondescript aspect of a man not greatly over thirty or thirty-five. As decades mounted up, this singular quality began to excite wide notice; but Curwen always explained it by saying that he came of hardy forefathers, and practised a simplicity of living which did not wear him out. How such simplicity could be reconciled with the inexplicable comings and goings of the secretive merchant, and with the queer gleaming of his windows at all hours of night, was not very clear to the townsfolk; and they were prone to assign other reasons for his continued youth and longevity. It was held, for the most part, that Curwen's incessant mixings and boilings of chemicals had much to do with his condition. Gossip spoke of the strange substances he brought from London and the Indies on his ships or purchased in Newport, Boston, and New York; and when old Dr. Jabez Bowen came from Rehoboth and opened his apothecary shop across the Great Bridge at the Sign of the Unicorn and Mortar, there was ceaseless talk of the drugs, acids, and metals that the taciturn recluse incessantly bought or ordered from him. Acting on the assumption that Curwen possessed a wondrous and secret medical skill, many sufferers of various sorts applied to him for aid; but though he appeared to encourage their belief in a non-committal way, and always gave them odd-coloured potions in response to their requests, it was observed that his ministrations to others seldom proved of benefit. At length, when over fifty years had passed since the stranger's advent, and without producing more than five years' apparent change in his face and physique, the people began to whisper more darkly; and to meet more than half way that desire for isolation which he had always shewn.

Private letters and diaries of the period reveal, too, a multitude of other reasons why Joseph Curwen was marvelled at, feared, and finally shunned like a plague. His passion for graveyards, in which he was glimpsed at all hours, and under all conditions, was notorious; though no one had witnessed any deed on his part which could actually be termed ghoulish. On the Pawtuxet Road he had a farm, at which he generally lived during the summer, and to which he would frequently be seen riding at various odd times of the day or night. Here his only visible servants, farmers, and caretakers were a sullen pair of aged Narragansett Indians; the husband dumb and curiously scarred, and the wife of a very repulsive cast of countenance, probably due to a mixture of negro blood. In the lean-to of this house was the laboratory where most of the chemical experiments were conducted. Curious porters and teamers who delivered bottles, bags, or boxes at the small rear door would exchange accounts of the fantastic flasks, crucibles, alembics, and furnaces they saw in the low shelved room; and prophesied in whispers that the close-mouthed "chymist"—by which they meant alchemist—would not be long in finding the Philosopher's Stone. The nearest neighbours to this farm—the Fenners, a quarter of a mile away—had still queerer things to tell of certain sounds which they insisted came from the Curwen place in the night. There were cries, they said, and sustained howlings; and they did not like the large number of livestock which thronged the pastures, for no such amount was needed to keep a lone old man and a very few servants in meat, milk, and wool. The identity of the stock seemed to change from week to week as new droves were purchased from the Kingstown farmers. Then, too, there was something very obnoxious about a certain great stone outbuilding with only high narrow slits for windows.

Great Bridge idlers likewise had much to say of Curwen's town house in Olney Court; not so much the fine new one built in 1761, when the man must have been nearly a century old, but the first low gambrel-roofed one with the windowless attic and shingled sides, whose timbers he took the peculiar precaution of burning after its demolition. Here there was less mystery, it is true; but the hours at which lights were seen, the secretiveness of the two swarthy foreigners who comprised the only menservants, the hideous indistinct mumbling of the incredibly aged French housekeeper, the large amounts of food seen to enter a door within which only four persons lived, and the quality of certain voices often heard in muffled conversation at highly unseasonable times, all combined with what was known of the Pawtuxet farm to give the place a bad name.

In choicer circles, too, the Curwen home was by no means undiscussed; for as the newcomer had gradually worked into the church and trading life of the town, he had naturally made acquaintances of the better sort, whose company and conversation he was well fitted by education to enjoy. His birth was known to be good, since the Curwens or Corwins of Salem needed no introduction in New England. It developed that Joseph Curwen had travelled much in very early life, living for a time in England and making at least two voyages to the Orient; and his speech, when he deigned to use it, was that of a learned and cultivated Englishman. But for some reason or other Curwen did not care for society. Whilst never actually rebuffing a visitor, he always reared such a wall of reserve that few could think of anything to say to him which would not sound inane.

There seemed to lurk in his bearing some cryptic, sardonic arrogance, as if he had come to find all human beings dull through having moved among stranger and more potent entities. When Dr. Checkley, the famous wit, came from Boston in 1738 to be rector of King's Church, he did not neglect calling on one of whom he soon heard so much; but left in a very short while because of some sinister undercurrent he detected in his host's discourse. Charles Ward told his father, when they discussed Curwen one winter evening, that he would give much to learn what the mysterious old man had said to the sprightly cleric, but that all diarists agree concerning Dr. Checkley's reluctance to repeat anything he had heard. The good man had been hideously shocked, and could never recall Joseph Curwen without a visible loss of the gay urbanity for which he was famed.

More definite, however, was the reason why another man of taste and breeding avoided the haughty hermit. In 1746 Mr. John Merritt, an elderly English gentleman of literary and scientific leanings, came from Newport to the town which was so rapidly overtaking it in standing, and built a fine country seat on the Neck in what is now the heart of the best residence section. He lived in considerable style and comfort, keeping

Weird Tales, May 1945

"They found the grave vacant—precisely as they had expected."

the first coach and liveried servants in town, and taking great pride in his telescope, his microscope, and his well-chosen library of English and Latin books. Hearing of Curwen as the owner of the best library in Providence, Mr. Merritt early paid him a call, and was more cordially received than most other callers at the house had been. His admiration for his host's ample shelves, which besides the Greek, Latin, and English classics were equipped with a remarkable battery of philosophical, mathematical, and scientific works including Paracelsus, Agricola, Van Helmont, Sylvius, Glauber, Boyle, Boerhaave, Becher, and Stahl, led Curwen to suggest a visit to the farmhouse and laboratory whither he had never invited anyone before; and the two drove out at once in Mr. Merritt's coach.

Mr. Merritt always confessed to seeing nothing really horrible at the farmhouse, but maintained that the titles of the books in the special library of thaumaturgical, alchemical, and theological subjects which Curwen kept in a front room were alone sufficient to inspire him with a lasting loathing. Perhaps, however, the facial expression of the owner in exhibiting them contributed much of the prejudice. This bizarre collection, besides a host of standard works which Mr. Merritt was not too alarmed to envy, embraced nearly all the cabbalists, daemonologists, and magicians known to man; and was a treasure-house of lore in the doubtful realms of alchemy and astrology. Hermes Trismegistus in Mesnard's edition, the *Turba Philosophorum*, Geber's *Liber Investigationis*, and Artephius's *Key of Wisdom* all were there; with the cabbalistic *Zohar*, Peter Jammy's set of *Albertus Magnus*, Raymond Lully's *Ars Magna et Ultima* in

Zetzner's edition, Roger Bacon's *Thesaurus Chemicus*, Fludd's *Clavis Alchimiae*, and Trithemius' *De Lapide Philosophico* crowding them close. Mediaeval Jews and Arabs were represented in profusion, and Mr. Merritt turned pale when, upon taking down a fine volume conspicuously labelled as the *Qanoon-e-Islam*, he found it was in truth the forbidden *Necronomicon* of the mad Arab Abdul Alhazred, of which he had heard such monstrous things whispered some years previously after the exposure of nameless rites at the strange little fishing village of Kingsport, in the Province of the Massachusetts-Bay.

But oddly enough, the worthy gentleman owned himself most impalpably disquieted by a mere minor detail. On the huge mahogany table there lay face downwards a badly worn copy of Borellus, bearing many cryptical marginalia and interlineations in Curwen's hand. The book was open at about its middle, and one paragraph displayed such thick and tremulous pen-strokes beneath the lines of mystic black-letter that the visitor could not resist scanning it through. Whether it was the nature of the passage underscored, or the feverish heaviness of the strokes which formed the underscoring, he could not tell; but something in that combination affected him very badly and very peculiarly. He recalled it to the end of his days, writing it down from memory in his diary and once trying to recite it to his close friend Dr. Checkley till he saw how greatly it disturbed the urbane rector. It read:

> *The essential Saltes of Animals may be so prepared and preserved, that an ingenious Man may have the whole Ark of Noah in his own Studie, and raise the fine Shape of an Animal out of its Ashes at his Pleasure; and by the lyke Method from the essential Saltes of humane Dust, a Philosopher may, without any criminal Necromancy, call up the Shape of any dead Ancestour from the Dust whereinto his Bodie has been incinerated.*

It was near the docks along the southerly part of the Town Street, however, that the worst things were muttered about Joseph Curwen. Sailors are superstitious folk; and the seasoned salts who manned the infinite rum, slave, and molasses sloops, the rakish privateers, and the great brigs of the Browns, Crawfords, and Tillinghasts, all made strange furtive signs of protection when they saw the slim, deceptively young-looking figure with its yellow hair and slight stoop entering the Curwen warehouse in Doubloon Street or talking with captains and supercargoes on the long quay where the Curwen ships rode restlessly. Curwen's own clerks and captains hated and feared him, and all his sailors were mongrel riff-raff from Martinique, St. Eustatius, Havana, or Port Royal. It was, in a way, the frequency with which these sailors were replaced which inspired the acutest and most tangible part of the fear in which the old man was held. A crew would be turned loose in the town on shore leave, some of its members perhaps charged with this errand or that; and when reassembled it would be almost sure to lack one or more men. That many of the errands had concerned the farm on the Pawtuxet Road, and that few of the sailors had ever been seen to return from that place, was not forgotten; so that in time it became exceedingly difficult for Curwen to keep his oddly assorted hands. Almost invariably several would desert soon after hearing the gossip of the Providence wharves, and their replacement in the West Indies became an increasingly great problem to the merchant.

By 1760 Joseph Curwen was virtually an outcast, suspected of vague horrors and daemoniac alliances which seemed all the more menacing because they could not be named, understood, or even proved to exist. The last straw may have come from the affair of the missing soldiers in 1758, for in March and April of that year two Royal regiments on their way to New France were quartered in Providence, and depleted by an inexplicable process far beyond the average rate of desertion. Rumour dwelt on the frequency with which Curwen was wont to be seen talking with the red-coated strangers; and as several of them began to be missed, people thought of the odd conditions among his own seamen. What would have happened if the regiments had not been ordered on, no one can tell.

Meanwhile the merchant's worldly affairs were prospering. He had a virtual monopoly of the town's trade in saltpetre, black pepper, and cinnamon, and easily led any other one shipping establishment save the Browns in his importation of brassware, indigo, cotton, woollens, salt, rigging, iron, paper, and English goods of every kind. Such shopkeepers as James Green, at the Sign of the Elephant in Cheapside, the Russells, at the Sign of the Golden Eagle across the Bridge, or Clark and Nightingale at the Frying-Pan and Fish near the New Coffee-House, depended almost wholly upon him for their stock; and his arrangements with the local distillers, the Narragansett dairymen and horse-breeders, and the Newport candle-makers, made him one of the prime exporters of the Colony.

Ostracised though he was, he did not lack for civic spirit of a sort. When the Colony House burned down, he subscribed handsomely to the lotteries by which the new brick one—still standing at the head of its parade in the old main street—was built in 1761. In that same year, too, he helped rebuild the Great Bridge after the October gale. He replaced many of the books of the public library consumed in the Colony House fire, and bought heavily in the lottery that gave the muddy Market Parade and deep-rutted Town Street their pavement of great round stones with a brick footwalk or "causey" in the middle. About this time, also, he built the plain but excellent new house whose doorway is still such a triumph of carving.

When the Whitefield adherents broke off from Dr. Cotton's hill church in 1743 and founded Deacon Snow's church across the Bridge, Curwen had gone with them; though his zeal and attendance soon abated. Now, however, he cultivated piety once more; as if to dispel the shadow which had thrown him into isolation and would soon begin to wreck his business fortunes if not sharply checked.

II.

The sight of this strange, pallid man, hardly middle-aged in aspect yet certainly not less than a full century old, seeking at last to emerge from a cloud of fright and detestation too vague to pin down or analyse, was at once a pathetic, a dramatic, and a contemptible thing. Such is the power of wealth and of surface gestures, however, that there came indeed a slight abatement in the visible aversion displayed toward him; especially after the rapid disappearances of his sailors abruptly ceased. He must likewise have begun to practice an extreme care and secrecy in his graveyard expeditions, for he was never again caught at such wanderings; whilst the rumours of uncanny sounds and manoeuvres at his Pawtuxet farm diminished in proportion. His rate of food consumption and cattle replacement remained abnormally high; but not until modern times, when Charles Ward examined a set of his accounts and invoices in the Shepley Library, did it occur to any person — save one embittered youth, perhaps — to make dark comparisons between the large number of Guinea blacks he imported until 1766, and the disturbingly small number for whom he could produce bona fide bills of sale either to slave-dealers at the Great Bridge or to the planters of the Narragansett Country. Certainly, the cunning and ingenuity of this abhorred character were uncannily profound, once the necessity for their exercise had become impressed upon him.

But of course the effect of all this belated mending was necessarily slight. Curwen continued to be avoided and distrusted, as indeed the one fact of his continued air of youth at a great age would have been enough to warrant; and he could see that in the end his fortunes would be likely to suffer. His elaborate studies and experiments, whatever they may have been, apparently required a heavy income for their maintenance; and since a change of environment would deprive him of the trading advantages he had gained, it would not have profited him to begin anew in a different region just then. Judgment demanded that he patch up his relations with the townsfolk of Providence, so that his presence might no longer be a signal for hushed conversation, transparent excuses of errands elsewhere, and a general atmosphere of constraint and uneasiness. His clerks, being now reduced to the shiftless and impecunious residue whom no one else would employ, were giving him much worry; and he held to his sea-captains and mates only by shrewdness in gaining some kind of ascendancy over them — a mortgage, a promissory note, or a bit of information very pertinent to their welfare. In many cases, diarists have recorded with some awe, Curwen shewed almost the power of a wizard in unearthing family secrets for questionable use. During the final five years of his life it seemed as though only direct talks with the long-dead could possibly have furnished some of the data which he had so glibly at his tongue's end.

About this time the crafty scholar hit upon a last desperate expedient to regain his footing in the community. Hitherto a complete hermit, he now determined to contract an advantageous marriage; securing as a bride some lady whose unquestioned position would make all ostracism of his home impossible. It may be that he also had deeper reasons for wishing an alliance; reasons so far outside the known cosmic sphere that only papers found a century and a half after his death caused anyone to suspect them; but of this nothing certain can ever be learned. Naturally he was aware of the horror and indignation with which any ordinary courtship of his would be received, hence he looked about for some likely candidate upon whose parents he might exert a suitable pressure. Such candidates, he found, were not at all easy to discover; since he had very particular requirements in the way of beauty, accomplishments, and social security. At length his survey narrowed down to the household of one of his best and oldest ship-captains, a widower of high birth and unblemished standing named Dutee Tillinghast, whose only daughter Eliza seemed dowered with every conceivable advantage save prospects as an heiress. Capt. Tillinghast was completely under the domination of Curwen; and consented, after a terrible interview in his cupolaed house on Power's Lane hill, to sanction the blasphemous alliance.

Eliza Tillinghast was at that time eighteen years of age, and had been reared as gently as the reduced circumstances of her father permitted. She had attended Stephen Jackson's school opposite the Court-House Parade; and had been diligently instructed by her mother, before the latter's death of smallpox in 1757, in all the arts and refinements of domestic life. A sampler of hers, worked in 1753 at the age of nine, may still be found in the rooms of the Rhode Island Historical Society. After her mother's death she had kept the house, aided only by one old black woman. Her arguments with her father concerning the proposed Curwen marriage must have been painful indeed; but of these we have no record. Certain it is that her engagement to young Ezra Weeden, second mate of the Crawford packet Enterprise, was dutifully broken off, and that her union with Joseph Curwen took place on the seventh of March, 1763, in the Baptist church, in the presence of one of the most distinguished assemblages which the town could boast; the ceremony being performed by the younger Samuel Winsor. The *Gazette* mentioned the event very briefly, and in most surviving copies the item in question seems to be cut or torn out. Ward found a single intact copy after much search in the archives of a private collector of note, observing with amusement the meaningless urbanity of the language:

> *Monday evening last, Mr. Joseph Curwen, of this Town, Merchant, was married to Miss Eliza Tillinghast, Daughter of Capt. Dutee Tillinghast, a young Lady who has real Merit, added to a beautiful Person, to grace the connubial State and perpetuate its Felicity.*

The collection of Durfee-Arnold letters, discovered by Charles Ward shortly before his first reputed madness in the private collection of Melville F. Peters, Esq., of George St., and covering this and a somewhat antecedent period, throws vivid light on the outrage done to public sentiment by this ill-assorted match. The social influence of the Tillinghasts, however, was not to be denied; and once more Joseph Curwen found his house frequented by persons whom he could never otherwise have induced to cross his threshold. His acceptance was by no means complete, and his bride was socially the sufferer through her forced venture; but at all events the wall of utter ostracism was somewhat worn down. In his treatment of his wife the strange bridegroom astonished both her and the community by displaying an extreme graciousness and consideration. The new house in Olney Court was now wholly free from disturbing manifestations, and although Curwen was much absent at the Pawtuxet farm which his wife never visited, he seemed more like a normal citizen than at any other time in his long years of residence. Only one person remained in open enmity with him, this being the youthful ship's officer whose engagement to Eliza Tillinghast had been so abruptly broken. Ezra Weeden had frankly vowed vengeance; and though of a quiet and ordinarily mild disposition, was now gaining a hate-bred, dogged purpose which boded no good to the usurping husband.

On the seventh of May, 1765, Curwen's only child Ann was born; and was christened by the Rev. John Graves of King's Church, of which both husband and wife had become communicants shortly after their marriage, in order to compromise between their respective Congregational and Baptist affiliations. The record of this birth, as well as that of the marriage two years before, was stricken from most copies of the church and town annals where it ought to appear; and Charles Ward located both with the greatest difficulty after his discovery of the widow's change of name had apprised him of his own relationship, and engendered the feverish interest which culminated in his madness. The birth entry, indeed, was found very curiously through correspondence with the heirs of the loyalist Dr. Graves, who had taken with him a duplicate set of records when he left his pastorate at the outbreak of the Revolution. Ward had tried this source because he knew that his great-great-grandmother Ann Tillinghast Potter had been an Episcopalian.

Shortly after the birth of his daughter, an event he seemed to welcome with a fervour greatly out of keeping with his usual coldness, Curwen resolved to sit for a portrait. This he had painted by a very gifted Scotsman named Cosmo Alexander, then a resident of Newport, and since famous as the early teacher of Gilbert Stuart. The likeness was said to have been executed on a wall-panel of the library of the house in Olney Court, but neither of the two old diaries mentioning it gave any hint of its ultimate disposition. At this period the erratic scholar shewed signs of unusual abstraction, and spent as much time as he possibly could at his farm on the Pawtuxet Road. He seemed, it was stated, in a condition of suppressed excitement or suspense; as if expecting some phenomenal thing or on the brink of some strange discovery. Chemistry or alchemy would appear to have played a great part, for he took from his house to the farm the greater number of his volumes on that subject.

His affectation of civic interest did not diminish, and he lost no opportunities for helping such leaders as Stephen Hopkins, Joseph Brown, and Benjamin West in their efforts to raise the cultural tone of the town, which was then much below the level of Newport in its patronage of the liberal arts. He had helped Daniel Jenckes found his bookshop in 1763, and was thereafter his best customer; extending aid likewise to the struggling *Gazette* that appeared each Wednesday at the Sign of Head. In politics he ardently supported Governor Hopkins against the Ward party whose prime strength was in Newport, and his really eloquent speech at Hacher's Hall in 1765 against the setting off of North Providence as a separate town with a pro-Ward vote in the General Assembly did more than any other one thing to wear down the prejudice against him. But Ezra Weeden, who watched him closely, sneered cynically at all this outward activity; and freely swore it was no more than a mask for some nameless traffick with the blackest gulfs of Tartarus. The revengeful youth began a systematic study of the man and his doings whenever he was in port; spending hours at night by the wharves with a dory in readiness when he saw lights in the Curwen warehouses, and following the small boat which would sometimes steal quietly off and down the bay. He also kept as close a watch as possible on the Pawtuxet farm, and was once severely bitten by the dogs the old Indian couple loosed upon him.

III.

In 1766 came the final change in Joseph Curwen. It was very sudden, and gained wide notice amongst the curious townsfolk; for the air of suspense and expectancy dropped like an old cloak, giving instant place to an ill-concealed exaltation of perfect triumph. Curwen seemed to have difficulty in restraining himself from public harangues on what he had found or learned or made; but apparently the need of secrecy was greater than the longing to share his rejoicing, for no explanation was ever offered by him. It was after this transition, which appears to have come early in July, that the sinister scholar began to astonish people by his possession of information which only their long-dead ancestors would seem to be able to impart.

But Curwen's feverish secret activities by no means ceased with this change. On the contrary, they tended rather to increase; so that more and more of his shipping business was handled by the captains whom he now bound to him by ties of fear as potent as those of bankruptcy had been. He altogether abandoned the slave trade, alleging that its profits were constantly decreasing. Every possible moment was spent at the Pawtuxet farm; though there were rumours now and then of his presence in places which, though not actually near graveyards, were yet so situated in relation to graveyards that thoughtful people wondered just how thorough the old merchant's change of habits really was. Ezra Weeden, though his periods of espionage were necessarily brief and intermittent on account of his sea voyaging, had a vindictive persistence which the bulk of the practical townsfolk and farmers lacked; and subjected Curwen's affairs to a scrutiny such as they had never had before.

Many of the odd manoeuvres of the strange merchant's vessels had been taken for granted on account of the unrest of the times, when every colonist seemed determined to resist the provisions of the Sugar Act which hampered a prominent traffick. Smuggling and evasion were the rule in Narragansett Bay, and nocturnal landings of illicit cargoes were continuous commonplaces. But Weeden, night after night following the lighters or small sloops which he saw steal off from the Curwen warehouses at the Town Street docks, soon felt assured that it was not merely His Majesty's armed ships which the sinister skulker was anxious to avoid. Prior to the change in 1766 these boats had for the most part contained chained negroes, who were carried down and across the bay and landed at an obscure point on the shore just north of Pawtuxet; being afterward driven up the bluff and across country to the Curwen farm, where they were locked in that enormous stone outbuilding which had only high narrow slits for windows. After that change, however, the whole programme was altered. Importation of slaves ceased at once, and for a time Curwen abandoned his midnight sailings. Then, about the spring of 1767, a new policy appeared. Once more the lighters grew wont to put out from the black, silent docks, and this time they would go down the bay some distance, perhaps as far as Namquit Point, where they would meet and receive cargo from strange ships of considerable size and widely varied appearance. Curwen's sailors would then deposit this cargo at the usual point on the shore, and transport it overland to the farm; locking it in the same cryptical stone building which had formerly received the negroes. The cargo consisted almost wholly of boxes and cases, of which a large proportion were oblong and heavy and disturbingly suggestive of coffins.

Weeden always watched the farm with unremitting assiduity; visiting it each night for long periods, and seldom letting a week go by without a sight except when the ground bore a footprint-revealing snow. Even then he would often walk as close as possible in the travelled road or on the ice of the neighbouring river to see what tracks others might have left. Finding his own vigils interrupted by nautical duties, he hired a tavern companion named Eleazar Smith to continue the survey during his absences; and between them the two could have set in motion some extraordinary rumours. That they did not do so was only because they knew the effect of publicity would be to warn their quarry and make further progress impossible. Instead, they wished to learn something definite before taking any action. What they did learn must have been startling indeed, and Charles Ward spoke many times to his parents of his regret at Weeden's later burning of his notebooks. All that can be told of their discoveries is what Eleazar Smith jotted down in a none too coherent diary, and what other diarists and letter-writers have timidly repeated from the statements which they finally made—and according to which the farm was only the outer shell of some vast and revolting menace, of a scope and depth too profound and intangible for more than shadowy comprehension.

It is gathered that Weeden and Smith became early convinced that a great series of tunnels and catacombs, inhabited by a very sizeable staff of persons besides the old Indian and his wife, underlay the farm. The house was an old peaked relic of the middle seventeenth century with enormous stack chimney and diamond-paned lattice windows, the laboratory being in a lean-to toward the north, where the roof came nearly to the ground. This building stood clear of any other; yet judging by the different voices heard at odd times within, it must have been accessible through secret passages beneath. These voices, before 1766, were mere mumblings and negro whisperings and frenzied screams, coupled with curious chants or invocations. After that date, however, they assumed a very singular and terrible cast as they ran the gamut betwixt dronings of dull acquiescence and explosions of frantic pain or fury, rumblings of conversation and whines of entreaty, pantings of eagerness and shouts of protest. They appeared to be in different languages, all known to Curwen, whose rasping accents were frequently distinguishable in reply, reproof, or threatening. Sometimes it seemed that several persons must be in the house; Curwen, certain captives, and the guards of those captives. There were voices of a sort that neither Weeden nor Smith had ever heard before despite their wide knowledge of foreign parts, and many that they did seem to place as belonging to this or that nationality. The nature of the conversations seemed always a kind of catechism, as if Curwen were extorting some sort of information from terrified or rebellious prisoners.

Weeden had many verbatim reports of overheard scraps in his notebook, for English, French, and Spanish, which he knew, were frequently used; but of these nothing has survived. He did, however, say that besides a few ghoulish dialogues in which the past affairs of Providence families were concerned, most of the questions and answers he could understand were historical or scientific; occasionally pertaining to very remote places and ages. Once, for example, an alternately raging and sullen figure was questioned in French about the Black Prince's massacre at Limoges in 1370, as if there were some hidden reason which he ought to know. Curwen asked the prisoner—if prisoner it were—whether the order to slay was given because of the Sign of the Goat found on the altar in the ancient Roman crypt beneath the Cathedral, or whether the Dark Man of the Haute Vienne Coven had spoken the Three Words. Failing to obtain replies, the inquisitor had seemingly resorted to extreme means; for there was a terrific shriek followed by silence and muttering and a bumping sound.

None of these colloquies was ever ocularly witnessed, since the windows were always heavily draped. Once, though, during a discourse in an unknown tongue, a shadow was seen on the curtain which startled Weeden exceedingly; reminding him of one of the puppets in a show he had seen in the autumn of 1764 in Hacher's Hall, when a man from Germantown, Pennsylvania, had given a clever mechanical spectacle advertised as "View of the Famous City of Jerusalem, in which are represented Jerusalem, the Temple of Solomon, his Royal Throne, the noted Towers, and Hills, likewise the Sufferings of Our Saviour from the Garden of Gethsemane to the Cross on the Hill of Golgotha; an artful piece of Statuary, Worthy to be seen by the Curious." It was on this occasion that the listener, who had crept close to the window of the front room whence the speaking proceeded, gave a start which roused the old Indian pair and caused them to loose the dogs on him. After that no more conversations were ever heard in the house, and Weeden and Smith concluded that Curwen had transferred his field of action to regions below.

That such regions in truth existed, seemed amply clear from many things. Faint cries and groans unmistakably came up now and then from what appeared to be the solid earth in places far from any structure; whilst hidden in the bushes along the river-bank in the rear, where the high ground sloped steeply down to the valley of the Pawtuxet, there was found an arched oaken door in a frame of heavy masonry, which was obviously an entrance to caverns within the hill. When or how these catacombs could have been constructed, Weeden was unable to say; but he frequently pointed out how easily the place might have been reached by bands of unseen workmen from the river. Joseph Curwen put his mongrel seamen to diverse uses indeed! During the heavy spring rains of 1769 the two watchers kept a sharp eye on the steep river-bank to see if any subterrene secrets might be washed to light, and were rewarded by the sight of a profusion of both human and animal bones in places where deep gullies had been worn in the banks. Naturally there might be many explanations of such things in the rear of a stock farm, and in a locality where old Indian burying-grounds were common, but Weeden and Smith drew their own inferences.

It was in January 1770, whilst Weeden and Smith were still debating vainly on what, if anything, to think or do about the whole bewildering business, that the incident of the Fortaleza occurred. Exasperated by the burning of the revenue sloop Liberty at Newport during the previous summer, the customs fleet under Admiral Wallace had adopted an increased vigilance concerning strange vessels; and on this occasion His Majesty's armed schooner Cygnet, under Capt. Charles Leslie, captured after a short pursuit one early morning the scow Fortaleza of Barcelona, Spain, under Capt. Manuel Arruda, bound according to its log from Grand Cairo, Egypt, to Providence. When searched for contraband material, this ship revealed the astonishing fact that its cargo consisted exclusively of Egyptian mummies, consigned to "Sailor A. B. C.," who would come to remove his goods in a lighter just off Namquit Point and whose identity Capt. Arruda felt himself in honour bound not to reveal. The Vice-Admiralty Court at Newport, at a loss what to do in view of the non-contraband nature of the cargo on the one hand and of the unlawful secrecy of the entry on the other hand, compromised on Collector Robinson's recommendation by freeing the ship but forbidding it a port in Rhode Island waters. There were later rumours of its having been seen in Boston Harbour, though it never openly entered the Port of Boston.

This extraordinary incident did not fail of wide remark in Providence, and there were not many who doubted the existence of some connexion between the cargo of mummies and the sinister Joseph Curwen. His exotic studies and his curious chemical importations being common knowledge, and his fondness for graveyards being common suspicion; it did not take much imagination to link him with a freakish importation which could not conceivably have been destined for anyone else in the town. As if conscious of this natural belief, Curwen took care to speak casually on several occasions of the chemical value of the balsams found in mummies; thinking perhaps that he might make the affair seem less unnatural, yet stopping just short of admitting his participation. Weeden and Smith, of course, felt no doubt whatsoever of the significance of the thing; and indulged in the wildest theories concerning Curwen and his monstrous labours.

The following spring, like that of the year before, had heavy rains; and the watchers kept careful track of the river-bank behind the Curwen farm. Large sections were washed away, and a certain number of bones discovered; but no glimpse was afforded of any actual subterranean chambers or burrows. Something was rumoured, however, at the village of Pawtuxet about a mile below, where the river flows in falls over a rocky terrace to join the placid landlocked cove. There, where quaint old cottages climbed the hill from the rustic bridge, and fishing-smacks lay anchored at their sleepy docks, a vague report went round of things that were floating down the river and flashing into sight for a minute as they went over the falls. Of course the Pawtuxet is a long river which winds through many settled regions abounding in graveyards, and of course the spring rains had been very heavy; but the fisherfolk about the bridge did not like the wild way that one of the things stared as it shot down to the still water below, or the way that another half cried out although its condition had greatly departed from that of objects which normally cry out. That rumour sent Smith — for Weeden was just then at sea — in haste to the river-bank behind the farm; where surely enough there remained the evidences of an extensive cave-in. There was, however, no trace of a passage into the steep bank; for the miniature avalanche had left behind a solid wall of mixed earth and shrubbery from aloft. Smith went to the extent of some experimental digging, but was deterred by lack of success — or perhaps by fear of possible success. It is interesting to speculate on what the persistent and revengeful Weeden would have done had he been ashore at the time.

IV.

By the autumn of 1770 Weeden decided that the time was ripe to tell others of his discoveries; for he had a large number of facts to link together, and a second eye-witness to refute the possible charge that jealousy and vindictiveness had spurred his fancy. As his first confidant he selected Capt. James Mathewson of the Enterprise, who on the one hand knew him well enough not to doubt his veracity, and on the other hand was sufficiently influential in the town to be heard in turn with respect. The colloquy took place in an upper room of Sabin's Tavern near the docks, with Smith present to corroborate virtually every statement; and it could be seen that Capt. Mathewson was tremendously impressed. Like nearly everyone else in the town, he had had black suspicions of his own anent Joseph Curwen; hence it needed only this confirmation and enlargement of data to convince him absolutely. At the end of the conference he was very grave, and enjoined strict silence upon the two younger men. He would, he said, transmit the information separately to some ten or so of the most learned and prominent citizens of Providence; ascertaining their views and following whatever advice they might have to offer. Secrecy would probably be essential in any case, for this was no matter that the town constables or militia could cope with; and above all else the excitable crowd must be kept in ignorance, lest there be enacted in these already troublous times a repetition of that frightful Salem panic of less than a century before which had first brought Curwen hither.

The right persons to tell, he believed, would be Dr. Benjamin West, whose pamphlet on the late transit of Venus proved him a scholar and keen thinker; Rev. James Manning, President of the College which had just moved up from Warren and was temporarily housed in the new King Street schoolhouse awaiting the completion of its building on the hill above Presbyterian-Lane; ex-Governor Stephen Hopkins, who had been a member of the Philosophical Society at Newport, and was a man of very broad perceptions; John Carter, publisher of the *Gazette*; all four of the Brown brothers, John, Joseph, Nicholas, and Moses, who formed the recognised local magnates, and of whom Joseph was an amateur scientist of parts; old Dr. Jabez Bowen, whose erudition was considerable, and who had much first-hand knowledge of Curwen's odd purchases; and Capt. Abraham Whipple, a privateersman of phenomenal boldness and energy who could be counted on to lead in any active measures needed. These men, if favourable, might eventually be brought together for collective deliberation; and with them would rest the responsibility of deciding whether or not to inform the Governor of the Colony, Joseph Wanton of Newport, before taking action.

The mission of Capt. Mathewson prospered beyond his highest expectations; for whilst he found one or two of the chosen confidants somewhat sceptical of the possible ghastly side of Weeden's tale, there was not one who did not think it necessary to take some sort of secret and coördinated action. Curwen, it was clear, formed a vague potential menace to the welfare of the town and Colony; and must be eliminated at any cost. Late in December 1770 a group of eminent townsmen met at the home of Stephen Hopkins and debated tentative measures. Weeden's notes, which he had given to Capt. Mathewson, were carefully read; and he and Smith were summoned to give testimony anent details. Something very like fear seized the whole assemblage before the meeting was over, though there ran through that fear a grim determination which Capt. Whipple's bluff and resonant profanity best expressed. They would not notify the Governor, because a more than legal course seemed necessary. With hidden powers of uncertain extent apparently at his disposal, Curwen was not a man who could safely be warned to leave town. Nameless reprisals might ensue, and even if the sinister creature complied, the removal would be no more than the shifting of an unclean burden to another place. The times were lawless, and men who had flouted the King's revenue forces for years were not the ones to balk at sterner things when duty impelled. Curwen must be surprised at his Pawtuxet farm by a large raiding-party of seasoned privateersmen and given one decisive chance to explain himself. If he proved a madman, amusing himself with shrieks and imaginary conversations in different voices, he would be properly confined. If something graver appeared, and if the underground horrors indeed turned out to be real, he and all with him must die. It could be done quietly, and even the widow and her father need not be told how it came about.

While these serious steps were under discussion there occurred in the town an incident so terrible and inexplicable that for a time little else was mentioned for miles around. In the middle of a moonlight January night with heavy snow underfoot there resounded over the river and up the hill a shocking series of cries which brought sleepy heads to every window; and people around Weybosset Point saw a great white thing plunging frantically along the badly cleared space in front of the Turk's Head. There was a baying of dogs in the distance, but this subsided as soon as the clamour of the awakened town became audible. Parties of men with lanterns and muskets hurried out to see what was happening, but nothing rewarded their search. The next morning, however, a giant, muscular body, stark naked, was found on the jams of ice around the southern piers of the Great Bridge, where the Long Dock stretched out beside Abbott's distil-house, and the identity of this object became a theme for endless speculation and whispering. It was not so much the younger as the older folk who whispered, for only in the patriarchs did that rigid face with horror-bulging eyes strike any chord of memory. They, shaking as they did so, exchanged furtive murmurs of wonder and fear; for in those stiff, hideous features lay a resemblance so marvellous as to be almost an identity—and that identity was with a man who had died full fifty years before.

Ezra Weeden was present at the finding; and remembering the baying of the night before, set out along Weybosset Street and across Muddy Dock Bridge whence the sound had come. He had a curious expectancy, and was not surprised when, reaching the edge of the settled district where the street merged into the Pawtuxet Road, he came upon some very curious tracks in the snow. The naked giant had been pursued by dogs and many booted men, and the returning tracks of the hounds and their masters could be easily traced. They had given up the chase upon coming too near the town. Weeden smiled grimly, and as a perfunctory detail traced the footprints back to their source. It was the Pawtuxet farm of Joseph Curwen, as he well knew it would be; and he would have given much had the yard been less confusingly trampled. As it was, he dared not seem too interested in full daylight. Dr. Bowen, to whom Weeden went at once with his report, performed an autopsy on the strange corpse, and discovered peculiarities which baffled him utterly. The digestive tracts of the huge man seemed never to have been in use, whilst the whole skin had a coarse, loosely knit texture impossible to account for. Impressed by what the old men whispered of this body's likeness to the long-dead blacksmith Daniel Green, whose great-grandson Aaron Hoppin was a supercargo in Curwen's employ, Weeden asked casual questions till he found where Green was buried. That night a party of ten visited the old North Burying Ground opposite Herrenden's Lane and opened a grave. They found it vacant, precisely as they had expected.

Meanwhile arrangements had been made with the post riders to intercept Joseph Curwen's mail, and shortly before the incident of the naked body there was found a letter from one Jedediah Orne of Salem which made the coöperating citizens think deeply. Parts of it, copied and preserved in the private archives of the Smith family where Charles Ward found it, ran as follows:

I delight that you continue in ye Gett'g at Olde Matters in your Way, and doe not think better was done at Mr. Hutchinson's in Salem-Village. Certainely, there was Noth'g butt ye liveliest Awfulness in that which H. rais'd upp from What he cou'd gather onlie a part of. What you sente, did not Worke, whether because of Any Thing miss'g, or because ye Wordes were not Righte from my Speak'g or yr Copy'g. I alone am at a Loss. I have not ye Chymicall art to followe Borellus, and owne my Self confounded by ye VII. Booke of ye Necronomicon that you recommende. But I wou'd have you Observe what was tolde to us aboute tak'g Care whom to calle up, for you are Sensible what Mr. Mather writ in ye Marginalia of— —, and can judge how truely that Horrendous thing is reported. I say to you againe, doe not call up Any that you can not put downe; by the Which I meane, Any that can in Turne call up somewhat against you, whereby your Powerfullest Devices may not be of use. Ask of the Lesser, lest the Greater shall not wish to Answer, and shall commande more than you. I was frighted when I read of your know'g what Ben Zariatnatmik hadde in his ebony Boxe, for I was conscious who must have tolde you. And againe I ask that you shalle write me as Jedediah and not Simon. In this Community a Man may not live too long, and you knowe my Plan by which I came back as my Son. I am desirous you will Acquaint me with what ye Blacke Man learnt from Sylvanus Cocidius in ye Vault, under ye Roman Wall, and will be oblig'd for ye Lend'g of ye MS. you speak of.

Another and unsigned letter from Philadelphia provoked equal thought, especially for the following passage:

I will observe what you say respecting the sending of Accounts only by yr Vessels, but can not always be certain when to expect them. In the Matter spoke of, I require onlie one more thing; but wish to be sure I apprehend you exactly. You inform me, that no Part must be missing if the finest Effects are to be had, but you can not but know how hard it is to be sure. It seems a great Hazard and Burthen to take away the whole Box, and in Town (i.e. St. Peter's, St. Paul's, St. Mary's, or Christ Church) it can scarce be done at all. But I know what Imperfections were in the one I rais'd up October last, and how many live Specimens you were forc'd to imploy before you hit upon the right Mode in the year 1766; so will be guided by you in all Matters. I am impatient for yr Brig, and inquire daily at Mr. Biddle's Wharf.

A third suspicious letter was in an unknown tongue and even an unknown alphabet. In the Smith diary found by Charles Ward a single oft-repeated combination of characters is clumsily copied; and authorities at Brown University have pronounced the alphabet Amharic or Abyssinian, although they do not recognise the word. None of these epistles was ever delivered to Curwen, though the disappearance of Jedediah Orne from Salem as recorded shortly afterward shewed that the Providence men took certain quiet steps. The Pennsylvania Historical Society also has some curious letters received by Dr. Shippen regarding the presence of an unwholesome character in Philadelphia. But more decisive steps were in the air, and it is in the secret assemblages of sworn and tested sailors and faithful old privateersmen in the Brown warehouses by night that we must look for the main fruits of Weeden's disclosures. Slowly and surely a plan of campaign was under development which would leave no trace of Joseph Curwen's noxious mysteries.

Curwen, despite all precautions, apparently felt that something was in the wind; for he was now remarked to wear an unusually worried look. His coach was seen at all hours in the town and on the Pawtuxet Road, and he dropped little by little the air of forced geniality with which he had latterly sought to combat the town's prejudice. The nearest neighbours to his farm, the Fenners, one night remarked a great shaft of light shooting into the sky from some aperture in the roof of that cryptical stone building with the high, excessively narrow windows; an event which they quickly communicated to John Brown in Providence. Mr. Brown had become the executive leader of the select group bent on Curwen's extirpation, and had informed the Fenners that some action was about to be taken. This he deemed needful because of the impossibility of their not witnessing the final raid; and he explained his course by saying that Curwen was known to be a spy of the customs officers at Newport, against whom the hand of every Providence shipper, merchant, and farmer was openly or clandestinely raised. Whether the ruse was wholly believed by neighbours who had seen so many queer things is not certain; but at any rate the Fenners were willing to connect any evil with a man of such queer ways. To them Mr. Brown had entrusted the duty of watching the Curwen farmhouse, and of regularly reporting every incident which took place there.

V.

The probability that Curwen was on guard and attempting unusual things, as suggested by the odd shaft of light, precipitated at last the action so carefully devised by the band of serious citizens. According to the Smith diary a company of about one hundred men met at 10 p.m. on Friday, April 12th, 1771, in the great room of Thurston's Tavern at the Sign of the Golden Lion on Weybosset Point across the Bridge. Of the guiding group of prominent men in addition to the leader John Brown there were present Dr. Bowen, with his case of surgical instruments, President Manning without the great periwig (the largest in the Colonies) for which he was noted, Governor Hopkins, wrapped in his dark cloak and accompanied by his seafaring brother Esek, whom he had initiated at the last moment with the permission of the rest, John Carter, Capt. Mathewson, and Capt. Whipple, who was to lead the actual raiding party. These chiefs conferred apart in a rear chamber, after which Capt. Whipple emerged to the great room and gave the gathered seamen their last oaths and instructions. Eleazar Smith was with the leaders as they sat in the rear apartment awaiting the arrival of Ezra Weeden, whose duty was to keep track of Curwen and report the departure of his coach for the farm.

About 10:30 a heavy rumble was heard on the Great Bridge, followed by the sound of a coach in the street outside; and at that hour there was no need of waiting for Weeden in order to know that the doomed man had set out for his last night of unhallowed wizardry. A moment later, as the receding coach clattered faintly over the Muddy Dock Bridge, Weeden appeared; and the raiders fell silently into military order in the street, shouldering the firelocks, fowling-pieces, or whaling harpoons which they had with them. Weeden and Smith were with the party, and of the deliberating citizens there were present for active service Capt. Whipple, the leader, Capt. Esek Hopkins, John Carter, President Manning, Capt. Mathewson, and Dr. Bowen; together with Moses Brown, who had come up at the eleventh hour though absent from the preliminary session in the tavern. All these freemen and their hundred sailors began the long march without delay, grim and a trifle apprehensive as they left the Muddy Dock behind and mounted the gentle rise of Broad Street toward the Pawtuxet Road. Just beyond Elder Snow's church some of the men turned back to take a parting look at Providence lying outspread under the early spring stars. Steeples and gables rose dark and shapely, and salt breezes swept up gently from the cove north of the Bridge. Vega was climbing above the great hill across the water, whose crest of trees was broken by the roof-line of the unfinished College edifice. At the foot of that hill, and along the narrow mounting lanes of its side, the old town dreamed; Old Providence, for whose safety and sanity so monstrous and colossal a blasphemy was about to be wiped out.

An hour and a quarter later the raiders arrived, as previously agreed, at the Fenner farmhouse; where they heard a final report on their intended victim. He had reached his farm over half an hour before, and the strange light had soon afterward shot once into the sky, but there were no lights in any visible windows. This was always the case of late. Even as this news was given another great glare arose toward the south, and the party realised that they had indeed come close to the scene of awesome and unnatural wonders. Capt. Whipple now ordered his force to separate into three divisions; one of twenty men under Eleazar Smith to strike across to the shore and guard the landing-place against possible reinforcements for Curwen until summoned by a messenger for desperate service, a second of twenty men under Capt. Esek Hopkins to steal down into the river valley behind the Curwen farm and demolish with axes or gunpowder the oaken door in the high, steep bank, and the third to close in on the house and adjacent buildings themselves. Of this division one third was to be led by Capt. Mathewson to the cryptical stone edifice with high narrow windows, another third to follow Capt. Whipple himself to the main farmhouse, and the remaining third to preserve a circle around the whole group of buildings until summoned by a final emergency signal.

The river party would break down the hillside door at the sound of a single whistle-blast, then waiting and capturing anything which might issue from the regions within. At the sound of two whistle-blasts it would advance through the aperture to oppose the enemy or join the rest of the raiding contingent. The party at the stone building would accept these respective signals in an analogous manner; forcing an entrance at the first, and at the second descending whatever passage into the ground might be discovered, and joining the general or focal warfare expected to take place within the caverns. A third or emergency signal of three blasts would summon the immediate reserve from its general guard duty; its twenty men dividing equally and entering the unknown depths through both farmhouse and stone building. Capt. Whipple's belief in the existence of catacombs was absolute, and he took no alternative into consideration when making his plans. He had with him a whistle of great power and shrillness, and did not fear any upsetting or misunderstanding of signals. The final reserve at the landing, of course, was nearly out of the whistle's range; hence would require a special messenger if needed for help. Moses Brown and John Carter went with Capt. Hopkins to the river-bank, while President Manning was detailed with Capt. Mathewson to the stone building. Dr. Bowen, with Ezra Weeden, remained in Capt. Whipple's party which was to storm the farmhouse itself. The attack was to begin as soon as a messenger from Capt. Hopkins had joined Capt. Whipple to notify him of the river party's readiness. The leader would then deliver the loud single blast, and the various advance parties would commence their simultaneous attack on three points. Shortly before 1 a.m. the three divisions left the Fenner farmhouse; one to guard the landing, another to seek the river valley and the hillside door, and the third to subdivide and attend to the actual buildings of the Curwen farm.

Eleazar Smith, who accompanied the shore-guarding party, records in his diary an uneventful march and a long wait on the bluff by the bay; broken once by what seemed to be the distant sound of the signal whistle and again by a peculiar muffled blend of roaring and crying and a powder blast which seemed to come from the same direction. Later on one man thought he caught some distant gunshots, and still later Smith himself felt the throb of titanic and thunderous words resounding in upper air. It was just before dawn that a single haggard messenger with wild eyes and a hideous unknown odour about his clothing appeared and told the detachment to disperse quietly to their homes and never again think or speak of the night's doings or of him who had been Joseph Curwen. Something about the bearing of the messenger carried a conviction which his mere words could never have conveyed; for though he was a seaman well known to many of them, there was something obscurely lost or gained in his soul which set him for evermore apart. It was the same later on when they met other old companions who had gone into that zone of horror. Most of them had lost or gained something imponderable and indescribable. They had seen or heard or felt something which was not for human creatures, and could not forget it. From them there was never any gossip, for to even the commonest of mortal instincts there are terrible boundaries. And from that single messenger the party at the shore caught a nameless awe which almost sealed their own lips. Very few are the rumours which ever came from any of them, and Eleazar Smith's diary is the only written record which has survived from that whole expedition which set forth from the Sign of the Golden Lion under the stars.

Charles Ward, however, discovered another vague sidelight in some Fenner correspondence which he found in New London, where he knew another branch of the family had lived. It seems that the Fenners, from whose house the doomed farm was distantly visible, had watched the departing columns of raiders; and had heard very clearly the angry barking of the Curwen dogs, followed by the first shrill blast which precipitated the attack. This blast had been followed by a repetition of the great shaft of light from the stone building, and in another moment, after a quick sounding of the second signal ordering a general invasion, there had come a subdued prattle of musketry followed by a horrible roaring cry which the correspondent Luke Fenner had represented in his epistle by the characters "Waaaahrrrrr-R'waaahrrr." This cry, however, had possessed a quality which no mere writing could convey, and the correspondent mentions that his mother fainted completely at the sound. It was later repeated less loudly, and further but more muffled evidences of gunfire ensued; together with a loud explosion of powder from the direction of the river. About an hour afterward all the dogs began to bark frightfully, and there were vague ground rumblings so marked that the candlesticks tottered on the mantelpiece. A strong smell of sulphur was noted; and Luke Fenner's father declared that he heard the third or emergency whistle signal, though the others failed to detect it. Muffled musketry sounded again, followed by a deep scream less piercing but even more horrible than those which had preceded it; a kind of throaty, nastily plastic cough or gurgle whose quality as a scream must have come more from its continuity and psychological import than from its actual acoustic value.

Then the flaming thing burst into sight at a point where the Curwen farm ought to lie, and the human cries of desperate and frightened men were heard. Muskets flashed and cracked, and the flaming thing fell to the ground. A second flaming thing appeared, and a shriek of human origin was plainly distinguished. Fenner wrote that he could even gather a few words belched in frenzy: "Almighty, protect thy lamb!" Then there were more shots, and the second flaming thing fell. After that came silence for about three-quarters of an hour; at the end of which time little Arthur Fenner, Luke's brother, exclaimed that he saw "a red fog" going up to the stars from the accursed farm in the distance. No one but the child can testify to this, but Luke admits the significant coincidence implied by the panic of almost convulsive fright which at the same moment arched the backs and stiffened the fur of the three cats then within the room.

Five minutes later a chill wind blew up, and the air became suffused with such an intolerable stench that only the strong freshness of the sea could have prevented its being noticed by the shore party or by any wakeful souls in Pawtuxet village. This stench was nothing which any of the Fenners had ever encountered before, and produced a kind of clutching, amorphous fear beyond that of the tomb or the charnel-house. Close upon it came the awful voice which no hapless hearer will ever be able to forget. It thundered out of the sky like a doom, and windows rattled as its echoes died away. It was deep and musical; powerful as a bass organ, but evil as the forbidden books of the Arabs. What it said no man can tell, for it spoke in an unknown tongue, but this is the writing Luke Fenner set down to portray the daemoniac intonations:

"DEESMEES — JESHET — BONEDOSEFE-DUVEMA — ENTTEMOSS."

Not till the year 1919 did any soul link this crude transcript with anything else in mortal knowledge, but Charles Ward paled as he recognised what Mirandola had denounced in shudders as the ultimate horror among black magic's incantations.

An unmistakably human shout or deep chorused scream seemed to answer this malign wonder from the Curwen farm, after which the unknown stench grew complex with an added odour equally intolerable. A wailing distinctly different from the scream now burst out, and was protracted ululantly in rising and falling paroxysms. At times it became almost articulate, though no auditor could trace any definite words; and at one point it seemed to verge toward the confines of diabolic and hysterical laughter. Then a yell of utter, ultimate fright and stark madness wrenched from scores of human throats — a yell which came strong and clear despite the depth from which it must have burst; after which darkness and silence ruled all things. Spirals of acrid smoke ascended to blot out the stars, though no flames appeared and no buildings were observed to be gone or injured on the following day.

Toward dawn two frightened messengers with monstrous and unplaceable odours saturating their clothing knocked at the Fenner door and requested a keg of rum, for which they paid very well indeed. One of them told the family that the affair of Joseph Curwen was over, and that the events of the night were not to be mentioned again. Arrogant as the order seemed, the aspect of him who gave it took away all resentment and lent it a fearsome authority; so that only these furtive letters of Luke Fenner, which he urged his Connecticut relative to destroy, remain to tell what was seen and heard. The non-compliance of that relative, whereby the letters were saved after all, has alone kept the matter from a merciful oblivion. Charles Ward had one detail to add as a result of a long canvass of Pawtuxet residents for ancestral traditions. Old Charles Slocum of that village said that there was known to his grandfather a queer rumour concerning a charred, distorted body found in the fields a week after the death of Joseph Curwen was announced. What kept the talk alive was the notion that this body, so far as could be seen in its burnt and twisted condition, was neither thoroughly human nor wholly allied to any animal which Pawtuxet folk had ever seen or read about.

VI.

Not one man who participated in that terrible raid could ever be induced to say a word concerning it, and every fragment of the vague data which survives comes from those outside the final fighting party. There is something frightful in the care with which these actual raiders destroyed each scrap which bore the least allusion to the matter. Eight sailors had been killed, but although their bodies were not produced their families were satisfied with the statement that a clash with customs officers had occurred. The same statement also covered the numerous cases of wounds, all of which were extensively bandaged and treated only by Dr. Jabez Bowen, who had accompanied the party. Hardest to explain was the nameless odour clinging to all the raiders, a thing which was discussed for weeks. Of the citizen leaders, Capt. Whipple and Moses Brown were most severely hurt, and letters of their wives testify the bewilderment which their reticence and close guarding of their bandages produced. Psychologically every participant was aged, sobered, and shaken. It is fortunate that they were all strong men of action and simple, orthodox religionists, for with more subtle introspectiveness and mental complexity they would have fared ill indeed. President Manning was the most disturbed; but even he outgrew the darkest shadow, and smothered memories in prayers. Every man of those leaders had a stirring part to play in later years, and it is perhaps fortunate that this is so. Little more than a twelvemonth afterward Capt. Whipple led the mob who burnt the revenue ship Gaspee, and in this bold act we may trace one step in the blotting out of unwholesome images.

There was delivered to the widow of Joseph Curwen a sealed leaden coffin of curious design, obviously found ready on the spot when needed, in which she was told her husband's body lay. He had, it was explained, been killed in a customs battle about which it was not politic to give details. More than this no tongue ever uttered of Joseph Curwen's end, and Charles Ward had only a single hint wherewith to construct a theory. This hint was the merest thread — a shaky underscoring of a passage in Jedediah Orne's confiscated letter to Curwen, as partly copied in Ezra Weeden's handwriting. The copy was found in the possession of Smith's descendants; and we are left to decide whether Weeden gave it to his companion after the end, as a mute clue to the abnormality which had occurred, or whether, as is more probable, Smith had it before, and added the underscoring himself from what he had managed to extract from his friend by shrewd guessing and adroit cross-questioning. The underlined passage is merely this:

> *I say to you againe, doe not call up Any that you can not put downe; by the which I meane, Any that can in turn call up somewhat against you, whereby your powerfullest Devices may not be of use. Ask of the Lesser, lest the Greater shall not wish to Answer, and shall commande more than you.*

In the light of this passage, and reflecting on what last unmentionable allies a beaten man might try to summon in his direst extremity, Charles Ward may well have wondered whether any citizen of Providence killed Joseph Curwen.

The deliberate effacement of every memory of the dead man from Providence life and annals was vastly aided by the influence of the raiding leaders. They had not at first meant to be so thorough, and had allowed the widow and her father and child to remain in ignorance of the true conditions; but Capt. Tillinghast was an astute man, and soon uncovered enough rumours to whet his horror and cause him to demand that his daughter and granddaughter change their name, burn the library and all remaining papers, and chisel the inscription from the slate slab above Joseph Curwen's grave. He knew Capt. Whipple well, and probably extracted more hints from that bluff mariner than anyone else ever gained respecting the end of the accursed sorcerer.

From that time on the obliteration of Curwen's memory became increasingly rigid, extending at last by common consent even to the town records and files of the *Gazette.* It can be compared in spirit only to the hush that lay on Oscar Wilde's name for a decade after his disgrace, and in extent only to the fate of that sinful King of Runazar in Lord Dunsany's tale, whom the Gods decided must not only cease to be, but must cease ever to have been.

Mrs. Tillinghast, as the widow became known after 1772, sold the house in Olney Court and resided with her father in Power's Lane till her death in 1817. The farm at Pawtuxet, shunned by every living soul, remained to moulder through the years; and seemed to decay with unaccountable rapidity. By 1780 only the stone and brickwork were standing, and by 1800 even these had fallen to shapeless heaps. None ventured to pierce the tangled shrubbery on the river-bank behind which the hillside door may have lain, nor did any try to frame a definite image of the scenes amidst which Joseph Curwen departed from the horrors he had wrought.

Only robust old Capt. Whipple was heard by alert listeners to mutter once in a while to himself, "Pox on that ——, but he had no business to laugh while he screamed. 'Twas as though the damn'd —— had some'at up his sleeve. For half a crown I'd burn his —— house."

PART THREE:

A SEARCH AND AN EVOCATION.

1.

Charles Ward, as we have seen, first learned in 1918 of his descent from Joseph Curwen. That he at once took an intense interest in everything pertaining to the bygone mystery is not to be wondered at; for every vague rumour that he had heard of Curwen now became something vital to himself, in whom flowed Curwen's blood. No spirited and imaginative genealogist could have done otherwise than begin forthwith an avid and systematic collection of Curwen data.

In his first delvings there was not the slightest attempt at secrecy; so that even Dr. Lyman hesitates to date the youth's madness from any period before the close of 1919. He talked freely with his family — though his mother was not particularly pleased to own an ancestor like Curwen — and with the officials of the various museums and libraries he visited. In applying to private families for records thought to be in their possession he made no concealment of his object, and shared the somewhat amused scepticism with which the accounts of the old diarists and letter-writers were regarded. He often expressed a keen wonder as to what really had taken place a century and a half before at that Pawtuxet farmhouse whose site he vainly tried to find, and what Joseph Curwen really had been.

When he came across the Smith diary and archives and encountered the letter from Jedediah Orne he decided to visit Salem and look up Curwen's early activities and connexions there, which he did during the Easter vacation of 1919. At the Essex Institute, which was well known to him from former sojourns in the glamorous old town of crumbling Puritan gables and clustered gambrel roofs, he was very kindly received, and unearthed there a considerable amount of Curwen data. He found that his ancestor was born in Salem-Village, now Danvers, seven miles from town, on the eighteenth of February (O.S.) 1662-3; and that he had run away to sea at the age of fifteen, not appearing again for nine years, when he returned with the speech, dress, and manners of a native Englishman and settled in Salem proper. At that time he had little to do with his family, but spent most of his hours with the curious books he had brought from Europe, and the strange chemicals which came for him on ships from England, France, and Holland. Certain trips of his into the country were the objects of much local inquisitiveness, and were whisperingly associated with vague rumours of fires on the hills at night.

Curwen's only close friends had been one Edward Hutchinson of Salem-Village and one Simon Orne of Salem. With these men he was often seen in conference about the Common, and visits among them were by no means infrequent. Hutchinson had a house well out toward the woods, and it was not altogether liked by sensitive people because of the sounds heard there at night. He was said to entertain strange visitors, and the lights seen from his windows were not always of the same colour. The knowledge he displayed concerning long-dead persons and long-forgotten events was considered distinctly unwholesome, and he disappeared about the time the witchcraft panic began, never to be heard from again. At that time Joseph Curwen also departed, but his settlement in Providence was soon learned of. Simon Orne lived in Salem until 1720, when his failure to grow visibly old began to excite attention. He thereafter disappeared, though thirty years later his precise counterpart and self-styled son turned up to claim his property. The claim was allowed on the strength of documents in Simon Orne's known hand, and Jedediah Orne continued to dwell in Salem till 1771, when certain letters from Providence citizens to the Rev. Thomas Barnard and others brought about his quiet removal to parts unknown.

Certain documents by and about all of these strange characters were available at the Essex Institute, the Court House, and the Registry of Deeds, and included both harmless commonplaces such as land titles and bills of sale, and furtive fragments of a more provocative nature. There were four or five unmistakable allusions to them on the witchcraft trial records; as when one Hepzibah Lawson swore on July 10, 1692, at the Court of Oyer and Terminen under Judge Hathorne, that "fortie Witches and the Blacke Man were wont to meete in the Woodes behind Mr. Hutchinson's house," and one Amity How declared at a session of August 8th before Judge Gedney that "Mr. G. B. (Rev. George Burroughs) on that Nighte putt ye Divell his Marke upon Bridget S., Jonathan A., Simon O., Deliverance W., Joseph C., Susan P., Mehitable C., and Deborah B." Then there was a catalogue of Hutchinson's uncanny library as found after his disappearance, and an unfinished manuscript in his handwriting, couched in a cipher none could read. Ward had a photostatic copy of this manuscript made, and began to work casually on the cipher as soon as it was delivered to him. After the following August his labours on the cipher became intense and feverish, and there is reason to believe from his speech and conduct that he hit upon the key before October or November. He never stated, though, whether or not he had succeeded.

But of greatest immediate interest was the Orne material. It took Ward only a short time to prove from identity of penmanship a thing he had already considered established from the text of the letter to Curwen; namely, that Simon Orne and his supposed son were one and the same person. As Orne had said to his correspondent, it was hardly safe to live too long in Salem, hence he resorted to a thirty-year sojourn abroad, and did not return to claim his lands except as a representative of a new generation. Orne had apparently been careful to destroy most of his correspondence, but the citizens who took action in 1771 found and preserved a few letters and papers which excited their wonder. There were cryptic formulae and diagrams in his and other hands which Ward now either copied with care or had photographed, and one extremely mysterious letter in a chirography that the searcher recognised from items in the Registry of Deeds as positively Joseph Curwen's.

This Curwen letter, though undated as to the year, was evidently not the one in answer to which Orne had written the confiscated missive; and from internal evidence Ward placed it not much later than 1750. It may not be amiss to give the text in full, as a sample of the style of one whose history was so dark and terrible. The recipient is addressed as "Simon," but a line (whether drawn by Curwen or Orne Ward could not tell) is run through the word.

Providence, 1 May

Brother:—

My honoured Antient friende, due Respects and earnest Wishes to Him whom we serve for yr eternall Power. I am just come upon that which you ought to knowe, concern'g the matter of the Laste Extremitie and what to doe regard' yt. I am not dispos'd to followe you in go' g Away on acct. of my yeares, for Providence hath not ye Sharpeness of ye Bay in hunt'g oute uncommon Things and bringinge to Tryall. I am ty'd up in Shippes and Goodes, and cou'd not doe as you did, besides the whiche my farme at Patuxet hath under it That you knowe, that wou'd not waite for my com'g Backe as an Other.

But I am not unreadie for harde ffortunes, as I haue tolde you, and haue longe work'd upon ye Way of get'g Backe after ye Laste. I laste Night strucke on ye Wordes that bringe up YOGGE-SOTHOTHE, and sawe for ye firste Time that fface spoke of by Ibn Schacabao in ye — — —. And IT said, that ye III Psalme in ye Liber-Damnatus holdes ye Clavicle. With Sunne in V House, Saturne in Trine, drawe ye Pentagram of Fire, and saye ye ninth Verse thrice. This Verse repeate eache Roodemas and Hallow's Eve; and ye Thing will breede in ye Outside Spheres.

And of ye Seede of Olde shal One be borne who shal looke Backe, tho' know'g not what he seekes.

Yett will this availe Nothing if there be no Heir, and if the Saltes, or the Way to make the Saltes bee not Readie for his Hands. And here I will owne, I have not taken needed Stepps nor found Much. Ye Process is plaguey harde to come neare, and it uses up such a Store of Specimens, I am harde putte to it to get Enough, notwithstand'g the Sailors I have from the Indies. Ye People aboute are become curious, but I can stande them off. Ye gentry are worse than the Populace, be'g more Circumstantiall in their Accts. and more believ'd in what they tell. That Parson and Mr. Merritt have talk'd some, I am fearfull, but no Thing soe far is Dangerous. Ye Chymical substances are easie of get'g, there be'g II. goode Chymists in Towne, Dr. Bowen and Sam Carew. I am foll'g oute what Borellus saith, and have Helpe in Abdool Al-Hazred his VII. Booke. Whatever I gette, you shal have. And in ye meane while, do not neglect to make use of ye Wordes I have here given. I have them Righte, but if you Desire to see HIM, imploy the Writinge on ye Piece of — — —, that I am putt'g in this Packet. Saye ye Verses every Roodemas and Hallow's Eve; and if yr Line runn not out, one shall bee in yeares to come that shal looke backe and use what Saltes or Stuff for Saltes you shal leave him. Job XIV. XIV.

I rejoice you are again at Salem, and hope I may see you not longe hence. I have a goode Stallion, and am think'g of get'g a Coach, there be'g one (Mr. Merritt's) in Providence alreadie, tho' ye Roades are bad. If you are dispos'd to travel, doe not pass me bye. From Boston take ye Poste Rd. thro' Dedham, Wrentham, and Attleborough, goode Taverns be'g at all these Townes. Stop at Mr. Bolcom's in Wrentham, where ye Beddes are finer than Mr. Hatch's, but eate at ye other House for their cooke is better. Turne into Providence by Patucket falls, and ye Rd. past Mr. Sayles's Tavern. My House opp. Mr. Epenetus Olney's Tavern off ye Towne Street, 1st on ye N. side of Olney's Court. Distance from Boston Store abt. XLIV miles.

Sir, I am yr olde and true ffriend and Servt. in Almonsin-Metraton.

—JOSEPHUS C.

To Mr. Simon Orne,
William's-Lane, in Salem.

This letter, oddly enough, was what first gave Ward the exact location of Curwen's Providence home; for none of the records encountered up to that time had been at all specific. The discovery was doubly striking because it indicated as the newer Curwen house, built in 1761 on the site of the old, a dilapidated building still standing in Olney Court and well known to Ward in his antiquarian rambles over Stampers' Hill. The place was indeed only a few squares from his own home on the great hill's higher ground, and was now the abode of a negro family much esteemed for occasional washing, house-cleaning, and furnace-tending services. To find, in distant Salem, such sudden proof of the significance of this familiar rookery in his own family history, was a highly impressive thing to Ward; and he resolved to explore the place immediately upon his return. The more mystical phases of the letter, which he took to be some extravagant kind of symbolism, frankly baffled him; though he noted with a thrill of curiosity that the Biblical passage referred to — Job 14:14 — was the familiar verse, "If a man die, shall he live again? All the days of my appointed time will I wait, till my change come."

II.

Young Ward came home in a state of pleasant excitement, and spent the following Saturday in a long and exhaustive study of the house in Olney Court. The place, now crumbling with age, had never been a mansion; but was a modest two-and-a-half story wooden town house of the familiar Providence colonial type, with plain peaked roof, large central chimney, and artistically carved doorway with rayed fanlight, triangular pediment, and trim Doric pilasters. It had suffered but little alteration externally, and Ward felt he was gazing on something very close to the sinister matters of his quest.

The present negro inhabitants were known to him, and he was very courteously shewn about the interior by old Asa and his stout wife Hannah. Here there was more change than the outside indicated, and Ward saw with regret that fully half of the fine scroll-and-urn overmantels and shell-carved cupboard linings were gone, whilst much of the fine wainscotting and bolection moulding was marked, hacked, and gouged, or covered up altogether with cheap wall-paper. In general, the survey did not yield as much as Ward had somehow expected; but it was at least exciting to stand within the ancestral walls which had housed such a man of horror as Joseph Curwen. He saw with a thrill that a monogram had been very carefully effaced from the ancient brass knocker.

From then until after the close of school Ward spent his time on the photostatic copy of the Hutchinson cipher and the accumulation of local Curwen data. The former still proved unyielding; but of the latter he obtained so much, and so many clues to similar data elsewhere, that he was ready by July to make a trip to New London and New York to consult old letters whose presence in those places was indicated. This trip was very fruitful, for it brought him the Fenner letters with their terrible description of the Pawtuxet farmhouse raid, and the Nightingale-Talbot letters in which he learned of the portrait painted on a panel of the Curwen library. This matter of the portrait interested him particularly, since he would have given much to know just what Joseph Curwen looked like; and he decided to make a second search of the house in Olney Court to see if there might not be some trace of the ancient features beneath peeling coats of later paint or layers of mouldy wall-paper.

Early in August that search took place, and Ward went carefully over the walls of every room sizeable enough to have been by any possibility the library of the evil builder. He paid especial attention to the large panels of such overmantels as still remained; and was keenly excited after about an hour, when on a broad area above the fireplace in a spacious ground-floor room he became certain that the surface brought out by the peeling of several coats of paint was sensibly darker than any ordinary interior paint or the wood beneath it was likely to have been. A few more careful tests with a thin knife, and he knew that he had come upon an oil portrait of great extent. With truly scholarly restraint the youth did not risk the damage which an immediate attempt to uncover the hidden picture with the knife might have done, but just retired from the scene of his discovery to enlist expert help. In three days he returned with an artist of long experience, Mr. Walter C. Dwight, whose studio is near the foot of College Hill; and that accomplished restorer of paintings set to work at once with proper methods and chemical substances. Old Asa and his wife were duly excited over their strange visitors, and were properly reimbursed for this invasion of their domestic hearth.

As day by day the work of restoration progressed, Charles Ward looked on with growing interest at the lines and shades gradually unveiled after their long oblivion. Dwight had begun at the bottom; hence since the picture was a three-quarter-length one, the face did not come out for some time. It was meanwhile seen that the subject was a spare, well-shaped man with dark-blue coat, embroidered waistcoat, black satin small-clothes, and white silk stockings, seated in a carved chair against the background of a window with wharves and ships beyond. When the head came out it was observed to bear a neat Albemarle wig, and to possess a thin, calm, undistinguished face which seemed somehow familiar to both Ward and the artist. Only at the very last, though, did the restorer and his client begin to gasp with astonishment at the details of that lean, pallid visage, and to recognise with a touch of awe the dramatic trick which heredity had played. For it took the final bath of oil and the final stroke of the delicate scraper to bring out fully the expression which centuries had hidden; and to confront the bewildered Charles Dexter Ward, dweller in the past, with his own living features in the countenance of his horrible great-great- great-grandfather.

Ward brought his parents to see the marvel he had uncovered, and his father at once determined to purchase the picture despite its execution on stationary panelling. The resemblance to the boy, despite an appearance of rather greater age, was marvellous; and it could be seen that through some trick of atavism the physical contours of Joseph Curwen had found precise duplication after a century and a half. Mrs. Ward's resemblance to her ancestor was not at all marked, though she could recall relatives who had some of the facial characteristics shared by her son and by the bygone Curwen. She did not relish the discovery, and told her husband that he had better burn the picture instead of bringing it home. There was, she averred, something unwholesome about it; not only intrinsically, but in its very resemblance to Charles. Mr. Ward, however, was a practical man of power and affairs — a cotton manufacturer with extensive mills at Riverpoint in the Pawtuxet Valley — and not one to listen to feminine scruples. The picture impressed him mightily with its likeness to his son, and he believed the boy deserved it as a present. In this opinion, it is needless to say, Charles most heartily concurred; and a few days later Mr. Ward located the owner of the house — a small rodent-featured person with a guttural accent — and obtained the whole mantel and overmantel bearing the picture at a curtly fixed price which cut short the impending torrent of unctuous haggling.

It now remained to take off the panelling and remove it to the Ward home, where provisions were made for its thorough restoration and installation with an electric mock-fireplace in Charles's third-floor study or library. To Charles was left the task of superintending this removal, and on the twenty-eighth of August he accompanied two expert workmen from the Crooker decorating firm to the house in Olney Court, where the mantel and portrait-bearing overmantel were detached with great care and precision for transportation in the company's motor truck. There was left a space of exposed brickwork marking the chimney's course, and in this young Ward observed a cubical recess about a foot square, which must have lain directly behind the head of the portrait. Curious as to what such a space might mean or contain, the youth approached and looked within; finding beneath the deep coatings of dust and soot some loose yellowed papers, a crude, thick copybook, and a few mouldering textile shreds which may have formed the ribbon binding the rest together. Blowing away the bulk of the dirt and cinders, he took up the book and looked at the bold inscription on its cover. It was in a hand which he had learned to recognise at the Essex Institute, and proclaimed the volume as the "Journall and Notes of Jos: Curwen, Gent., of Providence-Plantations, Late of Salem."

Excited beyond measure by his discovery, Ward shewed the book to the two curious workmen beside him. Their testimony is absolute as to the nature and genuineness of the finding, and Dr. Willett relies on them to help establish his theory that the youth was not mad when he began his major eccentricities. All the other papers were likewise in Curwen's handwriting, and one of them seemed especially portentous because of its inscription: "To Him Who Shal Come After, & How He May Gett Beyonde Time & ye Spheres." Another was in a cipher; the same, Ward hoped, as the Hutchinson cipher which had hitherto baffled him. A third, and here the searcher rejoiced, seemed to be a key to the cipher; whilst the fourth and fifth were addressed respectively to "Edw. Hutchinson, Armiger" and "Jedediah Orne, esq.," "or Their Heir or Heirs, or Those Represent'g Them." The sixth and last was inscribed: "Joseph Curwen his Life and Travells Bet'n ye yeares 1678 and 1687: Of Whither He Voyag'd, Where He Stay'd, Whom He Sawe, and What He Learnt."

III.

We have now reached the point from which the more academic school of alienists date Charles Ward's madness. Upon his discovery the youth had looked immediately at a few of the inner pages of the book and manuscripts, and had evidently seen something which impressed him tremendously. Indeed, in shewing the titles to the workmen, he appeared to guard the text itself with peculiar care, and to labour under a perturbation for which even the antiquarian and genealogical significance of the find could hardly account. Upon returning home he broke the news with an almost embarrassed air, as if he wished to convey an idea of its supreme importance without having to exhibit the evidence itself. He did not even shew the titles to his parents, but simply told them that he had found some documents in Joseph Curwen's handwriting, "mostly in cipher," which would have to be studied very carefully before yielding up their true meaning. It is unlikely that he would have shewn what he did to the workmen, had it not been for their unconcealed curiosity. As it was he doubtless wished to avoid any display of peculiar reticence which would increase their discussion of the matter.

That night Charles Ward sat up in his room reading the new-found book and papers, and when day came he did not desist. His meals, on his urgent request when his mother called to see what was amiss, were sent up to him; and in the afternoon he appeared only briefly when the men came to install the Curwen picture and mantelpiece in his study. The next night he slept in snatches in his clothes, meanwhile wrestling feverishly with the unravelling of the cipher manuscript. In the morning his mother saw that he was at work on the photostatic copy of the Hutchinson cipher, which he had frequently shewn her before; but in response to her query he said that the Curwen key could not be applied to it. That afternoon he abandoned his work and watched the men fascinatedly as they finished their installation of the picture with its woodwork above a cleverly realistic electric log, setting the mock-fireplace and overmantel a little out from the north wall as if a chimney existed, and boxing in the sides with panelling to match the room's. The front panel holding the picture was sawn and hinged to allow cupboard space behind it. After the workmen went he moved his work into the study and sat down before it with his eyes half on the cipher and half on the portrait which stared back at him like a year-adding and century-recalling mirror.

His parents, subsequently recalling his conduct at this period, give interesting details anent the policy of concealment which he practiced. Before servants he seldom hid any paper which he might be studying, since he rightly assumed that Curwen's intricate and archaic chirography would be too much for them. With his parents, however, he was more circumspect; and unless the manuscript in question were a cipher, or a mere mass of cryptic symbols and unknown ideographs (as that entitled "To Him Who Shal Come After, etc." seemed to be), he would cover it with some convenient paper until his caller had departed. At night he kept the papers under lock and key in an antique cabinet of his, where he also placed them whenever he left the room. He soon resumed fairly regular hours and habits, except that his long walks and other outside interests seemed to cease. The opening of school, where he now began his senior year, seemed a great bore to him; and he frequently asserted his determination never to bother with college. He had, he said, important special investigations to make, which would provide him with more avenues toward knowledge and the humanities than any university which the world could boast.

Naturally, only one who had always been more or less studious, eccentric, and solitary could have pursued this course for many days without attracting notice. Ward, however, was constitutionally a scholar and a hermit; hence his parents were less surprised than regretful at the close confinement and secrecy he adopted. At the same time, both his father and mother thought it odd that he would shew them no scrap of his treasure-trove, nor give any connected account of such data as he had deciphered. This reticence he explained away as due to a wish to wait until he might announce some connected revelation, but as the weeks passed without further disclosures there began to grow up between the youth and his family a kind of constraint; intensified in his mother's case by her manifest disapproval of all Curwen delvings.

During October Ward began visiting the libraries again, but no longer for the antiquarian matter of his former days. Witchcraft and magic, occultism and daemonology, were what he sought now; and when Providence sources proved unfruitful he would take the train for Boston and tap the wealth of the great library in Copley Square, the Widener Library at Harvard, or the Zion Research Library in Brookline, where certain rare works on Biblical subjects are available. He bought extensively, and fitted up a whole additional set of shelves in his study for newly acquired works on uncanny subjects; while during the Christmas holidays he made a round of out-of-town trips including one to Salem to consult certain records at the Essex Institute.

About the middle of January, 1920, there entered Ward's bearing an element of triumph which he did not explain, and he was no more found at work upon the Hutchinson cipher. Instead, he inaugurated a dual policy of chemical research and record-scanning; fitting up for the one a laboratory in the unused attic of the house, and for the latter haunting all the sources of vital statistics in Providence. Local dealers in drugs and scientific supplies, later questioned, gave astonishingly queer and meaningless catalogues of the substances and instruments he purchased; but clerks at the State House, the City Hall, and the various libraries agree as to the definite object of his second interest. He was searching intensely and feverishly for the grave of Joseph Curwen, from whose slate slab an older generation had so wisely blotted the name.

Little by little there grew upon the Ward family the conviction that something was wrong. Charles had had freaks and changes of minor interests before, but this growing secrecy and absorption in strange pursuits was unlike even him. His school work was the merest pretence; and although he failed in no test, it could be seen that the old application had all vanished. He had other concernments now; and when not in his new laboratory with a score of obsolete alchemical books, could be found either poring over old burial records down town or glued to his volumes of occult lore in his study, where the startlingly—one almost fancied increasingly—similar features of Joseph Curwen stared blandly at him from the great overmantel on the north wall.

Late in March Ward added to his archive-searching a ghoulish series of rambles about the various ancient cemeteries of the city. The cause appeared later, when it was learned from City Hall clerks that he had probably found an important clue. His quest had suddenly shifted from the grave of Joseph Curwen to that of one Naphthali Field; and this shift was explained when, upon going over the files that he had been over, the investigators actually found a fragmentary record of Curwen's burial which had escaped the general obliteration, and which stated that the curious leaden coffin had been interred "10 ft. S. and 5 ft. W. of Naphthali Field's grave in y— —." The lack of a specified burying-ground in the surviving entry greatly complicated the search, and Naphthali Field's grave seemed as elusive as that of Curwen; but here no systematic effacement had existed, and one might reasonably be expected to stumble on the stone itself even if its record had perished. Hence the rambles—from which St. John's (the former King's) Churchyard and the ancient Congregational burying-ground in the midst of Swan Point Cemetery were excluded, since other statistics had shewn that the only Naphthali Field (obiit 1729) whose grave could have been meant had been a Baptist.

IV.

It was toward May when Dr. Willett, at the request of the senior Ward, and fortified with all the Curwen data which the family had gleaned from Charles in his non-secretive days, talked with the young man. The interview was of little value or conclusiveness, for Willett felt at every moment that Charles was thoroughly master of himself and in touch with matters of real importance; but it at least forced the secretive youth to offer some rational explanation of his recent demeanour. Of a pallid, impassive type not easily shewing embarrassment, Ward seemed quite ready to discuss his pursuits, though not to reveal their object. He stated that the papers of his ancestor had contained some remarkable secrets of early scientific knowledge, for the most part in cipher, of an apparent scope comparable only to the discoveries of Friar Bacon and perhaps surpassing even those. They were, however, meaningless except when correlated with a body of learning now wholly obsolete; so that their immediate presentation to a world equipped only with modern science would rob them of all impressiveness and dramatic significance. To take their vivid place in the history of human thought they must first be correlated by one familiar with the background out of which they evolved, and to this task of correlation Ward was now devoting himself. He was seeking to acquire as fast as possible those neglected arts of old which a true interpreter of the Curwen data must possess, and hoped in time to make a full announcement and presentation of the utmost interest to mankind and to the world of thought. Not even Einstein, he declared, could more profoundly revolutionise the current conception of things.

As to his graveyard search, whose object he freely admitted, but the details of whose progress he did not relate, he said he had reason to think that Joseph Curwen's mutilated headstone bore certain mystic symbols — carved from directions in his will and ignorantly spared by those who had effaced the name — which were absolutely essential to the final solution of his cryptic system. Curwen, he believed, had wished to guard his secret with care; and had consequently distributed the data in an exceedingly curious fashion. When Dr. Willett asked to see the mystic documents, Ward displayed much reluctance and tried to put him off with such things as photostatic copies of the Hutchinson cipher and Orne formulae and diagrams; but finally shewed him the exteriors of some of the real Curwen finds — the "Journall and Notes," the cipher (title in cipher also), and the formula-filled message "To Him Who Shal Come After" — and let him glance inside such as were in obscure characters.

He also opened the diary at a page carefully selected for its innocuousness and gave Willett a glimpse of Curwen's connected handwriting in English. The doctor noted very closely the crabbed and complicated letters, and the general aura of the seventeenth century which clung round both penmanship and style despite the writer's survival into the eighteenth century, and became quickly certain that the document was genuine. The text itself was relatively trivial, and Willett recalled only a fragment:

> *Wedn. 16 Octr. 1754. My Sloope the* Wakeful *this Day putt in from London with XX newe Men pick'd up in ye Indies, Spaniards from Martineco and 2 Dutch Men from Surinam. Ye Dutch Men are like to Desert from have'g hearde Somewhat ill of these Ventures, but I will see to ye Inducing of them to Staye. ffor Mr. Knight Dexter of ye Bay and Book 120 Pieces Camblets, 100 Pieces Assrtd. Cambleteens, 20 Pieces blue Duffles, 100 Pieces Shalloons, 50 Pieces Calamancoes, 300 Pieces each, Shendsoy and Humhums. ffor Mr. Green at ye Elephant 50 Gallon Cyttles, 20 Warm'g Pannes, 15 Bake Cyttles, 10 pr. Smoke'g Tonges. ffor Mr. Perrigo 1 Sett of Awles. ffor Mr. Nightingale 50 Reames prime Foolscap. Say'd ye SABAOTH thrice last Nighte but None appear'd. I must heare more from Mr. H. in Transylvania, tho' it is Harde reach'g him and exceeding strange he can not give me the Use of what he hath so well us'd these hundred yeares. Simon hath not Writ these V. Weekes, but I expecte soon hear'g from him.*

When upon reaching this point Dr. Willett turned the leaf he was quickly checked by Ward, who almost snatched the book from his grasp. All that the doctor had a chance to see on the newly opened page was a brief pair of sentences; but these, strangely enough, lingered tenaciously in his memory. They ran:

> *Ye Verse from Liber-Damnatus be'g spoke V Roodmasses and IV Hallows-Eves, I am Hopeful ye Thing is breed'g Outside ye Spheres. It will drawe One who is to Come, if I can make sure he shal bee, and he shall think on Past thinges and looke back thro' all ye yeares, against ye which I must have ready ye Saltes or That to make 'em with.*

Willett saw no more, but somehow this small glimpse gave a new and vague terror to the painted features of Joseph Curwen which stared blandly down from the overmantel. Ever after that he entertained the odd fancy — which his medical skill of course assured him was only a fancy — that the eyes of the portrait had a sort of wish, if not an actual tendency, to follow young Charles Ward as he moved about the room. He stopped before leaving to study the picture closely, marvelling at its resemblance to Charles and memorising every minute detail of the cryptical, colourless face, even down to a slight scar or pit in the smooth brow above the right eye. Cosmo Alexander, he decided, was a painter worthy of the Scotland that produced Raeburn, and a teacher worthy of his illustrious pupil Gilbert Stuart.

Assured by the doctor that Charles's mental health was in no danger, but that on the other hand he was engaged in researches which might prove of real importance, the Wards were more lenient than they might otherwise have been when during the following June the youth made positive his refusal to attend college. He had, he declared, studies of much more vital importance to pursue; and intimated a wish to go abroad the following year in order to avail himself of certain sources of data not existing in America. The senior Ward, while denying this latter wish as absurd for a boy of only eighteen, acquiesced regarding the university; so that after a none too brilliant graduation from the Moses Brown School there ensued for Charles a three-year period of intensive occult study and graveyard searching. He became recognised as an eccentric, and dropped even more completely from the sight of his family's friends than he had been before; keeping close to his work and only occasionally making trips to other cities to consult obscure records. Once he went south to talk with a strange old mulatto who dwelt in a swamp and about whom a newspaper had printed a curious article. Again he sought a small village in the Adirondacks whence reports of certain odd ceremonial practices had come. But still his parents forbade him the trip to the Old World which he desired.

Coming of age in April, 1923, and having previously

inherited a small competence from his maternal grandfather, Ward determined at last to take the European trip hitherto denied him. Of his proposed itinerary he would say nothing save that the needs of his studies would carry him to many places, but he promised to write his parents fully and faithfully. When they saw he could not be dissuaded, they ceased all opposition and helped as best they could; so that in June the young man sailed for Liverpool with the farewell blessings of his father and mother, who accompanied him to Boston and waved him out of sight from the White Star pier in Charlestown. Letters soon told of his safe arrival, and of his securing good quarters in Great Russell Street, London; where he proposed to stay, shunning all family friends, till he had exhausted the resources of the British Museum in a certain direction. Of his daily life he wrote but little, for there was little to write. Study and experiment consumed all his time, and he mentioned a laboratory which he had established in one of his rooms. That he said nothing of antiquarian rambles in the glamorous old city with its luring skyline of ancient domes and steeples and its tangles of roads and alleys whose mystic convolutions and sudden vistas alternately beckon and surprise, was taken by his parents as a good index of the degree to which his new interests had engrossed his mind.

In June, 1924, a brief note told of his departure for Paris, to which he had before made one or two flying trips for material in the Bibliothèque Nationale. For three months thereafter he sent only postal cards, giving an address in the Rue St. Jacques and referring to a special search among rare manuscripts in the library of an unnamed private collector. He avoided acquaintances, and no tourists brought back reports of having seen him. Then came a silence, and in October the Wards received a picture card from Prague, Czecho-Slovakia, stating that Charles was in that ancient town for the purpose of conferring with a certain very aged man supposed to be the last living possessor of some very curious mediaeval information. He gave an address in the Neustadt, and announced no move till the following January; when he dropped several cards from Vienna telling of his passage through that city on the way toward a more easterly region whither one of his correspondents and fellow-delvers into the occult had invited him.

The next card was from Klausenburg in Transylvania, and told of Ward's progress toward his destination. He was going to visit a Baron Ferenczy, whose estate lay in the mountains east of Rakus; and was to be addressed at Rakus in the care of that nobleman. Another card from Rakus a week later, saying that his host's carriage had met him and that he was leaving the village for the mountains, was his last message for a considerable time; indeed, he did not reply to his parents' frequent letters until May, when he wrote to discourage the plan of his mother for a meeting in London, Paris, or Rome during the summer, when the elder Wards were planning to travel in Europe. His researches, he said, were such that he could not leave his present quarters; while the situation of Baron Ferenczy's castle did not favour visits. It was on a crag in the dark wooded mountains, and the region was so shunned by the country folk that normal people could not help feeling ill at ease. Moreover, the Baron was not a person likely to appeal to correct and conservative New England gentlefolk. His aspect and manners had idiosyncrasies, and his age was so great as to be disquieting. It would be better, Charles said, if his parents would wait for his return to Providence; which could scarcely be far distant.

That return did not, however, take place until May 1926, when after a few heralding cards the young wanderer quietly slipped into New York on the *Homeric* and traversed the long miles to Providence by motor-coach, eagerly drinking in the green rolling hills, the fragrant, blossoming orchards, and the white steepled towns of vernal Connecticut; his first taste of ancient New England in nearly four years. When the coach crossed the Pawcatuck and entered Rhode Island amidst the faery goldenness of a late spring afternoon his heart beat with quickened force, and the entry to Providence along Reservoir and Elmwood avenues was a breathless and wonderful thing despite the depths of forbidden lore to which he had delved. At the high square where Broad, Weybosset, and Empire Streets join, he saw before and below him in the fire of sunset the pleasant, remembered houses and domes and steeples of the old town; and his head swam curiously as the vehicle rolled down to the terminal behind the Biltmore, bringing into view the great dome and soft, roof-pierced greenery of the ancient hill across the river, and the tall colonial spire of the First Baptist Church limned pink in the magic evening light against the fresh springtime verdure of its precipitous background.

Old Providence! It was this place and the mysterious forces of its long, continuous history which had brought him into being, and which had drawn him back toward marvels and secrets whose boundaries no prophet might fix. Here lay the arcana, wondrous or dreadful as the case might be, for which all his years of travel and application had been preparing him. A taxicab whirled him through Post Office Square with its glimpse of the river, the old Market House, and the head of the bay, and up the steep curved slope of Waterman Street to Prospect, where the vast gleaming dome and sunset-flushed Ionic columns of the Christian Science Church beckoned northward. Then eight squares past the fine old estates his childish eyes had known, and the quaint brick sidewalks so often trodden by his youthful feet. And at last the little white overtaken farmhouse on the right, on the left the classic Adam porch and stately bayed facade of the great brick house where he was born. It was twilight, and Charles Dexter Ward had come home.

V.

A school of alienists slightly less academic than Dr. Lyman's assign to Ward's European trip the beginning of his true madness. Admitting that he was sane when he started, they believe that his conduct upon returning implies a disastrous change. But even to this claim

Dr. Willett refuses to accede. There was, he insists, something later; and the queernesses of the youth at this stage he attributes to the practice of rituals learned abroad — odd enough things, to be sure, but by no means implying mental aberration on the part of their celebrant. Ward himself, though visibly aged and hardened, was still normal in his general reactions; and in several talks with Willett displayed a balance which no madman — even an incipient one — could feign continuously for long. What elicited the notion of insanity at this period were the sounds heard at all hours from Ward's attic laboratory, in which he kept himself most of the time. There were chantings and repetitions, and thunderous declamations in uncanny rhythms; and although these sounds were always in Ward's own voice, there was something in the quality of that voice, and in the accents of the formulae it pronounced, which could not but chill the blood of every hearer. It was noticed that Nig, the venerable and beloved black cat of the household, bristled and arched his back perceptibly when certain of the tones were heard.

The odours occasionally wafted from the laboratory were likewise exceedingly strange. Sometimes they were very noxious, but more often they were aromatic, with a haunting, elusive quality which seemed to have the power of inducing fantastic images. People who smelled them had a tendency to glimpse momentary mirages of enormous vistas, with strange hills or endless avenues of sphinxes and hippogriffs stretching off into infinite distance.

Ward did not resume his old-time rambles, but applied himself diligently to the strange books he had brought home, and to equally strange delvings within his quarters; explaining that European sources had greatly enlarged the possibilities of his work, and promising great revelations in the years to come. His older aspect increased to a startling degree his resemblance to the Curwen portrait in his library; and Dr. Willett would often pause by the latter after a call, marvelling at the virtual identity, and reflecting that only the small pit above the picture's right eye now remained to differentiate the long-dead wizard from the living youth. These calls of Willett's, undertaken at the request of the senior Wards, were curious affairs. Ward at no time repulsed the doctor, but the latter saw that he could never reach the young man's inner psychology. Frequently he noted peculiar things about; little wax images of grotesque design on the shelves or tables, and the half-erased remnants of circles, triangles, and pentagrams in chalk or charcoal on the cleared central space of the large room. And always in the night those rhythms and incantations thundered, till it became very difficult to keep servants or suppress furtive talk of Charles's madness.

In January, 1927, a peculiar incident occurred. One night about midnight, as Charles was chanting a ritual whose weird cadence echoed unpleasantly through the house below, there came a sudden gust of chill wind from the bay, and a faint, obscure trembling of the earth which everyone in the neighbourhood noted. At the same time the cat exhibited phenomenal traces of fright, while dogs bayed for as much as a mile around. This was the prelude to a sharp thunderstorm, anomalous for the season, which brought with it such a crash that Mr. and Mrs. Ward believed the house had been struck. They rushed upstairs to see what damage had been done, but Charles met them at the door to the attic; pale, resolute, and portentous, with an almost fearsome combination of triumph and seriousness on his face. He assured them that the house had not really been struck, and that the storm would soon be over. They paused, and looking through a window saw that he was indeed right; for the lightning flashed farther and farther off, whilst the trees ceased to bend in the strange frigid gust from the water. The thunder sank to a sort of dull mumbling chuckle and finally died away. Stars came out, and the stamp of triumph on Charles Ward's face crystallised into a very singular expression.

For two months or more after this incident Ward was less confined than usual to his laboratory. He exhibited a curious interest in the weather, and made odd inquiries about the date of the spring thawing of the ground. One night late in March he left the house after midnight, and did not return till almost morning; when his mother, being wakeful, heard a rumbling motor draw up to the carriage entrance. Muffled oaths could be distinguished, and Mrs. Ward, rising and going to the window, saw four dark figures removing a long, heavy box from a truck at Charles's direction and carrying it within by the side door. She heard laboured breathing and ponderous footfalls on the stairs, and finally a dull thumping in the attic; after which the footfalls descended again, and the four men reappeared outside and drove off in their truck.

The next day Charles resumed his strict attic seclusion, drawing down the dark shades of his laboratory windows and appearing to be working on some metal substance. He would open the door to no one, and steadfastly refused all proffered food. About noon a wrenching sound followed by a terrible cry and a fall were heard, but when Mrs. Ward rapped at the door her son at length answered faintly, and told her that nothing had gone amiss. The hideous and indescribable stench now welling out was absolutely harmless and unfortunately necessary. Solitude was the one prime essential, and he would appear later for dinner. That afternoon, after the conclusion of some odd hissing sounds which came from behind the locked portal, he did finally appear; wearing an extremely haggard aspect and forbidding anyone to enter the laboratory upon any pretext. This, indeed, proved the beginning of a new policy of secrecy; for never afterward was any other person permitted to visit either the mysterious garret workroom or the adjacent storeroom which he cleaned out, furnished roughly, and added to his inviolably private domain as a sleeping apartment. Here he lived, with books brought up from his library beneath, till the time he purchased the Pawtuxet bungalow and moved to it all his scientific effects.

In the evening Charles secured the paper before the rest of the family and damaged part of it through an apparent accident. Later on Dr. Willett, having fixed the date from statements by various members of the household, looked up an intact copy at the *Journal* office and found that in the destroyed section the following small item had occurred:

NOCTURNAL DIGGERS
SURPRISED IN
NORTH BURIAL GROUND.

Robert Hart, night watchman at the North Burial Ground, this morning discovered a party of several men with a motor truck in the oldest part of the cemetery, but apparently frightened them off before they had accomplished whatever their object may have been.

The discovery took place at about four o'clock, when Hart's attention was attracted by the sound of a motor outside his shelter. Investigating, he saw a large truck on the main drive several rods away; but could not reach it before the sound of his feet on the gravel had revealed his approach. The men hastily placed a large box in the truck and drove away toward the street before they could be overtaken; and since no known grave was disturbed, Hart believes that this box was an object which they wished to bury.

The diggers must have been at work for a long while before detection, for Hart found an enormous hole dug at a considerable distance back from the roadway in the lot of Amasa Field, where most of the old stones have long ago disappeared. The hole, a place as large and deep as a grave, was empty; and did not coincide with any interment mentioned in the cemetery records.

Sergt. Riley of the Second Station viewed the spot and gave the opinion that the hole was dug by bootleggers rather gruesomely and ingeniously seeking a safe cache for liquor in a place not likely to be disturbed. In reply to questions Hart said he thought the escaping truck had headed up Rochambeau Avenue, though he could not be sure.

During the next few days Ward was seldom seen by his family. Having added sleeping quarters to his attic realm, he kept closely to himself there, ordering food brought to the door and not taking it in until after the servant had gone away. The droning of monotonous formulae and the chanting of bizarre rhythms recurred at intervals, while at other times occasional listeners could detect the sound of tinkling glass, hissing chemicals, running water, or roaring gas flames. Odours of the most unplaceable quality, wholly unlike any before noted, hung at times around the door; and the air of tension observable in the young recluse whenever he did venture briefly forth was such as to excite the keenest speculation. Once he made a hasty trip to the Athenaeum for a book he required, and again he hired a messenger to fetch him a highly obscure volume from Boston. Suspense was written portentously over the whole situation, and both the family and Dr. Willett confessed themselves wholly at a loss what to do or think about it.

VI.

Then on the fifteenth of April a strange development occurred. While nothing appeared to grow different in kind, there was certainly a very terrible difference in degree; and Dr. Willett somehow attaches great significance to the change. The day was Good Friday, a circumstance of which the servants made much, but which others quite naturally dismiss as an irrelevant coincidence. Late in the afternoon young Ward began repeating a certain formula in a singularly loud voice, at the same time burning some substance so pungent that its fumes escaped over the entire house. The formula was so plainly audible in the hall outside the locked door that Mrs. Ward could not help memorising it as she waited and listened anxiously, and later on she was able to write it down at Dr. Willett's request. It ran as follows, and experts have told Dr. Willett that its very close analogue can be found in the mystic writings of "Eliphas Levi," that cryptic soul who crept through a crack in the forbidden door and glimpsed the frightful vistas of the void beyond:

Per Adonai Eloim, Adonai Jehova,
Adonai Sabaoth, Metraton On Agla Mathon,
verbum pythonicum, mysterium salamandrae,
conventus sylvorum, antra gnomorum,
daemonia Coeli God, Almonsin, Gibor, Jehosua,
Evam, Zariatnatmik, veni, veni, veni.

This had been going on for two hours without change or intermission when over all the neighbourhood a pandaemoniac howling of dogs set in. The extent of this howling can be judged from the space it received in the papers the next day, but to those in the Ward household it was overshadowed by the odour which instantly followed it; a hideous, all-pervasive odour which none of them had ever smelt before or have ever smelt since. In the midst of this mephitic flood there came a very perceptible flash like that of lightning, which would have been blinding and impressive but for the daylight around; and then was heard the voice that no listener can ever forget because of its thunderous remoteness, its incredible depth, and its eldritch dissimilarity to Charles Ward's voice. It shook the house, and was clearly heard by at least two neighbours above the howling of the dogs. Mrs. Ward, who had been listening in despair outside her son's locked laboratory, shivered as she recognised its hellish import; for Charles had told her of its evil fame in dark books, and of the manner in which it had thundered, according to the Fenner letters, above the doomed Pawtuxet farmhouse on the night of Joseph Curwen's annihilation. There was no mistaking that nightmare phrase, for Charles had described it too vividly in the old days when he had talked frankly of his Curwen investigations. And yet it was only this fragment of an archaic and forgotten language: "DIES MIES JESCHET BOENE DOESEF DOUVEMA ENITEMAUS."

Close upon this thundering there came a momentary

darkening of the daylight, though sunset was still an hour distant, and then a puff of added odour different from the first but equally unknown and intolerable. Charles was chanting again now and his mother could hear syllables that sounded like "Yi-nash-Yog-Sothoth-he-lglb-fi-throdag"—ending in a "Yah!" whose maniacal force mounted in an ear-splitting crescendo. A second later all previous memories were effaced by the wailing scream which burst out with frantic explosiveness and gradually changed form to a paroxysm of diabolic and hysterical laughter. Mrs. Ward, with the mingled fear and blind courage of maternity, advanced and knocked affrightedly at the concealing panels, but obtained no sign of recognition. She knocked again, but paused nervelessly as a second shriek arose, this one unmistakably in the familiar voice of her son, and sounding concurrently with the still bursting cachinnations of that other voice. Presently she fainted, although she is still unable to recall the precise and immediate cause. Memory sometimes makes merciful deletions.

Mr. Ward returned from the business section at about quarter past six; and not finding his wife downstairs, was told by the frightened servants that she was probably watching at Charles's door, from which the sounds had been far stranger than ever before. Mounting the stairs at once, he saw Mrs. Ward stretched at full length on the floor of the corridor outside the laboratory; and realising that she had fainted, hastened to fetch a glass of water from a set bowl in a neighbouring alcove. Dashing the cold fluid in her face, he was heartened to observe an immediate response on her part, and was watching the bewildered opening of her eyes when a chill shot through him and threatened to reduce him to the very state from which she was emerging. For the seemingly silent laboratory was not as silent as it had appeared to be, but held the murmurs of a tense, muffled conversation in tones too low for comprehension, yet of a quality profoundly disturbing to the soul.

It was not, of course, new for Charles to mutter formulae; but this muttering was definitely different. It was so palpably a dialogue, or imitation of a dialogue, with the regular alteration of inflections suggesting question and answer, statement and response. One voice was undisguisedly that of Charles, but the other had a depth and hollowness which the youth's best powers of ceremonial mimicry had scarcely approached before. There was something hideous, blasphemous, and abnormal about it, and but for a cry from his recovering wife which cleared his mind by arousing his protective instincts it is not likely that Theodore Howland Ward could have maintained for nearly a year more his old boast that he had never fainted. As it was, he seized his wife in his arms and bore her quickly downstairs before she could notice the voices which had so horribly disturbed him. Even so, however, he was not quick enough to escape catching something himself which caused him to stagger dangerously with his burden. For Mrs. Ward's cry had evidently been heard by others than he, and there had come in response to it from behind the locked door the first distinguishable words which that masked and terrible colloquy had yielded. They were merely an excited caution in Charles's own voice, but somehow their implications held a nameless fright for the father who overheard them. The phrase was just this: "Sshh!-write!"

Mr. and Mrs. Ward conferred at some length after dinner, and the former resolved to have a firm and serious talk with Charles that very night. No matter how important the object, such conduct could no longer be permitted; for these latest developments transcended every limit of sanity and formed a menace to the order and nervous well-being of the entire household. The youth must indeed have taken complete leave of his senses, since only downright madness could have prompted the wild screams and imaginary conversations in assumed voices which the present day had brought forth. All this must be stopped, or Mrs. Ward would be made ill and the keeping of servants become an impossibility.

Mr. Ward rose at the close of the meal and started upstairs for Charles's laboratory. On the third floor, however, he paused at the sounds which he heard proceeding from the now disused library of his son. Books were apparently being flung about and papers wildly rustled, and upon stepping to the door Mr. Ward beheld the youth within, excitedly assembling a vast armful of literary matter of every size and shape. Charles's aspect was very drawn and haggard, and he dropped his entire load with a start at the sound of his father's voice. At the elder man's command he sat down, and for some time listened to the admonitions he had so long deserved. There was no scene. At the end of the lecture he agreed that his father was right, and that his noises, mutterings, incantations, and chemical odours were indeed inexcusable nuisances. He agreed to a policy of greater quiet, though insisting on a prolongation of his extreme privacy. Much of his future work, he said, was in any case purely book research; and he could obtain quarters elsewhere for any such vocal rituals as might be necessary at a later stage. For the fright and fainting of his mother he expressed the keenest contrition, and explained that the conversation later heard was part of an elaborate symbolism designed to create a certain mental atmosphere. His use of abstruse technical terms somewhat bewildered Mr. Ward, but the parting impression was one of undeniable sanity and poise despite a mysterious tension of the utmost gravity. The interview was really quite inconclusive, and as Charles picked up his armful and left the room Mr. Ward hardly knew what to make of the entire business. It was as mysterious as the death of poor old Nig, whose stiffening form had been found an hour before in the basement, with staring eyes and fear-distorted mouth.

Driven by some vague detective instinct, the bewildered parent now glanced curiously at the vacant shelves to see what his son had taken up to the attic. The youth's library was plainly and rigidly classified, so that one might tell at a glance the books or at least the kind of books which had been withdrawn. On this occasion Mr. Ward was astonished to find that nothing of the occult or the antiquarian, beyond what had been previously removed, was missing. These new withdrawals were all modern items; histories, scientific treatises, geographies, manuals of literature, philosophic works, and certain contemporary newspapers and magazines. It was a very curious shift from Charles Ward's recent run of reading, and the father paused in a growing vortex of perplexity and an engulfing sense of strangeness. The strangeness was a very poignant sensation, and almost clawed at his chest as he strove to see just what was wrong around him. Something was indeed wrong, and tangibly as well as spiritually so. Ever since he had been in this room he had known that something was amiss, and at last it dawned upon him what it was.

On the north wall rose still the ancient carved overmantel from the house in Olney Court, but to the cracked and precariously restored oils of the large Curwen portrait disaster had come. Time and unequal heating had done their work at last, and at some time since the room's last cleaning the worst had happened. Peeling clear of the wood, curling tighter and tighter, and finally crumbling into small bits with what must have been malignly silent suddenness, the portrait of Joseph Curwen had resigned forever its staring surveillance of the youth it so strangely resembled, and now lay scattered on the floor as a thin coating of fine bluish-grey dust.

PART FOUR:
A MUTATION AND A MADNESS.

1.

In the week following that memorable Good Friday Charles Ward was seen more often than usual, and was continually carrying books between his library and the attic laboratory. His actions were quiet and rational, but he had a furtive, hunted look which his mother did not like, and developed an incredibly ravenous appetite as gauged by his demands upon the cook. Dr. Willett had been told of those Friday noises and happenings, and on the following Tuesday had a long conversation with the youth in the library where the picture stared no more. The interview was, as always, inconclusive; but Willett is still ready to swear that the youth was sane and himself at the time. He held out promises of an early revelation, and spoke of the need of securing a laboratory elsewhere. At the loss of the portrait he grieved singularly little considering his first enthusiasm over it, but seemed to find something of positive humour in its sudden crumbling.

About the second week Charles began to be absent from the house for long periods, and one day when good old black Hannah came to help with the spring cleaning she mentioned his frequent visits to the old house in Olney Court, where he would come with a large valise and perform curious delvings in the cellar. He was always very liberal to her and to old Asa, but seemed more worried than he used to be; which grieved her very much, since she had watched him grow up from birth. Another report of his doings came from Pawtuxet, where some friends of the family saw him at a distance a surprising number of times. He seemed to haunt the resort and canoe-house of Rhodes-on-the-Pawtuxet, and subsequent inquiries by Dr. Willett at that place brought out the fact that his purpose was always to secure access to the rather hedged-in river-bank, along which he would walk toward the north, usually not reappearing for a very long while.

Late in May came a momentary revival of ritualistic sounds in the attic laboratory which brought a stern reproof from Mr. Ward and a somewhat distracted promise of amendment from Charles. It occurred one morning, and seemed to form a resumption of the imaginary conversation noted on that turbulent Good Friday. The youth was arguing or remonstrating hotly with himself, for there suddenly burst forth a perfectly distinguishable series of clashing shouts in differentiated tones like alternate demands and denials which caused Mrs. Ward to run upstairs and listen at the door. She could hear no more than a fragment whose only plain words were "must have it red for three months," and upon her knocking all sounds ceased at once. When Charles was later questioned by his father he said that there were certain conflicts of spheres of consciousness which only great skill could avoid, but which he would try to transfer to other realms.

About the middle of June a queer nocturnal incident occurred. In the early evening there had been some noise and thumping in the laboratory upstairs, and Mr. Ward was on the point of investigating when it suddenly quieted down. That midnight, after the family had retired, the butler was night-locking the front door when according to his statement Charles appeared somewhat blunderingly and uncertainly at the foot of the stairs with a large suitcase and made signs that he wished egress. The youth spoke no word, but the worthy Yorkshireman caught one sight of his fevered eyes and trembled causelessly. He opened the door and young Ward went out, but in the morning he presented his resignation to Mrs. Ward. There was, he said, something unholy in the glance Charles had fixed on him. It was no way for a young gentleman to look at an honest person, and he could not possibly stay another night. Mrs. Ward allowed the man to depart, but she did not value his statement highly. To fancy Charles in a savage state that night was quite ridiculous, for as long as she had remained awake she had heard faint sounds from the laboratory above; sounds as if of sobbing and pacing, and of a sighing which told only of despair's profoundest depths. Mrs. Ward had grown used to listening for sounds in the night, for the mystery of her son was fast driving all else from her mind.

The next evening, much as on another evening nearly three months before, Charles Ward seized the newspaper very early and accidentally lost the main section. The matter was not recalled till later, when Dr. Willett began checking up loose ends and searching out missing links here and there. In the *Journal* office he found the section which Charles had lost, and marked two items as of possible significance. They were as follows:

MORE CEMETERY DELVING.

It was this morning discovered by Robert Hart, night watchman at the North Burial Ground, that ghouls were again at work in the ancient portion of the cemetery. The grave of Ezra Weeden, who was born in 1740 and died in 1824 according to his uprooted and savagely splintered slate headstone, was found excavated and rifled, the work being evidently done with a spade stolen from an adjacent tool-shed.

Whatever the contents may have been after more than a century of burial, all was gone except a few slivers of decayed wood. There were no wheel tracks, but the police have measured a single set of footprints which they found in the vicinity, and which indicate the boots of a man of refinement.

Hart is inclined to link this incident with the digging discovered last March, when a party in a motor truck were frightened away after making a deep excavation; but Sergt. Riley of the Second Station discounts this theory and points to vital differences in the two cases. In March the digging had been in a spot where no grave was known; but this time a well-marked and cared-for grave had been rifled with every evidence of deliberate purpose, and with a conscious malignity expressed in the splintering of the slab which had been intact up to the day before.

Members of the Weeden family, notified of the happening, expressed their astonishment and regret; and were wholly unable to think of any enemy who would care to violate the grave of their ancestor. Hazard Weeden of 598 Angell Street recalls a family legend according to which Ezra Weeden was involved in some very peculiar circumstances, not dishonourable to himself, shortly before the Revolution; but of any modern feud or mystery he is frankly ignorant. Inspector Cunningham has been assigned to the case, and hopes to uncover some valuable clues in the near future.

DOGS NOISY IN PAWTUXET.

Residents of Pawtuxet were aroused about 3 a.m. today by a phenomenal baying of dogs which seemed to centre near the river just north of Rhodes-on-the-Pawtuxet. The volume and quality of the howling were unusually odd, according to most who heard it; and Fred Lemdin, night watchman at Rhodes, declares it was mixed with something very like the shrieks of a man in mortal terror and agony. A sharp and very brief thunderstorm, which seemed to strike somewhere near the bank of the river, put an end to the disturbance. Strange and unpleasant odours, probably from the oil tanks along the bay, are popularly linked with this incident; and may have had their share in exciting the dogs.

The aspect of Charles now became very haggard and hunted, and all agreed in retrospect that he may have wished at this period to make some statement or confession from which sheer terror withheld him. The morbid listening of his mother in the night brought out the fact that he made frequent sallies abroad under cover of darkness, and most of the more academic alienists unite at present in charging him with the revolting cases of vampirism which the press so sensationally reported about this time, but which have not yet been definitely traced to any known perpetrator. These cases, too recent and celebrated to need detailed mention, involved victims of every age and type and seemed to cluster around two distinct localities; the residential hill and the North End, near the Ward home, and the suburban districts across the Cranston line near Pawtuxet. Both late wayfarers and sleepers with open windows were attacked, and those who lived to tell the tale spoke unanimously of a lean, lithe, leaping monster with burning eyes which fastened its teeth in the throat or upper arm and feasted ravenously.

Dr. Willett, who refuses to date the madness of Charles Ward as far back as even this, is cautious in attempting to explain these horrors. He has, he declares, certain theories of his own; and limits his positive statements to a peculiar kind of negation: "I will not," he says, "state who or what I believe perpetrated these attacks and murders, but I will declare that Charles Ward was innocent of them. I have reason to be sure he was ignorant of the taste of blood, as indeed his continued anaemic decline and increasing pallor prove better than any verbal argument. Ward meddled with terrible things, but he has paid for it, and he was never a monster or a villain. As for now—I don't like to think. A change came, and I'm content to believe that the old Charles Ward died with it. His soul did, anyhow, for that mad flesh that vanished from Waite's hospital had another."

Willett speaks with authority, for he was often at the Ward home attending Mrs. Ward, whose nerves had begun to snap under the strain. Her nocturnal listening had bred some morbid hallucinations which she confided to the doctor with hesitancy, and which he ridiculed in talking to her, although they made him ponder deeply when alone. These delusions always concerned the faint sounds which she fancied she heard in the attic laboratory and bedroom, and emphasised the occurrence of muffled sighs and sobbings at the most impossible times. Early in July Willett ordered Mrs. Ward to Atlantic City for an indefinite recuperative sojourn, and cautioned both Mr. Ward and the haggard and elusive Charles to write her only cheering letters. It is probably to this enforced and reluctant escape that she owes her life and continued sanity.

II.

Not long after his mother's departure, Charles Ward began negotiating for the Pawtuxet bungalow. It was a squalid little wooden edifice with a concrete garage, perched high on the sparsely settled bank of the river slightly above Rhodes, but for some odd reason the youth would have nothing else. He gave the real-estate agencies no peace till one of them secured it for him at an exorbitant price from a somewhat reluctant owner, and as soon as it was vacant he took possession under cover of darkness, transporting in a great closed van the entire contents of his attic laboratory, including the books both weird and modern which he had borrowed from his study. He had this van loaded in the black small hours, and his father recalls only a drowsy realisation of stifled oaths and stamping feet on the night the goods were taken away. After that Charles moved back to his own old quarters on the third floor, and never haunted the attic again.

To the Pawtuxet bungalow Charles transferred all the secrecy with which he had surrounded his attic realm, save that he now appeared to have two sharers of his mysteries; a villainous-looking Portuguese half-caste from the South Main St. waterfront who acted as a servant, and a thin, scholarly stranger with dark glasses and a stubbly full beard of dyed aspect whose status was evidently that of a colleague. Neighbours vainly tried to engage these odd persons in conversation. The mulatto Gomes spoke very little English, and the bearded man, who gave his name as Dr. Allen, voluntarily followed his example. Ward himself tried to be more affable, but succeeded only in provoking curiosity with his rambling accounts of chemical research. Before long queer tales began to circulate regarding the all-night burning of lights; and somewhat later, after this burning had suddenly ceased, there rose still queerer tales of disproportionate orders of meat from the butcher's and of the muffled shouting, declamation, rhythmic chanting, and screaming supposed to come from some very deep cellar below the place. Most distinctly the new and strange household was bitterly disliked by the honest bourgeoisie of the vicinity, and it is not remarkable that dark hints were advanced connecting the hated establishment with the current epidemic of vampiristic attacks and murders; especially since the radius of that plague seemed now confined wholly to Pawtuxet and the adjacent streets of Edgewood.

Ward spent most of his time at the bungalow, but slept occasionally at home and was still reckoned a dweller beneath his father's roof. Twice he was absent from the city on week-long trips, whose destinations have not yet been discovered. He grew steadily paler and more emaciated even than before, and lacked some of his former assurance when repeating to Dr. Willett his old, old story of vital research and future revelations. Willett often waylaid him at his father's house, for the elder Ward was deeply worried and perplexed, and wished his son to get as much sound oversight as could be managed in the case of so secretive and independent an adult. The doctor still insists that the youth was sane even as late as this, and adduces many a conversation to prove his point.

About September the vampirism declined, but in the following January Ward almost became involved in serious trouble. For some time the nocturnal arrival and departure of motor trucks at the Pawtuxet bungalow had been commented upon, and at this juncture an unforeseen hitch exposed the nature of at least one item of their contents. In a lonely spot near Hope Valley had occurred one of the frequent sordid waylaying of trucks by "hi-jackers" in quest of liquor shipments, but this time the robbers had been destined to receive the greater shock. For the long cases they seized proved upon opening to contain some exceedingly gruesome things; so gruesome, in fact, that the matter could not be kept quiet amongst the denizens of the underworld. The thieves had hastily buried what they discovered, but when the State Police got wind of the matter a careful search was made. A recently arrested vagrant, under promise of immunity from prosecution on any additional charge, at last consented to guide a party of troopers to the spot; and there was found in that hasty cache a very hideous and shameful thing. It would not be well for the national—or even the international—sense of decorum if the public were ever to know what was uncovered by that awestruck party. There was no mistaking it, even by these far from studious officers; and telegrams to Washington ensued with feverish rapidity.

The cases were addressed to Charles Ward at his Pawtuxet bungalow, and State and Federal officials at once paid him a very forceful and serious call. They found him pallid and worried with his two odd companions, and received from him what seemed to be a valid explanation and evidence of innocence. He had needed certain anatomical specimens as part of a programme of research whose depth and genuineness anyone who had known him in the last decade could prove, and had ordered the required kind and number from agencies which he had thought as reasonably legitimate as such things can be. Of the identity of the specimens he had known absolutely nothing, and was properly shocked when the inspectors hinted at the monstrous effect on public sentiment and national dignity which a knowledge of the matter would produce. In this statement he was firmly sustained by his bearded colleague Dr. Allen, whose oddly hollow voice carried even more conviction than his own nervous tones; so that in the end the officials took no action, but carefully set down the New York name and address which Ward gave them as a basis for a search which came to nothing. It is only fair to add that the specimens were quickly and quietly restored to their proper places, and that the general public will never know of their blasphemous disturbance.

On February 9, 1928, Dr. Willett received a letter from Charles Ward which he considers of extraordinary importance, and about which he has frequently quarrelled with Dr. Lyman. Lyman believes that this note contains positive proof of a well-developed case of dementia praecox, but Willett on the other hand regards it as the last perfectly sane utterance of the hapless youth. He calls especial attention to the normal character of the penmanship; which though shewing traces of shattered nerves, is nevertheless distinctly Ward's own. The text in full is as follows:

100 Prospect St.
Providence, R.I.,

February 8, 1928.

Dear Dr. Willett:—

I feel that at last the time has come for me to make the disclosures which I have so long promised you, and for which you have pressed me so often. The patience you have shewn in waiting, and the confidence you have shewn in my mind and integrity, are things I shall never cease to appreciate.

And now that I am ready to speak, I must own with humiliation that no triumph such as I dreamed of can ever be mine. Instead of triumph I have found terror, and my talk with you will not be a boast of victory but a plea for help and advice in saving both myself and the world from a horror beyond all human conception or calculation. You recall what those Fenner letters said of the old raiding party at Pawtuxet. That must all be done again, and quickly. Upon us depends more than can be put into words — all civilisation, all natural law, perhaps even the fate of the solar system and the universe. I have brought to light a monstrous abnormality, but I did it for the sake of knowledge. Now for the sake of all life and Nature you must help me thrust it back into the dark again.

I have left that Pawtuxet place forever, and we must extirpate everything existing there, alive or dead. I shall not go there again, and you must not believe it if you ever hear that I am there. I will tell you why I say this when I see you. I have come home for good, and wish you would call on me at the very first moment that you can spare five or six hours continuously to hear what I have to say. It will take that long — and believe me when I tell you that you never had a more genuine professional duty than this. My life and reason are the very least things which hang in the balance.

I dare not tell my father, for he could not grasp the whole thing. But I have told him of my danger, and he has four men from a detective agency watching the house. I don't know how much good they can do, for they have against them forces which even you could scarcely envisage or acknowledge. So come quickly if you wish to see me alive and hear how you may help to save the cosmos from stark hell.

Any time will do — I shall not be out of the house. Don't telephone ahead, for there is no telling who or what may try to intercept you. And let us pray to whatever gods there be that nothing may prevent this meeting.

In utmost gravity and desperation,

— CHARLES DEXTER WARD.

P.S. Shoot Dr. Allen on sight and dissolve his body in acid. Don't burn it.

Dr. Willett received this note about 10:30 a.m., and immediately arranged to spare the whole late afternoon and evening for the momentous talk, letting it extend on into the night as long as might be necessary. He planned to arrive about four o'clock, and through all the intervening hours was so engulfed in every sort of wild speculation that most of his tasks were very mechanically performed. Maniacal as the letter would have sounded to a stranger, Willett had seen too much of Charles Ward's oddities to dismiss it as sheer raving. That something very subtle, ancient, and horrible was hovering about he felt quite sure, and the reference to Dr. Allen could almost be comprehended in view of what Pawtuxet gossip said of Ward's enigmatical colleague. Willett had never seen the man, but had heard much of his aspect and bearing, and could not but wonder what sort of eyes those much-discussed dark glasses might conceal.

Promptly at four Dr. Willett presented himself at the Ward residence, but found to his annoyance that Charles had not adhered to his determination to remain indoors. The guards were there, but said that the young man seemed to have lost part of his timidity. He had that morning done much apparently frightened arguing and protesting over the telephone, one of the detectives said, replying to some unknown voice with phrases such as "I am very tired and must rest a while," "I can't receive anyone for some time," "you'll have to excuse me," "Please postpone decisive action till we can arrange some sort of compromise," or "I am very sorry, but I must take a complete vacation from everything; I'll talk with you later." Then, apparently gaining boldness through meditation, he had slipped out so quietly that no one had seen him depart or knew that he had gone until he returned about one o'clock and entered the house without a word. He had gone upstairs, where a bit of his fear must have surged back; for he was heard to cry out in a highly terrified fashion upon entering his library, afterward trailing off into a kind of choking gasp. When, however, the butler had gone to inquire what the trouble was, he had appeared at the door with a great show of boldness, and had silently gestured the man away in a manner that terrified him unaccountably. Then he had evidently done some rearranging of his shelves, for a great clattering and thumping and creaking ensued; after which he had reappeared and left at once. Willett inquired whether or not any message had been left, but was told that there was none. The butler seemed queerly disturbed about something in Charles's appearance and manner, and asked solicitously if there was much hope for a cure of his disordered nerves.

For almost two hours Dr. Willett waited vainly in Charles Ward's library, watching the dusty shelves with their wide gaps where books had been removed, and smiling grimly at the panelled overmantel on the north wall, whence a year before the suave features of old Joseph Curwen had looked mildly down. After a time the shadows began to gather, and the sunset cheer gave place to a vague growing terror which flew shadow-like before the night. Mr. Ward finally arrived, and shewed much surprise and anger at his son's absence after all the pains which had been taken to guard him. He had not known of Charles's appointment, and promised to notify Willett when the youth returned. In bidding the doctor goodnight he

Weird Tales, May 1945

expressed his utter perplexity at his son's condition, and urged his caller to do all he could to restore the boy to normal poise. Willett was glad to escape from that library, for something frightful and unholy seemed to haunt it; as if the vanished picture had left behind a legacy of evil. He had never liked that picture; and even now, strong-nerved though he was, there lurked a quality in its vacant panel which made him feel an urgent need to get out into the pure air as soon as possible.

III.

The next morning Willett received a message from the senior Ward, saying that Charles was still absent. Mr. Ward mentioned that Dr. Allen had telephoned him to say that Charles would remain at Pawtuxet for some time, and that he must not be disturbed. This was necessary because Allen himself was suddenly called away for an indefinite period, leaving the researches in need of Charles's constant oversight. Charles sent his best wishes, and regretted any bother his abrupt change of plans might have caused. In listening to this message Mr. Ward heard Dr. Allen's voice for the first time, and it seemed to excite some vague and elusive memory which could not be actually placed, but which was disturbing to the point of fearfulness.

Faced by these baffling and contradictory reports, Dr. Willett was frankly at a loss what to do. The frantic earnestness of Charles's note was not to be denied, yet what could one think of its writer's immediate violation of his own expressed policy? Young Ward had written that his delvings had become blasphemous and menacing, that they and his bearded colleague must be extirpated at any cost, and that he himself would never return to their final scene; yet according to latest advices he had forgotten all this and was back in the thick of the mystery. Common sense bade one leave the youth alone with his freakishness, yet some deeper instinct would not permit the impression of that frenzied letter to subside. Willett read it over again, and could not make its essence sound as empty and insane as both its bombastic verbiage and its lack of fulfilment would seem to imply. Its terror was too profound and real, and in conjunction with what the doctor already knew evoked too vivid hints of monstrosities from beyond time and space to permit of any cynical explanation. There were nameless horrors abroad; and no matter how little one might be able to get at them, one ought to stand prepared for any sort of action at any time.

For over a week Dr. Willett pondered on the dilemma which seemed thrust upon him, and became more and more inclined to pay Charles a call at the Pawtuxet bungalow. No friend of the youth had ever ventured to storm this forbidden retreat, and even his father knew of its interior only from such descriptions as he chose to give; but Willett felt that some direct conversation with his patient was necessary. Mr. Ward had been receiving brief and non-committal typed notes from his son, and said that Mrs. Ward in her Atlantic City retirement had had no better word. So at length the doctor resolved to act; and despite a curious sensation inspired by old legends of Joseph Curwen, and by more recent revelations and warnings from Charles Ward, set boldly out for the bungalow on the bluff above the river.

Willett had visited the spot before through sheer curiosity, though of course never entering the house or proclaiming his presence; hence knew exactly the route to take. Driving out Broad Street one early afternoon toward the end of February in his small motor, he thought oddly of the grim party which had taken that selfsame road a hundred and fifty-seven years before on a terrible errand which none might ever comprehend.

The ride through the city's decaying fringe was short, and trim Edgewood and sleepy Pawtuxet presently spread out ahead. Willett turned to the right down Lockwood Street and drove his car as far along that rural road as he could, then alighted and walked north to where the bluff towered above the lovely bends of the river and the sweep of misty downlands beyond. Houses were still few here, and there was no mistaking the isolated bungalow with its concrete garage on a high point of land at his left. Stepping briskly up the neglected gravel walk he rapped at the door with a firm hand, and spoke without a tremor to the evil Portuguese mulatto who opened it to the width of a crack.

He must, he said, see Charles Ward at once on vitally important business. No excuse would be accepted, and a repulse would mean only a full report of the matter to the elder Ward. The mulatto still hesitated, and pushed against the door when Willett attempted to open it; but the doctor merely raised his voice and renewed his demands. Then there came from the dark interior a husky whisper which somehow chilled the hearer through and through though he did not know why he feared it. "Let him in, Tony," it said, "we may as well talk now as ever." But disturbing as was the whisper, the greater fear was that which immediately followed. The floor creaked and the speaker hove in sight — and the owner of those strange and resonant tones was seen to be no other than Charles Dexter Ward.

The minuteness with which Dr. Willett recalled and recorded his conversation of that afternoon is due to the importance he assigns to this particular period. For at last he concedes a vital change in Charles Dexter Ward's mentality, and believes that the youth now spoke from a brain hopelessly alien to the brain whose growth he had watched for six and twenty years. Controversy with Dr. Lyman has compelled him to be very specific, and he definitely dates the madness of Charles Ward from the time the typewritten notes began to reach his parents. Those notes are not in Ward's normal style; not even in the style of that last frantic letter to Willett. Instead, they are strange and archaic, as if the snapping of the writer's mind had released a flood of tendencies and impressions picked up unconsciously through boyhood antiquarianism. There is an obvious effort to be modern, but the spirit and occasionally the language are those of the past.

The past, too, was evident in Ward's every tone and gesture as he received the doctor in that shadowy bungalow. He bowed, motioned Willett to a seat, and began to speak abruptly in that strange whisper which he sought to explain at the very outset.

"I am grown phthisical," he began, "from this cursed river air. You must excuse my speech. I suppose you are come from my father to see what ails me, and I hope you will say nothing to alarm him."

Willett was studying these scraping tones with extreme care, but studying even more closely the face of the speaker. Something, he felt, was wrong; and he thought of what the family had told him about the fright of that Yorkshire butler one night. He wished it were not so dark, but did not request that any blind be opened. Instead, he merely asked Ward why he had so belied the frantic note of little more than a week before.

"I was coming to that," the host replied. "You must know, I am in a very bad state of nerves, and do and say queer things I cannot account for. As I have told you often, I am on the edge of great matters; and the bigness of them has a way of making me light-headed. Any man might well be frighted of what I have found, but I am not to be put off for long. I was a dunce to have that guard and stick at home; for having gone this far, my place is here. I am not well spoke of by my prying neighbours, and perhaps I was led by weakness to believe myself what they say of me. There is no evil to any in what I do, so long as I do it rightly. Have the goodness to wait six months, and I'll shew you what will pay your patience well."

"You may as well know I have a way of learning old matters from things surer than books, and I'll leave you to judge the importance of what I can give to history, philosophy, and the arts by reason of the doors I have access to. My ancestor had all this when those witless peeping Toms came and murdered him. I now have it again, or am coming very imperfectly to have a part of it. This time nothing must happen, and least of all through any idiot fears of my own. Pray forget all I writ you, Sir, and have no fear of this place or any in it. Dr. Allen is a man of fine parts, and I owe him an apology for anything ill I have said of him. I wish I had no need to spare him, but there were things he had to do elsewhere. His zeal is equal to mine in all those matters, and I suppose that when I feared the work I feared him too as my greatest helper in it."

Ward paused, and the doctor hardly knew what to say or think. He felt almost foolish in the face of this calm repudiation of the letter; and yet there clung to him the fact that while the present discourse was strange and alien and indubitably mad, the note itself had been tragic in its naturalness and likeness to the Charles Ward he knew. Willett now tried to turn the talk on early matters, and recall to the youth some past events which would restore a familiar mood; but in this process he obtained only the most grotesque results. It was the same with all the alienists later on. Important sections of Charles Ward's store of mental images, mainly those touching modern times and his own personal life, had been unaccountably expunged; whilst all the massed antiquarianism of his youth had welled up from some profound subconsciousness to engulf the contemporary and the individual. The youth's intimate knowledge of elder things was abnormal and unholy, and he tried his best to hide it. When Willett would mention some favourite object of his boyhood archaistic studies he often shed by pure accident such a light as no normal mortal could conceivably be expected to possess, and the doctor shuddered as the glib allusion glided by.

It was not wholesome to know so much about the way the fat sheriff's wig fell off as he leaned over at the play in Mr. Douglass's Histrionick Academy in King Street on the eleventh of February, 1762, which fell on a Thursday; or about how the actors cut the text of Steele's "Conscious Lover" so badly that one was almost glad the Baptist-ridden legislature closed the theatre a fortnight later. That Thomas Sabin's Boston coach was "damn'd uncomfortable" old letters may well have told; but what healthy antiquarian could recall how the creaking of Epenetus Olney's new signboard (the gaudy crown he set up after he took to calling his tavern the Crown Coffee House) was exactly like the first few notes of the new jazz piece all the radios in Pawtuxet were playing?

Ward, however, would not be quizzed long in this vein. Modern and personal topics he waved aside quite summarily, whilst regarding antique affairs he soon shewed the plainest boredom. What he wished clearly enough was only to satisfy his visitor enough to make him depart without the intention of returning. To this end he offered to shew Willett the entire house, and at once proceeded to lead the doctor through every room from cellar to attic. Willett looked sharply, but noted that the visible books were far too few and trivial ever to have filled the wide gaps on Ward's shelves at home, and that the meagre so-called "laboratory" was the flimsiest sort of a blind. Clearly, there were a library and a laboratory elsewhere; but just where, it was impossible to say.

Essentially defeated in his quest for something he could not name, Willett returned to town before evening and told the senior Ward everything which had occurred. They agreed that the youth must be definitely out of his mind, but decided that nothing drastic need be done just then. Above all, Mrs. Ward must be kept in as complete an ignorance as her son's own strange typed notes would permit.

Mr. Ward now determined to call in person upon his son, making it wholly a surprise visit. Dr. Willett took him in his car one evening, guiding him to within sight of the bungalow and waiting patiently for his return. The session was a long one, and the father emerged in a very saddened and perplexed state. His reception had developed much like Willett's, save that Charles had been an excessively long time in appearing after the visitor had forced his way into the hall and sent the Portuguese away with an imperative demand; and in the bearing of the altered son there was no trace of filial affection. The lights had been dim, yet even so the youth had complained that they dazzled him outrageously. He had not spoken out loud at all, averring that his throat was in very poor condition; but in his hoarse whisper there was a quality so vaguely disturbing that Mr. Ward could not banish it from his mind.

Now definitely leagued together to do all they could toward the youth's mental salvation, Mr. Ward and Dr. Willett set about collecting every scrap of data which the case might afford. Pawtuxet gossip was the first item they studied, and this was relatively easy to glean since both had friends in that region. Dr. Willett obtained the most rumours because people talked more frankly to him than to a parent of the central figure, and from all he heard he could tell that young Ward's life had become indeed a strange one. Common tongues would not dissociate his household from the vampirism of the previous summer, while the nocturnal comings and goings of the motor trucks provided their share of dark speculation. Local tradesmen spoke of the queerness of the orders brought them by the evil-looking mulatto, and in particular of the inordinate amounts of meat and fresh blood secured from the two butcher shops in the immediate neighbourhood. For a household of only three, these quantities were quite absurd.

Then there was the matter of the sounds beneath the earth. Reports of these things were harder to pin down, but all the vague hints tallied in certain basic essentials. Noises of a ritual nature positively existed, and at times when the bungalow was dark. They might, of course, have come from the known cellar; but rumour insisted that there were deeper and more spreading crypts. Recalling the ancient tales of Joseph Curwen's catacombs, and assuming for granted that the present bungalow had been selected because of its situation on the old Curwen site as revealed in one or another of the documents found behind the picture, Willett and Mr. Ward gave this phase of the gossip much attention; and searched many times without success for the door in the river-bank which old manuscripts mentioned. As to popular opinions of the bungalow's various inhabitants, it was soon plain that the Brava Portuguese was loathed, the bearded and spectacled Dr. Allen feared, and the pallid young scholar disliked to a profound extent. During the last week or two Ward had obviously changed much, abandoning his attempts at affability and speaking only in hoarse but oddly repellent whispers on the few occasions that he ventured forth.

Such were the shreds and fragments gathered here and there; and over these Mr. Ward and Dr. Willett held many long and serious conferences. They strove to exercise deduction, induction, and constructive imagination to their utmost extent; and to correlate every known fact of Charles's later life, including the frantic letter which the doctor now shewed the father, with the meagre documentary evidence available concerning old Joseph Curwen. They would have given much for a glimpse of the papers Charles had found, for very clearly the key to the youth's madness lay in what he had learned of the ancient wizard and his doings.

IV.

And yet, after all, it was from no step of Mr. Ward's or Dr. Willett's that the next move in this singular case proceeded. The father and the physician, rebuffed and confused by a shadow too shapeless and intangible to combat, had rested uneasily on their oars while the typed notes of young Ward to his parents grew fewer and fewer. Then came the first of the month with its customary financial adjustments, and the clerks at certain banks began a peculiar shaking of heads and telephoning from one to the other. Officials who knew Charles Ward by sight went down to the bungalow to ask why every cheque of his appearing at this juncture was a clumsy forgery, and were reassured less than they ought to have been when the youth hoarsely explained that his hand had lately been so much affected by a nervous shock as to make normal writing impossible. He could, he said, form no written characters at all except with great difficulty; and could prove it by the fact that he had been forced to type all his recent letters, even those to his father and mother, who would bear out the assertion.

What made the investigators pause in confusion was not this circumstance alone, for that was nothing unprecedented or fundamentally suspicious, nor even the Pawtuxet gossip, of which one or two of them had caught echoes. It was the muddled discourse of the young man which nonplussed them, implying as it did a virtually total loss of memory concerning important monetary matters which he had had at his fingertips only a month or two before. Something was wrong; for despite the apparent coherence and rationality of his speech, there could be no normal reason for this ill-concealed blankness on vital points. Moreover, although none of these men knew Ward well, they could not help observing the change in his language and manner. They had heard he was an antiquarian, but even the most hopeless antiquarians do not make daily use of obsolete phraseology and gestures. Altogether, this combination of hoarseness, palsied hands, bad memory, and altered speech and bearing must represent some disturbance or malady of genuine gravity, which no doubt formed the basis of the prevailing odd rumours; and after their departure the party of officials decided that a talk with the senior Ward was imperative.

So on the sixth of March, 1928, there was a long and serious conference in Mr. Ward's office, after which the utterly bewildered father summoned Dr. Willett in a kind of helpless resignation. Willett looked over the strained and awkward signatures of the cheques, and compared them in his mind with the penmanship of that last frantic note. Certainly, the change was radical and profound, and yet there was something damnably familiar about the new writing. It had crabbed and archaic tendencies of a very curious sort, and seemed to result from a type of stroke utterly different from that which the youth had always used. It was strange — but where had he seen it before? On the whole, it was obvious that Charles was insane. Of that there could be no doubt. And since it appeared unlikely that he could handle his property or continue to deal with the outside world much longer, something must quickly be done toward his oversight and possible cure. It was then that the alienists were called in, Drs. Peck and Waite of Providence and Dr. Lyman of Boston, to whom Mr. Ward and Dr. Willett gave the most exhaustive possible history of the case, and who conferred at length in the now unused library of their young patient, examining what books and papers of his were left in order to gain some further notion of his habitual mental cast. After scanning this material and examining the ominous note to Willett they all agreed that Charles Ward's studies had been enough to unseat or at least to warp any ordinary intellect, and wished most heartily that they could see his more intimate volumes and documents; but this latter they knew they could do, if at all, only after a scene at the bungalow itself. Willett now reviewed the whole case with febrile energy; it being at this time that he obtained the statements of the workmen who had seen Charles find the Curwen documents, and that he collated the incidents of the destroyed newspaper items, looking up the latter at the *Journal* office.

On Thursday, the eighth of March, Drs. Willett, Peck, Lyman, and Waite, accompanied by Mr. Ward, paid the youth their momentous call; making no concealment of their object and questioning the now acknowledged patient with extreme minuteness. Charles, though he was inordinately long in answering the summons and was still redolent of strange and noxious laboratory odours when he did finally make his agitated appearance, proved a far from recalcitrant subject; and admitted freely that his memory and balance had suffered somewhat from close application to abstruse studies. He offered no resistance when his removal to other quarters was insisted upon; and seemed, indeed, to display a high degree of intelligence as apart from mere memory. His conduct would have sent his interviewers away in bafflement had not the persistently archaic trend of his speech and unmistakable replacement of modern by ancient ideas in his consciousness marked him out as one definitely removed from the normal. Of his work he would say no more to the group of doctors than he had formerly said to his family and to Dr. Willett, and his frantic note of the previous month he dismissed as mere nerves and hysteria. He insisted that this shadowy bungalow possessed no library or laboratory beyond the visible ones, and waxed abstruse in explaining the absence from the house of such odours as now saturated all his clothing. Neighbourhood gossip he attributed to nothing more than the cheap inventiveness of baffled curiosity. Of the whereabouts of Dr. Allen he said he did not feel at liberty to speak definitely, but assured his inquisitors that the bearded and spectacled man would return when needed. In paying off the stolid Brava who resisted all questioning by the visitors, and in closing the bungalow which still seemed to hold such nighted secrets, Ward shewed no sign of nervousness save a barely noticed tendency to pause as though listening for something very faint. He was apparently animated by a calmly philosophic resignation, as if his removal were the merest transient incident which would cause the least trouble if facilitated and disposed of once and for all. It was clear that he trusted to his obviously unimpaired keenness of absolute mentality to overcome all the embarrassments into which his twisted memory, his lost voice and handwriting, and his secretive and eccentric behaviour had led him. His mother, it was agreed, was not to be told of the change; his father supplying typed notes in his name. Ward was taken to the restfully and picturesquely situated private hospital maintained by Dr. Waite on Conanicut Island in the bay, and subjected to the closest scrutiny and questioning by all the physicians connected with the case. It was then that the physical oddities were noticed; the slackened metabolism, the altered skin, and the disproportionate neural reactions. Dr. Willett was the most perturbed of the various examiners, for he had attended Ward all his life and could appreciate with terrible keenness the extent of his physical disorganisation. Even the familiar olive mark on his hip was gone, while on his chest was a great black mole or cicatrice which had never been there before, and which made Willett wonder whether the youth had ever submitted to any of the "witch markings" reputed to be inflicted at certain unwholesome nocturnal meetings in wild and lonely places. The doctor could not keep his mind off a certain transcribed witch-trial record from Salem which Charles had shewn him in the old non-secretive days, and which read: "Mr. G. B. on that Nighte putt ye Divell his Marke upon Bridget S., Jonathan A., Simon O., Deliverance W., Joseph C., Susan P., Mehitable C., and Deborah B." Ward's face, too, troubled him horribly, till at length he suddenly discovered why he was horrified. For above the young man's right eye was something which he had never previously noticed—a small scar or pit precisely like that in the crumbled painting of old Joseph Curwen, and perhaps attesting some hideous ritualistic inoculation to which both had submitted at a certain stage of their occult careers.

While Ward himself was puzzling all the doctors at the hospital a very strict watch was kept on all mail addressed either to him or to Dr. Allen, which Mr. Ward had ordered delivered at the family home. Willett had predicted that very little would be found, since any communications of a vital nature would probably have been exchanged by messenger; but in the latter part of March there did come a letter from Prague for Dr. Allen which gave both the doctor and the father deep thought. It was in a very crabbed and archaic hand; and though clearly not the effort of a foreigner, shewed almost as singular a departure from modern English as the speech of young Ward himself. It read:

Kleinstrasse 11, Altstadt, Prague,
11th Feby. 1928.

Brother in Almonsin-Metraton:—

I this day receiv'd yr mention of what came up from the Salts I sent you. It was wrong, and meanes clearly that ye Headstones had been chang'd when Barnabas gott me the Specimen. It is often so, as you must be sensible of from the Thing you gott from ye Kings Chapell ground in 1769 and what H. gott from Olde Bury'g Point in 1690, that was like to ende him. I gott such a Thing in Aegypt 75 yeares gone, from the which came that Scar ye Boy saw on me here in 1924. As I told you longe ago, do not calle up That which you can not put downe; either from dead Saltes or out of ye Spheres beyond. Have ye Wordes for laying at all times readie, and stopp not to be sure when there is any Doubte of Whom you have. Stones are all chang'd now in Nine groundes out of 10. You are never sure till you question. I this day heard from H., who has had Trouble with the Soldiers. He is like to be sorry Transylvania is pass'd from Hungary to Roumania, and wou'd change his Seat if the Castel weren't so fulle of What we Knowe. But of this he hath doubtless writ you. In my next Send'g there will be Somewhat from a Hill tomb from ye East that will delight you greatly. Meanwhile forget not I am desirous of B. F. if you can possibly get him for me. You know G. in Philada. better than I. Have him up firste if you will, but doe not use him soe hard he will be Difficult, for I must speake to him in ye End.

Yogg-Sothoth Neblod Zin

— SIMON O.

To Mr. J. C. in Providence.

Mr. Ward and Dr. Willett paused in utter chaos before this apparent bit of unrelieved insanity. Only by degrees did they absorb what it seemed to imply. So the absent Dr. Allen, and not Charles Ward, had come to be the leading spirit at Pawtuxet? That must explain the wild reference and denunciation in the youth's last frantic letter. And what of this addressing of the bearded and spectacled stranger as "Mr. J. C."? There was no escaping the inference, but there are limits to possible monstrosity. Who was "Simon O."; the old man Ward had visited in Prague four years previously? Perhaps, but in the centuries behind there had been another Simon O.— Simon Orne, alias Jedediah, of Salem, who vanished in 1771, and whose peculiar handwriting Dr. Willett now unmistakably recognised from the photostatic copies of the Orne formulae which Charles had once shewn him. What horrors and mysteries, what contradictions and contraventions of Nature, had come back after a century and a half to harass Old Providence with her clustered spires and domes?

The father and the old physician, virtually at a loss what to do or think, went to see Charles at the hospital and questioned him as delicately as they could about Dr. Allen, about the Prague visit, and about what he had learned of Simon or Jedediah Orne of Salem. To all these inquiries the youth was politely non-committal, merely barking in his hoarse whisper that he had found Dr. Allen to have a remarkable spiritual rapport with certain souls from the past, and that any correspondent the bearded man might have in Prague would probably be similarly gifted. When they left, Mr. Ward and Dr. Willett realised to their chagrin that they had really been the ones under catechism; and that without imparting anything vital himself, the confined youth had adroitly pumped them of everything the Prague letter had contained.

Drs. Peck, Waite, and Lyman were not inclined to attach much importance to the strange correspondence of young Ward's companion; for they knew the tendency of kindred eccentrics and monomaniacs to band together, and believed that Charles or Allen had merely unearthed an expatriated counterpart — perhaps one who had seen Orne's handwriting and copied it in an attempt to pose as the bygone character's reincarnation. Allen himself was perhaps a similar case, and may have persuaded the youth into accepting him as an avatar of the long-dead Curwen. Such things had been known before, and on the same basis the hard-headed doctors disposed of Willett's growing disquiet about Charles Ward's present handwriting, as studied from unpremeditated specimens obtained by various ruses. Willett thought he had placed its odd familiarity at last, and that what it vaguely resembled was the bygone penmanship of old Joseph Curwen himself; but this the other physicians regarded as a phase of imitativeness only to be expected in a mania of this sort, and refused to grant it any importance either favourable or unfavourable. Recognising this prosaic attitude in his colleagues, Willett advised Mr. Ward to keep to himself the letter which arrived for Dr. Allen on the second of April from Rakus, Transylvania, in a handwriting so intensely and fundamentally like that of the Hutchinson cipher that both father and physician paused in awe before breaking the seal. This read as follows:

Castle Ferenczy
7 March 1928.

Dear C.:—

Hadd a Squad of 20 Militia up to talk about what the Country Folk say. Must digg deeper and have less Hearde. These Roumanians plague me damnably, being officious and particular where you cou'd buy a Magyar off with a Drinke and ffood. Last monthe M. got me ye Sarcophagus of ye Five Sphinxes from ye Acropolis where He whome I call'd up say'd it wou'd be, and I have hadde 3 Talkes with What was therein inhum'd. It will go to S. O. in Prague directly, and thence to you. It is stubborn but you know ye Way with Such. You shew Wisdom in having lesse about than Before; for there was no Neede to keep the Guards in Shape and eat'g off their Heads, and it made Much to be founde in Case of Trouble, as you too welle knowe. You can now move and worke elsewhere with no Kill'g Trouble if needful, tho' I hope no Thing will soon force you to so Bothersome a Course. I rejoice that you traffick not so much with Those Outside; for there was ever a Mortall Peril in it, and you are sensible what it did when you ask'd Protection of One not dispos'd to give it. You excel me in gett'g ye fformulae so another may saye them with Success, but Borellus fancy'd it wou'd be so if just ye right Wordes were hadd. Does ye Boy use 'em often? I regret that he growes squeamish, as I fear'd he wou'd when I hadde him here nigh 15 Monthes, but am sensible you knowe how to deal with him. You can't saye him down with ye fformula, for that will Worke only upon such as ye other fformula hath call'd up from Saltes; but you still have strong Handes and Knife and Pistol, and Graves are not harde to digg, nor Acids loth to burne. O. sayes you have promis'd him B. F. I must have him after. B. goes to you soone, and may he give you what you wishe of that Darke Thing belowe Memphis. Imploy care in what you calle up, and beware of ye Boy. It will be ripe in a yeare's time to have up ye Legions from Underneath, and then there are no Boundes to what shal be oures. Have Confidence in what I saye, for you knowe O. and I have hadd these 150 yeares more than you to consulte these Matters in.

Nephreu — Ka nai Hadoth,

— EDW. H.

For J Curwen, Esq.
Providence.

But if Willett and Mr. Ward refrained from shewing this letter to the alienists, they did not refrain from acting upon it themselves. No amount of learned sophistry could controvert the fact that the strangely bearded and spectacled Dr. Allen, of whom Charles's frantic letter had spoken as such a monstrous menace, was in close and sinister correspondence with two inexplicable creatures whom Ward had visited in his travels and who plainly claimed to be survivals or avatars of Curwen's old Salem colleagues; that he was regarding himself as the reincarnation of Joseph Curwen, and that he entertained — or was at least advised to entertain — murderous designs against a "boy" who could scarcely be other than Charles Ward. There was organised horror afoot; and no matter who had started it, the missing Allen was by this time at the bottom of it. Therefore, thanking heaven that Charles was now safe in the hospital, Mr. Ward lost no time in engaging detectives to learn all they could of the cryptic, bearded doctor; finding whence he had come and what Pawtuxet knew of him, and if possible discovering his current whereabouts. Supplying the men with one of the bungalow keys which Charles yielded up, he urged them to explore Allen's vacant room which had been identified when the patient's belongings had been packed; obtaining what clues they could from any effects he might have left about. Mr. Ward talked with the detectives in his son's old library, and they felt a marked relief when they left it at last; for there seemed to hover about the place a vague aura of evil. Perhaps it was what they had heard of the infamous old wizard whose picture had once stared from the panelled overmantel, and perhaps it was something different and irrelevant; but in any case they all half sensed an intangible miasma which centred in that carven vestige of an older dwelling and which at times almost rose to the intensity of a material emanation.

PART FIVE:
A NIGHTMARE AND A CATACLYSM.

I.

And now swiftly followed that hideous experience which has left its indelible mark of fear on the soul of Marinus Bicknell Willett, and has added a decade to the visible age of one whose youth was even then far behind. Dr. Willett had conferred at length with Mr. Ward, and had come to an agreement with him on several points which both felt the alienists would ridicule. There was, they conceded, a terrible movement alive in the world, whose direct connexion with a necromancy even older than the Salem witchcraft could not be doubted. That at least two living men — and one other of whom they dared not think — were in absolute possession of minds or personalities which had functioned as early as 1690 or before was likewise almost unassailably proved even in the face of all known natural laws. What these horrible creatures — and Charles Ward as well — were doing or trying to do seemed fairly clear from their letters and from every bit of light both old and new which had filtered in upon the case. They were robbing the tombs of all the ages, including those of the world's wisest and greatest men, in the hope of recovering from the bygone ashes some vestige of the consciousness and lore which had once animated and informed them.

A hideous traffick was going on among these nightmare ghouls, whereby illustrious bones were bartered with the calm calculativeness of schoolboys swapping books; and from what was extorted from this centuried dust there was anticipated a power and a wisdom beyond anything which the cosmos had ever seen concentrated in one man or group. They had found unholy ways to keep their brains alive, either in the same body or different bodies; and had evidently achieved a way of tapping the consciousness of the dead whom they gathered together. There had, it seems, been some truth in chimerical old Borellus when he wrote of preparing from even the most antique remains certain "Essential Saltes" from which the shade of a long-dead living thing might be raised up. There was a formula for evoking such a shade, and another for putting it down; and it had now been so perfected that it could be taught successfully. One must be careful about evocations, for the markers of old graves are not always accurate.

Willett and Mr. Ward shivered as they passed from conclusion to conclusion. Things — presences or voices of some sort — could be drawn down from unknown places as well as from the grave, and in this process also one must be careful. Joseph Curwen had indubitably evoked many forbidden things, and as for Charles — what might one think of him? What forces "outside the spheres" had reached him from Joseph Curwen's day and turned his mind on forgotten things? He had been led to find certain directions, and he had used them. He had talked with the man of horror in Prague and stayed long with the creature in the mountains of Transylvania. And he must have found the grave of Joseph Curwen at last. That newspaper item and what his mother had heard in the night were too significant to overlook. Then he had summoned something, and it must have come. That mighty voice aloft on Good Friday, and those different tones in the locked attic laboratory. What were they like, with their depth and hollowness? Was there not here some awful foreshadowing of the dreaded stranger Dr. Allen with his spectral bass? Yes, that was what Mr. Ward had felt with vague horror in his single talk with the man — if man it were — over the telephone!

What hellish consciousness or voice, what morbid shade or presence, had come to answer Charles Ward's secret rites behind that locked door? Those voices heard in argument — "must have it red for three months" — Good God! Was not that just before the vampirism broke out? The rifling of Ezra Weeden's ancient grave, and the cries later at Pawtuxet — whose mind had planned the vengeance and rediscovered the shunned seat of elder blasphemies? And then the bungalow and the bearded stranger, and the gossip, and the fear. The final madness of Charles neither father nor doctor could attempt to explain, but they did feel sure that the mind of Joseph Curwen had come to earth again and was following its ancient morbidities. Was daemoniac possession in truth a possibility? Allen had something to do with it, and the detectives must find out more about one whose existence menaced the young man's life. In the meantime, since the existence of some vast crypt beneath the bungalow seemed virtually beyond dispute, some effort must be made to find it. Willett and Mr. Ward, conscious of the sceptical attitude of the alienists, resolved during their final conference to undertake a joint secret exploration of unparalleled thoroughness; and agreed to meet at the bungalow on the following morning with valises and with certain tools and accessories suited to architectural search and underground exploration.

The morning of April 6th dawned clear, and both explorers were at the bungalow by ten o'clock. Mr. Ward had the key, and an entry and cursory survey were made. From the disordered condition of Dr. Allen's room it was obvious that the detectives had been there before, and the later searchers hoped that they had found some clue which might prove of value. Of course the main business lay in the cellar; so thither they descended without much delay, again making the circuit which each had vainly made before in the presence of the mad young owner. For a time everything seemed baffling, each inch of the earthen floor and stone walls having so solid and innocuous an aspect that the thought of a yawning aperture was scarcely to be entertained. Willett reflected that since the original cellar was dug without knowledge of any catacombs beneath, the beginning of the passage would represent the strictly modern delving of young Ward and his associates, where they had probed for the ancient vaults whose rumour could have reached them by no wholesome means.

The doctor tried to put himself in Charles's place to see how a delver would be likely to start, but could not gain much inspiration from this method. Then he decided on elimination as a policy, and went carefully over the whole subterranean surface both vertical and horizontal, trying to account for every inch separately. He was soon substantially narrowed down, and at last had nothing left but the small platform before the washtubs, which he had tried once before in vain. Now experimenting in every possible way, and exerting a double strength, he finally found that the top did indeed turn and slide horizontally on a corner pivot. Beneath it lay a trim concrete surface with an iron manhole, to which Mr. Ward at once rushed with excited zeal. The cover was not hard to lift, and the father had quite removed it when Willett noticed the queerness of his aspect. He was swaying and nodding dizzily, and in the gust of noxious air which swept up from the black pit beneath the doctor soon recognised ample cause.

In a moment Dr. Willett had his fainting companion on the floor above and was reviving him with cold water. Mr. Ward responded feebly, but it could be seen that the mephitic blast from the crypt had in some way gravely sickened him. Wishing to take no chances, Willett hastened out to Broad Street for a taxicab and had soon dispatched the sufferer home despite his weak-voiced protests; after which he produced an electric torch, covered his nostrils with a band of sterile gauze, and descended once more to peer into the new-found depths. The foul air had now slightly abated, and Willett was able to send a beam of light down the Stygian hole. For about ten feet, he saw, it was a sheer cylindrical drop with concrete walls and an iron ladder; after which the hole appeared to strike a flight of old stone steps which must originally have emerged to earth somewhat southwest of the present building.

II.

Willett freely admits that for a moment the memory of the old Curwen legends kept him from climbing down alone into that malodorous gulf. He could not help thinking of what Luke Fenner had reported on that last monstrous night. Then duty asserted itself and he made the plunge, carrying a great valise for the removal of whatever papers might prove of supreme importance. Slowly, as befitted one of his years, he descended the ladder and reached the slimy steps below. This was ancient masonry, his torch told him; and upon the dripping walls he saw the unwholesome moss of centuries. Down, down, ran the steps; not spirally, but in three abrupt turns; and with such narrowness that two men could have passed only with difficulty. He had counted about thirty when a sound reached him very faintly; and after that he did not feel disposed to count any more.

It was a godless sound; one of those low-keyed, insidious outrages of Nature which are not meant to be. To call it a dull wail, a doom-dragged whine, or a hopeless howl of chorused anguish and stricken flesh without mind would be to miss its most quintessential loathsomeness and soul-sickening overtones. Was it for this that Ward had seemed to listen on that day he was removed? It was the most shocking thing that Willett had ever heard, and it continued from no determinate point as the doctor reached the bottom of the steps and cast his torchlight around on lofty corridor walls surmounted by Cyclopean vaulting and pierced by numberless black archways. The hall in which he stood was perhaps fourteen feet high to the middle of the vaulting and ten or twelve feet broad. Its pavement was of large chipped flagstones, and its walls and roof were of dressed masonry. Its length he could not imagine, for it stretched ahead indefinitely into the blackness. Of the archways, some had doors of the old six-panelled colonial type, whilst others had none.

Overcoming the dread induced by the smell and the howling, Willett began to explore these archways one by one; finding beyond them rooms with groined stone ceilings, each of medium size and apparently of bizarre uses. Most of them had fireplaces, the upper courses of whose chimneys would have formed an interesting study in engineering. Never before or since had he seen such instruments or suggestions of instruments as here loomed up on every hand through the burying dust and cobwebs of a century and a half, in many cases evidently shattered as if by the ancient raiders. For many of the chambers seemed wholly untrodden by modern feet, and must have represented the earliest and most obsolete phases of Joseph Curwen's experimentation. Finally there came a room of obvious modernity, or at least of recent occupancy. There were oil heaters, bookshelves and tables, chairs and cabinets, and a desk piled high with papers of varying antiquity and contemporaneousness. Candlesticks and oil lamps stood about in several places; and finding a match-safe handy, Willett lighted such as were ready for use.

In the fuller gleam it appeared that this apartment was nothing less than the latest study or library of Charles Ward. Of the books the doctor had seen many before, and a good part of the furniture had plainly come from the Prospect Street mansion. Here and there was a piece well known to Willett, and the sense of familiarity became so great that he half forgot the noisomeness and the wailing, both of which were plainer here than they had been at the foot of the steps. His first duty, as planned long ahead, was to find and seize any papers which might seem of vital importance; especially those portentous documents found by Charles so long ago behind the picture in Olney Court. As he searched he perceived how stupendous a task the final unravelling would be; for file on file was stuffed with papers in curious hands and bearing curious designs, so that months or even years might be needed for a thorough deciphering and editing. Once he found large packets of letters with Prague and Rakus postmarks, and in writing clearly recognisable as Orne's and Hutchinson's; all of which he took with him as part of the bundle to be removed in his valise.

At last, in a locked mahogany cabinet once gracing the Ward home, Willett found the batch of old Curwen papers; recognising them from the reluctant glimpse Charles had granted him so many years ago. The youth had evidently kept them together very much as they had been when first he found them, since all the titles recalled by the workmen were present except the papers addressed to Orne and Hutchinson, and the cipher with its key. Willett placed the entire lot in his valise and continued his examination of the files. Since young Ward's immediate condition was the greatest matter at stake, the closest searching was done among the most obviously recent matter; and in this abundance of contemporary manuscript one very baffling oddity was noted. The oddity was the slight amount in Charles's normal writing, which indeed included nothing more recent than two months before. On the other hand, there were literally reams of symbols and formulae, historical notes and philosophical comment, in a crabbed penmanship absolutely identical with the ancient script of Joseph Curwen, though of undeniably modern dating. Plainly, a part of the latter-day programme had been a sedulous imitation of the old wizard's writing, which Charles seemed to have carried to a marvellous state of perfection. Of any third hand which might have been Allen's there was not a trace. If he had indeed come to be the leader, he must have forced young Ward to act as his amanuensis.

In this new material one mystic formula, or rather pair of formulae, recurred so often that Willett had it by heart before he had half finished his quest. It consisted of two parallel columns, the left-hand one surmounted by the archaic symbol called "Dragon's Head" and used in almanacks to indicate the ascending node, and the right hand one headed by a corresponding sign of "Dragon's Tail" or descending node. The appearance of the whole was something like this, and almost unconsciously the doctor realised that the second half was no more than the first written syllabically backward with the exception of the final monosyllables and of the odd name Yog-Sothoth, which he had come to recognise under various spellings from other things he had seen in connexion with this horrible matter. The formulae were as follows — exactly so, as Willett is abundantly able to testify — and the first one struck an odd note of uncomfortable latent memory in his brain, which he recognised later when reviewing the events of that horrible Good Friday of the previous year.

☊

Y'AI 'NG'NGAH,
YOG-SOTHOTH
H'EE — L'GEB
F'AI THRODOG
UAAAH!

☋

OGTHROD AI'F
GEB'L — EE'H
YOG-SOTHOTH
'NGAH'NG AI'Y
ZHRO!

So haunting were these formulae, and so frequently did he come upon them, that before the doctor knew it he was repeating them under his breath. Eventually, however, he felt he had secured all the papers he could digest to advantage for the present; hence resolved to examine no more till he could bring the sceptical alienists en masse for an ampler and more systematic raid. He had still to find the hidden laboratory, so leaving his valise in the lighted room he emerged again into the black noisome corridor whose vaulting echoed ceaselessly with that dull and hideous whine.

The next few rooms he tried were all abandoned, or filled only with crumbling boxes and ominous-looking leaden coffins; but impressed him deeply with the magnitude of Joseph Curwen's original operations. He thought of the slaves and seamen who had disappeared, of the graves which had been violated in every part of the world, and of what that final raiding party must have seen; and then he decided it was better not to think any more. Once a great stone staircase mounted at his right, and he deduced that this must have reached to one of the Curwen outbuildings—perhaps the famous stone edifice with the high slit-like windows—provided the steps he had descended had led from the steep-roofed farmhouse. Suddenly the walls seemed to fall away ahead, and the stench and the wailing grew stronger. Willett saw that he had come upon a vast open space, so great that his torchlight would not carry across it; and as he advanced he encountered occasional stout pillars supporting the arches of the roof.

After a time he reached a circle of pillars grouped like the monoliths of Stonehenge, with a large carved altar on a base of three steps in the centre; and so curious were the carvings on that altar that he approached to study them with his electric light. But when he saw what they were he shrank away shuddering, and did not stop to investigate the dark stains which discoloured the upper surface and had spread down the sides in occasional thin lines. Instead, he found the distant wall and traced it as it swept round in a gigantic circle perforated by occasional black doorways and indented by a myriad of shallow cells with iron gratings and wrist and ankle bonds on chains fastened to the stone of the concave rear masonry. These cells were empty, but still the horrible odour and the dismal moaning continued, more insistent now than ever, and seemingly varied at times by a sort of slippery thumping.

III.

From that frightful smell and that uncanny noise Willett's attention could no longer be diverted. Both were plainer and more hideous in the great pillared hall than anywhere else, and carried a vague impression of being far below, even in this dark nether world of subterrene mystery. Before trying any of the black archways for steps leading further down, the doctor cast his beam of light about the stone-flagged floor. It was very loosely paved, and at irregular intervals there would occur a slab curiously pierced by small holes in no definite arrangement, while at one point there lay a very long ladder carelessly flung down. To this ladder, singularly enough, appeared to cling a particularly large amount of the frightful odour which encompassed everything. As he walked slowly about it suddenly occurred to Willett that both the noise and the odour seemed strongest directly above the oddly pierced slabs, as if they might be crude trap-doors leading down to some still deeper region of horror. Kneeling by one, he worked at it with his hands, and found that with extreme difficulty he could budge it. At his touch the moaning beneath ascended to a louder key, and only with vast trepidation did he persevere in the lifting of the heavy stone. A stench unnameable now rose up from below, and the doctor's head reeled dizzily as he laid back the slab and turned his torch upon the exposed square yard of gaping blackness.

If he had expected a flight of steps to some wide gulf of ultimate abomination, Willett was destined to be disappointed; for amidst that foetor and cracked whining he discerned only the brick-faced top of a cylindrical well perhaps a yard and a half in diameter and devoid of any ladder or other means of descent. As the light shone down, the wailing changed suddenly to a series of horrible yelps; in conjunction with which there came again that sound of blind, futile scrambling and slippery thumping. The explorer trembled, unwilling even to imagine what noxious thing might be lurking in that abyss, but in a moment mustered up the courage to peer over the rough-hewn brink; lying at full length and holding the torch downward at arm's length to see what might lie below. For a second he could distinguish nothing but the slimy, moss-grown brick walls sinking illimitably into that half-tangible miasma of murk and foulness and anguished frenzy; and then he saw that something dark was leaping clumsily and frantically up and down at the bottom of the narrow shaft, which must have been from twenty to twenty-five feet below the stone floor where he lay. The torch shook in his hand, but he looked again to see what manner of living creature might be immured there in the darkness of that unnatural well; left starving by young Ward through all the long month since the doctors had taken him away, and clearly only one of a vast number prisoned in the kindred wells whose pierced stone covers so thickly studded the floor of the great vaulted cavern. Whatever the things were, they could not lie down in their cramped spaces; but must have crouched and whined and waited and feebly leaped all those hideous weeks since their master had abandoned them unheeded.

But Marinus Bicknell Willett was sorry that he looked again; for surgeon and veteran of the dissecting-room though he was, he has not been the same since. It is hard to explain just how a single sight of a tangible object with measureable dimensions could so shake and change a man; and we may only say that there is about certain outlines and entities a power of symbolism and suggestion which acts frightfully on a sensitive thinker's perspective and whispers terrible hints of obscure cosmic relationships and unnameable realities behind the protective illusions of common vision. In that second look Willett saw such an outline or entity, for during the next few instants he was undoubtedly as stark mad as any inmate of Dr. Waite's private hospital. He dropped the electric torch from a hand drained of muscular power or nervous coördination, nor heeded the sound of crunching teeth which told of its fate at the bottom of the pit. He screamed and screamed and screamed in a voice whose falsetto panic no acquaintance of his would ever have recognised; and though he could not rise to his feet he crawled and rolled desperately away over the damp pavement where dozens of Tartarean wells poured forth their exhausted whining and yelping to answer his own insane cries. He tore his hands on the rough, loose stones, and many times bruised his head against the frequent pillars, but still he kept on. Then at last he slowly came to himself in the utter blackness and stench, and stopped his ears against the droning wail into which the burst of yelping had subsided. He was drenched with perspiration and without means of producing a light; stricken and unnerved in the abysmal blackness and horror, and crushed with a memory he never could efface. Beneath him dozens of those things still lived, and from one of the shafts the cover was removed. He knew that what he had seen could never climb up the slippery walls, yet shuddered at the thought that some obscure foot-hold might exist.

What the thing was, he would never tell. It was like some of the carvings on the hellish altar, but it was alive. Nature had never made it in this form, for it was too palpably unfinished. The deficiencies were of the most surprising sort, and the abnormalities of proportion could not be described. Willett consents only to say that this type of thing must have represented entities which Ward called up from imperfect salts, and which he kept for servile or ritualistic purposes. If it had not had a certain significance, its image would not have been carved on that damnable stone. It was not the worst thing depicted on that stone—but Willett never opened the other pits. At the time, the first connected idea in his mind was an idle paragraph from some of the old Curwen data he had digested long before; a phrase used by Simon or Jedediah Orne in that portentous confiscated letter to the bygone sorcerer: "Certainely, there was Noth'g but ye liveliest Awfulness in that which H. rais'd upp from What he cou'd gather onlie a part of."

Then, horribly supplementing rather than displacing this image, there came a recollection of those ancient lingering rumours anent the burned, twisted thing found in the fields a week after the Curwen raid. Charles Ward had once told the doctor what old Slocum said of that object; that it was neither thoroughly human, nor wholly allied to any animal which Pawtuxet folk had ever seen or read about.

These words hummed in the doctor's mind as he rocked to and fro, squatting on the nitrous stone floor. He tried to drive them out, and repeated the Lord's Prayer to himself; eventually trailing off into a mnemonic hodge-podge like the modernistic Waste Land of Mr. T. S. Eliot, and finally reverting to the oft-repeated dual formula he had lately found in Ward's underground library: "Y'ai 'ng'ngah, Yog-Sothoth" and so on till the final underlined "Zhro." It seemed to soothe him, and he staggered to his feet after a time; lamenting bitterly his fright-lost torch and looking wildly about for any gleam of light in the clutching inkiness of the chilly air. Think he would not; but he strained his eyes in every direction for some faint glint or reflection of the bright illumination he had left in the library. After a while he thought he detected a suspicion of a glow infinitely far away, and toward this he crawled in agonised caution on hands and knees amidst the stench and howling, always feeling ahead lest he collide with the numerous great pillars or stumble into the abominable pit he had uncovered.

Once his shaking fingers touched something which he knew must be the steps leading to the hellish altar, and from this spot he recoiled in loathing. At another time he encountered the pierced slab he had removed, and here his caution became almost pitiful. But he did not come upon the dread aperture after all, nor did anything issue from that aperture to detain him. What had been down there made no sound nor stir. Evidently its crunching of the fallen electric torch had not been good for it. Each time Willett's fingers felt a perforated slab he trembled. His passage over it would sometimes increase the groaning below, but generally it would produce no effect at all, since he moved very noiselessly. Several times during his progress the glow ahead diminished perceptibly, and he realised that the various candles and lamps he had left must be expiring one by one. The thought of being lost in utter darkness without matches amidst this underground world of nightmare labyrinths impelled him to rise to his feet and run, which he could safely do now that he had passed the open pit; for he knew that once the light failed, his only hope of rescue and survival would lie in whatever relief party Mr. Ward might send after missing him for a sufficient period. Presently, however, he emerged from the open space into the narrower corridor and definitely located the glow as coming from a door on his right. In a moment he had reached it and was standing once more in young Ward's secret library, trembling with relief, and watching the sputterings of that last lamp which had brought him to safety.

IV.

In another moment he was hastily filling the burned-out lamps from an oil supply he had previously noticed, and when the room was bright again he looked about to see if he might find a lantern for further exploration. For racked though he was with horror, his sense of grim purpose was still uppermost; and he was firmly determined to leave no stone unturned in his search for the hideous facts behind Charles Ward's bizarre madness. Failing to find a lantern, he chose the smallest of the lamps to carry; also filling his pockets with candles and matches, and taking with him a gallon can of oil, which he proposed to keep for reserve use in whatever hidden laboratory he might uncover beyond the terrible open space with its unclean altar and nameless covered wells. To traverse that space again would require his utmost fortitude, but he knew it must be done. Fortunately neither the frightful altar nor the opened shaft was near the vast cell-indented wall which bounded the cavern area, and whose black mysterious archways would form the next goals of a logical search.

So Willett went back to that great pillared hall of stench and anguished howling; turning down his lamp to avoid any distant glimpse of the hellish altar, or of the uncovered pit with the pierced stone slab beside it. Most of the black doorways led merely to small chambers, some vacant and some evidently used as storerooms; and in several of the latter he saw some very curious accumulations of various objects. One was packed with rotting and dust-draped bales of spare clothing, and the explorer thrilled when he saw that it was unmistakably the clothing of a century and a half before. In another room he found numerous odds and ends of modern clothing, as if gradual provisions were being made to equip a large body of men. But what he disliked most of all were the huge copper vats which occasionally appeared; these, and the sinister incrustations upon them. He liked them even less than the weirdly figured leaden bowls whose rims retained such obnoxious deposits and around which clung repellent odours perceptible above even the general noisomeness of the crypt. When he had completed about half the entire circuit of the wall he found another corridor like that from which he had come, and out of which many doors opened. This he proceeded to investigate; and after entering three rooms of medium size and of no significant contents, he came at last to a large oblong apartment whose business-like tanks and tables, furnaces and modern instruments, occasional books and endless shelves of jars and bottles proclaimed it indeed the long-sought laboratory of Charles Ward — and no doubt of old Joseph Curwen before him.

After lighting the three lamps which he found filled and ready, Dr. Willett examined the place and all its appurtenances with the keenest interest; noting from the relative quantities of various reagents on the shelves that young Ward's dominant concern must have been with some branch of organic chemistry. On the whole, little could be learned from the scientific ensemble, which included a gruesome-looking dissecting-table; so that the room was really rather a disappointment. Among the books was a tattered old copy of Borellus in black-letter, and it was weirdly interesting to note that Ward had underlined the same passage whose marking had so perturbed good Mr. Merritt at Curwen's farmhouse more than a century and a half before. That older copy, of course, must have perished along with the rest of Curwen's occult library in the final raid. Three archways opened off the laboratory, and these the doctor proceeded to sample in turn. From his cursory survey he saw that two led merely to small storerooms; but these he canvassed with care, remarking the piles of coffins in various stages of damage and shuddering violently at two or three of the few coffin-plates he could decipher. There was much clothing also stored in these rooms, and several new and tightly nailed boxes which he did not stop to investigate. Most interesting of all, perhaps, were some odd bits which he judged to be fragments of old Joseph Curwen's laboratory appliances. These had suffered damage at the hands of the raiders, but were still partly recognisable as the chemical paraphernalia of the Georgian period.

The third archway led to a very sizeable chamber entirely lined with shelves and having in the centre a table bearing two lamps. These lamps Willett lighted, and in their brilliant glow studied the endless shelving which surrounded him. Some of the upper levels were wholly vacant, but most of the space was filled with small odd-looking leaden jars of two general types; one tall and without handles like a Grecian lekythos or oil-jug, and the other with a single handle and proportioned like a Phaleron jug. All had metal stoppers, and were covered with peculiar-looking symbols moulded in low relief. In a moment the doctor noticed that these jugs were classified with great rigidity; all the lekythoi being on one side of the room with a large wooden sign reading "Custodes" above them, and all the Phalerons on the other, correspondingly labelled with a sign reading "Materia." Each of the jars or jugs, except some on the upper shelves that turned out to be vacant, bore a cardboard tag with a number apparently referring to a catalogue; and Willett resolved to look for the latter presently. For the moment, however, he was more interested in the nature of the array as a whole, and experimentally opened several of the lekythoi and Phalerons at random with a view to a rough generalisation. The result was invariable. Both types of jar contained a small quantity of a single kind of substance; a fine dusty powder of very light weight and of many shades of dull, neutral colour. To the colours which formed the only point of variation there was no apparent method of disposal; and no distinction between what occurred in the lekythoi and what occurred in the Phalerons. A bluish-grey powder might be by the side of a pinkish-white one, and any one in a Phaleron might have its exact counterpart in a lekythos. The most individual feature about the powders was their non-adhesiveness. Willett would pour one into his hand, and upon returning it to its jug would find that no residue whatever remained on its palm.

The meaning of the two signs puzzled him, and he wondered why this battery of chemicals was separated so radically from those in glass jars on the shelves of the laboratory proper. "Custodes," "Materia"; that was the Latin for "Guards" and "Materials," respectively — and then there came a flash of memory as to where he had seen that word "Guards" before in connexion with this dreadful mystery. It was, of course, in the recent letter to Dr. Allen purporting to be from old Edward Hutchinson; and the phrase had read: "There was no Neede to keep the Guards in Shape and eat'g off their Heads, and it made Much to be founde in Case of Trouble, as you too welle knowe." What did this signify? But wait — was there not still another reference to "guards" in this matter which he had failed wholly to recall when reading the Hutchinson letter? Back in the old non-secretive days Ward had told him of the Eleazar Smith diary recording the spying of Smith and Weeden on the Curwen farm, and in that dreadful chronicle there had been a mention of conversations overheard before the old wizard betook himself wholly beneath the earth. There had been, Smith and Weeden insisted, terrible colloquies wherein figured Curwen, certain captives of his, and the guards of those captives. Those guards, according to Hutchinson or his avatar, had "eaten their heads off," so that now Dr. Allen did not keep them in shape. And if not in shape, how save as the "salts" to which it appears this wizard band was engaged in reducing as many human bodies or skeletons as they could?

So that was what these lekythoi contained; the monstrous fruit of unhallowed rites and deeds, presumably won or cowed to such submission as to help, when called up by some hellish incantation, in the defence of their blasphemous master or the questioning of those who were not so willing? Willett shuddered at the thought of what he had been pouring in and out of his hands, and for a moment felt an impulse to flee in panic from that cavern of hideous shelves with their silent and perhaps watching sentinels. Then he thought of the "Materia"—in the myriad Phaleron jugs on the other side of the room. Salts too—and if not the salts of "guards," then the salts of what? God! Could it be possible that here lay the mortal relics of half the titan thinkers of all the ages; snatched by supreme ghouls from crypts where the world thought them safe, and subject to the beck and call of madmen who sought to drain their knowledge for some still wilder end whose ultimate effect would concern, as poor Charles had hinted in his frantic note, "all civilisation, all natural law, perhaps even the fate of the solar system and the universe"? And Marinus Bicknell Willett had sifted their dust through his hands!

Then he noticed a small door at the farther end of the room, and calmed himself enough to approach it and examine the crude sign chiselled above. It was only a symbol, but it filled him with vague spiritual dread; for a morbid, dreaming friend of his had once drawn it on paper and told him a few of the things it means in the dark abyss of sleep. It was the sign of Koth, that dreamers see fixed above the archway of a certain black tower standing alone in twilight—and Willett did not like what his friend Randolph Carter had said of its powers. But a moment later he forgot the sign as he recognised a new acrid odour in the stench-filled air. This was a chemical rather than animal smell, and came clearly from the room beyond the door. And it was, unmistakably, the same odour which had saturated Charles Ward's clothing on the day the doctors had taken him away. So it was here that the youth had been interrupted by the final summons? He was wiser than old Joseph Curwen, for he had not resisted. Willett, boldly determined to penetrate every wonder and nightmare this nether realm might contain, seized the small lamp and crossed the threshold. A wave of nameless fright rolled out to meet him, but he yielded to no whim and deferred to no intuition. There was nothing alive here to harm him, and he would not be stayed in his piercing of the eldritch cloud which engulfed his patient.

The room beyond the door was of medium size, and had no furniture save a table, a single chair, and two groups of curious machines with clamps and wheels, which Willett recognised after a moment as mediaeval instruments of torture. On one side of the door stood a rack of savage whips, above which were some shelves bearing empty rows of shallow pedestalled cups of lead shaped like Grecian kylikes. On the other side was the table; with a powerful Argand lamp, a pad and pencil, and two of the stoppered lekythoi from the shelves outside set down at irregular places as if temporarily or in haste. Willett lighted the lamp and looked carefully at the pad, to see what notes young Ward might have been jotting down when interrupted; but found nothing more intelligible than the following disjointed fragments in that crabbed Curwen chirography, which shed no light on the case as a whole:

B. dy'd not. Escap'd into walls and founde Place below.
Sawe olde V. saye ye Sabaoth and learnt ye Way.
Rais'd Yog-Sothoth thrice and was ye nexte Day deliver'd.
F. soughte to wipe out all know'g howe to raise Those from Outside.

As the strong Argand blaze lit up the entire chamber the doctor saw that the wall opposite the door, between the two groups of torturing appliances in the corners, was covered with pegs from which hung a set of shapeless-looking robes of a rather dismal yellowish-white. But far more interesting were the two vacant walls, both of which were thickly covered with mystic symbols and formulae roughly chiselled in the smooth dressed stone. The damp floor also bore marks of carving; and with but little difficulty Willett deciphered a huge pentagram in the centre, with a plain circle about three feet wide half way between this and each corner. In one of these four circles, near where a yellowish robe had been flung carelessly down, there stood a shallow kylix of the sort found on the shelves above the whip-rack; and just outside the periphery was one of the Phaleron jugs from the shelves in the other room, its tag numbered 118. This was unstoppered, and proved upon inspection to be empty; but the explorer saw with a shiver that the kylix was not. Within its shallow area, and saved from scattering only by the absence of wind in this sequestered cavern, lay a small amount of a dry, dull-greenish efflorescent powder which must have belonged in the jug; and Willett almost reeled at the implications that came sweeping over him as he correlated little by little the several elements and antecedents of the scene. The whips and the instruments of torture, the dust or salts from the jug of "Materia," the two lekythoi from the "Custodes" shelf, the robes, the formulae on the walls, the notes on the pad, the hints from letters and legends, and the thousand glimpses, doubts, and suppositions which had come to torment the friends and parents of Charles Ward—all these engulfed the doctor in a tidal wave of horror as he looked at that dry greenish powder outspread in the pedestalled leaden kylix on the floor.

With an effort, however, Willett pulled himself together and began studying the formulae chiselled on the walls. From the stained and incrusted letters it was obvious that they were carved in Joseph Curwen's time, and their text was such as to be vaguely familiar to one who had read much Curwen material or delved extensively into the history of magic. One the doctor clearly recognised as what Mrs. Ward heard her son chanting on that ominous Good Friday a year before, and what an authority had told him was a very terrible invocation addressed to secret gods outside the normal spheres. It was not spelled here exactly as Mrs. Ward had set it down from memory, nor yet as the authority had shewn it to him in the forbidden pages of "Eliphas Levi"; but its identity was unmistakable, and such words as Sabaoth, Metraton, Almonsin, and Zariatnatmik sent a shudder of fright through the searcher who had seen and felt so much of cosmic abomination just around the corner.

This was on the left-hand wall as one entered the room. The right-hand wall was no less thickly inscribed, and Willett felt a start of recognition as he came upon the pair of formulae so frequently occurring in the recent notes in the library. They were, roughly speaking, the same; with the ancient symbols of "Dragon's Head" and "Dragon's Tail" heading them as in Ward's scribblings. But the spelling differed quite widely from that of the modern versions, as if old Curwen had had a different way of recording sound, or as if later study had evolved more powerful and perfected variants of the invocations in question. The doctor tried to reconcile the chiselled version with the one which still ran persistently in his head, and found it hard to do. Where the script he had memorised began "Y'ai 'ng'ngah, Yog-Sothoth," this epigraph started out as "Aye, engengah, Yogge-Sothotha"; which to his mind would seriously interfere with the syllabification of the second word.

Ground as the later text was into his consciousness, the discrepancy disturbed him; and he found himself chanting the first of the formulae aloud in an effort to square the sound he conceived with the letters he found carved. Weird and menacing in that abyss of antique blasphemy rang his voice; its accents keyed to a droning sing-song either through the spell of the past and the unknown, or through the hellish example of that dull, godless wail from the pits whose inhuman cadences rose and fell rhythmically in the distance through the stench and the darkness.

> ☊
> *Y'AI 'NG'NGAH,*
> *YOG-SOTHOTH*
> *H'EE—L'GEB*
> *F'AI THRODOG*
> *UAAAH!"*

But what was this cold wind which had sprung into life at the very outset of the chant? The lamps were sputtering woefully, and the gloom grew so dense that the letters on the wall nearly faded from sight. There was smoke, too, and an acrid odour which quite drowned out the stench from the far-away wells; an odour like that he had smelt before, yet infinitely stronger and more pungent. He turned from the inscriptions to face the room with its bizarre contents, and saw that the kylix on the floor, in which the ominous efflorescent powder had lain, was giving forth a cloud of thick, greenish-black vapour of surprising volume and opacity. That powder—Great God! it had come from the shelf of "Materia"—what was it doing now, and what had started it? The formula he had been chanting—the first of the pair—Dragon's Head, ascending node—Blessed Saviour, could it be ....

The doctor reeled, and through his head raced wildly disjointed scraps from all he had seen, heard, and read of the frightful case of Joseph Curwen and Charles Dexter Ward. "I say to you againe, doe not call up Any that you can not put downe ... Have ye Wordes for laying at all times readie, and stopp not to be sure when there is any Doubte of Whom you have ... Three Talkes with What was therein inhum'd ..." Mercy of Heaven, what is that shape behind the parting smoke?

V.

Marinus Bicknell Willett has no hope that any part of his tale will be believed except by certain sympathetic friends, hence he has made no attempt to tell it beyond his most intimate circle. Only a few outsiders have ever heard it repeated, and of these the majority laugh and remark that the doctor surely is getting old. He has been advised to take a long vacation and to shun future cases dealing with mental disturbance. But Mr. Ward knows that the veteran physician speaks only a horrible truth. Did not he himself see the noisome aperture in the bungalow cellar? Did not Willett send him home overcome and ill at eleven o'clock that portentous morning? Did he not telephone the doctor in vain that evening, and again the next day, and had he not driven to the bungalow itself on that following noon, finding his friend unconscious but unharmed on one of the beds upstairs? Willett had been breathing stertorously, and opened his eyes slowly when Mr. Ward gave him some brandy fetched from the car. Then he shuddered and screamed, crying out, "That beard ... those eyes .... God, who are you?" A very strange thing to say to a trim, blue-eyed, clean-shaven gentleman whom he had known from the latter's boyhood.

In the bright noon sunlight the bungalow was unchanged since the previous morning. Willett's clothing bore no disarrangement beyond certain smudges and worn places at the knees, and only a faint acrid odour reminded Mr. Ward of what he had smelt on his son that day he was taken to the hospital. The doctor's flashlight was missing, but his valise was safely there, as empty as when he had brought it. Before indulging in any explanations, and obviously with great moral effort, Willett staggered dizzily down to the cellar and tried the fateful platform before the tubs. It was unyielding. Crossing to where he had left his yet unused tool satchel the day before, he obtained a chisel and began to pry up the stubborn planks one by one. Underneath the smooth concrete was still visible, but of any opening or perforation there was no longer a trace. Nothing yawned this time to sicken the mystified father who had followed the doctor downstairs; only the smooth concrete underneath the planks — no noisome well, no world of subterrene horrors, no secret library, no Curwen papers, no nightmare pits of stench and howling, no laboratory or shelves or chiselled formulae, no . . . . Dr. Willett turned pale, and clutched at the younger man. "Yesterday," he asked softly, "did you see it here . . . and smell it?" And when Mr. Ward, himself transfixed with dread and wonder, found strength to nod an affirmative, the physician gave a sound half a sigh and half a gasp, and nodded in turn. "Then I will tell you," he said.

So for an hour, in the sunniest room they could find upstairs, the physician whispered his frightful tale to the wondering father. There was nothing to relate beyond the looming up of that form when the greenish-black vapour from the kylix parted, and Willett was too tired to ask himself what had really occurred. There were futile, bewildered head-shakings from both men, and once Mr. Ward ventured a hushed suggestion, "Do you suppose it would be of any use to dig?" The doctor was silent, for it seemed hardly fitting for any human brain to answer when powers of unknown spheres had so vitally encroached on this side of the Great Abyss. Again Mr. Ward asked, "But where did it go? It brought you here, you know, and it sealed up the hole somehow." And Willett again let silence answer for him.

But after all, this was not the final phase of the matter. Reaching for his handkerchief before rising to leave, Dr. Willett's fingers closed upon a piece of paper in his pocket which had not been there before, and which was companioned by the candles and matches he had seized in the vanished vault. It was a common sheet, torn obviously from the cheap pad in that fabulous room of horror somewhere underground, and the writing upon it was that of an ordinary lead pencil — doubtless the one which had lain beside the pad. It was folded very carelessly, and beyond the faint acrid scent of the cryptic chamber bore no print or mark of any world but this. But in the text itself it did indeed reek with wonder; for here was no script of any wholesome age, but the laboured strokes of mediaeval darkness, scarcely legible to the laymen who now strained over it, yet having combinations of symbols which seemed vaguely familiar. The briefly scrawled message was this, and its mystery lent purpose to the shaken pair, who forthwith walked steadily out to the Ward car and gave orders to be driven first to a quiet dining place and then to the John Hay Library on the hill.

At the library it was easy to find good manuals of palaeography, and over these the two men puzzled till the lights of evening shone out from the great chandelier. In the end they found what was needed. The letters were indeed no fantastic invention, but the normal script of a very dark period. They were the pointed Saxon minuscules of the eighth or ninth century A.D., and brought with them memories of an uncouth time when under a fresh Christian veneer ancient faiths and ancient rites stirred stealthily, and the pale moon of Britain looked sometimes on strange deeds in the Roman ruins of Caerleon and Hexham, and by the towers along Hadrian's crumbling wall. The words were in such Latin as a barbarous age might remember — "Corvinus necandus est. Cadaver aq(ua) forti dissolvendum, nec aliq(ui)d retinendum. Tace ut potes." — which may roughly be translated, "Curwen must be killed. The body must be dissolved in aqua fortis, nor must anything be retained. Keep silence as best you are able."

Willett and Mr. Ward were mute and baffled. They had met the unknown, and found that they lacked emotions to respond to it as they vaguely believed they ought. With Willett, especially, the capacity for receiving fresh impressions of awe was well-nigh exhausted; and both men sat still and helpless till the closing of the library forced them to leave. Then they drove listlessly to the Ward mansion in Prospect Street, and talked to no purpose into the night. The doctor rested toward morning, but did not go home. And he was still there Sunday noon when a telephone message came from the detectives who had been assigned to look up Dr. Allen.

Mr. Ward, who was pacing nervously about in a dressing-gown, answered the call in person; and told the men to come up early the next day when he heard their report was almost ready. Both Willett and he were glad that this phase of the matter was taking form, for whatever the origin of the strange minuscule message, it seemed certain that the "Curwen" who must be destroyed could be no other than the bearded and spectacled stranger. Charles had feared this man, and had said in the frantic note that he must be killed and dissolved in acid. Allen, moreover, had been receiving letters from the strange wizards in Europe under the name of Curwen, and palpably regarded himself as an avatar of the bygone necromancer. And now from a fresh and unknown source had come a message saying that "Curwen" must be killed and dissolved in acid. The linkage was too unmistakable to be factitious; and besides, was not Allen planning to murder young Ward upon the advice of the creature called Hutchinson? Of course, the letter they had seen had never reached the bearded stranger; but from its text they could see that Allen had already formed plans for dealing with the youth if he grew too "squeamish." Without doubt, Allen must be apprehended; and even if the most drastic directions were not carried out, he must be placed where he could inflict no harm upon Charles Ward.

That afternoon, hoping against hope to extract some gleam of information anent the inmost mysteries from the only available one capable of giving it, the father and the doctor went down the bay and called on young Charles at the hospital. Simply and gravely Willett told him all he had found, and noticed how pale he turned as each description made certain the truth of the discovery. The physician employed as much dramatic effect as he could, and watched for a wincing on Charles's part when he approached the matter of the covered pits and the nameless hybrids within. But Ward did not wince. Willett paused, and his voice grew indignant as he spoke of how the things were starving. He taxed the youth with shocking inhumanity, and shivered when only a sardonic laugh came in reply. For Charles, having dropped as useless his pretence that the crypt did not exist, seemed to see some ghastly jest in this affair; and chuckled hoarsely at something which amused him. Then he whispered, in accents doubly terrible because of the cracked voice he used, "Damn 'em, they do eat, but they don't need to! That's the rare part! A month, you say, without food? Lud, Sir, you be modest! D'ye know, that was the joke on poor old Whipple with his virtuous bluster! Kill everything off, would he? Why, damme, he was half-deaf with the noise from Outside and never saw or heard aught from the wells! He never dreamed they were there at all! Devil take ye, those cursed things have been howling down there ever since Curwen was done for a hundred and fifty-seven years gone!"

But no more than this could Willett get from the youth. Horrified, yet almost convinced against his will, he went on with his tale in the hope that some incident might startle his auditor out of the mad composure he maintained. Looking at the youth's face, the doctor could not but feel a kind of terror at the changes which recent months had wrought. Truly, the boy had drawn down nameless horrors from the skies. When the room with the formulae and the greenish dust was mentioned, Charles shewed his first sign of animation. A quizzical look overspread his face as he heard what Willett had read on the pad, and he ventured the mild statement that those notes were old ones, of no possible significance to anyone not deeply initiated in the history of magic. "But," he added, "had you but known the words to bring up that which I had out in the cup, you had not been here to tell me this. 'Twas Number 118, and I conceive you would have shook had you looked it up in my list in t'other room. 'Twas never raised by me, but I meant to have it up that day you came to invite me hither."

Then Willett told of the formula he had spoken and of the greenish-black smoke which had arisen; and as he did so he saw true fear dawn for the first time on Charles Ward's face. "It came, and you be here alive?" As Ward croaked the words his voice seemed almost to burst free of its trammels and sink to cavernous abysses of uncanny resonance. Willett, gifted with a flash of inspiration, believed he saw the situation, and wove into his reply a caution from a letter he remembered. "No. 118, you say? But don't forget that stones are all changed now in nine grounds out of ten. You are never sure till you question!" And then, without warning, he drew forth the minuscule message and flashed it before the patient's eyes. He could have wished no stronger result, for Charles Ward fainted forthwith.

All this conversation, of course, had been conducted with the greatest secrecy lest the resident alienists accuse the father and the physician of encouraging a madman in his delusions. Unaided, too, Dr. Willett and Mr. Ward picked up the stricken youth and placed him on the couch. In reviving, the patient mumbled many times of some word which he must get to Orne and Hutchinson at once; so when his consciousness seemed fully back the doctor told him that of those strange creatures at least one was his bitter enemy, and had given Dr. Allen advice for his assassination. This revelation produced no visible effect, and before it was made the visitors could see that their host had already the look of a hunted man. After that he would converse no more, so Willett and the father departed presently; leaving behind a caution against the bearded Allen, to which the youth only replied that this individual was very safely taken care of, and could do no one any harm even if he wished. This was said with an almost evil chuckle very painful to hear. They did not worry about any communications Charles might indite to that monstrous pair in Europe, since they knew that the hospital authorities seized all outgoing mail for censorship and would pass no wild or outré-looking missive.

There is, however, a curious sequel to the matter of Orne and Hutchinson, if such indeed the exiled wizards were. Moved by some vague presentiment amidst the horrors of that period, Willett arranged with an international press-cutting bureau for accounts of notable current crimes and accidents in Prague and in eastern Transylvania; and after six months believed that he had found two very significant things amongst the multifarious items he received and had translated. One was the total wrecking of a house by night in the oldest quarter of Prague, and the disappearance of the evil old man called Josef Nadek, who had dwelt in it alone ever since anyone could remember. The other was a titan explosion in the Transylvanian mountains east of Rakus, and the utter extirpation with all its inmates of the ill-regarded Castle Ferenczy, whose master was so badly spoken of by peasants and soldiery alike that he would shortly have been summoned to Bucharest for serious questioning had not this incident cut off a career already so long as to antedate all common memory. Willett maintains that the hand which wrote those minuscules was able to wield stronger weapons as well; and that while Curwen was left to him to dispose of, the writer felt able to find and deal with Orne and Hutchinson itself. Of what their fate may have been the doctor strives sedulously not to think.

VI.

The following morning Dr. Willett hastened to the Ward home to be present when the detectives arrived. Allen's destruction or imprisonment — or Curwen's, if one might regard the tacit claim to reincarnation as valid — he felt must be accomplished at any cost, and he communicated this conviction to Mr. Ward as they sat waiting for the men to come. They were downstairs this time, for the upper parts of the house were beginning to be shunned because of a peculiar nauseousness which hung indefinitely about; a nauseousness which the older servants connected with some curse left by the vanished Curwen portrait.

At nine o'clock the three detectives presented themselves and immediately delivered all that they had to say. They had not, regrettably enough, located the Brava Tony Gomes as they had wished, nor had they found the least trace of Dr. Allen's source or present whereabouts; but they had managed to unearth a considerable number of local impressions and facts concerning the reticent stranger. Allen had struck Pawtuxet people as a vaguely unnatural being, and there was a universal belief that his thick sandy beard was either dyed or false — a belief conclusively upheld by the finding of such a false beard, together with a pair of dark glasses, in his room at the fateful bungalow. His voice, Mr. Ward could well testify from his one telephone conversation, had a depth and hollowness that could not be forgotten; and his glance seemed malign even through his smoked and horn-rimmed glasses. One shopkeeper, in the course of negotiations, had seen a specimen of his handwriting and declared it was very queer and crabbed; this being confirmed by pencilled notes of no clear meaning found in his room and identified by the merchant. In connexion with the vampirism rumours of the preceding summer, a majority of the gossips believed that Allen rather than Ward was the actual vampire. Statements were also obtained from the officials who had visited the bungalow after the unpleasant incident of the motor truck robbery. They had felt less of the sinister in Dr. Allen, but had recognised him as the dominant figure in the queer shadowy cottage. The place had been too dark for them to observe him clearly, but they would know him again if they saw him. His beard had looked odd, and they thought he had some slight scar above his dark spectacled right eye. As for the detectives' search of Allen's room, it yielded nothing definite save the beard and glasses, and several pencilled notes in a crabbed writing which Willett at once saw was identical with that shared by the old Curwen manuscripts and by the voluminous recent notes of young Ward found in the vanished catacombs of horror.

Dr. Willett and Mr. Ward caught something of a profound, subtle, and insidious cosmic fear from this data as it was gradually unfolded, and almost trembled in following up the vague, mad thought which had simultaneously reached their minds. The false beard and glasses — the crabbed Curwen penmanship — the old portrait and its tiny scar — and the altered youth in the hospital with such a scar — that deep, hollow voice on the telephone — was it not of this that Mr. Ward was reminded when his son barked forth those pitiable tones to which he now claimed to be reduced? Who had ever seen Charles and Allen together? Yes, the officials had once, but who later on? Was it not when Allen left that Charles suddenly lost his growing fright and began to live wholly at the bungalow? Curwen — Allen — Ward — in what blasphemous and abominable fusion had two ages and two persons become involved? That damnable resemblance of the picture to Charles — had it not used to stare and stare, and follow the boy around the room with its eyes? Why, too, did both Allen and Charles copy Joseph Curwen's handwriting, even when alone and off guard? And then the frightful work of those people — the lost crypt of horrors that had aged the doctor overnight; the starved monsters in the noisome pits; the awful formula which had yielded such nameless results; the message in minuscules found in Willett's pocket; the papers and the letters and all the talk of graves and "salts" and discoveries — whither did everything lead? In the end Mr. Ward did the most sensible thing. Steeling himself against any realisation of why he did it, he gave the detectives an article to be shewn to such Pawtuxet shopkeepers as had seen the portentous Dr. Allen. That article was a photograph of his luckless son, on which he now carefully drew in ink the pair of heavy glasses and the black pointed beard which the men had brought from Allen's room.

For two hours he waited with the doctor in the oppressive house where fear and miasma were slowly gathering as the empty panel in the upstairs library leered and leered and leered. Then the men returned. Yes. The altered photograph was a very passable likeness of Dr. Allen. Mr. Ward turned pale, and Willett wiped a suddenly dampened brow with his handkerchief. Allen — Ward — Curwen — it was becoming too hideous for coherent thought. What had the boy called out of the void, and what had it done to him? What, really, had happened from first to last? Who was this Allen who sought to kill Charles as too "squeamish," and why had his destined victim said in the postscript to that frantic letter that he must be so completely obliterated in acid? Why, too, had the minuscule message, of whose origin no one dared think, said that "Curwen" must be likewise obliterated? What was the change, and when had the final stage occurred? That day when his frantic note was received — he had been nervous all the morning, then there was an alteration. He had slipped out unseen and swaggered boldly in past the men hired to guard him. That was the time, when he was out. But no — had he not cried out in terror as he entered his study — this very room? What had he found there? Or wait — what had found him? That simulacrum which brushed boldly in without having been seen to go — was that an alien shadow and a horror forcing itself upon a trembling figure which had never gone out at all? Had not the butler spoken of queer noises?

Willett rang for the man and asked him some low-toned questions. It had, surely enough, been a bad business. There had been noises — a cry, a gasp, a choking, and a sort of clattering or creaking or thumping, or all of these. And Mr. Charles was not the same when he stalked out without a word. The butler shivered as he spoke, and sniffed at the heavy air that blew down from some open window upstairs. Terror had settled definitely upon the house, and only the business-like detectives failed to imbibe a full measure of it. Even they were restless, for this case had held vague elements in the background which pleased them not at all. Dr. Willett was thinking deeply and rapidly, and his thoughts were terrible ones. Now and then he would almost break into muttering as he ran over in his head a new, appalling, and increasingly conclusive chain of nightmare happenings.

Then Mr. Ward made a sign that the conference was over, and everyone save him and the doctor left the room. It was noon now, but shadows as of coming night seemed to engulf the phantom-haunted mansion. Willett began talking very seriously to his host, and urged that he leave a great deal of the future investigation to him. There would be, he predicted, certain obnoxious elements which a friend could bear better than a relative. As family physician he must have a free hand, and the first thing he required was a period alone and undisturbed in the abandoned library upstairs, where the ancient overmantel had gathered about itself an aura of noisome horror more intense than when Joseph Curwen's features themselves glanced slyly down from the painted panel.

Mr. Ward, dazed by the flood of grotesque morbidities and unthinkably maddening suggestions that poured in upon him from every side, could only acquiesce; and half an hour later the doctor was locked in the shunned room with the panelling from Olney Court. The father, listening outside, heard fumbling sounds of moving and rummaging as the moments passed; and finally a wrench and a creak, as if a tight cupboard door were being opened. Then there was a muffled cry, a kind of snorting choke, and a hasty slamming of whatever had been opened. Almost at once the key rattled and Willett appeared in the hall, haggard and ghastly, and demanding wood for the real fireplace on the south wall of the room. The furnace was not enough, he said; and the electric log had little practical use. Longing yet not daring to ask questions, Mr. Ward gave the requisite orders and a man brought some stout pine logs, shuddering as he entered the tainted air of the library to place them in the grate. Willett meanwhile had gone up to the dismantled laboratory and brought down a few odds and ends not included in the moving of the July before. They were in a covered basket, and Mr. Ward never saw what they were.

Then the doctor locked himself in the library once more, and by the clouds of smoke which rolled down past the windows from the chimney it was known that he had lighted the fire. Later, after a great rustling of newspapers, that odd wrench and creaking were heard again; followed by a thumping which none of the eavesdroppers liked. Thereafter two suppressed cries of Willett's were heard, and hard upon these came a swishing rustle of indefinable hatefulness. Finally the smoke that the wind beat down from the chimney grew very dark and acrid, and everyone wished that the weather had spared them this choking and venomous inundation of peculiar fumes. Mr. Ward's head reeled, and the servants all clustered together in a knot to watch the horrible black smoke swoop down. After an age of waiting the vapours seemed to lighten, and half-formless sounds of scraping, sweeping, and other minor operations were heard behind the bolted door. And at last, after the slamming of some cupboard within, Willett made his appearance — sad, pale, and haggard, and bearing the cloth-draped basket he had taken from the upstairs laboratory. He had left the window open, and into that once accursed room was pouring a wealth of pure, wholesome air to mix with a queer new smell of disinfectants. The ancient overmantel still lingered; but it seemed robbed of malignity now, and rose as calm and stately in its white panelling as if it had never borne the picture of Joseph Curwen. Night was coming on, yet this time its shadows held no latent fright, but only a gentle melancholy.

Of what he had done the doctor would never speak. To Mr. Ward he said, "I can answer no questions, but I will say that there are different kinds of magic. I have made a great purgation, and those in this house will sleep the better for it."

VII.

That Dr. Willett's "purgation" had been an ordeal almost as nerve-racking in its way as his hideous wandering in the vanished crypt is shewn by the fact that the elderly physician gave out completely as soon as he reached home that evening. For three days he rested constantly in his room, though servants later muttered something about having heard him after midnight on Wednesday, when the outer door softly opened and closed with phenomenal softness. Servants' imaginations, fortunately, are limited, else comment might have been excited by an item in Thursday's Evening Bulletin which ran as follows:

NORTH END GHOULS
AGAIN ACTIVE.

After a lull of ten months since the dastardly vandalism in the Weeden lot at the North Burial Ground, a nocturnal prowler was glimpsed early this morning in the same cemetery by Robert Hart, the night watchman. Happening to glance for a moment from his shelter at about 2 a.m., Hart observed the glow of a lantern or pocket torch not far to the northwest, and upon opening the door detected the figure of a man with a trowel very plainly silhouetted against a nearby electric light. At once starting in pursuit, he saw the figure dart hurriedly toward the main entrance, gaining the street and losing himself among the shadows before approach or capture was possible.

Like the first of the ghouls active during the past year, this intruder had done no real damage before detection. A vacant part of the Ward lot shewed signs of a little superficial digging, but nothing even nearly the size of a grave had been attempted, and no previous grave had been disturbed.

Hart, who cannot describe the prowler except as a small man probably having a full beard, inclines to the view that all three of the digging incidents have a common source; but police from the Second Station think otherwise on account of the savage nature of the second incident, where an ancient coffin was removed and its headstone violently shattered.

The first of the incidents, in which it is thought an attempt to bury something was frustrated, occurred a year ago last March, and has been attributed to bootleggers seeking a cache. It is possible, says Sergt. Riley, that this third affair is of similar nature. Officers at the Second Station are taking especial pains to capture the gang of miscreants responsible for these repeated outrages.

All day Thursday Dr. Willett rested as if recuperating from something past or nerving himself for something to come. In the evening he wrote a note to Mr. Ward, which was delivered the next morning and which caused the half-dazed parent to ponder long and deeply. Mr. Ward had not been able to go down to business since the shock of Monday with its baffling reports and its sinister "purgation," but he found something calming about the doctor's letter in spite of the despair it seemed to promise and the fresh mysteries it seemed to evoke.

10 Barnes St.,
Providence, R. I.

April 12, 1928.

Dear Theodore:—

I feel that I must say a word to you before doing what I am going to do tomorrow. It will conclude the terrible business we have been going through (for I feel that no spade is ever likely to reach that monstrous place we know of), but I'm afraid it won't set your mind at rest unless I expressly assure you how very conclusive it is.

You have known me ever since you were a small boy, so I think you will not distrust me when I hint that some matters are best left undecided and unexplored. It is better that you attempt no further speculation as to Charles's case, and almost imperative that you tell his mother nothing more than she already suspects. When I call on you tomorrow Charles will have escaped. That is all which need remain in anyone's mind. He was mad, and he escaped. You can tell his mother gently and gradually about the mad part when you stop sending the typed notes in his name. I'd advise you to join her in Atlantic City and take a rest yourself. God knows you need one after this shock, as I do myself. I am going South for a while to calm down and brace up.

So don't ask me any questions when I call. It may be that something will go wrong, but I'll tell you if it does. I don't think it will. There will be nothing more to worry about, for Charles will be very, very safe. He is now—safer than you dream. You need hold no fears about Allen, and who or what he is. He forms as much a part of the past as Joseph Curwen's picture, and when I ring your doorbell you may feel certain that there is no such person. And what wrote that minuscule message will never trouble you or yours.

But you must steel yourself to melancholy, and prepare your wife to do the same. I must tell you frankly that Charles's escape will not mean his restoration to you. He has been afflicted with a peculiar disease, as you must realise from the subtle physical as well as mental changes in him, and you must not hope to see him again. Have only this consolation—that he was never a fiend or even truly a madman, but only an eager, studious, and curious boy whose love of mystery and of the past was his undoing. He stumbled on things no mortal ought ever to know, and reached back through the years as no one ever should reach; and something came out of those years to engulf him.

And now comes the matter in which I must ask you to trust me most of all. For there will be, indeed, no uncertainty about Charles's fate. In about a year, say, you can if you wish devise a suitable account of the end; for the boy will be no more. You can put up a stone in your lot at the North Burial Ground exactly ten feet west of your father's and facing the same way, and that will mark the true resting-place of your son. Nor need you fear that it will mark any abnormality or changeling. The ashes in that grave will be those of your own unaltered bone and sinew—of the real Charles Dexter Ward whose mind you watched from infancy—the real Charles with the olive-mark on his hip and without the black witch-mark on his chest or the pit on his forehead. The Charles who never did actual evil, and who will have paid with his life for his "squeamishness."

That is all. Charles will have escaped, and a year from now you can put up his stone. Do not question me tomorrow. And believe that the honour of your ancient family remains untainted now, as it has been at all times in the past.

With profoundest sympathy, and exhortations to fortitude, calmness, and resignation, I am ever

Sincerely your friend,

—MARINUS B. WILLETT.

So on the morning of Friday, April 13, 1928, Marinus Bicknell Willett visited the room of Charles Dexter Ward at Dr. Waite's private hospital on Conanicut Island. The youth, though making no attempt to evade his caller, was in a sullen mood; and seemed disinclined to open the conversation which Willett obviously desired. The doctor's discovery of the crypt and his monstrous experience therein had of course created a new source of embarrassment, so that both hesitated perceptibly after the interchange of a few strained formalities. Then a new element of constraint crept in, as Ward seemed to read behind the doctor's mask-like face a terrible purpose which had never been there before. The patient quailed, conscious that since the last visit there had been a change whereby the solicitous family physician had given place to the ruthless and implacable avenger.

Ward actually turned pale, and the doctor was the first to speak. "More," he said, "has been found out, and I must warn you fairly that a reckoning is due."

"Digging again, and coming upon more poor starving pets?" was the ironic reply. It was evident that the youth meant to shew bravado to the last.

"No," Willett slowly rejoined, "this time I did not have to dig. We have had men looking up Dr. Allen, and they found the false beard and spectacles in the bungalow."

"Excellent," commented the disquieted host in an effort to be wittily insulting, "and I trust they proved more becoming than the beard and glasses you now have on!"

"They would become you very well," came the even and studied response, "as indeed they seem to have done."

As Willett said this, it almost seemed as though a cloud passed over the sun; though there was no change in the shadows on the floor. Then Ward ventured:

"And is this what asks so hotly for a reckoning? Suppose a man does find it now and then useful to be twofold?"

"No," said Willett gravely, "again you are wrong. It is no business of mine if any man seeks duality; provided he has any right to exist at all, and provided he does not destroy what called him out of space."

Ward now started violently. "Well, Sir, what have ye found, and what d'ye want with me?"

The doctor let a little time elapse before replying, as if choosing his words for an effective answer.

"I have found," he finally intoned, "something in a cupboard behind an ancient overmantel where a picture once was, and I have burned it and buried the ashes where the grave of Charles Dexter Ward ought to be."

The madman choked and sprang from the chair in which he had been sitting:

"Damn ye, who did ye tell — and who'll believe it was he after these full two full months, with me alive? What d'ye mean to do?"

Willett, though a small man, actually took on a kind of judicial majesty as he calmed the patient with a gesture.

"I have told no one. This is no common case — it is a madness out of time and a horror from beyond the spheres which no police or lawyers or courts or alienists could ever fathom or grapple with. Thank God some chance has left inside me the spark of imagination, that I might not go astray in thinking out this thing. You cannot deceive me, Joseph Curwen, for I know that your accursed magic is true!"

"I know how you wove the spell that brooded outside the years and fastened on your double and descendant; I know how you drew him into the past and got him to raise you up from your detestable grave; I know how he kept you hidden in his laboratory while you studied modern things and roved abroad as a vampire by night, and how you later shewed yourself in beard and glasses that no one might wonder at your godless likeness to him; I know what you resolved to do when he balked at your monstrous rifling of the world's tombs, and at what you planned afterward, and I know how you did it."

"You left off your beard and glasses and fooled the guards around the house. They thought it was he who went in, and they thought it was he who came out when you had strangled and hidden him. But you hadn't reckoned on the different contents of two minds. You were a fool, Curwen, to fancy that a mere visual identity would be enough. Why didn't you think of the speech and the voice and the handwriting? It hasn't worked, you see, after all. You know better than I who or what wrote that message in minuscules, but I will warn you it was not written in vain. There are abominations and blasphemies which must be stamped out, and I believe that the writer of those words will attend to Orne and Hutchinson. One of those creatures wrote you once, 'do not call up any that you can not put down'. You were undone once before, perhaps in that very way, and it may be that your own evil magic will undo you all again. Curwen, a man can't tamper with Nature beyond certain limits, and every horror you have woven will rise up to wipe you out."

But here the doctor was cut short by a convulsive cry from the creature before him. Hopelessly at bay, weaponless, and knowing that any show of physical violence would bring a score of attendants to the doctor's rescue, Joseph Curwen had recourse to his one ancient ally, and began a series of cabbalistic motions with his forefingers as his deep, hollow voice, now unconcealed by feigned hoarseness, bellowed out the opening words of a terrible formula. *"PER ADONAI ELOIM, ADONAI JEHOVA, ADONAI SABAOTH, METRATON . . . ."*

But Willett was too quick for him. Even as the dogs in the yard outside began to howl, and even as a chill wind sprang suddenly up from the bay, the doctor commenced the solemn and measured intonation of that which he had meant all along to recite. An eye for an eye — magic for magic — let the outcome shew how well the lesson of the abyss had been learned! So in a clear voice Marinus Bicknell Willett began the second of that pair of formulae whose first had raised the writer of those minuscules — the cryptic invocation whose heading was the Dragon's Tail, sign of the descending node —

☋
OGTHROD AI'F
GEB'L — EE'H
YOG-SOTHOTH
'NGAH'NG AI'Y
ZHRO!"

At the very first word from Willett's mouth the previously commenced formula of the patient stopped short. Unable to speak, the monster made wild motions with his arms until they too were arrested. When the awful name of Yog-Sothoth was uttered, the hideous change began. It was not merely a dissolution, but rather a transformation or recapitulation; and Willett shut his eyes lest he faint before the rest of the incantation could be pronounced.

But he did not faint, and that man of unholy centuries and forbidden secrets never troubled the world again. The madness out of time had subsided, and the case of Charles Dexter Ward was closed. Opening his eyes before staggering out of that room of horror, Dr. Willett saw that what he had kept in memory had not been kept amiss. There had, as he had predicted, been no need for acids. For like his accursed picture a year before, Joseph Curwen now lay scattered on the floor as a thin coating of fine bluish-grey dust.

The Colour out of Space

12,300-WORD NOVELETTE; 1927.

Many of the most serious H.P. Lovecraft fans consider "The Colour out of Space" to be his best story, and it was in later years his own personal favorite. It is one of his most truly cosmic horror stories, trading not at all on supernatural elements, relying for all its power on the idea of real forces and entities that humans are simply not equipped to fully perceive or understand.

Looking for new markets in the aftermath of several unexpected rejections of his work by Farnsworth Wright at Weird Tales, *Lovecraft sent "The Colour out of Space" to* Amazing Stories, *the groundbreaking "scienti-fiction" magazine edited by the now-legendary Hugo Gernsback. He was pleasantly surprised when it was accepted right away, and published just a few months later in the September 1927 issue; he was surprised again, less pleasantly this time, when he received the cheque for it: a whopping $25, roughly one-fifth of the payment he was expecting.*

Needless to say, Lovecraft never sent another story to Gernsback, and took to calling him "Hugo the Rat" (Wright, of Weird Tales, *was "Farny the Fox"). But seeing Lovecraft's by-line in a competing magazine did have the salutary effect of shaking Wright up a little and encouraging him to be more generous with his acceptance letters.*

West of Arkham the hills rise wild, and there are valleys with deep woods that no axe has ever cut. There are dark narrow glens where the trees slope fantastically, and where thin brooklets trickle without ever having caught the glint of sunlight. On the gentler slopes there are farms, ancient and rocky, with squat, moss-coated cottages brooding eternally over old New England secrets in the lee of great ledges; but these are all vacant now, the wide chimneys crumbling and the shingled sides bulging perilously beneath low gambrel roofs.

The old folk have gone away, and foreigners do not like to live there. French-Canadians have tried it, Italians have tried it, and the Poles have come and departed. It is not because of anything that can be seen or heard or handled, but because of something that is imagined. The place is not good for the imagination, and does not bring restful dreams at night. It must be this which keeps the foreigners away, for old Ammi Pierce has never told them of anything he recalls from the strange days. Ammi, whose head has been a little queer for years, is the only one who still remains, or who ever talks of the strange days; and he dares to do this because his house is so near the open fields and the travelled roads around Arkham.

There was once a road over the hills and through the valleys, that ran straight where the blasted heath is now; but people ceased to use it and a new road was laid curving far toward the south. Traces of the old one can still be found amidst the weeds of a returning wilderness, and some of them will doubtless linger even when half the hollows are flooded for the new reservoir. Then the dark woods will be cut down and the blasted heath will slumber far below blue waters whose surface will mirror the sky and ripple in the sun. And the secrets of the strange days will be one with the deep's secrets; one with the hidden lore of old ocean, and all the mystery of primal earth.

When I went into the hills and vales to survey for the new reservoir they told me the place was evil. They told me this in Arkham, and because that is a very old town full of witch legends I thought the evil must be something which grandams had whispered to children through centuries. The name "blasted heath" seemed to me very odd and theatrical, and I wondered how it had come into the folklore of a Puritan people. Then I saw that dark westward tangle of glens and slopes for myself, and ceased to wonder at anything besides its own elder mystery. It was morning when I saw it, but shadow lurked always there. The trees grew too thickly, and their trunks were too big for any healthy New England wood. There was too much silence in the dim alleys between them, and the floor was too soft with the dank moss and mattings of infinite years of decay.

In the open spaces, mostly along the line of the old road, there were little hillside farms; sometimes with all the buildings standing, sometimes with only one or two, and sometimes with only a lone chimney or fast-filling cellar. Weeds and briers reigned, and furtive wild things rustled in the undergrowth. Upon everything was a haze of restlessness and oppression; a touch of the unreal and the grotesque, as if some vital element of perspective or chiaroscuro were awry. I did not wonder that the foreigners would not stay, for this was no region to sleep in. It was too much like a landscape of Salvator Rosa; too much like some forbidden woodcut in a tale of terror.

But even all this was not so bad as the blasted heath. I knew it the moment I came upon it at the bottom of a spacious valley; for no other name could fit such a thing, or any other thing fit such a name. It was as if the poet had coined the phrase from having seen this one particular region. It must, I thought as I viewed it, be the outcome of a fire; but why had nothing new ever grown over those five acres of grey desolation that sprawled open to the sky like a great spot eaten by acid in the woods and fields? It lay largely to the north of the ancient road

Amazing Stories, September 1927

"... and in the fearsome instant of deeper darkness, the watchers saw wriggling at that treetop height, a thousand tiny points of faint and unhallowed radiance, ripping each bough like the fire of St. Elmo ... and all the while the shaft of phosphorescence from the well was getting brighter and brighter and bringing to the minds of the huddled men, a sense of doom and abnormalcy ... It was no longer shining out; it was pouring out; and as the shapeless stream of unplaceable colour left the well, it seemed to flow directly into the sky."

line, but encroached a little on the other side. I felt an odd reluctance about approaching, and did so at last only because my business took me through and past it. There was no vegetation of any kind on that broad expanse, but only a fine grey dust or ash which no wind seemed ever to blow about. The trees near it were sickly and stunted, and many dead trunks stood or lay rotting at the rim. As I walked hurriedly by I saw the tumbled bricks and stones of an old chimney and cellar on my right, and the yawning black maw of an abandoned well whose stagnant vapours played strange tricks with the hues of the sunlight. Even the long, dark woodland climb beyond seemed welcome in contrast, and I marvelled no more at the frightened whispers of Arkham people. There had been no house or ruin near; even in the old days the place must have been lonely and remote. And at twilight, dreading to repass that ominous spot, I walked circuitously back to the town by the curving road on the south. I vaguely wished some clouds would gather, for an odd timidity about the deep skyey voids above had crept into my soul.

In the evening I asked old people in Arkham about the blasted heath, and what was meant by that phrase "strange days" which so many evasively muttered. I could not, however, get any good answers except that all the mystery was much more recent than I had dreamed. It was not a matter of old legendry at all, but something within the lifetime of those who spoke. It had happened in the 'eighties, and a family had disappeared or was killed. Speakers would not be exact; and because they all told me to pay no attention to old Ammi Pierce's crazy tales, I sought him out the next morning, having heard that he lived alone in the ancient tottering cottage where the trees first begin to get very thick. It was a fearsomely archaic place, and had begun to exude the faint miasmal odour which clings about houses that have stood too long. Only with persistent knocking could I rouse the aged man, and when he shuffled timidly to the door I could tell he was not glad to see me. He was not so feeble as I had expected; but his eyes drooped in a curious way, and his unkempt clothing and white beard made him seem very worn and dismal.

Not knowing just how he could best be launched on his tales, I feigned a matter of business; told him of my surveying, and asked vague questions about the district. He was far brighter and more educated than I had been led to think, and before I knew it had grasped quite as much of the subject as any man I had talked with in Arkham. He was not like other rustics I had known in the sections where reservoirs were to be. From him there were no protests at the miles of old wood and farmland to be blotted out, though perhaps there would have been had not his home lain outside the bounds of the future lake. Relief was all that he shewed; relief at the doom of the dark ancient valleys through which he had roamed all his life. They were better under water now—better under water since the strange days. And with this opening his husky voice sank low, while his body leaned forward and his right forefinger began to point shakily and impressively.

It was then that I heard the story, and as the rambling voice scraped and whispered on I shivered again and again despite the summer day. Often I had to recall the speaker from ramblings, piece out scientific points which he knew only by a fading parrot memory of professors' talk, or bridge over gaps, where his sense of logic and continuity broke down. When he was done I did not wonder that his mind had snapped a trifle, or that the folk of Arkham would not speak much of the blasted heath. I hurried back before sunset to my hotel, unwilling to have the stars come out above me in the open; and the next day returned to Boston to give up my position. I could not go into that dim chaos of old forest and slope again, or face another time that grey blasted heath where the black well yawned deep beside the tumbled bricks and stones. The reservoir will soon be built now, and all those elder secrets will be safe forever under watery fathoms. But even then I do not believe I would like to visit that country by night—at least not when the sinister stars are out; and nothing could bribe me to drink the new city water of Arkham.

It all began, old Ammi said, with the meteorite. Before that time there had been no wild legends at all since the witch trials, and even then these western woods were not feared half so much as the small island in the Miskatonic where the devil held court beside a curious stone altar older than the Indians. These were not haunted woods, and their fantastic dusk was never terrible till the strange days. Then there had come that white noontide cloud, that string of explosions in the air, and that pillar of smoke from the valley far in the wood. And by night all Arkham had heard of the great rock that fell out of the sky and bedded itself in the ground beside the well at the Nahum Gardner place. That was the house which had stood where the blasted heath was to come—the trim white Nahum Gardner house amidst its fertile gardens and orchards.

Nahum had come to town to tell people about the stone, and had dropped in at Ammi Pierce's on the way. Ammi was forty then, and all the queer things were fixed very strongly in his mind. He and his wife had gone with the three professors from Miskatonic University who hastened out the next morning to see the weird visitor from unknown stellar space, and had wondered why Nahum had called it so large the day before. It had shrunk, Nahum said as he pointed out the big brownish mound above the ripped earth and charred grass near the archaic well-sweep in his front yard; but the wise men answered that stones do not shrink. Its heat lingered persistently, and Nahum declared it had glowed faintly in the night. The professors tried it with a geologist's hammer and found it was oddly soft. It was, in truth, so soft as to be almost plastic; and they gouged rather than chipped a specimen to take back to the college for testing. They took it in an old pail borrowed from Nahum's kitchen, for even the small piece refused to grow cool. On the trip back they stopped at Ammi's to rest, and seemed thoughtful when Mrs. Pierce remarked that the fragment was growing smaller and burning the bottom of the pail. Truly, it was not large, but perhaps they had taken less than they thought.

The day after that — all this was in June of '82 — the professors had trooped out again in a great excitement. As they passed Ammi's they told him what queer things the specimen had done, and how it had faded wholly away when they put it in a glass beaker. The beaker had gone, too, and the wise men talked of the strange stone's affinity for silicon. It had acted quite unbelievably in that well-ordered laboratory; doing nothing at all and shewing no occluded gases when heated on charcoal, being wholly negative in the borax bead, and soon proving itself absolutely non-volatile at any producible temperature, including that of the oxy-hydrogen blowpipe. On an anvil it appeared highly malleable, and in the dark its luminosity was very marked. Stubbornly refusing to grow cool, it soon had the college in a state of real excitement; and when upon heating before the spectroscope it displayed shining bands unlike any known colours of the normal spectrum there was much breathless talk of new elements, bizarre optical properties, and other things which puzzled men of science are wont to say when faced by the unknown.

Hot as it was, they tested it in a crucible with all the proper reagents. Water did nothing. Hydrochloric acid was the same. Nitric acid and even aqua regia merely hissed and spattered against its torrid invulnerability. Ammi had difficulty in recalling all these things, but recognized some solvents as I mentioned them in the usual order of use. There were ammonia and caustic soda, alcohol and ether, nauseous carbon disulphide and a dozen others; but although the weight grew steadily less as time passed, and the fragment seemed to be slightly cooling, there was no change in the solvents to shew that they had attacked the substance at all. It was a metal, though, beyond a doubt. It was magnetic, for one thing; and after its immersion in the acid solvents there seemed to be faint traces of the Widmanstätten figures found on meteoric iron. When the cooling had grown very considerable, the testing was carried on in glass; and it was in a glass beaker that they left all the chips made of the original fragment during the work. The next morning both chips and beaker were gone without trace, and only a charred spot marked the place on the wooden shelf where they had been.

All this the professors told Ammi as they paused at his door, and once more he went with them to see the stony messenger from the stars, though this time his wife did not accompany him. It had now most certainly shrunk, and even the sober professors could not doubt the truth of what they saw. All around the dwindling brown lump near the well was a vacant space, except where the earth had caved in; and whereas it had been a good seven feet across the day before, it was now scarcely five. It was still hot, and the sages studied its surface curiously as they detached another and larger piece with hammer and chisel. They gouged deeply this time, and as they pried away the smaller mass they saw that the core of the thing was not quite homogeneous.

They had uncovered what seemed to be the side of a large coloured globule imbedded in the substance. The colour, which resembled some of the bands in the meteor's strange spectrum, was almost impossible to describe; and it was only by analogy that they called it colour at all. Its texture was glossy, and upon tapping it appeared to promise both brittleness and hollowness. One of the professors gave it a smart blow with a hammer, and it burst with a nervous little pop. Nothing was emitted, and all trace of the thing vanished with the puncturing. It left behind a hollow spherical space about three inches across, and all thought it probable that others would be discovered as the enclosing substance wasted away.

Conjecture was vain; so after a futile attempt to find additional globules by drilling, the seekers left again with their new specimen — which proved, however, as baffling in the laboratory as its predecessor had been. Aside from being almost plastic, having heat, magnetism, and slight luminosity, cooling slightly in powerful acids, possessing an unknown spectrum, wasting away in air, and attacking silicon compounds with mutual destruction as a result, it presented no identifying features whatsoever; and at the end of the tests the college scientists were forced to own that they could not place it. It was nothing of this earth, but a piece of the great outside; and as such dowered with outside properties and obedient to outside laws.

That night there was a thunderstorm, and when the professors went out to Nahum's the next day they met with a bitter disappointment. The stone, magnetic as it had been, must have had some peculiar electrical property; for it had "drawn the lightning," as Nahum said, with a singular persistence. Six times within an hour the farmer saw the lightning strike the furrow in the front yard, and when the storm was over nothing remained but a ragged pit by the ancient well-sweep, half-choked with caved-in earth. Digging had borne no fruit, and the scientists verified the fact of the utter vanishment. The failure was total; so that nothing was left to do but go back to the laboratory and test again the disappearing fragment left carefully cased in lead. That fragment lasted a week, at the end of which nothing of value had been learned of it. When it had gone, no residue was left behind, and in time the professors felt scarcely sure they had indeed seen with waking eyes that cryptic vestige of the fathomless gulfs outside; that lone, weird message from other universes and other realms of matter, force, and entity.

As was natural, the Arkham papers made much of the incident with its collegiate sponsoring, and sent reporters to talk with Nahum Gardner and his family. At least one Boston daily also sent a scribe, and Nahum quickly became a kind of local celebrity. He was a lean, genial person of about fifty, living with his wife and three sons on the pleasant farmstead in the valley. He and Ammi exchanged visits frequently, as did their wives; and Ammi had nothing but praise for him after all these years. He seemed slightly proud of the notice his place had attracted, and talked often of the meteorite in the succeeding weeks. That July and August were hot; and Nahum worked hard at his haying in the ten-acre pasture across Chapman's Brook; his rattling wain wearing deep ruts in the shadowy lanes between. The labour tired him more than it had in other years, and he felt that age was beginning to tell on him.

Then fell the time of fruit and harvest. The pears and apples slowly ripened, and Nahum vowed that his orchards were prospering as never before. The fruit was growing to phenomenal size and unwonted gloss, and in such abundance that extra barrels were ordered to handle the future crop. But with the ripening came sore disappointment; for of all that gorgeous array of specious lusciousness not one single jot was fit to eat. Into the fine flavour of the pears and apples had crept a stealthy bitterness and sickishness, so that even the smallest of bites induced a lasting disgust. It was the same with the melons and tomatoes, and Nahum sadly saw that his entire crop was lost. Quick to connect events, he declared that the meteorite had poisoned the soil, and thanked Heaven that most of the other crops were in the upland lot along the road.

Winter came early, and was very cold. Ammi saw Nahum less often than usual, and observed that he had begun to look worried. The rest of his family, too, seemed to have grown taciturn; and were far from steady in their church-going or their attendance at the various social events of the countryside. For this reserve or melancholy no cause could be found, though all the household confessed now and then to poorer health and a feeling of vague disquiet. Nahum himself gave the most definite statement of anyone when he said he was disturbed about certain footprints in the snow. They were the usual winter prints of red squirrels, white rabbits, and foxes, but the brooding farmer professed to see something not quite right about their nature and arrangement. He was never specific, but appeared to think that they were not as characteristic of the anatomy and habits of squirrels and rabbits and foxes as they ought to be. Ammi listened without interest to this talk until one night when he drove past Nahum's house in his sleigh on the way back from Clark's Corners. There had been a moon, and a rabbit had run across the road, and the leaps of that rabbit were longer than either Ammi or his horse liked. The latter, indeed, had almost run away when brought up by a firm rein. Thereafter Ammi gave Nahum's tales more respect, and wondered why the Gardner dogs seemed so cowed and quivering every morning. They had, it developed, nearly lost the spirit to bark.

In February the McGregor boys from Meadow Hill were out shooting woodchucks, and not far from the Gardner place bagged a very peculiar specimen. The proportions of its body seemed slightly altered in a queer way impossible to describe, while its face had taken on an expression which no one ever saw in a woodchuck before. The boys were genuinely frightened, and threw the thing away at once, so that only their grotesque tales of it ever reached the people of the countryside. But the shying of the horses near Nahum's house had now become an acknowledged thing, and all the basis for a cycle of whispered legend was fast taking form.

People vowed that the snow melted faster around Nahum's than it did anywhere else, and early in March there was an awed discussion in Potter's general store at Clark's Corners. Stephen Rice had driven past Gardner's in the morning, and had noticed the skunk-cabbages coming up through the mud by the woods across the road. Never were things of such size seen before, and they held strange colours that could not be put into any words. Their shapes were monstrous, and the horse had snorted at an odour which struck Stephen as wholly unprecedented. That afternoon several persons drove past to see the abnormal growth, and all agreed that plants of that kind ought never to sprout in a healthy world. The bad fruit of the fall before was freely mentioned, and it went from mouth to mouth that there was poison in Nahum's ground. Of course it was the meteorite; and remembering how strange the men from the college had found that stone to be, several farmers spoke about the matter to them.

One day they paid Nahum a visit; but having no love of wild tales and folklore were very conservative in what they inferred. The plants were certainly odd, but all skunk-cabbages are more or less odd in shape and odour and hue. Perhaps some mineral element from the stone had entered the soil, but it would soon be washed away. And as for the footprints and frightened horses — of course this was mere country talk which such a phenomenon as the aërolite would be certain to start. There was really nothing for serious men to do in cases of wild gossip, for superstitious rustics will say and believe anything. And so all through the strange days the professors stayed away in contempt. Only one of them, when given two phials of dust for analysis in a police job over a year and a half later, recalled that the queer colour of that skunk-cabbage had been very like one of the anomalous bands of light shewn by the meteor fragment in the college spectroscope, and like the brittle globule found imbedded in the stone from the abyss. The samples in this analysis case gave the same odd bands at first, though later they lost the property.

The trees budded prematurely around Nahum's, and at night they swayed ominously in the wind. Nahum's second son Thaddeus, a lad of fifteen, swore that they swayed also when there was no wind; but even the gossips would not credit this. Certainly, however, restlessness was in the air. The entire Gardner family developed the habit of stealthy listening, though not for any sound which they could consciously name. The listening was, indeed, rather a product of moments when consciousness seemed half to slip away. Unfortunately such moments increased week by week, till it became common speech that "something was wrong with all Nahum's folks." When the early saxifrage came out it had another strange colour; not quite like that of the skunk-cabbage, but plainly related and equally unknown to anyone who saw it. Nahum took some blossoms to Arkham and shewed them to the editor of the *Gazette*, but that dignitary did no more than write a humorous article about them, in which the dark fears of rustics were held up to polite ridicule. It was a mistake of Nahum's to tell a stolid city man about the way the great, overgrown mourning-cloak butterflies behaved in connexion with these saxifrages.

April brought a kind of madness to the country folk, and began that disuse of the road past Nahum's which led to its ultimate abandonment. It was the vegetation. All the orchard trees blossomed forth in strange colours, and through the stony soil of the yard and adjacent pasturage there sprang up a bizarre growth which only a botanist could connect with the proper flora of the region. No sane wholesome colours were anywhere to be seen except in the green grass and leafage; but everywhere those hectic and prismatic variants of some diseased, underlying primary tone without a place among the known tints of earth. The "Dutchman's breeches" became a thing of sinister menace, and the bloodroots grew insolent in their chromatic perversion. Ammi and the Gardners thought that most of the colours had a sort of haunting familiarity, and decided that they reminded one of the brittle globule in the meteor. Nahum ploughed and sowed the ten-acre pasture and the upland lot, but did nothing with the land around the house. He knew it would be of no use, and hoped that the summer's strange growths would draw all the poison from the soil. He was prepared for almost anything now, and had grown used to the sense of something near him waiting to be heard. The shunning of his house by neighbors told on him, of course; but it told on his wife more. The boys were better off, being at school each day; but they could not help being frightened by the gossip. Thaddeus, an especially sensitive youth, suffered the most.

In May the insects came, and Nahum's place became a nightmare of buzzing and crawling. Most of the creatures seemed not quite usual in their aspects and motions, and their nocturnal habits contradicted all former experience. The Gardners took to watching at night — watching in all directions at random for something . . . they could not tell what. It was then that they all owned that Thaddeus had been right about the trees. Mrs. Gardner was the next to see it from the window as she watched the swollen boughs of a maple against a moonlit sky. The boughs surely moved, and there was no wind. It must be the sap. Strangeness had come into everything growing now.

Yet it was none of Nahum's family at all who made the next discovery. Familiarity had dulled them, and what they could not see was glimpsed by a timid windmill salesman from Bolton who drove by one night in ignorance of the country legends. What he told in Arkham was given a short paragraph in the *Gazette*; and it was there that all the farmers, Nahum included, saw it first.

The night had been dark and the buggy-lamps faint, but around a farm in the valley which everyone knew from the account must be Nahum's, the darkness had been less thick. A dim though distinct luminosity seemed to inhere in all the vegetation, grass, leaves, and blossoms alike, while at one moment a detached piece of the phosphorescence appeared to stir furtively in the yard near the barn.

The grass had so far seemed untouched, and the cows were freely pastured in the lot near the house, but toward the end of May the milk began to be bad. Then Nahum had the cows driven to the uplands, after which the trouble ceased. Not long after this the change in grass and leaves became apparent to the eye. All the verdure was going grey, and was developing a highly singular quality of brittleness. Ammi was now the only person who ever visited the place, and his visits were becoming fewer and fewer. When school closed the Gardners were virtually cut off from the world, and sometimes let Ammi do their errands in town. They were failing curiously both physically and mentally, and no one was surprised when the news of Mrs. Gardner's madness stole around.

It happened in June, about the anniversary of the meteor's fall, and the poor woman screamed about things in the air which she could not describe. In her raving there was not a single specific noun, but only verbs and pronouns. Things moved and changed and fluttered, and ears tingled to impulses which were not wholly sounds. Something was taken away — she was being drained of something — something was fastening itself on her that ought not to be — someone must make it keep off — nothing was ever still in the night — the walls and windows shifted. Nahum did not send her to the county asylum, but let her wander about the house as long as she was harmless to herself and others. Even when her expression changed he did nothing. But when the boys grew afraid of her, and Thaddeus nearly fainted at the way she made faces at him, he decided to keep her locked in the attic. By July she had ceased to speak and crawled on all fours, and before that month was over Nahum got the mad notion that she was slightly luminous in the dark, as he now clearly saw was the case with the nearby vegetation.

It was a little before this that the horses had stampeded. Something had aroused them in the night, and their neighing and kicking in their stalls had been terrible. There seemed virtually nothing to do to calm them, and when Nahum opened the stable door they all bolted out like frightened woodland deer. It took a week to track all four, and when found they were seen to be quite useless and unmanageable. Something had snapped in their brains, and each one had to be shot for its own good. Nahum borrowed a horse from Ammi for his haying, but found it would not approach the barn. It shied, balked, and whinnied, and in the end he could do nothing but drive it into the yard while the men used their own strength to get the heavy wagon near enough the hayloft for convenient pitching. And all the while the vegetation was turning grey and brittle. Even the flowers whose hues had been so strange were greying now, and the fruit was coming out grey and dwarfed and tasteless. The asters and golden-rod bloomed grey and distorted, and the roses and zinneas and hollyhocks in the front yard were such blasphemous-looking things that Nahum's oldest boy Zenas cut them down. The strangely puffed insects died about that time, even the bees that had left their hives and taken to the woods.

By September all the vegetation was fast crumbling to a

greyish powder, and Nahum feared that the trees would die before the poison was out of the soil. His wife now had spells of terrific screaming, and he and the boys were in a constant state of nervous tension. They shunned people now, and when school opened the boys did not go. But it was Ammi, on one of his rare visits, who first realised that the well water was no longer good. It had an evil taste that was not exactly fetid nor exactly salty, and Ammi advised his friend to dig another well on higher ground to use till the soil was good again. Nahum, however, ignored the warning, for he had by that time become calloused to strange and unpleasant things. He and the boys continued to use the tainted supply, drinking it as listlessly and mechanically as they ate their meagre and ill-cooked meals and did their thankless and monotonous chores through the aimless days. There was something of stolid resignation about them all, as if they walked half in another world between lines of nameless guards to a certain and familiar doom.

Thaddeus went mad in September after a visit to the well. He had gone with a pail and had come back empty-handed, shrieking and waving his arms, and sometimes lapsing into an inane titter or a whisper about "the moving colours down there." Two in one family was pretty bad, but Nahum was very brave about it. He let the boy run about for a week until he began stumbling and hurting himself, and then he shut him in an attic room across the hall from his mother's. The way they screamed at each other from behind their locked doors was very terrible, especially to little Merwin, who fancied they talked in some terrible language that was not of earth. Merwin was getting frightfully imaginative, and his restlessness was worse after the shutting away of the brother who had been his greatest playmate.

Almost at the same time the mortality among the livestock commenced. Poultry turned greyish and died very quickly, their meat being found dry and noisome upon cutting. Hogs grew inordinately fat, then suddenly began to undergo loathsome changes which no one could explain. Their meat was of course useless, and Nahum was at his wit's end. No rural veterinary would approach his place, and the city veterinary from Arkham was openly baffled. The swine began growing grey and brittle and falling to pieces before they died, and their eyes and muzzles developed singular alterations. It was very inexplicable, for they had never been fed from the tainted vegetation. Then something struck the cows. Certain areas or sometimes the whole body would be uncannily shrivelled or compressed, and atrocious collapses or disintegrations were common. In the last stages — and death was always the result — there would be a greying and turning brittle like that which beset the hogs. There could be no question of poison, for all the cases occurred in a locked and undisturbed barn. No bites of prowling things could have brought the virus, for what live beast of earth can pass through solid obstacles? It must be only natural disease — yet what disease could wreak such results was beyond any mind's guessing.

When the harvest came there was not an animal surviving on the place, for the stock and poultry were dead and the dogs had run away. These dogs, three in number, had all vanished one night and were never heard of again. The five cats had left some time before, but their going was scarcely noticed since there now seemed to be no mice, and only Mrs. Gardner had made pets of the graceful felines.

On the nineteenth of October Nahum staggered into Ammi's house with hideous news. The death had come to poor Thaddeus in his attic room, and it had come in a way which could not be told. Nahum had dug a grave in the railed family plot behind the farm, and had put therein what he found. There could have been nothing from outside, for the small barred window and locked door were intact; but it was much as it had been in the barn. Ammi and his wife consoled the stricken man as best they could, but shuddered as they did so. Stark terror seemed to cling round the Gardners and all they touched, and the very presence of one in the house was a breath from regions unnamed and unnamable. Ammi accompanied Nahum home with the greatest reluctance, and did what he might to calm the hysterical sobbing of little Merwin. Zenas needed no calming. He had come of late to do nothing but stare into space and obey what his father told him; and Ammi thought that his fate was very merciful. Now and then Merwin's screams were answered faintly from the attic, and in response to an inquiring look Nahum said that his wife was getting very feeble.

When night approached, Ammi managed to get away; for not even friendship could make him stay in that spot when the faint glow of the vegetation began and the trees may or may not have swayed without wind. It was really lucky for Ammi that he was not more imaginative. Even as things were, his mind was bent ever so slightly; but had he been able to connect and reflect upon all the portents around him he must inevitably have turned a total maniac. In the twilight he hastened home, the screams of the mad woman and the nervous child ringing horribly in his ears.

Three days later Nahum lurched into Ammi's kitchen in the early morning, and in the absence of his host stammered out a desperate tale once more, while Mrs. Pierce listened in a clutching fright. It was little Merwin this time. He was gone. He had gone out late at night with a lantern and pail for water, and had never come back. He'd been going to pieces for days, and hardly knew what he was about. Screamed at everything. There had been a frantic shriek from the yard then, but before the father could get to the door the boy was gone. There was no glow from the lantern he had taken, and of the child himself no trace. At the time Nahum thought the lantern and pail were gone too; but when dawn came, and the man had plodded back from his all-night search of the woods and fields, he had found some very curious things near the well. There was a crushed and apparently somewhat melted mass of iron which had certainly been the lantern; while a bent bail and twisted iron hoops beside it, both half-fused, seemed to hint at the remnants of the pail. That was all.

Nahum was past imagining, Mrs. Pierce was blank, and Ammi, when he had reached home and heard the tale, could give no guess. Merwin was gone, and there would be no use in telling the people around, who shunned all Gardners now. No use, either, in telling the city people at Arkham who laughed at everything. Thad was gone, and now Merwin was gone. Something was creeping and creeping and waiting to be seen and felt and heard. Nahum would go soon, and he wanted Ammi to look after his wife and Zenas if they survived him. It must all be a judgment of some sort; though he could not fancy what for, since he had always walked uprightly in the Lord's ways so far as he knew.

For over two weeks Ammi saw nothing of Nahum; and then, worried about what might have happened, he overcame his fears and paid the Gardner place a visit. There was no smoke from the great chimney, and for a moment the visitor was apprehensive of the worst. The aspect of the whole farm was shocking — greyish withered grass and leaves on the ground, vines falling in brittle wreckage from archaic walls and gables, and great bare trees clawing up at the grey November sky with a studied malevolence which Ammi could not but feel had come from some subtle change in the tilt of the branches. But Nahum was alive, after all. He was weak, and lying on a couch in the low-ceiled kitchen, but perfectly conscious and able to give simple orders to Zenas. The room was deadly cold; and as Ammi visibly shivered, the host shouted huskily to Zenas for more wood. Wood, indeed, was sorely needed; since the cavernous fireplace was unlit and empty, with a cloud of soot blowing about in the chill wind that came down the chimney. Presently Nahum asked him if the extra wood had made him any more comfortable, and then Ammi saw what had happened. The stoutest cord had broken at last, and the hapless farmer's mind was proof against more sorrow.

Questioning tactfully, Ammi could get no clear data at all about the missing Zenas. "In the well — he lives in the well —" was all that the clouded father would say. Then there flashed across the visitor's mind a sudden thought of the mad wife, and he changed his line of inquiry. "Nabby? Why, here she is!" was the surprised response of poor Nahum, and Ammi soon saw that he must search for himself. Leaving the harmless babbler on the couch, he took the keys from their nail beside the door and climbed the creaking stairs to the attic. It was very close and noisome up there, and no sound could be heard from any direction. Of the four doors in sight, only one was locked, and on this he tried various keys on the ring he had taken. The third key proved the right one, and after some fumbling Ammi threw open the low white door.

It was quite dark inside, for the window was small and half-obscured by the crude wooden bars; and Ammi could see nothing at all on the wide-planked floor. The stench was beyond enduring, and before proceeding further he had to retreat to another room and return with his lungs filled with breathable air. When he did enter he saw something dark in the corner, and upon seeing it more clearly he screamed outright. While he screamed he thought a momentary cloud eclipsed the window, and a second later he felt himself brushed as if by some hateful current of vapour. Strange colours danced before his eyes; and had not a present horror numbed him he would have thought of the globule in the meteor that the geologist's hammer had shattered, and of the morbid vegetation that had sprouted in the spring. As it was he thought only of the blasphemous monstrosity which confronted him, and which all too clearly had shared the nameless fate of young Thaddeus and the live-stock. But the terrible thing about this horror was that it very slowly and perceptibly moved as it continued to crumble.

Ammi would give me no added particulars to this scene, but the shape in the corner does not reappear in his tale as a moving object. There are things which cannot be mentioned, and what is done in common humanity is sometimes cruelly judged by the law. I gathered that no moving thing was left in that attic room, and that to leave anything capable of motion there would have been a deed so monstrous as to damn any accountable being to eternal torment. Anyone but a stolid farmer would have fainted or gone mad, but Ammi walked conscious through that low doorway and locked the accursed secret behind him. There would be Nahum to deal with now; he must be fed and tended, and removed to some place where he could be cared for.

Commencing his descent of the dark stairs, Ammi heard a thud below him. He even thought a scream had been suddenly choked off, and recalled nervously the clammy vapour which had brushed by him in that frightful room above. What presence had his cry and entry started up? Halted by some vague fear, he heard still further sounds below. Indubitably there was a sort of heavy dragging, and a most detestably sticky noise as of some fiendish and unclean species of suction. With an associative sense goaded to feverish heights, he thought unaccountably of what he had seen upstairs. Good God! What eldritch dream-world was this into which he had blundered? He dared move neither backward nor forward, but stood there trembling at the black curve of the boxed-in staircase. Every trifle of the scene burned itself into his brain. The sounds, the sense of dread expectancy, the darkness, the steepness of the narrow steps — and merciful Heaven! — the faint but unmistakable luminosity of all the woodwork in sight; steps, sides, exposed laths, and beams alike!

Then there burst forth a frantic whinny from Ammi's horse outside, followed at once by a clatter which told of a frenzied runaway. In another moment horse and buggy had gone beyond earshot, leaving the frightened man on the dark stairs to guess what had sent them. But that was not all. There had been another sound out there. A sort of liquid splash — water — it must have been the well. He had left Hero untied near it, and a buggy wheel must have brushed the coping and knocked in a stone.

And still the pale phosphorescence glowed in that detestably ancient woodwork. God! how old the house was! Most of it built before 1670, and the gambrel roof not later than 1730.

A feeble scratching on the floor downstairs now sounded distinctly, and Ammi's grip tightened on a heavy stick he had picked up in the attic for some purpose. Slowly nerving himself, he finished his descent and walked boldly toward the kitchen. But he did not complete the walk, because what he sought was no longer there. It had come to meet him, and it was still alive after a fashion. Whether it had crawled or whether it had been dragged by any external force, Ammi could not say; but the death had been at it. Everything had happened in the last half-hour, but collapse, greying, and disintegration were already far advanced. There was a horrible brittleness, and dry fragments were scaling off. Ammi could not touch it, but looked horrifiedly into the distorted parody that had been a face. "What was it, Nahum — what was it?" he whispered, and the cleft, bulging lips were just able to crackle out a final answer.

"Nothin' . . . nothin' . . . the colour . . . it burns . . . cold an' wet, but it burns . . . it lived in the well . . . I seen it . . . a kind of smoke . . . jest like the flowers last spring . . . the well shone at night . . . Thad an' Mernie an' Zenas . . . everything alive . . . suckin' the life out of everything . . . in that stone . . . it must a' come in that stone p'izened the whole place . . . dun't know what it wants . . . that round thing them men from the college dug outen the stone . . . they smashed it . . . it was that same colour . . . jest the same, like the flowers an' plants . . . must a' ben more of 'em . . . seeds . . . seeds . . . they growed . . . I seen it the fust time this week . . . must a' got strong on Zenas . . . he was a big boy, full o' life . . . it beats down your mind an' then gits ye . . . burns ye up . . . in the well water . . . you was right about that . . . evil water . . . Zenas never come back from the well . . . can't git away . . . draws ye . . . ye know summ'at's comin' but tain't no use . . . I seen it time an' agin senct Zenas was took . . . whar's Nabby, Ammi? . . . my head's no good . . . dun't know how long sence I fed her . . . it'll git her ef we ain't keerful . . . jest a colour . . . her face is gittin' to hev that colour sometimes towards night . . . an' it burns an' sucks . . . it come from some place whar things ain't as they is here . . . one o' them professors said so . . . he was right . . . look out, Ammi, it'll do sumthin' more . . . sucks the life out . . . ."

But that was all. That which spoke could speak no more because it had completely caved in. Ammi laid a red checked tablecloth over what was left and reeled out the back door into the fields. He climbed the slope to the ten-acre pasture and stumbled home by the north road and the woods. He could not pass that well from which his horse had run away. He had looked at it through the window, and had seen that no stone was missing from the rim. Then the lurching buggy had not dislodged anything after all — the splash had been something else — something which went into the well after it had done with poor Nahum.

When Ammi reached his house the horse and buggy had arrived before him and thrown his wife into fits of anxiety. Reassuring her without explanations, he set out at once for Arkham and notified the authorities that the Gardner family was no more. He indulged in no details, but merely told of the deaths of Nahum and Nabby, that of Thaddeus being already known, and mentioned that the cause seemed to be the same strange ailment which had killed the livestock. He also stated that Merwin and Zenas had disappeared. There was considerable questioning at the police station, and in the end Ammi was compelled to take three officers to the Gardner farm, together with the coroner, the medical examiner, and the veterinary who had treated the diseased animals. He went much against his will, for the afternoon was advancing and he feared the fall of night over that accursed place, but it was some comfort to have so many people with him.

The six men drove out in a democrat-wagon, following Ammi's buggy, and arrived at the pest-ridden farmhouse about four o'clock. Used as the officers were to gruesome experiences, not one remained unmoved at what was found in the attic and under the red checked tablecloth on the floor below. The whole aspect of the farm with its grey desolation was terrible enough, but those two crumbling objects were beyond all bounds. No one could look long at them, and even the medical examiner admitted that there was very little to examine. Specimens could be analysed, of course, so he busied himself in obtaining them — and here it develops that a very puzzling aftermath occurred at the college laboratory where the two phials of dust were finally taken. Under the spectroscope both samples gave off an unknown spectrum, in which many of the baffling bands were precisely like those which the strange meteor had yielded in the previous year. The property of emitting this spectrum vanished in a month, the dust thereafter consisting mainly of alkaline phosphates and carbonates.

Ammi would not have told the men about the well if he had thought they meant to do anything then and there. It was getting toward sunset, and he was anxious to be away. But he could not help glancing nervously at the stony curb by the great sweep, and when a detective questioned him he admitted that Nahum had feared something down there — so much so that he had never even thought of searching it for Merwin or Zenas. After that nothing would do but that they empty and explore the well immediately, so Ammi had to wait trembling while pail after pail of rank water was hauled up and splashed on the soaking ground outside. The men sniffed in disgust at the fluid, and toward the last held their noses against the foetor they were uncovering. It was not so long a job as they had feared it would be, since the water was phenomenally low.

There is no need to speak too exactly of what they found. Merwin and Zenas were both there, in part, though the vestiges were mainly skeletal. There were also a small deer and a large dog in about the same state, and a number of bones of smaller animals. The ooze and slime at the bottom seemed inexplicably porous and bubbling, and a man who descended on hand-holds with a long pole found that he could sink the wooden shaft to any depth in the mud of the floor without meeting any solid obstruction.

Twilight had now fallen, and lanterns were brought from the house. Then, when it was seen that nothing further could be gained from the well, everyone went indoors and conferred in the ancient sitting-room while the intermittent light of a spectral half-moon played wanly on the grey desolation outside. The men were frankly nonplussed by the entire case, and could find no convincing common element to link the strange vegetable conditions, the unknown disease of livestock and humans, and the unaccountable deaths of Merwin and Zenas in the tainted well. They had heard the common country talk, it is true; but could not believe that anything contrary to natural law had occurred. No doubt the meteor had poisoned the soil, but the illness of persons and animals who had eaten nothing grown in that soil was another matter. Was it the well water? Very possibly. It might be a good idea to analyze it. But what peculiar madness could have made both boys jump into the well? Their deeds were so similar — and the fragments shewed that they had both suffered from the grey brittle death. Why was everything so grey and brittle?

It was the coroner, seated near a window overlooking the yard, who first noticed the glow about the well. Night had fully set in, and all the abhorrent grounds seemed faintly luminous with more than the fitful moonbeams; but this new glow was something definite and distinct, and appeared to shoot up from the black pit like a softened ray from a searchlight, giving dull reflections in the little ground pools where the water had been emptied. It had a very queer colour, and as all the men clustered round the window Ammi gave a violent start. For this strange beam of ghastly miasma was to him of no unfamiliar hue. He had seen that colour before, and feared to think what it might mean. He had seen it in the nasty brittle globule in that aërolite two summers ago, had seen it in the crazy vegetation of the springtime, and had thought he had seen it for an instant that very morning against the small barred window of that terrible attic room where nameless things had happened. It had flashed there a second, and a clammy and hateful current of vapour had brushed past him — and then poor Nahum had been taken by something of that colour. He had said so at the last — said it was like the globule and the plants. After that had come the runaway in the yard and the splash in the well — and now that well was belching forth to the night a pale insidious beam of the same demoniac tint.

It does credit to the alertness of Ammi's mind that he puzzled even at that tense moment over a point which was essentially scientific. He could not but wonder at his gleaning of the same impression from a vapour glimpsed in the daytime, against a window opening on the morning sky, and from a nocturnal exhalation seen as a phosphorescent mist against the black and blasted landscape. It wasn't right — it was against Nature — and he thought of those terrible last words of his stricken friend, "It come from some place whar things ain't as they is here . . . one o' them professors said so . . . ."

All three horses outside, tied to a pair of shrivelled saplings by the road, were now neighing and pawing frantically. The wagon driver started for the door to do something, but Ammi laid a shaky hand on his shoulder. "Dun't go out thar," he whispered. "They's more to this nor what we know. Nahum said somethin' lived in the well that sucks your life out. He said it must be some'at growed from a round ball like one we all seen in the meteor stone that fell a year ago June. Sucks an' burns, he said, an' is jest a cloud of colour like that light out thar now, that ye can hardly see an' can't tell what it is. Nahum thought it feeds on everything livin' an' gits stronger all the time. He said he seen it this last week. It must be somethin' from away off in the sky like the men from the college last year says the meteor stone was. The way it's made an' the way it works ain't like no way o' God's world. It's some'at from beyond."

So the men paused indecisively as the light from the well grew stronger and the hitched horses pawed and whinnied in increasing frenzy. It was truly an awful moment; with terror in that ancient and accursed house itself, four monstrous sets of fragments — two from the house and two from the well — in the woodshed behind, and that shaft of unknown and unholy iridescence from the slimy depths in front. Ammi had restrained the driver on impulse, forgetting how uninjured he himself was after the clammy brushing of that coloured vapour in the attic room, but perhaps it is just as well that he acted as he did. No one will ever know what was abroad that night; and though the blasphemy from beyond had not so far hurt any human of unweakened mind, there is no telling what it might not have done at that last moment, and with its seemingly increased strength and the special signs of purpose it was soon to display beneath the half-clouded moonlit sky.

All at once one of the detectives at the window gave a short, sharp gasp. The others looked at him, and then quickly followed his own gaze upward to the point at which its idle straying had been suddenly arrested. There was no need for words. What had been disputed in country gossip was disputable no longer, and it is because of the thing which every man of that party agreed in whispering later on, that the strange days are never talked about in Arkham.

It is necessary to premise that there was no wind at that hour of the evening. One did arise not long afterward, but there was absolutely none then. Even the dry tips of the lingering hedge-mustard, grey and blighted, and the fringe on the roof of the standing democrat-wagon were unstirred. And yet amid that tense godless calm the high bare boughs of all the trees in the yard were moving. They were twitching morbidly and spasmodically, clawing in convulsive and epileptic madness at the moonlit clouds; scratching impotently in the noxious air as if jerked by some alien and bodiless line of linkage with subterrene horrors writhing and struggling below the black roots.

Not a man breathed for several seconds. Then a cloud of

darker depth passed over the moon, and the silhouette of clutching branches faded out momentarily. At this there was a general cry; muffled with awe, but husky and almost identical from every throat. For the terror had not faded with the silhouette, and in a fearsome instant of deeper darkness the watchers saw wriggling at that treetop height a thousand tiny points of faint and unhallowed radiance, tipping each bough like the fire of St. Elmo or the flames that came down on the apostles' heads at Pentecost. It was a monstrous constellation of unnatural light, like a glutted swarm of corpse-fed fireflies dancing hellish sarabands over an accursed marsh; and its colour was that same nameless intrusion which Ammi had come to recognize and dread. All the while the shaft of phosphorescence from the well was getting brighter and brighter, bringing to the minds of the huddled men a sense of doom and abnormality which far outraced any image their conscious minds could form. It was no longer shining out, it was pouring out; and as the shapeless stream of unplaceable colour left the well it seemed to flow directly into the sky.

The veterinary shivered, and walked to the front door to drop the heavy extra bar across it. Ammi shook no less, and had to tug and point for lack of a controllable voice when he wished to draw notice to the growing luminosity of the trees. The neighing and stamping of the horses had become utterly frightful, but not a soul of that group in the old house would have ventured forth for any earthly reward. With the moments the shining of the trees increased, while their restless branches seemed to strain more and more toward verticality. The wood of the well-sweep was shining now, and presently a policeman dumbly pointed to some wooden sheds and bee-hives near the stone wall on the west. They were commencing to shine, too, though the tethered vehicles of the visitors seemed so far unaffected. Then there was a wild commotion and clopping in the road, and as Ammi quenched the lamp for better seeing they realized that the span of frantic greys had broken their sapling and run off with the democrat-wagon.

The shock served to loosen several tongues, and embarrassed whispers were exchanged. "It spreads on everything organic that's been around here," muttered the medical examiner. No one replied, but the man who had been in the well gave a hint that his long pole must have stirred up something intangible. "It was awful," he added. "There was no bottom at all. Just ooze and bubbles and the feeling of something lurking under there." Ammi's horse still pawed and screamed deafeningly in the road outside, and nearly drowned its owner's faint quaver as he mumbled his formless reflections. "It come from that stone . . . it growed down thar . . . it got everything livin' . . . it fed itself on 'em, mind and body . . . Thad an' Mernie, Zenas an' Nabby . . . Nahum was the last . . . they all drunk the water . . . it got strong on 'em . . . it come from beyond, whar things ain't like they be here . . . now it's goin' home . . . ."

At this point, as the column of unknown colour flared suddenly stronger and began to weave itself into fantastic suggestions of shape which each spectator later described differently, there came from poor tethered Hero such a sound as no man before or since ever heard from a horse. Every person in that low-pitched sitting room stopped his ears, and Ammi turned away from the window in horror and nausea. Words could not convey it — when Ammi looked out again the hapless beast lay huddled inert on the moonlit ground between the splintered shafts of the buggy. That was the last of Hero till they buried him next day. But the present was no time to mourn, for almost at this instant a detective silently called attention to something terrible in the very room with them. In the absence of the lamplight it was clear that a faint phosphorescence had begun to pervade the entire apartment. It glowed on the broad-planked floor and the fragment of rag carpet, and shimmered over the sashes of the small-paned windows. It ran up and down the exposed corner-posts, coruscated about the shelf and mantel, and infected the very doors and furniture. Each minute saw it strengthen, and at last it was very plain that healthy living things must leave that house.

Ammi shewed them the back door and the path up through the fields to the ten-acre pasture. They walked and stumbled as in a dream, and did not dare look back till they were far away on the high ground. They were glad of the path, for they could not have gone the front way, by that well. It was bad enough passing the glowing barn and sheds, and those shining orchard trees with their gnarled, fiendish contours; but thank heaven the branches did their worst twisting high up. The moon went under some very black clouds as they crossed the rustic bridge over Chapman's Brook, and it was blind groping from there to the open meadows.

When they looked back toward the valley and the distant Gardner place at the bottom they saw a fearsome sight. All the farm was shining with the hideous unknown blend of colour; trees, buildings, and even such grass and herbage as had not been wholly changed to lethal grey brittleness. The boughs were all straining skyward, tipped with tongues of foul flame, and lambent tricklings of the same monstrous fire were creeping about the ridgepoles of the house, barn and sheds. It was a scene from a vision of Fuseli, and over all the rest reigned that riot of luminous amorphousness, that alien and undimensioned rainbow of cryptic poison from the well — seething, feeling, lapping, reaching, scintillating, straining, and malignly bubbling in its cosmic and unrecognizable chromaticism.

Then without warning the hideous thing shot vertically up toward the sky like a rocket or meteor, leaving behind no trail and disappearing through a round and curiously regular hole in the clouds before any man could gasp or cry out.

No watcher can ever forget that sight, and Ammi stared blankly at the stars of Cygnus, Deneb twinkling above the others, where the unknown colour had melted into the Milky Way. But his gaze was the next moment called swiftly to earth by the crackling in the valley. It was just that. Only a wooden ripping and crackling, and not an explosion, as so many others of the party vowed. Yet the outcome was the same, for in one feverish kaleidoscopic instant there burst up from that doomed

Famous Fantastic Mysteries, October 1941

"It was a monstrous constellation of unnatural light, like a glutted swarm of corpse-fed fireflies dancing hellish sarabandes . . . . The shaft of phosphorescence from the well grew brighter and brighter, bringing to the minds of the huddled men a sense of doom . . . ."

and accursed farm a gleamingly eruptive cataclysm of unnatural sparks and substance; blurring the glance of the few who saw it, and sending forth to the zenith a bombarding cloudburst of such coloured and fantastic fragments as our universe must needs disown. Through quickly re-closing vapours they followed the great morbidity that had vanished, and in another second they had vanished too. Behind and below was only a darkness to which the men dared not return, and all about was a mounting wind which seemed to sweep down in black, frore gusts from interstellar space. It shrieked and howled, and lashed the fields and distorted woods in a mad cosmic frenzy, till soon the trembling party realized it would be no use waiting for the moon to shew what was left down there at Nahum's.

Too awed even to hint theories, the seven shaking men trudged back toward Arkham by the north road. Ammi was worse than his fellows, and begged them to see him inside his own kitchen, instead of keeping straight on to town. He did not wish to cross the blighted, wind-whipped woods alone to his home on the main road. For he had had an added shock that the others were spared, and was crushed forever with a brooding fear he dared not even mention for many years to come. As the rest of the watchers on that tempestuous hill had stolidly set their faces toward the road, Ammi had looked back an instant at the shadowed valley of desolation so lately sheltering his ill-starred friend. And from that stricken, far-away spot he had seen something feebly rise, only to sink down again upon the place from which the great shapeless horror had shot into the sky. It was just a colour — but not any colour of our earth or heavens. And because Ammi recognized that colour, and knew that this last faint remnant must still lurk down there in the well, he has never been quite right since.

Ammi would never go near the place again. It is forty-four years now since the horror happened, but he has never been there, and will be glad when the new reservoir blots it out. I shall be glad, too, for I do not like the way the sunlight changed colour around the mouth of that abandoned well I passed. I hope the water will always be very deep — but even so, I shall never drink it. I do not think I shall visit the Arkham country hereafter.

Three of the men who had been with Ammi returned the next morning to see the ruins by daylight, but there were not any real ruins. Only the bricks of the chimney, the stones of the cellar, some mineral and metallic litter here and there, and the rim of that nefandous well. Save for Ammi's dead horse, which they towed away and buried, and the buggy which they shortly returned to him, everything that had ever been living had gone. Five eldritch acres of dusty grey desert remained, nor has anything ever grown there since. To this day it sprawls open to the sky like a great spot eaten by acid in the woods and fields, and the few who have ever dared glimpse it in spite of the rural tales have named it "the blasted heath."

The rural tales are queer. They might be even queerer if city men and college chemists could be interested enough to analyze the water from that disused well, or the grey dust that no wind seems ever to disperse. Botanists, too, ought to study the stunted flora on the borders of that spot, for they might shed light on the country notion that the blight is spreading — little by little, perhaps an inch a year. People say the colour of the neighboring herbage is not quite right in the spring, and that wild things leave queer prints in the light winter snow. Snow never seems quite so heavy on the blasted heath as it is elsewhere. Horses — the few that are left in this motor age — grow skittish in the silent valley; and hunters cannot depend on their dogs too near the splotch of greyish dust.

They say the mental influences are very bad, too; numbers went queer in the years after Nahum's taking, and always they lacked the power to get away. Then the stronger-minded folk all left the region, and only the foreigners tried to live in the crumbling old homesteads. They could not stay, though; and one sometimes wonders what insight beyond ours their wild, weird stories of whispered magic have given them. Their dreams at night, they protest, are very horrible in that grotesque country; and surely the very look of the dark realm is enough to stir a morbid fancy. No traveler has ever escaped a sense of strangeness in those deep ravines, and artists shiver as they paint thick woods whose mystery is as much of the spirit as of the eye. I myself am curious about the sensation I derived from my one lone walk before Ammi told me his tale. When twilight came I had vaguely wished some clouds would gather, for an odd timidity about the deep skyey voids above had crept into my soul.

Do not ask me for my opinion. I do not know — that is all. There was no one but Ammi to question; for Arkham people will not talk about the strange days, and all three professors who saw the aërolite and its coloured globule are dead. There were other globules — depend upon that. One must have fed itself and escaped, and probably there was another which was too late. No doubt it is still down the well — I know there was something wrong with the sunlight I saw above that miasmal brink. The rustics say the blight creeps an inch a year, so perhaps there is a kind of growth or nourishment even now. But whatever demon hatchling is there, it must be tethered to something or else it would quickly spread. Is it fastened to the roots of those trees that claw the air? One of the current Arkham tales is about fat oaks that shine and move as they ought not to do at night.

What it is, only God knows. In terms of matter I suppose the thing Ammi described would be called a gas, but this gas obeyed laws that are not of our cosmos. This was no fruit of such worlds and suns as shine on the telescopes and photographic plates of our observatories. This was no breath from the skies whose motions and dimensions our astronomers measure or deem too vast to measure. It was just a colour out of space — a frightful messenger from unformed realms of infinity beyond all Nature as we know it; from realms whose mere existence stuns the brain and numbs us with the black extra-cosmic gulfs it throws open before our frenzied eyes.

I doubt very much if Ammi consciously lied to me, and I

do not think his tale was all a freak of madness as the townfolk had forewarned. Something terrible came to the hills and valleys on that meteor, and something terrible — though I know not in what proportion — still remains. I shall be glad to see the water come.

Meanwhile I hope nothing will happen to Ammi. He saw so much of the thing — and its influence was so insidious. Why has he never been able to move away? How clearly he recalled those dying words of Nahum's — "Can't git away . . . draws ye . . . ye know summ'at's comin' but tain't no use . . . . " Ammi is such a good old man — when the reservoir gang gets to work I must write the chief engineer to keep a sharp watch on him. I would hate to think of him as the grey, twisted, brittle monstrosity which persists more and more in troubling my sleep.

The Descendant.

1,500-WORD FRAGMENT; 1927.

This short vignette appears to have been the beginning of a novelette or perhaps a longer piece, set in London rather than New England. It isn't clear when Lovecraft wrote it; but it is, essentially, the start of a rough draft. Lovecraft apparently decided, having gotten 1,500 words into it, not to continue; but he apparently felt that it was worth saving to possibly take up later on.

"The Descendant" was written sometime around April of 1927, and was published shortly after Lovecraft's death in Robert H. Barlow's amateur-press journal, Leaves, in the 1938 issue.

In London there is a man who screams when the church bells ring. He lives all alone with his streaked cat in Gray's Inn, and people call him harmlessly mad. His room is filled with books of the tamest and most puerile kind, and hour after hour he tries to lose himself in their feeble pages. All he seeks from life is not to think. For some reason thought is very horrible to him, and anything which stirs the imagination he flees as a plague. He is very thin and grey and wrinkled, but there are those who declare he is not nearly so old as he looks. Fear has its grisly claws upon him, and a sound will make him start with staring eyes and sweat-beaded forehead. Friends and companions he shuns, for he wishes to answer no questions. Those who once knew him as scholar and aesthete say it is very pitiful to see him now. He dropped them all years ago, and no one feels sure whether he left the country or merely sank from sight in some hidden byway. It is a decade now since he moved into Gray's Inn, and of where he had been he would say nothing till the night young Williams bought the *Necronomicon.*

Williams was a dreamer, and only twenty-three, and when he moved into the ancient house he felt a strangeness and a breath of cosmic wind about the grey wizened man in the next room. He forced his friendship where old friends dared not force theirs, and marvelled at the fright that sat upon this gaunt, haggard watcher and listener. For that the man always watched and listened no one could doubt. He watched and listened with his mind more than with his eyes and ears, and strove every moment to drown something in his ceaseless poring over gay, insipid novels. And when the church bells rang he would stop his ears and scream, and the grey cat that dwelt with him would howl in unison till the last peal died reverberantly away.

But try as Williams would, he could not make his neighbour speak of anything profound or hidden. The old man would not live up to his aspect and manner, but would feign a smile and a light tone and prattle feverishly and frantically of cheerful trifles; his voice every moment rising and thickening till at last it would split in a piping and incoherent falsetto. That his learning was deep and thorough, his most trivial remarks made abundantly clear; and Williams was not surprised to hear that he had been to Harrow and Oxford. Later it developed that he was none other than Lord Northam, of whose ancient hereditary castle on the Yorkshire coast so many odd things were told; but when Williams tried to talk of the castle, and of its reputed Roman origin, he refused to admit that there was anything unusual about it. He even tittered shrilly when the subject of the supposed under-crypts, hewn out of the solid crag that frowns on the North Sea, was brought up.

So matters went till that night when Williams brought home the infamous *Necronomicon* of the mad Arab Abdul Alhazred. He had known of the dreaded volume since his sixteenth year, when his dawning love of the bizarre had led him to ask queer questions of a bent old bookseller in Chandos Street; and he had always wondered why men paled when they spoke of it. The old bookseller had told him that only five copies were known to have survived the shocked edicts of the priests and lawgivers against it and that all of these were locked up with frightened care by custodians who had ventured to begin a reading of the hateful black-letter. But now, at last, he had not only found an accessible copy but had made it his own at a ludicrously low figure. It was at a Jew's shop in the squalid precincts of Clare Market, where he had often bought strange things before, and he almost fancied the gnarled old Levite smiled amidst tangles of beard as the great discovery was made. The bulky leather cover with the brass clasp had been so prominently visible, and the price was so absurdly slight.

The one glimpse he had had of the title was enough to send him into transports, and some of the diagrams set in the vague Latin text excited the tensest and most disquieting recollections in his brain. He felt it was highly necessary to get the ponderous thing home and begin deciphering it, and bore it out of the shop with such precipitate haste that the old Jew chuckled disturbingly behind him. But when at last it was safe in his room he found the combination of black-letter and debased idiom too much for his powers as a linguist, and reluctantly called on his strange, frightened friend for help with the twisted, mediaeval Latin. Lord Northam was simpering inanities to his streaked cat, and started violently when the young man entered. Then he saw the volume and shuddered wildly, and fainted altogether when Williams uttered the title. It was when he regained his senses that he told his story; told his fantastic figment of madness in frantic whispers, lest his friend be not quick to burn the accursed book and give wide scattering to its ashes.

There must, Lord Northam whispered, have been something wrong at the start; but it would never have come to a head if he had not explored too far. He was the nineteenth Baron of a line whose beginnings went uncomfortably far back into the past—unbelievably far, if vague tradition could be heeded, for there were family tales of a descent from pre-Saxon times, when a certain Cnaeus Gabinius Capito, military tribune in the Third Augustan Legion then stationed at Lindum in Roman Britain, had been summarily expelled from his command for participation in certain rites unconnected with any known religion. Gabinius had, the rumour ran, come upon a cliffside cavern where strange folk met together and made the Elder Sign in the dark; strange folk whom the Britons knew not save in fear, and who were the last to survive from a great land in the west that had sunk, leaving only the islands with the raths and circles and shrines of which Stonehenge was the greatest. There was no certainty, of course, in the legend that Gabinius had built an impregnable fortress over the forbidden cave and founded a line which Pict and Saxon, Dane and Norman were powerless to obliterate; or in the tacit assumption that from this line sprang the bold companion and lieutenant of the Black Prince whom Edward Third created Baron of Northam. These things were not certain, yet they were often told; and in truth the stonework of Northam Keep did look alarmingly like the masonry of Hadrian's Wall. As a child Lord Northam had had peculiar dreams when sleeping in the older parts of the castle, and had acquired a constant habit of looking back through his memory for half-amorphous scenes and patterns and impressions which formed no part of his waking experience. He became a dreamer who found life tame and unsatisfying; a searcher for strange realms and relationships once familiar, yet lying nowhere in the visible regions of earth.

Filled with a feeling that our tangible world is only an atom in a fabric vast and ominous, and that unknown demesnes press on and permeate the sphere of the known at every point, Northam in youth and young manhood drained in turn the founts of formal religion and occult mystery. Nowhere, however, could he find ease and content; and as he grew older the staleness and limitations of life became more and more maddening to him. During the 'nineties he dabbled in Satanism, and at all times he devoured avidly any doctrine or theory which seemed to promise escape from the close vistas of science and the dully unvarying laws of Nature. Books like Ignatius Donnelly's chimerical account of Atlantis he absorbed with zest, and a dozen obscure precursors of Charles Fort enthralled him with their vagaries. He would travel leagues to follow up a furtive village tale of abnormal wonder, and once went into the desert of Araby to seek a Nameless City of faint report, which no man has ever beheld. There rose within him the tantalising faith that somewhere an easy gate existed, which if one found would admit him freely to those outer deeps whose echoes rattled so dimly at the back of his memory. It might be in the visible world, yet it might be only in his mind and soul. Perhaps he held within his own half-explored brain that cryptic link which would awaken him to elder and future lives in forgotten dimensions; which would bind him to the stars, and to the infinities and eternities beyond them.

History of the Necronomicon.

600-WORD ESSAY;
1926.

This brief essay was penned by H.P. Lovecraft around 1926 as a reference document, so that he might keep his stories straight and in sync with one another when the Necronomicon *was brought into them, and for the other writers in his circle of friends who occasionally used it in their own stories.*

Although it was never intended for publication, in 1938 following Lovecraft's death fellow amateur journalist Wilson Shepherd published a "Limited Memorial Edition" of it as a stand-alone piece, a pamphlet-sized chapbook of sorts, under his Rebel Press imprint.

Original title *Al Azif* — "azif" being the word used by Arabs to designate that nocturnal sound (made by insects) suppos'd to be the howling of daemons.

Composed by Abdul Alhazred, a mad poet of Sanaá, in Yemen, who is said to have flourished during the period of the Ommiade caliphs, circa 700 A.D. He visited the ruins of Babylon and the subterranean secrets of Memphis and spent ten years alone in the great southern desert of Arabia — the Roba el Khaliyeh or "Empty Space" of the ancients — and "Dahna" or "Crimson" desert of the modern Arabs, which is held to be inhabited by protective evil spirits and monsters of death. Of this desert many strange and unbelievable marvels are told by those who pretend to have penetrated it. In his last years Alhazred dwelt in Damascus, where the *Necronomicon (Al Azif)* was written, and of his final death or disappearance (738 A.D.) many terrible and conflicting things are told. He is said by Ebn Khallikan (12th cent. biographer) to have been seized by an invisible monster in broad daylight and devoured horribly before a large number of fright-frozen witnesses. Of his madness many things are told. He claimed to have seen fabulous Irem, or City of Pillars, and to have found beneath the ruins of a certain nameless desert town the shocking annals and secrets of a race older than mankind. He was only an indifferent Moslem, worshipping unknown entities whom he called Yog-Sothoth and Cthulhu.

In A.D. 950 the *Azif*, which had gained a considerable tho' surreptitious circulation amongst the philosophers of the age, was secretly translated into Greek by Theodorus Philetas of Constantinople under the title *Necronomicon*. For a century it impelled certain experimenters to terrible attempts, when it was suppressed and burnt by the patriarch Michael. After this it is only heard of furtively, but (1228) Olaus Wormius made a Latin translation later in the Middle Ages, and the Latin text was printed twice — once in the fifteenth century in black-letter (evidently in Germany) and once in the seventeenth (prob. Spanish) — both editions being without identifying marks, and located as to time and place by internal typographical evidence only. The work both Latin and Greek was banned by Pope Gregory IX in 1232, shortly after its Latin translation, which called attention to it. The Arabic original was lost as early as Wormius' time, as indicated by his prefatory note; and no sight of the Greek copy — which was printed in Italy between 1500 and 1550 — has been reported since the burning of a certain Salem man's library in 1692. An English translation made by Dr. Dee was never printed, and exists only in fragments recovered from the original manuscript. Of the Latin texts now existing one (15th cent.) is known to be in the British Museum under lock and key, while another (17th cent.) is in the Bibliothèque Nationale at Paris. A seventeenth-century edition is in the Widener Library at Harvard, and in the library of Miskatonic University at Arkham. Also in the library of the University of Buenos Aires. Numerous other copies probably exist in secret, and a fifteenth-century one is persistently rumoured to form part of the collection of a celebrated American millionaire. A still vaguer rumour credits the preservation of a sixteenth-century Greek text in the Salem family of Pickman; but if it was so preserved, it vanished with the artist R. U. Pickman, who disappeared early in 1926. The book is rigidly suppressed by the authorities of most countries, and by all branches of organised ecclesiasticism. Reading leads to terrible consequences. It was from rumours of this book (of which relatively few of the general public know) that Robert W. Chambers is said to have derived the idea of his early novel *The King in Yellow*.

The Thing in the Moonlight.

BY H.P. LOVECRAFT
AND J. CHAPMAN MISKE

700-WORD FRAGMENT
1927.

"The Thing in the Moonlight" was published in the January 1941 issue of Bizarre, *and it is one of the shortest stories in this collection — weighing in at just 700 words. Like "The Very Old Folk," it is essentially an excerpt from a letter sent from Lovecraft to Donald Wandrei, which Wandrei published in J. Chapman Miske's amateur-press journal,* Scienti-Snaps, *after Lovecraft's death. Miske's contribution to the story was, essentially, just the frame story — that is, the story of the semi-literate Morgan. How much of the prose in the rest of the story is Lovecraft's, and how much is Donald Wandrei's, is not clear.*

The letter on which the story is based was written in late 1927.

ABOUT J. CHAPMAN MISKE (1920-2003).

J. Chapman Miske was the editor of Scienti-Snaps (later renamed Bizarre), which published several items under Lovecraft's by-line in the years following his death in 1937. One of them — "The Very Old Folk" — was actually written by him; the other — "The Thing in the Moonlight" — was a collaboration of sorts. Both were transcriptions of dreams Lovecraft had had, which he included in letters to Donald Wandrei; after his death, Wandrei sent both of them to Miske, who published the one verbatim, and the other with some modifications.

There was some confusion in later years, when Arkham House published "The Thing in the Moonlight" as a Lovecraft story. It's fairly clear what happened with it, and its provenance as a modified dream-transcription is obvious; but it's been frequently miscategorized as a fake Lovecraft story in the years since.

Morgan is not a literary man; in fact he cannot speak English with any degree of coherency. That is what makes me wonder about the words he wrote, though others have laughed.

He was alone the evening it happened. Suddenly an unconquerable urge to write came over him, and taking pen in hand he wrote the following:

My name is Howard Phillips. *I live at 66 College Street, in Providence, Rhode Island. On November 24, 1927 — for I know not even what the year may be now — I fell asleep and dreamed, since when I have been unable to awaken.*

My dream began in a dank, reed-choked marsh that lay under a grey autumn sky, with a rugged cliff of lichen-crusted stone rising to the north. Impelled by some obscure quest, I ascended a rift or cleft in this beetling precipice, noting as I did so the black mouths of many fearsome burrows extending from both walls into the depths of the stony plateau.

At several points the passage was roofed over by the choking of the upper parts of the narrow fissure; these places being exceeding dark, and forbidding the perception of such burrows as may have existed there. In one such dark space I felt conscious of a singular accession of fright, as if some subtle and bodiless emanation from the abyss were engulfing my spirit; but the blackness was too great for me to perceive the source of my alarm.

At length I emerged upon a table-land of moss-grown rock and scanty soil, lit by a faint moonlight which had replaced the expiring orb of day. Casting my eyes about, I beheld no living object, but was sensible of a very peculiar stirring far below me, amongst the whispering rushes of the pestilential swamp I had lately quitted.

After walking for some distance, I encountered the rusty tracks of a street railway, and the worm-eaten poles which still held the limp and sagging trolley wire. Following this line, I soon came upon a yellow, vestibuled car numbered 1852 — of a plain, double-trucked type common from 1900 to 1910. It was untenanted, but evidently ready to start; the trolley being on the wire and the air-brake now and then throbbing beneath the floor. I boarded it and looked vainly about for the light switch — noting as I did so the absence of the controller handle, which thus implied the brief absence of the motorman. Then I sat down in one of the cross seats of the vehicle. Presently I heard a swishing in the sparse grass toward the left, and saw the dark forms of two men looming up in the moonlight. They had the regulation caps of a railway company, and I could not doubt but that they were conductor and motorman. Then one of them sniffed with singular sharpness, and raised his face to howl to the moon. The other dropped on all fours to run toward the car.

I leaped up at once and raced madly out of that car and across endless leagues of plateau till exhaustion forced me to stop — doing this not because the conductor had dropped on all fours, but because the face of the motorman was a mere white cone tapering to one blood-red-tentacle . . . .

I was aware that I only dreamed, but the very awareness was not pleasant. Since that fearful night, I have prayed only for awakening — it has not come!

Instead I have found myself an inhabitant of this terrible dream-world! That first night gave way to dawn, and I wandered aimlessly over the lonely swamp-lands. When night came, I still wandered, hoping for awakening. But suddenly I parted the weeds and saw before me the ancient railway car — and to one side a cone-faced thing lifted its head and in the streaming moonlight howled strangely!

It has been the same each day. Night takes me always to that place of horror. I have tried not moving, with the coming of nightfall, but I must walk in my slumber, for always I awaken with the thing of dread howling before me in the pale moonlight, and I turn and flee madly.

God! when will I awaken?

That is what Morgan wrote. I would go to 66 College Street in Providence, but I fear for what I might find there.

with the $16 he'd paid for Lovecraft's services. It ran in the November 1928 issue.

Lovecraft never did manage to collect the $4 by which de Castro underpaid him for the job.

The Last Test.

BY ADOLPHE DE CASTRO AND H.P. LOVECRAFT

19,500-WORD NOVELLA; 1927.

When Adolphe de Castro was first introduced to H.P. Lovecraft, he was looking for help in revising two literary projects: a collection of short stories, and a memoir of his adventures with legendary American writer Ambrose Bierce.

The Last Test *started out as one of the short stories in that collection. When it was presented to Lovecraft, it was little more than an extended synopsis, raggily clothed in de Castro's usual wooden prose; and it was not in any sense a "weird tale": A scientist, working obsessively to find a cure for a terrible fever, has run out of patients because he's developed a bad reputation; desperate for a specimen, he tries to convince his own sister to sacrifice herself for "science."*

Lovecraft took on this drab little yarn, which was a mid-size novelette but seemed to drag on a great deal. Adding a little supernatural action to it and bringing some other characters on board, Lovecraft expanded it to just under 20,000 words, while tightening the plot so that no element was wasted.

Lovecraft delivered the finished product to de Castro in late 1927, shortly after writing "The Colour out of Space." Under his hands it had blossomed into a decent work — no masterpiece, but a competent and eminently saleable novella, which, although Lovecraft would never have released it under his own by-line, he was no doubt proud to present to de Castro. De Castro then sent Lovecraft a chequefor $16 — a fee calculated based on the word count of the original story rather than that of the considerably expanded finished product — along with a huge list of changes that the would-be author wanted made.

Lovecraft, ordinarily a very mellow character, found this display of chutzpah a little too much. He returned the cheque with an angry note, and de Castro decided to content himself with the revisions as delivered. He then offered the story to Weird Tales *magazine, which snapped it up for $175 — a princely payment, especially compared with the $16 he'd paid for Lovecraft's services. It ran in the November 1928 issue.*

ABOUT ADOLPHE DE CASTRO (1859-1959).

Adolphe de Castro was a fascinating man. Fascinating, and — as you have no doubt gathered — more than a little sharp of elbow. He spent a great deal of time trying to get several literary figures, including Lovecraft, to do revisory and editorial work for him for free in exchange for a cut of future anticipated revenues that everyone but de Castro seems to have known would never materialize.

De Castro's resume is almost mind-boggling. He was born Abram Dancygier, of Jewish parents living in Poland, in 1859. In 1877 he was ordained a rabbi, and in 1882 earned a Ph.D. in Oriental Philology at the University of Bonn — or, at any rate, so he later claimed. By 1884 he was living in San Francisco, working as a dentist (apparently his Ph.D. gave him the title of "doctor," and this was good enough in those rough frontier days) and occasionally doing a bit of freelance journalism.

In 1900 he moved to New York, abandoning his wife and children on the West Coast, to pursue a book publishing opportunity. There, he remade himself once again as an attorney; spent a year as vice-consul in Madrid; spent another year in Scotland; and entered a second (bigamous) marriage in 1907.

During the First World War, our hero — who had, years before, changed his name to Gustav Adolphe Danziger — changed it yet again, adopting a family name that sounded less German: Adolphe de Castro.

De Castro was not the brightest light in the literary firmament; although both his contributions to this collection are competent stories, that's largely attributable to Lovecraft, who extensively rewrote both of them. But he had the good sense to hitch his wagon to Ambrose Bierce's star when, in 1886, he had the chance to do so. He and Bierce collaborated on a translation of a German novella that de Castro subsequently represented as original fiction and published serially in the San Francisco Examiner *as* The Monk and the Hangman's Daughter; *subsequently he joined with Bierce and the West Coast poet Joaquin Miller to form a publishing company, the Western Authors Publishing Association. However, de Castro's handling of this business venture apparently led to him and Bierce parting ways under less-than-amicable circumstances.*

De Castro spent several years in Mexico as a small newspaper editor before returning to the U.S. to try to capitalize on his former association with Bierce by publishing a memoir. Accordingly, he sat down, churned out a long-winded, mendacious, autobiographical mess of a draft, and started looking for an editor to help him polish it up. It was this project that first brought him into contact with Lovecraft. His pitch was for Lovecraft to help him with the Bierce boondoggle in exchange for a cut of future revenues, and meanwhile he sort of eased him along with cash jobs from his collection of short story drafts — starting, of course, with The Last Test.

Lovecraft seems to have found the old rascal delightfully amusing, if frequently tiresome in his constant angling for advantage and for free services. "Old Dolph is a portly, sentimental, & gesticulating person given to egotistical rambling about old times & the great men he has intimately known," Lovecraft wrote to his aunt, Lillian Clark.

In another letter, he wrote, "As usual he boasted and haggled inconclusively, tried to persuade me to undertake work on a promissory basis, and regaled us with tedious anecdotes of how he secured the election of Roosevelt, Taft, & Harding as Presidents. According to himself, he is apparently America's foremost power behind the throne!"

De Castro wasn't all hot air. He produced several very competent works of scholarship, particularly in the area of religious studies. But he most certainly was a social engineer — a smooth, crafty operator of the "lovable rogue" sort. Lovecraft probably found him somewhat less lovable after de Castro short-changed him on The Last Test *and then sold the story to* Weird Tales *for $175; but it couldn't have been too bad, as he worked with de Castro twice more in later years. (The second story is "The Electric Executioner"; the third story has been lost.)*

Although already fairly elderly in 1927 when he met Lovecraft — nearly 70 years old — de Castro would outlive Lovecraft by more than 20 years, dying a few weeks shy of his 100th birthday in November 1959.

I.

Few persons know the inside of the Clarendon story, or even that there is an inside not reached by the newspapers. It was a San Francisco sensation in the days before the fire, both because of the panic and menace that kept it company, and because of its close linkage with the governor of the state. Governor Dalton, it will be recalled, was Clarendon's best friend, and later married his sister. Neither Dalton nor Mrs. Dalton would ever discuss the painful affair, but somehow the facts have leaked out to a limited circle. But for that and for the years which have given a sort of vagueness and impersonality to the actors, one would still pause before probing into secrets so strictly guarded at the time.

The appointment of Dr. Alfred Clarendon as medical director of San Quentin Penitentiary in 189- was greeted with the keenest enthusiasm throughout California. San Francisco had at last the honour of harbouring one of the greatest biologists and physicians of the period, and solid pathological leaders from all over the world might be expected to flock thither to study his methods, profit by his advice and researches, and learn how to cope with their own local problems. California, almost overnight, would become a centre of medical scholarship with earthwide influence and reputation.

Governor Dalton, anxious to spread the news in its fullest significance, saw to it that the press carried ample and dignified accounts of his new appointee. Pictures of Dr. Clarendon and his new home near old Goat Hill, sketches of his career and manifold honours, and popular accounts of his salient scientific discoveries were all presented in the principal California dailies, till the public soon felt a sort of reflected pride in the man whose studies of pyemia in India, of the pest in China, and of every sort of kindred disorder elsewhere would soon enrich the world of medicine with an antitoxin of revolutionary importance — a basic antitoxin combating the whole febrile principle at its very source, and ensuring the ultimate conquest and extirpation of fever in all its diverse forms.

Back of the appointment stretched an extended and not wholly unromantic history of early friendship, long separation, and dramatically renewed acquaintance. James Dalton and the Clarendon family had been friends in New York ten years before — friends and more than friends, since the doctor's only sister, Georgina, was the sweetheart of Dalton's youth, while the doctor himself had been his closest associate and almost his protégé in the days of school and college. The father of Alfred and Georgina, a Wall Street pirate of the ruthless elder breed, had known Dalton's father well; so well, indeed, that he had finally stripped him of all he possessed in a memorable afternoon's fight on the stock exchange. Dalton Senior, hopeless of recuperation and wishing to give his one adored child the benefit of his insurance, had promptly blown out his brains; but James had not sought to retaliate. It was, as he viewed it, all in the game; and he wished no harm to the father of the girl he meant to marry and of the budding young scientist whose admirer and protector he had been throughout their years of fellowship and study. Instead, he turned to the law, established himself in a small way, and in due course of time asked "Old Clarendon" for Georgina's hand.

Old Clarendon had refused very firmly and loudly, vowing that no pauper and upstart lawyer was fit to be his son-in-law; and a scene of considerable violence had occurred. James, telling the wrinkled freebooter at last what he ought to have been told long before, had left the house and the city in a high temper; and was embarked within a month upon the California life which was to lead him to the governorship through many a fight with ring and politician. His farewells to Alfred and Georgina had been brief, and he had never known the aftermath of that scene in the Clarendon library. Only by a day did he miss the news of Old Clarendon's death from apoplexy, and by so missing it, changed the course of his whole career. He had not written Georgina in the decade that followed; knowing her loyalty to her father, and waiting till his own fortune and position might remove all obstacles to the match. Nor had he sent any word to Alfred, whose calm indifference in the face of affection and hero-worship had always savoured of conscious destiny and the self-sufficiency of genius. Secure in the ties of a constancy rare even then, he had worked and risen with thoughts only of the future; still a bachelor, and with a perfect intuitive faith that Georgina also was waiting.

In this faith Dalton was not deceived. Wondering perhaps why no message ever came, Georgina found no romance save in her dreams and expectations; and in the course of time became busy with the new responsibilities brought by her brother's rise to greatness. Alfred's growth had not belied the promise of his youth, and the slim boy had darted quietly up the steps of science with a speed and permanence almost dizzying to contemplate. Lean and ascetic, with steel-rimmed pince-nez and pointed brown beard, Dr. Alfred Clarendon was an authority at twenty-five and an international figure at thirty. Careless of worldly affairs with the negligence of genius, he depended vastly on the care and management of his sister, and was secretly thankful that her memories of James had kept her from other and more tangible alliances.

Georgina conducted the business and household of the great bacteriologist, and was proud of his strides toward the conquest of fever. She bore patiently with his eccentricities, calmed his occasional bursts of fanaticism, and healed those breaches with his friends which now and then resulted from his unconcealed scorn of anything less than a single-minded devotion to pure truth and its progress. Clarendon was undeniably irritating at times to ordinary folk; for he never tired of depreciating the service of the individual as contrasted with the service of mankind as a whole, and in censuring men of learning who mingled domestic life or outside interests with their pursuit of abstract science. His enemies called him a bore; but his admirers, pausing before the white heat of ecstasy into which he would work himself, became almost ashamed of ever having any standards or aspirations outside the one divine sphere of unalloyed knowledge.

The doctor's travels were extensive and Georgina generally accompanied him on the shorter ones. Three times, however, he had taken long, lone jaunts to strange and distant places in his studies of exotic fevers and half-fabulous plagues; for he knew that it is out of the unknown lands of cryptic and immemorial Asia that most of the earth's diseases spring. On each of these occasions he had brought back curious mementoes which added to the eccentricity of his home, not least among which was the needlessly large staff of Thibetan servants picked up somewhere in U-tsang during an epidemic of which the world never heard, but amidst which Clarendon had discovered and isolated the germ of black fever. These men, taller than most Thibetans and clearly belonging to a stock but little investigated in the outside world, were of a skeletonic leanness which made one wonder whether the doctor had sought to symbolise in them the anatomical models of his college years. Their aspect, in the loose black silk robes of Bonpa priests which he chose to give them, was grotesque in the highest degree; and there was an unsmiling silence and stiffness in their motions which enhanced their air of fantasy and gave Georgina a queer, awed feeling of having stumbled into the pages of Vathek or the Arabian Nights.

But queerest of all was the general factotum or clinic-man, whom Clarendon addressed as Surama, and whom he had brought back with him after a long stay in Northern Africa, during which he had studied certain odd intermittent fevers among the mysterious Saharan Tuaregs, whose descent from the primal race of lost Atlantis is an old archaeological rumour. Surama, a man of great intelligence and seemingly inexhaustible erudition, was as morbidly lean as the Thibetan servants; with swarthy, parchment-like skin drawn so tightly over his bald pate and hairless face that every line of the skull stood out in ghastly prominence — this death's-head effect being heightened by lustrelessly burning black eyes set with a depth which left to common visibility only a pair of dark, vacant sockets. Unlike the ideal subordinate, he seemed despite his impassive features to spend no effort in concealing such emotions as he possessed. Instead, he carried about an insidious atmosphere of irony or amusement, accompanied at certain moments by a deep, guttural chuckle like that of a giant turtle which has just torn to pieces some furry animal and is ambling away toward the sea. His race appeared to be Caucasian, but could not be classified more closely than that. Some of Clarendon's friends thought he looked like a high-caste Hindoo notwithstanding his accentless speech, while many agreed with Georgina — who disliked him — when she gave her opinion that a Pharaoh's mummy, if miraculously brought to life, would form a very apt twin for this sardonic skeleton.

Dalton, absorbed in his uphill political battles and isolated from Eastern interests through the peculiar self-sufficiency of the old West, had not followed the meteoric rise of his former comrade; Clarendon had actually heard nothing of one so far outside his chosen world of science as the governor. Being of independent and even of abundant means, the Clarendons had for many years stuck to their old Manhattan mansion in East Nineteenth Street, whose ghosts must have looked sorely askance at the bizarrerie of Surama and the Thibetans. Then, through the doctor's wish to transfer his base of medical observation, the great change had suddenly come, and they had crossed the continent to take up a secluded life in San Francisco; buying the gloomy old Bannister place near Goat Hill, overlooking the bay, and establishing their strange household in a rambling, French-roofed relic of mid-Victorian design and gold-rush parvenu display, set amidst high-walled grounds in a region still half suburban.

Dr. Clarendon, though better satisfied than in New York, still felt cramped for lack of opportunities to apply and test his pathological theories. Unworldly as he was, he had never thought of using his reputation as an influence to gain public appointment; though more and more he realised that only the medical directorship of a government or a charitable institution — a prison, almshouse, or hospital — would give him a field of sufficient width to complete his researches and make his discoveries of the greatest use to humanity and science at large.

Then he had run into James Dalton by sheer accident one afternoon in Market Street as the governor was swinging out of the Royal Hotel. Georgina had been with him, and an almost instant recognition had heightened the drama of the reunion. Mutual ignorance of one another's progress had bred long explanation and histories, and Clarendon was pleased to find

"The deep chuckle ceased, and in its place came a frantic, ululant yelp as of a thousand ghouls in torment."

Weird Tales, November 1928

that he had so important an official for a friend. Dalton and Georgina, exchanging many a glance, felt more than a trace of their youthful tenderness; and a friendship was then and there revived which led to frequent calls and a fuller and fuller exchange of confidences.

James Dalton learned of his old protégé's need for political appointment, and sought, true to his protective role of school and college days, to devise some means of giving "Little Alf" the needed position and scope. He had, it is true, wide appointive powers; but the legislature's constant attacks and encroachments forced him to exercise these with the utmost discretion. At length, however, scarcely three months after the sudden reunion, the foremost institutional medical office in the state fell vacant. Weighing all the elements with care, and conscious that his friend's achievements and reputation would justify the most substantial rewards, the governor felt at last able to act. Formalities were few, and on the eighth of November, 189-, Dr. Alfred Schuyler Clarendon became medical director of the California State Penitentiary at San Quentin.

II.

In scarcely more than a month the hopes of Dr. Clarendon's admirers were amply fulfilled. Sweeping changes in methods brought to the prison's medical routine an efficiency never before dreamed of; and though the subordinates were naturally not without jealousy, they were obliged to admit the magical results of a really great man's superintendence. Then came a time where mere appreciation might well have grown to devout thankfulness at a providential conjunction of time, place, and man; for one morning Dr. Jones came to his new chief with a grave face to announce his discovery of a case which he could not but identify as that selfsame black fever whose germ Clarendon had found and classified.

Dr. Clarendon shewed no surprise, but kept on at the writing before him.

"I know," he said evenly; "I came across that case yesterday. I'm glad you recognised it. Put the man in a separate ward, though I don't believe this fever is contagious."

Dr. Jones, with his own opinion of the malady's contagiousness, was glad of this deference to caution; and hastened to execute the order. Upon his return Clarendon rose to leave, declaring that he would himself take charge of the case alone. Disappointed in his wish to study the great man's methods and technique, the junior physician watched his chief stride away toward the lone ward where he had placed the patient, more critical of the new regime than at any time since admiration had displaced his first jealous pangs.

Reaching the ward, Clarendon entered hastily, glancing at the bed and stepping back to see how far Dr. Jones's obvious curiosity might have led him. Then, finding the corridor still vacant, he shut the door and turned to examine the sufferer. The man was a convict of a peculiarly repulsive type, and seemed to be racked by the keenest throes of agony. His features were frightfully contracted, and his knees drawn sharply up in the mute desperation of the stricken. Clarendon studied him closely, raising his tightly shut eyelids, took his pulse and temperature, and finally dissolving a tablet in water, forced the solution between the sufferer's lips. Before long the height of the attack abated, as shewn by the relaxing body and returning normality of expression, and the patient began to breathe more easily. Then, by a soft rubbing of the ears, the doctor caused the man to open his eyes. There was life in them, for they moved from side to side, though they lacked the fine fire which we are wont to deem the image of the soul. Clarendon smiled as he surveyed the peace his help had brought, feeling behind him the power of an all-capable science. He had long known of this case, and had snatched the victim from death with the work of a moment. Another hour and this man would have gone—yet Jones had seen the symptoms for days before discovering them, and having discovered them, did not know what to do.

Man's conquest of disease, however, cannot be perfect. Clarendon, assuring the dubious trusty-nurses that the fever was not contagious, had had the patient bathed, sponged in alcohol, and put to bed; but was told the next morning that the case was lost. The man had died after midnight in the most intense agony, and with such cries and distortions of face that the nurses were driven almost to panic. The doctor took this news with his usual calm, whatever his scientific feelings may have been, and ordered the burial of the patient in quicklime. Then, with a philosophic shrug of the shoulders, he made the usual rounds of the penitentiary.

Two days later the prison was hit again. Three men came down at once this time, and there was no concealing the fact that a black fever epidemic was under way. Clarendon, having adhered so firmly to his theory of non-contagiousness, suffered a distinct loss of prestige, and was handicapped by the refusal of the trusty-nurses to attend the patients. Theirs was not the soul-free devotion of those who sacrifice themselves to science and humanity. They were convicts, serving only because of the privileges they could not otherwise buy, and when the price became too great they preferred to resign the privileges.

But the doctor was still master of the situation. Consulting with the warden and sending urgent messages to his friend the governor, he saw to it that special rewards in cash and in reduced terms were offered to the convicts for the dangerous nursing service; and by this method succeeded in getting a very fair quota of volunteers. He was steeled for action now, and nothing could shake his poise and determination. Additional cases brought only a curt nod, and he seemed a stranger to fatigue as he hastened from bedside to bedside all over the vast stone home of sadness and evil. More than forty cases developed within another week, and nurses had to be brought from the city. Clarendon went home very seldom at this stage, often sleeping on a cot in the warden's quarters, and always giving himself up with typical abandon to the service of medicine and of mankind.

Then came the first mutterings of that storm which was soon to convulse San Francisco. News will out, and the menace of black fever spread over the town like a fog from the bay. Reporters trained in the doctrine of "sensation first" used their imagination without restraint, and gloried when at last they were able to produce a case in the Mexican quarter which a local physician—fonder perhaps of money than of truth or civic welfare—pronounced black fever.

That was the last straw. Frantic at the thought of the crawling death so close upon them, the people of San Francisco went mad en masse, and embarked upon that historic exodus of which all the country was soon to hear over busy wires. Ferries and rowboats, excursion steamers and launches, railways and cable cars, bicycles and carriages, moving-vans and work carts, all were pressed into instant and frenzied service. Sausalito and Tamalpais, as lying in the direction of San Quentin, shared in the flight; while housing space in Oakland, Berkeley, and Alameda rose to fabulous prices. Tent colonies sprang up, and improvised villages lined the crowded southward highways from Millbrae to San Jose. Many sought refuge with friends in Sacramento, while the fright-shaken residue forced by various causes to stay behind could do little more than maintain the basic necessities of a nearly dead city.

Business, save for quack doctors with "sure cures" and "preventives" for use against the fever, fell rapidly to the vanishing-point. At first the saloons offered "medicated drinks," but soon found that the populace preferred to be duped by charlatans of more professional aspect. In strangely noiseless streets persons peered into one another's faces to glimpse possible plague symptoms, and shopkeepers began more and more to refuse admission to their clientele, each customer seeming to them a fresh fever menace. Legal and judicial machinery began to disintegrate as attorneys and county clerks succumbed one by one to the urge for flight. Even the doctors deserted in large numbers, many of them pleading the need of vacations among the mountains and the lakes in the northern part of the state. Schools and colleges, theatres and cafés, restaurants and saloons, all gradually closed their doors; and in a single week San Francisco lay prostrate and inert with only its light, power, and water service even half normal, with newspapers in skeletonic form, and with a crippled parody on transportation maintained by the horse and cable cars.

This was the lowest ebb. It could not last long, for courage and observation are not altogether dead in mankind; and sooner or later the non-existence of any widespread black fever epidemic outside San Quentin became too obvious a fact to deny, notwithstanding several actual cases and the undeniable spread of typhoid in the unsanitary suburban tent colonies. The leaders and editors of the community conferred and took action, enlisting in their service the very reporters whose energies had done so much to bring on the trouble, but now turning their "sensation first" avidity into more constructive channels. Editorials and fictitious interviews appeared, telling of Dr. Clarendon's complete control of the disease, and of the absolute impossibility of its diffusion beyond the prison walls. Reiteration and circulation slowly did their work, and gradually a slim backward trickle of urbanites swelled into a vigorous refluent stream. One of the first healthy symptoms was the start of a newspaper controversy of the approved acrimonious kind, attempting to fix blame for the panic wherever the various participants thought it belonged. The returning doctors, jealously strengthened by their timely vacations, began striking at Clarendon, assuring the public that they as well as he would keep the fever in leash, and censuring him for not doing even more to check its spread within San Quentin.

Clarendon had, they averred, permitted far more deaths than were necessary. The veriest tyro in medicine knew how to check fever contagion; and if this renowned savant did not do it, it was clearly because he chose for scientific reasons to study the final effects of the disease, rather than to prescribe properly and save the victims. This policy, they insinuated, might be proper enough among convicted murderers in a penal institution, but it would not do in San Francisco, where life was still a precious and sacred thing. Thus they went on, and the papers were glad to publish all they wrote, since the sharpness of the campaign, in which Dr. Clarendon would doubtless join, would help to obliterate confusion and restore confidence among the people.

But Clarendon did not reply. He only smiled, while his singular clinic-man Surama indulged in many a deep, testudinous chuckle. He was at home more nowadays, so that reporters began besieging the gate of the great wall the doctor had built around his house, instead of pestering the warden's office at San Quentin. Results, though, were equally meagre; for Surama formed an impassable barrier between the doctor and the outer world — even after the reporters had got into the grounds. The newspaper men getting access to the front hall had glimpses of Clarendon's singular entourage and made the best they could in a "write-up" of Surama and the queer skeletonic Thibetans. Exaggeration, of course, occurred in every fresh article, and the net effect of the publicity was distinctly adverse to the great physician. Most persons hate the unusual, and hundreds who could have excused heartlessness or incompetence stood ready to condemn the grotesque taste manifested in the chuckling attendant and the eight black-robed Orientals.

Early in January an especially persistent young man from the Observer climbed the moated eight-foot brick wall in the rear of the Clarendon grounds and began a survey of the varied outdoor appearances which trees concealed from the front walk. With quick, alert brain he took in everything — the rose-arbour, the aviaries, the animal cages where all sorts of mammalia from monkeys to guinea-pigs might be seen and heard, the stout wooden clinic building with barred windows in the northwest corner of the yard — and bent searching glances throughout the thousand square feet of intramural privacy. A great article was brewing, and he would have escaped unscathed but for the barking of Dick, Georgina Clarendon's gigantic and beloved St. Bernard. Surama, instant in his response, had the youth by the collar before a protest could be uttered, and was presently shaking him as a terrier shakes a rat, and dragging him through the trees to the front yard and the gate.

Breathless explanations and quavering demands to see Dr. Clarendon were useless. Surama only chuckled and dragged his victim on. Suddenly a positive fright crept over the dapper scribe, and he began to wish desperately that this unearthly creature would speak if only to prove that he really was a being of honest flesh and blood belonging to this planet. He became deathly sick, and strove not to glimpse the eyes which he knew must lie at the base of those gaping black sockets. Soon he heard the gate open and felt himself propelled violently through; in another moment waking rudely to the things of earth as he landed wetly and muddily in the ditch which Clarendon had had dug around the entire length of the wall. Fright gave a place to rage as he heard the massive gate slam shut, and he rose dripping to shake his fist at the forbidding portal. Then, as he turned to go, a soft sound grated behind him, and through a small wicket in the gate he felt the sunken eyes of Surama and heard the echoes of a deep-voiced, blood-freezing chuckle.

This young man, feeling perhaps justly that his handling had been rougher than he deserved, resolved to revenge himself upon the household responsible for his treatment. Accordingly he prepared a fictitious interview with Dr. Clarendon, supposed to be held in the clinic building, during which he was careful to describe the agonies of a dozen black fever patients whom his imagination ranged on orderly rows of couches. His masterstroke was the picture of one especially pathetic sufferer gasping for water, while the doctor held a glass of the sparkling fluid just out of his reach, in a scientific attempt to determine the effect of a tantalising emotion on the course of the disease. This invention was followed by paragraphs of insinuating comment so outwardly respectful that it bore a double venom. Dr. Clarendon was, the article ran, undoubtedly the greatest and most single-minded scientist in the world; but science is no friend to individual welfare, and one would not like to have one's gravest ills drawn out and aggravated merely to satisfy an investigator on some point of abstract truth. Life is too short for that.

Altogether, the article was diabolically skilful, and succeeded in horrifying nine readers out of ten against Dr. Clarendon and his supposed methods. Other papers were quick to copy and enlarge upon its substance, taking the cue it offered, and commencing a series of "faked" interviews which fairly ran the gamut of derogatory fantasy. In no case, however, did the doctor condescend to offer a contradiction. He had no time to waste on fools and liars, and cared little for the esteem of a thoughtless rabble he despised. When James Dalton telegraphed his regrets and offered aid, Clarendon replied with an almost boorish curtness. He did not heed the barking of dogs, and could not bother to muzzle them. Nor would he thank anyone for messing with a matter wholly beneath notice. Silent and contemptuous, he continued his duties with tranquil evenness.

But the young reporter's spark had done its work. San Francisco was insane again, and this time as much with rage as with fear. Sober judgment became a lost art; and though no second exodus occurred, there ensued a reign of vice and recklessness born of desperation, and suggesting parallel phenomena in mediaeval times of pestilence. Hatred ran riot against the man who had found the disease and was struggling to restrain it, and a light-headed public forgot his great services to knowledge in their efforts to fan the flames of resentment. They seemed, in their blindness, to hate him in person, rather than the plague which had come to their breeze-cleaned and usually healthy city.

Then the young reporter, playing in the Neronic fire he had kindled, added a crowning personal touch of his own. Remembering the indignities he had suffered at the hands of the cadaverous clinic-man, he prepared a masterly article on the home and environment of Dr. Clarendon, giving especial prominence to Surama, whose very aspect he declared sufficient to scare the healthiest person into any sort of fever. He tried to make the gaunt chuckler appear equally ridiculous and terrible, succeeding best, perhaps, in the latter half of his intention, since a tide of horror always welled up whenever he thought of his brief proximity to the creature. He collected all the rumours current about the man, elaborated on the unholy depth of his reputed scholarship, and hinted darkly that it could have been no godly realm of secret and aeon-weighted Africa wherein Dr. Clarendon had found him.

Georgina, who followed the papers closely, felt crushed and hurt by these attacks upon her brother, but James Dalton, who called often at the house, did his best to comfort her. In this he was warm and sincere; for he wished not only to console the woman he loved, but to utter some measure of the reverence he had always felt for the starward-bound genius who had been his youth's closest comrade. He told Georgina how greatness can never be exempted from the shafts of envy, and cited the long, sad list of splendid brains crushed beneath vulgar heels. The attacks, he pointed out, formed the truest of all proofs of Alfred's solid eminence.

"But they hurt just the same," she rejoined, "and all the more because I know that Al really suffers from them, no matter how indifferent he tries to be."

Dalton kissed her hand in a manner not then obsolete among well-born persons.

"And it hurts me a thousand times more, knowing that it hurts you and Alf. But never mind, Georgie, we'll stand together and pull through it!"

Thus it came about that Georgina came more and more to rely on the strength of the steel-firm, square-jawed governor who had been her youthful swain, and more and more to confide in him the things she feared. The press attacks and the epidemic were not quite all. There were aspects of the household which she did not like. Surama, cruel in equal measure to man and beast, filled her with the most unnamable repulsion; and she could not but feel that he meant some vague, indefinable harm to Alfred. She did not like the Thibetans, either, and thought it very peculiar that Surama was able to talk with them. Alfred would not tell her who or what Surama was, but had once explained rather haltingly that he was a much older man than would be commonly thought credible, and that he had mastered secrets and been through experiences calculated to make him a colleague of phenomenal value for any scientist seeking Nature's hidden mysteries.

Urged by her uneasiness, Dalton became a still more frequent visitor at the Clarendon home, though he saw that his presence was deeply resented by Surama. The bony clinic-man formed the habit of glaring peculiarly from those spectral sockets when admitting him, and would often, after closing the gate when he left, chuckle monotonously in a manner that made his flesh creep. Meanwhile Dr. Clarendon seemed oblivious of everything save his work at San Quentin, whither he went each day in his launch — alone save for Surama, who managed the wheel while the doctor read or collated his notes. Dalton welcomed these regular absences, for they gave him constant opportunities to renew his suit for Georgina's hand. When he would overstay and meet Alfred, however, the latter's greeting was always friendly despite his habitual reserve. In time the engagement of James and Georgina grew to be a definite thing, and the two awaited only a favourable chance to speak to Alfred.

The governor, whole-souled in everything and firm in his protective loyalty, spared no pains in spreading propaganda on his old friend's behalf. Press and officialdom both felt his influence, and he even succeeded in interesting scientists in the East, many of whom came to California to study the plague and investigate the anti-fever bacillus which Clarendon was so rapidly isolating and perfecting. These doctors and biologists, however, did not obtain the information they wished; so that several of them left with a very unfortunate impression. Not a few prepared articles hostile to Clarendon, accusing him of an unscientific and fame-seeking attitude, and intimating that he concealed his methods through a highly unprofessional desire for ultimate personal profit.

Others, fortunately, were more liberal in their judgments, and wrote enthusiastically of Clarendon and his work. They had seen the patients, and could appreciate how marvellously he held the dread disease in leash. His secrecy regarding the antitoxin they deemed quite justifiable, since its public diffusion in unperfected form could not but do more harm than good. Clarendon himself, whom many of their number had met before, impressed them more profoundly than ever, and they did not hesitate to compare him with Jenner, Lister, Koch, Pasteur, Metchnikoff, and the rest of those whose whole lives have served pathology and humanity. Dalton was careful to save for Alfred all the magazines that spoke well of him, bringing them in person as an excuse to see Georgina. They did not, however, produce much effect save a contemptuous smile; and Clarendon would generally throw them to Surama, whose deep, disturbing chuckle upon reading formed a close parallel to the doctor's own ironic amusement.

One Monday evening early in February Dalton called with the definite intention of asking Clarendon for his sister's hand. Georgina herself admitted him to the grounds, and as they walked toward the house he stopped to pat the great dog which rushed up and laid friendly fore paws on his breast. It was Dick, Georgina's cherished St. Bernard, and Dalton was glad to feel that he had the affection of a creature which meant so much to her.

Dick was excited and glad, and turned the governor nearly half about with his vigorous pressure as he gave a soft quick bark and sprang off through the trees toward the clinic. He did not vanish, though, but presently stopped and looked back, softly barking again as if he wished Dalton to follow. Georgina, fond of obeying her huge pet's playful whims, motioned to James to see what he wanted; and they both walked slowly after him as he trotted relievedly to the rear of the yard where the top of the clinic building stood silhouetted against the stars above the great brick wall.

The outline of lights within shewed around the edges of the dark window-curtains so they knew that Alfred and Surama were at work. Suddenly from the interior came a thin, subdued sound like a cry of a child — a plaintive call of "Mamma! Mamma!" at which Dick barked, while James and Georgina started perceptibly. Then Georgina smiled, remembering the parrots that Clarendon always kept for experimental uses, and patted Dick on the head either to forgive him for having fooled her and Dalton, or to console him for having been fooled himself.

As they turned slowly toward the house Dalton mentioned his resolve to speak to Alfred that evening about their engagement, and Georgina supplied no objection. She knew that her brother would not relish the loss of a faithful manager and companion, but believed his affection would place no barrier in the way of her happiness.

Later that evening Clarendon came into the house with a springy step and aspect less grim than usual. Dalton, seeing a good omen in this easy buoyancy, took heart as the doctor wrung his hand with a jovial "Ah, Jimmy, how's politics this year?" He glanced at Georgina, and she quietly excused herself, while the two men settled down to a chat on general subjects. Little by little, amidst many reminders of their old youthful days, Dalton worked toward his point; till at last he came out plainly with the crucial query.

"Alf, I want to marry Georgina. Have we your blessing?"

Keenly watching his old friend, Dalton saw a shadow steal over his face. The dark eyes flashed for a moment, then veiled themselves as wonted placidity returned. So science or selfishness was at work after all!

"You're asking an impossibility, James. Georgina isn't the aimless butterfly she was years ago. She has a place in the service of truth and mankind now, and that place is here. She's decided to devote her life to my work — to the household that makes my work possible — and there's no room for desertion or personal caprice."

Dalton waited to see if he had finished. The same old fanaticism — humanity versus the individual — and the doctor was going to let it spoil his sister's life! Then he tried to answer.

"But look here, Alf, do you mean to say that Georgina, in particular, is so necessary to your work that you must make a slave and martyr of her? Use your sense of proportion, man! If it were a question of Surama or somebody in the utter thick of your experiments it might be different; but after all, Georgina is only a housekeeper to you in the last analysis. She has promised to be my wife and says that she loves me. Have you the right to cut her off from the life that belongs to her? Have you the right — "

"That'll do, James!" Clarendon's face was set and white. "Whether or not I have the right to govern my own family is no business of an outsider."

"Outsider — you can say that to a man who — " Dalton almost choked as the steely voice of the doctor interrupted him again.

"An outsider to my family, and from now on an outsider to my home. Dalton, your presumption goes just a little too far! Good evening, Governor!"

And Clarendon strode from the room without extending his hand.

Dalton hesitated for a moment, almost at a loss what to do, when presently Georgina entered. Her face shewed that she had spoken with her brother, and Dalton took both her hands impetuously.

"Well, Georgie, what do you say? I'm afraid it's a choice between Alf and me. You know how I feel — you know how I felt before, when it was your father I was up against. What's your answer this time?"

He paused as she responded slowly.

"James, dear, do you believe that I love you?"

He nodded and pressed her hands expectantly.

"Then, if you love me, you'll wait a while. Don't think of

Al's rudeness. He's to be pitied. I can't tell you the whole thing now, but you know how worried I am — what with the strain of his work, the criticisms, and the staring and cackling of that horrible creature Surama! I'm afraid he'll break down — he shews the strain more than anyone outside the family could tell. I can see it, for I've watched him all my life. He's changing — slowly bending under his burdens — and he puts on his extra brusqueness to hide it. You can see what I mean, can't you, dear?"

She paused, and Dalton nodded again, pressing one of her hands to his breast. Then she concluded.

"So promise me, dear, to be patient. I must stand by him; I must! I must!"

Dalton did not speak for a while, but his head inclined in what was almost a bow of reverence. There was more of Christ in this devoted woman than he had thought any human being possessed; and in the face of such love and loyalty he could do no urging.

Words of sadness and parting were brief; and James, whose blue eyes were misty, scarcely saw the gaunt clinic-man as the gate to the street was at last opened to him. But when it slammed to behind him he heard that blood-curdling chuckle he had come to recognise so well, and knew that Surama was there — Surama, whom Georgina had called her brother's evil genius. Walking away with a firm step, Dalton resolved to be watchful, and to act at the first sign of trouble.

III.

Meanwhile in San Francisco, the epidemic still on the lips of all, seethed with anti-Clarendon feeling. Actually the cases outside the penitentiary were very few, and confined almost wholly to the lower Mexican element whose lack of sanitation was a standing invitation to disease of every kind; but politicians and the people needed no more than this to confirm the attacks made by the doctor's enemies. Seeing that Dalton was immovable in his championship of Clarendon, the malcontents, medical dogmatists, and ward-heelers turned their attention to the state legislature; lining up the anti-Clarendonists and the governor's old enemies with great shrewdness, and preparing to launch a law — with a veto-proof majority — transferring the authority for minor institutional appointments from the chief executive to the various boards or commissions concerned.

In the furtherance of this measure no lobbyist was more active than Clarendon's chief assistant, Dr. Jones. Jealous of his superior from the first, he now saw an opportunity for turning matters to his liking; and he thanked fate for the circumstance — responsible indeed for his present position — of his relationship to the chairman of the prison board. The new law, if passed, would certainly mean the removal of Clarendon and the appointment of himself in his stead; so, mindful of his own interest, he worked hard for it. Jones was all that Clarendon was not — a natural politician and sycophantic opportunist who served his own advancement first and science only incidentally. He was poor, and avid for salaried position, quite in contrast to the wealthy and independent savant he sought to displace. So with a rat-like cunning and persistence he laboured to undermine the great biologist above him, and was one day rewarded by the news that the new law was passed. Thenceforward the governor was powerless to make appointments to the state institutions, and the medical directorship of San Quentin lay at the disposal of the prison board.

Of all this legislative turmoil Clarendon was singularly oblivious. Wrapped wholly in matters of administration and research, he was blind to the treason of "that ass Jones" who worked by his side, and deaf to all the gossip of the warden's office. He had never in his life read the newspapers, and the banishment of Dalton from his house cut off his last real link with the world of outside events. With the naiveté of a recluse, he at no time thought of his position as insecure. In view of Dalton's loyalty, and of his forgiveness of even the greatest wrongs, as shewn in his dealings with the elder Clarendon who had crushed his father to death on the stock exchange, the possibility of a gubernatorial dismissal was, of course, out of the question; nor could the doctor's political ignorance envisage a sudden shift of power which might place the matter of retention or dismissal in very different hands. Thereupon he merely smiled with satisfaction when Dalton left for Sacramento; convinced that his place in San Quentin and his sister's place in his household were alike secure from disturbance. He was accustomed to having what he wanted, and fancied his luck was still holding out.

The first week in March, a day or so after the enactment of the new law, the chairman of the prison board called at San Quentin. Clarendon was out, but Dr. Jones was glad to shew the august visitor — his own uncle, incidentally — through the great infirmary, including the fever ward made so famous by press and panic. By this time converted against his will to Clarendon's belief in the fever's non-contagiousness, Jones smilingly assured his uncle that nothing was to be feared, and encouraged him to inspect the patients in detail — especially a ghastly skeleton, once a very giant of bulk and vigour, who was, he insinuated, slowly and painfully dying because Clarendon would not administer the proper medicine.

"Do you mean to say," cried the chairman, "that Dr. Clarendon refuses to let the man have what he needs, knowing his life could be saved?"

"Just that," snapped Dr. Jones, pausing as the door opened to admit none other than Clarendon himself. Clarendon nodded coldly to Jones and surveyed the visitor, whom he did not know, with disapproval.

"Dr. Jones, I thought you knew this case was not to be disturbed at all. And haven't I said that visitors aren't to be admitted except by special permission?"

But the chairman interrupted before his nephew could introduce him.

"Pardon me, Dr. Clarendon, but am I to understand that you refuse to give this man the medicine that would save him?" Clarendon glared coldly, and rejoined with steel in his voice.

"That's an impertinent question, sir. I am in authority here, and visitors are not allowed. Please leave the room at once."

The chairman, his sense of drama secretly tickled, answered with greater pomp and hauteur than were necessary.

"You mistake me, sir! I, not you, am master here. You are addressing the chairman of the prison board. I must say, moreover, that I deem your activity a menace to the welfare of the prisoners, and must request your resignation. Henceforth Dr. Jones will be in charge, and if you wish to remain until your formal dismissal you will take your orders from him."

It was Wilfred Jones's great moment. Life never gave him another such climax, and we need not grudge him this one. After all, he was a small rather than a bad man, and he had only obeyed a small man's code of looking to himself at all costs. Clarendon stood still, gazing at the speaker as if he thought him mad, till in another second the look of triumph on Dr. Jones's face convinced him that something important was indeed afoot. He was icily courteous as he replied.

"No doubt you are what you claim to be, sir. But fortunately my appointment came from the governor of the state, and can therefore be revoked only by him."

The chairman and his nephew both stared perplexedly, for they had not realised to what lengths unworldly ignorance can go. Then the older man, grasping the situation, explained at some length.

"Had I found that the current reports did you an injustice," he concluded, "I would have deferred action; but the case of this poor man and your own arrogant manner left me no choice. As it is — "

But Dr. Clarendon interrupted with a new razor-sharpness in his voice.

"As it is, I am the director in charge at present, and I ask you to leave this room at once."

The chairman reddened and exploded.

"Look here, sir, who do you think you're talking to? I'll have you chucked out of here — damn your impertinence!"

But he had time only to finish the sentence. Transformed by the insult to a sudden dynamo of hate, the slender scientist launched out with both fists in a burst of preternatural strength of which no one would have thought him capable. And if his strength was preternatural, his accuracy of aim was no less so; for not even a champion of the ring could have wrought a neater result. Both men — the chairman and Dr. Jones — were squarely hit; the one full in the face and the other on the point of the chin. Going down like felled trees, they lay motionless and unconscious on the floor; while Clarendon, now clear and completely master of himself, took his hat and cane and went out to join Surama in the launch. Only when seated in the moving boat did he at last give audible vent to the frightful rage that consumed him. Then, with face convulsed, he called down imprecations from the stars and the gulfs beyond the stars; so that even Surama shuddered, made an elder sign that no book of history records, and forgot to chuckle.

IV.

Georgina soothed her brother's hurt as best she could. He had come home mentally and physically exhausted and thrown himself on the library lounge; and in that gloomy room, little by little, the faithful sister had taken in the almost incredible news. Her consolations were instantaneous and tender, and she made him realise how vast, though unconscious, a tribute to his greatness the attacks, persecution, and dismissal all were. He had tried to cultivate the indifference she preached, and could have done so had personal dignity alone been involved. But the loss of scientific opportunity was more than he could calmly bear, and he sighed again and again as he repeated how three months more of study in the prison might have given him at last the long-sought bacillus which would make all fever a thing of the past.

Then Georgina tried another mode of cheering, and told him that surely the prison board would send for him again if the fever did not abate, or if it broke out with increased force. But even this was ineffective, and Clarendon answered only in a string of bitter, ironic, and half-meaningless little sentences whose tone shewed all too clearly how deeply despair and resentment had bitten.

"Abate? Break out again? Oh, it'll abate all right! At least, they'll think it has abated. They'd think anything, no matter what happens! Ignorant eyes see nothing, and bunglers are never discoverers. Science never shews her face to that sort. And they call themselves doctors! Best of all, fancy that ass Jones in charge!"

Ceasing with a quick sneer, he laughed so daemoniacally that Georgina shivered.

The days that followed were dismal ones indeed at the Clarendon mansion. Depression, stark and unrelieved, had taken hold of the doctor's usually tireless mind; and he would even have refused food had not Georgina forced it upon him. His great notebook of observations lay unopened on the library table, and his little gold syringe of anti-fever serum — a clever device of his own, with a self-contained reservoir, attached to a broad gold finger ring, and single-pressure action peculiar to itself — rested idly in a small leather case beside it. Vigour, ambition, and the desire for study and observation seemed to have died within him; and he made no inquiries about his clinic, where hundreds of germ cultures stood in their orderly phials awaiting his attention.

The countless animals held for experiments played, lively and well fed, in the early spring sunshine; and as Georgina strolled out through the rose-arbour to the cages she felt a strangely incongruous sense of happiness about her. She knew, though, how tragically transient that happiness must be; since the start of new work would soon make all these small creatures unwilling martyrs to science. Knowing this, she glimpsed a sort of compensating element in her brother's inaction, and encouraged him to keep on in a rest he needed so badly. The eight Thibetan servants moved noiselessly about, each as impeccably effective as usual; and Georgina saw to it that the order of the household did not suffer because of the master's relaxation.

Study and starward ambition laid aside in slippered and dressing-gowned indifference, Clarendon was content to let Georgina treat him as an infant. He met her maternal fussiness with a slow, sad smile, and always obeyed her multitude of orders and precepts. A kind of faint, wistful felicity came over the languid household, amidst which the only dissenting note was supplied by Surama. He indeed was miserable, and looked often with sullen and resentful eyes at the sunny serenity in Georgina's face. His only joy had been the turmoil of experiment, and he missed the routine of seizing the fated animals, bearing them to the clinic in clutching talons, and watching them with hot brooding gaze and evil chuckles as they gradually fell into the final coma with wide-opened, red-rimmed eyes, and swollen tongue lolling from froth-covered mouth.

Now he was seemingly driven to desperation by the sight of the carefree creatures in their cages, and frequently came to ask Clarendon if there were any orders. Finding the doctor apathetic and unwilling to begin work, he would go away muttering under his breath and glaring curses upon everything; stealing with cat-like tread to his own quarters in the basement, where his voice would sometimes ascend in deep, muffled rhythms of blasphemous strangeness and uncomfortably ritualistic suggestion.

All this wore on Georgina's nerves, but not by any means so gravely as her brother's continued lassitude itself. The duration of the state alarmed her, and little by little she lost the air of cheerfulness which had so provoked the clinic-man. Herself skilled in medicine, she found the doctor's condition highly unsatisfactory from an alienist's point of view; and she now feared as much from his absence of interest and activity as she had formerly feared from his fanatical zeal and overstudy. Was lingering melancholy about to turn the once brilliant man of intellect into an innocuous imbecile?

Then, toward the end of May, came the sudden change. Georgina always recalled the smallest details connected with it; details as trivial as the box delivered to Surama the day before, postmarked Algiers, and emitting a most unpleasant odour; and the sharp, sudden thunderstorm, rare in the extreme for California, which sprang up that night as Surama chanted his rituals behind his locked basement door in a droning chest-voice louder and more intense than usual.

It was a sunny day, and she had been in the garden gathering flowers for the dining-room. Re-entering the house, she glimpsed her brother in the library, fully dressed and seated at the table, alternately consulting the notes in his thick observation book, and making fresh entries with brisk assured strokes of the pen. He was alert and vital, and there was a satisfying resilience about his movements as he now and then turned a page, or reached for a book from the rear of the great table. Delighted and relieved, Georgina hastened to deposit her flowers in the dining-room and return; but when she reached the library again she found that her brother was gone.

She knew, of course, that he must be in the clinic at work, and rejoiced to think that his old mind and purpose had snapped back into place. Realising it would be of no use to delay the luncheon for him, she ate alone and set aside a bite to be kept warm in case of his return at an odd moment. But he did not come. He was making up for lost time, and was still in the great stout-planked clinic when she went for a stroll through the rose-arbour.

As she walked among the fragrant blossoms she saw Surama fetching animals for the test. She wished she could notice him less, for he always made her shudder; but her very dread had sharpened her eyes and ears where he was concerned. He always went hatless around the yard, and the total hairlessness of his head enhanced his skeleton-like aspect horribly. Now she heard a faint chuckle as he took a small monkey from its cage against the wall and carried it to the clinic, his long, bony fingers pressing so cruelly into its furry sides that it cried out in frightened anguish. The sight sickened her, and brought her walk to an end. Her inmost soul rebelled at the ascendancy this creature had gained over her brother, and she reflected bitterly that the two had almost changed places as master and servant.

Night came without Clarendon's return to the house, and Georgina concluded that he was absorbed in one of his very longest sessions, which meant total disregard of time. She hated to retire without a talk with him about his sudden recovery; but finally, feeling it would be futile to wait up, she wrote a cheerful note and propped it before his chair on the library table; then started resolutely for bed. She was not quite asleep when she heard the outer door open and shut. So it had not been an all-night session after all! Determined to see that her brother had a meal before retiring she rose, slipped on a robe, and descended to the library, halting only when she heard voices from behind the half-opened door. Clarendon and Surama were talking, and she waited till the clinic-man might go.

Surama, however, shewed no inclination to depart; and indeed, the whole heated tenor of the discourse seemed to bespeak absorption and promise length. Georgina, though she had not meant to listen, could not help catching a phrase now and then, and presently became aware of a sinister undercurrent which frightened her very much without being wholly clear to her. Her brother's voice, nervous, incisive, held her notice with disquieting persistence.

"But anyway," he was saying, "we haven't enough animals for another day, and you know how hard it is to get a decent supply at short notice. It seems silly to waste so much effort on comparative trash when human specimens could be had with just a little extra care."

Georgina sickened at the possible implication, and caught at the hall rack to steady herself. Surama was replying in that deep, hollow tone which seemed to echo with the evil of a thousand ages and a thousand planets.

"Steady, steady—what a child you are with your haste and impatience! You crowd things so! When you've lived as I have, so that a whole life will seem only an hour, you won't be so fretful about a day or week or month! You work too fast. You've plenty of specimens in the cages for a full week if you'll only go at a sensible rate. You might even begin on the older material if you'd be sure not to overdo it."

"Never mind my haste!" The reply was snapped out sharply. "I have my own methods. I don't want to use our material if I can help it, for I prefer them as they are. And you'd better be careful of them anyway—you know the knives those sly dogs carry."

Surama's deep chuckle came. "Don't worry about that. The brutes eat, don't they? Well, I can get you one any time you need it. But go slow—with the boy gone, there are only eight, and now that you've lost San Quentin it'll be hard to get new ones by the wholesale. I'd advise you to start in on Tsanpo—he's the least use to you as he is, and—"

But that was all Georgina heard. Transfixed by a hideous dread from the thoughts this talk excited, she nearly sank to the floor where she stood, and was scarcely able to drag herself up the stairs and into her room. What was the evil monster Surama planning? Into what was he guiding her brother? What monstrous circumstances lay behind these cryptic sentences? A thousand phantoms of darkness and menace danced before her eyes, and she flung herself upon the bed without hope of sleep. One thought above the rest stood out with fiendish prominence, and she almost screamed aloud as it beat itself into her brain with renewed force. Then Nature, kinder than she expected, intervened at last. Closing her eyes in a dead faint, she did not awake till morning, nor did any fresh nightmare come to join the lasting one which the overheard words had brought.

With the morning sunshine came a lessening of the tension. What happens in the night when one is tired often reaches the consciousness in distorted forms, and Georgina could see that her brain must have given strange colour to scraps of common medical conversation. To suppose her brother—only son of the gentle Frances Schuyler Clarendon—guilty of savage sacrifices in the name of science would be to do an injustice to their blood, and she decided to omit all mention of her trip downstairs, lest Alfred ridicule her fantastic notions. When she reached the breakfast table she found that Clarendon was already gone, and regretted that not even this second morning had given her a chance to congratulate him on his revived activity. Quietly taking the breakfast served by stone-deaf old Margarita, the Mexican cook, she read the morning paper and seated herself with some needlework by the sitting-room window overlooking the great yard. All was silent out there, and she could see that the last of the animal cages had been emptied. Science was served, and the lime-pit held all that was left of the once pretty and lively little creatures. This slaughter had always grieved her, but she had never complained, since she knew it was all for humanity. Being a scientist's sister, she used to say to herself, was like being the sister of a soldier who kills to save his countrymen from their foes.

After luncheon Georgina resumed her post by the window, and had been busily sewing for some time when the sound of a pistol shot from the yard caused her to look out in alarm. There, not far from the clinic, she saw the ghastly form of Surama, a revolver in his hand, and his skull-face twisted into a strange expression as he chuckled at a cowering figure robed in black silk and carrying a long Thibetan knife. It was the servant Tsanpo, and as she recognised the shrivelled face Georgina remembered horribly what she had overheard the night before. The sun flashed on the polished blade, and suddenly Surama's revolver spat once more. This time the knife flew from the Mongol's hand, and Surama glanced greedily at his shaking and bewildered prey.

Then Tsanpo, glancing quickly at his unhurt hand and at the fallen knife, sprang nimbly away from the stealthily approaching clinic-man and made a dash for the house. Surama, however, was too swift for him, and caught him in a single leap, seizing his shoulder and almost crushing him. For a moment the Thibetan tried to struggle, but Surama lifted him like an animal by the scruff of the neck and bore him off toward the clinic. Georgina heard him chuckling and taunting the man in his own tongue, and saw the yellow face of the victim twist and quiver with fright. Suddenly realising against her own will what was taking place, a great horror mastered her and she fainted for the second time within twenty-four hours.

When consciousness returned, the golden light of late afternoon was flooding the room. Georgina, picking up her fallen work-basket and scattered materials, was lost in a daze of doubt; but finally felt convinced that the scene which had overcome her must have been all too tragically real. Her worst fears, then, were horrible truths. What to do about it, nothing in her experience could tell her; and she was vaguely thankful that her brother did not appear. She must talk to him, but not now. She could not talk to anybody now. And, thinking shudderingly of the monstrous happening behind those barred clinic windows, she crept into bed for a long night of anguished sleeplessness.

Rising haggardly on the following day, Georgina saw the doctor for the first time since his recovery. He was bustling about preoccupiedly, circulating between the house and the clinic, and paying little attention to anything besides his work. There was no chance for the dreaded interview, and Clarendon did not even notice his sister's worn-out aspect and hesitant manner.

In the evening she heard him in the library, talking to himself in a fashion most unusual for him, and she felt that he was under a great strain which might culminate in the return of his apathy. Entering the room, she tried to calm him without referring to any trying subject, and forced a steadying cup of bouillon upon him. Finally she asked gently what was distressing him, and waited anxiously for his reply, hoping to hear that Surama's treatment of the poor Thibetan had horrified and outraged him.

There was a note of fretfulness in his voice as he responded.

"What's distressing me? Good God, Georgina, what isn't? Look at the cages and see if you have to ask again! Cleaned out — milked dry — not a cursed specimen left; and a line of the most important bacterial cultures incubating in their tubes without a chance to do an ounce of good! Days' work wasted — whole programme set back — it's enough to drive a man mad! How shall I ever get anywhere if I can't scrape up some decent subjects?"

Georgina stroked his forehead.

"I think you ought to rest a while, Al dear."

He moved away.

"Rest? That's good! That's damn good! What else have I been doing but resting and vegetating and staring blankly into space for the last fifty or a hundred or a thousand years? Just as I manage to shake off the clouds, I have to run short of material — and then I'm told to lapse back again into drooling stupefaction! God! And all the while some sneaking thief is probably working with my data and getting ready to come out ahead of me with the credit for my own work. I'll lose by a neck — some fool with the proper specimens will get the prize, when one week more with even half-adequate facilities would see me through with flying colours!"

His voice rose querulously, and there was an overtone of mental strain which Georgina did not like. She answered softly, yet not so softly as to hint at the soothing of a psychopathic case.

"But you're killing yourself with this worry and tension, and if you're dead, how can you do your work?"

He gave a smile that was almost a sneer.

"I guess a week or a month — all the time I need — wouldn't quite finish me, and it doesn't much matter what becomes of me or any other individual in the end. Science is what must be served — science — the austere cause of human knowledge. I'm like the monkeys and birds and guinea-pigs I use — just a cog in the machine, to be used to the advantage of the whole. They had to be killed — I may have to be killed — what of it? Isn't the cause we serve worth that and more?"

Georgina sighed. For a moment she wondered whether, after all, this ceaseless round of slaughter really was worth while.

"But are you absolutely sure your discovery will be enough of a boon to humanity to warrant these sacrifices?"

Clarendon's eyes flashed dangerously.

"Humanity! What the deuce is humanity? Science! Dolts! Just individuals over and over again! Humanity is made for preachers to whom it means the blindly credulous. Humanity is made for the predatory rich to whom it speaks in terms of dollars and cents. Humanity is made for the politician to whom it signifies collective power to be used to his advantage. What is humanity? Nothing! Thank God that crude illusion doesn't last! What a grown man worships is truth — knowledge — science — light — the rending of the veil and the pushing back of the shadow. Knowledge, the juggernaut! There is death in our own ritual. We must kill — dissect — destroy — and all for the sake of discovery — the worship of the ineffable light. The goddess Science demands it. We test a doubtful poison by killing. How else? No thought for self — just knowledge — the effect must be known."

His voice trailed off in a kind of temporary exhaustion, and Georgina shuddered slightly.

"But this is horrible, Al! You shouldn't think of it that way!"

Clarendon cackled sardonically, in a manner which stirred odd and repugnant associations in his sister's mind.

"Horrible? You think what I say is horrible? You ought to hear Surama! I tell you, things were known to the priests of Atlantis that would have you drop dead of fright if you heard a hint of them. Knowledge was knowledge a hundred thousand years ago, when our especial forbears were shambling about Asia as speechless semi-apes! They know something of it in the Hoggar region — there are rumours in the farther uplands of Thibet — and once I heard an old man in China calling on Yog-Sothoth — "

He turned pale, and made a curious sign in the air with his extended forefinger. Georgina felt genuinely alarmed, but became somewhat calmer as his speech took a less fantastic form.

"Yes, it may be horrible, but it's glorious too. The pursuit of knowledge, I mean. Certainly, there's no slovenly sentiment connected with it. Doesn't Nature kill — constantly and remorselessly — and are any but fools horrified at the struggle? Killings are necessary. They are the glory of science. We learn something from them, and we can't sacrifice learning to sentiment. Hear the sentimentalists howl against vaccination! They fear it will kill the child. Well, what if it does? How else can we discover the laws of disease concerned? As a scientist's sister you ought to know better than to prate sentiment. You ought to help my work instead of hindering it!"

"But, Al," protested Georgina, "I haven't the slightest intention of hindering your work. Haven't I always tried to help as much as I could? I am ignorant, I suppose, and can't help very actively; but at least I'm proud of you — proud for my own sake and for the family's sake — and I've always tried to smooth the way. You've given me credit for that many a time."

Clarendon looked at her keenly.

"Yes," he said jerkily as he rose and strode from the room, "you're right. You've always tried to help as best you knew. You may yet have a chance to help still more."

Georgina, seeing him disappear through the front door, followed him into the yard. Some distance away a lantern was shining through the trees, and as they approached it they saw Surama bending over a large object stretched on the ground. Clarendon, advancing, gave a short grunt; but when Georgina saw what it was she rushed up with a shriek. It was Dick, the great St. Bernard, and he was lying still with reddened eyes and protruding tongue.

"He's sick, Al!" she cried. "Do something for him, quick!"

The doctor looked at Surama, who had uttered something in a tongue unknown to Georgina.

"Take him to the clinic," he ordered; "I'm afraid Dick's caught the fever."

Surama took up the dog as he had taken poor Tsanpo the day before, and carried him silently to the building near the wall. He did not chuckle this time, but glanced at Clarendon with what appeared to be real anxiety. It almost seemed to Georgina that Surama was asking the doctor to save her pet.

Clarendon, however, made no move to follow, but stood still for a moment and then sauntered slowly toward the house. Georgina, astonished at such callousness, kept up a running fire of entreaties on Dick's behalf, but it was of no use. Without paying the slightest attention to her pleas he made directly for the library and began to read in a large old book which had lain face down on the table. She put her hand on his shoulder as he sat there, but he did not speak or turn his head. He only kept on reading, and Georgina, glancing curiously over his shoulder, wondered in what strange alphabet this brass-bound tome was written.

In the cavernous parlour across the hall, sitting alone in the dark a quarter of an hour later, Georgina came to her decision. Something was gravely wrong—just what, and to what extent, she scarcely dared formulate to herself—and it was time that she called in some stronger force to help her. Of course it must be James. He was powerful and capable, and his sympathy and affection would shew him the right thing to do. He had known Al always, and would understand.

It was by this time rather late, but Georgina had resolved on action. Across the hall the light still shone from the library, and she looked wistfully at the doorway as she quietly donned a hat and left the house. Outside the gloomy mansion and forbidding grounds, it was only a short walk to Jackson Street, where by good luck she found a carriage to take her to the Western Union telegraph office. There she carefully wrote out a message to James Dalton in Sacramento, asking him to come at once to San Francisco on a matter of the greatest importance to them all.

V.

Dalton was frankly perplexed by Georgina's sudden message. He had had no word from the Clarendons since that stormy February evening when Alfred had declared him an outsider to his home; and he in turn had studiously refrained from communicating, even when he had longed to express sympathy after the doctor's summary ousting from office. He had fought hard to frustrate the politicians and keep the appointive power, and was bitterly sorry to watch the unseating of a man who, despite recent estrangements, still represented to him the ultimate ideal of scientific competence.

Now, with this clearly frightened summons before him, he could not imagine what had happened. He knew, though, that Georgina was not one to lose her head or send forth a needless alarm; hence he wasted no time, but took the Overland which left Sacramento within the hour, going at once to his club and sending word to Georgina by a messenger that he was in town and wholly at her service.

Meanwhile things had been quiescent at the Clarendon home, notwithstanding the doctor's continued taciturnity and his absolute refusal to report on the dog's condition. Shadows of evil seemed omnipresent and thickening, but for the moment there was a lull. Georgina was relieved to get Dalton's message and learn that he was close at hand, and sent back word that she would call him when necessity arose. Amidst all the gathering tension some faint compensating element seemed manifest, and Georgina finally decided that it was the absence of the lean Thibetans, whose stealthy, sinuous ways and disturbing exotic aspect had always annoyed her. They had vanished all at once; and old Margarita, the sole visible servant left in the house, told her they were helping their master and Surama at the clinic.

The following morning—the twenty-eighth of May—long to be remembered—was dark and lowering, and Georgina felt the precarious calm wearing thin. She did not see her brother at all, but knew he was in the clinic hard at work at something despite the lack of specimens he had bewailed. She wondered how poor Tsanpo was getting along, and whether he had really been subjected to any serious inoculation, but it must be confessed that she wondered more about Dick. She longed to know whether Surama had done anything for the faithful dog amidst his master's oddly callous indifference. Surama's apparent solicitude on the night of Dick's seizure had impressed her greatly, giving her perhaps the kindliest feeling she had ever had for the detested clinic-man. Now, as the day advanced, she found herself thinking more and more of Dick; till at last her harassed nerves, finding in this one detail a sort of symbolic summation of the whole horror that lay upon the household, could stand the suspense no longer.

Up to that time she had always respected Alfred's imperious wish that he be never approached or disturbed at the clinic; but as this fateful afternoon advanced, her resolution to break through the barrier grew stronger and stronger. Finally she set out with determined face, crossing the yard and entering the unlocked vestibule of the forbidden structure with the fixed intention of discovering how the dog was or of knowing the reason for her brother's secrecy.

The inner door, as usual, was locked; and behind it she heard voices in heated conversation. When her knocking brought no response she rattled the knob as loudly as possible, but still the voices argued on unheeding. They belonged, of course, to Surama and her brother; and as she stood there trying to attract attention she could not help but catch something of their drift. Fate had made her for the second time an eavesdropper, and once more the matter she overheard seemed likely to tax her mental poise and nervous endurance to their ultimate bounds. Alfred and Surama were plainly quarrelling with increasing violence, and the purport of their speech was enough to arouse the wildest fears and confirm the gravest apprehensions. Georgina shivered as her brother's voice mounted shrilly to dangerous heights of fanatical tension.

"You, damn you—you're a fine one to talk defeat and moderation to me! Who started all this, anyway? Did I have any idea of your cursed devil-gods and elder world? Did I ever in my life think of your damned spaces beyond the stars and your crawling chaos Nyarlathotep? I was a normal scientific man, confound you, till I was fool enough to drag you out of the vaults with your devilish Atlantean secrets. You egged me on, and now you want to cut me off! You loaf around doing nothing and telling me to go slow when you might just as well as not be going out and getting material. You know damn well that I don't know how to go about such things, whereas you must have been an old hand at it before the earth was made. It's like you, you damned walking corpse, to start something you won't or can't finish!"

Surama's evil chuckle came.

"You're insane, Clarendon. That's the only reason I let you rave on when I could send you to hell in three minutes. Enough is enough, and you've certainly had enough material for any novice at your stage. You've had all I'm going to get you, anyhow! You're only a maniac on the subject now—what a cheap, crazy thing to sacrifice even your poor sister's pet dog, when you could have spared him as well as not! You can't look at any living thing now without wanting to jab that gold syringe into it. No—Dick had to go where the Mexican boy went—where Tsanpo and the other seven went—where all the animals went! What a pupil! You're no fun anymore—you've lost your nerve. You set out to control things, and they're controlling you. I'm about done with you, Clarendon. I thought you had the stuff in you, but you haven't. It's about time I tried somebody else. I'm afraid you'll have to go!"

In the doctor's shouted reply there was both fear and frenzy.

"Be careful, you —! There are powers against your powers—I didn't go to China for nothing, and there are things in Alhazred's Azif which weren't known in Atlantis! We've both meddled in dangerous things, but you needn't think you know all my resources. How about the Nemesis of Flame? I talked in Yemen with an old man who had come back alive from the Crimson Desert—he had seen Irem, the City of Pillars, and had worshipped at the underground shrines of Nug and Yeb—Iä! Shub-Niggurath!"

Through Clarendon's shrieking falsetto cut the deep chuckle of the clinic-man.

"Shut up, you fool! Do you suppose your grotesque nonsense has any weight with me? Words and formulae—words and formulae—what do they all mean to one who has the substance behind them? We're in a material sphere now, and subject to material laws. You have your fever; I have my revolver. You'll get no specimens, and I'll get no fever so long as I have you in front of me with this gun between!"

That was all Georgina could hear. She felt her senses reeling, and staggered out of the vestibule for a saving breath of the lowering outside air. She saw that the crisis had come at last, and that help must now arrive quickly if her brother was to be saved from the unknown gulfs of madness and mystery. Summoning up all her reserve energy, she managed to reach the house and get to the library, where she scrawled a hasty note for Margarita to take to James Dalton.

When the old woman had gone, Georgina had just strength enough to cross to the lounge and sink weakly down into a sort of semi-stupor. There she lay for what seemed like years, conscious only of the fantastic creeping up of the twilight from the lower corners of the great, dismal room, and plagued by a thousand shadowy shapes of terror which filed with phantasmal, half-limned pageantry through her tortured and stifled brain. Dusk deepened into darkness, and still the spell held. Then a firm tread sounded in the hall, and she heard someone enter the room and fumble at the match-safe. Her heart almost stopped beating as the gas-jets of the chandelier flared up one by one, but then she saw that the arrival was her brother. Relieved to the bottom of her heart that he was still alive, she gave vent to an involuntary sigh, profound, long-drawn, and tremulous, and lapsed at last into kindly oblivion.

At the sound of that sigh Clarendon turned in alarm toward the lounge, and was inexpressibly shocked to see the pale and unconscious form of his sister there. Her face had a death-like quality that frightened his inmost spirit, and he flung himself on his knees by her side, awake to a realisation of what her passing away would mean to him. Long unused to private practice amidst his ceaseless quest for truth, he had lost the physician's instinct of first aid, and could only call out her name and chafe her wrists mechanically as fear and grief possessed him. Then he thought of water, and ran to the dining-room for a carafe. Stumbling about in a darkness which seemed to harbour vague terrors, he was some time in finding what he sought; but at last he clutched it in shaking hand and hastened back to dash the cold fluid in Georgina's face. The method was crude but effective. She stirred, sighed a second time, and finally opened her eyes.

"You are alive!" he cried, and put his cheek to hers as she stroked his head maternally. She was almost glad she fainted, for the circumstance seemed to have dispelled the strange Alfred and brought her own brother back to her. She sat up slowly and tried to reassure him.

"I'm all right, Al. Just give me a glass of water. It's a sin to waste it this way—to say nothing of spoiling my waist! Is that the way to behave every time your sister drops off for a nap? You needn't think I'm going to be sick, for I haven't time for such nonsense!"

Alfred's eyes shewed that her cool, common-sense speech

had had its effect. His brotherly panic dissolved in an instant, and instead there came into his face a vague, calculating expression, as if some marvellous possibility had just dawned upon him. As she watched the subtle waves of cunning and appraisal pass fleetingly over his countenance she became less and less certain that her mode of reassurance had been a wise one, and before he spoke she found herself shivering at something she could not define. A keen medical instinct almost told her that his moment of sanity had passed, and that he was now once more the unrestrained fanatic for scientific research. There was something morbid in the quick narrowing of his eyes at her casual mention of good health. What was he thinking? To what unnatural extreme was his passion for experiment about to be pushed? Wherein lay the special significance of her pure blood and absolutely flawless organic state? None of these misgivings, however, troubled Georgina for more than a second, and she was quite natural and unsuspicious as she felt her brother's steady fingers at her pulse.

"You're a bit feverish, Georgie," he said in a precise, elaborately restrained voice as he looked professionally into her eyes.

"Why, nonsense, I'm all right," she replied. "One would think you were on the watch for fever patients just for the sake of shewing off your discovery! It would be poetic, though, if you could make your final proof and demonstration by curing your own sister!"

Clarendon started violently and guiltily. Had she suspected his wish? Had he muttered anything aloud? He looked at her closely, and saw that she had no inkling of the truth. She smiled up sweetly into his face and patted his hand as he stood by the side of the lounge. Then he took a small oblong leather case from his vest pocket, and taking out a little gold syringe, he began fingering it thoughtfully, pushing the piston speculatively in and out of the empty cylinder.

"I wonder," he began with suave sententiousness, "whether you would really be willing to help science in—something like that way—if the need arose? Whether you would have the devotion to offer yourself to the cause of medicine as a sort of Jephthah's daughter if you knew it meant the absolute perfection and completion of my work?"

Georgina, catching the odd and unmistakable glitter in her brother's eyes, knew at last that her worst fears were true. There was nothing to do now but keep him quiet at all hazards and to pray that Margarita had found James Dalton at his club.

"You look tired, Al dear," she said gently. "Why not take a little morphia and get some of the sleep you need so badly?"

He replied with a kind of crafty deliberation.

"Yes, you're right. I'm worn out, and so are you. Each of us needs a good sleep. Morphine is just the thing—wait till I go and fill the syringe and we'll both take a proper dose."

Still fingering the empty syringe, he walked softly out of the room. Georgina looked about her with the aimlessness of desperation, ears alert for any sign of possible help. She thought she heard Margarita again in the basement kitchen, and rose to ring the bell, in an effort to learn of the fate of her message.

The old servant answered her summons at once, and declared she had given the message at the club hours ago. Governor Dalton had been out, but the clerk had promised to deliver the note at the very moment of his arrival. Margarita waddled below stairs again, but still Clarendon did not reappear. What was he doing? What was he planning? She had heard the outer door slam, so knew he must be at the clinic. Had he forgotten his original intention with the vacillating mind of madness? The suspense grew almost unbearable, and Georgina had to keep her teeth clenched tightly to avoid screaming.

It was the gate bell, which rang simultaneously in house and clinic, that broke the tension at last. She heard the cat-like tread of Surama on the walk as he left the clinic to answer it; and then, with an almost hysterical sigh of relief, she caught the firm, familiar accents of Dalton in conversation with the sinister attendant. Rising, she almost tottered to meet him as he loomed up in the library doorway; and for a moment no word was spoken while he kissed her hand in his courtly, old-school fashion. Then Georgina burst forth into a torrent of hurried explanation, telling all that had happened, all she had glimpsed and overheard, and all she feared and suspected.

Dalton listened gravely and comprehendingly, his first bewilderment gradually giving place to astonishment, sympathy, and resolution. The message, held by a careless clerk, had been slightly delayed, and had found him appropriately enough in the midst of a warm lounging-room discussion about Clarendon. A fellow-member, Dr. MacNeil, had brought in a medical journal with an article well calculated to disturb the devoted scientist, and Dalton had just asked to keep the paper for future reference when the message was handed him at last. Abandoning his half-formed plan to take Dr. MacNeil into his confidence regarding Alfred, he called at once for his hat and stick, and lost not a moment in getting a cab for the Clarendon home.

Surama, he thought, appeared alarmed at recognising him; though he had chuckled as usual when striding off again toward the clinic. Dalton always recalled Surama's stride and chuckle on this ominous night, for he was never to see the unearthly creature again. As the chuckler entered the clinic vestibule his deep, guttural gurgles seemed to blend with some low mutterings of thunder which troubled the far horizon.

When Dalton had heard all Georgina had to say, and learned that Alfred was expected back at any moment with an hypodermic dose of morphine, he decided he had better talk with the doctor alone. Advising Georgina to retire to her room and await developments, he walked about the gloomy library, scanning the shelves and listening for Clarendon's nervous footstep on the clinic path outside. The vast room's corners were dismal despite the chandelier, and the closer Dalton looked at his friend's choice of books the less he liked them. It was not the balanced collection of a normal physician, biologist, or man of general culture. There were too many volumes on doubtful borderland themes; dark speculations and forbidden rituals of the Middle Ages, and strange exotic mysteries in alien alphabets both known and unknown.

The great notebook of observations on the table was unwholesome, too. The handwriting had a neurotic cast, and the spirit of the entries was far from reassuring. Long passages were inscribed in crabbed Greek characters, and as Dalton marshalled his linguistic memory for their translation he gave a sudden start, and wished his college struggles with Xenophon and Homer had been more conscientious. There was something wrong — something hideously wrong — here, and the governor sank limply into the chair by the table as he pored more and more closely over the doctor's barbarous Greek. Then a sound came, startlingly near, and he jumped nervously at a hand laid sharply on his shoulder.

"What, may I ask, is the cause of this intrusion? You might have stated your business to Surama."

Clarendon was standing icily by the chair, the little gold syringe in one hand. He seemed very calm and rational, and Dalton fancied for a moment that Georgina must have exaggerated his condition. How, too, could a rusty scholar be absolutely sure about these Greek entries? The governor decided to be very cautious in his interview, and thanked the lucky chance which had placed a specious pretext in his coat pocket. He was very cool and assured as he rose to reply.

"I didn't think you'd care to have things dragged before a subordinate, but I thought you ought to see this article at once."

He drew forth the magazine given him by Dr. MacNeil and handed it to Clarendon.

"On page 542 — you see the heading, 'Black Fever Conquered by New Serum.' It's by Dr. Miller of Philadelphia — and he thinks he's got ahead of you with your cure. They were discussing it at the club, and MacNeil thought the exposition very convincing. I, as a layman, couldn't pretend to judge; but at all events I thought you oughtn't to miss a chance to digest the thing while it's fresh. If you're busy, of course, I won't disturb you —"

Clarendon cut in sharply.

"I'm going to give my sister an hypodermic — she's not quite well — but I'll look at what that quack has to say when I get back. I know Miller — a damn sneak and incompetent — and I don't believe he has the brains to steal my methods from the little he's seen of them."

Dalton suddenly felt a wave of intuition warning him that Georgina must not receive that intended dose. There was something sinister about it. From what she had said, Alfred must have been inordinately long preparing it, far longer than was needed for the dissolving of a morphine tablet. He decided to hold his host as long as possible, meanwhile testing his attitude in a more or less subtle way. "I'm sorry Georgina isn't well. Are you sure that the injection will do her good? That it won't do her any harm?" Clarendon's spasmodic start shewed that something had been struck home.

"Do her harm?" he cried. "Don't be absurd! You know Georgina must be in the best of health — the very best, I say — in order to serve science as a Clarendon should serve it. She, at least, appreciates the fact that she is my sister. She deems no sacrifice too great in my service. She is a priestess of truth and discovery, as I am a priest."

He paused in his shrill tirade, wild-eyed, and somewhat out of breath. Dalton could see that his attention had been momentarily shifted. "But let me see what this cursed quack has to say," he continued. "If he thinks his pseudo-medical rhetoric can take a real doctor in, he is even simpler than I thought!"

Clarendon nervously found the right page and began reading as he stood there clutching his syringe. Dalton wondered what the real facts were. MacNeil had assured him that the author was a pathologist of the highest standing, and that whatever errors the article might have, the mind behind it was powerful, erudite, and absolutely honourable and sincere.

Watching the doctor as he read, Dalton saw the thin, bearded face grow pale. The great eyes blazed, and the pages crackled in the tenser grip of the long, lean fingers. A perspiration broke out on the high, ivory-white forehead where the hair was already thinning, and the reader sank gaspingly into the chair his visitor had vacated as he kept on with his devouring of the text. Then came a wild scream as from a haunted beast, and Clarendon lurched forward on the table, his outflung arms sweeping books and paper before them as consciousness went dark like a wind-quenched candle-flame.

Dalton, springing to help his stricken friend, raised the slim form and tilted it back in the chair. Seeing the carafe on the floor near the lounge, he dashed some water into the twisted face, and was rewarded by seeing the large eyes slowly open. They were sane eyes now — deep and sad and unmistakably sane — and Dalton felt awed in the presence of a tragedy whose ultimate depth he could never hope or dare to plumb.

The golden hypodermic was still clutched in the lean left hand, and as Clarendon drew a deep, shuddering breath he unclosed his fingers and studied the glittering thing that rolled about on his palm. Then he spoke — slowly, and with the ineffable sadness of utter, absolute despair.

"Thanks, Jimmy, I'm quite all right. But there's much to be done. You asked me a while back if this shot of morphia would do Georgie any harm. I'm in a position now to tell you that it won't."

He turned a small screw in the syringe and laid a finger on the piston, at the same time pulling with his left hand at the skin of his own neck. Dalton cried out in alarm as a lightning motion of his right hand injected the contents of the cylinder into the ridge of distended flesh.

"Good Lord, Al, what have you done?"

Clarendon smiled gently — a smile almost of peace and resignation, different indeed from the sardonic sneer of the past few weeks. "You ought to know, Jimmy, if you've still the judgment that made you a governor. You must have pieced together enough from my notes to realise that there's nothing else to do. With your marks in Greek back at Columbia I guess you couldn't have missed much. All I can say is that it's true.

"James, I don't like to pass blame along, but it's only right to tell you that Surama got me into this. I can't tell you who or what he is, for I don't fully know myself, and what I do know is stuff that no sane person ought to know; but I will say that I don't consider him a human being in the fullest sense, and that I'm not sure whether or not he's alive as we know life.

"You think I'm talking nonsense. I wish I were, but the whole hideous mess is damnably real. I started out in life with a clean mind and purpose. I wanted to rid the world of fever. I tried and failed—and I wish to God I had been honest enough to say that I'd failed. Don't let my old talk of science deceive you, James—I found no antitoxin and was never even half on the track of one!

"Don't look so shaken up, old fellow! A veteran politician-fighter like you must have seen plenty of unmaskings before. I tell you, I never had even the start of a fever cure. But my studies had taken me into some queer places, and it was just my damned luck to listen to the stories of some still queerer people. James, if you ever wish any man well, tell him to keep clear of the ancient, hidden places of the earth. Old backwaters are dangerous—things are handed down there that don't do healthy people any good. I talked too much with old priests and mystics, and got to hoping I might achieve things in dark ways that I couldn't achieve in lawful ways.

"I shan't tell you just what I mean, for if I did I'd be as bad as the old priests that were the ruin of me. All I need say is that after what I've learned I shudder at the thought of the world and what it's been through. The world is cursed old, James, and there have been whole chapters lived and closed before the dawn of our organic life and the geologic eras connected with it. It's an awful thought—whole forgotten cycles of evolution with beings and races and wisdom and diseases—all lived through and gone before the first amoeba ever stirred in the tropic seas geology tells us about.

"I said gone, but I didn't quite mean that. It would have been better that way, but it wasn't quite so. In places traditions have kept on—I can't tell you how—and certain archaic life-forms have managed to struggle thinly down the aeons in hidden spots. There were cults, you know—bands of evil priests in lands now buried under the sea. Atlantis was the hotbed. That was a terrible place. If heaven is merciful, no one will ever drag up that horror from the deep.

"It had a colony, though, that didn't sink; and when you get too confidential with one of the Tuareg priests in Africa, he's likely to tell you wild tales about it—tales that connect up with whispers you'll hear among the mad lamas and flighty yak-drivers on the secret table-lands of Asia. I'd heard all the common tales and whispers when I came on the big one. What that was, you'll never know—but it pertained to somebody or something that had come down from a blasphemously long time ago, and could be made to live again—or seem alive again—through certain processes that weren't very clear to the man who told me.

"Now, James, in spite of my confession about the fever, you know I'm not bad as a doctor. I plugged hard at medicine, and soaked up about as much as the next man—maybe a little more, because down there in the Hoggar country I did something no priest had ever been able to do. They led me blindfolded to a place that had been sealed up for generations—and I came back with Surama.

"Easy, James! I know what you want to say. How does he know all he knows?—why does he speak English—or any other language, for that matter—without an accent?—why did he come away with me?—and all that. I can't tell you altogether, but I can say that he takes in ideas and images and impressions with something besides his brain and senses. He had a use for me and my science. He told me things, and opened up vistas. He taught me to worship ancient, primordial, and unholy gods, and mapped out a road to a terrible goal which I can't even hint to you. Don't press me, James—it's for the sake of your sanity and the world's sanity!

"The creature is beyond all bounds. He's in league with the stars and all the forces of Nature. Don't think I'm still crazy, James—I swear to you I'm not! I've had too many glimpses to doubt. He gave me new pleasures that were forms of his palaeogene worship, and the greatest of those was the black fever.

"God, James! Haven't you seen through the business by this time? Do you still believe the black fever came out of Thibet, and that I learned about it there? Use your brains, man! Look at Miller's article here! He's found a basic antitoxin that will end all fever within half a century, when other men learn how to modify it for the different forms. He's cut the ground of my youth from under me—done what I'd have given my life to do—taken the wind out of all the honest sails I ever flung to the breeze of science! Do you wonder his article gave me a turn? Do you wonder it shocks me out of my madness back to the old dreams of my youth? Too late! Too late! But not too late to save others!

"I guess I'm rambling a bit now, old man. You know—the hypodermic. I asked you why you didn't tumble to the facts about black fever. How could you, though? Doesn't Miller say he's cured seven cases with his serum? A matter of diagnosis, James. He only thinks it is black fever. I can read between his lines. Here, old chap, on page 551, is the key to the whole thing. Read it again.

"You see, don't you? The fever cases from the Pacific Coast didn't respond to his serum. They puzzled him. They didn't even seem like any true fever he knew. Well, those were my cases! Those were the real black fever cases! And there can't ever be an antitoxin on earth that'll cure black fever!

"How do I know? Because black fever isn't of this earth! It's from somewhere else, James—and Surama alone knows where, because he brought it here. He brought it and I spread it! That's the secret, James! That's all I wanted the appointment for—that's all I ever did—just spread the fever that I carried in this gold syringe and in the deadlier finger-ring-pump-syringe you see on my index finger! Science? A blind! I wanted to kill, and kill, and kill! A single pressure on my finger, and the black fever was inoculated. I wanted to see living things writhe and squirm, scream and froth at the mouth. A single pressure of the pump-syringe and I could watch them as they died, and I couldn't live or think unless I had plenty to watch. That's why I jabbed everything in sight with the accursed hollow needle. Animals, criminals, children, servants — and the next would have been —"

Clarendon's voice broke, and he crumpled up perceptibly in his chair.

"That — that, James — was — my life. Surama made it so — he taught me, and kept me at it till I couldn't stop. Then — then it got too much even for him. He tried to check me. Fancy — he trying to check anybody in that line! But now I've got my last specimen. That is my last test. Good subject, James — I'm healthy — devilish healthy. Deuced ironic, though — the madness has gone now, so there won't be any fun watching the agony! Can't be — can't —"

A violent shiver of fever racked the doctor, and Dalton mourned amidst his horror-stupefaction that he could give no grief. How much of Alfred's story was sheer nonsense, and how much nightmare truth he could not say; but in any case he felt that the man was a victim rather than a criminal, and above all, he was a boyhood comrade and Georgina's brother. Thoughts of the old days came back kaleidoscopically. "Little Alf" — the yard at Phillips Exeter — the quadrangle at Columbia — the fight with Tom Cortland when he saved Alf from a pummeling . . . .

He helped Clarendon to the lounge and asked gently what he could do. There was nothing. Alfred could only whisper now, but he asked forgiveness for all his offences, and commended his sister to the care of his friend.

"You — you'll — make her happy," he gasped. "She deserves it. Martyr — to — a myth! Make it up to her, James. Don't — let — her — know — more — than she has to!"

His voice trailed off in a mumble, and he fell into a stupor. Dalton rang the bell, but Margarita had gone to bed, so he called up the stairs for Georgina. She was firm of step, but very pale. Alfred's scream had tried her sorely, but she had trusted James. She trusted him still as he shewed her the unconscious form on the lounge and asked her to go back to her room and rest, no matter what sounds she might hear. He did not wish her to witness the awful spectacle of delirium certain to come, but bade her kiss her brother a final farewell as he lay there calm and still, very like the delicate boy he had once been. So she left him — the strange, moonstruck, star-reading genius she had mothered so long — and the picture she carried away was a very merciful one.

Dalton must bear to his grave a sterner picture. His fears of delirium were not vain, and all through the black midnight hours his giant strength restrained the frenzied contortions of the mad sufferer. What he heard from those swollen, blackening lips he will never repeat. He has never been quite the same man since, and he knows that no one who hears such things can ever be wholly as he was before. So, for the world's good, he dares not speak, and he thanks God that his layman's ignorance of certain subjects makes many of the revelations cryptic and meaningless to him.

Toward morning Clarendon suddenly woke to a sane consciousness and began to speak in a firm voice.

"James, I didn't tell you what must be done — about everything. Blot out these entries in Greek and send my notebook to Dr. Miller. All my other notes, too, that you'll find in the files. He's the big authority today — his article proves it. Your friend at the club was right.

"But everything in the clinic must go. Everything without exception, dead or alive or — otherwise. All the plagues of hell are in those bottles on the shelves. Burn them — burn it all — if one thing escapes, Surama will spread black death throughout the world. And above all burn Surama! That — that thing — must not breathe the wholesome air of heaven. You know now — what I told you — you know why such an entity can't be allowed on earth. It won't be murder — Surama isn't human — if you're as pious as you used to be, James, I shan't have to urge you. Remember the old text — 'Thou shalt not suffer a witch to live' — or something of the sort.

"Burn him, James! Don't let him chuckle again over the torture of mortal flesh! I say, burn him — the Nemesis of Flame — that's all that can reach him, James, unless you can catch him asleep and drive a stake through his heart . . . Kill him — extirpate him — cleanse the decent universe of its primal taint — the taint I recalled from its age-long sleep . . ."

The doctor had risen on his elbow, and his voice was a piercing shriek toward the last. The effort was too much, however, and he lapsed very suddenly into a deep, tranquil coma. Dalton, himself fearless of fever, since he knew the dread germ to be non-contagious, composed Alfred's arms and legs on the lounge and threw a light afghan over the fragile form. After all, mightn't much of this horror be exaggeration and delirium? Mightn't old Doc MacNeil pull him through on a long chance? The governor strove to keep awake, and walked briskly up and down the room, but his energies had been taxed too deeply for such measures. A second's rest in the chair by the table took matters out of his hands, and he was presently sleeping soundly despite his best intentions.

Dalton started up as a fierce light shone in his eyes, and for a moment he thought the dawn had come. But it was not the dawn, and as he rubbed his heavy lids he saw that it was the glare of the burning clinic in the yard, whose stout planks flamed and roared and crackled heavenward in the most stupendous holocaust he had ever seen. It was indeed the "Nemesis of Flame" that Clarendon had wished, and Dalton felt that some strange combustibles must be involved in a blaze so much wilder than anything normal pine or redwood could afford. He glanced alarmedly at the lounge, but Alfred was not there. Starting up, he went to call Georgina, but met her in the hall, roused as he was by the mountain of living fire.

"The clinic's burning down!" she cried. "How is Al now?"

"He's disappeared — disappeared while I dropped asleep!" replied Dalton, reaching out a steadying arm to the form which faintness had begun to sway.

Gently leading her upstairs toward her room, he promised to search at once for Alfred, but Georgina slowly shook her head as the flames from outside cast a weird glow through the window on the landing.

"He must be dead, James — he could never live, sane and knowing what he did. I heard him quarrelling with Surama, and know that awful things were going on. He is my brother, but — it is best as it is."

Her voice had sunk to a whisper.

Suddenly through the open window came the sound of a deep, hideous chuckle, and the flames of the burning clinic took fresh contours till they half resembled some nameless, Cyclopean creatures of nightmare. James and Georgina paused hesitant, and peered out breathlessly through the landing window. Then from the sky came a thunderous peal, as a forked bolt of lightning shot down with terrible directness into the very midst of the blazing ruin. The deep chuckle ceased, and in its place came a frantic, ululant yelp as of a thousand ghouls and werewolves in torment. It died away with long, reverberant echoes, and slowly the flames resumed their normal shape.

The watchers did not move, but waited till the pillar of fire had shrunk to a smouldering glow. They were glad of a half-rusticity which had kept the firemen from trooping out, and of the wall that excluded the curious. What had happened was not for vulgar eyes — it involved too much of the universe's inner secrets for that.

In the pale dawn, James spoke softly to Georgina, who could do no more than put her head on his breast and sob.

"Sweetheart, I think he has atoned. He must have set the fire, you know, while I was asleep. He told me it ought to be burned — the clinic, and everything in it, Surama, too. It was the only way to save the world from the unknown horrors he had loosed upon it. He knew, and he did what was best.

"He was a great man, Georgie. Let's never forget that. We must always be proud of him, for he started out to help mankind, and was titanic even in his sins. I'll tell you more sometime. What he did, be it good or evil, was what no man ever did before. He was the first and last to break through certain veils, and even Apollonius of Tyana takes second place beside him. But we mustn't talk about that. We must remember him only as the Little Alf we knew — as the boy who wanted to master medicine and conquer fever."

In the afternoon the leisurely firemen overhauled the ruins and found two skeletons with bits of blackened flesh adhering — only two, thanks to the undisturbed lime-pits. One was of a man; the other is still a subject of debate among the biologists of the coast. It was not exactly an ape's or a saurian's skeleton, but it had disturbing suggestions of lines of evolution of which palaeontology has revealed no trace. The charred skull, oddly enough, was very human, and reminded people of Surama; but the rest of the bones were beyond conjecture. Only well-cut clothing could have made such a body look like a man.

But the human bones were Clarendon's. No one disputed this, and the world at large still mourns the untimely death of the greatest doctor of his age; the bacteriologist whose universal fever serum would have far eclipsed Dr. Miller's kindred anti-toxin had he lived to bring it to perfection. Much of Miller's late success, indeed, is credited to the notes bequeathed him by the hapless victim of the flames. Of the old rivalry and hatred almost none survived, and even Dr. Wilfred Jones has been known to boast of his association with the vanished leader.

James Dalton and his wife Georgina have always preserved a reticence which modesty and family grief might well account for. They published certain notes as a tribute to the great man's memory, but have never confirmed or contradicted either the popular estimate or the rare hints of marvels that a very few keen thinkers have been known to whisper. It was very subtly and slowly that the facts filtered out. Dalton probably gave Dr. MacNeil an inkling of the truth, and that good soul had not many secrets from his son.

The Daltons have led, on the whole, a very happy life; for their cloud of terror lies far in the background, and a strong mutual love has kept the world fresh for them. But there are things which disturb them oddly — little things, of which one would scarcely ever think of complaining. They cannot bear persons who are lean or deep-voiced beyond certain limits, and Georgina turns pale at the sound of any guttural chuckling. Senator Dalton has a mixed horror of occultism, travel, hypodermics, and strange alphabets which most find hard to unify, and there are still those who blame him for the vast proportion of the doctor's library that he destroyed with such painstaking completeness.

MacNeil, though, seemed to realise. He was a simple man, and he said a prayer as the last of Alfred Clarendon's strange books crumbled to ashes. Nor would anyone who had peered understandingly within those books wish a word of that prayer unsaid.

The Very Old Folk.

2,500-WORD SHORT STORY; 1927.

On Nov. 3, 1927, shortly after finishing his revision of The Last Test *for Adolphe de Castro, H.P. Lovecraft wrote a letter to Donald Wandrei in which the text of this story appears; it was an extensive description of a detailed dream. However, it's a particularly sinister dream, presented in such a way as to suggest that it might actually be an ancestral memory percolating through.*

As detailed in the introduction to "The Thing in the Moonlight," Wandrei, after Lovecraft's death, gave the text of the letter to J. Chapman Miske to publish in his fan magazine, Scienti-Snaps, *which he did in the Summer 1940 issue.*

It was a flaming sunset or late afternoon in the tiny provincial town of Pompelo, at the foot of the Pyrenees in Hispania Citerior. The year must have been in the late republic, for the province was still ruled by a senatorial proconsul instead of a prætorian legate of Augustus, and the day was the first before the Kalends of November. The hills rose scarlet and gold to the north of the little town, and the westering sun shone ruddily and mystically on the crude new stone and plaster buildings of the dusty forum and the wooden walls of the circus some distance to the east. Groups of citizens — broad-browed Roman colonists and coarse-haired Romanised natives, together with obvious hybrids of the two strains, alike clad in cheap woollen togas — and sprinklings of helmeted legionaries and coarse-mantled, black-bearded tribesmen of the circumambient Vascones — all thronged the few paved streets and forum; moved by some vague and ill-defined uneasiness.

I myself had just alighted from a litter, which the Illyrian bearers seemed to have brought in some haste from Calagurris, across the Iberus to the southward. It appeared that I was a provincial quæstor named L. Cælius Rufus, and that I had been summoned by the proconsul, P. Scribonius Libo, who had come from Tarraco some days before. The soldiers were the fifth cohort of the XIIth legion, under the military tribune Sex. Asellius; and the legatus of the whole region, Cn. Balbutius, had also come from Calagurris, where the permanent station was.

The cause of the conference was a horror that brooded on the hills. All the townsfolk were frightened, and had begged the presence of a cohort from Calagurris. It was the Terrible Season of the autumn, and the wild people in the mountains were preparing for the frightful ceremonies which only rumour told of in the towns. They were the very old folk who dwelt higher up in the hills and spoke a choppy language which the Vascones could not understand. One seldom saw them; but a few times a year they sent down little yellow, squint-eyed messengers (who looked like Scythians) to trade with the merchants by means of gestures, and every spring and autumn they held the infamous rites on the peaks, their howlings and altar-fires throwing terror into the villages. Always the same — the night before the Kalends of Maius and the night before the Kalends of November. Townsfolk would disappear just before these nights, and would never be heard of again. And there were whispers that the native shepherds and farmers were not ill-disposed toward the very old folk — that more than one thatched hut was vacant before midnight on the two hideous Sabbaths.

This year the horror was very great, for the people knew that the wrath of the very old folk was upon Pompelo. Three months previously five of the little squint-eyed traders had come down from the hills, and in a market brawl three of them had been killed. The remaining two had gone back wordlessly to their mountains — and this autumn not a single villager had disappeared. There was menace in this immunity. It was not like the very old folk to spare their victims at the Sabbath. It was too good to be normal, and the villagers were afraid.

For many nights there had been a hollow drumming on the hills, and at last the ædile Tib. Annæus Stilpo (half native in blood) had sent to Balbutius at Calagurris for a cohort to stamp out the Sabbath on the terrible night. Balbutius had carelessly refused, on the ground that the villagers' fears were empty, and that the loathsome rites of hill folk were of no concern to the Roman People unless our own citizens were menaced.

I, however, who seemed to be a close friend of Balbutius, had disagreed with him; averring that I had studied deeply in the black forbidden lore, and that I believed the very old folk capable of visiting almost any nameless doom upon the town, which after all was a Roman settlement and contained a great number of our citizens. The complaining ædile's own mother Helvia was a pure Roman, the daughter of M. Helvius Cinna, who had come over with Scipio's army. Accordingly I had sent a slave — a nimble little Greek called Antipater — to the proconsul with letters, and Scribonius had heeded my plea and ordered Balbutius to send his fifth cohort, under Asellius, to Pompelo; entering the hills at dusk on the eve of November's

Kalends and stamping out whatever nameless orgies he might find — bringing such prisoners as he might take to Tarraco for the next proprætor's court. Balbutius, however, had protested, so that more correspondence had ensued. I had written so much to the proconsul that he had become gravely interested, and had resolved to make a personal inquiry into the horror.

He had at length proceeded to Pompelo with his lictors and attendants; there hearing enough rumours to be greatly impressed and disturbed, and standing firmly by his order for the Sabbath's extirpation. Desirous of conferring with one who had studied the subject, he ordered me to accompany Asellius' cohort — and Balbutius had also come along to press his adverse advice, for he honestly believed that drastic military action would stir up a dangerous sentiment of unrest amongst the Vascones both tribal and settled.

So here we all were in the mystic sunset of the autumn hills — old Scribonius Libo in his toga prætexta, the golden light glancing on his shiny bald head and wrinkled hawk face, Balbutius with his gleaming helmet and breastplate, blue-shaven lips compressed in conscientiously dogged opposition, young Asellius with his polished greaves and superior sneer, and the curious throng of townsfolk, legionaries, tribesmen, peasants, lictors, slaves, and attendants. I myself seemed to wear a common toga, and to have no especially distinguishing characteristic. And everywhere horror brooded. The town and country folk scarcely dared speak aloud, and the men of Libo's entourage, who had been there nearly a week, seemed to have caught something of the nameless dread. Old Scribonius himself looked very grave, and the sharp voices of us later comers seemed to hold something of curious inappropriateness, as in a place of death or the temple of some mystic God.

We entered the prætorium and held grave converse. Balbutius pressed his objections, and was sustained by Asellius, who appeared to hold all the natives in extreme contempt while at the same time deeming it inadvisable to excite them. Both soldiers maintained that we could better afford to antagonise the minority of colonists and civilised natives by inaction, than to antagonise a probable majority of tribesmen and cottagers by stamping out the dread rites.

I, on the other hand, renewed my demand for action, and offered to accompany the cohort on any expedition it might undertake. I pointed out that the barbarous Vascones were at best turbulent and uncertain, so that skirmishes with them were inevitable sooner or later whichever course we might take; that they had not in the past proved dangerous adversaries to our legions, and that it would ill become the representatives of the Roman People to suffer barbarians to interfere with a course which the justice and prestige of the Republic demanded. That, on the other hand, the successful administration of a province depended primarily upon the safety and good-will of the civilized element in whose hands the local machinery of commerce and prosperity reposed, and in whose veins a large mixture of our own Italian blood coursed. These, though in numbers they might form a minority, were the stable element whose constancy might be relied on, and whose cooperation would most firmly bind the province to the Imperium of the Senate and the Roman People.

It was at once a duty and an advantage to afford them the protection due to Roman citizens; even (and here I shot a sarcastic look at Balbutius and Asellius) at the expense of a little trouble and activity, and of a slight interruption of the draught-playing and cock-fighting at the camp in Calagurris. That the danger to the town and inhabitants of Pompelo was a real one, I could not from my studies doubt. I had read many scrolls out of Syria and Ægyptus, and the cryptic towns of Etruria, and had talked at length with the bloodthirsty priest of Diana Aricina in his temple in the woods bordering Lacus Nemorensis.

There were shocking dooms that might be called out of the hills on the Sabbaths; dooms which ought not to exist within the territories of the Roman People; and to permit orgies of the kind known to prevail at Sabbaths would be but little in consonance with the customs of those whose forefathers, A. Postumius being consul, had executed so many Roman citizens for the practice of the Bacchanalia — a matter kept ever in memory by the Senatus Consultum de Bacchanalibus, graven upon bronze and set open to every eye.

Checked in time, before the progress of the rites might evoke anything with which the iron of a Roman pilum might not be able to deal, the Sabbath would not be too much for the powers of a single cohort. Only participants need be apprehended, and the sparing of a great number of mere spectators would considerably lessen the resentment which any of the sympathising country folk might feel. In short, both principle and policy demanded stern action; and I could not doubt but that Publius Scribonius, bearing in mind the dignity and obligations of the Roman People, would adhere to his plan of despatching the cohort, me accompanying, despite such objections as Balbutius and Asellius — speaking indeed more like provincials than Romans — might see fit to offer and multiply.

The slanting sun was now very low, and the whole hushed town seemed draped in an unreal and malign glamour. Then P. Scribonius the proconsul signified his approval of my words, and stationed me with the cohort in the provisional capacity of a centurio primipilus; Balbutius and Asellius assenting, the former with better grace than the latter. As twilight fell on the wild autumnal slopes, a measured, hideous beating of strange drums floated down from afar in terrible rhythm. Some few of the legionarii showed timidity, but sharp commands brought them into line, and the whole cohort was soon drawn up on the open plain east of the circus. Libo himself, as well as Balbutius, insisted on accompanying the cohort; but great difficulty was suffered in getting a native guide to point out the paths up the mountain. Finally a young man named Vercellius, the son of pure Roman parents, agreed to take us at least past the foothills.

We began to march in the new dusk, with the thin silver sickle of a young moon trembling over the woods on our left. That which disquieted us most was the fact that the Sabbath was to be held at all. Reports of the coming cohort must have reached the hills, and even the lack of a final decision could not make the rumour less alarming—yet there were the sinister drums as of yore, as if the celebrants had some peculiar reason to be indifferent whether or not the forces of the Roman People marched against them. The sound grew louder as we entered a rising gap in the hills, steep wooded banks enclosing us narrowly on either side, and displaying curiously fantastic tree-trunks in the light of our bobbing torches.

All were afoot save Libo, Balbutius, Asellius, two or three of the centuriones, and myself, and at length the way became so steep and narrow that those who had horses were forced to leave them; a squad of ten men being left to guard them, though robber bands were not likely to be abroad on such a night of terror. Once in a while it seemed as though we detected a skulking form in the woods nearby, and after a half-hour's climb the steepness and narrowness of the way made the advance of so great a body of men—over 300, all told—exceedingly cumbrous and difficult. Then with utter and horrifying suddenness we heard a frightful sound from below. It was from the tethered horses—they had screamed, not neighed, but screamed . . . and there was no light down there, nor the sound of any human thing, to show why they had done so. At the same moment bonfires blazed out on all the peaks ahead, so that terror seemed to lurk equally well before and behind us.

Looking for the youth Vercellius, our guide, we found only a crumpled heap weltering in a pool of blood. In his hand was a short sword snatched from the belt of D. Vibulanus, a subcenturio, and on his face was such a look of terror that the stoutest veterans turned pale at the sight. He had killed himself when the horses screamed . . . He, who had been born and lived all his life in that region, and knew what men whispered about the hills. All the torches now began to dim, and the cries of frightened legionaries mingled with the unceasing screams of the tethered horses. The air grew perceptibly colder, more suddenly so than is usual at November's brink, and seemed stirred by terrible undulations which I could not help connecting with the beating of huge wings.

The whole cohort now remained at a standstill, and as the torches faded I watched what I thought were fantastic shadows outlined in the sky by the spectral luminosity of the Via Lactea as it flowed through Perseus, Cassiopeia, Cepheus, and Cygnus. Then suddenly all the stars were blotted from the sky—even bright Deneb and Vega ahead, and the lone Altair and Fomalhaut behind us. And as the torches died out altogether, there remained above the stricken and shrieking cohort only the noxious and horrible altar-flames on the towering peaks; hellish and red, and now silhouetting the mad, leaping, and colossal forms of such nameless beasts as had never a Phrygian priest or Campanian grandam whispered of in the wildest of furtive tales.

And above the nighted screaming of men and horses that dæmonic drumming rose to louder pitch, whilst an ice-cold wind of shocking sentience and deliberateness swept down from those forbidden heights and coiled about each man separately, till all the cohort was struggling and screaming in the dark, as if acting out the fate of Laocoön and his sons. Only old Scribonius Libo seemed resigned. He uttered words amidst the screaming, and they echo still in my ears. "*Malitia vetus—malitia vetus est . . . venit . . . tandem venit . . .*"

And then I waked. It was the most vivid dream in years, drawing upon wells of the subconscious long untouched and forgotten. Of the fate of that cohort no record exists, but the town at least was saved—for encyclopædias tell of the survival of Pompelo to this day, under the modern Spanish name of Pompelona . . . .

Yrs for Gothick Supremacy—

—C. IVLIVS. VERVS.MAXIMINVS.

1928.

Bachelorhood Revisited.

For H.P. Lovecraft, 1928 was productive in ways other than the strictly literary. Having now firmly established his home base in Providence, and spent enough time there to feel comfortable in it, he set forth to do a little traveling. Along the way, he dashed off a solid horror story for ghostwriting client Zealia Bishop — "The Curse of Yig."

His first destination was New York, at the invitation of his wife, Sonia, who was making one last attempt to reanimate their shambling, undead marriage. Within just a few months, she, too, had given up, and by November was suggesting to Lovecraft that perhaps they should end it with an amicable divorce.

In New York, Lovecraft found his old literary circle, the Kalem Club, essentially defunct; shorn of its *de facto* leader by Lovecraft's return to Providence, the group had faded out. But its members were still around, and Lovecraft had a pretty good time for a month or two before setting out on a lengthy tour of the Eastern Seaboard in the company of various literary friends

While on this trip, Lovecraft spent several weeks in the Brattleboro area of Vermont as the guest of Vrest Orton, and learned much about Vermont provincial legends from Orton and from fellow writer Edith Miniter, which he would press into service following his return to Providence when writing *The Dunwich Horror*.

Sometime that summer, possibly for the entertainment of his old Kalem Club mates, he dashed off "Ibid," a lighthearted little spoof of an academic paper that's something of classics tour de force.

The Curse of Yig.

BY ZEALIA BISHOP
AND H.P. LOVECRAFT

7,000-WORD SHORT STORY;
1928.

This short story appears to be largely Lovecraft's work. Bishop, in her memoir, claimed she wrote the story and sent it to him and he was very impressed and helped her polish it; however, Lovecraft, in a letter to August Derleth, characterized it as "75 percent mine," and recalled that Bishop gave him only the bare outline of a story.

"There was no plot or motivation — no prologue or aftermath to the incident — so that one might say that the story, as a story, is wholly my own," Lovecraft wrote.

Readers familiar with Lovecraft's 1928 work will also recognize at least one significant element that this story shares with The Dunwich Horror, *which Lovecraft wrote just a few months later. More details cannot be divulged here without spoiling the ending.*

The story was finished in early 1928, and first published in the November 1929 issue of Weird Tales *magazine.*

ABOUT ZEALIA BISHOP
(1897-1968).

In early 1927, a 30-year-old divorcée studying journalism at Columbia University happened to mention to Samuel Loveman that she was looking for someone to help her break into fiction

writing, and Loveman introduced her to H.P. Lovecraft. The result: three beefy collaborative weird-fiction stories centered in Oklahoma.

Bishop, in her memoir, freely admits Lovecraft pushed her in ways she would not naturally have gone. Her hope had been to make a few extra bucks to support herself and her young son by writing breezy shopgirl romance stories. She quickly learned that she was working with the wrong teacher for that sort of thing. After a few of her forays into romantic fiction came back marked with comments like "No gentleman would dare kiss a girl in this fashion," she took the hint and stopped sending him such works.

Shortly after this, Bishop left Columbia and went back to live with her sister in Oklahoma. It was there that she first set about writing weird stories, with Lovecraft's long-distance assistance.

In 1925 I went into Oklahoma looking for snake lore, and I came out with a fear of snakes that will last me the rest of my life. I admit it is foolish, since there are natural explanations for everything I saw and heard, but it masters me none the less. If the old story had been all there was to it, I would not have been so badly shaken. My work as an American Indian ethnologist has hardened me to all kinds of extravagant legendry, and I know that simple white people can beat the redskins at their own game when it comes to fanciful inventions. But I can't forget what I saw with my own eyes at the insane asylum in Guthrie.

I called at that asylum because a few of the oldest settlers told me I would find something important there. Neither Indians nor white men would discuss the snake-god legends I had come to trace. The oil-boom newcomers, of course, knew nothing of such matters, and the red men and old pioneers were plainly frightened when I spoke of them. Not more than six or seven people mentioned the asylum, and those who did were careful to talk in whispers. But the whisperers said that Dr. McNeill could shew me a very terrible relic and tell me all I wanted to know. He could explain why Yig, the half-human father of serpents, is a shunned and feared object in central Oklahoma, and why old settlers shiver at the secret Indian orgies which make the autumn days and nights hideous with the ceaseless beating of tom-toms in lonely places.

It was with the scent of a hound on the trail that I went to Guthrie, for I had spent many years collecting data on the evolution of serpent-worship among the Indians. I had always felt, from well-defined undertones of legend and archaeology, that great Quetzalcoatl — benign snake-god of the Mexicans — had had an older and darker prototype; and during recent months I had well-nigh proved it in a series of researches stretching from Guatemala to the Oklahoma plains. But everything was tantalising and incomplete, for above the border the cult of the snake was hedged about by fear and furtiveness.

Now it appeared that a new and copious source of data was about to dawn, and I sought the head of the asylum with an eagerness I did not try to cloak. Dr. McNeill was a small, clean-shaven man of somewhat advanced years, and I saw at once from his speech and manner that he was a scholar of no mean attainments in many branches outside his profession. Grave and doubtful when I first made known my errand, his face grew thoughtful as he carefully scanned my credentials and the letter of introduction which a kindly old ex-Indian agent had given me.

"So you've been studying the Yig legend, eh?" he reflected sententiously. "I know that many of our Oklahoma ethnologists have tried to connect it with Quetzalcoatl, but I don't think any of them have traced the intermediate steps so well. You've done remarkable work for a man as young as you seem to be, and you certainly deserve all the data we can give.

"I don't suppose old Major Moore or any of the others told you what it is I have here. They don't like to talk about it, and neither do I. It is very tragic and very horrible, but that is all. I refuse to consider it anything supernatural. There's a story about it that I'll tell you after you see it — a devilish sad story, but one that I won't call magic. It merely shews the potency that belief has over some people. I'll admit there are times when I feel a shiver that's more than physical, but in daylight I set all that down to nerves. I'm not a young fellow any more, alas!

"To come to the point, the thing I have is what you might call a victim of Yig's curse — a physically living victim. We don't let the bulk of the nurses see it, although most of them know it's here. There are just two steady old chaps whom I let feed it and clean out its quarters — used to be three, but good old Stevens passed on a few years ago. I suppose I'll have to break in a new group pretty soon; for the thing doesn't seem to age or change much, and we old boys can't last forever. Maybe the ethics of the near future will let us give it a merciful release, but it's hard to tell.

"Did you see that single ground-glass basement window over in the east wing when you came up the drive? That's where it is. I'll take you there myself now. You needn't make any comment. Just look through the moveable panel in the door and thank God the light isn't any stronger. Then I'll tell you the story — or as much as I've been able to piece together."

We walked downstairs very quietly, and did not talk as we threaded the corridors of the seemingly deserted basement. Dr. McNeill unlocked a grey-painted steel door, but it was only a bulkhead leading to a further stretch of hallway. At length he paused before a door marked B-116, opened a small observation panel which he could use only by standing on tiptoe, and pounded several times upon the painted metal, as if to arouse the occupant, whatever it might be.

A faint stench came from the aperture as the doctor unclosed it, and I fancied his pounding elicited a kind of low, hissing response. Finally he motioned me to replace him at the peep-hole, and I did so with a causeless and increasing tremor. The barred, ground-glass window, close to the earth outside, admitted only a feeble and uncertain pallor; and I had to look into the malodourous den for several seconds before I could see what was crawling and wriggling about on the straw-covered floor, emitting every now and then a weak and vacuous hiss.

"B-but — but for God's sake what is it?"

Weird Tales, November 1929

Then the shadowed outlines began to take shape, and I perceived that the squirming entity bore some remote resemblance to a human form laid flat on its belly. I clutched at the door-handle for support as I tried to keep from fainting.

The moving object was almost of human size, and entirely devoid of clothing. It was absolutely hairless, and its tawny-looking back seemed subtly squamous in the dim, ghoulish light. Around the shoulders it was rather speckled and brownish, and the head was very curiously flat. As it looked up to hiss at me I saw that the beady little black eyes were damnably anthropoid, but I could not bear to study them long. They fastened themselves on me with a horrible persistence, so that I closed the panel gaspingly and left the creature to wriggle about unseen in its matted straw and spectral twilight. I must have reeled a bit, for I saw that the doctor was gently holding my arm as he guided me away. I was stuttering over and over again: "B-but for God's sake, what is it?"

Dr. McNeill told me the story in his private office as I sprawled opposite him in an easy-chair. The gold and crimson of late afternoon changed to the violet of early dusk, but still I sat awed and motionless. I resented every ring of the telephone and every whir of the buzzer, and I could have cursed the nurses and interns whose knocks now and then summoned the doctor briefly to the outer office. Night came, and I was glad my host switched on all the lights. Scientist though I was, my zeal for research was half forgotten amidst such breathless ecstasies of fright as a small boy might feel when whispered witch-tales go the rounds of the chimney-corner.

It seems that Yig, the snake-god of the central plains tribes — presumably the primal source of the more southerly Quetzalcoatl or Kukulcan — was an odd, half-anthropomorphic devil of highly arbitrary and capricious nature. He was not wholly evil, and was usually quite well-disposed toward those who gave proper respect to him and his children, the serpents; but in the autumn he became abnormally ravenous, and had to be driven away by means of suitable rites. That was why the tom-toms in the Pawnee, Wichita, and Caddo country pounded ceaselessly week in and week out in August, September, and October; and why the medicine-men made strange noises with rattles and whistles curiously like those of the Aztecs and Mayas.

Yig's chief trait was a relentless devotion to his children — a devotion so great that the redskins almost feared to protect themselves from the venomous rattlesnakes which thronged the region. Frightful clandestine tales hinted of his vengeance upon mortals who flouted him or wreaked harm upon his wriggling progeny; his chosen method being to turn his victim, after suitable tortures, to a spotted snake.

In the old days of the Indian Territory, the doctor went on, there was not quite so much secrecy about Yig. The plains tribes, less cautious than the desert nomads and Pueblos, talked quite freely of their legends and autumn ceremonies with the first Indian agents, and let considerable of the lore spread out through the neighbouring regions of white settlement. The great fear came in the land-rush days of '89, when some extraordinary incidents had been rumoured, and the rumours sustained, by what seemed to be hideously tangible proofs. Indians said that the new white men did not know how to get on with Yig, and afterward the settlers came to take that theory at face value. Now no old-timer in middle Oklahoma, white or red, could be induced to breathe a word about the snake-god except in vague hints. Yet after all, the doctor added with almost needless emphasis, the only truly authenticated horror had been a thing of pitiful tragedy rather than of bewitchment. It was all very material and cruel — even that last phase which had caused so much dispute.

Dr. McNeill paused and cleared his throat before getting down to his special story, and I felt a tingling sensation as when a theatre curtain rises. The thing had begun when Walker Davis and his wife Audrey left Arkansas to settle in the newly opened public lands in the spring of 1889, and the end had come in the country of the Wichitas — north of the Wichita River, in what is at present Caddo County. There is a small village called Binger there now, and the railway goes through; but otherwise the place is less changed than other parts of Oklahoma. It is still a section of farms and ranches — quite productive in these days — since the great oil-fields do not come very close.

Walker and Audrey had come from Franklin County in the Ozarks with a canvas-topped wagon, two mules, an ancient and useless dog called "Wolf," and all their household goods. They were typical hill-folk, youngish and perhaps a little more ambitious than most, and looked forward to a life of better returns for their hard work than they had had in Arkansas. Both were lean, raw-boned specimens; the man tall, sandy, and grey-eyed, and the woman short and rather dark, with a black straightness of hair suggesting a slight Indian admixture.

In general, there was very little of distinction about them, and but for one thing their annals might not have differed from those of thousands of other pioneers who flocked into the new country at that time. That thing was Walker's almost epileptic fear of snakes, which some laid to prenatal causes, and some said came from a dark prophecy about his end with which an old Indian squaw had tried to scare him when he was small. Whatever the cause, the effect was marked indeed; for despite his strong general courage the very mention of a snake would cause him to grow faint and pale, while the sight of even a tiny specimen would produce a shock sometimes bordering on a convulsion seizure.

The Davises started out early in the year, in the hope of being on their new land for the spring ploughing. Travel was slow; for the roads were bad in Arkansas, while in the Territory there were great stretches of rolling hills and red, sandy barrens without any roads whatever. As the terrain grew flatter, the change from their native mountains depressed them more, perhaps, than they realised; but they found the people at the Indian agencies very affable, while most of the settled Indians seemed friendly and civil. Now and then they encountered a fellow-pioneer, with whom crude pleasantries and expressions of amiable rivalry were generally exchanged.

Owing to the season, there were not many snakes in evidence, so Walker did not suffer from his special temperamental weakness. In the earlier stages of the journey, too, there were no Indian snake-legends to trouble him; for the transplanted tribes from the southeast do not share the wilder beliefs of their western neighbours. As fate would have it, it was a white man at Okmulgee in the Creek country who gave the Davises the first hint of Yig beliefs; a hint which had a curiously fascinating effect on Walker, and caused him to ask questions very freely after that.

Before long Walker's fascination had developed into a bad case of fright. He took the most extraordinary precautions at each of the nightly camps, always clearing away whatever vegetation he found, and avoiding stony places whenever he could. Every clump of stunted bushes and every cleft in the great, slab-like rocks seemed to him now to hide malevolent serpents, while every human figure not obviously part of a settlement or emigrant train seemed to him a potential snake-god till nearness had proved the contrary. Fortunately no troublesome encounters came at this stage to shake his nerves still further.

As they approached the Kickapoo country they found it

harder and harder to avoid camping near rocks. Finally it was no longer possible, and poor Walker was reduced to the puerile expedient of droning some of the rustic anti-snake charms he had learned in his boyhood. Two or three times a snake was really glimpsed, and these sights did not help the sufferer in his efforts to preserve composure.

On the twenty-second evening of the journey a savage wind made it imperative, for the sake of the mules, to camp in as sheltered a spot as possible; and Audrey persuaded her husband to take advantage of a cliff which rose uncommonly high above the dried bed of a former tributary of the Canadian River. He did not like the rocky cast of the place, but allowed himself to be overruled this once; leading the animals sullenly toward the protecting slope, which the nature of the ground would not allow the wagon to approach.

Audrey, examining the rocks near the wagon, meanwhile noticed a singular sniffing on the part of the feeble old dog. Seizing a rifle, she followed his lead, and presently thanked her stars that she had forestalled Walker in her discovery. For there, snugly nested in the gap between two boulders, was a sight it would have done him no good to see. Visible only as one convoluted expanse, but perhaps comprising as many as three or four separate units, was a mass of lazy wriggling which could not be other than a brood of new-born rattlesnakes.

Anxious to save Walker from a trying shock, Audrey did not hesitate to act, but took the gun firmly by the barrel and brought the butt down again and again upon the writhing objects. Her own sense of loathing was great, but it did not amount to a real fear. Finally she saw that her task was done, and turned to cleanse the improvised bludgeon in the red sand and dry, dead grass near by. She must, she reflected, cover the nest up before Walker got back from tethering the mules. Old Wolf, tottering relic of mixed shepherd and coyote ancestry that he was, had vanished, and she feared he had gone to fetch his master.

Footsteps at that instant proved her fear well founded. A second more, and Walker had seen everything. Audrey made a move to catch him if he should faint, but he did no more than sway. Then the look of pure fright on his bloodless face turned slowly to something like mingled awe and anger, and he began to upbraid his wife in trembling tones.

"Gawd's sake, Aud, but why'd ye go for to do that? Hain't ye heerd all the things they've been tellin' about this snake-devil Yig? Ye'd ought to a told me, and we'd a moved on. Don't ye know they's a devil-god what gets even if ye hurts his children? What for d'ye think the Injuns all dances and beats their drums in the fall about? This land's under a curse, I tell ye — nigh every soul we've a-talked to sence we come in's said the same. Yig rules here, an' he comes out every fall for to git his victims and turn 'em into snakes. Why, Aud, they won't none of them Injuns acrost the Canayjin kill a snake for love nor money!

"Gawd knows what ye done to yourself, gal, a-stompin' out a hull brood o' Yig's chillen. He'll git ye, sure, sooner or later, unlessen I kin buy a charm offen some o' the Injun medicine-men. He'll git ye, Aud, as sure's they's a Gawd in heaven — he'll come outa the night and turn ye into a crawlin' spotted snake!"

All the rest of the journey Walker kept up the frightened reproofs and prophecies. They crossed the Canadian near Newcastle, and soon afterward met with the first of the real plains Indians they had seen — a party of blanketed Wichitas, whose leader talked freely under the spell of the whiskey offered him, and taught poor Walker a long-winded protective charm against Yig in exchange for a quart bottle of the same inspiring fluid. By the end of the week the chosen site in the Wichita country was reached, and the Davises made haste to trace their boundaries and perform the spring ploughing before even beginning the construction of a cabin.

The region was flat, drearily windy, and sparse of natural vegetation, but promised great fertility under cultivation. Occasional outcroppings of granite diversified a soil of decomposed red sandstone, and here and there a great flat rock would stretch along the surface of the ground like a man-made floor. There seemed to be a very few snakes, or possible dens for them; so Audrey at last persuaded Walker to build the one-room cabin over a vast, smooth slab of exposed stone. With such a flooring and with a good-sized fireplace the wettest weather might be defied — though it soon became evident that dampness was no salient quality of the district. Logs were hauled in the wagon from the nearest belt of woods, many miles toward the Wichita Mountains.

Walker built his wide-chimneyed cabin and crude barn with the aid of some of the other settlers, though the nearest one was over a mile away. In turn, he helped his helpers at similar house-raisings, so that many ties of friendship sprang up between the new neighbours. There was no town worthy the name nearer than El Reno, on the railway thirty miles or more to the northeast; and before many weeks had passed, the people of the section had become very cohesive despite the wideness of their scattering. The Indians, a few of whom had begun to settle down on ranches, were for the most part harmless, though somewhat quarrelsome when fired by the liquid stimulation which found its way to them despite all government bans.

Of all the neighbours the Davises found Joe and Sally Compton, who likewise hailed from Arkansas, the most helpful and congenial. Sally is still alive, known now as Grandma Compton; and her son Clyde, then an infant in arms, has become one of the leading men of the state. Sally and Audrey used to visit each other often, for their cabins were only two miles apart; and in the long spring and summer afternoons they exchanged many a tale of old Arkansas and many a rumour about the new country.

Sally was very sympathetic about Walker's weakness regarding snakes, but perhaps did more to aggravate than cure the parallel nervousness which Audrey was acquiring through his incessant praying and prophesying about the curse of Yig. She was uncommonly full of gruesome snake stories, and produced a direfully strong impression with her acknowledged masterpiece — the tale of a man in Scott County who had been bitten by a whole horde of rattlers at once, and had swelled so monstrously from poison that his body had finally burst with a pop. Needless to say, Audrey did not repeat this anecdote to her husband, and she implored the Comptons to beware of starting it on the rounds of the countryside. It is to Joe's and Sally's credit that they heeded this plea with the utmost fidelity.

Walker did his corn-planting early, and in midsummer improved his time by harvesting a fair crop of the native grass of the region. With the help of Joe Compton he dug a well which gave a moderate supply of very good water, though he planned to sink an artesian later on. He did not run into many serious snake scares, and made his land as inhospitable as possible for wriggling visitors. Every now and then he rode over to the cluster of thatched, conical huts which formed the main village of the Wichitas, and talked long with the old men and shamans about the snake-god and how to nullify his wrath. Charms were always ready in exchange for whiskey, but much of the information he got was far from reassuring.

Yig was a great god. He was bad medicine. He did not forget things. In the autumn his children were hungry and wild, and Yig was hungry and wild, too. All the tribes made medicine against Yig when the corn harvest came. They gave him some corn, and danced in proper regalia to the sound of whistle, rattle, and drum. They kept the drums pounding to drive Yig away, and called down the aid of Tir, whose children men are, even as the snakes are Yig's children. It was bad that the squaw of Davis killed the children of Yig. Let Davis say the charms many times when the corn harvest comes. Yig is Yig. Yig is a great god.

By the time the corn harvest did come, Walker had succeeded in getting his wife into a deplorably jumpy state. His prayers and borrowed incantations came to be a nuisance; and when the autumn rites of the Indians began, there was always a distant wind-borne pounding of tom-toms to lend an added background of the sinister. It was maddening to have the muffled clatter always stealing over the wide red plains. Why would it never stop? Day and night, week on week, it was always going in exhaustless relays, as persistently as the red dusty winds that carried it. Audrey loathed it more than her husband did, for he saw in it a compensating element of protection. It was with this sense of a mighty, intangible bulwark against evil that he got in his corn crop and prepared cabin and stable for the coming winter.

The autumn was abnormally warm, and except for their primitive cookery the Davises found scant use for the stone fireplace Walker had built with such care. Something in the unnaturalness of the hot dust-clouds preyed on the nerves of all the settlers, but most of all on Audrey's and Walker's. The notions of a hovering snake-curse and the weird, endless rhythm of the distant Indian drums formed a bad combination which any added element of the bizarre went far to render utterly unendurable.

Notwithstanding this strain, several festive gatherings were held at one or another of the cabins after the crops were reaped; keeping naively alive in modernity those curious rites of the harvest-home which are as old as human agriculture itself. Lafayette Smith, who came from southern Missouri and had a cabin about three miles east of Walker's, was a very passable fiddler; and his tunes did much to make the celebrants forget the monotonous beating of the distant tom-toms. Then Hallowe'en drew near, and the settlers planned another frolic — this time, had they but known it, of a lineage older than even agriculture; the dread Witch-Sabbath of the primal pre-Aryans, kept alive through ages in the midnight blackness of secret woods, and still hinting at vague terrors under its latter-day mask of comedy and lightness. Hallowe'en was to fall on a Thursday, and the neighbours agreed to gather for their first revel at the Davis cabin.

It was on that thirty-first of October that the warm spell broke. The morning was grey and leaden, and by noon the incessant winds had changed from searingness to rawness. People shivered all the more because they were not prepared for the chill, and Walker Davis' old dog Wolf dragged himself wearily indoors to a place beside the hearth. But the distant drums still thumped on, nor were the white citizenry less inclined to pursue their chosen rites. As early as four in the afternoon the wagons began to arrive at Walker's cabin; and in the evening, after a memorable barbecue, Lafayette Smith's fiddle inspired a very fair-sized company to great feats of saltatory grotesqueness in the one good-sized but crowded room. The younger folk indulged in the amiable inanities proper to the season, and now and then old Wolf would howl with doleful and spine-tickling ominousness at some especially spectral strain from Lafayette's squeaky violin — a device he had never heard before. Mostly, though, this battered veteran slept through the merriment; for he was past the age of active interests and lived largely in his dreams. Tom and Jennie Rigby had brought their collie Zeke along, but the canines did not fraternise. Zeke seemed strangely uneasy over something, and nosed around curiously all the evening.

Audrey and Walker made a fine couple on the floor, and Grandma Compton still likes to recall her impression of their dancing that night. Their worries seemed forgotten for the nonce, and Walker was shaved and trimmed into a surprising degree of spruceness. By ten o'clock all hands were healthily tired, and the guests began to depart family by family with many handshakings and bluff assurances of what a fine time everybody had had. Tom and Jennie thought Zeke's eerie howls as he followed them to their wagon were marks of regret at having to go home; though Audrey said it must be the far-away tom-toms which annoyed him, for the distant thumping was surely ghastly enough after the merriment within.

The night was bitterly cold, and for the first time Walker put a great log in the fireplace and banked it with ashes to keep it smouldering till morning. Old Wolf dragged himself within the ruddy glow and lapsed into his customary coma. Audrey and Walker, too tired to think of charms or curses, tumbled into the rough pine bed and were asleep before the cheap alarm-clock on the mantel had ticked out three minutes. And from far away, the rhythmic pounding of those hellish tom-toms still pulsed on the chill night-wind.

Dr. McNeill paused here and removed his glasses, as if a blurring of the objective world might make the reminiscent vision clearer.

"You'll soon appreciate," he said, "that I had a great deal of difficulty in piecing out all that happened after the guests left. There were times, though — at first — when I was able to make a try at it." After a moment of silence he went on with the tale:

Audrey had terrible dreams of Yig, who appeared to her in the guise of Satan as depicted in cheap engravings she had seen. It was, indeed, from an absolute ecstasy of nightmare that she started suddenly awake to find Walker already conscious and sitting up in bed. He seemed to be listening intently to something, and silenced her with a whisper when she began to ask what had roused him.

"Hark, Aud!" he breathed. "Don't ye hear somethin' a-singin' and buzzin' and rustlin'? D'ye reckon it's the fall crickets?"

Certainly, there was distinctly audible within the cabin such a sound as he had described. Audrey tried to analyse it, and was impressed with some element at once horrible and familiar, which hovered just outside the rim of her memory. And beyond it all, waking a hideous thought, the monotonous beating of the distant tom-toms came incessantly across the black plains on which a cloudy half-moon had set.

"Walker — s'pose it's — the — the — curse o' Yig?"

She could feel him tremble.

"No, gal, I don't reckon he comes that away. He's shapen like a man, except ye look at him clost. That's what Chief Grey Eagle says. This here's some varmints come in outen the cold — not crickets, I calc'late, but summat like 'em. I'd orter git up and stomp 'em out afore they make much headway or git at the cupboard."

He rose, felt for the lantern that hung within easy reach, and rattled the tin match-box nailed to the wall beside it. Audrey sat up in bed and watched the flare of the match grow into the steady glow of the lantern. Then, as their eyes began to take in the whole of the room, the crude rafters shook with the frenzy of their simultaneous shriek. For the flat, rocky floor, revealed in the new-born illumination, was one seething, brown-speckled mass of wriggling rattlesnakes, slithering toward the fire, and even now turning their loathsome heads to menace the fright-blasted lantern-bearer.

It was only for an instant that Audrey saw the things. The reptiles were of every size, of uncountable numbers, and apparently of several varieties; and even as she looked, two or three of them reared their heads as if to strike at Walker. She did not faint — it was Walker's crash to the floor that extinguished the lantern and plunged her into blackness. He had not screamed a second time — fright had paralysed him, and he fell as if shot by a silent arrow from no mortal's bow. To Audrey the entire world seemed to whirl about fantastically, mingling with the nightmare from which she had started.

Voluntary motion of any sort was impossible, for will and the sense of reality had left her. She fell back inertly on her pillow, hoping that she would wake soon. No actual sense of what had happened penetrated her mind for some time. Then, little by little, the suspicion that she was really awake began to dawn on her; and she was convulsed with a mounting blend of panic and grief which made her long to shriek out despite the inhibiting spell which kept her mute.

Walker was gone, and she had not been able to help him. He had died of snakes, just as the old witch-woman had predicted when he was a little boy. Poor Wolf had not been able to help, either — probably he had not even awaked from his senile stupor. And now the crawling things must be coming for her, writhing closer and closer every moment in the dark, perhaps even now twining slipperily about the bedposts and oozing up over the coarse woollen blankets. Unconsciously she crept under the clothes and trembled.

It must be the curse of Yig. He had sent his monstrous children on All-Hallows' Night, and they had taken Walker first. Why was that — wasn't he innocent enough? Why not come straight for her — hadn't she killed those little rattlers alone?

Then she thought of the curse's form as told by the Indians. She wouldn't be killed — just turned to a spotted snake. Ugh! So she would be like those things she had glimpsed on the floor — those things which Yig had sent to get her and enroll her among their number! She tried to mumble a charm that Walker had taught her, but found she could not utter a single sound.

The noisy ticking of the alarm-clock sounded above the maddening beat of the distant tom-toms. The snakes were taking a long time — did they mean to delay on purpose to play on her nerves? Every now and then she thought she felt a steady, insidious pressure on the bedclothes, but each time it turned out to be only the automatic twitchings of her overwrought nerves. The clock ticked on in the dark, and a change came slowly over her thoughts.

Those snakes couldn't have taken so long! They couldn't be Yig's messengers after all, but just natural rattlers that were nested below the rock and had been drawn there by the fire. They weren't coming for her, perhaps — perhaps they had sated themselves on poor Walker. Where were they now? Gone? Coiled by the fire? Still crawling over the prone corpse of their victim? The clock ticked, and the distant drums throbbed on.

At the thought of her husband's body lying there in the pitch blackness a thrill of purely physical horror passed over Audrey. That story of Sally Compton's about the man back in Scott County! He, too, had been bitten by a whole bunch of rattlesnakes, and what had happened to him? The poison had rotted the flesh and swelled the whole corpse, and in the end the bloated thing had burst horribly—burst horribly with a detestable popping noise. Was that what was happening to Walker down there on the rock floor? Instinctively she felt she had begun to listen for something too terrible even to name to herself.

The clock ticked on, keeping a kind of mocking, sardonic time with the far-off drumming that the night-wind brought. She wished it were a striking clock, so that she could know how long this eldritch vigil must last. She cursed the toughness of fibre that kept her from fainting, and wondered what sort of relief the dawn could bring, after all. Probably neighbours would pass—no doubt somebody would call—would they find her still sane? Was she still sane now?

Morbidly listening, Audrey all at once became aware of something which she had to verify with every effort of her will before she could believe it; and which, once verified, she did not know whether to welcome or dread. The distant beating of the Indian tom-toms had ceased. They had always maddened her—but had not Walker regarded them as a bulwark against nameless evil from outside the universe? What were some of those things he had repeated to her in whispers after talking with Grey Eagle and the Wichita medicine-men?

She did not relish this new and sudden silence, after all! There was something sinister about it. The loud-ticking clock seemed abnormal in its new loneliness. Capable at last of conscious motion, she shook the covers from her face and looked into the darkness toward the window. It must have cleared after the moon set, for she saw the square aperture distinctly against the background of stars.

Then without warning came that shocking, unutterable sound—ugh!—that dull, putrid pop of cleft skin and escaping poison in the dark. God!—Sally's story—that obscene stench, and this gnawing, clawing silence! It was too much. The bonds of muteness snapped, and the black night waxed reverberant with Audrey's screams of stark, unbridled frenzy.

Consciousness did not pass away with the shock. How merciful if only it had! Amidst the echoes of her shrieking Audrey still saw the star-sprinkled square of window ahead, and heard the doom-boding ticking of that frightful clock. Did she hear another sound? Was that square window still a perfect square? She was in no condition to weigh the evidence of her senses or distinguish between fact and hallucination.

No—that window was not a perfect square. Something had encroached on the lower edge. Nor was the ticking of the clock the only sound in the room. There was, beyond dispute, a heavy breathing neither her own nor poor Wolf's. Wolf slept very silently, and his wakeful wheezing was unmistakable. Then Audrey saw against the stars the black, daemoniac silhouette of something anthropoid—the undulant bulk of a gigantic head and shoulders fumbling slowly toward her.

"Y'aaaah! Y'aaaah! Go away! Go away! Go away, snake-devil! Go 'way, Yig! I didn't mean to kill 'em—I was feared he'd be scairt of 'em. Don't, Yig, don't! I didn't go for to hurt yore chillen—don't come nigh me—don't change me into no spotted snake!"

But the half-formless head and shoulders only lurched onward toward the bed, very silently.

Everything snapped at once inside Audrey's head, and in a second she had turned from a cowering child to a raging madwoman. She knew where the axe was—hung against the wall on those pegs near the lantern. It was within easy reach, and she could find it in the dark. Before she was conscious of anything further it was in her hands, and she was creeping toward the foot of the bed—toward the monstrous head and shoulders that every moment groped their way nearer. Had there been any light, the look on her face would not have been pleasant to see.

"Take that, you! And that, and that, and that!"

She was laughing shrilly now, and her cackles mounted higher as she saw that the starlight beyond the window was yielding to the dim prophetic pallor of coming dawn.

Dr. McNeill wiped the perspiration from his forehead and put on his glasses again. I waited for him to resume, and as he kept silent I spoke softly.

"She lived? She was found? Was it ever explained?"

The doctor cleared his throat.

"Yes—she lived, in a way. And it was explained. I told you there was no bewitchment—only cruel, pitiful, material horror."

It was Sally Compton who had made the discovery. She had ridden over to the Davis cabin the next afternoon to talk over the party with Audrey, and had seen no smoke from the chimney. That was queer. It had turned very warm again, yet Audrey was usually cooking something at that hour. The mules were making hungry-sounding noises in the barn, and there was no sign of old Wolf sunning himself in the accustomed spot by the door.

Altogether, Sally did not like the look of the place, so was very timid and hesitant as she dismounted and knocked. She got no answer but waited some time before trying the crude door of split logs. The lock, it appeared, was unfastened; and she slowly pushed her way in. Then, perceiving what was there, she reeled back, gasped, and clung to the jamb to preserve her balance.

A terrible odour had welled out as she opened the door, but that was not what had stunned her. It was what she had seen. For within that shadowy cabin monstrous things had happened and three shocking objects remained on the floor to awe and baffle the beholder.

Near the burned-out fireplace was the great dog—purple decay on the skin left bare by mange and old age, and the whole carcass burst by the puffing effect of rattlesnake poison. It must have been bitten by a veritable legion of the reptiles.

To the right of the door was the axe-hacked remnant of what had been a man—clad in a nightshirt, and with the shattered bulk of a lantern clenched in one hand. He was totally free from any sign of snake-bite. Near him lay the ensanguined axe, carelessly discarded.

And wriggling flat on the floor was a loathsome, vacant-eyed thing that had been a woman, but was now only a mute mad caricature. All that this thing could do was to hiss, and hiss, and hiss.

Both the doctor and I were brushing cold drops from our foreheads by this time. He poured something from a flask on his desk, took a nip, and handed another glass to me. I could only suggest tremulously and stupidly:

"So Walker had only fainted that first time — the screams roused him, and the axe did the rest?"

"Yes." Dr. McNeill's voice was low. "But he met his death from snakes just the same. It was his fear working in two ways — it made him faint, and it made him fill his wife with the wild stories that caused her to strike out when she thought she saw the snake-devil."

I thought for a moment.

"And Audrey — wasn't it queer how the curse of Yig seemed to work itself out on her? I suppose the impression of hissing snakes had been fairly ground into her."

"Yes. There were lucid spells at first, but they got to be fewer and fewer. Her hair came white at the roots as it grew, and later began to fall out. The skin grew blotchy, and when she died — "

I interrupted with a start.

"Died? Then what was that — that thing downstairs?"

McNeill spoke gravely.

"That is what was born to her three-quarters of a year afterward. There were three more of them — two were even worse — but this is the only one that lived."

Ibid.

1,700-WORD SATIRICAL ESSAY; 1928.

H.P. Lovecraft included this humourous little faux-disquisition in a letter to Maurice Moe in the summer of 1928, shortly after he ghostwrote "The Curse of Yig" for Zealia Bishop; when exactly it was written is unknown.

Moe, when he received it, enjoyed it enormously, and considered submitting it to a national magazine on Lovecraft's behalf; but this was never done. It was not published until shortly after Lovecraft's death, when it appeared in the January 1938 issue of George W. Macauley's amateur journal, the O-Wash-Ta-Nong.

". . . as Ibid says in his famous Lives of the Poets."

— FROM A STUDENT THEME.

The erroneous idea that Ibid is the author of the *Lives* is so frequently met with, even among those pretending to a degree of culture, that it is worth correcting. It should be a matter of general knowledge that Cf. is responsible for this work. Ibid's masterpiece, on the other hand, was the famous Op. Cit. wherein all the significant undercurrents of Graeco-Roman expression were crystallised once for all — and with admirable acuteness, notwithstanding the surprisingly late date at which Ibid wrote. There is a false report — very commonly reproduced in modern books prior to von Schweinkopf's monumental Geschichte der Ostrogothen in Italien — that Ibid was a Romanised Visigoth of Ataulf's horde who settled in Placentia about 410 A. D. The contrary cannot be too strongly emphasised; for von Schweinkopf, and since his time Littlewit[1] and Bêtenoir[2] have shewn with irrefutable force that this strikingly isolated

1 *Rome and Byzantium: A Study in Survival (Waukesha, 1869), Vol. XX, p. 598.*

2 *Influences Romains dans le Moyen Age (Fond du Lac, 1877), Vol. XV, p. 720.*

figure was a genuine Roman — or at least as genuine a Roman as that degenerate and mongrelised age could produce — of whom one might well say what Gibbon said of Boethius, "that he was the last whom Cato or Tully could have acknowledged for their countryman." He was, like Boethius and nearly all the eminent men of his age, of the great Anician family, and traced his genealogy with much exactitude and self-satisfaction to all the heroes of the republic. His full name — long and pompous according to the custom of an age which had lost the trinomial simplicity of classic Roman nomenclature — is stated by von Schweinkopf[1] to have been Caius Anicius Magnus Furius Camillus Aemilianus Cornelius Valerius Pompeius Julius Ibidus; though Littlewit [4] rejects Aemilianus and adds Claudius Deciusfunianus; whilst Bêtenoir[2] differs radically, giving the full name as Magnus Furius Camillus Aurelius Antoninus Flavius Anicius Petronius Valentinianus Aegidus Ibidus.

The eminent critic and biographer was born in the year 486, shortly after the extinction of the Roman rule in Gaul by Clovis. Rome and Ravenna are rivals for the honour of his birth, though it is certain that he received his rhetorical and philosophical training in the schools of Athens — the extent of whose suppression by Theodosius a century before is grossly exaggerated by the superficial. In 512, under the benign rule of the Ostrogoth Theodoric, we behold him as a teacher of rhetoric at Rome, and in 516 he held the consulship together with Pompilius Numantius Bombastes Marcellinus Deodamnatus. Upon the death of Theodoric in 526, Ibidus retired from public life to compose his celebrated work (whose pure Ciceronian style is as remarkable a case of classic atavism as is the verse of Claudius Claudianus, who flourished a century before Ibidus); but he was later recalled to scenes of pomp to act as court rhetorician for Theodatus, nephew of Theodoric.

Upon the usurpation of Vitiges, Ibidus fell into disgrace and was for a time imprisoned; but the coming of the Byzantine-Roman army under Belisarius soon restored him to liberty and honours. Throughout the siege of Rome he served bravely in the army of the defenders, and afterward followed the eagles of Belisarius to Alba, Porto, and Centumcellae. After the Frankish siege of Milan, Ibidus was chosen to accompany the learned Bishop Datius to Greece, and resided with him at Corinth in the year 539. About 541 he removed to Constantinopolis, where he received every mark of imperial favour both from Justinianus and Justinus the Second. The Emperors Tiberius and Maurice did kindly honour to his old age, and contributed much to his immortality — especially Maurice, whose delight it was to trace his ancestry to old Rome notwithstanding his birth at Arabiscus, in Cappadocia. It was Maurice who, in the poet's 101st year, secured the adoption of his work as a textbook in the schools of the empire, an honour which proved a fatal tax on the aged rhetorician's emotions, since he passed away peacefully at his home near the church of St. Sophia on the sixth day before the Kalends of September, A. D. 587, in the 102nd year of his age.

His remains, notwithstanding the troubled state of Italy, were taken to Ravenna for interment; but being interred in the suburb of Classe, were exhumed and ridiculed by the Lombard Duke of Spoleto, who took his skull to King Autharis for use as a wassail-bowl. Ibid's skull was proudly handed down from king to king of the Lombard line. Upon the capture of Pavia by Charlemagne in 774, the skull was seized from the tottering Desiderius and carried in the train of the Frankish conqueror. It was from this vessel, indeed, that Pope Leo administered the royal unction which made of the hero-nomad a Holy Roman Emperor. Charlemagne took Ibid's skull to his capital at Aix, soon afterward presenting it to his Saxon teacher Alcuin, upon whose death in 804 it was sent to Alcuin's kinsfolk in England.

William the Conqueror, finding it in an abbey niche where the pious family of Alcuin had placed it (believing it to be the skull of a saint[3] who had miraculously annihilated the Lombards by his prayers), did reverence to its osseous antiquity; and even the rough soldiers of Cromwell, upon destroying Ballylough Abbey in Ireland in 1650 (it having been secretly transported thither by a devout Papist in 1539, upon Henry VII's dissolution of the English monasteries), declined to offer violence to a relic so venerable.

It was captured by the private soldier Read-'em-and-Weep Hopkins, who not long after traded it to Rest-in-Jehovah Stubbs for a quid of new Virginia weed. Stubbs, upon sending forth his son Zerubbabel to seek his fortune in New England in 1661 (for he thought ill of the Restoration atmosphere for a pious young yeoman), gave him St. Ibid's — or rather Brother Ibid's, for he abhorred all that was Popish — skull as a talisman. Upon landing in Salem Zerubbabel set it up in his cupboard beside the chimney, he having built a modest house near the town pump. However, he had not been wholly unaffected by the Restoration influence; and having become addicted to gaming, lost the skull to one Epenetus Dexter, a visiting freeman of Providence.

It was in the house of Dexter, in the northern part of the town near the present intersection of North Main and Olney Streets, on the occasion of Canonchet's raid of March 30, 1676, during King Philip's War; and the astute sachem, recognising it at once as a thing of singular venerableness and dignity, sent it as a symbol of alliance to a faction of the Pequots in Connecticut with whom he was negotiating. On April 4 he was captured by the colonists and soon after executed, but the austere head of Ibid continued on its wanderings.

The Pequots, enfeebled by a previous war, could give the now stricken Narragansetts no assistance; and in 1680 a Dutch furtrader of Albany, Petrus van Schaack, secured the

1 *Following Procopius, Goth. x.y.z.*

2 Following Jornandes, Codex Murat. xxj. 4144.

3 *Not till the appearance of von Schweinkopf's work in 1797 were St. Ibid and the rhetorician properly re-identified.*

distinguished cranium for the modest sum of two guilders, he having recognised its value from the half-effaced inscription carved in Lombardic minuscules (palaeography, it might be explained, was one of the leading accomplishments of New-Netherland fur-traders of the seventeenth century).

From van Schaack, sad to say, the relic was stolen in 1683 by a French trader, Jean Grenier, whose Popish zeal recognised the features of one whom he had been taught at his mother's knee to revere as St. Ibide. Grenier, fired with virtuous rage at the possession of this holy symbol by a Protestant, crushed van Schaack's head one night with an axe and escaped to the north with his booty; soon, however, being robbed and slain by the half-breed voyageur Michel Savard, who took the skull — despite the illiteracy which prevented his recognising it — to add to a collection of similar but more recent material.

Upon his death in 1701 his half-breed son Pierre traded it among other things to some emissaries of the Sacs and Foxes, and it was found outside the chief's tepee a generation later by Charles de Langlade, founder of the trading post at Green Bay, Wisconsin. De Langlade regarded this sacred object with proper veneration and ransomed it at the expense of many glass beads; yet after his time it found itself in many other hands, being traded to settlements at the head of Lake Winnebago, to tribes around Lake Mendota, and finally, early in the nineteenth century, to one Solomon Juneau, a Frenchman, at the new trading post of Milwaukee on the Menominee River and the shore of Lake Michigan.

Later traded to Jacques Caboche, another settler, it was in 1850 lost in a game of chess or poker to a newcomer named Hans Zimmerman; being used by him as a beer-stein until one day, under the spell of its contents, he suffered it to roll from his front stoop to the prairie path before his home — where, falling into the burrow of a prairie-dog, it passed beyond his power of discovery or recovery upon his awaking.

So for generations did the sainted skull of Caius Anicius Magnus Furius Camillus Aemilianus Cornelius Valerius Pompeius Julius Ibidus, consul of Rome, favourite of emperors, and saint of the Romish church, lie hidden beneath the soil of a growing town. At first worshipped with dark rites by the prairie-dogs, who saw in it a deity sent from the upper world, it afterward fell into dire neglect as the race of simple, artless burrowers succumbed before the onslaught of the conquering Aryan. Sewers came, but they passed by it. Houses went up — 2303 of them, and more — and at last one fateful night a titan thing occurred. Subtle Nature, convulsed with a spiritual ecstasy, like the froth of that region's quondam beverage, laid low the lofty and heaved high the humble — and behold! In the roseal dawn the burghers of Milwaukee rose to find a former prairie turned to a highland! Vast and far-reaching was the great upheaval. Subterrene arcana, hidden for years, came at last to the light. For there, full in the rifted roadway, lay bleached and tranquil in bland, saintly, and consular pomp the dome-like skull of Ibid!

The Dunwich Horror.

17,200-WORD NOVELLA; 1928.

The Dunwich Horror *is one of the more controversial of Lovecraft's later tales. It lends itself particularly well to a good-vs.-evil interpretation, and it's therefore not surprising that it was one of August Derleth's favorites. It also depends far more on supernatural elements than other, arguably better, Lovecraft stories from this period; one of the signal characteristics of Lovecraft's best stories is a sickening plausibility — a sense that the events of the story can be explained not merely by ghosts and supernatural fancies, but by real material beings and entities that our feeble senses can just barely begin to perceive. It's hard to see how that's the case with this story.*

Nonetheless, The Dunwich Horror *is a gripping tale, unpretentiously pulpy and a truly satisfying read. In fact, it may have been written as an experiment in balancing literary quality with pulp action writing, with an eye toward getting more stories into* Weird Tales *and other pulps; certainly it is far more reminiscent of one of his ghost-written tales (especially "The Curse of Yig," written a few months earlier) than of his own later by-lined work. Indeed,* The Dunwich Horror *borrows several plot elements from "The Curse of Yig," including one very important one that cannot be discussed here without spoiling the ending.*

Written in August of 1928, The Dunwich Horror *was of course pounced upon by Farnsworth Wright the very instant it was submitted to* Weird Tales. *It was also published quite promptly, in the April 1929 issue of the magazine.*

Gorgons and Hydras, and Chimaeras — dire stories of Celaeno and the Harpies — may reproduce themselves in the brain of superstition — but they were there before. They are transcripts, types — the archetypes are in us, and eternal. How else should the recital of that which we know in a waking sense to be false come to affect us at all? Is it that we naturally conceive terror from such objects, considered in their capacity of being able to inflict upon us bodily injury? O, least of all! These terrors are of older standing. They date beyond body — or without the body, they would have been the same . . . That the kind of fear here treated is purely spiritual — that it is strong in proportion as it is objectless on earth, that it predominates in the period of our sinless infancy — are difficulties the solution of which might afford some probable insight into our ante-mundane condition, and a peep at least into the shadowland of pre-existence.

— CHARLES LAMB: WITCHES AND OTHER NIGHT-FEARS.

I.

When a traveller in north central Massachusetts takes the wrong fork at the junction of Aylesbury pike just beyond Dean's Corners he comes upon a lonely and curious country.

The ground gets higher, and the brier-bordered stone walls press closer and closer against the ruts of the dusty, curving road. The trees of the frequent forest belts seem too large, and the wild weeds, brambles and grasses attain a luxuriance not often found in settled regions. At the same time the planted fields appear singularly few and barren; while the sparsely scattered houses wear a surprisingly uniform aspect of age, squalor, and dilapidation.

Without knowing why, one hesitates to ask directions from the gnarled solitary figures spied now and then on crumbling doorsteps or on the sloping, rock-strewn meadows. Those figures are so silent and furtive that one feels somehow confronted by forbidden things, with which it would be better to have nothing to do. When a rise in the road brings the mountains in view above the deep woods, the feeling of strange uneasiness is increased. The summits are too rounded and symmetrical to give a sense of comfort and naturalness, and sometimes the sky silhouettes with especial clearness the queer circles of tall stone pillars with which most of them are crowned.

Gorges and ravines of problematical depth intersect the way, and the crude wooden bridges always seem of dubious safety. When the road dips again there are stretches of marshland that one instinctively dislikes, and indeed almost fears at evening when unseen whippoorwills chatter and the fireflies come out in abnormal profusion to dance to the raucous, creepily insistent rhythms of stridently piping bull-frogs. The thin, shining line of the Miskatonic's upper reaches has an oddly serpent-like suggestion as it winds close to the feet of the domed hills among which it rises.

As the hills draw nearer, one heeds their wooded sides more than their stone-crowned tops. Those sides loom up so darkly and precipitously that one wishes they would keep their distance, but there is no road by which to escape them. Across a covered bridge one sees a small village huddled between the stream and the vertical slope of Round Mountain, and wonders at the cluster of rotting gambrel roofs bespeaking an earlier architectural period than that of the neighbouring region. It is not reassuring to see, on a closer glance, that most of the houses are deserted and falling to ruin, and that the broken-steepled church now harbours the one slovenly mercantile establishment of the hamlet. One dreads to trust the tenebrous tunnel of the bridge, yet there is no way to avoid it. Once across, it is hard to prevent the impression of a faint, malign odour about the village street, as of the massed mould and decay of centuries. It is always a relief to get clear of the place, and to follow the narrow road around the base of the hills and across the level country beyond till it rejoins the Aylesbury pike. Afterwards one sometimes learns that one has been through Dunwich.

Outsiders visit Dunwich as seldom as possible, and since a certain season of horror all the signboards pointing towards it have been taken down. The scenery, judged by an ordinary aesthetic canon, is more than commonly beautiful; yet there is no influx of artists or summer tourists. Two centuries ago, when talk of witch-blood, Satan-worship, and strange forest presences was not laughed at, it was the custom to give reasons for avoiding the locality. In our sensible age — since the Dunwich horror of 1928 was hushed up by those who had the town's and the world's welfare at heart — people shun it without knowing exactly why. Perhaps one reason — though it cannot apply to uninformed strangers — is that the natives are now repellently decadent, having gone far along that path of retrogression so common in many New England backwaters. They have come to form a race by themselves, with the well-defined mental and physical stigmata of degeneracy and inbreeding. The average of their intelligence is woefully low, whilst their annals reek of overt viciousness and of half-hidden murders, incests, and deeds of almost unnameable violence and perversity. The old gentry, representing the two or three armigerous families which came from Salem in 1692, have kept somewhat above the general level of decay; though many branches are sunk into the sordid populace so deeply that only their names remain as a key to the origin they disgrace. Some of the Whateleys and Bishops still send their eldest sons to Harvard and Miskatonic, though those sons seldom return to the mouldering gambrel roofs under which they and their ancestors were born.

No one, even those who have the facts concerning the recent horror, can say just what is the matter with Dunwich; though old legends speak of unhallowed rites and conclaves of the Indians, amidst which they called forbidden shapes of shadow out of the great rounded hills, and made wild orgiastic prayers that were answered by loud crackings and rumblings from the ground below. In 1747 the Reverend Abijah Hoadley, newly come to the Congregational Church at Dunwich Village, preached a memorable sermon on the close presence of Satan and his imps; in which he said:

It must be allow'd, that these Blasphemies of an infernall Train of Daemons are Matters of too common Knowledge to be deny'd; the cursed Voices of Azazel and Buzrael, of Beelzebub and Belial, being heard now from under Ground by above a Score of credible Witnesses now living. I myself did not more than a Fortnight ago catch a very

The Dunwich Horror

by H. P. LOVECRAFT

"Oh, oh, great Gawd . . . that . . . that!"

Weird Tales, April 1929

plain Discourse of evill Powers in the Hill behind my House; wherein there were a Rattling and Rolling, Groaning, Screeching, and Hissing, such as no Things of this Earth could raise up, and which must needs have come from those Caves that only black Magick can discover, and only the Divell unlock.

Mr. Hoadley disappeared soon after delivering this sermon, but the text, printed in Springfield, is still extant. Noises in the hills continued to be reported from year to year, and still form a puzzle to geologists and physiographers.

Other traditions tell of foul odours near the hill-crowning circles of stone pillars, and of rushing airy presences to be heard faintly at certain hours from stated points at the bottom of the great ravines; while still others try to explain the Devil's Hop Yard — a bleak, blasted hillside where no tree, shrub, or grass-blade will grow. Then, too, the natives are mortally afraid of the numerous whippoorwills which grow vocal on warm nights. It is vowed that the birds are psychopomps lying in wait for the souls of the dying, and that they time their eerie cries in unison with the sufferer's struggling breath. If they can catch the fleeing soul when it leaves the body, they instantly flutter away chittering in daemoniac laughter; but if they fail, they subside gradually into a disappointed silence.

These tales, of course, are obsolete and ridiculous; because they come down from very old times. Dunwich is indeed ridiculously old — older by far than any of the communities within thirty miles of it. South of the village one may still spy the cellar walls and chimney of the ancient Bishop house, which was built before 1700; whilst the ruins of the mill at the falls, built in 1806, form the most modern piece of architecture to be seen. Industry did not flourish here, and the nineteenth-century factory movement proved short-lived. Oldest of all are the great rings of rough-hewn stone columns on the hilltops, but these are more generally attributed to the Indians than to the settlers. Deposits of skulls and bones, found within these circles and around the sizeable table-like rock on Sentinel Hill, sustain the popular belief that such spots were once the burial-places of the Pocumtucks; even though many ethnologists, disregarding the absurd improbability of such a theory, persist in believing the remains Caucasian.

II.

It was in the township of Dunwich, in a large and partly inhabited farmhouse set against a hillside four miles from the village and a mile and a half from any other dwelling, that Wilbur Whateley was born at 5 a.m. on Sunday, the second of February, 1913. This date was recalled because it was Candlemas, which people in Dunwich curiously observe under another name; and because the noises in the hills had sounded, and all the dogs of the countryside had barked persistently, throughout the night before. Less worthy of notice was the fact that the mother was one of the decadent Whateleys, a somewhat deformed, unattractive albino woman of thirty-five, living with an aged and half-insane father about whom the most frightful tales of wizardry had been whispered in his youth. Lavinia Whateley had no known husband, but according to the custom of the region made no attempt to disavow the child; concerning the other side of whose ancestry the country folk might—and did—speculate as widely as they chose. On the contrary, she seemed strangely proud of the dark, goatish-looking infant who formed such a contrast to her own sickly and pink-eyed albinism, and was heard to mutter many curious prophecies about its unusual powers and tremendous future.

Lavinia was one who would be apt to mutter such things, for she was a lone creature given to wandering amidst thunderstorms in the hills and trying to read the great odorous books which her father had inherited through two centuries of Whateleys, and which were fast falling to pieces with age and wormholes. She had never been to school, but was filled with disjointed scraps of ancient lore that Old Whateley had taught her. The remote farmhouse had always been feared because of Old Whateley's reputation for black magic, and the unexplained death by violence of Mrs Whateley when Lavinia was twelve years old had not helped to make the place popular. Isolated among strange influences, Lavinia was fond of wild and grandiose day-dreams and singular occupations; nor was her leisure much taken up by household cares in a home from which all standards of order and cleanliness had long since disappeared.

There was a hideous screaming which echoed above even the hill noises and the dogs' barking on the night Wilbur was born, but no known doctor or midwife presided at his coming. Neighbours knew nothing of him till a week afterward, when Old Whateley drove his sleigh through the snow into Dunwich Village and discoursed incoherently to the group of loungers at Osborne's general store. There seemed to be a change in the old man—an added element of furtiveness in the clouded brain which subtly transformed him from an object to a subject of fear—though he was not one to be perturbed by any common family event. Amidst it all he showed some trace of the pride later noticed in his daughter, and what he said of the child's paternity was remembered by many of his hearers years afterward.

"I dun't keer what folks think—ef Lavinny's boy looked like his pa, he wouldn't look like nothin' ye expeck. Ye needn't think the only folks is the folks hereabouts. Lavinny's read some, an' has seed some things the most o' ye only tell abaout. I calc'late her man is as good a husban' as ye kin find this side of Aylesbury; an' ef ye knowed as much abaout the hills as I dew, ye wouldn't ast no better church weddin' nor her'n. Let me tell ye suthin—some day yew folks'll hear a child o' Lavinny's a-callin' its father's name on the top o' Sentinel Hill!"

The only person who saw Wilbur during the first month of his life were old Zechariah Whateley, of the undecayed Whateleys, and Earl Sawyer's common-law wife, Mamie Bishop. Mamie's visit was frankly one of curiosity, and her subsequent tales did justice to her observations; but Zechariah came to lead a pair of Alderney cows which Old Whateley had bought of his son Curtis. This marked the beginning of a course of cattle-buying on the part of small Wilbur's family which ended only in 1928, when the Dunwich horror came and went; yet at no time did the ramshackle Whateley barn seem overcrowded with livestock. There came a period when people were curious enough to steal up and count the herd that grazed precariously on the steep hillside above the old farm-house, and they could never find more than ten or twelve anaemic, bloodless-looking specimens. Evidently some blight or distemper, perhaps sprung from the unwholesome pasturage or the diseased fungi and timbers of the filthy barn, caused a heavy mortality amongst the Whateley animals. Odd wounds or sores, having something of the aspect of incisions, seemed to afflict the visible cattle; and once or twice during the earlier months certain callers fancied they could discern similar sores about the throats of the grey, unshaven old man and his slatternly, crinkly-haired albino daughter.

In the spring after Wilbur's birth Lavinia resumed her customary rambles in the hills, bearing in her misproportioned arms the swarthy child. Public interest in the Whateleys subsided after most of the country folk had seen the baby, and no one bothered to comment on the swift development which that newcomer seemed every day to exhibit. Wilbur's growth was indeed phenomenal, for within three months of his birth he had attained a size and muscular power not usually found in infants under a full year of age. His motions and even his vocal sounds showed a restraint and deliberateness highly peculiar in an infant, and no one was really unprepared when, at seven months, he began to walk unassisted, with falterings which another month was sufficient to remove.

It was somewhat after this time—on Hallowe'en—that

a great blaze was seen at midnight on the top of Sentinel Hill where the old table-like stone stands amidst its tumulus of ancient bones. Considerable talk was started when Silas Bishop — of the undecayed Bishops — mentioned having seen the boy running sturdily up that hill ahead of his mother about an hour before the blaze was remarked. Silas was rounding up a stray heifer, but he nearly forgot his mission when he fleetingly spied the two figures in the dim light of his lantern. They darted almost noiselessly through the underbrush, and the astonished watcher seemed to think they were entirely unclothed. Afterwards he could not be sure about the boy, who may have had some kind of a fringed belt and a pair of dark trunks or trousers on. Wilbur was never subsequently seen alive and conscious without complete and tightly buttoned attire, the disarrangement or threatened disarrangement of which always seemed to fill him with anger and alarm. His contrast with his squalid mother and grandfather in this respect was thought very notable until the horror of 1928 suggested the most valid of reasons.

The next January gossips were mildly interested in the fact that "Lavinny's black brat" had commenced to talk, and at the age of only eleven months. His speech was somewhat remarkable both because of its difference from the ordinary accents of the region, and because it displayed a freedom from infantile lisping of which many children of three or four might well be proud. The boy was not talkative, yet when he spoke he seemed to reflect some elusive element wholly unpossessed by Dunwich and its denizens. The strangeness did not reside in what he said, or even in the simple idioms he used; but seemed vaguely linked with his intonation or with the internal organs that produced the spoken sounds. His facial aspect, too, was remarkable for its maturity; for though he shared his mother's and grandfather's chinlessness, his firm and precociously shaped nose united with the expression of his large, dark, almost Latin eyes to give him an air of quasi-adulthood and well-nigh preternatural intelligence. He was, however, exceedingly ugly despite his appearance of brilliancy; there being something almost goatish or animalistic about his thick lips, large-pored, yellowish skin, coarse crinkly hair, and oddly elongated ears. He was soon disliked even more decidedly than his mother and grandsire, and all conjectures about him were spiced with references to the bygone magic of Old Whateley, and how the hills once shook when he shrieked the dreadful name of Yog-Sothoth in the midst of a circle of stones with a great book open in his arms before him. Dogs abhorred the boy, and he was always obliged to take various defensive measures against their barking menace.

III.

Meanwhile old Whateley continued to buy cattle without measurably increasing the size of his herd. He also cut timber and began to repair the unused parts of his house — a spacious, peak-roofed affair whose rear end was buried entirely in the rocky hillside, and whose three least-ruined ground-floor rooms had always been sufficient for himself and his daughter.

There must have been prodigious reserves of strength in the old man to enable him to accomplish so much hard labour; and though he still babbled dementedly at times, his carpentry seemed to show the effects of sound calculation. It had already begun as soon as Wilbur was born, when one of the many tool sheds had been put suddenly in order, clapboarded, and fitted with a stout fresh lock. Now, in restoring the abandoned upper storey of the house, he was a no less thorough craftsman. His mania showed itself only in his tight boarding-up of all the windows in the reclaimed section — though many declared that it was a crazy thing to bother with the reclamation at all.

Less inexplicable was his fitting up of another downstairs room for his new grandson — a room which several callers saw, though no one was ever admitted to the closely-boarded upper storey. This chamber he lined with tall, firm shelving, along which he began gradually to arrange, in apparently careful order, all the rotting ancient books and parts of books which during his own day had been heaped promiscuously in odd corners of the various rooms.

"I made some use of 'em," he would say as he tried to mend a torn black-letter page with paste prepared on the rusty kitchen stove, "but the boy's fitten to make better use of 'em. He'd orter hev 'em as well so as he kin, for they're goin' to be all of his larnin'."

When Wilbur was a year and seven months old — in September of 1914 — his size and accomplishments were almost alarming. He had grown as large as a child of four, and was a fluent and incredibly intelligent talker. He ran freely about the fields and hills, and accompanied his mother on all her wanderings. At home he would pore diligently over the queer pictures and charts in his grandfather's books, while Old Whateley would instruct and catechize him through long, hushed afternoons. By this time the restoration of the house was finished, and those who watched it wondered why one of the upper windows had been made into a solid plank door. It was a window in the rear of the east gable end, close against the hill; and no one could imagine why a cleated wooden runway was built up to it from the ground. About the period of this work's completion people noticed that the old tool-house, tightly locked and windowlessly clapboarded since Wilbur's birth, had been abandoned again. The door swung listlessly open, and when Earl Sawyer once stepped within after a cattle-selling call on Old Whateley he was quite discomposed by the singular odour he encountered — such a stench, he averred, as he had never before smelt in all his life except near the Indian circles on the hills, and which could not come from anything sane or of this earth.

But then, the homes and sheds of Dunwich folk have never been remarkable for olfactory immaculateness.

The following months were void of visible events, save that everyone swore to a slow but steady increase in the mysterious hill noises. On May Eve of 1915 there were tremors which even the Aylesbury people felt, whilst the following Hallowe'en produced an underground rumbling queerly synchronized with bursts of flame—"them witch Whateleys' doin's"—from the summit of Sentinel Hill. Wilbur was growing up uncannily, so that he looked like a boy of ten as he entered his fourth year. He read avidly by himself now; but talked much less than formerly. A settled taciturnity was absorbing him, and for the first time people began to speak specifically of the dawning look of evil in his goatish face. He would sometimes mutter an unfamiliar jargon, and chant in bizarre rhythms which chilled the listener with a sense of unexplainable terror. The aversion displayed towards him by dogs had now become a matter of wide remark, and he was obliged to carry a pistol in order to traverse the countryside in safety. His occasional use of the weapon did not enhance his popularity amongst the owners of canine guardians.

The few callers at the house would often find Lavinia alone on the ground floor, while odd cries and footsteps resounded in the boarded-up second storey. She would never tell what her father and the boy were doing up there, though once she turned pale and displayed an abnormal degree of fear when a jocose fish-pedlar tried the locked door leading to the stairway. That pedlar told the store loungers at Dunwich Village that he thought he heard a horse stamping on that floor above. The loungers reflected, thinking of the door and runway, and of the cattle that so swiftly disappeared. Then they shuddered as they recalled tales of Old Whateley's youth, and of the strange things that are called out of the earth when a bullock is sacrificed at the proper time to certain heathen gods. It had for some time been noticed that dogs had begun to hate and fear the whole Whateley place as violently as they hated and feared young Wilbur personally.

In 1917 the war came, and Squire Sawyer Whateley, as chairman of the local draft board, had hard work finding a quota of young Dunwich men fit even to be sent to development camp. The government, alarmed at such signs of wholesale regional decadence, sent several officers and medical experts to investigate; conducting a survey which New England newspaper readers may still recall. It was the publicity attending this investigation which set reporters on the track of the Whateleys, and caused the *Boston Globe* and *Arkham Advertiser* to print flamboyant Sunday stories of young Wilbur's precociousness, Old Whateley's black magic, and the shelves of strange books, the sealed second storey of the ancient farmhouse, and the weirdness of the whole region and its hill noises. Wilbur was four and a half then, and looked like a lad of fifteen. His lips and cheeks were fuzzy with a coarse dark down, and his voice had begun to break.

Earl Sawyer went out to the Whateley place with both sets of reporters and camera men, and called their attention to the queer stench which now seemed to trickle down from the sealed upper spaces. It was, he said, exactly like the smell he had found in the toolshed abandoned when the house was finally repaired; and like the faint odours which he sometimes thought he caught near the stone circle on the mountains. Dunwich folk read the stories when they appeared, and grinned over the obvious mistakes. They wondered, too, why the writers made so much of the fact that Old Whateley always paid for his cattle in gold pieces of extremely ancient date. The Whateleys had received their visitors with ill-concealed distaste, though they did not dare court further publicity by a violent resistance or refusal to talk.

IV.

For a decade the annals of the Whateleys sink indistinguishably into the general life of a morbid community used to their queer ways and hardened to their May Eve and All-Hallows orgies. Twice a year they would light fires on the top of Sentinel Hill, at which times the mountain rumblings would recur with greater and greater violence; while at all seasons there were strange and portentous doings at the lonely farm-house. In the course of time callers professed to hear sounds in the sealed upper storey even when all the family were downstairs, and they wondered how swiftly or how lingeringly a cow or bullock was usually sacrificed. There was talk of a complaint to the Society for the Prevention of Cruelty to Animals but nothing ever came of it, since Dunwich folk are never anxious to call the outside world's attention to themselves.

About 1923, when Wilbur was a boy of ten whose mind, voice, stature, and bearded face gave all the impressions of maturity, a second great siege of carpentry went on at the old house. It was all inside the sealed upper part, and from bits of discarded lumber people concluded that the youth and his grandfather had knocked out all the partitions and even removed the attic floor, leaving only one vast open void between the ground storey and the peaked roof. They had torn down the great central chimney, too, and fitted the rusty range with a flimsy outside tin stove-pipe.

In the spring after this event Old Whateley noticed the growing number of whippoorwills that would come out of Cold Spring Glen to chirp under his window at night. He seemed to regard the circumstance as one of great significance, and told the loungers at Osborn's that he thought his time had almost come.

"They whistle jest in tune with my breathin' naow," he said, "an' I guess they're gittin' ready to ketch my soul. They know it's a-goin' aout, an' dun't calc'late to miss it. Yew'll know, boys, arter I'm gone, whether they git me er not. Ef they dew, they'll keep up a-singin' an' laffin' till break o' day. Ef they dun't they'll kinder quiet daown like. I expeck them an' the souls they hunts fer hev some pretty tough tussles sometimes."

On Lammas Night, 1924, Dr Houghton of Aylesbury was

hastily summoned by Wilbur Whateley, who had lashed his one remaining horse through the darkness and telephoned from Osborn's in the village. He found Old Whateley in a very grave state, with a cardiac action and stentorous breathing that told of an end not far off. The shapeless albino daughter and oddly bearded grandson stood by the bedside, whilst from the vacant abyss overhead there came a disquieting suggestion of rhythmical surging or lapping, as of the waves on some level beach. The doctor, though, was chiefly disturbed by the chattering night birds outside; a seemingly limitless legion of whippoorwills that cried their endless message in repetitions timed diabolically to the wheezing gasps of the dying man. It was uncanny and unnatural — too much, thought Dr Houghton, like the whole of the region he had entered so reluctantly in response to the urgent call.

Towards one o'clock Old Whateley gained consciousness, and interrupted his wheezing to choke out a few words to his grandson.

"More space, Willy, more space soon. Yew grows — an' that grows faster. It'll be ready to serve ye soon, boy. Open up the gates to Yog-Sothoth with the long chant that ye'll find on page 751 of the complete edition, an' then put a match to the prison. Fire from airth can't burn it nohaow."

He was obviously quite mad. After a pause, during which the flock of whippoorwills outside adjusted their cries to the altered tempo while some indications of the strange hill noises came from afar off, he added another sentence or two.

"Feed it reg'lar, Willy, an' mind the quantity; but dun't let it grow too fast fer the place, fer ef it busts quarters or gits aout afore ye opens to Yog-Sothoth, it's all over an' no use. Only them from beyont kin make it multiply an' work . . . Only them, the old uns as wants to come back . . ."

But speech gave place to gasps again, and Lavinia screamed at the way the whippoorwills followed the change. It was the same for more than an hour, when the final throaty rattle came. Dr Houghton drew shrunken lids over the glazing grey eyes as the tumult of birds faded imperceptibly to silence. Lavinia sobbed, but Wilbur only chuckled whilst the hill noises rumbled faintly.

"They didn't git him," he muttered in his heavy bass voice.

Wilbur was by this time a scholar of really tremendous erudition in his one-sided way, and was quietly known by correspondence to many librarians in distant places where rare and forbidden books of old days are kept. He was more and more hated and dreaded around Dunwich because of certain youthful disappearances which suspicion laid vaguely at his door; but was always able to silence inquiry through fear or through use of that fund of old-time gold which still, as in his grandfather's time, went forth regularly and increasingly for cattle-buying. He was now tremendously mature of aspect, and his height, having reached the normal adult limit, seemed inclined to wax beyond that figure. In 1925, when a scholarly correspondent from Miskatonic University called upon him one day and departed pale and puzzled, he was fully six and three-quarters feet tall.

Through all the years Wilbur had treated his half-deformed albino mother with a growing contempt, finally forbidding her to go to the hills with him on May Eve and Hallowmass; and in 1926 the poor creature complained to Mamie Bishop of being afraid of him.

"They's more abaout him as I knows than I kin tell ye, Mamie," she said, "an' naowadays they's more nor what I know myself. I vaow afur Gawd, I dun't know what he wants nor what he's a-tryin' to dew."

That Hallowe'en the hill noises sounded louder than ever, and fire burned on Sentinel Hill as usual; but people paid more attention to the rhythmical screaming of vast flocks of unnaturally belated whippoorwills which seemed to be assembled near the unlighted Whateley farmhouse. After midnight their shrill notes burst into a kind of pandemoniac cachinnation which filled all the countryside, and not until dawn did they finally quiet down. Then they vanished, hurrying southward where they were fully a month overdue. What this meant, no one could quite be certain till later. None of the countryfolk seemed to have died — but poor Lavinia Whateley, the twisted albino, was never seen again.

In the summer of 1927 Wilbur repaired two sheds in the farmyard and began moving his books and effects out to them. Soon afterwards Earl Sawyer told the loungers at Osborn's that more carpentry was going on in the Whateley farmhouse. Wilbur was closing all the doors and windows on the ground floor, and seemed to be taking out partitions as he and his grandfather had done upstairs four years before. He was living in one of the sheds, and Sawyer thought he seemed unusually worried and tremulous. People generally suspected him of knowing something about his mother's disappearance, and very few ever approached his neighbourhood now. His height had increased to more than seven feet, and showed no signs of ceasing its development.

V.

The following winter brought an event no less strange than Wilbur's first trip outside the Dunwich region. Correspondence with the Widener Library at Harvard, the Bibliothèque Nationale in Paris, the British Museum, the University of Buenos Ayres, and the Library of Miskatonic University at Arkham had failed to get him the loan of a book he desperately wanted; so at length he set out in person, shabby, dirty, bearded, and uncouth of dialect, to consult the copy at Miskatonic, which was the nearest to him geographically. Almost eight feet tall, and carrying a cheap new valise from Osborne's general store, this dark and goatish gargoyle appeared one day in Arkham in quest of the dreaded volume kept under lock and key at the college library — the hideous *Necronomicon* of the mad Arab Abdul Alhazred in Olaus Wormius' Latin version, as printed in Spain in the seventeenth century. He had never seen a city before, but had no thought save to find his way to the university grounds; where indeed, he passed heedlessly by the great white-fanged watchdog that barked with unnatural fury and enmity, and tugged frantically at its stout chain.

Wilbur had with him the priceless but imperfect copy of Dr Dee's English version which his grandfather had bequeathed him, and upon receiving access to the Latin copy he at once began to collate the two texts with the aim of discovering a certain passage which would have come on the 751st page of his own defective volume. This much he could not civilly refrain from telling the librarian — the same erudite Henry Armitage (a.m. Miskatonic, Ph.D. Princeton, Litt.D. Johns Hopkins) who had once called at the farm, and who now politely plied him with questions. He was looking, he had to admit, for a kind of formula or incantation containing the frightful name Yog-Sothoth, and it puzzled him to find discrepancies, duplications, and ambiguities which made the matter of determination far from easy. As he copied the formula he finally chose, Dr. Armitage looked involuntarily over his shoulder at the open pages; the left-hand one of which, in the Latin version, contained such monstrous threats to the peace and sanity of the world.

Nor is it to be thought (ran the text as Armitage mentally translated it) that man is either the oldest or the last of earth's masters, or that the common bulk of life and substance walks alone. The Old Ones were, the Old Ones are, and the Old Ones shall be. Not in the spaces we know, but between them, they walk serene and primal, undimensioned and to us unseen. Yog-Sothoth knows the gate. Yog-Sothoth is the gate. Yog-Sothoth is the key and guardian of the gate. Past, present, future, all are one in Yog-Sothoth. He knows where the Old Ones broke through of old, and where They shall break through again. He knows where They had trod earth's fields, and where They still tread them, and why no one can behold Them as They tread. By Their smell can men sometimes know Them near, but of Their semblance can no man know, saving only in the features of those They have begotten on mankind; and of those are there many sorts, differing in likeness from man's truest eidolon to that shape without sight or substance which is Them. They walk unseen and foul in lonely places where the Words have been spoken and the Rites howled through at their Seasons. The wind gibbers with Their voices, and the earth mutters with Their consciousness. They bend the forest and crush the city, yet may not forest or city behold the hand that smites. Kadath in the cold waste hath known Them, and what man knows Kadath? The ice desert of the South and the sunken isles of Ocean hold stones whereon Their seal is engraved, but who hath seen the deep frozen city or the sealed tower long garlanded with seaweed and barnacles? Great Cthulhu is Their cousin, yet can he spy Them only dimly. Iä! Shub-Niggurath! As a foulness shall ye know Them. Their hand is at your throats, yet ye see Them not; and Their habitation is even one with your guarded threshold. Yog-Sothoth is the key to the gate, whereby the spheres meet. Man rules now where They ruled once; They shall soon rule where man rules now. After summer is winter, after winter summer. They wait patient and potent, for here shall They reign again.

Dr. Armitage, associating what he was reading with what he had heard of Dunwich and its brooding presences, and of Wilbur Whateley and his dim, hideous aura that stretched from a dubious birth to a cloud of probable matricide, felt a wave of fright as tangible as a draught of the tomb's cold clamminess. The bent, goatish giant before him seemed like the spawn of another planet or dimension; like something only partly of mankind, and linked to black gulfs of essence and entity that stretch like titan phantasms beyond all spheres of force and matter, space and time. Presently Wilbur raised his head and began speaking in that strange, resonant fashion which hinted at sound-producing organs unlike the run of mankind's.

"Mr. Armitage," he said, "I calc'late I've got to take that book home. They's things in it I've got to try under sarten conditions that I can't git here, en' it 'ud be a mortal sin to let a red-tape rule hold me up. Let me take it along, Sir, an' I'll swar they wun't nobody know the difference. I dun't need to tell ye I'll take good keer of it. It wan't me that put this Dee copy in the shape it is . . ."

He stopped as he saw firm denial on the librarian's face, and his own goatish features grew crafty. Armitage, half-ready to tell him he might make a copy of what parts he needed, thought suddenly of the possible consequences and checked himself. There was too much responsibility in giving such a being the key to such blasphemous outer spheres. Whateley saw how things stood, and tried to answer lightly.

"Wal, all right, ef ye feel that way abaout it. Maybe Harvard won't be so fussy as yew be.' And without saying more he rose and strode out of the building, stooping at each doorway.

Armitage heard the savage yelping of the great watchdog, and studied Whateley's gorilla-like lope as he crossed the bit of campus visible from the window. He thought of the wild tales he had heard, and recalled the old Sunday stories in the Advertiser; these things, and the lore he had picked up from Dunwich rustics and villagers during his one visit there. Unseen things not of earth — or at least not of tridimensional earth — rushed foetid and horrible through New England's glens, and brooded obscenely on the mountain tops. Of this he had long felt certain. Now he seemed to sense the close presence of some terrible part of the intruding horror, and to glimpse a hellish advance in the black dominion of the ancient and once passive nightmare. He locked away the *Necronomicon* with a shudder of disgust, but the room still reeked with an unholy and unidentifiable stench. "As a foulness shall ye know them," he quoted. Yes — the odour was the same as that which had sickened him at the Whateley farmhouse less than three years before. He thought of Wilbur, goatish and ominous, once again, and laughed mockingly at the village rumours of his parentage.

"Inbreeding?' Armitage muttered half-aloud to himself. "Great God, what simpletons! Show them Arthur Machen's

Great God Pan and they'll think it a common Dunwich scandal! But what thing—what cursed shapeless influence on or off this three-dimensional earth—was Wilbur Whateley's father? Born on Candlemas—nine months after May Eve of 1912, when the talk about the queer earth noises reached clear to Arkham—what walked on the mountains that May night? What Roodmas horror fastened itself on the world in half-human flesh and blood?"

During the ensuing weeks Dr Armitage set about to collect all possible data on Wilbur Whateley and the formless presences around Dunwich. He got in communication with Dr. Houghton of Aylesbury, who had attended Old Whateley in his last illness, and found much to ponder over in the grandfather's last words as quoted by the physician. A visit to Dunwich Village failed to bring out much that was new; but a close survey of the *Necronomicon*, in those parts which Wilbur had sought so avidly, seemed to supply new and terrible clues to the nature, methods, and desires of the strange evil so vaguely threatening this planet. Talks with several students of archaic lore in Boston, and letters to many others elsewhere, gave him a growing amazement which passed slowly through varied degrees of alarm to a state of really acute spiritual fear. As the summer drew on he felt dimly that something ought to be done about the lurking terrors of the upper Miskatonic valley, and about the monstrous being known to the human world as Wilbur Whateley.

VI.

The Dunwich Horror itself came between Lammas and the equinox in 1928, and Dr. Armitage was among those who witnessed its monstrous prologue. He had heard, meanwhile, of Whateley's grotesque trip to Cambridge, and of his frantic efforts to borrow or copy from the *Necronomicon* at the Widener Library. Those efforts had been in vain, since Armitage had issued warnings of the keenest intensity to all librarians having charge of the dreaded volume. Wilbur had been shockingly nervous at Cambridge; anxious for the book, yet almost equally anxious to get home again, as if he feared the results of being away long.

Early in August the half-expected outcome developed, and in the small hours of the third Dr. Armitage was awakened suddenly by the wild, fierce cries of the savage watchdog on the college campus. Deep and terrible, the snarling, half-mad growls and barks continued; always in mounting volume, but with hideously significant pauses. Then there rang out a scream from a wholly different throat—such a scream as roused half the sleepers of Arkham and haunted their dreams ever afterwards—such a scream as could come from no being born of earth, or wholly of earth.

Armitage, hastening into some clothing and rushing across the street and lawn to the college buildings, saw that others were ahead of him; and heard the echoes of a burglar-alarm still shrilling from the library. An open window showed black and gaping in the moonlight. What had come had indeed completed its entrance; for the barking and the screaming, now fast fading into a mixed low growling and moaning, proceeded unmistakably from within. Some instinct warned Armitage that what was taking place was not a thing for unfortified eyes to see, so he brushed back the crowd with authority as he unlocked the vestibule door. Among the others he saw Professor Warren Rice and Dr Francis Morgan, men to whom he had told some of his conjectures and misgivings; and these two he motioned to accompany him inside. The inward sounds, except for a watchful, droning whine from the dog, had by this time quite subsided; but Armitage now perceived with a sudden start that a loud chorus of whippoorwills among the shrubbery had commenced a damnably rhythmical piping, as if in unison with the last breaths of a dying man.

The building was full of a frightful stench which Dr Armitage knew too well, and the three men rushed across the hall to the small genealogical reading-room whence the low whining came. For a second nobody dared to turn on the light, then Armitage summoned up his courage and snapped the switch. One of the three—it is not certain which—shrieked aloud at what sprawled before them among disordered tables and overturned chairs. Professor Rice declares that he wholly lost consciousness for an instant, though he did not stumble or fall.

The thing that lay half-bent on its side in a foetid pool of greenish-yellow ichor and tarry stickiness was almost nine feet tall, and the dog had torn off all the clothing and some of the skin. It was not quite dead, but twitched silently and spasmodically while its chest heaved in monstrous unison with the mad piping of the expectant whippoorwills outside. Bits of shoe-leather and fragments of apparel were scattered about the room, and just inside the window an empty canvas sack lay where it had evidently been thrown. Near the central desk a revolver had fallen, a dented but undischarged cartridge later explaining why it had not been fired. The thing itself, however, crowded out all other images at the time. It would be trite and not wholly accurate to say that no human pen could describe it, but one may properly say that it could not be vividly visualized by anyone whose ideas of aspect and contour are too closely bound up with the common life-forms of this planet and of the three known dimensions. It was partly human, beyond a doubt, with very manlike hands and head, and the goatish, chinless face had the stamp of the Whateley's upon it. But the torso and lower parts of the body were teratologically fabulous, so that only generous clothing could ever have enabled it to walk on earth unchallenged or uneradicated.

Above the waist it was semi-anthropomorphic; though its chest, where the dog's rending paws still rested watchfully, had the leathery, reticulated hide of a crocodile or alligator. The back was piebald with yellow and black, and dimly suggested the squamous covering of certain snakes. Below the waist, though, it was the worst; for here all human resemblance left off and sheer phantasy began. The skin was thickly covered with coarse black fur, and from the abdomen a score of long greenish-grey tentacles with red sucking mouths protruded limply.

Their arrangement was odd, and seemed to follow the symmetries of some cosmic geometry unknown to earth or the solar system. On each of the hips, deep set in a kind of pinkish, ciliated orbit, was what seemed to be a rudimentary eye; whilst in lieu of a tail there depended a kind of trunk or feeler with purple annular markings, and with many evidences of being an undeveloped mouth or throat. The limbs, save for their black fur, roughly resembled the hind legs of prehistoric earth's giant saurians, and terminated in ridgy-veined pads that were neither hooves nor claws. When the thing breathed, its tail and tentacles rhythmically changed colour, as if from some circulatory cause normal to the non-human greenish tinge, whilst in the tail it was manifest as a yellowish appearance which alternated with a sickly grayish-white in the spaces between the purple rings. Of genuine blood there was none; only the foetid greenish-yellow ichor which trickled along the painted floor beyond the radius of the stickiness, and left a curious discoloration behind it.

As the presence of the three men seemed to rouse the dying thing, it began to mumble without turning or raising its head. Dr. Armitage made no written record of its mouthings, but asserts confidently that nothing in English was uttered. At first the syllables defied all correlation with any speech of earth, but towards the last there came some disjointed fragments evidently taken from the *Necronomicon*, that monstrous blasphemy in quest of which the thing had perished. These fragments, as Armitage recalls them, ran something like "N'gai, n'gha'ghaa, bugg-shoggog, y'hah: Yog-Sothoth, Yog-Sothoth .... "They trailed off into nothingness as the whippoorwills shrieked in rhythmical crescendos of unholy anticipation.

Then came a halt in the gasping, and the dog raised its head in a long, lugubrious howl. A change came over the yellow, goatish face of the prostrate thing, and the great black eyes fell in appallingly. Outside the window the shrilling of the whippoorwills had suddenly ceased, and above the murmurs of the gathering crowd there came the sound of a panic-struck whirring and fluttering. Against the moon vast clouds of feathery watchers rose and raced from sight, frantic at that which they had sought for prey.

All at once the dog started up abruptly, gave a frightened bark, and leaped nervously out of the window by which it had entered. A cry rose from the crowd, and Dr. Armitage shouted to the men outside that no one must be admitted till the police or medical examiner came. He was thankful that the windows were just too high to permit of peering in, and drew the dark curtains carefully down over each one. By this time two policemen had arrived; and Dr Morgan, meeting them in the vestibule, was urging them for their own sakes to postpone entrance to the stench-filled reading-room till the examiner came and the prostrate thing could be covered up.

Meanwhile frightful changes were taking place on the floor. One need not describe the kind and rate of shrinkage and disintegration that occurred before the eyes of Dr Armitage and Professor Rice; but it is permissible to say that, aside from the external appearance of face and hands, the really human element in Wilbur Whateley must have been very small. When the medical examiner came, there was only a sticky whitish mass on the painted boards, and the monstrous odour had nearly disappeared. Apparently Whateley had had no skull or bony skeleton; at least, in any true or stable sense. He had taken somewhat after his unknown father.

VII.

Yet all this was only the prologue of the actual Dunwich Horror. Formalities were gone through by bewildered officials, abnormal details were duly kept from press and public, and men were sent to Dunwich and Aylesbury to look up property and notify any who might be heirs of the late Wilbur Whateley. They found the countryside in great agitation, both because of the growing rumblings beneath the domed hills, and because of the unwonted stench and the surging, lapping sounds which came increasingly from the great empty shell formed by Whateley's boarded-up farmhouse. Earl Sawyer, who tended the horse and cattle during Wilbur's absence, had developed a woefully acute case of nerves. The officials devised excuses not to enter the noisome boarded place; and were glad to confine their survey of the deceased's living quarters, the newly mended sheds, to a single visit. They filed a ponderous report at the courthouse in Aylesbury, and litigations concerning heirship are said to be still in progress amongst the innumerable Whateleys, decayed and undecayed, of the upper Miskatonic valley.

An almost interminable manuscript in strange characters, written in a huge ledger and adjudged a sort of diary because of the spacing and the variations in ink and penmanship, presented a baffling puzzle to those who found it on the old bureau which served as its owner's desk. After a week of debate it was sent to Miskatonic University, together with the deceased's collection of strange books, for study and possible translation; but even the best linguists soon saw that it was not likely to be unriddled with ease. No trace of the ancient gold with which Wilbur and Old Whateley had always paid their debts has yet been discovered.

It was in the dark of September ninth that the horror broke loose. The hill noises had been very pronounced during the evening, and dogs barked frantically all night. Early risers on the tenth noticed a peculiar stench in the air. About seven o'clock Luther Brown, the hired boy at George Corey's, between Cold Spring Glen and the village, rushed frenziedly back from his morning trip to Ten-Acre Meadow with the cows. He was almost convulsed with fright as he stumbled into the kitchen; and in the yard outside the no less frightened herd were pawing and lowing pitifully, having followed the boy back in the panic they shared with him. Between gasps Luther tried to stammer out his tale to Mrs Corey.

"Up thar in the rud beyont the glen, Mis' Corey — they's suthin' ben thar! It smells like thunder, an' all the bushes an' little trees is pushed back from the rud like they'd a haouse ben moved along of it. An' that ain't the wust, nuther. They's prints in the rud, Mis' Corey — great raound prints as big as barrel-heads, all sunk daown deep like a elephant had ben along, only they's a sight more nor four feet could make! I looked at one or two afore I run, an' I see every one was covered with lines spreadin' aout from one place, like as if big palm-leaf fans — twict or three times as big as any they is — hed of ben paounded daown into the rud. An' the smell was awful, like what it is around Wizard Whateley's ol' haouse . . . ."

Here he faltered, and seemed to shiver afresh with the fright that had sent him flying home. Mrs Corey, unable to extract more information, began telephoning the neighbours; thus starting on its rounds the overture of panic that heralded the major terrors. When she got Sally Sawyer, housekeeper at Seth Bishop's, the nearest place to Whateley's, it became her turn to listen instead of transmit; for Sally's boy Chauncey, who slept poorly, had been up on the hill towards Whateley's, and had dashed back in terror after one look at the place, and at the pasturage where Mr. Bishop's cows had been left out all night.

"Yes, Mis' Corey," came Sally's tremulous voice over the party wire, "Cha'ncey he just come back a-postin', and couldn't half talk fer bein' scairt! He says Ol' Whateley's house is all bowed up, with timbers scattered raound like they'd ben dynamite inside; only the bottom floor ain't through, but is all covered with a kind o' tar-like stuff that smells awful an' drips daown offen the aidges onto the graoun' whar the side timbers is blowed away. An' they's awful kinder marks in the yard, tew — great raound marks bigger raound than a hogshead, an' all sticky with stuff like is on the browed-up haouse. Cha'ncey he says they leads off into the medders, whar a great swath wider'n a barn is matted daown, an' all the stun walls tumbled every whichway wherever it goes.

"An' he says, says he, Mis' Corey, as haow he sot to look fer Seth's caows, frightened ez he was an' faound 'em in the upper pasture nigh the Devil's Hop Yard in an awful shape. Haff on 'em's clean gone, an' nigh haff o' them that's left is sucked most dry o' blood, with sores on 'em like they's ben on Whateleys cattle ever senct Lavinny's black brat was born. Seth he's gone aout naow to look at 'em, though I'll vaow he won't keer ter git very nigh Wizard Whateley's! Cha'ncey didn't look keerful ter see whar the big matted-daown swath led arter it leff the pasturage, but he says he thinks it p'inted towards the glen rud to the village.

"I tell ye, Mis' Corey, they's suthin' abroad as hadn't orter be abroad, an' I for one think that black Wilbur Whateley, as come to the bad end he deserved, is at the bottom of the breedin' of it. He wa'n't all human hisself, I allus says to everybody; an' I think he an' Ol' Whateley must a raised suthin' in that there nailed-up haouse as ain't even so human as he was. They's allus ben unseen things araound Dunwich — livin' things — as ain't human an' ain't good fer human folks.

"The graoun' was a-talkin' las' night, an' towards mornin' Cha'ncey he heered the whippoorwills so laoud in Col' Spring Glen he couldn't sleep nun. Then he thought he heered another faint-like saound over towards Wizard Whateley's — a kinder rippin' or tearin' o' wood, like some big box er crate was bein' opened fur off. What with this an' that, he didn't git to sleep at all till sunup, an' no sooner was he up this mornin', but he's got to go over to Whateley's an' see what's the matter. He see enough I tell ye, Mis' Corey! This dun't mean no good, an' I think as all the men-folks ought to git up a party an' do suthin'. I know suthin' awful's abaout, an' feel my time is nigh, though only Gawd knows jest what it is.

"Did your Luther take accaount o' whar them big tracks led tew? No? Wal, Mis' Corey, ef they was on the glen rud this side o' the glen, an' ain't got to your haouse yet, I calc'late they must go into the glen itself. They would do that. I allus says Col' Spring Glen ain't no healthy nor decent place. The whippoorwills an' fireflies there never did act like they was creaters o' Gawd, an' they's them as says ye kin hear strange things a-rushin' an' a-talkin' in the air daown thar ef ye stand in the right place, atween the rock falls an' Bear's Den."

By that noon fully three-quarters of the men and boys of Dunwich were trooping over the roads and meadows between the newmade Whateley ruins and Cold Spring Glen, examining in horror the vast, monstrous prints, the maimed Bishop cattle, the strange, noisome wreck of the farmhouse, and the bruised, matted vegetation of the fields and roadside. Whatever had burst loose upon the world had assuredly gone down into the great sinister ravine; for all the trees on the banks were bent and broken, and a great avenue had been gouged in the precipice-hanging underbrush. It was as though a house, launched by an avalanche, had slid down through the tangled growths of the almost vertical slope. From below no sound came, but only a distant, undefinable foetor; and it is not to be wondered at that the men preferred to stay on the edge and argue, rather than descend and beard the unknown Cyclopean horror in its lair. Three dogs that were with the party had barked furiously at first, but seemed cowed and reluctant when near the glen. Someone telephoned the news to the Aylesbury Transcript; but the editor, accustomed to wild tales from Dunwich, did no more than concoct a humorous paragraph about it; an item soon afterwards reproduced by the Associated Press.

That night everyone went home, and every house and barn was barricaded as stoutly as possible. Needless to say, no cattle were allowed to remain in open pasturage. About two in the morning a frightful stench and the savage barking of the dogs awakened the household at Elmer Frye's, on the eastern edge of Cold Spring Glen, and all agreed that they could hear a sort of muffled swishing or lapping sound from somewhere outside. Mrs Frye proposed telephoning the neighbours, and Elmer was about to agree when the noise of splintering wood burst in upon their deliberations. It came, apparently, from the barn;

and was quickly followed by a hideous screaming and stamping amongst the cattle. The dogs slavered and crouched close to the feet of the fear-numbed family. Frye lit a lantern through force of habit, but knew it would be death to go out into that black farmyard. The children and the women-folk whimpered, kept from screaming by some obscure, vestigial instinct of defence which told them their lives depended on silence. At last the noise of the cattle subsided to a pitiful moaning, and a great snapping, crashing, and crackling ensued. The Fryes, huddled together in the sitting-room, did not dare to move until the last echoes died away far down in Cold Spring Glen. Then, amidst the dismal moans from the stable and the daemoniac piping of the late whippoorwills in the glen, Selina Frye tottered to the telephone and spread what news she could of the second phase of the horror.

The next day all the countryside was in a panic; and cowed, uncommunicative groups came and went where the fiendish thing had occurred. Two titan swaths of destruction stretched from the glen to the Frye farmyard, monstrous prints covered the bare patches of ground, and one side of the old red barn had completely caved in. Of the cattle, only a quarter could be found and identified. Some of these were in curious fragments, and all that survived had to be shot. Earl Sawyer suggested that help be asked from Aylesbury or Arkham, but others maintained it would be of no use. Old Zebulon Whateley, of a branch that hovered about halfway between soundness and decadence, made darkly wild suggestions about rites that ought to be practiced on the hill-tops. He came of a line where tradition ran strong, and his memories of chantings in the great stone circles were not altogether connected with Wilbur and his grandfather.

Darkness fell upon a stricken countryside too passive to organize for real defence. In a few cases closely related families would band together and watch in the gloom under one roof; but in general there was only a repetition of the barricading of the night before, and a futile, ineffective gesture of loading muskets and setting pitchforks handily about. Nothing, however, occurred except some hill noises; and when the day came there were many who hoped that the new horror had gone as swiftly as it had come. There were even bold souls who proposed an offensive expedition down in the glen, though they did not venture to set an actual example to the still reluctant majority.

When night came again the barricading was repeated, though there was less huddling together of families. In the morning both the Frye and the Seth Bishop households reported excitement among the dogs and vague sounds and stenches from afar, while early explorers noted with horror a fresh set of the monstrous tracks in the road skirting Sentinel Hill. As before, the sides of the road showed a bruising indicative of the blasphemously stupendous bulk of the horror; whilst the conformation of the tracks seemed to argue a passage in two directions, as if the moving mountain had come from Cold Spring Glen and returned to it along the same path. At the base of the hill a thirty-foot swath of crushed shrubbery saplings led steeply upwards, and the seekers gasped when they saw that even the most perpendicular places did not deflect the inexorable trail. Whatever the horror was, it could scale a sheer stony cliff of almost complete verticality; and as the investigators climbed round to the hill's summit by safer routes they saw that the trail ended — or rather, reversed — there.

It was here that the Whateleys used to build their hellish fires and chant their hellish rituals by the table-like stone on May Eve and Hallowmass. Now that very stone formed the centre of a vast space thrashed around by the mountainous horror, whilst upon its slightly concave surface was a thick and foetid deposit of the same tarry stickiness observed on the floor of the ruined Whateley farmhouse when the horror escaped. Men looked at one another and muttered. Then they looked down the hill. Apparently the horror had descended by a route much the same as that of its ascent. To speculate was futile. Reason, logic, and normal ideas of motivation stood confounded. Only old Zebulon, who was not with the group, could have done justice to the situation or suggested a plausible explanation.

Thursday night began much like the others, but it ended less happily. The whippoorwills in the glen had screamed with such unusual persistence that many could not sleep, and about 3 a.m. all the party telephones rang tremulously. Those who took down their receivers heard a fright-mad voice shriek out, "Help, oh, my Gawd! . . .' and some thought a crashing sound followed the breaking off of the exclamation. There was nothing more. No one dared do anything, and no one knew till morning whence the call came. Then those who had heard it called everyone on the line, and found that only the Fryes did not reply. The truth appeared an hour later, when a hastily assembled group of armed men trudged out to the Frye place at the head of the glen. It was horrible, yet hardly a surprise. There were more swaths and monstrous prints, but there was no longer any house. It had caved in like an egg-shell, and amongst the ruins nothing living or dead could be discovered. Only a stench and a tarry stickiness. The Elmer Fryes had been erased from Dunwich.

VIII.

In the meantime a quieter yet even more spiritually poignant phase of the horror had been blackly unwinding itself behind the closed door of a shelf-lined room in Arkham. The curious manuscript record or diary of Wilbur Whateley, delivered to Miskatonic University for translation had caused much worry and bafflement among the experts in language both ancient and modern; its very alphabet, notwithstanding a general resemblance to the heavily-shaded Arabic used in Mesopotamia, being absolutely unknown to any available authority. The final conclusion of the linguists was that the text represented an artificial alphabet, giving the effect of a cipher; though none of the usual methods of cryptographic solution seemed to furnish any clue, even when applied on the basis of every tongue the writer might conceivably have used.

The ancient books taken from Whateley's quarters, while absorbingly interesting and in several cases promising to open up new and terrible lines of research among philosophers and men of science, were of no assistance whatever in this matter. One of them, a heavy tome with an iron clasp, was in another unknown alphabet — this one of a very different cast, and resembling Sanskrit more than anything else. The old ledger was at length given wholly into the charge of Dr. Armitage, both because of his peculiar interest in the Whateley matter, and because of his wide linguistic learning and skill in the mystical formulae of antiquity and the middle ages.

Armitage had an idea that the alphabet might be something esoterically used by certain forbidden cults which have come down from old times, and which have inherited many forms and traditions from the wizards of the Saracenic world. That question, however, he did not deem vital; since it would be unnecessary to know the origin of the symbols if, as he suspected, they were used as a cipher in a modern language. It was his belief that, considering the great amount of text involved, the writer would scarcely have wished the trouble of using another speech than his own, save perhaps in certain special formulae and incantations. Accordingly he attacked the manuscript with the preliminary assumption that the bulk of it was in English.

Dr. Armitage knew, from the repeated failures of his colleagues, that the riddle was a deep and complex one; and that no simple mode of solution could merit even a trial. All through late August he fortified himself with the mass lore of cryptography; drawing upon the fullest resources of his own library, and wading night after night amidst the arcana of Trithemius' *Poligraphia*, Giambattista Porta's *De Furtivis Literarum Notis*, De Vigenere's *Traite des Chiffres*, Falconer's *Cryptomenysis Patefacta*, Davys' and Thicknesse's eighteenth-century treatises, and such fairly modern authorities as Blair, van Marten and Kluber's script itself, and in time became convinced that he had to deal with one of those subtlest and most ingenious of cryptograms, in which many separate lists of corresponding letters are arranged like the multiplication table, and the message built up with arbitrary key-words known only to the initiated. The older authorities seemed rather more helpful than the newer ones, and Armitage concluded that the code of the manuscript was one of great antiquity, no doubt handed down through a long line of mystical experimenters. Several times he seemed near daylight, only to be set back by some unforeseen obstacle. Then, as September approached, the clouds began to clear. Certain letters, as used in certain parts of the manuscript, emerged definitely and unmistakably; and it became obvious that the text was indeed in English.

On the evening of September 2, the last major barrier gave way, and Dr. Armitage read for the first time a continuous passage of Wilbur Whateley's annals. It was in truth a diary, as all had thought; and it was couched in a style clearly showing the mixed occult erudition and general illiteracy of the strange being who wrote it. Almost the first long passage that Armitage deciphered, an entry dated November 26, 1916, proved highly startling and disquieting. It was written,he remembered, by a child of three and a half who looked like a lad of twelve or thirteen.

"Today learned the Aklo for the Sabaoth," it ran, "which did not like, it being answerable from the hill and not from the air. That upstairs more ahead of me than I had thought it would be, and is not like to have much earth brain. Shot Elam Hutchins's collie Jack when he went to bite me, and Elam says he would kill me if he dast. I guess he won't. Grandfather kept me saying the Dho formula last night, and I think I saw the inner city at the 2 magnetic poles. I shall go to those poles when the earth is cleared off, if I can't break through with the Dho-Hna formula when I commit it. They from the air told me at Sabbat that it will be years before I can clear off the earth, and I guess grandfather will be dead then, so I shall have to learn all the angles of the planes and all the formulas between the Yr and the Nhhngr. They from outside will help, but they cannot take body without human blood. That upstairs looks it will have the right cast. I can see it a little when I make the Voorish sign or blow the powder of Ibn Ghazi at it, and it is near like them at May Eve on the Hill. The other face may wear off some. I wonder how I shall look when the earth is cleared and there are no earth beings on it. He that came with the Aklo Sabaoth said I may be transfigured there being much of outside to work on."

Morning found Dr. Armitage in a cold sweat of terror and a frenzy of wakeful concentration. He had not left the manuscript all night, but sat at his table under the electric light turning page after page with shaking hands as fast as he could decipher the cryptic text. He had nervously telephoned his wife he would not be home, and when she brought him a breakfast from the house he could scarcely dispose of a mouthful. All that day he read on, now and then halted maddeningly as a reapplication of the complex key became necessary. Lunch and dinner were brought him, but he ate only the smallest fraction of either. Toward the middle of the next night he drowsed off in his chair, but soon woke out of a tangle of nightmares almost as hideous as the truths and menaces to man's existence that he had uncovered.

On the morning of September 4 Professor Rice and Dr. Morgan insisted on seeing him for a while, and departed trembling and ashen-grey. That evening he went to bed, but slept only fitfully. Wednesday — the next day — he was back at the manuscript, and began to take copious notes both from the current sections and from those he had already deciphered. In the small hours of that night he slept a little in a easy chair in his office, but was at the manuscript again before dawn. Some time before noon his physician, Dr. Hartwell, called to see him and insisted that he cease work. He refused; intimating that it was of the most vital importance for him to complete the reading of the diary and promising an explanation in due course of time.

That evening, just as twilight fell, he finished his terrible perusal and sank back exhausted. His wife, bringing his dinner, found him in a half-comatose state; but he was conscious enough to warn her off with a sharp cry when he saw her eyes wander toward the notes he had taken. Weakly rising, he gathered up the scribbled papers and sealed them all in a great envelope, which he immediately placed in his inside coat pocket. He had sufficient strength to get home, but was so clearly in need of medical aid that Dr. Hartwell was summoned at once. As the doctor put him to bed he could only mutter over and over again, "But what, in God's name, can we do?"

Dr. Armitage slept, but was partly delirious the next day. He made no explanations to Hartwell, but in his calmer moments spoke of the imperative need of a long conference with Rice and Morgan. His wilder wanderings were very startling indeed, including frantic appeals that something in a boarded-up farmhouse be destroyed, and fantastic references to some plan for the extirpation of the entire human race and all animal and vegetable life from the earth by some terrible elder race of beings from another dimension. He would shout that the world was in danger, since the Elder Things wished to strip it and drag it away from the solar system and cosmos of matter into some other plane or phase of entity from which it had once fallen, vigintillions of aeons ago. At other times he would call for the dreaded *Necronomicon* and the *Daemonolatreia* of Remigius, in which he seemed hopeful of finding some formula to check the peril he conjured up.

"Stop them, stop them!" he would shout. "Those Whateleys meant to let them in, and the worst of all is left! Tell Rice and Morgan we must do something — it's a blind business, but I know how to make the powder . . . It hasn't been fed since the second of August, when Wilbur came here to his death, and at that rate . . ."

But Armitage had a sound physique despite his seventy-three years, and slept off his disorder that night without developing any real fever. He woke late Friday, clear of head, though sober with a gnawing fear and tremendous sense of responsibility. Saturday afternoon he felt able to go over to the library and summon Rice and Morgan for a conference, and the rest of that day and evening the three men tortured their brains in the wildest speculation and the most desperate debate. Strange and terrible books were drawn voluminously from the stack shelves and from secure places of storage; and diagrams and formulae were copied with feverish haste and in bewildering abundance. Of scepticism there was none. All three had seen the body of Wilbur Whateley as it lay on the floor in a room of that very building, and after that not one of them could feel even slightly inclined to treat the diary as a madman's raving.

Opinions were divided as to notifying the Massachusetts State Police, and the negative finally won. There were things involved which simply could not be believed by those who had not seen a sample, as indeed was made clear during certain subsequent investigations. Late at night the conference disbanded without having developed a definite plan, but all day Sunday Armitage was busy comparing formulae and mixing chemicals obtained from the college laboratory. The more he reflected on the hellish diary, the more he was inclined to doubt the efficacy of any material agent in stamping out the entity which Wilbur Whateley had left behind him — the earth threatening entity which, unknown to him, was to burst forth in a few hours and become the memorable Dunwich Horror.

Monday was a repetition of Sunday with Dr. Armitage, for the task in hand required an infinity of research and experiment. Further consultations of the monstrous diary brought about various changes of plan, and he knew that even in the end a large amount of uncertainty must remain. By Tuesday he had a definite line of action mapped out, and believed he would try a trip to Dunwich within a week. Then, on Wednesday, the great shock came. Tucked obscurely away in a corner of the *Arkham Advertiser* was a facetious little item from the Associated Press, telling what a record-breaking monster the bootleg whisky of Dunwich had raised up. Armitage, half stunned, could only telephone for Rice and Morgan. Far into the night they discussed, and the next day was a whirlwind of preparation on the part of them all. Armitage knew he would be meddling with terrible powers, yet saw that there was no other way to annul the deeper and more malign meddling which others had done before him.

IX.

Friday morning Armitage, Rice, and Morgan set out by motor for Dunwich, arriving at the village about one in the afternoon. The day was pleasant, but even in the brightest sunlight a kind of quiet dread and portent seemed to hover about the strangely domed hills and the deep, shadowy ravines of the stricken region. Now and then on some mountain top a gaunt circle of stones could be glimpsed against the sky. From the air of hushed fright at Osborn's store they knew something hideous had happened, and soon learned of the annihilation of the Elmer Frye house and family. Throughout that afternoon they rode around Dunwich, questioning the natives concerning all that had occurred, and seeing for themselves with rising pangs of horror the drear Frye ruins with their lingering traces of the tarry stickiness, the blasphemous tracks in the Frye yard, the wounded Seth Bishop cattle, and the enormous swaths of disturbed vegetation in various places. The trail up and down Sentinel Hill seemed to Armitage of almost cataclysmic significance, and he looked long at the sinister altar-like stone on the summit.

At length the visitors, apprised of a party of State Police which had come from Aylesbury that morning in response to the first telephone reports of the Frye tragedy, decided to seek out the officers and compare notes as far as practicable. This, however, they found more easily planned than performed; since no sign of the party could be found in any direction. There had been five of them in a car, but now the car stood empty near the ruins in the Frye yard. The natives, all of whom had talked with the policemen, seemed at first as perplexed as Armitage and his companions. Then old Sam Hutchins thought of something and turned pale, nudging Fred Farr and pointing to the dank, deep hollow that yawned close by.

"Gawd," he gasped, "I telled 'em not ter go daown into the glen, an' I never thought nobody'd dew it with them tracks an' that smell an' the whippoorwills a-screechin' daown thar in the dark o' noonday . . ."

A cold shudder ran through natives and visitors alike, and every ear seemed strained in a kind of instinctive, unconscious listening. Armitage, now that he had actually come upon the horror and its monstrous work, trembled with the responsibility he felt to be his. Night would soon fall, and it was then that the mountainous blasphemy lumbered upon its eldritch course. Negotium perambulans in tenebris . . . The old librarian rehearsed the formula he had memorized, and clutched the paper containing the alternative one he had not memorized. He saw that his electric flashlight was in working order. Rice, beside him, took from a valise a metal sprayer of the sort used in combating insects; whilst Morgan uncased the big-game rifle on which he relied despite his colleague's warnings that no material weapon would be of help.

Armitage, having read the hideous diary, knew painfully well what kind of a manifestation to expect; but he did not add to the fright of the Dunwich people by giving any hints or clues. He hoped that it might be conquered without any revelation to the world of the monstrous thing it had escaped. As the shadows gathered, the natives commenced to disperse homeward, anxious to bar themselves indoors despite the present evidence that all human locks and bolts were useless before a force that could bend trees and crush houses when it chose. They shook their heads at the visitors' plan to stand guard at the Frye ruins near the glen; and, as they left, had little expectancy of ever seeing the watchers again.

There were rumblings under the hills that night, and the whippoorwills piped threateningly. Once in a while a wind, sweeping up out of Cold Spring Glen, would bring a touch of ineffable foetor to the heavy night air; such a foetor as all three of the watchers had smelled once before, when they stood above a dying thing that had passed for fifteen years and a half as a human being. But the looked-for terror did not appear. Whatever was down there in the glen was biding its time, and Armitage told his colleagues it would be suicidal to try to attack it in the dark.

Morning came wanly, and the night-sounds ceased. It was a grey, bleak day, with now and then a drizzle of rain; and heavier and heavier clouds seemed to be piling themselves up beyond the hills to the north-west. The men from Arkham were undecided what to do. Seeking shelter from the increasing rainfall beneath one of the few undestroyed Frye outbuildings, they debated the wisdom of waiting, or of taking the aggressive and going down into the glen in quest of their nameless, monstrous quarry. The downpour waxed in heaviness, and distant peals of thunder sounded from far horizons. Sheet lightning shimmered, and then a forky bolt flashed near at hand, as if descending into the accursed glen itself. The sky grew very dark, and the watchers hoped that the storm would prove a short, sharp one followed by clear weather.

It was still gruesomely dark when, not much over an hour later, a confused babel of voices sounded down the road. Another moment brought to view a frightened group of more than a dozen men, running, shouting, and even whimpering hysterically. Someone in the lead began sobbing out words, and the Arkham men started violently when those words developed a coherent form.

"Oh, my Gawd, my Gawd," the voice choked out. "It's a-goin' agin, an' this time by day! It's aout—it's aout an' a-movin' this very minute, an' only the Lord knows when it'll be on us all!"

The speaker panted into silence, but another took up his message.

"Nigh on a haour ago Zeb Whateley here heered the 'phone a-ringin', an' it was Mis' Corey, George's wife, that lives daown by the junction. She says the hired boy Luther was aout drivin' in the caows from the storm arter the big bolt, when he see all the trees a-bendin' at the maouth o' the glen—opposite side ter this—an' smelt the same awful smell like he smelt when he faound the big tracks las' Monday mornin'. An' she says he says they was a swishin' lappin' saound, more nor what the bendin' trees an' bushes could make, an' all on a suddent the trees along the rud begun ter git pushed one side, an' they was a awful stompin' an' splashin' in the mud. But mind ye, Luther he didn't see nothin' at all, only just the bendin' trees an' underbrush.

"Then fur ahead where Bishop's Brook goes under the rud he heerd a awful creakin' an' strainin' on the bridge, an' says he could tell the saound o' wood a-startin' to crack an' split. An' all the whiles he never see a thing, only them trees an' bushes a-bendin'. An' when the swishin' saound got very fur off—on the rud towards Wizard Whateley's an' Sentinel Hill—Luther he had the guts ter step up whar he'd heerd it fust an' look at the graound. It was all mud an' water, an' the sky was dark, an' the rain was wipin' aout all tracks abaout as fast as could be; but beginnin' at the glen maouth, whar the trees hed moved, they was still some o' them awful prints big as bar'ls like he seen Monday."

At this point the first excited speaker interrupted.

"But that ain't the trouble naow—that was only the start. Zeb here was callin' folks up an' everybody was a-listenin' in when a call from Seth Bishop's cut in. His haousekeeper Sally was carryin' on fit to kill—she'd jest seed the trees a-bendin' beside the rud, an' says they was a kind o' mushy saound, like a elephant puffin' an' treadin', a-headin' fer the haouse. Then she up an' spoke suddent of a fearful smell, an' says her boy Cha'ncey was a-screamin' as haow it was jest like what he smelt up to the Whateley rewins Monday mornin'. An' the dogs was barkin' an' whinin' awful.

"An' then she let aout a turrible yell, an' says the shed daown the rud had jest caved in like the storm hed blowed it over, only the wind w'an't strong enough to dew that. Everybody was a-listenin', an' we could hear lots o' folks on the wire a-gaspin'. All to onct Sally she yelled again, an' says the front yard picket fence hed just crumbled up, though they wa'n't no sign o' what done it. Then everybody on the line could hear Cha'ncey an' old Seth Bishop a-yellin' tew, an' Sally was shriekin' aout that suthin' heavy hed struck the haouse — not lightnin' nor nothin', but suthin' heavy again' the front, that kep' a-launchin' itself agin an' agin, though ye couldn't see nothin' aout the front winders. An' then . . . an' then . . ."

Lines of fright deepened on every face; and Armitage, shaken as he was, had barely poise enough to prompt the speaker.

"An' then . . . Sally she yelled aout, "O help, the haouse is a-cavin' in . . . an' on the wire we could hear a turrible crashin' an' a hull flock o' screaming . . . jes like when Elmer Frye's place was took, only wuss . . ."

The man paused, and another of the crowd spoke.

"That's all — not a saound nor squeak over the 'phone arter that. Jest still-like. We that heerd it got aout Fords an' wagons an' rounded up as many able-bodied men-folks as we could git, at Corey's place, an' come up here ter see what yew thought best ter dew. Not but what I think it's the Lord's jedgment fer our iniquities, that no mortal kin ever set aside."

Armitage saw that the time for positive action had come, and spoke decisively to the faltering group of frightened rustics.

"We must follow it, boys." He made his voice as reassuring as possible. "I believe there's a chance of putting it out of business. You men know that those Whateleys were wizards — well, this thing is a thing of wizardry, and must be put down by the same means. I've seen Wilbur Whateley's diary and read some of the strange old books he used to read; and I think I know the right kind of spell to recite to make the thing fade away. Of course, one can't be sure, but we can always take a chance. It's invisible — I knew it would be — but there's powder in this long-distance sprayer that might make it show up for a second. Later on we'll try it. It's a frightful thing to have alive, but it isn't as bad as what Wilbur would have let in if he'd lived longer. You'll never know what the world escaped. Now we've only this one thing to fight, and it can't multiply. It can, though, do a lot of harm; so we mustn't hesitate to rid the community of it.

"We must follow it — and the way to begin is to go to the place that has just been wrecked. Let somebody lead the way — I don't know your roads very well, but I've an idea there might be a shorter cut across lots. How about it?"

The men shuffled about a moment, and then Earl Sawyer spoke softly, pointing with a grimy finger through the steadily lessening rain.

"I guess ye kin git to Seth Bishop's quickest by cuttin' across the lower medder here, wadin' the brook at the low place, an' climbin' through Carrier's mowin' an' the timber-lot beyont. That comes aout on the upper rud mighty nigh Seth's — a leetle t'other side."

Armitage, with Rice and Morgan, started to walk in the direction indicated; and most of the natives followed slowly. The sky was growing lighter, and there were signs that the storm had worn itself away. When Armitage inadvertently took a wrong direction, Joe Osborn warned him and walked ahead to show the right one. Courage and confidence were mounting, though the twilight of the almost perpendicular wooded hill which lay towards the end of their short cut, and among whose fantastic ancient trees they had to scramble as if up a ladder, put these qualities to a severe test.

At length they emerged on a muddy road to find the sun coming out. They were a little beyond the Seth Bishop place, but bent trees and hideously unmistakable tracks showed what had passed by. Only a few moments were consumed in surveying the ruins just round the bend. It was the Frye incident all over again, and nothing dead or living was found in either of the collapsed shells which had been the Bishop house and barn. No one cared to remain there amidst the stench and tarry stickiness, but all turned instinctively to the line of horrible prints leading on towards the wrecked Whateley farmhouse and the altar-crowned slopes of Sentinel Hill.

As the men passed the site of Wilbur Whateley's abode they shuddered visibly, and seemed again to mix hesitancy with their zeal. It was no joke tracking down something as big as a house that one could not see, but that had all the vicious malevolence of a daemon. Opposite the base of Sentinel Hill the tracks left the road, and there was a fresh bending and matting visible along the broad swath marking the monster's former route to and from the summit.

Armitage produced a pocket telescope of considerable power and scanned the steep green side of the hill. Then he handed the instrument to Morgan, whose sight was keener. After a moment of gazing Morgan cried out sharply, passing the glass to Earl Sawyer and indicating a certain spot on the slope with his finger. Sawyer, as clumsy as most non-users of optical devices are, fumbled a while; but eventually focused the lenses with Armitage's aid. When he did so his cry was less restrained than Morgan's had been.

"Gawd almighty, the grass an' bushes is a'movin'! It's a-goin' up — slow-like — creepin' — up ter the top this minute, heaven only knows what fur!"

Then the germ of panic seemed to spread among the seekers. It was one thing to chase the nameless entity, but quite another to find it. Spells might be all right — but suppose they weren't? Voices began questioning Armitage about what he knew of the thing, and no reply seemed quite to satisfy. Everyone seemed to feel himself in close proximity to phases of Nature and of being utterly forbidden and wholly outside the sane experience of mankind.

X.

In the end the three men from Arkham — old, white-bearded Dr. Armitage, stocky, iron-grey Professor Rice, and lean, youngish Dr. Morgan, ascended the mountain alone. After much patient instruction regarding its focusing and use, they left the telescope with the frightened group that remained in the road; and as they climbed they were watched closely by those among whom the glass was passed round. It was hard going, and Armitage had to be helped more than once. High above the toiling group the great swath trembled as its hellish maker repassed with snail-like deliberateness. Then it was obvious that the pursuers were gaining.

Curtis Whateley — of the undecayed branch — was holding the telescope when the Arkham party detoured radically from the swath. He told the crowd that the men were evidently trying to get to a subordinate peak which overlooked the swath at a point considerably ahead of where the shrubbery was now bending. This, indeed, proved to be true; and the party were seen to gain the minor elevation only a short time after the invisible blasphemy had passed it.

Then Wesley Corey, who had taken the glass, cried out that Armitage was adjusting the sprayer which Rice held, and that something must be about to happen. The crowd stirred uneasily, recalling that his sprayer was expected to give the unseen horror a moment of visibility. Two or three men shut their eyes, but Curtis Whateley snatched back the telescope and strained his vision to the utmost. He saw that Rice, from the party's point of advantage above and behind the entity, had an excellent chance of spreading the potent powder with marvellous effect.

Those without the telescope saw only an instant's flash of grey cloud — a cloud about the size of a moderately large building — near the top of the mountain. Curtis, who held the instrument, dropped it with a piercing shriek into the ankle-deep mud of the road. He reeled, and would have crumbled to the ground had not two or three others seized and steadied him. All he could do was moan half-inaudibly.

"Oh, oh, great Gawd . . . that . . . that . . ."

There was a pandemonium of questioning, and only Henry Wheeler thought to rescue the fallen telescope and wipe it clean of mud. Curtis was past all coherence, and even isolated replies were almost too much for him.

"Bigger'n a barn . . . all made o' squirmin' ropes . . . hull thing sort o' shaped like a hen's egg bigger'n anything with dozens o' legs like hogs-heads that haff shut up when they step . . . nothin' solid abaout it — all like jelly, an' made o' sep'rit wrigglin' ropes pushed clost together . . . great bulgin' eyes all over it . . . ten or twenty maouths or trunks a-stickin' aout all along the sides, big as stove-pipes an all a-tossin' an openin' an' shuttin' . . . all grey, with kinder blue or purple rings . . . an' Gawd it Heaven — that haff face on top . . ."

This final memory, whatever it was, proved too much for poor Curtis; and he collapsed completely before he could say more. Fred Farr and Will Hutchins carried him to the roadside and laid him on the damp grass. Henry Wheeler, trembling, turned the rescued telescope on the mountain to see what he might. Through the lenses were discernible three tiny figures, apparently running towards the summit as fast as the steep incline allowed. Only these — nothing more. Then everyone noticed a strangely unseasonable noise in the deep valley behind, and even in the underbrush of Sentinel Hill itself. It was the piping of unnumbered whippoorwills, and in their shrill chorus there seemed to lurk a note of tense and evil expectancy.

Earl Sawyer now took the telescope and reported the three figures as standing on the topmost ridge, virtually level with the altar-stone but at a considerable distance from it. One figure, he said, seemed to be raising its hands above its head at rhythmic intervals; and as Sawyer mentioned the circumstance the crowd seemed to hear a faint, half-musical sound from the distance, as if a loud chant were accompanying the gestures. The weird silhouette on that remote peak must have been a spectacle of infinite grotesqueness and impressiveness, but no observer was in a mood for aesthetic appreciation. "I guess he's sayin' the spell," whispered Wheeler as he snatched back the telescope. The whippoorwills were piping wildly, and in a singularly curious irregular rhythm quite unlike that of the visible ritual.

Suddenly the sunshine seemed to lessen without the intervention of any discernible cloud. It was a very peculiar phenomenon, and was plainly marked by all. A rumbling sound seemed brewing beneath the hills, mixed strangely with a concordant rumbling which clearly came from the sky. Lightning flashed aloft, and the wondering crowd looked in vain for the portents of storm. The chanting of the men from Arkham now became unmistakable, and Wheeler saw through the glass that they were all raising their arms in the rhythmic incantation. From some farmhouse far away came the frantic barking of dogs.

The change in the quality of the daylight increased, and the crowd gazed about the horizon in wonder. A purplish darkness, born of nothing more than a spectral deepening of the sky's blue, pressed down upon the rumbling hills. Then the lightning flashed again, somewhat brighter than before, and the crowd fancied that it had showed a certain mistiness around the altar-stone on the distant height. No one, however, had been using the telescope at that instant. The whippoorwills continued their irregular pulsation, and the men of Dunwich braced themselves tensely against some imponderable menace with which the atmosphere seemed surcharged.

Without warning came those deep, cracked, raucous vocal sounds which will never leave the memory of the stricken group who heard them. Not from any human throat were they born, for the organs of man can yield no such acoustic perversions. Rather would one have said they came from the pit itself, had not their source been so unmistakably the altar-stone on the peak. It is almost erroneous to call them sounds at all, since so much of their ghastly, infra-bass timbre spoke to dim seats of consciousness and terror far subtler than the ear; yet one must do so, since their form was indisputably though vaguely that of half-articulate words. They were loud — loud as the rumblings and the thunder above which they echoed — yet did they come from no visible being. And because imagination might suggest a conjectural source in the world of non-visible beings, the huddled crowd at the mountain's base huddled still closer, and winced as if in expectation of a blow.

"Ygnailh . . . ygnaiih . . . thflthkh'ngha . . . Yog-Sothoth . . ." rang the hideous croaking out of space. "Y'bthnk . . . h'ehye — n'grkdl'lh . . ."

The speaking impulse seemed to falter here, as if some frightful psychic struggle were going on. Henry Wheeler strained his eye at the telescope, but saw only the three grotesquely silhouetted human figures on the peak, all moving their arms furiously in strange gestures as their incantation drew near its culmination. From what black wells of Acherontic fear or feeling, from what unplumbed gulfs of extra-cosmic consciousness or obscure, long-latent heredity, were those half-articulate thunder-croakings drawn? Presently they began to gather renewed force and coherence as they grew in stark, utter, ultimate frenzy.

"Eh-y-ya-ya-yahaah — e'yayayaaaa . . . ngh'aaaaa . . . ngh'aaa . . . h'yuh . . . h'yuh . . . HELP! HELP! . . . ff — ff — ff — FATHER! FATHER! YOG-SOTHOTH!"

But that was all. The pallid group in the road, still reeling at the indisputably English syllables that had poured thickly and thunderously down from the frantic vacancy beside that shocking altar-stone, were never to hear such syllables again. Instead, they jumped violently at the terrific report which seemed to rend the hills; the deafening, cataclysmic peal whose source, be it inner earth or sky, no hearer was ever able to place. A single lightning bolt shot from the purple zenith to the altar-stone, and a great tidal wave of viewless force and indescribable stench swept down from the hill to all the countryside. Trees, grass, and under-brush were whipped into a fury; and the frightened crowd at the mountain's base, weakened by the lethal foetor that seemed about to asphyxiate them, were almost hurled off their feet. Dogs howled from the distance, green grass and foliage wilted to a curious, sickly yellow-grey, and over field and forest were scattered the bodies of dead whippoorwills.

The stench left quickly, but the vegetation never came right again. To this day there is something queer and unholy about the growths on and around that fearsome hill. Curtis Whateley was only just regaining consciousness when the Arkham men came slowly down the mountain in the beams of a sunlight once more brilliant and untainted. They were grave and quiet, and seemed shaken by memories and reflections even more terrible than those which had reduced the group of natives to a state of cowed quivering. In reply to a jumble of questions they only shook their heads and reaffirmed one vital fact.

"The thing has gone for ever," Armitage said. "It has been split up into what it was originally made of, and can never exist again. It was an impossibility in a normal world. Only the least fraction was really matter in any sense we know. It was like its father — and most of it has gone back to him in some vague realm or dimension outside our material universe; some vague abyss out of which only the most accursed rites of human blasphemy could ever have called him for a moment on the hills."

There was a brief silence, and in that pause the scattered senses of poor Curtis Whateley began to knit back into a sort of continuity; so that he put his hands to his head with a moan. Memory seemed to pick itself up where it had left off, and the horror of the sight that had prostrated him burst in upon him again.

"Oh, oh, my Gawd, that haff face — that haff face on top of it . . . that face with the red eyes an' crinkly albino hair, an' no chin, like the Whateleys . . . It was a octopus, centipede, spider kind o' thing, but they was a haff-shaped man's face on top of it, an' it looked like Wizard Whateley's, only it was yards an' yards acrost . . . ."

He paused exhausted, as the whole group of natives stared in a bewilderment not quite crystallized into fresh terror. Only old Zebulon Whateley, who wanderingly remembered ancient things but who had been silent heretofore, spoke aloud.

"Fifteen year' gone," he rambled, "I heered Ol' Whateley say as haow some day we'd hear a child o' Lavinny's a-callin' its father's name on the top o' Sentinel Hill . . ."

But Joe Osborn interrupted him to question the Arkham men anew.

"What was it, anyhaow, an' haowever did young Wizard Whateley call it aout o' the air it come from?"

Armitage chose his words very carefully.

"It was — well, it was mostly a kind of force that doesn't belong in our part of space; a kind of force that acts and grows and shapes itself by other laws than those of our sort of Nature. We have no business calling in such things from outside, and only very wicked people and very wicked cults ever try to. There was some of it in Wilbur Whateley himself — enough to make a devil and a precocious monster of him, and to make his passing out a pretty terrible sight. I'm going to burn his accursed diary, and if you men are wise you'll dynamite that altar-stone up there, and pull down all the rings of standing stones on the other hills. Things like that brought down the beings those Whateleys were so fond of — the beings they were going to let in tangibly to wipe out the human race and drag the earth off to some nameless place for some nameless purpose.

"But as to this thing we've just sent back — the Whateleys raised it for a terrible part in the doings that were to come. It grew fast and big from the same reason that Wilbur grew fast and big — but it beat him because it had a greater share of the outsideness in it. You needn't ask how Wilbur called it out of the air. He didn't call it out. It was his twin brother, but it looked more like the father than he did."

1929.

Poetry and Freedom.

For H.P. Lovecraft, 1929 was the year he came to fully inhabit the life that he would lead until his death just a few years later. But it seems almost certain that, had he been given twenty or thirty more years instead of just seven, he would have spent them in much the same way.

In March of 1929, Lovecraft's marriage to Sonia Haft Greene officially ended — mostly. (Much to her subsequent chagrin, he neglected to file the final decree.)

So the spring of 1929 found Lovecraft in the position of a free man, of broad leisure but slender means, with a nationwide network of friends and admirers all eager to play host during his summer travels. The best years of his life were upon him.

In the writing of his own weird fiction, 1929 was a bye year for Lovecraft. Other than the revision work he did on "The Electric Executioner" for Adolphe de Castro, he wrote no major fiction. But that summer he wrote a lengthy travelogue, "Travels in the Provinces of America"— the first of several similar works with which he would, over the next several years, re-live and commemorate his summer journeyings.

Then, at the very end of the year, Lovecraft took up poetry again for the first time in a decade. Although he'd spent most of the 1910s considering himself primarily a poet and essayist, he had all but abandoned poetry after meeting Clark Ashton Smith for the first time in September 1922. Lovecraft deemed Smith's talents as a poet to be far greater than his own — so much so that he hesitated to invite the comparison by producing current poetry. So his focus shifted fully onto fiction, and his poetic muse drifted off to sleep, to be awakened only once or twice with a sonnet or snatch of anapestic or dactylic verse for his own enjoyment or dedicated to a friend (or, in the case of "The Cats," friends).

Now, however, starting in November of 1929, he turned back to poetry and, in an intensely productive month or so, produced the best poems of his career — first warming up with "The Outpost" and "The Ancient Track," and finally producing the crowning achievement of his career as a poet, *Fungi from Yuggoth*, the legendary sonnet cycle pounded out in seven eventful days centered on New Year's Day 1930.

The Electric Executioner.

BY ADOLPHE DE CASTRO
AND H.P. LOVECRAFT

**8,000-WORD NOVELETTE;
1929.**

This short novelette was another of the stories Adolphe de Castro asked H.P. Lovecraft to revise for him. In this case, de Castro paid the full fee in advance — perhaps he was aware of the resentment his underpayment for The Last Test *had engendered.*

Lovecraft handled this story much as he had the other, but stuck more closely to the plot points and did not allow it to grow as the other had. He also took the opportunity to slip a few references to Cthulhu and Yog-Sothoth into it, very cleverly modifying the spelling to make them seem like Aztec variants of the same cosmic entities.

Lovecraft finished the revision in mid-1929, and de Castro successfully placed it in the August 1930 issue of Weird Tales *magazine.*

For one who has never faced the danger of legal execution, I have a rather queer horror of the electric chair as a subject. Indeed, I think the topic gives me more of a shudder than it gives many a man who has been on trial for his life. The reason is that I associate the thing with an incident of forty years ago — a very strange incident which brought me close to the edge of the unknown's black abyss.

In 1889 I was an auditor and investigator connected with the Tlaxcala Mining Company of San Francisco, which operated several small silver and copper properties in the San Mateo Mountains in Mexico. There had been some trouble at Mine No. 3, which had a surly, furtive assistant superintendent named Arthur Feldon; and on August 6th the firm received a telegram saying that Feldon had decamped, taking with him all the stock records, securities, and private papers, and leaving the whole clerical and financial situation in dire confusion. This development was a severe blow to the company, and late in the afternoon President McComb called me into his office to give orders for the recovery of the papers at any cost. There were, he knew, grave drawbacks. I had never seen Feldon, and there were only very indifferent photographs to go by. Moreover, my own wedding was set for Thursday of the following week — only nine days ahead — so that I was naturally not eager to be hurried off to Mexico on a man-hunt of indefinite length. The need, however, was so great that McComb felt justified in asking me to go at once; and I for my part decided that the effect on my status with the company would make ready acquiescence eminently worthwhile.

I was to start that night, using the president's private car as far as Mexico City, after which I would have to take a narrow-gauge railway to the mines. Jackson, the superintendent of No. 3, would give me all details and any possible clues upon my arrival; and then the search would begin in earnest — through the mountains, down to the coast, or among the byways of Mexico City, as the case might be.

I set out with a grim determination to get the matter done — and successfully done — as swiftly as possible; and tempered my discontent with pictures of an early return with papers and culprit, and of a wedding which would be almost a triumphal ceremony. Having notified my family, fiancée, and principal friends, and made hasty preparations for the trip, I met President McComb at eight p.m. at the Southern Pacific depot, received from him some written instructions and a cheque-book, and left in his car attached to the 8:15 eastbound transcontinental train.

The journey that followed seemed destined for uneventfulness, and after a good night's sleep I revelled in the ease of the private car so thoughtfully assigned me; reading my instructions with care, and formulating plans for the capture of Feldon and the recovery of the documents. I knew the Tlaxcala country quite well — probably much better than the missing man — hence had a certain amount of advantage in my search unless he had already used the railway.

According to the instructions, Feldon had been a subject of worry to Superintendent Jackson for some time; acting secretively, and working unaccountably in the company's laboratory at odd hours. That he was implicated with a Mexican boss and several peons in some thefts of ore was strongly suspected; but though the natives had been discharged, there was not enough evidence to warrant any positive step regarding the subtle official. Indeed, despite his furtiveness, there seemed to be more of defiance than of guilt in the man's bearing. He wore a chip on his shoulder, and talked as if the company were cheating him instead of his cheating the company. The obvious surveillance of his colleagues, Jackson wrote, appeared to irritate him increasingly; and now he had gone with everything of importance in the office. Of his possible whereabouts no guess could be made; though Jackson's final telegram suggested the wild slopes of the Sierra de Malinche, that tall, myth-surrounded peak with the corpse-shaped silhouette, from whose neighbourhood the thieving natives were said to have come.

The Electric Executioner

by Adolphe de Castro

"On the gravelly floor lay the horror."

Weird Tales, August 1930

At El Paso, which we reached at two a.m. of the night following our start, my private car was detached from the transcontinental train and joined to an engine specially ordered by telegraph to take it southward to Mexico City. I continued to drowse till dawn, and all the next day grew bored on the flat, desert Chihuahua landscape. The crew had told me we were due in Mexico City at noon Friday, but I soon saw that countless delays were wasting precious hours. There were waits on sidings all along the single-tracked route, and now and then a hot-box or other difficulty would further complicate the schedule.

At Torreón we were six hours late, and it was almost eight o'clock on Friday evening—fully twelve hours behind schedule—when the conductor consented to do some speeding in an effort to make up time. My nerves were on edge, and I could do nothing but pace the car in desperation. In the end I found that the speeding had been purchased at a high cost indeed, for within a half-hour the symptoms of a hot-box had developed in my car itself; so that after a maddening wait the crew decided that all the bearings would have to be overhauled after a quarter-speed limp ahead to the next station with shops — the factory town of Querétaro. This was the last straw, and I almost stamped like a child. Actually I sometimes caught myself pushing at my chair-arm as if trying to urge the train forward at a less snail-like pace.

It was almost ten in the evening when we drew into Querétaro, and I spent a fretful hour on the station platform while my car was sidetracked and tinkered at by a dozen native mechanics. At last they told me the job was too much for them, since the forward truck needed new parts which could not be obtained nearer than Mexico City. Everything indeed seemed against me, and I gritted my teeth when I thought of Feldon getting farther and farther away — perhaps to the easy cover of Veracruz with its shipping or Mexico City with its varied rail facilities — while fresh delays kept me tied and helpless. Of course Jackson had notified the police in all the cities around, but I knew with sorrow what their efficiency amounted to.

The best I could do, I soon found out, was to take the regular night express for Mexico City, which ran from Aguas Calientes and made a five-minute stop at Querétaro. It would be along at one a.m. if on time, and was due in Mexico City at five o'clock Saturday morning. When I purchased my ticket I found that the train would be made up of European compartment carriages instead of long American cars with rows of two-seat chairs. These had been much used in the early days of Mexican railroading, owing to the European construction interests back of the first lines; and in 1889 the Mexican Central was still running a fair number of them on its shorter trips. Ordinarily I prefer the American coaches, since I hate to have people facing me; but for this once I was glad of the foreign carriage. At such a time of night I stood a good chance of having a whole compartment to myself, and in my tired, nervously hypersensitive state I welcomed the solitude — as well as the comfortably upholstered seat with soft arm-rests and head-cushion, running the whole width of the vehicle. I bought a first-class ticket, obtained my valise from the side-tracked private car, telegraphed both President McComb and Jackson of what had happened, and settled down in the station to wait for the night express as patiently as my strained nerves would let me.

For a wonder, the train was only half an hour late; though even so, the solitary station vigil had about finished my endurance. The conductor, shewing me into a compartment, told me he expected to make up the delay and reach the capital on time; and I stretched myself comfortably on the forward-facing seat in the expectation of a quiet three-and-a-half-hour run. The light from the overhead oil lamp was soothingly dim, and I wondered whether I could snatch some much-needed sleep in spite of my anxiety and nerve-tension. It seemed, as the train jolted into motion, that I was alone; and I was heartily glad of it. My thoughts leaped ahead to my quest, and I nodded with the accelerating rhythm of the speeding string of carriages.

Then suddenly I perceived that I was not alone after all. In the corner diagonally opposite me, slumped down so that his face was invisible, sat a roughly clad man of unusual size, whom the feeble light had failed to reveal before. Beside him on the seat was a huge valise, battered and bulging, and tightly gripped even in his sleep by one of his incongruously slender hands. As the engine whistled sharply at some curve or crossing, the sleeper started nervously into a kind of watchful half-awakening; raising his head and disclosing a handsome face, bearded and clearly Anglo-Saxon, with dark, lustrous eyes. At sight of me his wakefulness became complete, and I wondered at the rather hostile wildness of his glance. No doubt, I thought, he resented my presence when he had hoped to have the compartment alone all the way; just as I was myself disappointed to find strange company in the half-lighted carriage. The best we could do, however, was to accept the situation gracefully; so I began apologising to the man for my intrusion. He seemed to be a fellow-American, and we could both feel more at ease after a few civilities. Then we could leave each other in peace for the balance of the journey.

To my surprise, the stranger did not respond to my courtesies with so much as a word. Instead, he kept staring at me fiercely and almost appraisingly, and brushed aside my embarrassed proffer of a cigar with a nervous lateral movement of his disengaged hand. His other hand still tensely clutched the great, worn valise, and his whole person seemed to radiate some obscure malignity. After a time he abruptly turned his face toward the window, though there was nothing to see in the dense blackness outside. Oddly, he appeared to be looking at something as intently as if there really were something to look at. I decided to leave him to his own curious devices and meditations without further annoyance; so settled back in my seat, drew the brim of my soft hat over my face, and closed my eyes in an effort to snatch the sleep I had half counted on.

I could not have dozed very long or very fully when my eyes fell open as if in response to some external force. Closing them again with some determination, I renewed my quest of a nap, yet wholly without avail. An intangible influence seemed bent on keeping me awake; so raising my head, I looked about the dimly lighted compartment to see if anything were amiss. All appeared normal, but I noticed that the stranger in the opposite corner was looking at me very intently — intently, though without any of the geniality or friendliness which would have implied a change from his former surly attitude. I did not attempt conversation this time, but leaned back in my previous sleepy posture; half closing my eyes as if I had dozed off once more, yet continuing to watch him curiously from beneath my down-turned hat brim. As the train rattled onward through the night I saw a subtle and gradual metamorphosis come over the expression of the staring man. Evidently satisfied that I was asleep, he allowed his face to reflect a curious jumble of emotions, the nature of which seemed anything but reassuring. Hatred, fear, triumph, and fanaticism flickered compositely over the lines of his lips and the angles of his eyes, while his gaze became a glare of really alarming greed and ferocity. Suddenly it dawned upon me that this man was mad, and dangerously so.

I will not pretend that I was anything but deeply and thoroughly frightened when I saw how things stood. Perspiration started out all over me, and I had hard work to maintain my attitude of relaxation and slumber. Life had many attractions for me just then, and the thought of dealing with a homicidal maniac — possibly armed and certainly powerful to a marvellous degree — was a dismaying and terrifying one. My disadvantage in any sort of struggle was enormous; for the man was a virtual giant, evidently in the best of athletic trim, while I have always been rather frail, and was then almost worn out with anxiety, sleeplessness, and nervous tension. It was undeniably a bad moment for me, and I felt pretty close to a horrible death as I recognised the fury of madness in the stranger's eyes. Events from the past came up into my consciousness as if for a farewell — just as a drowning man's whole life is said to resurrect itself before him at the last moment.

Of course I had my revolver in my coat pocket, but any motion of mine to reach and draw it would be instantly obvious. Moreover, if I did secure it, there was no telling what effect it would have on the maniac. Even if I shot him once or twice he might have enough remaining strength to get the gun from me and deal with me in his own way; or if he were armed himself he might shoot or stab without trying to disarm me. One can cow a sane man by covering him with a pistol, but an insane man's complete indifference to consequences gives him a strength and menace quite superhuman for the time being. Even in those pre-Freudian days I had a common-sense realisation of the dangerous power of a person without normal inhibitions. That the stranger in the corner was indeed about to start some murderous action, his burning eyes and twitching facial muscles did not permit me to doubt for a moment.

Suddenly I heard his breath begin to come in excited gasps, and saw his chest heaving with mounting excitement. The time for a showdown was close, and I tried desperately to think of the best thing to do. Without interrupting my pretence of sleep, I began to slide my right hand gradually and inconspicuously toward the pocket containing my pistol; watching the madman closely as I did so, to see if he would detect any move. Unfortunately he did — almost before he had time to register the fact in his expression. With a bound so agile and abrupt as to be almost incredible in a man of his size, he was upon me before I knew what had happened; looming up and swaying forward like a giant ogre of legend, and pinioning me with one powerful hand while with the other he forestalled me in reaching the revolver. Taking it from my pocket and placing it in his own, he released me contemptuously, well knowing how fully his physique placed me at his mercy. Then he stood up at his full height — his head almost touching the roof of the carriage — and stared down at me with eyes whose fury had quickly turned to a look of pitying scorn and ghoulish calculation.

I did not move, and after a moment the man resumed his seat opposite me; smiling a ghastly smile as he opened his great bulging valise and extracted an article of peculiar appearance — a rather large cage of semi-flexible wire, woven somewhat like a baseball catcher's mask, but shaped more like the helmet of a diving-suit. Its top was connected with a cord whose other end remained in the valise. This device he fondled with obvious affection, cradling it in his lap as he looked at me afresh and licked his bearded lips with an almost feline motion of the tongue. Then, for the first time, he spoke — in a deep, mellow voice of softness and cultivation startlingly at variance with his rough corduroy clothes and unkempt aspect.

"You are fortunate, sir. I shall use you first of all. You shall go into history as the first fruits of a remarkable invention. Vast sociological consequences — I shall let my light shine, as it were. I'm radiating all the time, but nobody knows it. Now you shall know. Intelligent guinea-pig. Cats and burros — it worked even with a burro . . ."

He paused, while his bearded features underwent a convulsive motion closely synchronised with a vigorous gyratory shaking of the whole head. It was as though he were shaking clear of some nebulous obstructing medium, for the gesture was followed by a clarification or subtilisation of expression which hid the more obvious madness in a look of suave composure through which the craftiness gleamed only dimly. I glimpsed the difference at once, and put in a word to see if I could lead his mind into harmless channels. "You seem to have a marvellously fine instrument, if I'm any judge. Won't you tell me how you came to invent it?" He nodded.

"Mere logical reflection, dear sir. I consulted the needs of the age and acted upon them. Others might have done the same had their minds been as powerful — that is, as capable of sustained concentration — as mine. I had the sense of conviction — the available will power — that is all. I realised, as no one else has yet realised, how imperative it is to remove everybody from the earth before Quetzalcoatl comes back, and realised also that it must be done elegantly. I hate butchery of any kind, and hanging is barbarously crude. You know last year the New York legislature voted to adopt electric execution for condemned men — but all the apparatus they have in mind is as primitive as Stephenson's 'Rocket' or Davenport's first electric engine. I knew of a better way, and told them so, but they paid no attention to me. God, the fools! As if I didn't know all there is to know about men and death and electricity — student, man, and boy — technologist and engineer — soldier of fortune . . ."

He leaned back and narrowed his eyes.

"I was in Maximilian's army twenty years and more ago. They were going to make me a nobleman. Then those damned greasers killed him and I had to go home. But I came back — back and forth, back and forth. I live in Rochester, New York . . ."

His eyes grew deeply crafty, and he leaned forward, touching me on the knee with the fingers of a paradoxically delicate hand. "I came back, I say, and I went deeper than any of them. I hate greasers, but I like Mexicans! A puzzle? Listen to me, young fellow — you don't think Mexico is really Spanish, do you? God, if you knew the tribes I know! In the mountains — in the mounains — Anahuac — Tenochtitlan — the Old Ones ..."

His voice changed to a chanting and not unmelodious howl.

"I?! Huitzilopotchli! ... Nahuatlacatl! Seven, seven, seven ... Xochimilca, Chalca, Tepaneca, Acolhua, Tlahuica, Tlascalteca, Azteca! ... I?! I?! I have been to the Seven Caves of Chicomoztoc, but no one shall ever know! I tell you because you will never repeat it."

He subsided, and resumed a conversational tone.

"It would surprise you to know what things are told in the mountains. Huitzilopotchli is coming back ... of that there can be no doubt. Any peon south of Mexico City can tell you that. But I meant to do nothing about it. I went home, as I tell you, again and again, and was going to benefit society with my electric executioner when that cursed Albany legislature adopted the other way. A joke, sir, a joke! Grandfather's chair — sit by the fireside — Hawthorne — "

The man was chuckling with a morbid parody of good nature.

"Why, sir, I'd like to be the first man to sit in their damned chair and feel their little two-bit battery current! It wouldn't make a frog's legs dance! And they expect to kill murderers with it — reward of merit — everything! But then, young man, I saw the uselessness — the pointless illogicality, as it were — of killing just a few. Everybody is a murderer — they murder ideas — steal inventions — stole mine by watching, and watching, and watching — "

The man choked and paused, and I spoke soothingly.

"I'm sure your invention was much the better, and probably they'll come to use it in the end."

Evidently my tact was not great enough, for his response shewed fresh irritation.

" 'Sure,' are you? Nice, mild, conservative assurance! Cursed lot you care — but you'll soon know! Why, damn you, all the good there ever will be in that electric chair will have been stolen from me. The ghost of Nezahualpilli told me that on the sacred mountain. They watched, and watched, and watched — "

He choked again, then gave another of those gestures in which he seemed to shake both his head and his facial expression. That seemed temporarily to steady him.

"What my invention needs is testing. That is it — here. The wire hood or head-net is flexible, and slips on easily. Neckpiece binds but doesn't choke. Electrodes touch forehead and base of cerebellum — all that's necessary. Stop the head, and what else can go? The fools up at Albany, with their carved oak easy-chair, think they've got to make it a head-to-foot affair. Idiots! — don't they know that you don't need to shoot a man through the body after you've plugged him through the brain? I've seen men die in battle — I know better. And then their silly high-power circuit — dynamos — all that. Why didn't they see what I've done with the storage-battery? Not a hearing — nobody knows — I alone have the secret — that's why I and Quetzalcoatl and Huitzilopotchli will rule the world alone — I and they, if I choose to let them ... But I must have experimental subjects — subjects — do you know whom I've chosen for the first?"

I tried jocoseness, quickly merging into friendly seriousness, as a sedative. Quick thought and apt words might save me yet.

"Well, there are lots of fine subjects among the politicians of San Francisco, where I come from! They need your treatment, and I'd like to help you introduce it! But really, I think I can help you in all truth. I have some influence in Sacramento, and if you'll go back to the States with me after I'm through with my business in Mexico, I'll see that you get a hearing."

He answered soberly and civilly.

"No — I can't go back. I swore not to when those criminals at Albany turned down my invention and set spies to watch me and steal from me. But I must have American subjects. Those greasers are under a curse, and would be too easy; and the full-blood Indians — the real children of the feathered serpent — are sacred and inviolate except for proper sacrificial victims ... and even those must be slain according to ceremony. I must have Americans without going back — and the first man I choose will be signally honoured. Do you know who he is?"

I temporised desperately. "Oh, if that's all the trouble, I'll find you a dozen first-rate Yankee specimens as soon as we get to Mexico City! I know where there are lots of small mining men who wouldn't be missed for days — "

But he cut me short with a new and sudden air of authority which had a touch of real dignity in it.

"That'll do — we've trifled long enough. Get up and stand erect like a man. You're the subject I've chosen, and you'll thank me for the honour in the other world, just as the sacrificial victim thanks the priest for transferring him to eternal glory. A new principle — no other man alive has dreamed of such a battery, and it might never again be hit on if the world experimented a thousand years. Do you know that atoms aren't what they seem? Fools! A century after this some dolt would be guessing if I were to let the world live!"

As I arose at his command, he drew additional feet of cord from the valise and stood erect beside me, the wire helmet outstretched toward me in both hands, and a look of real exaltation on his tanned and bearded face. For an instant he seemed like a radiant Hellenic mystagogue or hierophant.

"Here, O Youth — a libation! Wine of the cosmos — nectar of the starry spaces — Linos — Iacchus — Ialmenos — Zagreus — Dionysos — Atys — Hylas — sprung from Apollo and slain by the hounds of Argos — seed of Psamathe — child of the sun — Evoë! Evoë!"

He was chanting again, and this time his mind seemed far back amongst the classic memories of his college days. In my erect posture I noticed the nearness of the signal cord overhead, and wondered whether I could reach it through some gesture of ostensible response to his ceremonial mood. It was worth trying, so with an antiphonal cry of "Evoë!" I put my arms forward and upward toward him in a ritualistic fashion, hoping to give the cord a tug before he could notice the act. But it was useless. He saw my purpose, and moved one hand toward the right-hand coat pocket where my revolver lay. No words were needed, and we stood for a moment like carven figures. Then he quietly said, "Make haste!"

Again my mind rushed frantically about seeking avenues of escape. The doors, I knew, were not locked on Mexican trains; but my companion could easily forestall me if I tried to unlatch one and jump out. Besides, our speed was so great that success in that direction would probably be as fatal as failure. The only thing to do was to play for time. Of the three-and-a-half-hour trip a good slice was already worn away, and once we got to Mexico City the guards and police in the station would provide instant safety.

There would, I thought, be two distinct times for diplomatic stalling. If I could get him to postpone the slipping on of the hood, that much time would be gained. Of course I had no belief that the thing was really deadly; but I knew enough of madmen to understand what would happen when it failed to work. To his disappointment would be added a mad sense of my responsibility for the failure, and the result would be a red chaos of murderous rage. Therefore the experiment must be postponed as long as possible. Yet the second opportunity did exist, for if I planned cleverly I might devise explanations for the failure which would hold his attention and lead him into more or less extended searches for corrective influences. I wondered just how far his credulity went, and whether I could prepare in advance a prophecy of failure which would make the failure itself stamp me as a seer or initiate, or perhaps a god. I had enough of a smattering of Mexican mythology to make it worth trying; though I would try other delaying influences first and let the prophecy come as a sudden revelation. Would he spare me in the end if I could make him think me a prophet or divinity? Could I "get by" as Quetzalcoatl or Huitzilopotchli? Anything to drag matters out till five o'clock, when we were due in Mexico City.

But my opening "stall" was the veteran will-making ruse. As the maniac repeated his command for haste, I told him of my family and intended marriage, and asked for the privilege of leaving a message and disposing of my money and effects. If, I said, he would lend me some paper and agree to mail what I should write, I could die more peacefully and willingly. After some cogitation he gave a favourable verdict and fished in his valise for a pad, which he handed me solemnly as I resumed my seat. I produced a pencil, artfully breaking the point at the outset and causing some delay while he searched for one of his own. When he gave me this, he took my broken pencil and proceeded to sharpen it with a large, horn-handled knife which had been in his belt under his coat. Evidently a second pencil-breaking would not profit me greatly.

What I wrote, I can hardly recall at this date. It was largely gibberish, and composed of random scraps of memorised literature when I could think of nothing else to set down. I made my handwriting as illegible as I could without destroying its nature as writing; for I knew he would be likely to look at the result before commencing his experiment, and realised how he would react to the sight of obvious nonsense. The ordeal was a terrible one, and I chafed each second at the slowness of the train. In the past I had often whistled a brisk gallop to the sprightly "tac" of wheels on rails, but now the tempo seemed slowed down to that of a funeral march — my funeral march, I grimly reflected.

My ruse worked till I had covered over four pages, six by nine; when at last the madman drew out his watch and told me I could have but five minutes more. What should I do next? I was hastily going through the form of concluding the will when a new idea struck me. Ending with a flourish and handing him the finished sheets, which he thrust carelessly into his left-hand coat pocket, I reminded him of my influential Sacramento friends who would be so much interested in his invention.

"Oughtn't I to give you a letter of introduction to them?" I said. "Oughtn't I to make a signed sketch and description of your executioner so that they'll grant you a cordial hearing? They can make you famous, you know — and there's no question at all but that they'll adopt your method for the state of California if they hear of it through someone like me, whom they know and trust."

I was taking this tack on the chance that his thoughts as a disappointed inventor would let him forget the Aztec-religious side of his mania for a while. When he veered to the latter again, I reflected, I would spring the "revelation" and "prophecy."

The scheme worked, for his eyes glowed an eager assent, though he brusquely told me to be quick. He further emptied the valise, lifting out a queer-looking congeries of glass cells and coils to which the wire from the helmet was attached, and delivering a fire of running comment too technical for me to follow yet apparently quite plausible and straightforward. I pretended to note down all he said, wondering as I did so whether the queer apparatus was really a battery after all. Would I get a slight shock when he applied the device? The man surely talked as if he were a genuine electrician. Description of his own invention was clearly a congenial task for him, and I saw he was not as impatient as before. The hopeful grey of dawn glimmered red through the windows before he wound up, and I felt at last that my chance of escape had really become tangible.

But he, too, saw the dawn, and began glaring wildly again. He knew the train was due in Mexico City at five, and would certainly force quick action unless I could override all his judgment with engrossing ideas. As he rose with a determined air, setting the battery on the seat beside the open valise, I reminded him that I had not made the needed sketch; and asked him to hold the headpiece so that I could draw it near the battery. He complied and resumed his seat, with many admonitions to me to hurry. After another moment I paused for some information, asking him how the victim was placed for execution, and how his presumable struggles were overcome.

"Why," he replied, "the criminal is securely strapped to a post. It does not matter how much he tosses his head, for the helmet fits tightly and draws even closer when the current comes on. We turn the switch gradually — you see it here, a carefully arranged affair with a rheostat."

A new idea for delay occurred to me as the tilled fields and increasingly frequent houses in the dawn-light outside told of our approach to the capital at last.

"But," I said, "I must draw the helmet in place on a human head as well as beside the battery. Can't you slip it on yourself a moment so that I can sketch you with it? The papers as well as the officials will want all this, and they are strong on completeness."

I had, by chance, made a better shot than I had planned; for at my mention of the press the madman's eyes lit up afresh. "The papers? Yes — damn them, you can make even the papers give me a hearing! They all laughed at me and wouldn't print a word. Here, you, hurry up! We've not a second to lose!"

He had slipped the headpiece on and was watching my flying pencil avidly. The wire mesh gave him a grotesque, comic look as he sat there with nervously twitching hands.

"Now, curse 'em, they'll print pictures! I'll revise your sketch if you make any blunders — must be accurate at any cost. Police will find you afterward — they'll tell how it works. Associated Press item — back up your letter — immortal fame . . . Hurry, I say — hurry, confound you!" The train was lurching over the poorer roadbed near the city and we swayed disconcertingly now and then. With this excuse I managed to break the pencil again, but of course the maniac at once handed me my own which he had sharpened. My first batch of ruses was about used up, and I felt that I should have to submit to the headpiece in a moment. We were still a good quarter-hour from the terminal, and it was about time for me to divert my companion to his religious side and spring the divine prophecy.

Mustering up my scraps of Nahuan-Aztec mythology, I suddenly threw down pencil and paper and commenced to chant.

"I?! I?! Tloquenahuaque, Thou Who Art All In Thyself! Thou too, Ipalnemoan, By Whom We Live! I hear, I hear! I see, I see! Serpent-bearing Eagle, hail! A message! A message! Huitzilopotchli, in my soul echoes thy thunder!"

At my intonations the maniac stared incredulously through his odd mask, his handsome face shewn in a surprise and perplexity which quickly changed to alarm. His mind seemed to go blank a moment, and then to recrystallise in another pattern. Raising his hands aloft, he chanted as if in a dream.

"Mictlanteuctli, Great Lord, a sign! A sign from within thy black cave! I?! Tonatiuh-Metztli! Cthulhutl! Command, and I serve!"

Now in all this responsive gibberish there was one word which struck an odd chord in my memory. Odd, because it never occurs in any printed account of Mexican mythology, yet had been overheard by me more than once as an awestruck whisper amongst the peons in my own firm's Tlaxcala mines. It seemed to be part of an exceedingly secret and ancient ritual; for there were characteristic whispered responses which I had caught now and then, and which were as unknown as itself to academic scholarship. This maniac must have spent considerable time with the hill peons and Indians, just as he had said; for surely such unrecorded lore could have come from no mere book-learning. Realising the importance he must attach to this doubly esoteric jargon, I determined to strike at his most vulnerable spot and give him the gibberish responses the natives used.

"Ya-R'lyeh! Ya-R'lyeh!" I shouted. "Cthulhutl fhtaghn! Niguratl-Yig! Yog-Sototl — "

But I never had a chance to finish. Galvanised into a religious epilepsy by the exact response which his subconscious mind had probably not really expected, the madman scrambled down to a kneeling posture on the floor, bowing his wire-helmeted head again and again, and turning it to the right and left as he did so. With each turn his obeisances became more profound, and I could hear his foaming lips repeating the syllable "kill, kill, kill," in a rapidly swelling monotone. It occurred to me that I had overreached myself, and that my response had unloosed a mounting mania which would rouse him to the slaying-point before the train reached the station.

As the arc of the madman's turnings gradually increased, the slack in the cord from his headpiece to the battery had naturally been taken up more and more. Now, in an all-forgetting delirium of ecstasy, he began to magnify his turns to complete circles, so that the cord wound round his neck and began to tug at its moorings to the battery on the seat. I wondered what he would do when the inevitable would happen, and the battery would be dragged to presumable destruction on the floor.

Then came the sudden cataclysm. The battery, yanked over the seat's edge by the maniac's last gesture of orgiastic frenzy, did indeed fall; but it did not seem to have wholly broken. Instead, as my eye caught the spectacle in one too-fleeting instant, the actual impact was borne by the rheostat, so that the switch was jerked over instantly to full current. And the marvellous thing is that there was a current. The invention was no mere dream of insanity.

I saw a blinding blue auroral coruscation, heard an ululating shriek more hideous than any of the previous cries of that mad, horrible journey, and smelled the nauseous odour of burning flesh. That was all my overwrought consciousness could bear, and I sank instantly into oblivion.

When the train guard at Mexico City revived me, I found a crowd on the station platform around my compartment door. At my involuntary cry the pressing faces became curious and dubious, and I was glad when the guard shut out all but the trim doctor who had pushed his way through to me. My cry was a very natural thing, but it had been prompted by something more than the shocking sight on the carriage floor which

I had expected to see. Or I should say, by something less, because in truth there was not anything on the floor at all.

Nor, said the guard, had there been when he opened the door and found me unconscious within. My ticket was the only one sold for that compartment, and I was the only person found within it. Just myself and my valise, nothing more. I had been alone all the way from Querétaro. Guard, doctor, and spectators alike tapped their foreheads significantly at my frantic and insistent questions.

Had it all been a dream, or was I indeed mad? I recalled my anxiety and overwrought nerves, and shuddered. Thanking the guard and doctor, and shaking free of the curious crowd, I staggered into a cab and was taken to the Fonda Nacional, where, after telegraphing Jackson at the mine, I slept till afternoon in an effort to get a fresh grip on myself. I had myself called at one o'clock, in time to catch the narrow-gauge for the mining country, but when I got up I found a telegram under the door. It was from Jackson, and said that Feldon had been found dead in the mountains that morning, the news reaching the mine about ten o'clock. The papers were all safe, and the San Francisco office had been duly notified. So the whole trip, with its nervous haste and harrowing mental ordeal, had been for nothing!

Knowing that McComb would expect a personal report despite the course of events, I sent another wire ahead and took the narrow-gauge after all. Four hours later I was rattled and jolted into the station of Mine No. 3, where Jackson was waiting to give a cordial greeting. He was so full of the affair at the mine that he did not notice my still shaken and seedy appearance.

The superintendent's story was brief, and he told me it as he led me toward the shack up the hillside above the *arrastre*, where Feldon's body lay. Feldon, he said, had always been a queer, sullen character, ever since he was hired the year before; working at some secret mechanical device and complaining of constant espionage, and being disgustingly familiar with the native workmen. But he certainly knew the work, the country, and the people. He used to make long trips into the hills where the peons lived, and even to take part in some of their ancient, heathenish ceremonies. He hinted at odd secrets and strange powers as often as he boasted of his mechanical skill. Of late he had disintegrated rapidly; growing morbidly suspicious of his colleagues, and undoubtedly joining his native friends in ore-thieving after his cash got low. He needed unholy amounts of money for something or other — was always having boxes come from laboratories and machine shops in Mexico City or the States.

As for the final absconding with all the papers — it was only a crazy gesture of revenge for what he called "spying." He was certainly stark mad, for he had gone across country to a hidden cave on the wild slope of the haunted Sierra de Malinche, where no white men live, and had done some amazingly queer things. The cave, which would never have been found but for the final tragedy, was full of hideous old Aztec idols and altars; the latter covered with the charred bones of recent burnt-offerings of doubtful nature. The natives would tell nothing — indeed, they swore they knew nothing — but it was easy to see that the cave was an old rendezvous of theirs, and that Feldon had shared their practices to the fullest extent.

The searchers had found the place only because of the chanting and the final cry. It had been close to five that morning, and after an all-night encampment the party had begun to pack up for its empty-handed return to the mines. Then somebody had heard faint rhythms in the distance, and knew that one of the noxious old native rituals was being howled from some lonely spot up the slope of the corpse-shaped mountain. They heard the same old names — Mictlanteuctli, Tonatiuh-Metzli, Cthulhutl, Ya-R'lyeh, and all the rest — but the queer thing was that some English words were mixed with them. Real white man's English, and no greaser patter. Guided by the sound, they had hastened up the weed-entangled mountainside toward it, when after a spell of quiet the shriek had burst upon them. It was a terrible thing — a worse thing than any of them had ever heard before. There seemed to be some smoke, too, and a morbid acrid smell.

Then they stumbled on the cave, its entrance screened by scrub mesquites, but now emitting clouds of foetid smoke. It was lighted within, the horrible altars and grotesque images revealed flickeringly by candles which must have been changed less than a half-hour before; and on the gravelly floor lay the horror that made all the crowd reel backward. It was Feldon, head burned to a crisp by some odd device he had slipped over it — a kind of wire cage connected with a rather shaken-up battery which had evidently fallen to the floor from a nearby altar-pot. When the men saw it they exchanged glances, thinking of the "electric executioner" Feldon had always boasted of inventing — the thing which everyone had rejected, but had tried to steal and copy. The papers were safe in Feldon's open portmanteau which stood close by, and an hour later the column of searchers started back for No. 3 with a grisly burden on an improvised stretcher.

That was all, but it was enough to make me turn pale and falter as Jackson led me up past the *arrastre* to the shed where he said the body lay. For I was not without imagination, and knew only too well into what hellish nightmare this tragedy somehow supernaturally dovetailed. I knew what I should see inside that gaping door around which the curious miners clustered, and did not flinch when my eyes took in the giant form, the rough corduroy clothes, the oddly delicate hands, the wisps of burnt beard, and the hellish machine itself — battery slightly broken, and headpiece blackened by the charring of what was inside. The great, bulging portmanteau did not surprise me, and I quailed only at two things — the folded sheets of paper sticking out of the left-hand pocket, and the queer sagging of the corresponding right-hand pocket. In a moment when no one was looking I reached out and seized the too familiar sheets, crushing them in my hand without daring to look at their penmanship. I ought to be sorry now that a kind of panic fear made me burn them that night with averted eyes. They would have been a positive proof or disproof of something — but for that matter I could still have had proof by asking about the revolver the coroner afterward took from that sagging right-hand coat pocket. I never had the courage to ask about that — because my own revolver was missing after the night on the train. My pocket pencil, too, shewed signs of a crude and hasty sharpening unlike the precise pointing I had given it Friday afternoon on the machine in President McComb's private car.

So in the end I went home still puzzled — mercifully puzzled, perhaps. The private car was repaired when I got back to Querétaro, but my greatest relief was crossing the Rio Grande into El Paso and the States. By the next Friday I was in San Francisco again, and the postponed wedding came off the following week.

As to what really happened that night — as I've said, I simply don't dn I tell my story most people call me a plain liar. Others lay it to abnormal psychology — and heaven knows I was overwrought — while still others talk of "astral projection" of some sort. My zeal to catch Feldon certainly sent my thoughts ahead toward him, and with all his Indian magic he'd be about the first one to recognise and meet them. Was he in the railway carriage or was I in the cave on the corpse-shaped haunted mountain? What would have happened to me, had I not delayed him as I did? I'll confess I don't know, and I'm not sure that I want to know. I've never been in Mexico since — and as I said at the start, I don't enjoy hearing about electric executions.

The Outpost.

POETRY;
1929.

This evocative poem marks H.P. Lovecraft's return to the form, on Nov. 26, 1929. It was inspired by a visit with Edward Lloyd Sechrist, who had recently returned from Zimbabwe and had seen the ruins of an ancient city there.

Lovecraft submitted it to Weird Tales, *but editor Farnsworth Wright rejected it, saying it was too long. So Lovecraft gave it to amateur journalist Victor Edward Bacon to publish in his journal,* Bacon's Essays, *in the spring 1930 issue.*

When evening cools the yellow stream,
And shadows stalk the jungle's ways,
Zimbabwe's palace flares ablaze
For a great King who fears to dream.

For he alone of all mankind
Waded the swamp that serpents shun;
And struggling toward the setting sun,
Came on the veldt that lies behind.

No other eyes had vented there
Since eyes were lent for human sight —
But there, as sunset turned to night,
He found the Elder Secret's lair.

Strange turrets rose beyond the plain,
And walls and bastions spread around
The distant domes that fouled the ground
Like leprous fungi after rain.

A grudging moon writhed up to shine
Past leagues where life can have no home;
And paling far-off tower and dome,
Shewed each unwindowed and malign.

Then he who in his boyhood ran
Through vine-hung ruins free of fear,
Trembled at what he saw — for here
Was no dead, ruined seat of man.

Inhuman shapes, half-seen, half-guessed,
Half solid and half ether-spawned,
Seethed down from starless voids that yawned
In heav'n, to these blank walls of pest.

And voidward from that pest-mad zone
Amorphous hordes seethed darkly back,
Their dim claws laden with the wrack
Of things that men have dreamed and known.
The ancient Fishers from Outside —
Were there not tales the high-priest told,
Of how they found the worlds of old,
And took what pelf their fancy spied?

Their hidden, dread-ringed outposts brood
Upon a million worlds of space;
Abhorred by every living race,
Yet scatheless in their solitude.

Sweating with fright, the watcher crept
Back to the swamp that serpents shun,
So that he lay, by rise of sun,
Safe in the palace where he slept.

None saw him leave, or come at dawn,
Nor does his flesh bear any mark
Of what he met in that curs't dark —
Yet from his sleep all peace has gone.

When evening cools the yellow stream,
And shadows stalk the jungle's ways,
Zimbabwe's palace flares ablaze,
For a great King who fears to dream.

The Ancient Track.

POETRY;
1929.

This short piece in iambic quadrameter is widely regarded as the best individual poem among Lovecraft's 1929–1930 verses. Lovecraft wrote it in early December 1929; he submitted it to Weird Tales, *which readily accepted it and published it in the March 1930 issue.*

There was no hand to hold me back
That night I found the ancient track
Over the hill, and strained to see
The fields that teased my memory.
This tree, that wall — I knew them well,
And all the roofs and orchards fell

Familiarly upon my mind
As from a past not far behind.
I knew what shadows would be cast
When the late moon came up at last
From back of Zaman's Hill, and how
The vale would shine three hours from now.
And when the path grew steep and high,
And seemed to end against the sky,
I had no fear of what might rest
Beyond that silhouetted crest.
Straight on I walked, while all the night
Grew pale with phosphorescent light,
And wall and farmhouse gable glowed
Unearthly by the climbing road.
There was the milestone that I knew —
"Two miles to Dunwich" — now the view
Of distant spire and roofs would dawn
With ten more upward paces gone ....

There was no hand to hold me back
That night I found the ancient track,

And reached the crest to see outspread
A valley of the lost and dead:
And over Zaman's Hill the horn
Of a malignant moon was born,
To light the weeds and vines that grew
On ruined walls I never knew.
The fox-fire glowed in field and bog,
And unknown waters spewed a fog
Whose curling talons mocked the thought
That I had ever known this spot.
Too well I saw from the mad scene
That my loved past had never been—
Nor was I now upon the trail
Descending to that long-dead vale.
Around was fog—ahead, the spray
Of star-streams in the Milky Way . . . .

There was no hand to hold me back
That night I found the ancient track.

Fungi from Yuggoth.

36-POEM SONNET CYCLE;
1930.

H.P. Lovecraft wrote this remarkable sequence of sonnets all at once during a single highly productive week: Dec. 27, 1929, to Jan. 4, 1930. They are usually treated as a sonnet cycle, although they don't all fit together as a story or theme.

Nor do they all fit the same rhyme scheme. The majority are in the Petrarchan or modified Petrarchan form, but some are in the Shakespearean form, and all of them, whatever their style might otherwise be, finish with the classic final couplet.

Although individual sonnets from Fungi from Yuggoth *were published here and there in various amateur journals and in* Weird Tales, *the full set was not published until August Derleth collected all of them for* Beyond the Wall of Sleep, *published by Arkham House in 1943.*

I.
THE BOOK.

The place was dark and dusty and half-lost
In tangles of old alleys near the quays,
Reeking of strange things brought in from the seas,
And with queer curls of fog that west winds tossed.
Small lozenge panes, obscured by smoke and frost,
Just shewed the books, in piles like twisted trees,
Rotting from floor to roof—congeries
Of crumbling elder lore at little cost.
I entered, charmed, and from a cobwebbed heap
Took up the nearest tome and thumbed it through,
Trembling at curious words that seemed to keep
Some secret, monstrous if one only knew.
Then, looking for some seller old in craft,
I could find nothing but a voice that laughed.

Weird Tales, multiple dates (standing-head art)

II.
PURSUIT.

I held the book beneath my coat, at pains
To hide the thing from sight in such a place;
Hurrying through the ancient harbor lanes
With often-turning head and nervous pace.
Dull, furtive windows in old tottering brick
Peered at me oddly as I hastened by,
And thinking what they sheltered, I grew sick
For a redeeming glimpse of clean blue sky.
No one had seen me take the thing — but still
A blank laugh echoed in my whirling head,
And I could guess what nighted worlds of ill
Lurked in that volume I had coveted.
The way grew strange — the walls alike and madding —
And far behind me, unseen feet were padding.

III.
THE KEY.

I do not know what windings in the waste
Of those strange sea-lanes brought me home once more,
But on my porch I trembled, white with haste
To get inside and bolt the heavy door.
I had the book that told the hidden way
Across the void and through the space-hung screens
That hold the undimensioned worlds at bay,
And keep lost aeons to their own demesnes.
At last the key was mine to those vague visions
Of sunset spires and twilight woods that brood
Dim in the gulfs beyond this earth's precisions,
Lurking as memories of infinitude.
The key was mine, but as I sat there mumbling,
The attic window shook with a faint fumbling.

IV.
RECOGNITION.

The day had come again, when as a child
I saw — just once — that hollow of old oaks,
Grey with a ground-mist that enfolds and chokes
The slinking shapes which madness has defiled.
It was the same — an herbage rank and wild
Clings round an altar whose carved sign invokes
That Nameless One to whom a thousand smokes
Rose, aeons gone, from unclean towers up-piled.
I saw the body spread on that dank stone,
And knew those things which feasted were not men;
I knew this strange, grey world was not my own,
But Yuggoth, past the starry voids — and then
The body shrieked at me with a dead cry,
And all too late I knew that it was I!

V.
HOMECOMING.

The daemon said that he would take me home
To the pale, shadowy land I half recalled
As a high place of stair and terrace, walled
With marble balustrades that sky-winds comb,
While miles below a maze of dome on dome
And tower on tower beside a sea lies sprawled.
Once more, he told me, I would stand enthralled
On those old heights, and hear the far-off foam.
All this he promised, and through sunset's gate
He swept me, past the lapping lakes of flame,
And red-gold thrones of gods without a name
Who shriek in fear at some impending fate.
Then a black gulf with sea-sounds in the night:
"Here was your home," he mocked, "when you had sight!"

VI.

THE LAMP.

We found the lamp inside those hollow cliffs
Whose chiseled sign no priest in Thebes could read,
And from whose caverns frightened hieroglyphs
Warned every living creature of earth's breed.
No more was there — just that one brazen bowl
With traces of a curious oil within;
Fretted with some obscurely patterned scroll,
And symbols hinting vaguely of strange sin.
Little the fears of forty centuries meant
To us as we bore off our slender spoil,
And when we scanned it in our darkened tent
We struck a match to test the ancient oil.
It blazed — great God! . . . But the vast shapes we saw
In that mad flash have seared our lives with awe.

VII.

ZAMAN'S HILL.

The great hill hung close over the old town,
A precipice against the main street's end;
Green, tall, and wooded, looking darkly down
Upon the steeple at the highway bend.
Two hundred years the whispers had been heard
About what happened on the man-shunned slope —
Tales of an oddly mangled deer or bird,
Or of lost boys whose kin had ceased to hope.
One day the mail-man found no village there,
Nor were its folk or houses seen again;
People came out from Aylesbury to stare —
Yet they all told the mail-man it was plain
That he was mad for saying he had spied
The great hill's gluttonous eyes, and jaws stretched wide.

VIII.

THE PORT.

Ten miles from Arkham I had struck the trail
That rides the cliff-edge over Boynton Beach,
And hoped that just at sunset I could reach
The crest that looks on Innsmouth in the vale.
Far out at sea was a retreating sail,
White as hard years of ancient winds could bleach,
But evil with some portent beyond speech,
So that I did not wave my hand or hail.
Sails out of Innsmouth! echoing old renown
Of long-dead times. But now a too-swift night
Is closing in, and I have reached the height
Whence I so often scan the distant town.
The spires and roofs are there — but look! The gloom
Sinks on dark lanes, as lightless as the tomb!

IX.

THE COURTYARD.

It was the city I had known before;
The ancient, leprous town where mongrel throngs
Chant to strange gods, and beat unhallowed gongs
In crypts beneath foul alleys near the shore.
The rotting, fish-eyed houses leered at me
From where they leaned, drunk and half-animate,
As edging through the filth I passed the gate
To the black courtyard where the man would be.
The dark walls closed me in, and loud I cursed
That ever I had come to such a den,
When suddenly a score of windows burst
Into wild light, and swarmed with dancing men:
Mad, soundless revels of the dragging dead —
And not a corpse had either hands or head!

X.

THE PIGEON-FLYERS.

They took me slumming, where gaunt walls of brick
Bulge outward with a viscous stored-up evil,
And twisted faces, thronging foul and thick,
Wink messages to alien god and devil.
A million fires were blazing in the streets,
And from flat roofs a furtive few would fly
Bedraggled birds into the yawning sky
While hidden drums droned on with measured beats.
I knew those fires were brewing monstrous things,
And that those birds of space had been Outside —
I guessed to what dark planet's crypts they plied,
And what they brought from Thog beneath their wings.
The others laughed — till struck too mute to speak
By what they glimpsed in one bird's evil beak.

XI.

THE WELL.

Farmer Seth Atwood was past eighty when
He tried to sink that deep well by his door,
With only Eb to help him bore and bore.
We laughed, and hoped he'd soon be sane again.
And yet, instead, young Eb went crazy, too,
So that they shipped him to the county farm.
Seth bricked the well-mouth up as tight as glue —
Then hacked an artery in his gnarled left arm.
After the funeral we felt bound to get
Out to that well and rip the bricks away,
But all we saw were iron hand-holds set
Down a black hole deeper than we could say.
And yet we put the bricks back — for we found
The hole too deep for any line to sound.

XII.

THE HOWLER.

They told me not to take the Briggs' Hill path
That used to be the highroad through to Zoar,
For Goody Watkins, hanged in seventeen-four,
Had left a certain monstrous aftermath.
Yet when I disobeyed, and had in view
The vine-hung cottage by the great rock slope,
I could not think of elms or hempen rope,
But wondered why the house still seemed so new.
Stopping a while to watch the fading day,
I heard faint howls, as from a room upstairs,
When through the ivied panes one sunset ray
Struck in, and caught the howler unawares.
I glimpsed — and ran in frenzy from the place,
And from a four-pawed thing with human face.

XIII.

HESPERIA.

The winter sunset, flaming beyond spires
And chimneys half-detached from this dull sphere,
Opens great gates to some forgotten year
Of elder splendours and divine desires.
Expectant wonders burn in those rich fires,
Adventure-fraught, and not untinged with fear;
A row of sphinxes where the way leads clear
Toward walls and turrets quivering to far lyres.
It is the land where beauty's meaning flowers;
Where every unplaced memory has a source;
Where the great river Time begins its course
Down the vast void in starlit streams of hours.
Dreams bring us close — but ancient lore repeats
That human tread has never soiled these streets.

XIV.

STAR-WINDS.

it is a certain hour of twilight glooms,
Mostly in autumn, when the star-wind pours
Down hilltop streets, deserted out-of-doors,
But shewing early lamplight from snug rooms.
The dead leaves rush in strange, fantastic twists,
And chimney-smoke whirls round with alien grace,
Heeding geometries of outer space,
While Fomalhaut peers in through southward mists.
This is the hour when moonstruck poets know
What fungi sprout in Yuggoth, and what scents
And tints of flowers fill Nithon's continents,
Such as in no poor earthly garden blow.
Yet for each dream these winds to us convey,
A dozen more of ours they sweep away!

XV.

ANTARKTOS.

Deep in my dream the great bird whispered queerly
Of the black cone amid the polar waste;
Pushing above the ice-sheet lone and drearly,
By storm-crazed aeons battered and defaced.
Hither no living earth-shapes take their courses,
And only pale auroras and faint suns
Glow on that pitted rock, whose primal sources
Are guessed at dimly by the Elder Ones.
If men should glimpse it, they would merely wonder
What tricky mound of Nature's build they spied;
But the bird told of vaster parts, that under
The mile-deep ice-shroud crouch and brood and bide.
God help the dreamer whose mad visions shew
Those dead eyes set in crystal gulfs below!

XVI.

THE WINDOW.

The house was old, with tangled wings outthrown,
Of which no one could ever half keep track,
And in a small room somewhat near the back
Was an odd window sealed with ancient stone.
There, in a dream-plagued childhood, quite alone
I used to go, where night reigned vague and black;
Parting the cobwebs with a curious lack
Of fear, and with a wonder each time grown.
One later day I brought the masons there
To find what view my dim forbears had shunned,
But as they pierced the stone, a rush of air
Burst from the alien voids that yawned beyond.
They fled — but I peered through and found unrolled
All the wild worlds of which my dreams had told.

XVII.

A MEMORY.

There were great steppes, and rocky table-lands
Stretching half-limitless in starlit night,
With alien campfires shedding feeble light
On beasts with tinkling bells, in shaggy bands.
Far to the south the plain sloped low and wide
To a dark zigzag line of wall that lay
Like a huge python of some primal day
Which endless time had chilled and petrified.
I shivered oddly in the cold, thin air,
And wondered where I was and how I came,
When a cloaked form against a campfire's glare
Rose and approached, and called me by my name.
Staring at that dead face beneath the hood,
I ceased to hope — because I understood.

XVIII.
THE GARDENS OF YIN.

Beyond that wall, whose ancient masonry
Reached almost to the sky in moss-thick towers,
There would be terraced gardens, rich with flowers,
And flutter of bird and butterfly and bee.
There would be walks, and bridges arching over
Warm lotos-pools reflecting temple eaves,
And cherry-trees with delicate boughs and leaves
Against a pink sky where the herons hover.
All would be there, for had not old dreams flung
Open the gate to that stone-lanterned maze
Where drowsy streams spin out their winding ways,
Trailed by green vines from bending branches hung?
I hurried — but when the wall rose, grim and great,
I found there was no longer any gate.

XIX.
THE BELLS.

Year after year I heard that faint, far ringing
Of deep-toned bells on the black midnight wind;
Peals from no steeple I could ever find,
But strange, as if across some great void winging.
I searched my dreams and memories for a clue,
And thought of all the chimes my visions carried;
Of quiet Innsmouth, where the white gulls tarried
Around an ancient spire that once I knew.
Always perplexed I heard those far notes falling,
Till one March night the bleak rain splashing cold
Beckoned me back through gateways of recalling
To elder towers where the mad clappers tolled.
They tolled — but from the sunless tides that pour
Through sunken valleys on the sea's dead floor.

XX.
NIGHT-GAUNTS.

Out of what crypt they crawl, I cannot tell,
But every night I see the rubbery things,
Black, horned, and slender, with membraneous wings,
And tails that bear the bifid barb of hell.
They come in legions on the north wind's swell,
With obscene clutch that titillates and stings,
Snatching me off on monstrous voyagings
To grey worlds hidden deep in nightmare's well.
Over the jagged peaks of Thok they sweep,
Heedless of all the cries I try to make,
And down the nether pits to that foul lake
Where the puffed shoggoths splash in doubtful sleep.
But oh! If only they would make some sound,
Or wear a face where faces should be found!

XXI.
NYARLATHOTEP.

And at the last from inner Egypt came
The strange dark One to whom the fellahs bowed;
Silent and lean and cryptically proud,
And wrapped in fabrics red as sunset flame.
Throngs pressed around, frantic for his commands,
But leaving, could not tell what they had heard;
While through the nations spread the awestruck word
That wild beasts followed him and licked his hands.
Soon from the sea a noxious birth began;
Forgotten lands with weedy spires of gold;
The ground was cleft, and mad auroras rolled
Down on the quaking citadels of man.
Then, crushing what he chanced to mould in play,
The idiot Chaos blew Earth's dust away.

XXII.
AZATHOTH.

Out in the mindless void the daemon bore me,
Past the bright clusters of dimensioned space,
Till neither time nor matter stretched before me,
But only Chaos, without form or place.
Here the vast Lord of All in darkness muttered
Things he had dreamed but could not understand,
While near him shapeless bat-things flopped and fluttred
In idiot vortices that ray-streams fanned.
They danced insanely to the high, thin whining
Of a cracked flute clutched in a monstrous paw,
Whence flow the aimless waves whose chance combining
Gives each frail cosmos its eternal law.
"I am His Messenger," the daemon said,
As in contempt he struck his Master's head.

XXIII.
MIRAGE.

I do not know if ever it existed —
That lost world floating dimly on Time's stream —
And yet I see it often, violet-misted,
And shimmering at the back of some vague dream.
There were strange towers and curious lapping rivers,
Labyrinths of wonder, and low vaults of light,
And bough-crossed skies of flame, like that which quivers
Wistfully just before a winter's night.
Great moors led off to sedgy shores unpeopled,
Where vast birds wheeled, while on a windswept hill
There was a village, ancient and white-steepled,
With evening chimes for which I listen still.
I do not know what land it is — or dare
Ask when or why I was, or will be, there.

XXIV.

THE CANAL.

Somewhere in dream there is an evil place
Where tall, deserted buildings crowd along
A deep, black, narrow channel, reeking strong
Of frightful things whence oily currents race.
Lanes with old walls half meeting overhead
Wind off to streets one may or may not know,
And feeble moonlight sheds a spectral glow
Over long rows of windows, dark and dead.
There are no footfalls, and the one soft sound
Is of the oily water as it glides
Under stone bridges, and along the sides
Of its deep flume, to some vague ocean bound.
None lives to tell when that stream washed away
Its dream-lost region from the world of clay.

XXV.

ST. TOAD'S.

"Beware St. Toad's cracked chimes!" I heard him scream
As I plunged into those mad lanes that wind
In labyrinths obscure and undefined
South of the river where old centuries dream.
He was a furtive figure, bent and ragged,
And in a flash had staggered out of sight,
So still I burrowed onward in the night
Toward where more roof lines rose, malign and jagged.
No guide-book told of what was lurking here —
But now I heard another old man shriek:
"Beware St.Toad's cracked chimes!" And growing weak,
I paused, when a third greybeard croaked in fear:
"Beware St. Toad's cracked chimes!" Aghast, I fled —
Till suddenly that black spire loomed ahead.

XXVI.

THE FAMILIARS.

John Whateley lived about a mile from town,
Up where the hills begin to huddle thick;
We never thought his wits were very quick,
Seeing the way he let his farm run down.
He used to waste his time on some queer books
He'd found around the attic of his place,
Till funny lines got creased into his face,
And folks all said they didn't like his looks.
When he began those night-howls we declared
He'd better be locked up away from harm,
So three men from the Aylesbury town farm
Went for him — but came back alone and scared.
They'd found him talking to two crouching things
That at their step flew off on great black wings.

XXVII.

THE ELDER PHAROS.

From Leng, where rocky peaks climb bleak and bare
Under cold stars obscure to human sight,
There shoots at dusk a single beam of light
Whose far blue rays make shepherds whine in prayer.
They say (though none has been there) that it comes
Out of a pharos in a tower of stone,
Where the last Elder One lives on alone,
Talking to Chaos with the beat of drums.
The Thing, they whisper, wears a silken mask
Of yellow, whose queer folds appear to hide
A face not of this earth, though none dares ask
Just what those features are, which bulge inside.
Many, in man's first youth, sought out that glow,
But what they found, no one will ever know.

XXVIII.

EXPECTANCY.

I cannot tell why some things hold for me
A sense of unplumbed marvels to befall,
Or of a rift in the horizon's wall
Opening to worlds where only gods can be.
There is a breathless, vague expectancy,
As of vast ancient pomps I half recall,
Or wild adventures, uncorporeal,
Ecstacy-fraught, and as a day-dream free.
It is in sunsets and strange city spires,
Old villages and woods and misty downs,
South winds, the sea, low hills, and lighted towns,
Old gardens, half-heard songs, and the moon's fires.
But though its lure alone makes life worth living,
None gains or guesses what it hints at giving.

XXIX.

NOSTALGIA.

Once every year, in autumn's wistful glow,
The birds fly out over an ocean waste,
Calling and chattering in a joyous haste
To reach some land their inner memories know.
Great terraced gardens where bright blossoms blow,
And lines of mangoes luscious to the taste,
And temple-groves with branches interlaced
Over cool paths — all these their vague dreams shew.
They search the sea for marks of their old shore —
For the tall city, white and turreted —
But only empty waters stretch ahead,
So that at last they turn away once more.
Yet sunken deep where alien polyps throng,
The old towers miss their lost, remembered song.

XXX.
BACKGROUND.

I never can be tied to raw, new things,
For I first saw the light in an old town,
Where from my window huddled roofs sloped down
To a quaint harbour rich with visionings.
Streets with carved doorways where the sunset beams
Flooded old fanlights and small window-panes,
And Georgian steeples topped with gilded vanes—
These were the sights that shaped my childhood dreams.
Such treasures, left from times of cautious leaven,
Cannot but loose the hold of flimsier wraiths
That flit with shifting ways and muddled faiths
Across the changeless walls of earth and heaven.
They cut the moment's thongs and leave me free
To stand alone before eternity.

XXXI.
THE DWELLER.

It had been old when Babylon was new;
None knows how long it slept beneath that mound,
Where in the end our questing shovels found
Its granite blocks and brought it back to view.
There were vast pavements and foundation-walls,
And crumbling slabs and statues, carved to shew
Fantastic beings of some long ago
Past anything the world of man recalls.
And then we saw those stone steps leading down
Through a choked gate of graven dolomite
To some black haven of eternal night
Where elder signs and primal secrets frown.
We cleared a path—but raced in mad retreat
When from below we heard those clumping feet.

XXXII.
ALIENATION.

His solid flesh had never been away,
For each dawn found him in his usual place,
But every night his spirit loved to race
Through gulfs and worlds remote from common day.
He had seen Yaddith, yet retained his mind,
And come back safely from the Ghooric zone,
When one still night across curved space was thrown
That beckoning piping from the voids behind.
He waked that morning as an older man,
And nothing since has looked the same to him.
Objects around float nebulous and dim—
False, phantom trifles of some vaster plan.
His folk and friends are now an alien throng
To which he struggles vainly to belong.

XXXIII.
HARBOUR WHISTLES.

Over old roofs and past decaying spires
The harbour whistles chant all through the night;
Throats from strange ports, and beaches far and white,
And fabulous oceans, ranged in motley choirs.
Each to the other alien and unknown,
Yet all, by some obscurely focussed force
From brooding gulfs beyond the Zodiac's course,
Fused into one mysterious cosmic drone.
Through shadowy dreams they send a marching line
Of still more shadowy shapes and hints and views;
Echoes from outer voids, and subtle clues
To things which they themselves cannot define.
And always in that chorus, faintly blent,
We catch some notes no earth-ship ever sent.

XXXIV.
RECAPTURE.

The way led down a dark, half-wooded heath
Where moss-grey boulders humped above the mould,
And curious drops, disquieting and cold,
Sprayed up from unseen streams in gulfs beneath.
There was no wind, nor any trace of sound
In puzzling shrub, or alien-featured tree,
Nor any view before—till suddenly,
Straight in my path, I saw a monstrous mound.
Half to the sky those steep sides loomed upspread,
Rank-grassed, and cluttered by a crumbling flight
Of lava stairs that scaled the fear-topped height
In steps too vast for any human tread.
I shrieked—and knew what primal star and year
Had sucked me back from man's dream-transient sphere!

XXXV.
EVENING STAR.

I saw it from that hidden, silent place
Where the old wood half shuts the meadow in.
It shone through all the sunset's glories—thin
At first, but with a slowly brightening face.
Night came, and that lone beacon, amber-hued,
Beat on my sight as never it did of old;
The evening star—but grown a thousandfold
More haunting in this hush and solitude.
It traced strange pictures on the quivering air—
Half-memories that had always filled my eyes—
Vast towers and gardens; curious seas and skies
Of some dim life—I never could tell where.
But now I knew that through the cosmic dome
Those rays were calling from my far, lost home.

XXXVI.

CONTINUITY.

There is in certain ancient things a trace
Of some dim essence — more than form or weight;
A tenuous aether, indeterminate,
Yet linked with all the laws of time and space.
A faint, veiled sign of continuities
That outward eyes can never quite descry;
Of locked dimensions harbouring years gone by,
And out of reach except for hidden keys.
It moves me most when slanting sunbeams glow
On old farm buildings set against a hill,
And paint with life the shapes which linger still
From centuries less a dream than this we know.
In that strange light I feel I am not far
From the fixt mass whose sides the ages are.

1930.

The Traveller from Providence.

In 1930, H.P. Lovecraft continued relatively happily in the path he had followed since leaving New York. There was never any question of him moving away from Providence now; he had already declined several such offers. But he was now far from reclusive. The small income he received from his dwindling inheritance and from stingy editors and reluctant ghost-writing clients would be saved carefully away over each long and frugal winter so that he might have bus and train fare in the spring; then he would sally forth on excursions to visit literary friends who, knowing his straitened circumstances, would put him up, feed him, and take him on tours of local scenery. Then he would spend a few weeks writing a lengthy travelogue to commemorate his journey.

It was a good life.

In addition to the travelogues of 1930 (there were two: "An Account of Charleston" and "A Description of the Town of Quebeck"), Lovecraft continued with the outburst of poetry that he'd started in 1929, wrapping things up with *Fungi from Yuggoth* by Jan. 4.

Later that year, his ghostwriting practice yielded one of the best of his collaborative works, a novella titled *The Mound*—which, as was customary, ran under the by-line of his client, Zealia Bishop.

Lovecraft contributed only one work to his own canon in 1930, but it's rather a big one: *The Whisperer in Darkness*.

The summer of 1930 is also the time when Lovecraft started corresponding with fellow *Weird Tales* regular Robert E. Howard, a prolific and fairly successful weird-poetry and fiction writer who's known today as one of the "Three Musketeers of *Weird Tales*" (the other two being Lovecraft and Clark Ashton Smith). Howard, who is best known for his Conan the Barbarian stories, would soon be contributing his own derivative content to Lovecraft's great Cthulhu-Mythos sandbox.

For years it has been fashionable, among some Lovecraft fans, to regard Howard as a puerile hack, dashing out low-brow juvenile-fantasy stag-mag stories by the dozen along with occasional pastiches of Lovecraft under the Great One's mentorship. This attitude, when encountered, is always a sure sign of an incomplete familiarity with one or both authors.

After *The Whisperer in Darkness* was complete, Lovecraft spent the last several months of 1930 hammering out "A Description of the Town of Quebeck." By the time he finished, it was 75,000 words long, the longest piece he had ever written. Judging by word count alone, one could make the case that Lovecraft, in 1930, was a travel writer who occasionally wrote weird fiction, rather than the other way around.

The Mound.

BY ZEALIA BISHOP AND H.P. LOVECRAFT

30,000-WORD NOVELLA; 1930.

This dark novella is the longest and quite possibly the best of H.P. Lovecraft's revision works. Its plot is reminiscent of Lord Edward Bulwer-Lytton's popular classic novel The Coming Race, *which Lovecraft surely had read and which may have been part of the inspiration for it.*

Seasoned Lovecraft readers will also detect more than a little resemblance between The Mound *and* The Whisperer in Darkness, *which Lovecraft wrote a few months later.*

It is hard to know exactly how much of the story was Zealia Bishop's, and how much Lovecraft's; but it is probably safe to assume that it is largely his. Lovecraft wrote, in a letter to Robert Barlow, that Bishop merely told him of a legend of a strange Indian mound haunted by a headless ghost, which sometimes is a woman. But, that can't have been all, because he went on to say that he found her story "insufferably tame and flat"; for that to make sense, there would have had to be an actual story, not merely the germ of an idea.

Nonetheless, the execution is all classic Lovecraft — although as with all his collaborations, Lovecraft didn't put the same level of polish into The Mound *that he did on the stories that would run with his name on them.*

Unfortunately when Bishop submitted The Mound *to Farnsworth Wright, the editor of* Weird Tales, *it was rejected — it was, Wright said, too long to run in one shot, but not set up in such a way that it could be serialized. The real reason for the story's rejection may have been financial, as its length would mean a high price and the Depression was hitting* Weird Tales *hard at that time.*

Eventually the story was published, in abridged form, in the November 1940 issue — nearly 11 years after it was finished in early 1930.

I.

It is only within the last few years that most people have stopped thinking of the West as a new land. I suppose the idea gained ground because our own especial civilisation happens to be new there; but nowadays explorers are digging beneath the surface and bringing up whole chapters of life that rose and fell among these plains and mountains before recorded history began. We think nothing of a Pueblo village 2500 years old, and it hardly jolts us when archaeologists put the sub-pedregal culture of Mexico back to 17,000 or 18,000 B.C. We hear rumours of still older things, too — of primitive man contemporaneous with extinct animals and known today only through a few fragmentary bones and artefacts — so that the idea of newness is fading out pretty rapidly.

Europeans usually catch the sense of immemorial ancientness and deep deposits from successive life-streams better than we do. Only a couple of years ago a British author spoke of Arizona as a "moon-dim region, very lovely in its way, and stark and old — an ancient, lonely land."

Yet I believe I have a deeper sense of the stupefying — almost horrible — ancientness of the West than any European. It all comes from an incident that happened in 1928; an incident which I'd greatly like to dismiss as three-quarters hallucination, but which has left such a frightfully firm impression on my memory that I can't put it off very easily. It was in Oklahoma, where my work as an American Indian ethnologist constantly takes me and where I had come upon some devilishly strange and disconcerting matters before.

Make no mistake — Oklahoma is a lot more than a mere pioneers' and promoters' frontier. There are old, old tribes with old, old memories there; and when the tom-toms beat ceaselessly over brooding plains in the autumn the spirits of men are brought dangerously close to primal, whispered things. I am white and Eastern enough myself, but anybody is welcome to know that the rites of Yig, Father of Snakes, can get a real shudder out of me any day. I have heard and seen too much to be "sophisticated" in such matters. And so it is with this incident of 1928. I'd like to laugh it off — but I can't.

I had gone into Oklahoma to track down and correlate one of the many ghost tales which were current among the white settlers, but which had strong Indian corroboration, and — I felt sure — an ultimate Indian source. They were very curious, these open-air ghost tales; and though they sounded flat and prosaic in the mouths of the white people, they had earmarks of linkage with some of the richest and obscurest phases of native mythology. All of them were woven around the vast, lonely, artificial-looking mounds in the western part of the state, and all of them involved apparitions of exceedingly strange aspect and equipment.

The commonest, and among the oldest, became quite famous in 1892, when a government marshal named John Willis went into the mound region after horse-thieves and came out with a wild yarn of nocturnal cavalry horses in the air between great armies of invisible spectres — battles that involved the rush of hooves and feet, the thud of blows, the clank of metal on metal, the muffled cries of warriors, and the fall of human and equine bodies. These things happened by moonlight, and frightened his horse as well as himself. The sounds persisted an hour at a time; vivid, but subdued as if brought from a distance by a wind, and unaccompanied by any glimpse of the armies themselves. Later on Willis learned that the seat of the sounds was a notoriously haunted spot, shunned by settlers and Indians alike. Many had seen, or half seen, the warring horsemen in the sky, and had furnished dim, ambiguous descriptions. The settlers described the ghostly fighters as Indians, though of no familiar tribe, and having the most singular costumes and weapons. They even went so far as to say that they could not be sure the horses were really horses.

The Indians, on the other hand, did not seem to claim the spectres as kinsfolk. They referred to them as "those people," "the old people," or "they who dwell below," and appeared to hold them in too great a frightened veneration to talk much about them. No ethnologist had been able to pin any tale-teller down to a specific description of the beings, and apparently nobody had ever had a very clear look at them. The Indians had one or two old proverbs about these phenomena, saying that "men very old, make very big spirit; not so old, not so big; older than all time, then spirit he so big he near flesh; those old people and spirits they mix up — get all the same."

Now all of this, of course, is "old stuff" to an ethnologist of a piece with the persistent legends of rich hidden cities and buried races which abound among the Pueblo and plains Indians, and which lured Coronado centuries ago on his vain search for the fabled Quivira. What took me into western Oklahoma was something far more definite and tangible — a local and distinctive tale which, though really old, was wholly new to the outside world of research, and which involved the first clear descriptions of the ghosts which it treated of. There was an added thrill in the fact that it came from the remote town of Binger, in Caddo County, a place I had long known as the scene of a very terrible and partly inexplicable occurrence connected with the snake-god myth.

The tale, outwardly, was an extremely naive and simple one, and centred in a huge, lone mound or small hill that rose above the plain about a third of a mile west of the village — a mound which some thought a product of Nature, but which others believed to be a burial-place or ceremonial dais constructed by prehistoric tribes. This mound, the villagers said, was constantly haunted by two Indian figures which appeared in alternation: an old man who paced back and forth along the top from dawn till dusk, regardless of the weather and with only brief intervals of disappearance; and a squaw who took his place at night with a blue-flamed torch that glimmered quite continuously till morning. When the moon was bright the squaw's peculiar figure could be seen fairly plainly, and over half the villagers agreed that the apparition was headless.

Local opinion was divided as to the motives and relative ghostliness of the two visions. Some held that the man was not a ghost at all, but a living Indian who had killed and beheaded a squaw for gold and buried her somewhere on the mound. According to these theorists he was pacing the eminence through sheer remorse, bound by the spirit of his victim which took visible shape after dark. But other theorists, more uniform in their spectral beliefs, held that both man and woman were ghosts; the man having killed the squaw and himself as well at some very distant period. These and minor variant versions seemed to have been current ever since the settlement of the Wichita country in 1889, and were, I was told, sustained to an astonishing degree by still-existing phenomena which anyone might observe for himself. Not many ghost tales offer such free and open proof, and I was very eager to see what bizarre wonders might be lurking in this small, obscure village so far from the beaten path of crowds and from the ruthless searchlight of scientific knowledge. So, in the late summer of 1928 I took a train for Binger and brooded on strange mysteries as the cars rattled timidly along their single track through a lonelier and lonelier landscape.

Binger is a modest cluster of frame houses and stores in the midst of a flat windy region full of clouds of red dust. There are about 500 inhabitants besides the Indians on a neighbouring reservation; the principal occupation seeming to be agriculture. The soil is decently fertile, and the oil boom has not reached this part of the state. My train drew in at twilight, and I felt rather lost and uneasy — cut off from wholesome and everyday things — as it puffed away to the southward without me.

The station platform was filled with curious loafers, all of whom seemed eager to direct me when I asked for the man to whom I had letters of introduction. I was ushered along a commonplace main street whose ruled surface was red with the sandstone soil of the country, and finally delivered at the door of my prospective host.

Those who had arranged things for me had done well; for Mr. Compton was a man of high intelligence and local responsibility, while his mother — who lived with him and was familiarly known as "Grandma Compton" — was one of the first pioneer generation, and a veritable mine of anecdote and folklore.

That evening the Comptons summed up for me all the legends current among the villagers, proving that the phenomenon I had come to study was indeed a baffling and important one. The ghosts, it seems, were accepted almost as a matter of course by everyone in Binger. Two generations had been born and grown up within sight of that queer, lone tumulus and its restless figures. The neighbourhood of the mound was naturally feared and shunned, so that the village and the farms had not spread toward it in all four decades of settlement; yet venturesome individuals had several times visited it. Some had come back to report that they saw no ghosts at all when they neared

the dreaded hill; that somehow the lone sentinel had stepped out of sight before they reached the spot, leaving them free to climb the steep slope and explore the flat summit. There was nothing up there, they said — merely a rough expanse of underbrush. Where the Indian watcher could have vanished to, they had no idea. He must, they reflected, have descended the slope and somehow managed to escape unseen along the plain, although there was no convenient cover within sight. At any rate, there did not appear to be any opening into the mound, a conclusion which was reached after considerable exploration of the shrubbery and tall grass on all sides. In a few cases some of the more sensitive searchers declared that they felt a sort of invisible restraining presence; but they could describe nothing more definite than that. It was simply as if the air thickened against them in the direction they wished to move.

It is needless to mention that all these daring surveys were conducted by day. Nothing in the universe could have induced any human being, white or red, to approach that sinister elevation after dark; and indeed, no Indian would have thought of going near it even in the brightest sunlight.

But it was not from the tales of these sane, observant seekers that the chief terror of the ghost-mound sprang; indeed, had their experience been typical, the phenomenon would have bulked far less prominently in the local legendry. The most evil thing was the fact that many other seekers had come back strangely impaired in mind and body, or had not come back at all.

The first of these cases had occurred in 1891, when a young man named Heaton had gone with a shovel to see what hidden secrets he could unearth. He had heard curious tales from the Indians, and had laughed at the barren report of another youth who had been out to the mound and had found nothing. Heaton had watched the mound with a spy glass from the village while the other youth made his trip; and as the explorer neared the spot, he saw the sentinel Indian walk deliberately down into the tumulus as if a trap-door and staircase existed on the top.

The other youth had not noticed how the Indian disappeared, but had merely found him gone upon arriving at the mound.

When Heaton made his own trip he resolved to get to the bottom of the mystery, and watchers from the village saw him hacking diligently at the shrubbery atop the mound. Then they saw his figure melt slowly into invisibility, not to reappear for long hours, till after the dusk drew on, and the torch of the headless squaw glimmered ghoulishly on the distant elevation.

About two hours after nightfall he staggered into the village minus his spade and other belongings, and burst into a shrieking monologue of disconnected ravings. He howled of shocking abysses and monsters, of terrible carvings and statues, of inhuman captors and grotesque tortures, and of other fantastic abnormalities too complex and chimerical even to remember. "Old! Old! Old!" he would moan over and over again; "great God, they are older than the earth, and came here from somewhere else — they know what you think, and make you know what they think — they're half-man, half-ghost — crossed the line — melt and take shape again — getting more and more so, yet we're all descended from them in the beginning — children of Tulu — everything made of gold — monstrous animals, half-human — dead slaves — madness — Iä! Shub-Niggurath! — that white man — oh, my God, What they did to him!"

Heaton was the village idiot for about eight years, after which he died in an epileptic fit. Since his ordeal there had been two more cases of mound-madness, and eight of total disappearance. Immediately after Heaton's mad return, three desperate and determined men had gone out to the lone hill together, heavily armed, and with spades and pickaxes. Watching villagers saw the Indian ghost melt away as the explorers drew near, and afterward saw the men climb the mound and begin scouting around through the underbrush. All at once they faded into nothingness, and were never seen again. One watcher, with an especially powerful telescope, thought he saw other forms dimly materialise beside the hapless men and drag them down into the mound; but this account remained uncorroborated.

It is needless to say that no searching-party went out after the lost ones, and that for many years the mound was wholly unvisited. Only when the incidents of 1891 were largely forgotten did anybody dare to think of further explorations. Then, about 1910, a fellow too young to recall the old horrors made a trip to the shunned spot and found nothing at all.

By 1915 the acute dread and wild legendry of '91 had largely faded into the commonplace and unimaginative ghost-tales at present surviving — that is, had so faded among the white people. On the nearby reservation were old Indians who thought much and kept their own counsel.

About this time a second wave of active curiosity and

Weird Tales, November 1940 (both images)

adventuring developed, and several bold searchers made the trip to the mound and returned. Then came a trip of two Eastern visitors with spades and other apparatus — a pair of amateur archaeologists connected with a small college, who had been making studies among the Indians. No one watched this trip from the village, but they never came back. The searching-party that went out after them — among whom was my host, Clyde Compton — found nothing whatsoever amiss at the mound.

The next trip was the solitary venture of old Capt. Lawton, a grizzled pioneer who had helped to open up the region in 1889, but who had never been there since. He had recalled the mound and its fascination all through the years; and being now in comfortable retirement, resolved to have a try at solving the ancient riddle. Long familiarity with Indian myth had given him ideas rather stranger than those of the simple villagers, and he had made preparations for some extensive delving.

He ascended the mound on the morning of Thursday, May 11, 1916, watched through spy glasses by more than twenty people in the village and on the adjacent plain. His disappearance was very sudden, and occurred as he was hacking at the shrubbery with a brush-cutter. No one could say more than that he was there one moment and absent the next. For over a week no tidings of him reached Binger, and then — in the middle of the night — there dragged itself into the village the object about which dispute still rages.

It said it was — or had been — Capt. Lawton, but it was definitely younger by as much as forty years than the old man who had climbed the mound. Its hair was jet black, and its face — now distorted with nameless fright — free from wrinkles. But it did remind Grandma Compton most uncannily of the captain as he had looked back in '89. Its feet were cut off neatly at the ankles, and the stumps were smoothly healed to an extent almost incredible if the being really were the man who had walked upright a week before. It babbled of incomprehensible things, and kept repeating the name "George Lawton, George E. Lawton" as if trying to reassure itself of its own identity. The things it babbled of, Grandma Compton thought, were curiously like the hallucinations of poor young Heaton in '91; though there were minor differences. "The blue light! — the blue light! . . ." muttered the object. "Always down there, before there were any living things — older than the dinosaurs — always the same, only weaker — never death — brooding and brooding and brooding — the same people, half-man and half-gas — the dead that walk and work — oh, those beasts, those half-human unicorns — houses and cities of gold — old, old, old, older than time — came down from the stars — Great Tulu — Azathoth — Nyarlathotep — waiting, waiting . . ."

The object died before dawn.

Of course there was an investigation, and the Indians at the reservation were grilled unmercifully. But they knew nothing, and had nothing to say. At least, none of them had anything to say except old Grey Eagle, a Wichita chieftain whose more than a century of age put him above common fears. He alone deigned to grunt some advice.

"You let um 'lone, white man. No good — those people. All under here, all under there, them old ones. Yig, big father of snakes, he there. Yig is Yig. Tiráwa, big father of men, he there. Tiráwa is Tiráwa. No die. No get old. Just same like air. Just live and wait. One time they come out here, live and fight. Build um dirt tepee. Bring up gold — they got plenty. Go off and make new lodges. Me them. You them. Then big waters come. All change. Nobody come out, let nobody in. Get in, no get out. You let um 'lone, you have no bad medicine. Red man know, he no get catch. White man meddle, he no come back. Keep 'way little hills. No good. Grey Eagle say this."

If Joe Norton and Rance Wheelock had taken the old chief's advice, they would probably be here today; but they didn't. They were great readers and materialists, and feared nothing in heaven or earth; and they thought that some Indian fiends had a secret headquarters inside the mound. They had been to the mound before, and now they went again to avenge old Capt. Lawton — boasting that they'd do it if they had to tear the mound down altogether. Clyde Compton watched them with a pair of prism binoculars and saw them round the base of the sinister hill. Evidently they meant to survey their territory very gradually and minutely. Minutes passed, and they did not reappear. Nor were they ever seen again.

Once more the mound was a thing of panic fright, and only the excitement of the Great War served to restore it to the farther background of Binger folklore. It was unvisited from 1916 to 1919, and would have remained so but for the daredeviltry of some of the youths back from service in France. From 1919 to 1920, however, there was a veritable epidemic of mound-visiting among the prematurely hardened young veterans — an epidemic that waxed as one youth after another returned unhurt and contemptuous. By 1920 — so short is human memory — the mound was almost a joke; and the tame story of the murdered squaw began to displace darker whispers on everybody's tongues.

Then two reckless young brothers — the especially unimaginative and hard-boiled Clay boys — decided to go and dig up the buried squaw and the gold for which the old Indian had murdered her.

They went out on a September afternoon — about the time the Indian tom-toms begin their incessant annual beating over the flat, red-dusty plains. Nobody watched them, and their parents did not become worried at their non-return for several hours. Then came an alarm and a searching-party, and another resignation to the mystery of silence and doubt.

But one of them came back after all. It was Ed, the elder, and his straw-coloured hair and beard had turned an albino white for two inches from the roots. On his forehead was a queer scar like a branded hieroglyph. Three months after he and his brother Walker had vanished he skulked into his house at night, wearing nothing but a queerly patterned blanket which he thrust into the fire as soon as he had got into a suit of his own clothes. He told his parents that he and Walker had been captured by some strange Indians — not Wichitas or

Caddos — and held prisoners somewhere toward the west. Walker had died under torture, but he himself had managed to escape at a high cost. The experience had been particularly terrible, and he could not talk about it just then. He must rest — and anyway, it would do no good to give an alarm and try to find and punish the Indians. They were not of a sort that could be caught or punished, and it was especially important for the good of Binger — for the good of the world — that they be not pursued into their secret lair. As a matter of fact, they were not altogether what one could call real Indians — he would explain about that later. Meanwhile he must rest. Better not to rouse the village with the news of his return — he would go upstairs and sleep. Before he climbed the rickety flight to his room he took a pad and pencil from the living-room table, and an automatic pistol from his father's desk drawer.

Three hours later the shot rang out. Ed Clay had put a bullet neatly through his temples with a pistol clutched in his left hand, leaving a sparsely written sheet of paper on the rickety table near his bed. He had, it later appeared from the whittled pencil-stub and stove full of charred paper, originally written much more; but had finally decided not to tell what he knew beyond vague hints. The surviving fragment was only a mad warning scrawled in a curiously backhanded script — the ravings of a mind obviously deranged by hardships — and it read thus; rather surprisingly for the utterance of one who had always been stolid and matter-of-fact:

> *For gods sake never go nere that mound it is part of some kind of a world so devilish and old it cannot be spoke about me and Walker went and was took into the thing just melted at times and made up agen and the whole world outside is helpless alongside of what they can do — they what live forever young as they like and you cant tell if they are really men or just gostes — and what they do cant be spoke about and this is only 1 entrance — you cant tell how big the whole thing is — after what we seen I dont want to live aney more France was nothing besides this — and see that people always keep away o god they wood if they see poor walker like he was in the end.*
>
> *Yrs truely*
>
> — ED CLAY.

At the autopsy it was found that all of young Clay's organs were transposed from right to left within his body, as if he had been turned inside out. Whether they had always been so, no one could say at the time, but it was later learned from army records that Ed had been perfectly normal when mustered out of the service in May, 1919. Whether there was a mistake somewhere, or whether some unprecedented metamorphosis had indeed occurred, is still an unsettled question, as is also the origin of the hieroglyph-like scar on the forehead.

That was the end of the explorations of the mound. In the eight intervening years no one had been near the place, and few indeed had even cared to level a spyglass at it. From time to time people continued to glance nervously at the lone hill as it rose starkly from the plain against the western sky, and to shudder at the small dark speck that paraded by day and the glimmering will-o'-the-wisp that danced by night. The thing was accepted at face value as a mystery not to be probed, and by common consent the village shunned the subject. It was, after all, quite easy to avoid the hill; for space was unlimited in every direction, and community life always follows beaten trails. The mound side of the village was simply kept trailless, as if it had been water or swampland or desert. And it is a curious commentary on the stolidity and imaginative sterility of the human animal that the whispers with which children and strangers were warned away from the mound quickly sank once more into the flat tale of a murderous Indian ghost and his squaw victim. Only the tribesmen on the reservation, and thoughtful old-timers like Grandma Compton, remembered the overtones of unholy vistas and deep cosmic menace which clustered around the ravings of those who had come back changed and shattered.

It was very late, and Grandma Compton had long since gone upstairs to bed, when Clyde finished telling me this. I hardly knew what to think of the frightful puzzle, yet rebelled at any notion to conflict with sane materialism. What influence had brought madness, or the impulse of flight and wandering, to so many who had visited the mound? Though vastly impressed, I was spurred on rather than deterred. Surely I must get to the bottom of this matter, as well I might if I kept a cool head and an unbroken determination.

Compton saw my mood and shook his head worriedly. Then he motioned me to follow him outdoors.

We stepped from the frame house to the quiet side street or lane, and walked a few paces in the light of a waning August moon to where the houses were thinner. The half-moon was still low, and had not blotted many stars from the sky; so that I could see not only the weltering gleams of Altair and Vega, but the mystic shimmering of the Milky Way, as I looked out over the vast expanse of earth and sky in the direction that Compton pointed. Then all at once I saw a spark that was not a star — a bluish spark that moved and glimmered against the Milky Way near the horizon, and that seemed in a vague way more evil and malevolent than anything in the vault above. In another moment it was clear that this spark came from the top of a long distant rise in the outspread and faintly litten plain, and I turned to Compton with a question.

"Yes," he answered, "it's the blue ghost-light — and that is the mound. There's not a night in history that we haven't seen it — and not a living soul in Binger that would walk out over that plain toward it. It's a bad business, young man, and if you're wise you'll let it rest where it is. Better call your search off, son, and tackle some of the other Injun legends around here. We've plenty to keep you busy, heaven knows!"

II.

But I was in no mood for advice; and though Compton gave me a pleasant room, I could not sleep a wink through eagerness for the next morning with its chances to see the daytime ghost and to question the Indians at the reservation. I meant to go about the whole thing slowly and thoroughly, equipping myself with all available data both white and red before I commenced any actual archaeological investigations.

I rose and dressed at dawn, and when I heard others stirring I went downstairs. Compton was building the kitchen fire while his mother was busy in the pantry. When he saw me he nodded, and after a moment invited me out into the glamorous young sunlight. I knew where we were going, and as we walked along the lane I strained my eyes westward over the plains.

There was the mound — far away and very curious in its aspect of artificial regularity. It must have been from thirty to forty feet high, and all of a hundred yards from north to south as I looked at it. It was not as wide as that from east to west, Compton said, but had the contour of a rather thinnish ellipse. He, I knew, had been safely out to it and back several times.

As I looked at the rim silhouetted against the deep blue of the west I tried to follow its minor irregularities, and became impressed with a sense of something moving upon it. My pulse mounted a bit feverishly, and I seized quickly on the high-powered binoculars which Compton had quietly offered me. Focussing them hastily, I saw at first only a tangle of underbrush on the distant mound's rim — and then something stalked into the field.

It was unmistakably a human shape, and I knew at once that I was seeing the daytime "Indian ghost." I did not wonder at the description, for surely the tall, lean, darkly robed being with the filleted black hair and seamed, coppery, expressionless, aquiline face looked more like an Indian than anything else in my previous experience. And yet my trained ethnologist's eye told me at once that this was no redskin of any sort hitherto known to history, but a creature of vast racial variation and of a wholly different culture-stream. Modern Indians are brachycephalic — round-headed — and you can't find any dolichocephalic or long-headed skulls except in ancient Pueblo deposits dating back 2,500 years or more; yet this man's long-headedness was so pronounced that I recognised it at once, even at this vast distance and in the uncertain field of the binoculars. I saw, too, that the pattern of his robe represented a decorative tradition utterly remote from anything we recognise in southwestern native art. There were shining metal trappings, likewise, and a short sword or kindred weapon at his side, all wrought in a fashion wholly alien to anything I had ever heard of.

As he paced back and forth along the top of the mound I followed him for several minutes with the glass, noting the kinaesthetic quality of his stride and the poised way he carried his head; and there was borne in upon me the strong, persistent conviction that this man, whoever or whatever he might be, was certainly not a savage. He was the product of a civilisation, I felt instinctively, though of what civilisation I could not guess.

At length he disappeared beyond the farther edge of the mound, as if descending the opposite and unseen slope; and I lowered the glass with a curious mixture of puzzled feelings. Compton was looking quizzically at me, and I nodded non-committally. "What do you make of that?" he ventured. "This is what we've seen here in Binger every day of our lives."

That noon found me at the Indian reservation talking with old Grey Eagle — who, through some miracle, was still alive, though he must have been close to a hundred and fifty years old. He was a strange, impressive figure — this stern, fearless leader of his kind who had talked with outlaws and traders in fringed buckskin and French officials in knee-breeches and three-cornered hats — and I was glad to see that, because of my air of deference toward him, he appeared to like me. His liking, however, took an unfortunately obstructive form as soon as he learned what I wanted; for all he would do was to warn me against the search I was about to make.

"You good boy — you no bother that hill. Bad medicine. Plenty devil under there — catchum when you dig. No dig, no hurt. Go and dig, no come back. Just same when me boy, just same when my father and he father boy. All time buck he walk in day, squaw with no head she walk in night. All time since white man with tin coats they come from sunset and below big river — long way back — three, four times more back than Grey Eagle — two times more back than Frenchmen — all same after then. More back than that, nobody go near little hills nor deep valleys with stone caves. Still more back, those old ones no hide, come out and make villages. Bring plenty gold. Me them. You them. Then big waters come. All change. Nobody come out, let nobody in. Get in, no get out. They no die — no get old like Grey Eagle with valleys in face and snow on head. Just same like air — some man, some spirit. Bad medicine. Sometimes at night spirit come out on half-man-half-horse-with-horn and fight where men once fight. Keep 'way them place. No good. You good boy — go 'way and let them old ones 'lone."

That was all I could get out of the ancient chief, and the rest of the Indians would say nothing at all. But if I was troubled, Grey Eagle was clearly more so; for he obviously felt a real regret at the thought of my invading the region he feared so abjectly. As I turned to leave the reservation he stopped me for a final ceremonial farewell, and once more tried to get my promise to abandon my search. When he saw that he could not, he produced something half-timidly from a buckskin pouch he wore, and extended it toward me very solemnly. It was a worn but finely minted metal disc about two inches in diameter, oddly figured and perforated, and suspended from a leathern cord.

"You no promise, then Grey Eagle no can tell what get you. But if anything help um, this good medicine. Come from my father — he get from he father — he get from he father — all way back, close to Tiráwa, all men's father. My father say, 'You keep 'way from those old ones, keep 'way from little hills and valleys with stone caves. But if old ones they come out to get you, then you shew um this medicine. They know. They make him long way back. They look, then they no do such bad medicine maybe. But no can tell. You keep 'way, just same. Them no good. No tell what they do.'"

As he spoke, Grey Eagle was hanging the thing around my neck, and I saw it was a very curious object indeed. The more I looked at it, the more I marvelled; for not only was its heavy, darkish, lustrous, and richly mottled substance an absolutely strange metal to me, but what was left of its design seemed to be of a marvellously artistic and utterly unknown workmanship. One side, so far as I could see, had borne an exquisitely modelled serpent design; whilst the other side had depicted a kind of octopus or other tentacled monster. There were some half-effaced hieroglyphs, too, of a kind which no archaeologist could identify or even place conjecturally. With Grey Eagle's permission I later had expert historians, anthropologists, geologists, and chemists pass carefully upon the disc, but from them I obtained only a chorus of bafflement. It defied either classification or analysis. The chemists called it an amalgam of unknown metallic elements of heavy atomic weight, and one geologist suggested that the substance must be of meteoric origin, shot from unknown gulfs of interstellar space. Whether it really saved my life or sanity or existence as a human being I cannot attempt to say, but Grey Eagle is sure of it. He has it again, now, and I wonder if it has any connexion with his inordinate age. All his fathers who had it lived far beyond the century mark, perishing only in battle. Is it possible that Grey Eagle, if kept from accidents, will never die? But I am ahead of my story.

When I returned to the village I tried to secure more mound-lore, but found only excited gossip and opposition. It was really flattering to see how solicitous the people were about my safety, but I had to set their almost frantic remonstrances aside. I shewed them Grey Eagle's charm, but none of them had ever heard of it before, or seen anything even remotely like it. They agreed that it could not be an Indian relic, and imagined that the old chief's ancestors must have obtained it from some trader.

When they saw they could not deter me from my trip, the Binger citizens sadly did what they could to aid my outfitting. Having known before my arrival the sort of work to be done, I had most of my supplies already with me — machete and trench-knife for shrub-clearing and excavating, electric torches for any underground phase which might develop, rope, field-glasses, tape-measure, microscope, and incidentals for emergencies — as much, in fact, as might be comfortably stowed in a convenient handbag. To this equipment I added only the heavy revolver which the sheriff forced upon me, and the pick and shovel which I thought might expedite my work.

I decided to carry these latter things slung over my shoulder with a stout cord — for I soon saw that I could not hope for any helpers or fellow-explorers. The village would watch me, no doubt, with all its available telescopes and field-glasses; but it would not send any citizen so much as a yard over the flat plain toward the lone hillock. My start was timed for early the next morning, and all the rest of that day I was treated with the awed and uneasy respect which people give to a man about to set out for certain doom.

When morning came — a cloudy though not a threatening morning — the whole village turned out to see me start across the dust- blown plain. Binoculars shewed the lone man at his usual pacing on the mound, and I resolved to keep him in sight as steadily as possible during my approach.

At the last moment a vague sense of dread oppressed me, and I was just weak and whimsical enough to let Grey Eagle's talisman swing on my chest in full view of any beings or ghosts who might be inclined to heed it. Bidding *au revoir* to Compton and his mother, I started off at a brisk stride despite the bag in my left hand and the clanking pick and shovel strapped to my back, holding my field-glass in my right hand and taking a glance at the silent pacer from time to time. As I neared the mound I saw the man very clearly, and fancied I could trace an expression of infinite evil and decadence on his seamed, hairless features. I was startled, too, to see that his goldenly gleaming weapon-case bore hieroglyphs very similar to those on the unknown talisman I wore. All the creature's costume and trappings bespoke exquisite workmanship and cultivation. Then, all too abruptly, I saw him start down the farther side of the mound and out of sight. When I reached the place, about ten minutes after I set out, there was no one there.

There is no need of relating how I spent the early part of my search in surveying and circumnavigating the mound, taking measurements, and stepping back to view the thing from different angles. It had impressed me tremendously as I approached it, and there seemed to be a kind of latent menace in its too regular outlines. It was the only elevation of any sort on the wide, level plain; and I could not doubt for a moment that it was an artificial tumulus. The steep sides seemed wholly unbroken, and without marks of human tenancy or passage. There were no signs of a path toward the top; and, burdened as I was, I managed to scramble up only with considerable difficulty.

When I reached the summit I found a roughly level elliptical plateau about 300 by 50 feet in dimensions, uniformly covered with rank grass and dense underbrush, and utterly incompatible with the constant presence of a pacing sentinel. This condition gave me a real shock, for it shewed beyond question that the "Old Indian," vivid though he seemed, could not be other than a collective hallucination.

I looked about with considerable perplexity and alarm, glancing wistfully back at the village and the mass of black dots which I knew was the watching crowd. Training my glass upon them, I saw that they were studying me avidly with their glasses; so to reassure them I waved my cap in the air with a show of jauntiness which I was far from feeling. Then, settling to my work I flung down pick, shovel, and bag; taking my machete from the latter and commencing to clear away underbrush. It was a weary task, and now and then I felt a curious shiver as some perverse gust of wind arose to hamper my motion with a skill approaching deliberateness. At times it seemed as if a half-tangible force were pushing me back as I worked — almost as if the air thickened in front of me, or as if formless hands tugged at my wrists. My energy seemed used up without producing adequate results, yet for all that I made some progress.

By afternoon I had clearly perceived that, toward the northern end of the mound, there was a slight bowl-like depression in the root-tangled earth. While this might mean nothing, it would be a good place to begin when I reached the digging stage, and I made a mental note of it. At the same time I noticed another and very peculiar thing — namely, that the Indian talisman swinging from my neck seemed to behave oddly at a point about seventeen feet southeast of the suggested bowl. Its gyrations were altered whenever I happened to stoop around that point, and it tugged downward as if attracted by some magnetism in the soil. The more I noticed this, the more it struck me, till at length I decided to do a little preliminary digging there without further delay.

As I turned up the soil with my trench-knife I could not help wondering at the relative thinness of the reddish regional layer. The country as a whole was all red sandstone earth, but here I found a strange black loam less than a foot down. It was such soil as one finds in the strange, deep valleys farther west and south, and must surely have been brought from a considerable distance in the prehistoric age when the mound was reared. Kneeling and digging, I felt the leathern cord around my neck tugged harder and harder, as something in the soil seemed to draw the heavy metal talisman more and more. Then I felt my implements strike a hard surface, and wondered if a rock layer rested beneath. Prying about with the trench-knife, I found that such was not the case. Instead, to my intense surprise and feverish interest, I brought up a mould-clogged, heavy object of cylindrical shape — about a foot long and four inches in diameter — to which my hanging talisman clove with glue-like tenacity. As I cleared off the black loam my wonder and tension increased at the bas-reliefs revealed by that process. The whole cylinder, ends and all, was covered with figures and hieroglyphs; and I saw with growing excitement that these things were in the same unknown tradition as those on Grey Eagle's charm and on the yellow metal trappings of the ghost I had seen through my binoculars.

Sitting down, I further cleaned the magnetic cylinder against the rough corduroy of my knickerbockers, and observed that it was made of the same heavy, lustrous unknown metal as the charm — hence, no doubt, the singular attraction. The carvings and chasings were very strange and very horrible — nameless monsters and designs fraught with insidious evil — and all were of the highest finish and craftsmanship. I could not at first make head or tail of the thing, and handled it aimlessly until I spied a cleavage near one end. Then I sought eagerly for some mode of opening, discovering at last that the end simply unscrewed.

The cap yielded with difficulty, but at last it came off, liberating a curious aromatic odour. The sole contents was a bulky roll of a yellowish, paper-like substance inscribed in greenish characters, and for a second I had the supreme thrill of fancying that I held a written key to unknown elder worlds and abysses beyond time. Almost immediately, however, the unrolling of one end shewed that the manuscript was in Spanish — albeit the formal, pompous Spanish of a long-departed day. In the golden sunset light I looked at the heading and the opening paragraph, trying to decipher the wretched and ill-punctuated script of the vanished writer. What manner of relic was this? Upon what sort of a discovery had I stumbled? The first words set me in a new fury of excitement and curiosity, for instead of diverting me from my original quest they startlingly confirmed me in that very effort.

The yellow scroll with the green script began with a bold, identifying caption and a ceremoniously desperate appeal for belief in incredible revelations to follow:

RELACIÓN DE PÁNFILO DE ZAMACONA Y NUÑEZ, HIDALGO DE LUARCA EN ASTURIAS, TOCANTE AL MUNDO SOTERRÁNEO DE XINAIÁN, A.D. MDXLV

En el nombre de la santísima Trinidad, Padre, Hijo, y Espíritu-Santo, tres personas distintas y un solo. Dios verdadero, y de la santísima Virgen nuestra Señora, YO, PÁNFILO DE ZAMACONA, HIJO DE PEDRO GUZMAN Y ZAMACONA, HIDALGO, Y DE LA DOÑA YNÉS ALVARADO Y NUÑEZ, DE LUARCA EN ASTURIAS, juro para que todo que deco está verdadero como sacramento . . . .

I paused to reflect on the portentous significance of what I was reading. "The Narrative of Pánfilo de Zamacona y Nuñez, gentleman, of Luarca in Asturias, Concerning the Subterranean World of Xinaián, A. D. 1545" . . . Here, surely, was too much for any mind to absorb all at once. A subterranean world — again that persistent idea which filtered through all the Indian tales and through all the utterances of those who had come back from the mound. And the date — 1545 — what could this mean? In 1540 Coronado and his men had gone north from Mexico into the wilderness, but had they not turned back in 1542? My eye ran questingly down the opened part of the scroll, and almost at once seized on the name Francisco Vasquez de Coronado. The writer of this thing, clearly, was one of Coronado's men — but what had he been doing in this remote realm three years after his party had gone back? I must read further, for another glance told me that what was now unrolled was merely a summary of Coronado's northward march, differing in no essential way from the account known to history.

It was only the waning light which checked me before I

could unroll and read more, and in my impatient bafflement I almost forgot to be frightened at the onrush of night in this sinister place. Others, however, had not forgotten the lurking terror, for I heard a loud distant hallooing from a knot of men who had gathered at the edge of the town. Answering the anxious hail, I restored the manuscript to its strange cylinder — to which the disc around my neck still clung until I pried it off — and packed it and my smaller implements for departure. Leaving the pick and shovel for the next day's work, I took up my handbag, scrambled down the steep side of the mound, and in another quarter-hour was back in the village explaining and exhibiting my curious find. As darkness drew on, I glanced back at the mound I had so lately left, and saw with a shudder that the faint bluish torch of the nocturnal squaw-ghost had begun to glimmer.

It was hard work waiting to get at the bygone Spaniard's narrative; but I knew I must have quiet and leisure for a good translation, so reluctantly saved the task for the later hours of night. Promising the townsfolk a clear account of my findings in the morning, and giving them an ample opportunity to examine the bizarre and provocative cylinder, I accompanied Clyde Compton home and ascended to my room for the translating process as soon as I possibly could. My host and his mother were intensely eager to hear the tale, but I thought they had better wait till I could thoroughly absorb the text myself and give them the gist concisely and unerringly.

Opening my handbag in the light of a single electric bulb, I again took out the cylinder and noted the instant magnetism which pulled the Indian talisman to its carven surface. The designs glimmered evilly on the richly lustrous and unknown metal, and I could not help shivering as I studied the abnormal and blasphemous forms that leered at me with such exquisite workmanship. I wish now that I had carefully photographed all these designs — though perhaps it is just as well that I did not. Of one thing I am really glad, and that is that I could not then identify the squatting octopus-headed thing which dominated most of the ornate cartouches, and which the manuscript called "Tulu." Recently I have associated it, and the legends in the manuscript connected with it, with some new-found folklore of monstrous and unmentioned Cthulhu, a horror which seeped down from the stars while the young earth was still half-formed; and had I known of the connexion then, I could not have stayed in the same room with the thing. The secondary motif, a semi-anthropomorphic serpent, I did quite readily place as a prototype of the Yig, Quetzalcoatl, and Kukulcan conceptions.

Before opening the cylinder I tested its magnetic powers on metals other than that of Grey Eagle's disc, but found that no attraction existed. It was no common magnetism which pervaded this morbid fragment of unknown worlds and linked it to its kind.

At last I took out the manuscript and began translating — jotting down a synoptic outline in English as I went, and now and then regretting the absence of a Spanish dictionary when I came upon some especially obscure or archaic word or construction. There was a sense of ineffable strangeness in thus being thrown back nearly four centuries in the midst of my continuous quest — thrown back to a year when my own forbears were settled, homekeeping gentlemen of Somerset and Devon under Henry the Eighth, with never a thought of the adventure that was to take their blood to Virginia and the New World; yet when that new world possessed, even as now, the same brooding mystery of the mound which formed my present sphere and horizon. The sense of a throwback was all the stronger because I felt instinctively that the common problem of the Spaniard and myself was one of such abysmal timelessness — of such unholy and unearthly eternity — that the scant four hundred years between us bulked as nothing in comparison. It took no more than a single look at that monstrous and insidious cylinder to make me realise the dizzying gulfs that yawned between all men of the known earth and the primal mysteries it represented. Before that gulf Pánfilo de Zamacona and I stood side by side; just as Aristotle and I, or Cheops and I, might have stood.

III.

Of his youth in Luarca, a small, placid port on the Bay of Biscay, Zamacona told little. He had been wild, and a younger son, and had come to New Spain in 1532, when only twenty years old. Sensitively imaginative, he had listened spellbound to the floating rumours of rich cities and unknown worlds to the north — and especially to the tale of the Franciscan friar Marcos de Niza, who came back from a trip in 1539 with glowing accounts of fabulous Cíbola and its great walled towns with terraced stone houses. Hearing of Coronado's contemplated expedition in search of these wonders — and of the greater wonders whispered to lie beyond them in the land of buffaloes — young Zamacona managed to join the picked party of 300, and started north with the rest in 1540.

History knows the story of that expedition — how Cíbola was found to be merely the squalid Pueblo village of Zuñi, and how de Niza was sent back to Mexico in disgrace for his florid exaggerations; how Coronado first saw the Grand Canyon, and how at Cicuyé, on the Pecos, he heard from the Indian called El Turco of the rich and mysterious land of Quivira, far to the northeast, where gold, silver, and buffaloes abounded, and where there flowed a river two leagues wide. Zamacona told briefly of the winter camp at Tiguex on the Pecos, and of the northward start in April, when the native guide proved false and led the party astray amidst a land of prairie-dogs, salt pools, and roving, bison-hunting tribes.

When Coronado dismissed his larger force and made his final forty-two-day march with a very small and select detachment, Zamacona managed to be included in the advancing party. He spoke of the fertile country and of the great ravines with trees visible only from the edge of their steep banks; and of how all the men lived solely on buffalo-meat. And then came mention of the expedition's farthest limit—of the presumable but disappointing land of Quivira with its villages of grass houses, its brooks and rivers, its good black soil, its plums, nuts, grapes, and mulberries, and its maize-growing and copper-using Indians. The execution of El Turco, the false native guide, was casually touched upon, and there was a mention of the cross which Coronado raised on the bank of a great river in the autumn of 1541—a cross bearing the inscription, "Thus far came the great general, Francisco Vásquez de Coronado."

This supposed Quivira lay at about the fortieth parallel of north latitude, and I see that quite lately the New York archaeologist Dr. Hodge has identified it with the course of the Arkansas River through Barton and Rice Counties, Kansas. It is the old home of the Wichitas, before the Sioux drove them south into what is now Oklahoma, and some of the grass-house village sites have been found and excavated for artefacts. Coronado did considerable exploring hereabouts, led hither and thither by the persistent rumours of rich cities and hidden worlds which floated fearfully around on the Indians' tongues. These northerly natives seemed more afraid and reluctant to talk about the rumoured cities and worlds than the Mexican Indians had been; yet at the same time seemed as if they could reveal a good deal more than the Mexicans had they been willing or dared to do so. Their vagueness exasperated the Spanish leader, and after many disappointing searches he began to be very severe toward those who brought him stories. Zamacona, more patient than Coronado, found the tales especially interesting; and learned enough of the local speech to hold long conversations with a young buck named Charging Buffalo, whose curiosity had led him into much stranger places than any of his fellow-tribesmen had dared to penetrate.

It was Charging Buffalo who told Zamacona of the queer stone doorways, gates, or cave-mouths at the bottom of some of those deep, steep, wooded ravines which the party had noticed on the northward march. These openings, he said, were mostly concealed by shrubbery; and few had entered them for untold aeons. Those who went to where they led, never returned—or in a few cases returned mad or curiously maimed. But all this was legend, for nobody was known to have gone more than a limited distance inside any of them within the memory of the grandfathers of the oldest living men. Charging Buffalo himself had probably been farther than anyone else, and he had seen enough to curb both his curiosity and his greed for the rumoured gold below.

Beyond the aperture he had entered there was a long passage running crazily up and down and round about, and covered with frightful carvings of monsters and horrors that no man had ever seen. At last, after untold miles of windings and descents, there was a glow of terrible blue light; and the passage opened upon a shocking nether world. About this the Indian would say no more, for he had seen something that had sent him back in haste. But the golden cities must be somewhere down there, he added, and perhaps a white man with the magic of the thunder-stick might succeed in getting to them. He would not tell the big chief Coronado what he knew, for Coronado would not listen to Indian talk any more. Yes—he could shew Zamacona the way if the white man would leave the party and accept his guidance. But he would not go inside the opening with the white man. It was bad in there.

The place was about a five days' march to the south, near the region of great mounds. These mounds had something to do with the evil world down there—they were probably ancient closed-up passages to it, for once the Old Ones below had had colonies on the surface and had traded with men everywhere, even in the lands that had sunk under the big waters. It was when those lands had sunk that the Old Ones closed themselves up below and refused to deal with surface people. The refugees from the sinking places had told them that the gods of outer earth were against men, and that no men could survive on the outer earth unless they were daemons in league with the evil gods. That is why they shut out all surface folk, and did fearful things to any who ventured down where they dwelt. There had been sentries once at the various openings, but after ages they were no longer needed. Not many people cared to talk about the hidden Old Ones, and the legends about them would probably have died out but for certain ghostly reminders of their presence now and then. It seemed that the infinite ancientness of these creatures had brought them strangely near to the borderline of spirit, so that their ghostly emanations were more commonly frequent and vivid. Accordingly the region of the great mounds was often convulsed with spectral nocturnal battles reflecting those which had been fought in the days before the openings were closed.

The Old Ones themselves were half-ghost—indeed, it was said that they no longer grew old or reproduced their kind, but flickered eternally in a state between flesh and spirit. The change was not complete, though, for they had to breathe. It was because the underground world needed air that the openings in the deep valleys were not blocked up as the mound-openings on the plains had been. These openings, Charging Buffalo added, were probably based on natural fissures in the earth. It was whispered that the Old Ones had come down from the stars to the world when it was very young, and had gone inside to build their cities of solid gold because the surface was not then fit to live on. They were the ancestors of all men, yet none could guess from what star—or what place beyond the stars—they came. Their hidden cities were still full of gold and silver, but men had better let them alone unless protected by very strong magic.

They had frightful beasts with a faint strain of human blood, on which they rode, and which they employed for other purposes. The things, so people hinted, were carnivorous, and like their masters, preferred human flesh; so that although the Old Ones themselves did not breed, they had a sort of half-human slave-class which also served to nourish the human and animal population. This had been very oddly recruited, and was supplemented by a second slave-class of reanimated corpses.

The Old Ones knew how to make a corpse into an automaton which would last almost indefinitely and perform any sort of work when directed by streams of thought. Charging Buffalo said that the people had all come to talk by means of thought only; speech having been found crude and needless, except for religious devotions and emotional expression, as aeons of discovery and study rolled by. They worshipped Yig, the great father of serpents, and Tulu, the octopus-headed entity that had brought them down from the stars; appeasing both of these hideous monstrosities by means of human sacrifices offered up in a very curious manner which Charging Buffalo did not care to describe.

Zamacona was held spellbound by the Indian's tale, and at once resolved to accept his guidance to the cryptic doorway in the ravine. He did not believe the accounts of strange ways attributed by legend to the hidden people, for the experiences of the party had been such as to disillusion one regarding native myths of unknown lands; but he did feel that some sufficiently marvellous field of riches and adventure must indeed lie beyond the weirdly carved passages in the earth. At first he thought of persuading Charging Buffalo to tell his story to Coronado — offering to shield him against any effects of the leader's testy scepticism — but later he decided that a lone adventure would be better. If he had no aid, he would not have to share anything he found; but might perhaps become a great discoverer and owner of fabulous riches. Success would make him a greater figure than Coronado himself — perhaps a greater figure than anyone else in New Spain, including even the mighty viceroy Don Antonio de Mendoza.

On October 7, 1541, at an hour close to midnight, Zamacona stole out of the Spanish camp near the grass-house village and met Charging Buffalo for the long southward journey. He travelled as lightly as possible, and did not wear his heavy helmet and breastplate. Of the details of the trip the manuscript told very little, but Zamacona records his arrival at the great ravine on October 13th. The descent of the thickly wooded slope took no great time; and though the Indian had trouble in locating the shrubbery-hidden stone door again amidst the twilight of that deep gorge, the place was finally found. It was a very small aperture as doorways go, formed of monolithic sandstone jambs and lintel, and bearing signs of nearly effaced and now undecipherable carvings. Its height was perhaps seven feet, and its width not more than four. There were drilled places in the jambs which argued the bygone presence of a hinged door or gate, but all other traces of such a thing had long since vanished.

At sight of this black gulf Charging Buffalo displayed considerable fear, and threw down his pack of supplies with signs of haste. He had provided Zamacona with a good stock of resinous torches and provisions, and had guided him honestly and well; but refused to share in the venture that lay ahead. Zamacona gave him the trinkets he had kept for such an occasion, and obtained his promise to return to the region in a month; afterward shewing the way southward to the Pecos Pueblo villages. A prominent rock on the plain above them was chosen as a meeting-place; the one arriving first to pitch camp until the other should arrive.

In the manuscript Zamacona expressed a wistful wonder as to the Indian's length of waiting at the rendezvous — for he himself could never keep that tryst. At the last moment Charging Buffalo tried to dissuade him from his plunge into the darkness, but soon saw it was futile, and gestured a stoical farewell. Before lighting his first torch and entering the opening with his ponderous pack, the Spaniard watched the lean form of the Indian scrambling hastily and rather relievedly upward among the trees. It was the cutting of his last link with the world, though he did not know that he was never to see a human being — in the accepted sense of that term — again.

Zamacona felt no immediate premonition of evil upon entering that ominous doorway, though from the first he was surrounded by a bizarre and unwholesome atmosphere. The passage, slightly taller and wider than the aperture, was for many yards a level tunnel of Cyclopean masonry, with heavily worn flagstones underfoot, and grotesquely carved granite and sandstone blocks in sides and ceiling. The carvings must have been loathsome and terrible indeed, to judge from Zamacona's description, according to which most of them revolved around the monstrous beings Yig and Tulu. They were unlike anything the adventurer had ever seen before, though he added that the native architecture of Mexico came closest to them of all things in the outer world. After some distance the tunnel began to dip abruptly, and irregular natural rock appeared on all sides. The passage seemed only partly artificial, and decorations were limited to occasional cartouches with shocking bas-reliefs.

Following an enormous descent, whose steepness at times produced an acute danger of slipping and tobogganing, the passage became exceedingly uncertain in its direction and variable in its contour. At times it narrowed almost to a slit or grew so low that stooping and even crawling were necessary, while at other times it broadened out into sizeable caves or chains of caves. Very little human construction, it was plain, had gone into this part of the tunnel; though occasionally a sinister cartouche or hieroglyphic on the wall, or a blocked-up lateral passageway, would remind Zamacona that this was in truth the aeon-forgotten high-road to a primal and unbelievable world of living things.

For three days, as best he could reckon, Pánfilo de Zamacona scrambled down, up, along, and around, but always predominately downward, through this dark region of palaeogean night. Once in a while he heard some secret being of darkness patter or flap out of his way, and on just one occasion he half glimpsed a great, bleached thing that set him trembling. The quality of the air was mostly very tolerable, though foetid zones were now and then met with, while one great cavern of stalactites and stalagmites afforded a depressing dampness. This latter, when Charging Buffalo had come upon it, had quite seriously barred the way; since the limestone deposits of ages had built fresh pillars in the path of the primordial abyss-denizens. The Indian, however, had broken through these; so that Zamacona did not find his course impeded. It was an unconscious comfort to him to reflect that someone else from the outside world had been there before — and the Indian's careful descriptions had removed the element of surprise and unexpectedness. More — Charging Buffalo's knowledge of the tunnel had led him to provide so good a torch supply for the journey in and out, that there would be no danger of becoming stranded in darkness. Zamacona camped twice, building a fire whose smoke seemed well taken care of by the natural ventilation.

At what he considered the end of the third day — though his cocksure guesswork chronology is not at any time to be given the easy faith that he gave it — Zamacona encountered the prodigious descent and subsequent prodigious climb which Charging Buffalo had described as the tunnel's last phase. As at certain earlier points, marks of artificial improvement were here discernible; and several times the steep gradient was eased by a flight of rough-hewn steps. The torch shewed more and more of the monstrous carvings on the walls, and finally the resinous flare seemed mixed with a fainter and more diffusive light as Zamacona climbed up and up after the last downward stairway. At length the ascent ceased, and a level passage of artificial masonry with dark, basaltic blocks led straight ahead. There was no need for a torch now, for all the air was glowing with a bluish, quasi-electric radiance that flickered like an aurora. It was the strange light of the inner world that the Indian had described — and in another moment Zamacona emerged from the tunnel upon a bleak, rocky hillside which climbed above him to a seething, impenetrable sky of bluish coruscations, and descended dizzily below him to an apparently illimitable plain shrouded in bluish mist.

He had come to the unknown world at last, and from his manuscript it is clear that he viewed the formless landscape as proudly and exaltedly as ever his fellow-countryman Balboa viewed the new-found Pacific from that unforgettable peak in Darien. Charging Buffalo had turned back at this point, driven by fear of something which he would only describe vaguely and evasively as a herd of bad cattle, neither horse nor buffalo, but like the things the mound-spirits rode at night — but Zamacona could not be deterred by any such trifle. Instead of fear, a strange sense of glory filled him; for he had imagination enough to know what it meant to stand alone in an inexplicable nether world whose existence no other white man suspected.

The soil of the great hill that surged upward behind him and spread steeply downward below him was dark grey, rock-strewn, without vegetation, and probably basaltic in origin; with an unearthly cast which made him feel like an intruder on an alien planet. The vast distant plain, thousands of feet below, had no features he could distinguish; especially since it appeared to be largely veiled in a curling, bluish vapour. But more than hill or plain or cloud, the bluely luminous, coruscating sky impressed the adventurer with a sense of supreme wonder and mystery. What created this sky within a world he could not tell; though he knew of the northern lights, and had even seen them once or twice. He concluded that this subterraneous light was something vaguely akin to the aurora; a view which moderns may well endorse, though it seems likely that certain phenomena of radio-activity may also enter in.

At Zamacona's back the mouth of the tunnel he had traversed yawned darkly, defined by a stone doorway very like the one he had entered in the world above, save that it was of greyish-black basalt instead of red sandstone. There were hideous sculptures, still in good preservation and perhaps corresponding to those on the outer portal which time had largely weathered away. The absence of weathering here argued a dry, temperate climate; indeed, the Spaniard already began to note the delightfully spring-like stability of temperature which marks the air of the north's interior. On the stone jambs were works proclaiming the bygone presence of hinges, but of any actual door or gate no trace remained. Seating himself for rest and thought, Zamacona lightened his pack by removing an amount of food and torches sufficient to take him back through the tunnel. These he proceeded to cache at the opening, under a cairn hastily formed of the rock fragments which everywhere lay around. Then, readjusting his lightened pack, he commenced his descent toward the distant plain; preparing to invade a region which no living thing of outer earth had penetrated in a century or more, which no white man had ever penetrated, and from which, if legend were to be believed, no organic creature had ever returned sane.

Zamacona strode briskly along down the steep, interminable slope, his progress checked at times by the bad walking that came from loose rock fragments, or by the excessive precipitousness of the grade. The distance of the mist-shrouded plain must have been enormous, for many hours' walking brought him apparently no closer to it than he had been before. Behind him was always the great hill stretching upward into a bright aerial sea of bluish coruscations. Silence was universal; so that his own footsteps, and the fall of stones that he dislodged, struck on his ears with startling distinctness.

It was at what he regarded as about noon that he first saw the abnormal footprints which set him to thinking of Charging Buffalo's terrible hints, precipitate flight, and strangely abiding terror.

The rock-strewn nature of the soil gave few opportunities for tracks of any kind, but at one point a rather level interval had caused the loose detritus to accumulate in a ridge, leaving a considerable area of dark-grey loam absolutely bare. Here, in a rambling confusion indicating a large herd aimlessly wandering, Zamacona found the abnormal prints. It is to be regretted that he could not describe them more exactly, but the manuscript displayed far more vague fear than accurate observation. Just what it was that so frightened the Spaniard can only be inferred from his later hints regarding the beasts. He referred to the prints as "not hooves, nor hands, nor feet, nor precisely paws — nor so large as to cause alarm on that account." Just why or how long ago the things had been there, was not easy to guess. There was no vegetation visible, hence grazing was out of the question; but of course if the beasts were carnivorous they might well have been hunting smaller animals, whose tracks their own would tend to obliterate.

Glancing backward from this plateau to the heights above, Zamacona thought he detected traces of a great winding road which had once led from the tunnel downward to the plain. One could get the impression of this former highway only from a broad panoramic view, since a trickle of loose rock fragments had long ago obscured it; but the adventurer felt none the less certain that it had existed. It had not, probably, been an elaborately paved trunk route; for the small tunnel it reached seemed scarcely like a main avenue to the outer world. In choosing a straight path of descent Zamacona had not followed its curving course, though he must have crossed it once or twice. With his attention now called to it, he looked ahead to see if he could trace it downward toward the plain; and this he finally thought he could do. He resolved to investigate its surface when next he crossed it, and perhaps to pursue its line for the rest of the way if he could distinguish it.

Having resumed his journey, Zamacona came some time later upon what he thought was a bend of the ancient road. There were signs of grading and of some primal attempt at rock-surfacing, but not enough was left to make the route worth following. While rummaging about in the soil with his sword, the Spaniard turned up something that glittered in the eternal blue daylight, and was thrilled at beholding a kind of coin or medal of a dark, unknown, lustrous metal, with hideous designs on each side. It was utterly and bafflingly alien to him, and from his description I have no doubt but that it was a duplicate of the talisman given me by Grey Eagle almost four centuries afterward. Pocketing it after a long and curious examination, he strode onward; finally pitching camp at an hour which he guessed to be the evening of the outer world.

The next day Zamacona rose early and resumed his descent through this blue-litten world of mist and desolation and preternatural silence. As he advanced, he at last became able to distinguish a few objects on the distant plain below — trees, bushes, rocks, and a small river that came into view from the right and curved forward at a point to the left of his contemplated course. This river seemed to be spanned by a bridge connected with the descending roadway, and with care the explorer could trace the route of the road beyond it in a straight line over the plain. Finally he even thought he could detect towns scattered along the rectilinear ribbon; towns whose left-hand edges reached the river and sometimes crossed it. Where such crossings occurred, he saw as he descended, there were always signs of bridges either ruined or surviving. He was now in the midst of a sparse grassy vegetation, and saw that below him the growth became thicker and thicker. The road was easier to define now, since its surface discouraged the grass which the looser soil supported. Rock fragments were less frequent, and the barren upward vista behind him looked bleak and forbidding in contrast to his present milieu.

It was on this day that he saw the blurred mass moving over the distant plain. Since his first sight of the sinister footprints he had met with no more of these, but something about that slowly and deliberately moving mass peculiarly sickened him. Nothing but a herd of grazing animals could move just like that, and after seeing the footprints he did not wish to meet the things which had made them. Still, the moving mass was not near the road — and his curiosity and greed for fabled gold were great. Besides, who could really judge things from vague, jumbled footprints or from the panic-twisted hints of an ignorant Indian?

In straining his eyes to view the moving mass Zamacona became aware of several other interesting things. One was that on certain parts of the plain, unmistakable towns glittered oddly in the misty blue light. Another was that, besides the towns, several similarly glittering structures of a more isolated sort were scattered here and there along the road and over the plain. They seemed to be embowered in clumps of vegetation, and those off the road had small avenues leading to the highway. No smoke or other signs of life could be discerned about any of the towns or buildings. Finally Zamacona saw that the plain was not infinite in extent, though the half-concealing blue mists had hitherto made it seem so. It was bounded in the remote distance by a range of low hills, toward a gap in which the river and roadway seemed to lead. All this — especially the glittering of certain pinnacles in the towns — had become very vivid when Zamacona pitched his second camp amidst the endless blue day. He likewise noticed the flocks of high-soaring birds, whose nature he could not clearly make out.

The next afternoon — to use the language of the outer world, as the manuscript did at all times — Zamacona reached the silent plain and crossed the soundless, slow-running river on a curiously carved and fairly well-preserved bridge of black basalt. The water was clear, and contained large fishes of a wholly strange aspect. The roadway was now paved and somewhat overgrown with weeds and creeping vines, and its course was occasionally outlined by small pillars bearing obscure symbols. On every side the grassy level extended, with here and there a clump of trees or shrubbery, and with unidentifiable bluish flowers growing irregularly over the whole area. Now and then some spasmodic motion of the grass indicated the presence of serpents.

In the course of several hours the traveller reached a grove of old and alien-looking evergreen-trees which he knew, from distant viewing, protected one of the glittering-roofed isolated structures. Amidst the encroaching vegetation he saw the hideously sculptured pylons of a stone gateway leading off the road, and was presently forcing his way through briers above a moss-crusted tessellated walk lined with huge trees and low monolithic pillars.

At last, in this hushed green twilight, he saw the crumbling and ineffably ancient facade of the building—a temple, he had no doubt. It was a mass of nauseous bas-reliefs, depicting scenes and beings, objects and ceremonies, which could certainly have no place on this or any sane planet.

In hinting of these things Zamacona displays for the first time that shocked and pious hesitancy which impairs the informative value of the rest of his manuscript. We cannot help regretting that the Catholic ardour of Renaissance Spain had so thoroughly permeated his thought and feeling. The door of the place stood wide open, and absolute darkness filled the windowless interior. Conquering the repulsion which the mural sculptures had excited, Zamacona took out flint and steel, lighted a resinous torch, pushed aside curtaining vines, and sallied boldly across the ominous threshold.

For a moment he was quite stupefied by what he saw. It was not the all-covering dust and cobwebs of immemorial aeons, the fluttering winged things, the shriekingly loathsome sculptures on the walls, the bizarre form of the many basins and braziers, the sinister pyramidal altar with the hollow top, or the monstrous, octopus-headed abnormality in some strange, dark metal leering and squatting broodingly on its hieroglyphed pedestal, which robbed him of even the power to give a startled cry. It was nothing so unearthly as this—but merely the fact that, with the exception of the dust, the cobwebs, the winged things, and the gigantic emerald-eyed idol, every particle of substance in sight was composed of pure and evidently solid gold.

Even the manuscript, written in retrospect after Zamacona knew that gold is the most common structural metal of a nether world containing limitless lodes and veins of it, reflects the frenzied excitement which the traveller felt upon suddenly finding the real source of all the Indian legends of golden cities. For a time the power of detailed observation left him, but in the end his faculties were recalled by a peculiar tugging sensation in the pocket of his doublet. Tracing the feeling, he realised that the disc of strange metal he had found in the abandoned road was being attracted strongly by the vast octopus-headed, emerald-eyed idol on the pedestal, which he now saw to be composed of the same unknown exotic metal. He was later to learn that this strange magnetic substance—as alien to the inner world as to the outer world of men—is the one precious metal of the blue-lighted abyss. None knows what it is or where it occurs in Nature, and the amount of it on this planet came down from the stars with the people when great Tulu, the octopus-headed god, brought them for the first time to this earth. Certainly, its only known source was a stock of pre-existing artefacts, including multitudes of Cyclopean idols. It could never be placed or analysed, and even its magnetism was exerted only on its own kind. It was the supreme ceremonial metal of the hidden people, its use being regulated by custom in such a way that its magnetic properties might cause no inconvenience. A very weakly magnetic alloy of it with such base metals as iron, gold, silver, copper, or zinc, had formed the sole monetary standard of the hidden people at one period of their history.

Zamacona's reflections on the strange idol and its magnetism were disturbed by a tremendous wave of fear as, for the first time in this silent world, he heard a rumble of very definite and obviously approaching sound. There was no mistaking its nature. It was a thunderously charging herd of large animals; and, remembering the Indian's panic, the footprints, and the moving mass distantly seen, the Spaniard shuddered in terrified anticipation. He did not analyse his position, or the significance of this onrush of great lumbering beings, but merely responded to an elemental urge toward self-protection. Charging herds do not stop to find victims in obscure places, and on the outer earth Zamacona would have felt little or no alarm in such a massive, grove-girt edifice. Some instinct, however, now bred a deep and peculiar terror in his soul; and he looked about frantically for any means of safety.

There being no available refuge in the great, gold-patinaed interior, he felt that he must close the long-disused door; which still hung on its ancient hinges, doubled back against the inner wall. Soil, vines, and moss had entered the opening from outside, so that he had to dig a path for the great gold portal with his sword; but he managed to perform this work very swiftly under the frightful stimulus of the approaching noise. The hoofbeats had grown still louder and more menacing by the time he began tugging at the heavy door itself; and for a while his fears reached a frantic height, as hope of starting the age-clogged metal grew faint. Then, with a creak, the thing responded to his youthful strength, and a frenzied siege of pulling and pushing ensued. Amidst the roar of unseen stampeding feet success came at last, and the ponderous golden door clanged shut, leaving Zamacona in darkness but for the single lighted torch he had wedged between the pillars of a basin-tripod. There was a latch, and the frightened man blessed his patron saint that it was still effective.

Sound alone told the fugitive the sequel. When the roar grew very near it resolved itself into separate footfalls, as if the evergreen grove had made it necessary for the herd to slacken speed and disperse. But feet continued to approach, and it became evident that the beasts were advancing among the trees and circling the hideously carven temple walls. In the curious deliberation of their tread Zamacona found something very alarming and repulsive, nor did he like the scuffling sounds which were audible even through the thick stone walls and heavy golden door. Once the door rattled ominously on its archaic hinges, as if under a heavy impact, but fortunately it still held. Then, after a seemingly endless interval, he heard retreating steps and realised that his unknown visitors were leaving. Since the herds did not seem to be very numerous, it would have perhaps been safe to venture out within a half-hour or less; but Zamacona took no chances. Opening his pack, he prepared his camp on the golden tiles of the temple's floor, with the great door still securely latched against all comers; drifting eventually into a sounder sleep than he could have known in the blue-litten spaces outside. He did not even mind the hellish, octopus-headed bulk of great Tulu, fashioned of unknown metal and leering with fishy, sea-green eyes, which squatted in the blackness above him on its monstrously hieroglyphed pedestal.

Surrounded by darkness for the first time since leaving the tunnel, Zamacona slept profoundly and long. He must have more than made up the sleep he had lost at his two previous camps, when the ceaseless glare of the sky had kept him awake despite his fatigue, for much distance was covered by other living feet while he lay in his healthily dreamless rest. It is well that he rested deeply, for there were many strange things to be encountered in his next period of consciousness.

IV.

What finally roused Zamacona was a thunderous rapping at the door. It beat through his dreams and dissolved all the lingering mists of drowsiness as soon as he knew what it was. There could be no mistake about it — it was a definite, human, and peremptory rapping, performed apparently with some metallic object, and with all the measured quality of conscious thought or will behind it. As the awakening man rose clumsily to his feet, a sharp vocal note was added to the summons — someone calling out, in a not unmusical voice, a formula which the manuscript tries to represent as "oxi, oxi, giathcán yca relex." Feeling sure that his visitors were men and not daemons, and arguing that they could have no reason for considering him an enemy, Zamacona decided to face them openly and at once; and accordingly fumbled with the ancient latch till the golden door creaked open from the pressure of those outside.

As the great portal swung back, Zamacona stood facing a group of about twenty individuals of an aspect not calculated to give him alarm. They seemed to be Indians; though their tasteful robes and trappings and swords were not such as he had seen among any of the tribes of the outer world, while their faces had many subtle differences from the Indian type. That they did not mean to be irresponsibly hostile, was very clear; for instead of menacing him in any way they merely probed him attentively and significantly with their eyes, as if they expected their gaze to open up some sort of communication. The longer they gazed, the more he seemed to know about them and their mission; for although no one had spoken since the vocal summons before the opening of the door, he found himself slowly realising that they had come from the great city beyond the low hills, mounted on animals, and that they had been summoned by animals who had reported his presence; that they were not sure what kind of person he was or just where he had come from but that they knew he must be associated with that dimly remembered outer world which they sometimes visited in curious dreams. How he read all this in the gaze of the two or three leaders he could not possibly explain; though he learned why a moment later.

As it was, he attempted to address his visitors in the Wichita dialect he had picked up from Charging Buffalo; and after this failed to draw a vocal reply he successively tried the Aztec, Spanish, French, and Latin tongues — adding as many scraps of lame Greek, Galician, and Portuguese, and of the Bable peasant patois of his native Asturias, as his memory could recall. But not even this polyglot array — his entire linguistic stock — could bring a reply in kind. When, however, he paused in perplexity, one of the visitors began speaking in an utterly strange and rather fascinating language whose sounds the Spaniard later had much difficulty in representing on paper. Upon his failure to understand this, the speaker pointed first to his own eyes, then to his forehead, and then to his eyes again, as if commanding the other to gaze at him in order to absorb what he wanted to transmit.

Zamacona, obeying, found himself rapidly in possession of certain information. The people, he learned, conversed nowadays by means of unvocal radiations of thought; although they had formerly used a spoken language which still survived as the written tongue, and into which they still dropped orally for tradition's sake, or when strong feeling demanded a spontaneous outlet. He could understand them merely by concentrating his attention upon their eyes; and could reply by summoning up a mental image of what he wished to say, and throwing the substance of this into his glance. When the thought-speaker paused, apparently inviting a response, Zamacona tried his best to follow the prescribed pattern, but did not appear to succeed very well. So he nodded, and tried to describe himself and his journey by signs. He pointed upward, as if to the outer world, then closed his eyes and made signs as of a mole burrowing. Then he opened his eyes again and pointed downward, in order to indicate his descent of the great slope. Experimentally he blended a spoken word or two with his gestures — for example, pointing successively to himself and to all of his visitors and saying "un hombre," and then pointing to himself alone and very carefully pronouncing his individual name, Pánfilo de Zamacona.

Before the strange conversation was over, a good deal of data had passed in both directions. Zamacona had begun to learn how to throw his thoughts, and had likewise picked up several words of the region's archaic spoken language. His visitors, moreover, had absorbed many beginnings of an elementary Spanish vocabulary. Their own old language was utterly unlike anything the Spaniard had ever heard, though there were times later on when he was to fancy an infinitely remote linkage with the Aztec, as if the latter represented some far stage of corruption, or some very thin infiltration of loan-words. The underground world, Zamacona learned, bore an ancient name which the manuscript records as "Xinaián"; but which, from the writer's supplementary explanations and diacritical marks, could probably be best represented to Anglo-Saxon ears by the phonetic arrangement K'n-yan.

It is not surprising that this preliminary discourse did not go beyond the merest essentials, but those essentials were highly important. Zamacona learned that the people of K'n-yan were almost infinitely ancient, and that they had come from a distant part of space where physical conditions are much like those of the earth. All this, of course, was legend now; and one could not say how much truth was in it, or how much worship was really due to the octopus-headed being Tulu who had traditionally brought them hither and whom they still reverenced for aesthetic reasons. But they knew of the outer world, and were indeed the original stock who had peopled it as soon as its crust was fit to live on. Between glacial ages they had had some remarkable surface civilisations, especially one at the South Pole near the mountain Kadath.

At some time infinitely in the past most of the outer world had sunk beneath the ocean, so that only a few refugees remained to bear the news to K'n-yan. This was undoubtedly due to the wrath of space-devils hostile alike to men and to men's gods — for it bore out rumours of a primordially earlier sinking which had submerged the gods themselves, including great Tulu, who still lay prisoned and dreaming in the watery vaults of the half-cosmic city Relex. No man not a slave of the space-devils, it was argued, could live long on the outer earth; and it was decided that all beings who remained there must be evilly connected. Accordingly traffic with the lands of sun and starlight abruptly ceased. The subterraneous approaches to K'n-yan, or such as could be remembered, were either blocked up or carefully guarded; and all encroachers were treated as dangerous spies and enemies.

But this was long ago. With the passing of ages fewer and fewer visitors came to K'n-yan, and eventually sentries ceased to be maintained at the unblocked approaches. The mass of the people forgot, except through distorted memories and myths and some very singular dreams, that an outer world existed; though educated folk never ceased to recall the essential facts. The last visitors ever recorded — centuries in the past — had not even been treated as devil-spies, faith in the old legendry having long before died out. They had been questioned eagerly about the fabulous outer regions; for scientific curiosity in K'n-yan was keen, and the myths, memories, dreams, and historical fragments relating to the earth's surface had often tempted scholars to the brink of an external expedition which they had not quite dared to attempt. The only thing demanded of such visitors was that they refrain from going back and informing the outer world of K'n-yan's positive existence; for after all, one could not be sure about these outer lands. They coveted gold and silver, and might prove highly troublesome intruders. Those who had obeyed the injunction had lived happily, though regrettably briefly, and had told all they could about their world — little enough, however, since their accounts were all so fragmentary and conflicting that one could hardly tell what to believe and what to doubt. One wished that more of them would come. As for those who disobeyed and tried to escape — it was very unfortunate about them. Zamacona himself was very welcome, for he appeared to be a higher-grade man, and to know much more about the outer world, than anyone else who had come down within memory. He could tell them much — and they hoped he would be reconciled to his lifelong stay.

Many things which Zamacona learned about K'n-yan in that first colloquy left him quite breathless. He learned, for instance, that during the past few thousand years the phenomena of old age and death had been conquered; so that men no longer grew feeble or died except through violence or will. By regulating the system, one might be as physiologically young and immortal as he wished; and the only reason why any allowed themselves to age, was that they enjoyed the sensation in a world where stagnation and commonplaceness reigned. They could easily become young again when they felt like it. Births had ceased, except for experimental purposes, since a large population had been found needless by a master-race which controlled Nature and organic rivals alike. Many, however, chose to die after a while; since despite the cleverest efforts to invent new pleasures, the ordeal of consciousness became too dull for sensitive souls — especially those in whom time and satiation had blinded the primal instincts and emotions of self-preservation. All the members of the group before Zamacona were from 500 to 1500 years old; and several had seen surface visitors before, though time had blurred the recollection. These visitors, by the way, had often tried to duplicate the longevity of the underground race; but had been able to do so only fractionally, owing to evolutionary differences developing during the million or two years of cleavage.

These evolutionary differences were even more strikingly shewn in another particular — one far stranger than the wonder of immortality itself. This was the ability of the people of K'n-yan to regulate the balance between matter and abstract energy, even where the bodies of living organic beings were concerned, by the sheer force of the technically trained will. In other words, with suitable effort a learned man of K'n-yan could dematerialise and rematerialise himself — or, with somewhat greater effort and subtler technique, any other object he chose; reducing solid matter to free external particles and recombining the particles again without damage. Had not Zamacona answered his visitors' knock when he did, he would have discovered this accomplishment in a highly puzzling way; for only the strain and bother of the process prevented the twenty men from passing bodily through the golden door without pausing for a summons.

This art was much older than the art of perpetual life; and it could be taught to some extent, though never perfectly, to any intelligent person. Rumours of it had reached the outer world in past aeons; surviving in secret traditions and ghostly legendry. The men of K'n-yan had been amused by the primitive and imperfect spirit tales brought down by outer-world stragglers. In practical life this principle had certain industrial applications, but was generally suffered to remain neglected through lack of any particular incentive to its use. Its chief surviving form was in connexion with sleep, when for excitement's sake many dream-connoisseurs resorted to it to enhance the vividness of their visionary wanderings. By the aid of this method certain dreamers even paid half-material visits to a strange, nebulous realm of mounds and valleys and varying light which some believed to be the forgotten outer world. They would go thither on their beasts, and in an age of peace live over the old, glorious battles of their forefathers. Some philosophers thought that in such cases they actually coalesced with immaterial forces left behind by these warlike ancestors themselves.

The people of K'n-yan all dwelt in the great, tall city of Tsath beyond the mountains. Formerly several races of them had inhabited the entire underground world, which stretched down to unfathomable abysses and which included besides the blue-litten region a red-litten region called Yoth, where relics of a still older and non-human race were found by archaeologists. In the course of time, however, the men of Tsath had conquered and enslaved the rest; interbreeding them with certain horned and four-footed animals of the red-litten region, whose semi-human leanings were very peculiar, and which, though containing a certain artificially created element, may have been in part the degenerate descendants of those peculiar entities who had left the relics. As aeons passed, and mechanical discoveries made the business of life extremely easy, a concentration of the people of Tsath took place; so that all the rest of K'n-yan became relatively deserted.

It was easier to live in one place, and there was no object in maintaining a population of overflowing proportions. Many of the old mechanical devices were still in use, though others had been abandoned when it was seen that they failed to give pleasure, or that they were not necessary for a race of reduced numbers whose mental force could govern an extensive array of inferior and semihuman industrial organisms. This extensive slave-class was highly composite, being bred from ancient conquered enemies, from outer-world stragglers, from dead bodies curiously galvanised into effectiveness, and from the naturally inferior members of the ruling race of Tsath. The ruling type itself had become highly superior through selective breeding and social evolution — the nation having passed through a period of idealistic industrial democracy which gave equal opportunities to all, and thus, by raising the naturally intelligent to power, drained the masses of all their brains and stamina. Industry, being found fundamentally futile except for the supplying of basic needs and the gratification of inescapable yearnings, had become very simple. Physical comfort was ensured by an urban mechanisation of standardised and easily maintained pattern, and other elemental needs were supplied by scientific agriculture and stock-raising. Long travel was abandoned, and people went back to using the horned, half-human beasts instead of maintaining the profusion of gold, silver, and steel transportation machines which had once threaded land, water, and air. Zamacona could scarcely believe that such things had ever existed outside dreams, but was told he could see specimens of them in museums. He could also see the ruins of other vast magical devices by travelling a day's journey to the valley of Do-Hna, to which the race had spread during its period of greatest numbers. The cities and temples of this present plain were of a far more archaic period, and had never been other than religious and antiquarian shrines during the supremacy of the men of Tsath.

In government, Tsath was a kind of communistic or semi-anarchical state; habit rather than law determining the daily order of things. This was made possible by the age-old experience and paralysing ennui of the race, whose wants and needs were limited to physical fundamentals and to new sensations. An aeon-long tolerance not yet undermined by growing reaction had abolished all illusions of values and principles, and nothing but an approximation to custom was ever sought or expected. To see that the mutual encroachments of pleasure-seeking never crippled the mass life of the community — this was all that was desired. Family organisation had long ago perished, and the civil and social distinction of the sexes had disappeared. Daily life was organised in ceremonial patterns; with games, intoxication, torture of slaves, day-dreaming, gastronomic and emotional orgies, religious exercises, exotic experiments, artistic and philosophical discussions, and the like, as the principal occupations. Property — chiefly land, slaves, animals, shares in the common city enterprise of Tsath, and ingots of magnetic Tulu-metal, the former universal money standard — was allocated on a very complex basis which included a certain amount equally divided among all the freemen. Poverty was unknown, and labour consisted only of certain administrative duties imposed by an intricate system of testing and selection. Zamacona found difficulty in describing conditions so unlike anything he had previously known; and the text of his manuscript proved unusually puzzling at this point.

Art and intellect, it appeared, had reached very high levels in Tsath; but had become listless and decadent. The dominance of machinery had at one time broken up the growth of normal aesthetics, introducing a lifelessly geometrical tradition fatal to sound expression. This had soon been outgrown, but had left its mark upon all pictorial and decorative attempts; so that except for conventionalised religious designs, there was little depth or feeling in any later work. Archaistic reproductions of earlier work had been found much preferable for general enjoyment. Literature was all highly individual and analytical, so much so as to be wholly incomprehensible to Zamacona. Science had been profound and accurate, and all-embracing save in the one direction of astronomy. Of late, however, it was falling into decay, as people found it increasingly useless to tax their minds by recalling its maddening infinitude of details and ramifications. It was thought more sensible to abandon the deepest speculations and to confine philosophy to conventional forms. Technology, of course, could be carried on by rule of thumb. History was more and more neglected, but exact and copious chronicles of the past existed in the libraries. It was still an interesting subject, and there would be a vast number to rejoice at the fresh outer-world knowledge brought in by Zamacona. In general, though, the modern tendency was to feel rather than to think; so that men were now more highly esteemed for inventing new diversions than for preserving old facts or pushing back the frontier of cosmic mystery.

Religion was a leading interest in Tsath, though very few actually believed in the supernatural. What was desired was the aesthetic and emotional exaltation bred by the mystical moods and sensuous rites which attended the colourful ancestral faith. Temples to Great Tulu, a spirit of universal harmony anciently symbolised as the octopus-headed god who had brought all men down from the stars, were the most richly constructed objects in all K'n-yan; while the cryptic shrines of Yig, the principle of life symbolised as the Father of all Serpents, were almost as lavish and remarkable. In time Zamacona learned much of the orgies and sacrifices connected with this religion, but seemed piously reluctant to describe them in his manuscript. He himself never participated in any of the rites save those which he mistook for perversions of his own faith; nor did he ever lose an opportunity to try to convert the people to that faith of the Cross which the Spaniards hoped to make universal.

Prominent in the contemporary religion of Tsath was a revived and almost genuine veneration for the rare, sacred metal of Tulu — that dark, lustrous, magnetic stuff which was nowhere found in Nature, but which had always been with men in the form of idols and hieratic implements. From the earliest times any sight of it in its unalloyed form had impelled respect, while all the sacred archives and litanies were kept in cylinders wrought of its purest substance. Now, as the neglect of science and intellect was dulling the critically analytical spirit, people were beginning to weave around the metal once more that same fabric of awestruck superstition which had existed in primitive times.

Another function of religion was the regulation of the calendar, born of a period when time and speed were regarded as prime fetiches in man's emotional life. Periods of alternate waking and sleeping, prolonged, abridged, and inverted as mood and convenience dictated, and timed by the tail-beats of Great Yig, the Serpent, corresponded very roughly to terrestrial days and nights; though Zamacona's sensations told him they must actually be almost twice as long. The year-unit, measured by Yig's annual shedding of his skin, was equal to about a year and a half of the outer world. Zamacona thought he had mastered this calendar very well when he wrote his manuscript, whence the confidently given date of 1545; but the document failed to suggest that his assurance in this matter was fully justified.

As the spokesman of the Tsath party proceeded with his information, Zamacona felt a growing repulsion and alarm. It was not only what was told, but the strange, telepathic manner of telling, and the plain inference that return to the outer world would be impossible, that made the Spaniard wish he had never descended to this region of magic, abnormality, and decadence. But he knew that nothing but friendly acquiescence would do as a policy, hence decided to cooperate in all his visitors' plans and furnish all the information they might desire. They, on their part, were fascinated by the outer-world data which he managed haltingly to convey.

It was really the first draught of reliable surface information they had had since the refugees straggled back from Atlantis and Lemuria aeons before, for all their subsequent emissaries from outside had been members of narrow and local groups without any knowledge of the world at large — Mayas, Toltecs, and Aztecs at best, and mostly ignorant tribes of the plains. Zamacona was the first European they had ever seen, and the fact that he was a youth of education and brilliancy made him of still more emphatic value as a source of knowledge. The visiting party shewed their breathless interest in all he contrived to convey, and it was plain that his coming would do much to relieve the flagging interest of weary Tsath in matters of geography and history.

The only thing which seemed to displease the men of Tsath was the fact that curious and adventurous strangers were beginning to pour into those parts of the upper world where the passages to K'n-yan lay. Zamacona told them of the founding of Florida and New Spain, and made it clear that a great part of the world was stirring with the zest of adventure — Spanish, Portuguese, French, and English. Sooner or later Mexico and Florida must meet in one great colonial empire — and then it would be hard to keep outsiders from the rumoured gold and silver of the abyss. Charging Buffalo knew of Zamacona's journey into the earth. Would he tell Coronado, or somehow let a report get to the great viceroy, when he failed to find the traveller at the promised meeting-place? Alarm for the continued secrecy and safety of K'n-yan shewed in the faces of the visitors, and Zamacona absorbed from their minds the fact that from now on sentries would undoubtedly be posted once more at all the unblocked passages to the outside world which the men of Tsath could remember.

V.

The long conversation of Zamacona and his visitors took place in the green-blue twilight of the grove just outside the temple door. Some of the men reclined on the weeds and moss beside the half-vanished walk, while others, including the Spaniard and the chief spokesman of the Tsath party, sat on the occasional low monolithic pillars that lined the temple approach. Almost a whole terrestrial day must have been consumed in the colloquy, for Zamacona felt the need of food several times, and ate from his well-stocked pack while some of the Tsath party went back for provisions to the roadway, where they had left the animals on which they had ridden. At length the prime leader of the party brought the discourse to a close, and indicated that the time had come to proceed to the city.

There were, he affirmed, several extra beasts in the cavalcade, upon one of which Zamacona could ride. The prospect of mounting one of those ominous hybrid entities whose fabled nourishment was so alarming, and a single sight of which had set Charging Buffalo into such a frenzy of flight, was by no means reassuring to the traveller. There was, moreover, another point about the things which disturbed him greatly—the apparently preternatural intelligence with which some members of the previous day's roving pack had reported his presence to the men of Tsath and brought out the present expedition. But Zamacona was not a coward, hence followed the men boldly down the weed-grown walk toward the road where the things were stationed.

And yet he could not refrain from crying out in terror at what he saw when he passed through the great vine-draped pylons and emerged upon the ancient road. He did not wonder that the curious Wichita had fled in panic, and had to close his eyes a moment to retain his sanity. It is unfortunate that some sense of pious reticence prevented him from describing fully in his manuscript the nameless sight he saw. As it is, he merely hinted at the shocking morbidity of these great floundering white things, with black fur on their backs, a rudimentary horn in the centre of their foreheads, and an unmistakable trace of human or anthropoid blood in their flat-nosed, bulging-lipped faces. They were, he declared later in his manuscript, the most terrible objective entities he ever saw in his life, either in K'n-yan or in the outer world. And the specific quality of their supreme terror was something apart from any easily recognisable or describable feature. The main trouble was that they were not wholly products of Nature.

The party observed Zamacona's fright, and hastened to reassure him as much as possible. The beasts or gyaa-yothn, they explained, surely were curious things; but were really very harmless. The flesh they ate was not that of intelligent people of the master-race, but merely that of a special slave-class which had for the most part ceased to be thoroughly human, and which indeed was the principal meat stock of K'n-yan. They—or their principal ancestral element—had first been found in a wild state amidst the Cyclopean ruins of the deserted red-litten world of Yoth which lay below the blue-litten world of K'n-yan. That part of them was human, seemed quite clear; but men of science could never decide whether they were actually the descendants of the bygone entities who had lived and reigned in the strange ruins. The chief ground for such a supposition was the well-known fact that the vanished inhabitants of Yoth had been quadrupedal. This much was known from the very few manuscripts and carvings found in the vaults of Zin, beneath the largest ruined city of Yoth. But it was also known from these manuscripts that the beings of Yoth had possessed the art of synthetically creating life, and had made and destroyed several efficiently designed races of industrial and transportational animals in the course of their history—to say nothing of concocting all manner of fantastic living shapes for the sake of amusement and new sensations during the long period of decadence. The beings of Yoth had undoubtedly been reptilian in affiliations, and most physiologists of Tsath agreed that the present beasts had been very much inclined toward reptilianism before they had been crossed with the mammal slave-class of K'n-yan.

It argues well for the intrepid fire of those Renaissance Spaniards who conquered half the unknown world, that Pánfilo de Zamacona y Nuñez actually mounted one of the morbid beasts of Tsath and fell into place beside the leader of the cavalcade—the man named Gll'-Hthaa-Ynn, who had been most active in the previous exchange of information. It was a repulsive business; but after all, the seat was very easy, and the gait of the clumsy gyaa-yoth surprisingly even and regular. No saddle was necessary, and the animal appeared to require no guidance whatever.

The procession moved forward at a brisk gait, stopping only at certain abandoned cities and temples about which Zamacona was curious, and which Gll'Hthaa-Ynn was obligingly ready to display and explain. The largest of these towns, B'graa, was a marvel of finely wrought gold, and Zamacona studied the curiously ornate architecture with avid interest. Buildings tended toward height and slenderness, with roofs bursting into a multitude of pinnacles. The streets were narrow, curving, and occasionally picturesquely hilly, but Gll'-Hthaa-Ynn said that the later cities of K'n-yan were far more spacious and regular in design. All these old cities of the plain shewed traces of levelled walls—reminders of the archaic days when they had been successively conquered by the now dispersed armies of Tsath.

There was one object along the route which Gll'-Hthaa-Ynn exhibited on his own initiative, even though it involved a detour of about a mile along a vine-tangled side path. This was a squat, plain temple of black basalt blocks without a single carving, and containing only a vacant onyx pedestal. The remarkable thing about it was its story, for it was a link with a fabled elder world compared to which even cryptic Yoth was a thing of yesterday. It had been built in imitation of certain temples depicted in the vaults of Zin, to house a very terrible black toad-idol found in the red-litten world and called Tsathoggua in the Yothic manuscripts. It had been a potent and widely worshipped god, and after its adoption the people of K'n-yan had lent its name to the city which was later to become dominant in that region. Yothic legend said that it had come from a mysterious inner realm beneath the red-litten world—a black realm of peculiar-sensed beings which had no light at all, but which had had great civilisations and mighty gods before ever the reptilian quadrupeds of Yoth had come into being. Many images of Tsathoggua existed in Yoth, all of which were alleged to have come from the black inner realm, and which were supposed by Yothic archaeologists to represent the aeon-extinct race of that realm. The black realm called N'kai in the Yothic manuscripts had been explored as thoroughly as possible by these archaeologists, and singular stone troughs or burrows had excited infinite speculation.

When the men of K'n-yan discovered the red-litten world and deciphered its strange manuscripts, they took over the

Tsathoggua cult and brought all the frightful toad images up to the land of blue light — housing them in shrines of Yoth-quarried basalt like the one Zamacona now saw. The cult flourished until it almost rivalled the ancient cults of Yig and Tulu, and one branch of the race even took it to the outer world, where the smallest of the images eventually found a shrine at Olathoë, in the land of Lomar near the earth's north pole. It was rumoured that this outer-world cult survived even after the great ice-sheet and the hairy Gnophkehs destroyed Lomar, but of such matters not much was definitely known in K'n-yan. In that world of blue light the cult came to an abrupt end, even though the name of Tsath was suffered to remain.

What ended the cult was the partial exploration of the black realm of N'kai beneath the red-litten world of Yoth. According to the Yothic manuscripts, there was no surviving life in N'kai, but something must have happened in the aeons between the days of Yoth and the coming of men to the earth; something perhaps not unconnected with the end of Yoth. Probably it had been an earthquake, opening up lower chambers of the lightless world which had been closed against the Yothic archaeologists; or perhaps some more frightful juxtaposition of energy and electrons, wholly inconceivable to any sort of vertebrate minds, had taken place. At any rate, when the men of K'n-yan went down into N'kai's black abyss with their great atom-power searchlights they found living things — living things that oozed along stone channels and worshipped onyx and basalt images of Tsathoggua. But they were not toads like Tsathoggua himself. Far worse — they were amorphous lumps of viscous black slime that took temporary shapes for various purposes. The explorers of K'n-yan did not pause for detailed observations, and those who escaped alive sealed the passage leading from red-litten Yoth down into the gulfs of nether horror. Then all the images of Tsathoggua in the land of K'n-yan were dissolved into the ether by disintegrating rays, and the cult was abolished forever.

Aeons later, when naive fears were outgrown and supplanted by scientific curiosity, the old legends of Tsathoggua and N'kai were recalled and a suitably armed and equipped exploring party went down to Yoth to find the closed gate of the black abyss and see what might still lie beneath. But they could not find the gate, nor could any man ever do so in all the ages that followed. Nowadays there were those who doubted that any abyss had ever existed, but the few scholars who could still decipher the Yothic manuscripts believed that the evidence for such a thing was adequate, even though the middle records of K'n-yan, with accounts of the one frightful expedition into N'kai, were more open to question. Some of the later religious cults tried to suppress remembrance of N'kai's existence, and attached severe penalties to its mention; but these had not begun to be taken seriously at the time of Zamacona's advent to K'n-yan.

As the cavalcade returned to the old highway and approached the low range of mountains, Zamacona saw that the river was very close on the left. Somewhat later, as the terrain rose, the stream entered a gorge and passed through the hills, while the road traversed the gap at a rather higher level close to the brink. It was about this time that light rainfall came. Zamacona noticed the occasional drops and drizzle, and looked up at the coruscating blue air, but there was no diminution of the strange radiance. Gll'-Hthaa-Ynn then told him that such condensations and precipitations of water-vapour were not uncommon, and that they never dimmed the glare of the vault above. A kind of mist, indeed, always hung about the lowlands of K'n-yan, and compensated for the complete absence of true clouds.

The slight rise of the mountain pass enabled Zamacona, by looking behind, to see the ancient and deserted plain in panorama as he had seen it from the other side. He seems to have appreciated its strange beauty, and to have vaguely regretted leaving it; for he speaks of being urged by Gll'-Hthaa-Ynn to drive his beast more rapidly. When he faced frontward again he saw that the crest of the road was very near; the weed-grown way leading starkly up and ending against a blank void of blue light. The scene was undoubtedly highly impressive — a steep green mountain wall on the right, a deep river-chasm on the left with another green mountain wall beyond it, and ahead, the churning sea of bluish coruscations into which the upward path dissolved. Then came the crest itself, and with it the world of Tsath outspread in a stupendous forward vista.

Zamacona caught his breath at the great sweep of peopled landscape, for it was a hive of settlement and activity beyond anything he had ever seen or dreamed of. The downward slope of the hill itself was relatively thinly strown with small farms and occasional temples; but beyond it lay an enormous plain covered like a chess board with planted trees, irrigated by narrow canals cut from the river, and threaded by wide, geometrically precise roads of gold or basalt blocks. Great silver cables borne aloft on golden pillars linked the low, spreading buildings and clusters of buildings which rose here and there, and in some places one could see lines of partly ruinous pillars without cables. Moving objects shewed the fields to be under tillage, and in some cases Zamacona saw that men were ploughing with the aid of the repulsive, half-human quadrupeds.

But most impressive of all was the bewildering vision of clustered spires and pinnacles which rose afar off across the plain and shimmered flower-like and spectral in the coruscating blue light. At first Zamacona thought it was a mountain covered with houses and temples, like some of the picturesque hill cities of his own Spain, but a second glance shewed him that it was not indeed such. It was a city of the plain, but fashioned of such heaven-reaching towers that its outline was truly that of a mountain. Above it hung a curious greyish haze, through which the blue light glistened and took added overtones of radiance from the million golden minarets. Glancing at Gll'-Hthaa-Ynn, Zamacona knew that this was the monstrous, gigantic, and omnipotent city of Tsath.

As the road turned downward toward the plain, Zamacona felt a kind of uneasiness and sense of evil. He did not like the beast he rode, or the world that could provide such a beast, and he did not like the atmosphere that brooded over the distant city of Tsath. When the cavalcade began to pass occasional farms, the Spaniard noticed the forms that worked in the fields; and did not like their motions and proportions, or the mutilations he saw on most of them. Moreover, he did not like the way that some of these forms were herded in corrals, or the way they grazed on the heavy verdure. Gll'-Hthaa-Ynn indicated that these beings were members of the slave-class, and that their acts were controlled by the master of the farm, who gave them hypnotic impressions in the morning of all they were to do during the day. As semi-conscious machines, their industrial efficiency was nearly perfect. Those in the corrals were inferior specimens, classified merely as livestock.

Upon reaching the plain, Zamacona saw the larger farms and noted the almost human work performed by the repulsive horned gyaa-yothn. He likewise observed the more manlike shapes that toiled along the furrows, and felt a curious fright and disgust toward certain of them whose motions were more mechanical than those of the rest. These, Gll'-Hthaa-Ynn explained, were what men called the y'm-bhi — organisms which had died, but which had been mechanically reanimated for industrial purposes by means of atomic energy and thought-power. The slave-class did not share the immortality of the freemen of Tsath, so that with time the number of y'm-bhi had become very large. They were dog-like and faithful, but not so readily amenable to thought-commands as were living slaves. Those which most repelled Zamacona were those whose mutilations were greatest; for some were wholly headless, while others had suffered singular and seemingly capricious subtractions, distortions, transpositions, and graftings in various places. The Spaniard could not account for this condition, but Gll'-Hthaa-Ynn made it clear that these were slaves who had been used for the amusement of the people in some of the vast arenas; for the men of Tsath were connoisseurs of delicate sensation, and required a constant supply of fresh and novel stimuli for their jaded impulses. Zamacona, though by no means squeamish, was not favourably impressed by what he saw and heard.

Approached more closely, the vast metropolis became dimly horrible in its monstrous extent and inhuman height. Gll'-Hthaa-Ynn explained that the upper parts of the great towers were no longer used, and that many had been taken down to avoid the bother of maintenance. The plain around the original urban area was covered with newer and smaller dwellings, which in many cases were preferred to the ancient towers. From the whole mass of gold and stone a monotonous roar of activity droned outward over the plain, while cavalcades and streams of wagons were constantly entering and leaving over the great gold- or stone-paved roads.

Several times Gll'-Hthaa-Ynn paused to shew Zamacona some particular object of interest, especially the temples of Yig, Tulu, Nug, Yeb, and the Not-to-Be-Named One which lined the road at infrequent intervals, each in its embowering grove according to the custom of K'n-yan. These temples, unlike those of the deserted plain beyond the mountains, were still in active use, large parties of mounted worshippers coming and going in constant streams. Gll'Hthaa-Ynn took Zamacona into each of them, and the Spaniard watched the subtle orgiastic rites with fascination and repulsion. The ceremonies of Nug and Yeb sickened him especially — so much, indeed, that he refrained from describing them in his manuscript. One squat, black temple of Tsathoggua was encountered, but it had been turned into a shrine of Shub-Niggurath, the All-Mother and wife of the Not-to-Be-Named One. This deity was a kind of sophisticated Astarte, and her worship struck the pious Catholic as supremely obnoxious. What he liked least of all were the emotional sounds emitted by the celebrants — jarring sounds in a race that had ceased to use vocal speech for ordinary purposes.

Close to the compact outskirts of Tsath, and well within the shadow of its terrifying towers, Gll'-Hthaa-Ynn pointed out a monstrous circular building before which enormous crowds were lined up. This, he indicated, was one of the many amphitheatres where curious sports and sensations were provided for the weary people of K'n-yan. He was about to pause and usher Zamacona inside the vast curved facade, when the Spaniard, recalling the mutilated forms he had seen in the fields, violently demurred. This was the first of those friendly clashes of taste which were to convince the people of Tsath that their guest followed strange and narrow standards.

Tsath itself was a network of strange and ancient streets; and despite a growing sense of horror and alienage, Zamacona was enthralled by its intimations of mystery and cosmic wonder. The dizzy giganticism of its overawing towers, the monstrous surge of teeming life through its ornate avenues, the curious carvings on its doorways and windows, the odd vistas glimpsed from balustraded plazas and tiers of titan terraces, and the enveloping grey haze which seemed to press down on the gorge-like streets in low ceiling-fashion, all combined to produce such a sense of adventurous expectancy as he had never known before.

He was taken at once to a council of executives which held forth in a gold-and-copper palace behind a gardened and fountained park, and was for some time subjected to close, friendly questioning in a vaulted hall frescoed with vertiginous arabesques. Much was expected of him, he could see, in the way of historical information about the outside earth; but in return all the mysteries of K'n-yan would be unveiled to him. The one great drawback was the inexorable ruling that he might never return to the world of sun and stars and Spain which was his.

A daily programme was laid down for the visitor, with time apportioned judiciously among several kinds of activities. There were to be conversations with persons of learning in various places, and lessons in many branches of Tsathic lore. Liberal periods of research were allowed for, and all the libraries of K'n-yan both secular and sacred were to be thrown open to him as soon as he might master the written languages. Rites and spectacles were to be attended—except when he might especially object—and much time would be left for the enlightened pleasure-seeking and emotional titillation which formed the goal and nucleus of daily life. A house in the suburbs or an apartment in the city would be assigned him, and he would be initiated into one of the large affection-groups, including many noblewomen of the most extreme and art-enhanced beauty, which in latter-day K'n-yan took the place of family units. Several horned gyaa-yothn would be provided for his transportation and errand-running, and ten living slaves of intact body would serve to conduct his establishment and protect him from thieves and sadists and religious orgiasts on the public highways. There were many mechanical devices which he must learn to use, but Gll'-Hthaa-Ynn would instruct him immediately regarding the principal ones.

Upon his choosing an apartment in preference to a suburban villa, Zamacona was dismissed by the executives with great courtesy and ceremony, and was led through several gorgeous streets to a cliff-like carven structure of some seventy or eighty floors. Preparations for his arrival had already been instituted, and in a spacious ground-floor suite of vaulted rooms slaves were busy adjusting hangings and furniture. There were lacquered and inlaid tabourets, velvet and silk reclining-corners and squatting-cushions, and infinite rows of teakwood and ebony pigeon-holes with metal cylinders containing some of the manuscripts he was soon to read—standard classics which all urban apartments possessed. Desks with great stacks of membrane-paper and pots of the prevailing green pigment were in every room—each with graded sets of pigment brushes and other odd bits of stationery. Mechanical writing devices stood on ornate golden tripods, while over all was shed a brilliant blue light from energy-globes set in the ceiling. There were windows, but at this shadowy ground-level they were of scant illuminating value. In some of the rooms were elaborate baths, while the kitchen was a maze of technical contrivances. Supplies were brought, Zamacona was told, through the network of underground passages which lay beneath Tsath, and which had once accommodated curious mechanical transports. There was a stable on that underground level for the beasts, and Zamacona would presently be shewn how to find the nearest runway to the street.

Before his inspection was finished, the permanent staff of slaves arrived and were introduced; and shortly afterward there came some half dozen freemen and noblewomen of his future affection-group, who were to be his companions for several days, contributing what they could to his instruction and amusement. Upon their departure, another party would take their place, and so onward in rotation through a group of about fifty members.

VI.

Thus was Pánfilo de Zamacona y Nuñez absorbed for four years into the life of the sinister city of Tsath in the blue-litten nether world of K'n-yan. All that he learned and saw and did is clearly not told in his manuscript; for a pious reticence overcame him when he began to write in his native Spanish tongue, and he dared not set down everything. Much he consistently viewed with repulsion, and many things he steadfastly refrained from seeing or doing or eating. For other things he atoned by frequent countings of the beads of his rosary. He explored the entire world of K'n-yan, including the deserted machine-cities of the middle period on the gorse-grown plain of Nith, and made one descent into the red-litten world of Yoth to see the Cyclopean ruins. He witnessed prodigies of craft and machinery which left him breathless, and beheld human metamorphoses, dematerialisations, rematerialisations, and reanimations which made him cross himself again and again. His very capacity for astonishment was blunted by the plethora of new marvels which every day brought him.

But the longer he stayed, the more he wished to leave, for the inner life of K'n-yan was based on impulses very plainly outside his radius. As he progressed in historical knowledge, he understood more; but understanding only heightened his distaste. He felt that the people of Tsath were a lost and dangerous race—more dangerous to themselves than they knew—and that their growing frenzy of monotony-warfare and novelty-quest was leading them rapidly toward a precipice of disintegration and utter horror. His own visit, he could see, had accelerated their unrest; not only by introducing fears of outside invasion, but by exciting in many a wish to sally forth and taste the diverse external world he described. As time progressed, he noticed an increasing tendency of the people to resort to dematerialisation as an amusement; so that the apartments and amphitheatres of Tsath became a veritable Witches' Sabbath of transmutations, age-adjustments, death-experiments, and projections. With the growth of boredom and restlessness, he saw, cruelty and subtlety and revolt were growing apace. There was more and more cosmic abnormality, more and more curious sadism, more and more ignorance and superstition, and more and more desire to escape out of physical life into a half-spectral state of electronic dispersal.

All his efforts to leave, however, came to nothing. Persuasion was useless, as repeated trials proved; though the mature disillusion of the upper classes at first prevented them from resenting their guest's open wish for departure. In a year which he reckoned as 1543 Zamacona made an actual attempt to escape through the tunnel by which he had entered K'n-yan, but after a weary journey across the deserted plain he encountered forces in the dark passage which discouraged him from future attempts in that direction. As a means of sustaining hope and keeping the image of home in mind, he began about this time to make rough draughts of the manuscript relating his adventures;

delighting in the loved, old Spanish words and the familiar letters of the Roman alphabet. Somehow he fancied he might get the manuscript to the outer world; and to make it convincing to his fellows he resolved to enclose it in one of the Tulu-metal cylinders used for sacred archives. That alien, magnetic substance could not but support the incredible story he had to tell.

But even as he planned, he had little real hope of ever establishing contact with the earth's surface. Every known gate, he knew, was guarded by persons or forces that it were better not to oppose. His attempt at escape had not helped matters, for he could now see a growing hostility to the outer world he represented. He hoped that no other European would find his way in; for it was possible that later comers might not fare as well as he. He himself had been a cherished fountain of data, and as such had enjoyed a privileged status. Others, deemed less necessary, might receive rather different treatment. He even wondered what would happen to him when the sages of Tsath considered him drained dry of fresh facts; and in self-defence began to be more gradual in his talks on earth-lore, conveying whenever he could the impression of vast knowledge held in reserve.

One other thing which endangered Zamacona's status in Tsath was his persistent curiosity regarding the ultimate abyss of N'kai, beneath red-litten Yoth, whose existence the dominant religious cults of K'n-yan were more and more inclined to deny. When exploring Yoth he had vainly tried to find the blocked-up entrance; and later on he experimented in the arts of dematerialisation and projection, hoping that he might thereby be able to throw his consciousness downward into the gulfs which his physical eyes could not discover. Though never becoming truly proficient in these processes, he did manage to achieve a series of monstrous and portentous dreams which he believed included some elements of actual projection into N'kai; dreams which greatly shocked and perturbed the leaders of Yig and Tulu-worship when he related them, and which he was advised by friends to conceal rather than exploit. In time those dreams became very frequent and maddening; containing things which he dared not record in his main manuscript, but of which he prepared a special record for the benefit of certain learned men in Tsath.

It may have been unfortunate — or it may have been mercifully fortunate — that Zamacona practiced so many reticences and reserved so many themes and descriptions for subsidiary manuscripts. The main document leaves one to guess much about the detailed manners, customs, thoughts, language, and history of K'n-yan, as well as to form any adequate picture of the visual aspect and daily life of Tsath. One is left puzzled, too, about the real motivations of the people; their strange passivity and craven unwarlikeness, and their almost cringing fear of the outer world despite their possession of atomic and dematerialising powers which would have made them unconquerable had they taken the trouble to organise armies as in the old days. It is evident that K'n-yan was far along in its decadence — reacting with mixed apathy and hysteria against the standardised and time-tabled life of stultifying regularity which machinery had brought it during its middle period. Even the grotesque and repulsive customs and modes of thought and feeling can be traced to this source; for in his historical research Zamacona found evidence of bygone eras in which K'n-yan had held ideas much like those of the classic and renaissance outer world, and had possessed a national character and art full of what Europeans regard as dignity, kindness, and nobility.

The more Zamacona studied these things, the more apprehensive about the future he became; because he saw that the omnipresent moral and intellectual disintegration was a tremendously deep-seated and ominously accelerating movement. Even during his stay the signs of decay multiplied. Rationalism degenerated more and more into fanatical and orgiastic superstition, centring in a lavish adoration of the magnetic Tulu-metal, and tolerance steadily dissolved into a series of frenzied hatreds, especially toward the outer world of which the scholars were learning so much from him. At times he almost feared that the people might some day lose their age-long apathy and brokenness and turn like desperate rats against the unknown lands above them, sweeping all before them by virtue of their singular and still-remembered scientific powers. But for the present they fought their boredom and sense of emptiness in other ways; multiplying their hideous emotional outlets and increasing the mad grotesqueness and abnormality of their diversions. The arenas of Tsath must have been accursed and unthinkable places — Zamacona never went near them. And what they would be in another century, or even in another decade, he did not dare to think. The pious Spaniard crossed himself and counted his beads more often than usual in those days.

In the year 1545, as he reckoned it, Zamacona began what may well be accepted as his final series of attempts to leave K'n-yan. His fresh opportunity came from an unexpected source — a female of his affection-group who conceived for him a curious individual infatuation based on some hereditary memory of the days of monogamous wedlock in Tsath. Over this female — a noblewoman of moderate beauty and of at least average intelligence named T'la-yub — Zamacona acquired the most extraordinary influence; finally inducing her to help him in an escape, under the promise that he would let her accompany him. Chance proved a great factor in the course of events, for T'la-yub came of a primordial family of gatelords who had retained oral traditions of at least one passage to the outer world which the mass of people had forgotten even at the time of the great closing; a passage to a mound on the level plains of earth which had, in consequence, never been sealed up or guarded. She explained that the primordial gate-lords were not guards or sentries, but merely ceremonial and economic proprietors, half-feudal and baronial in status, of an era preceding the severance of surface-relations. Her own family had been so reduced at the time of the closing that their gate had been wholly overlooked; and they had ever afterward preserved the secret of its existence as a sort of hereditary secret — a source of pride, and of a sense of reserve power, to offset the feeling of vanished wealth and influence which so constantly irritated them.

Zamacona, now working feverishly to get his manuscript into final form in case anything should happen to him, decided to take with him on his outward journey only five beast-loads of unalloyed gold in the form of the small ingots used for minor decorations — enough, he calculated, to make him a personage of unlimited power in his own world. He had become somewhat hardened to the sight of the monstrous gyaa-yothn during his four years of residence in Tsath, hence did not shrink from using the creatures; yet he resolved to kill and bury them, and cache the gold, as soon as he reached the outer world, since he knew that even a glimpse of one of the things would drive any ordinary Indian mad. Later he could arrange for a suitable expedition to transport the treasure to Mexico. T'la-yub he would perhaps allow to share his fortunes, for she was by no means unattractive; though possibly he would arrange for her sojourn amongst the plains Indians, since he was not overanxious to preserve links with the manner of life in Tsath. For a wife, of course, he would choose a lady of Spain — or at worst, an Indian princess of normal outer-world descent and a regular and approved past. But for the present T'la-yub must be used as a guide. The manuscript he would carry on his own person, encased in a book-cylinder of the sacred and magnetic Tulu-metal.

The expedition itself is described in the addendum to Zamacona's manuscript, written later, and in a hand shewing signs of nervous strain. It set out amidst the most careful precautions, choosing a rest-period and proceeding as far as possible along the faintly lighted passages beneath the city. Zamacona and T'la-yub, disguised in slaves' garments, bearing provision-knapsacks, and leading the five laden beasts on foot, were readily taken for commonplace workers; and they clung as long as possible to the subterranean way — using a long and little-frequented branch which had formerly conducted the mechanical transports to the now ruined suburb of L'thaa. Amidst the ruins of L'thaa they came to the surface, thereafter passing as rapidly as possible over the deserted, blue-litten plain of Nith toward the Grh-yan range of low hills. There, amidst the tangled underbrush, T'la-yub found the long disused and half-fabulous entrance to the forgotten tunnel; a thing she had seen but once before — aeons in the past, when her father had taken her thither to shew her this monument to their family pride. It was hard work getting the laden gyaa-yothn to scrape through the obstructing vines and briers, and one of them displayed a rebelliousness destined to bear dire consequences — bolting away from the party and loping back toward Tsath on its detestable pads, golden burden and all.

It was nightmare work burrowing by the light of blue-ray torches upward, downward, forward, and upward again through a dank, choked tunnel that no foot had trodden since ages before the sinking of Atlantis; and at one point T'la-yub had to practice the fearsome art of dematerialisation on herself, Zamacona, and the laden beasts in order to pass a point wholly clogged by shifting earth-strata. It was a terrible experience for Zamacona; for although he had often witnessed dematerialisation in others, and even practiced it himself to the extent of dream-projection, he had never been fully subjected to it before. But T'la-yub was skilled in the arts of K'n-yan, and accomplished the double metamorphosis in perfect safety.

Thereafter they resumed the hideous burrowing through stalactited crypts of horror where monstrous carvings leered at every turn; alternately camping and advancing for a period which Zamacona reckoned as about three days, but which was probably less. At last they came to a very narrow place where the natural or only slightly hewn cave-walls gave place to walls of wholly artificial masonry, carved into terrible bas-reliefs. These walls, after about a mile of steep ascent, ended with a pair of vast niches, one on each side, in which monstrous, nitre-encrusted images of Yig and Tulu squatted, glaring at each other across the passage as they had glared since the earliest youth of the human world. At this point the passage opened into a prodigious vaulted and circular chamber of human construction; wholly covered with horrible carvings, and revealing at the farther end an arched passageway with the foot of a flight of steps. T'la-yub knew from family tales that this must be very near the earth's surface, but she could not tell just how near. Here the party camped for what they meant to be their last rest-period in the subterraneous world.

It must have been hours later that the clank of metal and the padding of beasts' feet awakened Zamacona and T'la-yub. A bluish glare was spreading from the narrow passage between the images of Yig and Tulu, and in an instant the truth was obvious. An alarm had been given at Tsath — as was later revealed, by the returning gyaa-yoth which had rebelled at the brier-choked tunnel-entrance — and a swift party of pursuers had come to arrest the fugitives. Resistance was clearly useless, and none was offered. The party of twelve beast-riders proved studiously polite, and the return commenced almost without a word or thought-message on either side.

It was an ominous and depressing journey, and the ordeal of dematerialisation and rematerialisation at the choked place was all the more terrible because of the lack of that hope and expectancy which had palliated the process on the outward trip. Zamacona heard his captors discussing the imminent clearing of this choked place by intensive radiations, since henceforward sentries must be maintained at the hitherto unknown outer portal. It would not do to let outsiders get within the passage, for then any who might escape without due treatment would have a hint of the vastness of the inner world and would perhaps be curious enough to return in greater strength. As with the other passages since Zamacona's coming, sentries must be stationed all along, as far as the very outermost gate; sentries drawn from amongst all the slaves, the dead-alive y'm-bhi, or the class of discredited freemen. With the overrunning of the

American plains by thousands of Europeans, as the Spaniard had predicted, every passage was a potential source of danger; and must be rigorously guarded until the technologists of Tsath could spare the energy to prepare an ultimate and entrance-hiding obliteration as they had done for many passages in earlier and more vigorous times.

Zamacona and T'la-yub were tried before three gn'agn of the supreme tribunal in the gold-and-copper palace behind the gardened and fountained park, and the Spaniard was given his liberty because of the vital outer-world information he still had to impart. He was told to return to his apartment and to his affection-group; taking up his life as before, and continuing to meet deputations of scholars according to the latest schedule he had been following. No restrictions would be imposed upon him so long as he might remain peacefully in K'n-yan—but it was intimated that such leniency would not be repeated after another attempt at escape. Zamacona had felt that there was an element of irony in the parting words of the chief gn'ag—an assurance that all of his gyaa-yothn, including the one which had rebelled, would be returned to him.

The fate of T'la-yub was less happy. There being no object in retaining her, and her ancient Tsathic lineage giving her act a greater aspect of treason than Zamacona's had possessed, she was ordered to be delivered to the curious diversions of the amphitheatre; and afterward, in a somewhat mutilated and half-dematerialised form, to be given the functions of a y'm-bhi or animated corpse-slave and stationed among the sentries guarding the passage whose existence she had betrayed. Zamacona soon heard, not without many pangs of regret he could scarcely have anticipated, that poor T'la-yub had emerged from the arena in a headless and otherwise incomplete state, and had been set as an outermost guard upon the mound in which the passage had been found to terminate. She was, he was told, a night-sentinel, whose automatic duty was to warn off all comers with a torch; sending down reports to a small garrison of twelve dead slave y'm-bhi and six living but partly dematerialised freemen in the vaulted, circular chamber if the approachers did not heed her warning. She worked, he was told, in conjunction with a day-sentinel— a living freeman who chose this post in preference to other forms of discipline for other offences against the state. Zamacona, of course, had long known that most of the chief gate-sentries were such discredited freemen.

It was now made plain to him, though indirectly, that his own penalty for another escape-attempt would be service as a gate-sentry— but in the form of a dead-alive y'm-bhi slave, and after amphitheatre-treatment even more picturesque than that which T'la-yub was reported to have undergone. It was intimated that he—or parts of him—would be reanimated to guard some inner section of the passage, within sight of others, where his abridged person might serve as a permanent symbol of the rewards of treason. But, his informants always added, it was of course inconceivable that he would ever court such a fate. So long as he remained peaceably in K'n-yan, he would continue to be a free, privileged, and respected personage.

Yet in the end Pánfilo de Zamacona did court the fate so direfully hinted to him. True, he did not really expect to encounter it; but the nervous latter part of his manuscript makes it clear that he was prepared to face its possibility. What gave him a final hope of scatheless escape from K'n-yan was his growing mastery of the art of dematerialisation. Having studied it for years, and having learned still more from the two instances in which he had been subjected to it, he now felt increasingly able to use it independently and effectively. The manuscript records several notable experiments in this art—minor successes accomplished in his apartment—and reflects Zamacona's hope that he might soon be able to assume the spectral form in full, attaining complete invisibility and preserving that condition as long as he wished.

Once he reached this stage, he argued, the outward way lay open to him. Of course he could not bear away any gold, but mere escape was enough. He would, though, dematerialise and carry away with him his manuscript in the Tulu-metal cylinder, even though it cost additional effort; for this record and proof must reach the outer world at all hazards. He now knew the passage to follow; and if he could thread it in an atom-scattered state, he did not see how any person or force could detect or stop him. The only trouble would be if he failed to maintain his spectral condition at all times. That was the one ever-present peril, as he had learned from his experiments. But must one not always risk death and worse in a life of adventure? Zamacona was a gentleman of Old Spain; of the blood that faced the unknown and carved out half the civilisation of the New World.

For many nights after his ultimate resolution Zamacona prayed to St. Pamphilus and other guardian saints, and counted the beads of his rosary. The last entry in the manuscript, which toward the end took the form of a diary more and more, was merely a single sentence—"Es más tarde de lo que pensaba—tengo que marcharme"... "It is later than I thought; I must go." After that, only silence and conjecture—and such evidence as the presence of the manuscript itself, and what that manuscript could lead to, might provide.

VII.

When I looked up from my half-stupefied reading and notetaking the morning sun was high in the heavens. The electric bulb was still burning, but such things of the real world—the modern outer world—were far from my whirling brain. I knew I was in my room at Clyde Compton's at Binger—but upon what monstrous vista had I stumbled? Was this thing a hoax or a chronicle of madness? If a hoax, was it a jest of the sixteenth century or of today? The manuscript's age looked appallingly genuine to my not-wholly-unpractised eyes, and the problem presented by the strange metal cylinder I dared not even think about.

Moreover, what a monstrously exact explanation it gave of all the baffling phenomena of the mound — of the seemingly meaningless and paradoxical actions of diurnal and nocturnal ghosts, and of the queer cases of madness and disappearance! It was even an accursedly plausible explanation — evilly consistent — if one could adopt the incredible. It must be a shocking hoax devised by someone who knew all the lore of the mound. There was even a hint of social satire in the account of that unbelievable nether world of horror and decay. Surely this was the clever forgery of some learned cynic — something like the leaden crosses in New Mexico, which a jester once planted and pretended to discover as a relique of some forgotten Dark Age colony from Europe.

Upon going down to breakfast I hardly knew what to tell Compton and his mother, as well as the curious callers who had already begun to arrive. Still in a daze, I cut the Gordian Knot by giving a few points from the notes I had made, and mumbling my belief that the thing was a subtle and ingenious fraud left there by some previous explorer of the mound — a belief in which everybody seemed to concur when told of the substance of the manuscript. It is curious how all that breakfast group — and all the others in Binger to whom the discussion was repeated — seemed to find a great clearing of the atmosphere in the notion that somebody was playing a joke on somebody. For the time we all forgot that the known, recent history of the mound presented mysteries as strange as any in the manuscript, and as far from acceptable solution as ever.

The fears and doubts began to return when I asked for volunteers to visit the mound with me. I wanted a larger excavating party — but the idea of going to that uncomfortable place seemed no more attractive to the people of Binger than it had seemed on the previous day. I myself felt a mounting horror upon looking toward the mound and glimpsing the moving speck which I knew was the daylight sentinel; for in spite of all my scepticism the morbidities of that manuscript stuck by me and gave everything connected with the place a new and monstrous significance. I absolutely lacked the resolution to look at the moving speck with my binoculars. Instead, I set out with the kind of bravado we display in nightmares — when, knowing we are dreaming, we plunge desperately into still thicker horrors, for the sake of having the whole thing over the sooner. My pick and shovel were already out there, so I had only my handbag of smaller paraphernalia to take. Into this I put the strange cylinder and its contents, feeling vaguely that I might possibly find something worth checking up with some part of the green-lettered Spanish text. Even a clever hoax might be founded on some actual attribute of the mound which a former explorer had discovered — and that magnetic metal was damnably odd! Grey Eagle's cryptic talisman still hung from its leathern cord around my neck.

I did not look very sharply at the mound as I walked toward it, but when I reached it there was nobody in sight. Repeating my upward scramble of the previous day, I was troubled by thoughts of what might lie close at hand if, by any miracle, any part of the manuscript were actually half-true. In such a case, I could not help reflecting, the hypothetical Spaniard Zamacona must have barely reached the outer world when overtaken by some disaster — perhaps an involuntary rematerialisation. He would naturally, in that event, have been seized by whichever sentry happened to be on duty at the time — either the discredited freeman, or, as a matter of supreme irony, the very T'la-yub who had planned and aided his first attempt at escape — and in the ensuing struggle the cylinder with the manuscript might well have been dropped on the mound's summit, to be neglected and gradually buried for nearly four centuries. But, I added, as I climbed over the crest, one must not think of extravagant things like that. Still, if there were anything in the tale, it must have been a monstrous fate to which Zamacona had been dragged back . . . the amphitheatre . . . mutilation . . . duty somewhere in the dank, nitrous tunnel as a dead-alive slave . . . a maimed corpse-fragment as an automatic interior sentry . . . .

It was a very real shock which chased this morbid speculation from my head, for upon glancing around the elliptical summit I saw at once that my pick and shovel had been stolen. This was a highly provoking and disconcerting development; baffling, too, in view of the seeming reluctance of all the Binger folk to visit the mound. Was this reluctance a pretended thing, and had the jokers of the village been chuckling over my coming discomfiture as they solemnly saw me off ten minutes before? I took out my binoculars and scanned the gaping crowd at the edge of the village. No — they did not seem to be looking for any comic climax; yet was not the whole affair at bottom a colossal joke in which all the villagers and reservation people were concerned — legends, manuscript, cylinder, and all? I thought of how I had seen the sentry from a distance, and then found him unaccountably vanished; thought also of the conduct of old Grey Eagle, of the speech and expressions of Compton and his mother, and of the unmistakable fright of most of the Binger people. On the whole, it could not very well be a village-wide joke. The fear and the problem were surely real, though obviously there were one or two jesting daredevils in Binger who had stolen out to the mound and made off with the tools I had left.

Everything else on the mound was as I had left it — brush cut by my machete, slight, bowl-like depression toward the north end, and the hole I had made with my trench-knife in digging up the magnetism-revealed cylinder. Deeming it too great a concession to the unknown jokers to return to Binger for another pick and shovel, I resolved to carry out my programme as best I could with the machete and trench-knife in my handbag; so extracting these, I set to work excavating the bowl-like depression which my eye had picked as the possible site of a former entrance to the mound. As I proceeded,

I felt again the suggestion of a sudden wind blowing against me which I had noticed the day before — a suggestion which seemed stronger, and still more reminiscent of unseen, formless, opposing hands laid on my wrists, as I cut deeper and deeper through the root-tangled red soil and reached the exotic black loam beneath. The talisman around my neck appeared to twitch oddly in the breeze — not in any one direction, as when attracted by the buried cylinder, but vaguely and diffusely, in a manner wholly unaccountable.

Then, quite without warning, the black, root-woven earth beneath my feet began to sink cracklingly, while I heard a faint sound of sifting, falling matter far below me. The obstructing wind, or forces, or hands now seemed to be operating from the very seat of the sinking, and I felt that they aided me by pushing as I leaped back out of the hole to avoid being involved in any cave-in. Bending down over the brink and hacking at the mould-caked root-tangle with my machete, I felt that they were against me again — but at no time were they strong enough to stop my work. The more roots I severed, the more falling matter I heard below. Finally the hole began to deepen of itself toward the centre, and I saw that the earth was sifting down into some large cavity beneath, so as to leave a good-sized aperture when the roots that had bound it were gone. A few more hacks of the machete did the trick, and with a parting cave-in and uprush of curiously chill and alien air the last barrier gave way. Under the morning sun yawned a huge opening at least three feet square, and shewing the top of a flight of stone steps down which the loose earth of the collapse was still sliding. My quest had come to something at last! With an elation of accomplishment almost overbalancing fear for the nonce, I replaced the trench-knife and machete in my handbag, took out my powerful electric torch, and prepared for a triumphant, lone, and utterly rash invasion of the fabulous nether world I had uncovered.

It was rather hard getting down the first few steps, both because of the fallen earth which had choked them and because of a sinister up-pushing of a cold wind from below. The talisman around my neck swayed curiously, and I began to regret the disappearing square of daylight above me. The electric torch shewed dank, water-stained, and salt-encrusted walls fashioned of huge basalt blocks, and now and then I thought I descried some trace of carving beneath the nitrous deposits. I gripped my handbag more tightly, and was glad of the comforting weight of the sheriff's heavy revolver in my right-hand coat pocket. After a time the passage began to wind this way and that, and the staircase became free from obstructions. Carvings on the walls were now definitely traceable, and I shuddered when I saw how clearly the grotesque figures resembled the monstrous bas-reliefs on the cylinder I had found. Winds and forces continued to blow malevolently against me, and at one or two bends I half fancied the torch gave glimpses of thin, transparent shapes not unlike the sentinel on the mound as my binoculars had shewed him. When I reached this stage of visual chaos I stopped for a moment to get a grip on myself. It would not do to let my nerves get the better of me at the very outset of what would surely be a trying experience, and the most important archaeological feat of my career.

But I wished I had not stopped at just that place, for the act fixed my attention on something profoundly disturbing. It was only a small object lying close to the wall on one of the steps below me, but that object was such as to put my reason to a severe test, and bring up a line of the most alarming speculations. That the opening above me had been closed against all material forms for generations was utterly obvious from the growth of shrub-roots and accumulation of drifting soil; yet the object before me was most distinctly not many generations old. For it was an electric torch much like the one I now carried — warped and encrusted in the tomb-like dampness, but none the less perfectly unmistakable.

I descended a few steps and picked it up, wiping off the evil deposits on my rough coat. One of the nickel bands bore an engraved name and address, and I recognised it with a start the moment I made it out. It read "Jas. C. Williams, 17 Trowbridge St., Cambridge, Mass." — and I knew that it had belonged to one of the two daring college instructors who had disappeared on June 28, 1915. Only thirteen years ago, and yet I had just broken through the sod of centuries! How had the thing got there? Another entrance — or was there something after all in this mad idea of dematerialisation and rematerialisation?

Doubt and horror grew upon me as I wound still farther down the seemingly endless staircase. Would the thing never stop? The carvings grew more and more distinct, and assumed a narrative pictorial quality which brought me close to panic as I recognised many unmistakable correspondences with the history of K'n-yan as sketched in the manuscript now resting in my handbag. For the first time I began seriously to question the wisdom of my descent, and to wonder whether I had not better return to the upper air before I came upon something which would never let me return as a sane man. But I did not hesitate long, for as a Virginian I felt the blood of ancestral fighters and gentlemen-adventurers pounding a protest against retreat from any peril known or unknown.

My descent became swifter rather than slower, and I avoided studying the terrible bas-reliefs and intaglios that had unnerved me. All at once I saw an arched opening ahead, and realised that the prodigious staircase had ended at last. But with that realisation came horror in mounting magnitude, for before me there yawned a vast vaulted crypt of all-too-familiar outline — a great circular space answering in every least particular to the carving-lined chamber described in the Zamacona manuscript.

It was indeed the place. There could be no mistake. And if any room for doubt yet remained, that room was abolished by what I saw directly across the great vault. It was a second arched opening, commencing a long, narrow passage and having at its mouth two huge opposite niches bearing loathsome and titanic images of shockingly familiar pattern. There in the dark unclean Yig and hideous Tulu squatted eternally, glaring at each other across the passage as they had glared since the earliest youth of the human world.

From this point onward I ask no credence for what I tell — for what I think I saw. It is too utterly unnatural, too utterly monstrous and incredible, to be any part of sane human experience or objective reality. My torch, though casting a powerful beam ahead, naturally could not furnish any general illumination of the Cyclopean crypt; so I now began moving it about to explore the giant walls little by little. As I did so, I saw to my horror that the space was by no means vacant, but was instead littered with odd furniture and utensils and heaps of packages which bespoke a populous recent occupancy — no nitrous reliques of the past, but queerly shaped objects and supplies in modern, every-day use. As my torch rested on each article or group of articles, however, the distinctness of the outlines soon began to grow blurred; until in the end I could scarcely tell whether the things belonged to the realm of matter or to the realm of spirit.

All this while the adverse winds blew against me with increasing fury, and the unseen hands plucked malevolently at me and snatched at the strange magnetic talisman I wore. Wild conceits surged through my mind. I thought of the manuscript and what it said about the garrison stationed in this place — twelve dead slave y'm-bhi and six living but partly dematerialised freemen — that was in 1545 — three hundred and eighty-three years ago . . . What since then? Zamacona had predicted change . . . subtle disintegration . . . more dematerialisation . . . weaker and weaker . . . was it Grey Eagle's talisman that held them at bay — their sacred Tulu-metal — and were they feebly trying to pluck it off so that they might do to me what they had done to those who had come before? . . . It occurred to me with shuddering force that I was building my speculations out of a full belief in the Zamacona manuscript — this must not be — I must get a grip on myself —

But, curse it, every time I tried to get a grip I saw some fresh sight to shatter my poise still further. This time, just as my will power was driving the half-seen paraphernalia into obscurity, my glance and torch-beam had to light on two things of very different nature; two things of the eminently real and sane world; yet they did more to unseat my shaky reason than anything I had seen before — because I knew what they were, and knew how profoundly, in the course of Nature, they ought not to be there. They were my own missing pick and shovel, side by side, and leaning neatly against the blasphemously carved wall of that hellish crypt. God in heaven — and I had babbled to myself about daring jokers from Binger!

That was the last straw. After that the cursed hypnotism of the manuscript got at me, and I actually saw the half-transparent shapes of the things that were pushing and plucking; pushing and plucking — those leprous palaeogean things with something of humanity still clinging to them — the complete forms, and the forms that were morbidly and perversely incomplete . . . all these, and hideous other entities — the four-footed blasphemies with ape-like face and projecting horn . . . and not a sound so far in all that nitrous hell of inner earth . . . .

Then there was a sound — a flopping; a padding; a dull, advancing sound which heralded beyond question a being as structurally material as the pickaxe and the shovel — something wholly unlike the shadow-shapes that ringed me in, yet equally remote from any sort of life as life is understood on the earth's wholesome surface. My shattered brain tried to prepare me for what was coming, but could not frame any adequate image. I could only say over and over again to myself, "It is of the abyss, but it is not dematerialised." The padding grew more distinct, and from the mechanical cast of the tread I knew it was a dead thing that stalked in the darkness. Then — oh, God, I saw it in the full beam of my torch; saw it framed like a sentinel in the narrow passage between the nightmare idols of the serpent Yig and the octopus Tulu . . . .

Let me collect myself enough to hint at what I saw; to explain why I dropped torch and handbag and fled empty-handed in the utter blackness, wrapped in a merciful unconsciousness which did not wear off until the sun and the distant yelling and the shouting from the village roused me as I lay gasping on the top of the accursed mound. I do not yet know what guided me again to the earth's surface. I only know that the watchers in Binger saw me stagger up into sight three hours after I had vanished; saw me lurch up and fall flat on the ground as if struck by a bullet. None of them dared to come out and help me; but they knew I must be in a bad state, so tried to rouse me as best they could by yelling in chorus and firing off revolvers.

It worked in the end, and when I came to I almost rolled down the side of the mound in my eagerness to get away from that black aperture which still yawned open. My torch and tools, and the handbag with the manuscript, were all down there; but it is easy to see why neither I nor anyone else ever went after them. When I staggered across the plain and into the village I dared not tell what I had seen. I only muttered vague things about carvings and statues and snakes and shaken nerves. And I did not faint again until somebody mentioned that the ghost-sentinel had reappeared about the time I had staggered half way back to town.

I left Binger that evening, and have never been there since, though they tell me the ghosts still appear on the mound as usual.

But I have resolved to hint here at last what I dared not hint to the people of Binger on that terrible August afternoon. I don't know yet just how I can go about it — and if in the end you think my reticence strange, just remember that to imagine such a horror is one thing, but to see it is another thing. I saw it. I think you'll recall my citing early in this tale the case of a bright young man named Heaton who went out to that mound one day in 1891 and came back at night as the village idiot, babbling for eight years about horrors and then dying in an epileptic fit. What he used to keep moaning was "That white man — oh, my God, what they did to him . . ."

Well, I saw the same thing that poor Heaton saw — and I saw it after reading the manuscript, so I know more of its history than he did. That makes it worse — for I know all that it implies; all that must be still brooding and festering and waiting down there. I told you it had padded mechanically toward me out of the narrow passage and had stood sentry-like at the entrance between the frightful eidola of Yig and Tulu. That was very natural and inevitable — because the thing was a sentry. It had been made a sentry for punishment, and it was quite dead — besides lacking head, arms, lower legs, and other customary parts of a human being. Yes — it had been a very human being once; and what is more, it had been white. Very obviously, if that manuscript was as true as I think it was, this being had been used for the diversions of the amphitheatre before its life had become wholly extinct and supplanted by automatic impulses controlled from outside.

On its white and only slightly hairy chest some letters had been gashed or branded — I had not stopped to investigate, but had merely noted that they were in an awkward and fumbling Spanish; an awkward Spanish implying a kind of ironic use of the language by an alien inscriber familiar neither with the idiom nor the Roman letters used to record it. The inscription had read "Secuestrado a la voluntad de Xinaián en el cuerpo decapitado de Tlayúb" — "Seized by the will of K'n-yan in the headless body of T'la-yub."

The Whisperer in Darkness.

26,000-WORD NOVELLA; 1930.

If The Dunwitch Horror *engendered any doubts about the trend of Lovecraft's horror fiction into a less-supernatural, more-science-fictionish direction,* The Whisperer in Darkness *put them definitively to rest. This deeply unsettling narrative blurs the line between and among weird fiction, dark fantasy, and science fiction, and arguably makes better use of its scholarly-but-a-little-thick professorial narrator to evoke subtextual horror than any previous work.*

By the time he was writing this story, Lovecraft was acutely aware that he and his primary literary outlet — Weird Tales *— were not exactly a match made in Valhalla. They had different literary goals in mind when approaching any given story.* Weird Tales *liked fairly conventional shudder-pulp tales, especially ones that delivered a big finish; and Lovecraft had learned by experience that if he let his writing get too subtle and sophisticated, it would be shot right back to him with an apologetic note from Farnsworth Wright.*

The Whisperer in Darkness *may have been his attempt to bridge these two worlds. It features plenty of pulpy action, to the point of getting roundly criticized by some Lovecraft fans for borrowing too much from writers like Robert E. Howard. And it does have that oft-parodied "final crowning horror" line, the last piece of evidence withheld until the very last sentence that reveals The Horrid Truth; but it is voiced by Professor Wilmarth, and for a careful reader (who has figured out the truth already, long since), it functions not so much as a crowning horror, but as a line that rings true to a character who we know really isn't as smart as he thinks he is.*

If such was Lovecraft's goal, it must be counted as a great success.

This story also takes greater advantage of the whole Cthulhu Mythos than most previous works. Clark Ashton Smith is incorporated into it (as an Atlantean priest, "Klarkash-Ton"), as is his toad-god Tsothoggua; August Derleth becomes "M. le Comte d'Erlette," the author of the dread tome Cultes des Goules. *The Cthulhu*

Mythos was starting to take shape as a real shared science-fiction universe from which Lovecraft and his friends could draw characters and references to enhance the realism of their weird tales.

Lovecraft started on this story on Feb. 24, 1930, just after finishing The Mound *for Zealia Bishop, and it's easy to draw parallels between the two — as with* The Dunwitch Horror's *relationship with "The Curse of Yig,"* The Mound *feels a bit like a long, highly polished warm-up exercise to* The Whisperer in Darkness.

Lovecraft took his time writing The Whisperer in Darkness; *by the time he finished it, on Sept. 26, he had also written "Medusa's Coil" for Zealia Bishop, as well as two more travelogues: "Account of a Visit to Charleston, S.C." and "An Account of Charleston, in His Maj'ty's Province of South-Carolina."*

The Whisperer in Darkness *was, of course, snatched right up by editor Farnsworth Wright of* Weird Tales, *despite its cumbersome length, and the cheque Lovecraft received for it was $350 — the most he'd ever be paid for a single story. It was published in the August 1931 issue.*

I.

Bear in mind closely that I did not see any actual visual horror at the end. To say that a mental shock was the cause of what I inferred — that last straw which sent me racing out of the lonely Akeley farmhouse and through the wild domed hills of Vermont in a commandeered motor at night — is to ignore the plainest facts of my final experience. Notwithstanding the deep things I saw and heard, and the admitted vividness of the impression produced on me by these things, I cannot prove even now whether I was right or wrong in my hideous inference. For after all Akeley's disappearance establishes nothing. People found nothing amiss in his house despite the bullet-marks on the outside and inside. It was just as though he had walked out casually for a ramble in the hills and failed to return. There was not even a sign that a guest had been there, or that those horrible cylinders and machines had been stored in the study. That he had mortally feared the crowded green hills and endless trickle of brooks among which he had been born and reared, means nothing at all, either; for thousands are subject to just such morbid fears. Eccentricity, moreover, could easily account for his strange acts and apprehensions toward the last.

The whole matter began, so far as I am concerned, with the historic and unprecedented Vermont floods of November 3, 1927. I was then, as now, an instructor of literature at Miskatonic University in Arkham, Massachusetts, and an enthusiastic amateur student of New England folklore. Shortly after the flood, amidst the varied reports of hardship, suffering, and organized relief which filled the press, there appeared certain odd stories of things found floating in some of the swollen rivers; so that many of my friends embarked on curious discussions and appealed to me to shed what light I could on the subject. I felt flattered at having my folklore study taken so seriously, and did what I could to belittle the wild, vague tales which seemed so clearly an outgrowth of old rustic superstitions. It amused me to find several persons of education who insisted that some stratum of obscure, distorted fact might underlie the rumors.

The tales thus brought to my notice came mostly through newspaper cuttings; though one yarn had an oral source and was repeated to a friend of mine in a letter from his mother in Hardwick, Vermont. The type of thing described was essentially the same in all cases, though there seemed to be three separate instances involved — one connected with the Winooski River near Montpelier, another attached to the West River in Windham County beyond Newfane, and a third centering in the Passumpsic in Caledonia County above Lyndonville. Of course many of the stray items mentioned other instances, but on analysis they all seemed to boil down to these three. In each case country folk reported seeing one or more very bizarre and disturbing objects in the surging waters that poured down from the unfrequented hills, and there was a widespread tendency to connect these sights with a primitive, half-forgotten cycle of whispered legend which old people resurrected for the occasion.

What people thought they saw were organic shapes not quite like any they had ever seen before. Naturally, there were many human bodies washed along by the streams in that tragic period; but those who described these strange shapes felt quite sure that they were not human, despite some superficial resemblances in size and general outline. Nor, said the witnesses, could they have been any kind of animal known to Vermont. They were pinkish things about five feet long; with crustaceous bodies bearing vast pairs of dorsal fins or membranous wings and several sets of articulated limbs, and with a sort of convoluted ellipsoid, covered with multitudes of very short antennae, where a head would ordinarily be. It was really remarkable how closely the reports from different sources tended to coincide; though the wonder was lessened by the fact that the old legends, shared at one time throughout the hill country, furnished a morbidly vivid picture which might well have coloured the imaginations of all the witnesses concerned. It was my conclusion that such witnesses — in every case naive and simple backwoods folk — had glimpsed the battered and bloated bodies of human beings or farm animals in the whirling currents; and had allowed the half-remembered folklore to invest these pitiful objects with fantastic attributes.

The ancient folklore, while cloudy, evasive, and largely forgotten by the present generation, was of a highly singular character, and obviously reflected the influence of still earlier Indian tales. I knew it well, though I had never been in Vermont, through the exceedingly rare monograph of Eli Davenport, which embraces material orally obtained prior to 1839 among the oldest people of the state. This material, moreover, closely coincided with tales which I had personally heard from elderly rustics in the mountains of New Hampshire. Briefly summarized, it hinted at a hidden race of monstrous beings which lurked somewhere among the remoter hills — in the deep woods of the highest peaks, and the dark valleys where streams trickle from unknown sources. These beings were seldom glimpsed, but evidences of their presence were reported by those who had ventured farther than usual up the slopes of certain mountains or into certain deep, steep-sided gorges that even the wolves shunned.

There were queer footprints or claw-prints in the mud of brook-margins and barren patches, and curious circles of stones, with the grass around them worn away, which did not seem to have been placed or entirely shaped by Nature. There were, too, certain caves of problematical depth in the sides of the hills; with mouths closed by boulders in a manner scarcely accidental, and with more than an average quota of the queer prints leading both toward and away from them — if indeed the direction of these prints could be justly estimated. And worst of all, there were the things which adventurous people had seen very rarely in the twilight of the remotest valleys and the dense perpendicular woods above the limits of normal hill-climbing.

It would have been less uncomfortable if the stray accounts of these things had not agreed so well. As it was, nearly all the rumors had several points in common; averring that the creatures were a sort of huge, light-red crab with many pairs of legs and with two great batlike wings in the middle of the back. They sometimes walked on all their legs, and sometimes on the hindmost pair only, using the others to convey large objects of indeterminate nature. On one occasion they were spied in considerable numbers, a detachment of them wading along a shallow woodland watercourse three abreast in evidently disciplined formation. Once a specimen was seen flying — launching itself from the top of a bald, lonely hill at night and vanishing in the sky after its great flapping wings had been silhouetted an instant against the full moon.

These things seemed content, on the whole, to let mankind alone; though they were at times held responsible for the disappearance of venturesome individuals — especially persons who built houses too close to certain valleys or too high up on certain mountains. Many localities came to be known as inadvisable to settle in, the feeling persisting long after the cause was forgotten. People would look up at some of the neighbouring mountain-precipices with a shudder, even when not recalling how many settlers had been lost, and how many farmhouses burnt to ashes, on the lower slopes of those grim, green sentinels.

But while according to the earliest legends the creatures would appear to have harmed only those trespassing on their privacy; there were later accounts of their curiosity respecting men, and of their attempts to establish secret outposts in the human world. There were tales of the queer claw-prints seen around farmhouse windows in the morning, and of occasional disappearances in regions outside the obviously haunted areas. Tales, besides, of buzzing voices in imitation of human speech which made surprising offers to lone travelers on roads and cart-paths in the deep woods, and of children frightened out of their wits by things seen or heard where the primal forest pressed close upon their door-yards. In the final layer of legends — the layer just preceding the decline of superstition and the abandonment of close contact with the dreaded places — there are shocked references to hermits and remote farmers who at some period of life appeared to have undergone a repellent mental change, and who were shunned and whispered about as mortals who had sold themselves to the strange beings. In one of the northeastern counties it seemed to be a fashion about 1800 to accuse eccentric and unpopular recluses of being allies or representatives of the abhorred things.

As to what the things were — explanations naturally varied. The common name applied to them was "those ones," or "the old ones," though other terms had a local and transient use. Perhaps the bulk of the Puritan settlers set them down bluntly as familiars of the devil, and made them a basis of awed theological speculation. Those with Celtic legendry in their heritage — mainly the Scotch-Irish element of New Hampshire, and their kindred who had settled in Vermont on Governor Wentworth's colonial grants — linked them vaguely with the malign fairies and "little people" of the bogs and raths, and protected themselves with scraps of incantation handed down through many generations. But the Indians had the most fantastic theories of all. While tribal legends differed, there was a marked consensus of belief in certain vital particulars; it being unanimously agreed that the creatures were not native to this earth.

The Pennacook myths, which were the most consistent and picturesque, taught that the Winged Ones came from the Great Bear in the sky, and had mines in our earthly hills whence they took a kind of stone they could not get on any other world. They did not live here, said the myths, but merely maintained outposts and flew back with vast cargoes of stone to their own stars in the north. They harmed only those earth-people who got too near them or spied upon them. Animals shunned them through instinctive hatred, not because of being hunted. They could not eat the things and animals of earth, but brought their own food from the stars. It was bad to get near them, and sometimes young hunters who went into their hills never came back. It was not good, either, to listen to what they whispered at night in the forest with voices like a bee's that tried to be like the voices of men. They knew the speech of all kinds of men — Pennacooks, Hurons, men of the Five Nations — but did not seem to have or need any speech of their own. They talked with their heads, which changed colour in different ways to mean different things.

All the legendry, of course, white and Indian alike, died down during the nineteenth century, except for occasional atavistical flareups. The ways of the Vermonters became settled; and once their habitual paths and dwellings were established according to a certain fixed plan, they remembered less and less what fears and avoidances had determined that plan, and even that there had been any fears or avoidances. Most people simply knew that certain hilly regions were considered as highly unhealthy, unprofitable, and generally unlucky to live in, and that the farther one kept from them the better off one usually was. In time the ruts of custom and economic interest became so deeply cut in approved places that there was no longer any reason for going outside them, and the haunted hills were left deserted by accident rather than by design. Save during infrequent local scares, only wonder-loving grandmothers and retrospective nonagenarians ever whispered of beings dwelling in those hills; and even such whispers admitted that there was not much to fear from those things now that they were used to the presence of houses and settlements, and now that human beings let their chosen territory severely alone.

All this I had long known from my reading, and from certain folk tales picked up in New Hampshire; hence when the flood-time rumours began to appear, I could easily guess what imaginative background had evolved them. I took great pains to explain this to my friends, and was correspondingly amused when several contentious souls continued to insist on a possible element of truth in the reports. Such persons tried to point out that the early legends had a significant persistence and uniformity, and that the virtually unexplored nature of the Vermont hills made it unwise to be dogmatic about what might or might not dwell among them; nor could they be silenced by my assurance that all the myths were of a well-known pattern common to most of mankind and determined by early phases of imaginative experience which always produced the same type of delusion.

It was of no use to demonstrate to such opponents that the Vermont myths differed but little in essence from those universal legends of natural personification which filled the ancient world with fauns and dryads and satyrs, suggested the kallikanzarai of modern Greece, and gave to wild Wales and Ireland their dark hints of strange, small, and terrible hidden races of troglodytes and burrowers. No use, either, to point out the even more startlingly similar belief of the Nepalese hill tribes in the dreaded Mi-Go or "Abominable Snow-Men" who lurk hideously amidst the ice and rock pinnacles of the Himalayan summits. When I brought up this evidence, my opponents turned it against me by claiming that it must imply some actual historicity for the ancient tales; that it must argue the real existence of some queer elder earth-race, driven to hiding after the advent and dominance of mankind, which might very conceivably have survived in reduced numbers to relatively recent times — or even to the present.

The more I laughed at such theories, the more these stubborn friends asseverated them; adding that even without the heritage of legend the recent reports were too clear, consistent,

Weird Tales, August 1931

"I let my flashlight return to the vacant easy-chair, then noticed for the first time the presence of certain objects in the seat."

detailed, and sanely prosaic in manner of telling, to be completely ignored. Two or three fanatical extremists went so far as to hint at possible meanings in the ancient Indian tales which gave the hidden beings a nonterrestrial origin; citing the extravagant books of Charles Fort with their claims that voyagers from other worlds and outer space have often visited the earth. Most of my foes, however, were merely romanticists who insisted on trying to transfer to real life the fantastic lore of lurking "little people" made popular by the magnificent horror-fiction of Arthur Machen.

II.

As was only natural under the circumstances, this piquant debating finally got into print in the form of letters to the *Arkham Advertiser*; some of which were copied in the press of those Vermont regions whence the flood-stories came. The *Rutland Herald* gave half a page of extracts from the letters on both sides, while the *Brattleboro Reformer* reprinted one of my long historical and mythological summaries in full, with some accompanying comments in "The Pendrifter's" thoughtful column, which supported and applauded my skeptical conclusions. By the spring of 1928 I was almost a well-known figure in Vermont, notwithstanding the fact that I had never set foot in the state. Then came the challenging letters from Henry Akeley which impressed me so profoundly, and which took me for the first and last time to that fascinating realm of crowded green precipices and muttering forest streams.

Most of what I know of Henry Wentworth Akeley was gathered by correspondence with his neighbours, and with his only son in California, after my experience in his lonely farmhouse. He was, I discovered, the last representative on his home soil of a long, locally distinguished line of jurists, administrators, and gentlemen-agriculturists. In him, however, the family mentally had veered away from practical affairs to pure scholarship; so that he had been a notable student of mathematics, astronomy, biology, anthropology, and folklore at the University of Vermont. I had never previously heard of him, and he did not give many autobiographical details in his communications; but from the first I saw he was a man of character, education, and intelligence, albeit a recluse with very little worldly sophistication.

Despite the incredible nature of what he claimed, I could not help at once taking Akeley more seriously than I had taken any of the other challengers of my views. For one thing, he was really close to the actual phenomena — visible and tangible — that he speculated so grotesquely about; and for another thing, he was amazingly willing to leave his conclusions in a tenative state like a true man of science. He had no personal preferences to advance, and was always guided by what he took to be solid evidence. Of course I began by considering him mistaken, but gave him credit for being intelligently mistaken; and at no time did I emulate some of his friends in attributing his ideas, and his fear of the lonely green hills, to insanity. I could see that there was a great deal to the man, and knew that what he reported must surely come from strange circumstance deserving investigation, however little it might have to do with the fantastic causes he assigned. Later on I received from him certain material proofs which placed the matter on a somewhat different and bewilderingly bizarre basis.

I cannot do better than transcribe in full, so far as is possible, the long letter in which Akeley introduced himself, and which formed such an important landmark in my own intellectual history. It is no longer in my possession, but my memory holds almost every word of its portentous message; and again I affirm my confidence in the sanity of the man who wrote it. Here is the text — a text which reached me in the cramped, archaic-looking scrawl of one who had obviously not mingled much with the world during his sedate, scholarly life.

> *R.F.D. #2,*
> *Townshend, Windham Co., Vermont.*
>
> *May 5,1928*
>
> *Albert N. Wilmarth, Esq.,*
> *118 Saltonstall St.,*
> *Arkham, Mass.*
>
> *My Dear Sir:*
>
> *I have read with great interest the* Brattleboro Reformer's *reprint (Apr. 23, '28) of your letter on the recent stories of strange bodies seen floating in our flooded streams last fall, and on the curious folklore they so well agree with. It is easy to see why an outlander would take the position you take, and even why "Pendrifter" agrees with you. That is the attitude generally taken by educated persons both in and out of Vermont, and was my own attitude as a young man (I am now 57) before my studies, both general and in Davenport's book, led me to do some exploring in parts of the hills hereabouts not usually visited.*
>
> *I was directed toward such studies by the queer old tales I used to hear from elderly farmers of the more ignorant sort, but now I wish I had let the whole matter alone. I might say, with all proper modesty, that the subject of anthropology and folklore is by no means strange to me. I took a good deal of it at college, and am familiar with most of the standard authorities such as Tylor, Lubbock, Frazer, Quatrefages, Murray, Osborn, Keith, Boule, G. Elliott Smith, and so on. It is no news to me that tales of hidden races are as old as all mankind. I have seen the reprints of letters from you, and those agreeing with you, in the Rutland Herald, and guess I know about where your controversy stands at the present time.*
>
> *What I desire to say now is, that I am afraid your adversaries are nearer right than yourself, even though all reason seems to be on your side. They are nearer right than they realise themselves — for of course they go only by theory, and cannot know what I know. If I knew as little of the matter as they, I would feel justified in believing as they do. I would be wholly on your side.*

You can see that I am having a hard time getting to the point, probably because I really dread getting to the point; but the upshot of the matter is that I have certain evidence that monstrous things do indeed live in the woods on the high hills which nobody visits. I have not seen any of the things floating in the rivers, as reported, but I have seen things like them under circumstances I dread to repeat. I have seen footprints, and of late have seen them nearer my own home (I live in the old Akeley place south of Townshend Village, on the side of Dark Mountain) than I dare tell you now. And I have overheard voices in the woods at certain points that I will not even begin to describe on paper.

At one place I heard them so much that I took a phonograph there with a dictaphone attachment and wax blank — and I shall try to arrange to have you hear the record I got. I have run it on the machine for some of the old people up here, and one of the voices had nearly scared them paralysed by reason of its likeness to a certain voice (that buzzing voice in the woods which Davenport mentions) that their grandmothers have told about and mimicked for them. I know what most people think of a man who tells about "hearing voices" — but before you draw conclusions just listen to this record and ask some of the older backwoods people what they think of it. If you can account for it normally, very well; but there must be something behind it. Ex nihilo nihil fit, *you know.*

Now my object in writing you is not to start an argument but to give you information which I think a man of your tastes will find deeply interesting. This is private. Publicly I am on your side, for certain things show me that it does not do for people to know too much about these matters. My own studies are now wholly private, and I would not think of saying anything to attract people's attention and cause them to visit the places I have explored. It is true — terribly true — that there are non-human creatures watching us all the time; with spies among us gathering information. It is from a wretched man who, if he was sane (as I think he was) was one of those spies, that I got a large part of my clues to the matter. He later killed himself, but I have reason to think there are others now.

The things come from another planet, being able to live in interstellar space and fly through it on clumsy, powerful wings which have a way of resisting the aether but which are too poor at steering to be of much use in helping them about on earth. I will tell you about this later if you do not dismiss me at once as a madman. They come here to get metals from mines that go deep under the hills, and I think I know where they come from. They will not hurt us if we let them alone, but no one can say what will happen if we get too curious about them. Of course a good army of men could wipe out their mining colony. That is what they are afraid of. But if that happened, more would come from outside — any number of them. They could easily conquer the earth, but have not tried so far because they have not needed to. They would rather leave things as they are to save bother.

I think they mean to get rid of me because of what I have discovered. There is a great black stone with unknown hieroglyphics half worn away which I found in the woods on Round Hill, east of here; and after I took it home everything became different. If they think I suspect too much they will either kill me or take me off the earth to where they come from. They like to take away men of learning once in a while, to keep informed on the state of things in the human world.

This leads me to my secondary purpose in addressing you — namely, to urge you to hush up the present debate rather than give it more publicity. People must be kept away from these hills, and in order to effect this, their curiosity ought not to be aroused any further. Heaven knows there is peril enough anyway, with promoters and real estate men flooding Vermont with herds of summer people to overrun the wild places and cover the hills with cheap bungalows.

I shall welcome further communication with you, and shall try to send you that phonograph record and black stone (which is so worn that photographs don't show much) by express if you are willing. I say "try" because I think those creatures have a way of tampering with things around here. There is a sullen furtive fellow named Brown, on a farm near the village, who I think is their spy. Little by little they are trying to cut me off from our world because I know too much about their world.

They have the most amazing way of finding out what I do. You may not even get this letter. I think I shall have to leave this part of the country and go live with my son in San Diego, Cal., if things get any worse, but it is not easy to give up the place you were born in, and where your family has lived for six generations. Also, I would hardly dare sell this house to anybody now that the creatures have taken notice of it. They seem to be trying to get the black stone back and destroy the phonograph record, but I shall not let them if I can help it. My great police dogs always hold them back, for there are very few here as yet, and they are clumsy in getting about. As I have said, their wings are not much use for short flights on earth. I am on the very brink of deciphering that stone — in a very terrible way — and with your knowledge of folklore you may be able to supply the missing links enough to help me. I suppose you know all about the fearful myths antedating the coming of man to the earth — the Yog-Sothoth and Cthulhu cycles — which are hinted at in the Necronomicon. *I had access to a copy of that once, and hear that you have one in your college library under lock and key.*

To conclude, Mr. Wilmarth, I think that with our respective studies we can be very useful to each other. I don't wish to put you in any peril, and suppose I ought to warn you that possession of the stone and the record won't be very safe; but I think you will find any risks worth running for the sake of knowledge. I will drive down to Newfane or Brattleboro to send whatever you authorize me to send, for the express offices there are more to be trusted.

I might say that I live quite alone now, since I can't keep hired help any more. They won't stay because of the things that try to get near the house at night, and that keep the dogs barking continually. I am glad I didn't get as deep as this into the business while my wife was alive, for it would have driven her mad.

Hoping that I am not bothering you unduly, and that you will decide to get in touch with me rather than throw this letter into the waste basket as a madman's raving, I am

Yrs. very truly,

— HENRY W. AKELEY.

P.S. I am making some extra prints of certain photographs taken by me, which I think will help to prove a number of the points I have touched on. The old people think they are monstrously true. I shall send you these very soon if you are interested. —H. W. A.

It would be difficult to describe my sentiments upon reading this strange document for the first time. By all ordinary rules, I ought to have laughed more loudly at these extravagances than at the far milder theories which had previously moved me to mirth; yet something in the tone of the letter made me take it with paradoxical seriousness. Not that I believed for a moment in the hidden race from the stars which my correspondent spoke of; but that, after some grave preliminary doubts, I grew to feel oddly sure of his sanity and sincerity, and of his confrontation by some genuine though singular and abnormal phenomenon which he could not explain except in this imaginative way. It could not be as he thought it, I reflected, yet on the other hand, it could not be otherwise than worthy of investigation. The man seemed unduly excited and alarmed about something, but it was hard to think that all cause was lacking. He was so specific and logical in certain ways—and after all, his yarn did fit in so perplexingly well with some of the old myths—even the wildest Indian legends.

That he had really overheard disturbing voices in the hills, and had really found the black stone he spoke about, was wholly possible despite the crazy inferences he had made—inferences probably suggested by the man who had claimed to be a spy of the outer beings and had later killed himself. It was easy to deduce that this man must have been wholly insane, but that he probably had a streak of perverse outward logic which made the naïve Akeley—already prepared for such things by his folklore studies—believe his tale. As for the latest developments—it appeared from his inability to keep hired help that Akeley's humbler rustic neighbours were as convinced as he that his house was besieged by uncanny things at night. The dogs really barked, too.

And then the matter of that phonograph record, which I could not but believe he had obtained in the way he said. It must mean something; whether animal noises deceptively like human speech, or the speech of some hidden, night-haunting human being decayed to a state not much above that of lower animals. From this my thoughts went back to the black hieroglyphed stone, and to speculations upon what it might mean. Then, too, what of the photographs which Akeley said he was about to send, and which the old people had found so convincingly terrible?

As I re-read the cramped handwriting I felt as never before that my credulous opponents might have more on their side than I had conceded. After all, there might be some queer and perhaps hereditarily misshapen outcasts in those shunned hills, even though no such race of star-born monsters as folklore claimed. And if there were, then the presence of strange bodies in the flooded streams would not be wholly beyond belief. Was it too presumptuous to suppose that both the old legends and the recent reports had this much of reality behind them? But even as I harboured these doubts I felt ashamed that so fantastic a piece of bizarrerie as Henry Akeley's wild letter had brought them up.

In the end I answered Akeley's letter, adopting a tone of friendly interest and soliciting further particulars. His reply came almost by return mail; and contained, true to promise, a number of Kodak views of scenes and objects illustrating what he had to tell. Glancing at these pictures as I took them from the envelope, I felt a curious sense of fright and nearness to forbidden things; for in spite of the vagueness of most of them, they had a damnably suggestive power which was intensified by the fact of their being genuine photographs—actual optical links with what they portrayed, and the product of an impersonal transmitting process without prejudice, fallibility, or mendacity.

The more I looked at them, the more I saw that my serious estimate of Akeley and his story had not been unjustified. Certainly, these pictures carried conclusive evidence of something in the Vermont hills which was at least vastly outside the radius of our common knowledge and belief. The worst thing of all was the footprint—a view taken where the sun shone on a mud patch somewhere in a deserted upland. This was no cheaply counterfeited thing, I could see at a glance; for the sharply defined pebbles and grassblades in the field of vision gave a clear index of scale and left no possibility of a tricky double exposure. I have called the thing a "footprint," but "claw-print" would be a better term. Even now I can scarcely describe it save to say that it was hideously crablike, and that there seemed to be some ambiguity about its direction. It was not a very deep or fresh print, but seemed to be about the size of an average man's foot. From a central pad, pairs of saw-toothed nippers projected in opposite directions—quite baffling as to function, if indeed the whole object were exclusively an organ of locomotion.

Another photograph—evidently a time-exposure taken in deep shadow—was of the mouth of a woodland cave, with a boulder of rounded regularity choking the aperture. On the bare ground in front of it, one could just discern a dense network of curious tracks, and when I studied the picture with a magnifier I felt uneasily sure that the tracks were like the one in the other view. A third pictured showed a druid-like circle of standing stones on the summit of a wild hill. Around the cryptic circle the grass was very much beaten down and worn away, though I could not detect any footprints even with the glass. The extreme remoteness of the place was apparent from the veritable sea of tenantless mountains which formed the background and stretched away toward a misty horizon.

But if the most disturbing of all the views was that of the footprint, the most curiously suggestive was that of the great black stone found in the Round Hill woods. Akeley had photographed it on what was evidently his study table, for I could see rows of books and a bust of Milton in the background. The thing, as nearly as one might guess, had faced the camera vertically with a somewhat irregularly curved surface of one by two feet; but to say anything definite about that surface, or about the general shape of the whole mass, almost defies the power of language. What outlandish geometrical principles had guided its cutting — for artificially cut it surely was — I could not even begin to guess; and never before had I seen anything which struck me as so strangely and unmistakably alien to this world. Of the hieroglyphics on the surface I could discern very few, but one or two that I did see gave rather a shock. Of course they might be fraudulent, for others besides myself had read the monstrous and abhorred *Necronomicon* of the mad Arab Abdul Alhazred; but it nevertheless made me shiver to recognise certain ideographs which study had taught me to link with the most blood-curdling and blasphemous whispers of things that had had a kind of mad half-existence before the earth and the other inner worlds of the solar system were made.

Of the five remaining pictures, three were of swamp and hill scenes which seemed to bear traces of hidden and unwholesome tenancy. Another was of a queer mark in the ground very near Akeley's house, which he said he had photographed the morning after a night on which the dogs had barked more violently than usual. It was very blurred, and one could really draw no certain conclusions from it; but it did seem fiendishly like that other mark or claw-print photographed on the deserted upland. The final picture was of the Akeley place itself: a trim white house of two stories and attic, about a century and a quarter old, and with a well-kept lawn and stone-bordered path leading up to a tastefully carved Georgian doorway. There were several huge police dogs on the lawn, squatting near a pleasant-faced man with a close-cropped grey beard whom I took to be Akeley himself — his own photographer, one might infer from the tube-connected bulb in his right hand.

From the pictures I turned to the bulky, closely-written letter itself; and for the next three hours was immersed in a gulf of unutterable horror. Where Akeley had given only outlines before, he now entered into minute details; presenting long transcripts of words overheard in the woods at night, long accounts of monstrous pinkish forms spied in thickets at twilight on the hills, and a terrible cosmic narrative derived from the application of profound and varied scholarship to the endless bygone discourses of the mad self-styled spy who had killed himself. I found myself faced by names and terms that I had heard elsewhere in the most hideous of connections — Yuggoth, Great Cthulhu, Tsathoggua, Yog Sothoth, R'lyeh, Nyarlathotep, Azathoth, Hastur, Yian, Leng, the Lake of Hali, Bethmoora, the Yellow Sign, L'mur-Kathulos, Bran, and the Magnum Innominandum — and was drawn back through nameless aeons and inconceivable dimensions to worlds of elder, outer entity at which the crazed author of the *Necronomicon* had only guessed in the vaguest way. I was told of the pits of primal life, and of the streams that had trickled down therefrom; and finally, of the tiny rivulets from one of those streams which had become entangled with the destinies of our own earth.

My brain whirled; and where before I had attempted to explain things away, I now began to believe in the most abnormal and incredible wonders. The array of vital evidence was damnably vast and overwhelming; and the cool, scientific attitude of Akeley — an attitude removed as far as imaginable from the demented, the fanatical, the hysterical, or even the. extravagantly speculative — had a tremendous effect on my thought and judgment. By the time I laid the frightful letter aside I could understand the fears he had come to entertain, and was ready to do anything in my power to keep people away from those wild, haunted hills. Even now, when time has dulled the impression and made me half-question my own experience and horrible doubts, there are things in that letter of Akeley's which I would not quote, or even form into words on paper. I am almost glad that the letter and record and photographs are gone now — and I wish, for reasons I shall soon make clear, that the new planet beyond Neptune had not been discovered.

With the reading of that letter my public debating about the Vermont horror permanently ended. Arguments from opponents remained unanswered or put off with promises, and eventually the controversy petered out into oblivion. During late May and June I was in constant correspondence with Akeley; though once in a while a letter would be lost, so that we would have to retrace our ground and perform considerable laborious copying. What we were trying to do, as a whole, was to compare notes in matters of obscure mythological scholarship and arrive at a clearer correlation of the Vermont horrors with the general body of primitive world legend.

For one thing, we virtually decided that these morbidities and the hellish Himalayan Mi-Go were one and the same order of incarnated nightmare. There were also absorbing zoological conjectures, which I would have referred to Professor Dexter in my own college but for Akeley's imperative command to tell no one of the matter before us. If I seem to disobey that command now, it is only because I think that at this stage a warning about those farther Vermont hills — and about those Himalayan peaks which bold explorers are more and more determined to ascend — is more conducive to public safety than silence would be. One specific thing we were leading up to was a deciphering of the hieroglyphics on that infamous black stone — a deciphering which might well place us in possession of secrets deeper and more dizzying than any formerly known to man.

III.

Toward the end of June the phonograph record came — shipped from Brattleboro, since Akeley was unwilling to trust conditions on the branch line north of there. He had begun to feel an increased sense of espionage, aggravated by the loss of some of our letters; and said much about the insidious deeds of certain men whom he considered tools and agents of the hidden beings. Most of all he suspected the surly farmer Walter Brown, who lived alone on a run-down hillside place near the deep woods, and who was often seen loafing around corners in Brattleboro, Bellows Falls, Newfane, and South Londonderry in the most inexplicable and seemingly unmotivated way. Brown's voice, he felt convinced, was one of those he had overheard on a certain occasion in a very terrible conversation; and he had once found a footprint or clawprint near Brown's house which might possess the most ominous significance. It had been curiously near some of Brown's own footprints—footprints that faced toward it.

So the record was shipped from Brattleboro, whither Akeley drove in his Ford car along the lonely Vermont back roads. He confessed in an accompanying note that he was beginning to be afraid of those roads, and that he would not even go into Townshend for supplies now except in broad daylight. It did not pay, he repeated again and again, to know too much unless one were very remote from those silent and problematical hills. He would be going to California pretty soon to live with his son, though it was hard to leave a place where all one's memories and ancestral feelings centered.

Before trying the record on the commercial machine which I borrowed from the college administration building I carefully went over all the explanatory matter in Akeley's various letters. This record, he had said, was obtained about 1 a.m. on the 1st of May, 1915, near the closed mouth of a cave where the wooded west slope of Dark Mountain rises out of Lee's swamp. The place had always been unusually plagued with strange voices, this being the reason he had brought the phonograph, dictaphone, and blank in expectation of results. Former experience had told him that May Eve—the hideous Sabbat-night of underground European legend—would probably be more fruitful than any other date, and he was not disappointed. It was noteworthy, though, that he never again heard voices at that particular spot.

Unlike most of the overheard forest voices, the substance of the record was quasi-ritualistic, and included one palpably human voice which Akeley had never been able to place. It was not Brown's, but seemed to be that of a man of greater cultivation. The second voice, however, was the real crux of the thing—for this was the accursed buzzing which had no likeness to humanity despite the human words which it uttered in good English grammar and with a scholarly accent.

The recording phonograph and dictaphone had not worked uniformly well, and had of course been at a great disadvantage because of the remote and muffled nature of the overheard ritual; so that the actual speech secured was very fragmentary. Akeley had given me a transcript of what he believed the spoken words to be, and I glanced through this again as I prepared the machine for action. The text was darkly mysterious rather than openly horrible, though a knowledge of its origin and manner of gathering gave it all the associative horror which any words could well possess. I will present it here in full as I remember it—and I am fairly confident that I know it correctly by heart, not only from reading the transcript, but from playing the record itself over and over again. It is not a thing which one might readily forget!

(Indistinguishable Sounds)

A CULTIVATED MALE HUMAN VOICE: . . . is the Lord of the Wood, even to . . . and the gifts of the men of Leng . . . so from the wells of night to the gulfs of space, and from the gulfs of space to the wells of night, ever the praises of Great Cthulhu, of Tsathoggua, and of Him Who is not to be Named. Ever Their praises, and abundance to the Black Goat of the Woods. Ia! Shub-Niggurath! The Goat with a Thousand Young!

A BUZZING IMITATION OF HUMAN SPEECH: Ia! Shub-Niggurath! The Black Goat of the Woods with a Thousand Young!

HUMAN VOICE: And it has come to pass that the Lord of the Woods, being . . . seven and nine, down the onyx steps . . . (tri)butes to Him in the Gulf, Azathoth, He of Whom Thou hast taught us marv(els) . . . on the wings of night out beyond space, out beyond th . . . to That whereof Yuggoth is the youngest child, rolling alone in black aether at the rim . . .

BUZZING VOICE: . . . go out among men and find the ways thereof, that He in the Gulf may know. To Nyarlathotep, Mighty Messenger, must all things be told. And He shall put on the semblance of men, the waxen mask and the robe that hides, and come down from the world of Seven Suns to mock . . .

HUMAN VOICE: Nyarlathotep, Great Messenger, bringer of strange joy to Yuggoth through the void, Father of the Million Favoured Ones, Stalker among . . .

(Speech Cut Off by End of Record)

Such were the words for which I was to listen when I started the phonograph. It was with a trace of genuine dread and reluctance that I pressed the lever and heard the preliminary scratching of the sapphire point, and I was glad that the first faint, fragmentary words were in a human voice—a mellow, educated voice which seemed vaguely Bostonian in accent, and which was certainly not that of any native of the Vermont hills. As I listened to the tantalisingly feeble rendering, I seemed to find the speech identical with Akeley's carefully prepared transcript. On it chanted, in that mellow Bostonian voice . . . "Ia! Shub-Niggurath! The Goat with a Thousand Young! . . ."

And then I heard the other voice. To this hour I shudder retrospectively when I think of how it struck me, prepared though I was by Akeley's accounts. Those to whom I have since described the record profess to find nothing but cheap imposture or madness in it; but could they have the accursed thing itself, or read the bulk of Akeley's correspondence, (especially that terrible and encyclopaedic second letter), I know they would think differently. It is, after all, a tremendous pity that I did not disobey Akeley and play the record for others—a tremendous pity, too, that all of his letters were lost. To me, with my first-hand impression of the actual sounds, and with my knowledge of the background and surrounding circumstances, the voice was a monstrous thing. It swiftly followed the human voice in ritualistic response, but in my imagination it was a morbid echo winging its way across unimaginable abysses from unimaginable outer hells. It is more than two years now since I last ran off that blasphemous waxen cylinder; but at this moment, and at all other moments, I can still hear that feeble, fiendish buzzing as it reached me for the first time.

"Ia! Shub-Niggurath! The Black Goat of the Woods with a Thousand Young!"

But though the voice is always in my ears, I have not even yet been able to analyse it well enough for a graphic description. It was like the drone of some loathsome, gigantic insect ponderously shaped into the articulate speech of an alien species, and I am perfectly certain that the organs producing it can have no resemblance to the vocal organs of man, or indeed to those of any of the mammalia. There were singularities in timbre, range, and overtones which placed this phenomenon wholly outside the sphere of humanity and earth-life. Its sudden advent that first time almost stunned me, and I heard the rest of the record through in a sort of abstracted daze. When the longer passage of buzzing came, there was a sharp intensification of that feeling of blasphemous infinity which had struck me during the shorter and earlier passage. At last the record ended abruptly, during an unusually clear speech of the human and Bostonian voice; but I sat stupidly staring long after the machine had automatically stopped.

I hardly need say that I gave that shocking record many another playing, and that I made exhaustive attempts at analysis and comment in comparing notes with Akeley. It would be both useless and disturbing to repeat here all that we concluded; but I may hint that we agreed in believing we had secured a clue to the source of some of the most repulsive primordial customs in the cryptic elder religions of mankind. It seemed plain to us, also, that there were ancient and elaborate alliances between the hidden outer creatures and certain members of the human race. How extensive these alliances were, and how their state today might compare with their state in earlier ages, we had no means of guessing; yet at best there was room for a limitless amount of horrified speculation. There seemed to be an awful, immemorial linkage in several definite stages betwixt man and nameless infinity. The blasphemies which appeared on earth, it was hinted, came from the dark planet Yuggoth, at the rim of the solar system; but this was itself merely the populous outpost of a frightful interstellar race whose ultimate source must lie far outside even the Einsteinian space-time continuum or greatest known cosmos.

Meanwhile we continued to discuss the black stone and the best way of getting it to Arkham—Akeley deeming it inadvisable to have me visit him at the scene of his nightmare studies. For some reason or other, Akeley was afraid to trust the thing to any ordinary or expected transportation route. His final idea was to take it across country to Bellows Falls and ship it on the Boston and Maine system through Keene and Winchendon and Fitchburg, even though this would necessitate his driving along somewhat lonelier and more forest-traversing hill roads than the main highway to Brattleboro. He said he had noticed a man around the express office at Brattleboro when he had sent the phonograph record, whose actions and expression had been far from reassuring. This man had seemed too anxious to talk with the clerks, and had taken the train on which the record was shipped. Akeley confessed that he had not felt strictly at ease about that record until he heard from me of its safe receipt.

About this time—the second week in July—another letter of mine went astray, as I learned through an anxious communication from Akeley. After that he told me to address him no more at Townshend, but to send all mail in care of the General Delivery at Brattleboro; whither he would make frequent trips either in his car or on the motor-coach line which had lately replaced passenger service on the lagging branch railway. I could see that he was getting more and more anxious, for he went into much detail about the increased barking of the dogs on moonless nights, and about the fresh claw-prints he sometimes found in the road and in the mud at the back of his farmyard when morning came. Once he told about a veritable army of prints drawn up in a line facing an equally thick and resolute line of dog-tracks, and sent a loathsomely disturbing Kodak picture to prove it. That was after a night on which the dogs had outdone themselves in barking and howling.

On the morning of Wednesday, July 18, I received a telegram from Bellows Falls, in which Akeley said he was expressing the black stone over the B. & M. on Train No. 5508, leaving Bellows Falls at 12:15 p.m., standard time, and due at the North Station in Boston at 4:12 p.m. It ought, I calculated, to get up to Arkham at least by the next noon; and accordingly I stayed in all Thursday morning to receive it. But noon came and went without its advent, and when I telephoned down to the express office I was informed that no shipment for me had arrived. My next act, performed amidst a growing alarm, was to give a long-distance call to the express agent at the Boston North Station; and I was scarcely surprised to learn that my consignment had not appeared. Train No. 5508 had pulled in only 35 minutes late on the day before, but had contained no box addressed to me. The agent promised, however, to institute a searching inquiry; and I ended the day by sending Akeley a night-letter outlining the situation.

With commendable promptness a report came from the Boston office on the following afternoon, the agent telephoning as soon as he learned the facts. It seemed that the railway express clerk on No. 5508 had been able to recall an incident which might have much bearing on my loss—an argument with a very curious-voiced man, lean, sandy, and rustic-looking, when the train was waiting at Keene, N. H., shortly after one o'clock standard time. The man, he said, was greatly excited about a heavy box which he claimed to expect, but which was neither on the train nor entered on the company's books. He had given the name of Stanley Adams, and had had such a queerly thick droning voice, that it made the clerk abnormally dizzy and sleepy to listen to him. The clerk could not remember quite how the conversation had ended, but recalled starting into a fuller awakeness when the train began to move. The Boston agent added that this clerk was a young man of wholly unquestioned veracity and reliability, of known antecedents and long with the company.

That evening I went to Boston to interview the clerk in person, having obtained his name and address from the office. He was a frank, prepossessing fellow, but I saw that he could add nothing to his original account. Oddly, he was scarcely sure that he could even recognise the strange inquirer again. Realising that he had no more to tell, I returned to Arkham and sat up till morning writing letters to Akeley, to the express company and to the police department and station agent in Keene. I felt that the strange-voiced man who had so queerly affected the clerk must have a pivotal place in the ominous business, and hoped that Keene station employees and telegraph-office records might tell something about him and about how he happened to make his inquiry when and where he did.

I must admit, however, that all my investigations came to nothing. The queer-voiced man had indeed been noticed around the Keene station in the early afternoon of July 18, and one lounger seemed to couple him vaguely with a heavy box; but he was altogether unknown, and had not been seen before or since. He had not visited the telegraph office or received any message so far as could be learned, nor had any message which might justly be considered a notice of the black stone's presence on No. 5508 come through the office for anyone. Naturally Akeley joined with me in conducting these inquiries, and even made a personal trip to Keene to question the people around the station; but his attitude toward the matter was more fatalistic than mine. He seemed to find the loss of the box a portentous and menacing fulfillment of inevitable tendencies, and had no real hope at all of its recovery. He spoke of the undoubted telepathic and hypnotic powers of the hill creatures and their agents, and in one letter hinted that he did not believe the stone was on this earth any longer. For my part, I was duly enraged, for I had felt there was at least a chance of learning profound and astonishing things from the old, blurred hieroglyphs. The matter would have rankled bitterly in my mind had not Akeley's immediately subsequent letters brought up a new phase of the whole horrible hill problem which at once seized all my attention.

IV.

The unknown things, Akeley wrote in a script grown pitifully tremulous, had begun to close in on him with a wholly new degree of determination. The nocturnal barking of the dogs whenever the moon was dim or absent was hideous now, and there had been attempts to molest him on the lonely roads he had to traverse by day. On the second of August, while bound for the village in his car, he had found a tree-trunk laid in his path at a point where the highway ran through a deep patch of woods; while the savage barking of the two great dogs he had with him told all too well of the things which must have been lurking near. What would have happened had the dogs not been there, he did not dare guess — but he never went out now without at least two of his faithful and powerful pack. Other road experiences had occurred on August fifth and sixth; a shot grazing his car on one occasion, and the barking of the dogs telling of unholy woodland presences on the other.

On August fifteenth I received a frantic letter which disturbed me greatly, and which made me wish Akeley could put aside his lonely reticence and call in the aid of the law. There had been frightful happening on the night of the 12-13th, bullets flying outside the farmhouse, and three of the twelve great dogs being found shot dead in the morning. There were myriads of claw-prints in the road, with the human prints of Walter Brown among them. Akeley had started to telephone to Brattleboro for more dogs, but the wire had gone dead before he had a chance to say much. Later he went to Brattleboro in his car, and learned there that linemen had found the main cable neatly cut at a point where it ran through the deserted hills north of Newfane. But he was about to start home with four fine new dogs, and several cases of ammunition for his big-game repeating rifle. The letter was written at the post office in Brattleboro, and came through to me without delay.

My attitude toward the matter was by this time quickly slipping from a scientific to an alarmedly personal one. I was afraid for Akeley in his remote, lonely farmhouse, and half afraid for myself because of my now definite connection with the strange hill problem. The thing was reaching out so. Would it suck me in and engulf me? In replying to his letter I urged him to seek help, and hinted that I might take action myself if he did not. I spoke of visiting Vermont in person in spite of his wishes, and of helping him explain the situation to the proper authorities. In return, however, I received only a telegram from Bellows Falls which read thus:

> *APPRECIATE YOUR POSITION BUT CAN DO NOTHING TAKE NO ACTION YOURSELF FOR IT COULD ONLY HARM BOTH WAIT FOR EXPLANATION HENRY AKELY*

But the affair was steadily deepening. Upon my replying to the telegram I received a shaky note from Akeley with the astonishing news that he had not only never sent the wire, but had not received the letter from me to which it was an obvious reply. Hasty inquiries by him at Bellows Falls had brought out that the message was deposited by a strange sandy-haired man with a curiously thick, droning voice, though more than this he could not learn. The clerk showed him the original text as scrawled in pencil by the sender, but the handwriting was wholly unfamiliar. It was noticeable that the signature was misspelled — A-K-E-L-Y, without the second "E." Certain conjectures were inevitable, but amidst the obvious crisis he did not stop to elaborate upon them.

He spoke of the death of more dogs and the purchase of still others, and of the exchange of gunfire which had become a settled feature each moonless night. Brown's prints, and the prints of at least one or two more shod human figures, were now found regularly among the claw-prints in the road, and at the back of the farmyard. It was, Akeley admitted, a pretty bad business; and before long he would probably have to go to live with his California son whether or not he could sell the old place. But it was not easy to leave the only spot one could really think of as home. He must try to hang on a little longer; perhaps he could scare off the intruders — especially if he openly gave up all further attempts to penetrate their secrets.

Writing Akeley at once, I renewed my offers of aid, and spoke again of visiting him and helping him convince the authorities of his dire peril. In his reply he seemed less set against that plan than his past attitude would have led one to predict, but said he would like to hold off a little while longer — long enough to get his things in order and reconcile himself to the idea of leaving an almost morbidly cherished birthplace. People looked askance at his studies and speculations and it would be better to get quietly off without setting the countryside in a turmoil and creating widespread doubts of his own sanity. He had had enough, he admitted, but he wanted to make a dignified exit if he could.

This letter reached me on the 28th of August, and I prepared and mailed as encouraging a reply as I could. Apparently the encouragement had effect, for Akeley had fewer terrors to report when he acknowledged my note. He was not very optimistic, though, and expressed the belief that it was only the full moon season which was holding the creatures off. He hoped there would not be many densely cloudy nights, and talked vaguely of boarding in Brattleboro when the moon waned. Again I wrote him encouragingly but on September 5th there came a fresh communication which had obviously crossed my letter in the mails; and to this I could not give any such hopeful response. In view of its importance I believe I had better give it in full — as best I can do from memory of the shaky script. It ran substantially as follows:

Monday

Dear Wilmarth:

A rather discouraging P. S. to my last. Last night was thickly cloudy — though no rain — and not a bit of moonlight got through. Things were pretty bad, and I think the end is getting near, in spite of all we have hoped. After midnight something landed on the roof of the house, and the dogs all rushed up to see what it was. I could hear them snapping and tearing around, and then one managed to get on the roof by jumping from the low ell. There was a terrible fight up there, and I heard a frightful buzzing which I'll never forget. And then there was a shocking smell. About the same time bullets came through the window and nearly grazed me. I think the main line of the hill creatures had got close to the house when the dogs divided because of the roof business. What was up there I don't know yet, but I'm afraid the creatures are learning to steer better with their space wings. I put out the light and used the windows for loopholes, and raked all around the house with rifle fire aimed just high enough not to hit the dogs. That seemed to end the business, but in the morning I found great pools of blood in the yard, besides pools of a green sticky stuff that had the worst odour I have ever smelled. I climbed up on the roof and found more of the sticky stuff there. Five of the dogs were killed — I'm afraid I hit one myself by aiming too low, for he was shot in the back. Now I am setting the panes the shots broke, and am going to Brattleboro for more dogs. I guess the men at the kennels think I am crazy. Will drop another note later. Suppose I'll be ready for moving in a week or two, though it nearly kills me to think of it.

Hastily —

— AKELEY.

But this was not the only letter from Akeley to cross mine. On the next morning — September 6th — still another came; this time a frantic scrawl which utterly unnerved me and put me at a loss what to say or do next. Again I cannot do better than quote the text as faithfully as memory will let me.

Tuesday

Clouds didn't break, so no moon again — and going into the wane anyhow. I'd have the house wired for electricity and put in a searchlight if I didn't know they'd cut the cables as fast as they could be mended.

I think I am going crazy. It may be that all I have ever written you is a dream or madness. It was bad enough before, but this time it is too much. They talked to me last night — talked in that cursed buzzing voice and told me things that I dare not repeat to you. I heard them plainly above the barking of the dogs, and once when they were drowned out a human voice helped them. Keep out of this, Wilmarth — it is worse than either you or I ever suspected. They don't mean to let me get to California now — they want to take me off alive, or what theoretically and mentally amounts to alive — not only to Yuggoth, but beyond that — away outside the galaxy and possibly beyond the last curved rim of space. I told them I wouldn't go where they wish, or in the terrible way they propose to take me, but I'm afraid it will be no use. My place is so far out that they may come by day as well as by night before long. Six more dogs killed, and I felt presences all along the wooded parts of the road when I drove to Brattleboro today. It was a mistake for me to try to send you that phonograph record and black stone. Better smash the record before it's too late. Will drop you another line tomorrow if I'm still here. Wish I could arrange to get my books and things to Brattleboro and board there. I would run off without anything if I could but something inside my mind holds me back. I can slip out to Brattleboro, where I ought to be safe, but I feel just as much a prisoner there as at the house. And I seem to know that I couldn't get much farther even if I dropped everything and tried. It is horrible — don't get mixed up in this.

Yrs —

— AKELEY.

I did not sleep at all the night after receiving this terrible thing, and was utterly baffled as to Akeley's remaining degree of sanity. The substance of the note was wholly insane, yet the manner of expression — in view of all that had gone before — had a grimly potent quality of convincingness. I made no attempt to answer it, thinking it better to wait until Akeley might have time to reply to my latest communication. Such a reply indeed came on the following day, though the fresh material in it quite overshadowed any of the points brought up by the letter nominally answered. Here is what I recall of the text, scrawled and blotted as it was in the course of a plainly frantic and hurried composition.

Wednesday

W.:—

Your letter came, but it's no use to discuss anything any more. I am fully resigned. Wonder that I have even enough will power left to fight them off. Can't escape even if I were willing to give up everything and run. They'll get me.

Had a letter from them yesterday — R.F.D. man brought it while I was at Brattleboro. Typed and postmarked Bellows Falls. Tells what they want to do with me — I can't repeat it. Look out for yourself, too! Smash that record. Cloudy nights keep up, and moon waning all the time. Wish I dared to get help — it might brace up my will power — but everyone who would dare to come at all would call me crazy unless there happened to be some proof. Couldn't ask people to come for no reason at all — am all out of touch with everybody and have been for years.

But I haven't told you the worst, Wilmarth. Brace up to read this, for it will give you a shock. I am telling the truth, though. It is this — I have seen and touched one of the things, or part of one of the things. God, man, but it's awful! It was dead, of course. One of the dogs had it, and I found it near the kennel this morning. I tried to save it in the woodshed to convince people of the whole thing, but it all evaporated in a few hours. Nothing left. You know, all those things in the rivers were seen only on the first morning after the flood. And here's the worst. I tried to photograph it for you, but when I developed the film there wasn't anything visible except the woodshed. What can the thing have been made of? I saw it and felt it, and they all leave footprints. It was surely made of matter — but what kind of matter? The shape can't be described. It was a great crab with a lot of pyramided fleshy rings or knots of thick, ropy stuff covered with feelers where a man's head would be. That green sticky stuff is its blood or juice. And there are more of them due on earth any minute.

Walter Brown is missing — hasn't been seen loafing around any of his usual corners in the villages hereabouts. I must have got him with one of my shots, though the creatures always seem to try to take their dead and wounded away.

Got into town this afternoon without any trouble, but am afraid they're beginning to hold off because they're sure of me. Am writing this in Brattleboro P. O. This may be goodbye — if it is, write my son George Goodenough Akeley, 176 Pleasant St., San Diego, Cal., but don't come up here. Write the boy if you don't hear from me in a week, and watch the papers for news.

I'm going to play my last two cards now — if I have the will power left. First to try poison gas on the things (I've got the right chemicals and have fixed up masks for myself and the dogs) and then if that doesn't work, tell the sheriff. They can lock me in a madhouse if they want to — it'll be better than what the other creatures would do. Perhaps I can get them to pay attention to the prints around the house — they are faint, but I can find them every morning. Suppose, though, police would say I faked them somehow; for they all think I'm a queer character.

Must try to have a state policeman spend a night here and see for himself — though it would be just like the creatures to learn about it and hold off that night. They cut my wires whenever I try to telephone in the night — the linemen think it is very queer, and may testify for me if they don't go and imagine I cut them myself. I haven't tried to keep them repaired for over a week now.

I could get some of the ignorant people to testify for me about the reality of the horrors, but everybody laughs at what they say, and anyway, they have shunned my place for so long that they don't know any of the new events. You couldn't get one of those rundown farmers to come within a mile of my house for love or money. The mail-carrier hears what they say and jokes me about it — God! If I only dared tell him how real it is! I think I'll try to get him to notice the prints, but he comes in the afternoon and they're usually about gone by that time. If I kept one by setting a box or pan over it, he'd think surely it was a fake or joke.

Wish I hadn't gotten to be such a hermit, so folks don't drop around as they used to. I've never dared show the black stone or the Kodak pictures, or play that record, to anybody but the ignorant people. The others would say I faked the whole business and do nothing but laugh. But I may yet try showing the pictures. They give those claw-prints clearly, even if the things that made them can't be photographed. What a shame nobody else saw that thing this morning before it went to nothing!

But I don't know as I care. After what I've been through, a madhouse is as good a place as any. The doctors can help me make up my mind to get away from this house, and that is all that will save me.

Write my son George if you don't hear soon. Goodbye, smash that record, and don't mix up in this.

Yrs —

— AKELEY.

This letter frankly plunged me into the blackest of terror. I did not know what to say in answer, but scratched off some incoherent words of advice and encouragement and sent them by registered mail. I recall urging Akeley to move to Brattleboro at once, and place himself under the protection of the authorities; adding that I would come to that town with the phonograph record and help convince the courts of his sanity. It was time, too, I think I wrote, to alarm the people generally against this thing in their midst. It will be observed that at this moment of stress my own belief in all Akeley had told and claimed was virtually complete, though I did think his failure to get a picture of the dead monster was due not to any freak of Nature but to some excited slip of his own.

V.

Then, apparently crossing my incoherent note and reaching me Saturday afternoon, September 8th, came that curiously different and calming letter neatly typed on a new machine; that strange letter of reassurance and invitation which must have marked so prodigious a transition in the whole nightmare drama of the lonely hills. Again I will quote from memory — seeking for special reasons to preserve as much of the flavour of the style as I can. It was postmarked Bellows Falls, and the signature as well as the body of the letter was typed — as is frequent with beginners in typing. The text, though, was marvellously accurate for a tyro's work; and I concluded that Akeley must have used a machine at some previous period — perhaps in college. To say that the letter relieved me would be only fair, yet beneath my relief lay a substratum of uneasiness. If Akeley had been sane in his terror, was he now sane in his deliverance? And the sort of "improved rapport" mentioned . . . what was it? The entire thing implied such a diametrical reversal of Akeley's previous attitude! But here is the substance of the text, carefully transcribed from a memory in which I take some pride.

Townshend, Vermont, Thursday, Sept. 6, 1928.

My dear Wilmarth: —

It gives me great pleasure to be able to set you at rest regarding all the silly things I've been writing you. I say "silly," although by that I mean my frightened attitude rather than my descriptions of certain phenomena. Those phenomena are real and important enough; my mistake had been in establishing an anomalous attitude toward them.

I think I mentioned that my strange visitors were beginning to communicate with me, and to attempt such communication. Last night this exchange of speech became actual. In response to certain signals I admitted to the house a messenger from those outside — a fellow-human, let me hasten to say. He told me much that neither you nor I had even begun to guess, and showed clearly how totally we had misjudged and misinterpreted the purpose of the Outer Ones in maintaining their secret colony on this planet.

It seems that the evil legends about what they have offered to men, and what they wish in connection with the earth, are wholly the result of an ignorant misconception of allegorical speech — speech, of course, moulded by cultural backgrounds and thought-habits vastly different from anything we dream of. My own conjectures, I freely own, shot as widely past the mark as any of the guesses of illiterate farmers and savage Indians. What I had thought morbid and shameful and ignominious is in reality awesome and mind-expanding and even glorious — my previous estimate being merely a phase of man's eternal tendency to hate and fear and shrink from the utterly different.

Now I regret the harm I have inflicted upon these alien and incredible beings in the course of our nightly skirmishes. If only I had consented to talk peacefully and reasonably with them in the first place! But they bear me no grudge, their emotions being organised very differently from ours. It is their misfortune to have had as their human agents in Vermont some very inferior specimens — the late Walter Brown, for example. He prejudiced me vastly against them. Actually, they have never knowingly harmed men, but have often been cruelly wronged and spied upon by our species. There is a whole secret cult of evil men (a man of your mystical erudition will understand me when I link them with Hastur and the Yellow Sign) devoted to the purpose of tracking them down and injuring them on behalf of monstrous powers from other dimensions. It is against these aggressors — not against normal humanity — that the drastic precautions of the Outer Ones are directed. Incidentally, I learned that many of our lost letters were stolen not by the Outer Ones but by the emissaries of this malign cult.

All that the Outer Ones wish of man is peace and non-molestation and an increasing intellectual rapport. This latter is absolutely necessary now that our inventions and devices are expanding our knowledge and motions, and making it more and more impossible for the Outer Ones' necessary outposts to exist secretly on this planet. The alien beings desire to know mankind more fully, and to have a few of mankind's philosophic and scientific leaders know more about them. With such an exchange of knowledge all perils will pass, and a satisfactory modus vivendi be established. The very idea of any attempt to enslave or degrade mankind is ridiculous.

As a beginning of this improved rapport, the Outer Ones have naturally chosen me — whose knowledge of them is already so considerable — as their primary interpreter on earth. Much was told me last night — facts of the most stupendous and vista-opening nature — and more will be subsequently communicated to me both orally and in writing. I shall not be called upon to make any trip outside just yet, though I shall probably wish to do so later on — employing special means and transcending everything which we have hitherto been accustomed to regard as human experience. My house will be besieged no longer. Everything has reverted to normal, and the dogs will have no further occupation. In place of terror I have been given a rich boon of knowledge and intellectual adventure which few other mortals have ever shared.

The Outer Beings are perhaps the most marvellous organic things in or beyond all space and time — members of a cosmos-wide race of which all other life-forms are merely degenerate variants. They are more vegetable than animal, if these terms can be applied to the sort of matter composing them, and have a somewhat fungoid structure; though the presence of a chlorophyll-like substance and a very singular nutritive system differentiate them altogether from true cormophytic fungi. Indeed, the type is composed of a form of matter totally alien to our part of space — with electrons having a wholly different vibration-rate. That is why the beings cannot be photographed on the ordinary camera films and plates of our known universe, even though our eyes can see them. With proper knowledge, however, any good chemist could make a photographic emulsion which would record their images.

The genus is unique in its ability to traverse the heatless and airless interstellar void in full corporeal form, and some of its variants cannot do this without mechanical aid or curious surgical transpositions. Only a few species have the ether-resisting wings characteristic of the Vermont variety. Those inhabiting certain remote peaks in the Old World were brought in other ways. Their external resemblance to animal life, and to the sort of structure we understand as material, is a matter of parallel evolution rather than of close kinship. Their brain-capacity exceeds that of any other surviving life-form, although the winged types of our hill country are by no means the most highly developed. Telepathy is their usual means of discourse, though we have rudimentary vocal organs which, after a slight operation (for surgery is an incredibly expert and everyday thing among them), can roughly duplicate the speech of such types of organism as still use speech.

Their main immediate abode is a still undiscovered and almost lightless planet at the very edge of our solar system — beyond Neptune, and the ninth in distance from the sun. It is, as we have inferred, the object mystically hinted at as "Yuggoth" in certain ancient and forbidden writings; and it will soon be the scene of a strange focussing of thought upon our world in an effort to facilitate mental rapport. I would not be surprised if astronomers become sufficiently sensitive to these thought-currents to discover Yuggoth when the Outer Ones wish them to do so. But Yuggoth, of course, is only the stepping-stone. The main body of the beings inhabits strangely organized abysses wholly beyond the utmost reach of any human imagination. The space-time globule which we recognize as the totality of all cosmic entity is only an atom in the genuine infinity which is theirs. And as much of this infinity as any human brain can hold is eventually to be opened up to me, as it has been to not more than fifty other men since the human race has existed.

You will probably call this raving at first, Wilmarth, but in time you will appreciate the titanic opportunity I have stumbled upon. I want you to share as much of it as is possible, and to that end must tell you thousands of things that won't go on paper. In the past I have warned you not to come to see me. Now that all is safe, I take pleasure in rescinding that warning and inviting you.

Can't you make a trip up here before your college term opens? It would be marvelously delightful if you could. Bring along the phonograph record and all my letters to you as consultative data — we shall need them in piecing together the whole tremendous story. You might bring the Kodak prints, too, since I seem to have mislaid the negatives and my own prints in all this recent excitement. But what a wealth of facts I have to add to all this groping and tentative material — and what a stupendous device I have to supplement my additions!

Don't hesitate — I am free from espionage now, and you will not meet anything unnatural or disturbing. Just come along and let my car meet you at the Brattleboro station — prepare to stay as long as you can, and expect many an evening of discussion of things beyond all human conjecture. Don't tell anyone about it, of course — for this matter must not get to the promiscuous public.

The train service to Brattleboro is not bad — you can get a timetable in Boston. Take the B. & M. to Greenfield, and then change for the brief remainder of the way. I suggest your taking the convenient 4:10 p.m. — standard — from Boston. This gets into Greenfield at 7:35, and at 9:19 a train leaves there which reaches Brattleboro at 10:01. That is weekdays. Let me know the date and I'll have my car on hand at the station.

Pardon this typed letter, but my handwriting has grown shaky of late, as you know, and I don't feel equal to long stretches of script. I got this new Corona in Brattleboro yesterday — it seems to work very well.

Awaiting word, and hoping to see you shortly with the phonograph record and all my letters — and the Kodak prints —

I am —

Yours in anticipation,

— HENRY W. AKELEY.

TO ALBERT N. WILMARTH, ESQ.,
MISKATONIC UNIVERSITY,
ARKHAM, MASS.

The complexity of my emotions upon reading, re-reading, and pondering over this strange and unlooked-for letter is past adequate description. I have said that I was at once relieved and made uneasy, but this expresses only crudely the overtones of diverse and largely subconscious feelings which comprised both the relief and the uneasiness. To begin with, the thing was so antipodally at variance with the whole chain of horrors preceding it — the change of mood from stark terror to cool complacency and even exultation was so unheralded, lightning-like, and complete! I could scarcely believe that a single day could so alter the psychological perspective of one who had written that final frenzied bulletin of Wednesday, no matter what relieving disclosures that day might have brought. At certain moments a sense of conflicting unrealities made me wonder whether this whole distantly reported drama of fantastic forces were not a kind of half-illusory dream created largely within my own mind. Then I thought of the phonograph record and gave way to still greater bewilderment.

The letter seemed so unlike anything which could have been expected! As I analysed my impression, I saw that it consisted of two distinct phases. First, granting that Akeley had been sane before and was still sane, the indicated change in the situation itself was so swift and unthinkable. And secondly, the change in Akeley's own manner, attitude, and language was so vastly beyond the normal or the predictable. The man's whole personality seemed to have undergone an insidious mutation — a mutation so deep that one could scarcely reconcile his two aspects with the supposition that both represented equal sanity. Word-choice, spelling — all were subtly different. And with my academic sensitiveness to prose style, I could trace profound divergences in his commonest reactions and rhythm-responses.

Certainly, the emotional cataclysm or revelation which could produce so radical an overturn must be an extreme one indeed! Yet in another way the letter seemed quite characteristic of Akeley. The same old passion for infinity — the same old scholarly inquisitiveness. I could not a moment — or more than a moment — credit the idea of spuriousness or malign substitution. Did not the invitation — the willingness to have me test the truth of the letter in person — prove its genuineness?

I did not retire Saturday night, but sat up thinking of the shadows and marvels behind the letter I had received. My mind, aching from the quick succession of monstrous conceptions it had been forced to confront during the last four months, worked upon this startling new material in a cycle of doubt and acceptance which repeated most of the steps experienced in facing the earlier wonders; till long before dawn a burning interest and curiosity had begun to replace the original storm of perplexity and uneasiness. Mad or sane, metamorphosed or merely relieved, the chances were that Akeley had actually encountered some stupendous change of perspective in his hazardous research; some change at once diminishing his danger — real or fancied — and opening dizzy new vistas of cosmic and superhuman knowledge. My own zeal for the unknown flared up to meet his, and I felt myself touched by the contagion of the morbid barrier-breaking. To shake off the maddening and wearying limitations of time and space and natural law — to be linked with the vast outside — to come close to the nighted and abysmal secrets of the infinite and the ultimate — surely such a thing was worth the risk of one's life, soul, and sanity! And Akeley had said there was no longer any peril — he had invited me to visit him instead of warning me away as before. I tingled at the thought of what he might now have to tell me — there was an almost paralysing fascination in the thought of sitting in that lonely and lately-beleaguered farmhouse with a man who had talked with actual emissaries from outer space; sitting there with the terrible record and the pile of letters in which Akeley had summarised his earlier conclusions.

So late Sunday morning I telegraphed Akeley that I would meet him in Brattleboro on the following Wednesday — September 12th — if that date were convenient for him. In only one respect did I depart from his suggestions, and that concerned the choice of a train. Frankly, I did not feel like arriving in that haunted Vermont region late at night; so instead of accepting the train he chose I telephoned the station and devised another arrangement. By rising early and taking the 8:07 A.M. (standard) into Boston, I could catch the 9:25 for Greenfield; arriving there at 12:22 noon. This connected exactly with a train reaching Brattleboro at 1:08 p.m. — a much more comfortable hour than 10:01 for meeting Akeley and riding with him into the close-packed, secret-guarding hills.

I mentioned this choice in my telegram, and was glad to learn in the reply which came toward evening that it had met with my prospective host's endorsement. His wire ran thus:

ARRANGEMENT SATISFACTORY WILL MEET ONE EIGHT TRAIN WEDNESDAY DONT FORGET RECORD AND LETTERS AND PRINTS KEEP DESTINATION QUIET EXPECT GREAT REVELATIONS AKELEY

Receipt of this message in direct response to one sent to Akeley — and necessarily delivered to his house from the Townshend station either by official messenger or by a restored telephone service — removed any lingering subconscious doubts I may have had about the authorship of the perplexing letter. My relief was marked — indeed, it was greater than I could account for at the time; since all such doubts had been rather deeply buried. But I slept soundly and long that night, and was eagerly busy with preparations during the ensuing two days.

VI.

On Wednesday I started as agreed, taking with me a valise full of simple necessities and scientific data, including the hideous phonograph record, the Kodak prints, and the entire file of Akeley's correspondence. As requested, I had told no one where I was going; for I could see that the matter demanded utmost privacy, even allowing for its most favourable turns. The thought of actual mental contact with alien, outside entities was stupefying enough to my trained and somewhat prepared mind; and this being so, what might one think of its effect on the vast masses of uninformed laymen? I do not know whether dread or adventurous expectancy was uppermost in me as I changed trains at Boston and began the long westward run out of familiar regions into those I knew less thoroughly. Waltham — Concord — Ayer — Fitchburg — Gardner — Athol —

My train reached Greenfield seven minutes late, but the northbound connecting express had been held. Transferring in haste, I felt a curious breathlessness as the cars rumbled on through the early afternoon sunlight into territories I had always read of but had never before visited. I knew I was entering an altogether older-fashioned and more primitive New England than the mechanised, urbanised coastal and southern areas where all my life had been spent; an unspoiled, ancestral New England without the foreigners and factory-smoke, bill-boards and concrete roads, of the sections which modernity has touched. There would be odd survivals of that continuous native life whose deep roots make it the one authentic outgrowth of the landscape — the continuous native life which keeps alive strange ancient memories, and fertilises the soil for shadowy, marvellous, and seldom-mentioned beliefs.

Now and then I saw the blue Connecticut River gleaming in the sun, and after leaving Northfield we crossed it. Ahead loomed green and cryptical hills, and when the conductor came around I learned that I was at last in Vermont. He told me to set my watch back an hour, since the northern hill country will have no dealings with new-fangled daylight time schemes. As

I did so it seemed to me that I was likewise turning the calendar back a century.

The train kept close to the river, and across in New Hampshire I could see the approaching slope of steep Wantastiquet, about which singular old legends cluster. Then streets appeared on my left, and a green island showed in the stream on my right. People rose and filed to the door, and I followed them. The car stopped, and I alighted beneath the long train-shed of the Brattleboro station.

Looking over the line of waiting motors I hesitated a moment to see which one might turn out to be the Akeley Ford, but my identity was divined before I could take the initiative. And yet it was clearly not Akeley himself who advanced to meet me with an outstretched hand and a mellowly phrased query as to whether I was indeed Mr. Albert N. Wilmarth of Arkham. This man bore no resemblance to the bearded, grizzled Akeley of the snapshot; but was a younger and more urbane person, fashionably dressed, and wearing only a small, dark moustache. His cultivated voice held an odd and almost disturbing hint of vague familiarity, though I could not definitely place it in my memory.

As I surveyed him I heard him explaining that he was a friend of my prospective host's who had come down from Townshend in his stead. Akeley, he declared, had suffered a sudden attack of some asthmatic trouble, and did not feel equal to making a trip in the outdoor air. It was not serious, however, and there was to be no change in plans regarding my visit. I could not make out just how much this Mr. Noyes — as he announced himself — knew of Akeley's researches and discoveries, though it seemed to me that his casual manner stamped him as a comparative outsider. Remembering what a hermit Akeley had been, I was a trifle surprised at the ready availability of such a friend; but did not let my puzzlement deter me from entering the motor to which he gestured me. It was not the small ancient car I had expected from Akeley's descriptions, but a large and immaculate specimen of recent pattern — apparently Noyes's own, and bearing Massachusetts license plates with the amusing "sacred codfish" device of that year. My guide, I concluded, must be a summer transient in the Townshend region.

Noyes climbed into the car beside me and started it at once. I was glad that he did not overflow with conversation, for some peculiar atmospheric tensity made me feel disinclined to talk. The town seemed very attractive in the afternoon sunlight as we swept up an incline and turned to the right into the main street. It drowsed like the older New England cities which one remembers from boyhood, and something in the collocation of roofs and steeples and chimneys and brick walls formed contours touching deep viol-strings of ancestral emotion. I could tell that I was at the gateway of a region half-bewitched through the piling-up of unbroken time-accumulations; a region where old, strange things have had a chance to grow and linger because they have never been stirred up.

As we passed out of Brattleboro my sense of constraint and foreboding increased, for a vague quality in the hill-crowded countryside with its towering, threatening, close-pressing green and granite slopes hinted at obscure secrets and immemorial survivals which might or might not be hostile to mankind. For a time our course followed a broad, shallow river which flowed down from unknown hills in the north, and I shivered when my companion told me it was the West River. It was in this stream, I recalled from newspaper items, that one of the morbid crablike beings had been seen floating after the floods.

Gradually the country around us grew wilder and more deserted. Archaic covered bridges lingered fearsomely out of the past in pockets of the hills, and the half-abandoned railway track paralleling the river seemed to exhale a nebulously visible air of desolation. There were awesome sweeps of vivid valley where great cliffs rose, New England's virgin granite showing grey and austere through the verdure that scaled the crests. There were gorges where untamed streams leaped, bearing down toward the river the unimagined secrets of a thousand pathless peaks. Branching away now and then were narrow, half-concealed roads that bored their way through solid, luxuriant masses of forest among whose primal trees whole armies of elemental spirits might well lurk. As I saw these I thought of how Akeley had been molested by unseen agencies on his drives along this very route, and did not wonder that such things could be.

The quaint, sightly village of Newfane, reached in less than an hour, was our last link with that world which man can definitely call his own by virtue of conquest and complete occupancy. After that we cast off all allegiance to immediate, tangible, and time-touched things, and entered a fantastic world of hushed unreality in which the narrow, ribbon-like road rose and fell and curved with an almost sentient and purposeful caprice amidst the tenantless green peaks and half-deserted valleys. Except for the sound of the motor, and the faint stir of the few lonely farms we passed at infrequent intervals, the only thing that reached my ears was the gurgling, insidious trickle of strange waters from numberless hidden fountains in the shadowy woods.

The nearness and intimacy of the dwarfed, domed hills now became veritably breath-taking. Their steepness and abruptness were even greater than I had imagined from hearsay, and suggested nothing in common with the prosaic objective world we know. The dense, unvisited woods on those inaccessible slopes seemed to harbour alien and incredible things, and I felt that the very outline of the hills themselves held some strange and aeon-forgotten meaning, as if they were vast hieroglyphs left by a rumoured titan race whose glories live only in rare, deep dreams. All the legends of the past, and all the stupefying imputations of Henry Akeley's letters and exhibits, welled up in my memory to heighten the atmosphere of tension and growing menace. The purpose of my visit, and the frightful abnormalities it postulated struck at me all at once with a chill sensation that nearly over-balanced my ardour for strange delvings.

My guide must have noticed my disturbed attitude; for as the road grew wilder and more irregular, and our motion slower and more jolting, his occasional pleasant comments expanded into a steadier flow of discourse. He spoke of the beauty and weirdness of the country, and revealed some acquaintance with the folklore studies of my prospective host. From his polite questions it was obvious that he knew I had come for a scientific purpose, and that I was bringing data of some importance; but he gave no sign of appreciating the depth and awfulness of the knowledge which Akeley had finally reached.

His manner was so cheerful, normal, and urbane that his remarks ought to have calmed and reassured me; but oddly enough, I felt only the more disturbed as we bumped and veered onward into the unknown wilderness of hills and woods. At times it seemed as if he were pumping me to see what I knew of the monstrous secrets of the place, and with every fresh utterance that vague, teasing, baffling familiarity in his voice increased. It was not an ordinary or healthy familiarity despite the thoroughly wholesome and cultivated nature of the voice. I somehow linked it with forgotten nightmares, and felt that I might go mad if I recognised it. If any good excuse had existed, I think I would have turned back from my visit. As it was, I could not well do so — and it occurred to me that a cool, scientific conversation with Akeley himself after my arrival would help greatly to pull me together.

Besides, there was a strangely calming element of cosmic beauty in the hypnotic landscape through which we climbed and plunged fantastically. Time had lost itself in the labyrinths behind, and around us stretched only the flowering waves of faery and the recaptured loveliness of vanished centuries — the hoary groves, the untainted pastures edged with gay autumnal blossoms, and at vast intervals the small brown farmsteads nestling amidst huge trees beneath vertical precipices of fragrant brier and meadow-grass. Even the sunlight assumed a supernal glamour, as if some special atmosphere or exhalation mantled the whole region. I had seen nothing like it before save in the magic vistas that sometimes form the backgrounds of Italian primitives. Sodoma and Leonardo conceived such expanses, but only in the distance, and through the vaultings of Renaissance arcades. We were now burrowing bodily through the midst of the picture, and I seemed to find in its necromancy a thing I had innately known or inherited and for which I had always been vainly searching.

Suddenly, after rounding an obtuse angle at the top of a sharp ascent, the car came to a standstill. On my left, across a well-kept lawn which stretched to the road and flaunted a border of whitewashed stones, rose a white, two-and-a-half-story house of unusual size and elegance for the region, with a congenes of contiguous or arcade-linked barns, sheds, and windmill behind and to the right. I recognised it at once from the snapshot I had received, and was not surprised to see the name of Henry Akeley on the galvanised-iron mailbox near the road. For some distance back of the house a level stretch of marshy and sparsely-wooded land extended, beyond which soared a steep, thickly-forested hillside ending in a jagged leafy crest. This latter, I knew, was the summit of Dark Mountain, half way up which we must have climbed already.

Alighting from the car and taking my valise, Noyes asked me to wait while he went in and notified Akeley of my advent. He himself, he added, had important business elsewhere, and could not stop for more than a moment. As he briskly walked up the path to the house I climbed out of the car myself, wishing to stretch my legs a little before settling down to a sedentary conversation. My feeling of nervousness and tension had risen to a maximum again now that I was on the actual scene of the morbid beleaguering described so hauntingly in Akeley's letters, and I honestly dreaded the coming discussions which were to link me with such alien and forbidden worlds.

Close contact with the utterly bizarre is often more terrifying than inspiring, and it did not cheer me to think that this very bit of dusty road was the place where those monstrous tracks and that foetid green ichor had been found after moonless nights of fear and death. Idly I noticed that none of Akeley's dogs seemed to be about. Had he sold them all as soon as the Outer Ones made peace with him? Try as I might, I could not have the same confidence in the depth and sincerity of that peace which appeared in Akeley's final and queerly different letter. After all, he was a man of much simplicity and with little worldly experience. Was there not, perhaps, some deep and sinister undercurrent beneath the surface of the new alliance?

Led by my thoughts, my eyes turned downward to the powdery road surface which had held such hideous testimonies. The last few days had been dry, and tracks of all sorts cluttered the rutted, irregular highway despite the unfrequented nature of the district. With a vague curiosity I began to trace the outline of some of the heterogeneous impressions, trying meanwhile to curb the flights of macabre fancy which the place and its memories suggested. There was something menacing and uncomfortable in the funereal stillness, in the muffled, subtle trickle of distant brooks, and in the crowding green peaks and black-wooded precipices that choked the narrow horizon.

And then an image shot into my consciousness which made those vague menaces and flights of fancy seem mild and insignificant indeed. I have said that I was scanning the miscellaneous prints in the road with a kind of idle curiosity — but all at once that curiosity was shockingly snuffed out by a sudden and paralysing gust of active terror. For though the dust tracks were in general confused and overlapping, and unlikely to arrest any casual gaze, my restless vision had caught certain details near the spot where the path to the house joined the highway; and had recognised beyond doubt or hope the frightful significance of those details. It was not for nothing, alas, that I had pored for hours over the Kodak views of the Outer Ones' claw-prints which Akeley had sent. Too well did I know the marks of those loathsome nippers, and that hint of ambiguous direction which stamped the horrors as no creatures of this planet. No chance had been left me for merciful mistake. Here, indeed, in objective form before my own eyes, and surely made not many hours ago, were at least three marks which stood out blasphemously among the surprising plethora of blurred footprints leading to and from the Akeley farmhouse. They were the hellish tracks of the living fungi from Yuggoth.

I pulled myself together in time to stifle a scream. After all, what more was there than I might have expected, assuming that I had really believed Akeley's letters? He had spoken of making peace with the things. Why, then, was it strange that some of them had visited his house? But the terror was stronger than the reassurance. Could any man be expected to look unmoved for the first time upon the claw-marks of animate beings from outer depths of space? Just then I saw Noyes emerge from the door and approach with a brisk step. I must, I reflected, keep command of myself, for the chances were that this genial friend knew nothing of Akeley's profoundest and most stupendous probings into the forbidden.

Akeley, Noyes hastened to inform me, was glad and ready to see me; although his sudden attack of asthma would prevent him from being a very competent host for a day or two. These spells hit him hard when they came, and were always accompanied by a debilitating fever and general weakness. He never was good for much while they lasted — had to talk in a whisper, and was very clumsy and feeble in getting about. His feet and ankles swelled, too, so that he had to bandage them like a gouty old beef-eater. Today he was in rather bad shape, so that I would have to attend very largely to my own needs; but he was none the less eager for conversation. I would find him in the study at the left of the front hall — the room where the blinds were shut. He had to keep the sunlight out when he was ill, for his eyes were very sensitive.

As Noyes bade me adieu and rode off northward in his car I began to walk slowly toward the house. The door had been left ajar for me; but before approaching and entering I cast a searching glance around the whole place, trying to decide what had struck me as so intangibly queer about it. The barns and sheds looked trimly prosaic enough, and I noticed Akeley's battered Ford in its capacious, unguarded shelter. Then the secret of the queerness reached me. It was the total silence. Ordinarily a farm is at least moderately murmurous from its various kinds of livestock, but here all signs of life were missing. What of the hens and the dogs? The cows, of which Akeley had said he possessed several, might conceivably be out to pasture, and the dogs might possibly have been sold; but the absence of any trace of cackling or grunting was truly singular.

I did not pause long on the path, but resolutely entered the open house door and closed it behind me. It had cost me a distinct psychological effort to do so, and now that I was shut inside I had a momentary longing for precipitate retreat. Not that the place was in the least sinister in visual suggestion; on the contrary, I thought the graceful late-colonial hallway very tasteful and wholesome, and admired the evident breeding of the man who had furnished it. What made me wish to flee was something very attenuated and indefinable. Perhaps it was a certain odd odour which I thought I noticed — though I well knew how common musty odours are in even the best of ancient farmhouses.

VII.

Refusing to let these cloudy qualms overmaster me, I recalled Noyes's instructions and pushed open the six-panelled, brass-latched white door on my left. The room beyond was darkened as I had known before; and as I entered it I noticed that the queer odour was stronger there. There likewise appeared to be some faint, half-imaginary rhythm or vibration in the air. For a moment the closed blinds allowed me to see very little, but then a kind of apologetic hacking or whispering sound drew my attention to a great easy-chair in the farther, darker corner of the room. Within its shadowy depths I saw the white blur of a man's face and hands; and in a moment I had crossed to greet the figure who had tried to speak. Dim though the light was, I perceived that this was indeed my host. I had studied the Kodak picture repeatedly, and there could be no mistake about this firm, weather-beaten face with the cropped, grizzled beard.

But as I looked again my recognition was mixed with sadness and anxiety; for certainly, his face was that of a very sick man. I felt that there must be something more than asthma behind that strained, rigid, immobile expression and unwinking glassy stare; and realised how terribly the strain of his frightful experiences must have told on him. Was it not enough to break any human being — even a younger man than this intrepid delver into the forbidden? The strange and sudden relief, I feared, had come too late to save him from something like a general breakdown. There was a touch of the pitiful in the limp, lifeless way his lean hands rested in his lap. He had on a loose dressing-gown, and was swathed around the head and high around the neck with a vivid yellow scarf or hood.

And then I saw that he was trying to talk in the same hacking whisper with which he had greeted me. It was a hard whisper to catch at first, since the grey moustache concealed all movements of the lips, and something in its timbre disturbed me greatly; but by concentrating my attention I could soon make out its purport surprisingly well. The accent was by no means a rustic one, and the language was even more polished than correspondence had led me to expect.

"Mr. Wilmarth, I presume? You must pardon my not rising. I am quite ill, as Mr. Noyes must have told you; but I could not resist having you come just the same. You know what I wrote in my last letter — there is so much to tell you tomorrow when I shall feel better. I can't say how glad I am to see you in person after all our many letters. You have the file with you, of course? And the Kodak prints and records? Noyes put your valise in the hall — I suppose you saw it. For tonight I fear you'll have to wait on yourself to a great extent. Your room is upstairs — the one over this — and you'll see the bathroom door open at the head of the staircase. There's a meal spread for you in the dining-room — right through this door at your right — which you can take whenever you feel like it. I'll be a better host tomorrow — but just now weakness leaves me helpless.

"Make yourself at home — you might take out the letters and pictures and records and put them on the table here before you go upstairs with your bag. It is here that we shall discuss them — you can see my phonograph on that corner stand.

"No, thanks — there's nothing you can do for me. I know these spells of old. Just come back for a little quiet visiting before night, and then go to bed when you please. I'll rest right here — perhaps sleep here all night as I often do. In the morning I'll be far better able to go into the things we must go into. You realise, of course, the utterly stupendous nature of the matter before us. To us, as to only a few men on this earth, there will be opened up gulfs of time and space and knowledge beyond anything within the conception of human science or philosophy.

"Do you know that Einstein is wrong, and that certain objects and forces can move with a velocity greater than that of light? With proper aid I expect to go backward and forward in time, and actually see and feel the earth of remote past and future epochs. You can't imagine the degree to which those beings have carried science. There is nothing they can't do with the mind and body of living organisms. I expect to visit other planets, and even other stars and galaxies. The first trip will be to Yuggoth, the nearest world fully peopled by the beings. It is a strange dark orb at the very rim of our solar system — unknown to earthly astronomers as yet. But I must have written you about this. At the proper time, you know, the beings there will direct thought-currents toward us and cause it to be discovered — or perhaps let one of their human allies give the scientists a hint.

"There are mighty cities on Yuggoth — great tiers of terraced towers built of black stone like the specimen I tried to send you. That came from Yuggoth. The sun shines there no brighter than a star, but the beings need no light. They have other subtler senses, and put no windows in their great houses and temples. Light even hurts and hampers and confuses them, for it does not exist at all in the black cosmos outside time and space where they came from originally. To visit Yuggoth would drive any weak man mad — yet I am going there. The black rivers of pitch that flow under those mysterious cyclopean bridges — things built by some elder race extinct and forgotten before the beings came to Yuggoth from the ultimate voids — ought to be enough to make any man a Dante or Poe if he can keep sane long enough to tell what he has seen.

"But remember — that dark world of fungoid gardens and windowless cities isn't really terrible. It is only to us that it would seem so. Probably this world seemed just as terrible to the beings when they first explored it in the primal age. You know they were here long before the fabulous epoch of Cthulhu was over, and remember all about sunken R'lyeh when it was above the waters. They've been inside the earth, too — there are openings which human beings know nothing of — some of them in these very Vermont hills — and great worlds of unknown life down there; blue-litten K'n-yan, red-litten Yoth, and black, lightless N'kai. It's from N'kai that frightful Tsathoggua came — you know, the amorphous, toad-like god-creature mentioned in the Pnakotic Manuscripts and the *Necronomicon* and the Commoriom myth-cycle preserved by the Atlantean high-priest Klarkash-Ton.

"But we will talk of all this later on. It must be four or five o'clock by this time. Better bring the stuff from your bag, take a bite, and then come back for a comfortable chat."

Very slowly I turned and began to obey my host; fetching my valise, extracting and depositing the desired articles, and finally ascending to the room designated as mine. With the memory of that roadside claw-print fresh in my mind, Akeley's whispered paragraphs had affected me queerly; and the hints of familiarity with this unknown world of fungous life — forbidden Yuggoth — made my flesh creep more than I cared to own. I was tremendously sorry about Akeley's illness, but had to confess that his hoarse whisper had a hateful as well as pitiful quality. If only he wouldn't gloat so about Yuggoth and its black secrets!

My room proved a very pleasant and well-furnished one, devoid alike of the musty odour and disturbing sense of vibration; and after leaving my valise there I descended again to greet Akeley and take the lunch he had set out for me. The dining-room was just beyond the study, and I saw that a kitchen ell extended still farther in the same direction. On the dining-table an ample array of sandwiches, cake, and cheese awaited me, and a Thermos-bottle beside a cup and saucer testified that hot coffee had not been forgotten. After a well-relished meal I poured myself a liberal cup of coffee, but found that the culinary standard had suffered a lapse in this one detail. My first spoonful revealed a faintly unpleasant acrid taste, so that I did not take more. Throughout the lunch I thought of Akeley sitting silently in the great chair in the darkened next room.

Once I went in to beg him to share the repast, but he whispered that he could eat nothing as yet. Later on, just before he slept, he would take some malted milk — all he ought to have that day.

After lunch I insisted on clearing the dishes away and washing them in the kitchen sink — incidentally emptying the coffee which I had not been able to appreciate. Then returning to the darkened study I drew up a chair near my host's corner and prepared for such conversation as he might feel inclined to conduct. The letters, pictures, and record were still on the large centre-table, but for the nonce we did not have to draw upon them. Before long I forgot even the bizarre odour and curious suggestions of vibration.

I have said that there were things in some of Akeley's letters — especially the second and most voluminous one — which I would not dare to quote or even form into words on paper. This hesitancy applies with still greater force to the things I heard whispered that evening in the darkened room among the lonely hills. Of the extent of the cosmic horrors unfolded by that raucous voice I cannot even hint. He had known hideous things before, but what he had learned since making his pact with the Outside Things was almost too much for sanity to bear. Even now I absolutely refused to believe what he implied about the constitution of ultimate infinity, the juxtaposition of dimensions, and the frightful position of our known cosmos of space and time in the unending chain of linked cosmos-atoms which makes up the immediate super-cosmos of curves, angles, and material and semi-material electronic organisation.

Never was a sane man more dangerously close to the arcana of basic entity — never was an organic brain nearer to utter annihilation in the chaos that transcends form and force and symmetry. I learned whence Cthulhu first came, and why half the great temporary stars of history had flared forth. I guessed — from hints which made even my informant pause timidly — the secret behind the Magellanic Clouds and globular nebulae, and the black truth veiled by the immemorial allegory of Tao. The nature of the Doels was plainly revealed, and I was told the essence (though not the source) of the Hounds of Tindalos. The legend of Yig, Father of Serpents, remained figurative no longer, and I started with loathing when told of the monstrous nuclear chaos beyond angled space which the *Necronomicon* had mercifully cloaked under the name of Azathoth. It was shocking to have the foulest nightmares of secret myth cleared up in concrete terms whose stark, morbid hatefulness exceeded the boldest hints of ancient and mediaeval mystics. Ineluctably I was led to believe that the first whisperers of these accursed tales must have had discourse with Akeley's Outer Ones, and perhaps have visited outer cosmic realms as Akeley now proposed visiting them.

I was told of the Black Stone and what it implied, and was glad that it had not reached me. My guesses about those hieroglyphics had been all too correct! And yet Akeley now seemed reconciled to the whole fiendish system he had stumbled upon; reconciled and eager to probe farther into the monstrous abyss. I wondered what beings he had talked with since his last letter to me, and whether many of them had been as human as that first emissary he had mentioned. The tension in my head grew insufferable, and I built up all sorts of wild theories about that queer, persistent odour and those insidious hints of vibration in the darkened room.

Night was falling now, and as I recalled what Akeley had written me about those earlier nights I shuddered to think there would be no moon. Nor did I like the way the farmhouse nestled in the lee of that colossal forested slope leading up to Dark Mountain's unvisited crest. With Akeley's permission I lighted a small oil lamp, turned it low, and set it on a distant bookcase beside the ghostly bust of Milton; but afterward I was sorry I had done so, for it made my host's strained, immobile face and listless hands look damnably abnormal and corpselike. He seemed half-incapable of motion, though I saw him nod stiffly once in awhile.

After what he had told, I could scarcely imagine what profounder secrets he was saving for the morrow; but at last it developed that his trip to Yuggoth and beyond — and my own possible participation in it — was to be the next day's topic. He must have been amused by the start of horror I gave at hearing a cosmic voyage on my part proposed, for his head wabbled violently when I showed my fear. Subsequently he spoke very gently of how human beings might accomplish — and several times had accomplished — the seemingly impossible flight across the interstellar void. It seemed that complete human bodies did not indeed make the trip, but that the prodigious surgical, biological, chemical, and mechanical skill of the Outer Ones had found a way to convey human brains without their concomitant physical structure.

There was a harmless way to extract a brain, and a way to keep the organic residue alive during its absence. The bare, compact cerebral matter was then immersed in an occasionally replenished fluid within an ether-tight cylinder of a metal mined in Yuggoth, certain electrodes reaching through and connecting at will with elaborate instruments capable of duplicating the three vital faculties of sight, hearing, and speech. For the winged fungus-beings to carry the brain-cylinders intact through space was an easy matter. Then, on every planet covered by their civilisation, they would find plenty of adjustable faculty-instruments capable of being connected with the encased brains; so that after a little fitting these travelling intelligences could be given a full sensory and articulate life — albeit a bodiless and mechanical one — at each stage of their journeying through and beyond the space-time continuum. It was as simple as carrying a phonograph record about and playing it wherever a phonograph of corresponding make exists. Of its success there could be no question. Akeley was not afraid. Had it not been brilliantly accomplished again and again?

For the first time one of the inert, wasted hands raised itself and pointed stiffly to a high shelf on the farther side of the room. There, in a neat row, stood more than a dozen cylinders of a metal I had never seen before — cylinders about a foot high and somewhat less in diameter, with three curious sockets set in an isosceles triangle over the front convex surface of each. One of them was linked at two of the sockets to a pair of singular-looking machines that stood in the background. Of their purport I did not need to be told, and I shivered as with ague. Then I saw the hand point to a much nearer corner where some intricate instruments with attached cords and plugs, several of them much like the two devices on the shelf behind the cylinders, were huddled together.

"There are four kinds of instruments here, Wilmarth," whispered the voice. "Four kinds — three faculties each — makes twelve pieces in all. You see there are four different sorts of beings represented in those cylinders up there. Three humans, six fungoid beings who can't navigate space corporeally, two beings from Neptune (God! if you could see the body this type has on its own planet!), and the rest entities from the central caverns of an especially interesting dark star beyond the galaxy.

In the principal outpost inside Round Hill you'll now and then find more cylinders and machines — cylinders of extra-cosmic brains with different senses from any we know — allies and explorers from the uttermost Outside — and special machines for giving them impressions and expression in the several ways suited at once to them and to the comprehensions of different types of listeners. Round Hill, like most of the beings' main outposts all through the various universes, is a very cosmopolitan place. Of course, only the more common types have been lent to me for experiment.

"Here — take the three machines I point to and set them on the table. That tall one with the two glass lenses in front — then the box with the vacuum tubes and sounding-board — and now the one with the metal disc on top. Now for the cylinder with the label 'B-67' pasted on it. Just stand in that Windsor chair to reach the shelf. Heavy? Never mind! Be sure of the number — B-67. Don't bother that fresh, shiny cylinder joined to the two testing instruments — the one with my name on it. Set B-67 on the table near where you've put the machines — and see that the dial switch on all three machines is jammed over to the extreme left.

"Now connect the cord of the lens machine with the upper socket on the cylinder — there! Join the tube machine to the lower left-hand socket, and the disc apparatus to the outer socket. Now move all the dial switches on the machine over to the extreme right — first the lens one, then the disc one, and then the tube one. That's right. I might as well tell you that this is a human being — just like any of us. I'll give you a taste of some of the others tomorrow."

To this day I do not know why I obeyed those whispers so slavishly, or whether I thought Akeley was mad or sane. After what had gone before, I ought to have been prepared for anything; but this mechanical mummery seemed so like the typical vagaries of crazed inventors and scientists that it struck a chord of doubt which even the preceding discourse had not excited. What the whisperer implied was beyond all human belief — yet were not the other things still farther beyond, and less preposterous only because of their remoteness from tangible concrete proof?

As my mind reeled amidst this chaos, I became conscious of a mixed grating and whirring from all three of the machines lately linked to the cylinder — a grating and whirring which soon subsided into a virtual noiselessness. What was about to happen? Was I to hear a voice? And if so, what proof would I have that it was not some cleverly concocted radio device talked into by a concealed but closely watched speaker? Even now I am unwilling to swear just what I heard, or just what phenomenon really took place before me. But something certainly seemed to take place.

To be brief and plain, the machine with the tubes and sound-box began to speak, and with a point and intelligence which left no doubt that the speaker was actually present and observing us. The voice was loud, metallic, lifeless, and plainly mechanical in every detail of its production. It was incapable of inflection or expressiveness, but scraped and rattled on with a deadly precision and deliberation.

"Mr. Wilmarth," it said, "I hope I do not startle you. I am a human being like yourself, though my body is now resting safely under proper vitalising treatment inside Round Hill, about a mile and a half east of here. I myself am here with you — my brain is in that cylinder and I see, hear, and speak through these electronic vibrators. In a week I am going across the void as I have been many times before, and I expect to have the pleasure of Mr. Akeley's company. I wish I might have yours as well; for I know you by sight and reputation, and have kept close track of your correspondence with our friend. I am, of course, one of the men who have become allied with the outside beings visiting our planet. I met them first in the Himalayas, and have helped them in various ways. In return they have given me experiences such as few men have ever had.

"Do you realise what it means when I say I have been on thirty-seven different celestial bodies — planets, dark stars, and less definable objects — including eight outside our galaxy and two outside the curved cosmos of space and time? All this has not harmed me in the least. My brain has been removed from my body by fissions so adroit that it would be crude to call the operation surgery. The visiting beings have methods which make these extractions easy and almost normal — and one's body never ages when the brain is out of it. The brain, I may add, is virtually immortal with its mechanical faculties and a limited nourishment supplied by occasional changes of the preserving fluid.

"Altogether, I hope most heartily that you will decide to come with Mr. Akeley and me. The visitors are eager to know men of knowledge like yourself, and to show them the great abysses that most of us have had to dream about in fanciful ignorance. It may seem strange at first to meet them, but I know you will be above minding that. I think Mr. Noyes will go along, too — the man who doubtless brought you up here in his car. He has been one of us for years — I suppose you recognised his voice as one of those on the record Mr. Akeley sent you."

At my violent start the speaker paused a moment before concluding. "So Mr. Wilmarth, I will leave the matter to you; merely adding that a man with your love of strangeness and folklore ought never to miss such a chance as this. There is nothing to fear. All transitions are painless; and there is much to enjoy in a wholly mechanised state of sensation. When the electrodes are disconnected, one merely drops off into a sleep of especially vivid and fantastic dreams.

"And now, if you don't mind, we might adjourn our session till tomorrow. Good night — just turn all the switches back to the left; never mind the exact order, though you might let the lens machine be last. Good night, Mr. Akeley — treat our guest well! Ready now with those switches?"

That was all. I obeyed mechanically and shut off all three switches, though dazed with doubt of everything that had occurred. My head was still reeling as I heard Akeley's whispering voice telling me that I might leave all the apparatus on the table just as it was. He did not essay any comment on what had happened, and indeed no comment could have conveyed much to my burdened faculties. I heard him telling me I could take the lamp to use in my room, and deduced that he wished to rest alone in the dark. It was surely time he rested, for his discourse of the afternoon and evening had been such as to exhaust even a vigorous man. Still dazed, I bade my host good night and went upstairs with the lamp, although I had an excellent pocket flashlight with me.

I was glad to be out of that downstairs study with the queer odour and vague suggestions of vibration, yet could not of course escape a hideous sense of dread and peril and cosmic abnormality as I thought of the place I was in and the forces I was meeting. The wild, lonely region, the black, mysteriously forested slope towering so close behind the house; the footprint in the road, the sick, motionless whisperer in the dark, the hellish cylinders and machines, and above all the invitations to strange surgery and stranger voyagings — these things, all so new and in such sudden succession, rushed in on me with a cumulative force which sapped my will and almost undermined my physical strength.

To discover that my guide Noyes was the human celebrant in that monstrous bygone Sabbat-ritual on the phonograph record was a particular shock, though I had previously sensed a dim, repellent familiarity in his voice. Another special shock came from my own attitude toward my host whenever I paused to analyse it; for much as I had instinctively liked Akeley as revealed in his correspondence, I now found that he filled me with a distinct repulsion. His illness ought to have excited my pity; but instead, it gave me a kind of shudder. He was so rigid and inert and corpselike — and that incessant whispering was so hateful and unhuman!

It occurred to me that this whispering was different from anything else of the kind I had ever heard; that, despite the curious motionlessness of the speaker's moustache-screened lips, it had a latent strength and carrying-power remarkable for the wheezing of an asthmatic. I had been able to understand the speaker when wholly across the room, and once or twice it had seemed to me that the faint but penetrant sounds represented not so much weakness as deliberate repression — for what reason I could not guess. From the first I had felt a disturbing quality in their timbre. Now, when I tried to weigh the matter, I thought I could trace this impression to a kind of subconscious familiarity like that which had made Noyes's voice so hazily ominous. But when or where I had encountered the thing it hinted at, was more than I could tell.

One thing was certain — I would not spend another night here. My scientific zeal had vanished amidst fear and loathing, and I felt nothing now but a wish to escape from this net of morbidity and unnatural revelation. I knew enough now. It must indeed be true that strange cosmic linkages do exist — but such things are surely not meant for normal human beings to meddle with.

Blasphemous influences seemed to surround me and press chokingly upon my senses. Sleep, I decided, would be out of the question; so I merely extinguished the lamp and threw myself on the bed fully dressed. No doubt it was absurd, but I kept ready for some unknown emergency; gripping in my right hand the revolver I had brought along, and holding the pocket flashlight in my left. Not a sound came from below, and I could imagine how my host was sitting there with cadaverous stiffness in the dark.

Somewhere I heard a clock ticking, and was vaguely grateful for the normality of the sound. It reminded me, though, of another thing about the region which disturbed me — the total absence of animal life. There were certainly no farm beasts about, and now I realised that even the accustomed night-noises of wild living things were absent. Except for the sinister trickle of distant unseen waters, that stillness was anomalous — interplanetary — and I wondered what star-spawned, intangible blight could be hanging over the region. I recalled from old legends that dogs and other beasts had always hated the Outer Ones, and thought of what those tracks in the road might mean.

VIII.

Do not ask me how long my unexpected lapse into slumber lasted, or how much of what ensued was sheer dream. If I tell you that I awakened at a certain time, and heard and saw certain things, you will merely answer that I did not wake then; and that everything was a dream until the moment when I rushed out of the house, stumbled to the shed where I had seen the old Ford, and seized that ancient vehicle for a mad, aimless race over the haunted hills which at last landed me — after hours of jolting and winding through forest-threatened labyrinths — in a village which turned out to be Townshend.

You will also, of course, discount everything else in my report; and declare that all the pictures, record-sounds, cylinder-and-machine sounds, and kindred evidences were bits of pure deception practiced on me by the missing Henry Akeley. You will even hint that he conspired with other eccentrics to carry out a silly and elaborate hoax — that he had the express shipment removed at Keene, and that he had Noyes make that terrifying wax record. It is odd, though, that Noyes has not ever yet been identified; that he was unknown at any of the villages near Akeley's place, though he must have been frequently in the region. I wish I had stopped to memorize the license-number of his car — or perhaps it is better after all that I did not. For I, despite all you can say, and despite all I sometimes try to say to myself, know that loathsome outside influences must be lurking there in the half-unknown hills — and that those influences have spies and emissaries in the world of men. To keep as far as possible from such influences and such emissaries is all that I ask of life in future.

When my frantic story sent a sheriff's posse out to the farmhouse, Akeley was gone without leaving a trace. His loose dressing gown, yellow scarf, and foot-bandages lay on the study floor near his corner easy-chair, and it could not be decided whether any of his other apparel had vanished with him. The dogs and livestock were indeed missing, and there were some curious bullet-holes both on the house's exterior and on some of the walls within; but beyond this nothing unusual could be detected. No cylinders or machines, none of the evidences I had brought in my valise, no queer odour or vibration-sense, no foot-prints in the road, and none of the problematical things I glimpsed at the very last.

I stayed a week in Brattleboro after my escape, making inquiries among people of every kind who had known Akeley; and the results convince me that the matter is no figment of dream or delusion. Akeley's queer purchase of dogs and ammunition and chemicals, and the cutting of his telephone wires, are matters of record; while all who knew him — including his son in California — concede that his occasional remarks on strange studies had a certain consistency. Solid citizens believe he was mad, and unhesitatingly pronounce all reported evidences mere hoaxes devised with insane cunning and perhaps abetted by eccentric associates; but the lowlier country folk sustain his statements in every detail. He had showed some of these rustics his photographs and black stone, and had played the hideous record for them; and they all said the footprints and buzzing voice were like those described in ancestral legends.

They said, too, that suspicious sights and sounds had been noticed increasingly around Akeley's house after he found the black stone, and that the place was now avoided by everybody except the mail man and other casual, tough-minded people. Dark Mountain and Round Hill were both notoriously haunted spots, and I could find no one who had ever closely explored either. Occasional disappearances of natives throughout the district's history were well attested, and these now included the semi-vagabond Walter Brown, whom Akeley's letters had mentioned. I even came upon one farmer who thought he had personally glimpsed one of the queer bodies at flood-time in the swollen West River, but his tale was too confused to be really valuable.

When I left Brattleboro I resolved never to go back to Vermont, and I feel quite certain I shall keep my resolution. Those wild hills are surely the outpost of a frightful cosmic race — as I doubt all the less since reading that a new ninth planet has been glimpsed beyond Neptune, just as those influences had said it would be glimpsed. Astronomers, with a hideous appropriateness they little suspect, have named this thing "Pluto." I feel, beyond question, that it is nothing less than nighted Yuggoth — and I shiver when I try to figure out the real reason why its monstrous denizens wish it to be known in this way at this especial time. I vainly try to assure myself that these daemoniac creatures are not gradually leading up to some new policy hurtful to the earth and its normal inhabitants.

But I have still to tell of the ending of that terrible night in the farmhouse. As I have said, I did finally drop into a troubled doze; a doze filled with bits of dream which involved monstrous landscape-glimpses. Just what awaked me I cannot yet say, but that I did indeed awake at this given point I feel very certain. My first confused impression was of stealthily creaking floor-boards in the hall outside my door, and of a clumsy, muffled fumbling at the latch. This, however, ceased almost at once; so that my really clear impressions begin with the voices heard from the study below. There seemed to be several speakers, and I judged that they were controversially engaged.

By the time I had listened a few seconds I was broad awake, for the nature of the voices was such as to make all thought of sleep ridiculous. The tones were curiously varied, and no one who had listened to that accursed phonograph record could harbour any doubts about the nature of at least two of them. Hideous though the idea was, I knew that I was under the same roof with nameless things from abysmal space; for those two voices were unmistakably the blasphemous buzzings which the Outside Beings used in their communication with men. The two were individually different — different in pitch, accent, and tempo — but they were both of the same damnable general kind.

A third voice was indubitably that of a mechanical utterance-machine connected with one of the detached brains in the cylinders. There was as little doubt about that as about the buzzings; for the loud, metallic, lifeless voice of the previous evening, with its inflectionless, expressionless scraping and rattling, and its impersonal precision and deliberation, had been utterly unforgettable. For a time I did not pause to question whether the intelligence behind the scraping was the identical one which had formerly talked to me; but shortly afterward I reflected that any brain would emit vocal sounds of the same quality if linked to the same mechanical speech-producer; the only possible differences being in language, rhythm, speed, and pronunciation. To complete the eldritch colloquy there were two actually human voices — one the crude speech of an unknown and evidently rustic man, and the other the suave Bostonian tones of my erstwhile guide Noyes.

As I tried to catch the words which the stoutly-fashioned floor so bafflingly intercepted, I was also conscious of a great deal of stirring and scratching and shuffling in the room below; so that I could not escape the impression that it was full of living beings — many more than the few whose speech I could single out. The exact nature of this stirring is extremely hard to describe, for very few good bases of comparison exist. Objects seemed now and then to move across the room like conscious entities; the sound of their footfalls having something about it like a loose, hard-surfaced clattering — as of the contact of ill-coordinated surfaces of horn or hard rubber. It was, to use a more concrete but less accurate comparison, as if people with loose, splintery wooden shoes were shambling and rattling about on the polished board floor. Of the nature and appearance of those responsible for the sounds, I did not care to speculate.

Before long I saw that it would be impossible to distinguish any connected discourse. Isolated words — including the names of Akeley and myself — now and then floated up, especially when uttered by the mechanical speech-producer; but their true significance was lost for want of continuous context. Today I refuse to form any definite deductions from them, and even their frightful effect on me was one of suggestion rather than of revelation. A terrible and abnormal conclave, I felt certain, was assembled below me; but for what shocking deliberations I could not tell. It was curious how this unquestioned sense of the malign and the blasphemous pervaded me despite Akeley's assurances of the Outsider's friendliness.

With patient listening I began to distinguish clearly between voices, even though I could not grasp much of what any of the voices said. I seemed to catch certain typical emotions behind some of the speakers. One of the buzzing voices, for example, held an unmistakable note of authority; whilst the mechanical voice, notwithstanding its artificial loudness and regularity, seemed to be in a position of subordination and pleading. Noyes's tones exuded a kind of conciliatory atmosphere. The others I could make no attempt to interpret. I did not hear the familiar whisper of Akeley, but well knew that such a sound could never penetrate the solid flooring of my room.

I will try to set down some of the few disjointed words and other sounds I caught, labelling the speakers of the words as best I know how. It was from the speech-machine that I first picked up a few recognisable phrases.

THE SPEECH-MACHINE: . . . brought it on myself . . . sent back the letters and the record . . . end on it . . . taken in . . . seeing and hearing . . . damn you . . . impersonal force, after all . . . fresh, shiny cylinder . . . great God . . .

FIRST BUZZING VOICE: . . . time we stopped . . . small and human . . . Akeley . . . brain . . . saying . . .

SECOND BUZZING VOICE: Nyarlathotep . . . Wilmarth . . . records and letters . . . cheap imposture . . .

NOYES: . . . (an unpronounceable word or name, possibly N'gah-Kthun) harmless . . . peace . . . couple of weeks . . . theatrical . . . told you that before . . .

FIRST BUZZING VOICE: . . . no reason . . . original plan . . . effects . . . Noyes can watch Round Hill . . . fresh cylinder . . . Noyes's car . . .

NOYES: . . . well . . . all yours . . . down here . . . rest . . . place . . .

(Several Voices at Once in Indistinguishable Speech)

(Many Footsteps, Including the Peculiar Loose Stirring or Clattering)

(A Curious Sort of Flapping Sound)

(The Sound of an Automobile Starting and Receding)

(Silence)

That is the substance of what my ears brought me as I lay rigid upon that strange upstairs bed in the haunted farmhouse among the daemoniac hills — lay there fully dressed, with a revolver clenched in my right hand and a pocket flashlight gripped in my left. I became, as I have said, broad awake; but a kind of obscure paralysis nevertheless kept me inert till long after the last echoes of the sounds had died away. I heard the wooden, deliberate ticking of the ancient Connecticut clock somewhere far below, and at last made out the irregular snoring of a sleeper. Akeley must have dozed off after the strange session, and I could well believe that he needed to do so.

Just what to think or what to do was more than I could decide After all, what had I heard beyond things which previous information might have led me to expect? Had I not known that the nameless Outsiders were now freely admitted to the farmhouse? No doubt Akeley had been surprised by an unexpected visit from them. Yet something in that fragmentary discourse had chilled me immeasurably, raised the most grotesque and horrible doubts, and made me wish fervently that I might wake up and prove everything a dream. I think my subconscious mind must have caught something which my consciousness has not yet recognised. But what of Akeley? Was he not my friend, and would he not have protested if any harm were meant me? The peaceful snoring below seemed to cast ridicule on all my suddenly intensified fears.

Was it possible that Akeley had been imposed upon and used as a lure to draw me into the hills with the letters and pictures and phonograph record? Did those beings mean to engulf us both in a common destruction because we had come to know too much? Again I thought of the abruptness and unnaturalness of that change in the situation which must have occurred between Akeley's penultimate and final letters. Something, my instinct told me, was terribly wrong. All was not as it seemed. That acrid coffee which I refused — had there not been an attempt by some hidden, unknown entity to drug it? I must talk to Akeley at once, and restore his sense of proportion. They had hypnotised him with their promises of cosmic revelations, but now he must listen to reason. We must get out of this before it would be too late. If he lacked the will power to make the break for liberty, I would supply it. Or if I could not persuade him to go, I could at least go myself. Surely he would let me take his Ford and leave it in a garage in Brattleboro. I had noticed it in the shed — the door being left unlocked and open now that peril was deemed past — and I believed there was a good chance of its being ready for instant use. That momentary dislike of Akeley which I had felt during and after the evening's conversation was all gone now. He was in a position much like my own, and we must stick together. Knowing his indisposed condition, I hated to wake him at this juncture, but I knew that I must. I could not stay in this place till morning as matters stood.

At last I felt able to act, and stretched myself vigorously to regain command of my muscles. Arising with a caution more impulsive than deliberate, I found and donned my hat, took my valise, and started downstairs with the flashlight's aid. In my nervousness I kept the revolver clutched in my right hand, being able to take care of both valise and flashlight with my left. Why I exerted these precautions I do not really know, since I was even then on my way to awaken the only other occupant of the house.

As I half-tiptoed down the creaking stairs to the lower hall I could hear the sleeper more plainly, and noticed that he must be in the room on my left — the living-room I had not entered. On my right was the gaping blackness of the study in which I had heard the voices. Pushing open the unlatched door of the living-room I traced a path with the flashlight toward the source of the snoring, and finally turned the beams on the sleeper's face. But in the next second I hastily turned them away and commenced a catlike retreat to the hall, my caution this time springing from reason as well as from instinct. For the sleeper on the couch was not Akeley at all, but my quondam guide Noyes.

Just what the real situation was, I could not guess; but common sense told me that the safest thing was to find out as much as possible before arousing anybody. Regaining the hall, I silently closed and latched the living-room door after me; thereby lessening the chances of awakening Noyes. I now cautiously entered the dark study, where I expected to find Akeley, whether asleep or awake, in the great corner chair which was evidently his favorite resting-place. As I advanced, the beams of my flashlight caught the great centre-table, revealing one of the hellish cylinders with sight and hearing machines attached, and with a speech machine standing close by, ready to be connected at any moment. This, I reflected, must be the encased brain I had heard talking during the frightful conference; and for a second I had a perverse impulse to attach the speech machine and see what it would say.

It must, I thought, be conscious of my presence even now; since the sight and hearing attachments could not fail to disclose the rays of my flashlight and the faint creaking of the floor beneath my feet. But in the end I did not dare meddle with the thing. I idly saw that it was the fresh shiny cylinder with Akeley's name on it, which I had noticed on the shelf earlier in the evening and which my host had told me not to bother. Looking back at that moment, I can only regret my timidity and wish that I had boldly caused the apparatus to speak. God knows what mysteries and horrible doubts and questions of identity it might have cleared up! But then, it may be merciful that I let it alone.

From the table I turned my flashlight to the corner where I thought Akeley was, but found to my perplexity that the great easy-chair was empty of any human occupant asleep or awake. From the seat to the floor there trailed voluminously the familiar old dressing-gown, and near it on the floor lay the yellow scarf and the huge foot-bandages I had thought so odd. As I hesitated, striving to conjecture where Akeley might be, and why he had so suddenly discarded his necessary sick-room garments, I observed that the queer odour and sense of vibration were no longer in the room. What had been their cause? Curiously it occurred to me that I had noticed them only in Akeley's vicinity. They had been strongest where he sat, and wholly absent except in the room with him or just outside the doors of that room. I paused, letting the flashlight wander about the dark study and racking my brain for explanations of the turn affairs had taken.

Would to Heaven I had quietly left the place before allowing that light to rest again on the vacant chair. As it turned out, I did not leave quietly; but with a muffled shriek which must have disturbed, though it did not quite awake, the sleeping sentinel across the hall. That shriek, and Noyes's still-unbroken snore, are the last sounds I ever heard in that morbidity-choked farmhouse beneath the black-wooded crest of haunted mountain — that focus of transcosmic horror amidst the lonely green hills and curse-muttering brooks of a spectral rustic land.

It is a wonder that I did not drop flashlight, valise, and revolver in my wild scramble, but somehow I failed to lose any of these. I actually managed to get out of that room and that house without making any further noise, to drag myself and my belongings safely into the old Ford in the shed, and to set that archaic vehicle in motion toward some unknown point of safety in the black, moonless night. The ride that followed was a piece of delirium out of Poe or Rimbaud or the drawings of Dore, but finally I reached Townshend. That is all. If my sanity is still unshaken, I am lucky. Sometimes I fear what the years will bring, especially since that new planet Pluto has been so curiously discovered.

As I have implied, I let my flashlight return to the vacant easy-chair after its circuit of the room; then noticing for the first time the presence of certain objects in the seat, made inconspicuous by the adjacent loose folds of the empty dressing-gown. These are the objects, three in number, which the investigators did not find when they came later on. As I said at the outset, there was nothing of actual visual horror about them. The trouble was in what they led one to infer. Even now I have my moments of half-doubt — moments in which I half-accept the scepticism of those who attribute my whole experience to dream and nerves and delusion.

The three things were damnably clever constructions of their kind, and were furnished with ingenious metallic clamps to attach them to organic developments of which I dare not form any conjecture. I hope — devoutly hope — that they were the waxen products of a master artist, despite what my inmost fears tell me. Great God! That whisperer in darkness with its morbid odour and vibrations! Sorcerer, emissary, changeling, outsider . . . that hideous repressed buzzing . . . and all the time in that fresh, shiny cylinder on the shelf . . . poor devil . . . "Prodigious surgical, biological, chemical, and mechanical skill . . ."

For the things in the chair, perfect to the last, subtle detail of microscopic resemblance — or identity — were the face and hands of Henry Wentworth Akeley.

Medusa's Coil.

BY ZEALIA BISHOP AND H.P. LOVECRAFT

17,000-WORD NOVELETTE; 1930.

Fresh from The Mound, *one of the best of Lovecraft's revision works, we now turn to what is widely regarded as one of his worst — or, at least, one of his most drastically flawed. "Medusa's Coil," although for the most part well-built and written with a fine atmosphere of eldritch horror, is so deeply flawed in one or two spots that it's hard not to at least wonder a little if it wasn't deliberate sabotage.*

The first thing about "Medusa's Coil" that must be acknowledged is the racism. It is unquestionably the most racist story in Lovecraft's canon. Part of that is intrinsic to the setting — an old Antebellum-South-style plantation in southern Missouri, complete with little colony of slave cabins populated with happy, banjo-picking black people who talk like Mammie in Gone with the Wind. *There are also a number of highly offensive racial slurs.*

In general, "Medusa's Coil" feels unfinished, like it's a second draft of a story with great potential but which doesn't really work yet. A couple of the plot developments, if looked at too closely, completely break the story's plausibility; and the final plot twist, apparently intended to supply the story's final crowning horror, will cause most modern readers to burst out in derisive laughter.

That said, it is a compelling story, and can be read with enjoyment if one is prepared to hold one's nose occasionally while doing so.

This story seems to have been more of Zealia Bishop's own work than was the case with The Mound. *Lovecraft's notes refer to the "original story" in several particulars, including the notorious final plot twist. However, her notes don't survive, and we can only speculate as to how much of this story must be charged against Lovecraft's reputation and how much to his client's.*

It is worth mentioning, though, that by the time Lovecraft had finished this story for Bishop — the last of his revisions for her — she owed him a fair amount of money. The knowledge that he was not very likely to ever see payment for the work he was doing may have had an impact, either consciously or subconsciously, with the quality of Lovecraft's contribution to this story.

He wrote it in mid-1930 during his summer travels, during the same time in which he was working on The Whisperer in Darkness; *but it was not published until several years later, in the January 1939 issue of* Weird Tales.

I.

The drive toward Cape Girardeau had been through unfamiliar country; and as the late afternoon light grew golden and half-dreamlike I realized that I must have directions if I expected to reach the town before night. I did not care to be wandering about these bleak southern Missouri lowlands after dark, for roads were poor and the November cold rather formidable in an open roadster. Black clouds, too, were massing on the horizon; so I looked about among the long grey and blue shadows that streaked the flat, brownish fields, hoping to glimpse some house where I might get the needed information.

It was a lonely and deserted country, but at last I spied a roof among a clump of trees near the small river on my right; perhaps a full half-mile from the road, and probably reachable by some path or drive which I would presently come upon. In the absence of any nearer dwelling, I resolved to try my luck there; and was glad when the bushes by the roadside revealed the ruin of a carved stone gateway, covered with dry, dead vines and choked with undergrowth which explained why I had not been able to trace the path across the fields in my first distant view. I saw that I could not drive the car in, so I parked it very carefully near the gate — where a thick evergreen would shield it in case of rain — and got out for the long walk to the house.

Traversing that brush-grown path in the gathering twilight I was conscious of a distinct sense of foreboding, probably induced by the air of sinister decay hovering about the gate and the former driveway. From the carvings on the old stone pillars I inferred that this place was once an estate of manorial dignity; and I could clearly see that the driveway had originally boasted guardian lines of linden trees, some of which had died, while others had lost their special identity among the wild scrub growths of the region.

As I ploughed onward, cockleburs and stickers clung to my clothes, and I began to wonder whether the place could be inhabited after all. Was I tramping on a vain errand? For a moment I was tempted to go back and try some farm farther along the road, when a view of the house ahead aroused my curiosity and stimulated my venturesome spirit.

There was something provocatively fascinating in the tree-girt, decrepit pile before me, for it spoke of the graces and spaciousness of a bygone era and a far more southerly environment. It was a typical wooden plantation house of the classic, early nineteenth-century pattern, with two and a half

Weird Tales, January 1939

stories and a great Ionic portico whose pillars reached up as far as the attic and supported a triangular pediment. Its state of decay was extreme and obvious; one of the vast columns having rotted and fallen to the ground, while the upper piazza or balcony had sagged dangerously low. Other buildings, I judged, had formerly stood near it.

As I mounted the broad stone steps to the low porch and the carved and fanlighted doorway I felt distinctly nervous, and started to light a cigarette — desisting when I saw how dry and inflammable everything about me was. Though now convinced that the house was deserted, I nevertheless hesitated to violate its dignity without knocking; so tugged at the rusty iron knocker until I could get it to move, and finally set up a cautious rapping which seemed to make the whole place shake and rattle. There was no response, yet once more I plied the cumbrous, creaking device — as much to dispel the sense of unholy silence and solitude as to arouse any possible occupant of the ruin.

Somewhere near the river I heard the mournful note of a dove, and it seemed as if the coursing water itself were faintly audible. Half in a dream, I seized and rattled the ancient latch, and finally gave the great six-panelled door a frank trying. It was unlocked, as I could see in a moment; and though it stuck and grated on its hinges I began to push it open, stepping through it into a vast shadowy hall as I did so.

But the moment I took this step I regretted it. It was not that a legion of spectres confronted me in that dim and dusty hall with the ghostly Empire furniture; but that I knew all at once that the place was not deserted at all. There was a creaking on the great curved staircase, and the sound of faltering footsteps slowly descending. Then I saw a tall, bent figure silhouetted for an instant against the great Palladian window on the landing.

My first start of terror was soon over, and as the figure descended the final flight I was ready to greet the householder whose privacy I had invaded. In the semi-darkness I could see him reach in his pocket for a match. There came a flare as he lighted a small kerosene lamp which stood on a rickety console table near the foot of the stairs. In the feeble glow was revealed the stooping figure of a very tall, emaciated old man; disordered as to dress and unshaved as to face, yet for all that with the bearing and expression of a gentleman.

I did not wait for him to speak, but at once began to explain my presence.

"You'll pardon my coming in like this, but when my knocking didn't raise anybody I concluded that no one lived here. What I wanted originally was to know the right road to Cape Girardeau — the shortest road, that is. I wanted to get there before dark, but now, of course — "

As I paused, the man spoke, in exactly the cultivated tone I had expected, and with a mellow accent as unmistakably Southern as the house he inhabited.

"Rather, you must pardon me for not answering your knock more promptly. I live in a very retired way, and am not usually expecting visitors. At first I thought you were a mere curiosity-seeker. Then when you knocked again I started to answer, but I am not well and have to move very slowly. Spinal neuritis — very troublesome case.

"But as for your getting to town before dark — it's plain you can't do that. The road you are on — for I suppose you came from the gate — isn't the best or shortest way. What you must do is to take your first left after you leave the gate — that is, the first real road to your left. There are three or four cart paths you can ignore, but you can't mistake the real road because of the extra large willow tree on the right just opposite it. Then when you've turned, keep on past two roads and turn to the right along the third. After that — "

"Please wait a moment! How can I follow all these clues in pitch darkness, without ever having been near here before, and with only an indifferent pair of headlights to tell me what is and what isn't a road? Besides, I think it's going to storm pretty soon, and my car is an open one. It looks as if I were in a bad fix if I want to get to Cape Girardeau tonight. The fact is, I don't think I'd better try to make it. I don't like to impose burdens, or anything like that — but in view of the circumstances, do you suppose you could put me up for the night? I won't be any trouble — no meals or anything. Just let me have a corner to sleep in till daylight, and I'm all right. I can leave the car in the road where it is — a bit of wet weather won't hurt it if worst comes to worst."

As I made my sudden request I could see the old man's face lose its former expression of quiet resignation and take on an odd, surprised look.

"Sleep — here?"

He seemed so astonished at my request that I repeated it.

"Yes, why not? I assure you I won't be any trouble. What else can I do? I'm a stranger hereabouts, these roads are a labyrinth in the dark, and I'll wager it'll be raining torrents outside of an hour — "

This time it was my host's turn to interrupt, and as he did so I could feel a peculiar quality in his deep, musical voice.

"A stranger — of course you must be, else you wouldn't think of sleeping here, wouldn't think of coming here at all. People don't come here nowadays."

He paused, and my desire to stay was increased a thousandfold by the sense of mystery his laconic words seemed to evoke. There was surely something alluringly queer about this place, and the pervasive musty smell seemed to cloak a thousand secrets. Again I noticed the extreme decrepitude of everything about me, manifest even in the feeble rays of the single small lamp. I felt woefully chilly, and saw with regret that no heating was provided, and yet so great was my curiosity that I still wished most ardently to stay and learn something of the recluse and his dismal abode.

"Let that be as it may," I replied. "I can't help about other people. But I surely would like to have a spot to stop till daylight. Still — if people don't relish this place, mayn't it be because it's getting so run-down? Of course I suppose it would take a fortune to keep such an estate up, but if the burden's too great why don't you look for smaller quarters? Why try to stick it out here in this way — with all the hardships and discomforts?"

The man did not seem offended, but answered me very gravely.

"Surely you may stay if you really wish to — you can come to no harm that I know of. But others claim there are certain peculiarly undesirable influences here. As for me — I stay here because I have to. There is something I feel it a duty to guard — something that holds me. I wish I had the money and health and ambition to take decent care of the house and grounds."

With my curiosity still more heightened, I prepared to take my host at his word; and followed him slowly upstairs when he motioned me to do so. It was very dark now, and a faint pattering outside told me that the threatened rain had come. I would have been glad of any shelter, but this was doubly welcome because of the hints of mystery about the place and its master. For an incurable lover of the grotesque, no more fitting haven could have been provided.

II.

There was a second-floor corner room in less unkempt shape than the rest of the house, and into this my host led me, setting down his small lamp and lighting a somewhat larger one. From the cleanliness and contents of the room, and from the books ranged along the walls, I could see that I had not guessed amiss in thinking the man a gentleman of taste and breeding. He was a hermit and eccentric, no doubt, but he still had standards and intellectual interests. As he waved me to a seat I began a conversation on general topics, and was pleased to find him not at all taciturn. If anything, he seemed glad of someone with whom to talk, and did not even attempt to swerve the discussion from personal topics.

He was, I learned, one Antoine de Russy, of an ancient, powerful, and cultivated line of Louisiana planters. More than a century ago his grandfather, a younger son, had migrated to southern Missouri and founded a new estate in the lavish ancestral manner, building this pillared mansion and surrounding it with all the accessories of a great plantation. There had been, at one time, as many as 200 negroes in the cabins which stood on the flat ground in the rear — ground that the river had now invaded — and to hear them singing and laughing and playing the banjo at night was to know the fullest charm of a civilization and social order now sadly extinct. In front of the house, where the great guardian oaks and willows stood, there had been a lawn like a broad green carpet, always watered and trimmed and with flagstoned, flower-bordered walks curving through it. "Riverside" — for such the place was called — had been a lovely and idyllic homestead in its day; and my host could recall it when many traces of its best period were not yet gone.

It was raining hard now, with dense sheets of water beating against the insecure roof, walls, and windows, and sending in drops through a thousand chinks and crevices. Moisture trickled down to the floor from unsuspected places, and the mounting wind rattled the rotting, loose-hinged shutters outside. But I minded none of this, for I saw that a story was coming. Incited to reminiscence, my host made a move to shew me to sleeping-quarters; but kept on recalling the older, better days. Soon, I saw, I would receive an inkling of why he lived alone in that ancient place, and why his neighbours thought it full of undesirable influences. His voice was very musical as he spoke on, and his tale soon took a turn which left me no chance to grow drowsy.

"Yes — Riverside was built in 1816, and my father was born in 1828. He'd be over a century old now if he were alive, but he died young — so young I can just barely remember him. In '64 that was — he was killed in the war, Seventh Louisiana Infantry C.S.A., for he went back to the old home to enlist. My grandfather was too old to fight, yet he lived on to be ninety-five, and helped my mother bring me up. A good bringing-up, too — I'll give them credit. We always had strong traditions — high notions of honour — and my grandfather saw to it that I grew up the way de Russys have grown up, generation after generation, ever since the Crusades. We weren't quite wiped out financially, but managed to get on very comfortable after the war. I went to a good school in Louisiana, and later to Princeton. Later on I was able to get the plantation on a fairly profitable basis — though you see what it's come to now.

"My mother died when I was twenty, and my grandfather two years later. It was rather lonely after that; and in '85 I married a distant cousin in New Orleans. Things might have been different if she'd lived, but she died when my son Denis was born. Then I had only Denis. I didn't try marriage again, but gave all my time to the boy. He was like me — like all the de Russys — darkish and tall and thin, and with the devil of a temper. I gave him the same training my grandfather had given me, but he didn't need much training when it came to points of honour. It was in him, I reckon. Never saw such high spirit — all I could do to keep him from running away to the Spanish War when he was eleven! Romantic young devil, too — full of high notions — you'd call 'em Victorian, now — no trouble at all to make him let the nigger wenches alone. I sent him to the same school I'd gone to, and to Princeton, too. He was Class of 1909.

"In the end he decided to be a doctor, and went a year to the Harvard Medical School. Then he hit on the idea of keeping to the old French tradition of the family, and argued me into sending him across to the Sorbonne. I did — and proudly enough, though I knew how lonely I'd be with him so far off. Would to God I hadn't! I thought he was the safest kind of boy to be in Paris. He had a room in the Rue St. Jacques — that's near the University in the 'Latin Quarter' — but according to his letters and his friends he didn't cut up with the gayer dogs at all. The people he knew were mostly young fellows from home — serious students and artists who thought more of their work than of striking attitudes and painting the town red.

"But of course there were lots of fellows who were on a sort of dividing line between serious studies and the devil. The aesthetes — the decadents, you know. Experiments in life and sensation — the Baudelaire kind of a chap. Naturally Denis ran up against a good many of these, and saw a good deal of their life. They had all sorts of crazy circles and cults — imitation devil-worship, fake Black Masses, and the like. Doubt if it did them much harm on the whole — probably most of'em forgot all about it in a year or two. One of the deepest in this queer stuff was a fellow Denis had known at school — for that matter, whose father I'd known myself. Frank Marsh, of New Orleans. Disciple of Lafcadio Hearn and Gauguin and Van Gogh — regular epitome of the yellow 'nineties. Poor devil — he had the makings of a great artist, at that.

"Marsh was the oldest friend Denis had in Paris, so as a matter of course they saw a good deal of each other — to talk over old times at St. Clair academy, and all that. The boy wrote me a good deal about him, and I didn't see any especial harm when he spoke of the group of mystics Marsh ran with. It seems there was some cult of prehistoric Egyptian and Carthaginian magic having a rage among the Bohemian element on the left bank — some nonsensical thing that pretended to reach back to forgotten sources of hidden truth in lost African civilisations — the great Zimbabwe, the dead Atlantean cities in the Haggar region of the Sahara — and they had a lot of gibberish concerned with snakes and human hair. At least, I called it gibberish, then. Denis used to quote Marsh as saying odd things about the veiled facts behind the legend of Medusa's snaky locks — and behind the later Ptolemaic myth of Berenice, who offered up her hair to save her husband-brother, and had it set in the sky as the constellation Coma Berenices.

"I don't think this business made much impression on Denis until the night of the queer ritual at Marsh's rooms when he met the priestess. Most of the devotees of the cult were young fellows, but the head of it was a young woman who called herself 'Tanit-Isis' — letting it be known that her real name — her name in this latest incarnation, as she put it — was Marceline Bedard. She claimed to be the left-handed daughter of Marquis de Chameaux, and seemed to have been both a petty artist and an artist's model before adopting this more lucrative magical game. Someone said she had lived for a time in the West Indies — Martinique, I think — but she was very reticent about herself. Part of her pose was a great show of austerity and holiness, but I don't think the more experienced students took that very seriously.

"Denis, though, was far from experienced, and wrote me fully ten pages of slush about the goddess he had discovered. If I'd only realised his simplicity I might have done something, but I never thought a puppy infatuation like that could mean much. I felt absurdly sure that Denis' touchy personal honour and family pride would always keep him out of the most serious complications.

"As time went, though, his letters began to make me nervous. He mentioned this Marceline more and more, and his friends less and less, and began talking about the 'cruel and silly way' they declined to introduce her to their mothers and sisters. He seems to have asked her no questions about herself, and I don't doubt but that she filled him full of romantic legendry concerning her origin and divine revelations and the way people slighted her. At length I could see that Denis was altogether cutting his own crowd and spending the bulk of his time with his alluring priestess. At her especial request he never told the old crowd of their continual meetings; so nobody over there tried to break the affair up.

"I suppose she thought he was fabulously rich; for he had the air of a patrician, and people of a certain class think all aristocratic Americans are wealthy. In any case, she probably thought this a rare chance to contract a genuine right-handed alliance with a really eligible young man. By the time my nervousness burst into open advice, it was too late. The boy had lawfully married her, and wrote that he was dropping his studies and bringing the woman home to Riverside. He said she had made a great sacrifice and resigned her leadership of the magical cult, and that henceforward she would be merely a private gentlewoman — the future mistress of Riverside, and mother of de Russys to come.

"Well, sir, I took it the best way I could. I knew that sophisticated Continentals have different standards from our old American ones — and anyway, I really knew nothing against the woman. A charlatan, perhaps, but why necessarily any worse? I suppose I tried to keep as naïve as possible about such things in those days, for the boy's sake. Clearly, there was nothing for a man of sense to do but let Denis alone so long as his new wife conformed to de Russy ways. Let her have a chance to prove herself — perhaps she wouldn't hurt the family as much as some might fear. So I didn't raise any objections or ask any penitence. The thing was done, and I stood ready to welcome the boy back, whatever he brought with him.

"They got here three weeks after the telegram telling of marriage. Marceline was beautiful — there was no denying that — and I could see how the boy might very well get foolish about her. She did have an air of breeding, and I think to this day she must have had some strains of good blood in her. She was apparently not much over twenty; of medium size, fairly slim, and as graceful as a tigress in posture and motion. Her complexion was a deep olive — like old ivory — and her eyes were large and very dark. She had small, classically regular features — though not quite clean-cut enough to suit my taste — and the most singular braid of jet black hair that I ever saw.

"I didn't wonder that she had dragged the subject of hair into her magical cult, for with that heavy profusion of it the idea must have occurred to her naturally. Coiled up, it made her look like some Oriental princess in a drawing of Aubrey Beardsley's. Hanging down her back, it came well below her knees and shone in the light as if it had possessed some separate, unholy vitality of its own. I would almost have thought of Medusa or Berenice myself — without having such things suggested to me — upon seeing and studying that hair.

"Sometimes I thought it moved slightly of itself, and tended to arrange itself in distinct ropes or strands, but this may have been sheer illusion. She braided it incessantly, and seemed to use some sort of preparation on it. I got the notion once — a curious, whimsical notion — that it was a living being which she had to feed in some strange way. All nonsense — but it added to my feeling of constraint about her and her hair.

"For I can't deny that I failed to like her wholly, no matter how hard I tried. I couldn't tell what the trouble was, but it was there. Something about her repelled me very subtly, and I could not help weaving morbid and macabre associations about everything connected with her. Her complexion called up thoughts of Babylon, Atlantis, Lemuria, and the terrible forgotten dominations of an elder world; her eyes struck me sometimes as the eyes of some unholy forest creature or animal goddess too immeasurably ancient to be fully human; and her hair — that dense, exotic, overnourished growth of oily inkiness — made one shiver as a great black python might have done. There was no doubt but that she realised my involuntary attitude — though I tried to hide it, and she tried to hide the fact that she noticed it.

"Yet the boy's infatuation lasted. He positively fawned on her, and overdid all the little gallantries of daily life to a sickening degree. She appeared to return the feeling, though I could see it took a conscious effort to make her duplicate his enthusiasms and extravagances. For one thing, I think she was piqued to learn we weren't as wealthy as she had expected.

"It was a bad business all told. I could see that sad undercurrents were arising. Denis was half-hypnotised with puppy-love, and began to grow away from me as he felt my shrinking from his wife. This kind of thing went on for months, and I saw that I was losing my only son — the boy who had formed the centre of all my thoughts and acts for the past quarter century. I'll own that I felt bitter about it — what father wouldn't? And yet I could do nothing.

"Marceline seemed to be a good wife enough in those early months, and our friends received her without any quibbling or questioning. I was always nervous, though, about what some of the young fellows in Paris might write home to their relatives after the news of the marriage spread around. Despite the woman's love of secrecy, it couldn't remain hidden forever — indeed, Denis had written a few of his closest friends, in strict confidence, as soon as he was settled with her at Riverside.

"I got to staying alone in my room more and more, with my failing health as an excuse. It was about that time that my present spinal neuritis began to develop — which made the excuse a pretty good one. Denis didn't seem to notice the trouble, or take any interest in me and my habits and affairs; and it hurt me to see how callous he was getting. I began to get sleepless, and often racked my brain in the night to try to find out what made my new daughter-in-law so repulsive and even dimly horrible to me. It surely wasn't her old mystical nonsense, for she had left all the past behind her and never mentioned it once. She didn't even do any painting, although I understood that she had once dabbled in art.

"Oddly, the only ones who seemed to share my uneasiness were the servants. The darkies around the house seemed very sullen in their attitude toward her, and in a few weeks all save the few who were strongly attached to our family had left. These few — old Scipio and his wife Sarah, the cook Delilah, and Mary, Scipio's daughter — were as civil as possible; but plainly revealed that their new mistress commanded their duty rather than their affection. They stayed in their own remote part of the house as much as possible. McCabe, our white chauffeur, was insolently admiring rather than hostile; and another exception was a very old Zulu woman, said to have been a sort of leader in her small cabin as a kind of family pensioner. Old Sophonisba always shewed reverence whenever Marceline came near her, and one time I saw her kiss the ground where her mistress had walked. Blacks are superstitious animals, and I wondered whether Marceline had been talking any of her mystical nonsense to our hands in order to overcome their evident dislike."

III.

"Well, that's how we went on for nearly half a year. Then, in the summer of 1916, things began to happen. Toward the middle of June Denis got a note from his old friend Frank Marsh, telling of a sort of nervous breakdown which made him want to take a rest in the country. It was postmarked New Orleans — for Marsh had gone home from Paris when he felt the collapse coming on — and seemed a very plain though polite bid for an invitation from us. Marsh, of course, knew that Marceline was here; and asked very courteously after her. Denis was sorry to hear of his trouble and told him at once to come along for an indefinite visit.

"Marsh came — and I was shocked to notice how he had changed since I had seen him in his earlier days. He was a smallish, lightish fellow, with blue eyes and an undecided chin; and now I could see the effects of drink and I don't know what else in his puffy eyelids, enlarged nose-pores, and heavy lines around the mouth. I reckon he had taken his dose of decadence pretty seriously, and set out to be as much of a Rimbaud, Baudelaire, or Lautreamont as he could. And yet he was delightful to talk to — for like all decadents he was exquisitely sensitive to the colour and atmosphere and names of things; admirably, thoroughly alive, and with whole records of conscious experience in obscure, shadowy fields of living and feeling which most of us pass over without knowing they exist. Poor young devil — if only his father had lived longer and taken him in hand! There was great stuff in the boy!

"I was glad of the visit, for I felt it would help to set up a normal atmosphere in the house again. And that's what it really seemed to do at first; for as I said, Marsh was a delight to have around. He was as sincere and profound an artist as I ever saw in my life, and I certainly believe that nothing on earth mattered to him except the perception and expression of beauty. When he saw an exquisite thing, or was creating one, his eyes would dilate until the light irises were nearly out of sight — leaving two mystical black pits in that weak, delicate, chalk-like face; black pits opening on strange worlds which none of us could guess about.

"When he reached here, though, he didn't have many chances to shew this tendency; for he had, as he told Denis, gone quite stale. It seems he had been very successful as an artist of a bizarre kind — like Fuseli or Goya or Sime or Clark Ashton Smith — but had suddenly become played out. The world of ordinary things around him had ceased to hold anything he could recognize as beauty — beauty, that is, of enough force and poignancy to arouse his creative faculty. He had often been this way before — all decadents are — but this time he could not invent any new, strange, or outré sensation or experience which would supply the needed illusion of fresh beauty or stimulatingly adventurous expectancy. He was like a Durtal or a des Esseintes at the most jaded point of his curious orbit.

"Marceline was away when Marsh arrived. She hadn't been enthusiastic about his coming, and had refused to decline an invitation from some of our friends in St. Louis which came about that time for her and Denis. Denis, of course, stayed to receive his guest; but Marceline had gone on alone. It was the first time they had ever been separated, and I hoped the interval would help to dispel the daze that was making such a fool of the boy. Marceline shewed no hurry to get back, but seemed to me to prolong her absence as much as she could. Denis stood it better than one would have expected from such a doting husband, and seemed more like his old self as he talked over other days with Marsh and tried to cheer the listless aesthete up.

"It was Marsh who seemed most impatient to see the woman; perhaps because he thought her strange beauty, or some phase of the mysticism which had gone into her one-time magical cult, might help to reawaken his interest in things and give him another start toward artistic creation. That there was no baser reason, I was absolutely certain from what I knew of Marsh's character. With all his weaknesses, he was a gentleman — and it had indeed relieved me when I first learned that he wanted to come here because his willingness to accept Denis' hospitality proved that there was no reason why he shouldn't.

"When, at last, Marceline did return, I could see that Marsh was tremendously affected. He did not attempt to make her talk of the bizarre thing which she had so definitely abandoned, but was unable to hide a powerful admiration which kept his eyes — now dilated in that curious way for the first time during his visit — riveted to her every moment she was in the room. She, however, seemed uneasy rather than pleased by his steady scrutiny — that is, she seemed so at first, though this feeling of hers wore away in a few days, and left the two on a basis of the most cordial and voluble congeniality. I could see Marsh studying her constantly when he thought no one was watching; and I wondered how long it would be that only the artist, and not the primitive man, would be aroused by her mysterious graces.

"Denis naturally felt some irritation at this turn of affairs; though he realised that his guest was a man of honour and that, as kindred mystics and aesthetes, Marceline and Marsh would naturally have things and interests to discuss in which a more or less conventional person could have no part. He didn't hold anything against anybody, but merely regretted that his own imagination was too limited and traditional to let him talk with Marceline as Marsh talked. At this stage of things I began to see more of the boy. With his wife otherwise busy, he had time to remember that he had a father — and a father who was ready to help him in any sort of perplexity or difficulty.

"We often sat together on the veranda watching Marsh and Marceline as they rode up or down the drive on horseback, or played tennis on the court that used to stretch south of the house. They talked mostly in French, which Marsh, though he hadn't more than a quarter-portion of French blood, handled more glibly than either Denis or I could speak it. Marceline's English, always academically correct, was rapidly improving in accent; but it was plain that she relished dropping back into her mother-tongue. As we looked at the congenial couple they made, I could see the boy's cheek and throat muscles tighten — though he wasn't a whit less ideal a host to Marsh, or a whit less considerate husband to Marceline.

"All this was generally in the afternoon; for Marceline rose very late, had breakfast in bed, and took an immense amount of time preparing to come downstairs. I never knew of anyone so wrapped up in cosmetics, beauty exercises, hair-oils, unguents, and everything of that kind. It was in these morning hours that Denis and Marsh did their real visiting, and exchanged the close confidences which kept their friendship up despite the strain that jealousy imposed.

"Well, it was in one of those morning talks on the veranda that Marsh made the proposition which brought on the end. I was laid up with some of my neuritis, but had managed to get downstairs and stretch out on the front parlour sofa near the long window. Denis and Marsh were just outside; so I couldn't help hearing all they said. They had been talking about art, and the curious, capricious elements needed to jolt an artist into producing the real article, when Marsh suddenly swerved from abstractions to the personal application he must have had in mind from the start.

" 'I suppose,' he was saying, 'that nobody can tell just what it is in some scenes or objects that makes them aesthetic stimuli for certain individuals. Basically, of course, it must have some reference to each man's background of stored-up mental associations, for no two people have the same scale of sensitiveness and responses. We decadents are artists for whom all ordinary things have ceased to have any emotional or imaginative significance, but no one of us responds in the same way to exactly the same extraordinary. Now take me, for instance . . .'

"He paused and resumed.

" 'I know, Denny, that I can say these things to you because you such a preternaturally unspoiled mind — clean, fine, direct, objective, and all that. You won't misunderstand as an oversubtilised, effete man of the world might.'

"He paused once more.

" 'The fact is, I think I know what's needed to set my imagination working again. I've had a dim idea of it ever since we were in Paris, but I'm sure now. It's Marceline, old chap — that face and that hair, and the train of shadowy images they bring up. Not merely visible beauty — though God knows there's enough of that — but something peculiar and individualised, that can't exactly be explained. Do you know, in the last few days I've felt the existence of such a stimulus so keenly that I honestly think I could outdo myself — break into the real masterpiece class if I could get ahold of paint and canvas at just the time when her face and hair set my fancy stirring and weaving. There's something weird and other-worldly about it — something joined up with the dim ancient thing Marceline represents. I don't know how much she's told you about that side of her, but I can assure you there's plenty of it. She has some marvellous links with the outside . . . .'

"Some change in Denis' expression must have halted the speaker here, for there was a considerable spell of silence before the words went on. I was utterly taken aback, for I'd expected no such overt development like this; and I wondered what my son could be thinking. My heart began to pound violently, and I strained my ears in the frankest of intentional eavesdropping. Then Marsh resumed.

" 'Of course you're jealous — I know how a speech like mine must sound — but I can swear to you that you needn't be.'

"Denis did not answer, and Marsh went on.

" 'To tell the truth, I could never be in love with Marceline — I couldn't even be a cordial friend of hers in the warmest sense. Why, damn it all, I felt like a hypocrite talking with her these days as I've been doing.

" 'The case simply is, that one phase of her half hypnotises me in a certain way — a very strange, fantastic, and dimly terrible way — just as another phase half hypnotises you in a much more normal way. I see something in her — or to be psychologically exact, something through her or beyond her — that you didn't see at all. Something that brings up a vast pageantry of shapes from forgotten abysses, and makes me want to paint incredible things whose outlines vanish the instant I try to envisage them clearly. Don't mistake, Denny, your wife is a magnificent being, a splendid focus of cosmic forces who has a right to be called divine if anything on earth has!'

"I felt a clearing of the situation at this point, for the abstract strangeness of Marsh's statement, plus the flattery he was now heaping on Marceline, could not fail to disarm and mollify one as fondly proud of his consort as Denis always was. Marsh evidently caught the change himself, for there was more confidence in his tone as he continued.

" 'I must paint her, Denny — must paint that hair — and you won't regret. There's something more than mortal about that hair — something more than beautiful —'

"He paused, and I wondered what Denis could be thinking. I wondered, indeed, what I was really thinking myself. Was Marsh's interest actually that of the artist alone, or was he merely infatuated as Denis had been? I had thought, in their schooldays, that he had envied my boy; and I dimly felt that it might be the same now. On the other hand, something in that talk of artistic stimulus had rung amazingly true; so that the more I pondered, the more I was inclined to take the stuff at face value. Denis seemed to do so, too, for although I could not catch his low-spoken reply, I could tell by the effect it produced that it must have been affirmative.

"There was a sound of someone slapping another on the back, and then a grateful speech from Marsh that I was long to remember.

" 'That's great, Denny, and just as I told you, you'll never regret it. In a sense, I'm half doing it for you. You'll be a different man when you see it. I'll put you back where you used to be — give you a waking-up and a sort of salvation — but you can't see what I mean as yet. Just remember old friendship, and don't get the idea that I'm not the same old bird!'

"I rose perplexedly as I saw the two stroll off across the lawn, arm in arm, and smoking in unison. What could Marsh have meant by his strange and almost ominous reassurance? The more my fears were quieted in one direction, the more they were aroused in another. Look at it any way I could, it seemed to be a rather bad business.

"But matters got started just the same. Denis fixed up an attic room with skylights, and Marsh sent for all sorts of painting equipment. Everyone was rather excited about the new venture, and I was at least glad that something was on foot to break the brooding tension. Soon the sittings began, and we all took them quite seriously — for we could see that Marsh regarded them as important artistic events. Denny and I used to go quietly about the house as though something sacred were occurring, and we knew that it was sacred as far as Marsh was concerned.

"With Marceline, though, it was a different matter, as I began to see at once. Whatever Marsh's reactions to the sittings may have been, hers were painfully obvious. Every possible way she betrayed a frank and commonplace infatuation for the artist, and would repulse Denis' marks of affection whenever she dared. Oddly, I noticed this more vividly than Denis himself, and tried to devise some plan for keeping the boy's mind easy until the matter could be straightened out. There was no use in having him excited about it if it could be helped.

"In the end I decided that Denis had better be away while the disagreeable situation existed. I could represent his interests well enough at this end, and sooner or later Marsh would finish the picture and go. My view of Marsh's honour was such that I did not look for any worse developments. When the matter had blown over, and Marceline had forgotten about her new infatuation, it would be time enough to have Denis on hand again.

"So I wrote a long letter to my marketing and financial agent in New York, and cooked up a plan to have the boy summoned there for an indefinite time. I had the agent write him that our affairs absolutely required one of us to go East, and of course my illness made it clear that I could not be the one. It was arranged that when Denis got to New York he would find enough plausible matters to keep him busy as long as I thought he ought to be away.

"The plan worked perfectly, and Denis started for New York without the least suspicion; Marceline and Marsh going with him in the car to Cape Girardeau, where he caught the afternoon train to St. Louis. They returned after dark, and as McCabe drove the car back to the stables I could hear them talking on the veranda — in those same chairs near the long parlour window where Marsh and Denis had sat when I overheard them talk about the portrait. This time I resolved to do some intentional eavesdropping, so quietly went down to the front parlour and stretched out on the sofa near the window.

"At first I could not hear anything but very shortly there came the sound of a chair being shifted, followed by a short, sharp breath and a sort of inarticulately hurt exclamation from Marceline. Then I heard Marsh speaking in a strained, almost formal voice.

" 'I'd enjoy working tonight if you aren't too tired.'

"Marceline's reply was in the same hurt tone which had marked her exclamation. She used English as he had done.

" 'Oh, Frank, is that really all you care about? Forever working! Can't we just sit out here in this glorious moonlight?'

"He answered impatiently, his voice shewing a certain contempt beneath the dominant quality of artistic enthusiasm.

" 'Moonlight! Good God, what cheap sentimentality! For a supposedly sophisticated person you surely do hang on to some of the crudest claptrap that ever escaped from the dime novels! With art at your elbow, you have to think of the moon — cheap as a spotlight at the varieties! Or perhaps it makes you think of the Roodmas dance around the stone pillars at Auteiul. Hell, how you used to make those goggle-eyed yaps stare! But not — I suppose you've dropped all that now. No more Atlantean magic or hair-snake rites for Madame de Russy! I'm the only one to remember the old things — the things that came down through the temples of Tanit and echoed on the ramparts of Zimbabwe. But I won't be cheated of that remembrance — all that is weaving itself into the thing on my canvas — the thing that is going to capture wonder and crystallise the secrets of 75,000 years . . .'

"Marceline interrupted in a voice full of mixed emotions.

" 'It's you who are cheaply sentimental now! You know well that the old things had better be let alone. All of you had better watch out if ever I chant the old rites or try to call up what lies hidden in Yuggoth, Zimbabwe, and R'lyeh. I thought you had more sense!

" 'You lack logic. You want me to be interested in this precious painting of yours, yet you never let me see what you're doing. Always that black cloth over it! It's of me — I shouldn't think it would matter if I saw it . . .'

"Marsh was interrupting this time, his voice curiously hard and strained.

" 'No. Not now. You'll see it in due course of time. You say it's of you — yes, it's that, but it's more. If you knew, you mightn't be so impatient. Poor Denis! My God, it's a shame!'

"My throat was suddenly dry as the words rose to an almost febrile pitch. What could Marsh mean? Suddenly I saw that he had stopped and was entering the house alone. I heard the front door slam, and listened as his footsteps ascended the stairs. Outside on the veranda I could still hear Marceline's heavy, angry breathing. I crept away sick at heart, feeling that there were grave things to ferret out before I could safely let Denis come back.

"After that evening the tension around the place was even worse than before. Marceline had always lived on flattery and fawning and the shock of those few blunt words from Marsh was too much for her temperament. There was no living in the house with her anymore, for with poor Denis gone she took out her abusiveness on everybody. When she could find no one indoors to quarrel with she would go out to Sophonisba's cabin and spend hours talking with the queer old Zulu woman. Aunt Sophy was the only person who would fawn abjectly enough to suit her, and when I tried once to overhear their conversation I found Marceline whispering about 'elder secrets' and 'unknown Kadath' while the negress rocked to and fro in her chair, making inarticulate sounds of reverence and admiration every now and then.

"But nothing could break her dog-like infatuation for Marsh. She would talk bitterly and sullenly to him, yet was getting more and more obedient to his wishes. It was very convenient for him, since he now became able to make her pose for the picture whenever he felt like painting. He tried to shew gratitude for this willingness, but I thought I could detect a kind of contempt or even loathing beneath his careful politeness. For my part, I frankly hated Marceline! There was no use in calling my attitude anything as mild as dislike these days. Certainly, I was glad Denis was away. His letters, not nearly so frequent as I wished, shewed signs of strain and worry.

"As the middle of August went by I gathered from Marsh's remarks that the portrait was nearly done. His mood seemed increasingly sardonic, though Marceline's temper improved a bit as the prospect of seeing the thing tickled her vanity. I can still recall the day when Marsh said he'd have everything finished within a week. Marceline brightened up perceptibly, though not without a venomous look at me. It seemed as if her coiled hair visibly tightened around her head.

" 'I'm to be the first to see it!' she snapped. Then, smiling at Marsh, she said, 'And if I don't like it I shall slash it to pieces!'

"Marsh's face took on the most curious look I have ever seen it wear as he answered her.

" 'I can't vouch for your taste, Marceline, but I swear it will be magnificent! Not that I want to take much credit — art creates itself — and this thing had to be done. Just wait!'

"During the next few days I felt a queer sense of foreboding, as if the completion of the picture meant a kind of catastrophe instead of a relief. Denis, too, had not written me, and my agent in New York said he was planning some trip to the country. I wondered what the outcome of the whole thing would be. What a queer mixture of elements — Marsh and Marceline, Denis and I! How would all these ultimately react on one another? When my fears grew too great I tried to lay them all to my infirmity, but that explanation never quite satisfied me."

IV.

"Well, the thing exploded on Tuesday, the twenty-sixth of August. I had risen at my usual time and had breakfast, but was not good for much because of the pain in my spine. It had been troubling me badly of late, and forcing me to take opiates when it got too unbearable; nobody else was downstairs except the servants, though I could hear Marceline moving about in her room. Marsh slept in the attic next his studio, and had begun to keep such late hours that he was seldom up till noon. About ten o'clock the pain got the better of me, so that I took a double dose of my opiate and lay down on the parlour sofa. The last I heard was Marceline's pacing overhead. Poor creature — if I had known! She must have been walking before the long mirror admiring herself. That was like her. Vain from start to finish — revelling in her own beauty, just as she revelled in all the little luxuries Denis was able to give her.

"I didn't wake up till near sunset, and knew instantly how long I had slept from the golden light and long shadows outside the long window. Nobody was about, and a sort of unnatural stillness seemed to be hovering over everything. From afar, though, I thought I could sense a faint howling, wild and intermittent, whose quality had a slight but baffling familiarity about it. I'm not much for psychic premonitions, but I was frightfully uneasy from the start. There had been dreams — even worse than the ones I had been dreaming in the weeks before — and this time they seemed hideously linked to some black and festering reality. The whole place had a poisonous air. Afterward I reflected that certain sounds must have filtered through into my unconscious brain during those hours of drugged sleep. My pain, though, was very much eased; and I rose and walked without difficulty.

"Soon enough I began to see that something was wrong. Marsh and Marceline might have been riding, but someone ought to have been getting dinner in the kitchen. Instead, there was only silence, except for that faint, distant howl or wail; and nobody answered when I pulled the old-fashioned bell-cord to summon Scipio. Then, chancing to look up, I saw the spreading stain on the ceiling — the bright red stain, that must have come through the floor of Marceline's room.

"In an instant I forgot my crippled back and hurried upstairs to find out the worst. Everything under the sun raced through my mind as I struggled with the dampness-warped door of that silent chamber, and most hideous of all was a terrible sense of malign fulfilment and fatal expectedness. I had, it struck me, known all along that nameless horrors were gathering; that something profoundly and cosmically evil had gained a foothold under my roof from which only blood and tragedy could result.

"The door gave at last, and I stumbled into the large room beyond — all dim from the branches of the great trees outside the windows. For a moment I could do nothing but flinch at the faint evil odour that immediately struck my nostrils. Then, turning on the electric light and glancing around, I glimpsed a nameless blasphemy on the yellow and blue rug.

"It lay face down in a great pool of dark, thickened blood, and had the gory print of a shod human foot in the middle of its naked back. Blood was spattered everywhere — on the walls, furniture, and floor. My knees gave way as I took in the sight, so that I had to stumble to a chair and slump down. The thing had obviously been a human being, though its identity was not easy to establish at first; since it was without clothes, and had most of its hair hacked and torn from the scalp in a very crude way. It was of a deep ivory colour, and I knew that it must have been Marceline. The shoe-print on the back made the thing seem all the more hellish. I could not even picture the strange, loathsome tragedy which must have taken place while I slept in the room below. When I raised my hand to wipe my dripping forehead I saw that my fingers were sticky with blood. I shuddered, then realised that it must have come from the knob of the door which the unknown murderer had forced shut behind him as he left. He had taken his weapon with him, it seemed, for no instrument of death was visible here.

"As I studied the floor I saw that a line of sticky footprints like the one on the body led away from the horror to the door. There was another blood-trail, too, and of a less easily explainable kind; a broadish, continuous line, as if marking the path of some huge snake. At first I concluded it must be due to something the murderer had dragged after him. Then, noting the way some of the footprints seemed to be superimposed on it, I was forced to believe that it could have been there when the murderer left. But what crawling entity could have been in that room with the victim and her assassin, leaving before the killer when the deed was done? As I asked myself this question I thought I heard fresh bursts of that faint, distant wailing.

"Finally, rousing myself from a lethargy of horror, I got on my feet again and began following the footprints. Who the murderer was, I could not even faintly guess, nor could I try to explain the absence of the servants. I vaguely felt that I ought to go up to Marsh's attic quarters, but before I had fully formulated the idea I saw that the bloody trail was indeed taking me there. Was he himself the murderer? Had he gone mad under the strain of the morbid situation and suddenly run amok?

"In the attic corridor the trail became faint, the prints almost ceasing as they merged with the dark carpet. I could still, however, discern the strange single path of the entity who had gone first; and this led straight to the closed door of Marsh's studio, disappearing beneath it at a point about half way from side to side. Evidently it had crossed the threshold at a time when the door was wide open.

"Sick at heart, I tried the knob and found the door unlocked. Opening it, I paused in the waning north light to see what fresh nightmare might be awaiting me. There was certainly something human on the floor, and I reached for the switch to turn on the chandelier.

"But as the light flashed up my gaze left the floor and its horror — that was Marsh, poor devil — to fix itself frantically and incredulously upon the living thing that cowered and stared in the open doorway leading to Marsh's bedroom. It was a tousled, wild-eyed thing, crusted with dried blood and carrying in its hand a wicked machete which had been one of the ornaments of the studio wall. Yet even in that awful moment I recognised it as one whom I had thought more than a thousand miles away. It was my own boy Denis — or the maddened wreck which had once been Denis.

"The sight of me seemed to bring back a trifle of sanity — or at least of memory — in the poor boy. He straightened up and began to toss his head about as if trying to shake free from some enveloping influence. I could not speak a word, but moved my lips in an effort to get back my voice. My eyes wandered for a moment to the figure on the floor in front of the heavily draped easel — the figure toward which the strange blood-trail led, and which seemed to be tangled in the coils of some dark, ropy object. The shifting of my glance apparently produced some impression in the twisted brain of the boy, for suddenly he began to mutter in a hoarse whisper whose purport I was soon able to catch.

" 'I had to exterminate her — she was the devil — the summit and high-priestess of all evil — the spawn of the pit — Marsh knew, and tried to warn me. Good old Frank — I didn't kill him, though I was ready to before I realised. But I went down there and killed her — then that cursed hair —'

"I listened in horror as Denis choked, paused, and began again.

" 'You didn't know — her letters got queer and I knew she was in love with Marsh. Then she nearly stopped writing. He never mentioned her — I felt something was wrong, and thought I ought to come back and find out. Couldn't tell you — your manner would have given it away. Wanted to surprise them. Got here about noon today — came in a cab and sent the house-servants all off — let the field hands alone, for their cabins are all out of earshot. Told McCabe to get me some things in Cape Girardeau and not bother to come back until tomorrow. Had all the niggers take the old car and let Mary drive them to Bend Village for a vacation — told 'em we were all going on some sort of outing and wouldn't need help. Said they'd better stay all night with Uncle Scip's cousin, who keeps that nigger boarding house.'

"Denis was getting very incoherent now, and I strained my ears to grasp every word. Again I thought I heard that wild, far-off wail, but the story had first place for the present.

" 'Saw you sleeping in the parlour, and took a chance you wouldn't wake up. Then went upstairs on the quiet to hunt up Marsh and . . .that woman!'

"The boy shuddered as he avoided pronouncing Marceline's name. At the same time I saw his eyes dilate in unison with a bursting of the distant crying, whose vague familiarity had now become very great.

" 'She was not in her room, so I went up to the studio. Door was shut, and I could hear voices inside. Didn't knock — just burst in and found her posing for the picture. Nude, but with the hellish hair all draped around her. And making all sorts of sheep's eyes at Marsh. He had the easel turned half away from the door, so I couldn't see the picture. Both of them were pretty well jolted when I shewed up, and Marsh dropped his brush. I was in a rage and told him he'd have to shew me the portrait, but he got calmer every minute. Told me it wasn't quite done, but would be in a day or two — said I could see it then — she — hadn't seen it.

" 'But that didn't go with me. I stepped up, and he dropped a velvet curtain over the thing before I could see it. He was ready to fight before letting me see it, but that — that — she — stepped up and sided with me. Said we ought to see it. Frank got horrible worked up, and gave me a punch when I tried to get at the curtain. I punched back and seemed to have knocked him out. Then I was almost knocked out myself by the shriek that — that creature — gave. She'd drawn aside the hangings herself, and caught a look at what Marsh had been painting. I wheeled around and saw her rushing like mad out of the room — then I saw the picture.'

"Madness flared up in the boy's eyes again as he got to this place, and I thought for a minute he was going to spring at me with his machete. But after a pause he partly steadied himself.

" 'Oh, God — that thing! Don't ever look at it! Burn it with the hangings around it and throw the ashes into the river! Marsh knew — and was warning me. He knew what it was — what that woman — that leopardess, or gorgon, or lamia, or whatever she was — actually represented. He'd tried to hint to me ever since I met her in his Paris studio, but it couldn't be told in words. I thought they all wronged her when they whispered horrors about her — she had me hypnotised so that I couldn't believe the plain facts — but this picture has caught the whole secret — the whole monstrous background!

" 'God, but Frank is an artist! That thing is the greatest piece any living soul has produced since Rembrandt! It's a crime to burn it — but it would be a greater crime to let it exist — just as it would have been an abhorrent sin to let — that she-daemon — exist any longer. The minute I saw it I understood what — she — was, and what part she played in the frightful secret that has come down from the days of Cthulhu and the Elder Ones — the secret that was nearly wiped out when Atlantis sank, but that kept half alive in hidden traditions and allegorical myths and furtive, midnight cult-practices. For you know she was the real thing. It wasn't any fake. It would have been merciful if it had been a fake. It was the old, hideous shadow that philosophers never dared mention — the thing hinted at in the *Necronomicon* and symbolised in the Easter Island colossi.

" 'She thought we couldn't see through — that the false front would hold till we had bartered away our immortal souls. And she was half right — she'd have got me in the end. She was only — waiting. But Frank — good old Frank — was too much for me. *He knew what it all meant, and painted it.* I don't wonder she shrieked and ran off when she saw it. It wasn't quite done, but God knows *enough was there.*

Weird Tales, May 1945

"'Then I knew I'd got to kill her—kill her, and everything connected with her. It was a taint that wholesome human blood couldn't bear. There was something else, too—but you'll never know that if you burn the picture without looking. I staggered down to her room with this machete that I got off the wall here, leaving Frank still knocked out. He was breathing, though, and I knew and thanked heaven I hadn't killed him.

"'I found her in front of the mirror braiding that accursed hair. She turned on me like a wild beast, and began spitting out her hatred of Marsh. The fact that she'd been in love with him—and I knew she had—only made it worse. For a minute I couldn't move, and she came within an ace of completely hypnotising me. Then I thought of the picture, and the spell broke. She saw the breaking in my eyes, and must have noticed the machete, too. I never saw anything give such a wild jungle beast look as she did then. She sprang for me with claws out like a leopard's, but I was too quick. I swung the machete, and it was all over.'

"Denis had to stop again, and I saw the perspiration running down his forehead through the spattered blood. But in a moment he hoarsely resumed.

"'I said it was all over—but God! some of it had only just begun! I felt I had fought the legions of Satan, and put my foot on the back of the thing I had annihilated. *Then I saw that blasphemous braid of coarse black hair begin to twist and squirm of itself.*

"'I might have known it. It was all in the old tales. That damnable hair had a life of its own, that couldn't be ended by killing the creature itself. I knew I'd have to burn it, so I started to hack it off with the machete. God, but it was devilish work! Tough—like iron wires—but I managed to do it. And it was loathsome the way the big braid writhed and struggled in my grasp.

"'About the time I had the last strand cut or pulled off I heard that eldritch wailing from behind the house. You know—it's still going off and on. I don't know what it is, but it must be something springing from this hellish business. It half seems like something I ought to know but can't quite place. It got my nerves the first time I heard it, and I dropped the severed braid in my fright. Then, I got a worse fright — for in another second the braid had turned on me and began to strike venomously with one of its ends which had knotted itself up like a sort of grotesque head. I struck out with the machete, and it turned away. Then, when I had my breath again, I saw that the monstrous thing was crawling along the floor by itself like a great black snake. I couldn't do anything for a while, but when it vanished through the door I managed to pull myself together and stumble after it. I could follow the broad, bloody trail, and I saw it led upstairs. It brought me here — and may heaven curse me if I didn't see it through the doorway, striking at poor dazed Marsh like a maddened rattler as it had struck at me, finally coiling around him as a python would. He had begun to come to, but that abominable serpent got him before he was on his feet. I knew that all of the woman's hatred was behind it, but I hadn't the power to pull it off. I tried, but it was too much for me. Even the machete was no good — I couldn't swing it freely or it would have slashed Frank to pieces. So I saw those monstrous coils tighten — saw poor Frank crushed to death before my eyes — and all the time that awful faint howling came from somewhere beyond the fields.

" 'That's all. I pulled the velvet cloth over the picture and hope it'll never be lifted. The thing must be burnt. I couldn't pry the coils off poor, dead Frank — they cling to him like a leach, and seem to have lost their motion altogether. It's as if that snaky rope of hair has a kind of perverse fondness for the man it killed — it's clinging to him — embracing him. You'll have to burn poor Frank with it — but for God's sake don't forget to see it in ashes. That and the picture. They must both go. The safety of the world demands that they go.

"Denis might have whispered more, but a fresh burst of distant wailing cut us short. For the first time we knew what it was, for a westerly veering wind brought articulate words at last. We ought to have known long before, since sounds much like it had often come from the same source. It was wrinkled Sophonisba, the ancient Zulu witch-woman who had fawned on Marceline, keening from her cabin in a way which crowned the horrors of this nightmare tragedy. We could both hear some of the things she howled, and knew that secret and primordial bonds linked this savage sorceress with that other inheritor of elder secrets who had just been extirpated. Some of the words she used betrayed her closeness to daemonic and palaeogean traditions.

" 'Iä! Iä! Shub-Niggurath! Ya-R'lyeh! N'gagi n'bulu bwana n'lolo! Ya, yo, poor Missy Tanit, poor Missy Isis! Marse Clooloo, come up outen de water an' git yo chile — she done daid! She done daid! De hair ain' got no missus no mo', Marse Clooloo. Ol' Sophy, she know! Ol' Sophy, she done got de black stone outen Big Zimbabwe in ol' Affriky! Ol' Sophy, she done dance in de moonshine roun' de crocodile-stone befo' de N'bangus cotch her and sell her to de ship folks! No mo' Tanit! No mo' Isis! No mo' witch-woman to keep de fire a-goin' in de big stone place! Ya, yo! *N'gagi n'bulu bwana n'lolo! Iä! Shub-Niggurath!* She daid! Ol' Sophy know!'

"That wasn't the end of the wailing, but it was all I could pay attention to. The expression on my boy's face shewed that it had reminded him of something frightful, and the tightening of his hand on the machete boded no good. I knew he was desperate, and sprang to disarm him before he could do anything more.

"But I was too late. An old man with a bad spine doesn't count for much physically. There was a terrible struggle, but he had done for himself before many seconds were over. I'm not sure yet but that he tried to kill me, too. His last panting words were something about the need of wiping out everything that had been connected with Marceline, either by blood or marriage."

V.

"I wonder to this day that I didn't go stark mad in that instant — or in the moments and hours afterward. In front of me was the slain body of my boy — the only human being I had to cherish — and ten feet away, in front of that shrouded easel, was the body of his best friend, with a nameless coil of horror wound around it. Below was the scalped corpse of that she-monster, about whom I was half-ready to believe anything. I was too dazed to analyse the probability of the hair story — and even if I had not been, that dismal howling coming from Aunt Sophy's cabin would have been enough to quiet doubt for the nonce.

"If I'd been wise, I'd have done just what poor Denis told me to — burned the picture and the body-grasping hair at once and without curiosity — but I was too shaken to be wise. I suppose I muttered foolish things over my boy — and then I remembered that the night was wearing on and that the servants would be back in the morning. It was plain that a matter like this could never be explained, and I knew that I must cover things up and invent a story.

"That coil of hair around Marsh was a monstrous thing. As I poked at it with a sword which I took from the wall I almost thought I felt it tighten its grip on the dead man. I didn't dare touch it — and the longer I looked at it the more horrible things I noticed about it. One thing gave me a start. I won't mention it — but it partly explained the need for feeding the hair with queer oils as Marceline had always done.

"In the end I decided to bury all three bodies in the cellar — with quicklime, which I knew we had in the storehouse. It was a night of hellish work. I dug three graves — my boy's a long way from the other two, for I didn't want him to be near either the woman's body or her hair. I was sorry I couldn't get the coil from around poor Marsh. It was terrible work getting them all down to the cellar. I used blankets in carting the woman and the poor devil with the coil around him. Then I had to get two barrels of lime from the storehouse. God must have given me strength, for I not only moved them but filled all three graves without a hitch.

"Some of the lime I made into whitewash. I had to take a stepladder and fix over the parlour ceiling where the blood had oozed through. And I burned nearly everything in Marceline's room, scrubbing the walls and floor and heavy furniture. I washed up the attic studio, too, and the trail and footprints that led there. And all the time I could hear old Sophy's wailing in the distance. The devil must have been in that creature to let her voice go on like that. But she always was howling queer things. That's why the field niggers didn't get scared or curious that night. I locked the studio door and took the key to my room. Then I burned all my stained clothes in the fireplace. By dawn the whole house looked quite normal so far as any casual eye could tell. I hadn't dared touch the covered easel, but meant to attend to that later.

"Well, the servants came back the next day, and I told them all the young folks had gone to St. Louis. None of the field hands seemed to have seen or heard anything, and old Sophonisba's wailing had stopped at the instant of sunrise. She was like a sphinx after that, and never let out a word of what had been on her brooding brain the day and night before.

"Later on I pretended that Denis and Marsh and Marceline had gone back to Paris and had a certain discreet agency mail me letters from there — letters I had fixed up in forged handwriting. It took a good deal of deceit and reticence in several things to various friends, and I knew people have secretly suspected me of holding something back. I had the deaths of Marsh and Denis reported during the war, and later said Marceline had entered a convent. Fortunately Marsh was an orphan whose eccentric ways had alienated him from his people in Louisiana. Things might have been patched up a good deal better for me if I had had the sense to burn the picture, sell the plantation, and give up trying to manage things with a shaken and overstrained mind. You see what my folly has brought me to. Failing crops — hands discharged one by one — place falling apart to ruin — and myself a hermit and a target for dozens of queer countryside stories. Nobody will come around here after dark anymore — or any other time if it can be helped. That's why I knew you must be a stranger.

"And why do I stay here? I can't wholly tell you that. It's bound up too closely with things at the very rim of sane reality. It wouldn't have been so, perhaps, if I hadn't looked at the picture. I ought to have done as poor Denis told me. I honestly meant to burn it when I went up to that locked studio a week after the horror, but I looked first — and that changed everything.

"No — there's no use telling what I saw. You can, in a way, see for yourself presently; though time and dampness have done their work. I don't think it can hurt you if you want to take a look, but it was different with me. I knew too much of what it all meant.

"Denis had been right — it was the greatest triumph of human art since Rembrandt, even though still unfinished. I grasped that at the start, and knew that poor Marsh had justified his decadent philosophy. He was to painting what Baudelaire was to poetry — and Marceline was the key that had unlocked his inmost stronghold of genius.

"The thing almost stunned me when I pulled aside the hangings — stunned me before I half knew what the whole thing was. You know, it's only partly a portrait. Marsh had been pretty literal when he hinted that he wasn't painting Marceline alone, but what he saw through her and beyond her.

"Of course she was in it — was the key to it, in a sense — but her figure only formed one point in a vast composition. She was nude except for that hideous web of hair spun around her, and was half-seated, half-reclining on a sort of bench or divan, carved in patterns unlike those of any known decorative tradition. There was a monstrously shaped goblet in one hand, from which was spilling fluid whose colour I haven't been able to place or classify to this day — I don't know where Marsh even got the pigments.

"The figure and the divan were in the left-hand foreground of the strangest sort of scene I ever saw in my life. I think there was a faint suggestion of its all being a kind of emanation from the woman's brain, yet there was also a directly opposite suggestion — as if she were just an evil image or hallucination conjured up by the scene itself.

"I can't tell you know whether it's an exterior or an interior — whether those hellish Cyclopean vaultings are seen from the outside or the inside, or whether they are indeed carven stone and not merely a morbid fungous arborescence. The geometry of the whole thing is crazy — one gets the acute and obtuse angles all mixed up.

"And God! The shapes of nightmare that float around in that perpetual daemon twilight! The blasphemies that lurk and leer and hold a Witches' Sabbat with that woman as a high-priestess! The black shaggy entities that are not quite goats — the crocodile-headed beast with three legs and a dorsal row of tentacles — and the flat-nosed Ægipans dancing in a pattern that Egypt's priests knew and called accursed!

"But the scene wasn't Egypt — it was *behind* Egypt; behind even Atlantis; behind fabled Mu, and myth-whispered Lemuria. It was the ultimate fountainhead of all horror on this earth, and the symbolism shewed only too clearly how integral a part of it Marceline was. I think it must be the unmentionable R'lyeh, that was not built by any creatures of this planet — the thing Marsh and Denis used to talk about in the shadows with hushed voices. In the picture it appears that the whole scene is deep under water — though everybody seems to be breathing freely.

"Well — I couldn't do anything but look and shudder, and finally I saw that Marceline was watching me craftily out of those monstrous, dilated eyes on the canvas. It was no mere superstition — Marsh had actually caught something of her horrible vitality in his symphonies of line and colour, so that she still brooded and hated, just as if most of her weren't down in the cellar under quicklime. *And it was worst of all when some of those Hecate-born snaky strands of hair began to lift themselves up from the surface and grope out into the room toward me.*

"Then it was that I knew the last final horror, and realised I was a guardian and a prisoner forever. She was the thing from which the first dim legends of Medusa and the Gorgons had sprung, and something in my shaken will had been captured and turned to stone at last. Never again would I be safe from those coiling snaky strands — the strands in the picture, and those that lay brooding under the lime near the wine casks. All too late I recalled the tales of the virtual indestructibility, even through centuries of burial, of the hair of the dead.

"My life since has been nothing but horror and slavery. Always there had lurked the fear of what broods down in the cellar. In less than a month the niggers began whispering about the great black snake that crawled around near the wine casks after dark, and about the curious way its trail would lead to another spot six feet away. Finally I had to move everything to another part of the cellar, for not a darky could be induced to go near the place where the snake was seen.

"Then the field hands began talking about the black snake that visited old Sophonisba's cabin every night after midnight. One of them shewed me its trail — and not long afterward I found out that Aunt Sophy herself had begun to pay strange visits to the cellar of the big house, lingering and muttering for hours in the very spot where none of the other blacks would go near. God, but I was glad when that old witch died! I honestly believe she had been a priestess of some ancient and terrible tradition back in Africa. She must have lived to be almost a hundred and fifty years old.

"Sometimes I think I hear something gliding around the house at night. There will be a queer noise on the stairs, where the boards are loose, and the latch of my room will rattle as if with an inward pressure. I always keep my door locked, of course. Then there are certain mornings when I seem to catch a sickish musty odour in the corridors, and notice a faint, ropy trail through the dust of the floors. I know I must guard the hair in the picture, for if anything were to happen to it, there are entities in this house which would take a sure and terrible revenge. I don't even dare to die — for life and death are all one to those in the clutch of what came out of R'lyeh. Something would be on hand to punish my neglect. Medusa's coil has got me, and it will always be the same. Never mix up with secret and ultimate horror, young man, if you value your immortal soul."

Weird Tales, January 1939

VI.

As the old man finished his story I saw that the small lamp had long since burned dry, and that the large one was nearly empty. It must, I knew, be near dawn, and my ears told me that the storm was over. The tale had held me in a half-daze, and I almost feared to glance at the door lest it reveal an inward pressure from some unnamable source. It would be hard to say which had the greatest hold on me — stark horror, incredulity, or a kind of morbid fantastic curiosity. I was wholly beyond speech and had to wait for my strange host to break the spell.

"Do you want to see — the thing?"

His voice was low and hesitant, and I saw he was tremendously in earnest. Of my various emotions, curiosity gained the upper hand; and I nodded silently. He rose, lighting a candle on a nearby table and holding it high before him as he opened the door.

"Come with me — upstairs."

I dreaded to brave those musty corridors again, but fascination downed all my qualms. The boards creaked beneath our feet, and I trembled once when I thought I saw a faint, rope-like line traced in the dust near the staircase.

The steps of the attic were noisy and rickety, with several of the treads missing. I was just glad of the need of looking sharply to my footing, for it gave me an excuse not to glance about. The attic corridor was pitch-black and heavily cobwebbed, and inch-deep with dust except where a beaten trail led to a door on the left at the farther end. As I noticed the rotting remains of a thick carpet I thought of the other feet which had pressed it in bygone decades — of these, and of one thing which did not have feet.

The old man took me straight to the door at the end of the beaten path, and fumbled a second with the rusty latch. I was acutely frightened now that I knew the picture was so close, yet dared not retreat at this stage. In another moment my host was ushering me into the deserted studio.

The candle light was very faint, yet served to shew most of the principal features. I noticed the low, slanting roof, the huge enlarged dormer, the curios and trophies hung on the wall — and most of all, the great shrouded easel in the centre of the floor. To that easel de Russy now walked, drawing aside the dusty velvet hangings on the side turned away from me, and motioning me silently to approach. It took a good deal of courage to make me obey, especially when I saw how my guide's eyes dilated in the wavering candle light as he looked at the unveiled canvas. But again curiosity conquered everything, and I walked around to where de Russy stood. Then I saw the damnable thing.

I did not faint — though no reader can possibly realise the effort it took to keep me from doing so. I did cry out, but stopped short when I saw the frightened look on the old man's face. As I had expected, the canvas was warped, mouldy, and scabrous from dampness and neglect; but for all that I could trace the monstrous hints of evil cosmic outsideness that lurked all through the nameless scene's morbid content and perverted geometry.

It was as the old man had said — a vaulted, columned hell of mingled Black Masses and Witches' Sabbaths — and what perfect completion could have added to it was beyond my power to guess. Decay had only increased the utter hideousness of its wicked symbolism and diseased suggestion, for the parts most affected by time were just those parts of the picture which in Nature — or in the extra-cosmic realm that mocked Nature — would be apt to decay and disintegrate.

The utmost horror of all, of course, was Marceline — and as I saw the bloated, discoloured flesh I formed the odd fancy that perhaps the figure on the canvas had some obscure, occult linkage with the figure which lay in quicklime under the cellar floor. Perhaps the lime had preserved the corpse instead of destroying it — but could it have preserved those black, malign eyes that glared and mocked at me from their painted hell?

And there was something else about the creature which I could not fail to notice — something which de Russy had not been able to put into words, but which perhaps had something to do with Denis' wish to kill all those of his blood who had dwelt under the same roof with her. Whether Marsh knew, or whether the genius in him painted it without his knowing, none could say. But Denis and his father could not have known till they saw the picture.

Surpassing all in horror was the streaming black hair — which covered the rotting body, but which was itself not even slightly decayed. All I had heard of it was amply verified. It was nothing human, this ropy, sinuous, half-oily, half-crinkly flood of serpent darkness. Vile, independent life proclaimed itself at every unnatural twist and convolution, and the suggestion of numberless *reptilian heads* at the out-turned ends was far too marked to be illusory or accidental.

The blasphemous thing held me like a magnet. I was helpless, and did not wonder at the myth of the gorgon's glance which turned all beholders to stone. Then I thought I saw a change come over the thing. The leering features perceptibly moved, so that the rotting jaw fell, allowing the thick, beast-like lips to disclose a row of pointed yellow fangs. The pupils of the fiendish eyes dilated, and the eyes themselves seemed to bulge outward. And the hair — that accursed hair! *It had begun to rustle and wave perceptibly, the snake-heads all turning toward de Russy and vibrating as if to strike!*

Reason deserted me altogether, and before I knew what I was doing I drew my automatic and sent a shower of twelve steel-jacketed bullets through the shocking canvas. The whole thing at once fell to pieces, even the frame toppling from the easel and clattering to the dust-covered floor. But though this horror was shattered, another had risen before me in the form of de Russy himself, whose maddened shrieks as he saw the picture vanish were almost as terrible as the picture itself had been.

With a half-articulate scream of "God, now you've done

it!" the frantic old man seized me violently by the arm and commenced to drag me out of the room and down the rickety stairs. He had dropped the candle in his panic; but dawn was near, and some faint grey light was filtering in through the dust-covered windows. I tripped and stumbled repeatedly, but never for a moment would my guide slacken his pace.

"Run!" he shrieked, "run for your life! You don't know what you've done! I never told you the whole thing! There were things I had to do — *the picture talked to me and told me.* I had to guard and keep it — now the worst will happen! *She and that hair will come up out of their graves, for God knows what purpose!*

"Hurry, man! For God's sake let's get out of here while there's time. If you have a car take me along to Cape Girardeau with you. It may well get me in the end, anywhere, but I'll give it a run for its money. Out of here — quick!"

As we reached the ground floor I became aware of a slow, curious thumping from the rear of the house, followed by a sound of a door shutting. De Russy had not heard the thumping, but the other noise caught his ear and drew from him the most terrible shriek that ever sounded in human throat.

"Oh, God — great God — that was the cellar door — she's coming — "

By this time I was desperately wrestling with the rusty latch and sagging hinges of the great front door — almost as frantic as my host now that I heard the slow, thumping tread approaching from the unknown rear rooms of the accursed mansion. The night's rain had warped the oaken planks, and the heavy door stuck and resisted even more strongly than it had when I forced an entrance the evening before.

Somewhere a plank creaked beneath the foot of whatever was walking, and the sound seemed to snap the last cord of sanity in the poor old man. With a roar like that of a maddened bull he released his grip on me and made a plunge to the right, through the open door of a room which I judged had been a parlour. A second later, just as I got the front door open and was making my own escape, I heard the tinkling clatter of broken glass and knew he had leapt through a window. And as I bounded off the sagging porch to commence my mad race down the long, weed-grown drive I thought I could catch the thud of dead, dogged footsteps which did not follow me, but which kept leadenly on through the door of the cobwebbed parlour.

I looked backward only twice as I plunged heedlessly through the burrs and briers of that abandoned drive, past the dying lindens and grotesque scrub-oaks, in the grey pallor of a cloudy November dawn. The first time was when an acrid smell overtook me, and I thought of the candle de Russy had dropped in the attic studio. By then I was comfortably near the road, on the high place from which the roof of the distant house was clearly visible above its encircling trees; and just as I expected, thick clouds of smoke were billowing out of the attic dormers and curling upward into the leaden heavens. I thanked the powers of creation that an immemorial curse was about to be purged by fire and blotted from the earth.

But in the next instant came that second backward look in which I glimpsed two other things — things that cancelled most of the relief and gave me a supreme shock from which I shall never recover. I have said that I was on a high part of the drive, from which much of the plantation behind me was visible. This vista included not only the house and its trees but some of the abandoned and partly flooded land beside the river, and several bends of the weed-choked drive I had been so hastily traversing. In both of these latter places I now beheld sights — or suspicions of sights — which I wish devoutly I could deny.

It was a faint, distant scream which made me turn back again, and as I did so I caught a trace of motion on the dull grey marshy plain behind the house. At that distance human figures are very small, yet I thought the motion resolved itself into two of these — pursuer and pursued. I even thought I saw the dark-clothed leading figure overtaken, seized, and dragged violently in the direction of the now burning house.

But I could not watch the outcome, for at once a nearer sight obtruded itself — a suggestion of motion among the underbrush at a point some distance back along the deserted drive. *Unmistakably, the weeds and bushes and briers were swaying as no wind could sway them; swaying as if some large, swift serpent were wriggling purposefully along on the ground in pursuit of me.*

That was all I could stand. I scrambled along madly for the gate, heedless of torn clothing and bleeding scratches, and jumped into the roadster parked under the great evergreen tree. It was a bedraggled, rain-drenched sight; but the works were unharmed and I had no trouble in starting the thing. I went on blindly in the direction the car was headed for; nothing was in my mind but to get away from that frightful region of nightmares and cacodaemons — to get away as quickly and as far as gasoline could take me.

About three or four miles along the road a farmer hailed me — a kindly, drawling fellow of middle age and considerable native intelligence. I was glad to slow down and ask directions, though I knew I must present a strange enough aspect. The man readily told me the way to Cape Girardeau, and inquired where I had come from in such a state at such an early hour. Thinking it best to say little, I merely mentioned that I had been caught in the night's rain and had taken shelter at a nearby farmhouse, afterward losing my way in the underbrush trying to find my car.

"At a farmhouse, eh? Wonder whose it could'a been. Ain't nothin' standin' this side o' Jim Ferris' place acrost Barker's Crick, an' that's all o' twenty miles by the rud."

I gave a start, and wondered what fresh mystery this portended. Then I asked my informant if he had overlooked the large ruined plantation house whose ancient gate bordered the road not far back.

"Funny ye sh'd recolleck that, stranger! Must a ben here afore some time. But that house ain't here now. Burnt down five or six years ago — and they did tell some queer stories about it."

I shuddered.

"You mean Riverside — ol' man de Russy's place. Queer goin's on there fifteen or twenty years ago. Ol' man's boy married a gal from abroad, and some folks thought she was a mighty odd sort. Didn't like the looks of her. then she and the boy went off sudden, and later on the ol' man said he was kilt in the war. But some o' the niggers hinted queer things. Got around at last that the ol' fellow fell in love with the gal himself and kilt her and the boy. That place was sure enough haunted by a black snake, mean that what it may.

"Then five or six years ago the ol' man disappeared and the house burned down. Some do say he was burnt up in it. It was a mornin' after a rainy night just like this, when lots o' folks heard an awful yellin' across the fields in old de Russy's voice. When they stopped and looked, they see the house goin' up in smoke quick as a wink — that place was all like tinder anyhow, rain or no rain. Nobody never seen the ol' man again, but onct in a while they tell of the ghost of that big black snake glidin' aroun'.

"What d'ye make of it, anyhow? You seem to hev knowed the place. Didn't ye ever hear tell of the de Russys? What d'ye reckon was the trouble with that gal young Denis married? She kinder made everybody shiver and feel hateful, though ye' couldn't never tell why."

I was trying to think, but that process was almost beyond me now. The house burned down years ago? Then where, and under what conditions, had I passed the night? And why did I know what I knew of these things? Even as I pondered I saw a hair on my coat sleeve — the short, grey hair of an old man.

In the end I drove on without telling anything. But did I hint that gossip was wronging the poor old planter who had suffered so much. I made it clear — as if from distant but authentic reports wafted among friends — that if anyone was to blame for the trouble at Riverside it was the woman, Marceline. She was not suited to Missouri ways, I said, and it was too bad that Denis had ever married her.

More I did not intimate, for I felt that the de Russys, with their proudly cherished honour and high, sensitive spirits, would not wish me to say more. They had borne enough, God knows, without the countryside guessing what a daemon of the pit — what a gorgon of the elder blasphemies — had come to flaunt their ancient and stainless name.

Nor was it right that the neighbours should know that other horror which my strange host of the night could not bring himself to tell me — that horror which he must have learned, as I learned it, from details in the lost masterpiece of poor Frank Marsh.

It would be too hideous if they knew that the one-time heiress of Riverside — the accursed gorgon or lamia whose hateful crinkly coil of serpent-hair must even now be brooding and twining vampirically around an artist's skeleton in a lime-packed grave beneath a charred foundation — was faintly, subtly, yet to the eyes of genius unmistakably the scion of Zimbabwe's most primal grovelers. No wonder she owned a link with that old witch-woman — for, though in deceitfully slight proportion, Marceline was a negress.

1931.

A Crisis of Confidence.

As 1931 began, H.P. Lovecraft's penchant for self-criticism was starting to become a real problem for him. Through his extensive travels and even more extensive correspondence, he'd become the center of a vast and growing circle of friends. His particular literary style was developing into something really special and virtually inimitable. But as fast as his abilities developed, his standards were rising even faster, so that it seemed to him that everything he did was derivative hackwork and hyperadjectival garbage. His sensitivity to criticism, always high, got even worse as the 1930s wore on, to the point that he actually produced barely anything of his own for the last three years of his life. He simply psyched himself out.

The worst of that was in the future, though. In 1931, Lovecraft was immersed in one of the longest, most intricate, and iconic of his tales: *At the Mountains of Madness*. Ironically, this story would be the one that would precipitate a true crisis of confidence in Lovecraft. Convinced that it was the best work of his life, he submitted it with pride to *Weird Tales*, only to have editor Farnsworth Wright reject it on the wafer-thin pretext of it being too long.

Lovecraft took this very hard. After getting Farnsworth's rejection, he announced plans to give up writing fiction entirely (luckily, he changed his mind later), and that summer he did almost as much moping as he did traveling, travel writing, and ghostwriting. Wright, who seems to have had no idea what he'd done, spent the subsequent five years trying to get Lovecraft to start sending him stories again.

But Lovecraft was so psyched out that, after he finished *The Shadow over Innsmouth* at the end of that year, only the timely intervention of August Derleth may have saved it from the match and furnace-grate.

H.P. Lovecraft had become his own most merciless critic. And the problem was not going to get better with time — although if he'd had a few years more, it might have.

At the Mountains of Madness.

41,000-WORD NOVEL; 1931.

It was ironic, but understandable, that At the Mountains of Madness *would be the story that would precipitate Lovecraft's late-stage crisis of confidence. It was, as he knew (and as most Lovecraft scholars agree) the best work of his life. He was fresh from the unalloyed success of* The Whisperer in Darkness, *in which he'd actually managed to successfully serve two masters — delivering a thrilling, unsubtle pulp ride to the high-school dropouts that Farnsworth Wright was convinced were his primary and exclusive readership as well as a complex and subtle subtextual literary experience for the more refined tastes of himself and his writerly friends. He may have thought he had done the same thing with* At the Mountains of Madness.

But when he submitted it to Weird Tales, *editor Farnsworth Wright rejected it, giving as his reason the prosaic and unsatisfying explanation that it was too long.*

It's not clear why this had the effect on Lovecraft that it did; Wright, as he well knew, was almost predictable in his reactions to unusual stories. He'd reject them, brood for a month or two, ask for them back and publish them. And sometimes he would do that in response not to the quality of the stories on offer, but to the always-touch-and-go financial situation of the moment at Weird Tales. *So Lovecraft should have been used to rejection slips from Wright.*

Lovecraft scholar S.T. Joshi suggests that this rejection hit Lovecraft unusually hard because a book publisher had just rejected a collection of his short stories that the publisher had actually solicited from him — something that happened several times in Lovecraft's life. But this particular rejection came with an explanatory letter claiming the stories had been too uniformly macabre and too unsubtle for consideration.

This last item was the cruelest cut, as Lovecraft justly prided himself on his skillful use of subtext, and he blamed Wright for encouraging him to dumb down his work to "Dunwitch Horror" levels so that the average Weird Tales *reader would not be confused. Thus, Joshi posits, when Wright rejected* At the Mountains of Madness *it came just as he was blaming Wright for ruining his chances at rising above the pulp markets. He'd remade himself for Farnsworth, which had caused the book publishers to reject him, and now Farnsworth was rejecting him too. And to make matters even worse, he was rejecting it for the most Phillistine reason imaginable.*

It's very likely Joshi is correct about this.

Joshi also suggests the fundamental problem afflicting Lovecraft in 1931 was that his work had become too science-fictiony for the weird-fiction publishers, and too weird-fictiony for the science-fiction publishers. He is almost certainly right about this as well.

Lovecraft wrote the story very quickly, starting on Feb. 24, 1931, and finishing on March 22. After its rejection by Wright, the typescript lay about for several years until Julius Schwartz, a friend who was trying to get into the literary-agency business, got it placed with Astounding Stories. *It ran in the February, March, and April 1936 issues, and was February's cover story (a distinction that Lovecraft never had with* Weird Tales*).*

I.

I am forced into speech because men of science have refused to follow my advice without knowing why. It is altogether against my will that I tell my reasons for opposing this contemplated invasion of the antarctic — with its vast fossil hunt and its wholesale boring and melting of the ancient ice caps. And I am the more reluctant because my warning may be in vain.

Doubt of the real facts, as I must reveal them, is inevitable; yet, if I suppressed what will seem extravagant and incredible, there would be nothing left. The hitherto withheld photographs, both ordinary and aerial, will count in my favor, for they are damnably vivid and graphic. Still, they will be doubted because of the great lengths to which clever fakery can be carried. The ink drawings, of course, will be jeered at as obvious impostures, notwithstanding a strangeness of technique which art experts ought to remark and puzzle over.

In the end I must rely on the judgment and standing of the few scientific leaders who have, on the one hand, sufficient independence of thought to weigh my data on its own hideously convincing merits or in the light of certain primordial and highly baffling myth-cycles; and on the other hand, sufficient influence to deter the exploring world in general from any rash and over-ambitious program in the region of those mountains of madness. It is an unfortunate fact that relatively obscure men like myself and my associates, connected only with a small university, have little chance of making an impression where matters of a wildly bizarre or highly controversial nature are concerned.

It is further against us that we are not, in the strictest sense, specialists in the fields which came primarily to be concerned. As a geologist, my object in leading the Miskatonic University Expedition was wholly that of securing deep-level specimens

CONTENTS COPYRIGHTED 1936

FEBRUARY 1936

ASTOUNDING STORIES

20¢

At the Mountains of Madness

by H. P. LOVECRAFT

of rock and soil from various parts of the antarctic continent, aided by the remarkable drill devised by Professor Frank H. Pabodie of our engineering department. I had no wish to be a pioneer in any other field than this, but I did hope that the use of this new mechanical appliance at different points along previously explored paths would bring to light materials of a sort hitherto unreached by the ordinary methods of collection.

Pabodie's drilling apparatus, as the public already knows from our reports, was unique and radical in its lightness, portability, and capacity to combine the ordinary artesian drill principle with the principle of the small circular rock drill in such a way as to cope quickly with strata of varying hardness. Steel head, jointed rods, gasoline motor, collapsible wooden derrick, dynamiting paraphernalia, cording, rubbish-removal auger, and sectional piping for bores five inches wide and up to one thousand feet deep all formed, with needed accessories, no greater load than three seven-dog sledges could carry. This was made possible by the clever aluminum alloy of which most of the metal objects were fashioned. Four large Dornier aeroplanes, designed especially for the tremendous altitude flying necessary on the antarctic plateau and with added fuel-warming and quick-starting devices worked out by Pabodie, could transport our entire expedition from a base at the edge of the great ice barrier to various suitable inland points, and from these points a sufficient quota of dogs would serve us.

We planned to cover as great an area as one antarctic season — or longer, if absolutely necessary — would permit, operating mostly in the mountain ranges and on the plateau south of Ross Sea; regions explored in varying degree by Shackleton, Amundsen, Scott, and Byrd. With frequent changes of camp, made by aeroplane and involving distances great enough to be of geological significance, we expected to unearth a quite unprecedented amount of material — especially in the pre-Cambrian strata of which so narrow a range of antarctic specimens had previously been secured. We wished also to obtain as great as possible a variety of the upper fossiliferous rocks, since the primal life history of this bleak realm of ice and death is of the highest importance to our knowledge of the earth's past. That the antarctic continent was once temperate and even tropical, with a teeming vegetable and animal life of which the lichens, marine fauna, arachnida, and penguins of the northern edge are the only survivals, is a matter of common information; and we hoped to expand that information in variety, accuracy, and detail. When a simple boring revealed fossiliferous signs, we would enlarge the aperture by blasting, in order to get specimens of suitable size and condition.

Our borings, of varying depth according to the promise held out by the upper soil or rock, were to be confined to exposed, or nearly exposed, land surfaces — these inevitably being slopes and ridges because of the mile or two-mile thickness of solid ice overlying the lower levels. We could not afford to waste drilling the depth of any considerable amount of mere glaciation, though Pabodie had worked out a plan for sinking copper electrodes in thick clusters of borings and melting off limited areas of ice with current from a gasoline-driven dynamo. It is this plan — which we could not put into effect except experimentally on an expedition such as ours — that the coming Starkweather-Moore Expedition proposes to follow, despite the warnings I have issued since our return from the antarctic.

The public knows of the Miskatonic Expedition through our frequent wireless reports to the *Arkham Advertiser* and Associated Press, and through the later articles of Pabodie and myself. We consisted of four men from the University — Pabodie, Lake of the biology department, Atwood of the physics department — also a meteorologist — and myself, representing geology and having nominal command — besides sixteen assistants: seven graduate students from Miskatonic and nine skilled mechanics. Of these sixteen, twelve were qualified aeroplane pilots, all but two of whom were competent wireless operators. Eight of them understood navigation with compass and sextant, as did Pabodie, Atwood, and I. In addition, of course, our two ships — wooden ex-whalers, reinforced for ice conditions and having auxiliary steam — were fully manned.

The Nathaniel Derby Pickman Foundation, aided by a few special contributions, financed the expedition; hence our preparations were extremely thorough, despite the absence of great publicity. The dogs, sledges, machines, camp materials, and unassembled parts of our five planes were delivered in Boston, and there our ships were loaded. We were marvelously well-equipped for our specific purposes, and in all matters pertaining to supplies, regimen, transportation, and camp construction we profited by the excellent example of our many recent and exceptionally brilliant predecessors. It was the unusual number and fame of these predecessors which made our own expedition — ample though it was — so little noticed by the world at large.

As the newspapers told, we sailed from Boston Harbor on September 2nd, 1930, taking a leisurely course down the coast and through the Panama Canal, and stopping at Samoa and Hobart, Tasmania, at which latter place we took on final supplies. None of our exploring party had ever been in the polar regions before, hence we all relied greatly on our ship captains — J. B. Douglas, commanding the brig Arkham, and serving as commander of the sea party, and Georg Thorfinnssen, commanding the barque Miskatonic — both veteran whalers in antarctic waters.

As we left the inhabited world behind, the sun sank lower and lower in the north, and stayed longer and longer above the horizon each day. At about 62° South Latitude we sighted our first icebergs — table-like objects with vertical sides — and just before reaching the antarctic circle, which we crossed on October 20th with appropriately quaint ceremonies, we were considerably troubled with field ice. The falling temperature bothered me considerably after our long voyage through the tropics, but I tried to brace up for the worse rigors to come. On many occasions the curious atmospheric effects enchanted me vastly; these including a strikingly vivid mirage — the first I had ever seen—in which distant bergs became the battlements of unimaginable cosmic castles.

Pushing through the ice, which was fortunately neither extensive nor thickly packed, we regained open water at South Latitude 67°, East Longitude 175° On the morning of October 26th a strong land blink appeared on the south, and before noon we all felt a thrill of excitement at beholding a vast, lofty, and snow-clad mountain chain which opened out and covered the whole vista ahead. At last we had encountered an outpost of the great unknown continent and its cryptic world of frozen death. These peaks were obviously the Admiralty Range discovered by Ross, and it would now be our task to round Cape Adare and sail down the east coast of Victoria Land to our contemplated base on the shore of McMurdo Sound, at the foot of the volcano Erebus in South Latitude 77° 9'.

The last lap of the voyage was vivid and fancy-stirring. Great barren peaks of mystery loomed up constantly against the west as the low northern sun of noon or the still lower horizon-grazing southern sun of midnight poured its hazy reddish rays over the white snow, bluish ice and water lanes, and black bits of exposed granite slope. Through the desolate summits swept raging, intermittent gusts of the terrible antarctic wind; whose cadences sometimes held vague suggestions of a wild and half-sentient musical piping, with notes extending over a wide range, and which for some subconscious mnemonic reason seemed to me disquieting and even dimly terrible. Something about the scene reminded me of the strange and disturbing Asian paintings of Nicholas Roerich, and of the still stranger and more disturbing descriptions of the evilly fabled plateau of Leng which occur in the dreaded *Necronomicon* of the mad Arab Abdul Alhazred. I was rather sorry, later on, that I had ever looked into that monstrous book at the college library.

On the 7th of November, sight of the westward range having been temporarily lost, we passed Franklin Island; and the next day descried the cones of Mts. Erebus and Terror on Ross Island ahead, with the long line of the Parry Mountains beyond. There now stretched off to the east the low, white line of the great ice barrier, rising perpendicularly to a height of two hundred feet like the rocky cliffs of Quebec, and marking the end of southward navigation. In the afternoon we entered McMurdo Sound and stood off the coast in the lee of smoking Mt. Erebus. The scoriac peak towered up some twelve thousand, seven hundred feet against the eastern sky, like a Japanese print of the sacred Fujiyama, while beyond it rose the white, ghostlike height of Mt. Terror, ten thousand, nine hundred feet in altitude, and now extinct as a volcano.

Puffs of smoke from Erebus came intermittently, and one of the graduate assistants—a brilliant young fellow named Danforth—pointed out what looked like lava on the snowy slope, remarking that this mountain, discovered in 1840, had undoubtedly been the source of Poe's image when he wrote seven years later:

The lavas that restlessly roll
Their sulphurous currents down Yaanek
In the ultimate climes of the pole—
That groan as they roll down Mount Yaanek
In the realms of the boreal pole.

Danforth was a great reader of bizarre material, and had talked a good deal of Poe. I was interested myself because of the antarctic scene of Poe's only long story—the disturbing and enigmatical Arthur Gordon Pym. On the barren shore, and on the lofty ice barrier in the background, myriads of grotesque penguins squawked and flapped their fins, while many fat seals were visible on the water, swimming or sprawling across large cakes of slowly drifting ice.

Using small boats, we effected a difficult landing on Ross Island shortly after midnight on the morning of the 9th, carrying a line of cable from each of the ships and preparing to unload supplies by means of a breeches-buoy arrangement. Our sensations on first treading Antarctic soil were poignant and complex, even though at this particular point the Scott and Shackleton expeditions had preceded us. Our camp on the frozen shore below the volcano's slope was only a provisional one, headquarters being kept aboard the Arkham. We landed all our drilling apparatus, dogs, sledges, tents, provisions, gasoline tanks, experimental ice-melting outfit, cameras, both ordinary and aerial, aeroplane parts, and other accessories, including three small portable wireless outfits—besides those in the planes—capable of communicating with the Arkham's large outfit from any part of the antarctic continent that we would be likely to visit. The ship's outfit, communicating with the outside world, was to convey press reports to the *Arkham Advertiser*'s powerful wireless station on Kingsport Head, Massachusetts. We hoped to complete our work during a single antarctic summer; but if this proved impossible, we would winter on the Arkham, sending the Miskatonic north before the freezing of the ice for another summer's supplies.

I need not repeat what the newspapers have already published about our early work: of our ascent of Mt. Erebus; our successful mineral borings at several points on Ross Island and the singular speed with which Pabodie's apparatus accomplished them, even through solid rock layers; our provisional test of the small ice-melting equipment; our perilous ascent of the great barrier with sledges and supplies; and our final assembling of five huge aeroplanes at the camp atop the barrier. The health of our land party—twenty men and fifty-five Alaskan sledge dogs—was remarkable, though of course we had so far encountered no really destructive temperatures or windstorms. For the most part, the thermometer varied between zero and 20° or 25° above, and our experience with New England winters had accustomed us to rigors of this sort. The barrier camp was semi-permanent, and destined to be a storage cache for gasoline, provisions, dynamite, and other supplies. Only four of our planes were needed to carry the actual exploring material, the fifth being left with a pilot and two men from the ships at the storage cache to form a means of reaching us from the Arkham in case all our exploring planes were lost. Later, when not using all the other planes for moving apparatus, we would employ one or two in a shuttle transportation service between this cache and another permanent base on the great plateau from six hundred to seven hundred miles southward, beyond Beardmore Glacier. Despite the almost unanimous accounts of appalling winds and tempests that pour down from the plateau, we determined to dispense with intermediate bases, taking our chances in the interest of economy and probable efficiency.

Wireless reports have spoken of the breathtaking, four-hour, nonstop flight of our squadron on November 21st over the lofty shelf ice, with vast peaks rising on the west, and the unfathomed silences echoing to the sound of our engines. Wind troubled us only moderately, and our radio compasses helped us through the one opaque fog we encountered. When the vast rise loomed ahead, between Latitudes 83° and 84°, we knew we had reached Beardmore Glacier, the largest valley glacier in the world, and that the frozen sea was now giving place to a frowning and mountainous coast line. At last we were truly entering the white, aeon-dead world of the ultimate south. Even as we realized it we saw the peak of Mt. Nansen in the eastern distance, towering up to its height of almost fifteen thousand feet.

The successful establishment of the southern base above the glacier in Latitude 86° 7', East Longitude 174° 23', and the phenomenally rapid and effective borings and blastings made at various points reached by our sledge trips and short aeroplane flights, are matters of history; as is the arduous and triumphant ascent of Mt. Nansen by Pabodie and two of the graduate students — Gedney and Carroll — on December 13-15. We were some eight thousand, five hundred feet above sea-level, and when experimental drillings revealed solid ground only twelve feet down through the snow and ice at certain points, we made considerable use of the small melting apparatus and sunk bores and performed dynamiting at many places where no previous explorer had ever thought of securing mineral specimens. The pre-Cambrian granites and beacon sandstones thus obtained confirmed our belief that this plateau was homogeneous, with the great bulk of the continent to the west, but somewhat different from the parts lying eastward below South America — which we then thought to form a separate and smaller continent divided from the larger one by a frozen junction of Ross and Weddell Seas, though Byrd has since disproved the hypothesis.

In certain of the sandstones, dynamited and chiseled after boring revealed their nature, we found some highly interesting fossil markings and fragments; notably ferns, seaweeds, trilobites, crinoids, and such mollusks as linguellae and gastropods — all of which seemed of real significance in connection with the region's primordial history. There was also a queer triangular, striated marking, about a foot in greatest diameter, which Lake pieced together from three fragments of slate brought up from a deep-blasted aperture. These fragments came from a point to the westward, near the Queen Alexandra Range; and Lake, as a biologist, seemed to find their curious marking unusually puzzling and provocative, though to my geological eye it looked not unlike some of the ripple effects reasonably common in the sedimentary rocks. Since slate is no more than a metamorphic formation into which a sedimentary stratum is pressed, and since the pressure itself produces odd distorting effects on any markings which may exist, I saw no reason for extreme wonder over the striated depression.

On January 6th, 1931, Lake, Pabodie, Danforth, the other six students, and myself flew directly over the south pole in two of the great planes, being forced down once by a sudden high wind, which, fortunately, did not develop into a typical storm. This was, as the papers have stated, one of several observation flights, during others of which we tried to discern new topographical features in areas unreached by previous explorers. Our early flights were disappointing in this latter respect, though they afforded us some magnificent examples of the richly fantastic and deceptive mirages of the polar regions, of which our sea voyage had given us some brief foretastes. Distant mountains floated in the sky as enchanted cities, and often the whole white world would dissolve into a gold, silver, and scarlet land of Dunsanian dreams and adventurous expectancy under the magic of the low midnight sun. On cloudy days we had considerable trouble in flying owing to the tendency of snowy earth and sky to merge into one mystical opalescent void with no visible horizon to mark the junction of the two.

At length we resolved to carry out our original plan of flying five hundred miles eastward with all four exploring planes and establishing a fresh sub-base at a point which would probably be on the smaller continental division, as we mistakenly conceived it. Geological specimens obtained there would be desirable for purposes of comparison. Our health so far had remained excellent — lime juice well offsetting the steady diet of tinned and salted food, and temperatures generally above zero enabling us to do without our thickest furs. It was now midsummer, and with haste and care we might be able to conclude work by March and avoid a tedious wintering through the long antarctic night. Several savage windstorms had burst upon us from the west, but we had escaped damage through the skill of Atwood in devising rudimentary aeroplane shelters and windbreaks of heavy snow blocks, and reinforcing the principal camp buildings with snow. Our good luck and efficiency had indeed been almost uncanny.

The outside world knew, of course, of our program, and was told also of Lake's strange and dogged insistence on a westward — or rather, northwestward — prospecting trip before our radical shift to the new base. It seems that he had pondered a great deal, and with alarmingly radical daring, over that triangular striated marking in the slate; reading into it certain contradictions in nature and geological period which whetted his curiosity to the utmost, and made him avid to sink more borings and blastings in the west-stretching formation to which the exhumed fragments evidently belonged. He was strangely convinced that the marking was the print of some bulky, unknown, and radically unclassifiable organism of considerably advanced evolution, notwithstanding that the rock which bore it was of so vastly ancient a date — Cambrian if not actually pre-Cambrian — as to preclude the probable existence not only of all highly evolved life, but of any life at all above the unicellular or at most the trilobite stage. These fragments, with their odd marking, must have been five hundred million to a thousand million years old.

II.

Popular imagination, I judge, responded actively to our wireless bulletins of Lake's start northwestward into regions never trodden by human foot or penetrated by human imagination, though we did not mention his wild hopes of revolutionizing the entire sciences of biology and geology. His preliminary sledging and boring journey of January 11th to 18th with Pabodie and five others — marred by the loss of two dogs in an upset when crossing one of the great pressure ridges in the ice — had brought up more and more of the Archaean slate; and even I was interested by the singular profusion of evident fossil markings in that unbelievably ancient stratum. These markings, however, were of very primitive life forms involving no great paradox except that any life forms should occur in rock as definitely pre-Cambrian as this seemed to be; hence I still failed to see the good sense of Lake's demand for an interlude in our time-saving program — an interlude requiring the use of all four planes, many men, and the whole of the expedition's mechanical apparatus. I did not, in the end, veto the plan, though I decided not to accompany the northwestward party despite Lake's plea for my geological advice. While they were gone, I would remain at the base with Pabodie and five men and work out final plans for the eastward shift. In preparation for this transfer, one of the planes had begun to move up a good gasoline supply from McMurdo Sound; but this could wait temporarily. I kept with me one sledge and nine dogs, since it is unwise to be at any time without possible transportation in an utterly tenantless world of aeon-long death.

Lake's sub-expedition into the unknown, as everyone will recall, sent out its own reports from the shortwave transmitters on the planes; these being simultaneously picked up by our apparatus at the southern base and by the Arkham at McMurdo Sound, whence they were relayed to the outside world on wave lengths up to fifty meters. The start was made January 22nd at 4 a.m., and the first wireless message we received came only two hours later, when Lake spoke of descending and starting a small-scale ice-melting and bore at a point some three hundred miles away from us. Six hours after that a second and very excited message told of the frantic, beaver-like work whereby a shallow shaft had been sunk and blasted, culminating in the discovery of slate fragments with several markings approximately like the one which had caused the original puzzlement.

Three hours later a brief bulletin announced the resumption of the flight in the teeth of a raw and piercing gale; and when I dispatched a message of protest against further hazards, Lake replied curtly that his new specimens made any hazard worth taking. I saw that his excitement had reached the point of mutiny, and that I could do nothing to check this headlong risk of the whole expedition's success; but it was appalling to think of his plunging deeper and deeper into that treacherous and sinister white immensity of tempests and unfathomed mysteries which stretched off for some fifteen hundred miles to the half-known, half-suspected coast line of Queen Mary and Knox Lands.

Then, in about an hour and a half more, came that doubly excited message from Lake's moving plane, which almost reversed my sentiments and made me wish I had accompanied the party:

> *10:05 P.M. On the wing. After snowstorm, have spied mountain range ahead higher than any hitherto seen. May equal Himalayas, allowing for height of plateau. Probable Latitude 76° 15', Longitude 113° 10' E. Reaches far as can see to right and left. Suspicion of two smoking cones. All peaks black and bare of snow. Gale blowing off them impedes navigation.*

After that Pabodie, the men and I hung breathlessly over the receiver. Thought of this titanic mountain rampart seven hundred miles away inflamed our deepest sense of adventure; and we rejoiced that our expedition, if not ourselves personally, had been its discoverers. In half an hour Lake called us again:

> *Moulton's plane forced down on plateau in foothills, but nobody hurt and perhaps can repair. Shall transfer essentials to other three for return or further moves if necessary, but no more heavy plane travel needed just now. Mountains surpass anything in imagination. Am going up scouting in Carroll's plane, with all weight out. You can't imagine anything like this. Highest peaks must go over thirty-five thousand feet. Everest out of the running. Atwood to work out height with theodolite while Carroll and I go up. Probably wrong about cones, for formations look stratified. Possibly pre-Cambrian slate with other strata mixed in. Queer skyline effects — regular sections of cubes clinging to highest peaks. Whole thing marvelous in red-gold light of low sun. Like land of mystery in a dream or gateway to forbidden world of untrodden wonder. Wish you were here to study.*

Though it was technically sleeping-time, not one of us listeners thought for a moment of retiring. It must have been a good deal the same at McMurdo Sound, where the supply cache and the Arkham were also getting the messages; for Captain Douglas gave out a call congratulating everybody on the important find, and Sherman, the cache operator, seconded his sentiments. We were sorry, of course, about the damaged aeroplane, but hoped it could be easily mended. Then, at 11 p.m., came another call from Lake:

Up with Carroll over highest foothills. Don't dare try really tall peaks in present weather, but shall later. Frightful work climbing, and hard going at this altitude, but worth it. Great range fairly solid, hence can't get any glimpses beyond. Main summits exceed Himalayas, and very queer. Range looks like pre-Cambrian slate, with plain signs of many other upheaved strata. Was wrong about volcanism. Goes farther in either direction than we can see. Swept clear of snow above about twenty-one thousand feet. Odd formations on slopes of highest mountains. Great low square blocks with exactly vertical sides, and rectangular lines of low, vertical ramparts, like the old Asian castles clinging to steep mountains in Roerich's paintings. Impressive from distance. Flew close to some, and Carroll thought they were formed of smaller separate pieces, but that is probably weathering. Most edges crumbled and rounded off as if exposed to storms and climate changes for millions of years. Parts, especially upper parts, seem to be of lighter-colored rock than any visible strata on slopes proper, hence of evidently crystalline origin. Close flying shows many cave-mouths, some unusually regular in outline, square or semicircular. You must come and investigate. Think I saw rampart squarely on top of one peak. Height seems about thirty thousand to thirty-five thousand feet. Am up twenty-one thousand, five hundred myself, in devilish, gnawing cold. Wind whistles and pipes through passes and in and out of caves, but no flying danger so far.

From then on for another half hour Lake kept up a running fire of comment, and expressed his intention of climbing some of the peaks on foot. I replied that I would join him as soon as he could send a plane, and that Pabodie and I would work out the best gasoline plan—just where and how to concentrate our supply in view of the expedition's altered character. Obviously, Lake's boring operations, as well as his aeroplane activities, would require a great deal for the new base which he planned to establish at the foot of the mountains; and it was possible that the eastward flight might not be made, after all, this season. In connection with this business I called Captain Douglas and asked him to get as much as possible out of the ships and up the barrier with the single dog team we had left there. A direct route across the unknown region between Lake and McMurdo Sound was what we really ought to establish.

Lake called me later to say that he had decided to let the camp stay where Moulton's plane had been forced down, and where repairs had already progressed somewhat. The ice sheet was very thin, with dark ground here and there visible, and he would sink some borings and blasts at that very point before making any sledge trips or climbing expeditions. He spoke of the ineffable majesty of the whole scene, and the queer state of his sensations at being in the lee of vast, silent pinnacles whose ranks shot up like a wall reaching the sky at the world's rim. Atwood's theodolite observations had placed the height of the five tallest peaks at from thirty thousand to thirty-four thousand feet. The windswept nature of the terrain clearly disturbed Lake, for it argued the occasional existence of prodigious gales, violent beyond anything we had so far encountered. His camp lay a little more than five miles from where the higher foothills rose abruptly. I could almost trace a note of subconscious alarm in his words—flashed across a glacial void of seven hundred miles—as he urged that we all hasten with the matter and get the strange, new region disposed of as soon as possible. He was about to rest now, after a continuous day's work of almost unparalleled speed, strenuousness, and results.

In the morning I had a three-cornered wireless talk with Lake and Captain Douglas at their widely separated bases. It was agreed that one of Lake's planes would come to my base for Pabodie, the five men, and myself, as well as for all the fuel it could carry. The rest of the fuel question, depending on our decision about an easterly trip, could wait for a few days, since Lake had enough for immediate camp heat and borings. Eventually the old southern base ought to be restocked, but if we postponed the easterly trip we would not use it till the next summer, and, meanwhile, Lake must send a plane to explore a direct route between his new mountains and McMurdo Sound.

Pabodie and I prepared to close our base for a short or long period, as the case might be. If we wintered in the antarctic we would probably fly straight from Lake's base to the Arkham without returning to this spot. Some of our conical tents had already been reinforced by blocks of hard snow, and now we decided to complete the job of making a permanent village. Owing to a very liberal tent supply, Lake had with him all that his base would need, even after our arrival. I wirelessed that Pabodie and I would be ready for the northwestward move after one day's work and one night's rest.

Our labors, however, were not very steady after 4 p.m., for about that time Lake began sending in the most extraordinary and excited messages. His working day had started unpropitiously, since an aeroplane survey of the nearly-exposed rock surfaces showed an entire absence of those Archaean and primordial strata for which he was looking, and which formed so great a part of the colossal peaks that loomed up at a tantalizing distance from the camp. Most of the rocks glimpsed were apparently Jurassic and Comanchian sandstones and Permian and Triassic schists, with now and then a glossy black outcropping suggesting a hard and slaty coal. This rather discouraged Lake, whose plans all hinged on unearthing specimens more than five hundred million years older. It was clear to him that in order to recover the Archaean slate vein in which he had found the odd markings, he would have to make a long sledge trip from these foothills to the steep slopes of the gigantic mountains themselves.

He had resolved, nevertheless, to do some local boring as part of the expedition's general program; hence he set up the drill and put five men to work with it while the rest finished settling the camp and repairing the damaged aeroplane. The softest visible rock—a sandstone about a quarter of a mile from the camp—had been chosen for the first sampling; and the drill made excellent progress without much supplementary blasting. It was about three hours afterward, following the first really heavy blast of the operation, that the shouting of the drill

Astounding Stories, February 1936

"It was a queer state of sensations — being in the lee of vast, silent pinnacles, where ranks shot up like a wall reaching the sky at the world's rim."

crew was heard; and that young Gedney — the acting foreman — rushed into the camp with the startling news.

They had struck a cave. Early in the boring the sandstone had given place to a vein of Comanchian limestone, full of minute fossil cephalopods, corals, echini, and spirifera, and with occasional suggestions of siliceous sponges and marine vertebrate bones — the latter probably of teleosts, sharks, and ganoids. This, in itself, was important enough, as affording the first vertebrate fossils the expedition had yet secured; but when shortly afterward the drill head dropped through the stratum into apparent vacancy, a wholly new and doubly intense wave of excitement spread among the excavators. A good-sized blast had laid open the subterrene secret; and now, through a jagged aperture perhaps five feet across and three feet thick, there yawned before the avid searchers a section of shallow limestone hollowing worn more than fifty million years ago by the trickling ground waters of a bygone tropic world.

The hollowed layer was not more than seven or eight feet deep but extended off indefinitely in all directions and had a fresh, slightly moving air which suggested its membership in an extensive subterranean system. Its roof and floor were abundantly equipped with large stalactites and stalagmites, some of which met in columnar form: but important above all else was the vast deposit of shells and bones, which in places nearly choked the passage. Washed down from unknown jungles of Mesozoic tree ferns and fungi, and forests of Tertiary cycads, fan palms, and primitive angiosperms, this osseous medley contained representatives of more Cretaceous, Eocene, and other animal species than the greatest paleontologist could have counted or classified in a year. Mollusks, crustacean armor, fishes, amphibians, reptiles, birds, and early mammals — great and small, known and unknown. No wonder Gedney ran back to the camp shouting, and no wonder everyone else dropped work and rushed headlong through the biting cold to where the tall derrick marked a new-found gateway to secrets of inner earth and vanished aeons.

When Lake had satisfied the first keen edge of his curiosity, he scribbled a message in his notebook and had young Moulton run back to the camp to dispatch it by wireless. This was my first word of the discovery, and it told of the identification of early shells, bones of ganoids and placoderms, remnants of labyrinthodonts and thecodonts, great mosasaur skull fragments, dinosaur vertebrae and armor plates, pterodactyl teeth and wing bones, Archaeopteryx debris, Miocene sharks' teeth, primitive bird skulls, and other bones of archaic mammals such as palaeotheres, Xiphodons, Eohippi, Oreodons, and titanotheres. There was nothing as recent as a mastodon, elephant, true camel, deer, or bovine animal; hence Lake concluded that the last deposits had occurred during the Oligocene Age, and that the hollowed stratum had lain in its present dried, dead, and inaccessible state for at least thirty million years.

On the other hand, the prevalence of very early life forms was singular in the highest degree. Though the limestone formation was, on the evidence of such typical imbedded fossils as ventriculites, positively and unmistakably Comanchian and not a particle earlier, the free fragments in the hollow space included a surprising proportion from organisms hitherto considered as peculiar to far older periods — even rudimentary fishes, mollusks, and corals as remote as the Silurian or Ordovician. The inevitable inference was that in this part of the world there had been a remarkable and unique degree of continuity between the life of over three hundred million years ago and that of only thirty million years ago. How far this continuity had extended beyond the Oligocene Age when the cavern was closed was of course past all speculation. In any event, the coming of the frightful ice in the Pleistocene some five hundred thousand years ago — a mere yesterday as compared with the age of this cavity — must have put an end to any of the primal forms which had locally managed to outlive their common terms.

Lake was not content to let his first message stand, but had another bulletin written and dispatched across the snow to the camp before Moulton could get back. After that Moulton stayed at the wireless in one of the planes, transmitting to me — and to the Arkham for relaying to the outside world — the frequent postscripts which Lake sent him by a succession of messengers. Those who followed the newspapers will remember the excitement created among men of science by that afternoon's reports — reports which have finally led, after all these years, to the organization of that very Starkweather-Moore Expedition which I am so anxious to dissuade from its purposes. I had better give the messages literally as Lake sent them, and as our base operator McTighe translated them from the pencil shorthand:

> *Fowler makes discovery of highest importance in sandstone and limestone fragments from blasts. Several distinct triangular striated prints like those in Archaean slate, proving that source survived from over six hundred million years ago to Comanchian times without more than moderate morphological changes and decrease in average size. Comanchian prints apparently more primitive or decadent, if anything, than older ones. Emphasize importance of discovery in press. Will mean to biology what Einstein has meant to mathematics and physics. Joins up with my previous work and amplifies conclusions. Appears to indicate, as I suspected, that earth has seen whole cycle or cycles of organic life before known one that begins with Archaeozoic cells. Was evolved and specialized not later than a thousand million years ago, when planet was young and recently uninhabitable for any life forms or normal protoplasmic structure. Question arises when, where, and how development took place.*

> *LATER. Examining certain skeletal fragments of large land and marine saurians and primitive mammals, find singular local wounds or injuries to bony structure not attributable to any known predatory or carnivorous animal of any period, of two sorts — straight, penetrant bores, and apparently hacking incisions. One or two cases of cleanly severed bones. Not many specimens affected. Am sending*

Astounding Stories, February 1936

"I've got to dissect one of these things before —"

to camp for electric torches. Will extend search area underground by hacking away stalactites.

STILL LATER. Have found peculiar soapstone fragment about six inches across and an inch and a half thick, wholly unlike any visible local formation — greenish, but no evidences to place its period. Has curious smoothness and regularity. Shaped like five-pointed star with tips broken off, and signs of other cleavage at inward angles and in center of surface. Small, smooth depression in center of unbroken surface. Arouses much curiosity as to source and weathering. Probably some freak of water action. Carroll, with magnifier, thinks he can make out additional markings of geologic significance. Groups of tiny dots in regular patterns. Dogs growing uneasy as we work, and seem to hate this soapstone. Must see if it has any peculiar odor. Will report again when Mills gets back with light and we start on underground area.

10:15 P.M. Important discovery. Orrendorf and Watkins, working underground at 9:45 with light, found monstrous barrel-shaped fossil of wholly unknown nature; probably vegetable unless overgrown specimen of unknown marine radiata. Tissue evidently preserved by mineral salts. Tough as leather, but astonishing flexibility retained in places. Marks of broken-off parts at ends and around sides. Six feet end to end, three and five-tenths feet central diameter, tapering to one foot at each end. Like a barrel with five bulging ridges in place of staves. Lateral breakages, as of thinnish stalks, are at equator in middle of these ridges. In furrows between ridges are curious growths — combs or wings that fold up and spread out like fans. All greatly damaged but one, which gives almost seven-foot wing spread. Arrangement reminds one of certain monsters of primal myth, especially fabled Elder Things in Necronomicon. *These wings seem to be membraneous, stretched on frame work of glandular tubing. Apparent minute orifices in frame tubing at wing tips. Ends of body shriveled, giving no clue to interior or to what has been broken off there. Must dissect when we get back to camp. Can't decide whether vegetable or animal. Many features obviously of almost incredible primitiveness. Have set all hands cutting stalactites and looking for further specimens. Additional scarred bones found, but these must wait. Having trouble with dogs. They can't endure the new specimen, and would probably tear it to pieces if we didn't keep it at a distance from them.*

11:30 P.M. Attention, Dyer, Pabodie, Douglas. Matter of highest — I might say transcendent — importance. Arkham must relay to Kingsport Head Station at once. Strange barrel growth is the Archaean thing that left prints in rocks. Mills, Boudreau, and Fowler discover cluster of thirteen more at underground point forty feet from aperture. Mixed with curiously rounded and configured soapstone fragments smaller than one previously found — star-shaped, but no marks of breakage except at some of the points. Of organic specimens, eight apparently perfect, with all appendages. Have brought all to surface, leading off dogs to distance. They cannot stand the things. Give close attention to description and repeat back for accuracy Papers must get this right.

Objects are eight feet long all over. Six-foot, five-ridged barrel torso three and five-tenths feet central diameter, one foot end diameters. Dark gray, flexible, and infinitely tough. Seven-foot membranous wings of same color, found folded, spread out of furrows between ridges. Wing framework tubular or glandular, of lighter gray, with orifices at wing tips. Spread wings have serrated edge. Around equator, one at central apex of each of the five vertical, stave-like ridges are five systems of light gray flexible arms or tentacles found tightly folded to torso but expansible to maximum length of over three feet. Like arms of primitive crinoid. Single stalks three inches diameter branch after six inches into five substalks, each of which branches after eight inches into small, tapering tentacles or tendrils, giving each stalk a total of twenty-five tentacles.

At top of torso blunt, bulbous neck of lighter gray, with gill-like suggestions, holds yellowish five-pointed starfish-shaped apparent head covered with three-inch wiry cilia of various prismatic colors. Head thick and puffy, about two feet point to point, with three-inch flexible yellowish tubes projecting from each point. Slit in exact center of top probably breathing aperture. At end of each tube is spherical expansion where yellowish membrane rolls back on handling to reveal glassy, red-irised globe, evidently an eye. Five slightly longer reddish tubes start from inner angles of starfish-shaped head and end in saclike swellings of same color which, upon pressure, open to bell-shaped orifices two inches maximum diameter and lined with sharp, white tooth like projections — probably mouths. All these tubes, cilia, and points of starfish head, found folded tightly down; tubes and points clinging to bulbous neck and torso. Flexibility surprising despite vast toughness.

At bottom of torso, rough but dissimilarly functioning counterparts of head arrangements exist. Bulbous light-gray pseudo-neck, without gill suggestions, holds greenish five-pointed starfish arrangement. Tough, muscular arms four feet long and tapering from seven inches diameter at base to about two and five-tenths at point. To each point is attached small end of a greenish five-veined membranous triangle eight inches long and six wide at farther end. This is the paddle, fin, or pseudofoot which has made prints in rocks from a thousand million to fifty or sixty million years old. From inner angles of starfish-arrangement project two-foot reddish tubes tapering from three inches diameter at base to one at tip. Orifices at tips. All these parts infinitely tough and leathery, but extremely flexible. Four-foot arms with paddles undoubtedly used for locomotion of some sort, marine or otherwise. When moved, display suggestions of exaggerated muscularity. As found, all these projections tightly folded over pseudoneck and end of torso, corresponding to projections at other end.

Cannot yet assign positively to animal or vegetable kingdom, but odds now favor animal. Probably represents incredibly advanced evolution of radiata without loss of certain primitive features. Echinoderm resemblances unmistakable despite local contradictory evidences. Wing structure puzzles in view of probable marine habitat, but may have use in water navigation. Symmetry is curiously vegetablelike, suggesting vegetable's essential up-and-down structure rather than animal's fore-and-aft structure. Fabulously early date of evolution, preceding even simplest Archaean protozoa hitherto known, baffles all conjecture as to origin.

Complete specimens have such uncanny resemblance to certain creatures of primal myth that suggestion of ancient existence outside antarctic becomes inevitable. Dyer and Pabodie have read Necronomicon *and seen Clark Ashton Smith's nightmare paintings based on text, and will understand when I speak of Elder Things supposed to have created all earth life as jest or mistake. Students have always thought conception formed from morbid imaginative treatment of very ancient tropical radiata. Also like prehistoric folklore things Wilmarth has spoken of — Cthulhu cult appendages, etc.*

Vast field of study opened. Deposits probably of late Cretaceous or early Eocene period, judging from associated specimens. Massive stalagmites deposited above them. Hard work hewing out, but toughness prevented damage. State of preservation miraculous, evidently owing to limestone action. No more found so far, but will resume search later. Job now to get fourteen huge specimens to camp without dogs, which bark furiously and can't be trusted near them. With nine men — three left to guard the dogs — we ought to manage the three sledges fairly well, though wind is bad. Must establish plane communication with McMurdo Sound and begin shipping material. But I've got to dissect one of these things before we take any rest. Wish I had a real laboratory here. Dyer better kick himself for having tried to stop my westward trip. First the world's greatest

Astounding Stories, February 1936

"First the world"

mountains, and then this. If this last isn't the high spot of the expedition, I don't know what is. We're made scientifically. Congrats, Pabodie, on the drill that opened up the cave. Now will Arkham please repeat description?

The sensations of Pabodie and myself at receipt of this report were almost beyond description, nor were our companions much behind us in enthusiasm. McTighe, who had hastily translated a few high spots as they came from the droning receiving set, wrote out the entire message from his shorthand version as soon as Lake's operator signed off. All appreciated the epoch-making significance of the discovery, and I sent Lake congratulations as soon as the Arkham's operator had repeated back the descriptive parts as requested; and my example was followed by Sherman from his station at the McMurdo Sound supply cache, as well as by Captain Douglas of the Arkham. Later, as head of the expedition, I added some remarks to be relayed through the Arkham to the outside world. Of course, rest was an absurd thought amidst this excitement; and my only wish was to get to Lake's camp as quickly as I could. It disappointed me when he sent word that a rising mountain gale made early aerial travel impossible.

But within an hour and a half interest again rose to banish

disappointment. Lake, sending more messages, told of the completely successful transportation of the fourteen great specimens to the camp. It had been a hard pull, for the things were surprisingly heavy; but nine men had accomplished it very neatly. Now some of the party were hurriedly building a snow corral at a safe distance from the camp, to which the dogs could be brought for greater convenience in feeding. The specimens were laid out on the hard snow near the camp, save for one on which Lake was making crude attempts at dissection.

This dissection seemed to be a greater task than had been expected, for, despite the heat of a gasoline stove in the newly raised laboratory tent, the deceptively flexible tissues of the chosen specimen — a powerful and intact one — lost nothing of their more than leathery toughness. Lake was puzzled as to how he might make the requisite incisions without violence destructive enough to upset all the structural niceties he was looking for. He had, it is true, seven more perfect specimens; but these were too few to use up recklessly unless the cave might later yield an unlimited supply. Accordingly he removed the specimen and dragged in one which, though having remnants of the starfish arrangements at both ends, was badly crushed and partly disrupted along one of the great torso furrows.

Results, quickly reported over the wireless, were baffling and provocative indeed. Nothing like delicacy or accuracy was possible with instruments hardly able to cut the anomalous tissue, but the little that was achieved left us all awed and bewildered. Existing biology would have to be wholly revised, for this thing was no product of any cell growth science knows about. There had been scarcely any mineral replacement, and despite an age of perhaps forty million years, the internal organs were wholly intact. The leathery, undeteriorative, and almost indestructible quality was an inherent attribute of the thing's form of organization, and pertained to some paleogean cycle of invertebrate evolution utterly beyond our powers of speculation. At first all that Lake found was dry, but as the heated tent produced its thawing effect, organic moisture of pungent and offensive odor was encountered toward the thing's uninjured side. It was not blood, but a thick, dark-green fluid apparently answering the same purpose. By the time Lake reached this stage, all thirty-seven dogs had been brought to the still uncompleted corral near the camp, and even at that distance set up a savage barking and show of restlessness at the acrid, diffusive smell.

Far from helping to place the strange entity, this provisional dissection merely deepened its mystery. All guesses about its external members had been correct, and on the evidence of these one could hardly hesitate to call the thing animal; but internal inspection brought up so many vegetable evidences that Lake was left hopelessly at sea. It had digestion and circulation, and eliminated waste matter through the reddish tubes of its starfish-shaped base. Cursorily, one would say that its respiration apparatus handled oxygen rather than carbon dioxide, and there were odd evidences of air-storage chambers and methods of shifting respiration from the external orifice to at least two other fully developed breathing systems — gills and pores. Clearly, it was amphibian, and probably adapted to long airless hibernation periods as well. Vocal organs seemed present in connection with the main respiratory system, but they presented anomalies beyond immediate solution. Articulate speech, in the sense of syllable utterance, seemed barely conceivable, but musical piping notes covering a wide range were highly probable. The muscular system was almost prematurely developed.

The nervous system was so complex and highly developed as to leave Lake aghast. Though excessively primitive and archaic in some respects, the thing had a set of ganglial centers and connectives arguing the very extremes of specialized development. Its five-lobed brain was surprisingly advanced, and there were signs of a sensory equipment, served in part through the wiry cilia of the head, involving factors alien to any other terrestrial organism. Probably it had more than five senses, so that its habits could not be predicted from any existing analogy. It must, Lake thought, have been a creature of keen sensitiveness and delicately differentiated functions in its primal world — much like the ants and bees of today. It reproduced like the vegetable cryptogams, especially the Pteridophyta, having spore cases at the tips of the wings and evidently developing from a thallus or prothallus.

But to give it a name at this stage was mere folly. It looked like a radiate, but was clearly something more. It was partly vegetable, but had three-fourths of the essentials of animal structure. That it was marine in origin, its symmetrical contour and certain other attributes clearly indicated; yet one could not be exact as to the limit of its later adaptations. The wings, after all, held a persistent suggestion of the aerial. How it could have undergone its tremendously complex evolution on a new-born earth in time to leave prints in Archaean rocks was so far beyond conception as to make Lake whimsically recall the primal myths about Great Old Ones who filtered down from the stars and concocted earth life as a joke or mistake; and the wild tales of cosmic hill things from outside told by a folklorist colleague in Miskatonic's English department.

Naturally, he considered the possibility of the pre-Cambrian prints having been made by a less evolved ancestor of the present specimens, but quickly rejected this too-facile theory upon considering the advanced structural qualities of the older fossils. If anything, the later contours showed decadence rather than higher evolution. The size of the pseudofeet had decreased, and the whole morphology seemed coarsened and simplified. Moreover, the nerves and organs just examined held singular suggestions of retrogression from forms still more complex. Atrophied and vestigial parts were surprisingly prevalent. Altogether, little could be said to have been solved; and Lake fell back on mythology for a provisional name — jocosely dubbing his finds "The Elder Ones."

At about 2:30 a.m., having decided to postpone further work and get a little rest, he covered the dissected organism with a tarpaulin, emerged from the laboratory tent, and studied the intact specimens with renewed interest. The ceaseless antarctic sun had begun to limber up their tissues a trifle, so that the head points and tubes of two or three showed signs of unfolding; but Lake did not believe there was any danger of immediate decomposition in the almost subzero air. He did, however, move all the undissected specimens close together and throw a spare tent over them in order to keep off the direct solar rays. That would also help to keep their possible scent away from the dogs, whose hostile unrest was really becoming a problem, even at their substantial distance and behind the higher and higher snow walls which an increased quota of the men were hastening to raise around their quarters. He had to weight down the corners of the tent cloth with heavy blocks of snow to hold it in place amidst the rising gale, for the titan mountains seemed about to deliver some gravely severe blasts. Early apprehensions about sudden antarctic winds were revived, and under Atwood's supervision precautions were taken to bank the tents, new dog corral, and crude aeroplane shelters with snow on the mountainward side. These latter shelters, begun with hard snow blocks during odd moments, were by no means as high as they should have been; and Lake finally detached all hands from other tasks to work on them.

It was after four when Lake at last prepared to sign off and advised us all to share the rest period his outfit would take when the shelter walls were a little higher. He held some friendly chat with Pabodie over the ether, and repeated his praise of the really marvelous drills that had helped him make his discovery. Atwood also sent greetings and praises. I gave Lake a warm word of congratulations, owning up that he was right about the western trip, and we all agreed to get in touch by wireless at ten in the morning. If the gale was then over, Lake would send a plane for the party at my base. Just before retiring I dispatched a final message to the Arkham with instructions about toning down the day's news for the outside world, since the full details seemed radical enough to rouse a wave of incredulity until further substantiated.

III.

None of us, I imagine, slept very heavily or continuously that morning. Both the excitement of Lake's discovery and the mounting fury of the wind were against such a thing. So savage was the blast, even where we were, that we could not help wondering how much worse it was at Lake's camp, directly under the vast unknown peaks that bred and delivered it. McTighe was awake at ten o'clock and tried to get Lake on the wireless, as agreed, but some electrical condition in the disturbed air to the westward seemed to prevent communication. We did, however, get the Arkham, and Douglas told me that he had likewise been vainly trying to reach Lake. He had not known about the wind, for very little was blowing at McMurdo Sound, despite its persistent rage where we were.

Throughout the day we all listened anxiously and tried to get Lake at intervals, but invariably without results. About noon a positive frenzy of wind stampeded out of the west, causing us to fear for the safety of our camp; but it eventually died down, with only a moderate relapse at 2 p.m. After three o'clock it was very quiet, and we redoubled our efforts to get Lake. Reflecting that he had four planes, each provided with an excellent short-wave outfit, we could not imagine any ordinary accident capable of crippling all his wireless equipment at once. Nevertheless the stony silence continued, and when we thought of the delirious force the wind must have had in his locality we could not help making the most direful conjectures.

By six o'clock our fears had become intense and definite, and after a wireless consultation with Douglas and Thorfinnssen I resolved to take steps toward investigation. The fifth aeroplane, which we had left at the McMurdo Sound supply cache with Sherman and two sailors, was in good shape and ready for instant use, and it seemed that the very emergency for which it had been saved was now upon us. I got Sherman by wireless and ordered him to join me with the plane and the two sailors at the southern base as quickly as possible, the air conditions being apparently highly favorable. We then talked over the personnel of the coming investigation party, and decided that we would include all hands, together with the sledge and dogs which I had kept with me. Even so great a load would not be too much for one of the huge planes built to our special orders for heavy machinery transportation. At intervals I still tried to reach Lake with the wireless, but all to no purpose.

Sherman, with the sailors Gunnarsson and Larsen, took off at 7:30, and reported a quiet flight from several points on the wing. They arrived at our base at midnight, and all hands at once discussed the next move. It was risky business sailing over the antarctic in a single aeroplane without any line of bases, but no one drew back from what seemed like the plainest necessity. We turned in at two o'clock for a brief rest after some preliminary loading of the plane, but were up again in four hours to finish the loading and packing.

At 7:15 a.m., January 25th, we started flying northwestward under McTighe's pilotage with ten men, seven dogs, a sledge, a fuel and food supply, and other items including the plane's wireless outfit. The atmosphere was clear, fairly quiet, and relatively mild in temperature, and we anticipated very little trouble in reaching the latitude and longitude designated by Lake as the site of his camp. Our apprehensions were over what we might find, or fail to find, at the end of our journey, for silence continued to answer all calls dispatched to the camp.

Every incident of that four-and-a-half-hour flight is burned into my recollection because of its crucial position in my life. It marked my loss, at the age of fifty-four, of all that peace and balance which the normal mind possesses through its accustomed conception of external nature and nature's laws. Thenceforward the ten of us — but the student Danforth and myself above all others — were to face a hideously amplified world of lurking horrors which nothing can erase from our emotions, and which we would refrain from sharing with mankind in general if we could. The newspapers have printed the bulletins we sent from the moving plane, telling of our non-stop course, our two battles with treacherous upper-air gales, our glimpse of the broken surface where Lake had sunk his mid-journey shaft three days before, and our sight of a group of those strange fluffy snow cylinders noted by Amundsen and Byrd as rolling in the wind across the endless leagues of frozen plateau. There came a point, though, when our sensations could not be conveyed in any words the press would understand, and a latter point when we had to adopt an actual rule of strict censorship.

The sailor Larsen was first to spy the jagged line of witch-like cones and pinnacles ahead, and his shouts sent everyone to the windows of the great cabined plane. Despite our speed, they were very slow in gaining prominence; hence we knew that they must be infinitely far off, and visible only because of their abnormal height. Little by little, however, they rose grimly into the western sky; allowing us to distinguish various bare, bleak, blackish summits, and to catch the curious sense of fantasy which they inspired as seen in the reddish antarctic light against the provocative background of iridescent ice-dust clouds. In the whole spectacle there was a persistent, pervasive hint of stupendous secrecy and potential revelation. It was as if these stark, nightmare spires marked the pylons of a frightful gateway into forbidden spheres of dream, and complex gulfs of remote time, space, and ultra-dimensionality. I could not help feeling that they were evil things — mountains of madness whose farther slopes looked out over some accursed ultimate abyss. That seething, half-luminous cloud background held ineffable suggestions of a vague, ethereal beyondness far more than terrestrially spatial, and gave appalling reminders of the utter remoteness, separateness, desolation, and aeon-long death of this untrodden and unfathomed austral world.

It was young Danforth who drew our notice to the curious regularities of the higher mountain skyline — regularities like clinging fragments of perfect cubes, which Lake had mentioned in his messages, and which indeed justified his comparison with the dreamlike suggestions of primordial temple ruins, on cloudy Asian mountaintops so subtly and strangely painted by Roerich. There was indeed something hauntingly Roerich-like about this whole unearthly continent of mountainous mystery. I had felt it in October when we first caught sight of Victoria Land, and I felt it afresh now. I felt, too, another wave of uneasy consciousness of Archaean mythical resemblances; of how disturbingly this lethal realm corresponded to the evilly famed plateau of Leng in the primal writings. Mythologists have placed Leng in Central Asia; but the racial memory of man — or of his predecessors — is long, and it may well be that certain tales have come down from lands and mountains and temples of horror earlier than Asia and earlier than any human world we know. A few daring mystics have hinted at a pre-Pleistocene origin for the fragmentary Pnakotic Manuscripts, and have suggested that the devotees of Tsathoggua were as alien to mankind as Tsathoggua itself. Leng, wherever in space or time it might brood, was not a region I would care to be in or near, nor did I relish the proximity of a world that had ever bred such ambiguous and Archaean monstrosities as those Lake had just mentioned. At the moment I felt sorry that I had ever read the abhorred *Necronomicon*, or talked so much with that unpleasantly erudite folklorist Wilmarth at the university.

This mood undoubtedly served to aggravate my reaction to the bizarre mirage which burst upon us from the increasingly opalescent zenith as we drew near the mountains and began to make out the cumulative undulations of the foothills. I had seen dozens of polar mirages during the preceding weeks, some of them quite as uncanny and fantastically vivid as the present sample; but this one had a wholly novel and obscure quality of menacing symbolism, and I shuddered as the seething labyrinth of fabulous walls and towers and minarets loomed out of the troubled ice vapors above our heads.

The effect was that of a Cyclopean city of no architecture known to man or to human imagination, with vast aggregations of night-black masonry embodying monstrous perversions of geometrical laws. There were truncated cones, sometimes terraced or fluted, surmounted by tall cylindrical shafts here and there bulbously enlarged and often capped with tiers of thinnish scalloped disks; and strange beetling, table-like constructions suggesting piles of multitudinous rectangular slabs or circular plates or five-pointed stars with each one overlapping the one beneath. There were composite cones and pyramids either alone or surmounting cylinders or cubes or flatter truncated cones and pyramids, and occasional needle-like spires in curious clusters of five. All of these febrile structures seemed knit together by tubular bridges crossing from one to the other at various dizzy heights, and the implied scale of the whole was terrifying and oppressive in its sheer gigantism. The general type of mirage was not unlike some of the wilder forms observed and drawn by the arctic whaler Scoresby in 1820, but at this time and place, with those dark, unknown mountain peaks soaring stupendously ahead, that anomalous elder-world discovery in our minds, and the pall of probable disaster enveloping the greater part of our expedition, we all seemed to find in it a taint of latent malignity and infinitely evil portent.

I was glad when the mirage began to break up, though in the process the various nightmare turrets and cones assumed distorted, temporary forms of even vaster hideousness. As the whole illusion dissolved to churning opalescence we began to look earthward again, and saw that our journey's end was not far off. The unknown mountains ahead rose dizzily up like a fearsome rampart of giants, their curious regularities showing with startling clearness even without a field-glass. We were over the lowest foothills now, and could see amidst the snow, ice, and bare patches of their main plateau a couple of darkish spots which we took to be Lake's camp and boring. The higher foothills shot up between five and six miles away, forming a range almost distinct from the terrifying line of more than Himalayan peaks beyond them. At length Ropes — the student who had relieved McTighe at the controls — began to head downward toward the left-hand dark spot whose size marked it as the camp. As he did so, McTighe sent out the last uncensored wireless message the world was to receive from our expedition.

Everyone, of course, has read the brief and unsatisfying bulletins of the rest of our antarctic sojourn. Some hours after our landing we sent a guarded report of the tragedy we found, and reluctantly announced the wiping out of the whole Lake party by the frightful wind of the preceding day, or of the night before that. Eleven known dead, young Gedney missing. People pardoned our hazy lack of details through realization of the shock the sad event must have caused us, and believed us when we explained that the mangling action of the wind had rendered all eleven bodies unsuitable for transportation outside. Indeed, I flatter myself that even in the midst of our distress, utter bewilderment, and soul-clutching horror, we scarcely went beyond the truth in any specific instance. The tremendous significance lies in what we dared not tell; what I would not tell now but for the need of warning others off from nameless terrors.

It is a fact that the wind had brought dreadful havoc. Whether all could have lived through it, even without the other thing, is gravely open to doubt. The storm, with its fury of madly driven ice particles, must have been beyond anything our expedition had encountered before. One aeroplane shelter — all, it seems, had been left in a far too flimsy and inadequate state — was nearly pulverized; and the derrick at the distant boring was entirely shaken to pieces. The exposed metal of the grounded planes and drilling machinery was bruised into a high polish, and two of the small tents were flattened despite their snow banking. Wooden surfaces left out in the blast were pitted and denuded of paint, and all signs of tracks in the snow were completely obliterated. It is also true that we found none of the Archaean biological objects in a condition to take outside as a whole. We did gather some minerals from a vast, tumbled pile, including several of the greenish soapstone fragments whose odd five-pointed rounding and faint patterns of grouped dots caused so many doubtful comparisons; and some fossil bones, among which were the most typical of the curiously injured specimens.

None of the dogs survived, their hurriedly built snow inclosure near the camp being almost wholly destroyed. The wind may have done that, though the greater breakage on the side next the camp, which was not the windward one, suggests an outward leap or break of the frantic beasts themselves. All three sledges were gone, and we have tried to explain that the wind may have blown them off into the unknown. The drill and ice-melting machinery at the boring were too badly damaged to warrant salvage, so we used them to choke up that subtly disturbing gateway to the past which Lake had blasted. We likewise left at the camp the two most shaken up of the planes; since our surviving party had only four real pilots — Sherman, Danforth, McTighe, and Ropes — in all, with Danforth in a poor nervous shape to navigate. We brought back all the books, scientific equipment, and other incidentals we could find, though much was rather unaccountably blown away. Spare tents and furs were either missing or badly out of condition.

It was approximately 4 p.m., after wide plane cruising had forced us to give Gedney up for lost, that we sent our guarded message to the Arkham for relaying; and I think we did well to keep it as calm and noncommittal as we succeeded in doing. The most we said about agitation concerned our dogs, whose frantic uneasiness near the biological specimens was to be expected from poor Lake's accounts. We did not mention, I think, their display of the same uneasiness when sniffing around the queer greenish soapstones and certain other objects in the disordered region — objects including scientific instruments, aeroplanes, and machinery, both at the camp and at the boring, whose parts had been loosened, moved, or otherwise tampered with by winds that must have harbored singular curiosity and investigativeness.

About the fourteen biological specimens, we were pardonably indefinite. We said that the only ones we discovered were damaged, but that enough was left of them to prove Lake's description wholly and impressively accurate. It was hard work keeping our personal emotions out of this matter — and we did not mention numbers or say exactly how we had found those which we did find. We had by that time agreed not to transmit anything suggesting madness on the part of Lake's men, and it surely looked like madness to find six imperfect monstrosities carefully buried upright in nine-foot snow graves under five-pointed mounds punched over with groups of dots in patterns exactly those on the queer greenish soapstones dug up from Mesozoic or Tertiary times. The eight perfect specimens mentioned by Lake seemed to have been completely blown away.

We were careful, too, about the public's general peace of mind; hence Danforth and I said little about that frightful trip over the mountains the next day. It was the fact that only a radically lightened plane could possibly cross a range of such height, which mercifully limited that scouting tour to the two of us. On our return at one a.m., Danforth was close to hysterics, but kept an admirably stiff upper lip. It took no persuasion to make him promise not to show our sketches and the other things we brought away in our pockets, not to say anything more to the others than what we had agreed to relay outside, and to hide our camera films for private development later on; so that part of my present story will be as new to Pabodie, McTighe, Ropes, Sherman, and the rest as it will be to the world in general. Indeed, Danforth is closer mouthed than I: for he saw, or thinks he saw, one thing he will not tell even me.

As all know, our report included a tale of a hard ascent — a confirmation of Lake's opinion that the great peaks are of Archaean slate and other very primal crumpled strata unchanged since at least middle Comanchian times; a conventional comment on the regularity of the clinging cube and rampart formations; a decision that the cave mouths indicate dissolved calcareous veins; a conjecture that certain slopes and passes would permit of the scaling and crossing of the entire range by seasoned mountaineers; and a remark that the mysterious other side holds a lofty and immense superplateau as ancient and unchanging as the mountains themselves — twenty thousand feet in elevation, with grotesque rock formations protruding through a thin glacial layer and with low gradual foothills between the general plateau surface and the sheer precipices of the highest peaks.

This body of data is in every respect true so far as it goes, and it completely satisfied the men at the camp. We laid our absence of sixteen hours — a longer time than our announced flying, landing, reconnoitering, and rock-collecting program called for — to a long mythical spell of adverse wind conditions, and told truly of our landing on the farther foothills. Fortunately our tale sounded realistic and prosaic enough not to tempt any of the others into emulating our flight. Had any tried to do that, I would have used every ounce of my persuasion to stop them — and I do not know what Danforth would have done. While we were gone, Pabodie, Sherman, Ropes, McTighe, and Williamson had worked like beavers over Lake's two best planes, fitting them again for use despite the altogether unaccountable juggling of their operative mechanism.

We decided to load all the planes the next morning and start back for our old base as soon as possible. Even though indirect, that was the safest way to work toward McMurdo Sound; for a straight-line flight across the most utterly unknown stretches of the aeon-dead continent would involve many additional hazards. Further exploration was hardly feasible in view of our tragic decimation and the ruin of our drilling machinery. The doubts and horrors around us — which we did not reveal — made us wish only to escape from this austral world of desolation and brooding madness as swiftly as we could.

As the public knows, our return to the world was accomplished without further disasters. All planes reached the old base on the evening of the next day — January 27th — after a swift non-stop flight; and on the 28th we made McMurdo Sound in two laps, the one pause being very brief, and occasioned by a faulty rudder in the furious wind over the ice shelf after we had cleared the great plateau. In five days more, the Arkham and Miskatonic, with all hands and equipment on board, were shaking clear of the thickening field ice and working up Ross Sea with the mocking mountains of Victoria Land looming westward against a troubled antarctic sky and twisting the wind's wails into a wide-ranged musical piping which chilled my soul to the quick. Less than a fortnight later we left the last hint of polar land behind us and thanked heaven that we were clear of a haunted, accursed realm where life and death, space and time, have made black and blasphemous alliances, in the unknown epochs since matter first writhed and swam on the planet's scarce-cooled crust.

Since our return we have all constantly worked to discourage antarctic exploration, and have kept certain doubts and guesses to ourselves with splendid unity and faithfulness. Even young Danforth, with his nervous breakdown, has not flinched or babbled to his doctors — indeed, as I have said, there is one thing he thinks he alone saw which he will not tell even me, though I think it would help his psychological state if he would consent to do so. It might explain and relieve much, though perhaps the thing was no more than the delusive aftermath of an earlier shock. That is the impression I gather after those rare, irresponsible moments when he whispers disjointed things to me — things which he repudiates vehemently as soon as he gets a grip on himself again.

It will be hard work deterring others from the great white south, and some of our efforts may directly harm our cause by drawing inquiring notice. We might have known from the first that human curiosity is undying, and that the results we announced would be enough to spur others ahead on the same age-long pursuit of the unknown. Lake's reports of those biological monstrosities had aroused naturalists and paleontologists to the highest pitch, though we were sensible enough not to show the detached parts we had taken from the actual buried specimens, or our photographs of those specimens as they were found. We also refrained from showing the more puzzling of the scarred bones and greenish soapstones; while Danforth and I have closely guarded the pictures we took or drew on the superplateau across the range, and the crumpled things we smoothed, studied in terror, and brought away in our pockets.

But now that Starkweather-Moore party is organizing, and with a thoroughness far beyond anything our outfit attempted. If not dissuaded, they will get to the innermost nucleus of the antarctic and melt and bore till they bring up that which we know may end the world. So I must break through all reticences at last — even about that ultimate, nameless thing beyond the mountains of madness.

IV.

It is only with vast hesitancy and repugnance that I let my mind go back to Lake's camp and what we really found there — and to that other thing beyond the mountains of madness. I am constantly tempted to shirk the details, and to let hints stand for actual facts and ineluctable deductions. I hope I have said enough already to let me glide briefly over the rest; the rest, that is, of the horror at the camp. I have told of the wind-ravaged terrain, the damaged shelters, the disarranged machinery, the varied uneasiness of our dogs, the missing sledges and other items, the deaths of men and dogs, the absence of Gedney, and the six insanely buried biological specimens, strangely sound in texture for all their structural injuries, from a world forty million years dead. I do not recall whether I mentioned that upon checking up the canine bodies we found one dog missing. We did not think much about that till later — indeed, only Danforth and I have thought of it at all.

The principal things I have been keeping back relate to

the bodies, and to certain subtle points which may or may not lend a hideous and incredible kind of rationale to the apparent chaos. At the time, I tried to keep the men's minds off those points; for it was so much simpler — so much more normal — to lay everything to an outbreak of madness on the part of some of Lake's party. From the look of things, that demon mountain wind must have been enough to drive any man mad in the midst of this center of all earthly mystery and desolation.

The crowning abnormality, of course, was the condition of the bodies — men and dogs alike. They had all been in some terrible kind of conflict, and were torn and mangled in fiendish and altogether inexplicable ways. Death, so far as we could judge, had in each case come from strangulation or laceration. The dogs had evidently started the trouble, for the state of their ill-built corral bore witness to its forcible breakage from within. It had been set some distance from the camp because of the hatred of the animals for those hellish Archaean organisms, but the precaution seemed to have been taken in vain. When left alone in that monstrous wind, behind flimsy walls of insufficient height, they must have stampeded — whether from the wind itself, or from some subtle, increasing odor emitted by the nightmare specimens, one could not say. Those specimens, of course, had been covered with a tent-cloth; yet the low antarctic sun had beat steadily upon that cloth, and Lake had mentioned that solar heat tended to make the strangely sound and tough tissues of the things relax and expand. Perhaps the wind had whipped the cloth from over them, and jostled them about in such a way that their more pungent olfactory qualities became manifest despite their unbelievable antiquity.

But whatever had happened, it was hideous and revolting enough. Perhaps I had better put squeamishness aside and tell the worst at last — though with a categorical statement of opinion, based on the first-hand observations and most rigid deductions of both Danforth and myself, that the then missing Gedney was in no way responsible for the loathsome horrors we found. I have said that the bodies were frightfully mangled. Now I must add that some were incised and subtracted from in the most curious, cold-blooded, and inhuman fashion. It was the same with dogs and men. All the healthier, fatter bodies, quadrupedal or bipedal, had had their most solid masses of tissue cut out and removed, as by a careful butcher; and around them was a strange sprinkling of salt — taken from the ravaged provision chests on the planes — which conjured up the most horrible associations. The thing had occurred in one of the crude aeroplane shelters from which the plane had been dragged out, and subsequent winds had effaced all tracks which could have supplied any plausible theory. Scattered bits of clothing, roughly slashed from the human incision subjects, hinted no clues. It is useless to bring up the half impression of certain faint snow prints in one shielded corner of the ruined inclosure — because that impression did not concern human prints at all, but was clearly mixed up with all the talk of fossil prints which poor Lake had been giving throughout the preceding weeks. One had to be careful of one's imagination in the lee of those overshadowing mountains of madness.

As I have indicated, Gedney and one dog turned out to be missing in the end. When we came on that terrible shelter we had missed two dogs and two men; but the fairly unharmed dissecting tent, which we entered after investigating the monstrous graves, had something to reveal. It was not as Lake had left it, for the covered parts of the primal monstrosity had been removed from the improvised table. Indeed, we had already realized that one of the six imperfect and insanely buried things we had found — the one with the trace of a peculiarly hateful odor — must represent the collected sections of the entity which Lake had tried to analyze. On and around that laboratory table were strewn other things, and it did not take long for us to guess that those things were the carefully though oddly and inexpertly dissected parts of one man and one dog. I shall spare the feelings of survivors by omitting mention of the man's identity. Lake's anatomical instruments were missing, but there were evidences of their careful cleansing. The gasoline stove was also gone, though around it we found a curious litter of matches. We buried the human parts beside the other ten men; and the canine parts with the other thirty-five dogs. Concerning the bizarre smudges on the laboratory table, and on the jumble of roughly handled illustrated books scattered near it, we were much too bewildered to speculate.

This formed the worst of the camp horror, but other things were equally perplexing. The disappearance of Gedney, the one dog, the eight uninjured biological specimens, the three sledges, and certain instruments, illustrated technical and scientific books, writing materials, electric torches and batteries, food and fuel, heating apparatus, spare tents, fur suits, and the like, was utterly beyond sane conjecture; as were likewise the spatter-fringed ink blots on certain pieces of paper, and the evidences of curious alien fumbling and experimentation around the planes and all other mechanical devices both at the camp and at the boring. The dogs seemed to abhor this oddly disordered machinery. Then, too, there was the upsetting of the larder, the disappearance of certain staples, and the jarringly comical heap of tin cans pried open in the most unlikely ways and at the most unlikely places. The profusion of scattered matches, intact, broken, or spent, formed another minor enigma — as did the two or three tent cloths and fur suits which we found lying about with peculiar and unorthodox slashings conceivably due to clumsy efforts at unimaginable adaptations. The maltreatment of the human and canine bodies, and the crazy burial of the damaged Archaean specimens, were all of a piece with this apparent disintegrative madness. In view of just such an eventuality as the present one, we carefully photographed all the main evidences of insane disorder at the camp; and shall use the prints to buttress our pleas against the departure of the proposed Starkweather-Moore Expedition.

Our first act after finding the bodies in the shelter was to photograph and open the row of insane graves with the five-pointed snow mounds. We could not help noticing the resemblance of these monstrous mounds, with their clusters of grouped dots, to poor Lake's descriptions of the strange greenish soapstones; and when we came on some of the soapstones themselves in the great mineral pile, we found the likeness very close indeed. The whole general formation, it must be made clear, seemed abominably suggestive of the starfish head of the Archaean entities; and we agreed that the suggestion must have worked potently upon the sensitized minds of Lake's overwrought party. Our own first sight of the actual buried entities formed a horrible moment, and sent the imaginations of Pabodie and myself back to some of the shocking primal myths we had read and heard. We all agreed that the mere sight and continued presence of the things must have coöperated with the oppressive polar solitude and daemon mountain wind in driving Lake's party mad.

For madness — centering in Gedney as the only possible surviving agent — was the explanation spontaneously adopted by everybody so far as spoken utterance was concerned; though I will not be so naive as to deny that each of us may have harbored wild guesses which sanity forbade him to formulate completely. Sherman, Pabodie, and McTighe made an exhaustive aeroplane cruise over all the surrounding territory in the afternoon, sweeping the horizon with field glasses in quest of Gedney and of the various missing things; but nothing came to light. The party reported that the titan barrier range extended endlessly to right and left alike, without any diminution in height or essential structure. On some of the peaks, though, the regular cube and rampart formations were bolder and plainer, having doubly fantastic similitudes to Roerich-painted Asian hill ruins. The distribution of cryptical cave mouths on the black snow-denuded summits seemed roughly even as far as the range could be traced.

In spite of all the prevailing horrors, we were left with enough sheer scientific zeal and adventurousness to wonder about the unknown realm beyond those mysterious mountains. As our guarded messages stated, we rested at midnight after our day of terror and bafflement — but not without a tentative plan for one or more range-crossing altitude flights in a lightened plane with aerial camera and geologist's outfit, beginning the following morning. It was decided that Danforth and I try it first, and we awaked at 7 a.m. intending an early flight; however, heavy winds — mentioned in our brief, bulletin to the outside world — delayed our start till nearly nine o'clock.

I have already repeated the noncommittal story we told the men at camp — and relayed outside — after our return sixteen hours later. It is now my terrible duty to amplify this account by filling in the merciful blanks with hints of what we really saw in the hidden transmontane world — hints of the revelations which have finally driven Danforth to a nervous collapse. I wish he would add a really frank word about the thing which he thinks he alone saw — even though it was probably a nervous delusion — and which was perhaps the last straw that put him where he is; but he is firm against that. All I can do is to repeat his later disjointed whispers about what set him shrieking as the plane soared back through the wind-tortured mountain pass after that real and tangible shock which I shared. This will form my last word. If the plain signs of surviving elder horrors in what I disclose be not enough to keep others from meddling with the inner antarctic — or at least from prying too deeply beneath the surface of that ultimate waste of forbidden secrets and inhuman, aeon-cursed desolation — the responsibility for unnamable and perhaps immeasurable evils will not be mine.

Danforth and I, studying the notes made by Pabodie in his afternoon flight and checking up with a sextant, had calculated that the lowest available pass in the range lay somewhat to the right of us, within sight of camp, and about twenty-three thousand or twenty-four thousand feet above sea level. For this point, then, we first headed in the lightened plane as we embarked on our flight of discovery. The camp itself, on foothills which sprang from a high continental plateau, was some twelve thousand feet in altitude; hence the actual height increase necessary was not so vast as it might seem. Nevertheless we were acutely conscious of the rarefied air and intense cold as we rose; for, on account of visibility conditions, we had to leave the cabin windows open. We were dressed, of course, in our heaviest furs.

As we drew near the forbidding peaks, dark and sinister above the line of crevasse-riven snow and interstitial glaciers, we noticed more and more the curiously regular formations clinging to the slopes; and thought again of the strange Asian paintings of Nicholas Roerich. The ancient and wind-weathered rock strata fully verified all of Lake's bulletins, and proved that these pinnacles had been towering up in exactly the same way since a surprisingly early time in earth's history — perhaps over fifty million years. How much higher they had once been, it was futile to guess; but everything about this strange region pointed to obscure atmospheric influences unfavorable to change, and calculated to retard the usual climatic processes of rock disintegration.

But it was the mountainside tangle of regular cubes, ramparts, and cave mouths which fascinated and disturbed us most. I studied them with a field glass and took aerial photographs while Danforth drove; and at times I relieved him at the controls — though my aviation knowledge was purely an amateur's — in order to let him use the binoculars. We could easily see that much of the material of the things was a lightish Archaean quartzite, unlike any formation visible over broad areas of the general surface; and that their regularity was extreme and uncanny to an extent which poor Lake had scarcely hinted.

As he had said, their edges were crumbled and rounded from untold aeons of savage weathering; but their preternatural solidity and tough material had saved them from obliteration. Many parts, especially those closest to the slopes, seemed identical in substance with the surrounding rock surface. The whole arrangement looked like the ruins of Macchu Picchu in the Andes, or the primal foundation walls of Kish as dug up by the Oxford Field Museum Expedition in 1929; and both Danforth and I obtained that occasional impression of separate Cyclopean blocks which Lake had attributed to his

Astounding Stories, March 1936

"It was, very clearly, the blasphemous city of the mirage — in stark, objective reality!"

flight-companion Carroll. How to account for such things in this place was frankly beyond me, and I felt queerly humbled as a geologist. Igneous formations often have strange regularities — like the famous Giants' Causeway in Ireland — but this stupendous range, despite Lake's original suspicion of smoking cones, was above all else non-volcanic in evident structure.

The curious cave mouths, near which the odd formations seemed most abundant, presented another albeit a lesser puzzle because of their regularity of outline. They were, as Lake's bulletin had said, often approximately square or semicircular; as if the natural orifices had been shaped to greater symmetry by some magic hand. Their numerousness and wide distribution were remarkable, and suggested that the whole region was honeycombed with tunnels dissolved out of limestone strata. Such glimpses as we secured did not extend far within the caverns, but we saw that they were apparently clear of stalactites and stalagmites. Outside, those parts of the mountain slopes adjoining the apertures seemed invariably smooth and regular;

and Danforth thought that the slight cracks and pittings of the weathering tended toward unusual patterns. Filled as he was with the horrors and strangenesses discovered at the camp, he hinted that the pittings vaguely resembled those baffling groups of dots sprinkled over the primeval greenish soapstones, so hideously duplicated on the madly conceived snow mounds above those six buried monstrosities.

We had risen gradually in flying over the higher foothills and along toward the relatively low pass we had selected. As we advanced we occasionally looked down at the snow and ice of the land route, wondering whether we could have attempted the trip with the simpler equipment of earlier days. Somewhat to our surprise we saw that the terrain was far from difficult as such things go; and that despite the crevasses and other bad spots it would not have been likely to deter the sledges of a Scott, a Shackleton, or an Amundsen. Some of the glaciers appeared to lead up to wind-bared passes with unusual continuity, and upon reaching our chosen pass we found that its case formed no exception.

Our sensations of tense expectancy as we prepared to round the crest and peer out over an untrodden world can hardly be described on paper; even though we had no cause to think the regions beyond the range essentially different from those already seen and traversed. The touch of evil mystery in these barrier mountains, and in the beckoning sea of opalescent sky glimpsed betwixt their summits, was a highly subtle and attenuated matter not to be explained in literal words. Rather was it an affair of vague psychological symbolism and aesthetic association — a thing mixed up with exotic poetry and paintings, and with archaic myths lurking in shunned and forbidden volumes. Even the wind's burden held a peculiar strain of conscious malignity; and for a second it seemed that the composite sound included a bizarre musical whistling or piping over a wide range as the blast swept in and out of the omnipresent and resonant cave mouths. There was a cloudy note of reminiscent repulsion in this sound, as complex and unplaceable as any of the other dark impressions.

We were now, after a slow ascent, at a height of twenty-three thousand, five hundred and seventy feet according to the aneroid; and had left the region of clinging snow definitely below us. Up here were only dark, bare rock slopes and the start of rough-ribbed glaciers — but with those provocative cubes, ramparts, and echoing cave-mouths to add a portent of the unnatural, the fantastic, and the dreamlike. Looking along the line of high peaks, I thought I could see the one mentioned by poor Lake, with a rampart exactly on top. It seemed to be half lost in a queer antarctic haze — such a haze, perhaps, as had been responsible for Lake's early notion of volcanism. The pass loomed directly before us, smooth and windswept between its jagged and malignly frowning pylons. Beyond it was a sky fretted with swirling vapors and lighted by the low polar sun — the sky of that mysterious farther realm upon which we felt no human eye had ever gazed.

A few more feet of altitude and we would behold that realm. Danforth and I, unable to speak except in shouts amidst the howling, piping wind that raced through the pass and added to the noise of the unmuffled engines, exchanged eloquent glances. And then, having gained those last few feet, we did indeed stare across the momentous divide and over the unsampled secrets of an elder and utterly alien earth.

V.

I think that both of us simultaneously cried out in mixed awe, wonder, terror, and disbelief in our own senses as we finally cleared the pass and saw what lay beyond. Of course, we must have had some natural theory in the back of our heads to steady our faculties for the moment. Probably we thought of such things as the grotesquely weathered stones of the Garden of the Gods in Colorado, or the fantastically symmetrical wind-carved rocks of the Arizona desert. Perhaps we even half thought the sight a mirage like that we had seen the morning before on first approaching those mountains of madness. We must have had some such normal notions to fall back upon as our eyes swept that limitless, tempest-scarred plateau and grasped the almost endless labyrinth of colossal, regular, and geometrically eurythmic stone masses which reared their crumbled and pitted crests above a glacial sheet not more than forty or fifty feet deep at its thickest, and in places obviously thinner.

The effect of the monstrous sight was indescribable, for some fiendish violation of known natural law seemed certain at the outset. Here, on a hellishly ancient table-land fully twenty thousand feet high, and in a climate deadly to habitation since a pre-human age not less than five hundred thousand years ago, there stretched nearly to the vision's limit a tangle of orderly stone which only the desperation of mental self-defense could possibly attribute to any but a conscious and artificial cause. We had previously dismissed, so far as serious thought was concerned, any theory that the cubes and ramparts of the mountainsides were other than natural in origin. How could they be otherwise, when man himself could scarcely have been differentiated from the great apes at the time when this region succumbed to the present unbroken reign of glacial death?

Yet now the sway of reason seemed irrefutably shaken, for this Cyclopean maze of squared, curved, and angled blocks had features which cut off all comfortable refuge. It was, very clearly, the blasphemous city of the mirage in stark, objective, and ineluctable reality. That damnable portent had had a material basis after all — there had been some horizontal stratum of ice dust in the upper air, and this shocking stone survival had projected its image across the mountains according to the simple laws of reflection, Of course, the phantom had been twisted and exaggerated, and had contained things which the real source did not contain; yet now, as we saw that real source, we thought it even more hideous and menacing than its distant image.

Only the incredible, unhuman massiveness of these vast

stone towers and ramparts had saved the frightful things from utter annihilation in the hundreds of thousands — perhaps millions — of years it had brooded there amidst the blasts of a bleak upland. "Corona Mundi — Roof of the World — " All sorts of fantastic phrases sprang to our lips as we looked dizzily down at the unbelievable spectacle. I thought again of the eldritch primal myths that had so persistently haunted me since my first sight of this dead antarctic world — of the demoniac plateau of Leng, of the Mi-Go, or abominable Snow-Men of the Himalayas, of the Pnakotic Manuscripts with their pre-human implications, of the Cthulhu cult, of the *Necronomicon*, and of the Hyperborean legends of formless Tsathoggua and the worse than formless star spawn associated with that semi-entity.

For boundless miles in every direction the thing stretched off with very little thinning; indeed, as our eyes followed it to the right and left along the base of the low, gradual foothills which separated it from the actual mountain rim, we decided that we could see no thinning at all except for an interruption at the left of the pass through which we had come. We had

Astounding Stories, March 1936

"The effect of the monstrous sight was indescribable! Some fiendish violation of natural laws!"

merely struck, at random, a limited part of something of incalculable extent. The foothills were more sparsely sprinkled with grotesque stone structures, linking the terrible city to the already familiar cubes and ramparts which evidently formed its mountain outposts. These latter, as well as the queer cave mouths, were as thick on the inner as on the outer sides of the mountains.

The nameless stone labyrinth consisted, for the most part, of walls from ten to one hundred and fifty feet in ice-clear height, and of a thickness varying from five to ten feet. It was composed mostly of prodigious blocks of dark primordial slate, schist, and sandstone — blocks in many cases as large as 4 × 6 × 8 feet — though in several places it seemed to be carved out of a solid, uneven bed-rock of pre-Cambrian slate. The buildings were far from equal in size, there being innumerable honeycomb arrangements of enormous extent as well as smaller separate structures. The general shape of these things tended to be conical, pyramidal, or terraced; though there were many perfect cylinders, perfect cubes, clusters of cubes, and other rectangular forms, and a peculiar sprinkling of angled edifices whose five-pointed ground plan roughly suggested modern fortifications. The builders had made constant and expert use of the principle of the arch, and domes had probably existed in the city's heyday.

The whole tangle was monstrously weathered, and the glacial surface from which the towers projected was strewn with fallen blocks and immemorial debris. Where the glaciation was transparent we could see the lower parts of the gigantic piles, and we noticed the ice-preserved stone bridges which connected the different towers at varying distances above the ground. On the exposed walls we could detect the scarred places where other and higher bridges of the same sort had existed. Closer inspection revealed countless largish windows; some of which were closed with shutters of a petrified material originally wood, though most gaped open in a sinister and menacing fashion. Many of the ruins, of course, were roofless, and with uneven though wind-rounded upper edges; whilst others, of a more sharply conical or pyramidal model or else protected by higher surrounding structures, preserved intact outlines despite the omnipresent crumbling and pitting. With the field glass we could barely make out what seemed to be sculptural decorations in horizontal bands — decorations including those curious groups of dots whose presence on the ancient soapstones now assumed a vastly larger significance.

In many places the buildings were totally ruined and the ice sheet deeply riven from various geologic causes. In other places the stonework was worn down to the very level of the glaciation. One broad swath, extending from the plateau's interior, to a cleft in the foothills about a mile to the left of the pass we had traversed, was wholly free from buildings. It probably represented, we concluded, the course of some great river which in Tertiary times — millions of years ago — had poured through the city and into some prodigious subterranean abyss of the great barrier range. Certainly, this was above all a region of caves, gulfs, and underground secrets beyond human penetration.

Looking back to our sensations, and recalling our dazedness at viewing this monstrous survival from aeons we had thought pre-human, I can only wonder that we preserved the semblance of equilibrium, which we did. Of course, we knew that something — chronology, scientific theory, or our own consciousness — was woefully awry; yet we kept enough poise to guide the plane, observe many things quite minutely, and take a careful series of photographs which may yet serve both us and the world in good stead. In my case, ingrained scientific habit may have helped; for above all my bewilderment and sense of menace, there burned a dominant curiosity to fathom more of this age-old secret — to know what sort of beings had built and lived in this incalculably gigantic place, and what relation to the general world of its time or of other times so unique a concentration of life could have had.

For this place could be no ordinary city. It must have formed the primary nucleus and center of some archaic and unbelievable chapter of earth's history whose outward ramifications, recalled only dimly in the most obscure and distorted myths, had vanished utterly amidst the chaos of terrene convulsions long before any human race we know had shambled out of apedom. Here sprawled a Palaeogaean megalopolis compared with which the fabled Atlantis and Lemuria, Commoriom and Uzuldaroum, and Olathoë in the land of Lomar, are recent things of today — not even of yesterday; a megalopolis ranking with such whispered pre-human blasphemies as Valusia, R'lyeh, Ib in the land of Mnar, and the Nameless city of Arabia Deserta. As we flew above that tangle of stark titan towers my imagination sometimes escaped all bounds and roved aimlessly in realms of fantastic associations — even weaving links betwixt this lost world and some of my own wildest dreams concerning the mad horror at the camp.

The plane's fuel tank, in the interest of greater lightness, had been only partly filled; hence we now had to exert caution in our explorations. Even so, however, we covered an enormous extent of ground — or, rather, air — after swooping down to a level where the wind became virtually negligible. There seemed to be no limit to the mountain range, or to the length of the frightful stone city which bordered its inner foothills. Fifty miles of flight in each direction showed no major change in the labyrinth of rock and masonry that clawed up corpse-like through the eternal ice. There were, though, some highly absorbing diversifications; such as the carvings on the canyon where that broad river had once pierced the foothills and approached its sinking place in the great range. The headlands at the stream's entrance had been boldly carved into Cyclopean pylons; and something about the ridgy, barrel-shaped designs stirred up oddly vague, hateful, and confusing semi-remembrances in both Danforth and me.

We also came upon several star-shaped open spaces, evidently public squares, and noted various undulations in the terrain. Where a sharp hill rose, it was generally hollowed out into some sort of rambling-stone edifice; but there were at least two exceptions. Of these latter, one was too badly weathered to disclose what had been on the jutting eminence, while the other still bore a fantastic conical monument carved out of the solid rock and roughly resembling such things as the well-known Snake Tomb in the ancient valley of Petra.

Flying inland from the mountains, we discovered that the city was not of infinite width, even though its length along the foothills seemed endless. After about thirty miles the grotesque stone buildings began to thin out, and in ten more miles we came to an unbroken waste virtually without signs of sentient artifice. The course of the river beyond the city seemed marked by a broad, depressed line, while the land assumed a somewhat greater ruggedness, seeming to slope slightly upward as it receded in the mist-hazed west.

So far we had made no landing, yet to leave the plateau without an attempt at entering some of the monstrous structures would have been inconceivable. Accordingly, we decided to find a smooth place on the foothills near our navigable pass, there grounding the plane and preparing to do some exploration on foot. Though these gradual slopes were partly covered with a scattering of ruins, low flying soon disclosed an ample number of possible landing-places. Selecting that nearest to the pass, since our flight would be across the great range and back to camp, we succeeded about 12:30 p.m. in effecting a landing on a smooth, hard snow-field wholly devoid of obstacles and well adapted to a swift and favorable take-off later on.

It did not seem necessary to protect the plane with a snow banking for so brief a time and in so comfortable an absence of high winds at this level; hence we merely saw that the landing skis were safely lodged, and that the vital parts of the mechanism were guarded against the cold. For our foot journey we discarded the heaviest of our flying furs, and took with us a small outfit consisting of pocket compass, hand camera, light provisions, voluminous notebooks and paper, geologist's hammer and chisel, specimen-bags, coil of climbing rope, and powerful electric torches with extra batteries; this equipment having been carried in the plane on the chance that we might be able to effect a landing, take ground pictures, make drawings and topographical sketches, and obtain rock specimens from some bare slope, outcropping, or mountain cave. Fortunately we had a supply of extra paper to tear up, place in a spare specimen-bag, and use on the ancient principle of hare-and-hounds for marking our course in any interior mazes we might be able to penetrate. This had been brought in case we found some cave system with air quiet enough to allow such a rapid and easy method in place of the usual rock-chipping method of trail-blazing.

Walking cautiously downhill over the crusted snow toward the stupendous stone labyrinth that loomed against the opalescent west, we felt almost as keen a sense of imminent marvels as we had felt on approaching the unfathomed mountain pass four hours previously. True, we had become visually familiar with the incredible secret concealed by the barrier peaks; yet the prospect of actually entering primordial walls reared by conscious beings perhaps millions of years ago — before any known race of men could have existed — was none the less awesome and potentially terrible in its implications of cosmic abnormality. Though the thinness of the air at this prodigious altitude made exertion somewhat more difficult than usual, both Danforth and I found ourselves bearing up very well, and felt equal to almost any task which might fall to our lot. It took only a few steps to bring us to a shapeless ruin worn level with the snow, while ten or fifteen rods farther on there was a huge, roofless rampart still complete in its gigantic five-pointed outline and rising to an irregular height of ten or eleven feet. For this latter we headed; and when at last we were actually able to touch its weathered Cyclopean blocks, we felt that we had established an unprecedented and almost blasphemous link with forgotten aeons normally closed to our species.

This rampart, shaped like a star and perhaps three hundred feet from point to point, was built of Jurassic sandstone blocks of irregular size, averaging 6 × 8 feet in surface. There was a row of arched loopholes or windows about four feet wide and five feet high, spaced quite symmetrically along the points of the star and at its inner angles, and with the bottoms about four feet from the glaciated surface. Looking through these, we could see that the masonry was fully five feet thick, that there were no partitions remaining within, and that there were traces of banded carvings or bas-reliefs on the interior walls — facts we had indeed guessed before, when flying low over this rampart and others like it. Though lower parts must have originally existed, all traces of such things were now wholly obscured by the deep layer of ice and snow at this point.

We crawled through one of the windows and vainly tried to decipher the nearly effaced mural designs, but did not attempt to disturb the glaciated floor. Our orientation flights had indicated that many buildings in the city proper were less ice-choked, and that we might perhaps find wholly clear interiors leading down to the true ground level if we entered those structures still roofed at the top. Before we left the rampart we photographed it carefully, and studied its mortarless Cyclopean masonry with complete bewilderment. We wished that Pabodie were present, for his engineering knowledge might have helped us guess how such titanic blocks could have been handled in that unbelievably remote age when the city and its outskirts were built up.

The half-mile walk downhill to the actual city, with the upper wind shrieking vainly and savagely through the skyward peaks in the background, was something of which the smallest details will always remain engraved on my mind. Only in fantastic nightmares could any human beings but Danforth and me conceive such optical effects. Between us and the churning vapors of the west lay that monstrous tangle of dark stone towers, its outré and incredible forms impressing us afresh at every new angle of vision. It was a mirage in solid stone, and were it not for the photographs, I would still doubt that such a thing could be. The general type of masonry was identical with that of the rampart we had examined; but the extravagant shapes which this masonry took in its urban manifestations were past all description.

Even the pictures illustrate only one or two phases of its endless variety, preternatural massiveness, and utterly alien exoticism. There were geometrical forms for which an Euclid would scarcely find a name — cones of all degrees of irregularity and truncation, terraces of every sort of provocative disproportion, shafts with odd bulbous enlargements, broken columns in curious groups, and five-pointed or five-ridged arrangements of mad grotesqueness. As we drew nearer we could see beneath certain transparent parts of the ice-sheet, and detect some of the tubular stone bridges that connected the crazily sprinkled structures at various heights. Of orderly streets there seemed to be none, the only broad open swath being a mile to the left, where the ancient river had doubtless flowed through the town into the mountains.

Our field-glasses showed the external, horizontal bands of nearly effaced sculptures and dot-groups to be very prevalent, and we could half imagine what the city must once have looked like — even though most of the roofs and tower tops had necessarily perished. As a whole, it had been a complex tangle of twisted lanes and alleys, all of them deep canyons, and some little better than tunnels because of the overhanging masonry or overarching bridges. Now, outspread below us, it loomed like a dream fantasy against a westward mist through whose northern end the low, reddish antarctic sun of early afternoon was struggling to shine; and when, for a moment, that sun encountered a denser obstruction and plunged the scene into temporary shadow, the effect was subtly menacing in a way I can never hope to depict. Even the faint howling and piping of the unfelt wind in the great mountain passes behind us took on a wilder note of purposeful malignity. The last stage of our descent to the town was unusually steep and abrupt, and a rock outcropping at the edge where the grade changed led us to think that an artificial terrace had once existed there. Under the glaciation, we believed, there must be a flight of steps or its equivalent.

When at last we plunged into the town itself, clambering over fallen masonry and shrinking from the oppressive nearness and dwarfing height of omnipresent crumbling and pitted walls, our sensations again became such that I marvel at the amount of self-control we retained. Danforth was frankly jumpy, and began making some offensively irrelevant speculations about the horror at the camp — which I resented all the more because I could not help sharing certain conclusions forced upon us by many features of this morbid survival from nightmare antiquity. The speculations worked on his imagination, too; for in one place — where a debris-littered alley turned a sharp corner — he insisted that he saw faint traces of ground markings which he did not like; whilst elsewhere he stopped to listen to a subtle, imaginary sound from some undefined point — a muffled musical piping, he said, not unlike that of the wind in the mountain caves, yet somehow disturbingly different. The ceaseless five-pointedness of the surrounding architecture and of the few distinguishable mural arabesques had a dimly sinister suggestiveness we could not escape, and gave us a touch of terrible subconscious certainty concerning the primal entities which had reared and dwelt in this unhallowed place.

Nevertheless, our scientific and adventurous souls were not wholly dead, and we mechanically carried out our program of chipping specimens from all the different rock types represented in the masonry. We wished a rather full set in order to draw better conclusions regarding the age of the place. Nothing in the great outer walls seemed to date from later than the Jurassic and Comanchian periods, nor was any piece of stone in the entire place of a greater recency than the Pliocene Age. In stark certainty, we were wandering amidst a death which had reigned at least five hundred thousand years, and in all probability even longer.

As we proceeded through this maze of stone-shadowed twilight we stopped at all available apertures to study interiors and investigate entrance possibilities. Some were above our reach, whilst others led only into ice-choked ruins as unroofed and barren as the rampart on the hill. One, though spacious and inviting, opened on a seemingly bottomless abyss without visible means of descent. Now and then we had a chance to study the petrified wood of a surviving shutter, and were impressed by the fabulous antiquity implied in the still discernible grain. These things had come from Mesozoic gymnosperms and conifers — especially Cretaceous cycads — and from fan palms and early angiosperms of plainly Tertiary date. Nothing definitely later than the Pliocene could be discovered. In the placing of these shutters — whose edges showed the former presence of queer and long-vanished hinges — usage seemed to be varied — some being on the outer and some on the inner side of the deep embrasures. They seemed to have become wedged in place, thus surviving the rusting of their former and probably metallic fixtures and fastenings.

After a time we came across a row of windows — in the bulges of a colossal five-edged cone of undamaged apex — which led into a vast, well-preserved room with stone flooring; but these were too high in the room to permit descent without a rope. We had a rope with us, but did not wish to bother with this twenty-foot drop unless obliged to — especially in this thin plateau air where great demands were made upon the heart action. This enormous room was probably a hall or concourse of some sort, and our electric torches showed bold, distinct, and potentially startling sculptures arranged round the walls in broad, horizontal bands separated by equally broad strips of conventional arabesques. We took careful note of this spot, planning to enter here unless a more easily gained interior were encountered.

Finally, though, we did encounter exactly the opening we wished; an archway about six feet wide and ten feet high, marking the former end of an aerial bridge which had spanned an alley about five feet above the present level of glaciation.

These archways, of course, were flush with upper-story floors, and in this case one of the floors still existed. The building thus accessible was a series of rectangular terraces on our left facing westward. That across the alley, where the other archway yawned, was a decrepit cylinder with no windows and with a curious bulge about ten feet above the aperture. It was totally dark inside, and the archway seemed to open on a well of illimitable emptiness.

Heaped debris made the entrance to the vast left-hand building doubly easy, yet for a moment we hesitated before taking advantage of the long-wished chance. For though we had penetrated into this tangle of archaic mystery, it required fresh resolution to carry us actually inside a complete and surviving building of a fabulous elder world whose nature was becoming more and more hideously plain to us. In the end, however, we made the plunge, and scrambled up over the rubble into the gaping embrasure. The floor beyond was of great slate slabs, and seemed to form the outlet of a long, high corridor with sculptured walls.

Observing the many inner archways which led off from it, and realizing the probable complexity of the nest of apartments within, we decided that we must begin our system of hare-and-hound trail-blazing. Hitherto our compasses, together with frequent glimpses of the vast mountain range between the towers in our rear, had been enough to prevent our losing our way; but from now on, the artificial substitute would be necessary. Accordingly we reduced our extra paper to shreds of suitable size, placed these in a bag to be carried by Danforth, and prepared to use them as economically as safety would allow. This method would probably gain us immunity from straying, since there did not appear to be any strong air currents inside the primordial masonry. If such should develop, or if our paper supply should give out, we could of course fall back on the more secure though more tedious and retarding method of rock-chipping.

Just how extensive a territory we had opened up, it was impossible to guess without a trial. The close and frequent connection of the different buildings made it likely that we might cross from one to another on bridges underneath the ice, except where impeded by local collapses and geologic rifts, for very little glaciation seemed to have entered the massive constructions. Almost all the areas of transparent ice had revealed the submerged windows as tightly shuttered, as if the town had been left in that uniform state until the glacial sheet came to crystallize the lower part for all succeeding time. Indeed, one gained a curious impression that this place had been deliberately closed and deserted in some dim, bygone aeon, rather than overwhelmed by any sudden calamity or even gradual decay. Had the coming of the ice been foreseen, and had a nameless population left en masse to seek a less doomed abode? The precise physiographic conditions attending the formation of the ice-sheet at this point would have to wait for later solution. It had not, very plainly, been a grinding drive. Perhaps the pressure of accumulated snows had been responsible, and perhaps some flood from the river, or from the bursting of some ancient glacial dam in the great range, had helped to create the special state now observable. Imagination could conceive almost anything in connection with this place.

VI.

It would be cumbrous to give a detailed, consecutive account of our wanderings inside that cavernous, aeon-dead honeycomb of primal masonry—that monstrous lair of elder secrets which now echoed for the first time, after uncounted epochs, to the tread of human feet. This is especially true because so much of the horrible drama and revelation came from a mere study of the omnipresent mural carvings. Our flashlight photographs of those carvings will do much toward proving the truth of what we are now disclosing, and it is lamentable that we had not a larger film supply with us. As it was, we made crude notebook sketches of certain salient features after all our films were used up.

The building which we had entered was one of great size and elaborateness, and gave us an impressive notion of the architecture of that nameless geologic past. The inner partitions were less massive than the outer walls, but on the lower levels were excellently preserved. Labyrinthine complexity, involving curiously irregular differences in floor levels, characterized the entire arrangement; and we should certainly have been lost at the very outset but for the trail of torn paper left behind us. We decided to explore the more decrepit upper parts first of all, hence climbed aloft in the maze for a distance of some one hundred feet, to where the topmost tier of chambers yawned snowily and ruinously open to the polar sky. Ascent was effected over the steep, transversely ribbed stone ramps or inclined planes which everywhere served in lieu of stairs. The rooms we encountered were of all imaginable shapes and proportions, ranging from five-pointed stars to triangles and perfect cubes. It might be safe to say that their general average was about 30 by 30 feet in floor area, and 20 feet in height, though many larger apartments existed. After thoroughly examining the upper regions and the glacial level, we descended, story by story, into the submerged part, where indeed we soon saw we were in a continuous maze of connected chambers and passages probably leading over unlimited areas outside this particular building. The Cyclopean massiveness and gigantism of everything about us became curiously oppressive; and there was something vaguely but deeply unhuman in all the contours, dimensions, proportions, decorations, and constructional nuances of the blasphemously archaic stonework. We soon realized, from what the carvings revealed, that this monstrous city was many million years old.

We cannot yet explain the engineering principles used in the anomalous balancing and adjustment of the vast rock masses, though the function of the arch was clearly much relied on. The rooms we visited were wholly bare of all portable contents, a circumstance which sustained our belief in the city's deliberate desertion. The prime decorative feature was the almost universal system of mural sculpture, which tended to run in continuous horizontal bands three feet wide and arranged from floor to ceiling in alternation with bands of equal width given over to geometrical arabesques. There were exceptions to this rule of arrangement, but its preponderance was overwhelming. Often, however, a series of smooth cartouches containing oddly patterned groups of dots would be sunk along one of the arabesque bands.

The technique, we soon saw, was mature, accomplished, and aesthetically evolved to the highest degree of civilized mastery, though utterly alien in every detail to any known art tradition of the human race. In delicacy of execution no sculpture I have ever seen could approach it. The minutest details of elaborate vegetation, or of animal life, were rendered with astonishing vividness despite the bold scale of the carvings; whilst the conventional designs were marvels of skillful intricacy. The arabesques displayed a profound use of mathematical principles, and were made up of obscurely symmetrical curves and angles based on the quantity of five. The pictorial bands followed a highly formalized tradition, and involved a peculiar treatment of perspective, but had an artistic force that moved us profoundly, notwithstanding the intervening gulf of vast geologic periods. Their method of design hinged on a singular juxtaposition of the cross-section with the two-dimensional silhouette, and embodied an analytical psychology beyond that of any known race of antiquity. It is useless to try to compare this art with any represented in our museums. Those who see our photographs will probably find its closest analogue in certain grotesque conceptions of the most daring futurists.

The arabesque tracery consisted altogether of depressed lines, whose depth on unweathered walls varied from one to two inches. When cartouches with dot-groups appeared — evidently as inscriptions in some unknown and primordial language and alphabet — the depression of the smooth surface was perhaps an inch and a half, and of the dots perhaps a half inch more. The pictorial bands were in countersunk low relief, their background being depressed about two inches from the original wall surface. In some specimens marks of a former coloration could be detected, though for the most part the untold aeons had disintegrated and banished any pigments which may have been applied. The more one studied the marvelous technique, the more one admired the things. Beneath their strict conventionalization one could grasp the minute and accurate observation and graphic skill of the artists; and indeed, the very conventions themselves served to symbolize and accentuate the real essence or vital differentiation of every object delineated. We felt, too, that besides these recognizable excellences there were others lurking beyond the reach of our perceptions. Certain touches here and there gave vague hints of latent symbols and stimuli which another mental and emotional background, and a fuller or different sensory equipment, might have made of profound and poignant significance to us.

The subject matter of the sculptures obviously came from the life of the vanished epoch of their creation, and contained a large proportion of evident history. It is this abnormal historic-mindedness of the primal race — a chance circumstance operating, through coincidence, miraculously in our favor — which made the carvings so awesomely informative to us, and which caused us to place their photography and transcription above all other considerations. In certain rooms the dominant arrangement was varied by the presence of maps, astronomical charts, and other scientific designs of an enlarged scale — these things giving a naive and terrible corroboration to what we gathered from the pictorial friezes and dadoes. In hinting at what the whole revealed, I can only hope that my account will not arouse a curiosity greater than sane caution on the part of those who believe me at all. It would be tragic if any were to be allured to that realm of death and horror by the very warning meant to discourage them.

Interrupting these sculptured walls were high windows and massive twelve-foot doorways; both now and then retaining the petrified wooden planks — elaborately carved and polished — of the actual shutters and doors. All metal fixtures had long ago vanished, but some of the doors remained in place and had to be forced aside as we progressed from room to room. Window-frames with odd transparent panes — mostly elliptical — survived here and there, though in no considerable quantity. There were also frequent niches of great magnitude, generally empty, but once in a while containing some bizarre object carved from green soapstone which was either broken or perhaps held too inferior to warrant removal. Other apertures were undoubtedly connected with bygone mechanical facilities — heating, lighting, and the like — of a sort suggested in many of the carvings. Ceilings tended to be plain, but had sometimes been inlaid with green soapstone or other tiles, mostly fallen now. Floors were also paved with such tiles, though plain stonework predominated.

As I have said, all furniture and other movables were absent; but the sculptures gave a clear idea of the strange devices which had once filled these tomb-like, echoing rooms. Above the glacial sheet the floors were generally thick with detritus, litter, and debris, but farther down this condition decreased. In some of the lower chambers and corridors there was little more than gritty dust or ancient incrustations, while occasional areas had an uncanny air of newly swept immaculateness. Of course, where rifts or collapses had occurred, the lower levels were as littered as the upper ones. A central court — as in other structures we had seen from the air — saved the inner regions from total darkness; so that we seldom had to use our electric torches in the upper rooms except when studying sculptured details. Below the ice cap, however, the twilight deepened; and in many parts of the tangled ground level there was an approach to absolute blackness.

To form even a rudimentary idea of our thoughts and feelings as we penetrated this aeon-silent maze of unhuman masonry, one must correlate a hopelessly bewildering chaos of fugitive moods, memories, and impressions. The sheer appalling antiquity and lethal desolation of the place were enough to overwhelm almost any sensitive person, but added to these elements were the recent unexplained horror at the camp, and the revelations all too soon effected by the terrible mural sculptures around us. The moment we came upon a perfect section of carving, where no ambiguity of interpretation could exist, it took only a brief study to give us the hideous truth — a truth which it would be naive to claim Danforth and I had not independently suspected before, though we had carefully refrained from even hinting it to each other. There could now be no further merciful doubt about the nature of the beings which had built and inhabited this monstrous dead city millions of years ago, when man's ancestors were primitive archaic mammals, and vast dinosaurs roamed the tropical steppes of Europe and Asia.

We had previously clung to a desperate alternative and insisted — each to himself — that the omnipresence of the five-pointed motifs meant only some cultural or religious exaltation of the Archaean natural object which had so patently embodied the quality of five-pointedness; as the decorative motifs of Minoan Crete exalted the sacred bull, those of Egypt the scarabaeus, those of Rome the wolf and the eagle, and those of various savage tribes some chosen totem animal. But this lone refuge was now stripped from us, and we were forced to face definitely the reason-shaking realization which the reader of these pages has doubtless long ago anticipated. I can scarcely bear to write it down in black and white even now, but perhaps that will not be necessary.

The things once rearing and dwelling in this frightful masonry in the age of dinosaurs were not indeed dinosaurs, but far worse. Mere dinosaurs were new and almost brainless objects — but the builders of the city were wise and old, and had left certain traces in rocks even then laid down well nigh a thousand million years — rocks laid down before the true life of earth had advanced beyond plastic groups of cells — rocks laid down before the true life of earth had existed at all. They were the makers and enslavers of that life, and above all doubt the originals of the fiendish elder myths which things like the Pnakotic Manuscripts and the *Necronomicon* affrightedly hint about. They were the great "Old Ones" that had filtered down from the stars when earth was young — the beings whose substance an alien evolution had shaped, and whose powers were such as this planet had never bred. And to think that only the day before Danforth and I had actually looked upon fragments of their millennially fossilized substance — and that poor Lake and his party had seen their complete outlines . . . .

It is of course impossible for me to relate in proper order the stages by which we picked up what we know of that monstrous chapter of pre-human life. After the first shock of the certain revelation, we had to pause a while to recuperate, and it was fully three o'clock before we got started on our actual tour of systematic research. The sculptures in the building we entered were of relatively late date — perhaps two million years ago — as checked up by geological, biological, and astronomical features — and embodied an art which would be called decadent in comparison with that of specimens we found in older buildings after crossing bridges under the glacial sheet. One edifice hewn from the solid rock seemed to go back forty or possibly even fifty million years — to the lower Eocene or upper Cretaceous — and contained bas-reliefs of an artistry surpassing anything else, with one tremendous exception, that we encountered. That was, we have since agreed, the oldest domestic structure we traversed.

Were it not for the support of those photographs soon to be made public, I would refrain from telling what I found and inferred, lest I be confined as a madman. Of course, the infinitely early parts of the patchwork tale — representing the pre-terrestrial life of the star-headed beings on other planets, in other galaxies, and in other universes — can readily be interpreted as the fantastic mythology of those beings themselves; yet such parts sometimes involved designs and diagrams so uncannily close to the latest findings of mathematics and astrophysics that I scarcely know what to think. Let others judge when they see the photographs I shall publish.

Naturally, no one set of carvings which we encountered told more than a fraction of any connected story, nor did we even begin to come upon the various stages of that story in their proper order. Some of the vast rooms were independent units so far as their designs were concerned, whilst in other cases a continuous chronicle would be carried through a series of rooms and corridors. The best of the maps and diagrams were on the walls of a frightful abyss below even the ancient ground level — a cavern perhaps two hundred feet square and sixty feet high, which had almost undoubtedly been an educational center of some sort. There were many provoking repetitions of the same material in different rooms and buildings, since certain chapters of experience, and certain summaries or phases of racial history, had evidently been favorites with different decorators or dwellers. Sometimes, though, variant versions of the same theme proved useful in settling debatable points and filling up gaps.

I still wonder that we deduced so much in the short time at our disposal. Of course, we even now have only the barest outline — and much of that was obtained later on from a study of the photographs and sketches we made. It may be the effect of this later study — the revived memories and vague impressions acting in conjunction with his general sensitiveness and with that final supposed horror-glimpse whose essence he will not reveal even to me — which has been the immediate source of Danforth's present breakdown. But it had to be; for we could not issue our warning intelligently without the fullest possible information, and the issuance of that warning is a prime necessity. Certain lingering influences in that unknown antarctic world of disordered time and alien natural law make it imperative that further exploration be discouraged.

VII.

The full story, so far as deciphered, will eventually appear in an official bulletin of Miskatonic University. Here I shall sketch only the salient highlights in a formless, rambling way. Myth or otherwise, the sculptures told of the coming of those star-headed things to the nascent, lifeless earth out of cosmic space — their coming, and the coming of many other alien entities such as at certain times embark upon spatial pioneering. They seemed able to traverse the interstellar ether on their vast membranous wings — thus oddly confirming some curious hill folklore long ago told me by an antiquarian colleague. They had lived under the sea a good deal, building fantastic cities and fighting terrific battles with nameless adversaries by means of intricate devices employing unknown principles of energy. Evidently their scientific and mechanical knowledge far surpassed man's today, though they made use of its more widespread and elaborate forms only when obliged to. Some of the sculptures suggested that they had passed through a stage of mechanized life on other planets, but had receded upon finding its effects emotionally unsatisfying. Their preternatural toughness of organization and simplicity of natural wants made them peculiarly able to live on a high plane without the more specialized fruits of artificial manufacture, and even without garments, except for occasional protection against the elements.

It was under the sea, at first for food and later for other purposes, that they first created earth-life — using available substances according to long-known methods. The more elaborate experiments came after the annihilation of various cosmic enemies. They had done the same thing on other planets, having manufactured not only necessary foods, but certain multicellular protoplasmic masses capable of molding their tissues into all sorts of temporary organs under hypnotic influence and thereby forming ideal slaves to perform the heavy work of the community. These viscous masses were without doubt what Abdul Alhazred whispered about as the "Shoggoths" in his frightful *Necronomicon*, though even that mad Arab had not hinted that any existed on earth except in the dreams of those who had chewed a certain alkaloidal herb. When the star-headed Old Ones on this planet had synthesized their simple food forms and bred a good supply of Shoggoths, they allowed other cell-groups to develop into other forms of animal and vegetable life for sundry purposes, extirpating any whose presence became troublesome.

With the aid of the Shoggoths, whose expansions could be made to lift prodigious weights, the small, low cities under the sea grew to vast and imposing labyrinths of stone not unlike those which later rose on land. Indeed, the highly adaptable Old Ones had lived much on land in other parts of the universe, and probably retained many traditions of land construction. As we studied the architecture of all these sculptured palaeogean cities, including that whose aeon-dead corridors we were even then traversing, we were impressed by a curious coincidence which we have not yet tried to explain, even to ourselves. The tops of the buildings, which in the actual city around us had, of course, been weathered into shapeless ruins ages ago, were clearly displayed in the bas-reliefs, and showed vast clusters of needle-like spires, delicate finials on certain cone and pyramid apexes, and tiers of thin, horizontal scalloped disks capping cylindrical shafts. This was exactly what we had seen in that monstrous and portentous mirage, cast by a dead city whence such skyline features had been absent for thousands and tens of thousands of years, which loomed on our ignorant eyes across the unfathomed mountains of madness as we first approached poor Lake's ill-fated camp.

Of the life of the Old Ones, both under the sea and after part of them migrated to land, volumes could be written. Those in shallow water had continued the fullest use of the eyes at the ends of their five main head tentacles, and had practiced the arts of sculpture and of writing in quite the usual way — the writing accomplished with a stylus on waterproof waxen surfaces. Those lower down in the ocean depths, though they used a curious phosphorescent organism to furnish light, pieced out their vision with obscure special senses operating through the prismatic cilia on their heads — senses which rendered all the Old Ones partly independent of light in emergencies. Their forms of sculpture and writing had changed curiously during the descent, embodying certain apparently chemical coating processes — probably to secure phosphorescence — which the bas-reliefs could not make clear to us. The beings moved in the sea partly by swimming — using the lateral crinoid arms — and partly by wriggling with the lower tier of tentacles containing the pseudo-feet. Occasionally they accomplished long swoops with the auxiliary use of two or more sets of their fan-like folding wings. On land they locally used the pseudofeet, but now and then flew to great heights or over long distances with their wings. The many slender tentacles into which the crinoid arms branched were infinitely delicate, flexible, strong, and accurate in muscular-nervous coordination — ensuring the utmost skill and dexterity in all artistic and other manual operations.

The toughness of the things was almost incredible. Even the terrific pressure of the deepest sea-bottoms appeared powerless to harm them. Very few seemed to die at all except by violence, and their burial-places were very limited. The fact that they covered their vertically inhumed dead with five-pointed inscribed mounds set up thoughts in Danforth and me which made a fresh pause and recuperation necessary after the sculptures revealed it. The beings multiplied by means of spores — like vegetable pteridophytes, as Lake had suspected — but, owing to their prodigious toughness and longevity, and consequent lack of replacement needs, they did not encourage the large-scale development of new prothallia except when they had new regions to colonize. The young matured swiftly, and received an education evidently beyond any standard we can imagine. The prevailing intellectual and

Astounding Stories, March 1936

"The toughness of the things was almost incredible. Even terrific pressures were powerless to harm them!"

aesthetic life was highly evolved, and produced a tenaciously enduring set of customs and institutions which I shall describe more fully in my coming monograph. These varied slightly according to sea or land residence, but had the same foundations and essentials.

Though able, like vegetables, to derive nourishment from inorganic substances, they vastly preferred organic and especially animal food. They ate uncooked marine life under the sea, but cooked their viands on land. They hunted game and raised meat herds — slaughtering with sharp weapons whose odd marks on certain fossil bones our expedition had noted. They resisted all ordinary temperatures marvelously, and in their natural state could live in water down to freezing. When the great chill of the Pleistocene drew on, however — nearly a million years ago — the land dwellers had to resort to special measures, including artificial heating — until at last the deadly cold appears to have driven them back into the sea. For their prehistoric flights through cosmic space, legend said, they absorbed certain chemicals and became almost independent of eating, breathing, or heat conditions — but by the time of the great cold they had lost track of the method. In any case they could not have prolonged the artificial state indefinitely without harm.

Being non-pairing and semi-vegetable in structure, the Old Ones had no biological basis for the family phase of mammal life, but seemed to organize large households on the principles of comfortable space-utility and — as we deduced from the pictured occupations and diversions of co-dwellers — congenial mental association. In furnishing their homes they kept everything in the center of the huge rooms, leaving all the wall spaces free for decorative treatment. Lighting, in the case of the land inhabitants, was accomplished by a device probably electro-chemical in nature. Both on land and under water they used curious tables, chairs and couches like cylindrical frames — for they rested and slept upright with folded-down tentacles — and racks for hinged sets of dotted surfaces forming their books.

Government was evidently complex and probably socialistic, though no certainties in this regard could be deduced from the sculptures we saw. There was extensive commerce, both local and between different cities — certain small, flat counters, five-pointed and inscribed, serving as money. Probably the smaller of the various greenish soapstones found by our expedition were pieces of such currency. Though the culture was mainly urban, some agriculture and much stock raising existed. Mining and a limited amount of manufacturing were also practiced. Travel was very frequent, but permanent migration seemed relatively rare except for the vast colonizing movements by which the race expanded. For personal locomotion no external aid was used, since in land, air, and water movement alike the Old Ones seemed to possess excessively vast capacities for speed. Loads, however, were drawn by beasts of burden — Shoggoths under the sea, and a curious variety of primitive vertebrates in the later years of land existence.

These vertebrates, as well as an infinity of other life forms — animal and vegetable, marine, terrestrial, and aerial — were the products of unguided evolution acting on life cells made by the Old Ones, but escaping beyond their radius of attention. They had been suffered to develop unchecked because they had not come in conflict with the dominant beings. Bothersome forms, of course, were mechanically exterminated. It interested us to see in some of the very last and most decadent sculptures a shambling, primitive mammal, used sometimes for food and sometimes as an amusing buffoon by the land dwellers, whose vaguely simian and human foreshadowings were unmistakable. In the building of land cities the huge stone blocks of the high towers were generally lifted by vast-winged pterodactyls of a species heretofore unknown to paleontology.

The persistence with which the Old Ones survived various geologic changes and convulsions of the earth's crust was little short of miraculous. Though few or none of their first cities seem to have remained beyond the Archaean Age, there was no interruption in their civilization or in the transmission of their records. Their original place of advent to the planet was the Antarctic Ocean, and it is likely that they came not long after the matter forming the moon was wrenched from the neighboring South Pacific. According to one of the sculptured maps the whole globe was then under water, with stone cities scattered farther and farther from the antarctic as aeons passed. Another map shows a vast bulk of dry land around the south pole, where it is evident that some of the beings made experimental settlements, though their main centers were transferred to the nearest sea bottom. Later maps, which display the land mass as cracking and drifting, and sending certain detached parts northward, uphold in a striking way the theories of continental drift lately advanced by Taylor, Wegener, and Joly.

With the upheaval of new land in the South Pacific tremendous events began. Some of the marine cities were hopelessly shattered, yet that was not the worst misfortune. Another race — a land race of beings shaped like octopi and probably corresponding to fabulous pre-human spawn of Cthulhu — soon began filtering down from cosmic infinity and precipitated a -monstrous war which for a time drove the Old Ones wholly back to the sea — a colossal blow in view of the increasing land settlements. Later peace was made, and the new lands were given to the Cthulhu spawn whilst the Old Ones held the sea and the older lands. New land cities were founded — the greatest of them in the antarctic, for this region of first arrival was sacred. From then on, as before, the antarctic remained the center of the Old Ones' civilization, and all the cities built there by the Cthulhu spawn were blotted out. Then suddenly the lands of the Pacific sank again, taking with them the frightful stone city of R'lyeh and all the cosmic octopi, so that the Old Ones were again supreme on the planet except for one shadowy fear about which they did not like to speak. At a rather later age their cities dotted all the land and water areas of the globe — hence the recommendation in my coming monograph that some archaeologist make systematic borings with Pabodie's type of apparatus in certain widely separated regions.

The steady trend down the ages was from water to land—a movement encouraged by the rise of new land masses, though the ocean was never wholly deserted. Another cause of the landward movement was the new difficulty in breeding and managing the Shoggoths upon which successful sea life depended. With the march of time, as the sculptures sadly confessed, the art of creating new life from inorganic matter had been lost, so that the Old Ones had to depend on the molding of forms already in existence. On land the great reptiles proved highly tractable; but the Shoggoths of the sea, reproducing by fission and acquiring a dangerous degree of accidental intelligence, presented for a time a formidable problem.

They had always been controlled through the hypnotic suggestions of the Old Ones, and had modeled their tough plasticity into various useful temporary limbs and organs; but now their self-modeling powers were sometimes exercised independently, and in various imitative forms implanted by past suggestion. They had, it seems, developed a semi-stable brain whose separate and occasionally stubborn volition echoed the will of the Old Ones without always obeying it. Sculptured images of these Shoggoths filled Danforth and me with horror and loathing. They were normally shapeless entities composed of a viscous jelly which looked like an agglutination of bubbles, and each averaged about fifteen feet in diameter when a sphere. They had, however, a constantly shifting shape and volume—throwing out temporary developments or forming apparent organs of sight, hearing, and speech in imitation of their masters, either spontaneously or according to suggestion.

They seem to have become peculiarly intractable toward the middle of the Permian Age, perhaps one hundred and fifty million years ago, when a veritable war of re-subjugation was waged upon them by the marine Old Ones. Pictures of this war, and of the headless, slime-coated fashion in which the Shoggoths typically left their slain victims, held a marvelously fearsome quality despite the intervening abyss of untold ages. The Old Ones had used curious weapons of molecular and atomic disturbances against the rebel entities, and in the end had achieved a complete victory. Thereafter the sculptures showed a period in which Shoggoths were tamed and broken by armed Old Ones as the wild horses of the American west were tamed by cowboys. Though during the rebellion the Shoggoths had shown an ability to live out of water, this transition was not encouraged—since their usefulness on land would hardly have been commensurate with the trouble of their management.

During the Jurassic Age the Old Ones met fresh adversity in the form of a new invasion from outer space—this time by half-fungous, half-crustacean creatures—creatures undoubtedly the same as those figuring in certain whispered hill legends of the north, and remembered in the Himalayas as the Mi-Go, or abominable Snow-Men. To fight these beings the Old Ones attempted, for the first time since their terrene advent, to sally forth again into the planetary ether; but, despite all traditional preparations, found it no longer possible to leave the earth's atmosphere. Whatever the old secret of interstellar travel had been, it was now definitely lost to the race. In the end the Mi-Go drove the Old Ones out of all the northern lands, though they were powerless to disturb those in the sea. Little by little the slow retreat of the elder race to their original antarctic habitat was beginning.

It was curious to note from the pictured battles that both the Cthulhu spawn and the Mi-Go seem to have been composed of matter more widely different from that which we know than was the substance of the Old Ones. They were able to undergo transformations and reintegrations impossible for their adversaries, and seem therefore to have originally come from even remoter gulfs of the cosmic space. The Old Ones, but for their abnormal toughness and peculiar vital properties, were strictly material, and must have had their absolute origin within the known space-time continuum—whereas the first sources of the other beings can only be guessed at with bated breath. All this, of course, assuming that the non-terrestrial linkages and the anomalies ascribed to the invading foes are not pure mythology. Conceivably, the Old Ones might have invented a cosmic framework to account for their occasional defeats, since historical interest and pride obviously formed their chief psychological element. It is significant that their annals failed to mention many advanced and potent races of beings whose mighty cultures and towering cities figure persistently in certain obscure legends.

The changing state of the world through long geologic ages appeared with startling vividness in many of the sculptured maps and scenes. In certain cases existing science will require revision, while in other cases its bold deductions are magnificently confirmed. As I have said, the hypothesis of Taylor, Wegener, and Joly that all the continents are fragments of an original antarctic land mass which cracked from centrifugal force and drifted apart over a technically viscous lower surface—an hypothesis suggested by such things as the complementary outlines of Africa and South America, and the way the great mountain chains are rolled and shoved up—receives striking support from this uncanny source.

Maps evidently showing the Carboniferous world of an hundred million or more years ago displayed significant rifts and chasms destined later to separate Africa from the once continuous realms of Europe (then the Valusia of primal legend), Asia, the Americas, and the antarctic continent. Other charts—and most significantly one in connection with the founding fifty million years ago of the vast dead city around us—showed all the present continents well differentiated. And in the latest discoverable specimen—dating perhaps from the Pliocene Age—the approximate world of today appeared quite clearly despite the linkage of Alaska with Siberia, of North America with Europe through Greenland, and of South America with the antarctic continent through Graham Land. In the Carboniferous map the whole globe—ocean floor and rifted land mass alike—bore symbols of the Old Ones' vast stone cities, but in the later charts the gradual recession toward the antarctic became very plain. The final Pliocene specimen showed no land cities except on the antarctic continent and the tip of South America, nor any ocean cities north of the fiftieth parallel of South Latitude. Knowledge and interest in the northern world, save for a study of coast-lines probably made during long exploration flights on those fan-like membranous wings, had evidently declined to zero among the Old Ones.

Destruction of cities through the upthrust of mountains, the centrifugal rending of continents, the seismic convulsions of land or sea-bottom, and other natural causes, was a matter of common record; and it was curious to observe how fewer and fewer replacements were made as the ages wore on. The vast dead megalopolis that yawned around us seemed to be the last general center of the race—built early in the Cretaceous Age after a titanic earth-buckling had obliterated a still vaster predecessor not far distant. It appeared that this general region was the most sacred spot of all, where reputedly the first Old Ones had settled on a primal sea-bottom. In the new city—many of whose features we could recognize in the sculptures, but which stretched fully a hundred miles along the mountain range in each direction beyond the farthest limits of our aerial survey—there were reputed to be preserved certain sacred stones forming part of the first sea-bottom city, which thrust up to light after long epochs in the course of the general crumpling of strata.

VIII.

Naturally, Danforth and I studied with especial interest and a peculiarly personal sense of awe everything pertaining to the immediate district in which we were. Of this local material there was naturally a vast abundance; and on the tangled ground level of the city we were lucky enough to find a house of very late date whose walls, though somewhat damaged by a neighboring rift, contained sculptures of decadent workmanship carrying the story of the region much beyond the period of the Pliocene map whence we derived our last general glimpse of the pre-human world. This was the last place we examined in detail, since what we found there gave us a fresh immediate objective.

Certainly, we were in one of the strangest, weirdest, and most terrible of all the corners of earth's globe. Of all existing lands, it was infinitely the most ancient. The conviction grew upon us that this hideous upland must indeed be the fabled nightmare plateau of Leng which even the mad author of the *Necronomicon* was reluctant to discuss. The great mountain chain was tremendously long—starting as a low range at Luitpold Land on the east coast of Weddell Sea and virtually crossing the entire continent. That really high part stretched in a mighty arc from about Latitude 82°, E. Longitude 60° to Latitude 70°, E. Longitude 115°, with its concave side toward our camp and its seaward end in the region of that long, ice-locked coast whose hills were glimpsed by Wilkes and Mawson at the antarctic circle.

Yet even more monstrous exaggerations of nature seemed disturbingly close at hand. I have said that these peaks are higher than the Himalayas, but the sculptures forbid me to say that they are earth's highest. That grim honor is beyond doubt reserved for something which half the sculptures hesitated to record at all, whilst others approached it with obvious repugnance and trepidation. It seems that there was one part of the ancient land—the first part that ever rose from the waters after the earth had flung off the moon and the Old Ones had seeped down, from the stars—which had come to be shunned as vaguely and namelessly evil. Cities built there had crumbled before their time, and had been found suddenly deserted. Then when the first great earth buckling had convulsed the region in the Comanchian Age, a frightful line of peaks had shot suddenly up amidst the most appalling din and chaos—and earth had received her loftiest and most terrible mountains.

If the scale of the carvings was correct, these abhorred things must have been much over forty thousand feet high—radically vaster than even the shocking mountains of madness we had crossed. They extended, it appeared, from about Latitude 77°, E. Longitude 70° to Latitude 70°, E. Longitude 100°—less than three hundred miles away from the dead city, so that we would have spied their dreaded summits in the dim western distance had it not been for that vague, opalescent haze. Their northern end must likewise be visible from the long antarctic circle coast line at Queen Mary Land.

Some of the Old Ones, in the decadent days, had made strange prayers to those mountains—but none ever went near them or dared to guess what lay beyond. No human eye had ever seen them, and as I studied the emotions conveyed in the carvings, I prayed that none ever might. There are protecting hills along the coast beyond them—Queen Mary and Kaiser Wilhelm Lands—and I thank Heaven no one has been able to land and climb those hills. I am not as sceptical about old tales and fears as I used to be, and I do not laugh now at the pre-human sculptor's notion that lightning paused meaningfully now and then at each of the brooding crests, and that an unexplained glow shone from one of those terrible pinnacles all through the long polar night. There may be a very real and very monstrous meaning in the old Pnakotic whispers about Kadath in the Cold Waste.

But the terrain close at hand was hardly less strange, even if less namelessly accursed. Soon after the founding of the city the great mountain range became the seat of the principal temples, and many carvings showed what grotesque and fantastic towers had pierced the sky where now we saw only the curiously clinging cubes and ramparts. In the course of ages the caves had appeared, and had been shaped into adjuncts of the temples.

With the advance of still later epochs, all the limestone veins of the region were hollowed out by ground waters, so that the mountains, the foothills, and the plains below them were a veritable network of connected caverns and galleries. Many graphic sculptures told of explorations deep underground, and of the final discovery of the Stygian sunless sea that lurked at earth's bowels.

This vast nighted gulf had undoubtedly been worn by the great river which flowed down from the nameless and horrible westward mountains, and which had formerly turned at the base of the Old Ones' range and flowed beside that chain into the Indian Ocean between Budd and Totten Lands on Wilkes's coast line. Little by little it had eaten away the limestone hill base at its turning, till at last its sapping currents reached the caverns of the ground waters and joined with them in digging a deeper abyss. Finally its whole bulk emptied into the hollow hills and left the old bed toward the ocean dry. Much of the later city as we now found it had been built over that former bed. The Old Ones, understanding what had happened, and exercising their always keen artistic sense, had carved into ornate pylons those headlands of the foothills where the great stream began its descent into eternal darkness.

This river, once crossed by scores of noble stone bridges, was plainly the one whose extinct course we had seen in our aeroplane survey. Its position in different carvings of the city helped us to orient ourselves to the scene as it had been at various stages of the region's age-long, aeon-dead history, so that we were able to sketch a hasty but careful map of the salient features — squares, important buildings, and the like — for guidance in further explorations. We could soon reconstruct in fancy the whole stupendous thing as it was a million or ten million or fifty million years ago, for the sculptures told us exactly what the buildings and mountains and squares and suburbs and landscape setting and luxuriant Tertiary vegetation had looked like. It must have had a marvelous and mystic beauty, and as I thought of it, I almost forgot the clammy sense of sinister oppression with which the city's inhuman age and massiveness and deadness and remoteness and glacial twilight had choked and weighed on my spirit. Yet according to certain carvings, the denizens of that city had themselves known the clutch of oppressive terror; for there was a somber and recurrent type of scene in which the Old Ones were shown in the act of recoiling affrightedly from some object — never allowed to appear in the design — found in the great river and indicated as having been washed down through waving, vine-draped cycad forests from those horrible westward mountains.

It was only in the one late-built house with the decadent carvings that we obtained any foreshadowing of the final calamity leading to the city's desertion. Undoubtedly there must have been many sculptures of the same age elsewhere, even allowing for the slackened energies and aspirations of a stressful and uncertain period; indeed, very certain evidence of the existence of others came to us shortly afterward. But this was the first and only set we directly encountered. We meant to look farther later on; but as I have said, immediate conditions dictated another present objective. There would, though, have been a limit — for after all hope of a long future occupancy of the place had perished among the Old Ones, there could not but have been a complete cessation of mural decoration. The ultimate blow, of course, was the coming of the great cold which once held most of the earth in thrall, and which has never departed from the ill-fated poles — the great cold that, at the world's other extremity, put an end to the fabled lands of Lomar and Hyperborea.

Just when this tendency began in the antarctic, it would be hard to say in terms of exact years. Nowadays we set the beginning of the general glacial periods at a distance of about five hundred thousand years from the present, but at the poles the terrible scourge must have commenced much earlier. All quantitative estimates are partly guesswork, but it is quite likely that the decadent sculptures were made considerably less than a million years ago, and that the actual desertion of the city was complete long before the conventional opening of the Pleistocene — five hundred thousand years ago — as reckoned in terms of the earth's whole surface.

In the decadent sculptures there were signs of thinner vegetation everywhere, and of a decreased country life on the part of the Old Ones. Heating devices were shown in the houses, and winter travelers were represented as muffled in protective fabrics. Then we saw a series of cartouches — the continuous band arrangement being frequently interrupted in these late carvings — depicting a constantly growing migration to the nearest refuges of greater warmth — some fleeing to cities under the sea off the far-away coast, and some clambering down through networks of limestone caverns in the hollow hills to the neighboring black abyss of subterrene waters.

In the end it seems to have been the neighboring abyss which received the greatest colonization. This was partly due, no doubt, to the traditional sacredness of this special region, but may have been more conclusively determined by the opportunities it gave for continuing the use of the great temples on the honeycombed mountains, and for retaining the vast land city as a place of summer residence and base of communication with various mines. The linkage of old and new abodes was made more effective by means of several gradings and improvements along the connecting routes, including the chiseling of numerous direct tunnels from the ancient metropolis to the black abyss — sharply down-pointing tunnels whose mouths we carefully drew, according to our most thoughtful estimates, on the guide map we were compiling. It was obvious that at least two of these tunnels lay within a reasonable exploring distance of where we were — both being on the mountainward edge of the city, one less than a quarter of a mile toward the ancient river-course, and the other perhaps twice that distance in the opposite direction.

The abyss, it seems, had shelving shores of dry land at certain places, but the Old Ones built their new city under water — no doubt because of its greater certainty of uniform warmth. The depth of the hidden sea appears to have been very great, so that the earth's internal heat could ensure its habitability for an indefinite period. The beings seemed to have had no trouble in adapting themselves to part-time — and eventually, of course, whole-time — residence under water, since they had never allowed their gill systems to atrophy. There were many sculptures which showed how they had always frequently visited their submarine kinsfolk elsewhere, and how they had habitually bathed on the deep bottom of their great river. The darkness of inner earth could likewise have been no deterrent to a race accustomed to long antarctic nights.

Decadent though their style undoubtedly was, these latest carvings had a truly epic quality where they told of the building of the new city in the cavern sea. The Old Ones had gone about it scientifically — quarrying insoluble rocks from the heart of the honeycombed mountains, and employing expert workers from the nearest submarine city to perform the construction according to the best methods. These workers brought with them all that was necessary to establish the new venture — Shoggoth tissue from which to breed stone lifters and subsequent beasts of burden for the cavern city, and other protoplasmic matter to mold into phosphorescent organisms for lighting purposes.

At last a mighty metropolis rose on the bottom of that Stygian sea, its architecture much like that of the city above, and its workmanship displaying relatively little decadence because of the precise mathematical element inherent in building operations. The newly bred Shoggoths grew to enormous size and singular intelligence, and were represented as taking and executing orders with marvelous quickness. They seemed to converse with the Old Ones by mimicking their voices — a sort of musical piping over a wide range, if poor Lake's dissection had indicated aright — and to work more from spoken commands than from hypnotic suggestions as in earlier times. They were, however, kept in admirable control. The phosphorescent organisms supplied light with vast effectiveness, and doubtless atoned for the loss of the familiar polar auroras of the outer-world night.

Art and decoration were pursued, though of course with a certain decadence. The Old Ones seemed to realize this falling off themselves, and in many cases anticipated the policy of Constantine the Great by transplanting especially fine blocks of ancient carving from their land city, just as the emperor, in a similar age of decline, stripped Greece and Asia of their finest art to give his new Byzantine capital greater splendors than its own people could create. That the transfer of sculptured blocks had not been more extensive was doubtless owing to the fact that the land city was not at first wholly abandoned. By the time total abandonment did occur — and it surely must have occurred before the polar Pleistocene was far advanced — the Old Ones had perhaps become satisfied with their decadent art — or had ceased to recognize the superior merit of the older carvings. At any rate, the aeon-silent ruins around us had certainly undergone no wholesale sculptural denudation, though all the best separate statues, like other movables, had been taken away.

The decadent cartouches and dadoes telling this story were, as I have said, the latest we could find in our limited search. They left us with a picture of the Old Ones shuttling back and forth betwixt the land city in summer and the sea-cavern city in winter, and sometimes trading with the sea-bottom cities off the antarctic coast. By this time the ultimate doom of the land city must have been recognized, for the sculptures showed many signs of the cold's malign encroachments. Vegetation was declining, and the terrible snows of the winter no longer melted completely even in midsummer. The saurian livestock were nearly all dead, and the mammals were standing it none too well. To keep on with the work of the upper world it had become necessary to adapt some of the amorphous and curiously cold-resistant Shoggoths to land life — a thing the Old Ones had formerly been reluctant to do. The great river was now lifeless, and the upper sea had lost most of its denizens except the seals and whales. All the birds had flown away, save only the great, grotesque penguins.

What had happened afterward we could only guess. How long had the new sea-cavern city survived? Was it still down there, a stony corpse in eternal blackness? Had the subterranean waters frozen at last? To what fate had the ocean-bottom cities of the outer world been delivered? Had any of the Old Ones shifted north ahead of the creeping ice cap? Existing geology shows no trace of their presence. Had the frightful Mi-Go been still a menace in the outer land world of the north? Could one be sure of what might or might not linger, even to this day, in the lightless and unplumbed abysses of earth's deepest waters? Those things had seemingly been able to withstand any amount of pressure — and men of the sea have fished up curious objects at times. And has the killer-whale theory really explained the savage and mysterious scars on antarctic seals noticed a generation ago by Borchgrevingk?

The specimens found by poor Lake did not enter into these guesses, for their geologic setting proved them to have lived at what must have been a very early date in the land city's history. They were, according to their location, certainly not less than thirty million years old, and we reflected that in their day the sea-cavern city, and indeed the cavern itself, had had no existence. They would have remembered an older scene, with lush Tertiary vegetation everywhere, a younger land city of flourishing arts around them, and a great river sweeping northward along the base of the mighty mountains toward a far-away tropic ocean.

And yet we could not help thinking about these specimens — especially about the eight perfect ones that were missing from Lake's hideously ravaged camp. There was something abnormal about that whole business — the strange things we had tried so hard to lay to somebody's madness — those frightful graves — the amount and nature of the missing material — Gedney — the unearthly toughness of those archaic monstrosities, and the queer vital freaks the sculptures now showed the race to have — Danforth and I had seen a good deal in the last few hours, and were prepared to believe and keep silent about many appalling and incredible secrets of primal nature.

IX.

I have said that our study of the decadent sculptures brought about a change in our immediate objective. This, of course, had to do with the chiseled avenues to the black inner world, of whose existence we had not known before, but which we were now eager to find and traverse. From the evident scale of the carvings we deduced that a steeply descending walk of about a mile through either of the neighboring tunnels would bring us to the brink of the dizzy, sunless cliffs above the great abyss; down whose sides paths, improved by the Old Ones, led to the rocky shore of the hidden and nighted ocean. To behold this fabulous gulf in stark reality was a lure which seemed impossible of resistance once we knew of the thing — yet we realized we must begin the quest at once if we expected to include it in our present trip.

It was now 8 p.m., and we did not have enough battery replacements to let our torches burn on forever. We had done so much studying and copying below the glacial level that our battery supply had had at least five hours of nearly continuous use, and despite the special dry cell formula, would obviously be good for only about four more — though by keeping one torch unused, except for especially interesting or difficult places, we might manage to eke out a safe margin beyond that. It would not do to be without a light in these Cyclopean catacombs, hence in order to make the abyss trip we must give up all further mural deciphering. Of course we intended to revisit the place for days and perhaps weeks of intensive study and photography — curiosity having long ago got the better of horror — but just now we must hasten. Our supply of trail-blazing paper was far from unlimited, and we were reluctant to sacrifice spare notebooks or sketching paper to augment it, but we did let one large notebook go. If worse came to worst we could resort to rock-chipping — and of course it would be possible, even in case of really lost direction, to work up to full daylight by one channel or another if granted sufficient time for plentiful trial and error. So at last we set off eagerly in the indicated direction of the nearest tunnel.

According to the carvings from which we had made our map, the desired tunnel-mouth could not be much more than a quarter of a mile from where we stood; the intervening space showing solid-looking buildings quite likely to be penetrable still at a sub-glacial level. The opening itself would be in the basement — on the angle nearest the foothills — of a vast five-pointed structure of evidently public and perhaps ceremonial nature, which we tried to identify from our aerial survey of the ruins. No such structure came to our minds as we recalled our flight, hence we concluded that its upper parts had been greatly damaged, or that it had been totally shattered in an ice rift we had noticed. In the latter case the tunnel would probably turn out to be choked, so that we would have to try the next nearest one — the one less than a mile to the north. The intervening river course prevented our trying any of the more southern tunnels on this trip; and indeed, if both of the neighboring ones were choked it was doubtful whether our batteries would warrant an attempt on the next northerly one — about a mile beyond our second choice.

As we threaded our dim way through the labyrinth with the aid of map and compass — traversing rooms and corridors in every stage of ruin or preservation, clambering up ramps, crossing upper floors and bridges and clambering down again, encountering choked doorways and piles of debris, hastening now and then along finely preserved and uncannily immaculate stretches, taking false leads and retracing our way (in such cases removing the blind paper trail we had left), and once in a while striking the bottom of an open shaft through which daylight poured or trickled down — we were repeatedly tantalized by the sculptured walls along our route. Many must have told tales of immense historical importance, and only the prospect of later visits reconciled us to the need of passing them by. As it was, we slowed down once in a while and turned on our second torch. If we had had more films, we would certainly have paused briefly to photograph certain bas-reliefs, but time-consuming hand-copying was clearly out of the question.

I come now once more to a place where the temptation to hesitate, or to hint rather than state, is very strong. It is necessary, however, to reveal the rest in order to justify my course in discouraging further exploration. We had wormed our way very close to the computed site of the tunnel's mouth — having crossed a second-story bridge to what seemed plainly the tip of a pointed wall, and descended to a ruinous corridor especially rich in decadently elaborate and apparently ritualistic sculptures of late workmanship — when, shortly before 8:30 p.m., Danforth's keen young nostrils gave us the first hint of something unusual. If we had had a dog with us, I suppose we would have been warned before. At first we could not precisely say what was wrong with the formerly crystal-pure air, but after a few seconds our memories reacted only too definitely. Let me try to state the thing without flinching. There was an odor — and that odor was vaguely, subtly, and unmistakably akin to what had nauseated us upon opening the insane grave of the horror poor Lake had dissected.

Of course the revelation was not as clearly cut at the time as it sounds now. There were several conceivable explanations, and we did a good deal of indecisive whispering. Most important of all, we did not retreat without further investigation; for having come this far, we were loath to be balked by anything short of certain disaster. Anyway, what we must have suspected was altogether too wild to believe. Such things did not happen in any normal world. It was probably sheer irrational instinct which made us dim our single torch — tempted no longer by the decadent and sinister sculptures that leered menacingly from the oppressive walls — and which softened our progress to a cautious tiptoeing and crawling over the increasingly littered floor and heaps of debris.

Danforth's eyes as well as nose proved better than mine, for it was likewise he who first noticed the queer aspect of the debris after we had passed many half-choked arches leading to chambers and corridors on the ground level. It did not look quite as it ought after countless thousands of years of desertion, and when we cautiously turned on more light we saw that a kind of swath seemed to have been lately tracked through it. The irregular nature of the litter precluded any definite marks, but in the smoother places there were suggestions of the dragging of heavy objects. Once we thought there was a hint of parallel tracks as if of runners. This was what made us pause again.

It was during that pause that we caught — simultaneously this time — the other odor ahead. Paradoxically, it was both a less frightful and more frightful odor — less frightful intrinsically, but infinitely appalling in this place under the known circumstances — unless, of course, Gedney — for the odor was the plain and familiar one of common petrol — every-day gasoline.

Our motivation after that is something I will leave to psychologists. We knew now that some terrible extension of the camp horrors must have crawled into this nighted burial place of the aeons, hence could not doubt any longer the existence of nameless conditions — present or at least recent — just ahead. Yet in the end we did let sheer burning curiosity — or anxiety — or autohypnotism — or vague thoughts of responsibility toward Gedney — or what not — drive us on. Danforth whispered again of the print he thought he had seen at the alley-turning in the ruins above; and of the faint musical piping — potentially of tremendous significance in the light of Lake's dissection report, despite its close resemblance to the cave-mouth echoes of the windy peaks — which he thought he had shortly afterward half heard from unknown depths below. I, in my turn, whispered of how the camp was left — of what had disappeared, and of how the madness of a lone survivor might have conceived the inconceivable — a wild trip across the monstrous mountains and a descent into the unknown, primal masonry — But we could not convince each other, or even ourselves, of anything definite. We had turned off all light as we stood still, and vaguely noticed that a trace of deeply filtered upper day kept the blackness from being absolute. Having automatically begun to move ahead, we guided ourselves by occasional flashes from our torch. The disturbed debris formed an impression we could not shake off, and the smell of gasoline grew stronger. More and more ruin met our eyes and hampered our feet, until very soon we saw that the forward way was about to cease. We had been all too correct in our pessimistic guess about that rift glimpsed from the air. Our tunnel quest was a blind one, and we were not even going to be able to reach the basement out of which the abyssward aperture opened.

The torch, flashing over the grotesquely carved walls of the blocked corridor in which we stood, showed several doorways in various states of obstruction; and from one of them the gasoline odor — quite submerging that other hint of odor — came with especial distinctness. As we looked more steadily, we saw that beyond a doubt there had been a slight and recent clearing away of debris from that particular opening. Whatever the lurking horror might be, we believed the direct avenue toward it was now plainly manifest. I do not think anyone will wonder that we waited an appreciable time before making any further motion.

And yet, when we did venture inside that black arch, our first impression was one of anticlimax. For amidst the littered expanse of that sculptured Crypt — a perfect cube with sides of about twenty feet — there remained no recent object of instantly discernible size; so that we looked instinctively, though in vain, for a farther doorway. In another moment, however, Danforth's sharp vision had descried a place where the floor debris had been disturbed; and we turned on both torches full strength. Though what we saw in that light was actually simple and trifling, I am none the less reluctant to tell of it because of what it implied. It was a rough leveling of the debris, upon which several small objects lay carelessly scattered, and at one corner of which a considerable amount of gasoline must have been spilled lately enough to leave a strong odor even at this extreme superplateau altitude. In other words, it could not be other than a sort of camp — a camp made by questing beings who, like us, had been turned back by the unexpectedly choked way to the abyss.

Let me be plain. The scattered objects were, so far as substance was concerned, all from Lake's camp; and consisted of tin cans as queerly opened as those we had seen at that ravaged place, many spent matches, three illustrated books more or less curiously smudged, an empty ink bottle with its pictorial and instructional carton, a broken fountain pen, some oddly snipped fragments of fur and tent-cloth, a used electric battery with circular of directions, a folder that came with our type of tent heater, and a sprinkling of crumpled papers. It was all bad enough but when we smoothed out the papers and looked at what was on them, we felt we had come to the worst. We had found certain inexplicably blotted papers at the camp which might have prepared us, yet the effect of the sight down there in the pre-human vaults of a nightmare city was almost too much to bear.

A mad Gedney might have made the groups of dots in imitation of those found on the greenish soapstones, just as the dots on those insane five-pointed grave-mounds might have been made; and he might conceivably have prepared rough, hasty sketches — varying in their accuracy or lack of it — which outlined the neighboring parts of the city and traced the way from a circularly represented place outside our previous route — a place we identified as a great cylindrical tower in the carvings and as a vast circular gulf glimpsed in our aerial survey — to the present five-pointed structure and the tunnel-mouth therein. He might, I repeat, have prepared such sketches; for those

Astounding Stories, March 1936

before us were quite obviously compiled, as our own had been, from late sculptures somewhere in the glacial labyrinth, though not from the ones which we had seen and used. But what that art-blind bungler could never have done was to execute those sketches in a strange and assured technique perhaps superior, despite haste and carelessness, to any of the decadent carvings from which they were taken — the characteristic and unmistakable technique of the Old Ones themselves in the dead city's heyday.

There are those who will say Danforth and I were utterly mad not to flee for our lives after that; since our conclusions were now — notwithstanding their wildness — completely fixed, and of a nature I need not even mention to those who have read my account as far as this. Perhaps we were mad — for have I not said those horrible peaks were mountains of madness? But I think I can detect something of the same spirit — albeit in a less extreme form — in the men who stalk deadly beasts through African jungles to photograph them or study their habits. Half-paralyzed with terror though we were, there was nevertheless fanned within us a blazing flame of awe and curiosity which triumphed in the end.

Of course we did not mean to face that — or those — which we knew had been there, but we felt that they must be gone by now. They would by this time have found the other neighboring entrance to the abyss, and have passed within, to whatever night-black fragments of the past might await them in the ultimate gulf—the ultimate gulf they had never seen. Or if that entrance, too, was blocked, they would have gone on to the north seeking another. They were, we remembered, partly independent of light.

Looking back to that moment, I can scarcely recall just what precise form our new emotions took—just what change of immediate objective it was that so sharpened our sense of expectancy. We certainly did not mean to face what we feared—yet I will not deny that we may have had a lurking, unconscious wish to spy certain things from some hidden vantage point. Probably we had not given up our zeal to glimpse the abyss itself, though there was interposed a new goal in the form of that great circular place shown on the crumpled sketches we had found. We had at once recognized it as a monstrous cylindrical tower figuring in the very earliest carvings, but appearing only as a prodigious round aperture from above. Something about the impressiveness of its rendering, even in these hasty diagrams, made us think that its sub-glacial levels must still form a feature of peculiar importance. Perhaps it embodied architectural marvels as yet unencountered by us. It was certainly of incredible age according to the sculptures in which it figured—being indeed among the first things built in the city. Its carvings, if preserved, could not but be highly significant. Moreover, it might form a good present link with the upper world—a shorter route than the one we were so carefully blazing, and probably that by which those others had descended.

At any rate, the thing we did was to study the terrible sketches—which quite perfectly confirmed our own—and start back over the indicated course to the circular place; the course which our nameless predecessors must have traversed twice before us. The other neighboring gate to the abyss would lie beyond that. I need not speak of our journey—during which we continued to leave an economical trail of paper—for it was precisely the same in kind as that by which we had reached the cul-de-sac; except that it tended to adhere more closely to the ground level and even descend to basement corridors. Every now and then we could trace certain disturbing marks in the debris or litter under-foot; and after we had passed outside the radius of the gasoline scent, we were again faintly conscious—spasmodically—of that more hideous and more persistent scent. After the way had branched from our former course, we sometimes gave the rays of our single torch a furtive sweep along the walls; noting in almost every case the well-nigh omnipresent sculptures, which indeed seem to have formed a main aesthetic outlet for the Old Ones.

About 9:30 p.m., while traversing a long, vaulted corridor whose increasingly glaciated floor seemed somewhat below the ground level and whose roof grew lower as we advanced, we began to see strong daylight ahead and were able to turn off our torch. It appeared that we were coming to the vast circular place, and that our distance from the upper air could not be very great. The corridor ended in an arch surprisingly low for these megalithic ruins, but we could see much through it even before we emerged. Beyond there stretched a prodigious round space—fully two hundred feet in diameter—strewn with debris and containing many choked archways corresponding to the one we were about to cross. The walls were—in available spaces—boldly sculptured into a spiral band of heroic proportions; and displayed, despite the destructive weathering caused by the openness of the spot, an artistic splendor far beyond anything we had encountered before. The littered floor was quite heavily glaciated, and we fancied that the true bottom lay at a considerably lower depth.

But the salient object of the place was the titanic stone ramp which, eluding the archways by a sharp turn outward into the open floor, wound spirally up the stupendous cylindrical wall like an inside counterpart of those once climbing outside the monstrous towers or ziggurats of antique Babylon. Only the rapidity of our flight, and the perspective which confounded the descent with the tower's inner wall, had prevented our noticing this feature from the air, and thus caused us to seek another avenue to the sub-glacial level. Pabodie might have been able to tell what sort of engineering held it in place, but Danforth and I could merely admire and marvel. We could see mighty stone corbels and pillars here and there, but what we saw seemed inadequate to the function performed. The thing was excellently preserved up to the present top of the tower—a highly remarkable circumstance in view of its exposure—and its shelter had done much to protect the bizarre and disturbing cosmic sculptures on the walls.

As we stepped out into the awesome half-daylight of this monstrous cylinder-bottom—fifty million years old, and without doubt the most primally ancient structure ever to meet our eyes—we saw that the ramp-traversed sides stretched dizzily up to a height of fully sixty feet. This, we recalled from our aerial survey, meant an outside glaciation of some forty feet; since the yawning gulf we had seen from the plane had been at the top of an approximately twenty-foot mound of crumbled masonry, somewhat sheltered for three-fourths of its circumference by the massive curving walls of a line of higher ruins. According to the sculptures, the original tower had stood in the center of an immense circular plaza, and had been perhaps five hundred or six hundred feet high, with tiers of horizontal disks near the top, and a row of needle-like spires along the upper rim. Most of the masonry had obviously toppled outward rather than inward—a fortunate happening, since otherwise the ramp might have been shattered and the whole interior choked. As it was, the ramp showed sad battering; whilst the choking was such that all the archways at the bottom seemed to have been recently cleared.

It took us only a moment to conclude that this was indeed the route by which those others had descended, and that this would be the logical route for our own ascent despite the long trail of paper we had left elsewhere. The tower's mouth was no farther from the foothills and our waiting plane than was the great terraced building we had entered, and any further sub-glacial exploration we might make on this trip would lie in this general region. Oddly, we were still thinking about possible later trips—even after all we had seen and guessed. Then, as we picked our way cautiously over the debris of the great floor, there came a sight which for the time excluded all other matters.

It was the neatly huddled array of three sledges in that farther angle of the ramp's lower and outward-projecting course which had hitherto been screened from our view. There they were—the three sledges missing from Lake's camp—shaken by a hard usage which must have included forcible dragging along great reaches of snowless masonry and debris, as well as much hand portage over utterly unnavigable places. They were carefully and intelligently packed and strapped, and contained things memorably familiar enough: the gasoline stove, fuel cans, instrument cases, provision tins, tarpaulins obviously bulging with books, and some bulging with less obvious contents—everything derived from Lake's equipment.

After what we had found in that other room, we were in a measure prepared for this encounter. The really great shock came when we stepped over and undid one tarpaulin whose outlines had peculiarly disquieted us. It seems that others as well as Lake had been interested in collecting typical specimens; for there were two here, both stiffly frozen, perfectly preserved, patched with adhesive plaster where some wounds around the neck had occurred, and wrapped with care to prevent further damage. They were the bodies of young Gedney and the missing dog.

X.

Many people will probably judge us callous as well as mad for thinking about the northward tunnel and the abyss so soon after our somber discovery, and I am not prepared to say that we would have immediately revived such thoughts but for a specific circumstance which broke in upon us and set up a whole new train of speculations. We had replaced the tarpaulin over poor Gedney and were standing in a kind of mute bewilderment when the sounds finally reached our consciousness—the first sounds we had heard since descending out of the open where the mountain wind whined faintly from its unearthly heights. Well known and mundane though they were, their presence in this remote world of death was more unexpected and unnerving than any grotesque or fabulous tones could possibly have been—since they gave a fresh upsetting to all our notions of cosmic harmony.

Had it been some trace of that bizarre musical piping over a wide range which Lake's dissection report had led us to expect in those others—and which, indeed, our overwrought fancies had been reading into every wind howl we had heard since coming on the camp horror—it would have had a kind of hellish congruity with the aeon-dead region around us. A voice from other epochs belongs in a graveyard of other epochs. As it was, however, the noise shattered all our profoundly seated adjustments—all our tacit acceptance of the inner antarctic as a waste utterly and irrevocably void of every vestige of normal life. What we heard was not the fabulous note of any buried blasphemy of elder earth from whose supernal toughness an age-denied polar sun had evoked a monstrous response. Instead, it was a thing so mockingly normal and so unerringly familiarized by our sea days off Victoria Land and our camp days at McMurdo Sound that we shuddered to think of it here, where such things ought not to be. To be brief—it was simply the raucous squawking of a penguin.

The muffled sound floated from sub-glacial recesses nearly opposite to the corridor whence we had come—regions manifestly in the direction of that other tunnel to the vast abyss. The presence of a living water-bird in such a direction—in a world whose surface was one of age-long and uniform lifelessness—could lead to only one conclusion; hence our first thought was to verify the objective reality of the sound. It was, indeed, repeated, and seemed at times to come from more than one throat. Seeking its source, we entered an archway from which much debris had been cleared; resuming our trail-blazing—with an added paper-supply taken with curious repugnance from one of the tarpaulin bundles on the sledges—when we left daylight behind.

As the glaciated floor gave place to a litter of detritus, we plainly discerned some curious, dragging tracks; and once Danforth found a distinct print of a sort whose description would be only too superfluous. The course indicated by the penguin cries was precisely what our map and compass prescribed as an approach to the more northerly tunnel-mouth, and we were glad to find that a bridgeless thoroughfare on the ground and basement levels seemed open. The tunnel, according to the chart, ought to start from the basement of a large pyramidal structure which we seemed vaguely to recall from our aerial survey as remarkably well-preserved. Along our path the single torch showed a customary profusion of carvings, but we did not pause to examine any of these.

Suddenly a bulky white shape loomed up ahead of us, and we flashed on the second torch. It is odd how wholly this new quest had turned our minds from earlier fears of what might lurk near. Those other ones, having left their supplies in the great circular place, must have planned to return after their scouting trip toward or into the abyss; yet we had now discarded all caution concerning them as completely as if they had never existed. This white, waddling thing was fully six feet high, yet we seemed to realize at once that it was not one of those others. They were larger and dark, and, according to the sculptures, their motion over land surfaces was a swift, assured matter despite the queerness of their sea-born tentacle equipment. But to say that the white thing did not profoundly frighten us would be vain. We were indeed clutched for an instant by a primitive dread almost sharper than the worst of our reasoned fears regarding those others. Then came a flash of anticlimax as the white shape sidled into a lateral archway to our left to join two others of its kind which had summoned it in raucous tones. For it was only a penguin — albeit of a huge, unknown species larger than the greatest of the known king penguins, and monstrous in its combined albinism and virtual eyelessness.

When we had followed the thing into the archway and turned both our torches on the indifferent and unheeding group of three, we saw that they were all eyeless albinos of the same unknown and gigantic species. Their size reminded us of some of the archaic penguins depicted in the Old Ones' sculptures, and it did not take us long to conclude that they were descended from the same stock — undoubtedly surviving through a retreat to some warmer inner region whose perpetual blackness had destroyed their pigmentation and atrophied their eyes to mere useless slits. That their present habitat was the vast abyss we sought, was not for a moment to be doubted; and this evidence of the gulf's continued warmth and habitability filled us with the most curious and subtly perturbing fancies.

We wondered, too, what had caused these three birds to venture out of their usual domain. The state and silence of the great dead city made it clear that it had at no time been an habitual seasonal rookery, whilst the manifest indifference of the trio to our presence made it seem odd that any passing party of those others should have startled them. Was it possible that those others had taken some aggressive action or tried to increase their meat supply? We doubted whether that pungent odor which the dogs had hated could cause an equal antipathy in these penguins, since their ancestors had obviously lived on excellent terms with the Old Ones — an amicable relationship which must have survived in the abyss below as long as any of the Old Ones remained. Regretting — in a flare-up of the old spirit of pure science — that we could not photograph these anomalous creatures, we shortly left them to their squawking and pushed on toward the abyss whose openness was now so positively proved to us, and whose exact direction occasional penguin tracks made clear.

Not long afterward a steep descent in a long, low, doorless, and peculiarly sculptureless corridor led us to believe that we were approaching the tunnel-mouth at last. We had passed two more penguins, and heard others immediately ahead. Then the corridor ended in a prodigious open space which made us gasp involuntarily — a perfect inverted hemisphere, obviously deep underground; fully a hundred feet in diameter and fifty feet high, with low archways opening around all parts of the circumference but one, and that one yawning cavernously with a black, arched aperture which broke the symmetry of the vault to a height of nearly fifteen feet. It was the entrance to the great abyss.

In this vast hemisphere, whose concave roof was impressively though decadently carved to a likeness of the primordial celestial dome, a few albino penguins waddled — aliens there, but indifferent and unseeing. The black tunnel yawned indefinitely off at a steep, descending grade, its aperture adorned with grotesquely chiseled jambs and lintel. From that cryptical mouth we fancied a current of slightly warmer air, and perhaps even a suspicion of vapor proceeded; and we wondered what living entities other than penguins the limitless void below, and the contiguous honeycombings of the land and the titan mountains, might conceal. We wondered, too, whether the trace of mountain-top smoke at first suspected by poor Lake, as well as the odd haze we had ourselves perceived around the rampart-crowned peak, might not be caused by the tortuous-channeled rising of some such vapor from the unfathomed regions of earth's core.

Entering the tunnel, we saw that its outline was — at least at the start — about fifteen feet each way — sides, floor, and arched roof composed of the usual megalithic masonry. The sides were sparsely decorated with cartouches of conventional designs in a late, decadent style; and all the construction and carving were marvelously well-preserved. The floor was quite clear, except for a slight detritus bearing outgoing penguin tracks and the inward tracks of these others. The farther one advanced, the warmer it became; so that we were soon unbuttoning our heavy garments. We wondered whether there were any actually igneous manifestations below, and whether the waters of that sunless sea were hot. After a short distance the masonry gave place to solid rock, though the tunnel kept the same proportions and presented the same aspect of carved regularity. Occasionally its varying grade became so steep that grooves were cut in the floor. Several times we noted the mouths of small lateral galleries not recorded in our diagrams; none of them such as to complicate the problem of our return, and all of them welcome as possible refuges in case we met unwelcome entities on their way back from the abyss. The nameless scent of such things was very distinct. Doubtless it was suicidally foolish to venture into that tunnel under the known conditions, but the lure of the unplumbed is stronger in certain persons than most suspect — indeed, it was just such a lure which had brought us to this unearthly polar waste in the first place. We saw several penguins as we passed along, and speculated on the distance we would have to traverse. The carvings had led us to expect a steep downhill walk of about a mile to the abyss, but our previous wanderings had shown us that matters of scale were not wholly to be depended on.

After about a quarter of a mile that nameless scent became greatly accentuated, and we kept very careful track of the various lateral openings we passed. There was no visible vapor as at the mouth, but this was doubtless due to the lack of contrasting cooler air. The temperature was rapidly ascending, and we were not surprised to come upon a careless heap of material shudderingly familiar to us. It was composed of furs and tent-cloth taken from Lake's camp, and we did not pause to study the bizarre forms into which the fabrics had been slashed. Slightly beyond this point we noticed a decided increase in the size and number of the side galleries, and concluded that the densely honeycombed region beneath the higher foothills must now have been reached. The nameless scent was now curiously mixed with another and scarcely less offensive odor — of what nature we could not guess, though we thought of decaying organisms and perhaps unknown subterranean fungi. Then came a startling expansion of the tunnel for which the carvings had not prepared us — a broadening and rising into a lofty, natural-looking elliptical cavern with a level floor, some seventy-five feet long and fifty broad, and with many immense side passages leading away into cryptical darkness.

Though this cavern was natural in appearance, an inspection with both torches suggested that it had been formed by the artificial destruction of several walls between adjacent honeycombings. The walls were rough, and the high, vaulted roof was thick with stalactites; but the solid rock floor had been smoothed off, and was free from all debris, detritus, or even dust to a positively abnormal extent. Except for the avenue through which we had come, this was true of the floors of all the great galleries opening off from it; and the singularity of the condition was such as to set us vainly puzzling. The curious new fetor which had supplemented the nameless scent was excessively pungent here; so much so that it destroyed all trace of the other. Something about this whole place, with its polished and almost glistening floor, struck us as more vaguely baffling and horrible than any of the monstrous things we had previously encountered.

The regularity of the passage immediately ahead, as well as the larger proportion of penguin-droppings there, prevented all confusion as to the right course amidst this plethora of equally great cave mouths. Nevertheless we resolved to resume our paper trailblazing if any further complexity should develop; for dust tracks, of course, could no longer be expected. Upon resuming our direct progress we cast a beam of torchlight over the tunnel walls — and stopped short in amazement at the supremely radical change which had come over the carvings in this part of the passage. We realized, of course, the great decadence of the Old Ones' sculpture at the time of the tunneling, and had indeed noticed the inferior workmanship of the arabesques in the stretches behind us. But now, in this deeper section beyond the cavern, there was a sudden difference wholly transcending explanation — a difference in basic nature as well as in mere quality, and involving so profound and calamitous a degradation of skill that nothing in the hitherto observed rate of decline could have led one to expect it.

This new and degenerate work was coarse, bold, and wholly lacking in delicacy of detail. It was countersunk with exaggerated depth in bands following the same general line as the sparse cartouches of the earlier sections, but the height of the reliefs did not reach the level of the general surface. Danforth had the idea that it was a second carving — a sort of palimpsest formed after the obliteration of a previous design. In nature it was wholly decorative and conventional, and consisted of crude spirals and angles roughly following the quintile mathematical tradition of the Old Ones, yet seemingly more like a parody than a perpetuation of that tradition. We could not get it out of our minds that some subtly but profoundly alien element had been added to the aesthetic feeling behind the technique — an alien element, Danforth guessed, that was responsible for the laborious substitution. It was like, yet disturbingly unlike, what we had come to recognize as the Old Ones' art; and I was persistently reminded of such hybrid things as the ungainly Palmyrene sculptures fashioned in the Roman manner. That others had recently noticed this belt of carving was hinted by the presence of a used flashlight battery on the floor in front of one of the most characteristic cartouches.

Since we could not afford to spend any considerable time in study, we resumed our advance after a cursory look; though frequently casting beams over the walls to see if any further decorative changes developed. Nothing of the sort was perceived, though the carvings were in places rather sparse because of the numerous mouths of smooth-floored lateral tunnels. We saw and heard fewer penguins, but thought we caught a vague suspicion of an infinitely distant chorus of them somewhere deep within the earth. The new and inexplicable odor was abominably strong, and we could detect scarcely a sign of that other nameless scent. Puffs of visible vapor ahead bespoke increasing contrasts in temperature, and the relative nearness of the sunless sea-cliffs of the great abyss. Then, quite unexpectedly, we saw certain obstructions on the polished floor ahead — obstructions which were quite definitely not penguins — and turned on our second torch after making sure that the objects were quite stationary.

XI.

Still another time have I come to a place where it is very difficult to proceed. I ought to be hardened by this stage; but there are some experiences and intimations which scar too deeply to permit of healing, and leave only such an added sensitiveness that memory reinspires all the original horror. We saw, as I have said, certain obstructions on the polished floor ahead; and I may add that our nostrils were assailed almost simultaneously by a very curious intensification of the strange prevailing fetor, now quite plainly mixed with the nameless stench of those others which had gone before. The light of the second torch left no doubt of what the obstructions were, and we dared approach them only because we could see, even from a distance, that they were quite as past all harming power as had been the six similar specimens unearthed from the monstrous star-mounded graves at poor Lake's camp.

They were, indeed, as lacking in completeness as most of those we had unearthed — though it grew plain from the thick, dark-green pool gathering around them that their incompleteness was of infinitely greater recency. There seemed to be only four of them, whereas Lake's bulletins would have suggested no less than eight as forming the group which had preceded us. To find them in this state was wholly unexpected, and we wondered what sort of monstrous struggle had occurred down here in the dark.

Penguins, attacked in a body, retaliate savagely with their

beaks, and our ears now made certain the existence of a rookery far beyond. Had those others disturbed such a place and aroused murderous pursuit? The obstructions did not suggest it, for penguins' beaks against the tough tissues Lake had dissected could hardly account for the terrible damage our approaching glance was beginning to make out. Besides, the huge blind birds we had seen appeared to be singularly peaceful.

Had there, then, been a struggle among those others, and were the absent four responsible? If so, where were they? Were they close at hand and likely to form an immediate menace to us? We glanced anxiously at some of the smooth-floored lateral passages as we continued our slow and frankly reluctant approach. Whatever the conflict was, it had clearly been that which had frightened the penguins into their unaccustomed wandering. It must, then, have arisen near that faintly heard rookery in the incalculable gulf beyond, since there were no signs that any birds had normally dwelt here. Perhaps, we reflected, there had been a hideous running fight, with the weaker party seeking to get back to the cached sledges when their pursuers finished them. One could picture the demoniac fray between namelessly monstrous entities as it surged out of the black abyss with great clouds of frantic penguins squawking and scurrying ahead.

I say that we approached those sprawling and incomplete obstructions slowly and reluctantly. Would to Heaven we had never approached them at all, but had run back at top speed out of that blasphemous tunnel with the greasily smooth floors and the degenerate murals aping and mocking the things they had superseded — run back, before we had seen what we did see, and before our minds were burned with something which will never let us breathe easily again!

Both of our torches were turned on the prostrate objects, so that we soon realized the dominant factor in their incompleteness. Mauled, compressed, twisted, and ruptured as they were, their chief common injury was total decapitation. From each one the tentacled starfish-head had been removed; and as we drew near we saw that the manner of removal looked more like some hellish tearing or suction than like any ordinary form of cleavage. Their noisome dark-green ichor formed a large, spreading pool; but its stench was half overshadowed by the newer and stranger stench, here more pungent than at any other point along our route. Only when we had come very close to the sprawling obstructions could we trace that second, unexplainable fetor to any immediate source — and the instant we did so Danforth, remembering certain very vivid sculptures of the Old Ones' history in the Permian Age one hundred and fifty million years ago, gave vent to a nerve-tortured cry which echoed hysterically through that vaulted and archaic passage with the evil, palimpsest carvings.

I came only just short of echoing his cry myself; for I had seen those primal sculptures, too, and had shudderingly admired the way the nameless artist had suggested that hideous slime coating found on certain incomplete and prostrate Old Ones — those whom the frightful Shoggoths had characteristically slain and sucked to a ghastly headlessness in the great war of re-subjugation. They were infamous, nightmare sculptures even when telling of age-old, bygone things; for Shoggoths and their work ought not to be seen by human beings or portrayed by any beings. The mad author of the *Necronomicon* had nervously tried to swear that none had been bred on this planet, and that only drugged dreamers had even conceived them. Formless protoplasm able to mock and reflect all forms and organs and processes — viscous agglutinations of bubbling cells — rubbery fifteen-foot spheroids infinitely plastic and ductile — slaves of suggestion, builders of cities — more and more sullen, more and more intelligent, more and more amphibious, more and more imitative! Great God! What madness made even those blasphemous Old Ones willing to use and carve such things?

And now, when Danforth and I saw the freshly glistening and reflectively iridescent black slime which clung thickly to those headless bodies and stank obscenely with that new, unknown odor whose cause only a diseased fancy could envisage — clung to those bodies and sparkled less voluminously on a smooth part of the accursedly resculptured wall in a series of grouped dots — we understood the quality of cosmic fear to its uttermost depths. It was not fear of those four missing others — for all too well did we suspect they would do no harm again. Poor devils! After all, they were not evil things of their kind. They were the men of another age and another order of being. Nature had played a hellish jest on them — as it will on any others that human madness, callousness, or cruelty may hereafter dig up in that hideously dead or sleeping polar waste — and this was their tragic homecoming. They had not been even savages — for what indeed had they done? That awful awakening in the cold of an unknown epoch — perhaps an attack by the furry, frantically barking quadrupeds, and a dazed defense against them and the equally frantic white simians with the queer wrappings and paraphernalia . . . poor Lake, poor Gedney . . . and poor Old Ones! Scientists to the last — what had they done that we would not have done in their place? God, what intelligence and persistence! What a facing of the incredible, just as those carven kinsmen and forbears had faced things only a little less incredible! Radiates, vegetables, monstrosities, star-spawn — whatever they had been, they were men!

They had crossed the icy peaks on whose templed slopes they had once worshipped and roamed among the tree-ferns. They had found their dead city brooding under its curse, and had read its carven latter days as we had done. They had tried to reach their living fellows in fabled depths of blackness they had never seen — and what had they found? All this flashed in unison through the thoughts of Danforth and me as we looked from those headless, slime-coated shapes to the loathsome palimpsest sculptures and the diabolical dot-groups of fresh slime on the wall beside them — looked and understood what must have triumphed and survived down there in the Cyclopean water-city of that nighted, penguin-fringed abyss, whence even now a sinister curling mist had begun to belch pallidly as if in answer to Danforth's hysterical scream.

The shock of recognizing that monstrous slime and headlessness had frozen us into mute, motionless statues, and it is only through later conversations that we have learned of the complete identity of our thoughts at that moment. It seemed aeons that we stood there, but actually it could not have been more than ten or fifteen seconds. That hateful, pallid mist curled forward as if veritably driven by some remoter advancing bulk — and then came a sound which upset much of what we had just decided, and in so doing broke the spell and enabled us to run like mad past squawking, confused penguins over our former trail back to the city, along ice-sunken megalithic corridors to the great open circle, and up that archaic spiral ramp in a frenzied, automatic plunge for the sane outer air and light of day.

The new sound, as I have intimated, upset much that we had decided; because it was what poor Lake's dissection had led us to attribute to those we had judged dead. It was, Danforth later told me, precisely what he had caught in infinitely muffled form when at that spot beyond the alley corner above the glacial level; and it certainly had a shocking resemblance to the wind-pipings we had both heard around the lofty mountain caves. At the risk of seeming puerile I will add another thing, too, if only because of the surprising way Danforth's impressions chimed with mine. Of course common reading is what prepared us both to make the interpretation, though Danforth has hinted at queer notions about unsuspected and forbidden sources to which Poe may have had access when writing his Arthur Gordon Pym a century ago. It will be remembered that in that fantastic tale there is a word of unknown but terrible and prodigious significance connected with the antarctic and screamed eternally by the gigantic spectrally snowy birds of that malign region's core. "Tekeli-li! Tekeli-li!" That, I may admit, is exactly what we thought we heard conveyed by that sudden sound behind the advancing white mist — that insidious musical piping over a singularly wide range.

We were in full flight before three notes or syllables had been uttered, though we knew that the swiftness of the Old Ones would enable any scream-roused and pursuing survivor of the slaughter to overtake us in a moment if it really wished to do so. We had a vague hope, however, that non-aggressive conduct and a display of kindred reason might cause such a being to spare us in case of capture, if only from scientific curiosity. After all, if such an one had nothing to fear for itself, it would have no motive in harming us. Concealment being futile at this juncture, we used our torch for a running glance behind, and perceived that the mist was thinning. Would we see, at last, a complete and living specimen of those others? Again came that insidious musical piping — "Tekeli-li! Tekeli-li!" Then, noting that we were actually gaining on our pursuer, it occurred to us that the entity might be wounded. We could take no chances, however, since it was very obviously approaching in answer to Danforth's scream, rather than in flight from any other entity. The timing was too close to admit of doubt. Of the whereabouts of that less conceivable and less mentionable nightmare — that fetid, unglimpsed mountain of slime-spewing protoplasm whose race had conquered the abyss and sent land pioneers to re-carve and squirm through the burrows of the hills — we could form no guess; and it cost us a genuine pang to leave this probably crippled Old One — perhaps a lone survivor — to the peril of recapture and a nameless fate.

Thank Heaven we did not slacken our run. The curling mist had thickened again, and was driving ahead with increased speed; whilst the straying penguins in our rear were squawking and screaming and displaying signs of a panic really surprising in view of their relatively minor confusion when we had passed them. Once more came that sinister, wide-ranged piping — "Tekeli-li! Tekeli-li!" We had been wrong. The thing was not wounded, but had merely paused on encountering the bodies of its fallen kindred and the hellish slime inscription above them. We could never know what that demon message was — but those burials at Lake's camp had shown how much importance the beings attached to their dead. Our recklessly used torch now revealed ahead of us the large open cavern where various ways converged, and we were glad to be leaving those morbid palimpsest sculptures — almost felt even when scarcely seen — behind. Another thought which the advent of the cave inspired was the possibility of losing our pursuer at this bewildering focus of large galleries. There were several of the blind albino penguins in the open space, and it seemed clear that their fear of the oncoming entity was extreme to the point of unaccountability. If at that point we dimmed our torch to the very lowest limit of traveling need, keeping it strictly in front of us, the frightened squawking motions of the huge birds in the mist might muffle our footfalls, screen our true course, and somehow set up a false lead. Amidst the churning, spiraling fog, the littered and unglistening floor of the main tunnel beyond this point, as differing from the other morbidly polished burrows, could hardly form a highly distinguishing feature; even, so far as we could conjecture, for those indicated special senses which made the Old Ones partly, though imperfectly, independent of light in emergencies. In fact, we were somewhat apprehensive lest we go astray ourselves in our haste. For we had, of course, decided to keep straight on toward the dead city; since the consequences of loss in those unknown foothill honeycombings would be unthinkable.

The fact that we survived and emerged is sufficient proof that the thing did take a wrong gallery whilst we providentially hit on the right one. The penguins alone could not have saved us, but in conjunction with the mist they seem to have done so. Only a benign fate kept the curling vapors thick enough at the right moment, for they were constantly shifting and threatening to vanish. Indeed, they did lift for a second just before we emerged from the nauseously re-sculptured tunnel into the cave; so that we actually caught one first and only half-glimpse of the oncoming entity as we cast a final, desperately fearful glance backward before dimming the torch and mixing with the penguins in the hope of dodging pursuit. If the fate which screened us was benign, that which gave us the half-glimpse was infinitely the opposite; for to that flash of semi-vision can be traced a full half of the horror which has ever since haunted us.

Our exact motive in looking back again was perhaps no more than the immemorial instinct of the pursued to gauge the nature and course of its pursuer; or perhaps it was an automatic attempt to answer a subconscious question raised by one of our senses. In the midst of our flight, with all our faculties centered on the problem of escape, we were in no condition to observe and analyze details; yet even so, our latent brain cells must have wondered at the message brought them by our nostrils. Afterward we realized what it was — that our retreat from the fetid slime-coating on those headless obstructions, and the coincident approach of the pursuing entity, had not brought us the exchange of stenches which logic called for. In the neighborhood of the prostrate things that new and lately unexplainable fetor had been wholly dominant; but by this time it ought to have largely given place to the nameless stench associated with those others. This it had not done — for instead, the newer and less bearable smell was now virtually undiluted, and growing more and more poisonously insistent each second.

So we glanced back — simultaneously, it would appear; though no doubt the incipient motion of one prompted the imitation of the other. As we did so we flashed both torches full strength at the momentarily thinned mist; either from sheer primitive anxiety to see all we could, or in a less primitive but equally unconscious effort to dazzle the entity before we dimmed our light and dodged among the penguins of the labyrinth-center ahead. Unhappy act! Not Orpheus himself, or Lot's wife, paid much more dearly for a backward glance. And again came that shocking, wide-ranged piping — "Tekeli-li! Tekeli-li!"

I might as well be frank — even if I cannot bear to be quite direct — in stating what we saw; though at the time we felt that it was not to be admitted even to each other. The words reaching the reader can never even suggest the awfulness of the sight itself. It crippled our consciousness so completely that I wonder we had the residual sense to dim our torches as planned, and to strike the right tunnel toward the dead city. Instinct alone must have carried us through — perhaps better than reason could have done; though if that was what saved us, we paid a high price. Of reason we certainly had little enough left.

Danforth was totally unstrung, and the first thing I remember of the rest of the journey was hearing him light-headedly chant an hysterical formula in which I alone of mankind could have found anything but insane irrelevance. It reverberated in falsetto echoes among the squawks of the penguins; reverberated through the vaultings ahead, and — thank God — through the now empty vaultings behind. He could not have begun it at once — else we would not have been alive and blindly racing. I shudder to think of what a shade of difference in his nervous reactions might have brought.

"South Station Under — Washington Under — Park Street Under — Kendall — Central — Harvard . . . ." The poor fellow was chanting the familiar stations of the Boston-Cambridge tunnel that burrowed through our peaceful native soil thousands of miles away in New England, yet to me the ritual had neither irrelevance nor home-feeling. It had only horror, because I knew unerringly the monstrous, nefandous analogy that had suggested it. We had expected, upon looking back, to see a terrible and incredible moving entity if the mists were thin enough; but of that entity we had formed a clear idea. What we did see — for the mists were indeed all too malignly thinned — was something altogether different, and immeasurably more hideous and detestable. It was the utter, objective embodiment of the fantastic novelist's "thing that should not be"; and its nearest comprehensible analogue is a vast, onrushing subway train as one sees it from a station platform — the great black front looming colossally out of infinite subterranean distance, constellated with strangely colored lights and filling the prodigious burrow as a piston fills a cylinder.

But we were not on a station platform. We were on the track ahead as the nightmare, plastic column of fetid black iridescence oozed tightly onward through its fifteen-foot sinus, gathering unholy speed and driving before it a spiral, re-thickening cloud of the pallid abyss-vapor. It was a terrible, indescribable thing vaster than any subway train — a shapeless congeries of protoplasmic bubbles, faintly self-luminous, and with myriads of temporary eyes forming and un-forming as pustules of greenish light all over the tunnel-filling front that bore down upon us, crushing the frantic penguins and slithering over the glistening floor that it and its kind had swept so evilly free of all litter. Still came that eldritch, mocking cry — "Tekeli-li! Tekeli-li!" and at last we remembered that the demoniac Shoggoths — given life, thought, and plastic organ patterns solely by the Old Ones, and having no language save that which the dot-groups expressed — had likewise no voice save the imitated accents of their bygone masters.

XII.

Danforth and I have recollections of emerging into the great sculptured hemisphere and of threading our back trail through the Cyclopean rooms and corridors of the dead city; yet these are purely dream-fragments involving no memory of volition, details, or physical exertion. It was as if we floated in a nebulous world or dimension without time, causation, or orientation. The gray half-daylight of the vast circular space sobered us somewhat; but we did not go near those cached sledges or look again at poor Gedney and the dog. They have a strange and titanic mausoleum, and I hope the end of this planet will find them still undisturbed.

It was while struggling up the colossal spiral incline that we first felt the terrible fatigue and short breath which our race through the thin plateau air had produced; but not even fear

Astounding Stories, April 1936

"And then came a sound — a horrible sound — which enabled us to run like mad for the sane outer air —"

of collapse could make us pause before reaching the normal outer realm of sun and sky. There was something vaguely appropriate about our departure from those buried epochs; for as we wound our panting way up the sixty-foot cylinder of primal masonry, we glimpsed beside us a continuous procession of heroic sculptures in the dead race's early and undecayed technique — a farewell from the Old Ones, written fifty million years ago.

Finally scrambling out at the top, we found ourselves on a great mound of tumbled blocks, with the curved walls of higher stonework rising westward, and the brooding peaks of the great mountains showing beyond the more crumbled structures toward the east. The low antarctic sun of midnight peered redly from the southern horizon through rifts in the jagged ruins, and the terrible age and deadness of the nightmare city seemed all the starker by contrast with such relatively known and accustomed things as the features of the polar landscape. The sky above was a churning and opalescent mass of tenuous ice-vapors, and the cold clutched at our vitals. Wearily resting the outfit-bags to which we had instinctively clung throughout our desperate flight, we rebuttoned our heavy garments for the stumbling climb down the mound and the walk through the aeon-old stone maze to the foothills where our aeroplane waited. Of what had set us fleeing from that darkness of earth's secret and archaic gulfs we said nothing at all.

In less than a quarter of an hour we had found the steep grade to the foothills — the probable ancient terrace — by which we had descended, and could see the dark bulk of our great plane amidst the sparse ruins on the rising slope ahead. Halfway uphill toward our goal we paused for a momentary breathing spell, and turned to look again at the fantastic tangle of incredible stone shapes below us — once more outlined mystically against an unknown west. As we did so we saw that the sky beyond had lost its morning haziness; the restless ice-vapors having moved up to the zenith, where their mocking outlines seemed on the point of settling into some bizarre pattern which they feared to make quite definite or conclusive.

There now lay revealed on the ultimate white horizon behind the grotesque city a dim, elfin line of pinnacled violet whose needle-pointed heights loomed dreamlike against the beckoning rose-color of the western sky. Up toward this shimmering rim sloped the ancient table-land, the depressed course of the bygone river traversing it as an irregular ribbon of shadow. For a second we gasped in admiration of the scene's unearthly cosmic beauty, and then vague horror began to creep into our souls. For this far violet line could be nothing else than the terrible mountains of the forbidden land — highest of earth's peaks and focus of earth's evil; harborers of nameless horrors and Archaean secrets; shunned and prayed to by those who feared to carve their meaning; untrodden by any living thing on earth, but visited by the sinister lightnings and sending strange beams across the plains in the polar night — beyond doubt the unknown archetype of that dreaded Kadath in the Cold Waste beyond abhorrent Leng, whereof primal legends hint evasively. We were the first human beings ever to see them — and I hope to God we may be the last.

If the sculptured maps and pictures in that pre-human city had told truly, these cryptic violet mountains could not be much less than three hundred miles away; yet none the less sharply did their dim elfin essence appear above that remote and snowy rim, like the serrated edge of a monstrous alien planet about to rise into unaccustomed heavens. Their height, then, must have been tremendous beyond all comparison — carrying them up into tenuous atmospheric strata peopled only by such gaseous wraiths as rash flyers have barely lived to whisper of after unexplainable falls. Looking at them, I thought nervously of certain sculptured hints of what the great bygone river had washed down into the city from their accursed slopes — and wondered how much sense and how much folly had lain in the fears of those Old Ones who carved them so reticently. I recalled how their northerly end must come near the coast at Queen Mary Land, where even at that moment Sir Douglas Mawson's expedition was doubtless working less than a thousand miles away; and hoped that no evil fate would give Sir Douglas and his men a glimpse of what might lie beyond the protecting coastal range. Such thoughts formed a measure of my overwrought condition at the time — and Danforth seemed to be even worse.

Yet long before we had passed the great star-shaped ruin and reached our plane, our fears had become transferred to the lesser but vast-enough range whose recrossing lay ahead of us. From these foothills the black, ruin-crusted slopes reared up starkly and hideously against the east, again reminding us of those strange Asian paintings of Nicholas Roerich; and when we thought of the frightful amorphous entities that might have pushed their fetidly squirming way even to the topmost hollow pinnacles, we could not face without panic the prospect of again sailing by those suggestive skyward cave-mouths where the wind made sounds like an evil musical piping over a wide range. To make matters worse, we saw distinct traces of local mist around several of the summits — as poor Lake must have done when he made that early mistake about volcanism — and thought shiveringly of that kindred mist from which we had just escaped; of that, and of the blasphemous, horror-fostering abyss whence all such vapors came.

All was well with the plane, and we clumsily hauled on our heavy flying furs. Danforth got the engine started without trouble, and we made a very smooth take-off over the nightmare city. Below us the primal Cyclopean masonry spread out as it had done when first we saw it — so short, yet infinitely long, a time ago — and we began rising and turning to test the wind for our crossing through the pass. At a very high level there must have been great disturbance, since the ice-dust clouds of the zenith were doing all sorts of fantastic things; but at twenty-four thousand feet, the height we needed for the pass, we found navigation quite practicable. As we drew close to the jutting peaks the wind's strange piping again became manifest, and I could see Danforth's hands trembling at the controls.

Rank amateur that I was, I thought at that moment that I might be a better navigator than he in effecting the dangerous crossing between pinnacles; and when I made motions to change seats and take over his duties he did not protest. I tried to keep all my skill and self-possession about me, and stared at the sector of reddish farther sky betwixt the walls of the pass — resolutely refusing to pay attention to the puffs of mountain-top vapor, and wishing that I had wax-stopped ears like Ulysses' men off the Siren's coast to keep that disturbing windpiping from my consciousness.

But Danforth, released from his piloting and keyed up to a dangerous nervous pitch, could not keep quiet. I felt him turning and wriggling about as he looked back at the terrible receding city, ahead at the cave-riddled, cube-barnacled peaks, sidewise at the bleak sea of snowy, rampart-strewn foothills, and upward at the seething, grotesquely clouded sky. It was then, just as I was trying to steer safely through the pass, that his mad shrieking brought us so close to disaster by shattering my tight hold on myself and causing me to fumble helplessly with the controls for a moment. A second afterward my resolution triumphed and we made the crossing safely — yet I am afraid that Danforth will never be the same again.

I have said that Danforth refused to tell me what final horror made him scream out so insanely — a horror which, I feel sadly sure, is mainly responsible for his present breakdown. We had snatches of shouted conversation above the wind's piping and the engine's buzzing as we reached the safe side of the range and swooped slowly down toward the camp, but that had mostly to do with the pledges of secrecy we had made as we prepared to leave the nightmare city. Certain things, we had agreed, were not for people to know and discuss lightly — and I would not speak of them now but for the need of heading off that Starkweather-Moore Expedition, and others, at any cost. It is absolutely necessary, for the peace and safety of mankind, that some of earth's dark, dead corners and unplumbed depths be let alone; lest sleeping abnormalities wake to resurgent life, and blasphemously surviving nightmares squirm and splash out of their black lairs to newer and wider conquests.

All that Danforth has ever hinted is that the final horror was a mirage. It was not, he declares, anything connected with the cubes and caves of those echoing, vaporous, wormily-honeycombed mountains of madness which we crossed; but a single fantastic, demoniac glimpse, among the churning zenith-clouds, of what lay back of those other violet westward mountains which the Old Ones had shunned and feared. It is very probable that the thing was a sheer delusion born of the previous stresses we had passed through, and of the actual though unrecognized mirage of the dead transmontane city experienced near Lake's camp the day before; but it was so real to Danforth that he suffers from it still.

He has on rare occasions whispered disjointed and irresponsible things about "The black pit," "the carven rim," "the proto-Shoggoths," "the windowless solids with five dimensions," "the nameless cylinder," "the elder Pharos," "Yog-Sothoth," "the primal white jelly," "the color out of space," "the wings," "the eyes in darkness," "the moon-ladder," "the original, the eternal, the undying," and other bizarre conceptions; but when he is fully himself he repudiates all this and attributes it to his curious and macabre reading of earlier years. Danforth, indeed, is known to be among the few who have ever dared go completely through that worm-riddled copy of the *Necronomicon* kept under lock and key in the college library.

The higher sky, as we crossed the range, was surely vaporous and disturbed enough; and although I did not see the zenith, I can well imagine that its swirls of ice dust may have taken strange forms. Imagination, knowing how vividly distant scenes can sometimes be reflected, refracted, and magnified by such layers of restless cloud, might easily have supplied the rest — and, of course, Danforth did not hint any of these specific horrors till after his memory had had a chance to draw on his bygone reading. He could never have seen so much in one instantaneous glance.

At the time, his shrieks were confined to the repetition of a single, mad word of all too obvious source: "Tekeli-li! Tekeli-li!"

The Trap.

BY HENRY S. WHITEHEAD AND H.P. LOVECRAFT

8,500-WORD NOVELETTE; 1931.

This short novelette is the one Lovecraft likely worked on with Whitehead while visiting at his Dunedin, Florida, home in the summer of 1931. S. T. Joshi, in I Am Providence, *suggests that the collaboration likely took the form of Whitehead writing the first third or so, and Lovecraft more or less taking it from there. He is likely right; there is a distinctive change in the tone of the story at about that point.*

It was first published in the March 1932 issue of Strange Tales of Mystery and Terror.

ABOUT HENRY S. WHITEHEAD (1882-1932).

Henry St. Clair Whitehead was an established author whose polished, urbane stories appeared not only in Weird Tales *but also in more upmarket pulp titles like* Adventure *and* Black Mask.

Whitehead's style as a writer was considerably different from Lovecraft's — it was urbane and polished and gentlemen's-clubbish, but without the intense plausibility of Lovecraft's work. The two of them, around 1930, became good friends and colleagues, and the following year Whitehead had Lovecraft over for a three-week visit at his home in Dunedin, Florida. Probably during that stay (or, possibly, a few weeks afterward) Lovecraft and Whitehead worked together on a story that Whitehead was doping out: "The Trap."

The two of them would only be able to collaborate on one more story (maybe) before Whitehead's death from some sort of digestive disorder in 1932.

It was on a certain Thursday morning in December that the whole thing began with that unaccountable motion I thought I saw in my antique Copenhagen mirror. Something, it seemed to me, stirred — something reflected in the glass, though I was alone in my quarters. I paused and looked intently, then, deciding that the effect must be a pure illusion, resumed the interrupted brushing of my hair.

I had discovered the old mirror, covered with dust and cobwebs, in an outbuilding of an abandoned estate-house in Santa Cruz's sparsely settled Northside territory, and had brought it to the United States from the Virgin Islands. The venerable glass was dim from more than two hundred years' exposure to a tropical climate, and the graceful ornamentation along the top of the gilt frame had been badly smashed. I had had the detached pieces set back into the frame before placing it in storage with my other belongings.

Now, several years later, I was staying half as a guest and half as a tutor at the private school of my old friend Browne on a windy Connecticut hillside — occupying an unused wing in one of the dormitories, where I had two rooms and a hallway to myself. The old mirror, stowed securely in mattresses, was the first of my possessions to be unpacked on my arrival; and I had set it up majestically in the living-room, on top of an old rosewood console which had belonged to my great-grandmother.

The door of my bedroom was just opposite that of the living-room, with a hallway between; and I had noticed that by looking into my chiffonier glass I could see the larger mirror through the two doorways — which was exactly like glancing down an endless, though diminishing, corridor. On this Thursday morning I thought I saw a curious suggestion of motion down that normally empty corridor — but, as I have said, soon dismissed the notion.

When I reached the dining-room I found everyone complaining of the cold, and learned that the school's heating-plant was temporarily out of order. Being especially sensitive to low temperatures, I was myself an acute sufferer; and at once decided not to brave any freezing schoolroom that day. Accordingly I invited my class to come over to my living-room for an informal session around my grate-fire — a suggestion which the boys received enthusiastically.

After the session one of the boys, Robert Grandison, asked if he might remain; since he had no appointment for the second morning period. I told him to stay, and welcome. He sat down to study in front of the fireplace in a comfortable chair.

It was not long, however, before Robert moved to another chair somewhat farther away from the freshly replenished blaze, this change bringing him directly opposite the old mirror. From my own chair in another part of the room I noticed how fixedly he began to look at the dim, cloudy glass, and, wondering what so greatly interested him, was reminded of my own experience earlier that morning. As time passed he continued to gaze, a slight frown knitting his brows.

At last I quietly asked him what had attracted his attention. Slowly, and still wearing the puzzled frown, he looked over and replied rather cautiously:

"It's the corrugations in the glass — or whatever they are, Mr. Canevin. I was noticing how they all seem to run from a certain point. Look — I'll show you what I mean."

Strange Tales of Mystery and Terror, March 1932

The boy jumped up, went over to the mirror, and placed his finger on a point near its lower left-hand corner.

"It's right here, sir," he explained, turning to look toward me and keeping his finger on the chosen spot.

His muscular action in turning may have pressed his finger against the glass. Suddenly he withdrew his hand as though with some slight effort, and with a faintly muttered "Ouch." Then he looked at the glass in obvious mystification.

"What happened?" I asked, rising and approaching.

"Why — it — " He seemed embarrassed. "It — I — felt — well, as though it were pulling my finger into it. Seems — er — perfectly foolish, sir, but — well — it was a most peculiar sensation." Robert had an unusual vocabulary for his fifteen years.

I came over and had him show me the exact spot he meant. "You'll think I'm rather a fool, sir," he said shamefacedly, "but — well, from right here I can't be absolutely sure. From the chair it seemed to be clear enough."

Now thoroughly interested, I sat down in the chair Robert had occupied and looked at the spot he selected on the mirror. Instantly the thing "jumped out at me." Unmistakably, from that particular angle, all the many whorls in the ancient glass appeared to converge like a large number of spread strings held in one hand and radiating out in streams.

Getting up and crossing to the mirror, I could no longer see the curious spot. Only from certain angles, apparently, was it visible. Directly viewed, that portion of the mirror did not even give back a normal reflection — for I could not see my face in it. Manifestly I had a minor puzzle on my hands.

Presently the school gong sounded, and the fascinated

Robert Grandison departed hurriedly, leaving me alone with my odd little problem in optics. I raised several window-shades, crossed the hallway, and sought for the spot in the chiffonier mirror's reflection. Finding it readily, I looked very intently and thought I again detected something of the "motion." I craned my neck, and at last, at a certain angle of vision, the thing again "jumped out at me."

The vague "motion" was now positive and definite—an appearance of torsional movement, or of whirling; much like a minute yet intense whirlwind or waterspout, or a huddle of autumn leaves dancing circularly in an eddy of wind along a level lawn. It was, like the earth's, a double motion—around and around, and at the same time inward, as if the whorls poured themselves endlessly toward some point inside the glass. Fascinated, yet realizing that the thing must be an illusion, I grasped an impression of quite distinct suction, and thought of Robert's embarrassed explanation: "I felt as though it were pulling my finger into it."

A kind of slight chill ran suddenly up and down my backbone. There was something here distinctly worth looking into. And as the idea of investigation came to me, I recalled the rather wistful expression of Robert Grandison when the gong called him to class. I remembered how he had looked back over his shoulder as he walked obediently out into the hallway, and resolved that he should be included in whatever analysis I might make of this little mystery.

Exciting events connected with that same Robert, however, were soon to chase all thoughts of the mirror from my consciousness for a time. I was away all that afternoon, and did not return to the school until the five-fifteen "Call-Over"—a general assembly at which the boys' attendance was compulsory. Dropping in at this function with the idea of picking Robert up for a session with the mirror, I was astonished and pained to find him absent—a very unusual and unaccountable thing in his case. That evening Browne told me that the boy had actually disappeared, a search in his room, in the gymnasium, and in all other accustomed places being unavailing, though all his belongings—including his outdoor clothing—were in their proper places.

He had not been encountered on the ice or with any of the hiking groups that afternoon, and telephone calls to all the school-catering merchants of the neighbourhood were in vain. There was, in short, no record of his having been seen since the end of the lesson periods at two-fifteen; when he had turned up the stairs toward his room in Dormitory Number Three.

When the disappearance was fully realized, the resulting sensation was tremendous throughout the school. Browne, as headmaster, had to bear the brunt of it; and such an unprecedented occurrence in his well-regulated, highly organized institution left him quite bewildered. It was learned that Robert had not run away to his home in western Pennsylvania, nor did any of the searching-parties of boys and masters find any trace of him in the snowy countryside around the school. So far as could be seen, he had simply vanished.

Robert's parents arrived on the afternoon of the second day after his disappearance. They took their trouble quietly, though, of course, they were staggered by this unexpected disaster. Browne looked ten years older for it, but there was absolutely nothing that could be done. By the fourth day the case had settled down in the opinion of the school as an insoluble mystery. Mr. and Mrs. Grandison went reluctantly back to their home, and on the following morning the ten days' Christmas vacation began.

Boys and masters departed in anything but the usual holiday spirit; and Browne and his wife were left, along with the servants, as my only fellow-occupants of the big place. Without the masters and boys it seemed a very hollow shell indeed.

That afternoon I sat in front of my grate-fire thinking about Robert's disappearance and evolving all sorts of fantastic theories to account for it. By evening I had acquired a bad headache, and ate a light supper accordingly. Then, after a brisk walk around the massed buildings, I returned to my living-room and took up the burden of thought once more.

A little after ten o'clock I awakened in my armchair, stiff and chilled, from a doze during which I had let the fire go out. I was physically uncomfortable, yet mentally aroused by a peculiar sensation of expectancy and possible hope. Of course it had to do with the problem that was harassing me. For I had started from that inadvertent nap with a curious, persistent idea—the odd idea that a tenuous, hardly recognizable Robert Grandison had been trying desperately to communicate with me. I finally went to bed with one conviction unreasoningly strong in my mind. Somehow I was sure that young Robert Grandison was still alive.

That I should be receptive of such a notion will not seem strange to those who know my long residence in the West Indies and my close contact with unexplained happenings there. It will not seem strange, either, that I fell asleep with an urgent desire to establish some sort of mental communication with the missing boy. Even the most prosaic scientists affirm, with Freud, Jung, and Adler, that the subconscious mind is most open to external impressions in sleep; though such impressions are seldom carried over intact into the waking state.

Going a step further and granting the existence of telepathic forces, it follows that such forces must act most strongly on a sleeper; so that if I were ever to get a definite message from Robert, it would be during a period of profoundest slumber. Of course, I might lose the message in waking; but my aptitude for retaining such things has been sharpened by types of mental discipline picked up in various obscure corners of the globe.

I must have dropped asleep instantaneously, and from the vividness of my dreams and the absence of wakeful intervals I judge that my sleep was a very deep one. It was six-forty-five when I awakened, and there still lingered with me certain impressions which I knew were carried over from the world of somnolent cerebration. Filling my mind was the vision of Robert Grandison strangely transformed to a boy of a dull greenish dark-blue colour; Robert desperately endeavouring to communicate with me by means of speech, yet finding some almost insuperable difficulty in so doing. A wall of curious spatial separation seemed to stand between him and me — a mysterious, invisible wall which completely baffled us both.

I had seen Robert as though at some distance, yet queerly enough he seemed at the same time to be just beside me. He was both larger and smaller than in real life, his apparent size varying directly, instead of inversely, with the distance as he advanced and retreated in the course of conversation. That is, he grew larger instead of smaller to my eye when he stepped away or backwards, and vice versa; as if the laws of perspective in his case had been wholly reversed. His aspect was misty and uncertain — as if he lacked sharp or permanent outlines; and the anomalies of his colouring and clothing baffled me utterly at first.

At some point in my dream Robert's vocal efforts had finally crystallized into audible speech — albeit speech of an abnormal thickness and dullness. I could not for a time understand anything he said, and even in the dream racked my brain for a clue to where he was, what he wanted to tell, and why his utterance was so clumsy and unintelligible. Then little by little I began to distinguish words and phrases, the very first of which sufficed to throw my dreaming self into the wildest excitement and to establish a certain mental connection which had previously refused to take conscious form because of the utter incredibility of what it implied.

I do not know how long I listened to those halting words amidst my deep slumber, but hours must have passed while the strangely remote speaker struggled on with his tale. There was revealed to me such a circumstance as I cannot hope to make others believe without the strongest corroborative evidence, yet which I was quite ready to accept as truth — both in the dream and after waking — because of my former contacts with uncanny things. The boy was obviously watching my face — mobile in receptive sleep — as he choked along; for about the time I began to comprehend him, his own expression brightened and gave signs of gratitude and hope.

Any attempt to hint at Robert's message, as it lingered in my ears after a sudden awakening in the cold, brings this narrative to a point where I must choose my words with the greatest care. Everything involved is so difficult to record that one tends to flounder helplessly. I have said that the revelation established in my mind a certain connection which reason had not allowed me to formulate consciously before. This connection, I need no longer hesitate to hint, had to do with the old Copenhagen mirror whose suggestions of motion had so impressed me on the morning of the disappearance, and whose whorl-like contours and apparent illusions of suction had later exerted such a disquieting fascination on both Robert and me.

Resolutely, though my outer consciousness had previously rejected what my intuition would have liked to imply, it could reject that stupendous conception no longer. What was fantasy in the tale of "Alice" now came to me as a grave and immediate reality. That looking-glass had indeed possessed a malign, abnormal suction; and the struggling speaker in my dream made clear the extent to which it violated all the known precedents of human experience and all the age-old laws of our three sane dimensions. It was more than a mirror — it was a gate; a trap; a link with spatial recesses not meant for the denizens of our visible universe, and realizable only in terms of the most intricate non-Euclidean mathematics. And in some outrageous fashion Robert Grandison had passed out of our ken into the glass and was there immured, waiting for release.

It is significant that upon awakening I harboured no genuine doubt of the reality of the revelation. That I had actually held conversation with a trans-dimensional Robert, rather than evoked the whole episode from my broodings about his disappearance and about the old illusions of the mirror, was as certain to my utmost instincts as any of the instinctive certainties commonly recognized as valid. The tale thus unfolded to me was of the most incredibly bizarre character. As had been clear on the morning of his disappearance, Robert was intensely fascinated by the ancient mirror. All through the hours of school, he had it in mind to come back to my living-room and examine it further. When he did arrive, after the close of the school day, it was somewhat later than two-twenty, and I was absent in town. Finding me out and knowing that I would not mind, he had come into my living-room and gone straight to the mirror; standing before it and studying the place where, as we had noted, the whorls appeared to converge.

Then, quite suddenly, there had come to him an overpowering urge to place his hand upon this whorl-center. Almost reluctantly, against his better judgment, he had done so; and upon making the contact had felt at once the strange, almost painful suction which had perplexed him that morning. Immediately thereafter — quite without warning, but with a wrench which seemed to twist and tear every bone and muscle in his body and to bulge and press and cut at every nerve — he had been abruptly drawn through and found himself inside.

Once through, the excruciatingly painful stress upon his entire system was suddenly released. He felt, he said, as though he had just been born — a feeling that made itself evident every time he tried to do anything; walk, stoop, turn his head, or utter speech. Everything about his body seemed a misfit.

These sensations wore off after a long while, Robert's body becoming an organized whole rather than a number of protesting parts. Of all the forms of expression, speech remained the most difficult; doubtless because it is complicated, bringing into play a number of different organs, muscles, and tendons. Robert's feet, on the other hand, were the first members to adjust themselves to the new conditions within the glass.

During the morning hours I rehearsed the whole reason-defying problem; correlating everything I had seen and heard, dismissing the natural scepticism of a man of sense, and scheming to devise possible plans for Robert's release from his incredible prison. As I did so a number of originally perplexing points became clear — or at least, clearer — to me.

There was, for example, the matter of Robert's colouring. His face and hands, as I have indicated, were a kind of dull greenish dark-blue; and I may add that his familiar blue Norfolk jacket had turned to a pale lemon-yellow while his trousers remained a neutral grey as before. Reflecting on this after waking, I found the circumstance closely allied to the reversal of perspective which made Robert seem to grow larger when receding and smaller when approaching. Here, too, was a physical reversal — for every detail of his colouring in the unknown dimension was the exact reverse or complement of the corresponding colour detail in normal life. In physics the typical complementary colours are blue and yellow, and red and green. These pairs are opposites, and when mixed yield grey. Robert's natural colour was a pinkish-buff, the opposite of which is the greenish-blue I saw. His blue coat had become yellow, while the grey trousers remained grey. This latter point baffled me until I remembered that grey is itself a mixture of opposites. There is no opposite for grey — or rather, it is its own opposite.

Another clarified point was that pertaining to Robert's curiously dulled and thickened speech — as well as to the general awkwardness and sense of misfit bodily parts of which he complained. This, at the outset, was a puzzle indeed; though after long thought the clue occurred to me. Here again was the same reversal which affected perspective and colouration. Anyone in the fourth dimension must necessarily be reversed in just this way — hands and feet, as well as colours and perspectives, being changed about. It would be the same with all the other dual organs, such as nostrils, ears, and eyes. Thus Robert had been talking with a reversed tongue, teeth, vocal cords, and kindred speech-apparatus; so that his difficulties in utterance were little to be wondered at.

As the morning wore on, my sense of the stark reality and maddening urgency of the dream-disclosed situation increased rather than decreased. More and more I felt that something must be done, yet realized that I could not seek advice or aid. Such a story as mine — a conviction based upon mere dreaming — could not conceivably bring me anything but ridicule or suspicions as to my mental state. And what, indeed, could I do, aided or unaided, with as little working data as my nocturnal impressions had provided? I must, I finally recognized, have more information before I could even think of a possible plan for releasing Robert. This could come only through the receptive conditions of sleep, and it heartened me to reflect that according to every probability my telepathic contact would be resumed the moment I fell into deep slumber again.

I accomplished sleeping that afternoon, after a midday dinner at which, through rigid self-control, I succeeded in concealing from Browne and his wife the tumultuous thoughts that crashed through my mind. Hardly had my eyes closed when a dim telepathic image began to appear; and I soon realized to my infinite excitement that it was identical with what I had seen before. If anything, it was more distinct; and when it began to speak I seemed able to grasp a greater proportion of the words.

During this sleep I found most of the morning's deductions confirmed, though the interview was mysteriously cut off long prior to my awakening. Robert had seemed apprehensive just before communication ceased, but had already told me that in his strange fourth-dimensional prison colours and spatial relationships were indeed reversed — black being white, distance increasing apparent size, and so on. He had also intimated that, notwithstanding his possession of full physical form and sensations, most human vital properties seemed curiously suspended. Nutriment, for example, was quite unnecessary — a phenomenon really more singular than the omnipresent reversal of objects and attributes, since the latter was a reasonable and mathematically indicated state of things. Another significant piece of information was that the only exit from the glass to the world was the entrance-way, and that this was permanently barred and impenetrably sealed, so far as egress was concerned.

That night I had another visitation from Robert; nor did such impressions, received at odd intervals while I slept receptively minded, cease during the entire period of his incarceration. His efforts to communicate were desperate and often pitiful; for at times the telepathic bond would weaken, while at other times fatigue, excitement, or fear of interruption would hamper and thicken his speech. I may as well narrate as a continuous whole all that Robert told me throughout the whole series of transient mental contacts — perhaps supplementing it at certain points with facts directly related after his release. The telepathic information was fragmentary and often nearly inarticulate, but I studied it over and over during the waking intervals of three intense days; classifying and cogitating with feverish diligence, since it was all that I had to go upon if the boy were to be brought back into our world.

The fourth-dimensional region in which Robert found himself was not, as in scientific romance, an unknown and infinite realm of strange sights and fantastic denizens; but was rather a projection of certain limited parts of our own terrestrial sphere within an alien and normally inaccessible aspect or direction of space. It was a curiously fragmentary, intangible, and heterogeneous world — a series of apparently dissociated scenes merging indistinctly one into the other; their constituent details having an obviously different status from that of an object drawn into the ancient mirror as Robert had been drawn. These scenes were like dream-vistas or magic-lantern images — elusive visual impressions of which the boy was not really a part, but which formed a sort of panoramic background or ethereal environment against which or amidst which he moved.

He could not touch any of the parts of these scenes — walls, trees, furniture, and the like — but whether this was because they were truly non-material, or because they always receded at his approach, he was singularly unable to determine. Everything seemed fluid, mutable, and unreal. When he walked, it appeared to be on whatever lower surface the visible scene might have — floor, path, greensward, or such; but upon analysis he always found that the contact was an illusion. There was never any difference in the resisting force met by his feet — and by his hands when he would stoop experimentally — no matter what changes of apparent surface might be involved. He could not describe this foundation or limiting plane on which he walked as anything more definite than a virtually abstract pressure balancing his gravity. Of definite tactile distinctiveness it had none, and supplementing it there seemed to be a kind of restricted levitational force which accomplished transfers of altitude. He could never actually climb stairs, yet would gradually walk up from a lower level to a higher.

Passage from one definite scene to another involved a sort of gliding through a region of shadow or blurred focus where the details of each scene mingled curiously. All the vistas were distinguished by the absence of transient objects, and the indefinite or ambiguous appearance of such semi-transient objects as furniture or details of vegetation. The lighting of every scene was diffuse and perplexing, and of course the scheme of reversed colours — bright red grass, yellow sky with confused black and grey cloud-forms, white tree-trunks, and green brick walls — gave to everything an air of unbelievable grotesquerie. There was an alteration of day and night, which turned out to be a reversal of the normal hours of light and darkness at whatever point on the earth the mirror might be hanging.

This seemingly irrelevant diversity of the scenes puzzled Robert until he realized that they comprised merely such places as had been reflected for long continuous periods in the ancient glass. This also explained the odd absence of transient objects, the generally arbitrary boundaries of vision, and the fact that all exteriors were framed by the outlines of doorways or windows. The glass, it appeared, had power to store up these intangible scenes through long exposure; though it could never absorb anything corporeally, as Robert had been absorbed, except by a very different and particular process.

But — to me at least — the most incredible aspect of the mad phenomenon was the monstrous subversion of our known laws of space involved in the relation of various illusory scenes to the actual terrestrial regions represented. I have spoken of the glass as storing up the images of these regions, but this is really an inexact definition. In truth, each of the mirror scenes formed a true and quasi-permanent fourth-dimensional projection of the corresponding mundane region; so that whenever Robert moved to a certain part of a certain scene, as he moved into the image of my room when sending his telepathic messages, he was actually in that place itself, on earth — though under spatial conditions which cut off all sensory communication, in either direction, between him and the present tri-dimensional aspect of the place.

Theoretically speaking, a prisoner in the glass could in a few moments go anywhere on our planet — into any place, that is, which had ever been reflected in the mirror's surface. This probably applied even to places where the mirror had not hung long enough to produce a clear illusory scene; the terrestrial region being then represented by a zone of more or less formless shadow. Outside the definite scenes was a seemingly limitless waste of neutral grey shadow about which Robert could never be certain, and into which he never dared stray far lest he become hopelessly lost to the real and mirror worlds alike.

Among the earliest particulars which Robert gave, was the fact that he was not alone in his confinement. Various others, all in antique garb, were in there with him — a corpulent middle-aged gentleman with tied queue and velvet knee-breeches who spoke English fluently though with a marked Scandinavian accent; a rather beautiful small girl with very blonde hair which appeared a glossy dark blue; two apparently mute Negroes whose features contrasted grotesquely with the pallor of their reversed-coloured skins; three young men; one young woman; a very small child, almost an infant; and a lean, elderly Dane of extremely distinctive aspect and a kind of half-malign intellectuality of countenance.

This last-named individual — Axel Holm, who wore the satin small-clothes, flared-skirted coat, and voluminous full-bottomed periwig of an age more than two centuries in the past was notable among the little band as being the one responsible for the presence of them all. He it was who, skilled equally in the arts of magic and glass working, had long ago fashioned this strange dimensional prison in which himself, his slaves, and those whom he chose to invite or allure thither were immured unchangingly for as long as the mirror might endure.

Holm was born early in the seventeenth century, and had followed with tremendous competence and success the trade of a glass-blower and molder in Copenhagen. His glass, especially in the form of large drawing-room mirrors, was always at a premium. But the same bold mind which had made him the first glazier of Europe also served to carry his interests and ambitions far beyond the sphere of mere material craftsmanship. He had studied the world around him, and chafed at the limitations of human knowledge and capability. Eventually he sought for dark ways to overcome those limitations, and gained more success than is good for any mortal.

He had aspired to enjoy something like eternity, the mirror being his provision to secure this end. Serious study of the fourth dimension was far from beginning with Einstein in our own era; and Holm, more than erudite in all the methods of his day, knew that a bodily entrance into that hidden phase of space would prevent him from dying in the ordinary physical sense. Research showed him that the principle of reflection undoubtedly forms the chief gate to all dimensions beyond our familiar three; and chance placed in his hands a small and very ancient glass whose cryptic properties he believed he could turn to advantage. Once "inside" this mirror according to the method he had envisaged, he felt that "life" in the sense of form and consciousness would go on virtually forever, provided the mirror could be preserved indefinitely from breakage or deterioration.

Holm made a magnificent mirror, such as would be prized and carefully preserved; and in it deftly fused the strange whorl-configured relic he had acquired. Having thus prepared his refuge and his trap, he began to plan his mode of entrance and conditions of tenancy. He would have with him both servitors and companions; and as an experimental beginning he sent before him into the glass two dependable Negro slaves brought from the West Indies. What his sensations must have been upon beholding this first concrete demonstration of his theories, only imagination can conceive.

Undoubtedly a man of his knowledge realized that absence from the outside world, if deferred beyond the natural span of life of those within, must mean instant dissolution at the first attempt to return to that world. But, barring that misfortune or accidental breakage, those within would remain forever as they were at the time of entrance. They would never grow old, and would need neither food nor drink. To make his prison tolerable he sent ahead of him certain books and writing materials, a chair and table of stoutest workmanship, and a few other accessories. He knew that the images which the glass would reflect or absorb would not be tangible, but would merely extend around him like a background of dream.

His own transition in 1687 was a momentous experience; and must have been attended by mixed sensations of triumph and terror. Had anything gone wrong, there were frightful possibilities of being lost in dark and inconceivable multiple dimensions.

For over fifty years he had been unable to secure any additions to the little company of himself and slaves, but later on he had perfected his telepathic method of visualizing small sections of the outside world close to the glass, and attracting certain individuals in those areas through the mirror's strange entrance. Thus Robert, influenced into a desire to press upon the "door," had been lured within. Such visualizations depended wholly on telepathy, since no one inside the mirror could see out into the world of men.

It was, in truth, a strange life that Holm and his company had lived inside the glass. Since the mirror had stood for fully a century with its face to the dusty stone wall of the shed where I found it, Robert was the first being to enter this limbo after all that interval. His arrival was a gala event, for he brought news of the outside world which must have been of the most startling impressiveness to the more thoughtful of those within. He, in his turn — young though he was — felt overwhelmingly the weirdness of meeting and talking with persons who had been alive in the seventeenth and eighteenth centuries.

The deadly monotony of life for the prisoners can only be vaguely conjectured. As mentioned, its extensive spatial variety was limited to localities which had been reflected in the mirror for long periods; and many of these had become dim and strange as tropical climates had made inroads on the surface. Certain localities were bright and beautiful, and in these the company usually gathered. But no scene could be fully satisfying; since the visible objects were all unreal and intangible, and often of perplexingly indefinite outline. When the tedious periods of darkness came, the general custom was to indulge in memories, reflections, or conversations. Each one of that strange, pathetic group had retained his or her personality unchanged and unchangeable, since becoming immune to the time effects of outside space. The number of inanimate objects within the glass, aside from the clothing of the prisoners, was very small; being largely limited to the accessories Holm had provided for himself. The rest did without even furniture, since sleep and fatigue had vanished along with most other vital attributes. Such inorganic things as were present, seemed as exempt from decay as the living beings. The lower forms of animal life were wholly absent.

Robert derived most of his information from Herr Thiele, the gentleman who spoke English with a Scandinavian accent. This portly Dane had taken a fancy to him, and talked at considerable length. The others, too, had received him with courtesy and goodwill; Holm himself, seeming well-disposed, had told him about various matters including the door of the trap.

The boy, as he told me later, was sensible enough never to attempt communication with me when Holm was nearby. Twice, while thus engaged, he had seen Holm appear; and had accordingly ceased at once. At no time could I see the world behind the mirror's surface. Robert's visual image, which included his bodily form and the clothing connected with it, was — like the aural image of his halting voice and like his own visualization of myself — a case of purely telepathic transmission; and did not involve true interdimensional sight. However, had Robert been as trained a telepathist as Holm, he might have transmitted a few strong images apart from his immediate person.

Throughout this period of revelation I had, of course, been desperately trying to devise a method for Robert's release. On the fourth day — the ninth after the disappearance — I hit on a solution. Everything considered, my laboriously formulated process was not a very complicated one; though I could not tell beforehand how it would work, while the possibility of ruinous consequences in case of a slip was appalling. This process depended, basically, on the fact that there was no possible exit from inside the glass. If Holm and his prisoners were permanently sealed in, then release must come wholly from outside. Other considerations included the disposal of the other prisoners, if any survived, and especially of Axel Holm. What Robert had told me of him was anything but reassuring; and I certainly did not wish him loose in my apartment, free once more to work his evil will upon the world. The telepathic messages had not made fully clear the effect of liberation on those who had entered the glass so long ago.

There was, too, a final though minor problem in case of success — that of getting Robert back into the routine of school life without having to explain the incredible. In case of failure, it was highly inadvisable to have witnesses present at the release operations — and lacking these, I simply could not attempt to relate the actual facts if I should succeed. Even to me the reality seemed a mad one whenever I let my mind turn from the data so compellingly presented in that tense series of dreams.

When I had thought these problems through as far as possible, I procured a large magnifying-glass from the school laboratory and studied minutely every square millimetre of that whorl-centre which presumably marked the extent of the original ancient mirror used by Holm. Even with this aid I could not quite trace the exact boundary between the old area and the surface added by the Danish wizard: but after a long study decided on a conjectural oval boundary which I outlined very precisely with a soft blue pencil. I then made a trip to Stamford, where I procured a heavy glass-cutting tool; for my primary idea was to remove the ancient and magically potent mirror from its later setting.

My next step was to figure out the best time of day to make the crucial experiment. I finally settled on two-thirty a.m. — both because it was a good season for uninterrupted work, and because it was the "opposite" of two-thirty p.m., the probable moment at which Robert had entered the mirror. This form of "oppositeness" may or may not have been relevant, but I knew at least that the chosen hour was as good as any — and perhaps better than most.

I finally set to work in the early morning of the eleventh day after the disappearance, having drawn all the shades of my living-room and closed and locked the door into the hallway. Following with breathless care the elliptical line I had traced, I worked around the whorl-section with my steel-wheeled cutting tool. The ancient glass, half an inch thick, crackled crisply under the firm, uniform pressure; and upon completing the circuit I cut around it a second time, crunching the roller more deeply into the glass.

Then, very carefully indeed, I lifted the heavy mirror down from its console and leaned it face-inward against the wall; prying off two of the thin, narrow boards nailed to the back. With equal caution I smartly tapped the cut-around space with the heavy wooden handle of the glass-cutter.

At the very first tap the whorl-containing section of glass dropped out on the Bokhara rug beneath. I did not know what might happen, but was keyed up for anything, and took a deep involuntary breath. I was on my knees for convenience at the moment, with my face quite near the newly made aperture; and as I breathed there poured into my nostrils a powerful dusty odour — a smell not comparable to any other I have ever encountered. Then everything within my range of vision suddenly turned to a dull grey before my failing eyesight as I felt myself overpowered by an invisible force which robbed my muscles of their power to function.

I remember grasping weakly and futilely at the edge of the nearest window drapery and feeling it rip loose from its fastening. Then I sank slowly to the floor as the darkness of oblivion passed over me.

When I regained consciousness I was lying on the Bokhara rug with my legs held unaccountably up in the air. The room was full of that hideous and inexplicable dusty smell — and as my eyes began to take in definite images I saw that Robert Grandison stood in front of me. It was he — fully in the flesh and with his colouring normal — who was holding my legs aloft to bring the blood back to my head as the school's first-aid course had taught him to do with persons who had fainted. For a moment I was struck mute by the stifling odour and by a bewilderment which quickly merged into a sense of triumph. Then I found myself able to move and speak collectedly.

I raised a tentative hand and waved feebly at Robert.

"All right, old man," I murmured, "you can let my legs down now. Many thanks. I'm all right again, I think. It was the smell — I imagine — that got me. Open that farthest window, please — wide — from the bottom. That's it — thanks. No — leave the shade down the way it was."

I struggled to my feet, my disturbed circulation adjusting itself in waves, and stood upright hanging to the back of a big chair. I was still "groggy," but a blast of fresh, bitterly cold air from the window revived me rapidly. I sat down in the big chair and looked at Robert, now walking toward me.

"First," I said hurriedly, "tell me, Robert — those others — Holm? What happened to them, when I — opened the exit?"

Robert paused half-way across the room and looked at me very gravely.

"I saw them fade away — into nothingness — Mr. Canevin," he said with solemnity; "and with them — everything. There isn't any more 'inside,' sir — thank God, and you, sir!"

And young Robert, at last yielding to the sustained strain which he had borne through all those terrible eleven days, suddenly broke down like a little child and began to weep hysterically in great, stifling, dry sobs.

I picked him up and placed him gently on my davenport, threw a rug over him, sat down by his side, and put a calming hand on his forehead. "Take it easy, old fellow," I said soothingly.

The boy's sudden and very natural hysteria passed as quickly as it had come on as I talked to him reassuringly about my plans for his quiet restoration to the school. The interest of the situation and the need of concealing the incredible truth beneath a rational explanation took hold of his imagination as I had expected; and at last he sat up eagerly, telling the details of his release and listening to the instructions I had thought out. He had, it seems, been in the "projected area" of my bedroom when I opened the way back, and had emerged in that actual room—hardly realizing that he was "out." Upon hearing a fall in the living-room he had hastened thither, finding me on the rug in my fainting spell.

I need mention only briefly my method of restoring Robert in a seemingly normal way—how I smuggled him out of the window in an old hat and sweater of mine, took him down the road in my quietly started car, coached him carefully in a tale I had devised, and returned to arouse Browne with the news of his discovery. He had, I explained, been walking alone on the afternoon of his disappearance; and had been offered a motor ride by two young men who, as a joke and over his protests that he could go no farther than Stamford and back, had begun to carry him past that town. Jumping from the car during a traffic stop with the intention of hitch-hiking back before Call-Over, he had been hit by another car just as the traffic was released—awakening ten days later in the Greenwich home of the people who had hit him. On learning the date, I added, he had immediately telephoned the school; and I, being the only one awake, had answered the call and hurried after him in my car without stopping to notify anyone.

Browne, who at once telephoned to Robert's parents, accepted my story without question; and forbore to interrogate the boy because of the latter's manifest exhaustion. It was arranged that he should remain at the school for a rest, under the expert care of Mrs. Browne, a former trained nurse. I naturally saw a good deal of him during the remainder of the Christmas vacation, and was thus enabled to fill in certain gaps in his fragmentary dream-story.

Now and then we would almost doubt the actuality of what had occurred; wondering whether we had not both shared some monstrous delusion born of the mirror's glittering hypnotism, and whether the tale of the ride and accident were not after all the real truth. But whenever we did so we would be brought back to belief by some monstrous and haunting memory; with me, of Robert's dream-figure and its thick voice and inverted colours; with him, of the whole fantastic pageantry of ancient people and dead scenes that he had witnessed. And then there was that joint recollection of that damnable dusty odour ... We knew what it meant: the instant dissolution of those who had entered an alien dimension a century and more ago.

There are, in addition, at least two lines of rather more positive evidence; one of which comes through my researches in Danish annals concerning the sorcerer, Axel Holm. Such a person, indeed, left many traces in folklore and written records; and diligent library sessions, plus conferences with various learned Danes, have shed much more light on his evil fame. At present I need say only that the Copenhagen glass-blower—born in 1612—was a notorious Luciferian whose pursuits and final vanishing formed a matter of awed debate over two centuries ago. He had burned with a desire to know all things and to conquer every limitation of mankind—to which end he had delved deeply into occult and forbidden fields ever since he was a child.

He was commonly held to have joined a coven of the dreaded witch-cult, and the vast lore of ancient Scandinavian myth—with its Loki the Sly One and the accursed Fenris-Wolf—was soon an open book to him. He had strange interests and objectives, few of which were definitely known, but some of which were recognized as intolerably evil. It is recorded that his two Negro helpers, originally slaves from the Danish West Indies, had become mute soon after their acquisition by him; and that they had disappeared not long before his own disappearance from the ken of mankind.

Near the close of an already long life the idea of a glass of immortality appears to have entered his mind. That he had acquired an enchanted mirror of inconceivable antiquity was a matter of common whispering; it being alleged that he had purloined it from a fellow-sorcerer who had entrusted it to him for polishing.

This mirror—according to popular tales a trophy as potent in its way as the better-known Aegis of Minerva or Hammer of Thor—was a small oval object called "Loki's Glass," made of some polished fusible mineral and having magical properties which included the divination of the immediate future and the power to show the possessor his enemies. That it had deeper potential properties, realizable in the hands of an erudite magician, none of the common people doubted; and even educated persons attached much fearful importance to Holm's rumoured attempts to incorporate it in a larger glass of immortality.

Then had come the wizard's disappearance in 1687, and the final sale and dispersal of his goods amidst a growing cloud of fantastic legendry. It was, altogether, just such a story as one would laugh at if possessed of no particular key; yet to me, remembering those dream messages and having Robert Grandison's corroboration before me, it formed a positive confirmation of all the bewildering marvels that had been unfolded.

But as I have said, there is still another line of rather positive evidence—of a very different character—at my disposal. Two days after his release, as Robert, greatly improved in strength and appearance, was placing a log on my living-room fire, I noticed a certain awkwardness in his motions and was struck by a persistent idea. Summoning him to my desk I suddenly asked him to pick up an ink-stand—and was scarcely surprised to note that, despite lifelong right-handedness, he obeyed unconsciously with his left hand. Without alarming him, I then asked that he unbutton his coat and let me listen to his cardiac action. What I found upon placing my ear to his chest—and what I did not tell him for some time afterward—was that his heart was beating on his right side.

He had gone into the glass right-handed and with all organs in their normal positions. Now he was left-handed and with organs reversed, and would doubtless continue so for the rest of his life. Clearly, the dimensional transition had been no illusion—for this physical change was tangible and unmistakable. Had there been a natural exit from the glass, Robert would probably have undergone a thorough re-reversal and emerged in perfect normality — as indeed the colour-scheme of his body and clothing did emerge. The forcible nature of his release, however, undoubtedly set something awry; so that dimensions no longer had a chance to right themselves as chromatic wave-frequencies still did.

I had not merely opened Holm's trap; I had destroyed it; and at the particular stage of destruction marked by Robert's escape some of the reversing properties had perished. It is significant that in escaping Robert had felt no pain comparable to that experienced in entering. Had the destruction been still more sudden, I shiver to think of the monstrosities of colour the boy would always have been forced to bear. I may add that after discovering Robert's reversal I examined the rumpled and discarded clothing he had worn in the glass, and found, as I had expected, a complete reversal of pockets, buttons, and all other corresponding details.

At this moment Loki's Glass, just as it fell on my Bokhara rug from the now patched and harmless mirror, weighs down a sheaf of papers on my writing-table here in St. Thomas, venerable capital of the Danish West Indies — now the American Virgin Islands. Various collectors of old Sandwich glass have mistaken it for an odd bit of that early American product — but I privately realize that my paper-weight is an antique of far subtler and more paleogean craftsmanship. Still, I do not disillusion such enthusiasts.

The Shadow over Innsmouth.

26,800-WORD NOVELLA; 1931.

This novella was inspired by a journey to Newburyport, Massachusetts, which in 1931 was much faded from its glory years as a shipbuilding, fishing, and trading center.

At the time, Lovecraft was trying to find his way forward as a literary man. The rejections he'd been hit with earlier in the year had convinced him that what he was doing was not going to take him to where he wanted to be — that his efforts to serve two masters had doomed him to rejection by both, and that a repudiation of the pulp market and a thoroughgoing purification and possibly transformation of his literary style was the only solution.

Accordingly, he spent November and December of 1931 preparing experimental drafts of this story in different styles. He rejected each in turn; none survives today. Eventually Lovecraft gave up and wrote the story in his regular style.

The protagonist of The Shadow over Innsmouth, *Robert Olmstead, is one of the most clearly autobiographically inspired characters in Lovecraft's work, a fact which has, given the events of the story, given armchair psychoanalysts a great deal to pontificate about over the years.*

By the time Lovecraft had finished writing the story for the fifth time, and then subjecting it to his usual round of revision and redrafting, he was so thoroughly sick of it that he had convinced himself that it was worthless. However, August Derleth badgered him to type it up, which he reluctantly did. Derleth surreptitiously submitted it to Weird Tales *— which promptly rejected it as too hard to serialize.*

When The Shadow Over Innsmouth *was published, however, it was in book form — the first and only time in his life that one of his stories was produced as a finished book. ("The Shunned House" remained unbound until well after his death.)*

It was published by William L. Crawford's startup publishing house, Visionary Publishing Co., in 1936, shortly before Lovecraft's death. The proofs were riddled with typos when Lovecraft reviewed them, and when the corrections were made they, too, were riddled

"Death Thumbs a Ride" by ROBERT ARTHUR

MAY

Weird Tales

20¢

A Thriller Classic

THE SHADOW OVER INNSMOUTH

by

H. P. LOVECRAFT

SEABURY QUINN • NELSON S. BOND

Canada edition, Weird Tales, May 1942

with typos. Lovecraft persuaded Crawford to print an errata sheet, which was, in turn, riddled with typos. The illustrations by Frank Upatel were excellent, but the rest of the enterprise was a bit of a mess.

Crawford planned a press run of 400, but was only able to have 200 of them bound. The other 200 unbound ones have been lost or destroyed, and the surviving bound editions are treasured collector's items; at the time of this writing, a decent copy retails for about $4,000.

During the winter of 1927-28 officials of the federal government made a strange and secret investigation of certain conditions in the ancient Massachusetts seaport of Innsmouth. The public first learned of it in February, when a vast series of raids and arrests occurred, followed by the deliberate burning and dynamiting — under suitable precautions — of an enormous number of crumbling, worm-eaten, and supposedly empty houses along the abandoned waterfront. Uninquiring souls let this occurrence pass as one of the major clashes in a spasmodic war on liquor.

Keener news-followers, however, wondered at the prodigious number of arrests, the abnormally large force of men used in making them, and the secrecy surrounding the disposal of the prisoners. No trials, or even definite charges were reported; nor were any of the captives seen thereafter in the regular gaols of the nation. There were vague statements about disease and concentration camps, and later about dispersal in various naval and military prisons, but nothing positive ever developed. Innsmouth itself was left almost depopulated, and it is even now only beginning to show signs of a sluggishly revived existence.

Complaints from many liberal organizations were met with long confidential discussions, and representatives were taken on trips to certain camps and prisons. As a result, these societies became surprisingly passive and reticent. Newspaper men were harder to manage, but seemed largely to cooperate with the government in the end. Only one paper — a tabloid always discounted because of its wild policy — mentioned the deep diving submarine that discharged torpedoes downward in the marine abyss just beyond Devil Reef. That item, gathered by chance in a haunt of sailors, seemed indeed rather far-fetched; since the low, black reef lay a full mile and a half out from Innsmouth Harbour.

People around the country and in the nearby towns muttered a great deal among themselves, but said very little to the outer world. They had talked about dying and half-deserted Innsmouth for nearly a century, and nothing new could be wilder or more hideous than what they had whispered and hinted at years before. Many things had taught them secretiveness, and there was no need to exert pressure on them. Besides, they really knew little; for wide salt marshes, desolate and unpeopled, kept neighbors off from Innsmouth on the landward side.

But at last I am going to defy the ban on speech about this thing. Results, I am certain, are so thorough that no public harm save a shock of repulsion could ever accrue from a hinting of what was found by those horrified men at Innsmouth. Besides, what was found might possibly have more than one explanation. I do not know just how much of the whole tale has been told even to me, and I have many reasons for not wishing to probe deeper. For my contact with this affair has been closer than that of any other layman, and I have carried away impressions which are yet to drive me to drastic measures.

It was I who fled frantically out of Innsmouth in the early morning hours of July 16, 1927, and whose frightened appeals for government inquiry and action brought on the whole reported episode. I was willing enough to stay mute while the affair was fresh and uncertain; but now that it is an old story, with public interest and curiosity gone, I have an odd craving to whisper about those few frightful hours in that ill-rumored and evilly-shadowed seaport of death and blasphemous abnormality. The mere telling helps me to restore confidence in my own faculties; to reassure myself that I was not the first to succumb to a contagious nightmare hallucination. It helps me, too, in making up my mind regarding a certain terrible step which lies ahead of me.

I never heard of Innsmouth till the day before I saw it for the first and — so far — last time. I was celebrating my coming of age by a tour of New England — sightseeing, antiquarian, and genealogical — and had planned to go directly from ancient Newburyport to Arkham, whence my mother's family was derived. I had no car, but was travelling by train, trolley and motor-coach, always seeking the cheapest possible route. In Newburyport they told me that the steam train was the thing to take to Arkham; and it was only at the station ticket-office, when I demurred at the high fare, that I learned about Innsmouth. The stout, shrewd-faced agent, whose speech shewed him to be no local man, seemed sympathetic toward my efforts at economy, and made a suggestion that none of my other informants had offered.

"You could take that old bus, I suppose," he said with a certain hesitation, "but it ain't thought much of hereabouts. It goes through Innsmouth — you may have heard about that — and so the people don't like it. Run by an Innsmouth fellow — Joe Sargent — but never gets any custom from here, or Arkham either, I guess. Wonder it keeps running at all. I s'pose it's cheap enough, but I never see mor'n two or three people in it — nobody but those Innsmouth folk. Leaves the square — front of Hammond's Drug Store — at 10 a.m. and 7 p.m. unless they've changed lately. Looks like a terrible rattletrap — I've never been on it."

That was the first I ever heard of shadowed Innsmouth. Any reference to a town not shown on common maps or listed in recent guidebooks would have interested me, and the agent's odd manner of allusion roused something like real curiosity. A town able to inspire such dislike in its neighbors, I thought, must be at least rather unusual, and worthy of a tourist's attention. If it came before Arkham I would stop off there and so I asked the agent to tell me something about it. He was very deliberate, and spoke with an air of feeling slightly superior to what he said.

"Innsmouth? Well, it's a queer kind of a town down at the mouth of the Manuxet. Used to be almost a city—quite a port before the War of 1812—but all gone to pieces in the last hundred years or so. No railroad now—B. and M. never went through, and the branch line from Rowley was given up years ago.

"More empty houses than there are people, I guess, and no business to speak of except fishing and lobstering. Everybody trades mostly either here or in Arkham or Ipswich. Once they had quite a few mills, but nothing's left now except one gold refinery running on the leanest kind of part time.

"That refinery, though, used to be a big thing, and old man Marsh, who owns it, must be richer'n Croesus. Queer old duck, though, and sticks mighty close in his home. He's supposed to have developed some skin disease or deformity late in life that makes him keep out of sight. Grandson of Captain Obed Marsh, who founded the business. His mother seems to've been some kind of foreigner—they say a South Sea islander—so everybody raised Cain when he married an

"One night, in a frightful dream, I met two Ancient Ones under the sea ...

Ipswich girl fifty years ago. They always do that about Innsmouth people, and folks here and hereabouts always try to cover up any Innsmouth blood they have in 'em. But Marsh's children and grandchildren look just like anyone else far's I can see. I've had 'em pointed out to me here — though, come to think of it, the elder children don't seem to be around lately. Never saw the old man.

"And why is everybody so down on Innsmouth? Well, young fellow, you mustn't take too much stock in what people here say. They're hard to get started, but once they do get started they never let up. They've been telling things about Innsmouth — whispering 'em, mostly — for the last hundred years, I guess, and I gather they're more scared than anything else. Some of the stories would make you laugh — about old Captain Marsh driving bargains with the devil and bringing imps out of hell to live in Innsmouth, or about some kind of devil-worship and awful sacrifices in some place near the wharves that people stumbled on around 1845 or thereabouts — but I come from Panton, Vermont, and that kind of story don't go down with me.

"You ought to hear, though, what some of the old-timers tell about the black reef off the coast — Devil Reef, they call it. It's well above water a good part of the time, and never much below it, but at that you could hardly call it an island.

Weird Tales, January 1942

... in a phosphorescent, many-terraced palace surrounded by gardens of strange, leprous corals."

The story is that there's a whole legion of devils seen sometimes on that reef — sprawled about, or darting in and out of some kind of caves near the top. It's a rugged, uneven thing, a good bit over a mile out, and toward the end of shipping days sailors used to make big detours just to avoid it.

"That is, sailors that didn't hail from Innsmouth. One of the things they had against old Captain Marsh was that he was supposed to land on it sometimes at night when the tide was right. Maybe he did, for I dare say the rock formation was interesting, and it's just barely possible he was looking for pirate loot and maybe finding it; but there was talk of his dealing with demons there. Fact is, I guess on the whole it was really the Captain that gave the bad reputation to the reef.

"That was before the big epidemic of 1846, when over half the folks in Innsmouth was carried off. They never did quite figure out what the trouble was, but it was probably some foreign kind of disease brought from China or somewhere by the shipping. It surely was bad enough — there was riots over it, and all sorts of ghastly doings that I don't believe ever got outside of town — and it left the place in awful shape. Never came back — there can't be more'n 300 or 400 people living there now.

"But the real thing behind the way folks feel is simply race prejudice — and I don't say I'm blaming those that hold it. I hate those Innsmouth folks myself, and I wouldn't care to go to their town. I s'pose you know — though I can see you're a Westerner by your talk — what a lot our New England ships used to have to do with queer ports in Africa, Asia, the South Seas, and everywhere else, and what queer kinds of people they sometimes brought back with 'em. You've probably heard about the Salem man that came home with a Chinese wife, and maybe you know there's still a bunch of Fiji Islanders somewhere around Cape Cod.

"Well, there must be something like that back of the Innsmouth people. The place always was badly cut off from the rest of the country by marshes and creeks and we can't be sure about the ins and outs of the matter; but it's pretty clear that old Captain Marsh must have brought home some odd specimens when he had all three of his ships in commission back in the twenties and thirties. There certainly is a strange kind of streak in the Innsmouth folks today — I don't know how to explain it but it sort of makes you crawl. You'll notice a little in Sargent if you take his bus. Some of 'em have queer narrow heads with flat noses and bulgy, starry eyes that never seem to shut, and their skin ain't quite right. Rough and scabby, and the sides of the necks are all shriveled or creased up. Get bald, too, very young. The older fellows look the worst — fact is, I don't believe I've ever seen a very old chap of that kind. Guess they must die of looking in the glass! Animals hate 'em — they used to have lots of horse trouble before the autos came in.

"Nobody around here or in Arkham or Ipswich will have anything to do with 'em, and they act kind of offish themselves when they come to town or when anyone tries to fish on their grounds. Queer how fish are always thick off Innsmouth Harbour when there ain't any anywhere else around — but just try to fish there yourself and see how the folks chase you off! Those people used to come here on the railroad — walking and taking the train at Rowley after the branch was dropped — but now they use that bus.

"Yes, there's a hotel in Innsmouth — called the Gilman House — but I don't believe it can amount to much. I wouldn't advise you to try it. Better stay over here and take the ten o'clock bus tomorrow morning; then you can get an evening bus there for Arkham at eight o'clock. There was a factory inspector who stopped at the Gilman a couple of years ago and he had a lot of unpleasant hints about the place. Seems they get a queer crowd there, for this fellow heard voices in other rooms — though most of 'em was empty — that gave him the shivers. It was foreign talk he thought, but he said the bad thing about it was the kind of voice that sometimes spoke. It sounded so unnatural — slopping like, he said — that he didn't dare undress and go to sleep. Just waited up and lit out the first thing in the morning. The talk went on most all night.

"This fellow — Casey, his name was — had a lot to say about how the Innsmouth folk watched him and seemed kind of on guard. He found the Marsh refinery a queer place — it's in an old mill on the lower falls of the Manuxet. What he said tallied up with what I'd heard. Books in bad shape, and no clear account of any kind of dealings. You know it's always been a kind of mystery where the Marshes get the gold they refine. They've never seemed to do much buying in that line, but years ago they shipped out an enormous lot of ingots.

"Used to be talk of a queer foreign kind of jewelry that the sailors and refinery men sometimes sold on the sly, or that was seen once or twice on some of the Marsh women-folks. People allowed maybe old Captain Obed traded for it in some heathen port, especially since he always ordered stacks of glass beads and trinkets such as seafaring men used to get for native trade. Others thought and still think he'd found an old pirate cache out on Devil Reef. But here's a funny thing. The old Captain's been dead these sixty years, and there's ain't been a good-sized ship out of the place since the Civil War; but just the same the Marshes still keep on buying a few of those native trade things — mostly glass and rubber gewgaws, they tell me. Maybe the Innsmouth folks like 'em to look at themselves — Gawd knows they've gotten to be about as bad as South Sea cannibals and Guinea savages.

"That plague of '46 must have taken off the best blood in the place. Anyway, they're a doubtful lot now, and the Marshes and other rich folks are as bad as any. As I told you, there probably ain't more'n 400 people in the whole town in spite of all the streets they say there are. I guess they're what they call 'white trash' down South — lawless and sly, and full of secret things. They get a lot of fish and lobsters and do exporting by truck. Queer how the fish swarm right there and nowhere else.

"Nobody can ever keep track of these people, and state

school officials and census men have a devil of a time. You can bet that prying strangers ain't welcome around Innsmouth. I've heard personally of more'n one business or government man that's disappeared there, and there's loose talk of one who went crazy and is out at Danvers now. They must have fixed up some awful scare for that fellow.

"That's why I wouldn't go at night if I was you. I've never been there and have no wish to go, but I guess a daytime trip couldn't hurt you — even though the people hereabouts will advise you not to make it. If you're just sightseeing, and looking for old-time stuff, Innsmouth ought to be quite a place for you."

And so I spent part of that evening at the Newburyport Public Library looking up data about Innsmouth. When I had tried to question the natives in the shops, the lunchroom, the garages, and the fire station, I had found them even harder to get started than the ticket agent had predicted; and realized that I could not spare the time to overcome their first instinctive reticence. They had a kind of obscure suspiciousness, as if there were something amiss with anyone too much interested in Innsmouth. At the Y.M.C.A., where I was stopping, the clerk merely discouraged my going to such a dismal, decadent place; and the people at the library shewed much the same attitude. Clearly, in the eyes of the educated, Innsmouth was merely an exaggerated case of civic degeneration.

The Essex County histories on the library shelves had very little to say, except that the town was founded in 1643, noted for shipbuilding before the Revolution, a seat of great marine prosperity in the early 19th century, and later a minor factory center using the Manuxet as power. The epidemic and riots of 1846 were very sparsely treated, as if they formed a discredit to the county.

References to decline were few, though the significance of the later record was unmistakable. After the Civil War all industrial life was confined to the Marsh Refining Company, and the marketing of gold ingots formed the only remaining bit of major commerce aside from the eternal fishing. That fishing paid less and less as the price of the commodity fell and large-scale corporations offered competition, but there was never a dearth of fish around Innsmouth Harbour. Foreigners seldom settled there, and there was some discreetly veiled evidence that a number of Poles and Portuguese who had tried it had been scattered in a peculiarly drastic fashion.

Most interesting of all was a glancing reference to the strange jewelry vaguely associated with Innsmouth. It had evidently impressed the whole countryside more than a little, for mention was made of specimens in the museum of Miskatonic University at Arkham, and in the display room of the Newburyport Historical Society. The fragmentary descriptions of these things were bald and prosaic, but they hinted to me an undercurrent of persistent strangeness. Something about them seemed so odd and provocative that I could not put them out of my mind, and despite the relative lateness of the hour I resolved to see the local sample — said to be a large, queerly-proportioned thing evidently meant for a tiara — if it could possibly be arranged.

The librarian gave me a note of introduction to the curator of the Society, a Miss Anna Tilton, who lived nearby, and after a brief explanation that ancient gentlewoman was kind enough to pilot me into the closed building, since the hour was not outrageously late. The collection was a notable one indeed, but in my present mood I had eyes for nothing but the bizarre object which glistened in a corner cupboard under the electric lights.

It took no excessive sensitiveness to beauty to make me literally gasp at the strange, unearthly splendour of the alien, opulent phantasy that rested there on a purple velvet cushion. Even now I can hardly describe what I saw, though it was clearly enough a sort of tiara, as the description had said. It was tall in front, and with a very large and curiously irregular periphery, as if designed for a head of almost freakishly elliptical outline. The material seemed to be predominantly gold, though a weird lighter lustrousness hinted at some strange alloy with an equally beautiful and scarcely identifiable metal. Its condition was almost perfect, and one could have spent hours in studying the striking and puzzlingly untraditional designs — some simply geometrical, and some plainly marine — chased or moulded in high relief on its surface with a craftsmanship of incredible skill and grace.

The longer I looked, the more the thing fascinated me; and in this fascination there was a curiously disturbing element hardly to be classified or accounted for. At first I decided that it was the queer other-worldly quality of the art which made me uneasy. All other art objects I had ever seen either belonged to some known racial or national stream, or else were consciously modernistic defiances of every recognized stream. This tiara was neither. It clearly belonged to some settled technique of infinite maturity and perfection, yet that technique was utterly remote from any — Eastern or Western, ancient or modern — which I had ever heard of or seen exemplified. It was as if the workmanship were that of another planet.

However, I soon saw that my uneasiness had a second and perhaps equally potent source residing in the pictorial and mathematical suggestion of the strange designs. The patterns all hinted of remote secrets and unimaginable abysses in time and space, and the monotonously aquatic nature of the reliefs became almost sinister. Among these reliefs were fabulous monsters of abhorrent grotesqueness and malignity — half ichthyic and half batrachian in suggestion — which one could not dissociate from a certain haunting and uncomfortable sense of pseudomemory, as if they called up some image from deep cells and tissues whose retentive functions are wholly primal and awesomely ancestral. At times I fancied that every contour of these blasphemous fish-frogs was over-flowing with the ultimate quintessence of unknown and inhuman evil.

In odd contrast to the tiara's aspect was its brief and prosy history as related by Miss Tilton. It had been pawned for a ridiculous sum at a shop in State Street in 1873, by a drunken

Innsmouth man shortly afterward killed in a brawl. The Society had acquired it directly from the pawnbroker, at once giving it a display worthy of its quality. It was labeled as of probable East-Indian or Indochinese provenance, though the attribution was frankly tentative.

Miss Tilton, comparing all possible hypotheses regarding its origin and its presence in New England, was inclined to believe that it formed part of some exotic pirate hoard discovered by old Captain Obed Marsh. This view was surely not weakened by the insistent offers of purchase at a high price which the Marshes began to make as soon as they knew of its presence, and which they repeated to this day despite the Society's unvarying determination not to sell.

As the good lady shewed me out of the building she made it clear that the pirate theory of the Marsh fortune was a popular one among the intelligent people of the region. Her own attitude toward shadowed Innsmouth—which she had never seen—was one of disgust at a community slipping far down the cultural scale, and she assured me that the rumours of devil-worship were partly justified by a peculiar secret cult which had gained force there and engulfed all the orthodox churches.

It was called, she said, "The Esoteric Order of Dagon," and was undoubtedly a debased, quasi-pagan thing imported from the East a century before, at a time when the Innsmouth fisheries seemed to be going barren. Its persistence among a simple people was quite natural in view of the sudden and permanent return of abundantly fine fishing, and it soon came to be the greatest influence in the town, replacing Freemasonry altogether and taking up headquarters in the old Masonic Hall on New Church Green.

All this, to the pious Miss Tilton, formed an excellent reason for shunning the ancient town of decay and desolation; but to me it was merely a fresh incentive. To my architectural and historical anticipations was now added an acute anthropological zeal, and I could scarcely sleep in my small room at the "Y" as the night wore away.

Shortly before ten the next morning I stood with one small valise in front of Hammond's Drug Store in old Market Square waiting for the Innsmouth bus. As the hour for its arrival drew near I noticed a general drift of the loungers to other places up the street, or to the Ideal Lunch across the square. Evidently the ticket-agent had not exaggerated the dislike which local people bore toward Innsmouth and its denizens. In a few moments a small motor-coach of extreme decrepitude and dirty grey colour rattled down State Street, made a turn, and drew up at the curb beside me. I felt immediately that it was the right one; a guess which the half-illegible sign on the windshield—Arkham-Innsmouth-Newburyport—soon verified.

There were only three passengers—dark, unkempt men of sullen visage and somewhat youthful cast—and when the vehicle stopped they clumsily shambled out and began walking up State Street in a silent, almost furtive fashion. The driver also alighted, and I watched him as he went into the drug store to make some purchase. This, I reflected, must be the Joe Sargent mentioned by the ticket-agent; and even before I noticed any details there spread over me a wave of spontaneous aversion which could be neither checked nor explained. It suddenly struck me as very natural that the local people should not wish to ride on a bus owned and driven by this man, or to visit any oftener than possible the habitat of such a man and his kinsfolk.

When the driver came out of the store I looked at him more carefully and tried to determine the source of my evil impression. He was a thin, stoop-shouldered man not much under six feet tall, dressed in shabby blue civilian clothes and wearing a frayed golf cap. His age was perhaps thirty-five, but the odd, deep creases in the sides of his neck made him seem older when one did not study his dull, expressionless face. He had a narrow head, bulging, watery-blue eyes that seemed never to wink, a flat nose, a receding forehead and chin, and singularly undeveloped ears. His long thick lip and coarse-pored, greyish cheeks seemed almost beardless except for some sparse yellow hairs that straggled and curled in irregular patches; and in places the surface seemed queerly irregular, as if peeling from some cutaneous disease. His hands were large and heavily veined, and had a very unusual greyish-blue tinge. The fingers were strikingly short in proportion to the rest of the structure, and seemed to have a tendency to curl closely into the huge palm. As he walked toward the bus I observed his peculiarly shambling gait and saw that his feet were inordinately immense. The more I studied them the more I wondered how he could buy any shoes to fit them.

A certain greasiness about the fellow increased my dislike. He was evidently given to working or lounging around the fish docks, and carried with him much of their characteristic smell. Just what foreign blood was in him I could not even guess. His oddities certainly did not look Asiatic, Polynesian, Levantine or negroid, yet I could see why the people found him alien. I myself would have thought of biological degeneration rather than alienage.

I was sorry when I saw there would be no other passengers on the bus. Somehow I did not like the idea of riding alone with this driver. But as leaving time obviously approached I conquered my qualms and followed the man aboard, extending him a dollar bill and murmuring the single word "Innsmouth." He looked curiously at me for a second as he returned forty cents change without speaking. I took a seat far behind him, but on the same side of the bus, since I wished to watch the shore during the journey.

At length the decrepit vehicle started with a jerk, and rattled noisily past the old brick buildings of State Street amidst a cloud of vapour from the exhaust. Glancing at the people on the sidewalks, I thought I detected in them a curious wish to avoid looking at the bus—or at least a wish to avoid seeming to look at it. Then we turned to the left into High Street, where the going was smoother; flying by stately old mansions of the early republic and still older colonial farmhouses, passing the Lower Green and Parker River, and finally emerging into a long, monotonous stretch of open shore country.

The day was warm and sunny, but the landscape of sand and sedge-grass, and stunted shrubbery became more and desolate as we proceeded. Out the window I could see the blue water and the sandy line of Plum Island, and we presently drew very near the beach as our narrow road veered off from the main highway to Rowley and Ipswich. There were no visible houses, and I could tell by the state of the road that traffic was very light hereabouts. The weather-worn telephone poles carried only two wires. Now and then we crossed crude wooden bridges over tidal creeks that wound far inland and promoted the general isolation of the region.

Once in a while I noticed dead stumps and crumbling foundation-walls above the drifting sand, and recalled the old tradition quoted in one of the histories I had read, that this was once a fertile and thickly-settled countryside. The change, it was said, came simultaneously with the Innsmouth epidemic of 1846, and was thought by simple folk to have a dark connection with hidden forces of evil. Actually, it was caused by the unwise cutting of woodlands near the shore, which robbed the soil of the best protection and opened the way for waves of wind-blown sand.

At last we lost sight of Plum Island and saw the vast expanse of the open Atlantic on our left. Our narrow course began to climb steeply, and I felt a singular sense of disquiet in looking at the lonely crest ahead where the rutted road-way met the sky. It was as if the bus were about to keep on in its ascent, leaving the sane earth altogether and merging with the unknown arcana of upper air and cryptical sky. The smell of the sea took on ominous implications, and the silent driver's bent, rigid back and narrow head became more and more hateful. As I looked at him I saw that the back of his head was almost as hairless as his face, having only a few straggling yellow strands upon a grey scabrous surface.

Then we reached the crest and beheld the outspread valley beyond, where the Manuxet joins the sea just north of the long line of cliffs that culminate in Kingsport Head and veer off toward Cape Ann. On the far misty horizon I could just make out the dizzy profile of the Head, topped by the queer ancient house of which so many legends are told; but for the moment all my attention was captured by the nearer panorama just below me. I had, I realized, come face to face with rumour-shadowed Innsmouth.

It was a town of wide extent and dense construction, yet one with a portentous dearth of visible life. From the tangle of chimney-pots scarcely a wisp of smoke came, and the three tall steeples loomed stark and unpainted against the seaward horizon. One of them was crumbling down at the top, and in that and another there were only black gaping holes where clock-dials should have been. The vast huddle of sagging gambrel roofs and peaked gables conveyed with offensive clearness the idea of wormy decay, and as we approached along the now descending road I could see that many roofs had wholly caved in. There were some large square Georgian houses, too, with hipped roofs, cupolas, and railed "widow's walks." These were mostly well back from the water, and one or two seemed to be in moderately sound condition. Stretching inland from among them I saw the rusted, grass-grown line of the abandoned railway, with leaning telegraph-poles now devoid of wires, and the half-obscured lines of the old carriage roads to Rowley and Ipswich.

The decay was worst close to the waterfront, though in its very midst I could spy the white belfry of a fairly well preserved brick structure which looked like a small factory. The harbour, long clogged with sand, was enclosed by an ancient stone breakwater; on which I could begin to discern the minute forms of a few seated fishermen, and at whose end were what looked like the foundations of a bygone lighthouse. A sandy tongue had formed inside this barrier and upon it I saw a few decrepit cabins, moored dories, and scattered lobster-pots. The only deep water seemed to be where the river poured out past the belfried structure and turned southward to join the ocean at the breakwater's end.

Here and there the ruins of wharves jutted out from the shore to end in indeterminate rottenness, those farthest south seeming the most decayed. And far out at sea, despite a high tide, I glimpsed a long, black line scarcely rising above the water yet carrying a suggestion of odd latent malignancy. This, I knew, must be Devil Reef. As I looked, a subtle, curious sense of beckoning seemed superadded to the grim repulsion; and oddly enough, I found this overtone more disturbing than the primary impression.

We met no one on the road, but presently began to pass deserted farms in varying stages of ruin. Then I noticed a few inhabited houses with rags stuffed in the broken windows and shells and dead fish lying about the littered yards. Once or twice I saw listless-looking people working in barren gardens or digging clams on the fishy-smelling beach below, and groups of dirty, simian-visaged children playing around weed-grown doorsteps. Somehow these people seemed more disquieting than the dismal buildings, for almost every one had certain peculiarities of face and motions which I instinctively disliked without being able to define or comprehend them. For a second I thought this typical physique suggested some picture I had seen, perhaps in a book, under circumstances of particular horror or melancholy; but this pseudo-recollection passed very quickly.

As the bus reached a lower level I began to catch the steady note of a waterfall through the unnatural stillness. The leaning, unpainted houses grew thicker, lined both sides of the road, and displayed more urban tendencies than did those we were leaving behind, the panorama ahead had contracted to a street scene, and in spots I could see where a cobblestone pavement and stretches of brick sidewalk had formerly existed. All the houses were apparently deserted, and there were occasional gaps where tumbledown chimneys and cellar walls told of buildings that had collapsed. Pervading everything was the most nauseous fishy odour imaginable.

Soon cross streets and junctions began to appear; those on the left leading to shoreward realms of unpaved squalor and decay, while those on the right shewed vistas of departed grandeur. So far I had seen no people in the town, but there now came signs of a sparse habitation — curtained windows here and there, and an occasional battered motorcar at the curb. Pavement and sidewalks were increasingly well-defined, and though most of the houses were quite old — wood and brick structures of the early 19th century — they were obviously kept fit for habitation. As an amateur antiquarian I almost lost my olfactory disgust and my feeling of menace and repulsion amidst this rich, unaltered survival from the past.

But I was not to reach my destination without one very strong impression of poignantly disagreeable quality. The bus had come to a sort of open concourse or radial point with churches on two sides and the bedraggled remains of a circular green in the centre, and I was looking at a large pillared hall on the right-hand junction ahead. The structure's once white paint was now gray and peeling and the black and gold sign on the pediment was so faded that I could only with difficulty make out the words "Esoteric Order of Dagon" This, then was the former Masonic Hall now given over to a degraded cult. As I strained to decipher this inscription my notice was distracted by the raucous tones of a cracked bell across the street, and I quickly turned to look out the window on my side of the coach.

The sound came from a squat stone church of manifestly later date than most of the houses, built in a clumsy Gothic fashion and having a disproportionately high basement with shuttered windows. Though the hands of its clock were missing on the side I glimpsed, I knew that those hoarse strokes were tolling the hour of eleven. Then suddenly all thoughts of time were blotted out by an onrushing image of sharp intensity and unaccountable horror which had seized me before I knew what it really was. The door of the church basement was open, revealing a rectangle of blackness inside. And as I looked, a certain object crossed or seemed to cross that dark rectangle; burning into my brain a momentary conception of nightmare which was all the more maddening because analysis could not shew a single nightmarish quality in it.

It was a living object — the first except the driver that I had seen since entering the compact part of the town — and had I been in a steadier mood I would have found nothing whatever of terror in it. Clearly, as I realised a moment later, it was the pastor; clad in some peculiar vestments doubtless introduced since the Order of Dagon had modified the ritual of the local churches. The thing which had probably caught my first subconscious glance and supplied the touch of bizarre horror was the tall tiara he wore; an almost exact duplicate of the one Miss Tilton had shown me the previous evening. This, acting on my imagination, had supplied namelessly sinister qualities to the indeterminate face and robed, shambling form beneath it. There was not, I soon decided, any reason why I should have felt that shuddering touch of evil pseudo-memory. Was it not natural that a local mystery cult should adopt among its regimentals an unique type of head-dress made familiar to the community in some strange way — perhaps a treasure-trove?

A very thin sprinkling of repellent-looking youngish people now became visible on the sidewalks — lone individuals, and silent knots of two or three. The lower floors of the crumbling houses sometimes harboured small shops with dingy signs, and I noticed a parked truck or two as we rattled along. The sound of waterfalls became more and more distinct, and presently I saw a fairly deep river-gorge ahead, spanned by a wide, iron-railed highway bridge beyond which a large square opened out. As we clanked over the bridge I looked out on both sides and observed some factory buildings on the edge of the grassy bluff or part way down. The water far below was very abundant, and I could see two vigorous sets of falls upstream on my right and at least one downstream on my left. From this point the noise was quite deafening. Then we rolled into the large semicircular square across the river and drew up on the right-hand side in front of a tall, cupola crowned building with remnants of yellow paint and with a half-effaced sign proclaiming it to be the Gilman House.

I was glad to get out of that bus, and at once proceeded to check my valise in the shabby hotel lobby. There was only one person in sight — an elderly man without what I had come to call the "Innsmouth look" and I decided not to ask him any of the questions which bothered me; remembering that odd things had been noticed in this hotel. Instead, I strolled out on the square, from which the bus had already gone, and studied the scene minutely and appraisingly.

On one side of the cobblestoned open space was the straight line of the river; on the other was a semicircle of slant-roofed brick buildings of about the 1800 period, from which several streets radiated away to the southeast, south, and southwest. Lamps were depressingly few and small — all low-powered incandescents — and I was glad that my plans called for departure before dark, even though I knew the moon would be bright. The buildings were all in fair condition, and included perhaps a dozen shops in current operation; of which one was a grocery of the First National chain, others a dismal restaurant, a drug store, and a wholesale fish-dealer's office, and still another, at the eastward extremity of the square near the river, an office of the town's only industry — the Marsh Refining Company. There were perhaps ten people visible, and four or five automobiles and motor trucks stood scattered about. I did not need to be told that this was the civic centre of Innsmouth. Eastward I could catch blue glimpses of the harbour, against which rose the decaying remains of three once beautiful Georgian steeples. And toward the shore on the opposite bank of the river I saw the white belfry surmounting what I took to be the Marsh refinery.

For some reason or other I chose to make my first inquiries at the chain grocery, whose personnel was not likely to be native to Innsmouth. I found a solitary boy of about seventeen in charge, and was pleased to note the brightness and affability which promised cheerful information. He seemed exceptionally eager to talk, and I soon gathered that he did not like the place, its fishy smell, or its furtive people. A word with any outsider was a relief to him. He hailed from Arkham, boarded with a family who came from Ipswich, and went back whenever he got a moment off. His family did not like him to work in Innsmouth, but the chain had transferred him there and he did not wish to give up his job.

There was, he said, no public library or chamber of commerce in Innsmouth, but I could probably find my way about. The street I had come down was Federal. West of that were the fine old residence streets — Broad, Washington, Lafayette, and Adams — and east of it were the shoreward slums. It was in these slums — along Main Street — that I would find the old Georgian churches, but they were all long abandoned. It would be well not to make oneself too conspicuous in such neighbourhoods — especially north of the river since the people were sullen and hostile. Some strangers had even disappeared.

Certain spots were almost forbidden territory, as he had learned at considerable cost. One must not, for example, linger much around the Marsh refinery, or around any of the still used churches, or around the pillared Order of Dagon Hall at New Church Green. Those churches were very odd — all violently disavowed by their respective denominations elsewhere, and apparently using the queerest kind of ceremonials and clerical vestments. Their creeds were heterodox and mysterious, involving hints of certain marvelous transformations leading to bodily immortality — of a sort — on this earth. The youth's own pastor — Dr. Wallace of Asbury M. E. Church in Arkham — had gravely urged him not to join any church in Innsmouth.

As for the Innsmouth people — the youth hardly knew what to make of them. They were as furtive and seldom seen as animals that live in burrows, and one could hardly imagine how they passed the time apart from their desultory fishing. Perhaps — judging from the quantities of bootleg liquor they consumed — they lay for most of the daylight hours in an alcoholic stupor. They seemed sullenly banded together in some sort of fellowship and understanding — despising the world as if they had access to other and preferable spheres of entity. Their appearance — especially those staring, unwinking eyes which one never saw shut — was certainly shocking enough; and their voices were disgusting. It was awful to hear them chanting in their churches at night, and especially during their main festivals or revivals, which fell twice a year on April 30th and October 31st.

They were very fond of the water, and swam a great deal in both river and harbour. Swimming races out to Devil Reef were very common, and everyone in sight seemed well able to share in this arduous sport. When one came to think of it, it was generally only rather young people who were seen about in public, and of these the oldest were apt to be the most tainted-looking. When exceptions did occur, they were mostly persons with no trace of aberrancy, like the old clerk at the hotel. One wondered what became of the bulk of the older folk, and whether the "Innsmouth look" were not a strange and insidious disease-phenomenon which increased its hold as years advanced.

Only a very rare affliction, of course, could bring about such vast and radical anatomical changes in a single individual after maturity — changes invoking osseous factors as basic as the shape of the skull — but then, even this aspect was no more baffling and unheard-of than the visible features of the malady as a whole. It would be hard, the youth implied, to form any real conclusions regarding such a matter; since one never came to know the natives personally no matter how long one might live in Innsmouth.

The youth was certain that many specimens even worse than the worst visible ones were kept locked indoors in some places. People sometimes heard the queerest kind of sounds. The tottering waterfront hovels north of the river were reputedly connected by hidden tunnels, being thus a veritable warren of unseen abnormalities. What kind of foreign blood — if any — these beings had, it was impossible to tell. They sometimes kept certain especially repulsive characters out of sight when government and others from the outside world came to town.

It would be of no use, my informant said, to ask the natives anything about the place. The only one who would talk was a very aged but normal looking man who lived at the poorhouse on the north rim of the town and spent his time walking about or lounging around the fire station. This hoary character, Zadok Allen, was 96 years old and somewhat touched in the head, besides being the town drunkard. He was a strange, furtive creature who constantly looked over his shoulder as if afraid of something, and when sober could not be persuaded to talk at all with strangers. He was, however, unable to resist any offer of his favorite poison; and once drunk would furnish the most astonishing fragments of whispered reminiscence.

After all, though, little useful data could be gained from him; since his stories were all insane, incomplete hints of impossible marvels and horrors which could have no source save in his own disordered fancy. Nobody ever believed him, but the natives did not like him to drink and talk with strangers; and it was not always safe to be seen questioning him. It was probably from him that some of the wildest popular whispers and delusions were derived.

Several non-native residents had reported monstrous glimpses from time to time, but between old Zadok's tales and the malformed inhabitants it was no wonder such illusions were current. None of the non-natives ever stayed out late at night, there being a widespread impression that it was not wise to do so. Besides, the streets were loathsomely dark.

As for business — the abundance of fish was certainly almost uncanny, but the natives were taking less and less advantage of it. Moreover, prices were falling and competition was growing. Of course the town's real business was the refinery, whose commercial office was on the square only a few doors east of where we stood. Old Man Marsh was never seen, but sometimes went to the works in a closed, curtained car.

There were all sorts of rumors about how Marsh had come to look. He had once been a great dandy; and people said he still wore the frock-coated finery of the Edwardian age curiously adapted to certain deformities. His son had formerly conducted the office in the square, but latterly they had been keeping out of sight a good deal and leaving the brunt of affairs to the younger generation. The sons and their sisters had come to look very queer, especially the elder ones; and it was said that their health was failing.

One of the Marsh daughters was a repellent, reptilian-looking woman who wore an excess of weird jewellery clearly of the same exotic tradition as that to which the strange tiara belonged. My informant had noticed it many times, and had heard it spoken of as coming from some secret hoard, either of pirates or of demons. The clergymen — or priests, or whatever they were called nowadays — also wore this kind of ornament as a headdress; but one seldom caught glimpses of them. Other specimens the youth had not seen, though many were rumoured to exist around Innsmouth.

The Marshes, together with the other three gently bred families of the town — the Waites, the Gilmans, and the Eliots — were all very retiring. They lived in immense houses along Washington Street, and several were reputed to harbour in concealment certain living kinsfolk whose personal aspect forbade public view, and whose deaths had been reported and recorded.

Warning me that many of the street signs were down, the youth drew for my benefit a rough but ample and painstaking sketch map of the town's salient features. After a moment's study I felt sure that it would be of great help, and pocketed it with profuse thanks. Disliking the dinginess of the single restaurant I had seen, I bought a fair supply of cheese crackers and ginger wafers to serve as a lunch later on. My program, I decided, would be to thread the principal streets, talk with any non-natives I might encounter, and catch the eight o'clock coach for Arkham. The town, I could see, formed a significant and exaggerated example of communal decay; but being no sociologist I would limit my serious observations to the field of architecture.

Thus I began my systematic though half-bewildered tour of Innsmouth's narrow, shadow-blighted ways. Crossing the bridge and turning toward the roar of the lower falls, I passed close to the Marsh refinery, which seemed to be oddly free from the noise of industry. The building stood on the steep river bluff near a bridge and an open confluence of streets which I took to be the earliest civic center, displaced after the Revolution by the present Town Square.

Re-crossing the gorge on the Main Street bridge, I struck a region of utter desertion which somehow made me shudder. Collapsing huddles of gambrel roofs formed a jagged and fantastic skyline, above which rose the ghoulish, decapitated steeple of an ancient church. Some houses along Main Street were tenanted, but most were tightly boarded up. Down unpaved side streets I saw the black, gaping windows of deserted hovels, many of which leaned at perilous and incredible angles through the sinking of part of the foundations. Those windows stared so spectrally that it took courage to turn eastward toward the waterfront. Certainly, the terror of a deserted house swells in geometrical rather than arithmetical progression as houses multiply to form a city of stark desolation. The sight of such endless avenues of fishy-eyed vacancy and death, and the thought of such linked infinities of black, brooding compartments given over to cob-webs and memories and the conqueror worm, start up vestigial fears and aversions that not even the stoutest philosophy can disperse.

Fish Street was as deserted as Main, though it differed in having many brick and stone warehouses still in excellent shape. Water Street was almost its duplicate, save that there were great seaward gaps where wharves had been. Not a living thing did I see except for the scattered fishermen on the distant break-water, and not a sound did I hear save the lapping of the harbour tides and the roar of the falls in the Manuxet. The town was getting more and more on my nerves, and I looked behind me furtively as I picked my way back over the tottering Water Street bridge. The Fish Street bridge, according to the sketch, was in ruins.

North of the river there were traces of squalid life — active fish-packing houses in Water Street, smoking chimneys and patched roofs here and there, occasional sounds from indeterminate sources, and infrequent shambling forms in the dismal streets and unpaved lanes — but I seemed to find this even more oppressive than the southerly desertion. For one thing, the people were more hideous and abnormal than those near the centre of the town; so that I was several times evilly reminded of something utterly fantastic which I could not quite place. Undoubtedly the alien strain in the Innsmouth folk was stronger here than farther inland — unless, indeed, the "Innsmouth look" were a disease rather than a blood stain, in which case this district might be held to harbour the more advanced cases.

One detail that annoyed me was the distribution of the few faint sounds I heard. They ought naturally to have come wholly from the visibly inhabited houses, yet in reality were often strongest inside the most rigidly boarded-up facades. There were creakings, scurryings, and hoarse doubtful noises; and I thought uncomfortably about the hidden tunnels suggested by the grocery boy. Suddenly I found myself wondering what the voices of those denizens would be like. I had heard no speech so far in this quarter, and was unaccountably anxious not to do so.

Pausing only long enough to look at two fine but ruinous

old churches at Main and Church streets, I hastened out of that vile waterfront slum. My next logical goal was New Church Green, but somehow or other I could not bear to repass the church in whose basement I had glimpsed the inexplicably frightening form of that strangely diademmed priest or pastor. Besides, the grocery youth had told me that churches, as well as the Order of Dagon Hall, were not advisable neighbourhoods for strangers.

Accordingly I kept north along Main to Martin, then turning inland, crossing Federal Street safely north of the Green, and entering the decayed patrician neighbourhood of northern Broad, Washington, Lafayette, and Adams streets. Though these stately old avenues were ill-surfaced and unkempt, their elm-shaded dignity had not entirely departed. Mansion after mansion claimed my gaze, most of them decrepit and boarded up amidst neglected grounds, but one or two in each street shewing signs of occupancy. In Washington Street there was a row of four or five in excellent repair and with finely-tended lawns and gardens. The most sumptuous of these—with wide terraced parterres extending back the whole way to Lafayette Street—I took to be the home of Old Man Marsh, the afflicted refinery owner.

In all these streets no living thing was visible, and I wondered at the complete absence of cats and dogs from Innsmouth. Another thing which puzzled and disturbed me, even in some of the best-preserved mansions, was the tightly shuttered condition of many third-story and attic windows. Furtiveness and secretiveness seemed universal in this hushed city of alienage and death, and I could not escape the sensation of being watched from ambush on every hand by sly, staring eyes that never shut.

I shivered as the cracked stroke of three sounded from a belfry on my left. Too well did I recall the squat church from which those notes came. Following Washington street toward the river, I now faced a new zone of former industry and commerce; noting the ruins of a factory ahead, and seeing others, with the traces of an old railway station and covered railway bridge beyond, up the gorge on my right.

The uncertain bridge now before me was posted with a warning sign, but I took the risk and crossed again to the south bank where traces of life reappeared. Furtive, shambling creatures stared cryptically in my direction, and more normal faces eyed me coldly and curiously. Innsmouth was rapidly becoming intolerable, and I turned down Paine Street toward the Square in the hope of getting some vehicle to take me to Arkham before the still-distant starting-time of that sinister bus.

It was then that I saw the tumbledown fire station on my left, and noticed the red faced, bushy-bearded, watery eyed old man in nondescript rags who sat on a bench in front of it talking with a pair of unkempt but not abnormal looking firemen. This, of course, must be Zadok Allen, the half-crazed, liquorish nonagenarian whose tales of old Innsmouth and its shadow were so hideous and incredible.

It must have been some imp of the perverse—or some sardonic pull from dark, hidden sources—which made me change my plans as I did. I had long before resolved to limit my observations to architecture alone, and I was even then hurrying toward the Square in an effort to get quick transportation out of this festering city of death and decay; but the sight of old Zadok Allen set up new currents in my mind and made me slacken my pace uncertainly.

I had been assured that the old man could do nothing but hint at wild, disjointed, and incredible legends, and I had been warned that the natives made it unsafe to be seen talking with him; yet the thought of this aged witness to the town's decay, with memories going back to the early days of ships and factories, was a lure that no amount of reason could make me resist. After all, the strangest and maddest of myths are often merely symbols or allegories based upon truth—and old Zadok must have seen everything which went on around Innsmouth for the last ninety years. Curiosity flared up beyond sense and caution, and in my youthful egotism I fancied I might be able to sift a nucleus of real history from the confused, extravagant outpouring I would probably extract with the aid of raw whiskey.

I knew that I could not accost him then and there, for the firemen would surely notice and object. Instead, I reflected, I would prepare by getting some bootleg liquor at a place where the grocery boy had told me it was plentiful. Then I would loaf near the fire station in apparent casualness, and fall in with old Zadok after he had started on one of his frequent rambles. The youth had said that he was very restless, seldom sitting around the station for more than an hour or two at a time.

A quart bottle of whiskey was easily, though not cheaply, obtained in the rear of a dingy variety-store just off the Square in Eliot Street. The dirty-looking fellow who waited on me had a touch of the staring "Innsmouth look," but was quite civil in his way; being perhaps used to the custom of such convivial strangers—truckmen, gold-buyers, and the like—as were occasionally in town.

Reentering the Square I saw that luck was with me; for—shuffling out of Paine street around the corner of the Gilman House—I glimpsed nothing less than the tall, lean, tattered form of old Zadok Allen himself. In accordance with my plan, I attracted his attention by brandishing my newly-purchased bottle: and soon realised that he had begun to shuffle wistfully after me as I turned into Waite Street on my way to the most deserted region I could think of.

I was steering my course by the map the grocery boy had prepared, and was aiming for the wholly abandoned stretch of southern waterfront which I had previously visited. The only people in sight there had been the fishermen on the distant breakwater; and by going a few squares south I could get beyond the range of these, finding a pair of seats on some abandoned wharf and being free to question old Zadok unobserved for an indefinite time. Before I reached Main Street I could hear a faint and wheezy "Hey, Mister!" behind me and I presently allowed the old man to catch up and take copious pulls from the quart bottle.

I began putting out feelers as we walked amidst the omnipresent desolation and crazily tilted ruins, but found that the aged tongue did not loosen as quickly as I had expected. At length I saw a grass-grown opening toward the sea between crumbling brick walls, with the weedy length of an earth-and-masonry wharf projecting beyond. Piles of moss-covered stones near the water promised tolerable seats, and the scene was sheltered from all possible view by a ruined warehouse on the north. Here, I thought was the ideal place for a long secret colloquy; so I guided my companion down the lane and picked out spots to sit in among the mossy stones. The air of death and desertion was ghoulish, and the smell of fish almost insufferable; but I was resolved to let nothing deter me.

About four hours remained for conversation if I were to catch the eight o'clock coach for Arkham, and I began to dole out more liquor to the ancient tippler; meanwhile eating my own frugal lunch. In my donations I was careful not to overshoot the mark, for I did not wish Zadok's vinous garrulousness to pass into a stupor. After an hour his furtive taciturnity shewed signs of disappearing, but much to my disappointment he still sidetracked my questions about Innsmouth and its shadow-haunted past. He would babble of current topics, revealing a wide acquaintance with newspapers and a great tendency to philosophise in a sententious village fashion.

Toward the end of the second hour I feared my quart of whiskey would not be enough to produce results, and was wondering whether I had better leave old Zadok and go back for more. Just then, however, chance made the opening which my questions had been unable to make; and the wheezing ancient's rambling took a turn that caused me to lean forward and listen alertly. My back was toward the fishy-smelling sea, but he was facing it and something or other had caused his wandering gaze to light on the low, distant line of Devil Reef, then showing plainly and almost fascinatingly above the waves. The sight seemed to displease him, for he began a series of weak curses which ended in a confidential whisper and a knowing leer. He bent toward me, took hold of my coat lapel, and hissed out some hints that could not be mistaken.

"Thar's whar it all begun — that cursed place of all wickedness whar the deep water starts. Gate o' hell — sheer drop daown to a bottom no saoundin'-line kin tech. Ol' Cap'n Obed done it — him that faound aout more'n was good fer him in the Saouth Sea islands.

"Everybody was in a bad way them days. Trade fallin' off, mills losin' business — even the new ones — an' the best of our menfolks kilt aprivateerin' in the War of 1812 or lost with the Elizy brig an' the Ranger scow — both on 'em Gilman venters. Obed Marsh he had three ships afloat — brigantine Columby, brig Hefty, an' barque Sumatry Queen. He was the only one as kep' on with the East-Injy an' Pacific trade, though Esdras Martin's barkentine Malay Bride made a venter as late as twenty-eight.

"Never was nobody like Cap'n Obed — old limb o' Satan! Heh, heh! I kin mind him a-tellin' abaout furren parts, an' callin' all the folks stupid for goin' to Christian meetin' an' bearin' their burdns meek an' lowly. Says they'd orter git better gods like some o' the folks in the Injies — gods as ud bring 'em good fishin' in return for their sacrifices, an' ud reely answer folks's prayers.

"Matt Eliot his fust mate, talked a lot too, only he was again' folks's doin' any heathen things. Told abaout an island east of Othaheite whar they was a lot o' stone ruins older'n anybody knew anying abaout, kind o' like them on Ponape, in the Carolines, but with carven's of faces that looked like the big statues on Easter Island. Thar was a little volcanic island near thar, too, whar they was other ruins with diff'rent carvin' — ruins all wore away like they'd ben under the sea onct, an' with picters of awful monsters all over 'em.

"Wal, Sir, Matt he says the natives anound thar had all the fish they cud ketch, an' sported bracelets an' armlets an' head rigs made aout o' a queer kind o' gold an' covered with picters o' monsters jest like the ones carved over the ruins on the little island — sorter fish-like frogs or froglike fishes that was drawed in all kinds o' positions likes they was human bein's. Nobody cud get aout o' them whar they got all the stuff, an' all the other natives wondered haow they managed to find fish in plenty even when the very next island had lean pickin's. Matt he got to wonderon' too an' so did Cap'n Obed. Obed he notices, besides, that lots of the hn'some young folks ud drop aout o' sight fer good from year to year, an' that they wan't many old folks around. Also, he thinks some of the folks looked dinned queer even for Kanakys.

"It took Obed to git the truth aout o' them heathen. I dun't know haow he done it, but be begun by tradin' fer the gold-like things they wore. Ast 'em whar they come from, an' ef they cud git more, an' finally wormed the story aout o' the old chief — Walakea, they called him. Nobody but Obed ud ever a believed the old yeller devil, but the Cap'n cud read folks like they was books. Heh, heh! Nobody never believes me naow when I tell 'em, an' I dun't s'pose you will, young feller — though come to look at ye, ye hev kind o' got them sharp-readin' eyes like Obed had."

The old man's whisper grew fainter, and I found myself shuddering at the terrible and sincere portentousness of his intonation, even though I knew his tale could be nothing but drunken phantasy.

"Wal, Sir, Obed he larnt that they's things on this arth as most folks never heerd about — an' wouldn't believe ef they did hear. It seems these Kanakys was sacrificin' heaps o' their young men an' maidens to some kind o' god-things that lived under the sea, an' gittin' all kinds o' favour in return. They met the things on the little islet with the queer ruins, an' it seems them awful picters o' frog-fish monsters was supposed to be picters o' these things. Mebbe they was the kind o' critters as got all the mermaid stories an' sech started.

"They had all kinds a' cities on the sea-bottom, an' this

island was heaved up from thar. Seem they was some of the things alive in the stone buildin's when the island come up sudden to the surface. That's how the Kanakys got wind they was daown thar. Made sign-talk as soon as they got over bein' skeert, an' pieced up a bargain afore long.

"Them things liked human sacrifices. Had had 'em ages afore, but lost track o' the upper world after a time. What they done to the victims it ain't fer me to say, an' I guess Obed wasn't none too sharp abaout askin'. But it was all right with the heathens, because they'd ben havin' a hard time an' was desp'rate abaout everything. They give a sarten number o' young folks to the sea-things twice every year — May-Eve an' Hallawe'en — reg'lar as cud be. Also give some a' the carved knick-knacks they made. What the things agreed to give in return was plenty a' fish — they druv 'em in from all over the sea — an' a few gold like things naow an' then.

"Wal, as I says, the natives met the things on the little volcanic islet — goin' thar in canoes with the sacrifices et cet'ry, and bringin' back any of the gold-like jools as was comin' to 'em. At fust the things didn't never go onto the main island, but arter a time they come to want to. Seems they hankered arter mixin' with the folks, an' havin' j'int ceremonies on the big days — May-Eve an' Hallowe'en. Ye see, they was able to live both in ant aout o' water — what they call amphibians, I guess. The Kanakys told 'em as haow folks from the other islands might wanta wipe 'an out if they got wind o' their bein' thar, but they says they dun't keer much, because they cud wipe aout the hull brood o' humans ef they was willin' to bother — that is, any as didn't be, sarten signs sech as was used onct by the lost Old Ones, whoever they was. But not wantin' to bother, they'd lay low when anybody visited the island.

"When it come to matin' with them toad-lookin' fishes, the Kanakys kind o' balked, but finally they larnt something as put a new face on the matter. Seems that human folks has got a kind a' relation to sech water-beasts — that everything alive come aout o' the water onct an' only needs a little change to go back agin. Them things told the Kanakys that ef they mixed bloods there'd be children as ud look human at fust, but later turn more'n more like the things, till finally they'd take to the water an' jine the main lot o' things daown har. An' this is the important part, young feller — them as turned into fish things an' went into the water wouldn't never die. Them things never died excep' they was kilt violent.

"Wal, Sir, it seems by the time Obed knowed them islanders they was all full o' fish blood from them deep water things. When they got old an' begun to shew it, they was kep' hid until they felt like takin' to the water an' quittin' the place. Some was more teched than others, an' some never did change quite enough to take to the water; but mosily they turned out jest the way them things said. Them as was born more like the things changed arly, but them as was nearly human sometimes stayed on the island till they was past seventy, though they'd usually go daown under for trial trips afore that. Folks as had took to the water gen'rally come back a good deal to visit, so's a man ud often be a'talkin' to his own five-times-great-grand-father who'd left the dry land a couple o' hundred years or so afore.

"Everybody got aout o' the idee o' dyin' — excep' in canoe wars with the other islanders, or as sacrifices to the sea-gods daown below, or from snakebite or plague or sharp gallopin' ailments or somethin' afore they cud take to the water — but simply looked forrad to a kind o' change that wa'n't a bit horrible arter a while. They thought what they'd got was well wuth all they'd had to give up — an' I guess Obed kind o' come to think the same hisself when he'd chewed over old Walakea's story a bit. Walakea, though, was one of the few as hadn't got none of the fish blood — bein' of a royal line that intermarried with royal lines on other islands.

"Walakea he shewed Obed a lot o' rites an' incantations as had to do with the sea things, an' let him see some o' the folks in the village as had changed a lot from human shape. Somehaow or other, though, he never would let him see one of the reg'lar things from right aout o' the water. In the end he give him a funny kind o' thingumajig made aout o' lead or something, that he said ud bring up the fish things from any place in the water whar they might be a nest o' 'em. The idee was to drop it daown with the right kind o' prayers an' sech. Walakea allowed as the things was scattered all over the world, so's anybody that looked abaout cud find a nest an' bring 'em up ef they was wanted.

"Matt he didn't like this business at all, an' wanted Obed shud keep away from the island; but the Cap'n was sharp fer gain, an' faound he cud get them gold-like things so cheap it ud pay him to make a specialty of them. Things went on that way for years an' Obed got enough o' that gold-like stuff to make him start the refinery in Waite's old run-daown fullin' mill. He didn't dass sell the pieces like they was, for folks ud be all the time askin' questions. All the same his crews ud get a piece an' dispose of it naow and then, even though they was swore to keep quiet; an' he let his women-folks wear some o' the pieces as was more human-like than most.

"Well, come abaout thutty-eight — when I was seven year' old — Obed he faound the island people all wiped aout between v'yages. Seems the other islanders had got wind o' what was goin' on, and had took matters into their own hands. S'pose they must a had, after all, them old magic signs as the sea things says was the only things they was afeard of. No tellin' what any o' them Kanakys will chance to git a holt of when the sea-bottom throws up some island with ruins older'n the deluge. Pious cusses, these was — they didn't leave nothin' standin' on either the main island or the little volcanic islet excep' what parts of the ruins was too big to knock daown. In some places they was little stones strewed abaout — like charms — with somethin' on 'em like what ye call a swastika naowadays. Prob'ly them was the Old Ones' signs. Folks all wiped aout no trace o' no gold-like things an' none the nearby Kanakys ud breathe a word abaout the matter. Wouldn't even admit they'd ever ben any people on that island.

"That naturally hit Obed pretty hard, seein' as his normal trade was doin' very poor. It hit the whole of Innsmouth, too, because in seafarint days what profited the master of a ship gen'lly profited the crew proportionate. Most of the folks araound the taown took the hard times kind o' sheep-like an' resigned, but they was in bad shape because the fishin' was peterin' aout an' the mills wan't doin' none too well.

"Then's the time Obed he begun a-cursin' at the folks fer bein' dull sheep an' prayin' to a Christian heaven as didn't help 'em none. He told 'em he'd knowed o' folks as prayed to gods that give somethin' ye reely need, an' says ef a good bunch o' men ud stand by him, he cud mebbe get a holt o' sarten paowers as ud bring plenty o' fish an' quite a bit of gold. O' course them as sarved on the Sumatry Queen, an' seed the island knowed what he meant, an' wa'n't none too anxious to get clost to sea-things like they'd heard tell on, but them as didn't know what 'twas all abaout got kind o' swayed by what Obed had to say, and begun to ast him what he cud do to sit 'em on the way to the faith as 'ud bring 'em results."

Here the old man faltered, mumbled, and lapsed into a moody and apprehensive silence; glancing nervously over his shoulder and then turning back to stare fascinatedly at the distant black reef. When I spoke to him he did not answer, so I knew I would have to let him finish the bottle. The insane yarn I was hearing interested me profoundly, for I fancied there was contained within it a sort of crude allegory based upon the strangeness of Innsmouth and elaborated by an imagination at once creative and full of scraps of exotic legend. Not for a moment did I believe that the tale had any really substantial foundation; but none the less the account held a hint of genuine terror if only because it brought in references to strange jewels clearly akin to the malign tiara I had seen at Newburyport. Perhaps the ornaments had, after all, come from some strange island; and possibly the wild stories were lies of the bygone Obed himself rather than of this antique toper.

I handed Zadok the bottle, and he drained it to the last drop. It was curious how he could stand so much whiskey, for not even a trace of thickness had come into his high, wheezy voice. He licked the nose of the bottle and slipped it into his pocket, then beginning to nod and whisper softly to himself. I bent close to catch any articulate words he might utter, and thought I saw a sardonic smile behind the stained bushy whiskers. Yes — he was really forming words, and I could grasp a fair proportion of them.

"Poor Matt — Matt he allus was agin it — tried to line up the folks on his side, an' had long talks with the preachers — no use — they run the Congregational parson aout o' taown, an' the Methodist feller quit — never did see Resolved Babcock, the Baptist parson, agin — Wrath o' Jehovy — I was a mightly little critter, but I heerd what I heerd an, seen what I seen — Dagon an' Ashtoreth — Belial an' Beelzebub — Golden Caff an' the idols o' Canaan an' the Philistines — Babylonish abominations — *mene, mene, tekel, upharsin* —"

He stopped again, and from the look in his watery blue eyes I feared he was close to a stupor after all. But when I gently shook his shoulder he turned on me with astonishing alertness and snapped out some more obscure phrases.

"Dun't believe me, hey? Hey, heh, heh — then jest tell me, young feller, why Cap'n Obed an' twenty odd other folks used to row aout to Devil Reef in the dead o' night an' chant things so laoud ye cud hear 'em all over taown when the wind was right? Tell me that, hey? An' tell me why Obed was allus droppin' heavy things daown into the deep water t'other side o' the reef whar the bottom shoots daown like a cliff lower'n ye kin saound? Tell me what he done with that funny-shaped lead thingumajig as Walakea give him? Hey, boy? An' what did they all haowl on May-Eve, an, agin the next Hallowe'en? An' why'd the new church parsons — fellers as used to be sailors — wear them queer robes an' cover their-selves with them gold-like things Obed brung? Hey?"

The watery blue eyes were almost savage and maniacal now, and the dirty white beard bristled electrically. Old Zadok probably saw me shrink back, for he began to cackle evilly.

"Heh, heh, heh, heh! Beginni'n to see hey? Mebbe ye'd like to a ben me in them days, when I seed things at night aout to sea from the cupalo top o' my haouse. Oh, I kin tell ye' little pitchers hev big ears, an' I wa'n't missin' nothin' o' what was gossiped abaout Cap'n Obed an' the folks aout to the reef! Heh, heh, heh! Haow abaout the night I took my pa's ship's glass up to the cupalo an' seed the reef a-bristlin' thick with shapes that dove off quick soon's the moon riz?

"Obed an' the folks was in a dory, but them shapes dove off the far side into the deep water an' never come up . . .

"Haow'd ye like to be a little shaver alone up in a cupola a-watchin' shapes as wa'n't human shapes? . . . Heh? . . . Heh, heh, heh . . ."

The old man was getting hysterical, and I began to shiver with a nameless alarm. He laid a gnarled claw on my shoulder, and it seemed to me that its shaking was not altogether that of mirth.

"S'pose one night ye seed somethin' heavy heaved offen Obed's dory beyond the reef — and then learned next day a young feller was missin' from home. Hey! Did anybody ever see hide or hair o' Hiram Gilman agin? Did they? An' Nick Pierce, an' Luelly Waite, an' Adoniram Saouthwick, an' Henry Garrison. Hey? Heh, heh, heh, heh . . . Shapes talkin' sign language with their hands . . . them as had reel hands . . .

"Wal, Sir, that was the time Obed begun to git on his feet agin. Folks see his three darters a-wearin' gold-like things as nobody'd never see on 'em afore, an' smoke stared comin' aout o' the refin'ry chimbly. Other folks was prosp'rin, too — fish begun to swarm into the harbour fit to kill, an' heaven knows what sized cargoes we begun to ship aout to Newb'ryport, Arkham, an' Boston. T'was then Obed got the ol' branch railrud put through. Some Kingsport fishermen heerd abaout the ketch an' come up in sloops, but they was all lost. Nobody never see 'em agin. An' jest then our folk organised the Esoteric Order o' Dagon, an' bought Masonic Hall offen Calvary Commandery for it . . . heh, heh, heh! Matt Eliot was a Mason an' agin the sellin', but he dropped aout o' sight jest then.

"Remember, I ain't sayin' Obed was set on hevin' things jest like they was on that Kanaky isle. I dun't think he aimed at fust to do no mixin', nor raise no younguns to take to the water an' turn into fishes with eternal life. He wanted them gold things, an' was willin' to pay heavy, an' I guess the others was satisfied fer a while . . .

"Come in' forty-six the taown done some lookin' an' thinkin' fer itself. Too many folks missin'—too much wild preachin' at meetin' of a Sunday—too much talk abaout that reef. I guess I done a bit by tellin' Selectman Mowry what I see from the cupalo. They was a party one night as follered Obed's craowd aout to the reef, an' I heerd shots betwixt the dories. Nex' day Obed and thutty-two others was in gaol, with everybody a-wonderin' jest what was afoot and jest what charge agin 'em cud he get to holt. God, ef anybody'd look'd ahead . . . a couple o' weeks later, when nothin' had ben throwed into the sea fer thet long . . ."

Zadok was shewing signs of fright and exhaustion, and I let him keep silence for a while, though glancing apprehensively at my watch. The tide had turned and was coming in now, and the sound of the waves seemed to arouse him. I was glad of that tide, for at high water the fishy smell might not be so bad. Again I strained to catch his whispers.

"That awful night . . . I seed 'em. I was up in the cupalo . . . hordes of 'em . . . swarms of 'em . . . all over the reef an' swimmin' up the harbour into the Manuxet . . . God, what happened in the streets of Innsmouth that night . . . they rattled our door, but pa wouldn't open . . . then he clumb aout the kitchen winder with his musket to find Selecman Mowry an' see what he cud do . . . Maounds o' the dead an' the dyin' . . . shots and screams . . . shaoutin' in Ol Squar an' Taown Squar an' New Church Green—gaol throwed open . . .—proclamation . . . treason . . . called it the plague when folks come in an' faoud haff our people missin' . . . nobody left but them as ud jine in with Obed an' them things or else keep quiet . . . never heard o' my pa no more . . ."

The old man was panting and perspiring profusely. His grip on my shoulder tightened.

"Everything cleaned up in the mornin'—but they was traces . . . Obed he kinder takes charge an' says things is goin' to be changed . . . others'll worship with us at meetin'-time, an' sarten haouses hez got to entertin guests . . . they wanted to mix like they done with the Kanakys, an' he for one didn't feel baound to stop 'em. Far gone, was Obed . . . jest like a crazy man on the subjeck. He says they brung us fish an' treasure, an' shud hev what they hankered after . . .

"Nothin' was to be diff'runt on the aoutsid; only we was to keep shy o' strangers ef we knowed what was good fer us.

"We all hed to take the Oath o' Dagon, an' later on they was secon' an' third oaths that some o' us took. Them as ud help special, ud git special rewards—gold an' sech—No use balkin', fer they was millions of 'em daown thar. They'd ruther not start risin' an' wipin' aout human-kind, but ef they was gave away an' forced to, they cud do a lot toward jest that. We didn't hev them old charms to cut 'em off like folks in the Saouth Sea did, an' them Kanakys wudu't never give away their secrets.

"Yield up enough sacrifices an' savage knick-knacks an' harbourage in the taown when they wanted it, an' they'd let well enough alone. Wudn't bother no strangers as might bear tales aoutside—that is, withaout they got pryin'. All in the band of the faithful—Order o' Dagon—an' the children shud never die, but go back to the Mother Hydra an' Father Dagon what we all come from onct . . . Ia! Ia! Cthulhu fhtagn! Ph'nglui mglw'nafh Cthulhu R'lyeh wgah-nagl fhtaga—"

Old Zadok was fast lapsing into stark raving, and I held my breath. Poor old soul—to what pitiful depths of hallucination had his liquor, plus his hatred of the decay, alienage, and disease around him, brought that fertile, imaginative brain? He began to moan now, and tears were coursing down his channelled cheeks into the depths of his beard.

"God, what I seen senct I was fifteen year' old—*mene, mene, tekel, upharsin!*—the folks as was missin', and them as kilt theirselves—them as told things in Arkham or Ipswich or sech places was all called crazy, like you're callin' me right naow—but God, what I seen—they'd a kilt me long ago fer' what I know, only I'd took the fust an' secon' Oaths o' Dagon offen Obed, so was pertected unlessen a jury of 'em proved I told things knowin' an' delib'rit . . . but I wudn't take the third Oath—I'd a died ruther'n take that—

"It got wuss araound Civil War time, when children born senct 'forty-six begun to grow up—some 'em, that is. I was afeared—never did no pryin' arter that awful night, an' never see one o'—them—clost to in all my life. That is, never no full-blooded one. I went to the war, an' ef I'd a had any guts or sense I'd a never come back, but settled away from here. But folks wrote me things wa'n't so bad. That, I s'pose, was because gov'munt draft men was in taown arter 'sixty-three. Arter the war it was jest as bad agin. People begun to fall off—mills an' shops shet daown—shippin' stopped an' the harbour choked up—railrud give up—but they . . . they never stopped swimmin' in an' aout o' the river from that cursed reef o' Satan—an' more an' more attic winders got a-boarded up, an' more an' more noises was heerd in haouses as wa'n't s'posed to hev nobody in 'em . . .

"Folks aoutside hev their stories abaout us—s'pose you've heerd a plenty on 'em, seein' what questions ye ast—stories abaout things they've seed naow an' then, an' abaout that queer joolry as still comes in from somewhars an' ain't quite all melted up—but nothin' never gits def'nite. Nobody'll believe nothin'. They call them gold-like things pirate loot, an' allaow the Innsmouth folks hez furren blood or is dis-tempered or somethin'. Beside, them that lives here shoo off as many strangers as they kin, an' encourage the rest not to git very cur'ous, specially raound night time. Beasts balk at the critters—hosses wuss'n mules—but when they got autos that was all right.

"In 'forty-six Cap'n Obed took a second wife that nobody in the taown never see—some says he didn't want to, but was made to by them as he'd called in—had three children by her — two as disappeared young, but one gal as looked like anybody else an' was eddicated in Europe. Obed finally got her married off by a trick to an Arkham feller as didn't suspect nothin'. But nobody aoutside'll hav nothin' to do with Innsmouth folks naow. Barnabas Marsh that runs the refin'ry now is Obed's grandson by his fust wife — son of Onesiphorus, his eldest son, but his mother was another o' them as wa'n't never seen aoutdoors.

"Right naow Barnabas is abaout changed. Can't shet his eyes no more, an' is all aout o' shape. They say he still wears clothes, but he'll take to the water soon. Mebbe he's tried it already — they do sometimes go daown for little spells afore they go daown for good. Ain't ben seed abaout in public fer nigh on ten year'. Dun't know haow his poor wife kin feel — she come from Ipiwich, an' they nigh lynched Barnabas when he courted her fifty odd year' ago. Obed he died in 'seventy-eight an' all the next gen'ration is gone naow — the fust wife's children dead, and the rest . . . God knows . . ."

The sound of the incoming tide was now very insistent, and little by little it seemed to change the old man's mood from maudlin tearfulness to watchful fear. He would pause now and then to renew those nervous glances over his shoulder or out toward the reef, and despite the wild absurdity of his tale, I could not help beginning to share his apprehensiveness. Zadok now grew shriller, seemed to be trying to whip up his courage with louder speech.

"Hey, yew, why dun't ye say somethin'? Haow'd ye like to be livin' in a taown like this, with everything a-rottin' an' dyin', an' boarded-up monsters crawlin' an' bleatin' an' barkin' an' hoppin' araoun' black cellars an' attics every way ye turn? Hey? Haow'd ye like to hear the haowlin' night arter night from the churches an' Order o' Dagon Hall, an' know what's doin' part o' the haowlin'? Haow'd ye like to hear what comes from that awful reef every May-Eve an' Hallowmass? Hey? Think the old man's crazy, eh? Wal, Sir, let me tell ye that ain't the wust!"

Zadok was really screaming now, and the mad frenzy of his voice disturbed me more than I care to own.

"Curse ye, dun't set thar a'starin' at me with them eyes — I tell Obed Marsh he's in hell, an, hez got to stay thar! Heh, heh . . . in hell, I says! Can't git me — I hain't done nothin' nor told nobody nothin' —

"Oh, you, young feller? Wal, even ef I hain't told nobody nothin' yet, I'm a'goin' to naow! Yew jest set still an' listen to me, boy — this is what I ain't never told nobody . . . I says I didn't get to do pryin' arter that night — but I faound things about jest the same!"

"Yew want to know what the reel horror is, hey? Wal, it's this — it ain't what them fish devils hez done, but what they're a-goin' to do! They're a-bringin' things up aout o' whar they come from into the taown — been doin' it fer years, an' slackenin' up lately. Them haouses north o' the river be-twixt Water an' Main Streets is full of 'em — them devils an' what they brung — an' when they git ready . . . I say, when they git . . . ever hear tell of a shoggoth?

"Hey, d'ye hear me? I tell ye I know what them things be — I seen 'em one night when . . . eh-ahhh-ah! e'yahhh . . ."

The hideous suddenness and inhuman frightfulness of the old man's shriek almost made me faint. His eyes, looking past me toward the malodorous sea, were positively starting from his head; while his face was a mask of fear worthy of Greek tragedy. His bony claw dug monstrously into my shoulder, and he made no motion as I turned my head to look at whatever he had glimpsed.

There was nothing that I could see. Only the incoming tide, with perhaps one set of ripples more local than the long-flung line of breakers. But now Zadok was shaking me, and I turned back to watch the melting of that fear-frozen face into a chaos of twitching eyelids and mumbling gums. Presently his voice came back — albeit as a trembling whisper.

"Git aout o' here! Get aout o' here! They seen us — git aout fer your life! Dun't wait fer nothin' — they know naow — Run fer it — quick — aout o' this taown — "

Another heavy wave dashed against the loosing masonry of the bygone wharf, and changed the mad ancient's whisper to another inhuman and blood-curdling scream. "E-yaahhhh! . . . Yheaaaaaa! . . ."

Before I could recover my scattered wits he had relaxed his clutch on my shoulder and dashed wildly inland toward the street, reeling northward around the ruined warehouse wall.

I glanced back at the sea, but there was nothing there. And when I reached Water Street and looked along it toward the north there was no remaining trace of Zadok Allen.

I can hardly describe the mood in which I was left by this harrowing episode — an episode at once mad and pitiful, grotesque and terrifying. The grocery boy had prepared me for it, yet the reality left me none the less bewildered and disturbed. Puerile though the story was, old Zadok's insane earnestness and horror had communicated to me a mounting unrest which joined with my earlier sense of loathing for the town and its blight of intangible shadow.

Later I might sift the tale and extract some nucleus of historic allegory; just now I wished to put it out of my head. The hour grown perilously late — my watch said 7:15, and the Arkham bus left Town Square at eight — so I tried to give my thoughts as neutral and practical a cast as possible, meanwhile walking rapidly through the deserted streets of gaping roofs and leaning houses toward the hotel where I had checked my valise and would find my bus.

Though the golden light of late afternoon gave the ancient roofs and decrepit chimneys an air of mystic loveliness and peace, I could not help glancing over my shoulder now and then. I would surely be very glad to get out of malodorous and fear-shadowed Innsmouth, and wished there were some other vehicle than the bus driven by that sinister-looking fellow Sargent. Yet I did not hurry too precipitately, for there were architectural details worth viewing at every silent corner; and

I could easily, I calculated, cover the necessary distance in a half-hour.

Studying the grocery youth's map and seeking a route I had not traversed before, I chose Marsh Street instead of State for my approach to Town Square. Near the corner of Fall street I began to see scattered groups of furtive whisperers, and when I finally reached the Square I saw that almost all the loiterers were congregated around the door of the Gilman House. It seemed as if many bulging, watery, unwinking eyes looked oddly at me as I claimed my valise in the lobby, and I hoped that none of these unpleasant creatures would be my fellow-passengers on the coach.

The bus, rather early, rattled in with three passengers somewhat before eight, and an evil-looking fellow on the sidewalk muttered a few indistinguishable words to the driver. Sargent threw out a mail-bag and a roll of newspapers, and entered the hotel; while the passengers — the same men whom I had seen arriving in Newburyport that morning — shambled to the sidewalk and exchanged some faint guttural words with a loafer in a language I could have sworn was not English. I boarded the empty coach and took the seat I had taken before, but was hardly settled before Sargent re-appeared and began mumbling in a throaty voice of peculiar repulsiveness.

I was, it appeared, in very bad luck. There had been something wrong with the engine, despite the excellent time made from Newburyport, and the bus could not complete the journey to Arkham. No, it could not possibly be repaired that night, nor was there any other way of getting transportation out of Innsmouth either to Arkham or elsewhere. Sargent was sorry, but I would have to stop over at the Gilman. Probably the clerk would make the price easy for me, but there was nothing else to do.

Almost dazed by this sudden obstacle, and violently dreading the fall of night in this decaying and half-unlighted town, I left the bus and reentered the hotel lobby; where the sullen queer-looking night clerk told me I could have Room 428 on next the top floor — large, but without running water — for a dollar.

Despite what I had heard of this hotel in Newburyport, I signed the register, paid my dollar, let the clerk take my valise, and followed that sour, solitary attendant up three creaking flights of stairs past dusty corridors which seemed wholly devoid of life. My room was a dismal rear one with two windows and bare, cheap furnishings. It overlooked a dingy court-yard otherwise hemmed in by low, deserted brick blocks, and commanded a view of decrepit westward-stretching roofs with a marshy countryside beyond. At the end of the corridor was a bathroom — a discouraging relique with ancient marble bowl, tin tub, faint electric light, and musty wooded paneling around all the plumbing fixtures.

It being still daylight, I descended to the Square and looked around for a dinner of some sort; noticing as I did so the strange glances I received from the unwholesome loafers. Since the grocery was closed, I was forced to patronise the restaurant I had shunned before; a stooped, narrow-headed man with staring, unwinking eyes, and a flat-nosed wench with unbelievably thick, clumsy hands being in attendance. The service was all of the counter type, and it relieved me to find that much was evidently served from cans and packages. A bowl of vegetable soup with crackers was enough for me, and I soon headed back for my cheerless room at the Gilman; getting a evening paper and a fly-specked magazine from the evil-visaged clerk at the rickety stand beside his desk.

As twilight deepened I turned on the one feeble electric bulb over the cheap, iron-framed bed, and tried as best I could to continue the reading I had begun. I felt it advisable to keep my mind wholesomely occupied, for it would not do to brood over the abnormalities of this ancient, blight-shadowed town while I was still within its borders. The insane yarn I had heard from the aged drunkard did not promise very pleasant dreams, and I felt I must keep the image of his wild, watery eyes as far as possible from my imagination.

Also, I must not dwell on what that factory inspector had told the Newburyport ticket-agent about the Gilman House and the voices of its nocturnal tenants — not on that, nor on the face beneath the tiara in the black church doorway; the face for whose horror my conscious mind could not account. It would perhaps have been easier to keep my thoughts from disturbing topics had the room not been so gruesomely musty. As it was, the lethal mustiness blended hideously with the town's general fishy odour and persistently focussed one's fancy on death and decay.

Another thing that disturbed me was the absence of a bolt on the door of my room. One had been there, as marks clearly shewed, but there were signs of recent removal. No doubt it had been out of order, like so many other things in this decrepit edifice. In my nervousness I looked around and discovered a bolt on the clothes press which seemed to be of the same size, judging from the marks, as the one formerly on the door. To gain a partial relief from the general tension I busied myself by transferring this hardware to the vacant place with the aid of a handy three-in-one device including a screw-driver which I kept on my key-ring. The bolt fitted perfectly, and I was somewhat relieved when I knew that I could shoot it firmly upon retiring. Not that I had any real apprehension of its need, but that any symbol of security was welcome in an environment of this kind. There were adequate bolts on the two lateral doors to connecting rooms, and these I proceeded to fasten.

I did not undress, but decided to read till I was sleepy and then lie down with only my coat, collar, and shoes off. Taking a pocket flash light from my valise, I placed it in my trousers, so that I could read my watch if I woke up later in the dark. Drowsiness, however, did not come; and when I stopped to analyse my thoughts I found to my disquiet that I was really unconsciously listening for something — listening for something which I dreaded but could not name. That inspector's story must have worked on my imagination more deeply than

I had suspected. Again I tried to read, but found that I made no progress.

After a time I seemed to hear the stairs and corridors creak at intervals as if with footsteps, and wondered if the other rooms were beginning to fill up. There were no voices, however, and it struck me that there was something subtly furtive about the creaking. I did not like it, and debated whether I had better try to sleep at all. This town had some queer people, and there had undoubtedly been several disappearances. Was this one of those inns where travelers were slain for their money? Surely I had no look of excessive prosperity. Or were the towns folk really so resentful about curious visitors? Had my obvious sightseeing, with its frequent map-consultations, aroused unfavorable notice? It occurred to me that I must be in a highly nervous state to let a few random creakings set me off speculating in this fashion — but I regretted none the less that I was unarmed.

At length, feeling a fatigue which had nothing of drowsiness in it, I bolted the newly outfitted hall door, turned off the light, and threw myself down on the hard, uneven bed — coat, collar, shoes, and all. In the darkness every faint noise of the night seemed magnified, and a flood of doubly unpleasant thoughts swept over me. I was sorry I had put out the light, yet was too tired to rise and turn it on again. Then, after a long, dreary interval, and prefaced by a fresh creaking of stairs and corridor, there came that soft, damnably unmistakable sound which seemed like a malign fulfillment of all my apprehensions. Without the least shadow of a doubt, the lock of my door was being tried — cautiously, furtively, tentatively — with a key.

My sensations upon recognising this sign of actual peril were perhaps less rather than more tumultuous because of my previous vague fears. I had been, albeit without definite reason, instinctively on my guard — and that was to my advantage in the new and real crisis, whatever it might turn out to be. Nevertheless the change in the menace from vague premonition to immediate reality was a profound shock, and fell upon me with the force of a genuine blow. It never once occurred to me that the fumbling might be a mere mistake. Malign purpose was all I could think of, and I kept deathly quiet, awaiting the would-be intruder's next move.

After a time the cautious rattling ceased, and I heard the room to the north entered with a pass key. Then the lock of the connecting door to my room was softly tried. The bolt held, of course, and I heard the floor creak as the prowler left the room. After a moment there came another soft rattling, and I knew that the room to the south of me was being entered. Again a furtive trying of a bolted connecting door, and again a receding creaking. This time the creaking went along the hall and down the stairs, so I knew that the prowler had realised the bolted condition of my doors and was giving up his attempt for a greater or lesser time, as the future would shew.

The readiness with which I fell into a plan of action proves that I must have been subconsciously fearing some menace and considering possible avenues of escape for hours. From the first I felt that the unseen fumbler meant a danger not to be met or dealt with, but only to be fled from as precipitately as possible. The one thing to do was to get out of that hotel alive as quickly as I could, and through some channel other than the front stairs and lobby.

Rising softly and throwing my flashlight on the switch, I sought to light the bulb over my bed in order to choose and pocket some belongings for a swift, valiseless flight. Nothing, however, happened; and I saw that the power had been cut off. Clearly, some cryptic, evil movement was afoot on a large scale — just what, I could not say. As I stood pondering with my hand on the now useless switch I heard a muffled creaking on the floor below, and thought I could barely distinguish voices in conversation. A moment later I felt less sure that the deeper sounds were voices, since the apparent hoarse barkings and loose-syllabled croakings bore so little resemblance to recognized human speech. Then I thought with renewed force of what the factory inspector had heard in the night in this mouldering and pestilential building.

Having filled my pockets with the flashlight's aid, I put on my hat and tiptoed to the windows to consider chances of descent. Despite the state's safety regulations there was no fire escape on this side of the hotel, and I saw that my windows commanded only a sheer three story drop to the cobbled court-yard. On the right and left, however, some ancient brick business blocks abutted on the hotel; their slant roofs coming up to a reasonable jumping distance from my fourth-story level. To reach either of these lines of buildings I would have to be in a room two from my own — in one case on the north and in the other case on the south — and my mind instantly set to work out what chances I had of making the transfer.

I could not, I decided, risk an emergence into the corridor; where my footsteps would surely be heard, and where the difficulties of entering the desired room would be insuperable. My progress, if it was to be made at all, would have to be through the less solidly-built connecting doors of the rooms; the locks and bolts of which I would have to force violently, using my shoulder as a battering-ram whenever they were set against me. This, I thought, would be possible owing to the rickety nature of the house and its fixtures; but I realised I could not do it noiselessly. I would have to count on sheer speed, and the chance of getting to a window before any hostile forces became coordinated enough to open the right door toward me with a pass-key. My own outer door I reinforced by pushing the bureau against it — little by little, in order to make a minimum of sound.

I perceived that my chances were very slender, and was fully prepared for any calamity. Even getting to another roof would not solve the problem for there would then remain the task of reaching the ground and escaping from the town. One thing in my favour was the deserted and ruinous state of the abutting building and the number of skylights gaping blackly open in each row.

Gathering from the grocery boy's map that the best route out of town was southward, I glanced first at the connecting door on the south side of the room. It was designed to open in my direction, hence I saw — after drawing the bolt and finding other fastening in place — it was not a favorable one for forcing. Accordingly abandoning it as a route, I cautiously moved the bedstead against it to hamper any attack which might be made on it later from the next room. The door on the north was hung to open away from me, and this — though a test proved it to be locked or bolted from the other side — I knew must be my route. If I could gain the roofs of the buildings in Paine Street and descend successfully to the ground level, I might perhaps dart through the courtyard and the adjacent or opposite building to Washington or Bates — or else emerge in Paine and edge around southward into Washington. In any case, I would aim to strike Washington somehow and get quickly out of the Town Square region. My preference would be to avoid Paine, since the fire station there might be open all night.

As I thought of these things I looked out over the squalid sea of decaying roofs below me, now brightened by the beams of a moon not much past full. On the right the black gash of the river-gorge clove the panorama, abandoned factories and railway station clinging barnacle-like to its sides. Beyond it the rusted railway and the Rowley road led off through a flat marshy terrain dotted with islets of higher and dryer scrub-grown land. On the left the creek-threaded country-side was nearer, the narrow road to Ipswich gleaming white in the moonlight. I could not see from my side of the hotel the southward route toward Arkham which I had determined to take.

I was irresolutely speculating on when I had better attack the northward door, and on how I could least audibly manage it, when I noticed that the vague noises underfoot had given place to a fresh and heavier creaking of the stairs. A wavering flicker of light shewed through my transom, and the boards of the corridor began to groan with a ponderous load. Muffled sounds of possible vocal origin approached, and at length a firm knock came at my outer door.

For a moment I simply held my breath and waited. Eternities seemed to elapse, and the nauseous fishy odour of my environment seemed to mount suddenly and spectacularly. Then the knocking was repeated — continuously, and with growing insistence. I knew that the time for action had come, and forthwith drew the bolt of the northward connecting door, bracing myself for the task of battering it open. The knocking waxed louder, and I hoped that its volume would cover the sound of my efforts. At last beginning my attempt, I lunged again and again at the thin paneling with my left shoulder, heedless of shock or pain. The door resisted even more than I expected, but I did not give in. And all the while the clamour at the outer door increased.

Finally the connecting door gave, but with such a crash that I knew those outside must have heard. Instantly the outside knocking became a violent battering, while keys sounded ominously in the hall doors of the rooms on both sides of me. Rushing through the newly opened connexion, I succeeded in bolting the northerly hall door before the lock could he turned; but even as I did so I heard the hall door of the third room — the one from whose window I had hoped to reach the roof below — being tried with a pass key.

For an instant I felt absolute despair, since my trapping in a chamber with no window egress seemed complete. A wave of almost abnormal horror swept over me, and invested with a terrible but unexplainable singularity the flashlight-glimpsed dust prints made by the intruder who had lately tried my door from this room. Then, with a dazed automatism which persisted despite hopelessness, I made for the next connecting door and performed the blind motion of pushing at it in an effort to get through and — granting that fastenings might be as providentially intact as in this second room — bolt the hall door beyond before the lock could be turned from outside.

Sheer fortunate chance gave me my reprieve — for the connecting door before me was not only unlocked but actually ajar. In a second I was though, and had my right knee and shoulder against a hall door which was visibly opening inward. My pressure took the opener off guard, for the thing shut as I pushed, so that I could slip the well-conditioned bolt as I had done with the other door. As I gained this respite I heard the battering at the two other doors abate, while a confused clatter came from the connecting door I had shielded with the bedstead. Evidently the bulk of my assailants had entered the southerly room and were massing in a lateral attack. But at the same moment a pass key sounded in the next door to the north, and I knew that a nearer peril was at hand.

The northward connecting door was wide open, but there was no time to think about checking the already turning lock in the hall. All I could do was to shut and bolt the open connecting door, as well as its mate on the opposite side — pushing a bedstead against the one and a bureau against the other, and moving a washstand in front of the hall door. I must, I saw, trust to such makeshift barriers to shield me till I could get out the window and on the roof of the Paine Street block. But even in this acute moment my chief horror was something apart from the immediate weakness of my defenses. I was shuddering because not one of my pursuers, despite some hideous panting, grunting, and subdued barkings at odd intervals, was uttering an unmuffled or intelligible vocal sound.

As I moved the furniture and rushed toward the windows I heard a frightful scurrying along the corridor toward the room north of me, and perceived that the southward battering had ceased. Plainly, most of my opponents were about to concentrate against the feeble connecting door which they knew must open directly on me. Outside, the moon played on the ridgepole of the block below, and I saw that the jump would be desperately hazardous because of the steep surface on which I must land.

Surveying the conditions, I chose the more southerly of the two windows as my avenue of escape; planning to land on the inner slope of the roof and make for the nearest sky-light. Once inside one of the decrepit brick structures I would have to reckon with pursuit; but I hoped to descend and dodge in and out of yawning doorways along the shadowed courtyard, eventually getting to Washington Street and slipping out of town toward the south.

The clatter at the northerly connecting door was now terrific, and I saw that the weak panelling was beginning to splinter. Obviously, the besiegers had brought some ponderous object into play as a battering-ram. The bedstead, however, still held firm; so that I had at least a faint chance of making good my escape. As I opened the window I noticed that it was flanked by heavy velour draperies suspended from a pole by brass rings, and also that there was a large projecting catch for the shutters on the exterior. Seeing a possible means of avoiding the dangerous jump, I yanked at the hangings and brought them down, pole and all; then quickly hooking two of the rings in the shutter catch and flinging the drapery outside. The heavy folds reached fully to the abutting roof, and I saw that the rings and catch would be likely to bear my weight. So, climbing out of the window and down the improvised rope ladder, I left behind me forever the morbid and horror-infested fabric of the Gilman House.

I landed safely on the loose slates of the steep roof, and succeeded in gaining the gaping black skylight without a slip. Glancing up at the window I had left, I observed it was still dark, though far across the crumbling chimneys to the north I could see lights ominously blazing in the Order of Dagon Hall, the Baptist church, and the Congregational church which I recalled so shiveringly. There had seemed to be no one in the courtyard below, and I hoped there would be a chance to get away before the spreading of a general alarm. Flashing my pocket lamp into the skylight, I saw that there were no steps down. The distance was slight, however, so I clambered over the brink and dropped; striking a dusty floor littered with crumbling boxes and barrels.

The place was ghoulish-looking, but I was past minding such impressions and made at once for the staircase revealed by my flashlight—after a hasty glance at my watch, which shewed the hour to be 2 a.m. The steps creaked, but seemed tolerably sound; and I raced down past a barnlike second storey to the ground floor. The desolation was complete, and only echoes answered my footfalls. At length I reached the lower hall at the end of which I saw a faint luminous rectangle marking the ruined Paine Street doorway. Heading the other way, I found the back door also open; and darted out and down five stone steps to the grass-grown cobblestones of the courtyard.

The moonbeams did not reach down here, but I could just see my way about without using the flashlight. Some of the windows on the Gilman House side were faintly glowing, and I thought I heard confused sounds within. Walking softly over to the Washington Street side I perceived several open doorways, and chose the nearest as my route out. The hallway inside was black, and when I reached the opposite end I saw that the street door was wedged immovably shut. Resolved to try another building, I groped my way back toward the courtyard, but stopped short when close to the doorway.

For out of an opened door in the Gilman House a large crowd of doubtful shapes was pouring—lanterns bobbing in the darkness, and horrible croaking voices exchanging low cries in what was certainly not English. The figures moved uncertainly, and I realized to my relief that they did not know where I had gone; but for all that they sent a shiver of horror through my frame. Their features were indistinguishable, but their crouching, shambling gait was abominably repellent. And worst of all, I perceived that one figure was strangely robed, and unmistakably surmounted by a tall tiara of a design altogether too familiar. As the figures spread throughout the courtyard, I felt my fears increase. Suppose I could find no egress from this building on the street side? The fishy odour was detestable, and I wondered I could stand it without fainting. Again groping toward the street, I opened a door off the hall and came upon an empty room with closely shuttered but sashless windows. Fumbling in the rays of my flashlight, I found I could open the shutters; and in another moment had climbed outside and was fully closing the aperture in its original manner.

I was now in Washington Street, and for the moment saw no living thing nor any light save that of the moon. From several directions in the distance, however, I could hear the sound of hoarse voices, of footsteps, and of a curious kind of pattering which did not sound quite like footsteps. Plainly I had no time to lose. The points of the compass were clear to me, and I was glad that all the street lights were turned off, as is often the custom on strongly moonlit nights in prosperous rural regions. Some of the sounds came from the south, yet I retained my design of escaping in that direction. There would, I knew, be plenty of deserted doorways to shelter me in case I met any person or group who looked like pursuers.

I walked rapidly, softly, and close to the ruined houses. While hatless and dishevelled after my arduous climb, I did not look especially noticeable; and stood a good chance of passing unheeded if forced to encounter any casual wayfarer.

At Bates Street I drew into a yawning vestibule while two shambling figures crossed in front of me, but was soon on my way again and approaching the open space where Eliot Street obliquely crosses Washington at the intersection of South. Though I had never seen this space, it had looked dangerous to me on the grocery youth's map; since the moonlight would have free play there. There was no use trying to evade it, for any alternative course would involve detours of possibly disastrous visibility and delaying effect. The only thing to do was to cross it boldly and openly; imitating the typical shamble of the Innsmouth folk as best I could, and trusting that no one—or at least no pursuer of mine—would be there.

Just how fully the pursuit was organised—and indeed, just what its purpose might be—I could form no idea. There seemed to be unusual activity in the town, but I judged that the news of my escape from the Gilman had not yet spread. I would, of course, soon have to shift from Washington to some other southward street; for that party from the hotel would doubtless be after me. I must have left dust prints in that last old building, revealing how I had gained the street.

The open space was, as I had expected, strongly moonlit; and I saw the remains of a parklike, iron-railed green in its center. Fortunately no one was about though a curious sort of buzz or roar seemed to be increasing in the direction of Town Square. South Street was very wide, leading directly down a slight declivity to the waterfront and commanding a long view out a sea; and I hoped that no one would be glancing up it from afar as I crossed in the bright moonlight.

My progress was unimpeded, and no fresh sound arose to hint that I had been spied. Glancing about me, I involuntarily let my pace slacken for a second to take in the sight of the sea, gorgeous in the burning moonlight at the street's end. Far out beyond the breakwater was the dim, dark line of Devil Reef, and as I glimpsed it I could not help thinking of all the hideous legends I had heard in the last twenty-four hours—legends which portrayed this ragged rock as a veritable gateway to realms of unfathomed horror and inconceivable abnormality.

Then, without warning, I saw the intermittent flashes of light on the distant reef. They were definite and unmistakable, and awaked in my mind a blind horror beyond all rational proportion. My muscles tightened for panic flight, held in only by a certain unconscious caution and half-hypnotic fascination. And to make matters worse, there now flashed forth from the lofty cupola of the Gilman House, which loomed up to the northeast behind me, a series of analogous though differently spaced gleams which could be nothing less than an answering signal.

Controlling my muscles, and realising afresh how plainly visible I was, I resumed my brisker and feignedly shambling pace; though keeping my eyes on that hellish and ominous reef as long as the opening of South Street gave me a seaward view. What the whole proceeding meant, I could not imagine; unless it involved some strange rite connected with Devil Reef, or unless some party had landed from a ship on that sinister rock. I now bent to the left around the ruinous green; still gazing toward the ocean as it blazed in the spectral summer moonlight, and watching the cryptical flashing of those nameless, unexplainable beacons.

It was then that the most horrible impression of all was borne in upon me—the impression which destroyed my last vestige of self-control and sent me running frantically southward past the yawning black doorways and fishily staring windows of that deserted nightmare street. For at a closer glance I saw that the moonlit waters between the reef and the shore were far from empty. They were alive with a teeming horde of shapes swimming inward toward the town; and even at my vast distance and in my single moment of perception I could tell that the bobbing heads and flailing arms were alien and aberrant in a way scarcely to be expressed or consciously formulated.

My frantic running ceased before I had covered a block, for at my left I began to hear something like the hue and cry of organised pursuit. There were footsteps and gutteral sounds, and a rattling motor wheezed south along Federal Street. In a second all my plans were utterly changed—for if the southward highway were blocked ahead of me, I must clearly find another egress from Innsmouth. I paused and drew into a gaping doorway, reflecting how lucky I was to have left the moonlit open space before these pursuers came down the parallel street.

A second reflection was less comforting. Since the pursuit was down another street, it was plain that the party was not following me directly. It had not seen me, but was simply obeying a general plan of cutting off my escape. This, however, implied that all roads leading out of Innsmouth were similarly patrolled; for the people could not have known what route I intended to take. If this were so, I would have to make my retreat across country away from any road; but how could I do that in view of the marshy and creek-riddled nature of all the surrounding region? For a moment my brain reeled—both from sheer hopelessness and from a rapid increase in the omnipresent fishy odour.

Then I thought of the abandoned railway to Rowley, whose solid line of ballasted, weed-grown earth still stretched off to the northwest from the crumbling station on the edge at the river-gorge. There was just a chance that the townsfolk would not think of that; since its briar-choked desertion made it half-impassable, and the unlikeliest of all avenues for a fugitive to choose. I had seen it clearly from my hotel window and knew about how it lay. Most of its earlier length was uncomfortably visible from the Rowley road, and from high places in the town itself; but one could perhaps crawl inconspicuously through the undergrowth. At any rate, it would form my only chance of deliverance, and there was nothing to do but try it.

Drawing inside the hall of my deserted shelter, I once more consulted the grocery boy's map with the aid of the flashlight. The immediate problem was how to reach the ancient railway; and I now saw that the safest course was ahead to Babson Street; then west to Lafayette—there edging around but not crossing an open space homologous to the one I had traversed—and subsequently back northward and westward in a zigzagging line through Lafayette, Bates, Adam, and Bank streets—the latter skirting the river gorge—to the abandoned and dilapidated station I had seen from my window. My reason for going ahead to Babson was that I wished neither to recross the earlier open space nor to begin my westward course along a cross street as broad as South.

Starting once more, I crossed the street to the right-hand side in order to edge around into Babson as inconspicuously as possible. Noises still continued in Federal Street, and as I glanced behind me I thought I saw a gleam of light near the building through which I had escaped. Anxious to leave Washington Street, I broke into a quiet dogtrot, trusting to luck not to encounter any observing eye. Next the corner of Babson Street I saw to my alarm that one of the houses was still inhabited, as attested by curtains at the window; but there were no lights within, and I passed it without disaster.

In Babson Street, which crossed Federal and might thus reveal me to the searchers, I clung as closely as possible to the sagging, uneven buildings; twice pausing in a doorway as the noises behind me momentarily increased. The open space ahead shone wide and desolate under the moon, but my route would not force me to cross it. During my second pause I began to detect a fresh distribution of vague sounds; and upon looking cautiously out from cover beheld a motor car darting across the open space, bound outward along Eliot Street, which there intersects both Babson and Lafayette.

As I watched — choked by a sudden rise in the fishy odour after a short abatement — I saw a band of uncouth, crouching shapes loping and shambling in the same direction; and knew that this must be the party guarding the Ipswich road, since that highway forms an extension of Eliot Street. Two of the figures I glimpsed were in voluminous robes, and one wore a peaked diadem which glistened whitely in the moonlight. The gait of this figure was so odd that it sent a chill through me — for it seemed to me the creature was almost hopping.

When the last of the band was out of sight I resumed my progress; darting around the corner into Lafayette Street, and crossing Eliot very hurriedly lest stragglers of the party be still advancing along that thoroughfare. I did hear some croaking and clattering sounds far off toward Town Square, but accomplished the passage without disaster. My greatest dread was in re-crossing broad and moonlit South Street — with its seaward view — and I had to nerve myself for the ordeal. Someone might easily be looking, and possible Eliot Street stragglers could not fail to glimpse me from either of two points. At the last moment I decided I had better slacken my trot and make the crossing as before in the shambling gait of an average Innsmouth native.

When the view of the water again opened out — this time on my right — I was half-determined not to look at it at all. I could not however, resist; but cast a sidelong glance as I carefully and imitatively shambled toward the protecting shadows ahead. There was no ship visible, as I had half-expected there would be. Instead, the first thing which caught my eye was a small rowboat pulling in toward the abandoned wharves and laden with some bulky, tarpaulin-covered object. Its rowers, though distantly and indistinctly seen, were of an especially repellent aspect. Several swimmers were still discernible; while on the far black reef I could see a faint, steady glow unlike the winking beacon visible before, and of a curious colour which I could not precisely identify. Above the slant roofs ahead and to the right there loomed the tall cupola of the Gilman House, but it was completely dark. The fishy odour, dispelled for a moment by some merciful breeze, now closed in again with maddening intensity.

I had not quite crossed the street when I heard a muttering band advancing along Washington from the north. As they reached the broad open space where I had had my first disquieting glimpse of the moonlit water I could see them plainly only a block away — and was horrified by the bestial abnormality of their faces and the doglike sub-humanness of their crouching gait. One man moved in a positively simian way, with long arms frequently touching the ground; while another figure — robed and tiaraed — seemed to progress in an almost hopping fashion. I judged this party to be the one I had seen in the Gilman's courtyard — the one, therefore, most closely on my trail. As some of the figures turned to look in my direction I was transfixed with fright, yet managed to preserve the casual, shambling gait I had assumed. To this day I do not know whether they saw me or not. If they did, my stratagem must have deceived them, for they passed on across the moonlit space without varying their course — meanwhile croaking and jabbering in some hateful guttural patois I could not identify.

Once more in shadow, I resumed my former dog-trot past the leaning and decrepit houses that stared blankly into the night. Having crossed to the western sidewalk I rounded the nearest corner into Bates Street where I kept close to the buildings on the southern side. I passed two houses shewing signs of habitation, one of which had faint lights in upper rooms, yet met with no obstacle. As I turned into Adams Street I felt measurably safer, but received a shock when a man reeled out of a black doorway directly in front of me. He proved, however, too hopelessly drunk to be a menace; so that I reached the dismal ruins of the Bank Street warehouses in safety.

No one was stirring in that dead street beside the river-gorge, and the roar of the waterfalls quite drowned my foot steps. It was a long dog-trot to the ruined station, and the great brick warehouse walls around me seemed somehow more terrifying than the fronts of private houses. At last I saw the ancient arcaded station — or what was left of it — and made directly for the tracks that started from its farther end.

The rails were rusty but mainly intact, and not more than half the ties had rotted away. Walking or running on such a surface was very difficult; but I did my best, and on the whole made very fair time. For some distance the line kept on along the gorge's brink, but at length I reached the long covered bridge where it crossed the chasm at a dizzying height. The condition of this bridge would determine my next step. If humanly possible, I would use it; if not, I would have to risk more street wandering and take the nearest intact highway bridge.

The vast, barnlike length of the old bridge gleamed spectrally in the moonlight, and I saw that the ties were safe for at least a few feet within. Entering, I began to use my flashlight, and was almost knocked down by the cloud of bats that flapped past me. About half-way across there was a perilous gap in the ties which I feared for a moment would halt me; but in the end I risked a desperate jump which fortunately succeeded.

I was glad to see the moonlight again when I emerged from that macabre tunnel. The old tracks crossed River Street at grade, and at once veered off into a region increasingly rural and with less and less of Innsmouth's abhorrent fishy odour. Here the dense growth of weeds and briers hindered me and cruelly tore at my clothes, but I was none the less glad that they were there to give me concealment in case of peril. I knew that much of my route must be visible from the Rowley road.

The marshy region began very abruptly, with the single track on a low, grassy embankment where the weedy growth was somewhat thinner. Then came a sort of island of higher ground, where the line passed through a shallow open cut choked with bushes and brambles. I was very glad of this partial shelter, since at this point the Rowley road was uncomfortably near according to my window view. At the end of the cut it would cross the track and swerve off to a safer distance; but meanwhile I must be exceedingly careful. I was by this time thankfully certain that the railway itself was not patrolled.

Just before entering the cut I glanced behind me, but saw no pursuer. The ancient spires and roofs of decaying Innsmouth gleamed lovely and ethereal in the magic yellow moonlight, and I thought of how they must have looked in the old days before the shadow fell. Then, as my gaze circled inland from the town, something less tranquil arrested my notice and held me immobile for a second.

What I saw — or fancied I saw — was a disturbing suggestion of undulant motion far to the south; a suggestion which made me conclude that a very large horde must be pouring out of the city along the level Ipswich road. The distance was great and I could distinguish nothing in detail; but I did not at all like the look of that moving column. It undulated too much, and glistened too brightly in the rays of the now westering moon. There was a suggestion of sound, too, though the wind was blowing the other way — a suggestion of bestial scraping and bellowing even worse than the muttering of the parties I had lately overheard.

All sorts of unpleasant conjectures crossed my mind. I thought of those very extreme Innsmouth types said to be hidden in crumbling, centuried warrens near the waterfront; I thought, too, of those nameless swimmers I had seen. Counting the parties so far glimpsed, as well as those presumably covering other roads, the number of my pursuers must be strangely large for a town as depopulated as Innsmouth.

Whence could come the dense personnel of such a column as I now beheld? Did those ancient, unplumbed warrens teem with a twisted, uncatalogued, and unsuspected life? Or had some unseen ship indeed landed a legion of unknown outsiders on that hellish reef? Who were they? Why were they here? And if such a column of them was scouring the Ipswich road, would the patrols on the other roads be likewise augmented?

I had entered the brush-grown cut and was struggling along at a very slow pace when that damnable fishy odour again waxed dominant. Had the wind suddenly changed eastward, so that it blew in from the sea and over the town? It must have, I concluded, since I now began to hear shocking guttural murmurs from that hitherto silent direction. There was another sound, too — a kind of wholesale, colossal flopping or pattering which somehow called up images of the most detestable sort. It made me think illogically of that unpleasantly undulating column on the far-off Ipswich road.

And then both stench and sounds grew stronger, so that I paused shivering and grateful for the cut's protection. It was here, I recalled, that the Rowley road drew so close to the old railway before crossing westward and diverging. Something was coming along that road, and I must lie low till its passage and vanishment in the distance. Thank heaven these creatures employed no dogs for tracking — though perhaps that would have been impossible amidst the omnipresent regional odour. Crouched in the bushes of that sandy cleft I felt reasonably safe, even though I knew the searchers would have to cross the track in front of me not much more than a hundred yards away. I would be able to see them, but they could not, except by a malign miracle, see me.

All at once I began dreading to look at them as they passed. I saw the close moonlit space where they would surge by, and had curious thoughts about the irredeemable pollution of that space. They would perhaps be the worst of all Innsmouth types — something one would not care to remember.

The stench waxed overpowering, and the noises swelled to a bestial babel of croaking, baying and barking without the least suggestion of human speech. Were these indeed the voices of my pursuers? Did they have dogs after all? So far I had seen none of the lower animals in Innsmouth. That flopping or pattering was monstrous — I could not look upon the degenerate creatures responsible for it. I would keep my eyes shut till the sound receded toward the west. The horde was very close now — air foul with their hoarse snarlings, and the ground almost shaking with their alien-rhythmed footfalls. My breath nearly ceased to come, and I put every ounce of will-power into the task of holding my eyelids down.

I am not even yet willing to say whether what followed was a hideous actuality or only a nightmare hallucination. The later action of the government, after my frantic appeals, would tend to confirm it as a monstrous truth; but could not an hallucination have been repeated under the quasi-hypnotic spell of that ancient, haunted, and shadowed town? Such places have strange properties, and the legacy of insane legend might well have acted on more than one human imagination amidst those dead, stench-cursed streets and huddles of rotting roofs and crumbling steeples. Is it not possible that the germ of an actual contagious madness lurks in the depths of that shadow over Innsmouth? Who can be sure of reality after hearing things like the tale of old Zadok Allen? The government men never found poor Zadok, and have no conjectures to make as to what became of him. Where does madness leave off and reality begin? Is it possible that even my latest fear is sheer delusion?

But I must try to tell what I thought I saw that night under the mocking yellow moon — saw surging and hopping down the Rowley road in plain sight in front of me as I crouched among the wild brambles of that desolate railway cut. Of course my resolution to keep my eyes shut had failed. It was foredoomed to failure — for who could crouch blindly while a legion of croaking, baying entities of unknown source flopped noisomely past, scarcely more than a hundred yards away?

I thought I was prepared for the worst, and I really ought to have been prepared considering what I had seen before.

My other pursuers had been accursedly abnormal — so should I not have been ready to face a strengthening of the abnormal element; to look upon forms in which there was no mixture of the normal at all? I did not open my eyes until the raucous clamour came loudly from a point obviously straight ahead. Then I knew that a long section of them must be plainly in sight where the sides of the cut flattened out and the road crossed the track — and I could no longer keep myself from sampling whatever horror that leering yellow moon might have to shew.

It was the end, for whatever remains to me of life on the surface of this earth, of every vestige of mental peace and confidence in the integrity of nature and of the human mind. Nothing that I could have imagined — nothing, even, that I could have gathered had I credited old Zadok's crazy tale in the most literal way — would be in any way comparable to the demoniac, blasphemous reality that I saw — or believe I saw. I have tried to hint what it was in order to postpone the horror of writing it down baldly. Can it be possible that this planet has actually spawned such things; that human eyes have truly seen, as objective flesh, what man has hitherto known only in febrile phantasy and tenuous legend?

And yet I saw them in a limitless stream — flopping, hopping, croaking, bleating — urging inhumanly through the spectral moonlight in a grotesque, malignant saraband of fantastic nightmare. And some of them had tall tiaras of that nameless whitish-gold metal . . . and some were strangely robed . . . and one, who led the way, was clad in a ghoulishly humped black coat and striped trousers, and had a man's felt hat perched on the shapeless thing that answered for a head.

I think their predominant colour was a greyish-green, though they had white bellies. They were mostly shiny and slippery, but the ridges of their backs were scaly. Their forms vaguely suggested the anthropoid, while their heads were the heads of fish, with prodigious bulging eyes that never closed. At the sides of their necks were palpitating gills, and their long paws were webbed. They hopped irregularly, sometimes on two legs and sometimes on four. I was somehow glad that they had no more than four limbs. Their croaking, baying voices, clearly used for articulate speech, held all the dark shades of expression which their staring faces lacked.

But for all of their monstrousness they were not unfamiliar to me. I knew too well what they must be — for was not the memory of the evil tiara at Newburyport still fresh? They were the blasphemous fish-frogs of the nameless design — living and horrible — and as I saw them I knew also of what that humped, tiaraed priest in the black church basement had fearsomely reminded me. Their number was past guessing. It seemed to me that there were limitless swarms of them and certainly my momentary glimpse could have shewn only the least fraction. In another instant everything was blotted out by a merciful fit of fainting; the first I had ever had.

It was a gentle daylight rain that awaked me from my stupor in the brush-grown railway cut, and when I staggered out to the roadway ahead I saw no trace of any prints in the fresh mud. The fishy odour, too, was gone, Innsmouth's ruined roofs and toppling steeples loomed up greyly toward the southeast, but not a living creature did I spy in all the desolate salt marshes around. My watch was still going, and told me that the hour was past noon.

The reality of what I had been through was highly uncertain in my mind, but I felt that something hideous lay in the background. I must get away from evil-shadowed Innsmouth — and accordingly I began to test my cramped, wearied powers of locomotion. Despite weakness, hunger, horror, and bewilderment I found myself after a time able to walk; so I started slowly along the muddy road to Rowley. Before evening I was in the village, getting a meal and providing myself with presentable clothes. I caught the night train to Arkham, and the next day talked long and earnestly with government officials there; a process I later repeated in Boston. With the main result of these colloquies the public is now familiar — and I wish, for normality's sake, there were nothing more to tell. Perhaps it is madness that is overtaking me — yet perhaps a greater horror — or a greater marvel — is reaching out.

As may well be imagined, I gave up most of the foreplanned features of the rest of my tour — the scenic, architectural, and antiquarian diversions on which I had counted so heavily. Nor did I dare look for that piece of strange jewelry said to be in the Miskatonic University Museum. I did, however, improve my stay in Arkham by collecting some genealogical notes I had long wished to possess; very rough and hasty data, it is true, but capable of good use later on when I might have time to collate and codify them. The curator of the historical society there — Mr. B. Lapham Peabody — was very courteous about assisting me, and expressed unusual interest when I told him I was a grandson of Eliza Orne of Arkham, who was born in 1867 and had married James Williamson of Ohio at the age of seventeen.

It seemed that a maternal uncle of mine had been there many years before on a quest much like my own; and that my grandmother's family was a topic of some local curiosity. There had, Mr. Peabody said, been considerable discussion about the marriage of her father, Benjamin Orne, just after the Civil War; since the ancestry of the bride was peculiarly puzzling. That bride was understood to have been an orphaned Marsh of New Hampshire — a cousin of the Essex County Marshes — but her education had been in France and she knew very little of her family. A guardian had deposited funds in a Boston bank to maintain her and her French governess; but that guardian's name was unfamiliar to Arkham people, and in time he dropped out of sight, so that the governess assumed the role by court appointment. The Frenchwoman — now long dead — was very taciturn, and there were those who said she would have told more than she did.

But the most baffling thing was the inability of anyone to

place the recorded parents of the young woman — Enoch and Lydia (Meserve) Marsh — among the known families of New Hampshire. Possibly, many suggested, she was the natural daughter of some Marsh of prominence — she certainly had the true Marsh eyes. Most of the puzzling was done after her early death, which took place at the birth of my grandmother — her only child.

Having formed some disagreeable impressions connected with the name of Marsh, I did not welcome the news that it belonged on my own ancestral tree; nor was I pleased by Mr. Peabody's suggestion that I had the true Marsh eyes myself. However, I was grateful for data which I knew would prove valuable; and took copious notes and lists of book references regarding the well-documented Orne family.

I went directly home to Toledo from Boston, and later spent a month at Maumee recuperating from my ordeal. In September I entered Oberlin for my final year, and from then till the next June was busy with studies and other wholesome activities — reminded of the bygone terror only by occasional official visits from government men in connexion with the campaign which my pleas and evidence had started. Around the middle of July — just a year after the Innsmouth experience — I spent a week with my late mother's family in Cleveland; checking some of my new genealogical data with the various notes, traditions, and bits of heirloom material in existence there, and seeing what kind of a connected chart I could construct.

I did not exactly relish this task, for the atmosphere of the Williamson home had always depressed me. There was a strain of morbidity there, and my mother had never encouraged my visiting her parents as a child, although she always welcomed her father when he came to Toledo. My Arkham-born grandmother had seemed strange and almost terrifying to me, and I do not think I grieved when she disappeared. I was eight years old then, and it was said that she had wandered off in grief after the suicide of my Uncle Douglas, her eldest son. He had shot himself after a trip to New England — the same trip, no doubt, which had caused him to be recalled at the Arkham Historical Society.

This uncle had resembled her, and I had never liked him either. Something about the staring, unwinking expression of both of them had given me a vague, unaccountable uneasiness. My mother and Uncle Walter had not looked like that. They were like their father, though poor little cousin Lawrence — Walter's son — had been an almost perfect duplicate of his grandmother before his condition took him to the permanent seclusion of a sanitarium at Canton. I had not seen him in four years, but my uncle once implied that his state, both mental and physical, was very bad. This worry had probably been a major cause of his mother's death two years before.

My grandfather and his widowed son Walter now comprised the Cleveland household, but the memory of older times hung thickly over it. I still disliked the place, and tried to get my researches done as quickly as possible. Williamson records and traditions were supplied in abundance by my grandfather; though for Orne material I had to depend on my uncle Walter, who put at my disposal the contents of all his files, including notes, letters, cuttings, heirlooms, photographs, and miniatures.

It was in going over the letters and pictures on the Orne side that I began to acquire a kind of terror of my own ancestry. As I have said, my grandmother and Uncle Douglas had always disturbed me. Now, years after their passing, I gazed at their pictured faces with a measurably heightened feeling of repulsion and alienation. I could not at first understand the change, but gradually a horrible sort of comparison began to obtrude itself on my unconscious mind despite the steady refusal of my consciousness to admit even the least suspicion of it. It was clear that the typical expression of these faces now suggested something it had not suggested before — something which would bring stark panic if too openly thought of.

But the worst shock came when my uncle shewed me the Orne jewelery in a downtown safe deposit vault. Some of the items were delicate and inspiring enough, but there was one box of strange old pieces descended from my mysterious great-grandmother which my uncle was almost reluctant to produce. They were, he said, of very grotesque and almost repulsive design, and had never to his knowledge been publicly worn; though my grandmother used to enjoy looking at them. Vague legends of bad luck clustered around them, and my great-grandmother's French governess had said they ought not to be worn in New England, though it would be quite safe to wear them in Europe.

As my uncle began slowly and grudgingly to unwrap the things he urged me not to be shocked by the strangeness and frequent hideousness of the designs. Artists and archaeologists who had seen them pronounced their workmanship superlatively and exotically exquisite, though no one seemed able to define their exact material or assign them to any specific art tradition. There were two armlets, a tiara, and a kind of pectoral; the latter having in high relief certain figures of almost unbearable extravagance.

During this description I had kept a tight rein on my emotions, but my face must have betrayed my mounting fears. My uncle looked concerned, and paused in his unwrapping to study my countenance. I motioned to him to continue, which he did with renewed signs of reluctance. He seemed to expect some demonstration when the first piece — the tiara — became visible, but I doubt if he expected quite what actually happened. I did not expect it, either, for I thought I was thoroughly forewarned regarding what the jewelery would turn out to be. What I did was to faint silently away, just as I had done in that brier choked railway cut a year before.

From that day on my life has been a nightmare of brooding and apprehension nor do I know how much is hideous truth and how much madness. My great-grandmother had been a Marsh of unknown source whose husband lived in Arkham — and did not old Zadok say that the daughter of Obed Marsh by a monstrous mother was married to an Arkham man through a trick? What was it the ancient toper had muttered about the line of my eyes to Captain Obed's? In Arkham, too, the curator had told me I had the true Marsh eyes. Was Obed Marsh my own great-great-grandfather? Who — or what — then, was my great-great-grandmother?

But perhaps this was all madness. Those whitish-gold ornaments might easily have been bought from some Innsmouth sailor by the father of my great-grandmother, whoever he was. And that look in the staring-eyed faces of my grandmother and self-slain uncle might be sheer fancy on my part — sheer fancy, bolstered up by the Innsmouth shadow which had so darkly coloured my imagination. But why had my uncle killed himself after an ancestral quest in New England?

For more than two years I fought off these reflections with partial success. My father secured me a place in an insurance office, and I buried myself in routine as deeply as possible.

In the winter of 1930–31, however, the dreams began. They were very sparse and insidious at first, but increased in frequency and vividness as the weeks went by. Great watery spaces opened out before me, and I seemed to wander through titanic sunken porticos and labyrinths of weedy cyclopean walls with grotesque fishes as my companions. Then the other shapes began to appear, filling me with nameless horror the moment I awoke. But during the dreams they did not horrify me at all — I was one with them; wearing their unhuman trappings, treading their aqueous ways, and praying monstrously at their evil sea-bottom temples.

There was much more than I could remember, but even what I did remember each morning would be enough to stamp me as a madman or a genius if ever I dared write it down. Some frightful influence, I felt, was seeking gradually to drag me out of the sane world of wholesome life into unnamable abysses of blackness and alienage; and the process told heavily on me. My health and appearance grew steadily worse, till finally I was forced to give up my position and adopt the static, secluded life of an invalid. Some odd nervous affliction had me in its grip, and I found myself at times almost unable to shut my eyes.

It was then that I began to study the mirror with mounting alarm. The slow ravages of disease are not pleasant to watch, but in my case there was something subtler and more puzzling in the background. My father seemed to notice it, too, for he began looking at me curiously and almost affrightedly. What was taking place in me? Could it be that I was coming to resemble my grandmother and uncle Douglas?

One night I had a frightful dream in which I met my grandmother under the sea. She lived in a phosphorescent palace of many terraces, with gardens of strange leprous corals and grotesque brachiate efflorescences, and welcomed me with a warmth that may have been sardonic. She had changed — as those who take to the water change — and told me she had never died. Instead, she had gone to a spot her dead son had learned about, and had leaped to a realm whose wonders — destined for him as well — he had spurned with a smoking pistol. This was to be my realm, too — I could not escape it. I would never die, but would live with those who had lived since before man ever walked the earth.

I met also that which had been her grandmother. For eighty thousand years Pth'thya-l'yi had lived in Y'ha-nthlei, and thither she had gone back after Obed Marsh was dead. Y'ha-nthlei was not destroyed when the upper-earth men shot death into the sea. It was hurt, but not destroyed. The Deep Ones could never be destroyed, even though the palaeogean magic of the forgotten Old Ones might sometimes check them. For the present they would rest; but some day, if they remembered, they would rise again for the tribute Great Cthulhu craved. It would be a city greater than Innsmouth next time. They had planned to spread, and had brought up that which would help them, but now they must wait once more. For bringing the upper-earth men's death I must do a penance, but that would not be heavy. This was the dream in which I saw a shoggoth for the first time, and the sight set me awake in a frenzy of screaming. That morning the mirror definitely told me I had acquired the Innsmouth look.

So far I have not shot myself as my uncle Douglas did. I bought an automatic and almost took the step, but certain dreams deterred me. The tense extremes of horror are lessening, and I feel queerly drawn toward the unknown sea-deeps instead of fearing them. I hear and do strange things in sleep, and awake with a kind of exaltation instead of terror. I do not believe I need to wait for the full change as most have waited. If I did, my father would probably shut me up in a sanitarium as my poor little cousin is shut up. Stupendous and unheard-of splendors await me below, and I shall seek them soon. Iä-R'lyeh! Cthulhu fhtagn! Iä! Iä! No, I shall not shoot myself — I cannot be made to shoot myself!

I shall plan my cousin's escape from that Canton mad-house, and together we shall go to marvel-shadowed Innsmouth. We shall swim out to that brooding reef in the sea and dive down through black abysses to Cyclopean and many-columned Y'ha-nthlei, and in that lair of the Deep Ones we shall dwell amidst wonder and glory for ever.

1932.

The Ghost Writer.

Despite H.P. Lovecraft's crisis of confidence the previous year, early in 1932 he set to work on another novelette: "The Dreams in the Witch-House."

Then in April, before leaving on his travels, Lovecraft found a new ghostwriting client, Hazel Heald. Heald was an attractive divorcee just half a dozen years younger than Lovecraft, and soon started getting interested in him romantically (or so neighbor Muriel Eddy claims); but when she tried to encourage him to make a move on her, he backed away, although he continued to work with her for some time afterward.

In May, Lovecraft started his summer travels, and they were very extensive in 1932. They took him all the way to New Orleans this time, on a visit to E. Hoffman Price; there, he helped Price revise "Tarbis of the Lake." He had hoped to meet Robert E. Howard there as well, but Howard was unable to make it down from his home in Cross Plains, Texas.

After leaving New Orleans, Lovecraft made his way back toward New England via Mobile, Montgomery, Atlanta, Richmond and Fredericksburg, running himself to the brink of exhaustion exploring museums and historic sites, visiting writer friends, and staying up all night talking about stories and plots. His journeys were cut short by the death of his aunt Lillian Clark.

In July, after his return to attend to his aunt's death, Lovecraft dashed off three pulpy short stories for Hazel Heald to submit to *Weird Tales*: "The Man of Stone," "Winged Death," and "The Horror in the Museum."

In November 1932, Lovecraft initiated the exchange of letters with Robert E. Howard that would turn into possibly the most famous epistolic exchange of either writer's life: the "civilization vs. barbarism" debate, in which Lovecraft advocated for civilization and Howard for barbarism as the highest and best state of humanity.

The Dreams in the Witch House.

14,700-WORD NOVELETTE; 1932.

H.P. Lovecraft arguably bit off more than he could chew when he set himself to write a story that would give scientific credibility to the legends of Salem witchcraft. And yet he does manage to pull it off, if with a few flaws here and there.

In February 1932 when "The Dreams in the Witch House" was completed, he sent out to his friends for critiques, and August Derleth, who really ought to have known better, was a little too blunt about his reaction to it. (In Derleth's defense, he was an active believing and practicing Catholic, and the story probably touched one or two of his spiritual nerves.)

Lovecraft, once again shorn of his tentatively budding confidence, promptly gave up on the thing. Fortunately, Derleth, perhaps regretting his bluntness, talked Lovecraft into letting him copy the manuscript, which he then surreptitiously slipped to Farnsworth Wright at Weird Tales. *Wright promptly contacted Lovecraft and bought the story. It was published in the July 1933 issue.*

But Lovecraft seems to have regarded this as either a fluke, or as further evidence that his muse was only good for pulp production. For the following year and a half, although he would produce plenty of ghostwritings and collaborations as well as more travelogues (including one ghost-written for his ex-wife, who had just returned from a trip to Europe), he would write no more original fiction under his own by-line in 1932.

Whether the dreams brought on the fever or the fever brought on the dreams Walter Gilman did not know. Behind everything crouched the brooding, festering horror of the ancient town, and of the mouldy, unhallowed garret gable where he wrote and studied and wrestled with figures and formulae when he was not tossing on the meagre iron bed. His ears were growing sensitive to a preternatural and intolerable degree, and he had long ago stopped the cheap mantel clock whose ticking had come to seem like a thunder of artillery. At night the subtle stirring of the black city outside, the sinister scurrying of rats in the wormy partitions, and the creaking of hidden timbers in the centuried house, were enough to give him a sense of strident pandemonium. The darkness always teemed with unexplained sound — and yet he sometimes shook with fear lest the noises he heard should subside and allow him to hear certain other fainter noises which he suspected were lurking behind them.

He was in the changeless, legend-haunted city of Arkham, with its clustering gambrel roofs that sway and sag over attics where witches hid from the King's men in the dark, olden years of the Province. Nor was any spot in that city more steeped in macabre memory than the gable room which harboured him — for it was this house and this room which had likewise harboured old Keziah Mason, whose flight from Salem Gaol at the last no one was ever able to explain. That was in 1692 — the gaoler had gone mad and babbled of a small white-fanged furry thing which scuttled out of Keziah's cell, and not even Cotton Mather could explain the curves and angles smeared on the grey stone walls with some red, sticky fluid.

Possibly Gilman ought not to have studied so hard. Non-Euclidean calculus and quantum physics are enough to stretch any brain, and when one mixes them with folklore, and tries to trace a strange background of multi-dimensional reality behind the ghoulish hints of the Gothic tales and the wild whispers of the chimney-corner, one can hardly expect to be wholly free from mental tension. Gilman came from Haverhill, but it was only after he had entered college in Arkham that he began to connect his mathematics with the fantastic legends of elder magic. Something in the air of the hoary town worked obscurely on his imagination. The professors at Miskatonic had urged him to slacken up, and had voluntarily cut down his course at several points. Moreover, they had stopped him from consulting the dubious old books on forbidden secrets that were kept under lock and key in a vault at the university library. But all these precautions came late in the day, so that Gilman had some terrible hints from the dreaded *Necronomicon* of Abdul Alhazred, the fragmentary *Book of Eibon*, and the suppressed *Unaussprechlicken Kulten* of von Junzt to correlate with his abstract formulae on the properties of space and the linkage of dimensions known and unknown.

He knew his room was in the old Witch-House — that, indeed, was why he had taken it. There was much in the Essex County records about Keziah Mason's trial, and what she had admitted under pressure to the Court of Oyer and Terminer had fascinated Gilman beyond all reason. She had told Judge Hathorne of lines and curves that could be made to point out directions leading through the walls of space to other spaces beyond, and had implied that such lines and curves were frequently used at certain midnight meetings in the dark valley of the white stone beyond Meadow Hill and on the unpeopled island in the river. She had spoken also of the Black Man, of her oath, and of her new secret name of Nahab. Then she had drawn those devices on the walls of her cell and vanished.

"The hideous crone seized Gilman by the shoulder, yanking him out of bed and into empty space."

Weird Tales, July 1933

Gilman believed strange things about Keziah, and had felt a queer thrill on learning that her dwelling was still standing after more than two hundred and thirty-five years. When he heard the hushed Arkham whispers about Keziah's persistent presence in the old house and the narrow streets, about the irregular human tooth-marks left on certain sleepers in that and other houses, about the childish cries heard near May-Eve, and Hallowmass, about the stench often noted in the old house's attic just after those dreaded seasons, and about the small, furry, sharp-toothed thing which haunted the mouldering structure and the town and nuzzled people curiously in the black hours before dawn, he resolved to live in the place at any cost.

A room was easy to secure, for the house was unpopular, hard to rent, and long given over to cheap lodgings. Gilman could not have told what he expected to find there, but he knew he wanted to be in the building where some circumstance had more or less suddenly given a mediocre old woman of the Seventeenth Century an insight into mathematical depths perhaps beyond the utmost modern delvings of Planck, Heisenberg, Einstein, and de Sitter.

He studied the timber and plaster walls for traces of cryptic designs at every accessible spot where the paper had peeled, and within a week managed to get the eastern attic room where Keziah was held to have practised her spells. It had been vacant from the first—for no one had ever been willing to stay there long—but the Polish landlord had grown wary about renting it. Yet nothing whatever happened to Gilman till about the time of the fever. No ghostly Keziah flitted through the sombre halls and chambers, no small furry thing crept into his dismal eyrie to nuzzle him, and no record of the witch's incantations rewarded his constant search. Sometimes he would take walks through shadowy tangles of unpaved musty-smelling lanes where eldritch brown houses of unknown age leaned and tottered and leered mockingly through narrow, small-paned windows. Here he knew strange things had happened once, and there was a faint suggestion behind the surface that everything of that monstrous past might not — at least in the darkest, narrowest, and most intricately crooked alleys — have utterly perished. He also rowed out twice to the ill-regarded island in the river, and made a sketch of the singular angles described by the moss-grown rows of grey standing stones whose origin was so obscure and immemorial.

Gilman's room was of good size but queerly irregular shape; the north wall slating perceptibly inward from the outer to the inner end, while the low ceiling slanted gently downward in the same direction. Aside from an obvious rat-hole and the signs of other stopped-up ones, there was no access — nor any appearance of a former avenue of access — to the space which must have existed between the slanting wall and the straight outer wall on the house's north side, though a view from the exterior showed where a window had been boarded up at a very remote date. The loft above the ceiling — which must have had a slanting floor — was likewise inaccessible. When Gilman climbed up a ladder to the cob-webbed level loft above the rest of the attic he found vestiges of a bygone aperture tightly and heavily covered with ancient planking and secured by the stout wooden pegs common in Colonial carpentry. No amount of persuasion, however, could induce the stolid landlord to let him investigate either of these two closed spaces.

As time wore along, his absorption in the irregular wall and ceiling of his room increased; for he began to read into the odd angles a mathematical significance which seemed to offer vague clues regarding their purpose. Old Keziah, he reflected, might have had excellent reasons for living in a room with peculiar angles; for was it not through certain angles that she claimed to have gone outside the boundaries of the world of space we know? His interest gradually veered away from the unplumbed voids beyond the slanting surfaces, since it now appeared that the purpose of those surfaces concerned the side he was on.

The touch of brain-fever and the dreams began early in February. For some time, apparently, the curious angles of Gilman's room had been having a strange, almost hypnotic effect on him; and as the bleak winter advanced he had found himself staring more and more intently at the corner where the down-slanting ceiling met the inward-slanting wall. About this period his inability to concentrate on his formal studies worried him considerably, his apprehensions about the mid-year examinations being very acute. But the exaggerated sense of hearing was scarcely less annoying. Life had become an insistent and almost unendurable cacophony, and there was that constant, terrifying impression of other sounds — perhaps from regions beyond life — trembling on the very brink of audibility. So far as concrete noises went, the rats in the ancient partitions were the worst. Sometimes their scratching seemed not only furtive but deliberate. When it came from beyond the slanting north wall it was mixed with a sort of dry rattling; and when it came from the century-closed loft above the slanting ceiling Gilman always braced himself as if expecting some horror which only bided its time before descending to engulf him utterly.

The dreams were wholly beyond the pale of sanity, and Gilman fell that they must be a result, jointly, of his studies in mathematics and in folklore. He had been thinking too much about the vague regions which his formulae told him must lie beyond the three dimensions we know, and about the possibility that old Keziah Mason — guided by some influence past all conjecture — had actually found the gate to those regions. The yellowed county records containing her testimony and that of her accusers were so damnably suggestive of things beyond human experience — and the descriptions of the darting little furry object which served as her familiar were so painfully realistic despite their incredible details.

That object — no larger than a good-sized rat and quaintly called by the townspeople "Brown Jenkin" — seemed to have been the fruit of a remarkable case of sympathetic herd-delusion, for in 1692 no less than eleven persons had testified to glimpsing it. There were recent rumours, too, with a baffling and disconcerting amount of agreement. Witnesses said it had long hair and the shape of a rat, but that its sharp-toothed, bearded face was evilly human while its paws were like tiny human hands. It took messages betwixt old Keziah and the devil, and was nursed on the witch's blood, which it sucked like a vampire. Its voice was a kind of loathsome titter, and it could speak all languages. Of all the bizarre monstrosities in Gilman's dreams, nothing filled him with greater panic and nausea than this blasphemous and diminutive hybrid, whose image flitted across his vision in a form a thousandfold more hateful than anything his waking mind had deduced from the ancient records and the modern whispers.

Gilman's dreams consisted largely in plunges through limitless abysses of inexplicably coloured twilight and baffingly disordered sound; abysses whose material and gravitational properties, and whose relation to his own entity, he could not even begin to explain. He did not walk or climb, fly or swim, crawl or wriggle; yet always experienced a mode of motion partly voluntary and partly involuntary. Of his own condition he could not well judge, for sight of his arms, legs, and torso seemed always cut off by some odd disarrangement of perspective; but he felt that his physical organization and faculties were somehow marvellously transmuted and obliquely projected — though not without a certain grotesque relationship to his normal proportions and properties.

The abysses were by no means vacant, being crowded with indescribably angled masses of alien-hued substance, some of which appeared to be organic while others seemed inorganic. A few of the organic objects tended to awake vague memories in the back of his mind, though he could form no conscious idea of what they mockingly resembled or suggested. In the later dreams he began to distinguish separate categories into which the organic objects appeared to be divided, and which seemed to involve in each case a radically different species of conduct-pattern and basic motivation. Of these categories one seemed to him to include objects slightly less illogical and irrelevant in their motions than the members of the other categories.

All the objects — organic and inorganic alike — were totally beyond description or even comprehension. Gilman sometimes compared the inorganic matter to prisms, labyrinths, clusters of cubes and planes, and Cyclopean buildings; and the organic things struck him variously as groups of bubbles, octopi, centipedes, living Hindoo idols, and intricate arabesques roused into a kind of ophidian animation. Everything he saw was unspeakably menacing and horrible; and whenever one of the organic entities appeared by its motions to be noticing him, he felt a stark, hideous fright which generally jolted him awake. Of how the organic entities moved, he could tell no more than of how he moved himself. In time he observed a further mystery — the tendency of certain entities to appear suddenly out of empty space, or to disappear totally with equal suddenness. The shrieking, roaring confusion of sound which permeated the abysses was past all analysis as to pitch, timbre or rhythm; but seemed to be synchronous with vague visual changes in all the indefinite objects, organic and inorganic alike. Gilman had a constant sense of dread that it might rise to some unbearable degree of intensity during one or another of its obscure, relentlessly inevitable fluctuations.

But it was not in these vortices of complete alienage that he saw Brown Jenkin. That shocking little horror was reserved for certain lighter, sharper dreams which assailed him just before he dropped into the fullest depths of sleep. He would be lying in the dark fighting to keep awake when a faint lambent glow would seem to shimmer around the centuried room, showing in a violet mist the convergence of angled planes which had seized his brain so insidiously. The horror would appear to pop out of the rat-hole in the corner and patter toward him over the sagging, wide-planked floor with evil expectancy in its tiny, bearded human face; but mercifully, this dream always melted away before the object got close enough to nuzzle him. It had hellishly long, sharp, canine teeth; Gilman tried to stop up the rat-hole every day, but each night the real tenants of the partitions would gnaw away the obstruction, whatever it might be. Once he had the landlord nail a tin over it, but the next night the rats gnawed a fresh hole, in making which they pushed or dragged out into the room a curious little fragment of bone.

Gilman did not report his fever to the doctor, for he knew he could not pass the examinations if ordered to the college infirmary when every moment was needed for cramming. As it was, he failed in Calculus D and Advanced General Psychology, though not without hope of making up lost ground before the end of the term.

It was in March when the fresh element entered his lighter preliminary dreaming, and the nightmare shape of Brown Jenkin began to be companioned by the nebulous blur which grew more and more to resemble a bent old woman. This addition disturbed him more than he could account for, but finally he decided that it was like an ancient crone whom he had twice actually encountered in the dark tangle of lanes near the abandoned wharves. On those occasions the evil, sardonic, and seemingly unmotivated stare of the beldame had set him almost shivering — especially the first time when an overgrown rat darting across the shadowed mouth of a neighbouring alley had made him think irrationally of Brown Jenkin. Now, he reflected, those nervous fears were being mirrored in his disordered dreams. That the influence of the old house was unwholesome he could not deny, but traces of his early morbid interest still held him there. He argued that the fever alone was responsible for his nightly fantasies, and that when the touch abated he would be free from the monstrous visions. Those visions, however, were of absorbing vividness and convincingness, and whenever he awaked he retained a vague sense of having undergone much more than he remembered. He was hideously sure that in unrecalled dreams he had talked with both Brown Jenkin and the old woman, and that they had been urging him to go somewhere with them and to meet a third being of greater potency.

Toward the end of March he began to pick up in his mathematics, though the other studies bothered him increasingly. He was getting an intuitive knack for solving Riemannian equations, and astonished Professor Upham by his comprehension of fourth-dimensional and other problems which had floored all the rest of the class. One afternoon there was a discussion of possible freakish curvatures in space, and of theoretical points of approach or even contact between our part of the cosmos and various other regions as distant as the farthest stars or the transgalactic gulfs themselves — or even as fabulously remote as the tentatively conceivable cosmic units beyond the whole Einsteinian space-time continuum. Gilman's handling of this theme filled everyone with admiration, even though some of his hypothetical illustrations caused an increase in the always plentiful gossip about his nervous and solitary eccentricity. What made the students shake their heads was his sober theory that a man might — given mathematical knowledge admittedly beyond all likelihood of human acquirement — step deliberately from the earth to any other celestial body which might lie at one of an infinity of specific points in the cosmic pattern.

Such a step, he said, would require only two stages; first, a passage out of the three-dimensional sphere we know, and second, a passage back to the three-dimensional sphere at another point, perhaps one of infinite remoteness. That this could be accomplished without loss of life was in many cases conceivable. Any being from any part of three-dimensional space could probably survive in the fourth dimension; and its survival of the second stage would depend upon what alien part of three-dimensional space it might select for its re-entry. Denizens of some planets might be able to live on certain others — even planets belonging to other galaxies, or to similar dimensional phases of other space-time continua — though of course there must be vast numbers of mutually uninhabitable even though mathematically juxtaposed bodies or zones of space.

It was also possible that the inhabitants of a given dimensional realm could survive entry to many unknown and incomprehensible realms of additional or indefinitely multiplied dimensions — be they within or outside the given space-time continuum — and that the converse would be likewise true. This was a matter for speculation, though one could be fairly certain that the type of mutation involved in a passage from any given dimensional plane to the next higher one would not be destructive of biological integrity as we understand it. Gilman could not be very clear about his reasons for this last assumption, but his haziness here was more than overbalanced by his clearness on other complex points. Professor Upham especially liked his demonstration of the kinship of higher mathematics to certain phases of magical lore transmitted down the ages from an ineffable antiquity — human or pre-human — whose knowledge of the cosmos and its laws was greater than ours.

Around 1 April Gilman worried considerably because his slow fever did not abate. He was also troubled by what some of his fellow lodgers said about his sleep-walking. It seemed that he was often absent from his bed and that the creaking of his floor at certain hours of the night was remarked by the man in the room below. This fellow also spoke of hearing the tread of shod feet in the night; but Gilman was sure he must have been mistaken in this, since shoes as well as other apparel were always precisely in place in the morning. One could develop all sorts of aural delusions in this morbid old house — for did not Gilman himself, even in daylight, now feel certain that noises other than rat-scratching came from the black voids beyond the slanting wall and above the slanting ceiling? His pathologically sensitive ears began to listen for faint footfalls in the immemorially sealed loft overhead, and sometimes the illusion of such things was agonizingly realistic.

However, he knew that he had actually become a somnambulist; for twice at night his room had been found vacant, though with all his clothing in place. Of this he had been assured by Frank Elwood, the one fellow-student whose poverty forced him to room in this squalid and unpopular house. Elwood had been studying in the small hours and had come up for help on a differential equation, only to find Gilman absent. It had been rather presumptuous of him to open the unlocked door after knocking had failed to rouse a response, but he had needed the help very badly and thought that his host would not mind a gentle prodding awake. On neither occasion, though, had Gilman been there; and when told of the matter he wondered where he could have been wandering, barefoot and with only his night clothes on. He resolved to investigate the matter if reports of his sleep-walking continued, and thought of sprinkling flour on the floor of the corridor to see where his footsteps might lead. The door was the only conceivable egress, for there was no possible foothold outside the narrow window.

As April advanced, Gilman's fever-sharpened ears were disturbed by the whining prayers of a superstitious loom-fixer named Joe Mazurewicz who had a room on the ground floor. Mazurewicz had told long, rambling stories about the ghost of old Keziah and the furry sharp-fanged, nuzzling thing, and had said he was so badly haunted at times that only his silver crucifix — given him for the purpose by Father Iwanicki of St. Stanislaus' Church — could bring him relief. Now he was praying because the Witches' Sabbath was drawing near. May Eve was Walpurgis Night, when hell's blackest evil roamed the earth and all the slaves of Satan gathered for nameless rites and deeds. It was always a very bad time in Arkham, even though the fine folks up in Miskatonic Avenue and High and Saltonstall Streets pretended to know nothing about it. There would be bad doings, and a child or two would probably be missing. Joe knew about such things, for his grandmother in the old country had heard tales from her grandmother. It was wise to pray and count one's beads at this season. For three months Keziah and Brown Jenkin had not been near Joe's room, nor near Paul Choynski's room, nor anywhere else — and it meant no good when they held off like that. They must be up to something.

Gilman dropped in at the doctor's office on the sixteenth of the month, and was surprised to find his temperature was not as high as he had feared. The physician questioned him sharply, and advised him to see a nerve specialist. On reflection, he was glad he had not consulted the still more inquisitive college doctor. Old Waldron, who had curtailed his activities before, would have made him take a rest — an impossible thing now that he was so close to great results in his equations. He was certainly near the boundary between the known universe and the fourth dimension, and who could say how much farther he might go?

But even as these thoughts came to him he wondered at the source of his strange confidence. Did all of this perilous sense of imminence come from the formulae on the sheets he covered day by day? The soft, stealthy, imaginary footsteps in the sealed loft above were unnerving. And now, too, there was a growing feeling that somebody was constantly persuading him to do something terrible which he could not do. How about the somnambulism? Where did he go sometimes in the night? And what was that faint suggestion of sound which once in a while seemed to trickle through the confusion of identifiable sounds even in broad daylight and full wakefulness? Its rhythm did not correspond to anything on earth, unless perhaps to the cadence of one or two unmentionable Sabbat-chants, and sometimes he feared it corresponded to certain attributes of the vague shrieking or roaring in those wholly alien abysses of dream.

The dreams were meanwhile getting to be atrocious. In the lighter preliminary phase the evil old woman was now of fiendish distinctness, and Gilman knew she was the one who had frightened him in the slums. Her bent back, long nose, and shrivelled chin were unmistakable, and her shapeless brown garments were like those he remembered. The expression on her face was one of hideous malevolence and exultation, and when he awaked he could recall a croaking voice that persuaded and threatened. He must meet the Black Man and go with them all to the throne of Azathoth at the centre of ultimate chaos. That was what she said. He must sign the book of Azathoth in his own blood and take a new secret name now that his independent delvings had gone so far. What kept him from going with her and Brown Jenkin and the other to the throne of Chaos where the thin flutes pipe mindlessly was the fact that he had seen the name "Azathoth" in the *Necronomicon*, and knew it stood for a primal evil too horrible for description.

The old woman always appeared out of thin air near the corner where the downward slant met the inward slant. She seemed to crystallize at a point closer to the ceiling than to the floor, and every night she was a little nearer and more distinct before the dream shifted. Brown Jenkin, too, was always a little nearer at the last, and its yellowish-white fangs glistened shockingly in that unearthly violet phosphorescence. Its shrill loathsome tittering struck more and more into Gilman's head, and he could remember in the morning how it had pronounced the words "Azathoth" and "Nyarlathotep."

In the deeper dreams everything was likewise more distinct, and Gilman felt that the twilight abysses around him were those of the fourth dimension. Those organic entities whose motions seemed least flagrantly irrelevant and unmotivated were probably projections of life-forms from our own planet, including human beings. What the others were in their own dimensional sphere or spheres he dared not try to think. Two of the less irrelevantly moving things — a rather large congeries of iridescent, prolately spheroidal bubbles and a very much smaller polyhedron of unknown colours and rapidly shifting surface angles — seemed to take notice of him and follow him about or float ahead as he changed position among the titan prisms, labyrinths, cube-and-plane clusters and quasi-buildings; and all the while the vague shrieking and roaring waxed louder and louder, as if approaching some monstrous climax of utterly unendurable intensity.

During the night of 19–20 April the new development occurred. Gilman was half involuntarily moving about in the twilight abysses with the bubble-mass and the small polyhedron floating ahead when he noticed the peculiarly regular angles formed by the edges of some gigantic neighbouring prism-clusters. In another second he was out of the abyss and standing tremulously on a rocky hillside bathed in intense, diffused green light. He was barefooted and in his nightclothes, and when he tried to walk discovered that he could scarcely lift his feet. A swirling vapour hid everything but the immediate sloping terrain from sight, and he shrank from the thought of the sounds, that might surge out of that vapour.

Then he saw the two shapes laboriously crawling toward him — the old woman and the little furry thing. The crone strained up to her knees and managed to cross her arms in a singular fashion, while Brown Jenkin pointed in a certain direction with a horribly anthropoid forepaw which it raised with evident difficulty. Spurred by an impulse he did not originate, Gilman dragged himself forward along a course determined by the angle of the old woman's arms and the direction of the small monstrosity's paw, and before he had shuffled three steps he was back in the twilight abysses. Geometrical shapes seethed around him, and he fell dizzily and interminably. At last he woke in his bed in the crazily angled garret of the eldritch old house.

He was good for nothing that morning, and stayed away from all his classes. Some unknown attraction was pulling his eyes in a seemingly irrelevant direction, for he could not help staring at a certain vacant spot on the floor. As the day advanced, the focus of his unseeing eyes changed position, and by noon he had conquered the impulse to stare at vacancy. About two o'clock he went out for lunch and as he threaded the narrow lanes of the city he found himself turning always to the southeast. Only an effort halted him at a cafeteria in Church Street, and after the meal he felt the unknown pull still more strongly.

He would have to consult a nerve specialist after all — perhaps there was a connection with his somnambulism — but meanwhile he might at least try to break the morbid spell himself. Undoubtedly he could still manage to walk away from the pull, so with great resolution he headed against it and dragged himself deliberately north along Garrison Street. By the time he had reached the bridge over the Miskatonic he was in a cold perspiration, and he clutched at the iron railing as he gazed upstream at the ill-regarded island whose regular lines of ancient standing stones brooded sullenly in the afternoon sunlight.

Then he gave a start. For there was a clearly visible living figure on that desolate island, and a second glance told him it was certainly the strange old woman whose sinister aspect had worked itself so disastrously into his dreams. The tall grass near her was moving, too, as if some other living thing were crawling close to the ground. When the old woman began to turn toward him he fled precipitately off the bridge and into the shelter of the town's labyrinthine waterfront alleys. Distant though the island was, he felt that a monstrous and invincible evil could flow from the sardonic stare of that bent, ancient figure in brown.

The southeastward pull still held, and only with tremendous resolution could Gilman drag himself into the old house and up the rickety stairs. For hours he sat silent and aimless, with his eyes shifting gradually westward. About six o'clock his sharpened ears caught the whining prayers of Joe Mazurewicz two floors below, and in desperation he seized his hat and walked out into the sunset-golden streets, letting the now directly southward pull carry him where it might. An hour later darkness found him in the open fields beyond Hangman's Brook, with the glimmering spring stars shining ahead. The urge to walk was gradually changing to an urge to leap mystically into space, and suddenly he realized just where the source of the pull lay.

It was in the sky. A definite point among the stars had a claim on him and was calling him. Apparently it was a point somewhere between Hydra and Argo Navis, and he knew that he had been urged toward it ever since he had awaked soon after dawn. In the morning it had been underfoot, and now it was roughly south but stealing toward the west. What was the meaning of this new thing? Was he going mad? How long would it last? Again mustering his resolution, Gilman turned and dragged himself back to the sinister old house.

Mazurewicz was waiting for him at the door, and seemed both anxious and reluctant to whisper some fresh bit of superstition. It was about the witch-light. Joe had been out celebrating the night before — and it was Patriots' Day in Massachusetts — and had come home after midnight. Looking up at the house from outside, he had thought at first that Gilman's window was dark, but then he had seen the faint violet glow within. He wanted to warn the gentleman about that glow, for everybody in Arkham knew it was Keziah's witch-light which played near Brown Jenkin and the ghost of the old crone herself. He had not mentioned this before, but now he must tell about it because it meant that Keziah and her long-toothed familiar were haunting the young gentleman. Sometimes he and Paul Choynski and Landlord Dombrowski thought they saw that light seeping out of cracks in the sealed loft above the young gentleman's room, but they had all agreed not to talk about that. However, it would be better for the gentleman to take another room and get a crucifix from some good priest like Father Iwanicki.

As the man rambled on, Gilman felt a nameless panic clutch at his throat. He knew that Joe must have been half drunk when he came home the night before; yet the mention of a violet light in the garret window was of frightful import. It was a lambent glow of this sort which always played about the old woman and the small furry thing in those lighter, sharper dreams which prefaced his plunge into unknown abysses, and the thought that a wakeful second person could see the dream-luminance was utterly beyond sane harborage. Yet where had the fellow got such an odd notion? Had he himself talked as well as walked around the house in his sleep? No, Joe said, he had not — but he must check up on this. Perhaps Frank Elwood could tell him something, though he hated to ask.

Fever — wild dreams — somnambulism — illusions of sounds — a pull toward a point in the sky — and now a suspicion of insane sleep-talking! He must stop studying, see a nerve specialist, and take himself in hand. When he climbed to the second storey he paused at Elwood's door but saw that the other youth was out. Reluctantly he continued up to his garret room and sat down in the dark. His gaze was still pulled to the southward, but he also found himself listening intently for some sound in the closed loft above, and half imagining that an evil violet light seeped down through an infinitesimal crack in the low, slanting ceiling.

That night as Gilman slept, the violet light broke upon him with heightened intensity, and the old witch and small furry thing, getting closer than ever before, mocked him with inhuman squeals and devilish gestures. He was glad to sink into the vaguely roaring twilight abysses, though the pursuit of that iridescent bubble-congeries and that kaleidoscopic little polyhedron was menacing and irritating. Then came the shift as vast converging planes of a slippery-looking substance loomed above and below him — a shift which ended in a flash of delirium and a blaze of unknown, alien light in which yellow, carmine, and indigo were madly and inextricably blended.

He was half lying on a high, fantastically balustraded terrace above a boundless jungle of outlandish, incredible peaks, balanced planes, domes, minarets, horizontal disks poised on pinnacles, and numberless forms of still greater wildness — some of stone and some of metal — which glittered gorgeously in the mixed, almost blistering glare from a poly-chromatic sky. Looking upward he saw three stupendous disks of flame, each of a different hue, and at a different height above an infinitely distant curving horizon of low mountains. Behind him tiers of higher terraces towered aloft as far as he could see. The city below stretched away to the limits of vision, and he hoped that no sound would well up from it.

The pavement from which he easily raised himself was a veined polished stone beyond his power to identify, and the tiles were cut in bizarre-angled shapes which struck him as less asymmetrical than based on some unearthly symmetry whose laws he could not comprehend. The balustrade was chest-high, delicate, and fantastically wrought, while along the rail were ranged at short intervals little figures of grotesque design and exquisite workmanship. They, like the whole balustrade, seemed to be made of some sort of shining metal whose colour could not be guessed in the chaos of mixed effulgences, and their nature utterly defied conjecture. They represented some ridged barrel-shaped objects with thin horizontal arms radiating spoke-like from a central ring and with vertical knobs or bulbs projecting from the head and base of the barrel. Each of these knobs was the hub of a system of five long, flat, triangularly tapering arms arranged around it like the arms of a starfish — nearly horizontal, but curving slightly away from the central barrel. The base of the bottom knob was fused to the long railing with so delicate a point of contact that several figures had been broken off and were missing. The figures were about four and a half inches in height, while the spiky arms gave them a maximum diameter of about two and a half inches.

When Gilman stood up, the tiles felt hot to his bare feet. He was wholly alone, and his first act was to walk to the balustrade and look dizzily down at the endless, Cyclopean city almost two thousand feet below. As he listened he thought a rhythmic confusion of faint musical pipings covering a wide tonal range welled up from the narrow streets beneath, and he wished he might discern the denizens of the place. The sight turned him giddy after a while, so that he would have fallen to the pavement had he not clutched instinctively at the lustrous balustrade. His right hand fell on one of the projecting figures, the touch seeming to steady him slightly. It was too much, however, for the exotic delicacy of the metal-work, and the spiky figure snapped off under his grasp. Still half dazed, he continued to clutch it as his other hand seized a vacant space on the smooth railing.

But now his over-sensitive ears caught something behind him, and he looked back across the level terrace. Approaching him softly though without apparent furtiveness were five figures, two of which were the sinister old woman and the fanged, furry little animal. The other three were what sent him unconscious; for they were living entities about eight feet high, shaped precisely like the spiky images on the balustrade, and propelling themselves by a spider-like wriggling of their lower set of starfish-arms.

Gilman awoke in his bed, drenched by a cold perspiration and with a smarting sensation in his face, hands and feet. Springing to the floor, he washed and dressed in frantic haste, as if it were necessary for him to get out of the house as quickly as possible. He did not know where he wished to go, but felt that once more he would have to sacrifice his classes. The odd pull toward that spot in the sky between Hydra and Argo had abated, but another of even greater strength had taken its place. Now he felt that he must go north — infinitely north. He dreaded to cross the bridge that gave a view of the desolate island in the Miskatonic, so went over the Peabody Avenue bridge. Very often he stumbled, for his eyes and ears were chained to an extremely lofty point in the blank blue sky.

After about an hour he got himself under better control, and saw that he was far from the city. All around him stretched the bleak emptiness of salt marshes, while the narrow road ahead led to Innsmouth — that ancient, half-deserted town which Arkham people were so curiously unwilling to visit. Though the northward pull had not diminished, he resisted it as he had resisted the other pull, and finally found that he could almost balance the one against the other. Plodding back to town and getting some coffee at a soda fountain, he dragged himself into the public library and browsed aimlessly among the lighter magazines. Once he met some friends who remarked how oddly sunburned he looked, but he did not tell them of his walk. At three o'clock he took some lunch at a restaurant, noting meanwhile that the pull had either lessened or divided itself. After that he killed the time at a cheap cinema show, seeing the inane performance over and over again without paying any attention to it.

About nine at night he drifted homeward and shuffled into the ancient house. Joe Mazurewicz was whining unintelligible prayers, and Gilman hastened up to his own garret chamber without pausing to see if Elwood was in. It was when he turned on the feeble electric light that the shock came. At once he saw there was something on the table which did not belong there, and a second look left no room for doubt. Lying on its side — for it could not stand up alone — was the exotic spiky figure which in his monstrous dream he had broken off the fantastic balustrade. No detail was missing. The ridged, barrel-shaped center, the thin radiating arms, the knobs at each end, and the flat, slightly outward-curving starfish-arms spreading from those knobs — all were there. In the electric light the colour seemed to be a kind of iridescent grey veined with green; and Gilman could see amidst his horror and bewilderment that one of the knobs ended in a jagged break, corresponding to its former point of attachment to the dream-railing.

Only his tendency toward a dazed stupor prevented him from screaming aloud. This fusion of dream and reality was too much to bear. Still dazed, he clutched at the spiky thing and staggered downstairs to Landlord Dombrowski's quarters. The whining prayers of the superstitious loom-fixer were still sounding through the mouldy halls, but Gilman did not mind them now.

The landlord was in, and greeted him pleasantly. No, he had not seen that thing before and did not know anything about it. But his wife had said she found a funny tin thing in one of the beds when she fixed the rooms at noon, and maybe that was it. Dombrowski called her, and she waddled in. Yes, that was the thing. She had found it in the young gentleman's bed — on the side next the wall. It had looked very queer to her, but of course the young gentleman had lots of queer things in his room — books and curios and pictures and markings on paper. She certainly knew nothing about it.

So Gilman climbed upstairs again in mental turmoil, convinced that he was either still dreaming or that his somnambulism had run to incredible extremes and led him to depredations in unknown places. Where had he got this outré thing? He did not recall seeing it in any museum in Arkham. It must have been somewhere, though; and the sight of it as he snatched it in his sleep must have caused the odd dream-picture of the balustraded terrace. Next day he would make some very guarded inquiries — and perhaps see the nerve specialist.

Meanwhile he would try to keep track of his somnambulism. As he went upstairs and across the garret hall he sprinkled about some flour which he had borrowed — with a frank admission as to its purpose — from the landlord. He had stopped at Elwood's door on the way, but had found all dark within. Entering his room, he placed the spiky thing on the table, and lay down in complete mental and physical exhaustion without pausing to undress. From the closed loft above the slating ceiling he thought he heard a faint scratching and padding, but he was too disorganized even to mind it. That cryptical pull from the north was getting very strong again, though it seemed now to come from a lower place in the sky.

In the dazzling violet light of dream the old woman and the fanged, furry thing came again and with a greater distinctness than on any former occasion. This time they actually reached him, and he felt the crone's withered claws clutching at him. He was pulled out of bed and into empty space, and for a moment he heard a rhythmic roaring and saw the twilight amorphousness of the vague abysses seething around him. But that moment was very brief, for presently he was in a crude, windowless little space with rough beams and planks rising to a peak just above his head, and with a curious slanting floor underfoot. Propped level on that floor were low cases full of books of every degree of antiquity and disintegration, and in the centre were a table and bench, both apparently fastened in place. Small objects of unknown shape and nature were ranged on the tops of the cases, and in the flaming violet light Gilman thought he saw a counterpart of the spiky image which had puzzled him so horribly. On the left the floor fell abruptly away, leaving a black triangular gulf out of which, after a second's dry rattling, there presently climbed the hateful little furry thing with the yellow fangs and bearded human face.

The evilly-grinning beldame still clutched him, and beyond the table stood a figure he had never seen before — a tall, lean man of dead black colouration but without the slightest sign of negroid features: wholly devoid of either hair or beard, and wearing as his only garment a shapeless robe of some heavy black fabric. His feet were indistinguishable because of the table and bench, but he must have been shod, since there was a clicking whenever he changed position. The man did not speak, and bore no trace of expression on his small, regular features. He merely pointed to a book of prodigious size which lay open on the table, while the beldame thrust a huge grey quill into Gilman's right hand. Over everything was a pall of intensely maddening fear, and the climax was reached when the furry thing ran up the dreamer's clothing to his shoulders and then down his left arm, finally biting him sharply in the wrist just below his cuff. As the blood spurted from this wound Gilman lapsed into a faint.

He awaked on the morning of the twenty-second with a pain in his left wrist, and saw that his cuff was brown with dried blood. His recollections were very confused, but the scene with the black man in the unknown space stood out vividly. The rats must have bitten him as he slept, giving rise to the climax of that frightful dream. Opening the door, he saw that the flour on the corridor floor was undisturbed except for the huge prints of the loutish fellow who roomed at the other end of the garret. So he had not been sleep-walking this time. But something would have to be done about those rats. He would speak to the landlord about them. Again he tried to stop up the hole at the base of the slanting wall, wedging in a candlestick which seemed of about the right size. His ears were ringing horribly, as if with the residual echoes of some horrible noise heard in dreams.

As he bathed and changed clothes he tried to recall what he had dreamed after the scene in the violet-litten space, but nothing definite would crystallize in his mind. That scene itself must have corresponded to the sealed loft overhead, which had begun to attack his imagination so violently, but later impressions were faint and hazy. There were suggestions of the vague, twilight abysses, and of still vaster, blacker abysses beyond them — abysses in which all fixed suggestions were absent. He had been taken there by the bubble-congeries and the little polyhedron which always dogged him; but they, like himself, had changed to wisps of mist in this farther void of ultimate blackness. Something else had gone on ahead — a larger wisp which now and then condensed into nameless approximations of form — and he thought that their progress had not been in a straight line, but rather along the alien curves and spirals of some ethereal vortex which obeyed laws unknown to the physics and mathematics of any conceivable cosmos. Eventually there had been a hint of vast, leaping shadows, of a monstrous, half-acoustic pulsing, and of the thin, monotonous piping of an unseen flute — but that was all. Gilman decided he had picked up that last conception from what he had read in the *Necronomicon* about the mindless entity Azathoth, which rules all time and space from a black throne at the centre of Chaos.

When the blood was washed away the wrist wound proved very slight, and Gilman puzzled over the location of the two tiny punctures. It occurred to him that there was no blood on the bedspread where he had lain — which was very curious in view of the amount on his skin and cuff. Had he been sleep-walking within his room, and had the rat bitten him as he sat in some chair or paused in some less rational position? He looked in every corner for brownish drops or stains, but did not find any. He had better, he thought, spinkle flour within the room as well as outside the door — though after all no further proof of his sleep-walking was needed. He knew he did walk and the thing to do now was to stop it. He must ask Frank Elwood for help. This morning the strange pulls from space seemed lessened, though they were replaced by another sensation even more inexplicable. It was a vague, insistent impulse to fly away from his present situation, but held not a hint of the specific direction in which he wished to fly. As he picked up the strange spiky image on the table he thought the older northward pull grew a trifle stronger; but even so, it was wholly overruled by the newer and more bewildering urge.

He took the spiky image down to Elwood's room, steeling himself against the whines of the loom-fixer which welled up from the ground floor. Elwood was in, thank heaven, and appeared to be stirring about. There was time for a little conversation before leaving for breakfast and college, so Gilman hurriedly poured forth an account of his recent dreams and fears. His host was very sympathetic, and agreed that something ought to be done. He was shocked by his guest's drawn, haggard aspect, and noticed the queer, abnormal-looking sunburn which others had remarked during the past week.

There was not much, though, that he could say. He had not seen Gilman on any sleep-walking expedition, and had no idea what the curious image could be. He had, though, heard the French-Canadian who lodged just under Gilman talking to Mazurewicz one evening. They were telling each other how badly they dreaded the coming of Walpurgis Night, now only a few days off; and were exchanging pitying comments about the poor, doomed young gentleman. Desrochers, the fellow under Gilman's room, had spoken of nocturnal footsteps shod and unshod, and of the violet light he saw one night when he had stolen fearfully up to peer through Gilman's keyhole. He had not dared to peer, he told Mazurewicz, after he had glimpsed that light through the cracks around the door. There had been soft talking, too — and as he began to describe it his voice had sunk to an inaudible whisper.

Elwood could not imagine what had set these superstitious creatures gossiping, but supposed their imaginations had been roused by Gilman's late hours and somnolent walking and talking on the one hand, and by the nearness of traditionally-feared May Eve on the other hand. That Gilman talked in his sleep was plain, and it was obviously from Desrochers' keyhole listenings that the delusive notion of the violet dream-light had got abroad. These simple people were quick to imagine they had seen any odd thing they had heard about. As for a plan of action — Gilman had better move down to Elwood's room and avoid sleeping alone. Elwood would, if awake, rouse him whenever he began to talk or rise in his sleep. Very soon, too, he must see the specialist. Meanwhile they would take the spiky image around to the various museums and to certain professors; seeking identification and stating that it had been found in a public rubbish-can. Also, Dombrowski must attend to the poisoning of those rats in the walls.

Braced up by Elwood's companionship, Gilman attended classes that day. Strange urges still tugged at him, but he could sidetrack them with considerable success. During a free period he showed the queer image to several professors, all of whom were intensely interested, though none of them could shed any light upon its nature or origin. That night he slept on a couch which Elwood had had the landlord bring to the second storey room, and for the first time in weeks was wholly free from disquieting dreams. But the feverishness still hung on, and the whines of the loom-fixer were an unnerving influence.

During the next few days Gilman enjoyed an almost perfect immunity from morbid manifestations. He had, Elwood said, showed no tendency to talk or rise in his sleep; and meanwhile the landlord was putting rat-poison everywhere. The only disturbing element was the talk among the superstitious foreigners, whose imaginations had become highly excited. Mazurewicz was always trying to make him get a crucifix, and finally forced one upon him which he said had been blessed by the good Father Iwanicki. Desrochers, too, had something to say; in fact, he insisted that cautious steps had sounded in the now vacant room above him on the first and second nights of Gilman's absence from it. Paul Choynski thought he heard sounds in the halls and on the stairs at night, and claimed that his door had been softly tried, while Mrs. Dombrowski vowed she had seen Brown Jenkin for the first time since All-Hallows. But such naïve reports could mean very little, and Gilman let the cheap metal crucifix hang idly from a knob on his host's dresser.

For three days Gilman and Elwood canvassed the local museums in an effort to identify the strange spiky image, but always without success. In every quarter, however, interest was intense; for the utter alienage of the thing was a tremendous challenge to scientific curiosity. One of the small radiating arms was broken off and subjected to chemical analysis. Professor Ellery found platinum, iron and tellurium in the strange alloy; but mixed with these were at least three other apparent elements of high atomic weight which chemistry was absolutely powerless to classify. Not only did they fail to correspond with any known element, but they did not even fit the vacant places reserved for probable elements in the periodic system. The mystery remains unsolved to this day, though the image is on exhibition at the museum of Miskatonic University.

On the morning of April twenty-seventh a fresh rat-hole appeared in the room where Gilman was a guest, but Dombrowski tinned it up during the day. The poison was not having much effect, for scratchings and scurryings in the walls were virtually undiminished.

Elwood was out late that night, and Gilman waited up for him. He did not wish to go to sleep in a room alone — especially since he thought he had glimpsed in the evening twilight the repellent old woman whose image had become so horribly transferred to his dreams. He wondered who she was, and what had been near her rattling the tin can in a rubbish-heap at the mouth of a squalid courtyard. The crone had seemed to notice him and leer evilly at him — though perhaps this was merely his imagination.

The next day both youths felt very tired, and knew they would sleep like logs when night came. In the evening they drowsily discussed the mathematical studies which had so completely and perhaps harmfully engrossed Gilman, and speculated about the linkage with ancient magic and folklore which seemed so darkly probable. They spoke of old Keziah Mason, and Elwood agreed that Gilman had good scientific grounds for thinking she might have stumbled on strange and significant information. The hidden cults to which these witches belonged often guarded and handed down surprising secrets from elder, forgotten eons; and it was by no means impossible that Keziah had actually mastered the art of passing through dimensional gates. Tradition emphasizes the uselessness of material barriers in halting a witch's notions, and who can say what underlies the old tales of broomstick rides through the night?

Whether a modern student could ever gain similar powers from mathematical research alone, was still to be seen. Success, Gilman added, might lead to dangerous and unthinkable situations, for who could foretell the conditions pervading an adjacent but normally inaccessible dimension? On the other hand, the picturesque possibilities were enormous. Time could not exist in certain belts of space, and by entering and remaining in such a belt one might preserve one's life and age indefinitely; never suffering organic metabolism or deterioration except for slight amounts incurred during visits to one's own or similar planes. One might, for example, pass into a timeless dimension and emerge at some remote period of the earth's history as young as before.

Whether anybody had ever managed to do this, one could hardly conjecture with any degree of authority. Old legends are hazy and ambiguous, and in historic times all attempts at crossing forbidden gaps seem complicated by strange and terrible alliances with beings and messengers from outside. There was the immemorial figure of the deputy or messenger of hidden and terrible powers — the "Black Man" of the witch-cult, and the "Nyarlathotep" of the *Necronomicon*. There was, too, the baffling problem of the lesser messengers or intermediaries — the quasi-animals and queer hybrids which legend depicts as witches' familiars. As Gilman and Elwood retired, too sleepy to argue further, they heard Joe Mazurewicz reel into the house half drunk, and shuddered at the desperate wildness of his whining prayers.

That night Gilman saw the violet light again. In his dream he had heard a scratching and gnawing in the partitions, and thought that someone fumbled clumsily at the latch. Then he saw the old woman and the small furry thing advancing toward him over the carpeted floor. The beldame's face was alight with inhuman exultation, and the little yellow-toothed morbidity tittered mockingly as it pointed at the heavily-sleeping form of Elwood on the other couch across the room. A paralysis of fear stifled all attempts to cry out. As once before, the hideous crone seized Gilman by the shoulders, yanking him out of bed and into empty space. Again the infinitude of the shrieking abysses flashed past him, but in another second he thought he was in a dark, muddy, unknown alley of foetid odors with the rotting walls of ancient houses towering up on every hand.

Ahead was the robed black man he had seen in the peaked space in the other dream, while from a lesser distance the old woman was beckoning and grimacing imperiously. Brown Jenkin was rubbing itself with a kind of affectionate playfulness around the ankles of the black man, which the deep mud largely concealed. There was a dark open doorway on the right, to which the black man silently pointed. Into this the grinning crone started, dragging Gilman after her by his pajama sleeves. There were evil-smelling staircases which creaked ominously, and on which the old woman seemed to radiate a faint violet light; and finally a door leading off a landing. The crone fumbled with the latch and pushed the door open, motioning to Gilman to wait, and disappearing inside the black aperture.

The youth's over-sensitive ears caught a hideous strangled cry, and presently the beldame came out of the room bearing a small, senseless form which she thrust at the dreamer as if ordering him to carry it. The sight of this form, and the expression on its face, broke the spell. Still too dazed to cry out, he plunged recklessly down the noisome staircase and into the mud outside, halting only when seized and choked by the waiting black man. As consciousness departed he heard the faint, shrill tittering of the fanged, rat-like abnormality.

On the morning of the twenty-ninth Gilman awaked into a maelstrom of horror. The instant he opened his eyes he knew something was terribly wrong, for he was back in his old garret room with the slanting wall and ceiling, sprawled on the now unmade bed. His throat was aching inexplicably, and as he struggled to a sitting posture he saw with growing fright that his feet and pajama bottoms were brown with caked mud. For the moment his recollections were hopelessly hazy, but he knew at least that he must have been sleep-walking. Elwood had been lost too deeply in slumber to hear and stop him. On the floor were confused muddy prints, but oddly enough they did not extend all the way to the door. The more Gilman looked at them, the more peculiar they seemed; for in addition to those he could recognize as his there were some smaller, almost round markings — such as the legs of a large chair or a table might make, except that most of them tended to be divided into halves. There were also some curious muddy rat-tracks leading out of a fresh hole and back into it again. Utter bewilderment and the fear of madness racked Gilman as he staggered to the door and saw that there were no muddy prints outside. The more he remembered of his hideous dream the more terrified he felt, and it added to his desperation to hear Joe Mazurewicz chanting mournfully two floors below.

Descending to Elwood's room he roused his still-sleeping host and began telling of how he had found himself, but Elwood could form no idea of what might really have happened. Where Gilman could have been, how he got back to his room without making tracks in the hall, and how the muddy, furniture-like prints came to be mixed with his in the garret chamber, were wholly beyond conjecture. Then there were those dark, livid marks on his throat, as if he had tried to strangle himself. He put his hands up to them, but found that they did not even approximately fit. While they were talking, Desrochers dropped in to say that he had heard a terrific clattering overhead in the dark small hours. No, there had been no one on the stairs after midnight, though just before midnight he had heard faint footfalls in the garret, and cautiously descending steps he did not like. It was, he added, a very bad time of year for Arkham. The young gentleman had better be sure to wear the crucifix Joe Mazurewicz had given him. Even the daytime was not safe, for after dawn there had been strange sounds in the house — especially a thin, childish wail hastily choked off.

Gilman mechanically attended classes that morning, but was wholly unable to fix his mind on his studies. A mood of hideous apprehension and expectancy had seized him, and he seemed to be awaiting the fall of some annihilating blow. At noon he lunched at the University spa, picking up a paper from the next seat as he waited for dessert. But he never ate that dessert; for an item on the paper's first page left him limp, wild-eyed, and able only to pay his check and stagger back to Elwood's room.

There had been a strange kidnapping the night before in Orne's Gangway, and the two-year-old child of a clod-like laundry worker named Anastasia Wolejko had completely vanished from sight. The mother, it appeared, had feared the event for some time; but the reasons she assigned for her fear were so grotesque that no one took them seriously. She had, she said, seen Brown Jenkin about the place now and then ever since early in March, and knew from its grimaces and titterings that little Ladislas must be marked for sacrifice at the awful Sabbat on Walpurgis Night. She had asked her neighbour Mary Czanek to sleep in the room and try to protect the child, but Mary had not dared. She could not tell the police, for they never believed such things. Children had been taken that way every year ever since she could remember. And her friend Pete Stowacki would not help because he wanted the child out of the way.

But what threw Gilman into a cold perspiration was the report of a pair of revellers who had been walking past the mouth of the gangway just after midnight. They admitted they had been drunk, but both vowed they had seen a crazily dressed trio furtively entering the dark passageway. There had, they said, been a huge robed negro, a little old woman in rags, and a young white man in his night-clothes. The old woman had been dragging the youth, while around the feet of the negro a tame rat was rubbing and weaving in the brown mud.

Gilman sat in a daze all the afternoon, and Elwood — who had meanwhile seen the papers and formed terrible conjectures from them — found him thus when he came home. This time neither could doubt but that something hideously serious was closing in around them. Between the phantasms of nightmare and the realities of the objective world a monstrous and unthinkable relationship was crystallizing, and only stupendous vigilance could avert still more direful developments. Gilman must see a specialist sooner or later, but not just now, when all the papers were full of this kidnapping business.

Just what had really happened was maddeningly obscure, and for a moment both Gilman and Elwood exchanged whispered theories of the wildest kind. Had Gilman unconsciously succeeded better than he knew in his studies of space and its dimensions? Had he actually slipped outside our sphere to points unguessed and unimaginable? Where — if anywhere — had he been on those nights of demoniac alienage? The roaring twilight abysses — the green hillside — the blistering terrace — the pulls from the stars — the ultimate black vortex — the black man — the muddy alley and the stairs — the old witch and the fanged, furry horror — the bubble-congeries and the little polyhedron — the strange sunburn — the wrist-wound — the unexplained image — the muddy feet — the throat marks — the tales and fears of the superstitious foreigners — what did all this mean? To what extent could the laws of sanity apply to such a case?

There was no sleep for either of them that night, but next day they both cut classes and drowsed. This was April thirtieth, and with the dusk would come the hellish Sabbat-time which all the foreigners and the superstitious old folk feared. Mazurewicz came home at six o'clock and said people at the mill were whispering that the Walpurgis revels would be held in the dark ravine beyond Meadow Hill where the old white stone stands in a place queerly devoid of all plant-life. Some of them had even told the police and advised them to look there for the missing Wolejko child, but they did not believe anything would be done. Joe insisted that the poor young gentleman wear his nickel-chained crucifix, and Gilman put it on and dropped it inside his shirt to humour the fellow.

Late at night the two youths sat drowsing in their chairs, lulled by the praying of the loom-fixer on the floor below. Gilman listened as he nodded, his preternaturally sharpened hearing seeming to strain for some subtle, dreaded murmur beyond the noises in the ancient house. Unwholesome recollections of things in the *Necronomicon* and the *Black Book* welled up, and he found himself swaying to infandous rhythms said to pertain to the blackest ceremonies of the Sabbat and to have an origin outside the time and space we comprehend.

Presently he realized what he was listening for — the hellish chant of the celebrants in the distant black valley. How did he know so much about what they expected? How did he know the time when Nahab and her acolyte were due to bear the brimming bowl which would follow the black cock and the black goat? He saw that Elwood had dropped asleep, and tried to call out and waken him. Something, however, closed his throat. He was not his own master. Had he signed the black man's book after all?

Then his fevered, abnormal hearing caught the distant, windborne notes. Over miles of hill and field and alley they came, but he recognized them none the less. The fires must be lit, and the dancers must be starting in. How could he keep himself from going? What was it that had enmeshed him? Mathematics — folklore — the house — old Keziah — Brown Jenkin . . . and now he saw that there was a fresh rat-hole in the wall near his couch. Above the distant chanting and the nearer praying of Joe Mazurewicz came another sound — a stealthy, determined scratching in the partitions. He hoped the electric lights would not go out. Then he saw the fanged, bearded little face in the rat-hole — the accursed little face which he at last realized bore such a shocking, mocking resemblance to old Keziah's — and heard the faint fumbling at the door.

The screaming twilight abysses flashed before him, and he felt himself helpless in the formless grasp of the iridescent bubble-congeries. Ahead raced the small, kaleidoscopic polyhedron and all through the churning void there was a heightening and acceleration of the vague tonal pattern which seemed to foreshadow some unutterable and unendurable climax. He seemed to know what was coming — the monstrous burst of Walpurgis-rhythm in whose cosmic timbre would be concentrated all the primal, ultimate space-time seethings which lie behind the massed spheres of matter and sometimes break forth in measured reverberations that penetrate faintly to every layer of entity and give hideous significance throughout the worlds to certain dreaded periods.

But all this vanished in a second. He was again in the cramped, violet-litten peaked space with the slanting floor, the low cases of ancient books, the bench and table, the queer objects, and the triangular gulf at one side. On the table lay a small white figure — an infant boy, unclothed and unconscious — while on the other side stood the monstrous, leering old woman with a gleaming, grotesque-hafted knife in her right hand, and a queerly proportioned pale metal bowl covered with curiously chased designs and having delicate lateral handles in her left. She was intoning some croaking ritual in a language which Gilman could not understand, but which seemed like something guardedly quoted in the *Necronomicon*.

As the scene grew clearer he saw the ancient crone bend forward and extend the empty bowl across the table — and unable to control his own emotions, he reached far forward and took it in both hands, noticing as he did so its comparative lightness. At the same moment the disgusting form of Brown Jenkin scrambled up over the brink of the triangular black gulf on his left. The crone now motioned him to hold the bowl in a certain position while she raised the huge, grotesque knife above the small white victim as high as her right hand could reach. The fanged, furry thing began tittering a continuation of the unknown ritual, while the witch croaked loathsome responses. Gilman felt a gnawing poignant abhorrence shoot through his mental and emotional paralysis, and the light metal bowl shook in his grasp. A second later the downward motion of the knife broke the spell completely, and he dropped the bowl with a resounding bell-like clangour while his hands darted out frantically to stop the monstrous deed.

In an instant he had edged up the slanting floor around the end of the table and wrenched the knife from the old woman's claws; sending it clattering over the brink of the narrow triangular gulf. In another instant, however, matters were reversed; for those murderous claws had locked themselves tightly around his own throat, while the wrinkled face was twisted with insane fury. He felt the chain of the cheap crucifix grinding into his neck, and in his peril wondered how the sight of the object itself would affect the evil creature. Her strength was altogether superhuman, but as she continued her choking he reached feebly in his shirt and drew out the metal symbol, snapping the chain and pulling it free.

At sight of the device the witch seemed struck with panic, and her grip relaxed long enough to give Gilman a chance to break it entirely. He pulled the steel-like claws from his neck, and would have dragged the beldame over the edge of the gulf had not the claws received a fresh access of strength and closed in again. This time he resolved to reply in kind, and his own hands reached out for the creature's throat. Before she saw what he was doing he had the chain of the crucifix twisted about her neck, and a moment later he had tightened it enough to cut off her breath. During her last struggle he felt something bite at his ankle, and saw that Brown Jenkin had come to her aid. With one savage kick he sent the morbidity over the edge of the gulf and heard it whimper on some level far below.

Whether he had killed the ancient crone he did not know, but he let her rest on the floor where she had fallen. Then, as he turned away, he saw on the table a sight which nearly snapped the last thread of his reason. Brown Jenkin, tough of sinew and with four tiny hands of demoniac dexterity, had been busy while the witch was throttling him, and his efforts had been in vain. What he had prevented the knife from doing to the victim's chest, the yellow fangs of the furry blasphemy had done to a wrist — and the bowl so lately on the floor stood full beside the small lifeless body.

In his dream-delirium Gilman heard the hellish alien-rhythmed chant of the Sabbat coming from an infinite distance, and knew the black man must be there. Confused memories mixed themselves with his mathematics, and he believed his subconscious mind held the angles which he needed to guide him back to the normal world alone and unaided for the first time. He felt sure he was in the immemorially sealed loft above his own room, but whether he could ever escape through the slanting floor or the long-stooped egress he doubted greatly. Besides, would not an escape from a dream-loft bring him merely into a dream-house — an abnormal projection of the actual place he sought? He was wholly bewildered as to the relation betwixt dream and reality in all his experiences.

The passage through the vague abysses would be frightful, for the Walpurgis-rhythm would be vibrating, and at last he would have to hear that hitherto-veiled cosmic pulsing which he so mortally dreaded. Even now he could detect a low, monstrous shaking whose tempo he suspected all too well. At Sabbat-time it always mounted and reached through to the worlds to summon the initiate to nameless rites. Half the chants of the Sabbat were patterned on this faintly overheard pulsing which no earthly ear could endure in its unveiled spatial fulness. Gilman wondered, too, whether he could trust his instincts to take him back to the right part of space. How could he be sure he would not land on that green-litten hillside of a far planet, on the tessellated terrace above the city of tentacled monsters somewhere beyond the galaxy or in the spiral black vortices of that ultimate void of Chaos where reigns the mindless demon-sultan Azathoth?

Just before he made the plunge the violet light went out and left him in utter blackness. The witch — old Keziah — Nahab — that must have meant her death. And mixed with the distant chant of the Sabbat and the whimpers of Brown Jenkin in the gulf below he thought he heard another and wilder whine from unknown depths. Joe Mazurewicz — the prayers against the Crawling Chaos now turning to an inexplicably triumphant shriek — worlds of sardonic actuality impinging on vortices of febrile dream — Iä! Shub-Niggurath! The Goat with a Thousand Young . . . .

They found Gilman on the floor of his queerly-angled old garret room long before dawn, for the terrible cry had brought Desrochers and Choynski and Dombrowski and Mazurewicz at once, and had even wakened the soundly sleeping Elwood in his chair. He was alive, and with open, staring eyes, but seemed largely unconscious. On his throat were the marks of murderous hands, and on his left ankle was a distressing rat-bite. His clothing was badly rumpled and Joe's crucifix was missing, Elwood trembled, afraid even to speculate what new form his friend's sleep-walking had taken. Mazurewicz seemed half dazed because of a "sign" he said he had had in response to his prayers, and he crossed himself frantically when the squealing and whimpering of a rat sounded from beyond the slanting partition.

When the dreamer was settled on his couch in Elwood's room they sent for Doctor Malkowski — a local practitioner who would repeat no tales where they might prove embarrassing — and he gave Gilman two hypodermic injections which caused him to relax in something like natural drowsiness. During the day the patient regained consciousness at times and whispered his newest dream disjointedly to Elwood. It was a painful process, and at its very start brought out a fresh and disconcerting fact.

Gilman — whose ears had so lately possessed an abnormal sensitiveness — was now stone-deaf. Doctor Malkowski, summoned again in haste, told Elwood that both ear-drums were ruptured, as if by the impact of some stupendous sound intense beyond all human conception or endurance. How such a sound could have been heard in the last few hours without arousing all the Miskatonic Valley was more than the honest physician could say.

Elwood wrote his part of the colloquy on paper, so that a fairly easy communication was maintained. Neither knew what to make of the whole chaotic business, and decided it would be better if they thought as little as possible about it. Both, though, agreed that they must leave this ancient and accursed house as soon as it could be arranged. Evening papers spoke of a police raid on some curious revellers in a ravine beyond Meadow Hill just before dawn, and mentioned that the white stone there was an object of age-long superstitious regard. Nobody had been caught, but among the scattering fugitives had been glimpsed a huge negro. In another column it was stated that no trace of the missing child Ladislas Wolejko had been found.

The crowning horror came that very night. Elwood will never forget it, and was forced to stay out of college the rest of the term because of the resulting nervous breakdown. He had thought he heard rats in the partition all the evening, but paid little attention to them. Then, long after both he and Gilman had retired, the atrocious shrieking began. Elwood jumped up, turned on the lights and rushed over to his guest's couch. The occupant was emitting sounds of veritably inhuman nature, as if racked by some torment beyond description. He was writhing under the bedclothes, and a great stain was beginning to appear on the blankets.

Elwood scarcely dared to touch him, but gradually the screaming and writhing subsided. By this time Dombrowski, Choynski, Desrochers, Mazurewicz, and the top-floor lodger were all crowding into the doorway, and the landlord had sent his wife back to telephone for Doctor Malkowski. Everybody shrieked when a large rat-like form suddenly jumped out from beneath the ensanguined bedclothes and scuttled across the floor to a fresh, open hole close by. When the doctor arrived and began to pull down those frightful covers Walter Gilman was dead.

It would be barbarous to do more than suggest what had killed Gilman. There had been virtually a tunnel through his body — something had eaten his heart out. Dombrowski, frantic at the failure of his rat-poisoning efforts, cast aside all thought of his lease and within a week had moved with all his older lodgers to a dingy but less ancient house in Walnut Street. The worst thing for a while was keeping Joe Mazurewicz quiet; for the brooding loom-fixer would never stay sober, and was constantly whining and muttering about spectral and terrible things.

It seems that on that last hideous night Joe had stooped to look at the crimson rat-tracks which led from Gilman's couch to the near-by hole. On the carpet they were very indistinct, but a piece of open flooring intervened between the carpet's edge and the baseboard. There Mazurewicz had found something monstrous — or thought he had, for no one else could quite agree with him despite the undeniable queerness of the prints. The tracks on the flooring were certainly vastly unlike the average prints of a rat but even Choynski and Desrochers would not admit that they were like the prints of four tiny human hands.

The house was never rented again. As soon as Dombrowski left it the pall of its final desolation began to descend, for people shunned it both on account of its old reputation and because of the new foetid odour. Perhaps the ex-landlord's rat-poison had worked after all, for not long after his departure the place became a neighbourhood nuisance. Health officials traced the smell to the closed spaces above and beside the eastern garret room, and agreed that the number of dead rats must be enormous. They decided, however, that it was not worth their while to hew open and disinfect the long-sealed spaces; for the foetor would soon be over, and the locality was not one which encouraged fastidious standards. Indeed, there were always vague local tales of unexplained stenches upstairs in the Witch-House just after May-Eve and Hallowmass. The neighbours acquiesced in the inertia — but the foetor none the less formed an additional count against the place. Toward the last the house was condemned as a habitation by the building inspector.

Gilman's dreams and their attendant circumstances have never been explained. Elwood, whose thoughts on the entire episode are sometimes almost maddening, came back to college the next autumn and was graduated in the following June. He found the spectral gossip of the town much disminished, and it is indeed a fact that — notwithstanding certain reports of a ghostly tittering in the deserted house which lasted almost as long as that edifice itself — no fresh appearances either of Old Keziah or of Brown Jenkin have been muttered of since Gilman's death.

It is rather fortunate that Elwood was not in Arkham in that later year when certain events abruptly renewed the local whispers about elder horrors. Of course he heard about the matter afterward and suffered untold torments of black and bewildered speculation; but even that was not as bad as actual nearness and several possible sights would have been.

In March, 1931, a gale wrecked the roof and great chimney of the vacant Witch-House, so that a chaos of crumbling bricks, blackened, moss-grown shingles, and rotting planks and timbers crashed down into the loft and broke through the floor beneath. The whole attic storey was choked with debris from above, but no one took the trouble to touch the mess before the inevitable razing of the decrepit structure. That ultimate step came in the following December, and it was when Gilman's old room was cleared out by reluctant, apprehensive workmen that the gossip began.

Among the rubbish which had crashed through the ancient slanting ceiling were several things which made the workmen pause and call in the police. Later the police in turn called in the coroner and several professors from the university. There were bones — badly crushed and splintered, but clearly recognizable as human — whose manifestly modern date conflicted puzzlingly with the remote period at which their only possible lurking place, the low, slant-floored loft overhead, had supposedly been sealed from all human access. The coroner's physician decided that some belonged to a small child, while certain others — found mixed with shreds of rotten brownish cloth — belonged to a rather undersized, bent female of advanced years. Careful sifting of debris also disclosed many tiny bones of rats caught in the collapse, as well as older rat-bones gnawed by small fangs in a fashion now and then highly productive of controversy and reflection.

Other objects found included the mangled fragments of many books and papers, together with a yellowish dust left from the total disintegration of still older books and papers. All, without exception, appeared to deal with black magic in its most advanced and horrible forms; and the evidently recent date of certain items is still a mystery as unsolved as that of the modern human bones. An even greater mystery is the absolute homogeneity of the crabbed, archaic writing found on a wide range of papers whose conditions and watermarks suggest age differences of at least one hundred and fifty to two hundred years. To some, though, the greatest mystery of all is the variety of utterly inexplicable objects — objects whose shapes, materials, types of workmanship, and purposes baffle all conjecture — found scattered amidst the wreckage in evidently diverse states of injury. One of these things — which excited several Miskatonic professors profoundly — is a badly damaged monstrosity plainly resembling the strange image which Gilman gave to the college museum, save that it is large, wrought of some peculiar bluish stone instead of metal, and possessed of a singularly angled pedestal with undecipherable hieroglyphics.

Archaeologists and anthropologists are still trying to explain the bizarre designs chased on a crushed bowl of light metal whose inner side bore ominous brownish stains when found. Foreigners and credulous grandmothers are equally garrulous about the modern nickel crucifix with broken chain mixed in the rubbish and shiveringly identified by Joe Mazurewicz as that which he had given poor Gilman many years before. Some believe this crucifix was dragged up to the sealed loft by rats, while others think it must have been on the floor in some corner of Gilman's old room at the time. Still others, including Joe himself, have theories too wild and fantastic for sober credence.

When the slanting wall of Gilman's room was torn out, the once-sealed triangular space between that partition and the house's north wall was found to contain much less structural debris, even in proportion to its size, than the room itself, though it had a ghastly layer of older materials which paralyzed the wreckers with horror. In brief, the floor was a veritable ossuary of the bones of small children — some fairly modern, but others extending back in infinite gradations to a period so remote that crumbling was almost complete. On this deep bony layer rested a knife of great size, obvious antiquity, and grotesque, ornate, and exotic design — above which the debris was piled.

In the midst of this debris, wedged between a fallen plank and a cluster of cemented bricks from the ruined chimney, was an object destined to cause more bafflement, veiled fright, and openly superstitious talk in Arkham than anything else discovered in the haunted and accursed building.

This object was the partly crushed skeleton of a huge diseased rat, whose abnormalities of form are still a topic of debate and source of singular reticence among the members of Miskatonic's department of comparative anatomy. Very little concerning this skeleton has leaked out, but the workmen who found it whisper in shocked tones about the long, brownish hairs with which it was associated.

The bones of the tiny paws, it is rumoured, imply prehensile characteristics more typical of a diminutive monkey than of a rat, while the small skull with its savage yellow fangs is of the utmost anomalousness, appearing from certain angles like a miniature, monstrously degraded parody of a human skull. The workmen crossed themselves in fright when they came upon this blasphemy, but later burned candles of gratitude in St. Stanislaus' Church because of the shrill, ghostly tittering they felt they would never hear again.

Bothon.

(ALTERNATE TITLE: THE BRUISE)

BY HENRY S. WHITEHEAD
AND H.P. LOVECRAFT

**10,500-WORD NOVELETTE;
1932.**

This is the story on which Lovecraft was helping Whitehead at the time of his death — or, at least, it purports to be. We know that the two of them were working on a story answering to the description of "Bothon" — they called it "The Bruise" — at that time. But this story was not published until 1946, when it appeared in both Amazing Stories *magazine and August Derleth's second Arkham House collection of Whitehead's stories,* West India Lights. *The "conspiracy theory" is that Derleth, unable to find the original of the story and wanting to include it in the collection, simply created a pastiche that answered the same general description, then sent it to* Amazing Stories *for initial publication so that its previously-unpublished status wouldn't draw suspicion.*

And this may very well be what happened. The story really doesn't show any evidence of Lovecraft having taken an active hand in writing it, and its narrative construction shows a markedly un-Lovecraftian lack of tightness. Some of that lack of tightness results from "noob mistakes" that Whitehead wouldn't have been likely to make either. For example, in the story (and this can be discussed without fear of spoilers) the character asks a doctor for a sleeping medication, and the doctor reluctantly obliges, warning him carefully that the preparation is dangerous if too large a dose is taken. The patient thanks the doctor, takes a prudent dose, it works exactly as intended, and nothing further is heard about the medicine or its dangers. This is a blatant violation of the "Chekov's Gun" rule of storytelling, the idea that if you introduce a gun in Act I, it has to have gone off by the end. How likely is it that either Lovecraft or Whitehead would make such a basic mistake?

However, absence of evidence is not evidence of absence, and in a case like this where there is an absence of evidence, it's logical to assume things are what they purport to be. Therefore the story is presented here — but with the caveat that not every Lovecraft scholar, and certainly not the one whose words you're reading right now, believes it's really his work.

Powers Meredith, at his shower-bath before dinner in the bathroom adjoining his room in his New York City club, allowed the cake of soap to drop on the tiled floor. Stooping to recover it he rapped the side of his head against the marble sidewall. The resulting bruise was painful, and almost at once puffed up into a noticeable lump ....

Meredith dined in the grill that evening. Having no after-dinner engagement he went into the quiet library of the club, empty at this hour, and settled himself with a new book beside a softly-shaded reading lamp.

From time to time a slight, inadvertent pressure of his head against the chair's leather upholstered back would remind him unpleasantly of his accident in the shower-bath. This, after it happened several times, became an annoyance, and Meredith shifted himself into a preventive attitude with his legs draped over one of the chair's rounded arms.

No one else came into the library. Faint, clicking noises came in from the nearby billiard-room where a couple of men were playing, but, absorbed in his book, he did not notice these. The only perceptible sound was that of the gentle, steady rain outside. This, in the form of a soothing, continuous murmur, came through the partly-opened, high windows. He read on.

Precisely as he turned over the ninety-sixth page of his book, he heard a dull sound, like a very large explosion coming from a vast distance.

Alert now, his finger holding his place in the book, he listened. Then he heard a rumbling roar, as though countless tons of wrecked masonry were falling; falling; clearly, unmistakably, the remote thunder of some catastrophic ruin. He dropped his book, and, obeying an almost automatic impulse, started for the door.

He met nobody as he rushed down the stairs. At the coatroom, which he had to pass on his way to the doorway, two fellow members were chatting easily as they took their checks. Meredith glanced at them, surprised. He rushed on, to the doorway, and out into the street, where he paused. An empty street!

The rain, reduced now to a mere drizzle, made the asphalt shimmer in the street lights. Over towards Broadway, certainly, there must be clamour! But when he reached it he found only the compound eleven o'clock bedlam of Times Square.

Along Sixth Avenue, countless taxi-cabs weaved in a many-hued stream, jockeying for position in the maëlstrom of the night-traffic about the Hippodrome. On the corner, a solitary rubber-coated policeman swung long efficient arms like a pair of mechanical semaphores, and skilfully directed the crawling traffic. To his ever-increasing wonderment, everything seemed normal. But what then had been that catastrophic sound?

Returning to the club entrance, he hesitated, a frown

creasing his brow. He mounted the three steps hesitatingly, and entered, pausing at the door-man's desk.

"Send me up an 'extra,' please, if one comes out," he told the clerk. Then he went up to his bedroom completely puzzled.

Half an hour later as he lay in bed wakeful and trying to compose in his thoughts the varying, incongruous aspect of this strange affair, he was all at once acutely conscious of a distant, thin, confused, roaring hum. The most prominent element in this sound was the deep, soft, and insistently penetrating blending of countless voices. Through it ran a kind of dominant note—a note of horror. The sound chilled his blood. It was eerie. He found himself holding his breath as he listened,

"She stood aghast as the monster wave rolled in ...."

straining every faculty to take in that faint, distant, terrible clamour of fear and despair.

Of just when he fell asleep he had no recollection, but when he awakened the next morning there hung over his mind a shadow of remembered horror, not wholly dissipated until he had bathed and begun to dress. He heard none of the sounds at the time of his awakening.

No "extra" lay outside his bedroom door, and a little later at breakfast he opened expectantly and scanned several newspapers vainly and with a mounting sense of wonderment for any account of a catastrophe which could have caused the sounds. Gradually the implication grew upon him. He had, actually, heard the convincing, unmistakable evidence of such a catastrophe — and no one else knew anything about it!

He fell asleep immediately after turning in.

The following morning was Sunday. The reading-room was full, and he carried his book up to his bed-room after late breakfast to read the rest of it in peace. Soon after he became immersed in it, his attention was distracted by the tapping of a window-shade, blown in and out by the breeze. It was annoying and he paused in his reading, intending to rise and adjust the shade.

As he withdrew his eyes, and part of his attention, from his book, all at once he heard a new sound. It was precisely as though a distant, sound-proof door had been abruptly opened.

As he listened, fascinated, there came back to him and grew upon him a paralyzing, cold fear. There seemed to be no stopping it. The faint penumbra of a slight nausea shook him. He could distinguish overtones now, high tones, cries of battle; the impact of a charge against a resistant horde; noise of plied weapons.

The window-shade tapped again against the window casing. He snapped back into the familiar environment of his bedroom. He felt a little sick and weak. He rose shakily, walked across the room and into the bathroom, and, noisily splashing the water about, washed his hands and face.

Then he paused, suddenly, to listen again, a towel gripped between clenched hands. But he could hear nothing now, nothing except the tapping of that window-shade in the fresh breeze blowing through the open window. He hung the towel on its porcelain rod and walked back to his chair.

Astounding Stories, August 1946

It was an hour too early for lunch, but he wanted urgently to be where there were people about, even waiters, people who were not "hearing things"!

In order to prolong his companionship with old Cavanagh, the only other early luncher, Meredith ate somewhat more than usual. The unaccustomed heavy meal at such an hour made him drowsy, and after lunch he stretched out on a davenport before one of the two open fireplaces in the now unoccupied reading-room, and fell at once into an uneasy sleep.

A little before three he awakened, stale, and as he came to conscious wakefulness he began to hear, at first quite distinctly, and then with increasing loudness and clarity—as though a steady hand were opening up a loudspeaker—that same sound of fire and human conflict, and the dreadful, menacing roar of a thunderous ocean's incalculable anger.

Then, Old Cavanagh, napping on the other davenport, struggled with senile deliberation to his feet with many accompanying "hum"s and "ha"s, and began lumbering across the room towards him.

"Lord's sake, what's the matter?" he demanded.

Kindly goodwill looked out of the old man's distorted countenance. Meredith, unable to control himself any longer, stammered out his incredible story.

"Hm! Strange . . ." was the old man's comment when Meredith ended. He produced, lighted deliberately, and puffed upon an enormous cigar. He seemed to cogitate as the two sat side by side in a pregnant silence of many minutes. At last he spoke.

"You're upset, my boy, naturally. But, you can hear everything that's going on around you, can't you? Your actual hearing's all right, then. Hm! This other 'hearing' starts up and goes on only when everything's perfectly quiet. First time, you were here reading; second time, in bed; third time, reading again; this time—if I wasn't snoring—you were in perfect quiet once more. Let's test that out, now. Keep perfectly still, and I'll do the same. Let's see if you hear anything."

They fell silent once more, and for a while Meredith could hear nothing of the strange sounds. Then, as the silence deepened, once again came that complex of sounds indicating devastating battle, murder, and sudden death.

He nodded silently at Cavanagh, and at the old man's acquiescent murmur the sounds ceased abruptly.

It took urging before Meredith could be persuaded to consult an aurist. Medical men, Cavanagh reminded him, would keep quiet about anything strange or embarrassing. Professional ethics . . . .

They went uptown together that afternoon to Dr. Gatefield, a noted specialist. The doctor heard the story with close-lipped, professional attention. Then he tested Meredith's hearing with various delicate instruments. Finally he gave an opinion.

"We are familiar with various 'ear-noises' Mr. Meredith. In some cases the location of one of the arteries too close to the ear-drum gives 'roaring' noises. There are others, similar. I have eliminated everything of that kind. Your physical organism is in excellent condition, and unusually acute. There is nothing wrong with your hearing. This is a case for a psychiatrist.

"I am not suggesting anything like mental derangement, you will please understand! But I recommend Dr. Cowlington. This seems to be a clear case of what is sometimes called 'clairaudience,' or something similar—his department; not mine. The aural equivalent of 'clairvoyance' is what I am indicating, you see what I mean. 'Second-sight' has to do with the eyes, of course, but it is mental, although there is often some physical background, I have no knowledge of those phenomena. I hope you will take my advice and allow Dr. Cowling—"

"All right!" interrupted Meredith. "Where does he live? I might as well go through with the thing now as later."

Dr. Gatefield showed traces of sympathy under his rather frosty professional exterior. He dropped the diagnostician, became the obliging, courteous gentleman. He telephoned to his colleague, the psychiatrist, and then surprised both Meredith and Cavanagh by accompanying them to Dr. Cowlington's.

The psychiatrist proved to be a tall, thin, and rather kindly person, with heavy, complex spectacles on a prominent nose, and then, sand-coloured wisps of hair in a complication of cowlicks. He showed marked interest in the case from the start. After hearing Meredith's story and the aurist's report he subjected Meredith to an examination of more than an hour, from which, feeling more or less as though he had been dissected, he nevertheless derived a considerable sense of relief.

It was decided that Meredith should arrange at once to take several days off, come to Dr. Cowlington's house, and remain "under observation."

He arrived at the doctor's the next morning and was given a pleasant, upstairs room, with many books and a comfortable davenport on which, in a recumbent position, the psychiatrist suggested, he should spend most of his waking hours, reading.

During Monday and Tuesday, Meredith, now after Dr. Cowlington's skillful reassurances no longer upset at hearing the strange sounds, listened carefully for whatever might reach him from what seemed like another—and very restless—world! He heard as he listened for long periods uninterrupted by any aural distractions, the drama of a great community in the paralyzing grip of fear—fighting for its corporate life—against irresistible, impending, dreadful doom.

He began, about this time, at Dr. Cowlington's suggestion, to write down some of the syllabification of the cries and shouts as well as he could manage it, on a purely phonetic basis. The sounds corresponded to no language known to him. The words and phrases were blurred and marred by the continuous uproar of the fury of waters. This was invariably, and continued to be, the sustained, distinctive background for every sound he heard during the periods while he remained passive and quiet. The various words and phrases were entirely unintelligible. His notes looked like nothing which either he or Cowlington could relate to any modern or ancient tongue. When read aloud they made nothing but gibberish.

These strange terms were studied over very carefully by Dr. Cowlington, by Meredith himself, and by no less than three professors of Archaeology and Comparative Philology — one of whom, the Archaeologist, was a friend of Cowlington's, and the other two called in by him. All of these experts on ancient and obsolete languages listened with the greatest courtesy to Meredith's attempt to explain the apparent setting of the sounds — most of them were in the nature of battle — cries and what Meredith took to be fragments of desperately uttered prayer, some of the material having come to him in the form of uncouth, raucous howls — and with the greatest interest to his attempts at reproducing them orally. They studied his written notes with the most meticulous care. The verdict was unanimous, even emphatic on the part of the younger and more dogmatic philologist. These sounds were quite utterly at variance with any known speech, including Sanskrit, Indo-Iranian, and even the conjectural Akkadian and Sumerian spoken tongues. The transcribed syllables corresponded to nothing in any known language, ancient or modern. Emphatically they were not Japanese.

The three professors took their departure, and Meredith and the psychiatrist Dr. Cowlington went over the list again.

Meredith had written: "I, I, I, I; — R'ly-eh! — Ieh nya, Ieh nya; — zoh, zoh-an-nuh!" There was only one grouping of the words which formed anything like a section of continuous speech, or sentence, and which Meredith had been able to capture more or less intact and write down — "Ióth, Ióth, — natcal-o, do yan kho thútthut."

There were many other cries and, as he believed, desperately uttered prayers quite as strange and off the beaten tracks of recognized human speech as those noted down.

It was quite possibly because of his concentration on this affair of the remembered words — his own interest in them being naturally enhanced by Dr. Cowlington's and that of the three experts — that Meredith's dream-state impressions just at this time, and suddenly, became markedly acute. These dreams had been continuous and consecutive since their beginning several nights before, but on this night after the rather elaborate investigation of the words and syllables, Meredith began in earnest to get the affair of his environment in the strange city of the flames and conflicts and confusion and of a roaring ocean, cleared up with a startling abruptness. His dream impression that night was so utterly vivid, so acutely identical with the terms of the waking state, that he couldn't tell the difference between his dream slumber and wakeful consciousness!

Everything that he had derived mentally out of that night's sleep was clearly and definitely present in his mind. It seemed to him precisely as though he had not been asleep; that he had not emerged from an ordinary night's rest into the accustomed circumstances of an early morning's awakening. It was, rather, as though he had very abruptly passed out of one quite definite life into another; as though, as it came to him afterwards, he had walked out of a theatre into the wholly unrelated after-theatre life of Times Square.

One of the radical phases of this situation was not only that the succession of dream experiences had been continuous, with time-allowances for the intervening periods of those days — in between which he had spent here in Dr. Cowlington's quiet house; not only that, extraordinary as this realization seemed to him. The nearly consecutive dream experiences had been the events of the past few days in a life of thirty-two years, spent in that same environment and civilization of which the cataclysmic conditions which he had been envisaging appeared to presage a direful end.

He was, to set out plainly what he had brought out of that last night's dream-experience, one Bothon, general of the military forces of the great district of Ludekta, the south-westerly provincial division of the continent of Atlantis, which had been colonized, as every Atlantean school child was well aware, some eighteen hundred years before by a series of emigrations from the mother continent. The Naacal language — with minor variations not unlike the differences between American speech and "English English" — was the common language of both continents.

From his native Ludekta the General Bothon had made several voyages to the mother land. The first of these had been to Ghua, the central eastern province, a kind of grand tour made just after his finishing, at the age of twenty-two, his professional course in the Ludekta College of Military Training. He was thus familiar by experience, as were many other cultivated Atlanteans of the upper classes, with the very highly developed civilization of the mother continent. These cultural contacts had been aided by his second visit, and further enhanced not long before the present period of the dream-experiences when, at the age of thirty-one, Bothon, already of the rank of general, had been sent out as Ambassador to Aglad-Dho, joint capital of the confederated south-eastern provinces of Yish, Knan, and Buathon, one of the most strategic diplomatic posts, and the second most important provincial confederation of the mother continent.

He had served in his ambassadorial capacity for only four months, and then had been abruptly recalled without explanation, but, as he had soon discovered upon his arrival home, because of the privately communicated request of the Emperor himself. His diplomatic superiors at home offered him no censure. Such Imperial requests were not unknown. These gentlemen were, actually, quite unaware of the reasons behind the Imperial request. No explanations had been given them, but there had been no Imperial censure of any kind.

But the General, Bothon, knew the reasons very well, although he kept them strictly to himself. There was, indeed, only one reason, as he was acutely and very well aware.

The requirements of his office had taken him rather

frequently to Alu, the continental capital, metropolis of the civilized world.

Here in the great city of Alu were assembled from all known parts of the terrestrial globe the world's diplomats, artists, philosophers, traders and shipmasters. Here in the great warehouses of solid stone and along the innumerable wharves were piled the world's goods — fabrics and perfumes; strange animals for the delectation of the untraveled curious. Here in the endless stalls and markets were dyed stuffs and silks, tubas and cymbals and musical rattles and lyres, choice woods and implements for the toilet-strigils, and curiously carved hand-fitting little blocks of soapstone, and oils innumerable for the freshening of beards and the anointing of bodies. Here were tunics and sandals and belts and thongs of soft-tanned, variously perfumed leathers. Here were displayed carved and cunningly wrought pieces of household furniture — glowing, burnished wall-mirrors of copper and tin and steel, bedsteads of an infinite range and design, cushions of swans' feathers, tables of plain and polished artisanship and of intarsia with metal scrolls set flush to their levels; marquetry work of contrasting woods — chairs and stools and cupboards and chests and footrests. Here were ornaments innumerable — fire-screens, and spindles for parchment-rolls, and tongs, and shades for lamps made of the scraped skins of animals; metal lamps of every design, and vegetable oils for the lamps in earthenware jars of many sizes and shapes. Here were foods and wines and dried fruits, and honey of many flavours; grains and dried meats and loaves of barley and wheat-meal past computation. Here in the great street of the armorers were maces and axes and swords and daggers of all the world's varieties and designs; armour of plate and chain-hauberks, and greaves and bassinets, and shelves with rows and rows of the heavy plate and helmets standardized for the use of such fighting men as Bothon himself commanded in their thousands.

Here were to be seen and examined costly canopies and the elaborate litters in which the slaves of the rich carried their masters through the narrow streets and broad, airy avenues of Alu. Rugs there were in an endless profusion of size and shape and design; rugs from distant Lemuria and from Atlantis and from tropical Antillea, and from the mountainous interior regions of the mother continent itself, where thousands of cunning weavers of fabrics worked at their looms; ordinary rugs of pressed felt, and gorgeous glowing rugs of silk from the southern regions where the mulberry trees grew; rugs, too, and thin, soft draperies of complex patterns made of the wool of lambs and of the long, silk-like hair of the mountain sheep.

Here in Alu, centre of the world's culture, were philosophers with their groups of disciples, small or great, propounding their systems on the corners of streets and in the public squares, wrangling incessantly over the end of man, and the greatest good, and the origin of material things. Here were vast libraries containing the essence of all that had been written down concerning science and religion and engineering and the innumerable fine arts, of the civilization of forty thousand years. Here were the temples of religion where the hierarchs propounded the principles of life, colleges of priests studying incessantly more and more deeply into the mysteries of the four principles; teaching the people the endless applications of these esoteric affairs to their conduct and daily lives.

Into this fascinating treasure house of a great civilization the ambassador Bothon had penetrated as often as possible. The excellence of his family background, his own character and personal qualities, and his official position, all combined to make him a welcome guest in the mansions of the members of the emperor's court and of the highest stratum of social life in Alu.

An impressionable young man, most of whose life previous to his appointment as ambassador had been spent in hard training for his military duties and in the rigorous prosecution of these as he rose rapidly grade by grade by hard man's work in camp and field during his many campaigns in the standing army of Ludekta, the general, Bothon, revelled in these many high social contacts. Very soon he found within himself and growing apace, the strong and indeed natural desire for a type of life to which his backgrounds and achievements had amply entitled him, but of which he had been, so far, deprived because of the well-nigh incessant demands upon him of his almost continuous military service.

In short, the ambassador from Ludekta very greatly came to desire marriage, with some lady of his own caste and, preferably, of this metropolitan city of Alu with its sophistication and wide culture; a lady who might preside graciously over his ambassadorial establishment; who, when his term of office was concluded, would return with him to his native Ludekta in Atlantis, there permanently to grace the fine residence he had in his mind's eye when, a little later, he should retire from the Ludektan army and settle down as a senator into the type of life which he envisaged for his middle years.

He had been both fortunate and unfortunate in his actual falling in love. The lady, who reciprocated his ardent advances, was the Netvissa Ledda, daughter of the Netvis Toldon who was the emperor's brother. The fortunate aspect of this intense and sudden love affair which set all social Alu to commenting upon it, was the altogether human one of a virtually perfect compatibility between the two. Their initial mutual attraction had become a settled regard for each other almost overnight. Within a few days thereafter they were very deeply in love. Humanly considered, the affair was perfection itself. Every circumstance save one, and that a merely artificial side of the case, gave promise of an ideal union.

The single difficulty in the way of this marriage was, however, most unfortunately, an insuperable one. The Netvissa Ledda, niece of the emperor, belonged of right to the very highest social caste of the empire. The rank and degree of Netvis lay next to Royalty itself, and in the case of the family of the Netvis Toldon partook of royalty. Against this fact, basic in the structure of the empire's long-established custom, the Ambassador, General Bothon of Ludekta — although a gentleman of the very highest attainments, character, and worth, whose family record reached back a thousand years into the dim past before the colonization of Atlantis, whose reputation was second to none in the empire — the General, Bothon, was a commoner. As such, according to the rigid system prevalent at the court in Alu, capital of the Empire, he was hopelessly ineligible. The marriage was simply out of the question.

The Emperor being called upon to settle this awkward affair, acted summarily, quite in the spirit of one who destroys a hopelessly wounded and suffering creature as an act of mercy. The Emperor took the one course open to him under these circumstances, and the General, Bothon, without any choice being open to him save submission to an Imperial request which had the force of law, took ship for Ludekta, leaving behind him in Alu the highest and dearest hope of his life, irreparably shattered.

For the subsequent conduct of the General Bothon, recently Ludektan Ambassador to Aglad-Dho, there were three very definite contributing reasons. Of these the first and most prominent was the depth and intensity and genuineness of his love for the Netvissa Ledda. Beyond all possible things, he wanted her; and the proud soul of Bothon was very grievously racked and torn at the sudden unexpected and arbitrary separation from her which the Imperial request had brought about.

The voyage from Aglad-Dho to Ludekta, across two sections of the globe's great oceans and through the ship canals and lakes which bisected the southern continent of the western hemisphere, occupied seven weeks. During this period of enforced inaction the bitter chagrin and deep disappointment of Bothon crystallized itself by means of the sustained reflection inevitable under the circumstances. General Bothon arrived in Ludekta in a state of mind which made him ready for anything, provided only it was action. This state of mind was the second of these contributory factors. The third was the immediate satisfaction of his desire for activity. During the course of his voyage home the ghoulish and, indeed, sub-human factory slaves, the shockingly simian Gyaa-Hua, had inaugurated a revolt. This had spread, by the time of Bothon's arrival, throughout the entire province of Ludekta. The state sorely needed the efficient services of this, the youngest and most brilliant of its generals, and his reception on landing was more nearly that of a saviour of his country than what a virtually disgraced diplomat might expect.

Into this campaign, which he prosecuted with the utmost vigor and a thoroughgoing military effectiveness, Bothon threw himself with an abounding energy which even his most ardent Ludektan admirers had not anticipated. At the end of an intensive campaign of less than three weeks, with this very dangerous revolt completely crushed and the leaders of the Gyaa-Hua hanging to a man by great hooks through their neck muscles in dreadful rows along the outer city walls on either side of the great archway that pierced the defence of Ludekta's capital, the General Bothon found himself the hero of Ludekta and the idol of his admiring troops. A rigid disciplinarian; the attitude of the officers and men of the Ludektan standing army towards this general had hitherto been based upon the respect which his great abilities had always commanded. Now he found himself the recipient of something almost like worship because of this last brilliant campaign of his. It had been a tour de force.

Although it is highly probable that they would have advanced him because of this achievement in any event, the actual occasion for the action of the Ludektan Senate in rewarding Bothon with the supreme command of the standing army was the speech before that body of the aging generalissimo Tarba. Old Tarba ended his notable panegyric by laying his truncheon, emblem of the supreme command, on the great marble slab before the presiding senator, with a dramatic gesture.

Bothon thus found himself suddenly possessed of that intensive hero worship which would cause the state to acquiesce in anything which its object might suggest. He was, at the same time, in supreme command of the largest sectional standing army of the entire continent of Atlantis; an army, thanks chiefly to his own efficiency, probably the best trained and most effective fighting unit then extant.

Under the combined effect of the contributing causes and his new authority General Bothon made up his mind. On the eleventh day after his triumphal entry into Ludekta's capital city, forty-seven Ludektan war vessels freshly outfitted, their oar-slaves supplemented by a reserve of the Gyaa-Hua, selected for the power and endurance of their gorilla-like bodies, with new skin sails throughout the fleet, and the flower of the Ludektan army on board, sailed out from Ludekta westward for Alu under the command of the General Bothon.

It was precisely simultaneous with the arrival of this war fleet off the shores of the great city of Alu that there began unprecedented natural disturbances affecting the entire area of the mother continent. These were comparable to nothing recorded in the capital's carefully kept slate and parchment records, which went back over a period of thousands of years.

The first presage of these impending calamities took the form of a coppery tinge which replaced the blue of the sky. Without any warning the long ground-swell of this Western Ocean changed abruptly, along with the colour of the water, into a kind of dull brick-grey, to short, choppy, spray-capped waves. These tossed even the great Ludektan war galleys so violently as to shatter many of the sweeps. The wind, to the consternation of several of Bothon's captains, appeared to come from every quarter at once! It tore the heavy skin sails of the Ludektan galleys away from their copper rings and bolts in some cases. In others it split the sails in clean straight lines as though they had been slit with sharp knives.

Undaunted by these manifestations and the reports of his augurs who had cast their lots and slain their sheep and fowls in a hasty series of divinations to account, if possible, for this unfavourable reception at the hands of the elements, the indomitable will of Bothon forced his fleet to an orderly landing. He sent forthwith as his herald to the Emperor himself, his highest ranking sub-general, accompanied by an imposing guard of honour. On slate tablets Bothon had set forth his demand in his own hand. This was in the form of a set of alternatives. The Emperor was asked to receive him as Generalissimo of the military forces of Ludekta, and to consent to his immediate marriage with the Netvissa Ledda; or, he, Bothon, would proceed forthwith to the siege of Alu and take the lady of his heart by force and arms.

The message prayed the Emperor to elect the first alternative. It also set forth briefly and in formal heraldic terms the status of the ancient family of Bothon.

The Emperor had been very seriously annoyed at this challenge, as he chose to regard it. He felt that his office and dignity had been outraged. He crucified Bothon's entire delegation.

The siege of Alu began forthwith under that menacing copper-tinted sky and to the accompaniment of a rumbling series of little earthquakes.

Not only not within the memory of living men, but, as the records indicated, during its entire history over thousands of years as the metropolis of the civilized world, had there been any previous hostile manifestations against the great city of Alu. That anything like this terrible campaign which the renowned General Bothon of Ludekta set in motion against her might come to pass, had never even remotely occurred to anyone in Alu. So promptly did Bothon launch his attack that the tortured bodies of the members of his delegation to the Emperor had not' yet ceased writhing on their row of crosses before he had penetrated, at the head of his trained legionaries, to a point within two squares of the Imperial Palace which stood at the centre of the great city.

There had been virtually no resistance. This intensive campaign would have been triumphantly concluded within twenty minutes, the Emperor probably captured along with all his Palace guards and household, the person of the Lady Ledda secured by this ardent lover of hers, and the entire objective of the expedition accomplished, save for what in modern legal phraseology would have been described as An Act of God.

The premonitory earth-shakings which had accompanied this armed invasion culminated, at that point in the advance of Bothon's army, in a terrific seismic cataclysm. The stone-paved streets opened in great gaping fissures. Massive buildings crashed tumultuously all about and upon the triumphantly advancing Ludektans. The General, Bothon, at the head of his troops, dazed and deafened and hurled violently upon the ground, retained consciousness long enough to see three quarters of his devoted following engulfed, smashed, torn to fragments, crushed into unrecognizable heaps of bloody pulp; and this holocaust swiftly and mercifully obliterated from before his failing vision by the drifting dust from millions of tons of crumbled masonry.

He awakened in the innermost keep of the dungeon in Alu's citadel.

Coming quietly into Meredith's bedroom about ten o'clock in the morning, Dr. Cowlington, who had made up his mind overnight on a certain matter, quietly led his initial conversation with his observation-patient around to the subject which had been most prominent in his mind since their conference of yesterday over the strange linguistic terms which Meredith had noted down.

"It has occurred to me that I might very well tell you about something quite out of the ordinary which came under my notice seven or eight years ago," he said. "It happened while I was chief intern in the Connecticut State Hospital for the Insane. I served there for two years under Dr. Floyd Haviland before I went into private practice. We had a few private patients in the hospital, and one of these, who was in my particular charge, was a gentleman of middle-age who had come to us because of Haviland's enormous reputation, without commitment. This gentleman, whom I will call 'Smith,' was neither legally nor actually 'insane.' His difficulty, which had interfered very seriously with the course of his life and affairs, would ordinarily be classified as 'delusions.' He was with us for nearly two months. As a voluntary patient of the institution, and being a man of means, he had private rooms. He was in every way normal except for his intensive mental preoccupation with what I have called his delusions. In daily contact with him during this period I became convinced that Mr. Smith was not suffering from anything like a delusive affection of the mind.

"I diagnosed his difficulty — and Dr. Haviland agreed with me — that this patient, Smith, was suffering mentally from the effects of an ancestral memory.

"Such a case is so rare as to be virtually unique. The average psychiatrist would go through a life-time working at his speciality without encountering anything of the sort. There are, however, recorded cases. We were able to send our patient home in a mental condition of almost complete normality. As sometimes occurs in mental cases, his virtual cure was accomplished by making our diagnosis very clear to him — impressing upon his mind through reiterated and very positive statements that he was in no sense of the word demented, and that his condition, while unusual, was not outside the range and limitations of complete normality."

"It must have been a very interesting case," said Meredith. His reply was dictated by nothing deeper than a desire to be courteous. For his mind was full of the affairs of the General, Bothon, raging now in his prison-chamber; his mind harried, anxious over the fate of his surviving soldiers; that lurid glare, dimmed by the remoteness of his flame-tinted prison-chamber, in his eyes; his mind tortured and his keen sense of hearing stultified by the sustained, dreadful roaring of that implacable sea. He, Meredith, for reasons far too deep for his own analysis, felt utterly incapable of telling Dr. Cowlington what was transpiring in those dreams of his. All his inmost basic instincts were warning him, though subconsciously, that what he might tell now, if he would, could not possibly be believed!

Dr. Cowlington, looking at his patient, saw a face drawn and lined as though from some devastating mental stress; a deeply introspective expression in the eyes, which, professionally speaking, he did not like. The doctor considered a moment before resuming, erect in his chair, his knees crossed, his fingertips joined in a somewhat judicial attitude.

"Frankly, Meredith, I emphasized the fact that the man I have called Smith was in no sense insane because I feel that I must go farther and tell you that the nature of his apparent 'delusions' was, in one striking particular, related to your own case. I did not wish to give you the slightest alarm over the perfect soundness of your own mentality! To put the matter plainly, Mr. Smith remembered, although rather vaguely and dimly, certain phases of those ancestral memories I mentioned, and was able to reproduce a number of the terms of some unknown and apparently prehistoric language. Meredith"— the doctor turned and looked intensely into the eyes of his now interested patient — "there were three or four of Smith's words identical with yours!"

"Good God!" Meredith exclaimed, "What were the words, Doctor? Did you make notes of them?"

"Yes, I have them here," answered the psychiatrist.

Meredith was out of his chair and leaning eagerly over the doctor's shoulder long before Cowlington had his papers arranged. He gazed with a consuming intensity at the words and phrases carefully typed on several sheets of foolscap; listened, with an almost tremulous attention, while Dr. Cowlington carefully reproduced the sounds of these uncouth terms. Then, taking the sheets and resuming his chair, he read through all that had been written down, pronouncing the words, though very quietly, under his breath, his lips barely moving.

He was pale, and shaking from head to foot, when he rose at last and handed back, hands trembling, the thin fascicle of papers to its owner. Dr. Cowlington looked at him anxiously, his professional mind alert, his fears somewhat aroused over the wisdom of this experiment of his in bringing his former case thus abruptly to his patient's attention. Dr. Cowlington felt, if he had cared to put his impression into words, somewhat baffled. He could not, despite his long and careful training in dealing with mental, nervous, and "borderland" cases, quite put his acute professional finger upon just which one of the known simple and complex emotions was, for this moment, dominating this very interesting patient of his.

Dr. Cowlington would have been even more completely puzzled if he had known.

For Meredith, reading through the strange babblings of the patient, Smith, had recognized all the words and terms, and had lit upon the phrase:

"Our beloved Bothon has disappeared."

Dr. Cowlington, sensing accurately that it might be unwise to prolong this particular interview, concluded wisely that Meredith would most readily regain his normal poise and equanimity if left alone to cope with whatever, for the time-being, held possession of his mind, and rose quietly and walked over to the bedroom door.

He paused there, however, for an instant, before leaving the room, and looked back at the man. Meredith had not, apparently, so much as noted the doctor's movements towards departure. His mind, very obviously, was turned inward. He was, it appeared, entirely oblivious to his surroundings.

And Dr, Cowlington, whose professional outward deportment, acquired through years of contact with abnormal people, had not wholly obliterated a kindly disposition, noted with a certain emotion of his own that there were unchecked tears plainly visible in his patient's inward-gazing eyes.

Summoned back to Meredith's room an hour later by one of his house nurses, Dr. Cowlington found his patient restored to his accustomed urbane normality.

"I asked you to come up for a moment, Doctor," began Meredith, "because I wanted to inquire if there is anything that you would care to give a patient to induce sleep." Then, with a deprecating smile: "The only such things I know about are morphine and laudanum! I don't know very much about medicine and naturally you wouldn't want to give me one of those any more than I would want to take it."

Dr. Cowlington resumed his judicial manner. He thought rapidly about this unexpected request. He took into consideration how his story about the patient, Smith, had appeared to upset Meredith. He deliberately refrained from inquiring why Meredith wanted a sleeping potion. Then he nodded his head.

"I use a very simple preparation;" he said. "It is non-habit-forming; based on a rather dangerous drug, chloral; but, as I use it for my patients, compounded with an aromatic syrup and diluted with half a tumbler of water, it works very well. I will send some up to you but remember, please, four teaspoonfuls of the syrup is the outside dose. Two will probably be enough. Never more than four at any time, and not more than one dose in twenty-four hours."

Dr. Cowlington rose, came over to Meredith, and looked at the place where he had struck the side of his head against the marble wall of his shower-bath. The bruise was still there. The doctor passed his fingers lightly over the contusion.

"It's beginning to go down," he remarked. Then he smiled pleasantly, again nodded his head at Meredith, and started to leave. Meredith stopped him as he was about to go out of the room.

"I wanted to ask you," said Meredith, "I wanted to ask you, Doctor, if you would be willing to put me in touch with the man to whom you referred as "Smith'?"

The doctor shook his head. "I'm sorry, Mr. Smith died two years ago."

In ten minutes the house nurse fetched in a small tray. On it was a tumbler, a mixing spoon, and a freshly put up eight-ounce bottle containing a reddish coloured, pleasant tasting syrup.

Twenty minutes later, Meredith, who had compromised on three teaspoons, was deeply asleep on his bed; and the General, Bothon, in the innermost dungeon chamber of the great citadel of Alu, was standing poised in the centre of that dungeon's smooth stone floor, tensed to leap in any direction; while all about him the rending crashes of thousands of tons of the riven and falling masonry of the citadel itself was deafening him against all other sounds except the incessant and indescribably thunderous fury of the now utterly maddened ocean. The lurid glare of the fires from without had been markedly heightened. Detonation after detonation came to Bothon's ears at frequent intervals. The Aluans were blowing up this central portion of their great city, in order to check the advance of the conflagration which had raged for days and nights and was utterly beyond control. These detonations seemed actually faint to the alert man in that prison room against the hideous crashing of the sections of the citadel itself, and the sustained roar of the ocean.

Abruptly the crisis for which he had been waiting arrived. The stone flooring beneath his feet buckled and sagged at his right. He whirled about and leaped far in the other direction, pressing himself, hands and arms stretched out above his head, against the wall of the prison-chamber, his heart pounding wildly, his breath coming in great gasps and sobs as the stifling, earthquake-deadened air about him shrank to a sudden and devastating attenuation. Then the solid wall opposite split in a tearing gap from top to bottom, and an even more stifling cloud of white dust sifted abruptly through the room as the ceiling was riven asunder.

Stifling, choking, fighting for breath and life, the General, Bothon, lowered his arms and whirled about again in the direction of this thunderous breakage, and groped his way across the now precarious flooring in the faint hope of discovering an avenue of escape. He struggled up a steep mound of débris through the grey darkness of the hanging dust where a few seconds before there had been a level floor of solid masonry. He groped his way through thicker clouds of the drifting, settling stone-dust, skirted the irregular edges of yawning holes and toiled up and down mounded heaps of rubble, far past the place where the confining wall of his dungeon had stood, onward and forward resolutely towards that vague goal of freedom.

At last, the resources of his mighty body spent, his eyes two tortured red holes, his mouth and throat one searing pain, Bothon emerged across the last hill of rubbish which had been the citadel of Alu and came out upon the corner edge of one of the largest of the city's great public squares.

For the first time in the course of his progress out of that death trap, Bothon suddenly trod on something soft and yielding. He paused. He could hardly see, and he crouched and felt with his hands, under the thickly mounded dust.

It was the body of a man, in chain mail. Bothon, exhaled a painful breath of satisfaction. He rolled the body over, freeing it from the pounds of dust upon it, and slid his hand along the copper-studded leather belt to where a short, heavy, one-handed battle-axe was attached. This he drew from its sheath.

Then from the dead man's silken tunic he tore off a large section and cleansed his eyes and mouth and wiped the sweat-caked dust from his face.

Finally he took from the corpse a heavy leathern purse. He lay down for a few moments beside the dead soldier on the soft dust for a brief rest. Some ten minutes later he rose, stretched himself, testing the heavy axe with three or four singing strokes through the clearing air, and dusted out and readjusted his garments, finally tightening a loosened sandal thong.

He stood free now in the center of Alu. He was adequately armed. A great gust of energy surged through him. He oriented himself; then he turned with an instinct as sure as a homing bee's in the direction he had been seeking, and began to march at the unhurrying, space-devouring pace of a Ludektan legionary, straight for the Imperial Palace.

Bothon had thoroughly settled in his mind the answer to a question which, for the first few days of his captivity, had puzzled him greatly. Why had he been left alone and undisturbed in that confinement; food and water brought to him at regular intervals in accordance with the ordinary routine of the citadel? Why, to put the matter plainly, having been obviously captured by the Emperor's retainers while lying unconscious within two squares of the Imperial Palace, had he not been summarily crucified? His keen trained mind had apprised him that the answer was to be found in the hideous turmoil of the raging sea and in the fearful sounds of a disintegrating city. The Emperor had been too greatly occupied by those cataclysms even to command the punishment of this leader of such an armed attack against the world's metropolis as had not been known in all the long history of the mother continent.

Skirting its enormous outer walls, Bothon came at last to the massive chief entrance-way to the Imperial Palace. This enormous structure, its basic walls eight feet thick, stood massive, magnificent, intact. Without any hesitation he began mounting the many broad steps straight towards the magnificent entrance-gates of copper and gold and porphyry.

Before these gates, in the rigid line and under the command of an officer beneath whose corselet appeared the pale blue tunic of the Emperor's household guards, stood a dozen fully armed soldiers. One of these, at a word from the officer, ran down the steps to turn back this intruder. Bothon slew him with a single crashing stroke and continued to mount the steps.

At this a shouted command of the officer sent the entire troop down the steps upon him in close order. Bothon paused, and waiting until the foremost was no more than the space of two of the broad steps above him, leaped lightly to his right. Then as the foremost four of the soldiers passed beyond him under the impetus of their downward charge, Bothon as lightly leaped back again, his heavy axe falling upon the troop's flank with deadly, short, quick-swinging blows.

Before they could collect themselves the officer and five of his men lay dead upon the steps. Leaving the demoralized remainder to gather themselves together as best they might, Bothon leaped up the intervening steps and was through the great entrance-doors, and, with a pair of lightning-like right-and-left strokes of his axe, had disposed of the two men-at-arms stationed just inside the doorway.

His way into the Palace now entirely unobstructed, Bothon sped through well-remembered rooms and along broad corridors into the heart of the Imperial Palace of Alu.

Within thirty seconds he had located the entrance to the brother of the Emperor, Netvis Toldon's apartments, and had passed through the doorway.

He discovered the family reclining about the horse-shoe-shaped table in the refectory, for it was the hour of the evening meal. He paused in the doorway, was met with surprised glances, and bowed low to the Netvis Toldon.

"I beseech you to pardon this intrusion, my Lord Netvis. It would be inexcusable under other circumstances, at a more favourable time." The nobleman returned no answer, only stared in surprise. Then, the dear lady of his heart, the Netvissa Ledda, rose to her feet from her place at her father's table, her eyes wide with wonderment. A dawning realization of what this strange invasion might mean, made her lovely face suddenly the hue of the Aluan roses. She looked at this heroically formed lover of hers, her soul in her eyes.

"Come, my lady Ledda," said Bothon quickly, and as lightly as a deer the Netvissa Ledda ran to him.

He took her arm, very quietly, and, before the assembled members of the family of Toldon had recovered from their surprise, the two were hastening along the corridor towards the palace entrance.

From around the first corner before them came then abrupt sounds of armed men. They paused, listening, and Bothon shifted his axe into his right hand and stepped before the lady Ledda, but she laid firm hands upon his left arm. "This way, swiftly" she whispered, and led him down a narrow passageway at the wide corridor's left. This they traversed in haste, and had barely negotiated a sharp turn when they heard the guard-troop rush along the main corridor, and a voice, commanding:

"To the apartment of my Lord, the Netvis Toldon!"

The narrow passage-way led them past cook-rooms and scullery-chambers, and ended at a small door which opened upon a narrow court. Rapidly traversing this, they emerged upon a square at the west side of the palace, and well before any pursuit could have traced their course, were indistinguishable among the vast concourse of the people who thronged the wide avenues of Alu.

Bothon now resumed the direction of their course of escape. Leading the way across a larger adjacent square, he reached the secluded corner, mounded about with débris, where he had secured his weapon. It was not yet past the early dusk of a mid-summer evening, and now there was nothing to interfere with his keen vision.

Yes, it was as he had guessed from the quality of that torn fragment of silken tunic with which he had wiped his tortured eyes free of the stone-dust. The dead man was an officer of one of the Imperial Legions.

Seating the Lady Ledda upon a block of granite and requesting her to watch, Bothon knelt swiftly beside the dead body and busied himself upon it.

At the end of two intensive minutes the Netvissa Ledda looked up at his touch upon her shoulder to see her lover apparelled from head to foot in the uniform, armour, and accoutrements of an Elton of the Imperial Legion of the Hawk.

Then they hurried southward, side by side, across the great square with its desolation of shattered buildings, towards one of the few remaining residences of the rich before which four coal-black slaves in the livery of their household were lowering an ornamental litter to the ground.

From the luxurious vehicle, as they arrived beside it, there emerged a stout citizen who stared at them inquiringly, his initial fear disappearing at recognition of the Emperor's niece and the uniform of an Imperial Legion.

"We request the loan of your litter, my lord," said Bothon.

"Most willingly," returned the citizen, bowing. Bothon expressed thanks, handed his companion into the litter, distributed a handful of silver among the four slaves, and gave the destination to the Negro who stood beside the forward left-hand pole. Then he climbed in himself and drew the red silk curtains together.

The strong litter-poles strained and creaked as the load was hoisted to four brawny shoulders, and then the litter swung away from the residence of its still bowing and smirking owner towards the military enclosure which housed and guarded the flying-vessels of the Aluvian standing army.

"You may have observed how very completely I have entrusted my Imperial person to you," remarked the Netvissa Ledda, smiling. She was very well aware of the reasons for the Imperial request which had sent Bothon back to Ludekta, and for the first armed invasion against the Aluvian metropolis. "I have not so much as inquired as to our destination!"

"It is my intention to seek safety to the northwest," answered Bothon gravely. "I am convinced the prediction of Bal, Lord of Fields, as to the destruction of the Mother Continent, is not a mere classic to be learned, as we learned it in our childhood, as a formal exercise in rhetoric. Here, all about us, is the evidence. More, my four augurs warned me of the continent's danger ere I brought my war-galleys up upon the beaches of Alu. The four great forces, they insisted, were in collusion to that end. Do we not see and hear them at work? Fire raging through the land; earth shaking mightily; winds such as never were encountered hitherto upon the planet, else the old records lie! Water, the commotion of which surpasses all experiences;—is it not so, my beloved? Am I not constrained to speak thus to be heard amidst this hellish tumult?"

The Lady Ledda nodded, grave now in her turn.

"There are many deafened in the palace," she remarked. "Where are we to go for refuge?"

"We depart straight this night, for the great mountains of 'A-Wah-Ii," answered Bothon, "if so be the four great forces allow us possession of a war chariot. And, to that end, your ring, my beloved."

The Lady Ledda nodded again, understandingly, and removed from the middle finger of her right hand the ring of the two suns and the eight-pointed star which, as a member of the Royal Family, she was entitled to wear. Bothon received it, and slipped it upon the little finger of his right hand.

The sentinel on guard before the barracks of the officer commanding the military enclosure of the Aluvian supply-barracks, saluted the commanding looking Elton of the Legion of the Hawk who stepped down from the ornamented litter. The Elton addressed him in formal military phrases.

"Report at once to the Ka-Kalbo Netro, the arrival of the Elton Barko of the Legion of the Hawk, conveying a member of the Imperial household into exile. I am requisitioning one battle-chariot of capacity for two persons, and officer's rations sufficient for fourteen days, together with the medicinal supply for a full kit-va of men. My authority, the Imperial Signet. Behold!"

The sentinel saluted the sun-and-star ring of the Emperor, repeated his orders like an efficient automaton, saluted the Elton of the Hawk Legion, and departed at the double to fetch the commandant, the Ka-Kalbo Netro.

The Ka-Kalbo arrived promptly in answer to this summons. He saluted the Imperial Signet, and, as a Ka-Kalbo outranked an Elton by one full grade, was punctiliously saluted according to military usage by the Elton Barko of the Legion of the Hawk, an officer whose personal acquaintance he had not previously made.

Within ten minutes the Netvissa Ledda had been ceremoniously carried to and placed upon her seat in the commandeered battle-chariot, and the Elton Barko had taken his place beside her. Then, the dozen sweating mechanicians who had carried out their commandant's orders in record time standing in a stiff, saluting row, the battle-chariot started off at a stiff gallop, the driver standing and plying his long thong with loud, snapping reports over the horses' backs, while at the great chariot's rear the spare-horse leader whistled continuously to the four relay animals which galloped behind.

The heights of 'A-Wah-Ii, to the northwest, gave some promise, in Bothon's opinion, of security from the anciently predicted submersion of the continent. Those towering mountains would, at least, be among the last sections to sink, should the gas belts, hypothecated by the scientists of the mother continent, explode, and remove the undersea support of this great land of the globe's most ancient and noble civilization.

Shortly after daybreak, and accurately, according to the map and careful explanations of the painstaking Ka-Kalbo Netro, the chariot paused in the centre of a great level tableland one quarter of the way to his destination. The country was utterly uninhabited. They were relatively safe here in a region only lightly visited by the earthquakes, and not at all by fire. The roar of the north wind troubled the Netvissa Ledda severely. Bothon barely noticed it. He was now convinced that he was losing his sense of hearing.

They ate and slept and resumed their journey at noon after a readjustment of the provisions and a change of the now rested animals.

Their four days' journey steadily northwest was uneventful. The charioteer drove onward steadily. On the fourth day, as the coppery ball which was the smoking sun reached and touched a flat horizon, they caught their first view of the lofty summits of the 'A-Wah-Ii region, a goal of a possible immunity.

Dr. Cowlington, an anxious look on his face, was standing beside Meredith's bed when he awakened in mid-morning. He had slept twenty hours. However, what the doctor thought of as his patient's mental condition was so entirely normal, and his cheerfulness so pronounced after his protracted sleep, that Dr. Cowlington was reassured, and changed his mind about removing the bottle of sleeping medicine. Plainly it had had an excellent effect on Meredith.

Stretched out in his usual quiet-inducing attitude on the davenport just before lunch, Meredith suddenly ceased reading and put down his magazine. It had occurred to him that he had heard none of the turmoil of Alu during that waking period. He sat up, puzzled. Bothon, he remembered, had been hearing the sounds about him only dimly, a strange, perhaps a significant, coincidence.

He felt the bruise behind his right ear. It was no longer even slightly painful to the touch. He pressed his finger-tips firmly against the place. The contusion was now barely perceptible to the sense of touch.

He reported the apparent loss of what the ear-specialist Gatefield had named his "clairaudience" to Dr. Cowlington after lunch.

"Your bruise is going down," said the doctor significantly. He examined the posterior edge of Meredith's right temporal area.

"I thought so," remarked the doctor, nodding. "Your secondary 'hearing' began with that injury to your head. As it goes down, some obscure stimulation of the auditory apparatus, which accounts for your ability to hear those sounds, diminishes accordingly. You could probably hear only some stupendous sound from there now. And in a day or so I predict that you will be hearing nothing more, and then you can go home!"

And, within an hour came the "stupendous sound" in very truth. It broke in upon Meredith's quiet reading once more as though someone had opened that sound-proof door.

A curious, secondary, mental vision accompanied it. It was as though Meredith, in his own proper person, yet through the strange connection of his personality with the General, Bothon, stood on the heights of Tharan-Yud, overlooking the stricken city of Alu. The utter fury of mountainous waves accompanied the now titanic rumblings of malignant earth, the wholesale crashing of the cyclopean masonry of Alu as the vast city crumbled and melted beneath his horrified eyes. With these hellish horrors went the wild roaring of ravaging flame, and the despairing, hysterical cacophony of Alu's doomed millions.

Then there came, at last, a sound as of the veritable yawning of the nethermost watery gulf of earth, and the high sun itself was blotted out by a monstrous green wall of advancing death. The sea rose up and fell upon accursed Alu, drowning forever the shrieks of utter despair, the piping and chittering of the obscurely gnawing Gyaa-Hua distracted at last from their loathsome banquet — hissings, roarings, shriekings, whinings, tearings, seethings — a cacophony more than human ears might bear, a sight of utter devastation more onerous than man might look upon, and live.

There came to Meredith a merciful stupor, as the waters of Mu-Iadon closed in forever over the mother continent, and as his consciousness failed him, he emerged once more out of that quiet bedroom — away from his overlooking of the world's major catastrophe and, as Bothon, walked beside the Lady Ledda along a wooded ravine in 'A-Wah-Ii, goal of safety, among laden fruit trees, yet not, it seemed, upon the towering heights of those noble mountains but upon an island about the shores of which rolled and roared a brown and viscid ocean choked with the mud which had been the soil of the mother continent.

"We are safe here, it would appear, my Bothon," said the Netvissa Ledda. "Let us lie down and sleep, for I am very weary."

And after watching for a little space while the Lady Ledda reclined and slept, Bothon lay down beside her and fell at once into the deep and dreamless slumber of utter physical exhaustion.

Meredith awakened on his davenport. The room was dark, and when he had risen, switched on the lights and looked at his watch, he found that it was four o'clock in the morning. He undressed and went to bed and awakened three hours later without having dreamed.

A world and an era had come to its cataclysmic end, and he had been witness of it.

The contusion on his head had disappeared, Dr. Cowlington observed later in the morning.

"I think you can go home now, you'll never hear again," said the doctor, in his judicial manner. "But, by the way, Meredith, what, if you can remember, was the name of that 'mother continent' of yours?"

"We called it Mu," said Meredith. The doctor was silent for a while; then he nodded his head. He had made up his mind.

"I thought so," said he, gravely.

"Why?" Meredith asked.

"Because *Smith* called it that," replied the doctor.

Tarbis of the Lake.

BY E. HOFFMAN PRICE
AND H.P. LOVECRAFT

**5,400-WORD SHORT STORY;
1932.**

The day H.P. Lovecraft arrived in New Orleans, and E. Hoffman Price met up with him in the lobby of his cheap hotel on St. Charles Street, the two authors stayed up late into the night talking and comparing notes while Lovecraft guzzled cup after cup of super-sweet coffee. Much of that time was spent talking about this story.

"Tarbis of the Lake" was one of Price's first stories written specifically for a professional audience — he'd been publishing regularly in the amateur-press journals for some time, and was just in the process of taking his business to the next level.

"There was a magnificent hair-splitting wrangle over each comma," Price recalls, in a reminiscent essay titled "The Man Who Was Lovecraft." "He felt that the element of coincidence entered into the meeting of the hero and the mysterious Tarbis . . . He insisted that the entire background should be presented, and while he did not put it in so many words, I knew that he had in mind a treatment comparable to that deliberate and generous development characteristic of his Arkham stories."

That was in June 1932. "Tarbis of the Lake" was published a year and a half later, in the February 1934 issue of Weird Tales *magazine.*

ABOUT E. HOFFMAN PRICE (1896-1988).

Edgar Hoffman Price was the kind of writer most sought after by pulp titles like Adventure *and* The Argosy. *As a surprisingly young teenager, he'd fought with U.S. forces in the Philippines, Mexico and France just before and during the First World War. He'd subsequently attended and graduated from West Point.*

In the early 1920s, Price started writing stories for Weird Tales *magazine, and it was through that connection that he got in touch with H.P. Lovecraft — but that connection didn't happen until 1932, years after Price had first started following Lovecraft's by-line.*

In that year, Lovecraft paid a visit to New Orleans, where Price was living at the time. Robert E. Howard telegraphed Price to let him know Lovecraft was coming to town, and Price met up with him and the two of them spent a couple weeks together.

Price was a particular fan of "The Silver Key," and urged Lovecraft to write a sequel to it. Whether Lovecraft was receptive to this idea or not is unknown — although it seems unlikely; Lovecraft's high levels of self-criticism made him tend to be loath to revisit his earlier works.

However, when Price wrote a sequel and proposed that Lovecraft collaborate with him on it, Lovecraft acceded, albeit with noticeable reluctance; the result was "Through the Gates of the Silver Key."

Price and Lovecraft corresponded regularly by letter until Lovecraft's death. Along the way, a proposal was floated for the two of them to form a writing team; but nothing came of this.

"My son," said white-haired Father Peytral to his companion, whose steel-grey eyes seemed far older than his rugged, bronzed features, "suppose that you abandon this hypothetical *friend* of yours and tell what is worrying you. Never mind what I'll think. Just express yourself."

John Rankin started. His face darkened for an instant; then he smiled as he caught the kindly expression in the old priest's eyes.

"I might have known you'd see through it, Father Peytral. But before I go any further, tell me who — what — well, *was* there ever a woman named Tarbis? I mean, other than—"

Rankin abruptly checked his speech, stared at the earth and at the heels of the unending throng of pilgrims who passed along the Esplanade.

Father Peytral's scrutiny of Rankin became keener at the mention of Tarbis.

"What's that?" he demanded. *"Tarbis?"* The priest frowned as he groped for a moment for a thought that was evading him, then resumed, "There is an old tradition to the effect that Tarbis, Queen of Ethiopia —"

"Ethiopia?" interrupted Rankin. "Why — *she* is as white as I am."

Father Peytral's eyebrows rose. Then, instead of asking the question that was on his lips, he explained, "Ethiopia in those days was the upper kingdom of Egypt. A queen of that country was no more negro than Rameses the Great.

"And Tarbis," he continued, "offered her hand and crown to Moses, who declined both. The pride of the queen and the woman being sorely wounded, she abandoned her throne and set sail, wandering until she reached France. She founded not only the city of Tarbes, which to this day bears her name, but also its neighbour Lapurdum — our modern Lourdes which God has so signally honoured in selecting it as the place for the apparition of the Holy Virgin to appear.

"They say that the site of the original Lapurdum was three kilometres from here. Its inhabitants practiced black magic.

The place became a den of necromancers, an affront to God, man, and nature. But instead of following the Scriptural precedent, and destroying Lapurdum with fire, the Almighty caused a flood to rise out of the earth and overwhelm the city, whence the present lake, not far from the outskirts of the modern city of Lourdes.

"All of which," concluded Father Peytral, "is to be found in the archives of Lourdes."

Weird Tales, February 1934

"She was one flight below and centuries away."

"Good God!" muttered Rankin. "Worse and worse! You've just succeeded in confirming my outrageous fancy — the thing I've tried to deny . . . ."

Rankin suddenly sat bolt-upright. His bronzed cheeks had become sickly yellow. His eyes were burning with an unnatural light, and his face was drawn and haggard as he regarded the priest for a moment before continuing, "That Ethiopian queen never died. *She is living in Lourdes, on the street that leads to the chateau.* I knew — I sensed — and now you have confirmed it!"

Father Peytral recognized solemn-voiced knowledge.

"My son," he said in a low, even voice, "that any human being, man or woman, could attain everlasting physical life is denied both by the Church and by science. Whatever the source of your obsession, you must forget such fantastic thoughts!"

"Forget them?" exclaimed Rankin. "I've tried that for several years. You've often tried to get me to open up. I evaded your queries, but my fear finally got the best of me. First it was a lover's fancy, that idea that Tarbis Dulac had in the dim past discovered the secret of eternal youth. That didn't alarm me. It was just a quaint conceit, a whimsical fancy about a girl I think a great deal of. But at last I found that I was telling myself that I didn't believe anything of the kind."

"Which," said the priest, "assured you that you did believe just that, and it frightened you."

Rankin nodded.

"So I left Lourdes. I roamed all over Asia, trying to forget. And when I finally succeeded in driving her antique smile from my conscious memory, and with it the idea that she was someone who had lived for ages, she returned and haunted me in nightmarish dreams. She made statuesque gestures, like — you've seen them, sculptured —"

"*Mais oui,*" agreed Father Peytral. "In the Louvre, for instance."

"She wore a tall, curious head-dress. She murmured words that I could not understand, except in momentary flashes. And what I understood troubled me more than what I didn't. I'm afraid of Tarbis — and I'm in love with her."

He raised his eyes and made a despairing gesture of his hand, then let his head droop wearily. Father Peytral murmured to himself as he contemplated the hopelessly baffled expression of Rankin's rugged features.

"And now you tell me a legend of a Tarbis who was a queen, Lord knows how many centuries ago," muttered Rankin. "And of the lake — her very name today, Dulac . . . *du Lac* . . ." Then, jerking himself erect: "What do you say? Am I utterly insane?"

"No," replied the priest as he grasped Rankin by the shoulder. "On the contrary, your doubts prove your sanity. An insane person is assured that everyone but himself is unbalanced. Your denying this delusion is your best assurance."

"Well, what am I to do?" demanded Rankin, taking heart. "I can't stand being near a woman who I know is an uncanny creature that should have died ages ago. And neither can I stay away from her. I've tried both!"

For a moment neither spoke. Then Father Peytral's frown of perplexed pondering was replaced by a smile of calm assurance.

"You have unwittingly taken the right course," he said, "in speaking your thought aloud instead of letting it be an inner murmuring that has poisoned your mind. See this Tarbis Dulac, look her in the eye, speak to her and tell her your thought. Never mind what she thinks of your sanity. Face her unflinchingly and express yourself. Ask her solemnly who and what she is, and tell her why you ask. If she cares for you, she will not be harsh in her judgment."

"Father Peytral, I can't do that!" protested Rankin. "She'll think —" He regarded the priest with outraged amazement.

"You seem to forget —"

Father Peytral shook his grey head. His smile was a tale of time-mellowed grief.

"My son," he said in a voice that was none the less authoritative for being low, "I do not forget. I *know*. If she cares for you, she will not judge harshly. And once you have enunciated this outrageous thought, you will have conquered it. Your fear and your furtive denials have fostered this obsession, even as your speaking boldly will burn it out."

Rankin pondered for a moment. He rose from the stone bench and stood erect. His eyes were less haggard, and his drawn face had relaxed.

"Thank you, Father," he said. "I'll see her tonight, and I'll follow your advice."

Rankin lifted his hat and bowed. Then, to himself, as he strode down the Esplanade, "Fine old man . . . not a sign of a sermon . . . seems perfectly natural to call him *Father* . . . ."

Like those pilgrims who flock toward Lourdes, Rankin had crossed land and sea for the good of his soul, even though he had not come to pray, or to drink the water of the spring that had miraculously burst forth from the grotto of the great black rock of Massabielle. But, though Father Peytral's assurance gave Rankin a new grip on himself, and a weapon with which to combat his obsession, the priest's words had at the same time strengthened Rankin's ever-present feeling that he was dealing with one whose name was written on the first pages of the archives of that city which had not always been a holy place, comparable to Rome, Jerusalem, or Mecca.

That evening Rankin sat once more in the luxuriously furnished reception room of that outwardly unprepossessing house which was perched on the steep slope of the hill whose high-walled fortress and square donjon built by the Moslem conquerors commanded the valley of the Gave.

"It is good to see you again, mon ami," she said as she regarded Rankin with her smouldering, long-lashed eyes. "Incurable nomad, you tried to forget Tarbis, didn't you?"

"But I couldn't," Rankin admitted sombrely. The assurance that he had gained from Father Peytral was slowly melting before the loveliness of Tarbis Dulac. "And I know now that I never shall. You've haunted me. Your memory followed me and made a madness of my dreams. So I've returned."

"I knew that you would, some day," murmured the girl. "I've been expecting you."

She smiled that slow, archaic smile that had haunted Rankin; but her eyes were dolorous and incredibly ancient. They contradicted the youthful freshness of her skin and the gracious contours of her throat and shoulders. Tarbis was uncommonly lovely, and anyone but Rankin would have accepted her without undue wonderings and fancies.

Then Rankin nerved himself for the assault.

"I've returned to solve the riddle," said Rankin. "You've evaded me and mocked me with that sphinx smile of yours, and your eyes have laughed at me. I've wondered entirely too long who and what you are. So I've returned to find out, once and for all," he concluded.

The girl's eyebrows rose in Moorish arches, and she made a fleeting gesture of her slender hand. That damnable, haunting gesture! That insidious suggestion of sculptured fingers on the granite of deserted temples and rifled tombs!

"Insatiable, aren't you?" she chided. "What more do you want? What have I ever denied you?"

Tarbis was right. Any sane man should have been content. Yet there was that same evasion which had always left Rankin baffled. Rankin knew that he had flinched from the assault; that he had failed solemnly to demand who and what she was.

"Tarbis, how old are you?" he asked in blunt-spoken desperation.

"Such a question, *mon ami*!" Her laugh was light. She refused to take him seriously. Then she answered, "I'm ever so much older than you suspect, John. But would I be any more pleasing if you could catalogue me like a piece of antique furniture, a bit of jade, a Persian carpet?"

Rankin had to admit that Tarbis was right. And to consider her as a normal woman was the sane and logical thing; yet there would be no peace until she had answered the solemn adjuration he was to make.

"I wonder," she continued, "if you are sure that you want to know. Did you ever stop to think that you might have long regrets?"

Worse and yet worse! She was hinting at the very thought that he had sought to disown.

"You know," said Tarbis after a long pause during which her lips were alternately smiling and grave, "I could just as well question you, and wonder why you've left me several times, with never a quarrel or any apparent necessity. And I do know that you've always cared for me — a great deal. There is nothing to prevent your staying in Lourdes. You know I'd not seek any claim on you. Yet you've always left."

"Yes, and always returned!" he retorted, stung by the memory of his resolutions to forget her, and his inevitable relapse from his determination. "But this time I'm going to get the answer. You're so much more than you appear to be. You're not one woman but a world of women in one, and you are withholding a hundredfold more than you'll ever reveal."

"Such versatility should be pleasing," suggested Tarbis with a lightness that belied her unsmiling eyes.

Rankin decided that she was not mocking him, but he would no longer accept evasion. He rose abruptly and seized her by the wrist.

"Let's not fence any longer! Just because I've not found words to express myself — "

Rankin stopped short. He had found words, but he dared not use them.

"Then tell me what is on your mind, John," said Tarbis. "Maybe I'll understand."

She spoke very solemnly now. Her voice was grave, and her eyes were unsmiling and age-old. Rankin released her wrist and stared at the golden-olive tint that crept back to erase the white imprint of his grasp. She regarded him intently for a long moment, then spoke again.

"Can't you forget your morbid curiosity?" she pleaded. "Can't you take me for what I am, and without question? Kiss me, and love me for the sake of the evening, and for myself. And if you do care enough to be jealous, stay here in Lourdes, always, and watch me as closely as any Turk ever guarded his harem."

Rankin saw the gleam of tears in her great lustrous eyes. He knew that he was about to weaken as he had so many times before. At the moment, his thoughts seemed outrageous and insane beyond expression. And then he thought of the obsession that had overwhelmed him and affronted every trace of reason. No matter what she thought of his sanity, he had to declare himself. It would be better for her to think him utterly mad than for him to become so in fact. He nerved himself for the final plunge.

"Tarbis, do you know that most of the time I've been resisting the thought that you are not a woman at all, but *something* — "

"Must you know *all* about me?" she interrupted, recoiling from the implication of his last word, and eager to prevent his expressing that which she sensed would follow. "John, can't you take anything for granted? Have I ever — "

"No, I can't," declared Rankin, evading her attempted change of subject. "I've reached the verge of madness, telling myself, arguing with myself to prove that you are not older than any woman has a right to be. In my own mind I've denied breaths of rumours and hints that no rational person would bother to deny."

"Oh, those damnable, meddling priests and villagers!" exclaimed Tarbis with a despairing, impersonal bitterness. "Can't they live and let live? Can't they be content to go their placid, ordained ways and leave me in peace?"

"But they didn't talk about you," protested Rankin.

"No, but they spoke of *her*," countered Tarbis. "John, can't you forget all this? You do care for me, don't you? Or am I just another riddle that your insatiable mind must solve lest it perish of unsatisfied vanity? Must you know *everything?*"

"Not everything. Tarbis. But this one thing, yes; for the good of my soul and my sanity. Who and what are you?" he demanded desperately, steeling himself to resist the appeal that he read in her eyes.

She was about to yield. He could not now relent.

"Since you insist, I'll tell you," she finally assented. "No, I'll show you, and let you draw your own conclusion. I will let you meet my rival face to face."

"*Your* rival?" gasped Rankin, amazed at that turn. "You mean *my* rival, don't you?"

"No, I mean what I said: *my* rival," affirmed Tarbis. "My rival, and my damnation. She will drive you away. She will everlastingly destroy the happiness I have stolen — we have stolen. But since it must be —"

She took Rankin by the hand, and half turned toward the winding stairway. Then she paused and reached for her wine-glass.

"A toast, John," she proposed, with the air of one gallantly drinking to impending doom. "To my rival and to her damnation!"

Rankin drained his glass. Tarbis barely moistened her lips, and set the stemmed glass back on the old lace runner that crossed the table. Then she led the way upstairs.

As Rankin passed the carved newel post and followed her up through the dim light, it seemed that he was marching toward a perilous rendezvous. For a moment he wanted to take the steps three at a bound, seize her and carry her back to the warmth and light of that familiar living-room, to fight those torturing fancies on the level ground of sanity. But Rankin remembered his resolve, and stifled the sadness that was mingled with his sense of impending peril.

Tarbis halted at the head of the stairs. Her blue-black hair glistened under the glow of a shaded oil lamp. Queer, how this luxurious house of hers should be so obsolete in some details. The square-cut emerald on her finger was phosphorescent as the eyes of a beast of prey. Rankin knew why he observed and made mental comment on such irrelevancies . . . once, in crossing a courtyard to face a firing-squad, he had noted the pattern of the tiles and had observed that the colour scheme was clashing . . . .

"She is waiting for us," he heard Tarbis saying. "Here, in my own room."

Rankin fought the raging impulse to retreat and let well enough alone. He followed her into the dimness of that familiar room with its canopied bed and its dressing table. A hand-mirror lay, as always, face down, the twining golden serpents of its handle gleaming in the faint light. Rankin wondered again why that mirror was never face up.

Then, in a niche in the masonry of the wall he saw a mummy-case whose gilded features stared vacantly at him.

"She is here," said Tarbis. "I will leave you with her. Her last words were spoken far back in the first youth of time. Her lips are silent, but she will speak to your mind. And when you know, you may return to the living-room. I'll probably be asleep on the divan."

She paused and regarded him intently for a moment; then she continued, "Perhaps, when she tells you who I am, and how old I am, you'll pass quietly on, without even a word of farewell. But, perhaps — the memories we share — I hope —"

She turned, without expressing her hope. The door closed behind her, leaving Rankin with his strange companion. The loneliness of the room oppressed him. The departure of Tarbis made it appallingly like a tomb.

He felt in his vest pocket for cigarettes, but found none. Well, no matter; although a smoke would be company while he sat there, seeking the point of the tableau she had arranged. Then he saw a silver case among the combs and perfume vials and powder boxes. It was half filled with long, slender cigarettes. He struck light to one. It was ever so faintly scented and had a curious but not unpleasant aroma. That exotic tobacco was appropriate to Tarbis. Rankin snapped his lighter closed and leaned back in his chair to contemplate the gilded features of the sycamore case and its rows of painted hieroglyphs.

Through the gray wisps of smoke he regarded the gilded mask, at first idly, then with an intentness that he sought to deny himself. Something new was stirring disquietingly in his mind. He forced himself to think of Tarbis whose slender length was now stretched out on the Shemaka rug that covered the divan. Tarbis du Lac . . . Tarbis of the Lake . . . asleep or awake, she would be smiling in whimsical mockery of her latest lover.

Even though she had never once hinted that he had any predecessors in her affections, Rankin knew that Tarbis must have had many lovers before him. He knew that she must have learned ever so long ago that illusion is more alluring than candour.

And this thought slowly but certainly brought his consciousness back to the gilded face before him. The convictions that had haunted him so long became stronger than ever before. Had the occupant of that sycamore case lived until today, she too would have learned from experience that no lover cares for candour about his predecessors. *Had she lived* —

Then Rankin surrendered to a new madness which was more perturbing than that which he had sought to conquer that evening. It was terrifying. He shivered and sat erect in his chair. The scented poison of the cigarette curled unheeded around his fingers and stained them.

If the carver had given life and animation to those long almond-shaped eyes, they would be the eyes of Tarbis. The fire of the cigarette ate into his fingers and momentarily broke the spell. He ground the butt into the rug beneath his feet and struck light to another smoke. But the distraction was not enough to stop the surge of surmise that had become knowledge. That curved, antique smile of gilt was Tarbis herself staring at him, mocking the wooden conventions of Egyptian carving and fighting through the gold leaf into faithful portraiture.

He knew now what Tarbis had intended to convey to him. He had been haunted by the outlandish idea that Tarbis, ages ago, had discovered the secret of everlasting youth. Rankin had considered such a fancy outrageous, and any woman who inspired the like, uncanny. But now—

Tarbis had become something infinitely more terrifying: she was not one who had, ages ago, discovered the secret of eternal youth, but rather the product of an Egyptian magic which had enabled dead Tarbis to materialize and present the semblance of a physical woman.

Rankin clutched the arms of his chair. Every memory of Tarbis and her amorous encircling arms denied the conviction carried by that gilded smile; yet as he stared, Rankin began to remember things which he wished that he had never learned. To distract himself from the fancy that Tarbis was age-old, he had listened to adepts in High Asia, who muttered of Tibetan lore, and the lost magic of Egypt, never suspecting that he was acquiring a knowledge that would in the end be more horrible than the whim he sought to cast out.

He wondered when she emerged from the painted case with its painted hieroglyphs. He wondered what she had done with her endless yards of linen bandages, and how she had escaped their firm embrace. Then, bit by bit, there came back to Rankin the words of that slant-eyed adept he had befriended.

"There are nine elements which when fused into a unit make what your eye sees as a single human body: the physical, flesh-and-blood body; the shadow; the double, or astral counterpart called the *ka*; the soul, or *ba*; the heart; a spirit called *khu*; a Power; a Name; and a ninth component which is a motivating force . . . . And all these, mark you, are used in a mystical, or esoteric sense. Yet this knowledge if truly interpreted and rightly used can serve to work all the wonders of the hidden Egyptian magic that was codified by Thoth . . . ."

The embalmed physical body of Tarbis was in the case before Rankin; and that which had seemed to him to be a living woman was but an aggregation of elements that had joined the *ka*, which lingers near the physical body until it utterly disintegrates.

Every whimsical speech and mannerism of Tarbis came trooping back to confirm Rankin's dismaying conviction. His brain reeled at the recollection of her avoidance of daylight.

"My dear," she had murmured one evening, "you sit up to the most unusual hours making love to me— oh, ever so charmingly!—and then you marvel that I'd rather not spend the following day strolling along the Esplanade, or scaling Pic de Jer. And it's one of my pet vanities, *tu comprends*, this being seen only at my best, at night, by my own lighting . . . ."

It was clear, now. That ancient necromancy had not been able to restore the missing *shadow*, so that Tarbis could not appear by the shadow-casting sun. The Name, the Power, the *ka* . . . perhaps all but the one missing irreplaceable element were present.

Then Rankin's sanity revolted. He fought the urge to wrench the lid from the sycamore case. He dared not yield to the demand to find out what was behind that gilded, smiling mask. If indeed it was empty, that would mean that that dead, bandage-swathed thing emerged from its cell to offer him the unholy semblance of a living woman.

Rankin shivered as though a breath of the abysmal outer spaces had been exhaled into his veins and was chilling his blood.

"It can't be empty!" his mind screamed to his *self.* "Good God, if it's empty—!"

He dared not complete the utterance. He refused to think of the slender, shapely arms of Tarbis and her curved, carmine smile.

"But if *it* is in there, then she's an illusion—a shadow from the tomb. That is as bad—or is it worse?"

Rankin forced his brain to cease that insistent surging that would end by cracking his skull. The veins in his temples would in another moment burst like rotted fire-hose.

Then the strokes of the cathedral bell mercifully interrupted the dread that he could neither accept nor deny. And during the moment of respite accorded him by that sound from the outer world, he noted for the first time the possible significance of the peculiar aroma of the cigarettes Tarbis had left in her case. It was reminiscent of something they smoked in Persia and Hindustan.

He smiled at the gilded mask. The last rich note of the cathedral bell reminded him that Lourdes was a holy city. He envied the calm priests and the pious pilgrims, and was glad that they were there, not far from the foot of the hill.

"Tarbis, you devil, and your cigarettes!" he exulted, gratefully ascribing his dreadful fancies to the influence of *charras*, or whatever other like drug they might have contained thus to upset his mind. He sighed with relief and weariness. "But maybe I deserve it."

He rose and found that he still trembled violently. His legs barely supported his weight; but his brain no longer rocked and quivered from clamourings from beyond the Border.

Tarbis would be waiting for him in the living-room. She would see the mark of terror still branding his features. But he forgave her the ghastly jest. He could be generous, now that he had conquered his obsession by expressing it in words. He had asked her: and she had answered by showing him in her oblique way that there were fancies infinitely more disturbing than that of her possessing everlasting youth. Only Tarbis could have devised such an answer: slender, alluring Tarbis curled up on the Shemaka rug.

But as he reached the door, a lurking residue of the evening's horror returned to remind him that his conquest had not been complete. He knew that in the end he would begin to wonder anew whether that case was or was not empty, and whether Tarbis was a revenant imprisoned by day, but loose at night to fascinate him with her archaic, Egyptian smile. And Rankin's dreadful surmises marched once more in a circle that was started afresh by his glance of premature triumph at that gilded mask. That subtle, gilded smile! That hint of a hidden jest!

He retraced his steps. With an effort he grasped the cover.

And then he slowly withdrew his hands. He knew that his sanity demanded that he refrain from giving any physical expression to that question. But, as he was about to step back, he knew what would become of his regained reason if he retreated without having learned, forever and always, what the case contained, whose names and titles were depicted in painted hieroglyphs upon that carven sycamore.

Rankin thrust the cover aside. And then he tore the crumbling linen bandages that swathed the features of the dead. He had ceased thinking; he had nerved himself to the task and he could not stop. His mind was dead, but his fingers lived. They tore another layer of bandages, and another.

Something forced him to look at that face. A blind instinct and a compelling terror urged him to learn the truth, whatever it might be. The dust of centuries mingled with the dust of crumbled linen and pungent spices and choked him. Then he stepped back and regarded the shrunken, hideously life-like features. The gilded mask had been a portrait; *but here he faced Tarbis herself!*

He gasped for breath. He sought to deny his eyes, refute the evidence of his senses, prove that he had not felt the burning ardour of those shrivelled lips. This was the supreme horror, the utterly worst outrage.

Rankin forced his eyes at last to leave that mockery of the loveliness of Tarbis. He saw what was worse: the final link in the evidence that bound Tarbis to that which had lived and died, ages ago. On the now exposed breast of the mummy he could see a knife scar: that same scar that marred the perfection of the living Tarbis — or the one that he had thought was living.

Rankin was bereft of all sensation but a terrific whirring in his ears and a drumming at his temples. He leaped back and flung open the door of the room. For a moment he thought of flight — flight in any direction whatsoever. Then he knew that he could never escape that which he had seen face to face, never elude the recollection of an Egyptian magic that was based on the reassembling of the scattered nine elements of a corpse. Rankin had penetrated the veil; he had pried, and loosed upon himself a doom. He thought for an instant of the day when he met Tarbis, a living, lovely woman. Each move that he had made had taken him further from the woman he loved; yet the knowledge that there was no refuge from that which stared at him drove him to his final desperate resource!

Rankin snatched the oil lamp from its bracket and unscrewed its top. Then he poured the contents of the bowl over the mummy. He applied the still-burning wick to the linen bandages. That would settle it, once and for all: decide now and forever who and what was waiting for him in that living-room, one flight below, and centuries away.

As the flames enveloped the bandaged figure, he heard the voice of Tarbis screaming from the anguish of the dissolution of the bonds that tied the spiritual essences to the mummified body. He heard that awful cry from the living-room and knew that that fascinating simulacrum was in the agony of a second and final separation from its body. And the horror of having loved a shadow from the tomb was drowned in the greater horror of having caused the everlasting extinction of one who had loved life so well that she had returned from the dead.

Rankin dared not pass through that lower room to escape. And escape he must! Instantly, or never; yet to see beloved Tarbis — beloved though she was but the *khu*, the *ka*, the Name, and the Power assembled by a forgotten necromancer — to see her being consumed by the astral counterpart of the flames which enveloped the linen-bandaged body —

Rankin burst through the window at the head of the stairs. As he leaped, he heard above the crash and tinkle of glass a scream of mortal misery and despair more acute than any flame could wrench from her lips. He heard her very clearly pronounce his name.

She knew. As much of her as still remained knew that no power could ever restore her; that Rankin had destroyed her.

Rankin picked himself from the ground and fled blindly, without thought or sensation, and maddened by that final cry of agony. In his flight down the steep slope of the street leading from the hill of the citadel to the level of the city, Rankin stumbled and pitched headlong in a heap against a wall.

The impact numbed his senses and for the moment dulled the misery of his mind. Then a man's voice pronounced his name, and a firm hand helped him to his feet.

In the moonlight he recognized Father Peytral. The old priest's usually placid features were tense, as with a reflected terror that he read in Rankin's staring eyes.

"My son," said Father Peytral in a low, trembling voice, "I was watching across the street. I heard, and I saw the flames . . . . You have freed her earthbound soul . . . no, don't try to explain . . . . Little as I know, it is too much. But she is released from an abomination.

"I understand your grief," the old man continued, as he took Rankin's arm. "Let us pray for her soul, and the healing of yours."

"Too late," muttered Rankin in a strained, hoarse voice. The unutterable grief of Tarbis rang again through his memory. "My soul is damned beyond the redemption of time, or your prayers."

Rankin bowed; and the priest did not seek to detain him as he turned and strode down the slope.

common is a certain shameless, extravagant campiness that makes them, frankly, a lot of fun to read. One gets the impression that Lovecraft was having great fun when he wrote them.

And in mid-1932, Lovecraft really needed some fun in his writing life. He had just finished "The Dreams in the Witch-House" a few months earlier; but the rejection of At the Mountains of Madness *had shaken his confidence badly the year before. Having a not-too-picky client for whom he could pound out stories without fear of being judged for them was surely a real balm to his wounded soul.*

The Man of Stone.

BY HAZEL HEALD AND H.P. LOVECRAFT

6,500-WORD SHORT STORY; 1932.

H.P. Lovecraft apparently wrote this story based on a synopsis supplied by Hazel Heald. The key thing to remember, while reading it, is that the story plays to some of Lovecraft's most notable weaknesses as a writer — in particular dialogue and romantic tension; the story actually involves a love triangle, a thing that Lovecraft would never have introduced into a story on his own. Nonetheless, with the help of a framing story involving a diary, he pulls it off better than might be expected.

This is one of the first three Hazel Heald stories; it, "Winged Death," and "The Horror in the Museum" were written at roughly the same time, in mid-1932. It was published very quickly thereafter, in the October 1932 issue of Wonder Stories.

ABOUT HAZEL HEALD (1896-1961).

Hazel Heald first engaged Lovecraft's services as a "revisionist" — which, as with Zealia Bishop, really meant "ghost-writer" — in mid-1932, when she was in her late 30s; she was six years Lovecraft's junior. She was an attractive divorcée, and at one point apparently tried to encourage him to make a move on her romantically; but nothing came of this.

Lovecraft collaborated with Heald on five titles, all relatively short magazine stories. All five are solid, readable, enjoyable works. What they share in

HAZEL HEALD

(from Wonder Stories, October 1932)

Ben Hayden was always a stubborn chap, and once he had heard about those strange statues in the upper Adirondacks, nothing could keep him from going to see them. I had been his closest acquaintance for years, and our Damon and Pythias friendship made us inseparable at all times. So when Ben firmly decided to go — well, I had to trot along too, like a faithful collie.

"Jack," he said, "you know Henry Jackson, who was up in a shack beyond Lake Placid for that beastly spot in his lung? Well, he came back the other day nearly cured, but had a lot to say about some devilish queer conditions up there. He ran into the business all of a sudden and can't be sure yet that it's anything more than a case of bizarre sculpture; but just the same his uneasy impression sticks.

"It seems he was out hunting one day, and came across a cave with what looked like a dog in front of it. Just as he was expecting the dog to bark he looked again, and saw that the thing wasn't alive at all. It was a stone dog — such a perfect image, down to the smallest whisker, that he couldn't decide whether it was a supernaturally clever statue or a petrified animal. He was almost afraid to touch it, but when he did he realised it was surely made of stone.

"After a while he nerved himself up to go into the cave — and there he got a still bigger jolt. Only a little way in there was another stone figure — or what looked like it — but this time it was a man's. It lay on the floor, on its side, wore clothes, and had a peculiar smile on its face. This time Henry didn't stop to do any touching, but beat it straight for the village, Mountain Top, you know. Of course he asked questions — but they did not get him very far. He found he was on a ticklish subject, for the natives only shook their heads, crossed their fingers, and muttered something about a 'Mad Dan' — whoever he was.

"It was too much for Jackson, so he came home weeks ahead of his planned time. He told me all about it because he knows how fond I am of strange things — and oddly enough, I was able to fish up a recollection that dovetailed pretty neatly with his yarn. Do you remember Arthur Wheeler, the sculptor who was such a realist that people began calling him nothing but a solid photographer? I think you knew him slightly. Well, as a matter of fact, he ended up in that part of the Adirondacks himself. Spent a lot of time there, and then dropped out of sight. Never heard from again. Now if stone statues that look like men and dogs are turning up around there, it looks to me as if they might be his work — no matter what the rustics say, or refuse to say, about them. Of course a fellow with Jackson's nerves might easily get flighty and disturbed over things like that; but I'd have done a lot of examining before running away.

"In fact, Jack, I'm going up there now to look things over — and you're coming along with me. It would mean a lot to find Wheeler — or any of his work. Anyhow, the mountain air will brace us both up."

So less than a week later, after a long train ride and a jolting bus trip through breathlessly exquisite scenery, we arrived at Mountain Top in the late, golden sunlight of a June evening. The village comprised only a few small houses, a hotel, and the general store at which our bus drew up; but we knew that the latter would probably prove a focus for such information. Surely enough, the usual group of idlers was gathered around the steps; and when we represented ourselves as health-seekers in search of lodgings they had many recommendations to offer.

Though we had not planned to do any investigating till the next day, Ben could not resist venturing some vague, cautious questions when he noticed the senile garrulousness of one of the ill-clad loafers. He felt, from Jackson's previous experience, that it would be useless to begin with references to the queer statues; but decided to mention Wheeler as one whom we had known, and in whose fate we consequently had a right to be interested.

The crowd seemed uneasy when Sam stopped his whittling and started talking, but they had slight occasion for alarm. Even this barefoot old mountain decadent tightened up when he heard Wheeler's name, and only with difficulty could Ben get anything coherent out of him. "Wheeler?" he had finally wheezed. "Oh, yeh — that feller as was all the time blastin' rocks and cuttin' 'em up into statues. So yew knowed him, hey? Wal, they ain't much we kin tell ye, and mebbe that's too much. He stayed out to Mad Dan's cabin in the hills — but not so very long. Got so he wa'nt wanted no more . . . by Dan, that is. Kinder soft-spoken and got around Dan's wife till the old devil took notice. Pretty sweet on her, I guess. But he took the trail sudden, and nobody's seen hide nor hair of him since. Dan must a told him sumthin' pretty plain — bad feller to get agin ye, Dan is! Better keep away from thar, boys, for they ain't no good in that part of the hills. Dan's ben workin' up a worse and worse mood, and ain't seen about no more. Nor his wife, neither. Guess he's penned her up so's nobody else kin make eyes at her!"

As Sam resumed his whittling after a few more observations, Ben and I exchanged glances. Here, surely, was a new lead which deserved intensive following up. Deciding to lodge at the hotel, we settled ourselves as quickly as possible; planning for a plunge into the wild hilly country on the next day.

At sunrise we made our start, each bearing a knapsack laden with provisions and such tools as we thought we might need. The day before us had an almost stimulating air of invitation — through which only a faint undercurrent of the sinister ran. Our rough mountain road quickly became steep and winding, so that before long our feet ached considerably.

After about two miles we left the road — crossing a stone wall on our right near a great elm and striking off diagonally toward a steeper slope according to the chart and directions which Jackson had prepared for us. It was rough and briery travelling, but we knew that the cave could not be far off.

In the end we came upon the aperture quite suddenly — a black, bush-grown crevice where the ground shot abruptly upward, and beside it, near a shallow rock pool, a small, still figure stood rigid — as if rivalling its own uncanny petrification.

It was a grey dog — or a dog's statue — and as our simultaneous gasp died away we scarcely knew what to think. Jackson had exaggerated nothing, and we could not believe that any sculptor's hand had succeeded in producing such perfection. Every hair of the animal's magnificent coat seemed distinct, and those on the back were bristled up as if some unknown thing had taken him unaware. Ben, at last half-kindly touching the delicate stony fur, gave vent to an exclamation.

"Good God, Jack, but this can't be any statue! Look at it — all the little details, and the way the hair lies! None of Wheeler's technique here! This is a real dog — though heaven only knows how he ever got in this state. Just like stone — feel for yourself. Do you suppose there's any strange gas that sometimes comes out of the cave and does this to animal life? We ought to have looked more into the local legends. And if this is a real dog — or was a real dog — then that man inside must be the real thing too."

It was with a good deal of genuine solemnity — almost dread — that we finally crawled on hands and knees through the cave-mouth, Ben leading. The narrowness looked hardly three feet, after which the grotto expanded in every direction to form a damp, twilight chamber floored with rubble and detritus. For a time we could make out very little, but as we rose to our feet and strained our eyes we began slowly to descry a recumbent figure amidst the greater darkness ahead. Ben fumbled with his flashlight, but hesitated for a moment before turning it on the prostrate figure. We had little doubt that the stony thing was what had once been a man, and something in the thought unnerved us both.

When Ben at last sent forth the electric beam we saw that the object lay on its side, back toward us. It was clearly of the same material as the dog outside, but was dressed in the mouldering and unpetrified remains of rough sport clothing. Braced as we were for a shock, we approached quite calmly to examine the thing; Ben going around to the other side to glimpse the averted face.

Neither could possibly have been prepared for what Ben

Wonder Stories, October 1932

(Illustration by Paul)

"In the chair was the form of a man; on the floor lay a woman's figure. We made no move to approach these petrified bodies."

saw when he flashed the light on those stony features. His cry was wholly excusable, and I could not help echoing it as I leaped to his side and shared the sight. Yet it was nothing hideous or intrinsically terrifying. It was merely a matter of recognition, for beyond the least shadow of a doubt this chilly rock figure with its half-frightened, half-bitter expression had at one time been our old acquaintance, Arthur Wheeler.

Some instinct sent us staggering and crawling out of the cave, and down the tangled slope to a point whence we could not see the ominous stone dog. We hardly knew what to think, for our brains were churning with conjectures and apprehensions. Ben, who had known Wheeler well, was especially upset; and seemed to be piecing together some threads I had overlooked.

Again and again as we paused on the green slope he repeated "Poor Arthur, poor Arthur!" but not till he muttered the name "Mad Dan" did I recall the trouble into which, according to old Sam Poole, Wheeler had run just before his disappearance. Mad Dan, Ben implied, would doubtless be glad to see what had happened. For a moment it flashed over both of us that the jealous host might have been responsible for the sculptor's presence in this evil cave, but the thought went as quickly as it came.

The thing that puzzled us most was to account for the phenomenon itself. What gaseous emanation or mineral vapour could have wrought this change in so relatively short a time was utterly beyond us. Normal petrification, we know, is a slow chemical replacement process requiring vast ages for completion; yet here were two stone images which had been living things — or at least Wheeler had — only a few weeks before. Conjecture was useless. Clearly, nothing remained but to notify the authorities and let them guess what they might; and yet at the back of Ben's head that notion about Mad Dan still persisted. Anyhow, we clawed our way back to the road, but Ben did not turn toward the village, but looked along upward toward where old Sam had said Dan's cabin lay. It was the second house from the village, the ancient loafer had wheezed, and lay on the left far back from the road in a thick copse of scrub oaks. Before I knew it Ben was dragging me up the sandy highway past a dingy farmstead and into a region of increasing wildness.

It did not occur to me to protest, but I felt a certain sense of mounting menace as the familiar marks of agriculture and civilisation grew fewer and fewer. At last the beginning of a narrow, neglected path opened up on our left, while the peaked roof of a squalid, unpainted building shewed itself beyond a sickly growth of half-dead trees. This, I knew, must be Mad Dan's cabin; and I wondered that Wheeler had ever chosen so unprepossessing a place for his headquarters. I dreaded to walk up that weedy, uninviting path, but could not lag behind when Ben strode determinedly along and began a vigorous rapping at the rickety, musty-smelling door.

There was no response to the knock, and something in its echoes sent a series of shivers through one. Ben, however, was quite unperturbed; and at once began to circle the house in quest of unlocked windows. The third that he tried — in the rear of the dismal cabin — proved capable of opening, and after a boost and a vigorous spring he was safely inside and helping me after him.

The room in which we landed was full of limestone and granite blocks, chiselling tools and clay models, and we realised at once that it was Wheeler's erstwhile studio. So far we had not met with any sign of life, but over everything hovered a damnably ominous dusty odour. On our left was an open door evidently leading to a kitchen on the chimney side of the house, and through this Ben started, intent on finding anything he could concerning his friend's last habitat. He was considerably ahead of me when he crossed the threshold, so that I could not see at first what brought him up short and wrung a low cry of horror from his lips.

In another moment, though, I did see — and repeated his cry as instinctively as I had done in the cave. For here in this cabin — far from any subterranean depths which could breed strange gases and work strange mutations — were two stony figures which I knew at once were no products of Arthur Wheeler's chisel. In a rude armchair before the fireplace, bound in position by the lash of a long rawhide whip, was the form of a man — unkempt, elderly, and with a look of fathomless horror on its evil, petrified face.

On the floor beside it lay a woman's figure; graceful, and with a face betokening considerable youth and beauty. Its expression seemed to be one of sardonic satisfaction, and near its outflung right hand was a large tin pail, somewhat stained on the inside, as with a darkish sediment.

We made no move to approach those inexplicably petrified bodies, nor did we exchange any but the simplest conjectures. That this stony couple had been Mad Dan and his wife we could not well doubt, but how to account for their present condition was another matter. As we looked horrifiedly around we saw the suddenness with which the final development must have come — for everything about us seemed, despite a heavy coating of dust, to have been left in the midst of commonplace household activities.

The only exception to this rule of casualness was on the kitchen table; in whose cleared centre, as if to attract attention, lay a thin, battered, blank-book weighted down by a sizeable tin funnel. Crossing to read the thing, Ben saw that it was a kind of diary or set of dated entries, written in a somewhat cramped and none too practiced hand. The very first words riveted my attention, and before ten seconds had elapsed he was breathlessly devouring the halting text — I avidly following as I peered over his shoulder. As we read on — moving as we did so into the less loathsome atmosphere of the adjoining room — many obscure things became terribly clear to us, and we trembled with a mixture of complex emotions.

This is what we read — and what the coroner read later on. The public has seen a highly twisted and sensationalised version in the cheap newspapers, but not even that has more than a fraction of the genuine terror which the simple original held for us as we puzzled it out alone in that musty cabin among the wild hills, with two monstrous stone abnormalities lurking in the death-like silence of the next room. When we had finished Ben pocketed the book with a gesture half of repulsion, and his first words were "Let's get out of here." Silently and nervously we stumbled to the front of the house, unlocked the door, and began the long tramp back to the village.

There were many statements to make and questions to answer in the days that followed, and I do not think that either Ben or I can ever shake off the effects of the whole harrowing experience. Neither can some of the local authorities and city reporters who flocked around — even though they burned a certain book and many papers found in attic boxes, and destroyed considerable apparatus in the deepest part of that sinister hillside cave. But here is the text itself:

"NOVEMBER 5 — My name is Daniel Morris. Around here they call me 'Mad Dan' because I believe in powers that nobody else believes in nowadays. When I go up on Thunder Hill to keep the Feast of the Foxes they think I am crazy — all except the back country folks that are afraid of me. They try to stop me from sacrificing the Black Goat at Hallow Eve, and always prevent my doing the Great Rite that would open the gate. They ought to know better, for they know I am a Van Kauran on my mother's side, and anybody this side of the Hudson can tell what the Van Kaurans have handed down. We come from Nicholas Van Kauran, the wizard, who was hanged in Wijtgaart in 1587, and everybody knows he had made the bargain with the Black Man.

"The soldiers never got his *Book of Eibon* when they burned his house, and his grandson, William Van Kauran, brought it over when he came to Rensselaerwyck and later crossed the river to Esopus. Ask anybody in Kingston or Hurley about what the William Van Kauran line could do to people that got in their way. Also, ask them if my Uncle Hendrik didn't manage to keep hold of the *Book of Eibon* when they ran him out of town and he went up the river to this place with his family.

"I am writing this — and am going to keep writing this — because I want people to know the truth after I am gone. Also, I am afraid I shall really go mad if I don't set things down in plain black and white. Everything is going against me, and if it keeps up I shall have to use the secrets in the Book and call in certain Powers. Three months ago that sculptor Arthur Wheeler came to Mountain Top, and they sent him up to me because I am the only man in the place who knows anything except farming, hunting, and fleecing summer boarders. The fellow seemed to be interested in what I had to say, and made a deal to stop here for $13.00 a week with meals. I gave him the back room beside the kitchen for his lumps of stone and his chiselling, and arranged with Nate Williams to tend to his rock blasting and haul his big pieces with a drag and yoke of oxen.

"That was three months ago. Now I know why that cursed son of hell took so quick to the place. It wasn't my talk at all, but the looks of my wife Rose, that is Osborne Chandler's oldest girl. She is sixteen years younger than I am, and is always casting sheep's eyes at the fellows in town. But we always managed to get along fine enough till this dirty rat shewed up, even if she did balk at helping me with the Rites on Roodmas and Hallowmass. I can see now that Wheeler is working on her feelings and getting her so fond of him that she hardly looks at me, and I suppose he'll try to elope with her sooner or later.

"But he works slow like all sly, polished dogs, and I've got plenty of time to think up what to do about it. They don't either of them know I suspect anything, but before long they'll both realise it doesn't pay to break up a Van Kauran's home. I promise them plenty of novelty in what I'll do.

"NOVEMBER 25 — Thanksgiving Day! That's a pretty good joke! But at that I'll have something to be thankful for when I finish what I've started. No question but that Wheeler is trying to steal my wife. For the time being, though, I'll let him keep on being a star boarder. Got the *Book of Eibon* down from Uncle Hendrik's old trunk in the attic last week, and am looking up something good which won't require sacrifices that I can't make around here. I want something that'll finish these two sneaking traitors, and at the same time get me into no trouble. If it has a twist of drama in it, so much the better. I've thought of calling in the emanation of Yoth, but that needs a child's blood and I must be careful about the neighbours. The Green Decay looks promising, but that would be a bit unpleasant for me as well as for them. I don't like certain sights and smells.

"DECEMBER 10 — Eureka! I've got the very thing at last! Revenge is sweet — and this is the perfect climax! Wheeler, the sculptor — this is too good! Yes, indeed, that damned sneak is going to produce a statue that will sell quicker than any of the things he's been carving these past weeks! A realist, eh? Well — the new statuary won't lack any realism! I found the formula in a manuscript insert opposite page 679 of the Book. From the handwriting I judge it was put there by my great-grandfather Bareut Picterse Van Kauran — the one who disappeared from New Paltz in 1839. Iä! Shub-Niggurath! The Goat with a Thousand Young!

"To be plain, I've found a way to turn those wretched rats into stone statues. It's absurdly simple, and really depends more on plain chemistry than on the Outer Powers. If I can get hold of the right stuff I can brew a drink that'll pass for home-made wine, and one swig ought to finish any ordinary being short of an elephant. What it amounts to is a kind of petrification infinitely speeded up. Shoots the whole system full of calcium and barium salts and replaces living cells with mineral matter so fast that nothing can stop it. It must have been one of those things great-grandfather got at the Great Sabbat on Sugar-Loaf in the Catskills. Queer things used to go on there. Seems to me I heard of a man in New Paltz — Squire Hasbrouck — turned to stone or something like that, in 1834. He was an enemy of the Van Kaurans. First thing I must do is order the five chemicals I need from Albany and Montreal. Plenty of time later to experiment. When everything is over I'll round up all the statues and sell them as Wheeler's work to pay for his overdue board bill! He always was a realist and an egoist — wouldn't it be natural for him to make a self-portrait in stone, and to use my wife for another model — as indeed he's really been doing for the past fortnight? Trust the dull public not to ask what quarry the queer stone came from!

"DECEMBER 25 — Christmas. Peace on earth, and so forth! These two swine are goggling at each other as if I didn't exist. They must think I'm deaf, dumb, and blind! Well, the barium sulphate and calcium chloride came from Albany last Thursday, and the acids, catalytics, and instruments are due from Montreal any day now. The mills of the gods — and all that! I'll do the work in Allen's Cave near the lower wood lot, and at the same time will be openly making some wine in the cellar here. There ought to be some excuse for offering a new drink — though it won't take much planning to fool those moonstruck nincompoops. The trouble will be to make Rose take wine, for she pretends not to like it. Any experiments that I make on animals will be down at the cave, and nobody ever thinks of going there in winter. I'll do some wood-cutting to account for my time away. A small load or two brought in will keep him off the track.

"JANUARY 20 — It's harder work than I thought. A lot depends on the exact proportions. The stuff came from Montreal, but I had to send again for some better scales and an acetylene lamp. They're getting curious down at the village. Wish the express office weren't in Steenwyck's store. Am trying various mixtures on the sparrows that drink and bathe in the pool in front of the cave — when it's melted. Sometimes it kills them, but sometimes they fly away. Clearly, I've missed some important reaction. I suppose Rose and that upstart are making the most of my absence — but I can afford to let them. There can be no doubt of my success in the end.

"FEBRUARY 11 — Have got it at last! Put a fresh lot in the little pool — which is well melted today — and the first bird that drank toppled over as if he were shot. I picked him up a second later, and he was a perfect piece of stone, down to the smallest claws and feather. Not a muscle changed since he was poised for drinking, so he must have died the instant any of the stuff got to his stomach. I didn't expect the petrification to come so soon. But a sparrow isn't a fair test of the way the thing would act with a large animal. I must get something bigger to try it on, for it must be the right strength when I give it to those swine. I guess Rose's dog Rex will do. I'll take him along the next time and say a timber wolf got him. She thinks a lot of him, and I shan't be sorry to give her something to sniffle over before the big reckoning. I must be careful where I keep this book. Rose sometimes pries around in the queerest places.

"FEBRUARY 15 — Getting warm! Tried it on Rex and it worked like a charm with only double the strength. I fixed the rock pool and got him to drink. He seemed to know something queer had hit him, for he bristled and growled, but he was a piece of stone before he could turn his head. The solution ought to have been stronger, and for a human being ought to be very much stronger. I think I'm getting the hang of it now, and am about ready for that cur Wheeler. The stuff seems to be tasteless, but to make sure I'll flavour it with the new wine I'm making up at the house. Wish I were surer about the tastelessness, so I could give it to Rose in water without trying to urge wine on her. I'll get the two separately — Wheeler out here and Rose at home. Have just fixed a strong solution and cleared away all strange objects in front of the cave. Rose whimpered like a puppy when I told her a wolf had got Rex, and Wheeler gurgled a lot of sympathy.

"MARCH 1 — Iä R'lyeh! Praise the Lord Tsathoggua! I've got the son of hell at last! Told him I'd found a new ledge of friable limestone down this way, and he trotted after me like the yellow cur he is! I had the wine-flavoured stuff in a bottle on my hip, and he was glad of a swig when we got here. Gulped it down without a wink — and dropped in his tracks before you could count three. But he knows I've had my vengeance, for I made a face at him that he couldn't miss. I saw the look of understanding come into his face as he keeled over. In two minutes he was solid stone.

"I dragged him into the cave and put Rex's figure outside again. That bristling dog shape will help to scare people off. It's getting time for the spring hunters, and besides, there's a damned 'lunger' named Jackson in a cabin over the hill who does a lot of snooping around in the snow. I wouldn't want my laboratory and storeroom to be found just yet! When I got home I told Rose that Wheeler had found a telegram at the village summoning him suddenly home. I don't know whether she believed me or not but it doesn't matter. For form's sake, I packed Wheeler's things and took them down the hill, telling her I was going to ship them after him. I put them in the dry well at the abandoned Rapelye place. Now for Rose!

"MARCH 3 — Can't get Rose to drink any wine. I hope that stuff is tasteless enough to go unnoticed in water. I tried it in tea and coffee, but it forms a precipitate and can't be used that way. If I use it in water I'll have to cut down the dose and trust to a more gradual action. Mr. and Mrs. Hoog dropped in this noon, and I had hard work keeping the conversation away from Wheeler's departure. It mustn't get around that we say he was called back to New York when everybody at the village knows no telegram came, and that he didn't leave on the bus. Rose is acting damned queer about the whole thing. I'll have to pick a quarrel with her and keep her locked in the attic. The best way is to try to make her drink that doctored wine — and if she does give in, so much better.

"MARCH 7 — Have started in on Rose. She wouldn't drink the wine so I took a whip to her and drove her up in the attic. She'll never come down alive. I pass her a platter of salty bread and salt meat, and a pail of slightly doctored water, twice a day. The salt food ought to make her drink a lot, and it can't be long before the action sets in. I don't like the way she shouts about Wheeler when I'm at the door. The rest of the time she is absolutely silent.

"MARCH 9 — It's damned peculiar how slow that stuff is in getting hold of Rose. I'll have to make it stronger — probably she'll never taste it with all the salt I've been feeding her. Well, if it doesn't get her there are plenty of other ways to fall back on. But I would like to carry this neat statue plan through! Went to the cave this morning and all is well there. I sometimes hear Rose's steps on the ceiling overhead, and I think they're getting more and more dragging. The stuff is certainly working, but it's too slow. Not strong enough. From now on I'll rapidly stiffen up the dose.

"MARCH 11 — It is very queer. She is still alive and moving. Tuesday night I heard her piggling with a window, so went up and gave her a rawhiding. She acts more sullen than frightened, and her eyes look swollen. But she could never drop to the ground from that height and there's nowhere she could climb down. I have had dreams at night, for her slow, dragging pacing on the floor above gets on my nerves. Sometimes I think she works at the lock on the door.

"MARCH 15 — Still alive, despite all the strengthening of the dose. There's something queer about it. She crawls now, and doesn't pace very often. But the sound of her crawling is horrible. She rattles the windows, too, and fumbles with the door. I shall have to finish her off with the rawhide if this keeps up. I'm getting very sleepy. Wonder if Rose has got on her guard somehow. But she must be drinking the stuff. This sleepiness is abnormal — I think the strain is telling on me. I'm sleepy . . ."

(Here the cramped handwriting trails out in a vague scrawl, giving place to a note in a firmer, evidently feminine handwriting, indicative of great emotional tension.)

"MARCH 16 — 4 A.M. — This is added by Rose C. Morris, about to die. Please notify my father, Osborne E. Chandler, Route 2, Mountain Top, N.Y. I have just read what the beast has written. I felt sure he had killed Arthur Wheeler, but did not know how till I read this terrible notebook. Now I know what I escaped. I noticed the water tasted queer, so took none of it after the first sip. I threw it all out of the window. That one sip has half paralysed me, but I can still get about. The thirst was terrible, but I ate as little as possible of the salty food and was able to get a little water by setting some old pans and dishes that were up here under places where the roof leaked. There were two great rains. I thought he was trying to poison me, though I didn't know what the poison was like. What he has written about himself and me is a lie. We were never happy together and I think I married him only under one of those spells that he was able to lay on people. I guess he hypnotised both my father and me, for he was always hated and feared and suspected of dark dealings with the devil. My father once called him The Devil's Kin, and he was right.

"No one will ever know what I went through as his wife. It was not simply common cruelty — though God knows he was cruel enough, and beat me often with a leather whip. It was more — more than anyone in this age can ever understand. He was a monstrous creature, and practiced all sorts of hellish ceremonies handed down by his mother's people. He tried to make me help in the rites — and I don't dare even hint what they were. I would not, so he beat me. It would be blasphemy to tell what he tried to make me do. I can say he was a murderer even then, for I know what he sacrificed one night on Thunder Hill. He was surely the Devil's Kin. I tried four times to run away, but he always caught and beat me. Also, he had a sort of hold over my mind, and even over my father's mind.

"About Arthur Wheeler I have nothing to be ashamed of. We did come to love each other, but only in an honourable way. He gave me the first kind treatment I had ever had since leaving my father's, and meant to help me get out of the clutches of that fiend. He had several talks with my father, and was going to help me get out west. After my divorce we would have been married.

"Ever since that brute locked me in the attic I have planned to get out and finish him. I always kept the poison overnight in case I could escape and find him asleep and give it to him somehow. At first he waked easily when I worked on the lock of the door and tested the conditions at the windows, but later he began to get more tired and sleep sounder. I could always tell by his snoring when he was asleep.

"Tonight he was so fast asleep I forced the lock without waking him. It was hard work getting downstairs with my partial paralysis, but I did. I found him here with the lamp burning — asleep at the table, where he had been writing in this book. In the corner was the long rawhide whip he had so often beaten me with. I used it to tie him to the chair so he could not move a muscle. I lashed his neck so that I could pour anything down his throat without his resisting.

"He waked up just as I was finishing and I guess he saw right off that he was done for. He shouted frightful things and tried to chant mystical formulas, but I choked him off with a dish towel from the sink. Then I saw this book he had been writing in, and stopped to read it. The shock was terrible, and I almost fainted four or five times. My mind was not ready for such things. After that I talked to that fiend for two or three hours steady. I told him everything I had wanted to tell him through all the years I had been his slave, and a lot of other things that had to do with what I had read in this awful book.

"He looked almost purple when I was through, and I think he was half delirious. Then I got a funnel from the cupboard and jammed it into his mouth after taking out the gag. He knew what I was going to do, but was helpless. I had brought down the pail of poisoned water, and without a qualm, I poured a good half of it into the funnel.

"It must have been a very strong dose, for almost at once I saw that brute begin to stiffen and turn a dull stony grey. In ten minutes I knew he was solid stone. I could not bear to touch him, but the tin funnel clinked horribly when I pulled it out of his mouth. I wish I could have given that Kin of the Devil a more painful, lingering death, but surely this was the most appropriate he could have had.

"There is not much more to say. I am half-paralysed, and with Arthur murdered I have nothing to live for. I shall make things complete by drinking the rest of the poison after placing this book where it will be found. In a quarter of an hour I shall be a stone statue. My only wish is to be buried beside the statue that was Arthur — when it is found in that cave where the fiend left it. Poor trusting Rex ought to lie at our feet. I do not care what becomes of the stone devil tied in the chair . . ."

Winged Death.

BY HAZEL HEALD AND H.P. LOVECRAFT

10,000-WORD NOVELETTE; 1932.

This novelette will win no awards for subtlety or cosmic plausibility, but it's a remarkably satisfying read nonetheless. It is, like "The Man of Stone," a sort of epistolary narrative presented in the point of view of the villain — this being accomplished with the use of the negligible frame story of four men reading his journal.

One of the first three Hazel Heald stories, "Winged Death" was written in mid-1932 and first published in the March 1934 issue of Weird Tales *magazine.*

I.

The Orange Hotel stands in High Street near the railway station in Bloemfontein, South Africa. On Sunday, January 24, 1932, four men sat shivering from terror in a room on its third floor. One was George C. Titteridge, proprietor of the hotel; another was police constable Ian De Witt of the Central Station; a third was Johannes Bogaert, the local coroner; the fourth, and apparently the least disorganised of the group, was Dr. Cornelius Van Keulen, the coroner's physician. On the floor, uncomfortably evident amidst the stifling summer heat, was the body of a dead man — but this was not what the four were afraid of. Their glances wandered from the table, on which lay a curious assortment of things, to the ceiling overhead, across whose smooth whiteness a series of huge, faltering alphabetical characters had somehow been scrawled in ink; and every now and then Dr. Van Keulen would glance half-furtively at a worn leather blank-book which he held in his left hand. The horror of the four seemed about equally divided among the blank-book, the scrawled words on the ceiling, and a dead fly of peculiar aspect which floated in a bottle of ammonia on the table. Also on the table were an open inkwell, a pen and writing-pad, a physician's medical case, a bottle of hydrochloric acid, and a tumbler about a quarter full of black oxide of manganese.

"I am utterly engulfed in horror. The thing has touched me, and I am a helpless victim."

Weird Tales, March 1934

The worn leather book was the journal of the dead man on the floor, and had at once made it clear that the name "Frederick N. Mason, Mining Properties, Toronto, Canada," signed in the hotel register, was a false one. There were other things—terrible things—which it likewise made clear; and still other things of far greater terror at which it hinted hideously without making them clear or even fully believable. It was the half-belief of the four men, fostered by lives spent close to the black, settled secrets of brooding Africa, which made them shiver so violently in spite of the searing January heat.

The blank-book was not a large one, and the entries were in a fine handwriting, which, however, grew careless and nervous-looking toward the last. It consisted of a series of jottings at first rather irregularly spaced, but finally becoming daily. To call it a diary would not be quite correct, for it chronicled only one set of its writer's activities. Dr. Van Keulen recognised the name of the dead man the moment he opened the cover, for it was that of an eminent member of his own profession who had been largely connected with African matters. In another moment he was horrified to find this name linked with a dastardly crime, officially unsolved, which had filled the newspapers some four months before. And the farther he read, the deeper grew his horror, awe, and sense of loathing and panic. Here, in essence, is the text which the doctor read aloud in that sinister and increasingly noisome room while the three men around him breathed hard, fidgeted in their chairs, and darted frightened glances at the ceiling, the table, the thing on the floor, and one another:

JOURNAL OF THOMAS SLAUENWITE, M.D.:

Touching punishment of Henry Sargent Moore, Ph.D., of Brooklyn, New York, Professor of Invertebrate Biology in Columbia University, New York, N.Y. Prepared to be read after my death, for the satisfaction of making public the accomplishment of my revenge, which may otherwise never be imputed to me even if it succeeds.

JANUARY 5, 1929—I have now fully resolved to kill Dr. Henry Moore, and a recent incident has shewn me how I shall do it. From now on, I shall follow a consistent line of action; hence the beginning of this journal. It is hardly necessary to repeat the circumstances which have driven me to this course, for the informed part of the public is familiar with all the salient facts. I was born in Trenton, New Jersey, on April 12, 1885, the son of Dr. Paul Slauenwite, formerly of Pretoria, Transvaal, South Africa. Studying medicine as part of my family tradition, I was led by my father (who died in 1916, while I was serving in France in a South African regiment) to specialise in African fevers; and after my graduation from Columbia spent much time in researches which took me from Durban, in Natal, up to the equator itself. In Mombasa I worked out my new theory of the transmission and development of remittent fever, aided only slightly by the papers of the late government physician, Sir Norman Sloane, which I found in the house I occupied. When I published my results I became at a single stroke a famous authority. I was told of the probability of an almost supreme position in the South African health service, and even a probable knighthood, in the event of my becoming a naturalised citizen, and accordingly I took the necessary steps. Then occurred the incident for which I am about to kill Henry Moore.

This man, my classmate and friend of years in America and Africa, chose deliberately to undermine my claim to my own theory; alleging that Sir Norman Sloane had anticipated me in every essential detail, and implying that I had probably found more of his papers than I had stated in my account of the matter. To buttress this absurd accusation he produced certain personal letters from Sir Norman which indeed shewed that the older man had been over my ground, and that he would have published his results very soon but for his sudden death. This much I could only admit with regret. What I could not excuse was the jealous suspicion that I had stolen the theory from Sir Norman's papers. The British government, sensibly enough, ignored these aspersions, but withheld the half-promised appointment and knighthood on the ground that my theory, while original with me, was not in fact new. I could soon see that my career in Africa was perceptibly checked; though I had placed all my hopes on such a career, even to the point of resigning American citizenship. A distinct coolness toward me had arisen among the Government set in Mombasa, especially among those who had known Sir Norman. It was then that I resolved to be even with Moore sooner or later, though I did not know how. He had been jealous of my early celebrity, and had taken advantage of his old correspondence with Sir Norman to ruin me. This from the friend whom I had myself led to take an interest in Africa—whom I had coached and inspired till he achieved his present moderate fame as an authority on African entomology. Even now, though, I will not deny that his attainments are profound. I made him, and in return he has ruined me. Now—some day—I shall destroy him.

When I saw myself losing ground in Mombasa, I applied for my present situation in the interior—at M'gonga, only fifty miles from the Uganda line. It is a cotton and ivory trading-post, with only eight white men besides myself. A beastly hole, almost on the equator, and full of every sort of fever known to mankind. Poisonous snakes and insects everywhere, and niggers with diseases nobody ever heard of outside medical college. But my work is not hard, and I have always had plenty of time to plan things to do to Henry Moore. It amuses me to give his *Diptera of Central and Southern Africa* a prominent place on my shelf. I suppose it actually is a standard manual—they use it at Columbia, Harvard, and the U. of Wis.—but my own suggestions are really responsible for half its strong points.

Last week I encountered the thing which decided me how to kill Moore. A party from Uganda brought in a black with a queer illness which I can't yet diagnose. He was lethargic, with a very low temperature, and shuffled in a peculiar way. Most of the others were afraid of him and said he was under some kind of witch-doctor spell; but Gobo, the interpreter, said he had been bitten by an insect. What it was, I can't imagine—for there is only a slight puncture on the arm. It is bright red, though, with a purple ring around it. Spectral-looking—I don't wonder the boys lay it to black magic. They seem to have seen cases like it before, and say there's really nothing to do about it. Old N'Kuru, one of the Galla boys at the post, says it must be the bite of a devil-fly, which makes its victim waste away gradually and die, and then takes hold of his soul and personality if it is still alive itself—flying around with all his likes, dislikes, and consciousness. A queer legend—and I don't know of any local insect deadly enough to account for it.

I gave this sick black—his name is Mevana—a good shot of quinine and took a sample of his blood for testing, but haven't made much progress. There is certainly a strange germ present, but I can't even remotely identify it. The nearest thing to it is the bacillus one finds in oxen, horses, and dogs that the tsetse-fly has bitten; but tsetse-flies don't infect human beings, and this is too far north for them anyway. However — the important thing is that I've decided how to kill Moore. If this interior region has insects as poisonous as the natives say, I'll see that he gets a shipment of them from a source he won't suspect, and with plenty of assurances that they are harmless. Trust him to throw overboard all caution when it comes to studying an unknown species — and then we'll see how Nature takes its course! It ought not to be hard to find an insect that scares the blacks so much. First to see how poor Mevana turns out — and then to find my envoy of death.

JANUARY 7 — Mevana is no better, though I have injected all the antitoxins I know of. He has fits of trembling, in which he rants affrightedly about the way his soul will pass when he dies into the insect that bit him, but between them he remains in a kind of half-stupor. Heart action still strong, so I may pull him through. I shall try to, for he can probably guide me better than anyone else to the region where he was bitten. Meanwhile I'll write to Dr. Lincoln, my predecessor here, for Allen, the head factor, says he had a profound knowledge of the local sicknesses. He ought to know about the death-fly if any white man does. He's at Nairobi now, and a black runner ought to get me a reply in a week — using the railway for half the trip.

JANUARY 10 — Patient unchanged, but I have found what I want! It was in an old volume of the local health records, which I've been going over diligently while waiting to hear from Lincoln. Thirty years ago there was an epidemic that killed off thousands of natives in Uganda, and it was definitely traced to a rare fly called *Glossina palpalis* — a sort of cousin of the *Glossina marsitans*, or tsetse. It lives in the bushes on the shores of lakes and rivers, and feeds on the blood of crocodiles, antelopes, and large mammals. When these food animals have the germ of trypanosomiasis, or sleeping-sickness, it picks it up and develops acute infectivity after an incubation period of thirty-one days. Then for seventy-five days it is sure death to anyone or anything it bites. Without doubt, this must be the "devil-fly" the niggers talk about. Now I know what I'm heading for. Hope Mevana pulls through. Ought to hear from Lincoln in four or five days — he has a great reputation for success in things like this. My worst problem will be to get the flies to Moore without his recognising them. With his cursed plodding scholarship it would be just like him to know all about them, since they're actually on record.

JANUARY 15 — Just heard from Lincoln, who confirms all that the records say about *Glossina palpalis*. He has a remedy for sleeping-sickness which has succeeded in a great number of cases when not given too late. Intermuscular injections of tryparsamide. Since Mevana was bitten about two months ago, I don't know how it will work — but Lincoln says that cases have been known to drag on eighteen months, so possibly I'm not too late. Lincoln sent over some of his stuff, so I've just given Mevana a stiff shot. In a stupor now. They've brought his principal wife from the village, but he doesn't even recognise her. If he recovers, he can certainly shew me where the flies are. He's a great crocodile hunter, according to report, and knows all Uganda like a book. I'll give him another shot tomorrow.

JANUARY 16 — Mevana seems a little brighter today, but his heart action is slowing up a bit. I'll keep up the injections, but not overdo them.

JANUARY 17 — Recovery really pronounced today. Mevana opened his eyes and shewed signs of actual consciousness, though dazed, after the injection. Hope Moore doesn't know about tryparsamide. There's a good chance he won't, since he never leaned much toward medicine. Mevana's tongue seemed paralysed, but I fancy that will pass off if I can only wake him up. Wouldn't mind a good sleep myself, but not of this kind!

JANUARY 25 — Mevana nearly cured! In another week I can let him take me into the jungle. He was frightened when he first came to — about having the fly take his personality after he died — but brightened up finally when I told him he was going to get well. His wife, Ugowe, takes good care of him now, and I can rest a bit. Then for the envoys of death!

FEBRUARY 3 — Mevana is well now, and I have talked with him about a hunt for flies. He dreads to go near the place where they got him, but I am playing on his gratitude. Besides, he has an idea that I can ward off disease as well as cure it. His pluck would shame a white man — there's no doubt that he'll go. I can get off by telling the head factor the trip is in the interest of local health work.

MARCH 12 — In Uganda at last! Have five boys besides Mevana, but they are all Gallas. The local blacks couldn't be hired to come near the region after the talk of what had happened to Mevana. This jungle is a pestilential place — steaming with miasmal vapours. All the lakes look stagnant. In one spot we came upon a trace of Cyclopean ruins which made even the Gallas run past in a wide circle. They say these megaliths are older than man, and that they used to be a haunt or outpost of "The Fishers from Outside" — whatever that means — and of the evil gods Tsadogwa and Clulu. To this day they are said to have a malign influence, and to be connected somehow with the devil-flies.

MARCH 15 — Struck Lake Mlolo this morning — where Mevana was bitten. A hellish, green-scummed affair, full of crocodiles. Mevana has fixed up a fly-trap of fine wire netting baited with crocodile meat. It has a small entrance, and once the quarry get in, they don't know enough to get out. As stupid as they are deadly, and ravenous for fresh meat or a bowl of blood. Hope we can get a good supply. I've decided that I must experiment with them — finding a way to change their appearance so that Moore won't recognise them. Possibly I can cross them with some other species, producing a strange hybrid whose infection-carrying capacity will be undiminished. We'll see. I must wait, but am in no hurry now. When I get ready I'll have Mevana get me some infected meat to feed my envoys of death — and then for the post-office. Ought to be no trouble getting infection, for this country is a veritable pest-hole.

MARCH 16 — Good luck. Two cages full. Five vigorous specimens with wings glistening like diamonds. Mevana is emptying them into a large can with a tightly meshed top, and I think we caught them in the nick of time. We can get them to M'gonga without trouble. Taking plenty of crocodile meat for their food. Undoubtedly all or most of it is infected.

APRIL 20 — Back at M'gonga and busy in the laboratory. Have sent to Dr. Joost in Pretoria for some tsetse-flies for hybridisation experiments. Such a crossing, if it will work at all, ought to produce something pretty hard to recognise yet at the same time just as deadly as the *palpalis*. If this doesn't work, I shall try certain other *diptera* from the interior, and I have sent to Dr. Vandervelde at Nyangwe for some of the Congo types. I shan't have to send Mevana for more tainted meat after all; for I find I can keep cultures of the germ *Trypanosoma gambiense*, taken from the meat we got last month, almost indefinitely in tubes. When the time comes, I'll taint some fresh meat and feed my winged envoys a good dose — then bon voyage to them!

JUNE 18 — My tsetse-flies from Joost came today. Cages for breeding were all ready long ago, and I am now making selections. Intend to use ultra-violet rays to speed up the life-cycle. Fortunately I have the needed apparatus in my regular equipment. Naturally I tell no one what I'm doing. The ignorance of the few men here makes it easy for me to conceal my aims and pretend to be merely studying existing species for medical reasons.

JUNE 29 — The crossing is fertile! Good deposits of eggs last Wednesday, and now I have some excellent larvae. If the mature insects look as strange as these do, I need do nothing more. Am preparing separate numbered cages for the different specimens.

JULY 7 — New hybrids are out! Disguise is excellent as to shape, but sheen of wings still suggests *palpalis*. Thorax has faint suggestions of the stripes of the tsetse. Slight variation in individuals. Am feeding them all on tainted crocodile meat, and after infectivity develops will try them on some of the blacks — apparently, of course, by accident. There are so many mildly venomous flies around here that it can easily be done without exciting suspicion. I shall loose an insect in my tightly screened dining-room when Batta, my house-boy, brings in breakfast — keeping well on guard myself. When it has done its work I'll capture or swat it — an easy thing because of its stupidity — or asphyxiate it by filling the room with chlorine gas. If it doesn't work the first time, I'll try again until it does. Of course, I'll have the tryparsamide handy in case I get bitten myself — but I shall be careful to avoid biting, for no antidote is really certain.

AUGUST 10 — Infectivity mature, and managed to get Batta stung in fine shape. Caught the fly on him, returning it to its cage. Eased up the pain with iodine, and the poor devil is quite grateful for the service. Shall try a variant specimen on Gamba, the factor's messenger, tomorrow. That will be all the tests I shall dare to make here, but if I need more I shall take some specimens to Ukala and get additional data.

AUGUST 11 — Failed to get Gamba, but recaptured the fly alive. Batta still seems as well as usual, and has no pain in the back where he was stung. Shall wait before trying to get Gamba again.

AUGUST 14 — Shipment of insects from Vandervelde at last. Fully seven distinct species, some more or less poisonous. Am keeping them well fed in case the tsetse crossing doesn't work. Some of these fellows look very unlike the *palpalis*, but the trouble is that they may not make a fertile cross with it.

AUGUST 17 — Got Gamba this afternoon, but had to kill the fly on him. It nipped him in the left shoulder. I dressed the bite, and Gamba is as grateful as Batta was. No change in Batta.

AUGUST 20 — Gamba unchanged so far — Batta too. Am experimenting with a new form of disguise to supplement the hybridisation — some sort of dye to change the telltale glitter of the *palpalis*' wings. A bluish tint would be best — something I could spray on a whole batch of insects. Shall begin by investigating things like Prussian and Turnbull's blue — iron and cyanogen salts.

AUGUST 25 — Batta complained of a pain in his back today — things may be developing.

SEPTEMBER 3 — Have made fair progress in my experiments. Batta shews signs of lethargy, and says his back aches all the time. Gamba beginning to feel uneasy in his bitten shoulder.

SEPTEMBER 24 — Batta worse and worse, and beginning to get frightened about his bite. Thinks it must be a devil-fly, and entreated me to kill it — for he saw me cage it — until I pretended to him that it had died long ago. Said he didn't want his soul to pass into it upon his death. I give him shots of plain water with a hypodermic to keep his morale up. Evidently the fly retains all the properties of the *palpalis*. Gamba down, too, and repeating all of Batta's symptoms. I may decide to give him a chance with tryparsamide, for the effect of the fly is proved well enough. I shall let Batta go on, however, for I want a rough idea of how long it takes to finish a case. Dye experiments coming along finely. An isomeric form of ferrous ferrocyanide, with some admixture of potassium salts, can be dissolved in alcohol and sprayed on the insects with splendid effect. It stains the wings blue without affecting the dark thorax much, and doesn't wear off when I sprinkle the specimens with water. With this disguise, I think I can use the present tsetse hybrids and avoid bothering with any more experiments. Sharp as he is, Moore couldn't recognise a blue-winged fly with a half-tsetse thorax. Of course, I keep all this dye business strictly under cover. Nothing must ever connect me with the blue flies later on.

OCTOBER 9 — Batta is lethargic and has taken to his bed. Have been giving Gamba tryparsamide for two weeks, and fancy he'll recover.

OCTOBER 25 — Batta very low, but Gamba nearly well.

NOVEMBER 18 — Batta died yesterday, and a curious thing happened which gave me a real shiver in view of the native legends and Batta's own fears. When I returned to the laboratory after the death I heard the most singular buzzing and thrashing in cage 12, which contained the fly that bit Batta. The creature seemed frantic, but stopped still when I appeared — lighting on the wire netting and looking at me in the oddest way. It reached its legs through the wires as if it were bewildered. When I came back from dining with Allen, the thing was dead. Evidently it had gone wild and beaten its life out on the sides of the cage. It certainly is peculiar that this should happen just as Batta died. If any black had seen it, he'd have laid it at once to the absorption of the poor devil's soul. I shall start my blue-stained hybrids on their way before long now. The hybrid's rate of killing seems a little ahead of the pure *palpalis'* rate, if anything. Batta died three months and eight days after infection — but of course there is always a wide margin of uncertainty. I almost wish I had let Gamba's case run on.

DECEMBER 5 — Busy planning how to get my envoys to Moore. I must have them appear to come from some disinterested entomologist who has read his *Diptera of Central and Southern Africa* and believes he would like to study this "new and unidentifiable species." There must also be ample assurances that the blue-winged fly is harmless, as proved by the natives' long experience. Moore will be off his guard, and one of the flies will surely get him sooner or later — though one can't tell just when. I'll have to rely on the letters of New York friends — they still speak of Moore from time to time — to keep me informed of early results, though I dare say the papers will announce his death. Above all, I must shew no interest in his case. I shall mail the flies while on a trip, but must not be recognised when I do it. The best plan will be to take a long vacation in the interior, grow a beard, mail the package at Ukala while passing as a visiting entomologist, and return here after shaving off the beard.

APRIL 12, 1930 — Back in M'gonga after my long trip. Everything has come off finely — with clockwork precision. Have sent the flies to Moore without leaving a trace. Got a Christmas vacation Dec. 15th, and set out at once with the proper stuff. Made a very good mailing container with room to include some germ-tainted crocodile meat as food for the envoys. By the end of February I had beard enough to shape into a close Van Dyke. Shewed up at Ukala March 9th and typed a letter to Moore on the trading-post machine. Signed it "Nevil Wayland-Hall" — supposed to be an entomologist from London. Think I took just the right tone — interest of a brother-scientist, and all that. Was artistically casual in emphasising the "complete harmlessness" of the specimens. Nobody suspected anything. Shaved the beard as soon as I hit the bush, so that there wouldn't be any uneven tanning by the time I got back here. Dispensed with native bearers except for one small stretch of swamp — I can do wonders with one knapsack, and my sense of direction is good. Lucky I'm used to such travelling. Explained my protracted absence by pleading a touch of fever and some mistakes in direction when going through the bush. But now comes the hardest part psychologically — waiting for news of Moore without shewing the strain. Of course, he may possibly escape a bite until the venom is played out — but with his recklessness the chances are one hundred to one against him. I have no regrets; after what he did to me, he deserves this and more.

JUNE 30 — Hurrah! The first step worked! Just heard casually from Dyson of Columbia that Moore had received some new blue-winged flies from Africa, and that he is badly puzzled over them! No word of any bite — but if I know Moore's slipshod ways as I think I do, there'll be one before long!

AUGUST 27 — Letter from Morton in Cambridge. He says Moore writes of feeling very run-down, and tells of an insect bite on the back of his neck — from a curious new specimen that he received about the middle of June. Have I succeeded? Apparently Moore doesn't connect the bite with his weakness. If this is the real stuff, then Moore was bitten well within the insect's period of infectivity.

SEPTEMBER 12 — Victory! Another line from Dyson says that Moore is really in an alarming shape. He now traces his illness to the bite, which he received around noon on June 19, and is quite bewildered about the identity of the insect. Is trying to get in touch with the "Nevil Wayland-Hall" who sent him the shipment. Of the hundred-odd that I sent, about twenty-five seem to have reached him alive. Some escaped at the time of the bite, but several larvae have appeared from eggs laid since the time of mailing. He is, Dyson says, carefully incubating these larvae. When they mature I suppose he'll identify the tsetse-*palpalis* hybridisation — but that won't do him much good now. He'll wonder, though, why the blue wings aren't transmitted by heredity!

NOVEMBER 8 — Letters from half a dozen friends tell of Moore's serious illness. Dyson's came today. He says Moore is utterly at sea about the hybrids that came from the larvae and is beginning to think that the parents got their blue wings in some artificial way. Has to stay in bed most of the time now. No mention of using tryparsamide.

FEBRUARY 13, 1931 — Not so good! Moore is sinking, and seems to know no remedy, but I think he suspects me. Had a very chilly letter from Morton last month, which told nothing of Moore; and now Dyson writes — also rather constrainedly — that Moore is forming theories about the whole matter. He's been making a search for "Wayland-Hall" by telegraph — at London, Ukala, Nairobi, Mombasa, and other places — and of course finds nothing. I judge that he's told Dyson whom he suspects, but that Dyson doesn't believe it yet. Fear Morton does believe it. I see that I'd better lay plans for getting out of here and effacing my identity for good. What an end to a career that started out so well! More of Moore's work — but this time he's paying for it in advance! Believe I'll go back to South Africa — and meanwhile will quietly deposit funds there to the credit of my new self — "Frederick Nasmyth Mason of Toronto, Canada, broker in mining properties." Will establish a new signature for identification. If I never have to take the step, I can easily re-transfer the funds to my present self.

AUGUST 15 — Half a year gone, and still suspense. Dyson and Morton — as well as several other friends — seem to have stopped writing me. Dr. James of San Francisco hears from Moore's friends now and then, and says Moore is in an almost continuous coma. He hasn't been able to walk since May. As long as he could talk he complained of being cold. Now he can't talk, though it is thought he still has glimmers of consciousness. His breathing is short and quick, and can be heard some distance away. No question but that *Trypanosoma gambiense* is feeding on him — but he holds out better than the niggers around here. Three months and eight days finished Batta, and here Moore is alive over a year after his biting. Heard rumours last month of an intensive search around Ukala for "Wayland-Hall." Don't think I need to worry yet, though, for there's absolutely nothing in existence to link me with this business.

OCTOBER 7 — It's over at last! News in the *Mombasa Gazette*. Moore died September 20 after a series of trembling fits and with a temperature vastly below normal. So much for that! I said I'd get him, and I did! The paper had a three-column report of his long illness and death, and of the futile search for "Wayland-Hall." Obviously, Moore was a bigger character in Africa than I had realised. The insect that bit him has now been fully identified from the surviving specimens and developed larvae, and the wing-staining is also detected. It is universally realised that the flies were prepared and shipped with intent to kill. Moore, it appears, communicated certain suspicions to Dyson, but the latter — and the police — are maintaining secrecy because of absence of proof. All of Moore's enemies are being looked up, and the Associated Press hints that "an investigation, possibly involving an eminent physician now abroad, will follow."

One thing at the very end of the report — undoubtedly, the cheap romancing of a yellow journalist — gives me a curious shudder in view of the legends of the blacks and the way the fly happened to go wild when Batta died. It seems that an odd incident occurred on the night of Moore's death; Dyson having been aroused by the buzzing of a blue-winged fly — which immediately flew out the window — just before the nurse telephoned the death news from Moore's home, miles away in Brooklyn.

But what concerns me most is the African end of the matter. People at Ukala remember the bearded stranger who typed the letter and sent the package, and the constabulary are combing the country for any blacks who may have carried him. I didn't use many, but if officers question the Ubandes who took me through the N'Kini jungle belt I'll have more to explain than I like. It looks as if the time has come for me to vanish; so tomorrow I believe I'll resign and prepare to start for parts unknown.

NOVEMBER 9 — Hard work getting my resignation acted on, but release came today. I didn't want to aggravate suspicion by decamping outright. Last week I heard from James about Moore's death — but nothing more than is in the papers. Those around him in New York seem rather reticent about details, though they all talk about a searching investigation. No word from any of my friends in the East. Moore must have spread some dangerous suspicions around before he lost consciousness — but there isn't an iota of proof he could have adduced. Still, I am taking no chances. On Thursday I shall start for Mombasa, and when there will take a steamer down the coast to Durban. After that I shall drop from sight — but soon afterward the mining properties' broker Frederick Nasmyth Mason, from Toronto, will turn up in Johannesburg. Let this be the end of my journal. If in the end I am not suspected, it will serve its original purpose after my death and reveal what would otherwise not be known. If, on the other hand, these suspicions do materialise and persist, it will confirm and clarify the vague charges, and fill in many important and puzzling gaps. Of course, if danger comes my way I shall have to destroy it.

Well, Moore is dead — as he amply deserves to be. Now Dr. Thomas Slauenwite is dead, too. And when the body formerly belonging to Thomas Slauenwite is dead, the public may have this record.

II.

JANUARY 15, 1932—A new year—and a reluctant reopening of this journal. This time I am writing solely to relieve my mind, for it would be absurd to fancy that the case is not definitely closed. I am settled in the Vaal Hotel, Johannesburg, under my new name, and no one has so far challenged my identity. Have had some inconclusive business talks to keep up my part as a mine broker, and believe I may actually work myself into that business. Later I shall go to Toronto and plant a few evidences for my fictitious past. But what is bothering me is an insect that invaded my room around noon today. Of course I have had all sorts of nightmares about blue flies of late, but those were only to be expected in view of my prevailing nervous strain. This thing, however, was a waking actuality, and I am utterly at a loss to account for it. It buzzed around my bookshelf for fully a quarter of an hour, and eluded every attempt to catch or kill it. The queerest thing was its colour and aspect—for it had blue wings and was in every way a duplicate of my hybrid envoys of death. How it could possibly be one of these, in fact, I certainly don't know. I disposed of all the hybrids—stained and unstained—that I didn't send to Moore, and can't recall any instance of escape. Can this be wholly an hallucination? Or could any of the specimens that escaped in Brooklyn when Moore was bitten have found their way back to Africa? There was that absurd story of the blue fly that waked Dyson when Moore died—but after all, the survival and return of some of the things is not impossible. It is perfectly plausible that the blue should stick to their wings, too, for the pigment I devised was almost as good as tattooing for permanence. By elimination, that would seem to be the only rational explanation for this thing; though it is very curious that the fellow has come as far south as this. Possibly it's some hereditary homing instinct inherent in the tsetse strain. After all, that side of him belongs to South Africa. I must be on my guard against a bite. Of course the original venom—if this is actually one of the flies that escaped from Moore—was worn out ages ago; but the fellow must have fed as he flew back from America, and he may well have come through Central Africa and picked up a fresh infectivity. Indeed, that's more probable than not; for the *palpalis* half of his heredity would naturally take him back to Uganda, and all the *trypanosomiasis* germs. I still have some of the tryparsamide left—I couldn't bear to destroy my medicine case, incriminating though it may be—but since reading up on the subject I am not so sure about the drug's action as I was. It gives one a fighting chance—certainly it saved Gamba—but there's always a large probability of failure.

It's devilish queer that this fly should have happened to come into my room—of all places in the wide expanse of Africa! Seems to strain coincidence to the breaking-point. I suppose that if it comes again, I shall certainly kill it. I'm surprised that it escaped me today, for ordinarily these fellows are extremely stupid and easy to catch. Can it be a pure illusion after all? Certainly the heat is getting me of late as it never did before—even up around Uganda.

JANUARY 16—Am I going insane? The fly came again this noon, and acted so anomalously that I can't make head or tail of it. Only delusion on my part could account for what that buzzing pest seemed to do. It appeared from nowhere, and went straight to my bookshelf—circling again and again to front a copy of Moore's *Diptera of Central and Southern Africa*. Now and then it would light on top or back of the volume, and occasionally it would dart forward toward me and retreat before I could strike at it with a folded paper. Such cunning is unheard of among the notoriously stupid African *diptera*. For nearly half an hour I tried to get the cursed thing, but at last it darted out the window through a hole in the screen that I hadn't noticed. At times I fancied it deliberately mocked me by coming within reach of my weapon and then skilfully sidestepping as I struck out. I must keep a tight hold of my consciousness.

JANUARY 17—Either I am mad or the world is in the grip of some sudden suspension of the laws of probability as we know them. That damnable fly came in from somewhere just before noon and commenced buzzing around the copy of Moore's *Diptera* on my shelf. Again I tried to catch it, and again yesterday's experience was repeated. Finally the pest made for the open inkwell on my table and dipped itself in—just the legs and thorax, keeping its wings clear. Then it sailed up to the ceiling and lit—beginning to crawl around in a curved patch and leaving a trail of ink. After a time it hopped a bit and made a single ink spot unconnected with the trail—then it dropped squarely in front of my face, and buzzed out of sight before I could get it. Something about this whole business struck me as monstrously sinister and abnormal—more so than I could explain to myself.

When I looked at the ink-trail on the ceiling from different angles, it seemed more and more familiar to me, and it dawned on me suddenly that it formed an absolutely perfect question-mark. What device could be more malignly appropriate? It is a wonder that I did not faint. So far the hotel attendants have not noticed it.

Have not seen the fly this afternoon and evening, but am keeping my inkwell securely closed. I think my extermination of Moore must be preying on me, and giving me morbid hallucinations. Perhaps there is no fly at all.

JANUARY 18—Into what strange hell of living nightmare am I plunged? What occurred today is something which could not normally happen—and yet an hotel attendant has seen the marks on the ceiling and concedes their reality. About eleven o'clock this morning, as I was writing on a manuscript, something darted down to the inkwell for a second and flashed aloft again before I could see what it was. Looking up, I saw that hellish fly on the ceiling as it had been before—crawling along and tracing another trail of curves and turns. There was nothing I could do, but I folded a newspaper in readiness to get the creature if it should fly near enough. When it had made several turns on the ceiling it flew into a dark corner and disappeared, and as I looked upward at the doubly defaced plastering I saw that the new ink-trail was that of a huge and unmistakable figure 5! For a time I was almost unconscious from a wave of nameless menace for which I could not fully account. Then I summoned up my resolution and took an active step. Going out to a chemist's shop I purchased some gum and other things necessary for preparing a sticky trap—also a duplicate inkwell. Returning to my room, I filled the new inkwell with the sticky mixture and set it where the old one had been, leaving it open. Then I tried to concentrate my mind on some reading. About three o'clock I heard the accursed insect again, and saw it circling around the new inkwell. It descended to the sticky surface but did not touch it, and afterward sailed straight toward me—retreating before I could hit it. Then it went to the bookshelf and circled around Moore's treatise. There is something profound and diabolic about the way the intruder hovers near that book.

The worst part was the last. Leaving Moore's book, the insect flew over to the open window and began beating itself rhythmically against the wire screen. There would be a series of beats and then a series of equal length and another pause, and so on. Something about this performance held me motionless for a couple of moments, but after that I went over to the window and tried to kill the noxious thing. As usual, no use. It merely flew across the room to a lamp and began beating the same tattoo on the stiff cardboard shade. I felt a vague desperation, and proceeded to shut all the doors as well as the window whose screen had the imperceptible hole. It seemed very necessary to kill this persistent being, whose hounding was rapidly unseating my mind. Then, unconsciously counting, I began to notice that each of its series of beatings contained just five strokes. Five—the same number that the thing had traced in ink on the ceiling in the morning! Could there be any conceivable connexion? The notion was maniacal, for that would argue a human intellect and a knowledge of written figures in the hybrid fly. A human intellect—did not that take one back to the most primitive legends of the Uganda blacks? And yet there was that infernal cleverness in eluding me as contrasted with the normal stupidity of the breed.

As I laid aside my folded paper and sat down in growing horror, the insect buzzed aloft and disappeared through a hole in the ceiling where the radiator pipe went to the room above. The departure did not soothe me, for my mind had started on a train of wild and terrible reflections. If this fly had a human intelligence, where did that intelligence come from? Was there any truth in the native notion that these creatures acquire the personality of their victims after the latter's death? If so, whose personality did this fly bear? I had reasoned out that it must be one of those which escaped from Moore at the time he was bitten. Was this the envoy of death which had bitten Moore? If so, what did it want with me? What did it want with me anyway? In a cold perspiration I remembered the actions of the fly that had bitten Batta when Batta died. Had its own personality been displaced by that of its dead victim? Then there was that sensational news account of the fly that waked Dyson when Moore died. As for that fly that was hounding me—could it be that a vindictive human personality drove it on? How it hovered around Moore's book!—I refused to think any farther than that.

All at once I began to feel sure that the creature was indeed infected, and in the most virulent way. With a malign deliberation so evident in every act, it must surely have charged itself on purpose with the deadliest bacilli in all Africa. My mind, thoroughly shaken, was now taking the thing's human qualities for granted. I now telephoned the clerk and asked for a man to stop up the radiator pipehole and other possible chinks in my room. I spoke of being tormented by flies, and he seemed to be quite sympathetic. When the man came, I shewed him the ink-marks on the ceiling, which he recognised without difficulty. So they are real! The resemblance to a question-mark and a figure 5 puzzled and fascinated him. In the end he stopped up all the holes he could find, and mended the window-screen, so that I can now keep both windows open. He evidently thought me a bit eccentric, especially since no insects were in sight while he was here. But I am past minding that. So far the fly has not appeared this evening. God knows what it is, what it wants, or what will become of me!

JANUARY 19—I am utterly engulfed in horror. The thing has touched me. Something monstrous and daemoniac is at work around me, and I am a helpless victim. In the morning, when I returned from breakfast, that winged fiend from hell brushed into the room over my head, and began beating itself against the window-screen as it did yesterday. This time, though, each series of beats contained only four strokes. I rushed to the window and tried to catch it, but it escaped as usual and flew over to Moore's treatise, where it buzzed around mockingly. Its vocal equipment is limited, but I noticed that its spells of buzzing came in groups of four. By this time I was certainly mad, for I called out to it, "Moore, Moore, for God's sake, what do you want?" When I did so, the creature suddenly ceased its circling, flew toward me, and made a low, graceful dip in the air, somehow suggestive of a bow. Then it flew back to the book. At least, I seemed to see it do all this—though I am trusting my senses no longer. And then the worst thing happened. I had left my door open, hoping the monster would leave if I could not catch it; but about 11:30 I shut the door, concluding it had gone. Then I settled down to read. Just at noon I felt a tickling on the back of my neck, but when I put my hand up nothing was there. In a moment I felt the tickling again—and before I could move, that nameless spawn of hell sailed into view from behind, did another of those mocking, graceful dips in the air, and flew out through the keyhole — which I had never dreamed was large enough to allow its passage. That the thing had touched me, I could not doubt. It had touched me without injuring me — and then I remembered in a sudden cold fright that Moore had been bitten on the back of the neck at noon.

No invasion since then — but I have stuffed all the keyholes with paper and shall have a folded paper ready for use whenever I open the door to leave or enter.

JANUARY 20 — I cannot yet believe fully in the supernatural, yet I fear none the less that I am lost. The business is too much for me. Just before noon today that devil appeared outside the window and repeated its beating operations; but this time in series of three. When I went to the window it flew off out of sight.

I still have resolution enough to take one more defensive step. Removing both window-screens, I coated them with my sticky preparation — the one I used in the inkwell — outside and inside, and set them back in place. If that creature attempts another tattoo, it will be its last! Rest of the day in peace. Can I weather this experience without becoming a maniac?

JANUARY 21 — On board train for Bloemfontein. I am routed. The thing is winning. It has a diabolic intelligence against which all my devices are powerless. It appeared outside the window this morning, but did not touch the sticky screen. Instead, it sheered off without lighting and began buzzing around in circles — two at a time, followed by a pause in the air. After several of these performances it flew off out of sight over the roofs of the city. My nerves are just about at the breaking-point, for these suggestions of numbers are capable of a hideous interpretation. Monday the thing dwelt on the figure five; Tuesday it was four; Wednesday it was three; and now today it is two. Five, four, three, two — what can this be save some monstrous and unthinkable counting-off of days? For what purpose, only the evil powers of the universe can know. I spent all the afternoon packing and arranging about my trunks, and now I have taken the night express for Bloemfontein. Flight may be useless, but what else can one do?

JANUARY 22 — Settled at the Orange Hotel, Bloemfontein — a comfortable and excellent place — but the horror followed me. I had shut all the doors and windows, stopped all the keyholes, looked for any possible chinks, and pulled down all the shades — but just before noon I heard a dull tap on one of the window-screens. I waited — and after a long pause another tap came. A second pause, and still another single tap. Raising the shade, I saw that accursed fly, as I had expected. It described one large, slow circle in the air, and then flew out of sight. I was left as weak as a rag, and had to rest on the couch. One! This was clearly the burden of the monster's present message. One tap, one circle. Did this mean one more day for me before some unthinkable doom? Ought I to flee again, or entrench myself here by sealing up the room?

After an hour's rest I felt able to act, and ordered a large reserve supply of canned and packaged food — also linen and towels — sent in. Tomorrow I shall not under any circumstances open any crevice of door or window. When the food and linen came the black looked at me queerly, but I no longer care how eccentric — or insane — I may appear. I am hounded by powers worse than the ridicule of mankind.

Having received my supplies, I went over every square millimetre of the walls, and stopped up every microscopic opening I could find. At last I feel able to get real sleep.

(Handwriting here becomes irregular, nervous, and very difficult to decipher)

JANUARY 23 — It is just before noon, and I feel that something very terrible is about to happen. Didn't sleep as late as I expected, even though I got almost no sleep on the train the night before. Up early, and have had trouble getting concentrated on anything — reading or writing. That slow, deliberate counting-off of days is too much for me. I don't know which has gone wild — Nature or my head. Until about eleven I did very little except walk up and down the room. Then I heard a rustle among the food packages brought in yesterday, and that daemoniac fly crawled out before my eyes. I grabbed something flat and made passes at the thing despite my panic fear, but with no more effect than usual. As I advanced, that blue-winged horror retreated as usual to the table where I had piled my books, and lit for a second on Moore's *Diptera of Central and Southern Africa*. Then as I followed, it flew over to the mantel clock and lit on the dial near the figure 12. Before I could think up another move it had begun to crawl around the dial very slowly and deliberately — in the direction of the hands. It passed under the minute hand, curved down and up, passed under the hour hand, and finally came to a stop exactly at the figure 12. As it hovered there it fluttered its wings with a buzzing noise.

Is this a portent of some sort? I am getting as superstitious as the blacks. The hour is now a little after eleven. Is twelve the end?

I have just one last resort, brought to my mind through utter desperation. Wish I had thought of it before. Recalling that my medicine case contains both of the substances necessary to generate chlorine gas, I have resolved to fill the room with that lethal vapour — asphyxiating the fly while protecting myself with an ammonia-sealed handkerchief tied over my face. Fortunately I have a good supply of ammonia. This crude mask will probably neutralise the acrid chlorine fumes till the insect is dead — or at least helpless enough to crush. But I must be quick. How can I be sure that the thing will not suddenly dart for me before my preparations are complete? I ought not to be stopping to write in this journal.

LATER — Both chemicals — hydrochloric acid and manganese dioxide — on the table all ready to mix. I've tied the handkerchief over my nose and mouth, and have a bottle of ammonia ready to keep it soaked until the chlorine is gone. Have battened down both windows. But I don't like the actions of that hybrid daemon. It stays on the clock, but is very slowly crawling around backward from the 12 mark to meet the gradually advancing minute-hand. Is this to be my last entry in this journal? It would be useless to try to deny what I suspect. Too often a grain of incredible truth lurks behind the wildest and most fantastic of legends. Is the personality of Henry Moore trying to get at me through this blue-winged devil? Is this the fly that bit him, and that in consequence absorbed his consciousness when he died? If so, and if it bites me, will my own personality displace Moore's and enter that buzzing body when I die of the bite later on? Perhaps, though, I need not die even if it gets me. There is always a chance with tryparsamide. And I regret nothing. Moore had to die, be the outcome what it will.

SLIGHTLY LATER — The fly has paused on the clock-dial near the 45-minute mark. It is now 11:30. I am saturating the handkerchief over my face with ammonia, and keeping the bottle handy for further applications. This will be the final entry before I mix the acid and manganese and liberate the chlorine. I ought not to be losing time, but it steadies me to get things down on paper. But for this record, I'd have lost all my reason long ago. The fly seems to be getting restless, and the minute-hand is approaching it. Now for the chlorine . . . .

(End of the journal)

On Sunday, Jan. 24, 1932, after repeated knocking had failed to gain any response from the eccentric man in Room 303 of the Orange Hotel, a black attendant entered with a pass key and at once fled shrieking downstairs to tell the clerk what he had found. The clerk, after notifying the police, summoned the manager; and the latter accompanied Constable De Witt, Coroner Bogaert, and Dr. Van Keulen to the fatal room. The occupant lay dead on the floor — his face upward, and bound with a handkerchief which smelled strongly of ammonia. Under this covering the features shewed an expression of stark, utter fear which transmitted itself to the observers. On the back of the neck Dr. Van Keulen found a virulent insect bite — dark red, with a purple ring around it — which suggested a tsetse-fly or something less innocuous. An examination indicated that death must be due to heart-failure induced by sheer fright rather than to the bite — though a subsequent autopsy indicated that the germ of trypanosomiasis had been introduced into the system. On the table were several objects — a worn leather blank-book containing the journal just described, a pen, writing-pad, and open inkwell, a doctor's medicine case with the initials "T. S." marked in gold, bottles of ammonia and hydrochloric acid, and a tumbler about a quarter full of black manganese dioxide. The ammonia bottle demanded a second look because something besides the fluid seemed to be in it. Looking closer, Coroner Bogaert saw that the alien occupant was a fly. It seemed to be some sort of hybrid with vague tsetse affiliations, but its wings — shewing faintly blue despite the action of the strong ammonia — were a complete puzzle. Something about it waked a faint memory of newspaper reading in Dr. Van Keulen — a memory which the journal was soon to confirm. Its lower parts seemed to have been stained with ink, so thoroughly that even the ammonia had not bleached them. Possibly it had fallen at one time into the inkwell, though the wings were untouched. But how had it managed to fall into the narrow-necked ammonia bottle? It was as if the creature had deliberately crawled in and committed suicide!

But the strangest thing of all was what Constable De Witt noticed on the smooth white ceiling overhead as his eyes roved about curiously. At his cry the other three followed his gaze — even Dr. Van Keulen, who had for some time been thumbing through the worn leather book with an expression of mixed horror, fascination, and incredulity. The thing on the ceiling was a series of shaky, straggling ink-tracks, such as might have been made by the crawling of some ink-drenched insect. At once everyone thought of the stains on the fly so oddly found in the ammonia bottle. But these were no ordinary ink-tracks. Even a first glance revealed something hauntingly familiar about them, and closer inspection brought gasps of startled wonder from all four observers. Coroner Bogaert instinctively looked around the room to see if there were any conceivable instrument or arrangement of piled-up furniture which could make it possible for those straggling marks to have been drawn by human agency. Finding nothing of the sort, he resumed his curious and almost awestruck upward glance. For beyond a doubt these inky smudges formed definite letters of the alphabet — letters coherently arranged in English words. The doctor was the first to make them out clearly, and the others listened breathlessly as he recited the insane-sounding message so incredibly scrawled in a place no human hand could reach:

"SEE MY JOURNAL — IT GOT ME FIRST — I DIED — THEN I SAW I WAS IN IT — THE BLACKS ARE RIGHT — STRANGE POWERS IN NATURE — NOW I WILL DROWN WHAT IS LEFT —"

Presently, amidst the puzzled hush that followed, Dr. Van Keulen commenced reading aloud from the worn leather journal.

The Horror in the Museum.

BY HAZEL HEALD AND H.P. LOVECRAFT

11,000-WORD NOVELETTE; 1932.

It is hard to know quite what to think of "The Horror in the Museum." In I Am Providence, *S.T. Joshi expresses hope that it was written as a self-parody. It certainly has a strong dose of that overcooked aura of deliberate extravagance that would characterize one; on the other hand, it's equally possible that Lovecraft was just having some ironic, campy fun.*

One of the first three stories written for Hazel Heald, "The Horror in the Museum" was written in late 1932, and promptly published in the July 1933 issue of Weird Tales.

I.

It was languid curiosity which first brought Stephen Jones to Rogers' Museum. Someone had told him about the queer underground place in Southwark Street across the river, where waxen things so much more horrible than the worst effigies at Madame Tussaud's were shown, and he had strolled in one April day to see how disappointing he would find it. Oddly, he was not disappointed. There was something different and distinctive here, after all.

Of course, the usual gory commonplaces were present—Landru, Dr. Crippen, Madame Demers, Rizzio, Lady Jane Grey, endless maimed victims of war and revolution, and monsters like Gilles de Rais and Marquis de Sade—but there were other things which had made him breathe faster and stay till the ringing of the closing bell. The man who had fashioned this collection could be no ordinary mountebank. There was imagination—even a kind of diseased genius—in some of this stuff.

Later he had learned about George Rogers. The man had been on the Tussaud staff, but some trouble had developed which led to his discharge. There were aspersions on his sanity and tales of his crazy forms of secret worship—though latterly his success with his own basement museum had dulled the edge of some criticisms while sharpening the insidious point of others. Teratology and the iconography of nightmare were his hobbies, and even he had had the prudence to screen off some of his worst effigies in a special alcove for adults only. It was this alcove which had fascinated Jones so much. There were lumpish hybrid things which only fantasy could spawn, moulded with devilish skill, and coloured in a horribly life-like fashion.

Some were the figures of well-known myth—gorgons, chimeras, dragons, cyclops, and all their shuddersome congeners. Others were drawn from darker and more furtively whispered cycles of subterranean legend—black, formless Tsathoggua, many-tentacled Cthulhu, proboscidian Chaugnar Faugn, and other rumoured blasphemies from forbidden books like the *Necronomicon*, the *Book of Eibon*, or the *Unaussprechlichen Kulten* of von Junzt. But the worst were wholly original with Rogers, and represented shapes which no tale of antiquity had ever dared to suggest. Several were hideous parodies on forms of organic life we know, while others seemed to be taken from feverish dreams of other planets and galaxies. The wilder paintings of Clark Ashton Smith might suggest a few—but nothing could suggest the effect of poignant, loathsome terror created by their great size and fiendishly cunning workmanship, and by the diabolically clever lighting conditions under which they were exhibited.

Stephen Jones, as a leisurely connoisseur of the bizarre in art, had sought out Rogers himself in the dingy office and workroom behind the vaulted museum chamber— an evil-looking crypt lighted dimly by dusty windows set slit-like and horizontal in the brick wall on a level with the ancient cobblestones of a hidden courtyard. It was here that the images were repaired—here, too, where some of them had been made. Waxen arms, legs, heads and torsos lay in grotesque array on various benches, while on high tiers of shelves matted wigs, ravenous-looking teeth, and glassy, staring eyes were indiscriminately scattered. Costumes of all sorts hung from hooks, and in one alcove were great piles of flesh-coloured wax-cakes and shelves filled with paint-cans and brushes of every description. In the centre of the room was a large melting-furnace used to prepare the wax for melding, its fire-box topped by a huge iron container on hinges, with a spout which permitted the pouring of melted wax with the merest touch of a finger.

Other things in the dismal crypt were less describable—isolated parts of problematical entities whose assembled forms were the phantoms of delirium. At one end was a door of heavy plank, fastened by an unusually large padlock and with a very peculiar symbol painted over it. Jones, who had once had access to the dreaded *Necronomicon*, shivered involuntarily as he recognized that symbol. This showman, he reflected, must indeed be a person of disconcertingly wide scholarship in dark and dubious fields.

Nor did the conversation of Rogers disappoint him. The man was tall, lean, and rather unkempt, with large black eyes which gazed combustively from a pallid and usually stubble-covered face. He did not resent Jones' intrusion, but seemed to welcome the chance of unburdening himself to an interested person. His voice was of singular depth and resonance, and harboured a sort of repressed intensity bordering on the feverish. Jones did not wonder that many had thought him mad.

With every successive call — and such calls became a habit as the weeks went by — Jones had found Rogers more communicative and confidential. From the first there had been hints of strange faiths and practices on the showman's part, and later on those hints expanded into tales — despite a few odd corroborative photographs — whose extravagance was almost comic.

It was some time in June, on a night when Jones had brought a bottle of good whisky and plied his host somewhat freely, that the really demented talk first appeared. Before that there had been wild enough stories — accounts of mysterious trips to Tibet, the African interior, the Arabian desert, the Amazon valley, Alaska, and certain little-known islands of the South Pacific, plus claims of having read such monstrous and half-fabulous books as the prehistoric Pnakotic fragments and the Dhol chants attributed to malign and non-human Leng — but nothing in all this had been so unmistakably insane as what had cropped out that June evening under the spell of the whisky.

To be plain, Rogers began making vague boasts of having found certain things in nature that no one had found before, and of having brought back tangible evidences of such discoveries. According to his bibulous harangue, he had gone farther than anyone else in interpreting the obscure and primal books he studied, and had been directed by them to certain remote places where strange survivals are hidden — survivals of aeons and life-cycles earlier than mankind, and in some case connected with other dimensions and other worlds, communication with which was frequent in the forgotten pre-human days. Jones marvelled at the fancy which could conjure up such notions, and wondered just what Rogers' mental history had been. Had his work amidst the morbid grotesqueries of Madame Tussaud's been the start of his imaginative flights, or was the tendency

Weird Tales, July 1933

"He spoke not a word, but put every ounce of energy into the defense of his life."

innate, so that his choice of occupation was merely one of its manifestations? At any rate, the man's work was clearly very closely linked with his notions. Even now there was no mistaking the trend of his blackest hints about the nightmare monstrosities in the screened-off "adults only" alcove. Heedless of ridicule, he was trying to imply that not all of these demoniac abnormalities were artificial.

It was Jones' frank scepticism and amusement at these irresponsible claims which broke up the growing cordiality. Rogers, it was clear, took himself very seriously; for he now became morose and resentful, continuing to tolerate Jones only through a dogged urge to break down his wall of urbane and complacent incredulity. Wild tales and suggestions of rites and sacrifices to nameless elder gods continued, and now and then Rogers would lead his guest to one of the hideous blasphemies in the screen-off alcove and point out features difficult to reconcile with even the finest human craftsmanship. Jones continued his visits through sheer fascination, though he knew he had forfeited his host's regards. At times he would humour Rogers with pretended assent to some mad hint or assertion, but the gaunt showman was seldom to be deceived by such tactics.

The tension came to a head later in September. Jones had casually dropped into the museum one afternoon, and was wandering through the dim corridors whose horrors were now so familiar, when he heard a very peculiar sound from the general direction of Rogers' workroom. Others heard it too, and started nervously as the echoes reverberated through the great vaulted basement. The three attendants exchanged odd glances; and one of them, a dark, taciturn, foreign-looking fellow who always served Rogers as a repairer and assistant designer, smiled in a way which seemed to puzzle his colleagues and which grated very harshly on some facet of Jones' sensibilities. It was the yelp or scream of a dog, and was such a sound as could be made only under conditions of the utmost fright and agony combined. Its stark, anguished frenzy was appalling to hear, and in this setting of grotesque abnormality it held a double hideousness. Jones remembered that no dogs were allowed in the museum.

He was about to go to the door leading into the workroom, when the dark attendant stopped him with a word and a gesture. Mr. Rogers, the man said in a soft, somewhat accented voice at once apologetic and vaguely sardonic, was out, and there were standing orders to admit no one to the workroom during his absence. As for that yelp, it was undoubtedly something out in the courtyard behind the museum. This neighbourhood was full of stray mongrels, and their fights were sometimes shockingly noisy. There were no dogs in any part of the museum. But if Mr. Jones wished to see Mr. Rogers he might find him just before closing-time.

After this Jones climbed the old stone steps to the street outside and examined the squalid neighbourhood curiously. The leaning, decrepit buildings — once dwellings but now largely shops and warehouses — were very ancient indeed. Some of them were of a gabled type seeming to go back to Tudor times, and a faint miasmatic stench hung subtly about the whole region. Beside the dingy house whose basement held the museum was a low archway pierced by a dark cobbled alley, and this Jones entered in a vague wish to find the courtyard behind the workroom and settle the affair of the dog comfortably in his mind. The courtyard was dim in the late afternoon light, hemmed in by rear walls even uglier and more intangibly menacing than the crumbling facades of the evil old houses. Not a dog was in sight, and Jones wondered how the aftermath of such a frantic turmoil could have completely vanished so soon.

Despite the assistant's statement that no dog had been in the museum, Jones glanced nervously at the three small windows of the basement workroom — narrow, horizontal rectangles close to the grass-grown pavement, with grimy panes that stared repulsively and incuriously like the eyes of dead fish. To their left a worn flight of stairs led to an opaque and heavily bolted door. Some impulse urged him to crouch low on the damp, broken cobblestones and peer in, on the chance that the thick green shades, worked by long cords that hung down to a reachable level, might not be drawn. The outer surfaces were thick with dirt, but as he rubbed them with his handkerchief he saw there was no obscuring curtain in the way of his vision.

So shadowed was the cellar from the inside that not much could be made out, but the grotesque working paraphernalia now and then loomed up spectrally as Jones tried each of the windows in turn. It seemed evident at first that no one was within; yet when he peered through the extreme right-hand window — the one nearest the entrance alley — he saw a glow of light at the farther end of the apartment which made him pause in bewilderment. There was no reason why any light should be there. It was an inner side of the room, and he could not recall any gas or electric fixture near that point. Another look defined the glow as a large vertical rectangle, and a thought occurred to him. It was in that direction that he had always noticed the heavy plank door with the abnormally large padlock — the door which was never opened, and above which was crudely smeared that hideous cryptic symbol from the fragmentary records of forbidden elder magic. It must be open now — and there was a light inside. All his former speculation as to where that door led, and as to what lay behind it, were now renewed with trebly disquieting force.

Jones wandered aimlessly around the dismal locality till close to six o'clock, when he returned to the museum to make the call on Rogers. He could hardly tell why he wished so especially to see the man just then, but there must have been some subconscious misgivings about that terribly unplaceable canine scream of the afternoon, and about the glow of light in that disturbing and usually unopened inner doorway with the heavy padlock.

The attendants were leaving as he arrived, and he thought that Orabona — the dark foreign-looking assistant — eyed him with something like sly, repressed amusement. He did not relish that look—even though he had seen the fellow turn it on his employer many times.

The vaulted exhibition room was ghoulish in its desertion, but he strode quickly through it and rapped at the door of the office and workroom. Response was slow in coming, though there were footsteps inside. Finally, in response to a second knock, the lock rattled, and the ancient six-panelled portal creaked reluctantly open to reveal the slouching, feverish-eyed form of George Rogers.

From the first it was clear that the showman was in an unusual mood. There was a curious mixture of reluctance and actual gloating in his welcome, and his talk at once veered to extravagances of the most hideous and incredible sort.

Surviving elder gods—nameless sacrifices—the other-than-artificial nature of some of the alcove horrors—all the usual boasts, but uttered in a tone of peculiarly increasing confidence. Obviously, Jones reflected, the poor fellow's madness was gaining on him. From time to time Rogers would send furtive glances toward the heavy, padlocked inner door at the end of the room, or toward a piece of coarse burlap on the floor not far from it, beneath which some small object appeared to be lying. Jones grew more nervous as the moments passed, and began to feel as hesitant about mentioning the afternoon's oddities as he had formerly been anxious to do so.

Rogers' sepulchrally resonant bass almost cracked under the excitement of his fevered rambling.

"Do you remember," he shouted, "what I told you about that ruined city in Indo-China where the Tcho-Tchos lived? You had to admit I'd been there when you saw the photographs, even if you did think I made that oblong swimmer in darkness out of wax. If you'd seen it writhing in the underground pools as I did ....

"Well, this is bigger still. I never told you about this, because I wanted to work out the later parts before making any claim. When you see the snapshots you'll know the geography couldn't have been faked, and I fancy I have another way of proving It isn't any waxed concoction of mine. You've never seen It, for the experiments wouldn't let me keep It on exhibition."

The showman glanced queerly at the padlocked door.

"It all comes from that long ritual in the eighth Pnakotic fragment. When I got it figured out I saw it could only have one meaning. There were things in the north before the land of Lomar—before mankind existed—and this was one of them. It took us all the way to Alaska, and up the Nootak from Fort Morton, but the thing was there as we knew it would be. Great cyclopean ruins, acres of them. There was less left than we had hoped for, but after three million years what could one expect? And weren't the Eskimo legends all in the right direction? We couldn't get one of the beggars to go with us, and had to sledge all the way back to Nome for Americans. Orabona was no good up in that climate—it made him sullen and hateful.

"I'll tell you later how we found It. When we got the ice blasted out of the pylons of the central ruin the stairway was just as we knew it would be. Some carvings still there, and it was no trouble keeping the Yankees from following us in. Orabona shivered like a leaf—you'd never think it from the damned insolent way he struts around here. He knew enough of the Elder Lore to be properly afraid. The eternal light was gone, but our torches showed enough. We saw the bones of others who had been before us aeons ago, when the climate was warm. Some of those bones were of things you couldn't even imagine. At the third level down we found the ivory throne the fragments said so much about—and I may as well tell you it wasn't empty.

"The thing on the throne didn't move—and we knew then that It needed the nourishment of sacrifice. But we didn't want to wake It then. Better to get It to London first. Orabona and I went to the surface for the big box, but when we had packed it we couldn't get It up the three flights of steps. These steps weren't made for human beings, and their size bothered us. Anyway, it was devilish heavy. We had to have the Americans down to get It out. They weren't anxious to go into the place, but of course the worst thing was safely inside the box. We told them it was a batch of ivory carving—archaeological stuff; and after seeing the carved throne they probably believed us. It's a wonder they didn't suspect hidden treasure and demand a share. They must have told queer tales around Nome later on; though I doubt if they ever went back to those ruins, even for the ivory throne."

Rogers paused, felt around in his desk, and produced an envelope of good-sized photographic prints. Extracting one and laying it face down before him, he handed the rest to Jones. The set was certainly an odd one: ice-clad hills, dog sledges, men in furs, and vast tumbled ruins against a background of snow—ruins whose bizarre outlines and enormous stone blocks could hardly be accounted for. One flashlight view showed an incredible interior chamber with wild carvings and a curious throne whose proportions could not have been designed for a human occupant. The carvings of the gigantic masonry—high walls and peculiar vaulting overhead—were mainly symbolic, and involved both wholly unknown designs and certain hieroglyphs darkly cited in obscene legends. Over the throne loomed the same dreadful symbol which was now painted on the workroom wall above the padlocked plank door. Jones darted a nervous glance at the closed portal. Assuredly, Rogers had been to strange places and had seen strange things. Yet this mad interior picture might easily be a fraud—taken from a very clever stage setting. One must not be too credulous. But Rogers was continuing:

"Well, we shipped the box from Nome and got to London without any trouble. That was the first time we'd ever brought back anything that had a chance of coming alive. I didn't put It on display, because there were more important things to do for It. It needed the nourishment of sacrifice, for It was a god. Of course I couldn't get It the sort of sacrifices which It used to have in Its day, for such things don't exist now. But there were other things which might do. The blood is the life, you know. Even the lemures and elementals that are older than the earth will come when the blood of men or beasts is offered under the right conditions."

The expression on the narrator's face was growing very alarming and repulsive, so that Jones fidgeted involuntarily in his chair. Rogers seemed to notice his guest's nervousness, and continued with a distinctly evil smile.

"It was last year that I got It, and ever since then I've been trying rites and sacrifices. Orabona hasn't been much help, for he was always against the idea of waking It. He hates It — probably because he's afraid of what It will come to mean. He carries a pistol all the time to protect himself — fool, as if there were human protection against It! If I ever see him draw that pistol, I'll strangle him. He wanted me to kill It and make an effigy of It. But I've stuck by my plans, and I'm coming out on top in spite of all the cowards like Orabona and damned sniggering sceptics like you, Jones! I've chanted the rites and made certain sacrifices, and last week the transition came. The sacrifice was — received and enjoyed!"

Rogers actually licked his lips, while Jones held himself uneasily rigid. The showman paused and rose, crossing the room to the piece of burlap at which he had glanced so often. Bending down, he took hold of one corner as he spoke again.

"You've laughed enough at my work — now it's time for you to get some facts. Orabona tells me you heard a dog screaming around here this afternoon. Do you know what that meant?"

Jones started. For all his curiosity he would have been glad to get out without further light on the point which had so puzzled him. But Rogers was inexorable, and began to lift the square of burlap. Beneath it lay a crushed, almost shapeless mass which Jones was slow to classify. Was it a once-living thing which some agency had flattened, sucked dry of blood, punctured in a thousand places, and wrung into a limp, broken-boned heap of grotesqueness? After a moment Jones realized what it must be. It was what was left of a dog — a dog, perhaps of considerable size and whitish colour. Its breed was past recognition, for distortion had come in nameless and hideous ways. Most of the hair was burned off as by some pungent acid, and the exposed, bloodless skin was riddled by innumerable circular wounds or incisions. The form of torture necessary to cause such results was past imagining.

Electrified with a pure loathing which conquered his mounting disgust, Jones sprang with a cry.

"You damned sadist — you madman — you do a thing like this and dare to speak to a decent man!"

Rogers dropped the burlap with a malignant sneer and faced his oncoming guest. His words held an unnatural calm.

"Why, you fool, do you think I did this? What of it? It is not human and does not pretend to be. To sacrifice is merely to offer. I gave the dog to It. What happened is It's work, not mine. It needed the nourishment of the offering, and took it in Its own way. But let me show you what It looks like."

As Jones stood hesitating, the speaker had returned to his desk and took up the photograph he had laid face down without showing. Now he extended it with a curious look. Jones took it and glanced at it in an almost mechanical way. After a moment the visitor's glance became sharper and more absorbed, for the utterly satanic force of the object depicted had an almost hypnotic effect. Certainly, Rogers had outdone himself in modelling the eldritch nightmare which the camera had caught. The thing was a work of sheer, infernal genius, and Jones wondered how the public would react when it was placed on exhibition. So hideous a thing had no right to exist — probably the mere contemplation of it, after it was done, had completed the unhinging of its maker's mind and led him to worship it with brutal sacrifices. Only a stout sanity could resist the insidious suggestion that the blasphemy was — or had once been — some morbid and exotic form of actual life.

The thing in the picture squatted or was balanced on what appeared to be a clever reproduction of the monstrously carved throne in the other curious photograph. To describe it with any ordinary vocabulary would be impossible, for nothing even roughly corresponding to it has ever come within the imagination of sane mankind. It represented something meant perhaps to be roughly connected with the vertebrates of this planet — though one could not be too sure of that. Its bulk was cyclopean, for even squatted it towered to almost twice the height of Orabona, who was shown beside it. Looking sharply, one might trace its approximations toward the bodily features of the higher vertebrates.

There was an almost globular torso, with six long, sinuous limbs terminating in crab-like claws. From the upper end a subsidiary globe bulged forth bubble-like; its triangle of three staring, fishy eyes, its foot-long and evidently flexible proboscis, and a distended lateral system analogous to gills, suggesting that it was a head. Most of the body was covered with what at first appeared to be fur, but which on closer examination proved to be a dense growth of dark, slender tentacles or sucking filaments, each tipped with a mouth suggesting the head of an asp. On the head and below the proboscis the tentacles tended to be longer and thicker, marked with spiral stripes — suggesting the traditional serpent-locks of Medusa. To suggest that such a thing could have an expression seems paradoxical; yet Jones felt that that triangle of bulging fish eyes and that obliquely poised proboscis all bespoke a blend of hate, greed and sheer cruelty incomprehensible to mankind because it was mixed with other emotions not of the world or this solar system. Into this bestial abnormality, he reflected, Rogers must have poured at once all his malignant insanity and all his uncanny sculptural genius. The thing was incredible — and yet the photograph proved that it existed.

Rogers interrupted his reveries.

"Well — what do you think of It? Now do you wonder what crushed the dog and sucked it dry with a million mouths? It needed nourishment — and It will need more. It is a god, and I am the first priest of Its latter-day hierarchy. Iä! Shub-Niggurath! The Goat with a Thousand Young!"

Jones lowered the photograph in disgust and pity.

"See here, Rogers, this won't do. There are limits, you know. It's a great piece of work, and all that, but it isn't good for you. Better not see it any more — let Orabona break it up, and try to forget about it. And let me tear this beastly picture up, too."

With a snarl, Rogers snatched the photograph and returned it to the desk.

"Idiot — you — and you still think It's a fraud! You still think I made It, and you still think my figures are nothing but lifeless wax! Why, damn you, you're going to know. Not just now, for It is resting after the sacrifice — but later. Oh, yes — you will not doubt the power of It then."

As Rogers glanced toward the padlocked inner door Jones retrieved his hat and stick from a near-by bench.

"Very well, Rogers, let it be later. I must be going now, but I'll call round tomorrow afternoon. Think my advice over and see if it doesn't sound sensible. Ask Orabona what he thinks, too."

Rogers bared his teeth in wild-beast fashion.

"Must be going now, eh? Afraid, after all! Afraid, for all your bold talk! You say the effigies are only wax, and yet you run away when I begin to prove that they aren't. You're like the fellows who take my standing bet that they daren't spend the night in the museum — they come boldly enough, but after an hour they shriek and hammer to get out! Want me to ask Orabona, eh? You two — always against me! You want to break down the coming earthly reign of It!"

Jones preserved his calm.

"No, Rogers — there's nobody against you. And I'm not afraid of your figures, either, much as I admire your skill. But we're both a bit nervous tonight, and I fancy some rest will do us good."

Again Rogers checked his guest's departure.

"Not afraid, eh? — then why are you so anxious to go? Look here — do you or don't you dare to stay alone here in the dark? What's your hurry if you don't believe in It?"

Some new idea seemed to have struck Rogers, and Jones eyed him closely.

"Why, I've no special hurry — but what would be gained by my staying here alone? What would it prove? My only objection is that it isn't very comfortable for sleeping. What good would it do either of us?"

This time it was Jones who was struck with an idea. He continued in a tone of conciliation.

"See here, Rogers — I've just asked you what it would prove if I stayed, when we both knew. It would prove that your effigies are just effigies, and that you oughtn't to let your imagination go the way it's been going lately. Suppose I do stay. If I stick it out till morning, will you agree to take a new view of things — go on a vacation for three months or so and let Orabona destroy that new thing of yours? Come, now — isn't that fair?"

The expression on the showman's face was hard to read. It was obvious that he was thinking quickly, and that of sundry conflicting emotions, malign triumph was getting the upper hand. His voice held a choking quality as he replied.

"Fair enough! If you do stick it out, I'll take your advice. We'll go out for dinner and come back. I'll lock you in the display room and go home. In the morning I'll come down ahead of Orabona — he comes half an hour before the rest — and see how you are. But don't try it unless you are very sure of your scepticism. Others have backed out — you have that chance. And I suppose a pounding on the outer door would always bring a constable. You may not like it so well after a while — you'll be in the same building, though not in the same room with It."

As they left the rear door into the dingy courtyard, Rogers took with him the piece of burlap — weighted with a gruesome burden. Near the centre of the court was a manhole, whose cover the showman lifted quietly, and with a shuddersome suggestion of familiarity. Burlap and all, the burden went down to the oblivion of a cloacal labyrinth. Jones shuddered, and almost shrank from the gaunt figure at his side as they emerged into the street.

By unspoken mutual consent, they did not dine together, but agreed to meet in front of the museum at eleven.

Jones hailed a cab, and breathed more freely when he had crossed Waterloo Bridge and was approaching the brilliantly lighted Strand. He dined at a quiet café, and subsequently went to his home in Portland Place to bathe and get a few things. Idly he wondered what Rogers was doing. He had heard that the man had a vast, dismal house in the Walworth Road, full of obscure and forbidden books, occult paraphernalia, and wax images which he did not choose to place on exhibition. Orabona, he understood, lived in separate quarters in the same house.

At eleven Jones found Rogers waiting by the basement door in Southwark Street. Their words were few, but each seemed taut with a menacing tension. They agreed that the vaulted exhibition room alone should form the scene of the vigil, and Rogers did not insist that the watcher sit in the special adult alcove of supreme horrors. The showman, having extinguished all the lights with switches in the workroom, locked the door of that crypt with one of the keys on his crowded ring. Without shaking hands he passed out the street door, locked it after him, and passed up the worn steps to the sidewalk outside. As his tread receded, Jones realized that the long, tedious vigil had commenced.

II.

Later, in the utter blackness of the great arched cellar, Jones cursed the childish naïveté which had brought him there. For the first half-hour he had kept flashing his pocket-light at intervals, but now just sitting in the dark on one of the visitor's benches had become a more nerve-wracking thing. Every time the beam shot out it lighted up some morbid, grotesque object — a guillotine, a nameless hybrid monster, a pasty-bearded face crafty with evil, a body with red torrents streaming from a severed throat. Jones knew that no sinister reality was attached to these things, but after that first half-hour he preferred not to see them.

Why he had bothered to humour that madman he could scarcely imagine. It would have been much simpler merely to have let him alone, or to have called in a mental specialist. Probably, he reflected, it was the fellow-feeling of one artist for another. There was so much genius in Rogers that he deserved every possible chance to be helped quietly out of his growing mania. Any man who could imagine and construct the incredibly life-like things that he had produced was not far from actual greatness. He had the fancy of a Sime or a Doré joined to the minute, scientific craftsmanship of a Blatschka. Indeed, he had done for the world of nightmare what the Blatschkas with their marvellously accurate plant models of finely wrought and coloured glass had done for the world of botany.

At midnight the strokes of a distant clock filtered through the darkness, and Jones felt cheered by the message from a still-surviving outside world. The vaulted museum chamber was like a tomb — ghastly in its utter solitude. Even a mouse would be cheering company; yet Rogers had once boasted that — for "certain reasons," as he said — no mice or even insects ever came near the place. That was very curious, yet it seemed to be true. The deadness and silence were virtually complete. If only something would make a sound! He shuffled his feet, and the echoes came spectrally out of the absolute stillness. He coughed, but there was something mocking in the staccato reverberations. He could not, he vowed, begin talking to himself. That meant nervous disintegration. Time seemed to pass with abnormal and disconcerting slowness. He could have sworn that hours had elapsed since he last flashed the light on his watch, yet here was only the stroke of midnight.

He wished that his senses were not so preternaturally keen. Something in the darkness and stillness seemed to have sharpened them, so that they responded to faint intimations hardly strong enough to be called true impressions. His ears seemed at times to catch a faint, elusive susurrus which could not quite be identified with the nocturnal hum of the squalid streets outside, and he thought of vague, irrelevant things like the music of the spheres and the unknown, inaccessible life of alien dimensions pressing on our own. Rogers often speculated about such things.

The floating specks of light in his blackness-drowned eyes seemed inclined to take on curious symmetries of pattern and motion. He had often wondered about those strange rays from the unplumbed abyss which scintillate before us in the absence of all earthly illumination, but he had never known any that behaved just as these were behaving. They lacked the restful aimlessness of ordinary light-specks, suggesting some will and purpose remote from any terrestrial conception.

Then there was that suggestion of odd stirrings. Nothing was open, yet in spite of the general draftlessness Jones felt that the air was not uniformly quiet. There were intangible variations in pressure — not quite decided enough to suggest the loathsome pawings of unseen elementals. It was abnormally chilly, too. He did not like any of this. The air tasted salty, as if it were mixed with the brine of dark subterrene waters, and there was a bare hint of some odour of ineffable mustiness. In the daytime he had never noticed that the waxen figures had an odour. Even now that half-received hint was not the way wax figures ought to smell. It was more like the faint smell of specimens in a natural-history museum. Curious, in view of Rogers' claims that his figures were not all artificial — indeed, it was probably that claim which made one's imagination conjure up the olfactory suspicion. One must guard against excesses of imagination — had not such things driven poor Rogers mad?

But the utter loneliness of this place was frightful. Even the distant chimes seemed to come from across cosmic gulfs. It made Jones think of that insane picture which Rogers had showed him — the wildly carved chamber with the cryptic throne which the fellow had claimed was part of a three-million-year-old ruin in the shunned and inaccessible solitudes of the Arctic. Perhaps Rogers had been to Alaska, but that picture was certainly nothing but stage scenery. It couldn't normally be otherwise, with all that carving and those terrible symbols. And that monstrous shape supposed to have been found on that throne — what a flight of diseased fancy! Jones wondered just how far he actually was from the insane masterpiece in wax — probably it was kept behind that heavy, padlocked plank door leading somewhere out of the workroom. But it would never do to brood about a waxen image. Was not the present room full of such things, some of them scarcely less horrible than the dreadful "IT"? And beyond a thin canvas screen on the left was the "Adults only" alcove with its nameless phantoms of delirium.

The proximity of the numberless waxen shapes began to get on Jones' nerves more and more as the quarter-hours wore on. He knew the museum so well that he could not get rid of their usual images even in the total darkness. Indeed, the darkness had the effect of adding to the remembered images certain very disturbing imaginative overtones. The guillotine seemed to creak, and the bearded face of Landru — slayer of his fifty wives — twisted itself into expressions of monstrous menace. From the severed throat of Madame Demers a hideous bubbling sound seemed to emanate, while the headless, legless victim of a trunk murder tried to edge closer and closer on its gory stumps. Jones began shutting his eyes to see if that would dim the images, but found it was useless. Besides, when he shut his eyes the strange, purposeful patterns of light-specks became more disturbingly pronounced.

Then suddenly he began trying to keep the hideous images he had formerly been trying to banish. He tried to keep them because they were giving place to still more hideous ones. In spite of himself his memory began reconstructing the utterly non-human blasphemies that lurked in the obscurer corners, and these lumpish hybrid growths oozed and wriggled toward him as though hunting him down in a circle. Black Tsathoggua moulded itself from a toad-like gargoyle to a long, sinuous line with hundreds of rudimentary feet, and a lean, rubbery night-gaunt spread its wings as if to advance and smother the watcher. Jones braced himself to keep from screaming. He knew he was reverting to the traditional terrors of his childhood, and resolved to use his adult reason to keep the phantoms at bay. It helped a bit, he found, to flash the light again. Frightful as were the images it showed, these were not as bad as what his fancy called out of the utter blackness.

But there were drawbacks. Even in the light of his torch he could not help suspecting a slight, furtive trembling on the part of the canvas partition screening off the terrible "Adults only" alcove. He knew what lay beyond, and shivered. Imagination called up the shocking forms of fabulous Yog-Sothoth — only a congeries of iridescent globes, yet stupendous in its malign suggestiveness. What was this accursed mass slowly floating toward him and bumping on the partition that stood in the way? A small bulge in the canvas far to the right suggested the sharp horn of Gnoph-keh, the hairy myth-thing of the Greenland ice, that walked sometimes on two legs, sometimes on four, and sometimes on six.

To get this stuff out of his head Jones walked boldly toward the hellish alcove with torch burning steadily. Of course, none of his fears was true. Yet were not the long, facial tentacles of great Cthulhu actually swaying, slowly and insidiously? He knew they were flexible, but he had not realised that the draft caused by his advance was enough to set them in motion.

Returning to his former seat outside the alcove, he shut his eyes and let the symmetrical light-specks do their worst. The distant clock boomed a single stroke. Could it be only one? He flashed the light on his watch and saw that it was precisely that hour. It would be hard indeed waiting for the morning. Rogers would be down at about eight o'clock, ahead of even Orabona. It would be light outside in the main basement long before that, but none of it could penetrate here. All the windows in this basement had been bricked up but the three small ones facing the court. A pretty bad wait, all told.

His ears were getting most of the hallucinations now — for he could swear he heard stealthy, plodding footsteps in the workroom beyond the closed and locked door. He had no business thinking of that unexhibited horror which Rogers called "It." The thing was a contamination — it had driven its maker mad, and now even its picture was calling up imaginative terrors. It was very obviously beyond that padlocked door of heavy planking. Those steps were certainly pure imagination.

Then he thought he heard the key turn in the workroom door. Flashing on his torch, he saw nothing but the ancient six-paneled portal in its proper position. Again he tried darkness and closed his eyes, but there followed a harrowing illusion of creaking — not the guillotine this time, but the slow, furtive opening of the workroom door. He would not scream. Once he screamed, he would be lost. There was a sort of padding or shuffling audible now, and it was slowly advancing toward him. He must retain command of himself. Had he not done so when the nameless brain-shape tried to close in on him? The shuffling crept nearer, and his resolution failed. He did not scream but merely gulped out a challenge.

"Who goes there? Who are you? What do you want?"

There was no answer, but the shuffling kept on. Jones did not know which he feared most to do — turn on his flashlight or stay in the dark while the thing crept upon him. This thing was different, he felt profoundly, from the other terrors of the evening. His fingers and throat worked spasmodically. Silence was impossible, and the suspense of utter blackness was beginning to be the most intolerable of all conditions. Again he cried out hysterically — "Halt! Who goes there?" — as he switched on the revealing beam of his torch. Then, paralyzed by what he saw, he dropped the flashlight and screamed — not once but many times.

Shuffling toward him in the darkness was the gigantic, blasphemous form of a black thing not wholly ape and not wholly insect. Its hide hung loosely upon its frame, and its rugose, dead-eyed rudiment of a head swayed drunkenly from side to side. Its forepaws were extended, with talons spread wide, and its whole body was taut with murderous malignity despite its utter lack of facial expression. After the screams and the final coming of darkness it leaped, and in a moment had Jones pinned to the floor. There was no struggle, for the watcher had fainted.

Jones' fainting spell could not have lasted more than a moment, for the nameless thing was apishly dragging him through the darkness when he began recovering consciousness. What started him fully awake were the sounds which the thing was making — or rather, the voice with which it was making them. That voice was human, and it was familiar. Only one living being could be behind the hoarse, feverish accents which were chanting to an unknown horror.

"Iä! Iä!" it was howling. "I am coming, O Rhan-Tegoth, coming with the nourishment. You have waited long and fed ill, but now you shall have what was promised. That and more, for instead of Orabona it will be one of high degree who has doubted you. You shall crush and drain him, with all his doubts, and grow strong thereby. And ever after among men he shall be shown as a monument to your glory. Rhan-Tegoth, infinite and invincible, I am your slave and high-priest. You are hungry, and I shall provide. I read the sign and have led you forth. I shall feed you with blood, and you shall feed me with power. Iä! Shub-Niggurath! The Goat with a Thousand Young!"

In an instant all the terrors of the night dropped from Jones like a discarded cloak. He was again master of his mind, for he knew the very earthly and material peril he had to deal with. This was no monster of fable, but a dangerous madman. It was Rogers, dressed in some nightmare covering of his own insane designing, and about to make a frightful sacrifice to the devil-god he had fashioned out of wax. Clearly, he must have entered the workroom from the rear courtyard, donned his disguise, and then advanced to seize his neatly-trapped and fear-broken victim. His strength was prodigious, and if he was to be thwarted, one must act quickly. Counting on the madman's confidence in his unconsciousness he determined to take him by surprise, while his grip was relatively lax. The feel of a threshold told him he was crossing into the pitch-black workroom.

With the strength of mortal fear Jones made a sudden spring from the half-recumbent posture in which he was being dragged. For an instant he was free of the astonished maniac's hands, and in another instant a lucky lunge in the dark had put his own hands at his captor's weirdly concealed throat. Simultaneously Rogers gripped him again, and without further preliminaries the two were locked in a desperate struggle of life and death. Jones' athletic training, without doubt, was his sole salvation; for his mad assailant, freed from every inhibition of fair play, decency, or even self-preservation, was an engine of savage destruction as formidable as a wolf or panther.

Guttural cries sometimes punctured the hideous tussle in the dark. Blood spurted, clothing ripped, and Jones at last felt the actual throat of the maniac, shorn of its spectral mask. He spoke not a word, but put every ounce of energy into the defence of his life. Rogers kicked, gouged, butted, bit, clawed, and spat—yet found strength to yelp out actual sentences at times. Most of his speech was in a ritualistic jargon full of references to "It" or "Rhan-Tegoth," and to Jones' overwrought nerves it seemed as if the cries echoed from an infinite distance of demoniac snortings and bayings. Toward the last they were rolling on the floor, overturning benches or striking against the walls and the brick foundations of the central melting-furnace. Up to the very end Jones could not be certain of saving himself, but chance finally intervened in his favour. A jab of his knee against Rogers' chest produced a general relaxation, and a moment later he knew he had won.

Though hardly able to hold himself up, Jones rose and stumbled about the walls seeking the light-switch—for his flashlight was gone, together with most of his clothing. As he lurched along he dragged his limp opponent with him, fearing a sudden attack when the madman came to. Finding the switch-box, he fumbled till he had the right handle. Then, as the wildly disordered workroom burst into sudden radiance, he set about binding Rogers with such cords and belts as he could easily find. The fellow's disguise—or what was left of it—seemed to be made of a puzzling queer sort of leather. For some reason it made Jones' flesh crawl to touch it, and there seemed to be an alien, rusty odour about it. In the normal clothes beneath it was Rogers' key-ring, and this the exhausted victor seized as his final passport to freedom. The shades at the small, slit-like windows were all securely drawn, and he let them remain so.

Washing off the blood of battle at a convenient sink, Jones donned the most ordinary-looking and least ill-fitting clothes he could find on the costume hooks. Testing the door to the courtyard, he found it fastened with a spring-lock which did not require a key from the inside. He kept the key-ring, however, to admit him on his return with aid—for plainly, the thing to do was to call in an alienist. There was no telephone in the museum, but it would not take long to find an all-night restaurant or chemist's shop where one could be had. He had almost opened the door when a torrent of hideous abuse from across the room told him that Rogers—whose visible injuries were confined to a long, deep scratch down the left cheek—had regained consciousness.

"Fool! Spawn of Noth-Yidik and effluvium of K'thun! Son of the dogs that howl in the maelstrom of Azathoth! You would have been sacred and immortal, and now you are betraying It and Its priest! Beware—for It is hungry! It would have been Orabona—that damned treacherous dog ready to turn against me and It—but I give you the honour instead. Now you must both beware, for It is not gentle without Its priest.

"Iä! Iä! Vengeance is at hand! Do you know you would have been immortal? Look at the furnace! There is a fire ready to light, and there is wax in the kettle. I would have done with you as I have done with other once living forms. Hei! You, who have vowed all my effigies are waxen, would have become a waxen effigy yourself! The furnace was already! When It had had its fill, and you were like that dog I showed you, I would have made your flattened, punctured fragments immortal! Wax would have done it. Haven't you said I'm a great artist? Wax in every pore—wax over every square inch of you—Iä! Iä! And ever after the world would have looked at your mangled carcass and wondered how I ever imagined and made such a thing! Hei! and Orabona would have come next, and others after him—and thus would my waxen family have grown!

"Dog—do you still think I made all my effigies? Why not say preserved? You know by this time the strange places I've been to, and the strange things I've brought back. Coward—you could never face the dimensional shambler whose hide I put on to scare you—the mere sight of it alive, or even the full-fledged thought of it, would kill you instantly with fright! Iä! Iä! It waits hungry for the blood that is the life!"

Rogers, propped against the wall, swayed to and fro in his bonds.

"See here, Jones—if I let you go will you let me go? It must be taken care of by Its high priest. Orabona will be enough to keep It alive—and when he is finished I will make his fragments immortal in wax for the world to see. It could have been you, but you have rejected the honour. I won't bother you again. Let me go, and I will share with you the power that It will bring me. Iä! Iä! Great is Rhan-Tegoth! Let me go! Let me go! It is starving down there beyond that door, and if It dies the Old Ones can never come back. Hei! Hei! Let me go!"

Jones merely shook his head, though the hideousness of the showman's imaginings revolted him. Rogers, now staring wildly at the padlocked plank door, thumped his head again and again against the brick wall and kicked with his tightly bound ankles. Jones was afraid he would injure himself, and advanced to bind him more firmly to some stationary object. Writhing, Rogers edged away from him and set up a series of frenetic ululations whose utter, monstrous unhumanness was appalling, and whose sheer volume was almost incredible. It seemed impossible that any human throat could produce noises so loud and piercing, and Jones felt that if this continued there would be no need to telephone for aid. It could not be long before a constable would investigate, even granting that there were no listening neighbours in this deserted warehouse district.

"Wza-y'ei! Wza-y'ei!" howled the madman. "Y'kaa haa ho-ii, Rhan-Tegoth-Cthulhu fthagn-Ei! Ei! Ei! Ei!-Rhan-Tegoth. Rhan-Tegoth, Rhan-Tegoth!"

The tautly trussed creature, who had started squirming his way across the littered floor, now reached the padlocked plank door and commenced knocking his head thunderously against it. Jones dreaded the task of binding him further, and wished he were not so exhausted from his previous struggle. This violent aftermath was getting hideously on his nerves, and he began to feel a return of the nameless qualms he had felt in the dark. Everything about Rogers and his museum was so hellishly morbid and suggestive of black vistas beyond life! It was loathsome to think of the waxen masterpiece of abnormal genius which must at this very moment be lurking close at hand in the blackness beyond the heavy, padlocked door.

And now something happened which sent an addition chill down Jones' spine, and caused every hair — even the tiny growth on the backs of his hands — to bristle with a vague fright beyond classification. Rogers had suddenly stopped screaming and beating his head against the stout plank door, and was straining up to a sitting position, head cocked on one side as if listening intently for something. All at once a smile of devilish triumph overspread his face, and he began speaking intelligibly again — this time in a hoarse whisper contrasting oddly with his former stentorian howling.

"Listen, fool! Listen hard! It has heard me, and is coming. Can't you hear It splashing out of Its tank down there at the end of the runway? I dug it deep, because there was nothing too good for It. It is amphibious, you know — you saw the gills in the picture. It came to the earth from lead-gray Yuggoth, where the cities are under the warm deep sea. It can't stand up in there — too tall — has to sit down or crouch. Let me get my keys — we must let It out and kneel down before it. Then we will go out and find a dog or cat — or perhaps a drunken man — to give It the nourishment It needs."

It was not what the madman said, but the way he said it, that disorganized Jones so badly. The utter, insane confidence and sincerity in that crazed whisper were damnably contagious. Imagination, such a stimulus, could find an active menace in the devilish wax figure that lurked unseen just beyond the heavy planking. Eyeing the door in unholy fascination, Jones noticed that it bore several distinct cracks, though no marks of violent treatment were visible on this side. He wondered how large a room or closet lay behind it, and how the waxen figure was arranged. The maniac's idea of a tank and runway was as clever as all his other imaginings.

Then, in one terrible instant, Jones completely lost the power to draw a breath. The leather belt he had seized for Rogers' further strapping fell from his limp hands, and a spasm of shivering convulsed him from head to foot. He might have known the place would drive him mad as it had driven Rogers — and now he was mad. He was mad, for he now harboured hallucinations more weird than any which had assailed him earlier that night. The madman was bidding him hear the splashing of a mythical monster in a tank beyond the door — and now, God help him, he did hear it!

Rogers saw the spasm of horror reach Jones' face and transform it to a staring mask of fear. He cackled.

"At last, fool, you believe! At last you know! You hear It and It comes! Get me my keys, fool — we must do homage and serve It!"

But Jones was past paying attention to any human words, mad or sane. Phobic paralysis held him immobile and half conscious, with wild images racing phantasmagorically through his helpless imagination. There was a splashing. There was padding or shuffling, as of great wet paws on a solid surface. Something was approaching. Into his nostrils, from the cracks in that nightmare plank door, poured a noisome animal stench like and yet unlike that of the mammal cages at the zoological gardens in Regent's Park.

He did not know now whether Rogers was talking or not. Everything real had faded away, and he was a statue obsessed with dreams and hallucinations so unnatural that they became almost objective and remote from him. He thought he heard a sniffing or snorting from the unknown gulf beyond the door, and when a sudden baying, trumpeting noise assailed his ears he could not feel sure that it came from the tightly bound maniac whose image swam uncertainly in his shaken vision. The photograph of that accursed, unseen wax thing persisted in floating through his consciousness. Such a thing had no right to exist. Had it not driven him mad?

Even as he reflected, a fresh evidence of madness beset him. Something, he thought, was fumbling with the latch of the heavy padlocked door. It was patting and pawing and pushing at the planks. There was a thudding on the stout wood, which grew louder and louder. The stench was horrible. And now the assault on that door from the inside was a malign, determined pounding like the strokes of a battering-ram. There was an ominous cracking — a splintering — a welling fetor — a falling plank — a black paw ending in a crab-like claw . . . .

"Help! Help! God help me! . . . Aaaaaaa!"

With intense effort Jones is today able to recall a sudden bursting of his fear-paralysis into the liberation of frenzied automatic flight. What he evidently did must have paralleled curiously the wild, plunging flights of maddest nightmares; for he seems to have leaped across the disordered crypt at almost a single bound, yanked open the outside door, which closed and locked itself after him with a clatter, sprung up the worn stone steps three at a time, and raced frantically and aimlessly out of that dark cobblestoned court and through the squalid streets of Southwark.

Here the memory ends. Jones does not know how he got home, and there is no evidence of his having hired a cab. Probably he raced all the way by blind instinct—over Waterloo Bridge, along the Strand and Charing Cross and up Haymarket and Regent Street to his own neighbourhood. He still had on the queer melange of museum costumes when he grew conscious enough to call the doctor.

A week later the nerve specialists allowed him to leave his bed and walk in the open air.

But he had not told the specialists much. Over his whole experience hung a pall of madness and nightmare, and he felt that silence was the only course. When he was up, he scanned intently all the papers which had accumulated since that hideous night, but found no reference to anything queer at the museum. How much, after all, had been reality? Where did reality end and morbid dream begin? Had his mind gone wholly to pieces in that dark exhibition chamber, and had the whole fight with Rogers been a phantasm of fever? It would help to put him on his feet if he could settle some of these maddening points. He must have seen that damnable photograph of the wax image called "It," for no brain but Rogers' could ever have conceived such a blasphemy.

It was a fortnight before he dared to enter Southwark Street again. He went in the middle of the morning, when there was the greatest amount of sane, wholesome activity around the ancient, crumbling shops and warehouses. The museum's sign was still there, and as he approached he saw that the place was still open. The gateman nodded in pleasant recognition as he summoned up the courage to enter, and in the vaulted chamber below an attendant touched his cap cheerfully. Perhaps everything had been a dream. Would he dare to knock at the door of the workroom and look for Rogers?

Then Orabona advanced to greet him. His dark, sleek face was a trifle sardonic, but Jones felt that he was not unfriendly. He spoke with a trace of accent.

"Good morning, Mr. Jones. It is some time since we have seen you here. Did you wish Mr. Rogers? I'm sorry, but he is away. He had word of business in America, and had to go. Yes, it was very sudden. I am in charge now—here, and at the house. I try to maintain Mr. Rogers' high standard—till he is back."

The foreigner smiled—perhaps from affability alone. Jones scarcely knew how to reply, but managed to mumble out a few inquiries about the day after his last visit. Orabona seemed greatly amused by the questions, and took considerable care in framing his replies.

"Oh, yes, Mr. Jones—the 28th of last month. I remember it for many reasons. In the morning—before Mr. Rogers got here, you understand—I found the workroom in quite a mess. There was a great deal of—cleaning up—to do. There had been—late work, you see. Important new specimen given its secondary baking process. I took complete charge when I came.

"It was a hard specimen to prepare—but of course Mr. Rogers had taught me a great deal. He is, as you know, a very great artist. When he came he helped me complete the specimen—helped very materially, I assure you—but he left soon without even greeting the men. As I tell you, he was called away suddenly. There were important chemical reactions involved. They made loud noises—in fact, some teamsters in the court outside fancy they heard several pistol shots—very amusing idea!

"As for the new specimen—that matter is very unfortunate. It is a great masterpiece—designed and made, you understand, by Mr. Rogers. He will see about it when he gets back."

Again Orabona smiled.

"The police, you know. We put it on display a week ago, and there were two or three faintings. One poor fellow had an epileptic fit in front of it. You see, it's a trifle—stronger—than the rest. Larger, for one thing. Of course, it was in the adult alcove. The next day a couple of men from Scotland Yard looked it over and said it was too morbid to be shown. Said we'd have to remove it. It was a tremendous shame—such a masterpiece of art—but I didn't feel justified in appealing to the courts in Mr. Rogers' absence. He would not like so much publicity with the police now—but when he gets back—when he gets back—"

For some reason or other Jones felt a mounting tide of uneasiness and repulsion. But Orabona was continuing.

"You are a connoisseur, Mr. Jones. I am sure I violate no law in offering you a private view. It may be—subject of course, to Mr. Rogers' wishes—that we shall destroy the specimen some day—but that would be a crime."

Jones had a powerful impulse to refuse the sight and flee precipitately, but Orabona was leading him forward by the arm with an artist's enthusiasm. The adult alcove, crowded with nameless horrors, held no visitors. In the farther corner a large niche had been curtained off, and to this the smiling assistant advanced.

"You must know, Mr. Jones, that the title of this specimen is 'The Sacrifice to Rhan-Tegoth.'"

Jones started violently, but Orabona appeared not to notice.

"The shapeless, colossal god is a feature in certain obscure legends which Mr. Rogers had studied. All nonsense, of course, as you've so often assured, Mr. Rogers. It is supposed to have come from outer space, and to have lived in the Arctic three million years ago. It treated its sacrifices rather peculiarly and horribly, as you shall see. Mr. Rogers had made it fiendishly life-like—even to the face of the victim."

Now trembling violently, Jones clung to the brass railing in front of the curtained niche. He almost reached out to stop Orabona when he saw the curtain beginning to swing aside, but some conflicting impulse held him back. The foreigner smiled triumphantly.

"Behold!"

Jones reeled in spite of his grip on the railing.

"God!—great god!"

Fully ten feet high despite a shambling, crouching attitude expressive of infinite cosmic malignancy, a monstrosity of unbelievable horror was shewn starting forward from a cyclopean ivory throne covered with grotesque carvings. In the central pair of its six legs it bore a crushed, flattened, distorted, bloodless thing, riddled with a million punctures, and in places seared as with some pungent acid. Only the mangled head of the victim, lolling upside down at one side, revealed that it represented something once human.

The monster itself needed no title for one who had seen a certain hellish photograph. That damnable print had been all too faithful; yet it could not carry the full horror which lay in the gigantic actuality. The globular torso—the bubble-like suggestion of a head—the three fishy eyes—the foot-long proboscis—the bulging gills—the monstrous capillation of asp-like suckers—the six sinuous limbs with their black paws and crab-like claws—God! the familiarity of the black paw ending in a crab-like claw! . . .

Orabona's smile was utterly damnable. Jones choked, and stared at the hideous exhibit with a mounting fascination which perplexed and disturbed him. What half-revealed horror was holding and forcing him to look longer and search out details? This had driven Rogers mad . . . Rogers, supreme artist . . . said they weren't artificial . . . .

Then he localized the thing that held him. It was the crushed waxen victim's lolling head, and something that it implied. This head was not entirely devoid of a face, and that face was familiar. It was like the mad face of poor Rogers. Jones peered closer, hardly knowing why he was driven to do so. Wasn't it natural for a mad egotist to mould his own features into his masterpiece? Was there anything more that subconscious vision had seized on and suppressed in sheer terror?

The wax of the mangled face had been handled with boundless dexterity. Those punctures—how perfectly they reproduced the myriad wounds somehow inflicted on that poor dog! But there was something more. On the left cheek one could trace an irregularity which seemed outside the general scheme—as if the sculptor had sought to cover up a defect of his first modelling. The more Jones looked at it, the more mysteriously it horrified him—and then, suddenly, he remembered a circumstance which brought his horror to a head. That night of hideousness—the tussle—the bound madman—and the long, deep scratch down the left cheek of the actual living Rogers . . . .

Jones, releasing his desperate clutch on the railing, sank in a total faint.

Orabona continued to smile.

Weird Tales, September 1935

1933.

Literary High Camp, Revisited.

A combination of Lovecraft's discouragement and a deluge of ghostwriting and collaboration work kept Lovecraft's output fairly low again in 1933.

Early in the year, he somewhat reluctantly worked with E. Hoffman Price on a sequel to "The Silver Key," titled "Through the Gates of the Silver Key," which was published under a joint by-line in *Weird Tales* the following year. He also ghostwrote two more campy horror-pulp stories for Hazel Heald: "Out of the Aeons," possibly the best of his short collaborations; and "The Horror in the Burying-Ground," which was unquestionably the campiest. And he helped a new young protege, Robert H. Barlow, with two slight pieces of juvenilia: "The Slaying of the Monster" and "The Hoard of the Wizard-Beast."

All but the last of these were handled in the first eight months of 1933, leaving Lovecraft with little time to work on his own projects.

During that year, Lovecraft and his one surviving aunt were forced by the continuing deterioration of their financial situation to move yet again, into a smaller residence. Lovecraft was not displeased, because the new house — although their quarters in it were considerably smaller — was more architecturally interesting than the old.

In August, Lovecraft finally turned to work of his own, and wrote "The Thing on the Doorstep," which he then sent along the rounds of his writer friends for critique, as his habit had latterly become. Some of their comments were diffident enough that Lovecraft shelved the whole thing for two years; it wasn't offered for publication until 1935, at which time it was snapped right up by *Weird Tales*.

The only other fiction Lovecraft wrote under his own name was a dream-transcript, "The Wicked Clergyman," and it hardly counts; it was included in a letter to a friend, and the friend submitted it for publication.

Another interesting thing happened to Lovecraft in 1933 — for the first time in his life, he got drunk. On New Year's Eve, one of Samuel Loveman's more rascally friends spiked the lifelong teetotaler's drink. Lovecraft, as it turned out, was rather the life of the party when he had a few drinks on board.

brought up. There is a menacing, portentous quality in the tones which they use to describe very ordinary events — a seemingly unjustified tendency to assume a furtive, suggestive, confidential air, and to fall into awesome whispers at certain points — which insidiously disturbs the listener. Old Yankees often talk like that; but in this case the melancholy aspect of the half-mouldering village, and the dismal nature of the story unfolded, give these gloomy, secretive mannerisms an added significance. One feels profoundly the quintessential horror that lurks behind the isolated Puritan and his strange repressions — feels it, and longs to escape precipitately into clearer air.

The loungers whisper impressively that the shuttered house is that of old Miss Sprague — Sophie Sprague, whose brother Tom was buried on the seventeenth of June, back in '86. Sophie was never the same after that funeral — that and the other thing which happened the same day — and in the end she took to staying in all the time. Won't even be seen now, but leaves notes under the back-door mat and has her things brought from the store by Ned Peck's boy. Afraid of something — the old Swamp Hollow burying-ground most of all. Never could be dragged near there since her brother — and the other one — were laid away.

Not much wonder, though, seeing the way crazy Johnny Dow rants. He hangs around the burying-ground all day and sometimes at night, and claims he talks with Tom — and the other. Then he marches by Sophie's house and shouts things at her — that's why she began to keep the shutters closed. He says things are coming from somewhere to get her sometime. Ought to be stopped, but one can't be too hard on poor Johnny. Besides, Steve Barbour always had his opinions.

Johnny does his talking to two of the graves. One of them is Tom Sprague's. The other, at the opposite end of the graveyard, is that of Henry Thorndike, who was buried on the same day. Henry was the village undertaker — the only one in miles — and never liked around Stillwater. A city fellow from Rutland — been to college and full of book learning. Read queer things nobody else ever heard of, and mixed chemicals for no good purpose. Always trying to invent something new — some new-fangled embalming-fluid or some foolish kind of medicine. Some folks said he had tried to be a doctor but failed in his studies and took to the next best profession. Of course, there wasn't much undertaking to do in a place like Stillwater, but Henry farmed on the side.

Mean, morbid disposition — and a secret drinker if you could judge by the empty bottles in his rubbish heap. No wonder Tom Sprague hated him and blackballed him from the Masonic lodge, and warned him off when he tried to make up to Sophie. The way he experimented on animals was against Nature and Scripture. Who could forget the state that collie dog was found in, or what happened to old Mrs. Akeley's cat? Then there was the matter of Deacon Leavitt's calf, when Tom had led a band of the village boys to demand an accounting. The curious thing

Weird Tales, May 1937

"Then there was that awful 'Comin' again some day,' in a death-like squawk."

was that the calf came alive after all in the end, though Tom had found it as stiff as a poker. Some said the joke was on Tom, but Thorndike probably thought otherwise, since he had gone down under his enemy's fist before the mistake was discovered.

Tom, of course, was half drunk at the time. He was a vicious brute at best, and kept his poor sister half cowed with threats. That's probably why she is such a fear-racked creature still. There were only the two of them, and Tom would never let her leave because that meant splitting the property. Most of the fellows were too afraid of him to shine up to Sophie — he stood six feet one in his stockings — but Henry Thorndike was a sly cuss who had ways of doing things behind folk's backs. He wasn't much to look at, but Sophie never discouraged him any. Mean and ugly as he was, she'd have been glad if anybody could have freed her from her brother. She may not have stopped to wonder how she could get clear of him after he got her clear of Tom.

Well, that was the way things stood in June of '86. Up to this point, the whispers of the loungers at Peck's store are not so unbearably portentous; but as they continue, the element of secretiveness and malign tension grows. Tom Sprague, it appears, used to go to Rutland on periodic sprees, his absences being Henry Thorndike's great opportunities. He was always in bad shape when he got back, and old Dr. Pratt, deaf and half blind though he was, used to warn him about his heart, and about the danger of delirium tremens. Folks could always tell by the shouting and cursing when he was home again.

It was on the ninth of June—on a Wednesday, the day after young Joshua Goodenough finished building his new-fangled silo—that Tom started out on his last and longest spree. He came back the next Tuesday morning and folks at the store saw him lashing his bay stallion the way he did when whiskey had a hold of him. Then there came shouts and shrieks and oaths from the Sprague house, and the first thing anybody knew Sophie was running over to old Dr. Pratt's at top speed.

The doctor found Thorndike at Sprague's when he got there, and Tom was on the bed in his room, with eyes staring and foam around his mouth. Old Pratt fumbled around and gave the usual tests, then shook his head solemnly and told Sophie she had suffered a great bereavement—that her nearest and dearest had passed through the pearly gates to a better land, just as everybody knew he would if he didn't let up on his drinking.

Sophie kind of sniffled, but didn't seem to take on much. Thorndike didn't do anything but smile—perhaps at the ironic fact that he, always an enemy, was now the only person who could be of any use to Thomas Sprague. He shouted something in old Dr. Pratt's half-good ear about the need of having the funeral early on account of Tom's condition. Drunks like that were always doubtful subjects, and any extra delay—with merely rural facilities—would entail consequences, visual and otherwise, hardly acceptable to the deceased's loving mourners. The doctor had muttered that Tom's alcoholic career ought to have embalmed him pretty well in advance, but Thorndike assured him to the contrary, at the same time boasting of his own skill, and of the superior methods he had devised through his experiments.

It is here that the whispers of the loungers grow acutely disturbing. Up to this point the story is usually told by Ezra Davenport, or Luther Fry, if Ezra is laid up with chilblains, as he is apt to be in winter; but from there on old Calvin Wheeler takes up the thread, and his voice has a damnably insidious way of suggesting hidden horror. If Johnny Dow happens to be passing by there is always a pause, for Stillwater does not like to have Johnny talk too much with strangers.

Calvin edges close to the traveller and sometimes seizes a coat-lapel with his gnarled, mottled hand while he half shuts his watery blue eyes.

"Well, sir," he whispers, "Henry he went home an' got his undertaker's fixin's—crazy Johnny Dow lugged most of 'em, for he was always doin' chores for Henry—an' says as Doc Pratt an' crazy Johnny should help lay out the body. Doc always did say as how he thought Henry talked too much—a-boastin' what a fine workman he was, an' how lucky it was that Stillwater had a reg'lar undertaker instead of buryin' folks jest as they was, like they do over to Whitby.

" 'Suppose,' says he, 'some fellow was to be took with some of them paralysin' cramps like you read about. How'd a body like it when they lowered him down and begun shovelin' the dirt back? How'd he like it when he was chokin' down there under the new headstone, scratchin' an' tearin' if he chanced to get back the power, but all the time knowin' it wasn't no use? No, sir, I tell you it's a blessin' Stillwater's got a smart doctor as knows when a man's dead and when he ain't, and a trained undertaker who can fix a corpse so he'll stay put without no trouble.'

"That was the way Henry went on talkin', most like he was talkin' to poor Tom's remains; and old Doc Pratt he didn't like what he was able to catch of it, even though Henry did call him a smart doctor. Crazy Johnny kept watchin' of the corpse, and it didn't make it none too pleasant the way he'd slobber about things like, 'He ain't cold, Doc,' or 'I see his eyelids move,' or 'There's a hole in his arm jest like the ones I git when Henry gives me a syringe full of what makes me feel good.' Thorndike shut him up on that, though we all knowed he'd been givin' poor Johnny drugs. It's a wonder the poor fellow ever got clear of the habit.

"But the worst thing, accordin' to the doctor, was the way the body jerked up when Henry began to shoot it full of embalmin'-fluid. He'd been boastin' about what a fine new formula he'd got practicin' on cats and dogs, when all of a sudden Tom's corpse began to double up like it was alive and fixin' to wrassle. Land of Goshen, but Doc says he was scared stiff, though he knowed the way corpses act when the muscles begin to stiffen. Well, sir, the long and short of it is, that the corpse sat up an' grabbed a holt of Thorndike's syringe so that it got stuck in Henry hisself, an' give him as neat a dose of his own embalmin'-fluid as you'd wish to see. That got Henry pretty scared, though he yanked the point out and managed to get the body down again and shot full of the fluid. He kept measurin' more of the stuff out as though he wanted to be sure there was enough, and kept reassurin' himself as not much had got into him, but crazy Johnny begun singin' out, 'That's what you give Lige Hopkins's dog when it got all dead an' stiff an' then waked up agin. Now you're a-going to get dead an' stiff like Tom Sprague be! Remember it don't set to work till after a long spell if you don't get much.'

"Sophie, she was downstairs with some of the neighbours—my wife Matildy, she that's dead an' gone this thirty year, was one of them. They were all tryin' to find out whether Thorndike was over when Tom came home, and whether findin' him there was what set poor Tom off. I may as well say as some folks thought it mighty funny that Sophie didn't carry on more, nor mind the way Thorndike had smiled. Not as anybody was hintin' that Henry helped Tom off with some of his queer cooked-up fluids and syringes, or that Sophie would keep still if she thought so—but you know how folks will guess behind a body's back. We all knowed the nigh crazy way Thorndike had hated Tom—not without reason, at that—and Emily Barbour says to my Matildy as how Henry was lucky to have ol' Doc Pratt right on the spot with a death certificate as didn't leave no doubt for nobody."

When old Calvin gets to this point he usually begins to mumble indistinguishably in his straggling, dirty white beard. Most listeners try to edge away from him, and he seldom appears to heed the gesture. It is generally Fred Peck, who was a very small boy at the time of the events, who continues the tale.

Thomas Sprague's funeral was held on Thursday, June 17th, only two days after his death. Such haste was thought almost indecent in remote and inaccessible Stillwater, where long distances had to be covered by those who came, but Thorndike had insisted that the peculiar condition of the deceased demanded it. The undertaker had seemed rather nervous since preparing the body, and could be seen frequently feeling his pulse. Old Dr. Pratt thought he must be worrying about the accidental dose of embalming-fluid. Naturally, the story of the "laying out" had spread, so that a double zest animated the mourners who assembled to glut their curiosity and morbid interest.

Thorndike, though he was obviously upset, seemed intent on doing his professional duty in magnificent style. Sophie and others who saw the body were most startled by its utter life-likeness, and the mortuary virtuoso made doubly sure of his job by repeating certain injections at stated intervals. He almost wrung a sort of reluctant admiration from the townsfolk and visitors, though he tended to spoil that impression by his boastful and tasteless talk. Whenever he administered to his silent charge he would repeat that eternal rambling about the good luck of having a first-class undertaker. What—he would say as if directly addressing the body—if Tom had had one of those careless fellows who bury their subjects alive? The way he harped on the horrors of premature burial was truly barbarous and sickening.

Services were held in the stuffy best room—opened for the first time since Mrs. Sprague died. The tuneless little parlour organ groaned disconsolately, and the coffin, supported on trestles near the hall door, was covered with sickly-smelling flowers. It was obvious that a record-breaking crowd was assembling from far and near, and Sophie endeavoured to look properly grief-stricken for their benefit. At unguarded moments she seemed both puzzled and uneasy, dividing her scrutiny between the feverish-looking undertaker and the life-like body of her brother. A slow disgust at Thorndike seemed to be brewing within her, and neighbours whispered freely that she would soon send him about his business now that Tom was out of the way—that is, if she could, for such a slick customer was sometimes hard to deal with. But with her money and remaining looks she might be able to get another fellow, and he'd probably take care of Henry well enough.

As the organ wheezed into *Beautiful Isle of Somewhere* the Methodist church choir added their lugubrious voices to the gruesome cacophony, and everyone looked piously at Deacon Leavitt—everyone, that is, except crazy Johnny Dow, who kept his eyes glued to the still form beneath the glass of the coffin. He was muttering softly to himself.

Stephen Barbour—from the next farm—was the only one who noticed Johnny. He shivered as he saw that the idiot was talking directly to the corpse, and even making foolish signs with his fingers as if to taunt the sleeper beneath the plate glass. Tom, he reflected, had kicked poor Johnny around on more than one occasion, though probably not without provocation. Something about this whole event was getting on Stephen's nerves. There was a suppressed tension and brooding abnormality in the air for which he could not account. Johnny ought not to have been allowed in the house—and it was curious what an effort Thorndike seemed to be making not to look at the body. Every now and then the undertaker would feel his pulse with an odd air.

The Reverend Silas Atwood droned on in a plaintive monotone about the deceased—about the striking of Death's sword in the midst of this little family, breaking the earthly tie between this loving brother and sister. Several of the neighbours looked furtively at one another from beneath lowered eyelids, while Sophie actually began to sob nervously. Thorndike moved to her side and tried to reassure her, but she seemed to shrink curiously away from him. His motions were distinctly uneasy, and he seemed to feel acutely the abnormal tension permeating the air. Finally, conscious of his duty as master of ceremonies, he stepped forward and announced in a sepulchral voice that the body might be viewed for the last time.

Slowly the friends and neighbours filed past the bier, from which Thorndike roughly dragged crazy Johnny away. Tom seemed to be resting peacefully. That devil had been handsome in his day. A few genuine sobs—and many feigned ones—were heard, though most of the crowd were content to stare curiously and whisper afterward. Steve Barbour lingered long and attentively over the still face, and moved away shaking his head. His wife, Emily, following after him, whispered that Henry Thorndike had better not boast so much about his work, for Tom's eyes had come open. They had been shut when the services began, for she had been up and looked. But they certainly looked natural—not the way one would expect after two days.

When Fred Peck gets this far he usually pauses as if he did not like to continue. The listener, too, tends to feel that something unpleasant is ahead. But Peck reassures his audience with the statement that what happened isn't as bad as folks like to hint. Even Steve never put into words what he may have thought, and crazy Johnny, of course, can't be counted at all.

It was Luella Morse — the nervous old maid who sang in the choir — who seems to have touched things off. She was filing past the coffin like the rest, but stopped to peer a little closer than anyone else except the Barbours had peered. And then, without warning, she gave a shrill scream and fell in a dead faint.

Naturally, the room was at once a chaos of confusion. Old Dr. Pratt elbowed his way to Luella and called for some water to throw in her face, and others surged up to look at her and the coffin. Johnny Dow began chanting to himself, "He knows, he knows, he kin hear all we're a-sayin' and see all we're a-doin', and they'll bury him that way" — but no one stopped to decipher his mumbling except Steve Barbour.

In a very few moments Luella began to come out of her faint, and could not tell exactly what had startled her. All she could whisper was, "The way he looked — the way he looked." But to other eyes the body seemed exactly the same. It was a gruesome sight, though, with those open eyes and that high colouring.

And then the bewildered crowed noticed something which put both Luella and the body out of their minds for a moment. It was Thorndike — on whom the sudden excitement and jostling crowd seemed to be having a curiously bad effect. He had evidently been knocked down in the general bustle, and was on the floor trying to drag himself to a sitting posture. The expression on his face was terrifying in the extreme, and his eyes were beginning to take on a glazed, fishy expression. He could scarcely speak aloud, but the husky rattle of his throat held an ineffable desperation which was obvious to all.

"Get me home, quick, and let me be. That fluid I got in my arm by mistake . . . heart action . . . the damned excitement . . . too much . . . wait . . . wait . . . don't think I'm dead if I seem to . . . only the fluid — just get me home and wait . . . I'll come to later, don't know how long . . . all the time I'll be conscious and know what's going on . . . don't be deceived . . ."

As his words trailed off into nothingness old Dr. Pratt reached him and felt his pulse — watching a long time and finally shaking his head. "No use doing anything — he's gone. Heart no good — and that fluid he got in his arm must have been bad stuff. I don't know what it is."

A kind of numbness seemed to fall on all the company. New death in the chamber of death! Only Steve Barbour thought to bring up Thorndike's last choking words. Was he surely dead, when he himself had said he might falsely seem so? Wouldn't it be better to wait a while and see what would happen? And for that matter, what harm would it do if Doc Pratt were to give Tom Sprague another looking over before burial?

Crazy Johnny was moaning, and had flung himself on Thorndike's body like a faithful dog. "Don't ye bury him, don't ye bury him! He ain't dead no more nor Lige Hopkins's dog nor Deacon Leavitt's calf was when he shot 'em full. He's got some stuff he puts into ye to make ye seem like dead when ye ain't! Ye seem like dead but ye know everything what's a-goin' on, and the next day ye come to as good as ever. Don't ye bury him — he'll come to under the earth an' he can't scratch up! He's a good man, an' not like Tom Sprague. Hope to Gawd Tom scratches an' chokes for hours an' hours . . ."

But no one save Barbour was paying any attention to poor Johnny. Indeed, what Steve himself had said had evidently fallen on deaf ears. Uncertainly was everywhere. Old Doc Pratt was applying final tests and mumbling about death certificate blanks, and unctuous Elder Atwood was suggesting that something be done about a double interment. With Thorndike dead there was no undertaker this side of Rutland, and it would mean a terrible expense if one were to be brought from there, and if Thorndike were not embalmed in this hot June weather — well, one couldn't tell. And there were no relatives or friends to be critical unless Sophie chose to be — but Sophie was on the other side of the room, staring silently, fixedly, and almost morbidly into her brother's coffin.

Deacon Leavitt tried to restore a semblance of decorum, and had poor Thorndike carried across the hall to the sitting-room, meanwhile sending Zenas Wells and Walter Perkins over to the undertaker's house for a coffin of the right size. The key was in Henry's trousers pocket. Johnny continued to whine and paw at the body, and Elder Atwood busied himself with inquiring about Thorndike's denomination — for Henry had not attended local services. When it was decided that his folks in Rutland — all dead now — had been Baptists, the Reverend Silas decided that Deacon Leavitt had better offer the brief prayer.

It was a gala day for the funeral-fanciers of Stillwater and vicinity. Even Luella had recovered enough to stay. Gossip, murmured and whispered, buzzed busily while a few composing touches were given to Thorndike's cooling, stiffening form. Johnny had been cuffed out of the house, as most agreed he should have been in the first place, but his distant howls were now and then wafted gruesomely in.

When the body was encoffined and laid out beside that of Thomas Sprague, the silent, almost frightening-looking Sophie gazed intently at it as she had gazed at her brother's. She had not uttered a word for a dangerously long time, and the mixed expression on her face was past all describing or interpreting. As the others withdrew to leave her alone with the dead she managed to find a sort of mechanical speech, but no one could make out the words, and she seemed to be talking first to one body and then the other.

And now, with what would seem to an outsider the acme of gruesome unconscious comedy, the whole funeral mummery of the afternoon was listlessly repeated. Again the organ wheezed, again the choir screeched and scraped, again a droning incantation arose, and again the morbidly curious spectators filed past a macabre object — this time a dual array of mortuary repose. Some of the more sensitive people shivered at the whole proceeding, and again Stephen Barbour felt an underlying note of eldritch horror and daemoniac abnormality. God, how life-like both of those corpses were . . . and how in earnest poor

Thorndike had been about not wanting to be judged dead . . . and how he hated Tom Sprague . . . but what could one do in the face of common sense — a dead man was a dead man, and there was old Doc Pratt with his years of experience . . . if nobody else bothered, why should one bother oneself? . . . Whatever Tom had got he had probably deserved . . . and if Henry had done anything to him, the score was even now . . . well, Sophie was free at last . . . .

As the peering procession moved at last toward the hall and the outer door, Sophie was alone with the dead once more. Elder Atwood was out in the road talking to the hearse-driver from Lee's livery stable, and Deacon Leavitt was arranging for a double quota of pall-bearers. Luckily the hearse would hold two coffins. No hurry — Ed Plummer and Ethan Stone were going ahead with shovels to dig the second grave. There would be three livery hacks and any number of private rigs in the cavalcade — no use trying to keep the crowd away from the graves.

Then came that frantic scream from the parlour where Sophie and the bodies were. Its suddenness almost paralysed the crowd and brought back the same sensation which had surged up when Luella had screamed and fainted. Steve Barbour and Deacon Leavitt started to go in, but before they could enter the house Sophie was bursting forth, sobbing and gasping about "That face at the window! . . . that face at the window!"

At the same time a wild-eyed figure rounded the corner of the house, removing all mystery from Sophie's dramatic cry. It was, very obviously, the face's owner — poor crazy Johnny, who began to leap up and down, pointing at Sophie and shrieking, "She knows! She knows! I seen it in her face when she looked at 'em and talked to 'em! She knows, and she's a-lettin' 'em go down in the earth to scratch and claw for air . . . But they'll talk to her so's she kin hear 'em . . . they'll talk to her, an' appear to her . . . and some day they'll come back an' git her!"

Zenas Wells dragged the shrieking half-wit to a woodshed behind the house and bolted him in as best he could. His screams and poundings could be heard at a distance, but nobody paid him any further attention. The procession was made up, and with Sophie in the first hack it slowly covered the short distance past the village to the Swamp Hollow burying-ground.

Elder Atwood made appropriate remarks as Thomas Sprague was laid to rest, and by the time he was through, Ed and Ethan had finished Thorndike's grave on the other side of the cemetery — to which the crowd was presently shifted. Deacon Leavitt then spoke ornamentally, and the lowering process was repeated. People had begun to drift off in knots, and the clatter of receding buggies and carryalls was quite universal, when the shovels began to fly again. As the earth thudded down on the coffin-lids, Thorndike's first, Steve Barbour noticed the queer expressions flitting over Sophie Sprague's face. He couldn't keep track of them all, but behind the rest there seemed to lurk a sort of wry, perverse, half-suppressed look of vague triumph. He shook his head.

Zenas had run ahead and let crazy Johnny out of the woodshed before Sophie got home, and the poor fellow at once made frantically for the graveyard. He arrived before the shovelmen were through, and while many of the curious mourners were still lingering about. What he shouted into Tom Sprague's partly filled grave, and how he clawed at the loose earth of Thorndike's freshly finished mound across the cemetery, surviving spectators still shudder to recall. Jotham Blake, the constable, had to take him back to the town farm by force, and his screams waked dreadful echoes.

This is where Fred Peck usually leaves off the story. What more, he asks, is there to tell? It was a gloomy tragedy, and one can scarcely wonder that Sophie grew queer after that. That is all one hears if the hour is so late that old Calvin Wheeler has tottered home, but when he is still around he breaks in again with that damnably suggestive and insidious whisper. Sometimes those who hear him dread to pass either the shuttered house or the graveyard afterward, especially after dark.

"Heh, heh . . . Fred was only a little shaver then, and don't remember no more than half of what was goin' on! You want to know why Sophie keeps her house shuttered, and why crazy Johnny still keeps a-talkin' to the dead and a-shoutin' at Sophie's windows? Well, sir, I don't know's I know all there is to know, but I hear what I hear."

Here the old man ejects his cud of tobacco and leans forward to buttonhole the listener.

"It was that same night, mind ye — toward mornin', and just eight hours after them burials — when we heard the first scream from Sophie's house. Woke us all up — Steve and Emily Barbour and me and Matildy goes over hot-footin', all in night gear, and finds Sophie all dressed and dead fainted on the settin'-room floor. Lucky she hadn't locked the door. When we got her to she was shakin' like a leaf, and wouldn't let on by so much as a word what was ailin' her. Matildy and Emily done what they could to quiet her down, but Steve whispered things to me as didn't make me none too easy. Come about an hour when we allowed we'd be goin' home soon, that Sophie she begun to tip her head on one side like she was a-listenin' to somethin'. Then on a sudden she screamed again, and keeled over in another faint.

"Well, sir, I'm tellin' what I'm tellin', and won't do no guessin' like Steve Barbour would a done if he dared. He always was the greatest hand for hintin' things . . . died ten years ago of pneumony . . . .

"What we heard so faint-like was just poor crazy Johnny, of course. 'Taint more than a mile to the buryin'-ground, and he must a got out of the window where they'd locked him up at the town farm — even if Constable Blake says he didn't get out that night. From that day to this he hangs around them graves a-talkin' to the both of them — cussin' and kickin' at Tom's mound, and puttin' posies and things on Henry's. And when he ain't a-doin' that he's hangin' around Sophie's shuttered windows howlin' about what's a-comin' soon to git her.

"She wouldn't never go near the buryin'-ground, and now she won't come out of the house at all nor see nobody. Got to sayin' there was a curse on Stillwater — and I'm dinged if she ain't half right, the way things is a-goin' to pieces these days. There certainly was somethin' queer about Sophie right along. Once when Sally Hopkins was a'callin' on her — in '97 or '98, I think it was — there was an awful rattlin' at her winders — and Johnny was safe locked up at the time — at least, so Constable Dodge swore up and down. But I ain't takin' no stock in their stories about noises every seventeenth of June, or about faint shinin' figures a-tryin' Sophie's door and winders every black mornin' about two o'clock.

"You see, it was about two o'clock in the mornin' that Sophie heard the sounds and keeled over twice that first night after the buryin'. Steve and me, and Matildy and Emily, heard the second lot, faint as it was, just like I told you. And I'm a-tellin' you again as how it must a been crazy Johnny over to the buryin'-ground, let Jotham Blake claim what he will. There ain't no tellin' the sound of a man's voice so far off, and with our heads full of nonsense it ain't no wonder we thought there was two voices — and voices that hadn't ought to be speakin' at all.

"Steve, he claimed to have heard more than I did. I verily believe he took some stock in ghosts. Matildy and Emily was so scared they didn't remember what they heard. And curious enough, nobody else in town — if anybody was awake at the ungodly hour — never said nothin' about hearin' no sounds at all.

"Whatever it was, was so faint it might have been the wind if there hadn't been words. I made out a few, but don't want to say as I'd back up all Steve claimed to have caught . . . .

" 'She-devil' . . . 'all the time' . . . 'Henry' . . . and 'alive' was plain . . . and so was 'you know' . . . 'said you'd stand by' . . . 'get rid of him' and 'bury me' . . . in a kind of changed voice . . . Then there was that awful 'comin' again some day' — in a death-like squawk . . . but you can't tell me Johnny couldn't have made those sounds . . . .

"Hey, you! What's takin' you off in such a hurry? Mebbe there's more I could tell you if I had a mind . . ."

The Slaying of the Monster.

BY ROBERT H. BARLOW AND H.P. LOVECRAFT

300-WORD SHORT STORY; 1933.

This tiny sketch is either a very short short story or a very long ironic jest. It is the first story Barlow ever sent to Lovecraft, several years after he first started corresponding with him as a fan; and Lovecraft immediately saw the potential in the 15-year-old stripling. He replied with an encouraging letter and a revision of the story, and encouraged Barlow to publish it in one of the amateur-press journals — which he never did. S.T. Joshi, who has perused and examined more of Lovecraft's writing than probably any other person alive today, estimates its ratio of Lovecraft to Barlow at 30-70.

"The Slaying of the Monster" was not published in Barlow's lifetime; it did not see print until it was included in The Hoard of the Wizard-Beast and One Other, *a book published by Necronomicon Press in 1994.*

ABOUT ROBERT H. BARLOW (1918-1951).

Robert Haywood Barlow was just 13 years old when he first wrote to Lovecraft in 1931. Lovecraft took an early shine to the lad — although he had no idea how young he really was at first. He was initially more a fan of fantasy than weird fiction, and among his favorites were Lord Dunsany and Clark Ashton Smith.

Over the subsequent six years, Barlow and Lovecraft kept up a running correspondence, and Lovecraft came to see him as a sort of child prodigy.

When it Became clear that his death was at hand, Lovecraft chose Barlow to be his literary executor. Unfortunately he did not let his other friends know this, and many of them — including Barlow's most admired living author, Clark Ashton Smith — assumed that his promptness in taking possession of Lovecraft's effects (intending to deposit them in the Brown University archive, although Smith did not know that at the time) amounted to opportunistic theft.

In any case, when August Derleth formed Arkham House and commenced the publication of the first of about 40 years' worth of collected, modified, "posthumously collaborated-upon" and outright fabricated Lovecraftiana, Barlow seemed happy to hand over the keys and bow out of the whole mess. He moved to Mexico and took a job at Mexico City College, where he became a leading authority on Native Mexican anthropology. But like a lot of gay men in that era, he lived on a razor's edge. In 1951, convinced that a disgruntled student was on the point of denouncing him for homosexuality, he locked himself in his home and took an overdose of seconal. He was just 32 years old.

Great was the clamour in Laen; for smoke had been spied in the Hills of the Dragon. That surely meant the Stirrings of the Monster — the Monster who spat lava and shook the earth as he writhed in its depths. And when the men of Laen spoke together they swore to slay the Monster and keep his fiery breath from searing their minaret-studded city and toppling their alabaster domes.

So it was that by torch-light gathered fully a hundred of the little people, prepared to battle the Evil One in his hidden fast-hold. With the coming of night they began marching in ragged columns into the foot-hills beneath the fulgent lunar rays. Ahead a burning cloud shone clearly through the purple dusk, a guide to their goal.

For the sake of truth it is to be recorded that their spirits sank low long ere they sighted the foe, and as the moon grew dim and the coming of the dawn was heralded by gaudy clouds they wished themselves more than ever at home, dragon or no dragon. But as the sun rose they cheered up slightly, and, shifting their spears, resolutely trudged the remaining distance.

Clouds of sulphurous smoke hung pall-like over the world, darkening even the new-risen sun, and always replenished by sullen puffs from the mouth of the Monster. Little tongues of hungry flame made the Laenians move swiftly over the hot stones. "But where is the dragon?" whispered one — fearfully and hoping it would not accept the query as an invitation. In vain they looked — there was nothing solid enough to slay.

So shouldering their weapons, they wearily returned home and there set up a stone tablet graven to this effect —

BEING TROUBLED BY A FIERCE MONSTER THE BRAVE CITIZENS OF LAEN DID SET UPON IT AND SLAY IT IN ITS FEARFUL LAIR SAVING THE LAND FROM A DREADFUL DOOM.

These words were hard to read when we dug that stone from its deep, ancient layers of encrusting lava.

Through the Gates of the Silver Key.

BY E. HOFFMAN PRICE AND H.P. LOVECRAFT

14,00-WORD NOVELETTE; 1933.

This longish novelette actually started life as a 6,000-word short story, which E. Hoffman Price dashed off and sent to H.P. Lovecraft after Lovecraft's June 1932 visit to Price at his New Orleans home. The original story, titled "The Lord of Illusion," sought to pick up where Lovecraft's 1926 short story "The Silver Key" left off. With it Price included a note asking if Lovecraft would be willing to revise the story, and suggesting that perhaps it could be published as a collaboration.

Lovecraft appears to have been somewhat reluctant to take this on, but no doubt felt obligated by having received such excellent hospitality from Price on his visit the previous year; so he obliged.

The resulting story feels a little confused in parts, as Price's style of hard-charging action and Lovecraft's of darksome contemplativeness make for an odd mixture. Perhaps not surprisingly, Farnsworth Wright, editor of Weird Tales, *initially declined to publish it; but several months later, apparently having second thoughts, he wrote to ask for it to be sent back to him, and accepted it. It was published in the July 1934 issue.*

I.

In a vast room hung with strangely figured arras and carpeted with Bonkhata rugs of impressive age and workmanship, four men were sitting around a document-strewn table. From the far corners, where odd tripods of wrought iron were now and then replenished by an incredibly aged Negro in somber livery, came the hypnotic fumes of olibanum; while in a deep niche on one side there ticked a curious, coffin-shaped clock whose dial bore baffling hieroglyphs and whose four hands did not move in consonance with any time system known on this planet. It was a singular and disturbing room, but well fitted to the business then at hand. For there, in the New Orleans home of this continent's greatest mystic, mathematician and orientalist, there was being settled at last the estate of a scarcely less great mystic, scholar, author and dreamer who had vanished from the face of the earth four years before.

Randolph Carter, who had all his life sought to escape from the tedium and limitations of waking reality in the beckoning vistas of dreams and fabled avenues of other dimensions, disappeared from the sight of man on the seventh of October, 1928, at the age of fifty-four. His career had been a strange and lonely one, and there were those who inferred from his curious novels many episodes more bizarre than any in his recorded history. His association with Harley Warren, the South Carolina mystic whose studies in the primal Naacal language of the Himalayan priests had led to such outrageous conclusions, had been close. Indeed, it was he who — one mist-mad, terrible night in an ancient graveyard — had seen Warren descend into a dank and nitrous vault, never to emerge. Carter lived in Boston, but it was from the wild, haunted hills behind hoary and witch-accursed Arkham that all his forebears had come. And it was amid these ancient, cryptically brooding hills that he had ultimately vanished.

His old servant, Parks — who died early in 1930 — had spoken of the strangely aromatic and hideously carven box he had found in the attic, and of the indecipherable parchments and queerly figured silver key which that box had contained: matters of which Carter had also written to others. Carter, he said, had told him that this key had come down from his ancestors, and that it would help him to unlock the gates to his lost boyhood, and to strange dimensions and fantastic realms which he had hitherto visited only in vague, brief, and elusive dreams. Then one day Carter took the box and its contents and rode away in his car, never to return.

Later on, people found the car at the side of an old, grass-grown road in the hills behind crumbling Arkham — the hills where Carter's forebears had once dwelt, and where the ruined cellar of the great Carter homestead still gaped to the sky. It was in a grove of tall elms near by that another of the Carters had mysteriously vanished in 1781, and not far away was the half-rotted cottage where Goody Fowler, the witch, had brewed her ominous potions still earlier. The region had been settled in 1692 by fugitives from the witchcraft trials in Salem, and even now it bore a name for vaguely ominous things scarcely to be envisaged. Edmund Carter had fled from the shadow of Gallows Hill just in time, and the tales of his sorceries were many. Now, it seemed, his lone descendant had gone somewhere to join him.

In the car they found the hideously carved box of fragrant wood, and the parchment which no man could read. The silver key was gone — presumably with Carter. Further than that there was no certain clue. Detectives from Boston said that the fallen timbers of the old Carter place seemed oddly disturbed, and somebody found a handkerchief on the rock-ridged, sinisterly wooded slope behind the ruins near the dreaded cave called the Snake Den.

It was then that the country legends about the Snake Den gained a new vitality. Farmers whispered of the blasphemous uses to which old Edmund Carter the wizard had put that horrible grotto, and added later tales about the fondness which Randolph Carter himself had had for it when a boy. In Carter's boyhood the venerable gambrel-roofed homestead was still standing and tenanted by his great-uncle Christopher. He had visited there often, and had talked singularly about the Snake Den. People remembered what he had said about a deep fissure and an unknown inner cave beyond, and speculated on the change he had shown after spending one whole memorable day in the cavern when he was nine. That was in October, too — and ever after that he had seemed to have a uncanny knack at prophesying future events.

It had rained late in the night that Carter vanished, and no one was quite able to trace his footprints from the car. Inside the Snake Den all was amorphous liquid mud, owing to the copious seepage. Only the ignorant rustics whispered about the prints they thought they spied where the great elms overhang the road, and on the sinister hillside near the Snake Den, where the handkerchief was found. Who could pay attention to whispers that spoke of stubby little tracks like those which Randolph Carter's square-toed boots made when he was a small boy? It was as crazy a notion as that other whisper — that the tracks of old Benijah Corey's peculiar heelless boots had met the stubby little tracks in the road. Old Benijah had been the Carters' hired man when Randolph was young; but he had died thirty years ago.

It must have been these whispers plus Carter's own statement to Parks and others that the queerly arabesqued silver key would help him unlock the gates of his lost boyhood — which caused a number of mystical students to declare that the missing man had actually doubled back on the trail of time and returned through forty-five years to that other October day in 1883 when he had stayed in the Snake Den as a small boy. When he came out that night, they argued, he had somehow made the whole trip to 1928 and back; for did he not thereafter know of things which were to happen later? And yet he had never spoken of anything to happen after 1928.

One student — an elderly eccentric of Providence, Rhode Island, who had enjoyed a long and close correspondence with Carter — had a still more elaborate theory, and believed that Carter had not only returned to boyhood, but achieved a further liberation, roving at will through the prismatic vistas of boyhood dream. After a strange vision this man published a tale of Carter's vanishing in which he hinted that the lost one now reigned as king on the opal throne of Ilek-Vad, that fabulous town of turrets atop the hollow cliffs of glass overlooking the twilight sea wherein the bearded and finny Gnorri build their singular labyrinths.

"Below him the ground was festering with gigantic Dholes."

Weird Tales, July 1934

Through the Gates of the Silver Key

By H. P. LOVECRAFT and E. HOFFMANN PRICE

A colossal story of cosmic scope by two of the greatest writers of weird fiction in the world today

It was this old man, Ward Phillips, who pleaded most loudly against the apportionment of Carter's estate to his heirs — all distant cousins — on the ground that he was still alive in another time-dimension and might well return some day. Against him was arrayed the legal talent of one of the cousins, Ernest K. Aspinwall of Chicago, a man ten years Carter's senior, but keen as a youth in forensic battles. For four years the contest had raged, but now the time for apportionment had come, and this vast, strange room in New Orleans was to be the scene of the arrangement.

It was the home of Carter's literary and financial executor — the distinguished Creole student of mysteries and Eastern antiquities, Étienne-Laurent de Marigny. Carter had met de Marigny during the war, when they both served in the French Foreign Legion, and had at once cleaved to him because of their similar tastes and outlook. When, on a memorable joint furlough, the learned young Creole had taken the wistful Boston dreamer to Bayonne, in the south of France, and had shown him certain terrible secrets in the nighted and immemorial crypts that burrow beneath that brooding, eon-weighted city, the friendship was forever sealed. Carter's will had named de Marigny as executor, and now that avid scholar was reluctantly presiding over the settlement of the estate. It was sad work for him, for like the old Rhode Islander he did not believe that Carter was dead. But what weight had the dreams of mystics against the harsh wisdom of the world?

Around the table in that strange room in the old French Quarter sat the men who claimed an interest in the proceedings. There had been the usual legal advertisements of the conference in papers wherever Carter's heirs were thought to live; yet only four now sat listening to the abnormal ticking of that coffin-shaped clock which told no earthly time, and to the bubbling of the courtyard fountain beyond half-curtained, fan-lighted windows. As the hours wore on, the faces of the four were half shrouded in the curling fumes from the tripods, which, piled recklessly with fuel, seemed to need less and less attention from the silently gliding and increasingly nervous old Negro.

There was Étienne de Marigny himself — slim, dark, handsome, mustached, and still young. Aspinwall, representing the heirs, was white-haired, apoplectic-faced, side-whiskered, and portly. Phillips, the Providence mystic, was lean, gray, long-nosed, clean-shaven, and stoop-shouldered. The fourth man was non-committal in age — lean, with a dark, bearded, singularly immobile face of very regular contour, bound with the turban of a high-caste Brahman and having night-black, burning, almost irisless eyes which seemed to gaze out from a vast distance behind the features. He had announced himself as the Swami Chandraputra, an adept from Benares, with important information to give; and both de Marigny and Phillips — who had corresponded with him — had been quick to recognize the genuineness of his mystical pretensions. His speech had an oddly forced, hollow, metallic quality, as if the use of English taxed his vocal apparatus; yet his language was as easy, correct and idiomatic as any native Anglo-Saxon's. In general attire he was the normal European civilian, but his loose clothes sat peculiarly badly on him, while his bushy black beard, Eastern turban, and large, white mittens gave him an air of exotic eccentricity.

De Marigny, fingering the parchment found in Carter's car, was speaking.

"No, I have not been able to make anything of the parchment. Mr. Phillips, here, also gives it up. Colonel Churchward declares it is not Naacal, and it looks nothing at all like the hieroglyphics on that Easter Island war-club. The carvings on that box, though, do strangely suggest Easter Island images. The nearest thing I can recall to these parchment characters — notice how all the letters seem to hang down from horizontal word-bar — is the writing in a book poor Harley Warren once had. It came from India while Carter and I were visiting him in 1919, and he never would tell us anything about it — said it would be better if we didn't know, and hinted that it might have come originally from some place other than the Earth. He took it with him in December, when he went down into the vault in that old graveyard — but neither he nor the book ever came to the surface again. Some time ago I sent our friend here — the Swami Chandraputra — a memory-sketch of some of those letters, and also a photostatic copy of the Carter parchment. He believes he may be able to shed light on them after certain references and consultations.

"But the key — Carter sent me a photograph of that. Its curious arabesques were not letters, but seem to have belonged to the same culture-tradition as the parchment. Carter always spoke of being on the point of solving the mystery, though he never gave details. Once he grew almost poetic about the whole business. That antique silver key, he said, would unlock the successive doors that bar our free march down the mighty corridors of space and time to the very Border which no man has crossed since Shaddad with his terrific genius built and concealed in the sands of Arabia Pettraea the prodigious domes and uncounted minarets of thousand-pillared Irem. Half-starved dervishes — wrote Carter — and thirst-crazed nomads have returned to tell of that monumental portal, and of the hand that is sculptured above the keystone of the arch, but no man has passed and retraced his steps to say that his footprints on the garnet-strewn sands within bear witness to his visit. The key, he surmised, was that for which the cyclopean sculptured hand vainly grasps.

"Why Carter didn't take the parchment as well as the key, we can not say. Perhaps he forgot it — or perhaps he forbore to take it through recollection of one who had taken a book of like characters into a vault and never returned. Or perhaps it was really immaterial to what he wished to do."

As de Marigny paused, old Mr. Phillips spoke in a harsh, shrill voice.

"We can know of Randolph Carter's wandering only what we dream. I have been to many strange places in dreams, and have heard many strange and significant things in Ulthar, beyond the River Skai. It does not appear that the parchment was needed, for certainly Carter reentered the world of his boyhood dreams, and is now a king in Ilek-Vad."

Mr. Aspinwall grew doubly apoplectic-looking as he sputtered: "Can't somebody shut the old fool up? We've had enough of these moonings. The problem is to divide the property, and it's about time we got to it."

For the first time Swami Chandraputra spoke in his queerly alien voice.

"Gentlemen, there is more to this matter than you think. Mr. Aspinwall does not do well to laugh at the evidence of dreams. Mr. Phillips has taken an incomplete view—perhaps because he has not dreamed enough. I, myself, have done much dreaming. We in India have always done that, just as all the Carters seem to have done it. You, Mr. Aspinwall, as a maternal cousin, are naturally not a Carter. My own dreams, and certain other sources of information, have told me a great deal which you still find obscure. For example, Randolph Carter forgot that parchment which he couldn't decipher—yet it would have been well for him had he remembered to take it. You see, I have really learned pretty much what happened to Carter after he left his car with the silver key at sunset on that seventh of October, four years ago."

Aspinwall audibly sneered, but the others sat up with heightened interest. The smoke from the tripods increased, and the crazy ticking of that coffin-shaped clock seemed to fall into bizarre patterns like the dots and dashes of some alien and insoluble telegraph message from outer space. The Hindoo leaned back, half closed his eyes, and continued in that oddly labored yet idiomatic speech, while before his audience there began to float a picture of what had happened to Randolph Carter.

II.

The hills beyond Arkham are full of a strange magic—something, perhaps, which the old wizard Edmund Carter called down from the stars and up from the crypts of nether earth when he fled there from Salem in 1692. As soon as Randolph Carter was back among them he knew that he was close to one of the gates which a few audacious, abhorred and alien-souled men have blasted through titan walls betwixt the world and the outside absolute. Here, he felt, and on this day of the year, he could carry out with success the message he had deciphered months before from the arabesques of that tarnished and incredibly ancient silver key. He knew now how it must be rotated, and how it must be held up to the setting sun, and what syllables of ceremony must be intoned into the void at the ninth and last turning. In a spot as close to a dark polarity and induced gate as this, it could not fail in its primary functions. Certainly, he would rest that night in the lost boyhood for which he had never ceased to mourn.

He got out of the car with the key in his pocket, walking up-hill deeper and deeper into the shadowy core of that brooding, haunted countryside of winding road, vine-grown stone wall, black woodland, gnarled, neglected orchard, gaping-windowed, deserted farm-house, and nameless ruin. At the sunset hour, when the distant spires of Kingsport gleamed in the ruddy blaze, he took out the key and made the needed turnings and intonations. Only later did he realize how soon the ritual had taken effect.

Then in the deepening twilight he had heard a voice out of the past: Old Benijah Corey, his great-uncle's hired man. Had not old Benijah been dead for thirty years? Thirty years before when. What was time? Where had he been? Why was it strange that Benijah should be calling him on this seventh of October 1883? Was he not out later than Aunt Martha had told him to stay? What was this key in his blouse pocket, where his little telescope—given him by his father on his ninth birthday, two months before—ought to be? Had he found it in the attic at home? Would it unlock the mystic pylon which his sharp eye had traced amidst the jagged rocks at the back of that inner cave behind the Snake Den on the hill? That was the place they always coupled with old Edmund Carter the wizard. People wouldn't go there, and nobody but him had ever noticed or squirmed through the root-choked fissure to that great black inner chamber with the pylon. Whose hands had carved that hint of a pylon out of the living rock? Old Wizard Edmund's—or others that he had conjured up and commanded?

That evening little Randolph ate supper with Uncle Chris and Aunt Martha in the old gambrel-roofed farm-house.

Next morning he was up early and out through the twisted-boughed apple orchard to the upper timber lot where the mouth of the Snake Den lurked black and forbidding amongst grotesque, overnourished oaks. A nameless expectancy was upon him, and he did not even notice the loss of his handkerchief as he fumbled in his blouse pocket to see if the queer silver key was safe. He crawled through the dark orifice with tense, adventurous assurance, lighting his way with matches taken from the sitting-room. In another moment he had wriggled through the root-choked fissure at the farther end, and was in the vast, unknown inner grotto whose ultimate rock wall seemed half like a monstrous and consciously shapen pylon. Before that dank, dripping wall he stood silent and awestruck, lighting one match after another as he gazed. Was that stony bulge above the keystone of the imagined arch really a gigantic sculptured hand? Then he drew forth the silver key, and made motions and intonations whose source he could only dimly remember. Was anything forgotten? He knew only that he wished to cross the barrier to the untrammeled land of his dreams and the gulfs where all dimensions dissolved in the absolute.

III.

What happened then is scarcely to be described in words. It is full of those paradoxes, contradictions and anomalies which have no place in waking life, but which fill our more fantastic dreams and are taken as matters of course till we return to our narrow, rigid, objective world of limited causation and tri-dimensional logic. As the Hindoo continued his tale, he had difficulty in avoiding what seemed—even more than the notion of a man transferred through the years to boyhood—an air of trivial, puerile extravagance. Mr. Aspinwall, in disgust, gave an apoplectic snort and virtually stopped listening.

For the rite of the silver key, as practiced by Randolph Carter in that black, haunted cave within a cave, did not prove unavailing. From the first gesture and syllable an aura of strange, awesome mutation was apparent — a sense of incalculable disturbance and confusion in time and space, yet one which held no hint of what we recognize as motion and duration. Imperceptibly, such things as age and location ceased to have any significance whatever. The day before, Randolph Carter had miraculously leaped a gulf of years. Now there was no distinction between boy and man. There was only the entity Randolph Carter, with a certain store of images which had lost all connection with terrestrial scenes and circumstances of acquisition. A moment before, there had been an inner cave with vague suggestions of a monstrous arch and gigantic sculptured hand on the farther wall. Now there was neither cave nor absence of cave; neither wall nor absence of wall. There was only a flux of impressions not so much visual as cerebral, amidst which the entity that was Randolph Carter experienced perceptions or registrations of all that his mind revolved on, yet without any clear consciousness of the way in which he received them.

By the time the rite was over, Carter knew that he was in no region whose place could be told by Earth's geographers, and in no age whose date history could fix; for the nature of what was happening was not wholly unfamiliar to him. There were hints of it in the cryptical Pnakotic fragments, and a whole chapter in the forbidden *Necronomicon* of the mad Arab, Abdul Alhazred, had taken on significance when he had deciphered the designs graven on the silver key. A gate had been unlocked — not, indeed, the Ultimate Gate, but one leading from Earth and time to that extension of Earth which is outside time, and from which in turn the Ultimate Gate leads fearsomely and perilously to the last Void which is outside all earths, all universes, and all matter.

There would be a Guide — and a very terrible one; a Guide who had been an entity of Earth millions of years before, when man was undreamed of, and when forgotten shapes moved on a steaming planet building strange cities among whose last, crumbling ruins the first mammals were to play. Carter remembered what the monstrous *Necronomicon* had vaguely and disconcertingly adumbrated concerning that Guide:

"And while there are those," the mad Arab had written, "who have dared to seek glimpses beyond the Veil, and to accept HIM as guide, they would have been more prudent had they avoided commerce with HIM; for it is written in the Book of Thoth how terrific is the price of a single glimpse. Nor may those who pass ever return, for in the vastnesses transcending our world are shapes of darkness that seize and bind. The Affair that shambleth about in the night, the evil that defieth the Elder Sign, the Herd that stand watch at the secret portal each tomb is known to have and that thrive on that which groweth out of the tenants thereof: — all these Blacknesses are lesser than HE WHO guardeth the Gateway: HE WHO will guide the rash one beyond all the worlds into the Abyss of unnamable devourers. For He is 'UMR AT-TAWIL, the Most Ancient One, which the scribe rendereth as THE PROLONGED OF LIFE."

Memory and imagination shaped dim half-pictures with uncertain outlines amidst the seething chaos, but Carter knew that they were of memory and imagination only. Yet he felt that it was not chance which built these things in his consciousness, but rather some vast reality, ineffable and undimensioned, which surrounded him and strove to translate itself into the only symbols he was capable of grasping. For no mind of Earth may grasp the extensions of shape which interweave in the oblique gulfs outside time and the dimensions we know.

There floated before Carter a cloudy pageantry of shapes and scenes which he somehow linked with Earth's primal, eon-forgotten past. Monstrous living things moved deliberately through vistas of fantastic handiwork that no sane dream ever held, and landscapes bore incredible vegetation and cliffs and mountains and masonry of no human pattern. There were cities under the sea, and denizens thereof; and towers in great deserts where globes and cylinders and nameless winged entities shot off into space, or hurtled down out of space. All this Carter grasped, though the images bore no fixed relation to one another or to him. He himself had no stable form or position, but only such shifting hints of form and position as his whirling fancy supplied.

He had wished to find the enchanted regions of his boyhood dreams, where galleys sail up the river Oukranos past the gilded spires of Thran, and elephant caravans tramp through perfumed jungles in Kied, beyond forgotten palaces with veined ivory columns that sleep lovely and unbroken under the moon. Now, intoxicated with wider visions, he scarcely knew what he sought. Thoughts of infinite and blasphemous daring rose in his mind, and he knew he would face the dreaded Guide without fear, asking monstrous and terrible things of him.

All at once the pageant of impressions seemed to achieve a vague kind of stabilization. There were great masses of towering stone, carven into alien and incomprehensible designs and disposed according to the laws of some unknown, inverse geometry. Light filtered from a sky of no assignable colour in baffling, contradictory directions, and played almost sentiently over what seemed to be a curved line of gigantic hieroglyphed pedestals more hexagonal than otherwise, and surmounted by cloaked, ill-defined shapes.

There was another shape, too, which occupied no pedestal, but which seemed to glide or float over the cloudy, floor-like lower level. It was not exactly permanent in outline, but held transient suggestions of something remotely preceding or paralleling the human form, though half as large again as an ordinary man. It seemed to be heavily cloaked, like the shapes on the pedestals, with some neutral-coloured fabric; and Carter could not detect any eye-holes through which it might gaze. Probably it did not need to gaze, for it seemed to belong to an order of beings far outside the merely physical in organization and faculties.

A moment later Carter knew that this was so, for the Shape

had spoken to his mind without sound or language. And though the name it uttered was a dreaded and terrible one, Randolph Carter did not flinch in fear.

Instead, he spoke back, equally without sound or language, and made those obeisances which the hideous *Necronomicon* had taught him to make. For this shape was nothing less than that which all the world has feared since Lomar rose out of the sea, and the Children of the Fire Mist came to Earth to teach the Elder Lore to man. It was indeed the frightful Guide and Guardian of the Gate—'UMR AT-TAWIL, the ancient one, which the scribe rendereth the PROLONGED OF LIFE.

The Guide knew, as he knew all things, of Carter's quest and coming, and that this seeker of dreams and secrets stood before him unafraid. There was no horror or malignity in what he radiated, and Carter wondered for a moment whether the mad Arab's terrific blasphemous hints came from envy and a baffled wish to do what was now about to be done. Or perhaps the Guide reserved his horror and malignity for those who feared. As the radiations continued, Carter eventually interpreted them in the form of words.

"I am indeed that Most Ancient One," said the Guide, "of whom you know. We have awaited you—the Ancient Ones and I. You are welcome, even though long delayed. You have the key, and have unlocked the First Gate. Now the Ultimate Gate is ready for your trial. If you fear, you need not advance. You may still go back unharmed, the way you came. But if you chose to advance—"

The pause was ominous, but the radiations continued to be friendly. Carter hesitated not a moment, for a burning curiosity drove him on.

"I will advance," he radiated back, "and I accept you as my Guide."

At this reply the Guide seemed to make a sign by certain motions of his robe which may or may not have involved the lifting of an arm or some homologous member. A second sign followed, and from his well-learned lore Carter knew that he was at last very close to the Ultimate Gate. The light now changed to another inexplicable colour, and the shapes on the quasi-hexagonal pedestals became more clearly defined. As they sat more erect, their outlines became more like those of men, though Carter knew that they could not be men. Upon their cloaked heads there now seemed to rest tall, uncertainly coloured miters, strangely suggestive of those on certain nameless figures chiseled by a forgotten sculptor along the living cliffs of a high, forbidden mountain in Tartary; while grasped in certain folds of their swathings were long sceptres whose carven heads bodied forth a grotesque and archaic mystery.

Carter guessed what they were and whence they came, and Whom they served; and guessed, too, the price of their service. But he was still content, for at one mighty venture he was to learn all. Damnation, he reflected, is but a word bandied about by those whose blindness leads them to condemn all who can see, even with a single eye. He wondered at the vast conceit of those who had babbled of the malignant Ancient Ones, as if They could pause from their everlasting dreams to wreak a wrath on mankind. As well, he thought, might a mammoth pause to visit frantic vengeance on an angleworm. Now the whole assemblage on the vaguely hexagonal pillars was greeting him with a gesture of those oddly carven sceptres and radiating a message which he understood:

"We salute you, Most Ancient One, and you, Randolph Carter, whose daring has made you one of us."

Carter saw now that one of the pedestals was vacant, and a gesture of the Most Ancient One told him it was reserved for him. He saw also another pedestal, taller than the rest, and at the center of the oddly curved line—neither semicircle nor ellipse, parabola nor hyperbola—which they formed. This, he guessed, was the Guide's own throne. Moving and rising in a manner hardly definable, Carter took his seat; and as he did so he saw that the Guide had seated himself.

Gradually and mistily it became apparent that the Most Ancient One was holding something—some object clutched in the outflung folds of his robe as if for the sight, or what answered for sight, of the cloaked Companions. It was a large sphere, or apparent sphere, of some obscurely iridescent metal, and as the Guide put it forward a low, pervasive half-impression of sound began to rise and fall in intervals which seemed to be rhythmic even though they followed no rhythm of Earth. There was a suggestion of chanting or what human imagination might interpret as chanting. Presently the quasi-sphere began to grow luminous, and as it gleamed up into a cold, pulsating light of unassignable colour, Carter saw that its flickerings conformed to the alien rhythm of the chant. Then all the mitered, sceptre-bearing Shapes on the pedestals commenced a slight, curious swaying in the same inexplicable rhythm, while nimbuses of unclassifiable light—resembling that of the quasi-sphere—played around their shrouded heads.

The Hindoo paused in his tale and looked curiously at the tall, coffin-shaped clock with the four hands and hieroglyphed dial, whose crazy ticking followed no known rhythm of Earth.

"You, Mr. de Marigny," he suddenly said to his learned host, "do not need to be told the particularly alien rhythm to which those cowled Shapes on the hexagonal pillars chanted and nodded. You are the only one else—in America—who has had a taste of the Outer Extension. That clock—I suppose it was sent to you by the Yogi poor Harley Warren used to talk about—the seer who said that he alone of living men had been to Yian-Ho, the hidden legacy of eon-old Leng, and had borne certain things away from that dreadful and forbidden city. I wonder how many of its subtler properties you know? If my dreams and readings be correct, it was made by those who knew much of the First Gateway. But let me go on with my tale."

At last, continued the Swami, the swaying and the suggestion of chanting ceased, the lambent nimbuses around the now drooping and motionless heads faded, while the cloaked shapes slumped curiously on their pedestals. The quasi-sphere, however, continued to pulsate with inexplicable light. Carter felt that the Ancient Ones were sleeping as they had been when he first saw them, and he wondered out of what cosmic dreams his coming had aroused them. Slowly there filtered into his mind the truth that this strange chanting ritual had been one of instruction, and that the Companions had been chanted by the Most Ancient One into a new and peculiar kind of sleep in order that their dreams might open the Ultimate Gate to which the silver key was a passport. He knew that in the profundity of this deep sleep they were contemplating unplumbed vastnesses of utter and absolute outsideness, and that they were to accomplish that which his presence had demanded.

The Guide did not share this sleep, but seemed still to be giving instructions in some subtle, soundless way. Evidently he was implanting images of those things which he wished the Companions to dream: and Carter knew that as each of the Ancient Ones pictured the prescribed thought, there would be born the nucleus of a manifestation visible to his earthly eyes. When the dreams of all the Shapes had achieved a oneness, that manifestation would occur, and everything he required be materialized, through concentration. He had seen such things on Earth — in India, where the combined, projected will of a circle of adepts can make a thought take tangible substance, and in hoary Atlaanat, of which few even dare speak.

Just what the Ultimate Gate was, and how it was to be passed, Carter could not be certain; but a feeling of tense expectancy surged over him. He was conscious of having a kind of body, and of holding the fateful silver key in his hand. The masses of towering stone opposite him seemed to possess the evenness of a wall, toward the centre of which his eyes were irresistibly drawn. And then suddenly he felt the mental currents of the Most Ancient One cease to flow forth.

For the first time Carter realized how terrific utter silence, mental and physical, may be. The earlier moments had never failed to contain some perceptible rhythm, if only the faint, cryptical pulse of the Earth's dimensional extension, but now the hush of the abyss seemed to fall upon everything. Despite his intimations of body, he had no audible breath, and the glow of 'Umr at-Tawil's quasi-sphere had grown petrifiedly fixed and unpulsating. A potent nimbus, brighter than those which had played round the heads of the Shapes, blazed frozenly over the shrouded skull of the terrible Guide.

A dizziness assailed Carter, and his sense of lost orientation waxed a thousandfold. The strange lights seemed to hold the quality of the most impenetrable blacknesses heaped upon blacknesses while about the Ancient Ones, so close on their pseudo-hexagonal thrones, there hovered an air of the most stupefying remoteness. Then he felt himself wafted into immeasurable depths, with waves of perfumed warmth lapping against his face. It was as if he floated in a torrid, rose-tinctured sea; a sea of drugged wine whose waves broke foaming against shores of brazen fire. A great fear clutched him as he half saw that vast expanse of surging sea lapping against its far off coast. But the moment of silence was broken — the surgings were speaking to him in a language that was not of physical sound or articulate words.

"The Man of Truth is beyond good and evil," intoned the voice that was not a voice. "The Man of Truth has ridden to All-Is-One. The Man of Truth has learned that Illusion is the One Reality, and that Substance is the Great Impostor."

And now, in that rise of masonry to which his eyes had been so irresistibly drawn, there appeared the outline of a titanic arch not unlike that which he thought he had glimpsed so long ago in that cave within a cave, on the far, unreal surface of the three-dimensioned Earth. He realized that he had been using the silver key — moving it in accord with an unlearned and instinctive ritual closely akin to that which had opened the Inner Gate. That rose-drunken sea which lapped his cheeks was, he realized, no more or less than the adamantine mass of the solid wall yielding before his spell, and the vortex of thought with which the Ancient Ones had aided his spell. Still guided by instinct and blind determination, he floated forward — and through the Ultimate Gate.

IV.

Randolph Carter's advance through the cyclopean bulk of masonry was like a dizzy precipitation through the measureless gulfs between the stars. From a great distance he felt triumphant, godlike surges of deadly sweetness, and after that the rustling of great wings, and impressions of sound like the chirpings and murmurings of objects unknown on Earth or in the solar system. Glancing backward, he saw not one gate alone but a multiplicity of gates, at some of which clamoured Forms he strove not to remember.

And then, suddenly, he felt a greater terror than that which any of the Forms could give — a terror from which he could not flee because it was connected with himself. Even the First Gateway had taken something of stability from him, leaving him uncertain about his bodily form and about his relationship to the mistily defined objects around him, but it had not disturbed his sense of unity. He had still been Randolph Carter, a fixed point in the dimensional seething. Now, beyond the Ultimate Gateway, he realized in a moment of consuming fright that he was not one person, but many persons.

He was in many places at the same time. On Earth, on October 7, 1883, a little boy named Randolph Carter was leaving the Snake Den in the hushed evening light and running down the rocky slope, and through the twisted-boughed orchard toward his Uncle Christopher's house in the hills beyond Arkham; yet at that same moment, which was also somehow in the earthly year of 1928, a vague shadow not less Randolph

Carter was sitting on a pedestal among the Ancient Ones in Earth's transdimensional extension. Here, too, was a third Randolph Carter, in the unknown and formless cosmic abyss beyond the Ultimate Gate. And elsewhere, in a chaos of scenes whose infinite multiplicity and monstrous diversity brought him close to the brink of madness, were a limitless confusion of beings which he knew were as much himself as the local manifestation now beyond the Ultimate Gate.

There were Carters in settings belonging to every known and suspected age of Earth's history, and to remoter ages of earthly entity transcending knowledge, suspicion, and credibility; Carters of forms both human and non-human, vertebrate and invertebrate, conscious and mindless, animal and vegetable. And more, there were Carters having nothing in common with earthly life, but moving outrageously amidst backgrounds of other planets and systems and galaxies and cosmic continua; spores of eternal life drifting from world to world, universe to universe, yet all equally himself. Some of the glimpses recalled dreams — both faint and vivid, single and persistent — which he had had through the long years since he first began to dream; and a few possessed a haunting, fascinating and almost horrible familiarity which no earthly logic could explain.

Faced with this realization, Randolph Carter reeled in the clutch of supreme horror — horror such as had not been hinted even at the climax of that hideous night when two had ventured into an ancient and abhorred necropolis under a waning moon and only one had emerged. No death, no doom, no anguish can arouse the surpassing despair which flows from a loss of identity. Merging with nothingness is peaceful oblivion; but to be aware of existence and yet to know that one is no longer a definite being distinguished from other beings — that one no longer has a self — that is the nameless summit of agony and dread.

He knew that there had been a Randolph Carter of Boston, yet could not be sure whether he — the fragment or facet of an entity beyond the Ultimate Gate — had been that one or some other. His self had been annihilated; and yet he — if indeed there could, in view of that utter nullity of individual existence, be such a thing as he — was equally aware of being in some inconceivable way a legion of selves. It was as though his body had been suddenly transformed into one of those many-limbed and many-headed effigies sculptured in Indian temples, and he contemplated the aggregation in a bewildered attempt to discern which was the original and which the additions — if indeed (supremely monstrous thought!) there were any original as distinguished from other embodiments.

Then, in the midst of these devastating reflections, Carter's beyond-the-gate fragment was hurled from what had seemed the nadir of horror to black, clutching pits of a horror still more profound. This time it was largely external — a force of personality which at once confronted and surrounded and pervaded him, and which in addition to its local presence, seemed also to be a part of himself, and likewise to be co-existent with all time and conterminous with all space. There was no visual image, yet the sense of entity and the awful concept of combined localism and identity and infinity lent a paralyzing terror beyond anything which any Carter-fragment had hitherto deemed capable of existing.

In the face of that awful wonder, the quasi-Carter forgot the horror of destroyed individuality. It was an All-in-One and One-in-All of limitless being and self — not merely a thing of one space-time continuum, but allied to the ultimate animating essence of existence's whole unbounded sweep — the last, utter sweep which has no confines and which outreaches fancy and mathematics alike. It was perhaps that which certain secret cults of Earth had whispered of as Yog-Sothoth, and which has been a deity under other names; that which the crustaceans of Yuggoth worship as the Beyond-One, and which the vaporous brains of the spiral nebulae know by an untranslatable sign — yet in a flash the Carter-facet realized how slight and fractional all these conceptions are.

And now the Being was addressing the Carter-facet in prodigious waves that smote and burned and thundered — a concentration of energy that blasted its recipient with well-nigh unendurable violence, and that paralleled in an unearthly rhythm the curious swaying of the Ancient Ones, and the flickering of the monstrous lights, in that baffling region beyond the First Gate. It was as though suns and worlds and universes had converged upon one point whose very position in space they had conspired to annihilate with an impact of resistless fury. But amidst the greater terror one lesser terror was diminished; for the searing waves appeared somehow to isolate the Beyond-the-Gate Carter from his infinity of duplicates — to restore, as it were, a certain amount of the illusion of identity. After a time the hearer began to translate the waves into speech-forms known to him, and his sense of horror and oppression waned. Fright became pure awe, and what had seemed blasphemously abnormal seemed now only ineffably majestic.

"Randolph Carter," it seemed to say, "my manifestations on your planet's extension, the Ancient Ones, have sent you as one who would lately have returned to small lands of dream which he had lost, yet who with greater freedom has risen to greater and nobler desires and curiosities. You wished to sail up golden Oukranos, to search out forgotten ivory cities in orchid-heavy Kied, and to reign on the opal throne of Ilek-Vad, whose fabulous towers and numberless domes rise mighty toward a single red star in a firmament alien to your Earth and to all matter. Now, with the passing of two Gates, you wish loftier things. You would not flee like a child from a scene disliked to a dream beloved, but would plunge like a man into that last and inmost of secrets which lies behind all scenes and dreams.

"What you wish, I have found good; and I am ready to grant that which I have granted eleven times only to beings of your planet — five times only to those you call men, or those resembling them. I am ready to show you the Ultimate Mystery, to look on which is to blast a feeble spirit. Yet before you gaze full at that last and first of secrets you may still wield a free choice, and return if you will through the two Gates with the Veil still unrent before our eyes."

V.

A sudden shutting-off of the waves left Carter in a chilling and awesome silence full of the spirit of desolation. On every hand pressed the illimitable vastness of the void; yet the seeker knew that the Being was still there. After a moment he thought of words whose mental substance he flung into the abyss: "I accept. I will not retreat."

The waves surged forth again, and Carter knew that the Being had heard. And now there poured from that limitless Mind a flood of knowledge and explanation which opened new vistas to the seeker, and prepared him for such a grasp of the cosmos as he had never hoped to possess. He was told how childish and limited is the notion of a tri-dimensional world, and what an infinity of directions there are besides the known directions of up-down, forward-backward, right-left. He was shown the smallness and tinsel emptiness of the little Earth gods, with their petty, human interests and connections — their hatreds, rages, loves and vanities; their craving for praise and sacrifice, and their demands for faiths contrary to reason and nature.

While most of the impressions translated themselves to Carter as words there were others to which other senses gave interpretation. Perhaps with eyes and perhaps with imagination he perceived that he was in a region of dimensions beyond those conceivable to the eye and brain of man. He saw now, in the brooding shadows of that which had been first a vortex of power and then an illimitable void, a sweep of creation that dizzied his senses. From some inconceivable vantagepoint he looked upon prodigious forms whose multiple extensions transcended any conception of being, size and boundaries which his mind had hitherto been able to hold, despite a lifetime of cryptical study. He began to understand dimly why there could exist at the same time the little boy Randolph Carter in the Arkham farm-house in 1883, the misty form on the vaguely hexagonal pillar beyond the First Gate, the fragment now facing the Presence in the limitless abyss, and all the other Carters his fancy or perception envisaged.

Then the waves increased in strength and sought to improve his understanding, reconciling him to the multiform entity of which his present fragment was an infinitesimal part. They told him that every figure of space is but the result of the intersection by a plane of some corresponding figure of one more dimension — as a square is cut from a cube, or a circle from a sphere. The cube and sphere, of three dimensions, are thus cut from corresponding forms of four dimensions, which men know only through guesses and dreams; and these in turn are cut from forms of five dimensions, and so on up to the dizzy and reachless heights of archetypal infinity. The world of men and of the gods of men is merely an infinitesimal phase of an infinitesimal thing — the three-dimensional phase of that small wholeness reached by the First Gate, where 'Umr at-Tawil dictates dreams to the Ancient Ones. Though men hail it as reality, and brand thoughts of its many-dimensioned original as unreality, it is in truth the very opposite. That which we call substance and reality is shadow and illusion, and that which we call shadow and illusion is substance and reality.

Time, the waves went on, is motionless, and without beginning or end. That it has motion and is the cause of change is an illusion. Indeed, it is itself really an illusion, for except to the narrow sight of beings in limited dimensions there are no such things as past, present and future. Men think of time only because of what they call change, yet that too is illusion. All that was, and is, and is to be, exists simultaneously.

These revelations came with a god like solemnity which left Carter unable to doubt. Even though they lay almost beyond his comprehension, he felt that they must be true in the light of that final cosmic reality which belies all local perspectives and narrow partial views; and he was familiar enough with profound speculations to be free from the bondage of local and partial conceptions. Had his whole quest not been based upon a faith in the unreality of the local and partial?

After an impressive pause the waves continued, saying that what the denizens of few-dimensioned zones call change is merely a function of their consciousness, which views the external world from various cosmic angles. As the shapes produced by the cutting of a cone seem to vary with the angles of cutting — being circle, ellipse, parabola or hyperbola according to that angle, yet without any change in the cone itself — so do the local aspects of an unchanged and endless reality seem to change with the cosmic angle of regarding. To this variety of angles of consciousness the feeble beings of the inner worlds are slaves, since with rare exceptions they can not learn to control them. Only a few students of forbidden things have gained inklings of this control, and have thereby conquered time and change. But the entities outside the Gates command all angles, and view the myriad parts of the cosmos in terms of fragmentary change-involving perspective, or of the changeless totality beyond perspective, in accordance with their will.

As the waves paused again, Carter began to comprehend, vaguely and terrifiedly, the ultimate background of that riddle of lost individuality which had at first so horrified him. His intuition pieced together the fragments of revelation, and brought him closer and closer to a grasp of the secret. He understood that much of the frightful revelation would have come upon him — splitting up his ego amongst myriads of earthly counterparts inside the First Gate, had not the magic of 'Umr at-Tawil kept it from him in order that he might use the silver key with precision for the Ultimate Gate's opening. Anxious for clearer knowledge, he sent out waves of thought, asking more of the exact relationship between his various facets — the fragment now beyond the Ultimate Gate, the fragment still on the quasi-hexagonal pedestal beyond the First Gate, the boy of 1883, the man of 1928, the various ancestral beings who had formed his heritage and the bulwark of his ego, amid the nameless denizens of the other eons and other worlds which that first hideous flash of ultimate perception had identified with him. Slowly the waves of the Being surged out in reply, trying to make plain what was almost beyond the reach of an earthly mind.

All descended lines of beings of the finite dimensions, continued the waves, and all stages of growth in each one of these beings, are merely manifestations of one archetypal and eternal being in the space outside dimensions. Each local being — son, father, grandfather, and so on — and each stage of individual being — infant, child, boy, man — is merely one of the infinite phases of that same archetypal and eternal being, caused by a variation in the angle of the consciousness-plane which cuts it. Randolph Carter at all ages; Randolph Carter and all his ancestors, both human and pre-human, terrestrial and pre-terrestrial; all these were only phases of one ultimate, eternal "Carter" outside space and time — phantom projections differentiated only by the angle at which the plane of consciousness happened to cut the eternal archetype in each case.

A slight change of angle could turn the student of today into the child of yesterday; could turn Randolph Carter into that wizard, Edmund Carter who fled from Salem to the hills behind Arkham in 1692, or that Pickman Carter who in the year 2169 would use strange means in repelling the Mongol hordes from Australia; could turn a human Carter into one of those earlier entities which had dwelt in primal Hyperborea and worshipped black, plastic Tsathoggua after flying down from Kythamil, the double planet that once revolved around Arcturus; could turn a terrestrial Carter to a remotely ancestral and doubtfully shaped dweller on Kythamil itself, or a still remoter creature of trans-galactic Stronti, or a four-dimensioned gaseous consciousness in an older space-time continuum, or a vegetable brain of the future on a dark, radioactive comet of inconceivable orbit — so on, in endless cosmic cycle.

The archetype, throbbed the waves, are the people of the Ultimate Abyss — formless, ineffable, and guessed at only by rare dreamers on the low-dimensioned worlds. Chief among such was this informing Being itself . . . which indeed was Carter's own archetype. The zeal of Carter and all his forebears for forbidden cosmic secrets was a natural result of derivation from the Supreme Archetype. On every world all great wizards, all great thinkers, all great artists, are facets of It.

Almost stunned with awe, and with a kind of terrifying delight, Randolph Carter's consciousness did homage to that transcendent Entity from which it was derived. As the waves paused again he pondered in the mighty silence, thinking of strange tributes, stranger questions, and still stranger requests. Curious concepts flowed conflictingly through a brain dazed with unaccustomed vistas and unforeseen disclosures. It occurred to him that, if these disclosures were literally true, he might bodily visit all those infinitely distant ages and parts of the universe which he had hitherto known only in dreams, could he but command the magic to change the angle of his consciousness-plane. And did not the silver key supply that magic? Had it not first changed him from a man in 1928 to a boy in 1883, and then to something quite outside time? Oddly, despite his present apparent absence of body; he knew that the key was still with him.

While the silence still lasted, Randolph Carter radiated forth the thoughts and questions which assailed him. He knew that in this ultimate abyss he was equidistant from every facet of his archetype — human or non-human, terrestrial or extra-terrestrial, galactic or trans-galactic; and his curiosity regarding the other phases of his being — especially those phases which were farthest from an earthly 1928 in time and space, or which had most persistently haunted his dreams throughout life — was at fever heat. He felt that his archetypal Entity could at will send him bodily to any of these phases of bygone and distant life by changing his consciousness-plane and despite the marvels he had undergone he burned for the further marvel of walking in the flesh through those grotesque and incredible scenes which visions of the night had fragmentarily brought him.

Without definite intention he was asking the Presence for access to a dim, fantastic world whose five multi-coloured suns, alien constellations, dizzily black crags, clawed, tapir-snouted denizens, bizarre metal towers, unexplained tunnels, and cryptical floating cylinders had intruded again and again upon his slumbers. That world, he felt vaguely, was in all the conceivable cosmos the one most freely in touch with others; and he longed to explore the vistas whose beginnings he had glimpsed, and to embark through space to those still remoter worlds with which the clawed, snouted denizens trafficked. There was no time for fear. As at all crises of his strange life, sheer cosmic curiosity triumphed over everything else.

When the waves resumed their awesome pulsing, Carter knew that his terrible request was granted. The Being was telling him of the nighted gulfs through which he would have to pass, of the unknown quintuple star in an unsuspected galaxy around which the alien world revolved, and of the burrowing inner horrors against which the clawed, snouted race of that world perpetually fought. It told him, too, of how the angle of his personal consciousness-plane, and the angle of his consciousness-plane regarding the space-time elements of the sought-for world, would have to be tilted simultaneously in order to restore to that world the Carter-facet which had dwelt there.

The Presence wanted him to be sure of his symbols if he wished ever to return from the remote and alien world he had chosen, and he radiated back an impatient affirmation; confident that the silver key, which he felt was with him and which he knew had tilted both world and personal planes in throwing him back to 1883, contained those symbols which were meant. And now the Being, grasping his impatience, signified its readiness to accomplish the monstrous precipitation. The waves abruptly ceased, and there supervened a momentary stillness tense with nameless and dreadful expectancy.

Then, without warning, came a whirring and drumming that swelled to a terrific thundering. Once again Carter felt himself the focal point of an intense concentration of energy which smote and hammered and seared unbearably in the now-familiar rhythm of outer space, and which he could not classify as either the blasting heat of a blazing star, or the all-petrifying cold of the ultimate abyss. Bands and rays of colour utterly foreign to any spectrum of our universe played and wove and interlaced before him, and he was conscious of a frightful velocity of motion. He caught one fleeting glimpse of a figure sitting alone upon a cloudy throne more hexagonal than otherwise . . . .

VI.

As the Hindoo paused in his story he saw that de Marigny and Phillips were watching him absorbedly. Aspinwall pretended to ignore the narrative and kept his eyes ostentatiously on the papers before him. The alien-rhythmed ticking of the coffin-shaped clock took on a new and portentous meaning, while the fumes from the choked, neglected tripods wove themselves into fantastic and inexplicable shapes, and formed disturbing combinations with the grotesque figures of the draft-swayed tapestries. The old Negro who had tended them was gone—perhaps some growing tension had frightened him out of the house. An almost apologetic hesitancy hampered the speaker as he resumed in his oddly labored yet idiomatic voice.

"You have found these things of the abyss hard to believe," he said, "but you will find the tangible and material things ahead still harder. That is the way of our minds. Marvels are doubly incredible when brought into three dimensions from the vague regions of possible dream. I shall not try to tell you much— that would be another and very different story. I will tell only what you absolutely have to know."

Carter, after that final vortex of alien and polychromatic rhythm, had found himself in what for a moment he thought was his old insistent dream. He was, as many a night before, walking amidst throngs of clawed, snouted beings through the streets of a labyrinth of inexplicably fashioned metal under a palate of diverse solar colour; and as he looked down he saw that his body was like those of the others—rugose, partly squamous, and curiously articulated in a fashion mainly insect-like yet not without a caricaturish resemblance to the human outline. The silver key was still in his grasp, though held by a noxious-looking claw.

In another moment the dream-sense vanished, and he felt rather as one just awakened from a dream. The ultimate abyss— the Being— the entity of an absurd, outlandish race called Randolph Carter on a world of the future not yet born—some of these things were parts of the persistent recurrent dreams of the wizard Zkauba on the planet Yaddith. They were too persistent—they interfered with his duties in weaving spells to keep the frightful Dholes in their burrows, and became mixed up with his recollections of the myriad real worlds he had visited in light-beam envelopes. And now they had become quasi-real as never before. This heavy, material silver key in his right upper claw, exact image of one he had dreamt about meant no good. He must rest and reflect, and consult the tablets of Nhing for advice on what to do. Climbing a metal wall in a lane off the main concourse, he entered his apartment and approached the rack of tablets.

Seven day-fractions later Zkauba squatted on his prism in awe and half despair, for the truth had opened up a new and conflicting set of memories. Nevermore could he know the peace of being one entity. For all time and space he was two: Zkauba the wizard of Yaddith, disgusted with the thought of the repellent earth-mammal Carter that he was to be and had been, and Randolph Carter, of Boston on the Earth, shivering with fright at the clawed, mantel thing which he had once been, and had become again.

The time units spent on Yaddith, croaked the Swami—whose laboured voice was beginning to show signs of fatigue—made a tale in themselves which could not be related in brief compass. There were trips to Stronti and Mthura and Kath, and other worlds in the twenty-eight galaxies accessible to the light-beam envelopes of the creatures of Yaddith, and trips back and forth through eons of time with the aid of the silver key and various other symbols known to Yaddith's wizards. There were hideous struggles with the bleached viscous Dholes in the primal tunnels that honeycombed the planet. There were awed sessions in libraries amongst the massed lore of ten thousand worlds living and dead. There were tense conferences with other minds of Yaddith, including that of the Arch-Ancient Buo. Zkauba told no one of what had befallen his personality, but when the Randolph Carter facet was uppermost he would study furiously every possible means of returning to the Earth and to human form, and would desperately practice human speech with the alien throat-organs so ill adapted to it.

The Carter-facet had soon learned with horror that the silver key was unable to effect his return to human form. It was, as he deduced too late from things he remembered, things he dreamed, and things he inferred from the lore of Yaddith, a product of Hyperborea on Earth; with power over the personal consciousness-angles of human beings alone. It could, however, change the planetary angle and send the user at will through time in an unchanged body. There had been an added spell which gave it limitless powers it otherwise lacked; but this, too, was a human discovery—peculiar to a spatially unreachable region, and not to be duplicated by the wizards of Yaddith. It had been written on the undecipherable parchment in the hideously carven box with the silver key, and Carter bitterly lamented that he had left it behind. The now inaccessible Being of the abyss had warned him to be sure of his symbols, and had doubtless thought he lacked nothing.

As time wore on he strove harder and harder to utilize the monstrous lore of Yaddith in finding a way back to the abyss and the omnipotent Entity. With his new knowledge be could have done much toward reading the cryptic parchment; but that power, under present conditions, was merely ironic. There were times, however, when the Zkauba-facet was uppermost and when he strove to erase the conflicting Carter-memories which troubled him.

Thus long spaces of time wore on — ages longer than the brain of man could grasp, since the beings of Yaddith die only after prolonged cycles. After many hundreds of revolutions the Carter-facet seemed to gain on the Zkauba-facet, and would spend vast periods calculating the distance of Yaddith in space and time from the human Earth that was to be. The figures were staggering eons of light-years beyond counting but the immemorial lore of Yaddith fitted Carter to grasp such things. He cultivated the power of dreaming himself momentarily Earthward, and learned many things about our planet that he had never known before. But he could not dream the needed formula on the missing parchment.

Then at last he conceived a wild plan of escape from Yaddith — which began when be found a drug that would keep his Zkauba-facet always dormant, yet with out dissolution of the knowledge and memories of Zkauba. He thought that his calculations would let him perform a voyage with a light-wave envelope such as no being of Yaddith had ever performed — a bodily voyage through nameless eons and across incredible galactic reaches to the solar system and the Earth itself.

Once on Earth, though in the body of a clawed, snouted thing, he might be able somehow to find and finish deciphering, the strangely hieroglyphed parchment he had left in the car at Arkham; and with its aid — and the key's — resume his normal terrestrial semblance.

He was not blind to the perils of the attempt. He knew that when he had brought the planet-angle to the right eon (a thing impossible to do while hurtling through space), Yaddith would be a dead world dominated by triumphant Dholes, and that his escape in the light-wave envelope would be a matter of grave doubt. Likewise was he aware of how he must achieve suspended animation, in the manner of an adept, to endure the eon long flight through fathomless abysses. He knew, too, that — assuming his voyage succeeded — he must immunize himself to the bacterial and other earthly conditions hostile to a body from Yaddith. Furthermore, he must provide a way of feigning human shape on Earth until he might recover and decipher the parchment and resume that shape in truth. Otherwise he would probably be discovered and destroyed by the people in horror as a thing that should not be. And there must be some gold — luckily obtainable on Yaddith — to tide him over that period of quest.

Slowly Carter's plans went forward. He prepared a light-wave envelope of abnormal toughness, able to stand both the prodigious time-transition and the unexampled flight through space. He tested all his calculations, and sent forth his Earthward dreams again and again, bringing them as close as possible to 1928. He practiced suspended animation with marvelous success. He discovered just the bacterial agent he needed, and worked out the varying gravity-stresses to which he must become used. He artfully fashioned a waxen mask and loose costume enabling him to pass among men as a human being of a sort, and devised a doubly potent spell with which to hold back the Dholes at the moment of his starting from the dead, black Yaddith of the inconceivable future. He took care, too, to assemble a large supply of the drugs — unobtainable on Earth — which would keep his Zkauba-facet in abeyance till he might shed the Yaddith body, nor did he neglect a small store of gold for earthly use.

The starting-day was a time of doubt and apprehension. Carter climbed up to his envelope-platform, on the pretext of sailing for the triple star Nython, and crawled into the sheath of shining metal. He had just room to perform the ritual of the silver key, and as he did so he slowly started the levitation of his envelope. There was an appalling seething and darkening of the day, and hideous racking of pain. The cosmos seemed to reel irresponsibly, and the other constellations danced in a black sky.

All at once Carter felt a new equilibrium. The cold of interstellar gulfs gnawed at the outside of his envelope, and he could see that he floated free in space — the metal building from which he had started having decayed years before. Below him the ground was festering with gigantic Dholes; and even as he looked, one reared up several hundred feet and leveled a bleached, viscous end at him. But his spells were effective, and in another moment he was falling away from Yaddith, unharmed.

VII.

In that bizarre room in New Orleans, from which the old black servant had instinctively fled, the odd voice of Swami Chandraputra grew hoarser still.

"Gentlemen," he continued, "I will not ask you to believe these things until I have shown you special proof. Accept it, then, as a myth, when I tell you of the thousands of light-years — thousands of years of time, and uncounted billions of miles that Randolph Carter hurtled through space as a nameless, alien entity in a thin envelope of electron-activated metal. He timed his period of suspended animation with utmost care, planning to have it end only a few years before the time of landing on the Earth in or near 1928.

"He will never forget that awakening. Remember, gentlemen, that before that eon long sleep he had lived consciously for thousands of terrestrial years amidst the alien and horrible wonders of Yaddith. There was a hideous gnawing of cold, a cessation of menacing dreams, and a glance through the eye-plates of the envelope. Stars, clusters, nebulae, on every hand — and at last their outline bore some kinship to the constellations of Earth that he knew.

"Some day his descent into the solar system may be told. He saw Kynath and Yuggoth on the rim, passed close to Neptune and glimpsed the hellish white fungi that spot it, learned an untellable secret from the close glimpsed mists of Jupiter, and saw the horror on one of the satellites, and gazed at the cyclopean ruins that sprawl over Mars' ruddy disc. When the Earth drew near he saw it as a thin crescent which swelled alarmingly in size. He slackened speed, though his sensations of homecoming made him wish to lose not a moment. I will not try to tell you of these sensations as I learned them from Carter.

"Well, toward the last Carter hovered about in the Earth's upper air waiting till daylight came over the Western Hemisphere. He wanted to land where he had left—near the Snake Den in the hills behind Arkham. If any of you have been away from home long—and I know one of you has—I leave it to you how the sight of New England's rolling hills and great elms and gnarled orchards and ancient stone walls must have affected him.

"He came down at dawn in the lower meadow of the old Carter place, and was thankful for the silence and solitude. It was autumn, as when he had left, and the smell of the hills was balm to his soul. He managed to drag the metal envelope up the slope of the timber lot into the Snake Den, though it would not go through the weed-choked fissure to the inner cave. It was there also that he covered his alien body with the human clothing and waxen mask which would be necessary. He kept the envelope here for over a year, till certain circumstances made a new hiding-place necessary.

"He walked to Arkham—incidentally practicing the management of his body in human posture and against terrestrial gravity—and had his gold changed to money at a bank. He also made some inquiries—posing as a foreigner ignorant of much English—and found that the year was 1930, only two years after the goal he had aimed at.

"Of course, his position was horrible. Unable to assert his identity, forced to live on guard every moment, with certain difficulties regarding food, and with a need to conserve the alien drug which kept his Zkauba-facet dormant, he felt that he must act as quickly as possible. Going to Boston and taking a room in the decaying West End, where he could live cheaply and inconspicuously, he at once established inquiries concerning Randolph Carter's estate and effects. It was then that he learned how anxious Mr. Aspinwall, here, was to have the estate divided, and how valiantly Mr. de Marigny and Mr. Phillips strove to keep it intact."

The Hindoo bowed, though no expression crossed his dark, tranquil, and thickly bearded face.

"Indirectly," he continued, "Carter secured a good copy of the missing parchment and began working on its deciphering. I am glad to say that I was able to help in all this—for he appealed to me quite early, and through me came in touch with other mystics throughout the world. I went to live with him in Boston—a wretched place in Chambers Street. As for the parchment—I am pleased to help Mr. de Marigny in his perplexity. To him let me say that the language of those hieroglyphics is not Naacal, but R'lyehian, which was brought to Earth by the spawn of Cthulhu countless ages ago. It is, of course, a translation—there was a Hyperborean original millions of years earlier in the primal tongue of Tsath-yo.

"There was more to decipher than Carter had looked for, but at no time did he give up hope. Early this year he made great strides through a book he imported from Nepal, and there is no question but that he will win before long. Unfortunately, however, one handicap has developed—the exhaustion of the alien drug which keeps the Zkauba-facet dormant. This is not, however, as great a calamity as was feared. Carter's personality is gaining in the body, and when Zkauba comes upper most—for shorter and shorter periods, and now only when evoked by some unusual excitement—he is generally too dazed to undo any of Carter's work. He can not find the metal envelope that would take him back to Yaddith, for although he almost did, once, Carter hid it anew at a time when the Zkanba-facet was wholly latent. All the harm he has done is to frighten a few people and create certain nightmare rumors among the Poles and Lithuanians of Boston's West End. So far, he had never injured the careful disguise prepared by the Carter-facet, though he sometimes throws it off so that parts have to be replaced. I have seen what lies beneath—and it is not good to see.

"A month ago Carter saw the advertisement of this meeting, and knew that he must act quickly to save his estate. He could not wait to decipher the parchment and resume his human form. Consequently he deputed me to act for him.

"Gentlemen, I say to you that Randolph Carter is not dead; that he is temporarily in an anomalous condition, but that within two or three months at the outside he will be able to appear in proper form and demand the custody of his estate. I am prepared to offer proof if necessary. Therefore I beg that you will adjourn this meeting for an indefinite period."

VIII.

De Marigny and Phillips stared at the Hindoo as if hypnotized, while Aspinwall emitted a series of snorts and bellows. The old attorney's disgust had by now surged into open rage and he pounded the table with an apoplectically veined fist. When he spoke, it was in a kind of bark.

"How long is this foolery to be borne? I've listened an hour to this madman—this faker—and now he has the damned effrontery to say Randolph Carter is alive—to ask us to postpone the settlement for no good reason! Why don't you throw the scoundrel out, de Marigny? Do you mean to make us all the butts of a charlatan or idiot?"

De Marigny quietly raised his hand and spoke softly.

"Let us think slowly and dearly. This has been a very singular tale, and there are things in it which I, as a mystic not altogether ignorant, recognize as far from impossible. Furthermore—since 1930 I have received letters from the Swami which tally with his account."

As he paused, old Mr. Phillips ventured a word.

"Swami Chandraputra spoke of proofs. I, too, recognize much that is significant in this story, and I have myself had many oddly corroborative letters from the Swami during the last two years; but some of these statements are very extreme. Is there not something tangible which can be shown?"

At last the impassive-faced Swami replied, slowly and hoarsely, and drawing an object from the pocket of his loose coat as he spoke.

"While none of you here has ever seen the silver key itself, Messrs. de Marigny and Phillips have seen photographs of it. Does this look familiar to you?"

He fumblingly laid on the table, with his large, white-mittened hand, a heavy key of tarnished silver — nearly five inches long, of unknown and utterly exotic workmanship, and covered from end to end with hieroglyphs of the most bizarre description. De Marigny and Phillips gasped.

"That's it!" cried de Marigny. "The camera doesn't lie. I couldn't be mistaken!"

But Aspinwall had already launched a reply.

"Fools! What does it prove? If that's really the key that belonged to my cousin, it's up to this foreigner — this damned nigger — to explain how he got it! Randolph Carter vanished with the key four years ago. How do we know he wasn't robbed and murdered? He was half crazy himself, and in touch with still crazier people.

"Look here, you nigger — where did you get that key? Did you kill Randolph Carter?"

The Swami's features, abnormally placid, did not change; but the remote, irisless black eyes behind them blazed dangerously. He spoke with great difficulty.

"Please control yourself, Mr. Aspinwall. There is another form of poof that I could give, but its effect upon everybody would not be pleasant. Let us be reasonable. Here are some papers obviously written since 1930, and in the unmistakable style of Randolph Carter."

He clumsily drew a long envelope from inside his loose coat and handed it to the sputtering attorney as de Marigny and Phillips watched with chaotic thoughts and a dawning feeling of supernal wonder.

"Of course the handwriting is almost illegible — but remember that Randolph Carter now has no hands well adapted to forming human script."

Aspinwall looked through the papers hurriedly, and was visibly perplexed, but he did not change his demeanor. The room was tense with excitement and nameless dread and the alien rhythm of the coffin-shaped clock had an utterly diabolic sound to de Marigny and Phillips, though the lawyer seemed affected not at all.

Aspinwall spoke again. "These look like clever forgeries. If they aren't, they may mean that Randolph Carter has been brought under the control of people with no good purpose. There's only one thing to do — have this faker arrested. De Marigny, will you telephone for the police?"

"Let us wait," answered their host. "I do not think this case calls for the police. I have a certain idea. Mr. Aspinwall, this gentleman is a mystic of real attainments. He says he is in the confidence of Randolph Carter. Will it satisfy you if he can answer certain questions which could be answered only by one in such confidence? I know Carter, and can ask such questions. Let me get a book which I think will make a good test."

He turned toward the door to the library, Phillips dazedly following in a kind of automatic way. Aspinwall remained where he was, studying closely the Hindoo who confronted him with abnormally impassive face. Suddenly, as Chandraputra clumsily restored the silver key to his pocket the lawyer emitted a guttural shout.

"Hey, by Heaven I've got it! This rascal is in disguise. I don't believe he's an East Indian at all. That face — it isn't a face, but a mask! I guess his story put that into my head, but it's true. It never moves, and that turban and beard hide the edges. This fellow's a common crook! He isn't even a foreigner — I've been watching his language. He's a Yankee of some sort. And look at those mittens — he knows his fingerprints could be spotted. Damn you, I'll pull that thing off — "

"Stop!" The hoarse, oddly alien voice of the Swami held a tone beyond all mere earthly fright. "I told you there was another form of proof which I could give if necessary, and I warned you not to provoke me to it. This red-faced old meddler is right; I'm not really an East Indian. This face is a mask, and what it covers is not human. You others have guessed — I felt that minutes ago. It wouldn't be pleasant if I took that mask off — let it alone. Ernest, I may as well tell you that I am Randolph Carter."

No one moved. Aspinwall snorted and made vague motions. De Marigny and Phillips, across the room, watched the workings of the red face and studied the back of the turbaned figure that confronted him. The clock's abnormal ticking was hideous and the tripod fumes and swaying arras danced a dance of death. The half-choking lawyer broke the silence.

"No you don't, you crook — you can't scare me! You've reasons of your own for not wanting that mask off. Maybe we'd know who you are. Off with it — "

As he reached forward, the Swami seized his hand with one of his own clumsily mittened members, evoking a curious cry of mixed pain and surprise. De Marigny started toward the two, but paused confused as the pseudo-Hindoo's shout of protest changed to a wholly inexplicable rattling and buzzing sound. Aspinwall's red face was furious, and with his free hand he made another lunge at his opponent's bushy beard. This time he succeeded in getting a hold, and at his frantic tug the whole waxen visage came loose from the turban and clung to the lawyer's apoplectic fist.

As it did so, Aspinwall uttered a frightful gurgling cry, and Phillips and de Maigny saw his face convulsed with a wilder, deep and more hideous epilepsy of stark panic than ever they had seen on human countenance before. The pseudo-Swami had meanwhile released his other hand and was standing as if dazed, making buzzing noises of a most abnormal quality. Then the turbaned figure slumped oddly into a posture scarcely human, and began a curious, fascinated sort of shuffle toward the coffin-shaped clock that ticked out its cosmic and abnormal rhythm. His now uncovered face was turned away, and de Marigny and Phillips could not see what the lawyer's act had disclosed. Then their attention was turned to Aspinwall, who was sinking ponderously to the floor. The spell was broken-but when they reached the old man he was dead.

Turning quickly to the shuffling Swami's receding back, de Marigny saw one of the great white mittens drop listlessly off a dangling arm. The fumes of the olibanum were thick, and all that could be glimpsed of the revealed hand was something long and black . . . Before the Creole could reach the retreating figure, old Mr. Phillips laid a hand on his shoulder.

"Don't!" he whispered, "We don't know what we're up against. That other facet, you know — Zkauba, the wizard of Yaddith . . ."

The turbaned figure had now reached the abnormal clock, and the watchers saw though the dense fumes a blurred black claw fumbling with the tall, hieroglyphed door. The fumbling made a queer, clicking sound. Then the figure entered the coffin-shaped case and pulled the door shut after it.

De Marigny could no longer be restrained, but when he reached and opened the clock it was empty. The abnormal ticking went on, beating out the dark, cosmic rhythm which underlies all mystical gate-openings. On the floor the great white mitten, and the dead man with a bearded mask clutched in his hand, had nothing further to reveal.

A year passed, and nothing has been heard of Randolph Carter. His estate is still unsettled. The Boston address from which one "Swami Chandraputra" sent inquiries to various mystics in 1930-1932 was indeed tenanted by a strange Hindoo, but he left shortly before the date of the New Orleans conference and has never been seen since. He was said to be dark, expressionless, and bearded, and his landlord thinks the swarthy mask — which was duly exhibited — looked very much like him. He was never, however, suspected of any connection with the nightmare apparitions whispered of by local Slavs. The hills behind Arkham were searched for the "metal envelope," but nothing of the sort was ever found. However, a clerk in Arkham's First National Bank does recall a queer turbaned man who cashed an odd bit of gold bullion in October, 1930.

De Marigny and Phillips scarcely know what to make of the business. After all, what was proved?

There was a story. There was a key which might have been forged from one of the pictures Carter had freely distributed in 1928. There were papers — all indecisive. There was a masked stranger, but who now living saw behind the mask? Amidst the strain and the olibanum fumes that act of vanishing in the clock might easily have been a dual hallucination. Hindoos know much of hypnotism. Reason proclaims the "Swami" a criminal with designs on Randolph Carter's estate. But the autopsy said that Aspinwall had died of shock. Was it rage alone which caused it? And some things in that story . . . .

In a vast room hung with strangely figured arras and filled with olibanum fumes, Étienne Laurent de Marigny often sits listening with vague sensations to the abnormal rhythm of that hieroglyphed, coffin-shaped clock.

Out of the Aeons.

BY HAZEL HEALD
AND H.P. LOVECRAFT

10,000-WORD NOVELETTE;
1933.

Of the five Hazel Heald ghostwritings Lovecraft performed, "Out of the Aeons" is the finest, and holds up well against some of the best of Lovecraft's by-lined work.

One of the more interesting aspects of this story is how long it takes the museum officials to realize what's really going on. At a certain point, one has to wonder if, in truth, they've already guessed, and are so eager for the scientific knowledge that might be gleaned that they are hiding behind a wall of willful ignorance — and that we are about to vicariously "experience" in close first-person perspective the perpetration of one of the most evil acts one human being can perform on another.

That is probably all that can be said without spoiling the story.

This story was written in mid-1933, right around the same time Lovecraft was writing "The Thing on the Doorstep," and published in the April 1935 issue of Weird Tales.

(Manuscript found among the effects of the late Richard H. Johnson, Ph.D., curator of the Cabot Museum of Archaeology, Boston, Mass.)

I.

It is not likely that anyone in Boston — or any alert reader elsewhere — will ever forget the strange affair of the Cabot Museum. The newspaper publicity given to that hellish mummy, the antique and terrible rumours vaguely linked with it, the morbid wave of interest and cult activities during 1932, and the frightful fate of the two intruders on December 1st of that year, all combined to form one of those classic mysteries which go down for generations as folklore and become the nuclei of whole cycles of horrific speculation.

Everyone seems to realise, too, that something very vital and unutterably hideous was suppressed in the public accounts of the culminant horrors. Those first disquieting hints as to the condition of one of the two bodies were dismissed and ignored too abruptly — nor were the singular modifications in the mummy given the following-up which their news value would normally prompt. It also struck people as queer that the mummy was never restored to its case. In these days of expert taxidermy the excuse that its disintegrating condition made exhibition impracticable seemed a peculiarly lame one.

As curator of the museum I am in a position to reveal all the suppressed facts, but this I shall not do during my lifetime. There are things about the world and universe which it is better for the majority not to know, and I have not departed from the opinion in which all of us — museum staff, physicians, reporters, and police — concurred at the period of the horror itself. At the same time it seems proper that a matter of such overwhelming scientific and historic importance should not remain wholly unrecorded — hence this account which I have prepared for the benefit of serious students. I shall place it among various papers to be examined after my death, leaving its fate to the discretion of my executors. Certain threats and unusual events during the past weeks have led me to believe that my life — as well as that of other museum officials — is in some peril through the enmity of several widespread secret cults of Asiatics, Polynesians, and heterogeneous mystical devotees; hence it is possible that the work of the executors may not be long postponed.

(Executor's note: Dr. Johnson died suddenly and rather mysteriously of heart-failure on April 22, 1933. Wentworth Moore, taxidermist of the museum, disappeared around the middle of the preceding month. On February 18 of the same year Dr. William Minot, who superintended a dissection connected with the case, was stabbed in the back, dying the following day.)

The real beginning of the horror, I suppose, was in 1879 — long before my term as curator — when the museum acquired that ghastly, inexplicable mummy from the Orient Shipping Company. Its very discovery was monstrous and menacing, for it came from a crypt of unknown origin and fabulous antiquity on a bit of land suddenly upheaved from the Pacific's floor.

On May 11, 1878, Capt. Charles Weatherbee of the freighter Eridanus, bound from Wellington, New Zealand, to Valparaiso, Chile, had sighted a new island unmarked on any chart and evidently of volcanic origin. It projected quite boldly out of the sea in the form of a truncated cone. A landing-party under Capt. Weatherbee noted evidences of long submersion on the rugged slopes which they climbed, while at the summit there were signs of recent destruction, as by an earthquake. Among the scattered rubble were massive stones of manifestly artificial shaping, and a little examination disclosed the presence of some of that prehistoric Cyclopean masonry found on certain

Pacific islands and forming a perpetual archaeological puzzle.

Finally the sailors entered a massive stone crypt—judged to have been part of a much larger edifice, and to have originally lain far underground—in one corner of which the frightful mummy crouched. After a short period of virtual panic, caused partly by certain carvings on the walls, the men were induced to move the mummy to the ship, though it was only with fear and loathing that they touched it. Close to the body, as if once thrust into its clothes, was a cylinder of an unknown metal containing a roll of thin, bluish-white membrane of equally unknown nature, inscribed with peculiar characters in a greyish, indeterminable pigment. In the centre of the vast stone floor was a suggestion of a trap-door, but the party lacked apparatus sufficiently powerful to move it.

The Cabot Museum, then newly established, saw the meagre reports of the discovery and at once took steps to acquire the mummy and the cylinder. Curator Pickman made a personal trip to Valparaiso and outfitted a schooner to search for the crypt where the thing had been found, though meeting with failure in this matter. At the recorded position of the island nothing but the sea's unbroken expanse could be discerned, and the seekers realised that the same seismic forces which had suddenly thrust the island up had carried it down again to the watery darkness where it had brooded for untold aeons. The secret of that immovable trap-door would never be solved. The mummy and the cylinder, however, remained—and the former was placed on exhibition early in November, 1879, in the museum's hall of mummies.

The Cabot Museum of Archaeology, which specialises in such remnants of ancient and unknown civilisations as do not fall within the domain of art, is a small and scarcely famous institution, though one of high standing in scientific circles. It stands in the heart of Boston's exclusive Beacon Hill district—in Mt. Vernon Street, near Joy—housed in a former private mansion with an added wing in the rear, and was a source of pride to its austere neighbours until the recent terrible events brought it an undesirable notoriety. The hall of mummies on the western side of the original mansion (which was designed by Bulfinch and erected in 1819), on the second floor, is justly esteemed by historians and anthropologists as harbouring the greatest collection of its kind in America. Here may be found typical examples of Egyptian embalming from the earliest Sakkarah specimens to the last Coptic attempts of the eighth century; mummies of other cultures, including the prehistoric Indian specimens recently found in the Aleutian Islands; agonised Pompeian figures moulded in plaster from tragic hollows in the ruin-choking ashes; naturally mummified bodies from mines and other excavations in all parts of the earth—some surprised by their terrible entombment in the grotesque postures caused by their last, tearing death-throes—everything, in short, which any collection of the sort could well be expected to contain. In 1879, of course, it was much less ample than it is now; yet even then it was remarkable.

But that shocking thing from the primal Cyclopean crypt on an ephemeral sea-spawned island was always its chief attraction and most impenetrable mystery.

The mummy was that of a medium-sized man of unknown race, and was cast in a peculiar crouching posture. The face, half shielded by claw-like hands, had its under jaw thrust far forward, while the shrivelled features bore an expression of fright so hideous that few spectators could view them unmoved. The eyes were closed, with lids clamped down tightly over eyeballs apparently bulging and prominent. Bits of hair and beard remained, and the colour of the whole was a sort of dull neutral grey. In texture the thing was half leathery and half stony, forming an insoluble enigma to those experts who sought to ascertain how it was embalmed. In places bits of its substance were eaten away by time and decay. Rags of some peculiar fabric, with suggestions of unknown designs, still clung to the object.

Just what made it so infinitely horrible and repulsive one could hardly say. For one thing, there was a subtle, indefinable sense of limitless antiquity and utter alienage which affected one like a view from the brink of a monstrous abyss of unplumbed blackness—but mostly it was the expression of crazed fear on the puckered, prognathous, half-shielded face. Such a symbol of infinite, inhuman, cosmic fright could not help communicating the emotion to the beholder amidst a disquieting cloud of mystery and vain conjecture.

Among the discriminating few who frequented the Cabot Museum this relic of an elder, forgotten world soon acquired an unholy fame, though the institution's seclusion and quiet policy prevented it from becoming a popular sensation of the "Cardiff Giant" sort. In the last century the art of vulgar ballyhoo had not invaded the field of scholarship to the extent it has now succeeded in doing. Naturally, savants of various kinds tried their best to classify the frightful object, though always without success. Theories of a bygone Pacific civilisation, of which the Easter Island images and the megalithic masonry of Ponape and Nan-Matol are conceivable vestiges, were freely circulated among students, and learned journals carried varied and often conflicting speculations on a possible former continent whose peaks survive as the myriad islands of Melanesia and Polynesia. The diversity in dates assigned to the hypothetical vanished culture—or continent—was at once bewildering and amusing; yet some surprisingly relevant allusions were found in certain myths of Tahiti and other islands.

Meanwhile the strange cylinder and its baffling scroll of unknown hieroglyphs, carefully preserved in the museum library, received their due share of attention. No question could exist as to their association with the mummy; hence all realised that in the unravelling of their mystery the mystery of the shrivelled horror would in all probability be unravelled as well. The cylinder, about four inches long by seven-eighths of an inch in diameter, was of a queerly iridescent metal utterly defying chemical analysis and seemingly impervious to all reagents. It was tightly fitted with a cap of the same substance, and bore engraved figurings of an evidently decorative and possibly symbolic nature—conventional designs which seemed to follow

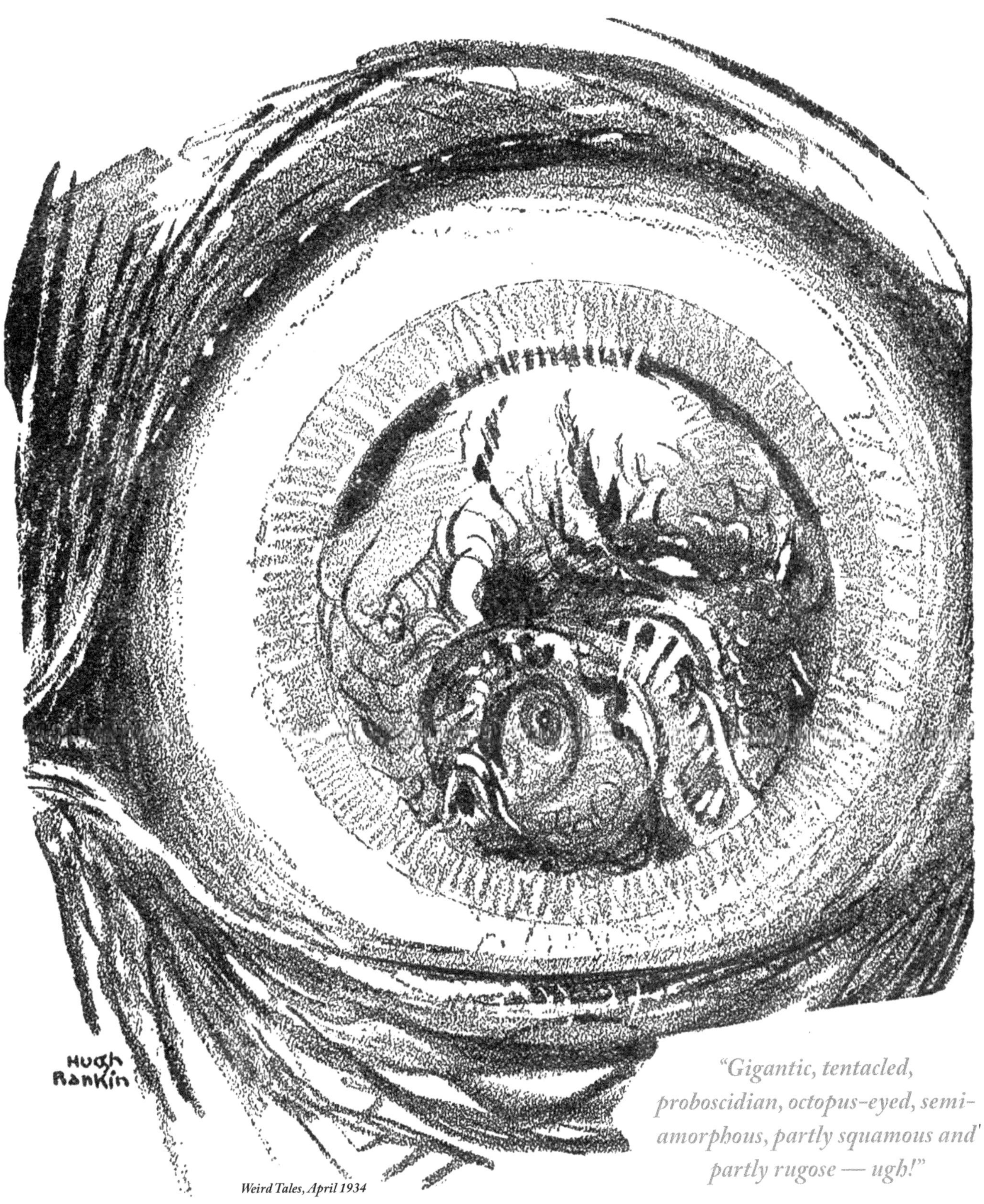

"Gigantic, tentacled, proboscidian, octopus-eyed, semi-amorphous, partly squamous and partly rugose — ugh!"

Weird Tales, April 1934

a peculiarly alien, paradoxical, and doubtfully describable system of geometry.

Not less mysterious was the scroll it contained — a neat roll of some thin, bluish-white, unanalysable membrane, coiled round a slim rod of metal like that of the cylinder, and unwinding to a length of some two feet. The large, bold hieroglyphs, extending in a narrow line down the centre of the scroll and penned or painted with a grey pigment defying analysts, resembled nothing known to linguists and palaeographers, and could not be deciphered despite the transmission of photographic copies to every living expert in the given field.

It is true that a few scholars, unusually versed in the

literature of occultism and magic, found vague resemblances between some of the hieroglyphs and certain primal symbols described or cited in two or three very ancient, obscure, and esoteric texts such as the *Book of Eibon*, reputed to descend from forgotten Hyperborea; the Pnakotic Fragments, alleged to be pre-human; and the monstrous and forbidden *Necronomicon* of the mad Arab Abdul Alhazred. None of these *resemblances*, however, was beyond dispute; and because of the prevailing low estimation of occult studies, no effort was made to circulate copies of the hieroglyphs among mystical specialists. Had such circulation occurred at this early date, the later history of the case might have been very different; indeed, a glance at the hieroglyphs by any reader of von Junzt's horrible *Nameless Cults* would have established a linkage of unmistakable significance. At this period, however, the readers of that monstrous blasphemy were exceedingly few; copies having been incredibly scarce in the interval between the suppression of the original Dusseldorf edition (1839) and of the Bridewell translation (1845) and the publication of the expurgated reprint by the Golden Goblin Press in 1909. Practically speaking, no occultist or student of the primal past's esoteric lore had his attention called to the strange scroll until the recent outburst of sensational journalism which precipitated the horrible climax.

II.

Thus matters glided along for a half-century following the installation of the frightful mummy at the museum. The gruesome object had a local celebrity among cultivated Bostonians, but no more than that; while the very existence of the cylinder and scroll — after a decade of futile research — was virtually forgotten. So quiet and conservative was the Cabot Museum that no reporter or feature writer ever thought of invading its uneventful precincts for rabble-tickling material.

The invasion of ballyhoo commenced in the spring of 1931, when a purchase of somewhat spectacular nature — that of the strange objects and inexplicably preserved bodies found in crypts beneath the almost vanished and evilly famous ruins of Chateau Faussesflammes, in Averoigne, France — brought the museum prominently into the news columns. True to its "hustling" policy, the *Boston Pillar* sent a Sunday feature writer to cover the incident and pad it with an exaggerated general account of the institution itself; and this young man — Stuart Reynolds by name — hit upon the nameless mummy as a potential sensation far surpassing the recent acquisitions nominally forming his chief assignment. A smattering of theosophical lore, and a fondness for the speculations of such writers as Colonel Churchward and Lewis Spence concerning lost continents and primal forgotten civilisations, made Reynolds especially alert toward any aeonian relic like the unknown mummy.

At the museum the reporter made himself a nuisance through constant and not always intelligent questionings and endless demands for the movement of encased objects to permit photographs from unusual angles. In the basement library room he pored endlessly over the strange metal cylinder and its membraneous scroll, photographing them from every angle and securing pictures of every bit of the weird hieroglyphed text. He likewise asked to see all books with any bearing whatever on the subject of primal cultures and sunken continents — sitting for three hours taking notes, and leaving only in order to hasten to Cambridge for a sight (if permission were granted) of the abhorred and forbidden *Necronomicon* at the Widener Library.

On April 5th the article appeared in the Sunday Pillar, smothered in photographs of mummy, cylinder, and hieroglyphed scroll, and couched in the peculiarly simpering, infantile style which the *Pillar* affects for the benefit of its vast and mentally immature clientele. Full of inaccuracies, exaggerations, and sensationalism, it was precisely the sort of thing to stir the brainless and fickle interest of the herd — and as a result the once-quiet museum began to be swarmed with chattering and vacuously staring throngs such as its stately corridors had never known before.

There were scholarly and intelligent visitors, too, despite the puerility of the article — the pictures had spoken for themselves — and many persons of mature attainments sometimes see the Pillar by accident. I recall one very strange character who appeared during November — a dark, turbaned, and bushily bearded man with a laboured, unnatural voice, curiously expressionless face, clumsy hands covered with absurd white mittens, who gave a squalid West End address and called himself "Swami Chandraputra." This fellow was unbelievably erudite in occult lore and seemed profoundly and solemnly moved by the resemblance of the hieroglyphs on the scroll to certain signs and symbols of a forgotten elder world about which he professed vast intuitive knowledge.

By June, the fame of the mummy and scroll had leaked far beyond Boston, and the museum had inquiries and requests for photographs from occultists and students of arcana all over the world. This was not altogether pleasing to our staff, since we are a scientific institution without sympathy for fantastic dreamers; yet we answered all questions with civility. One result of these catechisms was a highly learned article in *The Occult Review* by the famous New Orleans mystic Étienne-Laurent de Marigny, in which was asserted the complete identity of some of the odd geometrical designs on the iridescent cylinder, and of several of the hieroglyphs on the membranous scroll, with certain ideographs of horrible significance (transcribed from primal monoliths or from the secret rituals of hidden bands of esoteric students and devotees) reproduced in the hellish and suppressed *Black Book* or *Nameless Cults* of von Junzt.

De Marigny recalled the frightful death of von Junzt in 1840, a year after the publication of his terrible volume at Düsseldorf, and commented on his blood-curdling and partly suspected sources of information. Above all, he emphasised the enormous relevance of the tales with which von Junzt linked most of the monstrous ideographs he had reproduced. That these tales, in which a cylinder and scroll were expressly mentioned, held a remarkable suggestion of relationship to the things at the museum, no one could deny; yet they were of such breath-taking extravagance — involving such unbelievable sweeps of time and such fantastic anomalies of a forgotten elder world — that one could much more easily admire than believe them.

Admire them the public certainly did, for copying in the press was universal. Illustrated articles sprang up everywhere, telling or purporting to tell the legends in the *Black Book*, expatiating on the horror of the mummy, comparing the cylinder's designs and the scroll's hieroglyphs with the figures reproduced by von Junzt, and indulging in the wildest, most sensational, and most irrational theories and speculations. Attendance at the museum was trebled, and the widespread nature of the interest was attested by the plethora of mail on the subject — most of it inane and superfluous — received at the museum. Apparently the mummy and its origin formed — for imaginative people — a close rival to the Depression as chief topic of 1931 and 1932. For my own part, the principal effect of the *furore* was to make me read von Junzt's monstrous volume in the Golden Goblin edition — a perusal which left me dizzy and nauseated, yet thankful that I had not seen the utter infamy of the unexpurgated text.

III.

The archaic whispers reflected in the *Black Book*, and linked with designs and symbols so closely akin to what the mysterious scroll and cylinder bore, were indeed of a character to hold one spellbound and not a little awestruck. Leaping an incredible gulf of time — behind all the civilisations, races, and lands we know — they clustered round a vanished nation and a vanished continent of the misty, fabulous dawn-years . . . that to which legend has given the name of Mu, and which old tablets in the primal Naacal tongue speak of as flourishing 200,000 years ago, when Europe harboured only hybrid entities, and lost Hyperborea knew the nameless worship of black amorphous Tsathoggua.

There was mention of a kingdom or province called K'naa in a very ancient land where the first human people had found monstrous ruins left by those who had dwelt there before — vague waves of unknown entities which had filtered down from the stars and lived out their aeons on a forgotten, nascent world. K'naa was a sacred place, since from its midst the bleak basalt cliffs of Mount Yaddith-Gho soared starkly into the sky, topped by a gigantic fortress of Cyclopean stone, infinitely older than mankind and built by the alien spawn of the dark planet Yuggoth, which had colonised the earth before the birth of terrestrial life.

The spawn of Yuggoth had perished aeons before, but had left behind them one monstrous and terrible living thing which could never die — their hellish god or patron daemon Ghatanothoa, which glowered and brooded eternally though unseen in the crypts beneath that fortress on Yaddith-Gho. No human creature had ever climbed Yaddith-Gho or seen that blasphemous fortress except as a distant and geometrically abnormal outline against the sky; yet most agreed that Ghatanothoa was still there, wallowing and burrowing in unsuspected abysses beneath the megalithic walls. There were always those who believed that sacrifices must be made to Ghatanothoa, lest it crawl out of its hidden abysses and waddle horribly through the world of men as it had once waddled through the primal world of the Yuggoth-spawn.

People said that if no victims were offered, Ghatanothoa would ooze up to the light of day and lumber down the basalt cliffs of Yaddith-Gho bringing doom to all it might encounter. For no living thing could behold Ghatanothoa, or even a perfect graven image of Ghatanothoa, however small, without suffering a change more horrible than death itself. Sight of the god, or its image, as all the legends of the Yuggoth-spawn agreed, meant paralysis and petrifaction of a singularly shocking sort, in which the victim was turned to stone and leather on the outside, while the brain within remained perpetually alive — horribly fixed and prisoned through the ages, and maddeningly conscious of the passage of interminable epochs of helpless inaction till chance and time might complete the decay of the petrified shell and leave it exposed to die. Most brains, of course, would go mad long before this aeon-deferred release could arrive. No human eyes, it was said, had ever glimpsed Ghatanothoa, though the danger was as great now as it had been for the Yuggoth-spawn.

And so there was a cult in K'naa which worshipped Ghatanothoa and each year sacrificed to it twelve young warriors and twelve young maidens. These victims were offered up on flaming altars in the marble temple near the mountain's base, for none dared climb Yaddith-Gho's basalt cliffs or draw near to the Cyclopean pre-human stronghold on its crest. Vast was the power of the priests of Ghatanothoa, since upon them alone depended the preservation of K'naa and of all the land of Mu from the petrifying emergence of Ghatanothoa out of its unknown burrows.

There were in the land a hundred priests of the Dark God, under Imash-Mo the High-Priest, who walked before King Thabon at the Nath-feast, and stood proudly whilst the King knelt at the Dhoric shrine. Each priest had a marble house, a chest of gold, two hundred slaves, and a hundred concubines, besides immunity from civil law and the power of life and death over all in K'naa save the priests of the King. Yet in spite of these defenders there was ever a fear in the land lest Ghatanothoa slither up from the depths and lurch viciously down the mountain to bring horror and petrification to mankind. In the latter years the priests forbade men even to guess or imagine what its frightful aspect might be.

It was in the Year of the Red Moon (estimated as B.C. 173,148 by von Junzt) that a human being first dared to breathe defiance against Ghatanothoa and its nameless menace. This bold heretic was T'yog, High-Priest of Shub-Niggurath and guardian of the copper temple of the Goat with a Thousand Young. T'yog had thought long on the powers of the various gods, and had had strange dreams and revelations touching the life of this and earlier worlds. In the end he felt sure that the gods friendly to man could be arrayed against the hostile gods, and believed that Shub-Niggurath, Nug, and Yeb, as well as Yig the Serpent-god, were ready to take sides with man against the tyranny and presumption of Ghatanothoa.

Inspired by the Mother Goddess, T'yog wrote down a strange formula in the hieratic Naacal of his order, which he believed would keep the possessor immune from the Dark God's petrifying power. With this protection, he reflected, it might be possible for a bold man to climb the dreaded basalt cliffs and — first of all human beings — enter the Cyclopean fortress beneath which Ghatanothoa reputedly brooded. Face to face with the god, and with the power of Shub-Niggurath and her sons on his side, T'yog believed that he might be able to bring it to terms and at last deliver mankind from its brooding menace. With humanity freed through his efforts, there would be no limits to the honours he might claim. All the honours of the priests of Ghatanothoa would perforce be transferred to him; and even kingship or godhood might conceivably be within his reach.

So T'yog wrote his protective formula on a scroll of pthagon membrane (according to von Junzt, the inner skin of the extinct ya-kith lizard) and enclosed it in a carven cylinder of lagh metal — the metal brought by the Elder Ones from Yuggoth, and found in no mine of earth. This charm, carried in his robe, would make him proof against the menace of Ghatanothoa — it would even restore the Dark God's petrified victims if that monstrous entity should ever emerge and begin its devastations. Thus he proposed to go up the shunned and man-untrodden mountain, invade the alien-angled citadel of Cyclopean stone, and confront the shocking devil-entity in its lair. Of what would follow, he could not even guess; but the hope of being mankind's saviour lent strength to his will.

He had, however, reckoned without the jealousy and self-interest of Ghatanothoa's pampered priests. No sooner did they hear of his plan than — fearful for their prestige and privilege in case the Daemon-God should be dethroned — they set up a frantic clamour against the so-called sacrilege, crying that no man might prevail against Ghatanothoa, and that any effort to seek it out would merely provoke it to a hellish onslaught against mankind which no spell or priestcraft could hope to avert. With those cries they hoped to turn the public mind against T'yog; yet such was the people's yearning for freedom from Ghatanothoa, and such their confidence in the skill and zeal of T'yog, that all the protestations came to naught. Even the King, usually a puppet of the priests, refused to forbid T'yog's daring pilgrimage.

It was then that the priests of Ghatanothoa did by stealth what they could not do openly. One night Imash-Mo, the High-Priest, stole to T'yog in his temple chamber and took from his sleeping form the metal cylinder; silently drawing out the potent scroll and putting in its place another scroll of great similitude, yet varied enough to have no power against any god or daemon. When the cylinder was slipped back into the sleeper's cloak Imash-Mo was content, for he knew T'yog was little likely to study that cylinder's contents again. Thinking himself protected by the true scroll, the heretic would march up the forbidden mountain and into the Evil Presence — and Ghatanothoa, unchecked by any magic, would take care of the rest.

It would no longer be needful for Ghatanothoa's priests to preach against the defiance. Let T'yog go his way and meet his doom. And secretly, the priests would always cherish the stolen scroll — the true and potent charm — handing it down from one High-Priest to another for use in any dim future when it might be needful to contravene the Devil-God's will. So the rest of the night Imash-Mo slept in great peace, with the true scroll in a new cylinder fashioned for its harbourage.

It was dawn on the Day of the Sky-Flames (nomenclature undefined by von Junzt) that T'yog, amidst the prayers and chanting of the people and with King Thabon's blessing on his head, started up the dreaded mountain with a staff of tlath-wood in his right hand. Within his robe was the cylinder holding what he thought to be the true charm — for he had indeed failed to find out the imposture. Nor did he see any irony in the prayers which Imash-Mo and the other priests of Ghatanothoa intoned for his safety and success.

All that morning the people stood and watched as T'yog's dwindling form struggled up the shunned basalt slope hitherto alien to men's footsteps, and many stayed watching long after he had vanished where a perilous ledge led round to the mountain's hidden side. That night a few sensitive dreamers thought they heard a faint tremor convulsing the hated peak; though most ridiculed them for the statement. Next day vast crowds watched the mountain and prayed, and wondered how soon T'yog would return. And so the next day, and the next. For weeks they hoped and waited, and then they wept. Nor did anyone ever see T'yog, who would have saved mankind from fears, again.

Thereafter men shuddered at T'yog's presumption, and tried not to think of the punishment his impiety had met. And the priests of Ghatanothoa smiled to those who might resent the god's will or challenge its right to the sacrifices. In later years the ruse of Imash-Mo became known to the people; yet the knowledge availed not to change the general feeling that Ghatanothoa were better left alone. None ever dared to defy it again.

And so the ages rolled on, and King succeeded King, and High-Priest succeeded High-Priest, and nations rose and decayed, and lands rose above the sea and returned into the sea. And with many millennia decay fell upon K'naa — till at last on a hideous day of storm and thunder, terrific rumbling, and mountain-high waves, all the land of Mu sank into the sea forever.

Yet down the later aeons thin streams of ancient secrets trickled. In distant lands there met together grey-faced fugitives who had survived the sea-fiend's rage, and strange skies drank the smoke of altars reared to vanished gods and daemons. Though none knew to what bottomless deep the sacred peak and Cyclopean fortress of dreaded Ghatanothoa had sunk, there were still those who mumbled its name and offered to it nameless sacrifices lest it bubble up through leagues of ocean and shamble among men spreading horror and petrifaction.

Around the scattered priests grew the rudiments of a dark and secret cult — secret because the people of the new lands had other gods and devils, and thought only evil of elder and alien ones — and within that cult many hideous things were done, and many strange objects cherished. It was whispered that a certain line of elusive priests still harboured the true charm against Ghatanothoa which Imash-Mo stole from the sleeping T'yog; though none remained who could read or understand the cryptic syllables, or who could even guess in what part of the world the lost K'naa, the dreaded peak of Yaddith-Gho, and the titan fortress of the Devil-God had lain.

Though it flourished chiefly in those Pacific regions around which Mu itself had once stretched, there were rumours of the hidden and detested cult of Ghatanothoa in ill-fated Atlantis, and on the abhorred plateau of Leng. Von Junzt implied its presence in the fabled subterrene kingdom of K'n-yan, and gave clear evidence that it had penetrated Egypt, Chaldaea, Persia, China, the forgotten Semite empires of Africa, and Mexico and Peru in the New World. That it had a strong connexion with the witchcraft movement in Europe, against which the bulls of popes were vainly directed, he more than strongly hinted. The West, however, was never favourable to its growth; and public indignation — aroused by glimpses of hideous rites and nameless sacrifices — wholly stamped out many of its branches. In the end it became a hunted, doubly furtive underground affair — yet never could its nucleus be quite exterminated. It always survived somehow, chiefly in the Far East and on the Pacific Islands, where its teachings became merged into the esoteric lore of the Polynesian Areoi.

Von Junzt gave subtle and disquieting hints of actual contact with the cult; so that as I read I shuddered at what was rumoured about his death. He spoke of the growth of certain ideas regarding the appearance of the Devil-God — a creature which no human being (unless it were the too-daring T'yog, who had never returned) had ever seen — and contrasted this habit of speculation with the taboo prevailing in ancient Mu against any attempt to imagine what the horror looked like. There was a peculiar fearfulness about the devotees' awed and fascinated whispers on this subject — whispers heavy with morbid curiosity concerning the precise nature of what T'yog might have confronted in that frightful pre-human edifice on the dreaded and now-sunken mountains before the end (if it was an end) finally came — and I felt oddly disturbed by the German scholar's oblique and insidious references to this topic.

Scarcely less disturbing were von Junzt's conjectures on the whereabouts of the stolen scroll of cantrips against Ghatanothoa, and on the ultimate uses to which this scroll might be put. Despite all my assurance that the whole matter was purely mythical, I could not help shivering at the notion of a latter-day emergence of the monstrous god, and at the picture of a humanity turned suddenly to a race of abnormal statues, each encasing a living brain doomed to inert and helpless consciousness for untold aeons of futurity. The old Dusseldorf savant had a poisonous way of suggesting more than he stated, and I could understand why his damnable book was suppressed in so many countries as blasphemous, dangerous, and unclean.

I writhed with repulsion, yet the thing exerted an unholy fascination; and I could not lay it down till I had finished it. The alleged reproductions of designs and ideographs from Mu were marvellously and startlingly like the markings on the strange cylinder and the characters on the scroll, and the whole account teemed with details having vague, irritating suggestions of resemblance to things connected with the hideous mummy. The cylinder and scroll — the Pacific setting — the persistent notion of old Capt. Weatherbee that the Cyclopean crypt where the mummy was found had once lain under a vast building . . . somehow I was vaguely glad that the volcanic island had sunk before that massive suggestion of a trapdoor could be opened.

IV.

What I read in the *Black Book* formed a fiendishly apt preparation for the news items and closer events which began to force themselves upon me in the spring of 1932. I can scarcely recall just when the increasingly frequent reports of police action against the odd and fantastical religious cults in the Orient and elsewhere commenced to impress me; but by May or June I realised that there was, all over the world, a surprising and unwonted burst of activity on the part of bizarre, furtive, and esoteric mystical organisations ordinarily quiescent and seldom heard from.

It is not likely that I would have connected these reports with either the hints of von Junzt or the popular *furore* over the mummy and cylinder in the museum, but for certain significant syllables and persistent resemblances — sensationally dwelt upon by the press — in the rites and speeches of the various secret celebrants brought to public attention. As it was, I could not help remarking with disquiet the frequent recurrence of a name — in various corrupt forms — which seemed to constitute a focal point of all the cult worship, and which was obviously regarded with a singular mixture of reverence and terror. Some of the forms quoted were G'tanta, Tanotah, Than-Tha, Gatan, and Ktan-Tah — and it did not require the suggestions of my now numerous occultist correspondents to make me see in these variants a hideous and suggestive kinship to the monstrous name rendered by von Junzt as Ghatanothoa.

There were other disquieting features, too. Again and again the reports cited vague, awestruck references to a "true scroll"—something on which tremendous consequences seemed to hinge, and which was mentioned as being in the custody of a certain "Nagob," whoever and whatever he might be. Likewise, there was an insistent repetition of a name which sounded like Tog, Tiok, Yog, Zob, or Yob, and which my more and more excited consciousness involuntarily linked with the name of the hapless heretic T'yog as given in the *Black Book*. This name was usually uttered in connexion with such cryptical phrases as "It is none other than he," "He had looked upon its face," "He knows all, though he can neither see nor feel," "He has brought the memory down through the aeons," "The true scroll will release him," "Nagob has the true scroll," "He can tell where to find it."

Something very queer was undoubtedly in the air, and I did not wonder when my occultist correspondents, as well as the sensational Sunday papers, began to connect the new abnormal stirrings with the legends of Mu on the one hand, and with the frightful mummy's recent exploitation on the other hand. The widespread articles in the first wave of press publicity, with their insistent linkage of the mummy, cylinder, and scroll with the tale in the *Black Book*, and their crazily fantastic speculations about the whole matter, might very well have roused the latent fanaticism in hundreds of those furtive groups of exotic devotees with which our complex world abounds. Nor did the papers cease adding fuel to the flames—for the stories on the cult-stirrings were even wilder than the earlier series of yarns.

As the summer drew on, attendants noticed a curious new element among the throngs of visitors which—after a lull following the first burst of publicity—were again drawn to the museum by the second *furore*. More and more frequently there were persons of strange and exotic aspect—swarthy Asiatics, long-haired nondescripts, and bearded brown men who seemed unused to European clothes—who would invariably inquire for the hall of mummies and would subsequently be found staring at the hideous Pacific specimen in a veritable ecstasy of fascination. Some quiet, sinister undercurrent in this flood of eccentric foreigners seemed to impress all the guards, and I myself was far from undisturbed. I could not help thinking of the prevailing cult-stirrings among just such exotics as these—and the connexion of those stirrings with myths all too close to the frightful mummy and its cylinder scroll.

At times I was half tempted to withdraw the mummy from exhibition—especially when an attendant told me that he had several times glimpsed strangers making odd obeisances before it, and had overheard singsong mutterings which sounded like chants or rituals addressed to it at hours when the visiting throngs were somewhat thinned. One of the guards acquired a queer nervous hallucination about the petrified horror in the lone glass case, alleging that he could see from day to day certain vague, subtle, and infinitely slight changes in the frantic flexion of the bony claws, and in the fear-crazed expression of the leathery face. He could not get rid of the loathsome idea that those horrible, bulging eyes were about to pop suddenly open.

It was early in September, when the curious crowds had lessened and the hall of mummies was sometimes vacant, that the attempt to get at the mummy by cutting the glass of its case was made. The culprit, a swarthy Polynesian, was spied in time by a guard, and was overpowered before any damage occurred. Upon investigation the fellow turned out to be a Hawaiian notorious for his activity in certain underground religious cults, and having a considerable police record in connexion with abnormal and inhuman rites and sacrifices. Some of the papers found in his room were highly puzzling and disturbing, including many sheets covered with hieroglyphs closely resembling those on the scroll at the museum and in the *Black Book* of von Junzt; but regarding these things he could not be prevailed upon to speak.

Scarcely a week after this incident, another attempt to get at the mummy—this time by tampering with the lock of his case—resulted in a second arrest. The offender, a Cingalese, had as long and unsavoury a record of loathsome cult activities as the Hawaiian had possessed, and displayed a kindred unwillingness to talk to the police. What made this case doubly and darkly interesting was that a guard had noticed this man several times before, and had heard him addressing to the mummy a peculiar chant containing unmistakable repetitions of the word "T'yog." As a result of this affair I doubled the guards in the hall of mummies, and ordered them never to leave the now notorious specimen out of sight, even for a moment.

As may well be imagined, the press made much of these two incidents, reviewing its talk of primal and fabulous Mu, and claiming boldly that the hideous mummy was none other than the daring heretic T'yog, petrified by something he had seen in the pre-human citadel he had invaded, and preserved intact through 175,000 years of our planet's turbulent history. That the strange devotees represented cults descended from Mu, and that they were worshipping the mummy—or perhaps even seeking to awaken it to life by spells and incantations—was emphasised and reiterated in the most sensational fashion.

Writers exploited the insistence of the old legends that the brain of Ghatanothoa's petrified victims remained conscious and unaffected—a point which served as a basis for the wildest and most improbable speculations. The mention of a "true scroll" also received due attention—it being the prevailing popular theory that T'yog's stolen charm against Ghatanothoa was somewhere in existence, and that cult-members were trying to bring it into contact with T'yog himself for some purpose of their own.

One result of this exploitation was that a third wave of gaping visitors began flooding the museum and staring at the hellish mummy which served as a nucleus for the whole strange and disturbing affair.

It was among this wave of spectators—many of whom made repeated visits—that talk of the mummy's vaguely changing aspect first began to be widespread. I suppose—despite the disturbing notion of the nervous guard some months before—that the museum's personnel was too well used to the constant sight of odd shapes to pay close attention to details; in any case, it was the excited whispers of visitors which at length aroused the guards to the subtle mutation which was apparently in progress. Almost simultaneously the press got hold of it—with blatant results which can well be imagined.

Naturally, I gave the matter my most careful observation, and by the middle of October decided that a definite disintegration of the mummy was under way. Through some chemical or physical influence in the air, the half-stony, half-leathery fibres seemed to be gradually relaxing, causing distinct variations in the angles of the limbs and in certain details of the fear-twisted facial expression. After a half-century of perfect preservation this was a highly disconcerting development, and I had the museum's taxidermist, Dr. Moore, go carefully over the gruesome object several times. He reported a general relaxation and softening, and gave the thing two or three astringent sprayings, but did not dare to attempt anything drastic lest there be a sudden crumbling and accelerated decay.

The effect of all this upon the gaping crowds was curious. Heretofore each new sensation sprung by the press had brought fresh waves of staring and whispering visitors, but now—though the papers blathered endlessly about the mummy's changes—the public seemed to have acquired a definite sense of fear which outranked even its morbid curiosity. People seemed to feel that a sinister aura hovered over the museum, and from a high peak the attendance fell to a level distinctly below normal. This lessened attendance gave added prominence to the stream of freakish foreigners who continued to infest the place, and whose numbers seemed in no way diminished.

On November 18th a Peruvian of Indian blood suffered a strange hysterical or epileptic seizure in front of the mummy, afterward shrieking from his hospital cot, "It tried to open its eyes!—T'yog tried to open his eyes and stare at me!"

I was by this time on the point of removing the object from exhibition, but permitted myself to be overruled at a meeting of our very conservative directors. However, I could see that the museum was beginning to acquire an unholy reputation in its austere and quiet neighbourhood. After this incident I gave instructions that no one be allowed to pause before the monstrous Pacific relic for more than a few minutes at a time.

It was on November 24th, after the museum's five o'clock closing, that one of the guards noticed a minute opening of the mummy's eyes. The phenomenon was very slight—nothing but a thin crescent of cornea being visible in either eye—but it was none the less of the highest interest. Dr. Moore, having been summoned hastily, was about to study the exposed bits of eyeball with a magnifier when his handling of the mummy caused the leathery lids to fall tightly shut again. All gentle efforts to open them failed, and the taxidermist did not dare to apply drastic measures. When he notified me of all this by telephone I felt a sense of mounting dread hard to reconcile with the apparently simple event concerned. For a moment I could share the popular impression that some evil, amorphous blight from unplumbed deeps of time and space hung murkily and menacingly over the museum.

Two nights later a sullen Filipino was trying to secrete himself in the museum at closing time. Arrested and taken to the station, he refused even to give his name, and was detained as a suspicious person. Meanwhile the strict surveillance of the mummy seemed to discourage the odd hordes of foreigners from haunting it. At least, the number of exotic visitors distinctly fell off after the enforcement of the "move along" order.

It was during the early morning hours of Thursday, December 1st, that a terrible climax developed. At about one o'clock horrible screams of mortal fright and agony were heard issuing from the museum, and a series of frantic telephone calls from neighbours brought to the scene quickly and simultaneously a squad of police and several museum officials, including myself. Some of the policemen surrounded the building while others, with the officials, cautiously entered. In the main corridor we found the night watchman strangled to death—a bit of East Indian hemp still knotted around his neck—and realised that despite all precautions some darkly evil intruder or intruders had gained access to the place. Now, however, a tomblike silence enfolded everything and we almost feared to advance upstairs to the fateful wing where we knew the core of the trouble must lurk. We felt a bit more steadied after flooding the building with light from the central switches in the corridor, and finally crept reluctantly up the curving staircase and through a lofty archway to the hall of mummies.

V.

It is from this point onward that reports of the hideous case have been censored—for we have all agreed that no good can be accomplished by a public knowledge of those terrestrial conditions implied by the further developments. I have said that we flooded the whole building with light before our ascent. Now beneath the beams that beat down on the glistening cases and their gruesome contents, we saw outspread a mute horror whose baffling details testified to happenings utterly beyond our comprehension. There were two intruders—who we afterward agreed must have hidden in the building before closing time—but they would never be executed for the watchman's murder. They had already paid the penalty.

One was a Burmese and the other a Fiji-Islander—both known to the police for their share in frightful and repulsive cult activities. They were dead, and the more we examined them the more utterly monstrous and unnamable we felt their manner of death to be. On both faces was a more wholly frantic and inhuman look of fright than even the oldest policeman had ever seen before; yet in the state of the two bodies there were vast and significant differences.

The Burmese lay collapsed close to the nameless mummy's case, from which a square of glass had been neatly cut. In his right hand was a scroll of bluish membrane which I at once saw was covered with greyish hieroglyphs — almost a duplicate of the scroll in the strange cylinder in the library downstairs, though later study brought out subtle differences. There was no mark of violence on the body, and in view of the desperate, agonised expression on the twisted face we could only conclude that the man died of sheer fright.

It was the closely adjacent Fijian, though, that gave us the profoundest shock. One of the policemen was the first to feel of him, and the cry of fright he emitted added another shudder to that neighbourhood's night of terror. We ought to have known from the lethal greyness of the once-black, fear-twisted face, and of the bony hands — one of which still clutched an electric torch — that something was hideously wrong; yet every one of us was unprepared for what that officer's hesitant touch disclosed. Even now I can think of it only with a paroxysm of dread and repulsion. To be brief — the hapless invader, who less than an hour before had been a sturdy living Melanesian bent on unknown evils, was now a rigid, ash-grey figure of stony, leathery petrification, in every respect identical with the crouching, aeon-old blasphemy in the violated glass case.

Yet that was not the worst. Crowning all other horrors, and indeed seizing our shocked attention before we turned to the bodies on the floor, was the state of the frightful mummy. No longer could its changes be called vague and subtle, for it had now made radical shifts of posture. It had sagged and slumped with a curious loss of rigidity; its bony claws had sunk until they no longer even partly covered its leathery, fearcrazed face; and — God help us! — its hellish bulging eyes had popped wide open, and seemed to be staring directly at the two intruders who had died of fright or worse.

That ghastly, dead-fish stare was hideously mesmerising, and it haunted us all the time we were examining the bodies of the invaders. Its effect on our nerves was damnably queer, for we somehow felt a curious rigidity creeping over us and hampering our simplest motions — a rigidity which later vanished very oddly when we passed the hieroglyphed scroll around for inspection. Every now and then I felt my gaze drawn irresistibly toward those horrible bulging eyes in the case, and when I returned to study them after viewing the bodies I thought I detected something very singular about the glassy surface of the dark and marvellously well-preserved pupils. The more I looked, the more fascinated I became; and at last I went down to the office — despite that strange stiffness in my limbs — and brought up a strong multiple magnifying glass. With this I commenced a very close and careful survey of the fishy pupils, while the others crowded expectantly around.

I had always been rather sceptical of the theory that scenes and objects become photographed on the retina of the eye in cases of death or coma; yet no sooner did I look through the lens than I realised the presence of some sort of image other than the room's reflection in the glassy, bulging optics of this nameless spawn of the aeons. Certainly, there was a dimly outlined scene on the age-old retinal surface, and I could not doubt that it formed the last thing on which those eyes had looked in life — countless millennia ago. It seemed to be steadily fading, and I fumbled with the magnifier in order to shift another lens into place. Yet it must have been accurate and clear-cut; even if infinitesimally small, when — in response to some evil spell or act connected with their visit — it had confronted those intruders who were frightened to death. With the extra lens I could make out many details formerly invisible, and the awed group around me hung on the flood of words with which I tried to tell what I saw.

For here, in the year 1932, a man in the city of Boston was looking on something which belonged to an unknown and utterly alien world — a world that vanished from existence and normal memory aeons ago. There was a vast room — a chamber of Cyclopean masonry — and I seemed to be viewing it from one of its corners. On the walls were carvings so hideous that even in this imperfect image their stark blasphemousness and bestiality sickened me. I could not believe that the carvers of these things were human, or that they had ever seen human beings when they shaped the frightful outlines which leered at the beholder. In the centre of the chamber was a colossal trap-door of stone, pushed upward to permit the emergence of some object from below. The object should have been clearly visible — indeed, must have been when the eyes first opened before the fear-stricken intruders — though under my lenses it was merely a monstrous blur.

As it happened, I was studying the right eye only when I brought the extra magnification into play. A moment later I wished fervently that my search had ended there. As it was, however, the zeal of discovery and revelation was upon me, and I shifted my powerful lenses to the mummy's left eye in the hope of finding the image less faded on that retina. My hands, trembling with excitement and unnaturally stiff from some obscure influence, were slow in bringing the magnifier into focus, but a moment later I realised that the image was less faded than in the other eye. I saw in a morbid flash of half-distinctness the insufferable thing which was welling up through the prodigious trap-door in that Cyclopean, immemorially archaic crypt of a lost world — and fell fainting with an inarticulate shriek of which I am not even ashamed.

By the time I revived there was no distinct image of anything in either eye of the monstrous mummy. Sergeant Keefe of the police looked with my glass, for I could not bring myself to face that abnormal entity again. And I thanked all the powers of the cosmos that I had not looked earlier than I did. It took all my resolution, and a great deal of solicitation, to make me relate what I had glimpsed in the hideous moment of revelation. Indeed, I could not speak till we had all adjourned to the office below, out of sight of that daemoniac thing which could not be. For I had begun to harbour the most terrible and fantastic notions about the mummy and its glassy, bulging eyes — that it had a kind of hellish consciousness, seeing all that occurred before it and trying vainly to communicate some frightful message from the gulfs of time. That meant madness — but at last I thought I might be better off if I told what I had half seen.

After all, it was not a long thing to tell. Oozing and surging up out of that yawning trap-door in the Cyclopean crypt I had glimpsed such an unbelievable behemothic monstrosity that I could not doubt the power of its original to kill with its mere sight. Even now I cannot begin to suggest it with any words at my command. I might call it gigantic — tentacled — proboscidian — octopus-eyed — semi-amorphous — plastic — partly squamous and partly rugose — ugh! But nothing I could say could even adumbrate the loathsome, unholy, non-human, extra-galactic horror and hatefulness and unutterable evil of that forbidden spawn of black chaos and illimitable night. As I write these words the associated mental image causes me to lean back faint and nauseated. As I told of the sight to the men around me in the office, I had to fight to preserve the consciousness I had regained.

Nor were my hearers much less moved. Not a man spoke above a whisper for a full quarter-hour, and there were awed, half-furtive references to the frightful lore in the *Black Book*, to the recent newspaper tales of cult-stirrings, and to the sinister events in the museum. Ghatanothoa . . . Even its smallest perfect image could petrify — T'yog — the false scroll — he never came back — the true scroll which could fully or partly undo the petrification — did it survive? — the hellish cults — the phrases overheard — "It is none other than he" — "He had looked upon its face" — "He knows all, though he can neither see nor feel" — "He had brought the memory down through the aeons" — "The true scroll will release him" — "Nagob has the true scroll" — "He can tell where to find it."

Only the healing greyness of the dawn brought us back to sanity; a sanity which made of that glimpse of mine a closed topic — something not to be explained or thought of again.

We gave out only partial reports to the press, and later on cooperated with the papers in making other suppressions. For example, when the autopsy shewed the brain and several other internal organs of the petrified Fijian to be fresh and unpetrified, though hermetically sealed by the petrification of the exterior flesh — an anomaly about which physicians are still guardedly and bewilderedly debating — we did not wish a *furore* to be started. We knew too well what the yellow journals, remembering what was said of the intact-brained and still-conscious state of Ghatanothoa's stony-leathery victims, would make of this detail.

As matters stood, they pointed out that the man who had held the hieroglyphed scroll — and who had evidently thrust it at the mummy through the opening in the case — was not petrified, while the man who had not held it was. When they demanded that we make certain experiments — applying the scroll both to the stony-leathery body of the Fijian and to the mummy itself — we indignantly refused to abet such superstitious notions. Of course, the mummy was withdrawn from public view and transferred to the museum laboratory awaiting a really scientific examination before some suitable medical authority. Remembering past events, we kept it under a strict guard; but even so, an attempt was made to enter the museum at 2:25 a.m. on December 5th. Prompt working of the burglar alarm frustrated the design, though unfortunately the criminal or criminals escaped.

That no hint of anything further ever reached the public, I am profoundly thankful. I wish devoutly that there were nothing more to tell. There will, of course, be leaks, and if anything happens to me I do not know what my executors will do with this manuscript; but at least the case will not be painfully fresh in the multitude's memory when the revelation comes. Besides, no one will believe the facts when they are finally told. That is the curious thing about the multitude. When their yellow press makes hints, they are ready to swallow anything; but when a stupendous and abnormal revelation is actually made, they laugh it aside as a lie. For the sake of general sanity it is probably better so.

I have said that a scientific examination of the frightful mummy was planned. This took place on December 8th, exactly a week after the hideous culmination of events, and was conducted by the eminent Dr. William Minot, in conjunction with Wentworth Moore, Sc.D., taxidermist of the museum. Dr. Minot had witnessed the autopsy of the oddly petrified Fijian the week before. There were also present Messrs. Lawrence Cabot and Dudley Saltonstall of the museum's trustees, Drs. Mason, Wells, and Carver of the museum staff, two representatives of the press, and myself. During the week the condition of the hideous specimen had not visibly changed, though some relaxation of its fibres caused the position of the glassy, open eyes to shift slightly from time to time. All of the staff dreaded to look at the thing — for its suggestion of quiet, conscious watching had become intolerable — and it was only with an effort that I could bring myself to attend the examination.

Dr. Minot arrived shortly after 1:00 p.m., and within a few minutes began his survey of the mummy. Considerable disintegration took place under his hands, and in view of this — and of what we told him concerning the gradual relaxation of the specimen since the first of October — he decided that a thorough dissection ought to be made before the substance was further impaired. The proper instruments being present in the laboratory equipment, he began at once; exclaiming aloud at the odd, fibrous nature of the grey, mummified substance.

But his exclamation was still louder when he made the first deep incision, for out of that cut there slowly trickled a thick crimson stream whose nature — despite the infinite ages dividing this hellish mummy's lifetime from the present — was utterly unmistakable. A few more deft strokes revealed various organs in astonishing degrees of non-petrified preservation — all, indeed, being intact except where injuries to the petrified exterior had brought about malformation or destruction. The resemblance of this condition to that found in the fright-killed

Fiji-Islander was so strong that the eminent physician gasped in bewilderment. The perfection of those ghastly bulging eyes was uncanny, and their exact state with respect to petrification was very difficult to determine.

At 3:30 p.m. the brain-case was opened — and ten minutes later our stunned group took an oath of secrecy which only such guarded documents as this manuscript will ever modify. Even the two reporters were glad to confirm the silence.

For the opening had revealed a pulsing, living brain.

The Thing on the Doorstep.

10,700-WORD NOVELETTE; 1933.

If H.P. Lovecraft was trying to, in a sense, square the circle of high-literary-value pulp storytelling, "The Thing on the Doorstep" most probably was an attempt to capture the pulp spirit in isolation. Or perhaps it was an attempt to take a tip from Robert E. Howard and dash off something quick and easy with a market in mind. It was written around the same time as Howard's "middle period" Conan the Cimmerian tales, which Howard dashed off in haste to keep the wolves of the Great Depression from his door. "Middle Period" Conan stories are the ones on which the stereotypes are based — they invariably involve some ancient ruins, a shapely damsel in distress, a supernatural force to be defeated with barbarian ninja-craft, and an ending scene with Conan, arm around the just-rescued damsel, loudly and happily looking forward to the next adventure. Perhaps Lovecraft, also feeling the economic pinch, decided to try something similar, cashing in on his own writing tropes — Deep Ones, Great Cthulhu, ancestral horrors, burying-grounds, ambulatory corpses, and insane asylums; all of them are represented in this compact, delightfully pulpy romp of a story.

By the standards of Weird Tales *stories, "The Thing on the Doorstep" is excellent. Its literary merits, measured by subtlety and skillful use of subtext, are not up to the standards of Lovecraft's other works; but as a plot-driven work of action-packed pulp storytelling, it's hard to beat. Women will have to grit their teeth a bit, though, as this is by far the most sexist work in Lovecraft's canon.*

Lovecraft dashed it off in just a few days, between Aug. 21 and 24. Once he was done with it, though, he felt very discouraged about its prospects — or maybe he had second thoughts about letting himself get so pulpy under his own by-line. He shelved it unsubmitted, and got busy forgetting all about it. Its publication was a total accident; Lovecraft included it in a letter to his friend Bernard Austin Dwyer, who took the next steps. It was published just before his death, in the January 1937 issue of Weird Tales.

I.

It is true that I have sent six bullets through the head of my best friend, and yet I hope to show by this statement that I am not his murderer. At first I shall be called a madman — madder than the man I shot in his cell at the Arkham Sanitarium. Later some of my readers will weigh each statement, correlate it with the known facts, and ask themselves how I could have believed otherwise than I did after facing the evidence of that horror — that thing on the doorstep.

Until then I also saw nothing but madness in the wild tales I have acted on. Even now I ask myself whether I was misled — or whether I am not mad after all. I do not know — but others have strange things to tell of Edward and Asenath Derby, and even the stolid police are at their wits' ends to account for that last terrible visit. They have tried weakly to concoct a theory of a ghastly jest or warning by discharged servants, yet they know in their hearts that the truth is something infinitely more terrible and incredible.

So I say that I have not murdered Edward Derby. Rather have I avenged him, and in so doing purged the earth of a horror whose survival might have loosed untold terrors on all mankind. There are black zones of shadow close to our daily paths, and now and then some evil soul breaks a passage through. When that happens, the man who knows must strike before reckoning the consequences.

I have known Edward Pickman Derby all his life. Eight years my junior, he was so precocious that we had much in common from the time he was eight and I was sixteen. He was the most phenomenal child scholar I have ever known, and at seven was writing verse of a sombre, fantastic, almost morbid cast which astonished the tutors surrounding him. Perhaps his private education and coddled seclusion had something to do with his premature flowering. An only child, he had organic weaknesses which startled his doting parents and caused them to keep him closely chained to their side. He was never allowed out without his nurse, and seldom had a chance to play unconstrainedly with other children. All this doubtless fostered a strange secretive life in the boy, with imagination as his one avenue of freedom.

At any rate, his juvenile learning was prodigious and bizarre; and his facile writings such as to captivate me despite my greater age. About that time I had leanings toward art of a somewhat grotesque cast, and I found in this younger child a rare kindred spirit. What lay behind our joint love of shadows and marvels was, no doubt, the ancient, mouldering, and subtly fearsome town in which we live — witch-cursed, legend-haunted Arkham, whose huddled, sagging gambrel roofs and crumbling Georgian balustrades brood out the centuries beside the darkly muttering Miskatonic.

As time went by I turned to architecture and gave up my design of illustrating a book of Edward's demoniac poems, yet our comradeship suffered no lessening. Young Derby's odd genius developed remarkably, and in his eighteenth year his collected nightmare-lyrics made a real sensation when issued under the title Azathoth and Other Horrors. He was a close correspondent of the notorious Baudelairean poet Justin Geoffrey, who wrote The People of the Monolith and died screaming in a madhouse in 1926 after a visit to a sinister, ill-regarded village in Hungary.

In self-reliance and practical affairs, however, Derby was greatly retarded because of his coddled existence. His health had improved, but his habits of childish dependence were fostered by over-careful parents, so that he never travelled alone, made independent decisions, or assumed responsibilities. It was early seen that he would not be equal to a struggle in the business or professional arena, but the family fortune was so ample that this formed no tragedy. As he grew to years of manhood he retained a deceptive aspect of boyishness. Blond and blue-eyed, he had the fresh complexion of a child; and his attempt to raise a moustache were discernible only with difficulty. His voice was soft and light, and his unexercised life gave him a juvenile chubbiness rather than the paunchiness of premature middle age. He was of good height, and his handsome face would have made him a notable gallant had not his shyness held him to seclusion and bookishness.

Derby's parents took him abroad every summer, and he was quick to seize on the surface aspects of European thought and expression. His Poe-like talents turned more and more toward the decadent, and other artistic sensitiveness and yearnings were half-aroused in him. We had great discussions in those days. I had been through Harvard, had studied in a Boston architect's office, had married, and had finally returned to Arkham to practise my profession — settling in the family homestead in Saltonstall Street since my father had moved to Florida for his health. Edward used to call almost every evening, till I came to regard him as one of the household. He had a characteristic way of ringing the doorbell or sounding the knocker that grew to be a veritable code signal, so that after dinner I always listened for the familiar three brisk strokes followed by two more after a pause. Less frequently I would visit at his house and note with envy the obscure volumes in his constantly growing library.

Derby went through Miskatonic University in Arkham since his parents would not let him board away from them. He entered at sixteen and completed his course in three years, majoring in English and French literature and receiving high marks in everything but mathematics and the sciences. He mingled very little with the other students, though looking enviously at the "daring" or "Bohemian" set — whose superficially "smart" language and meaningless ironic pose he aped, and whose dubious conduct he wished he dared adopt.

What he did do was to become an almost fanatical devotee of subterranean magical lore, for which Miskatonic's library was and is famous. Always a dweller on the surface of phantasy and strangeness, he now delved deep into the actual runes and riddles left by a fabulous past for the guidance or puzzlement of posterity. He read things like the frightful *Book of Eibon*, the *Unaussprechlichen Kulten* of von Junzt, and the forbidden *Necronomicon* of the mad Arab Abdul Alhazred, though he did not tell his parents he had seen them. Edward was twenty when my son and only child was born, and seemed pleased when I named the newcomer Edward Derby Upton after him.

By the time he was twenty-five Edward Derby was a prodigiously learned man and a fairly well known poet and *fantaisiste* though his lack of contacts and responsibilities had slowed down his literary growth by making his products derivative and over-bookish. I was perhaps his closest friend — finding him an inexhaustible mine of vital theoretical topics, while he relied on me for advice in whatever matters he did not wish to refer to his parents. He remained single — more through shyness, inertia, and parental protectiveness than through inclination — and moved in society only to the slightest and most perfunctory extent. When the war came both health and ingrained timidity kept him at home. I went to Plattsburg for a commission but never got overseas.

So the years wore on. Edward's mother died when he was thirty four and for months he was incapacitated by some odd psychological malady. His father took him to Europe, however, and he managed to pull out of his trouble without visible effects. Afterward he seemed to feel a sort of grotesque exhilaration, as if of partial escape from some unseen bondage. He began to mingle in the more "advanced" college set despite his middle age, and was present at some extremely wild doings — on one occasion paying heavy blackmail (which he borrowed of me) to keep his presence at a certain affair from his father's notice. Some of the whispered rumors about the wild Miskatonic set were extremely singular. There was even talk of black magic and of happenings utterly beyond credibility.

II.

Edward was thirty-eight when he met Asenath Waite. She was, I judge, about twenty-three at the time; and was taking a special course in mediaeval metaphysics at Miskatonic. The daughter of a friend of mine had met her before — in the Hall School at Kingsport — and had been inclined to shun her because of her odd reputation. She was dark, smallish, and very good-looking except for overprotuberant eyes; but something in her expression alienated extremely sensitive people. It was, however, largely her origin and conversation which caused average folk to avoid her. She was one of the Innsmouth Waites, and dark legends have clustered for generations about crumbling, half-deserted Innsmouth and its people. There are tales of horrible bargains about the year 1850, and of a strange element "not quite human" in the ancient families of the run-down fishing port — tales such as only old-time Yankees can devise and repeat with proper awesomeness.

Asenath's case was aggravated by the fact that she was Ephraim Waite's daughter — the child of his old age by an unknown wife who always went veiled. Ephraim lived in a half-decayed mansion in Washington Street, Innsmouth, and those who had seen the place (Arkham folk avoid going to Innsmouth whenever they can) declared that the attic windows were always boarded, and that strange sounds sometimes floated from within as evening drew on. The old man was known to have been a prodigious magical student in his day, and legend averred that he could raise or quell storms at sea according to his whim. I had seen him once or twice in my youth as he came to Arkham to consult forbidden tomes at the college library, and had hated his wolfish, saturnine face with its tangle of iron-grey beard. He had died insane — under rather queer circumstances — just before his daughter (by his will made a nominal ward of the principal) entered the Hall School, but she had been his morbidly avid pupil and looked fiendishly like him at times.

The friend whose daughter had gone to school with Asenath Waite repeated many curious things when the news of Edward's acquaintance with her began to spread about. Asenath, it seemed, had posed as a kind of magician at school; and had really seemed able to accomplish some highly baffling marvels. She professed to be able to raise thunderstorms, though her seeming success was generally laid to some uncanny knack at prediction. All animals markedly disliked her, and she could make any dog howl by certain motions of her right hand. There were times when she displayed snatches of knowledge and language very singular — and very shocking — for a young girl; when she would frighten her schoolmates with leers and winks of an inexplicable kind, and would seem to extract an obscene zestful irony from her present situation.

Most unusual, though, were the well-attested cases of her influence over other persons. She was, beyond question, a genuine hypnotist. By gazing peculiarly at a fellow-student she would often give the latter a distinct feeling of exchanged personality — as if the subject were placed momentarily in the magician's body and able to stare half across the room at her real body, whose eyes blazed and protruded with an alien expression. Asenath often made wild claims about the nature of consciousness and about its independence of the physical frame — or at least from the life-processes of the physical frame. Her crowning rage, however, was that she was not a man; since she believed a male brain had certain unique and far-reaching cosmic powers. Given a man's brain, she declared, she could not only equal but surpass her father in mastery of unknown forces.

Edward met Asenath at a gathering of "intelligentsia" held in one of the students' rooms, and could talk of nothing else when he came to see me the next day. He had found her full of the interests and erudition which engrossed him most, and was in addition wildly taken with her appearance. I had never seen the young woman, and recalled casual references only faintly, but I knew who she was. It seemed rather regrettable that Derby should become so upheaved about her; but I said nothing to discourage him, since infatuation thrives on opposition. He was not, he said, mentioning her to his father.

In the next few weeks I heard of very little but Asenath

Weird Tales, January 1937

"The pit of the Shoggoths! Down the six thousand steps ... the abomination of abominations."

from young Derby. Others now remarked Edward's autumnal gallantry, though they agreed that he did not look even nearly his actual age, or seem at all inappropriate as an escort for his bizarre divinity. He was only a trifle paunchy despite his indolence and self-indulgence, and his face was absolutely without lines. Asenath, on the other hand, had the premature crow's feet which come from the exercises of an intense will.

About this time Edward brought the girl to call on me, and I at once saw that his interest was by no means one-sided. She eyed him continually with an almost predatory air, and I perceived that their intimacy was beyond untangling. Soon afterward I had a visit from old Mr. Derby, whom I had always admired and respected. He had heard the tales of his son's new friendship, and had wormed the whole truth out of "the boy." Edward meant to marry Asenath, and had even been looking at houses in the suburbs. Knowing my usually great influence with his son, the father wondered if I could help to break the ill-advised affair off; but I regretfully expressed my doubts. This time it was not a question of Edward's weak will but of the woman's strong will. The perennial child had transferred his dependence from the parental image to a new and stronger image, and nothing could be done about it.

The wedding was performed a month later — by a justice of the peace, according to the bride's request. Mr. Derby, at my advice, offered no opposition, and he, my wife, my son, and I attended the brief ceremony — the other guests being wild young people from the college. Asenath had bought the old Crowninshield place in the country at the end of High Street, and they proposed to settle there after a short trip to Innsmouth, whence three servants and some books and household goods were to be brought. It was probably not so much consideration for Edward and his father as a personal wish to be near the college, its library, and its crowd of "sophisticates," that made Asenath settle in Arkham instead of returning permanently home.

When Edward called on me after the honeymoon I thought he looked slightly changed. Asenath had made him get rid of the undeveloped moustache, but there was more than that. He looked soberer and more thoughtful, his habitual pout of childish rebelliousness being exchanged for a look almost of genuine sadness. I was puzzled to decide whether I liked or disliked the change. Certainly he seemed for the moment more normally adult than ever before. Perhaps the marriage was a good thing — might not the change of dependence form a start toward actual neutralisation, leading ultimately to responsible independence? He came alone, for Asenath was very busy. She had brought a vast store of books and apparatus from Innsmouth (Derby shuddered as he spoke the name), and was finishing the restoration of the Crowninshield house and grounds.

Her home — in that town — was a rather disgusting place, but certain objects in it had taught him some surprising things. He was progressing fast in esoteric lore now that he had Asenath's guidance. Some of the experiments she proposed were very daring and radical — he did not feel at liberty to describe them — but he had confidence in her powers and intentions. The three servants were very queer — an incredibly aged couple who had been with old Ephraim and referred occasionally to him and to Asenath's dead mother in a cryptic way, and a swarthy young wench who had marked anomalies of feature and seemed to exude a perpetual odour of fish.

III.

For the next two years I saw less and less of Derby. A fortnight would sometimes slip by without the familiar three-and-two strokes at the front door; and when he did call — or when, as happened with increasing infrequency, I called on him — he was very little disposed to converse on vital topics. He had become secretive about those occult studies which he used to describe and discuss so minutely, and preferred not to talk of his wife. She had aged tremendously since her marriage, till now — oddly enough — she seemed the elder of the two. Her face held the most concentratedly determined expression I had ever seen, and her whole aspect seemed to gain a vague, unplaceable repulsiveness. My wife and son noticed it as much as I, and we all ceased gradually to call on her — for which, Edward admitted in one of his boyishly tactless moments, she was unmitigatedly grateful. Occasionally the Derbys would go on long trips — ostensibly to Europe, though Edward sometimes hinted at obscurer destinations.

It was after the first year that people began talking about the change in Edward Derby. It was very casual talk, for the change was purely psychological; but it brought up some interesting points. Now and then, it seemed Edward was observed to wear an expression and to do things wholly incompatible with his usual flabby nature. For example — although in the old days he could not drive a car, he was now seen occasionally to dash into or out of the old Crowninshield driveway with Asenath's powerful Packard, handling it like a master, and meeting traffic entanglements with a skill and determination utterly alien to his accustomed nature. In such cases he seemed always to be just back from some trip or just starting on one — what sort of trip, no one could guess, although he mostly favoured the Innsmouth road.

Oddly, the metamorphosis did not seem altogether pleasing. People said he looked too much like his wife, or like old Ephraim Waite himself, in these moments — or perhaps these moments seemed unnatural because they were so rare. Sometimes, hours after starting out in this way, he would return listlessly sprawled on the rear seat of the car while an obviously hired chauffeur or mechanic drove. Also, his preponderant aspect on the streets during his decreasing round of social contacts (including, I may say, his calls on me) was the old-time indecisive one — its irresponsible childishness even more marked than in the past. While Asenath's face aged, Edward — aside from those exceptional occasions — actually relaxed into a kind of exaggerated immaturity, save when a trace of the new sadness or understanding would flash across it. It was really very puzzling. Meanwhile the Derbys almost dropped out of the gay college circle — not through their own disgust, we heard, but because something about their present studies shocked even the most callous of the other decadents.

It was in the third year of the marriage that Edward began to hint openly to me of a certain fear and dissatisfaction. He would let fall remarks about things "going too far," and would talk darkly about the need of "gaining his identity." At first I ignored such references, but in time I began to question him guardedly, remembering what my friend's daughter had said about Asenath's hypnotic influence over the other girls at school — the cases where students had thought they were in her body looking across the room at themselves. This questioning seemed to make him at once alarmed and grateful, and once he mumbled something about having a serious talk with me later. About this time old Mr. Derby died, for which I was afterward very thankful. Edward was badly upset, though by no means disorganized. He had seen astonishingly little of his parent since his marriage, for Asenath had concentrated in herself all his vital sense of family linkage. Some called him callous in his loss — especially since those jaunty and confident moods in the car began to increase. He now wished to move back into the old family mansion, but Asenath insisted on staying in the Crowninshield house to which she had become well adjusted.

Not long afterward my wife heard a curious thing from a friend—one of the few who had not dropped the Derbys. She had been out to the end of High Street to call on the couple, and had seen a car shoot briskly out of the drive with Edward's oddly confident and almost sneering face above the wheel. Ringing the bell, she had been told by the repulsive wench that Asenath was also out; but had chanced to look at the house in leaving. There, at one of Edward's library windows, she had glimpsed a hastily withdrawn face—a face whose expression of pain, defeat, and wistful hopelessness was poignant beyond description. It was—incredibly enough in view of its usual domineering cast—Asenath's; yet the caller had vowed that in that instant the sad, muddled eyes of poor Edward were gazing out from it.

Edward's calls now grew a trifle more frequent, and his hints occasionally became concrete. What he said was not to be believed, even in centuried and legend-haunted Arkham; but he threw out his dark lore with a sincerity and convincingness which made one fear for his sanity. He talked about terrible meetings in lonely places, of cyclopean ruins in the heart of the Maine woods beneath which vast staircases led down to abysses of nighted secrets, of complex angles that led through invisible walls to other regions of space and time, and of hideous exchanges of personality that permitted explorations in remote and forbidden places, on other worlds, and in different space-time continua.

He would now and then back up certain crazy hints by exhibiting objects which utterly nonplussed me—elusively coloured and bafflingly textured objects like nothing ever heard of on earth, whose insane curves and surfaces answered no conceivable purpose, and followed no conceivable geometry. These things, he said, came "from outside"; and his wife knew how to get them. Sometimes—but always in frightened and ambiguous whisper—he would suggest things about old Ephraim Waite, whom he had seen occasionally at the college library in the old days. These adumbrations were never specific, but seemed to revolve around some especially horrible doubt as to whether the old wizard were really dead—in a spiritual as well as corporeal sense.

At times Derby would halt abruptly in his revelations, and I wondered whether Asenath could possibly have divined his speech at a distance and cut him off through some unknown sort of telepathic mesmerism—some power of the kind she had displayed at school. Certainly, she suspected that he told me things, for as the weeks passed she tried to stop his visits with words and glances of a most inexplicable potency. Only with difficulty could he get to see me, for although he would pretend to be going somewhere else, some invisible force would generally clog his motions or make him forget his destination for the time being. His visits usually came when Asenath was away—"away in her own body," as he once oddly put it. She always found out later—the servants watched his goings and coming—but evidently she thought it inexpedient to do anything drastic.

IV.

Derby had been married more than three years on that August day when I got that telegram from Maine. I had not seen him for two months, but had heard he was away "on business." Asenath was supposed to be with him, though watchful gossip declared there was someone upstairs in the house behind the doubly curtained windows. They had watched the purchases made by the servants. And now the town marshal of Chesuncook had wired of the draggled madman who stumbled out of the woods with delirious ravings and screamed to me for protection. It was Edward—and he had been just able to recall his own name and address.

Chesuncook is close to the wildest, deepest, and least explored forest belt in Maine, and it took a whole day of feverish jolting through fantastic and forbidding scenery to get there in a car. I found Derby in a cell at the town farm, vacillating between frenzy and apathy. He knew me at once, and began pouring out a meaningless, half-incoherent torrent of words in my direction.

"Dan, for God's sake! The pit of the shoggoths! Down the six thousand steps . . . the abomination of abominations . . . I never would let her take me, and then I found myself there—Ia! Shub-Niggurath!—The shape rose up from the altar, and there were five hundred that howled—The Hooded Thing bleated 'Kamog! Kamog!'—that was old Ephraim's secret name in the coven—I was there, where she promised she wouldn't take me—A minute before I was locked in the library, and then I was there where she had gone with my body—in the place of utter blasphemy, the unholy pit where the black realm begins and the watcher guards the gate—I saw a shoggoth—it changed shape—I can't stand it—I'll kill her if she ever sends me there again—I'll kill that entity—her, him, it—I'll kill it! I'll kill it with my own hands!"

It took me an hour to quiet him, but he subsided at last. The next day I got him decent clothes in the village, and set out with him for Arkham. His fury of hysteria was spent, and he was inclined to be silent, though he began muttering darkly to himself when the car passed through Augusta—as if the sight of a city aroused unpleasant memories. It was clear that he did not wish to go home; and considering the fantastic delusions he seemed to have about his wife—delusions undoubtedly springing from some actual hypnotic ordeal to which he had been subjected—I thought it would be better if he did not. I would, I resolved, put him up myself for a time; no matter what unpleasantness it would make with Asenath. Later I would help him get a divorce, for most assuredly there were mental factors which made this marriage suicidal for him.

When we struck open country again Derby's muttering faded away, and I let him nod and drowse on the seat beside me as I drove.

During our sunset dash through Portland the muttering commenced again, more distinctly than before, and as I listened I caught a stream of utterly insane drivel about Asenath. The extent to which she had preyed on Edward's nerves was plain, for he had woven a whole set of hallucinations around her. His present predicament, he mumbled furtively, was only one of a long series. She was getting hold of him, and he knew that some day she would never let go. Even now she probably let him go only when she had to, because she couldn't hold on long at a time. She constantly took his body and went to nameless places for nameless rites, leaving him in her body and locking him upstairs—but sometimes she couldn't hold on, and he would find himself suddenly in his own body again in some far-off, horrible, and perhaps unknown place. Sometimes she'd get hold of him again and sometimes she couldn't. Often he was left stranded somewhere as I had found him—time and again he had to find his way home from frightful distances, getting somebody to drive the car after he found it.

The worst thing was that she was holding on to him longer and longer at a time. She wanted to be a man—to be fully human—that was why she got hold of him. She had sensed the mixture of fine-wrought brain and weak will in him. Some day she would crowd him out and disappear with his body—disappear to become a great magician like her father and leave him marooned in that female shell that wasn't even quite human. Yes, he knew about the Innsmouth blood now. There had been traffick with things from the sea—it was horrible ... And old Ephraim—he had known the secret, and when he grew old did a hideous thing to keep alive—he wanted to live forever—Asenath would succeed—one successful demonstration had taken place already.

As Derby muttered on I turned to look at him closely, verifying the impression of change which an earlier scrutiny had given me. Paradoxically, he seemed in better shape than usual—harder, more normally developed, and without the trace of sickly flabbiness caused by his indolent habits. It was as if he had been really active and properly exercised for the first time in his coddled life, and I judged that Asenath's force must have pushed him into unwonted channels of motion and alertness. But just now his mind was in a pitiable state; for he was mumbling wild extravagances about his wife, about black magic, about old Ephraim, and about some revelation which would convince even me. He repeated names which I recognized from bygone browsings in forbidden volumes, and at times made me shudder with a certain thread of mythological consistency—or convincing coherence—which ran through his maundering. Again and again he would pause, as if to gather courage for some final and terrible disclosure.

"Dan, Dan, don't you remember him—wild eyes and the unkempt beard that never turned white? He glared at me once, and I never forgot it. Now she glares that way. And I know why! He found it in the *Necronomicon*—the formula. I don't dare tell you the page yet, but when I do you can read and understand. Then you will know what has engulfed me. On, on, on, on—body to body to body—he means never to die. The life-glow—he knows how to break the link ... it can flicker on a while even when the body is dead. I'll give you hints and maybe you'll guess. Listen, Dan—do you know why my wife always takes such pains with that silly backhand writing? Have you ever seen a manuscript of old Ephraim's? Do you want to know why I shivered when I saw some hasty notes Asenath had jotted down?

"Asenath—is there such a person? Why did they half-think there was poison in old Ephraim's stomach? Why do the Gilmans whisper about the way he shrieked—like a frightened child—when he went mad and Asenath locked him up in the padded attic room where—the other—had been? Was it old Ephraim's soul that was locked in? Who locked in whom? Why had he been looking for months for someone with a fine mind and a weak will?—Why did he curse that his daughter wasn't a son? Tell me, Daniel Upton—what devilish exchange was perpetrated in the house of horror where that blasphemous monster had his trusting, weak-willed half-human child at his mercy? Didn't he make it permanent—as she'll do in the end with me? Tell me why that thing that calls itself Asenath writes differently off guard, so that you can't tell its script from—"

Then the thing happened. Derby's voice was rising to a thin treble scream as he raved, when suddenly it was shut off with an almost mechanical click. I thought of those other occasions at my home when his confidences had abruptly ceased—when I had half-fancied that some obscure telepathic wave of Asenath's mental force was intervening to keep him silent. This, though, was something altogether different—and, I felt, infinitely more horrible. The face beside me was twisted almost unrecognizably for a moment, while through the whole body there passed a shivering motion—as if all the bones, organs, muscles, nerves, and glands were adjusting themselves to a radically different posture, set of stresses, and general personality.

Just where the supreme horror lay, I could not for my life tell; yet there swept over me such a swamping wave of sickness and repulsion—such a freezing, petrifying sense of utter alienage and abnormality—that my grasp of the wheel grew feeble and uncertain. The figure beside me seemed less like a lifelong friend than like some monstrous intrusion from outer space—some damnable, utterly accursed focus of unknown and malign cosmic forces.

I had faltered only a moment, but before another moment was over my companion had seized the wheel and forced me to change places with him. The dusk was now very thick, and the lights of Portland far behind, so I could not see much of his face. The blaze of his eyes, though, was phenomenal; and I knew that he must now be in that queerly energized state—so unlike his usual self—which so many people had noticed. It seemed odd and incredible that listless Edward Derby—he who could never assert himself, and who had never learned to drive — should be ordering me about and taking the wheel of my own car, yet that was precisely what had happened. He did not speak for some time, and in my inexplicable horror I was glad he did not.

In the lights of Biddeford and Saco I saw his firmly set mouth, and shivered at the blaze of his eyes. The people were right — he did look damnably like his wife and like old Ephraim when in these moods. I did not wonder that the moods were disliked — there was certainly something unnatural in them, and I felt the sinister element all the more because of the wild ravings I had been hearing. This man, for all my lifelong knowledge of Edward Pickman Derby, was a stranger — an intrusion of some sort from the black abyss.

He did not speak until we were on a dark stretch of road, and when he did his voice seemed utterly unfamiliar. It was deeper, firmer, and more decisive than I had ever known it to be; while its accent and pronunciation were altogether changed — though vaguely, remotely, and rather disturbingly recalling something I could not quite place. There was, I thought, a trace of very profound and very genuine irony in the timbre — not the flashy, meaninglessly jaunty pseudo-irony of the callow "sophisticate," which Derby had habitually affected, but something grim, basic, pervasive, and potentially evil. I marvelled at the self-possession so soon following the spell of panic-struck muttering.

"I hope you'll forget my attack back there, Upton," he was saying. "You know what my nerves are, and I guess you can excuse such things. I'm enormously grateful, of course, for this lift home.

"And you must forget, too, any crazy things I may have been saying about my wife — and about things in general. That's what comes from overstudy in a field like mine. My philosophy is full of bizarre concepts, and when the mind gets worn out it cooks up all sorts of imaginary concrete applications. I shall take a rest from now on — you probably won't see me for some time, and you needn't blame Asenath for it.

"This trip was a bit queer, but it's really very simple. There are certain Indian relics in the north wood — standing stones, and all that — which mean a good deal in folklore, and Asenath and I are following that stuff up. It was a hard search, so I seem to have gone off my head. I must send somebody for the car when I get home. A month's relaxation will put me on my feet."

I do not recall just what my own part of the conversation was, for the baffling alienage of my seatmate filled all my consciousness. With every moment my feeling of elusive cosmic horror increased, till at length I was in a virtual delirium of longing for the end of the drive. Derby did not offer to relinquish the wheel, and I was glad of the speed with which Portsmouth and Newburyport flashed by.

At the junction where the main highway runs inland and avoids Innsmouth, I was half-afraid my driver would take the bleak shore road that goes through that damnable place. He did not, however, but darted rapidly past Rowley and Ipswich toward our destination. We reached Arkham before midnight, and found the lights still on at the old Crowninshield house. Derby left the car with a hasty repetition of his thanks, and I drove home alone with a curious feeling of relief. It had been a terrible drive — all the more terrible because I could not quite tell why — and I did not regret Derby's forecast of a long absence from my company.

The next two months were full of rumours. People spoke of seeing Derby more and more in his new energized state, and Asenath was scarcely ever in to her callers. I had only one visit from Edward, when he called briefly in Asenath's car — duly reclaimed from wherever he had left it in Maine — to get some books he had lent me. He was in his new state, and paused only long enough for some evasively polite remarks. It was plain that he had nothing to discuss with me when in this condition — and I noticed that he did not even trouble to give the old three-and-two signal when ringing the doorbell. As on that evening in the car, I felt a faint, infinitely deep horror which I could not explain; so that his swift departure was a prodigious relief.

In mid-September Derby was away for a week, and some of the decadent college set talked knowingly of the matter — hinting at a meeting with a notorious cult-leader, lately expelled from England, who had established headquarters in New York. For my part I could not get that strange ride from Maine out of my head. The transformation I had witnessed had affected me profoundly, and I caught myself again and again trying to account for the thing — and for the extreme horror it had inspired in me.

But the oddest rumours were those about the sobbing in the old Crowninshield house. The voice seemed to be a woman's, and some of the younger people thought it sounded like Asenath's. It was heard only at rare intervals, and would sometimes be choked off as if by force. There was talk of an investigation, but this was dispelled one day when Asenath appeared in the streets and chatted in a sprightly way with a large number of acquaintances — apologizing for her recent absence and speaking incidentally about the nervous breakdown and hysteria of a guest from Boston. The guest was never seen, but Asenath's appearance left nothing to be said. And then someone complicated matters by whispering that the sobs had once or twice been in a man's voice.

One evening in mid-October, I heard the familiar three-and-two ring at the front door. Answering it myself, I found Edward on the steps, and saw in a moment that his personality was the old one which I had not encountered since the day of his ravings on that terrible ride from Chesuncook. His face was twitching with a mixture of odd emotions in which fear and triumph seemed to share dominion, and he looked furtively over his shoulder as I closed the door behind him.

Following me clumsily to the study, he asked for some whiskey to steady his nerves. I forbore to question him, but waited till he felt like beginning whatever he wanted to say. At length he ventured some information in a choking voice.

"Asenath has gone, Dan. We had a long talk last night while the servants were out, and I made her promise to stop preying on me. Of course I had certain — certain occult defences I never told you about. She had to give in, but got frightfully angry. Just packed up and started for New York — walked right out to catch the eight-twenty in to Boston. I suppose people will talk, but I can't help that. You needn't mention that there was any trouble — just say she's gone on a long research trip.

"She's probably going to stay with one of her horrible groups of devotees. I hope she'll go west and get a divorce — anyhow, I've made her promise to keep away and let me alone. It was horrible, Dan — she was stealing my body — crowding me out — making a prisoner of me. I lay low and pretended to let her do it, but I had to be on the watch. I could plan if I was careful, for she can't read my mind literally, or in detail. All she could read of my planning was a sort of general mood of rebellion — and she always thought I was helpless. Never thought I could get the best of her . . . but I had a spell or two that worked."

Derby looked over his shoulder and took some more whiskey.

"I paid off those damned servants this morning when they got back. They were ugly about it, and asked questions, but they went. They're her kin — Innsmouth people — and were hand and glove with her. I hope they'll let me alone — I didn't like the way they laughed when they walked away. I must get as many of Dad's old servants again as I can. I'll move back home now.

"I suppose you think I'm crazy, Dan — but Arkham history ought to hint at things that back up what I've told you — and what I'm going to tell you. You've seen one of the changes, too — in your car after I told you about Asenath that day coming home from Maine. That was when she got me — drove me out of my body. The last thing I remember was when I was all worked up trying to tell you what that she-devil is. Then she got me, and in a flash I was back at the house — in the library where those damned servants had me locked up — and in that cursed fiend's body that isn't even human . . . You know it was she you must have ridden home with — that preying wolf in my body — You ought to have known the difference!"

I shuddered as Derby paused. Surely, I had known the difference — yet could I accept an explanation as insane as this? But my distracted caller was growing even wilder.

"I had to save myself — I had to, Dan! She'd have got me for good at Hallowmass — they hold a Sabbat up there beyond Chesuncook, and the sacrifice would have clinched things. She'd have got me for good — she'd have been I, and I'd have been she — forever — too late — My body'd have been hers for good — She'd have been a man, and fully human, just as she wanted to be — I suppose she'd have put me out of the way — killed her own ex-body with me in it, damn her, just as she did before — just as she did, or it did before — " Edward's face was now atrociously distorted, and he bent it uncomfortably close to mine as his voice fell to a whisper.

"You must know what I hinted in the car — that she isn't Asenath at all, but really old Ephraim himself. I suspected it a year and a half ago, and I know it now. Her handwriting shows it when she goes off guard — sometimes she jots down a note in writing that's just like her father's manuscripts, stroke for stroke — and sometimes she says things that nobody but an old man like Ephraim could say. He changed forms with her when he felt death coming — she was the only one he could find with the right kind of brain and a weak enough will — he got her body permanently, just as she almost got mine, and then poisoned the old body he'd put her into. Haven't you seen old Ephraim's soul glaring out of that she-devil's eyes dozens of times — and out of mine when she has control of my body?"

The whisperer was panting, and paused for breath. I said nothing; and when he resumed his voice was nearer normal. This, I reflected, was a case for the asylum, but I would not be the one to send him there. Perhaps time and freedom from Asenath would do its work. I could see that he would never wish to dabble in morbid occultism again.

"I'll tell you more later — I must have a long rest now. I'll tell you something of the forbidden horrors she led me into — something of the age-old horrors that even now are festering in out-of-the-way corners with a few monstrous priests to keep them alive. Some people know things about the universe that nobody ought to know, and can do things that nobody ought to be able to do. I've been in it up to my neck, but that's the end. Today I'd burn that damned *Necronomicon* and all the rest if I were librarian at Miskatonic.

"But she can't get me now. I must get out of that accursed house as soon as I can, and settle down at home. You'll help me, I know, if I need help. Those devilish servants, you know — and if people should get too inquisitive about Asenath. You see, I can't give them her address . . . Then there are certain groups of searchers — certain cults, you know — that might misunderstand our breaking up . . . some of them have damnably curious ideas and methods. I know you'll stand by me if anything happens — even if I have to tell you a lot that will shock you . . ."

I had Edward stay and sleep in one of the guest-chambers that night, and in the morning he seemed calmer. We discussed certain possible arrangements for his moving back into the Derby mansion, and I hoped he would lose no time in making the change. He did not call the next evening, but I saw him frequently during the ensuing weeks. We talked as little as possible about strange and unpleasant things, but discussed the renovation of the old Derby house, and the travels which Edward promised to take with my son and me the following summer.

Of Asenath we said almost nothing, for I saw that the subject was a peculiarly disturbing one. Gossip, of course, was rife; but that was no novelty in connection with the strange menage at the old Crowninshield house. One thing I did not like was what Derby's banker let fall in an over-expansive mood at the Miskatonic Club — about the cheques Edward was sending regularly to a Moses and Abigail Sargent and a Eunice Babson in Innsmouth. That looked as if those evil-faced servants were extorting some kind of tribute from him — yet he had not mentioned the matter to me.

I wished that the summer — and my son's Harvard vacation — would come, so that we could get Edward to Europe. He was not, I soon saw, mending as rapidly as I had hoped he would; for there was something a bit hysterical in his occasional exhilaration, while his moods of fright and depression were altogether too frequent. The old Derby house was ready by December, yet Edward constantly put off moving. Though he hated and seemed to fear the Crowninshield place, he was at the same time queerly enslaved by it. He could not seem to begin dismantling things, and invented every kind of excuse to postpone action. When I pointed this out to him he appeared unaccountably frightened. His father's old butler — who was there with other reacquired servants — told me one day that Edward's occasional prowlings about the house, and especially down in the cellar, looked odd and unwholesome to him. I wondered if Asenath had been writing disturbing letters, but the butler said there was no mail which could have come from her.

It was about Christmas that Derby broke down one evening while calling on me. I was steering the conversation toward next summer's travels when he suddenly shrieked and leaped up from his chair with a look of shocking, uncontrollable fright — a cosmic panic and loathing such as only the nether gulfs of nightmare could bring to any sane mind.

"My brain! My brain! God, Dan — it's tugging — from beyond — knocking — clawing — that she-devil — even now — Ephraim — Kamog! Kamog! — The pit of the shoggoths — Ia! Shub-Niggurath! The Goat with a Thousand Young! . . .

"The flame — the flame — beyond body, beyond life — in the earth — oh, God!"

I pulled him back to his chair and poured some wine down his throat as his frenzy sank to a dull apathy. He did not resist, but kept his lips moving as if talking to himself. Presently I realized that he was trying to talk to me, and bent my ear to his mouth to catch the feeble words.

"Again, again — she's trying — I might have known — nothing can stop that force; not distance nor magic, nor death — it comes and comes, mostly in the night — I can't leave — it's horrible — oh, God, Dan, if you only knew as I do just how horrible it is . . ."

When he had slumped down into a stupor I propped him with pillows and let normal sleep overtake him. I did not call a doctor, for I knew what would be said of his sanity, and wished to give nature a chance if I possibly could. He waked at midnight, and I put him to bed upstairs, but he was gone by morning. He had let himself quietly out of the house — and his butler, when called on the wire, said he was at home pacing about the library.

Edward went to pieces rapidly after that. He did not call again, but I went daily to see him. He would always be sitting in his library, staring at nothing and having an air of abnormal listening. Sometimes he talked rationally, but always on trivial topics. Any mention of his trouble, of future plans, or of Asenath would send him into a frenzy. His butler said he had frightful seizures at night, during which he might eventually do himself harm.

I had a long talk with his doctor, banker, and lawyer, and finally took the physician with two specialist colleagues to visit him. The spasms that resulted from the first questions were violent and pitiable — and that evening a closed car took his poor struggling body to the Arkham Sanitarium. I was made his guardian and called on him twice weekly — almost weeping to hear his wild shrieks, awesome whispers, and dreadful, droning repetitions of such phrases as "I had to do it — I had to do it — it'll get me — it'll get me — down there — down there in the dark — Mother! Mother! Dan! Save me — save me — "

How much hope of recovery there was, no one could say, but I tried my best to be optimistic. Edward must have a home if he emerged, so I transferred his servants to the Derby mansion, which would surely be his sane choice. What to do about the Crowninshield place with its complex arrangements and collections of utterly inexplicable objects I could not decide, so left it momentarily untouched — telling the Derby household to go over and dust the chief rooms once a week, and ordering the furnace man to have a fire on those days.

The final nightmare came before Candlemas — heralded, in cruel irony, by a false gleam of hope. One morning late in January the sanitarium telephoned to report that Edward's reason had suddenly come back. His continuous memory, they said, was badly impaired; but sanity itself was certain. Of course he must remain some time for observation, but there could be little doubt of the outcome. All going well, he would surely be free in a week.

I hastened over in a flood of delight, but stood bewildered when a nurse took me to Edward's room. The patient rose to greet me, extending his hand with a polite smile; but I saw in an instant that he bore the strangely energized personality which had seemed so foreign to his own nature — the competent personality I had found so vaguely horrible, and which Edward himself had once vowed was the intruding soul of his wife. There was the same blazing vision — so like Asenath's and old Ephraim's — and the same firm mouth; and when he spoke I could sense the same grim, pervasive irony in his voice — the deep irony so redolent of potential evil. This was the person who had driven my car through the night five months before — the person I had not seen since that brief call when he had forgotten the oldtime doorbell signal and stirred such nebulous fears in me — and now he filled me with the same dim feeling of blasphemous alienage and ineffable cosmic hideousness.

He spoke affably of arrangements for release — and there was nothing for me to do but assent, despite some remarkable gaps in his recent memories. Yet I felt that something was terribly, inexplicably wrong and abnormal. There were horrors in this thing that I could not reach. This was a sane person — but was it indeed the Edward Derby I had known? If not, who or what was it—and where was Edward? Ought it to be free or confined—or ought it to be extirpated from the face of the earth? There was a hint of the abysmally sardonic in everything the creature said—the Asenath-like eyes lent a special and baffling mockery to certain words about the early liberty earned by an especially close confinement! I must have behaved very awkwardly, and was glad to beat a retreat.

All that day and the next I racked my brain over the problem. What had happened? What sort of mind looked out through those alien eyes in Edward's face? I could think of nothing but this dimly terrible enigma, and gave up all efforts to perform my usual work. The second morning the hospital called up to say that the recovered patient was unchanged, and by evening I was close to a nervous collapse—a state I admit, though others will vow it coloured my subsequent vision. I have nothing to say on this point except that no madness of mine could account for all the evidence.

V.

It was in the night—after that second evening—that stark, utter horror burst over me and weighted my spirit with a black, clutching panic from which it can never shake free. It began with a telephone call just before midnight. I was the only one up, and sleepily took down the receiver in the library. No one seemed to be on the wire, and I was about to hang up and go to bed when my ear caught a very faint suspicion of sound at the other end. Was someone trying under great difficulties to talk? As I listened I thought I heard a sort of half-liquid bubbling noise—"glub... glub... glub"—which had an odd suggestion of inarticulate, unintelligible word and syllable divisions. I called "Who is it?" But the only answer was "glub... glub... glub-glub." I could only assume that the noise was mechanical; but fancying that it might be a case of a broken instrument able to receive but not to send, I added, "I can't hear you. Better hang up and try Information." Immediately I heard the receiver go on the hook at the other end.

This, I say, was just about midnight. When the call was traced afterward it was found to come from the old Crowninshield house, though it was fully half a week from the housemaid's day to be there. I shall only hint what was found at that house—the upheaval in a remote cellar storeroom, the tracks, the dirt, the hastily rifled wardrobe, the baffling marks on the telephone, the clumsily used stationery, and the detestable stench lingering over everything. The police, poor fools, have their smug little theories, and are still searching for those sinister discharged servants—who have dropped out of sight amidst the present furore. They speak of a ghoulish revenge for things that were done, and say I was included because I was Edward's best friend and adviser.

Idiots! Do they fancy those brutish clowns could have forged that handwriting? Do they fancy they could have brought what later came? Are they blind to the changes in that body that was Edward's? As for me, I now believe all that Edward Derby ever told me. There are horrors beyond life's edge that we do not suspect, and once in a while man's evil prying calls them just within our range. Ephraim—Asenath—that devil called them in, and they engulfed Edward as they are engulfing me.

Can I be sure that I am safe? Those powers survive the life of the physical form. The next day—in the afternoon, when I pulled out of my prostration and was able to walk and talk coherently—I went to the madhouse and shot him dead for Edward's and the world's sake, but can I be sure till he is cremated? They are keeping the body for some silly autopsies by different doctors—but I say he must be cremated. He must be cremated—he who was not Edward Derby when I shot him. I shall go mad if he is not, for I may be the next. But my will is not weak—and I shall not let it be undermined by the terrors I know are seething around it. One life—Ephraim, Asenath, and Edward—who now? I will not be driven out of my body... I will not change souls with that bullet-ridden lich in the madhouse!

But let me try to tell coherently of that final horror. I will not speak of what the police persistently ignored—the tales of that dwarfed, grotesque, malodorous thing met by at least three wayfarers in High Street just before two o'clock, and the nature of the single footprints in certain places. I will say only that just about two the doorbell and knocker waked me—doorbell and knocker both, applied alternately and uncertainly in a kind of weak desperation, and each trying to keep Edward's old signal of three-and-two strokes.

Roused from sound sleep, my mind leaped into a turmoil. Derby at the door—and remembering the old code! That new personality had not remembered it... was Edward suddenly back in his rightful state? Why was he here in such evident stress and haste? Had he been released ahead of time, or had he escaped? Perhaps, I thought as I flung on a robe and bounded downstairs, his return to his own self had brought raving and violence, revoking his discharge and driving him to a desperate dash for freedom. Whatever had happened, he was good old Edward again, and I would help him!

When I opened the door into the elm-arched blackness a gust of insufferably foetid wind almost flung me prostrate. I choked in nausea, and for a second scarcely saw the dwarfed, humped figure on the steps. The summons had been Edward's, but who was this foul, stunted parody? Where had Edward had time to go? His ring had sounded only a second before the door opened.

The caller had on one of Edward's overcoats—its bottom almost touching the ground, and its sleeves rolled back yet still covering the hands. On the head was a slouch hat pulled low, while a black silk muffler concealed the face. As I stepped unsteadily forward, the figure made a semi-liquid sound like that I had heard over the telephone—"glub... glub..."—and thrust at me a large, closely written paper impaled on the end of a long pencil. Still reeling from the morbid and unaccountable foetor, I seized the paper and tried to read it in the light from the doorway.

Beyond question, it was in Edward's script. But why had he written when he was close enough to ring — and why was the script so awkward, coarse and shaky? I could make out nothing in the dim half light, so edged back into the hall, the dwarf figure clumping mechanically after but pausing on the inner door's threshold. The odour of this singular messenger was really appalling, and I hoped (not in vain, thank God!) that my wife would not wake and confront it.

Then, as I read the paper, I felt my knees give under me and my vision go black. I was lying on the floor when I came to, that accursed sheet still clutched in my fear-rigid hand. This is what it said.

Dan — go to the sanitarium and kill it. Exterminate it. It isn't Edward Derby any more. She got me — it's Asenath — and she has been dead three months and a half. I lied when I said she had gone away. I killed her. I had to. It was sudden, but we were alone and I was in my right body. I saw a candlestick and smashed her head in. She would have got me for good at Hallowmass.

I buried her in the farther cellar storeroom under some old boxes and cleaned up all the traces. The servants suspected next morning, but they have such secrets that they dare not tell the police. I sent them off, but God knows what they — and others of the cult — will do.

I thought for a while I was all right, and then I felt the tugging at my brain. I knew what it was — I ought to have remembered. A soul like hers — or Ephraim's — is half detached, and keeps right on after death as long as the body lasts. She was getting me — making me change bodies with her-seizing my body and putting me in that corpse of hers buried in the cellar.

I knew what was coming — that's why I snapped and had to go to the asylum. Then it came — I found myself choked in the dark — in Asenath's rotting carcass down there in the cellar under the boxes where I put it. And I knew she must be in my body at the sanitarium — permanently, for it was after Hallowmass, and the sacrifice would work even without her being there — sane, and ready for release as a menace to the world. I was desperate, and in spite of everything I clawed my way out.

I'm too far gone to talk — I couldn't manage to telephone — but I can still write. I'll get fixed up somehow and bring this last word and warning. Kill that fiend if you value the peace and comfort of the world. See that it is cremated. If you don't, it will live on and on, body to body forever, and I can't tell you what it will do. Keep clear of black magic, Dan, it's the devil's business. Goodbye — you've been a great friend. Tell the police whatever they'll believe — and I'm damnably sorry to drag all this on you. I'll be at peace before long — this thing won't hold together much more. Hope you can read this. And kill that thing — kill it.

Yours —

Ed.

It was only afterward that I read the last half of this paper, for I had fainted at the end of the third paragraph. I fainted again when I saw and smelled what cluttered up the threshold where the warm air had struck it. The messenger would not move or have consciousness any more.

The butler, tougher-fibred than I, did not faint at what met him in the hall in the morning. Instead, he telephoned the police. When they came I had been taken upstairs to bed, but the — other mass — lay where it had collapsed in the night. The men put handkerchiefs to their noses.

What they finally found inside Edward's oddly-assorted clothes was mostly liquescent horror. There were bones, too — and a crushed-in skull. Some dental work positively identified the skull as Asenath's.

The Hoard of the Wizard-Beast.

BY ROBERT H. BARLOW
AND H.P. LOVECRAFT

2,200-WORD SHORT STORY; 1933.

This story was a sort of sequel to an entry in Barlow's Annals of the Jinns, a series of tiny short stories which he had written for publication in fantasy-fan magazines.

Lovecraft's reaction when Barlow forwarded the story to him was positive and encouraging. He pointed out several structural issues with it, and made some suggestions for changes. These suggestions and modifications added up; S. T. Joshi estimates that this story was about 60 percent Lovecraft's work by the time they were done.

"The Hoard of the Wizard-Beast" was written late in 1933, and although it was published in an amateur-press title shortly thereafter, the details of that publication are unknown.

There had happened in the teeming and many-towered city of Zeth one of those incidents which are prone to take place in all capitals of all worlds. Nor, simply because Zeth lies on a planet of strange beasts and stranger vegetation, did this incident differ greatly from what might have occurred in London or Paris or any of the great governing towns we know. Through the cleverly concealed dishonesty of an aged but shrewd official, the treasury was exhausted. No shining phrulder, as of old, lay stacked about the strong-room; and over empty coffers the sardonic spider wove webs of mocking design. When, at last, the giphath Yalden entered that obscure vault and discovered the thefts, there were left only some phlegmatic rats which peered sharply at him as at an alien intruder.

There had been no accountings since Kishan the old keeper had died many moon-turns before, and great was Yalden's dismay to find this emptiness instead of the expected wealth. The indifference of the small creatures in the cracks between the flagstones could not spread itself to him. This was a very grave matter, and would have to be met in a very prompt and serious way. Clearly, there was nothing to do but consult Oorn, and Oorn was a highly portentous being.

Oorn, though a creature of extremely doubtful nature, was the virtual ruler of Zeth. It obviously belonged somewhere in the outer abyss, but had blundered into Zeth one night and suffered capture by the shamith priests. The coincidence of Its excessively bizarre aspect and Its innate gift of mimicry had impressed the sacred brothers as offering vast possibilities, hence in the end they had set It up as a god and an oracle, organising a new brotherhood to serve It — and incidentally to suggest the edicts It should utter and the replies It should give. Like the Delphi and Dodona of a later world, Oorn grew famous as a giver of judgments and solver of riddles; nor did Its essence differ from them save that It lay infinitely earlier in Time, and upon an elder world where all things might happen.

And now Yalden, being not above the credulousness of his day and planet, had set out for the close-guarded and richly-fitted hall wherein Oorn brooded and mimicked the promptings of the priests.

When Yalden came within sight of the Hall, with its tower of blue tile, he became properly religious, and entered the building acceptably, in a humble manner which greatly impeded progress. According to custom, the guardians of the deity acknowledged his obeisance and pecuniary offering, and retired behind heavy curtains to ignite the thuribles. After everything was in readiness, Yalden murmured a conventional prayer and bowed low before a curious empty dais studded with exotic jewels. For a moment — as the ritual prescribed — he stayed in this abased position, and when he arose the dais was no longer empty. Unconcernedly munching something the priests had given It was a large pudgy creature very hard to describe, and covered with short grey fur. Whence It had come in so brief a time only the priests might tell, but the suppliant knew that It was Oorn.

Hesitantly Yalden stated his unfortunate mission and asked advice; weaving into his discourse the type of flattery which seemed to him most discreet. Then, with anxiety, he awaited the oracle's response. Having tidily finished Its food, Oorn raised three small reddish eyes to Yalden and uttered certain words in a tone of vast decisiveness: "Gumay ere hfotuol leheht teg." After this It vanished suddenly in a cloud of pink smoke which seemed to issue from behind the curtain where the acolytes were.

The acolytes then came forth from their hiding-place and spoke to Yalden, saying: "Since you have pleased the deity with your concise statement of a very deplorable state of affairs, we are honoured by interpreting its directions. The aphorism you heard signifies no less than the equally mystic phrase 'Go thou unto thy destination' or more properly speaking, you are to slay the monster-wizard Anathas, and replenish the treasury with its fabled hoard."

With this Yalden was dismissed from the temple. It may

not be said in veracity that he was fearless, for in truth, he was openly afraid of the monster Anathas, as were all the inhabitants of Ullathia and the surrounding land. Even those who doubted its actuality would not have chosen to reside in the immediate neighbourhood of the Cave of Three Winds wherein it was said to dwell.

But the prospect was not without romantic appeal, and Yalden was young and consequently unwise. He knew, among other things, that there was always the hope of rescuing some feminine victim of the monster's famed and surprising erotic taste. Of the true aspect of Anathas none could be certain; tales of a widely opposite nature being commonly circulated. Many vowed it had been seen from afar in the form of a giant black shadow peculiarly repugnant to human taste, while others alleged it was a mound of gelatinous substance that oozed hatefully in the manner of putrescent flesh. Still others claimed they had seen it as a monstrous insect with astonishing supernumerary appurtenances. But in one thing all coincided; namely, that it was advisable to have as little traffic as possible with Anathas.

With due supplications to his gods and to their messenger Oorn, Yalden set out for the Cave of Three Winds. In his bosom were mixed an ingrained, patriotic sense of duty, and a thrill of adventurous expectancy regarding the unknown mysteries he faced. He had not neglected such preparations as a sensible man might make, and a wizard of old repute had furnished him with certain singular accessories. He had, for example, a charm which prevented his thirsting or hungering, and wholly did away with his need for provisions. There was likewise a glistening cape to counteract the evil emanations of a mineral that lay scattered over the rocky ground along his course. Other warnings and safeguards dealt with certain gaudy land-crustaceans, and with the deathly-sweet mists which arise at certain points until dispersed by heliotropism.

Thus shielded, Yalden fared without incident until he came to the place of the White Worm. Here of necessity he delayed to make preparations for finding the rest of his way. With patient diligence he captured the small colourless maggot, and surrounded it with a curious mark made with green paint. As was prophesied, the Lord of Worms, whose name was Sarall, made promise of certain things in return for its freedom. Then Yalden released it, and it crawled away after directing him on the course he was to follow.

The sere and fruitless land through which he now travelled was totally uninhabited. Not even the hardier of the beasts were to be seen beyond the edge of that final plateau which separated him from his goal. Far off, in a purplish haze, rose the mountains amidst which dwelt Anathas. It lived not solitary, despite the lonely region around, for strange pets resided with it — some the fabled elder monsters, and others unique beings created by its own fearful craft.

At the heart of its cave, legend said, Anathas had concealed an enormous hoard of jewels, gold, and other things of fabulous value. Why so potent a wonder-worker should care for such gauds, or revel in the counting of money, was by no means clear; but many things attested the truth of these tastes. Great numbers of persons of stronger will and wit than Yalden had died in remarkable manners while seeking the hoard of the wizard-beast, and their bones were laid in a strange pattern before the mouth of the cave, as a warning to others.

When, after countless vicissitudes, Yalden came at last into sight of the Cave of Winds amid the glistening boulders, he knew indeed that report had not lied concerning the isolation of Anathas' lair. The cavern-mouth was well-concealed, and over everything an ominous quiet lowered. There was no trace of habitation, save of course the ossuary ornamentation in the front yard. With his hand on the sword that had been sanctified by a priest of Oorn, Yalden tremblingly advanced. When he had attained the very opening of the lair, he hesitated no longer, for it was evident that the monster was away.

Deeming this the best of all times to prosecute his business, Yalden plunged at once within the cave. The interior was very cramped and exceedingly dirty, but the roof glittered with an innumerable array of small, varicoloured lights, the source of which was not to be perceived. In the rear yawned another opening, either natural or artificial; and to this black, low-arched burrow Yalden hastened, crawling within it on hands and knees. Before long a faint blue radiance glowed at the farther end, and presently the searcher emerged into an ampler space. Straightening up, he beheld a most singular change in his surroundings. This second cavern was tall and domed as if it had been shapen by supernatural powers, and a soft blue and silver light infused the gloom. Anathas, thought Yalden, lived indeed in comfort; for this room was finer than anything in the Palace of Zeth, or even in the Temple of Oorn, upon which had been lavished unthinkable wealth and beauty. Yalden stood agape, but not for long, since he desired most of all to seek the object of his quest and depart before Anathas should return from wherever it might be. For Yalden did not wish to encounter the monster-sorcerer of which so many tales were told.

Leaving therefore this second cave by a narrow cleft which he saw, the seeker followed a devious and unlit way far down through the solid rock of the plateau. This, he felt, would take him to that third and ultimate cavern where his business lay. As he progressed, he glimpsed ahead of him a curious glow; and at last, without warning, the walls receded to reveal a vast open space paved solidly with blazing coals above which flapped and shrieked an obscene flock of wyvern-headed birds. Over the fiery surface green monstrous salamanders slithered, eyeing the intruder with malignant speculation. And on the far side rose the stairs of a metal dais, encrusted with jewels, and piled high with precious objects: the hoard of the wizard-beast.

At sight of this unattainable wealth, Yalden's fervour well-nigh overcame him; and chaffing at his futility, he searched the sea of flame for some way of crossing. This, he soon perceived, was not readily to be found; for in all that glowing crypt there was only a slight crescent of flooring near the entrance which a mortal man might hope to walk on. Desperation, however, possessed him; so that at last he resolved to risk all and try the fiery pavement. Better to die in the quest than to return empty-handed. With teeth set, he started toward the sea of flame, heedless of what might follow.

As it was, surprise seared him almost as vehemently as he had expected the flames to do — for with his advance, the glowing floor divided to form a narrow lane of safe cool earth leading straight to the golden throne. Half dazed, and heedless of whatever might underlie such curiously favouring magic, Yalden drew his sword and strode boldly betwixt the walls of flame that rose from the rifted pavement. The heat hurt him not at all, and the wyvern-creatures drew back, hissing, and did not molest him.

The hoard now glistened close at hand, and Yalden thought of how he would return to Zeth, laden with fabulous spoils and worshipped by throngs as a hero. In his joy he forgot to wonder at Anathas' lax care of its treasures; nor did the very friendly behaviour of the fiery pavement seem in any way remarkable. Even the huge arched opening behind the dais, so oddly invisible from across the cavern, failed to disturb him seriously. Only when he had mounted the broad stair of the dais and stood ankle-deep amid the bizarre golden reliques of other ages and other worlds, and the lovely, luminous gems from unknown mines and of unknown natures and meanings, did Yalden begin to realise that anything was wrong.

But now he perceived that the miraculous passage through the flaming floor was closing again, leaving him marooned on the dais with the glittering treasure he had sought. And when it had fully closed, and his eyes had circled round vainly for some way of escape, he was hardly reassured by the shapeless jelly-like shadow which loomed colossal and stinking in the great archway behind the dais. He was not permitted to faint, but was forced to observe that this shadow was infinitely more hideous than anything hinted in any popular legend, and that its seven iridescent eyes were regarding him with placid amusement.

Then Anathas the wizard-beast rolled fully out of the archway, mighty in necromantic horror, and jested with the small frightened conqueror before allowing that horde of slavering and peculiarly hungry green salamanders to complete their slow, anticipatory ascent of the dais.

The Wicked Clergyman.

1,700-WORD SHORT STORY;
1933.

This short story is simply a dream-transcript. Lovecraft included it in a letter to Bernard Austin Dwyer dated Oct. 22 ,1933; after Lovecraft's death, Dwyer packaged it up as a story, gave it a title, and submitted it to Weird Tales. *It was published in the April 1939 issue.*

"The Wicked Clergyman" is often referred to as "The Evil Clergyman," the alternative title given to it by August Derleth when he republished it in 1965 in Dagon and Other Macabre Tales.

I was shewn into the attic chamber by a grave, intelligent-looking man with quiet clothes and an iron-gray beard, who spoke to me in this fashion:

"Yes, he lived here — but I don't advise your doing anything. Your curiosity makes you irresponsible. We never come here at night, and it's only because of his will that we keep it this way. You know what he did. That abominable society took charge at last, and we don't know where he is buried. There was no way the law or anything else could reach the society.

"I hope you won't stay till after dark. And I beg of you to let that thing on the table — the thing that looks like a match-box — alone. We don't know what it is, but we suspect it has something to do with what he did. We even avoid looking at it very steadily."

After a time the man left me alone in the attic room. It was very dingy and dusty, and only primitively furnished, but it had a neatness which showed it was not a slum-denizen's quarters. There were shelves full of theological and classical books, and another bookcase containing treatises on magic — Paracelsus, Albertus Magnus, Trithemius, Hermes Trismegistus, Borellus, and others in a strange alphabet whose titles I could not decipher. The furniture was very plain. There was a door, but it led only into a closet. The only egress was the aperture in the floor up to which the crude, steep staircase led. The windows were of bull's-eye pattern, and the black oak beams bespoke unbelievable antiquity. Plainly, this house was of the Old World. I seemed to know where I was, but cannot recall what I then knew. Certainly the town was not London. My impression is of a small seaport.

The small object on the table fascinated me intensely. I seemed to know what to do with it, for I drew a pocket electric light—or what looked like one—out of my pocket and nervously tested its flashes. The light was not white but violet, and seemed less like true light than like some radioactive bombardment. I recall that I did not regard it as a common flashlight—indeed, I had a common flashlight in another pocket.

It was getting dark, and the ancient roofs and chimney-pots outside looked very queer through the bull's-eye window-panes. Finally I summoned up courage and propped the small object up on the table against a book—then turned the rays of the peculiar violet light upon it. The light seemed now to be more like a rain of hail or small violet particles than like a continuous beam. As the particles struck the glassy surface at the center of the strange device, they seemed to produce a crackling noise like the sputtering of a vacuum tube through which sparks are passed. The dark glassy surface displayed a pinkish glow, and a vague white shape seemed to be taking form at its center. Then I noticed that I was not alone in the room—and put the ray-projector back in my pocket.

But the newcomer did not speak—nor did I hear any sound whatever during all the immediately following moments. Everything was shadowy pantomime, as if seen at a vast distance through some intervening haze—although on the other hand the newcomer and all subsequent comers loomed large and close, as if both near and distant, according to some abnormal geometry.

The newcomer was a thin, dark man of medium height attired in the clerical garb of the Anglican church. He was apparently about thirty years old, with a sallow, olive complexion and fairly good features, but an abnormally high forehead. His black hair was well cut and neatly brushed, and he was clean-shaven though blue-chinned with a heavy growth of beard. He wore rimless spectacles with steel bows. His build and lower facial features were like other clergymen I had seen, but he had a vastly higher forehead, and was darker and more intelligent-looking—also more subtly and concealedly evil-looking. At the present moment—having just lighted a faint oil lamp—he looked nervous, and before I knew it he was casting all his magical books into a fireplace on the window side of the room (where the wall slanted sharply) which I had not noticed before. The flames devoured the volumes greedily—leaping up in strange colors and emitting indescribably hideous odors as the strangely hieroglyphed leaves and wormy bindings succumbed to the devastating element. All at once I saw there were others in the room—grave-looking men in clerical costume, one of whom wore the bands and knee-breeches of a bishop. Though I could hear nothing, I could see that they were bringing a decision of vast import to the first-comer. They seemed to hate and fear him at the same time, and he seemed to return these sentiments. His face set itself into a grim expression, but I could see his right hand shaking as he tried to grip the back of a chair. The bishop pointed to the empty case and to the fireplace (where the flames had died down amidst a charred, non-committal mass), and seemed filled with a peculiar loathing. The first-comer then gave a wry smile and reached out with his left hand toward the small object on the table. Everyone then seemed frightened. The procession of clerics began filing down the steep stairs through the trapdoor in the floor, turning and making menacing gestures as they left. The bishop was last to go.

The first-comer now went to a cupboard on the inner side of the room and extracted a coil of rope. Mounting a chair, he attached one end of the rope to a hook in the great exposed central beam of black oak, and began making a noose with the other end. Realizing he was about to hang himself, I started forward to dissuade or save him. He saw me and ceased his preparations, looking at me with a kind of triumph which puzzled and disturbed me. He slowly stepped down from the chair and began gliding toward me with a positively wolfish grin on his dark, thin-lipped face.

I felt somehow in deadly peril, and drew out the peculiar ray-projector as a weapon of defense. Why I thought it could help me, I do not know. I turned it on—full in his face, and saw the sallow features glow first with violet and then with pinkish light. His expression of wolfish exultation began to be crowded aside by a look of profound fear—which did not, however, wholly displace the exultation. He stopped in his tracks—then, flailing his arms wildly in the air, began to stagger backwards. I saw he was edging toward the open stair-well in the floor, and tried to shout a warning, but he did not hear me. In another instant he had lurched backward through the opening and was lost to view.

I found difficulty in moving toward the stair-well, but when I did get there I found no crushed body on the floor below. Instead there was a clatter of people coming up with lanterns, for the spell of phantasmal silence had broken, and I once more heard sounds and saw figures as normally tri-dimensional. Something had evidently drawn a crowd to this place. Had there been a noise I had not heard?

Presently the two people (simple villagers, apparently) farthest in the lead saw me—and stood paralyzed. One of them shrieked loudly and reverberantly:

"Ahrrh! . . . It be'ee, zur? Again?"

Then they all turned and fled frantically. All, that is, but one. When the crowd was gone I saw the grave-bearded man who had brought me to this place—standing alone with a lantern. He was gazing at me gaspingly and fascinatedly, but did not seem afraid. Then he began to ascend the stairs, and joined me in the attic. He spoke:

"So you didn't let it alone! I'm sorry. I know what has happened. It happened once before, but the man got frightened and shot himself. You ought not to have made him come back. You know what he wants. But you mustn't get frightened like the other man he got. Something very strange and terrible has happened to you, but it didn't get far enough to hurt your mind and personality. If you'll keep cool, and accept the need for making certain radical readjustments in your life, you can keep right on enjoying the world, and the fruits of your scholarship. But you can't live here — and I don't think you'll wish to go back to London. I'd advise America.

"You mustn't try anything more with that — thing. Nothing can be put back now. It would only make matters worse to do — or summon — anything. You are not as badly off as you might be — but you must get out of here at once and stay away. You'd better thank Heaven it didn't go further . . . .

"I'm going to prepare you as bluntly as I can. There's been a certain change — in your personal appearance. He always causes that. But in a new country you can get used to it. There's a mirror up at the other end of the room, and I'm going to take you to it. You'll get a shock — though you will see nothing repulsive."

I was now shaking with a deadly fear, and the bearded man almost had to hold me up as he walked me across the room to the mirror, the faint lamp (i.e., that formerly on the table, not the still fainter lantern he had brought) in his free hand. This is what I saw in the glass:

A thin, dark man of medium stature attired in the clerical garb of the Anglican church, apparently about thirty, and with rimless, steel-bowed glasses glistening beneath a sallow, olive forehead of abnormal height.

It was the silent first-comer who had burned his books.

For all the rest of my life, in outward form, I was to be that man!

The Book.

1,200-WORD SHORT STORY;
1933/1934.

Readers familiar with the first four poems of Fungi from Yuggoth will feel a sense of deja vu when reading "The Book."

S. T. Joshi has suggested that the story is an artifact of the painful period of late 1933 and early 1934, during which Lovecraft's well of inspiration was running dry and he was desperately trying to jump-start something by cannibalizing old ideas. Although this is, of course, speculation, it seems very likely.

"The Book" was probably written sometime in late 1933 or early 1934, although no one knows for sure. It was first published in Robert H. Barlow's amateur-press journal, Leaves, *in the 1938 issue.*

My memories are very confused. There is even much doubt as to where they begin; for at times I feel appalling vistas of years stretching behind me, while at other times it seems as if the present moment were an isolated point in a grey, formless infinity. I am not even certain how I am communicating this message. While I know I am speaking, I have a vague impression that some strange and perhaps terrible mediation will be needed to bear what I say to the points where I wish to be heard. My identity, too, is bewilderingly cloudy. I seem to have suffered a great shock — perhaps from some utterly monstrous outgrowth of my cycles of unique, incredible experience.

These cycles of experience, of course, all stem from that worm-riddled book. I remember when I found it — in a dimly lighted place near the black, oily river where the mists always swirl. That place was very old, and the ceiling-high shelves full of rotting volumes reached back endlessly through windowless inner rooms and alcoves. There were, besides, great formless heaps of books on the floor and in crude bins; and it was in one of these heaps that I found the thing. I never learned its title, for the early pages were missing; but it fell open toward the end and gave me a glimpse of something which sent my senses reeling.

There was a formula — a sort of list of things to say and do — which I recognised as something black and forbidden; something which I had read of before in furtive paragraphs of mixed abhorrence and fascination penned by those strange ancient delvers into the universe's guarded secrets whose decaying texts I loved to absorb. It was a key — a guide — to certain gateways and transitions of which mystics have dreamed and whispered since the race was young, and which lead to freedoms and discoveries beyond the three dimensions and realms of life and matter that we know. Not for centuries had any man recalled its vital substance or known where to find it, but this book was very old indeed. No printing-press, but the hand of some half-crazed monk, had traced these ominous Latin phrases in uncials of awesome antiquity.

I remember how the old man leered and tittered, and made a curious sign with his hand when I bore it away. He had refused to take pay for it, and only long afterward did I guess why. As I hurried home through those narrow, winding, mist-choked waterfront streets I had a frightful impression of being stealthily followed by softly padding feet. The centuried, tottering houses on both sides seemed alive with a fresh and morbid malignity — as if some hitherto closed channel of evil understanding had abruptly been opened. I felt that those walls and overhanging gables of mildewed brick and fungous plaster and timber — with fishy, eye-like, diamond-paned windows that leered — could hardly desist from advancing and crushing me . . . yet I had read only the least fragment of that blasphemous rune before closing the book and bringing it away.

I remember how I read the book at last — white-faced, and locked in the attic room that I had long devoted to strange searchings. The great house was very still, for I had not gone up till after midnight. I think I had a family then — though the details are very uncertain — and I know there were many servants. Just what the year was, I cannot say; for since then I have known many ages and dimensions, and have had all my notions of time dissolved and refashioned. It was by the light of candles that I read — I recall the relentless dripping of the wax — and there were chimes that came every now and then from distant belfries. I seemed to keep track of those chimes with a peculiar intentness, as if I feared to hear some very remote, intruding note among them.

Then came the first scratching and fumbling at the dormer window that looked out high above the other roofs of the city. It came as I droned aloud the ninth verse of that primal lay, and I knew amidst my shudders what it meant. For he who passes the gateways always wins a shadow, and never again can he be alone. I had evoked — and the book was indeed all I had suspected. That night I passed the gateway to a vortex of twisted time and vision, and when morning found me in the attic room I saw in the walls and shelves and fittings that which I had never seen before.

Nor could I ever after see the world as I had known it. Mixed with the present scene was always a little of the past and a little of the future, and every once-familiar object loomed alien in the new perspective brought by my widened sight. From then on I walked in a fantastic dream of unknown and half-known shapes; and with each new gateway crossed, the less plainly could I recognise the things of the narrow sphere to which I had so long been bound. What I saw about me none else saw; and I grew doubly silent and aloof lest I be thought mad. Dogs had a fear of me, for they felt the outside shadow which never left my side. But still I read more — in hidden, forgotten books and scrolls to which my new vision led me — and pushed through fresh gateways of space and being and life-patterns toward the core of the unknown cosmos.

I remember the night I made the five concentric circles of fire on the floor, and stood in the innermost one chanting that monstrous litany the messenger from Tartary had brought. The walls melted away, and I was swept by a black wind through gulfs of fathomless grey with the needle-like pinnacles of unknown mountains miles below me. After a while there was utter blackness, and then the light of myriad stars forming strange, alien constellations. Finally I saw a green-litten plain far below me, and discerned on it the twisted towers of a city built in no fashion I had ever known or read of or dreamed of. As I floated closer to that city I saw a great square building of stone in an open space, and felt a hideous fear clutching at me. I screamed and struggled, and after a blankness was again in my attic room, sprawled flat over the five phosphorescent circles on the floor. In that night's wandering there was no more of strangeness than in many a former night's wandering; but there was more of terror because I knew I was closer to those outside gulfs and worlds than I had ever been before. Thereafter I was more cautious with my incantations, for I had no wish to be cut off from my body and from the earth in unknown abysses whence I could never return.

1934.

In the Gathering Darkness.

H.P. Lovecraft continued to enjoy a glut of business in his ghost-writing operations in 1934, so much so that he started farming the work out to talented friends; yet he still wasn't making enough money from the business to live on. It's unfortunate that among all his friends there apparently wasn't one with enough business sense to advise him on this; perhaps if he'd had a decent income, he could have varied his diet enough to avoid the intestinal cancer that would eventually take his life.

Late in 1933, Lovecraft wrote to Robert Barlow that he was having trouble with his muse. Every artist occasionally experiences a dry spell, during which nothing seems to work and the well of inspiration runs dry. Typically these dry spells engender periods of agonized soul-searching, accompanied by fears that one's best years are in the past and that perhaps one isn't really much good anyway, and only just got lucky that one time . . . .

Lovecraft was in the grip of just such a spell of discouragement as 1933 ripened into 1934, around the time he is thought to have written "The Book"; and that may explain the low level of his creative output that year.

In any case, Lovecraft's fiction output for 1934 was negligible. He kept himself busy with an unusually ambitious summer travel itinerary, including a bicycle tour of Nantucket, and several accompanying travelogues; and he scratched his weird-fiction itch by helping his latest young epistolary protegé, Duane W. Rimel, with "The Tree on the Hill" and "The Sorcery of Aphlar." Rimel would later achieve literary success and fame (or, depending on your point of view, notoriety) as a prolific writer of porno-shop paperbacks under the pseudonym "Rex Weldon."

Finally, on Nov. 10, 1934, his travels and the associated travelogues all finished, Lovecraft tucked into one of his very best novellas, *The Shadow out of Time*. He worked on it all the rest of that year, and at the end of the year was still only about halfway done with it.

that one had to go to a porno shop (or, as they usually style themselves, an "adult bookstore") to purchase.

This literary legacy may be why Duane Weldon Rimel gets scant respect from some Lovecraft scholars. Many of them are already a little resentful about the fact that Lovecraft's highly literary work is constantly being lumped in with that of pulp-fiction "hacks" like Seabury Quinn and Hugh B. Cave; rounding out the reference group with one of the most prolific writers of sleazy paperback hardcore would be, perhaps, just a little too much for these proud scholars to take.

The Tree on the Hill.

BY DUANE W. RIMEL AND H.P. LOVECRAFT

4,200-WORD SHORT STORY; 1934.

This short story is one of the earliest of Duane Rimel's writings, which he sent to Lovecraft in early 1934. Lovecraft replied with a graceful note and some substantial suggestions for revision; but Rimel didn't place it for publication until 1940, when it ran in the fan magazine Polaris.

The story is clearly intended to be set in the Snake River country of eastern Washington and northern Idaho, although the reference to the "Salmon River gorge" is confusing and there is no such town as Hampden; possibly he was trying to do something like what Lovecraft had done with Arkham, Massachusetts, and the Miskatonic River, blending real and fictional geographic elements.

ABOUT DUANE W. RIMEL (1915-1996).

Duane Weldon Rimel was one of several young budding writers interested in weird fiction who reached out to Lovecraft in the 1930s. He was 18 or 19 years old when he wrote to Lovecraft, living in Asotin, a tiny town in the state of Washington — just across the border from Lewiston, Idaho.

Rimel, after Lovecraft's death ended their association, went on to a fairly successful career as a genre-fiction writer. He wrote four detective novels of the "hard-boiled" type, one science-fiction novel, and numerous short stories and novelettes in science fiction, weird fiction, and fantasy.

But it was under his pseudonym, Rex Weldon, that Rimel put up his real numbers. "Rex Weldon" cranked out dozens of undeniably popular titles throughout the 1960s and 1970s and beyond — titles with names like Sex Week, Stud for Hire, Bed Slave, *and* Hot to Swap, *not to mention* Reluctant Lesbian, The Two-Way Amazon, *and* Your Wife for Mine. *These were the kind of books*

I.

Southeast of Hampden, near the tortuous Salmon River gorge, is a range of steep, rocky hills which have defied all efforts of sturdy homesteaders. The canyons are too deep and the slopes too precipitous to encourage anything save seasonal livestock grazing. The last time I visited Hampden the region — known as Hell's Acres — was part of the Blue Mountain Forest Reserve. There are no roads linking this inaccessible locality with the outside world, and the hill-folk will tell you that it is indeed a spot transplanted from His Satanic Majesty's front yard. There is a local superstition that the area is haunted — but by what or by whom no one seems to know. Natives will not venture within its mysterious depths, for they believe the stories handed down to them by the Nez Percé Indians, who have shunned the region for untold generations, because, according to them, it is a playground of certain giant devils from the Outside. These suggestive tales made me very curious.

My first excursion — and my last, thank God! — into those hills occurred while Constantine Theunis and I were living in Hampden the summer of 1938. He was writing a treatise on Egyptian mythology, and I found myself alone much of the time, despite the fact that we shared a modest cabin on Beacon Street, within sight of the infamous Pirate House, built by Exer Jones over sixty years ago.

The morning of June 23rd found me walking in those oddly shaped hills, which had, since seven o'clock, seemed very ordinary indeed. I must have been about seven miles north of Hampden before I noticed anything unusual. I was climbing a grassy ridge overlooking a particularly deep canyon, when I came upon an area totally devoid of the usual bunch-grass and greaseweed. It extended southward, over numerous hills and valleys. At first I thought the spot had been burned over the previous fall, but upon examining the turf, I found no signs of a blaze. The nearby slopes and ravines looked terribly scarred and seared, as if some gigantic torch had blasted them, wiping away all vegetation. And yet there was no evidence of fire . . . .

I moved on over rich, black soil in which no grass flourished. As I headed for the approximate centre of this desolate area, I began to notice a strange silence. There were no larks, no rabbits, and even the insects seemed to have deserted the place. I gained the summit of a lofty knoll and tried to guess at the size of that bleak, inexplicable region. Then I saw the lone tree.

It stood on a hill somewhat higher than its companions, and attracted the eye because it was so utterly unexpected. I had seen no trees for miles: thorn and hackberry bushes clustered the shallower ravines, but there had been no mature trees. Strange to find one standing on the crest of the hill.

I crossed two steep canyons before I came to it; and a surprise awaited me. It was not a pine tree, nor a fir tree, nor a hackberry tree. I had never, in all my life, seen one to compare with it — and I never have to this day, for which I am eternally thankful!

More than anything it resembled an oak. It had a huge, twisted trunk, fully a yard in diameter, and the large limbs began spreading outward scarcely seven feet from the ground. The leaves were round, and curiously alike in size and design. It might have been a tree painted on a canvas, but I will swear that it was real. I shall always know that it was real, despite what Theunis said later.

I recall that I glanced at the sun and judged the time to be about ten o'clock a.m., although I did not look at my watch. The day was becoming warm, and I sat for a while in the welcome shade of the huge tree. Then I regarded the rank grass that flourished beneath it — another singular phenomenon when I remembered the bleak terrain through which I had passed. A wild maze of hills, ravines, and bluffs hemmed me in on all sides, although the rise on which I sat was rather higher than any other within miles. I looked far to the east — and I jumped to my feet, startled and amazed. Shimmering though a blue haze of distance were the Bitterroot Mountains! There is no other range of snow-capped peaks within three hundred miles of Hampden; and I knew — at this altitude — that I shouldn't be seeing them at all. For several minutes I gazed at the marvel; then I became drowsy. I lay in the rank grass, beneath the tree. I unstrapped my camera, took off my hat, and relaxed, staring skyward through the green leaves. I closed my eyes.

Then a curious phenomenon began to assail me — a vague, cloudy sort of vision — glimpsing or day-dreaming seemingly without relevance to anything familiar. I thought I saw a great temple by a sea of ooze, where three suns gleamed in a pale red sky. The vast tomb, or temple, was an anomalous colour — a nameless blue-violet shade. Large beasts flew in the cloudy sky, and I seemed to hear the pounding of their scaly wings. I went nearer the stone temple, and a huge doorway loomed in front of me. Within that portal were swirling shadows that seemed to dart and leer and try to snatch me inside that awful darkness. I thought I saw three flaming eyes in the shifting void of a doorway, and I screamed with mortal fear. In that noisome depth, I knew, lurked utter destruction — a living hell even worse than death. I screamed again. The vision faded.

I saw the round leaves and the sane earthly sky. I struggled to rise. I was trembling; cold perspiration beaded my brow. I had a mad impulse to flee; run insanely from that sinister tree on the hill — but I checked the absurd intuition and sat down, trying to collect my senses. Never had I dreamed anything so realistic, so horrifying. What had caused the vision? I had been reading several of Theunis' tomes on ancient Egypt . . . I mopped my forehead, and decided that it was time for lunch. But I did not feel like eating.

Then I had an inspiration. I would take a few snapshots of the tree, for Theunis. They might shock him out of his habitual air of unconcern. Perhaps I would tell him about the dream . . . Opening my camera, I took half a dozen shots of the tree. Also, I included one of the gleaming, snow-crested peaks. I might want to return, and these photos would help.

Folding the camera, I returned to my cushion of soft grass. Had that spot beneath the tree a certain alien enchantment? I know that I was reluctant to leave it . . . .

I gazed upward at the curious round leaves. I closed my eyes. A breeze stirred the branches, and their whispered music lulled me into tranquil oblivion. And suddenly I saw again the pale red sky and the three suns. The land of three shadows! Again the great temple came into view. I seemed to be floating on the air — a disembodied spirit exploring the wonders of a mad, multi-dimensional world! The temple's oddly angled cornices frightened me, and I knew that this place was one that no man on earth had ever seen in his wildest dreams.

Again the vast doorway yawned before me; and I was sucked within that black, writhing cloud. I seemed to be staring at space unlimited. I saw a void beyond my vocabulary to describe; a dark, bottomless gulf teeming with nameless shapes and entities — things of madness and delirium, as tenuous as a mist from Shamballah.

My soul shrank. I was terribly afraid. I screamed and screamed, and felt that I would soon go mad. Then in my dream I ran and ran in a fever of utter terror, but I did not know what I was running from . . . I left that hideous temple and that hellish void, yet I knew I must, barring some miracle, return . . . .

At last my eyes flew open. I was not beneath the tree. I was sprawled on a rocky slope, my clothing torn and disordered. My hands were bleeding. I stood up; pain stabbing through me. I recognized the spot — the ridge where I had first seen the blasted area! I must have walked miles — unconscious! The tree was not in sight, and I was glad . . . Even the knees of my trousers were torn, as if I had crawled part of the way.

I glanced at the sun. Late afternoon! *Where* had I been? I snatched out my watch. It had stopped at 10:34.

II.

"So you have the snapshots?" Theunis drawled. I met his grey eyes across the breakfast table. Three days had slipped by since my return from Hell's Acres. I had told him about the dream beneath the tree, and he had laughed.

"Yes," I replied. "They came last night. Haven't had a chance to open them yet. Give 'em a good, careful study — if they aren't all failures. Perhaps you'll change your mind."

Theunis smiled; sipped his coffee. I gave him the unopened envelope and he quickly broke the seal and withdrew the pictures. He glanced at the first one, and the smile faded from his leonine face. He crushed out his cigarette.

"My God, man! Look at this!"

I seized the glossy rectangle. It was the first picture of the tree, taken at a distance of fifty feet or so. The cause of Theunis' excitement escaped me. There it was, standing boldly on the hill, while below it grew the jungle of grass where I had lain. In the distance were my snow-capped mountains!

"There you are," I cried. "The proof of my story — "

"Look at it!" Theunis snapped. "The shadows — there are three for every rock, bush, and tree!"

He was right . . . below the tree, spread in fanlike incongruity, lay three overlapping shadows. Suddenly I realized that the picture held an abnormal and inconsistent element. The leaves on the thing were too lush for the work of sane nature, while the trunk was bulged and knotted in the most abhorrent shapes. Theunis dropped the picture on the table.

"There is something wrong," I muttered. "The tree I saw didn't look as repulsive as that — "

"Are you sure?" Theunis grated. "The fact is, you may have seen many things not recorded on this film."

"It shows more than I saw!"

"That's the point. There is something damnably out of place in this landscape; something I can't understand. The tree seems to suggest a thought — beyond my grasp . . . it is too misty; too uncertain; too unreal to be natural!" He rapped nervous fingers on the table. He snatched the remaining films and shuffled through them, rapidly.

I reached for the snapshot he had dropped, and sensed a touch of bizarre uncertainty and strangeness as my eyes absorbed its every detail. The flowers and weeds pointed at varying angles, while some of the grass grew in the most bewildering fashion. The tree seemed too veiled and clouded to be readily distinguished, but I noted the huge limbs and the half-bent flower stems that were ready to fall over, yet did not fall. And the many, overlapping shadows . . . They were, altogether, very disquieting shadows — too long or short when compared to the stems they fell below to give one a feeling of comfortable normality. The landscape hadn't shocked me the day of my visit . . . There was a dark familiarity and mocking suggestion of it; something tangible, yet distant as the stars beyond the galaxy.

Theunis came back to earth. "Did you mention *three* suns in your dreaming orgy?"

I nodded, frankly puzzled. Then it dawned on me. My fingers trembled slightly as I stared at the picture again. My dream! Of course —

"The others are just like it," Theunis said. "That same uncertainness; that *suggestion*. I should be able to catch the mood of the thing; see it in its real light, but it is too . . . Perhaps later I shall find out, if I look at it long enough."

We sat in silence for some time. A thought came to me, suddenly, prompted by a strange, inexplicable longing to visit the tree again. "Let's make an excursion. I think I can take you there in half a day."

"You'd better stay away," replied Theunis, thoughtfully. "I doubt if you could find the place again if you wanted to."

"Nonsense," I replied. "Surely, with these photos to guide us — "

"Do you see any familiar landmarks in them?"

His observation was uncanny. After looking through the remaining snaps carefully, I had to admit that there were none.

Theunis muttered under his breath and drew viciously on his cigarette. "A perfectly normal or nearly so — picture of a spot apparently dropped from nowhere. Seeing mountains at this low altitude is preposterous . . . but wait!"

He sprang from the chair as a hunted animal and raced from the room. I could hear him moving about in our makeshift library, cursing volubly. Before long he reappeared with an old, leather-bound volume. Theunis opened it reverently, and peered over the odd characters.

"What do you call that?" I inquired.

"This is an early English translation of the *Chronicle of Nath*, written by Rudolf Yergler, a German mystic and alchemist who borrowed some of his lore from Hermes Trismegistus, the ancient Egyptian sorcerer. There is a passage here that might interest you — might make you understand why this business is even further from the natural than you suspect. Listen:

" 'So in the year of the Black Goat there came unto Nath a shadow that should not be on Earth, and that had no form known to the eyes of Earth. And it fed on the souls of men; they that it gnawed being lured and blinded with dreams till the horror and the endless night lay upon them. Nor did they see that which gnawed them; for the shadow took false shapes that men know or dream of, and only freedom seemed waiting in the Land of the Three Suns. But it was told by priests of the Old Book that he who could see the shadow's true shape, and live after the seeing, might shun its doom and send it back to the starless gulf of its spawning. This none could do save through the Gem; wherefore did Ka-Nefer the High-Priest keep that gem sacred in the temple. And when it was lost with Phrenes, he who braved the horror and was never seen more, there was weeping in Nath. Yet did the Shadow depart sated at last, nor shall it hunger again till the cycles roll back to the year of the Black Goat.' "

Theunis paused while I stared, bewildered. Finally he spoke. "Now, Single, I suppose you can guess how this all links up. There is no need of going deep into the primal lore behind this business, but I may as well tell you that according to the old legends this is the so-called "Year of the Black Goat" — when certain horrors from the fathomless Outside are supposed to visit the earth and do infinite harm. We don't know how they'll be manifest, but there's reason to think that strange mirages and hallucinations will be mixed up in the matter. I don't like the thing you've run up against — the story or the pictures. It may be pretty bad, and I warn you to look out. But first I must try to do what old Yergler says — to see if I can glimpse the matter as it is. Fortunately the old Gem he mentions has been rediscovered — I know where I can get at it. We must use it on the photograph and see what we see.

"It's more or less like a lens or prism, though one can't take photographs with it. Someone of peculiar sensitiveness might look through and sketch what he sees. There's a bit of danger, and the looker may have his consciousness shaken a trifle; for the real shape of the shadow isn't pleasant and doesn't belong on this earth. But it would be a lot more dangerous not to do anything about it. Meanwhile, if you value your life and your sanity, keep away from that hill — and from the thing you think is a tree on it."

I was more bewildered than ever. "How can there be organized beings from the Outside in our midst?" I cried. "How do we know that such things exist?"

"You reason in terms of this tiny earth," Theunis said. "Surely you don't think that the world is a rule for measuring the universe. There are entities we never dream of floating under our very noses. Modern science is thrusting back the borderland of the unknown and proving that the mystics were not so far off the track — "

Suddenly I knew I did not want to look at the picture again; I wanted to destroy it. I wanted to run from it. Theunis was suggesting something beyond . . . A trembling, cosmic fear gripped me and drew me away from the hideous picture, for I was afraid I would recognize some object in it . . . .

I glanced at my friend. He was poring over the ancient book, a strange expression on his face. He sat up straight. "Let's call the thing off for today. I'm tired of this endless guessing and wondering. I must get the loan of the gem from the museum where it is, and do what is to be done."

"As you say," I replied. "Will you have to go to Croydon?"

He nodded.

"Then we'll both go home," I said decisively.

III.

I need not chronicle the events of the fortnight that followed. With me they formed a constant and enervating struggle between a mad longing to return to the cryptic tree of dreams and freedom, and a frenzied dread of that self-same thing and all connected with it. That I did not return is perhaps less a matter of my own will than a matter of pure chance. Meanwhile I knew that Theunis was desperately active in some investigation of the strangest nature — something which included a mysterious motor trip and a return under circumstances of the greatest secrecy. By hints over the telephone I was made to understand that he had somewhere borrowed the obscure and primal object mentioned in the ancient volume as "The Gem," and that he was busy devising a means of applying it to the photographs I had left with him. He spoke fragmentarily of "refraction," "polarization," and "unknown angles of space and time," and indicated that he was building a kind of box or camera obscura for the study of the curious snapshots with the gem's aid.

It was on the sixteenth day that I received the startling message from the hospital in Croydon. Theunis was there, and wanted to see me at once. He had suffered some odd sort of seizure; being found prone and unconscious by friends who found their way into his house after hearing certain cries of mortal agony and fear. Though still weak and helpless, he had now regained his senses and seemed frantic to tell me something and have me perform certain important duties. This much the hospital informed me over the wire; and within half an hour I was at my friend's bedside, marvelling at the inroads which worry and tension had made on his features in so brief a time.

His first act was to move away the nurses in order to speak in utter confidence.

"Single — I saw it!" His voice was strained and husky. "You must destroy them all — those pictures. I sent it back by seeing it, but the pictures had better go. That tree will never be seen on the hill again — at least, I hope not — till thousands of aeons bring back the Year of the Black Goat. You are safe now — mankind is safe." He paused, breathing heavily, and continued.

"Take the Gem out of the apparatus and put it in the safe — you know the combination. It must go back where it came from, for there's a time when it may be needed to save the world. They won't let me leave here yet, but I can rest if I know it's safe. Don't look through the box as it is — it would fix you as it's fixed me. And burn those damned photographs . . . the one in the box and the others . . ." But Theunis was exhausted now, and the nurses advanced and motioned me away as he leaned back and closed his eyes.

In another half-hour I was at his house and looking curiously at the long black box on the library table beside the overturned chair. Scattered papers blew about in a breeze from the open window, and close to the box I recognized with a queer sensation the envelope of pictures I had taken. It required only a moment for me to examine the box and detach at one end my earliest picture of the tree, and at the other end a strange bit of amber-coloured crystal, cut in devious angles impossible to classify. The touch of the glass fragment seemed curiously warm and electric, and I could scarcely bear to put it out of sight in Theunis' wall safe. The snapshot I handled with a disconcerting mixture of emotions. Even after I had replaced it in the envelope with the rest I had a morbid longing to save it and gloat over it and rush out and up the hill toward its original. Peculiar line-arrangements sprang out of its details to assault and puzzle my memory . . . pictures behind pictures . . . secrets lurking in half-familiar shapes . . . But a saner contrary instinct, operating at the same time, gave me the vigor and avidity of unplaceable fear as I hastily kindled a fire in the grate and watched the problematic envelope burn to ashes. Somehow I felt that the earth had been purged of a horror on whose brink I had trembled, and which was none the less monstrous because I did not know what it was.

Of the source of Theunis' terrific shock I could form no coherent guess, nor did I dare to think too closely about it. It is notable that I did not at any time have the least impulse to look through the box before removing the gem and photograph. What was shown in the picture by the antique crystal's lens or prism-like power was not, I felt curiously certain, anything that a normal brain ought to be called upon to face. Whatever it was, I had myself been close to it — had been completely under the spell of its allurement — as it brooded on that remote hill in the form of a tree and an unfamiliar landscape. And I did not wish to know what I had so narrowly escaped.

Would that my ignorance might have remained complete! I could sleep better at night. As it was, my eye was arrested before I left the room by the pile of scattered papers rustling on the table beside the black box. All but one were blank, but that one bore a crude drawing in pencil. Suddenly recalling what Theunis had once said about sketching the horror revealed by the gem, I strove to turn away; but sheer curiosity defeated my sane design. Looking again almost furtively, I observed the nervous haste of the stroke, and the unfinished edge left by the sketcher's terrified seizure. Then, in a burst of perverse boldness, I looked squarely at the dark and forbidden design — and fell in a faint.

I shall never describe fully what I saw. After a time I regained my senses, thrust the sheet into the dying fire, and staggered out through the quiet streets to my home. I thanked God that I had not looked through the crystal at the photograph, and prayed fervently that I might forget the drawing's terrible hint of what Theunis had beheld. Since then I have never been quite the same. Even the fairest scenes have seemed to hold some vague, ambiguous hint of the nameless blasphemies which may underlie them and form their masquerading essence. And yet the sketch was so slight — so little indicative of all that Theunis, to judge from his guarded accounts later on, must have discerned!

Only a few basic elements of the landscape were in the thing. For the most part a cloudy, exotic-looking vapour dominated the view. Every object that might have been familiar was seen to be part of something vague and unknown and altogether un-terrestrial — something infinitely vaster than any human eye could grasp, and infinitely alien, monstrous, and hideous, as guessed from the fragment within range.

Where I had, in the landscape itself, seen the twisted, half-sentient tree, there was here visible only a gnarled, terrible hand or talon with fingers or feelers shockingly distended and evidently groping toward something on the ground or in the spectator's direction. And squarely below the writhing, bloated digits I thought I saw an outline in the grass where a man had lain.

But the sketch was hasty, and I could not be sure.

The Battle that Ended the Century.

BY ROBERT H. BARLOW AND H.P. LOVECRAFT

1,300-WORD SHORT STORY; 1934.

This pint-size parody started out as Barlow's plan to write something silly that would name-check every person he could think of in the world of professional magazine writers, illustrators and publishers. Initially he used their names directly; but when he read the project, Lovecraft suggested that they should be disguised punnishly to make things more fun. He himself therefore became "Horse Power Hateart"; Miles G. Breuer became "M. Gin Brewery"; Seabury Quinn became "Teaberry Quince"; and Edward G. Huey became "Goofy Hooey."

Readers who are familiar with Robert E. Howard's humorously hyperbolic boxing stories, especially those starring the sailor Steve Costigan, will immediately recognize and appreciate the parody in this exaggerated boxing story.

Lovecraft really got into the project, and ended up name-checking scores of colleagues. Some of these references are somewhat obscure and difficult to track down today, more than 85 years on. (In the text that follows, where they could be puzzled out, they are identified in brackets.)

Barlow and Lovecraft ran about 50 copies of this story off on legal-size paper, using a mimeograph machine, and had them mailed anonymously to members of the clique. The chief effect seems to have been to separate the sheep from the goats with regard to Lovecraft Circle members' senses of humor. Donald Wandrei, in particular, was reportedly not amused.

On the eve of the year 2001 a vast crowd of interested spectators were present amidst the romantic ruins of Cohen's Garage, on the former site of New York, to witness a fistic encounter between two renowned champions of the strange-story firmament — Two-Gun Bob [Robert E.

Howard], the Terror of the Plains, and Knockout Bernie [Bernard Austin Dwyer], the Wild Wolf of West Shokan. The Wolf was fresh from his correspondence course in physical training, sold to him by Mr. Arthur Leeds [real name].

Before the battle the auguries were determined by the venerated Thibetan Lama Bill Lum Li [William Lumley], who evoked the primal serpent-god of Valusia [a reference to The Shadow Kingdom by Robert E. Howard] and found unmistakable signs of victory for both sides. Cream-puffs were inattentively vended by Wladislaw Brenryk [Andrew Brosnatch] — the partakers being treated by the official surgeons, Drs. D. H. Killer [David H. Keller] and M. Gin Brewery [Miles G. Breuer].

The gong was sounded at 39 o'clock, after which the air grew red with the gore of battle, lavishly flung about by the mighty Texas slaughterer. Very shortly the first actual damage occurred — the loosening of several teeth in both participants. One, bouncing out from the Wolf's mouth after a casual tap from Two-Gun, described a parabola toward Yucatan; being retrieved in a hasty expedition by Messrs. A. Hijacked Barrell [A. Hyatt Verrill] and G. A. Scotland [George Allan England]. This incident was used by the eminent sociologist and ex-poet Frank Chimesleep Short, Jr., [Frank Belknap Long, Jr.] as the basis of a ballad of proletarian propaganda with three intentionally defective lines. Meanwhile a potentate from a neighbouring kingdom, the Effjay of Akkamin [Forrest J. Ackerman] (also known to himself as an amateur critic), expressed his frenzied disgust at the technique of the combatants, at the same time peddling photographs of the fighters (with himself in the foreground) at five cents each.

In round two the Shokan Soaker's sturdy right crashed through the Texan's ribs and became entangled in sundry viscera; thereby enabling Two-Gun to get in several telling blows on his opponent's unprotected chin. Bob was greatly annoyed by the effeminate squeamishness shewn by several onlookers as muscles, glands, gore, and bits of flesh were spattered over the ringside. During this round the eminent magazine-cover anatomist Mrs. M. Blunderage [Margaret Brundage] portrayed the battlers as a pair of spirited nudes behind a thin veil of conveniently curling tobacco-smoke, while the late Mr. C. HalfCent [C.C. Cenf] provided a sketch of three Chinamen clad in silk hats and galoshes — this being his own original conception of the affray. Among the amateur sketches made was one by Mr. Goofy Hooey [Edward G. Huey] which later gained fame in the annual Cubist exhibit as "Abstraction of an Eradicated Pudding."

In the third round the fight grew really rough; several ears and other appurtenances being wholly or partially detached from the frontier battler by the Shokan Shocker. Somewhat irritated, Two-Gun countered with some exceptionally sharp blows; severing many fragments from his aggressor, who continued to fight with all his remaining members. At this stage the audience gave signs of much nervous excitement — instances of trampling and goring being frequent. The more enthusiastic members were placed in the custody of Mr. Harry Brobst [real name] of the Butler Hospital for Mental Diseases.

The entire affair was reported by Mr. W. Lablache Talcum [Wilfred Blanch Talman], his copy being revised by Horse Power Hateart [H.P. Lovecraft]. Throughout the event notes were taken by M. le Comte d'Erlette [August Derleth] for a 200-volume novel-cycle in the Proustian manner, to be entitled *Morning in September*, with illustrations by Mrs. Blunderage. Mr. J. Caesar Warts [Julius Schwartz] frequently interviewed both battlers and all the more important spectators; obtaining as souvenirs (after a spirited struggle with the Effjay) an autographed quarter-rib of Two-Gun's, in an excellent state of preservation, and three finger-nails from the Wild Wolf. Lighting effects were supplied by the Electrical Testing Laboratories under the supervision of H. Kanebrake [H.C. Koenig].

The fourth round was prolonged eight hours at the request of the official artist, Mr. H. Wanderer [Howard Wandrei], who wished to put certain shadings of fantasy into his representation of the Wolf's depleted physiognomy, which included several supernumerary details supplied by the imagination.

The climax came in round five, when the Texas Tearer's left passed entirely through Battling Bernie's face and brought both sluggers to the mat. This was adjudged a finish by the referee — Robertieff Essovitch Karovsky, [Robert S. Carr], the Muscovite Ambassador — who, in view of the Shokan Shocker's gory state, declared the latter to be essentially liquidated according to the Marxian ideology. The Wild Wolf entered an official protest, which was promptly overruled on the ground that all the points necessary to technical death were theoretically present.

The gonfalons sounded a fanfare of triumph for the victor, while the technically vanquished was committed to the care of the official mortician, Mr. Teaberry Quince. [Seabury Quinn]. During the ceremonies the theoretical corpse strolled away for a bite of bologna, but a tasteful cenotaph was supplied to furnish a focus for the rites. The funeral procession was headed by a gaily bedecked hearse driven by Malik Taus [E. Hoffman Price], the Peacock Sultan, who sat on the box in West Point uniform and turban, and steered an expert course over several formidable hedges and stone walls. About half way to the cemetery the cortege was rejoined by the corpse, who sat beside Sultan Malik on the box and finished his bologna sandwich — his ample girth having made it impossible to enter the hastily selected cenotaph. An appropriate dirge was rendered by Maestro Sing Lee Bawledout [Franklin Lee Baldwin] on the piccolo; Messrs. De Silva, Brown, and Henderson's celebrated aria, "Never Swat a Fly," from the old cantata *Just Imagine*, being chosen for the occasion. The only detail omitted from the funeral was the interment, which was interrupted by the disconcerting news that the official gate-taker — the celebrated financier and publisher Ivar K. Rodent, Esq. [Ivar Kruger] — had absconded with the entire proceeds. This omission was regretted chiefly by the Rev. D. Vest Wind [David Van Bush], who was thereby forced to leave unspoken a long and moving sermon revised expressly for the celebration from a former discourse delivered at the burial of a favourite horse.

Mr. Talcum's report of the event, illustrated by the well-known artist Klarkash-Ton [Clark Ashton Smith] (who esoterically depicted the fighters as boneless fungi), was printed after repeated rejections by the discriminating editor of the *Windy City Grab-Bag* [*Weird Tales*] — as a broadside by W. Peter Chef [W. Paul Cook] (with typographical supervision by Vrest Orton [real name]). This, through the efforts of Otis Adelbert Kline [real name], was finally placed on sale in the bookshop of Smearum & Weep [Dauber & Pine], three and a half copies finally being disposed of through the alluring catalogue description supplied by Samuelus Philanthropus, Esq. [Samuel Loveman]

In response to this wide demand, the text was finally reprinted by Mr. Demerit [Abraham Merritt] in the polychromatic pages of *Wurst's Weakly Americana* [Hearst's The American Weekly] under the title "Has Science Been Outmoded? or, The Millers in the Garage." No copies, however, remain in circulation; since all which were not snapped up by fanatical bibliophiles were seized by the police in connexion with the libel suit of the Wild Wolf, who was, after several appeals ending with the World Court, adjudged not only officially alive but the clear winner of the combat.

The Sorcery of Aphlar.

BY DUANE W. RIMEL
AND H.P. LOVECRAFT

900-WORD SHORT STORY;
1934.

If some Lovecraft scholars have expressed skepticism that Duane Rimel's later story, "The Disinterment," is really Rimel's work, others have voiced doubts that "The Sorcery of Aphlar" contains any of Lovecraft's. It is clearly a Dunsanian story, almost to the point of being a pastiche of Dunsanian-era Lovecraft.

It's a tiny thing, at just 900 words, and, as Lord Dunsany knockoffs go, quite good. It was originally titled, "The Sorcery of Alfred"; but Lovecraft advised his young protégé that using an ordinary English name in a Dunsanian fantasy was a bad idea, so he changed it to Aphlar.

Written in early 1934, "The Sorcery of Aphlar" was published later that year, in the December 1934 issue of Fantasy Fan.

The Council of Twelve seated on the jewelled celestial dais ordered that Aphlar be cast from the gates of Bel-haz-en. He sat too much alone, they decreed, and brooded when toil should have been his lot. And in his obscure and hidden delvings he read all too frequently those papyri of Elder aeons which reposed in the Guothic shrine and were to be consulted only for rare and special purposes.

The twilight city of Bel-haz-en had climbed backward in its knowledge. No longer did philosophers sit upon street corners speaking wise words to the populace, for stupid ignorance ruled within the crumbling and immemorially ancient walls. Where once the wisdom of the stars abounded, only feebleness and desolation now lay upon the place, spreading like a monstrous blight and sucking foul nurture from the stupid dwellers. And out of the waters of the Oll that meandered from the mountains of Azlakka to pass by the aged city, there rose often great clouds of pestilence that racked the people sorely, leaving them pale and near to dying. All this their loss of wisdom brought. And now the council had sent their last and greatest wise man from them.

Aphlar wandered to the mountains far above the city and built a cavern for protection from the summer heat and winter chill. There he read his scrolls in silence and told his mighty wisdom to the wind about the crags and to the swallows on the wing. All day he sat and watched below or drew queer drawings on small bits of stone and chanted to them, for he knew that someday men would seek the cave and slay him. The cunning of the twelve did not mislead him. Had not the last exiled wise man's screams rent the night two moon-rounds before when people thought him safely gone? Had not his own eyes seen the priest's sword-slashed form floating by in the poison waters? He knew no lion had killed old Azik, let the council say what they might. Does a lion slash with a sword and leave his prey uneaten?

Through many seasons Aphlar sat upon the mountain, gazing at the muddy Oll as it wound into the misty distance to the land where none ever ventured. He spoke his words of wisdom to the snails that worked in the ground by his feet. They seemed to understand, and waved their slimy feelers before they sank beneath the sand again. On moonlit nights he climbed the hill above his cave and made strange offerings to the moon-God Ale; and when the night-birds heard the sound they drew close and listened to the whispering. And when queer winged things flapped across the darkened sky and loomed up dimly against the moon Aphlar was content. Those which he had addressed had heeded his beckoning. His thoughts were always far away, and his prayers were offered to the pale fancies of dusk.

Then one day past noontide Aphlar rose from his earthen chair and strode down the rock mountainside. His eyes, heeding not the rotten, stone-walled city, held steadfast to the river. When he drew near its muddy brink he paused and looked up the bosom of the stream. A small object floated near the rushes, and this Aphlar rescued with tender and curious care. Then, wrapping the thing in the folds of his robe, he climbed up again to his cave in the hills. All day he sat and gazed upon the object; rummaging now and then in his musty chronicles, and muttering awful syllables as he drew faint figures on a piece of parchment.

That night the gibbous moon rose high, but Aphlar did not climb above his dwelling. Queer night-birds flew past the cavern's mouth, chirped eerily, and fled away into the shadows.

Many days passed before the council sent their messengers of murder; but at last the time was thought ripe, and seven dark-browed men stole away to the hills. Yet when that grim seven ventured within the cave they saw not the wise man Aphlar. Instead, small blades of grass were sprouting in his natural chair of earth. All about lay papyri dim and musty, with faint figures drawn upon them.

The seven shuddered and left forthwith when they beheld these things, but as the last man tremblingly withdrew he saw a round and unknown thing lying on the ground. He picked it up, and his fellows drew close in curiosity; but they saw upon it only alien symbols which they could not read, yet which made them shrink and quaver without knowing why. Then he who had found it cast it quickly over the steep precipice beside him, but no sound came from the slope below whereon it should have fallen. And the thrower trembled, fearing many things that are not known but only whispered about. Then, when he told how the sphere he had held was without the weight a thing of stone should have; how it was like to have floated on air as the thistledown floats; he and the six with him slunk as one from the spot and swore it was a place accursed.

But after they had gone a snail crawled slowly from a sandy crevice and slid intently over to where the blades of grass were growing. And when it reached the spot, two slimy feelers stretched forth and bent oddly downward, as if eager to watch forever the winding river.

Till A' the Seas.

BY ROBERT H. BARLOW
AND H.P. LOVECRAFT

**3,300-WORD SHORT STORY;
1934.**

This short story is a gloomy, pensive "last man living at the end of the world" story, set far into the future after "a' the seas" have evaporated away and everyone in the world save one man has died of thirst. It is a bleak story and it revels in its bleakness; at the death of the world, there can be no room for "happily ever after."

Lovecraft provided a tweak here and a word-change there, helping Barlow — who by this time was starting to get quite good; and he supplied the concluding paragraph, after the inevitable and ironic end, putting the whole human race into the context of a cold and unfeeling universe.

Written in late 1934, "Till A' The Seas" was first published in the Summer 1935 issue of The Californian.

I.

Upon an eroded cliff-top rested the man, gazing far across the valley. Lying thus, he could see a great distance, but in all the sere expanse there was no visible motion. Nothing stirred the dusty plain, the disintegrated sand of long-dry river-beds, where once coursed the gushing streams of Earth's youth.

There was little greenery in this ultimate world, this final stage of mankind's prolonged presence upon the planet. For unnumbered aeons the drought and sandstorms had ravaged all the lands. The trees and bushes had given way to small, twisted shrubs that persisted long through their sturdiness; but these, in turn, perished before the onslaught of coarse grasses and stringy, tough vegetation of strange evolution.

The ever-present heat, as Earth drew nearer to the sun, withered and killed with pitiless rays. It had not come at once; long aeons had gone before any could feel the change. And all through those first ages man's adaptable form had followed the slow mutation and modelled itself to fit the more and more torrid air.

Then the day had come when men could bear their hot cities but ill, and a gradual recession began, slow yet deliberate. Those towns and settlements closest to the equator had been first, of course, but later there were others. Man, softened and exhausted, could cope no longer with the ruthlessly mounting heat. It seared him as he was, and evolution was too slow to mould new resistances in him.

Yet not at first were the great cities of the equator left to the spider and the scorpion. In the early years there were many who stayed on, devising curious shields and armours against the heat and the deadly dryness. These fearless souls, screening certain buildings against the encroaching sun, made miniature worlds of refuge wherein no protective armour was needed. They contrived marvellously ingenious things, so that for a while men persisted in the rusting towers, hoping thereby to cling to old lands till the searing should be over. For many would not believe what the astronomers said, and looked for a coming of the mild olden world again.

But one day the men of Dath, from the new city of Niyara, made signals to Yuanario, their immemorially ancient capital, and gained no answer from the few who remained therein. And when explorers reached that millennial city of bridge-linked towers they found only silence. There was not even the horror of corruption, for the scavenger lizards had been swift.

Only then did the people fully realize that these cities were lost to them; know that they must forever abandon them to nature. The other colonists in the hot lands fled from their brave posts, and total silence reigned within the high basalt walls of a thousand empty towns. Of the dense throngs and multitudinous activities of the past, nothing finally remained. There now loomed against the rainless deserts only the blistered towers of vacant houses, factories, and structures of every sort, reflecting the sun's dazzling radiance and parching in the more and more intolerable heat.

Many lands, however, had still escaped the scorching blight, so that the refugees were soon absorbed in the life of a newer world. During strangely prosperous centuries the hoary deserted cities of the equator grew half-forgotten and entwined with fantastic fables. Few thought of those spectral rotting towers . . . those huddles of shabby walls and cactus-choked streets, darkly silent and abandoned . . . Wars came, sinful and prolonged, but the times of peace were greater. Yet always the swollen sun increased its radiance as Earth drew closer to its fiery parent. It was as if the planet meant to return to that source whence it was snatched, aeons ago, through the accidents of cosmic growth.

After a time the blight crept outward from the central belt. Southern Yarat burned as a tenantless desert — and then the north. In Perath and Baling, those ancient cities where brooding centuries dwelt, there moved only the scaly shapes of the serpent and the salamander, and at last Loton echoed only to the fitful falling of tottering spires and crumbling domes.

Steady, universal, and inexorable was the great eviction of man from the realms he had always known. No land within the widening stricken belt was spared; no people left unrouted. It was an epic, a titan tragedy whose plot was unrevealed to the actors — this wholesale desertion of the cities of men. It took not years or even centuries, but millennia of ruthless change. And still it kept on — sullen, inevitable, savagely devastating.

Agriculture was at a standstill; the world fast became too arid for crops. This was remedied by artificial substitutes, soon universally used. And as the old places that had known the great things of mortals were left, the loot salvaged by the fugitives grew smaller and smaller. Things of the greatest value and importance were left in dead museums — lost amid the centuries — and in the end the heritage of the immemorial past was abandoned.

A degeneracy both physical and cultural set in with the insidious heat. For man had so long dwelt in comfort and security that this exodus from past scenes was difficult. Nor were these events received phlegmatically; their very slowness was terrifying. Degradation and debauchery were soon common; government was disorganized, and the civilizations aimlessly slid back toward barbarism.

When, forty-nine centuries after the blight from the equatorial belt, the whole western hemisphere was left unpeopled, chaos was complete. There was no trace of order or decency in the last scenes of this titanic, wildly impressive migration. Madness and frenzy stalked through them, and fanatics screamed of an Armageddon close at hand.

Mankind was now a pitiful remnant of the elder races, a fugitive not only from the prevailing conditions, but from his own degeneracy. Into the northland and the Antarctic went those who could; the rest lingered for years in an incredible saturnalia, vaguely doubting the forthcoming disasters. In the city of Borligo a wholesale execution of the new prophets took place, after months of unfulfilled expectations. They thought the flight to the northland unnecessary, and looked no longer for the threatened ending.

How they perished must have been terrible indeed — those vain, foolish creatures who thought to defy the universe. But the blackened, scorched towns are mute ....

These events, however, must not be chronicled — for there are larger things to consider than this complex and unhastening downfall of a lost civilization. During a long period morale was at lowest ebb among the courageous few who settled upon the alien Arctic and Antarctic shores, now mild as were those of southern Yarat in the long-dead past. But here there was respite. The soil was fertile, and forgotten pastoral arts were called into use anew. There was, for a long time, a contented little epitome of the lost lands; though here were no vast throngs or great buildings. Only a sparse remnant of humanity survived the aeons of change and peopled those scattered villages of the later world.

How many millennia this continued is not known. The sun was slow in invading this last retreat; and as the eras passed there developed a sound, sturdy race, bearing no memories or legends of the old, lost lands. Little navigation was practiced by this new people, and the flying machine was wholly forgotten. Their devices were of the simplest type, and their culture was simple and primitive. Yet they were contented, and accepted the warm climate as something natural and accustomed.

But unknown to these simple peasant-folk, still further rigours of nature were slowly preparing themselves. As the generations passed, the waters of the vast and unplumbed ocean wasted slowly away; enriching the air and the desiccated soil, but sinking lower and lower each century. The splashing surf still glistened bright, and the swirling eddies were still there, but a doom of dryness hung over the whole watery expanse. However, the shrinkage could not have been detected save by instruments more delicate than any then known to the race. Even had the people realized the ocean's contraction, it is not likely that any vast alarm or great disturbance would have resulted, for the losses were so slight, and the seas so great ... Only a few inches during many centuries — but in many centuries; increasing—

So at last the oceans went, and water became a rarity on a globe of sun-baked drought. Man had slowly spread over all the Arctic and Antarctic lands; the equatorial cities, and many of later habitation, were forgotten even to legend.

And now again the peace was disturbed, for water was scarce, and found only in deep caverns. There was little enough, even of this; and men died of thirst wandering in far places. Yet so slow were these deadly changes, that each new generation of man was loath to believe what it heard from its parents. None would admit that the heat had been less or the water more plentiful in the old days, or take warning that days of bitterer burning and drought were to come. Thus it was even at the end, when only a few hundred human creatures panted for breath beneath the cruel sun; a piteous huddled handful out of all the unnumbered millions who had once dwelt on the doomed planet.

And the hundreds became small, till man was to be reckoned only in tens. These tens clung to the shrinking dampness of the caves, and knew at last that the end was near. So slight was their range that none had ever seen the tiny, fabled spots of ice left close to the planet's poles — if such indeed remained. Even had they existed and been known to man, none could have reached them across the trackless and formidable deserts. And so the last pathetic few dwindled ....

It cannot be described, this awesome chain of events that depopulated the whole Earth; the range is too tremendous for any to picture or encompass. Of the people of Earth's fortunate ages, billions of years before, only a few prophets and madmen could have conceived that which was to come — could have grasped visions of the still, dead lands, and long-empty sea-beds. The rest would have doubted ... doubted alike the shadow of change upon the planet and the shadow of doom upon the race. For man has always thought himself the immortal master of natural things . . . .

II.

When he had eased the dying pangs of the old woman, Ull wandered in a fearful daze out into the dazzling sands. She had been a fearsome thing, shrivelled and so dry; like withered leaves. Her face had been the colour of the sickly yellow grasses that rustled in the hot wind, and she was loathsomely old.

But she had been a companion; someone to stammer out vague fears to, to talk to about this incredible thing; a comrade to share one's hopes for succour from those silent other colonies beyond the mountains. He could not believe none lived elsewhere, for Ull was young, and not certain as are the old.

For many years he had known none but the old woman — her name was Mladdna. She had come that day in his eleventh year, when all the hunters went to seek food, and did not return. Ull had no mother that he could remember, and there were few women in the tiny group. When the men vanished, those three women, the young one and the two old, had screamed fearfully, and moaned long. Then the young one had gone mad, and killed herself with a sharp stick. The old ones buried her in a shallow hole dug with their nails, so Ull had been alone when this still old Mladdna came.

She walked with the aid of a knotty pole, a priceless relique of the old forests, hard and shiny with years of use. She did not say whence she came, but stumbled into the cabin while the young suicide was being buried. There she waited till the two returned, and they accepted her incuriously.

That was the way it had been for many weeks, until the two fell sick, and Mladdna could not cure them. Strange that those younger two should have been stricken, while she, infirm and ancient, lived on. Mladdna had cared for them many days, and at length they died, so that Ull was left with only the stranger. He screamed all the night, so she became at length out of patience, and threatened to die too. Then, hearkening, he became quiet at once; for he was not desirous of complete solitude. After that he lived with Mladdna and they gathered roots to eat.

Mladdna's rotten teeth were ill suited to the food they gathered, but they contrived to chop it up till she could manage it. This weary routine of seeking and eating was Ull's childhood.

Now he was strong, and firm, in his nineteenth year, and the old woman was dead. There was naught to stay for, so he determined at once to seek out those fabled huts beyond the mountains, and live with the people there.

There was nothing to take on the journey. Ull closed the door of his cabin — why, he could not have told, for no animals had been there for many years — and left the dead woman within.

Half-dazed, and fearful at his own audacity, he walked long hours in the dry grasses, and at length reached the first of the foothills. The afternoon came, and he climbed until he was weary, and lay down on the grasses. Sprawled there, he thought of many things. He wondered at the strange life, passionately anxious to seek out the lost colony beyond the mountains; but at last he slept.

When he awoke there was starlight on his face, and he felt refreshed. Now that the sun was gone for a time, he travelled more quickly, eating little, and determining to hasten before the lack of water became difficult to bear. He had brought none; for the last people, dwelling in one place and never having occasion to bear their precious water away, made no vessels of any kind. Ull hoped to reach his goal within a day, and thus escape thirst; so he hurried on beneath the bright stars, running at times in the warm air, and at other times lapsing into a dogtrot.

So he continued until the sun arose, yet still he was within the small hills, with three great peaks looming ahead. In their shade he rested again. Then he climbed all the morning, and at mid-day surmounted the first peak, where he lay for a time, surveying the space before the next range.

Upon an eroded cliff-top rested the man, gazing far across the valley. Lying thus he could see a great distance, but in all the sere expanse there was no visible motion . . . .

The second night came, and found Ull amid the rough peaks, the valley and the place where he had rested far behind. He was nearly out of the second range now, and hurrying still. Thirst had come upon him that day, and he regretted his folly. Yet he could not have stayed there with the corpse, alone in the grasslands. He sought to convince himself thus, and hastened ever on, tiredly straining.

And now there were only a few steps before the cliff wall would part and allow a view of the land beyond. Ull stumbled wearily down the stony way, tumbling and bruising himself even more. It was nearly before him, this land where men were rumoured to have dwelt; this land of which he had heard tales in his youth. The way was long, but the goal was great. A boulder of giant circumference cut off his view; upon this he scrambled anxiously. Now at last he could behold by the sinking orb his long-sought destination, and his thirst and aching muscles were forgotten as he saw joyfully that a small huddle of buildings clung to the base of the farther cliff.

Ull rested not; but, spurred on by what he saw, ran and staggered and crawled the half mile remaining. He fancied that he could detect forms among the rude cabins. The sun was nearly gone; the hateful, devastating sun that had slain humanity. He could not be sure of details, but soon the cabins were near.

They were very old, for clay blocks lasted long in the still dryness of the dying world. Little, indeed, changed but the living things — the grasses and these last men.

Before him an open door swung on rude pegs. In the fading

light Ull entered, weary unto death, seeking painfully the expected faces.

Then he fell upon the floor and wept, for at the table was propped a dry and ancient skeleton.

He rose at last, crazed by thirst, aching unbearably, and suffering the greatest disappointment any mortal could know. He was, then, the last living thing upon the globe. His the heritage of the Earth . . . all the lands, and all to him equally useless. He staggered up, not looking at the dim white form in the reflected moonlight, and went through the door. About the empty village, spectrally preserved by the changeless air, he wandered. Here there was a dwelling, there a rude place where things had been made — clay vessels holding only dust, and nowhere any liquid to quench his burning thirst.

Then, in the centre of the little town, Ull saw a well-curb. He knew what it was, for he had heard tales of such things from Mladdna. With pitiful joy, he reeled forward and leaned upon the edge. There, at last, was the end of his search. Water — slimy, stagnant, and shallow, but water — before his sight.

Ull cried out in the voice of a tortured animal, groping for the chain and bucket. His hand slipped on the slimy edge; and he fell upon his chest across the brink. For a moment he lay there — then soundlessly his body was precipitated down the black shaft.

There was a slight splash in the murky shallowness as he struck some long-sunken stone, dislodged aeons ago from the massive coping. The disturbed water subsided into quietness.

And now at last the Earth was dead. The final pitiful survivor had perished. All the teeming billions; the slow aeons; the empires and civilizations of mankind were summed up in this poor twisted form — and how titanically meaningless it had all been! Now indeed had come an end and climax to all the efforts of humanity — how monstrous and incredible a climax in the eyes of those poor complacent fools in the prosperous days! Not ever again would the planet know the thunderous tramping of human millions — or even the crawling of lizards and the buzz of insects, for they, too, had gone. Now was come the reign of sapless branches and endless fields of tough grasses. Earth, like its cold, imperturbable moon, was given over to silence and blackness forever.

The stars whirled on; the whole careless plan would continue for infinities unknown. This trivial end of a negligible episode mattered not to distant nebulae or to suns new-born, flourishing, and dying. The race of man, too puny and momentary to have a real function or purpose, was as if it had never existed. To such a conclusion the aeons of its farcically toilsome evolution had led.

But when the deadly sun's first rays darted across the valley, a light found its way to the weary face of a broken figure that lay in the slime.

1935.

Swan Song.

H.P. Lovecraft's literary output was not vast in 1935, although it included one of the very best stories of the 20th century: the novella *The Shadow out of Time.*

The Shadow out of Time was finished up in February 1935 And after that, only one more story flowed off Lovecraft's weird-fiction pen: "The Haunter of the Dark." "The Haunter of the Dark" would be not only the last by-lined Lovecraft prose fiction to come out in 1935, but the last one he would write in his life.

But Lovecraft was hardly inactive in 1935. In that year, he participated in five collaborative efforts, representing varying degrees of involvement from some desultory round-robin fun with Robert Barlow to a full-on ghostwriting with William Lumley on "The Diary of Alonzo Typer." He also worked with Duane Rimel on the stunningly Lovecraftian "The Disinterment" and with C.L. Moore, A. Merritt, Frank Belknap Long, and Robert E. Howard on "The Challenge from Beyond."

Nor did he neglect his summer travels. Lovecraft in 1935 journeyed down the Eastern Seaboard to Florida once again, this time to spend several weeks with Robert H. Barlow.

And in October of 1935, two of his unplaced novellas — *At the Mountains of Madness* and *The Shadow out of Time* — found a publisher in *Astounding Stories.* Things were looking up — or, at least, they seemed to be.

The Shadow out of Time.

25,200-WORD NOVELLA; 1935.

Many Lovecraft scholars rank The Shadow out of Time *together with* At the Mountains of Madness *as H.P. Lovecraft's best work. For any Lovecraft fan, it is a bit bittersweet. It distinctly hints that Lovecraft was starting to come out of the crisis of confidence sparked by the rejection of* At the Mountains of Madness *several years before; it is, arguably, his most deftly crafted work, welding together pulp action and literary craftsmanship better than anything he'd ever done before. But it is, essentially, his swan song.*

H.P. Lovecraft had been stewing on the basic story of The Shadow out of Time *for years. It wasn't until late 1934 that he finally sat down to execute it.*

It was not an easy job. If his previous tale, the endearingly campy "The Thing on the Doorstep," had taken him three days to produce, this more serious work would take him well over three months. He finished it on Feb. 22, 1935.

Upon its completion, Lovecraft was once again very unsure of its quality. So he set the manuscript aside. Then he mailed it off to August Derleth to look at.

Derleth did not get to it for several months. So in July, Lovecraft asked him to forward it to him in care of Robert H. Barlow in Florida, where he was then sojourning; Barlow had expressed an enthusiastic desire to read it when Derleth was through, and Lovecraft figured if Derleth wasn't through by now, after sitting on it for five months, he'd missed his chance.

By August Lovecraft was getting annoyed with Barlow as well. It seemed that he, too, was sitting on the manuscript. Then, unexpectedly, his young protege presented him with a surprise: a typescript. Barlow had not only read the story, he'd been typing it up, as a gift to Lovecraft.

There were quite a few typos, and Barlow hadn't made any carbon copies. Still it was a magnificent gift. Lovecraft made the necessary corrections and sent it on the rounds of his friends to read.

One of the friends on the list was Donald Wandrei, who at the time was in contact with the editor of Astounding Stories, *F. Orlin Tremaine. Wandrei passed it to Tremaine, who promptly bought it for $280. It was the cover story in the June 1936 issue.*

I.

After twenty-two years of nightmare and terror, saved only by a desperate conviction of the mythical source of certain impressions, I am unwilling to vouch for the truth of that which I think I found in Western Australia on the night of 17-18 July 1935. There is reason to hope that my experience was wholly or partly an hallucination — for which, indeed, abundant causes existed. And yet, its realism was so hideous that I sometimes find hope impossible.

If the thing did happen, then man must be prepared to accept notions of the cosmos, and of his own place in the seething vortex of time, whose merest mention is paralysing. He must, too, be placed on guard against a specific, lurking peril which, though it will never engulf the whole race, may impose monstrous and unguessable horrors upon certain venturesome members of it.

It is for this latter reason that I urge, with all the force of my being, final abandonment of all the attempts at unearthing those fragments of unknown, primordial masonry which my expedition set out to investigate.

Assuming that I was sane and awake, my experience on that night was such as has befallen no man before. It was, moreover, a frightful confirmation of all I had sought to dismiss as myth and dream. Mercifully there is no proof, for in my fright I lost the awesome object which would — if real and brought out of that noxious abyss — have formed irrefutable evidence.

When I came upon the horror I was alone — and I have up to now told no one about it. I could not stop the others from digging in its direction, but chance and the shifting sand have so far saved them from finding it. Now I must formulate some definite statement — not only for the sake of my own mental balance, but to warn such others as may read it seriously.

These pages — much in whose earlier parts will be familiar to close readers of the general and scientific press — are written in the cabin of the ship that is bringing me home. I shall give them to my son, Professor Wingate Peaslee of Miskatonic University — the only member of my family who stuck to me after my queer amnesia of long ago, and the man best informed on the inner facts of my case. Of all living persons, he is least likely to ridicule what I shall tell of that fateful night.

I did not enlighten him orally before sailing, because I think he had better have the revelation in written form. Reading and re-reading at leisure will leave with him a more convincing picture than my confused tongue could hope to convey.

He can do anything that he thinks best with this account — showing it, with suitable comment, in any quarters where it will be likely to accomplish good. It is for the sake of such readers as are unfamiliar with the earlier phases of my case that I am prefacing the revelation itself with a fairly ample summary of its background.

My name is Nathaniel Wingate Peaslee, and those who recall the newspaper tales of a generation back — or the letters and articles in psychological journals six or seven years ago — will know who and what I am. The press was filled with the details of my strange amnesia in 1908-13, and much was made of the traditions of horror, madness, and witchcraft which lurked behind the ancient Massachusetts town then and now forming my place of residence. Yet I would have it known that there is nothing whatever of the mad or sinister in my heredity and early life. This is a highly important fact in view of the shadow which fell so suddenly upon me from outside sources.

It may be that centuries of dark brooding had given to crumbling, whisper-haunted Arkham a peculiar vulnerability as regards such shadows — though even this seems doubtful in the light of those other cases which I later came to study. But the chief point is that my own ancestry and background are altogether normal. What came, came from somewhere else — where I even now hesitate to assert in plain words.

I am the son of Jonathan and Hannah (Wingate) Peaslee, both of wholesome old Haverhill stock. I was born and reared in Haverhill — at the old homestead in Boardman Street near Golden Hill — and did not go to Arkham till I entered Miskatonic University as instructor of political economy in 1895.

For thirteen years more my life ran smoothly and happily. I married Alice Keezar of Haverhill in 1896, and my three children, Robert, Wingate and Hannah were born in 1898, 1900, and 1903, respectively. In 1898 I became an associate professor, and in 1902 a full professor. At no time had I the least interest in either occultism or abnormal psychology.

It was on Thursday, 14 May 1908, that the queer amnesia came. The thing was quite sudden, though later I realized that certain brief, glimmering visions of several hours previous — chaotic visions which disturbed me greatly because they were so unprecedented — must have formed premonitory symptoms. My head was aching, and I had a singular feeling — altogether new to me — that some one else was trying to get possession of my thoughts.

The collapse occurred about 10.20 a.m., while I was conducting a class in Political Economy VI — history and present tendencies of economics — for juniors and a few

CONTENTS COPYRIGHTED 1936

JUNE 1936

ASTOUNDING STORIES

20¢

The Shadow Out of Time

H. P. Lovecraft

also: Schachner, Van Lorne, Coblentz, Corbett, Williamson

sophomores. I began to see strange shapes before my eyes, and to feel that I was in a grotesque room other than the classroom.

My thoughts and speech wandered from my subject, and the students saw that something was gravely amiss. Then I slumped down, unconscious, in my chair, in a stupor from which no one could arouse me. Nor did my rightful faculties again look out upon the daylight of our normal world for five years, four months, and thirteen days.

It is, of course, from others that I have learned what followed. I showed no sign of consciousness for sixteen and a half hours though removed to my home at 27 Crane Street, and given the best of medical attention.

At 3 a.m. 15 May my eyes opened and I began to speak, but before long the doctor and my family were thoroughly frightened by the trend of my expression and language. It was clear that I had no remembrance of my identity and my past, though for some reason I seemed anxious to conceal this lack of knowledge. My eyes glazed strangely at the persons around me, and the flections of my facial muscles were altogether unfamiliar.

Even my speech seemed awkward and foreign. I used my vocal organs clumsily and gropingly, and my diction had a curiously stilted quality, as if I had laboriously learned the English language from books. The pronunciation was barbarously alien, whilst the idiom seemed to include both scraps of curious archaism and expressions of a wholly incomprehensible cast.

Of the latter, one in particular was very potently—even terrifiedly—recalled by the youngest of the physicians twenty years afterward. For at that late period such a phrase began to have an actual currency—first in England and then in the United States—and though of much complexity and indisputable newness, it reproduced in every least particular the mystifying words of the strange Arkham patient of 1908.

Physical strength returned at once, although I required an odd amount of re-education in the use of my hands, legs, and bodily apparatus in general. Because of this and other handicaps inherent in the mnemonic lapse, I was for some time kept under strict medical care.

When I saw that my attempts to conceal the lapse had failed, I admitted it openly, and became eager for information of all sorts. Indeed, it seemed to the doctors that I lost interest in my proper personality as soon as I found the case of amnesia accepted as a natural thing.

They noticed that my chief efforts were to master certain points in history, science, art, language, and folklore—some of them tremendously abstruse, and some childishly simple—which remained, very oddly in many cases, outside my consciousness.

At the same time they noticed that I had an inexplicable command of many almost unknown sorts of knowledge—a command which I seemed to wish to hide rather than display. I would inadvertently refer, with casual assurance, to specific events in dim ages outside of the range of accepted history—passing off such references as a jest when I saw the surprise they created. And I had a way of speaking of the future which two or three times caused actual fright.

These uncanny flashes soon ceased to appear, though some observers laid their vanishment more to a certain furtive caution on my part than to any waning of the strange knowledge behind them. Indeed, I seemed anomalously avid to absorb the speech, customs, and perspectives of the age around me; as if I were a studious traveller from a far, foreign land.

As soon as permitted, I haunted the college library at all hours; and shortly began to arrange for those odd travels, and special courses at American and European Universities, which evoked so much comment during the next few years.

I did not at any time suffer from a lack of learned contacts, for my case had a mild celebrity among the psychologists of the period. I was lectured upon as a typical example of secondary personality—even though I seemed to puzzle the lecturers now and then with some bizarre symptoms or some queer trace of carefully veiled mockery.

Of real friendliness, however, I encountered little. Something in my aspect and speech seemed to excite vague fears and aversions in every one I met, as if I were a being infinitely removed from all that is normal and healthful. This idea of a black, hidden horror connected with incalculable gulfs of some sort of distance was oddly widespread and persistent.

My own family formed no exception. From the moment of my strange waking my wife had regarded me with extreme horror and loathing, vowing that I was some utter alien usurping the body of her husband. In 1910 she obtained a legal divorce, nor would she ever consent to see me even after my return to normality in 1913. These feelings were shared by my elder son and my small daughter, neither of whom I have ever seen since.

Only my second son, Wingate, seemed able to conquer the terror and repulsion which my change aroused. He indeed felt that I was a stranger, but though only eight years old held fast to a faith that my proper self would return. When it did return he sought me out, and the courts gave me his custody. In succeeding years he helped me with the studies to which I was driven, and today, at thirty-five, he is a professor of psychology at Miskatonic.

But I do not wonder at the horror caused—for certainly, the mind, voice, and facial expression of the being that awakened on 15 May 1908, were not those of Nathaniel Wingate Peaslee.

I will not attempt to tell much of my life from 1908 to 1913, since readers may glean the outward essentials—as I largely had to do—from files of old newspapers and scientific journals.

I was given charge of my funds, and spent them slowly and on the whole wisely, in travel and in study at various centres of learning. My travels, however, were singular in the extreme, involving long visits to remote and desolate places.

In 1909 I spent a month in the Himalayas, and in 1911 roused much attention through a camel trip into the unknown

Astounding Stories, June 1936

"They spoke by the clicking or scraping of huge paws."

deserts of Arabia. What happened on those journeys I have never been able to learn.

During the summer of 1912 I chartered a ship and sailed in the Arctic, north of Spitzbergen, afterward showing signs of disappointment.

Later in that year I spent weeks — alone beyond the limits of previous or subsequent exploration in the vast limestone cavern systems of western Virginia — black labyrinths so complex that no retracing of my steps could even be considered.

My sojourns at the universities were marked by abnormally rapid assimilation, as if the secondary personality had an intelligence enormously superior to my own. I have found, also, that my rate of reading and solitary study was phenomenal. I could master every detail of a book merely by glancing over it as fast as I could turn the leaves; while my skill at interpreting complex figures in an instant was veritably awesome.

At times there appeared almost ugly reports of my power to influence the thoughts and acts of others, though I seemed to have taken care to minimize displays of this faculty.

Other ugly reports concerned my intimacy with leaders of occultist groups, and scholars suspected of connection with nameless bands of abhorrent elder-world hierophants. These rumours, though never proved at the time, were doubtless stimulated by the known tenor of some of my reading — for the consultation of rare books at libraries cannot be effected secretly.

There is tangible proof — in the form of marginal notes — that I went minutely through such things as the Comte d'Erlette's *Cultes des Goules*, Ludvig Prinn's *De Vermis Mysteriis*, the *Unaussprechlichen Kulten* of von Junzt, the surviving fragments of the puzzling *Book of Eibon*, and the dreaded *Necronomicon* of the mad Arab Abdul Alhazred. Then, too, it is undeniable that a fresh and evil wave of underground cult activity set in about the time of my odd mutation.

In the summer of 1913 I began to display signs of ennui and flagging interest, and to hint to various associates that a change might soon be expected in me. I spoke of returning memories of my earlier life — though most auditors judged me insincere, since all the recollections I gave were casual, and such as might have been learned from my old private papers.

About the middle of August I returned to Arkham and re-opened my long-closed house in Crane Street. Here I installed a mechanism of the most curious aspect, constructed piecemeal by different makers of scientific apparatus in Europe and America, and guarded carefully from the sight of any one intelligent enough to analyse it.

Those who did see it — a workman, a servant, and the new housekeeper — say that it was a queer mixture of rods, wheels, and mirrors, though only about two feet tall, one foot wide, and one foot thick. The central mirror was circular and convex. All this is borne out by such makers of parts as can be located.

On the evening of Friday, 26 September, I dismissed the housekeeper and the maid until noon of the next day. Lights burned in the house till late, and a lean, dark, curiously foreign-looking man called in an automobile.

It was about one a.m. that the lights were last seen. At 2.15 a.m. a policeman observed the place in darkness, but the stranger's motor still at the curb. By 4 o'clock the motor was certainly gone.

It was at 6 o'clock that a hesitant, foreign voice on the telephone asked Dr Wilson to call at my house and bring me out of a peculiar faint. This call — a long-distance one — was later traced to a public booth in the North Station in Boston, but no sign of the lean foreigner was ever unearthed.

When the doctor reached my house he found me unconscious in the sitting room — in an easy-chair with a table drawn up before it. On the polished top were scratches showing where some heavy object had rested. The queer machine was gone, nor was anything afterward heard of it. Undoubtedly the dark, lean foreigner had taken it away.

In the library grate were abundant ashes, evidently left from the burning of the every remaining scrap of paper on which I had written since the advent of the amnesia. Dr Wilson found my breathing very peculiar, but after a hypodermic injection it became more regular.

At 11.15 a.m., 27 September, I stirred vigorously, and my hitherto masklike face began to show signs of expression. Dr Wilson remarked that the expression was not that of my secondary personality, but seemed much like that of my normal self. About 11.30 I muttered some very curious syllables — syllables which seemed unrelated to any human speech. I appeared, too, to struggle against something. Then, just after noon — the housekeeper and the maid having meanwhile returned — I began to mutter in English.

"— of the orthodox economists of that period, Jevons typifies the prevailing trend toward scientific correlation. His attempt to link the commercial cycle of prosperity and depression with the physical cycle of the solar spots forms perhaps the apex of — "

Nathaniel Wingate Peaslee had come back — a spirit in whose time scale it was still Thursday morning in 1908, with the economics class gazing up at the battered desk on the platform.

II.

My reabsorption into normal life was a painful and difficult process. The loss of over five years creates more complications than can be imagined, and in my case there were countless matters to be adjusted.

What I heard of my actions since 1908 astonished and disturbed me, but I tried to view the matter as philosophically as I could. At last, regaining custody of my second son, Wingate, I settled down with him in the Crane Street house and endeavoured to resume my teaching — my old professorship having been kindly offered me by the college.

I began work with the February, 1914, term, and kept at

it just a year. By that time I realized how badly my experience had shaken me. Though perfectly sane — I hoped — and with no flaw in my original personality, I had not the nervous energy of the old days. Vague dreams and queer ideas continually haunted me, and when the outbreak of the World War turned my mind to history I found myself thinking of periods and events in the oddest possible fashion.

My conception of time, my ability to distinguish between consecutiveness and simultaneousness — seemed subtly disordered so that I formed chimerical notions about living in one age and casting one's mind all over eternity for knowledge of past and future ages.

The war gave me strange impressions of remembering some of its far-off consequences — as if I knew how it was coming out and could look back upon it in the light of future information. All such quasi-memories were attended with much pain, and with a feeling that some artificial psychological barrier was set against them.

When I diffidently hinted to others about my impressions I met with varied responses. Some persons looked uncomfortably at me, but men in the mathematics department spoke of new developments in those theories of relativity — then discussed only in learned circles — which were later to become so famous. Dr. Albert Einstein, they said, was rapidly reducing time to the status of a mere dimension.

But the dreams and disturbed feelings gained on me, so that I had to drop my regular work in 1915. Certainly the impressions were taking an annoying shape — giving me the persistent notion that my amnesia had formed some unholy sort of exchange; that the secondary personality had indeed suffered displacement.

Thus I was driven to vague and frighted speculations concerning the whereabouts of my true self during the years that another had held my body. The curious knowledge and strange conduct of my body's late tenant troubled me more and more as I learned further details from persons, papers, and magazines.

Queernesses that had baffled others seemed to harmonize terribly with some background of black knowledge which festered in the chasms of my subconscious. I began to search feverishly for every scrap of information bearing on the studies and travels of that other one during the dark years.

Not all of my troubles were as semi-abstract as this. There were the dreams — and these seemed to grow in vividness and concreteness. Knowing how most would regard them, I seldom mentioned them to anyone but my son or certain trusted psychologists, but eventually I commenced a scientific study of other cases in order to see how typical or nontypical such visions might be among amnesia victims.

My results, aided by psychologists, historians, anthropologists, and mental specialists of wide experience, and by a study that included all records of split personalities from the days of daemonic-possession legends to the medically realistic present, at first bothered me more than they consoled me.

I soon found that my dreams had, indeed, no counterpart in the overwhelming bulk of true amnesia cases. There remained, however, a tiny residue of accounts which for years baffled and shocked me with their parallelism to my own experience. Some of them were bits of ancient folklore; others were case histories in the annals of medicine; one or two were anecdotes obscurely buried in standard histories.

It thus appeared that, while my special kind of affliction was prodigiously rare, instances of it had occurred at long intervals ever since the beginning of men's annals. Some centuries might contain one, two, or three cases, others none — or at least none whose record survived.

The essence was always the same — a person of keen thoughtfulness seized a strange secondary life and leading for a greater or lesser period an utterly alien existence typified at first by vocal and bodily awkwardness, and later by a wholesale acquisition of scientific, historic, artistic, and anthropologic knowledge; an acquisition carried on with feverish zest and with a wholly abnormal absorptive power. Then a sudden return of rightful consciousness, intermittently plagued ever after with vague unplaceable dreams suggesting fragments of some hideous memory elaborately blotted out.

And the close resemblance of those nightmares to my own — even in some of the smallest particulars — left no doubt in my mind of their significantly typical nature. One or two of the cases had an added ring of faint, blasphemous familiarity, as if I had heard of them before through some cosmic channel too morbid and frightful to contemplate. In three instances there was specific mention of such an unknown machine as had been in my house before the second change.

Another thing that worried me during my investigation was the somewhat greater frequency of cases where a brief, elusive glimpse of the typical nightmares was afforded to persons not visited by the well-defined amnesia.

These persons were largely of mediocre mind or less — some so primitive that they could scarcely be thought of as vehicles for abnormal scholarship and preternatural mental acquisitions. For a second they would be fired with alien force — then a backward lapse, and a thin, swift-fading memory of unhuman horrors.

There had been at least three such cases during the past half century — one only fifteen years before. Had something been groping blindly through time from some unsuspected abyss in Nature? Were these faint cases monstrous, sinister experiments of a kind and authorship utterly beyond sane belief?

Such were a few of the formless speculations of my weaker hours — fancies abetted by myths which my studies uncovered. For I could not doubt but that certain persistent legends of immemorial antiquity, apparently unknown to the victims and physicians connected with recent amnesia cases, formed a striking and awesome elaboration of memory lapses such as mine.

Of the nature of the dreams and impressions which were growing so clamorous I still almost fear to speak. They seemed to savor of madness, and at times I believed I was indeed going mad. Was there a special type of delusion afflicting those who had suffered lapses of memory? Conceivably, the efforts of the subconscious mind to fill up a perplexing blank with pseudo-memories might give rise to strange imaginative vagaries.

This indeed—though an alternative folklore theory finally seemed to me more plausible—was the belief of many of the alienists who helped me in my search for parallel cases, and who shared my puzzlement at the exact resemblances sometimes discovered.

They did not call the condition true insanity, but classed it rather among neurotic disorders. My course in trying to track down and analyze it, instead of vainly seeking to dismiss or forget it, they heartily endorsed as correct according to the best psychological principles. I especially valued the advice of such physicians as had studied me during my possession by the other personality.

My first disturbances were not visual at all, but concerned the more abstract matters which I have mentioned. There was, too, a feeling of profound and inexplicable horror concerning myself. I developed a queer fear of seeing my own form, as if my eyes would find it something utterly alien and inconceivably abhorrent.

When I did glance down and behold the familiar human shape in quiet grey or blue clothing, I always felt a curious relief, though in order to gain this relief I had to conquer an infinite dread. I shunned mirrors as much as possible, and was always shaved at the barber's.

It was a long time before I correlated any of these disappointed feelings with the fleeting, visual impressions which began to develop. The first such correlation had to do with the odd sensation of an external, artificial restraint on my memory.

I felt that the snatches of sight I experienced had a profound and terrible meaning, and a frightful connexion with myself, but that some purposeful influence held me from grasping that meaning and that connexion. Then came that queerness about the element of time, and with it desperate efforts to place the fragmentary dream-glimpses in the chronological and spatial pattern.

The glimpses themselves were at first merely strange rather than horrible. I would seem to be in an enormous vaulted chamber whose lofty stone groinings were well-nigh lost in the shadows overhead. In whatever time or place the scene might be, the principle of the arch was known as fully and used as extensively as by the Romans.

There were colossal, round windows and high, arched doors, and pedestals or tables each as tall as the height of an ordinary room. Vast shelves of dark wood lined the walls, holding what seemed to be volumes of immense size with strange hieroglyphs on their backs.

The exposed stonework held curious carvings, always in curvilinear mathematical designs, and there were chiselled inscriptions in the same characters that the huge books bore. The dark granite masonry was of a monstrous megathic type, with lines of convex-topped blocks fitting the concave-bottomed courses which rested upon them.

There were no chairs, but the tops of the vast pedestals were littered with books, papers, and what seemed to be writing materials—oddly figured jars of a purplish metal, and rods with stained tips. Tall as the pedestals were, I seemed at times able to view them from above. On some of them were great globes of luminous crystal serving as lamps, and inexplicable machines formed of vitreous tubes and metal rods.

The windows were glazed, and latticed with stout-looking bars. Though I dared not approach and peer out them, I could see from where I was the waving tops of singular fern-like growths. The floor was of massive octagonal flagstones, while rugs and hangings were entirely lacking.

Later I had visions of sweeping through Cyclopean corridors of stone, and up and down gigantic inclined planes of the same monstrous masonry. There were no stairs anywhere, nor was any passageway less than thirty feet wide. Some of the structures through which I floated must have towered in the sky for thousands of feet.

There were multiple levels of black vaults below, and never-opened trap-doors, sealed down with metal bands and holding dim suggestions of some special peril.

I seemed to be a prisoner, and horror hung broodingly over everything I saw. I felt that the mocking curvilinear hieroglyphs on the walls would blast my soul with their message were I not guarded by a merciful ignorance.

Still later my dreams included vistas from the great round windows, and from the titanic flat roof, with its curious gardens, wide barren area, and high, scalloped parapet of stone, to which the topmost of the inclined planes led.

There were almost endless leagues of giant buildings, each in its garden, and ranged along paved roads fully 200 feet wide. They differed greatly in aspect, but few were less than 500 feet square or a thousand feet high. Many seemed so limitless that they must have had a frontage of several thousand feet, while some shot up to mountainous altitudes in the grey, steamy heavens.

They seemed to be mainly of stone or concrete, and most of them embodied the oddly curvilinear type of masonry noticeable in the building that held me. Roofs were flat and garden-covered, and tended to have scalloped parapets. Sometimes there were terraces and higher levels, and wide, cleared spaces amidst the gardens. The great roads held hints of motion, but in the earlier visions I could not resolve this impression into details.

In certain places I beheld enormous dark cylindrical towers which climbed far above any of the other structures. These appeared to be of a totally unique nature and shewed signs of prodigious age and dilapidation. They were built of a bizarre type of square-cut basalt masonry, and tapered slightly toward their rounded tops. Nowhere in any of them could the least traces of windows or other apertures save huge doors be found. I noticed also some lower buildings—all crumbling with the weathering of aeons—which resembled these dark, cylindrical towers in basic architecture. Around all these aberrant piles of square-cut masonry there hovered an inexplicable aura of menace and concentrated fear, like that bred by the sealed trap-doors.

The omnipresent gardens were almost terrifying in their strangeness, with bizarre and unfamiliar forms of vegetation nodding over broad paths lined with curiously carven monoliths. Abnormally vast fern-like growths predominated — some green, and some of a ghastly, fungoid pallor.

Among them rose great spectral things resembling calamites, whose bamboo-like trunks towered to fabulous heights. Then there were tufted forms like fabulous cycads, and grotesque dark-green shrubs and trees of coniferous aspect.

Flowers were small, colourless, and unrecognizable, blooming in geometrical beds and at large among the greenery.

In a few of the terrace and roof-top gardens were larger and more blossoms of most offensive contours and seeming to suggest artificial breeding. Fungi of inconceivable size, outlines, and colours speckled the scene in patterns bespeaking some unknown but well-established horticultural tradition. In the larger gardens on the ground there seemed to be some attempt to preserve the irregularities of Nature, but on the roofs there was more selectiveness, and more evidences of the topiary art.

The skies were almost always moist and cloudy, and sometimes I would seem to witness tremendous rains. Once in a while, though, there would be glimpses of the sun — which looked abnormally large — and of the moon, whose markings held a touch of difference from the normal that I could never quite fathom. When very rarely the night sky was clear to any extent, I beheld constellations which were nearly beyond recognition. Known outlines were sometimes approximated, but seldom duplicated; and from the position of the few groups I could recognize, I felt I must be in the earth's southern hemisphere, near the Tropic of Capricorn.

The far horizon was always steamy and indistinct, but I could see that great jungles of unknown tree-ferns, calamites, lepidodendra, and sigillaria lay outside the city, their fantastic frondage waving mockingly in the shifting vapours. Now and then there would be suggestions of motion in the sky, but these my early visions never resolved.

By the autumn of 1914 I began to have infrequent dreams of strange floatings over the city and through the regions around it. I saw interminable roads through forests of fearsome growths with mottled, fluted, and banded trunks, and past other cities as strange as the one which persistently haunted me.

I saw monstrous constructions of black or iridescent tone in glades and clearings where perpetual twilight reigned, and traversed long causeways over swamps so dark that I could tell but little of their moist, towering vegetation.

Once I saw an area of countless miles strewn with age-blasted basaltic ruins whose architecture had been like that of the few windowless, round-topped towers in the haunting city.

And once I saw the sea — a boundless, steamy expanse beyond the colossal stone piers of an enormous town of domes and arches. Great shapeless suggestions of shadow moved over it, and here and there its surface was vexed with anomalous spoutings.

III.

As I have said, it was not immediately that these wild visions began to hold their terrifying quality. Certainly, many persons have dreamed intrinsically stranger things — things compounded of unrelated scraps of daily life, pictures, and reading, and arranged in fantastically novel forms by the unchecked caprices of sleep.

For some time I accepted the visions as natural, even though I had never before been an extravagant dreamer. Many of the vague anomalies, I argued, must have come from trivial sources too numerous to track down; while others seemed to reflect a common text book knowledge of the plants and other conditions of the primitive world of a hundred and fifty million years ago — the world of the Permian or Triassic age.

In the course of some months, however, the element of terror did figure with accumulating force. This was when the dreams began so unfailingly to have the aspect of memories, and when my mind began to link them with my growing abstract disturbances — the feeling of mnemonic restraint, the curious impressions regarding time, and sense of a loathsome exchange with my secondary personality of 1908-13, and, considerably later, the inexplicable loathing of my own person.

As certain definite details began to enter the dreams, their horror increased a thousandfold — until by October, 1915, I felt I must do something. It was then that I began an intensive study of other cases of amnesia and visions, feeling that I might thereby objectivise my trouble and shake clear of its emotional grip.

However, as before mentioned, the result was at first almost exactly opposite. It disturbed me vastly to find that my dreams had been so closely duplicated; especially since some of the accounts were too early to admit of any geological knowledge — and therefore of any idea of primitive landscapes — on the subjects' part.

What is more, many of these accounts supplied very horrible details and explanations in connexion with the visions of great buildings and jungle gardens — and other things. The actual sights and vague impressions were bad enough, but what was hinted or asserted by some of the other dreamers savored of madness and blasphemy. Worst of all, my own pseudo-memory was aroused to wilder dreams and hints of coming revelations. And yet most doctors deemed my course, on the whole, an advisable one.

I studied psychology systematically, and under the prevailing stimulus my son Wingate did the same — his studies leading eventually to his present professorship. In 1917 and 1918 I took special courses at Miskatonic. Meanwhile, my examination of medical, historical, and anthropological records became indefatigable, involving travels to distant libraries, and finally including even a reading of the hideous books of forbidden elder lore in which my secondary personality had been so disturbingly interested.

Some of the latter were the actual copies I had consulted in my altered state, and I was greatly disturbed by certain marginal notations and ostensible corrections of the hideous text in a script and idiom which somehow seemed oddly unhuman.

These markings were mostly in the respective languages of the various books, all of which the writer seemed to know with equal, though obviously academic, facility. One note appended to von Junzt's *Unaussprechlichen Kulten*, however, was alarmingly otherwise. It consisted of certain curvilinear hieroglyphs in the same ink as that of the German corrections, but following no recognized human pattern. And these hieroglyphs were closely and unmistakably akin to the characters constantly met with in my dreams — characters whose meaning I would sometimes momentarily fancy I knew, or was just on the brink of recalling.

To complete my black confusion, my librarians assured me that, in view of previous examinations and records of consultation of the volumes in question, all of these notations must have been made by myself in my secondary state. This despite the fact that I was and still am ignorant of three of the languages involved.

Piecing together the scattered records, ancient and modern, anthropological and medical, I found a fairly consistent mixture of myth and hallucination whose scope and wildness left me utterly dazed. Only one thing consoled me, the fact that the myths were of such early existence. What lost knowledge could have brought pictures of the Palaeozoic or Mesozoic landscape into these primitive fables, I could not even guess; but the pictures had been there. Thus, a basis existed for the formation of a fixed type of delusion.

Cases of amnesia no doubt created the general myth pattern — but afterward the fanciful accretions of the myths must have reacted on amnesia sufferers and coloured their pseudo-memories. I myself had read and heard all the early tales during my memory lapse — my quest had amply proved that. Was it not natural, then, for my subsequent dreams and emotional impressions to become coloured and moulded by what my memory subtly held over from my secondary state?

A few of the myths had significant connexions with other cloudy legends of the pre-human world, especially those Hindu tales involving stupefying gulfs of time and forming part of the lore of modern theosopists.

Primal myth and modern delusion joined in their assumption that mankind is only one — perhaps the least — of the highly evolved and dominant races of this planet's long and largely unknown career. Things of inconceivable shape, they implied, had reared towers to the sky and delved into every secret of Nature before the first amphibian forbear of man had crawled out of the hot sea 300 million years ago.

Some had come down from the stars; a few were as old as the cosmos itself, others had arisen swiftly from terrene germs as far behind the first germs of our life-cycle as those germs are behind ourselves. Spans of thousands of millions of years, and linkages to other galaxies and universes, were freely spoken of. Indeed, there was no such thing as time in its humanly accepted sense.

But most of the tales and impressions concerned a relatively late race, of a queer and intricate shape, resembling no life-form known to science, which had lived till only fifty million years before the advent of man. This, they indicated, was the greatest race of all because it alone had conquered the secret of time.

It had learned all things that ever were known or ever would be known on the earth, through the power of its keener minds to project themselves into the past and future, even through gulfs of millions of years, and study the lore of every age. From the accomplishments of this race arose all legends of prophets, including those in human mythology.

In its vast libraries were volumes of texts and pictures holding the whole of earth's annals — histories and descriptions of every species that had ever been or that ever would be, with full records of their arts, their achievements, their languages, and their psychologies.

With this aeon-embracing knowledge, the Great Race chose from every era and life-form such thoughts, arts, and processes as might suit its own nature and situation. Knowledge of the past, secured through a kind of mind-casting outside the recognized senses, was harder to glean than knowledge of the future.

In the latter case the course was easier and more material. With suitable mechanical aid a mind would project itself forward in time, feeling its dim, extra-sensory way till it approached the desired period. Then, after preliminary trials, it would seize on the best discoverable representative of the highest of that period's life-forms. It would enter the organism's brain and set up therein its own vibrations, while the displaced mind would strike back to the period of the displacer, remaining in the latter's body till a reverse process was set up.

The projected mind, in the body of the organism of the future, would then pose as a member of the race whose outward form it wore, learning as quickly as possible all that could be learned of the chosen age and its massed information and techniques.

Meanwhile the displaced mind, thrown back to the displacer's age and body, would be carefully guarded. It would be kept from harming the body it occupied, and would be drained of all its knowledge by trained questioners. Often it could be questioned in its own language, when previous quests into the future had brought back records of that language.

If the mind came from a body whose language the Great Race could not physically reproduce, clever machines would be made, on which the alien speech could be played as on a musical instrument.

The Great Race's members were immense rugose cones ten feet high, and with head and other organs attached to foot-thick, distensible limbs spreading from the apexes. They spoke by the clicking or scraping of huge paws or claws attached to the end of two of their four limbs, and walked by the expansion and contraction of a viscous layer attached to their vast, ten-foot bases.

When the captive mind's amazement and resentment had worn off, and when — assuming that it came from a body vastly different from the Great Race's — it had lost its horror at its unfamiliar temporary form, it was permitted to study its new environment and experience a wonder and wisdom approximating that of its displacer.

With suitable precautions, and in exchange for suitable services, it was allowed to rove all over the habitable world in titan airships or on the huge boatlike atomic-engined vehicles which traversed the great roads, and to delve freely into the libraries containing the records of the planet's past and future.

This reconciled many captive minds to their lot; since none were other than keen, and to such minds the unveiling of hidden mysteries of earth — closed chapters of inconceivable pasts and dizzying vortices of future time which include the years ahead of their own natural ages — forms always, despite the abysmal horrors often unveiled, the supreme experience of life.

Now and then certain captives were permitted to meet other captive minds seized from the future — to exchange thoughts with consciousnesses living a hundred or a thousand or a million years before or after their own ages. And all were urged to write copiously in their own languages of themselves and their respective periods; such documents to be filed in the great central archives.

It may be added that there was one special type of captive whose privileges were far greater than those of the majority. These were the dying permanent exiles, whose bodies in the future had been seized by keen-minded members of the Great Race who, faced with death, sought to escape mental extinction.

Such melancholy exiles were not as common as might be expected, since the longevity of the Great Race lessened its love of life — especially among those superior minds capable of projection. From cases of the permanent projection of elder minds arose many of those lasting changes of personality noticed in later history — including mankind's.

As for the ordinary cases of exploration — when the displacing mind had learned what it wished in the future, it would build an apparatus like that which had started its flight and reverse the process of projection. Once more it would be in its own body in its own age, while the lately captive mind would return to that body of the future to which it properly belonged.

Only when one or the other of the bodies had died during the exchange was this restoration impossible. In such cases, of course, the exploring mind had — like those of the death-escapers — to live out an alien-bodied life in the future; or else the captive mind — like the dying permanent exiles — had to end its days in the form and past age of the Great Race.

This fate was least horrible when the captive mind was also of the Great Race — a not infrequent occurrence, since in all its periods that race was intensely concerned with its own future. The number of dying permanent exiles of the Great Race was very slight — largely because of the tremendous penalties attached to displacements of future Great Race minds by the moribund.

Through projection, arrangements were made to inflict these penalties on the offending minds in their new future bodies — and sometimes forced re-exchanges were effected.

Complex cases of the displacement of exploring or already captive minds by minds in various regions of the past had been known and carefully rectified. In every age since the discovery of mind projection, a minute but well-recognised element of the population consisted of Great Race minds from past ages, sojourning for a longer or shorter while.

When a captive mind of alien origin was returned to its own body in the future, it was purged by an intricate mechanical hypnosis of all it had learned in the Great Race's age — this because of certain troublesome consequences inherent in the general carrying forward of knowledge in large quantities.

The few existing instances of clear transmission had caused, and would cause at known future times, great disasters. And it was largely in consequence of two cases of this kind — said the old myths — that mankind had learned what it had concerning the Great Race.

Of all things surviving physically and directly from that aeon-distant world, there remained only certain ruins of great stones in far places and under the sea, and parts of the text of the frightful Pnakotic Manuscripts.

Thus the returning mind reached its own age with only the faintest and most fragmentary visions of what it had undergone since its seizure. All memories that could be eradicated were eradicated, so that in most cases only a dream-shadowed blank stretched back to the time of the first exchange. Some minds recalled more than others, and the chance joining of memories had at rare times brought hints of the forbidden past to future ages.

There probably never was a time when groups or cults did not secretly cherish certain of these hints. In the *Necronomicon* the presence of such a cult among human beings was suggested — a cult that sometimes gave aid to minds voyaging down the aeons from the days of the Great Race.

And, meanwhile, the Great Race itself waxed well-nigh omniscient, and turned to the task of setting up exchanges with the minds of other planets, and of exploring their pasts and futures. It sought likewise to fathom the past years and origin of that black, aeon-dead orb in far space whence its own mental heritage had come — for the mind of the Great Race was older than its bodily form.

The beings of a dying elder world, wise with the ultimate secrets, had looked ahead for a new world and species wherein they might have long life; and had sent their minds en masse into that future race best adapted to house them — the cone-shaped beings that peopled our earth a billion years ago.

Thus the Great Race came to be, while the myriad minds sent backward were left to die in the horror of strange shapes. Later the race would again face death, yet would live through another forward migration of its best minds into the bodies of others who had a longer physical span ahead of them.

Such was the background of intertwined legend and hallucination. When, around 1920, I had my researches in coherent shape, I felt a slight lessening of the tension which their earlier stages had increased. After all, and in spite of the fancies prompted by blind emotions, were not most of my phenomena readily explainable? Any chance might have turned my mind to dark studies during the amnesia — and then I read the forbidden legends and met the members of ancient and ill-regarded cults. That, plainly, supplied the material for the dreams and disturbed feelings which came after the return of memory.

As for the marginal notes in dream-hieroglyphs and languages unknown to me, but laid at my door by librarians — I might easily have picked up a smattering of the tongues during my secondary state, while the hieroglyphs were doubtless coined by my fancy from descriptions in old legends, and afterward woven into my dreams. I tried to verify certain points through conversation with known cult leaders, but never succeeded in establishing the right connexions.

At times the parallelism of so many cases in so many distant ages continued to worry me as it had at first, but on the other hand I reflected that the excitant folklore was undoubtedly more universal in the past than in the present.

Probably all the other victims whose cases were like mine had had a long and familiar knowledge of the tales I had learned only when in my secondary state. When these victims had lost their memory, they had associated themselves with the creatures of their household myths — the fabulous invaders supposed to displace men's minds — and had thus embarked upon quests for knowledge which they thought they could take back to a fancied, non-human past.

Then, when their memory returned, they reversed the associative process and thought of themselves as the former captive minds instead of as the displacers. Hence the dreams and pseudo-memories following the conventional myth pattern.

Despite the seeming cumbrousness of these explanations, they came finally to supersede all others in my mind — largely because of the greater weakness of any rival theory. And a substantial number of eminent psychologists and anthropologists gradually agreed with me.

The more I reflected, the more convincing did my reasoning seem; till in the end I had a really effective bulwark against the visions and impressions which still assailed me. Suppose I did see strange things at night? These were only what I had heard and read of. Suppose I did have odd loathings and perspectives and pseudo-memories? These, too, were only echoes of myths absorbed in my secondary state. Nothing that I might dream, nothing that I might feel, could be of any actual significance.

Fortified by this philosophy, I greatly improved in nervous equilibrium, even though the visions — rather than the abstract impressions — steadily became more frequent and more disturbingly detailed. In 1922 I felt able to undertake regular work again, and put my newly gained knowledge to practical use by accepting an instructorship in psychology at the university.

My old chair of political economy had long been adequately filled — besides which, methods of teaching economics had changed greatly since my heyday. My son was at this time just entering on the post-graduate studies leading to his present professorship, and we worked together a great deal.

IV.

I continued, however, to keep a careful record of the outré dreams which crowded upon me so thickly and vividly. Such a record, I argued, was of genuine value as a psychological document. The glimpses still seemed damnably like memories, though I fought off this impression with a goodly measure of success.

In writing, I treated the phantasmata as things seen; but at all other times I brushed them aside like any gossamer illusions of the night. I had never mentioned such matters in common conversation; though reports of them, filtering out as such things will, had aroused sundry rumors regarding my mental health. It is amusing to reflect that these rumors were confined wholly to laymen, without a single champion among physicians or psychologists.

Of my visions after 1914 I will here mention only a few, since fuller accounts and records are at the disposal of the serious student. It is evident that with time the curious inhibitions somewhat waned, for the scope of my visions vastly increased. They have never, though, become other than disjointed fragments seemingly without clear motivation.

Within the dreams I seemed gradually to acquire a greater and greater freedom of wandering. I floated through many strange buildings of stone, going from one to the other along mammoth underground passages which seemed to form the common avenues of transit. Sometimes I encountered those gigantic sealed trap-doors in the lowest level, around which such an aura of fear and forbiddenness clung.

I saw tremendously tessellated pools, and rooms of curious and inexplicable utensils of myriad sorts. Then there were colossal caverns of intricate machinery whose outlines and purpose were wholly strange to me, and whose sound manifested itself only after many years of dreaming. I may here remark that sight and sound are the only senses I have ever exercised in the visionary world.

The real horror began in May, 1915, when I first saw the living things. This was before my studies had taught me what, in view of the myths and case histories, to expect. As mental barriers wore down, I beheld great masses of thin vapour in various parts of the building and in the streets below.

These steadily grew more solid and distinct, till at last I could trace their monstrous outlines with uncomfortable ease. They seemed to be enormous, iridescent cones, about ten feet high and ten feet wide at the base, and made up of some ridgy, scaly, semi-elastic matter. From their apexes projected four flexible, cylindrical members, each a foot thick, and of a ridgy substance like that of the cones themselves.

These members were sometimes contracted almost to nothing, and sometimes extended to any distance up to about ten feet. Terminating two of them were enormous claws or nippers. At the end of a third were four red, trumpetlike appendages. The fourth terminated in an irregular yellowish globe some two feet in diameter and having three great dark eyes ranged along its central circumference.

Surmounting this head were four slender grey stalks bearing flower-like appendages, whilst from its nether side dangled eight greenish antennae or tentacles. The great base of the central cone was fringed with a rubbery, grey substance which moved the whole entity through expansion and contraction.

Their actions, though harmless, horrified me even more than their appearance — for it is not wholesome to watch monstrous objects doing what one had known only human beings to do. These objects moved intelligently about the great rooms, getting books from the shelves and taking them to the great tables, or vice versa, and sometimes writing diligently with a peculiar rod gripped in the greenish head tentacles. The huge nippers were used in carrying books and in conversation-speech consisting of a kind of clicking and scraping.

The objects had no clothing, but wore satchels or knapsacks suspended from the top of the conical trunk. They commonly carried their head and its supporting member at the level of the cone top, although it was frequently raised or lowered.

The other three great members tended to rest downward at the sides of the cone, contracted to about five feet each when not in use. From their rate of reading, writing, and operating their machines — those on the tables seemed somehow connected with thought — I concluded that their intelligence was enormously greater than man's.

Afterward I saw them everywhere; swarming in all the great chambers and corridors, tending monstrous machines in vaulted crypts, and racing along the vast roads in gigantic, boat-shaped cars. I ceased to be afraid of them, for they seemed to form supremely natural parts of their environment.

Individual differences amongst them began to be manifest, and a few appeared to be under some kind of restraint. These latter, though shewing no physical variation, had a diversity of gestures and habits which marked them off not only from the majority, but very largely from one another.

They wrote a great deal in what seemed to my cloudy vision a vast variety of characters — never the typical curvilinear hieroglyphs of the majority. A few, I fancied, used our own familiar alphabet. Most of them worked much more slowly than the general mass of the entities.

All this time my own part in the dreams seemed to be that of a disembodied consciousness with a range of vision wider than the normal, floating freely about, yet confined to the ordinary avenues and speeds of travel. Not until August, 1915, did any suggestions of bodily existence begin to harass me. I say harass, because the first phase was a purely abstract, though infinitely terrible, association of my previously noted body loathing with the scenes of my visions.

For a while my chief concern during dreams was to avoid looking down at myself, and I recall how grateful I was for the total absence of large mirrors in the strange rooms. I was mightily troubled by the fact that I always saw the great tables — whose height could not be under ten feet — from a level not below that of their surfaces.

And then the morbid temptation to look down at myself became greater and greater, till one night I could not resist it. At first my downward glance revealed nothing whatever. A moment later I perceived that this was because my head lay at the end of a flexible neck of enormous length. Retracting this neck and gazing down very sharply, I saw the scaly, rugose, iridescent bulk of a vast cone ten feet tall and ten feet wide at the base. That was when I waked half of Arkham with my screaming as I plunged madly up from the abyss of sleep.

Only after weeks of hideous repetition did I grow half-reconciled to these visions of myself in monstrous form. In the dreams I now moved bodily among the other unknown entities, reading terrible books from the endless shelves and writing for hours at the great tables with a stylus managed by the green tentacles that hung down from my head.

Snatches of what I read and wrote would linger in my memory. There were horrible annals of other worlds and other universes, and of stirrings of formless life outside of all universes. There were records of strange orders of beings which had peopled the world in forgotten pasts, and frightful chronicles of grotesque-bodied intelligences which would people it millions of years after the death of the last human being.

I learned of chapters in human history whose existence no scholar of today has ever suspected. Most of these writings were in the language of the hieroglyphs; which I studied in a queer way with the aid of droning machines, and which was evidently an agglutinative speech with root systems utterly unlike any found in human languages.

Other volumes were in other unknown tongues learned in the same queer way. A very few were in languages I knew. Extremely clever pictures, both inserted in the records and forming separate collections, aided me immensely. And all the time I seemed to be setting down a history of my own age in English. On waking, I could recall only minute and meaningless scraps of the unknown tongues which my dream-self had mastered, though whole phrases of the history stayed with me.

I learned — even before my waking self had studied the parallel cases or the old myths from which the dreams doubtless

"Of the animals I saw I could write volumes!"

sprang — that the entities around me were of the world's greatest race, which had conquered time and had sent exploring minds into every age. I knew, too, that I had been snatched from my age while another used my body in that age, and that a few of the other strange forms housed similarly captured minds. I seemed to talk, in some odd language of claw clickings, with exiled intellects from every corner of the solar system.

There was a mind from the planet we know as Venus, which would live incalculable epochs to come, and one from an outer moon of Jupiter six million years in the past. Of earthly minds there were some from the winged, star-headed, half-vegetable race of palaeogean Antarctica; one from the reptile people of fabled Valusia; three from the furry pre-human Hyperborean worshippers of Tsathoggua; one from the wholly abominable Tcho-Tchos; two from the arachnid denizens of earth's last age; five from the hardy coleopterous species immediately following mankind, to which the Great Race was some day to transfer its keenest minds en masse in the face of horrible peril; and several from different branches of humanity.

Astounding Stories, June 1936

I talked with the mind of Yiang-Li, a philosopher from the cruel empire of Tsan-Chan, which is to come in 5,000 A.D.; with that of a general of the greatheaded brown people who held South Africa in 50,000 B.C.; with that of a twelfth-century Florentine monk named Bartolomeo Corsi; with that of a king of Lomar who had ruled that terrible polar land one hundred thousand years before the squat, yellow Inutos came from the west to engulf it.

I talked with the mind of Nug-Soth, a magician of the dark conquerors of 16,000 A.D.; with that of a Roman named Titus Sempronius Blaesus, who had been a quaestor in Sulla's time; with that of Khephnes, an Egyptian of the 14th Dynasty, who told me the hideous secret of Nyarlathotep, with that of a priest of Atlantis' middle kingdom; with that of a Suffolk gentleman of Cromwell's day, James Woodville; with that of a court astronomer of pre-Inca Peru; with that of the Australian physicist Nevil Kingston-Brown, who will die in 2,518 A.D.; with that of an archimage of vanished Yhe in the Pacific; with that of Theodotides, a Greco-Bactrian official of 200 B.C.; with that of an aged Frenchman of Louis XIII's time named Pierre-Louis Montagny; with that of Crom-Ya, a Cimmerian chieftain of 15,000 B.C.; and with so many others that my brain cannot hold the shocking secrets and dizzying marvels I learned from them.

I awaked each morning in a fever, sometimes frantically trying to verify or discredit such information as fell within the range of modern human knowledge. Traditional facts took on new and doubtful aspects, and I marvelled at the dream-fancy which could invent such surprising addenda to history and science.

I shivered at the mysteries the past may conceal, and trembled at the menaces the future may bring forth. What was hinted in the speech of post-human entities of the fate of mankind produced such an effect on me that I will not set it down here.

After man there would be the mighty beetle civilisation, the bodies of whose members the cream of the Great Race would seize when the monstrous doom overtook the elder world. Later, as the earth's span closed, the transferred minds would again migrate through time and space — to another stopping-place in the bodies of the bulbous vegetable entities of Mercury. But there would be races after them, clinging pathetically to the cold planet and burrowing to its horror-filled core, before the utter end.

Meanwhile, in my dreams, I wrote endlessly in that history of my own age which I was preparing — half voluntarily and half through promises of increased library and travel opportunities — for the Great Race's central archives. The archives were in a colossal subterranean structure near the city's center, which I came to know well through frequent labors and consultations. Meant to last as long as the race, and to withstand the fiercest of earth's convulsions, this titan repository surpassed all other buildings in the massive, mountain-like firmness of its construction.

The records, written or printed on great sheets of a curiously tenacious cellulose fabric, were bound into books that opened from the top, and were kept in individual cases of a strange, extremely light, rustless metal of greyish hue, decorated with mathematical designs and bearing the title in the Great Race's curvilinear hieroglyphs.

These cases were stored in tiers of rectangular vaults — like closed, locked shelves — wrought of the same rustless metal and fastened by knobs with intricate turnings. My own history was assigned a specific place in the vaults of the lowest or vertebrate level — the section devoted to the culture of mankind and of the furry and reptilian races immediately preceding it in terrestrial dominance.

But none of the dreams ever gave me a full picture of daily life. All were the merest misty, disconnected fragments, and it is certain that these fragments were not unfolded in their rightful sequence. I have, for example, a very imperfect idea of my own living arrangements in the dream-world; though I seem to have possessed a great stone room of my own. My restrictions as a prisoner gradually disappeared, so that some of the visions included vivid travels over the mighty jungle roads, sojourns in strange cities, and explorations of some of the vast, dark, windowless ruins from which the Great Race shrank in curious fear. There were also long sea voyages in enormous, many-decked boats of incredible swiftness, and trips over wild regions in closed projectile-like airships lifted and moved by electrical repulsion.

Beyond the wide, warm ocean were other cities of the Great Race, and on one far continent I saw the crude villages of the black-snouted, winged creatures who would evolve as a dominant stock after the Great Race had sent its foremost minds into the future to escape the creeping horror. Flatness and exuberant green life were always the keynote of the scene. Hills were low and sparse, and usually displayed signs of volcanic forces.

Of the animals I saw, I could write volumes. All were wild; for the Great Race's mechanised culture had long since done away with domestic beasts, while food was wholly vegetable or synthetic. Clumsy reptiles of great bulk floundered in steaming morasses, fluttered in the heavy air, or spouted in the seas and lakes; and among these I fancied I could vaguely recognise lesser, archaic prototypes of many forms — dinosaurs, pterodactyls, ichthyosaurs, labyrinthodonts, plesiosaurs, and the like — made familiar through palaeontology. Of birds or mammals there were none that I could discover.

The ground and swamps were constantly alive with snakes, lizards, and crocodiles while insects buzzed incessantly among the lush vegetation. And far out at sea, unspied and unknown monsters spouted mountainous columns of foam into the vaporous sky. Once I was taken under the ocean in a gigantic submarine vessel with searchlights, and glimpsed some living horrors of awesome magnitude. I saw also the ruins of incredible sunken cities, and the wealth of crinoid, brachiopod, coral, and ichthyic life which everywhere abounded.

Of the physiology, psychology, folkways, and detailed history of the Great Race my visions preserved but little information, and many of the scattered points I here set down were gleaned from my study of old legends and other cases rather than from my own dreaming.

For in time, of course, my reading and research caught up with and passed the dreams in many phases, so that certain dream-fragments were explained in advance and formed verifications of what I had learned. This consolingly established my belief that similar reading and research, accomplished by my secondary self, had formed the source of the whole terrible fabric of pseudomemories.

The period of my dreams, apparently, was one somewhat less than 150,000,000 years ago, when the Palaeozoic age was giving place to the Mesozoic. The bodies occupied by the Great Race represented no surviving — or even scientifically known — line of terrestrial evolution, but were of a peculiar, closely homogeneous, and highly specialised organic type inclining as much as to the vegetable as to the animal state.

Cell action was of an unique sort almost precluding fatigue, and wholly eliminating the need of sleep. Nourishment, assimilated through the red trumpet-like appendages on one of the great flexible limbs, was always semi-fluid and in many aspects wholly unlike the food of existing animals.

The beings had but two of the senses which we recognise — sight and hearing, the latter accomplished through the flower-like appendages on the grey stalks above their heads. Of other and incomprehensible senses — not, however, well utilizable by alien captive minds inhabiting their bodies — they possessed many. Their three eyes were so situated as to give them a range of vision wider than the normal. Their blood was a sort of deep-greenish ichor of great thickness.

They had no sex, but reproduced through seeds or spores which clustered on their bases and could be developed only under water. Great, shallow tanks were used for the growth of their young — which were, however, reared only in small numbers on account of the longevity of individuals — four or five thousand years being the common life span.

Markedly defective individuals were quickly disposed of as soon as their defects were noticed. Disease and the approach of death were, in the absence of a sense of touch or of physical pain, recognised by purely visual symptoms.

The dead were incinerated with dignified ceremonies. Once in a while, as before mentioned, a keen mind would escape death by forward projection in time; but such cases were not numerous. When one did occur, the exiled mind from the future was treated with the utmost kindness till the dissolution of its unfamiliar tenement.

The Great Race seemed to form a single, loosely knit nation or league, with major institutions in common, though there were four definite divisions. The political and economic system of each unit was a sort of fascistic socialism, with major resources rationally distributed, and power delegated to a small governing board elected by the votes of all able to pass certain educational and psychological tests. Family organisation was not overstressed, though ties among persons of common descent were recognised, and the young were generally reared by their parents.

Resemblances to human attitudes and institutions were, of course, most marked in those fields where on the one hand highly abstract elements were concerned, or where on the other hand there was a dominance of the basic, unspecialised urges common to all organic life. A few added likenesses came through conscious adoption as the Great Race probed the future and copied what it liked.

Industry, highly mechanised, demanded but little time from each citizen; and the abundant leisure was filled with intellectual and aesthetic activities of various sorts.

The sciences were carried to an unbelievable height of development, and art was a vital part of life, though at the period of my dreams it had passed its crest and meridian. Technology was enormously stimulated through the constant struggle to survive, and to keep in existence the physical fabric of great cities, imposed by the prodigious geologic upheavals of those primal days.

Crime was surprisingly scant, and was dealt with through highly efficient policing. Punishments ranged from privilege deprivation and imprisonment to death or major emotion wrenching, and were never administered without a careful study of the criminal's motivations.

Warfare, largely civil for the last few millennia though sometimes waged against reptilian or octopodic invaders, or against the winged, star-headed Old Ones who centered in the antarctic, was infrequent though infinitely devastating. An enormous army, using camera-like weapons which produced tremendous electrical effects, was kept on hand for purposes seldom mentioned, but obviously connected with the ceaseless fear of the dark, windowless elder ruins and of the great sealed trap-doors in the lowest subterranean levels.

This fear of the basalt ruins and trap-doors was largely a matter of unspoken suggestion — or, at most, of furtive quasi-whispers. Everything specific which bore on it was significantly absent from such books as were on the common shelves. It was the one subject lying altogether under a taboo among the Great Race, and seemed to be connected alike with horrible bygone struggles, and with that future peril which would some day force the race to send its keener minds ahead en masse in time.

Imperfect and fragmentary as were the other things presented by dreams and legends, this matter was still more bafflingly shrouded. The vague old myths avoided it — or perhaps all allusions had for some reason been excised. And in the dreams of myself and others, the hints were peculiarly few. Members of the Great Race never intentionally referred to the matter, and what could be gleaned came only from some of the more sharply observant captive minds.

According to these scraps of information, the basis of the fear was a horrible elder race of half-polypous, utterly alien entities which had come through space from immeasurably distant universes and had dominated the earth and three other solar planets about 600 million years ago. They were only partly material — as we understand matter — and their type of consciousness and media of perception differed widely from those of terrestrial organisms. For example, their senses did not include that of sight; their mental world being a strange, non-visual pattern of impressions.

They were, however, sufficiently material to use implements of normal matter when in cosmic areas containing it; and they required housing — albeit of a peculiar kind. Though their senses could penetrate all material barriers, their substance could not; and certain forms of electrical energy could wholly destroy them. They had the power of aërial motion, despite the absence of wings or any other visible means of levitation. Their minds were of such texture that no exchange with them could be effected by the Great Race.

When these things had come to the earth they had built mighty basalt cities of windowless towers, and had preyed horribly upon the beings they found. Thus it was when the minds of the Great Race sped across the void from that obscure, trans-galactic world known in the disturbing and debatable Eltdown Shards as Yith.

The newcomers, with the instruments they created, had

found it easy to subdue the predatory entities and drive them down to those caverns of inner earth which they had already joined to their abodes and begun to inhabit.

Then they had sealed the entrances and left them to their fate, afterward occupying most of their great cities and preserving certain important buildings for reasons connected more with superstition than with indifference, boldness, or scientific and historical zeal.

But as the aeons passed there came vague, evil signs that the elder things were growing strong and numerous in the inner world. There were sporadic irruptions of a particularly hideous character in certain small and remote cities of the Great Race, and in some of the deserted elder cities which the Great Race had not peopled — places where the paths to the gulfs below had not been properly sealed or guarded.

After that greater precautions were taken, and many of the paths were closed forever — though a few were left with sealed trap-doors for strategic use in fighting the elder things if ever they broke forth in unexpected places.

The irruptions of the elder things must have been shocking beyond all description, since they had permanently coloured the psychology of the Great Race. Such was the fixed mood of horror that the very aspect of the creatures was left unmentioned. At no time was I able to gain a clear hint of what they looked like.

There were veiled suggestions of a monstrous plasticity, and of temporary lapses of visibility, while other fragmentary whispers referred to their control and military use of great winds. Singular whistling noises, and colossal footprints made up of five circular toe marks, seemed also to be associated with them.

It was evident that the coming doom so desperately feared by the Great Race — the doom that was one day to send millions of keen minds across the chasm of time to strange bodies in the safer future — had to do with a final successful irruption of the elder beings.

Mental projections down the ages had clearly foretold such a horror, and the Great Race had resolved that none who could escape should face it. That the foray would be a matter of vengeance, rather than an attempt to reoccupy the outer world, they knew from the planet's later history — for their projections shewed the coming and going of subsequent races untroubled by the monstrous entities.

Perhaps these entities had come to prefer earth's inner abysses to the variable, storm-ravaged surface, since light meant nothing to them. Perhaps, too, they were slowly weakening with the aeons. Indeed, it was known that they would be quite dead in the time of the post-human beetle race which the fleeing minds would tenant.

Meanwhile, the Great Race maintained its cautious vigilance, with potent weapons ceaselessly ready despite the horrified banishing of the subject from common speech and visible records. And always the shadow of nameless fear hung bout the sealed trap-doors and the dark, windowless elder towers.

V.

That is the world of which my dreams brought me dim, scattered echoes every night. I cannot hope to give any true idea of the horror and dread contained in such echoes, for it was upon a wholly intangible quality — the sharp sense of pseudo-memory — that such feelings mainly depended.

As I have said, my studies gradually gave me a defence against these feelings in the form of rational psychological explanations; and this saving influence was augmented by the subtle touch of accustomedness which comes with the passage of time. Yet in spite of everything the vague, creeping terror would return momentarily now and then. It did not, however, engulf me as it had before; and after 1922 I lived a very normal life of work and recreation.

In the course of years I began to feel that my experience — together with the kindred cases and the related folklore — ought to be definitely summarised and published for the benefit of serious students; hence I prepared a series of articles briefly covering the whole ground and illustrated with crude sketches of some of the shapes, scenes, decorative motifs, and hieroglyphs remembered from the dreams.

These appeared at various times during 1928 and 1929 in the *Journal of the American Psychological Society*, but did not attract much attention. Meanwhile I continued to record my dreams with the minutest care, even though the growing stack of reports attained troublesomely vast proportions. On July 10, 1934, there was forwarded to me by the Psychological Society the letter which opened the culminating and most horrible phase of the whole mad ordeal. It was postmarked Pilbarra, Western Australia, and bore the signature of one whom I found, upon inquiry, to be a mining engineer of considerable prominence. Enclosed were some very curious snapshots. I will reproduce the text in its entirety, and no reader can fail to understand how tremendous an effect it and the photographs had upon me.

I was, for a time, almost stunned and incredulous; for although I had often thought that some basis of fact must underlie certain phases of the legends which had coloured my dreams, I was none the less unprepared for anything like a tangible survival from a lost world remote beyond all imagination. Most devastating of all were the photographs — for here, in cold, incontrovertible realism, there stood out against a background of sand certain worn-down, water-ridged, storm-weathered blocks of stone whose slightly convex tops and slightly concave bottoms told their own story.

And when I studied them with a magnifying glass I could see all too plainly, amidst the batterings and pittings, the traces of those vast curvilinear designs and occasional hieroglyphs whose significance had become so hideous to me. But here is the letter, which speaks for itself.

49, Dampier St.,
Pilbarra, W. Australia

May 18, 1934.

Prof. N. W Peaslee,
c/o Am. Psychological Society,
30 E. 41st St.
New York City, U.S.A.

My Dear Sir:—

A recent conversation with Dr. E. M. Boyle of Perth, and some papers with your articles which he has just sent me, make it advisable for me to tell you about certain things I have seen in the Great Sandy Desert east of our gold field here. It would seem, in view of the peculiar legends about old cities with huge stonework and strange designs and hieroglyphs which you describe, that I have come upon something very important.

The blackfellows have always been full of talk about "great stones with marks on them," and seem to have a terrible fear of such things. They connect them in some way with their common racial legends about Buddai, the gigantic old man who lies asleep for ages underground with his head on his arm, and who will some day awake and eat up the world.

There are some very old and half-forgotten tales of enormous underground huts of great stones, where passages lead down and down, and where horrible things have happened. The blackfellows claim that once some warriors, fleeing in battle, went down into one and never came back, but that frightful winds began to blow from the place soon after they went down. However, there usually isn't much in what these natives say.

But what I have to tell is more than this. Two years ago, when I was prospecting about 500 miles east in the desert, I came on a lot of queer pieces of dressed stone perhaps 3 × 2 × 2 feet in size, and weathered and pitted to the very limit.

At first I couldn't find any of the marks the blackfellows told about, but when I looked close enough I could make out some deeply carved lines in spite of the weathering. There were peculiar curves, just like what the blackfellows had tried to describe. I imagine there must have been thirty or forty blocks, some nearly buried in the sand, and all within a circle perhaps a quarter of a mile in diameter.

When I saw some, I looked around closely for more, and made a careful reckoning of the place with my instruments. I also took pictures of ten or twelve of the most typical blocks, and will enclose the prints for you to see.

I turned my information and pictures over to the government at Perth, but they have done nothing about them.

Then I met Dr. Boyle, who had read your articles in the Journal of the American Psychological Society, *and, in time, happened to mention the stones. He was enormously interested, and became quite excited when I shewed him my snapshots, saying that the stones and the markings were just like those of the masonry you had dreamed about and seen described in legends.*

He meant to write you, but was delayed. Meanwhile, he sent me most of the magazines with your articles, and I saw at once, from your drawings and descriptions, that my stones are certainly the kind you mean. You can appreciate this from the enclosed prints. Later on you will hear directly from Dr. Boyle.

Now I can understand how important all this will be to you. Without question we are faced with the remains of an unknown civilization older than any dreamed of before, and forming a basis for your legends.

As a mining engineer, I have some knowledge of geology, and can tell you that these blocks are so ancient they frighten me. They are mostly sandstone and granite, though one is almost certainly made of a queer sort of cement or concrete.

They bear evidence of water action, as if this part of the world had been submerged and come up again after long ages—all since those blocks were made and used. It is a matter of hundreds of thousands of years—or heaven knows how much more. I don't like to think about it.

In view of your previous diligent work in tracking down the legends and everything connected with them, I cannot doubt but that you will want to lead an expedition to the desert and make some archaeological excavations. Both Dr. Boyle and I are prepared to cooperate in such work if you—or organizations known to you—can furnish the funds.

I can get together a dozen miners for the heavy digging—the blackfellows would be of no use, for I've found that they have an almost maniacal fear of this particular spot. Boyle and I are saying nothing to others, for you very obviously ought to have precedence in any discoveries or credit.

The place can be reached from Pilbarra in about four days by motor tractor—which we'd need for our apparatus. It is somewhat west and south of Warburton's path of 1873, and 100 miles southeast of Joanna Spring. We could float things up the De Grey River instead of starting from Pilbarra—but all that can be talked over later.

Roughly the stones lie at a point about 22° 3' 14" South Latitude, 125° 0' 39" East Longitude. The climate is tropical, and the desert conditions are trying.

I shall welcome further correspondence upon this subject, and am keenly eager to assist in any plan you may devise. After studying your articles I am deeply impressed with the profound significance of the whole matter. Dr. Boyle will write later. When rapid communication is needed, a cable to Perth can be relayed by wireless.

Hoping profoundly for an early message,
Believe me,
Most faithfully yours,

— ROBERT B.F. MACKENZIE.

Of the immediate aftermath of this letter, much can be learned from the press. My good fortune in securing the backing of Miskatonic University was great, and both Mr. Mackenzie and Dr. Boyle proved invaluable in arranging matters at the Australian end. We were not too specific with the public about our objects, since the whole matter would have lent itself unpleasantly to sensational and jocose treatment by the cheaper newspapers. As a result, printed reports were sparing; but enough appeared to tell of our quest for reported Australian ruins and to chronicle our various preparatory steps.

Professor William Dyer of the college's geology department—leader of the Miskatonic Antarctic Expedition Of 1930-31—Ferdinand C. Ashley of the department of ancient history, and Tyler M. Freeborn of the department of anthropology—together with my son Wingate—accompanied me.

My correspondent, Mackenzie, came to Arkham early in 1935 and assisted in our final preparations. He proved to be a tremendously competent and affable man of about fifty, admirably well-read, and deeply familiar with all the conditions of Australian travel.

He had tractors waiting at Pilbarra, and we chartered a tramp steamer sufficiently small to get up the river to that point. We were prepared to excavate in the most careful and scientific fashion, sifting every particle of sand, and disturbing nothing which might seem to be in or near its original situation.

Sailing from Boston aboard the wheezy Lexington on March 28, 1935, we had a leisurely trip across the Atlantic and Mediterranean, through the Suez Canal, down the Red Sea, and across the Indian Ocean to our goal. I need not tell how the sight of the low, sandy West Australian coast depressed me, and how I detested the crude mining town and dreary gold fields where the tractors were given their last loads.

Dr. Boyle, who met us, proved to be elderly, pleasant, and intelligent—and his knowledge of psychology led him into many long discussions with my son and me.

Discomfort and expectancy were oddly mingled in most of us when at length our party of eighteen rattled forth over the arid leagues of sand and rock. On Friday, May 31st, we forded a branch of the De Grey and entered the realm of utter desolation. A certain positive terror grew on me as we advanced to this actual site of the elder world behind the legends—a terror, of course, abetted by the fact that my disturbing dreams and pseudo-memories still beset me with unabated force.

It was on Monday, June 3rd, that we saw the first of the half-buried blocks. I cannot describe the emotions with which I actually touched—in objective reality—a fragment of Cyclopean masonry in every respect like the blocks in the walls of my dream-buildings. There was a distinct trace of carving—and my hands trembled as I recognised part of a curvilinear decorative scheme made hellish to me through years of tormenting nightmare and baffling research.

A month of digging brought a total of some 1250 blocks in varying stages of wear and disintegration. Most of these were carven megaliths with curved tops and bottoms. A minority were smaller, flatter, plain-surfaced, and square or octagonally cut-like those of the floors and pavements in my dreams—while a few were singularly massive and curved or slanted in such a manner as to suggest use in vaulting or groining, or as parts of arches or round window casings.

The deeper—and the farther north and east—we dug, the more blocks we found; though we still failed to discover any trace of arrangement among them. Professor Dyer was appalled at the measureless age of the fragments, and Freeborn found traces of symbols which fitted darkly into certain Papuan and Polynesian legends of infinite antiquity. The condition and scattering of the blocks told mutely of vertiginous cycles of time and geologic upheavals of cosmic savagery.

We had an aëroplane with us, and my son Wingate would often go up to different heights and scan the sand-and-rock waste for signs of dim, large-scale outlines—either differences of level or trails of scattered blocks. His results were virtually negative; for whenever he would one day think he had glimpsed some significant trend, he would on his next trip find the impression replaced by another equally insubstantial—a result of the shifting, wind-blown sand.

One or two of these ephemeral suggestions, though, affected me queerly and disagreeably. They seemed, after a fashion, to dovetail horribly with something I had dreamed or read, but which I could no longer remember. There was a terrible familiarity about them—which somehow made me look furtively and apprehensively over the abominable, sterile terrain toward the north and northeast.

Around the first week in July I developed an unaccountable set of mixed emotions about that general northeasterly region. There was horror, and there was curiosity—but more than that, there was a persistent and perplexing illusion of memory.

I tried all sorts of psychological expedients to get these notions out of my head, but met with no success. Sleeplessness also gained upon me, but I almost welcomed this because of the resultant shortening of my dream-periods. I acquired the habit of taking long, lone walks in the desert late at night—usually to the north or northeast, whither the sum of my strange new impulses seemed subtly to pull me.

Sometimes, on these walks, I would stumble over nearly buried fragments of the ancient masonry. Though there were fewer visible blocks here than where we had started, I felt sure that there must be a vast abundance beneath the surface. The ground was less level than at our camp, and the prevailing high winds now and then piled the sand into fantastic temporary hillocks—exposing low traces of the elder stones while it covered other traces.

I was queerly anxious to have the excavations extend to this territory, yet at the same time dreaded what might be revealed. Obviously, I was getting into a rather bad state—all the worse because I could not account for it.

An indication of my poor nervous health can be gained from my response to an odd discovery which I made on one of my nocturnal rambles. It was on the evening of July 11th, when the moon flooded the mysterious hillocks with a curious pallor.

Wandering somewhat beyond my usual limits, I came upon a great stone which seemed to differ markedly from any we had yet encountered. It was almost wholly covered, but I stooped and cleared away the sand with my hands, later studying the object carefully and supplementing the moonlight with my electric torch.

Unlike the other very large rocks, this one was perfectly

square-cut, with no convex or concave surface. It seemed, too, to be of a dark basaltic substance, wholly dissimilar to the granite and sandstone and occasional concrete of the now familiar fragments.

Suddenly I rose, turned, and ran for the camp at top speed. It was a wholly unconscious and irrational flight, and only when I was close to my tent did I fully realise why I had run. Then it came to me. The queer dark stone was something which I had dreamed and read about, and which was linked with the uttermost horrors of the aeon-old legendry.

It was one of the blocks of that basaltic elder masonry which the fabled Great Race held in such fear — the tall, windowless ruins left by those brooding, half-material, alien things that festered in earth's nether abysses and against whose wind-like, invisible forces the trap-doors were sealed and the sleepless sentinels posted.

I remained awake all night, but by dawn realised how silly I had been to let the shadow of a myth upset me. Instead of being frightened, I should have had a discoverer's enthusiasm.

The next forenoon I told the others about my find, and Dyer, Freeborn, Boyle, my son, and I set out to view the anomalous block. Failure, however, confronted us. I had formed no clear idea of the stone's location, and a late wind had wholly altered the hillocks of shifting sand.

VI.

I come now to the crucial and most difficult part of my narrative — all the more difficult because I cannot be quite certain of its reality. At times I feel uncomfortably sure that I was not dreaming or deluded; and it is this feeling in view of the stupendous implications which the objective truth of my experience would raise — which impels me to make this record.

My son — a trained psychologist with the fullest and most sympathetic knowledge of my whole case — shall be the primary judge of what I have to tell.

First let me outline the externals of the matter, as those at the camp know them. On the night of July 17-18, after a windy day, I retired early but could not sleep. Rising shortly before eleven, and afflicted as usual with that strange feeling regarding the northeastward terrain, I set out on one of my typical nocturnal walks; seeing and greeting only one person — an Australian miner named Tupper — as I left our precincts.

The moon, slightly past full, shone from a clear sky, and drenched the ancient sands with a white, leprous radiance which seemed to me somehow infinitely evil. There was no longer any wind, nor did any return for nearly five hours, as amply attested by Tupper and others who saw me walking rapidly across the pallid, secret-guarding hillocks toward the northeast.

About 3:30 a.m. a violent wind blew up, waking everyone in camp and felling three of the tents. The sky was unclouded, and the desert still blazed with that leprous moonlight. As the party saw to the tents my absence was noted, but in view of my previous walks this circumstance gave no one alarm. And yet, as many as three men — all Australians — seemed to feel something sinister in the air.

Mackenzie explained to Professor Freeborn that this was a fear picked up from blackfellow folklore — the natives having woven a curious fabric of malignant myth about the high winds which at long intervals sweep across the sands under a clear sky. Such winds, it is whispered, blow out of the great stone huts under the ground, where terrible things have happened — and are never felt except near places where the big marked stones are scattered. Close to four the gale subsided as suddenly as it had begun, leaving the sand hills in new and unfamiliar shapes.

It was just past five, with the bloated, fungoid moon sinking in the west, when I staggered into camp — hatless, tattered, features scratched and ensanguined, and without my electric torch. Most of the men had returned to bed, but Professor Dyer was smoking a pipe in front of his tent. Seeing my winded and almost frenzied state, he called Dr. Boyle, and the two of them got me on my cot and made me comfortable. My son, roused by the stir, soon joined them, and they all tried to force me to lie still and attempt sleep.

But there was no sleep for me. My psychological state was very extraordinary — different from anything I had previously suffered. After a time I insisted upon talking — nervously and elaborately explaining my condition. I told them I had become fatigued, and had lain down in the sand for a nap. There had, I said, been dreams even more frightful than usual — and when I was awaked by the sudden high wind my overwrought nerves had snapped. I had fled in panic, frequently falling over half-buried stones and thus gaining my tattered and bedraggled aspect. I must have slept long — hence the hours of my absence.

Of anything strange either seen or experienced I hinted absolutely nothing — exercising the greatest self-control in that respect. But I spoke of a change of mind regarding the whole work of the expedition, and urged a halt in all digging toward the northeast. My reasoning was patently weak — for I mentioned a dearth of blocks, a wish not to offend the superstitious miners, a possible shortage of funds from the college, and other things either untrue or irrelevant. Naturally, no one paid the least attention to my new wishes — not even my son, whose concern for my health was obvious.

The next day I was up and around the camp, but took no part in the excavations. Seeing that I could not stop the work, I decided to return home as soon as possible for the sake of my nerves, and made my son promise to fly me in the plane to Perth — a thousand miles to the southwest — as soon as he had surveyed the region I wished let alone.

If, I reflected, the thing I had seen was still visible, I might decide to attempt a specific warning even at the cost of ridicule. It was just conceivable that the miners who knew the local folklore might back me up. Humouring me, my son made the survey that very afternoon, flying over all the terrain my walk could possibly have covered. Yet nothing of what I had found remained in sight.

It was the case of the anomalous basalt block all over again — the shifting sand had wiped out every trace. For an instant I half regretted having lost a certain awesome object in my stark fright — but now I know that the loss was merciful. I can still believe my whole experience an illusion — especially if, as I devoutly hope, that hellish abyss is never found.

Wingate took me to Perth on July 20th, though declining to abandon the expedition and return home. He stayed with me until the 25th, when the steamer for Liverpool sailed. Now, in the cabin of the Empress, I am pondering long and frantically upon the entire matter, and have decided that my son at least must be informed. It shall rest with him whether to diffuse the matter more widely.

In order to meet any eventuality I have prepared this summary of my background — as already known in a scattered way to others — and will now tell as briefly as possible what seemed to happen during my absence from the camp that hideous night.

Nerves on edge, and whipped into a kind of perverse eagerness by that inexplicable, dread-mingled, mnemonic urge toward the northeast, I plodded on beneath the evil, burning moon. Here and there I saw, half shrouded by sand, those primal Cyclopean blocks left from nameless and forgotten aeons.

The incalculable age and brooding horror of this monstrous waste began to oppress me as never before, and I could not keep from thinking of my maddening dreams, of the frightful legends which lay behind them, and of the present fears of natives and miners concerning the desert and its carven stones.

And yet I plodded on as if to some eldritch rendezvous — more and more assailed by bewildering fancies, compulsions, and pseudo-memories. I thought of some of the possible contours of the lines of stones as seen by my son from the air, and wondered why they seemed at once so ominous and so familiar. Something was fumbling and rattling at the latch of my recollection, while another unknown force sought to keep the portal barred.

The night was windless, and the pallid sand curved upward and downward like frozen waves of the sea. I had no goal, but somehow ploughed along as if with fate-bound assurance. My dreams welled up into the waking world, so that each sand-embedded megalith seemed part of endless rooms and corridors of pre-human masonry, carved and hieroglyphed with symbols that I knew too well from years of custom as a captive mind of the Great Race.

At moments I fancied I saw those omniscient, conical horrors moving about at their accustomed tasks, and I feared to look down lest I find myself one with them in aspect. Yet all the while I saw the sand-covered blocks as well as the rooms and corridors; the evil, burning moon as well as the lamps of luminous crystal; the endless desert as well as the waving ferns beyond the windows. I was awake and dreaming at the same time.

I do not know how long or how far — or indeed, in just what direction — I had walked when I first spied the heap of blocks bared by the day's wind. It was the largest group in one place that I had seen so far, and so sharply did it impress me that the visions of fabulous aeons faded suddenly away.

Again there were only the desert and the evil moon and the shards of an unguessed past. I drew close and paused, and cast the added light of my electric torch over the tumbled pile. A hillock had blown away, leaving a low, irregularly round mass of megaliths and smaller fragments some forty feet across and from two to eight feet high.

From the very outset I realized that there was some utterly unprecedented quality about those stones. Not only was the mere number of them quite without parallel, but something in the sandworn traces of design arrested me as I scanned them under the mingled beams of the moon and my torch.

Not that any one differed essentially from the earlier specimens we had found. It was something subtler than that. The impression did not come when I looked at one block alone, but only when I ran my eye over several almost simultaneously.

Then, at last, the truth dawned upon me. The curvilinear patterns on many of those blocks were closely related — parts of one vast decorative conception. For the first time in this aeon-shaken waste I had come upon a mass of masonry in its old position — tumbled and fragmentary, it is true, but none the less existing in a very definite sense.

Mounting at a low place, I clambered laboriously over the heap; here and there clearing away the sand with my fingers, and constantly striving to interpret varieties of size, shape, and style, and relationships of design.

After a while I could vaguely guess at the nature of the bygone structure, and at the designs which had once stretched over the vast surfaces of the primal masonry. The perfect identity of the whole with some of my dream-glimpses appalled and unnerved me.

This was once a Cyclopean corridor thirty feet tall, paved with octagonal blocks and solidly vaulted overhead. There would have been rooms opening off on the right, and at the farther end one of those strange inclined planes would have wound down to still lower depths.

I started violently as these conceptions occurred to me, for there was more in them than the blocks themselves had supplied. How did I know that this level should have been far underground? How did I know that the plane leading upward should have been behind me? How did I know that the long subterrene passage to the Square of Pillars ought to lie on the left one level above me?

How did I know that the room of machines and the rightward-leading tunnel to the central archives ought to lie two levels below? How did I know that there would be one of those horrible, metal-banded trap-doors at the very bottom four levels down? Bewildered by this intrusion from the dream-world, I found myself shaking and bathed in a cold perspiration.

Then, as a last, intolerable touch, I felt that faint, insidious stream of cool air trickling upward from a depressed place near the center of the huge heap. Instantly, as once before, my visions faded, and I saw again only the evil moonlight, the brooding desert, and the spreading tumulus of palaeogean masonry. Something real and tangible, yet fraught with infinite suggestions of nighted mystery, now confronted me. For that stream of air could argue but one thing — a hidden gulf of great size beneath the disordered blocks on the surface.

My first thought was of the sinister blackfellow legends of vast underground huts among the megaliths where horrors happen and great winds are born. Then thoughts of my own dreams came back, and I felt dim pseudo-memories tugging at my mind. What manner of place lay below me? What primal, inconceivable source of age-old myth-cycles and haunting nightmares might I be on the brink of uncovering?

It was only for a moment that I hesitated, for more than curiosity and scientific zeal was driving me on and working against my growing fear.

I seemed to move almost automatically, as if in the clutch of some compelling fate. Pocketing my torch, and struggling with a strength that I had not thought I possessed, I wrenched aside first one titan fragment of stone and then another, till there welled up a strong draught whose dampness contrasted oddly with the desert's dry air. A black rift began to yawn, and at length — when I had pushed away every fragment small enough to budge — the leprous moonlight blazed on an aperture of ample width to admit me.

I drew out my torch and cast a brilliant beam into the opening. Below me was a chaos of tumbled masonry, sloping roughly down toward the north at an angle of about forty-five degrees, and evidently the result of some bygone collapse from above.

Between its surface and the ground level was a gulf of impenetrable blackness at whose upper edge were signs of gigantic, stress-heaved vaulting. At this point, it appeared, the desert's sands lay directly upon a floor of some titan structure of earth's youth — how preserved through aeons of geologic convulsion I could not then and cannot now even attempt to guess.

In retrospect, the barest idea of a sudden, lone descent into such a doubtful abyss — and at a time when one's whereabouts were unknown to any living soul — seems like the utter apex of insanity. Perhaps it was — yet that night I embarked without hesitancy upon such a descent.

Again there was manifest that lure and driving of fatality which had all along seemed to direct my course. With torch flashing intermittently to save the battery, I commenced a mad scramble down the sinister, Cyclopean incline below the opening — sometimes facing forward as I found good hand- and foot-holds, and at other times turning to face the heap of megaliths as I clung and fumbled more precariously.

In two directions beside me distant walls of carven, crumbling masonry loomed dimly under the direct beams of my torch. Ahead, however, was only unbroken darkness.

I kept no track of time during my downward scramble. So seething with baffling hints and images was my mind that all objective matters seemed withdrawn into incalculable distances. Physical sensation was dead, and even fear remained as a wraith-like, inactive gargoyle leering impotently at me.

Eventually, I reached a level floor strewn with fallen blocks, shapeless fragments of stone, and sand and detritus of every kind. On either side — perhaps thirty feet apart — rose massive walls culminating in huge groinings. That they were carved I could just discern, but the nature of the carvings was beyond my perception.

What held me the most was the vaulting overhead. The beam from my torch could not reach the roof, but the lower parts of the monstrous arches stood out distinctly. And so perfect was their identity with what I had seen in countless dreams of the elder world, that I trembled actively for the first time.

Behind and high above, a faint luminous blur told of the distant moonlit world outside. Some vague shred of caution warned me that I should not let it out of my sight, lest I have no guide for my return.

I now advanced toward the wall at my left, where the traces of carving were plainest. The littered floor was nearly as hard to traverse as the downward heap had been, but I managed to pick my difficult way.

At one place I heaved aside some blocks and brushed away the detritus to see what the pavement was like, and shuddered at the utter, fateful familiarity of the great octagonal stones whose buckled surface still held roughly together.

Reaching a convenient distance from the wall, I cast the searchlight slowly and carefully over its worn remnants of carving. Some bygone influx of water seemed to have acted on the sandstone surface, while there were curious incrustations which I could not explain.

In places the masonry was very loose and distorted, and I wondered how many aeons more this primal, hidden edifice could keep its remaining traces of form amidst earth's heavings.

But it was the carvings themselves that excited me most. Despite their time-crumbled state, they were relatively easy to trace at close range; and the complete, intimate familiarity of every detail almost stunned my imagination.

That the major attributes of this hoary masonry should be familiar, was not beyond normal credibility.

Powerfully impressing the weavers of certain myths, they had become embodied in a stream of cryptic lore which, somehow, coming to my notice during the amnesic period, had evoked vivid images in my subconscious mind.

But how could I explain the exact and minute fashion in which each line and spiral of these strange designs tallied with what I had dreamed for more than a score of years? What obscure, forgotten iconography could have reproduced each subtle shading and nuance which so persistently, exactly, and unvaryingly besieged my sleeping vision night after night?

For this was no chance or remote resemblance. Definitely and absolutely, the millennially ancient, aeon-hidden corridor in which I stood was the original of something I knew in sleep as intimately as I knew my own house in Crane Street, Arkham. True, my dreams shewed the place in its undecayed prime; but the identity was no less real on that account. I was wholly and horribly oriented.

The particular structure I was in was known to me. Known, too, was its place in that terrible elder city of dreams. That I could visit unerringly any point in that structure or in that city which had escaped the changes and devastations of uncounted ages, I realized with hideous and instinctive certainty. What in heaven's name could all this mean? How had I come to know what I knew? And what awful reality could lie behind those antique tales of the beings who had dwelt in this labyrinth of primordial stone?

Words can convey only fractionally the welter of dread and bewilderment which ate at my spirit. I knew this place. I knew what lay before me, and what had lain overhead before the myriad towering stories had fallen to dust and debris and the desert. No need now, I thought with a shudder, to keep that faint blur of moonlight in view.

I was torn betwixt a longing to flee and a feverish mixture of burning curiosity and driving fatality. What had happened to this monstrous megalopolis of old in the millions of years since the time of my dreams? Of the subterrene mazes which had underlain the city and linked all the titan towers, how much had still survived the writhings of earth's crust?

Had I come upon a whole buried world of unholy archaism? Could I still find the house of the writing master, and the tower where S'gg'ha, the captive mind from the star-headed vegetable carnivores of Antarctica, had chiselled certain pictures on the blank spaces of the walls?

Would the passage at the second level down, to the hall of the alien minds, be still unchoked and traversable? In that hall the captive mind of an incredible entity — a half-plastic denizen of the hollow interior of an unknown trans-Plutonian planet eighteen million years in the future — had kept a certain thing which it had modelled from clay.

I shut my eyes and put my hand to my head in a vain, pitiful effort to drive these insane dream-fragments from my consciousness. Then, for the first time, I felt acutely the coolness, motion, and dampness of the surrounding air. Shuddering, I realized that a vast chain of aeon-dead black gulfs must indeed be yawning somewhere beyond and below me.

I thought of the frightful chambers and corridors and inclines as I recalled them from my dreams. Would the way to the central archives still be open? Again that driving fatality tugged insistently at my brain as I recalled the awesome records that once lay cased in those rectangular vaults of rustless metal.

There, said the dreams and legends, had reposed the whole history, past and future, of the cosmic space-time continuum — written by captive minds from every orb and every age in the solar system. Madness, of course — but had I not now stumbled into a nighted world as mad as I?

I thought of the locked metal shelves, and of the curious knob twistings needed to open each one. My own came vividly into my consciousness. How often had I gone through that intricate routine of varied turns and pressures in the terrestrial vertebrate section on the lowest level! Every detail was fresh and familiar.

If there were such a vault as I had dreamed of, I could open it in a moment. It was then that madness took me utterly. An instant later, and I was leaping and stumbling over the rocky debris toward the well-remembered incline to the depths below.

VII.

From that point forward my impressions are scarcely to be relied on — indeed, I still possess a final, desperate hope that they all form parts of some daemonic dream or illusion born of delirium. A fever raged in my brain, and everything came to me through a kind of haze — sometimes only intermittently.

The rays of my torch shot feebly into the engulfing blackness, bringing phantasmal flashes of hideously familiar walls and carvings, all blighted with the decay of ages. In one place a tremendous mass of vaulting had fallen, so that I had to clamber over a mighty mound of stones reaching almost to the ragged, grotesquely stalactited roof.

It was all the ultimate apex of nightmare, made worse by the blasphemous tug of pseudo-memory. One thing only was unfamiliar, and that was my own size in relation to the monstrous masonry. I felt oppressed by a sense of unwonted smallness, as if the sight of these towering walls from a mere human body was something wholly new and abnormal. Again and again I looked nervously down at myself, vaguely disturbed by the human form I possessed.

Onward through the blackness of the abyss I leaped, plunged, and staggered — often falling and bruising myself, and once nearly shattering my torch. Every stone and corner of that daemonic gulf was known to me, and at many points I stopped to cast beams of light through choked and crumbling, yet familiar, archways.

Some rooms had totally collapsed; others were bare, or debris-filled. In a few I saw masses of metal — some fairly intact, some broken, and some crushed or battered — which I recognised as the colossal pedestals or tables of my dreams. What they could in truth have been, I dared not guess.

I found the downward incline and began its descent — though after a time halted by a gaping, ragged chasm whose narrowest point could not be much less than four feet across. Here the stonework had fallen through, revealing incalculable inky depths beneath.

I knew there were two more cellar levels in this titan

edifice, and trembled with fresh panic as I recalled the metal-clamped trap-door on the lowest one. There could be no guards now — for what had lurked beneath had long since done its hideous work and sunk into its long decline. By the time of the posthuman beetle race it would be quite dead. And yet, as I thought of the native legends, I trembled anew.

It cost me a terrible effort to vault that yawning chasm, since the littered floor prevented a running start — but madness drove me on. I chose a place close to the left-hand wall — where the rift was least wide and the landing-spot reasonably clear of dangerous debris — and after one frantic moment reached the other side in safety.

At last, gaining the lower level, I stumbled on past the archway of the room of machines, within which were fantastic ruins of metal, half buried beneath fallen vaulting. Everything was where I knew it would be, and I climbed confidently over the heaps which barred the entrance of a vast transverse corridor. This, I realised, would take me under the city to the central archives.

Endless ages seemed to unroll as I stumbled, leaped, and crawled along that debris-cluttered corridor. Now and then I could make out carvings on the ages-stained walls — some familiar, others seemingly added since the period of my dreams. Since this was a subterrene house-connecting highway, there were no archways save when the route led through the lower levels of various buildings.

At some of these intersections I turned aside long enough to look down well-remembered corridors and into well-remembered rooms. Twice only did I find any radical changes from what I had dreamed of — and in one of these cases I could trace the sealed-up outlines of the archway I remembered.

I shook violently, and felt a curious surge of retarding weakness, as I steered a hurried and reluctant course through the crypt of one of those great windowless, ruined towers whose alien, basalt masonry bespoke a whispered and horrible origin.

This primal vault was round and fully two hundred feet across, with nothing carved upon the dark-hued stonework. The floor was here free from anything save dust and sand, and I could see the apertures leading upward and downward. There were no stairs or inclines — indeed, my dreams had pictured those elder towers as wholly untouched by the fabulous Great Race. Those who had built them had not needed stairs or inclines.

In the dreams, the downward aperture had been tightly sealed and nervously guarded. Now it lay open-black and yawning, and giving forth a current of cool, damp air. Of what limitless caverns of eternal night might brood below, I would not permit myself to think.

Later, clawing my way along a badly heaped section of the corridor, I reached a place where the roof had wholly caved in. The debris rose like a mountain, and I climbed up over it, passing through a vast, empty space where my torchlight could reveal neither walls nor vaulting. This, I reflected, must be the cellar of the house of the metal-purveyors, fronting on the third square not far from the archives. What had happened to it I could not conjecture.

I found the corridor again beyond the mountain of detritus and stone, but after a short distance encountered a wholly choked place where the fallen vaulting almost touched the perilously sagging ceiling. How I managed to wrench and tear aside enough blocks to afford a passage, and how I dared disturb the tightly packed fragments when the least shift of equilibrium might have brought down all the tons of superincumbent masonry to crush me to nothingness, I do not know.

It was sheer madness that impelled and guided me — if, indeed, my whole underground adventure was not — as I hope — a hellish delusion or phase of dreaming. But I did make — or dream that I made — a passage that I could squirm through. As I wiggled over the mound of debris — my torch, switched continuously on, thrust deeply in my mouth — I felt myself torn by the fantastic stalactites of the jagged floor above me.

I was now close to the great underground archival structure which seemed to form my goal. Sliding and clambering down the farther side of the barrier, and picking my way along the remaining stretch of corridor with hand-held, intermittently flashing torch, I came at last to a low, circular crypt with arches — still in a marvelous state of preservation — opening off on every side.

The walls, or such parts of them as lay within reach of my torchlight, were densely hieroglyphed and chiselled with typical curvilinear symbols — some added since the period of my dreams.

This, I realised, was my fated destination, and I turned at once through a familiar archway on my left. That I could find a clear passage up and down the incline to all the surviving levels, I had, oddly, little doubt. This vast, earth-protected pile, housing the annals of all the solar system, had been built with supernal skill and strength to last as long as that system itself.

Blocks of stupendous size, poised with mathematical genius and bound with cements of incredible toughness, had combined to form a mass as firm as the planet's rocky core. Here, after ages more prodigious than I could sanely grasp, its buried bulk stood in all its essential contours, the vast, dust-drifted floors scarce sprinkled with the litter elsewhere so dominant.

The relatively easy walking from this point onward went curiously to my head. All the frantic eagerness hitherto frustrated by obstacles now took itself out in a kind of febrile speed, and I literally raced along the low-roofed, monstrously well-remembered aisles beyond the archway.

I was past being astonished by the familiarity of what I saw. On every hand the great hieroglyphed metal shelf-doors loomed monstrously; some yet in place, others sprung open, and still others bent and buckled under bygone geological stresses not quite strong enough to shatter the titan masonry.

Here and there a dust-covered heap beneath a gaping, empty shelf seemed to indicate where cases had been shaken

Astounding Stories, August 1946

"Never before had human feet pressed upon those immortal pavements!"

down by earth tremors. On occasional pillars were great symbols or letters proclaiming classes and subclasses of volumes.

Once I paused before an open vault where I saw some of the accustomed metal cases still in position amidst the omnipresent gritty dust. Reaching up, I dislodged one of the thinner specimens with some difficulty, and rested it on the floor for inspection. It was titled in the prevailing curvilinear hieroglyphs, though something in the arrangement of the characters seemed subtly unusual.

The odd mechanism of the hooked fastener was perfectly well known to me, and I snapped up the still rustless and workable lid and drew out the book within. The latter, as expected, was some twenty by fifteen inches in area, and two inches thick; the thin metal covers opening at the top.

Its tough cellulose pages seemed unaffected by the myriad cycles of time they had lived through, and I studied the queerly pigmented, brush-drawn letters of the text-symbols unlike either the usual curved hieroglyphs or any alphabet known to human scholarship—with a haunting, half-aroused memory.

It came to me that this was the language used by a captive mind I had known slightly in my dreams—a mind from a large asteroid on which had survived much of the archaic life and lore of the primal planet whereof it formed a fragment. At the same time I recalled that this level of the archives was devoted to volumes dealing with the non-terrestrial planets.

As I ceased poring over this incredible document I saw that the light of my torch was beginning to fail, hence quickly inserted the extra battery I always had with me. Then, armed with the stronger radiance, I resumed my feverish racing through unending tangles of aisles and corridors—recognising now and then some familiar shelf, and vaguely annoyed by the acoustic conditions which made my footfalls echo incongruously in these catacombs.

The very prints of my shoes behind me in the millennially untrodden dust made me shudder. Never before, if my mad dreams held anything of truth, had human feet pressed upon those immemorial pavements.

Of the particular goal of my insane racing, my conscious mind held no hint. There was, however, some force of evil potency pulling at my dazed will and buried recollection, so that I vaguely felt I was not running at random.

I came to a downward incline and followed it to profounder depths. Floors flashed by me as I raced, but I did not pause to explore them. In my whirling brain there had begun to beat a certain rhythm which set my right hand twitching in unison. I wanted to unlock something, and felt that I knew all the intricate twists and pressures needed to do it. It would be like a modern safe with a combination lock.

Dream or not, I had once known and still knew. How any dream—or scrap of unconsciously absorbed legend—could have taught me a detail so minute, so intricate, and so complex, I did not attempt to explain to myself. I was beyond all coherent thought. For was not this whole experience—this shocking familiarity with a set of unknown ruins, and this monstrously exact identity of everything before me with what only dreams and scraps of myth could have suggested—a horror beyond all reason?

Probably it was my basic conviction then—as it is now during my saner moments—that I was not awake at all, and that the entire buried city was a fragment of febrile hallucination.

Eventually, I reached the lowest level and struck off to the right of the incline. For some shadowy reason I tried to soften my steps, even though I lost speed thereby. There was a space I was afraid to cross on this last, deeply buried floor.

As I drew near it I recalled what thing in that space I feared. It was merely one of the metal-barred and closely guarded trap-doors. There would be no guards now, and on that account I trembled and tiptoed as I had done in passing through that black basalt vault where a similar trap-door had yawned.

I felt a current of cool, damp air as I had felt there, and wished that my course led in another direction. Why I had to take the particular course I was taking, I did not know.

When I came to the space I saw that the trap-door yawned widely open. Ahead, the shelves began again, and I glimpsed on the floor before one of them a heap very thinly covered with dust, where a number of cases had recently fallen. At the same moment a fresh wave of panic clutched me, though for some time I could not discover why.

Heaps of fallen cases were not uncommon, for all through the aeons this lightless labyrinth had been racked by the heavings of earth and had echoed at intervals of the deafening clatter of toppling objects. It was only when I was nearly across the space that I realized why I shook so violently.

Not the heap, but something about the dust of the level floor was troubling me. In the light of my torch it seemed as if that dust were not as even as it ought to be—there were places where it looked thinner, as if it had been disturbed not many months before. I could not be sure, for even the apparently thinner places were dusty enough; yet a certain suspicion of regularity in the fancied unevenness was highly disquieting.

When I brought the torchlight close to one of the queer places I did not like what I saw—for the illusion of regularity became very great. It was as if there were regular lines of composite impressions—impressions that went in threes, each slightly over a foot square, and consisting of five nearly circular three-inch prints, one in advance of the other four.

These possible lines of foot-square impressions appeared to lead in two directions, as if something had gone somewhere and returned. They were, of course, very faint, and may have been illusions or accidents; but there was an element of dim, fumbling terror about the way I thought they ran. For at one end of them was the heap of cases which must have clattered down not long before, while at the other end was the ominous trap-door with the cool, damp wind, yawning unguarded down to abysses past imagination.

VIII.

That my strange sense of compulsion was deep and overwhelming is shewn by its conquest of my fear. No rational motive could have drawn me on after that hideous suspicion of prints and the creeping dream-memories it excited. Yet my right hand, even as it shook with fright, still twitched rhythmically in its eagerness to turn a lock it hoped to find. Before I knew it I was past the heap of lately fallen cases and running on tiptoe through aisles of utterly unbroken dust toward a point which I seemed to know morbidly, horribly well.

My mind was asking itself questions whose origin and relevancy I was only beginning to guess. Would the shelf be reachable by a human body? Could my human hand master all the aeon-remembered motions of the lock? Would the lock be undamaged and workable? And what would I do—what dare I do with what—as I now commenced to realise—I both hoped and feared to find? Would it prove the awesome, brain-shattering truth of something past normal conception, or shew only that I was dreaming?

The next I knew I had ceased my tiptoed racing and was standing still, staring at a row of maddeningly familiar hieroglyphed shelves. They were in a state of almost perfect preservation, and only three of the doors in this vicinity had sprung open.

My feelings toward these shelves cannot be described — so utter and insistent was the sense of old acquaintance. I was looking high up at a row near the top and wholly out of my reach, and wondering how I could climb to best advantage. An open door four rows from the bottom would help, and the locks of the closed doors formed possible holds for hands and feet. I would grip the torch between my teeth, as I had in other places where both hands were needed. Above all I must make no noise.

How to get down what I wished to remove would be difficult, but I could probably hook its movable fastener in my coat collar and carry it like a knapsack. Again I wondered whether the lock would be undamaged. That I could repeat each familiar motion I had not the least doubt. But I hoped the thing would not scrape or creak — and that my hand could work it properly.

Even as I thought these things I had taken the torch in my mouth and begun to climb. The projecting locks were poor supports; but, as I had expected, the opened shelf helped greatly. I used both the swinging door and the edge of the aperture itself in my ascent, and managed to avoid any loud creaking.

Balanced on the upper edge of the door, and leaning far to my right, I could just reach the lock I sought. My fingers, half numb from climbing, were very clumsy at first; but I soon saw that they were anatomically adequate. And the memory-rhythm was strong in them.

Out of unknown gulfs of time the intricate, secret motions had somehow reached my brain correctly in every detail — for after less than five minutes of trying there came a click whose familiarity was all the more startling because I had not consciously anticipated it. In another instant the metal door was slowly swinging open with only the faintest grating sound.

Dazedly I looked over the row of greyish case ends thus exposed, and felt a tremendous surge of some wholly inexplicable emotion. Just within reach of my right hand was a case whose curving hieroglyphs made me shake with a pang infinitely more complex than one of mere fright. Still shaking, I managed to dislodge it amidst a shower of gritty flakes, and ease it over toward myself without any violent noise.

Like the other case I had handled, it was slightly more than twenty by fifteen inches in size, with curved mathematical designs in low relief. In thickness it just exceeded three inches.

Crudely wedging it between myself and the surface I was climbing, I fumbled with the fastener and finally got the hook free. Lifting the cover, I shifted the heavy object to my back, and let the hook catch hold of my collar. Hands now free, I awkwardly clambered down to the dusty floor, and prepared to inspect my prize.

Kneeling in the gritty dust, I swung the case around and rested it in front of me. My hands shook, and I dreaded to draw out the book within almost as much as I longed — and felt compelled — to do so. It had very gradually become clear to me what I ought to find, and this realisation nearly paralysed my faculties.

If the thing were there — and if I were not dreaming — the implications would be quite beyond the power of the human spirit to bear. What tormented me most was my momentary inability to feel that my surroundings were a dream. The sense of reality was hideous — and again becomes so as I recall the scene.

At length I tremblingly pulled the book from its container and stared fascinatedly at the well-known hieroglyphs on the cover. It seemed to be in prime condition, and the curvilinear letters of the title held me in almost as hypnotised a state as if I could read them. Indeed, I cannot swear that I did not actually read them in some transient and terrible access of abnormal memory.

I do not know how long it was before I dared to lift that thin metal cover. I temporized and made excuses to myself. I took the torch from my mouth and shut it off to save the battery. Then, in the dark, I collected my courage finally lifting the cover without turning on the light. Last of all, I did indeed flash the torch upon the exposed page — steeling myself in advance to suppress any sound no matter what I should find.

I looked for an instant, then collapsed. Clenching my teeth, however, I kept silent. I sank wholly to the floor and put a hand to my forehead amidst the engulfing blackness. What I dreaded and expected was there. Either I was dreaming, or time and space had become a mockery.

I must be dreaming — but I would test the horror by carrying this thing back and shewing it to my son if it were indeed a reality. My head swam frightfully, even though there were no visible objects in the unbroken gloom to swirl about me. Ideas and images of the starkest terror — excited by vistas which my glimpse had opened up — began to throng in upon me and cloud my senses.

I thought of those possible prints in the dust, and trembled at the sound of my own breathing as I did so. Once again I flashed on the light and looked at the page as a serpent's victim may look at his destroyer's eyes and fangs.

Then, with clumsy fingers, in the dark, I closed the book, put it in its container, and snapped the lid and the curious, hooked fastener. This was what I must carry back to the outer world if it truly existed — if the whole abyss truly existed — if I, and the world itself, truly existed.

Just when I tottered to my feet and commenced my return I cannot be certain. It comes to me oddly — as a measure of my sense of separation from the normal world — that I did not even once look at my watch during those hideous hours underground.

Torch in hand, and with the ominous case under one arm, I eventually found myself tiptoeing in a kind of silent panic past the draught-giving abyss and those lurking suggestions of prints. I lessened my precautions as I climbed up the endless inclines, but could not shake off a shadow of apprehension which I had not felt on the downward journey.

I dreaded having to repass through the black basalt crypt that was older than the city itself, where cold draughts welled up from unguarded depths. I thought of that which the Great Race had feared, and of what might still be lurking — be it ever so weak and dying — down there. I thought of those five-circle prints and of what my dreams had told me of such prints — and of strange winds and whistling noises associated with them. And I thought of the tales of the modern blackfellows, wherein the horror of great winds and nameless subterrene ruins was dwelt upon.

I knew from a carven wall symbol the right floor to enter, and came at last after passing that other book I had examined — to the great circular space with the branching archways. On my right, and at once recognisable, was the arch through which I had arrived. This I now entered, conscious that the rest of my course would be harder because of the tumbled state of the masonry outside the archive building. My new metal-cased burden weighed upon me, and I found it harder and harder to be quiet as I stumbled among debris and fragments of every sort.

Then I came to the ceiling-high mound of debris through which I had wrenched a scanty passage. My dread at wriggling through again was infinite, for my first passage had made some noise, and I now — after seeing those possible prints — dreaded sound above all things. The case, too, doubled the problem of traversing the narrow crevice.

But I clambered up the barrier as best I could, and pushed the case through the aperture ahead of me. Then, torch in mouth, I scrambled through myself — my back torn as before by stalactites.

As I tried to grasp the case again, it fell some distance ahead of me down the slope of the debris, making a disturbing clatter and arousing echoes which sent me into a cold perspiration. I lunged for it at once, and regained it without further noise — but a moment afterward the slipping of blocks under my feet raised a sudden and unprecedented din.

The din was my undoing. For, falsely or not, I thought I heard it answered in a terrible way from spaces far behind me. I thought I heard a shrill, whistling sound, like nothing else on earth, and beyond any adequate verbal description. If so, what followed has a grim irony — since, save for the panic of this thing, the second thing might never have happened.

As it was, my frenzy was absolute and unrelieved. Taking my torch in my hand and clutching feebly at the case, I leaped and bounded wildly ahead with no idea in my brain beyond a mad desire to race out of these nightmare ruins to the waking world of desert and moonlight which lay so far above.

I hardly knew it when I reached the mountain of debris which towered into the vast blackness beyond the caved-in roof, and bruised and cut myself repeatedly in scrambling up its steep slope of jagged blocks and fragments.

Then came the great disaster. Just as I blindly crossed the summit, unprepared for the sudden dip ahead, my feet slipped utterly and I found myself involved in a mangling avalanche of sliding masonry whose cannon-loud uproar split the black cavern air in a deafening series of earth-shaking reverberations.

I have no recollection of emerging from this chaos, but a momentary fragment of consciousness shows me as plunging and tripping and scrambling along the corridor amidst the clangour — case and torch still with me.

Then, just as I approached that primal basalt crypt I had so dreaded, utter madness came. For as the echoes of the avalanche died down, there became audible a repetition of that frightful alien whistling I thought I had heard before. This time there was no doubt about it — and what was worse, it came from a point not behind but ahead of me.

Probably I shrieked aloud then. I have a dim picture of myself as flying through the hellish basalt vault of the elder things, and hearing that damnable alien sound piping up from the open, unguarded door of limitless nether blacknesses. There was a wind, too — not merely a cool, damp draught, but a violent, purposeful blast belching savagely and frigidly from that abominable gulf whence the obscene whistling came.

There are memories of leaping and lurching over obstacles of every sort, with that torrent of wind and shrieking sound growing moment by moment, and seeming to curl and twist purposefully around me as it struck out wickedly from the spaces behind and beneath.

Though in my rear, that wind had the odd effect of hindering instead of aiding my progress; as if it acted like a noose or lasso thrown around me. Heedless of the noise I made, I clattered over a great barrier of blocks and was again in the structure that led to the surface.

I recall glimpsing the archway to the room of machines and almost crying out as I saw the incline leading down to where one of those blasphemous trap-doors must be yawning two levels below. But instead of crying out I muttered over and over to myself that this was all a dream from which I must soon awake. Perhaps I was in camp — perhaps I was at home in Arkham. As these hopes bolstered up my sanity I began to mount the incline to the higher level.

I knew, of course, that I had the four-foot cleft to re-cross, yet was too racked by other fears to realise the full horror until I came almost upon it. On my descent, the leap across had been easy — but could I clear the gap as readily when going uphill, and hampered by fright, exhaustion, the weight of the metal case, and the anomalous backward tug of that daemon wind? I thought of these things at the last moment, and thought also of the nameless entities which might be lurking in the black abysses below the chasm.

My wavering torch was growing feeble, but I could tell by

some obscure memory when I neared the cleft. The chill blasts of wind and the nauseous whistling shrieks behind me were for the moment like a merciful opiate, dulling my imagination to the horror of the yawning gulf ahead. And then I became aware of the added blasts and whistling in front of me — tides of abomination surging up through the cleft itself from depths unimagined and unimaginable.

Now, indeed, the essence of pure nightmare was upon me. Sanity departed — and, ignoring everything except the animal impulse of flight, I merely struggled and plunged upward over the incline's debris as if no gulf had existed. Then I saw the chasm's edge, leaped frenziedly with every ounce of strength I possessed, and was instantly engulfed in a pandaemoniae vortex of loathsome sound and utter, materially tangible blackness.

This is the end of my experience, so far as I can recall. Any further impressions belong wholly to the domain of phantasmagoria delirium. Dream, madness, and memory merged wildly together in a series of fantastic, fragmentary delusions which can have no relation to anything real.

There was a hideous fall through incalculable leagues of viscous, sentient darkness, and a babel of noises utterly alien to all that we know of the earth and its organic life. Dormant, rudimentary senses seemed to start into vitality within me, telling of pits and voids peopled by floating horrors and leading to sunless crags and oceans and teeming cities of windowless, basalt towers upon which no light ever shone.

Secrets of the primal planet and its immemorial aeons flashed through my brain without the aid of sight or sound, and there were known to me things which not even the wildest of my former dreams had ever suggested. And all the while cold fingers of damp vapor clutched and picked at me, and that eldritch, damnable whistling shrieked fiendishly above all the alternations of babel and silence in the whirlpools of darkness around.

Afterward there were visions of the Cyclopean city of my dreams — not in ruins, but just as I had dreamed of it. I was in my conical, non-human body again, and mingled with crowds of the Great Race and the captive minds who carried books up and down the lofty corridors and vast inclines.

Then, superimposed upon these pictures, were frightful, momentary flashes of a non-vistial consciousness involving desperate struggles, a writhing free from clutching tentacles of whistling wind, an insane, bat-like flight through half-solid air, a feverish burrowing through the cyclone-whipped dark, and a wild stumbling and scrambling over fallen masonry.

Once there was a curious, intrusive flash of half sight — a faint, diffuse suspicion of bluish radiance far overhead. Then there came a dream of wind — pursued climbing and crawling — of wriggling into a blaze of sardonic moonlight through a jumble of debris which slid and collapsed after me amidst a morbid hurricane. It was the evil, monotonous beating of that maddening moonlight which at last told me of the return of what I had once known as the objective, waking world.

I was clawing prone through the sands of the Australian desert, and around me shrieked such a tumult of wind as I had never before known on our planet's surface. My clothing was in rags, and my whole body was a mass of bruises and scratches.

Full consciousness returned very slowly, and at no time could I tell just where delirious dream left off and true memory began. There had seemed to be a mound of titan blocks, an abyss beneath it, a monstrous revelation from the past, and a nightmare horror at the end — but how much of this was real?

My flashlight was gone, and likewise any metal case I may have discovered. Had there been such a case — or any abyss — or any mound? Raising my head, I looked behind me, and saw only the sterile, undulant sands of the desert.

The daemon wind died down, and the bloated, fungoid moon sank reddeningly in the west. I lurched to my feet and began to stagger southwestward toward the camp. What in truth had happened to me? Had I merely collapsed in the desert and dragged a dream-racked body over miles of sand and buried blocks? If not, how could I bear to live any longer?

For, in this new doubt, all my faith in the myth-born unreality of my visions dissolved once more into the hellish older doubting. If that abyss was real, then the Great Race was real — and its blasphemous reachings and seizures in the cosmos-wide vortex of time were no myths or nightmares, but a terrible, soul-shattering actuality.

Had I, in full, hideous fact, been drawn back to a pre-human world of a hundred and fifty million years ago in those dark, baffling days of the amnesia? Had my present body been the vehicle of a frightful alien consciousness from palaeogean gulfs of time?

Had I, as the captive mind of those shambling horrors, indeed known that accursed city of stone in its primordial heyday, and wriggled down those familiar corridors in the loathsome shape of my captor? Were those tormenting dreams of more than twenty years the offspring of stark, monstrous memories?

Had I once veritably talked with minds from reachless corners of time and space, learned the universe's secrets, past and to come, and written the annals of my own world for the metal cases of those titan archives? And were those others — those shocking elder things of the mad winds and daemon pipings — in truth a lingering, lurking menace, waiting and slowly weakening in black abysses while varied shapes of life drag out their multimillennial courses on the planet's age-racked surface?

I do not know. If that abyss and what I held were real, there is no hope. Then, all too truly, there lies upon this world of man a mocking and incredible shadow out of time. But, mercifully, there is no proof that these things are other than fresh phases of my myth-born dreams. I did not bring back the metal case that would have been a proof, and so far those subterrene corridors have not been found.

If the laws of the universe are kind, they will never be found. But I must tell my son what I saw or thought I saw, and let him use his judgment as a psychologist in gauging the reality of my experience, and communicating this account to others.

I have said that the awful truth behind my tortured years of dreaming hinges absolutely upon the actuality of what I thought I saw in those Cyclopean, buried ruins. It has been hard for me, literally, to set down that crucial revelation, though no reader can have failed to guess it. Of course, it lay in that book within the metal case — the case which I pried out of its lair amidst the dust of a million centuries.

No eye had seen, no hand had touched that book since the advent of man to this planet. And yet, when I flashed my torch upon it in that frightful abyss, I saw that the queerly pigmented letters on the brittle, aeon-browned cellulose pages were not indeed any nameless hieroglyphs of earth's youth. They were, instead, the letters of our familiar alphabet, spelling out the words of the English language in my own handwriting.

Astounding Stories, June 1936

Collapsing Cosmoses.

BY ROBERT H. BARLOW
AND H.P. LOVECRAFT

600-WORD FRAGMENT; 1935.

This tiny little snippet of story is the result of what you might call an extreme round-robin experiment conducted by Barlow and Lovecraft. Each would write a paragraph, then send it off for the other to continue. It was Lovecraft who started the thing off, introducing us to the characters Dam Bor and Hack Ni engaged in a great big Edmond Hamilton-style space opera. (The character names were meant to satirize Captain Jan Tor and Engineer Hal Kur of Interplanetary Patrol Cruiser 79388, the main characters in a popular series of far-future interplanetary science-fiction stories by Hamilton, which regularly appeared in Weird Tales.*)*

The snippet goes on for some 600 words, never really getting anywhere but being rather funny doing it ("At the sound, which was something like that of a rusty sewing-machine, only more horrible, Hak Ni too raised his snout in defiance . . ."). At a certain point, apparently one or both authors simply got bored with it and moved on to other things.

It was published, shortly after Lovecraft's death, in the winter 1938 issue of Barlow's journal, Leaves.

Dam Bor glued each of his six eyes to the lenses of the cosmoscope. His nasal tentacles were orange with fear, and his antennae buzzed hoarsely as he dictated his report to the operator behind him.

"It has come!" he cried. "That blur in the ether can be nothing less than a fleet from outside the space-time continuum we know. Nothing like this has ever appeared before. It must be an enemy. Give the alarm to the Inter-Cosmic Chamber of Commerce. There's no time to lose—at this rate they'll be upon us in less than six centuries. Hak Ni must have a chance to get the fleet in action at once."

I glanced up from the *Windy City Grab-Bag*, which had beguiled my inactive peace-time days in the Super-Galactic Patrol. The handsome young vegetable, with whom I had shared my bowl of caterpillar custard since earliest infancy, and with whom I had been thrown out of every joint in the intra-dimensional city of Kastor-Ya, had really a worried look upon his lavender face. After he had given the alarm we jumped on our ether-bikes and hastened across to the outer planet on which the Chamber held its sessions.

Within the Great Council Chamber, which measured twenty-eight square feet (with quite a high ceiling), were gathered delegates from all the thirty-seven galaxies of our immediate universe. Oll Stof, President of the Chamber and representative of the Milliner's Soviet, raised his eyeless snout with dignity and prepared to address the assembled multitude. He was a highly developed protozoan organism from Nov-Kas, and spoke by emitting alternate waves of heat and cold.

"Gentlemen," he radiated, "a terrible peril has come upon us which I feel I must bring to your attention."

Everybody applauded riotously, as a wave of excitement rippled through the variegated audience; those who were handless slithering their tentacles together. He continued: "Hak Ni, crawl upon the dais!"

There was a thunderous silence, during which a faint prompting was heard from the dizzy summit of the platform. Hak Ni, the yellow-furred and valorous commander of our ranks through numerous instalments, ascended to the towering peak inches above the floor.

"My friends —" he began, with an eloquent scraping of his posterior limbs, "these treasured walls and pillars shall not mourn on my account . . ." At this point, one of his numerous relatives cheered. "Well do I remember when . . ."

Oll Stof interrupted him. "You have anticipated my thoughts and orders. Go forth and win for dear old Inter-Cosmic."

Two paragraphs later found us soaring out past innumerable stars toward where a faint blur half a million light-years long marked the presence of the hated enemy, whom we had not seen. What monsters of malformed grotesqueness seethed out there among the moons of infinity, we really didn't know, but there was a malign menace in the glow that steadily increased until it spanned the entire heavens. Very soon we made out separate objects in the blur. Before all my horror-stricken vision-areas there spread an endless array of scissors-shaped space-ships of totally unfamiliar form.

Then from the direction of the enemy there came a terrifying sound, which I soon recognised as a hail and a challenge. An answering thrill crept through me as I met with uplifted antennae this threat of battle with a monstrous intrusion upon our fair system from unknown outside abysses.

At the sound, which was something like that of a rusty sewing-machine, only more horrible, Hak Ni too raised his snout in defiance, radiating a masterful order to the captains of the fleet. Instantly the huge space-ships swung into battle formation, with only a hundred or two of them many light-years out of line.

The Challenge from Beyond.

BY ROBERT E. HOWARD, FRANK BELKNAP LONG, H.P. LOVECRAFT, A. MERRITT, AND C.L. MOORE

6,000-WORD SHORT STORY; 1935.

In all of H.P. Lovecraft's collaborations and revisions, only once did he get involved in an intended-for-publication project that involved more than one other writer. That was in 1935, when he was dragooned into participating in a round-robin story bearing the vague and turgid title of "The Challenge from Beyond."

"The Challenge from Beyond" was instigated by Julius Schwartz, the editor of Fantasy Magazine. *His idea was to put together two "teams" of writers to create round-robin stories. There would be a science-fiction story, and a weird-fiction one.*

For each story, he persuaded an impressive list of professional writers to participate. On the sci-fi side, he got E.E. "Doc" Smith, Donald Wandrei, Stanley G. Weinbaum, Harl Vincent, and Stanley Leinster. On the weird-fiction side, he signed up C.L. Moore, A. Merritt, Robert E. Howard, Frank Belknap Long, and, of course, H.P. Lovecraft.

ABOUT C.L. MOORE (1911-1987).

Catherine Lucille Moore is, today, known as a seminal figure in the world of science fiction and fantasy. In 1935, though, she was still new on the scene; her professional career had just started to take off. Her sci-fi series starring Northwest Smith — whose similarities to Han Solo of the Star Wars franchise have been frequently remarked upon and are almost certainly not coincidental — had debuted in late 1933 in Weird Tales, *and her sword-and-sorcery story "The Black God's Kiss" had just clinched the front cover of* Weird Tales *in November 1934, with an illustration by Margaret Brundage. She was just hitting her stride, and plainly destined for greatness, when she paused to participate in this little fanzine project.*

ABOUT A. MERRITT (1884-1943).

Of all the writers tapped for this project, Abraham Grace Merritt was the most prominent. In 1935, he was the assistant editor at Hearst's American Weekly, *a general lifestyle magazine inserted as a Sunday supplement in all the Hearst newspapers nationwide; the following year he would be promoted to editor. In addition, he had more pulp-magazine credits than any other writer on the project (with the possible exception of Howard), many of them in high-end pulp titles like* The Argosy *and* All-Story Weekly *as well as* Weird Tales.

Merritt was best known for adventure fiction, with lost civilizations and monsters and scheming Russian villains; and for his lush, evocative storytelling style.

ABOUT ROBERT E. HOWARD (1906-1936).

Robert Ervin Howard was a Texan and a prolific pulp-story writer with a remarkable talent for evoking action in his writing. He, too, had a vast catalog of writing credits to his name. He is best known for his "Conan the Cimmerian" character, and, to a lesser degree, for his humorous Sailor Steve Costigan boxing stories and his El Borak tales about a Texas gunfighter in Afghanistan.

Of all the writers tapped for this project, Robert E. Howard was the only full-time professional fiction writer. Every other participant had a "day job" — Moore at an insurance company, Merritt as a magazine editor, Lovecraft as a revisionist, and Long as a freelance nonfiction writer — but Howard was paying all his bills with his fiction output, and by 1935 doing fairly well at it.

ABOUT FRANK BELKNAP LONG (1901-1994).

In the years to follow, the volume of Frank Belknap Long's literary output would surpass that of all the other writers in this group; but that was in the future. In 1934, he was the junior member of the crew, although his publishing record was nothing to sneer at; he'd been a full-time writer since the early 1920s, with many credits in Weird Tales *and other low-end pulps and even a published book of poetry to his name.*

Like Howard, Long was a professional writer, paying his bills with his pen; but unlike Howard, he didn't restrict himself to fiction writing. Long was an active and prolific freelance nonfiction writer and journalist.

THE PROJECT.

In a classic round-robin story, several writers take turns contributing to the story, letting it go where it will. Each writer contributes his or her paragraph, or chapter, or whatever; and then hands it off to the next writer. This can lead to hard feelings when different writers have different expectations for the story; and that is exactly what actually happened in this case.

Editor Schwartz tapped C.L. Moore to start things off, and she wrote and submitted her part professionally and without drama, then handed it off to Frank Belknap Long for Part 2. Long, however, took the story in a direction that ruined A. Merritt's plans for Part 3, and Merritt, who probably didn't really want to be involved in this fan project anyway, balked. He insisted that if he was going to be involved, Long's contribution would have to be thrown out, and he would go second.

Merritt was the biggest name in the room. So, unreasonable though this request was, Schwartz felt he had to grant it. At this, Long stormed off angrily, and Merritt took the floor and wrote his installment.

Then it was Lovecraft's turn. Lovecraft developed most of the actual story; his contribution is much longer than anyone else's. He borrowed the basic concept from his novella The Shadow out of Time.

Then it was Robert E. Howard's turn, and, true to his reputation, Howard turned the story from one of breathless cosmic horror into a saga of savage and bloody conquest.

For the last installment, Frank Belknap Long, having cooled off a little, agreed to finish the story off, and did so with reasonable smoothness.

As a story, "The Challenge from Beyond" is pretty light stuff. But the contrast among the writers' differing styles, and especially between Lovecraft's and Howard's, makes it well worth the few minutes it takes to read it.

I.
(BY C.L. MOORE)

George Campbell opened sleep-fogged eyes upon darkness and lay gazing out of the tent flap upon the pale August night for some minutes before he roused enough even to wonder what had wakened him. There was in the keen, clear air of these Canadian woods a soporific as potent as any drug. Campbell lay quiet for a moment, sinking slowly back into the delicious borderlands of sleep, conscious of an exquisite weariness, an unaccustomed sense of muscles well used, and relaxed now into perfect ease. These were vacation's most delightful moments, after all — rest, after toil, in the clear, sweet forest night.

Luxuriously, as his mind sank backward into oblivion, he assured himself once more that three long months of freedom lay before him — freedom from cities and monotony, freedom from pedagogy and the University and students with no rudiments of interest in the geology he earned his daily bread by dinning into their obdurate ears. Freedom from —

Abruptly the delightful somnolence crashed about him. Somewhere outside the sound of tin shrieking across tin slashed into his peace. George Campbell sat up jerkily and reached for his flashlight. Then he laughed and put it down again, straining his eyes through the midnight gloom outside where among the tumbling cans of his supplies a dark anonymous little night beast was prowling. He stretched out a long arm and groped about among the rocks at the tent door for a missile. His fingers closed on a large stone, and he drew back his hand to throw.

But he never threw it. It was such a queer thing he had come upon in the dark. Square, crystal smooth, obviously artificial, with dull rounded corners. The strangeness of its rock surfaces to his fingers was so remarkable that he reached again for his flashlight and turned its rays upon the thing he held.

All sleepiness left him as he saw what it was he had picked up in his idle groping. It was clear as rock crystal, this queer, smooth cube. Quartz, unquestionably, but not in its usual hexagonal crystallized form. Somehow — he could not guess the method — it had been wrought into a perfect cube, about four inches in measurement over each worn face. For it was incredibly worn. The hard, hard crystal was rounded now until its corners were almost gone and the thing was beginning to assume the outlines of a sphere. Ages and ages of wearing, years almost beyond counting, must have passed over this strange clear thing.

But the most curious thing of all was that shape he could make out dimly in the heart of the crystal. For imbedded in its center lay a little disc of a pale and nameless substance with characters incised deep upon its quartz-enclosed surface. Wedge-shaped characters, faintly reminiscent of cuneiform writing.

George Campbell wrinkled his brows and bent closer above the little enigma in his hands, puzzling helplessly. How could such a thing as this have imbedded in pure rock crystal? Remotely a memory floated through his mind of ancient legends that called quartz crystals ice which had frozen too hard to melt again. Ice — and wedge-shaped cuneiforms — yes, didn't that sort of writing originate among the Sumerians who came down from the north in history's remotest beginnings to settle in the primitive Mesopotamian valley? Then hard sense regained control and he laughed. Quartz, of course, was formed in the earliest of earth's geological periods, when there was nothing anywhere but heat and heaving rock. Ice had not come for tens of millions of years after this thing must have been formed.

And yet — that writing. Man-made, surely, although its characters were unfamiliar save in their faint hinting at cuneiform shapes. Or could there, in a Paleozoic world, have been things with a written language who might have graven these cryptic wedges upon the quartz-enveloped disc he held? Or — might a thing like this have fallen meteor-like out of space into the unformed rock of a still molten world? Could it —

Then he caught himself up sharply and felt his ears going hot at the luridness of his own imagination. The silence and the solitude and the queer thing in his hands were conspiring to play tricks with his common sense. He shrugged and laid the crystal down at the edge of his pallet, switching off the light. Perhaps morning and a clear head would bring him an answer to the questions that seemed so insoluble now.

But sleep did not come easily. For one thing, it seemed to him as he flashed off the light, that the little cube had shone for a moment as if with sustained light before it faded into the surrounding dark. Or perhaps he was wrong. Perhaps it had been only his dazzled eyes that seemed to see the light forsake it reluctantly, glowing in the enigmatic deeps of the thing with queer persistence.

He lay there unquietly for a long while, turning the unanswered questions over and over in his mind. There was something about this crystal cube out of the unmeasured past, perhaps from the dawn of all history, that constituted a challenge that would not let him sleep.

II.

(BY A. MERRITT)

He lay there, it seemed to him, for hours. It had been the lingering light, the luminescence that seemed so reluctant to die, which held his mind. It was as though something in the heart of the cube had awakened, stirred drowsily, become suddenly alert . . . and intent upon him.

Sheer fantasy, this. He stirred impatiently and flashed his light upon his watch. Close to one o'clock; three hours more before the dawn. The beam fell and was focused upon the warm crystal cube. He held it there closely, for minutes. He snapped it out, then watched.

There was no doubt about it now. As his eyes accustomed themselves to the darkness, he saw that the strange crystal was glimmering with tiny fugitive lights deep within it like threads of sapphire lightnings. They were at its center and they seemed to him to come from the pale disk with its disturbing markings. And the disc itself was becoming larger . . . the markings shifting shapes . . . the cube was growing . . . was it illusion brought about by the tiny lightnings . . . . ?

He heard a sound. It was the very ghost of a sound, like the ghosts of harp strings being plucked with ghostly fingers. He bent closer. It came from the cube . . . .

There was squeaking in the underbrush, a flurry of bodies and an agonized wailing like a child in death throes and swiftly stilled. Some small tragedy of the wilderness, killer and prey. He stepped over to where it had been enacted, but could see nothing. He again snapped off the flash and looked toward his tent. Upon the ground was a pale blue glimmering. It was the cube. He stooped to pick it up; then obeying some obscure warning, drew back his hand.

And again, he saw, its glow was dying. The tiny sapphire lightnings flashing fitfully, withdrawing to the disc from which they had come. There was no sound from it.

He sat, watching the luminescence glow and fade, glow and fade, but steadily becoming dimmer. It came to him that two elements were necessary to produce the phenomenon. The electric ray itself, and his own fixed attention. His mind must travel along the ray, fix itself upon the cube's heart, if its beat were to wax, until . . . what?

He felt a chill of spirit, as though from contact with some alien thing. It was alien, he knew it; not of this earth. Not of earth's life. He conquered his shrinking, picked up the cube and took it into the tent. It was neither warm nor cold; except for its weight he would not have known he held it. He put it upon the table, keeping the torch turned from it; then stepped to the flap of the tent and closed it.

He went back to the table, drew up the camp chair, and turned the flash directly upon the cube, focusing it so far as he could upon its heart. He sent all his will, all his concentration, along it; focusing will and sight upon the disc as he had the light.

As though at command, the sapphire lightnings burned forth. They burst from the disc into the body of the crystal cube, then beat back, bathing the disc and the markings. Again these began to change, shifting, moving, advancing, and retreating in the blue gleaming. They were no longer cuneiform. They were things . . . objects.

He heard the murmuring music, the plucked harp strings. Louder grew the sound and louder, and now all the body of the cube vibrated to their rhythm. The crystal walls were melting, growing misty as though formed of the mist of diamonds. And the disc itself was growing . . . the shapes shifting, dividing and multiplying as though some door had been opened and into it companies of phantasms were pouring while brighter, more bright grew the pulsing light.

He felt swift panic, tried to withdraw sight and will, dropped the flash. The cube had no need now of the ray . . . and he could not withdraw . . . could not withdraw? Why, he himself was being sucked into that disc which was now a globe within which unnameable shapes danced to a music that bathed the globe with steady radiance.

There was no tent. There was only a vast curtain of sparkling mist behind which shone the globe . . . He felt himself drawn through that mist, sucked through it as if by a mighty wind, straight for the globe.

III.

(BY H. P. LOVECRAFT)

As the mist-blurred light of the sapphire suns grew more and more intense, the outlines of the globe ahead wavered and dissolved to a churning chaos. Its pallor and its motion and its music all blended themselves with the engulfing mist — bleaching it to a pale steel-colour and setting it undulantly in motion. And the sapphire suns, too, melted imperceptibly into the greying infinity of shapeless pulsation.

Meanwhile the sense of forward, outward motion grew intolerably, incredibly, cosmically swift. Every standard of speed known to earth seemed dwarfed, and Campbell knew that any such flight in physical reality would mean instant death to a human being. Even as it was — in this strange, hellish hypnosis or nightmare — the quasi-visual impression of meteor-like hurtling almost paralyzed his mind. Though there were no real points of reference in the grey, pulsing void, he felt that he was approaching and passing the speed of light itself. Finally his consciousness did go under — and merciful blackness swallowed everything.

It was very suddenly, and amidst the most impenetrable darkness, that thoughts and ideas again came to George Campbell. Of how many moments — or years — or eternities — had elapsed since his flight through the grey void, he could form no estimate. He knew only that he seemed to be at rest and without pain. Indeed, the absence of all physical sensation was the salient quality of his condition. It made even the blackness seem less solidly black — suggesting as it did that he was rather a disembodied intelligence in a state beyond physical senses, than a corporeal being with senses deprived of their accustomed objects of perception. He could think sharply and quickly — almost preternaturally so — yet could form no idea whatsoever of his situation.

Half by instinct, he realised that he was not in his own tent. True, he might have awaked there from a nightmare to a world equally black; yet he knew this was not so. There was no camp cot beneath him — he had no hands to feel the blankets and canvas surface and flashlight that ought to be around him — there was no sensation of cold in the air — no flap through which he could glimpse the pale night outside... something was wrong, dreadfully wrong.

He cast his mind backward and thought of the fluorescent cube which had hypnotised him — of that, and all which had followed. He had known that his mind was going, yet had been unable to draw back. At the last moment there had been a shocking, panic fear — a subconscious fear beyond even that caused by the sensation of daemonic flight. It had come from some vague flash or remote recollection — just what, he could not at once tell. Some cell-group in the back of his head had seemed to find a cloudily familiar quality in the cube — and that familiarity was fraught with dim terror. Now he tried to remember what the familiarity and the terror were.

Little by little it came to him. Once — long ago, in connection with his geological life-work — he had read of something like that cube. It had to do with those debatable and disquieting clay fragments called the Eltdown Shards, dug up from pre-carboniferous strata in southern England thirty years before. Their shape and markings were so queer that a few scholars hinted at artificiality, and made wild conjectures about them and their origin. They came, clearly, from a time when no human beings could exist on the globe — but their contours and figurings were damnably puzzling. That was how they got their name.

It was not, however, in the writings of any sober scientist that Campbell had seen that reference to a crystal, disc-holding globe. The source was far less reputable, and infinitely more vivid. About 1912 a deeply learned Sussex clergyman of occultist leanings — the Reverend Arthur Brooke Winters-Hall — had professed to identify the markings on the Eltdown Shards with some of the so-called "pre-human hieroglyphs" persistently cherished and esoterically handed down in certain mystical circles, and had published at his own expense what purported to be a "translation" of the primal and baffling "inscriptions" — a "translation" still quoted frequently and seriously by occult writers. In this "translation" — a surprisingly long brochure in view of the limited number of "shards" existing — had occurred the narrative, supposedly of pre-human authorship, containing the now frightening reference.

As the story went, there dwelt on a world — and eventually on countless other worlds — of outer space a mighty order of worm-like beings whose attainments and whose control of nature surpassed anything within the range of terrestrial imagination. They had mastered the art of interstellar travel early in their career, and had peopled every habitable planet in their own galaxy — killing off the races they found.

Beyond the limits of their own galaxy — which was not ours — they could not navigate in person; but in their quest for knowledge of all space and time they discovered a means of spanning certain transgalactic gulfs with their minds. They devised peculiar objects — strangely energized cubes of a curious crystal containing hypnotic talismen and enclosed in space-resisting spherical envelopes of an unknown substance — which could be forcibly expelled beyond the limits of their universe, and which would respond to the attraction of cool solid matter only.

These, of which a few would necessarily land on various inhabited worlds in outside universes, formed the ether-bridges needed for mental communication. Atmospheric friction burned away the protecting envelope, leaving the cube exposed and subject to discovery by the intelligent minds of the world where it fell. By its very nature, the cube would attract and rivet attention. This, when coupled with the action of light, was sufficient to set its special properties working.

The mind that noticed the cube would be drawn into it by the power of the disc, and would be sent on a thread of obscure energy to the place whence the disc had come — the remote world of the worm-like space-explorers across stupendous galactic abysses. Received in one of the machines to which each cube was attuned, the captured mind would remain suspended without body or senses until examined by one of the dominant race. Then it would, by an obscure process of interchange, be pumped of all its contents. The investigator's mind would now occupy the strange machine while the captive mind occupied the interrogator's worm-like body. Then, in another interchange, the interrogator's mind would leap across boundless space to the captive's vacant and unconscious body on the trans-galactic world — animating the alien tenement as best it might, and exploring the alien world in the guise of one of its denizens.

When done with exploration, the adventurer would use the cube and its disc in accomplishing his return — and sometimes the captured mind would be restored safely to its own remote world. Not always, however, was the dominant race so kind. Sometimes, when a potentially important race capable of space travel was found, the worm-like folk would employ the cube to capture and annihilate minds by the thousands, and would extirpate the race for diplomatic reasons — using the exploring minds as agents of destruction.

In other cases sections of the worm-folk would permanently occupy a trans-galactic planet — destroying the captured minds and wiping out the remaining inhabitants preparatory to settling down in unfamiliar bodies. Never, however, could the parent civilization be quite duplicated in such a case; since the new planet would not contain all the materials necessary for the worm-race's arts. The cubes, for example, could be made only on the home planet.

Only a few of the numberless cubes sent forth ever found a landing and response on an inhabited world — since there was no such thing as aiming them at goals beyond sight or knowledge. Only three, ran the story, had ever landed on peopled worlds in our own particular universe. One of these had struck a planet near the galactic rim two thousand billion years ago, while another had lodged three billion years ago on a world near the centre of the galaxy. The third — and the only one ever known to have invaded the solar system — had reached our own earth 150,000,000 years ago.

It was with this latter that Dr. Winters-Hall's "translation" chiefly dealt. When the cube struck the earth, he wrote, the ruling terrestrial species was a huge, cone-shaped race surpassing all others before or since in mentality and achievements. This race was so advanced that it had actually sent minds abroad in both space and time to explore the cosmos, hence recognised something of what had happened when the cube fell from the sky and certain individuals had suffered mental change after gazing at it.

Realising that the changed individuals represented invading minds, the race's leaders had them destroyed — even at the cost of leaving the displaced minds exiled in alien space. They had had experience with even stranger transitions. When, through a mental exploration of space and time, they formed a rough idea of what the cube was, they carefully hid the thing from light and sight, and guarded it as a menace. They did not wish to destroy a thing so rich in later experimental possibilities. Now and then some rash, unscrupulous adventurer would furtively gain access to it and sample its perilous powers despite the consequences — but all such cases were discovered, and safely and drastically dealt with.

Of this evil meddling the only bad result was that the worm-like outside race learned from the new exiles what had happened to their explorers on earth, and conceived a violent hatred of the planet and all its life-forms. They would have depopulated it if they could, and indeed sent additional cubes into space in the wild hope of striking it by accident in unguarded places — but that accident never came to pass.

The cone-shaped terrestrial beings kept the one existing cube in a special shrine as a relique and basis for experiments, till after aeons it was lost amidst the chaos of war and the destruction of the great polar city where it was guarded. When, fifty million years ago, the beings sent their minds ahead into the infinite future to avoid a nameless peril of inner earth, the whereabouts of the sinister cube from space were unknown.

This much, according to the learned occultist, the Eltdown Shards had said. What now made the account so obscurely frightful to Campbell was the minute accuracy with which the alien cube had been described. Every detail tallied — dimensions, consistency, hieroglyphed central disc, hypnotic effects. As he thought the matter over and over amidst the darkness of his strange situation, he began to wonder whether his whole experience with the crystal cube — indeed, its very existence — were not a nightmare brought on by some freakish subconscious memory of this old bit of extravagant, charlatanic reading. If so, though, the nightmare must still be in force; since his present apparently bodiless state had nothing of normality in it.

Of the time consumed by this puzzled memory and reflection, Campbell could form no estimate. Everything about his state was so unreal that ordinary dimensions and measurements became meaningless. It seemed an eternity, but perhaps it was not really long before the sudden interruption came. What happened was as strange and inexplicable as the blackness it succeeded. There was a sensation — of the mind rather than of the body — and all at once Campbell felt his thoughts swept or sucked beyond his control in tumultuous and chaotic fashion.

Memories arose irresponsibly and irrelevantly. All that he knew — all his personal background, traditions, experiences, scholarship, dreams, ideas, and inspirations — welled up abruptly and simultaneously, with a dizzying speed and abundance which soon made him unable to keep track of any separate concept. The parade of all his mental contents became an avalanche, a cascade, a vortex. It was as horrible and vertiginous as his hypnotic flight through space when the crystal cube pulled him. Finally it sapped his consciousness and brought on fresh oblivion.

Another measureless blank — and then a slow trickle of sensation. This time it was physical, not mental. Sapphire light, and a low rumble of distant sound. There were tactile impressions — he could realise that he was lying at full length on something, though there was a baffling strangeness about the feel of his posture. He could not reconcile the pressure of the supporting surface with his own outlines — or with the outlines of the human form at all. He tried to move his arms, but found no definite response to the attempt. Instead, there were little, ineffectual nervous twitches all over the area which seemed to mark his body.

He tried to open his eyes more widely, but found himself unable to control their mechanism. The sapphire light came in a diffused, nebulous manner, and could nowhere be voluntarily focussed into definiteness. Gradually, though, visual images began to trickle in curiously and indecisively. The limits and qualities of vision were not those which he was used to, but he could roughly correlate the sensation with what he had known as sight. As this sensation gained some degree of stability, Campbell realised that he must still be in the throes of nightmare.

He seemed to be in a room of considerable extent—of medium height, but with a large proportionate area. On every side—and he could apparently see all four sides at once—were high, narrowish slits which seemed to serve as combined doors and windows. There were singular low tables or pedestals, but no furniture of normal nature and proportions. Through the slits streamed floods of sapphire light, and beyond them could be mistily seen the sides and roofs of fantastic buildings like clustered cubes. On the walls—in the vertical panels between the slits—were strange markings of an oddly disquieting character. It was some time before Campbell understood why they disturbed him so—then he saw that they were, in repeated instances, precisely like some of the hieroglyphs on the crystal cube's disc.

The actual nightmare element, though, was something more than this. It began with the living thing which presently entered through one of the slits, advancing deliberately toward him and bearing a metal box of bizarre proportions and glassy, mirror-like surfaces. For this thing was nothing human—nothing of earth—nothing even of man's myths and dreams. It was a gigantic, pale-grey worm or centipede, as large around as a man and twice as long, with a disc-like, apparently eyeless, cilia-fringed head bearing a purple central orifice. It glided on its rear pairs of legs, with its fore part raised vertically—the legs, or at least two pairs of them, serving as arms. Along its spinal ridge was a curious purple comb, and a fan-shaped tail of some grey membrane ended its grotesque bulk. There was a ring of flexible red spikes around its neck, and from the twistings of these came clicking, twanging sounds in measured, deliberate rhythms.

Here, indeed, was outré nightmare at its height—capricious fantasy at its apex. But even this vision of delirium was not what caused George Campbell to lapse a third time into unconsciousness. It took one more thing—one final, unbearable touch—to do that. As the nameless worm advanced with its glistening box, the reclining man caught in the mirror-like surface a glimpse of what should have been his own body. Yet—horribly verifying his disordered and unfamiliar sensations—it was not his own body at all that he saw reflected in the burnished metal. It was, instead, the loathsome, pale-grey bulk of one of the great centipedes.

IV.

(BY ROBERT E. HOWARD)

From that final lap of senselessness, he emerged with a full understanding of his situation. His mind was imprisoned in the body of a frightful native of an alien planet, while, somewhere on the other side of the universe, his own body was housing the monster's personality.

He fought down an unreasoning horror. Judged from a cosmic standpoint, why should his metamorphosis horrify him? Life and consciousness were the only realities in the universe. Form was unimportant. His present body was hideous only according to terrestrial standards. Fear and revulsion were drowned in the excitement of titanic adventure.

What was his former body but a cloak, eventually to be cast off at death anyway? He had no sentimental illusions about the life from which he had been exiled. What had it ever given him save toil, poverty, continual frustration and repression? If this life before him offered no more, at least it offered no less. Intuition told him it offered more—much more.

With the honesty possible only when life is stripped to its naked fundamentals, he realized that he remembered with pleasure only the physical delights of his former life. But he had long ago exhausted all the physical possibilities contained in that earthly body. Earth held no new thrills. But in the possession of this new, alien body he felt promises of strange, exotic joys.

A lawless exultation rose in him. He was a man without a world, free of all conventions or inhibitions of Earth, or of this strange planet, free of every artificial restraint in the universe. He was a god! With grim amusement he thought of his body moving in earth's business and society, with all the while an alien monster staring out of the windows that were George Campbell's eyes on people who would flee if they knew.

Let him walk the earth slaying and destroying as he would. Earth and its races no longer had any meaning to George Campbell. There he had been one of a billion nonentities, fixed in place by a mountainous accumulation of conventions, laws and manners, doomed to live and die in his sordid niche. But in one blind bound he had soared above the commonplace. This was not death, but re-birth—the birth of a full-grown mentality, with a new-found freedom that made little of physical captivity on Yekub.

He started. Yekub! It was the name of this planet, but how had he known? Then he knew, as he knew the name of him whose body he occupied—Tothe. Memory, deep grooved in Tothe's brain, was stirring in him—shadows of the knowledge Tothe had. Carved deep in the physical tissues of the brain, they spoke dimly as implanted instincts to George Campbell; and his human consciousness seized them and translated them to show him the way not only to safety and freedom, but to the power his soul, stripped to its primitive impulses, craved. Not as a slave would he dwell on Yekub, but as a king! Just as of old barbarians had sat on the throne of lordly empires.

For the first time he turned his attention to his surroundings. He still lay on the couch-like thing in the midst of that fantastic room, and the centipede man stood before him, holding the polished metal object, and clashing its neck-spikes. Thus it spoke to him, Campbell knew, and what it said he dimly understood, through the implanted thought processes of Tothe, just as he knew the creature was Yukth, supreme lord of science.

But Campbell gave no heed, for he had made his desperate plan, a plan so alien to the ways of Yekub that it was beyond Yukth's comprehension and caught him wholly unprepared. Yukth, like Campbell, saw the sharp-pointed metal shard on a nearby table, but to Yukth it was only a scientific implement.

He did not even know it could be used as a weapon. Campbell's earthly mind supplied the knowledge and the action that followed, driving Tothe's body into movements no man of Yekub had ever made before.

Campbell snatched the pointed shard and struck, ripping savagely upward. Yukth reared and toppled, his entrails spilling on the floor. In an instant Campbell was streaking for a door. His speed was amazing, exhilarating, first fulfillment of the promise of novel physical sensations.

As he ran, guided wholly by the instinctive knowledge implanted in Tothe's physical reflexes, it was as if he were borne by a separate consciousness in his legs. Tothe's body was bearing him along a route it had traversed ten thousand times when animated by Tothe's mind.

Down a winding corridor he raced, up a twisted stair, through a carved door, and the same instincts that had brought him there told him he had found what he sought. He was in a circular room with a domed roof from which shone a livid blue light. A strange structure rose in the middle of the rainbow-hued floor, tier on tier, each of a separate, vivid color. The ultimate tier was a purple cone, from the apex of which a blue smoky mist drifted upward to a sphere that poised in mid-air — a sphere that shone like translucent ivory.

This, the deep-grooved memories of Tothe told Campbell, was the god of Yekub, though why the people of Yekub feared and worshipped it had been forgotten a million years. A worm-priest stood between him and the altar which no hand of flesh had ever touched. That it could be touched was a blasphemy that had never occurred to a man of Yekub. The worm-priest stood in frozen horror until Campbell's shard ripped the life out of him.

On his centipede-legs Campbell clambered the tiered altar, heedless of its sudden quiverings, heedless of the change that was taking place in the floating sphere, heedless of the smoke that now billowed out in blue clouds. He was drunk with the feel of power. He feared the superstitions of Yekub no more than he feared those of earth. With that globe in his hands he would be king of Yekub. The worm men would dare deny him nothing, when he held their god as hostage. He reached a hand for the ball — no longer ivory-hued, but red as blood . . . .

V.

(BY FRANK BELKNAP LONG)

Out of the tent into the pale August night walked the body of George Campbell. It moved with a slow, wavering gait between the bodies of enormous trees, over a forest path strewed with sweet scented pine needles. The air was crisp and cold. The sky was an inverted bowl of frosted silver flecked with stardust, and far to the north the Aurora Borealis splashed streamers of fire.

The head of the walking man lolled hideously from side to side. From the corners of his lax mouth drooled thick threads of amber froth, which fluttered in the night breeze. He walked upright at first, as a man would walk, but gradually as the tent receded, his posture altered. His torso began almost imperceptibly to slant, and his limbs to shorten.

In a far-off world of outer space the centipede creature that was George Campbell clasped to its bosom a god whose lineaments were red as blood, and ran with insect-like quiverings across a rainbow-hued hall and out through massive portals into the bright glow of alien suns.

Weaving between the trees of earth in an attitude that suggested the awkward loping of a werebeast, the body of George Campbell was fulfilling a mindless destiny. Long, claw-tipped fingers dragged leaves from a carpet of odorous pine needles as it moved toward a wide expanse of gleaming water.

In the far-off, extra-galactic world of the worm people, George Campbell moved between cyclopean blocks of black masonry down long, fern-planted avenues holding aloft the round red god.

There was a harsh animal cry in the underbrush near the gleaming lake on earth where the mind of a worm creature dwelt in a body swayed by instinct. Human teeth sank into soft animal fur, tore at black animal flesh. A little silver fox sank its fangs in frantic retaliation into a furry human wrist, and thrashed about in terror as its blood spurted. Slowly the body of George Campbell arose, its mouth splashed with fresh blood. With upper limbs swaying oddly it moved towards the waters of the lake.

As the vermiform creature that was George Campbell crawled between the black blocks of stone thousands of worm-shapes prostrated themselves in the scintillating dust before it. A godlike power seemed to emanate from its weaving body as it moved with a slow, undulant motion toward a throne of spiritual empire transcending all the sovereignties of earth.

A trapper stumbling wearily through the dense woods of earth near the tent where the worm-creature dwelt in the body of George Campbell came to the gleaming waters of the lake and discerned something dark floating there. He had been lost in the woods all night, and weariness enveloped him like a leaden cloak in the pale morning light.

But the shape was a challenge that he could not ignore. Moving to the edge of the water he knelt in the soft mud and reached out toward the floating bulk. Slowly he pulled it to the shore.

Far off in outer space the worm-creature holding the glowing red god ascended a throne that gleamed like the constellation Cassiopeia under an alien vault of hyper-suns. The great deity that he held aloft energized his worm tenement, burning away in the white fire of a supermundane spirituality all animal dross.

On earth the trapper gazed with unutterable horror into the blackened and hairy face of the drowned man. It was a bestial face, repulsively anthropoid in contour, and from its twisted, distorted mouth black ichor poured.

"He who sought your body in the abysses of Time will

occupy an unresponsive tenement," said the red god. "No spawn of Yekub can control the body of a human.

"On all earth, living creatures rend one another, and feast with unutterable cruelty on their kith and kin. No worm-mind can control a bestial man-body when it yearns to raven. Only man-minds instinctively conditioned through the course of ten thousand generations can keep the human instincts in thrall. Your body will destroy itself on earth, seeking the blood of its animal kin, seeking the cool water where it can wallow at its ease. Seeking eventually destruction, for the death-instinct is more powerful in it than the instincts of life and it will destroy itself in seeking to return to the slime from which it sprang."

Thus spoke the round red god of Yekub in a far-off segment of the space-time continuum to George Campbell as the latter, with all human desire purged away, sat on a throne and ruled an empire of worms more wisely, kindly, and benevolently than any man of earth had ever ruled an empire of men.

The Disinterment.

BY DUANE W. RIMEL AND H.P. LOVECRAFT

4,600-WORD SHORT STORY; 1935.

When Duane Rimel sent this story to Lovecraft for feedback in early 1935, the reaction must have been very gratifying; Lovecraft was quite enthusiastic about it. The story itself is rather magnificent. It's such solid work that many Lovecraft scholars have speculated on the possibility that Rimel — who maintained firmly and strongly that it was his story with some minor but critical revisions by Lovecraft — might have been lying, and that it really was ghost written by the great one himself.

"The Disinterment" is very reminiscent of Lovecraft's story "The Outsider" — which is a fairly good argument for it not being his work, as Lovecraft tended to be far too critical of his own backlist to revisit anything on it this closely; moreover, he several times expressed himself dissatisfied with "The Outsider" in particular, claiming that its plotting was too mechanical and its writing too baroque. Assuming it really is Rimel's work, it is remarkably Lovecraftian in every way.

As a side note, it is easy to read this story as being placed in Hampden, Massachusetts — the town on which Lovecraft modeled his fictional village of Dunwitch; but it appears to have been the same made-up town in the Snake River wilderness that Rimel introduced in "The Tree on the Hill."

It was first published in the Summer 1935 issue of The Californian.

I awoke abruptly from a horrible dream and stared wildly about. Then, seeing the high, arched ceiling and the narrow stained windows of my friend's room, a flood of uneasy revelation coursed over me; and I knew that all of Andrews' hopes had been realized.

I lay supine in a large bed, the posts of which reared upward in dizzy perspective; while on vast shelves about the chamber were the familiar books and antiques I was accustomed to seeing in that secluded corner of the crumbling and ancient mansion which had formed our joint home for many years. On a table by the wall stood a huge candelabrum of early workmanship and design, and the usual light window-curtains had been replaced by hangings of sombre black, which took on a faint, ghostly lustre in the dying light.

I recalled forcibly the events preceding my confinement and seclusion in this veritable medieval fortress. They were not pleasant, and I shuddered anew when I remembered the couch that had held me before my tenancy of the present one — the couch that everyone supposed would be my last. Memory burned afresh regarding those hideous circumstances which had compelled me to choose between a true death and a hypothetical one — with a later re-animation by therapeutic methods known only to my comrade, Marshall Andrews.

The whole thing had begun when I returned from the Orient a year before and discovered, to my utter horror, that I had contracted leprosy while abroad. I had known that I was taking grave chances in caring for my stricken brother in the Philippines, but no hint of my own affliction appeared until I returned to my native land. Andrews himself had made the discovery, and kept it from me as long as possible; but our close acquaintance soon disclosed the awful truth.

At once I was quartered in our ancient abode atop the crags overlooking crumbling Hampden, from whose musty halls and quaint, arched doorways I was never permitted to go forth. It was a terrible existence, with the yellow shadow hanging constantly over me; yet my friend never faltered in his faith, taking care not to contract the dread scourge, but meanwhile making life as pleasant and comfortable as possible. His widespread though somewhat sinister fame as a surgeon prevented any authority from discovering my plight and shipping me away.

It was after nearly a year of this seclusion — late in August — that Andrews decided on a trip to the West Indies — to study "native" medical methods, he said. I was left in care of venerable Simes, the household factotum. So far no outward signs of the disease had developed, and I enjoyed a tolerable though almost completely private existence during my colleague's absence.

It was during this time that I read many of the tomes Andrews had acquired in the course of his twenty years as a surgeon, and learned why his reputation, though locally of the highest, was just a bit shady. For the volumes included any number of fanciful subjects hardly related to modern medical knowledge: treatises and unauthoritative articles on monstrous experiments in surgery; accounts of the bizarre effects of glandular transplantation and rejuvenation in animals and men alike; brochures on attempted brain transference; and a host of other fanatical speculations not countenanced by orthodox physicians. It appeared, too, that Andrews was an authority on obscure medicaments; some of the few books I waded through revealing that he had spent much time in chemistry and in the search for new drugs which might be used as aids in surgery. Looking back at those studies now, I find them hellishly suggestive when associated with his later experiments.

Andrews was gone longer than I expected, returning early in November, almost four months later; and when he did arrive, I was quite anxious to see him, since my condition was at last on the brink of becoming noticeable. I had reached a point where I must seek absolute privacy to keep from being discovered. But my anxiety was slight as compared with his exuberance over a certain new plan he had hatched while in the Indies — a plan to be carried out with the aid of a curious drug he had learned of from a native "doctor" in Haiti. When he explained that his idea concerned me, I became somewhat alarmed, though in my position there could be little to make my plight worse. I had, indeed, considered more than once the oblivion that would come with a revolver or a plunge from the roof to the jagged rocks below.

On the day after his arrival, in the seclusion of the dimly lit study, he outlined the whole grisly scheme. He had found in Haiti a drug, the formula for which he would develop later, which induced a state of profound sleep in anyone taking it; a trance so deep that death was closely counterfeited — with all muscular reflexes, even the respiration and heart-beat, completely stilled for the time being. Andrews had, he said, seen it demonstrated on natives many times. Some of them remained somnolent for days at a time, wholly immobile and as much like death as death itself. This suspended animation, he explained further, would even pass the closest examination of any medical man. He himself, according to all known laws, would have to report as dead a man under the influence of such a drug. He stated, too, that the subject's body assumed the precise appearance of a corpse — even a slight *rigor mortis* developing in prolonged cases.

For some time his purpose did not seem wholly clear, but when the full import of his words became apparent I felt weak and nauseated. Yet in another way I was relieved; for the thing meant at least a partial escape from my curse, an escape from the banishment and shame of an ordinary death of the dread leprosy. Briefly, his plan was to administer a strong dose of the drug to me and call the local authorities, who would immediately pronounce me dead, and see that I was buried within a very short while. He felt assured that with their careless examination they would fail to notice my leprosy symptoms, which in truth had hardly appeared. Only a trifle over fifteen months had passed since I had caught the disease, whereas the corruption takes seven years to run its entire course.

Later, he said, would come resurrection. After my interment in the family graveyard — beside my centuried dwelling and barely a quarter-mile from his own ancient pile — the appropriate steps would be taken. Finally, when my estate was settled and my decease widely known, he would secretly open the tomb and bring me to his own abode again, still alive and none the worse for my adventure.

It seemed a ghastly and daring plan, but to me it offered the only hope for even a partial freedom; so I accepted his proposition, but not without a myriad of misgivings. What if the effect of the drug should wear off while I was in my tomb? What if the coroner should discover the awful ruse, and fail to inter me? These were some of the hideous doubts which assailed me before the experiment. Though death would have been a release from my curse, I feared it even worse than the yellow scourge; feared it even when I could see its black wings constantly hovering over me.

Fortunately I was spared the horror of viewing my own funeral and burial rites. They must, however, have gone just as Andrews had planned, even to the subsequent disinterment; for after the initial dose of the poison from Haiti I lapsed into a semi-paralytic state and from that to a profound, night-black sleep. The drug had been administered in my room, and Andrews had told me before giving it that he would recommend to the coroner a verdict of heart failure due to nerve strain. Of course, there was no embalming — Andrews saw to that — and the whole procedure, leading up to my secret transportation from the graveyard to his crumbling manor, covered a period of three days. Having been buried late in the afternoon of the third day, my body was secured by Andrews that very night. He had replaced the fresh sod just as it had been when the workmen left. Old Simes, sworn to secrecy, had helped Andrews in his ghoulish task.

Later I had lain for over a week in my old familiar bed. Owing to some unexpected effect of the drug, my whole body was completely paralyzed, so that I could move my head only slightly. All my senses, however, were fully alert, and by another week's time I was able to take nourishment in good quantities. Andrews explained that my body would gradually regain its former sensibilities; though owing to the presence of the leprosy it might take considerable time. He seemed greatly interested in analysing my daily symptoms, and always asked if there was any feeling present in my body.

Many days passed before I was able to control any part of my anatomy, and much longer before the paralysis crept from my enfeebled limbs so that I could feel the ordinary bodily reactions. Lying and staring at my numb hulk was like having it injected with a perpetual anesthetic. There was a total alienation I could not understand, considering that my head and neck were quite alive and in good health.

Andrews explained that he had revived my upper half first and could not account for the complete bodily paralysis; though my condition seemed to trouble him little considering the damnably intent interest he centred upon my reactions and stimuli from the very beginning. Many times during lulls in our conversation I would catch a strange gleam in his eyes as he viewed me on the couch — a glint of victorious exultation which, queerly enough, he never voiced aloud; though he seemed to be quite glad that I had run the gauntlet of death and had come through alive. Still, there was that horror I was to meet in less than six years, which added to my desolation and melancholy during the tedious days in which I awaited the return of normal bodily functions. But I would be up and about, he assured me, before very long, enjoying an existence few men had ever experienced. The words did not, however, impress me with their true and ghastly meaning until many days later.

During that awful siege in bed Andrews and I became somewhat estranged. He no longer treated me so much like a friend as like an implement in his skilled and greedy fingers. I found him possessed of unexpected traits — little examples of baseness and cruelty, apparent even to the hardened Simes, which disturbed me in a most unusual manner. Often he would display extraordinary cruelty to live specimens in his laboratory, for he was constantly carrying on various hidden projects in glandular and muscular transplantation on guinea-pigs and rabbits. He had also been employing his newly discovered sleeping potion in curious experiments with suspended animation. But of these things he told me very little, though old Simes often let slip chance comments which shed some light on the proceedings. I was not certain how much the old servant knew, but he had surely learned considerable, being a constant companion to both Andrews and myself.

With the passage of time, a slow but consistent feeling began creeping into my disabled body; and at the reviving symptoms Andrews took a fanatical interest in my case. He still seemed more coldly analytical than sympathetic toward me, taking my pulse and heart-beat with more than usual zeal. Occasionally, in his fevered examinations, I saw his hands tremble slightly — an uncommon sight with so skilled a surgeon — but he seemed oblivious of my scrutiny. I was never allowed even a momentary glimpse of my full body, but with the feeble return of the sense of touch, I was aware of a bulk and heaviness which at first seemed awkward and unfamiliar.

Gradually I regained the use of my hands and arms; and with the passing of the paralysis came a new and terrible sensation of physical estrangement. My limbs had difficulty in following the commands of my mind, and every movement was jerky and uncertain. So clumsy were my hands, that I had to become accustomed to them all over again. This must, I thought, be due to my disease and the advance of the contagion in my system. Being unaware of how the early symptoms affected the victim (my brother's being a more advanced case), I had no means of judging; and since Andrews shunned the subject, I deemed it better to remain silent.

One day I asked Andrews — I no longer considered him a friend — if I might try rising and sitting up in bed. At first he objected strenuously, but later, after cautioning me to keep the blankets well up around my chin so that I would not be chilled, he permitted it. This seemed strange, in view of the comfortable temperature. Now that late autumn was slowly turning into winter, the room was always well heated. A growing chilliness at night, and occasional glimpses of a leaden sky through the window, had told me of the changing season; for no calendar was ever in sight upon the dingy walls.

With the gentle help of Simes I was eased to a sitting position, Andrews coldly watching from the door to the laboratory. At my success a slow smile spread across his leering features, and he turned to disappear from the darkened doorway. His mood did nothing to improve my condition. Old Simes, usually so regular and consistent, was now often late in his duties, sometimes leaving me alone for hours at a time.

The terrible sense of alienation was heightened by my new position. It seemed that the legs and arms inside my gown were hardly able to follow the summoning of my mind, and it became mentally exhausting to continue movement for any length of time. My fingers, woefully clumsy, were wholly unfamiliar to my inner sense of touch, and I wondered vaguely if I were to be accursed the rest of my days with an awkwardness induced by my dread malady.

It was on the evening following my half-recovery that the dreams began. I was tormented not only at night but during the day as well. I would awaken, screaming horribly, from some frightful nightmare I dared not think about outside the realm of sleep. These dreams consisted mainly of ghoulish things; graveyards at night, stalking corpses, and lost souls amid a chaos of blinding light and shadow. The terrible reality of the visions disturbed me most of all: it seemed that some inside influence was inducing the grisly vistas of moonlit tombstones and endless catacombs of the restless dead. I could not place their source; and at the end of a week I was quite frantic with abominable thoughts which seemed to obtrude themselves upon my unwelcome consciousness.

By that time a slow plan was forming whereby I might escape the living hell into which I had been propelled. Andrews cared less and less about me, seeming intent only on my progress and growth and recovery of normal muscular reactions. I was becoming every day more convinced of the nefarious doings going on in that laboratory across the threshold — the animal cries were shocking, and rasped hideously on my overwrought nerves. And I was gradually beginning to think that Andrews had not saved me from deportation solely for my own benefit, but for some accursed reason of his own. Simes's attention was slowly becoming slighter and slighter, and I was convinced that the aged servitor had a hand in the deviltry somewhere. Andrews no longer eyed me as a friend, but as an object of experimentation; nor did I like the way he fingered his scalpel when he stood in the narrow doorway and stared at me with crafty alertness. I had never before seen such a transformation come over any man. His ordinarily handsome features were now lined and whisker-grown, and his eyes gleamed as if some imp of Satan were staring from them. His cold, calculating gaze made me shudder horribly, and gave me a fresh determination to free myself from his bondage as soon as possible.

I had lost track of time during my dream-orgy, and had no way of knowing how fast the days were passing. The curtains were often drawn in the daytime, the room being lit by waxen cylinders in the large candelabrum. It was a nightmare of living horror and unreality; though through it all I was gradually becoming stronger. I always gave careful responses to Andrews' inquiries concerning my returning physical control, concealing the fact that a new life was vibrating through me with every passing day — an altogether strange sort of strength, but one which I was counting on to serve me in the coming crisis.

Finally, one chilly evening when the candles had been extinguished, and a pale shaft of moonlight fell through the dark curtains upon my bed, I determined to rise and carry out my plan of action. There had been no movement from either of my captors for several hours, and I was confident that both were asleep in adjoining bedchambers. Shifting my cumbersome weight carefully, I rose to a sitting position and crawled cautiously out of bed, down upon the floor. A vertigo gripped me momentarily, and a wave of weakness flooded my entire being. But finally strength returned, and by clutching at a bed-post I was able to stand upon my feet for the first time in many months. Gradually a new strength coursed through me, and I donned the dark robe which I had seen hanging on a nearby chair. It was quite long, but served as a cloak over my nightdress. Again came that feeling of awful unfamiliarity which I had experienced in bed; that sense of alienation, and of difficulty in making my limbs perform as they should. But there was need for haste before my feeble strength might give out. As a last precaution in dressing, I slipped some old shoes over my feet; but though I could have sworn they were my own, they seemed abnormally loose, so that I decided they must belong to the aged Simes.

Seeing no other heavy objects in the room, I seized from the table the huge candelabrum, upon which the moon shone with a pallid glow, and proceeded very quietly toward the laboratory door.

My first steps came jerkily and with much difficulty, and in the semi-darkness I was unable to make my way very rapidly. When I reached the threshold, a glance within revealed my former friend seated in a large overstuffed chair; while beside him was a smoking-stand upon which were assorted bottles and a glass. He reclined half-way in the moonlight through the large window, and his greasy features were creased in a drunken smirk. An opened book lay in his lap — one of the hideous tomes from his private library.

For a long moment I gloated over the prospect before me, and then, stepping forward suddenly, I brought the heavy weapon down upon his unprotected head. The dull crunch was followed by a spurt of blood, and the fiend crumpled to the floor, his head laid half open. I felt no contrition at taking the man's life in such a manner. In the hideous, half-visible specimens of his surgical wizardry scattered about the room in various stages of completion and preservation, I felt there was enough evidence to blast his soul without my aid. Andrews had gone too far in his practices to continue living, and as one of his monstrous specimens — of that I was now hideously certain — it was my duty to exterminate him.

Simes, I realized, would be no such easy matter; indeed, only unusual good fortune had caused me to find Andrews unconscious. When I finally reeled up to the servant's bedchamber door, faint from exhaustion, I knew it would take all my remaining strength to complete the ordeal.

The old man's room was in utmost darkness, being on the north side of the structure, but he must have seen me silhouetted in the doorway as I came in. He screamed hoarsely, and I aimed the candelabrum at him from the threshold. It struck something soft, making a sloughing sound in the darkness; but the screaming continued. From that time on events became hazy and jumbled together, but I remember grappling with the man and choking the life from him little by little. He gibbered a host of awful things before I could lay hands on him — cried and begged for mercy from my clutching fingers. I hardly realized my own strength in that mad moment which left Andrews' associate in a condition like his own.

Retreating from the darkened chamber, I stumbled for the stairway door, sagged through it, and somehow reached the landing below. No lamps were burning, and my only light was a filtering of moonbeams coming from the narrow windows in the hall. But I made my jerky way over the cold, damp slabs of stone, reeling from the terrible weakness of my exertion, and reached the front door after ages of fumbling and crawling about in the darkness.

Vague memories and haunting shadows came to taunt me in that ancient hallway; shadows once friendly and understandable, but now grown alien and unrecognizable, so that I stumbled down the worn steps in a frenzy of something more than fear. For a moment I stood in the shadow of the giant stone manor, viewing the moonlit trail down which I must go to reach the home of my forefathers, only a quarter of a mile distant. But the way seemed long, and for a while I despaired of ever traversing the whole of it.

At last I grasped a piece of dead wood as a cane and set out down the winding road. Ahead, seemingly only a few rods away in the moonlight, stood the venerable mansion where my ancestors had lived and died. Its turrets rose spectrally in the shimmering radiance, and the black shadow cast on the beetling hillside appeared to shift and waver, as if belonging to a castle of unreal substance. There stood the monument of half a century; a haven for all my family old and young, which I had deserted many years ago to live with the fanatical Andrews. It stood empty on that fateful night, and I hope that it may always remain so.

In some manner I reached the aged place; though I do not remember the last half of the journey at all. It was enough to be near the family cemetery, among whose moss-covered and crumbling stones I would seek the oblivion I had desired. As I approached the moonlit spot the old familiarity — so absent during my abnormal existence — returned to plague me in a wholly unexpected way. I drew close to my own tombstone, and the feeling of homecoming grew stronger; with it came a fresh flood of that awful sense of alienation and disembodiment which I knew so well. I was satisfied that the end was drawing near; nor did I stop to analyse emotions till a little later, when the full horror of my position burst upon me.

Intuitively I knew my own tombstone; for the grass had scarcely begun to grow between the pieces of sod. With feverish haste I began clawing at the mound, and scraping the wet earth from the hole left by the removal of the grass and roots. How long I worked in the nitrous soil before my fingers struck the coffin-lid, I can never say; but sweat was pouring from me and my nails were but useless, bleeding hooks.

At last I threw out the last bit of loose earth, and with trembling fingers tugged on the heavy lid. It gave a trifle; and I was prepared to lift it completely open when a fetid and nauseous odour assailed my nostrils. I started erect, horrified. Had some idiot placed my tombstone on the wrong grave, causing me to unearth another body? For surely there could be no mistaking that awful stench. Gradually a hideous uncertainty came over me and I scrambled from the hole. One look at the newly made headpiece was enough. This was indeed my own grave . . . but what fool had buried within it another corpse?

All at once a bit of the unspeakable truth propelled itself upon my brain. The odour, in spite of its putrescence, seemed somehow familiar — horribly familiar . . . Yet I could not credit my senses with such an idea. Reeling and cursing, I fell into the black cavity once more, and by the light of a hastily lit match, lifted the long lid completely open. Then the light went out, as if extinguished by a malignant hand, and I clawed my way out of that accursed pit, screaming in a frenzy of fear and loathing.

When I regained consciousness I was lying before the door of my own ancient manor, where I must have crawled after that hideous rendezvous in the family cemetery. I realized that dawn was close at hand, and rose feebly, opening the aged portal before me and entering the place which had known no footsteps for over a decade. A fever was ravaging my weakened body, so that I was hardly able to stand, but I made my way slowly through the musty, dimly lit chambers and staggered into my own study — the study I had deserted so many years before.

When the sun has risen, I shall go to the ancient well beneath the old willow tree by the cemetery and cast my deformed self into it. No other man shall ever view this blasphemy which has survived life longer than it should have. I do not know what people will say when they see my disordered grave, but this will not trouble me if I can find oblivion from that which I beheld amidst the crumbling, moss-crusted stones of the hideous place.

I know now why Andrews was so secretive in his actions; so damnably gloating in his attitude toward me after my artificial death. He had meant me for a specimen all the time — a specimen of his greatest feat of surgery, his masterpiece of unclean witchery . . . an example of perverted artistry for him alone to see. Where Andrews obtained that other with which I lay accursed in his mouldering mansion I shall probably never know; but I am afraid that it was brought from Haiti along with his fiendish medicine. At least these long hairy arms and horrible short legs are alien to me . . . alien to all natural and sane laws of mankind. The thought that I shall be tortured with that other during the rest of my brief existence is another hell.

Now I can but wish for that which once was mine; that which every man blessed of God ought to have at death; that which I saw in that awful moment in the ancient burial ground when I raised the lid on the coffin — my own shrunken, decayed, and headless body.

The Diary of Alonzo Typer.

BY WILLIAM LUMLEY AND H.P. LOVECRAFT

8,200-WORD NOVELETTE; 1935.

This short novelette is one of the most flat-out fun-to-read stories in Lovecraft's canon. It is almost entirely his work; the draft of the story which Lumley supplied him with was, to put it bluntly, terrible.

Lovecraft took the draft and rewrote it, trying to preserve Lumley's prose style as much as possible while infusing it with some actual clutching horror. The result — well, it is certainly not Lovecraft's best work, but it is uncommonly fun.

It was written late in 1935, but was not published until the February 1938 issue of Weird Tales *magazine.*

ABOUT WILLIAM LUMLEY (1880-1960).

H.P. Lovecraft once wrote, in a letter to R.H. Barlow, that he made a point of helping, at no charge, two broad categories of people: Promising beginners who need encouragement and help to get a start; and "certain old or handicapped people who are pathetically in need of some cheering influence — these, even when I recognize them as incapable of improvement. In my opinion, the good accomplished by giving these poor souls a little more to live for, vastly overbalances any harm which could be wrought through their popular overestimation. Old Bill Lumley and old Doc Kuntz are typical cases of this sort."

William Lumley might not have appreciated this characterization of himself as, essentially, a literary charity case; but it really wasn't far from the truth. He was an eccentric gentleman who, although only a decade older than Lovecraft, was thought of as elderly. When he first made Lumley's acquaintance, Lovecraft reported with great amusement that the old gentleman actually believed in Yog-Sothoth and Cthulhu; it's not clear to what extent that was really the case, but Lumley was a believer in mysticism.

He enjoyed the companionship of the Lovecraft Circle, but really didn't have the chops to be a part of it.

Luckily for us, though, he had enough of a sense of story and plot to supply Lovecraft with a rough draft that, awful though it was, would inspire him to write one of the most entertaining of all his revisions: "The Diary of Alonzo Typer."

EDITOR'S NOTE.

Alonzo Hasbrouch Typer of Kingston, New York, was last seen and recognized on April 17, 1908, around noon, at the Hotel Richmond in Batavia. He was the only survivor of an ancient Ulster Country family, and was fifty-three years old at the time of his disappearance.

Mr. Typer was educated privately and at Columbia and Heidelberg universities. All his life was spent as a student, the field of his researches including many obscure and generally feared borderlands of human knowledge. His papers on vampirism, ghouls and poltergeist phenomena were privately printed after rejection by many publishers. He resigned from the Society for Psychical Research in 1900 after a series of peculiarly bitter controversies.

At various times Mr. Typer travelled extensively, sometimes dropping out of sight for long periods. He is known to have visited obscure spots in Nepal, India, Tibet, and Indo-China, and passed most of the year 1899 on mysterious Easter Island. The extensive search for Mr. Typer after his disappearance yielded no results, and his estate was divided among distant cousins in New York City.

The diary herewith presented was allegedly found in the ruins of a large country house near Attica, N.Y., which had borne a curiously sinister reputation for generations before its collapse. The edifice was very old, antedating the general white settlement of the region, and had formed the home of a strange and secretive family named van der Heyl, which had migrated from Albany in 1746 under a curious cloud of witchcraft suspicion. The structure probably dated from about 1760.

Of the history of the van der Heyls very little is known. They remained entirely aloof from their normal neighbours, employed negro servants brought directly from Africa and speaking little English, and educated their children privately and at European colleges. Those of them who went out into the world were soon lost to sight, though not before gaining evil repute for association with Black Mass groups and cults of even darker significance.

Around the dreaded house a straggling village arose, populated by Indians and later by renegades from the surrounding country, which bore the dubious name of Chorazin. Of the singular hereditary strains which afterward appeared in the mixed Chorazin villagers, several monographs have been written by ethnologists. Just behind the village, and in sight of the van der Heyl house, is a steep hill crowned with a peculiar ring of ancient standing stones which the Iroquois always regarded with fear and loathing. The origin and nature of the stones, whose date, according to archaeological and climatological evidence, must be fabulously early, is a problem still unsolved.

From about 1795 onward, the legends of the incoming pioneers and later population have much to say about strange cries and chants proceeding at certain seasons from Chorazin and from the great house and hill of standing stones; though there is reason to suppose that the noises ceased about 1872, when the entire van der Heyl household— servants and all— suddenly and simultaneously disappeared.

Thenceforward the house was deserted; for other disastrous events— including three unexplained deaths, five disappearances, and four cases of sudden insanity— occurred when later owners and interested visitors attempted to stay in it. The house, village, and extensive rural areas on all sides reverted to the state and were auctioned off in the absence of discoverable van der Heyl heirs. Since about 1890 the owners (successively the late Charles A. Shields and his son Oscar S. Shields, of Buffalo) have left the entire property in a state of absolute neglect, and have warned all inquirers not to visit the region.

Of those known to have approached the house during the last forty years, most were occult students, police officers, newspaper men, and odd characters from abroad. Among the latter was a mysterious Eurasian, probably from Chochin-China, whose later appearance with blank mind and bizarre mutilations excited wide press notice in 1903.

Mr. Typer's diary— a book about 6 x 3 1/2 inches in size, with tough paper and an oddly durable binding of thin sheet metal— was discovered in the possession of one of the decadent Chorazin villagers on November 16, 1935, by a state policeman sent to investigate the rumoured collapse of the deserted van der Heyl mansion. The house had indeed fallen, obviously from sheer age and decrepitude, in the severe gale of November 12. Disintegration was peculiarly complete, and no thorough search of the ruins could be made for several weeks. John Eagle, the swarthy, simian-faced, Indian-like villager who had the diary, said that he found the book quite near the surface of the debris, in what must have been an upper front room.

Very little of the contents of the house could be identified, though an enormous and astonishingly solid brick vault in the cellar (whose ancient iron door had to be blasted open because of the strangely figured and perversely tenacious lock) remained intact and presented several puzzling features. For one thing, the walls were covered with still undeciphered hieroglyphs roughly incised in the brickwork. Another peculiarity was a huge circular aperture in the rear of the vault, blocked by a cave-in evidently caused by the collapse of the house.

But strangest of all was the apparently recent deposit of some foetid, slimy, pitch-black substance on the flagstone floor, extending in a yard-broad, irregular line with one end at the blocked circular aperture. Those who first opened the vault declared that the place smelled like the snake-house at a zoo.

The diary, which was apparently designed solely to cover an investigation of the dreaded van der Heyl house, by the vanished Mr. Typer, has been proved by handwriting experts to be genuine. The script shows signs of increasing nervous strain as it progresses toward the end, in places becoming almost illegible. Chorazin villagers — whose stupidity and taciturnity baffle all students of the region and its secrets — admit no recollection of Mr. Typer as distinguished from other rash visitors to the dreaded house.

The text of the diary is here given verbatim and without comment. (Passages that have proven impossible to read are here represented as fully as possible, with dashes substituting for undecipherable letters.) How to interpret it, and what, other than the writer's madness, to infer from it, the reader must decide for himself. Only the future can tell what its value may be in solving a generation-old mystery. It may be remarked that genealogists confirm Mr. Typer's belated memory in the matter of Adriaen Sleght.

THE DIARY.

ARRIVED HERE about 6 p.m. Had to walk all the way from Attica in the teeth of an oncoming storm, for no one would rent me a horse or rig, and I can't run an automobile. This place is even worse than I had expected, and I dread what is coming, even though I long at the same time to learn the secret. All too soon will come the night — the old Walpurgis Sabbat horror — and after that time in Wales I know what to look for. Whatever comes, I shall not flinch. Prodded by some unfathomable urge, I have given my whole life to the quest of unholy mysteries. I came here for nothing else, and will not quarrel with fate.

It was very dark when I got here, though the sun had by no means set. The storm clouds were the densest I had ever seen, and I could not have found my way but for the lightning-flashes. The village is a hateful little back-water, and its few inhabitants no better than idiots. One of them saluted me in a queer way, as if he knew me. I could see very little of the landscape — just a small, swamp valley of strange brown weed-stalks and dead fungi surrounded by scraggly, evilly twisted trees with bare boughs. But behind the village is a dismal-looking hill on whose summit is a circle of great stones with another stone at the center. That, without question, is the vile primordial thing V—— told me about the N—— estbat.

The great house lies in the midst of a park all overgrown with curious-looking briars. I could scarcely break through, and when I did the vast age and decrepitude of the building almost stopped me from entering. The place looked filthy and diseased, and I wondered how so leprous a building could hang together. It is wooden; and though its original lines are hidden by a bewildering tangle of wings added at various dates, I think it was first built in the square colonial fashion of New England. Probably that was easier to build than a Dutch stone house — and then, too, I recall that Dirck van der Heyl's wife was from Salem, a daughter of the unmentionable Abaddon Corey. There was a small pillared porch, and I got under it just as the storm burst. It was a fiendish tempest — black as midnight, with rain in sheets, thunder and lightning like the day of general dissolution, and a wind that actually clawed at me.

The door was unlocked, so I took out my electric torch and went inside. Dust was inches thick on floor and furniture, and the place smelled like a mould-caked tomb. There was a hall reaching all the way through, and a curving staircase on the right.

I ploughed my way upstairs and selected this front room to camp out in. The whole place seems fully furnished, though most of the furniture is breaking down. This is written at 8 o'clock, after a cold meal from my traveling-case. After this the village people will bring me supplies, though they won't agree to come any closer than the ruins of the park gate until (as they say) later. I wish I could get rid of an unpleasant feeling of familiarity with this place.

LATER — I am conscious of several presences in this house. One in particular is decidedly hostile toward me — a malevolent will which is seeking to break down my own and overcome me. I must not countenance this for an instant, but must use all my forces to resist it. It is appallingly evil, and definitely nonhuman. I think it must be allied to powers outside Earth — powers in the spaces behind time and beyond the universe. It towers like a colossus, bearing out what is said in the Aklo writings. There is such a feeling of vast size connected with it that I wonder these chambers can contain its bulk — and yet it has no visible bulk. Its age must be unutterably vast — shockingly, indescribably so.

APRIL 18 — Slept very little last night. At 3 a.m. a strange, creeping wind began to pervade the whole region, ever rising until the house rocked as if in a typhoon. As I went down the staircase to see the rattling front door the darkness took half-visible forms in my imagination. Just below the landing I was pushed violently from behind — by the wind, I suppose, though I could have sworn I saw the dissolving outlines of a gigantic black paw as I turned quickly about. I did not lose my footing, but safely finished the descent and shot the heavy bolt of the dangerously shaking door.

I had not meant to explore the house before dawn; yet now, unable to sleep again, and fired with mixed terror and curiosity, I felt reluctant to postpone my search. With my powerful torch I ploughed through the dust to the great south parlour, where I knew the portraits would be. There they were, just as V—— had said, and as I seemed to know from some obscurer source as well. Some were so blackened and dust-clouded that I could make little or nothing of them, but from those I could trace I recognized that they were indeed of the hateful line of the van der Heyls. Some of the paintings seemed to suggest faces I had known; but just what faces, I could not recall.

The outlines of that frightful hybrid Joris — spawned in 1773 by Dirck's youngest daughter — were clearest of all, and I could trace the green eyes and the serpent look in his face.

Every time I shut off the flashlight that face would seem to glow in the dark until I half fancied it shone with a faint, greenish light of its own. The more I looked, the more evil it seemed, and I turned away to avoid hallucinations of changing expression.

But that to which I turned was even worse. The long, dour face, small, closely set eyes, and swine-like features identified it at once, even though the artist had striven to make the snout look as human as possible. This was what V—— had whispered about. As I stared in horror, I thought the eyes took on a reddish glow, and for a moment the background seemed replaced by an alien and seemingly irrelevant scene—a lone, bleak moor beneath a dirty yellow sky, whereon grew a wretched-looking blackthorn bush. Fearing for my sanity, I rushed from that accursed gallery to the dust-cleared corner upstairs where I have my "camp."

LATER—Decided to explore some more of the labyrinthine wings of the house by daylight. I cannot be lost, for my footprints are distinct in the ankle-deep dust, and I can trace other identifying marks when necessary. It is curious how easily I learn the intricate windings of the corridors. Followed a long, outflung northerly "ell" to its extremity, and came to a locked door, which I forced. Beyond was a very small room quite crowded with furniture, and with the panelling badly worm-eaten. On the outer wall I spied a black space behind the rotting woodwork, and discovered a narrow secret passage leading downward to unknown inky depths. It was a steeply inclined chute or tunnel without steps or handholds, and I wondered what its use could have been.

Above the fireplace was a mouldy painting, which I found on close inspection to be that of a young woman in the dress of the late eighteenth century. The face is of classic beauty, yet with the most fiendishly evil expression which I have ever known the human countenance to bear. Not merely callousness, greed, and cruelty, but some quality hideous beyond human comprehension seems to sit upon those finely carved features. And as I looked it seemed to me that the artist—or the slow processes of mold and decay—had imparted to that pallid complexion a sickly greenish cast, and the least suggestion of an almost imperceptibly scaly texture.

Later I ascended to the attic, where I found several chests of strange books—many of utterly alien aspects in letters and in physical form alike. One contained variants of the Aklo formulae which I had never known to exist. I have not yet examined the books on the dusty shelves downstairs.

APRIL 19—There are certainly unseen presences here, even though the dust bears no footprints but my own. Cut a path through the briars yesterday to the park gate where my supplies are left, but this morning I found it closed. Very odd, since the bushes are barely stirring with spring sap. Again I had that feeling of something at hand so colossal that the chambers can scarcely contain it. This time I feel more than one of the presences is of such a size, and I know now that the third Aklo ritual—which I found in that book in the attic yesterday—would make such being solid and visible. Whether I shall dare to try this materialization remains to be seen. The perils are great.

Last night I began to glimpse evanescent shadow-faces and forms in the dim corners of the halls and chambers—faces and forms so hideous and loathsome that I dare not describe them. They seemed allied in substance to that titanic paw which tried to push me down the stairs night before last, and must of course be phantoms of my disturbed imagination. What I am seeking would not be quite like these things. I have seen the paw again, sometimes alone and sometimes with its mate, but I have resolved to ignore all such phenomena.

Early this afternoon I explored the cellar for the first time, descending by a ladder found in a store-room, since the wooden steps had rotted away. The whole place is a mass of nitrous encrustations, with amorphous mounds marking the spots where various objects have disintegrated. At the farther end is a narrow passage which seems to extend under the northerly "ell" where I found the little locked room, and at the end of this is a heavy brick wall with a locked iron door. Apparently belonging to a vault of some sort, this wall and door bear evidences of Eighteenth-Century workmanship and must be contemporary with the oldest additions to the house—clearly pre-Revolutionary. On the lock, which is obviously older than the rest of the ironwork, are engraved certain symbols which I cannot decipher.

V—— had not told me about this vault. It fills me with a greater disquiet than anything else I have seen, for every time I approach it I have an almost irresistible impulse to listen for something. Hitherto no untoward sounds have marked my stay in this malign place. As I left the cellar I wished devoutly that the steps were still there; for my progress up the ladder seemed maddeningly slow. I do not want to go down there again—and yet some evil genius urges me to try it at night if I would learn what is to be learned.

APRIL 20—I have sounded the depths of horror—only to be made aware of still lower depths. Last night the temptation was too strong, and in the black small hours I descended once more into that nitrous, hellish cellar with my flashlight, tiptoeing among the amorphous heaps to that terrible brick wall and locked door. I made no sound, and refrained from whispering any of the incantations I knew, but I listened with mad intentness.

At last I heard the sounds from beyond those barred plates of sheet iron, the menacing padding and muttering as of gigantic night-things within. Then, too, there was a damnable slithering, as of a vast serpent or sea-beast dragging its monstrous folds over a paved floor. Nearly paralyzed with fright, I glanced at the huge rusty lock, and at the alien, cryptic hieroglyphs graven upon it. They were signs I could not recognize, and something in their vaguely Mongoloid technique hinted at a blasphemous and indescribable antiquity. At times I fancied I could see them glowing with a greenish light.

I turned to flee, but found that vision of the titan paws before me, the great talons seeming to swell and become more tangible as I gazed. Out of the cellar's evil blackness they stretched, with shadowy hints of scaly wrists beyond them, and with a waxing, malignant will guiding their horrible gropings. Then I heard from behind me — within that abominable vault — a fresh burst of muffled reverberations which seemed to echo from far horizons like distant thunder. Impelled by this greater fear, I advanced toward the shadowy paws with my flashlight and saw them vanish before the full force of the electric beam. Then up the ladder I raced, torch between my teeth, nor did I rest till I had regained my upstairs "camp."

What is to be my ultimate end, I dare not imagine. I came as a seeker, but now I know that something is seeking me. I could not leave if I wished. This morning I tried to go to the gate for my supplies, but found the briars twisted tightly in my path. It was the same in every direction — behind and on all sides of the house. In places the brown, barbed vines had uncurled to astonishing heights, forming a steel-like hedge against my egress. The villagers are connected with all this. When I went indoors I found my supplies in the great front hall, though without any clue as to how they came there. I am sorry now that I swept the dust away. I shall scatter some more and see what prints are left.

This afternoon I read some of the books in the great shadowy library at the rear of the ground floor, and formed certain suspicions which I cannot bear to mention. I had never seen the text of the Pnakotic Manuscripts or of the Eltdown Shards before, and would not have come here had I known what they contain. I believe it is too late now — for the awful Sabbat is only ten days away. It is for that night of horror that they are saving me.

APRIL 21 — I have been studying the portraits again. Some have names attached, and I noticed one — of an evil-faced woman, painted some two centuries ago — which puzzled me. It bore the name of Trintje van der Heyl Sleght, and I have a distinct impression that I once met the name of Sleght before, in some significant connection. It was not horrible then, though it becomes so now. I must rack my brain for the clue.

The eyes of the pictures haunt me. Is it possible that some of them are emerging more distinctly from their shrouds of dust and decay and mold? The serpent-faced and swine-faced warlocks stare horribly at me from their blackened frames, and a score of other hybrid faces are beginning to peer out of shadowy backgrounds. There is a hideous look of family resemblance in them all, and that which is human is more horrible than that which is non-human. I wish they reminded me less of other faces — faces I have known in the past. They were an accursed line, and Cornelis of Leydon was the worst of them. It was he who broke down the barrier after his father had found that other key. I am sure that V— — knows only a fragment of the horrible truth, so that I am indeed unprepared and defenceless. What of the line before old Class? What he did in 1591 could never have been done without generations of evil heritage, or some link with the outside. And what of the branches this monstrous line has sent forth? Are they scattered over the world, all awaiting their common heritage of horror? I must recall the place where I once so particularly noticed the name of Sleght.

I wish I could be sure that those pictures stay always in their frames. For several hours now I have been seeing momentary presences like the earlier paws and shadow-faces and forms, but closely duplicating some of the ancient portraits. Somehow I can never glimpse a presence and the portrait it resembles at the same time — the light is always wrong for one or the other, or else the presence and the portrait are in different rooms.

Perhaps, as I have hoped, the presences are mere figments of imagination, but I cannot be sure now. Some are female, and of the same helling beauty as the picture in the little locked room. Some are like no portrait I have seen, yet make me feel that their painted features lurk unrecognized beneath the mold and soot of canvases I cannot decipher. A few, I desperately fear, have approached materialization in solid or semi-solid form — and some have a dreaded and unexplained familiarity.

There is one woman who in full loveliness excels all the rest. Her poisonous charms are like a honeyed flower growing on the brink of hell. When I look at her closely she vanishes, only to reappear later. Her face has a greenish cast, and now and then I fancy I can spy a suspicion of the squamous in its smooth texture. Who is she? Is she that being who dwelt in the little locked room a century and more ago?

My supplies were again left in the front hall — that, clearly, is to be the custom. I had sprinkled dust about to catch footprints, but this morning the whole hall was swept clean by some unknown agency.

APRIL 22 — This has been a day of horrible discovery. I explored the cobwebbed attic again, and found a carved, crumbling chest — plainly from Holland — full of blasphemous books and papers far older than any hitherto encountered here. There was a Greek *Necronomicon*, a Norman-French *Livre d'Eibon*, and a first edition of old Ludvig Prinn's *De Vermis Mysteriis*. But the old bound manuscript was the worst. It was in low Latin, and full of the strange, crabbed handwriting of Claes van der Heyl, being evidently the diary or notebook kept by him between 1560 and 1580. When I unfastened the blackened silver clasp and opened the yellowed leaves a coloured drawing fluttered out — the likeness of a monstrous creature resembling nothing so much as a squid, beaked and tentacled, with great yellow eyes, and with certain abominable approximations to the human form in its contours.

I had never before seen so utterly loathsome and nightmarish a form. On the paws, feet, and head-tentacles were curious claws — reminding me of the colossal shadow-shapes which had groped so horribly in my path — while the entity as a whole sat upon a great throne-like pedestal inscribed with unknown hieroglyphs of vaguely Chinese cast. About both writing and image there hung an air of sinister evil so profound and pervasive that I could not think it the product of any one world or age. Rather must that monstrous shape be a focus for all the evil in unbounded space, throughout the eons past and to come — and those eldritch symbols be vile sentient ikons endowed with a morbid life of their own and ready to wrest themselves from the parchment for the reader's destruction. To the meaning of that monster and of those hieroglyphs I had no clue, but I knew that both had been traced with a hellish precision and for no nameable purpose. As I studied the leering characters, their kinship to the symbols on that ominous lock in the cellar became more and more manifest. I left the picture in the attic, for never could sleep come to me with such a thing nearby.

All the afternoon and evening I read in the manuscript book of old Claes van der Heyl; and what I read will cloud and make horrible whatever period of life lies ahead of me. The genesis of the world, and of previous worlds, unfolded itself before my eyes. I learned of the city Shamballah, built by the Lemurians fifty million years ago, yet inviolate still behind its wall of psychic force in the eastern desert. I learned of the *Book of Dzyan*, whose first six chapters antedate the Earth, and which was old when the lords of Venus came through space in their ships to civilize our planet. And I saw recorded in writing for the first time that name which others had spoken to me in whispers, and which I had known in a closer and more horrible way — the shunned and dread name of Yian-Ho.

In several places I was held up by passages requiring a key. Eventually, from various allusions, I gathered that old Claes had not dared to embody all his knowledge in one book, but had left certain points for another. Neither volume can be wholly intelligible without its fellow; hence I have resolved to find the second one if it lies anywhere within this accursed house. Though plainly a prisoner, I have not lost my lifelong zeal for the unknown; and am determined to probe the cosmos as deeply as possible before doom comes.

APRIL 23 — Searched all the morning for the second diary, and found it about noon in a desk in the little locked room. Like the first, it is in Claes van der Heyl's barbarous Latin, and it seems to consist of disjointed notes referring to various sections of the other. Glancing through the leaves, I spied at once the abhorred name of Yian-Ho — of Yian-Ho, that lost and hidden city wherein brood aeon-old secrets, and of which dim memories older than the body lurk behind the minds of all men. It was repeated many times, and the text around it was strewn with crudely-drawn hieroglyphs plainly akin to those on the pedestal in that hellish drawing I had seen. Here, clearly, lay the key to that monstrous tentacled shape and its forbidden message. With this knowledge I ascended the creaking stairs to the attic of cobwebs and horror.

When I tried to open the attic door it stuck as never before. Several times it resisted every effort to open it, and when at last it gave way I had a distinct feeling that some colossal unseen shape had suddenly released it — a shape that soared away on non-material but audibly beating wings. When I found the horrible drawing I felt that it was not precisely where I left it. Applying the key in the other book, I soon saw that the latter was no instant guide to the secret. It was only a clue — a clue to a secret too black to be left lightly guarded. It would take hours — perhaps days — to extract the awful message.

Shall I live long enough to learn the secret? The shadowy black arms and paws haunt my vision more and more now, and seem even more titanic than at first. Nor am I ever long free from those vague, unhuman presences whose nebulous bulk seems too vast for the chambers to contain. And now and then the grotesque, evanescent faces and forms, and the mocking portrait-shapes, troop before me in bewildering confusion.

Truly, there are terrible primal arcana of Earth which had better be left unknown and unevoked; dread secrets which have nothing to do with man, and which man may learn only in exchange for peace and sanity; cryptic truths which make the knower evermore an alien among his kind, and cause him to walk alone on Earth. Likewise there are dread survivals of things older and more potent than man; things that have blasphemously straggled down through the aeons to ages never meant for them; monstrous entities that have lain sleeping endlessly in incredible crypts and remote caverns, outside the laws of reason and causation, and ready to be waked by such blasphemers as shall know their dark forbidden signs and furtive passwords.

APRIL 24 — Studied the picture and the key all day in the attic. At sunset I heard strange sounds, of a sort not encountered before and seeming to come from far away. Listening, I realized that they must flow from that queer abrupt hill with the circle of standing stones, which lies behind the village and some distance north of the house. I had heard that there was a path from the house leading up that hill to the primal cromlech, and had suspected that at certain seasons the van der Heyls had much occasion to use it; but the whole matter had hitherto lain latent in my consciousness. The present sounds consisted of a shrill piping intermingled with a peculiar and hideous sort of hissing or whistling, a bizarre, alien kind of music, like nothing which the annals of Earth describe. It was very faint, and soon faded, but the matter has set me thinking. It is toward the hill that the long, northerly "ell" with the secret chute, and the locked brick vault under it, extend. Can there be any connection which has so far eluded me?

APRIL 25 — I have made a peculiar and disturbing discovery about the nature of my imprisonment. Drawn toward the hill by a sinister fascination, I found the briars giving way before me, but in that direction only. There is a ruined gate, and beneath the bushes the traces of an old path no doubt exist. The briars extend part-way up and all around the hill, though

Weird Tales, February 1938

"To the meaning of that monster and those hieroglyphs I had no clue."

the summit with the standing stones bears only a curious growth of moss and stunted grass. I climbed the hill and spent several hours there, noticing a strange wind which seems always to sweep around the forbidding monoliths and which sometimes seems to whisper in an oddly articulate though darkly cryptic fashion.

These stones, both in colour and texture, resemble nothing I have seen elsewhere. They are neither brown nor grey, but rather of a dirty yellow merging into an evil green and having a suggestion of chameleon-like variability. Their texture is queerly like that of a scaled serpent, and is inexplicably nauseous to the touch — being as cold and clammy as the skin of a toad or other reptile. Near the central menhir is a singular stone-rimmed hollow which I cannot explain, but which may possibly form the entrance to a long-choked well or tunnel. When I sought to descend the hill at points away from the house I found the briars intercepting me as before, though the path toward the house was easily retraceable.

APRIL 26 — Up on the hill again this evening, and found that windy whispering much more distinct. The almost angry humming came close to actual speech, of a vague, sibilant sort, and reminded me of the strange piping chant I had heard from afar. After sunset there came a curious flash of premature summer lightning on the northern horizon, followed almost at once by a queer detonation high in the fading sky. Something about this phenomenon disturbed me greatly, and I could not escape the impression that the noise ended in a kind of unhuman hissing speech which trailed off into guttural cosmic laughter. Is my mind tottering at last, or has my unwarranted curiosity evoked unheard-of horrors from the twilight spaces? The Sabbat is close at hand now. What will be the end?

APRIL 27 — At last my dreams are to be realized! Whether or not my life or spirit or body will be claimed, I shall enter the gateway! Progress in deciphering those crucial hieroglpyhs in the picture has been slow, but this afternoon I hit upon the final clue. By evening I knew their meaning — and that meaning can apply in only one way to the things I have encountered in this house.

There is beneath this house — sepulchred I know not where — an Ancient One Who will show me the gateway I would enter, and give me the lost signs and words I shall need. How long It has lain buried here, forgotten save by those who reared the stone on the hill, and by those who later sought out this place and built this house, I cannot conjecture. It was in search of this Thing, beyond question, that Hendrik van der Heyl came to New Netherland in 1638. Men of this Earth know It not, save in the secret whispers of the fear-shaken few who have found or inherited the key. No human eye has even yet glimpsed It — unless, perhaps, the vanished wizards of this house delved farther than has been guessed.

With knowledge of the symbols came likewise a mastery of the Seven Lost Signs of Terror, and a tacit recognition of the hideous and unutterable Words of Fear. All that remains for me to accomplish is the Chant which will transfigure that Forgotten One who is Guardian of the Ancient Gateway. I marvel much at the Chant. It is composed of strange and repellent gutturals and disturbing sibilants resembling no language I have ever encountered, even in the blackest chapters of the *Livre d'Eibon*. When I visited the hill at sunset I tried to read it aloud, but evoked in response only a vague, sinister rumbling on the far horizon, and a thin cloud of elemental dust that writhed and whirled like some evil living thing. Perhaps I do not pronounce the alien syllables correctly, or perhaps it is only on the Sabbat — that hellish Sabbat for which the Powers in this house are without question holding me — that the great Transfiguration can occur.

Had an odd spell of fright this morning. I thought for a moment that I recalled where I had seen that baffling name of Sleght before, and the prospect of realization filled me with unutterable horror.

APRIL 28 — Today dark ominous clouds have hovered intermittently over the circle on this hill. I have noticed such clouds several times before, but their contours and arrangements now hold a fresh significance. They are snake-like and fantastic, and curiously like the evil shadow-shapes I have seen in the house. They float in a circle around the primal cromlech, revolving repeatedly as though endowed with a sinister life and purpose. I could swear that they give forth an angry murmuring. After some fifteen minutes they sail slowly away, ever to the eastward, like the units of a straggling battalion. Are they indeed those dread Ones whom Solomon knew of old — those giant black beings whose number is legion and whose tread doth shake the earth?

I have been rehearsing the Chant that will transfigure the Nameless Thing; yet strange fears assail me even when I utter the syllables under my breath. Piecing all evidence together, I have now discovered that the only way to It is through the locked cellar vault. That vault was built with a hellish purpose, and must cover the hidden burrow leading to the Immemorial Lair. What guardians live endlessly within, flourishing from century to century on an unknown nourishment, only the mad may conjecture. The warlocks of this house, who called them out of inner Earth, have known them only too well, as the shocking portraits and memories of the place reveal.

What troubles me most is the limited nature of the Chant. It evokes the Nameless One, yet provides no method for the control of That Which is evoked. There are, of course, the general signs and gestures, but whether they will prove effective toward such a One remains to be seen. Still, the rewards are great enough to justify any danger, and I could not retreat if I would, since an unknown force plainly urges me on.

I have discovered one more obstacle. Since the locked cellar vault must be traversed, the key to that place must be found. The lock is far too strong for forcing. That the key is somewhere hereabouts cannot be doubted, but the time before the Sabbat is very short. I must search diligently and thoroughly. It will take courage to unlock that iron door, for what prisoned horrors may not lurk within?

LATER — I have been shunning the cellar for the past day or two, but late this afternoon I again descended to those forbidding precincts.

At first all was silent, but within five minutes the menacing padding and muttering began once more beyond the iron door. This time it was loud and more terrifying than on any previous occasion, and I likewise recognized the slithering that bespoke some monstrous sea-beast — now swifter and nervously intensified, as if the thing were striving to force its way through the portal where I stood.

As the pacing grew louder, more restless, and more sinister, there began to pound through it those hellish and more unidentifiable reverberations which I had heard on my second visit to the cellar — those muffled reverberations which seemed to echo from far horizons like distant thunder. Now, however, their volume was magnified a hundredfold, and their timbre freighted with new and terrifying implications. I can compare the sound to nothing more aptly than the roar of some dread monster of the vanished saurian age, when primal horrors roamed the Earth, and Valusia's serpent-men laid the foundation-stones of evil magic. To such a roar — but swelled to deafening heights reached by no known organic throat — was this shocking sound akin. Dare I unlock the door and face the onslaught of what lies beyond?

APRIL 29 — The key to the vault is found. I came upon it this noon in the little locked room — buried beneath rubbish in a drawer of the ancient desk, as if some belated effort to conceal it had been made. It was wrapped in a crumbling newspaper dated October 31, 1872; but there was an inner wrapping of dried skin — evidently the hide of some unknown reptile — which bore a Low Latin message in the same crabbed writing as that of the notebooks I found. As I had thought, the lock and key were vastly older than the vault. Old Claes van der Heyl had them ready for something he or his descendants meant to do — and how much older than he they were I could not estimate. Deciphering the Latin message, I trembled in a fresh access of clutching terror and nameless awe.

"The secrets of the monstrous primal Ones;" ran the crabbed text, "whose cryptic words relate the hidden things that were before man; the things no one of Earth should learn, lest peace be for ever forfeited; shall by me never suffer revelation. To Yian-Ho, that lost and forbidden city of countless aeons whose place may not be told, I have been in the veritable flesh of this body, as none other among the living has been. Therein have I found, and thence have I borne away, that knowledge which I would gladly lose, though I may not. I have learnt to bridge a gap that should not be bridged, and must call out of the Earth That which should not be waked nor called. And what is sent to follow me will not sleep till I or those after me have found and done what is to be found and done.

"That which I have awaked and borne away with me, I may not part with again. So it is written in the Book of Hidden Things. That which I have willed to be has twined its dreadful shape around me, and — if I live not to do its bidding — around those children born and unborn who shall come after me, until the bidding be done. Strange may be their joinings, and awful the aid they may summon till the end be reached. Into lands unknown and dim must the seeking go, and a house must be built for the outer guardians.

"This is the key to that lock which was given me in the dreadful, aeon-old and forbidden city of Yian-Ho; the lock which I or mine must place upon the vestibule of That Which is to be found. And may the Lords of Yaddith succor me — or him — who must set that lock in place or turn the key thereof."

Such was the message — a message which, once I had read it, I seemed to have known before. Now, as I write these words, the key is before me. I gaze on it with mixed dread and longing, and cannot find words to describe its aspect. It is of the same unknown, subtly greenish frosted metal as the lock; a metal best compared to brass tarnished with verdigris. Its design is alien and fantastic, and the coffin-shaped end of the ponderous bulk leaves no doubt of the lock it was meant to fit. The handle roughly forms a strange, nonhuman image, whose exact outlines and identity cannot now be traced. Upon holding it for any length of time I seem to feel an alien, anomalous life in the cold metal — a quickening or pulsing too feeble for ordinary recognition.

Below the eidolon is graven a faint, eon-worn legend in those blasphemous, Chinese-like hieroglyphs I have come to know so well. I can only make out the beginning — the words: "My vengeance lurks . . ." — before the text fades to indistinctness. There is some fatality in this timely finding of the key — for tomorrow night comes the hellish Sabbat. But strangely enough, amidst all this hideous expectancy, that question of the Sleght name bothers me more and more. Why should I dread to find it linked with the van der Heyls?

WALPURGIS-EVE — APRIL 30 — The time has come. I waked last night to see the key glowing with a lurid greenish radiance — that same morbid green which I have seen in the eyes and skin of certain portraits here, on the shocking lock and key, on the monstrous menhirs of the hill, and in a thousand other recesses of my consciousness. There were strident whispers in the air — sibilant whisperings like those of the wind around that dreadful cromlech. Something spoke to me out of the frore aether of space, and it said, "The hour falls." It is an omen, and I laugh at my own fears. Have I not the dread words and the Seven Lost Signs of Terror — the power coercive of any Dweller in the cosmos or in the unknown darkened spaces? I will no longer hesitate.

The heavens are very dark, as if a terrific storm were coming on — a storm even greater than that of the night when I reached here, nearly a fortnight ago. From the village, less than a mile away, I hear a queer and unwonted babbling. It is as I thought — these poor degraded idiots are within the secret, and keep the awful Sabbat on the hill.

Here in the house the shadows gather densely. In the darkness the sky before me almost glows with a greenish light of its own. I have not yet been to the cellar. It is better that I wait, lest the sound of that muttering and padding — those slitherings and muffled reverberations — unnerve me before I can unlock the fateful door.

Of what I shall encounter, and what I must do, I have only the most general idea. Shall I find my task in the vault itself, or must I burrow deeper into the nighted heart of our planet? There are things I do not yet understand — or at least, prefer not to understand — despite a dreadful, increasing and inexplicable sense of bygone familiarity with this fearsome house. That chute, for instance, leading down from the little locked room. But I think I know why the wing with the vault extends toward the hill.

6 P.M. — Looking out the north windows, I can see a group of villagers on the hill. They seem unaware of the lowering sky, and are digging near the great central menhir. It occurs to me that they are working on that stone-rimmed hollow place

which looks like a long-choked tunnel entrance. What is to come? How much of the olden Sabbat rites have these people retained? That key glows horribly — it is not imagination. Dare I use it as it must be used? Another matter has greatly disturbed me. Glancing nervously through a book in the library I came upon an ampler form of the name that has teased my memory so sorely: "Trintje, wife of Adriaen Sleght." The Adriaen leads me to the very brink of recollection.

MIDNIGHT — Horror is unleashed, but I must not weaken. The storm has broken with pandemoniac fury, and lightning has struck the hill three times, yet the hybrid, malformed villagers are gathering within the cromlech. I can see them in the almost constant flashes. The great standing stones loom up shockingly, and have a dull green luminosity that reveals them even when the lightning is not there. The peals of thunder are deafening, and every one seems to be horribly answered from some indeterminate direction. As I write, the creatures on the hill have begun to chant and howl and scream in a degraded, half-simian version of the ancient ritual. Rain pours down like a flood, yet they leap and emit sounds in a kind of diabolic ecstasy.

"Iä! Shub-Niggurath! The Goat with a Thousand Young!"

But the worst thing is within the house. Even at this height, I have begun to hear sounds from the cellar. It is the padding and muttering and slithering and muffled reverberations within the vault . . . .

Memories come and go. That name Adriaen Sleght pounds oddly at my consciousness. Dirck van der Heyl's son-in-law . . . his child old Dirck's granddaughter and Abaddon Corey's great-granddaughter . . . .

LATER — Merciful God! At last I know where I saw that name. I know, and am transfixed with horror. All is lost . . . .

The key has begun to feel warm as my left hand nervously clutches it. At times that vague quickening or pulsing is so distinct that I can almost feel the living metal move. It came from Yian-Ho for a terrible purpose, and to me — who all too late know the thin stream of van der Heyl blood that trickles down through the Sleghts into my own lineage — has descended the hideous task of fulfilling that purpose . . . .

My courage and curiousity wane. I know the horror that lies beyond that iron door. What if Claes van der Heyl was my ancestor — need I expiate his nameless sin? I will not — I swear I will not! . . . *[the writing here grows indistinct]* . . . too late — cannot help self — black paws materialize — am dragged away toward the cellar . . . .

The Haunter of the Dark.

9,200-WORD NOVELETTE; 1935.

This short novelette is the last weird-fiction story H.P. Lovecraft ever wrote, and it was part of a playful pact with fellow weird-fiction writer Robert Bloch — the man who today is most famous as the author of Psycho. *It started when Bloch's story "The Shambler from the Stars," was published in the September 1935 issue of* Weird Tales. *In Bloch's story, a "mystic dreamer" in Providence accidentally reads aloud from an eldritch spell book, thereby conjuring a Thing from Beyond, which seizes him in its tentacles and sucks out all his blood. The "mystic dreamer" was obviously modeled on Lovecraft, and a* Weird Tales *reader suggested in a letter to the editor the following month that Lovecraft respond in kind — with a story involving Bloch meeting an equally horrible fate.*

Lovecraft's jovial riposte was "The Haunter of the Dark," a fabulous dark tale of the demise of one "Robert Blake."

It was written between November 5 and 9, just after Lovecraft finished revising "The Diary of Alonzo Typer" for William Lumley. It was published in the December 1936 issue of Weird Tales.

I have seen the dark universe yawning,
Where the black planets roll without aim,
Where they roll in their horror unheeded,
Without knowledge or lustre or name.

— NEMESIS.

Cautious investigators will hesitate to challenge the common belief that Robert Blake was killed by lightning, or by some profound nervous shock derived from an electrical discharge. It is true that the window he faced was unbroken, but nature has shown herself capable of many freakish performances. The expression on his face may easily have arisen from some obscure muscular source unrelated to anything he saw, while the entries in his diary are clearly the result of a fantastic imagination aroused by certain local superstitions and by certain old matters he had uncovered. As for the anomalous conditions at the deserted church of Federal Hill—the shrewd analyst is not slow in attributing them to some charlatanry, conscious or unconscious, with at least some of which Blake was secretly connected.

For after all, the victim was a writer and painter wholly devoted to the field of myth, dream, terror, and superstition, and avid in his quest for scenes and effects of a bizarre, spectral sort. His earlier stay in the city—a visit to a strange old man as deeply given to occult and forbidden lore as he—had ended amidst death and flame, and it must have been some morbid instinct which drew him back from his home in Milwaukee. He may have known of the old stories despite his statements to the contrary in the diary, and his death may have nipped in the bud some stupendous hoax destined to have a literary reflection.

Among those, however, who have examined and correlated all this evidence, there remain several who cling to less rational and commonplace theories. They are inclined to take much of Blake's diary at its face value, and point significantly to certain facts such as the undoubted genuineness of the old church record, the verified existence of the disliked and unorthodox Starry Wisdom sect prior to 1877, the recorded disappearance of an inquisitive reporter named Edwin M. Lillibridge in 1893, and—above all—the look of monstrous, transfiguring fear on the face of the young writer when he died. It was one of these believers who, moved to fanatical extremes, threw into the bay the curiously angled stone and its strangely adorned metal box found in the old church steeple—the black windowless steeple, and not the tower where Blake's diary said those things originally were. Though widely censured both officially and unofficially, this man—a reputable physician with a taste for odd folklore—averred that he had rid the earth of something too dangerous to rest upon it.

Between these two schools of opinion the reader must judge for himself. The papers have given the tangible details from a sceptical angle, leaving for others the drawing of the picture as Robert Blake saw it—or thought he saw it—or pretended to see it. Now studying the diary closely, dispassionately, and at leisure, let us summarize the dark chain of events from the expressed point of view of their chief actor.

Young Blake returned to Providence in the winter of 1934-5, taking the upper floor of a venerable dwelling in a grassy court off College Street—on the crest of the great eastward hill near the Brown University campus and behind the marble John Hay Library. It was a cosy and fascinating place, in a little garden oasis of village-like antiquity where huge, friendly cats sunned themselves atop a convenient shed. The square Georgian house had a monitor roof, classic doorway with fan carving, small-paned windows, and all the other earmarks of early nineteenth century workmanship. Inside were six-panelled doors, wide floor-boards, a curving colonial staircase, white Adam-period mantels, and a rear set of rooms three steps below the general level.

Blake's study, a large southwest chamber, overlooked the front garden on one side, while its west windows—before one of which he had his desk—faced off from the brow of the hill and commanded a splendid view of the lower town's outspread roofs and of the mystical sunsets that flamed behind them. On the far horizon were the open countryside's purple slopes. Against these, some two miles away, rose the spectral hump of Federal Hill, bristling with huddled roofs and steeples whose remote outlines wavered mysteriously, taking fantastic forms as the smoke of the city swirled up and enmeshed them. Blake had a curious sense that he was looking upon some unknown, ethereal world which might or might not vanish in dream if ever he tried to seek it out and enter it in person.

Having sent home for most of his books, Blake bought some antique furniture suitable for his quarters and settled down to write and paint—living alone, and attending to the simple housework himself. His studio was in a north attic room, where the panes of the monitor roof furnished admirable lighting. During that first winter he produced five of his best-known short stories—"The Burrower Beneath," "The Stairs in the Crypt," "Shaggai," "In the Vale of Pnath," and "The Feaster from the Stars"—and painted seven canvases; studies of nameless, unhuman monsters, and profoundly alien, non-terrestrial landscapes.

At sunset he would often sit at his desk and gaze dreamily off at the outspread west—the dark towers of Memorial Hall just below, the Georgian court-house belfry, the lofty pinnacles of the downtown section, and that shimmering, spire-crowned mound in the distance whose unknown streets and labyrinthine gables so potently provoked his fancy. From his few local acquaintances he learned that the far-off slope was a vast Italian quarter, though most of the houses were remnants of older Yankee and Irish days. Now and then he would train his field-glasses on that spectral, unreachable world beyond the curling smoke; picking out individual roofs and chimneys and steeples, and speculating upon the bizarre and curious mysteries they might house. Even with optical aid Federal Hill seemed somehow alien, half fabulous, and linked to the unreal, intangible marvels of Blake's own tales and pictures. The feeling would persist long after the hill had faded into the violet, lamp-starred twilight, and the court-house floodlights and the red Industrial Trust beacon had blazed up to make the night grotesque.

Of all the distant objects on Federal Hill, a certain huge, dark church most fascinated Blake. It stood out with especial distinctness at certain hours of the day, and at sunset the great tower and tapering steeple loomed blackly against the flaming sky. It seemed to rest on especially high ground; for the grimy façade, and the obliquely seen north side with sloping roof and the tops of great pointed windows, rose boldly above the tangle of surrounding ridgepoles and chimney-pots. Peculiarly grim and austere, it appeared to be built of stone, stained and weathered with the smoke and storms of a century and more. The style, so far as the glass could show, was that earliest experimental form of Gothic revival which preceded the stately Upjohn period and held over some of the outlines and proportions of the Georgian age. Perhaps it was reared around 1810 or 1815.

As months passed, Blake watched the far-off, forbidding structure with an oddly mounting interest. Since the vast windows were never lighted, he knew that it must be vacant. The longer he watched, the more his imagination worked, till at length he began to fancy curious things. He believed that a vague, singular aura of desolation hovered over the place, so that even the pigeons and swallows shunned its smoky eaves. Around other towers and belfries his glass would reveal great flocks of birds, but here they never rested. At least, that is what he thought and set down in his diary. He pointed the place out to several friends, but none of them had even been on Federal Hill or possessed the faintest notion of what the church was or had been.

In the spring a deep restlessness gripped Blake. He had begun his long-planned novel — based on a supposed survival of the witch-cult in Maine — but was strangely unable to make progress with it. More and more he would sit at his westward window and gaze at the distant hill and the black, frowning steeple shunned by the birds. When the delicate leaves came out on the garden boughs the world was filled with a new beauty, but Blake's restlessness was merely increased. It was then that he first thought of crossing the city and climbing bodily up that fabulous slope into the smoke-wreathed world of dream.

Late in April, just before the aeon-shadowed Walpurgis time, Blake made his first trip into the unknown. Plodding through the endless downtown streets and the bleak, decayed squares beyond, he came finally upon the ascending avenue of century-worn steps, sagging Doric porches, and blear-paned cupolas which he felt must lead up to the long-known, unreachable world beyond the mists. There were dingy blue-and-white street signs which meant nothing to him, and presently he noted the strange, dark faces of the drifting crowds, and the foreign signs over curious shops in brown, decade-weathered buildings. Nowhere could he find any of the objects he had seen from afar; so that once more he half fancied that the Federal Hill of that distant view was a dream-world never to be trod by living human feet.

Now and then a battered church façade or crumbling spire came in sight, but never the blackened pile that he sought. When he asked a shopkeeper about a great stone church the man smiled and shook his head, though he spoke English freely. As Blake climbed higher, the region seemed stranger and stranger, with bewildering mazes of brooding brown alleys leading eternally off to the south. He crossed two or three broad avenues, and once thought he glimpsed a familiar tower. Again he asked a merchant about the massive church of stone, and this time he could have sworn that the plea of ignorance was feigned. The dark man's face had a look of fear which he tried to hide, and Blake saw him make a curious sign with his right hand.

Then suddenly a black spire stood out against the cloudy sky on his left, above the tiers of brown roofs lining the tangled southerly alleys. Blake knew at once what it was, and plunged toward it through the squalid, unpaved lanes that climbed from the avenue. Twice he lost his way, but he somehow dared not ask any of the patriarchs or housewives who sat on their doorsteps, or any of the children who shouted and played in the mud of the shadowy lanes.

At last he saw the tower plain against the southwest, and a huge stone bulk rose darkly at the end of an alley. Presently he stood in a wind-swept open square, quaintly cobblestoned, with a high bank wall on the farther side. This was the end of his quest; for upon the wide, iron-railed, weed-grown plateau which the wall supported — a separate, lesser world raised fully six feet above the surrounding streets — there stood a grim, titan bulk whose identity, despite Blake's new perspective, was beyond dispute.

The vacant church was in a state of great decrepitude. Some of the high stone buttresses had fallen, and several delicate finials lay half lost among the brown, neglected weeds and grasses. The sooty Gothic windows were largely unbroken, though many of the stone mullions were missing. Blake wondered how the obscurely painted panes could have survived so well, in view of the known habits of small boys the world over. The massive doors were intact and tightly closed. Around the top of the bank wall, fully enclosing the grounds, was a rusty iron fence whose gate — at the head of a flight of steps from the square — was visibly padlocked. The path from the gate to the building was completely overgrown. Desolation and decay hung like a pall above the place, and in the birdless eaves and black, ivyless walls Blake felt a touch of the dimly sinister beyond his power to define.

There were very few people in the square, but Blake saw a policeman at the northerly end and approached him with questions about the church. He was a great wholesome Irishman, and it seemed odd that he would do little more than make the sign of the cross and mutter that people never spoke of that building. When Blake pressed him he said very hurriedly that the Italian priest warned everybody against it, vowing that a monstrous evil had once dwelt there and left its mark. He himself had heard dark whispers of it from his father, who recalled certain sounds and rumours from his boyhood.

There had been a bad sect there in the old days — an outlaw sect that called up awful things from some unknown gulf of night. It had taken a good priest to exorcise what had come, though there did be those who said that merely the light could do it. If Father O'Malley were alive there would be many a thing he could tell. But now there was nothing to do but let it alone. It hurt nobody now, and those that owned it were dead or far away. They had run away like rats after the threatening talk in '77, when people began to mind the way folks vanished now and then in the neighbourhood. Some day the city would step in and take the property for lack of heirs, but little good would come of anybody's touching it. Better it be left alone for the years to topple, lest things be stirred that ought to rest forever in their black abyss.

After the policeman had gone Blake stood staring at the sullen steepled pile. It excited him to find that the structure seemed as sinister to others as to him, and he wondered what grain of truth might lie behind the old tales the bluecoat had repeated. Probably they were mere legends evoked by the evil look of the place, but even so, they were like a strange coming to life of one of his own stories.

The afternoon sun came out from behind dispersing clouds, but seemed unable to light up the stained, sooty walls of the old temple that towered on its high plateau. It was odd that the green of spring had not touched the brown, withered growths in the raised, iron-fenced yard. Blake found himself edging nearer the raised area and examining the bank wall and rusted fence for possible avenues of ingress. There was a terrible lure about the blackened fane which was not to be resisted. The fence had no opening near the steps, but round on the north side were some missing bars. He could go up the steps and walk round on the narrow coping outside the fence till he came to the gap. If the people feared the place so wildly, he would encounter no interference.

He was on the embankment and almost inside the fence before anyone noticed him. Then, looking down, he saw the few people in the square edging away and making the same sign with their right hands that the shopkeeper in the avenue had made. Several windows were slammed down, and a fat woman darted into the street and pulled some small children inside a rickety, unpainted house. The gap in the fence was very easy to pass through, and before long Blake found himself wading amidst the rotting, tangled growths of the deserted yard. Here and there the worn stump of a headstone told him that there had once been burials in the field; but that, he saw, must have been very long ago. The sheer bulk of the church was oppressive now that he was close to it, but he conquered his mood and approached to try the three great doors in the façade. All were securely locked, so he began a circuit of the Cyclopean building in quest of some minor and more penetrable opening. Even then he could not be sure that he wished to enter that haunt of desertion and shadow, yet the pull of its strangeness dragged him on automatically.

A yawning and unprotected cellar window in the rear furnished the needed aperture. Peering in, Blake saw a subterrene gulf of cobwebs and dust faintly litten by the western sun's filtered rays. Debris, old barrels, and ruined boxes and furniture of numerous sorts met his eye, though over everything lay a shroud of dust which softened all sharp outlines. The rusted remains of a hot-air furnace showed that the building had been used and kept in shape as late as mid-Victorian times.

Acting almost without conscious initiative, Blake crawled through the window and let himself down to the dust-carpeted and debris-strewn concrete floor. The vaulted cellar was a vast one, without partitions; and in a corner far to the right, amid dense shadows, he saw a black archway evidently leading upstairs. He felt a peculiar sense of oppression at being actually within the great spectral building, but kept it in check as he cautiously scouted about—finding a still-intact barrel amid the dust, and rolling it over to the open window to provide for his exit. Then, bracing himself, he crossed the wide, cobweb-festooned space toward the arch. Half-choked with the omnipresent dust, and covered with ghostly gossamer fibres, he reached and began to climb the worn stone steps which rose into the darkness. He had no light, but groped carefully with his hands. After a sharp turn he felt a closed door ahead, and a little fumbling revealed its ancient latch. It opened inward, and beyond it he saw a dimly illumined corridor lined with worm-eaten panelling.

Once on the ground floor, Blake began exploring in a rapid fashion. All the inner doors were unlocked, so that he freely passed from room to room. The colossal nave was an almost eldritch place with its driffs and mountains of dust over box pews, altar, hour-glass pulpit, and sounding-board and its titanic ropes of cobweb stretching among the pointed arches of the gallery and entwining the clustered Gothic columns. Over all this hushed desolation played a hideous leaden light as the declining afternoon sun sent its rays through the strange, half-blackened panes of the great apsidal windows.

The paintings on those windows were so obscured by soot that Blake could scarcely decipher what they had represented, but from the little he could make out he did not like them. The designs were largely conventional, and his knowledge of obscure symbolism told him much concerning some of the ancient patterns. The few saints depicted bore expressions distinctly open to criticism, while one of the windows seemed to show merely a dark space with spirals of curious luminosity scattered about in it. Turning away from the windows, Blake noticed that the cobwebbed cross above the altar was not of the ordinary kind, but resembled the primordial ankh or crux ansata of shadowy Egypt.

In a rear vestry room beside the apse Blake found a rotting desk and ceiling-high shelves of mildewed, disintegrating books. Here for the first time he received a positive shock of objective horror, for the titles of those books told him much. They were the black, forbidden things which most sane people have never even heard of, or have heard of only in furtive, timorous whispers; the banned and dreaded repositories of equivocal secret and immemorial formulae which have trickled down the stream of time from the days of man's youth, and the dim, fabulous days before man was. He had himself read many of them—a Latin version of the abhorred *Necronomicon*, the sinister *Liber Ivonis*, the infamous *Cultes des Goules* of Comte d'Erlette, the *Unaussprechlichen Kulten* of von Junzt, and old Ludvig Prinn's hellish *De Vermis Mysteriis*. But there were others he had known merely by reputation or not at all—the Pnakotic Manuscripts, the *Book of Dzyan*, and a crumbling volume of wholly unidentifiable characters yet with certain symbols and diagrams shudderingly recognizable to the occult student. Clearly, the lingering local rumours had not lied. This place had once been the seat of an evil older than mankind and wider than the known universe.

In the ruined desk was a small leather-bound record-book filled with entries in some odd cryptographic medium. The manuscript writing consisted of the common traditional symbols used today in astronomy and anciently in alchemy, astrology, and other dubious arts — the devices of the sun, moon, planets, aspects, and zodiacal signs — here massed in solid pages of text, with divisions and paragraphings suggesting that each symbol answered to some alphabetical letter.

In the hope of later solving the cryptogram, Blake bore off this volume in his coat pocket. Many of the great tomes on the shelves fascinated him unutterably, and he felt tempted to borrow them at some later time. He wondered how they could have remained undisturbed so long. Was he the first to conquer the clutching, pervasive fear which had for nearly sixty years protected this deserted place from visitors?

Having now thoroughly explored the ground floor, Blake ploughed again through the dust of the spectral nave to the front vestibule, where he had seen a door and staircase presumably leading up to the blackened tower and steeple — objects so long familiar to him at a distance. The ascent was a choking experience, for dust lay thick, while the spiders had done their worst in this constricted place. The staircase was a spiral with high, narrow wooden treads, and now and then Blake passed a clouded window looking dizzily out over the city. Though he had seen no ropes below, he expected to find a bell or peal of bells in the tower whose narrow, louvre-boarded lancet windows his field-glass had studied so often. Here he was doomed to disappointment; for when he attained the top of the stairs he found the tower chamber vacant of chimes, and clearly devoted to vastly different purposes.

The room, about fifteen feet square, was faintly lighted by four lancet windows, one on each side, which were glazed within their screening of decayed louvre-boards. These had been further fitted with tight, opaque screens, but the latter were now largely rotted away. In the centre of the dust-laden floor rose a curiously angled stone pillar some four feet in height and two in average diameter, covered on each side with bizarre, crudely incised and wholly unrecognizable hieroglyphs. On this pillar rested a metal box of peculiarly asymmetrical form; its hinged lid thrown back, and its interior holding what looked beneath the decade-deep dust to be an egg-shaped or irregularly spherical object some four inches through. Around the pillar in a rough circle were seven high-backed Gothic chairs still largely intact, while behind them, ranging along the dark-panelled walls, were seven colossal images of crumbling, black-painted plaster, resembling more than anything else the cryptic carven megaliths of mysterious Easter Island. In one corner of the cobwebbed chamber a ladder was built into the wall, leading up to the closed trap door of the windowless steeple above.

As Blake grew accustomed to the feeble light he noticed odd bas-reliefs on the strange open box of yellowish metal. Approaching, he tried to clear the dust away with his hands and handkerchief, and saw that the figurings were of a monstrous and utterly alien kind; depicting entities which, though seemingly alive, resembled no known life-form ever evolved on this planet. The four-inch seeming sphere turned out to be a nearly black, red-striated polyhedron with many irregular flat surfaces; either a very remarkable crystal of some sort or an artificial object of carved and highly polished mineral matter. It did not touch the bottom of the box, but was held suspended by means of a metal band around its centre, with seven queerly-designed supports extending horizontally to angles of the box's inner wall near the top. This stone, once exposed, exerted upon Blake an almost alarming fascination. He could scarcely tear his eyes from it, and as he looked at its glistening surfaces he almost fancied it was transparent, with half-formed worlds of wonder within. Into his mind floated pictures of alien orbs with great stone towers, and other orbs with titan mountains and no mark of life, and still remoter spaces where only a stirring in vague blacknesses told of the presence of consciousness and will.

When he did look away, it was to notice a somewhat singular mound of dust in the far corner near the ladder to the steeple. Just why it took his attention he could not tell, but something in its contours carried a message to his unconscious mind. Ploughing toward it, and brushing aside the hanging cobwebs as he went, he began to discern something grim about it. Hand and handkerchief soon revealed the truth, and Blake gasped with a baffling mixture of emotions. It was a human skeleton, and it must have been there for a very long time. The clothing was in shreds, but some buttons and fragments of cloth bespoke a man's grey suit. There were other bits of evidence — shoes, metal clasps, huge buttons for round cuffs, a stickpin of bygone pattern, a reporter's badge with the name of the old *Providence Telegram*, and a crumbling leather pocketbook. Blake examined the latter with care, finding within it several bills of antiquated issue, a celluloid advertising calendar for 1893, some cards with the name "Edwin M. Lillibridge," and a paper covered with pencilled memoranda.

This paper held much of a puzzling nature, and Blake read it carefully at the dim westward window. Its disjointed text included such phrases as the following:

Prof. Enoch Bowen home from Egypt May 1844 — buys old Free-Will Church in July — his archaeological work & studies in occult well known.

Dr. Drowne of 4th Baptist warns against Starry Wisdom in sermon 29 Dec. 1844.

Congregation 97 by end of '45.

1846 — 3 disappearances — first mention of Shining Trapezohedron.

7 disappearances 1848 — stories of blood sacrifice begin.

Investigation 1853 comes to nothing — stories of sounds.

Fr. O'Malley tells of devil-worship with box found in great Egyptian ruins — says they call up something that can't exist in light. Flees a little light, and banished by strong light. Then has to be summoned again. Probably got this from deathbed confession of Francis X. Feeney, who had joined Starry Wisdom in '49. These people say the Shining Trapezohedron shows them heaven & other worlds, & that the Haunter of the Dark tells them secrets in some way.

Story of Orrin B. Eddy 1857. They call it up by gazing at the crystal, & have a secret language of their own.

200 or more in cong. 1863, exclusive of men at front.

Irish boys mob church in 1869 after Patrick Regan's disappearance.

Veiled article in J. 14 March '72, but people don't talk about it.

6 disappearances 1876 — secret committee calls on Mayor Doyle.

Action promised Feb. 1877 — church closes in April.

Gang — Federal Hill Boys — threaten Dr — and vestrymen in May.

181 persons leave city before end of '77 — mention no names.

Ghost stories begin around 1880 — try to ascertain truth of report that no human being has entered church since 1877.

Ask Lanigan for photograph of place taken 1851 . . .

Restoring the paper to the pocketbook and placing the latter in his coat, Blake turned to look down at the skeleton in the dust. The implications of the notes were clear, and there could be no doubt but that this man had come to the deserted edifice forty-two years before in quest of a newspaper sensation which no one else had been bold enough to attempt. Perhaps no one else had known of his plan — who could tell? But he had never returned to his paper. Had some bravely-suppressed fear risen to overcome him and bring on sudden heart-failure? Blake stooped over the gleaming bones and noted their peculiar state. Some of them were badly scattered, and a few seemed oddly dissolved at the ends. Others were strangely yellowed, with vague suggestions of charring. This charring extended to some of the fragments of clothing. The skull was in a very peculiar state — stained yellow, and with a charred aperture in the top as if some powerful acid had eaten through the solid bone. What had happened to the skeleton during its four decades of silent entombment here Blake could not imagine.

Before he realized it, he was looking at the stone again, and letting its curious influence call up a nebulous pageantry in his mind. He saw processions of robed, hooded figures whose outlines were not human, and looked on endless leagues of desert lined with carved, sky-reaching monoliths. He saw towers and walls in nighted depths under the sea, and vortices of space where wisps of black mist floated before thin shimmerings of cold purple haze. And beyond all else he glimpsed an infinite gulf of darkness, where solid and semisolid forms were known only by their windy stirrings, and cloudy patterns of force seemed to superimpose order on chaos and hold forth a key to all the paradoxes and arcana of the worlds we know.

Then all at once the spell was broken by an access of gnawing, indeterminate panic fear. Blake choked and turned away from the stone, conscious of some formless alien presence close to him and watching him with horrible intentness. He felt entangled with something — something which was not in the stone, but which had looked through it at him — something which would ceaselessly follow him with a cognition that was not physical sight.

Plainly, the place was getting on his nerves — as well it might in view of his gruesome find. The light was waning, too, and since he had no illuminant with him he knew he would have to be leaving soon.

It was then, in the gathering twilight, that he thought he saw a faint trace of luminosity in the crazily angled stone. He had tried to look away from it, but some obscure compulsion drew his eyes back. Was there a subtle phosphorescence of radio-activity about the thing? What was it that the dead man's notes had said concerning a Shining Trapezohedron? What, anyway, was this abandoned lair of cosmic evil? What had been done here, and what might still be lurking in the bird-shunned shadows? It seemed now as if an elusive touch of foetor had arisen somewhere close by, though its source was not apparent. Blake seized the cover of the long-open box and snapped it down. It moved easily on its alien hinges, and closed completely over the unmistakably glowing stone.

At the sharp click of that closing a soft stirring sound seemed to come from the steeple's eternal blackness overhead, beyond the trap-door. Rats, without question — the only living things to reveal their presence in this accursed pile since he had entered it. And yet that stirring in the steeple frightened him horribly, so that he plunged almost wildly down the spiral stairs, across the ghoulish nave, into the vaulted basement, out amidst the gathering dust of the deserted square, and down through the teeming, fear-haunted alleys and avenues of Federal Hill towards the sane central streets and the home-like brick sidewalks of the college district.

During the days which followed, Blake told no one of his expedition. Instead, he read much in certain books, examined long years of newspaper files downtown, and worked feverishly at the cryptogram in that leather volume from the cobwebbed vestry room. The cipher, he soon saw, was no simple one; and after a long period of endeavour he felt sure that its language could not be English, Latin, Greek, French, Spanish, Italian, or German. Evidently he would have to draw upon the deepest wells of his strange erudition.

Every evening the old impulse to gaze westwards returned, and he saw the black steeple as of yore amongst the bristling roofs of a distant and half-fabulous world. But now it held a fresh note of terror for him. He knew the heritage of evil lore it masked, and with the knowledge his vision ran riot in queer new ways. The birds of spring were returning, and as he watched their sunset flights he fancied they avoided the gaunt, lone spire as never before. When a flock of them approached it, he thought, they would wheel and scatter in panic confusion — and he could guess at the wild twitterings which failed to reach him across the intervening miles.

It was in June that Blake's diary told of his victory over the cryptogram. The text was, he found, in the dark Aklo language used by certain cults of evil antiquity, and known to him in a halting way through previous researches. The diary is strangely reticent about what Blake deciphered, but he was patently awed and disconcerted by his results. There are references to a Haunter of the Dark awaked by gazing into the Shining Trapezohedron, and insane conjectures about the black gulfs of chaos from which it was called. The being is spoken of as holding all knowledge, and demanding monstrous sacrifices. Some of Blake's entries show fear lest the thing, which he seemed to regard as summoned, stalk abroad; though he adds that the streetlights form a bulwark which cannot be crossed.

Of the Shining Trapezohedron he speaks often, calling it a window on all time and space, and tracing its history from the days it was fashioned on dark Yuggoth, before ever the Old Ones brought it to earth. It was treasured and placed in its curious box by the crinoid things of Antarctica, salvaged from their ruins by the serpent-men of Valusia, and peered at aeons later in Lemuria by the first human beings. It crossed strange lands and stranger seas, and sank with Atlantis before a Minoan fisher meshed it in his net and sold it to swarthy merchants from nighted Khem. The Pharaoh Nephren-Ka built around it a temple with a windowless crypt, and did that which caused his name to be stricken from all monuments and records. Then it slept in the ruins of that evil fane which the priests and the new Pharaoh destroyed, till the delver's spade once more brought it forth to curse mankind.

Early in July the newspapers oddly supplement Blake's entries, though in so brief and casual a way that only the diary has called general attention to their contribution. It appears that a new fear had been growing on Federal Hill since a stranger had entered the dreaded church. The Italians whispered of unaccustomed stirrings and bumpings and scrapings in the dark windowless steeple, and called on their priests to banish an entity which haunted their dreams. Something, they said, was constantly watching at a door to see if it were dark enough to venture forth. Press items mentioned the longstanding local superstitions, but failed to shed much light on the earlier background of the horror. It was obvious that the young reporters of today are no antiquarians. In writing of these things in his diary, Blake expresses a curious kind of remorse, and talks of the duty of burying the Shining Trapezohedron and of banishing what he had evoked by letting daylight into the hideous jutting spire. At the same time, however, he displays the dangerous extent of his fascination, and admits a morbid longing — pervading even his dreams — to visit the accursed tower and gaze again into the cosmic secrets of the glowing stone.

Then something in the *Journal* on the morning of 17 July threw the diarist into a veritable fever of horror. It was only a variant of the other half-humorous items about the Federal hill restlessness, but to Blake it was somehow very terrible indeed. In the night a thunderstorm had put the city's lighting-system out of commission for a full hour, and in that black interval the Italians had nearly gone mad with fright. Those living near the dreaded church had sworn that the thing in the steeple had taken advantage of the street lamps' absence and gone down into the body of the church, flopping and bumping around in a viscous, altogether dreadful way. Towards the last it had bumped up to the tower, where there were sounds of the shattering of glass. It could go wherever the darkness reached, but light would always send it fleeing.

When the current blazed on again there had been a shocking commotion in the tower, for even the feeble light trickling through the grime-blackened, louvre-boarded windows was too much for the thing. It had bumped and slithered up into its tenebrous steeple just in time — for a long dose of light would have sent it back into the abyss whence the crazy stranger had called it. During the dark hour praying crowds had clustered round the church in the rain with lighted candles and lamps somehow shielded with folded paper and umbrellas — a guard of light to save the city from the nightmare that stalks in darkness. Once, those nearest the church declared, the outer door had rattled hideously.

But even this was not the worst. That evening in the Bulletin Blake read of what the reporters had found. Aroused at last to the whimsical news value of the scare, a pair of them had defied the frantic crowds of Italians and crawled into the church through the cellar window after trying the doors in vain. They found the dust of the vestibule and of the spectral nave ploughed up in a singular way, with bits of rotted cushions and satin pew-linings scattered curiously around. There was a bad odour everywhere, and here and there were bits of yellow stain and patches of what looked like charring. Opening the door to the tower, and pausing a moment at the suspicion of a scraping sound above, they found the narrow spiral stairs wiped roughly clean.

In the tower itself a similarly half-swept condition existed. They spoke of the heptagonal stone pillar, the overturned Gothic chairs, and the bizarre plaster images; though strangely enough the metal box and the old mutilated skeleton were not mentioned. What disturbed Blake the most — except for the hints of stains and charring and bad odours — was the final detail that explained the crashing glass. Every one of the tower's lancet windows was broken, and two of them had been darkened in a crude and hurried way by the stuffing of satin pew-linings and cushion-horsehair into the spaces between the slanting exterior louvre-boards. More satin fragments and bunches of horsehair lay scattered around the newly swept floor, as if someone had been interrupted in the act of restoring the tower to the absolute blackness of its tightly curtained days.

Yellowish stains and charred patches were found on the ladder to the windowless spire, but when a reporter climbed up, opened the horizontally-sliding trap-door and shot a feeble flashlight beam into the black and strangely foetid space, he saw nothing but darkness, and a heterogeneous litter of shapeless fragments near the aperture. The verdict, of course, was charlatanry. Somebody had played a joke on the superstitious hill-dwellers, or else some fanatic had striven to bolster up their fears for their own supposed good. Or perhaps some of the younger and more sophisticated dwellers had staged an elaborate

Weird Tales, December 1936

hoax on the outside world. There was an amusing aftermath when the police sent an officer to verify the reports. Three men in succession found ways of evading the assignment, and the fourth went very reluctantly and returned very soon without adding to the account given by the reporters.

From this point onwards Blake's diary shows a mounting tide of insidious horror and nervous apprehension. He upbraids himself for not doing something, and speculates wildly on the consequences of another electrical breakdown. It had been verified that on three occasions — during thunderstorms — he telephoned the electric light company in a frantic vein and asked that desperate precautions against a lapse of power be taken. Now and then his entries show concern over the failure of the reporters to find the metal box and stone, and the strangely marred old skeleton, when they explored the shadowy tower room. He assumed that these things had been removed — whither, and by whom or what, he could only guess. But his worst fears concerned himself, and the kind of unholy rapport he felt to exist between his mind and that lurking horror in the distant steeple — that monstrous thing of night which his rashness had called out of the ultimate black spaces. He seemed to feel a constant tugging at his will, and callers of that period remember how he would sit abstractedly at his desk and stare out of the west window at that far-off spire-bristling mound beyond the swirling smoke of the city. His entries dwell monotonously on certain terrible dreams, and of a strengthening of the unholy rapport in his sleep. There is mention of a night when he awakened to find himself fully dressed, outdoors, and headed automatically down College Hill towards the west. Again and again he dwells on the fact that the thing in the steeple knows where to find him.

The week following 30 July is recalled as the time of Blake's partial breakdown. He did not dress, and ordered all his food by telephone. Visitors remarked the cords he kept near his bed, and he said that sleep-walking had forced him to bind his ankles every night with knots which would probably hold or else waken him with the labour of untying. In his diary he told of the hideous experience which had brought the collapse. After retiring on the night of the 30th, he had suddenly found himself groping about in an almost black space. All he could see were short, faint, horizontal streaks of bluish light, but he could smell an overpowering foetor and hear a curious jumble of soft, furtive sounds above him. Whenever he moved he stumbled over something, and at each noise there would come a sort of answering sound from above — a vague stirring, mixed with the cautious sliding of wood on wood.

Once his groping hands encountered a pillar of stone with a vacant top, whilst later he found himself clutching the rungs of a ladder built into the wall, and fumbling his uncertain way upwards towards some region of intenser stench where a hot, searing blast beat down against him. Before his eyes a kaleidoscopic range of phantasmal images played, all of them dissolving at intervals into the picture of a vast, unplumbed abyss of night wherein whirled suns and worlds of an even profounder blackness. He thought of the ancient legends of Ultimate Chaos, at whose centre sprawls the blind idiot god Azathoth, Lord of All Things, encircled by his flopping horde of mindless and amorphous dancers, and lulled by the thin monotonous piping of a demoniac flute held in nameless paws.

Then a sharp report from the outer world broke through his stupor and roused him to the unutterable horror of his position. What it was, he never knew — perhaps it was some belated peal from the fireworks heard all summer on Federal Hill as the dwellers hail their various patron saints, or the saints of their native villages in Italy. In any event he shrieked aloud, dropped frantically from the ladder, and stumbled blindly across the obstructed floor of the almost lightless chamber that encompassed him.

He knew instantly where he was, and plunged recklessly down the narrow spiral staircase, tripping and bruising himself at every turn. There was a nightmare flight through a vast cobwebbed nave whose ghostly arches reached up to realms of leering shadow, a sightless scramble through a littered basement, a climb to regions of air and street lights outside, and a mad racing down a spectral hill of gibbering gables, across a grim, silent city of tall black towers, and up the steep eastward precipice to his own ancient door.

On regaining consciousness in the morning he found himself lying on his study floor fully dressed. Dirt and cobwebs covered him, and every inch of his body seemed sore and bruised. When he faced the mirror he saw that his hair was badly scorched while a trace of strange evil odour seemed to cling to his upper outer clothing. It was then that his nerves broke down. Thereafter, lounging exhaustedly about in a dressing-gown, he did little but stare from his west window, shiver at the threat of thunder, and make wild entries in his diary.

The great storm broke just before midnight on 8 August. Lightning struck repeatedly in all parts of the city, and two remarkable fireballs were reported. The rain was torrential, while a constant fusillade of thunder brought sleeplessness to thousands. Blake was utterly frantic in his fear for the lighting system, and tried to telephone the company around 1 a.m. though by that time service had been temporarily cut off in the interests of safety. He recorded everything in his diary — the large, nervous, and often undecipherable, hieroglyphs telling their own story of growing frenzy and despair, and of entries scrawled blindly in the dark.

He had to keep the house dark in order to see out of the window, and it appears that most of his time was spent at his desk, peering anxiously through the rain across the glistening miles of downtown roofs at the constellation of distant lights marking Federal Hill. Now and then he would fumblingly make an entry in his diary, so that detached phrases such as "The lights must not go"; "It knows where I am"; "I must destroy it"; and "it is calling to me, but perhaps it means no injury this time"; are found scattered down two of the pages.

Then the lights went out all over the city. It happened at 2.12 a.m. according to power-house records, but Blake's diary gives no indication of the time. The entry is merely, "Lights out — God help me."

On Federal Hill there were watchers as anxious as he, and rain-soaked knots of men paraded the square and alleys around the evil church with umbrella-shaded candles, electric flashlights, oil lanterns, crucifixes, and obscure charms of the many sorts common to southern Italy. They blessed each flash of lightning, and made cryptical signs of fear with their right hands when a turn in the storm caused the flashes to lessen and finally to cease altogether. A rising wind blew out most of the candles, so that the scene grew threateningly dark. Someone roused Father Merluzzo of Spirito Santo Church, and he hastened to the dismal square to pronounce whatever helpful syllables he could. Of the restless and curious sounds in the blackened tower, there could be no doubt whatever.

For what happened at 2.35 we have the testimony of the priest, a young, intelligent, and well-educated person; of Patrolman William J. Monohan of the Central Station, an officer of the highest reliability who had paused at that part of his beat to inspect the crowd; and of most of the seventy-eight men who had gathered around the church's high bank wall — especially those in the square where the eastward façade was visible. Of course there was nothing which can be proved as being outside the order of Nature. The possible causes of such an event are many. No one can speak with certainty of the obscure chemical processes arising in a vast, ancient, ill-aired, and long-deserted building of heterogeneous contents. Mephitic vapours — spontaneous combustion — pressure of gases born of long decay — any one of numberless phenomena might be responsible. And then, of course, the factor of conscious charlatanry can by no means be excluded. The thing was really quite simple in itself, and covered less than three minutes of actual time. Father Merluzzo, always a precise man, looked at his watch repeatedly.

It started with a definite swelling of the dull fumbling sounds inside the black tower. There had for some time been a vague exhalation of strange, evil odours from the church, and this had now become emphatic and offensive. Then at last there was a sound of splintering wood and a large, heavy object crashed down in the yard beneath the frowning easterly façade. The tower was invisible now that the candles would not burn, but as the object neared the ground the people knew that it was the smoke-grimed louvre-boarding of that tower's east window.

Immediately afterwards an utterly unbearable foetor welled forth from the unseen heights, choking and sickening the trembling watchers, and almost prostrating those in the square. At the same time the air trembled with a vibration as of flapping wings, and a sudden east-blowing wind more violent than any previous blast snatched off the hats and wrenched the dripping umbrellas from the crowd. Nothing definite could be seen in the candleless night, though some upward-looking spectators thought they glimpsed a great spreading blur of denser blackness against the inky sky — something like a formless cloud of smoke that shot with meteorlike speed towards the east.

That was all. The watchers were half numbed with fright, awe, and discomfort, and scarcely knew what to do, or whether to do anything at all. Not knowing what had happened, they did not relax their vigil; and a moment later they sent up a prayer as a sharp flash of belated lightning, followed by an earsplitting crash of sound, rent the flooded heavens. Half an hour later the rain stopped, and in fifteen minutes more the street lights sprang on again, sending the weary, bedraggled watchers relievedly back to their homes.

The next day's papers gave these matters minor mention in connection with the general storm reports. It seems that the great lightning flash and deafening explosion which followed the Federal Hill occurrence were even more tremendous farther east, where a burst of the singular foetor was likewise noticed. The phenomenon was most marked over College Hill, where the crash awakened all the sleeping inhabitants and led to a bewildered round of speculations. Of those who were already awake only a few saw the anomalous blaze of light near the top of the hill, or noticed the inexplicable upward rush of air which almost stripped the leaves from the trees and blasted the plants in the gardens. It was agreed that the lone, sudden lightning-bolt must have struck somewhere in this neighbourhood, though no trace of its striking could afterwards be found. A youth in the Tau Omega fraternity house thought he saw a grotesque and hideous mass of smoke in the air just as the preliminary flash burst, but his observation has not been verified. All of the few observers, however, agree as to the violent gust from the west and the flood of intolerable stench which preceded the belated stroke, whilst evidence concerning the momentary burned odour after the stroke is equally general.

These points were discussed very carefully because of their probable connection with the death of Robert Blake. Students in the Psi Delta house, whose upper rear windows looked into Blake's study, noticed the blurred white face at the westward window on the morning of the ninth, and wondered what was wrong with the expression. When they saw the same face in the same position that evening, they felt worried, and watched for the lights to come up in his apartment. Later they rang the bell of the darkened flat, and finally had a policeman force the door.

The rigid body sat bolt upright at the desk by the window, and when the intruders saw the glassy, bulging eyes, and the marks of stark, convulsive fright on the twisted features, they turned away in sickened dismay. Shortly afterwards the coroner's physician made an examination, and despite the unbroken window reported electrical shock, or nervous tension induced by electrical discharge, as the cause of death. The hideous expression he ignored altogether, deeming it a not improbable result of the profound shock as experienced by a person of such abnormal imagination and unbalanced emotions. He deduced these latter qualities from the books, paintings, and manuscripts found in the apartment, and from the blindly scrawled entries in the diary on the desk. Blake had prolonged his frenzied jottings to the last, and the broken-pointed pencil was found clutched in his spasmodically contracted right hand.

The entries after the failure of the lights were highly disjointed, and legible only in part. From them certain investigators have drawn conclusions differing greatly from the materialistic official verdict, but such speculations have little chance for belief among the conservative. The case of these imaginative theorists has not been helped by the action of superstitious Doctor Dexter, who threw the curious box and angled stone — an object certainly self-luminous as seen in the black windowless steeple where it was found — into the deepest channel of Narragansett Bay. Excessive imagination and neurotic unbalance on Blake's part, aggravated by knowledge of the evil bygone cult whose startling traces he had uncovered, form the dominant interpretation given those final frenzied jottings. These are the entries — or all that can be made of them:

Lights still out — must be five minutes now. Everything depends on lightning. Yaddith grant it will keep up! . . . Some influence seems beating through it . . . Rain and thunder and wind deafen . . . The thing is taking hold of my mind . . .

Trouble with memory. I see things I never knew before. Other worlds and other galaxies . . . Dark . . . The lightning seems dark and the darkness seems light . . .

It cannot be the real hill and church that I see in the

pitch-darkness. Must be retinal impression left by flashes. Heaven grant the Italians are out with their candles if the lightning stops!

What am I afraid of? Is it not an avatar of Nyarlathotep, who in antique and shadowy Khem even took the form of man? I remember Yuggoth, and more distant Shaggai, and the ultimate void of the black planets . . .

The long, winging flight through the void . . . cannot cross the universe of light . . . re-created by the thoughts caught in the Shining Trapezohedron . . . send it through the horrible abysses of radiance . . .

My name is Blake — Robert Harrison Blake of 620 East Knapp Street, Milwaukee, Wisconsin . . . I am on this planet . . .

Azathoth have mercy! — the lightning no longer flashes — horrible — I can see everything with a monstrous sense that is not sight — light is dark and dark is light . . . those people on the hill . . . guard . . . candles and charms . . . their priests . . .

Sense of distance gone — far is near and near is far. No light — no glass — see that steeple — that tower — window — can hear — Roderick Usher — am mad or going mad — the thing is stirring and fumbling in the tower.

I am it and it is I — I want to get out . . . must get out and unify the forces . . . it knows where I am . . .

I am Robert Blake, but I see the tower in the dark. There is a monstrous odour . . . senses transfigured . . . boarding at that tower window cracking and giving way . . . Iä . . . ngai . . . ygg . . .

I see it — coming here — hell-wind — titan blur — black wing — Yog Sothoth save me — the three-lobed burning eye . . .

1936.

Twilight.

Early in 1935, after Lovecraft's struggles with The *Shadow out of Time* yielded yet another sub-optimal (to his view) result, H.P. Lovecraft wrote despondently in a letter to E. Hoffman Price that he he feared that his fiction-writing career was now over, terminated by the hostile reception to *At the Mountains of Madness*. He added that, in hopes that his muse would deign to return to him, he intended to take another hiatus from fiction writing, like the one he took in 1908.

In 1936, he appeared to be doing just that.

Lovecraft did work on two major pieces of revision work in 1936: "In the Walls of Eryx," with Kenneth J. Sterling, and "The Night Ocean," by Robert H. Barlow. He wrote, of course, his usual copious volume of letters. And he also wrote several poems for friends.

It was one of these poems that became the last piece of weird writing ever penned by H.P. Lovecraft — a sonnet penned (or, more likely, typed, as his physical condition was by that time extremely frail) in December 1936, dedicated to his old California friend Clark Ashton Smith — who would, three months hence, be the sole surviving member of the "Three Musketeers of *Weird Tales*." (Robert E. Howard had shot himself six months before.)

In the Walls of Eryx.

BY KENNETH J. STERLING AND H.P. LOVECRAFT

12,000-WORD NOVELETTE; 1936.

This mid-sized novelette is the only piece of outright planet fiction in the Lovecraft canon, taking place on the planet Venus. It started out as a 6,000-word short story, which Sterling, a science fiction fan, dashed off and showed to Lovecraft — who, at this point, was already starting to suffer from the symptoms of the intestinal cancer that would shortly kill him. Lovecraft, as Sterling remembers it, revised the story so thoroughly that the finished product was almost entirely his work; but it doesn't really read like a Lovecraft story, and it's likely that he was at considerable pains to make sure it retained Sterling's ideas and writing style.

Written in early 1936, the story doesn't age well from a predicting-the-future standpoint; it depends for its plot on a complete absence of portable radio communication devices, and of course the surface of Venus is now known to be far too hot for life as we know it. But as 1930s planet-fiction goes, it's good stuff. It was well received when it was published in Weird Tales *in the October 1939 issue.*

ABOUT KENNETH J. STERLING (1921-1995).

In march of 1935, a 14-year-old Jewish boy who had just moved to Providence marched out of his house, made his way to 66 College Street, and rang the bell.

This was young Kenneth Sterling. Kenneth was a member of the Science Fiction League, and knew H.P. Lovecraft's work well; so when his family moved to Providence, he lost no time in meeting his new neighbor.

"Damn me if the little imp didn't talk like a man of 30," Lovecraft wrote in a letter to R.H. Barlow. "He's already sold a story to Wonder *[*Stories *magazine]... Hope he won't prove a nuisance—but I wouldn't for the world discourage him in his endeavors. He really does seem like an astonishingly promising brat."*

Sterling wasn't in Lovecraft's orbit for long. The following year, at the ripe old age of 15, he was admitted to Harvard, which took him away from Providence and from Lovecraft; subsequently he went to Johns Hopkins and became a medical doctor and medical-school professor, a calling that would channel his energies into entirely new and different directions. But before they did, he wrote "In the Walls of Eryx," with Lovecraft's help.

Before I try to rest I will set down these notes in preparation for the report I must make. What I have found is so singular, and so contrary to all past experience and expectations, that it deserves a very careful description.

I reached the main landing on Venus, March 18, terrestrial time; VI, 9 of the planet's calendar. Being put in the main group under Miller, I received my equipment—watch tuned to Venus's slightly quicker rotation—and went through the usual mask drill. After two days I was pronounced fit for duty.

Leaving the Crystal Company's post at Terra Nova around dawn, VI, 12, I followed the southerly route which Anderson had mapped out from the air. The going was bad, for these jungles are always half impassable after a rain. It must be the moisture that gives the tangled vines and creepers that leathery toughness, a toughness so great that a knife has to work ten minutes on some of them. By noon it was drier—the vegetation getting soft and rubbery so that my knife went through it easily, but even then I could not make much speed. These Carter oxygen masks are too heavy—just carrying one half wears an ordinary man out. A Dubois mask with sponge-reservoir instead of tubes would give just as good air at half the weight.

The crystal-detector seemed to function well, pointing steadily in a direction verifying Anderson's report. It is curious how that principle of affinity works—without any of the fakery of the old "divining rods" back home. There must be a great deposit of crystals within a thousand miles, though I suppose those damnable man-lizards always watch and guard it. Possibly they think we are just as foolish for coming to Venus to hunt the stuff as we think they are for grovelling in the mud whenever they see a piece of it, or for keeping that great mass on a pedestal in their temple. I wish they'd get a new religion, for they have no use for the crystals except to pray to them. Barring theology, they would let us take all we want—and even if they learned to tap them for power there'd be more than enough for their planet and the earth besides. I for one am tired of passing up the main deposits and merely seeking separate crystals out of jungle river-beds. Sometime I'll urge the wiping-out of these scaly beggars by a good stiff army from home. About twenty ships could bring enough troops across to turn the trick.

One can't call the damned things men for all their "cities" and towers. They haven't any skill except building—and using swords and poison darts—and I don't believe their so-called "cities" mean much more than ant-hills or beaver-dams. I doubt if they even have a real language—all the talk about psychological communication through those tentacles down their chests strikes me as bunk. What misleads people is their upright posture; just an accidental physical resemblance to terrestrial man.

I'd like to go through a Venus jungle for once without having to watch out for skulking groups of them or dodge their cursed darts. They may have been all right before we began to take the crystals, but they're certainly a bad enough nuisance now—with their dart-shooting and their cutting of our water pipes. More and more I come to believe that they have a special sense like our crystal-detectors. No one ever knew them to bother a man—apart from long-distance sniping—who didn't have crystals on him.

Around 1 p.m. a dart nearly took my helmet off, and I thought for a second one of my oxygen tubes was punctured. The sly devils hadn't made a sound, but three of them were closing in on me. I got them all by sweeping in a circle with my flame pistol, for even though their colour blended with the jungle, I could spot the moving creepers. One of them was fully eight feet tall, with a snout like a tapir's. The other two were average seven-footers. All that makes them hold their own is sheer numbers—even a single regiment of flame throwers could raise hell with them. It is curious, though, how they've come to be dominant on the planet. Not another living thing higher than the wriggling akmans and skorahs, or the flying tukahs of the other continent—unless of course those holes in the Dionaean Plateau hide something.

About two o'clock my detector veered westward, indicating isolated crystals ahead on the right. This checked up with Anderson, and I turned my course accordingly. It was harder going—not only because the ground was rising, but because the animal life and carnivorous plants were thicker. I was always slashing ugrats and stepping on skorahs, and my leather suit was all speckled from the bursting darohs which struck it from all sides. The sunlight was all the worse because of the mist, and did not seem to dry up the mud in the least. Every time I stepped my feet sank down five or six inches, and there was a sucking sort of "blup" every time I pulled them out. I wish somebody would invent a safe kind of suiting other than leather for this climate. Cloth of course would rot; but some thin metallic tissue that couldn't tear—like the surface of this revolving decay-proof record scroll—ought to be feasible sometime.

I ate about 3:30—if slipping these wretched food tablets through my mask can be called eating. Soon after that I noticed a decided change in the landscape—the bright,

Weird Tales, October 1939

"As he touched the gleaming surface he shuddered involuntarily."

poisonous-looking flowers shifting in colour and getting wraith-like. The outlines of everything shimmered rhythmically, and bright points of light appeared and danced in the same slow, steady tempo. After that the temperature seemed to fluctuate in unison with a peculiar rhythmic drumming.

The whole universe seemed to be throbbing in deep, regular pulsations that filled every corner of space and flowed through my body and mind alike. I lost all sense of equilibrium and staggered dizzily, nor did it change things in the least when I shut my eyes and covered my ears with my hands. However, my mind was still clear, and in a very few minutes I realized what had happened.

I had encountered at last one of those curious mirage-plants about which so many of our men told stories. Anderson had warned me of them, and described their appearance very closely — the shaggy stalk, the spiky leaves, and the mottled blossoms whose gaseous, dream-breeding exhalations penetrate every existing make of mask.

Recalling what happened to Bailey three years ago, I fell into a momentary panic, and began to dash and stagger about in the crazy, chaotic world which the plant's exhalations had woven around me. Then good sense came back, and I realized all I need do was retreat from the dangerous blossoms — heading away from the source of the pulsations, and cutting a path blindly — regardless of what might seem to swirl around me — until safely out of the plant's effective radius.

Although everything was spinning perilously, I tried to start in the right direction and hack my way ahead. My route must have been far from straight, for it seemed hours before I was free of the mirage-plant's pervasive influence. Gradually the dancing lights began to disappear, and the shimmering spectral scenery began to assume the aspect of solidity. When I did get wholly clear I looked at my watch and was astonished to find that the time was only 4:20. Though eternities had seemed to pass, the whole experience could have consumed little more than a half-hour.

Every delay, however, was irksome, and I had lost ground in my retreat from the plant. I now pushed ahead in the uphill direction indicated by the crystal-detector, bending every energy toward making better time. The jungle was still thick, though there was less animal life. Once a carnivorous blossom engulfed my right foot and held it so tightly that I had to hack it free with my knife; reducing the flower to strips before it let go.

In less than an hour I saw that the jungle growths were thinning out, and by five o'clock — after passing through a belt of tree-ferns with very little underbrush — I emerged on a broad mossy plateau. My progress now became rapid, and I saw by the wavering of my detector-needle that I was getting relatively close to the crystal I sought. This was odd, for most of the scattered, egg-like spheroids occurred in jungle streams of a sort not likely to be found on this treeless upland.

The terrain sloped upward, ending in a definite crest. I reached the top about 5:30 and saw ahead of me a very extensive plain with forests in the distance. This, without question, was the plateau mapped by Matsugawa from the air fifty years ago, and called on our maps "Eryx" or the "Erycinian Highland." But what made my heart leap was a smaller detail, whose position could not have been far from the plain's exact centre. It was a single point of light, blazing through the mist and seeming to draw a piercing, concentrated luminescence from the yellowish, vapour-dulled sunbeams. This, without doubt, was the crystal I sought — a thing possibly no larger than a hen's egg, yet containing enough power to keep a city warm for a year. I could hardly wonder, as I glimpsed the distant glow, that those miserable man-lizards worship such crystals. And yet they have not the least notion of the powers they contain.

Breaking into a rapid run, I tried to reach the unexpected prize as soon as possible; and was annoyed when the firm moss gave place to a thin, singularly detestable mud studded with occasional patches of weeds and creepers. But I splashed on heedlessly — scarcely thinking to look around for any of the skulking man-lizards. In this open space I was not very likely to be waylaid.

As I advanced, the light ahead seemed to grow in size and brilliancy, and I began to notice some peculiarity in its situation. Clearly, this was a crystal of the very finest quality, and my elation grew with every spattering step.

It is now that I must begin to be careful in making my report, since what I shall henceforward have to say involves unprecedented — though fortunately verifiable —matters. I was racing ahead with mounting eagerness, and had come within a hundred yards or so of the crystal — whose position on a sort of raised place in the omnipresent slime seemed very odd — when a sudden, overpowering force struck my chest and the knuckles of my clenched fists and knocked me over backward into the mud. The splash of my fall was terrific, nor did the softness of the ground and the presence of some slimy weeds and creepers save my head from a bewildering jarring. For a moment I lay supine, too utterly startled to think. Then I half mechanically stumbled to my feet and began to scrape the worst of the mud and scum from my leather suit.

Of what I had encountered I could not form the faintest idea. I had seen nothing which could have caused the shock, and I saw nothing now. Had I, after all, merely slipped in the mud? My sore knuckles and aching chest forbade me to think so. Or was this whole incident an illusion brought on by some hidden mirage-plant? It hardly seemed probable, since I had none of the usual symptoms, and since there was no place nearby where so vivid and typical a growth could lurk unseen. Had I been on the earth, I would have suspected a barrier of N-force laid down by some government to mark a forbidden zone, but in this humanless region such a notion would have been absurd.

Finally pulling myself together, I decided to investigate in a cautious way. Holding my knife as far as possible ahead of me, so that it might be first to feel the strange force, I started once more for the shining crystal — preparing to advance step by step with the greatest deliberation. At the third step I was brought up short by the impact of the knife-point on an apparently solid surface — a solid surface where my eyes saw nothing.

After a moment's recoil I gained boldness. Extending my gloved left hand I verified the presence of invisible solid matter — or a tactile illusion of solid matter — ahead of me. Upon moving my hand I found that the barrier was of substantial extent, and of an almost glassy smoothness, with no evidence of the joining of separate blocks. Nerving myself for further experiments, I removed a glove and tested the thing with my bare hand. It was indeed hard and glassy, and of a curious coldness as contrasted with the air around. I strained my eyesight to the utmost in an effort to glimpse some trace of the obstructing substance, but could discern nothing whatsoever. There was not even any evidence of refractive power as judged by the aspect of the landscape ahead. Absence of reflective power was proved by the lack of a glowing image of the sun at any point.

Burning curiosity began to displace all other feelings, and I enlarged my investigations as best I could. Exploring with my hands, I found that the barrier extended from the ground to some level higher than I could reach, and that it stretched off indefinitely on both sides. It was, then, a wall of some kind — though all guesses as to its materials and its purpose were beyond me. Again I thought of the mirage-plant and the dreams it induced, but a moment's reasoning put this out of my head.

Knocking sharply on the barrier with the hilt of my knife, and kicking at it with my heavy boots, I tried to interpret the sounds thus made. There was something suggestive of cement or concrete in these reverberations, though my hands had found the surface more glassy or metallic in feel. Certainly, I was confronting something strange beyond all previous experience.

The next logical move was to get some idea of the wall's dimensions. The height problem would be hard, if not insoluble, but the length and shape problem could perhaps be sooner dealt with. Stretching out my arms and pressing close to the barrier, I began to edge gradually to the left—keeping very careful track of the way I faced. After several steps I concluded that the wall was not straight, but that I was following part of some vast circle or ellipse. And then my attention was distracted by something wholly different— something connected with the still-distant crystal which had formed the object of my quest.

I have said that even from a great distance the shining object's position seemed indefinably queer—on a slight mound rising from the slime. Now—at about a hundred yards— I could see plainly despite the engulfing mist just what that mound was. It was the body of a man in one of the Crystal Company's leather suits, lying on his back, and with his oxygen mask half buried in the mud a few inches away. In his right hand, crushed convulsively against his chest, was the crystal which had led me here—a spheroid of incredible size, so large that the dead fingers could scarcely close over it. Even at the given distance I could see that the body was a recent one. There was little visible decay, and I reflected that in this climate such a thing meant death not more than a day before. Soon the hateful farnoth-flies would begin to cluster about the corpse. I wondered who the man was. Surely no one I had seen on this trip. It must have been one of the old-timers absent on a long roving commission, who had come to this especial region independently of Anderson's survey. There he lay, past all trouble, and with the rays of the great crystal streaming out from between his stiffened fingers.

For fully five minutes I stood there staring in bewilderment and apprehension. A curious dread assailed me, and I had an unreasonable impulse to run away. It could not have been done by those slinking man-lizards, for he still held the crystal he had found. Was there any connexion with the invisible wall? Where had he found the crystal? Anderson's instrument had indicated one in this quarter well before this man could have perished. I now began to regard the unseen barrier as something sinister, and recoiled from it with a shudder. Yet I knew I must probe the mystery all the more quickly and thoroughly because of this recent tragedy.

Suddenly—wrenching my mind back to the problem I faced— I thought of a possible means of testing the wall's height, or at least of finding whether or not it extended indefinitely upward. Seizing a handful of mud, I let it drain until it gained some coherence and then flung it high in the air toward the utterly transparent barrier. At a height of perhaps fourteen feet it struck the invisible surface with a resounding splash, disintegrating at once and oozing downward in disappearing streams with surprising rapidity. Plainly, the wall was a lofty one. A second handful, hurled at an even sharper angle, hit the surface about eighteen feet from the ground and disappeared as quickly as the first.

I now summoned up all my strength and prepared to throw a third handful as high as I possibly could. Letting the mud drain, and squeezing it to maximum dryness, I flung it up so steeply that I feared it might not reach the obstructing surface at all. It did, however, and this time it crossed the barrier and fell in the mud beyond with a violent spattering. At last I had a rough idea of the height of the wall, for the crossing had evidently occurred some twenty or twenty-one feet aloft.

With a nineteen—or twenty-foot vertical wall of glassy flatness, ascent was clearly impossible. I must, then, continue to circle the barrier in the hope of finding a gate, an ending, or some sort of interruption. Did the obstacle form a complete round or other closed figure, or was it merely an arc or semicircle? Acting on my decision, I resumed my slow leftward circling, moving my hands up and down over the unseen surface on the chance of finding some window or other small aperture. Before starting, I tried to mark my position by kicking a hole in the mud, but found the slime too thin to hold any impression. I did, though, gauge the place approximately by noting a tall cycad in the distant forest which seemed just on a line with the gleaming crystal a hundred yards away. If no gate or break existed I could now tell when I had completely circumnavigated the wall.

I had not progressed far before I decided that the curvature indicated a circular enclosure of about a hundred yards' diameter—provided the outline was regular. This would mean that the dead man lay near the wall at a point almost opposite the region where I had started. Was he just inside or just outside the enclosure? This I would soon ascertain.

As I slowly rounded the barrier without finding any gate, window, or other break, I decided that the body was lying within. On closer view the features of the dead man seemed vaguely disturbing. I found something alarming in his expression, and in the way the glassy eyes stared. By the time I was very near I believed I recognized him as Dwight, a veteran whom I had never known, but who was pointed out to me at the post last year. The crystal he clutched was certainly a prize—the largest single specimen I had ever seen.

I was so near the body that I could—but for the barrier—have touched it, when my exploring left hand encountered a corner in the unseen surface. In a second I had learned that there was an opening about three feet wide, extending from the ground to a height greater than I could reach. There was no door, nor any evidence of hinge marks bespeaking a former door. Without a moment's hesitation I stepped through and advanced two paces to the prostrate body—which lay at right angles to the hallway I had entered, in what seemed to be an intersecting doorless corridor. It gave me a fresh curiosity to find that the interior of this vast enclosure was divided by partitions.

Bending to examine the corpse, I discovered that it bore

no wounds. This scarcely surprised me, since the continued presence of the crystal argued against the pseudo-reptilian natives. Looking about for some possible cause of death, my eyes lit upon the oxygen mask lying close to the body's feet. Here, indeed, was something significant. Without this device no human being could breathe the air of Venus for more than thirty seconds, and Dwight—if it were he—had obviously lost his. Probably it had been carelessly buckled, so that the weight of the tubes worked the straps loose—a thing which could not happen with a Dubois sponge-reservoir mask. The half-minute of grace had been too short to allow the man to stoop and recover his protection—or else the cyanogen content of the atmosphere was abnormally high at the time. Probably he had been busy admiring the crystal—wherever he may have found it. He had, apparently, just taken it from the pouch in his suit, for the flap was unbuttoned.

I now proceeded to extricate the huge crystal from the dead prospector's fingers—a task which the body's stiffness made very difficult. The spheroid was larger than a man's fist, and glowed as if alive in the reddish rays of the weltering sun. As I touched the gleaming surface I shuddered involuntarily—as if by taking this precious object I had transferred to myself the doom which had overtaken its earlier bearer. However, my qualms soon passed, and I carefully buttoned the crystal into the pouch of my leather suit. Superstition has never been one of my failings.

Placing the man's helmet over his dead, staring face, I straightened up and stepped back through the unseen doorway to the entrance hall of the great enclosure. All my curiosity about the strange edifice now returned, and I racked my brains with speculations regarding its material, origin, and purpose.

That the hands of men had reared it I could not for a moment believe. Our ships first reached Venus only seventy-two years ago, and the only human beings on the planet have been those at Terra Nova. Nor does human knowledge include any perfectly transparent, non-refractive solid such as the substance of this building. Prehistoric human invasions of Venus can be pretty well ruled out, so that one must turn to the idea of native construction. Did a forgotten race of highly-evolved beings precede the man-lizards as masters of Venus? Despite their elaborately-built cities, it seemed hard to credit the pseudo-reptiles with anything of this kind. There must have been another race aeons ago, of which this is perhaps the last relique. Or will other ruins of kindred origin be found by future expeditions? The purpose of such a structure passes all conjecture—but its strange and seemingly non-practical material suggests a religious use.

Realizing my inability to solve these problems, I decided that all I could do was to explore the invisible structure itself. That various rooms and corridors extended over the seemingly unbroken plain of mud I felt convinced; and I believed that a knowledge of their plan might lead to something significant. So, feeling my way back through the doorway and edging past the body, I began to advance along the corridor toward those interior regions whence the dead man had presumably come. Later on I would investigate the hallway I had left.

Groping like a blind man despite the misty sunlight, I moved slowly onward. Soon the corridor turned sharply and began to spiral in toward the centre in ever-diminishing curves. Now and then my touch would reveal a doorless intersecting passage, and I several times encountered junctions with two, three, and four diverging avenues. In these latter cases I always followed the inmost route, which seemed to form a continuation of the one I had been traversing. There would be plenty of time to examine the branches after I had reached and returned from the main regions. I can scarcely describe the strangeness of the experience—threading the unseen ways of an invisible structure reared by forgotten hands on an alien planet!

At last, still stumbling and groping, I felt the corridor end in a sizeable open space. Fumbling about, I found I was in a circular chamber about ten feet across; and from the position of the dead man against certain distant forest landmarks I judged that this chamber lay at or near the centre of the edifice. Out of it opened five corridors besides the one through which I had entered, but I kept the latter in mind by sighting very carefully past the body to a particular tree on the horizon as I stood just within the entrance.

There was nothing in this room to distinguish it—merely the floor of thin mud which was everywhere present. Wondering whether this part of the building had any roof, I repeated my experiment with an upward-flung handful of mud, and found at once that no covering existed. If there had ever been one, it must have fallen long ago, for not a trace of debris or scattered blocks ever halted my feet. As I reflected, it struck me as distinctly odd that this apparently primordial structure should be so devoid of tumbling masonry, gaps in the walls, and other common attributes of dilapidation.

What was it? What had it ever been? Of what was it made? Why was there no evidence of separate blocks in the glassy, bafflingly homogenous walls? Why were there no traces of doors, either interior or exterior? I knew only that I was in a round, roofless, doorless edifice of some hard, smooth, perfectly transparent, non-refractive and non-reflective material, a hundred yards in diameter, with many corridors, and with a small circular room at the centre. More than this I could never learn from a direct investigation.

I now observed that the sun was sinking very low in the west—a golden-ruddy disc floating in a pool of scarlet and orange above the mist-clouded trees of the horizon. Plainly, I would have to hurry if I expected to choose a sleeping-spot on dry ground before dark. I had long before decided to camp for the night on the firm, mossy rim of the plateau near the crest whence I had first spied the shining crystal, trusting to my usual luck to save me from an attack by the man-lizards. It has always been my contention that we ought to travel in parties of two or more, so that someone can be on guard during sleeping hours, but the really small number of night attacks makes the Company careless about such things. Those scaly wretches seem to have difficulty in seeing at night, even with their curious glow-torches.

Having picked out again the hallway through which I had come, I started to return to the structure's entrance. Additional exploration could wait for another day. Groping a course as best I could through the spiral corridors—with only general sense, memory, and a vague recognition of some of the ill-defined weed patches on the plain as guides—I soon found myself once more in close proximity to the corpse. There were now one or two farnoth flies swooping over the helmet-covered face, and I knew that decay was setting in. With a futile instinctive loathing I raised my hand to brush away his vanguard of the scavengers—when a strange and astonishing thing became manifest. An invisible wall, checking the sweep of my arm, told me that—notwithstanding my careful retracing of the way—I had not indeed returned to the corridor in which the body lay. Instead, I was in a parallel hallway, having no doubt taken some wrong turn or fork among the intricate passages behind.

Hoping to find a doorway to the exit hall ahead, I continued my advance, but presently came to a blank wall. I would, then, have to return to the central chamber and steer my course anew. Exactly where I had made my mistake I could not tell. I glanced at the ground to see if by any miracle guiding footprints had remained, but at once realized that the thin mud held impressions only for a very few moments. There was little difficulty in finding my way to the centre again, and once there I carefully reflected on the proper outward course. I had kept too far to the right before. This time I must take a more leftward fork somewhere—just where, I could decide as I went.

As I groped ahead a second time I felt quite confident of my correctness, and diverged to the left at a junction I was sure I remembered. The spiralling continued, and I was careful not to stray into any intersecting passages. Soon, however, I saw to my disgust that I was passing the body at a considerable distance; this passage evidently reached the outer wall at a point much beyond it. In the hope that another exit might exist in the half of the wall I had not yet explored, I pressed forward for several paces, but eventually came once more to a solid barrier. Clearly, the plan of the building was even more complicated than I had thought.

I now debated whether to return to the centre again or whether to try some of the lateral corridors extending toward the body. If I chose this second alternative, I would run the risk of breaking my mental pattern of where I was; hence I had better not attempt it unless I could think of some way of leaving a visible trail behind me. Just how to leave a trail would be quite a problem, and I ransacked my mind for a solution. There seemed to be nothing about my person which could leave a mark on anything, nor any material which I could scatter—or minutely subdivide and scatter.

My pen had no effect on the invisible wall, and I could not lay a trail of my precious food tablets. Even had I been willing to spare the latter, there would not have been even nearly enough—besides which the small pellets would have instantly sunk from sight in the thin mud. I searched my pockets for an old-fashioned note-book—often used unofficially on Venus despite the quick rotting-rate of paper in the planet's atmosphere—whose pages I could tear up and scatter, but could find none. It was obviously impossible to tear the tough, thin metal of this revolving decay-proof record scroll, nor did my clothing offer any possibilities. In Venus's peculiar atmosphere I could not safely spare my stout leather suit, and underwear had been eliminated because of the climate.

I tried to smear mud on the smooth, invisible walls after squeezing it as dry as possible, but found that it slipped from sight as quickly as did the height-testing handfuls I had previously thrown. Finally I drew out my knife and attempted to scratch a line on the glassy, phantom surface—something I could recognize with my hand, even though I would not have the advantage of seeing it from afar. It was useless, however, for the blade made not the slightest impression on the baffling, unknown material.

Frustrated in all attempts to blaze a trail, I again sought the round central chamber through memory. It seemed easier to act back to this room than to steer a definite, predetermined course away from it, and I had little difficulty in finding it anew. This time I listed on my record scroll every turn I made—drawing a crude hypothetical diagram of my route, and marking all diverging corridors. It was, of course, maddeningly slow work when everything had to be determined by touch, and the possibilities of error were infinite; but I believed it would pay in the long run.

The long twilight of Venus was thick when I reached the central room, but I still had hopes of gaining the outside before dark. Comparing my fresh diagram with previous recollections, I believed I had located my original mistake, so once more set out confidently along the invisible hall-ways. I veered further to the left than during my previous attempts, and tried to keep track of my turnings on the records scroll in case I was still mistaken. In the gathering dusk I could see the dim line of the corpse, now the centre of a loathsome cloud of farnoth-flies. Before long, no doubt, the mud-dwelling sificlighs would be oozing in from the plain to complete the ghastly work. Approaching the body with some reluctance I was preparing to step past it when a sudden collision with a wall told me I was again astray.

I now realized plainly that I was lost. The complications of this building were too much for offhand solution, and I would probably have to do some careful checking before I could hope to emerge. Still, I was eager to get to dry ground before total darkness set in; hence I returned once more to the centre and began a rather aimless series of trials and errors—making notes by the light of my electric lamp. When I used this device I noticed with interest that it produced no reflection—not even the faintest glistening—in the transparent walls around me. I was, however, prepared for this; since the sun had at no time formed a gleaming image in the strange material.

I was still groping about when the dusk became total. A

heavy mist obscured most of the stars and planets, but the earth was plainly visible as a glowing, bluish-green point in the southeast. It was just past opposition, and would have been a glorious sight in a telescope. I could even make out the moon beside it whenever the vapours momentarily thinned. It was now impossible to see the corpse—my only landmark—so I blundered back to the central chamber after a few false turns. After all, I would have to give up hope of sleeping on dry ground. Nothing could be done till daylight, and I might as well make the best of it here. Lying down in the mud would not be pleasant, but in my leather suit it could be done. On former expeditions I had slept under even worse conditions, and now sheer exhaustion would help to conquer repugnance.

So here I am, squatting in the slime of the central room and making these notes on my record scroll by the light of the electric lamp. There is something almost humorous in my strange, unprecedented plight. Lost in a building without doors—a building which I cannot see! I shall doubtless get out early in the morning, and ought to be back at Terra Nova with the crystal by late afternoon. It certainly is a beauty— with surprising lustre even in the feeble light of this lamp. I have just had it out examining it. Despite my fatigue, sleep is slow in coming, so I find myself writing at great length. I must stop now. Not much danger of being bothered by those cursed natives in this place. The thing I like least is the corpse—but fortunately my oxygen mask saves me from the worst effects. I am using the chlorate cubes very sparingly. Will take a couple of food tablets now and turn in. More later.

LATER—AFTERNOON: VI, 13—There has been more trouble than I expected. I am still in the building, and will have to work quickly and wisely if I expect to rest on dry ground tonight. It took me a long time to get to sleep, and I did not wake till almost noon today. As it was, I would have slept longer but for the glare of the sun through the haze. The corpse was a rather bad sight—wriggling with sificlighs, and with a cloud of farnoth-flies around it. Something had pushed the helmet away from the face, and it was better not to look at it. I was doubly glad of my oxygen mask when I thought of the situation.

At length I shook and brushed myself dry, took a couple of food tablets, and put a new potassium chlorate cube in the electrolyser of the mask. I am using these cubes slowly, but wish I had a larger supply. I felt much better after my sleep, and expected to get out of the building very shortly.

Consulting the notes and sketches I had jotted down, I was impressed by the complexity of the hallways, and by the possibility that I had made a fundamental error. Of the six openings leading out of the central space, I had chosen a certain one as that by which I had entered—using a sighting-arrangement as a guide. When I stood just within the opening, the corpse fifty yards away was exactly in line with a particular lepidodendron in the far-off forest. Now it occurred to me that this sighting might not have been of sufficient accuracy—the distance of the corpse making its difference of direction in relation to the horizon comparatively slight when viewed from the openings next to that of my first ingress. Moreover, the tree did not differ as distinctly as it might from other lepidodendra on the horizon.

Putting the matter to a test, I found to my chagrin that I could not be sure which of three openings was the right one. Had I traversed a different set of windings at each attempted exit? This time I would be sure. It struck me that despite the impossibility of trail-blazing there was one marker I could leave. Though I could not spare my suit, I could—because of my thick head of hair—spare my helmet; and this was large and light enough to remain visible above the thin mud. Accordingly I removed the roughly hemi-spherical device and laid it at the entrance of one of the corridors—the right-hand one of the three I must try.

I would follow this corridor on the assumption that it was correct; repeating what I seemed to recall as the proper turns, and constantly consulting and making notes. If I did not get out, I would systematically exhaust all possible variations; and if these failed, I would proceed to cover the avenues extending from the next opening in the same way— continuing to the third opening if necessary. Sooner or later I could not avoid hitting the right path to the exit, but I must use patience. Even at worst, I could scarcely fail to reach the open plain in time for a dry night's sleep.

Immediate results were rather discouraging, though they helped me eliminate the right-hand opening in little more than an hour. Only a succession of blind alleys, each ending at a great distance from the corpse, seemed to branch from this hallway; and I saw very soon that it had not figured at all in the previous afternoon's wanderings. As before, however, I always found it relatively easy to grope back to the central chamber.

About 1 p.m. I shifted my helmet marker to the next opening and began to explore the hallways beyond it. At first I thought I recognized the turnings, but soon found myself in a wholly unfamiliar set of corridors. I could not get near the corpse, and this time seemed cut off from the central chamber as well, even though I thought I had recorded every move I made. There seemed to be tricky twists and crossings too subtle for me to capture in my crude diagrams, and I began to develop a kind of mixed anger and discouragement. While patience would of course win in the end, I saw that my searching would have to be minute, tireless and long-continued.

Two o'clock found me still wandering vainly through strange corridors—constantly feeling my way, looking alternately at my helmet and at the corpse, and jotting data on my scroll with decreasing confidence. I cursed the stupidity and idle curiosity which had drawn me into this tangle of unseen walls— reflecting that if I had let the thing alone and headed back as soon as I had taken the crystal from the body, I would even now be safe at Terra Nova.

Suddenly it occurred to me that I might be able to tunnel under the invisible walls with my knife, and thus effect a short cut to the outside — or to some outward-leading corridor. I had no means of knowing how deep the building's foundations were, but the omnipresent mud argued the absence of any floor save the earth. Facing the distant and increasingly horrible corpse, I began a course of feverish digging with the broad, sharp blade.

There was about six inches of semi-liquid mud, below which the density of the soil increased sharply. This lower soil seemed to be of a different colour — a greyish clay rather like the formations near Venus's north pole. As I continued downward close to the unseen barrier I saw that the ground was getting harder and harder. Watery mud rushed into the excavation as fast as I removed the clay, but I reached through it and kept on working. If I could bore any kind of a passage beneath the wall, the mud would not stop my wriggling out.

About three feet down, however, the hardness of the soil halted my digging seriously. Its tenacity was beyond anything I had encountered before, even on this planet, and was linked with an anomalous heaviness. My knife had to split and chip the tightly packed clay, and the fragments I brought up were like solid stones or bits of metal. Finally even this splitting and chipping became impossible, and I had to cease my work with no lower edge of wall in reach.

The hour-long attempt was a wasteful as well as futile one, for it used up great stores of my energy and forced me both to take an extra food tablet, and to put an additional chlorate cube in the oxygen mask. It has also brought a pause in the day's gropings, for I am still much too exhausted to walk. After cleaning my hands and arms of the worst of the mud I sat down to write these notes — leaning against an invisible wall and facing away from the corpse.

That body is simply a writhing mass of vermin now — the odour has begun to draw some of the slimy akmans from the far-off jungle. I notice that many of the efjeh-weeds on the plain are reaching out necrophagous feelers toward the thing; but I doubt if any are long enough to reach it. I wish some really carnivorous organisms like the skorahs would appear, for then they might scent me and wriggle a course through the building toward me. Things like that have an odd sense of direction. I could watch them as they came, and jot down their approximate route if they failed to form a continuous line. Even that would be a great help. When I met any the pistol would make short work of them.

But I can hardly hope for as much as that. Now that these notes are made I shall rest a while longer, and later will do some more groping. As soon as I get back to the central chamber — which ought to be fairly easy — I shall try the extreme left-hand opening. Perhaps I can get outside by dusk after all.

NIGHT: VI, 13 — New trouble. My escape will be tremendously difficult, for there are elements I had not suspected. Another night here in the mud, and a fight on my hands tomorrow. I cut my rest short and was up and groping again by four o'clock. After about fifteen minutes I reached the central chamber and moved my helmet to mark the last of the three possible doorways. Starting through this opening, I seemed to find the going more familiar, but was brought up short less than five minutes by a sight that jolted me more than I can describe.

It was a group of four or five of those detestable man-lizards emerging from the forest far off across the plain. I could not see them distinctly at that distance, but thought they paused and turned toward the trees to gesticulate, after which they were joined by fully a dozen more. The augmented party now began to advance directly toward the invisible building, and as they approached I studied them carefully. I had never before had a close view of the things outside the steamy shadows of the jungle.

The resemblance to reptiles was perceptible, though I knew it was only an apparent one, since these beings have no point of contact with terrestrial life. When they drew nearer they seemed less truly reptilian — only the flat head and the green, slimy, frog-like skin carrying out the idea. They walked erect on their odd, thick stumps, and their suction-discs made curious noises in the mud. These were average specimens, about seven feet in height, and with four long, ropy pectoral tentacles. The motions of those tentacles — if the theories of Fogg, Ekberg, and Janat are right, which I formerly doubted but am now more ready to believe — indicate that the things were in animated conversation.

I drew my flame pistol and was ready for a hard fight. The odds were bad, but the weapon gave me a certain advantage. If the things knew this building they would come through it after me, and in this way would form a key to getting out; just as carnivorous skorahs might have done. That they would attack me seemed certain; for even though they could not see the crystal in my pouch, they could divine its presence through that special sense of theirs.

Yet, surprisingly enough, they did not attack me. Instead they scattered and formed a vast circle around me — at a distance which indicated that they were pressing close to the unseen wall. Standing there in a ring, the beings stared silently and inquisitively at me, waving their tentacles and sometimes nodding their heads and gesturing with their upper limbs. After a while I saw others issue from the forest, and these advanced and joined the curious crowd. Those near the corpse looked briefly at it but made no move to disturb it. It was a horrible sight, yet the man-lizards seemed quite unconcerned. Now and then one of them would brush away the farnoth-flies with its limbs or tentacles, or crush a wriggling sificligh or akman, or an out-reaching efjeh-weed, with the suction discs on its stumps.

Staring back at these grotesque and unexpected intruders, and wondering uneasily why they did not attack me at once,

I lost for the time being the will-power and nervous energy to continue my search for a way out. Instead I leaned limply against the invisible wall of the passage where I stood, letting my wonder merge gradually into a chain of the wildest speculations. A hundred mysteries which had previously baffled me seemed all at once to take on a new and sinister significance, and I trembled with an acute fear unlike anything I had experienced before.

I believed I knew why these repulsive beings were hovering expectantly around me. I believed, too, that I had the secret of the transparent structure at last. The alluring crystal which I had seized, the body of the man who had seized it before me — all these things began to acquire a dark and threatening meaning.

It was no common series of mischances which had made me lose my way in this roofless, unseen tangle of corridors. Far from it. Beyond doubt, the place was a genuine maze — a labyrinth deliberately built by these hellish things whose craft and mentality I had so badly underestimated. Might I not have suspected this before, knowing of their uncanny architectural skill? The purpose was all too plain. It was a trap — a trap set to catch human beings, and with the crystal spheroid as bait. These reptilian things, in their war on the takers of crystals, had turned to strategy and were using our own cupidity against us.

Dwight — if this rotting corpse were indeed he — was a victim. He must have been trapped some time ago, and had failed to find his way out. Lack of water had doubtless maddened him, and perhaps he had run out of chlorate cubes as well. Probably his mask had not slipped accidentally after all. Suicide was a likelier thing. Rather than face a lingering death he had solved the issue by removing the mask deliberately and letting the lethal atmosphere do its work at once. The horrible irony of his fate lay in his position — only a few feet from the saving exit he had failed to find. One minute more of searching and he would have been safe.

And now I was trapped as he had been. Trapped, and with this circling herd of curious starers to mock at my predicament. The thought was maddening, and as it sank in I was seized with a sudden flash of panic which set me running aimlessly through the unseen hallways. For several moments I was essentially a maniac — stumbling, tripping, bruising myself on the invisible walls, and finally collapsing in the mud as a panting, lacerated heap of mindless, bleeding flesh.

The fall sobered me a bit, so that when I slowly struggled to my feet I could notice things and exercise my reason. The circling watchers were swaying their tentacles in an odd, irregular way suggestive of sly, alien laughter, and I shook my fist savagely at them as I rose. My gesture seemed to increase their hideous mirth — a few of them clumsily imitating it with their greenish upper limbs. Shamed into sense, I tried to collect my faculties and take stock of the situation.

After all, I was not as badly off as Dwight has been. Unlike him, I knew what the situation was — and forewarned is forearmed. I had proof that the exit was attainable in the end, and would not repeat his tragic act of impatient despair. The body — or skeleton, as it would soon be — was constantly before me as a guide to the sought — for aperture, and dogged patience would certainly take me to it if I worked long and intelligently enough.

I had, however, the disadvantage of being surrounded by these reptilian devils. Now that I realized the nature of the trap — whose invisible material argued a science and technology beyond anything on earth — I could no longer discount the mentality and resources of my enemies. Even with my flame-pistol I would have a bad time getting away — though boldness and quickness would doubtless see me through in the long run.

But first I must reach the exterior — unless I could lure or provoke some of the creatures to advance toward me. As I prepared my pistol for action and counted over my generous supply of ammunition it occurred to me to try the effect of its blasts on the invisible walls. Had I overlooked a feasible means of escape? There was no clue to the chemical composition of the transparent barrier, and conceivably it might be something which a tongue of fire could cut like cheese. Choosing a section facing the corpse, I carefully discharged the pistol at close range and felt with my knife where the blast had been aimed. Nothing was changed. I had seen the flame spread when it struck the surface, and now I realized that my hope had been vain. Only a long, tedious search for the exit would ever bring me to the outside.

So, swallowing another food tablet and putting another cube in the elecrolyser of my mask, I recommenced the long quest; retracing my steps to the central chamber and starting out anew. I constantly consulted my notes and sketches, and made fresh ones — taking one false turn after another, but staggering on in desperation till the afternoon light grew very dim. As I persisted in my quest I looked from time to time at the silent circle of mocking stares, and noticed a gradual replacement in their ranks. Every now and then a few would return to the forest, while others would arrive to take their places. The more I thought of their tactics the less I liked them, for they gave me a hint of the creatures' possible motives. At any time these devils could have advanced and fought me, but they seemed to prefer watching my struggles to escape. I could not but infer that they enjoyed the spectacle — and this made me shrink with double force from the prospect of falling into their hands.

With the dark I ceased my searching, and sat down in the mud to rest. Now I am writing in the light of my lamp, and will soon try to get some sleep. I hope tomorrow will see me out; for my canteen is low, and lacol tablets are a poor substitute for water. I would hardly dare to try the moisture in this slime, for none of the water in the mud-regions is potable except when distilled. That is why we run such long pipe lines to the yellow clay regions — or depend on rain-water when those devils find and cut our pipes. I have none too many chlorate cubes either, and must try to cut down my oxygen consumption as much as I can. My tunnelling attempt of the early afternoon, and my later panic flight, burned up a perilous amount of air. Tomorrow I will reduce physical exertion to the barest minimum until I meet the reptiles and have to deal with them. I must have a good cube supply for the journey back to Terra Nova. My enemies are still on hand; I can see a circle of their feeble glow-torches around me. There is a horror about those lights which will keep me awake.

NIGHT: VI, 14 — Another full day of searching and still no way out! I am beginning to be worried about the water problem, for my canteen went dry at noon. In the afternoon there was a burst of rain, and I went back to the central chamber for the helmet which I had left as a marker — using this as a bowl and getting about two cupfuls of water. I drank most of it, but have put the slight remainder in my canteen. Lacol tablets make little headway against real thirst, and I hope there will be more rain in the night. I am leaving my helmet bottom up to catch any that falls. Food tablets are none too plentiful, but not dangerously low. I shall halve my rations from now on. The chlorate cubes are my real worry, for even without violent exercise the day's endless tramping burned a dangerous number. I feel weak from my forced economies in oxygen, and from my constantly mounting thirst. When I reduce my food I suppose I shall feel still weaker.

There is something damnable — something uncanny — about this labyrinth. I could swear that I had eliminated certain turns through charting, and yet each new trial belies some assumption I had thought established. Never before did I realize how lost we are without visual landmarks. A blind man might do better — but for most of us sight is the king of the senses. The effect of all these fruitless wanderings is one of profound discouragement. I can understand how poor Dwight must have felt. His corpse is now just a skeleton, and the sificlighs and akmans and farnoth-flies are gone. The efjen-weeds are nipping the leather clothing to pieces, for they were longer and faster-growing than I had expected. And all the while those relays of tentacled starers stand gloatingly around the barrier laughing at me and enjoying my misery. Another day and I shall go mad if I do not drop dead from exhaustion.

However, there is nothing to do but persevere. Dwight would have got out if he had kept on a minute longer. It is just possible that somebody from Terra Nova will come looking for me before long, although this is only my third day out. My muscles ache horribly, and I can't seem to rest at all lying down in this loathesome mud. Last night, despite my terrific fatigue, I slept only fitfully, and tonight I fear will be no better. I live in an endless nightmare — poised between waking and sleeping, yet neither truly awake nor truly asleep. My hand shakes, I can write no more for the time being. That circle of feeble glow-torches is hideous.

LATE AFTERNOON: VI, 15 — Substantial progress! Looks good. Very weak, and did not sleep much till daylight. Then I dozed till noon, though without being at all rested. No rain, and thirst leaves me very weak. Ate an extra food tablet to keep me going, but without water it didn't help much. I dared to try a little of the slime water just once, but it made me violently sick and left me even thirstier than before. Must save chlorate cubes, so am nearly suffocating for lack of oxygen. Can't walk much of the time, but manage to crawl in the mud. About 2 p.m. I thought I recognized some passages, and got substantially nearer to the corpse — or skeleton — than I had been since the first day's trials. I was sidetracked once in a blind alley, but recovered the main trail with the aid of my chart and notes. The trouble with these jottings is that there are so many of them. They must cover three feet of the record scroll, and I have to stop for long periods to untangle them.

My head is weak from thirst, suffocation, and exhaustion, and I cannot understand all I have set down. Those damnable green things keep staring and laughing with their tentacles, and sometimes they gesticulate in a way that makes me think they share some terrible joke just beyond my perception.

It was three o'clock when I really struck my stride. There was a doorway which, according to my notes, I had not traversed before; and when I tried it I found I could crawl circuitously toward the weed-twined skeleton. The route was a sort of spiral, much like that by which I had first reached the central chamber. Whenever I came to a lateral doorway or junction I would keep to the course which seemed best to repeat that original journey. As I circled nearer and nearer to my gruesome landmark, the watchers outside intensified their cryptic gesticulations and sardonic silent laughter. Evidently they saw something grimly amusing in my progress — perceiving no doubt how helpless I would be in any encounter with them. I was content to leave them to their mirth; for although I realized my extreme weakness, I counted on the flame pistol and its numerous extra magazines to get me through the vile reptilian phalanx.

Hope now soared high, but I did not attempt to rise to my feet. Better crawl now, and save my strength for the coming encounter with the man-lizards. My advance was very slow, and the danger of straying into some blind alley very great, but nonetheless I seemed to curve steadily toward my osseous goal. The prospect gave me new strength, and for the nonce I ceased to worry about my pain, my thirst, and my scant supply of cubes. The creatures were now all massing around the entrance — gesturing, leaping, and laughing with their tentacles. Soon, I reflected, I would have to face the entire horde — and perhaps such reinforcements as they would receive from the forest.

I am now only a few yards from the skeleton, and am pausing to make this entry before emerging and breaking through the noxious band of entities. I feel confident that with my last ounce of strength I can put them to flight despite their numbers, for the range of this pistol is tremendous. Then a camp on the dry moss at the plateau's edge, and in the morning a weary trip through the jungle to Terra Nova. I shall be glad to see living men and the buildings of human beings again. The teeth of that skull gleam and grin horribly.

TOWARD NIGHT: VI, 15 — Horror and despair. Baffled again! After making the previous entry I approached still closer to the skeleton, but suddenly encountered an intervening wall. I had been deceived once more, and was apparently back where I had been three days before, on my first futile attempt to leave the labyrinth. Whether I screamed aloud I do not know — perhaps I was too weak to utter a sound. I merely lay dazed in the mud for a long period, while the greenish things outside leaped and laughed and gestured.

After a time I became more fully conscious. My thirst and weakness and suffocation were fast gaining on me, and with my last bit of strength I put a new cube in the electrolyser — recklessly, and without regard for the needs of my journey to Terra Nova. The fresh oxygen revived me slightly, and enabled me to look about more alertly.

It seemed as if I were slightly more distant from poor Dwight than I had been at that first disappointment, and I dully wondered if I could be in some other corridor a trifle more remote. With this faint shadow of hope I laboriously dragged myself forward — but after a few feet encountered a dead end as I had on the former occasion.

This, then, was the end. Three days had taken me nowhere, and my strength was gone. I would soon go mad from thirst, and I could no longer count on cubes enough to get me back. I feebly wondered why the nightmare things had gathered so thickly around the entrance as they mocked me. Probably this was part of the mockery — to make me think I was approaching an egress which they knew did not exist.

I shall not last long, though I am resolved not to hasten matters as Dwight did. His grinning skull has just turned toward me, shifted by the groping of one of the efjeh-weeds that are devouring his leather suit. The ghoulish stare of those empty eye-sockets is worse than the staring of those lizard horrors. It lends a hideous meaning to that dead, white-toothed grin.

I shall lie very still in the mud and save all the strength I can. This record — which I hope may reach and warn those who come after me — will soon be done. After I stop writing I shall rest a long while. Then, when it is too dark for those frightful creatures to see, I shall muster up my last reserves of strength and try to toss the record scroll over the wall and the intervening corridor to the plain outside. I shall take care to send it toward the left, where it will not hit the leaping band of mocking beleaguers. Perhaps it will be lost forever in the thin mud — but perhaps it will land in some widespread clump of weeds and ultimately reach the hands of men.

If it does survive to be read, I hope it may do more than merely warn men of this trap. I hope it may teach our race to let those shining crystals stay where they are. They belong to Venus alone. Our planet does not truly need them, and I believe we have violated some obscure and mysterious law — some law buried deep in the arcana of the cosmos — in our attempts to take them. Who can tell what dark, potent, and widespread forces spur on these reptilian things who guard their treasure so strangely? Dwight and I have paid, as others have paid and will pay. But it may be that these scattered deaths are only the prelude of greater horrors to come. Let us leave to Venus that which belongs only to Venus.

I am very near death now, and fear I may not be able to throw the scroll when dusk comes. If I cannot, I suppose the man-lizards will seize it, for they will probably realize what it is. They will not wish anyone to be warned of the labyrinth — and they will not know that my message holds a plea in their own behalf. As the end approaches I feel more kindly towards the things. In the scale of cosmic entity who can say which species stands higher, or more nearly approaches a space-wide organic norm — theirs or mine?

I have just taken the great crystal out of my pouch to look at in my last moments. It shines fiercely and menacingly in the red rays of the dying day. The leaping horde have noticed it, and their gestures have changed in a way I cannot understand. I wonder why they keep clustered around the entrance instead of concentrating at a still closer point in the transparent wall.

I am growing numb and cannot write much more. Things whirl around me, yet I do not lose consciousness. Can I throw this over the wall? That crystal glows so, yet the twilight is deepening.

Dark. Very weak. They are still laughing and leaping around the doorway, and have started those hellish glow-torches.

Are they going away? I dreamed I heard a sound . . . light in the sky.

REPORT OF WESLEY P. MILLER
SUPT. GROUP A
VENUS CRYSTAL CO.
(TERRA NOVA ON VENUS)
VI, 16:

Our operative A-49, Kenton J. Stanfield of 5317 Marshall Street, Richmond, Va., left Terra Nova early on VI, 12, for a short-term trip indicated by detector. Due back 13th or 14th. Did not appear by evening of 15th, so Scouting Plane FR-58 with five men under my command set out at 8 P.M. to follow route with detector. Needle showed no change from earlier readings.

Followed needle to Erycinian Highland, played strong searchlights all the way. Triple-range flame-guns and D-radiation cylinders could have dispersed any ordinary hostile force of natives, or any dangerous aggregation of carnivorous skorahs.

When over the open plain on Eryx we saw a group of moving lights which we knew were native glow-torches. As we approached, they scattered into the forest. Probably seventy-five to a hundred in all. Detector indicated crystal on spot where they had been. Sailing low over this spot, our lights picked out objects on the ground. Skeleton tangled in efjeh-weeds, and complete body ten feet from it. Brought plane down near bodies, and corner of wing crashed on unseen obstruction.

Approaching bodies on foot, we came up short against a smooth, invisible barrier which puzzled us enormously. Feeling along it near the skeleton, we struck an opening, beyond which was a space with another opening leading to the skeleton. The latter, though robbed of clothing by weeds, had one of the company's numbered metal helmets beside it. It was Operative B-9, Frederick N. Dwight of Koenig's division, who had been out of Terra Nova for two months on a long commission.

Between this skeleton and the complete body there seemed to be another wall, but we could easily identify the second man as Stanfield. He had a record scroll in his left hand and a pen in his right, and seemed to have been writing when he died. No crystal was visible, but the detector indicated a huge specimen near Stanfield's body.

We had great difficulty in getting at Stanfield, but finally succeeded. The body was still warm, and a great crystal lay beside it, covered by the shallow mud. We at once studied the record scroll in the left hand, and prepared to take certain steps based on its data. The contents of the scroll forms the long narrative prefixed to this report; a narrative whose main descriptions we have verified, and which we append as an explanation of what was found. The later parts of this account show mental decay, but there is no reason to doubt the bulk of it. Stanfield obviously died of a combination of thirst, suffocation, cardiac strain, and psychological depression. His mask was in place, and freely generating oxygen despite an alarmingly low cube supply.

Our plane being damaged, we sent a wireless and called out Anderson with Repair Plane PG-7, a crew of wreckers, and a set of blasting materials. By morning FH-58 was fixed, and went back under Anderson carrying the two bodies and the crystal. We shall bury Dwight and Stanfield in the company graveyard, and ship the crystal to Chicago on the next earth-bound liner. Later, we shall adopt Stanfield's suggestion — the sound one in the saner, earlier part of his report — and bring across enough troops to wipe out the natives altogether. With a clear field, there can be scarcely any limit to the amount of crystal we can secure.

In the afternoon we studied the invisible building or trap with great care, exploring it with the aid of long guiding cords, and preparing a complete chart for our archives. We were much impressed by the design, and shall keep specimens of the substance for chemical analysis. All such knowledge will be useful when we take over the various cities of the natives. Our type C diamond drills were able to bite into the unseen material, and wreckers are now planting dynamite preparatory to a thorough blasting. Nothing will be left when we are done. The edifice forms a distinct menace to aerial and other possible traffic.

In considering the plan of the labyrinth one is impressed not only with the irony of Dwight's fate, but with that of Stanfield as well. When trying to reach the second body from the skeleton, we could find no access on the right, but Markheim found a doorway from the first inner space some fifteen feet past Dwight and four or five past Stanfield. Beyond this was a long hall which we did not explore till later, but on the right-hand side of that hall was another doorway leading directly to the body. Stanfield could have reached the outside entrance by walking twenty-two or twenty-three feet if he had found the opening which lay directly behind him — an opening which he overlooked in his exhaustion and despair.

The Night Ocean.

BY ROBERT H. BARLOW AND H.P. LOVECRAFT

10,000-WORD NOVELETTE; 1936.

This novelette is a remarkable piece of writing, and definitely shows that Robert Barlow — who was still just 18 years old when he wrote it — was on track to become a truly exceptional writer. It's a slow-burning atmospheric story in which very little actually happens physically — but what does happen is steeped in subtextual horror.

Lovecraft himself gushed over the tale: "Holy Yuggoth, but it's a masterpiece!" he wrote. "Magnificent stuff — will bear comparison to the best of [Clark Ashton Smith]! Splendid rhythm, poetic imagery, emotional modulation and atmospheric power."

Not all readers will enjoy "The Night Ocean." But all — or nearly all — will be forced to admit it's a masterful piece of writing, especially in light of the fact that it came from the pen of an 18-year-old boy.

Barlow finished the story in August of 1936 while he was in Providence for an extended visit. It was first published in the Winter 1936 issue of The Californian.

I went to Ellston Beach not only for the pleasures of sun and ocean, but to rest a weary mind. Since I knew no person in the little town, which thrives on summer vacationists and presents only blank windows during most of the year, there seemed no likelihood that I might be disturbed. This pleased me, for I did not wish to see anything but the expanse of pounding surf and the beach lying before my temporary home.

My long work of the summer was completed when I left the city, and the large mural design produced by it had been entered in the contest. It had taken me the bulk of the year to finish the painting, and when the last brush was cleaned I was no longer reluctant to yield to the claims of health and find rest and seclusion for a time. Indeed, when I had been a week on the beach I recalled only now and then the work whose success had so recently seemed all-important. There was no longer the old concern with a hundred complexities of colour and ornament; no longer the fear and mistrust of my ability to render a mental image actual, and turn by my own skill alone the dim-conceived idea into the careful draught of a design. And yet that which later befell me by the lonely shore may have grown solely from the mental constitution behind such concern and fear and mistrust. For I have always been a seeker, a dreamer, and a ponderer on seeking and dreaming; and who can say that such a nature does not open latent eyes sensitive to unsuspected worlds and orders of being?

Now that I am trying to tell what I saw I am conscious of a thousand maddening limitations. Things seen by the inward sight, like those flashing visions which come as we drift into the blankness of sleep, are more vivid and meaningful to us in that form than when we have sought to weld them with reality. Set a pen to a dream, and the colour drains from it. The ink with which we write seems diluted with something holding too much of reality, and we find that after all we cannot delineate the incredible memory. It is as if our inward selves, released from the bonds of daytime and objectivity, revelled in prisoned emotions which are hastily stifled when we would translate them. In dreams and visions lie the greatest creations of man, for on them rests no yoke of line or hue. Forgotten scenes, and lands more obscure than the golden world of childhood, spring into the sleeping mind to reign until awakening puts them to rout. Amid these may be attained something of the glory and contentment for which we yearn, some adumbration of sharp beauties suspected but not before revealed, which are to us as the Grail to holy spirits of the mediaeval world. To shape these things on the wheel of art, to seek to bring some faded trophy from that intangible realm of shadow and gossamer, requires equal skill and memory. For although dreams are in all of us, few hands may grasp their moth-wings without tearing them.

Such skill this narrative does not have. If I might, I would reveal to you the hinted events which I perceived dimly, like one who peers into an unlit realm and glimpses forms whose motion is concealed. In my mural design, which then lay with a multitude of others in the building for which they were planned, I had striven equally to catch a trace of this elusive shadow-world, and had perhaps succeeded better than I shall now succeed. My stay in Ellston was to await the judging of that design; and when days of unfamiliar leisure had given me perspective, I discovered that — in spite of those weaknesses which a creator always detects most clearly — I had indeed managed to retain in line and colour some fragments snatched from the endless world of imagining. The difficulties of the process, and the resulting strain on all my powers, had undermined my health and brought me to the beach during this period of waiting.

Since I wished to be wholly alone, I rented (to the delight of the incredulous owner) a small house some distance from the village of Ellston — which, because of the waning season, was alive with a moribund bustle of tourists, uniformly uninteresting to me. The house, dark from the sea-wind though it had not been painted, was not even a satellite of the village; but swung below it on the coast like a pendulum beneath a still clock, quite alone upon a hill of weed-grown sand. Like a solitary warm animal it crouched facing the sea, and its inscrutable dirty windows stared upon a lonely realm of earth and sky and enormous sea. It will not do to use too much imagining in a narrative whose facts, could they be augmented and fitted into a mosaic, would be strange enough in themselves; but I thought the little house was lonely when I saw it, and that like myself, it was conscious of its meaningless nature before the great sea.

I took the place in late August, arriving a day before I was expected, and encountering a van and two workingmen unloading the furniture provided by the owner. I did not know then how long I would stay, and when the truck that brought the goods had left I settled my small luggage and locked the door (feeling very proprietary about having a house after months of a rented room) to go down the weedy hill and on the beach. Since it was quite square and had but one room, the house required little exploration. Two windows in each side provided a great quantity of light, and somehow a door had been squeezed in as an afterthought on the oceanward wall. The place had been built about ten years previously, but on account of its distance from Ellston village was difficult to rent even during the active summer season. There being no fireplace, it stood empty and alone from October until far into spring. Though actually less than a mile below Ellston, it seemed more remote; since a bend in the coast caused one to see only grassy dunes in the direction of the village.

The first day, half-gone when I was installed, I spent in the enjoyment of sun and restless water — things whose quiet majesty made the designing of murals seem distant and tiresome. But this was the natural reaction to a long concern with one set of habits and activities. I was through with my work and my vacation was begun. This fact, while elusive for the moment, showed in everything which surrounded me that afternoon of my arrival; and in the utter change from old scenes. There was an effect of bright sun upon a shifting sea of waves whose mysteriously impelled curves were strewn with what appeared to be rhinestones. Perhaps a watercolour might have caught the solid masses of intolerable light which lay upon the beach where the sea mingled with the sand. Although the ocean bore her own hue, it was dominated wholly and incredibly by the enormous glare. There was no other person near me, and I enjoyed the spectacle without the annoyance of any alien object upon the stage. Each of my senses was touched in a different way, but sometimes it seemed that the roar of the sea was akin to that great brightness, or as if the waves were glaring instead of the sun, each of these being so vigorous and insistent that impressions coming from them were mingled. Curiously, I saw no one bathing near my little square house during that or succeeding afternoons, although the curving shore included a wide beach even more inviting than that at the village, where the surf was dotted with random figures. I supposed that this was because of the distance and because there had never been other houses below the town. Why this unbuilt stretch existed, I could not imagine; since many dwellings straggled along the northward coast, facing the sea with aimless eyes.

I swam until the afternoon had gone, and later, having rested, walked into the little town. Darkness hid the sea from me as I entered, and I found in the dingy lights of the streets tokens of a life which was not even conscious of the great, gloom-shrouded thing lying so close. There were painted women in tinsel adornments, and bored men who were no longer young — a throng of foolish marionettes perched on the lip of the ocean-chasm; unseeing, unwilling to see what lay above them and about, in the multitudinous grandeur of the stars and the leagues of the night ocean.

I walked along that darkened sea as I went back to the bare little house, sending the beams of my flashlight out upon the naked and impenetrable void. In the absence of the moon, this light made a solid bar athwart the walls of the uneasy tide; and I felt an indescribable emotion born of the noise of the waters and the perception of my inconceivable smallness as I cast that tiny beam upon a realm immense in itself, yet only the black border of the earthly deep. That nighted deep, upon which ships were moving alone in the darkness where I could not see them, gave off the murmur of a distant, angry rabble.

When I reached my high residence I knew that I had passed no one during the mile's walk from the village, and yet there somehow lingered an impression that I had been all the while accompanied by the spirit of the lonely sea. It was, I thought, personified in a shape which was not revealed to me, but which moved quietly about beyond my range of comprehension. It was like those actors who wait behind darkened scenery in readiness for the lines which will shortly call them before our eyes to move and speak in the sudden revelation of the footlights. At last I shook off this fancy and sought my key to enter the place, whose bare walls gave a sudden feeling of security.

My cottage was entirely free of the village, as if it had wandered down the coast and was unable to return; and there I heard nothing of the disturbing clamour when I returned each night after supper. I generally stayed but a short while upon the streets of Ellston, though sometimes I went into the place for the sake of the walk it provided. There were all the multitude of curio-shops and falsely regal theatre-fronts that clutter vacation towns, but I never went into these; and the place seemed useful only for its restaurants. It was astonishing the number of useless things people found to do.

There was a succession of sun-filled days at first. I rose early, and beheld the grey sky agleam with promise of sunrise; a prophecy fulfilled as I stood witness. Those dawns were cold, and their colours faint in comparison to that uniform radiance of day which gives to every hour the quality of white noon. That great light, so apparent the first day, made each succeeding day a yellow page in the book of time. I noticed that many of the beach-people were displeased by the inordinate sun, whereas I sought it. After grey months of toil the lethargy induced by a physical existence in a region governed by the simple things — the wind and light and water — had a prompt effect upon me; and since I was anxious to continue this healing process, I spent all my time outdoors in the sunlight. This induced a state at once impassive and submissive, and gave me a feeling of security against the ravenous night. As darkness is akin to death, so is light to vitality. Through the heritage of a million years ago, when men were closer to the mother sea, and when the creatures of which we are born lay languid in the shallow, sun-pierced water, we still seek the primal things when we are tired, steeping ourselves within their lulling security like those early half-mammals which had not yet ventured upon the oozy land.

The monotony of the waves gave repose, and I had no other occupation than witnessing myriad ocean moods. There is a ceaseless change in the waters — colours and shades pass over them like the insubstantial expressions of a well-known face; and these are at once communicated to us by half-recognized senses. When the sea is restless, remembering old ships that have gone over her chasms, there comes up silently in our hearts the longing for a vanished horizon. But when she forgets, we forget also. Though we know her a lifetime, she must always hold an alien air, as if something too vast to have shape were lurking in the universe to which she is a door. The morning ocean, glimmering with a reflected mist of blue-white cloud and expanding diamond foam, has the eyes of one who ponders on strange things, and her intricately woven webs, through which dart myriad coloured fishes, hold the air of some great idle thing which will arise presently from the hoary immemorial chasms and stride upon the land.

I was content for many days, and glad that I had chosen the lonely house which sat like a small beast upon those rounded cliffs of sand. Among the pleasantly aimless amusements fostered by such a life, I took to following the edge of the tide (where the waves left a damp irregular outline rimmed with evanescent foam) for long distances; and sometimes I found curious bits of shell in the chance litter of the sea. There was an astonishing lot of debris on that inward-curving coast which my bare little house overlooked, and I judged that currents whose courses diverge from the village beach must reach that spot. At any rate, my pockets — when I had any — generally held vast stores of trash; most of which I threw away an hour or two after picking it up, wondering why I had kept it. Once, however, I found a small bone whose nature I could not identify, save that it was certainly nothing out of a fish; and I kept this, along with a large metal bead whose minutely carven design was rather unusual. This latter depicted a fishy thing against a patterned background of seaweed instead of the usual floral or geometrical designs, and was still clearly traceable though worn with years of tossing in the surf. Since I had never seen anything like it, I judged that it represented some fashion, now forgotten, of a previous year at Ellston, where similar fads were common.

I had been there perhaps a week when the weather began a gradual change. Each stage of this progressive darkening was followed by another subtly intensified, so that in the end the entire atmosphere surrounding me had shifted from day to evening. This was more obvious to me in a series of mental impressions than in what I actually witnessed, for the small house was lonely under the grey skies, and there was sometimes a beating wind that came out of the ocean bearing moisture. The sun was displaced by long intervals of cloudiness — layers of grey mist beyond whose unknown depth the sun lay cut off. Though it might glare with the old intensity above that enormous veil, it could not penetrate. The beach was a prisoner in a hueless vault for hours at a time, as if something of the night were welling into other hours.

Although the wind was invigorating and the ocean whipped into little churning spirals of activity by the vagrant flapping, I found the water growing chill, so that I could not stay in it as long as I had done previously, and thus I fell into the habit of long walks, which — when I was unable to swim — provided the exercise that I was so careful to obtain. These walks covered a greater range of sea-edge than my previous wanderings, and since the beach extended in a stretch of miles beyond the tawdry village, I often found myself wholly isolated upon an endless area of sand as evening drew close. When this occurred, I would stride hastily along the whispering sea-border, following the outline so that I should not wander inland and lose my way. And sometimes, when these walks were late (as they grew increasingly to be) I would come upon the crouching house that looked like a harbinger of the village. Insecure upon the wind-gnawed cliffs, a dark blot upon the morbid hues of the ocean sunset, it was more lonely than by the full light of either orb; and seemed to my imagination like a mute, questioning face turned toward me expectant of some action. That the place was isolated I have said, and this at first pleased me; but in that brief evening hour when the sun left a gore-splattered decline and darkness lumbered on like an expanding shapeless blot, there was an alien presence about the place: a spirit, a mood, an impression that came from the surging wind, the gigantic sky, and that sea which drooled blackening waves upon a beach grown abruptly strange. At these times I felt an uneasiness which had no very definite cause, although my solitary nature had made me long accustomed to the ancient silence and the ancient voice of nature.

These misgivings, to which I could have put no sure name, did not affect me long; yet I think now that all the while a gradual consciousness of the ocean's immense loneliness crept upon me, a loneliness that was made subtly horrible by intimations — which were never more than such — of some animation or sentience preventing me from being wholly alone.

The noisy, yellow streets of the town, with their curiously unreal activity, were very far away, and when I went there for my evening meal (mistrusting a diet entirely of my own ambiguous cooking) I took increasing and quite unreasonable care that I should return to the cottage before the late darkness, although I was often abroad until ten or so.

You will say that such action is unreasonable; that if I had feared the darkness in some childish way, I would have entirely avoided it. You will ask me why I did not leave the place since its loneliness was depressing me. To all this I have no reply, save that whatever unrest I felt, whatever of remote disturbance there was to me in brief aspects of the darkening sun or in the eager salt-brittle wind or in the robe of the dark sea that lay crumpled like an enormous garment so close to me, was something which had an origin half in my own heart, which showed itself only at fleeting moments, and which had no very long effect upon me. In the recurrent days of diamond light, with sportive waves flinging blue peaks at the basking shore, the memory of dark moods seemed rather incredible; yet only an hour or two afterward I might again experience those moods, and descend to a dim region of despair.

Perhaps these inward emotions were only a reflection of the sea's own mood; for although half of what we see is coloured by the interpretation placed upon it by our minds, many of our feelings are shaped quite distinctly by external, physical things. The sea can bind us to her many moods, whispering to us by the subtle token of a shadow or a gleam upon the waves, and hinting in these ways of her mournfulness or rejoicing. Always, she is remembering old things, and these memories, though we may not grasp them, are imparted to us, so that we share her gaiety or remorse. Since I was doing no work, seeing no person that I knew, I was perhaps susceptible to shades of her cryptic meaning which would have been overlooked by another. The ocean ruled my life during the whole of that late summer; demanding it as recompense for the healing she had brought me.

There were drownings at the beach that year, and while I heard of these only casually (such is our indifference to a death which does not concern us, and to which we are not witness), I knew that their details were unsavoury. The people who died—some of them swimmers of a skill beyond the average—were sometimes not found until many days had elapsed, and the hideous vengeance of the deep had scourged their rotten bodies. It was as if the sea had dragged them into a chasm-lair and had mulled them about in the darkness until, satisfied that they were no longer of any use, she had floated them ashore in a ghastly state. No one seemed to know what had caused these deaths. Their frequency excited alarm among the timid, since the undertow at Ellston was not strong, and since there were known to be no sharks at hand. Whether the bodies showed marks of any attacks I did not learn, but the dread of a death which moves among the waves and comes on lone people from a lightless, motionless place is a dread which men know and do not like. They must quickly find a reason for such a death, even if there are no sharks. Since sharks formed only a suspected cause, and one never to my knowledge confirmed, the swimmers who continued during the rest of the season were on guard against treacherous tides rather than against any possible sea-animal. Autumn, indeed, was not a great distance off, and some people used this as an excuse for leaving the sea, where men were snared by death, and going to the security of inland fields, where one cannot even hear the ocean.

So August ended, and I had been at the beach many days.

There had been a threat of a storm since the fourth of the new month, and on the sixth, when I set out for a walk in the damp wind, there was a mass of formless cloud, colourless and oppressive, above the ruffled leaden sea. The motion of the wind, directed toward no especial goal but stirring uneasily, provided a sensation of coming animation—a hint of life in the elements which might be the long-expected storm. I had eaten my luncheon at Ellston, and though the heavens seemed the closing lid of a great casket, I ventured far down the beach and away from both the town and my no-longer-to-be-seen house. As the universal grey became spotted with a carrion purple—curiously brilliant despite its sombre hue—I found that I was several miles from any possible shelter. This, however, did not seem very important; for despite the dark skies with their added glow of unknown presage I was in a curious mood of detachment paralleling that glow—a mood which flashed through a body grown suddenly alert and sensitive to the outline of shapes and meanings that were previously dim. Obscurely, a memory came to me; suggested by the likeness of the scene to one I had imagined when a story was read to me in childhood. That tale—of which I had not thought for many years—concerned a woman who was loved by the dark-bearded king of an underwater realm of blurred cliffs where fish-things lived, and who was taken from the golden-haired youth of her troth by a dark being crowned with a priest-like mitre and having the features of a withered ape. What had remained in the corner of my fancy was the image of cliffs beneath the water against the hueless, dusky no-sky of such a realm; and this, though I had forgotten most of the story, was recalled quite unexpectedly by the same pattern of cliff and sky which I then beheld. The sight was similar to what I had imagined in a year now lost save for random, incomplete impressions.

Suggestions of this story may have lingered behind certain irritating unfinished memories, and in certain values hinted to my senses by scenes whose actual worth was bafflingly small. Frequently, in flashes of momentary perception (the conditions more than the object being significant), we feel that certain isolated scenes and arrangements—a feathery landscape, a woman's dress along the curve of a road by afternoon, or the solidity of a century-defying tree against the pale morning sky—hold something precious, some golden virtue that we must grasp. And yet when such a scene or arrangement is viewed later, or from another point, we find that it has lost its value and meaning for us. Perhaps this is because the thing we see does not hold that elusive quality, but only suggests to the mind some very different thing which remains unremembered. The baffled mind, not wholly sensing the cause of its flashing appreciation, seizes on the object exciting it, and is surprised when there is nothing of worth therein. Thus it was when I beheld the purpling clouds. They held the stateliness and mystery of old monastery towers at twilight, but their aspect was also that of the cliffs in the old fairy-tale. Suddenly reminded of this lost image, I half expected to see, in the fine-spun dirty foam and among the waves which were now as if they had been poured of flawed black glass, the horrid figure of that ape-faced creature, wearing a mitre old with verdigris, advancing from its kingdom in some lost gulf to which those waves were sky.

I did not see any such creature from the realm of imagining, but as the chill wind veered, slitting the heavens like a rustling knife, there lay in the gloom of merging cloud and water only a grey object, like a piece of driftwood, tossing obscurely on the foam. This was a considerable distance out, and since it vanished shortly, may not have been wood, but a porpoise coming to the troubled surface.

I soon found that I had stayed too long contemplating the rising storm and linking my early fancies with its grandeur, for an icy rain began spotting down, bringing a more uniform gloom upon a scene already too dark for the hour. Hurrying along the grey sand, I felt the impact of cold drops upon my back, and before many moments my clothing was soaked throughout.

At first I had run, put to flight by the colourless drops whose pattern hung in long linking strands from an unseen sky, but after I saw that refuge was too far to reach in anything like a dry state, I slackened my pace, and returned home as if I had walked under clear skies. There was not much reason to hurry, although I did not idle as upon previous occasions. The constraining wet garments were cold upon me; and with the gathering darkness, and the wind that rose endlessly from the ocean, I could not repress a shiver. Yet there was, beside the discomfort of the precipitous rain, an exhilaration latent in the purplish ravelled masses of cloud and the stimulated reactions of my body. In a mood half of exultant pleasure from resisting the rain (which streamed from me now, and filled my shoes and pockets) and half of strange appreciation of those morbid, dominant skies which hovered with dark wings above the shifting eternal sea, I tramped along the grey corridor of Ellston Beach.

More rapidly than I had expected the crouching house showed in the oblique, flapping rain, and all the weeds of the sand cliff writhed in accompaniment to the frantic wind, as if they would uproot themselves to join the far-travelling element. Sea and sky had altered not at all, and the scene was that which had accompanied me, save that there was now painted upon it the hunching roof that seemed to bend from the assailing rain. I hurried up the insecure steps, and let myself into a dry room, where, unconsciously surprised that I was free of the nagging wind, I stood for a moment with water rilling from every inch of me.

There are two windows in the front of that house, one on each side, and these face nearly straight upon the ocean; which I now saw half obscured by the combined veils of the rain and of the imminent night. From these windows I looked as I dressed myself in a motley array of dry garments seized from convenient hangers and from a chair too laden to sit upon. I was prisoned on all sides by an unnaturally increased dusk which had filtered down at some undefined hour under cover of the storm. How long I had been on the reaches of wet grey sand, or what the real time was, I could not tell, though a moment's search produced my watch — fortunately left behind and thus avoiding the uniform wetness of my clothing. I half guessed the hour from the dimly seen hands, which were only slightly less indecipherable than the surrounding figures. In another moment my sight penetrated the gloom (greater in the house than beyond the bleared window) and saw that it was 6:45.

There had been no one upon the beach as I came in, and naturally I expected to see no further swimmers that night. Yet when I looked again from the window there appeared surely to be figures blotting the grime of the wet evening. I counted three moving about in some incomprehensible manner, and close to the house another — which may not have been a person, but a wave-ejected log, for the surf was now pounding fiercely. I was startled to no little degree, and wondered for what purpose those hardy persons stayed out in such a storm. And then I thought that perhaps like myself they had been caught unintentionally in the rain and had surrendered to the watery gusts. In another moment, prompted by a certain civilised hospitality which overcame my love of solitude, I stepped to the door and emerged momentarily (at the cost of another wetting, for the rain promptly descended upon me in exultant fury) on the small porch, gesticulating toward the people. But whether they did not see me, or did not understand, they made no returning signal. Dim in the evening, they stood as if half-surprised, or as if they awaited some other action from me. There was in their attitude something of that cryptic blankness, signifying anything or nothing, which the house wore about itself as seen in the morbid sunset. Abruptly there came to me a feeling that a sinister quality lurked about those unmoving figures who chose to stay in the rainy night upon a beach deserted by all people, and I closed the door with a surge of annoyance which sought all too vainly to disguise a deeper emotion of fear; a consuming fright that welled up from the shadows of my consciousness. A moment later, when I had stepped to the window, there seemed to be nothing outside but the portentous night.

Vaguely puzzled, and even more vaguely frightened — like one who has seen no alarming thing, but is apprehensive of what may be found in the dark street he is soon compelled to cross — I decided that I had very possibly seen no one, and that the murky air had deceived me.

The aura of isolation about the place increased that night, though just out of sight on the northward beach a hundred houses rose in the rainy darkness, their light bleared and yellow above streets of polished glass, like goblin-eyes reflected in an oily forest pool. Yet because I could not see them, or even reach them in bad weather — since I had no car nor any way to leave the crouching house except by walking in the figure-haunted darkness — I realized quite suddenly that I was, to all intents, alone with the dreary sea that rose and subsided unseen, unkenned, in the mist. And the voice of the sea had become a hoarse groan, like that of something wounded which shifts about before trying to rise.

Fighting away the prevalent gloom with a soiled lamp — for the darkness crept in at my windows and sat peering obscurely at me from the corners like a patient animal — I prepared my food, since I had no intention of going to the village. The hour seemed incredibly advanced, though it was not yet nine o'clock when I went to bed. Darkness had come early and furtively, and throughout the remainder of my stay lingered evasively over each scene and action which I beheld. Something had settled out of the night — something forever undefined, but stirring a latent sense within me, so that I was like a beast expecting the momentary rustle of an enemy.

There were hours of wind, and sheets of the downpour flapped endlessly on the meagre walls barring it from me. Lulls came in which I heard the mumbling sea, and I could guess that large formless waves jostled one another in the pallid whine of the winds, and flung on the beach a spray bitter with salt. Yet in the very monotony of the restless elements I found a lethargic note, a sound that beguiled me, after a time, into slumber grey and colourless as the night. The sea continued its mad monologue, and the wind her nagging, but these were shut out by the walls of unconsciousness, and for a time the night ocean was banished from a sleeping mind.

Morning brought an enfeebled sun — a sun like that which men will see when the earth is old, if there are any men left: a sun more weary than the shrouded, moribund sky. Faint echo of its old image, Phoebus strove to pierce the ragged, ambiguous clouds as I awoke, at moments sending a wash of pale gold rippling across the northwestern interior of my house, at others waning till it was only a luminous ball, like some incredible plaything forgotten on the celestial lawn. After a while the falling rain — which must have continued throughout the previous night — succeeded in washing away those vestiges of purple cloud which had been like the ocean-cliffs in an old fairy-tale. Cheated alike of the setting and rising sun, that day merged with the day before, as if the intervening storm had not ushered a long darkness into the world, but had swollen and subsided into one long afternoon. Gaining heart, the furtive sun exerted all his force in dispelling the old mist, streaked now like a dirty window, and cast it from his realm. The shallow blue day advanced as those grimy wisps retreated, and the loneliness which had encircled me welled back into a watchful place of retreat, whence it went no farther, but crouched and waited.

The ancient brightness was now once more upon the sun, and the old glitter on the waves, whose playful blue shapes had flocked upon that coast ere man was born, and would rejoice unseen when he was forgotten in the sepulchre of time. Influenced by these thin assurances, like one who believes the smile of friendship on an enemy's features, I opened my door, and as it swung outward, a black spot upon the inward burst of light, I saw the beach washed clean of any track, as if no foot before mine had disturbed the smooth sand. With the quick lift of spirit that follows a period of uneasy depression, I felt — in a purely yielding fashion and without volition — that my own memory was washed clean of all the mistrust and suspicion and disease-like fear of a lifetime, just as the filth of the water's edge succumbs to a particularly high tide, and is carried out of sight. There was a scent of soaked, brackish grass, like the mouldy pages of a book, commingled with a sweet odour born of the hot sunlight upon inland meadows, and these were borne into me like an exhilarating drink, seeping and tingling through my veins as if they would convey to me something of their own impalpable nature, and float me dizzily in the aimless breeze. And conspiring with these things, the sun continued to shower upon me, like the rain of yesterday, an incessant array of bright spears; as if it also wished to hide that suspected background presence which moved beyond my sight and was betrayed only by a careless rustle on the borders of my consciousness, or by the aspect of blank figures staring out of an ocean void.

That sun, a fierce ball solitary in the whirlpool of infinity, was like a horde of golden moths against my upturned face. A bubbling white grail of fire divine and incomprehensible, it withheld from me a thousand promised mirages where it granted one. For the sun did actually seem to indicate realms, secure and fanciful, where if I but knew the path I might wander in this curious exultation. Such things come of our own natures, for life has never yielded for one moment her secrets; and it is only in our interpretation of their hinted images that we may find ecstasy or dullness, according to a deliberately induced mood. Yet ever and again we must succumb to her deceptions, believing for the moment that we may this time find the with-held joy.

And in this way the fresh sweetness of the wind, on a morning following the haunted darkness (whose evil intimations had given me a greater uneasiness than any menace to my body), whispered to me of ancient mysteries only half-linked with earth, and of pleasures that were the sharper because I felt that I might experience only a part of them. The sun and wind and that scent that rose upon them told me of festivals of gods whose senses are a millionfold more poignant than man's and whose joys are a millionfold more subtle and prolonged. These things, they hinted, could be mine if I gave myself wholly into their bright deceptive power. And the sun, a crouching god with naked celestial flesh, an unknown, too-mighty furnace upon which eye might not look, seemed almost sacred in the glow of my newly sharpened emotions. The ethereal thunderous light it gave was something before which all things must worship astonished. The slinking leopard in his green-chasmed forest must have paused briefly to consider its leaf-scattered rays, and all things nurtured by it must have cherished its bright message on such a day. For when it is absent in the far reaches of eternity, earth will be lost and black against an illimitable void. That morning, in which I shared the fire of life, and whose brief moment of pleasure is secure against the ravenous years, was astir with the beckoning of strange things whose elusive names can never be written.

As I made my way toward the village, wondering how it might look after a long-needed scrubbing by the industrious rain, I saw, tangled in a glimmer of sunlit moisture that was poured over it like a yellow vintage, a small object like a hand, some twenty feet ahead of me, and touched by the repetitious foam. The shock and disgust born in my startled mind when I saw that it was indeed a piece of rotten flesh overcame my new contentment and engendered a shocked suspicion that it might actually be a hand. Certainly, no fish, or part of one, could assume that look, and I thought I saw mushy fingers wed in decay. I turned the thing over with my foot, not wishing to touch so foul an object, and it adhered stickily to the leather shoe, as if clutching with the grasp of corruption. The thing, whose shape was nearly lost, held too much resemblance to what I feared it might be; and I pushed it into the willing grasp of a seething wave, which took it from sight with an alacrity not often shown by those ravelled edges of the sea. Perhaps I should have reported my find, yet its nature was too ambiguous to make action natural. Since it had been partly eaten by some ocean-dwelling monstrousness, I did not think it identifiable enough to form evidence of an unknown but possible tragedy. The numerous drownings, of course, came into my mind — as well as other things lacking in wholesomeness, some of which remained only as possibilities. Whatever the storm-dislodged fragment may have been, and whether it were fish or some animal akin to man, I have never spoken of it until now. After all, there was no proof that it had not merely been distorted by rottenness into that shape.

I approached the town, sickened by the presence of such an object amidst the apparent beauty of the clean beach, though it was horribly typical of the indifference of death in a nature which mingles rottenness with beauty, and perhaps loves the former more. In Ellston I heard of no recent drowning or other mishap of the sea, and found no reference to such in the columns of the local paper — the only one I read during my stay.

It is difficult to describe the mental state in which succeeding days found me. Always susceptible to morbid emotions whose dark anguish might be induced by things outside myself, or might spring from the abysses of my own spirit, I was ridden by a feeling which was not of fear or despair, or anything akin to these, but was rather a perception of the brief hideousness and underlying filth of life — a feeling partly a reflection of my internal nature and partly a result of broodings induced by that gnawed rotten object which may have been a hand. In those days my mind was a place of shadowed cliffs and dark moving figures, like the ancient unsuspected realm which the fairy-tale recalled to me. I felt, in brief agonies of disillusionment, the gigantic blackness of this overwhelming universe, in which my days and the days of my race were as nothing to the shattered stars; a universe in which each action is vain and even the emotion of grief a wasted thing. The hours I had previously spent in something of regained health, contentment and physical well-being were given now (as if those days of the previous week were something definitely ended) to an indolence like that of a man who no longer cares to live. I was engulfed by a piteous lethargic fear of some ineluctable doom which would be, I felt, the completed hate of the peering stars and of the black enormous waves that hoped to clasp my bones within them — the vengeance of all the indifferent, horrendous majesty of the night ocean.

Something of the darkness and restlessness of the sea had penetrated my heart, so that I lived in an unreasoning, unperceiving torment, a torment none the less acute because of the subtlety of its origin and the strange, unmotivated quality of its vampiric existence. Before my eyes lay the phantasmagoria of the purpling clouds, the strange silver bauble, the recurrent stagnant foam, the loneliness of that bleak-eyed house, and the mockery of the puppet town. I no longer went to the village, for it seemed only a travesty of life. Like my own soul, it stood upon a dark, enveloping sea — a sea grown slowly hateful to me. And among these images, corrupt and festering, dwelt that of an object whose human contours left ever smaller the doubt of what it once had been.

These scribbled words can never tell of the hideous loneliness (something I did not even wish assuaged, so deeply was it embedded in my heart) which had insinuated itself within me, mumbling of terrible and unknown things stealthily circling nearer. It was not a madness: rather it was a too clear and naked perception of the darkness beyond this frail existence, lit by a momentary sun no more secure than ourselves: a realization of futility that few can experience and ever again touch the life about them: a knowledge that turn as I might, battle as I might with all the remaining power of my spirit, I could neither win an inch of ground from the inimical universe, nor hold for even a moment the life entrusted to me. Fearing death as I did life, burdened with a nameless dread yet unwilling to leave the scenes evoking it, I awaited whatever consummating horror was shifting itself in the immense region beyond the walls of consciousness.

Thus autumn found me, and what I had gained from the sea was lost back into it. Autumn on the beaches — a drear time betokened by no scarlet leaf nor any other accustomed sign. A frightening sea which changes not, though man changes. There was only a chilling of the waters, in which I no longer cared to enter — a further darkening of the pall-like sky, as if eternities of snow were waiting to descend upon the ghastly waves. Once that descent began, it would never cease, but would continue beneath the white and the yellow and the crimson sun and beneath that ultimate small ruby which shall yield only to the futilities of night. The once friendly waters babbled meaningfully at me, and eyed me with a strange regard; yet whether the darkness of the scene were a reflection of my own broodings, or whether the gloom within me were caused by what lay without, I could not have told. Upon the beach and me alike had fallen a shadow, like that of a bird which flies silently overhead — a bird whose watching eyes we do not suspect till the image on the ground repeats the image in the sky, and we look suddenly upward to find that something has been circling above us hitherto unseen. The day was in late September, and the town had closed the resorts where mad frivolity ruled empty, fear-haunted lives, and where raddled puppets performed their summer antics. The puppets were cast aside, smeared with the painted smiles and frowns they had last assumed, and there were not a hundred people left in the town. Again the gaudy, stucco-fronted buildings lining the shore were permitted to crumble undisturbed in the wind. As the month advanced to the day of which I speak, there grew in me the light of a grey, infernal dawn, wherein I felt some dark thaumaturgy would be completed. Since I feared such a thaumaturgy less than a continuance of my horrible suspicions — less than the too-elusive hints of something monstrous lurking behind the great stage — it was with more speculation than actual fear that I waited unendingly for the day of horror which seemed to be nearing.

The day, I repeat, was late in September, though whether the 22nd or 23rd I am uncertain. Such details have fled before the recollection of those uncompleted happenings — episodes with which no orderly existence should be plagued, because of the damnable suggestions (and only suggestions) they contain. I knew the time with an intuitive distress of spirit — a recognition too deep for me to explain. Throughout those daylight hours I was expectant of the night; impatient, perhaps, so that the sunlight passed like a half-glimpsed reflection in rippled water — a day of whose events I recall nothing. It was long since that portentous storm had cast a shadow over the beach, and I had determined, after hesitations caused by nothing tangible, to leave Ellston, since the year was chilling and there was no return to my earlier contentment. When a telegram came for me (lying two days in the Western Union office before I was located, so little was my name known) saying that my design had been accepted — winning above all others in the contest — I set a date for leaving. This news, which earlier in the year would have affected me strongly, I now received with a curious apathy. It seemed as unrelated to the unreality about me, as little pertinent to me, as if it were directed to another person whom I did not know, and whose message had come to me through some accident. None the less, it was that which forced me to complete my plans and leave the cottage by the shore.

There were only four nights of my stay remaining when there occurred the last of those events whose meaning lies more in the darkly sinister impression surrounding them than in anything obviously threatening. Night had settled over Ellston and the coast, and a pile of soiled dishes attested both to my recent meal and to my lack of industry. Darkness came as I sat with a cigarette before the seaward window, and it was a liquid which gradually filled the sky, washing in a floating moon, monstrously elevated. The flat sea bordering upon the gleaming sand, the utter absence of tree or figure or life of any sort, and the regard of that high moon made the vastness of my surroundings abruptly clear. There were only a few stars pricking through, as if to accentuate by their smallness the majesty of the lunar orb and of the restless, shifting tide.

I had stayed indoors, fearing somehow to go out before the sea on such a night of shapeless portent, but I heard it mumbling secrets of an incredible lore. Borne to me on a wind out of nowhere was the breath of some strange and palpitant life — the embodiment of all I had felt and of all I had suspected — stirring now in the chasms of the sky or beneath the mute waves. In what place this mystery turned from an ancient, horrible slumber I could not tell, but like one who stands by a figure lost in sleep, knowing that it will awake in a moment, I crouched by the windows, holding a nearly burnt-out cigarette, and faced the rising moon.

Gradually there passed into that never-stirring landscape a brilliance intensified by the overhead glimmerings, and I seemed more and more under some compulsion to watch whatever might follow. The shadows were draining from the beach, and I felt that they took with them all which might have been a harbour for my thoughts when the hinted thing should come. Where any of them did remain they were ebon and blank: still lumps of darkness sprawling beneath the cruel brilliant rays. The endless tableau of the lunar orb — dead now, whatever her past was, and cold as the unhuman sepulchres she bears amid the ruin of dusty centuries older than man — and the sea — astir, perhaps, with some unkenned life, some forbidden sentience — confronted me with a horrible vividness. I arose and shut the window; partly because of an inward prompting, but mostly, I think, as an excuse for transferring momentarily the stream of thought.

No sound came to me now as I stood before the closed panes. Minutes or eternities were alike. I was waiting, like my own fearing heart and the motionless scene beyond, for the token of some ineffable life. I had set the lamp upon a box in the western corner of the room, but the moon was brighter, and her bluish rays invaded places where the lamplight was faint. The ancient glow of the round silent orb lay upon the beach as it had lain for aeons, and I waited in a torment of expectancy made doubly acute by the delay in fulfillment, and the uncertainty of what strange completion was to come.

Outside the crouching hut a white illumination suggested vague spectral forms whose unreal, phantasmal motions seemed to taunt my blindness, just as unheard voices mocked my eager listening. For countless moments I was still, as if Time and the tolling of her great bell were hushed into nothingness. And yet there was nothing which I might fear: the moon-chiselled shadows were unnatural in no contour, and veiled nothing from my eyes. The night was silent — I knew that despite my closed window — and all the stars were fixed mournfully in a listening heaven of dark grandeur. No motion from me then, or word now, could reveal my plight, or tell of the fear-racked brain imprisoned in flesh which dared not break the silence, for all the torture it brought. As if expectant of death, and assured that nothing could serve to banish the soul-peril I confronted, I crouched with a forgotten cigarette in my hand. A silent world gleamed beyond the cheap, dirty windows, and in one corner of the room a pair of dirty oars, placed there before my arrival, shared the vigil of my spirit. The lamp burned endlessly, yielding a sick light hued like a corpse's flesh. Glancing at it now and again, for the desperate distraction it gave, I saw that many bubbles unaccountably rose and vanished in the kerosene-filled base. Curiously enough, there was no heat from the wick. And suddenly I became aware that the night as a whole was neither warm nor cold, but strangely neutral — as if all physical forces were suspended, and all the laws of a calm existence disrupted.

Then, with an unheard splash which sent from the silver water to the shore a line of ripples echoed in fear by my heart, a swimming thing emerged beyond the breakers. The figure may have been that of a dog, a human being, or something more strange. It could not have known that I watched — perhaps it did not care — but like a distorted fish it swam across the mirrored stars and dived beneath the surface. After a moment it came up again, and this time, since it was closer, I saw that it was carrying something across its shoulder. I knew, then, that it could be no animal, and that it was a man or something like a man, which came toward the land from a dark ocean. But it swam with a horrible ease. As I watched, dread-filled and passive, with the fixed stare of one who awaits death in another yet knows he cannot avert it, the swimmer approached the shore — though too far down the southward beach for me to discern its outlines or features. Obscurely loping, with sparks of moonlit foam scattered by its quick gait, it emerged and was lost among the inland dunes.

Now I was possessed by a sudden recurrence of fear, which had died away in the previous moments. There was a tingling coldness all over me — though the room, whose window I dared not open now, was stuffy. I thought it would be very horrible if something were to enter a window which was not closed. Now that I could no longer see the figure, I felt that it lingered somewhere in the close shadows, or peered hideously at me from whatever window I did not watch. And so I turned my gaze, eagerly and frantically, to each successive pane; dreading that I might indeed behold an intrusive regarding face, yet unable to keep myself from the terrifying inspection. But though I watched for hours, there was no longer anything upon the beach.

So the night passed, and with it began the ebbing of that strangeness — a strangeness which had surged up like an evil brew within a pot, had mounted to the very rim in a breathless moment, had paused uncertainly there, and had subsided, taking with it whatever unknown message it had borne. Like the stars that promise the revelation of terrible and glorious memories, goad us into worship by this deception, and then impart nothing. I had come frighteningly near to the capture of an old secret which ventured close to man's haunts and lurked cautiously just beyond the edge of the known. Yet in the end I had nothing, I was given only a glimpse of the furtive thing; a glimpse made obscure by the veils of ignorance. I cannot even conceive what might have shown itself had I been too close to that swimmer who went shoreward instead of into the ocean. I do not know what might have come if the brew had passed the rim of the pot and poured outward in a swift cascade of revelation. The night ocean withheld whatever it had nurtured. I shall know nothing more.

Even yet I do not know why the ocean holds such a fascination for me. But then, perhaps none of us can solve those things — they exist in defiance of all explanation. There are men, and wise men, who do not like the sea and its lapping surf on yellow shores; and they think us strange who love the mystery of the ancient and unending deep. Yet for me there is a haunting and inscrutable glamour in all the ocean's moods. It is in the melancholy silver foam beneath the moon's waxen corpse; it hovers over the silent and eternal waves that beat on naked shores; it is there when all is lifeless save for unknown shapes that glide through sombre depths. And when I behold the awesome billows surging in endless strength, there comes upon me an ecstasy akin to fear; so that I must abase myself before this mightiness, that I may not hate the clotted waters and their overwhelming beauty. Vast and lonely is the ocean, and even as all things came from it, so shall they return thereto. In the shrouded depths of time none shall reign upon the earth, nor shall any motion be, save in the eternal waters. And these shall beat on dark shores in thunderous foam, though none shall remain in that dying world to watch the cold light of the enfeebled moon playing on the swirling tides and coarse-grained sand. On the deep's margin shall rest only a stagnant foam, gathering about the shells and bones of perished shapes that dwelt within the waters. Silent, flabby things will toss and roll along empty shores, their sluggish life extinct. Then all shall be dark, for at last even the white moon on the distant waves shall wink out. Nothing shall be left, neither above nor below the sombre waters. And until that last millennium, as after it, the sea will thunder and toss throughout the dismal night.

To Clark Ashton Smith, Esq., upon His Phantastick Tales, Verses, Pictures, and Sculptures.

Sonnet;
1936.

This sonnet was penned and posted in December 1936, probably after H.P. Lovecraft knew he was about to die. As the title suggests, it is a tribute to his West Coast friend and colleague, whom he never met in person but considered one of his best friends. Other than a few letters and his "death diary," it is the last thing he wrote.

A TIME-BLACK TOWER against dim banks of cloud;
Around its base the pathless, pressing wood.
Shadow and silence, moss and mould, enshroud
Grey, age-fell'd slabs that once as cromlechs stood.
No fall of foot, no song of bird awakes
The lethal aisles of sempiternal night,
Tho' oft with stir of wings the dense air shakes,
As in the tower there glows a pallid light.
For here, apart, dwells one whose hands have wrought
Strange eidola that chill the world with fear;
Whose graven runes in tones of dread have taught
What things beyond the star-gulfs lurk and leer.
    Dark Lord of Averoigne—whose windows stare
    On pits of dream no other gaze could bear!

1937.

The Ides of March are Come . . . and Gone.

H.P. Lovecraft had spent the last few months of 1936 in an increasingly miserable state. He'd always been gaunt, except for that one year when Sonia had tried to fatten him up a bit; but now his cancer was interfering with his body's ability to draw nourishment from his meager food (meals typically consisted of a half-can of beans, a hunk of bread, and some cheese) and leaving him chronically constipated to boot. His failing energy left him unable to keep up his former pace of reading and work. And the death by suicide of his friend and colleague Robert E. Howard — a chronic depressive who once said he only chose to remain alive to spare his mother the pain his suicide would cause her — hit Lovecraft very hard at a time when his own personal resources were ebbing.

But although no surviving weird fiction or poetry flowed from his pen in 1937, it was not exactly inactive. Lovecraft seems to have known what was coming; in January of 1937, he started an actual death-diary, chronicling his deteriorating condition. He also revised a story for Duane W. Rimel, a tale titled "From the Sea." This story, the last weird-fiction work Lovecraft did in his life, has been lost.

By late February of 1937, Lovecraft was spending whole days in bed propped up with pillows, too weak to get up. A doctor, called in, found him sitting in bathwater, which gave him some relief from the chronic pain. On March 2, a specialist confirmed what the doctor had come to suspect: cancer. Advanced, metastasized and inoperable.

Lovecraft was checked into the Jane Brown Memorial Hospital, where, loaded with pain medication and being fed intravenously, he said goodbye to his friends and waited for death.

Finally, in the early morning hours of March 15, it came.

It seems likely that Lovecraft, an antiquarian with a great love for ancient Rome, would have derived at least a little satisfaction from having his death-date fall on the Ides of March, had he known. But, of course, that is one thing he could not write about.

APPENDIX.

Timeline of H.P. Lovecraft's Life and Work.

1890:

20 Aug 1890, 9 a.m.: HPL born in the Phillips home at 194 Angell Street, Providence, Rhode Island

1893:

Apr 1893: Father, Winfield Scott Lovecraft, committed to Butler Mental Hospital

1896:

26 Jan 1896: Grandmother Robie Phillips dies; family goes into mourning

1897:

08 Nov 1897: HPL writes his first known item, "The Young Folks' Ulysses," at age 7, as part of a catalogue of titles for the "Providence Press Co."

1898:

1898: Earliest known HPL fiction writings start appearing, undated, mostly styled after dime novels. "The Little Glass Bottle," "The Secret Cave; or, John Lees Adventure," The Mystery of the Grave-Yard; or, A Dead Man's Revenge," "The Noble Eavesdropper." Others were written but don't survive

1899:

04 Mar 1899: HPL launches The Scientific Gazette *as a one-page daily journal, although it quickly becomes a weekly*

1902:

1902: HPL writes "The Mysterious Ship"

1903:

02 Aug 1903: Using a hectograph, HPL publishes Vol. 1 No. 1 of the weekly Rhode Island Journal of Astronomy, *the first of 69 issues*

1904:

28 Mar 1904: Grandfather Whipple dies of a stroke. Family fortunes decline sharply as a result, and the Lovecrafts are forced to move from their mansion to a small duplex

Sep 1904: HPL enters Hope Street English and Classical High School

1905:

21 Apr 1905: HPL writes "The Beast in the Cave"

1906:

03 Jun 1906: First of HPL's letters-to-editor, "No Transit of Mars," appears in Providence Sunday Journal

27 Jul 1906: First of HPL's monthly astronomy columns in Pawtuxet Valley Gleaner *is published (run through end of 1906)*

01 Aug 1906: First of HPL's monthly astronomy columns in Providence Tribune *is published (run through 01 Jun 1908)*

1908:

Early 1908: HPL writes "The Alchemist"

Summer 1908: HPL suffers nervous breakdown, drops out of high school, becomes a near-recluse, studying chemistry and astronomy and writing Georgian poetry

1911:

Feb 1911: HPL's first letter to the editor of Argosy *is published*

1913:

11 Jan 1913: "Fishhead" by Irwin S. Cobb is published in All-Story Cavalier. *HPL responds with a letter to editor praising it. Its influence can be seen in later HPL stories*

Sep 1913: HPL initiates the "Fred Jackson Wars" in Argosy *with a cutting, erudite, sarcastic slam of author Jackson's syrupy romance stories. The "wars" rage on for at least two solid years and turn into a war of poets between HPL and John Russell*

1914:

01 Jan 1914: HPL starts a monthly astronomy column in Providence Evening News, *which runs through May 1918*

06 Apr 1914: HPL joins United Amateur Press Association, at the invitation of Edward F. Daas, official editor of UAPA, who noticed the poetry battle in Argosy. *His principal Jackson Wars sparring partner, Russell, joins too*

Oct 1914: HPL and Russell co-write a poem declaring a truce, which is published in Argosy

1915:

Apr 1915: The first of 13 issues of HPL's journal, The Conservative, *is published*

26 Apr 1915: Aunt Lillian Clark's husband dies (Uncle Franklin)

Jul 1915: HPL elected First Vice-President of UAPA

1916:

Oct 1916: First mention of HPL's revisory business, then called Symphony Literary Service (with Anne Tillery Renshaw and one of her friends)

Nov 1916: "The Alchemist" is published in *United Amateur*, the first published work of HPL's weird fiction

31 Dec 1916: Cousin Phillips dies of tuberculosis (Aunt Annie Gamwell's boy)

1917:

Jan 1917: HPL wins a movie-review contest roasting a movie called "The Image Maker"

18 Feb 1917: David Van Bush requests rates for HPL's revisory services from Symphony Literary Service

02 Apr 1917: U.S. enters First World War; HPL starts in writing patriotic doggerel

May 1917: HPL tries to join the Rhode Island National Guard. Mother, Sarah Susan Lovecraft, throws a fit

May 1917: HPL appointed Official Editor of United Amateur

Jun 1917: HPL resumes fiction writing with "The Tomb"

Jul 1917: HPL elected president of UAPA
Jul 1917: HPL writes "Dagon"
Aug 1917: HPL writes "A Reminiscence of Dr. Samuel Johnson"
Sep 1917: "A Reminiscence of Dr. Samuel Johnson" published in United Amateur
Mid-Sep 1917: W. Paul Cook visits HPL for first time; his mother thinks he's a tramp or something. Later Rheinhart Kleiner visits and is cordially received, since he's better dressed. Every hour or so mother appears with a glass of milk for HPL
Dec 1917: At mother's insistence HPL self-certifies unfit for draft

1918:

1918: HPL and Winifred Jackson develop what appears to have been a platonic romance
01 Feb 1918: "The Volunteer" patriotic poem first published in Providence Evening News; subsequently picked up by National Enquirer 07 Feb; also Appleton Post; St. Petersburg Evening Independent; and Trench and Camp (army paper in San Antonio)
Jun 1918: "The Beast in the Cave" published in The Vagrant
Jun 1918: HPL writes "Psychopompos"
Summer 1918: HPL's term as UAPA president expires
Summer 1918: HPL writes "Polaris" (after an exchange of letters with Maurice Moe in May 1918, describing the dream it's based on)
Summer 1918: HPL writes and circulates Hesperia (a manuscript magazine, now lost)
Aug 1918: HPL outlines plot for "The Tree" in a letter to Alfred Galpin
Oct 1918: "Psychopompos" published in The Vagrant
Nov 1918: Uncle Edwin (mother Sarah Susan Lovecraft's brother) dies. Sarah Susan goes into a steady decline

1919:

Jan. 1919: HPL's mother has a nervous breakdown, goes to stay with friends
13 Mar 1919: HPL's mother checks into Butler Hospital. HPL takes it hard
Spring 1919: HPL writes "Beyond the Wall of Sleep"
Spring 1919: HPL writes "Memory"
May 1919: HPL writes "The Green Meadow" (from dream in late 1918) with Winifred V. Jackson
Jun 1919: "Memory" published in United Co-Operative
Jul 1919: Volstead Act goes into effect; nationwide Prohibition begins
Jul 1919: HPL writes "Old Bugs" for Alfred Galpin, who told HPL he bought and drank some booze just before Prohibition kicked in just to try it out
4 Jul 1919: HPL's first trip to Boston for Hub Club stuff
Aug 1919: HPL and Maurice Moe desultorily launch a "literary partnership" to crack the pro markets. It doesn't go anywhere
Sep 1919: HPL discovers Lord Dunsany
16 Sep 1919: HPL writes "The Transition of Juan Romero"
Oct 1919: HPL writes "The White Ship"
Oct 1919: "Beyond the Wall of Sleep" published in Pine Cones
Nov 1919: "The White Ship" published in United Amateur
Nov 1919: "Dagon" published in The Vagrant
Nov or Dec 1919: HPL writes "The Street"
3 Dec 1919: HPL writes "The Doom that Came to Sarnath"
Late 1919: HPL starts keeping a commonplace book to jot down germs of ideas for weird stories
Late Dec 1919 or early Jan 1920: HPL writes "The Statement of Randolph Carter"

1920:

1920ish: David Van Bush becomes a very regular client
1920ish: HPL writes "Life and Death" (lost or apocryphal, or possibly an alternative title of "Ex Oblivione")
1920ish: HPL writes "Ex Oblivione" (but see "Life and Death" entry above)
Early 1920: HPL writes "The Tree"
28 Jan 1920: HPL writes "The Terrible Old Man"
May 1920: "The Statement of Randolph Carter" published in The Vagrant
Jun 1920: "The Doom that Came to Sarnath" published in The Scot

14 Jun 1920: HPL writes "The Cats of Ulthar"
Summer 1920: HPL elected Official Editor of United Amateur
Summer 1920: HPL writes "The Temple"
Summer 1920: HPL helps Anna Helen Crofts write "Poetry and the Gods"
Late summer 1920: HPL writes "Facts Concerning Arthur Jermyn and his Family"
Sep 1920: "Poetry and the Gods" published in United Amateur
Nov 1920: "The Cats of Ulthar" published in Tryout
Nov 1920: HPL writes "Celephaïs"
16 Nov 1920: HPL writes "From Beyond"
Dec 1920: "Polaris" published in The Philosopher
Dec 1920: "The Street" published in Wolverine
Late 1920: HPL writes "Nyarlarthotep"
Nov 1920 (but issue was several months late): "Nyarlarthotep" published in United Amateur
Dec 1920: HPL writes "The Crawling Chaos" with Winifred V. Jackson
12 Dec 1920: HPL writes "The Picture in the House" (in which the Miskatonic River is first mentioned)

1921:

1921: Second issue of Hesperia *(manuscript magazine) released (also lost)*
Jan 1921: First of three "In Defence of Dagon" essays sent out on the Transatlantic Circulator (manuscript-magazine circuit)
Late Jan 1921: HPL writes "The Nameless City"
22 Feb 1921: HPL delivers speech: "What Amateurdom and I have Done for Each Other" at Boston conference of amateur journos
28 Feb 1921: HPL writes "The Quest of Iranon"
Mar 1921: HPL writes "The Moon Bog"
Mar 1921: "Ex Oblivione" published in United Amateur *under Ward Phillips pseudonym*
Mar 1921: Part 1 of "Facts Concerning Arthur Jermyn and his Family" published in Wolverine
Apr 1921: Second of three "Defence of Dagon" essays sent out on Transatlantic Circulator
Apr 1921: "The Crawling Chaos" published in United Cooperative
24 May 1921: Sarah Susan Phillips Lovecraft dies
Jun 1921: Part 2 of "Facts Concerning Arthur Jermyn and his Family" published in Wolverine
Early summer-ish 1921: HPL writes "The Outsider"
Summer 1921: HPL's term as Official Editor ends; he is reelected
Summer 1921: "The Picture in the House" published in the "Jul 1919" issue of National Amateur (the issue was very late)
Jul 1921: "The Terrible Old Man" published in Tryout
Jul 1921: HPL meets Sonia Haft Greene at a NAPA convention
Aug 1921: HPL travels to visit Charles "Tryout" Smith, Myrta Alice Little, Harold Munroe, and others; does lots of sightseeing
14 Aug 1921: HPL writes "The Other Gods." Joshi points to this story as the spot at which the interconnectedness of HPL stories starts to manifest
Sep 1921: Third of three "In Defence of Dagon" essays out on Transatlantic Circulator
Sep 1921: George Julian Houtain prepares to launch Home Brew.
4 Sep 1921: Sonia comes to Providence to visit.
Oct 1921: "The Tree" published in Tryout.
Oct 1921: HPL writes Herbert West, Reanimator *parts 1 and 2 (in which Miskatonic University is first mentioned)*
Nov 1921: "The Nameless City" published in Wolverine
Dec 1921: HPL writes "The Music of Erich Zann"

1922:

1922ish: HPL writes "Sweet Ermengarde" (although it may have been a much older story pulled up and refreshed for a friend's journal to publish)
Feb 1922: Herbert West, Reanimator *publication starts, serialized, in* Home Brew
Mar 1922: HPL writes Herbert West, Reanimator *part 4*
Mar 1922: "The Music of Erich Zann" published in National Amateur
Mar 1922: HPL writes "Hypnos"

Mar 1922: "The Tomb" published in The Vagrant

06-12 Apr 1922: HPL spends a week in NYC with Sonia flirting with him

May 1922: "Celephaïs" first published in Sonia Haft Greene's journal Rainbow

Late May 1922: HPL goes on a trip to New Hampshire

Jun 1922: HPL writes "Azathoth"

Jun 1922: HPL writes Herbert West, Reanimator *part 6*

05 Jun 1922: HPL writes "What the Moon Brings"

26 Jun-5 Jul 1922: HPL journeys to Cambridge and Boston, then Magnolia to visit Sonia. They hash out "The Horror at Martins Beach." Sonia plants one on HPL, levelling up relationship. Sonia writes "Four O'Clock," with or without HPL's help

Jul 1922: Sixth and final installment of Herbert West, Reanimator *runs in* Home Brew

26 Jul-15 Oct 1922: HPL in NYC and Cleveland visiting Sonia again, as well as Alfred Galpin and Sam Loveman & al.

Sep 1922ish: HPL initiates correspondence with Clark Ashton Smith. His poetry writing virtually ceases, likely because he recognizes his skills in that area as embarrassingly shy of Smith's

Summer 1922: HPL's term as Official Editor ends; he's feuding with the "anti-literary" clique of amateurs

Oct 1922: HPL writes "The Hound" (in which the Necronomicon *is first mentioned)*

Nov 1922: HPL writes The Lurking Fear

30 Nov 1922: HPL appointed president of NAPA

Dec 1922: HPL travels to Boston, Salem, Marblehead

1923:

Jan-Apr 1923: The Lurking Fear *published serially in* Home Brew.

Early Feb: Another visit to Salem-Marblehead

Mar 1923: Yet another trip to Salem-Marblehead, an overnighter this time

Mar 1923: Weird Tales *starts publication*

Apr 1923: HPL takes a five-day trip to attend Hub Club and scope old New England stuff

May 1923: "Hypnos" published in National Amateur

May 1923: "What the Moon Brings" published in National Amateur

Summer 1923: NAPA presidency term ends; Sonia elected president of UAPA; HPL reelected to Official Editorship. Factions still feuding

Summer 1923: HPL discovers Arthur Machen

3-4 Jul 1923: Boston Hub Club trip

15-17 Jul 1923: Sonia visits

Aug 1923: HPL meets Clifford and Muriel Eddy

10 Aug 1923: HPL leaves on a sort of tour. Boston, New Hampshire, Marblehead, Pascoag, etc. 3 days.

Jul 1923ish: HPL submits five stories to Weird Tales, *initiating his publishing relationship there.*

Early Sep 1923: HPL writes "The Rats in the Walls"

Oct 1923ish: HPL helps Clifford Eddy with "Ashes" and "The Ghost Eater"

Oct 1923ish: HPL writes "The Unnamable"

Oct 1923: HPL writes "The Festival"

Oct 1923: "Dagon" published in Weird Tales *with a note reading, "This is the First of a Series of Remarkable Stories that H.P. LOVECRAFT is Writing for WEIRD TALES. The Second Will Appear in an Early Issue."*

Nov 1923: "The Horror at Martin's Beach" published in Weird Tales *as "The Invisible Monster"*

Late 1923: HPL helps Clifford Eddy with "The Loved Dead"

1924:

Feb 1924: "The Hound published in Weird Tales

Feb 1924ish: HPL helps Clifford Eddy with "Deaf, Dumb and Blind"

Mar 1924: "Ashes" (by Eddy) published in Weird Tales

Mar 1924: "The Rats in the Walls" published in Weird Tales

2 Mar 1924: HPL moves to NYC

3 Mar 1924: HPL marries Sonia Haft Greene

4 Mar 1924: HPL ghostwrites "Under the Pyramids" (a.k.a. "Imprisoned with the Pharaohs") for Harry Houdini (retyped on wedding night)

10 Mar 1924: HPL interviews at The Reading Lamp *with Gertrude Tucker*
21 Mar 1924: HPL receives $100 for "Under the Pyramids"
Mid-Mar 1924: JC Henneberger offers HPL editorship of Weird Tales *if he'll move to Chicago. He declines.*
Apr 1924: "The Ghost Eater" published in Weird Tales
May 1924: HPL and Sonia buy a home lot in Bryn Mawr Park
May 1924: "The Loved Dead" and "Under the Pyramids" published in Weird Tales. *Farnsworth Wright takes over as editor*
Summer 1924: HPL reelected Official Editor at UAPA but UAPA folds quietly sometime in 1926.
Jul 1924: Sonia having quit her job and opened a hat shop, experiences business failure. HPL gets a job selling collection-agency services and immediately loses it
Summer 1924: HPL fruitlessly seeks employment in NYC
7 Sep 1924: JC Henneberger "hires" HPL for a new magazine, which never materializes
Fall 1924: Kalem Club forms. HPL seemingly resigned to not getting a job; spends rest of year exploring NYC, hanging around cafeterias with friends, grasshoppering, and increasingly neglecting Sonia
10 Oct 1924: HPL visits Elizabethtown, loves it
17 Oct 1924: HPL, inspired by his visit to Elizabethtown, writes "The Shunned House"
20 Oct. 1924: Sonia hospitalized with gastric-nervous breakdown
09-14 Nov 1924: HPL travels to Philly to check out its antiquities
01 Dec 1924: Aunt Lillian spends a month in NYC helping
31 Dec 1924: Sonia moves to Cincinnati for job; HPL alone in NYC

1925:

Jan 1925: "The Festival" published in Weird Tales
Feb 1925: "The Statement of Randolph Carter" published in Weird Tales
Feb 1925: Sonia back in NYC for 6 weeks
26 Mar 1925: HPL has his silhouette done; today it is in frequent use and is one of the most iconic images of HPL
Apr 1925: "Deaf, Dumb and Blind" published in Weird Tales
May 1925: "The Music of Erich Zann" published in Weird Tales
24 May 1925: Burglars break in and steal three suits and HPL's overcoat. HPL spends the next five months tracking down and buying suitable cheap suits, one for summer and one for winter
Jun 1925: Sonia back in NYC for another stretch
Jun 1925: HPL tries copywriting with Arthur Leeds, but business fails
Jul 1925: "The Unnamable" published in Weird Tales
Jul 1925: HPL starts reading Providence in Colonial Times *(book), finds it inspirational. He begins planning for his return*
July-Sep 1925: HPL tries to save UAPA but it doesn't work
24 Jul 1925: Sonia back to Cleveland
2 Aug 1925: HPL writes "The Horror at Red Hook"
10 Aug 1925: HPL writes "He"
12 Aug 1925: HPL develops outline for "The Call of Cthulhu"
Sep 1925: "The Temple" published in Weird Tales
18 Sep 1925: HPL writes "In the Vault"
Nov 1925: "In the Vault" published in Tryout
Nov 1925: HPL spends 4 days revising an article on salesmanship for Sonia
Dec 1925: HPL starts work on Supernatural Horror in Literature

1926:

Jan 1926: HPL writes Supernatural Horror in Literature *chapters 1-4*
*Feb 1926: HPL writes "Cool Air" (his first post-*Supernatural Horror *title)*
Mar 1926: HPL writes Supernatural Horror in Literature *chapters 5-7*
27 Mar 1926: HPL invited to return to Providence
15 Mar-5 Apr: Sonia in town
Apr 1926: HPL writes Supernatural Horror in Literature *chapters 8-10*
Apr 1926: "The Outsider" published in Weird Tales.
17 Apr 1926: HPL returns to Providence

Jun 1926: "The Moon Bog" published in Weird Tales.
Jul 1926: August Derleth writes to HPL for first time.
Aug 1926: HPL writes "The Call of Cthulhu"
Sep 1926: "He" published in Weird Tales
Early Sep 1926: HPL writes "Pickman's Model"
13 Sep 1926: HPL back in NYC at Sonia's behest; stays, journeys to Philly, returns 25 Sep
Oct 1926: HPL helps Wilfred Blanch Talman write "Two Black Bottles" (which Talman started several months before)
Oct 1926: HPL, Eddy and Houdini collaborate on "The Cancer of Superstition," an anti-astrology screed, now lost
31 Oct 1926: Houdini dies
Nov 1926: HPL writes "The Silver Key"
9 Nov 1926: HPL writes "The Strange High House in the Mist"
Late 1926: Donald Wandrei first writes to HPL.

1927:

1927ish: UAPA now being dead, HPL starts to coordinate the Lovecraft Circle.
Jan 1927: HPL writes The Dream-Quest of Unknown Kadath
Jan 1927: "The Horror at Red Hook" published in Weird Tales
29 Jan–01 Mar 1927: HPL writes The Case of Charles Dexter Ward
Feb 1927: HPL edits a collection of John Ravenor Bullen's poetry (came out early 1928)
Mar 1927: HPL writes "The Colour out of Space"
Spring 1927: "The Green Meadow" published in The Vagrant
Apr 1927-ish: HPL writes "The Descendant"
Apr 1927-ish: HPL writes "The History of the Necronomicon*"*
May 1927: Zealia Bishop becomes a client
20 Jun 1927: HPL visits Chicago, meets Farnsworth Wright
12 Jul 1927: Donald Wandrei visits, is squired around.
Summer 1927: Lots of correspondents come to Providence to be squired around town by HPL. Frank Long, W. Paul Cook, James F. Morton, etc.
Summer 1927: HPL writes his first travelogue, "The Trip of Theobald," later published in Tryout
Aug 1927: "Two Black Bottles" published in Weird Tales
19 Aug 1927: HPL travels upcountry: New Hampshire, Vermont, Maine, Massachusetts.
Sep 1927: "The Colour out of Space" published in Amazing Stories
2 Sep 1927: HPL back from upcountry trip
29 Sep 1927: HPL writes a second travelogue based on upcountry trip: "Vermont—A First Impression"
Oct. 1927: "Pickman's Model" published in Weird Tales
Nov-ish 1927: Adolphe de Castro becomes a client; HPL revises "The Last Test" for him
Nov 1927: HPL writes a letter to Donald Wandrei that was published as "The Thing in the Moonlight."
Nov 1927: HPL reads Wandrei's Sonnets of the Midnight Hours, *is inspired by it (later would influence* Fungi from Yuggoth*)*
03 Nov 1927: HPL includes the story that would be published as "The Very Old Folk" in a letter to Donald Wandrei
Dec 1927: Farnsworth Wright proposes a story collection. Nothing happens.
Late 1927: HPL gets published in You'll Need a Night Light *with "The Horror at Red Hook" — the first appearance of HPL in hardcover*

1928:

1928: "The Colour out of Space" recognized on Edward O'Brien's Best Short Stories.
Early 1928: HPL works on Maurice Moe's Doorways to Poetry *as editor*
Feb 1928: "The Call of Cthulhu" published in Weird Tales
Mar 1928: "Cool Air" published in Tales of Magic and Mystery
Mar 1928: HPL writes "The Curse of Yig" for Zealia Bishop
Spring 1928: W. Paul Cook says "The Shunned House" book is printed, but not yet bound
Apr 1928: HPL returns to NYC to help Sonia set up a new hat shop, spends next six weeks gallivanting around with old friends while complaining about how much he hates NYC
10 Jun 1928: HPL and Vrest Orton come to Orton's new Vermont Country Store, stay until 24th exploring Brattleboro area

29 Jun 1928: HPL travels to Wilbraham to visit Edith Miniter, learns about the legend of whippoorwills as psychopomps
Summer 1928: HPL writes "Ibid"
Jul 1928: HPL returns to Providence, starts on his first large-scale travelogue, Observations on Several Parts of America."
Aug 1928: HPL writes The Dunwich Horror
Nov 1928: "The Last Test" is published in Weird Tales *(in which "Iä! Shub-Niggurath!" appears for the first time)*
Late 1928: Sonia pressing for a divorce

1929:

Early 1929: HPL starts to develop his critique of machine-culture/mass culture
Jan 1929: Loveman comes to town, travels around for a few days with HPL
Jan 1929: "The Silver Key" published in Weird Tales
Feb 1929: Divorce hearings
Apr 1929: The Dunwich Horror *published in* Weird Tales*; HPL paid $240 for it*
04 Apr 1929: HPL starts spring travels, all over NY and New England
May 20ish: HPL back from spring travels (10 states, first taste of the south in Richmond)
Jun 1929ish: HPL writes "Travels in the Provinces of America" (spring travelogue, 18k words)
Summer 1929: Wilfred Talman designs a bookplate for HPL
Jul 1929: HPL rewrites "The Electric Executioner" for Adolphe de Castro
Aug 1929: Several short excursions including an airplane ride on the 17th
Fall 1929: "The Call of Cthulhu" appears in Beware After Dark *anthology*
Nov 1929: "The Curse of Yig" published in Weird Tales
Mid-Dec 1929: HPL writes "The Ancient Track" (poem)
27 Dec 1929–4 Jan 1930: HPL writes Fungi from Yuggoth. *The sonnets would be published one by one over the next 2 years in* Weird Tales, *the* Providence Journal, *and Walter Coates'* Driftwind *as well as other amateur journals*

1930:

1930: "Sleepy Hollow To-Day" included in Macmillan grade-school textbook
Jan 1930: HPL ghostwrites The Mound *for Zealia Bishop*
04 Jan 1930: New York World mentions HPL in Bolitho's column
24 Feb 1930: HPL starts on The Whisperer in Darkness
Mar 1930: "The Ancient Track" published in Weird Tales
Late Apr 1930: HPL starts his summer travels with Richmond and Charleston
May 1930: HPL ghostwrites "Medusa's Coil" for Zealia Bishop (written while on the road in Richmond)
20 May 1930: Simon & Schuster solicits a novel
Late May 1930: HPL visits Roerich Museum in NYC
Jun 1930: Robert E. Howard connects with HPL
13 Jun 1930: HPL finally home from travels, for a bit
Mid-1930: HPL revises another DeCastro story, now lost, never published
03-05 Jul 1930: HPL attends NAPA convention in NYC
Aug 1930: "The Electric Executioner" published in Weird Tales
15-17 Aug 1930: HPL stays with Longs at Cape Cod
30 Aug 1930: HPL entrains for Quebec for a 3-day whirlwind tour
26 Sep 1930: The Whisperer in Darkness *is finished*
Late 1930: HPL starts corresponding with Henry S. Whitehead

1931:

1931ish: HPL starts corresponding with RH Barlow
Jan 1931: HPL writes "A Description of the Town of Quebeck, in New-France . . ."
Jan 1931: HPL starts showing evidence of changing political views
24 Feb 1931: HPL starts on At the Mountains of Madness
Late Feb 1931: HPL first articulates repudiation of the supernatural in favour of a merging of sci-fi and weird fiction; scientific justification is, he posits, required for true horror

14 Mar 1931: Discovery of Pluto announced in New York Times*; HPL is very excited. "It is probably Yuggoth," he says.*

22 Mar 1931: At the Mountains of Madness *is finished*

Spring 1931: Putnam editor ditches plan for a book, saying HPL's writing is not subtle enough. HPL, devastated, blames Wright for demanding dumb pulp stuff for Weird Tales.

May 1931: HPL starts corresponding with Bill Lumley, a nutty old mystic-believer who says he's witnessed monstrous rites in deserted cities, slept in pre-human ruins and awakened 20 years later, seen strange elemental spirits, conversed with ancient wizards, and so forth.

2 May 1931: HPL finishes typing At the Mountains of Madness, *leaves for St. Augustine, Fla., via NYC, DC, Richmond, Charlotte, etc.*

21 May 1931: HPL heads for Dunedin to stay with Henry Whitehead

June-ish 1931: HPL helps Whitehead write "The Trap."

10 Jun 1931: HPL gets a couple revision cheques, enabling him to continue traveling; heads south to Key West

16 Jun 1931: HPL back from Key West, in St. Augustine, starts a new story

20 Jun 1931: HPL learns Farnsworth "Farny the Fox" Wright has rejected At the Mountains of Madness, *becomes discouraged, drops his new story (it's now lost)*

23 Jun 1931: HPL heads north: Charleston, Richmond, Fredericksburg, Philly, NYC

Summer 1931: Henry Whitehead writes "Cassius" based on HPL's commonplace book entry.

6 Jul 1931: "Gang" meets at Talman's pad; Seabury Quinn visits

20 Jul 1931: HPL home in Providence; next day James Morton visits

Mid-1931: HPL's new "scienti-weird" style rubs his more traditionally devout friends wrong. They get more critical. He starts doubting himself.

Aug 1931: The Whisperer in Darkness *published in* Weird Tales*; HPL gets $350 for it*

Oct 1931: "The Strange High House in the Mist" published in Weird Tales

Early Oct 1931: HPL visits Boston, Newburyport, Haverhill, with Cook

Early Nov 1931: HPL visits Boston, Salem, Marblehead, Newburyport, Portsmouth with Cook

Nov 1931: "Cassius" (Whitehead's story) published in Strange Tales

Nov-Dec 1931: HPL writes The Shadow Over Innsmouth

1932:

Feb 1932: HPL writes "The Dreams in the Witch House"

Mar 1932: "The Trap" published in Strange Tales

Spring 1932: Hazel Heald becomes a client

Apr 1932: HPL and Whitehead working on "The Bruise" (either published as "Bothon," or lost and re-created as a pastiche by Arkham House personnel years later)

18 May 1932: HPL leaves for his summer travels: NYC a week, Washington, Knoxville, Chattanooga, Vicksburg, Natchez, finally New Orleans by end of month

12 Jun 1932: HPL meets E. Hoffman Price; helps him with "Tarbis of the Lake"

25 Jun 1932: HPL back in NYC, via Mobile, Montgomery, Atlanta, Richmond, Fredericksburg, etc.

01 Jul 1932: Telegram reaches HPL stating that aunt Lillian is dying. HPL cuts travels short and hurries home

Jul 1932: HPL writes "The Man of Stone" for Hazel Heald.

Jul 1932: HPL writes "Winged Death" for Hazel Heald

Jul 1932: HPL writes "The Horror in the Museum" for Hazel Heald

Jul 1932: HPL cited as a "great writer" in an article in American Author, *a writer's journal*

30 Aug 1932: HPL visits Cook in Boston, goes to see total solar eclipse, then Quebec; returns exhausted and looking like a zombie

Sep 1932 sometime: Harold Farnese sets "Mirage" and "The Elder Pharos" to music, swaps letters from HPL. One of these letters will cause trouble in 1937 when Farnese imperfectly describes it to August Derleth.

Oct 1932: "The Man of Stone" published in Wonder Stories

Oct 1932: E. Hoffman Price asks HPL to collaborate on "Through the Gates of the Silver Key"

07 Nov 1932: HPL initiates "civilization vs. barbarism" debate with Robert E. Howard

23 Nov 1932: Henry Whitehead dies

26 Dec 1932: HPL spends a week visiting the Longs in NYC for Christmastime

1933:

1933ish: HPL writes "The Horror in the Burying-Ground" for Hazel Heald

Feb 1933: HPL helps Robert Barlow with "The Slaying of the Monster" (apparently unpublished until 1994)

22 Feb 1933: HPL writes "Repetitions on the Times," calling for direct government intervention in the economy (a la New Deal)

11 Mar 1933: HPL sees Sonia for last time, on a 2-day trip to Hartford; he refuses to kiss her goodbye

Spring 1933: Correspondence with Robert Bloch starts

Apr 1933: HPL writes "Through the Gates of the Silver Key" with E. Hoffman Price

15 May 1933: HPL and aunt Annie Gamwell move into 66 College St

14 Jun 1933: Aunt Annie breaks her ankle, hospitalized

30 Jun 1933: Price visits for four days with a car; Frank Long and James Morton also visit later in July

Summer 1933: Richard Searight correspondence starts; Helen B. Sully comes to visit; HPL scares her in the churchyard with a spooky story

Jul 1933: "The Dreams in the Witch House" published in Weird Tales *after Derleth submitted it*

Jul 1933: "The Horror in the Museum" published in Weird Tales

Jul 1933: HPL named chairman of Bureau of Critics at NAPA

05 Jul 1933: Annie home from hospital

Aug 1933: HPL writes "Out of the Æons" for Hazel Heald.

01 Aug 1933: Allen Ullman of Knopf asks to see some stories; HPL sends a bunch; Ullman says no thanks

21 Aug 1933: HPL writes "The Thing on the Doorstep"

Sep 1933: HPL helps Robert Barlow with "The Hoard of the Wizard-Beast" (published later that year in an unknown amateur journal)

Sep 1933: Fantasy Fan magazine starts publication, with a fierce anti-Clark Ashton Smith letter from Forrest J. Ackerman

02 Sep 1933: HPL travels to Quebec for a week

Fall 1933: F. Lee Baldwin correspondence starts; Herman C. Koenig correspondence starts

22 Oct 1933: HPL writes "The Wicked Clergyman" (alt. tit. "The Evil Clergyman")

23 Nov 1933: HPL writes "Some Notes on a Nonentity" (autobiography)

Nov 1933: CL Moore is first published in Weird Tales

Nov 1933: "The Other Gods" is published in Fantasy Fan

24 Nov 1933: HPL travels to Plymouth to spend Thanksgiving there

Late 1933: HPL, struggling with a dry spell, writes "The Book," attempting to use the first poems of Fungi from Yuggoth *as inspiration for a new story.*

26 Dec 1933: HPL in NYC visiting friends

31 Dec 1933: HPL reportedly drinks spiked punch

1934:

Early 1934: Duane Rimel correspondence starts

08 Jan 1934: HPL meets A. Merritt

Mar 1934: "Winged Death" published in Weird Tales

13 Apr 1934: HPL writes 4000-word letter to editor of Providence Journal *defending New Deal*

17 Apr 1934: HPL leaves on 3-month trip to visit Barlow in Florida, via NYC and Charleston

May 1934: HPL helps Duane Rimel write "The Tree on the Hill"

Jun 1934: "From Beyond" published in Fantasy Fan

Jun 1934: HPL and Robert Barlow write, publish and distribute "The Battle that Ended the Century"

08 Jun 1934: Edith Miniter dies

Summer 1934: HPL discovers William Hope Hodgson books

Jul 1934: "Through the Gates of the Silver Key" published in Weird Tales

Jul 1934: HPL dragooned into serving another year as chairman of NAPA Bureau of Critics

Jul 1934: HPL helps Duane Rimel with "The Sorcery of Aphlar"

Jul 1934: HPL writes "Homes and Shrines of Poe" and "Some Notes on Interplanetary Fiction" for The Californian

10 Jul 1934: HPL finally home from Florida trip

4 Aug 1934: HPL on 3-day trip to Buttonwoods, RI

23 Aug 1934: HPL makes short trip to Boston, Salem, Marblehead, etc

31 Aug 1934: HPL visits Nantucket for a week
10 Nov 1934: HPL starts writing The Shadow Out of Time
Dec 1934: "The Sorcery of Aphlar" published in Fantasy Fan
11 Dec 1934: HPL writes an article about Roman architecture
30 Dec 1934: HPL travels to NYC for New Year

1935:

1935: Donald Wollheim takes over Phantagraph, *publishes lots of HPL stuff in it*
1 Jan 1935: HPL helps Robert Barlow with "Till A' the Seas"
8 Jan 1935: HPL home from NYC
Feb 1935: Fantasy Fan *publishes last issue, then folds, leaving* Supernatural Horror in Literature *half published*
Mid-Feb 1935: Derleth pitches his publishers, Loring & Mussey, on a HPL collection
22 Feb 1935: HPL finishes writing The Shadow out of Time *and sends it to Derleth*
Spring 1935: "What Belongs in Verse" published in Perspective Review
Mar 1935: Kenneth Sterling introduces himself to HPL
Apr 1935: "Out of the Æons" published in Weird Tales
Apr 1935: HPL initiates correspondence with C.L. Moore re. Barlow plan to publish a collection of her work
27 Apr 1935: Robert Moe visits; travels and explorations ensue
03 May 1935: HPL goes to Boston to sightsee with Edward Cole
25 May 1935: Charles Hornig visits, gets the tour
05 Jun 1935: HPL embarks on trip to Florida to visit Barlow, via NYC, Fredericksburg, Charleston, Jacksonville; arrives Jun 9. He helps creosote a cabin and helps Barlow set type and print "The Goblin Tower" by Frank Belknap Long. The two of them also write "Collapsing Cosmoses" during this time. Barlow also surprises HPL with a typescript of The Shadow out of Time.
Summer 1935: "Till A' the Seas" published in The Californian
Jul 1935: Loring & Mussey publishers reject Derleth's proposal for a HPL story collection
Jul-Aug 1935: "The Quest of Iranon" published in the journal Galleon.
18 Aug: HPL leaves Barlow's place, drifting northward
Late Aug: HPL participates in "The Challenge from Beyond"
Sep 1935: "The Challenge from Beyond" published in Fantasy Magazine
Sep 1935: HPL helps Duane Rimel with "The Disinterment"; Weird Tales rejects, later accepts
14 Sep 1935: HPL finally home again
20 Sep 1935: HPL travels to MA to scatter ashes of Edith Miniter's mother
8 Oct 1935: HPL and Aunt Annie visit New Haven
16 Oct 1935: HPL and Sam Loveman visit Boston
Mid-Oct 1935: HPL rewrites "Diary of Alonzo Typer" for William Lumley
Late Oct 1935: Julius Schwartz sells At the Mountains of Madness *to F. Orlin Tremaine of Astounding Stories for HPL, gets him $350 for it (less an agent fee of $35)*
Early Nov 1935: Donald Wandrei sells The Shadow Out of Time *to Tremaine for HPL, gets him $280. HPL subsequently writes that he was never closer to the bread line than just before these two cheques came in.*
5-9 Nov 1935: HPL writes "The Haunter of the Dark"
29 Dec 1935: HPL visits Long & Co. in NYC for holiday

1936:

Early 1936: William Crawford launches publication of The Shadow over Innsmouth *book*
7 Jan 1936: HPL home from holiday visit in NYC
Feb 1936: HPL revises "In the Walls of Eryx" for Kenneth Sterling
Feb 1936: At the Mountains of Madness *serialization starts in* Astounding Stories
Feb 1936: HPL basically admits his fiction career is over, ended by the hostile reception to At the Mountains of Madness *in 1931, in a letter to E. Hoffman Price*
28 Feb 1936: Anne Tillery Renshaw hires HPL to revise her self-help book, Well-Bred Speech, *which turns into a boondoggle*
17 Mar 1936: Aunt Annie has mastectomy. Finances get terrible. HPL back to eating cold canned beans.

Apr 1936: The Shadow over Innsmouth *published in book form (Visionary Publishing), and it's a hot mess of typos*
Jun 1936: The Shadow out of Time *printed in* Astounding Stories, *and it's also a hot mess of typos, but garnished with a generous dollop of bad copy-editing decisions*
19 Jun 1936: HPL learns of Robert E. Howard's suicide
Jul 1936: HPL submits "The Thing on Doorstep" and "The Haunter of the Dark" to Weird Tales, *first sub since 1931 when* At the Mountains of Madness *was rejected; both are accepted instantly, to his surprise*
08 Jul 1936: HPL renounces his hidebound tory-ism in a letter to Jennie Plaisier
18 Jul 1936: Maurice Moe visits with a car; they sightsee in it
28 Jul 1936: RH Barlow comes to town, moves into local boardinghouse, visits constantly
5 Aug 1936: De Castro visits, hangs out with HPL and Barlow; they write Edgar Allan Poe sonnets; DeCastro submits his to Weird Tales, *which accepts it; HPL and Barlow submit theirs but Weird Tales only wants one*
Mid-Aug 1936: HPL and Barlow work on "The Night Ocean"
1 Sep 1936: Barlow leaves town
11 Sep 1936: James Morton visits
19 Sep 1936: Robert Moe visits
Fall 1936: Kenneth Sterling heads off to Harvard
1 Oct 1936: Deadline for Well Bred Speech*; HPL stays up for 60 hours working to meet it*
Nov 1936: HPL starts correspondence with Fritz Leiber
30 Nov 1936: HPL writes a sonnet to Virgil Finlay "upon his drawing for Mr. Bloch's Tale, The Faceless God." It's his penultimate weird piece.
Dec 1936: HPL writes his last piece, "To Clark Ashton Smith, Esq., upon His Phantastick Tales, Verses, Pictures and Sculptures"
Dec 1936: "The Haunter of the Dark" published in Weird Tales
Christmas 1936: Willis Conover sends HPL a human skull, not knowing he was dying; HPL, probably also not knowing that, is super pleased.
Winter 1936: "The Night Ocean" published in The Californian

1937:

Jan 1937: "The Thing on the Doorstep" published in Weird Tales
Jan 1937: "The Disinterment" published in Weird Tales
Early Jan 1937: HPL starting to complain of "bum digestion." He starts a "death diary."
27 Jan 1937: HPL revises a story for Duane Rimel, "From the Sea," which does not survive; it's his last revision.
16 Feb 1937: HPL consults a doctor, learns he's gonna for sure die.
Mar 1937: HPL and Barlow's Poe sonnets run in Science-Fantasy Correspondent
15 Mar 1937, 7:15 a.m.: HPL pronounced dead.

16 Mar 1937: New York Times publishes HPL's obituary under headline "Writer charts fatal malady" (in reference to HPL's death diary); best friend Frank Belknap Long learns of his death by reading it.
18 Mar 1937: HPL's funeral.
Late Mar 1937: August Derleth maps out plans that would develop into Arkham House, enlisting Donald Wandrei to help.
26 Mar 1937: Aunt Annie Gamwell makes HPL's written wishes legally official by appointing Barlow his literary executor
May 1937: "The Horror in the Burying-Ground" published in Weird Tales
May 1937: DeCastro's Poe sonnet published in Weird Tales
Oct 1937: "The Shunned House" published in Weird Tales

1938:

1938: "The History of the Necronomicon*" published in* The Rebel Press
Jan 1938: "Ibid" published in O-Wash-Ta-Nong
Feb 1938: "The Diary of Alonzo Typer" published in Weird Tales
Summer 1938: "The Book," "Azathoth," "Collapsing Cosmoses," and "The Descendant" published in Leaves

1939:

Jan 1939: "Medusa's Coil" published in Weird Tales
Apr 1939: "The Wicked Clergyman" published in Weird Tales

Oct 1939: "In the Walls of Eryx" published in Weird Tales
Dec 1939: The Outsider and Others *published, inaugurating August Derleth's Arkham House*

1940:

Summer 1940: "The Very Old Folk" published in Scienti-Snaps
Sep 1940: "The Tree on the Hill" published in Polaris
Nov 1940: "The Mound" published in Weird Tales

1941:

Jan 1941: "The Thing in the Moonlight" published in Bizarre

1943:

1943: "Sweet Ermengarde" published in Beyond the Wall of Sleep *(Arkham House)*
1943: The Dream-Quest of Unknown Kadath *published (Arkham House)*

1944:

1944: "The Transition of Juan Romero" published in Marginalia *(Arkham House)*

1949:

1949: "Four O'Clock" published in Something About Cats and Other Pieces *(Arkham House)*

1959:

1959: "Old Bugs" published in The Shuttered Room and Other Pieces *(Arkham House)*

www.ingramcontent.com/pod-product-compliance
Lightning Source LLC
Chambersburg PA
CBHW081133300726
48982CB00005B/947

* 9 7 8 1 6 3 5 9 1 3 6 1 3 *